Places of Importance to Anglophone Women Writers of Africa, Asia, and Australia

COMPILED BY DEBORAH KENNEDY

The Norton Anthology of Literature by Women

THIRD EDITION
VOLUME 2
EARLY TWENTIETH CENTURY THROUGH CONTEMPORARY

The Norton Anthology of Literature by Women
The Traditions in English

THIRD EDITION

VOLUME 2

EARLY TWENTIETH CENTURY THROUGH
CONTEMPORARY

Sandra M. Gilbert
UNIVERSITY OF CALIFORNIA, DAVIS

Susan Gubar
INDIANA UNIVERSITY

W · W · NORTON & COMPANY · *New York* · *London*

W. W. Norton & Company has been independent since its founding in 1923, when William Warder Norton and Mary D. Herter Norton first published lectures delivered at the People's Institute, the adult education division of New York City's Cooper Union. The Nortons soon expanded their program beyond the Institute, publishing books by celebrated academics from America and abroad. By mid-century, the two major pillars of Norton's publishing program—trade books and college texts—were firmly established. In the 1950s, the Norton family transferred control of the company to its employees, and today—with a staff of four hundred and a comparable number of trade, college, and professional titles published each year—W. W. Norton & Company stands as the largest and oldest publishing house owned wholly by its employees.

Copyright © 2007, 1996, 1985 By Sandra M. Gilbert and Susan Gubar
All rights reserved.
Printed in the United States of America.

Composition by Binghamton Valley Composition.
Manufacturing by Lakeside Book Company, Crawfordsville.
Book design by Antonina Krass.
Project editor: Lory A. Frenkel.
Production manager: Benjamin Reynolds.

Library of Congress Cataloging-in-Publication Data

The Norton anthology of literature by women : the traditions in English / [compiled by] Sandra M. Gilbert, Susan Gubar.—3rd ed.
  p. cm.
Includes bibliographical references and index.
ISBN-13: 978-0-393-93013-9 (v. 1 : pbk.)
ISBN-10: 0-393-93013-0 (v. 1 : pbk.)
ISBN-13: 978-0-393-93014-6 (v. 2 : pbk.)
ISBN-10: 0-393-93014-9 (v. 2 : pbk.)

1. American literature—Women authors. 2. English literature—Women authors. 3. Women—Literary collections. I. Gilbert, Sandra M. II. Gubar, Susan, 1944–
PS508.W7N67 2007
820.8'09287—dc22
                        2006101170

W. W. Norton & Company, Inc., 500 Fifth Avenue, New York, N.Y. 10110
www.wwnorton.com
W. W. Norton & Company Ltd., 15 Carlisle Street, London W1D 3BS

1 2 3 4 5 6 7 8 9 0

Contents

PREFACE • xxi
ACKNOWLEDGMENTS • xxix

Early-Twentieth-Century Literature • 1

EDITH WHARTON (1862–1937) • 29
   The Angel at the Grave   31
   The Other Two   43

SUI SIN FAR (EDITH MAUD EATON [1865–1914]) • 56
   Mrs. Spring Fragrance   57

MARY AUSTIN (1868–1934) • 66
   The Walking Woman   66

CHARLOTTE MEW (1869–1928) • 72
   A White Night   73
   The Farmer's Bride   84
   The Quiet House   86

HENRY HANDEL RICHARDSON (1870–1946) • 87
   Two Hanged Women   88

WILLA CATHER (1873–1947) • 91
   Coming, Aphrodite!   93

DOROTHY RICHARDSON (1873–1957) • 120
   Death   122
   Women and the Future   123
      The Essential Egoist   125
      Women in the Future   127

AMY LOWELL (1874–1925) • 128
   The Letter   129
   Venus Transiens   130
   Madonna of the Evening Flowers   131
   The Weather-Cock Points South   131
   Opal   132
   Decade   132
   Summer Rain   132
   A Critical Fable   133
      [On T. S. Eliot and Ezra Pound]   133
   The Sisters   137

v

GERTRUDE STEIN (1874–1946) — 141
   The Gentle Lena   143
   Picasso   163
   Ada   165

ALICE DUNBAR-NELSON (1875–1935) — 166
   Mr. Baptiste   167
   I Sit and Sew   171

ANNA HEMPSTEAD BRANCH (1875–1937) — 172
   Sonnets from a Lock Box   172
      XIV ("What witchlike spell weaves here its deep design")   172
      XXV ("Into the void behold my shuddering flight")   173
      XXXI ("I say that words are men and when we spell")   173

ZITKALA ŠA (GERTRUDE SIMMONS BONNIN [1876–1938]) — 173
   The Trial Path   174

SUSAN GLASPELL (1876–1948) — 177
   Trifles   178

RADCLYFFE HALL (1880–1943) — 187
   Miss Ogilvy Finds Herself   188

ANZIA YEZIERSKA (ca. 1880?–1970) — 201
   The Lost "Beautifulness"   201

VIRGINIA WOOLF (1882–1941) — 212
   22 Hyde Park Gate   217
   Jane Eyre and *Wuthering Heights*   227
   A Woman's College from Outside   231
   Moments of Being   233
      "Slater's Pins Have No Points"   233
   A Room of One's Own   237
      [Shakespeare's Sister]   237
   Professions for Women   244
   The Death of the Moth   248

MINA LOY (1882–1966) — 250
   Gertrude Stein   250
   Three Moments in Paris   251
      One O'Clock at Night   251
   The Widow's Jazz   251
   Omen of Victory   253
   Photo after Pogrom   253
   Songge Byrd   254
   Portrait of a Nun   254
   Feminist Manifesto   255

ANNE SPENCER (1882–1975) — 258
   Before the Feast at Shushan   258
   White Things   259
   Lady, Lady   260

Letter to My Sister   260
Innocence   261

KATHARINE SUSANNAH PRICHARD (1883–1969)   261
The Cooboo   262

ANNA WICKHAM (EDITH ALICE MARY HARPER [1884–1947])   265
Meditation at Kew   265
The Affinity   266
Divorce   267
Dedication of the Cook   267

ELINOR WYLIE (1885–1928)   268
The Eagle and the Mole   269
Atavism   270
Wild Peaches   270
Full Moon   272
Let No Charitable Hope   272
One Person   273
   XII ("In our content, before the autumn came")   273
To a Lady's Countenance   273
Pastiche   274

ISAK DINESEN (1885–1962)   274
The Blank Page   276

H. D. (HILDA DOOLITTLE [1886–1961])   280
Orchard   283
Oread   284
Sea Poppies   284
Garden   285
Eurydice   285
Fragment Thirty-six   289
Helen   291
The Master   291

EDITH SITWELL (1887–1964)   300
En Famille   301
Sir Beelzebub   302
Aubade   303
Lullaby   304
Serenade: Any Man to Any Woman   305
Still Falls the Rain   306

MARIANNE MOORE (1887–1972)   307
Sojourn in the Whale   309
Those Various Scalpels   310
Poetry   311
A Grave   312
An Egyptian Pulled Glass Bottle in the Shape of a Fish   313
Silence   313
To a Snail   314

No Swan So Fine   314
The Steeple-Jack   315
The Paper Nautilus   317
His Shield   318
O to Be a Dragon   318

KATHERINE MANSFIELD (1888–1923)   319
The Daughters of the Late Colonel   321
The Fly   335

KATHERINE ANNE PORTER (1890–1980)   339
The Jilting of Granny Weatherall   340

ZORA NEALE HURSTON (1891–1960)   347
Sweat   349
How It Feels to Be Colored Me   357

NELLA LARSEN (1891–1964)   360
Quicksand   362

EDNA ST. VINCENT MILLAY (1892–1950)   444
First Fig   445
Second Fig   445
[Oh, oh, you will be sorry for that word!]   445
[I, being born a woman and distressed]   446
Sonnets from an Ungrafted Tree   446
The Buck in the Snow   452
To Inez Milholland   452
[Women have loved before as I love now]   453
[Oh, sleep forever in the Latmian cave]   453
Childhood Is the Kingdom Where Nobody Dies   454
Apostrophe to Man   455
Rendezvous   455
The Fitting   456
[I too beneath your moon, almighty Sex]   457
[The courage that my mother had]   457
An Ancient Gesture   457
[I will put Chaos into fourteen lines]   458

DJUNA BARNES (1892–1982)   458
How It Feels to Be Forcibly Fed   460
Cassation   463

REBECCA WEST (1892–1983)   468
Indissoluble Matrimony   469

DOROTHY PARKER (1893–1967)   487
Résumé   487
One Perfect Rose   488
News Item   488
Song of One of the Girls   488

    A Pig's-Eye View of Literature   489
        Oscar Wilde   489
        Harriet Beecher Stowe   489
        D. G. Rossetti   489
        Thomas Carlyle   490
        Alfred, Lord Tennyson   490
        Walter Savage Landor   490
        George Sand   490
    The Waltz   490

GENEVIEVE TAGGARD (1894–1948)   494
    Everyday Alchemy   494
    With Child   495
    The Quiet Woman   495
    Leave Me Alone a Little   496
    A Middle-aged, Middle-class Woman at Midnight   496
    At Last the Women are Moving   497
    Mill Town   497
    Demeter   498

JEAN RHYS (1894?–1979)   498
    Mannequin   499

LOUISE BOGAN (1897–1970)   504
    Medusa   505
    The Crows   505
    Women   506
    Cassandra   506
    The Crossed Apple   507
    Evening in the Sanitarium   507
    Several Voices out of a Cloud   508
    The Dream   509

KATE O'BRIEN (1897–1974)   509
    From Santa Teresa   510
    No Pasarán   515
        [On Bullfighting]   515

RUTH PITTER (1897–1992)   520
    The Military Harpist   520
    The Irish Patriarch   521
    Old Nelly's Birthday   522
    Yorkshire Wife's Saga   523

MARITA BONNER (1899–1971)   524
    On Being Young—a Woman—and Colored   524

ELIZABETH BOWEN (1899–1973)   528
    The Demon Lover   528

MERIDEL LE SUEUR (1900–1996)   533
    Annunciation   534

LAURA RIDING (1901–1991)   541
    The Map of Places   542
    Death as Death   543
    The Troubles of a Book   543
    Eve's Side of It   544
        Commentary [on "Eve's Side of It"]   548

Later-Twentieth-Century and Contemporary Literature   553

STEVIE SMITH (1902–1971)   580
    Papa Love Baby   580
    This Englishwoman   581
    Lord Barrenstock   581
    Dear Female Heart   582
    Souvenir de Monsieur Poop   582
    Human Affection   583
    The Wanderer   584
    Our Bog Is Dood   584
    Lightly Bound   585
    Not Waving but Drowning   585
    How Cruel Is the Story of Eve   585

ANAÏS NIN (1903–1977)   587
    Birth   588

DILYS LAING (1906–1960)   591
    Sonnet to a Sister in Error   591
    The Double Goer   592
    Let Them Ask Their Husbands   593
    Prayer of an Ovulating Female   593

DOROTHY LIVESAY (1909–1996)   594
    Green Rain   594
    Eve   595
    The Three Emily's   596
    The Children's Letters   596

EUDORA WELTY (1909– 2001)   597
    A Worn Path   598

ELIZABETH BISHOP (1911–1979)   604
    The Man-Moth   605
    Roosters   606
    The Fish   610
    Invitation to Miss Marianne Moore   612
    First Death in Nova Scotia   613
    In the Waiting Room   614
    One Art   617

Pink Dog   617
[Gender and Art]   618

MARY LAVIN (1912–1996)   619
   In a Café   619

MARY McCARTHY (1912–1989)   630
   Memories of a Catholic Girlhood   631
     Names   631

MAY SARTON (1912–1995)   637
   My Sisters, O My Sisters   638
   Letter from Chicago   642
   The Muse as Medusa   643

MURIEL RUKEYSER (1913–1980)   644
   Boy with His Hair Cut Short   645
   More of a Corpse than a Woman   645
   Who in One Lifetime   646
   Letter to the Front   647
     VII ("To be a Jew in the twentieth century")   647
   Night Feeding   647
   The Birth of Venus   648
   The Power of Suicide   648
   The Poem as Mask   649
   Käthe Kollwitz   649
   Myth   653
   Along History   654

MAY SWENSON (1913–1989)   654
   The Centaur   655
   Women   657
   Blue   657
   Bleeding   658

TILLIE OLSEN (b. ca. 1913)   659
   Tell Me a Riddle   660

JAMES TIPTREE JR. (ALICE B. SHELDON [1915–1987])   686
   The Women Men Don't See   687

RUTH STONE (b. 1915)   708
   In an Iridescent Time   709
   Periphery   709
   The Song of Absinthe Granny   710
   Second-Hand Coat   712
   Names   712
   Things I Say to Myself While Hanging Laundry   713
   At Eighty-Three She Lives Alone   714
   Sorrow   714
   Cousin Francis Speaks Out   715
   From Outer Space   715
   The Barrier   716
   The Jewels   716

MARGARET WALKER (1915–1998)   717
    Dark Blood   717
    Lineage   718
    Molly Means   718
    Kissie Lee   720
    Whores   721
    For Malcolm X   721

JUDITH WRIGHT (1915–2000)   722
    Half-Caste Girl   723
    Woman to Man   723
    The Sisters   724
    Ishtar   724
    Request to a Year   725
    To Another Housewife   726
    Eve to Her Daughters   726
    Naked Girl and Mirror   728
    "Rosina Alcona to Julius Brenzaida"   729
    Two Dreamtimes   730
    Some Words   733
    Counting in Sevens   734

P. K. PAGE (b. 1916)   735
    The Stenographers   736
    Typists   737
    Planet Earth   737

CARSON McCULLERS (1917–1967)   739
    The Ballad of the Sad Café   740

GWENDOLYN BROOKS (1917–2000)   780
    the mother   781
    a song in the front yard   782
    The Sundays of Satin-Legs Smith   782
    The Rites for Cousin Vit   786
    The Womanhood   786
       3 ("Stand off, daughter of the dusk")   786
    The Bean Eaters   787
    We Real Cool   787
    Bronzeville Woman in a Red Hat   787
    The Last Quatrain of the Ballad of Emmett Till   789
    Malcolm X   790

MURIEL SPARK (1918–2006)   790
    The Black Madonna   791

LOUISE BENNETT (1919–2006)   804
    Pass Fe White   805
    Colonisation in Reverse   806
    Jamaica Oman   808

DORIS LESSING (b. 1919)   809
    One off the Short List   810

OODGEROO NOONUCCAL (KATH WALKER [1920–1993])   828
We Are Going   828
Understand, Old One   829
Municipal Gum   830

GWEN HARWOOD (1920–1995)   831
In the Park   832
The Sea Anemones   832
Mother Who Gave Me Life   832
Mid-Channel   834

HISAYE YAMAMOTO (b. 1921)   834
Seventeen Syllables   835

MAVIS GALLANT (b. 1922)   844
Mlle. Dias de Corta   845

GRACE PALEY (b. 1922)   852
My Father Addresses Me on the Facts of Old Age   853

DENISE LEVERTOV (1923–1997)   859
The Goddess   860
Song for Ishtar   861
Hypocrite Women   862
In Mind   862
The Ache of Marriage   863
Eros at Temple Stream   863
Abel's Bride   864
The Son   864
Stepping Westward   865
The Mutes   866
What Were They Like?   868
Canción   868
Divorcing   869
The Dragonfly-Mother   869
Ancient Airs and Dances   871
Evening Train   872

NADINE GORDIMER (b. 1923)   873
The Moment before the Gun Went Off   874

SHIRLEY KAUFMAN (b. 1923)   877
His Wife   878
Mothers, Daughters   878
Abishag   879
Stones   880
Longing for Prophets   881
Intifada   881
   The Status Quo   881
   Peace March   882
   Decisions   882

PATRICIA BEER (1924–1999)   883
Witch   883
Brunhild   884

The Bull 885
In Memory of Constance Markiewicz 885
Mating Calls 886
Transvestism in the Novels of Charlotte Brontë 886

JANET FRAME (1924–2004) 887
Keel and Kool 888

FLANNERY O'CONNOR (1925–1964) 892
Good Country People 893

CAROLYN KIZER (b. 1925) 907
Pro Femina 908
Three ("I will speak about women of letters, for I'm in the racket") 908
Semele Recycled 909
Second Time Around 911

MAXINE W. KUMIN (b. 1925) 912
Making the Jam without You 913
The Envelope 915
How It Is 915
Skinnydipping with William Wordsworth 916
Women and Horses 917
Sonnet in So Many Words 918

ANNE SEXTON (1928–1974) 918
Her Kind 919
The Moss of His Skin 920
Housewife 921
Woman with Girdle 921
Somewhere in Africa 922
Sylvia's Death 923
In Celebration of My Uterus 924

MAYA ANGELOU (1928–2014) 926
I Know Why the Caged Bird Sings 926
[The Peckerwood Dentist and Momma's Incredible Powers] 926

CYNTHIA OZICK (b. 1928) 931
The Shawl 932

U. A. FANTHORPE (b. 1929) 935
For Saint Peter 936
Only Here for the Bier 936
1. Mother-in-Law 936
2. King's Daughter 937
Women Laughing 938
From the Third Storey 939

URSULA K. LE GUIN (b. 1929) 940
Sur 941
She Unnames Them 953

PAULE MARSHALL (b. 1929)   955
   Poets in the Kitchen   955

ADRIENNE RICH (b. 1929)   962
   Aunt Jennifer's Tigers   965
   Snapshots of a Daughter-in-Law   965
   "I Am in Danger—Sir—"   969
   Diving into the Wreck   970
   Power   972
   Twenty-one Love Poems   973
     XI ("Every peak is a crater")   973
     (The Floating Poem, Unnumbered)   973
     XXI ("The dark lintels, the blue and foreign stones")   973
   Phantasia for Elvira Shatayev   974
   Final Notations   975
   From Eastern War Time   976
   In Those Years   977
   To the Days   977
   Fox   978
   The School among the Ruins   979
   When We Dead Awaken: Writing as Re-Vision (1971)   982

TONI MORRISON (b. 1931)   994
   Recitatif   996
   From Unspeakable Things Unspoken   1009

ALICE MUNRO (b. 1931)   1026
   Floating Bridge   1026

SYLVIA PLATH (1932–1963)   1044
   The Disquieting Muses   1047
   The Colossus   1048
   You're   1049
   Mirror   1050
   The Bee Meeting   1050
   The Arrival of the Bee Box   1052
   Stings   1053
   The Swarm   1054
   Wintering   1056
   Daddy   1057
   Ariel   1059
   Nick and the Candlestick   1060
   Lady Lazarus   1062
   Words   1064
   Edge   1065

EDNA O'BRIEN (b. 1932)   1065
   Brother   1066

AUDRE LORDE (1934–1992)   1069
   Coal   1070
   On a Night of the Full Moon   1071

Now That I Am Forever with Child 1072
From the House of Yemanjá 1072
The Women of Dan Dance with Swords in Their Hands to Mark the
 Time When They Were Warriors 1074
Kitchen Linoleum 1075
The Electric Slide Boogie 1075
Zami: A New Spelling of My Name 1076
 [Origins] 1076

FLEUR ADCOCK (b. 1934) 1078
For a Five-Year-Old 1079
Miss Hamilton in London 1079
Against Coupling 1080
The Voyage Out 1081
On the Border 1082
Street Song 1083

DIANE DI PRIMA (b. 1934) 1084
Song for Baby-O, Unborn 1084
April Fool Birthday Poem for Grandpa 1085
Poem in Praise of My Husband (Taos) 1086
Letter to Jeanne (at Tassajara) 1087
Narrow Path into the Back Country 1087
Annunciation 1089
Thirteen Nightmares 1090
 Nightmare 7 1090
 Nightmare 12 1091
Loba 1092
 The Loba Priestess as Bag Lady Utters Ragged Warnings 1092

JUNE JORDAN (1936–2002) 1093
The Wedding 1093
The Reception 1094
Poem about Police Violence 1095
A Runaway Lil Bit Poem 1096
DeLiza Spend the Day in the City 1097

A. S. BYATT (b. 1936) 1097
A Stone Woman 1098

LUCILLE CLIFTON (b. 1936) 1119
admonitions 1119
the lost baby poem 1120
if our grandchild be a girl 1121
my dream about being white 1121
Poem to My Uterus 1122
To My Last Period 1122
Leda 3 1123

ANITA DESAI (b. 1937) 1123
Royalty 1124

CARYL CHURCHILL (b. 1938) 1136
Top Girls 1137

JOYCE CAROL OATES (b. 1938)   1191
  Where Are You Going, Where Have You Been?   1192

MARGARET ATWOOD (b. 1939)   1203
  This Is a Photograph of Me   1204
  Spelling   1205
  Waiting   1206
  Asparagus   1208
  Marsh Languages   1209
  Morning in the Burned House   1209
  Rape Fantasies   1210
  There Was Once   1217
  The Little Red Hen Tells All   1219

ANGELA CARTER (1940–1992)   1220
  The Company of Wolves   1221

MAXINE HONG KINGSTON (b. 1940)   1228
  No Name Woman   1229

BHARATI MUKHERJEE (b. 1940)   1238
  The Management of Grief   1238

LYN HEJINIAN (b. 1941)   1250
  From My Life   1250

GLORIA ANZALDÚA (1942–2004)   1254
  Tlilli, Tlapalli / The Path of the Red and Black Ink   1255

AMA ATA AIDOO (b. 1942)   1263
  The Message   1263

MARILYN HACKER (b. 1942)   1269
  Ballad of Ladies Lost and Found   1269
  Runaways Café I   1273
  Runaways Café II   1273
  From Cancer Winter   1273
  The Boy   1275
  Crepuscule with Muriel   1276
  Migraine Sonnets   1277

SHARON OLDS (b. 1942)   1278
  The Death of Marilyn Monroe   1279
  The Language of the Brag   1279
  Rite of Passage   1280
  The One Girl at the Boys' Party   1281
  This   1281
  The Mortal One   1282

LOUISE GLÜCK (b. 1943)   1283
  The School Children   1283
  The Drowned Children   1284
  Dedication to Hunger   1284
    4. The Deviation   1284
  Widows   1285

Terminal Resemblance   1286
First Memory   1287
Lullaby   1287
Vita Nova   1287

EAVAN BOLAND (b. 1944)   1288
In His Own Image   1289
Anorexic   1290
The Muse Mother   1291
Degas's Laundresses   1292
The Pomegranate   1293
Against Love Poetry   1295

ALICE WALKER (b. 1944)   1295
In Search of Our Mothers' Gardens   1296

LYNN FREED (b. 1945)   1303
Under the House   1304

OCTAVIA BUTLER (1947–2006)   1306
Bloodchild   1307

LORNA GOODISON (b. 1947)   1321
Guinea Woman   1321
Nanny   1323
Mother the Great Stones Got to Move   1324
Annie Pengelly   1325
After the Green Gown of My Mother Gone Down   1328
To Mr. William Wordsworth, Distributor of Stamps for Westmoreland   1330
Change If You Must Just Change Slow   1331

LESLIE MARMON SILKO (b. 1948)   1332
Yellow Woman   1332

JAMAICA KINCAID (b. 1949)   1339
Girl   1339

JULIA ALVAREZ (b. 1950)   1341
Bilingual Sestina   1341
The Master Bed   1342
Storm Windows   1343
33   1343
    [Where are the girls who were beautiful?]   1343
    [Sometimes the words are so close I am]   1344
On Not Shoplifting Louise Bogan's *The Blue Estuaries*   1344

ANNE CARSON (b. 1950)   1346
From The Glass Essay   1347
Lazarus Standup: Shooting Script   1361

CAROLYN FORCHÉ (b. 1950)   1363
The Colonel   1364
Elegy   1365

MEDBH McGUCKIAN (b. 1950)   1366
    The Flitting   1366
    Visiting Rainer Maria   1367
    Black Virgin   1368
    She is in the Past, She has this Grace   1369

GRACE NICHOLS (b. 1950)   1371
    The Assertion   1371
    The Fat Black Woman Remembers   1372
    Tropical Death   1372
    Out of Africa   1373

JORIE GRAHAM (b. 1951)   1374
    History   1374
    Orpheus and Eurydice   1375

JOY HARJO (b. 1951)   1377
    Deer Dancer   1377
    Mourning Song   1379
    The Naming   1380
    The Path to the Milky Way Leads through Los Angeles   1382
    Morning Song   1382
    When the World As We Knew It Ended   1383

RITA DOVE (b. 1952)   1384
    The House Slave   1385
    Parsley   1385
    Thomas and Beulah   1387
       The Great Palaces of Versailles   1387
       Wingfoot Lake   1388
    Persephone, Falling   1389
    Sonnet in Primary Colors   1390
    Rosa   1390
    "I have been a stranger in a strange land"   1391

LUCI TAPAHONSO (b. 1953)   1392
    Blue Horses Rush In   1392
    Leda and the Cowboy   1393

KIM ADDONIZIO (b. 1954)   1394
    "What Do Women Want?"   1395
    Generations   1396
    Last Call   1397
    31-Year-Old Lover   1398
    You Don't Know What Love Is   1398
    Sonnenizio on a Line from Drayton   1399

SANDRA CISNEROS (b. 1954)   1399
    Woman Hollering Creek   1400

LOUISE ERDRICH (b. 1954)   1408
    The Shawl   1409

HELENA MARÍA VIRAMONTES (b. 1954)   1414
    The Moths   1414

MARILYN CHIN (b. 1955)   1418
    How I Got That Name   1419
    That Half Is Almost Gone   1421
    The True Story of Mortar and Pestle   1422

CAROL ANN DUFFY (b. 1955)   1423
    Warming Her Pearls   1424
    Litany   1425
    September, 1997   1425
    Circe   1426
    Mrs Lazarus   1427

PAULA MEEHAN (b. 1955)   1428
    Child Burial   1429
    The View from under the Table   1429
    Thunder in the House   1430
    "Would you jump into my grave as quick?"   1431

REBECCA BROWN (b. 1956)   1432
    Forgiveness   1432

GISH JEN (b. 1956)   1436
    Who's Irish?   1437

JEANETTE WINTERSON (b. 1959)   1445
    The Poetics of Sex   1446

MARGARET EDSON (b. 1961)   1453
    Wit   1454

JACKIE KAY (b. 1961)   1487
    In My Country   1488
    Finger   1489
    Hottentot Venus   1489
    Paw Broon on the Starr Report   1491
    Big Milk   1492

JHUMPA LAHIRI (b. 1967)   1498
    A Temporary Matter   1498

SELECTED BIBLIOGRAPHIES   1511

PERMISSIONS ACKNOWLEDGMENTS   1555

INDEX   1565

Preface

> I think I was enchanted
> When first a sombre Girl -
> I read that Foreign Lady -
> The Dark - felt beautiful -

So wrote the brilliant American poet Emily Dickinson in the mid–nineteenth century, as she contemplated the literary achievements of "that Foreign Lady," the great British poet Elizabeth Barrett Browning, then living in exile in Italy. We begin our preface to the Third Edition of *The Norton Anthology of Literature by Women* with this tribute from one woman of letters to another because it emphasizes the international intellectual bonds that link readers and writers across time and space. In 1985, we began our Preface to the First Edition with Virginia Woolf's remark in *A Room of One's Own* that "books continue each other." Woolf, we noted, was urging her audience to contemplate the connections between the Restoration iconoclast Aphra Behn, the eighteenth-century lyricist Anne Finch, and the four great novelists of the nineteenth century—Jane Austen, Charlotte Brontë, Emily Brontë, and George Eliot—but by implication she was also arguing for the places occupied in her "fairly long series" by such American writers as Harriet Beecher Stowe and Dickinson. It was the tradition constituted by this series that the First Edition brought to a new audience of students and general readers.

Today, however, we can see more clearly just how complex and multifaceted Woolf's set of women writers really is. For during the years that have intervened between editions, the interlocked fields of women's studies, gender studies, feminist theory, queer theory, and cultural studies have evolved in ways we might not have anticipated in 1985. Throughout the past two decades, scholars have continued the excavation and assessment that provisionally defined women's literary history in the 1970s and '80s, and we are grateful to them for newly recovered works of literature, better edited texts, and new historical writings. In particular, however, we owe to them contributions that enrich the original pages of this anthology so dramatically as to have invited a crucial emendation in our subtitle: originally subtitled "The Tradition in English," with the Second Edition we began subtitling it "The Traditions in English" to signal a commitment to both mirror and serve the range of scholarly, critical, and pedagogic viewpoints that have enlivened feminist studies in a globalized era. Diversity itself has shaped the evolution of feminist criticism, from its early preoccupation with women's shared experiences to its more recent absorption in the complex issues and assumptions informing English-language texts by women writers of diverse geographical, cultural, racial, sexual, religious, and class origins and influences, just as diversity shaped the revisions of this anthology. The section-by-section changes noted below convey the diversity in genre, in ethnic and geographical origins, and in representation of individual writers that characterize the Third Edition.

At the same time, this Third Edition of *The Norton Anthology of Literature by Women* continues to remind readers of Woolf's affirmation that "books continue each other." Like all historically oriented Norton anthologies, our volumes provide a broad chronological overview of their subject—an overview that enables readers to fully appreciate the female literary traditions that, for several centuries, have coexisted with, revised, and influenced male literary models. With 219 writers (61 new to the Third Edition), *The Norton Anthology of Literature by Women* chronicles both the evolution in and the revolutions of women's literature in the British Isles, the United States, Canada, Australia, India, Africa, the Caribbean, and other English-speaking regions from the fourteenth century to the present.

As what is essentially a course-in-a-book, the anthology maintains its original commitment to offering major works in their entirety. To Charlotte Brontë's *Jane Eyre* and Kate Chopin's *The Awakening*, both included complete, we have added a third novel, *Quicksand* by Nella Larsen. We offer a wealth of complete longer prose fictions—Aphra Behn's *Oroonoko*, Eliza Haywood's *Fantomina*, Maria Edgeworth's *The Grateful Negro*, Jane Austen's *Love and Freindship*, George Eliot's *The Lifted Veil*, Rebecca Harding Davis's *Life in the Iron-Mills*, Willa Cather's *Coming, Aphrodite!*, and Carson McCullers's *Ballad of the Sad Café*. Drama has been similarly strengthened. To Susan Glaspell's pioneering *Trifles* and Caryl Churchill's innovative *Top Girls*, we add Margaret Edson's powerful and poignant full-length play, *Wit*. Longer verse selections include new versions of two narratives by Marie de France, translated by Dorothy Gilbert into rhymed octosyllabics especially for this volume, along with a number of complete long poems or poem cycles—notably Christina Rossetti's *Goblin Market*, H. D.'s "The Master," Edna St. Vincent Millay's *Sonnets from an Ungrafted Tree*, Muriel Rukeyser's "Käthe Kollwitz," Gwendolyn Brooks's "The Sundays of Satin-Legs Smith," Sylvia Plath's "Bee" sequence, and Marilyn Hacker's "Ballad of Ladies Lost and Found."

Taking into account the suggestions of countless teachers and students who used the anthology in many different educational settings, we have strengthened the representation of many "classic" or "standard" women writers. In some cases, we replaced earlier selections with more resonant texts; we now offer, for example, new prose works by such widely read authors as Elizabeth Gaskell, Louisa May Alcott, Sarah Orne Jewett, Mary E. Wilkins Freeman, Jean Rhys, Grace Paley, Nadine Gordimer, and Edna O'Brien. In other instances, we expanded representation of key authors such as Anne Bradstreet, Charlotte Smith, Frances Burney, Dorothy Wordsworth, Fanny Fern, George Eliot, Frances E. W. Harper, Charlotte Perkins Gilman, Charlotte Mew, Marianne Moore, Stevie Smith, Elizabeth Bishop, Margaret Walker, Ruth Stone, Judith Wright, Gwendolyn Brooks, Maxine Kumin, Adrienne Rich, Lucille Clifton, Eavan Boland, Rita Dove, and Louise Erdrich.

Section-by-Section Revisions
We have continued to organize these diverse writings chronologically, for we still believe that although conventional literary periodization does not always suit women's aesthetic past, the history of women's literary traditions does have significant historical phases of its own. Thus, here as in earlier editions, we have for the most part omitted references to the usual literary "ages" (i.e., Augustan, Romantic, Victorian) and instead have organized our authors by birth date into six eras, which our period introductions discuss in a way that makes clear the historical and thematic coherence of the material within each section. Since all of these periods are so dramatically affected by the manifold literary "traditions in English" that we represent, it will be useful to summarize the additions to each section, as well as to highlight the scope of each volume in the new two-volume format.

Volume 1
Literature of the Middle Ages and the Renaissance. Included for the first time are Marie de France's influential rhymed romances "Bisclavret" and "Yönec," in Dorothy Gilbert's lively and accessible new translations; Anne Askew's famous Newgate ballad; Martha Moulsworth's "Memorandum"; and Rachel Speght's passionate polemic against "Melastomus," the "cynical baiter of and foul-mouthed barker against Eve's sex." In addition, we have significantly expanded and enriched our representation of Julian of Norwich and Margery Kempe.

Literature of the Seventeenth and Eighteenth Centuries. Prose offerings newly include Sarah Kemble Knight's seventeenth-century "Journal of the Journey from Boston to N.Y.," and Judith Sargent Murray's polemic "On the Equality of the Sexes." Verse offerings have been greatly strengthened with the addition of eight new poets—Anne Ingram, Mary Leapor, Lucy Terry, Mary Alcock, Hannah More, Sarah Wentworth Morton, Helen Maria Williams, and Joanna Baillie—as well as expanded selections for Katherine Philips, Aphra Behn, Charlotte Smith, Lady Mary Wortley Montagu, and Phillis Wheatley.

Literature of the Nineteenth Century. This section has been enriched by three new poets whose popularity in their era gives them crucial historical importance: Felicia Hemans, Letitia Elizabeth Landon ("L.E.L"), and Adah Isaacs Menken. New prose works include Elizabeth Gaskell's "The Old Nurse's Story" and George Eliot's "Silly Novels by Lady Novelists," which highlights the conflicting forces that shaped the literary marketplace in which women poets and "lady novelists" were gaining ground in this period. New selections by Fanny Fern ("Blackwell Island") and Louisa May Alcott ("How I Went Out to Service") offer insights into the lives of working-class women in the era; and expanded selections by Harriet Jacobs and Frances E. W. Harper facilitate the study of race relations and literary representation. Finally, the texts for Emily Dickinson poems are now those of the newly established Franklin edition, with the Johnson numbering retained for reference.

Turn-of-the-Century Literature. Major additions here include works by two African American writers: the theorist of education Anna Julia Cooper and the pioneering novelist, playwright, and journalist Pauline E. Hopkins. A diverse group of new poets has been newly added: the American Sarah

Morgan Bryan Piatt, the Victorian Augusta Webster, and the collaborative couple known as "Michael Field" (Katherine Harris Bradley and Edith Emma Cooper). Other, equally striking additions are two poets in the Jewish traditions—the American Emma Lazarus and the English Amy Levy—and the Native Canadian Pauline Johnson, a poet and writer of fiction.

Volume 2

Early-Twentieth-Century Literature. A new centerpiece of this section is Nella Larsen's eminently teachable short novel *Quicksand*. Larsen is joined by three other important new fiction writers: the Asian American writer Sui Sin Far (Edith Maud Eaton), and the British writer Charlotte Mew (hitherto represented only by poetry), as well as new fiction by Jean Rhys. In addition, the section includes the American poet-activist Genevieve Taggard, the Irish novelist and travel writer Kate O'Brien, and the American poet-critic Laura Riding—long absent because of her theoretical stance against anthologies, but now represented by verse and by the brilliant prose monologue "Eve's Side of It."

Later-Twentieth-Century and Contemporary Literature. As the table of contents moves toward the present moment, richly diverse writers of "global English" proliferate: the Jamaican poets Louise Bennett and Lorna Goodison, the aboriginal Australian poet Oodgeroo Noonuccal (Kath Walker), the American Israeli artist Shirley Kaufman, the Italian American Beat Generation writer Diane di Prima, the African American feminist June Jordan, the Dominican American writer Julia Alvarez, the Canadian experimentalist Anne Carson, the Irish poet Medbh McGuckian, the Guyanese-born British writer Grace Nichols, the Native American poet Joy Harjo, the Chinese American novelist and short story writer Gish Jen, the Italian American poet Kim Addonizio, the Chicana writers Sandra Cisneros and Helen María Viramontes, the Asian American poet Marilyn Chin, the British poet Carol Ann Duffy, the Irish poet Paula Meehan, the British writer of lesbian fiction Jeanette Winterson, the American playwright Margaret Edson, the Scottish poet Jackie Kay, and the Indian American short story writer Jhumpa Lahiri. Included for the first time, these artists help us foreground both the vitality and the variety of recent achievements by contemporary literary women, whose global English radiates around the world, as if to support the claim made by Julia Alvarez in her witty "Bilingual Sestina" that not everything gets said in the supposed mainstream of "snowy, blue-eyed, gum-chewing English."

The geographic diversity above is matched by the greater diversity of genres, including science fiction and fantasy by James Tiptree Jr. (Alice Sheldon) and Octavia Butler, the experimental poetry of Lyn Hejinian, and Toni Morrison's influential critical essay "Unspeakable Things Unspoken." This section also looks afresh at many widely taught women writers, offering revised and expanded selections for Stevie Smith, Elizabeth Bishop, Ruth Stone, Carolyn Kizer, Maxine Kumin, Adrienne Rich, and Rita Dove, as well as newly anthologized stories by Mavis Gallant, Grace Paley, Nadine Gordimer, Janet Frame, A. S. Byatt, and Anita Desai.

Of course, no anthology can pretend to completeness. Editors inevitably find themselves unable to trace the ongoing evolution of every literary movement and tradition. In addition, permissions problems sometimes lead to the exclusion of important texts, as do space limitations. Thus we regret that inability to secure permission or financial constraints have made it impossible to reprint certain works we very much wanted, among them Virginia Woolf's *A Room of One's Own,* Adrienne Kennedy's play *A Movie Star Has to Star in Black and White,* and Toni Morrison's novel *The Bluest Eye.* Finally, we regret that we have not had room to include texts by countless women writers whose achievements we much admire. We are convinced, however, that the texts we have chosen will expand the contours of the canon. In addition, we continue to believe that whatever the subject, form, or provenance of our anthology's texts, we here reprint works whose historical, intellectual, or aesthetic significance clearly merits their inclusion.

Editorial Procedures
Adopting editorial procedures that have proved helpful in other Norton anthologies, we have in every case used what seemed to us the most accurate texts. In some instances, in order to make a work more easily accessible to the reader, we have modernized spelling and Americanized punctuation; otherwise, the spelling and punctuation of our texts is that of their authors or—as in the case of, say, Emily Brontë or Emily Dickinson—their best editors. After every selection we have indicated the date of first periodical or book publication (and, when appropriate, the date of a revised printing) on the right; whenever the facts are available, we have also indicated the date of composition on the left. Difficult allusions, foreign phrases, unfamiliar idioms, and arcane words have been glossed in annotations, many newly revised and expanded in this edition, at the bottom of the page. Whenever we found it necessary to present a text only in part, we have indicated internal cuts by three asterisks and prefaced the title of the work by the word "from." If we have supplied our own title for an excerpt, that title is enclosed in square brackets. Selected Bibliographies, extensively updated for this edition, are provided at the end of each volume to encourage and expedite further reading and research by students. Prepared by Deborah Kennedy, Saint Mary's University, and drawn by Adrian Kitzinger, three new endpaper maps, highlighting places of importance to women writers in the British Isles and North America and to women writers in English worldwide, provide a useful visual reference to the anthology's emphasis on global English literature. Finally, we have adopted a bolder typeface and redesigned the page, so as to make the text more readable.

We have tried to compose (and revise) headnotes and period introductions that are as lucid and informative as possible, providing necessary historical and biographical background without interposing our own critical interpretations between the reader and the text. Following our usual collaborative procedures, each of the two editors drafted approximately half of the headnotes, then exchanged and helped revise the drafts of the other editor. Two period introductions—those on the Literature of the Middle Ages and the Renaissance and on Later-Twentieth-Century and Contemporary Literature—originally written collaboratively, were revised separately, while the other period introductions were composed individually, then exchanged and revised: Susan Gubar drafted the introductions to the Seventeenth and Eighteenth Centuries and Turn-of-the-Century Literature, and revised the introduction to Later-Twentieth-Century and Contemporary Literature; Sandra

Gilbert drafted the introductions to Literature of the Nineteenth Century and Early-Twentieth-Century Literature, and revised the introduction to the Literature of the Middle Ages and the Renaissance.

Additional Resources

Following the model of several other Norton anthologies, the Third Edition introduces a two-volume format that has been welcomed by instructors and students for its flexibility and portability. The two-volume set accommodates the many instructors who use the anthology in a one-semester survey; it also opens up possibilities for using the individual volumes 1 or 2 for a variety of courses organized by period or topic, at levels from introductory to advanced.

Two new features give instructors even more flexibility: first, the publisher is making available the full list of 180 Norton Critical Editions, including the most frequently assigned novels—among them, Jane Austen's *Pride and Prejudice* and *Emma,* Mary Shelley's *Frankenstein,* Emily Brontë's *Wuthering Heights,* Edith Wharton's *The House of Mirth,* and Jean Rhys's *Wide Sargasso Sea*—to be packaged with the two-volume Third Edition, or either individual volume, for a low supplemental cost. Students thus can receive an authoritative, carefully annotated text accompanied by rich contextual and critical materials.

Second, in response to the call from adopters for more critical and theoretical texts, we have collaboratively edited a new companion reader, *Feminist Literary Theory and Criticism: A Norton Reader.* The *Reader,* the first anthology to trace the historical evolution of feminist writing about literature in English from the Middle Ages to the twenty-first century, includes more than one hundred writers in its three-part structure: Part 1, "Women Writers: On Writing," spans six centuries of historical documents (by 45 writers) about female literary creativity—from Christine de Pizan to Eavan Boland. Part 2, "Theory: On Gender and Culture," which focuses on the theoretical debates in the half century since Simone de Beauvoir articulated the idea of "alterity" in 1949, includes selections by 42 scholars and theorists. Part 3, "Practice: Representative Readings and Analyses," gathers contemporary critical interpretations of key literary works in six mini-casebooks: On Medieval Women, On Aphra Behn's *Oroonoko,* On Charlotte Brontë's *Jane Eyre,* On Emily Dickinson, On the Harlem Renaissance, and On Sylvia Plath. The casebooks have been tailored to be integrated with central texts and authors in *The Norton Anthology of Literature by Women.* Flexibly designed both to aid instructors who want to integrate more criticism and theory into their literature survey and to serve as a core text for feminist theory and criticism courses, this reader may be packaged with the anthology at a substantial discount to students or ordered on its own.

With their passwords, students also gain access to a site specifically developed to support *The Norton Anthology of Literature by Women*. This website will feature six online topics focusing on cultural and literary contexts of the works in the anthology. Each cluster illuminates a key cultural or literary development by providing a tightly cohesive group of texts and images, annotated web links, and questions for writing and discussion.

Teaching with The Norton Anthology of Literature by Women: *A Guide for Instructors*, Third Edition, by Laura Runge, University of South Florida, has been reconceived and rewritten virtually from beginning to end to reflect the new scholarship and new approaches (cultural studies, colonial/postcolonial, psychoanalytic, etc.) to teaching women's literature; it also offers inventive, carefully developed suggestions for organizing thematic and genre-based courses. This guide is a more practical, easy-to-use reference than past versions; its author/work entries include an introductory teaching hook, a quick read section, teaching suggestions, and discussion questions and projects or research ideas. Teaching links between the anthology and the reader are highlighted throughout. A selected bibliography completes the guide.

We began these prefatory remarks with references to Emily Dickinson's tribute to Elizabeth Barrett Browning and Virginia Woolf's pioneering essay on women and fiction; we want to now acknowledge our deep intellectual indebtedness to the hundreds of teachers worldwide who have for the past several decades responded to Woolf's impassioned explanation that "we think back through our mothers if we are women" by laboring to recover the female literary inheritance that we have attempted to reconstitute here. For these additions, we are indebted not just to new scholarship but also to the suggestions of countless teachers and students who have used the earlier editions of the anthology in many different educational settings. To be more specific about our methods: through questionnaires completed by a broad range of colleagues, we ascertained which texts, because infrequently assigned, could be replaced by others in greater demand.

We have included a separate list of acknowledgments in which we thank the many teachers, critics, and scholars who prepared detailed critiques of our material, offered special textual suggestions, and took time to respond to the detailed questionnaire. Their ideas—like our own—seem to us to be a part of a larger and ongoing collective enterprise on the part of countless researchers to whom we must all be profoundly grateful.

We also want to express our gratitude to a number of research and secretarial assistants, institutions, colleagues, friends, and relatives whose aid facilitated our work on this edition. Specifically, we thank Jamie Horrocks, Augustus Rose, and Julie Wise for invaluable research assistance. A number of readers and reviewers helped us with suggestions, including Alison Booth, Mary Favret, Susan Fraiman, Linda Gardiner, Marilyn Hacker, Tricia Lootens, Deidre Lynch, Andrew Miller, Celeste Schenck, Hollis Seamon, and Yung-Sing Wu. At W. W. Norton, Annie Abrams, Eileen Connell, Lory Frenkel, Rivka Genesen, Neil Ryder Hoos, Debra Morton Hoyt, Benjamin Reynolds, Nancy Rodwan, and Catherine Spencer were consistently helpful. As always, moreover, we are grateful to our home institutions—the University of California, Davis, and Indiana University—for financial and secretarial support. In addition, we wish to thank a number of colleagues and friends—Joanna Feit Diehl, Dorothy Gilbert, Kenneth Gros Louis, Kieran Setiya, Mary Jo Weaver—for advice and assistance. Sandra Gilbert wishes to thank the University of California, Davis, Humanities Institute and the Bogliasco Foundation for research and secretarial support; Susan Gubar would like to thank the Indiana University Distinguished Professors' fund for similar support, as well as Dean Kumble Subbaswamy and the College Arts and Humanities Institute. And we are as usual grateful to members of our innermost circles: our children—Roger, Katherine, and Susanna Gilbert and Marah and Simone Gubar—and our life companions—David Gale and Donald Gray.

Finally, though, our greatest debt is to several co-workers who in some sense helped author this book. Alice Falk's meticulous and scrupulous scholarship facilitated wise and detailed revisions of our annotations. Julia Reidhead's unflagging enthusiasm, support, and guidance buoyed us up at even our rockiest moments and made much of our work a great pleasure. The perpetually sagacious example of M. H. Abrams, Class of 1916 Professor Emeritus at Cornell and adviser on Norton anthologies, offered us a continual model of pedagogical and critical good sense. And perhaps most important of all, the late John Benedict, our first editor at Norton, continued to function (the way he always did) as a kind of muse whose spirit hovered over and sustained this project. His editorial expertise and personal brilliance inspired whatever was best in the First Edition, and it is to his memory that we rededicate our work on this Third Edition of *The Norton Anthology of Literature by Women*.

Acknowledgments

Among our many advisers and friends, the following were of special help in providing critiques of particular periods: Carolyn Dinshaw (New York University); Tricia Lootens (University of Georgia); Anne Mellor (University of California, Los Angeles); and Ruth Perry (MIT). We would also like to express appreciation to the teachers who provided reviews: Antoinette M. Aleccia (Montgomery College); Sharon Anthony (Montgomery College); Phyllis Ballata (Century College); Paula Barbour (Florida State University); Maria Belen Bistue (University of California, Davis); Perle Besserman (Illinois State University); Elyse M. Blankley (California State University–Long Beach); Suzanne Bost (Southern Methodist University); Paula R. Buck (Florida Southern College); Anne Charles (University of New Orleans); Nora Chase (Kingsboro Community College); Linda Daigle (Houston Community College); Michelle M. Davidson (Ivy Tech Community College–Columbus); Ron Di Constanzo (Long Beach City College); Angela Di Pace (Sacred Heart University); Regina Dilgen (Palm Beach Community College–Lake Worth); Cynthia Doherty (Harrisburg Area Community College); Helen Dunn (Sonoma State University); Nancy Fitzgerald (College of St. Scholastica); Katie Freeman (West Virginia Northern Community College); Cynthia Huff (University of Oklahoma); Norma Gillespie (Seminole State College); Christine Goold (Fort Lewis College); Pam Hardman (Western Washington University); Kathy Hickok (Iowa State University); Ondee Lerman Israel (Pace University); Nancy E. Johnson (SUNY—New Paltz); Dana Kinnison (University of Missouri); Diane Krantz (Weber State University); Ausra Kubilius (Southern New Hampshire University); Winifred Moranville (Simpson College); Rachel Nash (University of the Cariboo, British Columbia); Ann Norton (Saint Anselm College); Ellen Peel (San Francisco State University); Cathy Peppers (Idaho State University); Cathy Preston (University of Colorado); Jeanne M. Purdy (University of Minnesota–Morris); Lisa Robson (Brandon University, Manitoba); Deborah Sarbin (Clarion University); Bonnie Kime Scott (San Diego State University); Kathryn L. Seidel (University of Central Florida); Judy Slagle (East Tennessee State University); Marie Trevino (Michigan State University); Linda Wagner-Martin (University of North Carolina, Chapel Hill); Mary Katherine Wainwright (Manatee Community College); Kari Winter (University of Vermont); Teresa Winterhalter (Armstrong Atlantic State University); Yung-Hsing Wu (University of Louisiana at Lafayette); Sharon Yang (Worcester State College); and Bonnie Zimmerman (San Diego State University).

The Norton Anthology
of Literature by Women

THIRD EDITION
VOLUME 2
Early Twentieth Century through
Contemporary

Early-Twentieth-Century Literature

MEN AND WOMEN IN A NEW AGE

In *Everybody's Autobiography* (1937), the experimental writer Gertrude Stein recalled a conversation with the mystery novelist Dashiell Hammett. "In the nineteenth century men were confident, the women were not," she reports Hammett as having observed, "but in the twentieth century the men have no confidence." Hammett's comment summarizes a major change in social dynamics that characterized the life and literature of almost all English-speaking countries in the era (roughly between 1914 and 1939) that is usually called the "modernist" period. More generally, however, many literary men experienced the first half of this century as what W. H. Auden was to call an "age of anxiety," while many of their female counterparts experienced the time—to be sure, with important qualifications—as an era of exuberance. One reason for such different reactions was the increase in female power that marked the new culture of the twentieth century. In the second two decades of the century, women on both sides of the Atlantic not only achieved the vote after a seventy-five-year struggle but also entered all the professions in ever greater numbers. "The modern young man," wrote the British novelist D. H. Lawrence in his essay "Matriarchy" (1929), talks "rather feebly about man being master again. He knows perfectly well that he will never be master again."

Between the years 1914 and 1939 there were of course many reasons for both sexes to feel anxious about the rapidly changing world in which they lived. The phenomenon that has been called the "shock of the new" was profoundly disturbing to people who had been born and brought up in what had come to seem comparatively serene late Victorian times, for "the new" in this period included a scientific revolution that largely transformed the physical and social landscapes of England and America while producing a technology of destruction that shaped World War I, the deadliest war yet fought in Europe. In addition, because "the new" in these years also implied a complete disruption of the few traditional ideas about God and human nature that had emerged intact from the onslaughts of nineteenth-century skepticism, it was responsible for a widespread sense of intellectual doubt and social alienation. Finally, because the scientific revolution that shocked early-twentieth-century culture also meant the development of mass communication systems on a startling scale, it greatly intensified the rift between so-called high culture and so-called low (or "mass") culture, leading to what seemed an unbridgeable gulf between serious artists and popular, commercial artists. Inevitably, a number of literary figures responded with trepidation

to these changes. But because women had never perceived themselves as
the heirs of a stable and orderly society, it was male thinkers in particular
who felt themselves to be living in unprecedentedly threatening times.
Assaulted in public by the machinery of a new age and haunted in private
by women who would no longer stay in their traditional places, a number of
men saw themselves as increasingly marginal and powerless.

BEGINNINGS OF THE "MODERN" WORLD

The Georgian Afternoon

Despite the drastic cultural transformations that would soon become obvious
to many observers, the years that were to be known as the modernist period
began, at least in England, with what is often described as a long "Georgian"
afternoon; the accession to the throne in 1910 of King George V seemed to
usher in a kind of extension of the Victorian era in which large social changes
were disguised by smug and apparently secure continuations of traditional
modes and manners. Thus, while experimental painters, poets, and musicians wrote manifestos, mounted art shows, and performed concerts that
clamored for attention in Paris, London, and New York, much business—in
the provinces and even, to some extent, in the cities—went on as usual.

Between 1910 and 1918, for instance, traditional class stratifications persisted. The American novelists Edith Wharton and Henry James as well as
the more radical English writer Virginia Woolf recorded the doings of an
upper-class pre–World War I society that continued to be concerned with
conventional tea parties and elegant libraries, while the American novelist
Willa Cather, the British novelists Arnold Bennett and D. H. Lawrence, and
the Irish novelists George Moore and James Joyce portrayed bourgeois and
working-class figures whose motivations were no less monetary than were
those of characters in middle- and late-nineteenth-century works by Charles
Dickens, Thomas Hardy, and Theodore Dreiser. At the same time, literary
tastes appeared to change rather little: in England, for example, the editor
Edward Marsh's *Georgian Anthologies* (1912, 1915, 1917, 1919, 1922)
offered the public verses by such poets as John Masefield and Walter de la
Mare that generally celebrated bucolic landscapes or recounted romantic
stories.

The New Technology

Nevertheless, even while the long Georgian afternoon suggested that old
customs could still be preserved, the swift growth of a new technology, a
long-term consequence of the Industrial Revolution, was eroding traditional
ways of life. The first decade of the century saw the invention of radio, the
introduction of nickelodeons (theaters for the showing of moving pictures),
the development of a viable airplane, and the production (by Henry Ford) of
an inexpensive automobile that a few years later would be manufactured on
what was for the first time called an "assembly line." Along with such late-nineteenth-century innovations as the phonograph, the typewriter, the telephone, and the telegraph, these new devices were to have far-reaching effects
on travel, business, and communication.

To begin with, a number of artists on both sides of the Atlantic hailed the industrial inventiveness of the age in much the way that their nineteenth-century predecessors had welcomed the powers promised by, in William Wordsworth's phrase, "steamboats, viaducts, and railways." It is perhaps not surprising that the best-selling British writer Rudyard Kipling, often considered an apologist for the ambitions of the empire, should have exulted in the glamour of modern railroads ("Romance brings up the 9:15"), nor is it surprising that a wealthy novelist like Edith Wharton was the devoted owner of an expensive motorcar, but the early reactions to technology from a range of passionately revolutionary artists are somewhat more startling. In the June 1914 issue of the short-lived little magazine *Blast*, for instance, such rebels against the old order as the British painter-writer Wyndham Lewis and the American poet Ezra Pound signed a series of manifestos declaring that "machinery is the greatest Earth-medium." Within a decade or two, their enthusiasm would be seconded by two important American poets: in "Overture to a Dance of Locomotives" (1921), William Carlos Williams portrayed the exuberance of train travel from a perspective remarkably similar to Kipling's, and in *The Bridge* (1930), Hart Crane characterized the engineering marvel of the Brooklyn Bridge as a "harp and altar" of the future. As late as 1945, moreover, the iconoclastic Gertrude Stein proclaimed that "America began to live in the twentieth century in the [eighteen] eighties with the Ford car."

While many writers were eulogizing modern technology as the harbinger of a transfigured world, others were beginning to examine its darker implications; indeed, some of those who had originally been most optimistic were eventually to express skepticism. If such mass media as radio and film turned people into mere disembodied voices or images, these thinkers argued, mass manufacturing methods like the assembly line made individuals into interchangeable parts or robots. In addition, they claimed that the capitalist system which had fostered such developments severely widened the gap between what the Victorian writer Thomas Carlyle had called the "captains of industry" and the working classes whose labor served their needs. Thus, from the teens of the century on, critiques of the effects of technology and the intentions of industrial capitalism multiplied, focusing both on the psychology of the economic "masters" whose business triumphs were remaking society and the sociology of the alienated masses whose lives were being remade. In *The Financier* (1912), *The Titan* (1914), and *The Stoic* (not published until 1947), for instance, three novels that he called his *Trilogy of Desire*, Theodore Dreiser examined the power of what one critic has called "the businessman as buccaneer." At around the same time, the English novelist-poet D. H. Lawrence was producing a series of books that studied not only the lives of coal miners and factory workers in the industrial Midlands but also the minds of the magnates who shaped their fates. In particular, *Sons and Lovers* (1912), *Women in Love* (1921), and *Lady Chatterley's Lover* (1928) analyzed the deadened and deadening consciousness of the modern "captain of industry" while vividly dramatizing the "soulless ugliness of the coal-and-iron Midlands[,] . . . the cruelty of iron and the smoke of coal, and the endless, endless greed that drove it all."

Even more extravagant than the hostile critiques of novelists were the attacks of poets on the alienated world produced by modern technology. Though T. S. Eliot's despairing depiction of contemporary culture is not confined simply to a portrayal of the effects of mercantile industrialism, his *The Waste Land* (1922) includes perhaps the most famous scenes of alienation that were created in this period, notably its almost hallucinatory vision of a zombielike mass of urban pedestrians ("A crowd flowed over London Bridge, so many, / I had not thought death had undone so many"). Similarly, Eliot's friend and mentor Ezra Pound, who had originally joined Wyndham Lewis in welcoming the new age of the machine, soon saw the negative implications of an era of mechanization. "The 'age demanded' chiefly a mould in plaster," he noted in his sardonic "Hugh Selwyn Mauberley" (1920), "Made with no loss of time, / A prose kinema [cinema], not, not assuredly, alabaster / Or the 'sculpture' of rhyme." Later, in his radically experimental long poem called the *Cantos* (published serially between 1925 and 1959), Pound would go on to attack the foundations of the economic system, which he identified as "Usura" (usury), that had fostered such vulgarity.

Verse attacks like those by Eliot and Pound were both anticipated and echoed by a number of other poets. As if predicting Eliot's *Waste Land* vision of a deadened London crowd, the American poet Carl Sandburg wrote in a 1916 poem called "Halsted Street Car" of the blank faces—"Tired of wishes, / Empty of dreams"—of working-class passengers on a Chicago trolley; in a 1920 verse titled "Manual System," he described the workday of a telephone operator: "Mary has a thingamajig clamped on her ears / And sits all day taking plugs out and sticking plugs in," while in his brief "Modern Prayer," D. H. Lawrence summarized the culture of greedy materialism that had fostered such alienation:

> Almighty Mammon, make me rich!
> Make me rich quickly, with never a hitch
> in my fine prosperity! Kick those in the ditch
> who hinder me, Mammon, great son of a bitch!

Finally, beginning in 1930, such English poets as W. H. Auden, Stephen Spender, and Louis MacNeice produced a rich range of work based on the apocalyptic assumption that modern technology might in effect self-destruct. Though Auden, for instance, had begged in one early poem for "new styles of architecture, a change of heart," he and his contemporaries soon saw the "new" technology as wholly pernicious.

What particularly fostered the disillusionment of the Auden group was the economic depression that had struck both England and America at around the time these writers were beginning their literary careers, a transatlantic calamity that had been precipitated, especially in America, by the dangerous practice of buying stocks "on margin" (for a fraction of their real price)—a practice that resulted in the great New York stock market crash of 1929. The effects of the crash included breadlines, soup kitchens, and "tent cities" of the unemployed; and though both the British and American governments struggled to counteract the disaster by instituting such social welfare programs as Franklin Delano Roosevelt's 1933 New Deal, the Great Depression persisted in both countries throughout the 1930s. Its dismal consequences are reflected in the works of Auden, Spender, and others, who vividly depicted a ruined and ruinous industrial landscape—in Auden's words, "Smokeless chimneys, damaged bridges, rotting wharves and choked canals." At the same time, adopting a Marxist belief in the inevitability of a revolution that would replace industrial capitalism with a new order, these writers predicted the end of the "businessman as buccaneer." Auden's warning to captains of industry in "Consider This and in Our Time" (1930) was marked by a grimly prophetic exhilaration that permeated the verse of many of his contemporaries both in England and America:

> Financier, leaving your little room
> Where the money is made but not spent,
> You'll need your typist and your boy no more;
> The game is up for you and for the others.

World War I

In a sense, a technological apocalypse—a seeming end to the known world—had already occurred in Europe, for World War I, defined by leaders as "the war to end all wars" but experienced by participants as an unprecedented triumph of death-dealing military technology, functioned in these years as an extraordinary historical turning point. The critic Paul Fussell has shown that many of the young men who went to the front during World War I were imbued with almost chivalric ideals of heroism, ideals that were rapidly destroyed by the horror of the conflict, only to be replaced by the kind of pervasive irony that Ezra Pound expressed in his "Hugh Selwyn Mauberley" (1920):

> There died a myriad,
> And of the best, among them,
> For an old bitch gone in the teeth,
> For a botched civilization.

But even in the minds of those who might have thought culture still deserved defense, the new technological realities of trenches and poison gas, land mines and machine guns subverted idealism: expressly invented for this "Great War," these devices of destruction led to a higher military fatality rate than has ever been seen in any war before or since.

As the historian Eric Leed has observed, the practice of digging trenches to hold established positions left foot soldiers with the feeling that they were living in a realm of pollution. Buried beneath the soil, assaulted by the continuous rumble of big guns, threatened by mines from below and poison gas from above, these young men experienced themselves as helpless rather than heroic, and they saw the apparently empty landscape of the battlefield—a landscape that was really, as Leed puts it, "saturated" with enemies who were enclosed in trenches of their own—as nightmarishly threatening, even uncanny. Moreover, as the war veteran and poet Robert Graves reported, "the average life expectancy of an infantry subaltern [lieutenant] on the western front was, at some stages of the war, only about three months," the despairing anxiety of such combatants was more than justified.

Many responded with a form of nervous breakdown called "shell shock." Others became permanently embittered and alienated. Some blamed civilians, often—like the English poet Siegfried Sassoon in his "Glory of Women" (1918)—reproaching women because "you love us when we're heroes, home on leave. . . . You worship decorations. . . . You make us shells." Some—like the English poet Wilfred Owen (who was killed at the front in 1918)—held not only women civilians but "fathers" responsible for the conflict, arguing, as Owen did in his "Dulce et Decorum Est" (1920), that "if . . . you [could see] the white eyes writhing in [the] face" of a victim of poison gas, "you would not tell with such high zest / To children ardent for some desperate glory, / The old Lie: Dulce et decorum est / Pro patria mori" (It is sweet and proper to die for one's country).

As the comments of noncombatants like Pound reveal, even civilians were profoundly affected by the enormity of the catastrophe. In England, figures as diverse as the poet-suffragist Alice Meynell and the colonial apologist Rudyard Kipling shared Owen's belief that "fathers"—meaning an avaricious male ruling class—were responsible for the disaster. In "A Father of Women" (1917), Meynell reproached the "million living fathers of the war," while in "Common Form," one of his *Epitaphs of the War* (1914–18), Kipling—whose son was killed in an early battle—imagined a dead soldier saying, "If any question why we died, / Tell them, because our fathers lied." Though the United States did not enter the war until 1917—and only then after considerable national debate about the issue—a number of American writers expressed equal revulsion toward the conflict, with pacifists such as the activist-feminist writers Charlotte Perkins Gilman and Crystal Eastman holding a patriarchal system accountable for its horrors in much the way that Meynell had.

Much of the most intensely disillusioned World War I literature, however, was written not during but after the war. Ernest Hemingway's *The Sun Also Rises* (1926), a portrait of an artist made impotent by a war wound, as well as Lawrence's *Lady Chatterley's Lover* and Virginia Woolf's *Mrs. Dalloway* (1925), a profile of a society lady shadowed by a portrait of a young man made mad by the war, suggest the many ways in which this apocalyptic European crisis had deadened or sickened both participants and onlookers. For many thinkers, moreover, such alienation triggered a deeper sense of cultural fragmentation. As the Viennese psychoanalyst Sigmund Freud (1856–1939) wrote in 1915, before the war, "he who was not by stress of circumstances confined to one spot, could also confer upon himself . . . a new, a wider fatherland, wherein he moved unhindered and unsuspected," but after the war "that civilized cosmopolitan [stood] helpless in a world grown strange to him—his all-embracing patrimony disintegrated, the common estates in it laid waste, the fellow-citizens embroiled and debased!"

Intellectual Anxiety

Interestingly, Freud's own theories about the human psyche, as well as the ideas of such fellow analysts as Alfred Adler (1870–1937) and the speculations of such contemporary scientists as Albert Einstein (1879–1955), had dramatically contributed to the alienation that Freud thought had been fostered by the war. Though Freud's and Einstein's radically disruptive scientific theories were formulated early in the twentieth century, they had their most powerful impact between 1910 and 1940, and we are still feeling their effects today. Specifically, Freud's concept of psychoanalysis, first definitively set out in *The Interpretation of Dreams* (1900) and then elaborated in a series of studies published through the 1930s, implied that what the human mind experiences as "knowable" is not necessarily all that there is of the mind: the self, argued Freud, is constituted not only by the conscious personality (the "ego") but also by the warring forces of the desirous unconscious (the "id") and the moralistic, socially learned "upper"-conscious (the "superego").

More problematic still, this complex and layered self is, in Freud's view, constructed out of an interaction between the voracious, primitive infant and an adult world represented by parents whose repressive or seductive actions inexorably shape the child's development. Somewhat in the way that Charles Darwin's account of human evolution from animal forms (in *The Origin of Species*, 1859) had seemed to destroy the concept of human singularity, Freud's vision of an essentially amoral secret self, together with his insistence that this self was helplessly conditioned by external influences, seemed to subvert traditional beliefs in free will and morality; and this subversion was intensified by the claims of such other thinkers as Freud's former colleague Alfred Adler, who argued that the individual was driven by a "will to power" and—failing to achieve sufficient parental support—subject to disorders like the "inferiority complex."

The new physics outlined by Albert Einstein and other scientists mirrored these disturbing concepts of the "inner" world with equally troublesome visions of the "outer" world, while new philosophical ideas further fractured traditional notions of time, reality, experience, and language. Einstein's special theory of relativity (1905), followed by his general theory of relativity (1916), invited doubts about even such apparently absolute categories as space and time, implying that the physical universe was far more complex than earlier Newtonian physics had asserted it was. And diverse as they were, the questionings of received reality produced by the speculations of Henri Bergson (1859–1941), Edmund Husserl (1859–1938), and Martin Heidegger (1889–1976); the revisions of logic and mathematics undertaken by Alfred North Whitehead (1861–1947); and the linguistic analyses of Ludwig Wittgenstein (1889–1951) also tended to undercut the confidence of intellectuals in both the "knowability" of a material world and the plausibility of a moral order.

To complicate matters further, new research by ethnologists and archaeologists led to a cultural relativism that fostered skepticism about the nature of human society itself. Increasingly, investigators of so-called primitive societies and ancient artifacts had come to the conclusion that neither the origin nor the structure of society was necessarily patriarchal and that indeed there was no one fixed social system that governed the behavior of human groups around the world. By the turn of the century, the work of such figures as the British anthropologist Sir James Frazer (1854–1941) and his classicist colleague Jane Ellen Harrison (1850–1928) suggested—to the distress of many religious readers—that Western Christianity was as deeply shaped by the codes of archaic fertility cults as was any supposedly primitive theology. In particular, Frazer's *The Golden Bough* (1890) implied a connection between the figure of the Christian Messiah and the "dying and rising god" of such cults. Extensively revised between 1911 and 1915 and issued in an abridged edition in 1922, the book had an enormous impact on a number of modernist writers. Similarly influential were the speculations of Freud's former associate the psychoanalyst Carl Jung (1875–1961), who postulated that human thought was shaped by primitive "archetypal" images drawn from a "collective unconscious," and the work of Frazer's disciple Jessie Weston (1850–1928), whose *From Ritual to Romance* (1920)—a study of the relationship between fertility religions and the medieval cult of the Holy Grail—was adopted by T. S. Eliot to help provide a narrative framework for *The Waste Land*. Indeed, from Eliot's *The Waste Land* and Joyce's *Ulysses* (1922) to Hemingway's *The Sun Also Rises* and H. D.'s *Trilogy* (1944–46), many twentieth-century works were inspired by anthropological and mythographical research.

At the same time, a number of literary figures welcomed the annihilation of traditional faith that was brought about by all these scientific and philosophical movements. In his meditative "Sunday Morning" (1923), the American poet Wallace Stevens celebrated "the heavenly fellowship / Of men that perish and of summer morn," rejecting the old pieties of paradise, while in England, D. H. Lawrence vigorously redefined God as no more than "the great urge that has not yet found a body," and in Ireland, the poet William Butler Yeats concluded that "we are blest by everything, / Everything we look upon is blest." The case of Yeats is a telling one, however, for before affirming the blessedness of material reality, this poet had struggled for years to define a redemptive spiritual reality; repudiating traditional Christian dogma, he studied the occult, engaged in psychic research, and sought to strengthen his art with images of transcendence.

In this last respect, Yeats's early career was surprisingly similar to the later careers of such disparate poets as T. S. Eliot and W. H. Auden, both of whom—after periods of skepticism—found in orthodox Christianity a refuge from what seemed to them a culture of disbelief. Following the publication of *The Waste Land*, that classic of modernist despair, Eliot became increasingly religious, as if proposing that the best way to allay the intellectual anxieties of the twentieth century was to revive the verities of former ages. At the same time, in keeping with his conscious orthodoxy, his politics and his social views became notably conservative, even reactionary, charting a course that would be followed in various ways by such American writers as the poet-critics John Crowe Ransom and Allen Tate. Manifesting itself during the 1930s, the conservatism of these figures represented one major response to skepticism about reality and signaled a deep political split between two sets of twentieth-century writers, a split that would become more significant as the 1920s darkened into the 1930s, and as the intellectual anxiety fueled by contemporary science and philosophy was coupled with a more specifically political anxiety fostered by a new series of critical international developments.

International Anxiety

World War I was not the only disturbing international event that marked the years between 1914 and 1939, though it was the most striking. Specifically, this period saw the continuing decline of the British Empire; the intensification of isolationism in the United States; the growth of such revolutionary movements as anarchism, socialism, and communism; the worldwide trauma caused by the Russian Revolution of 1917; and the rise of international fascism, first manifested by Benito Mussolini's takeover of Italy (1922) and Adolf Hitler's accession to dictatorship in Germany (1933), and then most vividly dramatized by the Spanish civil war (1936–39).

In a sense, the slow but inexorable disintegration of the British Empire may have served as a portent of things to come, foreshadowing what the

German historian Oswald Spengler was to call, in a gloomy theoretical work, *The Decline of the West* (1918–22). In the once-crucial British colony of Ireland, the Easter Rising of 1916 was followed first by what came to be called the Irish "troubles"—guerrilla warfare, between British troops known as the Black and Tans and Irish rebels, that lasted from 1918 to 1920—and then by the establishment of the Irish Free State in 1921. At about the same time, agitation for freedom began in India, where Mohandas K. Gandhi returned from years spent in England and South Africa to lead an independence movement in 1915. The nation was not to achieve Gandhi's goal until 1949, but his radicalism—though manifested by "passive resistance" rather than overt violence—was so threatening that he was imprisoned by the British from 1930 to 1931 and again from 1942 to 1944. English anxiety about the disturbing "otherness" now asserting itself in a major colony was brilliantly represented in E. M. Forster's *A Passage to India* (1924). Other subject domains also gradually freed themselves from England in this period: Egypt achieved independence in 1923, while the establishment of the British Commonwealth in 1931 granted equal and independent status to Canada, Australia, and New Zealand.

Perhaps in part because of the monitory example of Britain's decline, the mood in the United States became increasingly conservative and isolationist in these years. The white supremacist Ku Klux Klan gained strength in the South and the Midwest as well as in such northern states as Maine and Oregon. Founded in 1915 (though taking the name of a white supremacist organization of the Reconstruction era), the Klan grew in membership to a peak in the mid-1920s; its power was symbolic of a widespread American racism that also led to the controversial 1931 trial of the so-called Scottsboro boys, nine young black men from Alabama who were accused (unjustly, in the view of many liberals) of having raped two young white women. But even in the supposedly egalitarian North, anxiety about African Americans was intensified when, between 1910 and 1920, the mass migration of southern blacks to New York City made the upper Manhattan neighborhood of Harlem one of the largest black communities in the United States and—because of poor living conditions and the underemployment of many of its citizens—the site of racial unrest throughout the 1920s and 1930s.

Besides feeling assaulted from within, many conservative Americans felt threatened from without. In response to the country's isolationist mood, the government sought to stem the tide of immigration that brought thirty-eight million new citizens to the land between 1820 and 1930. In 1917, a literacy requirement was imposed on all immigrants, and in 1921 and 1924 quota systems were established, severely restricting the number of southern and eastern Europeans and Asians who could enter the country. Still, despite such measures, American anxiety about international involvement was largely responsible for the reluctance of President Woodrow Wilson (who was elected on a platform of neutrality) to enter World War I; it was responsible, too, for a terror of Communist infiltration—a "Red scare"—that dominated the 1920s.

It was not the American 1920s alone that were haunted by the threat of such revolutionary movements as anarchism, socialism, and communism. A number of British socialists became such respected figures as the playwright George Bernard Shaw, the novelist H. G. Wells, the journalist Rebecca

West, and the writer-editor Leonard Woolf (husband of Virginia Woolf), whereas in the United States, anarchism and rebellion were usually associated with immigrants who were perceived as both unsavory and lawless. Such a perception in America fostered the passage of the Volstead Act (1918), which instituted the prohibition of liquor sales in the United States until its repeal in 1933, for the consumption of alcohol was often connected with just the immigrant groups that, during the Prohibition years, bootlegged sales of "bathtub" wine and gin. More specifically, this attitude led to the persecution in America of radical immigrants, including Emma Goldman, Nicola Sacco, and Bartolomeo Vanzetti.

The political agitator and free-love advocate Emma Goldman was a Russian Jew popularly called "Red Emma" and "the Queen of the Anarchists"; her *Living My Life* (1931) recorded a brilliant but controversial career as a rebel against oppression, a career for which she was deported to Russia in 1919. The Italian-born left-wing labor agitators Nicola Sacco and Bartolomeo Vanzetti, who were tried in 1920 and executed in 1927 for an alleged payroll robbery, were the focus of fierce American debate throughout the 1920s because it was believed by radicals and liberals alike that they were innocent, and that their "alien" ethnic origins and their political convictions had led to their deaths.

Even before the deportation of Emma Goldman and the Sacco-Vanzetti case had aroused American political passions, the Russian Revolution of 1917 had brought anxieties about left-wing agitation to a climax. To many thinkers, it appeared that the assassination of the czar and his family represented an apotheosis of the anarchy that had been troubling Europe for more than a century, ever since the French Revolution of 1789, and especially after Karl Marx and Friedrich Engels had produced their *Communist Manifesto* (1848). Certainly for William Butler Yeats the 1917 turmoil in Russia constituted a historical crux, a moment when he felt obliged to concede that what Spengler had called "the decline of the West" was a reality. In his famous poem "The Second Coming" (1920), Yeats suggested that the historical cycle represented by Western Christianity had at last come to an end: "Things fall apart; the centre cannot hold," he wrote. "Mere anarchy is loosed upon the world, / The blood-dimmed tide is loosed"; and later, according to one scholar, he "accepted the poem" not only as a comment on the Russian Revolution but as "an unconscious prophecy of the rise of fascism."

Again, Yeats is emblematic here, for despite his later repudiation of fascism, in 1934 he had composed a sequence of poems intended to be inspiring to the Irish fascist movement. His gesture revealed a political ambivalence that was characteristic of a number of the major modernists. In 1926, for instance, D. H. Lawrence published a novel fantasizing the redemption of Mexico by what he called a "blood-brotherhood" of revolutionaries whose common creed was based on the assumption that natural leaders must always command unquestioning loyalty from their subordinates; and in 1933, just before Hitler was to rise to power in Germany with the plan of finding a "final solution" to the "Jewish problem," T. S. Eliot gave a series of lectures titled *After Strange Gods*, declaring that populations "should be homogeneous" both in race and in religion, and adding that "reasons of race and religion combine to make any large number of free-thinking Jews undesirable," so that "a spirit of excessive tolerance is to be deprecated."

Yet even while these writers were flirting with fascism, another group of modernists were passionately attacking their reactionary orthodoxy. With its radical double assault on patriarchal culture and fascist ideology, *Three Guineas* (1938), by Eliot's friend and sometime publisher Virginia Woolf, was perhaps this period's fiercest critique of the intertwined Nazi notions of leadership and the Fatherland. But during the 1930s the Englishmen W. H. Auden and George Orwell, and the Americans John Dos Passos, John Steinbeck, Langston Hughes, Edna St. Vincent Millay, and Muriel Rukeyser, also wrote novels and poems that mourned the oppression of what the poet Carl Sandburg had once called "the people, yes" while advocating strong rebellion against both fascist and capitalist domination. On both sides of the Atlantic, moreover, many younger artists—including Ernest Hemingway, George Orwell, and Virginia Woolf's nephew Julian Bell—journeyed to Spain to fight on the side of the Loyalists (Republicans) against Franco's Falangists (Fascists). Speaking for all these activists, Auden's "Spain" (1937) concluded: "We are left alone with our day, and the time is short and / History to the defeated / May say Alas but cannot help or pardon."

Artistic Innovation

Many modern artists responded to the era of rapid change in which they found themselves with an urgent sense that new aesthetic modes were needed to mirror the newness of the century, and many gathered into informal communities for which the creation of such modes became a kind of group project. Three intertwined phenomena were associated with the development of these radical intellectual communities. First, because the new availability and speed of steamships, railroads, and motorcars had made long-range travel easy, a number of artists chose to journey abroad: Americans became expatriates in London and Paris; English writers settled in Paris, Mexico, Berlin, and the United States; German, Russian, and Spanish artists traveled to Paris or New York—and wherever they went, these figures tended to establish cosmopolitan groups that shared innovative aesthetic ideas. Second, because so many of these groups were held together by common artistic goals, a number of "little magazines" and anthologies sprang up in these years, disseminating a range of new literary views. Third, the availability of such periodicals fostered the development of the genre of the "manifesto," a statement in which groups of artists outlined their aesthetic principles, usually in revolutionary language.

Charting the movements of twentieth-century writers, painters, and musicians can be dizzying. Ezra Pound, T. S. Eliot, Robert Frost, and H. D. (Hilda Doolittle) established themselves in London during the first two decades of the century, but though Eliot was by and large to remain in England for the rest of his life, Pound was later to travel to Italy (where he would broadcast pro-Fascist propaganda for the Mussolini government), Frost was eventually to return to his New England home, and after the 1920s H. D. was to live intermittently in Switzerland. The same complexities mark the itineraries of many other writers. Though Gertrude Stein—perhaps the century's most famous expatriate—moved to Paris in 1903, where she settled permanently, as did Edith Wharton (who hardly left France after 1914), Ernest Hemingway, Sherwood Anderson, Henry Miller, Djuna Barnes, and Anaïs Nin lived in Paris (where Hemingway and Anderson, in particular, were members of the "Stein circle") during the 1920s and 1930s but then departed for points elsewhere. Similarly, though James Joyce was ultimately to settle in Paris, he did not do so until he had spent some years living in Trieste and Zurich, while W. B. Yeats, though he was deeply identified with the so-called Irish Renaissance, actually spent most of his life journeying between London, Paris, Dublin, and western Ireland. All these travelers produced a literature that is always singularly cosmopolitan even while it expresses a deep sense of uprootedness.

To be sure, little magazines did provide writers with aesthetic "homes" of a sort. *Poetry* and *The Little Review* in Chicago; *Broom* and the *Dial* in New York; *Blast,* the *Egoist,* and the *Criterion* in London; and *transition* in Paris, along with such annual collections as *The Imagist Anthology* (edited first by Ezra Pound, then by Amy Lowell) and *Wheels* (edited by Edith Sitwell), offered experimental writers a rich range of outlets for their talents as well as an array of pages that could be filled with manifestos explaining the new aesthetic assumptions on which these artists operated. The *Blast* manifestos of 1914, quoted earlier, were typical of these productions, but the "Imagist Manifesto" of 1915, written to justify the sharply chiseled free verse that had been composed from 1908 on by Pound and H. D., was more crucially influential, with its admonitions to "employ always the *exact* word," "to create new rhythms—as the expression of new moods," "to present an image," and "to produce poetry that is hard and clear" because "concentration is of the very essence of poetry."

Having slightly less impact on poetry in English, but almost equally representative in their radical repudiation of old forms and their enthusiasm for shockingly new methods, were the "Surrealist Manifesto" (1924) and "Manifesto: The Revolution of the Word," which was published in *transition* in 1929. In the first, the French poet André Breton confided that the "Secrets of the Magical / Surrealist Art"—an art based on dreams and visions, wild associations and images of the world that were "sur" (or super) real—included automatic writing, for the poet must "trust . . . the inexhaustible nature of the murmur." In the second, a series of axioms attacking linguistic and narrative "realism," such diverse figures as Kay Boyle and Hart Crane agreed that "THE LITERARY CREATOR HAS THE RIGHT TO DISINTEGRATE THE PRIMAL MATTER OF WORDS."

A number of individual writers produced critical statements of their own that also functioned as manifestos. Quite early in his career, for instance, Ezra Pound had advised all his contemporaries to "make it new" and paid tribute to Walt Whitman, the nineteenth-century American poet who virtually pioneered free verse, with the words "it was you that broke the new wood." Similarly, in a lecture called "Composition as Explanation" (1926), Gertrude Stein sought both to justify her use of what she called "the continuous present" and to account for what seemed the obscurity of her avantgarde writing with the observation that "the creator of the new composition in the arts is an outlaw until he is a classic." In an article titled "Modern Fiction" (1919), Virginia Woolf insisted that it is "the task of the novelist to convey" a "varying . . . unknown and uncircumscribed spirit" rather than fixed and discrete external realities, while in "The Novel Démeublé" (1936; *démeublé* means "unfurnished") Willa Cather argued for a fiction stripped of the stuffy furniture of circumstantial detail that had cluttered the works of "naturalists" and Victorians alike. Though the statements of other modernists were not quite so hortatory, their critical analyses of literature past and present often acted as equally passionate personal manifestos. Certainly Eliot's "Tradition and the Individual Talent" (1919) or his "The Metaphysical Poets" (1921) can be read in such a way, as can William Carlos Williams's prose collection titled *In the American Grain* (1925) and his essay praising the brilliance with which the American poet Marianne Moore cut "soiled words" out of "greasy" traditional contexts.

The experimental impulses articulated in both group and personal literary manifestos were strengthened by the intense experimentation that was being conducted by artists in other media. Since the late nineteenth century, painters from Auguste Renoir, Mary Cassatt, Marie Laurencin, and Edvard Munch to Georges Bracque and Pablo Picasso had used the techniques of impressionism, expressionism, and cubism to break down traditional modes of representing the material world, substituting for strictly pictorial images more abstract forms that were either determined by unique individual perceptions or governed by larger principles of design. It was during the modernist period, however, that the innovations of these artists began to seem most compelling to their literary contemporaries. Picasso, in particular, became a hero of the avant-garde: Gertrude Stein, one of the first great collectors of modern art and the subject of what was perhaps the Spanish painter's most famous portrait, wrote in an ironic understatement that he was "one whom some were certainly following." Similarly exhilarating to many literary figures were the daring works of such composers as Igor Stravinsky (whose 1913 ballet *Le Sacre du Printemps—The Rite of Spring—* shocked even cosmopolitan Paris with its ferocious primitivism) and Arnold Schoenberg (whose theory of the "twelve-tone row" seemed to many conservatives to threaten to replace traditional melodies with mathematical formulas).

Both the poetry and the fiction produced by writers who participated in this experimental culture were also often unnervingly controversial. To some, the Imagists' liberation of verse from traditional rhyme and rhythm, along with their turn toward such alien forms as the Japanese haiku, seemed to signal the end of poetry; to others, such liberation—particularly as it appeared in the beautifully crafted poems of H. D. and the early Pound— promised the beginning of a style that might, as William Carlos Williams thought, capture the inflections of the voice (and especially the American voice) more accurately than any conventional meter ever had. Similarly, to some the fragmented narratives of such ambitious works as Eliot's *The Waste Land*, Pound's *Cantos*, H. D.'s *Trilogy*, and Williams's *Paterson* (1946–58), as well as the more modest poems of Marianne Moore, together with these artists' use of literary allusions—quotations from writings in a range of languages—appeared willfully obscurantist, while to others the freeing of poetry from a straightforward narrative or argumentative line promised a new richness in the art.

Equally crucial but controversial innovations marked the development of modernist fiction. Most notable perhaps was the development in this period of the so-called stream-of-consciousness novel, a genre that seemed to many readers quite as obscure as the fragmented and allusive poetry of Eliot and Pound but that was destined to become no less influential. First defined by the English writer May Sinclair, who borrowed the phrase "stream of consciousness" from the American philosopher William James (1842–1910), this kind of novel generally focused on the thoughts, responses, and interior emotional experiences of a single central character, although sometimes the writer switched points of view among several key figures. Reflecting the concerns of an era obsessed by the hypotheses of Sigmund Freud and other psychoanalysts, the novelists who worked in this mode strove to represent not just the fluid movements of what might be considered the surface of the mind but also the irrational disruptions of thought that signaled the explosions of unconscious material into the consciousness.

James Joyce's *Ulysses* was unquestionably the most famous work in this mode; indeed, with its searching examinations of the phases of the mind of its protagonist Leopold Bloom and its equally innovative dramatizations of the thoughts of Bloom's counterhero Stephen Daedalus, the book represented a turning point in modern novelistic technique. But this important work's strategies were prepared for not only by Joyce's earlier *A Portrait of the Artist as a Young Man* (1916), a bildungsroman (development novel) that traced Stephen Daedalus's growth to maturity, but also by such equally radical experimentations as Dorothy Richardson's *Pointed Roofs* (1915), the first novel in a series called *Pilgrimage* that explored the mental evolution of its heroine, Miriam Henderson. Comparable stream-of-consciousness techniques were implemented in the work of such artists as May Sinclair, whose *Mary Olivier* (1919) was only one of several fictions by this writer that explored the lights and shadows of a protagonist's mind; Virginia Woolf, whose *Mrs. Dalloway, To the Lighthouse* (1927), and *The Waves* (1933) were particularly notable examples of what Woolf called a "tunneling" technique through which she "excavated" the dreams and desires of her characters; and William Faulkner, whose *The Sound and the Fury* (1929) and *As I Lay Dying* (1930) consisted of brilliantly sewn together "interior monologues."

Modernist fiction writers also undertook other revisionary strategies. What the critic Michael Hoffman has called Gertrude Stein's "abstractionism"— a method of emphasizing language itself rather than its narrative components—led not only to the experiment in "the continuous present" of Stein's own *Three Lives* (1909) but also, because of the force of Stein's personality and example, to the highly stylized and spare repetitions of Ernest Hemingway's *The Sun Also Rises* and *A Farewell to Arms* (1929). In the writings of Joyce (*Dubliners*, 1916), D. H. Lawrence, and Katherine Mansfield ("The Garden Party," 1922), moreover, this period saw what was in effect the invention of the modern short story. Influenced by the work of the Continental artists Guy de Maupassant, Ivan Turgenev, and Anton Chekhov, these writers struggled to create a genre whose plot would reflect not the complexity of an extended chain of causes and effects but the purity of what Woolf called a "timeless moment" or, in Joyce's words, an "epiphany" (a revelation) that functions as the turning point of a life. Finally, theatrical writing and production were marked by comparable innovation. In Ireland, Yeats, along with his patroness Lady Augusta Gregory and several other prominent literary figures, founded Dublin's Abbey Theatre, which presented often sensationally controversial or radically experimental plays by John Millington Synge, Padraic Colum, and Yeats himself. And in the United States a group of experimental dramatists—notably those associated with the Provincetown Players, headquartered both on Cape Cod and in Greenwich Village—sought to import new life into drama. Both Eugene O'Neill and Susan Glaspell produced plays that were striking for such "expressionistic" techniques as the use of archaic masks and symbols (in O'Neill's *The Emperor Jones*, 1922) or for their oblique, even mysterious narrative forms (in Glaspell's *Trifles*, 1916), while in her avant-garde *Machinal* (1928), Sophie Treadwell used pointedly nonrealistic scenes to present a feminist parable about an everywoman character called the Young Woman.

Even while these largely elite artists were formulating manifestos, experimenting with different styles, and pioneering new genres, a number of more popular literary modes and movements were developing. Perhaps the most impressive of these was what came to be known as the Harlem Renaissance, a movement led by the American black writers Jean Toomer, Nella Larsen, Langston Hughes, Countee Cullen, and Zora Neale Hurston, all of whom agreed, despite their major philosophical differences, that it was now essential for African Americans to become conscious of, and write about, their uniquely rich culture. Along with the bohemian quarter of Greenwich Village, Harlem had in any case become a center of New York's aesthetic life in the 1920s, for the increasingly fascinating new musical form of jazz, with its improvisational intensity, had forced many white intellectuals to pay attention to their black contemporaries. Now, therefore, it seemed possible for these writers to explore not only what Cullen called in "Heritage" (1925) the history of Africa's lost "copper sun or scarlet sea"—the history of a forgotten past—but also the distinctive pain of the black mother who represents the oppression of all her people when she tells her child in Hughes's "Mother to Son" (1922) that "life for me ain't been no crystal stair." Although the work of these writers clearly had an impact on that of their white contemporaries, it was to be most dramatically carried on in the writing of their black descendants Imamu Amiri Baraka (LeRoi Jones), Ishmael Reed, Toni Morrison, Paule Marshall, Audre Lorde, and Alice Walker.

Other movements that major modernists sometimes defined as "popular" also had important effects. Joyce, Stein, Woolf, and Lawrence, for instance, may have in various ways scorned such vulgar genres as science fiction and the detective novel along with radio, musical comedy, and film. Yet the rapid development of all those modes inevitably impinged on the careers of these artists as well as on the styles of their descendants. For one thing, the commercial appeal of best-selling thrillers and hit musicals contrasted sharply with the small sales achieved by the works of elite modernists, whose difficult experimental novels and poems often earned little money even when they were greeted with critical praise. Thus the gap between the aesthetically ambitious artist and the hack writer, first perceived in the nineteenth century, widened in these years, intensifying the sense of alienation experienced by many serious novelists and poets.

Modernist writers could not simply ignore the rise of mass media, however. Some actually led double lives, supporting themselves by writing for money while doing their "real" work on the side. Thus William Faulkner, F. Scott Fitzgerald, and Dorothy Parker went to Hollywood to write for the movies. In addition, a number of supposedly hack writers who produced commercial works were ultimately perceived as more serious than they had at first seemed. H. L. Mencken and George Jean Nathan's *Black Mask* magazine developed the talents of the influential artist Dashiell Hammett, whose style and subject matter have been frequently compared with those of Ernest Hemingway. In addition, this period—often referred to as the "golden age" of detective fiction—fostered the work of such mystery writers as Agatha Christie and Dorothy L. Sayers, novelists whose plots and characters left indelible marks on the consciousness of the era. Ultimately, as much as the innovations of the so-called high modernists, the pioneering contributions of these artists may represent the transfigurative quality of an age whose literary no less than its intellectual and social changes were among the most radical experienced in Western history.

MODERNIST IMAGES OF WOMEN

Perhaps because of the sense of cultural cataclysm inspired by the new technology, together with the widespread male anxiety about a female "takeover" that characterized the early years of the twentieth century, the images of women produced by modernist men (and even some produced by their female contemporaries) were often negative. To be sure, a number of writers created attractive female characters (and a number depicted unpleasant male characters), but by and large much literature of the period is notable for its obsession with what women should—and should not—be. In particular, threatened by suffragists, immobilized and unmanned by the war, alienated from both the industrial modes and the commercial media of what seemed an increasingly hectic society, many male novelists and poets tended to blame women for the sense of lost mastery that Lawrence outlined in his essay "Matriarchy." If man would never, in Lawrence's words, "be master again," these writers implied, that was because women had in effect conspired with the new technology to render their male contemporaries socially and even sexually impotent. Thus, where late-nineteenth-century literary men had become obsessed by the figure of the femme fatale, a merciless siren whose wiles were associated with the deadly potential of nature, modernist men were haunted by a new kind of destructive female: the flapper, a figure whose daunting ease with technology and unnerving sexual freedom were manifested by her short skirts and bobbed hair, her feverish dancing and wild drinking, her skillful driving and willful wandering.

Among the most destructive flappers in modernist fiction were Brett Ashley, the antiheroine of Ernest Hemingway's *The Sun Also Rises,* and Daisy Buchanan, the equally problematic heroine of F. Scott Fitzgerald's *The Great Gatsby* (1925). A "damned good-looking" woman whose almost mechanically sleek sexuality is emphasized by the narrator's notation that she "was built with curves like the hull of a racing yacht," Hemingway's Brett rules over a novel whose hero, Jake Barnes, has been rendered literally impotent by a World War I wound and whose other male characters are shown to be in one way or another figuratively impotent. Similarly seductive, Fitzgerald's narcissistic Daisy is a rich and faithless young married woman who incarnates the corrupted morals of the society over which she presides: her voice "was full of money—that was the inexhaustible charm that rose and fell in it, the jingle of it, the cymbals' song of it," and her mechanistic deathliness reaches a climax when she casually slams her lover's expensive automobile into her husband's mistress in a hit-and-run accident that leads not only to the woman's death but later to the deaths of two men.

While few other flappers were quite as metaphorically murderous as Brett Ashley and Daisy Buchanan, many were characterized as either decadent or dangerous. In Richard Aldington's World War I novel *The Death of a Hero* (1929), for instance, the soldier-protagonist's wife and mistress—indifferent to his suffering in the trenches—are described as "terribly at ease upon the Zion of sex, abounding in masochism, Lesbianism, sodomy, etcetera," while in T. S. Eliot's *The Waste Land* the loveless and even anaesthetized sexuality of a "typist home at teatime" is echoed by the robotlike eroticism of a number of other female figures, all of whom the poet sees as having been liberated from traditional moral standards to no good end. Moreover, in countless bitterly misogynistic poems and stories written toward the close of his life, D. H. Lawrence held newly energetic women responsible for most social ills, implying that the apocalypse of modernism had been set in motion by what he variously defined as "energetic women," "dominant women," and "volcanic Venuses," for, as he explained in one verse, "Vengeance is mine, saith the Lord, / but the women are my favorite vessels of wrath."

In picturing women as such "vessels of wrath," Lawrence was moving to a more general concept of the destructiveness implicit in all female ambition. Particularly the newly liberated intellectual or literary woman—the figure whom turn-of-the-century observers had labeled "the New Woman"—was seen by this writer and others as a flawed and potentially evil personage. Gudrun Brangwen, one of the two female protagonists of his *Women in Love*, for example, is no flapper but a serious artist. Yet her commitment to her works is frequently represented as narcissistic, while her consciousness is often characterized as coldly "glittering" and her turbulent love affair with Gerald Crich, one of the book's major male figures, leads directly to his death. In creating such a deadly female intellectual Lawrence was expressing an attitude that would also permeate the writings of W. B. Yeats, Ernest Hemingway, William Faulkner, and Nathanael West.

Imagining ideal womanhood in his "A Prayer for My Daughter" (1919), Yeats transcribed his own ambivalence toward the activism of Maude Gonne, the Irish actress and revolutionary whom he had loved almost all his life, with the imperative "let her [his infant daughter] think opinions are accursed" and then with the comment

> Have I not seen the loveliest woman born
> Out of the mouth of Plenty's horn,
> Because of her opinionated mind
> Barter that horn and every good
> By quiet natures understood
> For an old bellows full of angry wind?

A similar ambivalence toward the female intellect appears in West's *Miss Lonelyhearts* (1933), in which a group of male reporters curse lady writers with three names: "Mary Roberts Wilcox, Ella Wheeler Catheter . . . what they all needed was a good rape." As for suffragists, many were characterized as insane man-haters, and if they were not seen as mad, many—along with female intellectuals and New Women—were often labeled as lesbians. If they actually *were* lesbians, moreover, they were almost always described with horror or nervous scorn: in his *Autobiography* (1952), William Carlos Williams recalls a visit to the salon of the lesbian expatriate Natalie Barney, where women were "sneaking off together into a side room while casting surreptitious glances about them," and was reminded of the behavior of a French deputy who, confronted with the same scene, "undid his pants buttons, took out his tool and, shaking it right and left, yelled out in a rage, 'Have you never seen one of these?'"

Single women who did not define themselves as New Women or intellectuals fared little better at the hands of twentieth-century male artists, for the Victorian myth of the frustrated spinster lingered on, at least through the 1930s. Faulkner's short story "A Rose for Emily" (written in 1931) told the morbid tale of an unmarried southern heiress who keeps the skeleton of her lover in her bed for decades after his death while she herself grows increasingly bloated, as if fattening on his decay. In an equally savage vein, Auden's ballad "Miss Gee" (1937) recounted the case history of a churchgoing spinster who wears "her clothes buttoned up to her neck" and gets cancer from sexual frustration; the medical men who operate on her find the sight of her sick body hilarious:

> They laid her on the table,
> The students began to laugh;
> And Mr. Rose the surgeon
> He cut Miss Gee in half.

Even the images of women who had dutifully married did not necessarily escape such opprobrium, for widows were often depicted as prissy, fussy creatures. Wallace Stevens's "A High-Toned Old Christian Woman" (1923), for instance, complained that the joy generated by the "supreme fiction" of poetry "will make widows wince," but defiantly contended that "fictive things / Wink as they will. Wink most when widows wince."

Nor can the male modernists' portrayals of "properly" heterosexual women—married women, mothers, mistresses, whores—have been very much more inspiring for female readers. Perhaps the most famous female character in early-twentieth-century fiction was Molly Bloom, the heroine of *Ulysses*, an insatiably lusty earth-goddess who never gets out of bed in the course of the novel, and whose last words in the book—"yes I said yes I will Yes"—express her passionate acquiescence in her purely sexual destiny. From Lawrence's desirous Lady Chatterley to the obscene female figures in Samuel Beckett's poem "Whoroscope" (1929) to the prostitutes who haunt Henry Miller's *Tropic of Cancer* (1934) and his *Tropic of Capricorn* (1939), Molly Bloom's descendants proliferated in twentieth-century fiction, frequently described in terms of body parts, with Miller's whores usually appraised as "cunts." Even the former Victorian ideals of mothers and motherhood were now castigated, moreover, for psychoanalysts increasingly tended to blame the sins of the mothers for the neuroses of the sons. By 1942, the American writer Philip Wylie was to inveigh in *Generation of Vipers* against "the destroying mother," arguing that "we must face the dynasty of the dames at once."

Finally, with perhaps a few exceptions—Mrs. Wilcox and Margaret Schlegel in Forster's *Howards End* (1912) come to mind, for instance—it began to seem that the only "good" women in male-authored modern literature were, on the one hand, little girls who had not yet *become* women, and, on the other hand, adults who were willing to sacrifice themselves completely to the imperatives of male desire and need. An example of the first group is "Littless," the prepubescent tomboy heroine of Hemingway's "The Last Good Country" (published in 1972), Nick Adams's younger sister, who is beloved by the hero partly for her impassioned loyalty and partly for her intense innocence. Examples of the second group would include the nameless heroine of Lawrence's "The Woman Who Rode Away" (1923), a white woman who is stripped and sacrificed by American Indian priests so that their people can "regain the mastery that man must hold," and Rose of Sharon, the daughter of the Joads in John Steinbeck's *The Grapes of Wrath* (1939), who offers her milk-filled breast to a starving tramp she has never seen before. What distinguishes both these groups of women is their absence of self-will, their passivity and dutiful instrumentality—qualities that evidently seemed to their creators increasingly lacking in the behavior of real women.

WOMEN'S NEW LIVES

When Virginia Woolf meditated in her essay "Mr. Bennett and Mrs. Brown" (1924) on the change in "human character" that took place "on or about December, 1910," her examples were telling. First, she noted that while the "Victorian cook lived like a leviathan in the lower depths . . . the Georgian cook is a creature of sunshine and fresh air." Then, she observed that contemporary readers of Aeschylus's drama *Agamemnon* will find that their "sympathies are . . . almost entirely with Clytemnestra," a traditionally vilified figure whose vengeful murder of her husband Agamemnon was motivated by rage at his sacrificial slaughter of their daughter Iphigenia. Finally, she argued that readers who study the biographies of the Victorian sage Thomas Carlyle and his wife will dislike "the horrible domestic tradition" that confined "a woman of genius" like Jane Carlyle to the kitchen. For, declared Woolf, "all human relations have shifted"—and especially, as her images of change indicate, the relations between the sexes.

Woolf's analysis was characteristically acute, for the technological and intellectual innovations of the early twentieth century had a striking impact on women of all classes. Though workers on both sides of the Atlantic continued to suffer from economic exploitation—and in particular from the effects of widespread postwar unemployment in the 1920s and of the Great Depression in the 1930s—trade unionism and social welfare programs had begun to insulate them to some extent from the horrors experienced by, for instance, Victorian women in the mines or sweatshops, while universal public education, together with new systems of mass communication, gave them access to cultural institutions from which they had earlier been excluded. Similarly, both middle- and upper-class women, no longer bound by the preceding century's ideology of femininity, entered universities and professions in ever-increasing numbers while exulting in a new intellectual and sexual freedom. Finally, after nearly a century of struggle, women of all classes in both England and America at last gained the right to vote, a right that—at least in law—for the first time acknowledged their full citizenship in the human community.

Just before England entered the Great War in the summer of 1914, suffragist militancy had reached a new intensity. In 1913, British feminists, led by the Pankhursts, engaged in hunger strikes, window smashings, and other radical actions, and five thousand American feminists, led by Alice Paul, marched on Washington. When war broke out, however, British suffrage societies immediately suspended their protests, and the government issued an amnesty to all its hunger-striking female prisoners. Although a splinter group of pacifist women, led by the socialist Sylvia Pankhurst, refused to support "this capitalist war," most suffrage workers abandoned their struggle for the vote in favor of war work on the home front; major figures in the Women's Social and Political Union (WSPU)—most notably Sylvia Pankhurst's mother, Emmeline Pankhurst, and her sister, Christabel Pankhurst—became passionately patriotic, supporting (in the words of the historian Sheila Rowbotham) "military conscription for men, industrial conscription for women." In fact, the suffrage battle did not resume in England until 1916, when the National Union of Women's Suffrage Societies, led by Millicent Garrett Fawcett, pressured Parliament to introduce the new Franchise Bill and managed at last to win the support of prominent politicians. In June 1917, the House of Commons actually passed a women's suffrage bill, and by January 1918, the more conservative House of Lords had also accepted the bill.

Although the United States did not enter the war until 1917, events to some extent paralleled those in Great Britain. To be sure, between 1914 and 1916 the struggle for suffrage did not lapse in America as it had in England; on the contrary, two parties with rather different philosophies pressed the issue vigorously. Led by Carrie Chapman Catt, the National American Woman Suffrage Association (NAWSA) organized state referenda while also proselytizing for an amendment to the Constitution. At the same time, the Congressional Union (later the Woman's Party) under Alice Paul directed its energies entirely toward the passage of a constitutional amendment, and—in doing so—adopted increasingly militant tactics. As it had in England, the tide of political opinion began to turn in America in 1916 and 1917, although, again as in England, the already-divided women's movement split further over the issue of America's entrance into the war: the NAWSA—like the WSPU—patriotically supported war work, and the Woman's Party—like Sylvia Pankhurst's faction—took a pacifist line. Despite these rifts, however, the Nineteenth Amendment, granting women the vote, finally came before the House of Representatives in January 1918 and, with the support of President Woodrow Wilson, passed by a two-thirds majority while cheering throngs in the galleries and corridors of the Capitol sang the hymn "Old Hundred." Although another year and a half of struggle—including elaborate maneuvers in the Senate and arduous state-by-state campaigning—was necessary before the amendment became law, thirty-six states had finally ratified it by August 1920.

Most historians agree that in addition to decades of struggle and hard work, a major factor in achieving the right to vote was women's contribution to the war effort. For, in fact, one of the most striking discontinuities between male and female experience in the modernist period was generated by the Great War. Specifically, as young men were sent off to a front where their chances for survival were often slim and as they became increasingly immured in the muck and blood of "No Man's Land," their mothers, wives, sisters, and daughters on the home front seemed to become ever more powerful. Filling the places soldiers had left behind in mines and munitions factories, farms and railroads, women found themselves confronted for the first time with opportunities to do remunerative and meaningful work in the public sphere. By 1918, a visitor to London observed that "England was a world of women—women in uniforms," and the English poet Nina Macdonald proudly proclaimed that "Girls are doing things / They've never done before.... All the world is topsy-turvy / Since the War began."

That the world *was* in some sense "topsy-turvy" contributed, of course, to the soldiers' sickened sense of anxiety and exclusion from the homes they had left behind. Nevertheless, despite the massive tragedy that the conflict represented for thousands of grieving wives and mothers, such a reversal of the old order contributed enormously to the liberation—and the new exuberance—of women, who felt for the first time not only needed but appreciated. The American writer Harriot Stanton Blatch declared that war "make[s] the blood course through the veins" because, by compelling "women to work," it sends them "over the top[,] ... up the scaling-ladder, and out into 'All Man's Land.'" Similarly, women who were for the first time invited to work as nurses and ambulance drivers at the front itself found their experiences exhilarating as well as painful: the English novelist May Sinclair—an ambulance driver in Belgium—confided that "[you think] 'What a fool I would have been if I hadn't come. I wouldn't have missed this run for the world.'"

By the end of the war, the number of working women had increased by almost 50 percent in England, and seven hundred thousand of the women employed had directly replaced men in the workforce; similar statistics obtained in the United States. In both countries, moreover, it was not only working-class women who delighted in new usefulness and prosperity; many a middle- or upper-class woman could rejoice with the English doctor Caroline Matthews, who asserted that because her medical services were needed at last, "life was worth living in those days." Prime Minister Asquith, repudiating his former opposition to women's suffrage, admitted that women "have aided in the most effective way in the prosecution of the war," while President Wilson declared that "the services of the women—services rendered in every sphere ... wherever men have worked, and upon the very skirts and edges of the battle itself," should be rewarded with the full rights of citizenship.

There were a number of other ways in which the social disruption fostered by the war seemed also to help facilitate the liberation of women. Although nineteenth-century factory and farm workers had always had more freedom of movement than their upper-class counterparts, "war girls" were among the first "respectable" female groups in Western history who could stroll the public streets unescorted, go to theaters and dances without chaperones, and even travel on their own without incurring the suspicion that they were "fallen" women. In addition, such female workers were the first group to shed traditional women's costumes in significant numbers: though the American suffragist Amelia Bloomer had advocated the divided skirt (known as "the bloomer") in the mid–nineteenth century, that garment had been only a passing fad among radical freethinkers; now, however, impelled by the necessities of hard labor on the land, at the front, or in factories, most women shortened their skirts, and many took to wearing breeches or overalls. Even after the war, the trend they pioneered proved irreversible. As one historian has observed, flappers' clothing—short skirts, brassieres instead of corsets, silk stockings—"weighed one-tenth as much as [women's clothing] in the Victorian period."

Of course some of the most crucial social changes that marked women's lives in this era had already been set in motion by turn-of-the-century feminists; the birth control movement as well as the free love and child care movements, for example, had prewar origins. Nevertheless, all three came to considerable prominence in the years between 1914 and 1921. In 1914, the American nurse and birth control advocate Margaret Sanger founded a journal, *The Woman Rebel*, that was designed to give working women advice on birth control, and in 1916 she established the first birth control clinic in America. Also in 1916, the anarchist and free love theorist Emma Goldman was arrested in New York for lecturing on birth control; in 1918 the British suffragist and scientist Marie Stopes published her *Married Love,* a book offering contraceptive advice, and in 1921 she opened a London birth control clinic. Margaret Sanger summarized the long-standing feminist assumptions of all these women when she declared in *Woman and the New Race* (1920) that "the most far-reaching social development of modern times is the revolt of women against sex servitude."

Besides the advocacy of birth control, other elements of this revolt were agitation for communal child care centers (and in some cases communal domestic centers) and proselytizing for free love or at least for the sort of egalitarian conjugal relationship that came to be called "companionate marriage." In 1914, the British feminist Sylvia Pankhurst opened a small nursery for the children of factory workers which became so successful that it was moved to a pub formerly called the Gunmaker's Arms and now renamed the Mother's Arms. At around the same time, free love advocates in England and the United States, ranging from the activist Emma Goldman and the writer Neith Boyce to the self-proclaimed male feminists Bertrand Russell and Floyd Dell, championed the cause of sexual liberation. At the turn of the century, such sexologists as Edward Carpenter and Havelock Ellis had fought for women's rights, including the right to sexual pleasure. In *Love's Coming-of-Age* (1906) Carpenter celebrated "the sex-passion," noting that someday "the state of enforced celibacy in which vast numbers of women live to-day will be looked upon as a national wrong, almost as grievous as that of prostitution—of which latter evil indeed it is in some degree the counterpart or necessary accompaniment," and elsewhere in the book he preached his influential doctrine of "the intermediate sex," laying the groundwork for what would eventually become movements for the liberation of gay and lesbian desire. Similarly, in *Studies in the Psychology of* Sex (6 volumes, 1897–1910) and *Sexual Inversion* (1896, 1903) Havelock Ellis sought to demystify sexuality, arguing, as Carpenter would, that homosexuality was neither abnormal nor criminal. The work of these theorists clearly influenced the thinking of the British suffragist Dora Russell, wife of the philosopher Bertrand Russell, who declared in her *Hypatia* (1925) that "sex, even without children and without marriage is . . . a thing of dignity, beauty, and delight."

The views of Carpenter, Ellis, Russell, and others were distinctively new both in their departure from the Victorian ideal of what the scholar Nancy

Cott has called female "passionlessness" and in their repudiation of the vision of male sexual brutality implicit in the writings of turn-of-the-century feminists like Charlotte Perkins Gilman. Yet this new view was quickly to become characteristic of an age marked by the publication of some of the earliest marriage manuals to emphasize female pleasure: not only Marie Stopes's *Married Love* but also Theodore Hendrik van de Velde's *Ideal Marriage: Its Physiology and Technique* (1928, trans. 1930) for the first time encouraged women, the way Dora Russell did, to experience sex as a "thing of . . . delight" rather than an act of submission; and as researchers subsequently discovered, countless women did just that. The psychologist Lewis Terman found in 1938 that among 777 middle-class wives, 74 percent of those born between 1890 and 1900 remained virgins until marriage, but only 31.7 percent of those born after 1910 did so.

What contributed to the feelings of female autonomy that fostered such a new emphasis on women's sexual desires may, paradoxically enough, have been the fact that—in Virginia Woolf's phrase—"professions for women" seemed finally to have become seriously possible. The historian William Chafe has noted that in America during the first two decades of the twentieth century "female enrollment increased 1,000 per cent in public colleges and 485 per cent in private schools," and "the number of women employed in the professions increased by over 450,000 and in business by over 100,000." While the figures for England were not quite so dramatic, they were almost equally impressive to contemporary observers. Certainly, among activists, an increasing number seem to have been professional women. Of seventeen female contributors to a symposium titled "These Modern Women" sponsored by *The Nation* in 1927–28, four had Ph.D.s, two were lawyers, one was an artist, one was a cartoonist, one was a politician, and three were journalists, while the editor of *The Nation*, Freda Kirchwey, was herself a successful professional woman. In addition, during these years a number of other professional women rose to national prominence on both sides of the Atlantic, including the anthropologists Margaret Mead, Ruth Benedict, and Zora Neale Hurston; the psychologists Lorine Pruette and Lillian Gilbreth; and the psychoanalysts Karen Horney, Helene Deutsch, and Melanie Klein.

Despite all these advances, however, the 1920s and 1930s saw the inauguration of what the literary critic Elaine Showalter has called "feminism's awkward age." As Chafe has observed, the statistics representing American women's professional advances were misleading, for despite some gains, most career women tended to gravitate toward such traditionally "feminine" occupations as teaching and nursing, while the number of female medical students "actually diminished" between 1902–03 and 1926; in addition, women academics rarely achieved the status of full professor, and "prospects for career women" actually "grew worse rather than better" during the economic difficulties of the 1930s. Similarly, many vocational opportunities for English women closed down in the postwar years, a fact for which some female workers wrongly tended to blame themselves. By 1925, moreover, the feminist movement had significantly disintegrated, for the suffragists' utopian expectation that the achievement of the vote would mark a turning point into a better world was proven wrong when most female voters either failed to register or, if they did vote, cast ballots for the candidates recommended by husbands and fathers. Many sometime suffragists discovered, too, that "anti-feminism" was, in the words of Rebecca West, "strikingly the correct fashion [among] the intellectuals" in this period.

Even the ideal of companionate marriage now appeared to collapse; a number of women realized, with Crystal Eastman, that a woman "wants work of her own" but she also "wants husband, home, and children"—for whose care she was still obliged to bear primary responsibility—so that "how to reconcile these two desires in real life" was a perplexing question. As for the freedom of costume in which "war girls" had delighted, flappers learned that, as Sheila Rowbotham puts it, "going out to work in short skirts and fragile shoes was a problem," and the exhortations of a booming cosmetics industry along with the rise of "beauty parlors" threatened to turn even the most liberated New Woman back into a revised version of the living doll who had been the goal of her Victorian grandmother. Indeed, the masklike faces of such movie stars as Mary Pickford, Jean Harlow, and Clara Bow symbolized a return to the artificial ideal of "femininity" that was rapidly replacing the assertive ideas of feminism.

Nevertheless, the dreams and demands of feminists from Mary Wollstonecraft to Elizabeth Cady Stanton still lived in some quarters. Virginia Woolf's *A Room of One's Own* (1929) was no doubt the most brilliant contemporary analysis of woman's situation, while her *Orlando* (1928)—with its portrait of a four-hundred-year-old heroine who changes her sex from male to female in the late seventeenth century—was probably the wittiest contemporary dramatization of the feminist desire to revise and reconstruct history as what some recent writers have called "herstory." But neither work was anomalous. From Elizabeth Robins's *Ancilla's Share* (1924) and Dora Russell's *Hypatia* (1925) to the feminist essays included in V. F. Calverton and Samuel Schmalhausen's *Woman's Coming of Age* (1931), women continued to express the wish for a transformed society. From Ray Strachey's *The Cause* (1928) to Mary Beard's *On Understanding Women* (1931), I. B. O'Malley's *Women in Subjection* (1933), and Winifred Holtby's *Women and a Changing Civilization* (1935), women historians—both amateurs and professionals—continued to excavate and reconstruct a feminist past. Furthermore, in spite of the setbacks that fragmented the women's movement in the 1920s and 1930s, all these thinkers would have agreed with Woolf that they *were* living astonishingly new lives. "Am I the Christian gentlewoman my mother slaved to make me?" asked the poet Genevieve Taggard, and answered her own question with vehemence: "No indeed. I am a poet, a wine-bibber, a radical; a non-churchgoer who will no longer sing in the choir or lead prayer-meeting with a testimonial." In the same vein, the politician Cornelia Bryce Pinchot declared that "my feminism tells me that woman can bear children, charm her lovers, boss a business, swim the Channel, stand at Armageddon and battle for the Lord—all in the day's work!"

FEMINISM AND MODERNISM: THE NEW WOMAN'S LITERARY HISTORY

The exuberance of feminists such as Woolf and Russell, Taggard and Pinchot suggests that although the women's movement per se had suffered a series of defeats in the 1920s, a significant number of individuals felt themselves to be in possession of a new source of strength, a source that did not entirely depend on the vagaries of contemporary politics. Given the concern with "herstory" that permeated the writings of so many theorists who continued to espouse the feminist cause in the face of increasingly widespread indifference or hostility, what seems to have functioned as a wellspring of energy was a new realization that women did have a history, and particularly a history of cultural achievement. "We think back through our mothers if we are women," wrote Virginia Woolf in *A Room of One's Own,* explaining that a crucial problem of early-nineteenth-century women novelists was "that they had no tradition behind them, or one so short and partial that it was of little help." Elsewhere, she contrasted her own situation with that of her literary ancestresses: "The road [to female literary accomplishment] was cut many years ago . . . [by] many famous women, and many more unknown and forgotten have been before me, making the path smooth, and regulating my steps." In other words, the very existence of the nineteenth century's golden age of women's writing seems to have made a difference in Woolf's self-definition as a woman writer. For if women *had* written, and written successfully, women *could* write, and it was no longer necessary to ask, with the eighteenth-century poet Anne Finch, "How are we fallen, fallen by mistaken rules?" The poet or novelist "in" a woman was no longer what Aphra Behn had called "my masculine part"; rather, "it" was a powerful female self for whom Emily and Charlotte Brontë, Elizabeth Barrett Browning, and Emily Dickinson (as well as Finch and Behn themselves) provided patterns.

Of course, as the critic Harold Bloom has argued, the high achievements of literary precursors can in themselves constitute a source of anxiety for writers: Virginia Woolf and other literary women of her generation may well have wondered if their art could ever be as successful as the art of their great predecessors. In addition, women in Woolf's era had to contend with an intense male reaction not only against the present triumphs of suffragists but also against the past cultural achievements of women, whose history was now for the first time being adequately recounted. On balance, however, the records of women who had made the way "smooth" for Woolf and her peers seem to have been empowering rather than intimidating, and they seem to have persuaded writers of the teens, twenties, and thirties that any talented woman could be, in Taggard's words, "a poet, a wine-bibber, a radical."

Perhaps, too, the distinction between women writers' exuberant recognition that they at last had a strong female past and men writers' anxiety about the turmoil of the present accounts for the subtle but significant ways in which the texts produced by the two sexes often differ in this period. To be sure, as in earlier periods, women worked in most of the same modes and genres as their male contemporaries. The popular novelists Edith Wharton, Willa Cather, Katharine Susannah Prichard, Dorothy Sayers, and Agatha Christie had their counterparts in Sinclair Lewis, F. Scott Fitzgerald, John Galsworthy, Ellery Queen, and Rex Stout. The fictional experiments of Gertrude Stein, Dorothy Richardson, Virginia Woolf, and Djuna Barnes paralleled the fictional experiments of James Joyce, D. H. Lawrence, Ernest Hemingway, and William Faulkner. Women poets who employed traditional forms and meters—Anna Wickham, Edna St. Vincent Millay, Eleanor Wylie, Ruth Pitter, and Anne Spencer—were matched by male poets who employed comparable strategies—John Masefield, Stephen Vincent Benét, Robert Frost, and Countee Cullen. Finally, women innovators in verse—H. D., Marianne Moore, and Edith Sitwell—were influenced by (and influenced) the experiments of male innovators—Ezra Pound, T. S. Eliot, and William Carlos Williams. Nevertheless, both in theme and in technique the works of modernist women in all four categories frequently swerved from the works of modernist men.

Popular women novelists and memoirists, for instance, ranging from the best-selling writers Wharton and Cather to the autobiographer Vera Brittain and the mystery writer Christie, were distinctly concerned to explore the dynamics, and often the triumphs, of female lives. In the modernist period, Wharton, who had criticized the social system that sacrificed her heroine Lily Bart in her early *The House of Mirth* (1905), moved increasingly toward an affirmation of female strength. Ellen Olenska, the heroine of Wharton's Pulitzer Prize–winning *The Age of Innocence* (1920), expatriates herself to Paris (as her author, too, did during these years) and becomes an emblem of independence for the book's self-imprisoned hero, Newland Archer. Although Willa Cather often wrote novels and stories with male protagonists (for instance, "Coming, Aphrodite!" 1920), in *My Ántonia* (1918) she spoke through a male narrator to explore the almost matriarchal energies of Ántonia Shimerda Cusack, a pioneer woman whose genius for survival transforms her into a symbol of natural endurance and fertility. Working in a different mode and with entirely different materials, Vera Brittain developed a surprisingly similar theme: her *Testament of Youth* (1933), a memoir of the World War I years, recounted her discovery of her own capacities, her commitment to service in the world, and her ability to surmount the tragedies of the war. Even the detective story writers Sayers and Christie—women who might seem to have been merely producing entertainment for a popular market—created and celebrated strong women characters: Sayers's Harriet Vane, the heroine of *Gaudy Night* (1935), a mystery set in one of Oxford's women's colleges, is at least as smart and tough as Lord Peter Wimsey, the novel's detective hero; and Christie's Miss Jane Marple, the brilliant detective heroine of a series of novels, is arguably smarter and tougher than Christie's detective hero Hercule Poirot, who is often portrayed as foppish and effete.

Women who composed more consciously experimental books elaborated similar ideas about female power. From Virginia Woolf and Katherine Mansfield to Gertrude Stein and Zora Neale Hurston, such artists excavated the lives and strengths of heroines and their ancestresses. Woolf's Clarissa Dalloway, the protagonist of her *Mrs. Dalloway,* and her Mrs. Ramsay, the mystical and mysterious mother in *To the Lighthouse,* become emblems of authority and endurance as resonant as Ellen Olenska or Ántonia Cusack, while Mansfield's Mrs. Fairfield, the grandmother who presides over a group of fine stories about the author's New Zealand childhood, is equally energetic and inspiring. Similarly, the figure of St. Therese in Stein's libretto for the opera *Four Saints in Three Acts* (1927) is characterized as magically charismatic, and Janie, the heroine of Hurston's *Their Eyes Were Watching God* (1937), is depicted as a triumphant survivor.

To be sure, the fictions and poems authored by women writers in these years were not by any means consistent in representing triumphant heroines. Wharton's Ellen Olenska can find no place for herself in American society, while Woolf's Lily Briscoe fears that she is "no woman" because she repudiates the notion of marriage. Hurston's Janie survives by literally killing Tea Cake, the man she loves, and Nella Larsen's mixed-race Helga Crane is not only torn between two cultures but ultimately trapped in a "quagmire" of domestic servitude. Radclyffe Hall's Miss Ogilvy "finds herself" and her sexuality only to lose her life, while the "daughters of the late Colonel" who are the eponymous protagonists of one of Katherine Mansfield's best-known stories never find any strength at all. Still, even in dramatizing the conflicts—and defeats—endured by these fictional figures, their creators imply empowering alternatives that wouldn't have been available to nineteenth-century heroines. Lily Briscoe might, after all, find a way to marry, mother, *and* paint, just as, for instance, Woolf's sister Vanessa Bell did. Helga Crane's story is painful precisely because she sought to find a way out, as her author did. Miss Ogilvy did find a strong self during the war—and hence she dreamed of forging (as Radclyffe Hall did) relationships in which her erotic desires for other women could flourish.

In literary essays and experiments, the women writers who recorded and explored these complex dilemmas often meditated on the cultural situations that gave rise to such problems as well as on fundamental questions having to do with the nature of writing itself. Indeed, the issues they sometimes self-reflexively explored ranged from the kind of language a woman author inherited to the kinds of aesthetic traditions and conventions that were passed down to her. In *A Room of One's Own,* for example, Woolf explored both the pain and possibility of female tradition while calling for "a woman's sentence" that would be different from the "common sentence[,] . . . [the] man's sentence" that female writers had learned from "Thackeray, . . . Dickens, De Quincey"; for, she observed, "the weight, the pace, the stride of a man's mind are too unlike" those of female minds for women "to lift anything substantial" from male precursors. Whether or not they had read Woolf's proposal, her contemporaries Dorothy Richardson, Gertrude Stein, and Djuna Barnes—writing in very different ways—attempted stylistic innovations that would meet the need she expressed. *Pilgrimage,* Richardson's ambitious sequence of novels (published between 1915 and 1935), was composed in a freely flowing language that transcribed her heroine's stream of consciousness so effectively that Woolf thought this writer *had* "invented the psychological sentence of the feminine gender." In the meantime, Gertrude Stein, experimenting in Paris, sought to subvert the grammatical and narrative conventions of what she called "patriarchal poetry" by putting words together in an entirely unprecedented (and often enigmatic) fashion because, as she argued in "Composition as Explanation," "composition is the difference which makes each and all of them then different from other generations." Less drastically but perhaps just as dramatically, Djuna Barnes, in *Nightwood* (1937) and other works, wrote in an ornate and archaic style, as if by doing so she could create a new ancestral past for herself and other women. All these prose writers were employing the experimental strategies of male modernists to achieve distinctively feminist goals and doing so by remaking language so that it might more accurately reflect female experience, while revising conventions so that female artists might, as Stein put it, "Reject" what was oppressive in tradition, "Rejoice" in what was possible for the future, and "Rejuvenate" what was stale in the present.

Many of the women poets who were their contemporaries used a variety of techniques toward the same ends. The poets Wylie, Millay, Spencer, and Pitter, for instance—none of whom was consciously experimental—nevertheless emphasized women's experiences and female perspectives. In producing ambitious sonnet sequences, Millay and Wylie appropriated and revised a genre traditionally used by male writers to praise a female beloved in order to express the dreams and desires of a female writer about a male beloved. Similarly, Spencer and Pitter used apparently conventional forms to record the unconventional feelings of passionate women or to recount the case histories of obscure but unique heroines. As for the more experimental poets H. D., Marianne Moore, and Edith Sitwell, all quested with the same urgency that marked the work of Woolf and Stein for styles and forms that would free them from the burdensome conventions infecting "patriarchal poetry." Each in her own way sought to annihilate the inherited forms and formulas of tradition so as to release her individual talent—Moore slyly and sardonically, Sitwell with jazzy exuberance, and H. D. through overt recreations of matriarchal images as well as through inventive wordplay.

Finally, then, while many feminist modernists worked to excavate a specifically female past, all modernist women, even those who were not consciously feminists, strove to bring into being what H. D. called in *Trilogy* "the unwritten book of the new." Besides manifesting itself in linguistic experimentation and in the development of uniquely female perspectives, moreover, that "book of the new" now included a number of frank and forceful writings from artists working in the suddenly burgeoning lesbian tradition (including Radclyffe Hall and Amy Lowell); in newly rich African American, ethnic, and working-class traditions (including Nella Larsen, Anzia Yezierska, and Meridel Le Sueur); in a growing postcolonial tradition (including Jean Rhys and Katharine Susannah Prichard); and in a lively tradition of revisionary feminist mythmaking (including Isak Dinesen and Laura Riding Jackson).

As she so often did, Virginia Woolf summarized at least one aspect of the project on which so many of these artists were engaged. Toward the end of *A Room of One's Own*, she described a novel by an imaginary female author named Mary Carmichael, who had "broken the sequence" of traditional fiction because instead of focusing on a conventional romance between hero and heroine, she had written about a friendship between two women: " 'Chloe liked Olivia,' I read," noted Woolf. "And then it struck me how immense a change was there. Chloe liked Olivia perhaps for the first time in literature." Almost as significant, from Woolf's point of view, was the occupation that had fostered the new friendship of these two characters: "They shared a laboratory together." Entering the new world of the professions, as Woolf and many of her contemporaries saw, women were no longer to be defined primarily through their erotic relationships with men. Thus the task of the woman writer was, for the first time, the task of tracing the prospects and problems of an expanding female intellectual community. In 1932, in the first serious study of Virginia Woolf's work, the novelist and essayist Winifred Holtby summarized this point in a statement about the author of *A Room of One's Own* and *Mrs. Dalloway* that has resonant implications for our understanding of most female modernists: "When Virginia Woolf wrote of women," declared Holtby, "she wrote of a generation as adventurous in its exploration of experience as the Elizabethan men had been in their exploration of the globe. The women whom Mrs. Woolf knew were exploring the professional world, the political world, the world of business, discovering that they themselves had legs as well as wombs, brains as well as nerves, reason as well as sensibility; their Americas lay within themselves, and altered the map as profoundly as any added by Cabot or Columbus."

EDITH WHARTON
1862–1937

When Edith Wharton was forty-five, at the height of her considerable personal and literary powers, her longtime mentor and friend, the American novelist Henry James, began to characterize her (as he would for the rest of his life) in a series of striking phrases: as Wharton's biographer Cynthia Griffin Wolff reports, he called her "the whirling princess, the great and glorious pendulum, the gyrator, the devil-dancer, the golden eagle, the Fire Bird, the Shining One, the angel of desolation or of devastation, the historic ravager." Already the author of twelve books—including collections of poems, essays, and short stories as well as successful major novels and novellas such as *The House of Mirth* (1905) and *Madame de Trêymes* (1907)—Wharton, as James understood, was well on her way to becoming a major force in American literature. Within a few decades, in fact, she would be the highest-paid novelist in the country. Yet only a few years earlier, in 1898 (when she was thirty-six), this "whirling princess" had suffered a severe mental breakdown; in the words of her biographer R. W. B. Lewis, she had experienced a "terrible and long drawn-out period . . . of paralyzing melancholy, extreme exhaustion, constant fits of nausea, and no capacity whatever to make choices and decisions."

Born in New York City to a wealthy family, Edith Newbold Jones was raised to be a decorous, even aristocratic, young lady. Long established in high society, her parents summered in the elite resort community of Newport, Rhode Island, and, when Edith was three, took her to live abroad—in Italy, France, and Germany—because their income had been reduced by the economic depression that followed the American Civil War. Educated at home by a governess, the girl made her debut at seventeen. But even while following the course that had been plotted for debutantes by generations of conservative forebears, this novelist-to-be was transforming herself into an artist. At sixteen, she wrote a volume of poetry that her parents arranged to have privately printed, although they generally disapproved of literary activity. Even earlier, she had begun to read voraciously, sensing that her genteel education was inadequate to her intellectual ambitions. If she had not had "the leave to range in my father's library," she later remembered, "my mind would have starved at the age when the mental muscles are most in need of feeding," adding that "I was enthralled by *words*. . . . Wherever I went, they sang to me like the birds in an enchanted forest."

Despite her consciousness of literary "enthrallment," however, the tension between what appeared to be Edith Jones's social role and what she had gradually begun to understand were her creative aspirations continued well into her twenties and thirties. In 1885, at the age of twenty-three, she married Edward Robbins Wharton (known as Teddy), a wealthy Bostonian who was thirteen years older than she, and the couple settled into a life of conventional gentility, dividing their time between New York, Boston, Newport, and Europe, where they moved in politely idle circles. A kind and decent but not especially intellectual man, Teddy Wharton had little sympathy for his wife's literary interests, and it soon became clear that their childless marriage was not happy, though they preserved a facade of compatibility for many years. In fact, what Wharton herself called "the slow, stammering beginnings" of her artistic career did not seriously manifest themselves until she and her husband returned in 1888 from a yacht tour of the Aegean. At this point, perhaps energized by new insights and experiences, the young woman began to write with fresh vigor and even to publish verses and stories in such well-known periodicals as *Scribner's, Harper's,* and the *Century.* A few years later, she collaborated with Ogden Codman Jr., a Boston architect, on *The Decoration of Houses* (1897). But despite her increasing productivity, she was evidently conflicted about yielding herself entirely to her newly awakened ambition, for it was at about this time that she sought and received S. Weir Mitchell's "rest cure" treatment for the "paralyzing melancholy" that suddenly afflicted her.

By 1899, however, when she published two collections of short stories, Wharton had recovered from her nervous illness and definitively committed herself to the world of letters. From then on, she was to publish, on the average, a book a year for the rest of her life. As the critic Louis Auchincloss observes, her "major period" began with her composition of *The House of Mirth,* which appeared in 1905. Tracing the decline of Lily Bart, an elegant young lady in straitened circumstances who cannot bring herself to marry for money and consequently falls into hopeless poverty and alienation, this haunting masterpiece exposes the hypocrisies of the old New York society that its author had been educated to honor and obey. In particular, the novel examines both the problems associated with the artificial construction of woman-as-ornament and the pains inflicted by the secret but often savage dynamics of the marriage market on which such a decorative creature is supposed to be an object of exchange, a realm of social trade in which even the links of Lily's bracelet seem "like manacles chaining her to her fate."

In the novels that followed *The House of Mirth,* Wharton continued to dissect the pretensions and conventions of the civilization that destroyed Lily Bart. *The Reef* (1912), *The Custom of the Country* (1913), and *The Age of Innocence* (1920), for instance, all deal in one way or another with the imprisonment of unorthodox or even rebellious women by the social "manacles chaining" them to their fates. Often considered a female Henry James, Wharton explored in these works the social and psychological nuances that were of such compelling interest to that artful novelist. At the same time, she began to become a kind of modern mythologist. Studying the symbolist fictions of the Polish-born British novelist Joseph Conrad and admiring the innovative music of the Russian composer Igor Stravinsky, she wrote starkly structured, almost legendary tales of people whose fierce but forgotten lives were lived largely outside the urbane society in which she herself traveled with authority. *Ethan Frome* (1911) and *Summer* (1917) are her two most important novels in this mode; but she also composed a number of ghost stories, which reveal an abiding interest in the uncanny, the supernatural, the asocial.

Throughout this period of intense productivity, Wharton's marriage was slowly but inexorably deteriorating. During her middle forties, as the biographers Lewis and Wolff have revealed, she had a passionate affair with Morton Fullerton, a literary man who was also one of Henry James's protégés, an affair that may well have forced her and her husband to confront the inadequacies of their marriage. In 1910, as the relationship worsened, they sold The Mount, a lavish mansion they had built together near Lenox, Massachusetts, and moved to France, where Teddy had a nervous breakdown and was sent to a Swiss sanitorium. Then, in 1913, the couple divorced, and Wharton settled permanently in Europe, eventually purchasing two beautifully maintained French houses, where she was to spend the rest of her life.

Wharton clearly experienced her single state as a liberation. Traveling, entertaining, and writing, she formed friendships with many well-known men of letters, including— along with Henry James—the critic Percy Lubbock and the art historian Bernard Berenson. In addition, she became far more active in public affairs than she had been earlier. Most notably, during World War I, she organized shelters and workrooms for refugees and did much other charitable work. In the view of some critics, however, her writings—with a few exceptions—declined in quality during the 1920s.

Nevertheless, in the last decades of her life Wharton was at the peak of her fame. She was awarded the badge of the French Legion of Honor for her wartime philanthropic activities, won the Pulitzer Prize for *The Age of Innocence* (1920), and in 1923 became the first woman to receive an honorary doctorate from Yale. In 1930 she was elected to the National Institute of Arts and Letters, and in 1934 to the American Academy of Arts and Letters. When she died of a stroke at the age of seventy-five, she had produced a body of work that is impressive in its range and richness. Though they date from comparatively early in her career, "The Angel at the Grave" (1901) and "The Other Two" (1904) reveal in miniature the sardonic skill with which she could analyze the social pressures that had produced even her own complex personality. Each is, in a phrase she herself used to describe a successful short fiction, "a shaft driven straight into the heart of experience." More specifically, each is a dissection of the female condition: "The Angel at the Grave" examines the nature of a woman inheritor's problematic relationship to the male literary tradition she feels she has been appointed to carry on, and "The Other Two"—a tale Lewis has called "very likely the best story Mrs. Wharton ever wrote"—explores the artifice of the supposedly romantic process by which a woman is constructed as a "perfect wife." Scholars have customarily assumed that James applied epithets like "the whirling princess" and "the Fire Bird" to Wharton because of the energy with which she traveled and entertained. Yet, despite their sometimes coolly ironic surfaces, stories like these, along with novels from *The House of Mirth* and *Ethan Frome* to *Summer* and *The Age of Innocence*, have a fiercely subversive force that more than justifies such phrases.

The Angel at the Grave

I

The House stood a few yards back from the elm-shaded village street, in that semi-publicity sometimes cited as a democratic protest against old-world standards of domestic exclusiveness. This candid exposure to the public eye is more probably a result of the gregariousness which, in the New England bosom, oddly coexists with a shrinking from direct social contact; most of the inmates of such houses preferring that furtive intercourse which is the result of observations through shuttered windows and a categorical acquaintance with the neighboring clothes-lines. The House, however, faced its public with a difference. For sixty years it had written itself with a capital letter, had self-consciously squared itself in the eye of an admiring nation. The most searching inroads of village intimacy hardly counted in a household that opened on the universe; and a lady whose door-bell was at any moment liable to be rung by visitors from London or Vienna was not likely to flutter up-stairs when she observed a neighbor "stepping over."

The solitary inmate of the Anson House owed this induration[1] of the social texture to the most conspicuous accident in her annals: the fact that she was the only granddaughter of the great Orestes Anson.[2] She had been born, as it were, into a museum, and cradled in a glass case with a label; the first

---

1. Process of growing hard.
2. Probably intended to evoke Orestes Brownson (1803–1870), a prominent New England clergyman, editor, and writer who was interested in Transcendentalism.

foundations of her consciousness being built on the rock of her grandfather's celebrity. To a little girl who acquires her earliest knowledge of literature through a *Reader* embellished with fragments of her ancestor's prose, that personage necessarily fills an heroic space in the foreground of life. To communicate with one's past through the impressive medium of print, to have, as it were, a footing in every library in the country, and an acknowledged kinship with that world-diffused clan, the descendants of the great, was to be pledged to a standard of manners that amazingly simplified the lesser relations of life. The village street on which Paulina Anson's youth looked out led to all the capitals of Europe; and over the roads of intercommunication unseen caravans bore back to the elm-shaded House the tribute of an admiring world.

Fate seemed to have taken a direct share in fitting Paulina for her part as the custodian of this historic dwelling. It had long been secretly regarded as a "visitation"[3] by the great man's family that he had left no son and that his daughters were not "intellectual." The ladies themselves were the first to lament their deficiency, to own that nature had denied them the gift of making the most of their opportunities. A profound veneration for their parent and an unswerving faith in his doctrines had not amended their congenital incapacity to understand what he had written. Laura, who had her moments of mute rebellion against destiny, had sometimes thought how much easier it would have been if their progenitor had been a poet; for she could recite, with feeling, portions of *The Culprit Fay* and of the poems of Mrs. Hemans;[4] and Phoebe, who was more conspicuous for memory than imagination, kept an album filled with "selections." But the great man was a philosopher; and to both daughters respiration was difficult on the cloudy heights of metaphysic. The situation would have been intolerable but for the fact that, while Phoebe and Laura were still at school, their father's fame had passed from the open ground of conjecture to the chill privacy of certitude. Dr. Anson had in fact achieved one of those anticipated immortalities not uncommon at a time when people were apt to base their literary judgments on their emotions, and when to affect plain food and despise England went a long way toward establishing a man's intellectual pre-eminence. Thus, when the daughters were called on to strike a filial attitude about their parent's pedestal, there was little to do but to pose gracefully and point upward; and there are spines to which the immobility of worship is not a strain. A legend had by this time crystallized about the great Orestes, and it was of more immediate interest to the public to hear what brand of tea he drank, and whether he took off his boots in the hall, than to rouse the drowsy echo of his dialectic. A great man never draws so near his public as when it has become unnecessary to read his books and is still interesting to know what he eats for breakfast.

As recorders of their parent's domestic habits, as pious scavengers of his waste-paper basket, the Misses Anson were unexcelled. They always had an interesting anecdote to impart to the literary pilgrim, and the tact with which, in later years, they intervened between the public and the growing inacces-

---

3. An affliction.
4. Felicia Hemans (1793–1835), popular English poet; see p.000. *The Culprit Fay* (1835), a long poem by the American poet Joseph Stedman Drake.

sibility of its idol, sent away many an enthusiast satisfied to have touched the veil before the sanctuary. Still it was felt, especially by old Mrs. Anson, who survived her husband for some years, that Phoebe and Laura were not worthy of their privileges. There had been a third daughter so unworthy of hers that she had married a distant cousin, who had taken her to live in a new Western community where the *Works of Orestes Anson* had not yet become a part of the civic consciousness; but of this daughter little was said, and she was tacitly understood to be excluded from the family heritage of fame. In time, however, it appeared that the traditional penny with which she had been cut off had been invested to unexpected advantage; and the interest on it, when she died, returned to the Anson House in the shape of a granddaughter who was at once felt to be what Mrs. Anson called a "compensation." It was Mrs. Anson's firm belief that the remotest operations of nature were governed by the centripetal force of her husband's greatness and that Paulina's exceptional intelligence could be explained only on the ground that she was designed to act as the guardian of the family temple.

The House, by the time Paulina came to live in it, had already acquired the publicity of a place of worship; not the perfumed chapel of a romantic idolatry but the cold clean empty meetinghouse of ethical enthusiasms. The ladies lived on its outskirts, as it were, in cells that left the central fane[5] undisturbed. The very position of the furniture had come to have a ritual significance: the sparse ornaments were the offerings of kindred intellects, the steel engravings by Raphael Morghen marked the Via Sacra[6] of a European tour, and the black-walnut desk with its bronze inkstand modelled on the Pantheon was the altar of this bleak temple of thought.

To a child compact of[7] enthusiasms, and accustomed to pasture them on the scanty herbage of a new social soil, the atmosphere of the old house was full of floating nourishment. In the compressed perspective of Paulina's outlook it stood for a monument of ruined civilizations, and its white portico opened on legendary distances. Its very aspect was impressive to eyes that had first surveyed life from the jig-saw "residence" of a raw-edged Western town. The high-ceilinged rooms, with their panelled walls, their polished mahogany, their portraits of triple-stocked[8] ancestors and of ringleted "females" in crayon, furnished the child with the historic scenery against which a young imagination constructs its vision of the past. To other eyes the cold spotless thinly-furnished interior might have suggested the shuttered mind of a maiden-lady who associates fresh air and sunlight with dust and discoloration; but it is the eye which supplies the coloring-matter, and Paulina's brimmed with the richest hues.

Nevertheless, the House did not immediately dominate her. She had her confused out-reachings toward other centers of sensation, her vague intuition of a heliocentric system; but the attraction of habit, the steady pressure of example, gradually fixed her roving allegiance and she bent her neck to the yoke. Vanity had a share in her subjugation; for it had early been discovered that she was the only person in the family who could read her grandfather's works. The fact that she had perused them with delight at an age

---

5. Temple. "Meetinghouse": house of worship.
6. Holy Road (Latin). Morghen (1758–1833), Italian engraver.
7. Composed of.
8. Wearing multiple neck cloths.

when (even presupposing a metaphysical bias) it was impossible for her to understand them, seemed to her aunts and grandmother sure evidence of predestination. Paulina was to be the interpreter of the oracle, and the philosophic fumes so vertiginous to meaner minds would throw her into the needed condition of clairvoyance. Nothing could have been more genuine than the emotion on which this theory was based. Paulina, in fact, delighted in her grandfather's writings. His sonorous periods,[9] his mystic vocabulary, his bold flights into the rarefied air of the abstract, were thrilling to a fancy unhampered by the need of definitions. This purely verbal pleasure was supplemented later by the excitement of gathering up crumbs of meaning from the rhetorical board. What could have been more stimulating than to construct the theory of a girlish world out of the fragments of this Titanic cosmogony? Before Paulina's opinions had reached the stage when ossification sets in their form was fatally predetermined.

The fact that Dr. Anson had died and that his apotheosis had taken place before his young priestess's induction to the temple, made her ministrations easier and more inspiring. There were no little personal traits—such as the great man's manner of helping himself to salt, or the guttural cluck that started the wheels of speech—to distract the eye of young veneration from the central fact of his divinity. A man whom one knows only through a crayon portrait and a dozen yellowing tomes on free-will and intuition is at least secure from the belittling effects of intimacy.

Paulina thus grew up in a world readjusted to the fact of her grandfather's greatness; and as each organism draws from its surroundings the kind of nourishment most needful to its growth, so from this somewhat colorless conception she absorbed warmth, brightness and variety. Paulina was the type of woman who transmutes thought into sensation and nurses a theory in her bosom like a child.

In due course Mrs. Anson "passed away"—no one died in the Anson vocabulary—and Paulina became more than ever the foremost figure of the commemorative group. Laura and Phoebe, content to leave their father's glory in more competent hands, placidly lapsed into needlework and fiction, and their niece stepped into immediate prominence as the chief "authority" on the great man. Historians who were "getting up" the period wrote to consult her and to borrow documents; ladies with inexplicable yearnings begged for an interpretation of phrases which had "influenced" them, but which they had not quite understood; critics applied to her to verify some doubtful citation or to decide some disputed point in chronology; and the great tide of thought and investigation kept up a continuous murmur on the quiet shores of her life.

An explorer of another kind disembarked there one day in the shape of a young man to whom Paulina was primarily a kissable girl, with an afterthought in the shape of a grandfather. From the outset it had been impossible to fix Hewlett Winsloe's attention on Dr. Anson. The young man behaved with the innocent profanity of infants sporting on a tomb. His excuse was that he came from New York, a Cimmerian[1] outskirt which survived in Paulina's geography only because Dr. Anson had gone there once or twice to

---

9. Sentences, especially well-proportioned ones with several clauses.

1. Gloomy; from the Homeric myth of a country of perpetual fog and darkness.

lecture. The curious thing was that she should have thought it worth while to find excuses for young Winsloe. The fact that she did so had not escaped the attention of the village; but people, after a gasp of awe, said it was the most natural thing in the world that a girl like Paulina Anson should think of marrying. It would certainly seem a little odd to see a man in the House, but young Winsloe would of course understand that the Doctor's books were not to be disturbed, and that he must go down to the orchard to smoke—. The village had barely framed this *modus vivendi*[2] when it was convulsed by the announcement that young Winsloe declined to live in the House on any terms. Hang going down to the orchard to smoke! He meant to take his wife to New York. The village drew its breath and watched.

Did Persephone,[3] snatched from the warm fields of Enna, peer half-consentingly down the abyss that opened at her feet? Paulina it must be owned, hung a moment over the black gulf of temptation. She would have found it easy to cope with a deliberate disregard of her grandfather's rights; but young Winsloe's unconsciousness of that shadowy claim was as much a natural function as the falling of leaves on a grave. His love was an embodiment of the perpetual renewal which to some tender spirits seems a crueller process than decay.

On women of Paulina's mould this piety toward implicit demands, toward the ghosts of dead duties walking unappeased among usurping passions, has a stronger hold than any tangible bond. People said that she gave up young Winsloe because her aunts disapproved of her leaving them; but such disapproval as reached her was an emanation from the walls of the House, from the bare desk, the faded portraits, the dozen yellowing tomes that no hand but hers ever lifted from the shelf.

II

After that the House possessed her. As if conscious of its victory, it imposed a conqueror's claims. It had once been suggested that she should write a life of her grandfather, and the task from which she had shrunk as from a too-oppressive privilege now shaped itself into a justification of her course. In a burst of filial pantheism she tried to lose herself in the vast ancestral consciousness. Her one refuge from scepticism was a blind faith in the magnitude and the endurance of the idea to which she had sacrificed her life, and with a passionate instinct of self-preservation she labored to fortify her position.

The preparations for the *Life* led her through byways that the most scrupulous of the previous biographers had left unexplored. She accumulated her material with a blind animal patience unconscious of fortuitous risks. The years stretched before her like some vast blank page spread out to receive the record of her toil; and she had a mystic conviction that she would not die till her work was accomplished.

The aunts, sustained by no such high purpose, withdrew in turn to their respective divisions of the Anson "plot,"[4] and Paulina remained alone with

2. Way of living. (Latin).
3. In Greek mythology, the queen of the underworld, abducted by Hades while she was gathering flowers.
4. Burial plot.

her task. She was forty when the book was completed. She had travelled little in her life, and it had become more and more difficult to her to leave the House even for a day; but the dread of entrusting her document to a strange hand made her decide to carry it herself to the publisher. On the way to Boston she had a sudden vision of the loneliness to which this last parting condemned her. All her youth, all her dreams, all her renunciations lay in that neat bundle on her knee. It was not so much her grandfather's life as her own that she had written; and the knowledge that it would come back to her in all the glorification of print was of no more help than, to a mother's grief, the assurance that the lad she must part with will return with epaulets.[5]

She had naturally addressed herself to the firm which had published her grandfather's works. Its founder, a personal friend of the philosopher's, had survived the Olympian[6] group of which he had been a subordinate member, long enough to bestow his octogenarian approval on Paulina's pious undertaking. But he had died soon afterward; and Miss Anson found herself confronted by his grandson, a person with a brisk commercial view of his trade, who was said to have put "new blood" into the firm.

This gentleman listened attentively, fingering her manuscript as though literature were a tactile substance; then, with a confidential twist of his revolving chair, he emitted the verdict: "We ought to have had this ten years sooner."

Miss Anson took the words as an allusion to the repressed avidity of her readers. "It has been a long time for the public to wait," she solemnly assented.

The publisher smiled. "They haven't waited," he said.

She looked at him strangely. "Haven't waited?"

"No—they've gone off; taken another train. Literature's like a big railway-station now, you know: there's a train starting every minute. People are not going to hang round the waiting-room. If they can't get to a place when they want to they go somewhere else."

The application of this parable cost Miss Anson several minutes of throbbing silence. At length she said: "Then I am to understand that the public is no longer interested in—in my grandfather?" She felt as though heaven must blast the lips that risked such a conjecture.

"Well, it's this way. He's a name still, of course. People don't exactly want to be caught not knowing who he is; but they don't want to spend two dollars finding out, when they can look him up for nothing in any biographical dictionary."

Miss Anson's world reeled. She felt herself adrift among mysterious forces, and no more thought of prolonging the discussion than of opposing an earthquake with argument. She went home carrying the manuscript like a wounded thing. On the return journey she found herself travelling straight toward a fact that had lurked for months in the background of her life, and that now seemed to await her on the very threshold: the fact that fewer visitors came to the House. She owned to herself that for the last four or five years the number had steadily diminished. Engrossed in her work, she had noted the change only to feel thankful that she had fewer interruptions.

---

5. Shoulder ornaments worn by soldiers.
6. I.e., godlike. Olympus is the mountain where Greek gods live.

There had been a time when, at the travelling season, the bell rang continuously, and the ladies of the House lived in a chronic state of "best silks" and expectancy. It would have been impossible then to carry on any consecutive work; and she now saw that the silence which had gathered round her task had been the hush of death.

Not of *his* death! The very walls cried out against the implication. It was the world's enthusiasm, the world's faith, the world's loyalty that had died. A corrupt generation that had turned aside to worship the brazen serpent.[7] Her heart yearned with a prophetic passion over the lost sheep straying in the wilderness. But all great glories had their interlunar period; and in due time her grandfather would once more flash full-orbed upon a darkling world.

The few friends to whom she confided her adventure reminded her with tender indignation that there were other publishers less subject to the fluctuations of the market; but much as she had braved for her grandfather she could not again brave that particular probation. She found herself, in fact, incapable of any immediate effort. She had lost her way in a labyrinth of conjecture where her worst dread was that she might put her hand upon the clue.

She locked up the manuscript and sat down to wait. If a pilgrim had come just then the priestess would have fallen on his neck; but she continued to celebrate her rites alone. It was a double solitude; for she had always thought a great deal more of the people who came to see the House than of the people who came to see her. She fancied that the neighbors kept a keen eye on the path to the House; and there were days when the figure of a stranger strolling past the gate seemed to focus upon her the scorching sympathies of the village. For a time she thought of travelling; of going to Europe, or even to Boston; but to leave the House now would have seemed like deserting her post. Gradually her scattered energies centred themselves in the fierce resolve to understand what had happened. She was not the woman to live long in an unmapped country or to accept as final her private interpretation of phenomena. Like a traveller in unfamiliar regions she began to store for future guidance the minutest natural signs. Unflinchingly she noted the accumulating symptoms of indifference that marked her grandfather's descent toward posterity. She passed from the heights on which he had been grouped with the sages of his day to the lower level where he had come to be "the friend of Emerson," "the correspondent of Hawthorne,"[8] or (later still) "the Dr. Anson" mentioned in their letters. The change had taken place as slowly and imperceptibly as a natural process. She could not say that any ruthless hand had stripped the leaves from the tree: it was simply that, among the evergreen glories of his group, her grandfather's had proved deciduous.

She had still to ask herself why. If the decay had been a natural process, was it not the very pledge of renewal? It was easier to find such arguments than to be convinced by them. Again and again she tried to drug her solicitude with analogies; but at last she saw that such expedients were but the expression of a growing incredulity. The best way of proving her faith in her grandfather was not to be afraid of critics. She had no notion where these

---

7. I.e., false idol.
8. Nathaniel Hawthorne (1804–1864), American fiction writer. Ralph Waldo Emerson (1803–1882), American poet and essayist, founder of the Transcendentalist movement.

shadowy antagonists lurked; for she had never heard of the great man's doctrine being directly combated. Oblique assaults there must have been, however, Parthian shots[9] at the giant that none dared face; and she thirsted to close with such assailants. The difficulty was to find them. She began by re-reading the *Works*; thence she passed to the writers of the same school, those whose rhetoric bloomed perennial in *First Readers* from which her grandfather's prose had long since faded. Amid that clamor of far-off enthusiasms she detected no controversial note. The little knot of Olympians held their views in common with an early-Christian promiscuity.[1] They were continually proclaiming their admiration for each other, the public joining as chorus in this guileless antiphon[2] of praise; and she discovered no traitor in their midst.

What then had happened? Was it simply that the main current of thought had set another way? Then why did the others survive? Why were they still marked down as tributaries to the philosophic stream? This question carried her still farther afield, and she pressed on with the passion of a champion whose reluctance to know the worst might be construed into a doubt of his cause. At length—slowly but inevitably—an explanation shaped itself. Death had overtaken the doctrines about which her grandfather had draped his cloudy rhetoric. They had disintegrated and been re-absorbed, adding their little pile to the dust drifted about the mute lips of the Sphinx.[3] The great man's contemporaries had survived not by reason of what they taught, but of what they were; and he, who had been the mere mask through which they mouthed their lesson, the instrument on which their tune was played, lay buried deep among the obsolete tools of thought.

The discovery came to Paulina suddenly. She looked up one evening from her reading and it stood before her like a ghost. It had entered her life with stealthy steps, creeping close before she was aware of it. She sat in the library, among the carefully-tended books and portraits; and it seemed to her that she had been walled alive into a tomb hung with the effigies of dead ideas. She felt a desperate longing to escape into the outer air, where people toiled and loved, and living sympathies went hand in hand. It was the sense of wasted labor that oppressed her; of two lives consumed in that ruthless process that uses generations of effort to build a single cell. There was a dreary parallel between her grandfather's fruitless toil and her own unprofitable sacrifice. Each in turn had kept vigil by a corpse.

III

The bell rang—she remembered it afterward—with a loud thrilling note. It was what they used to call the "visitor's ring"; not the tentative tinkle of a neighbor dropping in to borrow a sauce-pan or discuss parochial incidents, but a decisive summons from the outer world.

Miss Anson put down her knitting and listened. She sat upstairs now,

---

9. Shots delivered while retreating (in the manner of archers from Parthia, in southwest Asia).
1. I.e., like the early Christians, who banded together without distinction.
2. Verses sung responsively.

3. In Greek mythology, a monster who killed all who could not answer her riddles; here, a figure for inscrutable mysteries (perhaps alluding as well to the statue of the Sphinx in the desert in Egypt).

making her rheumatism an excuse for avoiding the rooms below. Her interests had insensibly adjusted themselves to the perspective of her neighbors' lives, and she wondered—as the bell re-echoed—if it could mean that Mrs. Heminway's baby had come. Conjecture had time to ripen into certainty, and she was limping toward the closet where her cloak and bonnet hung, when her little maid fluttered in with the announcement: "A gentleman to see the house."

"The *House?*"

"Yes, m'm. I don't know what he means," faltered the messenger, whose memory did not embrace the period when such announcements were a daily part of the domestic routine.

Miss Anson glanced at the proffered card. The name it bore—*Mr. George Corby*—was unknown to her, but the blood rose to her languid cheek. "Hand me my Mechlin[4] cap, Katy," she said, trembling a little, as she laid aside her walking stick. She put her cap on before the mirror, with rapid unsteady touches. "Did you draw up the library blinds?" she breathlessly asked.

She had gradually built up a wall of commonplace between herself and her illusions, but at the first summons of the past filial passion swept away the frail barriers of expediency.

She walked down-stairs so hurriedly that her stick clicked like a girlish heel; but in the hall she paused, wondering nervously if Katy had put a match to the fire. The autumn air was cold and she had the reproachful vision of a visitor with elderly ailments shivering by her inhospitable hearth. She thought instinctively of the stranger as a survivor of the days when such a visit was a part of the young enthusiast's itinerary.

The fire was unlit and the room forbiddingly cold; but the figure which, as Miss Anson entered, turned from a lingering scrutiny of the book-shelves, was that of a fresh-eyed sanguine youth clearly independent of any artificial caloric.[5] She stood still a moment, feeling herself the victim of some anterior impression that made this robust presence an insubstantial thing; but the young man advanced with an air of genial assurance which rendered him at once more real and more reminiscent.

"Why this, you know," he exclaimed, "is simply immense!"

The words, which did not immediately present themselves as slang to Miss Anson's unaccustomed ear, echoed with an odd familiarity through the academic silence.

"The room, you know, I mean," he explained with a comprehensive gesture. "These jolly portraits, and the books—that's the old gentleman himself over the mantelpiece, I suppose—and the elms outside, and—and the whole business. I do like a congruous background—don't you?"

His hostess was silent. No one but Hewlett Winsloe had ever spoken of her grandfather as "the old gentleman."

"It's a hundred times better than I could have hoped," her visitor continued, with a cheerful disregard of her silence. "The seclusion, the remoteness, the philosophic atmosphere—there's so little of that kind of flavor left! I should have simply hated to find that he lived over a grocery, you know.—I

---

4. A delicate lace.
5. An imaginary fluid thought to produce and transfer heat.

had the deuce of a time finding out where he *did* live," he began again, after another glance of parenthetical enjoyment. "But finally I got on the trail through some old book on Brook Farm.[6] I was bound I'd get the environment right before I did my article."

Miss Anson, by this time, had recovered sufficient self-possession to seat herself and assign a chair to her visitor.

"Do I understand," she asked slowly, following his rapid eye about the room, "that you intend to write an article about my grandfather?"

"That's what I'm here for," Mr. Corby genially responded; "that is, if you're willing to help me; for I can't get on without your help," he added with a confident smile.

There was another pause, during which Miss Anson noticed a fleck of dust on the faded leather of the writing-table and a fresh spot of discoloration in the right-hand upper corner of Raphael Morghen's "Parnassus."

"Then you believe in him?" she said, looking up. She could not tell what had prompted her; the words rushed out irresistibly.

"Believe in him?" Corby cried, springing to his feet. "Believe in Orestes Anson? Why, I believe he's simply the greatest—the most stupendous—the most phenomenal figure we've got!"

The color rose to Miss Anson's brow. Her heart was beating passionately. She kept her eyes fixed on the young man's face, as though it might vanish if she looked away.

"You—you mean to say this in your article?" she asked.

"Say it? Why, the facts will say it," he exulted. "The baldest kind of a statement would make it clear. When a man is as big as that he doesn't need a pedestal!"

Miss Anson sighed. "People used to say that when I was young," she murmured. "But now—"

Her visitor stared. "When you were young? But how did they know—when the thing hung fire[7] as it did? When the whole edition was thrown back on his hands?"

"The whole edition—what edition?" It was Miss Anson's turn to stare.

"Why, of his pamphlet—*the* pamphlet—the one thing that counts, that survives, that makes him what he is! For heaven's sake," he tragically adjured her, "don't tell me there isn't a copy of it left!"

Miss Anson was trembling slightly. "I don't think I understand what you mean," she faltered, less bewildered by his vehemence than by the strange sense of coming on an unexplored region in the very heart of her dominion.

"Why, his account of the *amphioxus*,[8] of course! You can't mean that his family didn't know about it—that *you* don't know about it? I came across it by the merest accident myself, in a letter of vindication that he wrote in 1830 to an old scientific paper; but I understood there were journals—early journals; there must be references to it somewhere in the 'twenties. He must have been at least ten or twelve years ahead of Yarrell; and he saw the whole significance of it, too—he saw where it led to. As I understand it, he actually anticipated in his pamphlet Saint Hilaire's theory of the universal type,[9]

---

6. A cooperative community (1841–47) founded by the Transcendentalist Bronson Alcott, father of Louisa May Alcott.
7. Was delayed; remained unresolved.
8. A primitive organism.
9. The French naturalist Étienne Geoffroy Saint-Hilaire (1772–1844) argued that all animals had a single structural plan.

and supported the hypothesis by describing the notochord of the *amphioxus* as a cartilaginous vertebral column. The specialists of the day jeered at him, of course, as the specialists in Goethe's time jeered at the plant-metamorphosis.[1] As far as I can make out, the anatomists and zoologists were down on Dr. Anson to a man; that was why his cowardly publishers went back on their bargain. But the pamphlet must be here somewhere—he writes as though, in his first disappointment, he had destroyed the whole edition; but surely there must be at least one copy left?"

His scientific jargon was as bewildering as his slang; and there were even moments in his discourse when Miss Anson ceased to distinguish between them; but the suspense with which he continued to gaze on her acted as a challenge to her scattered thoughts.

"The *amphioxus*," she murmured, half-rising. "It's an animal, isn't it—a fish? Yes, I think I remember." She sank back with the inward look of one who retraces some lost line of association.

Gradually the distance cleared, the details started into life. In her researches for the biography she had patiently followed every ramification of her subject, and one of these overgrown paths now led her back to the episode in question. The great Orestes's title of "Doctor" had in fact not been merely the spontaneous tribute of a national admiration; he had actually studied medicine in his youth, and his diaries, as his granddaughter now recalled, showed that he had passed through a brief phase of anatomical ardor before his attention was diverted to super-sensual problems. It had indeed seemed to Paulina, as she scanned those early pages, that they revealed a spontaneity, a freshness of feeling somehow absent from his later lucubrations[2]—as though this one emotion had reached him directly, the others through some intervening medium. In the excess of her commemorative zeal she had even struggled through the unintelligible pamphlet to which a few lines in the journal had bitterly directed her. But the subject and the phraseology were alien to her and unconnected with her conception of the great man's genius; and after a hurried perusal she had averted her thoughts from the episode as from a revelation of failure. At length she rose a little unsteadily, supporting herself against the writing-table. She looked hesitatingly about the room; then she drew a key from her old fashioned reticule[3] and unlocked a drawer beneath one of the book-cases. Young Corby watched her breathlessly. With a tremulous hand she turned over the dusty documents that seemed to fill the drawer. "Is this it?" she said, holding out a thin discolored volume.

He seized it with a gasp. "Oh, by George," he said, dropping into the nearest chair.

She stood observing him strangely as his eye devoured the moldy pages.

"Is this the only copy left?" he asked at length, looking up for a moment as a thirsty man lifts his head from his glass.

"I think it must be. I found it long ago, among some old papers that my aunts were burning up after my grandmother's death. They said it was of no use—that he'd always meant to destroy the whole edition and that I ought

---

1. Johann Wolfgang von Goethe (1749–1832),: the German poet, developed a controversial botanical theory.
2. Laborious studies.
3. Woman's small handbag.

to respect his wishes. But it was something *he* had written; to burn it was like shutting the door against his voice—against something he had once wished to say, and that nobody had listened to. I wanted him to feel that I was always here, ready to listen, even when others hadn't thought it worth while; and so I kept the pamphlet, meaning to carry out his wish and destroy it before my death."

Her visitor gave a groan of retrospective anguish. "And but for me—but for today—you would have?"

"I should have thought it my duty."

"Oh, by George—by George," he repeated, subdued afresh by the inadequacy of speech.

She continued to watch him in silence. At length he jumped up and impulsively caught her by both hands.

"He's bigger and bigger!" he almost shouted. "He simply leads the field! You'll help me go to the bottom of this, won't you? We must turn out all the papers—letters, journals, memoranda. He must have made notes. He must have left some record of what led up to this. We must leave nothing unexplored. By Jove," he cried, looking up at her with his bright convincing smile, "do you know you're the granddaughter of a Great Man?"

Her color flickered like a girl's. "Are you—sure of him?" she whispered, as though putting him on his guard against a possible betrayal of trust.

"Sure! Sure! My dear lady—" he measured her again with his quick confident glance. "Don't *you* believe in him?"

She drew back with a confused murmur. "I—used to." She had left her hands in his: their pressure seemed to send a warm current to her heart. "It ruined my life!" she cried with sudden passion. He looked at her perplexedly.

"I gave up everything," she went on wildly, "to keep *him* alive. I sacrificed myself—others—I nursed his glory in my bosom and it died—and left me—left me here alone." She paused and gathered her courage with a gasp. "Don't make the same mistake!" she warned him.

He shook his head, still smiling. "No danger of that! You're not alone, my dear lady. He's here with you—he's come back to you today. Don't you see what's happened? Don't you see that it's your love that has kept him alive? If you'd abandoned your post for an instant—let things pass into other hands—if your wonderful tenderness hadn't perpetually kept guard—this might have been—must have been—irretrievably lost." He laid his hand on the pamphlet. "And then—then he *would* have been dead!"

"Oh," she said, "don't tell me too suddenly!" And she turned away and sank into a chair.

The young man stood watching her in an awed silence. For a long time she sat motionless, with her face hidden, and he thought she must be weeping.

At length he said, almost shyly: "You'll let me come back, then? You'll help me work this thing out?"

She rose calmly and held out her hand. "I'll help you," she declared.

"I'll come tomorrow, then. Can we get to work early?"

"As early as you please."

"At eight o'clock, then," he said briskly. "You'll have the papers ready?"

"I'll have everything ready." She added with a half-playful hesitancy: "And the fire shall be lit for you."

He went out with his bright nod. She walked to the window and watched his buoyant figure hastening down the elm-shaded street. When she turned back into the empty room she looked as though youth had touched her on the lips.

1901

The Other Two[1]

I

Waythorn, on the drawing-room hearth, waited for his wife to come down to dinner.

It was their first night under his own roof, and he was surprised at his thrill of boyish agitation. He was not so old, to be sure—his glass[2] gave him little more than the five-and-thirty years to which his wife confessed—but he had fancied himself already in the temperate zone; yet here he was listening for her step with a tender sense of all it symbolized, with some old trail of verse about the garlanded nuptial doorposts floating through his enjoyment of the pleasant room and the good dinner just beyond it.

They had been hastily recalled from their honeymoon by the illness of Lily Haskett, the child of Mrs. Waythorn's first marriage. The little girl, at Waythorn's desire, had been transferred to his house on the day of her mother's wedding, and the doctor, on their arrival, broke the news that she was ill with typhoid, but declared that all the symptoms were favorable. Lily could show twelve years of unblemished health, and the case promised to be a light one. The nurse spoke as reassuringly, and after a moment of alarm Mrs. Waythorn had adjusted herself to the situation. She was very fond of Lily— her affection for the child had perhaps been her decisive charm in Waythorn's eyes—but she had the perfectly balanced nerves which her little girl had inherited, and no woman ever wasted less tissue in unproductive worry. Waythorn was therefore quite prepared to see her come in presently, a little late because of a last look at Lily, but as serene and well-appointed as if her good-night kiss had been laid on the brow of health. Her composure was restful to him; it acted as ballast to his somewhat unstable sensibilities. As he pictured her bending over the child's bed he thought how soothing her presence must be in illness: her very step would prognosticate recovery.

His own life had been a gray one, from temperament rather than circumstance, and he had been drawn to her by the unperturbed gaiety which kept her fresh and elastic at an age when most woman's activities are growing either slack or febrile. He knew what was said about her; for, popular as she was, there had always been a faint undercurrent of detraction. When she had appeared in New York, nine or ten years earlier, as the pretty Mrs. Haskett whom Gus Varick had unearthed somewhere—was it in Pittsburgh or Utica?—society, while promptly accepting her, had reserved the right to cast a doubt on its own indiscrimination. Inquiry, however, established her undoubted connection with a socially reigning family, and explained her

---

1. First published by Scribner's in the 1904 collection *The Descent of Man and Other Stories*, the source of the present text.
2. Mirror.

recent divorce as the natural result of a runaway match at seventeen; and as nothing was known of Mr. Haskett it was easy to believe the worst of him.

Alice Haskett's remarriage with Gus Varick was a passport to the set whose recognition she coveted, and for a few years the Varicks were the most popular couple in town. Unfortunately the alliance was brief and stormy, and this time the husband had his champions. Still, even Varick's stanchest supporters admitted that he was not meant for matrimony, and Mrs. Varick's grievances were of a nature to bear the inspection of the New York courts.[3] A New York divorce is in itself a diploma of virtue, and in the semi-widowhood of this second separation Mrs. Varick took on an air of sanctity, and was allowed to confide her wrongs to some of the most scrupulous ears in town. But when it was known that she was to marry Waythorn there was a momentary reaction. Her best friends would have preferred to see her remain in the role of the injured wife, which was as becoming to her as crape to a rosy complexion. True, a decent time had elapsed, and it was not even suggested that Waythorn had supplanted his predecessor. People shook their heads over him, however, and one grudging friend, to whom he affirmed that he took the step with his eyes open, replied oracularly: "Yes—and with your ears shut."

Waythorn could afford to smile at these innuendoes. In the Wall Street phrase, he had "discounted" them. He knew that society has not yet adapted itself to the consequences of divorce, and that till the adaptation takes place every woman who uses the freedom the law accords her must be her own social justification. Waythorn had an amused confidence in his wife's ability to justify herself. His expectations were fulfilled, and before the wedding took place Alice Varick's group had rallied openly to her support. She took it all imperturbably: she had a way of surmounting obstacles without seeming to be aware of them, and Waythorn looked back with wonder at the trivialities over which he had worn his nerves thin. He had the sense of having found refuge in a richer, warmer nature than his own, and his satisfaction, at the moment, was humorously summed up in the thought that his wife, when she had done all she could for Lily, would not be ashamed to come down and enjoy a good dinner.

The anticipation of such enjoyment was not, however, the sentiment expressed by Mrs. Waythorn's charming face when she presently joined him. Though she had put on her most engaging teagown she had neglected to assume the smile that went with it, and Waythorn thought he had never seen her look so nearly worried.

"What is it?" he asked. "Is anything wrong with Lily?"

"No; I've just been in and she's still sleeping." Mrs. Waythorn hesitated. "But something tiresome has happened."

He had taken her two hands, and now perceived that he was crushing a paper between them.

"This letter?"

"Yes—Mr. Haskett has written—I mean his lawyer has written."

Waythorn felt himself flush uncomfortably. He dropped his wife's hands.

"What about?"

"About seeing Lily. You know the courts—"

"Yes, yes," he interrupted nervously.

---

3. Divorce in New York State could then be granted only on the grounds of adultery.

Nothing was known about Haskett in New York. He was vaguely supposed to have remained in the outer darkness from which his wife had been rescued, and Waythorn was one of the few who were aware that he had given up his business in Utica and followed her to New York in order to be near his little girl. In the days of his wooing, Waythorn had often met Lily on the doorstep, rosy and smiling, on her way "to see papa."

"I am so sorry," Mrs. Waythorn murmured.

He roused himself. "What does he want?"

"He wants to see her. You know she goes to him once a week."

"Well—he doesn't expect her to go to him now, does he?"

"No—he has heard of her illness; but he expects to come here."

"*Here?*"

Mrs. Waythorn reddened under his gaze. They looked away from each other.

"I'm afraid he has the right. . . . You'll see. . . ." She made a proffer of the letter.

Waythorn moved away with a gesture of refusal. He stood staring about the softly-lighted room, which a moment before had seemed so full of bridal intimacy.

"I'm so sorry," she repeated. "If Lily could have been moved—"

"That's out of the question," he returned impatiently.

"I suppose so."

Her lip was beginning to tremble, and he felt himself a brute.

"He must come, of course," he said. "When is—his day?"

"I'm afraid—to-morrow."

"Very well. Send a note in the morning."

The butler entered to announce dinner.

Waythorn turned to his wife. "Come—you must be tired. It's beastly, but try to forget about it," he said, drawing her hand through his arm.

"You're so good, dear. I'll try," she whispered back.

Her face cleared at once, and as she looked at him across the flowers, between the rosy candle-shades, he saw her lips waver back into a smile.

"How pretty everything is!" she sighed luxuriously.

He turned to the butler. "The champagne at once, please. Mrs. Waythorn is tired."

In a moment or two their eyes met above the sparkling glasses. Her own were quite clear and untroubled: he saw that she had obeyed his injunction and forgotten.

II

Waythorn, the next morning, went downtown earlier than usual. Haskett was not likely to come till the afternoon, but the instinct of flight drove him forth. He meant to stay away all day—he had thoughts of dining at his club. As his door closed behind him he reflected that before he opened it again it would have admitted another man who had as much right to enter it as himself, and the thought filled him with a physical repugnance.

He caught the "elevated"[4] at the employees' hour, and found himself crushed between two layers of pendulous humanity. At Eighth Street the

---

4. Elevated railway.

man facing him wriggled out, and another took his place. Waythorn glanced up and saw that it was Gus Varick. The men were so close together that it was impossible to ignore the smile of recognition on Varick's handsome overblown face. And after all—why not? They had always been on good terms, and Varick had been divorced before Waythorn's attentions to his wife began. The two exchanged a word on the perennial grievance of the congested trains, and when a seat at their side was miraculously left empty the instinct of self-preservation made Waythorn slip into it after Varick.

The latter drew the stout man's breath of relief. "Lord—I was beginning to feel like a pressed flower." He leaned back, looking unconcernedly at Waythorn. "Sorry to hear that Sellers is knocked out again."

"Sellers?" echoed Waythorn, starting at his partner's name.

Varick looked surprised. "You didn't know he was laid up with the gout?"

"No. I've been away—I only got back last night." Waythorn felt himself reddening in anticipation of the other's smile.

"Ah—yes; to be sure. And Sellers' attack came on two days ago. I'm afraid he's pretty bad. Very awkward for me, as it happens, because he was just putting through a rather important thing for me."

"Ah?" Waythorn wondered vaguely since when Varick had been dealing in "important things." Hitherto he had dabbled only in the shallow pools of speculation, with which Waythorn's office did not usually concern itself.

It occurred to him that Varick might be talking at random, to relieve the strain of their propinquity. That strain was becoming momentarily more apparent to Waythorn, and when, at Cortlandt Street, he caught sight of an acquaintance and had a sudden vision of the picture he and Varick must present to an initiated eye, he jumped up with a muttered excuse.

"I hope you'll find Sellers better," said Varick civilly, and he stammered back: "If I can be of any use to you—" and let the departing crowd sweep him to the platform.

At his office he heard that Sellers was in fact ill with the gout, and would probably not be able to leave the house for some weeks.

"I'm sorry it should have happened so, Mr. Waythorn," the senior clerk said with affable significance. "Mr. Sellers was very much upset at the idea of giving you such a lot of extra work just now."

"Oh, that's no matter," said Waythorn hastily. He secretly welcomed the pressure of additional business, and was glad to think that, when the day's work was over, he would have to call at his partner's on the way home.

He was late for luncheon, and turned in at the nearest restaurant instead of going to his club. The place was full, and the waiter hurried him to the back of the room to capture the only vacant table. In the cloud of cigar-smoke Waythorn did not at once distinguish his neighbors: but presently, looking about him, he saw Varick seated a few feet off. This time, luckily, they were too far apart for conversation, and Varick, who faced another way, had probably not even seen him; but there was an irony in their renewed nearness.

Varick was said to be fond of good living, and as Waythorn sat dispatching his hurried luncheon he looked across half enviously at the other's leisurely degustation of his meal. When Waythorn first saw him he had been helping himself with critical deliberation to a bit of Camembert at the ideal point of liquefaction, and now, the cheese removed, he was just pouring his *café double* from its little two-storied earthen pot. He poured slowly, his ruddy profile bent over the task, and one beringed white hand steadying the lid of the coffee-pot; then he stretched his other hand to the decanter of cognac at his elbow, filled a liqueur glass, took a tentative sip, and poured the brandy into his coffee-cup.

Waythorn watched him in a kind of fascination. What was he thinking of—only of the flavor of the coffee and the liqueur? Had the morning's meeting left no more trace in his thoughts than on his face? Had his wife so completely passed out of his life that even this odd encounter with her present husband, within a week after her remarriage, was no more than an incident in his day? And as Waythorn mused, another idea struck him: had Haskett ever met Varick as Varick and he had just met? The recollection of Haskett perturbed him, and he rose and left the restaurant, taking a circuitous way out to escape the placid irony of Varick's nod.

It was after seven when Waythorn reached home. He thought the footman who opened the door looked at him oddly.

"How is Miss Lily?" he asked in haste.

"Doing very well, sir. A gentleman—"

"Tell Barlow to put off dinner for half an hour," Waythorn cut him off, hurrying upstairs.

He went straight to his room and dressed without seeing his wife. When he reached the drawing-room she was there, fresh and radiant. Lily's day had been good; the doctor was not coming back that evening.

At dinner Waythorn told her of Sellers' illness and of the resulting complications. She listened sympathetically, adjuring him not to let himself be overworked, and asking vague feminine questions about the routine of the office. Then she gave him the chronicle of Lily's day; quoted the nurse and doctor, and told him who had called to inquire. He had never seen her more serene and unruffled. It struck him, with a curious pang, that she was very happy in being with him, so happy that she found a childish pleasure in rehearsing the trivial incidents of her day.

After dinner they went to the library, and the servant put the coffee and liqueurs on a low table before her and left the room. She looked singularly soft and girlish in her rosy pale dress, against the dark leather of one of his bachelor armchairs. A day earlier the contrast would have charmed him.

He turned away now, choosing a cigar with affected deliberation.

"Did Haskett come?" he asked, with his back to her.

"Oh, yes—he came."

"You didn't see him, of course?"

She hesitated a moment. "I let the nurse see him."

That was all. There was nothing more to ask. He swung round toward her, applying a match to his cigar. Well, the thing was over for a week, at any rate. He would try not to think of it. She looked up at him, a trifle rosier than usual, with a smile in her eyes.

"Ready for your coffee, dear?"

He leaned against the mantelpiece, watching her as she lifted the coffee-pot. The lamplight struck a gleam from her bracelets and tipped her soft hair with brightness. How light and slender she was, and how each gesture flowed into the next! She seemed a creature all compact of harmonies. As the thought of Haskett receded, Waythorn felt himself yielding again to the joy of possessorship. They were his, those white hands with their flitting motions, his the light haze of hair, the lips and eyes. . . .

She set down the coffee-pot, and reaching for the decanter of cognac, measured off a liqueur-glass and poured it into his cup.

Waythorn uttered a sudden exclamation.

"What is the matter?" she said, startled.

"Nothing; only—I don't take cognac in my coffee."

"Oh, how stupid of me," she cried.

Their eyes met, and she blushed a sudden agonized red.

III

Ten days later, Mr. Sellers, still house-bound, asked Waythorn to call on his way down town.

The senior partner, with his swaddled foot propped up by the fire, greeted his associate with an air of embarrassment.

"I'm sorry, my dear fellow; I've got to ask you to do an awkward thing for me."

Waythorn waited, and the other went on, after a pause apparently given to the arrangement of his phrases: "The fact is, when I was knocked out I had just gone into a rather complicated piece of business for—Gus Varick."

"Well?" said Waythorn, with an attempt to put him at his ease.

"Well—it's this way: Varick came to me the day before my attack. He had evidently had an inside tip from somebody, and had made about a hundred thousand. He came to me for advice, and I suggested his going in with Vanderlyn."

"Oh, the deuce!" Waythorn exclaimed. He saw in a flash what had happened. The investment was an alluring one, but required negotiation. He listened quietly while Sellers put the case before him, and, the statement ended, he said: "You think I ought to see Varick?"

"I'm afraid I can't as yet. The doctor is obdurate. And this thing can't wait. I hate to ask you, but no one else in the office knows the ins and outs of it."

Waythorn stood silent. He did not care a farthing for the success of Varick's venture, but the honor of the office was to be considered, and he could hardly refuse to oblige his partner.

"Very well," he said, "I'll do it."

That afternoon, apprised by telephone, Varick called at the office. Waythorn, waiting in his private room, wondered what the others thought of it. The newspapers, at the time of Mrs. Waythorn's marriage, had acquainted their readers with every detail of her previous matrimonial ventures, and Waythorn could fancy the clerks smiling behind Varick's back as he was ushered in.

Varick bore himself admirably. He was easy without being undignified, and Waythorn was conscious of cutting a much less impressive figure. Varick had no experience of business, and the talk prolonged itself for nearly an hour while Waythorn set forth with scrupulous precision the details of the proposed transaction.

"I'm awfully obliged to you," Varick said as he rose. "The fact is I'm not used to having much money to look after, and I don't want to make an ass of myself—" He smiled, and Waythorn could not help noticing that there was something pleasant about his smile. "It feels uncommonly queer to have enough cash to pay one's bills. I'd have sold my soul for it a few years ago!"

Waythorn winced at the allusion. He had heard it rumored that a lack of funds had been one of the determining causes of the Varick separation, but it did not occur to him that Varick's words were intentional. It seemed more likely that the desire to keep clear of embarrassing topics had fatally drawn him into one. Waythorn did not wish to be outdone in civility.

"We'll do the best we can for you," he said. "I think this is a good thing you're in."

"Oh, I'm sure it's immense. It's awfully good of you—" Varick broke off, embarrassed. "I suppose the thing's settled now—but if—"

"If anything happens before Sellers is about, I'll see you again," said Waythorn quietly. He was glad, in the end, to appear the more self-possessed of the two.

The course of Lily's illness ran smooth, and as the days passed Waythorn grew used to the idea of Haskett's weekly visit. The first time the day came round, he stayed out late, and questioned his wife as to the visit on his return. She replied at once that Haskett had merely seen the nurse downstairs, as the doctor did not wish any one in the child's sick-room till after the crisis.

The following week Waythorn was again conscious of the recurrence of the day, but had forgotten it by the time he came home to dinner. The crisis of the disease came a few days later, with a rapid decline of fever, and the little girl was pronounced out of danger. In the rejoicing which ensued the thought of Haskett passed out of Waythorn's mind, and one afternoon, letting himself into the house with a latch-key, he went straight to his library without noticing a shabby hat and umbrella in the hall.

In the library he found a small effaced-looking man with a thinnish gray beard sitting on the edge of a chair. The stranger might have been a piano-tuner, or one of those mysteriously efficient persons who are summoned in emergencies to adjust some detail of the domestic machinery. He blinked at Waythorn through a pair of gold-rimmed spectacles and said mildly: "Mr. Waythorn, I presume? I am Lily's father."

Waythorn flushed. "Oh—" he stammered uncomfortably. He broke off, disliking to appear rude. Inwardly he was trying to adjust the actual Haskett to the image of him projected by his wife's reminiscences. Waythorn had been allowed to infer that Alice's first husband was a brute.

"I am sorry to intrude," said Haskett, with his over-the-counter politeness.

"Don't mention it," returned Waythorn, collecting himself. "I suppose the nurse has been told?"

"I presume so. I can wait," said Haskett. He had a resigned way of speaking, as though life had worn down his natural powers of resistance.

Waythorn stood on the threshold, nervously pulling off his gloves.

"I'm sorry you've been detained. I will send for the nurse," he said; and as he opened the door he added with an effort: "I'm glad we can give you a good report of Lily." He winced as the *we* slipped out, but Haskett seemed not to notice it.

"Thank you, Mr. Waythorn. It's been an anxious time for me."

"Ah, well, that's past. Soon she'll be able to go to you." Waythorn nodded and passed out.

In his own room he flung himself down with a groan. He hated the womanish sensibility which made him suffer so acutely from the grotesque chances of life. He had known when he married that his wife's former husbands were both living, and that amid the multiplied contacts of modern existence there were a thousand chances to one that he would run against one or the other, yet he found himself as much disturbed by his brief encounter with Haskett as though the law had not obligingly removed all difficulties in the way of their meeting.

Waythorn sprang up and began to pace the room nervously. He had not suffered half as much from his two meetings with Varick. It was Haskett's presence in his own house that made the situation so intolerable. He stood still, hearing steps in the passage.

"This way, please," he heard the nurse say. Haskett was being taken upstairs, then: not a corner of the house but was open to him. Waythorn dropped into another chair, staring vaguely ahead of him. On his dressing table stood a photograph of Alice, taken when he had first known her. She was Alice Varick then—how fine and exquisite he had thought her! Those were Varick's pearls about her neck. At Waythorn's instance they had been returned before her marriage. Had Haskett ever given her any trinkets—and what had become of them, Waythorn wondered? He realized suddenly that he knew very little of Haskett's past or present situation; but from the man's appearance and manner of speech he could reconstruct with curious precision the surroundings of Alice's first marriage. And it startled him to think that she had, in the background of her life, a phase of existence so different from anything with which he had connected her. Varick, whatever his faults, was a gentleman, in the conventional, traditional sense of the term: the sense which at that moment seemed, oddly enough, to have most meaning to Waythorn. He and Varick had the same social habits, spoke the same language, understood the same allusions. But this other man . . . it was grotesquely uppermost in Waythorn's mind that Haskett had worn a made-up tie attached with an elastic. Why should that ridiculous detail symbolize the whole man? Waythorn was exasperated by his own paltriness, but the fact of the tie expanded, forced itself on him, became as it were the key to Alice's past. He could see her, as Mrs. Haskett, sitting in a "front parlor" furnished in plush, with a pianola, and a copy of *"Ben Hur"*[5] on the center-table. He could see her going to the theater with Haskett—or perhaps even to a "Church Sociable"—she in a "picture hat" and Haskett in a black frock coat, a little creased, with the made-up tie on an elastic. On the way home they would stop and look at the illuminated shop windows, lingering over the photographs of New York actresses. On Sunday afternoons Haskett would take her for a walk, pushing Lily ahead of them in a white enamelled perambulator, and Waythorn had a vision of the people they would stop and talk to. He could fancy how pretty Alice must have looked, in a dress adroitly constructed from the hints of a New York fashion-paper, and how she must

---

5. *Ben-Hur: A Tale of the Christ* (1880), an immensely popular, rather melodramatic romance by the American novelist and diplomat Lew Wallace; "Pianola": a player piano.

have looked down on the other women, chafing at her life, and secretly feeling that she belonged in a bigger place.

For the moment his foremost thought was one of wonder at the way in which she had shed the phase of existence which her marriage with Haskett implied. It was as if her whole aspect, every gesture, every inflection, every allusion, were a studied negation of that period of her life. If she had denied being married to Haskett she could hardly have stood more convicted of duplicity than in this obliteration of the self which had been his wife.

Waythorn started up, checking himself in the analysis of her motives. What right had he to create a fantastic effigy of her and then pass judgment on it? She had spoken vaguely of her first marriage as unhappy, had hinted, with becoming reticence, that Haskett had wrought havoc among her young illusions. . . . It was a pity for Waythorn's peace of mind that Haskett's very inoffensiveness shed a new light on the nature of those illusions. A man would rather think that his wife has been brutalized by her first husband than that the process has been reversed.

IV

"Mr. Waythorn, I don't like that French governess of Lily's."

Haskett, subdued and apologetic, stood before Waythorn in the library, revolving his shabby hat in his hand.

Waythorn, surprised in his armchair over the evening paper, stared back perplexedly at his visitor.

"You'll excuse me asking to see you," Haskett continued. "But this is my last visit, and I thought if I could have a word with you it would be a better way than writing to Mrs. Waythorn's lawyer."

Waythorn rose uneasily. He did not like the French governess either; but that was irrelevant.

"I am not so sure of that," he returned stiffly; "but since you wish it I will give your message to—my wife." He always hesitated over the possessive pronoun in addressing Haskett.

The latter sighed. "I don't know as that will help much. She didn't like it when I spoke to her."

Waythorn turned red. "When did you see her?" he asked.

"Not since the first day I came to see Lily—right after she was taken sick. I remarked to her then that I didn't like the governess."

Waythorn made no answer. He remembered distinctly that, after the first visit, he had asked his wife if she had seen Haskett. She had lied to him then, but she had respected his wishes since; and the incident cast a curious light on her character. He was sure she would not have seen Haskett that first day if she had divined that Waythorn would object, and the fact that she did not divine it was almost as disagreeable to the latter as the discovery that she had lied to him.

"I don't like the woman," Haskett was repeating with mild persistency. "She ain't straight, Mr. Waythorn—she'll teach the child to be underhand. I've noticed a change in Lily—she's too anxious to please—and she don't always tell the truth. She used to be the straightest child, Mr. Waythorn—" He broke off, his voice a little thick. "Not but what I want her to have a stylish education," he ended.

Waythorn was touched. "I'm sorry, Mr. Haskett; but frankly, I don't quite see what I can do."

Haskett hesitated. Then he laid his hat on the table, and advanced to the hearth-rug, on which Waythorn was standing. There was nothing aggressive in his manner, but he had the solemnity of a timid man resolved on a decisive measure.

"There's just one thing you can do, Mr. Waythorn," he said. "You can remind Mrs. Waythorn that, by the decree of the courts, I am entitled to have a voice in Lily's bringing-up." He paused, and went on more deprecatingly: "I'm not the kind to talk about enforcing my rights, Mr. Waythorn. I don't know as I think a man is entitled to rights he hasn't known how to hold on to; but this business of the child is different. I've never let go there—and I never mean to."

The scene left Waythorn deeply shaken. Shamefacedly, in indirect ways, he had been finding out about Haskett; and all that he learned was favorable. The little man, in order to be near his daughter, had sold out his share in a profitable business in Utica, and accepted a modest clerkship in a New York manufacturing house. He boarded in a shabby street and had few acquaintances. His passion for Lily filled his life. Waythorn felt that this exploration of Haskett was like groping about with a dark-lantern in his wife's past; but he saw now that there were recesses his lantern had not explored. He had never enquired into the exact circumstances of his wife's first matrimonial rupture. On the surface all had been fair. It was she who had obtained the divorce, and the court had given her the child. But Waythorn knew how many ambiguities such a verdict might cover. The mere fact that Haskett retained a right over his daughter implied an unsuspected compromise. Waythorn was an idealist. He always refused to recognize unpleasant contingencies till he found himself confronted with them, and then he saw them followed by a spectral train of consequences. His next days were thus haunted, and he determined to try to lay the ghosts by conjuring them up in his wife's presence.

When he repeated Haskett's request a flame of anger passed over her face; but she subdued it instantly and spoke with a slight quiver of outraged motherhood.

"It is very ungentlemanly of him," she said.

The word grated on Waythorn. "That is neither here nor there. It's a bare question of rights."

She murmured: "It's not as if he could ever be a help to Lily—"

Waythorn flushed. This was even less to his taste. "The question is," he repeated, "what authority has he over her?"

She looked downward, twisting herself a little in her seat. "I am willing to see him—I thought you objected," she faltered.

In a flash he understood that she knew the extent of Haskett's claims. Perhaps it was not the first time she had resisted them.

"My objecting has nothing to do with it," he said coldly; "if Haskett has a right to be consulted you must consult him."

She burst into tears, and he saw that she expected him to regard her as a victim.

Haskett did not abuse his rights. Waythorn had felt miserably sure that he would not. But the governess was dismissed, and from time to time the little man demanded an interview with Alice. After the first outburst she accepted the situation with her usual adaptability. Haskett had once reminded Waythorn of the piano-tuner, and Mrs. Waythorn, after a month or two, appeared to class him with that domestic familiar. Waythorn could not but respect the father's tenacity. At first he had tried to cultivate the suspicion that Haskett might be "up to" something, that he had an object in securing a foothold in the house. But in his heart Waythorn was sure of Haskett's single-mindedness; he even guessed in the latter a mild contempt for such advantages as his relation with the Waythorns might offer. Haskett's sincerity of purpose made him invulnerable, and his successor had to accept him as a lien on the property.

Mr. Sellers was sent to Europe to recover from his gout, and Varick's affairs hung on Waythorn's hands. The negotiations were prolonged and complicated; they necessitated frequent conferences between the two men, and the interests of the firm forbade Waythorn's suggesting that his client should transfer his business to another office.

Varick appeared well in the transaction. In moments of relaxation his coarse streak appeared, and Waythorn dreaded his geniality; but in the office he was concise and clear-headed, with a flattering deference to Waythorn's judgment. Their business relations being so affably established, it would have been absurd for the two men to ignore each other in society. The first time they met in a drawing-room, Varick took up their intercourse in the same easy key, and his hostess's grateful glance obliged Waythorn to respond to it. After that they ran across each other frequently, and one evening at a ball Waythorn, wandering through the remoter rooms, came upon Varick seated beside his wife. She colored a little, and faltered in what she was saying; but Varick nodded to Waythorn without rising, and the latter strolled on.

In the carriage, on the way home, he broke out nervously: "I didn't know you spoke to Varick."

Her voice trembled a little. "It's the first time—he happened to be standing near me; I didn't know what to do. It's so awkward, meeting everywhere—and he said you had been very kind about some business."

"That's different," said Waythorn.

She paused a moment. "I'll do just as you wish," she returned pliantly. "I thought it would be less awkward to speak to him when we meet."

Her pliancy was beginning to sicken him. Had she really no will of her own—no theory about her relation to these men? She had accepted Haskett—did she mean to accept Varick? It was "less awkward," as she had said, and her instinct was to evade difficulties or to circumvent them. With sudden vividness Waythorn saw how the instinct had developed. She was "as easy as an old shoe"—a shoe that too many feet had worn. Her elasticity was the result of tension in too many different directions. Alice Haskett—Alice Varick—Alice Waythorn—she had been each in turn, and had left hanging to each name a little of her privacy, a little of her personality, a little of the inmost self where the unknown god abides.

"Yes—it's better to speak to Varick," said Waythorn wearily.

V

The winter wore on, and society took advantage of the Waythorns' acceptance of Varick. Harassed hostesses were grateful to them for bridging over a social difficulty, and Mrs. Waythorn was held up as a miracle of good taste. Some experimental spirits could not resist the diversion of throwing Varick and his former wife together, and there were those who thought he found a zest in the propinquity. But Mrs. Waythorn's conduct remained irreproachable. She neither avoided Varick nor sought him out. Even Waythorn could not but admit that she had discovered the solution of the newest social problem.

He had married her without giving much thought to that problem. He had fancied that a woman can shed her past like a man. But now he saw that Alice was bound to hers both by the circumstances which forced her into continued relation with it, and by the traces it had left on her nature. With grim irony Waythorn compared himself to a member of a syndicate. He held so many shares in his wife's personality and his predecessors were his partners in the business. If there had been any element of passion in the transaction he would have felt less deteriorated by it. The fact that Alice took her change of husbands like a change of weather reduced the situation to mediocrity. He could have forgiven her for blunders, for excesses; for resisting Haskett, for yielding to Varick; for anything but her acquiescence and her tact. She reminded him of a juggler tossing knives; but the knives were blunt and she knew they would never cut her.

And then, gradually, habit formed a protecting surface for his sensibilities. If he paid for each day's comfort with the small change of his illusions, he grew daily to value the comfort more and set less store upon the coin. He had drifted into a dulling propinquity with Haskett and Varick and he took refuge in the cheap revenge of satirizing the situation. He even began to reckon up the advantages which accrued from it, to ask himself if it were not better to own a third of a wife who knew how to make a man happy than a whole one who had lacked opportunity to acquire the art. For it *was* an art, and made up, like all others, of concessions, eliminations and embellishments; of lights judiciously thrown and shadows skillfully softened. His wife knew exactly how to manage the lights, and he knew exactly to what training she owed her skill. He even tried to trace the source of his obligations, to discriminate between the influences which had combined to produce his domestic happiness: he perceived that Haskett's commonness had made Alice worship good breeding, while Varick's liberal construction of the marriage bond had taught her to value the conjugal virtues; so that he was directly indebted to his predecessors for the devotion which made his life easy if not inspiring.

From this phrase he passed into that of complete acceptance. He ceased to satirize himself because time dulled the irony of the situation and the joke lost its humor with its sting. Even the sight of Haskett's hat on the hall table had ceased to touch the springs of epigram. The hat was often seen there now, for it had been decided that it was better for Lily's father to visit her than for the little girl to go to his boarding-house. Waythorn, having acquiesced in this arrangement, had been surprised to find how little difference it made. Haskett was never obtrusive, and the few visitors who met him on the stairs were unaware of his identity. Waythorn did not know how often he saw Alice, but with himself Haskett was seldom in contact.

One afternoon, however, he learned on entering that Lily's father was waiting to see him. In the library he found Haskett occupying a chair in his usual provisional way. Waythorn always felt grateful to him for not leaning back.

"I hope you'll excuse me, Mr. Waythorn," he said rising. "I wanted to see Mrs. Waythorn about Lily, and your man asked me to wait here till she came in."

"Of course," said Waythorn, remembering that a sudden leak had that morning given over the drawing-room to the plumbers.

He opened his cigar-case and held it out to his visitor, and Haskett's acceptance seemed to mark a fresh stage in their intercourse. The spring evening was chilly, and Waythorn invited his guest to draw up his chair to the fire. He meant to find an excuse to leave Haskett in a moment; but he was tired and cold, and after all the little man no longer jarred on him.

The two were enclosed in the intimacy of their blended cigar smoke when the door opened and Varick walked into the room. Waythorn rose abruptly. It was the first time that Varick had come to the house, and the surprise of seeing him, combined with the singular inopportuneness of his arrival, gave a new edge to Waythorn's blunted sensibilities. He stared at his visitor without speaking.

Varick seemed too preoccupied to notice his host's embarrassment.

"My dear fellow," he exclaimed in his most expansive tone, "I must apologize for tumbling in on you in this way, but I was too late to catch you downtown, and so I thought—"

He stopped short, catching sight of Haskett, and his sanguine color deepened to a flush which spread vividly under his scant blond hair. But in a moment he recovered himself and nodded slightly. Haskett returned the bow in silence, and Waythorn was still groping for speech when the footman came in carrying a tea-table.

The intrusion offered a welcome vent to Waythorn's nerves. "What the deuce are you bringing this here for?" he said sharply.

"I beg your pardon, sir, but the plumbers are still in the drawing-room, and Mrs. Waythorn said she would have tea in the library." The footman's perfectly respectful tone implied a reflection on Waythorn's reasonableness.

"Oh, very well," said the latter resignedly, and the footman proceeded to open the folding tea-table and set out its complicated appointments. While this interminable process continued the three men stood motionless, watching it with a fascinated stare, till Waythorn, to break the silence, said to Varick: "Won't you have a cigar?"

He held out the case he had just tendered to Haskett, and Varick helped himself with a smile. Waythorn looked about for a match, and finding none, proffered a light from his own cigar. Haskett, in the background, held his ground mildly, examining his cigar-tip now and then, and stepping forward at the right moment to knock its ashes into the fire.

The footman at last withdrew, and Varick immediately began: "If I could just say half a word to you about this business—"

"Certainly," stammered Waythorn; "in the dining room—"

But as he placed his hand on the door it opened from without, and his wife appeared on the threshold.

She came in fresh and smiling, in her street dress and hat, shedding a fragrance from the boa which she loosened in advancing.

"Shall we have tea in here, dear?" she began; and then she caught sight of Varick. Her smile deepened, veiling a slight tremor of surprise.

"Why, how do you do?" she said with a distinct note of pleasure.

As she shook hands with Varick she saw Haskett standing behind him. Her smile faded for a moment, but she recalled it quickly, with a scarcely perceptible side-glance at Waythorn.

"How do you do, Mr. Haskett?" she said, and shook hands with him a shade less cordially.

The three men stood awkwardly before her, till Varick, always the most self-possessed, dashed into an explanatory phrase.

"We—I had to see Waythorn a moment on business," he stammered, brick-red from chin to nape.

Haskett stepped forward with his air of mild obstinacy. "I am sorry to intrude; but you appointed five o'clock—" he directed his resigned glance to the timepiece on the mantel.

She swept aside their embarrassment with a charming gesture of hospitality.

"I'm so sorry—I'm always late; but the afternoon was so lovely." She stood drawing off her gloves, propitiatory and graceful, diffusing about her a sense of ease and familiarity in which the situation lost its grotesqueness. "But before talking business," she added brightly, "I'm sure every one wants a cup of tea."

She dropped into her low chair by the tea-table, and the two visitors, as if drawn by her smile, advanced to receive the cups she held out.

She glanced about for Waythorn, and he took the third cup with a laugh.

1904

SUI SIN FAR (EDITH MAUD EATON)
1863–1914

"I give my right hand to the Occidentals and my left to the Orientals," declared the Asian American writer who published under the pseudonym Sui Sin Far, adding her hope that "between them they will not utterly destroy the insignificant 'connecting link.' " The daughter of a British father and a Chinese mother, Eaton was born in England and came to the New World at the age of seven, when the family settled first in Hudson City, New York, then near Montreal. The oldest of fourteen children, young Edith was educated at home after the age of eleven, and she was also obliged to help bring in money by selling her father's artwork on the streets along with lacework that she herself crocheted. At eighteen, she took a job as a typesetter for a Montreal newspaper but soon began to publish newspaper articles and stories to supplement her income. Writing as Sui Sin Far ("water lily," in Chinese), she produced pioneering tales of Asian American culture that eventually granted her a place as a "spiritual foremother of contemporary Eurasian authors." A number of critics have noted that it took "great determination and courage" for her to "champion the Chinese and working-class women and to identify herself as such, publicly and in print."

As Sui, Eaton worked in an era when Chinese immigrants had to confront deeply oppressive stereotypes that cast the Asian woman as (in the words of her biographer Amy Ling) a "sing-song girl, prostitute, or inmate of an opium den." The subtlety and sensitivity with which she delineates the dilemmas of Mrs. Spring Fragrance in the story of that name underline her commitment to what she hoped would be an accurate representation of the frequently misrepresented Chinese American community in which she grew up. The tale became the title piece of her only book, a collection published in 1912, just a few years before she died from what were evidently the consequences of childhood rheumatic fever. Sadly, the volume was out of print until 1995, when Amy Ling and Annette White-Parks produced a new edition. Yet as "Mrs. Spring Fragrance" reveals, Sui Sin Far had a prophetic grasp of issues that scholars of Asian American culture have only recently begun to study.

Mrs. Spring Fragrance

I

When Mrs. Spring Fragrance first arrived in Seattle, she was unacquainted with even one word of the American language. Five years later her husband, speaking of her, said: "There are no more American words for her learning." And everyone who knew Mrs. Spring Fragrance agreed with Mr. Spring Fragrance.

Mr. Spring Fragrance, whose business name was Sing Yook, was a young curio merchant. Though conservatively Chinese in many respects, he was at the same time what is called by the Westerners, "Americanized." Mrs. Spring Fragrance was even more "Americanized."

Next door to the Spring Fragrances lived the Chin Yuens. Mrs. Chin Yuen was much older than Mrs. Spring Fragrance; but she had a daughter of eighteen with whom Mrs. Spring Fragrance was on terms of great friendship. The daughter was a pretty girl whose Chinese name was Mai Gwi Far (a rose) and whose American name was Laura. Nearly everybody called her Laura, even her parents and Chinese friends. Laura had a sweetheart, a youth named Kai Tzu. Kai Tzu, who was American-born, and as ruddy and stalwart as any young Westerner, was noted amongst baseball players as one of the finest pitchers on the Coast. He could also sing, "Drink to me only with thine eyes,"[1] to Laura's piano accompaniment.

Now the only person who knew that Kai Tzu loved Laura and that Laura loved Kai Tzu, was Mrs. Spring Fragrance. The reason for this was that, although the Chin Yuen parents lived in a house furnished in American style, and wore American clothes, yet they religiously observed many Chinese customs, and their ideals of life were the ideals of their Chinese forefathers. Therefore, they had betrothed their daughter, Laura, at the age of fifteen, to

---

1. The poem "To Celia" (1616) by Ben Jonson, set to music in the 18th century.

the eldest son of the Chinese Government school-teacher in San Francisco. The time for the consummation of the betrothal was approaching.

Laura was with Mrs. Spring Fragrance and Mrs. Spring Fragrance was trying to cheer her.

"I had such a pretty walk today," said she. "I crossed the banks above the beach and came back by the long road. In the green grass the daffodils were blowing,[2] in the cottage gardens the currant bushes were flowering, and in the air was the perfume of the wallflower. I wished, Laura, that you were with me."

Laura burst into tears. "That is the walk," she sobbed, "Kai Tzu and I so love; but never, ah, never, can we take it together again."

"Now, Little Sister," comforted Mrs. Spring Fragrance, "you really must not grieve like that. Is there not a beautiful American poem written by a noble American named Tennyson, which says:

> " 'Tis better to have loved and lost,
> Than never to have loved at all?"[3]

Mrs. Spring Fragrance was unaware that Mr. Spring Fragrance, having returned from the city, tired with the day's business, had thrown himself down on the bamboo settee on the veranda, and that although his eyes were engaged in scanning the pages of the *Chinese World*, his ears could not help receiving the words which were borne to him through the open window.

> " 'Tis better to have loved and lost,
> Than never to have loved at all,"

repeated Mr. Spring Fragrance. Not wishing to hear more of the secret talk of women, he arose and sauntered around the veranda to the other side of the house. Two pigeons circled around his head. He felt in his pocket for a li-chi[4] which he usually carried for their pecking. His fingers touched a little box. It contained a jadestone pendant, which Mrs. Spring Fragrance had particularly admired the last time she was down town. It was the fifth anniversary of Mr. and Mrs. Spring Fragrance's wedding day.

Mr. Spring Fragrance pressed the little box down into the depths of his pocket.

A young man came out of the back door of the house at Mr. Spring Fragrance's left. The Chin Yuen house was at his right.

"Good evening," said the young man. "Good evening," returned Mr. Spring Fragrance. He stepped down from his porch and went and leaned over the railing which separated this yard from the yard in which stood the young man.

"Will you please tell me," said Mr. Spring Fragrance, "the meaning of two lines of an American verse which I have heard?"

"Certainly," returned the young man with a genial smile. He was a star student at the University of Washington, and had not the slightest doubt that he could explain the meaning of all things in the universe.

"Well," said Mr. Spring Fragrance, "it is this:

---

2. Blooming.
3. From *In Memoriam A. H. H.* (1850), by the British poet Alfred, Lord Tennyson (1809–1892).
4. I.e., lychee (the fruit of a Chinese tree).

" 'Tis better to have loved and lost,
Than never to have loved at all."

"Ah!" responded the young man with an air of profound wisdom. "That, Mr. Spring Fragrance, means that it is a good thing to love anyway—even if we can't get what we love, or, as the poet tells us, lose what we love. Of course, one needs experience to feel the truth of this teaching."

The young man smiled pensively and reminiscently. More than a dozen young maidens "loved and lost" were passing before his mind's eye.

"The truth of the teaching!" echoed Mr. Spring Fragrance, a little testily. "There is no truth in it whatever. It is disobedient to reason. Is it not better to have what you do not love than to love what you do not have?"

"That depends," answered the young man, "upon temperament."

"I thank you. Good evening," said Mr. Spring Fragrance. He turned away to muse upon the unwisdom of the American way of looking at things.

Meanwhile, inside the house, Laura was refusing to be comforted.

"Ah, no! no!" cried she. "If I had not gone to school with Kai Tzu, nor talked nor walked with him, nor played the accompaniments to his songs, then I might consider with complacency, or at least without horror, my approaching marriage with the son of Man You. But as it is—oh, as it is—!"

The girl rocked herself to and fro in heartfelt grief.

Mrs. Spring Fragrance knelt down beside her, and clasping her arms around her neck, cried in sympathy:

"Little Sister, oh, Little Sister! Dry your tears—do not despair. A moon has yet to pass before the marriage can take place. Who knows what the stars may have to say to one another during its passing? A little bird has whispered to me—"

For a long time Mrs. Spring Fragrance talked. For a long time Laura listened. When the girl arose to go, there was a bright light in her eyes.

II

Mrs. Spring Fragrance, in San Francisco on a visit to her cousin, the wife of the herb doctor of Clay Street,[5] was having a good time. She was invited everywhere that the wife of an honorable Chinese merchant could go. There was much to see and hear, including more than a dozen babies who had been born in the families of her friends since she last visited the city of the Golden Gate. Mrs. Spring Fragrance loved babies. She had had two herself, but both had been transplanted into the spirit land before the completion of even one moon. There were also many dinners and theatre-parties given in her honor. It was at one of the theatre-parties that Mrs. Spring Fragrance met Ah Oi, a young girl who had the reputation of being the prettiest Chinese girl in San Francisco, and the naughtiest. In spite of gossip, however, Mrs. Spring Fragrance took a great fancy to Ah Oi and invited her to a tête-à-tête picnic on the following day. This invitation Ah Oi joyfully accepted. She was a sort of bird girl and never felt so happy as when out in the park or woods.

On the day after the picnic Mrs. Spring Fragrance wrote to Laura Chin Yuen thus:

---

5. A main street in San Francisco's Chinatown.

My Precious Laura,—May the bamboo ever wave. Next week I accompany Ah Oi to the beauteous town of San José. There will we be met by the son of the Illustrious Teacher, and in a little Mission, presided over by a benevolent American priest, the little Ah Oi and the son of the Illustrious Teacher will be joined together in love and harmony—two pieces of music made to complete one another.

The Son of the Illustrious Teacher, having been through an American Hall of Learning, is well able to provide for his orphan bride and fears not the displeasure of his parents, now that he is assured that your grief at his loss will not be inconsolable. He wishes me to waft to you and to Kai Tzu—and the little Ah Oi joins with him—ten thousand rainbow wishes for your happiness.

My respects to your honorable parents, and to yourself, the heart of your loving friend,

JADE SPRING FRAGRANCE

To Mr. Spring Fragrance, Mrs. Spring Fragrance also indited a letter:

Great and Honored Man;—Greeting from your plum blossom,[6] who is desirous of hiding herself from the sun of your presence for a week of seven days more. My honorable cousin is preparing for the Fifth Moon Festival,[7] and wishes me to compound for the occasion some American "fudge," for which delectable sweet, made by my clumsy hands, you have sometimes shown a slight prejudice. I am enjoying a most agreeable visit, and American friends, as also our own, strive benevolently for the accomplishment of my pleasure. Mrs. Samuel Smith, an American Lady, known to my cousin, asked for my accompaniment to a magniloquent lecture the other evening. The subject was "America, the Protector of China!" It was most exhilarating, and the effect of so much expression of benevolence leads me to beg of you to forget to remember that the barber charges you one dollar for a shave while he humbly submits to the American man a bill of fifteen cents. And murmur no more because your honored elder brother, on a visit to this country, is detained under the roof-tree of this great Government instead of under your own humble roof. Console him with the reflection that he is protected under the wing of the Eagle, the Emblem of Liberty. What is the loss of ten hundred years or ten thousand times ten dollars compared with the happiness of knowing oneself so securely sheltered? All of this I have learned from Mrs. Samuel Smith, who is as brilliant and great of mind as one of your own superior sex.

For me it is sufficient to know that the Golden Gate Park is most enchanting, and the seals on the rock at the Cliff House extremely entertaining and amiable. There is much feasting and merry-making under the lanterns in honor of your Stupid Thorn.

I have purchased for your smoking a pipe with an amber mouth. It is

---

6. The plum blossom is the Chinese flower of virtue. It has been adopted by the Japanese, just in the same way as they have adopted the Chinese national flower, the chrysanthemum [Sui Sin Far's note].

7. The Dragon Boat Festival, held on the fifth day of the fifth lunar month (which falls sometime between late May and the last third of June).

said to be very sweet to the lips and to emit a cloud of smoke fit for the gods to inhale.

Awaiting, by the wonderful wire of the telegram message, your gracious permission to remain for the celebration of the Fifth Moon Festival and the making of American "fudge," I continue for ten thousand times ten thousand years,

Your ever loving obedient woman,

JADE

P.S. Forget not to care for the cat, the birds, and the flowers. Do not eat too quickly nor fan too vigorously now that the weather is warming.

Mrs. Spring Fragrance smiled as she folded this last epistle. Even if he were old-fashioned, there was never a husband so good and kind as hers. Only on one occasion since their marriage had he slighted her wishes. That was when, on the last anniversary of their wedding, she had signified a desire for a certain jadestone pendant, and he had failed to satisfy that desire.

But Mrs. Spring Fragrance, being of a happy nature, and disposed to look upon the bright side of things, did not allow her mind to dwell upon the jadestone pendant. Instead, she gazed complacently down upon her bejeweled fingers and folded in with her letter to Mr. Spring Fragrance a bright little sheaf of condensed love.

III

Mr. Spring Fragrance sat on his doorstep. He had been reading two letters, one from Mrs. Spring Fragrance, and the other from an elderly bachelor cousin in San Francisco. The one from the elderly bachelor cousin was a business letter, but contained the following postscript:

> Tsen Hing, the son of the Government school-master, seems to be much in the company of your young wife. He is a good-looking youth, and pardon me, my dear cousin; but if women are allowed to stray at will from under their husbands' mulberry roofs, what is to prevent them from becoming butterflies?

"Sing Foon is old and cynical," said Mr. Spring Fragrance to himself. "Why should I pay any attention to him? This is America, where a man may speak to a woman, and a woman listen, without any thought of evil."

He destroyed his cousin's letter and re-read his wife's. Then he became very thoughtful. Was the making of American fudge sufficient reason for a wife to wish to remain a week longer in a city where her husband was not?

The young man who lived in the next house came out to water the lawn.

"Good evening," said he. "Any news from Mrs. Spring Fragrance?"

"She is having a very good time," returned Mr. Spring Fragrance.

"Glad to hear it. I think you told me she was to return the end of this week."

"I have changed my mind about her," said Mr. Spring Fragrance. "I am bidding her remain a week longer, as I wish to give a smoking party during her absence. I hope I may have the pleasure of your company."

"I shall be delighted," returned the young fellow. "But, Mr. Spring Fragrance, don't invite any other white fellows. If you do not I shall be able to get in a scoop. You know, I'm a sort of honorary reporter for the *Gleaner*."

"Very well," absently answered Mr. Spring Fragrance.

"Of course, your friend the Consul will be present. I shall call it 'A high-class Chinese stag party!'"

In spite of his melancholy mood, Mr. Spring Fragrance smiled.

"Everything is 'high-class' in America," he observed.

"Sure!" cheerfully assented the young man. "Haven't you ever heard that all Americans are princes and princesses, and just as soon as a foreigner puts his foot upon our shores, he also becomes of the nobility—I mean, the royal family."

"What about my brother in the Detention Pen?"[8] dryly inquired Mr. Spring Fragrance.

"Now, you've got me," said the young man, rubbing his head. "Well, that is a shame—'a beastly shame,' as the Englishman says. But understand, old fellow, we that are real Americans are up against that—even more than you. It is against our principles."

"I offer the real Americans my consolations that they should be compelled to do that which is against their principles."

"Oh, well, it will all come right some day. We're not a bad sort, you know. Think of the indemnity money returned to the Dragon by Uncle Sam."[9]

Mr. Spring Fragrance puffed his pipe in silence for some moments. More than politics was troubling his mind.

At last he spoke. "Love," said he, slowly and distinctly, "comes before the wedding in this country, does it not?"

"Yes, certainly."

Young Carman knew Mr. Spring Fragrance well enough to receive with calmness his most astounding queries.

"Presuming," continued Mr. Spring Fragrance—"presuming that some friend of your father's, living—presuming—in England—has a daughter that he arranges with your father to be your wife. Presuming that you have never seen that daughter, but that you marry her, knowing her not. Presuming that she marries you, knowing you not.—After she marries you and knows you, will that woman love you?"

"Emphatically, no," answered the young man.

"That is the way it would be in America—that the woman who marries the man like that—would not love him?"

"Yes, that is the way it would be in America. Love, in this country, must be free, or it is not love at all."

"In China, it is different!" mused Mr. Spring Fragrance.

"Oh, yes, I have no doubt that in China it is different."

"But the love is in the heart all the same," went on Mr. Spring Fragrance.

"Yes, all the same. Everybody falls in love some time or another. Some"—pensively—"many times."

---

8. I.e., at Angel Island Immigration Center, in San Francisco Bay. Between 1910 and 1940, thousands of Chinese immigrants were sent there, after arriving in San Francisco, for interrogation and often long detention, and many were deported.
9. After the Boxer Uprising (1898–1900), a rebellion of Chinese against foreign influence in their country, China was forced to pay compensation to the foreign nations whose citizens lost their property and, in some cases, their lives; the United States used part of its share to provide scholarships for Chinese students.

Mr. Spring Fragrance arose.

"I must go down town," said he.

As he walked down the street he recalled the remark of a business acquaintance who had met his wife and had had some conversation with her: "She is just like an American woman."

He had felt somewhat flattered when this remark had been made. He looked upon it as a compliment to his wife's cleverness; but it rankled in his mind as he entered the telegraph office. If his wife was becoming as an American woman, would it not be possible for her to love as an American woman—a man to whom she was not married? There also floated in his memory the verse which his wife had quoted to the daughter of Chin Yuen. When the telegraph clerk handed him a blank, he wrote this message:

"Remain as you wish, but remember that ' 'Tis better to have loved and lost, than never to have loved at all.' "

When Mrs. Spring Fragrance received this message, her laughter tinkled like falling water. How droll! How delightful! Here was her husband quoting American poetry in a telegram. Perhaps he had been reading her American poetry books since she had left him! She hoped so. They would lead him to understand her sympathy for her dear Laura and Kai Tzu. She needed no longer keep from him their secret. How joyful! It had been such a hardship to refrain from confiding in him before. But discreetness had been most necessary, seeing that Mr. Spring Fragrance entertained as old-fashioned notions concerning marriage as did the Chin Yuen parents. Strange that that should be so, since he had fallen in love with her picture before *ever* he had seen her, just as she had fallen in love with his! And when the marriage veil was lifted and each beheld the other for the first time in the flesh, there had been no disillusion—no lessening of the respect and affection, which those who had brought about the marriage had inspired in each young heart.

Mrs. Spring Fragrance began to wish she could fall asleep and wake to find the week flown, and she in her own little home pouring tea for Mr. Spring Fragrance.

IV

Mr. Spring Fragrance was walking to business with Mr. Chin Yuen. As they walked they talked.

"Yes," said Mr. Chin Yuen, "the old order is passing away, and the new order is taking its place, even with us who are Chinese. I have finally consented to give my daughter in marriage to young Kai Tzu."

Mr. Spring Fragrance expressed surprise. He had understood that the marriage between his neighbor's daughter and the San Francisco schoolteacher's son was all arranged.

"So 'twas," answered Mr. Chin Yuen; "but it seems the young renegade, without consultation or advice, has placed his affections upon some untrustworthy female, and is so under her influence that he refuses to fulfill his parents' promise to me for him."

"So!" said Mr. Spring Fragrance. The shadow on his brow deepened.

"But," said Mr. Chin Yuen, with affable resignation, "it is all ordained by

Heaven. Our daughter, as the wife of Kai Tzu, for whom she has long had a loving feeling, will not now be compelled to dwell with a mother-in-law and where her own mother is not. For that, we are thankful, as she is our only one and the conditions of life in this Western country are not as in China. Moreover, Kai Tzu, though not so much of a scholar as the teacher's son, has a keen eye for business and that, in America, is certainly much more desirable than scholarship. What do you think?"

"Eh! What!" exclaimed Mr. Spring Fragrance. The latter part of his companion's remarks had been lost upon him.

That day the shadow which had been following Mr. Spring Fragrance ever since he had heard his wife quote, " 'Tis better to have loved," etc., became so heavy and deep that he quite lost himself within it.

At home in the evening he fed the cat, the bird, and the flowers. Then, seating himself in a carved black chair—a present from his wife on his last birthday—he took out his pipe and smoked. The cat jumped into his lap. He stroked it softly and tenderly. It had been much fondled by Mrs. Spring Fragrance, and Mr. Spring Fragrance was under the impression that it missed her. "Poor thing!" said he. "I suppose you want her back!" When he arose to go to bed he placed the animal carefully on the floor, and thus apostrophized it:

"O Wise and Silent One, your mistress returns to you, but her heart she leaves behind her, with the Tommies[1] in San Francisco."

The Wise and Silent One made no reply. He was not a jealous cat.

Mr. Spring Fragrance slept not that night; the next morning he ate not. Three days and three nights without sleep and food went by.

There was a springlike freshness in the air on the day that Mrs. Spring Fragrance came home. The skies overhead were as blue as Puget Sound stretching its gleaming length toward the mighty Pacific, and all the beautiful green world seemed to be throbbing with springing life.

Mrs. Spring Fragrance was never so radiant.

"Oh," she cried light-heartedly, "is it not lovely to see the sun shining so clear, and everything so bright to welcome me?"

Mr. Spring Fragrance made no response. It was the morning after the fourth sleepless night.

Mrs. Spring Fragrance noticed his silence, also his grave face.

"Everything—everyone is glad to see me but you," she declared, half seriously, half jestingly.

Mr. Spring Fragrance set down her valise. They had just entered the house.

"If my wife is glad to see me," he quietly replied, "I also am glad to see her!"

Summoning their servant boy, he bade him look after Mrs. Spring Fragrance's comfort.

"I must be at the store in half an hour," said he, looking at his watch. "There is some very important business requiring attention."

"What is the business?" inquired Mrs. Spring Fragrance, her lip quivering with disappointment.

"I cannot just explain to you," answered her husband.

Mrs. Spring Fragrance looked up into his face with honest and earnest

---

1. I.e., British Americans (usually slang for the British).

eyes. There was something in his manner, in the tone of her husband's voice, which touched her.

"Yen," said she, "you do not look well. You are not well. What is it?"

Something arose in Mr. Spring Fragrance's throat which prevented him from replying.

"O darling one! O sweetest one!" cried a girl's joyous voice. Laura Chin Yuen ran into the room and threw her arms around Mrs. Spring Fragrance's neck.

"I spied you from the window," said Laura, "and I couldn't rest until I told you. We are to be married next week, Kai Tzu and I. And all through you, all through you—the sweetest jade jewel in the world!"

Mr. Spring Fragrance passed out of the room.

"So the son of the Government teacher and little Happy Love are already married," Laura went on, relieving Mrs. Spring Fragrance of her cloak, her hat, and her folding fan.

Mr. Spring Fragrance paused upon the doorstep.

"Sit down, Little Sister, and I will tell you all about it," said Mrs. Spring Fragrance, forgetting her husband for a moment.

When Laura Chin Yuen had danced away, Mr. Spring Fragrance came in and hung up his hat.

"You got back very soon," said Mrs. Spring Fragrance, covertly wiping away the tears which had begun to fall as soon as she thought herself alone.

"I did not go," answered Mr. Spring Fragrance. "I have been listening to you and Laura."

"But if the business is very important, do not you think you should attend to it?" anxiously queried Mrs. Spring Fragrance.

"It is not important to me now," returned Mr. Spring Fragrance. "I would prefer to hear again about Ah Oi and Man You and Laura and Kai Tzu."

"How lovely of you to say that!" exclaimed Mrs. Spring Fragrance, who was easily made happy. And she began to chat away to her husband in the friendliest and wifeliest fashion possible. When she had finished she asked him if he were not glad to hear that those who loved as did the young lovers whose secrets she had been keeping, were to be united; and he replied that indeed he was; that he would like every man to be as happy with a wife as he himself had ever been and ever would be.

"You did not always talk like that," said Mrs. Spring Fragrance slyly. "You must have been reading my American poetry books!"

"American poetry!" ejaculated Mr. Spring Fragrance almost fiercely, "American poetry is detestable, *abhorrable!*"

"Why! why!" exclaimed Mrs. Spring Fragrance, more and more surprised.

But the only explanation which Mr. Spring Fragrance vouchsafed was a jadestone pendant.

1910, 1912

MARY AUSTIN
1868–1934

Ecologist, ethnographer, feminist, fiction writer, journalist, mystic—Mary Austin wrote hundreds of articles and more than thirty books, many focused on the American West, but she was born and raised in Carlinville, Illinois. After the untimely deaths of her father and sister, the young Mary Hunter was brought up by a mother very active in the Women's Christian Temperance Union, an organization important in the nineteenth-century evolution of the women's movement. At the age of twenty, after graduating from Blackburn College, the aspiring writer moved to California with her family and began publishing her first short stories. In 1891 she married Stafford Wallace Austin, and they settled in the Owens Valley, northwest of Bakersfield, where she gave birth to a daughter, Ruth, who proved to be retarded. The Austins were divorced in 1914; Ruth died in an institution four years later.

Austin's most famous work, *The Land of Little Rain* (1903), was inspired by the Mojave Desert and her residence with her husband in a succession of desert towns. Since its publication, this collection of sketches has been celebrated as a western classic. During the years following her move to Carmel, California, Austin maintained a long and productive literary career. Some of her work focuses on American Indian legends: *The Basket Woman* (1905) is a collection of realistic short stories, and *The Arrow-Maker* (1910) is a play about a female shaman. A number of her nonfictional studies, for example *The American Rhythm* (1923), examine the influence of Indian song on written poetry. The problem novels she produced explore the relationship between gender and creativity; her novel *A Woman of Genius* (1912) was based on her own early conflicts about her developing imaginative energies, as was her autobiography, *Earth Horizon* (1932). But Austin remains most revered for the love and respect with which she depicted the American desert as well as the Latino and Native American folk arts that flourished throughout the region. "The Walking Woman," one of her most frequently anthologized stories, captures the resonant mystery Austin found in rural solitaries attempting to follow nature's dictates in the quiet obscurity or seclusion they have chosen. An active, ardent advocate of environmental responsibility, Austin settled in Santa Fe, New Mexico. It seems fitting that Willa Cather wrote her paean to the physical beauties of the Southwest, *Death Comes for the Archbishop* (1927), in Austin's house.

The Walking Woman

The first time of my hearing of her was at Temblor.[1] We had come all one day between blunt, whitish bluffs rising from mirage water, with a thick, pale wake of dust billowing from the wheels, all the dead wall of the foothills sliding and shimmering with heat, to learn that the Walking Woman had passed us somewhere in the dizzying dimness, going down to the Tulares on her own feet. We heard of her again in the Carrisal, and again at Adobe Station, where she had passed a week before the shearing, and at last I had a glimpse of her at the Eighteen-Mile House as I went hurriedly northward on the Mojave stage; and afterward, sheepherders at whose camps she slept, and cowboys at rodeos, told me as much of her way of life as they could

---

1. A town in the Mojave Desert in California. All the places named in the story are located in or near this region.

understand. Like enough they told her as much of mine. That was very little. She was the Walking Woman, and no one knew her name, but because she was a sort of whom men speak respectfully, they called her to her face Mrs. Walker, and she answered to it if she was so inclined. She came and went about our western world on no discoverable errand, and whether she had some place of refuge where she lay by in the interim, or whether between her seldom, unaccountable appearances in our quarter she went on steadily walking, was never learned. She came and went, oftenest in a kind of muse[2] of travel which the untrammelled space begets, or at rare intervals flooding wondrously with talk, never of herself, but of things she had known and seen. She must have seen some rare happenings, too—by report. She was at Maverick the time of the Big Snow, and at Tres Piños when they brought home the body of Morena; and if anybody could have told whether De Borba killed Mariana for spite or defence, it would have been she, only she could not be found when most wanted. She was at Tunawai at the time of the cloud-burst, and if she had cared for it could have known most desirable things of the ways of trail-making, burrow-habiting small things.

All of which should have made her worth meeting, though it was not, in fact, for such things I was wishful to meet her; and as it turned out, it was not of these things we talked when at last we came together. For one thing, she was a woman, not old, who had gone about alone in a country where the number of women is as one in fifteen. She had eaten and slept at the herder's camps, and laid by for days at one-man stations whose masters had no other touch of human kind than the passing of chance prospectors, or the halting of the tri-weekly stage. She had been set on her way by teamsters[3] who lifted her out of white, hot desertness and put her down at the crossing of unnamed ways, days distant from anywhere. And through all this she passed unarmed and unoffended. I had the best testimony to this, the witness of the men themselves. I think they talked of it because they were so much surprised at it. It was not, on the whole, what they expected of themselves.

Well I understand that nature which wastes its borders with too eager burning, beyond which rim of desolation it flares forever quick and white, and have had some inkling of the isolating calm of a desire too high to stoop to satisfaction. But you could not think of these things pertaining to the Walking Woman; and if there were ever any truth in the exemption from offence residing in a frame of behavior called ladylike, it should have been inoperative here. What this really means is that you get no affront so long as your behavior in the estimate of the particular audience invites none. In the estimate of the immediate audience—conduct which affords protection in Mayfair[4] gets you no consideration in Maverick. And by no canon could it be considered ladylike to go about on your own feet, with a blanket and a black bag and almost no money in your purse, in and about the haunts of rude and solitary men.

There were other things that pointed the wish for a personal encounter with the Walking Woman. One of them was the contradiction of reports of her—as to whether she was comely, for example. Report said yes, and again, plain to the point of deformity. She had a twist to her face, some said; a

---

2. State of dreamy abstraction.
3. Those who drive teams of horses, mules, or oxen.
4. A fashionable part of London.

hitch to one shoulder; they averred she limped as she walked. But by the distance she covered she should have been straight and young. As to sanity, equal incertitude. On the mere evidence of her way of life she was cracked; not quite broken, but unserviceable. Yet in her talk there was both wisdom and information, and the word she brought about trails and water-holes was as reliable as an Indian's.

By her own account she had begun by walking off an illness. There had been an invalid to be taken care of for years, leaving her at last broken in body, and with no recourse but her own feet to carry her out of that predicament. It seemed there had been, besides the death of her invalid, some other worrying affairs, upon which, and the nature of her illness, she was never quite clear, so that it might very well have been an unsoundness of mind which drove her to the open, sobered and healed at last by the large soundness of nature. It must have been about that time that she lost her name. I am convinced that she never told it because she did not know it herself. She was the Walking Woman, and the country people called her Mrs. Walker. At the time I knew her, though she wore short hair and a man's boots, and had a fine down over all her face from exposure to the weather, she was perfectly sweet and sane.

I had met her occasionally at ranch-houses and road-stations, and had got as much acquaintance as the place allowed; but for the things I wished to know there wanted a time of leisure and isolation. And when the occasion came we talked altogether of other things.

It was at Warm Spring in the Little Antelope I came upon her in the heart of a clear forenoon. The spring lies off a mile from the main trail, and has the only trees about it known in that country. First you come upon a pool of waste full of weeds of a poisonous dark green, every reed ringed about the water-level with a muddy white incrustation. Then the three oaks appear staggering on the slope, and the spring sobs and blubbers below them in ashy-colored mud. All the hills of that country have the down plunge toward the desert and back abruptly toward the Sierra. The grass is thick and brittle and bleached straw-color toward the end of the season. As I rode up the swale[5] of the spring I saw the Walking Woman sitting where the grass was deepest, with her black bag and blanket, which she carried on a stick, beside her. It was one of those days when the genius of talk flows as smoothly as the rivers of mirage through the blue hot desert morning.

You are not to suppose that in my report of a Borderer[6] I give you the words only, but the full meaning of the speech. Very often the words are merely the punctuation of thought; rather, the crests of the long waves of intercommunicative silences. Yet the speech of the Walking Woman was fuller than most.

The best of our talk that day began in some dropped word of hers from which I inferred that she had had a child. I was surprised at that, and then wondered why I should have been surprised, for it is the most natural of all experiences to have children. I said something of that purport, and also that it was one of the perquisites of living I should be least willing to do without. And that led to the Walking Woman saying that there were three things

---

5. Low-lying and often wet stretch of land.
6. I.e., one who lives in what Austin calls the "country of lost borders."

which if you had known you could cut out all the rest, and they were good any way you got them, but best if, as in her case, they were related to and grew each one out of the others. It was while she talked that I decided that she really did have a twist to her face, a sort of natural warp or skew into which it fell when it was worn merely as a countenance, but which disappeared the moment it became the vehicle of thought or feeling.

The first of the experiences the Walking Woman had found most worth while had come to her in a sand-storm on the south slope of Tehachapi in a dateless spring. I judged it should have been about the time she began to find herself, after the period of worry and loss in which her wandering began. She had come, in a day pricked full of intimations of a storm, to the camp of Filon Geraud, whose companion shepherd had gone a three days' *pasear*[7] to Mojave for supplies. Geraud was of great hardihood, red-blooded, of a full laughing eye, and an indubitable spark for women. It was the season of the year when there is a soft bloom on the days, but the nights are cowering cold and the lambs tender, not yet flockwise. At such times a sand-storm works incalculable disaster. The lift of the wind is so great that the whole surface of the ground appears to travel upon it slantwise, thinning out miles high in air. In the intolerable smother the lambs are lost from the ewes; neither dogs nor man make headway against it.

The morning flared through a horizon of yellow smudge, and by midforenoon the flock broke.

"There were but the two of us to deal with the trouble," said the Walking Woman. "Until that time I had not known how strong I was, nor how good it is to run when running is worth while. The flock travelled down the wind, the sand bit our faces; we called, and after a time heard the words broken and beaten small by the wind. But after a little we had not to call. All the time of our running in the yellow dusk of day and the black dark of night, I knew where Filon was. A flock-length away, I knew him. Feel? What should I feel? I knew. I ran with the flock and turned it this way and that as Filon would have.

"Such was the force of the wind that when we came together we held by one another and talked a little between pantings. We snatched and ate what we could as we ran. All that day and night until the next afternoon the camp kit was not out of the cayaques.[8] But we held the flock. We herded them under a butte[9] when the wind fell off a little, and the lambs sucked; when the storm rose they broke, but we kept upon their track and brought them together again. At night the wind quieted, and we slept by turns; at least Filon slept. I lay on the ground when my turn was and beat with the storm. I was no more tired than the earth was. The sand filled in the creases of the blanket, and where I turned, dripped back upon the ground. But we saved the sheep. Some ewes there were that would not give down their milk because of the worry of the storm, and the lambs died. But we kept the flock together. And I was not tired."

The Walking Woman stretched out her arms and clasped herself, rocking in them as if she would have hugged the recollection to her breast.

"For you see," said she, "I worked with a man, without excusing, without

---

7. Walk (Spanish).
8. Saddlebags. "Camp kit": supplies.

9. Isolated hill or rocky formation.

any burden on me of looking or seeming. Not fiddling or fumbling as women work, and hoping it will all turn out for the best. It was not for Filon to ask, Can you, or Will you. He said, Do, and I did. And my work was good. We held the flock. And that," said the Walking Woman, the twists coming in her face again, "is one of the things that make you able to do without the others."

"Yes," I said; and then, "What others?"

"Oh," she said, as if it pricked her, "the looking and the seeming."

And I had not thought until that time that one who had the courage to be the Walking Woman would have cared! We sat and looked at the pattern of the thick crushed grass on the slope, wavering in the fierce noon like the waterings in the coat of a tranquil beast; the ache of a world-old bitterness sobbed and whispered in the spring. At last—

"It is by the looking and the seeming," said I, "that the opportunity finds you out."

"Filon found out," said the Walking Woman. She smiled; and went on from that to tell me how, when the wind went down about four o'clock and left the afternoon clear and tender, the flock began to feed, and they had out the kit from the cayaques, and cooked a meal. When it was over, and Filon had his pipe between his teeth, he came over from his side of the fire, of his own notion, and stretched himself on the ground beside her. Of his own notion. There was that in the way she said it that made it seem as if nothing of the sort had happened before to the Walking Woman, and for a moment I thought she was about to tell me one of the things I wished to know; but she went on to say what Filon had said to her of her work with the flock. Obvious, kindly things, such as any man in sheer decency would have said, so that there must have something more gone with the words to make them so treasured of the Walking Woman.

"We were very comfortable," said she, "and not so tired as we expected to be. Filon leaned up on his elbow. I had not noticed until then how broad he was in the shoulders, and how strong in the arms. And we had saved the flock together. We felt that. There was something that said together, in the slope of his shoulders toward me. It was around his mouth and on the cheek high up under the shine of his eyes. And under the shine the look—the look that said, 'We are one sort and one mind'—his eyes that were the color of the flat water in the tulares[1]—do you know the look?"

"I know it."

"The wind was stopped and all the earth smelled of dust, and Filon understood very well that what I had done with him I could not have done so well with another. And the look—the look in the eyes—"

"Ah-ah—!"

I have always said, I will say again, I do not know why at this point the Walking Woman touched me. If it were merely a response to my unconscious throb of sympathy, or the unpremeditated way of her heart to declare that this, after all, was the best of all indispensable experiences; or if in some flash of forward vision, encompassing the unimpassioned years, the stir, the movement of tenderness were for *me*—but no; as often as I have thought of it, I have thought of a different reason, but no conclusive one, why the Walking Woman should have put out her hand and laid it on my arm.

---

1. Marshy places overgrown with bulrushes ("tules").

"To work together, to love together," said the Walking Woman, withdrawing her hand again; "there you have two of the things; the other you know."

"The mouth at the breast," said I.

"The lips and the hands," said the Walking Woman. "The little, pushing hands and the small cry." There ensued a pause of fullest understanding, while the land before us swam in the noon, and a dove in the oaks behind the spring began to call. A little red fox came out of the hills and lapped delicately at the pool.

"I stayed with Filon until the fall," said she. "All that summer in the Sierra, until it was time to turn south on the trail. It was a good time, and longer than he could be expected to have loved one like me. And besides, I was no longer able to keep the trail. My baby was born in October."

Whatever more there was to say to this, the Walking Woman's hand said it, straying with remembering gesture to her breast. There are so many ways of loving and working, but only one way of the first-born. She added after an interval, that she did not know if she would have given up her walking to keep at home and tend him, or whether the thought of her son's small feet running beside her in the trails would have driven her to the open again. The baby had not stayed long enough for that. "And whenever the wind blows in the night," said the Walking Woman, "I wake and wonder if he is well covered."

She took up her black bag and her blanket; there was the ranch-house of Dos Palos to be made before night, and she went as outliers do, without a hope expressed of another meeting and no word of good-bye. She was the Walking Woman. That was it. She had walked off all sense of society-made values, and, knowing the best when the best came to her, was able to take it. Work—as I believed; love—as the Walking Woman had proved it; a child—as you subscribe to it. But look you: it was the naked thing the Walking Woman grasped, not dressed and tricked out, for instance, by prejudices in favor of certain occupations; and love, man love, taken as it came, not picked over and rejected if it carried no obligation of permanency; and a child; *any* way you get it, a child is good to have, say nature and the Walking Woman; to have it and not to wait upon a proper concurrence of so many decorations that the event may not come at all.

At least one of us is wrong. To work and to love and to bear children. *That* sounds easy enough. But the way we live establishes so many things of much more importance.

Far down the dim, hot valley I could see the Walking Woman with her blanket and the black bag over her shoulder. She had a queer, sidelong gait, as if in fact she had a twist all through her.

Recollecting suddenly that people called her lame, I ran down to the open space below the spring where she had passed. There in the bare, hot sand the track of her two feet bore evenly and white.

1909

CHARLOTTE MEW
1869–1928

When Charlotte Mew died in 1928, she was so obscure that one newspaper report of her death described her as "Charlotte New [*sic*], said to be a writer." Yet in her earlier years Mew had been a well-known literary woman whose works were admired by a number of contemporaries, including such notable artists as John Masefield, Walter de la Mare, and Thomas Hardy. Even during her lifetime, however, Mew was a paradoxical figure. The author of vividly detailed dramatic monologues that were surprising in their era for their frank depictions of both female and male sexuality, she was rigorous in maintaining her own moral standards and would, as one scholar explains, "drop anyone whom scandal had touched." Raised by genteel parents as a typical Victorian lady, she was, according to her friend Alida Monroe, "passionately attached to another woman," and she became virtually a transvestite in middle age, dressing in a tweed topcoat, a porkpie hat, and "size-two custom-made boots."

Mew was born in London into a large, comfortable middle-class family. But the pleasures of her youth were short-lived: three siblings died in childhood, and two others became mentally ill and were confined to asylums. Moreover, her father's death, when she was in her late twenties, left Charlotte, her remaining sister, and her mother nearly impoverished, for, as she later recollected, he had "spent all his available capital on living." To support themselves and their mother, Charlotte and her sister attempted various odd jobs; most notably, Charlotte wrote stories and poems for *The Egoist, The English Woman, The Yellow Book,* and other journals. But despite a modicum of literary success, she always had to economize and never recaptured the gaiety of her childhood home. In addition, the sexual orientation that she never openly discussed led in at least one case to public humiliation; in 1913, she evidently fell in love with the novelist May Sinclair, who admired her writing but decisively rejected her romantic overtures, then circulated cruel stories about an unpleasant bedroom scene.

Mew's most important verses appeared in a 1916 collection, *The Farmer's Bride,* whose title poem is still much anthologized. In this monologue, as in the equally powerful "The Quiet House," she demonstrates the vitality and inventiveness that must have especially appealed to a fellow dramatic poet like Thomas Hardy, who declared that she was "the least pretentious but undoubtedly the best woman poet of our day." At the same time, though, both pieces suggest the intensity with which she herself may have secretly rebelled against the veneer of docility she had been taught to cultivate. When the speaker of "The Quiet House" exclaims, "I think that my soul is red / Like the soul of a sword or a scarlet flower," one feels that she may be expressing Mew's own sexual and emotional frustrations. Similarly, when the same speaker wistfully and wishfully looks forward to the day when "I *shall* not think; I shall not be," one fears that her nihilistic desire predicts the day when Mew herself, alone and impoverished, put an end to her conflicted life by drinking a bottle of Lysol. With its powerful imagery of living burial, her chilling story, "A White Night," might be read as equally prophetic.

Yet despite her isolation—or perhaps because of it—Mew was thought by her contemporaries to be not only a great poet but a great performer of her own poems. When she read her verse aloud, notes the critic Michael Newton, she was said to "go into a trance, from which at the end of the reading she would have, with some difficulty to be summoned back," so that she "intoxicated her audience," with one observer remarking that listening to her was like "having whiskey with my tea."

A White Night

"The incident," said Cameron, "is spoiled inevitably in the telling, by its merely accidental quality of melodrama, its sensational machinery, which, to the view of anyone who didn't witness it, is apt to blur the finer outlines of the scene. The subtlety, or call it the significance, is missed, and unavoidably, as one attempts to put the thing before you, in a certain casual crudity, and inessential violence of fact. Make it a medieval matter—put it back some centuries—and the affair takes on its proper tone immediately, is tinctured with the sinister solemnity which actually enveloped it. But as it stands, a recollection, an experience, a picture, well, it doesn't reproduce; one must have the original if one is going to hang it on one's wall."

In spite of which I took it down the night he told it and, thanks to a trick of accuracy, I believe you have the story as I heard it, almost word for word.

It was in the spring of 1876, a rainless spring, as I remember it, of white roads and brown crops and steely skies.

Sent out the year before on mining business, I had been then some eighteen months in Spain. My job was finished; I was leaving the Black Country, planning a vague look round, perhaps a little sport among the mountains, when a letter from my sister Ella laid the dust of doubtful schemes.

She was on a discursive[1] honeymoon. They had come on from Florence to Madrid, and disappointed with the rank modernity of their last halt, wished to explore some of the least known towns of the interior: "Something unique, untrodden, and uncivilized," she indicated modestly. Further, if I were free and amiable, and so on, they would join me anywhere in Andalusia. I was in fact to show them round.

I did "my possible;" we roughed it pretty thoroughly, but the young person's passion for the strange bore her robustly through the risks and discomforts of those wilder districts which at best, perhaps, are hardly woman's ground.

King, on occasion nursed anxiety, and mourned his little luxuries; Ella accepted anything that befell, from dirt to danger, with a humorous composure dating back to nursery days—she had the instincts and the physique of a traveller, with a brilliancy of touch and a decision of attack on human instruments which told. She took our mule-drivers in hand with some success. Later, no doubt, their wretched beasts were made to smart for it, in the reaction from a lull in that habitual brutality which makes the animals of Spain a real blot upon the gay indifferentism of its people.

It pleased her to devise a lurid *Dies Irae*[2] for these affable barbarians, a special process of reincarnation for the Spaniard generally, whereby the space of one dog's life at least should be ensured to him.

And on the day I'm coming to, a tedious, dislocating journey in a springless cart had brought her to the verge of quite unusual weariness, a weariness of spirit only, she protested, waving a hand toward our man who lashed and sang alternately, fetching at intervals a sunny smile for the poor lady's vain remonstrances before he lashed again.

---

1. Running hither and thither.
2. Day of Wrath (Latin); i.e., Judgment Day, the subject of a famous medieval hymn that begins with these words.

The details of that day—our setting forth, our ride, and our arrival—all the minor episodes stand out with singular distinctness, forming a background in one's memory to the eventual, central scene.

We left our inn—a rough *posada*[3]—about sunrise, and our road, washed to a track by winter rains, lay first through wide half-cultivated slopes, capped everywhere with orange trees and palm and olive patches, curiously bare of farms or villages, till one recalls the lawless state of those outlying regions and the absence of communication between them and town.

Abruptly, blotted in blue mist, vineyards and olives, with the groups of aloes marking off field boundaries, disappeared. We entered on a land of naked rock, peak after peak of it, cutting a jagged line against the clear intensity of the sky.

This passed again, with early afternoon our straight, white road grew featureless, a dusty stretch, save far ahead the sun-tipped ridge of a sierra, and the silver ribbon of the river twisting among the barren hills. Toward the end we passed one of the wooden crosses set up on these roads to mark some spot of violence or disaster. These are the only signposts one encounters, and as we came up with it, our beasts were goaded for the last ascent.

Irregular grey walls came into view; we skirted them and turned in through a Roman gateway and across a bridge into a maze of narrow stone-pitched streets, spanned here and there by Moorish arches,[4] and execrably rough to rattle over.

A strong illusion of the Orient, extreme antiquity and dreamlike stillness marked the place.

Crossing the grey arcaded Plaza, just beginning at that hour to be splashed with blots of gaudy colour moving to the tinkling of the mule-bells, we were soon upon the outskirts of the town—the most untouched, remote and, I believe, the most remarkable that we had dropped upon.

In its neglect and singularity, it made a claim to something like supremacy of charm. There was the quality of diffidence belonging to unrecognized abandoned personalities in that appeal.

That's how it's docketed in memory—a city with a claim, which, as it happened, I was not to weigh.

Our inn, a long, one-storeyed building with caged windows, most of them unglazed, had been an old palacio;[5] its broken fortunes hadn't robbed it of its character, its air.

The spacious place was practically empty, and the shuttered rooms, stone-flagged and cool, after our shadeless ride, invited one to a prolonged siesta; but Ella wasn't friendly to a pause. Her buoyancy survived our meal. She seemed even to face the morrow's repetition of that indescribable experience with serenity. We found her in the small paved garden, sipping chocolate and airing Spanish with our host, a man of some distinction, possibly of broken fortunes too.

The conversation, delicately edged with compliment on his side, was on hers a little blunted by a limited vocabulary, and left us both presumably a margin for imagination.

---

3. Lodging, inn (Spanish).
4. Andalusia, which covers most of southern Spain, was long a Roman province (2nd c. B.C.E.–5th c. C.E.); rule by the Moors—Muslim Berbers—began in 711, was restricted to Granada (in the south) in the 13th century, and ended in 1492.
5. Palace (Spanish).

Sí, la Señora,[6] he explained as we came up, knew absolutely nothing of fatigue, and the impetuosity of the *Señora*, this attractive eagerness to make acquaintance with it, did great honour to his much forgotten, much neglected town. He spoke of it with rather touching ardour, as a place unvisited, but *"digno de renombre illustre,"* worthy of high fame.

It has stood still, it was perhaps too stationary; innovation was repellent to the Spaniard, yet this conservatism, lack of enterprise, the virtue or the failing of his country—as we pleased—had its aesthetic value. Was there not, he would appeal to the *Señora*, *"una belleza de reposo"* a beauty of quiescence a dignity above prosperity? *"Muy bien."*[7] Let the *Señora* judge, you had it there!

We struck out from the town, perhaps insensibly toward the landmark of a Calvary,[8] planted a mile or so beyond the walls, its three black shafts above the mass of roofs and pinnacles, in sharp relief against the sky, against which suddenly a flock of vultures threw the first white cloud. With the descending sun, the clear persistence of the blue was losing permanence, a breeze sprang up and birds began to call.

The Spanish evening has unique effects and exquisite exhilarations: this one led us on some distance past the Calvary and the last group of scattered houses—many in complete decay—which straggle, thinning outwards from the city boundaries into the *campo*.[9]

Standing alone, after a stretch of crumbling wall, a wretched little *venta*,[1] like a stop to some meandering sentence, closed the broken line.

The place was windowless, but through the open door an oath or two—the common blend of sacrilege and vileness—with a smell of charcoal, frying oil-cakes[2] and an odour of the stable, drifted out into the freshness of the evening air.

Immediately before us lay a dim expanse of treeless plain: behind, clear cut against a smokeless sky, the flat roof lines and towers of the city, seeming, as we looked back on them, less distant than in fact they were.

We took a road which finally confronted us with a huge block of buildings, an old church and convent, massed in the shadow of a hill and standing at the entrance to three cross-roads.

The convent, one of the few remaining in the south, not fallen into ruin, nor yet put, as far as one could judge, to worldly uses, was exceptionally large. We counted over thirty windows in a line upon the western side below the central tower with its pointed turret; the eastern wing, an evidently older part, was cut irregularly with a few square gratings.

The big, grey structure was impressive in its loneliness, its blank negation of the outside world, its stark expressionless detachment.

The church, of darker stone, was massive too; its only noticeable feature a small cloister with Romanesque[3] arcades joining the nave on its southwestern wall.

A group of peasant women coming out from vespers passed us and went

---

6. Yes, the lady (Spanish).
7. Very well (Spanish).
8. The hill where Jesus was crucified.
9. Countryside, field (Spanish).
1. Roadside inn (Spanish).

2. I.e., donut-like fried dough.
3. A highly ornamental style of architecture, dominant in Europe from the 10th to the mid-12th century.

chattering up the road, the last, an aged creature shuffling painfully some yards behind the rest still muttering her

> *Madre purisima,*
> *Madre catisima,*
> *Ruega por nosostros,*[4]

in a kind of automatic drone.

We looked in, as one does instinctively: the altar lights which hang like sickly stars in the profound obscurity of Spanish churches were being quickly blotted out.

We didn't enter then, but turned back to the convent gate, which stood half open, showing a side of the uncorniced cloisters, and a crowd of flowers, touched to an intensity of brilliance and fragrance by the twilight. Six or seven dogs, the sandy-coloured lurchers of the country, lean and wolfish-looking hounds, were sprawling round the gateway; save for this dejected crew, the place seemed resolutely lifeless; and this absence of a human note was just. One didn't want its solitude or silence touched, its really fine impersonality destroyed.

We hadn't meant—there wasn't light enough—to try the church again, but as we passed it, we turned into the small cloister. King, who had come to his last match, was seeking shelter from the breeze which had considerably freshened, and at the far end we came upon a little door, unlocked. I don't know why we tried it, but mechanically, as the conscientious tourist will, we drifted in and groped round. Only the vaguest outlines were discernible; the lancets of the lantern at the transept crossing, and a large rose window at the western end seemed, at a glance, the only means of light, and this was failing, leaving fast the fading panes.

One half-detected, almost guessed, the blind triforium,[5] but the enormous width of the great building made immediate mark. The darkness, masking as it did distinctive features, emphasized the sense of space, which, like the spirit of a shrouded form, gained force, intensity, from its material disguise.

We stayed not more than a few minutes, but on reaching the small door again we found it fast; bolted or locked undoubtedly in the short interval. Of course we put our backs to it and made a pretty violent outcry, hoping the worthy sacristan was hanging round or somewhere within call. Of course he wasn't. We tried two other doors; both barred, and there was nothing left for it but noise. We shouted, I suppose, for half an hour, intermittently, and King persisted hoarsely after I had given out.

The echo of the vast, dark, empty place caught up our cries, seeming to hold them in suspension for a second in the void invisibility of roof and arches, then to fling them down in hollow repetition with an accent of unearthly mimicry which struck a little grimly on one's ear; and when we paused the silence seemed alert, expectant, ready to repel the first recurrence of unholy clamour. Finally, we gave it up; the hope of a release before the dawn, at earliest, was too forlorn. King, explosive and solicitous, was solemnly perturbed, but Ella faced the situation with an admirable tranquility. Some chocolate and a muff would certainly, for her, she said, have made it

---

4. Mother most pure, Mother most chaste, pray for us (Spanish).

5. The gallery forming the upper story of the church aisle.

more engaging, but poor dear men, the really tragic element resolved itself into—No matches, no cigar!

Unluckily we hadn't even this poor means of temporary light. Our steps and voices sounded loud, almost aggressive, as we groped about; the darkness then was shutting down and shortly it grew absolute. We camped eventually in one of the side chapels on the south side of the chancel, and kept a conversation going for a time, but gradually it dropped. The temperature, the fixed obscurity, and possibly a curious oppression in the spiritual atmosphere relaxed and forced it down.

The scent of incense clung about; a biting chillness crept up through the aisles; it got intensely cold. The stillness too became insistent; it was literally deathlike, rigid, exclusive, even awfully remote. It shut us out and held aloof; our passive presences, our mere vitality, seemed almost a disturbance of it; quiet as we were, we breathed, but it was breathless, and as time went on, one's impulse was to fight the sort of shapeless personality it presently assumed, to talk, to walk about and make a definite attack on it. Its influence on the others was presumably more soothing, obviously they weren't that way inclined.

Five or six hours must have passed. Nothing had marked them, and they hadn't seemed to move. The darkness seemed to thicken, in a way, to muddle thought and filter through into one's brain, and waiting, cramped and cold for it to lift, the soundlessness again impressed itself unpleasantly—it was intense, unnatural, acute.

And then it stirred.

The break in it was vague but positive; it might have been that, scarcely audible, the wind outside was rising, and yet not precisely that. I barely caught, and couldn't localize the sound.

Ella and King were dozing, they had had some snatches of uncomfortable sleep; I, I suppose, was preternaturally awake. I heard a key turn, and the swing back of a door, rapidly followed by a wave of voices breaking in. I put my hand out and touched King, and in a moment, both of them waked and started up.

I can't say how, but it at once occurred to us that quiet was our cue, that we were in for something singular.

The place was filling slowly with a chant, and then, emerging from the eastern end of the north aisle and travelling down just opposite, across the intervening dark, a line of light came into view, crossing the opening of the arches, cut by the massive piers, a moving, flickering line, advancing and advancing with the voices.

The outlines of the figures in the long procession weren't perceptible, the faces, palely lit and level with the tapers they were carrying, one rather felt than saw; but unmistakably the voices were men's voices, and the chant, the measured, reiterated cadences, prevailed over the wavering light.

Heavy and sombre as the stillness which it broke, vaguely akin to it, the chant swept in and gained upon the silence with a motion of the tide. It was a music neither of the senses, nor the spirit, but the mind, as set, as stately, almost as inanimate as the dark aisles through which it echoed; even, colourless and cold.

And then, quite suddenly, against its grave and passionless inflections something clashed, a piercing intermittent note, an awful discord, shrilling out and dying down and shrilling out again—a cry—a scream.

The chant went on; the light, from where we stood, was steadily retreating, and we ventured forward. Judging our whereabouts as best we could, we made towards the choir and stumbled up some steps, placing ourselves eventually behind one of the pillars of the apse. And from this point, the whole proceeding was apparent.

At the west end the line of light was turning; fifty or sixty monks (about—and at a venture) habited in brown and carrying tapers, walking two and two, were moving up the central aisle towards us, headed by three, one with the cross between two others bearing heavy silver candlesticks with tapers, larger than those carried by the rest.

Reaching the chancel[6] steps, they paused; the three bearing the cross and candlesticks stood facing the altar, while those following diverged to right and left and lined the aisle. The first to take up this position were quite young, some almost boys; they were succeeded gradually by older men, those at the tail of the procession being obviously aged and infirm.

And then a figure, white and slight, erect—a woman's figure—struck a startling note at the far end of the brown line, a note as startling as the shrieks which jarred recurrently, were jarring still against the chant.

A pace or two behind her walked two priests in surplices, and after them another, vested in a cope. And on the whole impassive company her presence, her disturbance, made no mark. For them, in fact, she wasn't there.

Neither was she aware of them. I doubt if to her consciousness, or mine, as she approached, grew definite, there was a creature in the place besides herself.

She moved and uttered her successive cries as if both sound and motion were entirely mechanical—more like a person in some trance of terror or of anguish than a voluntary rebel; her cries bespoke a physical revulsion into which her spirit didn't enter; they were not her own—they were outside herself; there was no discomposure in her carriage, nor, when we presently saw it, in her face. Both were distinguished by a certain exquisite hauteur, and this detachment of her personality from her distress impressed one curiously. She wasn't altogether real, she didn't altogether live, and yet her presence there was the supreme reality of the unreal scene, and lent to it, at least as I was viewing it, its only element of life.

She had, one understood, her part to play; she wasn't, for the moment, quite prepared; she played it later with superb effect.

As she came up with the three priests, the monks closed in and formed a semi-circle round them, while the priests advanced and placed themselves behind the monks who bore the cross and candle-sticks, immediately below the chancel steps, facing the altar. They left her standing some few paces back, in the half-ring of sickly light shed by the tapers.

Now one saw her face. It was striking beauty, but its age? One couldn't say. It had the tints, the purity of youth—it might have been extremely young, matured merely by the moment; but for a veil of fine repression which only years, it seemed, could possibly have woven. And it was itself—this face—a mask, one of the loveliest that spirit ever wore. It kept the spirit's counsel. Though what stirred it then, in that unique emergency, one saw—to what

---

6. The part of the church containing the altar.

had stirred it, or might stir it gave no clue. It threw one back on vain conjecture.

Put the match of passion to it—would it burn? Touch it with grief and would it cloud, contract? With joy—and could it find, or had it ever found, a smile? Again, one couldn't say.

Only, as she stood there, erect and motionless, it showed the faintest flicker of distaste, disgust, as if she shrank from some repellent contact. She was clad, I think I said, from head to foot in a white linen garment; head and ears were covered too, the oval of the face alone was visible, and this was slightly flushed. Her screams were changing into little cries or moans, like those of a spent animal, from whom the momentary pressure of attack has been removed. They broke from her at intervals, unnoticed, unsuppressed, and now on silence, for the monks had ceased their chanting.

As they did so one realized the presence of these men, who, up to now, had scarcely taken shape as actualities, been more than an accompaniment—a drone. They shifted from a mass of voices to a row of pallid faces, each one lit by its own taper, hung upon the dark, or thrown abruptly, as it were, upon a screen; all different; all, at first distinct, but linked together by a subtle likeness, stamped with that dye which blurs the print of individuality—the signet of the cloister.

Taking them singly, though one did it roughly, rapidly enough, it wasn't difficult at starting to detect varieties of natural and spiritual equipment. There they were, spread out for sorting, nonentities and saints and devils, side by side, and what was queerer, animated by one purpose, governed by one law.

Some of the faces touched upon divinity; some fell below humanity; some were, of course, merely a blotch of book and bell,[7] and all were set impassively toward the woman standing there.

And then one lost the sense of their diversity in their resemblance; the similarity persisted and persisted till the row of faces seemed to merge into one face—the face of nothing human—of a system, of a rule. It framed the woman's and one felt the force of it: she wasn't in the hands of men.

There was a pause filled only by her cries, a space of silence which they hardly broke; and then one of the monks stepped forward, slid into the chancel and began to light up the high altar. The little yellow tongues of flame struggled and started up, till first one line and then another starred the gloom.

Her glance had followed him; her eyes were fixed upon that point of darkness growing to a blaze. There was for her, in that illumination, some intense significance, and as she gazed intently on the patch of brilliance, her cries were suddenly arrested—quelled. The light had lifted something, given back to her an unimpaired identity. She was at last in full possession of herself. The flicker of distaste had passed and left her face to its inflexible, inscrutable repose.

She drew herself to her full height and turned towards the men behind her with an air of proud surrender, of magnificent disdain. I think she made some sign.

---

7. The accessories of a religious ceremony.

Another monk stepped out, extinguished and laid down his taper, and approached her.

I was prepared for something singular, for something passably bizarre, but not for what immediately occurred. He touched her eyes and closed them; then her mouth, and made a feint of closing that, while one of the two priests threw over his short surplice a black stole and started audibly with a *Sub venite*.[8] The monks responded. Here and there I caught the words or sense of a response. The prayers for the most part were unintelligible: it was no doubt the usual office[9] for the dead, and if it was, no finer satire for the work in hand could well have been devised. Loudly and unexpectedly above his unctuous monotone a bell clanged out three times. An *Ave* followed, after which two bells together, this time muffled, sounded out again three times. The priest proceeded with a *Miserere*,[1] during which they rang the bells alternately, and there was something curiously suggestive and determinate about this part of the performance. The real action had, one felt, begun.

At the first stroke of the first bell her eyelids fluttered, but she kept them down; it wasn't until later at one point in the response, "*Non intres in judicium cum ancilla tua Domine*,"[2] she yielded to an impulse of her lips, permitted them the shadow of a smile. But for this slip she looked the thing of death they reckoned to have made her—detached herself, with an inspired touch, from all the living actors in the solemn farce, from all apparent apprehension of the scene. I, too, was quite incredibly outside it all.

I hadn't even asked myself precisely what was going to take place. Possibly I had caught the trick of her quiescence, acquiescence, and I went no further than she went; I waited—waited with her, as it were, to see it through. And I experienced a vague, almost resentful sense of interruption, incongruity, when King broke in to ask me what was up. He brought me back to Ella's presence, to the consciousness that this, so far as the spectators were concerned, was not a woman's comedy.

I made it briefly plain to them, as I knew something of the place and people, that any movement on our side would probably prove more than rash, and turned again to what was going forward.

They were clumsily transforming the white figure. Two monks had robed her in a habit of their colour of her order, I suppose, and were now putting on the scapular and girdle. Finally they flung over her the long white-hooded cloak and awkwardly arranged the veil, leaving her face uncovered; then they joined her hands and placed between them a small cross.

This change of setting emphasized my first impression of her face; the mask was lovelier now and more complete.

Two voices started sonorously, "*Libera me, Domine*,"[3] the monks took up the chant, the whole assembly now began to move, the muffled bells to ring again at intervals, while the procession formed and filed into the choir. The monks proceeded to their stalls, the younger taking places in the rear. The

---

8. Assist (Latin): the first words of a prayer that begins, "Come to [our] assistance, Saints of God." "Stole": an ecclesiastical vestment.
9. Rite.
1. Have mercy (Latin): the first word of the Latin version of Psalm 51, which begins, "Have mercy upon me, O God." "*Ave*": hail (Latin), the beginning of an invocation to the Virgin Mary.

2. Do not enter into judgment against your maidservant, Lord (Latin): the beginning of a prayer that is part of the traditional Roman Catholic service for the dead.
3. Free me, Lord (Latin): the beginning of the responsory traditionally sung at Roman Catholic funerals.

two who had assisted at the robing led the passive figure to the centre of the chancel, where the three who bore the cross and candlesticks turned round and stood a short way off confronting her. Two others, carrying the censer and *bénitier*,[4] stationed themselves immediately behind her with the priests and the officiant, who now, in a loud voice, began his recitations.

They seemed, with variations, to be going through it all again. I caught the *"Non intres in judicium"* and the *"Sub venite"* recurring with the force of a refrain. It was a long elaborate affair. The grave deliberation of its detail heightened its effect. Not to be tedious, I give it you in brief. It lasted altogether possibly two hours.

The priest assisting the officiant, lifting the border of his cope, attended him when he proceeded first to sprinkle, then to incense the presumably dead figure, with the crucifix confronting it, held almost like a challenge to its sightless face. They made the usual inclinations to the image as they passed it, and repeated the performance of the incensing and sprinkling with extreme formality at intervals, in all, I think, three times.

There was no break in the continuous drone proceeding from the choir; they kept it going; none of them looked up—or none at least of whom I had a view—when four young monks slid out, and, kneeling down in the clear space between her and the crucifix, dislodged a stone which must have previously been loosened in the paving of the chancel, and disclosed a cavity, the depth of which I wasn't near enough to see.

For this I wasn't quite prepared, and yet I wasn't discomposed. I can't attempt to make it clear under what pressure I accepted this impossible *dénouement*, but I did accept it. More than that, I was exclusively absorbed in her reception of it. Though she couldn't, wouldn't see, she must have been aware of what was happening. But on the other hand, she was prepared, dispassionately ready, for the end.

All through the dragging length of the long offices, although she hadn't stirred or given any sign (except that one faint shadow of a smile) of consciousness, I felt the force of her intense vitality, the tension of its absolute impression. The life of those enclosing presences seemed to have passed into her presence, to be concentrated there. For to my view it was these men who held her in death's grip who didn't live, and she alone who was absorbently alive.

The candles, burning steadily on either side the crucifix, the soft illumination of innumerable altar lights confronting her, intensified the darkness which above her and behind her—everywhere beyond the narrow confines of the feeble light in which she stood—prevailed.

This setting lent to her the aspect of an unsubstantial, almost supernatural figure, suddenly arrested in its passage through the dark.

She stood compliantly and absolutely still. If she had swayed, or given any hint of wavering, of an appeal to God or man, I must have answered it magnetically. It was she who had the key to what I might have done but didn't do. Make what you will of it—we were inexplicably *en rapport*.[5]

But failing failure I was backing her; it hadn't once occurred to me, without her sanction, to step in, to intervene; that I had anything to do with it

---

4. Basin containing holy water (French).   5. In harmony (French).

beyond my recognition of her—of her part, her claim to play it as she pleased. And now it was—a thousand years too late!

They managed the illusion for themselves and me magnificently. She had come to be a thing of spirit only, not in any sort of clay. She was already in the world of shades; some power as sovereign and determinate as Death itself had lodged her there, past rescue or the profanation of recall.

King was in the act of springing forward; he had got out his revolver; meant, if possible, to shoot her before closing with the rest. It was the right and only workable idea. I held him back, using the first deterrent that occurred to me, reminding him of Ella, and the notion of her danger may have hovered on the outskirts of my mind. But it was not for her at all that I was consciously concerned. I was impelled to stand aside, to force him, too, to stand aside and see it through.

What followed, followed as such things occur in dreams; the senses seize, the mind, or what remains of it, accepts mechanically the natural or unnatural sequence of events.

I saw the grave surrounded by the priests and blessed; and then the woman and the grave repeatedly, alternately, incensed and sprinkled with deliberate solemnity; and heard, as if from a great distance, the recitations of the prayers, and chanting of interminable psalms.

At the last moment, with their hands upon her, standing for a second still erect, before she was committed to the darkness, she unclosed her eyes, sent one swift glance towards the light, a glance which caught it, flashed it back, recaptured it and kept it for the lighting of her tomb. And then her face was covered with her veil.

The final act was the supreme illusion of the whole. I watched the lowering of the passive figure as if I had been witnessing the actual entombment of the dead.

The grave was sprinkled and incensed again, the stone replaced and fastened down. A long sequence of prayers said over it succeeded, at the end of which, the monks put out their tapers, only one or two remaining lit with those beside the Crucifix.

The priests and the officiant at length approached the altar, kneeling and prostrating there some minutes and repeating *"Pater Nosters,"*[6] followed by the choir.

Finally in rising, the officiant pronounced alone and loudly *"Requiescat in pace."*[7] The monks responded sonorously, "Amen."

The altar lights were one by one extinguished; at a sign, preceded by the cross, the vague, almost invisible procession formed and travelled down the aisle, reciting quietly the *"De Profundis"*[8] and guided now, by only, here and there, a solitary light. The quiet recitation, growing fainter, was a new and unfamiliar impression; I felt that I was missing something—what? I missed, in fact, the chanting; then quite suddenly and certainly I missed—the scream. In place of it there was this *"De Profundis"* and her silence. Out of her deep I realized it, dreamily, of course she would not call.

The door swung to; the church was dark and still again—immensely dark and still.

---

6. Our Fathers (Latin, with an English plural); i.e., the Lord's Prayer (Matthew 6.9–13).
7. May she rest in peace (Latin).
8. Out of the depths (Latin): the first words in the Latin version of Psalm 130, traditionally sung by Roman Catholics when the dead are buried.

There was a pause, in which we didn't move or speak; in which I doubted for a second the reality of the incredibly remote, yet almost present scene, trying to reconstruct it in imagination, pit the dream against the fact, the fact against the dream.

"Good God!" said King at length, "what are we going to do?"

His voice awoke me forcibly to something nearer daylight, to the human and inhuman elements in the remarkable affair, which hitherto had missed my mind; they struck against it now with a tremendous shock, and mentally I rubbed my eyes. I saw what King had all along been looking at, the sheer, unpicturesque barbarity. What *were* we going to do?

She breathed perhaps, perhaps she heard us—something of us—we were standing not more than a yard or so away; and if she did, she waited, that was the most poignant possibility, for our decision, our attack.

Ella was naturally unstrung: we left her crouching by the pillar; later I think she partially lost consciousness. It was well—it left us free.

Striking, as nearly as we could, the centre of the altar, working from it, we made a guess at the position of the stone, and on our hands and knees felt blindly for some indication of its loosened edge. But everywhere the paving, to our touch, presented an unevenness of surface, and we picked at random, chiefly for the sake of doing something. In that intolerable darkness there was really nothing to be done but wait for dawn or listen for some guidance from below. For that we listened breathless and alert enough, but nothing stirred. The stillness had become again intense, acute, and now a grim significance attached to it.

The minutes, hours, dragged; time wasn't as it had been, stationary, but desperately, murderously slow.

Each moment of inaction counted—counted horribly, as we stood straining ears and eyes for any hint of sound, of light.

At length the darkness lifted, almost imperceptibly at first; the big rose window to the west became a scarcely visible grey blot; the massive piers detached themselves from the dense mass of shadow and stood out, immense and vague; the windows of the lantern just above us showed a ring of slowly lightening panes; and with the dawn, we found the spot and set to work.

The implements we improvised we soon discovered to be practically useless. We loosened, but we couldn't move the stone.

At intervals we stopped and put our ears to the thin crevices. King thought, and still-believes, he heard some sound or movement; but I didn't. I was somehow sure, for that, it was too late.

For everything it was too late, and we returned reluctantly to a consideration of our own predicament; we had, if possible, to get away unseen. And this time luck was on our side. The sacristan, who came in early by the cloister door which we had entered by, without perceiving us, proceeded to the sacristy.

We made a rapid and effectual escape.

We sketched out and elaborated, on our way back to the town, the little scheme of explanation to be offered to our host, which was to cover an announcement of abrupt departure. He received it with polite credulity, profound regret. He ventured to believe that the *Señora* was not of the crowd, and he had hoped she would be able to remain.

Nothing, however, would induce her to remain for more than a few hours. We must push on without delay and put the night's occurrences before the nearest British Consul. She made no comments and admitted no fatigue, but on this point she was persistent to perversity. She carried it.

The Consul proved hospitable and amiable. He heard the story and was suitably impressed. It was a truly horrible experience—remarkably dramatic—yes. He added it—we saw him doing it—to his collection of strange tales.

The country was, he said, extremely rich in tragic anecdote; and men in his position earned their reputation for romance. But as to *doing* anything in this case, as in others even more remarkable, why, there was absolutely nothing to be done!

The laws of Spain were theoretically admirable, but practically, well—the best that could be said of them was that they had their comic side.

And this was not a civil matter, where the wheels might often, certainly, be oiled. The wheel ecclesiastic was more intractable.

He asked if we were leaving Spain immediately. We said, "Perhaps in a few days." "Take my advice," said he, "and make it a few hours."

We did.

Ella would tell you that the horror of those hours hasn't ever altogether ceased to haunt her, that it visits her in dreams and poisons sleep.

She hasn't ever understood, or quite forgiven me my attitude of temporary detachment. She refuses to admit that, after all, what one is pleased to call reality is merely the intensity of one's illusion. My illusion was intense.

"Oh, for you," she says, and with a touch of bitterness, "it was a spectacle. The woman didn't really count."

For me it was a spectacle, but more than that: it was an acquiescence in a rather splendid crime.

On looking back I see that, at the moment in my mind, the woman didn't really count. She saw herself she didn't. That's precisely what she made me see.

What counted chiefly with her, I suspect, was something infinitely greater to her vision than the terror of men's dreams.

She lies, one must remember, in the very centre of the sanctuary—has a place uniquely sacred to her order, the traditions of her kind. It was this honour, satisfying, as it did, some pride of spirit or of race, which bore her honourably through.

She had, one way or other, clogged the wheels of an inflexible machine. But for the speck of dust she knew herself to be, she was—oh horribly, I grant you!—yet not lightly, not dishonourably, swept away.

1903

The Farmer's Bride

    Three Summers since I chose a maid,
    Too young maybe—but more's to do
    At harvest-time than bide and woo.
        When us was wed she turned afraid
5   Of love and me and all things human;

> Like the shut of a winter's day
> Her smile went out, and 'twadn't a woman—
> > More like a little frightened fay.[1]
> > One night, in the Fall, she runned away.
>
> 10 "Out 'mong the sheep, her be," they said,
> Should properly have been abed;
> But sure enough she wadn't there
> Lying awake with her wide brown stare.
> So over seven-acre field and up-along across the down[2]
> 15 We chased her, flying like a hare
> Before our lanterns. To Church-Town
> > All in a shiver and a scare
> We caught her, fetched her home at last
> > And turned the key upon her, fast.
>
> 20 She does the work about the house
> As well as most, but like a mouse:
> > Happy enough to chat and play
> > With birds and rabbits and such as they,
> > So long as men-folk keep away.
> 25 "Not near, not near!" her eyes beseech
> When one of us comes within reach.
> > The women say that beasts in stall
> > Look round like children at her call.
> > I've hardly heard her speak at all.
>
> 30 Shy as a leveret,[3] swift as he,
> Straight and slight as a young larch tree,
> Sweet as the first wild violets, she,
> To her wild self. But what to me?
>
> The short days shorten and the oaks are brown,
> 35   The blue smoke rises to the low gray sky,
> One leaf in the still air falls slowly down,
>   A magpie's spotted feathers lie
> On the black earth spread white with rime,
> The berries redden up to Christmas-time.
> 40   What's Christmas-time without there be
>   Some other in the house than we!
>
> > She sleeps up in the attic there
> > Alone, poor maid. 'Tis but a stair
> Betwixt us. Oh! my God! the down,
> 45 The soft young down of her, the brown,
> The brown of her—her eyes, her hair, her hair!

1916

---

1. Fairy.
2. Meadow used for grazing.
3. A young hare.

The Quiet House

When we were children old Nurse used to say,
The house was like an auction or a fair
Until the lot of us were safe in bed.
It has been quiet as the country-side
Since Ted and Janey and then Mother died
And Tom crossed[1] Father and was sent away.
After the lawsuit he could not hold up his head,
Poor Father, and he does not care
For people here, or to go anywhere.

To get away to Aunt's for that week-end
Was hard enough; (since then, a year ago,
He scarcely lets me slip out of his sight—)
At first I did not like my cousin's friend,
I did not think I should remember him:
His voice has gone, his face is growing dim
And if I like him now I do not know.
He frightened me before he smiled—
He did not ask me if he might—
He said that he would come one Sunday night,
He spoke to me as if I were a child.

No year has been like this that has just gone by;
It may be that what Father says is true,
If things are so it does not matter why:
But everything has burned, and not quite through.
The colors of the world have turned
To flame, the blue, the gold has burned
In what used to be such a leaden sky.
When you are burned quite through you die.

Red is the strangest pain to bear;
In Spring the leaves on the budding trees;
In Summer the roses are worse than these,
More terrible than they are sweet:
A rose can stab you across the street
Deeper than any knife:
And the crimson haunts you everywhere—
Thin shafts of sunlight, like the ghosts of reddened swords
have struck our stair
As if, coming down, you had spilt your life.

I think that my soul is red
Like the soul of a sword or a scarlet flower:
But when these are dead
They have had their hour.

---

1. Disobeyed.

    I shall have had mine, too,
        For from head to feet
45 I am burned and stabbed half through,
        And the pain is deadly sweet.

    The things that kill us seem
        Blind to the death they give:
    It is only in our dream
50   The things that kill us live.

    The room is shut where Mother died,
        The other rooms are as they were,
    The world goes on the same outside,
        The sparrows fly across the Square,
55   The children play as we four did there,
        The trees grow green and brown and bare,
    The sun shines on the dead Church spire,
        And nothing lives here but the fire.
    While Father watches from his chair
60   Day follows day
    The same, now and then a different gray,
        Till, like his hair,
    Which Mother said was wavy once and bright,
        They will all turn white.
65   Tonight I heard a bell again—
    Outside it was the same mist of fine rain,
    The lamps just lighted down the long, dim street,
        No one for me—
    I think it is myself I go to meet:
70 I do not care; some day I *shall* not think; I shall not be.

                                                    1916

HENRY HANDEL RICHARDSON
1870–1946

Named Ethel Florence Lindsay Richardson at her birth, the writer who called herself H. H. Richardson left Australia at the age of seventeen, returning only once in 1912 for "a flying six-weeks' visit." Yet she has been claimed as one of Australia's most important novelists. Her trilogy, *The Fortunes of Richard Mahony* (1917, 1925, 1929), describes the psychological impact of colonialism on a character based on her father: a Dublin-born physician, he reestablished his practice in a series of provincial Australian towns, but he eventually lost his sanity. Her mother, who supported the family as postmaster in Koroit, is sympathetically presented as resourcefully practical in *The Getting of Wisdom* (1910). This satiric novel, which was produced as a film in 1977, provides a fictional portrait of the author as she moved at the age of twelve from her home to the Presbyterian Ladies' College in Melbourne. Richardson's surrogate, Laura Ramsbotham, is a rebellious, imaginative adolescent who is unable—no matter how she tries—to conform to the mindless proprieties of the school or to stifle her artistic creativity.

Laura's musical accomplishments reflect Richardson's training as a concert pianist in Leipzig in 1887. There she met and married J. G. Robertson, who subsequently became a professor of German languages at the University of London. Two works—*Maurice Guest* (1908) and *The Young Cosima* (1939)—deal directly with the development of musical genius, a subject of central importance to a literary artist who took Handel as her middle name. The best-selling *Ultima Thule* (1929), the final volume of the trilogy *The Fortunes of Richard Mahoney*, brought Richardson international fame. After the death of her husband, Richardson survived the bombings of Sussex during World War II, but she did not live to complete her autobiography, *Myself When Young* (1948).

"Two Hanged Women" portrays with economy the same competition between heterosexuality and female bonding that *The Getting of Wisdom* traces in its divided heroine. In doing so, it offers a subtle analysis of the ways in which society discourages public demonstrations of affection between same-sex couples while encouraging romantic displays between men and women. Thus it supplements the remarkably frank treatment of sexuality in *Maurice Guest* as well as in some of the other stories Richardson collected in *The End of Childhood* (1934).

Two Hanged Women

Hand in hand the youthful lovers sauntered along the esplanade. It was a night in midsummer; a wispy moon had set, and the stars glittered. The dark mass of the sea, at flood, lay tranquil, slothfully lapping the shingle.[1]

"Come on, let's make for the usual," said the boy.

But on nearing their favorite seat they found it occupied. In the velvety shade of the overhanging sea-wall, the outlines of two figures were visible.

"Oh, blast!" said the lad. "That's torn it. What now, Baby?"

"Why, let's stop here, Pincher, right close up, till we frighten 'em off."

And very soon loud, smacking kisses, amatory pinches and ticklings, and skittish squeals of pleasure did their work. Silently the intruders rose and moved away.

But the boy stood gaping after them, open-mouthed.

"Well, I'm damned! If it wasn't just two hanged[2] women!"

Retreating before a salvo of derisive laughter, the elder of the girls said: "We'll go out on the breakwater."[3] She was tall and thin, and walked with a long stride.

Her companion, shorter than she by a bobbed head of straight flaxen hair, was hard put to it to keep pace. As she pegged along she said doubtfully, as if in self-excuse: "Though I really ought to go home. It's getting late. Mother will be angry."

They walked with finger-tips lightly in contact; and at her words she felt what was like an attempt to get free, on the part of the fingers crooked in hers. But she was prepared for this, and held fast, gradually working her own up till she had a good half of the other hand in her grip.

---

1. Beach gravel.
2. Confounded (British expletive).
3. Barrier protecting the shore from strong waves.

For a moment neither spoke. Then, in a low, muffled voice, came the question: "Was she angry last night, too?"

The little fair girl's reply had an unlooked-for vehemence. "You know she wasn't!" And, mildly despairing: "But you never will understand. Oh, what's the good of . . . of anything!"

And on sitting down she let the prisoned hand go, even putting it from her with a kind of push. There it lay, palm upwards, the fingers still curved from her hold, looking like a thing with a separate life of its own; but a life that was ebbing.

On this remote seat, with their backs turned on lovers, lights, the town, the two girls sat and gazed wordlessly at the dark sea, over which great Jupiter was flinging a thin gold line. There was no sound but the lapping, sucking, sighing, of the ripples at the edge of the breakwater, and the occasional screech of an owl in the tall trees on the hillside.

But after a time, having stolen more than one side glance at her companion, the younger seemed to take heart of grace. With a childish toss of the head that set her loose hair swaying, she said, in a tone of meaning emphasis: "I like Fred."

The only answer was a faint, contemptuous shrug.

"I tell you I *like* him!"

"Fred? Rats!"

"No it isn't . . . that's just where you're wrong, Betty. But you think you're so wise. Always."

"I know what I know."

"Or imagine you do! But it doesn't matter. Nothing you can say makes any difference. I like him and always shall. In heaps of ways. He's so big and strong, for one thing: it gives you such a safe sort of feeling to be with him . . . as if nothing could happen while you were. Yes, it's . . . it's . . . well, I can't help it, Betty, there's something *comfy* in having a boy to go about with—like other girls do. One they'd eat their hats to get, too! I can see it in their eyes when we pass; Fred with his great long legs and broad shoulders—I don't nearly come up to them—and his blue eyes with the black lashes, and his shiny black hair. And I like his tweeds, the Harris smell of them, and his dirty old pipe, and the way he shows his teeth—he's got *topping*[4] teeth—when he laughs and says ra-*ther*! And other people, when they see us, look . . . well I don't quite know how to say it, but they look sort of pleased; and they make room for us and let us into the dark corner-seats at the pictures, just as if we'd a right to them. And they never laugh. (Oh, I can't *stick*[5] being laughed at!—and that's the truth.) Yes, it's so comfy, Betty darling . . . such a warm cosy comfy feeling. Oh, *won't* you understand?"

"Gawd! why not make a song of it?" But a moment later, very fiercely: "And who is it's taught you to think all this? Who's hinted it and suggested it till you've come to believe it? . . . believe it's what you really feel?"

"She hasn't! Mother's never said a word . . . about Fred."

"Words?—why waste words? . . . when she can do it with a cock of the

---

4. First-rate, excellent (British slang). "Harris": popular type of tweed clothing made of cloth hand-woven on Harris and other islands in Scotland's Outer Hebrides.
5. Bear.

eye. For your Fred, that!" and the girl called Betty held her fingers aloft and snapped them viciously. "But your mother's a different proposition."

"I think you're simply horrid."

To this there was no reply.

"*Why* have you such a down on her? What's she ever done to you? . . . except not get ratty when I stay out late with Fred. And I don't see how you can expect . . . being what she is . . . and with nobody but me—after all she *is* my mother . . . you can't alter that. I know very well—and you know, too— I'm not *too* putrid-looking. But"—beseechingly—"I'm *nearly* twenty-five now, Betty. And other girls . . . well, she sees them, every one of them, with a boy of their own, even though they're ugly, or fat, or have legs like sausages— they've only got to ogle them a bit—the girls, I mean . . . and there they are. And Fred's a good sort—he is, really!—and he dances well, and doesn't drink, and so . . . so why *shouldn't* I like him? . . . and off my own bat . . . without it having to be all Mother's fault, and me nothing but a parrot, and without any will of my own?"

"Why? Because I know her too well, my child! I can read her as you'd never dare to . . . even if you could. She's sly, your mother is, so sly there's no coming to grips with her . . . one might as well try to fill one's hand with cobwebs. But she's got a hold on you, a stranglehold, that nothing'll loosen. Oh! mothers aren't fair—I mean it's not fair of nature to weigh us down with them and yet expect us to be our own true selves. The handicap's too great. All those months, when the same blood's running through two sets of veins— there's no getting away from that, ever after. Take yours. As I say, does she need to open her mouth? Not she! She's only got to let it hang at the corners, and you reek, you drip with guilt."

Something in these words seemed to sting the younger girl. She hit back. "I know what it is, you're jealous, that's what you are! . . . and you've no other way of letting it out. But I tell you this. If ever I marry—yes, *marry!*—it'll be to please myself, and nobody else. Can you imagine me doing it to oblige her?"

Again silence.

"If I only think what it would be like to be fixed up and settled, and able to live in peace, without this eternal dragging two ways . . . just as if I was being torn in half. And see Mother smiling and happy again, like she used to be. Between the two of you I'm nothing but a punch-ball. Oh, I'm fed up with it! . . . fed up to the neck. As for you . . . And yet you can sit there as if you were made of stone! Why don't you *say* something? *Betty!* Why won't you speak?"

But no words came.

"I can *feel* you sneering. And when you sneer I hate you more than any one on earth. If only I'd never seen you!"

"Marry your Fred, and you'll never need to again."

"I will, too! I'll marry him, and have a proper wedding like other girls, with a veil and bridesmaids and bushels of flowers. And I'll live in a house of my own, where I can do as I like, and be left in peace, and there'll be no one to badger and bully me—Fred wouldn't . . . ever! Besides, he'll be away all day. And when he came back at night, he'd . . . I'd . . . I mean I'd—" But here the flying words gave out; there came a stormy breath and a cry of: "Oh, Betty, Betty! . . . I couldn't, no, I couldn't! It's when I think of *that* . . . Yes, it's quite true! I like him all right, I do indeed, but only as long as he doesn't come too near. If he even sits too close, I have to screw myself up to bear it"—and flinging herself down over her companion's lap, she hid her face. "And if he tries to touch me, Betty, or even takes my arm or puts his round me . . . And then his face . . . when it looks like it does sometimes . . . all wrong . . . as if it had gone all wrong—oh! then I feel I shall have to scream—out loud. I'm afraid of him . . . when he looks like that. Once . . . when he kissed me . . . I could have died with the horror of it. His breath . . . his breath . . . and his mouth—like fruit pulp—and the black hairs on his wrists . . . and the way he looked—and . . . and everything! No, I can't, I can't . . . nothing will make me . . . I'd rather die twice over. But what am I to do? Mother'll *never* understand. Oh, why has it got to be like this? I want to be happy, like other girls, and to make her happy, too . . . and everything's all wrong. You tell me, Betty darling, you help me, you're older . . . you *know* . . . and you can help me, if you will . . . if you only will!" And locking her arms round her friend she drove her face deeper into the warmth and darkness, as if, from the very fervor of her clasp, she could draw the aid and strength she needed.

Betty had sat silent, unyielding, her sole movement being to loosen her own arms from her sides and point her elbows outwards, to hinder them touching the arms that lay round her. But at this last appeal she melted; and gathering the young girl to her breast, she held her fast.—And so for long she continued to sit, her chin resting lightly on the fair hair, that was silky and downy as an infant's, and gazing with somber eyes over the stealthily heaving sea.

1934

WILLA CATHER
1873–1947

Willa Cather's novels commemorate an obdurate, primordial landscape that had almost been erased by the time she began writing. Her fictional frontiers—the shaggy midwestern plains of *O Pioneers!* (1913) or the cliffs, canyons, and caves of the Southwest in *The Professor's House* (1925)—evoke the grandeur of eternal, mysterious forces that call forth the exertions characteristic of her early settlers. But the pioneer is only one type of the determined, willful character who absorbed Cather throughout her highly successful career. Another is the artist, whom she portrayed first in the opera singer of *The Song of the Lark* (1915) and later in the actresses and vocalists of "Coming, Aphrodite!" (1920), *My Mortal Enemy* (1926), and *Lucy Gayheart* (1940). Whether she focused on pioneering settlers or pioneering artists, however, Cather was frequently drawn to powerful female figures.

Possibly the most momentous event in Cather's early life was the move from Virginia to Nebraska that her family undertook in 1883. For her first nine years, she lived in a spacious, three-story, brick farmhouse near Winchester, Virginia. Wilella Cather was the first of seven children born to Charles Cather, an easygoing farmer who turned to real estate in later life, and Mary Virginia (Boak) Cather, an imperious woman remembered with some ambivalence by her daughter. But Willie, as she liked to call herself, was primarily educated by her maternal grandmother, whose portrait she lovingly drew in the short story "Old Mrs. Harris" (1932). When the family moved to Webster County, Nebraska, Cather must have experienced the same shock at the primitive sod houses and the ice-encrusted wilderness that her narrator Jim Burden expresses in *My Ántonia* (1918). Less a country than the vast "material out of which countries are made," the land on which her family settled was, in her own words, "naked as the back of your hand."

Like Jim, too, when Cather moved with her family to neighboring Red Cloud, a town of twenty-five hundred situated on the Burlington railroad line, she identified with other uprooted immigrants: Swedish, Bohemian, and Russian settlers struggling to make a new life in the New World while preserving the cultural traditions of the Old World. In school at Red Cloud, as Sharon O'Brien has shown, Cather frequently dressed in boyish clothes, dreamed of becoming William Cather, M.D., and began equating artistry with masculinity. At home she read widely in British and American literature in her parents' library and in French and German translations at her neighbors'. At the University of Nebraska in Lincoln, she began studying the classics while publishing her writing in the undergraduate literary magazine. Before and after graduation in 1895, she reviewed cultural events for the Lincoln newspaper and then moved to Pittsburgh to edit the *Home Monthly* magazine for another year.

Cather's personal life during her ten-year residence in Pittsburgh is no less shrouded in obscurity than her later life in New York, because she burned as many of her letters as she could and because in her will she forbade publication of the surviving letters. Her biographers James Woodress and Leon Edel have argued, however, that what saved Cather from loneliness in those years was her relationship with Isabelle McClung. This daughter of a conservative Pittsburgh judge invited Cather to live in her house, where the two shared a bedroom. Cather began writing her fiction in an attic room in the McClung house, while she continued to work at the *Pittsburgh Daily Leader*. As music, drama, and book reviewer, Cather wrote about the Pittsburgh symphony's performance of Dvořák's *New World Symphony*, Helen Modjeska's acting in *Mary Stuart*, and Kate Chopin's predilection for romanticism in *The Awakening*. As a freelance artist, she composed the verse that would appear in *April Twilights* (1903) and the stories collected in *The Troll Garden* (1905).

In 1906 Cather moved to New York to join the staff of *McClure's Magazine*. An assignment in Boston led to a meaningful friendship with Sarah Orne Jewett: in subsequent essays, Cather praised Jewett's sparse but evocative prose style, a style she would strive toward in her own later fiction. In New York, Cather lived in a studio apartment at 60 South Washington Square, a building that also housed the woman who would become her lifelong companion, Edith Lewis. Cather decided to resign as managing editor of *McClure's* after her first novel, *Alexander's Bridge*, was serialized in the 1912 issues. From the architect Alexander, she moved on to the pioneer Alexandra in her next novel, *O Pioneers!*, which she dedicated to Jewett. Although Cather wrote both *O Pioneers!* and *The Song of the Lark* during stays in Isabelle McClung's house, by 1913 she had moved to 5 Bank Street with Edith Lewis. Cather was apparently extremely upset at Isabelle McClung's decision to marry in 1915. Yet she and Edith Lewis had already become close friends. Indeed, they had embarked on a series of trips to the Southwest, which would shape the writer's novels.

My Ántonia, the next novel Cather composed, was strongly autobiographical. Although it presents her memories of her Nebraskan childhood through a male narrator, its main subject is Ántonia, a female character who survives the suicide of her father, arduous farmwork, town employment as a hired girl, and an illegitimate pregnancy, to become "a rich mine of life, like the founders of early races." The tension between Ántonia's sturdy earthiness and Jim Burden's commitment to the sophistication and learning he associates with the East would inform a number of Cather's finest stories as well as later works like her Pulitzer Prize–winning war novel, *One of Ours* (1922). Yet, although she was gaining a literary reputation, Cather was becoming disillusioned with modern life. "The world was broken in two in 1922 or thereabouts," she wrote in her collected essays, *Not under Forty* (1936), expressing her distress over poor health, her disappointment about her books' receptions, and her growing contempt for contemporary values. From this point on, she would turn with nostalgia to historically remote periods.

Later novels such as *The Professor's House* (1925), *Death Comes for the Archbishop* (1927), and *Shadows on the Rock* (1931) continue to explore the individual's withdrawal from society, frequently depicting a quest for integrity through male characters who are often placed in a Catholic context. Typical in this respect are the European missionaries in New Mexico of *Death Comes for the Archbishop* and the seventeenth-century French Canadian settlers of *Shadows on the Rock*. With her last novel, however, Cather returned to the questions about female identity that had absorbed her earlier in her career. *Sapphira and the Slave Girl* (1940) focuses on the Shenandoah Valley of the writer's early childhood and on the reconciliation of a domineering mother with her equally willful daughter. As in Cather's earlier fiction, romantic plot elements are far less important than suggestive tableaux in which the self is tested and shaped by experience. As Toni Morrison has noted about this historical novel set in slave times, it charts "the reckless, unabated power of a white woman gathering identity unto herself from the wholly available and serviceable lives of Africanist others."

Cather had already received a number of honorary degrees and literary prizes when, in 1937, she prepared a complete edition of her works for Scribner's. "Coming, Aphrodite!," which appeared in her collection *Youth and the Bright Medusa*, (1920), integrates mythic material and social analysis to explore both the triumphs and the irrevocable personal costs of the artistic ambition that clearly propelled Cather's own career.

Coming, Aphrodite![1]

I

Don Hedger had lived for four years on the top floor of an old house on the south side of Washington Square,[2] and nobody had ever disturbed him. He occupied one big room with no outside exposure except on the north, where he had built in a many-paned studio window that looked upon a court and upon the roofs and walls of other buildings. His room was very cheerless, since he never got a ray of direct sunlight; the south corners were always in shadow. In one of the corners was a clothes closet, built against the partition, in another a wide divan, serving as a seat by day and a bed by night. In the front corner, the one farther from the window, was a sink, and a table with two gas burners where he sometimes cooked his food. There, too, in the perpetual dusk, was the dog's bed, and often a bone or two for his comfort.

The dog was a Boston bull terrier, and Hedger explained his surly disposition by the fact that he had been bred to the point where it told on his nerves. His name was Caesar III, and he had taken prizes at very exclusive dog shows. When he and his master went out to prowl about University Place or to promenade along West Street, Caesar III was invariably fresh and shining. His pink skin showed through his mottled coat, which glistened as if it

---

1. The Greek goddess of love.
2. In the Greenwich Village section of New York City.

had just been rubbed with olive oil, and he wore a brass-studded collar, bought at the smartest saddler's. Hedger, as often as not, was hunched up in an old striped blanket coat, with a shapeless felt hat pulled over his bushy hair, wearing black shoes that had become gray, or brown ones that had become black, and he never put on gloves unless the day was biting cold.

Early in May, Hedger learned that he was to have a new neighbor in the rear apartment—two rooms, one large and one small, that faced the west. His studio was shut off from the larger of these rooms by double doors, which, though they were fairly tight, left him a good deal at the mercy of the occupant. The rooms had been leased, long before he came there, by a trained nurse who considered herself knowing in old furniture. She went to auction sales and bought up mahogany and dirty brass and stored it away here, where she meant to live when she retired from nursing. Meanwhile, she sublet her rooms, with their precious furniture, to young people who came to New York to "write" or to "paint"—who proposed to live by the sweat of the brow rather than of the hand, and who desired artistic surroundings. When Hedger first moved in, these rooms were occupied by a young man who tried to write plays,—and who kept on trying until a week ago, when the nurse had put him out for unpaid rent.

A few days after the playwright left, Hedger heard an ominous murmur of voices through the bolted double doors: the lady-like intonation of the nurse—doubtless exhibiting her treasures—and another voice, also a woman's, but very different; young, fresh, unguarded, confident. All the same, it would be very annoying to have a woman in there. The only bathroom on the floor was at the top of the stairs in the front hall, and he would always be running into her as he came or went from his bath. He would have to be more careful to see that Caesar didn't leave bones about the hall, too; and she might object when he cooked steak and onions on his gas burner.

As soon as the talking ceased and the women left, he forgot them. He was absorbed in a study of paradise fish at the Aquarium, staring out at people through the glass and green water of their tank. It was a highly gratifying idea; the incommunicability of one stratum of animal life with another,— though Hedger pretended it was only an experiment in unusual lighting. When he heard trunks knocking against the sides of the narrow hall, then he realized that she was moving in at once. Toward noon, groans and deep gasps and the creaking of ropes, made him aware that a piano was arriving. After the tramp of the movers died away down the stairs, somebody touched off a few scales and chords on the instrument, and then there was peace. Presently he heard her lock her door and go down the hall humming something; going out to lunch, probably. He stuck his brushes in a can of turpentine and put on his hat, not stopping to wash his hands. Caesar was smelling along the crack under the bolted doors; his bony tail stuck out hard as a hickory withe, and the hair was standing up about his elegant collar.

Hedger encouraged him. "Come along, Caesar. You'll soon get used to a new smell."

In the hall stood an enormous trunk, behind the ladder that led to the roof, just opposite Hedger's door. The dog flew at it with a growl of hurt amazement. They went down three flights of stairs and out into the brilliant May afternoon.

Behind the Square, Hedger and his dog descended into a basement oyster house where there were no tablecloths on the tables and no handles on the coffee cups, and the floor was covered with sawdust, and Caesar was always welcome,—not that he needed any such precautionary flooring. All the carpets of Persia would have been safe for him. Hedger ordered steak and onions absentmindedly, not realizing why he had an apprehension that this dish might be less readily at hand hereafter. While he ate, Caesar sat beside his chair, gravely disturbing the sawdust with his tail.

After lunch Hedger strolled about the Square for the dog's health and watched the stages[3] pull out;—that was almost the very last summer of the old horse stages on Fifth Avenue. The fountain had but lately begun operations for the season and was throwing up a mist of rainbow water which now and then blew south and sprayed a bunch of Italian babies that were being supported on the outer rim by older, very little older, brothers and sisters. Plump robins were hopping about on the soil; the grass was newly cut and blindingly green. Looking up the Avenue through the Arch, one could see the young poplars with their bright, sticky leaves, and the Brevoort[4] glistening in its spring coat of paint, and shining horses and carriages,— occasionally an automobile, mis-shapen and sullen, like an ugly threat in a stream of things that were bright and beautiful and alive.

While Caesar and his master were standing by the fountain, a girl approached them, crossing the Square. Hedger noticed her because she wore a lavender cloth suit and carried in her arms a big bunch of fresh lilacs. He saw that she was young and handsome,—beautiful, in fact, with a splendid figure and good action. She, too, paused by the fountain and looked back through the Arch up the Avenue. She smiled rather patronizingly as she looked, and at the same time seemed delighted. Her slowly curving upper lip and half-closed eyes seemed to say: "You're gay, you're exciting, you are quite the right sort of thing; but you're none too fine for me!"

In the moment she tarried, Caesar stealthily approached her and sniffed at the hem of her lavender skirt, then, when she went south like an arrow, he ran back to his master and lifted a face full of emotion and alarm, his lower lip twitching under his sharp white teeth and his hazel eyes pointed with a very definite discovery. He stood thus, motionless, while Hedger watched the lavender girl go up the steps and through the door of the house in which he lived.

"You're right, my boy, it's she! She might be worse looking, you know."

When they mounted to the studio, the new lodger's door, at the back of the hall, was a little ajar, and Hedger caught the warm perfume of lilacs just brought in out of the sun. He was used to the musty smell of the old hall carpet. (The nurse-lessee had once knocked at his studio door and complained that Caesar must be somewhat responsible for the particular flavor of that mustiness, and Hedger had never spoken to her since.) He was used to the old smell, and he preferred it to that of the lilacs, and so did his companion, whose nose was so much more discriminating. Hedger shut his door vehemently, and fell to work.

Most young men who dwell in obscure studios in New York have had a

---

3. Public horse-drawn vehicles.
4. A fashionable hotel. "The Arch": the triumphal arch, dedicated in 1895, replaced a temporary arch erected in 1889 to commemorate the centennial of George Washington's inauguration in New York City.

beginning, come out of something, have somewhere a home town, a family, a paternal roof. But Don Hedger had no such background. He was a foundling, and had grown up in a school for homeless boys, where book-learning was a negligible part of the curriculum. When he was sixteen, a Catholic priest took him to Greensburg, Pennsylvania, to keep house for him. The priest did something to fill in the large gaps in the boy's education,—taught him to like "Don Quixote" and "The Golden Legend,"[5] and encouraged him to mess with paints and crayons in his room up under the slope of the mansard. When Don wanted to go to New York to study at the Art League, the priest got him a night job as packer in one of the big department stores. Since then, Hedger had taken care of himself; that was his only responsibility. He was singularly unencumbered; had no family duties, no social ties, no obligations toward any one but his landlord. Since he travelled light, he had travelled rather far. He had got over a good deal of the earth's surface, in spite of the fact that he never in his life had more than three hundred dollars ahead at any one time, and he had already outlived a succession of convictions and revelations about his art.

Though he was now but twenty-six years old, he had twice been on the verge of becoming a marketable product; once through some studies of New York streets he did for a magazine, and once through a collection of pastels he brought home from New Mexico, which Remington,[6] then at the height of his popularity, happened to see, and generously tried to push. But on both occasions Hedger decided that this was something he didn't wish to carry further,—simply the old thing over again and got nowhere,—so he took enquiring dealers experiments in a "later manner," that made them put him out of the shop. When he ran short of money, he could always get any amount of commercial work; he was an expert draughtsman and worked with lightning speed. The rest of his time he spent in groping his way from one kind of painting into another, or travelling about without luggage, like a tramp, and he was chiefly occupied with getting rid of ideas he had once thought very fine.

Hedger's circumstances, since he had moved to Washington Square, were affluent compared to anything he had ever known before. He was now able to pay advance rent and turn the key on his studio when he went away for four months at a stretch. It didn't occur to him to wish to be richer than this. To be sure, he did without a great many things other people think necessary, but he didn't miss them, because he had never had them. He belonged to no clubs, visited no houses, had no studio friends, and he ate his dinner alone in some decent little restaurant, even on Christmas and New Year's. For days together he talked to nobody but his dog and the janitress and the lame oysterman.

After he shut the door and settled down to his paradise fish on that first Tuesday in May, Hedger forgot all about his new neighbor. When the light failed, he took Caesar out for a walk. On the way home he did his marketing on West Houston Street, with a one-eyed Italian woman who always cheated him. After he had cooked his beans and scallopini, and drunk half a bottle

---

5. A long dramatic poem (1851) of medieval chivalry by Henry Wadsworth Longfellow. "Don Quixote": the famous novel (1605–15) of an aging knight longing for adventure, by Miguel de Cervantes.
6. Frederic Remington (1861–1909), popular American painter.

of Chianti, he put his dishes in the sink and went up on the roof to smoke. He was the only person in the house who ever went to the roof, and he had a secret understanding with the janitress about it. He was to have "the privilege of the roof," as she said, if he opened the heavy trapdoor on sunny days to air out the upper hall, and was watchful to close it when rain threatened. Mrs. Foley was fat and forty and hated to climb stairs,—besides, the roof was reached by a perpendicular iron ladder, definitely inaccessible to a woman of her bulk, and the iron door at the top of it was too heavy for any but Hedger's stong arm to lift. Hedger was not above medium height, but he practiced with weights and dumb-bells, and in the shoulders he was as strong as a gorilla.

So Hedger had the roof to himself. He and Caesar often slept up there on hot nights, rolled in blankets he had brought home from Arizona. He mounted with Caesar under his left arm. The dog had never learned to climb a perpendicular ladder, and never did he feel so much his master's greatness and his own dependence upon him, as when he crept under his arm for this perilous ascent. Up there was even gravel to scratch in and a dog could do whatever he liked, so long as he did not bark. It was a kind of Heaven, which no one was strong enough to reach but his great paint-smelling master.

On this blue May night there was a slender girlish looking young moon in the west, playing with a whole company of silver stars. Now and then one of them darted away from the ground and shot off into the gauzy blue with a soft little trail of light, like laughter. Hedger and his dog were delighted when a star did this. They were quite lost in watching the glittering game, when they were suddenly diverted by a sound,—not from the stars, though it was music. It was not the Prologue to Pagliacci,[7] which rose ever and anon on hot evenings from an Italian tenement on Thompson Street, with the gasps of the corpulent baritone who got behind it; nor was it the hurdy-gurdy[8] man, who often played at the corner in the balmy twilight. No, this was a woman's voice, singing the tempestuous, over-lapping phrases of Signor Puccini,[9] then comparatively new in the world, but already so popular that even Hedger recognized his unmistakable gusts of breath. He looked about over the roofs; all was blue and still, with the well-built chimneys that were never used now standing up dark and mournful. He moved softly toward the yellow quadrangle where the gas from the hall shone up through the half-lifted trapdoor. Oh yes! It came up through the hole like a strong draught, a big, beautiful voice, and it sounded rather like a professional's. A piano had arrived in the morning, Hedger remembered. This might be a very great nuisance. It would be pleasant enough to listen to, if you could turn it on and off as you wished; but you couldn't. Caesar, with the gas light shining on his collar and his ugly but sensitive face, panted and looked up for information. Hedger put down a reassuring hand.

"I don't know. We can't tell yet. It may not be so bad."

He stayed on the roof until all was still below, and finally descended, with quite a new feeling about his neighbor. Her voice, like her figure, inspired respect,—if one did not choose to call it admiration. Her door was shut, the

---

7. Popular Italian opera (1892) by Ruggero Leoncavallo.
8. Portable instrument that plays popular tunes when a crank is turned.
9. Giacomo Puccini (1858–1924), popular Italian opera composer.

transom was dark; nothing remained of her but the obtrusive trunk, unrightfully taking up room in the narrow hall.

II

For two days Hedger didn't see her. He was painting eight hours a day just then, and only went out to hunt for food. He noticed that she practiced scales and exercises for about an hour in the morning; then she locked her door, went humming down the hall, and left him in peace. He heard her getting her coffee ready at about the same time he got his. Earlier still, she passed his room on her way to her bath. In the evening she sometimes sang, but on the whole she didn't bother him. When he was working well he did not notice anything much. The morning paper lay before his door until he reached out for his milk bottle, then he kicked the sheet inside and it lay on the floor until evening. Sometimes he read it and sometimes he did not. He forgot there was anything of importance going on in the world outside of his third floor studio. Nobody had ever taught him that he ought to be interested in other people; in the Pittsburgh steel strike, in the Fresh Air Fund,[1] in the scandal about the Babies' Hospital. A gray wolf, living in a Wyoming canyon, would hardly have been less concerned about these things than was Don Hedger.

One morning he was coming out of the bath-room at the front end of the hall, having just given Caesar his bath and rubbed him into a glow with a heavy towel. Before the door, lying in wait for him, as it were, stood a tall figure in a flowing blue silk dressing gown that fell away from her marble arms. In her hands she carried various accessories of the bath.

"I wish," she said distinctly, standing in his way, "I wish you wouldn't wash your dog in the tub. I never heard of such a thing! I've found his hair in the tub, and I've smelled a doggy smell, and now I've caught you at it. It's an outrage!"

Hedger was badly frightened. She was so tall and positive, and was fairly blazing with beauty and anger. He stood blinking, holding on to his sponge and dog-soap, feeling that he ought to bow very low to her. But what he actually said was:

"Nobody has ever objected before. I always wash the tub,—and, anyhow, he's cleaner than most people."

"Cleaner than me?" her eyebrows went up, her white arms and neck and her fragrant person seemed to scream at him like a band of outraged nymphs. Something flashed through his mind about a man who was turned into a dog, or was pursued by dogs, because he unwittingly intruded upon the bath of beauty.[2]

"No, I didn't mean that," he muttered, turning scarlet under the bluish stubble of his muscular jaws. "But I know he's cleaner than I am."

"That I don't doubt!" Her voice sounded like a soft shivering of crystal, and with a smile of pity she drew the folds of her voluminous blue robe close about her and allowed the wretched man to pass. Even Caesar was fright-

---

1. New York charity (founded 1877) that sends city children to the country.
2. In Greek myth, the hunter Actaeon was punished by the goddess Artemis when he spied on her while she was bathing; he was turned into a stag and torn apart by his own hounds.

ened; he darted like a streak down the hall, through the door and to his own bed in the corner among the bones.

Hedger stood still in the doorway, listening to indignant sniffs and coughs and a great swishing of water about the sides of the tub. He had washed it; but as he had washed it with Caesar's sponge, it was quite possible that a few bristles remained; the dog was shedding now. The playwright had never objected, nor had the jovial illustrator who occupied the front apartment,— but he, as he admitted, "was usually pye-eyed,[3] when he wasn't in Buffalo." He went home to Buffalo sometimes to rest his nerves.

It had never occurred to Hedger that any one would mind using the tub after Caesar;—but then, he had never seen a beautiful girl caparisoned[4] for the bath before. As soon as he beheld her standing there, he realized the unfitness of it. For that matter, she ought not to step into a tub that any other mortal had bathed in; the illustrator was sloppy and left cigarette ends on the moulding.

All morning as he worked he was gnawed by a spiteful desire to get back at her. It rankled that he had been so vanquished by her disdain. When he heard her locking her door to go out for lunch, he stepped quickly into the hall in his messy painting coat, and addressed her.

"I don't wish to be exigent, Miss,"—he had certain grand words that he used upon occasion—"but if this is your trunk, it's rather in the way here."

"Oh, very well!" she exclaimed carelessly, dropping her keys into her hand-bag. "I'll have it moved when I can get a man to do it," and she went down the hall with her free, roving stride.

Her name, Hedger discovered from her letters, which the postman left on the table in the lower hall, was Eden Bower.

III

In the closet that was built against the partition separating his room from Miss Bower's, Hedger kept all his wearing apparel, some of it on hooks and hangers, some of it on the floor. When he opened his closet door now-a-days, little dust-colored insects flew out on downy wing, and he suspected that a brood of moths were hatching in his winter overcoat. Mrs. Foley, the janitress, told him to bring down all his heavy clothes and she would give them a beating and hang them in the court. The closet was in such disorder that he shunned the encounter, but one hot afternoon he set himself to the task. First he threw out a pile of forgotten laundry and tied it up in a sheet. The bundle stood as high as his middle when he had knotted the corners. Then he got his shoes and overshoes together. When he took his over-coat from its place against the partition, a long ray of yellow light shot across the dark enclosure,—a knot hole, evidently, in the high wainscoting of the west room. He had never noticed it before, and without realizing what he was doing, he stooped and squinted through it.

Yonder, in a pool of sunlight, stood his new neighbor, wholly unclad, doing exercises of some sort before a long gilt mirror. Hedger did not happen to think how unpardonable it was of him to watch her. Nudity was not improper to any one who had worked so much from the figure, and he continued to

3. Drunk.   4. Adorned.

look, simply because he had never seen a woman's body so beautiful as this one,—positively glorious in action. As she swung her arms and changed from one pivot of motion to another, muscular energy seemed to flow through her from her toes to her finger-tips. The soft flush of exercise and the gold of afternoon sun played over her flesh together, enveloped her in a luminous mist which, as she turned and twisted, made now an arm, now a shoulder, now a thigh, dissolve in pure light and instantly recover its outline with the next gesture. Hedger's fingers curved as if he were holding a crayon; mentally he was doing the whole figure in a single running line, and the charcoal seemed to explode in his hand at the point where the energy of each gesture was discharged into the whirling disc of light, from a foot or shoulder, from the up-thrust chin or the lifted breasts.

He could not have told whether he watched her for six minutes or sixteen. When her gymnastics were over, she paused to catch up a lock of hair that had come down, and examined with solicitude a little reddish mole that grew under her left arm-pit. Then, with her hand on her hip, she walked unconcernedly across the room and disappeared through the door into her bedchamber.

Disappeared—Don Hedger was crouching on his knees, staring at the golden shower which poured in through the west windows, at the lake of gold sleeping on the faded Turkish carpet. The spot was enchanted; a vision out of Alexandria, out of the remote pagan past, had bathed itself there in Helianthine fire.[5]

When he crawled out of his closet, he stood blinking at the gray sheet stuffed with laundry, not knowing what had happened to him. He felt a little sick as he contemplated the bundle. Everything here was different; he hated the disorder of the place, the gray prison light, his old shoes and himself and all his slovenly habits. The black calico curtains that ran on wires over his big window were white with dust. There were three greasy frying pans in the sink, and the sink itself—He felt desperate. He couldn't stand this another minute. He took up an armful of winter clothes and ran down four flights into the basement.

"Mrs. Foley," he began, "I want my room cleaned this afternoon, thoroughly cleaned. Can you get a woman for me right away?"

"Is it company you're having?" the fat, dirty janitress enquired. Mrs. Foley was the widow of a useful Tammany man, and she owned real estate in Flatbush.[6] She was huge and soft as a feather bed. Her face and arms were permanently coated with dust, grained like wood where the sweat had trickled.

"Yes, company. That's it."

"Well, this is a queer time of the day to be asking for a cleaning woman. It's likely I can get you old Lizzie, if she's not drunk. I'll send Willy round to see."

Willy, the son of fourteen, roused from the stupor and stain of his fifth box of cigarettes by the gleam of a quarter, went out. In five minutes he returned with old Lizzie,—she smelling strong of spirits and wearing several

---

5. Fire of the sun. Alexandria: a great classical center of learning and trade, founded in 322 B.C.E. by Alexander the Great.

6. A section of Brooklyn. "Tammany man": i.e., member of the Tammany Society, a corrupt New York political organization.

jackets which she had put on one over the other, and a number of skirts, long and short, which made her resemble an animated dish-clout. She had, of course, to borrow her equipment from Mrs. Foley, and toiled up the long flights, dragging mop and pail and broom. She told Hedger to be of good cheer, for he had got the right woman for the job, and showed him a great leather strap she wore about her wrist to prevent dislocation of tendons. She swished about the place, scattering dust and splashing soapsuds, while he watched her in nervous despair. He stood over Lizzie and made her scour the sink, directing her roughly, then paid her and got rid of her. Shutting the door on his failure, he hurried off with his dog to lose himself among the stevedores and dock laborers on West Street.

A strange chapter began for Don Hedger. Day after day, at that hour in the afternoon, the hour before his neighbor dressed for dinner, he crouched down in his closet to watch her go through her mysterious exercises. It did not occur to him that his conduct was detestable; there was nothing shy or retreating about this unclad girl,—a bold body, studying itself quite coolly and evidently well pleased with itself, doing all this for a purpose. Hedger scarcely regarded his action as conduct at all; it was something that had happened to him. More than once he went out and tried to stay away for the whole afternoon, but at about five o'clock he was sure to find himself among his old shoes in the dark. The pull of that aperture was stronger than his will,—and he had always considered his will the strongest thing about him. When she threw herself upon the divan and lay resting, he still stared, holding his breath. His nerves were so on edge that a sudden noise made him start and brought out the sweat on his forehead. The dog would come and tug at his sleeve, knowing that something was wrong with his master. If he attempted a mournful whine, those strong hands closed about his throat.

When Hedger came slinking out of his closet, he sat down on the edge of the couch, sat for hours without moving. He was not painting at all now. This thing, whatever it was, drank him up as ideas had sometimes done, and he sank into a stupor of idleness as deep and dark as the stupor of work. He could not understand it; he was no boy, he had worked from models for years, and a woman's body was no mystery to him. Yet now he did nothing but sit and think about one. He slept very little, and with the first light of morning he awoke as completely possessed by this woman as if he had been with her all the night before. The unconscious operations of life went on in him only to perpetuate this excitement. His brain held but one image now— vibrated, burned with it. It was a heathenish feeling; without friendliness, almost without tenderness.

Women had come and gone in Hedger's life. Not having had a mother to begin with, his relations with them, whether amorous or friendly, had been casual. He got on well with janitresses and wash-women, with Indians and with the peasant women of foreign countries. He had friends among the silk-skirt factory girls who came to eat their lunch in Washington Square, and he sometimes took a model for a day in the country. He felt an unreasoning antipathy toward the well-dressed women he saw coming out of big shops, or driving in the Park. If, on his way to the Art Museum,[7] he noticed a pretty

---

7. I.e., the Metropolitan Museum of Art, founded in 1870 and located since 1880 on Fifth Avenue at 82nd Street.

girl standing on the steps of one of the houses on upper Fifth Avenue, he frowned at her and went by with his shoulders hunched up as if he were cold. He had never known such girls, or heard them talk, or seen the inside of the houses in which they lived; but he believed them all to be artificial and, in an aesthetic sense, perverted. He saw them enslaved by desire of merchandise and manufactured articles, effective only in making life complicated and insincere and in embroidering it with ugly and meaningless trivialities. They were enough, he thought, to make one almost forget woman as she existed in art, in thought, and in the universe.

He had no desire to know the woman who had, for the time at least, so broken up his life,—no curiosity about her every-day personality. He shunned any revelation of it, and he listened for Miss Bower's coming and going, not to encounter, but to avoid her. He wished that the girl who wore shirt-waists and got letters from Chicago would keep out of his way, that she did not exist. With her he had naught to make. But in a room full of sun, before an old mirror, on a little enchanted rug of sleeping colors, he had seen a woman who emerged naked through a door, and disappeared naked. He thought of that body as never having been clad, or as having worn the stuffs and dyes of all the centuries but his own. And for him she had no geographical associations; unless with Crete, or Alexandria, or Veronese's[8] Venice. She was the immortal conception, the perennial theme.

The first break in Hedger's lethargy occurred one afternoon when two young men came to take Eden Bower out to dine. They went into her music room, laughed and talked for a few minutes, and then took her away with them. They were gone a long while, but he did not go out for food himself; he waited for them to come back. At last he heard them coming down the hall, gayer and more talkative than when they left. One of them sat down at the piano, and they all began to sing. This Hedger found absolutely unendurable. He snatched up his hat and went running down the stairs. Caesar leaped beside him, hoping that old times were coming back. They had supper in the oysterman's basement and then sat down in front of their own doorway. The moon stood full over the Square, a thing of regal glory; but Hedger did not see the moon; he was looking, murderously, for men. Presently two, wearing straw hats and white trousers and carrying canes, came down the steps from his house. He rose and dogged them across the Square. They were laughing and seemed very much elated about something. As one stopped to light a cigarette, Hedger caught from the other:

"Don't you think she has a beautiful talent?"

His companion threw away his match. "She has a beautiful figure." They both ran to catch the stage.

Hedger went back to his studio. The light was shining from her transom. For the first time he violated her privacy at night, and peered through that fatal aperture. She was sitting fully dressed, in the window, smoking a cigarette and looking out over the housetops. He watched her until she rose, looked about her with a disdainful, crafty smile, and turned out the light.

The next morning, when Miss Bower went out Hedger followed her. Her white skirt gleamed ahead of him as she sauntered about the Square. She sat down behind the Garibaldi[9] statue and opened a music book she carried.

---

8. Paolo Veronese (1528–1588), Venetian painter.
9. Giuseppe Garibaldi (1807–1882), Italian patriot and champion of independence.

She turned the leaves carelessly, and several times glanced in his direction. He was on the point of going over to her, when she rose quickly and looked up at the sky. A flock of pigeons had risen from somewhere in the crowded Italian quarter to the south, and were wheeling rapidly up through the morning air, soaring and dropping, scattering and coming together, now gray, now white as silver, as they caught or intercepted the sunlight. She put up her hand to shade her eyes and followed them with a kind of defiant delight in her face.

Hedger came and stood beside her. "You've surely seen them before?"

"Oh, yes," she replied, still looking up. "I see them every day from my windows. They always come home about five o'clock. Where do they live?"

"I don't know. Probably some Italian raises them for the market. They were here long before I came, and I've been here four years."

"In that same gloomy room? Why didn't you take mine when it was vacant?"

"It isn't gloomy. That's the best light for painting."

"Oh, is it? I don't know anything about painting. I'd like to see your pictures sometime. You have such a lot in there. Don't they get dusty, piled up against the wall like that?"

"Not very. I'd be glad to show them to you. Is your name really Eden Bower? I've seen your letters on the table."

"Well, it's the name I'm going to sing under. My father's name is Bowers, but my friend Mr. Jones, a Chicago newspaper man who writes about music, told me to drop the 's.' He's crazy about my voice."

Miss Bower didn't usually tell the whole story,—about anything. Her first name, when she lived in Huntington, Illinois, was Edna, but Mr. Jones had persuaded her to change it to one which he felt would be worthy of her future. She was quick to take suggestions, though she told him she "didn't see what was the matter with 'Edna.'"

She explained to Hedger that she was going to Paris to study. She was waiting in New York for Chicago friends who were to take her over but who had been detained. "Did you study in Paris?" she asked.

"No, I've never been in Paris. But I was in the south of France all last summer, studying with C———.[1] He's the biggest man among the moderns,— at least I think so."

Miss Bower sat down and made room for him on the bench. "Do tell me about it. I expected to be there by this time, and I can't wait to find out what it's like."

Hedger began to relate how he had seen some of this Frenchman's work in an exhibition, and deciding at once that this was the man for him, he had taken a boat for Marseilles the next week going over steerage. He proceeded at once to the little town on the coast where his painter lived, and presented himself. The man never took pupils, but because Hedger had come so far he let him stay. Hedger lived at the master's house and every day they went out together to paint, sometimes on the blazing rocks down by the sea. They wrapped themselves in light woollen blankets and didn't feel the heat. Being there and working with C——— was being in Paradise, Hedger concluded; he learned more in three months than in all his life before.

Eden Bower laughed. "You're a funny fellow. Didn't you do anything but

---

1. Perhaps a reference to the French painter Paul Cézanne (1839–1906).

work? Are the women very beautiful? Did you have awfully good things to eat and drink?"

Hedger said some of the women were fine looking, especially one girl who went about selling fish and lobsters. About the food there was nothing remarkable,—except the ripe figs, he liked those. They drank sour wine, and used goat-butter, which was strong and full of hair, as it was churned in a goat skin.

"But don't they have parties or banquets? Aren't there any fine hotels down there?"

"Yes, but they are all closed in summer, and the country people are poor. It's a beautiful country, though."

"How, beautiful?" she persisted.

"If you want to go in, I'll show you some sketches, and you'll see."

Miss Bower rose. "All right. I won't go to my fencing lesson this morning. Do you fence? Here comes your dog. You can't move but he's after you. He always makes a face at me when I meet him in the hall, and shows his nasty little teeth as if he wanted to bite me."

In the studio Hedger got out his sketches, but to Miss Bower, whose favorite pictures were Christ Before Pilate and a redhaired Magdalen of Henner,[2] these landscapes were not at all beautiful, and they gave her no idea of any country whatsoever. She was careful not to commit herself, however. Her vocal teacher had already convinced her that she had a great deal to learn about many things.

"Why don't we go out to lunch somewhere?" Hedger asked, and began to dust his fingers with a handkerchief—which he got out of sight as swiftly as possible.

"All right, the Brevoort," she said carelessly. "I think that's a good place, and they have good wine. I don't care for cocktails."

Hedger felt his chin uneasily. "I'm afraid I haven't shaved this morning. If you could wait for me in the Square? It won't take me ten minutes."

Left alone, he found a clean collar and handkerchief, brushed his coat and blacked his shoes, and last of all dug up ten dollars from the bottom of an old copper kettle he had brought from Spain. His winter hat was of such complexion that the Brevoort hall boy winked at the porter as he took it and placed it on the rack in a row of fresh straw ones.[3]

IV

That afternoon Eden Bower was lying on the couch in her music room, her face turned to the window, watching the pigeons. Reclining thus she could see none of the neighboring roofs, only the sky itself and the birds that crossed and recrossed her field of vision, white as scraps of paper blowing in the wind. She was thinking that she was young and handsome and had had a good lunch, that a very easy-going, light-hearted city lay in the streets below her; and she was wondering why she found this queer painter chap, with his

---

2. A painting of Mary Magdalen, a reformed prostitute in the New Testament, by Jean-Jacques Henner (1829–1905), French painter of religious subjects. Pilate is the judge who permitted Christ's crucifixion.

3. I.e., summer hats.

lean, bluish cheeks and heavy black eyebrows, more interesting than the smart young men she met at her teacher's studio.

Eden Bower was, at twenty, very much the same person that we all know her to be at forty, except that she knew a great deal less. But one thing she knew: that she was to be Eden Bower. She was like some one standing before a great show window full of beautiful and costly things, deciding which she will order. She understands that they will not all be delivered immediately, but one by one they will arrive at her door. She already knew some of the many things that were to happen to her; for instance, that the Chicago millionaire who was going to take her abroad with his sister as chaperone, would eventually press his claim in quite another manner. He was the most circumspect of bachelors, afraid of everything obvious, even of women who were too flagrantly handsome. He was a nervous collector of pictures and furniture, a nervous patron of music, and a nervous host; very cautious about his health, and about any course of conduct that might make him ridiculous. But she knew that he would at last throw all his precautions to the winds.

People like Eden Bower are inexplicable. Her father sold farming machinery in Huntington, Illinois, and she had grown up with no acquaintances or experiences outside of that prairie town. Yet from her earliest childhood she had not one conviction or opinion in common with the people about her,— the only people she knew. Before she was out of short dresses she had made up her mind that she was going to be an actress, that she would live far away in great cities, that she would be much admired by men and would have everything she wanted. When she was thirteen, and was already singing and reciting for church entertainments, she read in some illustrated magazine a long article about the late Czar of Russia,[4] then just come to the throne or about to come to it. After that, lying in the hammock on the front porch on summer evenings, or sitting through a long sermon in the family pew, she amused herself by trying to make up her mind whether she would or would not be the Czar's mistress when she played in his Capital. Now Edna had met this fascinating word only in the novels of Ouida,[5]—her hard-worked little mother kept a long row of them in the upstairs store-room, behind the linen chest. In Huntington, women who bore that relation to men were called by a very different name, and their lot was not an enviable one; of all the shabby and poor, they were the shabbiest. But then, Edna had never lived in Huntington, not even before she began to find books like "Sapho" and "Mademoiselle de Maupin,"[6] secretly sold in paper covers throughout Illinois. It was as if she had come into Huntington, into the Bowers family, on one of the trains that puffed over the marshes behind their back fence all day long, and was waiting for another train to take her out.

As she grew older and handsomer, she had many beaux, but these small-town boys didn't interest her. If a lad kissed her when he brought her home from a dance, she was indulgent and she rather liked it. But if he pressed her further, she slipped away from him, laughing. After she began to sing in Chicago, she was consistently discreet. She stayed as a guest in rich people's

---

4. Nicholas II (1868–1918; czar, 1894–1917), executed by the Bosheviks after the Russian Revolution.
5. Pseudonym of Louise de la Ramée (1839–1908), English author of popular romantic novels.
6. *Mademoiselle de Maupin* (1835), by Théophile Gautier, and *Sapho* (1884), by Alphonse Daudet, novels whose heroines are, respectively, a bisexual cross-dresser and a courtesan (one of whose affairs is with a woman).

houses, and she knew that she was being watched like a rabbit in a laboratory. Covered up in bed, with the lights out, she thought her own thoughts, and laughed.

This summer in New York was her first taste of freedom. The Chicago capitalist, after all his arrangements were made for sailing, had been compelled to go to Mexico to look after oil interests. His sister knew an excellent singing master in New York. Why should not a discreet, well-balanced girl like Miss Bower spend the summer there, studying quietly? The capitalist suggested that his sister might enjoy a summer on Long Island; he would rent the Griffiths' place for her, with all the servants, and Eden could stay there. But his sister met this proposal with a cold stare. So it fell out, that between selfishness and greed, Eden got a summer all her own,—which really did a great deal toward making her an artist and whatever else she was afterward to become. She had time to look about, to watch without being watched; to select diamonds in one window and furs in another, to select shoulders and moustaches in the big hotels where she went to lunch. She had the easy freedom of obscurity and the consciousness of power. She enjoyed both. She was in no hurry.

While Eden Bower watched the pigeons, Don Hedger sat on the other side of the bolted doors, looking into a pool of dark turpentine, at his idle brushes, wondering why a woman could do this to him. He, too, was sure of his future and knew that he was a chosen man. He could not know, of course, that he was merely the first to fall under a fascination which was to be disastrous to a few men and pleasantly stimulating to many thousands. Each of these two young people sensed the future, but not completely. Don Hedger knew that nothing much would ever happen to him. Eden Bower understood that to her a great deal would happen. But she did not guess that her neighbor would have more tempestuous adventures sitting in his dark studio than she would find in all the capitals of Europe, or in all the latitude of conduct she was prepared to permit herself.

V

One Sunday morning Eden was crossing the Square with a spruce young man in a white flannel suit and a panama hat. They had been breakfasting at the Brevoort and he was coaxing her to let him come up to her rooms and sing for an hour.

"No, I've got to write letters. You must run along now. I see a friend of mine over there, and I want to ask him about something before I go up."

"That fellow with the dog? Where did you pick him up?" The young man glanced toward the seat under a sycamore where Hedger was reading the morning paper.

"Oh, he's an old friend from the West," said Eden easily. "I won't introduce you, because he doesn't like people. He's a recluse. Good-bye. I can't be sure about Tuesday. I'll go with you if I have time after my lesson." She nodded, left him, and went over to the seat littered with newspapers. The young man went up the Avenue without looking back.

"Well, what are you going to do today? Shampoo this animal all morning?" Eden enquired teasingly.

Hedger made room for her on the seat. "No, at twelve o'clock I'm going out to Coney Island.[7] One of my models is going up in a balloon this afternoon. I've often promised to go and see her, and now I'm going."

Eden asked if models usually did such stunts. No, Hedger told her, but Molly Welch added to her earnings in that way. "I believe," he added, "she likes the excitement of it. She's got a good deal of spirit. That's why I like to paint her. So many models have flaccid bodies."

"And she hasn't, eh? Is she the one who comes to see you? I can't help hearing her, she talks so loud."

"Yes, she has a rough voice, but she's a fine girl. I don't suppose you'd be interested in going?"

"I don't know," Eden sat tracing patterns on the asphalt with the end of her parasol. "Is it any fun? I got up feeling I'd like to do something different today. It's the first Sunday I've not had to sing in church. I had that engagement for breakfast at the Brevoort, but it wasn't very exciting. That chap can't talk about anything but himself."

Hedger warmed a little. "If you've never been to Coney Island, you ought to go. It's nice to see all the people; tailors and bar-tenders and prize-fighters with their best girls, and all sorts of folks taking a holiday."

Eden looked sidewise at him. So one ought to be interested in people of that kind, ought one? He was certainly a funny fellow. Yet he was never, somehow, tiresome. She had seen a good deal of him lately, but she kept wanting to know him better, to find out what made him different from men like the one she had just left—whether he really was as different as he seemed. "I'll go with you," she said at last, "if you'll leave that at home." She pointed to Caesar's flickering ears with her sunshade.

"But he's half the fun. You'd like to hear him bark at the waves when they come in."

"No, I wouldn't. He's jealous and disagreeable if he sees you talking to any one else. Look at him now."

"Of course, if you make a face at him. He knows what that means, and he makes a worse face. He likes Molly Welch, and she'll be disappointed if I don't bring him."

Eden said decidedly that he couldn't take both of them. So at twelve o'clock when she and Hedger got on the boat at Desbrosses street, Caesar was lying on his pallet, with a bone.

Eden enjoyed the boat-ride. It was the first time she had been on the water, and she felt as if she were embarking for France. The light warm breeze and the plunge of the waves made her very wide awake, and she liked crowds of any kind. They went to the balcony of a big, noisy restaurant and had a shore dinner,[8] with tall steins of beer. Hedger had got a big advance from his advertising firm since he first lunched with Miss Bower ten days ago, and he was ready for anything.

After dinner they went to the tent behind the bathing beach, where the tops of two balloons bulged out over the canvas. A red-faced man in a linen suit stood in front of the tent, shouting in a hoarse voice and telling the people that if the crowd was good for five dollars more, a beautiful young woman would risk her life for their entertainment. Four little boys in dirty

---

7. Amusement center and neighborhood in Brooklyn, on the Atlantic Ocean.

8. I.e., a dinner of seafood.

red uniforms ran about taking contributions in their pill-box hats. One of the balloons was bobbing up and down in its tether and people were shoving forward to get nearer the tent.

"Is it dangerous, as he pretends?" Eden asked.

"Molly says it's simple enough if nothing goes wrong with the balloon. Then it would be all over, I suppose."

"Wouldn't you like to go up with her?"

"I? Of course not. I'm not fond of taking foolish risks."

Eden sniffed. "I shouldn't think sensible risks would be very much fun."

Hedger did not answer, for just then every one began to shove the other way and shout, "Look out. There she goes!" and a band of six pieces commenced playing furiously.

As the balloon rose from its tent enclosure, they saw a girl in green tights standing in the basket, holding carelessly to one of the ropes with one hand and with the other waving to the spectators. A long rope trailed behind to keep the balloon from blowing out to sea.

As it soared, the figure in green tights in the basket diminished to a mere spot, and the balloon itself, in the brilliant light, looked like a big silver-gray bat, with its wings folded. When it began to sink, the girl stepped through the hole in the basket to a trapeze that hung below, and gracefully descended through the air, holding to the rod with both hands, keeping her body taut and her feet close together. The crowd, which had grown very large by this time, cheered vociferously. The men took off their hats and waved, little boys shouted, and fat old women, shining with the heat and a beer lunch, murmured admiring comments upon the balloonist's figure. "Beautiful legs, she has!"

"That's so," Hedger whispered. "Not many girls would look well in that position." Then, for some reason, he blushed a slow, dark, painful crimson.

The balloon descended slowly, a little way from the tent, and the red-faced man in the linen suit caught Molly Welch before her feet touched the ground, and pulled her to one side. The band struck up "Blue Bell"[9] by way of welcome, and one of the sweaty pages ran forward and presented the balloonist with a large bouquet of artificial flowers. She smiled and thanked him, and ran back across the sand to the tent.

"Can't we go inside and see her?" Eden asked. "You can explain to the door man. I want to meet her." Edging forward, she herself addressed the man in the linen suit and slipped something from her purse into his hand.

They found Molly seated before a trunk that had a mirror in the lid and a "make-up" outfit spread upon the tray. She was wiping the cold cream and powder from her neck with a discarded chemise.

"Hello, Don," she said cordially. "Brought a friend?"

Eden liked her. She had an easy, friendly manner, and there was something boyish and devil-may-care about her.

"Yes, it's fun. I'm mad about it," she said in reply to Eden's questions. "I always want to let go, when I come down on the bar. You don't feel your weight at all, as you would on a stationary trapeze."

The big drum boomed outside, and the publicity man began shouting to newly arrived boat-loads. Miss Welch took a last pull at her cigarette. "Now

---

9. The "Blue Bell March" (1904), music by Theodore F. Morse and lyrics by Edward Madden.

you'll have to get out, Don. I change for the next act. This time I go up in a black evening dress, and lose the skirt in the basket before I start down."

"Yes, go along," said Eden. "Wait for me outside the door. I'll stay and help her dress."

Hedger waited and waited, while women of every build bumped into him and begged his pardon, and the red pages ran about holding out their caps for coins, and the people ate and perspired and shifted parasols against the sun. When the band began to play a two-step, all the bathers ran up out of the surf to watch the ascent. The second balloon bumped and rose, and the crowd began shouting to the girl in a black evening dress who stood leaning against the ropes and smiling. "It's a new girl," they called. "It ain't the Countess this time. You're a peach, girlie!"

The balloonist acknowledged these compliments, bowing and looking down over the sea of upturned faces,—but Hedger was determined she should not see him, and he darted behind the tent-fly. He was suddenly dripping with cold sweat, his mouth was full of the bitter taste of anger and his tongue felt stiff behind his teeth. Molly Welch, in a shirt-waist and a white tam-o'-shanter cap, slipped out from the tent under his arm and laughed up in his face. "She's a crazy one you brought along. She'll get what she wants!"

"Oh, I'll settle with you, all right!" Hedger brought out with difficulty.

"It's not my fault, Donnie. I couldn't do anything with her. She bought me off. What's the matter with you? Are you soft on her? She's safe enough. It's as easy as rolling off a log, if you keep cool." Molly Welch was rather excited herself, and she was chewing gum at a high speed as she stood beside him, looking up at the floating silver cone. "Now watch," she exclaimed suddenly. "She's coming down on the bar. I advised her to cut that out, but you see she does it first-rate. And she got rid of the skirt, too. Those black tights show off her legs very well. She keeps her feet together like I told her, and makes a good line along the back. See the light on those silver slippers,—that was a good idea I had. Come along to meet her. Don't be a grouch; she's done it fine!"

Molly tweaked his elbow, and then left him standing like a stump, while she ran down the beach with the crowd.

Though Hedger was sulking, his eye could not help seeing the low blue welter of the sea, the arrested bathers, standing in the surf, their arms and legs stained red by the dropping sun, all shading their eyes and gazing upward at the slowly falling silver star.

Molly Welch and the manager caught Eden under the arms and lifted her aside, a red page dashed up with a bouquet, and the band struck up "Blue Bell." Eden laughed and bowed, took Molly's arm, and ran up the sand in her black tights and silver slippers, dodging the friendly old women, and the gallant sports[1] who wanted to offer their homage on the spot.

When she emerged from the tent, dressed in her own clothes, that part of the beach was almost deserted. She stepped to her companion's side and said carelessly: "Hadn't we better try to catch this boat? I hope you're not sore at me. Really, it was lots of fun."

---

1. Jaunty young men.

Hedger looked at his watch. "Yes, we have fifteen minutes to get to the boat," he said politely.

As they walked toward the pier, one of the pages ran up panting. "Lady, you're carrying off the bouquet," he said, aggrievedly.

Eden stopped and looked at the bunch of spotty cotton roses in her hand. "Of course. I want them for a souvenir. You gave them to me yourself."

"I give 'em to you for looks, but you can't take 'em away. They belong to the show."

"Oh, you always use the same bunch?"

"Sure we do. There ain't too much money in this business."

She laughed and tossed them back to him.

"Why are you angry?" she asked Hedger. "I wouldn't have done it if I'd been with some fellows, but I thought you were the sort who wouldn't mind. Molly didn't for a minute think you would."

"What possessed you to do such a fool thing?" he asked roughly.

"I don't know. When I saw her coming down, I wanted to try it. It looked exciting. Didn't I hold myself as well as she did?"

Hedger shrugged his shoulders, but in his heart he forgave her.

The return boat was not crowded, though the boats that passed them, going out, were packed to the rails. The sun was setting. Boys and girls sat on the long benches with their arms about each other, singing. Eden felt a strong wish to propitiate her companion, to be alone with him. She had been curiously wrought up by her balloon trip; it was a lark, but not very satisfying unless one came back to something after the flight. She wanted to be admired and adored. Though Eden said nothing, and sat with her arms limp on the rail in front of her, looking languidly at the rising silhouette of the city and the bright path of the sun, Hedger felt a strange drawing near to her. If he but brushed her white skirt with his knee, there was an instant communication between them, such as there had never been before. They did not talk at all, but when they went over the gangplank she took his arm and kept her shoulder close to his. He felt as if they were enveloped in a highly charged atmosphere, an invisible network of subtle, almost painful sensibility. They had somehow taken hold of each other.

An hour later, they were dining in the back garden of a little French hotel on Ninth Street, long since passed away. It was cool and leafy there, and the mosquitoes were not very numerous. A party of South Americans at another table were drinking champagne, and Eden murmured that she thought she would like some, if it were not too expensive. "Perhaps it will make me think I am in the balloon again. That was a very nice feeling. You've forgiven me, haven't you?"

Hedger gave her a quick straight look from under his black eyebrows, and something went over her that was like a chill, except that it was warm and feathery. She drank most of the wine: her companion was indifferent to it. He was talking more to her tonight than he had ever done before. She asked him about a new picture she had seen in his room; a queer thing full of stiff, supplicating female figures. "It's Indian, isn't it?"

"Yes. I call it Rain Spirits, or maybe, Indian Rain. In the Southwest, where I've been a good deal, the Indian traditions make women have to do with the rain-fall. They were supposed to control it, somehow, and to be able to find springs and make moisture come out of the earth. You see I'm trying to learn to paint what people think and feel; to get away from all that photographic stuff. When I look at you, I don't see what a camera would see, do I?"

"How can I tell?"

"Well, if I should paint you, I could make you understand what I see." For the second time that day Hedger crimsoned unexpectedly, and his eyes fell and steadily contemplated a dish of little radishes. "That particular picture I got from a story a Mexican priest told me; he said he found it in an old manuscript book in a monastery down there, written by some Spanish Missionary, who got his stories from the Aztecs. This one he called 'The Forty Lovers of the Queen,' and it was more or less about rain-making."

"Aren't you going to tell it to me?" Eden asked.

Hedger fumbled among the radishes. "I don't know if it's the proper kind of story to tell a girl."

She smiled; "Oh, forget about that! I've been balloon riding today. I like to hear you talk."

Her low voice was flattering. She had seemed like clay in his hands ever since they got on the boat to come home. He leaned back in his chair, forgot his food, and, looking at her intently, began to tell his story, the theme of which he somehow felt was dangerous tonight.

The tale began, he said, somewhere in Ancient Mexico, and concerned the daughter of a king. The birth of this Princess was preceded by unusual portents. Three times her mother dreamed that she was delivered of serpents, which betokened that the child she carried would have power with the rain gods. The serpent was the symbol of water. The Princess grew up dedicated to the gods, and wise men taught her the rain-making mysteries. She was with difficulty restrained from men and was guarded at all times, for it was the law of the Thunder that she be maiden until her marriage. In the years of her adolescence, rain was abundant with her people. The oldest man could not remember such fertility. When the Princess had counted eighteen summers, her father went to drive out a war party that harried his borders on the north and troubled his prosperity. The King destroyed the invaders and brought home many prisoners. Among the prisoners was a young chief, taller than any of his captors, of such strength and ferocity that the King's people came a day's journey to look at him. When the Princess beheld his great stature, and saw that his arms and breast were covered with the figures of wild animals, bitten into the skin and colored, she begged his life from her father. She desired that he should practice his art upon her, and prick upon her skin the signs of Rain and Lightning and Thunder, and stain the wounds with herb-juices, as they were upon his own body. For many days, upon the roof of the King's house, the Princess submitted herself to the bone needle, and the women with her marvelled at her fortitude. But the Princess was without shame before the Captive, and it came about that he threw from him his needles and his stains, and fell upon the Princess to violate her honor; and her women ran down from the roof screaming, to call the guard which stood at the gateway of the King's house, and none stayed to protect their mistress. When the guard came, the Captive was thrown into bonds, and he was gelded, and his tongue was torn out, and he was given for a slave to the Rain Princess.

The country of the Aztecs to the east was tormented by thirst, and their king, hearing much of the rain-making arts of the Princess, sent an embassy to her father, with presents and an offer of marriage. So the Princess went from her father to be the Queen of the Aztecs, and she took with her the Captive, who served her in everything with entire fidelity and slept upon a mat before her door.

The King gave his bride a fortress on the outskirts of the city, whither she retired to entreat the rain gods. This fortress was called the Queen's House, and on the night of the new moon the Queen came to it from the palace. But when the moon waxed and grew toward the round, because the god of Thunder had had his will of her, then the Queen returned to the King. Drout abated in the country and rain fell abundantly by reason of the Queen's power with the stars.

When the Queen went to her own house she took with her no servant but the Captive, and he slept outside her door and brought her food after she had fasted. The Queen had a jewel of great value, a turquoise that had fallen from the sun, and had the image of the sun upon it. And when she desired a young man whom she had seen in the army or among the slaves, she sent the Captive to him with the jewel, for a sign that he should come to her secretly at the Queen's House upon business concerning the welfare of all. And some, after she had talked with them, she sent away with rewards; and some she took into her chamber and kept them by her for one night or two. Afterward she called the Captive and bade him conduct the youth by the secret way he had come, underneath the chambers of the fortress. But for the going away of the Queen's lovers the Captive took out the bar that was beneath a stone in the floor of the passage, and put in its stead a rush-reed, and the youth stepped upon it and fell through into a cavern that was the bed of an underground river, and whatever was thrown into it was not seen again. In this service nor in any other did the Captive fail the Queen.

But when the Queen sent for the Captain of the Archers, she detained him four days in her chamber, calling often for food and wine, and was greatly content with him. On the fourth day she went to the Captive outside her door and said:

"Tomorrow take this man up by the sure way, by which the King comes, and let him live."

In the Queen's door were arrows, purple and white. When she desired the King to come to her publicly, with his guard, she sent him a white arrow; but when she sent the purple, he came secretly, and covered himself with his mantle to be hidden from the stone gods at the gate. On the fifth night that the Queen was with her lover, the Captive took a purple arrow to the King, and the King came secretly and found them together. He killed the Captain with his own hand, but the Queen he brought to public trial. The Captive, when he was put to the question, told on his fingers forty men that he had let through the underground passage into the river. The Captive and the Queen were put to death by fire, both on the same day, and afterward there was scarcity of rain.

Eden Bower sat shivering a little as she listened. Hedger was not trying to please her, she thought, but to antagonize and frighten her by his brutal story. She had often told herself that his lean, big-boned lower jaw was like his bull-dog's, but tonight his face made Caesar's most savage and determined expression seem an affectation. Now she was looking at the man he really was. Nobody's eyes had ever defied her like this. They were searching her and seeing everything; all she had concealed from Livingston, and from the millionaire and his friends, and from the newspaper men. He was testing her, trying her out, and she was more ill at ease than she wished to show.

"That's quite a thrilling story," she said at last, rising and winding her scarf about her throat. "It must be getting late. Almost every one has gone."

They walked down the Avenue like people who have quarrelled, or who wish to get rid of each other. Hedger did not take her arm at the street crossings, and they did not linger in the Square. At her door he tried none of the old devices of the Livingston boys. He stood like a post, having forgotten to take off his hat, gave her a harsh, threatening glance, muttered "goodnight," and shut his own door noisily.

There was no question of sleep for Eden Bower. Her brain was working like a machine that would never stop. After she undressed, she tried to calm her nerves by smoking a cigarette, lying on the divan by the open window. But she grew wider and wider awake, combating the challenge that had flamed all evening in Hedger's eyes. The balloon had been one kind of excitement, the wine another; but the thing that had roused her, as a blow rouses a proud man, was the doubt, the contempt, the sneering hostility with which the painter had looked at her when he told his savage story. Crowds and balloons were all very well, she reflected, but woman's chief adventure is man. With a mind over active and a sense of life over strong, she wanted to walk across the roofs in the starlight, to sail over the sea and face at once a world of which she had never been afraid.

Hedger must be asleep; his dog had stopped sniffing under the double doors. Eden put on her wrapper and slippers and stole softly down the hall over the old carpet; one loose board creaked just as she reached the ladder. The trap-door was open, as always on hot nights. When she stepped out on the roof she drew a long breath and walked across it, looking up at the sky. Her foot touched something soft; she heard a low growl, and on the instant Caesar's sharp little teeth caught her ankle and waited. His breath was like steam on her leg. Nobody had ever intruded upon his roof before, and he panted for the movement or the word that would let him spring his jaw. Instead, Hedger's hand seized his throat.

"Wait a minute. I'll settle with him," he said grimly. He dragged the dog toward the manhole and disappeared. When he came back, he found Eden standing over by the dark chimney, looking away in an offended attitude.

"I caned him unmercifully," he panted. "Of course you didn't hear anything; he never whines when I beat him. He didn't nip you, did he?"

"I don't know whether he broke the skin or not," she answered aggrievedly, still looking off into the west.

"If I were one of your friends in white pants, I'd strike a match to find whether you were hurt, though I know you are not, and then I'd see your ankle, wouldn't I?"

"I suppose so."

He shook his head and stood with his hands in the pockets of his old painting jacket. "I'm not up to such boy-tricks. If you want the place to yourself, I'll clear out. There are plenty of places where I can spend the night, what's left of it. But if you stay here and I stay here—" He shrugged his shoulders.

Eden did not stir, and she made no reply. Her head drooped slightly, as if she were considering. But the moment he put his arms about her they began to talk, both at once, as people do in an opera. The instant avowal brought out a flood of trivial admissions. Hedger confessed his crime, was reproached and forgiven, and now Eden knew what it was in his look that she had found so disturbing of late.

Standing against the black chimney, with the sky behind and blue shadows before, they looked like one of Hedger's own paintings of that period; two figures, one white and one dark, and nothing whatever distinguishable about them but that they were male and female. The faces were lost, the contours blurred in shadow, but the figures were a man and a woman, and that was their whole concern and their mysterious beauty,—it was the rhythm in which they moved, at last, along the roof and down into the dark hole; he first, drawing her gently after him. She came down very slowly. The excitement and bravado and uncertainty of that long day and night seemed all at once to tell upon her. When his feet were on the carpet and he reached up to lift her down, she twined her arms about his neck as after a long separation, and turned her face to him, and her lips, with their perfume of youth and passion.

One Saturday afternoon Hedger was sitting in the window of Eden's music room. They had been watching the pigeons come wheeling over the roofs from their unknown feeding grounds.

"Why," said Eden suddenly, "don't we fix those big doors into your studio so they will open? Then, if I want you, I won't have to go through the hall. That illustrator is loafing about a good deal of late."

"I'll open them, if you wish. The bolt is on your side."

"Isn't there one on yours, too?"

"No. I believe a man lived there for years before I came in, and the nurse used to have these rooms herself. Naturally, the lock was on the lady's side."

Eden laughed and began to examine the bolt. "It's all stuck up with paint." Looking about, her eye lighted upon a bronze Buddah which was one of the nurse's treasures. Taking him by his head, she struck the bolt a blow with his squatting posteriors. The two doors creaked, sagged, and swung weakly inward a little way, as if they were too old for such escapades. Eden tossed the heavy idol into a stuffed chair. "That's better," she exclaimed exultantly. "So the bolts are always on the lady's side? What a lot society takes for granted!"

Hedger laughed, sprang up and caught her arms roughly. "Whoever takes you for granted—Did anybody, ever?"

"Everybody does. That's why I'm here. You are the only one who knows anything about me. Now I'll have to dress if we're going out for dinner."

He lingered, keeping his hold on her. "But I won't always be the only one, Eden Bower. I won't be the last."

"No, I suppose not," she said carelessly. "But what does that matter? You are the first."

As a long, despairing whine broke in the warm stillness, they drew apart. Caesar, lying on his bed in the dark corner, had lifted his head at this invasion of sunlight, and realized that the side of his room was broken open, and his whole world shattered by change. There stood his master and this woman, laughing at him! The woman was pulling the long black hair of this mightiest of men, who bowed his head and permitted it.

VI

In time they quarrelled, of course, and about an abstraction,—as young people often do, as mature people almost never do. Eden came in late one afternoon. She had been with some of her musical friends to lunch at Burton Ives' studio, and she began telling Hedger about its splendors. He listened a moment and then threw down his brushes. "I know exactly what it's like," he said impatiently. "A very good department-store conception of a studio. It's one of the show places."

"Well, it's gorgeous, and he said I could bring you to see him. The boys tell me he's awfully kind about giving people a lift,[2] and you might get something out of it."

Hedger started up and pushed his canvas out of the way. "What could I possibly get from Burton Ives? He's almost the worst painter in the world; the stupidest, I mean."

Eden was annoyed. Burton Ives had been very nice to her and had begged her to sit for him. "You must admit that he's a very successful one," she said coldly.

"Of course he is! Anybody can be successful who will do that sort of thing. I wouldn't paint his pictures for all the money in New York."

"Well, I saw a lot of them, and I think they are beautiful."

Hedger bowed stiffly.

"What's the use of being a great painter if nobody knows about you?" Eden went on persuasively. "Why don't you paint the kind of pictures people can understand, and then, after you're successful, do whatever you like?"

"As I look at it," said Hedger brusquely, "I am successful."

Eden glanced about. "Well, I don't see any evidences of it," she said, biting her lip. "He has a Japanese servant and a wine cellar, and keeps a riding horse."

Hedger melted a little. "My dear, I have the most expensive luxury in the world, and I am much more extravagant than Burton Ives, for I work to please nobody but myself."

"You mean you could make money and don't? That you don't try to get a public?"

"Exactly. A public only wants what has been done over and over. I'm painting for painters—who haven't been born."

"What would you do if I brought Mr. Ives down here to see your things?"

"Well, for God's sake, don't! Before he left I'd probably tell him what I thought of him."

Eden rose. "I give you up. You know very well there's only one kind of success that's real."

"Yes, but it's not the kind you mean. So you've been thinking me a scrub painter, who needs a helping hand from some fashionable studio man? What the devil have you had anything to do with me for, then?"

"There's no use talking to you," said Eden walking slowly toward the door.

---

2. I.e., help.

"I've been trying to pull wires for you all afternoon, and this is what it comes to." She had expected that the tidings of a prospective call from the great man would be received very differently, and had been thinking as she came home in the stage how, as with a magic wand, she might gild Hedger's future, float him out of his dark hole on a tide of prosperity, see his name in the papers and his pictures in the windows on Fifth Avenue.

Hedger mechanically snapped the midsummer leash on Caesar's collar and they ran downstairs and hurried through Sullivan Street off toward the river. He wanted to be among rough, honest people, to get down where the big drays bumped over stone paving blocks and the men wore corduroy trowsers and kept their shirts open at the neck. He stopped for a drink in one of the sagging bar-rooms on the water front. He had never in his life been so deeply wounded; he did not know he could be so hurt. He had told this girl all his secrets. On the roof, in these warm, heavy summer nights, with her hands locked in his, he had been able to explain all his misty ideas about an unborn art the world was waiting for; had been able to explain them better than he had ever done to himself. And she had looked away to the chattels of this uptown studio and coveted them for him! To her he was only an unsuccessful Burton Ives.

Then why, as he had put it to her, did she take up with him? Young, beautiful, talented as she was, why had she wasted herself on a scrub? Pity? Hardly; she wasn't sentimental. There was no explaining her. But in this passion that had seemed so fearless and so fated to be, his own position now looked to him ridiculous; a poor dauber without money or fame,—it was her caprice to load him with favors. Hedger ground his teeth so loud that his dog, trotting beside him, heard him and looked up.

While they were having supper at the oysterman's, he planned his escape. Whenever he saw her again, everything he had told her, that he should never have told any one, would come back to him; ideas he had never whispered even to the painter whom he worshipped and had gone all the way to France to see. To her they must seem his apology for not having horses and a valet, or merely the puerile boastfulness of a weak man. Yet if she slipped the bolt tonight and came through the doors and said, "Oh, weak man, I belong to you!" what could he do? That was the danger. He would catch the train out to Long Beach tonight, and tomorrow he would go on to the north end of Long Island, where an old friend of his had a summer studio among the sand dunes. He would stay until things came right in his mind. And she could find a smart painter, or take her punishment.

When he went home, Eden's room was dark; she was dining out somewhere. He threw his things into a hold-all he had carried about the world with him, strapped up some colors and canvases, and ran downstairs.

VII

Five days later Hedger was a restless passenger on a dirty, crowded Sunday train, coming back to town. Of course he saw now how unreasonable he had been in expecting a Huntington girl to know anything about pictures; here was a whole continent full of people who knew nothing about pictures and he didn't hold it against them. What had such things to do with him and Eden Bower? When he lay out on the dunes, watching the moon come up out of the sea, it had seemed to him that there was no wonder in the world like the wonder of Eden Bower. He was going back to her because she was older than art, because she was the most overwhelming thing that had ever come into his life.

He had written her yesterday, begging her to be at home this evening, telling her that he was contrite, and wretched enough.

Now that he was on his way to her, his stronger feeling unaccountably changed to a mood that was playful and tender. He wanted to share everything with her, even the most trivial things. He wanted to tell her about the people on the train, coming back tired from their holiday with bunches of wilted flowers and dirty daisies; to tell her that the fish-man, to whom she had often sent him for lobsters, was among the passengers, disguised in a silk shirt and a spotted tie, and how his wife looked exactly like a fish, even to her eyes on which cataracts were forming. He could tell her, too, that he hadn't as much as unstrapped his canvases,—that ought to convince her.

In those days passengers from Long Island came into New York by ferry. Hedger had to be quick about getting his dog out of the express car in order to catch the first boat. The East River, and the bridges, and the city to the west, were burning in the conflagration of the sunset; there was that great home-coming reach of evening in the air.

The car changes from Thirty-fourth Street were too many and too perplexing; for the first time in his life Hedger took a hansom cab[3] for Washington Square. Caesar sat bolt upright on the worn leather cushion beside him, and they jogged off, looking down on the rest of the world.

It was twilight when they drove down lower Fifth Avenue into the Square, and through the Arch behind them were the two long rows of pale violet lights that used to bloom so beautifully against the gray stone and asphalt. Here and yonder about the Square hung globes that shed a radiance not unlike the blue mists of evening, emerging softly when daylight died, as the stars emerged in the thin blue sky. Under them the sharp shadows of the trees fell on the cracked pavement and the sleeping grass. The first stars and the first lights were growing silver against the gradual darkening, when Hedger paid his driver and went into the house,—which, thank God, was still there! On the hall table lay his letter of yesterday, unopened.

He went upstairs with every sort of fear and every sort of hope clutching at his heart; it was as if tigers were tearing him. Why was there no gas burning in the top hall? He found matches and the gas bracket. He knocked, but got no answer; nobody was there. Before his own door were exactly five bottles of milk, standing in a row. The milk-boy had taken spiteful pleasure in thus reminding him that he forgot to stop his order.

Hedger went down to the basement; it, too, was dark. The janitress was taking her evening airing on the basement steps. She sat waving a palm-leaf fan majestically, her dirty calico dress open at the neck. She told him at once that there had been "changes." Miss Bower's room was to let again, and the piano would go tomorrow. Yes, she left yesterday, she sailed for Europe with friends from Chicago. They arrived on Friday, heralded by many telegrams. Very rich people they were said to be, though the man had refused to pay the nurse a month's rent in lieu of notice,—which would have been only right, as the young lady had agreed to take the rooms until October. Mrs. Foley had observed, too, that he didn't overpay her or Willy for their trouble,

---

3. A two-wheeled covered carriage, with the driver's seat raised behind.

and a great deal of trouble they had been put to, certainly. Yes, the young lady was very pleasant, but the nurse said there were rings on the mahogany table where she had put tumblers and wine glasses. It was just as well she was gone. The Chicago man was uppish in his ways, but not much to look at. She supposed he had poor health, for there was nothing to him inside his clothes.

Hedger went slowly up the stairs—never had they seemed so long, or his legs so heavy. The upper floor was emptiness and silence. He unlocked his room, lit the gas, and opened the windows. When he went to put his coat in the closet, he found, hanging among his clothes, a pale, flesh-tinted dressing gown he had liked to see her wear, with a perfume—oh, a perfume that was still Eden Bower! He shut the door behind him and there, in the dark, for a moment he lost his manliness. It was when he held this garment to him that he found a letter in the pocket.

The note was written with a lead pencil, in haste: She was sorry that he was angry, but she still didn't know just what she had done. She had thought Mr. Ives would be useful to him; she guessed he was too proud. She wanted awfully to see him again, but Fate came knocking at her door after he had left her. She believed in Fate. She would never forget him, and she knew he would become the greatest painter in the world. Now she must pack. She hoped he wouldn't mind her leaving the dressing gown; somehow, she could never wear it again.

After Hedger read this, standing under the gas, he went back into the closet and knelt down before the wall; the knot hole had been plugged up with a ball of wet paper,—the same blue note-paper on which her letter was written.

He was hard hit. Tonight he had to bear the loneliness of a whole lifetime. Knowing himself so well, he could hardly believe that such a thing had ever happened to him, that such a woman had lain happy and contented in his arms. And now it was over. He turned out the light and sat down on his painter's stool before the big window. Caesar, on the floor beside him, rested his head on his master's knee. We must leave Hedger thus, sitting in his tank with his dog, looking up at the stars.

COMING, APHRODITE! This legend, in electric lights over the Lexington Opera House, had long announced the return of Eden Bower to New York after years of spectacular success in Paris. She came at last, under the management of an American Opera Company, but bringing her own *chef d'orchestre*.[4]

One bright December afternoon Eden Bower was going down Fifth Avenue in her car, on the way to her broker, in Williams Street. Her thoughts were entirely upon stocks,—Cerro de Pasco,[5] and how much she should buy of it,—when she suddenly looked up and realized that she was skirting Washington Square. She had not seen the place since she rolled out of it in an old-fashioned four-wheeler to seek her fortune, eighteen years ago.

"*Arrêtez, Alphonse. Attendez moi*,"[6] she called, and opened the door before

---

4. Orchestra leader. *Aphrodite* (1906) is an opera by Camille Erlanger (1863–1919), based on Pierre Louÿ's novel *Aphrodite* (1896).

5. An important mining center in central Peru.
6. Stop, Alphonse. Wait for me (French).

he could reach it. The children who were streaking over the asphalt on roller skates saw a lady in a long fur coat, and short, high-heeled shoes, alight from a French car and pace slowly about the Square, holding her muff to her chin. This spot, at least, had changed very little, she reflected; the same trees, the same fountain, the white arch, and over yonder, Garibaldi, drawing the sword for freedom. There, just opposite her, was the old red brick house.

"Yes, that is the place," she was thinking. "I can smell the carpets now, and the dog,—what was his name? That grubby bathroom at the end of the hall, and that dreadful Hedger—still, there was something about him, you know—" She glanced up and blinked against the sun. From somewhere in the crowded quarter south of the Square a flock of pigeons rose, wheeling quickly upward into the brilliant blue sky. She threw back her head, pressed her muff closer to her chin, and watched them with a smile of amazement and delight. So they still rose, out of all that dirt and noise and squalor, fleet and silvery, just as they used to rise that summer when she was twenty and went up in a balloon on Coney Island!

Alphonse opened the door and tucked her robes about her. All the way down town her mind wandered from Cerro de Pasco, and she kept smiling and looking up at the sky.

When she had finished her business with the broker, she asked him to look in the telephone book for the address of M. Gaston Jules, the picture dealer, and slipped the paper on which he wrote it into her glove. It was five o'clock when she reached the French Galleries, as they were called. On entering she gave the attendant her card, asking him to take it to M. Jules. The dealer appeared very promptly and begged her to come into his private office, where he pushed a great chair toward his desk for her and signalled his secretary to leave the room.

"How good your lighting is in here," she observed, glancing about. "I met you at Simon's studio, didn't I? Oh, no! I never forget anybody who interests me." She threw her muff on his writing table and sank into the deep chair. "I have come to you for some information that's not in my line. Do you know anything about an American painter named Hedger?"

He took the seat opposite her. "Don Hedger? But, certainly! There are some very interesting things of his in an exhibition at V——'s. If you would care to—"

She held up her hand. "No, no. I've no time to go to exhibitions. Is he a man of any importance?"

"Certainly. He is one of the first men among the moderns. That is to say, among the very moderns. He is always coming up with something different. He often exhibits in Paris, you must have seen—"

"No, I tell you I don't go to exhibitions. Has he had great success? That is what I want to know."

M. Jules pulled at his short gray moustache. "But, Madame, there are many kinds of success," he began cautiously.

Madame gave a dry laugh. "Yes, so he used to say. We once quarrelled on that issue. And how would you define his particular kind?"

M. Jules grew thoughtful. "He is a great name with all the young men, and he is decidedly an influence in art. But one can't definitely place a man who is original, erratic, and who is changing all the time."

She cut him short. "Is he much talked about at home? In Paris, I mean?

Thanks. That's all I want to know." She rose and began buttoning her coat. "One doesn't like to have been an utter fool, even at twenty."

"*Mais, non!*"[7] M. Jules handed her her muff with a quick, sympathetic glance. He followed her out through the carpeted show-room, now closed to the public and draped in cheesecloth, and put her into her car with words appreciative of the honor she had done him in calling.

Leaning back in the cushions, Eden Bower closed her eyes, and her face, as the street lamps flashed their ugly orange light upon it, became hard and settled, like a plaster cast; so a sail, that has been filled by a strong breeze, behaves when the wind suddenly dies. Tomorrow night the wind would blow again, and this mask would be the golden face of Aphrodite. But a "big" career takes its toll, even with the best of luck.

1920

7. No, of course not! (French).

DOROTHY RICHARDSON
1873–1957

"She has invented a sentence that we might call the psychological sentence of the feminine gender," wrote Virginia Woolf about Dorothy Richardson's fluid and flexible transcriptions of female consciousness. She is "the greatest woman genius of our time," asserted the writer John Cowper Powys. Yet though Richardson's authorship of a groundbreaking, thirteen-volume novel sequence titled *Pilgrimage* won her such acclaim from intellectuals as well as the financial patronage of the novelist Bryher (Winifred Ellerman, a shipping heiress who was the close friend of the poet H. D.), she lived and worked in comparative obscurity. She earned minimal royalties from her books, which, after her death, were largely overlooked except by literary historians, who regarded them as experimental curiosities. Her ambition, however, was extraordinary: in the thirteen volumes of *Pilgrimage*, each a self-contained text yet all intricately interrelated, Richardson set out to recount the subtlest details of the living-and-learning process by which her heroine, Miriam Henderson, forges an identity.

As many contemporary critics observed, Miriam Henderson *was* in some sense Dorothy Richardson, or at least a crucial "aspect" of that artist, for Richardson endowed her protagonist with a family background and an early life almost exactly the equivalent of her own. Born in Abingdon, in the English county of Berkshire, Richardson, like Miriam Henderson, was the third of four daughters. Her father was a proud, independently wealthy man who lost most of his money during the 1890s; her mother was charming but mentally fragile. In 1895, while Dorothy was staying with her in the seaside resort of Hastings, where the two had gone for the sake of Mrs. Richardson's health, the older woman committed suicide in an episode that Richardson records with hallucinatory vividness at the end of *Honeycomb* (1917), the third book of *Pilgrimage*. Even before this drastic event, however, the young writer-to-be had had to confront a number of difficulties. Because of her father's bankruptcy, she had accepted two arduous teaching jobs—one at a girls' school in Germany, another at a school in the north of London; again, both situations are described with subtlety and sensitivity, in this case in the two first books of *Pilgrimage: Pointed Roofs* (1915) and *Backwater* (1916).

After her mother's death, Richardson moved to London, where she found an inexpensive "room of her own" in Bloomsbury and worked for eight years as a dental assistant. Here she began to write sketches, articles, and reviews; she encountered a number of London intellectuals who were to be lifelong friends; she became involved in the feminist and socialist movements; and—perhaps most important—she met the rising novelist H. G. Wells. The husband of one of Richardson's schoolfriends, Wells grew intensely interested in this lively and thoughtful young woman, and soon the two had entered into a prolonged affair, which Richardson used as the basis for a later volume of *Pilgrimage*.

In 1912, Richardson embarked on the composition of what was to become *Pilgrimage*. A few years earlier, she had left her job as dental assistant and begun to eke out a thin living as a writer, publishing sketches, reviews, and social commentaries in the mode of "Women and the Future" as well as articles about dentistry in a number of journals; in addition, she produced several books about Quakerism, a subject that fascinated her throughout her career. For the most part, however, after 1912, staying sometimes in London and sometimes in country cottages lent her by friends, she devoted herself with special passion to the massive work that would take her three decades to complete. Shortly after the first volume (*Pointed Roofs*) appeared, she met and, in 1917, married the artist Allan Odle. A skillful illustrator who was widely regarded as the heir of the sardonic turn-of-the-century aesthete Aubrey Beardsley, Odle was considerably younger than Richardson and evidently almost ethereally frail, so that her feelings for him appear to have been mostly maternal. Yet—despite some ambivalence on Richardson's part—the marriage was a strong one, lasting until Odle died of a heart attack in 1948.

In an early review of *Pointed Roofs*, the novelist May Sinclair borrowed a phrase from the American philosopher William James to describe Richardson's literary technique. "Every definite image of the mind is steeped and dyed in the free water that flows around it," James had written, adding, "Let us call [that water] the stream of thought, of consciousness, or of subjective life." Though Richardson herself objected to what she called the "label" of stream of consciousness, the phrase became standard for historians of modernism seeking to characterize not only her work but also the work of such major contemporaries as James Joyce, Virginia Woolf, and Sinclair herself. As the critic Walter Allen remarks of Richardson's ambitious novel sequence, "Reading *Pilgrimage*, we are within Miriam as in life we are within ourselves; we share in her extraordinary capacity for continuous and never-blunted response to current existence, the ultimate astonisher." Similarly, in "Death"—a brief tale that nevertheless demonstrates Richardson's technique in miniature—we share in the fluidity, the ceaseless streaming, of her protagonist's gradually lapsing consciousness, as well as in the brilliant perceptions with which the author endows the dying woman in her final crisis.

In 1957, Dorothy Richardson died in a nursing home in southeast London where she had been residing for some five years. Despite the influence she had had on novelists such as Sinclair and Woolf, no one at the home had ever heard of her; when she claimed to be a writer, the nurses, according to her biographer Gloria Fromm, "believed at first that she had delusions." Yet in recent years critics and scholars have begun to reread *Pilgrimage*, to recognize the significance both of its contribution to a modernist aesthetic and of its feminist emphasis on a single *woman's* mind, and thus to acknowledge the importance of Dorothy Richardson. For interestingly, in recounting the process by which Miriam Henderson forged her identity, Richardson had also forged an indelible identity for herself: though her given name was really Dorothy Miller Richardson, her tombstone—through an error that seems uncanny—was inscribed "To the Memory of Dorothy *Miriam* Odle, Authoress D. M. Richardson."

Death

 This was death this time, no mistake. Her cheeks flushed at the indecency of being seen, dying and then dead. If only she could get it over and lay herself out decent before anyone came in to see and meddle. Mrs. Gworsh winning, left out there in the easy world, coming in to see her dead and lay her out and talk about her. . . . While there's life there's hope. Perhaps she wasn't dying. Only afraid. People can be so mighty bad and get better. But no. Not after that feeling rolling up within, telling her in words, her whom it knew, that this time she was going to be overwhelmed. That was the beginning, the warning and the certainty. To be more and more next time, any minute, increasing till her life flowed out for all to see. Her heart thumped. The rush of life beating against the walls of her body, making her head spin, numbed the pain and brought a mist before her eyes. Death. What she'd always feared so shocking, and put away. But no one knows what it is, how awful beyond everything, till they're in for it. Nobody knows death is this rush of life in all your parts.

 The mist cleared. Her face was damp. The spinning in her head had ceased. She drew a careful breath. Without pain. Some of the pain had driven through her without feeling. But she was heavier. It wasn't gone either. Only waiting. She saw the doctor on his way. Scorn twisted her lips against her empty gums. Scores of times she'd waited for him. Felt him drive fear away. Joked. This time he'd say nothing. Watch, for her secret life to come up and out. When his turn came he'd know what it was like letting your life out; and all of them out there. No good telling. You can't know till you're in for it. They're all in for it, rich and poor alike. No help. The great enormous creature driving your innards up, what nobody knows. What *you* don't know. . . . Life ain't worth death.

 It's got to be stuck, shame or no . . . but how do you do it?

 She lay still and listened for footsteps. They knew next door by now. That piece[1] would never milk Snowdrop dry. Less cream, less butter. Everything going back. Slip-slop, go as you please, and never done. Where'd us be to now if I hadn't? That's it. What they don't think of. Slip-slop. Grinning and singing enough to turn the milk. I've got a tongue. I know it. You've got to keep on and keep on at them. Or nothing done. I been young, but never them silly ways. Snowdrop'll go back; for certain. . . .

 But I shan't ever *see* it no more . . . the thought flew lifting through her mind. See no more. Work no more. Worry no more. Then what had been the good of it? Why had she gone on year in year out since Tom died and she began ailing, tramping all weathers up to the field, toiling and aching, and black as thunder most times. What was the good? Nobody knew her. Tom never had. And now there was only that piece downstairs, and what she did didn't matter any more. Except to herself, and she'd go on being slip-slop; not knowing she was in for death that makes it all one whatever you do. Good and bad they're all dying and don't know it's the most they've got to do.

 Her mind looked back up and down her life. Tom. What a fool she'd been to think him any different. Then when he died she'd thought him the same

---

1. Girl (pejorative).

as at first, and cried because she'd let it all all slip in the worries. Little Joe. Tearing her open, then snuggled in her arms, sucking. And all outside bright and peaceful; better than the beginning with Tom. But they'd all stop if they knew where it led. Joe, and his wife, and his little ones, in for all of it, getting the hard of it now, and death waiting for them. She could tell them all now what it was like, all of them, the squire, all the same. All going the same way, rich and poor.

The Bible was right, "Remember now thy Creator in the days of thy youth."[2] What she had always wanted. She had always wanted to be good. Now it was too late. Nothing mattering, having it all lifted away, made the inside of you come back as it was at the first, ready to begin. Too late. Shocking she had thought it when parson said prepare for death, live as if you were going to die tonight. But it's true. If every moment was your last on earth you could be yourself. You'd dare. Everybody would dare. People is themselves when they are children, and not again till they know they'm dying. But conscience knows all the time. I've a heavy bill for all my tempers. God forgive me. But why should He? He was having his turn now, anyhow, with all this dying to do. Death must be got through as life had been, just somehow. But how?

When the doctor had gone she knew she was left to do it alone. While there's life there's hope. But the life in her was too much smaller than the great weight and pain. He made her easier, numb. Trying to think and not thinking. Everything unreal. The piece coming up and downstairs like something in another world. Perhaps God would let her go easy. Then it was all over? Just fading to nothing with everything still to do. . . .

The struggle came unexpectedly. She heard her cries, and then the world leapt upon her and grappled, and even in the midst of the agony of pain was the surprise of her immense strength. The strength that struggled against the huge stifling, the body that leapt and twisted against the heavy darkness, a shape within her shape, that she had not known. Her unknown self rushing forward through all her limbs to fight. Leaping out and curving in a great sweep away from where she lay to the open sill, yet pinned back, unwrenchable from the bed. Back and back she slid, down a long tunnel at terrific speed, cool, her brow cool and wet, with wind blowing upon it. Darkness in front. Back and back into her own young body, alone. In front on the darkness came the garden, the old garden in April, the crab-apple blossom, all as it was before she began, but brighter. . . .

1924

Women and the Future

Most of the prophecies born of the renewed moral visibility of woman, though superficially at war with each other, are united at their base. They meet and sink, in the sands of the assumption that we are, today, confronted with a new species of woman.

---

2. Ecclesiastes 12.1.

Nearly all of the prophets, nearly all of those who are at work constructing hells, or heavens, upon this loose foundation, are men. And their crying up, or down, of the woman of today, as contrasted to the woman of the past, is easily understood when we consider how difficult it is, even for the least prejudiced, to *think* the feminine past, to escape the images that throng the mind from the centuries of masculine expressiveness on the eternal theme: expressiveness that has so rarely reached beyond the portrayal of woman, whether Madonna, Diana, or Helen,[1] in her moments of relationship to the world as it is known to men.

Even the pioneers of feminism, Mill, Buckle,[2] and their followers, looked only to woman as she was to be in the future, making, for her past, polite, question-begging excuses. The poets, with one exception, accepted the old readings. There is little to choose between the vision of Catholic Rossetti and Swinburne the Pagan. Tennyson,[3] it is true, crowns woman, elaborately, and withal a little irritably, and with much logic-chopping. But he never escapes patronage, and leaves her leaning heavily, albeit most elegantly, upon the arm of man. Browning stands apart, and Stopford Brooke[4] will not be alone in asking what women themselves think of Browning's vision of woman as both queen and lord, outstripping man not only in the wisdom of the heart, but in that of the brain also.

And there is Meredith[5]—with his shining reputation for understanding; a legend that by far outruns his achievement. Glimpses of woman as a full cup unto herself, he certainly had. And he reveals much knowledge of men as they appear in the eyes of such women. This it is that has been accounted unto him for righteousness. He never sees that he is demanding the emancipation of that which he has shown to be independent of bonds. Hardy, his brother pagan and counterpart, is Perseus[6] hastening to Andromeda, seeking the freedom of the bound.

Since the heyday of Meredith and Hardy, battalions of women have become literate and, in the incandescence of their revelations, masculine illusions are dying like flies. But, even today, most men are scarcely aware of the searchlight flung by these revelations across the past. These modern women, they say, are a new type.

It does not greatly matter to women that men cling to this idea. The truth about the past can be trusted to look after itself. There is, however, no illusion more wasteful than the illusion of beginning all over again; nothing more misleading than the idea of being divorced from the past. It is, nevertheless,

---

1. These figures—the Virgin Mary, the Roman goddess of the moon, and Helen of Troy—stand, respectively, for the female stereotypes of mother, virgin, and whore.
2. Henry Thomas Buckle (1821–1862), British historian of civilization. John Stuart Mill (1806–1873), philosopher and economist who worked for political and social reform and wrote *The Subjection of Women* (1869).
3. Alfred, Lord Tennyson (1809–1892) showed "patronage" perhaps most clearly in *The Princess* (1850), a fantasy on women's education. Dante Gabriel Rossetti (1828–1882), in both his poetry and painting, showed his great interest in women's beauty. Algernon Charles Swinburne (1837–1909), a "pagan" both in his rebellion against Christianity and in his interest in Greek literature, created in his poetry some memorably powerful but horrifying women.
4. Brooke (1832–1916) poses this question in his *Poetry of Robert Browning* (1902). Robert Browning (1812–1889), British poet in whose work women display remarkable variety.
5. George Meredith (1828–1909), whose reputation was earned by poems such as *Modern Love* (1862) and novels such as *The Egoist* (1879).
6. In Greek legend, the hero Perseus rescued Andromeda, who had been bound on a rock as a sacrifice to a sea monster. Thomas Hardy (1840–1928), British poet and novelist; in this context, see especially *Tess of the D'Urbervilles* (1891).

quite probable that feminine insistence on exhuming hatchets is not altogether a single-hearted desire to avoid waste and error.

Many men, moreover, are thoroughly disconcerted by the "Modern Woman." They sigh for ancient mystery and inscrutability. For La Giaconda[7] . . . And the most amazing thing in the history of Leonardo's masterpiece is their general failure to recognize that Lisa stands alone in feminine portraiture because she is centered, unlike her nearest peers, those dreamful, passionately blossoming imaginations of Rossetti, neither upon humanity nor upon the consolations of religion.

The Essential Egoist

It is because she is so completely *there* that she draws men like a magnet. Never was better artistic bargain driven than between Leonardo and this lady who sat to him for years; who sat so long that she grew at home in her place, and the deepest layer of her being, her woman's enchanted domestication within the sheer marvel of existing, came forth and shone through the mobile mask of her face. Leonardo of the innocent eye, his genius concentrated upon his business of making a good picture, caught her, unawares, on a gleeful, cosmic holiday. And in seeking the highest, in going on till he got what he wanted, he reaped also the lesser things. For there is in Lisa more than the portrayal of essential womanhood. The secondary life of the lady is clearly visible. Her traffic with familiar webs, with her household and the external shapings of life. When Pater[8] said that her eyelids were a little weary, he showed himself observant. But he misinterpreted the weariness.

On the part of contemporary artists, there are, here and there, attempts to resuscitate man's ancient mystery woman, the beloved-hated abyss. The intensest and the most affrighted of these essayists are D. H. Lawrence and Augustus John.[9] Perhaps they are nearer salvation than they know.

For the essential characteristic of women is egoism. Let it at once be admitted that this is a masculine discovery. It has been offered as the worst that can be said of the sex as a whole. It is both the worst and the best. Egoism is at once the root of shameless selfishness and the ultimate dwelling place of charity. Many men, of whom Mr. Wells[1] is the chief spokesman, read the history of woman's past influence in public affairs as one long story of feminine egoism. They regard her advance with mixed feelings, and face her with a neat dilemma. Either, they say, you must go on being Helens and Cinderellas, or you must drop all that and play the game, in so far as your disabilities allow, as we play it. They look forward to the emergence of an army of civilized, docile women, following modestly behind the vanguard of males at work upon the business of reducing chaos to order.

Another group of thinkers sees the world in process of feminization, the savage wilderness, where men compete and fight, turned into a home. Over

---

7. The painting (ca. 1506) by Leonardo da Vinci (1452–1519), also known as the *Mona Lisa*.
8. Walter Pater (1839–1894), British essayist and critic; the observation is from his essay on Leonardo da Vinci in *The Renaissance* (1893).
9. British painter and etcher (1879–1961). Richardson may be alluding not only to his reliance on women as muses for his art but also to his remarkably tangled personal life. Lawrence (1885–1930), British poet, essayist, and novelist, who was notoriously concerned with relationships between the sexes, and particularly with powerful women.
1. H. G. Wells (1866–1946), writer of fiction and social criticism (whose views are more commonly seen as feminist).

against them are those who view the opening prospect with despair. To them, feminism is the invariable accompaniment of degeneration. They draw back in horror before the oncoming flood of mediocrity. They see ahead a democratized world, overrun by hordes of inferior beings, organized by majorities for material ends; with primitive, uncivilizable woman rampant in the midst.

Serenely apart from these small camps is a large class of delightful beings, the representatives of average masculinity at its best, drawing much comfort from the spectacle of contradictory, mysterious woman at last bidding fair to become something recognizably like itself. Women, they say, are beginning to take life like men; are finding in life the things men have found. They make room for her. They are charming. Their selfishness is social, gregarious. Woman is to be the jolly companion; to co-operate with man in the great business of organizing the world for jollity. But have any of these so variously grouped males any idea of the depth and scope of feminine egoism? Do they not confound it with masculine selfishness? Do they realize anything of the vast difference between these two things?

It is upon the perception of this difference that any verdict as to the result of woman's arrival "in the world" ultimately rests. Though, it is true, certain of these masculine forecasts are being abundantly realized. There is abroad in life a growing army of man-trained women, brisk, positive, rational creatures with no nonsense about them, living from the bustling surfaces of the mind; sharing the competitive partisanships of men; subject, like men, to fear; subject to national panic; to international, and even to cosmic panic. There is also an army let loose of the daughters of the horse-leech;[2] part of the organization of the world for pleasure. These types have always existed. The world of the moment particularly favors them. But their egoism is as nothing to the egoism of the womanly woman, the beloved-hated abyss, at once the refuge and the despair of man.

For the womanly woman lives, all her life, in the deep current of eternity, an individual, self-centered. Because she is one with life, past, present, and future are together in her, unbroken. Because she thinks flowingly, with her feelings, she is relatively indifferent to the fashions of men, to the momentary arts, religions, philosophies, and sciences, valuing them only in so far as she is aware of their importance in the evolution of the beloved. It is man's incomplete individuality that leaves him at the mercy of that subtle form of despair which is called ambition, and accounts for his apparent selfishness. Only completely self-centered consciousness can attain to unselfishness—the celebrated unselfishness of the womanly woman. Only a complete self, carrying all its goods in its own hands, can go out, perfectly, to others, move freely in any direction. Only a complete self can afford to man the amusing spectacle of the chameleon woman.

Apart from the saints, the womanly woman is the only human being free to try to be as good as she wants to be. And it is to this inexorable creature, whom even Nietzsche[3] was constrained to place ahead of man, that man

---

2. I.e., insatiably greedy women. See Proverbs 30.15: "The horseleech hath two daughters, crying, Give, give."
3. This is an unusual reading of the Germany philosopher Friedrich Nietzsche (1844–1900), who is generally highly critical of the "eternal feminine." However, in *Beyond Good and Evil* (1886) he finds woman inspiring respect and "even fear" because of "her *nature*, which is more 'natural' than man's," and because of "the naïveté of her egoism."

returns from his wanderings with those others in the deserts of agnosticism. She is rare. But wherever she is found, there also are found the dependent hosts.

But is not the material of this intuitive creature strictly limited? Is she not fettered by sex? Seeking man, while man, freed by nature for his divine purpose, seeks God, through blood and tears, through trial and error, in every form of civilization? He for God only, she for God in him?[4] She is. She does. When man announces that the tree at the door of the cave is God, she excels him in the dark joy of the discovery. When he reaches the point of saying that God is a Spirit and they that worship him must worship him in spirit and in truth, she is there waiting for him, ready to parrot any formula that shows him aware of the amazing fact of life.

And it is this creature who is now on the way to be driven out among the practical affairs of our world, together with the "intelligent" woman; i.e., with the woman who is intelligible to men. For the first time. Unwillingly. The results cannot be exactly predicted. But her gift of imaginative sympathy, her capacity for vicarious living, for being simultaneously in all the warring camps, will tend to make her within the council of nations what the Quaker[5] is within the council of religions.

Women in the Future

Public concerted action must always be a compromise. But there is all the difference between having things roughly arranged *ad hoc* by father, however strong his sense of abstract justice, and having them arranged by father prompted by mother, under the unseen presidency[6] of desire to do the best regardless, in the woman's regardless, unprincipled, miracle-working way, for all concerned.

The world at large is swiftly passing from youthful freebooting.[7] It is on the way to find itself married. That is to say, in for startling changes. Shaken up. Led by the nose and liking it. A question arises. How will his apparently lessened state react on man? In how far has he been dependent on his illusion of supremacy? Perhaps the answer to this is the superiority of men in talent, in constructive capacity. It is the talent of man, his capacity to *do* most things better than women, backed up by the genius of woman. The capacity to *see* that is carrying life forward to the levels opening out ahead.

1924

---

4. John Milton's *Paradise Lost* (1667, 1674), 4.299 (where "he" and "she" are Adam and Eve).
5. Or a member of the Society of Friends. Quakers emphasize the importance of each individual's understanding as guided by inner light; they are pacifists who traditionally have been active in reform and philanthropic movements.
6. I.e., act of presiding.
7. Piracy, plundering.

AMY LOWELL
1874–1925

"I am ugly, fat, conspicuous & dull," Amy Lowell confided to her diary when she was fifteen, adding, soon after, that "I should like best of anything to be literary." Although she *was* overweight, Lowell's adolescent self-definition was otherwise quite inaccurate. As the daughter of a prominent Boston family, she had inherited a confident manner bred by generations of privilege: her grandfathers on both sides had founded important textile businesses; one of her cousins was the poet James Russell Lowell; her father was a member of the governing board of the Massachusetts Institute of Technology; her brother Percival was the founder of the Lowell Observatory at Harvard; and her brother Abbott Lawrence was a president of Harvard. She herself, moreover, was evidently a gifted child who discovered that she liked best "to be literary" mainly by ranging through her father's excellent library. By the time she was in her early teens she had begun to read the Romantic poets, and she had produced a first book titled *Dream Drops, or Stories from Fairy Land, by a Dreamer* (1887), which her mother arranged for her to sell at a charity bazaar.

To be sure, as the daughter of a distinguished family Amy Lowell was expected to lead a genteel life. "My family did not consider that it was necessary for girls to learn either Greek or Latin," she later remembered, and described her formal education as not amounting to "a hill of beans." After making her debut in society, she took several long trips abroad, and at one point she almost became engaged to a "proper" Bostonian. In addition, both before and after the deaths of her parents in the last years of the century, she served on numerous civic boards and committees. At the same time, however, she continued to be tormented by personal problems; she suffered from bouts of "nervous prostration" and was intransigently overweight despite countless attempts at severe dieting, even while, persistently "literary," she converted several rooms of Sevenels—the Lowell family mansion, so named because seven Lowells lived there—into what one biographer has called "a baronial library."

It was during the Boston theater season of 1902 that this ambivalent former debutante first seriously defined herself as a poet. She experienced her literary awakening because of an encounter with Eleanora Duse, the Italian actress, who was appearing in a play written by her lover, the poet Gabriel D'Annunzio. Lowell attended the work's opening-night performance, where she was so overcome by Duse's dramatic presence that she returned home and wrote, as she later remembered, "seventy-one lines of bad blank verse," including a tribute to the actress's "woman's soul" and "woman's heart." After this, and after attending all the other performances of the D'Annunzio play, Lowell claimed to know that verse writing was her true vocation. Struggling to perfect her art, she read, studied, founded a little theater group, and in 1912 published her first collection, a somewhat derivative volume titled *A Dome of Many-Coloured Glass* in deference to "Adonais," the Romantic poet Percy Bysshe Shelley's elegy for her beloved John Keats.

Shortly before *A Dome* appeared and ten years after her crucial encounter with Duse, Lowell met another woman who was to inspire her even more than the Italian celebrity had. Ada Dwyer Russell, a divorced actress eleven years Lowell's senior, was introduced to the poet at a women's "lunch club," and the attraction between the two was evidently both mutual and instantaneous. By 1914, Ada Russell had moved into Sevenels, where she was to live with Amy Lowell for the rest of the writer's life, acting—the way Alice B. Toklas did for Gertrude Stein—as beloved companion, general amanuensis, resident critic, and nurturing muse. For her, Lowell composed many of her most poignant love poems, including "Madonna of the Evening Flowers," "The Letter," "Venus Transiens," and "Opal." At the same time, the relationship between the two women was evidently so deeply collaborative that Lowell sometimes joked that they should put up a sign above the doorway at Sevenels reading "Lowell & Russell, Makers of Fine Poems."

Also significantly influential on Lowell's evolving art was the founding in 1912 of *Poetry* magazine. Edited in Chicago by the innovative woman of letters Harriet Monroe, this journal immediately began to publish the works of Ezra Pound, T. S. Eliot, D. H. Lawrence, John Gould Fletcher, Richard Aldington, and H. D. (Hilda Doolittle), among others. Upon Lowell, H. D.'s free verse, with its irregular lines and crisp, Greek-inspired images, had the greatest impact; as one critic observes, "When in the January 1913 number [of *Poetry*] she saw the signature 'H. D., Imagiste,' she recognized in a flash her own as yet unrealized poetic identity," for she felt that she too ought to be writing verse in the deliberately stripped, cool, vividly pictorial style employed by the group of aesthetic radicals who, under the leadership of the revolutionary Ezra Pound, called themselves "Imagists." Journeying to London in 1913, Lowell and Russell met Pound; the following year, just before the outbreak of World War I, the pair returned to England to make the acquaintance of John Gould Fletcher, H. D., Henry James, D. H. Lawrence, and Robert Frost. With Lawrence and Frost, in particular, Lowell formed important, long-lasting friendships, though, as is clear in the sardonic couplets of her *A Critical Fable* (an updating of a similar poem by her uncle James Russell Lowell), her responses to other writers were not uniformly positive.

Nevertheless, no doubt encouraged by her participation in innovative aesthetic circles as well as by her relationship with Ada Russell, Lowell now began to produce and edit volumes of poetry and criticism at an increasingly energetic pace. Works such as *Can Grande's Castle* (1918) and *Pictures of the Floating World* (1919) firmly established her reputation as a leader of the Imagist movement, which its founder, Ezra Pound, sarcastically renamed "Amygism." Such books as *Tendencies in Modern American Poetry* (1917) gave her an equally solid reputation as a critic. Eccentric in her personal behavior—she was, for instance, famous for smoking what most people thought were "big black cigars" (really slim cigarillos)—she became a celebrity.

During her last years, Lowell's lifetime of ambitious activity combined with being seriously overweight led to ill health. In 1918, she had the first of a series of operations (for an umbilical hernia) that drastically weakened her. Still, she continued indefatigably writing, lecturing, reviewing, and maintaining many friendships. Her most important project in the early 1920s was a massive biography of John Keats, the Romantic poet she had admired since her youth. Published early in 1925, the book aroused much controversy, especially in England, and the author was planning to travel to London to defend it when she died of a cerebral hemorrhage in May 1925, at fifty-one. The following year her posthumously published volume of poems, *What's O'Clock*, was awarded the Pulitzer Prize. The honor, as her biographer Jean Gould observes, was fitting, for this collection featured a number of Lowell's finest verses, including her long meditation on the lot of female poets titled "The Sisters," a work that might well stand as a vindication of the rights of women like Amy Lowell to abandon genteel New England society and, instead, create poems, compose criticism, edit anthologies, write biographies, love women like Ada Russell, and smoke slim, elegant cigarillos.

The Letter

    Little cramped words scrawling all over the paper
    Like draggled fly's legs,
    What can you tell of the flaring moon
    Through the oak leaves?
5   Or of my uncurtained window and the bare floor

        Spattered with moonlight?
        Your silly quirks and twists have nothing in them
        Of blossoming hawthorns,
        And this paper is dull, crisp, smooth, virgin of loveliness
10   Beneath my hand.

        I am tired, Beloved, of chafing my heart against
        The want of you;
        Of squeezing it into little inkdrops,
        And posting[1] it.
15   And I scald alone, here, under the fire
        Of the great moon.

                                                    1919

Venus Transiens[1]

        Tell me,
        Was Venus more beautiful
        Than you are,
        When she topped
5   The crinkled waves,
        Drifting shoreward
        On her plaited shell?
        Was Botticelli's vision[2]
        Fairer than mine;
10   And were the painted rosebuds
        He tossed his lady,
        Of better worth
        Than the words I blow about you
        To cover your too great loveliness
15   As with a gauze
        Of misted silver?
        For me,
        You stand poised
        In the blue and buoyant air,
20   Cinctured by bright winds,
        Treading the sunlight.
        And the waves which precede you
        Ripple and stir
        The sands at my feet.

                                                    1919

---

1. Mailing.
1. Venus passing over (Latin). Venus is the Roman equivalent of Aphrodite, the: Greek goddess of love.
2. Sandro Botticelli (1444–1510) executed a famous painting called *The Birth of Venus* (ca. 1485), in which the goddess stands on a large scalloped seashell riding on the ocean waves. According to classical mythology, she was born from the sea foam.

Madonna[1] of the Evening Flowers

All day long I have been working,
Now I am tired.
I call: "Where are you?"
But there is only the oak-tree rustling in the wind.
5 The house is very quiet,
The sun shines in on your books,
On your scissors and thimble just put down,
But you are not there.
Suddenly I am lonely:
10 Where are you?
I go about searching.

Then I see you,
Standing under a spire of pale blue larkspur,
With a basket of roses on your arm.
15 You are cool, like silver,
And you smile.
I think the Canterbury bells[2] are playing little tunes.

You tell me that the peonies need spraying,
That the columbines have overrun all bounds,
20 That the pyrus japonica should be cut back and rounded.
You tell me these things.
But I look at you, heart of silver,
White heart-flame of polished silver,
Burning beneath the blue steeples of the larkspur,
25 And I long to kneel instantly at your feet,
While all about us peal the loud, sweet *Te Deums*[3] of the Canterbury bells.

1919

The Weather-Cock Points South

I put your leaves aside,
One by one:
The stiff, broad outer leaves;
The smaller ones,
5 Pleasant to touch, veined with purple;
The glazed inner leaves.
One by one
I parted you from your leaves,
Until you stood up like a white flower
10 Swaying slightly in the evening wind.

---

1. My lady. In Italian painting, the phrase is applied to the Virgin Mary.
2. Bellflowers (with a joking allusion to the famous cathedral in Canterbury, England.
3. The beginning of an ancient Christian Latin hymn: "Te deum laudamus" (We praise thee, God).

White flower,
Flower of wax, of jade, of unstreaked agate;
Flower with surfaces of ice,
With shadows faintly crimson.
15 Where in all the garden is there such a flower?
The stars crowd through the lilac leaves
To look at you.
The low moon brightens you with silver.

The bud is more than the calyx.
20 There is nothing to equal a white bud,
Of no color, and of all,
Burnished by moonlight,
Thrust upon by a softly-swinging wind.

1919

Opal

You are ice and fire,
The touch of you burns my hands like snow.
You are cold and flame.
You are the crimson of amaryllis,
5 The silver of moon-touched magnolias.
When I am with you,
My heart is a frozen pond
Gleaming with agitated torches.

1919

Decade

When you came, you were like red wine and honey,
And the taste of you burnt my mouth with its sweetness.
Now you are like morning bread,
Smooth and pleasant.
5 I hardly taste you at all for I know your savour,
But I am completely nourished.

1919

Summer Rain

All night our room was outer-walled with rain.
Drops fell and flattened on the tin roof,
And rang like little disks of metal.
Ping!—Ping!—and there was not a pinpoint of silence between them.
5 The rain rattled and clashed,

And the slats of the shutters danced and glittered.
But to me the darkness was red-gold and crocus-colored
With your brightness,
And the words you whispered to me
10 Sprang up and flamed—orange torches against the rain.
Torches against the wall of cool, silver rain!

1919

From A Critical Fable

[*On T. S. Eliot and Ezra Pound*]

* * *

To start off again with my tale: "The expatriates
2380 Come next," I began, "but the man who expatiates
Upon them must go all yclad in cold steel
Since these young men are both of them most *difficile*,[1]
And each is possessed of a gift for satire.
Their forked barbs would pierce any usual attire.
2385 In order of merit, if not of publicity,
I will take Eliot first, though it smacks of duplicity
To award Ezra Pound[2] the inferior place
As he simply won't run if not first in a race.
Years ago, 'twould have been the other way round,
2390 With Eliot a rather bad second to Pound.
But Pound has been woefully free with the mustard[3]
And so occupied has quite ruined his custard.
No poems from his pen, just spleen[4] on the loose,
And a man who goes on in that way cooks his goose.
2395 T. S. Eliot's a very unlike proposition,
He has simply won through by process of attrition.
Where Pound played the fool, Eliot acted the wiseacre;
Eliot works in his garden, Pound stultifies his acre.
Eliot's always engaged digging fruit out of dust;
2400 Pound was born in an orchard,[5] but his trees have the rust.
Eliot's mind is perpetually fixed and alert;
Pound goes off anywhere, anyhow, like a squirt.
Pound believes he's a thinker, but he's far too romantic;
Eliot's sure he's a poet when he's only pedantic.
2405 But Eliot has raised pedantry to a pitch,
While Pound has upset romance into a ditch.
Eliot fears to abandon an old masquerade;
Pound's one perfect happiness is to parade.
Eliot's learning was won at a very great price;
2410 What Pound calls his learning he got in a trice.
Eliot knows what he knows, though he cannot digest it;
Pound knows nothing at all, but has frequently guessed it.

---

1. Difficult (French). "Yclad": dressed (archaic).
2. The American poets T. S. Eliot (1888–1965) and Ezra Pound (1885–1972); each came to England in his twenties.
3. I.e., strong, pungent words.
4. Ill temper, spitefulness.
5. Pound was born on the frontier, in Idaho.

Eliot builds up his essays by a process of massing;
Pound's are mostly hot air, what the vulgar call 'gassing.'
Eliot lives like a snail in his shell, pen protruding;
Pound struts like a cock, self-adored, self-deluding.
Pound's darling desire is his ego's projection;
Eliot tortures his soul with a dream of perfection.
Pound's an ardent believer in the value of noise;
Eliot strains every nerve to attain a just poise.
Each despises his fellows, for varying reasons;
Each one is a traitor, but with different treasons.
Each has left his own country, but Pound is quite sick of it,
While for Eliot's sojourn, he is just in the nick of it.
Pound went gunning for trouble, and got it, for cause;
Eliot, far more astute, has deserved his applause.
Each has more brain than heart, but while one man's a critic
The other is more than two-thirds tympanitic.[6]
Both of them are book-men, but where Eliot has found
A horizon in letters, Pound has only found Pound.
Each man feels himself so little complete
That he dreads the least commerce with the man in the street;
Each imagines the world to be leagued in a dim pact
To destroy his immaculate taste by its impact.
To conceive such a notion, one might point out slyly,
Would scarcely occur to an author more highly
Original; such men seldom bother their wits
With outsiders at all, whether fits or misfits.
Where they are, whom they see, is a matter of sheer
Indifference to a poet with his own atmosphere
To exist in, and such have no need to be preachy
Anent commonplaceness since they can't write a *cliché*—
In toto,[7] at least, and it's *toto* that grounds
All meticulous poets like the Eliots and Pounds.
Taking up Eliot's poetry, it's a blend of intensive
And elegant satire with a would-be offensive
Kind of virulent diatribe, and neither sort's lacking
In the high type of polish we demand of shoe-blacking.
Watteau if you like, arm in arm with Laforgue,[8]
And both of these worthies laid out in a morgue.
The poems are expert even up to a vice,
But they're chilly and dead like corpses on ice.
Now a man who's reluctant to heat his work through,
I submit, is afraid of what that work will do
On its own, with its muscles and sinews unfrozen.
Something, I must think, which he would not have chosen.
Is there barely a clue here that the action of heat
Might reveal him akin to the man in the street?
For his brain—there's no doubt that is up on a steeple,
But his heart might betray him as one of the people.

---

6. I.e., Pound beats his own drum.
7. On the whole (Latin). "Anent": concerning.
8. Jules L. Laforgue (1860–1887), French symbolist poet who wrote in free verse. Antoine Watteau (1684–1721), French painter.

A fearful dilemma! We can hardly abuse him
For hiding the damaging fact and excuse him
If it really be so, and we've more than a hint of it,
Although I, for one, like him better by dint of it.
2465 Since the poet's not the half of him, we must include
The critical anchorite of his 'Sacred Wood.'
'This slim duodecimo[9] you must have your eye on
If you'd be up to date,' say his friends. He's a sly one.
To have chosen this format—the book's heavy as iron.
2470 I'm acutely aware that its grave erudition
Is quite in the line of a certain tradition,
That one which is commonly known as tuition.
To read it is much like a lengthy sojourning
In at least two or three institutions of learning.
2475 But, being no schoolboy, I find I'm not burning
For this sort of instruction, and vote for adjourning.
What the fellow's contrived to stuff into his skull
May be certainly classed as a pure miracle,
But the way he imparts it is terribly dull.
2480 This may not be fair, for I've only begun it,
And one should not pronounce on a book till one's done it,
But I've started so often, in so many places,
I think, had there been any livelier spaces
I must have encountered at least one of those
2485 Before falling, I say it with shame, in a doze.
We must take Ezra Pound from a different angle:
He's a belfry of excellent chimes run to jangle
By being too often and hurriedly tugged at,
And even, when more noise was wanted, just slugged at
2490 And hammered with anything there was lying round.
Such delicate bells could not stand so much Pound.
Few men have to their credit more excellent verses
Than he used to write, and even his worse is
Much better than most people's good. He'd a flair
2495 For just the one word indispensably there,
But which few could have hit on. Another distinction
Was the way he preserved fledgeling poets from extinction.[1]
Had he never consented to write when the urge
To produce was not on him, he'd have been on the verge
2500 Of a great reputation by now, but his shoulder
Had always its chip, and Ezra's a scolder.
Off he flew, giving nerves and brain up to the business
In a crowing excitement not unmixed with dizziness,
Whenever he could get any sort of newspaper
2505 To lend him a column and just let him vapor.
But while he was worrying his gift of invention

---

9. A small book size. "Sacred Wood": a book of critical essays (1920).
1. Pound promoted avant-garde movements, notably Imagism and Vorticism; the writers he encouraged included H. D. as well as Eliot.

        For adequate means to ensure the prevention
        Of any one's getting what he had not got,
        His uncherished talent succumbed to dry rot.
2510 When, after the battle, he would have employed her,
        He learnt, to his cost, that he had destroyed her.
        Now he does with her ghost, and the ghosts of the hosts
        Of troubadors, minstrels, and kings, for he boasts
        An acquaintance with persons of whose very names
2515 I am totally ignorant, likewise their fames.
        The foremost, of course, is Bertrand de Born,[2]
        He's a sort of pervasively huge leprecawn
        Popping out from Pound's lines where you never expect him.
        He is our poet's chief lar,[3] so we must not neglect him.
2520 There is Pierre de Maensac,[4] and Pierre won the singing—
        Where or how I can't guess, but Pound sets his fame ringing
        Because he was *dreitz hom* (whatever that is)
        And had De Tierci's wife; what happened to his
        We don't know, in fact we know nothing quite clearly,
2525 For Pound always treats his ghosts cavalierly.
        There is John Borgia's bath, and be sure that he needed it;
        Aurunculeia's shoe, but no one much heeded it.
        There's a chap named Navighero and another Barabello,
        Who prods a Pope's elephant; and one Mozarello;
2530 Savairic Mauleon—Good Lord, what a dance
        Of impossible names![5] First I think we're in France,
        Then he slides in Odysseus, and Eros, and Atthis—
        But I'm not to be fooled in my Greek, that's what that is.
        Yet, look, there's Italian sticking out in italics
2535 And French in plain type, the foreign vocalics
        Do give one the feeling of infinite background,
        When it's all just a trick of that consummate quack, Pound,
        To cheat us to thinking there's something behind it.
        But, when nothing's to find, it's a hard job to find it.
2540 The tragedy lies in the fact that the man
        Had a potentiality such as few can
        Look back or forward to; had he but kept it,
        There's no bar in all poetry but he might have leapt it.
        Even now, I believe, if he'd let himself grow,
2545 He might start again . . . ." "We will have no 'although'
        In your gamut of poets. Your man is a victim
        Of expatriation, and, as usual, it's licked him.
        It has happened more times than I care to reflect,
        And the general toll is two countries' neglect."

                                1922

---

2. Bertrans de Born (ca. 1140–c. 1215), a viscount, was a celebrated Provençal troubadour (as well as a soldier). Pound wrote of him in "Sestina: Altaforte" (1909) and "Near Perigord" (1911) and translated him in "Planh for the Young English King" (1909) and "A War Song" (1910).

3. Spirit guarding a Roman household.
4. Provençal troubadour (fl. ca. 1200).
5. These "impossible names" are in *Canto* 5 (1921), except Odysseus, who first appears in *Canto* 1 (a version was published in 1917).

The Sisters

    Taking us by and large, we're a queer lot
    We women who write poetry. And when you think
    How few of us there've been, it's queerer still.
    I wonder what it is that makes us do it,
5   Singles us out to scribble down, man-wise,
    The fragments of ourselves. Why are we
    Already mother-creatures, double-bearing,
    With matrices in body and in brain?
    I rather think that there is just the reason
10 We are so sparse a kind of human being;
    The strength of forty thousand Atlases[1]
    Is needed for our every-day concerns.
    There's Sapho,[2] now I wonder what was Sapho.
    I know a single slender thing about her:
15 That, loving, she was like a burning birch-tree
    All tall and glittering fire, and that she wrote
    Like the same fire caught up to Heaven and held there,
    A frozen blaze before it broke and fell.
    Ah, me! I wish I could have talked to Sapho,
20 Surprised her reticences by flinging mine
    Into the wind. This tossing off of garments
    Which cloud the soul is none too easy doing
    With us today. But still I think with Sapho
    One might accomplish it, were she in the mood
25 To bare her loveliness of words and tell
    The reasons, as she possibly conceived them,
    Of why they are so lovely. Just to know
    How she came at them, just to watch
    The crisp sea sunshine playing on her hair,
30 And listen, thinking all the while 'twas she
    Who spoke and that we two were sisters
    Of a strange, isolated little family.
    And she is Sapho—Sapho—not Miss or Mrs.,
    A leaping fire we call so for convenience;
35 But Mrs. Browning[3]—who would ever think
    Of such presumption as to call her "Ba."
    Which draws the perfect line between sea-cliffs
    And a close-shuttered room in Wimpole Street.
    Sapho could fly her impulses like bright
40 Balloons tip-tilting to a morning air
    And write about it. Mrs. Browning's heart
    Was squeezed in stiff conventions. So she lay
    Stretched out upon a sofa, reading Greek
    And speculating, as I must suppose,

---

1. In Greek mythology, Atlas was one of a giant race called the Titans; he was assigned the task of holding up the earth.
2. Or Sappho (b.ca. 612 B.C.E.), Greek lyric poet.
3. Elizabeth Barrett Browning (1806–1861), English poet known familiarly as "Ba"; she lived as an invalid in her father's house in Wimpole Street, until the poet Robert Browning courted and married her (see Vol. 1, p. 521).

45   In just this way on Sapho; all the need,
     The huge, imperious need of loving, crushed
     Within the body she believed so sick.
     And it was sick, poor lady, because words
     Are merely simulacra after deeds
50   Have wrought a pattern; when they take the place
     Of actions they breed a poisonous miasma
     Which, though it leave the brain, eats up the body.
     So Mrs. Browning, aloof and delicate,
     Lay still upon her sofa, all her strength
55   Going to uphold her over-topping brain.
     It seems miraculous, but she escaped
     To freedom and another motherhood
     Than that of poems. She was a very[4] woman
     And needed both.
                    If I had gone to call,
60   Would Wimpole Street have been the kindlier place,
     Or Casa Guidi,[5] in which to have met her?
     I am a little doubtful of that meeting,
     For Queen Victoria[6] was very young and strong
     And all-pervading in her apogee
65   At just that time. If we had stuck to poetry,
     Sternly refusing to be drawn off by mesmerism
     Or Roman revolutions,[7] it might have done.
     For, after all, she is another sister,
     But always, I rather think, an older sister
70   And not herself so curious a technician
     As to admit newfangled modes of writing—
     "Except, of course, in Robert, and that is neither
     Here nor there for Robert is a genius."
     I do not like the turn this dream is taking,
75   Since I am very fond of Mrs. Browning
     And very much indeed should like to hear her
     Graciously asking me to call her "Ba."
     But then the Devil of Verisimilitude
     Creeps in and forces me to know she wouldn't.
80   Convention again, and how it chafes my nerves,
     For we are such a little family
     Of singing sisters, and as if I didn't know
     What those years felt like tied down to the sofa.
     Confound Victoria, and the slimy inhibitions
85   She loosed on all us Anglo-Saxon creatures!
     Suppose there hadn't been a Robert Browning,
     No *Sonnets from the Portuguese*[8] would have been written.
     They are the first of all her poems to be,
     One might say, fertilized. For, after all,
90   A poet is flesh and blood as well as brain

---

4. True.
5. The house in Florence where the Brownings resided after their marriage.
6. Queen of England (1819–1901; r. 1837–1901).
7. At the time of the Brownings' residence, Italy was struggling for independence from foreign rule. "Mesmerism": hypnotism, which greatly interested Barrett Browning; she also was "drawn off" by spiritualism more generally.
8. A sequence of love sonnets (1850) by Barrett Browning addressed to her husband, Robert.

And Mrs. Browning, as I said before,
Was very, very woman. Well, there are two
Of us, and vastly unlike that's for certain.
Unlike at least until we tear the veils
95   Away which commonly gird souls. I scarcely think
Mrs. Browning would have approved the process
In spite of what had surely been relief;
For speaking souls must always want to speak
Even when bat-eyed, narrow-minded Queens
100 Set prudishness to keep the keys of impulse.
Then do the frowning Gods invent new banes
And make the need of sofas. But Sapho was dead
And I, and others, not yet peeped above
The edge of possibility. So that's an end
105 To speculating over tea-time talks
Beyond the movement of pentameters
With Mrs. Browning.
                    But I go dreaming on,
In love with these my spiritual relations.
I rather think I see myself walk up
110 A flight of wooden steps and ring a bell
And send a card in to Miss Dickinson.[9]
Yet that's a very silly way to do.
I should have taken the dream twist-ends about
And climbed over the fence and found her deep
115 Engrossed in the doings of a humming-bird
Among nasturtiums. Not having expected strangers,
She might forget to think me one, and holding up
A finger say quite casually: "Take care.
Don't frighten him, he's only just begun."
120 "Now this," I well believe I should have thought,
"Is even better than Sapho. With Emily
You're really here, or never anywhere at all
In range of mind." Wherefore, having begun
In the strict center we could slowly progress
125 To various circumferences,[1] as we pleased.
We could, but should we? That would quite depend
On Emily. I think she'd be exacting,
Without intention possibly, and ask
A thousand tight-rope tricks of understanding.
130 But, bless you, I would somersault all day
If by so doing I might stay with her.
I hardly think that we should mention souls
Although they might just round the corner from us
In some half-quizzical, half-wistful metaphor.
135 I'm very sure that I should never seek
To turn her parables to stated fact.
Sapho would speak, I think, quite openly,
And Mrs. Browning guard a careful silence,

---

9. Emily Dickinson (1830–1886), American poet; see Vol. 1, p. 1027.
1. Dickinson famously wrote "My Business is Circumference," and the metaphor is key to her writing.

But Emily would set doors ajar and slam them
And love you for your speed of observation.

Strange trio of my sisters, most diverse,
And how extraordinarily unlike
Each is to me, and which way shall I go?
Sapho spent and gained; and Mrs. Browning,
After a miser girlhood, cut the strings
Which tied her money-bags and let them run;
But Emily hoarded—hoarded—only giving
Herself to cold, white paper.[2] Starved and tortured,
She cheated her despair with games of patience[3]
And fooled herself by winning. Frail little elf,
The lonely brain-child of a gaunt maturity,
She hung her womanhood upon a bough
And played ball with the stars—too long—too long—
The garment of herself hung on a tree
Until at last she lost even the desire
To take it down. Whose fault? Why let us say,
To be consistent, Queen Victoria's.
But really, not to over-rate the queen,
I feel obliged to mention Martin Luther,[4]
And behind him the long line of Church Fathers
Who draped their prurience like a dirty cloth
About the naked majesty of God.
Good-bye, my sisters, all of you are great,
And all of you are marvellously strange,
And none of you has any word for me.
I cannot write like you, I cannot think
In terms of Pagan or of Christian now.
I only hope that possibly some day
Some other woman with an itch for writing
May turn to me as I have turned to you
And chat with me a brief few minutes. How
We lie, we poets! It is three good hours
I have been dreaming. Has it seemed so long
To you? And yet I thank you for the time
Although you leave me sad and self-distrustful,
For older sisters are very sobering things.
Put on your cloaks, my dears, the motor's waiting.
No, you have not seemed strange to me, but near,
Frightfully near, and rather terrifying.
I understand you all, for in myself—
Is that presumption? Yet indeed it's true—
We are one family. And still my answer
Will not be any one of yours, I see.
Well, never mind that now. Good night! Good night!

1925

---

2. This sentence relies on a sexual as well as a financial metaphor: "to spend" also means to have an orgasm.

3. Solitaire card games.
4. German monk (1483–1546), leader of the Protestant Reformation.

GERTRUDE STEIN
1874–1946

In paintings by Pablo Picasso (1906) and Pavel Tchelitchew (1930), sculptures by Jacques Lipchitz (1920) and Jo Davidson (1920), and the many photographs by Carl Van Vechten and Cecil Beaton, Gertrude Stein sometimes looks like the Roman emperor Ernest Hemingway took her to be and sometimes like the great Jewish Buddha many of her other friends thought she resembled. Whether, in a reference to the derisively experimental movement called "dadaism," she was hailed as the "the Mama of dada" or ridiculed as "the Mother Goose of Montparnasse," Stein herself was hardly embarrassed about her growing celebrity, for she believed that "Einstein was the creative philosophic mind of the century and I have been the creative literary mind of the century." But as late in her career as 1937 she admitted, "It always did bother me that the American public were more interested in me than in my work." If her oeuvre has been neglected as sometimes seeming opaque or even incomprehensible, this is because it includes short stories, portraits, novels, autobiographies, dramas, and poems that develop the radical linguistic experimentation associated with modernism.

Stein was a first-generation American, the youngest of seven children. In 1841, her German Jewish father, Daniel Stein, emigrated from Bavaria to Baltimore, where he established a profitable clothing business and married Amelia (Keyser) Stein before moving to Allegheny, Pennsylvania, in 1862 to start his family. Stein's earliest memories dated from the age of four, when the family lived in Austria and Paris before settling down in Oakland, California, in 1879. Although she had prattled in German and French, she soon began reading English poetry and fiction and, more idiosyncratically, congressional records and constitutional histories of England. After the death of her mother in 1888 and the death of her father three years later, she and her closest sibling, Leo, traveled to Baltimore, where they were cared for by their mother's sister, Fannie Bachrach, and provided for by an independent income secured for them by their eldest brother, Michael.

Stein's identification with Leo continued to inform her early development. After Leo transferred from the University of California to Harvard, Gertrude enrolled as a special student at the Annex that would become Radcliffe College. There she studied with the philosopher George Santayana and the psychologist William James. With the encouragement of James, she joined Leo in Baltimore in 1897 to pursue a medical education at Johns Hopkins, where her formal class training was supplemented by obstetrical work and by her friendship with Claribel and Etta Cone, two well-to-do and well-educated young women. But after two years, Stein abandoned her plans to complete the medical degree. She was probably depressed by her involvement in an erotic triangle with Mabel Haynes and May Bookstaver: Stein fictionalized her sense of misery at the futility of this relationship in *Q.E.D. or Things as They Are,* a work published posthumously in 1950. In 1902, she joined Leo, who had been studying in Italy with the art critic Bernard Berenson. After a summer in Bloomsbury and a winter in New York, she again returned to Leo, who occupied rooms at 27 rue de Fleurus that would soon become famous as a center of avant-garde activity in Paris.

It was from this early period in Paris that Stein's fascination with modern art dated. Attached by a courtyard to the rooms the Steins shared was an atelier (a studio), which was quickly filled with the many paintings they purchased from art dealers like Amboise Vollard. Stein herself recounted how they found Matisse's *La Femme au Chapeau* at the Petit Palais show, where some viewers were so infuriated by this picture that they laughed and tried to scratch off the paint. What attracted Stein to the impressionist and postimpressionist work of Cézanne, Renoir, Rousseau, Braque, Matisse, and Picasso was their effort to use deformation to intensify and clarify visual effect. Soon she began her own efforts to intensify and clarify English so as to liberate language from representation. The three stories that make up *Three Lives* (1909)—"The Good Anna," "Melanctha," and "The Gentle Lena"—were composed while the writer studied Cézanne's portrait of his wife and while she sat for Picasso's portrait of her. They are what she called "the first definite step away from the nineteenth century and into the twentieth century in literature." Early in her career, moreover, Stein began working in "the continuous present": derived from William James, her notion of time as a series of discrete moments, rather than a linear progression, enabled her to move toward a language drained of conventional meaning and charged, through repetition, with the insistent, recurrent obsessions of her characters' consciousnesses. Reliant as they are on commonplace American ethnic vocabularies, the stories have been both praised as sensitive analyses of stereotypes and criticized as insensitive promulgations of stereotypes.

When Stein finally found a publisher for *Three Lives,* she willingly allowed her new friend, Alice B. Toklas, to proofread the manuscript for her. Just arrived from California, Alice quickly supplanted Leo both in Gertrude's affections and in the atelier. Much later, Stein would cheerfully explain that she stopped being interested in Leo when it became clear that "it was I who was the genius, there was no reason for it but I was, and he was not." For the American Diane Wakoski, Stein and Toklas epitomize the genius and the devoted wife: Stein's "craggy, grand / stony ideas" were in some sense made possible by Toklas's embroidery, baking, and secretarial skills. Yet the Stein-Toklas relationship was not based just on Toklas's renunciatory adulation or Stein's energetic egotism. Stein's earlier depression in Baltimore was ended by the lifelong companionship of Toklas, who created the Plain Edition Press to publish Stein when she was feeling "a little bitter" about all her unpublished manuscripts. Even more important, Toklas helped free Stein's style. In the early experimental portrait "Ada" as well as in the long poem *Lifting Belly* (1915–17), Stein developed an encoded language to articulate the erotic and linguistic play she associated with Toklas. Indeed, in her first commercial success, Stein even wrote using Toklas's voice: in *The Autobiography of Alice B. Toklas* (1933), Gertrude's Alice describes the formative influence Stein had on younger writers such as Ernest Hemingway and Sherwood Anderson, even as she provides titillating gossip about the postimpressionists and modernists who populated the Stein-Toklas salon.

The books Stein completed before and after World War I are markedly different from each other and from works produced in the realistic tradition in fiction. Her thousand-page history, *The Making of Americans* (1925), attempted to delineate every sort of American "who ever can or is or was or will be living," while the prose poems of *Tender Buttons* (1914) supplied impressionistic definitions that are sometimes sardonic ("A White Hunter: A white hunter is nearly crazy") and sometimes enigmatic ("Cream: Cream cut. Any where crumb. Left hop chambers"). Within a small circle of artists, Stein was gaining a reputation as a prolific and daring inventor of new forms. Judging from *The Autobiography,* the Great War was a great adventure for Toklas and Stein, who enlisted in an American ambulance unit in France. After the war, they reestablished their salon, which was frequented by many American expatriates and visitors. Stein continued to produce experimental poems, but she also began writing plays (*Four Saints in Three Acts,* 1934) and giving lectures at Oxford and Cambridge, speeches that issued in—among other works—*Composition as Explanation* (1926), which was published by the Woolfs' Hogarth Press. In the 1930s, Stein profited from the commercial success of both the *Autobiography of Alice B. Toklas* and Virgil Thompson's opera version of her play *Four Saints in Three Acts,* which led to a long American lecture tour and a contract that ensured her continued publication in America.

During the German occupation of France in the early 1940s, Stein and Toklas were forced to take refuge in the area around Bilignin, where they had a summer house. Always productive, Stein continued to write novels (*Ida, a Novel,* 1941), plays (*The

Mother of Us All, 1947), and memoirs (*Wars I Have Seen*, 1945). Generous and friendly to the many GIs still in Paris after 1944, she was by this time a celebrity in the American press. Two years after her return to Paris, she entered the American Hospital at Neuilly-sur-Seine because of an abdominal tumor. On her deathbed, she was said to have asked, "What is the answer?" When no one spoke, she replied to herself with characteristic aplomb: "What is the question?" Alice B. Toklas, who died twenty-one years later, was buried beside Stein in the cemetery of Père-Lachaise in Paris.

The Gentle Lena

Lena was patient, gentle, sweet and german. She had been a servant for four years and had liked it very well.

Lena had been brought from Germany to Bridgepoint by a cousin and had been in the same place there for four years.

This place Lena had found very good. There was a pleasant, unexacting mistress and her children, and they all liked Lena very well.

There was a cook there who scolded Lena a great deal but Lena's german patience held no suffering and the good incessant woman really only scolded so for Lena's good.

Lena's german voice when she knocked and called the family in the morning was as awakening, as soothing, and as appealing, as a delicate soft breeze in midday, summer. She stood in the hallway every morning a long time in her unexpectant and unsuffering german patience calling to the young ones to get up. She would call and wait a long time and then call again, always even, gentle, patient, while the young ones fell back often into that precious, tense, last bit of sleeping that gives a strength of joyous vigor in the young, over them that have come to the readiness of middle age, in their awakening.

Lena had good hard work all morning, and on the pleasant, sunny afternoons she was sent out into the park to sit and watch the little two year old girl baby of the family.

The other girls, all them that make the pleasant, lazy crowd, that watch the children in the sunny afternoons out in the park, all liked the simple, gentle, german Lena very well. They all, too, liked very well to tease her, for it was so easy to make her mixed and troubled, and all helpless, for she could never learn to know just what the other quicker girls meant by the queer things they said.

The two or three of these girls, the ones that Lena always sat with, always worked together to confuse her. Still it was pleasant, all this life for Lena.

The little girl fell down sometimes and cried, and then Lena had to soothe her. When the little girl would drop her hat, Lena had to pick it up and hold it. When the little girl was bad and threw away her playthings, Lena told her she could not have them and took them from her to hold until the little girl should need them.

It was all a peaceful life for Lena, almost as peaceful as a pleasant leisure. The other girls, of course, did tease her, but then that only made a gentle stir within her.

Lena was a brown and pleasant creature, brown as blonde races often have them brown, brown, not with the yellow or the red or the chocolate brown of sun burned countries, but brown with the clear color laid flat on the light toned skin beneath, the plain, spare brown that makes it right to have been made with hazel eyes, and not too abundant straight, brown hair, hair that only later deepens itself into brown from the straw yellow of a german childhood.

Lena had the flat chest, straight back and forward falling shoulders of the patient and enduring working woman, though her body was now still in its milder girlhood and work had not yet made these lines too clear.

The rarer feeling that there was with Lena, showed in all the even quiet of her body movements, but in all it was the strongest in the patient, old-world ignorance, and earth made pureness of her brown, flat, soft featured face. Lena had eyebrows that were a wondrous thickness. They were black, and spread, and very cool, with their dark color and their beauty, and beneath them were her hazel eyes, simple and human, with the earth patience of the working, gentle, german woman.

Yes it was all a peaceful life for Lena. The other girls, of course, did tease her, but then that only made a gentle stir within her.

"What you got on your finger Lena," Mary, one of the girls she always sat with, one day asked her. Mary was good natured, quick, intelligent and Irish.

Lena had just picked up the fancy paper made accordion that the little girl had dropped beside her, and was making it squeak sadly as she pulled it with her brown strong, awkward finger.

"Why, what is it, Mary, paint?" said Lena, putting her finger to her mouth to taste the dirt spot.

"That's awful poison Lena, don't you know?" said Mary, "that green paint that you just tasted."

Lena had sucked a good deal of the green paint from her finger. She stopped and looked hard at the finger. She did not know just how much Mary meant by what she said.

"Ain't it poison, Nellie, that green paint, that Lena sucked just now," said Mary. "Sure it is Lena, its real poison, I ain't foolin' this time anyhow."

Lena was a little troubled. She looked hard at her finger where the paint was, and she wondered if she had really sucked it.

It was still a little wet on the edges and she rubbed it off a long time on the inside of her dress, and in between she wondered and looked at the finger and thought, was it really poison that she had just tasted.

"Ain't it too bad, Nellie, Lena should have sucked that," Mary said.

Nellie smiled and did not answer. Nellie was dark and thin, and looked Italian. She had a big mass of black hair that she wore high up on her head, and that made her face look very fine.

Nellie always smiled and did not say much, and then she would look at Lena to perplex her.

And so they all three sat with their little charges in the pleasant sunshine a long time. And Lena would often look at her finger and wonder if it was really poison that she had just tasted and then she would rub her finger on her dress a little harder.

Mary laughed at her and teased her and Nellie smiled a little and looked queerly at her.

Then it came time, for it was growing cooler, for them to drag together the little ones, who had begun to wander, and to take each one back to its own mother. And Lena never knew for certain whether it was really poison, that green stuff that she had tasted.

During these four years of service, Lena always spent her Sundays out at the house of her aunt, who had brought her four years before to Bridgepoint.

This aunt, who had brought Lena, four years before, to Bridgepoint, was a hard, ambitious, well meaning, german woman. Her husband was a grocer in the town, and they were very well to do. Mrs. Haydon, Lena's aunt, had two daughters who were just beginning as young ladies, and she had a little boy who was not honest and who was very hard to manage.

Mrs. Haydon was a short, stout, hard built, german woman. She always hit the ground very firmly and compactly as she walked. Mrs. Haydon was all a compact and well hardened mass, even to her face, reddish and darkened from its early blonde, with its hearty, shiny, cheeks, and doubled chin well covered over with the up-roll from her short, square neck.

The two daughters, who were fourteen and fifteen, looked like unkneaded, unformed mounds of flesh beside her.

The elder girl, Mathilda, was blonde, and slow, and simple, and quite fat. The younger, Bertha, who was almost as tall as her sister, was dark, and quicker, and she was heavy, too, but not really fat.

These two girls the mother had brought up very firmly. They were well taught for their position. They were always both well dressed, in the same kinds of hats and dresses, as is becoming in two german sisters. The mother liked to have them dressed in red. Their best clothes were red dresses, made of good heavy cloth, and strongly trimmed with braid of a glistening black. They had stiff, red felt hats, trimmed with black velvet ribbon, and a bird. The mother dressed matronly, in a bonnet and in black, always sat between her two big daughters, firm, directing, and repressed.

The only weak spot in this good german woman's conduct was the way she spoiled her boy, who was not honest and who was very hard to manage.

The father of this family was a decent, quiet, heavy, and uninterfering german man. He tried to cure the boy of his bad ways, and make him honest, but the mother could not make herself let the father manage, and so the boy was brought up very badly.

Mrs. Haydon's girls were now only just beginning as young ladies, and so to get her niece, Lena, married, was just then the most important thing that Mrs. Haydon had to do.

Mrs. Haydon had four years before gone to Germany to see her parents, and had taken the girls with her. This visit had been for Mrs. Haydon most successful, though her children had not liked it very well.

Mrs. Haydon was a good and generous woman, and she patronized her parents grandly, and all the cousins who came from all about to see her. Mrs. Haydon's people were of the middling class of farmers. They were not peasants, and they lived in a town of some pretension, but it all seemed very poor and smelly to Mrs. Haydon's american born daughters.

Mrs. Haydon liked it all. It was familiar, and then here she was so wealthy and important. She listened and decided, and advised all of her relations how to do things better. She arranged their present and their future for them, and showed them how in the past they had been wrong in all their methods.

Mrs. Haydon's only trouble was with her two daughters, whom she could not make behave well to her parents. The two girls were very nasty to all their numerous relations. Their mother could hardly make them kiss their grandparents, and every day the girls would get a scolding. But then Mrs. Haydon was so very busy that she did not have time to really manage her stubborn daughters.

These hard working, earth-rough german cousins were to these american born children, ugly and dirty and as far below them as were italian or negro workmen, and they could not see how their mother could ever bear to touch them, and then all the women dressed so funny, and were worked all rough and different.

The two girls stuck up their noses at them all, and always talked in english to each other about how they hated all these people and how they wished their mother would not do so. The girls could talk some german, but they never chose to use it.

It was her eldest brother's family that most interested Mrs. Haydon. Here there were eight children, and out of the eight, five of them were girls.

Mrs. Haydon thought it would be a fine thing to take one of these girls back with her to Bridgepoint and get her well started. Everybody liked that she should do so and they were all willing that it should be Lena.

Lena was the second girl in her large family. She was at this time just seventeen years old. Lena was not an important daughter in the family. She was always sort of dreamy and not there. She worked hard and went very regularly at it, but even good work never seemed to bring her near.

Lena's age just suited Mrs. Haydon's purpose. Lena could first go out to service, and learn how to do things, and then, when she was a little older, Mrs. Haydon could get her a good husband. And then Lena was so still and docile, she would never want to do things her own way. And then, too, Mrs. Haydon, with all her hardness had wisdom, and she could feel the rarer strain there was in Lena.

Lena was willing to go with Mrs. Haydon. Lena did not like her german life very well. It was not the hard work but the roughness that disturbed her. The people were not gentle, and the men when they were glad were very boisterous, and would lay hold of her and roughly tease her. They were good people enough around her, but it was all harsh and dreary for her.

Lena did not really know that she did not like it. She did not know that she was always dreamy and not there. She did not think whether it would be different for her away off there in Bridgepoint. Mrs. Haydon took her and got her different kinds of dresses, and then took her with them to the steamer. Lena did not really know what it was that had happened to her.

Mrs. Haydon, and her daughters, and Lena traveled second class on the steamer. Mrs. Haydon's daughters hated that their mother should take Lena. They hated to have a cousin, who was to them, little better than a nigger, and then everybody on the steamer there would see her. Mrs. Haydon's daughters said things like this to their mother, but she never stopped to hear them, and the girls did not dare to make their meaning very clear. And so they could only go on hating Lena hard, together. They could not stop her from going back with them to Bridgepoint.

Lena was very sick on the voyage. She thought, surely before it was over that she would die. She was so sick she could not even wish that she had not started. She could not eat, she could not moan, she was just blank and scared, and sure that every minute she would die. She could not hold herself in, nor help herself in her trouble. She just staid where she had been put, pale, and scared, and weak, and sick, and sure that she was going to die.

Mathilda and Bertha Haydon had no trouble from having Lena for a cousin on the voyage, until the last day that they were on the ship, and by that time they had made their friends and could explain.

Mrs. Haydon went down every day to Lena, gave her things to make her better, held her head when it was needful, and generally was good and did her duty by her.

Poor Lena had no power to be strong in such trouble. She did not know how to yield to her sickness nor endure. She lost all her little sense of being in her suffering. She was so scared, and then at her best, Lena, who was patient, sweet and quiet, had not self-control, nor any active courage.

Poor Lena was so scared and weak, and every minute she was sure that she would die.

After Lena was on land again a little while, she forgot all her bad suffering. Mrs. Haydon got her the good place, with the pleasant unexacting mistress, and her children, and Lena began to learn some English and soon was very happy and content.

All her Sundays out Lena spent at Mrs. Haydon's house. Lena would have liked much better to spend her Sundays with the girls she always sat with, and who often asked her, and who teased her and made a gentle stir within her, but it never came to Lena's unexpectant and unsuffering german nature to do something different from what was expected of her, just because she would like it that way better. Mrs. Haydon had said that Lena was to come to her house every other Sunday, and so Lena always went there.

Mrs. Haydon was the only one of her family who took any interest in Lena. Mr. Haydon did not think much of her. She was his wife's cousin and he was good to her, but she was for him stupid, and a little simple, and very dull, and sure some day to need help and to be in trouble. All young poor relations, who were brought from Germany to Bridgepoint were sure, before long, to need help and to be in trouble.

The little Haydon boy was always very nasty to her. He was a hard child for any one to manage, and his mother spoiled him very badly. Mrs. Haydon's daughters as they grew older did not learn to like Lena any better. Lena never knew that she did not like them either. She did not know that she was only happy with the other quicker girls, she always sat with in the park, and who laughed at her and always teased her.

Mathilda Haydon, the simple, fat, blonde, older daughter felt very badly that she had to say that this was her cousin Lena, this Lena who was little better for her than a nigger. Mathilda was an overgrown, slow, flabby, blonde, stupid, fat girl, just beginning as a woman; thick in her speech and dull and simple in her mind, and very jealous of all her family and of other girls, and proud that she could have good dresses and new hats and learn music, and hating very badly to have a cousin who was a common servant. And then Mathilda remembered very strongly that dirty nasty place that Lena came from and that Mathilda had so turned up her nose at, and where she had been made so angry because her mother scolded her and liked all those rough cow-smelly people.

Then, too, Mathilda would get very mad when her mother had Lena at their parties, and when she talked about how good Lena was, to certain german mothers in whose sons, perhaps, Mrs. Haydon might find Lena a good husband. All this would make the dull, blonde, fat Mathilda very angry. Sometimes she would get so angry that she would, in her thick, slow way, and with jealous anger blazing in her light blue eyes, tell her mother that she did not see how she could like that nasty Lena; and then her mother would scold Mathilda, and tell her that she knew her cousin Lena was poor and Mathilda must be good to poor people.

Mathilda Haydon did not like relations to be poor. She told all her girl friends what she thought of Lena, and so the girls would never talk to Lena at Mrs. Haydon's parties. But Lena in her unsuffering and unexpectant patience never really knew that she was slighted. When Mathilda was with her girls in the street or in the park and would see Lena, she always turned up her nose and barely nodded to her, and then she would tell her friends how funny her mother was to take care of people like that Lena, and how, back in Germany, all Lena's people lived just like pigs.

The younger daughter, the dark, large, but not fat, Bertha Haydon, who was very quick in her mind, and in her ways, and who was the favorite with her father, did not like Lena, either. She did not like her because for her Lena was a fool and so stupid, and she would let those Irish and Italian girls laugh at her and tease her, and everybody always made fun of Lena, and Lena never got mad, or even had sense enough to know that they were all making an awful fool of her.

Bertha Haydon hated people to be fools. Her father, too, thought Lena was a fool, and so neither the father nor the daughter ever paid any attention to Lena, although she came to their house every other Sunday.

Lena did not know how all the Haydons felt. She came to her aunt's house all her Sunday afternoons that she had out, because Mrs. Haydon had told her she must do so. In the same way Lena always saved all of her wages. She never thought of any way to spend it. The german cook, the good woman who always scolded Lena, helped her to put it in the bank each month, as soon as she got it. Sometimes before it got into the bank to be taken care of, somebody would ask Lena for it. The little Haydon boy sometimes asked and would get it, and sometimes some of the girls, the ones Lena always sat with, needed some more money; but the german cook, who always scolded Lena, saw to it that this did not happen very often. When it did happen she would scold Lena very sharply, and for the next few months she would not let Lena touch her wages, but put it in the bank for her on the same day that Lena got it.

So Lena always saved her wages, for she never thought to spend them, and she always went to her aunt's house for her Sundays because she did not know that she could do anything different.

Mrs. Haydon felt more and more every year that she had done right to bring Lena back with her, for it was all coming out just as she had expected. Lena was good and never wanted her own way, she was learning English, and saving all her wages, and soon Mrs. Haydon would get her a good husband.

All these four years Mrs. Haydon was busy looking around among all the german people that she knew for the right man to be Lena's husband, and now at last she was quite decided.

The man Mrs. Haydon wanted for Lena was a young german-american tailor, who worked with his father. He was good and all the family were very saving, and Mrs. Haydon was sure that this would be just right for Lena, and then too, this young tailor always did whatever his father and his mother wanted.

This old german tailor and his wife, the father and the mother of Herman Kreder, who was to marry Lena Mainz, were very thrifty, careful people. Herman was the only child they had left with them, and he always did everything they wanted. Herman was now twenty-eight years old, but he had never stopped being scolded and directed by his father and his mother. And now they wanted to see him married.

Herman Kreder did not care much to get married. He was a gentle soul and a little fearful. He had a sullen temper, too. He was obedient to his father and his mother. He always did his work well. He often went out on Saturday nights and on Sundays, with other men. He liked it with them but he never became really joyous. He liked to be with men and he hated to have women with them. He was obedient to his mother, but he did not care much to get married.

Mrs. Haydon and the elder Kreders had often talked the marriage over. They all three liked it very well. Lena would do anything that Mrs. Haydon wanted, and Herman was always obedient in everything to his father and his mother. Both Lena and Herman were saving and good workers and neither of them ever wanted their own way.

The elder Kreders, everybody knew, had saved up all their money, and they were hard, good german people, and Mrs. Haydon was sure that with these people Lena would never be in any trouble. Mr. Haydon would not say anything about it. He knew old Kreder had a lot of money and owned some good houses, and he did not care what his wife did with that simple, stupid Lena, so long as she would be sure never to need help or to be in trouble.

Lena did not care much to get married. She liked her life very well where she was working. She did not think much about Herman Kreder. She thought he was a good man and she always found him very quiet. Neither of them ever spoke much to the other. Lena did not care much just then about getting married.

Mrs. Haydon spoke to Lena about it very often. Lena never answered anything at all. Mrs. Haydon thought, perhaps Lena did not like Herman Kreder. Mrs. Haydon could not believe that any girl not even Lena, really had no feeling about getting married.

Mrs. Haydon spoke to Lena very often about Herman. Mrs. Haydon sometimes got very angry with Lena. She was afraid that Lena, for once, was going to be stubborn, now when it was all fixed right for her to be married.

"Why you stand there so stupid, why don't you answer, Lena," said Mrs. Haydon one Sunday, at the end of a long talking that she was giving Lena about Herman Kreder, and about Lena's getting married to him.

"Yes ma'am," said Lena, and then Mrs. Haydon was furious with this stupid Lena. "Why don't you answer with some sense, Lena, when I ask you if you don't like Herman Kreder. You stand there so stupid and don't answer just like you ain't heard a word what I been saying to you. I never see anybody like you, Lena. If you going to burst out at all, why don't you burst out sudden instead of standing there so silly and don't answer. And here I am so good to you, and find you a good husband so you can have a place to live in all your own. Answer me, Lena, don't you like Herman Kreder? He is a fine young fellow, almost too good for you, Lena, when you stand there so stupid and don't make no answer. There ain't many poor girls that get the chance you got now to get married."

"Why, I do anything you say, Aunt Mathilda. Yes, I like him. He don't say much to me, but I guess he is a good man, and I do anything you say for me to do."

"Well then Lena, why you stand there so silly all the time and not answer when I asked you."

"I didn't hear you say you wanted I should say anything to you. I didn't know you wanted me to say nothing. I do whatever you tell me it's right for me to do. I marry Herman Kreder, if you want me."

And so for Lena Mainz the match was made.

Old Mrs. Kreder did not discuss the matter with her Herman. She never thought that she needed to talk such things over with him. She just told him about getting married to Lena Mainz who was a good worker and very saving and never wanted her own way, and Herman made his usual little grunt in answer to her.

Mrs. Kreder and Mrs. Haydon fixed the day and made all the arrangements for the wedding and invited everybody who ought to be there to see them married.

In three months Lena Mainz and Herman Kreder were to be married.

Mrs. Haydon attended to Lena's getting all the things that she needed. Lena had to help a good deal with the sewing. Lena did not sew very well. Mrs. Haydon scolded because Lena did not do it better, but then she was very good to Lena, and she hired a girl to come and help her. Lena still stayed on with her pleasant mistress, but she spent all her evenings and her Sundays with her aunt and all the sewing.

Mrs. Haydon got Lena some nice dresses. Lena liked that very well. Lena liked having new hats even better, and Mrs. Haydon had some made for her by a real milliner who made them very pretty.

Lena was nervous these days, but she did not think much about getting married. She did not know really what it was, that, which was always coming nearer.

Lena liked the place where she was with the pleasant mistress and the good cook, who always scolded, and she liked the girls she always sat with. She did not ask if she would like being married any better. She always did whatever her aunt said and expected, but she was always nervous when she saw the Kreders with their Herman. She was excited and she liked her new hats, and everybody teased her and every day her marrying was coming nearer, and yet she did not really know what it was, this that was about to happen to her.

Herman Kreder knew more what it meant to be married and he did not like it very well. He did not like to see girls and he did not want to have to have one always near him. Herman always did everything that his father and his mother wanted and now they wanted that he should be married.

Herman had a sullen temper; he was gentle and he never said much. He liked to go out with other men, but he never wanted that there should be any women with them. The men all teased him about getting married. Herman did not mind the teasing but he did not like very well the getting married and having a girl always with him.

Three days before the wedding day, Herman went away to the country to be gone over Sunday. He and Lena were to be married Tuesday afternoon. When the day came Herman had not been seen or heard from.

The old Kreder couple had not worried much about it. Herman always did everything they wanted and he would surely come back in time to get married. But when Monday night came, and there was no Herman, they went to Mrs. Haydon to tell her what had happened.

Mrs. Haydon got very much excited. It was hard enough to work so as to get everything all ready, and then to have that silly Herman go off that way, so no one could tell what was going to happen. Here was Lena and everything all ready, and now they would have to make the wedding later so that they would know that Herman would be sure to be there.

Mrs. Haydon was very much excited, and then she could not say much to the old Kreder couple. She did not want to make them angry, for she wanted very badly now that Lena should be married to their Herman.

At last it was decided that the wedding should be put off a week longer. Old Mr. Kreder would go to New York to find Herman, for it was very likely that Herman had gone there to his married sister.

Mrs. Haydon sent word around, about waiting until a week from that Tuesday, to everybody that had been invited, and then Tuesday morning she sent for Lena to come down to see her.

Mrs. Haydon was very angry with poor Lena when she saw her. She scolded her hard because she was so foolish, and now Herman had gone off and nobody could tell where he had gone to, and all because Lena always was so dumb and silly. And Mrs. Haydon was just like a mother to her, and Lena always stood there so stupid and did not answer what anybody asked her, and Herman was so silly too, and now his father had to go and find him. Mrs. Haydon did not think that any old people should be good to their children. Their children always were so thankless, and never paid any attention, and older people were always doing things for their good. Did Lena think it gave Mrs. Haydon any pleasure, to work so hard to make Lena happy, and get her a good husband, and then Lena was so thankless and never did anything that anybody wanted. It was a lesson to poor Mrs. Haydon not to do things any more for anybody. Let everybody take care of themselves and never come to her with any troubles; she knew better now than to meddle to make other people happy. It just made trouble for her and her husband did not like it. He always said she was too good, and nobody ever thanked her for it, and there Lena was always standing stupid and not answering anything anybody wanted. Lena could always talk enough to those silly girls she liked so much, and always sat with, but who never did anything for her except to take away her money, and here was her aunt who tried so hard and was so good to her and treated her just like one of her own children and Lena stood there, and never made any answer and never tried to please her aunt, or to do anything that her aunt wanted. "No, it ain't no use your standin' there and cryin', now, Lena. Its too late now to care about that Herman. You should have cared some before, and then you wouldn't have to stand and cry now, and be a disappointment to me, and then I get scolded by my husband for taking care of everybody, and nobody ever thankful. I am glad you got the sense to feel sorry now, Lena, anyway, and I try to do what I can to help you out in your trouble, only you don't deserve to have anybody take any trouble for you. But perhaps you know better next time. You go home now and take care you don't spoil your clothes and that new hat, you had no business to be wearin' that this morning, but you ain't got no sense at all, Lena. I never in my life see anybody be so stupid."

Mrs. Haydon stopped and poor Lena stood there in her hat, all trimmed with pretty flowers, and the tears coming out of her eyes, and Lena did not know what it was that she had done, only she was not going to be married and it was a disgrace for a girl to be left by a man on the very day she was to be married.

Lena went home all alone, and cried in the street car.

Poor Lena cried very hard all alone in the street car. She almost spoiled her new hat with her hitting it against the window in her crying. Then she remembered that she must not do so.

The conductor was a kind man and he was very sorry when he saw her crying. "Don't feel so bad, you get another feller, you are such a nice girl," he said to make her cheerful. "But Aunt Mathilda said now, I never get married," poor Lena sobbed out for her answer. "Why you really got trouble like that," said the conductor, "I just said that now to josh you. I didn't ever think you really was left by a feller. He must be a stupid feller. But don't you worry, he wasn't much good if he could go away and leave you, lookin' to be such a nice girl. You just tell all your trouble to me, and I help you." The car was empty and the conductor sat down beside her to put his arm around her, and to be a comfort to her. Lena suddenly remembered where she was, and if she did things like that her aunt would scold her. She moved away from the man into the corner. He laughed, "Don't be scared," he said, "I wasn't going to hurt you. But you just keep up your spirit. You are a real nice girl, and you'll be sure to get a real good husband. Don't you let nobody fool you. You're all right and I don't want to scare you."

The conductor went back to his platform to help a passenger get on the car. All the time Lena stayed in the street car, he would come in every little while and reassure her, about her not to feel so bad about a man who hadn't no more sense than to go away and leave her. She'd be sure yet to get a good man, she needn't be so worried, he frequently assured her.

He chatted with the other passenger who had just come in, a very well dressed old man, and then with another who came in later, a good sort of a working man, and then another who came in, a nice lady, and he told them all about Lena's having trouble, and it was too bad there were men who treated a poor girl so badly. And everybody in the car was sorry for poor Lena and the workman tried to cheer her, and the old man looked sharply at her, and said she looked like a good girl, but she ought to be more careful and not be so careless, and things like that would not happen to her, and the nice lady went and sat beside her and Lena liked it, though she shrank away from being near her.

So Lena was feeling a little better when she got off the car, and the conductor helped her, and he called out to her, "You be sure you keep up a good heart now. He wasn't no good that feller and you were lucky for to lose him. You'll get a real man yet, one that will be better for you. Don't you be worried, you're a real nice girl as I ever see in such trouble," and the conductor shook his head and went back into his car to talk it over with the other passengers he had there.

The german cook, who always scolded Lena, was very angry when she heard the story. She never did think Mrs. Haydon would do so much for Lena, though she was always talking so grand about what she could do for everybody. The good german cook always had been a little distrustful to her. People who always thought they were so much never did really do things right for anybody. Not that Mrs. Haydon wasn't a good woman. Mrs. Haydon was a real, good, german woman, and she did really mean to do well by her niece Lena. The cook knew that very well, and she had always said so, and she always had liked and respected Mrs. Haydon, who always acted very proper to her, and Lena was so backward, when there was a man to talk to, Mrs. Haydon did have hard work when she tried to marry Lena. Mrs. Haydon was a good woman, only she did talk sometimes too grand. Perhaps this trouble would make her see it wasn't always so easy to do, to make everybody do everything just like she wanted. The cook was very sorry now for Mrs. Haydon. All this must be such a disappointment, and such a worry to her, and she really had always been very good to Lena. But Lena had better go and put on her other clothes and stop with all that crying. That wouldn't do nothing now to help her, and if Lena would be a good girl, and just be real patient, her aunt would make it all come out right yet for her. "I just tell Mrs. Aldrich, Lena, you stay here yet a little longer. You know she is always so good to you, Lena, and I know she let you, and I tell her all about that stupid Herman Kreder. I got no patience, Lena, with anybody who can be so stupid. You just stop now with your crying, Lena, and take off them good clothes and put them away so you don't spoil them when you need them, and you can help me with the dishes and everything will come off better for you. You see if I ain't right by what I tell you. You just stop crying now Lena quick, or else I scold you."

Lena still choked a little and was very miserable inside her but she did everything just as the cook told her.

The girls Lena always sat with were very sorry to see her look so sad with her trouble. Mary the Irish girl sometimes got very angry with her. Mary was always very hot when she talked of Lena's aunt Mathilda, who thought she was so grand, and had such stupid, stuck up daughters. Mary wouldn't be a fat fool like that ugly tempered Mathilda Haydon, not for anything anybody could ever give her. How Lena could keep on going there so much when they all always acted as if she was just dirt to them, Mary never could see. But Lena never had any sense of how she should make people stand round for her, and that was always all the trouble with her. And poor Lena, she was so stupid to be sorry for losing that gawky fool who didn't ever know what he wanted and just said "ja"[1] to his mamma and his papa, like a baby, and was scared to look at a girl straight, and then sneaked away the last day like as if somebody was going to do something to him. Disgrace, Lena talking about disgrace! It was a disgrace for a girl to be seen with the likes of him, let alone to be married to him. But that poor Lena, she never did know how to show herself off for what she was really. Disgrace to have him go away and leave her. Mary would just like to get a chance to show him. If Lena wasn't worth fifteen like Herman Kreder, Mary would just eat her own head all up. It was a good riddance Lena had of that Herman Kreder and his stingy,

---

1. Yes (German).

dirty parents, and if Lena didn't stop crying about it,—Mary would just naturally despise her.

Poor Lena, she knew very well how Mary meant it all, this she was always saying to her. But Lena was very miserable inside her. She felt the disgrace it was for a decent german girl that a man should go away and leave her. Lena knew very well that her aunt was right when she said the way Herman had acted to her was a disgrace to everyone that knew her. Mary and Nellie and the other girls she always sat with were always very good to Lena but that did not make her trouble any better. It was a disgrace the way Lena had been left, to any decent family, and that could never be made any different to her.

And so the slow days wore on, and Lena never saw her Aunt Mathilda. At last on Sunday she got word by a boy to go and see her aunt Mathilda. Lena's heart beat quick for she was very nervous now with all this that had happened to her. She went just as quickly as she could to see her Aunt Mathilda.

Mrs. Haydon quick, as soon as she saw Lena, began to scold her for keeping her aunt waiting so long for her, and for not coming in all the week to see her, to see if her aunt should need her, and so her aunt had to send a boy to tell her. But it was easy, even for Lena, to see that her aunt was not really angry with her. It wasn't Lena's fault, went on Mrs. Haydon, that everything was going to happen all right for her. Mrs. Haydon was very tired taking all this trouble for her, and when Lena couldn't even take trouble to come and see her aunt, to see if she needed anything to tell her. But Mrs. Haydon really never minded things like that when she could do things for anybody. She was tired now, all the trouble she had been taking to make things right for Lena, but perhaps now Lena heard it she would learn a little to be thankful to her. "You get all ready to be married Tuesday. Lena, you hear me," said Mrs. Haydon to her. "You come here Tuesday morning and I have everything all ready for you. You wear your new dress I got you, and your hat with all them flowers on it, and you be very careful coming you don't get your things all dirty, you so careless all the time, Lena, and not thinking, and you act sometimes you never got no head at all on you. You go home now, and you tell your Mrs. Aldrich that you leave her Tuesday. Don't you go forgetting now, Lena, anything I ever told you what you should do to be careful. You be a good girl, now Lena. You get married Tuesday to Herman Kreder." And that was all Lena ever knew of what had happened all this week to Herman Kreder. Lena forgot there was anything to know about it. She was really to be married Tuesday, and her Aunt Mathilda said she was a good girl, and now there was no disgrace left upon her.

Lena now fell back into the way she always had of being always dreamy and not there, the way she always had been, except for the few days she was so excited, because she had been left by a man the very day she was to have been married. Lena was a little nervous all these last days, but she did not think much about what it meant for her to be married.

Herman Kreder was not so content about it. He was quiet and was sullen and he knew he could not help it. He knew now he just had to let himself get married. It was not that Herman did not like Lena Mainz. She was as good as any other girl could be for him. She was a little better perhaps than other girls he saw, she was so very quiet, but Herman did not like to always have to have a girl around him. Herman had always done everything that his mother and his father wanted. His father had found him in New York, where Herman had gone to be with his married sister.

Herman's father when he had found him coaxed Herman a long time and went on whole days with his complaining to him, always troubled but gentle and quite patient with him, and always he was worrying to Herman about what was the right way his boy Herman should always do, always whatever it was his mother ever wanted from him, and always Herman never made him any answer.

Old Mr. Kreder kept on saying to him, he did not see how Herman could think now, it could be any different. When you make a bargain you just got to stick right to it, that was the only way old Mr. Kreder could ever see it, and saying you would get married to a girl and she got everything all ready, that was a bargain just like one you make in business and Herman he had made it, and now Herman he would just have to do it, old Mr. Kreder didn't see there was any other way a good boy like his Herman had, to do it. And then too that Lena Mainz was such a nice girl and Herman hadn't ought to really give his father so much trouble and make him pay out all that money, to come all the way to New York just to find him, and they both lose all that time from their working, when all Herman had to do was just to stand up, for an hour, and then he would be all right married, and it would be all over for him, and then everything at home would never be any different to him.

And his father went on; there was his poor mother saying always how her Herman always did everything before she ever wanted, and now just because he got notions in him, and wanted to show people how he could be stubborn, he was making all this trouble for her, and making them pay all that money just to run around and find him. "You got no idea Herman, how bad mama is feeling about the way you been acting Herman," said old Mr. Kreder to him. "She says she never can understand how you can be so thankless Herman. It hurts her very much you been so stubborn, and she find you such a nice girl for you, like Lena Mainz who is always just so quiet and always saves up all her wages, and she never wanting her own way at all like some girls are always all the time to have it, and your mama trying so hard, just so you could be comfortable Herman to be married, and then you act so stubborn Herman. You like all young people Herman, you think only about yourself, and what you are just wanting, and your mama she is thinking only what is good for you to have, for you in the future. Do you think your mama wants to have a girl around to be a bother, for herself, Herman. Its just for you Herman she is always thinking, and she talks always about how happy she will be, when she sees her Herman married to a nice girl, and then when she fixed it all up so good for you, so it never would be any bother to you, just the way she wanted you should like it, and you say yes all right, I do it, and then you go away like this act stubborn, and make all this trouble everybody to take for you, and we spend money, and I got to travel all round to find you. You come home now with me Herman and get married, and I tell your mama she better not say anything to you about how much it cost me to come all the way to look for you—Hey Herman," said his father coaxing, "Hey, you come home now and get married. All you got to do Herman is just to stand up for an hour Herman, and then you don't never to have any more bother to it—Hey Herman!—you come home with me to-morrow and get married. Hey Herman."

Herman's married sister liked her brother Herman, and she had always tried to help him, when there was anything she knew he wanted. She liked it that he was so good and always did everything that their father and their mother wanted, but still she wished it could be that he could have more his own way, if there was anything he ever wanted.

But now she thought Herman with his girl was very funny. She wanted that Herman should be married. She thought it would do him lots of good to get married. She laughed at Herman when she heard the story. Until his father came to find him, she did not know why it was Herman had come just then to New York to see her. When she heard the story she laughed a good deal at her brother Herman and teased him a good deal about his running away, because he didn't want to have a girl to be all the time around him.

Herman's married sister liked her brother Herman, and she did not want him not to like to be with women. He was good, her brother Herman, and it would surely do him good to get married. It would make him stand up for himself stronger. Herman's sister always laughed at him and always she would try to reassure him. "Such a nice man as my brother Herman acting like as if he was afraid of women. Why the girls all like a man like you Herman, if you didn't always run away when you saw them. It do you good really Herman to get married, and then you got somebody you can boss around when you want to. It do you good Herman to get married, you see if you don't like it, when you really done it. You go along home now with papa, Herman and get married to that Lena. You don't know how nice you like it Herman when you try once how you can do it. You just don't be afraid of nothing, Herman. You good enough for any girl to marry, Herman. Any girl be glad to have a man like you to be always with them Herman. You just go along home with papa and try it what I say, Herman. Oh you so funny Herman, when you sit there, and then run away and leave your girl behind you. I know she is crying like anything Herman for to lose you. Don't be bad to her Herman. You go along home with papa now and get married Herman. I'd be awful ashamed Herman, to really have a brother didn't have spirit enough to get married, when a girl is just dying for to have him. You always like me to be with you Herman. I don't see why you say you don't want a girl to be all the time around you. You always been good to me Herman, and I know you always be good to that Lena, and you soon feel just like as if she had always been there with you. Don't act like as if you wasn't a nice strong man, Herman. Really I laugh at you Herman, but you know I like awful well to see you real happy. You go home and get married to that Lena, Herman. She is a real pretty girl and real nice and good and quiet and she make my brother Herman very happy. You just stop your fussing now with Herman, papa. He go with you to-morrow papa, and you see he like it so much to be married, he make everybody laugh just to see him be so happy. Really truly, that's the way it will be with you Herman. You just listen to me what I tell you Herman." And so his sister laughed at him and reassured him, and his father kept on telling what the mother always said about her Herman, and he coaxed him and Herman never said anything in answer, and his sister packed his things up and was very cheerful with him, and she kissed him, and then she laughed and then she kissed him, and his father went and brought the tickets for the train, and at last late on Sunday he brought Herman back to Bridgepoint with him.

It was always very hard to keep Mrs. Kreder from saying what she thought, to her Herman, but her daughter had written her a letter, so as to warn her not to say anything about what he had been doing, to him, and her husband came in with Herman and said, "Here we are come home mama, Herman and me, and we are very tired it was so crowded coming," and then he whispered to her. "You be good to Herman, mama, he didn't mean to make us so much trouble," and so old Mrs. Kreder, held in what she felt was so strong in her to say to her Herman. She just said very stiffly to him, "I'm glad to see you come home to-day, Herman." Then she went to arrange it all with Mrs. Haydon.

Herman was now again just like he always had been, sullen and very good, and very quiet, and always ready to do whatever his mother and his father wanted. Tuesday morning came, Herman got his new clothes on and went with his father and his mother to stand up for an hour and get married. Lena was there in her new dress, and her hat with all the pretty flowers, and she was very nervous for now she knew she was really very soon to be married. Mrs. Haydon had everything all ready. Everybody was there just as they should be and very soon Herman Kreder and Lena Mainz were married.

When everything was really over, they went back to the Kreder house together. They were all now to live together, Lena and Herman and the old father and the old mother, in the house where Mr. Kreder had worked so many years as a tailor, with his son Herman always there to help him.

Irish Mary had often said to Lena she never did see how Lena could ever want to have anything to do with Herman Kreder and his dirty stingy parents. The old Kreders were to an Irish nature, a stingy, dirty couple. They had not the free-hearted, thoughtless, fighting, mud bespattered, ragged, peat-smoked cabin dirt that irish Mary knew and could forgive and love. Theirs was the german dirt of saving, of being dowdy and loose and foul in your clothes so as to save them and yourself in washing, having your hair greasy to save it in the soap and drying, having your clothes dirty, not in freedom, but because so it was cheaper, keeping the house close and smelly because so it cost less to get it heated, living so poorly not only so as to save money but so they should never even know themselves that they had it, working all the time not only because from their nature they just had to and because it made them money but also that they never could be put in any way to make them spend their money.

This was the place Lena now had for her home and to her it was very different than it could be for an irish Mary. She too was german and was thrifty, though she was always so dreamy and not there. Lena was always careful with things and she always saved her money, for that was the only way she knew how to do it. She never had taken care of her own money and she never had thought how to use it.

Lena Mainz had been, before she was Mrs. Herman Kreder, always clean and decent in her clothes and in her person, but it was not because she ever thought about it or really needed so to have it, it was the way her people did in the german country where she came from, and her Aunt Mathilda and the good german cook who always scolded, had kept her on and made her, with their scoldings, always more careful to keep clean and to wash real often. But there was no deep need in all this for Lena and so, though Lena did not like the old Kreders, though she really did not know that, she did not think about their being stingy dirty people.

Herman Kreder was cleaner than the old people, just because it was his nature to keep cleaner, but he was used to his mother and his father, and he never thought that they should keep things cleaner. And Herman too always saved all his money, except for that little beer he drank when he went out with other men of an evening the way he always liked to do it, and he never thought of any other way to spend it. His father had always kept all the money for them and he always was doing business with it. And then too Herman really had no money, for he always had worked for his father, and his father had never thought to pay him.

And so they began all four to live in the Kreder house together, and Lena began soon with it to look careless and a little dirty, and to be more lifeless with it, and nobody ever noticed much what Lena wanted, and she never really knew herself what she needed.

The only real trouble that came to Lena with their living all four there together, was the way old Mrs. Kreder scolded. Lena had always been used to being scolded, but this scolding of old Mrs. Kreder was very different from the way she ever before had had to endure it.

Herman, now he was married to her, really liked Lena very well. He did not care very much about her but she never was a bother to him being there around him, only when his mother worried and was nasty to them because Lena was so careless, and did not know how to save things right for them with their eating, and all the other ways with money, that the old woman had to save it.

Herman Kreder had always done everything his mother and his father wanted but he did not really love his parents very deeply. With Herman it was always only that he hated to have any struggle. It was all always all right with him when he could just go along and do the same thing over every day with his working, and not to hear things, and not to have people make him listen to their anger. And now his marriage, and he just knew it would, was making trouble for him. It made him hear more what his mother was always saying, with her scolding. He had to really hear it now because Lena was there, and she was so scared and dull always when she heard it. Herman knew very well with his mother, it was all right if one ate very little and worked hard all day and did not learn her when she scolded, the way Herman always had done before they were so foolish about his getting married and having a girl there to be all the time around him, and now he had to help her so the girl could learn too, not to hear it when his mother scolded, and not to look so scared, and not to eat much, and always to be sure to save it.

Herman really did not know very well what he could do to help Lena to understand it. He could never answer his mother back to help Lena, that never would make things any better for her, and he never could feel in himself any way to comfort Lena, to make her strong not to hear his mother, in all the awful ways she always scolded. It just worried Herman to have it like that all the time around him. Herman did not know much about how a man could make a struggle with a mother, to do much to keep her quiet, and indeed Herman never knew much how to make a struggle against anyone who really wanted to have anything very badly. Herman all his life never wanted anything so badly, that he would really make a struggle against any one to get it. Herman all his life only wanted to live regular and quiet, and not talk much and to do the same way every day like every other with his working. And now his mother had made him get married to this Lena and now with his mother making all that scolding, he had all this trouble and this worry always on him.

Mrs. Haydon did not see Lena now very often. She had not lost her interest in her niece Lena, but Lena could not come much to her house to see her, it would not be right, now Lena was a married woman. And then too Mrs. Haydon had her hands full just then with her two daughters, for she was getting them ready to find them good husbands, and then too her own husband now worried her very often about her always spoiling that boy of hers, so he would be sure to turn out no good and be a disgrace to a german family, and all because his mother always spoiled him. All these things were very worrying now to Mrs. Haydon, but still she wanted to be good to Lena, though she could not see her very often. She only saw her when Mrs. Haydon went to call on Mrs. Kreder or when Mrs. Kreder came to see Mrs. Haydon, and that never could be very often. Then too these days Mrs. Haydon could not scold Lena, Mrs. Kreder was always there with her, and it would not be right to scold Lena when Mrs. Kreder was there, who had now the real right to do it. And so her aunt always said nice things now to Lena, and though Mrs. Haydon sometimes was a little worried when she saw Lena looking sad and not careful, she did not have time just then to really worry much about it.

Lena now never any more saw the girls she always used to sit with. She had no way now to see them and it was not in Lena's nature to search out ways to see them, nor did she now ever think much of the days when she had been used to see them. They never any of them had come to the Kreder house to see her. Not even Irish Mary had ever thought to come to see her. Lena had been soon forgotten by them. They had soon passed away from Lena and now Lena never thought any more that she had ever known them.

The only one to her old friends who tried to know what Lena liked and what she needed, and who always made Lena come to see her, was the good german cook who had always scolded. She now scolded Lena hard for letting herself go so, and going out when she was looking so untidy. "I know you going to have a baby Lena, but that's no way for you to be looking. I am ashamed most to see you come and sit here in my kitchen, looking so sloppy and like you never used to Lena. I never see anybody like you Lena. Herman is very good to you, you always say so, and he don't treat you bad ever though you don't deserve to have anybody good to you, you so careless all the time, Lena, letting yourself go like you never had anybody tell you what was the right way you should know how to be looking. No, Lena, I don't see no reason you should let yourself go so and look so untidy Lena, so I am ashamed to see you sit there looking so ugly, Lena. No Lena that ain't no way ever I see a woman make things come out better, letting herself go so every way and crying all the time like as if you had real trouble. I never wanted to see you marry Herman Kreder, Lena, I knew what you got to stand with that old woman always, and that old man, he is so stingy too and he don't say things out but he ain't any better in his heart than his wife with her bad ways, I know that Lena, I know they don't hardly give you enough to eat, Lena, I am real sorry for you Lena, you know that Lena, but that ain't any way to be going round so untidy Lena, even if you have got all that trouble. You never see me do like that Lena, though sometimes I got a headache so I can't see to stand to be working hardly, and nothing comes right with all my cooking, but I always see Lena, I look decent. That's the only way a german girl can make things come out right Lena. You hear me what I am saying to you Lena. Now you eat something nice Lena, I got it all ready for you, and you wash up and be careful Lena and the baby will come all right to you, and then I make your Aunt Mathilda see that you live in a house soon all alone with Herman and your baby, and then everything go better for you. You hear me what I say to you Lena. Now don't let me ever see you come looking like this any more Lena, and you just stop with that always crying. You ain't got no reason to be sitting there now with all that crying, I never see anybody have trouble it did them any good to be the way you are doing, Lena. You hear me Lena. You go home now and you be good the way I tell you Lena, and I see what I can do. I make your Aunt Mathilda make old Mrs. Kreder let you be till you get your baby all right. Now don't you be scared and so silly Lena. I don't like to see you act so Lena when really you got a nice man and so many things really any girl should be grateful to be having. Now you go home Lena to-day and you do the way I say, to you, and I see what I can do to help you."

"Yes Mrs. Aldrich" said the good german woman to her mistress later, "Yes Mrs. Aldrich that's the way it is with them girls when they want so to get married. They don't know when they got it good Mrs. Aldrich. They never know what it is they're really wanting when they got it, Mrs. Aldrich. There's that poor Lena, she just been here crying and looking so careless so I scold her, but that was no good that marrying for that poor Lena, Mrs. Aldrich. She do look so pale and sad now Mrs. Aldrich, it just break my heart to see her. She was a good girl was Lena, Mrs. Aldrich, and I never had no trouble with her like I got with so many young girls nowadays, Mrs. Aldrich, and I never see any girl any better to work right than our Lena, and now she got to stand it all the time with that old woman Mrs. Kreder. My! Mrs. Aldrich, she is a bad old woman to her. I never see Mrs. Aldrich how old people can be so bad to young girls and not have no kind of patience with them. If Lena could only live with her Herman, he ain't so bad the way men are, Mrs. Aldrich, but he is just the way always his mother wants him, he ain't got no spirit in him, and so I don't really see no help for that poor Lena. I know her aunt, Mrs. Haydon, meant it all right for her Mrs. Aldrich, but poor Lena, it would be better for her if her Herman had stayed there in New York that time he went away to leave her. I don't like it the way Lena is looking now, Mrs. Aldrich. She looks like as if she don't have no life left in her hardly, Mrs. Aldrich, she just drags around and looks so dirty and after all the pains I always took to teach her and to keep her nice in her ways and looking. It don't do no good to them, for them girls to get married Mrs. Aldrich, they are much better when they only know it, to stay in a good place when they got it, and keep on regular with their working. I don't like it the way Lena looks now Mrs. Aldrich. I wish I knew some way to help that poor Lena, Mrs. Aldrich, but she is a bad old woman, that old Mrs. Kreder, Herman's mother. I speak to Mrs. Haydon real soon, Mrs. Aldrich, I see what we can do now to help that poor Lena."

These were really bad days for poor Lena. Herman always was real good to her and now he even sometimes tried to stop his mother from scolding Lena. "She ain't well now mama, you let her be now you hear me. You tell me what it is you want she should be doing, I tell her. I see she does it right just the way you want it mama. You let be, I say now mama, with that always scolding Lena. You let be, I say now, you wait till she is feeling better." Herman was getting really strong to struggle, for he could see that Lena with that baby working hard inside her, really could not stand it any longer with his mother and the awful ways she always scolded.

It was a new feeling Herman now had inside him that made him feel he was strong to make a struggle. It was new for Herman Kreder really to be wanting something, but Herman wanted strongly now to be a father, and he wanted badly that his baby should be a boy and healthy. Herman never had cared really very much about his father and his mother, though always, all his life, he had done everything just as they wanted, and he had never really cared much about his wife, Lena, though he always had been very good to her, and had always tried to keep his mother off her, with the awful way she always scolded, but to be really a father of a little baby, that feeling took hold of Herman very deeply. He was almost ready, so as to save his baby from all trouble, to really make a strong struggle with his mother and with his father, too, if he would not help him to control his mother.

Sometimes Herman even went to Mrs. Haydon to talk all this trouble over. They decided then together, it was better to wait there all four together for the baby, and Herman could make Mrs. Kreder stop a little with her scolding, and then when Lena was a little stronger, Herman should have his own house for her, next door to his father, so he could always be there to help him in his working, but so they could eat and sleep in a house where the old woman could not control them and they could not hear her awful scolding.

And so things went on, the same way, a little longer. Poor Lena was not feeling any joy to have a baby. She was scared the way she had been when she was so sick on the water. She was scared now every time when anything would hurt her. She was scared and still and lifeless, and sure that every minute she would die. Lena had no power to be strong in this kind of trouble, she could only sit still and be scared, and dull, and lifeless, and sure that every minute she would die.

Before very long, Lena had her baby. He was a good, healthy little boy, the baby. Herman cared very much to have the baby. When Lena was a little stronger he took a house next door to the old couple, so he and his own family could eat and sleep and do the way they wanted. This did not seem to make much change now for Lena. She was just the same as when she was waiting with her baby. She just dragged around and was careless with her clothes and all lifeless, and she acted always and lived on just as if she had no feeling. She always did everything regular with the work, the way she always had had to do it, but she never got back any spirit in her. Herman was always good and kind, and always helped her with her working. He did everything he knew to help her. He always did all the active new things in the house and for the baby. Lena did what she had to do the way she always had been taught it. She always just kept going now with her working, and she was always careless, and dirty, and a little dazed, and lifeless. Lena never got any better in herself of this way of being that she had had ever since she had been married.

Mrs. Haydon never saw any more of her niece, Lena. Mrs. Haydon had now so much trouble with her own house, and her daughters getting married, and her boy, who was growing up, and who always was getting so much worse to manage. She knew she had done right by Lena. Herman Kreder was a good man, she would be glad to get one so good, sometimes, for her own daughters, and now they had a home to live in together, separate from the old people, who had made their trouble for them. Mrs. Haydon felt she had done very well by her niece, Lena, and she never thought now she needed any more to go and see her. Lena would do very well now without her aunt to trouble herself any more about her.

The good german cook who had always scolded, still tried to do her duty like a mother to poor Lena. It was very hard now to do right by Lena. Lena never seemed to hear now what anyone was saying to her. Herman was always doing everything he could to help her. Herman always, when he was home, took good care of the baby. Herman loved to take care of his baby. Lena never thought to take him out or to do anything she didn't have to.

The good cook sometimes made Lena come to see her. Lena would come with her baby and sit there in the kitchen, and watch the good woman cooking, and listen to her sometimes a little, the way she used to, while the good german woman scolded her for going around looking so careless when now she had no trouble, and sitting there so dull, and always being just so thankless. Sometimes Lena would wake up a little and get back into her face her old, gentle, patient, and unsuffering sweetness, but mostly Lena did not seem to hear much when the good german woman scolded. Lena always liked it when Mrs. Aldrich her good mistress spoke to her kindly, and then Lena would seem to go back and feel herself to be like she was when she had been in service. But mostly Lena just lived along and was careless in her clothes, and dull, and lifeless.

By and by Lena had two more little babies. Lena was not so much scared now when she had the babies. She did not seem to notice very much when they hurt her, and she never seemed to feel very much now about anything that happened to her.

They were very nice babies, all these three that Lena had, and Herman took good care of them always. Herman never really cared much about his wife, Lena. The only things Herman ever really cared for were his babies. Herman always was very good to his children. He always had a gentle, tender way when he held them. He learned to be very handy with them. He spent all the time he was not working, with them. By the by he began to work all day in his own home so that he could have his children always in the same room with him.

Lena always was more and more lifeless and Herman now mostly never thought about her. He more and more took all the care of their three children. He saw to their eating right and their washing, and he dressed them every morning, and he taught them the right way to do things, and he put them to their sleeping, and he was now always every minute with them. Then there was to come to them, a fourth baby. Lena went to the hospital near by to have the baby. Lena seemed to be going to have much trouble with it. When the baby was come out at last, it was like its mother lifeless. While it was coming, Lena had grown very pale and sicker. When it was all over Lena had died, too, and nobody knew just how it had happened to her.

The good german cook who had always scolded Lena, and had always to the last day tried to help her, was the only one who ever missed her. She remembered how nice Lena had looked all the time she was in service with her, and how her voice had been so gentle and sweet-sounding, and how she always was a good girl, and how she never had to have any trouble with her, the way she always had with all the other girls who had been taken into the house to help her. The good cook sometimes spoke so of Lena when she had time to have a talk with Mrs. Aldrich, and this was all the remembering there now ever was of Lena.

Herman Kreder now always lived very happy, very gentle, very quiet, very well content alone with his three children. He never had a woman any more to be all the time around him. He always did all his own work in his house, when he was through every day with the work he was always doing for his father. Herman always was alone, and he always worked alone, until his little ones were big enough to help him. Herman Kreder was very well content now and he always lived very regular and peaceful, and with every day just like the next one, always alone now with his three good, gentle children.

FINIS[2]

1909

Picasso[1]

One whom some were certainly following was one who was completely charming. One whom some were certainly following was one who was charming. One whom some were following was one who was completely charming. One whom some were following was one who was certainly completely charming.

Some were certainly following and were certain that the one they were then following was one working and was one bringing out of himself then something. Some were certainly following and were certain that the one they were then following was one bringing out of himself then something that was coming to be a heavy thing, a solid thing and a complete thing.

One whom some were certainly following was one working and certainly was one bringing something out of himself then and was one who had been all his living had been one having something coming out of him.

Something had been coming out of him, certainly it had been coming out of him, certainly it was something, certainly it had been coming out of him and it had meaning, a charming meaning, a solid meaning, a struggling meaning, a clear meaning.

One whom some were certainly following and some were certainly following him, one whom some were certainly following was one certainly working.

One whom some were certainly following was one having something coming out of him something having meaning and this one was certainly working then.

This one was working and something was coming then, something was coming out of this one then. This one was one and always there was something coming out of this one and always there had been something coming out of this one. This one had never been one not having something coming

2. The end (Latin).
1. Stein became a friend of the Spanish artist Pablo Picasso (1881–1973) when she lived in Paris.

out of this one. This one was one having something coming out of this one. This one had been one whom some were following. This one was one whom some were following. This one was being one whom some were following. This one was one who was working.

This one was one who was working. This one was one being one having something being coming out of him. This one was one going on having something come out of him. This one was one going on working. This one was one whom some were following. This one was one who was working.

This one always had something being coming out of this one. This one was working. This one always had been working. This one was always having something that was coming out of this one that was a solid thing, a charming thing, a lovely thing, a perplexing thing, a disconcerting thing, a simple thing, a clear thing, a complicated thing, an interesting thing, a disturbing thing, a repellant thing, a very pretty thing. This one was one certainly being one having something coming out of him. This one was one whom some were following. This one was one who was working.

This one was one who was working and certainly this one was needing to be working so as to be one being working. This one was one having something coming out of him. This one would be one all his living having something coming out of him. This one was working and then this one was working and this one was needing to be working, not to be one having something coming out of him something having meaning, but was needing to be working so as to be one working.

This one was certainly working and working was something this one was certain this one would be doing and this one was doing that thing, this one was working. This one was not one completely working. This one was not ever completely working. This one certainly was not completely working.

This one was one having always something being coming out of him, something having completely a real meaning. This one was one whom some were following. This one was one who was working. This one was one who was working and he was one needing this thing needing to be working so as to be one having some way of being one having some way of working. This one was one who was working. This one was one having something come out of him something having meaning. This one was one always having something come out of him and this thing the thing coming out of him always had real meaning. This one was one who was working. This one was one who was almost always working. This one was not one completely working. This one was one not ever completely working. This one was not one working to have anything come out of him. This one did have something having meaning that did come out of him. He always did have something come out of him. He was working, he was not ever completely working. He did have some following. They were always following him. Some were certainly following him. He was one who was working. He was one having something coming out of him something having meaning. He was not ever completely working.

1912, 1934

Ada[1]

Barnes Colhard did not say he would not do it but he did not do it. He did it and then he did not do it, he did not ever think about it. He just thought some time he might do something.

His father Mr. Abram Colhard spoke about it to every one and very many of them spoke to Barnes Colhard about it and he always listened to them.

Then Barnes fell in love with a very nice girl and she would not marry him. He cried then, his father Mr. Abram Colhard comforted him and they took a trip and Barnes promised he would do what his father wanted him to be doing. He did not do the thing, he thought he would do another thing, he did not do the other thing, his father Mr. Colhard did not want him to do the other thing. He really did not do anything then. When he was a good deal older he married a very rich girl. He had thought perhaps he would not propose to her but his sister wrote to him that it would be a good thing. He married the rich girl and she thought he was the most wonderful man and one who knew everything. Barnes never spent more than the income of the fortune he and his wife had then, that is to say they did not spend more than the income and this was a surprise to very many who knew about him and about his marrying the girl who had such a large fortune. He had a happy life while he was living and after he was dead his wife and children remembered him.

He had a sister who also was successful enough in being one being living. His sister was one who came to be happier than most people come to be in living. She came to be a completely happy one. She was twice as old as her brother. She had been a very good daughter to her mother. She and her mother had always told very pretty stories to each other. Many old men loved to hear her tell these stories to her mother. Every one who ever knew her mother liked her mother. Many were sorry later that not every one liked the daughter. Many did like the daughter but not every one as every one had liked the mother. The daughter was charming inside in her, it did not show outside in her to every one, it certainly did to some. She did sometimes think her mother would be pleased with a story that did not please her mother, when her mother later was sicker the daughter knew that there were some stories she could tell her that would not please her mother. Her mother died and really mostly altogether the mother and the daughter had told each other stories very happily together.

The daughter then kept house for her father and took care of her brother. There were many relations who lived with them. The daughter did not like them to live with them and she did not like them to die with them. The daughter, Ada they had called her after her grandmother who had delightful ways of smelling flowers and eating dates and sugar, did not like it at all then as she did not like so much dying and she did not like any of the living she was doing then. Every now and then some old gentlemen told delightful stories to her. Mostly then there were not nice stories told by any one then in her living. She told her father Mr. Abram Colhard that she did not like it at all being one being living then. He never said anything. She was afraid

---

1. The character Ada is probably based on Stein's companion Alice B. Toklas (1887–1967).

then, she was one needing charming stories and happy telling of them and not having that thing she was always trembling. Then every one who could live with them were dead and there were then the father and the son a young man then and the daughter coming to be that one then. Her grandfather had left some money to them each one of them. Ada said she was going to use it to go away from them. The father said nothing then, then he said something and she said nothing then, then they both said nothing and then it was that she went away from them. The father was quite tender then, she was his daughter then. He wrote her tender letters then, she wrote him tender letters then, she never went back to live with him. He wanted her to come and she wrote him tender letters then. He liked the tender letters she wrote to him. He wanted her to live with him. She answered him by writing tender letters to him and telling very nice stories indeed in them. He wrote nothing and then he wrote again and there was some waiting and then he wrote tender letters again and again.

She came to be happier than anybody else who was living then. It is easy to believe this thing. She was telling some one, who was loving every story that was charming. Some one who was living was almost always listening. Some one who was loving[2] was almost always listening. That one who was loving was almost always listening. That one who was loving was telling about being one then listening. That one being loving was then telling stories having a beginning and a middle and an ending. That one was then one always completely listening. Ada was then one and all her living then one completely telling stories that were charming, completely listening to stories having a beginning and a middle and an ending. Trembling was all living, living was all loving, some one was then the other one. Certainly this one was loving this Ada then. And certainly Ada all her living then was happier in living than any one else who ever could, who was, who is, who ever will be living.

1909–10   1922

2. Implicitly, Stein herself.

ALICE DUNBAR-NELSON
1875–1935

Short-story writer, poet, teacher, diarist, journalist, and political activist, Alice Dunbar-Nelson was born Alice Ruth Moore in New Orleans, Louisiana, the second daughter of a seaman father and a seamstress mother. Like many in Creole society, she counted among her ancestors blacks, whites, and Native Americans. After attending a two-year teachers' training program, she had her first book, *Violets and Other Tales*—a collection of twelve poems and seventeen sketches—privately printed in 1895. When one of the poems in this volume was first published in the Boston *Monthly Review,* it caught the fancy of the youthful African American poet Paul Laurence Dunbar, who began to correspond with her. A few years later, the pair met and married, and Alice Dunbar began teaching in the New York City school system while also serving as recording secretary of the National Association of Colored Women. In 1899, her second book, *The Goodness of St. Rocque and Other Stories,* appeared, and in 1902, after she and Dunbar separated (later to divorce), she began teaching at the Howard High School in Wilmington, Delaware, where she was to be a popular instructor and the head of the English department for eighteen years.

In 1916, Alice Moore Dunbar remarried; her second husband, Robert John Nelson, was the publisher of the *Wilmington Advocate,* a weekly newspaper dedicated to the cause of black rights. Continually energetic, she edited several anthologies in these years—*Masterpieces of Negro Eloquence* (1914) and *The Dunbar Speaker and Entertainer* (1920)—and, besides working on many councils and committees, wrote a regular column for the *Washington Eagle.* In 1920, she risked—and lost—her teaching position because she insisted (despite her school district's rules forbidding employees to engage in political activity) on attending a meeting at which the presidential candidate Warren Harding's racial policies were to be formulated. From 1928 to 1931, she served as executive secretary of the American Interracial Peace Committee, a group sponsored by the American Friends Service Committee, which worked to encourage black support for world peace. Not coincidentally, "I Sit and Sew," one of the comparatively few verses she wrote, expresses Nelson's distinctively female frustration at the "wasted fields" of a world at war, a world she consistently tried to improve. "Mr. Baptiste" captures her sympathy for the African American and Creole characters about whom she often writes. In doing so, it illustrates a commitment to social activism that also motivated and shaped her journalism, her personal diary, and her work for antilynching as well as suffrage and educational campaigns.

Mr. Baptiste

He might have had another name: we never knew. Someone had christened him Mr. Baptiste long ago in the dim past, and it sufficed. No one had ever been known who had the temerity to ask him for another cognomen, for though he was a mild-mannered little man, he had an uncomfortable way of shutting up oyster-wise and looking disagreeable when approached concerning his personal history.

He was small: most Creole men are small when they are old. It is strange, but a fact. It must be that age withers them sooner and more effectually than those of un-Latinized extraction. Mr. Baptiste was, furthermore, very much wrinkled and lame. Like the Son of Man,[1] he had nowhere to lay his head, save when some kindly family made room for him in a garret or a barn. He subsisted by doing odd jobs, whitewashing, cleaning yards, doing errands, and the like.

The little old man was a frequenter of the levee.[2] Never a day passed that his quaint little figure was not seen moving up and down about the ships. Chiefly did he haunt the Texas and Pacific warehouses and the landing-place of the Morgan-line steamships. This seemed like madness, for these spots are almost the busiest on the levee, and the rough seamen and 'longshoremen have least time to be bothered with small weak folks. Still there was method in the madness of Mr. Baptiste. The Morgan steamships, as everyone knows, ply between New Orleans and Central and South American ports, doing the

---
1. Jesus.
2. An embankment that serves as a landing place on a river.

major part of the fruit trade; and many were the baskets of forgotten fruit that Mr. Baptiste took away with him unmolested. Sometimes, you know, bananas and mangoes and oranges and citrons will half spoil, particularly if it has been a bad voyage over the stormy Gulf, and the officers of the ships will give away stacks of fruit, too good to go into the river, too bad to sell to the fruit-dealers.

You could see Mr. Baptiste trudging up the street with his quaint one-sided walk, bearing his dilapidated basket on one shoulder, a nondescript head-cover pulled over his eyes, whistling cheerily. Then he would slip in at the back door of one of his clients with a brisk,—

"Ah, bonjour, madame. Now here ees jus' a lil' bit fruit, some bananas. Perhaps madame would cook some for Mr. Baptiste?"

And madame, who understood and knew his ways, would fry him some of the bananas, and set it before him, a tempting dish, with a bit of madame's bread and meat and coffee thrown in for lagniappe;[3] and Mr. Baptiste would depart, filled and contented, leaving the load of fruit behind as madame's pay. Thus did he eat, and his clients were many, and never too tired or too cross to cook his meals and get their pay in baskets of fruit.

One day he slipped in at Madame Garcia's kitchen door with such a woe-begone air, and slid a small sack of nearly ripe plantains on the table with such a misery-laden sigh, that madame, who was fat and excitable, threw up both hands and cried out:

"Mon Dieu, Mistare Baptiste, fo' w'y you look lak dat? What ees de mattare?"

For answer, Mr. Baptiste shook his head gloomily and sighed again. Madame Garcia moved heavily about the kitchen, putting the plantains in a cool spot and punctuating her footsteps with sundry "Mon Dieux" and "Misères."[4]

"Dose cotton!" ejaculated Mr. Baptiste, at last.

"Ah, mon Dieu!" groaned Madame Garcia, rolling her eyes heavenwards.

"Hit will drive de fruit away!" he continued.

"Misère!" said Madame Garcia.

"Hit will."

"Oui, oui"[5] said Madame Garcia. She had carefully inspected the plantains, and seeing that they were good and wholesome, was inclined to agree with anything Mr. Baptiste said.

He grew excited. "Yaas, dose cotton-yardmans,[6] dose 'longsho'mans, dey go out on one strik'. Dey t'row down dey tool an' say dey work no mo' wid niggers. Les veseaux,[7] dey lay in de river, no work, no cargo, yaas. Den de fruit ship, dey can' mak' lan, de mans, dey t'reaten an' say t'ings. Dey mak' big fight, yaas. Dere no mo' work on de levee, lak dat. Ever'body jus' walk roun' an' say cuss word, yaas!"

"Oh, mon Dieu, mon Dieu!" groaned Madame Garcia, rocking her guinea-blue-clad self to and fro.

Mr. Baptiste picked up his nondescript head-cover and walked out through

---

3. A little something extra, given to a customer.
4. Miseries (French). "Mon Dieux": my Gods (French).
5. Yes, yes (French).
6. Those hired to load cotton.
7. The vessels (French).

the brick-reddened alley, talking excitedly to himself. Madame Garcia called after him to know if he did not want his luncheon, but he shook his head and passed on.

Down on the levee it was even as Mr. Baptiste had said. The 'longshoremen, the cotton-yardmen, and the stevedores had gone out on a strike. The levee lay hot and unsheltered under the glare of a noonday sun. The turgid Mississippi scarce seemed to flow, but gave forth a brazen gleam from its yellow bosom. Great vessels lay against the wharf, silent and unpopulated. Excited groups of men clustered here and there among bales of uncompressed cotton, lying about in disorderly profusion. Cargoes of molasses and sugar gave out a sticky sweet smell, and now and then the fierce rays of the sun would kindle tiny blazes in the cotton and splinter-mixed dust underfoot.

Mr. Baptiste wandered in and out among the groups of men, exchanging a friendly salutation here and there. He looked the picture of woe-begone misery.

"Hello, Mr. Baptiste," cried a big, brawny Irishman, "sure an' you look, as if you was about to be hanged."

"Ah, mon Dieu," said Mr. Baptiste, "dose fruit ship be ruined fo' dees strik'."

"Damn the fruit!" cheerily replied the Irishman, artistically disposing of a mouthful of tobacco juice. "It ain't the fruit we care about, it's the cotton."

"Hear! hear!" cried a dozen lusty comrades.

Mr. Baptiste shook his head and moved sorrowfully away.

"Hey, by howly St. Patrick, here's that little fruit-eater!" called the center of another group of strikers perched on cotton-bales.

"Hello! Where—" began a second; but the leader suddenly held up his hand for silence, and the men listened eagerly.

It might not have been a sound, for the levee lay quiet and the mules on the cotton-drays[8] dozed languidly, their ears pitched at varying acute angles. But the practiced ears of the men heard a familiar sound stealing up over the heated stillness.

"Oh—ho—ho—humph—humph—humph—ho—ho—ho—oh—o—o—humph!"

Then the faint rattle of chains, and the steady thump of a machine pounding.

If ever you go on the levee you'll know that sound, the rhythmic song of the stevedores heaving cotton-bales, and the steady thump, thump, of the machine compressing them within the hold of the ship.

Finnegan, the leader, who had held up his hand for silence, uttered an oath.

"Scabs![9] Men, come on!"

There was no need for a further invitation. The men rose in sullen wrath and went down the levee, the crowd gathering in numbers as it passed along. Mr. Baptiste followed in its wake, now and then sighing a mournful protest which was lost in the roar of the men.

---

8. Carts, usually without sides, used to haul cotton.

9. Those who work while others (in the same jobs) are striking.

"Scabs!" Finnegan had said; and the word was passed along, until it seemed that the half of the second District knew and had risen to investigate.

"Oh—ho—ho—humph—humph—humph—oh—ho—ho—oh—o—o—humph!"

The rhythmic chorus sounded nearer, and the cause manifested itself when the curve of the levee above the French Market was passed. There rose a White Star steamer, insolently settling itself to the water as each consignment of cotton bales was compressed into her hold.

"Niggers!" roared Finnegan wrathily.

"Niggers! niggers! Kill'em, scabs!" chorused the crowd.

With muscles standing out like cables through their blue cotton shirts, and sweat rolling from glossy black skins, the Negro stevedores were at work steadily laboring at the cotton, with the rhythmic song swinging its cadence in the hot air. The roar of the crowd caused the men to look up with momentary apprehension, but at the overseer's reassuring word they bent back to work.

Finnegan was a Titan.[1] With livid face and bursting veins he ran into the street facing the French Market, and uprooted a huge block of paving stone. Staggering under its weight, he rushed back to the ship, and with one mighty effort hurled it into the hold.

The delicate poles of the costly machine tottered in the air, then fell forward with a crash as the whole iron framework in the hold collapsed.

"Damn ye," shouted Finnegan, "now yez can pack yer cotton!"

The crowd's cheers at this changed to howls, as the Negroes, infuriated at their loss, for those costly machines belong to the laborers and not to the ship-owners, turned upon the mob and began to throw brickbats, pieces of iron, chunks of wood, anything that came to hand. It was pandemonium turned loose over a turgid stream, with a malarial sun to heat the passions to fever point.

Mr. Baptiste had taken refuge behind a bread-stall on the outside of the market. He had taken off his cap, and was weakly cheering the Negroes on.

"Bravo!" cheered Mr. Baptiste.

"Will yez look at that damned fruit-eatin' Frinchman!" howled McMahon. "Cheerin' the niggers, are you?" and he let fly a brickbat in the direction of the bread-stall.

"Oh, mon Dieu, mon Dieu!" wailed the bread-woman.

Mr. Baptiste lay very still, with a great ugly gash in his wrinkled brown temple. Fishmen and vegetable marchands[2] gathered around him in a quick, sympathetic mass. The individual, the concrete bit of helpless humanity, had more interest for them than the vast, vague fighting mob beyond.

The noon-hour pealed from the brazen throats of many bells, and the numerous hoarse whistles of the steam-boats called the unheeded luncheon-time to the levee workers. The war waged furiously, and groans of the wounded mingled with curses and roars from the combatants.

"Killed instantly," said the surgeon, carefully lifting Mr. Baptiste into the ambulance.

---

1. A giant. 2. Merchants (French).

Tramp, tramp, tramp, sounded the militia steadily marching down Decatur Street.

"Whist! do yez hear!" shouted Finnegan; and the conflict had ceased ere the yellow river could reflect the sun from the polished bayonets.

You remember, of course, how long the strike lasted, and how many battles were fought and lives lost before the final adjustment of affairs. It was a fearsome war, and many forgot afterwards whose was the first life lost in the struggle,—poor little Mr. Baptiste's, whose body lay at the Morgue unclaimed for days before it was finally dropped unnamed into Potter's Field.[3]

1899

I Sit and Sew

I sit and sew—a useless task it seems,
My hands grown tired, my head weighed down with dreams—
The panoply of war, the martial tread of men,
Grim-faced, stern-eyed, gazing beyond the ken[1]
5 Of lesser souls, whose eyes have not seen Death
Nor learned to hold their lives but as a breath—
But—I must sit and sew.

I sit and sew—my heart aches with desire—
That pageant terrible, that fiercely pouring fire
10 On wasted fields, and writhing grotesque things
Once men. My soul in pity flings
Appealing cries, yearning only to go
There in that holocaust of hell, those fields of woe[2]—
But—I must sit and sew.

The little useless seam, the idle patch;
15 Why dream I here beneath my homely thatch,
When there they lie in sodden mud and rain,
Pitifully calling me, the quick[3] ones and the slain?
You need me, Christ! It is no roseate dream
20 That beckons me—this pretty futile seam,
It stifles me—God, must I sit and sew?

1920

---

3. Public burying place for the poor, unknown, and criminals (from Matthew 27.7).
1. Range of vision.
2. I.e., the trenches of World War I.
3. Living.

ANNA HEMPSTEAD BRANCH
1875–1937

The daughter of a comfortable professional family—her father was a lawyer, her mother a poet and writer of children's books—Anna Hempstead Branch was born in New London, Connecticut. After graduating from Smith College in 1897, she achieved a considerable reputation in the early years of the century with two collections of verse, *The Shoes That Danced* (1905) and *Rose of the Wind* (1910), both of which were significantly influenced by the art of the English Pre-Raphaelites, especially by the poetry of Christina Rossetti. Later her reputation was enhanced by *Sonnets from a Lock Box* (1929), a volume that is generally considered her finest book. Throughout her career, she was both devout and philosophical, pursuing studies of mysticism and numerology as well as more orthodox Christian theology, so that at least one critic felt that some of her work was reminiscent not only of Rossetti's devotional poetry but also of the meditative verse produced by the seventeenth-century Anglican lyricist George Herbert.

Putting her religious principles into practice, Branch devoted much energy to social service at Christadora House, a settlement house on New York's Lower East Side. In the belief that poetry was a sacred and redemptive activity that would foster human fellowship, she organized a series of readings at the house as well as at a successful youth club; then, along with Edwin Arlington Robinson, William Rose Benét, and other notable writers, she become a founding member of the Poets' Guild, an organization whose classes, readings, and dramatic performances lent what one scholar describes as a special "intellectual aura" to the house. Yet though a number of Branch's poems brood on the "stolid, homely, visible things" that manifest divinity, pieces such as the poems in *Sonnets from a Lock Box,* excerpted here, reveal a deeply rebellious and unorthodox strain in her thinking.

From Sonnets from a Lock Box

XIV

What witchlike spell weaves here its deep design,
And sells its pattern to the ignorant buyer.
Oh lacelike cruelty with stitches fine—
Which stings the flesh with its sharp mesh of fire.
5 God of the Thief and Patron of the Liar,[1]
I think that it is best not to inquire
Upon whose wheel was spun this mortal thread;
What dyed this curious robe so rich a red;
With shivering hues it is embroidered.
10 With changing colors like unsteady eyes.
I think the filigree is Medea's wreath.[2]
Oh, treacherous splendor! In this lustrous prize
Of gold and silver weaving, madness lies.
Who purchases this garment—Sire—buys death.

---

1. The Greek god Hermes, messenger of Zeus and herald of the other gods.
2. Medea was a sorceress who helped Jason, a Greek hero, win the Golden Fleece. She became his wife and bore him two sons, but when they returned to Greece, Jason took a new wife, Creusa. In revenge, Medea sent Creusa a splendid "wreath" or tiara and wedding robes; when Creusa put them on, they clung to her flesh and killed her.

XXV

Into the void behold my shuddering flight,
Plunging straight forward through unhuman space,
My wild hair backward blown and my white face
Set like a wedge of ice. My chattering teeth
Cut like sharp knives my swiftly freezing breath.
Perched upon straightness I seek a wilder zone.
My Flying Self—on this black steed alone—
Drives out to God or else to utter death.
Beware straight lines which do subdue man's pride!
'Tis on a broomstick that great witches ride.
Wild, dangerous and holy are the runes
Which shift the whirling atoms with their tunes.
Oh like a witch accursed shall she be burned
Who having flown on straightness has returned.

XXXI

I say that words are men and when we spell
In alphabets we deal with living things;
With feet and thighs and breasts, fierce heads, strong wings;
Material Powers, great Bridals, Heaven and Hell.
There is a menace in the tales we tell.
From out the throne from which all language springs
Voices proceed and fires and thunderings.
Oh when we speak, Great God, let us speak well.
Beware of shapes, beware of letterings,
For in them lies such magic as alters dream,
Shakes cities down and moves the inward scheme.
Beware the magic of the coin that sings.
These coins are graved with supernatural powers
And magic wills that are more strong than ours.

1929

ZITKALA ŠA (GERTRUDE SIMMONS BONNIN)
1876–1938

Born in South Dakota and given the name of her mother's second husband, Gertrude Simmons took the tribal name Zitkala Ša (Red Bird). Her mother was a Yankton-Nakota Sioux, her father a white man who deserted the family. She lived on the reservation until her eighth year, when she was sent to a Quaker missionary school in Wabash, Indiana. Although, after returning home, she felt dislocated by her experience, she continued to seek educational opportunities elsewhere, first traveling back to the institute; then enrolling for two years at Earlham College in Richmond, Indiana; next teaching at the Indian school at Carlisle, Pennsylvania and finally studying violin at the Boston Conservatory of Music. Throughout this period, she felt divided between the Native American and Euro-American worlds. At the turn of the century, she began publishing her autobiographical essays and stories in the *Atlantic Monthly* and *Harper's Monthly*. Her *Old Indian Legends* (1902) attempted to "transplant the native spirit . . . into the English language."

After marriage to Raymond Talesfase Bonnin, another Yankton Sioux, in 1902 the author moved to Utah, where she raised their son, continued to teach, and become involved in Native American rights activism. In 1916 Zitkala Ša moved with her family to Washington, D.C., eventually becoming president of the National Council of American Indians. Beside lecturing on Indian rights, she edited the *American Indian Magazine*; published another collection, *American Indian Stories* (1921); and collaborated on the composition of an opera, *The Sun Dance* (1913). A pioneering individualist, she often explained, "I will say just what I think. I fear no man—sometimes I think I do not even fear God."

The Trial Path

It was an autumn night on the plain. The smoke-lapels of the cone-shaped tepee flapped gently in the breeze. From the low night sky, with its myriad fire points, a large bright star peeped in at the smoke-hole of the wigwam between its fluttering lapels, down upon two Dakotas talking in the dark. The mellow stream from the star above, a maid of twenty summers, on a bed of sweetgrass, drank in with her wakeful eyes. On the opposite side of the tepee, beyond the center fireplace, the grandmother spread her rug. Though once she had lain down, the telling of a story has aroused her to a sitting posture.

Her eyes are tight closed. With a thin palm she strokes her wind-shorn hair.

"Yes, my grandchild, the legend says the large bright stars are wise old warriors, and the small dim ones are handsome young braves," she reiterates, in a high, tremulous voice.

"Then this one peeping in at the smoke-hole yonder is my dear old grandfather," muses the young woman, in long-drawn-out words.

Her soft rich voice floats through the darkness within the tepee, over the cold ashes heaped on the center fire, and passes into the ear of the toothless old woman, who sits dumb in silent reverie. Thence it flies on swifter wing over many winter snows, till at last it cleaves the warm light atmosphere of her grandfather's youth. From there her grandmother made answer:

"Listen! I am young again. It is the day of your grandfather's death. The elder one, I mean, for there were two of them. They were like twins, though they were not brothers. They were friends, inseparable! All things, good and bad, they shared together, save one, which made them mad. In that heated frenzy the younger man slew his most intimate friend. He killed his elder brother, for long had their affection made them kin."

The voice of the old woman broke. Swaying her stooped shoulders to and fro as she sat upon her feet, she muttered vain exclamations beneath her breath. Her eyes, closed tight against the night, beheld behind them the light of bygone days. They saw again a rolling black cloud spread itself over the land. Her ear heard the deep rumbling of a tempest in the west. She bent low a cowering head, while angry thunder-birds shrieked across the sky.

"Heyä! heyä!" (No! no!) groaned the toothless grandmother at the fury she had awakened. But the glorious peace afterward, when yellow sunshine made the people glad, now lured her memory onward through the storm.

"How fast, how loud my heart beats as I listen to the messenger's horrible tale!" she ejaculates. "From the fresh grave of the murdered man he hurried to our wigwam. Deliberately crossing his bare shins, he sat down unbidden beside my father, smoking a long-stemmed pipe. He had scarce caught his breath when, panting, he began:

" 'He was an only son, and a much-adored brother.'

"With wild, suspecting eyes he glanced at me as if I were in league with the man-killer, my lover. My father, exhaling sweet-scented smoke, assented—'How.' Then interrupting the 'Eya' on the lips of the round-eyed talebearer, he asked, 'My friend, will you smoke?' He took the pipe by its red-stone bowl, and pointed the long slender stem toward the man. 'Yes, yes, my friend,' replied he, and reached out a long brown arm.

"For many heart-throbs he puffed out the blue smoke, which hung like a cloud between us. But even through the smoke-mist I saw his sharp black eyes glittering toward me. I longed to ask what doom awaited the young murderer, but dared not open my lips, lest I burst forth into screams instead. My father plied the question. Returning the pipe, the man replied: 'Oh, the chieftain and his chosen men have had counsel together. They have agreed it is not safe to allow a man-killer loose in our midst. He who kills one of our tribe is an enemy, and must suffer the fate of a foe.'

"My temples throbbed like a pair of hearts!

"While I listened, a crier passed by my father's tepee. Mounted, and swaying with his pony's steps, he proclaimed in a loud voice these words (hark! I hear them now!): 'Ho-po! Give ear, all you people. A terrible deed is done. Two friends—ay, brothers in heart—have quarreled together. Now one lies buried on the hill, while the other sits, a dreaded man-killer, within his dwelling. Says our chieftain: "He who kills one of our tribe commits the offense of an enemy. As such he must be tried. Let the father of the dead man choose the mode of torture or taking of life. He has suffered livid pain, and he alone can judge how great the punishment must be to avenge his wrong." It is done.

" 'Come, every one, to witness the judgment of a father upon him who was once his son's best friend. A wild pony is now lassoed. The man-killer must mount and ride the ranting beast. Stand you all in two parallel lines from the center tepee of the bereaved family to the wigwam opposite in the great outer ring. Between you, in the wide space, is the given trailway. From the outer circle the rider must mount and ride his pony toward the center tepee. If, having gone the entire distance, the man-killer gains the center tepee still sitting on the pony's back, his life is spared and pardon given. But should he fall, then he himself has chosen death.'

"The crier's words now cease. A lull holds the village breathless. Then hurrying feet tear along, swish, swish, through the tall grass. Sobbing women hasten toward the trailway. The muffled groan of the round camp-ground is unbearable. With my face hid in the folds of my blanket, I run with the crowd toward the open place in the outer circle of our village. In a moment the two long files of solemn-faced people mark the path of the public trial. Ah! I see strong men trying to lead the lassoed pony, pitching and rearing, with white foam flying from his mouth. I choke with pain as I recognize my handsome lover desolately alone, striding with set face toward the lassoed pony. 'Do not fall! Choose life and me!' I cry in my breast, but over my lips I hold my thick blanket.

"In an instant he has leaped astride the frightened beast, and the men have let go their hold. Like an arrow sprung from a strong bow, the pony, with extended nostrils, plunges halfway to the center tepee. With all his might the rider draws the strong reins in. The pony halts with wooden legs. The rider is thrown forward by force, but does not fall. Now the maddened creature pitches, with flying heels. The line of men and women sways outward. Now it is back in place, safe from the kicking, snorting thing.

"The pony is fierce, with its large black eyes bulging out of their sockets. With humped back and nose to the ground, it leaps into the air. I shut my eyes. I can not see him fall.

"A loud shout goes up from the hoarse throats of men and women. I look. So! The wild horse is conquered. My lover dismounts at the doorway of the center wigwam. The pony, wet with sweat and shaking with exhaustion, stands like a guilty dog at his master's side. Here at the entranceway of the tepee sit the bereaved father, mother, and sister. The old warrior father rises. Stepping forward two long strides, he grasps the hand of the murderer of his only son. Holding it so the people can see, he cries, with compassionate voice, 'My son!' A murmur of surprise sweeps like a puff of sudden wind along the lines.

"The mother, with swollen eyes, with her hair cut square with her shoulders, now rises. Hurrying to the young man, she takes his right hand. 'My son!' she greets him. But on the second word her voice shook, and she turned away in sobs.

"The young people rivet their eyes upon the young woman. She does not stir. With bowed head, she sits motionless. The old warrior speaks to her. 'Shake hands with the young brave, my little daughter. He was your brother's friend for many years. Now he must be both friend and brother to you.'

"Hereupon the girl rises. Slowly reaching out her slender hand, she cries, with twitching lips, 'My brother!' The trial ends."

"Grandmother!" exploded the girl on the bed of sweet-grass. "Is this true?"

"Tosh!" answered the grandmother, with a warmth in her voice. "It is all true. During the fifteen winters of our wedded life many ponies passed from our hands, but this little winner, Ohiyesa, was a constant member of our family. At length, on that sad day your grandfather died, Ohiyesa was killed at the grave."

Though the various groups of stars which move across the sky, marking the passing of time, told how the night was in its zenith, the old Dakota woman ventured an explanation of the burial ceremony.

"My grandchild, I have scarce ever breathed the sacred knowledge in my heart. Tonight I must tell you one of them. Surely you are old enough to understand.

"Our wise medicine-man said I did well to hasten Ohiyesa after his master. Perchance on the journey along the ghostpath your grandfather will weary, and in his heart wish for his pony. The creature, already bound on the spirit-trail, will be drawn by that subtle wish. Together master and beast will enter the next camp-ground."

The woman ceased her talking. But only the deep breathing of the girl broke the quiet, for now the night wind had lulled itself to sleep.

"Hinnu! hinnu! Asleep! I have been talking in the dark, unheard. I did wish the girl would plant in her heart this sacred tale," muttered she, in a querulous voice.

Nestling into her bed of sweet scented grass, she dozed away into another dream. Still the guardian star in the night sky beamed compassionately down upon the little tepee on the plain.

1901, 1921

SUSAN GLASPELL
1876–1948

Cofounder in 1915 of the Provincetown Players, Susan Glaspell was also a noted dramatist and prolific fiction writer. Her full-length play *The Verge* (1921), which experimented with the psychological portrayal of character, focused on the feminism of the New Woman, while her Pulitzer Prize–winning drama *Alison's House* (1930) presented a fictionalized portrait of a woman artist modeled on Emily Dickinson. She published ten novels and more than forty short stories. "A Jury of Her Peers"—a short story version of her one-act play *Trifles* (1916)—was included in E. J. O'Brien's edition of *The Best Short Stories of 1917*.

The daughter of Elmer S. Glaspell, a feed dealer, and Alice (Keating) Glaspell, an emigrant from Dublin, Susan Glaspell was born and raised in Davenport, Iowa. After graduating from Drake University in 1899, she worked on the staff of the *Des Moines Daily News* until she could support herself by writing fiction. Her stories appeared in such magazines as *Harper's* and the *Ladies' Home Journal,* and her early novels were popular examples of regionalism. In 1911, Glaspell moved to Greenwich Village in New York City with a friend, and two years later she married George Cram Cook, a Harvard graduate from her hometown who was soon to become known as a charismatic director. They spent their winters in the Village and their summers in Provincetown, a small town on Cape Cod. Together they organized a group of Provincetown actors who performed one-act plays in a wharf theater (and later in Greenwich Village). Eugene O'Neill, Edna St. Vincent Millay, John Reed, Michael Gold, and Susan Glaspell were to become the leading playwrights of that group and in the Playwrights' Theater Glaspell also helped found in the Village. Determinedly anticommercial and avant-garde, Glaspell's and Cook's productions fostered the first experimental drama in America. Indeed, when their theaters grew commercially successful, Cook became disillusioned, and he and his wife lived in Greece from 1922 until his death in 1924. In 1925 she married the novelist and playwright Norman Matson, whom she was to divorce in 1932. The rest of her life was spent in Provincetown, where she wrote novels that continued to explore the major subject of *Trifles,* the confining environments that frustrate the full development of human potential as well as the impact of gender on the complex process by which we read and interpret not only literary but also social texts.

Trifles

Characters

GEORGE HENDERSON, *County Attorney*　　MRS. PETERS
HENRY PETERS, *Sheriff*　　MRS. HALE
LEWIS HALE, *A Neighboring Farmer*

SCENE.　*The kitchen in the now abandoned farmhouse of John Wright, a gloomy kitchen, and left without having been put in order—unwashed pans under the sink, a loaf of bread outside the breadbox, a dish towel on the table—other signs of incompleted work. At the rear the outer door opens and the* SHERIFF *comes in followed by the* COUNTY ATTORNEY *and* HALE. *The* SHERIFF *and* HALE *are men in middle life, the* COUNTY ATTORNEY *is a young man; all are much bundled up and go at once to the stove. They are followed by two women—the* SHERIFF'S WIFE *first; she is a slight wiry woman, a thin nervous face.* MRS. HALE *is larger and would ordinarily be called more comfortable looking, but she is disturbed now and looks fearfully about as she enters. The women have come in slowly, and stand close together near the door.*

COUNTY ATTORNEY [*Rubbing his hands.*]　This feels good. Come up to the fire, ladies.
MRS. PETERS [*After taking a step forward.*]　I'm not—cold.
SHERIFF [*Unbuttoning his overcoat and stepping away from the stove as if to mark the beginning of official business.*]　Now, Mr. Hale, before we move things about, you explain to Mr. Henderson just what you saw when you came here yesterday morning.
COUNTY ATTORNEY　By the way, has anything been moved? Are things just as you left them yesterday?
SHERIFF [*Looking about.*]　It's just the same. When it dropped below zero last night I thought I'd better send Frank out this morning to make a fire for us—no use getting pneumonia with a big case on, but I told him not to touch anything except the stove—and you know Frank.
COUNTY ATTORNEY　Somebody should have been left here yesterday.
SHERIFF　Oh—yesterday. When I had to send Frank to Morris Center for that man who went crazy—I want you to know I had my hands full yesterday, I knew you could get back from Omaha by today and as long as I went over everything here myself—
COUNTY ATTORNEY　Well, Mr. Hale, tell just what happened when you came here yesterday morning.
HALE　Harry and I had started to town with a load of potatoes. We came along the road from my place and as I got here I said, "I'm going to see if I can't get John Wright to go in with me on a party telephone."[1] I spoke to Wright about it once before and he put me off, saying folks talked too much anyway, and all he asked was peace and quiet—I guess you know about how much he talked himself; but I thought maybe if I went to the house and talked about it before his wife, though I said to Harry that I didn't know as what his wife wanted made much difference to John—

---

1. I.e., a single telephone line shared by two or four households.

COUNTY ATTORNEY   Let's talk about that later, Mr. Hale. I do want to talk about that, but tell now just what happened when you got to the house.
HALE   I didn't hear or see anything; I knocked at the door, and still it was all quiet inside. I knew they must be up, it was past eight o'clock. So I knocked again, and I thought I heard somebody say, "Come in." I wasn't sure, I'm not sure yet, but I opened the door—this door [*Indicating the door by which the two women are still standing*] and there in that rocker—[*Pointing to it.*] sat Mrs. Wright.
   [*They all look at the rocker.*]
COUNTY ATTORNEY   What—was she doing?
HALE   She was rockin' back and forth. She had her apron in her hand and was kind of—pleating it.
COUNTY ATTORNEY   And how did she—look?
HALE   Well, she looked queer.
COUNTY ATTORNEY   How do you mean—queer?
HALE   Well, as if she didn't know what she was going to do next. And kind of done up.
COUNTY ATTORNEY   How did she seem to feel about your coming?
HALE   Why, I don't think she minded—one way or other. She didn't pay much attention. I said, "How do, Mrs. Wright, it's cold, ain't it?" And she said, "Is it?"—and went on kind of pleating at her apron. Well, I was surprised; she didn't ask me to come up to the stove, or to set down, but just sat there, not even looking at me, so I said, "I want to see John." And then she—laughed. I guess you would call it a laugh. I thought of Harry and the team outside, so I said a little sharp: "Can't I see John?" "No," she says, kind o' dull like. "Ain't he home?" says I. "Yes," says she, "he's home." "Then why can't I see him?" I asked her, out of patience. " 'Cause he's dead," says she. *"Dead?"* says I. She just nodded her head, not getting a bit excited, but rockin' back and forth. "Why—where is he?" says I, not knowing what to say. She just pointed upstairs—like that [*Himself pointing to the room above*]. I got up, with the idea of going up there. I walked from there to here—then I says, "Why, what did he die of?" "He died of a rope round his neck," says she, and just went on pleatin' at her apron. Well, I went out and called Harry. I thought I might—need help. We went upstairs and there he was lyin'—
COUNTY ATTORNEY   I think I'd rather have you go into that upstairs, where you can point it all out. Just go on now with the rest of the story.
HALE   Well, my first thought was to get that rope off. It looked . . . [*Stops, his face twitches.*] . . . but Harry, he went up to him, and he said, "No, he's dead all right, and we'd better not touch anything." So we went back down stairs. She was still sitting that same way. "Has anybody been notified?" I asked. "No," says she, unconcerned. "Who did this, Mrs. Wright?" said Harry. He said it businesslike—and she stopped pleatin' of her apron. "I don't know," she says. "You don't *know*?" says Harry. "No," says she. "Weren't you sleepin' in the bed with him?" says Harry. "Yes," says she, "but I was on the inside." "Somebody slipped a rope round his neck and strangled him and you didn't wake up?" says Harry. "I didn't wake up," she said after him. We must 'a looked as if we didn't see how that could be, for after a minute she said, "I sleep sound." Harry was going to ask her more questions but I said maybe we ought to let her tell

her story first to the coroner, or the sheriff, so Harry went fast as he could to Rivers' place, where there's a telephone.

COUNTY ATTORNEY And what did Mrs. Wright do when she knew that you had gone for the coroner?

HALE She moved from that chair to this one over here [*Pointing to a small chair in the corner.*] and just sat there with her hands held together and looking down. I got a feeling that I ought to make some conversation, so I said I had come in to see if John wanted to put in a telephone, and at that she started to laugh, and then she stopped and looked at me— scared. [*The* COUNTY ATTORNEY, *who has had his notebook out, makes a note.*] I dunno, maybe it wasn't scared. I wouldn't like to say it was. Soon Harry got back, and then Dr. Lloyd came, and you, Mr. Peters, and so I guess that's all I know that you don't.

COUNTY ATTORNEY [*Looking around.*] I guess we'll go upstairs first—and then out to the barn and around there. [*To the* SHERIFF.] You're convinced that there was nothing important here—nothing that would point to any motive.

SHERIFF Nothing here but kitchen things.

[*The* COUNTY ATTORNEY, *after again looking around the kitchen, opens the door of a cupboard closet. He gets up on a chair and looks on a shelf. Pulls his hand away, sticky.*]

COUNTY ATTORNEY Here's a nice mess.

[*The women draw nearer.*]

MRS. PETERS [*To the other woman.*] Oh, her fruit; it did freeze. [*To the* COUNTY ATTORNEY.] She worried about that when it turned so cold. She said the fire'd go out and her jars would break.

SHERIFF Well, can you beat the women! Held for murder and worryin' about her preserves.

COUNTY ATTORNEY I guess before we're through she may have something more serious than preserves to worry about.

HALE Well, women are used to worrying over trifles.

[*The two women move a little closer together.*]

COUNTY ATTORNEY [*With the gallantry of a young politician.*] And yet, for all their worries, what would we do without the ladies? [*The women do not unbend. He goes to the sink, takes a dipperful of water from the pail and pouring it into a basin, washes his hands. Starts to wipe them on the roller towel, turns it for a cleaner place.*] Dirty towels! [*Kicks his foot against the pans under the sink.*] Not much of a housekeeper, would you say, ladies?

MRS. HALE [*Stiffly.*] There's a great deal of work to be done on a farm.

COUNTY ATTORNEY To be sure. And yet [*With a little bow to her.*] I know there are some Dickson county farmhouses which do not have such roller towels.

[*He gives it a pull to expose its full length again.*]

MRS. HALE Those towels get dirty awful quick. Men's hands aren't always as clean as they might be.

COUNTY ATTORNEY Ah, loyal to your sex, I see. But you and Mrs. Wright were neighbors. I suppose you were friends, too.

MRS. HALE [*Shaking her head.*] I've not seen much of her of late years. I've not been in this house—it's more than a year.

COUNTY ATTORNEY   And why was that? You didn't like her?
MRS. HALE   I liked her all well enough. Farmers' wives have their hands full, Mr. Henderson. And then—
COUNTY ATTORNEY   Yes—?
MRS. HALE [*Looking about.*]   It never seemed a very cheerful place.
COUNTY ATTORNEY   No—it's not cheerful. I shouldn't say she had the homemaking instinct.
MRS. HALE   Well, I don't know as Wright had, either.
COUNTY ATTORNEY   You mean that they didn't get on very well?
MRS. HALE   No, I don't mean anything. But I don't think a place'd be any cheerfuller for John Wright's being in it.
COUNTY ATTORNEY   I'd like to talk more of that a little later. I want to get the lay of things upstairs now.
   [*He goes to the left, where three steps lead to a stair door.*]
SHERIFF   I suppose anything Mrs. Peter does'll be all right. She was to take in some clothes for her, you know, and a few little things. We left in such a hurry yesterday.
COUNTY ATTORNEY   Yes, but I would like to see what you take, Mrs. Peters, and keep an eye out for anything that might be of use to us.
MRS. PETERS   Yes, Mr. Henderson.
   [*The women listen to the men's steps on the stairs, then look about the kitchen.*]
MRS. HALE   I'd hate to have men coming into my kitchen, snooping around and criticizing.
   [*She arranges the pans under sink which the* COUNTY ATTORNEY *had shoved out of place.*]
MRS. PETERS   Of course it's no more than their duty.
MRS. HALE   Duty's all right, but I guess that deputy sheriff that came out to make the fire might have got a little of this on. [*Gives the roller towel a pull.*] Wish I'd thought of that sooner. Seems mean to talk about her for not having things slicked up when she had to come away in such a hurry.
MRS. PETERS [*Who has gone to a small table in the left rear corner of the room, and lifted one end of a towel that covers a pan.*]   She had bread set.
   [*Stands still.*]
MRS. HALE [*Eyes fixed on a loaf of bread beside the breadbox, which is on a low shelf at the other side of the room. Moves slowly toward it.*]   She was going to put this in there. [*Picks up loaf, then abruptly drops it. In a manner of returning to familiar things.*] It's a shame about her fruit. I wonder if it's all gone. [*Gets up on the chair and looks.*] I think there's some here that's all right, Mrs. Peters. Yes—here; [*Holding it toward the window.*] this is cherries, too. [*Looking again.*] I declare I believe that's the only one. [*Gets down, bottle in her hand. Goes to the sink and wipes it off on the outside.*] She'll feel awful bad after all her hard work in the hot weather. I remember the afternoon I put up my cherries last summer.
   [*She puts the bottle on the big kitchen table, center of the room. With a sigh, is about to sit down in the rocking-chair. Before she is seated realizes what chair it is; with a slow look at it, steps back. The chair which she has touched rocks back and forth.*]

MRS. PETERS   Well, I must get those things from the front room closet. [*She goes to the door at the right, but after looking into the other room, steps back.*] You coming with me, Mrs. Hale? You could help me carry them.

    [*They go in the other room; reappear,* MRS. PETERS *carrying a dress and skirt,* MRS. HALE *following with a pair of shoes.*]

MRS. PETERS   My, it's cold in there.

    [*She puts the clothes on the big table, and hurries to the stove.*]

MRS. HALE [*Examining her skirt.*]   Wright was close. I think maybe that's why she kept so much to herself. She didn't even belong to the Ladies Aid. I suppose she felt she couldn't do her part, and then you don't enjoy things when you feel shabby. She used to wear pretty clothes and be lively, when she was Minnie Foster, one of the town girls singing in the choir. But that—oh, that was thirty years ago. This all you was to take in?

MRS. PETERS   She said she wanted an apron. Funny thing to want, for there isn't much to get you dirty in jail, goodness knows. But I suppose just to make her feel more natural. She said they was in the top drawer in this cupboard. Yes, here. And then her little shawl that always hung behind the door. [*Opens stair door and looks.*] Yes, here it is.

    [*Quickly shuts door leading upstairs.*]

MRS. HALE [*Abruptly moving toward her.*]   Mrs. Peters?

MRS. PETERS   Yes, Mrs. Hale?

MRS. HALE   Do you think she did it?

MRS. PETERS [*In a frightened voice.*]   Oh, I don't know.

MRS. HALE   Well, I don't think she did. Asking for an apron and her little shawl. Worrying about her fruit.

MRS. PETERS [*Starts to speak, glances up, where footsteps are heard in the room above. In a low voice.*]   Mr. Peters says it looks bad for her. Mr. Henderson is awful sarcastic in a speech and he'll make fun of her sayin' she didn't wake up.

MRS. HALE   Well, I guess John Wright didn't wake when they was slipping that rope under his neck.

MRS. PETERS   No, it's strange. It must have been done awful crafty and still. They say it was such a—funny way to kill a man, rigging it all up like that.

MRS. HALE   That's just what Mr. Hale said. There was a gun in the house. He says that's what he can't understand.

MRS. PETERS   Mr. Henderson said coming out that what was needed for the case was a motive; something to show anger, or—sudden feeling.

MRS. HALE [*Who is standing by the table.*]   Well, I don't see any signs of anger around here. [*She puts her hand on the dish towel which lies on the table, stands looking down at table, one half of which is clean, the other half messy.*] It's wiped to here. [*Makes a move as if to finish work, then turns and looks at loaf of bread outside the breadbox. Drops towel. In that voice of coming back to familiar things.*] Wonder how they are finding things upstairs. I hope she had it a little more red-up[2] up there. You know, it seems kind of sneaking. Locking her up in town and then coming out here and trying to get her own house to turn against her!

---

2. Tidied up.

MRS. PETERS   But Mrs. Hale, the law is the law.
MRS. HALE   I s'pose 'tis. [*Unbuttoning her coat.*] Better loosen up your things, Mrs. Peters. You won't feel them when you go out.
   [MRS. PETERS *takes off her fur tippet, goes to hang it on hook at back of room, stands looking at the under part of the small corner table.*]
MRS. PETERS   She was piecing a quilt.
   [*She brings the large sewing basket and they look at the bright pieces.*]
MRS. HALE   It's log cabin pattern. Pretty, isn't it? I wonder if she was goin' to quilt it or just knot it?
   [*Footsteps have been heard coming down the stairs. The* SHERIFF *enters followed by* HALE *and the* COUNTY ATTORNEY.]
SHERIFF   They wonder if she was going to quilt it or just knot it!
   [*The men laugh; the women look abashed.*]
COUNTY ATTORNEY [*Rubbing his hands over the stove.*]   Frank's fire didn't do much up there, did it? Well, let's go out to the barn and get that cleared up.
   [*The men go outside.*]
MRS. HALE [*Resentfully.*]   I don't know as there's anything so strange, our takin' up our time with little things while we're waiting for them to get the evidence. [*She sits down at the big table smoothing out a block with decision.*] I don't see as it's anything to laugh about.
MRS. PETERS [*Apologetically.*]   Of course they've got awful important things on their minds.
   [*Pulls up a chair and joins* MRS. HALE *at the table.*]
MRS. HALE [*Examining another block.*]   Mrs. Peters, look at this one. Here, this is the one she was working on, and look at the sewing! All the rest of it has been so nice and even. And look at this! It's all over the place! Why, it looks as if she didn't know what she was about!
   [*After she has said this they look at each other, then start to glance back at the door. After an instant* MRS. HALE *has pulled at a knot and ripped the sewing.*]
MRS. PETERS   Oh, what are you doing, Mrs. Hale?
MRS. HALE [*Mildly.*]   Just pulling out a stitch or two that's not sewed very good. [*Threading a needle.*] Bad sewing always made me fidgety.
MRS. PETERS [*Nervously.*]   I don't think we ought to touch things.
MRS. HALE   I'll just finish up this end. [*Suddenly stopping and leaning forward.*] Mrs. Peters?
MRS. PETERS   Yes, Mrs. Hale?
MRS. HALE   What do you suppose she was so nervous about?
MRS. PETERS   Oh—I don't know. I don't know as she was nervous. I sometimes sew awful queer when I'm just tired. [MRS. HALE *starts to say something, looks at* MRS. PETERS, *then goes on sewing.*] Well, I must get these things wrapped up. They may be through sooner than we think. [*Putting apron and other things together.*] I wonder where I can find a piece of paper, and string.
MRS. HALE   In that cupboard, maybe.
MRS. PETERS [*Looking in cupboard.*]   Why, here's a birdcage. [*Holds it up.*] Did she have a bird, Mrs. Hale?
MRS. HALE   Why, I don't know whether she did or not—I've not been here for so long. There was a man around last year selling canaries cheap, but

I don't know as she took one; maybe she did. She used to sing real pretty herself.

MRS. PETERS [*Glancing around.*]   Seems funny to think of a bird here. But she must have had one, or why would she have a cage? I wonder what happened to it.

MRS. HALE   I s'pose maybe the cat got it.

MRS. PETERS   No, she didn't have a cat. She's got that feeling some people have about cats—being afraid of them. My cat got in her room and she was real upset and asked me to take it out.

MRS. HALE   My sister Bessie was like that. Queer, ain't it?

MRS. PETERS [*Examining the cage.*]   Why, look at this door. It's broke. One hinge is pulled apart.

MRS. HALE [*Looking too.*]   Looks as if someone must have been rough with it.

MRS. PETERS   Why, yes.

[*She brings the cage forward and puts it on the table.*]

MRS. HALE   I wish if they're going to find any evidence they'd be about it. I don't like this place.

MRS. PETERS   But I'm awful glad you came with me, Mrs. Hale. It would be lonesome for me sitting here alone.

MRS. HALE   It would, wouldn't it? [*Dropping her sewing.*] But I tell you what I do wish, Mrs. Peters. I wish I had come over sometimes when she was here. I—[*Looking around the room.*]—wish I had.

MRS. PETERS   But of course you were awful busy, Mrs. Hale—your house and your children.

MRS. HALE   I could've come. I stayed away because it weren't cheerful—and that's why I ought to have come. I—I've never liked this place. Maybe because it's down in a hollow and you don't see the road. I dunno what it is but it's a lonesome place and always was. I wish I had come over to see Minnie Foster sometimes. I can see now—

[*Shakes her head.*]

MRS. PETERS   Well, you mustn't reproach yourself, Mrs. Hale. Somehow we just don't see how it is with other folks until—something comes up.

MRS. HALE   Not having children makes less work—but it makes a quiet house, and Wright out to work all day, and no company when he did come in. Did you know John Wright, Mrs. Peters?

MRS. PETERS   Not to know him; I've seen him in town. They say he was a good man.

MRS. HALE   Yes—good; he didn't drink, and kept his word as well as most, I guess, and paid his debts. But he was a hard man, Mrs. Peters. Just to pass the time of day with him—[*Shivers.*] Like a raw wind that gets to the bone. [*Pauses, her eye falling on the cage.*] I should think she would 'a wanted a bird. But what do you suppose went with it?

MRS. PETERS   I don't know, unless it got sick and died.

[*She reaches over and swings the broken door, swings it again. Both women watch it.*]

MRS. HALE   You weren't raised round here, were you? [MRS. PETERS *shakes her head.*] You didn't know—her?

MRS. PETERS   Not till they brought her yesterday.

MRS. HALE   She—come to think of it, she was kind of like a bird herself—real sweet and pretty, but kind of timid and—fluttery. How—she—did—change. [*Silence; then as if struck by a happy thought and relieved to get back to every day things.*] Tell you what, Mrs. Peters, why don't you take the quilt in with you? It might take up her mind.

MRS. PETERS   Why, I think that's a real nice idea, Mrs. Hale. There couldn't possibly be any objection to it, could there? Now, just what would I take? I wonder if her patches are in here—and her things.

[*They look in the sewing basket.*]

MRS. HALE   Here's some red. I expect this has got sewing things in it. [*Brings out a fancy box.*] What a pretty box. Looks like something somebody would give you. Maybe her scissors are in here. [*Opens box. Suddenly puts her hand to her nose.*] Why—[MRS. PETERS *bends nearer, then turns her face away.*] There's something wrapped up in this piece of silk.

MRS. PETERS   Why, this isn't her scissors.

MRS. HALE [*Lifting the silk.*]   Oh, Mrs. Peters—it's—

[MRS. PETERS *bends closer.*]

MRS. PETERS   It's the bird.

MRS. HALE [*Jumping up.*]   But, Mrs. Peters—look at it! Its neck! Look at its neck! It's all—other side to.

MRS. PETERS   Somebody—wrung—its—neck.

[*Their eyes meet. A look of growing comprehension, of horror. Steps are heard outside.* MRS. HALE *slips box under quilt pieces, and sinks into her chair. Enter* SHERIFF *and* COUNTY ATTORNEY. MRS. PETERS *rises.*]

COUNTY ATTORNEY [*As one turning from serious things to little pleasantries.*]   Well, ladies, have you decided whether she was going to quilt it or knot it?

MRS. PETERS   We think she was going to—knot it.

COUNTY ATTORNEY   Well, that's interesting, I'm sure. [*Seeing the birdcage.*] Has the bird flown?

MRS. HALE [*Putting more quilt pieces over the box.*]   We think the—cat got it.

COUNTY ATTORNEY [*Preoccupied.*]   Is there a cat?

[MRS. HALE *glances in a quick covert way at* MRS. PETERS.]

MRS. PETERS   Well, not now. They're superstitious, you know. They leave.

COUNTY ATTORNEY [*To* SHERIFF PETERS, *continuing an interrupted conversation.*]   No sign at all of anyone having come from the outside. Their own rope. Now let's go up again and go over it piece by piece. [*They start upstairs.*] It would have to have been someone who knew just the—

[MRS. PETERS *sits down. The two women sit there not looking at one another, but as if peering into something and at the same time holding back. When they talk now it is in the manner of feeling their way over strange ground, as if afraid of what they are saying, but as if they can not help saying it.*]

MRS. HALE   She liked the bird. She was going to bury it in that pretty box.

MRS. PETERS [*In a whisper.*]   When I was a girl—my kitten—there was a boy took a hatchet, and before my eyes—and before I could get there— [*Covers her face an instant.*] If they hadn't held me back I would have—

[*Catches herself, looks upstairs where steps are heard, falters weakly.*]—hurt him.

MRS. HALE [*With a slow look around her.*]   I wonder how it would seem never to have had any children around. [*Pause.*] No, Wright wouldn't like the bird—a thing that sang. She used to sing. He killed that, too.

MRS. PETERS [*Moving uneasily.*]   We don't know who killed the bird.

MRS. HALE   I knew John Wright.

MRS. PETERS   It was an awful thing was done in this house that night, Mrs. Hale. Killing a man while he slept, slipping a rope around his neck that choked the life out of him.

MRS. HALE   His neck. Choked the life out of him.

[*Her hand goes out and rests on the birdcage.*]

MRS. PETERS [*With rising voice.*]   We don't know who killed him. We don't know.

MRS. HALE [*Her own feeling not interrupted.*]   If there'd been years and years of nothing, then a bird to sing to you, it would be awful—still, after the bird was still.

MRS. PETERS [*Something within her speaking.*]   I know what stillness is. When we homesteaded in Dakota, and my first baby died—after he was two years old, and me with no other then—

MRS. HALE [*Moving.*]   How soon do you suppose they'll be through, looking for the evidence?

MRS. PETERS   I know what stillness is. [*Pulling herself back.*] The law has got to punish crime, Mrs. Hale.

MRS. HALE [*Not as if answering that.*]   I wish you'd seen Minnie Foster when she wore a white dress with blue ribbons and stood up there in the choir and sang. [*A look around the room.*] Oh, I wish I'd come over here once in a while! That was a crime! That was a crime! Who's going to punish that?

MRS. PETERS [*Looking upstairs.*]   We mustn't—take on.

MRS. HALE   I might have known she needed help! I know how things can be—for women. I tell you, it's queer, Mrs. Peters. We live close together and we live far apart. We all go through the same things—it's all just a different kind of the same thing. [*Brushes her eyes; noticing the bottle of fruit, reaches out for it.*] If I was you I wouldn't tell her her fruit was gone. Tell her it ain't. Tell her it's all right. Take this in to prove it to her. She—she may never know whether it was broke or not.

MRS. PETERS [*Takes the bottle, looks about for something to wrap it in; takes petticoat from the clothes brought from the other room, very nervously begins winding this around the bottle. In a false voice.*]   My, it's a good thing the men couldn't hear us. Wouldn't they just laugh! Getting all stirred up over a little thing like a—dead canary. As if that could have anything to do with—with—wouldn't they laugh!

[*The men are heard coming down stairs.*]

MRS. HALE [*Under her breath.*]   Maybe they would—maybe they wouldn't.

COUNTY ATTORNEY   No, Peters, it's all perfectly clear except a reason for doing it. But you know juries when it comes to women. If there was some definite thing. Something to show—something to make a story about—a thing that would connect up with this strange way of doing it—

[*The women's eyes meet for an instant. Enter* HALE *from outer door.*]

HALE   Well, I've got the team around. Pretty cold out there.
COUNTY ATTORNEY   I'm going to stay here a while by myself. [*To the* SHERIFF.] You can send Frank out for me, can't you? I want to go over everything. I'm not satisfied that we can't do better.
SHERIFF   Do you want to see what Mrs. Peters is going to take in?
   [*The* COUNTY ATTORNEY *goes to the table, picks up the apron, laughs.*]
COUNTY ATTORNEY   Oh, I guess they're not very dangerous things the ladies have picked out. [*Moves a few things about, disturbing the quilt pieces which cover the box. Steps back.*] No, Mrs. Peters doesn't need supervising. For that matter, a sheriff's wife is married to the law. Ever think of it that way, Mrs. Peters?
MRS. PETERS   Not—just that way.
SHERIFF   [*Chuckling.*]   Married to the law. [*Moves toward the other room.*] I just want you to come in here a minute, George. We ought to take a look at these windows.
COUNTY ATTORNEY [*Scoffingly.*]   Oh, windows!
SHERIFF   We'll be right out, Mr. Hale.
   [HALE *goes outside. The* SHERIFF *follows the* COUNTY ATTORNEY *into the other room. Then* MRS. HALE *rises, hands tight together, looking intensely at* MRS. PETERS, *whose eyes make a slow turn, finally meeting* MRS. HALE'S. *A moment* MRS. HALE *holds her, then her own eyes point the way to where the box is concealed. Suddenly* MRS. PETERS *throws back quilt pieces and tries to put the box in the bag she is wearing. It is too big. She opens box, starts to take bird out, cannot touch it, goes to pieces, stands there helpless. Sound of a knob turning in the other room.* MRS. HALE *snatches the box and puts it in the pocket of her big coat. Enter* COUNTY ATTORNEY *and* SHERIFF.]
COUNTY ATTORNEY [*Facetiously.*]   Well, Henry, at least we found out that she was not going to quilt it. She was going to—what is it you call it, ladies?
MRS. HALE [*Her hand against her pocket.*]   We call it—knot it, Mr. Henderson.

CURTAIN

1916

RADCLYFFE HALL
1880–1943

Una, Lady Troubridge, who was Radclyffe Hall's lover for twenty-seven years, supplied in her biography (1945) most of the scanty facts we have about the early life of this pioneering lesbian novelist. Marguerite Radclyffe-Hall was born in Bournemouth, Hampshire. She was neglected by her father, who left the family when she was three, and alienated from her American-born mother, who remarried an Italian singing teacher as insensitive to her daughter as she was. By the time she attended day schools and, for one year, King's College in London, Radclyffe Hall was calling herself "Peter" or "John," as if to express her desire to forge a new sexual identity for herself. At twenty-one, she inherited a fortune from the Radclyffe-Hall Trust, and moved to Kensington with the only affectionate relative she had ever known, her maternal grandmother. Six years later, she began the affair that would really provide her education. Mabel Veronica Batten ("Ladye") was a cultivated patroness of music. Twenty-three years older than Hall, she encouraged her young lover to relinquish sports for more intellectual pursuits, horses and dogs for books. After the death of Ladye in 1916, Hall turned to Una Troubridge for consolation, and they lived together for the rest of Hall's life.

Handsome in her tweed suits and cropped hair, Radclyffe Hall had published several volumes of verse and two novels before *Adam's Breed* (1926) won the Femina Vie Heureuse Prize and the James Tait Black Memorial Book Prize. But she became famous because of the trial and scandal that greeted her next book, *The Well of Loneliness* (1928). Introduced by the psychologist Havelock Ellis, Radclyffe Hall's novel focused on a heroine named Stephen Gordon, a girl brought up by a father who wanted a boy. Stephen lives and loves heroically, engaging in passionate affairs with other women and working in the London Ambulance Column during World War I. Feeling herself to be a man trapped in a female body, however, she suffers the frustrations of the "congenital invert." Through its reliance on this concept of the "invert," *The Well of Loneliness* presents lesbianism as a biological tragedy and has, therefore, been criticized by a number of contemporary historians of lesbian culture. Yet it nevertheless protests against the persecution of lesbians with unusual explicitness, even as it presents a broodingly attractive portrait of a young woman who aspires to the courage and verve she associates with masculinity. Although Radclyffe Hall responded to the banning of *The Well of Loneliness* in England by going on to write several religious novels, her contribution to literary history is still measured by her portrait of the conflicted but androgynous Stephen, who seems "to combine the strength of a man with the gentler and more subtle strength of a woman." "Miss Ogilvy Finds Herself" meditates on the same themes that inform Hall's lesbian classic, which was banned in England as obscene until 1949. *The Well of Loneliness* and stories like "Miss Ogilvy Finds Herself" have made Hall into what Terry Castle calls "the most important English lesbian writer of the first half of the twentieth century."

Miss Ogilvy Finds Herself

Miss Ogilvy stood on the quay at Calais and surveyed the disbanding of her Unit, the Unit that together with the coming of war[1] had completely altered the complexion of her life, at all events for three years.

Miss Ogilvy's thin, pale lips were set sternly and her forehead was puckered in an effort of attention, in an effort to memorize every small detail of every old war-weary battered motor on whose side still appeared the merciful emblem[2] that had set Miss Ogilvy free.

Miss Ogilvy's mind was jerking a little, trying to regain its accustomed balance, trying to readjust itself quickly to this sudden and paralyzing change. Her tall, awkward body with its queer look of strength, its broad, flat bosom and thick legs and ankles, as though in response to her jerking mind, moved uneasily, rocking backwards and forwards. She had this trick of rocking on her feet in moments of controlled agitation. As usual, her hands were thrust deep into her pockets, they seldom seemed to come out of her pockets unless

---

1. World War I, in 1914. 2. A Red Cross symbol of the ambulance corps.

it were to light a cigarette, and as though she were still standing firm under fire while the wounded were placed in her ambulances, she suddenly straddled her legs very slightly and lifted her head and listened. She was standing firm under fire at that moment, the fire of a desperate regret.

Some girls came towards her, young, tired-looking creatures whose eyes were too bright from long strain and excitement. They had all been members of that glorious Unit, and they still wore the queer little forage-caps[3] and the short, clumsy tunics of the French Militaire. They still slouched in walking and smoked Caporals in emulation of the Poilus.[4] Like their founder and leader these girls were all English, but like her they had chosen to serve England's ally, fearlessly thrusting right up to the trenches in search of the wounded and dying. They had seen some fine things in the course of three years, not the least fine of which was the cold, hard-faced woman who, commanding, domineering, even hectoring at times, had yet been possessed of so dauntless a courage and of so insistent a vitality that it vitalized the whole Unit.

"It's rotten!" Miss Ogilvy heard someone saying. "It's rotten, this breaking up of our Unit!" And the high, rather childish voice of the speaker sounded perilously near to tears.

Miss Ogilvy looked at the girl almost gently, and it seemed, for a moment, as though some deep feeling were about to find expression in words. But Miss Ogilvy's feelings had been held in abeyance so long that they seldom dared become vocal, so she merely said "Oh?" on a rising inflection—her method of checking emotion.

They were swinging the ambulance cars in midair, those of them that were destined to go back to England, swinging them up like sacks of potatoes, then lowering them with much clanging of chains to the deck of the waiting steamer. The porters were shoving and shouting and quarreling, pausing now and again to make meaningless gestures; while a pompous official was becoming quite angry as he pointed at Miss Ogilvy's own special car—it annoyed him, it was bulky and difficult to move.

"Bon Dieu! Mais dépêchez-vous donc!"[5] he bawled, as though he were bullying the motor.

Then Miss Ogilvy's heart gave a sudden, thick thud to see this undignified, pitiful ending; and she turned and patted the gallant old car as though she were patting a well-beloved horse, as though she would say: "Yes, I know how it feels—never mind, we'll go down together."

2

Miss Ogilvy sat in the railway carriage on her way from Dover to London. The soft English landscape sped smoothly past: small homesteads, small churches, small pastures, small lanes with small hedges; all small like England itself, all small like Miss Ogilvy's future. And sitting there still arrayed in her tunic, with her forage-cap resting on her knees, she was conscious of a sense of complete frustration; thinking less of those glorious years

---

3. Caps worn by infantry soldiers.
4. French soldiers.
5. Good God! Move along, then! (French).

at the Front and of all that had gone to the making of her, than of all that had gone to the marring of her from the days of her earliest childhood.

She saw herself as a queer little girl, aggressive and awkward because of her shyness; a queer little girl who loathed sisters and dolls, preferring the stable-boys as companions, preferring to play with footballs and tops, and occasional catapults. She saw herself climbing the tallest beech trees, arrayed in old breeches illicitly come by. She remembered insisting with tears and some temper that her real name was William and not Wilhelmina. All these childish pretences and illusions she remembered, and the bitterness that came after. For Miss Ogilvy had found as her life went on that in this world it is better to be one with the herd, that the world has no wish to understand those who cannot conform to its stereotyped pattern. True enough, in her youth she had gloried in her strength, lifting weights, swinging clubs and developing muscles, but presently this had grown irksome to her; it had seemed to lead nowhere, she being a woman, and then as her mother had often protested: muscles looked so appalling in evening dress—a young girl ought not to have muscles.

Miss Ogilvy's relation to the opposite sex was unusual and at that time added much to her worries, for no less than three men had wished to propose, to the genuine amazement of the world and her mother. Miss Ogilvy's instinct made her like and trust men, for whom she had a pronounced fellow-feeling; she would always have chosen them as her friends and companions in preference to girls or women; she would dearly have loved to share in their sports, their business, their ideas and their wide-flung interests. But men had not wanted her, except the three who had found in her strangeness a definite attraction, and those would-be suitors she had actually feared, regarding them with aversion. Towards young girls and women she was shy and respectful, apologetic and sometimes admiring. But their fads and their foibles, none of which she could share, while amusing her very often in secret, set her outside the sphere of their intimate lives, so that in the end she must blaze a lone trail through the difficulties of her nature.

"I can't understand you," her mother had said, "you're a very odd creature—now when I was your age . . ."

And her daughter had nodded, feeling sympathetic. There were two younger girls who also gave trouble, though in their case the trouble was fighting for husbands who were scarce enough even in those days. It was finally decided, at Miss Ogilvy's request, to allow her to leave the field clear for her sisters. She would remain in the country with her father when the others went up for the Season.[6]

Followed long, uneventful years spent in sport, while Sarah and Fanny toiled, sweated and gambled in the matrimonial market. Neither ever succeeded in netting a husband, and when the Squire died leaving very little money, Miss Ogilvy found to her great surprise that they looked upon her as a brother. They had so often jibed at her in the past, that at first she could scarcely believe her senses, but before very long it became all too real: she it was who must straighten out endless muddles, who must make the dreary arrangements for the move, who must find a cheap but genteel house in

---

6. The social season in London.

London and, once there, who must cope with the family accounts which she only, it seemed, could balance.

It would be: "You might see to that, Wilhelmina; you write, you've got such a good head for business." Or: "I wish you'd go down and explain to that man that we really can't pay his account till next quarter." Or: "This money for the grocer is five shillings short. Do run over my sum, Wilhelmina."

Her mother, grown feeble, discovered in this daughter a staff upon which she could lean with safety. Miss Ogilvy genuinely loved her mother, and was therefore quite prepared to be leaned on; but when Sarah and Fanny began to lean too with the full weight of endless neurotic symptoms incubated in resentful virginity, Miss Ogilvy found herself staggering a little. For Sarah and Fanny were grown hard to bear, with their mania for telling their symptoms to doctors, with their unstable nerves and their acrid tongues and the secret dislike they now felt for their mother. Indeed, when old Mrs. Ogilvy died, she was unmourned except by her eldest daughter who actually felt a void in her life—the unforeseen void that the ailing and weak will not infrequently leave behind them.

At about this time an aunt also died, bequeathing her fortune to her niece Wilhelmina who, however, was too weary to gird up her loins and set forth in search of exciting adventure—all she did was to move her protesting sisters to a little estate she had purchased in Surrey. This experiment was only a partial success, for Miss Ogilvy failed to make friends of her neighbors; thus at fifty-five she had grown rather dour, as is often the way with shy, lonely people.

When the war came she had just begun settling down—people do settle down in their fifty-sixth year—she was feeling quite glad that her hair was gray, that the garden took up so much of her time, that, in fact, the beat of her blood was slowing. But all this was changed when war was declared; on that day Miss Ogilvy's pulses throbbed wildly.

"My God! If only I were a man!" she burst out, as she glared at Sarah and Fanny, "if only I had been born a man!" Something in her was feeling deeply defrauded.

Sarah and Fanny were soon knitting socks and mittens and mufflers and Jaeger trench-helmets.[7] Other ladies were busily working at depots, making swabs at the Squire's, or splints at the Parson's; but Miss Ogilvy scowled and did none of these things—she was not at all like other ladies.

For nearly twelve months she worried officials with a view to getting a job out in France—not in their way but in hers, and that was the trouble. She wished to go up to the front-line trenches, she wished to be actually under fire, she informed the harassed officials.

To all her enquiries she received the same answer: "We regret that we cannot accept your offer." But once thoroughly roused she was hard to subdue, for her shyness had left her as though by magic.

Sarah and Fanny shrugged angular shoulders: "There's plenty of work here at home," they remarked, "though of course it's not quite so melodramatic!"

"Oh . . . ?" queried their sister on a rising note of impatience—and she promptly cut off her hair: "That'll jar them!" she thought with satisfaction.

---

7. Woolen caps worn in the trenches, where much of World War I was fought.

Then she went up to London, formed her admirable unit and finally got it accepted by the French, despite renewed opposition.

In London she had found herself quite at her ease, for many another of her kind was in London doing excellent work for the nation. It was really surprising how many cropped heads had suddenly appeared as it were out of space; how many Miss Ogilvies, losing their shyness, had come forward asserting their right to serve, asserting their claim to attention.

There followed those turbulent years at the front, full of courage and hardship and high endeavor; and during those years Miss Ogilvy forgot the bad joke that Nature seemed to have played her. She was given the rank of a French lieutenant and she lived in a kind of blissful illusion; appalling reality lay on all sides and yet she managed to live in illusion. She was competent, fearless, devoted and untiring. What then? Could any man hope to do better? She was nearly fifty-eight, yet she walked with a stride, and at times she even swaggered a little.

Poor Miss Ogilvy sitting so glumly in the train with her manly trench-boots and her forage-cap! Poor all the Miss Ogilvies back from the war with their tunics, their trench-boots, and their childish illusions! Wars come and wars go but the world does not change: it will always forget an indebtedness which it thinks it expedient not to remember.

3

When Miss Ogilvy returned to her home in Surrey it was only to find that her sisters were ailing from the usual imaginary causes, and this to a woman who had seen the real thing was intolerable, so that she looked with distaste at Sarah and then at Fanny. Fanny was certainly not prepossessing, she was suffering from a spurious attack of hay fever.

"Stop sneezing!" commanded Miss Ogilvy, in the voice that had so much impressed the Unit. But as Fanny was not in the least impressed, she naturally went on sneezing.

Miss Ogilvy's desk was piled mountain-high with endless tiresome letters and papers: circulars, bills, months-old correspondence, the gardener's accounts, an agent's report on some fields that required land-draining. She seated herself before this collection; then she sighed, it all seemed so absurdly trivial.

"Will you let your hair grow again?" Fanny enquired . . . she and Sarah had followed her into the study. "I'm certain the Vicar would be glad if you did."

"Oh?" murmured Miss Ogilvy, rather too blandly.

"Wilhelmina!"

"Yes?"

"You will do it, won't you?"

"Do what?"

"Let your hair grow; we all wish you would."

"Why should I?"

"Oh, well, it will look less odd, especially now that the war is over—in a small place like this people notice such things."

"I entirely agree with Fanny;" announced Sarah.

Sarah had become very self-assertive, no doubt through having mismanaged the estate during the years of her sister's absence. They had quite a heated dispute one morning over the south herbaceous border.

"Whose garden is this?" Miss Ogilvy asked sharply. "I insist on auricula-eyed sweet Williams! I even took the trouble to write from France, but it seems that my letter has been ignored."

"Don't shout," rebuked Sarah, "you're not in France now!"

Miss Ogilvy could gladly have boxed her ears: "I only wish to God I were," she muttered.

Another dispute followed close on its heels, and this time it happened to be over the dinner. Sarah and Fanny were living on weeds—at least that was the way Miss Ogilvy put it.

"We've become vegetarians," Sarah said grandly.

"You've become two damn tiresome cranks!" snapped their sister.

Now it never had been Miss Ogilvy's way to indulge in acid recriminations, but somehow, these days, she forgot to say: "Oh?" quite so often as expediency demanded. It may have been Fanny's perpetual sneezing that had got on her nerves; or it may have been Sarah, or the gardener, or the Vicar, or even the canary; though it really did not matter very much what it was just so long as she found a convenient peg upon which to hang her growing irritation.

"This won't do at all," Miss Ogilvy thought sternly, "life's not worth so much fuss, I must pull myself together." But it seemed this was easier said than done; not a day passed without her losing her temper and that over some trifle: "No, this won't do at all—it just mustn't be," she thought sternly.

Everyone pitied Sarah and Fanny: "Such a dreadful, violent old thing," said the neighbors.

But Sarah and Fanny had their revenge: "Poor darling, it's shell shock,[8] you know," they murmured.

Thus Miss Ogilvy's prowess was whittled away until she herself was beginning to doubt it. Had she ever been that courageous person who had faced death in France with such perfect composure? Had she ever stood tranquilly under fire, without turning a hair, while she issued her orders? Had she ever been treated with marked respect? She herself was beginning to doubt it.

Sometimes she would see an old member of the Unit, a girl who, more faithful to her than the others, would take the trouble to run down to Surrey. These visits, however, were seldom enlivening.

"Oh, well . . . here we are . . ." Miss Ogilvy would mutter.

But one day the girl smiled and shook her blond head: "I'm not—I'm going to be married."

Strange thoughts had come to Miss Ogilvy, unbidden, thoughts that had stayed for many an hour after the girl's departure. Alone in her study she had suddenly shivered, feeling a sense of complete desolation. With cold hands she had lighted a cigarette.

"I must be ill or something," she had mused, as she stared at her trembling fingers.

After this she would sometimes cry out in her sleep, living over in dreams

---

8. A mental illness suffered by some soldiers during World War I, brought on by combat experience (i.e., posttraumatic stress disorder).

God knows what emotions; returning, maybe to the battlefield of France. Her hair turned snow-white; it was not unbecoming yet she fretted about it.

"I'm growing very old," she would sigh as she brushed her thick mop before the glass; and then she would peer at her wrinkles.

For now that it had happened she hated being old; it no longer appeared such an easy solution of those difficulties that had always beset her. And this she resented most bitterly, so that she became the prey of self-pity, and of other undesirable states in which the body will torment the mind, and the mind, in its turn, the body. Then Miss Ogilvy straightened her ageing back, in spite of the fact that of late it had ached with muscular rheumatism, and she faced herself squarely and came to a resolve.

"I'm off!" she announced abruptly one day; and that evening she packed her kit-bag.

4

Near the south coast of Devon there exists a small island that is still very little known to the world, but which nevertheless can boast an hotel, the only building upon it. Miss Ogilvy had chosen this place quite at random, it was marked on her map by scarcely more than a dot, but somehow she had liked the look of that dot and had set forth alone to explore it.

She found herself standing on the mainland one morning looking at a vague blur of green through the mist, a vague blur of green that rose out of the Channel like a tidal wave suddenly suspended. Miss Ogilvy was filled with a sense of adventure; she had not felt like this since the ending of war.

"I was right to come here, very right indeed. I'm going to shake off all my troubles," she decided.

A fisherman's boat was parting the mist, and before it was properly beached, in she bundled.

"I hope they're expecting me?" she said gaily.

"They du be expecting you," the man answered.

The sea, which is generally rough off that coast, was indulging itself in an oily ground-swell; the broad, glossy swells struck the side of the boat, then broke and sprayed over Miss Ogilvy's ankles.

The fisherman grinned: "Feeling all right?" he queried. "It du be tiresome most times about these parts." But the mist had suddenly drifted away and Miss Ogilvy was staring wide-eyed at the island.

She saw a long shoal of jagged black rocks, and between them the curve of a small sloping beach, and above that the lift of the island itself, and above that again, blue heaven. Near the beach stood the little two-storied hotel which was thatched, and built entirely of timber; for the rest she could make out no signs of life apart from a host of white sea-gulls.

Then Miss Ogilvy said a curious thing. She said: "On the south-west side of that place there was once a cave—a very large cave. I remember that it was some way from the sea."

"There du be a cave still," the fisherman told her, "but it's just above highwater level."

"A-ah," murmured Miss Ogilvy thoughtfully, as though to herself; then she looked embarrassed.

The little hotel proved both comfortable and clean, the hostess both pleasant and comely. Miss Ogilvy started unpacking her bag, changed her mind and went for a stroll round the island. The island was covered with turf and thistles and traversed by narrow green paths thick with daisies. It had four rock-bound coves of which the south-western was by far the most difficult of access. For just here the island descended abruptly as though it were hurtling down to the water; and just here the shale was most treacherous and the tide-swept rocks most aggressively pointed. Here it was that the seagulls, grown fearless of man by reason of his absurd limitations, built their nests on the ledges and reared countless young who multiplied, in their turn, every season. Yes, and here it was that Miss Ogilvy, greatly marveling, stood and stared across at a cave; much too near the crumbling edge for her safety, but by now completely indifferent to caution.

"I remember . . . I remember . . ." she kept repeating. Then: "That's all very well, but what do I remember?"

She was conscious of somehow remembering all wrong, of her memory being distorted and colored—perhaps by the endless things she had seen since her eyes had last rested upon that cave. This worried her sorely, far more than the fact that she should be remembering the cave at all, she who had never set foot on the island before that actual morning. Indeed, except for the sense of wrongness when she struggled to piece her memories together, she was steeped in a very profound contentment which surged over her spirit, wave upon wave.

"It's extremely odd," pondered Miss Ogilvy. Then she laughed, so pleased did she feel with its oddness.

5

That night after supper she talked to her hostess who was only too glad, it seemed, to be questioned. She owned the whole island and was proud of the fact, as she very well might be, decided her boarder. Some curious things had been found on the island, according to comely Mrs. Nanceskivel: bronze arrow-heads, pieces of ancient stone celts;[9] and once they had dug up a man's skull and thigh-bone—this had happened while they were sinking a well. Would Miss Ogilvy care to have a look at the bones? They were kept in a cupboard in the scullery.

Miss Ogilvy nodded.

"Then I'll fetch him this moment," said Mrs. Nanceskivel, briskly.

In less than two minutes she was back with the box that contained those poor remnants of a man, and Miss Ogilvy, who had risen from her chair, was gazing down at those remnants. As she did so her mouth was sternly compressed, but her face and her neck flushed darkly.

Mrs. Nanceskivel was pointing to the skull: "Look, miss, he was killed," she remarked rather proudly, "and they tell me that the axe that killed him was bronze. He's thousands and thousands of years old, they tell me. Our local doctor knows a lot about such things and he wants me to send these bones to an expert; they ought to belong to the Nation, he says. But I know what would happen, they'd come digging up my island, and I won't have people digging up my island, I've got enough worry with the rabbits as it is."

---

9. Prehistoric stone axes.

But Miss Ogilvy could no longer hear the words for the pounding of the blood in her temples.

She was filled with a sudden, inexplicable fury against the innocent Mrs. Nanceskivel: "You . . . you . . ." she began, then checked herself, fearful of what she might say to the woman.

For her sense of outrage was overwhelming as she stared at those bones that were kept in the scullery; moreover, she knew how such men had been buried, which made the outrage seem all the more shameful. They had buried such men in deep, well-dug pits surmounted by four stout stones at their corners—four stout stones there had been and a covering stone. And all this Miss Ogilvy knew as by instinct, having no concrete knowledge on which to draw. But she knew it right down in the depths of her soul, and she hated Mrs. Nanceskivel.

And now she was swept by another emotion that was even more strange and more devastating: such a grief as she had not conceived could exist; a terrible unassuageable grief, without hope, without respite, without palliation, so that with something akin to despair she touched the long gash in the skull. Then her eyes, that had never wept since her childhood, filled slowly with large, hot, difficult tears. She must blink very hard, then close her eyelids, turn away from the lamp and say rather loudly:

"Thanks, Mrs. Nanceskivel. It's past eleven—I think I'll be going upstairs."

6

Miss Ogilvy closed the door of her bedroom, after which she stood quite still to consider: "Is it shell shock?" she muttered incredulously. "I wonder, can it be shell shock?"

She began to pace slowly about the room, smoking a Caporal. As usual her hands were deep in her pockets; she could feel small, familiar things in those pockets and she gripped them, glad of their presence. Then all of a sudden she was terribly tired, so tired that she flung herself down on the bed, unable to stand any longer.

She thought that she lay there struggling to reason, that her eyes were closed in the painful effort, and that as she closed them she continued to puff the inevitable cigarette. At least that was what she thought at one moment—the next, she was out in a sunset evening, and a large red sun was sinking slowly to the rim of a distant sea.

Miss Ogilvy knew that she was herself, that is to say she was conscious of her being, and yet she was not Miss Ogilvy at all, nor had she a memory of her. All that she now saw was very familiar, all that she now did was what she should do, and all that she now was seemed perfectly natural. Indeed, she did not think of these things; there seemed no reason for thinking about them.

She was walking with bare feet on turf that felt springy and was greatly enjoying the sensation; she had always enjoyed it, ever since as an infant she had learned to crawl on this turf. On either hand stretched rolling green uplands, while at her back she knew that there were forests; but in front, far away, lay the gleam of the sea towards which the big sun was sinking. The air was cool and intensely still, with never so much as a ripple or bird song. It was wonderfully pure—one might almost say young—but Miss Ogilvy thought of it merely as air. Having always breathed it she took it for granted, as she took the soft turf and the uplands.

She pictured herself as immensely tall; she was feeling immensely tall at the moment. As a matter of fact she was five feet eight which, however, was quite a considerable height when compared to that of her fellow tribesmen. She was wearing a single garment of pelts which came to her knees and left her arms sleeveless. Her arms and her legs, which were closely tattooed with blue zig-zag lines, were extremely hairy. From a leathern thong twisted about her waist there hung a clumsily made stone weapon, a celt, which in spite of its clumsiness was strongly hafted and useful for killing.

Miss Ogilvy wanted to shout aloud from a glorious sense of physical well-being, but instead she picked up a heavy, round stone which she hurled with great force at some distant rocks.

"Good! Strong!" she exclaimed. "See how far it goes!"

"Yes, strong. There is no one so strong as you. You are surely the strongest man in our tribe," replied her little companion.

Miss Ogilvy glanced at this little companion and rejoiced that they two were all alone together. The girl at her side had a smooth brownish skin, oblique black eyes and short, sturdy limbs. Miss Ogilvy marveled because of her beauty. She also was wearing a single garment of pelts, new pelts, she had made it that morning. She had stitched at it diligently for hours with short lengths of gut and her best bone needle. A strand of black hair hung over her bosom, and this she was constantly stroking and fondling; then she lifted the strand and examined her hair.

"Pretty," she remarked with childish complacence.

"Pretty," echoed the young man at her side.

"For you," she told him, "all of me is for you and none other. For you this body has ripened."

He shook back his own coarse hair from his eyes; he had sad brown eyes like those of a monkey. For the rest he was lean and steel-strong of loin, broad of chest, and with features not too uncomely. His prominent cheekbones were set rather high, his nose was blunt, his jaw somewhat bestial; but his mouth, though full-lipped, contradicted his jaw, being very gentle and sweet in expression. And now he smiled, showing big, square, white teeth.

"You . . . woman," he murmured contentedly, and the sound seemed to come from the depths of his being.

His speech was slow and lacking in words when it came to expressing a vital emotion, so one word must suffice and this he now spoke, and the word that he spoke had a number of meanings. It meant: "Little spring of exceedingly pure water." It meant: "Hut of peace for a man after battle." It meant: "Ripe red berry sweet to the taste." It meant: "Happy small home of future generations." All these things he must try to express by a word, and because of their loving she understood him.

They paused, and lifting her up he kissed her. Then he rubbed his large shaggy head on her shoulder; and when he released her she knelt at his feet.

"My master; blood of my body," she whispered. For with her it was different, love had taught her love's speech, so that she might turn her heart into sounds that her primitive tongue could utter.

After she had pressed her lips to his hands, and her cheek to his hairy and powerful forearm, she stood up and they gazed at the setting sun, but with bowed heads, gazing under their lids, because this was very sacred.

A couple of mating bears padded toward them from a thicket, and the female rose to her haunches. But the man drew his celt and menaced the beast, so that she dropped down noiselessly and fled, and her mate also fled, for here was the power that few dared to withstand by day or by night, on the uplands or in the forests. And now from across to the left where a river would presently lose itself in the marshes, came a rhythmical thudding, as a herd of red deer with wide nostrils and starting eyes thundered past, disturbed in their drinking by the bears.

After this the evening returned to its silence, and the spell of its silence descended on the lovers, so that each felt very much alone, yet withal more closely united to the other. But the man became restless under that spell, and he suddenly laughed; then grasping the woman he tossed her above his head and caught her. This he did many times for his own amusement and because he knew that his strength gave her joy. In this manner they played together for a while, he with his strength and she with her weakness. And they cried out, and made many guttural sounds which were meaningless save only to themselves. And the tunic of pelts slipped down from her breasts, and her two little breasts were pear-shaped.

Presently, he grew tired of their playing, and he pointed toward a cluster of huts and earthworks that lay to the eastward. The smoke from these huts rose in thick straight lines, bending neither to right nor left in its rising, and the thought of sweet burning rushes and brushwood touched his consciousness, making him feel sentimental.

"Smoke," he said.

And she answered: "Blue smoke."

He nodded: "Yes, blue smoke—home."

Then she said: "I have ground much corn since the full moon. My stones are too smooth. You make me new stones."

"All you have need of, I make," he told her.

She stole closer to him, taking his hand: "My father is still a black cloud full of thunder. He thinks that you wish to be head of our tribe in his place, because he is now very old. He must not hear of these meetings of ours, if he did I think he would beat me!"

So he asked her: "Are you unhappy, small berry?"

But at this she smiled: "What is being unhappy? I do not know what that means any more."

"I do not either," he answered.

Then as though some invisible force had drawn him, his body swung around and he stared at the forests where they lay and darkened, fold upon fold; and his eyes dilated with wonder and terror, and he moved his head quickly from side to side as a wild thing will do that is held between bars and whose mind is pitifully bewildered.

"Water!" he cried hoarsely, "great water—look, look! Over there. This land is surrounded by water!"

"What water?" she questioned.

He answered: "The sea." And he covered his face with his hands.

"Not so," she consoled, "big forests, good hunting. Big forests in which you hunt boar and aurochs.[1] No sea over there but only the trees."

He took his trembling hands from his face: "You are right . . . only trees," he said dully.

But now his face had grown heavy and brooding and he started to speak of a thing that oppressed him: "The Roundheaded-ones, they are devils," he growled, while his bushy black brows met over his eyes, and when this happened it changed his expression which became a little sub-human.

"No matter," she protested, for she saw that he forgot her and she wished him to think an talk only of love. "No matter. My father laughs at your fears. Are we not friends with the Roundheaded-ones? We are friends, so why should we fear them?"

"Our forts, very old, very weak," he went on, "and the Roundheaded-ones have terrible weapons. Their weapons are not made of good stone like ours, but of some dark, devilish substance."

"What of that?" she said lightly. "They would fight on our side, so why need we trouble about their weapons?"

But he looked away, not appearing to hear her. "We must barter all, all for their celts and arrows and spears, and then we must learn their secret. They lust after our women, they lust after our lands. We must barter all, all for their sly brown celts."

"Me . . . bartered?" she queried, very sure of his answer, otherwise she had not dared to say this.

"The Roundheaded-ones may destroy my tribe and yet I will not part with you," he told her. Then he spoke very gravely: "But I think they desire to slay us, and me they will try to slay first because they well know how much I mistrust them—they have seen my eyes fixed many times on their camps."

She cried: "I will bite out the throats of these people if they so much as scratch your skin!"

And at this his mood changed and he roared with amusement: "You . . . woman!" he roared. "Little foolish white teeth. Your teeth were made for nibbling wild cherries, not for tearing the throats of the Roundheaded-ones!"

"Thoughts of war always make me afraid," she whimpered, still wishing him to talk about love.

He turned his sorrowful eyes upon her, the eyes that were sad even when he was merry, and although his mind was often obtuse, yet he clearly perceived how it was with her then. And his blood caught fire from the flame in her blood, so that he strained her against his body.

"You . . . mine . . ." he stammered.

"Love," she said, trembling, "this is love."

And he answered: "Love."

Then their faces grew melancholy for a moment, because dimly, very dimly in their dawning souls, they were conscious of a longing for something more vast than their earthly passion could compass.

Presently, he lifted her like a child and carried her quickly southward and westward till they came to a place where a gentle descent led down to a marshy valley. Far away, at the line where the marshes ended, they discerned

---

1. Extinct long-horned wild oxen.

the misty line of the sea; but the sea and the marshes were become as one substance, merging, blending, folding together; and since they were lovers they also would be one, even as the sea and the marshes.

And now they reached the mouth of a cave that was set in the quiet hillside. There was bright green verdure beside the cave, and a number of small, pink, thick-stemmed flowers that when they were crushed smelt of spices. And within the cave there was bracken newly gathered and heaped together for a bed; while beyond, from some rocks, came a low liquid sound as a spring dripped out through a crevice. Abruptly, he set the girl on her feet, and she knew that the days of her innocence were over. And she thought of the anxious virgin soil that was rent and sown to bring forth fruit in season, and she gave a quick little gasp of fear:

"No . . . no . . ." she gasped. For, divining his need, she was weak with the longing to be possessed, yet the terror of love lay heavy upon her. "No . . . no . . ." she gasped.

But he caught her wrist and she felt the great strength of his rough, gnarled fingers, the great strength of the urge that leapt in his loins, and again she must give the quick gasp of fear, the while she clung close to him lest he should spare her.

The twilight was engulfed and possessed by darkness, which in turn was transfigured by the moonrise, which in turn was fulfilled and consumed by dawn. A mighty eagle soared up from his eyrie,[2] cleaving the air with his masterful wings, and beneath him from the rushes that harbored their nests, rose other great birds, crying loudly. Then the heavy-horned elks appeared on the uplands, bending their burdened heads to the sod; while beyond in the forests the fierce wild aurochs stamped as they bellowed their love songs.

But within the dim cave the lord of these creatures had put by his weapon and his instinct for slaying. And he lay there defenseless with tenderness, thinking no longer of death but of life as he murmured the word that had so many meanings. That meant: "Little spring of exceedingly pure water." That meant: "Hut of peace for a man after battle." That meant: "Ripe red berry sweet to the taste." That meant: "Happy small home of future generations."

7

They found Miss Ogilvy the next morning; the fisherman saw her and climbed to the ledge. She was sitting at the mouth of the cave. She was dead, with her hands thrust deep into her pockets.

1926, 1934

---

2. Nest on a cliff or mountaintop.

ANZIA YEZIERSKA
ca. 1880?–1970

Anzia Yezierska's novel *Bread Givers* (1925) dramatizes the ambivalence of a girl who confronts the misogyny of Jewish laws and learning in the Torah (the first five books of the Bible): "Women were always the curse of men," the girl's pious father proclaims, "but when they get older they're devils and witches." Angered though she is, later in the novel, after she rejects a lucrative marriage proposal that would have turned her into "another piece of property," this same daughter believes that her integrity comes from her father's "wiser-than-the-world kind of wisdom," for "he had given up worldly success to drink the wisdom of the Torah." Many of Yezierska's characters are similarly caught between the old world of their fathers, the shtetl (village) of Europe transplanted to the Lower East Side of New York, and the New World of America with its promise of advancement through education and economic mobility, a world that, ironically enough, inexorably isolates them from those origins that are the source of their energies. Yezierska's protagonists often long for the education, the language, the clothing, the manners that would make them American, but that very longing inflicts painfully acute moments of self-hatred and despair.

Born in the village of Plinsk in Poland, Yezierska emigrated with her parents and eight siblings to America in the early 1890s. Although her father continued to maintain the honorable poverty associated with the study of the Talmud (the ancient writings of rabbis), she sought to escape laundry and sweatshop work through advancement in night school. A scholarship enabled her to obtain a degree in domestic science from Teachers College at Columbia University. Married twice, once for a few months in 1910, and soon again for three years, she eventually decided to leave her only child, a daughter, with her second husband. Her fiction, which began appearing in 1915, won quick acclaim; "The Fat of the Land" was awarded the Edward J. O'Brien prize and her collection *Hungry Hearts* (1920) was purchased by the Hollywood producer Samuel Goldwyn for $10,000. Although she published story collections (like *Children of Loneliness,* 1923) and novels (like *Salome of the Tenements,* 1923) throughout the 1920s, her success had cut her off from the people who had inspired her writing in the first place. For all of the filth, poverty, ignorance, degrading toil, and misogyny of the ghetto, Jewish immigrant culture provided the familiar cadences of the Yiddish language and the warmth of familial customs that animated her fiction.

By the 1930s and 1940s, Yezierska had difficulties finding a publisher for her writing. She was quite poor and more than eighty years old when readers began to rediscover her work. But by the time she died, she was being recognized as a sensitive interpreter of the assimilation process.

The Lost "Beautifulness"

"Oi weh![1] How it shines the beautifulness!" exulted Hanneh Hayyeh over her newly painted kitchen. She cast a glance full of worship and adoration at the picture of her son in uniform; eyes like her own, shining with eagerness, with joy of life, looked back at her.

"Aby will not have to shame himself to come back to his old home," she rejoiced, clapping her hands—hands blistered from the paintbrush and cal-

---

1. Oh, pain! (Yiddish); usually a general expression of distress or despair.

loused from rough toil. "Now he'll be able to invite all the grandest friends he made in the army."

The smell of the paint was suffocating, but she inhaled in it huge draughts of hidden beauty. For weeks she had dreamed of it and felt in each tin of paint she was able to buy, in each stroke of the brush, the ecstasy of loving service for the son she idolized.

Ever since she first began to wash the fine silks and linens for Mrs. Preston, years ago, it had been Hanneh Hayyeh's ambition to have a white-painted kitchen exactly like that in the old Stuyvesant Square[2] mansion. Now her own kitchen was a dream come true.

Hanneh Hayyeh ran in to her husband, a stoop-shouldered, care-crushed man who was leaning against the bed, his swollen feet outstretched, counting the pennies that totaled his day's earnings.

"Jake Safransky!" she cried excitedly, "you got to come in and give a look on my painting before you go to sleep."

"Oi, let me alone. Give me only a rest."

Too intoxicated with the joy of achievement to take no for an answer, she dragged him into the doorway. "Nu?[3] How do you like it? Do I know what beautiful is?"

"But how much money did you spend out on that paint?"

"It was my own money," she said, wiping the perspiration off her face with a corner of her apron. "Every penny I earned myself from the extra washing."

"But you had ought save it up for the bad times. What'll you do when the cold weather starts in and the pushcart will not wheel itself out?"

"I save and pinch enough for myself. This I done in honor for my son. I want my Aby to lift up his head in the world. I want him to be able to invite even the President from America to his home and shame himself."

"You'd pull the bananas off a blind man's pushcart to bring to your Aby. You know nothing from holding tight to a dollar and saving a penny to a penny like poor people should."

"What do I got from living if I can't have a little beautifulness in my life? I don't allow for myself the ten cents to go to a moving picture that I'm crazy to see. I never yet treated myself to an ice-cream soda even for a holiday. Shining up the house for Aby is my only pleasure."

"Yah, but it ain't your house. It's the landlord's."

"Don't I live in it? I soak in pleasure from every inch of my kitchen. Why, I could kiss the grand white color on the walls. It lights up my eyes like sunshine in the room."

Her glance traveled from the newly painted walls to the geranium on the window-sill, and back to her husband's face.

"Jake!" she cried, shaking him, "ain't you got eyes? How can you look on the way it dances the beautifulness from every corner and not jump in the air from happiness?"

"I'm only thinking on the money you spent out on the landlord's house. Look only on me! I'm black from worry, but no care lays on your head. It only dreams itself in you how to make yourself for an American and lay in every penny you got on fixing out the house like the rich."

---

2. A historic district of New York; at its center is a park between East 15th and East 17th streets, bisected by Second Avenue.
3. Well? (Yiddish).

"I'm sick of living like a pig with my nose to the earth, all the time only pinching and scraping for bread and rent. So long my Aby is with America, I want to make myself for an American. I could tear the stars out from heaven for my Aby's wish."

Her sunken cheeks were flushed and her eyes glowed with light as she gazed about her.

"When I see myself around the house how I fixed it up with my own hands, I forget I'm only a nobody. It makes me feel I'm also a person like Mrs. Preston. It lifts me with high thoughts."

"Why didn't you marry yourself to a millionaire? You always want to make yourself like Mrs. Preston who got millions laying in the bank."

"But Mrs. Preston does make me feel that I'm alike with her," returned Hanneh Hayyeh, proudly. "Don't she talk herself out to me like I was her friend? Mrs. Preston says this war[4] is to give everybody a chance to lift up his head like a person. It is to bring together the people on top who got everything and the people on the bottom who got nothing. She's been telling me about a new word—democracy. It got me on fire. Democracy means that everybody in America is going to be with everybody alike."

"Och! Stop your dreaming out of your head. Close up your mouth from your foolishness. Women got long hair and small brains," he finished, muttering as he went to bed.

At the busy gossiping hour of the following morning when the butcher shop was crowded with women in dressing-sacks and wrappers covered over with shawls, Hanneh Hayyeh elbowed her way into the clamorous babel of her neighbors.

"What are you so burning? What are you so flaming?"

"She's always on fire with the wonders of her son."

"The whole world must stop still to listen to what news her son writes to her."

"She thinks her son is the only one soldier by the American army."

"My Benny is also one great wonder from smartness, but I ain't such a crazy mother like she."

The voices of her neighbors rose from every corner, but Hanneh Hayyeh, deaf to all, projected herself forward.

"What are you pushing yourself so wild? You ain't going to get your meat first. Ain't it, Mr. Sopkin, all got to wait their turn?"

Mr. Sopkin glanced up in the midst of cutting apart a quarter of meat. He wiped his knife on his greasy apron and leaned across the counter.

"Nu? Hanneh Hayyeh?" his ruddy face beamed. "Have you another letter from little Aby in France? What good news have you got to tell us?"

"No—it's not a letter," she retorted, with a gesture of impatience. "The good news is that I got done with the painting of my kitchen—and you all got to come and give a look how it shines in my house like in a palace."

Mr. Sopkin resumed cutting the meat.

"Oi weh!" clamored Hanneh Hayyeh, with feverish breathlessness. "Stop with your meat already and quick come. The store ain't going to run away from you! It will take only a minute. With one step you are upstairs in my house." She flung out her hands. "And everybody got to come along."

4. World War I.

"Do you think I can make a living from looking on the wonders you turn over in your house?" remonstrated the butcher, with a twinkle in his eye.

"Making money ain't everything in life. My new-painted kitchen will light up your heart with joy."

Seeing that Mr. Sopkin still made no move, she began to coax and wheedle, woman-fashion. "Oi weh! Mr. Sopkin! Don't be so mean. Come only. Your customers ain't going to run away from you. If they do, they only got to come back, because you ain't a skinner.[5] You weigh the meat honest."

How could Mr. Sopkin resist such seductive flattery?

"Hanneh Hayyeh!" he laughed. "You're crazy up in the air, but nobody can say no to anything you take into your head."

He tossed his knife down on the counter. "Everybody!" he called; "let us do her the pleasure and give a look on what she got to show us."

"Oi weh! I ain't got no time," protested one. "I left my baby alone in the house locked in."

"And I left a pot of eating on the stove boiling. It must be all burned away by this time."

"But you all got time to stand around here and chatter like a box of monkeys, for hours," admonished Mr. Sopkin. "This will only take a minute. You know Hanneh Hayyeh. We can't tear ourselves away from her till we do what wills itself in her mind."

Protesting and gesticulating, they all followed Mr. Sopkin as Hanneh Hayyeh led the way. Through the hallway of a dark, ill-smelling tenement, up two flights of crooked, rickety stairs, they filed. When Hanneh Hayyeh opened the door there were exclamations of wonder and joy: "Oi! Oi!" and "Ay! Ay! Takeh! Takeh!"[6]

"Gold is shining from every corner!"

"Like for a holiday!"

"You don't need to light up the gas, so it shines!"

"I wish I could only have it so grand!"

"You ain't got worries on your head, so it lays in your mind to make it so fancy."

Mr. Sopkin stood with mouth open, stunned with wonder at the transformation.

Hanneh Hayyeh shook him by the sleeve exultantly. "Nu? Why ain't you saying something?"

"Grand ain't the word for it! What a whiteness! And what a cleanliness! It tears out the eyes from the head! Such a tenant the landlord ought to give out a medal or let down the rent free. I saw the rooms before and I see them now. What a difference from one house to another."

"Ain't you coming in?" Hanneh Hayyeh besought her neighbors.

"God from the world! To step with our feet on this new painted floor?"

"Shah!"[7] said the butcher, taking off his apron and spreading it on the floor. "You can all give a step on my apron. It's dirty, anyhow."

They crowded in on the outspread apron and vied with one another in their words of praise.

---

5. A cheat, a swindler.
6. Oh! (exclamation of surprise), indeed (Yiddish).
7. Quiet! (Yiddish).

"May you live to see your son married from this kitchen, and may we all be invited to the wedding!"

"May you live to eat here cake and wine on the feasts of your grandchildren!"

"May you have the luck to get rich and move from here into your own bought house!"

"Amen!" breathed Hanneh Hayyeh. "May we all forget from our worries for rent!"

Mrs. Preston followed with keen delight Hanneh Hayyeh's every movement as she lifted the wash from the basket and spread it on the bed. Hanneh Hayyeh's rough, toil-worn hands lingered lovingly, caressingly over each garment. It was as though the fabrics held something subtly animate in their texture that penetrated to her very finger-tips.

"Hanneh Hayyeh! You're an artist!" There was reverence in Mrs. Preston's low voice that pierced the other woman's inmost being. "You do my laces and batistes[8] as no one else ever has. It's as if you breathed part of your soul into it."

The hungry-eyed, ghetto woman drank in thirstily the beauty and goodness that radiated from Mrs. Preston's person. None of the cultured elegance of her adored friend escaped Hanneh Hayyeh. Her glance traveled from the exquisite shoes to the flawless hair of the well-poised head.

"Your things got so much fineness. I'm crazy for the feel from them. I do them up so light in my hands like it was thin air I was handling."

Hanneh Hayyeh pantomimed as she spoke and Mrs. Preston, roused from her habitual reserve, put her fine, white hand affectionately over Hanneh Hayyeh's gnarled, roughened ones.

"Oi-i-i-i! Mrs. Preston! You always make me feel so grand!" said Hanneh Hayyeh, a mist of tears in her wistful eyes. "When I go away from you I could just sit down and cry. I can't give it out in words what it is. It chokes me so—how good you are to me—You ain't at all like a rich lady. You're so plain from the heart. You make the lowest nobody feel he's somebody."

"You are not a 'nobody,' Hanneh Hayyeh. You are an artist—an artist laundress."

"What mean you an artist?"

"An artist is so filled with love for the beautiful that he has to express it in some way. You express it in your washing just as a painter paints it in a picture."

"Paint?" exclaimed Hanneh Hayyeh. "If you could only give a look how I painted up my kitchen! It lights up the whole tenement house for blocks around. The grocer and the butcher and all the neighbors were jumping in the air from wonder and joy when they seen how I shined up my house."

"And all in honor of Aby's home-coming?" Mrs. Preston smiled, her thoughts for a moment on her own son, the youngest captain in his regiment whose home-coming had been delayed from week to week.

"Everything I do is done for my Aby," breathed Hanneh Hayyeh, her hands clasping her bosom as if feeling again the throb of his babyhood at her heart. "But this painting was already dreaming itself in my head for years. You remember the time the hot iron fell on my foot and you came to see me and

---

8. Fine sheer fabrics.

brought me a red flower-pot wrapped around with green crêpe paper? That flower-pot opened up the sky in my kitchen." The words surged from the seething soul of her. "Right away I saw before my eyes how I could shine up my kitchen like a parlor by painting the walls and sewing up new curtains for the window. It was like seeing before me your face every time I looked on your flowers. I used to talk to it like it could hear and feel and see. And I said to it: 'I'll show you what's in me. I'll show you that I know what beautiful is.'"

Her face was aglow with an enthusiasm that made it seem young, like a young girl's face.

"I begged myself by the landlord to paint up my kitchen, but he would n't listen to me. So I seen that if I ever hoped to fix up my house, I'd have to spend out my own money. And I began to save a penny to a penny to have for the paint. And when I seen the painters, I always stopped them to ask where and how to buy it so that it should come out the cheapest. By day and by night it burned in me the picture—my kitchen shining all white like yours, till I could n't rest till I done it."

With all her breeding, with all the restraint of her Anglo-Saxon forbears, Mrs. Preston was strangely shaken by Hanneh Hayyeh's consuming passion for beauty. She looked deep into the eyes of the Russian Jewess as if drinking in the secret of their hidden glow.

"I am eager to see that wonderful kitchen of yours," she said, as Hanneh Hayyeh bade her good-bye.

Hanneh Hayyeh walked home, her thoughts in a whirl with the glad anticipation of Mrs. Preston's promised visit. She wondered how she might share the joy of Mrs. Preston's presence with the butcher and all the neighbors. "I'll bake up a shtrudel cake," she thought to herself. "They will all want to come to get a taste of the cake and then they'll give a look on Mrs. Preston."

Thus smiling and talking to herself she went about her work. As she bent over the wash-tub rubbing the clothes, she visualized the hot, steaming shtrudel just out of the oven and the exclamations of pleasure as Mrs. Preston and the neighbors tasted it. All at once there was a knock at the door. Wiping her soapy hands on the corner of her apron, she hastened to open it.

"Oi! Mr. Landlord! Come only inside," she urged. "I got the rent for you, but I want you to give a look around how I shined up my flat."

The Prince Albert[9] that bound the protruding stomach of Mr. Benjamin Rosenblatt was no tighter than the skin that encased the smooth-shaven face. His mouth was tight. Even the small, popping eyes held a tight gleam.

"I got no time. The minutes is money," he said, extending a claw-like hand for the rent.

"But I only want you for a half a minute." And Hanneh Hayyeh dragged the owner of her palace across the threshold. "Nu? Ain't I a good painter? And all this I done while other people were sleeping themselves, after I'd come home from my day's work."

"Very nice," condescended Mr. Benjamin Rosenblatt, with a hasty glance around the room. "You certainly done a good job. But I got to go. Here's your receipt." And the fingers that seized Hanneh Hayyeh's rent-money seemed like pincers for grasping molars.

---

9. Double-breasted frock coat.

Two weeks later Jake Safransky and his wife Hanneh Hayyeh sat eating their dinner, when the janitor came in with a note.

"From the landlord," he said, handing it to Hanneh Hayyeh, and walked out.

"The landlord?" she cried, excitedly. "What for can it be?" With trembling fingers she tore open the note. The slip dropped from her hand. Her face grew livid, her eyes bulged with terror. "Oi weh!" she exclaimed, as she fell back against the wall.

"Gewalt!" cried her husband, seizing her limp hand, "you look like struck dead."

"Oi-i-i! The murderer! He raised me the rent five dollars a month."

"Good for you! I told you to listen to me. Maybe he thinks we got money laying in the bank when you got so many dollars to give out on paint."

She turned savagely on her husband. "What are you tearing yet my flesh? Such a money-grabber! How could I imagine for myself that so he would thank me for laying in my money to painting up his house?"

She seized her shawl, threw it over her head, and rushed to the landlord's office.

"Oi weh! Mr. Landlord! Where is your heart? How could you raise me my rent when you know my son is yet in France? And even with the extra washing I take in I don't get enough when the eating is so dear?"

"The flat is worth five dollars more," answered Mr. Rosenblatt, impatiently. "I can get another tenant any minute."

"Have pity on me! I beg you! From where I can squeeze out the five dollars more for you?"

"That don't concern me. If you can't pay, somebody else will. I got to look out for myself. In America everybody looks out for himself."

"Is it nothing by you how I painted up your house with my own blood-money?"

"You did n't do it for me. You done it for yourself," he sneered. "It's nothing to me how the house looks, so long as I get my rent in time. You wanted to have a swell house, so you painted it. That's all."

With a wave of his hand he dismissed her.

"I beg by your conscience! Think on God!" Hanneh Hayyeh wrung her hands. "Ain't your house worth more to you to have a tenant clean it out and paint it out so beautiful like I done?"

"Certainly," snarled the landlord. "Because the flat is painted new, I can get more money for it. I got no more time for you."

He turned to his stenographer and resumed the dictation of his letters.

Dazedly Hanneh Hayyeh left the office. A choking dryness contracted her throat as she staggered blindly, gesticulating and talking to herself.

"Oi weh! The sweat, the money I laid into my flat and it should all go to the devil. And I should be turned out and leave all my beautifulness. And from where will I get the money for moving? When I begin to break myself up to move, I got to pay out money for the moving man, money for putting up new lines,[1] money for new shelves and new hooks besides money for the rent. I got to remain where I am. But from where can I get together the five dollars for the robber? Should I go to Moisheh Itzek, the pawn-broker, or

---

1. I.e., for drying laundry.

should I maybe ask Mrs. Preston? No—She should n't think I got her for a friend only to help me. Oi weh! Where should I turn with my bitter heart?"

Mechanically she halted at the butcher-shop. Throwing herself on the vacant bench, she buried her face in her shawl and burst out in a loud, heart-piercing wail: "Woe is me! Bitter is me!"

"Hanneh Hayyeh! What to you happened?" cried Mr. Sopkin in alarm.

His sympathy unlocked the bottom depths of her misery.

"Oi-i-i! Black is my luck! Dark is for my eyes!"

The butcher and the neighbors pressed close in upon her.

"Gewalt! What is it? Bad news from Aby in France?"

"Oi-i-i! The murderer! The thief! His gall should burst as mine is bursting! His heart should break as mine is breaking! It remains for me nothing but to be thrown out in the gutter. The landlord raised me five dollars a month rent. And he ripped yet my wounds by telling me he raised me the rent because my painted-up flat is so much more worth."

"The dogs! The blood-sucking landlords! They are the new czars from America!"

"What are you going to do?"

"What should I do? Aby is coming from France any day, and he's got to have a home to come to. I will have to take out from my eating the meat and the milk to save together the extra five dollars. People! Give me an advice! What else can I do? If a wild wolf falls on you in the black night, will crying help you?"

With a gesture of abject despair, she fell prone upon the bench. "Gottuniu![2] If there is any justice and mercy on this earth, then may the landlord be tortured like he is torturing me! May the fires burn him and the waters drown him! May his flesh be torn from him in pieces and his bones be ground in the teeth of wild dogs!"

Two months later, a wasted, haggard Hanneh Hayyeh stood in the kitchen, folding Mrs. Preston's wash in her basket, when the janitor—the servant of her oppressor—handed her another note.

"From the landlord," he said in his toneless voice.

Hanneh Hayyeh paled. She could tell from his smirking sneer that it was a second notice of increased rental.

It grew black before her eyes. She was too stunned to think. Her first instinct was to run to her husband; but she needed sympathy—not nagging. And then in her darkness she saw a light—the face of her friend, Mrs. Preston. She hurried to her.

"Oi—friend! The landlord raised me my rent again," she gasped, dashing into the room like a thing hounded by wild beasts.

Mrs. Preston was shocked by Hanneh Hayyeh's distraught appearance. For the first time she noticed the ravages of worry and hunger.

"Hanneh Hayyeh! Try to calm yourself. It is really quite inexcusable the way the landlords are taking advantage of the situation. There must be a way out. We'll fix it up somehow."

"How fix it up?" Hanneh Hayyeh flared.

"We'll see that you get the rent you need." There was reassurance and confidence in Mrs. Preston's tone.

2. Dear God! (Yiddish).

Hanneh Hayyeh's eyes flamed. Too choked for utterance, her breath ceased for a moment.

"I want no charity! You think maybe I came to beg? No—I want justice!"

She shrank in upon herself, as though to ward off the raised whip of her persecutor. "You know how I feel?" Her voice came from the terrified depths of her. "It's as if the landlord pushed me in a corner and said to me: 'I want money, or I'll squeeze from you your life!' I have no money, so he takes my life.

"Last time, when he raised me my rent, I done without meat and without milk. What more can I do without?"

The piercing cry stirred Mrs. Preston as no mere words had done.

"Sometimes I get so weak for a piece of meat, I could tear the world to pieces. Hunger and bitterness are making a wild animal out of me. I ain't no more the same Hanneh Hayyeh I used to be."

The shudder that shook Hanneh Hayyeh communicated itself to Mrs. Preston. "I know the prices are hard to bear," she stammered, appalled.

"There used to be a time when poor people could eat cheap things," the toneless voice went on. "But now there ain't no more cheap things. Potatoes—rice—fish—even dry bread is dear. Look on my shoes! And I who used to be so neat with myself. I can't no more have my torn shoes fixed up. A pair of shoes or a little patch is only for millionaires."

"Something must be done," broke in Mrs. Preston, distraught for the first time in her life. "But in the meantime, Hanneh Hayyeh, you must accept this to tide you over." She spoke with finality as she handed her a bill.

Hanneh Hayyeh thrust back the money. "Ain't I hurt enough without you having to hurt me yet with charity? You want to give me hush money to swallow down an unrightness that burns my flesh? I want justice."

The woman's words were like bullets that shot through the static security of Mrs. Preston's life. She realized with a guilty pang that while strawberries and cream were being served at her table in January, Hanneh Hayyeh had doubtless gone without a square meal in months.

"We can't change the order of things overnight," faltered Mrs. Preston, baffled and bewildered by Hanneh Hayyeh's defiance of her proffered aid.

"Change things? There's got to be a change!" cried Hanneh Hayyeh with renewed intensity. "The world as it is not to live in any longer. If only my Aby would get back quick. But until he comes, I'll fight till all America will have to stop and listen to me. You was always telling me that the lowest nobody got something to give to America. And that's what I got to give to America—the last breath in my body for justice. I'll wake up America from its sleep. I'll go myself to the President with my Aby's soldier picture and ask him was all this war to let loose a bunch of blood-suckers to suck the marrow out from the people?"

"Hanneh Hayyeh," said Mrs. Preston, with feeling, "these laws are far from just, but they are all we have so far. Give us time. We are young. We are still learning. We're doing our best."

Numb with suffering the woman of the ghetto looked straight into the eyes of Mrs. Preston. "And you too—you too hold by the landlord's side?—Oi—I see! Perhaps you too got property out by agents."

A sigh that had in it the resignation of utter hopelessness escaped from her. "Nothing can hurt me no more—And you always stood out to me in my dreams as the angel from love and beautifulness. You always made-believe to me that you're only for democracy."

Tears came to Mrs. Preston's eyes. But she made no move to defend herself or reply and Hanneh Hayyeh walked out in silence.

A few days later the whole block was astir with the news that Hanneh Hayyeh had gone to court to answer her dispossess summons.

From the windows, the stoop, from the hallway, and the doorway of the butcher-shop the neighbors were talking and gesticulating while waiting for Hanneh Hayyeh's return.

Hopeless and dead, Hanneh Hayyeh dragged herself to the butcher-shop. All made way for her to sit on the bench. She collapsed in a heap, not uttering a single sound, nor making a single move.

The butcher produced a bottle of brandy and, hastily filling a small glass, brought it to Hanneh Hayyeh.

"Quick, take it to your lips," he commanded. Weak from lack of food and exhausted by the ordeal of the court-room, Hanneh Hayyeh obeyed like a child.

Soon one neighbor came in with a cup of hot coffee; another brought bread and herring with onion over it.

Tense, breathless, with suppressed curiosity quivering on their lips, they waited till Hanneh Hayyeh swallowed the coffee and ate enough to regain a little strength.

"Nu? What became in the court?"

"What said the judge?"

"Did they let you talk yourself out like you said you would?"

"Was the murderer there to say something?"

Hanneh Hayyeh wagged her head and began talking to herself in a low, toneless voice as if continuing her inward thought. "The judge said the same as Mrs. Preston said: the landlord has the right to raise our rent or put us out."

"Oi weh! If Hanneh Hayyeh with her fire in her mouth could n't get her rights, then where are we?"

"To whom should we go? Who more will talk for us now?"

"Our life lays in their hands."

"They can choke us so much as they like!"

"Nobody cares. Nobody hears our cry!"

Out of this babel of voices there flashed across Hanneh Hayyeh's deadened senses the chimera that to her was the one reality of her aspiring soul—"Oi-i-i-i! My beautiful kitchen!" she sighed as in a dream.

The butcher's face grew red with wrath. His eyes gleamed like sharp, darting steel. "I would n't give that robber the satisfaction to leave your grand painted house," he said, turning to Hanneh Hayyeh. "I'd smash down everything for spite. You got nothing to lose. Such a murderer! I would learn him a lesson! 'An eye for an eye and a tooth for a tooth.'"[3]

Hanneh Hayyeh, hair disheveled, clothes awry, the nails of her fingers dug in her scalp, stared with the glazed, impotent stare of a mad-woman. With unseeing eyes she rose and blindly made her way to her house.

As she entered her kitchen she encountered her husband hurrying in.

"Oi weh! Oi weh!" he whined. "I was always telling you your bad end.

---

3. See Exodus 21.24; Leviticus 24.20; Deuteronomy 19.21.

Everybody is already pointing their fingers on me! and all because you, a meshugeneh yideneh, a starved beggerin,[4] talked it into your head that you got to have for yourself a white-painted kitchen alike to Mrs. Preston. Now you'll remember to listen to your husband. Now, when you'll be laying in the street to shame and to laughter for the whole world."

"Out! Out from my sight! Out from my house!" shrieked Hanneh Hayyeh. In her rage she seized a flat-iron and Jake heard her hurl it at the slammed door as he fled downstairs.

It was the last night before the eviction. Hanneh Hayyeh gazed about her kitchen with tear-glazed eyes. "Some one who got nothing but only money will come in here and get the pleasure from all this beautifulness that cost me the blood from my heart. Is this already America? What for was my Aby fighting? Was it then only a dream—all these millions people from all lands and from all times, wishing and hoping and praying that America is? Did I wake myself from my dreaming to see myself back in the black times of Russia under the czar?"

Her eager, beauty-loving face became distorted with hate. "No—the landlord ain't going to get the best from me! I'll learn him a lesson. 'An eye for an eye'—"

With savage fury, she seized the chopping-axe and began to scratch down the paint, breaking the plaster on the walls. She tore up the floor-boards. She unscrewed the gas-jets, turned on the gas full force so as to blacken the white-painted ceiling. The night through she raged with the frenzy of destruction.

Utterly spent she flung herself on the lounge, but she could not close her eyes. Her nerves quivered. Her body ached, and she felt her soul ache there—inside her—like a thing killed that could not die.

The first grayness of dawn filtered through the air-shaft window of the kitchen. The room was faintly lighted, and as the rays of dawn got stronger and reached farther, one by one the things she had mutilated in the night started, as it were, into consciousness. She looked at her dish-closet, once precious, that she had scratched and defaced; the uprooted geranium-box on the window-sill; the marred walls. It was unbearable all this waste and desolation that stared at her. "Can it be I who done all this?" she asked herself. "What devil got boiling in me?"

What had she gained by her rage for vengeance? She had thought to spite the landlord, but it was her own soul she had killed. These walls that stared at her in their ruin were not just walls. They were animate—they throbbed with the pulse of her own flesh. For every inch of the broken plaster there was a scar on her heart. She had destroyed that which had taken her so many years of prayer and longing to build up. But this demolished beauty like her own soul, though killed, still quivered and ached with the unstilled pain of life. "Oi weh!" she moaned, swaying to and fro. "So much lost beautifulness—"

Private Abraham Safransky, with the look in his eyes and the swing of his shoulders of all the boys who come back from overseas, edged his way through the wet Delancey Street[5] crowds with the skill of one born to these

---

4. Beggar. "Meshugeneh yideneh": crazy old Jewish woman (both Yiddish).

5. A main street of the Lower East Side, where many tenements were located.

streets and the assurance of the United States Army. Fresh from the ship, with a twenty-four-hour leave stowed safely in his pocket, he hastened to see his people after nearly two years' separation.

On Private Safransky's left shoulder was the insignia of the Statue of Liberty. The three gold service stripes on his left arm and the two wound stripes of his right were supplemented by the Distinguished Service Medal on his left breast bestowed by the United States Government.

As he pictured his mother's joy when he would surprise her in her spotless kitchen, the soldier broke into the double-quick.

All at once he stopped; on the sidewalk before their house was a heap of household things that seemed familiar and there on the curbstone a woman huddled, cowering, broken.—Good God—his mother! His own mother—and all their worldly belongings dumped there in the rain.

1920

VIRGINIA WOOLF
1882–1941

In a memoir titled "A Sketch of the Past" (1939), the mature Virginia Woolf asked "Who was I . . . ? Adeline Virginia Stephen, the second daughter of Leslie and Julia Prinsep Stephen, born on 25th January 1882, descended from a great many people, some famous, others obscure; born into a large connection, born not of rich parents, but of well-to-do parents, born into a very communicative, literate, letter writing, visiting, articulate, late-nineteenth-century world." At the height of her fame as a novelist, essayist, editor, feminist, and influential force in English life and letters, Woolf had moved far from the Victorian origins she outlined in her reminiscence, yet—as she herself understood with greater clarity than many of her contemporaries—what her first biographer, Winifred Holtby, had called "the advantages of being Virginia Stephen" had consistently shaped both her consciousness and her career.

Woolf's father, Leslie Stephen, was a distinguished literary man, the editor first of *The Cornhill Magazine* and then of *The Dictionary of National Biography*, as well as the author of numerous critical, biographical, and philosophical studies. His friends, frequent visitors to the Stephen household, included the American poet and ambassador James Russell Lowell, the English novelist-poet George Meredith, and the American novelist Henry James. Woolf's lively and beautiful mother, Julia Stephen, also had artistic connections. As a girl, Julia had spent much time at Little Holland House, the Kensington estate where the painters William Holman Hunt, Edward Burne-Jones, and G. F. Watts, the actress Ellen Terry, and the poet Alfred, Lord Tennyson frequently gathered; and as a young widow she had seriously devoted herself to the profession of nursing, about which she wrote a useful and witty little book titled *Notes from Sick Rooms* (1883).

The union of these two was the second for both. As a young man, Leslie Stephen had been married to a daughter of the Victorian novelist William Makepeace Thackeray, by whom he had one child, a retarded girl who lived at home with the Stephen family during the years when Virginia was growing up. For her part, his wife Julia had been married at the age of nineteen to a promising attorney, Herbert Duckworth, by whom she had three children—Stella, George, and Gerald—who were to figure resonantly in Virginia's life. Widower and widow, the pair met and eventually wed when they were neighbors, living in an upper-middle-class quarter near London's Hyde Park Gate. Together, they had four more children: Vanessa (who became a painter), Thoby (who died at the age of twenty-six, after a promising university career), Virginia, and Adrian (who became a physician).

Woolf's childhood at 22 Hyde Park Gate was for the most part rich and exhilarating but, at times, bewildering. As she recalled in another memoir, the house itself consisted "of innumerable small oddly shaped rooms built to accommodate not one family but three" (the two Stephen families along with the Duckworths), and here "eleven people aged between eight and sixty lived . . . and were waited upon by seven servants," so that "the place seemed tangled and matted with emotion." Nevertheless, many of the children's activities were perfectly normal for their class and era. Summers the family spent at Talland House in Cornwall, a late-nineteenth-century country home of which Woolf has left an idyllic record in her 1927 novel *To the Lighthouse*. Winters in London were occupied with standard Victorian pedagogical routines: the boys were sent away to school, while the girls were taught at home by their mother and by a series of tutors and governesses, an inequitable education that was later to inspire considerable bitterness in Woolf. Still, despite such familial adherence to convention, the novelist's childhood was distinctively intellectual: not only was she continually brought in touch with what she once called the "old men of recognized genius" who were her father's friends, but she was also early given the freedom of her father's well-stocked library. She began, too, when she was quite young, to demonstrate her own imaginative talents, writing stories that her mother proudly circulated to friends and editing (at first with her brother Thoby and later alone) a family bulletin called *The Hyde Park Gate News*.

Although she had some traumatic childhood experiences—notably, as she was later to report, disturbing sexual advances from her stepbrothers Gerald and George Duckworth—Woolf identified the death in 1895 of her adored mother as possibly the most significant trauma of her life, an event from which she would not recover until she had in effect exorcized her mother's ghost through her characterization of Julia Stephen as Mrs. Ramsay in *To the Lighthouse*. "With mother's death the merry, various family life which she had held in being shut for ever," Woolf later remembered. "In its place a dark cloud settled over us. . . . A finger seemed laid on one's lips." To make matters worse, the girl's older half-sister, Stella Duckworth, who had become hostess and surrogate mother in the Stephen house, married within two years of Julia Stephen's death and died from complications of pregnancy worsened by appendicitis, three months after her marriage. For the next seven years, Virginia and her sister Vanessa were to be left largely at the mercy of their lugubrious father, now a mournful and deaf old man, and their social-climbing half brother George Duckworth, the central subject of her scathing autobiographical sketch "22 Hyde Park Gate."

Perhaps because of these difficulties, or perhaps, as she herself speculated, because of inherited sensitivities, it was in this period that the novelist-to-be suffered the first of a series of mental breakdowns that were to mark and mar the rest of her life. These episodes were characterized by what recent scholars and psychiatrists have defined as symptoms of manic depression, as well as by auditory hallucinations. On one famous occasion, for instance, Woolf claimed to have heard birds singing to her in Greek; on others, according to her husband, she "talked almost without stopping for 2 or 3 days, paying no attention to anyone in the room or anything said to her." As she herself observed in a letter to the composer Ethel Smyth, in these states "my brains went up in a shower of fireworks." Yet ironically enough, she added, such painful derangement was curiously productive: "As an experience, madness is terrific I can assure you. . . . [I]n its lava I still find most of the things I write about. It shoots out of one everything shaped, final, not in mere driblets as sanity does."

Bereavement did not always trigger Woolf's manic depression, however. Although she loved Leslie Stephen, for instance, she experienced his death in 1904 as a kind of liberation. Years later she remarked in her diary that had her father lived, "His life would have entirely ended mine. What would have happened? No writing, no books;—inconceivable." Certainly, after Stephen's demise, the ambition manifested by "writing" and "books" became possible for her as it had never been before. Packing up the relics of 22 Hyde Park Gate that they still wished to keep, the four youngest Stephens—Thoby, Vanessa, Virginia, and Adrian—left Kensington and settled at 46 Gordon Square in Bloomsbury, where the two young women, at last freed from the constraints of the Victorian society George Duckworth had so cherished, quickly became acquainted with a group of their brother Thoby's most brilliant Cambridge friends: Lytton Strachey, Saxon Sydney-Turner, John Maynard Keynes, Clive Bell, Leonard Woolf, Duncan Grant, and, eventually, E. M. Forster.

Many of these young men had been members of a college group known as the "Apostles," and a number were to become prominent in English intellectual circles, Strachey as an iconoclastic biographer, Keynes as a groundbreaking economist, Forster as a novelist, and Leonard Woolf as a man of letters, a socialist politician, and the husband of Virginia Stephen. But in these early Bloomsbury years, they functioned primarily as messengers of a freedom that Virginia, in particular, seems hardly to have allowed herself to imagine before she met them. From late-night discussions of beauty and truth, the group moved to frank analyses of their own sexuality, especially of the homosexuality that had characterized many of the men's secondary school and college careers. For the young woman who was to become the novelist Virginia Woolf, the Victorian period, with its covert suppression of the female intellect and its overt disapproval of everybody's sexuality, seemed definitively to have ended.

Just before and right after the move to Gordon Square, Virginia Stephen had also been actively engaged in a number of radical projects, studying Greek (at that time still an unusual undertaking for a young woman), teaching in a working women's college in south London, doing office chores for the suffrage movement, and writing reviews for the prestigious *Times Literary Supplement*. She was already quite aware that her vocation was to be a literary one, and already quite conscious, too, of her own deeply feminist inclinations. Yet still another trauma was to darken her life in this period: her brother Thoby's sudden death from typhoid fever on a trip that the four Stephens took to Greece in 1906. Like the loss of her mother, this family calamity may well have slowed Woolf's aesthetic growth; certainly it weakened her own mental and physical health for a time (in fact, she herself had a bad case of the illness that killed Thoby). Perhaps for this reason, it was not until after her marriage to Leonard Woolf in 1912 that she was able to focus on finishing her first novel, *The Voyage Out* (1915), a book on which she had been working for seven years when it was finally published.

Only a year before her wedding, Virginia Stephen had brooded on the contrast between her sister Vanessa—now married, a mother, and a productive painter—and herself: "To be 29 and unmarried—to be a failure—childless—insane too, no writer." But when she married Woolf, after the fiasco of a twenty-four-hour engagement to the homosexual Lytton Strachey, she appears to have felt that she had found a husband with whom she could be perfectly happy. Although their relationship may have been in some ways unusual—it seems hardly to have existed sexually, for example—the "Woolves," as Leonard and Virginia were called in their circle, were for the most part an exceptionally compatible couple. A former colonial administrator and, in his wife's words, a "penniless Jew," Leonard Woolf was passionately devoted to the sensitive yet powerfully ambitious literary woman he had married, nursing her through her episodes of mental illness, guarding her time and supporting her work when she was well. As a combination of Jewish "outsider" and Cambridge "insider," moreover, he may have provided the former Virginia Stephen with just the oblique perspective on her culture that she needed. Thus, although her physicians had advised her and her husband against starting a family and her childlessness did sometimes continue to trouble her, Woolf was in most ways satisfied, indeed sustained, by her relationship with Leonard.

With his support, Woolf worked steadily and intensely at the craft of fiction, publishing a series of novels that made her, by the mid-1920s, one of the best-known and most innovative literary artists in England. *The Voyage Out* was followed in 1919 by *Night and Day,* an exploration of the trials of a young woman who was, like the writer herself, a kind of anxious literary heiress. Comparatively conventional in form and substance, this book gave little indication of the more profoundly experimental works that were to come: *Jacob's Room* (1922), a deliberately fragmented meditation on the life and death of a young man who seemed, like Woolf's brother Thoby, to have been a confident inheritor of the patriarchal culture represented by institutions like Cambridge and Oxford; *Mrs. Dalloway* (1925), a daringly structured analysis of post–World War I London society that shifts from one character's mind to another's even while it focuses on a single day in the life of Clarissa Dalloway, a wellborn Westminster hostess, and Septimus Warren Smith, a shell-shocked veteran who paradoxically functions as a kind of other self for her; and *To the Lighthouse,* partly a nostalgic memoir of Woolf's own childhood summers at Talland House and partly a critique of the Victorian mores that made Talland House both a stimulating and a suffocating environment, especially for girls like the rebellious Virginia Stephen.

In the period when she was writing these books, Woolf and her husband also undertook to found a press. The Hogarth Press, as they called it, began at first as a hobby, an attempt on Leonard Woolf's part to offer his wife a species of what would today be labeled occupational therapy. But the enterprise quickly grew into a serious publishing venture; the Woolves produced editions of, among other important works, the poems of T. S. Eliot, the short stories of Katherine Mansfield, and the writings of Sigmund Freud in translation. Dominating what had come to be called the Bloomsbury Group both with her art and with her press, Leslie Stephen's youngest daughter had become, in her own right, an intellectual force to be reckoned with.

Yet central as she was to London literary life, Woolf continued to perceive herself as in many ways an outsider, and specifically as an outsider because she was a woman. From the first—as the critical essays included here suggest—she had been obsessed with reconstructing a uniquely female aesthetic heritage that she implicitly opposed to the predominantly male tradition represented by her father's *Dictionary of National Biography,* and that she was eventually to define as, at least in its inceptions, one of marginality. But when, in the early 1920s, Woolf met and fell in love with a younger writer named Victoria Sackville-West, her commitment to women's lives and works was dramatically intensified. The daughter of an old aristocratic family, Sackville-West was a lesbian poet-novelist who had been married for some years to Harold Nicolson, a literarily inclined diplomat who was evidently an unusually congenial and sympathetic husband. The mother of two sons, she nevertheless quite frankly led what she and Woolf called a "Sapphic" life, though over the years the ambiguity of her sexual identity had sometimes been troublesome.

Despite the comfort of her marriage to Leonard, Woolf's relationship with Vita, as she was called, became, in one biographer's words, the "great passion" of the older novelist's career, and it inspired at least one book: *Orlando* (1928), a parodic biography of a four-hundred-year-old character who changes from male to female in the late seventeenth century and whose fantastic, centuries-long development represents not only the history of the Sackville-West family but also the evolution of English literature from the Renaissance to the twentieth century. In addition, Woolf's feelings for Sackville-West may have energized her composition of a text that is in a sense *Orlando's* "sister" book: *A Room of One's Own* (1929), a luminous extended essay on "women and fiction" that is among the major achievements of feminist criticism in the English language.

After the exuberant blossoming represented by *Orlando* and *A Room of One's Own,* Woolf's life and work slowly darkened. Though her friendship with Vita was never entirely disrupted, it gradually dissolved, never to be replaced by another truly erotic passion. In some ways, *The Waves* (1931) represents Woolf at the height of her avant-garde experimental powers. A "poem-play," as she described it, this innovative novel consists of a series of gravely elegiac monologues spoken by six central characters: each figure is, in one way or another, an aspect of the central human self, and all are haunted by the untimely death of an ambiguously heroic youth named Percival, who is reminiscent of Woolf's lost brother Thoby. Following *The Waves*, Woolf achieved great popular success with what would now be called a "family chronicle" novel, *The Years* (1937), a book that traced the lives of the upper-class Pargiter clan from the Victorian 1880s to "the present moment" in the 1930s. But as Europe began to sink beneath the shadow of fascism, her own existence became increasingly grim. During the 1930s, her nephew Julian Bell, the oldest son of her sister Vanessa, was killed in the Spanish civil war, and she herself had never, in any case, struggled free of recurrent mental illness. Her last novel, *Between the Acts* (posthumously published in 1941), was written at a time when she was precariously balanced between health and disease. A few years earlier, she had produced her most radically feminist work, *Three Guineas* (1938), whose title referred to money she had been asked to contribute to various political causes. The book had taken years—and three scrapbooks full of notes and clippings—to compose, and in its examination of the modes of social oppression, it made overt what Woolf saw as the covert connections between the West's patriarchal social structures and Hitler's jackbooted Nazis marching for the Fatherland.

As German planes began to appear over the once bucolic Sussex countryside where the Woolves had a weekend home in the small village of Rodmell, Virginia Woolf became increasingly anxious, not only about her own sanity but about her society's health. Her physician brother, Adrian, had provided her and Leonard with a painless poison, in case of a German invasion (which would, of course, have been a particularly disastrous event for the couple, given Leonard's Jewish origins). But she feared that no doctor could offer her a cure for the "voices" she had begun to hear; no one could provide a panacea to prevent, in her words, "another of those terrible times" when she would sink into madness. On March 28, 1941, she weighted her pockets with stones and walked into the river Ouse, not far from her cottage at Rodmell, leaving a note for Leonard that explained, "I feel certain I am going mad again," but concluded with the reassurance that "If anyone could have saved me it would have been you. . . . I don't think two people could have been happier than we have been."

Dramatic and disturbing as it was, Woolf's suicide should not be taken as her life's culminating gesture. Certainly, when one sets that gray, precarious moment in 1941—a moment when the sky above Sussex was heavy with bombers and the novelist's own head buzzing with voices—against this artist's lifetime of energetic achievement, the defeat manifested in that bleak instant somewhat dissipates. Had Woolf lived, she would surely have written more and just as well, revising *Between the Acts* and perhaps reworking such other posthumously published works included here as "22 Hyde Park Gate." Yet stories like "The New Dress" and "Slater's Pins Have No Points," along with essays like "Professions for Women" or "Jane Eyre and Wuthering Heights," demonstrate that her vitality was continually intense, while a seemingly casual sketch like "The Death of the Moth" documents her intense attentiveness to—and empathy with—even the most radical otherness. "The advantages of being Virginia Stephen," after all, had been manifold, having taught her not only how to write but how to think and how *not* to think: not to think like a Victorian, not to think like an "insider," not to think like what she called "a patriarch." Instead, defining herself, the way she had in *Three Guineas*, as the founder of a "Society of Outsiders," Woolf had spent most of her life setting herself against both literal and figurative death: the death of the mind symbolized by mental illness as well as the death of the soul manifested by deadening social structures. The last line of *The Waves*, spoken by a character who is perhaps her most significant alter ego—the novelist Bernard—summarizes the determination that shaped her finest achievements: "Against you I will fling myself, unvanquished and unyielding, O Death!"

22 Hyde Park Gate[1]

As I have said, the drawing room at Hyde Park Gate was divided by black folding doors picked out with thin lines of raspberry red. We were still much under the influence of Titian. Mounds of plush, Watts'[2] portraits, busts shrined in crimson velvet, enriched the gloom of a room naturally dark and thickly shaded in summer by showers of Virginia Creeper.

But it is of the folding doors that I wish to speak. How could family life have been carried on without them? As soon dispense with water-closets or bathrooms as with folding doors in a family of nine men and women, one of whom into the bargain was an idiot.[3] Suddenly there would be a crisis—a servant dismissed, a lover rejected, pass books[4] opened, or poor Mrs. Tyndall who had lately poisoned her husband by mistake come for consolation. On one side of the door Cousin Adeline, Duchess of Bedford, perhaps would be on her knees—the Duke had died tragically at Woburn; Mrs. Dolmetsch would be telling how she had found her husband in bed with the parlor-maid or Lisa Stillman would be sobbing that Walter Headlam[5] had chalked her nose with a billiard cue—"which," she cried, "is what comes of smoking a pipe before gentlemen"—and my mother had much ado to persuade her that life had still to be faced, and the flower of virginity was still unplucked in spite of a chalk mark on the nose.

Though dark and agitated on one side, the other side of the door, especially on Sunday afternoons, was cheerful enough. There round the oval tea table with its pink china shell full of spice buns would be found old General Beadle, talking of the Indian Mutiny;[6] or Mr. Haldane, or Sir Frederick Pollock—talking of all things under the sun; or old C. B. Clarke, whose name is given to three excessively rare Himalayan ferns; and Professor Wolstenholme, capable, if you interrupted him, of spouting two columns of tea not unmixed with sultanas through his nostrils; after which he would relapse into a drowsy ursine[7] torpor, the result of eating opium to which he had been driven by the unkindness of his wife and the untimely death of his son Oliver who was eaten, somewhere off the coast of Coromandel, by a shark. These gentlemen came and came again; and they were often reinforced by Mr. Frederick Gibbs, sometime tutor to the Prince of Wales, whose imperturbable common sense and fund of information about the colonies in general and Canada in particular were a perpetual irritation to my father who used to wonder whether a brain fever at college in the year 1863 had not something to do with it. These old gentlemen were generally to be found, eating very slowly, staying very late and making themselves agreeable at Christmas-

---

1. Written by Woolf to be read aloud to the Memoir Club, a group consisting of the members of the famous Bloomsbury circle. All members of the club were expected to read memoirs characterized by "absolute frankness." This house, where Woolf was born, was in Kensington, a prosperous part of London.
2. George Frederick Watts (1817–1904), English painter strongly influenced by Titian—Tiziano Veacelli (ca. 1490–1576), Venetian painter of rich, dark interiors.
3. An allusion to Laura Stephen, Woolf's half sister, who eventually was sent to an asylum.
4. Bankbooks.
5. British classicist (1866–1908), a friend of Leslie Stephen.
6. A yearlong revolt of Indian troops in the British army that started in 1857, characterized by violent reprisals on both sides; it marked the beginning of direct British rule of the subcontinent and the end of the British East Indian Company.
7. Bearlike. "Sultanas": raisins.

time with curious presents of Indian silver work, and hand bags made from the skin of the ornithorhynchus[8]—as I seem to remember.

The tea table however was also fertilized by a ravishing stream of female beauty—the three Miss Lushingtons, the three Miss Stillmans, and the three Miss Montgomeries—all triplets, all ravishing, but of the nine the paragon for wit, grace, charm and distinction was undoubtedly the lovely Kitty Lushington—now Mrs. Leo Maxse. (Their engagement under the jackmanii in the Love Corner at St. Ives was my first introduction to the passion of love.) At the time I speak of she was in process of disengaging herself from Lord Morpeth, and had, I suspect, to explain her motives to my mother, a martinet[9] in such matters, for first promising to marry a man and then breaking it off. My mother believed that all men required an infinity of care. She laid all the blame, I feel sure, upon Kitty. At any rate I have a picture of her as she issued from the secret side of the folding doors bearing on her delicate pink cheeks two perfectly formed pear-shaped crystal tears. They neither fell nor in the least dimmed the luster of her eyes. She at once became the life and soul of the tea table—perhaps Leo Maxse was there—perhaps Ronny Norman—perhaps Esmé Howard—perhaps Arthur Studd, for the gentlemen were not all old, or all professors by any means—and when my father groaned beneath his breath but very audibly, "Oh Gibbs, what a bore you are!" it was Kitty whom my mother instantly threw into the breach. "Kitty wants to tell you how much she loved your lecture," my mother would cry, and Kitty still with the tears on her cheeks would improvise with the utmost gallantry some compliment or opinion which pacified my father who was extremely sensitive to female charm and largely depended upon female praise. Repenting of his irritation he would press poor Gibbs warmly by the hand and beg him to come soon again—which needless to say, poor Gibbs did.

And then there would come dancing into the room rubbing his hands, wrinkling his forehead, the most remarkable figure, as I sometimes think, that our household contained. I have alluded to a grisly relic of another age which we used to disinter from the nursery wardrobe—Herbert Duckworth's wig. (Herbert Duckworth had been a barrister.[1]) Herbert Duckworth's son—George Herbert—was by no means grisly. His hair curled naturally in dark crisp ringlets; he was six foot high; he had been in the Eton Eleven; he was now cramming at Scoones[2] in the hope of passing the Foreign Office examination. When Miss Willett of Brighton saw him "throwing off his ulster" in the middle of her drawing room she was moved to write an Ode Comparing George Duckworth to the Hermes of Praxiteles[3]—which Ode my mother kept in her writing table drawer, along with a little Italian medal that George had won for saving a peasant from drowning. Miss Willett was reminded of the Hermes; but if you looked at him closely you noticed that one of his ears was pointed; and the other round; you also noticed that though he had the curls of a God and the ears of a faun he had unmistakably the eyes of a pig. So strange a compound can seldom have existed. And in the days I speak of,

---

8. Duck-billed platypus.
9. Strict disciplinarian.
1. I.e., a lawyer who argues cases in court; while so doing, British barristers wear white or off-white horsehair wigs. Herbert Duckworth (1833–1870) was Woolf's mother's first husband.

2. I.e., intensively preparing for examinations at a "cram school." "Eton Eleven": i.e., on the cricket team at Eton, a prestigious English boys' school.
3. Athenian sculptor (4th c. B.C.E.); Hermes is the Greek messenger god, also associated with commerce and thieves. "Ulster": long, loose overcoat.

God, faun and pig were all in all alive, all in opposition, and in their conflicts producing the most astonishing eruptions.

To begin with the God—well, he was only a plaster cast perhaps of Miss Willett's Hermes, but I cannot deny that the benign figure of George Duckworth teaching his small half-brothers and sisters by the hour on a strip of coconut matting to play forward with a perfectly straight bat[4] had something Christlike about it. He was certainly Christian rather than Pagan in his divinity, for it soon became clear that this particular forward stroke to be applied to every ball indifferently, was a symbol of moral rectitude, and that one could neither slog nor bowl a sneak[5] without paltering rather dangerously (as poor Gerald Duckworth used to do) with the ideals of a sportsman and an English gentleman. Then, he would run miles to fetch cushions; he was always shutting doors and opening windows; it was always George who said the tactful thing, and broke bad news, and braved my father's irritation, and read aloud to us when we had the whooping cough, and remembered the birthdays of aunts, and sent turtle soup to the invalids, and attended funerals, and took children to the pantomime—oh yes, whatever else George might be he was certainly a saint.

But then there was the faun. Now this animal was at once sportive and demonstrative and thus often at variance with the self-sacrificing nature of the God. It was quite a common thing to come into the drawing room and find George on his knees with his arms extended, addressing my mother, who might be adding up the weekly books, in tones of fervent adoration. Perhaps he had been staying with the Chamberlains for the week-end. But he lavished caresses, endearments, enquiries and embraces as if, after forty years in the Australian bush, he had at last returned to the home of his youth and found an aged mother still alive to welcome him. Meanwhile we gathered round—the dinner bell had already rung—awkward, but appreciative. Few families, we felt, could exhibit such a scene as this. Tears rushed to his eyes with equal abandonment. For example when he had a tooth out he flung himself into the cook's arms in a paroxysm of weeping. When Judith Blunt refused him he sat at the head of the table sobbing loudly, but continuing to eat. He cried when he was vaccinated. He was fond of sending telegrams which began "My darling mother" and went on to say that he would be dining out. (I copied this style of his, I regret to say, with disastrous results on one celebrated occasion. "She is an angel" I wired, on hearing that Flora Russell had accepted him, and signed my nickname "Goat." "She is an aged Goat" was the version that arrived, at Islay, and had something to do, George said, with Flora's reluctance to ally herself with the Stephen family.) But all this exuberance of emotion was felt to be wholly to George's credit. It proved not only how deep and warm his feelings were, but how marvellously he had kept the open heart and simple manners of a child.

But when nature refused him two pointed ears and gave him only one she knew, I think, what she was about. In his wildest paroxysms of emotion, when he bellowed with grief, or danced round the room, leaping like a kid, and flung himself on his knees before the Dowager Lady Carnarvon there was always something self conscious, a little uneasy about him, as though

---

4. I.e., to properly use a cricket bat.   5. Unsportsmanlike strategies in cricket.

he were not quite sure of the effect—as though the sprightly faun had somehow been hobbled together with a timid and conventional old sheep.

It is true that he was abnormally stupid. He passed the simplest examinations with incredible difficulty. For years he was crammed by Mr. Scoones; and again and again he failed to pass the Foreign Office examination. He had existed all his life upon jobs found for him by his friends. His small brown eyes seemed perpetually to be boring into something too hard for them to penetrate. But when one compares them to the eyes of a pig, one is alluding not merely to their stupidity, or to their greed—George, I have been told, had the reputation of being the greediest young man in London ball-rooms—but to something obstinate and pertinacious in their expression as if the pig were grouting for truffles with his snout and would by sheer persistency succeed in unearthing them. Never shall I forget the pertinacity with which he learned "Love in the Valley" by heart in order to impress Flora Russell; or the determination with which he mastered the first volume of *Middlemarch*[6] for the same purpose; and how immensely he was relieved when he left the second volume in a train and got my father, whose set was ruined, to declare that in his opinion one volume of *Middlemarch* was enough. Had his obstinacy been directed solely to self-improvement there would have been no call for us to complain. I myself might even have been of use to him. But it gradually became clear that he was muddling out a scheme, a plan of campaign, a system of life—I scarcely know what to call it—and then we had every reason to feel the earth tremble beneath our feet and the heavens darken. For George Duckworth had become after my mother's death, for all practical purposes, the head of the family. My father was deaf, eccentric, absorbed in his work, and entirely shut off from the world. The management of affairs fell upon George. It was usually said that he was father and mother, sister and brother in one—and all the old ladies of Kensington and Belgravia added with one accord that Heaven had blessed those poor Stephen girls beyond belief, and it remained for them to prove that they were worthy of such devotion.

But what was George Duckworth thinking and what was there alarming in the sight of him as he sat in the red leather arm-chair after dinner, mechanically stroking the dachshund Schuster, and lugubriously glancing at the pages of George Eliot? Well, he might be thinking about the crest on the post office notepaper, and how nice it would look picked out in red (he was now Austen Chamberlain's[7] private secretary) or he might be thinking how the Duchess of St. Albans had given up using fish knives at dinner; or how Mrs. Grenfell had asked him to stay and he had created as he thought a good impression by refusing; at the same time he was revolving in the slow whirlpool of his brain schemes of the utmost thoughtfulness—plans for sending us for treats; for providing us with riding lessons; for finding jobs for some of poor Augusta Croft's innumerable penniless children. But the alarming thing was that he looked not merely muddled and emotional but obstinate. He looked as if he had made up his mind about something and would refuse to budge an inch. At the time it was extremely difficult to say what he had

---

6. Long novel (1871–72) by George Eliot, originally published in four volumes. "Love in the Valley": a poem (1851), more than 200 lines long, by George Meredith.

7. British politician (1863–1937), a member of Parliament (1892–1937) who held high office in several governments.

made up his mind to, but after the lapse of many years I think it may be said brutally and baldly, that George had made up his mind to rise in the social scale. He had a curious inborn reverence for the British aristocracy; the beauty of our great aunts had allied us in the middle of the nineteenth century with, I think I am right in saying, two dukes and quite a number of earls and countesses. They naturally showed no particular wish to remember the connection but George did his best to live up to it. His reverence for the symbols of greatness now that he was attached to a Cabinet Minister had fuller scope. His talk was all of ivory buttons that the coachmen of Cabinet Ministers wear in their coats; of having the entrée at Court; of baronies descending in the female line; of countesses secreting the diamonds of Marie Antoinette[8] in black boxes under their beds. His secret dreams as he sat in the red leather chair stroking Schuster were all of marrying a wife with diamonds, and having a coachman with a button, and having the entrée at Court. But the danger was that his dreams were secret even to himself. Had you told him—and I think Vanessa did once—that he was a snob, he would have burst into tears. What he liked, he explained, was to know "nice people"; Lady Jeune was nice; so were Lady Sligo, Lady Carnarvon and Lady Leitrim. Poor Mrs. Clifford, on the other hand, was not; nor was old Mr. Wolstenholme; of all our old friends, Kitty Maxse, who might have been Lady Morpeth, came nearest to his ideal. It was not a question of birth or wealth; it was—and then if you pressed him further he would seize you in his arms and cry out that he refused to argue with those he loved. "Kiss me, kiss me, you beloved," he would vociferate; and the argument was drowned in kisses. Everything was drowned in kisses. He lived in the thickest emotional haze, and as his passions increased and his desires became more vehement—he lived, Jack Hills[9] assured me, in complete chastity until his marriage—one felt like an unfortunate minnow shut up in the same tank with an unwieldy and turbulent whale.

Nothing stood in the way of his advancement. He was a bachelor of prepossessing appearance though inclined to fat, aged about thirty years, with an independent income of something over a thousand a year. As private secretary to Austen Chamberlain he was as a matter of course invited to all the great parties of all the great peers. Hostesses had no time to remember, if they had ever known, that the Duckworths had made their money in cotton, or coal, not a hundred years ago, and did not really rank, as George made out, among the ancient families of Somersetshire. For I have it on the best authority that when the original Duckworth acquired Orchardleigh about the year 1810 he filled it with casts from the Greek to which he had attached not merely fig leaves for the Gods but aprons for the Goddesses— much to the amusement of the Lords of Longleat who never forgot that old Duckworth had sold cotton by the yard and probably bought his aprons cheap. George, as I say, could have mounted alone to the highest pinnacles of London society. His mantelpiece was a gallery of invitation cards from every house in London. Why then did he insist upon cumbering himself with a couple of half-sisters who were more than likely to drag him down? It is probably useless to enquire. George's mind swam and steamed like a caul-

---

8. Wife of Louis XVI of France (1755–1793), guillotined after the French Revolution.

9. Husband of Woolf's half sister Stella Duckworth.

dron of rich Irish stew. He believed that aristocratic society was possessed of all the virtues and all the graces. He believed that his family had been entrusted to his care. He believed that it was his sacred duty—but when he reached that point his emotions overcame him; he began to sob; he flung himself on his knees; he seized Vanessa in his arms; he implored her in the name of her mother, of her grandmother, by all that was sacred in the female sex and holy in the traditions of our family to accept Lady Arthur Russell's invitation to dinner, to spend the week-end with the Chamberlains at Highbury.

I cannot conceal my own opinion that Vanessa was to blame; not indeed that she could help herself, but if, I sometimes think, she had been born with one shoulder higher than another, with a limp, with a squint, with a large mole on her left cheek, both our lives would have been changed for the better. As it was, George had a good deal of reason on his side. It was plain that Vanessa in her white satin dress made by Mrs. Young, wearing a single flawless amethyst round her neck, and a blue enamel butterfly in her hair—the gifts, of course, of George himself—beautiful, motherless, aged only eighteen, was a touching spectacle, an ornament for any dinner table, a potential peeress, anything might be made of such precious material as she was—outwardly at least; and to be seen hovering round her, providing her with jewels, and Arab horses, and expensive clothes, whispering encouragement, lavishing embraces which were not entirely concealed from the eyes of strangers, redounded to the credit of George himself and invested his figure with a pathos which it would not otherwise have had in the eyes of the dowagers of Mayfair. Unfortunately, what was inside Vanessa did not altogether correspond with what was outside. Underneath the necklaces and the enamel butterflies was one passionate desire—for paint and turpentine, for turpentine and paint. But poor George was no psychologist. His perceptions were obtuse. He never saw within. He was completely at a loss when Vanessa said she did not wish to stay with the Chamberlains at Highbury; and would not dine with Lady Arthur Russell—a rude, tyrannical old woman, with a bloodstained complexion and the manners of a turkey cock. He argued, he wept, he complained to Aunt Mary Fisher, who said that she could not believe her ears. Every battery was turned upon Vanessa. She was told that she was selfish, unwomanly, callous and incredibly ungrateful considering the treasures of affection that had been lavished upon her—the Arab horse she rode and the slabs of bright blue enamel which she wore. Still she persisted. She did not wish to dine with Lady Arthur Russell. As the season wore on, every morning brought its card of invitation for Mr. Duckworth and Miss Stephen; and every evening witnessed a battle between them. For the first year or so George, I suppose, was usually the victor. Off they went, in the hansom cab of those days and late at night Vanessa would come into my room complaining that she had been dragged from party to party, where she knew no one, and had been bored to death by the civilities of young men from the Foreign Office and the condescensions of old ladies of title. The more Vanessa resisted, the more George's natural obstinacy persisted. At last there was a crisis. Lady Arthur Russell was giving a series of select parties on Thursday evenings in South Audley Street. Vanessa had sat through one entire evening without opening her lips. George insisted that she must go next week and make amends, or he said, "Lady Arthur will never ask you to her house again." They argued until it was getting too late to dress. At last Vanessa, more in desperation than in concession, rushed upstairs, flung on her clothes and announced that she was ready to go. Off they went. What happened in the cab will never be known. But whenever they reached 2 South Audley Street—and they reached it several times in the course of the evening—one or the other was incapable of getting out. George refused to enter with Vanessa in such a passion; and Vanessa refused to enter with George in tears. So the cabman had to be told to drive once more round the Park. Whether they ever managed to alight I do not know.

But next morning as I was sitting spelling out my Greek George came into my room carrying in his hand a small velvet box. He presented me with the jewel it contained—a Jews' harp made of enamel with a pinkish blob of matter swinging in the center which I regret to say only fetched a few shillings when I sold it the other day. But his face showed that he had come upon a different errand. His face was sallow and scored with innumerable wrinkles, for his skin was as loose and flexible as a pug dog's, and he would express his anguish in the most poignant manner by puckering lines, folds, and creases from forehead to chin. His manner was stern. His bearing rigid. If Miss Willett of Brighton could have seen him then she would certainly have compared him to Christ on the cross. After giving me the Jews' harp he stood before the fire in complete silence. Then, as I expected, he began to tell me his version of the preceding night—wrinkling his forehead more than ever, but speaking with a restraint that was at once bitter and manly. Never, never again, he said, would he ask Vanessa to go out with him. He had seen a look in her eyes which positively frightened him. It should never be said of him that he made her do what she did not wish to do. Here he quivered, but checked himself. Then he went on to say that he had only done what he knew my mother would have wished him to do. His two sisters were the most precious things that remained to him. His home had always meant more to him—more than he could say, and here he became agitated, struggled for composure, and then burst into a statement which was at once dark and extremely lurid. We were driving Gerald from the house, he cried—when a young man was not happy at home—he himself had always been content—but if his sisters—if Vanessa refused to go out with him—if he could not bring his friends to the house—in short, it was clear that the chaste, the immaculate George Duckworth would be forced into the arms of whores. Needless to say he did not put it like that; and I could only conjure up in my virgin consciousness, dimly irradiated by having read the "Symposium"[1] with Miss Case, horrible visions of the vices to which young men were driven whose sisters did not make them happy at home. So we went on talking for an hour or two. The end of it was that he begged me, and I agreed, to go a few nights later to the Dowager Marchioness of Sligo's ball. I had already been to May Week[2] at Cambridge, and my recollections of gallopading round the room with Hawtrey, or sitting on the stairs and quizzing the dancers with Clive,[3] were such as to make me wonder why Vanessa found dances in Lon-

---

1. Janet Case (1862–1937), who began teaching Woolf Greek in 1902 and became a lifelong friend. "Symposium": dialogue on the subject of love—heterosexual, homosexual, and the love of beauty—by the Greek philosopher Plato (ca. 427–ca. 347 B.C.E.).
2. The festive week (in June) of intercollegiate boat races at the English university.
3. Clive Bell (1881–1964), later to be Vanessa's husband. "Quizzing": mocking.

don so utterly detestable. A few nights later I discovered for myself. After two hours of standing about in Lady Sligo's ball-room, of waiting to be introduced to strange young men, of dancing a round with Conrad Russell or with Esmé Howard, of dancing very badly, of being left without a partner, of being told by George that I looked lovely but must hold myself upright, I retired to an ante-room and hoped that a curtain concealed me. For some time it did. At length old Lady Sligo discovered me, judged the situation for herself and being a kind old peeress with a face like a rubicund sow's carried me off to the dining room, cut me a large slice of iced cake, and left me to devour it by myself in a corner.

On that occasion George was lenient. We left about two o'clock, and on the way home he praised me warmly, and assured me that I only needed practice to be a great social success. A few days later he told me that the Dowager Countess of Carnarvon particularly wished to make my acquaintance, and had invited me to dinner. As we drove across the Park he stroked my hand, and told me how he hoped that I should make friends with Elsie—for so both he and Vanessa had called her for some time at her own request—how I must not be frightened—how though she had been vice-reine of Canada and vice-reine of Ireland she was simplicity itself—always since the death of her husband dressed in black—refused to wear any of her jewels though she had inherited the diamonds of Marie Antoinette—and was the one woman, he said, with a man's sense of honor. The portrait he drew was of great distinction and bereavement. There would also be present her sister, Mrs. Popham of Littlecote, a lady also of distinction and also bereaved, for her husband, Dick Popham of Littlecote, came of an ancient unhappy race, cursed in the reign of Henry the Eighth, since which time the property had never descended from father to son. Sure enough Mary Popham was childless, and Dick Popham was in a lunatic asylum. I felt that I was approaching a house of grandeur and desolation, and was not a little impressed. But I could see nothing alarming either in Elsie Carnarvon or in Mrs. Popham of Littlecote. They were a couple of spare prim little women, soberly dressed in high black dresses, with gray hair strained off their foreheads, rather prominent blue eyes, and slightly protruding front teeth. We sat down to dinner.

The conversation was mild and kindly. Indeed I soon felt that I could not only reply to their questions—was I fond of painting?—was I fond of reading?—did I help my father in his work?—but could initiate remarks of my own. George had always complained of Vanessa's silence. I would prove that I could talk. So off I started. Heaven knows what devil prompted me—or why to Lady Carnarvon and Mrs. Popham of Littlecote of all people in the world I, a chit of eighteen, should have chosen to discourse upon the need of expressing the emotions! That, I said, was the great lack of modern life. The ancients, I said, discussed everything in common. Had Lady Carnarvon ever read the dialogues of Plato? "We—both men and women—" once launched it was difficult to stop, nor was I sure that my audacity was not holding them spell-bound with admiration. I felt that I was earning George's gratitude for ever. Suddenly a twitch, a shiver, a convulsion of amazing expressiveness, shook the Countess by my side; her diamonds, of which she wore a chaste selection, flashed in my eyes; and stopping, I saw George Duckworth blushing crimson on the other side of the table. I realized that I had committed some unspeakable impropriety. Lady Carnarvon and Mrs.

Popham began at once to talk of something entirely different; and directly dinner was over George, pretending to help me on with my cloak, whispered in my ear in a voice of agony, "They're not used to young women saying anything—." And then as if to apologize to Lady Carnarvon for my ill breeding, I saw him withdraw with her behind a pillar in the hall, and though Mrs. Popham of Littlecote tried to attract my attention to a fine specimen of Moorish metal work which hung on the wall, we both distinctly heard them kiss. But the evening was not over. Lady Carnarvon had taken tickets for the French actors, who were then appearing in some play whose name I have forgotten. We had stalls[4] of course, and filed soberly to our places in the very center of the crowded theater. The curtain went up. Snubbed, shy, indignant, and uncomfortable, I paid little attention to the play. But after a time I noticed that Lady Carnarvon on one side of me, and Mrs. Popham on the other, were both agitated by the same sort of convulsive twitching which had taken them at dinner. What could be the matter? They were positively squirming in their seats. I looked at the stage. The hero and heroine were pouring forth a flood of voluble French which I could not disentangle. Then they stopped. To my great astonishment the lady leapt over the back of a sofa; the gentleman followed her. Round and round the stage they dashed, the lady shrieking, the man groaning and grunting in pursuit. It was a fine piece of realistic acting. As the pursuit continued, the ladies beside me held to the arms of their stalls with claws of iron. Suddenly, the actress dropped exhausted upon the sofa, and the man with a howl of gratification, loosening his clothes quite visibly, leapt on top of her. The curtain fell. Lady Carnarvon, Mrs. Popham of Littlecote and George Duckworth rose simultaneously. Not a word was said. Out we filed. And as our procession made its way down the stalls I saw Arthur Cane leap up in his seat like a jack-in-the-box, amazed and considerably amused that George Duckworth and Lady Carnarvon of all people should have taken a girl of eighteen to see the French actors copulate upon the stage.

The brougham[5] was waiting, and Mrs. Popham of Littlecote, without speaking a word or even looking at me, immediately secreted herself inside it. Nor could Lady Carnarvon bring herself to face me. She took my hand, and said in a tremulous voice—her elderly cheeks were flushed with emotion—"I do hope, Miss Stephen, that the evening has not tired you very much." Then she stepped into the carriage, and the two bereaved ladies returned to Bruton Street. George meanwhile had secured a cab. He was much confused, and yet very angry. I could see that my remarks at dinner upon the dialogues of Plato rankled bitterly in his mind. And he told the cabman to go, not back to Hyde Park Gate as I hoped, but on to Melbury Road.

"It's quite early still," he said in his most huffy manner as he sat down. "And I think you want a little practice in how to behave to strangers. It's not your fault of course, but you have been out much less than most girls of your age." So it appeared that my education was to be continued, and that I was about to have another lesson in the art of behaviour at the house of Mrs. Holman Hunt.[6] She was giving a large evening party. Melbury Road was

---

4. Expensive seats.
5. Closed carriage.
6. Wife of William Holman Hunt (1827–1910), well-known Victorian painter; one of his most famous paintings is *The Light of the World* (1851–53).

lined with hansoms, four-wheelers, hired flies, and an occasional carriage drawn by a couple of respectable family horses. "A very *dritte*[7] crowd," said George disdainfully as we took our place in the queue. Indeed all our old family friends were gathered together in the Moorish Hall, and directly I came in I recognized the Stillmans, the Lushingtons, the Montgomeries, the Morrises, the Burne-Joneses—Mr. Gibbs, Professor Wolstenholme and General Beadle would certainly have been there too had they not all been sleeping for many years beneath the sod. The effect of the Moorish Hall, after Bruton Street, was garish, a little eccentric, and certainly very dowdy. The ladies were intense and untidy; the gentlemen had fine foreheads and short evening trousers, in some cases revealing a pair of bright red Pre-Raphaelite socks. George stepped among them like a Prince in disguise. I soon attached myself to a little covey of Kensington ladies who were being conveyed by Gladys Holman Hunt across the Moorish Hall to the studio. There we found old Holman Hunt himself dressed in a long Jaeger dressing gown, holding forth to a large gathering about the ideas which had inspired him in painting "The Light of the World," a copy of which stood upon an easel. He sipped cocoa and stroked his flowing beard as he talked, and we sipped cocoa and shifted our shawls—for the room was chilly—as we listened. Occasionally some of us strayed off to examine with reverent murmurs other bright pictures upon other easels, but the tone of the assembly was devout, high-minded, and to me after the tremendous experiences of the evening, soothingly and almost childishly simple. George was never lacking in respect for old men of recognized genius, and he now advanced with his opera hat pressed beneath his arm; drew his feet together, and made a profound bow over Holman Hunt's hand. Holman Hunt had no notion who he was, or indeed who any of us were; but went on sipping his cocoa, stroking his beard, and explaining what ideas had inspired him in painting "The Light of the World," until we left.

At last—at last—the evening was over.

I went up to my room, took off my beautiful white satin dress, and unfastened the three pink carnations which had been pinned to my breast by the Jews' harp. Was it really possible that tomorrow I should open my Greek dictionary and go on spelling out the dialogues of Plato with Miss Case? I felt I knew much more about the dialogues of Plato than Miss Case could ever do. I felt old and experienced and disillusioned and angry, amused and excited, full of mystery, alarm and bewilderment. In a confused whirlpool of sensation I stood slipping off my petticoats, withdrew my long white gloves, and hung my white silk stockings over the back of a chair. Many different things were whirling round in my mind—diamonds and countesses, copulations, the dialogues of Plato, Mad Dick Popham and "The Light of the World." Ah, how pleasant it would be to stretch out in bed, fall asleep and forget them all!

Sleep had almost come to me. The room was dark. The house silent. Then, creaking stealthily, the door opened; treading gingerly, someone entered. "Who?" I cried. "Don't be frightened," George whispered. "And don't turn

---

7. Third (German); i.e., third-rate.

on the light, oh beloved. Beloved—" and he flung himself on my bed, and took me in his arms.

Yes, the old ladies of Kensington and Belgravia never knew that George Duckworth was not only father and mother, brother and sister to those poor Stephen girls; he was their lover also.

1921?   1976

Jane Eyre and Wuthering Heights[1]

Of the hundred years that have passed since Charlotte Brontë was born, she, the center now of so much legend, devotion, and literature, lived but thirty-nine. It is strange to reflect how different those legends might have been had her life reached the ordinary human span. She might have become, like some of her famous contemporaries, a figure familiarly met with in London and elsewhere, the subject of pictures and anecdotes innumerable, the writer of many novels, of memoirs possibly, removed from us well within the memory of the middle-aged in all the splendor of established fame. She might have been wealthy, she might have been prosperous. But it is not so. When we think of her we have to imagine some one who had no lot in our modern world; we have to cast our minds back to the 'fifties of the last century, to a remote parsonage upon the wild Yorkshire moors. In that parsonage, and on those moors, unhappy and lonely, in her poverty and her exaltation, she remains for ever.

These circumstances, as they affected her character, may have left their traces on her work. A novelist, we reflect, is bound to build up his structure with much very perishable material which begins by lending it reality and ends by cumbering it with rubbish. As we open *Jane Eyre* once more we cannot stifle the suspicion that we shall find her world of imagination as antiquated, mid-Victorian, and out of date as the parsonage on the moor, a place only to be visited by the curious, only preserved by the pious. So we open *Jane Eyre;* and in two pages every doubt is swept clean from our minds.

> Folds of scarlet drapery shut in my view to the right hand; to the left were the clear panes of glass, protecting, but not separating me from the drear November day. At intervals, while turning over the leaves of my book, I studied the aspect of that winter afternoon. Afar, it offered a pale blank of mist and cloud; near, a scene of wet lawn and storm-beat shrub, with ceaseless rain sweeping away wildly before a long and lamentable blast.

There is nothing there more perishable than the moor itself, or more subject to the sway of fashion than the "long and lamentable blast." Nor is this exhilaration short-lived. It rushes us through the entire volume, without giving us time to think, without letting us lift our eyes from the page. So intense is our absorption that if some one moves in the room the movement seems

---

1. Two famous novels published in 1847, the first by Charlotte Brontë (1816–1855), the second by her sister Emily Brontë (1818–1848); see Vol. 1, pp. 633, 959.

to take place not there but up in Yorkshire. The writer has us by the hand, forces us along her road, makes us see what she sees, never leaves us for a moment or allows us to forget her.[2] At the end we are steeped through and through with the genius, the vehemence, the indignation of Charlotte Brontë. Remarkable faces, figures of strong outline and gnarled feature have flashed upon us in passing; but it is through her eyes that we have seen them. Once she is gone, we seek for them in vain. Think of Rochester and we have to think of Jane Eyre. Think of the moor, and again, there is Jane Eyre. Think of the drawing-room, even, those "white carpets on which seemed laid brilliant garlands of flowers," that "pale Parian mantelpiece" with its Bohemia glass of "ruby red" and the "general blending of snow and fire"—what is all that except Jane Eyre?

The drawbacks of being Jane Eyre are not far to seek. Always to be a governess and always to be in love is a serious limitation in a world which is full, after all, of people who are neither one nor the other. The characters of a Jane Austen or of a Tolstoi[3] have a million facets compared with these. They live and are complex by means of their effect upon many different people who serve to mirror them in the round. They move hither and thither whether their creators watch them or not, and the world in which they live seems to us an independent world which we can visit, now that they have created it, by ourselves. Thomas Hardy[4] is more akin to Charlotte Brontë in the power of his personality and the narrowness of his vision. But the differences are vast. As we read *Jude the Obscure* we are not rushed to a finish; we brood and ponder and drift away from the text in plethoric trains of thought which build up round the characters an atmosphere of question and suggestion of which they are themselves, as often as not, unconscious. Simple peasants as they are, we are forced to confront them with destinies and questionings of the hugest import, so that often it seems as if the most important characters in a Hardy novel are those which have no names. Of this power, of this speculative curiosity, Charlotte Brontë has no trace. She does not attempt to solve the problems of human life; she is even unaware that such problems exist; all her force, and it is the more tremendous for being constricted, goes into the assertion, "I love," "I hate," "I suffer."

For the self-centered and self-limited writers have a power denied the more catholic[5] and broad-minded. Their impressions are close packed and strongly stamped between their narrow walls. Nothing issues from their minds which has not been marked with their own impress. They learn little from other writers, and what they adopt they cannot assimilate. Both Hardy and Charlotte Brontë appear to have founded their styles upon a stiff and decorous journalism. The staple of their prose is awkward and unyielding. But both

---

2. Charlotte and Emily Brontë had much the same sense of colour. ". . . we saw—ah! it was beautiful—a splendid place carpeted with crimson, and crimson-covered chairs and tables, and a pure white ceiling bordered by gold, a shower of glass drops hanging in silver chains from the centre, and shimmering with little soft tapers" (*Wuthering Heights*). Yet it was merely a very pretty drawing-room, and within it a boudoir, both spread with white carpets, on which seemed laid brilliant garlands of flowers; both ceiled with snowy mouldings of white grapes and vine leaves, beneath which glowed in rich contrast crimson couches and ottomans; while the ornaments on the pale Parian mantelpiece were of sparkling Bohemia glass, ruby red; and between the windows large mirrors repeated the general blending of snow and fire [Woolf's note].
3. Count Leo Tolstoy (1828–1910), Russian novelist. Austen (1775–1817), English novelist; see Vol. 1, p. 459.
4. English novelist and poet (1840–1928), author of *Jude the Obscure* (1895).
5. Universal.

with labor and the most obstinate integrity by thinking every thought until it has subdued words to itself, have forged for themselves a prose which takes the mould of their minds entire; which has, into the bargain, a beauty, a power, a swiftness of its own. Charlotte Brontë, at least, owed nothing to the reading of many books. She never learned the smoothness of the professional writer, or acquired his ability to stuff and sway his language as he chooses. "I could never rest in communication with strong, discreet, and refined minds, whether male or female," she writes, as any leader-writer[6] in a provincial journal might have written; but gathering fire and speed goes on in her own authentic voice "till I had passed the outworks of conventional reserve and crossed the threshold of confidence, and won a place by their hearts' very hearthstone." It is there that she takes her seat; it is the red and fitful glow of the heart's fire which illumines her page. In other words, we read Charlotte Brontë not for exquisite observation of character—her characters are vigorous and elementary; not for comedy—hers is grim and crude; not for a philosophic view of life—hers is that of a country parson's daughter; but for her poetry. Probably that is so with all writers who have, as she has, an overpowering personality, who, as we should say in real life, have only to open the door to make themselves felt. There is in them some untamed ferocity perpetually at war with the accepted order of things which makes them desire to create instantly rather than to observe patiently. This very ardor, rejecting half shades and other minor impediments, wings its way past the daily conduct of ordinary people and allies itself with their more inarticulate passions. It makes them poets, or, if they choose to write in prose, intolerant of its restrictions. Hence it is that both Emily and Charlotte are always invoking the help of nature. They both feel the need of some more powerful symbol of the vast and slumbering passions in human nature than words or actions can convey. It is with a description of a storm that Charlotte ends her finest novel *Villette*. "The skies hang full and dark—a wrack[7] sails from the west; the clouds cast themselves into strange forms." So she calls in nature to describe a state of mind which could not otherwise be expressed. But neither of the sisters observed nature accurately as Dorothy Wordsworth observed it, or painted it minutely as Tennyson[8] painted it. They seized those aspects of the earth which were most akin to what they themselves felt or imputed to their characters, and so their storms, their moors, their lovely spaces of summer weather are not ornaments applied to decorate a dull page of display the writer's powers of observation—they carry on the emotion and light up the meaning of the book.

The meaning of a book, which lies so often apart from what happens and what is said and consists rather in some connection which things in themselves different have had for the writer, is necessarily hard to grasp. Especially this is so when, like the Brontës, the writer is poetic, and his meaning inseparable from his language, and itself rather a mood than a particular observation. *Wuthering Heights* is a more difficult book to understand than *Jane Eyre*, because Emily was a greater poet than Charlotte. When Charlotte wrote she said with eloquence and splendor and passion "I love," "I hate," "I

---

6. Editorial writer.
7. Wrecked ship. *Villette*, the last novel Brontë wrote, was published in 1853.

8. Alfred, Lord Tennyson (1809–1892), English poet. Wordsworth (1771–1855), English poet and diarist; see Vol. 1, p. 447.

suffer." Her experience, though more intense, is on a level with our own. But there is no "I" in *Wuthering Heights*. There are no governesses. There are no employers. There is love, but it is not the love of men and women. Emily was inspired by some more general conception. The impulse which urged her to create was not her own suffering or her own injuries. She looked out upon a world cleft into gigantic disorder and felt within her the power to unite it in a book. That gigantic ambition is to be felt throughout the novel—a struggle, half thwarted but of superb conviction, to say something through the mouths of her characters which is not merely "I love" or "I hate," but "we, the whole human race" and "you, the eternal powers . . ." the sentence remains unfinished. It is not strange that it should be so; rather it is astonishing that she can make us feel what she had it in her to say at all. It surges up in the half-articulate words of Catherine Earnshaw,[9] "If all else perished and he remained, I should still continue to be; and if all else remained and he were annihilated, the universe would turn to a mighty stranger; I should not seem part of it." It breaks out again in the presence of the dead. "I see a repose that neither earth nor hell can break, and I feel an assurance of the endless and shadowless hereafter—the eternity they have entered—where life is boundless in its duration, and love in its sympathy and joy in its fulness." It is this suggestion of power underlying the apparitions of human nature, and lifting them up into the presence of greatness that gives the book its huge stature among other novels. But it was not enough for Emily Brontë to write a few lyrics, to utter a cry, to express a creed. In her poems she did this once and for all, and her poems will perhaps outlast her novel. But she was novelist as well as poet. She must take upon herself a more laborious and a more ungrateful task. She must face the fact of other existences, grapple with the mechanism of external things, build up, in recognisable shape, farms and houses and report the speeches of men and women who existed independently of herself. And so we reach these summits of emotion not by rant or rhapsody but by hearing a girl sing old songs to herself as she rocks in the branches of a tree; by watching the moor sheep crop the turf; by listening to the soft wind breathing through the grass. The life at the farm with all its absurdities and its improbability is laid open to us. We are given every opportunity of comparing *Wuthering Heights* with a real farm and Heathcliff with a real man. How, we are allowed to ask, can there be truth or insight or the finer shades of emotion in men and women who so little resemble what we have seen ourselves? But even as we ask it we see in Heathcliff the brother that a sister of genius might have seen; he is impossible, we say, but nevertheless no boy in literature has so vivid an existence as his. So it is with the two Catherines; never could women feel as they do or act in their manner, we say. All the same, they are the most lovable women in English fiction. It is as if she could tear up all that we know human beings by, and fill these unrecognizable transparences with such a gust of life that they transcend reality. Hers, then, is the rarest of all powers. She could free life from its dependence on facts; with a few touches indicate the spirit of a face so that it needs no body; by speaking of the moor make the wind blow and the thunder roar.

1925

---

9. The central female character of *Wuthering Heights*; the "he" in her speech is Heathcliff, her adoptive brother and lover. She dies after the birth of her daughter, also named Catherine.

A Woman's College from Outside

The feathery-white moon never let the sky grow dark; all night the chestnut blossoms were white in the green, and dim was the cow-parsley in the meadows. Neither to Tartary nor to Arabia went the wind of the Cambridge courts, but lapsed dreamily in the midst of gray-blue clouds over the roofs of Newnham.[1] There, in the garden, if she needed space to wander, she might find it among the trees; and as none but women's faces could meet her face, she might unveil it, blank, featureless, and gaze into rooms where at that hour, blank, featureless, eyelids white over eyes, ringless hands extended upon sheets, slept innumerable women. But here and there a light still burned.

A double light one might figure in Angela's room, seeing how bright Angela herself was, and how bright came back the reflection of herself from the square glass. The whole of her was perfectly delineated—perhaps the soul. For the glass held up an untrembling image—white and gold, red slippers, pale hair with blue stones in it, and never a ripple or shadow to break the smooth kiss of Angela and her reflection in the glass, as if she were glad to be Angela. Anyhow the moment was glad—the bright picture hung in the heart of night, the shrine hollowed in the nocturnal blackness. Strange indeed to have this visible proof of the rightness of things; this lily floating flawless upon Time's pool, fearless, as if this were sufficient—this reflection. Which meditation she betrayed by turning, and the mirror held nothing at all, or only the brass bedstead, and she, running here and there, patting, and darting, became like a woman in a house, and changed again, pursing her lips over a black book and marking with her finger what surely could not be a firm grasp of the science of economics. Only Angela Williams was at Newnham for the purpose of earning her living, and could not forget even in moments of impassioned adoration the checks of her father at Swansea: her mother washing in the scullery: pink frocks out to dry on the line; tokens that even the lily no longer floats flawless upon the pool, but has a name on a card like another.

A. Williams—one may read it in the moonlight; and next to it some Mary or Eleanor, Mildred, Sarah, Phoebe upon square cards on their doors. All names, nothing but names. The cool white light withered them and starched them until it seemed as if the only purpose of all these names was to rise martially in order should there be a call on them to extinguish a fire, suppress an insurrection, or pass an examination. Such is the power of names written upon cards pinned upon doors. Such too the resemblance, what with tiles, corridors, and bedroom doors, to dairy or nunnery, a place of seclusion or discipline, where the bowl of milk stands cool and pure and there's a great washing of linen.

At that very moment soft laughter came from behind a door. A prim-voiced clock struck the hour—one, two. Now if the clock were issuing his commands, they were disregarded. Fire, insurrection, examination, were all snowed under by laughter, or softly uprooted, the sound seeming to bubble up from the depths and gently waft away the hour, rules, discipline. The bed was strewn with cards. Sally was on the floor. Helena in the chair. Good Bertha clasping her hands by the fire-place. A. Williams came in yawning.

---

1. The second oldest woman's college of Cambridge University.

"Because it's utterly and intolerably damnable," said Helena.

"Damnable," echoed Bertha. Then yawned.

"We're not eunuchs."

"I saw her slipping in by the back gate with that old hat on. They don't want us to know."

"They?" said Angela. "She."

Then the laughter.

The cards were spread, falling with their red and yellow faces on the table, and hands were dabbled in the cards. Good Bertha, leaning with her head against the chair, sighed profoundly. For she would willingly have slept, but since night is free pasturage, a limitless field, since night is unmolded richness, one must tunnel into its darkness. One must hang it with jewels. Night was shared in secret, day browsed on by the whole flock. The blinds were up. A mist was on the garden. Sitting on the floor by the window (while the others played), body, mind, both together, seemed blown through the air, to trail across the bushes. Ah, but she desired to stretch out in bed and to sleep! She believed that no one felt her desire for sleep; she believed humbly—sleepily—with sudden nods and lurchings, that other people were wide awake. When they laughed all together a bird chirped in its sleep out in the garden, as if the laughter—

Yes, as if the laughter (for she dozed now) floated out much like mist and attached itself by soft elastic shreds to plants and bushes, so that the garden was vaporous and clouded. And then, swept by the wind, the bushes would bow themselves and the white vapors blow off across the world.

From all the rooms where women slept this vapor issued, attaching itself to shrubs, like mist, and then blew freely out into the open. Elderly women[2] slept, who would on waking immediately clasp the ivory rod of office. Now smooth and colorless, reposing deeply, they lay surrounded, lay supported, by the bodies of youth recumbent or grouped at the window; pouring forth into the garden this bubbling laughter, this irresponsible laughter: this laughter of mind and body floating away rules, hours, discipline: immensely fertilising, yet formless, chaotic, trailing and straying and tufting the rose-bushes with shreds of vapor.

"Ah," breathed Angela, standing at the window in her nightgown. Pain was in her voice. She leant her head out. The mist was cleft as if her voice parted it. She had been talking, while the others played, to Alice Avery, about Bamborough Castle;[3] the color of the sands at evening; upon which Alice said she would write and settle the day, in August, and stooping, kissed her, at least touched her head with her hand, and Angela, positively unable to sit still, like one possessed of a wind-lashed sea in her heart, roamed up and down the room (the witness of such a scene) throwing her arms out to relieve this excitement, this astonishment at the incredible stooping of the miraculous tree with the golden fruit at its summit—hadn't it dropped into her arms? She held it glowing to her breast, a thing not to be touched, thought of, or spoken about, but left to glow there. And then, slowly putting there her stockings, there her slippers, folding her petticoat neatly on top, Angela, her other name being Williams, realized—how could she express it?—that

---

2. I.e., college administrators (the ceremonial staff or mace is a symbol of authority).

3. A medieval castle on the northeastern coast of England.

after the dark churning of myriad ages here was light at the end of the tunnel; life; the world. Beneath her it lay—all good; all lovable. Such was her discovery.

Indeed, how could one then feel surprise if, lying in bed, she could not close her eyes?—something irresistibly unclosed them—if in the shallow darkness chair and chest of drawers looked stately, and the looking-glass precious with its ashen hint of day? Sucking her thumb like a child (her age nineteen last November), she lay in this good world, this new world, this world at the end of the tunnel, until a desire to see it or forestall it drove her, tossing her blankets, to guide herself to the window, and there, looking out upon the garden, where the mist lay, all the windows open, one fiery-bluish, something murmuring in the distance, the world of course, and the morning coming, "Oh," she cried, as if in pain.

1926, 1977

Moments of Being
"Slater's Pins Have No Points"

"Slater's pins have no points—don't you always find that?" said Miss Craye, turning round as the rose fell out of Fanny Wilmot's dress, and Fanny stooped, with her ears full of the music, to look for the pin on the floor.

The words gave her an extraordinary shock, as Miss Craye struck the last chord of the Bach fugue. Did Miss Craye actually go to Slater's and buy pins then, Fanny Wilmot asked herself, transfixed for a moment. Did she stand at the counter waiting like anybody else, and was she given a bill with coppers wrapped in it, and did she slip them into her purse and then, an hour later, stand by her dressing table and take out the pins? What need had she of pins? For she was not so much dressed as cased, like a beetle compactly in its sheath, blue in winter, green in summer. What need had she of pins— Julia Craye—who lived, it seemed, in the cool glassy world of Bach fugues, playing to herself what she liked, and only consenting to take one or two pupils at the Archer Street College of Music (so the Principal, Miss Kingston, said) as a special favor to herself, who had "the greatest admiration for her in every way." Miss Craye was left badly off, Miss Kingston was afraid, at her brother's death. Oh, they used to have such lovely things, when they lived at Salisbury, and her brother Julius was, of course, a very well-known man: a famous archaeologist. It was a great privilege to stay with them, Miss Kingston said ("My family had always known them—they were regular Canterbury[1] people," Miss Kingston said), but a little frightening for a child; one had to be careful not to slam the door or bounce into the room unexpectedly. Miss Kingston, who gave little character sketches like this on the first day of term while she received checks and wrote out receipts for them, smiled here. Yes, she had been rather a tomboy; she had bounced in and set all those green Roman glasses and things jumping in their case. The Crayes were not used to children. The Crayes were none of them married. They kept cats;

---

1. A city in southern England.

the cats, one used to feel, knew as much about the Roman urns and things as anybody.

"Far more than I did!" said Miss Kingston brightly, writing her name across the stamp in her dashing, cheerful, full-bodied hand, for she had always been practical. That was how she made her living, after all.

Perhaps then, Fanny Wilmot thought, looking for the pin, Miss Craye said that about "Slater's pins having no points," at a venture. None of the Crayes had ever married. She knew nothing about pins—nothing whatever. But she wanted to break the spell that had fallen on the house; to break the pane of glass which separated them from other people. When Polly Kingston, that merry little girl, had slammed the door and made the Roman vases jump, Julius, seeing that no harm was done (that would be his first instinct) looked, for the case was stood in the window, at Polly skipping home across the fields; looked with the look his sister often had, that lingering, driving[2] look.

"Stars, sun, moon," it seemed to say, "the daisy in the grass, fires, frost on the window pane, my heart goes out to you. But," it always seemed to add, "you break, you pass, you go." And simultaneously it covered the intensity of both these states of mind with "I can't reach you—I can't get at you," spoken wistfully, frustratedly. And the stars faded, and the child went. That was the kind of spell that was the glassy surface, that Miss Craye wanted to break by showing, when she had played Bach beautifully as a reward to a favorite pupil (Fanny Wilmot knew that she was Miss Craye's favorite pupil), that she, too, knew, like other people, about pins. Slater's pins had no points.

Yes, the "famous archaeologist" had looked like that too. "The famous archaeologist"—as she said that, endorsing cheques, ascertaining the day of the month, speaking so brightly and frankly, there was in Miss Kingston's voice an indescribable tone which hinted at something odd; something queer in Julius Craye; it was the very same thing that was odd perhaps in Julia too. One could have sworn, thought Fanny Wilmot, as she looked for the pin, that at parties, meetings (Miss Kingston's father was a clergyman), she had picked up some piece of gossip, or it might only have been a smile, or a tone when his name was mentioned, which had given her "a feeling" about Julius Craye. Needless to say, she had never spoken about it to anybody. Probably she scarcely knew what she meant by it. But whenever she spoke of Julius, or heard him mentioned, that was the first thing that came to mind; and it was a seductive thought; there was something odd about Julius Craye.

It was so that Julia looked too, as she sat half turned on the music stool, smiling. It's on the field, it's on the pane, it's in the sky—beauty; and I can't get at it; I can't have it—I, she seemed to add, with that little clutch of the hand which was so characteristic, who adore it so passionately, would give the whole world to possess it! And she picked up the carnation which had fallen on the floor, while Fanny searched for the pin. She crushed it, Fanny felt, voluptuously in her smooth veined hands stuck about with water-colored rings set in pearls. The pressure of her fingers seemed to increase all that was most brilliant in the flower; to set it off; to make it more frilled, fresh, immaculate. What was odd in her, and perhaps in her brother, too, was that this crush and grasp of the finger was combined with a perpetual frustration.

---

2. The text printed here is from *A Haunted House and Other Stories* (1944), edited by Leonard Woolf. In the original version published in *Forum* (1928), this word was "desiring."

So it was even now with the carnation. She had her hands on it; she pressed it; but she did not possess it, enjoy it, not entirely and altogether.

None of the Crayes had married, Fanny Wilmot remembered. She had in mind how one evening when the lesson had lasted longer than usual and it was dark, Julia Craye had said "it's the use of men, surely, to protect us," smiling at her that same odd smile, as she stood fastening her cloak, which made her, like the flower, conscious to her finger tips of youth and brilliance, but, like the flower, too, Fanny suspected, made her feel awkward.

"Oh, but I don't want protection," Fanny had laughed, and when Julia Craye, fixing on her that extraordinary look, had said she was not so sure of that, Fanny positively blushed under the admiration in her eyes.

It was the only use of men, she had said. Was it for that reason then, Fanny wondered, with her eyes on the floor, that she had never married? After all, she had not lived all her life in Salisbury. "Much the nicest part of London," she had said once, "(but I'm speaking of fifteen or twenty years ago) is Kensington.[3] One was in the Gardens in ten minutes—it was like the heart of the country. One could dine out in one's slippers without catching cold. Kensington—it was like a village then, you know," she had said.

Here she broke off, to denounce acridly the draughts in the Tubes.[4]

"It was the use of men," she had said, with a queer wry acerbity. Did that throw any light on the problem why she had not married? One could imagine every sort of scene in her youth, when with her good blue eyes, her straight firm nose, her air of cool distinction, her piano playing, her rose flowering with chaste passion in the bosom of her muslin dress, she had attracted first the young men to whom such things, the china tea cups and the silver candlesticks and the inlaid table, for the Crayes had such nice things, were wonderful; young men not sufficiently distinguished; young men of the cathedral town with ambitions. She had attracted them first, and then her brother's friends from Oxford or Cambridge. They would come down in the summer; row her on the river; continue the argument about Browning[5] by letter; and arrange perhaps, on the rare occasions when she stayed in London, to show her—Kensington Gardens?

"Much the nicest part of London—Kensington (I'm speaking of fifteen or twenty years ago)," she had said once. One was in the gardens in ten minutes—in the heart of the country. One could make that yield what one liked, Fanny Wilmot thought, single out, for instance, Mr. Sherman, the painter, an old friend of hers; make him call for her, by appointment, one sunny day in June; take her to have tea under the trees. (They had met, too, at those parties to which one tripped in slippers without fear of catching cold.) The aunt or other elderly relative was to wait there while they looked at the Serpentine.[6] They looked at the Serpentine. He may have rowed her across. They compared it with the Avon.[7] She would have considered the comparison very furiously. Views of rivers were important to her. She sat hunched a little, a little angular, though she was graceful then, steering. At the critical moment, for he had determined that he must speak now—it was his only chance of getting her alone—he was speaking with his head turned

---

3. A fashionable district of London with an elegant park.
4. The London subway.
5. Robert Browning (1812–1889), English poet.
6. An artificial body of water in Hyde Park, London.
7. An English river.

at an absurd angle, in his great nervousness, over his shoulder—at that very moment she interrupted fiercely. He would have them into the Bridge,[8] she cried. It was a moment of horror, of disillusionment, of revelation, for both of them. I can't have it, I can't possess it, she thought. He could not see why she had come then. With a great splash of his oar he pulled the boat round. Merely to snub him? He rowed her back and said good-bye to her.

The setting of that scene could be varied as one chose, Fanny Wilmot reflected. (Where had that pin fallen?) It might be Ravenna; or Edinburgh, where she had kept house for her brother. The scene could be changed; and the young man and the exact manner of it all, but one thing was constant—her refusal, and her frown, and her anger with herself afterwards, and her argument, and her relief—yes, certainly her immense relief. The very next day, perhaps, she would get up at six, put on her cloak, and walk all the way from Kensington to the river. She was so thankful that she had not sacrificed her right to go and look at things when they are at their best—before people are up, that is to say she could have her breakfast in bed if she liked. She had not sacrificed her independence.

Yes, Fanny Wilmot smiled, Julia had not endangered her habits. They remained safe; and her habits would have suffered if she had married. "They're ogres," she had said one evening, half laughing, when another pupil, a girl lately married, suddenly bethinking her that she would miss her husband, had rushed off in haste.

"They're ogres," she had said, laughing grimly. An ogre would have interfered perhaps with breakfast in bed; with walks at dawn down to the river. What would have happened (but one could hardly conceive this) had she had children. She took astonishing precautions against chills, fatigue, rich food, the wrong food, draughts, heated rooms, journeys in the Tube, for she could never determine which of these it was exactly that brought on those terrible headaches that gave her life the semblance of a battlefield. She was always engaged in outwitting the enemy, until it seemed as if the pursuit had its interest; could she have beaten the enemy finally she would have found life a little dull. As it was, the tug-of-war was perpetual—on the one side the nightingale or the view which she loved with passion—yes, for views and birds she felt nothing less than passion; on the other the damp path or the horrid long drag up a steep hill which would certainly make her good for nothing next day and bring on one of her headaches. When, therefore, from time to time, she managed her forces adroitly and brought off a visit to Hampton Court[9] the week the crocuses—those glossy bright flowers were her favorite—were at their best, it was a victory. It was something that lasted; something that mattered for ever. She strung the afternoon on the necklace of memorable days, which was not too long for her to be able to recall this one or that one; this view, that city; to finger it, to feel it, to savour, sighing, the quality that made it unique.

"It was so beautiful last Friday," she said, "that I determined I must go there." So she had gone off to Waterloo[1] on her great undertaking—to visit Hampton Court—alone. Naturally, but perhaps foolishly, one pitied her for the thing she never asked pity for (indeed she was reticent habitually, speaking of her health only as a warrior might speak of his foe)—one pitied her

---

8. I.e., they were about to run into the bridge.
9. Former royal residence with extensive gardens located on the Thames, 15 miles from London.
1. One of London's railway stations.

for always doing everything alone. Her brother was dead. Her sister was asthmatic. She found the climate of Edinburgh good for her. It was too bleak for Julia. Perhaps, too, she found the associations painful, for her brother, the famous archaeologist, had died there; and she had loved her brother. She lived in a little house off the Brompton Road entirely alone.

Fanny Wilmot saw the pin; she picked it up. She looked at Miss Craye. Was Miss Craye so lonely? No, Miss Craye was steadily, blissfully, if only for that moment, a happy woman. Fanny had surprised her in a moment of ecstasy. She sat there, half turned away from the piano, with her hands clasped in her lap holding the carnation upright, while behind her was the sharp square of the window, uncurtained, purple in the evening, intensely purple after the brilliant electric lights which burned unshaded in the bare music room. Julia Craye, sitting hunched and compact holding her flower, seemed to emerge out of the London night, seemed to fling it like a cloak behind her, it seemed, in its bareness and intensity, the effluence of her spirit, something she had made which surrounded her. Fanny stared.

All seemed transparent, for a moment, to the gaze of Fanny Wilmot, as if looking through Miss Craye, she saw the very fountain of her being spurting its pure silver drops. She saw back and back into the past behind her. She saw the green Roman vases stood in their case; heard the choristers playing cricket; saw Julia quietly descend the curving steps on to the lawn; then saw her pour out tea beneath the cedar tree; softly enclosed the old man's hand in hers; saw her going round and about the corridors of that ancient Cathedral dwelling place with towels in her hand to mark them;[2] lamenting, as she went, the pettiness of daily life; and slowly ageing, and putting away clothes when summer came, because at her age they were too bright to wear; and tending her father's sickness; and cleaving her way ever more definitely as her will stiffened towards her solitary goal; traveling frugally; counting the cost and measuring out of her tight shut purse the sum needed for this journey or for that old mirror; obstinately adhering, whatever people might say, in choosing her pleasures for herself. She saw Julia——

Julia blazed. Julia kindled. Out of the night she burnt like a dead white star. Julia opened her arms. Julia kissed her on the lips. Julia possessed it.[3]

"Slater's pins have no points," Miss Craye said, laughing queerly and relaxing her arms as Fanny Wilmot pinned the flower to her breast with trembling fingers.

1928, 1944

From A Room of One's Own

[Shakespeare's Sister][1]

It was disappointing not to have brought back in the evening some important statement, some authentic fact. Women are poorer than men because— this or that. Perhaps now it would be better to give up seeking for the truth,

---

2. I.e., mark them for the laundry.
3. In the 1928 version, this paragraph reads: "She saw Julia open her arms; saw her blaze; saw her kindle. Out of the night she burnt like a dead white star. Julia kissed her. Julia possessed her."

1. This selection is taken from chapter 3 and the conclusion of the final chapter. In the previous chapter Woolf visits the British Museum library in an attempt to trace the different fates of men and women in history.

and receiving on one's head an avalanche of opinion hot as lava, discolored as dishwater. It would be better to draw the curtains; to shut out distractions; to light the lamp; to narrow the inquiry and to ask the historian, who records not opinions but facts, to describe under what conditions women lived, not throughout the ages, but in England, say in the time of Elizabeth.

For it is a perennial puzzle why no woman wrote a word of that extraordinary literature when every other man, it seemed, was capable of song or sonnet. What were the conditions in which women lived, I asked myself; for fiction, imaginative work that is, is not dropped like a pebble upon the ground, as science may be; fiction is like a spider's web, attached ever so lightly perhaps, but still attached to life at all four corners. Often the attachment is scarcely perceptible; Shakespeare's plays, for instance, seem to hang there complete by themselves. But when the web is pulled askew, hooked up at the edge, torn in the middle, one remembers that these webs are not spun in midair by incorporeal creatures, but are the work of suffering human beings, and are attached to grossly material things, like health and money and the houses we live in.

I went, therefore, to the shelf where the histories stand and took down one of the latest, Professor Trevelyan's *History of England*.[2] Once more I looked up Women, found "position of," and turned to the pages indicated. "Wife-beating," I read, "was a recognized right of man, and was practiced without shame by high as well as low. . . . Similarly," the historian goes on, "the daughter who refused to marry the gentleman of her parents' choice was liable to be locked up, beaten, and flung about the room, without any shock being inflicted on public opinion. Marriage was not an affair of personal affection, but of family avarice, particularly in the 'chivalrous' upper classes. . . . Betrothal often took place while one or both of the parties was in the cradle, and marriage when they were scarely out of the nurses' charge." That was about 1470, soon after Chaucer's time. The next reference to the position of women is some two hundred years later, in the time of the Stuarts. "It was still the exception for women of the upper and middle class to choose their own husbands, and when the husband had been assigned, he was lord and master, so far at least as law and custom could make him. Yet even so," Professor Trevelyan concludes, "neither Shakespeare's women nor those of authentic seventeenth-century memoirs, like the Verneys and the Hutchinsons,[3] seem wanting in personality and character." Certainly, if we consider it, Cleopatra must have had a way with her; Lady Macbeth, one would suppose, had a will of her own; Rosalind,[4] one might conclude, was an attractive girl. Professor Trevelyan is speaking no more than the truth when he remarks that Shakespeare's women do not seem wanting in personality and character. Not being a historian, one might go even further and say that women have burned like beacons in all the works of all the poets from the beginning of time—Clytemnestra, Antigone, Cleopatra, Lady Macbeth, Phèdre, Cressida, Rosalind, Desdemona, the Duchess of Malfi, among the dramatists; then

---

2. G. M. Trevelyan's *History of England* (1926), then the standard one-volume history.
3. Lucy Hutchinson wrote a biography of her husband, Colonel John Hutchinson (1616–1684). "The ideal family life of the period [1640–1650] that ended in such tragic political division has been recorded once and for all in the *Memoirs of the Verney Family*" (Trevelyan, *History of England*).
4. Heroines of three plays by Shakespeare—*Antony and Cleopatra, Macbeth,* and *As You Like It,* respectively.

among the prose writers: Millamant, Clarissa, Becky Sharp, Anna Karenina, Emma Bovary, Madame de Guermantes[5]—the names flock to mind, nor do they recall women "lacking in personality and character." Indeed, if woman had no existence save in the fiction written by men, one would imagine her a person of the utmost importance; very various; heroic and mean; splendid and sordid; infinitely beautiful and hideous in the extreme; as great as a man, some think even greater.[6] But this is woman in fiction. In fact, as Professor Trevelyan points out, she was locked up, beaten, and flung about the room.

A very queer, composite being thus emerges. Imaginatively she is of the highest importance; practically she is completely insignificant. She pervades poetry from cover to cover; she is all but absent from history. She dominates the lives of kings and conquerors in fiction; in fact she was the slave of any boy whose parents forced a ring upon her finger. Some of the most inspired words, some of the most profound thoughts in literature fall from her lips; in real life she could hardly read, could scarcely spell, and was the property of her husband.

It was certainly an odd monster that one made up by reading the historians first and the poets afterwards—a worm winged like an eagle; the spirit of life and beauty in a kitchen chopping up suet. But these monsters, however amusing to the imagination, have no existence in fact. What one must do to bring her to life was to think poetically and prosaically at one and the same moment, thus keeping in touch with fact—that she is Mrs. Martin, aged thirty-six, dressed in blue, wearing a black hat and brown shoes; but not losing sight of fiction either—that she is a vessel in which all sorts of spirits and forces are coursing and flashing perpetually. The moment, however, that one tries this method with the Elizabethan woman, one branch of illumination fails; one is held up by the scarcity of facts. One knows nothing detailed, nothing perfectly true and substantial about her. History scarcely mentions her. And I turned to Professor Trevelyan again to see what history meant to him. I found by looking at his chapter headings that it meant—

"The Manor Court and the Methods of Open-Field Agriculture . . . The Cistercians and Sheep-Farming . . . The Crusades . . . The University . . . The House of Commons . . . The Hundred Years' War . . . The Wars of the Roses . . . The Renaissance Scholars . . . The Dissolution of the Monasteries . . . Agrarian and Religious Strife . . . The Origin of English Sea-Power . . . The Armada . . ." and so on. Occasionally an individual woman is mentioned,

---

5. Characters in, respectively, Aeschylus's *Agamemnon*; Sophocles' *Antigone*; Shakespeare's *Antony and Cleopatra* and *Macbeth*; Racine's *Phèdre*; Shakespeare's *Troilus and Cressida, As You Like It*, and *Othello*; Webster's *The Duchess of Malfi*; Congreve's *The Way of the World* (not prose but drama); Richardson's *Clarissa*; Thackeray's *Vanity Fair*; Tolstoy's *Anna Karenina*; Flaubert's *Madame Bovary*; and Proust's *A la recherche du temps perdu*.

6. "It remains a strange and almost inexplicable fact that in Athena's city, where women were kept in almost Oriental suppression as odalisques or drudges, the stage should yet have produced figures like Clytemnestra and Cassandra, Atossa and Antigone, Phèdre and Medea, and all the other heroines who dominate play after play of the 'misogynist' Euripides. But the paradox of this world where in real life a respectable woman could hardly show her face alone in the street, and yet on the stage woman equals or surpasses man, has never been satisfactorily explained. In modern tragedy the same predominance exists. At all events, a very cursory survey of Shakespeare's work (similarly with Webster, though not with Marlowe or Jonson) suffices to reveal how this dominance, this initiative of women, persists from Rosalind to Lady Macbeth. So too in Racine; six of his tragedies bear their heroines' names; and what male characters of his shall we set against Hermione and Andromaque, Bérénice and Roxane, Phèdre and Athalie? So again with Ibsen; what men shall we match with Solveig and Nora, Hedda and Hilda Wangel and Rebecca West?"—F. L. Lucas, *Tragedy*, pp. 114–15" [Woolf's note].

an Elizabeth, or a Mary;[7] a queen or a great lady. But by no possible means could middle-class women with nothing but brains and character at their command have taken part in any one of the great movements which, brought together, constitute the historian's view of the past. Nor shall we find her in any collection of anecdotes. Aubrey[8] hardly mentions her. She never writes her own life and scarcely keeps a diary; there are only a handful of her letters in existence. She left no plays or poems by which we can judge her. What one wants, I thought—and why does not some brilliant student at Newnham or Girton[9] supply it?—is a mass of information; at what age did she marry; how many children had she as a rule; what was her house like; had she a room to herself; did she do the cooking; would she be likely to have a servant? All these facts lie somewhere, presumably, in parish registers and account books; the life of the average Elizabethan woman must be scattered about somewhere, could one collect it and make a book of it. It would be ambitious beyond my daring, I thought, looking about the shelves for books that were not there, to suggest to the students of those famous colleges that they should rewrite history, though I own that it often seems a little queer as it is, unreal, lopsided; but why should they not add a supplement to history? calling it, of course, by some inconspicuous name so that women might figure there without impropriety? For one often catches a glimpse of them in the lives of the great, whisking away into the background, concealing, I sometimes think, a wink, a laugh, perhaps a tear. And, after all, we have lives enough of Jane Austen; it scarcely seems necessary to consider again the influence of the tragedies of Joanna Baillie upon the poetry of Edgar Allan Poe; as for myself, I should not mind if the homes and haunts of Mary Russell Mitford[1] were closed to the public for a century at least. But what I find deplorable, I continued, looking about the bookshelves again, is that nothing is known about women before the eighteenth century. I have no model in my mind to turn about this way and that. Here am I asking why women did not write poetry in the Elizabethan age, and I am not sure how they were educated; whether they were taught to write; whether they had sitting rooms to themselves; how many women had children before they were twenty-one; what, in short, they did from eight in the morning till eight at night. They had no money evidently; according to Professor Trevelyan they were married whether they liked it or not before they were out of the nursery, at fifteen or sixteen very likely. It would have been extremely odd, even upon this showing, had one of them suddenly written the plays of Shakespeare, I concluded, and I thought of that old gentleman, who is dead now, but was a bishop, I think, who declared that it was impossible for any woman, past, present, or to come, to have the genius of Shakespeare. He wrote to the papers about it. He also told a lady who applied to him for information that cats do not as a matter of fact go to heaven, though they have, he added, souls of a sort. How much thinking those old gentlemen used to save one! How the borders

---

7. I.e., a queen: Elizabeth (1533–1603), queen of England (1558–1603), or Mary Stuart (1542–1587), queen of Scotland (1542–1587).
8. John Aubrey (1626–1697), English diarist.
9. The first two women's colleges of Cambridge University.

1. English poet and novelist (1787–1855), best known for her sketches of rural life. Austen (1775–1817), English novelist; see Vol. 1, p. 459. Baillie (1762–1851), English poet and dramatist; see Vol. 1, p. 400. Poe (1809–1849), American poet and short story writer.

of ignorance shrank back at their approach! Cats do not go to heaven. Women cannot write the plays of Shakespeare.

Be that as it may, I could not help thinking, as I looked at the works of Shakespeare on the shelf, that the bishop was right at least in this; it would have been impossible, completely and entirely, for any woman to have written the plays of Shakespeare in the age of Shakespeare. Let me imagine, since facts are so hard to come by, what would have happened had Shakespeare had a wonderfully gifted sister, called Judith, let us say. Shakespeare himself went, very probably—his mother was an heiress—to grammar school, where he may have learnt Latin—Ovid, Virgil, and Horace[2]—and the elements of grammar and logic. He was, it is well known, a wild boy who poached rabbits, perhaps shot a deer, and had, rather sooner than he should have done, to marry a woman in the neighborhood, who bore him a child rather quicker than was right. That escapade sent him to seek his fortune in London. He had, it seemed, a taste for the theater; he began by holding horses at the stage door. Very soon he got work in the theater, became a successful actor, and lived at the hub of the universe, meeting everybody, knowing everybody, practicing his art on the boards, exercising his wits in the streets, and even getting access to the palace of the queen. Meanwhile his extraordinarily gifted sister, let us suppose, remained at home. She was as adventurous, as imaginative, as agog to see the world as he was. But she was not sent to school. She had no chance of learning grammar and logic, let alone of reading Horace and Virgil. She picked up a book now and then, one of her brother's perhaps, and read a few pages. But then her parents came in and told her to mend the stockings or mind the stew and not moon about with books and papers. They would have spoken sharply but kindly, for they were substantial people who knew the conditions of life for a woman and loved their daughter—indeed, more likely than not she was the apple of her father's eye. Perhaps she scribbled some pages up in an apple loft on the sly, but was careful to hide them or set fire to them. Soon, however, before she was out of her teens, she was to be betrothed to the son of a neighboring wool-stapler.[3] She cried out that marriage was hateful to her, and for that she was severely beaten by her father. Then he ceased to scold her. He begged her instead not to hurt him, not to shame him in this matter of her marriage. He would give her a chain of beads or a fine petticoat, he said; and there were tears in his eyes. How could she disobey him? How could she break his heart? The force of her own gift alone drove her to it. She made up a small parcel of her belongings, let herself down by a rope one summer's night, and took the road to London. She was not seventeen. The birds that sang in the hedge were not more musical than she was. She had the quickest fancy, a gift like her brother's, for the tune of words. Like him, she had a taste for the theater. She stood at the stage door; she wanted to act, she said. Men laughed in her face. The manager—a fat, loose-lipped man—guffawed. He bellowed something about poodles dancing and women acting—no woman, he said, could possibly be an actress. He hinted—you can imagine what. She could get no training in her craft. Could she even seek her dinner

---

2. Three Latin poets of the Augustan age (27 B.C.E.–14 C.E.) whose works were part of the standard curriculum in boys' schools.

3. A merchant who buys wool from producers and sells it to manufacturers.

in a tavern or roam the streets at midnight? Yet her genius was for fiction and lusted to feed abundantly upon the lives of men and women and the study of their ways. At last—for she was very young, oddly like Shakespeare the poet in her face, with the same gray eyes and rounded brows—at last Nick Greene the actor-manager took pity on her; she found herself with child by that gentleman and so—who shall measure the heat and violence of the poet's heart when caught and tangled in a woman's body?—killed herself one winter's night and lies buried at some crossroads where the omnibuses now stop outside the Elephant and Castle![4]

That, more or less, is how the story would run, I think, if a woman in Shakespeare's day had had Shakespeare's genius. But for my part, I agree with the deceased bishop, if such he was—it is unthinkable that any woman in Shakespeare's day should have had Shakespeare's genius. For genius like Shakespeare's is not born among laboring, uneducated, servile people. It was not born in England among the Saxons and the Britons. It is not born today among the working classes. How, then, could it have been born among women whose work began, according to Professor Trevelyan, almost before they were out of the nursery, who were forced to it by their parents and held to it by all the power of law and custom? Yet genius of a sort must have existed among women as it must have existed among the working classes. Now and again an Emily Brontë or a Robert Burns[5] blazes out and proves its presence. But certainly it never got itself on to paper. When, however, one reads of a witch being ducked, of a woman possessed by devils, of a wise woman selling herbs, or even of a very remarkable man who had a mother, then I think we are on the track of a lost novelist, a suppressed poet, of some mute and inglorious[6] Jane Austen, some Emily Brontë who dashed her brains out on the moor or mopped and mowed about the highways crazed with the torture that her gift had put her to. Indeed, I would venture to guess that Anon, who wrote so many poems without signing them, was often a woman. It was a woman Edward Fitzgerald,[7] I think, suggested who made the ballads and the folk songs, crooning them to her children, beguiling her spinning with them, or the length of the winter's night.

This may be true or it may be false—who can say?—but what is true in it, so it seemed to me, reviewing the story of Shakespeare's sister as I had made it, is that any woman born with a great gift in the sixteenth century would certainly have gone crazed, shot herself, or ended her days in some lonely cottage outside the village, half witch, half wizard, feared and mocked at. For it needs little skill in psychology to be sure that a highly gifted girl who had tried to use her gift for poetry would have been so thwarted and hindered by other people, so tortured and pulled asunder by her own contrary instincts, that she must have lost her health and sanity to a certainty. No girl could have walked to London and stood at a stage door and forced her way into the presence of actor-managers without doing herself a violence and suffering an anguish which may have been irrational—for chastity may

---

4. A tavern located at a busy crossroads in south London. Suicides were commonly buried at crossroads.
5. A working-class Scottish poet (1759–1796) who wrote in his native dialect. Brontë (1818–1848), English poet and novelist; see Vol. 1, p. 959.
6. An echo of Thomas Gray's "Elegy Written in a Country Churchyard" (1751): "Some mute inglorious Milton here may rest (line 59)."
7. English poet and translator (1809–1883).

be a fetish invented by certain societies for unknown reasons—but were none the less inevitable. Chastity had then, it has even now, a religious importance in a woman's life, and has so wrapped itself round with nerves and instincts that to cut it free and bring it to the light of day demands courage of the rarest. To have lived a free life in London in the sixteenth century would have meant for a woman who was poet and playwright a nervous stress and dilemma which might well have killed her. Had she survived, whatever she had written would have been twisted and deformed, issuing from a strained and morbid imagination. And undoubtedly, I thought, looking at the shelf where there are no plays by women, her work would have gone unsigned. That refuge she would have sought certainly. It was the relic of the sense of chastity that dictated anonymity to women even so late as the nineteenth century. Currer Bell, George Eliot, George Sand,[8] all the victims of inner strife as their writings prove, sought ineffectively to veil themselves by using the name of a man. Thus they did homage to the convention, which if not implanted by the other sex was liberally encouraged by them (the chief glory of a woman is not to be talked of, said Pericles,[9] himself a much-talked-of man), that publicity in women is detestable. Anonymity runs in their blood. The desire to be veiled still possesses them.

* * *

I told you in the course of this paper that Shakespeare had a sister; but do not look for her in Sir Sidney Lee's[1] life of the poet. She died young—alas, she never wrote a word. She lies buried where the omnibuses now stop, opposite the Elephant and Castle. Now my belief is that this poet who never wrote a word and was buried at the crossroads still lives. She lives in you and in me, and in many other women who are not here tonight, for they are washing up the dishes and putting the children to bed. But she lives; for great poets do not die; they are continuing presences; they need only the opportunity to walk among us in the flesh. This opportunity, as I think, it is now coming within your power to give her. For my belief is that if we live another century or so—I am talking of the common life which is the real life and not of the little separate lives which we live as individuals—and have five hundred a year[2] each of us and rooms of our own; if we have the habit of freedom and the courage to write exactly what we think; if we escape a little from the common sitting room and see human beings not always in their relation to each other but in relation to reality; and the sky, too, and the trees or whatever it may be in themselves; if we look past Milton's[3] bogey, for no human being should shut out the view; if we face the fact, for it is a fact, that there is no arm to cling to, but that we go alone and that our relation is to the world of reality and not only to the world of men and women, then the opportunity will come and the dead poet who was Shakespeare's sister will put on the body which she has so often laid down. Drawing her life from the lives of the unknown who were her forerunners, as her brother did before

---

8. Male pen names of the novelists Charlotte Brontë, (1816–1855; see Vol. 1, p. 633), Marian Evans (1819–1880; see Vol. 1, p. 975), and Aurore Dupin (1804–1876).
9. Athenian statesman and orator (495–429 B.C.E.); this statement comes from his funeral oration (Thucydides 2.4).

1. Biographer of Shakespeare (1859–1926).
2. Woolf has suggested in chapter 2 that £500 a year is necessary for financial independence.
3. John Milton (1608–1674), English poet; his epic poem *Paradise Lost* retells the story of Genesis 2–3, and portrays Eve as morally and intellectually secondary to Adam.

her, she will be born. As for her coming without that preparation, without that effort on our part, without that determination that when she is born again she shall find it possible to live and write her poetry, that we cannot expect, for that would be impossible. But I maintain that she would come if we worked for her, and that so to work, even in poverty and obscurity, is worth while.

1929

Professions for Women[1]

When your secretary invited me to come here, she told me that your Society is concerned with the employment of women and she suggested that I might tell you something about my own professional experiences. It is true that I am a woman; it is true I am employed; but what professional experiences have I had? It is difficult to say. My profession is literature; and in that profession there are fewer experiences for women than in any other, with the exception of the stage—fewer, I mean, that are peculiar to women. For the road was cut many years ago—by Fanny Burney, by Aphra Behn, by Harriet Martineau, by Jane Austen, by George Eliot[2]—many famous women, and many more unknown and forgotten, have been before me, making the path smooth, and regulating my steps. Thus, when I came to write, there were very few material obstacles in my way. Writing was a reputable and harmless occupation. The family peace was not broken by the scratching of a pen. No demand was made upon the family purse. For ten[3] and sixpence one can buy paper enough to write all the plays of Shakespeare—if one has a mind that way. Pianos and models, Paris, Vienna, and Berlin, masters and mistresses, are not needed by a writer. The cheapness of writing paper is, of course, the reason why women have succeeded as writers before they have succeeded in the other professions.

But to tell you my story—it is a simple one. You have only got to figure to yourselves a girl in a bedroom with a pen in her hand. She had only to move that pen from left to right—from ten o'clock to one. Then it occurred to her to do what is simple and cheap enough after all—to slip a few of those pages into a envelope, fix a penny stamp in the corner, and drop the envelope into the red box at the corner. It was thus that I became a journalist; and my effort was rewarded on the first day of the following month—a very glorious day it was for me—by a letter from an editor containing a check for one pound ten shillings and sixpence. But to show you how little I deserve to be called a professional woman, how little I know of the struggles and difficulties of such lives, I have to admit that instead of spending that sum upon bread and butter, rent, shoes and stockings, or butcher's bills, I went out and bought a cat—a beautiful cat, a Persian cat, which very soon involved me in bitter disputes with my neighbors.

---

1. A paper read to the Women's Service League [Woolf's note].
2. English novelist (1819–1880). Burney (1752–1840), English novelist. Behn (1640–1689), English poet, playwright, and novelist. Martineau (1802–1876), English economist, journalist, and novelist. Austen (1775–1817), English novelist. All except Martineau are included in this anthology.
3. I.e., 10 shillings.

What could be easier than to write articles and to buy Persian cats with the profits? But wait a moment. Articles have to be about something. Mine, I seem to remember, was about a novel by a famous man. And while I was writing this review, I discovered that if I were going to review books I should need to do battle with a certain phantom. And the phantom was a woman, and when I came to know her better I called her after the heroine of a famous poem, The Angel in the House.[4] It was she who used to come between me and my paper when I was writing reviews. It was she who bothered me and wasted my time and so tormented me that at last I killed her. You who come of a younger and happier generation may not have heard of her—you may not know what I mean by The Angel in the House. I will describe her as shortly as I can. She was intensely sympathetic. She was immensely charming. She was utterly unselfish. She excelled in the difficult arts of family life. She sacrificed herself daily. If there was chicken, she took the leg; if there was a draft she sat in it—in short she was so constituted that she never had a mind or a wish of her own, but preferred to sympathize always with the minds and wishes of others. Above all—I need not say it—she was pure. Her purity was supposed to be her chief beauty—her blushes, her great grace. In those days—the last of Queen Victoria[5]—every house had its Angel. And when I came to write I encountered her with the very first words. The shadow of her wings fell on my page; I heard the rustling of her skirts in the room. Directly, that is to say, I took my pen in my hand to review that novel by a famous man, she slipped behind me and whispered: "My dear, you are a young woman. You are writing about a book that has been written by a man. Be sympathetic; be tender; flatter; deceive; use all the arts and wiles of our sex. Never let anybody guess that you have a mind of your own. Above all, be pure." And she made as if to guide my pen. I now record the one act for which I take some credit to myself, though the credit rightly belongs to some excellent ancestors of mine who left me a certain sum of money—shall we say five hundred pounds a year?[6]—so that it was not necessary for me to depend solely on charm for my living. I turned upon her and caught her by the throat. I did my best to kill her. My excuse, if I were to be had up in a court of law, would be that I acted in self-defense. Had I not killed her she would have killed me. She would have plucked the heart out of my writing. For, as I found, directly I put pen to paper, you cannot review even a novel without having a mind of your own, without expressing what you think to be the truth about human relations, morality, sex. And all these questions, according to the Angel of the House, cannot be dealt with freely and openly by women; they must charm, they must conciliate, they must—to put it bluntly—tell lies if they are to succeed. Thus, whenever I felt the shadow of her wing or the radiance of her halo upon my page, I took up the inkpot and flung it at her. She died hard. Her fictitious nature was of great assistance to her. It is far harder to kill a phantom than a reality. She was always creeping back when I thought I had despatched her. Though I flatter myself that I killed her in the end, the struggle was severe; it took much time that had better have been spent upon learning Greek grammar; or in roaming the

---

4. A popular Victorian poem of idealized domestic life by Coventry Patmore (1858).
5. Victoria (1819–1901) reigned from 1837 to 1901.

6. In *A Room of One's Own* (1929), Woolf names the same amount as crucial for Independence (she herself had inherited £2500 from an aunt in 1909).

world in search of adventures. But it was a real experience; it was an experience that was bound to befall all women writers at that time. Killing the Angel in the House was part of the occupation of a woman writer.

But to continue my story. The Angel was dead; what then remained? You may sat that what remained was a simple and common object—a young woman in a bedroom with an inkpot. In other words, now that she had rid herself of falsehood, that young woman had only to be herself. Ah, but what is "herself"? I mean, what is a woman? I assure you, I do not know. I do not believe that you know. I do not believe that anybody can know until she has expressed herself in all the arts and professions open to human skill. That indeed is one of the reasons why I have come here—out of respect for you, who are in process of showing us by your experiments what a woman is, who are in process of providing us, by your failures and successes, with that extremely inportant piece of information.

But to continue the story of my professional experiences. I made one pound ten and six by my first review; and I bought a Persian cat with the proceeds. Then I grew ambitious. A Persian cat is all very well, I said; but a Persian cat is not enough. I must have a motorcar. And it was thus that I became a novelist—for it is a very strange thing that people will give you a motorcar if you will tell them a story. It is a still stranger thing that there is nothing so delightful in the world as telling stories. It is far pleasanter than writing reviews of famous novels. And yet, if I am to obey your secretary and tell you my professional experiences as a novelist, I must tell you about a very strange experience that befell me as a novelist. And to understand it you must try first to imagine a novelist's state of mind. I hope I am not giving away professional secrets if I say that a novelist's chief desire is to be as unconscious as possible. He has to induce in himself a state of perpetual lethargy. He wants life to proceed with the utmost quiet and regularity. He wants to see the same faces, to read the same books, to do the same things day after day, month after month, while he is writing, so that nothing may break the illusion in which he is living—so that nothing may disturb or disquiet the mysterious nosings about, feelings around, darts, dashes, and sudden discoveries of that very shy and illusive spirit, the imagination. I suspect that this state is the same both for men and women. Be that as it may, I want you to imagine me writing a novel in a state of trance. I want you to figure to yourselves a girl sitting with a pen in her hand, which for minutes, and indeed for hours, she never dips into the inkpot. The image that comes to my mind when I think of this girl is the image of a fisherman lying sunk in dreams on the verge of a deep lake with a rod held out over the water. She was letting her imagination sweep unchecked round every rock and cranny of the world that lies submerged in the depths of our unconscious being. Now came the experience that I believe to be far commoner with women writers than with men. The line raced through the girl's fingers. Her imagination had rushed away. It had sought the pools, the depths, the dark places where the largest fish slumber. And then there was a smash. There was an explosion. There was foam and confusion. The imagination had dashed itself against something hard. The girl was roused from her dream. She was indeed in a state of the most acute and difficult distress. To speak without figure, she had thought of something, something about the body, about the passions which it was unfitting for her as a woman to say. Men, her reason told her, would be shocked. The consciousness of what men will say of a woman who speaks the truth about her passions had roused her from her artist's state of unconsciousness. She could write no more. The trance was over. Her imagination could work no longer. This I believe to be a very common experience with women writers—they are impeded by the extreme conventionality of the other sex. For though men sensibly allow themselves great freedom in these respects, I doubt that they realize or can control the extreme severity with which they condemn such freedom in women.

These then were two very genuine experiences of my own. These were two of the adventures of my professional life. The first—killing The Angel in the House—I think I solved. She died. But the second, telling the truth about my own experiences as a body, I do not think I solved. I doubt that any woman has solved it yet. The obstacles against her are still immensely powerful—and yet they are very difficult to define. Outwardly, what is simpler than to write books? Outwardly, what obstacles are there for a woman rather than for a man? Inwardly, I think, the case is very different; she has still many ghosts to fight, many prejudices to overcome. Indeed it will be a long time still, I think, before a woman can sit down to write a book without finding a phantom to be slain, a rock to be dashed against. And if this is so in literature, the freest of all professions for women, how is it in the new professions which you are now for the first time entering?

Those are the questions that I should like, had I time, to ask you. And indeed, if I have laid stress upon these professional experiences of mine, it is because I believe that they are, though in different forms, yours also. Even when the path is nominally open—when there is nothing to prevent a woman from being a doctor, a lawyer, a civil servant—there are many phantoms and obstacles, as I believe, looming in her way. To discuss and define them is I think of great value and importance; for thus only can the labor be shared, the difficulties be solved. But besides this, it is necessary also to discuss the ends and the aims for which we are fighting, for which we are doing battle with these formidable obstacles. Those aims cannot be taken for granted; they must be perpetually questioned and examined. The whole position, as I see it—here in this hall surrounded by women practicing for the first time in history I know not how many different professions—is one of extraordinary interest and importance. You have won rooms of your own in the house hitherto exclusively owned by men. You are able, though not without great labor and effort, to pay the rent. You are earning your five hundred pounds a year. But this freedom is only a beginning; the room is your own, but it is still bare. It has to be furnished; it has to be decorated; it has to be shared. How are you going to furnish it, how are you going to decorate it? With whom are you going to share it, and upon what terms? These, I think are questions of the utmost importance and interest. For the first time in history you are able to ask them; for the first time you are able to decide for yourselves what the answers should be. Willingly would I stay and discuss those questions and answers—but not tonight. My time is up; and I must cease.

1942

The Death of the Moth

Moths that fly by day are not properly to be called moths; they do not excite that pleasant sense of dark autumn nights and ivy-blossom which the commonest yellow-underwing asleep in the shadow of the curtain never fails to rouse in us. They are hybrid creatures, neither gay like butterflies nor somber like their own species. Nevertheless the present specimen, with his narrow hay-colored wings, fringed with a tassel of the same color, seemed to be content with life. It was a pleasant morning, mid-September, mild, benignant, yet with a keener breath than that of the summer months. The plow was already scoring the field opposite the window, and where the share[1] had been, the earth was pressed flat and gleamed with moisture. Such vigor came rolling in from the fields and the down beyond that it was difficult to keep the eyes strictly turned upon the book. The rooks[2] too were keeping one of their annual festivities; soaring round the tree tops until it looked as if a vast net with thousands of black knots in it had been cast up into the air; which, after a few moments sank slowly down upon the trees until every twig seemed to have a knot at the end of it. Then, suddenly, the net would be thrown into the air again in a wider circle this time, with the utmost clamor and vociferation, as though to be thrown into the air and settle slowly down upon the tree tops were a tremendously exciting experience.

The same energy which inspired the rooks, the plow-men, the horses, and even, it seemed, the lean bare-backed downs, sent the moth fluttering from side to side of his square of the window-pane. One could not help watching him. One was, indeed, conscious of a queer feeling of pity for him. The possibilities of pleasure seemed that morning so enormous and so various that to have only a moth's part in life, and a day moth's at that, appeared a hard fate, and his zest in enjoying his meager opportunities to the full, pathetic. He flew vigorously to one corner of his compartment, and, after waiting there a second, flew across to the other. What remained for him but to fly to a third corner and then to a fourth? That was all he could do, in spite of the size of the downs, the width of the sky, the far-off smoke of houses, and the romantic voice, now and then, of a steamer out at sea. What he could do he did. Watching him, it seemed as if a fiber, very thin but pure, of the enormous energy of the world had been thrust into his frail and diminutive body. As often as he crossed the pane, I could fancy that a thread of vital light became visible. He was little or nothing but life.

Yet, because he was so small, and so simple a form of the energy that was rolling in at the open window and driving its way through so many narrow and intricate corridors in my own brain and in those of other human beings, there was something marvelous as well as pathetic about him. It was as if someone had taken a tiny bead of pure life and decking it as lightly as possible with down and feathers, had set it dancing and zigzagging to show us the true nature of life. Thus displayed one could not get over the strangeness of it. One is apt to forget all about life, seeing it humped and bossed[3] and garnished and cumbered so that it has to move with the greatest circum-

---

1. I.e., plowshare.
2. Crows.
3. Ornamented.

spection and dignity. Again, the thought of all that life might have been had he been born in any other shape caused one to view his simple activities with a kind of pity.

After a time, tired by his dancing apparently, he settled on the window ledge in the sun, and, the queer spectacle being at an end, I forgot about him. Then, looking up, my eye was caught by him. He was trying to resume his dancing, but seemed either so stiff or so awkward that he could only flutter to the bottom of the window-pane; and when he tried to fly across it he failed. Being intent on other matters I watched these futile attempts for a time without thinking, unconsciously waiting for him to resume his flight, as one waits for a machine, that has stopped momentarily, to start again without considering the reason of its failure. After perhaps a seventh attempt he slipped from the wooden ledge and fell, fluttering his wings, on to his back on the window sill. The helplessness of his attitude roused me. It flashed upon me that he was in difficulties; he could no longer raise himself; his legs struggled vainly. But, as I stretched out a pencil, meaning to help him to right himself, it came over me that the failure and awkwardness were the approach of death. I laid the pencil down again.

The legs agitated themselves once more. I looked as if for the enemy against which he struggled. I looked out of doors. What had happened there? Presumably it was midday, and work in the fields had stopped. Stillness and quiet had replaced the previous animation. The birds had taken themselves off to feed in the brooks. The horses stood still. Yet the power was there all the same, massed outside indifferent, impersonal, not attending to anything in particular. Somehow it was opposed to the little hay-colored moth. It was useless to try to do anything. One could only watch the extraordinary efforts made by those tiny legs against an oncoming doom which could, had it chosen, have submerged an entire city, not merely a city, but masses of human beings; nothing, I knew had any chance against death. Nevertheless after a pause of exhaustion the legs fluttered again. It was superb this last protest, and so frantic that he succeeded at last in righting himself. One's sympathies, of course, were all on the side of life. Also, when there was nobody to care or to know, this gigantic effort on the part of an insignificant little moth, against a power of such magnitude, to retain what no one else valued or desired to keep, moved one strangely. Again, somehow, one saw life, a pure bead. I lifted the pencil again, useless though I knew it to be. But even as I did so, the unmistakable tokens of death showed themselves. The body relaxed, and instantly grew stiff. The struggle was over. The insignificant little creature now knew death. As I looked at the dead moth, this minute wayside triumph of so great a force over so mean an antagonist filled me with wonder. Just as life had been strange a few minutes before, so death was now as strange. The moth having righted himself now lay most decently and uncomplainingly composed. O yes, he seemed to say, death is stronger than I am.

1942

MINA LOY
1882–1966

"Women," declaimed Mina Loy in her unpublished "Feminist Manifesto" (1914), "if you want to realize yourselves (for you are on the brink of a devastating psychological upheaval) all your pet illusions must be unmasked. The lies of centuries have got to be discarded." An avant-garde writer and painter at various times associated with radically innovative aesthetic movements (futurism, dadaism) as well as with the social protests of feminism, Mina Loy refused throughout her career to abide by the rules of what she elsewhere called "the rubbish heap of tradition." "Nothing short of Absolute Demolition will bring about reform," she declared, identifying her project with the experimental works produced by such contemporaries as Gertrude Stein, Djuna Barnes, and Marianne Moore.

Born Mina Gertrude Lowy in London, she shortened her name to Loy when she married the painter Stephen Haweis and moved to Paris in 1903. The couple had three children; they lived for a while in Paris and for a while in Florence, moving in expatriate modernist circles. In 1916, however, Loy emigrated alone to New York, where she acted with the Provincetown Players, exhibited paintings, published in little magazines, and was defined by one newspaper as a typical "modern woman." In 1917, she divorced her first husband and soon married Arthur Craven, a somewhat shady "proto-Dadaist" and "master of disguise" who mysteriously disappeared within a year, leaving Loy pregnant. In the 1920s, after bearing the child, she returned to Europe, where she resided for many years in Florence, Berlin, and Paris, painting, writing poetry, and supporting herself by designing and manufacturing lampshades. In 1953, she moved again, this time to Aspen, Colorado, where she lived in seclusion and comparative obscurity near her only surviving children (two daughters) until her death in 1966.

Loy published few books in her lifetime: *Lunar Baedecker* (1923), a collection of diverse writings, had no successor until *Lunar Baedecker and Time-Tables* appeared, virtually unnoticed, in 1958. Yet major contemporaries and descendants from Ezra Pound and T. S. Eliot to William Carlos Williams and Denise Levertov deeply admired her rigorous experimentalism, sexual frankness, and severe commitment to precisely the search for the "radium of the word" that she herself praised in the works of Gertrude Stein.

Gertrude Stein[1]

Curie[2]
of the laboratory
of vocabulary
she crushed
5   the tonnage
of consciousness
congealed to phrases
to extract
a radium of the word

1914, 1925

---

1. American writer (1874–1946), whose prose and poetry reflect her interest in radical linguistic experimentation; see p. 141.

2. Marie Curie (1867–1934), physicist, chemist, and codiscoverer of radium.

From Three Moments in Paris
One O'Clock at Night

    Though you have never possessed me
    I have belonged to you since the beginning of time
    And sleepily I sit on your chair beside you
    Leaning against your shoulder
5   And your careless arm across my back gesticulates
    As your indisputable male voice roars
    Through my brain and my body
    Arguing "Dynamic Decomposition"
    Of which I understand nothing
10 Sleepily
    And the only less male voice of your brother pugilist of the intellect
    Booms   as it seems to me   so sleepy
    Across an interval of a thousand miles
    An interim of a thousand years
15 But you who make more noise than any man in the world when you
       clear your throat
    Deafening   wake me
    And I catch the thread of the argument
    Immediately assuming my personal mental attitude
    And cease to be a woman

20 Beautiful halfhour of being a mere woman
    The animal woman
    Understanding nothing of man
    But mastery   and the security of imparted physical heat
    Indifferent to cerebral gymnastics
25 Or regarding them as the self-indulgent play of children
    Or the thunder of alien gods
    But you wake me up
    Anyhow   who am I that I should criticize
       your theories of "Plastic Velocity"
    "Let us go home   she is tired   and
       wants to go to bed."

                                              1915

The Widow's Jazz

        The white flesh quakes to the negro soul
        Chicago! Chicago!

        An uninterpretable wail
        stirs in a tangle of pale snakes

5   to the lethargic ecstasy of steps
        backing into primeval goal

        White man quit his actin' wise
        colored folk hab de moon in dere eyes

        Haunted by wind instruments
10   in groves of grace

        the maiden saplings
        slant to the oboes

        and shampooed gigolos
        prowl to the sobbing taboos.

15   An electric crown
        crashes the furtive cargoes of the floor.

        the pruned contours
        dissolve
        in the brazen shallows of dissonance
20   revolving mimes

        of the encroaching Eros[1]
        in adolescence

        The black brute-angels
        in their human gloves
25   bellow through a monstrous growth of metal trunks

        and impish musics
        crumble the ecstatic loaf
        before a swooning flock of doves.

        Cravan
30   colossal absentee
        the substitute dark
        rolls to the incandescent memory

        of love's survivor
        on this rich suttee

35   seared by the flames of sound
        the widowed urn

        holds impotently
        your murdered laughter

        Husband
40   how secretly you cuckold me with death

        while this cajoling jazz
        blows with its tropic breath

---

1. Sexual love (literally, the Greek god of love).

```
            among the echoes of the flesh
            a synthesis
45          of racial caress

            The seraph and the ass
            in this unerring esperanto²
            of the earth
            converse
50          of everlit delight

            as my desire
            receded
            to the distance of the dead

            searches
55          the opaque silence
            of unpeopled space.
```

                                                                    1931

Omen of Victory

```
            Women in uniform
            relaxed for tea
            under a shady garden tree
            discover
5           a dove's feather
            fallen in the sugar.
```

                                                                    1958

Photo after Pogrom[1]

```
            Arrangement by rage
            of human rubble
            the false-eternal statues of the slain
            until they putrify:

5           Tossed on a pile of dead,
            one woman,
            her body hacked to utter beauty,
            oddly, by murder,

            attains the absolute smile
10          of dispossession:
            the marble pause before the extinct haven.
```

---

2. I.e., universal language. "Seraph": angel.   1. An organized massacre of Jews.

Death's drear
erasure of fear,
the unassumed
15   composure,

the purposeless peace
sealing the faces
of corpses.

Corpses are virgin.

1961

Songge Byrd

for isadora duncan[1]

Gossip-blown songstress
you flew upon men
caressed them
with the feathers of your eyes
5   seeing without the censor of surprise
that like yourself
descended from the skies
so many gods.

1982

Portrait of a Nun

The smile folded as a marriage-veil
hoarded in heaven
Over her abdomen
the hands crossed: consequence
5   of a mystic conception

The nostril: arched for incense—

The mourning and the starching
of her body's concealing:
a cloth coffin

10   Her face wrapping: a white napkin—

The round halo rising
through her flesh shining:
virgin apple to angels' offering

---

1. Innovator in expressionistic dance based on Greek forms (1878–1927).

The ascensional eyes:
15 pointed skyward as a crown
or now   cast down.

A nun
seeing no one
but Jesus
20 is gentle to us

1982

Feminist Manifesto

The feminist movement as at present instituted is
Inadequate
Women if you want to realise yourselves—you are on the eve of a devastating psychological upheaval—all your pet illusions must be unmasked—the lies of centuries have got to go—are you prepared for the **Wrench**—? There is no half-measure—NO scratching on the surface of the rubbish heap of tradition, will bring about **Reform**, the only method is
Absolute Demolition

Cease to place your confidence in economic legislation, vice-crusades & uniform education—you are glossing over
Reality.
Professional & commercial careers are opening up for you—
Is that all you want?
And if you honestly desire to find your level without prejudice—be **Brave** & deny at the outset—that pathetic clap-trap war cry **Woman is the equal of man**—
She is **NOT!** for
The man who lives a life in which his activities conform to a social code which is a protectorate of the feminine element—
——is no longer **masculine**

The women who adapt themselves to a theoretical valuation of their sex as a **relative impersonality**, are not yet **Feminine**

Leave off looking to men to find out what you are **not**—seek within yourselves to find out what you **are**

As conditions are at present constituted—you have the choice between **Parasitism, & Prostitution** —or **Negation**

Men & women are enemies, with the enmity of the exploited for the parasite, the parasite for the exploited—at present they are at the mercy of the advantage that each can take of the others sexual dependence—. The only point at which the interests of the sexes merge—is the sexual embrace.

The first illusion it is to your interest to demolish is the division of women into two classes **the mistress, & the mother** every well-balanced & developed woman knows that is not true, Nature has endowed the complete woman with a faculty for expressing herself through all her functions—there are **no restrictions** the woman who is so incompletely evolved as to be un-self-conscious in sex, will prove a restrictive influence on the temperamental expansion of the next generation; the woman who is a poor mistress will be an incompetent mother—an inferior mentality—& will enjoy an inadequate apprehension of **Life** .

To obtain results you must make sacrifices & the first & greatest sacrifice you have to make is of your "virtue" The fictitious value of woman as identified with her physical purity—is too easy a stand-by——rendering her lethargic in the acquisition of intrinsic merits of character by which she could obtain a concrete value—therefore, the first self-enforced law for the female sex, as a protection against the man made bogey[1] of virtue—which is the principal instrument of her subjection, would be the unconditional surgical destruction of virginity through-out the female population at puberty—.

The value of man is assessed entirely according to his use or interest to the community, the value of woman, depends entirely on chance, her success or insuccess in maneuvering a man into taking the life-long responsibility of her—

---

1. Source of fear or harassment.

The advantages of marriage are too ridiculously ample—
compared to all other trades—for under modern conditions a
woman can accept preposterously luxurious support from a
man (with-out return of any sort—even offspring)—as a thank
offering for her virginity
The woman who has not succeeded in striking that
advantageous bargain—is prohibited from any but
surreptitious re-action to Life-stimuli—**& entirely
<u>debarred</u> maternity.**
Every woman has a right to maternity—
Every woman of superior intelligence should realize her race-
responsibility, in producing children in adequate proportion to
the unfit or degenerate members of her sex—

Each child of a superior woman should be the result of a
definite period of psychic development in her life—& not
necessarily of a possibly irksome & outworn continuance of an
alliance—spontaneously adapted for vital creation in the
beginning but not necessarily harmoniously balanced as the
parties to it—follow their individual lines of personal
evolution—
For the harmony of the race, each individual should be the
expression of an easy & ample interpenetration of the male &
female temperaments—free of stress
Woman must become more responsible for the child than
man—
Women must destroy in themselves, the desire to be loved—

The feeling that it is a personal insult when a man transfers
his attentions from her to another woman
The desire for comfortable protection instead of an intelligent
curiosity & courage in meeting & resisting the pressure of life
sex or so called love must be reduced to its initial element,
honour, grief, sentimentality, pride & consequently jealousy
must be detached from it.
Woman for her happiness must retain her deceptive fragility of
appearance, combined with indomitable will, irreducible
courage, & abundant health the outcome of sound nerves—
Another great illusion that woman must use all her
introspective clear-sightedness & unbiased bravery to
destroy—for the sake of her <u>self respect</u> is the impurity of sex
the realisation in defiance of superstition that there is <u>nothing
impure in sex</u>—except in the mental attitude to it—will
constitute an incalculable & wider social regeneration than it
is possible for our generation to imagine.

1914   1982

ANNE SPENCER
1882–1975

Although she lived her entire life in relative obscurity and never collected her verse into a volume, Anne Spencer produced a number of the finest poems published during the Harlem Renaissance. Born on a Virginia plantation, Anne Bethel Scales Bannister witnessed with some dismay the incompatibility of her parents, free African Americans whose disputes ended in a separation around 1887. Mother and daughter moved to Bramwell, West Virginia, where Anne was educated at home until she entered the Virginia Seminary at fourteen years of age. After marrying a seminary schoolmate, Edward Spencer, she resided with her husband and mother in Lynchburg, Virginia, where she raised three children, helped organize black citizens for civil rights, cultivated a beautiful garden, and corresponded with a number of prominent literary men of her time, including James Weldon Johnson. It was Johnson who published "Before the Feast of Shushan" in *Crisis*. With his help, she placed other poems in such influential anthologies as Charles S. Johnson's *Ebony and Topaz* (1927) and Countee Cullen's *Caroling Dusk* (1927). A recluse after her husband's death in 1964, Spencer published fewer than thirty poems during her lifetime. For many years, editors who anthologized her verse praised her for writing about nonracial themes with imagistic precision and economy; however, the selections printed here illustrate the subtlety of her thinking about the impact of overvaluations of whiteness and devaluations of blackness in Western culture.

Before the Feast at Shushan

Garden of Shushan![1]
After Eden, all terrace, pool, and flower recollect thee:
Ye weavers in saffron and haze and Tyrian purple,[2]
Tell yet what range in color wakes the eye;
5 Sorcerer, release the dreams born here when
Drowsy, shifting palm-shade enspells the brain;
And sound! ye with harp and flute ne'er essay
Before these star-noted birds escaped from paradise awhile to
Stir all dark, and dear, and passionate desire, till mine
10 Arms go out to be mocked by the softly kissing body of the wind—
Slave, send Vashti[3] to her King!

The fiery wattles of the sun startle into flame
The marbled towers of Shushan:
So at each day's wane, two peers—the one in
15 Heaven, the other on earth—welcome with their
Splendor the peerless beauty of the Queen.

Cushioned at the Queen's feet and upon her knee
Finding glory for mine head,—still, nearly shamed

---

1. Ancient city in southwest Iran, named in the Book of Esther (1.2) as the site of the palace of Ahasuerus, king of Persia (i.e., Xerxes, r. 486–465 B.C.E.).
2. An expensive dye made from shellfish found off the Phoenician coast.
3. Wife of Ahasuerus, who was banished from his presence for refusing to appear as the king had commanded (Esther 1.10–22).

Am I, the King, to bend and kiss with sharp
20   Breath the olive-pink of sandaled toes between;
Or lift me high to the magnet of a gaze, dusky,
Like the pool when but the moon-ray strikes to its depth;
Or closer press to crush a grape 'gainst lips redder
25   Than the grape, a rose in the night of her hair;
Then—Sharon's Rose[4] in my arms.

And I am hard to force the petals wide;
And you are fast to suffer and be sad.
Is any prophet come to teach a new thing
Now in a more apt time?
30   Have him 'maze[5] how you say love is sacrament;
How says Vashti, love is both bread and wine;
How to the altar may not come to break and drink,
Hulky flesh nor fleshly spirit!

I, thy lord, like not manna for meat as a Judahn;[6]
35   I, thy master, drink, and red wine, plenty, and when
I thirst. Eat meat, and full, when I hunger.
I, thy King, teach you and leave you, when I list.
No woman in all Persia sets out strange action
To confuse Persia's lord—
40   Love is but desire and thy purpose fulfillment;
I, thy King, so say!

1920

White Things

Most things are colorful things—the sky, earth, and sea.
    Black men are most men; but the white are free!
White things are rare things; so rare, so rare
They stole from out a silvered world—somewhere.
5   Finding earth-plains fair plains, save greenly grassed,
They strewed white feathers of cowardice,[1] as they passed;
    The golden stars with lances fine
    The hills all red and darkened pine,
They blanched with their wand of power;
10   And turned the blood in a ruby rose
To a poor white poppy-flower.

They pyred a race of black, black men,
And burned them to ashes white; then,
Laughing, a young one claimed a skull,

---

4. The Rose of Sharon is a flowering plant, similarly identified with a woman in an erotic context in Song of Solomon 2.1.
5. I.e., amazed at.
6. I.e., I am not satisfied with the manna sent by God (Exodus 16) to feed the Jews (descendants of Judah, son of Jacob).
1. The association of white feathers with cowardice is traditional (from cockfighting: a white feather was seen as a sign of degenerate stock).

15   For the skull of a black is white, not dull,
         But a glistening awful thing;
         Made, it seems, for this ghoul to swing
In the face of God with all his might,
And swear by the hell that siréd him:
20   "Man-maker, make white!"

1923

Lady, Lady

Lady, Lady, I saw your face,
Dark as night withholding a star . . .
The chisel fell, or it might have been
You had borne so long the yoke of men.
5 Lady, Lady, I saw your hands,
Twisted, awry, like crumpled roots,
Bleached poor white in a sudsy tub,
Wrinkled and drawn from your rub-a-dub.
Lady, Lady, I saw your heart,
10 And altared there in its darksome place
Where the good God sits to spangle through.

1925

Letter to My Sister

It is dangerous for a woman to defy the gods;
To taunt them with the tongue's thin tip,
Or strut in the weakness of mere humanity,
Or draw a line daring them to cross;
5 The gods own the searing lightning,
The drowning waters, tormenting fears
And anger of red sins.

Oh, but worse still if you mince timidly—
Dodge this way or that, or kneel or pray,
10 Be kind, or sweat agony drops
Or lay your quick body over your feeble young;
If you have beauty or none, if celibate
Or vowed—the gods are Juggernaut,[1]
Passing over . . . over . . .

15 This you may do:
Lock your heart, then, quietly,
And lest they peer within,

---

1. A force that crushes everything in its path.

Light no lamp when dark comes down
Raise no shade for sun;
20 Breathless must your breath come through
If you'd die and dare deny
The gods their god-like fun.

1927

Innocence

She tripped and fell against a star,
A lady we all have known;
Just what the villagers lusted for
To claim her one of their own;
5 Fallen but once the lower felt she,
So turned her face and died,—
With never a hounding fool to see
'Twas a star-lance in her side!

1927

KATHARINE SUSANNAH PRICHARD
1883–1969

"With Henry Handel Richardson she pioneered the Australian novel as [an] art form," wrote one critic of Katharine Susannah Prichard. The author of thirteen novels, twelve plays, a number of short story collections, two volumes of verse, and a series of Marxist political pamphlets, Prichard is still little known outside Australia, yet her groundbreaking contribution to that nation's literary development was crucial; in addition, as "The Cooboo" reveals, her art transcended regional issues to focus on universal questions of exploitation and justice, freedom and survival.

Born in Levuka, Fiji, Prichard was the daughter of conservative middle-class parents. Her father was a Melbourne journalist who had published a novel in 1891, and the family lived in moderate comfort until his newspaper went out of business and their household goods were sold to pay debts, an event that may have fostered Prichard's later consciousness of economic inequities. Nevertheless, despite straitened circumstances, she was a precocious child who wrote and published her first story at the age of sixteen, and continued to write and publish short stories thereafter. According to her son, Ric Throssell, she later claimed that she had been born "with ink in her veins." In 1908, she journeyed to England, where she spent a year studying and writing journalism, a career she continued to pursue when she returned to Australia. In 1915, her novel *The Pioneers* won a major Australian literary prize and, as one biographer reports, she "was accorded public honors unprecedented for a native born writer."

Shortly after the 1917 Russian Revolution, Prichard became a committed Marxist; and in 1919, the year after she married Captain Hugo Throssell, an Australian World War I hero who had distinguished himself at Gallipoli, she joined the Communist

Party; its ideology was to influence her worldview for the next few decades. In particular, *Working Bullocks* (1926) and *Coonardoo* (1929) were marked by her newly passionate interest in the lives of the working classes and of the Australian Aborigines. But this period of literary productivity was shadowed by a grievous loss. In 1933—during the Depression, out of work and plagued with debts—her husband shot himself, leaving her desolate; she was eventually to memorialize the sufferings of that era in her novel *Intimate Strangers* (1939).

Among Prichard's later novels, the so-called goldfields trilogy—*The Roaring Nineties* (1946), *Golden Miles* (1948), and *Winged Seeds* (1950)—is widely regarded as her most significant achievement, partly for its historically realistic exploration of west Australia's prospecting era and partly for its vivid portrayal of an implicitly feminist heroine, Sally Gough. But "The Cooboo," too, suggests the skill with which this productively political artist could render the social dynamics that shadowed the lives of Australian Aborigines and half-castes while shaping the society of settlers who might seem to have traveled far from the oppressions of civilization.

The Cooboo[1]

They had been mustering[2] all day on the wide plains of Murndoo station. Over the red earth, black with ironstone pebbles, through mulga and curari bush, across the ridges which make a blue wall along the horizon. And the rosy, garish light of sunset was on plains, hills, moving cattle, men and horses.

Through red dust the bullocks mooched, restless and scary still, a wild mob from the hills. John Gray, in the rear with Arra, the boy who was his shadow; Wongana, on the right with his gin,[3] Rose; Frank, the half-caste, on the left with Minni.

A steer breaking from the mob before Rose, she wheeled and went after him. Faint and wailing, a cry followed her, as though her horse had stepped on and crushed some small creature. But the steer was getting away. Arra went after him, stretched along his horse's neck, rounded the beast and rode him back to the mob, sulky and blethering.[4] The mob swayed; it had broken three times that day, but was settling to the road.

John Gray called: "Yienda (you) damn fool, Rosey. Finish!"

The gin, on her slight, rough-haired horse, pulled up scowling.

"Tell Meetchie, Thirty Mile, to-morrow," John Gray said. "Miah, new moon."

Rose slewed[5] her horse away from the mob of men and cattle. That wailing, thin and hard as hair-string, moved with her.

"Minni!"

John Gray jerked his head towards Rose. Minni's bare heels struck her horse's belly; with a turn of the wrist she swung her horse off from the mob, turned, leaned forward, rising in her stirrups, and came up with Rose.

Thin, dark figures on their wiry station-bred horses, the gins rode into the haze of sunset towards the hills. The dull, dirty blue of the trousers wrapped round their legs was torn; their short, fairish hair tousled by the wind. But the glitter and tumult of Rose's eyes, Minni looked away from them.

---

1. Baby (Australian Aborigine dialect).
2. Rounding up cattle.
3. Native Australian wife or woman.
4. Muttering, grumbling.
5. Swung.

At a little distance, when men and cattle were a moving cloud of red dust, Rose's anger gushed after them.

"Koo!"[6]

Fierce as the cry of a hawk flew her last note of derision and defiance.

A far-away rattle of laughter drifted back across country. Alone they would have been afraid, as darkness coming up behind, was hovering near them, secreting itself among the low, writhen trees, and bushes; afraid of the evil spirits who wander over the plains and stony ridges when the light of day is withdrawn. But together they were not so afraid. Twenty miles away, over there, below that dent in the hills where Nyedee Creek made a sandy bed for itself among white-bodied gums, was Murndoo homestead and the uloo[7] of their people.

There was no track; and in the first darkness, which would be thick as wool after the glow of sunset faded, only their instinct would keep them moving in the direction of the homestead and their own low, round huts of bagging, rusty tin and dead boughs.

Both were Wongana's women: Rose, tall, gaunt and masterful; Minni, younger, fat and jolly. Rose had been a good stockman[8] in her day: one of the best. Minni did not ride or track nearly as well as Rose.

And yet, as they rode along, Minni pattered complacently of how well she had worked that day; of how she was flashed, this way and that, heading-off breakaways, dashing after them, turning them back to the mob so smartly that John had said, "Good man, Minni!" There was the white bullock—he had rushed near the yards. Had Rose seen the chestnut mare stumble in a crab-hole and send Arra flying? But Minni had chased the white bullock, chased him for a couple of miles, and brought him back to the yards. No doubt there would be nammery for her and a new gina-gina[9] when the men came in from the muster.

She pulled a pipe from her belt, shook the ashes out, and with reins looped over one arm stuffed the bowl with tobacco from a tin tied to her belt. Stooping down, she struck a match on her stirrup-iron, guarded the flame to the pipe between her short, white teeth, and smoked contentedly.

The scowl on Rose's face deepened, darkened. That thin, fretted wailing came from her breast.

She unslung from her neck the rag rope by which the baby had been against her body, and gave him a sagging breast to suck. Holding him with one arm, she rode slowly, her horse picking his way over the rough, stony earth.

It had been a hard day. The gins were mustering with the men at sunrise. Camped at Nyedee well the night before, in order to get a good start, they had been riding through the timbered ridges all the morning, rounding up the wild cows, calves and young bullocks, and driving them to the yards at Nyedee, where John Gray cut out the fats, left old Jimmy and a couple of boys to brand calves, turn the cows and calves back to the ridge again while he took on the mob for trucking at Meekatharra. The bullocks were as wild as birds: needed watching all day. And all the time that small, whimpering bundle against her breast had hampered Rose's movements.

There was nothing the gins liked better than a muster, riding after cattle.

---

6. An Aborigine cry.
7. Camp.
8. Herder.
9. Dress. "Nammery": reward.

And they could ride, were quicker in their movements, more alert than the men; sharper at picking up tracks. They did not go mustering very often nowadays when there was work to do at the homestead. Since John Gray had married, and there was a woman on Murndoo, she found plenty of washing, scrubbing and sweeping for the gins to do; would not spare them often to go after cattle. But John was short-handed. He had said he must have Rose and Minni to muster Nyedee. And all day her baby's crying had irritated Rose. The cooboo had wailed and wailed as she rode with him tied to her body.

The cooboo was responsible for the wrong things she had done all day. Stupid things. Rose was furious. The men had yelled at her. Wongana, her man, blackguarding her before everybody, had called her "a hen who did not know where she laid her eggs." And John Gray, with his "Yienda, damn fool, Rosey. Finish!" had sent her home like a naughty child.

Now, here was Minni jabbering of the tobacco she would get and the new gina-gina. How pleased Wongana would be with her! And the cooboo, wailing, wailing. He wailed as he chewed Rose's empty breast, squirming against her; wailed and gnawed.

She cried out with hurt and impatience. Rage, irritated to madness, rushed through her; rushed like waters coming down the dry creek-beds after heavy rain. Rose wrenched the cooboo from her breast and flung him from her to the ground. There was a crack as of twigs breaking.

Minni glanced aside. "Wiah!"[1] she gasped with widening eyes. But Rose rode on, gazing ahead over the rosy, garish plains and wall of the hills, darkening from the blue to purple and indigo.

When the women came into the station kitchen, earth, hills and trees were dark; the sky heavy with stars. Minni gave John's wife his message: that he would be home with the new moon, in about a fortnight.

Meetchie, as the blacks called Mrs. John Gray, could not make out why the gins were so stiff and quiet: why Rose stalked scowling and sulky-fellow, somber eyes just glancing, and away again. Meetchie wanted to ask about the muster, what sort of condition the bullocks had on; how many were on the road; if many calves had been branded at Nyedee. But she knew them too well to ask questions when they looked like that.

Only when she had given them bread and a tin of jam, cut off hunks of corned beef for them, filled their billies[2] with strong black tea, put sugar in their empty tins, and they were going off to the uloo, she was surprised to see Rose without her baby.

"Why, Rose," she exclaimed, "where's the cooboo?"

Rose stalked off into the night. Minni glanced back with scared eyes, and followed Rose.

In the dawn, when a cry, remote and anguished flew through the clear air, Meetchie wondered who was dead in the camp by the creek. She remembered Rose: how she had looked the night before. And the cooboo—where was he?

Then she knew that it was Rose wailing for her cooboo in the dawn: Rose cutting herself with stones until her body bled: Rose screaming in a fury of unavailing grief.

1932

---

1. Ho!   2. Cylindrical tin containers with close-fitting lids.

ANNA WICKHAM (EDITH ALICE MARY HARPER) 1884–1947

"I have to thank God I'm a woman," wrote Anna Wickham in a poem titled "The Affinity," explaining with some irony that "in these ordered days a woman only / Is free to be very hungry, very lonely." That terse, sardonic couplet defines the difficult liberty that was achieved in verse by this distinctively feminist poet who has now been largely forgotten. Born Edith Alice Mary Harper in Wimbledon, just outside London, Wickham emigrated with her family to Brisbane, Australia, at the age of six, where she was evidently raised in a freer environment than that of her English contemporaries. When she was twenty-one, she returned to Europe and studied opera singing in Paris, then married Parick Hepburn and bore two sons. Her marriage was conflicted, however. As one critic observes, she "was considered a 'rebellious' wife, a woman who lived by her own rules"; and according to her recent biographer, Jennifer Vaughan Jones, her husband was so infuriated by her rebelliousness that at one point he had her institutionalized for several months. Yet these problems appear to have energized her art, for she soon began to write poetry at an extraordinary pace. Her first collection was privately printed in 1911 under the title *Sons of John Oland,* and it was followed by three more volumes—*The Contemplative Quarry* (1915), *The Man with a Hammer* (1916), and *The Little Old House* (1921). The three books were signed by Anna Wickham, a name the writer adopted to memorialize Wickham Terrace, in Brisbane, where her father had urged her to vow that she would become a poet. All in all, in one four-year period of intense creative activity, she produced nine hundred poems.

Among London intellectuals of her era, Wickham was well known, especially in a circle that included the writers T. E. Hulme and D. H. Lawrence as well as the artists Gaudier-Brzeska and Jacob Epstein. In Paris in the twenties, too, Wickham became part of the glamorous lesbian expatriate community that had formed around the American millionaire Natalie Clifford Barney, with whom, according to Jones, the poet fell unrequitedly in love. Yet despite Wickham's productivity and her reputation as, in the words of the poet-editor Louis Untermeyer, "a magnificent gypsy of a woman," her verse is often as bitterly explicit about the impediments to female achievement as were the critical writings of her contemporary Virginia Woolf. In "Dedication of the Cook," for instance, Wickham declares, "If any ask why there's no great She-Poet, / Let him come live with me, and he will know it." At the same time, a number of her works, like "The Affinity," celebrate the aesthetic freedom made possible by woman's status as what Woolf called an "outsider."

Meditation at Kew[1]

Alas! for all the pretty women who marry dull men,
Go into the suburbs and never come out again,
Who lose their pretty faces, and dim their pretty eyes,
Because no one has skill or courage to organize.

5   What do these pretty women suffer when they marry?
They bear a boy who is like Uncle Harry,
A girl, who is like Aunt Eliza, and not new,
These old, dull races must breed true.

---

1. A west London suburb.

I would enclose a common[2] in the sun,
And let the young wives out to laugh and run;
I would steal their dull clothes and go away,
And leave the pretty naked things to play.

Then I would make a contract with hard Fate
That they see all the men in the world and choose a mate,
And I would summon all the pipers in the town
That they dance with Love at a feast, and dance him down.

From the gay unions of choice
We'd have a race of splendid beauty, and of thrilling voice.
The World whips frank, gay love with rods,
But frankly, gayly shall we get the gods.

1915

The Affinity

I have to thank God I'm a woman,
For in these ordered days a woman only
Is free to be very hungry, very lonely.

It is sad for Feminism, but still clear
That man, more often than woman, is pioneer.
If I would confide a new thought,
First to a man must it be brought.

Now, for our sins, it is my bitter fate
That such a man wills soon to be my mate,
And so of friendship is quick end:
When I have gained a love I lose a friend.

It is well within the order of things
That man should listen when his mate sings;
But the true male never yet walked
Who liked to listen when his mate talked.

I would be married to a full man,
As would all women since the world began;
But from a wealth of living I have proved
I must be silent, if I would be loved.

Now of my silence I have much wealth,
I have to do my thinking all by stealth.
My thoughts may never see the day;
My mind is like a catacomb where early Christians pray.

And of my silence I have much pain,
But of these pangs I have great gain;

---

2. A piece of land for public use; a park.

For I must take to drugs or drink,
Or I must write the things I think.

If my sex would let me speak,
I would be very lazy and most weak;
30 I should speak only, and the things I spoke
Would fill the air awhile, and clear like smoke.

The things I think now I write down,
And some day I will show them to the Town.
When I am sad I make thought clear;
35 I can re-read it all next year.

I have to thank God I'm a woman,
For in these ordered days a woman only
Is free to be very hungry, very lonely.

1915

Divorce

A voice from the dark is calling me.
In the close house I nurse a fire.
Out in the dark, cold winds rush free,

To the rock heights of my desire.
5 I smother in the house in the valley below,
Let me out to the night, let me go, let me go!

Spirits that ride the sweeping blast,
Frozen in rigid tenderness,
Wait! For I leave the fire at last,
10 My little-love's warm loneliness.
I smother in the house in the valley below,
Let me out in the night, let me go, let me go!

High on the hills are beating drums,
Clear from a line of marching men
15 To the rock's edge the hero comes.
He calls me, and he calls again.
On the hill there is fighting, victory, or quick death,
In the house is the fire, which I fan with sick breath
I smother in the house in the valley below,
20 Let me out in the dark, let me go, let me go!

1916

Dedication of the Cook

If any ask why there's no great She-Poet,
Let him come live with me, and he will know it:

If I'd indite an ode or mend a sonnet,
I must go choose a dish or tie a bonnet;
5 For she who serves in forced virginity
Since I am wedded will not have me free;
And those new flowers my garden is so rich in
Must die for clammy odors of my kitchen.

Yet had I chosen Dian's[1] barrenness
10 I'm not full woman, and I can't be less,
So could I state no certain truth for life,
Can I survive and be my good man's wife?

Yes! I will make the servant's cause my own
That she in pity leave me hours alone
15 So I will tend her mind and feed her wit
That she in time have her own joy of it;
And count it pride that not a sonnet's spoiled
Lacking her choice betwixt the baked and boiled.
20 So those young flowers my garden is so rich in
Will blossom from the ashes of my kitchen!

1922

1. Diana, the Roman virgin goddess of the moon and of the hunt.

ELINOR WYLIE
1885–1928

During her lifetime, Elinor Wylie seemed to the writer Carl Van Doren like a "white queen"—pale, elegantly dressed, dazzlingly successful, dominating the literary world with glittering poems and eloquent talk—while the critic Edmund Wilson regarded her as "one of the most steadily industrious and most productive writers of my acquaintance." Yet more recently at least one essayist has declared that her work "holds little interest; the poems include far too many references to goldfish, moonbeams, and snowflakes for modern taste." The woman who inspired such mixed opinions was born Elinor Hoyt in Somerville, New Jersey, the eldest of five children in a distinguished family, and her early years were marked by what one biographer calls "unruffled gentility." In 1905, at the age of twenty, she married Philip Hichborn, the son of a prominent admiral; but five years later she left him and her young son, Philip, to elope with Horace Wylie, a married lawyer seventeen years older than she. The ensuing scandal altered the wellborn young woman's sense of herself and of the world, imbuing her poetry with an enduring irony about society. Wylie's wife refused to grant him a divorce, and though the lovers sought anonymity in England, they were long considered notorious.

When the couple returned to the United States in 1916, just after the outbreak of World War I, they legally married, then settled in 1919 in Washington, D.C., where Horace had a government job and Elinor began seriously to publish poetry with the sponsorship of new friends, including the novelist Sinclair Lewis and the poet William Rose Benét. In 1912, she had had a small collection of verse, *Incidental Numbers*, privately printed in England, but she regarded the book as marred by "incredible immaturity." Wylie's first really ambitious volume was *Nets to Catch the Wind* (1921), a book that achieved instantaneous success with what the anthologist Louis Untermeyer called its "brilliance of moonlight coruscating on a plain of ice." At around the time that *Nets to Catch the Wind* appeared, she had moved to New York, where she became increasingly close to William Rose Benét, the editor of the prestigious *Saturday Review of Literature*. In 1922 she herself became literary editor of *Vanity Fair* and in 1923, she divorced Wylie to marry Benét. Also in 1923 she published another successful collection of verse, *Black Armour*, and a well-received first novel, *Jennifer Lorn: A Sedate Extravaganza*. In the following years she was to publish three more novels, including *The Venetian Glass Nephew* (1925), generally considered her strongest work of fiction, and *The Orphan Angel* (1926), a Book-of-the-Month Club selection.

Though later Wylie traveled to England, where she resided for long periods in the late 1920s and where, as she confided to Carl Van Doren, she found someone she really loved "for the first time" (the mysterious beloved to whom her sonnets in the sequence *One Person* are addressed), her marriage to Benét seems on the whole to have been good. She had returned to live with him just before she died of a stroke on the day that she finished correcting proofs for her last collection of verse, *Angels and Earthly Creatures* (posthumously published in 1929). And her years in New York had been triumphantly productive: besides publishing her novels and several collections of verse, she had become a literary personage; wealthy, beautiful, and fashionably dressed, she had also become a public personality, a friend of key intellectuals, and a patron saint to such younger writers as the poet Edna St. Vincent Millay, who movingly elegized her.

Despite her successes, however, Wylie's finest poetry is marked by an austere lyricism that suggests a deeply pessimistic cast of mind. "I was, being human, born alone," she confesses in one verse, adding, "I am, being woman, hard beset." Elsewhere, moreover, she reveals an ironic consciousness that her admirers may be mythologizing her, musing that "the woman [might be] molded by your wish." Perhaps some of the recent rejection of her work as disfigured by "too many references to goldfish [and] moonbeams" is the consequence of such mythologizing, an inability to separate the worldly glamour of the woman from the aesthetic severity of the poet.

The Eagle and the Mole

Avoid the reeking herd,
Shun the polluted flock,
Live like that stoic bird,
The eagle of the rock.

5   The huddled warmth of crowds
Begets and fosters hate;
He keeps, above the clouds,
His cliff inviolate.

When flocks are folded warm,
10   And herds to shelter run,
He sails above the storm,
He stares into the sun.

If in the eagle's track
Your sinews cannot leap,

15 Avoid the lathered pack,
    Turn from the steaming sheep.

    If you would keep your soul
    From spotted sight or sound,
    Live like the velvet mole;
20 Go burrow underground.

    And there hold intercourse
    With roots of trees and stones,
    With rivers at their source,
    And disembodied bones.

                                            1921

Atavism[1]

   I always was afraid of Somes's Pond:
   Not the little pond, by which the willow stands,
   Where laughing boys catch alewives[2] in their hands
   In brown, bright shallows; but the one beyond.
5 There, when the frost makes all the birches burn
   Yellow as cow-lilies, and the pale sky shines
   Like a polished shell between black spruce and pines,
   Some strange thing tracks us, turning where we turn.

   You'll say I dream it, being the true daughter
10 Of those who in old times endured this dread.
   Look! Where the lily-stems are showing red
   A silent paddle moves below the water,
   A sliding shape has stirred them like a breath;
   Tall plumes surmount a painted mask of death.

                                            1921

Wild Peaches

1

   When the world turns completely upside down
   You say we'll emigrate to the Eastern Shore[1]
   Aboard a river-boat from Baltimore;
   We'll live among wild peach trees, miles from town,
5 You'll wear a coonskin cap, and I a gown
   Homespun, dyed butternut's dark gold color.
   Lost, like your lotus-eating ancestor,[2]
   We'll swim in milk and honey till we drown.

---

1. Recurrence in an organism of genetic typical of an ancestral form.
2. An Atlantic fish of the herring family.
1. I.e., of Maryland, east of the Chesapeake Bay.

2. In Homer's *Odyssey* (book 9) the lotus-eaters remain in a state of drugged contentment because of the fruit they consume.

The winter will be short, the summer long,
10 The autumn amber-hued, sunny and hot,
    Tasting of cider and of scuppernong;[3]
    All seasons sweet, but autumn best of all.
    The squirrels in their silver fur will fall
    Like falling leaves, like fruit, before your shot.

2

15 The autumn frosts will lie upon the grass
    Like bloom on grapes of purple-brown and gold.
    The misted early mornings will be cold;
    The little puddles will be roofed with glass.
    The sun, which burns from copper into brass,
20 Melts these at noon, and makes the boys unfold
    Their knitted mufflers; full as they can hold,
    Fat pockets dribble chestnuts as they pass.

    Peaches grow wild, and pigs can live in clover;
    A barrel of salted herrings lasts a year;
25 The spring begins before the winter's over.
    By February you may find the skins
    Of garter snakes and water moccasins
    Dwindled and harsh, dead-white and cloudy-clear.

3

    When April pours the colors of a shell
30 Upon the hills, when every little creek
    Is shot with silver from the Chesapeake
    In shoals new-minted by the ocean swell,
    When strawberries go begging, and the sleek
    Blue plums lie open to the blackbird's beak,
35 We shall live well—we shall live very well.

    The months between the cherries and the peaches
    Are brimming cornucopias which spill
    Fruits red and purple, somber-bloomed and black;
    Then, down rich fields and frosty river beaches
40 We'll trample bright persimmons, while you kill
    Bronze partridge, speckled quail, and canvasback.

4

    Down to the Puritan marrow of my bones
    There's something in this richness that I hate.
    I love the look, austere, immaculate,
45 Of landscapes drawn in pearly monotones.
    There's something in my very blood that owns
    Bare hills, cold silver on a sky of slate,

---

3. A sweet golden wine made from grapes native to America.

A thread of water, churned to milky spate,[4]
Streaming through slanted pastures fenced with stones.

50 I love those skies, thin blue or snowy gray,
Those fields sparse-planted, rendering meager sheaves:
That spring, briefer than apple-blossom's breath,
Summer, so much too beautiful to stay,
Swift autumn, like a bonfire of leaves,
55 And sleepy winter, like the sleep of death.

                                                                1921

Full Moon

My bands of silk and miniver[1]
Momently grew heavier;
The black gauze was beggarly thin;
The ermine muffled mouth and chin;
5 I could not suck the moonlight in.

Harlequin in lozenges
Of love and hate, I walked in these
Striped and ragged rigmaroles;
Along the pavement my footsoles
10 Trod warily on living coals.
Shouldering the thoughts I loathed,
In their corrupt disguises clothed,
Mortality I could not tear
From my ribs, to leave them bare
15 Ivory in silver air.

There I walked, and there I raged;
The spiritual savage caged
Within my skeleton, raged afresh
To feel, behind a carnal mesh,
20 The clean bones crying in the flesh.

                                                                1923

Let No Charitable Hope

Now let no charitable hope
Confuse my mind with images
Of eagle and of antelope:
I am in nature none of these.

5 I was, being human, born alone;
I am, being woman, hard beset;

---

4. Flood or freshet.   1. A white fur.

I live by squeezing from a stone
The little nourishment I get.

In masks outrageous and austere
The years go by in single file;[1]
But none has merited my fear,
And none has quite escaped my smile.

1923

From One Person[1]

XII

In our content, before the autumn came
To shower sallow droppings on the mold,
Sometimes you have permitted me to fold
Your grief in swaddling-bands, and smile to name
Yourself my infant, with an infant's claim
To utmost adoration as of old,
Suckled with kindness, fondled from the cold,
And loved beyond philosophy or shame.

I dreamt I was the mother of a son
Who had deserved a manger for a crib;
Torn from your body, furbished from your rib,[2]
I am the daughter of your skeleton,
Born of your bitter and excessive pain:
I shall not dream you are my child again.

1929

To a Lady's Countenance

This unphilosophic sight;
This silly mask of silken white;
This thing which has, to hide its grief,
Less than a rose's lesser leaf;
This web a spider might have spun
With patience and precision;
This veil concealing sorrow's face,
Arranged with coquetry and grace,
Which shall remain, when all is said,
After sorrow itself is dead;
In color, a camellia flower;
In shape, a whim of the glass-blower;

---

1. Possibly an echo of Ralph Waldo Emerson's poem "Days" (1857): "Daughters of Time, the hypocritic Days, / Muffled and dumb like barefoot dervishes, / And marching single in an endless file."

1. A sonnet sequence.
2. In the Bible God fashions Eve from one of Adam's ribs (Genesis 2.21–22). The son with a manger for a crib was Jesus.

      The mind's eye hollowed and made blind,
      But not the brow above the mind;
15 And, whatsoever may be starved,
      The little lips uncut, uncarved;
      God's power has disdained to mold
      This clay so delicate and cold;
      Perchance he took it for the flesh
20 Of mushrooms, or the silkworm's mesh;
      Stuff too slight to bear the fine
      Finger-tip of the divine
      In lines of noble heritage;
      And so, you do not show your age.

1929

Pastiche

  Is not the woman molded by your wish
  A cockatrice[1] a most intricate kind?
  You have, my friend, the high fantastic mind
  To clasp the cold enamel of a fish
5 As breastplate for a bosom tigerish;
  To make a dove a dragon; or to bind
  A panther skin upon the escaping hind:
  You mix ambiguous spices in your dish.
  Will there remain, when thus embellished I
10 Sprout wings, or am by cloven heels improved,
  An atom of the lady that you loved?
  Does Christ or Lucifer seal this alchemy?
  Is there not lacking from your synthesis
  Someone you may occasionally miss?

1932

1. Legendary monster with the head, wings, and legs of a cock and the body of a serpent; its glance was fatal.

ISAK DINESEN
1885–1962

Isak Dinesen's writing career did not begin until she reached her late forties, when she believed that she had left her real life behind, although she would survive another thirty years to produce several brilliant volumes of short stories, as well as a fascinating autobiography, a novel, and a collection of essays. She had lost her coffee plantation in Africa, her husband, her health, and her lover when she returned to what she considered the stultifying confinement of her mother's house at Rungstedlund in Denmark. "All sorrows," she believed, "can be borne if you put them into a story or tell a story about them." And she was, by her own admission, "une conteuse, et rien qu'une conteuse" (a storyteller and nothing but a storyteller). As a storyteller who transformed the sorrows of her life through the sorcery of her art, she could see herself in her past youth and her future old age as a magical witch or wise sibyl.

Christened Karen Christentze Dinesen in 1885, Dinesen viewed her matrilineage with dislike, associating her mother, Ingeborg (Westenholz) Dinesen, with bourgeois practicality and puritanical morality. Tanne, as she was called, condescended to her mother and romanticized her father, Wilhelm Dinesen, as the representative of adventurous, aristocratic ancestors, erotically daring in their restless search for intense experiences in love and war. The author of *Letters from the Hunt* (1889), Wilhelm Dinesen had fought in the Dano-Prussian War of 1864; suffered the death of his first "great passion," an eighteen-year-old cousin; and wandered as far as America. Tanne was the second of five children in the family, all of whom must have been shocked by Wilhelm Dinesen's suicide in 1895. Her father left a note admitting that while he knew his other two daughters would fend for themselves, "my heart aches for Tanne." Certainly, the nine-year-old Tanne felt herself to be especially bereaved, and as her biographer Judith Thurman has shown, by fifteen Dinesen was obsessed with a fantasy of union with her father that would inform not only her subsequent relationships with men but also her sense of herself as an artist.

Educated in the schoolroom at Rungstedlund with her two sisters while her brothers were sent to boarding school, Dinesen wrote witty essays on Danish proverbs and the French Revolution, plays in which she took the part of Pierrot, and fantasies in which she was a romantic Lord Byron. In 1899, she went with her sisters and mother to Switzerland, where the girls entered the École Bénét and where Dinesen began painting. Although after this her formal education was supposed to be complete, back at home she read the plays of Shakespeare, the poetry of Heine and Shelley, and the novels of Laurence Sterne, as well as Danish writers such as the novelist Meïr Aaron Goldschmidt, the lyricist Johannes Ewald, and the storyteller Hans Christian Andersen. Over the objections of her family, moreover, she left for Copenhagen to enroll in the private art classes girls had to take for admission into the Royal Academy of Fine Arts. In 1904, she began work on a group of tales called *Likely Stories,* two of which were published in the Danish journal *Tilskueren* under the pseudonym Osceola, chosen to commemorate a rebellious leader of the Seminole Indians.

After five semesters at the Royal Academy, Dinesen returned home and fell in love with Hans Blixen-Finecke, a distant and dashing cousin on her father's side. When he did not respond, she married his twin brother, Bror, and convinced her family to support Bror's purchase of several hundred acres of land for a coffee plantation near Nairobi. Embarking in 1913 on the thirteen-day passage to British East Africa, neither Bror nor Tanne knew that the acreage was too acidic and too high in altitude for successful coffee growing. In *Out of Africa* (1937), Dinesen described the beauty of the Ngong hills around Nairobi, the dignified customs of the Masai and the Somali, her passionate love of safari life, and her enjoyment at playing the role of the aristocratic baroness to intelligent servants like Farah Aden, her steward. "Here I am where I ought to be," she explained, an affirmation that has been questioned by readers disturbed by the white privileges on which she clearly capitalized. Yet *Out of Africa* is still appreciated by others as a pastoral, although it is reticent about the personal problems she confronted on the farm.

The worst of these presented itself as a recurrent malady that she diagnosed as malaria, although it turned out to be syphilis contracted from her husband. Though she managed to treat her symptoms during a trip to Copenhagen in 1910, the disease would recur throughout her life, causing her repeated "lumbago," shooting pains "like a toothache" in her ears, and spinal degeneration. While she had no desire to separate from Bror, she soon fell in love with another adventurous aristocrat, the handsome, thirty-two-year-old Denys Finch-Hatton. Son of the earl of Winchilsea and Nottingham, Finch-Hatton had become a farmer, trader, flyer, and safari leader in East Africa in 1912, after an Eton and Oxford education. For a while, her lover and her husband shared a bedroom at Ngong, each using it while the other was on safari. But Bror began an affair with a woman he would eventually marry, and by 1922 Tanne had to agree to the divorce he wanted. For ten years, the woman who relished being called "the Lioness" managed the farm alone, although her visiting brother Thomas helped her face the droughts, fires, and disappointing harvests that eventually made it impossible for her to stay. Just before Dinesen's departure, in 1931, Finch-Hatton died in a plane crash and was buried in the Ngong hills.

Dinesen had begun reading Rudyard Kipling, Oscar Wilde, and Robert Louis Stevenson on the African farm, where she also wrote romances for her lover. On her return to Denmark, when she had to rescue herself from bankruptcy, she chose to write in Finch-Hatton's language to distance herself from her Danish surroundings, just as she used the pseudonym Isak, "the one who laughs," to cope with her sorrow. In *Seven Gothic Tales* (1934) and *Winter Tales* (1942), she focused with ironic wit on the charades and masquerades that liberate the self from the constraints of a fixed identity. Similarly, she created a myth of herself through her extravagant costumes—a gown that she named Sappho, for example, or a suit she called Sober Truth. Identifying her disease with her fallen father, whose suicide, she had reason to believe, was related to a case of syphilis, she considered "it was worth while having syphilis in order to become a Baroness." As one of the last representatives of the aristocratic spirit, then, she saw herself as a quixotic rebel opposed to a dreary bourgeois realism. In her later years, she was active in Danish intellectual life as a patroness of avant-garde artists, as a hostess of a lively salon, and as a speaker on the radio. Like many of the characters in her parables and fables, Dinesen delighted in her personal and artistic power even in the bleakest of historical moments.

Between the appearance of her thriller *The Angelic Avengers* (1944), published under the pseudonym Pierre Andrezel, and her next volume of stories, *Last Tales* (1957), Dinesen suffered from the syphilis that was now beyond treatment. Nevertheless, with the help of her companion and secretary, Clara Svendsen, she continued to travel—to America in 1959, for instance, where her books were greeted enthusiastically by admirers like Carson McCullers. After an operation on her spinal cord, and another on her stomach, however, Dinesen would never again weigh more than eighty-five pounds. "The doctor tells me that I have all the symptoms of a concentration camp prisoner," she explained during the time she lived on asparagus, fruit juice, oysters, and dry biscuits. She died of malnutrition.

The Blank Page

By the ancient city gate sat an old coffee-brown, black-veiled woman who made her living by telling stories.

She said:

"You want a tale, sweet lady and gentleman? Indeed I have told many tales, one more than a thousand,[1] since that time when I first let young men tell me, myself, tales of a red rose, two smooth lily buds, and four silky, supple, deadly entwining snakes. It was my mother's mother, the black-eyed dancer, the often-embraced, who in the end—wrinkled like a winter apple and crouching beneath the mercy of the veil—took upon herself to teach me the art of story-telling. Her own mother's mother had taught it to her, and both were better story-tellers than I am. But that, by now, is of no consequence,

---

1. A reference to *The Thousand and One Nights*, a collection of ancient tales in Arabic, arranged in its present form in the 15th century; the discrete stories are supposedly told by Scheherezade, a bride trying to delay her execution at the hands of her husband, the Sultan.

since to the people they and I have become one, and I am most highly honored because I have told stories for two hundred years."

Now if she is well paid and in good spirits, she will go on.

"With my grandmother," she said, "I went through a hard school. 'Be loyal to the story,' the old hag would say to me. 'Be eternally and unswervingly loyal to the story.' 'Why must I be that, Grandmother?' I asked her. 'Am I to furnish you with reasons, baggage?' she cried. 'And you mean to be a story-teller! Why, you are to become a story-teller, and I shall give you my reasons! Hear then: Where the story-teller is loyal, eternally and unswervingly loyal to the story, there, in the end, silence will speak. Where the story has been betrayed, silence is but emptiness. But we, the faithful, when we have spoken our last word, will hear the voice of silence. Whether a small snotty lass understands it or not.'

"Who then," she continues, "tells a finer tale than any of us? Silence does. And where does one read a deeper tale than upon the most perfectly printed page of the most precious book? Upon the blank page. When a royal and gallant pen, in the moment of its highest inspiration, has written down its tale with the rarest ink of all—where, then, may one read a still deeper, sweeter, merrier and more cruel tale than that? Upon the blank page."

The old beldame[2] for a while says nothing, only giggles a little and munches with her toothless mouth.

"We," she says at last, "the old women who tell stories, we know the story of the blank page. But we are somewhat averse to telling it, for it might well, among the uninitiated, weaken our own credit. All the same, I am going to make an exception with you, my sweet and pretty lady and gentleman of the generous hearts. I shall tell it to you."

High up in the blue mountains of Portugal there stands an old convent for sisters of the Carmelite order, which is an illustrious and austere order. In ancient times the convent was rich, the sisters were all noble ladies, and miracles took place there. But during the centuries highborn ladies grew less keen on fasting and prayer, the great dowries flowed scantily into the treasury of the convent, and today the few portionless[3] and humble sisters live in but one wing of the vast crumbling structure, which looks as if it longed to become one with the gray rock itself. Yet they are still a blithe and active sisterhood. They take much pleasure in their holy meditations, and will busy themselves joyfully with that one particular task which did once, long, long ago, obtain for the convent a unique and strange privilege: they grow the finest flax and manufacture the most exquisite linen of Portugal.

The long field below the convent is plowed with gentle-eyed, milk-white bullocks, and the seed is skillfully sown out by labor-hardened virginal hands with mold under the nails. At the time when the flax field flowers, the whole valley becomes air-blue, the very color of the apron which the blessed virgin put on to go out and collect eggs within St. Anne's poultry yard, the moment before the Archangel Gabriel in mighty wing-strokes lowered himself onto the threshold of the house,[4] and while high, high up a dove, neck-feathers raised and wings vibrating, stood like a small clear silver star in the sky. During this month the villagers many miles round raise their eyes to the flax

---

2. Aged woman (often disparaging).
3. Without dowries.
4. I.e., to announce that Mary would bear the son of God (Luke 1.26–38). Anne was Mary's mother.

field and ask one another: "Has the convent been lifted into heaven? Or have our good little sisters succeeded in pulling down heaven to them?"

Later in due course the flax is pulled, scutched and hackled;[5] thereafter the delicate thread is spun, and the linen woven, and at the very end the fabric is laid out on the grass to bleach, and is watered time after time, until one may believe that snow has fallen round the convent walls. All this work is gone through with precision and piety and with such sprinklings and litanies as are the secret of the convent. For these reasons the linen, baled high on the backs of small gray donkeys and sent out through the convent gate, downwards and ever downwards to the towns, is as flower-white, smooth and dainty as was my own little foot when, fourteen years old, I had washed it in the brook to go to a dance in the village.

Diligence, dear Master and Mistress, is a good thing, and religion is a good thing, but the very first germ of a story will come from some mystical place outside the story itself. Thus does the linen of the Convento Velho draw its true virtue from the fact that the very first linseed was brought home from the Holy Land itself by a crusader.

In the Bible, people who can read may learn about the lands of Lecha and Maresha, where flax is grown. I myself cannot read, and have never seen this book of which so much is spoken. But my grandmother's grandmother as a little girl was the pet of an old Jewish rabbi, and the learning she received from him has been kept and passed on in our family. So you will read, in the book of Joshua, of how Achsah the daughter of Caleb lighted from her ass and cried unto her father: "Give me a blessing! For thou hast now given me land; give me also the blessing of springs of water!" And he gave her the upper springs and the nether springs.[6] And in the fields of Lecha and Maresha lived, later on, the families of them that wrought the finest linen of all. Our Portuguese crusader, whose own ancestors had once been great linen weavers of Tomar, as he rode through these same fields was struck by the quality of the flax, and so tied a bag of seeds to the pommel of his saddle.

From this circumstance originated the first privilege of the convent, which was to procure bridal sheets for all the young princesses of the royal house.

I will inform you, dear lady and gentleman, that in the country of Portugal in very old and noble families a venerable custom has been observed. On the morning after the wedding of a daughter of the house, and before the morning gift had yet been handed over, the Chamberlain or High Steward from a balcony of the palace would hang out the sheet of the night and would solemnly proclaim: *Virginem eam tenemus*—"we declare her to have been a virgin." Such a sheet was never afterwards washed or again lain on.

This time-honored custom was nowhere more strictly upheld than within the royal house itself, and it has there subsisted till within living memory.

Now for many hundred years the convent in the mountains, in appreciation of the excellent quality of the linen delivered, has held its second high privilege: that of receiving back that central piece of the snow-white sheet which bore witness to the honor of a royal bride.

In the tall main wing of the convent, which overlooks an immense landscape of hills and valleys, there is a long gallery with a black-and-white marble floor. On the walls of the gallery, side by side, hangs a long row of heavy,

---

5. Beaten and combed.   6. Joshua 15.18–19.

gilt frames, each of them adorned with a coroneted plate of pure gold, on which is engraved the name of a princess: Donna Christina, Donna Ines, Donna Jacintha Lenora, Donna Maria. And each of these frames encloses a square cut from a royal wedding sheet.

Within the faded markings of the canvases people of some imagination and sensibility may read all the signs of the zodiac: the Scales, the Scorpion, the Lion, the Twins. Or they may there find pictures from their own world of ideas: a rose, a heart, a sword—or even a heart pierced through with a sword.

In days of old it would occur that a long, stately, richly colored procession wound its way through the stone-gray mountain scenery, upwards to the convent. Princesses of Portugal, who were now queens or queen dowagers of foreign countries, Archduchesses, or Electresses,[7] with their splendid retinue, proceeded here on a pilgrimage which was by nature both sacred and secretly gay. From the flax field upwards the road rises steeply; the royal-lady would have to descend from her coach to be carried this last bit of the way in a palanquin[8] presented to the convent for the very same purpose.

Later on, up to our own day, it has come to pass—as it comes to pass when a sheet of paper is being burnt, that after all other sparks have run along the edge and died away, one last clear little spark will appear and hurry along after them—that a very old highborn spinster undertakes the journey to Convento Velho. She has once, a long long time ago, been playmate, friend and maid-of-honor to a young princess of Portugal. As she makes her way to the convent she looks round to see the view widen to all sides. Within the building a sister conducts her to the gallery and to the plate bearing the name of the princess she has once served, and there takes leave of her, aware of her wish to be alone.

Slowly, slowly a row of recollections passes through the small, venerable, skull-like head under its mantilla[9] of black lace, and it nods to them in amicable recognition. The loyal friend and confidante looks back upon the young bride's elevated married life with the elected royal consort. She takes stock of happy events and disappointments—coronations and jubilees, court intrigues and wars, the birth of heirs to the throne, the alliances of younger generations of princes and princesses, the rise or decline of dynasties. The old lady will remember how once, from the markings on the canvas, omens were drawn; now she will be able to compare the fulfillment to the omen, sighing a little and smiling a little. Each separate canvas with its coroneted name-plate has a story to tell, and each has been set up in loyalty to the story.

But in the midst of the long row there hangs a canvas which differs from the others. The frame of it is as fine and as heavy as any, and as proudly as any carries the golden plate with the royal crown. But on this one plate no name is inscribed, and the linen within the frame is snow-white from corner to corner, a blank page.

I beg of you, you good people who want to hear stories told: look at this page, and recognize the wisdom of my grandmother and of all old story-telling women!

---

7. Wives or widows of the German princes entitled to choose the Holy Roman Emperor.

8. Enclosed litter carried on poles.

9. A light shawl (mantle).

For with what eternal and unswerving loyalty has not this canvas been inserted in the row! The story-tellers themselves before it draw their veils over their faces and are dumb. Because the royal papa and mama who once ordered this canvas to be framed and hung up, had they not had the tradition of loyalty in their blood, might have left it out.

It is in front of this piece of pure white linen that the old princesses of Portugal—worldly wise, dutiful, long-suffering queens, wives and mothers—and their noble old playmates, bridesmaids and maids-of-honor have most often stood still.

It is in front of the blank page that old and young nuns, with the Mother Abbess herself, sink into deepest thought.

1957

H. D. (HILDA DOOLITTLE)
1886–1961

"Take care, do not know me," H. D. warned her readers in her book-length poem *Trilogy* (1944–46); "shun me; for this reality / is infectious—ecstasy." The infectious ecstasy that H. D. dared to express was an alternative to what she considered the senseless violence of the modern world. Writing, in her periods of greatest productivity, during the two world wars, H. D. rejected the nightmare of history, substituting for it a personal, spiritual quest for resurrection. In search of "what men say is-not," she recovered eternal, mythic patterns in everyday events through what she called "spiritual realism." At their most problematic, H. D.'s equivalencies can be dizzyingly associative, for she traced the multiple meanings of related words, decoding such signs as if they were hieroglyphs. At their most powerful, the images of her poetry transformed her own life and the life of her times into a palimpsest, a record that retains traces of a still visible and viable ancient script.

Until the 1970s, H. D. was remembered for a handful of short, intense poems that helped define the literary movement the modernist poet Ezra Pound dubbed Imagism. But the pioneering works of the critics Norman Holmes Pearson, Susan Stanford Friedman, and Louis Martz have illuminated the later development of this major modernist. The early Imagist lyrics written at the beginning of the twentieth century were followed by long poetic narratives composed at midcentury. In part, H. D.'s development as a poet was the result of the Greek translations, prose fiction, and film criticism she produced throughout the 1920s and 1930s. In part, too, it was indebted to a series of illustrious men who functioned as "initiators" for the poet. If, as the literary critic Rachel Blau DuPlessis has shown, H. D. sometimes seemed inextricably drawn to a relationship of "romantic thralldom" with such men, what she took away from them was transformed into a revisionary mythology that reflected her lifelong effort to understand her identity as a woman and a poet.

The only surviving daughter in a prominent family that included five sons, Hilda Doolittle lived the first eight years of her life in Bethlehem, Pennsylvania. Her father, Charles Doolittle, was professor of mathematics and astronomy at Lehigh University. In her autobiographical prose, H. D. recurrently associated him with authority and knowledge, for he charted the course of the stars in his study, where the maps and instruments impressed her as sacred symbols. Artistically talented, H. D.'s mother, Helen (Wolle) Doolittle, was a member of the Moravian brotherhood, a Protestant sect noted for its mysticism, and she maintained a close relationship with her own mother and with her father, who was the head of the Moravian seminary. The community had brought with them from Germany a doctrine that taught faith in a direct, sensuous illumination of God. Indeed, for H. D., the "gift" of vision and spiritual wisdom that the Moravians traced from generation to generation was an aspect of her own poetic gift.

In 1895, when H. D.'s father became Flower Professor of Astronomy and director of the Flower Observatory at the University of Pennsylvania, the family moved to a suburb of Philadelphia. Hilda lived at home while attending first the Gordon School, then the Friends Central School, and, finally, Bryn Mawr. She soon left college, however, after failing English and suffering from a breakdown. In her autobiographical novel *HERmione* (1923, published 1981), she analyzed the conflict she experienced at this time between her relationship with the young Ezra Pound, to whom she became engaged, and her growing attachment to a girlfriend, Frances Gregg. An early admirer, the poet William Carlos Williams described the beauty of the youthful H. D. (which Pound celebrated in his series of poems titled "Hilda's Book") as well as her nervous isolation within her family (which H. D. attributed to her relationship with Frances). By 1911, she had decided to sail to Europe with Frances and Mrs. Gregg, a trip that resulted in her reunion with Pound in London and the beginning of a lifelong expatriation.

Through Pound, H. D. met D. H. Lawrence, William Butler Yeats, May Sinclair, and the poet-translator Richard Aldington. It was at Pound's suggestion, too, that she submitted her first poems to Harriet Monroe's magazine, *Poetry*. Indeed, in the tearoom of the British Museum in August 1912, Pound signed Hilda Doolittle's poems with the pseudonym "H. D. Imagiste." As the promoter of early Imagism, he defined the poetic principles he saw embodied in H. D.'s verse: direct treatment of the subject, no inessential words, and musical (rather than strictly regular) rhythms. H. D.'s strikingly minimalist poems from this period were collected in her first volume of verse, *Sea Garden* (1916). Before this happened, however, her relationship with Pound had become troubled by his magisterial willfulness and his infidelities. Influenced by Aldington, who had succeeded Pound as the editor of *The New Freewoman* (soon to become *The Egoist*), H. D. had begun to concentrate on her own poetic education, studying Greek lyrics, the French symbolists, and the troubadours of medieval Provence. In 1913, she married Aldington.

While Pound went on from Imagism to another experimental movement, Vorticism, and from H. D. to Dorothy Shakespear, whom he married in 1914, H. D. and Aldington were befriended by the wealthy American poet Amy Lowell, who published three anthologies and a critical book publicizing both Imagism and H. D. in America. At this time, the couple became intimate with D. H. and Frieda Lawrence. Much has been written about this relationship: Lawrence fictionalized H. D. as the bohemian Julia in *Aaron's Rod* (1922); H. D. portrayed Lawrence in the unpublished "Pilate's Wife" (1924–29) and in *Bid Me to Live* (1939, published 1960); and Aldington wrote a biography of D. H. Lawrence titled *Portrait of a Genius, But . . .* (1950). Lawrence and H. D., who met on the eve of World War I, shared a common revulsion against the war. Both were convinced of the necessity for spiritual rebirth, which they sought to attain through writing that drew on esoteric mythology and imagery grounded in the physical details of a natural world. From H. D.'s point of view, however, Lawrence sometimes seemed to represent an oppressively masculine smugness. Whether or not Lawrence withdrew from the sexual relationship H. D. was led to expect, as she implied in *Bid Me to Live*, she continued to wrestle in writing with her admiration and fear of his creative potency.

By 1915, when H. D. suffered a miscarriage, the catastrophes she identified with World War I had begun. In 1917, when the Lawrences lived in H. D.'s London flat, Aldington, who was training to become an army officer, began an affair with one of H. D.'s acquaintances. In 1918, he was sent to the French front, and at about the same time, H. D.'s brother Gilbert was killed in the war. The next year her father died, and she found herself pregnant after a trip to Cornwall with Cecil Gray, a wealthy young man who would go on to become a well-known music critic. After she contracted double pneumonia, H. D. was terrified that either she or her child would die. As she explains in the novel *Palimpsest* (1926), which fictionalizes much of this autobiographical material, she was "saved" from this crisis by the intercession of the twenty-four-year-old woman who would befriend her for the rest of her life, the writer Winifred Ellerman—or "Bryher," as she called herself (after one of the Scilly Isles).

Bryher was the illegitimate daughter of the richest of England's shipping magnates, a rebellious girl who wanted to be a boy and grew up to write historical adventure novels about boys. She had memorized all of *Sea Garden* before she met H. D., and she subsidized the publication of *Hymen* (1921), H. D.'s next volume of verse; continued to pay many of H. D.'s bills; and eventually adopted H. D.'s daughter, Perdita. In 1919 and 1920, Bryher fulfilled a promise to take H. D. to Greece, where H. D. had one of her first psychic or visionary experiences. She saw what she later called "writing on the wall" projected in her hotel room, pictographic images of the helmeted face of a dead airman, a tripod, and then the winged figure of Niké, goddess of victory. When H. D. was too exhausted to sustain her concentration, Bryher described the last vision, the union of Niké with the god of the sun, Helios. The two women felt they had glimpsed a narrative line that, moving beyond the destruction of modern culture to a vision of female regeneration, would inform H. D.'s later poetry. The visit to Corfu was the most dramatic of a series of trips that took them to Egypt (1923), Paris (1924), and America (1921, 1926).

Although H. D. published *Heliodora and Other Poems* in 1924, her *Collected Poems* in 1925, *Red Roses for Bronze* in 1931, and several novels, short stories, and Greek translations during the late 1930s, she was troubled by what she considered a decline in her creativity, a decline that she related both to her personal problems and to the confusion of the times. While H. D. resided, for the most part, in London and Switzerland, Bryher twice embarked on marriages of convenience. H. D., who had an affair with Bryher's second husband, Kenneth MacPherson, became interested in film through his journal *Close-Up;* however, her tremulous performance in MacPherson's movie *Borderline* (1930) seems to dramatize her sense of anxiety during this period. Already acquainted with the psychologists Hans Sachs and Havelock Ellis, H. D. decided to confront her writing difficulties and her dread of an impending world war by journeying to 19 Bergasse in Vienna, where she would undergo the still relatively new process of psychoanalysis with the famous psychotherapist Sigmund Freud.

H. D.'s 1933 and 1934 sessions with Freud are brilliantly portrayed in her impressionistic *Tribute to Freud* (1944, 1956). As "The Master" indicates, the poet accepted Freud's insights into the associative, imagistic workings of the unconscious, as well as his conviction about the importance of the childhood of the individual and the infancy of the race. But she viewed herself as more intuitive, more attuned to spiritual realities, than Freud was. Analyzing visions like those she had seen in Greece, he diagnosed H. D.'s "symptoms" in terms of her unresolved attachment to her mother, implying that she was a victim of penis envy; however, she went on to explore the "inspiration" she associated with the excavation of the maternal principle. With Bryher, H. D. helped Freud leave Vienna for London when the Nazis took control of Austria.

After surviving the bombings of London in World War II, H. D. composed two major epics about war, *Trilogy* and *Helen in Egypt* (1961). The former begins with the wasteland of war-torn London in *The Walls Do Not Fall* and moves backward first in *Tribute to the Angels* and then in *The Flowering of the Rod* to the birth of Christ, which is understood as a miracle of female creativity, for in the last of these books H. D. meditates on the crucial roles of the prostitute Mary Magdalene and the virgin mother Mary. Similarly, *Helen in Egypt* focuses on Helen of Troy as the scapegoat of a war that reveals the nihilism of a culture based on masculine values. Helen, who has been reviled as the cause of the war, must recover a less punitive sense of her self. H. D.'s two Marys and her Helen are each helped in their quests by mentors who resemble Freud: Kaspar, one of the three wise men to visit the Christ child in

Trilogy, and Theseus, in *Helen in Egypt,* provide the ancient wisdom that empowers female rebirth.

After the war, H. D. suffered a mental breakdown and moved from London to Küsnacht, Switzerland, but she continued to work on *Helen in Egypt* and on a coda to it titled *Hermetic Definition* (1972). She also wrote a number of prose and verse narratives that remain unpublished. Neither her interest in spiritualism nor her propensity for "romantic thralldom" was diminished in her later years. She continued working on occult material, specifically with tarot cards, Moravian rituals, and astrology. During World War II, she had become emotionally attached to Sir Hugh Carswell Dowding, chief air marshal of the Royal Air Force Fighter Command, and in her seventies she fell in love with Lionel Durand, a Haitian journalist. Yet, as her memoir of her earlier relationship with Pound, *End to Torment* (1979), indicates, she had come to believe that while "there was always a challenge" in the creativity of the men whom she admired or even adored, "the mother is the Muse, the Creator." The pseudonym H. D., which had begun as Pound's invention, had transformed itself into the mirror image of D. H. (Lawrence) and the replication of H(ugh) D(owding); however, by the end of the artist's life it seems to have stood for the hermetic definition of Hermes; for her mother, Helen; and for the spirit of Hellas.

In 1960, H. D. visited the United States for the last time, to accept the Award of Merit Medal for Poetry from the American Academy of Arts and Letters. The poets Robert Duncan and Denise Levertov were among her earliest admirers because, as Levertov succinctly explained, H. D.'s poetry offers "doors, ways in, tunnels through" the "hiddenness before which man must shed his arrogance."

Orchard[1]

I saw the first pear
as it fell—
the honey-seeking, golden-banded,
the yellow swarm
was not more fleet than I,
(spare us from loveliness)
and I fell prostrate
crying:
you have flayed us
with your blossoms,
spare us the beauty
of fruit-trees.

The honey-seeking
paused not,
the air thundered their song,
and I alone was prostrate.

O rough-hewn
god of the orchard,
I bring you an offering—
do you, alone unbeautiful,
son of the god,
spare us from loveliness:

---

1. When first published in *Poetry* (1913), this poem was titled "Priapus/Keeper of Orchards."

these fallen hazel-nuts,
stripped late of their green sheaths,
grapes, red-purple,
their berries
dripping with wine,
pomegranates already broken,
and shrunken figs
and quinces untouched,
I bring you as offering.

                                      1913, 1916

Oread[1]

Whirl up, sea—
whirl your pointed pines,
splash your great pines
on our rocks,
hurl your green over us,
cover us with your pools of fir.

                                      1914, 1925

Sea Poppies

Amber husk
fluted with gold,
fruit on the sand
marked with a rich grain,

treasure
spilled near the shrub-pines
to bleach on the boulders:

your stalk has caught root
among wet pebbles
and drift flung by the sea
and grated shells
and split conch-shells.

Beautiful, wide-spread,
fire upon leaf,
what meadow yields
so fragrant a leaf
as your bright leaf?

                                      1916

---

1. A mountain nymph.

Garden

I

You are clear
O rose, cut in rock,
hard as the descent of hail.

I could scrape the color
from the petals
like spilt dye from a rock.

If I could break you
I could break a tree.

If I could stir
I could break a tree—
I could break you.

II

O wind, rend open the heat,
cut apart the heat,
rend it to tatters.

Fruit cannot drop
through this thick air—
fruit cannot fall into heat
that presses up and blunts
the points of pears
and rounds the grapes.

Cut the heat—
plough through it,
turning it on either side
of your path.

1916

Eurydice[1]

I

So you have swept me back,
I who could have walked with the live souls
above the earth,
I who could have slept among the live flowers
at last;

---

1. According to Greek myth, the wife of the Greek poet Orpheus. Through his song, he managed to win her freedom from Hades after she died; but because he failed to keep the condition that he not look at her until they had both left the underworld, he lost her again.

       so for your arrogance
       and your ruthlessness
       I am swept back
       where dead lichens drip
10   dead cinders upon moss of ash;

       so for your arrogance
       I am broken at last,
       I who had lived unconscious,
       who was almost forgot;

15   if you had let me wait
       I had grown from listlessness into peace,
       if you had let me rest with the dead,
       I had forgot you
       and the past.

II

20   Here only flame upon flame
       and black among the red sparks,
       streaks of black and light
       grown colorless;

       why did you turn back,
25   that hell should be reinhabited
       of myself thus
       swept into nothingness?

       why did you turn?
       why did you glance back?
30   why did you hesitate for that moment?
       why did you bend your face
       caught with the flame of the upper earth,
       above my face?

       what was it that crossed my face
35   with the light from yours
       and your glance?
       what was it you saw in my face?
       the light of your own face,
       the fire of your own presence?

40   What had my face to offer
       but reflex of the earth,
       hyacinth color
       caught from the raw fissure in the rock
       where the light struck,
45   and the color of azure crocuses
       and the bright surface of gold crocuses
       and of the wind-flower,
       swift in its veins as lightning
       and as white.

III

50 Saffron from the fringe of the earth,
wild saffron that has bent
over the sharp edge of earth,
all the flowers that cut through the earth,
all, all the flowers are lost;

55 everything is lost,
everything is crossed with black,
black upon black
and worse than black,
this colorless light.

IV

60 Fringe upon fringe
of blue crocuses,
crocuses, walled against blue of themselves,
blue of that upper earth,
blue of the depth upon depth of flowers,
65 lost;

flowers,
if I could have taken once my breath of them,
enough of them,
more than earth,
70 even than of the upper earth,
had passed with me
beneath the earth;

if I could have caught up from the earth,
the whole of the flowers of the earth,
75 if once I could have breathed into myself
the very golden crocuses
and the red,
and the very golden hearts of the first saffron,
the whole of the golden mass,
80 the whole of the great fragrance,
I could have dared the loss.

V

So for your arrogance
and your ruthlessness
I have lost the earth
85 and the flowers of the earth,
and the live souls above the earth,
and you who passed across the light
and reached
ruthless;

>   90 you who have your own light,
>   who are to yourself a presence,
>   who need no presence;
>
>   yet for all your arrogance
>   and your glance,
>   95 I tell you this:
>
>   such loss is no loss,
>   such terror, such coils and strands and
>   pitfalls
>   of blackness,
>   such terror
>   100 is no loss;
>
>   hell is no worse than your earth
>   above the earth,
>   hell is no worse,
>   no, nor your flowers
>   105 nor your veins of light
>   nor your presence,
>   a loss;
>
>   my hell is no worse than yours
>   though you pass among the flowers and speak
>   110 with the spirits above earth.

VI

>   Against the black
>   I have more fervor
>   than you in all the splendor of that place,
>   against the blackness
>   115 and the stark gray
>   I have more light;
>
>   and the flowers,
>   if I should tell you,
>   you would turn from your own fit paths
>   120 toward hell,
>   turn again and glance back
>   and I would sink into a place
>   even more terrible than this.

VIII

>   At least I have the flowers of myself,
>   125 and my thoughts, no god
>   can take that;
>   I have the fervor of myself for a presence
>   and my own spirit for light;

and my spirit with its loss
knows this;
though small against the black,
small against the formless rocks,
hell must break before I am lost;

before I am lost,
hell must open like a red rose
for the dead to pass.

1917, 1925

Fragment Thirty-six

I know not what to do: my mind is divided.
—Sappho.[1]

I know not what to do,
my mind is reft:
is song's gift best?
is love's gift loveliest?
I know not what to do,
now sleep has pressed
weight on your eyelids.

Shall I break your rest,
devouring, eager?
is love's gift best?
nay, song's the loveliest:
yet were you lost,
what rapture
could I take from song?
what song were left?

I know not what to do:
to turn and slake
the rage that burns,
with my breath burn
and trouble your cool breath?
so shall I turn and take
snow in my arms?
(is love's gift best?)
yet flake on flake
of snow were comfortless,
did you lie wondering,
wakened yet unawake.

---

1. This fragment by the Greek poet Sappho (d. ca. 612 B.C.E.), Bergk 36, has, as H. D. states, been "reworked freely" in the poem (the epigraph is its literal translation).

>   Shall I turn and take
>   comfortless snow within my arms?
> 30   press lips to lips
>   that answer not,
>   press lips to flesh
>   that shudders not nor breaks?
>
>   Is love's gift best?
> 35   shall I turn and slake
>   all the wild longing?
>   O I am eager for you!
>   as the Pleiads[2] shake
>   white light in whiter water
> 40   so shall I take you?
>
>   My mind is quite divided,
>   my minds hesitate,
>   so perfect matched,
>   I know not what to do:
> 45   each strives with each
>   as two white wrestlers
>   standing for a match,
>   ready to turn and clutch
>   yet never shake muscle nor nerve nor tendon;
> 50   so my mind waits
>   to grapple with my mind,
>   yet I lie quiet,
>   I would seem at rest.
>
>   I know not what to do:
> 55   strain upon strain,
>   sound surging upon sound
>   makes my brain blind;
>   as a wave-line may wait to fall
>   yet (waiting for its falling)
> 60   still the wind may take
>   from off its crest,
>   white flake on flake of foam,
>   that rises,
>   seeming to dart and pulse
> 65   and rend the light,
>   so my mind hesitates
>   above the passion
>   quivering yet to break,
>   so my mind hesitates
> 70   above my mind,
>   listening to song's delight.

---

2. Seven sister nymphs who, according to Greek legend, were turned into stars (in the constellation Taurus).

I know not what to do:
will the sound break,
rending the night
with rift on rift of rose
and scattered light?
will the sound break at last
as the wave hesitant,
or will the whole night pass
and I lie listening awake?

1924

Helen[1]

All Greece hates
the still eyes in the white face,
the lustre as of olives
where she stands,
and the white hands.

All Greece reviles
the wan face when she smiles,
hating it deeper still
when it grows wan and white,
remembering past enchantments
and past ills.

Greece sees unmoved,
God's daughter, born of love,
the beauty of cool feet
and slenderest knees,
could love indeed the maid,
only if she were laid,
white ash amid funereal cypresses.

1924

The Master[1]

I

He was very beautiful,
the old man,
and I knew wisdom,
I found measureless truth
in his words,
his command
was final;

---

1. The wife of the Greek king Menelaus and the most beautiful woman in the world; according to classical mythology, she was given to the Trojan prince Paris by Aphrodite and thus blamed by the Greeks for the Trojan War waged to regain her.

1. Identified with Sigmund Freud (1856–1939), the founder of psychoanalysis, with whom H. D. underwent analysis (see headnote, p. 280).

(how did he understand?)

when I traveled to Miletus[2]
to get wisdom,
I left all else behind,
I fasted,
I worked late,
rose early;
whether I wore simple garments
or intricate
nothing was lost,
each vestment had meaning,
"every gesture is wisdom,"
he taught;
"nothing is lost,"[3]
he said;
I went late to bed
or early,
I caught the dream
and rose dreaming,
and we wrought philosophy on the dream content,[4]
I was content;

nothing was lost
for God is all
and the dream is God;
only to us,
to us
is small wisdom,
but great enough
to know God everywhere;

O he was fair,
even when I flung his words in his teeth,
he said,
"I will soon be dead
I must learn from the young";

his tyranny was absolute,
for I had to love him then,
I had to recognize that he was beyond all-men,
nearer to God
(he was so old)
I had to claim
pardon,
which he granted

---

2. Ancient city on the west coast of Asia Minor (modern Turkey).
3. An allusion to the Freudian notion that what seems to be forgotten has actually been repressed and remains in the unconscious.
4. Analysis of the contents of dreams is central to Freud's methods.

50   with his old head
so wise,
so beautiful
with his mouth so young
and his eyes—

55   O God,
let there be some surprise in heaven for him,
for no one but you could devise
anything suitable
for him,
60   so beautiful.

II

I don't know what to suggest,
I can hardly suggest things to God
who with a nod
says, "rise Olympos,
65   sink into the sea,
O Pelion,
Ossa,[5]
be still";

I do not know what to say to God,
70   for the hills
answer his nod,
and the sea
when he tells his daughter,
white Mother
75   of green
leaves
and green rills
and silver,
to still
80   tempest
or send peace
and surcease of peril
when a mountain has spit fire:

I did not know how to differentiate
85   between volcanic desire,
anemones like embers
and purple fire
of violets
like red heat,
90   and the cold
silver
of her feet:

---

5. All mountains in Greece: Olympus was said to be the home of the gods, and Ossa was famously piled on Pelion by the giants who were attempting to reach the heavens and storm Olympus.

I had two loves separate;
God who loves all mountains,
95 alone knew why
and understood
and told the old man
to explain
the impossible,

100 which he did.[6]

III

What can God give the old man,
who made this possible?

for a woman
breathes fire
105 and is cold,
a woman sheds snow from ankles
and is warm;
white heat
melts into snow-flake
110 and violets
turn to pure amethysts,
water-clear:

no,
I did not falter,
115 I saw the whole miracle,
I knew that the old man made this tenable,
but how could he have foreseen
the impossible?

how could he have known
120 how each gesture of this dancer
would be hieratic?[7]
words were scrawled on papyrus,
words were written most carefully,
each word was separate
125 yet each word led to another word,
and the whole made a rhythm
in the air,
till now unguessed at,
unknown.

---

6. H. D. wrote to Bryher of Freud's "terribly exciting" explanation of her writer's block: "It appears that I am that all-but extinct phenomena, the perfect bi-."
7. Highly stylized; priestly.

IV

130 I was angry at the old man,
I wanted an answer,
a neat answer,
when I argued and said, "well, tell me,
you will soon be dead,
135 the secret lies with you,"
he said,
"you are a poet";

I do not wish to be treated like a child, a weakling,
so I said,
140 (I was angry)
"you can not last forever,
the fire of wisdom dies with you,
I have traveled far to Miletus,
you can not stay long now with us,
145 I came for an answer";

I was angry with the old man
with his talk of the man-strength,
I was angry with his mystery, his mysteries,
I argued till day-break;

150 O, it was late,
and God will forgive me, my anger,
but I could not accept it.

I could not accept from wisdom
what love taught,
155 *woman is perfect.*

V

She is a woman,
yet beyond woman,
yet in woman,
her feet are the delicate pulse of the narcissus bud,
160 pushing from earth
(ah, where is your man-strength?)
her arms are the waving of the young
male,
tentative,
165 reaching out
that first evening
alone in a forest;

she is woman,
her thighs are frail yet strong,
170 she leaps from rock to rock
(it was only a small circle for her dance)

and the hills dance,

she conjures the hills;
"rhododendrons[8]
175   awake,"
her feet
pulse,
the rhododendrons
wake
180   there is purple flower
between her marble, her birch-tree white
thighs,
or there is a red flower,

there is a rose flower
185   parted wide,
as her limbs fling wide in dance
ecstatic
Aphrodite,[9]
there is a frail lavender flower
190   hidden in grass;

O God, what is it,
this flower
that in itself had power over the whole earth?
for she needs no man,
195   herself
is that dart and pulse of the male,
hands, feet, thighs,
herself perfect.

VI

Let the old man lie in the earth
200   (he has troubled men's thought long enough)
let the old man die,
let the old man be of the earth
he is earth,
Father,
205   O beloved
you are the earth,
he is the earth, Saturn,[1] wisdom,
rock, (O his bones are hard, he is strong, that old man)
let him create a new earth,
210   and from the rocks of this re-birth
the whole world

---

8. Greek, the word *rhodon* has the primary meaning "rose"; it can also refer to female genitalia.
9. Greek goddess of love.

1. Roman deity identified with Cronos, the Greek Titan who was the father of Zeus.

    must suffer,
    only we
    who are free,

215 may foretell,
    may prophesy,
    he,
    (it is he the old man
    who will bring a new world to birth)
220 it is he,
    it is he
    who already has formed a new earth.

VII

    He will trouble the thoughts of men
    yet for many an aeon,
225 they will travel far and wide,
    they will discuss all his written words,
    his pen will be sacred
    they will build a temple
    and keep all his sacred writings safe,
230 and men will come
    and men will quarrel
    but he will be safe;

    they will found temples in his name,
    his fame
235 will be so great
    that anyone who has known him
    will also be hailed as master,
    seer,
    interpreter;

240 only I,
    I will escape.

VIII

    And it was he himself, he who set me free
    to prophesy,

    he did not say
250 "stay,
    my disciple,"
    he did not say,
    "write,
    each word I say is sacred,"
255 he did not say, "teach"
    he did not say,

>   "heal
>   or seal
>   documents in my name,"
>
> 260   no,
>   he was rather casual,
>   "we won't argue about that"
>   (he said)
>   "you are a poet."

IX

> 265   So I went forth
>   blinded a little with the sort of terrible tears
>   that won't fall;
>   I said good-bye
>   and saw his old head
> 270   as he turned,
>   as he left the room
>   leaving me alone
>   with all his old trophies,[2]
>   the marbles, the vases, the stone Sphynx,
> 275   the old, old jars from Egypt;
>   he left me alone with these things
>   and his old back was bowed;
>
>   O God,
>   those tears didn't come,
> 280   how could they?
>   I went away,
>   I said,
>   "I won't have this tyranny
>   of an old man
> 285   he is too old,
>   I will die,
>   if I love him;
>
>   I can not love him
>   he is too near
> 290   too precious to God."

X

>   But one does not forget him
>   who makes all things feasible,
>   one does not forgive him
>   who makes God-in-all
> 295   possible,
>   for that is unbearable.

---

2. Freud had an extensive collection of antiquities; in his study and consulting room were more than two thousand Egyptian, Greek, Roman, Near Eastern, and Asian objects.

XI

Now can I bear even God,
for a woman's laughter
prophesies
happiness:
(not man, not men,
only one, the old man,
sacred to God);

no man will be present in those mysteries,
yet all men will kneel,
no man will be potent,
important,
yet all men will feel
what it is to be a woman,
will yearn,
burn,
turn from easy pleasure
to hardship
of the spirit,

men will see how long they have been blind,
poor men
poor man-kind
how long
how long
this thought of the man-pulse has tricked them,
has weakened them,
shall see woman,
perfect.

XII

And they did;
I was not the only one that cried
madly,
madly,
we were together,
we were one;

we were together
we were one;
sun-worshipers,
we flung
as one voice
our cry
Rhodocleia;[3]

---

3. H. D. seems to be making a number of allusions with this made-up name: to Rhodos, daughter of Aphrodite and wife of Helios (the sun); to *rhodon* (see n. 8, p. 296); to the Greek noun *kleis*, which means "key"; and to the verb *kleien*, "to praise or announce."

> Rhodocleia,
> near to the sun,
> we did not say
> "pity us,"
> we did not say, "look at us,"
> we cried,
> "O heart of the sun
> rhododendron,
> Rhodocleia,
> we are unworthy your beauty,
>
> you are near beauty the sun,
> you are that Lord become woman."

1934–35   1981

EDITH SITWELL
1887–1964

The daughter of an aristocratic English family, brought up in a sumptuous home, Edith Sitwell nevertheless began her life by feeling that "I was unpopular with my parents from the moment of my birth." Tall and slim, with a markedly aquiline nose for which a London orthopedist provided a special "contraption [turning] the organ in question . . . very firmly to the opposite way which Nature had intended," she must as a girl have seemed an unlikely candidate for the glamorous reputation she later achieved. According to one biographer, her mother was "neglectful, sometimes cruel, and often drunk," while her father was "interested only in sons." Yet, with the help of a supportive grandmother, a kind nurse, and an encouraging governess, Helen Rootham, who later became her closest companion, Sitwell began early to read and write poetry, dismissing her eccentric, scholarly father as a foolish man and her mother as a woman who cared only about a "silly daily life of bridge and watching the golfers on the golf course." Despite financial difficulties—including a series of debts that at one point sent the extravagant Lady Ida Sitwell to prison—Edith Sitwell settled in London in 1914, sharing a flat with Rootham, and in 1916 began editing *Wheels*, an avant-garde literary anthology featuring experimental writings that shocked conservative critics who might have expected greater decorum from an upper-class heiress.

Sitwell had from the first enjoyed the admiration and respect of her younger brothers, Osbert and Sacheverell, each of whom became a distinguished literary man in his own right, and those powerful ties with her siblings also clearly energized her. Yet that she was innately strong-willed, vigorous, and imaginative is plain from the innovative verse she began to publish during her *Wheels* period. The volumes *Clown's Houses* (1918), *The Wooden Pegasus* (1920), and *Façade* (1922) followed each other in rapid succession, proposing surprising alternatives to the more traditional work included in the comparatively sedate *Georgian Anthology* (1911–20)—an annual collection of poems by such writers as Rupert Brooke, Walter de la Mare, and John Masefield—against which Sitwell was reacting with some violence. Deliberately stylized, even rebelliously artificial, these early works seemed, according to a contemporary critic, to be composed for "the xylophone," written by "a virtuoso in the communication of a half-wooden, half-glassy tone which is seldom without brilliance." The musical analogy is apt, for *Façade* is a jazzy poem sequence whose syncopated linguistic rhythms are echoed by the background music that the British composer Sir William Walton wrote for it: when the pair first performed this joint production in public—Walton conducting the orchestra, Sitwell reading the poems from behind a screen—the controversial work was, according to one observer, a "sensation."

In her later years, Edith Sitwell became an increasingly dramatic figure on the London literary and artistic scene. As an aristocratic infant she had been painted in a Sitwell family portrait by the renowned American artist John Singer Sargent, but as a more compellingly aquiline adult she was the subject of photographs by Cecil Beaton and paintings by Roger Fry, Alvaro Guevara, Wyndham Lewis, Felix Topolski, and her close friend Pavel Tchelitchew; the Guevara hangs today in London's Tate Gallery. Toward the end of her career, too, she accumulated numerous awards and prizes: indeed, as honorary doctorates piled up, she referred to herself occasionally as "Edith Sitwell, D. Litt., D. Litt., D. Litt." More important, though, she continued to shine in major aesthetic circles, discovering and befriending the young Dylan Thomas and associating with such writers as Virginia Woolf.

During the grim years of World War II, when London was blitzed by German planes, Sitwell began to write poems that were less stylized, more macabre than any of her earlier works. Yet pieces such as "Lullaby" and "Serenade: Any Man to Any Woman" retain the metallic edge—the "xylophone" quality—that had marked even the verses of the lighthearted *Façade*, as if Sitwell had decided, when she was quite young, that her supposedly privileged world was no more and no less than, in the words of *Façade*'s Sir Beelzebub, a "hotel in Hell." At the same time, her famous "Still Falls the Rain" suggests a desperate, late-life preoccupation with the powerful narratives of the Roman Catholic Church, whose doctrines she had accepted in 1955, nearly a decade before her death of a cerebral hemorrhage in 1964.

En Famille[1]

    In the early springtime, after their tea,
    Through the young fields of the springing Bohea,[2]
    Jemima, Jocasta, Dinah, and Deb
    Walked with their father Sir Joshua Jebb—
5   An admiral red, whose only notion
    (A butterfly poised on a pigtailed ocean),
    Is of the peruked[3] sea whose swell
    Breaks on the flowerless rocks of Hell.
    Under the thin trees, Deb and Dinah,
10   Jemima, Jocasta walked, and finer
    Their black hair seemed (flat-sleek to see)
    Than the young leaves of the springing Bohea;
    Their cheeks were like nutmeg-flowers when swells

---

1. As a family (French).
2. A black Chinese tea.
3. Wearing an 18th-century periwig.

The rain into foolish silver bells.
They said, "If the door you would only slam,
Or if, Papa, you would once say 'Damn'—
Instead of merely roaring 'Avast'[4]
Or boldly invoking the nautical Blast—
We should now stand in the street of Hell

Watching siesta shutters that fell
With a noise like amber softly sliding;
Our moon-like glances through these gliding
Would see at her table preened and set
Myrrhina[5] sitting at her toilette
With eyelids closed as soft as the breeze
That flows from gold flowers on the incense-trees."

The Admiral said, "You could never call—
I assure you it would not do at all!
She gets down from table without saying 'Please,'
Forgets her prayers and to cross her T's,
In short, her scandalous reputation
Has shocked the whole of the Hellish nation;
And every turbaned Chinoiserie,[6]
With whom we should sip our black Bohea,
Would stretch out her simian fingers thin
To scratch you, my dears, like a mandoline;
For Hell is just as properly proper
As Greenwich, or as Bath, or Joppa!"[7]

1922

Sir Beelzebub[1]

When
Sir
Beelzebub called for his syllabub[2] in the hotel in Hell
    Where Proserpine[3] first fell,
Blue as the gendarmerie[4] were the waves of the sea

    (Rocking and shocking the bar-maid).

Nobody comes to give him his rum but the
Rim of the sky hippopotamus-glum

---

4. Stop! (nautical command).
5. Possibly a variation on "Myrrha," who in Greek myth was transformed into a myrrh tree by the gods because of her incestuous love for her father (their son was Adonis).
6. A term denoting European adaptations of Chinese forms and customs; here, it may simply refer to Chinese people.
7. The ancient name of the Israeli city of Jaffa, the center of many religious battles. Greenwich and Bath are cities in England.
1. One of the fallen angels who was cast into hell with Satan; also, another name for the Devil.
2. A dessert made of sweetened cream and wine or liquor.
3. In Roman myth, queen of the underworld and wife of Pluto, who abducted her while she was gathering flowers in a meadow.
4. The French police force.

Enhances the chances to bless with a benison
10 Alfred Lord Tennyson crossing the bar[5] laid
With cold vegetation from pale deputations
Of temperance workers (all signed In Memoriam[6])
Hoping with glory to trip up the Laureate's[7] feet

    (Moving in classical meters) . . .

15 Like Balaclava,[8] the lava came down from the
Roof, and the sea's blue wooden gendarmerie
Took them in charge while Beelzebub roared for his rum.

    . . . None of them come!

                                              1922

Aubade[1]

Jane, Jane,
Tall as a crane,
The morning light creaks down again;

Comb your cockscomb-ragged hair,
5 Jane, Jane, come down the stair.

Each dull blunt wooden stalactite
Of rain creaks, hardened by the light,

Sounding like an overtone
From some lonely world unknown.

10 But the creaking empty light
Will never harden into sight,

Will never penetrate your brain
With overtones like the blunt rain.

The light would show (if it could harden)
15 Eternities of kitchen garden,[2]

Cockscomb flowers that none will pluck,
And wooden flowers that 'gin to cluck.

---

5. A narrow ridge of sand near a harbor or beach. Tennyson (1809–1892) wrote a late poem called "Crossing the Bar" (1889), in which he said that he hoped "to see [his] Pilot face to face."
6. The title of Tennyson's long elegy (1850) for his friend Arthur Hallam.
7. In 1850 Tennyson succeeded William Wordsworth as poet laureate, an honorific title bestowed on English poets by the Crown.
8. Site of a battle during the Crimean War in 1854, described by Tennyson in "The Charge of the Light Brigade" (1854).
1. Dawn poem.
2. Small back gardens used by cooks to grow herbs and vegetables.

In the kitchen you must light
Flames as staring, red and white,

As carrots or as turnips, shining
Where the cold dawn light lies whining.

Cockscomb hair on the cold wind
Hangs limp, turns the milk's weak mind. . . .

    Jane, Jane,
    Tall as a crane,
The morning light creaks down again!

1923

Lullaby[1]

Though the world has slipped and gone,
Sounds my loud discordant cry
Like the steel birds' song on high:
"Still one thing is left—the Bone!"
Then out danced the Babioun.[2]

She sat in the hollow of the sea—
A socket whence the eye's put out—
She sang to the child a lullaby
(The steel birds' nest was thereabout).

"Do, do, do, do—
Thy mother's hied to the vaster race:
The Pterodactyl made its nest
And laid a steel egg in her breast—
Under the Judas[3]-colored sun.
She'll work no more, nor dance, nor moan,
And I am come to take her place
Do, do.

There's nothing left but earth's low bed—
(The Pterodactyl fouls its nest):
But steel wings fan thee to thy rest,
And wingless truth and larvae lie
And eyeless hope and handless fear—
All these for thee as toys are spread,
Do—do—

---

1. Written in reaction to World War II.
2. The phrase "out-dance the Babioun" occurs in an Epigram by Ben Jonson [Sitwell's note]. "Epigram 129: To Mime" (1616), by the English poet and dramatist Jonson (1572–1637).
3. The apostle who betrayed Jesus. "Pterodactyl": prehistoric flying reptile.

25   Red is the bed of Poland, Spain,[4]
      And thy mother's breast, who has grown wise
      In that fouled nest. If she could rise.
      Give birth again,
      In wolfish pelt she'd hide thy bones
30   To shield thee from the world's long cold,
      And down on all fours shouldst thou crawl
      For thus from no height canst thou fall—
      Do, do.

      She'd give no hands: there's nought to hold
35   And nought to make: there's dust to sift,
      But no food for the hands to lift.
      Do, do.

      Heed my ragged lullaby,
      Fear not living, fear not chance;
40   All is equal—blindness, sight,
      There is no depth, there is no height:
      Do, do.

      The Judas-colored sun is gone,
      And with the Ape thou art alone—
      Do,
45   Do."

                        1942

Serenade: Any Man to Any Woman

      Dark angel who art clear and straight
      As cannon shining in the air,
      Your blackness doth invade my mind,
      And thunderous as the armored wind
5   That rained on Europe is your hair;

      And so I love you till I die—
      (Unfaithful I, the cannon's mate):
      Forgive my love of such brief span,
      But fickle is the flesh of man,
10   And death's cold puts the passion out.

      I'll woo you with a serenade—
      The wolfish howls the starving made;
      And lies shall be your canopy
      To shield you from the freezing sky.

15   Yet when I clasp you in my arms—
      Who are my sleep, the zero hour

---

4. Countries that had recently come under fascist rule.

>   That clothes, instead of flesh, my heart—
>   You in my heaven have no part,
>   For you, my mirage broken in flower,
>
> 20 Can never see what dead men know!
>   Then die with me and be my love:[1]
>   The grave shall be your shady grove,
>   And in your pleasaunce[2] rivers flow
>
>   (To ripen this new Paradise)
> 25 From a more universal Flood
>   Than Noah knew: but yours is blood.
>
>   Yet still you will imperfect be
>   That in my heart like death's chill grows,
>   —A rainbow[3] shining in the night,
> 30 Born of my tears . . . your lips, the bright
>   Summer-old folly of the rose.

1942

Still Falls the Rain

The Raids,[1] 1940. Night and Dawn

> Still falls the Rain—
> Dark as the world of man, black as our loss—
> Blind as the nineteen hundred and forty nails
> Upon the Cross.
>
> 5 Still falls the Rain
>   With a sound like the pulse of the heart that is changed to the hammer-beat
>   In the Potter's Field,[2] and the sound of the impious feet
>
>   On the Tomb:
>   Still falls the Rain
>   In the Field of Blood where the small hopes breed and the
> 10   human brain
>   Nurtures its greed, that worm with the brow of Cain.[3]
>
>   Still falls the Rain
>   At the feet of the Starved Man[4] hung upon the Cross.
>   Christ that each day, each night, nails there, have mercy on us—

---

1. An ironic variation of a line from Christopher Marlowe's 1599 poem "The Passionate Shepherd to His Love": "Come live with me, and be my love."
2. Pleasure ground.
3. The rainbow was the sign God gave to Noah of the covenant after the Flood (Genesis 9.12–17).
1. I.e., the air raids on London.
2. A public burial place for criminals, the unidentified, and the indigent; the first potter's field was bought for this purpose with the 30 silver pieces given to Judas for betraying Jesus, and it was therefore renamed the field of blood (Matthew 27.7–8).
3. The first murderer, who killed his brother, Abel, and was marked by God (Genesis 4.8–15).
4. I.e., Jesus.

15   On Dives and on Lazarus:[5]
     Under the Rain the sore and the gold are as one.

     Still falls the Rain—
     Still falls the Blood from the Starved Man's wounded Side:[6]
     He bears in His Heart all wounds—those of the light that died,
20   The last faint spark
        In the self-murdered heart, the wounds of the sad uncompre-
            hending dark,
     The wounds of the baited bear—
     The blind and weeping bear whom the keepers beat
     On his helpless flesh . . . the tears of the hunted hare.

25   Still falls the Rain—
     Then—O Ile leape up to my God: who pulles me doune—[7]
     See, see where Christ's blood streames in the firmament:
     It flows from the Brow we nailed upon the tree
     Deep to the dying, to the thirsting heart
30   That holds the fires of the world—dark-smirched with pain
     As Caesar's laurel crown.[8]

     Then sounds the voice of One who like the heart of man
     Was once a child who among beasts has lain—
     'Still do I love, still shed my innocent light, my Blood, for thee.'

                                                         1942

---

5. A beggar, "full of sores," who lay outside the door of a rich man (popularly given the name Dives—Latin for "rich"), in a parable of Jesus (Luke 16.19–31).
6. After his side was pierced by a soldier's spear (John 19.34).
7. From Christopher Marlowe's *The Tragicall History of Dr. Faustus* (1604), scene 13.
8. I.e., the wreath worn as a sign of military victory. *Caesar* was a title used by the Roman emperors; more generally, it refers to temporal power (see Matthew 22.21).

MARIANNE MOORE
1887–1972

"I, too, dislike it," Marianne Moore once remarked about poetry, explaining, "There are things that are important beyond all this fiddle." Yet even as she wrote those words, this reserved and obscure sometime librarian was beginning to earn a distinctive reputation as a poet, and by the end of her career she had become one of the most famous—and famously eccentric—American writers of her generation. Wearing her legendary three-cornered hat, she appeared at baseball games, of which she was notoriously fond, like some character out of a fairy tale. Brooding in her Brooklyn apartment, she thought up names for a new Ford car—"The Resilient Bullet," "Mongoose Civique," "Turcotingo," "Utopian Turtletop"—that was eventually, despite her fanciful suggestions, to be called the Edsel, in honor of the company's former president. Even as a somewhat austere young writer, moreover, she had been praised by such major literary men as William Carlos Williams and T. S. Eliot, and praised not for public idiosyncrasies but for private inspiration. In a way, the contradictions in

Moore's history—between early reticence and later reputation, between impassioned aesthetic rigor and ironically eccentric self-presentation—are emblematic of both her life and art.

Born in Kirkwood, Missouri, near St. Louis, Moore spent her earliest years with her mother and brother in the home of her grandfather, a clergyman for whom her mother acted as housekeeper; her father, whom she never met, had been hospitalized following a mental breakdown before her birth. In 1894, after her grandfather died, the poet-to-be moved with her mother and brother to Carlisle, Pennsylvania. There she studied, and her mother taught, at the Metzger Institute. Later she attended Bryn Mawr College, where she found biology classes particularly "exhilarating" and where the poet H. D. (Hilda Doolittle) was a fellow student. After graduating from Bryn Mawr in 1908, Moore took courses in business at the Carlisle Commercial College, traveled to Europe with her mother, and from 1911 to 1915 taught shorthand, typing, and commercial law at the U.S. Industrial Indian School at Carlisle. In 1915, her verse began to appear in *The Egoist* in London and *Poetry* in Chicago, and by the end of the decade she had won a small but distinguished reputation.

Unassuming and shy, Moore continued to live with her mother, as she would throughout most of her life, and the pair moved first to New Jersey, then to Greenwich Village, and finally to Brooklyn, so that they could be near the poet's brother, a Presbyterian minister to whom she was also exceptionally close. Yet, even this early, friends could perceive the paradoxes in her personality. Presenting herself as a kind of anachronism—a dutiful, neo-Victorian daughter, an old-fashioned "lady"—she nevertheless struck William Carlos Williams as a pillar of modernism or, as he put it, "a rafter holding up the superstructure of our uncompleted building, a caryatid, her red hair plaited and wound twice about the fine skull[;] . . . she was surely one of the main supports of the new order." And indeed, though Moore earned her living at conventional jobs—secretary in a girls' school, part-time assistant in a New York City branch library—she was mingling socially with a group of avant-garde painters and writers who were connected with the experimental little magazine *Others*; more important, she was herself beginning to compose disruptive verse, with lines consistently organized into unusual stanza forms and language frequently freed from traditional associations, that would demonstrate her commitment to "the new order." Nevertheless, her first book appeared only because her former schoolmate H. D. and the writer Bryher (Winifred Ellerman), H. D.'s companion, conspired without her knowledge to have the volume, simply titled *Poems*, issued in London in 1921. After that, Moore herself arranged the publication of *Observations* (1924), which won the prestigious *Dial* award for that year; in the following year she herself became editor of *The Dial*, a position she held from 1925 to 1929.

A major New York literary magazine, *The Dial* brought Moore into even closer touch with a number of important figures, including Ezra Pound (whose work she printed in the same issue with work by the neo-Victorian essayist George Saintsbury), Hart Crane (whose poems she attempted to rigorously edit), and James Joyce (portions of whose *Finnegans Wake* she rejected because they seemed to her to be morally and linguistically "offensive"). Although she largely abandoned her own verse writing during her period with this journal, her editorial experience strengthened her aesthetic self-confidence and enriched her imagination. When she began to write and publish again, she produced one of her most significant books, *Selected Poems* (1935), a volume that appeared with a laudatory introduction from T. S. Eliot and that included among other major works "The Jerboa" and "Poetry."

Shortly before the publication of *Selected Poems*, Marianne Moore was sought out by a young poet, Elizabeth Bishop, then a student at Vassar, who was to become a lifelong friend and who later remembered the older writer as "not very tall and not in the least intimidating." At that time, however, Moore was composing some of her most formidable verse, carefully constructed stanzas bristling with erudite allusions, which were soon to strike the editor Louis Untermeyer as "frankly puzzling" because they "seem to erect a barrier of jagged clauses [and] barbed quotations . . . between herself and her audience." Yet about her characteristic, even notorious, use of quotations, Moore herself explained that "I was just trying to be honorable and not to steal things," and about her apparently "jagged" stanza forms, she insisted that "words cluster like chromosomes, determining the procedure [though] I may influence an arrangement or thin it, then try to have successive stanzas identical with the first."

Moore had perhaps more forthrightly formulated her personal aesthetic in her poem "To a Snail" (1924), where, defining " 'compression [as] the first grace of style,' " she added that "contractility is a virtue / as modesty is a virtue," a motto that seems eminently suitable to the quasi-Victorian spinster she so often pretended to be. Still, self-consciously "modest" and compressed as many of Moore's most ambitious early- and middle-period poems are, their serious implications become clear on close reading. Many, for instance, take animals, often quite exotic ones, as their overt subjects. But this poet appears to identify deeply with the ironically "humble" creatures who populate her distinctive bestiary, especially with those who are in their way as carefully camouflaged or fancifully armored as her own verse. In 1963, responding to a questionnaire from *Esquire* magazine, she explained that her "most paradoxical quality" was her desire "to be inconspicuous but look well." Her customary costume of cape and tricorn hat (an outfit she had ordered in imitation of "Washington crossing the Delaware") may not have been exactly "inconspicuous," but it was neither luxurious nor flashy.

Self-effacing though she was, however, Moore's later years were increasingly characterized by honors—including the Pulitzer Prize in 1951 and the Bollingen Prize in 1953—and by the kind of public adulation that led to her being asked, at one point, to throw out the ball to open the Brooklyn Dodgers' baseball season. During World War II, her poetry had become more frankly passionate; pieces like "The Paper Nautilus" openly addressed themselves to issues of love and survival that she might earlier have treated more obliquely. After her mother died in 1947, she continued for many years to live in the Brooklyn apartment that the pair had shared since the late 1920s, but in 1965 she moved to Manhattan, where she settled in Greenwich Village, remaining indomitably active almost to the end and for the most part enjoying, as Elizabeth Bishop put it, "an unusually fortunate old age." Indeed, in 1969, besides earning an honorary doctorate from Harvard, she was named "Senior Citizen of the Year" at a New York conference on aging. Yet even Bishop, her admirer and close friend, was mystified by the contradictions between the career and personality of this radically innovative old-fashioned "lady" who made such a mark on modern poetry. "When I try to summarize her life," confessed the younger woman, "I become foolishly bemused: I have a sort of subliminal glimpse of the capital letter *M* multiplying . . . Marianne's monogram; mother; manners; morals; and I catch myself murmuring, 'Manners and morals; manners *as* morals? or is it morals *as* manners?' "

Sojourn in the Whale[1]

Trying to open locked doors with a sword, threading
    the points of needles, planting shade trees
        upside down; swallowed by the opaqueness of one whom the
                                            seas
love better than they love you, Ireland—

---

1. An allusion to the biblical story of the prophet Jonah, who was swallowed by a whale because he disobeyed God and then released after he prayed for help (Jonah 1–2).

5   you have lived and lived on every kind of shortage.[2]
        You have been compelled by hags to spin
            gold thread from straw[3] and have heard men say:
    "There is a feminine temperament in direct contrast to ours:

    which makes her do these things. Circumscribed by a
10   heritage of blindness and native
            incompetence, she will become wise and will be forced to
                give in.
    Compelled by experience, she will turn back;

    water seeks its own level":
        and you have smiled. "Water in motion is far
            from level."[4] You have seen it, when obstacles happened
15   to bar
    the path, rise automatically.

                                                    1917, 1935

Those Various Scalpels,

those
various sounds consistently indistinct, like intermingled echoes
    struck from thin glasses successively at random—
        the inflection disguised: your hair, the tails of two
5   fighting-cocks head to head in stone—
        like sculptured scimitars repeating the curve of your ears in
                                                    reverse order:

        your eyes, flowers of ice and snow

sown by tearing winds on the cordage of disabled ships; your
                                                    raised hand,
10 an ambiguous signature: your cheeks, those rosettes
        of blood on the stone floors of French châteaux,[1]
    with regard to which the guides are so affirmative—
        your other hand,

    a bundle of lances all alike, partly hid by emeralds from Persia
15   and the fractional magnificence of Florentine
            goldwork—a collection of little objects—
    sapphires set with emeralds, and pearls with a moonstone,
                                                    made fine
    with enamel in gray, yellow, and dragonfly blue;
20   a lemon, a pear

    and three bunches of grapes, tied with silver: your dress, a
                                                    magnificent square

---

2. Most notoriously, the shortage of food in Ireland's great potato famine (1845–50), which killed a million or more people.
3. An allusion to the folktale "Rumplestiltskin" (collected by the Grimm brothers), in which a king commands a maiden to spin straw into gold.
4. *Literary Digest* [Moore's note].
1. Castles.

cathedral tower of uniform
and at the same time diverse appearance—a
species of vertical vineyard rustling in the storm
of conventional opinion. Are they weapons or scalpels?
Whetted to brilliance

by the hard majesty of that sophistication which is superior to
opportunity,
these things are rich instruments with which to experiment.
But why dissect destiny with instruments
more highly specialized than components of destiny itself?

1917, 1935

Poetry[1]

I, too, dislike it: there are things that are important beyond all
this fiddle.
Reading it, however, with a perfect contempt for it, one
discovers in
it after all, a place for the genuine.
Hands that can grasp, eyes
that can dilate, hair that can rise
if it must, these things are important not because a

high-sounding interpretation can be put upon them but because
they are
useful. When they become so derivative as to become
unintelligible,
the same thing may be said for all of us, that we
do not admire what
we cannot understand: the bat
holding on upside down or in quest of something to

eat, elephants pushing, a wild horse taking a roll, a tireless
wolf under
a tree, the immovable critic twitching his skin like a horse
that feels a flea, the base-
ball fan, the statistician—
nor is it valid
to discriminate against 'business documents and

school-books';[2] all these phenomena are important. One must
make a distinction

---

1. Moore revised this poem a number of times after its first publication in 1921. In her *Complete Poems* (1967), it is reduced to the first two sentences of the version printed here, which is taken from *Selected Poems* (1935).
2. *Diary of Tolstoy* (Dutton), p. 84. "Where the boundary between prose and poetry lies, I shall never be able to understand. The question is raised in manuals of style, yet the answer to it lies beyond me. Poetry is verse; prose is not verse. Or else poetry is everything with the exception of business documents and school books" [Moore's note]. Count Leo Tolstoy (1828–1910), Russian novelist and moral philosopher.

however: when dragged into prominence by half poets, the
        result is not poetry,
nor till the poets among us can be
    'literalists of
        the imagination'[3]—above
            insolence and triviality and can present

for inspection, imaginary gardens with real toads in them, shall
        we have
    it. In the meantime, if you demand on the one hand,
        the raw material of poetry in
            all its rawness and
                that which is on the other hand
                    genuine, then you are interested in poetry.

1921, 1935

A Grave

Man looking into the sea,
taking the view from those who have as much right to it as you
        have to it yourself,
it is human nature to stand in the middle of a thing,
but you cannot stand in the middle of this;
the sea has nothing to give but a well excavated grave.
The firs stand in a procession, each with an emerald turkey-foot
        at the top,
reserved as their contours, saying nothing;
repression, however, is not the most obvious characteristic of
        the sea;
the sea is a collector, quick to return a rapacious look.
There are others besides you who have worn that look—
whose expression is no longer a protest; the fish no longer
        investigate them
for their bones have not lasted:
men lower nets, unconscious of the fact that they are desecrating
        a grave,
and row quickly away—the blades of the oars
moving together like the feet of water-spiders as if there were
        no such thing as death.
The wrinkles progress upon themselves in a phalanx—beautiful
        under networks of foam,
and fade breathlessly while the sea rustles in and out of the
        seaweed;
the birds swim through the air at top speed, emitting cat-calls
        as heretofore—

---

3. Yeats: *Ideas of Good and Evil* (A. H. Bullen [1903]), p. 182. "The limitation of his [the poet William Blake's] view was from the very intensity of his vision; he was a too literal realist of the imagination, as others are of nature; and because he believed that the figures seen by the mind's eye, when exalted by inspiration, were 'eternal essences,' symbols of divine essences, he hated every grace of style that might obscure their lineaments" [Moore's note]. William Butler Yeats (1865–1939), Irish poet.

>   the tortoise-shell scourges about the feet of the cliffs, in motion
>   beneath them;
> 20 and the ocean, under the pulsation of lighthouses and noise of
>   bell-buoys,
>   advances as usual, looking as if it were not that ocean in which
>   dropped things are bound to sink—
>   in which if they turn and twist, it is neither with volition nor
>   consciousness.

1921, 1935

An Egyptian Pulled Glass Bottle in the Shape of a Fish

>   Here we have thirst
>   and patience, from the first,
>   and art, as in a wave held up for us to see
>   in its essential perpendicularity;
>
> 5   not brittle but
>   intense—the spectrum, that
>   spectacular and nimble animal the fish,
>   whose scales turn aside the sun's sword by their polish.

1921, 1967

Silence

>   My father used to say,
>   "Superior people never make long visits,
>   have to be shown Longfellow's grave
>   or the glass flowers at Harvard.[1]
> 5   Self-reliant like the cat—
>   that takes it prey to privacy,
>   the mouse's limp tail hanging like a shoelace from its mouth—
>   they sometimes enjoy solitude,
>   and can be robbed of speech
> 10 by speech which has delighted them.
>   The deepest feeling always shows itself in silence;
>   not in silence, but restraint."
>   Nor was he insincere in saying, "Make my house your inn."[2]
>   Inns are not residences.

1921, 1967

---

1. "My father used to say, 'Superior people never make long visits. When I am visiting, I like to go about by myself. I never had to be shown Longfellow's grave or the glass flowers at Harvard.' Miss A. M. Homans" [Moore's note]. The Botanical Museum of Harvard began its famous glass flower collection in 1887. The American poet Henry Wadsworth Longfellow (1807–1882) is buried in the Mount Auburn Cemetery in Cambridge, Mass.
2. Edmund Burke, in *Burke's Life*, by Sir James Prior (1872). " 'Throw yourself into a coach,' said he. 'Come down and make my house your inn' " [Moore's note]. Burke (1729–1797), British statesman and political writer.

To a Snail

If "compression is the first grace of style,"[1]
you have it. Contractility is a virtue
as modesty is a virtue.
It is not the acquisition of any one thing
that is able to adorn,
or the incidental quality that occurs
as a concomitant of something well said,
that we value in style,
but the principle that is hid:
in the absence of feet, "a method of
conclusions";
"a knowledge of principles,"
in the curious phenomenon of your
occipital[2] horn.

1924, 1967

No Swan So Fine

"No water so still as the
    dead fountains of Versailles."[1] No swan,
with swart blind look askance
and gondoliering legs, so fine
    as the chintz china one with fawn-
brown eyes and toothed gold
collar on to show whose bird it was.

Lodged in the Louis Fifteenth
    candelabrum-tree of cockscomb-
tinted buttons, dahlias,
sea urchins, and everlastings,
    it perches on the branching foam
of polished sculptured
flowers—at ease and tall. The king is dead.

1932, 1967

---

1. "The very first grace of style is that which comes from compression." *Demetrius on Style*, translated by William Hamilton Fyfe. Heinemann, 1932 [Moore's note]. A major Greek treatise on style (written perhaps in the 1st c. B.C.E.) was incorrectly ascribed by medieval scholars to the philosopher and statesman Demetrius of Phalerum (b. ca. 350 B.C.E.).

2. I.e., located near the back of the head.

1. "A pair of Louis XV candelabra with Dresden figures of swans belonging to Lord Balfour. 'There is no water so still as in the dead fountains of Versailles.' Percy Phillip, *New York Times Magazine*, May 10, 1931" [Moore's note]. Louis XV (1710–1774; r. 1715–74), the king of France, held court at the opulent palace of Versailles.

The Steeple-Jack

Dürer[1] would have seen a reason for living
   in a town like this, with eight stranded whales
to look at; with the sweet sea air coming into your house
on a fine day, from water etched
5   with waves as formal as the scales
on a fish.

One by one in two's and three's, the seagulls keep
   flying back and forth over the town clock,
or sailing around the lighthouse without moving their wings—
10 rising steadily with a slight
   quiver of the body—or flock
mewing where

a sea the purple of the peacock's neck is
   paled to greenish azure as Dürer changed
15 the pine green of the Tyrol to peacock blue and guinea
gray. You can see a twenty-five-
   pound lobster; and fish nets arranged
to dry. The

whirlwind fife-and-drum of the storm bends the salt
20   marsh grass, disturbs stars in the sky and the
star on the steeple; it is a privilege to see so
much confusion. Disguised by what
   might seem the opposite, the seaside flowers and

25 trees are favoured by the fog so that you have
   the tropics at first hand: the trumpet vine,
foxglove, giant snapdragon, a salpiglossis that has
spots and stripes; morning-glories, gourds,
   or moon-vines trained on fishing twine
30 at the back door:

cattails, flags, blueberries and spiderwort,
   striped grass, lichens, sunflowers, asters, daisies—
yellow and crab-claw ragged sailors with green bracts—toad-
   plant,
petunias, ferns; pink lilies, blue
35   ones, tigers; poppies; black sweet-peas.
The climate

is not right for the banyan, frangipani, or
   jack-fruit trees; or for exotic serpent
life. Ring lizard and snakeskin for the foot, if you see fit;

---

1. Albrecht Dürer (1471–1528), German painter and engraver; he passed through Tyrol or Tirol, a region of the Alps in west Austria (and, since 1919, Italy), when he traveled to Italy in 1494.

40   but here they've cats, not cobras, to
          keep down the rats. The diffident
    little newt

    with white pin-dots on black horizontal spaced-
          out bands lives here; yet there is nothing that
45   ambition can buy or take away. The college student
    named Ambrose sits on the hillside
          with his not-native books and hat
    and sees boats

    at sea progress white and rigid as if in
50   a groove. Liking an elegance of which
    the source is not bravado, he knows by heart the antique
    sugar-bowl shaped summerhouse of
          interlacing slats, and the pitch
    of the church

55   spire, not true, from which a man in scarlet lets
          down a rope as a spider spins a thread;
    he might be part of a novel, but on the sidewalk a
    sign says C. J. Poole, Steeple Jack,
60   in black and white; and one in red
    and white says

    Danger. The church portico has four fluted
          columns, each a single piece of stone, made
    modester by whitewash. This would be a fit haven for
65   waifs, children, animals, prisoners,
          and presidents who have repaid
    sin-driven

    senators by not thinking about them. The
          place has a schoolhouse, a post-office in a
    store, fish-houses, hen-houses, a three-masted
70   schooner on
    the stocks. The hero, the student,
          the steeple-jack, each in his way,
    is at home.

    It could not be dangerous to be living
75   in a town like this, of simple people,
    who have a steeple-jack placing danger signs by the church
    while he is gilding the solid-
          pointed star, which on a steeple
    stands for hope.

                                        1932, 1961

---

1. A marine mollusk (closely related to the octopus), also known as the argonaut. The female builds a fragile shell to contain her eggs, carrying it on the surface of the water with two of her eight tentacles, once thought to serve as sails—hence the name *nautilus,* which means "sailor."

The Paper Nautilus[1]

For authorities whose hopes
are shaped by mercenaries?
　　Writers entrapped by
　　teatime fame and by
5　　commuters' comforts? Not for these
　　the paper nautilus
　　constructs her thin glass shell.

　　Giving her perishable
souvenir of hope, a dull
10　　white outside and smooth-
　　edged inner surface
glossy as the sea, the watchful
　　maker of it guards it
　　day and night; she scarcely

15　　eats until the eggs are hatched.
Buried eightfold in her eight
　　arms, for she is in
　　a sense a devil-
fish, her glass ram's-horn-cradled freight
20　　is hid but is not crushed;
　　as Hercules, bitten

by a crab loyal to the hydra,[2]
was hindered to succeed,
　　the intensively
25　　watched eggs coming from
the shell free it when they are freed—
　　leaving its wasp-nest flaws
　　of white on white, and close-

laid Ionic chiton[3]-folds
30　　like the lines in the mane of
　　a Parthenon horse,[4]
　　round which the arms had
wound themselves as if they knew love
　　is the only fortress
35　　strong enough to trust to.

　　　　　　　　　　　　　　1940, 1941

---

2. In classical myth, a many-headed monster subdued by the hero Hercules. As he fought the monster, a crab bit him, and he crushed it underfoot.

3. Ancient Greek tunic.
4. I.e., represented in the frieze on the Parthenon, the main temple on the Acropolis in Athens.

His Shield

    The pin-swin or spine-swine
        (the edgehog miscalled hedgehog) with all his edges out,
      echidna and echinoderm[1] in distressed-
    pin-cushion thorn-fur coats, the spiny pig or porcupine,
5   the rhino with horned snout—
      everything is battle-dressed.

    Pig-fur won't do, I'll wrap
        myself in salamander-skin like Presbyter John.[2]
      A lizard in the midst of flames, a firebrand
10 that is life, asbestos-eyed asbestos-eared, with tattooed nap
        and permanent pig on
      the instep; he can withstand

    fire and won't drown. In his
        unconquerable country of unpompous gusto,
15   gold was so common none considered it; greed
    and flattery were unknown. Though rubies large as tennis
        balls conjoined in streams so
      that the mountain seemed to bleed,

    the inextinguishable
20   salamander styled himself but presbyter. His shield
      was his humility. In Carpasian
    linen[3] coat, flanked by his household lion cubs and sable
        retinue, he revealed
      a formula safer than

25 an armorer's: the power of relinquishing
        what one would keep; that is freedom. Become dinosaur-
      skulled, quilled or salamander-wooled, more ironshod
    and javelin-dressed than a hedgehog battalion of steel, but be
        dull. Don't be envied or
30   armed with a measuring-rod.

                                            1951

O to Be a Dragon[1]

      If I, like Solomon,[2] . . .
      could have my wish—

---

1. I.e., spiny-skin. "Echidna": another species of porcupine.
2. A legendary Christian monarch (12th century), who was said to perform marvels of all kinds. "Salamander": a lizard traditionally fabled to live in fire. "Presbyter": priest.
3. A fireproof material—probably asbestos—from Carpasia in Cyprus (see Pausanias 1.26.7).

1. See secondary symbols, Volume II of *The Tao of Painting*, translated and edited by Mai-mai Sze, Bollingen Series 49 (New York: Pantheon, 1956; Modern Library edition, p. 57) [Moore's note].
2. Solomon's wish: "an understanding heart." 1 Kings 3.9 [Moore's note].

> my wish . . . O to be a dragon,
> a symbol of the power of Heaven—of silkworm
> size or immense; at times invisible.
> Felicitous phenomenon!

1957

KATHERINE MANSFIELD
1888–1923

When she was thirty years old, Katherine Mansfield described the two motives of what she called her "writing game" with striking clarity and conviction: "*One* is joy," she explained in a letter to her husband, the critic J. Middleton Murry, adding that in this state of being "in some perfectly blissful way *at peace*," something like a flower "seems to open before my eyes." The other "kick off" consisted of "*a cry against corruption*" that she associated with the hopeless sense that "everything [is] doomed to disaster." It is hardly surprising that the New Zealand–born Kathleen Beauchamp should have felt divided about her identity as a London literary figure called Katherine Mansfield. She came from a conventional Victorian family, but she lived the bohemian life of a New Woman. She referred to herself as a "child" and liked to play with dolls, kittens, and imaginary babies, but she suffered from gonorrhea, had one miscarriage, and seems to have had an abortion. She repeatedly protested that she wanted nothing more than a home of her own, but she spent her life restlessly traveling from England to France and Italy, and back again. She said she adored her husband, but she never relinquished her close ties to her "wife," Ida Baker. Finally, and most tragically, while she searched for spiritual health, she suffered the debilitating consequences of the tuberculosis that killed her at the age of thirty-five.

Kathleen Beauchamp's father, Harold Beauchamp, was an enterprising Wellington businessman who would go on to become a prominent director of the Bank of New Zealand. Her mother, Annie (Dyer) Beauchamp, was a delicate woman who brought her own mother to live in the household. This grandmother provided the affectionate protection that Kathleen's self-absorbed, frail mother and upwardly mobile father could not supply. After the birth of her only brother, Kathleen was sent with her sisters to a series of New Zealand schools; then, at fifteen, she traveled with her family to London, where she studied for three years at Queen's College. By the time she unwillingly returned to New Zealand, she was reading the fiction of Oscar Wilde, Elizabeth Robins, the Brontës, and Leo Tolstoy, and she was beginning to receive payment for vignettes appearing in *The Native Companion*, a New Zealand journal. This sign of success was sufficient to persuade her father to allow her to go back to London.

Kathleen had already begun to establish the divided emotional loyalties that would inform the rest of her life. On the one hand, she was writing love letters to the son of her Wellington music teacher, Tom Trowell, whose twin, Garnet, would become her fiancé when she finally managed to return to England. On the other hand, an early journal entry indicates that she felt guilty about her passion for a Wellington schoolfriend, Maata Mahupuku, a Maori (native New Zealand) heiress. At Queen's College, moreover, she met Ida Constance Baker, a motherless girl whose father was to become the model for the tyrannical paterfamilias in "The Daughters of the Late Colonel." Ida eventually became known as L. M. (Leslie Moore) and Kathleen called herself Katherine Mansfield. When Katherine was rejected by Garnet Trowell's parents and decided on the spur of the moment to marry a new acquaintance, George Bowden, it was L. M. who accompanied the twenty-one-year-old bride, dressed all in black, to the Registry Office; it was also to L. M. that the bride fled on her wedding night. At this point, however, Mrs. Beauchamp arrived in London and packed Katherine off to a German hotel. There, according to her biographer Antony Alpers, she was "treated" for her lesbianism with cold baths, and she suffered a miscarriage.

Mansfield's early stories were first published individually in A. R. Orage's *New Age* and then collected in the caustic volume titled *In a German Pension* (1911). After she sent one tale, "The Woman at the Store," to a new review, *Rhythm*, she was visited by its literary editor, J. Middleton Murry, an Oxford undergraduate who came from what Alpers calls "the very bottom of the lower middle class." One year younger than Mansfield, he became in 1912 first a lodger in her flat and then her lover. Although *Rhythm* would soon go bankrupt, Mansfield continued to publish stories to supplement the modest allowance provided by her father, and Murry began earning money from critical essays and reviews.

Their lives, like everyone else's, were shattered by World War I. While L. M. worked as a machinist in an airplane factory, Murry took a job in military intelligence. For Mansfield, however, the reality of the war was brought home by the death of her brother, Leslie, who was "blown to bits" in France. In *Prelude* (1918) and "At the Bay" (1921), Mansfield went on to reconstruct the "undiscovered country" she had shared with Leslie Beauchamp in stories that depart from conventional narration to convey the mysterious radiance of childhood as it is perceived by a community of women and children. Near the end of her life, moreover, she wrote the startling antiwar story "The Fly" (1922) to express her outrage at the sacrifice of a generation of sons by their fathers, the architects of the war.

When she was not traveling or living on the Continent, Mansfield was befriended by a number of literary celebrities in London, including, most importantly, the novelists D. H. Lawrence and Virginia Woolf. These last two relationships illuminate the tensions in the writer's literary career. Throughout her journal and her numerous letters, Mansfield expressed her admiration for Lawrence, her sense that they were "unthinkably alike" not only in temperament but in their artistic efforts to capture the sensuous feeling of life. Yet she was horrified by the violent, public bickering in which Lawrence and his wife, Frieda, engaged, and she may have also understood that Lawrence was really searching for what he called a "blood brotherhood" with Murry, to whom he was greatly attracted. Even if she did not recognize herself and Murry in Lawrence's portraits of the self-conscious miniaturist Gudrun and her masterfully attractive but flawed lover Gerald in *Women in Love* (1920), Mansfield had been alienated by a shocking letter Lawrence wrote her in 1920: "You revolt me, stewing in your consumption."

Significant as Mansfield's relationship with Lawrence was, her friendship with Virginia Woolf was perhaps equally crucial. In 1918, the "Woolves" published *Prelude* at their Hogarth Press, and Mansfield and Woolf began visiting and writing each other. Sometimes the older, wealthier Woolf criticized Mansfield's bohemian promiscuity, but she nevertheless admitted that beyond Mansfield's "commonness" was an "inscrutable" intelligence. Analyzing their similar literary aims, Mansfield wrote Woolf, "We have the same job, Virginia." After Mansfield died, moreover, Woolf recorded in her diary that Mansfield had produced "the only writing I have ever been jealous of." Although Woolf did not understand why their relationship deteriorated, it is clear from Mansfield's letters that the younger writer envied a woman who had her own home, her own possessions, and her own man within call, for Mansfield's rootlessness was related to her uneasy alliance with Murry.

Mansfield sustained a relationship with Murry from the time she was twenty-four until her death. While she admired the critical intelligence shown in his book on Dostoyevsky, she knew the "sham" side of Murry's personality, when he seemed "to uncover" himself "and quiver" in an ecstasy of self-pity. Mansfield was also aware of Murry's physical revulsion against and impatience with her tuberculosis, a reaction she presents brilliantly in her short story "The Man without a Temperament" (1920). Mansfield's continual search for a healthy place to recuperate meant long separations, and her letters complain of her husband's monetary and emotional stinginess as well as of her loneliness. The sicker she became, the more she relied on L. M.'s services as a traveling companion, a home nurse, and a cook, but her dependence bred resentment, and L. M. came to seem like "The Albatross" or "a revolting hysterical ghoul." Mansfield's letters from this period remain difficult to interpret, for they were, like her *Journal*, heavily edited by Murry.

After 1918, Mansfield increasingly suffered from night terrors, insomnia, difficulty walking, pains in the chest, and a nausea that made it difficult for her to eat. The complex relationship between illness and creativity in Mansfield's career has been the source of much critical attention. At the onset of her physical problems Mansfield began writing the stories that would be published in *Bliss and Other Stories* (1920) as well as many reviews for Murry's journal, the *Atheneum*. Always short of money, she nevertheless began a series of cures that included stays in nursing homes, radium treatments, and X-rays. By 1922, when *The Garden Party and Other Stories* was published to critical acclaim, she was reading P. D. Ouspensky's *Cosmic Anatomy* and contemplating spiritual cures for the physical problems her physicians could not alleviate. Then she became acquainted through Orage with the Armenian Greek spiritualist Georgei Ivanovitch Gurdjieff. He was just establishing his Institute for the Harmonious Development of Man at Fontainebleau, where he recommended drastic shifts in habit, unsettling alterations in living conditions, and rhythmic exercises and dances to accomplish a "centering" that would result in a new self and a new way of seeing. In 1922, Mansfield secretly joined Gurdjieff's community, but soon she invited Murry to visit her. By that time, she had been installed in a hayloft where she could breathe the exhalation of cows, drink fresh milk, and gaze at the ceiling and walls, which were decorated with paintings of flowers, birds, and animals. On the night of Murry's visit, Mansfield suffered a hemorrhage and died almost instantly.

During her short lifetime, the former Kathleen Beauchamp had been recognized for the sardonic, often cynical stories that she wrote as a cry against the corruption of modern English society. But, midway in her career, she had also begun composing joyous narratives, peaceful memories of a blissful New Zealand childhood. For the last few years of her life, she brilliantly integrated her satiric and sympathetic impulses in portraits of impoverished, single women and imaginative children that transformed the art of the short story. Frequently compared with Anton Chekhov, whom she greatly admired, Mansfield practiced her art with strenuous discipline, for it was a reprieve from the pain of her life.

The Daughters of the Late Colonel

1

The week after was one of the busiest weeks of their lives. Even when they went to bed it was only their bodies that lay down and rested; their minds went on, thinking things out, talking things over, wondering, deciding, trying to remember where . . .

Constantia lay like a statue, her hands by her sides, her feet just overlapping each other, the sheet up to her chin. She stared at the ceiling.

"Do you think father would mind if we gave his top-hat to the porter?"[1]

---

1. In England, a male servant; originally a gatekeeper.

"The porter?" snapped Josephine. "Why ever the porter? What a very extraordinary idea!"

"Because," said Constantia slowly, "he must often have to go to funerals. And I noticed at—at the cemetery that he only had a bowler." She paused. "I thought then how very much he'd appreciate a top-hat. We ought to give him a present, too. He was always very nice to father."

"But," cried Josephine, flouncing on her pillow and staring across the dark at Constantia, "father's head!" And suddenly, for one awful moment, she nearly giggled. Not, of course, that she felt in the least like giggling. It must have been habit. Years ago, when they had stayed awake at night talking, their beds had simply heaved. And now the porter's head, disappearing, popped out, like a candle, under father's hat. . . . The giggle mounted, mounted; she clenched her hands; she fought it down; she frowned fiercely at the dark and said "Remember" terribly sternly.

"We can decide tomorrow," she sighed.

Constantia had noticed nothing; she sighed.

"Do you think we ought to have our dressing-gowns dyed as well?"

"Black?" almost shrieked Josephine.

"Well, what else?" said Constantia. "I was thinking—it doesn't seem quite sincere, in a way, to wear black out of doors and when we're fully dressed, and then when we're at home—"

"But nobody sees us," said Josephine. She gave the bedclothes such a twitch that both her feet became uncovered, and she had to creep up the pillows to get them well under again.

"Kate does," said Constantia. "And the postman very well might."

Josephine thought of her dark-red slippers, which matched her dressing-gown, and of Constantia's favorite indefinite green ones which went with hers. Black! Two black dressing-gowns and two pairs of black woolly slippers, creeping off to the bathroom like black cats.

"I don't think it's absolutely necessary," said she.

Silence. Then Constantia said, "We shall have to post the papers with the notice in them tomorrow to catch the Ceylon mail. . . . How many letters have we had up till now?"

"Twenty-three."

Josephine had replied to them all, and twenty-three times when she came to "We miss our dear father so much" she had broken down and had to use her handkerchief, and on some of them even to soak up a very light-blue tear with an edge of blotting-paper. Strange! She couldn't have put it on—but twenty-three times. Even now, though when she said over to herself sadly. "We miss our dear father *so* much" she could have cried if she'd wanted to.

"Have you got enough stamps?" came from Constantia.

"Oh, how can I tell?" said Josephine crossly. "What's the good of asking me that now?"

"I was just wondering," said Constantia mildly.

Silence again. There came a little rustle, a scurry, a hop.

"A mouse," said Constantia.

"It can't be a mouse because there aren't any crumbs," said Josephine.

"But it doesn't know there aren't," said Constantia.

A spasm of pity squeezed her heart. Poor little thing! She wished she'd left a tiny piece of biscuit on the dressing-table. It was awful to think of it not finding anything. What would it do?

"I can't think how they manage to live at all," she said slowly.

"Who?" demanded Josephine.

And Constantia said more loudly than she meant to, "Mice."

Josephine was furious. "Oh, what nonsense, Con!" she said. "What have mice got to do with it? You're asleep."

"I don't think I am," said Constantia. She shut her eyes to make sure. She was.

Josephine arched her spine, pulled up her knees, folded her arms so that her fists came under her ears, and pressed her cheek hard against the pillow.

2

Another thing which complicated matters was they had Nurse Andrews staying on with them that week. It was their own fault; they had asked her. It was Josephine's idea. On the morning—well, on the last morning, when the doctor had gone, Josephine had said to Constantia, "Don't you think it would be rather nice if we asked Nurse Andrews to stay on for a week as our guest?"

"Very nice," said Constantia.

"I thought," went on Josephine quickly, "I should just say this afternoon, after I've paid her, 'My sister and I would be very pleased, after all you've done for us, Nurse Andrews, if you would stay on for a week as our guest.' I'd have to put that in about being our guest in case—"

"Oh, but she could hardly expect to be paid!" cried Constantia.

"One never knows," said Josephine sagely.

Nurse Andrews had, of course, jumped at the idea. But it was a bother. It meant they had to have regular sit-down meals at the proper times, whereas if they'd been alone they could just have asked Kate if she wouldn't have minded bringing them a tray wherever they were. And meal-times now that the strain was over were rather a trial.

Nurse Andrews was simply fearful about butter. Really they couldn't help feeling that about butter, at least, she took advantage of their kindness. And she had that maddening habit of asking for just an inch more bread to finish what she had on her plate, and then, at the last mouthful, absent-mindedly—of course it wasn't absent-mindedly—taking another helping. Josephine got very red when this happened, and she fastened her small, bead-like eyes on the tablecloth as if she saw a minute strange insect creeping through the web of it. But Constantia's long, pale face lengthened and set, and she gazed away—away—far over the desert, to where that line of camels unwound like a thread of wool....

"When I was with Lady Tukes," said Nurse Andrews, "she had such a dainty little contrayvance for the buttah. It was a silvah Cupid balanced on the—on the bordah of a glass dish, holding a tayny fork. And when you wanted some buttah you simply pressed his foot and he bent down and speared you a piece. It was quite a gayme."

Josephine could hardly bear that. But "I think those things are very extravagant" was all she said.

"But whey?" asked Nurse Andrews, beaming through her eye-glasses. "No one, surely, would take more buttah than one wanted—would one?"

"Ring, Con," cried Josephine. She couldn't trust herself to reply.

And proud young Kate, the enchanted princess, came in to see what the old tabbies wanted now. She snatched away their plates of mock something or other and slapped down a white, terrified blancmange.[2]

"Jam, please, Kate," said Josephine kindly.

Kate knelt and burst open the sideboard, lifted the lid of the jam-pot, saw it was empty, put it on the table, and stalked off.

"I'm afraid," said Nurse Andrews a moment later, "there isn't any."

"Oh, what a bother!" said Josephine. She bit her lip. "What had we better do?"

Constantia looked dubious. "We can't disturb Kate again," she said softly.

Nurse Andrews waited, smiling at them both. Her eyes wandered, spying at everything behind her eye-glasses. Constantia in despair went back to her camels. Josephine frowned heavily—concentrated. If it hadn't been for this idiotic woman she and Con would, of course, have eaten their blancmange without. Suddenly the idea came.

"I know," she said. "Marmalade. There's some marmalade in the sideboard. Get it, Con."

"I hope," laughed Nurse Andrews, and her laugh was like a spoon tinkling against a medicine-glass—"I hope it's not very bittah marmalayde."

3

But, after all, it was not long now, and then she'd be gone for good. And there was no getting over the fact that she had been very kind to father. She had nursed him day and night at the end. Indeed, both Constantia and Josephine felt privately she had rather overdone the not leaving him at the very last. For when they had gone in to say good-bye Nurse Andrews had sat beside his bed the whole time, holding his wrist and pretending to look at her watch. It couldn't have been necessary. It was so tactless, too. Supposing father had wanted to say something—something private to them. Not that he had. Oh, far from it! He lay there, purple, a dark angry purple in the face, and never even looked at them when they came in. Then, as they were standing there, wondering what to do, he had suddenly opened one eye. Oh, what a difference it would have made, what a difference to their memory of him, how much easier to tell people about it, if he had only opened both! But no—one eye only. It glared at them a moment and then . . . went out.

4

It had made it very awkward for them when Mr. Farolles, of St. John's, called the same afternoon.

"The end was quite peaceful, I trust?" were the first words he said as he glided towards them through the dark drawing-room.

"Quite," said Josephine faintly. They both hung their heads. Both of them felt certain that eye wasn't at all a peaceful eye.

---

2. A sweet pudding.

"Won't you sit down?" said Josephine.

"Thank you, Miss Pinner," said Mr. Farolles gracefully. He folded his coat-tails and began to lower himself into father's armchair, but just as he touched it he almost sprang up and slid into the next chair instead.

He coughed. Josephine clasped her hands; Constantia looked vague.

"I want you to feel, Miss Pinner," said Mr. Farolles, "and you Miss Constantia, that I'm trying to be helpful. I want to be helpful to you both, if you will let me. These are the times," said Mr. Farolles, very simple and earnestly, "when God means us to be helpful to one another."

"Thank you very much, Mr. Farolles," said Josephine and Constantia.

"Not at all," said Mr. Farolles gently. He drew his kid gloves through his fingers and leaned forward. "And if either of you would like a little Communion,[3] either or both of you, here *and* now, you have only to tell me. A little Communion is often very help—a great comfort," he added tenderly.

But the idea of a little Communion terrified them. What! In the drawing-room by themselves—with no—no altar or anything! The piano would be much too high, thought Constantia, and Mr. Farolles could not possibly lean over it with the chalice. And Kate would be sure to come bursting in and interrupt them, thought Josephine. And supposing the bell rang in the middle? It might be somebody important—about their mourning. Would they get up reverently and go out, or would they have to wait . . . in torture?

"Perhaps you will send round a note by your good Kate if you would care for it later," said Mr. Farolles.

"Oh yes, thank you very much!" they both said.

Mr. Farolles got up and took his black straw hat from the round table.

"And about the funeral," he said softly. "I may arrange that—as your dear father's old friend and yours, Miss Pinner—and Miss Constantia?"

Josephine and Constantia got up too.

"I should like it to be quite simple," said Josephine firmly, "and not too expensive. At the same time, I should like—"

"A good one that will last," thought dreamy Constantia, as if Josephine were buying a nightgown. But of course Josephine didn't say that. "One suitable to our father's position." She was very nervous.

"I'll run round to our good friend Mr. Knight," said Mr. Farolles soothingly. "I will ask him to come and see you. I am sure you will find him very helpful indeed."

5

Well, at any rate, all that part of it was over, though neither of them could possibly believe that father was never coming back. Josephine had had a moment of absolute terror at the cemetery, while the coffin was lowered, to think that she and Constantia had done this thing without asking his permission. What would father say when he found out? For he was bound to find out sooner or later. He always did. "Buried. You two girls had me *buried!*" She heard his stick thumping. Oh, what would they say? What possible excuse could they make? It sounded such an appallingly heartless thing to

---

3. The ceremony in which sacramental wine and bread symbolizing the blood and body of Christ are consumed.

do. Such a wicked advantage to take of a person because he happened to be helpless at the moment. The other people seemed to treat it all as a matter of course. They were strangers; they couldn't be expected to understand that father was the very last person for such a thing to happen to. No, the entire blame for it all would fall on her and Constantia. And the expense, she thought, stepping into the tight-buttoned cab. When she had to show him the bills. What would he say then?

She heard him absolutely roaring. "And do you expect me to pay for this gimcrack excursion of yours?"

"Oh," groaned poor Josephine aloud, "we shouldn't have done it, Con!"

And Constantia, pale as a lemon in all that blackness, said in a frightened whisper, "Done what, Jug?"

"Let them bu-bury father like that," said Josephine, breaking down and crying into her new, queer-smelling mourning handkerchief.

"But what else could we have done?" asked Constantia wonderingly. "We couldn't have kept him, Jug—we couldn't have kept him unburied. At any rate, not in a flat[4] that size."

Josephine blew her nose; the cab was dreadfully stuffy.

"I don't know," she said forlornly. "It is all so dreadful. I feel we ought to have tried to, just for a time at least. To make perfectly sure. One thing's certain"—and her tears sprang out again—"father will never forgive us for this—never!"

6

Father would never forgive them. That was what they felt more than ever when, two mornings later, they went into his room to go through his things. They had discussed it quite calmly. It was even down on Josephine's list of things to be done. *Go through father's things and settle about them.* But that was a very different matter from saying after breakfast:

"Well, are you ready, Con?"

"Yes, Jug—when you are."

"Then I think we'd better get it over."

It was dark in the hall. It had been a rule for years never to disturb father in the morning, whatever happened. And now they were going to open the door without knocking even.... Constantia's eyes were enormous at the idea; Josephine felt weak in the knees.

"You—you go first," she gasped, pushing Constantia.

But Constantia said, as she always had said on those occasions, "No, Jug, that's not fair. You're eldest."

Josephine was just going to say—what at other times she wouldn't have owned to for the world—what she kept for her very last weapon, "But you're tallest," when they noticed that the kitchen door was open, and there stood Kate....

"Very stiff," said Josephine, grasping the door-handle and doing her best to turn it. As if anything ever deceived Kate!

It couldn't be helped. That girl was ... Then the door was shut behind them, but—but they weren't in father's room at all. They might have sud-

---

4. Room or suite of rooms.

denly walked through the wall by mistake into a different flat altogether. Was the door just behind them? They were too frightened to look. Josephine knew that if it was it was holding itself tight shut; Constantia felt that, like the doors in dreams, it hadn't any handle at all. It was the coldness which made it so awful. Or the whiteness—which? Everything was covered. The blinds were down, a cloth hung over the mirror, a sheet hid the bed; a huge fan of white paper filled the fireplace. Constantia timidly put out her hand; she almost expected a snowflake to fall. Josephine felt a queer tingling in her nose, as if her nose was freezing. Then a cab klop-klopped over the cobbles below, and the quiet seemed to shake into little pieces.

"I had better pull up a blind," said Josephine bravely.

"Yes, it might be a good idea," whispered Constantia.

They only gave the blind a touch, but it flew up and the cord flew after, rolling round the blindstick, and the little tassel tapped as if trying to get free. That was too much for Constantia.

"Don't you think—don't you think we might put it off for another day?" she whispered.

"Why?" snapped Josephine, feeling, as usual, much better now that she knew for certain that Constantia was terrified. "It's got to be done. But I do wish you wouldn't whisper, Con."

"I didn't know I was whispering," whispered Constantia.

"And why do you keep on staring at the bed?" said Josephine, raising her voice almost defiantly. "There's nothing *on* the bed."

"Oh, Jug, don't say so!" said poor Connie. "At any rate, not so loudly."

Josephine felt herself that she had gone too far. She took a wide swerve over to the chest of drawers, put out her hand, but quickly drew it back again.

"Connie!" she gasped, and she wheeled round and leaned with her back against the chest of drawers.

"Oh, Jug—what?"

Josephine could only glare. She had the most extraordinary feeling that she had just escaped something simply awful. But how could she explain to Constantia that father was in the chest of drawers? He was in the top drawer with his handkerchiefs and neckties, or in the next with his shirts and pyjamas, or in the lowest of all with his suits. He was watching there, hidden away—just behind the door-handle—ready to spring.

She pulled a funny old-fashioned face at Constantia, just as she used to in the old days when she was going to cry.

"I can't open," she nearly wailed.

"No, don't, Jug," whispered Constantia earnestly. "It's much better not to. Don't let's open anything. At any rate, not for a long time."

"But—but it seems so weak," said Josephine, breaking down.

"But why not be weak for once, Jug?" argued Constantia, whispering quite fiercely. "If it is weak." And her pale stare flew from the locked writing-table—so safe—to the huge glittering wardrobe, and she began to breathe in a queer, panting way. "Why shouldn't we be weak for once in our lives, Jug? It's quite excusable. Let's be weak—be weak, Jug. It's much nicer to be weak than to be strong."

And then she did one of those amazingly bold things that she'd done about twice before in their lives; she marched over to the wardrobe, turned the key, and took it out of the lock. Took it out of the lock and held it up to Josephine, showing Josephine by her extraordinary smile that she knew what she'd done, she'd risked deliberately father being in there among his overcoats.

If the huge wardrobe had lurched forward, had crashed down on Constantia, Josephine wouldn't have been surprised. On the contrary, she would have thought it the only suitable thing to happen. But nothing happened. Only the room seemed quieter than ever, and bigger flakes of cold air fell on Josephine's shoulders and knees. She began to shiver.

"Come, Jug," said Constantia, still with that awful callous smile, and Josephine followed just as she had that last time, when Constantia had pushed Benny into the round pond.

7

But the strain told on them when they were back in the dining-room. They sat down, very shaky, and looked at each other.

"I don't feel I can settle to anything," said Josephine, "until I've had something. Do you think we could ask Kate for two cups of hot water?"

"I really don't see why we shouldn't," said Constantia carefully. She was quite normal again. "I won't ring. I'll go to the kitchen door and ask her."

"Yes, do," said Josephine, sinking down into a chair. "Tell her, just two cups, Con, nothing else—on a tray."

"She needn't even put the jug on, need she?" said Constantia, as though Kate might very well complain if the jug had been there.

"Oh no, certainly not! The jug's not at all necessary. She can pour it direct out of the kettle," cried Josephine, feeling that would be a labor-saving indeed.

Their cold lips quivered at the greenish brims. Josephine curved her small red hands round the cup; Constantia sat up and blew on the wavy stream, making it flutter from one side to the other.

"Speaking of Benny," said Josephine.

And though Benny hadn't been mentioned Constantia immediately looked as though he had.

"He'll expect us to send him something of father's, of course. But it's so difficult to know what to send to Ceylon."

"You mean things get unstuck so on the voyage," murmured Constantia.

"No, lost," said Josephine sharply. "You know there's no post. Only runners."

Both paused to watch a black man in white linen drawers running through the pale fields for dear life, with a large brown-paper parcel in his hands. Josephine's black man was tiny; he scurried along glistening like an ant. But there was something blind and tireless about Constantia's tall, thin fellow, which made him, she decided, a very unpleasant person indeed. . . . On the veranda, dressed all in white and wearing a cork helmet, stood Benny. His right hand shook up and down, as father's did when he was impatient. And behind him, not in the least interested, sat Hilda, the unknown sister-in-law. She swung in a cane rocker and flicked over the leaves of the *Tatler*.

"I think his watch would be the most suitable present," said Josephine.

Constantia looked up; she seemed surprised.

"Oh, would you trust a gold watch to a native?"

"But of course I'd disguise it," said Josephine. "No one would know it was a watch." She liked the idea of having to make a parcel such a curious shape that no one could posssibly guess what it was. She even thought for a moment of hiding the watch in a narrow cardboard corset-box that she'd kept by her for a long time, waiting for it to come in for something. It was such beautiful firm cardboard. But, no, it wouldn't be appropriate for this occasion. It had lettering on it: *Medium Women's 28. Extra Firm Busks.*[5] It would be almost too much of a surprise for Benny to open that and find father's watch inside.

"And of course it isn't as though it would be going—ticking, I mean," said Constantia, who was still thinking of the native love of jewelry. "At least," she added, "it would be very strange if after all that time it was."

8

Josephine made no reply. She had flown off on one of her tangents. She had suddenly thought of Cyril. Wasn't it more usual for the only grandson to have the watch? And then dear Cyril was so appreciative, and a gold watch meant so much to a young man. Benny, in all probability, had quite got out of the habit of watches; men so seldom wore waistcoats in those hot climates.[6] Whereas Cyril in London wore them from year's end to year's end. And it would be so nice for her and Constantia, when he came to tea, to know it was there. "I see you've got on grandfather's watch, Cyril." It would be somehow so satisfactory.

Dear boy! What a blow his sweet, sympathetic little note had been! Of course they quite understood; but it was most unfortunate.

"It would have been such a point, having him," said Josephine.

"And he would have enjoyed it so," said Constantia, not thinking what she was saying.

However, as soon as he got back he was coming to tea with his aunties. Cyril to tea was one of their rare treats.

"Now, Cyril, you mustn't be frightened of our cakes. Your Auntie Con and I bought them at Buszard's this morning. We know what a man's appetite is. So don't be ashamed of making a good tea."

Josephine cut recklessly into the rich dark cake that stood for her winter gloves or the soling and heeling of Constantia's only respectable shoes. But Cyril was most unmanlike in appetite.

"I say, Aunt Josephine, I simply can't. I've only just had lunch, you know."

"Oh, Cyril, that can't be true! It's after four," cried Josephine. Constantia sat with her knife poised over the chocolate-roll.

"It is all the same," said Cyril. "I had to meet a man at Victoria[7] and he kept me hanging about till . . . there was only time to get lunch and to come on here. And he gave me—phew"—Cyril put his hand to his forehead—"a terrific blow-out," he said.

It was disappointing—today of all days. But still he couldn't be expected to know.

"But you'll have a meringue, won't you, Cyril?" said Aunt Josephine.

---

5. Ridged strips that stiffen a corset.
6. This is a pocket watch, usually worn in a small pocket of a vest to which it is attached with a fob.
7. A railroad station in London.

"These meringues were bought specially for you. Your dear father was so fond of them. We were sure you are, too."

"I *am*, Aunt Josephine," cried Cyril ardently. "Do you mind if I take half to begin with?"

"Not at all, dear boy; but we mustn't let you off with that."

"Is your dear father still so fond of meringues?" asked Auntie Con gently. She winced faintly as she broke through the shell of hers.

"Well, I don't quite know, Auntie Con," said Cyril breezily.

At that they both looked up.

"Don't know?" almost snapped Josephine. "Don't know a thing like that about your own father, Cyril?"

"Surely," said Auntie Con softly.

Cyril tried to laugh if off. "Oh well," he said, "it's such a long time since—"

He faltered. He stopped. Their faces were too much for him.

"Even *so*," said Josephine.

And Auntie Con looked.

Cyril put down his teacup. "Wait a bit," he cried. "Wait a bit, Aunt Josephine. What am I thinking of?"

He looked up. They were beginning to brighten. Cyril slapped his knee.

"Of course," he said, "it was meringues. How could I have forgotten? Yes, Aunt Josephine, you're perfectly right. Father's most frightfully keen on meringues."

They didn't only beam. Aunt Josephine went scarlet with pleasure; Auntie Con gave a deep, deep sigh.

"And now, Cyril, you must come and see father," said Josephine. "He knows you were coming to-day."

"Right," said Cyril, very firmly and heartily. He got up from his chair; suddenly he glanced at the clock.

"I say, Auntie Con, isn't your clock a bit slow? I've got to meet a man at—at Paddington[8] just after five. I'm afraid I shan't be able to stay very long with grandfather."

"Oh, he won't expect you to stay *very* long!" said Aunt Josephine.

Constantia was still gazing at the clock. She couldn't make up her mind if it was fast or slow. It was one or the other, she felt almost certain of that. At any rate, it had been.

Cyril still lingered. "Aren't you coming along, Auntie Con?"

"Of course," said Josephine, "we shall all go. Come on, Con."

9

They knocked at the door, and Cyril followed his aunts into grandfather's hot, sweetish room.

"Come on," said Grandfather Pinner. "Don't hang about. What is it? What've you been up to?"

He was sitting in front of the roaring fire, clasping his stick. He had a thick rug over his knees. On his lap there lay a beautiful pale yellow silk handkerchief.

---

8. Another London railroad station.

"It's Cyril, father," said Josephine shyly. And she took Cyril's hand and led him forward.

"Good afternoon, grandfather," said Cyril, trying to take his hand out of Aunt Josephine's. Grandfather Pinner shot his eyes at Cyril in the way he was famous for. Where was Auntie Con? She stood on the other side of Aunt Josephine; her long arms hung down in front of her; her hands were clasped. She never took her eyes off grandfather.

"Well," said Grandfather Pinner, beginning to thump, "what have you got to tell me?"

What had he, what had he got to tell him? Cyril felt himself smiling like a perfect imbecile. The room was stifling, too.

But Aunt Josephine came to the rescue. She cried brightly, "Cyril says his father is still very fond of meringues, father dear."

"Eh?" said Grandfather Pinner, curving his hand like a purple meringue-shell over one ear.

Josephine repeated, "Cyril says his father is still very fond of meringues."

"Can't hear," said old Colonel Pinner. And he waved Josephine away with his stick, then pointed with his stick to Cyril. "Tell me what she's trying to say," he said.

(My God) "Must I?" said Cyril, blushing and staring at Aunt Josephine.

"Do, dear," she smiled. "It will please him so much."

"Come on, out with it!" cried Colonel Pinner testily, beginning to thump again.

And Cyril leaned forward and yelled, "Father's still very fond of meringues."

At that Grandfather Pinner jumped as though he had been shot.

"Don't shout!" he cried. "What's the matter with the boy? *Meringues!* What about 'em?"

"Oh, Aunt Josephine, must we go on?" groaned Cyril desperately.

"It's quite all right, dear boy," said Aunt Josephine, as though he and she were at the dentist's together. "He'll understand in a minute." And she whispered to Cyril, "He's getting a bit deaf, you know." Then she leaned forward and really bawled at Grandfather Pinner, "Cyril only wanted to tell you, father dear, that *his* father is still very fond of meringues."

Colonel Pinner heard that time, heard and brooded, looking Cyril up and down.

"What an esstrordinary thing!" said old Grandfather Pinner. "What an esstrordinary thing to come all this way here to tell me!"

And Cyril felt it *was*.

"Yes, I shall send Cyril the watch," said Josephine.

"That would be very nice," said Constantia. "I seem to remember last time he came there was some little trouble about the time."

10

They were interrupted by Kate bursting through the door in her usual fashion, as though she had discovered some secret panel in the wall.

"Fried or boiled?" asked the bold voice.

Fried or boiled? Josephine and Constantia were quiet bewildered for the moment. They could hardly take it in.

"Fried or boiled what, Kate?" asked Josephine, trying to begin to concentrate.

Kate gave a loud sniff. "Fish."

"Well, why didn't you say so immediately?" Josephine reproached her gently. "How could you expect us to understand, Kate? There are a great many things in this world, you know, which are fried or boiled." And after such a display of courage she said quite brightly to Constantia, "Which do you prefer, Con?"

"I think it might be nice to have it fried," said Constantia. "On the other hand, of course boiled fish is very nice. I think I prefer both equally well . . . Unless you . . . In that case—"

"I shall fry it," said Kate, and she bounced back, leaving their door open and slamming the door of her kitchen.

Josephine gazed at Constantia; she raised her pale eyebrows until they rippled away into her pale hair. She got up. She said in a very lofty, imposing way, "Do you mind following me into the drawing-room, Constantia? I've something of great importance to discuss with you."

For it was always to the drawing-room they retired when they wanted to talk over Kate.

Josephine closed the door meaningly. "Sit down, Constantia," she said, still very grand. She might have been receiving Constantia for the first time. And Con looked round vaguely for a chair, as though she felt indeed quite a stranger.

"Now the question is," said Josephine, bending forward, "whether we shall keep her or not."

"That is the question," agreed Constantia.

"And this time," said Josephine firmly. "we must come to a definite decision."

Constantia looked for a moment as though she might begin going over all the other times, but she pulled herself together and said, "Yes, Jug."

"You see, Con," explained Josephine, "everything is so changed now." Constantia looked up quickly. "I mean," went on Josephine, "we're not dependent on Kate as we were." And she blushed faintly. "There's not father to cook for."

"That is perfectly true," agreed Constantia. "Father certainly doesn't want any cooking now, whatever else—"

Josephine broke in sharply. "You're not sleepy, are you, Con?"

"Sleepy, Jug?" Constantia was wide-eyed.

"Well, concentrate more," said Josephine sharply, and she returned to the subject. "What it comes to is, if we did"—and this she barely breathed, glancing at the door—"give Kate notice"—she raised her voice again—"we could manage our own food."

"Why not?" cried Constantia. She couldn't help smiling. The idea was so exciting. She clasped her hands. "What should we live on, Jug?"

"Oh, eggs in various forms!" said Jug, lofty again. "And, besides, there are all the cooked foods."

"But I've always heard," said Constantia, "they are considered so very expensive."

"Not if one buys them in moderation," said Josephine. But she tore herself away from this fascinating bypath and dragged Constantia after her.

"What we've got to decide now, however, is whether we really do trust Kate or not."

Constantia leaned back. Her flat little laugh flew from her lips.

"Isn't it curious, Jug," said she, "that just on this one subject I've never been able to quite make up my mind?"

11

She never had. The whole difficulty was to prove anything. How did one prove things, how could one? Suppose Kate had stood in front of her and deliberately made a face. Mightn't she very well have been in pain? Wasn't it impossible, at any rate, to ask Kate if she was making a face at her? If Kate answered "No"—and of course she would say "No"—what a position! How undignified! Then again Constantia suspected, she was almost certain that Kate went to her chest of drawers when she and Josephine were out, not to take things but to spy. Many times she had come back to find her amethyst cross in the most unlikely places, under her lace ties or on top of her evening Bertha.[9] More than once she had laid a trap for Kate. She had arranged things in a special order and then called Josephine to witness.

"You see, Jug?"

"Quite, Con."

"Now we shall be able to tell."

But, oh dear, when she did go to look, she was as far off from a proof as ever! If anything was displaced, it might so very well have happened as she closed the drawer; a jolt might have done it so easily.

"You come, Jug, and decide. I really can't. It's too difficult."

But after a pause and a long glare Josephine would sigh, "Now you've put the doubt into my mind, Con, I'm sure I can't tell myself."

"Well, we can't postpone it again," said Josephine. "If we postpone it this time—"

12

But at that moment in the street below a barrel-organ struck up. Josephine and Constantia sprang to their feet together.

"Run, Con," said Josephine. "Run quickly. There's sixpence on the—"

Then they remembered. It didn't matter. They would never have to stop the organ-grinder again. Never again would she and Constantia be told to make that monkey take his noise somewhere else. Never would sound that loud, strange bellow when father thought they were not hurrying enough. The organ-grinder might play there all day and the stick would not thump.

It never will thump again.
It never will thump again,

played the barrel-organ.

What was Constantia thinking? She had such a strange smile; she looked different. She couldn't be going to cry.

---

9. A detachable lace collar for low-necked dresses.

"Jug, Jug," said Constantia softly, pressing her hands together. "Do you know what day it is? It's Saturday. It's a week to-day, a whole week."

A week since father died,
A week since father died,

cried the barrel-organ. And Josephine, too, forgot to be practical and sensible; she smiled faintly, strangely. On the Indian carpet there fell a square of sunlight, pale red; it came and went and came—and stayed, deepened—until it shone almost golden.

"The sun's out," said Josephine, as though it really mattered.

A perfect fountain of bubbling notes shook from the barrel-organ, round, bright notes, carelessly scattered.

Constantia lifted her big, cold hands as if to catch them, and then her hands fell again. She walked over to the mantelpiece to her favorite Buddha. And the stone and gilt image, whose smile always gave her such a queer feeling, almost a pain and yet a pleasant pain, seemed today to be more than smiling. He knew something; he had a secret. "I know something that you don't know," said her Buddah. Oh, what was it, what could it be? And yet she had always felt there was . . . something.

The sunlight pressed through the windows, thieved its way in, flashed its light over the furniture and the photographs. Josephine watched it. When it came to mother's photograph, the enlargement over the piano, it lingered as though puzzled to find so little remained of mother, except the earrings shaped like tiny pagodas and a black feather boa. Why did the photographs of dead people always fade so? wondered Josephine. As soon as a person was dead their photograph died too. But, of course, this one of mother was very old. It was thirty-five years old. Josephine remembered standing on a chair and pointing out that feather boa to Constantia and telling her that it was a snake that had killed their mother in Ceylon. . . . Would everything have been different if mother hadn't died? She didn't see why. Aunt Florence had lived with them until they had left school, and they had moved three times and had their yearly holiday and . . . and there'd been changes of servants, of course.

Some little sparrows, young sparrows they sounded, chirped on the window-ledge. *Yeep—eyeep—yeep.* But Josephine felt they were not sparrows, not on the window-ledge. It was inside her, that queer little crying noise. *Yeep—eyeep—yeep.* Ah, what was it crying, so weak and forlorn?

If mother had lived, might they have married? But there had been nobody for them to marry. There had been father's Anglo-Indian friends before he quarreled with them. But after that she and Constantia never met a single man except clergymen. How did one meet men? Or even if they'd met them, how could they have got to know men well enough to be more than strangers? One read of people having adventures, being followed, and so on. But nobody had ever followed Constantia and her. Oh yes, there had been one year at Eastbourne[1] a mysterious man at their boarding-house who had put a note on the jug of hot water outside their bedroom door! But by the time Connie had found it the steam had made the writing too faint to read; they couldn't even make out to which of them it was addressed. And he had left next day.

---

1. A seaside resort in the south of England.

And that was all. The rest had been looking after father, and at the same time keeping out of father's way. But now? But now? The thieving sun touched Josephine gently. She lifted her face. She was drawn over to the window by gentle beams. . . .

Until the barrel-organ stopped playing Constantia stayed before the Buddha, wondering, but not as usual, not vaguely. This time her wonder was like longing. She remembered the times she had come in here, crept out of bed in her nightgown when the moon was full, and lain on the floor with her arms outstretched, as though she was crucified. Why? The big, pale moon had made her do it. The horrible dancing figures on the carved screen had leered at her and she hadn't minded. She remembered too how, whenever they were at the seaside, she had gone off by herself and got as close to the sea as she could, and sung something, something she had made up, while she gazed all over that restless water. There had been this other life, running out, bringing things home in bags, getting things on approval, discussing them with Jug, and taking them back to get more things on approval, and arranging father's trays and trying not to annoy father. But it all seemed to have happened in a kind of tunnel. It wasn't real. It was only when she came out of the tunnel into the moonlight or by the sea or into a thunderstorm that she really felt herself. What did it mean? What was it she was always wanting? What did it all lead to? Now? Now?

She turned away from the Buddha with one of her vague gestures. She went over to where Josephine was standing. She wanted to say something to Josephine, something frightfully important, about—about the future and what . . .

"Don't you think perhaps—" she began.

But Josephine interrupted her. "I was wondering if now—" she murmured. They stopped; they waited for each other.

"Go on, Con," said Josephine.

"No, no, Jug; after you," said Constantia.

"No, say what you were going to say. You began," said Josephine.

"I . . . I'd rather hear what you were going to say first," said Constantia.

"Don't be absurd, Con."

"Really, Jug."

"Connie!"

"Oh, *Jug!*"

A pause. Then Constantia said faintly, "I can't say what I was going to say, Jug, because I've forgotten what it was . . . that I was going to say."

Josephine was silent for a moment. She stared at a big cloud where the sun had been. Then she replied shortly, "I've forgotten too."

1922

The Fly

"Y'are very snug in here," piped old Mr. Woodifield, and he peered out of the great, green-leather armchair by his friend the boss's desk as a baby peers out of its pram. His talk was over; it was time for him to be off. But he did not want to go. Since he had retired, since his . . . stroke, the wife and the girls kept him boxed up in the house every day of the week except Tuesday. On Tuesday he was dressed and brushed and allowed to cut back to the City[1] for the day. Though what he did there the wife and girls couldn't imagine. Made a nuisance of himself to his friends, they supposed. . . . Well, perhaps so. All the same, we cling to our last pleasures as the tree clings to its last leaves. So there sat old Woodifield, smoking a cigar and staring almost greedily at the boss, who rolled in his office chair, stout, rosy, five years older than he, and still going strong, still at the helm. It did one good to see him.

Wistfully, admiringly, the old voice added, "It's snug in here, upon my word!"

"Yes, it's comfortable enough," agreed the boss, and he flipped the *Financial Times* with a paper-knife. As a matter of fact he was proud of his room; he liked to have it admired, especially by old Woodifield. It gave him a feeling of deep, solid satisfaction to be planted there in the midst of it in full view of that frail old figure in the muffler.

"I've had it done up lately," he explained, as he had explained for the past— how many?—weeks. "New carpet," and he pointed to the bright red carpet with a pattern of large white rings. "New furniture," and he nodded towards the massive bookcase and the table with legs like twisted treacle.[2] "Electric heating!" He waved almost exultantly towards the five transparent, pearly sausages glowing so softly in the tilted copper pan.

But he did not draw old Woodifield's attention to the photograph over the table of a grave-looking boy in uniform standing in one of those spectral photographers' parks with photographers' storm-clouds behind him. It was not new. It had been there for over six years.

"There was something I wanted to tell you," said old Woodifield, and his eyes grew dim remembering. "Now what was it? I had it in my mind when I started out this morning." His hands began to tremble, and patches of red showed above his beard.

Poor old chap, he's on his last pins, thought the boss. And, feeling kindly, he winked at the old man, and said jokingly, "I tell you what. I've got a little drop of something here that'll do you good before you go out into the cold again. It's beautiful stuff. It wouldn't hurt a child." He took a key off his watch-chain, unlocked a cupboard below his desk, and drew forth a dark, squat bottle. "That's the medicine," said he. "And the man from whom I got it told me on the strict Q.T.[3] it came from the cellars at Windsor Castle."

Old Woodifield's mouth fell open at the sight. He couldn't have looked more surprised if the boss had produced a rabbit.

"It's whisky, ain't it?" he piped feebly.

The boss turned the bottle and lovingly showed him the label. Whisky it was.

"D'you know," said he, peering up at the boss wonderingly, "they won't let me touch it at home." And he looked as though he was going to cry.

"Ah, that's where we know a bit more than the ladies," cried the boss, swooping across for two tumblers that stood on the table with the water-

---

1. I.e., the City of London; used more generally of London's business and financial interests.
2. Light molasses.
3. With complete secrecy ("Q.T." stands for "quiet").

bottle, and pouring a generous finger into each. "Drink it down. It'll do you good. And don't put any water with it. It's sacrilege to tamper with stuff like this. Ah!" He tossed off his, pulled out his handkerchief, hastily wiped his moustaches, and cocked an eye at old Woodifield, who was rolling his in his chaps.

The old man swallowed, was silent a moment, and then said faintly, "It's nutty!"

But it warmed him; it crept into his chill old brain—he remembered.

"That was it," he said, heaving himself out of his chair. "I thought you'd like to know. The girls were in Belgium last week having a look at poor Reggie's grave, and they happened to come across your boy's. They're quite near each other, it seems."

Old Woodifield paused, but the boss made no reply. Only a quiver in his eyelids showed that he heard.

"The girls were delighted with the way the place is kept," piped the old voice. "Beautifully looked after. Couldn't be better if they were at home. You've not been across, have yer?"

"No, no!" For various reasons the boss had not been across.

"There's miles of it," quavered old Woodifield, "and it's all as neat as a garden. Flowers growing on all the graves. Nice broad paths." It was plain from his voice how much he liked a nice broad path.

The pause came again. Then the old man brightened wonderfully.

"D'you know what the hotel made the girls pay for a pot of jam?" he piped. "Ten francs! Robbery, I call it. It was a little pot, so Gertrude says, no bigger than a half-crown. And she hadn't taken more than a spoonful when they charged her ten francs. Gertrude brought the pot away with her to teach 'em a lesson. Quite right, too; it's trading on our feelings. They think because we're over there having a look round we're ready to pay anything. That's what it is." And he turned towards the door.

"Quite right, quite right!" cried the boss, though what was quite right he hadn't the least idea. He came round by his desk, followed the shuffling footsteps to the door, and saw the old fellow out. Woodifield was gone.

For a long moment the boss stayed, staring at nothing, while the gray-haired office messenger, watching him, dodged in and out of his cubby-hole like a dog that expects to be taken for a run. Then: "I'll see nobody for half an hour, Macey," said the boss. "Understand? Nobody at all."

"Very good, sir."

The door shut, the firm heavy steps recrossed the bright carpet, the fat body plumped down in the spring chair, and leaning forward, the boss covered his face with his hands. He wanted, he intended, he had arranged to weep. . . .

It had been a terrible shock to him when old Woodifield sprang that remark upon him about the boy's grave. It was exactly as though the earth had opened and he had seen the boy lying there with Woodifield's girls staring down at him. For it was strange. Although over six years had passed away, the boss never thought of the boy except as lying unchanged, unblemished in his uniform, asleep for ever. "My son!" groaned the boss. But no tears came yet. In the past, in the first months and even years after the boy's death, he had only to say those words to be overcome by such grief that nothing short of a violent fit of weeping could relieve him. Time, he had declared then, he had told everybody, could make no difference. Other men perhaps might recover, might live their loss down, but not he. How was it possible? His boy was an only son. Ever since his birth the boss had worked at building up this business for him; it had no other meaning if it was not for the boy. Life itself had come to have no other meaning. How on earth could he have slaved, denied himself, kept going all those years without the promise for ever before him of the boy's stepping into his shoes and carrying on where he left off?

And that promise had been so near being fulfilled. The boy had been in the office learning the ropes for a year before the war. Every morning they had started off together; they had come back by the same train. And what congratulations he had received as the boy's father! No wonder; he had taken to it marvelously. As to his popularity with the staff, every man jack of them down to old Macey couldn't make enough of the boy. And he wasn't in the least spoilt. No, he was just his bright natural self, with the right word for everybody, with that boyish look and his habit of saying, "Simply splendid!"

But that was all over and done with as though it never had been. The day had come when Macey had handed him the telegram that brought the whole place crashing about his head. "Deeply regret to inform you . . ." And he had left the office a broken man, with his life in ruins.

Six years ago, six years. . . . How quickly time passed! It might have happened yesterday. The boss took his hands from his face; he was puzzled. Something seemed to be wrong with him. He wasn't feeling as he wanted to feel. He decided to get up and have a look at the boy's photograph. But it wasn't a favorite photograph of his; the expression was unnatural. It was cold, even stern-looking. The boy had never looked like that.

At that moment the boss noticed that a fly had fallen into his broad inkpot, and was trying feebly but desperately to clamber out again. Help! help! said those struggling legs. But the sides of the inkpot were wet and slippery; it fell back again and began to swim. The boss took up a pen, picked the fly out of the ink, and shook it on to a piece of blotting-paper. For a fraction of a second it lay still on the dark patch that oozed round it. Then the front legs waved, took hold, and, pulling its small, sodden body up, it began the immense task of cleaning the ink from its wings. Over and under, over and under, went a leg along a wing as the stone goes over and under the scythe. Then there was a pause, while the fly, seeming to stand on the tips of its toes, tried to expand first one wing and then the other. It succeeded at last, and, sitting down, it began, like a minute cat, to clean its face. Now one could imagine that the little front legs rubbed against each other lightly, joyfully. The horrible danger was over; it had escaped; it was ready for life again.

But just then the boss had an idea. He plunged his pen back into the ink, leaned his thick wrist on the blotting-paper, and as the fly tried its wings down came a great heavy blot. What would it make of that? What indeed! The little beggar seemed absolutely cowed, stunned, and afraid to move because of what would happen next. But then, as if painfully, it dragged itself forward. The front legs waved, caught hold, and, more slowly this time, the task began from the beginning.

He's a plucky little devil, thought the boss, and he felt a real admiration for the fly's courage. That was the way to tackle things; that was the right spirit. Never say die; it was only a question of . . . But the fly had again finished its laborious task, and the boss had just time to refill his pen, to shake fair and square on the new-cleaned body yet another dark drop. What about it this time? A painful moment of suspense followed. But behold, the front legs were again waving; the boss felt a rush of relief. He leaned over the fly and said to it tenderly, "You artful little b . . ." And he actually had the brilliant notion of breathing on it to help the drying process. All the same, there was something timid and weak about its efforts now, and the boss decided that this time should be the last, as he dipped the pen deep into the inkpot.

It was. The last blot fell on the soaked blotting-paper, and the draggled fly lay in it and did not stir. The back legs were stuck to the body; the front legs were not to be seen.

"Come on," said the boss. "Look sharp!" And he stirred it with his pen—in vain. Nothing happened or was likely to happen. The fly was dead.

The boss lifted the corpse on the end of the paper-knife and flung it into the waste-paper basket. But such a grinding feeling of wretchedness seized him that he felt positively frightened. He started forward and pressed the bell for Macey.

"Bring me some fresh blotting-paper," he said sternly, "and look sharp about it." And while the old dog padded away he fell to wondering what it was he had been thinking about before. What was it? It was . . . He took out his handkerchief and passed it inside his collar. For the life of him he could not remember.

1922   1923

KATHERINE ANNE PORTER
1890–1980

Writing in her journal, Katherine Anne Porter observed in 1936 that the "constant exercise of memory seems to be the chief occupation of my mind, and all my experience seems to be simply memory, with continuity, marginal notes, constant revision and comparison of one thing with another." When "thousands of memories converge, harmonize, arrange themselves around a central ideal in a coherent form," she continued, "I write a story." Through the memories that are transformed in her twenty-seven works of short fiction and her one novel, *Ship of Fools* (1962), Porter established herself as a fine stylist who could convey what she called "the thumbprint"—the distinctive individuality—of characters "who populate all these enormous migrations, calamities; who fight wars and furnish life for the future; these beings without which, one by one, all the 'broad movements of history' could never take place." Curiously, however, despite her "constant exercise of memory," the episodes from the past that Porter recalled in interviews and autobiographical sketches contain contradictory evidence about her family's religion, her medical history, and her literary career.

Porter's parents and siblings lived in a small log house in Indian Creek, Texas, but before she was two years old her mother died and the family moved to Kyle, into the household of her paternal grandmother, Catherine Anne Porter. According to this strong-willed woman, the young Callie Russell Porter (as she was called then) was "precocious, nervous, rebellious, unteachable, and made life very uncomfortable" for everyone. Porter's biographer Joan Givner has described the house as disorderly and cramped; however, Porter's grandmother was a storyteller who, in Givner's words, "laid the foundation for Porter's literary gifts." After her grandmother died in 1901, the destitute family eventually settled in San Antonio. Although Porter disliked the convent schools she attended, she later boasted that already at this point in her life she was reading Shakespeare, Dante, and Homer as well as French poetry in translation. At sixteen, she ran away; married John Henry Koontz, a railroad clerk; and converted to her husband's religion, Catholicism. Eight years later, she left Koontz to try an acting career in the movies, and in 1915 they divorced.

For several years, Porter worked on newspapers in Chicago; Fort Worth, Texas; and Denver, Colorado; and she also traveled around the South singing ballads and acting in little theater groups. After a long bout with tuberculosis in 1915 and a transformative trip to Mexico City in 1919, Porter produced her first published story while living in Greenwich Village; "María Concepción" was published in *Century* magazine in 1922. Fascinated by Mexican folk art, Porter would return to Mexico in such stories as "The Mexican Trinity" (1921), "Flowering Judas" (1930), and "Hacienda" (1934), where she studied the "*chance* of salvation" in Mexican culture as well as the dissolution of that chance for expatriated Americans.

Although throughout the 1920s and 1930s Porter traveled, wrote book reviews for *The New Republic* and *The Nation,* and collected her stories in the volume *Flowering Judas* (1930), a succession of unsatisfying love affairs and brief marriages made her personal life tormenting. *Noon Wine* (1937), *Pale Horse, Pale Rider* (1939), and *The Leaning Tower, and Other Stories* (1944) firmly established her reputation as a cosmopolitan writer of brilliant short stories, one who drew on her travels throughout New England, Bermuda, New York, Mexico, and Europe. After several years living in Paris, Porter returned to the United States in 1936. When her novel *Ship of Fools* was published in 1962, it was an instant best seller. Soon after, Porter received the National Book Award and the Pulitzer Prize for her *Collected Stories* (1954). In 1970, she published an expanded version of her essays.

Influenced by Willa Cather, Katherine Mansfield, James Joyce, and Virginia Woolf, Porter produced fictionalized accounts of herself and her childhood memories of her grandmother in such stories as "The Source," "The Grave," "Old Mortality," and "The Jilting of Granny Weatherall." "The Jilting of Granny Weatherall" is less overtly autobiographical than those stories in which Porter figures as the character Miranda; however, it presents a strong-willed, older woman who has reared a large family. And, as in so much of her fiction, Porter manages here to convey how past and present events mingle in the consciousness of a character who experiences an epiphany that is linked to her confrontation with death.

The Jilting of Granny Weatherall

She flicked her wrist neatly out of Doctor Harry's pudgy careful fingers and pulled the sheet up to her chin. The brat ought to be in knee breeches. Doctoring around the country with spectacles on his nose! "Get along now, take your schoolbooks and go. There's nothing wrong with me."

Doctor Harry spread a warm paw like a cushion on her forehead where the forked green vein danced and made her eyelids twitch. "Now, now, be a good girl, and we'll have you up in no time."

"That's no way to speak to a woman nearly eighty years old just because she's down. I'd have you respect your elders, young man."

"Well, Missy, excuse me." Doctor Harry patted her cheek. "But I've got to warn you, haven't I? You're a marvel, but you must be careful or you're going to be good and sorry."

"Don't tell me what I'm going to be. I'm on my feet now, morally speaking. It's Cornelia. I had to go to bed to get rid of her."

Her bones felt loose, and floated around in her skin, and Doctor Harry floated like a balloon around the foot of the bed. He floated and pulled down his waistcoat and swung his glasses on a cord. "Well, stay where you are, it certainly can't hurt you."

"Get along and doctor your sick," said Granny Weatherall. "Leave a well woman alone. I'll call for you when I want you. . . . Where were you forty years ago when I pulled through milk-leg[1] and double pneumonia? You weren't even born. Don't let Cornelia lead you on," she shouted, because Doctor Harry appeared to float up to the ceiling and out. "I pay my own bills, and I don't throw my money away on nonsense!"

She meant to wave good-by, but it was too much trouble. Her eyes closed of themselves, it was like a dark curtain drawn around the bed. The pillow rose and floated under her, pleasant as a hammock in a light wind. She listened to the leaves rustling outside the window. No, somebody was swishing newspapers: no, Cornelia and Doctor Harry were whispering together. She leaped broad awake, thinking they whispered in her ear.

"She was never like this, never like this!" "Well, what can we expect?" "Yes, eighty years old. . . ."

Well, and what if she was? She still had ears. It was like Cornelia to whisper around doors. She always kept things secret in such a public way. She was always being tactful and kind. Cornelia was dutiful; that was the trouble with her. Dutiful and good: "So good and dutiful," said Granny, "that I'd like to spank her." She saw herself spanking Cornelia and making a fine job of it.

"What'd you say, Mother?"

Granny felt her face tying up in hard knots.

"Can't a body think, I'd like to know?"

"I thought you might want something."

"I do. I want a lot of things. First off, go away and don't whisper."

She lay and drowsed, hoping in her sleep that the children would keep out and let her rest a minute. It had been a long day. Not that she was tired. It was always pleasant to snatch a minute now and then. There was always so much to be done, let me see: tomorrow.

Tomorrow was far away and there was nothing to trouble about. Things were finished somehow when the time came; thank God there was always a little margin over for peace: then a person could spread out the plan of life and tuck in the edges orderly. It was good to have everything clean and folded away, with the hair brushes and tonic bottles sitting straight on the white embroidered linen: the day started without fuss and the pantry shelves laid out with rows of jelly glasses and brown jugs and white stone-china jars with blue whirligigs and words painted on them: coffee, tea, sugar, ginger, cinnamon, allspice: and the bronze clock with the lion on top nicely dusted off. The dust that lion could collect in twenty-four hours! The box in the attic with all those letters tied up, well, she'd have to go through that tomorrow.

---

1. Swelling of the legs after childbirth.

All those letters—George's letters and John's letters and her letters to them both—lying around for the children to find afterwards made her uneasy. Yes, that would be tomorrow's business. No use to let them know how silly she had been once.

While she was rummaging around she found death in her mind and it felt clammy and unfamiliar. She had spent so much time preparing for death there was no need for bringing it up again. Let it take care of itself now. When she was sixty she had felt very old, finished, and went around making farewell trips to see her children and grandchildren, with a secret in her mind: This is the very last of your mother, children! Then she made her will and came down with a long fever. That was all just a notion like a lot of other things, but it was lucky too, for she had once for all got over the idea of dying for a long time. Now she couldn't be worried. She hoped she had better sense now. Her father had lived to be one hundred and two years old and had drunk a noggin of strong hot toddy on his last birthday. He told the reporters it was his daily habit, and he owed his long life to that. He had made quite a scandal and was very pleased about it. She believed she'd just plague Cornelia a little.

"Cornelia! Cornelia!" No footsteps, but a sudden hand on her cheek. "Bless you, where have you been?"

"Here, Mother."

"Well, Cornelia, I want a noggin of hot toddy."

"Are you cold, darling?"

"I'm chilly, Cornelia. Lying in bed stops the circulation. I must have told you that a thousand times."

Well, she could just hear Cornelia telling her husband that Mother was getting a little childish and they'd have to humor her. The thing that most annoyed her was that Cornelia thought she was deaf, dumb, and blind. Little hasty glances and tiny gestures tossed around her and over her head saying, "Don't cross her, let her have her way, she's eighty years old," and she sitting there as if she lived in a thin glass cage. Sometimes Granny almost made up her mind to pack up and move back to her own house where nobody could remind her every minute that she was old. Wait, wait, Cornelia, till your own children whisper behind your back!

In her day she had kept a better house and had got more work done. She wasn't too old yet for Lydia to be driving eighty miles for advice when one of the children jumped the track, and Jimmy still dropped in and talked things over: "Now, Mammy, you've a good business head, I want to know what you think of this? . . ." Old. Cornelia couldn't change the furniture around without asking. Little things, little things! They had been so sweet when they were little. Granny wished the old days were back again with the children young and everything to be done over. It had been a hard pull, but not too much for her. When she thought of all the food she had cooked, and all the clothes she had cut and sewed, and all the gardens she had made— well, the children showed it. There they were, made out of her, and they couldn't get away from that. Sometimes she wanted to see John again and point to them and say, Well, I didn't do so badly, did I? But that would have to wait. That was for tomorrow. She used to think of him as a man, but now all the children were older than their father, and he would be a child beside her if she saw him now. It seemed strange and there was something wrong in the idea. Why, he couldn't possibly recognize her. She had fenced in a hundred acres once, digging the post holes herself and clamping the wires with just a negro boy to help. That changed a woman. John would be looking for a young woman with the peaked Spanish comb in her hair and the painted fan. Digging post holes changed a woman. Riding country roads in the winter when women had their babies was another thing: sitting up nights with sick horses and sick negroes and sick children and hardly ever losing one. John, I hardly ever lost one of them! John would see that in a minute, that would be something he could understand, she wouldn't have to explain anything!

It made her feel like rolling up her sleeves and putting the whole place to rights again. No matter if Cornelia was determined to be everywhere at once, there were a great many things left undone on this place. She would start tomorrow and do them. It was good to be strong enough for everything, even if all you made melted and changed and slipped under your hands, so that by the time you finished you almost forgot what you were working for. What was it I set out to do? she asked herself intently, but she could not remember. A fog rose over the valley, she saw it marching across the creek swallowing the trees and moving up the hill like an army of ghosts. Soon it would be at the near edge of the orchard, and then it was time to go in and light the lamps. Come in, children, don't stay out in the night air.

Lighting the lamps had been beautiful. The children huddled up to her and breathed like little calves waiting at the bars[2] in the twilight. Their eyes followed the match and watched the flame rise and settle in a blue curve, then they moved away from her. The lamp was lit, they didn't have to be scared and hang on to Mother any more. Never, never never more. God, for all my life I thank Thee. Without Thee, my God, I could never have done it. Hail, Mary, full of grace.[3]

I want you to pick all the fruit this year and see that nothing is wasted. There's always someone who can use it. Don't let good things rot for want of using. You waste life when you waste good food. Don't let things get lost. It's bitter to lose things. Now, don't let me get to thinking, not when I am tired and taking a little nap before supper....

The pillow rose about her shoulders and pressed against her heart and the memory was being squeezed out of it: oh, push down the pillow, somebody; it would smother her if she tried to hold it. Such a fresh breeze blowing and such a green day with no threats in it. But he had not come, just the same. What does a woman do when she has put on the white veil and set out the white cake for a man and he doesn't come? She tried to remember. No, I swear he never harmed me but in that. He never harmed me but in that . . . and what if he did? There was the day, the day, but a whirl of dark smoke rose and covered it, crept up and over into the bright field where everything was planted so carefully in orderly rows. That was hell, she knew hell when she saw it. For sixty years she had prayed against remembering him and against losing her soul in the deep pit of hell, and now the two things were mingled in one and the thought of him was a smoky cloud from hell that moved and crept in her head when she had just got rid of Doctor Harry and was trying to rest a minute. Wounded vanity, Ellen, said a sharp voice in the

---

2. Pasture gates.
3. The best-known Catholic prayer to the Virgin Mary; its repetition is the main component of saying the rosary.

top of her mind. Don't let your wounded vanity get the upper hand of you. Plenty of girls get jilted. You were jilted, weren't you? Then stand up to it. Her eyelids wavered and let in streamers of blue-gray light like tissue paper over her eyes. She must get up and pull the shades down or she'd never sleep. She was in bed again and the shades were not down. How could that happen? Better turn over, hide from the light, sleeping in the light gave you nightmares. "Mother, how do you feel now?" and a stinging wetness on her forehead. But I don't like having my face washed in cold water!

Hapsy? George? Lydia? Jimmy? No, Cornelia, and her features were swollen and full of little puddles. "They're coming, darling, they'll all be here soon." Go wash your face, child, you look funny.

Instead of obeying, Cornelia knelt down and put her head on the pillow. She seemed to be talking but there was no sound. "Well, are you tongue-tied? Whose birthday is it? Are you going to give a party?"

Cornelia's mouth moved urgently in strange shapes. "Don't do that, you bother me, daughter."

"Oh, no, Mother. Oh, no...."

Nonsense. It was strange about children. They disputed your every word. "No what, Cornelia?"

"Here's Doctor Harry."

"I won't see that boy again. He just left five minutes ago."

"That was this morning, Mother. It's night now. Here's the nurse."

"This is Doctor Harry, Mrs. Weatherall. I never saw you look so young and happy!"

"Ah, I'll never be young again—but I'd be happy if they'd let me lie in peace and get rested."

She thought she spoke up loudly, but no one answered. A warm weight on her forehead, a warm bracelet on her wrist, and a breeze went on whispering, trying to tell her something. A shuffle of leaves in the everlasting hand of God, He blew on them and they danced and rattled. "Mother, don't mind, we're going to give you a little hypodermic." "Look here, daughter, how do ants get in this bed? I saw sugar ants yesterday." Did you send for Hapsy too?

It was Hapsy she really wanted. She had to go a long way back through a great many rooms to find Hapsy standing with a baby on her arm. She seemed to herself to be Hapsy also, and the baby on Hapsy's arm was Hapsy and himself and herself, all at once, and there was no surprise in the meeting. Then Hapsy melted from within and turned flimsy as gray gauze and the baby was a gauzy shadow, and Hapsy came up close and said, "I thought you'd never come," and looked at her very searchingly and said, "You haven't changed a bit!" They leaned forward to kiss, when Cornelia began whispering from a long way off, "Oh, is there anything you want to tell me? Is there anything I can do for you?"

Yes, she had changed her mind after sixty years and she would like to see George. I want you to find George. Find him and be sure to tell him I forgot him. I want him to know I had my husband just the same and my children and my house like any other woman. A good house too and a good husband that I loved and fine children out of him. Better than I hoped for even. Tell him I was given back everything he took away and more. Oh, no, oh, God, no, there was something else besides the house and the man and the children. Oh, surely they were not all? What was it? Something not given back. . . . Her breath crowded down under her ribs and grew into a monstrous frightening shape with cutting edges; it bored up into her head, and the agony was unbelievable: Yes, John, get the Doctor now, no more talk, my time has come.

When this one was born it should be the last. The last. It should have been born first, for it was the one she had truly wanted. Everything came in good time. Nothing left out, left over. She was strong, in three days she would be as well as ever. Better. A woman needed milk in her to have her full health.

"Mother, do you hear me?"

"I've been telling you—"

"Mother, Father Connolly's here."

"I went to Holy Communion only last week. Tell him I'm not so sinful as all that."

"Father just wants to speak to you."

He could speak as much as he pleased. It was like him to drop in and inquire about her soul as if it were a teething baby, and then stay on for a cup of tea and a round of cards and gossip. He always had a funny story of some sort, usually about an Irishman who made his little mistakes and confessed them, and the point lay in some absurd thing he would blurt out in the confessional showing his struggles between native piety and original sin. Granny felt easy about her soul. Cornelia, where are your manners? Give Father Connolly a chair. She had her secret comfortable understanding with a few favorite saints who cleared a straight road to God for her. All as surely signed and sealed as the papers for the new Forty Acres. Forever . . . heirs and assigns forever. Since the day the wedding cake was not cut, but thrown out and wasted. The whole bottom dropped out of the world, and there she was blind and sweating with nothing under her feet and the walls falling away. His hand had caught her under the breast, she had not fallen, there was the freshly polished floor with the green rug on it, just as before. He had cursed like a sailor's parrot and said, "I'll kill him for you." Don't lay a hand on him, for my sake leave something to God. "Now, Ellen, you must believe what I tell you. . . ."

So there was nothing, nothing to worry about any more, except sometimes in the night one of the children screamed in a nightmare, and they both hustled out shaking and hunting for the matches and calling, "There, wait a minute, here we are!" John, get the doctor now, Hapsy's time has come. But there was Hapsy standing by the bed in a white cap. "Cornelia, tell Hapsy to take off her cap. I can't see her plain."

Her eyes opened very wide and the room stood out like a picture she had seen somewhere. Dark colors with the shadows rising towards the ceiling in long angles. The tall black dresser gleamed with nothing on it but John's picture, enlarged from a little one, with John's eyes very black when they should have been blue. You never saw him, so how do you know how he looked? But the man insisted the copy was perfect, it was very rich and handsome. For a picture, yes, but it's not my husband. The table by the bed had a linen cover and a candle and a crucifix. The light was blue from Cornelia's silk lampshades. No sort of light at all, just frippery. You had to live forty years with kerosene lamps to appreciate honest electricity. She felt very strong and she saw Doctor Harry with a rosy nimbus around him.

"You look like a saint, Doctor Harry, and I vow that's as near as you'll ever come to it."

"She's saying something."

"I heard you, Cornelia. What's all this carrying-on?"

"Father Connolly's saying—"

Cornelia's voice staggered and bumped like a cart in a bad road. It rounded corners and turned back again and arrived nowhere. Granny stepped up in the cart very lightly and reached for the reins, but a man sat beside her and she knew him by his hands, driving the cart. She did not look in his face, for she knew without seeing, but looked instead down the road where the trees leaned over and bowed to each other and a thousand birds were singing a Mass. She felt like singing too, but she put her hand in the bosom of her dress and pulled out a rosary, and Father Connolly murmured Latin in a very solemn voice and tickled her feet.[4] My God, will you stop that nonsense? I'm a married woman. What if he did run away and leave me to face the priest by myself? I found another a whole world better. I wouldn't have exchanged my husband for anybody except St. Michael himself,[5] and you may tell him that for me with a thank you in the bargain.

Light flashed on her closed eyelids, and a deep roaring shook her. Cornelia, is that lightning? I hear thunder. There's going to be a storm. Close all the windows. Call the children in. . . . "Mother, here we are, all of us." "Is that you, Hapsy?" "Oh, no, I'm Lydia. We drove as fast as we could." Their faces drifted above her, drifted away. The rosary fell out of her hands and Lydia put it back. Jimmy tried to help, their hands fumbled together, and Granny closed two fingers around Jimmy's thumb. Beads wouldn't do, it must be something alive. She was so amazed her thoughts ran round and round. So, my dear Lord, this is my death and I wasn't even thinking about it. My children have come to see me die. But I can't, it's not time. Oh, I always hated surprises. I wanted to give Cornelia the amethyst set—Cornelia, you're to have the amethyst set, but Hapsy's to wear it when she wants, and, Doctor Harry, do shut up. Nobody sent for you. Oh, my dear Lord, do wait a minute. I meant to do something about the Forty Acres, Jimmy doesn't need it and Lydia will later on, with that worthless husband of hers. I meant to finish the altar cloth and send six bottles of wine to Sister Borgia for her dyspepsia. I want to send six bottles of wine to Sister Borgia, Father Connolly, now don't let me forget.

Cornelia's voice made short turns and tilted over and crashed. "Oh, Mother, oh, Mother, oh, Mother. . . ."

"I'm not going, Cornelia. I'm taken by surprise. I can't go."

You'll see Hapsy again. What about her? "I thought you'd never come." Granny made a long journey outward, looking for Hapsy. What if I don't find her? What then? Her heart sank down and down, there was no bottom to death, she couldn't come to the end of it. The blue light from Cornelia's lampshade drew into a tiny point in the center of her brain, it flickered and winked like an eye, quietly it fluttered and dwindled. Granny lay curled down within herself, amazed and watchful, staring at the point of light that was

---

4. He is anointing her feet with oil as he administers last rites.
5. St. Michael the archangel is traditionally credited with rescuing the souls of the faithful, especially at death.

herself; her body was now only a deeper mass of shadow in an endless darkness and this darkness would curl around the light and swallow it up. God, give a sign!

For the second time there was no sign. Again no bridegroom and the priest in the house.[6] She could not remember any other sorrow because this grief wiped them all away. Oh, no, there's nothing more cruel than this—I'll never forgive it. She stretched herself with a deep breath and blew out the light.

1930

6. In Christ's parable of the wise and foolish virgins, salvation is compared to the arrival of a bridegroom (Matthew 25.1–13).

ZORA NEALE HURSTON
1891–1960

Zora Neale Hurston once claimed that she had escaped punishment when arrested for crossing against a red light by explaining to the authorities that "I had seen white folks pass on green and therefore assumed the red light was for me." Both the humor and the audacity of this incident were typical of her. Like a number of her female characters, Hurston was a strong woman, determined to "wrassle me up a future, or die trying," and she was encouraged by another strong woman, her mother, who advised her to "jump at de sun." Not only did Hurston profit from a mother who refused to "squinch" the girl's spirits, she also gained self-confidence from her hometown, the first incorporated, self-governing, all-black town in the United States. Her father, John Hurston, a Baptist preacher, was elected to three terms as the mayor of Eatonville, Florida. Although Eatonville later inspired Hurston to preserve in her creative and anthropological works the linguistic exuberance, the protective community, and the spiritual traditions of southern black culture, when her mother died the nine-year-old girl saw herself as a wanderer. Alienated by her father's remarriage, she worked at fourteen as a wardrobe girl in a traveling Gilbert and Sullivan troupe until—with one dress and one change of underwear—she enrolled at Morgan Academy in Baltimore. There, and later at Howard University in Washington, D.C., she supported herself in jobs ranging from manicurist to maid.

After 1925, when Hurston moved to New York City, she became a frequent guest at the writer Carl Van Vechten's parties, where many distinguished Harlem artists mingled with wealthy whites. She worked first as a secretary and then as a chauffeur and companion to the popular white novelist Fannie Hurst. Early writings at Howard had brought her to the attention of Alain Locke, whose anthology *The New Negro* (1925) hailed the coming of a "new soul" for black America. Hurston contributed a story to Locke's influential volume, and she also helped edit the quarterly *Fire!!*, which the authors Langston Hughes and Wallace Thurman created in 1926. In addition, a number of her plays and stories won literary awards. Although Hughes and Hurston quarreled in 1931 after they tried to collaborate on the play *Mule Bone*, during the two and a half years that Hurston actively participated in the Harlem Renaissance she was appreciated by Hughes and his friends as a flamboyant dresser and a great teller of folktales.

During her early New York years, Hurston also enrolled at Barnard College, where she studied anthropology on a scholarship. Barnard's only black student, she received her degree in 1928 after working with the noted anthropologist Franz Boas. One year earlier, however, she had already embarked on folklore research in her hometown of Eatonville, research sponsored by Mrs. R. Osgood Mason, a white patron who subsidized a number of other artists besides Hurston. Generous though Mrs. Mason was, both Hurston's biographer Robert Hemenway and the literary critic Mary Helen Washington have shown that Hurston was placed in a situation of childlike dependency on a "godmother" who prohibited the young writer and scholar from publishing both her fiction and her anthropological findings. In addition, Hurston had to write her patroness adulatory letters to get her to agree even to the purchase of a much-needed pair of shoes. In 1932, when Mrs. Mason claimed ownership of the material Hurston had collected, the relationship collapsed.

During the period in which she published her most important work, Hurston taught at Bethune-Cookman College (1934), enrolled at Columbia University on a fellowship for graduate study in anthropology (1935), did dramatic coaching for the Federal Theater Project in New York (1935–36), traveled in the Caribbean on Guggenheim fellowships (1936 and 1937), and worked as an editor for the Federal Writers' Project in Florida. In 1927, she was briefly married, to Herbert Sheen, a medical student she had met at Howard University, and, at the end of the 1930s, she was again briefly married to Albert Price, a younger man. Among the most successful of the works she composed in this time, her collection of folklore *Mules and Men* (1935) and her novel *Their Eyes Were Watching God* (1937), were reissued in paperback in 1978 after years of critical neglect.

These two books established Hurston as an important twentieth-century writer. *Mules and Men* was based on Hurston's anthropological studies in Florida and Louisiana. During her earlier travels, Hurston had participated in hoodoo initiation ceremonies in New Orleans, spending sixty-nine hours, on one occasion, nude on a conjurer's couch, with her navel touching a snakeskin. Hoodoo ceremonies and tall-tale sessions reappear, vividly dramatized, in *Mules and Men,* along with descriptions of such hoodoo rites as "Eulalia—Ritual to Get a Man." Through her recounting of initiation, cursing, and conjuring ceremonies, Hurston demonstrated that hoodoo was "a suppressed religion" and not "just superstition," even while she rescued black expression from ridicule by illustrating its metaphoric inventiveness. Similarly, *Their Eyes Were Watching God* celebrated the uniqueness of black cultural roots. Hurston's heroine, Janie Woods, is warned by her grandmother that "de nigger woman is de mule uh de world." Yet Janie manages to live the text of a sermon her grandmother had wanted to preach, "a great sermon about colored women sittin' on high." Through her heroine's progress, Hurston charted the evolution of African American culture from subjugation through identification with whites and, finally, into autonomous racial identity and self-celebration.

Hurston received remarkably good reviews not only for these two books but for her novel *Jonah's Gourd Vine* (1934); for her play *Singing Steel* (1934), which attempted to debunk "the current mammy-song-Jolson conception of the Southern Negro"; and for her autobiography *Dust Tracks on a Road* (1942); however, she came under attack throughout the 1940s and 1950s. As early as 1937, the celebrated black novelist Richard Wright had criticized *Their Eyes Were Watching God* as a "minstrel" novel intended to make white people laugh at blacks. Her former teacher and friend Alain Locke called *Moses, Man of the Mountain* (1939)—a novel that takes Moses out of the Judeo-Christian tradition by portraying him as an African—"caricature instead of portraiture." Such critics were also opposed to the conservative cast of the political and social essays Hurston published in predominantly white magazines. Yet the basis for Hurston's rejection of northern liberalism was clarified by a letter she wrote to the editor of a Florida newspaper, in which she attacked the Supreme Court school desegregation decision (1954), for Hurston argued that integration denied the value of already-existing black institutions. By the 1950s, like many other journalists, Hurston was publishing anticommunist essays. While Hemenway has attributed Hurston's growing conservatism to her inability "to admit that one could both celebrate Afro-American culture and deplore many of the conditions that helped shape it," Washington has associated Hurston's decision to ignore the brutal side of black experience with a refusal to submit to political pressures on black writers, who were expected throughout this period to protest against racism by portraying blacks as degraded or victimized.

In any case, by the time Hurston published her last novel, *Seraph on the Suwanee* (1948), she was beginning to experience the insecurity and pain that would characterize the rest of her life. Although she continued to teach and travel, she began to suffer from gallbladder attacks and an ulcer. In 1948, she was accused in New York of impairing the morals of a minor, a charge that was dismissed but that nevertheless horrified her. In 1950, she was working as a maid in Miami until the woman who employed her discovered an article Hurston had published in the *Saturday Evening Post*. Subsequent freelance writing earned her some savings, and she managed to spend several years in a house in Eau Gallie, Florida, during the early 1950s. But her fiction was being rejected by publishing houses, and in 1956, she was evicted after her landlord decided to sell the property. After a stroke in 1959, she entered the St. Lucie County Welfare Home. Three months later she died penniless, and her body was placed in an unmarked grave.

Like the short story "Sweat," the essay "How It Feels to Be Colored Me" multiplies definitions of blackness and whiteness, as the critic Barbara Johnson has brilliantly demonstrated. Both were published before Hurston attained national visibility as a folklorist and a novelist. Their vitality is typical and helps explain why the contemporary black writer Alice Walker—the editor of a Zora Neale Hurston reader—admires Hurston's vision of "racial health—a sense of black people as complete, complex, *undiminished* human beings."

Sweat

It was eleven o'clock of a Spring night in Florida. It was Sunday. Any other night, Delia Jones would have been in bed for two hours by this time. But she was a washwoman, and Monday morning meant a great deal to her. So she collected the soiled clothes on Saturday when she returned the clean things. Sunday night after church, she sorted them and put the white things to soak. It saved her almost a half day's start. A great hamper in the bedroom held the clothes that she brought home. It was so much neater than a number of bundles lying around.

She squatted in the kitchen floor beside the great pile of clothes, sorting them into small heaps according to color, and humming a song in a mournful key, but wondering through it all where Sykes, her husband, had gone with her horse and buckboard.[1]

Just then something long, round, limp and black fell upon her shoulders and slithered to the floor beside her. A great terror took hold of her. It softened her knees and dried her mouth so that it was a full minute before she could cry out or move. Then she saw that it was the big bull whip her husband liked to carry when he drove.

She lifted her eyes to the door and saw him standing there bent over with laughter at her fright. She screamed at him.

---

1. An open wagon.

"Sykes, what you throw dat whip on me like dat? You know it would skeer me—looks just like a snake, an' you knows how skeered Ah is of snakes."

"Course Ah knowed it! That's how come Ah done it." He slapped his leg with his hand and almost rolled on the ground in his mirth. "If you such a big fool dat you got to have a fit over a earth worm or a string, Ah don't keer how bad Ah skeer you."

"You aint got no business doing it. Gawd knows it's a sin. Some day Ah'm gointuh drop dead from some of yo' foolishness. 'Nother thing, where you been wid mah rig? Ah feeds dat pony. He aint fuh you to be drivin' wid no bull whip."

"You sho is one aggravatin' nigger woman!" he declared and stepped into the room. She resumed her work and did not answer him at once. "Ah done tole you time and again to keep them white folks' clothes outa dis house."

He picked up the whip and glared down at her. Delia went on with her work. She went out into the yard and returned with a galvanized tub and set it on the washbench. She saw that Sykes had kicked all of the clothes together again, and now stood in her way truculently, his whole manner hoping, *praying,* for an argument. But she walked calmly around him and commenced to re-sort the things.

"Next time, Ah'm gointer kick 'em outdoors," he threatened as he struck a match along the leg of his corduroy breeches.

Delia never looked up from her work, and her thin, stooped shoulders sagged further.

"Ah aint for no fuss t'night, Sykes. Ah just come from taking sacrament at the church house."

He snorted scornfully. "Yeah, you just come from de church house on a Sunday night, but heah you is gone to work on them clothes. You ain't nothing but a hypocrite. One of them amen-corner Christians—sing, whoop, and shout, then come home and wash white folks' clothes on the Sabbath."

He stepped roughly upon the whitest pile of things, kicking them helter-skelter as he crossed the room. His wife gave a little scream of dismay, and quickly gathered them together again.

"Sykes, you quit grindin' dirt into these clothes! How can Ah git through by Sat'day if Ah don't start on Sunday?"

"Ah don't keer if you never git through. Anyhow, Ah done promised Gawd and a couple of other men, Ah aint gointer have it in mah house. Don't gimme no lip neither, else Ah'll throw 'em out and put mah fist up side yo' head to boot."

Delia's habitual meekness seemed to slip from her shoulders like a blown scarf. She was on her feet; her poor little body, her bare knuckly hands bravely defying the strapping hulk before her.

"Looka heah, Sykes, you done gone too fur. Ah been married to you fur fifteen years, and Ah been takin' in washin' fur fifteen years. Sweat, sweat, sweat! Work and sweat, cry and sweat, pray and sweat!"

"What's that got to do with me?" he asked brutally.

"What's it got to do with you, Sykes? Mah tub of suds is filled yo' belly with vittles more times than yo' hands is filled it. Mah sweat is done paid for this house and Ah reckon Ah kin keep on sweatin' in it."

She seized the iron skillet from the stove and struck a defensive pose, which act surprised him greatly, coming from her. It cowed him and he did not strike her as he usually did.

"Naw you won't," she panted, "that ole snaggle-toothed black woman you runnin' with aint comin' heah to pile up on mah sweat and blood. You aint paid for nothin' on this place, and Ah'm gointer stay right heah till Ah'm toted out foot foremost."

"Well, you better quit gittin' me riled up, else they'll be totin' you out sooner than you expect. Ah'm so tired of you Ah don't know whut to do. Gawd! how Ah hates skinny wimmen!"

A little awed by this new Delia, he sidled out of the door and slammed the back gate after him. He did not say where he had gone, but she knew too well. She knew very well that he would not return until nearly daybreak also. Her work over, she went on to bed but not to sleep at once. Things had come to a pretty pass!

She lay awake, gazing upon the debris that cluttered their matrimonial trail. Not an image left standing along the way. Anything like flowers had long ago been drowned in the salty stream that had been pressed from her heart. Her tears, her sweat, her blood. She had brought love to the union and he had brought a longing after the flesh. Two months after the wedding, he had given her the first brutal beating. She had the memory of his numerous trips to Orlando[2] with all of his wages when he had returned to her penniless, even before the first year had passed. She was young and soft then, but now she thought of her knotty, muscled limbs, her harsh knuckly hands, and drew herself up into an unhappy little ball in the middle of the big feather bed. Too late now to hope for love, even if it were not Bertha it would be someone else. This case differed from the others only in that she was bolder than the others. Too late for everything except her little home. She had built it for her old days, and planted one by one the trees and flowers there. It was lovely to her, lovely.

Somehow, before sleep came, she found herself saying aloud: "Oh well, whatever goes over the Devil's back, is got to come under his belly. Sometime or ruther, Sykes, like everybody else, is gointer reap his sowing." After that she was able to build a spiritual earthworks[3] against her husband. His shells could no longer reach her. *Amen.* She went to sleep and slept until he announced his presence in bed by kicking her feet and rudely snatching the covers away.

"Gimme some kivah heah, an' git yo' damn foots over on yo' own side! Ah oughter mash you in yo' mouf fuh drawing dat skillet on me."

Delia went clear to the rail without answering him. A triumphant indifference to all that he was or did.

The week was as full of work for Delia as all other weeks, and Saturday found her behind her little pony, collecting and delivering clothes.

It was a hot, hot day near the end of July. The village men on Joe Clarke's porch even chewed cane listlessly. They did not hurl the caneknots as usual. They let them dribble over the edge of the porch. Even conversation had collapsed under the heat.

"Heah come Delia Jones," Jim Merchant said, as the shaggy pony came 'round the bend of the road toward them. The rusty buckboard was heaped with baskets of crisp, clean laundry.

---

2. City in Florida. 3. I.e., fortifications.

"Yep," Joe Lindsay agreed. "Hot or col', rain or shine, jes ez reg'lar ez de weeks roll roun' Delia carries 'em an' fetches 'em on Sat'day."

"She better if she wanter eat," said Moss. "Syke Jones aint wuth de shot an' powder hit would tek tuh kill 'em. Not to huh he aint."

"He sho' aint," Walter Thomas chimed in. "It's too bad, too, cause she wuz a right pritty lil trick when he got huh. Ah'd uh mah'ied huh mahseff if he hadnter beat me to it."

Delia nodded briefly at the men as she drove past.

"Too much knockin' will ruin any 'oman. He done beat huh 'nough tuh kill three women, let 'lone change they looks," said Elijah Moseley. "How Syke kin stommuck dat big black greasy Mogul he's layin' roun' wid, gits me. Ah swear dat eight-rock[4] couldn't kiss a sardine can Ah done thowed out de back do 'way las' yeah."

"Aw, she's fat, thass how come. He's allus been crazy 'bout fat women," put in Merchant. "He'd a' been tied up wid one long time ago if he could a' found one tuh have him. Did Ah tell yuh 'bout him come sidlin' roun' *mah* wife—bringin' her a basket uh peecans outa his yard fuh a present? Yessir, mah wife! She tol' him tuh take em right straight back home, cause Delia works so hard ovah dat wash tub she reckon everything on de place taste lak sweat an' soapsuds. Ah jus' wisht Ah'd a caught 'im 'roun' dere! Ah'd a' made his hips ketch on fiah down dat shell road."

"Ah know he done it, too. Ah sees 'im grinnin' at every 'oman dat passes," Walter Thomas said. "But even so, he useter eat some mighty big hunks uh humble pie tuh git dat lil' 'oman he got. She wuz ez pritty ez a speckled pup! Dat wuz fifteen yeahs ago. He useter be so skeered uh losin' huh, she could make him do some parts of a husband's duty. Dey never wuz de same in de mind."

"There oughter be a law about him," said Lindsay. "He aint fit tuh carry guts tuh a bear."

Clarke spoke for the first time. "Taint no law on earth dat kin make a man be decent if it aint in 'im. There's plenty men dat takes a wife lak dey do a joint uh sugar-cane. It's round, juicy an' sweet when dey gits it. But dey squeeze an' grind, squeeze an' grind an' wring tell dey wring every drop uh pleasure dat's in 'em out. When dey's satisfied dat dey is wrung dry, dey treats 'em jes lak dey do a cane-chew. Dey thows 'em away. Dey knows whut dey is doin' while dey is at it, an' hates theirselves fuh it but they keeps on hangin' after huh tell she's empty. Den dey hates huh fuh bein' a cane-chew an' in de way."

"We oughter take Syke an' dat stray 'oman uh his'n down in Lake Howell swamp an' lay on de rawhide till they cain't say Lawd a' mussy.' He allus wuz uh ovahbearin' niggah, but since dat white 'oman from up north done teached 'im how to run a automobile, he done got too biggety[5] to live—an' we oughter kill 'im." Old Man Anderson advised.

A grunt of approval went around the porch. But the heat was melting their civic virtue and Elijah Moseley began to bait Joe Clarke.

"Come on, Joe, git a melon outa dere an' slice it up for yo' customers. We'se all sufferin' wid de heat. De bear's done got *me!*"

---

4. Derogatory term for a very dark-skinned black person. "Mogul": i.e., big woman.

5. I.e., full of himself.

"Thass right, Joe, a watermelon is jes' whut Ah needs tuh cure de eppi-zudicks,"[6] Walter Thomas joined forces with Moseley. "Come on dere, Joe. We all is steady customers an' you aint set us up in a long time. Ah chooses dat long, bowlegged Floridy favorite."

"A god, an' be dough. You all gimme twenty cents and slice way," Clarke retorted. "Ah needs a col' slice m'self. Heah, everybody chip in. Ah'll lend y'll mah meat knife."

The money was quickly subscribed and the huge melon brought forth. At that moment, Sykes and Bertha arrived. A determined silence fell on the porch and the melon was put away again.

Merchant snapped down the blade of his jackknife and moved toward the store door.

"Come on in, Joe, an' gimme a slab uh sow belly an' uh pound uh coffee—almost fuhgot 'twas Sat'day. Got to git on home." Most of the men left also.

Just then Delia drove past on her way home, as Sykes was ordering magnificently for Bertha. It pleased him for Delia to see.

"Git whutsoever yo' heart desires, Honey. Wait a minute, Joe. Give huh two bottles uh strawberry soda-water, uh quart uh parched ground-peas, an' a block uh chewin' gum."

With all this they left the store, with Sykes reminding Bertha that this was his town and she could have it if she wanted it.

The men returned soon after they left, and held their watermelon feast.

"Where did Syke Jones git da 'oman from nohow?" Lindsay asked.

"Ovah Apopka. Guess dey musta been cleanin' out de town when she lef'. She don't look lak a thing but a hunk uh liver wid hair on it."

"Well, she sho' kin squall," Dave Carter contributed. "When she gits ready tuh laff, she jes' opens huh mouf an' latches it back tuh de las' notch. No ole grandpa alligator down in Lake Bell ain't got nothin' on huh."

Bertha had been in town three months now. Sykes was still paying her room rent at Della Lewis'—the only house in town that would have taken her in. Sykes took her frequently to Winter Park to "stomps."[7] He still assured her that he was the swellest man in the state.

"Sho' you kin have dat lil' ole house soon's Ah kin git dat 'oman outa dere. Everything b'longs tuh me an' you sho' kin have it. Ah sho' 'bominates uh skinny 'oman. Lawdy, you sho' is got one portly shape on you! You kin git *anything* you wants. Dis is mah town an' you sho' kin have it."

Delia's work-worn knees crawled over the earth in Gethsemane and up the rocks of Calvary[8] many, many times during these months. She avoided the villagers and meeting places in her efforts to be blind and deaf. But Bertha nullified this to a degree, by coming to Delia's house to call Sykes out to her at the gate.

Delia and Sykes fought all the time now with no peaceful interludes. They slept and ate in silence. Two or three times Delia had attempted a timid friendliness, but she was repulsed each time. It was plain that the breaches must remain agape.

---

6. I.e., "epizootic," used of a disease that attacks a large number of animals at once.
7. Jazz dances.

8. The hill where Jesus was crucified. Gethsemane is the garden where he was betrayed (Matthew 26.36–47).

The sun had burned July to August. The heat streamed down like a million hot arrows, smiting all things living upon the earth. Grass withered, leaves browned, snakes went blind in shedding and men and dogs went mad. Dog days!

Delia came home one day and found Sykes there before her. She wondered, but started to go on into the house without speaking, even though he was standing in the kitchen door and she must either stoop under his arm or ask him to move. He made no room for her. She noticed a soap box beside the steps, but paid no particular attention to it, knowing that he must have brought it there. As she was stooping to pass under his outstretched arm, he suddenly pushed her backward, laughingly.

"Look in de box dere Delia, Ah done brung yuh somethin'!"

She nearly fell upon the box in her stumbling, and when she saw what it held, she all but fainted outright.

"Syke! Syke, mah Gawd! You take dat rattlesnake 'way from heah! You *gottuh*. Oh, Jesus, have mussy!"

"Ah aint gut tuh do nuthin' uh de kin'—fact is Ah aint got tuh do nothin' but die. Taint no use uh you puttin' on airs makin' out lak you skeered uh dat snake—he's gointer stay right heah tell he die. He wouldn't bite me cause Ah knows how tuh handle 'im. Nohow he wouldn't risk breakin' out his fangs 'gin yo' skinny laigs."

"Naw, now Syke, don't keep dat thing 'roun' heah tuh skeer me tuh death. You knows Ah'm even feared uh earth worms. Thass de biggest snake Ah evah did see. Kill 'im Syke, please."

"Doan ast me tuh do nothin' fuh yuh. Goin' 'roun' tryin' tuh be so damn asterperious.[9] Naw, Ah aint gonna kill it. Ah think uh damn sight mo' uh him dan you! Dat's a nice snake an' anybody doan lak 'im kin jes' hit de grit."

The village soon heard that Sykes had the snake, and came to see and ask questions.

"How de hen-fire did you ketch dat six-foot rattler, Syke?" Thomas asked.

"He's full uh frogs so he caint hardly move, thass how Ah eased up on 'm. But Ah'm a snake charmer an' knows how tuh handle 'em. Shux, dat aint nothin'. Ah could ketch one eve'y day if Ah so wanted tuh."

"Whut he needs is a heavy hick'ry club leaned real heavy on his head. Dat's de bes 'way tuh charm a rattlesnake."

"Naw, Walt, y'll jes' don't understand dese diamon' backs lak Ah do," said Sykes in a superior tone of voice.

The village agreed with Walter, but the snake stayed on. His box remained by the kitchen door with its screen wire covering. Two or three days later it had digested its meal of frogs and literally came to life. It rattled at every movement in the kitchen or the yard. One day as Delia came down the kitchen steps she saw his chalky-white fangs curved like scimitars hung in the wire meshes. This time she did not run away with averted eyes as usual. She stood for a long time in the doorway in a red fury that grew bloodier for every second that she regarded the creature that was her torment.

That night she broached the subject as soon as Sykes sat down to the table.

"Syke, Ah wants you tuh take dat snake 'way fum heah. You done starved

---

9. I.e., obstreperous (unruly).

me an' Ah put up widcher, you done beat me an Ah took dat, but you done kilt all mah insides bringin' dat varmint heah."

Sykes poured out a saucer full of coffee and drank it deliberately before he answered her.

"A whole lot Ah keer 'bout how you feels inside uh out. Dat snake aint goin' no damn wheah till Ah gits ready fuh 'im tuh go. So fur as beatin' is concerned, yuh aint took near all dat you gointer take ef yuh stay 'roun' me."

Delia pushed back her plate and got up from the table. "Ah hates you, Sykes," she said calmly. "Ah hates you tuh de same degree dat Ah useter love yuh. Ah done took an' took till mah belly is full up tuh mah neck. Dat's de reason Ah got mah letter fum de church an' moved mah membership tuh Woodbridge—so Ah don't haftuh take no sacrament wid yuh. Ah don't wantuh see yuh 'roun' me atall. Lay 'roun' wid dat 'oman all yuh wants tuh, but gwan 'way fum me an' mah house. Ah hates yuh lak uh suck-egg dog."

Sykes almost let the huge wad of corn bread and collard greens he was chewing fall out of his mouth in amazement. He had a hard time whipping himself up to the proper fury to try to answer Delia.

"Well, Ah'm glad you does hate me. Ah'm sho' tiahed uh you hangin' ontuh me. Ah don't want yuh. Look at yuh stringey ole neck! Yo' rawbony laigs an' arms is enough tuh cut uh man tuh death. You looks jes' lak de devvul's doll-baby tuh me. You cain't hate me no worse dan Ah hates you. Ah been hatin' you fuh years."

"Yo' ole black hide don't look lak nothin' tuh me, but uh passle uh wrinkled up rubber, wid yo' big ole yeahs flappin' on each side lak uh paih uh buzzard wings. Don't think Ah'm gointuh be run 'way fum mah house neither. Ah'm goin' tuh de white folks bout you, mah young man, de very nex' time you lay yo' han's on me. Mah cup is done run ovah."

Delia said this with no signs of fear and Sykes departed from the house, threatening her, but made not the slightest move to carry out any of them.

That night he did not return at all, and the next day being Sunday, Delia was glad she did not have to quarrel before she hitched up her pony and drove the four miles to Woodbridge.

She stayed to the night service—"love feast"—which was very warm and full of spirit. In the emotional winds her domestic trials were borne far and wide so that she sang as she drove homeward,

> "Jurden water,[1] black an' col'
> Chills de body, not de soul
> An' Ah wantah cross Jurden in uh calm time."

She came from the barn to the kitchen door and stopped.

"Whut's de mattah, ol' satan, you aint kickin' up yo' racket?" She addressed the snake's box. Complete silence. She went on into the house with a new hope in its birth struggles. Perhaps her threat to go to the white folks had frightened Sykes! Perhaps he was sorry! Fifteen years of misery and suppression had brought Delia to the place where she would hope *anything* that looked towards a way over or through her wall of inhibitions.

---

1. The Jordan River, the eastern border of Israel, which the Israelites had to cross to reach the promised land (Joshua 3).

She felt in the match safe behind the stove at once for a match. There was only one there.

"Dat niggah wouldn't fetch nothin' heah tuh save his rotten neck, but he kin run thew whut Ah brings quick enough. Now he done toted off nigh on tuh haff uh box uh matches. He done had dat 'oman heah in mah house too."

Nobody but a woman could tell how she knew this even before she struck the match. But she did and it put her into a new fury.

Presently she brought in the tubs to put the white things to soak. This time she decided she need not bring the hamper out of the bedroom: she would go in there and do the sorting. She picked up the pot-bellied lamp and went in. The room was small and the hamper stood hard by the foot of the white iron bed. She could sit and reach through the bedposts—resting as she worked.

"Ah wantah cross Jurden in uh calm time." She was singing again. The mood of the "love feast" had returned. She threw back the lid of the basket almost gaily. Then, moved by both horror and terror, she sprang back toward the door. *There lay the snake in the basket!* He moved sluggishly at first, but even as she turned round and round, jumped up and down in an insanity of fear, he began to stir vigorously. She saw him pouring his awful beauty from the basket upon the bed, then she seized the lamp and ran as fast as she could to the kitchen. The wind from the open door blew out the light and the darkness added to her terror. She sped to the darkness of the yard, slamming the door after her before she thought to set down the lamp. She did not feel safe even on the ground, so she climbed up in the hay barn.

There for an hour or more she lay sprawled upon the hay a gibbering wreck.

Finally she grew quiet, and after that, coherent thought. With this, stalked through her a cold, bloody rage. Hours of this. A period of introspection, a space of retrospection, then a mixture of both. Out of this an awful calm.

"Well, Ah done de bes' Ah could. If things aint right, Gawd knows taint mah fault."

She went to sleep—a twitch sleep—and woke up to a faint gray sky. There was a loud hollow sound below. She peered out. Sykes was at the wood-pile, demolishing a wire-covered box.

He hurried to the kitchen door, but hung outside there some minutes before he entered, and stood some minutes more inside before he closed it after him.

The gray in the sky was spreading. Delia descended without fear now, and crouched beneath the low bedroom window. The drawn shade shut out the dawn, shut in the night. But the thin walls held back no sound.

"Dat ol' scratch is woke up now!" She mused at the tremendous whirr inside, which every woodsman knows, is one of the sound illusions. The rattler is a ventriloquist. His whirr sounds to the right, to the left, straight ahead, behind, close under foot—everywhere but where it is. Woe to him who guesses wrong unless he is prepared to hold up his end of the argument! Sometimes he strikes without rattling at all.

Inside, Sykes heard nothing until he knocked a pot lid off the stove while trying to reach the match safe in the dark. He had emptied his pockets at Bertha's.

The snake seemed to wake up under the stove and Sykes made a quick leap into the bedroom. In spite of the gin he had had, his head was clearing now.

"Mah Gawd!" he chattered, "ef Ah could on'y strack uh light!"

The rattling ceased for a moment as he stood paralyzed. He waited. It seemed that the snake waited also.

"Oh, fuh de light! Ah thought he'd be too sick"—Sykes was muttering to himself when the whirr began again, closer, right underfoot this time. Long before this, Sykes' ability to think had been flattened down to primitive instinct and he leaped—onto the bed.

Outside Delia heard a cry that might have come from a maddened chimpanzee, a stricken gorilla. All the terror, all the horror, all the rage that man possibly could express, without a recognizable human sound.

A tremendous stir inside there, another series of animal screams, the intermittent whirr of the reptile. The shade torn violently down from the window, letting in the red dawn, a huge brown hand seizing the window stick, great dull blows upon the wooden floor punctuating the gibberish of sound long after the rattle of the snake had abruptly subsided. All this Delia could see and hear from her place beneath the window, and it made her ill. She crept over to the four-o'clocks[2] and stretched herself on the cool earth to recover.

She lay there. "Delia, Delia!" She could hear Sykes calling in a most despairing tone as one who expected no answer. The sun crept on up, and he called. Delia could not move—her legs were gone flabby. She never moved, he called, and the sun kept rising.

"Mah Gawd!" She heard him moan, "Mah Gawd fum Heben!" She heard him stumbling about and got up from her flower-bed. The sun was growing warm. As she approached the door she heard him call out hopefully, "Delia, is dat you Ah heah?"

She saw him on his hands and knees as soon as she reached the door. He crept an inch or two toward her—all that he was able, and she saw his horribly swollen neck and his one open eye shining with hope. A surge of pity too strong to support bore her away from that eye that must, could not, fail to see the tubs. He would see the lamp. Orlando with its doctors was too far. She could scarcely reach the Chinaberry tree, where she waited in the growing heat while inside she knew the cold river was creeping up and up to extinguish that eye which must know by now that she knew.

1926

How It Feels to Be Colored Me

I am colored but I offer nothing in the way of extenuating circumstances except the fact that I am the only Negro in the United States whose grandfather on the mother's side was not an Indian chief.

I remember the very day that I became colored. Up to my thirteenth year I lived in the little Negro town of Eatonville, Florida. It is exclusively a col-

---

2. Tropical plants with tubular flowers.

ored town. The only white people I knew passed through the town going to or coming from Orlando. The native whites rode dusty horses, the Northern tourists chugged down the sandy village road in automobiles. The town knew the Southerners and never stopped cane chewing[1] when they passed. But the Northerners were something else again. They were peered at cautiously from behind curtains by the timid. The more venturesome would come out on the porch to watch them go past and got just as much pleasure out of the tourists as the tourists got out of the village.

The front porch might seem a daring place for the rest of the town, but it was a gallery seat for me. My favorite place was atop the gate-post. Proscenium box for a born first-nighter. Not only did I enjoy the show, but I didn't mind the actors knowing that I liked it. I usually spoke to them in passing. I'd wave at them and when they returned my salute, I would say something like this: "Howdy-do-well-I-thank-you-where-you-goin'?" Usually automobile or the horse paused at this, and after a queer exchange of compliments, I would probably "go a piece of the way" with them, as we say in farthest Florida. If one of my family happened to come to the front in time to see me, of course negotiations would be rudely broken off. But even so, it is clear that I was the first "welcome-to-our-state" Floridian, and I hope the Miami Chamber of Commerce will please take notice.

During this period, white people differed from colored to me only in that they rode through town and never lived there. They liked to hear me "speak pieces" and sing and wanted to see me dance the parse-me-la, and gave me generously of their small silver for doing these things, which seemed strange to me for I wanted to do them so much that I needed bribing to stop. Only they didn't know it. The colored people gave no dimes. They deplored any joyful tendencies in me, but I was their Zora nevertheless. I belonged to them, to the nearby hotels, to the county—everybody's Zora.

But changes came in the family when I was thirteen, and I was sent to school in Jacksonville. I left Eatonville, the town of the oleanders, as Zora. When I disembarked from the river-boat at Jacksonville, she was no more. It seemed that I had suffered a sea change. I was not Zora of Orange County any more, I was now a little colored girl. I found it out in certain ways. In my heart as well as in the mirror, I became a fast brown—warranted not to rub nor run.

But I am not tragically colored. There is no great sorrow dammed up in my soul, nor lurking behind my eyes. I do not mind at all. I do not belong to the sobbing school of Negrohood who hold that nature somehow has given them a lowdown dirty deal and whose feelings are all hurt about it. Even in the helter-skelter skirmish that is my life, I have seen that the world is to the strong regardless of a little pigmentation more or less. No, I do not weep at the world—I am too busy sharpening my oyster knife.[2]

Someone is always at my elbow reminding me that I am the granddaughter of slaves. It fails to register depression with me. Slavery is sixty years in the past. The operation was successful and the patient is doing well, thank you. The terrible struggle that made me an American out of a potential slave said "On the line!" The Reconstruction[3] said "Get set!"; and the generation before

---

1. Chewing sugarcane.
2. A reference to the popular expression "The world is my oyster."
3. The period immediately following the Civil War ("the terrible struggle") when federal control of the South brought the newly freed slaves economic, political, and educational opportunities.

said "Go!" I am off to a flying start and I must not halt in the stretch to look behind and weep. Slavery is the price I paid for civilization, and the choice was not with me. It is a bully adventure and worth all that I have paid through my ancestors for it. No one on earth ever had a greater chance for glory. The world to be won and nothing to be lost. It is thrilling to think—to know that for any act of mine, I shall get twice as much praise or twice as much blame. It is quite exciting to hold the center of the national stage, with the spectators not knowing whether to laugh or to weep.

The position of my white neighbor is much more difficult. No brown specter pulls up a chair beside me when I sit down to eat. No dark ghost thrusts its leg against mine in bed. The game of keeping what one has is never so exciting as the game of getting.

I do not always feel colored. Even now I often achieve the unconscious Zora of Eatonville before the Hegira.[4] I feel most colored when I am thrown against a sharp white background.

For instance at Barnard. "Beside the waters of the Hudson"[5] I feel my race. Among the thousand white persons, I am a dark rock surged upon, and overswept, but through it all, I remain myself. When covered by the waters, I am; and the ebb but reveals me again.

Sometimes it is the other way around. A white person is set down in our midst, but the contrast is just as sharp for me. For instance, when I sit in the drafty basement that is The New World Cabaret[6] with a white person, my color comes. We enter chatting about any little nothing that we have in common and are seated by the jazz waiters. In the abrupt way that jazz orchestras have, this one plunges into a number. It loses no time in circumlocutions, but gets right down to business. It constricts the thorax and splits the heart with its tempo and narcotic harmonies. This orchestra grows rambunctious, rears on its hind legs and attacks the tonal veil with primitive fury, rending it, clawing it until it breaks through to the jungle beyond. I follow those heathen—follow them exultingly. I dance wildly inside myself; I yell within, I whoop; I shake my assegai[7] above my head, I hurl it true to the mark *yeeeeooww!* I am in the jungle and living in the jungle way. My face is painted red and yellow and my body is painted blue. My pulse is throbbing like a war drum. I want to slaughter something—give pain, give death to what, I do not know. But the piece ends. The men of the orchestra wipe their lips and rest their fingers. I creep back slowly to the veneer we call civilization with the last tone and find the white friend sitting motionless in his seat, smoking calmly.

"Good music they have here," he remarks, drumming the table with his fingertips.

Music. The great blobs of purple and red emotion have not touched him. He has only heard what I felt. He is far away and I see him but dimly across the ocean and the continent that have fallen between us. He is so pale with his whiteness then and I am so colored.

At certain times I have no race, I am me. When I set my hat at a certain

---

4. The flight of Muhammed from Mecca in 622 C.E.; thus, any journey, especially one undertaken to escape from a dangerous or undesirable situation.
5. Compare Psalm 137: "By the rivers of Babylon," where the exiled Israelites wept. Barnard, a women's college, is part of Columbia University in New York City.
6. Harlem nightclub popular in the 1920s.
7. A light spear used by tribesmen in southern Africa.

angle and saunter down Seventh Avenue, Harlem City, feeling as snooty as the lions in front of the Forty-Second Street Library,[8] for instance. So far as my feelings are concerned, Peggy Hopkins Joyce on the Boule Mich[9] with her gorgeous raiment, stately carriage, knees knocking together in a most aristocratic manner, has nothing on me. The cosmic Zora emerges. I belong to no race nor time. I am the eternal feminine with its string of beads.

I have no separate feeling about being an American citizen and colored. I am merely a fragment of the Great Soul that surges within the boundaries. My country, right or wrong.[1]

Sometimes, I feel discriminated against, but it does not make me angry. It merely astonishes me. How can any deny themselves the pleasure of my company? It's beyond me.

But in the main, I feel like a brown bag of miscellany propped against a wall. Against a wall in company with other bags, white, red and yellow. Pour out the contents, and there is discovered a jumble of small things priceless and worthless. A first-water[2] diamond, an empty spool, bits of broken glass, lengths of string, a key to a door long since crumbled away, a rusty knifeblade, old shoes saved for a road that never was and never will be, a nail bent under the weight of things too heavy for any nail, a dried flower or two still a little fragrant. In your hand is the brown bag. On the ground before you is the jumble it held—so much like the jumble in the bags, could they be emptied, that all might be dumped in a single heap and the bags refilled without altering the content of any greatly. A bit of colored glass more or less would not matter. Perhaps that is how the Great Stuffer of Bags filled them in the first place—who knows?

1928

8. The main branch of the New York Public Library, on Fifth Avenue.
9. The Boulevard Saint-Michel, a street in Paris's student quarter. Joyce (1893–1957), an American performer, beauty, and fashion setter in the 1920s.

1. Cf. Carl Schurz, speaking on the floor of the U.S. Senate in 1872: "My country, right or wrong; if right, to be kept right; and if wrong, to be set right."
2. Of the purest luster.

NELLA LARSEN
1891–1964

When Carl Van Vechten included Nella Larsen in his project of photographing pioneering African American artists of the Harlem Renaissance, one of his portraits featured vertiginous patterns of black and white: not only does the novelist wear a polka-dot dress, but the background before which she stands displays a dizzying pattern of white against black lines that seem to box her in. Larsen's brooding eyes, which appear to gaze sideways and up beyond the space enclosed by the image, add to the sense of disquietude or distrust. Enigmatic and conflicted, this version of Van Vechten's Larsen forecasts the characterization of her heroines as mixed-up, illegitimate, neurotic, and morbid, attributes thought to typify what we now take to be a stereotype of the tragic mulatto: a creature doomed to self-destruction because of conflicting racial identifications. Early critics of Larsen often ignored the social dimension of her fiction or faulted her as a traitor to her race because they viewed her and her central characters as flawed by divided sexual, racial, or class allegiances, while even a number of later readers failed to appreciate the complexities she managed to negotiate in a self-defined identity decidedly neither white nor black but instead white and black.

The protagonist of Larsen's first novel, *Quicksand* (1928), is born of a Danish mother whose black husband abandoned her. Throughout the plot, Helga Crane finds herself alienated from segregated black and white societies in part because of what can be interpreted as her psychological ambivalence but in part, too, because of the stultifying limitations that segregation places on both black and white cultures. From the southern college Naxos (an anagram of [Anglo-] Saxon) to Chicago, New York, Copenhagen, and finally back to the deep South, her journey provides a succession of social masks that stifle or deform a personal sense of authenticity or integrity. It is impossible not to wonder how autobiographical this first novel might be, though information about Larsen's life is only now being recovered, most recently by her biographer George Hutchinson in *In Search of Nella Larsen: A Biography of the Color Line*. Not unlike Helga, Larsen was the child of a Danish immigrant and a West Indian father whose death was followed by the mother's second marriage, this time to a white man; she attended a school connected to Fisk University in Nashville, the Normal School for teacher training; moved to Copenhagen for a three-or four-year stay with relatives; and returned to the United States, where she trained as a nurse before marrying. After marriage she continued as a public health nurse and then went into librarianship.

But unlike Helga and her smugly ignorant mate, Larsen and her husband, a research physicist, became quite active in the cultural activities associated with the extraordinary productivity of black writers, painters, and philosophers in the Harlem Renaissance. Before meeting Van Vechten, she had cut her hours working as the head of the children's division in the 135th Street public library in order to devote more time to her writing. With Van Vechten's friendship, encouragement, and connections, as well as the financial support of her husband, she published both *Quicksand* and *Passing* (1929) with Alfred A. Knopf, and won a Guggenheim Fellowship in 1930. As its title indicates, Larsen's second (and last) novel also analyzes mixed race characters, in this case two women light-skinned enough to pass as white. With this book, Larsen contributed to a rich tradition of meditations on cross-racial impersonation that stretches from the fiction of James Weldon Johnson's *Autobiography of an Ex-Colored Man* (1912) and Fanny Hurst's *Imitation of Life* (1933) to the new journalism of John Howard Griffin's *Black Like Me* (1961) and the contemporary performance art of Adrian Piper.

Nella Larsen's life during the years from 1930 until her death in 1964 remains shrouded in obscurity, though some scholars believe she stopped writing and returned to nursing because of a charge of plagiarism leveled at a short story titled "Sanctuary." Others believe that a growing alienation from her husband led to deepening depression. Yet the plagiarism scandal is curious on two counts. First, "Sanctuary"—which George Hutchinson calls her "blackest" or "folksiest" story—is actually a transmutation of a white author's English tale: it was thought to be based on Sheila Kaye-Smith's "Mrs. Adis." Second, Larsen's plagiarism or copying was a problem that earlier fiction had brilliantly confronted—specifically, the dangerous allure of personal inauthenticity and mimicry for women of color who find themselves anxiously navigating the perplexities of what Kimberlé Crenshaw has called the "intersectionality" of racism and sexism. In any case, by the time of Larsen's divorce and then her death, the two novels that had made her famous were out of print. Rutgers University Press reprinted them in 1986 with an introduction by Deborah E. McDowell, and they quickly became touchstone texts for students interested in the evolution of fiction, of interracial relationships, and of the transnationalism as well as the hybridity of American culture between the two world wars.

Quicksand

> My old man died in a fine big house.
> My ma died in a shack.
> I wonder where I'm gonna die,
> Being neither white nor black?
> —Langston Hughes[1]

One

Helga Crane sat alone in her room, which at that hour, eight in the evening, was in soft gloom. Only a single reading lamp, dimmed by a great black and red shade, made a pool of light on the blue Chinese carpet, on the bright covers of the books which she had taken down from their long shelves, on the white pages of the opened one selected, on the shining brass bowl crowded with many-colored nasturtiums beside her on the low table, and on the oriental silk which covered the stool at her slim feet. It was a comfortable room, furnished with rare and intensely personal taste, flooded with Southern sun in the day, but shadowy just then with the drawn curtains and single shaded light. Large, too. So large that the spot where Helga sat was a small oasis in a desert of darkness. And eerily quiet. But that was what she liked after her taxing day's work, after the hard classes, in which she gave willingly and unsparingly of herself with no apparent return. She loved this tranquillity, this quiet, following the fret and strain of the long hours spent among fellow members of a carelessly unkind and gossiping faculty, following the strenuous rigidity of conduct required in this huge educational community of which she was an insignificant part. This was her rest, this intentional isolation for a short while in the evening, this little time in her own attractive room with her own books. To the rapping of other teachers, bearing fresh scandals, or seeking information, or other more concrete favors, or merely talk, at that hour Helga Crane never opened her door.

An observer would have thought her well fitted to that framing of light and shade. A slight girl of twenty-two years, with narrow, sloping shoulders and delicate, but well-turned, arms and legs, she had, none the less, an air of radiant, careless health. In vivid green and gold negligee and glistening brocaded mules, deep sunk in the big high-backed chair, against whose dark tapestry her sharply cut face, with skin like yellow satin, was distinctly outlined, she was—to use a hackneyed word—attractive. Black, very broad brows over soft, yet penetrating, dark eyes, and a pretty mouth, whose sensitive and sensuous lips had a slight questioning petulance and a tiny dissatisfied droop, were the features on which the observer's attention would fasten; though her nose was good, her ears delicately chiseled, and her curly blue-black hair plentiful and always straying in a little wayward, delightful way. Just then it was tumbled, falling unrestrained about her face and on to her shoulders.

Helga Crane tried not to think of her work and the school as she sat there.

---

1. The final lines of "Cross" (1925) by Hughes (1902–1967), an important writer of the Harlem Renaissance.

Ever since her arrival in Naxos[2] she had striven to keep these ends of the days from the intrusion of irritating thoughts and worries. Usually she was successful. But not this evening. Of the books which she had taken from their places she had decided on Marmaduke Pickthall's *Saïd the Fisherman*.[3] She wanted forgetfulness, complete mental relaxation, rest from thought of any kind. For the day had been more than usually crowded with distasteful encounters and stupid perversities. The sultry hot Southern spring had left her strangely tired, and a little unnerved. And annoying beyond all other happenings had been that affair of the noon period, now again thrusting itself on her already irritated mind.

She had counted on a few spare minutes in which to indulge in the sweet pleasure of a bath and a fresh, cool change of clothing. And instead her luncheon time had been shortened, as had that of everyone else, and immediately after the hurried gulping down of a heavy hot meal the hundreds of students and teachers had been herded into the sun-baked chapel to listen to the banal, the patronizing, and even the insulting remarks of one of the renowned white preachers of the state.

Helga shuddered a little as she recalled some of the statements made by that holy white man of God to the black folk sitting so respectfully before him.

This was, he had told them with obvious sectional pride, the finest school for Negroes anywhere in the country, north or south; in fact, it was better even than a great many schools for white children. And he had dared any Northerner to come south and after looking upon this great institution to say that the Southerner mistreated the Negro. And he had said that if all Negroes would only take a leaf out of the book of Naxos and conduct themselves in the manner of the Naxos products, there would be no race problem, because Naxos Negroes knew what was expected of them. They had good sense and they had good taste. They knew enough to stay in their places, and that, said the preacher, showed good taste. He spoke of his great admiration for the Negro race, no other race in so short a time had made so much progress, but he had urgently besought them to know when and where to stop. He hoped, he sincerely hoped, that they wouldn't become avaricious and grasping, thinking only of adding to their earthly goods, for that would be a sin in the sight of Almighty God. And then he had spoken of contentment, embellishing his words with scriptural quotations and pointing out to them that it was their duty to be satisfied in the estate to which they had been called, hewers of wood and drawers of water.[4] And then he had prayed.

Sitting there in her room, long hours after, Helga again felt a surge of hot anger and seething resentment. And again it subsided in amazement at the memory of the considerable applause which had greeted the speaker just before he had asked his God's blessing upon them.

The South. Naxos. *Negro* education. Suddenly she hated them all. Strange, too, for this was the thing which she had ardently desired to share in, to be

---

2. Also the name of the Greek island on which, according to classical mythology, Theseus abandoned Ariadne after she had betrayed her father and helped him find his way through the Minotaur's labyrinth.
3. Novel (1903) by Marmaduke William Pickthall (1875–1936), a British Islamic scholar, novelist, and journalist.
4. Moses tells the children of Israel that among those standing before God are "the stranger that is in thy camp, from the hewer of thy wood unto the drawer of thy water" (Deuteronomy 29.11).

a part of this monument to one man's genius and vision. She pinned a scrap of paper about the bulb under the lamp's shade, for, having discarded her book in the certainty that in such a mood even Saïd and his audacious villainy could not charm her, she wanted an even more soothing darkness. She wished it were vacation, so that she might get away for a time.

"No, forever!" she said aloud.

The minutes gathered into hours, but still she sat motionless, a disdainful smile or an angry frown passing now and then across her face. Somewhere in the room a little clock ticked time away. Somewhere outside, a whippoorwill wailed. Evening died. A sweet smell of early Southern flowers rushed in on a newly-risen breeze which suddenly parted the thin silk curtains at the opened windows. A slender, frail glass vase fell from the sill with a tingling crash, but Helga Crane did not shift her position. And the night grew cooler, and older.

At last she stirred, uncertainly, but with an overpowering desire for action of some sort. A second she hesitated, then rose abruptly and pressed the electric switch with determined firmness, flooding suddenly the shadowy room with a white glare of light. Next she made a quick nervous tour to the end of the long room, paused a moment before the old bow-legged secretary that held with almost articulate protest her school-teacher paraphernalia of drab books and papers. Frantically Helga Crane clutched at the lot and then flung them violently, scornfully toward the wastebasket. It received a part, allowing the rest to spill untidily over the floor. The girl smiled ironically, seeing in the mess a simile of her own earnest endeavor to inculcate knowledge into her indifferent classes.

Yes, it was like that; a few of the ideas which she tried to put into the minds behind those baffling ebony, bronze, and gold faces reached their destination. The others were left scattered about. And, like the gay, indifferent wastebasket, it wasn't their fault. No, it wasn't the fault of those minds back of the diverse colored faces. It was, rather, the fault of the method, the general idea behind the system. Like her own hurried shot at the basket, the aim was bad, the material drab and badly prepared for its purpose.

This great community, she thought, was no longer a school. It had grown into a machine. It was now a show place in the black belt, exemplification of the white man's magnanimity, refutation of the black man's inefficiency. Life had died out of it. It was, Helga decided, now only a big knife with cruelly sharp edges ruthlessly cutting all to a pattern, the white man's pattern. Teachers as well as students were subjected to the paring process, for it tolerated no innovations, no individualisms. Ideas it rejected, and looked with open hostility on one and all who had the temerity to offer a suggestion or ever so mildly express a disapproval. Enthusiasm, spontaneity, if not actually suppressed, were at least openly regretted as unladylike or ungentlemanly qualities. The place was smug and fat with self-satisfaction.

A peculiar characteristic trait, cold, slowly accumulated unreason in which all values were distorted or else ceased to exist, had with surprising ferociousness shaken the bulwarks of that self-restraint which was also, curiously, a part of her nature. And now that it had waned as quickly as it had risen, she smiled again, and this time the smile held a faint amusement, which wiped away the little hardness which had congealed her lovely face. Nevertheless she was soothed by the impetuous discharge of violence, and a sigh of relief came from her.

She said aloud, quietly, dispassionately: "Well, I'm through with that," and, shutting off the hard, bright blaze of the overhead lights, went back to her chair and settled down with an odd gesture of sudden soft collapse, like a person who had been for months fighting the devil and then unexpectedly had turned round and agreed to do his bidding.

Helga Crane had taught in Naxos for almost two years, at first with the keen joy and zest of those immature people who have dreamed dreams of doing good to their fellow men. But gradually this zest was blotted out, giving place to a deep hatred for the trivial hypocrisies and careless cruelties which were, unintentionally perhaps, a part of the Naxos policy of uplift.[5] Yet she had continued to try not only to teach, but to befriend those happy singing children, whose charm and distinctiveness the school was so surely ready to destroy. Instinctively Helga was aware that their smiling submissiveness covered many poignant heartaches and perhaps much secret contempt for their instructors. But she was powerless. In Naxos between teacher and student, between condescending authority and smoldering resentment, the gulf was too great, and too few had tried to cross it. It couldn't be spanned by one sympathetic teacher. It was useless to offer her atom of friendship, which under the existing conditions was neither wanted nor understood.

Nor was the general atmosphere of Naxos, its air of self-rightness and intolerant dislike of difference, the best of mediums for a pretty, solitary girl with no family connections. Helga's essentially likable and charming personality was smudged out. She had felt this for a long time. Now she faced with determination that other truth which she had refused to formulate in her thoughts, the fact that she was utterly unfitted for teaching, even for mere existence, in Naxos. She was a failure here. She had, she conceded now, been silly, obstinate, to persist for so long. A failure. Therefore, no need, no use, to stay longer. Suddenly she longed for immediate departure. How good, she thought, to go now, tonight!—and frowned to remember how impossible that would be. "The dignitaries," she said, "are not in their offices, and there will be yards and yards of red tape to unwind, gigantic, impressive spools of it."

And there was James Vayle to be told, and much-needed money to be got. James, she decided, had better be told at once. She looked at the clock racing indifferently on. No, too late. It would have to be tomorrow.

She hated to admit that money was the most serious difficulty. Knowing full well that it was important, she nevertheless rebelled at the unalterable truth that it could influence her actions, block her desires. A sordid necessity to be grappled with. With Helga it was almost a superstition that to concede to money its importance magnified its power. Still, in spite of her reluctance and distaste, her financial situation would have to be faced, and plans made, if she were to get away from Naxos with anything like the haste which she now so ardently desired.

Most of her earnings had gone into clothes, into books, into the furnishings of the room which held her. All her life Helga Crane had loved and longed for nice things. Indeed, it was this craving, this urge for beauty which

---

5. The policy dedicated to improving the condition of African Americans through education, which would lead to economic self-sufficiency; its most notable advocate at the turn of the century was Booker T. Washington.

had helped to bring her into disfavor in Naxos—"pride" and "vanity" her detractors called it.

The sum owing to her by the school would just a little more than buy her ticket back to Chicago. It was too near the end of the school term to hope to get teaching-work anywhere. If she couldn't find something else, she would have to ask Uncle Peter for a loan. Uncle Peter was, she knew, the one relative who thought kindly, or even calmly, of her. Her step-father, her step-brothers and sisters, and the numerous cousins, aunts, and other uncles could not be even remotely considered. She laughed a little, scornfully, reflecting that the antagonism was mutual, or, perhaps, just a trifle keener on her side than on theirs. They feared and hated her. She pitied and despised them. Uncle Peter was different. In his contemptuous way he was fond of her. Her beautiful, unhappy mother had been his favorite sister. Even so, Helga Crane knew that he would be more likely to help her because her need would strengthen his oft-repeated conviction that because of her Negro blood she would never amount to anything, than from motives of affection or loving memory. This knowledge, in its present aspect of truth, irritated her to an astonishing degree. She regarded Uncle Peter almost vindictively, although always he had been extraordinarily generous with her and she fully intended to ask his assistance. "A beggar," she thought ruefully, "cannot expect to choose."

Returning to James Vayle, her thoughts took on the frigidity of complete determination. Her resolution to end her stay in Naxos would of course inevitably end her engagement to James. She had been engaged to him since her first semester there, when both had been new workers, and both were lonely. Together they had discussed their work and problems in adjustment, and had drifted into a closer relationship. Bitterly she reflected that James had speedily and with entire ease fitted into his niche. He was now completely "naturalized," as they used laughingly to call it. Helga, on the other hand, had never quite achieved the unmistakable Naxos mold, would never achieve it, in spite of much trying. She could neither conform, nor be happy in her unconformity. This she saw clearly now, and with cold anger at all the past futile effort. What a waste! How pathetically she had struggled in those first months and with what small success. A lack somewhere. Always she had considered it a lack of understanding on the part of the community, but in her present new revolt she realized that the fault had been partly hers. A lack of acquiescence. She hadn't really wanted to be made over. This thought bred a sense of shame, a feeling of ironical disillusion. Evidently there were parts of her she couldn't be proud of. The revealing picture of her past striving was too humiliating. It was as if she had deliberately planned to steal an ugly thing, for which she had no desire, and had been found out.

Ironically she visualized the discomfort of James Vayle. How her maladjustment had bothered him! She had a faint notion that it was behind his ready assent to her suggestion anent a longer engagement than, originally, they had planned. He was liked and approved of in Naxos and loathed the idea that the girl he was to marry couldn't manage to win liking and approval also. Instinctively Helga had known that secretly he had placed the blame upon her. How right he had been! Certainly his attitude had gradually changed, though he still gave her his attentions. Naxos pleased him and he had become content with life as it was lived there. No longer lonely, he was now one of the community and so beyond the need or the desire to discuss its affairs and its failings with an outsider. She was, she knew, in a queer indefinite way, a disturbing factor. She knew too that a something held him, a something against which he was powerless. The idea that she was in but one nameless way necessary to him filled her with a sensation amounting almost to shame. And yet his mute helplessness against that ancient appeal by which she held him pleased her and fed her vanity—gave her a feeling of power. At the same time she shrank away from it, subtly aware of possibilities she herself couldn't predict.

Helga's own feelings defeated inquiry, but honestly confronted, all pretense brushed aside, the dominant one, she suspected, was relief. At least, she felt no regret that tomorrow would mark the end of any claim she had upon him. The surety that the meeting would be a clash annoyed her, for she had no talent for quarreling—when possible she preferred to flee. That was all.

The family of James Vayle, in near-by Atlanta, would be glad. They had never liked the engagement, had never liked Helga Crane. Her own lack of family disconcerted them. No family. That was the crux of the whole matter. For Helga, it accounted for everything, her failure here in Naxos, her former loneliness in Nashville. It even accounted for her engagement to James. Negro society, she had learned, was as complicated, and as rigid in its ramifications as the highest strata of white society. If you couldn't prove your ancestry and connections, you were tolerated, but you didn't "belong." You could be queer, or even attractive, or bad, or brilliant, or even love beauty and such nonsense if you were a Rankin, or a Leslie, or a Scoville; in other words, if you had a family. But if you were just plain Helga Crane, of whom nobody had ever heard, it was presumptuous of you to be anything but inconspicuous and conformable.

To relinquish James Vayle would most certainly be social suicide, for the Vayles were people of consequence. The fact that they were a "first family" had been one of James's attractions for the obscure Helga. She had wanted social background, but—she had not imagined that it could be so stuffy.

She made a quick movement of impatience and stood up. As she did so, the room whirled about her in an impish, hateful way. Familiar objects seemed suddenly unhappily distant. Faintness closed about her like a vise. She swayed, her small, slender hands gripping the chair arms for support. In a moment the faintness receded, leaving in its wake a sharp resentment at the trick which her strained nerves had played upon her. And after a moment's rest she got hurriedly into bed, leaving her room disorderly for the first time.

Books and papers scattered about the floor, fragile stockings and underthings and the startling green and gold negligee dripping about on chairs and stool, met the encounter of the amazed eyes of the girl who came in the morning to awaken Helga Crane.

Two

She woke in the morning unrefreshed and with that feeling of half-terrified apprehension peculiar to Christmas and birthday mornings. A long moment she lay puzzling under the sun streaming in a golden flow through the yellow curtains. Then her mind returned to the night before. She had decided to leave Naxos. That was it.

Sharply she began to probe her decision. Reviewing the situation carefully, frankly, she felt no wish to change her resolution. Except—that it would be inconvenient. Much as she wanted to shake the dust of the place from her feet forever, she realized that there would be difficulties. Red tape. James Vayle. Money, Other work. Regretfully she was forced to acknowledge that it would be vastly better to wait until June, the close of the school year. Not so long, really. Half of March, April, May, some of June. Surely she could endure for that much longer conditions which she had borne for nearly two years. By an effort of will, her will, it could be done.

But this reflection, sensible, expedient, though it was, did not reconcile her. To remain seemed too hard. Could she do it? Was it possible in the present rebellious state of her feelings? The uneasy sense of being engaged with some formidable antagonist, nameless and un-understood, startled her. It wasn't, she was suddenly aware, merely the school and its ways and its decorous stupid people that oppressed her. There was something else, some other more ruthless force, a quality within herself, which was frustrating her, had always frustrated her, kept her from getting the things she had wanted. Still wanted.

But just what did she want? Barring a desire for material security, gracious ways of living, a profusion of lovely clothes, and a goodly share of envious admiration, Helga Crane didn't know, couldn't tell. But there was, she knew, something else. Happiness, she supposed. Whatever that might be. What, exactly, she wondered, was happiness. Very positively she wanted it. Yet her conception of it had no tangibility. She couldn't define it, isolate it, and contemplate it as she could some other abstract things. Hatred, for instance. Or kindness.

The strident ringing of a bell somewhere in the building brought back the fierce resentment of the night. It crystallized her wavering determination.

From long habit her biscuit-coloured feet had slipped mechanically out from under the covers at the bell's first unkind jangle. Leisurely she drew them back and her cold anger vanished as she decided that, now, it didn't at all matter if she failed to appear at the monotonous distasteful breakfast which was provided for her by the school as part of her wages.

In the corridor beyond her door was a medley of noises incident to the rising and preparing for the day at the same hour of many schoolgirls— foolish giggling, indistinguishable snatches of merry conversation, distant gurgle of running water, patter of slippered feet, low-pitched singing, good-natured admonitions to hurry, slamming of doors, clatter of various unnamable articles, and—suddenly—calamitous silence.

Helga ducked her head under the covers in the vain attempt to shut out what she knew would fill the pregnant silence—the sharp sarcastic voice of the dormitory matron. It came.

"Well! Even if every last one of you did come from homes where you weren't taught any manners, you might at least try to pretend that you're capable of learning some here, now that you have the opportunity. Who slammed the shower-baths door?"

Silence.

"Well, you needn't trouble to answer. It's rude, as all of you know. But it's just as well, because none of you can tell the truth. Now hurry up. Don't let me hear of a single one of you being late for breakfast. If I do there'll be extra work for everybody on Saturday. And *please* at least try to act like ladies and not like savages from the backwoods."

On her side of the door, Helga was wondering if it had ever occurred to the lean and desiccated Miss MacGooden that most of her charges had actually come from the backwoods. Quite recently too. Miss MacGooden, humorless, prim, ugly, with a face like dried leather, prided herself on being a "lady" from one of the best families—an uncle had been a congressman in the period of the Reconstruction.[6] She was therefore, Helga Crane reflected, perhaps unable to perceive that the inducement to act like a lady, her own acrimonious example, was slight, if not altogether negative. And thinking on Miss MacGooden's "ladyness," Helga grinned a little as she remembered that one's expressed reason for never having married, or intending to marry. There were, so she had been given to understand, things in the matrimonial state that were of necessity entirely too repulsive for a lady of delicate and sensitive nature to submit to.

Soon the forcibly shut-off noises began to be heard again, as the evidently vanishing image of Miss MacGooden evaporated from the short memories of the ladies-in-making. Preparations for the intake of the day's quota of learning went on again. Almost naturally.

"So much for that!" said Helga, getting herself out of bed.

She walked to the window and stood looking down into the great quadrangle below, at the multitude of students streaming from the six big dormitories which, two each, flanked three of its sides, and assembling into neat phalanxes preparatory to marching in military order to the sorry breakfast in Jones Hall on the fourth side. Here and there a male member of the faculty, important and resplendent in the regalia of an army officer, would pause in his prancing or strutting, to jerk a negligent or offending student into the proper attitude or place. The massed phalanxes increased in size and number, blotting out pavements, bare earth, and grass. And about it all was a depressing silence, a sullenness almost, until with a horrible abruptness the waiting band blared into "The Star Spangled Banner." The goose-step began. Left, right. Left, right. Forward! March! The automatons moved. The squares disintegrated into fours. Into twos. Disappeared into the gaping doors of Jones Hall. After the last pair of marchers had entered, the huge doors were closed. A few unlucky late-comers, apparently already discouraged, tugged half-heartedly at the knobs, and finding, as they had evidently expected, that they were indeed barred out, turned resignedly away.

Helga Crane turned away from the window, a shadow dimming the pale amber loveliness of her face. Seven o'clock it was now. At twelve those children who by some accident had been a little minute or two late would have their first meal after five hours of work and so-called education. Discipline, it was called.

There came a light knocking on her door.

"Come in," invited Helga unenthusiastically. The door opened to admit

---

6. Between 1868 and 1901, two black senators and twenty-two black representatives from eight southern states served in the U.S. Congress; Reconstruction (the period immediately following the Civil War, when federal control of the South the newly freed slaves economic, political, and educational opportunities) ended in 1877.

Margaret Creighton, another teacher in the English department and to Helga the most congenial member of the whole Naxos faculty. Margaret, she felt, appreciated her.

Seeing Helga still in night robe seated on the bedside in a mass of cushions, idly dangling a mule across bare toes like one with all the time in the world before her, she exclaimed in dismay: "Helga Crane, do you know what time it is? Why, it's long after half past seven. The students—"

"Yes, I know," said Helga defiantly, "the students are coming out from breakfast. Well, let them. I, for one, wish that there was some way that they could forever stay out from the poisonous stuff thrown at them, literally thrown at them, Margaret Creighton, for food. Poor things."

Margaret laughed. "That's just ridiculous sentiment, Helga, and you know it. But you haven't had any breakfast, yourself. Jim Vayle asked if you were sick. Of course nobody knew. You never tell anybody anything about yourself. I said I'd look in on you."

"Thanks awfully," Helga responded, indifferently. She was watching the sunlight dissolve from thick orange into pale yellow. Slowly it crept across the room, wiping out in its path the morning shadows. She wasn't interested in what the other was saying.

"If you don't hurry, you'll be late to your first class. Can I help you?" Margaret offered uncertainly. She was a little afraid of Helga. Nearly everyone was.

"No. Thanks all the same." Then quickly in another, warmer tone: "I do mean it. Thanks, a thousand times, Margaret. I'm really awfully grateful, but—you see, it's like this, I'm not going to be late to my class. I'm not going to be there at all."

The visiting girl, standing in relief, like old walnut against the buff-colored wall, darted a quick glance at Helga. Plainly she was curious. But she only said formally: "Oh, then you *are* sick." For something there was about Helga which discouraged questionings.

No, Helga wasn't sick. Not physically. She was merely disgusted. Fed up with Naxos. If that could be called sickness. The truth was that she had made up her mind to leave. That very day. She could no longer abide being connected with a place of shame, lies, hypocrisy, cruelty, servility, and snobbishness. "It ought," she concluded, "to be shut down by law."

"But, Helga, you can't go now. Not in the middle of the term." The kindly Margaret was distressed.

"But I can. And I am. Today."

"They'll never let you," prophesied Margaret.

"*They* can't stop me. Trains leave here for civilization every day. All that's needed is money," Helga pointed out.

"Yes, of course. Everybody knows that. What I mean is that you'll only hurt yourself in your profession. They won't give you a reference if you jump up and leave like this now. At this time of the year. You'll be put on the black list. And you'll find it hard to get another teaching-job. Naxos has enormous influence in the South. Better wait till school closes."

"Heaven forbid," answered Helga fervently, "that I should ever again want work anywhere in the South! I hate it." And fell silent, wondering for the hundredth time just what form of vanity it was that had induced an intelligent girl like Margaret Creighton to turn what was probably nice live crinkly hair, perfectly suited to her smooth dark skin and agreeable round features, into a dead straight, greasy, ugly mass.

Looking up from her watch, Margaret said: "Well, I've really got to run, or I'll be late myself. And since I'm staying—Better think it over, Helga. There's no place like Naxos, you know. Pretty good salaries, decent rooms, plenty of men, and all that. Ta-ta." The door slid to behind her.

But in another moment it opened. She was back. "I do wish you'd stay. It's nice having you here, Helga. We all think so. Even the dead ones. We need a few decorations to brighten our sad lives." And again she was gone.

Helga was unmoved. She was no longer concerned with what anyone in Naxos might think of her, for she was now in love with the piquancy of leaving. Automatically her fingers adjusted the Chinese-looking pillows on the low couch that served for her bed. Her mind was busy with plans for departure. Packing, money, trains, and—could she get a berth?

Three

On one side of the long, white, hot sand road that split the flat green, there was a little shade, for it was bordered with trees. Helga Crane walked there so that the sun could not so easily get at her. As she went slowly across the empty campus she was conscious of a vague tenderness for the scene spread out before her. It was so incredibly lovely, so appealing, and so facile. The trees in their spring beauty sent through her restive mind a sharp thrill of pleasure. Seductive, charming, and beckoning as cities were, they had not this easy unhuman loveliness. The trees, she thought, on city avenues and boulevards, in city parks and gardens, were tamed, held prisoners in a surrounding maze of human beings. Here they were free. It was human beings who were prisoners. It was too bad. In the midst of all this radiant life. They weren't, she knew, even conscious of its presence. Perhaps there was too much of it, and therefore it was less than nothing.

In response to her insistent demand she had been told that Dr. Anderson could give her twenty minutes at eleven o'clock. Well, she supposed that she could say all that she had to say in twenty minutes, though she resented being limited. Twenty minutes. In Naxos, she was as unimportant as that.

He was a new man, this principal, for whom Helga remembered feeling unaccountably sorry, when last September he had first been appointed to Naxos as its head. For some reason she had liked him, although she had seen little of him; he was so frequently away on publicity and money-raising tours. And as yet he had made but few and slight changes in the running of the school. Now she was a little irritated at finding herself wondering just how she was going to tell him of her decision. What did it matter to him? Why should she mind if it did? But there returned to her that indistinct sense of sympathy for the remote silent man with the tired gray eyes, and she wondered again by what fluke of fate such a man, apparently a humane and understanding person, had chanced into the command of this cruel educational machine. Suddenly, her own resolve loomed as an almost direct unkindness. This increased her annoyance and discomfort. A sense of defeat, of being cheated of justification, closed down on her. Absurd!

She arrived at the administration building in a mild rage, as unreasonable as it was futile, but once inside she had a sudden attack of nerves at the prospect of traversing that great outer room which was the workplace of some twenty odd people. This was a disease from which Helga had suffered at intervals all her life, and it was a point of honor, almost, with her never to give way to it. So, instead of turning away, as she felt inclined, she walked on, outwardly indifferent. Half-way down the long aisle which divided the room, the principal's secretary, a huge black man, surged toward her.

"Good-morning, Miss Crane, Dr. Anderson will see you in a few moments. Sit down right here."

She felt the inquiry in the shuttered eyes. For some reason this dissipated her self-consciousness and restored her poise. Thanking him, she seated herself, really careless now of the glances of the stenographers, bookkeepers, clerks. Their curiosity and slightly veiled hostility no longer touched her. Her coming departure had released her from the need for conciliation which had irked her for so long. It was pleasant to Helga Crane to be able to sit calmly looking out of the window on to the smooth lawn, where a few leaves quite prematurely fallen dotted the grass, for once uncaring whether the frock which she wore roused disapproval or envy.

Turning from the window, her gaze wandered contemptuously over the dull attire of the women workers. Drab colors, mostly navy blue, black, brown; unrelieved, save for a scrap of white or tan about the hands and necks. Fragments of a speech made by the dean of women floated through her thoughts—"Bright colors are vulgar"—"Black, gray, brown, and navy blue are the most becoming colors for colored people"—"Dark-complected people shouldn't wear yellow, or green or red."—The dean was a woman from one of the "first families"—a great "race" woman;[7] she, Helga Crane, a despised mulatto, but something intuitive, some unanalyzed driving spirit of loyalty to the inherent racial need for gorgeousness told her that bright colours *were* fitting and that dark-complexioned people *should* wear yellow, green, and red. Black, brown, and gray were ruinous to them, actually destroyed the luminous tones lurking in their dusky skins. One of the loveliest sights Helga had ever seen had been a sooty black girl decked out in a flaming orange dress, which a horrified matron had next day consigned to the dyer. Why, she wondered, didn't someone write *A Plea for Color*?

These people yapped loudly of race, of race consciousness, of race pride, and yet suppressed its most delightful manifestations, love of color, joy of rhythmic motion, naïve, spontaneous laughter. Harmony, radiance, and simplicity, all the essentials of spiritual beauty in the race they had marked for destruction.

She came back to her own problems. Clothes had been one of her difficulties in Naxos. Helga Crane loved clothes, elaborate ones. Nevertheless, she had tried not to offend. But with small success, for, although she had affected the deceptively simple variety, the hawk eyes of dean and matrons had detected the subtle difference from their own irreproachably conventional garments. Too, they felt that the colors were queer; dark purples, royal blues, rich greens, deep reds, in soft, luxurious woolens, or heavy, clinging silks. And the trimmings—when Helga used them at all—seemed to them odd. Old laces, strange embroideries, dim brocades. Her faultless, slim shoes

---

7. I.e., a strong advocate of "race consciousness" and "race pride" (see the following paragraph), dedicated to working on behalf on African Americans.

made them uncomfortable and her small plain hats seemed to them positively indecent. Helga smiled inwardly at the thought that whenever there was an evening affair for the faculty, the dear ladies probably held their breaths until she had made her appearance. They existed in constant fear that she might turn out in an evening dress. The proper evening wear in Naxos was afternoon attire. And one could, if one wished, garnish the hair with flowers.

Quick, muted footfalls sounded. The secretary had returned.

"Dr. Anderson will see you now, Miss Crane."

She rose, followed, and was ushered into the guarded sanctum, without having decided just what she was to say. For a moment she felt behind her the open doorway and then the gentle impact of its closing. Before her at a great desk her eyes picked out the figure of a man, at first blurred slightly in outline in that dimmer light. At his "Miss Crane?" her lips formed for speech, but no sound came. She was aware of inward confusion. For her the situation seemed charged, unaccountably, with strangeness and something very like hysteria. An almost overpowering desire to laugh seized her. Then, miraculously, a complete ease, such as she had never known in Naxos, possessed her. She smiled, nodded in answer to his questioning salutation, and with a gracious "Thank you" dropped into the chair which he indicated. She looked at him frankly now, this man still young, thirty-five perhaps, and found it easy to go on in the vein of a simple statement.

"Dr. Anderson, I'm sorry to have to confess that I've failed in my job here. I've made up my mind to leave. Today."

A short, almost imperceptible silence, then a deep voice of peculiarly pleasing resonance, asking gently: "You don't like Naxos, Miss Crane?"

She evaded. "Naxos, the place? Yes, I like it. Who wouldn't like it? It's so beautiful. But I—well—I don't seem to fit here."

The man smiled, just a little. "The school? You don't like the school?"

The words burst from her. "No, I don't like it. I hate it!"

"Why?" The question was detached, too detached.

In the girl blazed a desire to wound. There he sat, staring dreamily out of the window, blatantly unconcerned with her or her answer. Well, she'd tell him. She pronounced each word with deliberate slowness.

"Well, for one thing, I hate hypocrisy. I hate cruelty to students, and to teachers who can't fight back. I hate backbiting, and sneaking, and petty jealousy. Naxos? It's hardly a place at all. It's more like some loathsome, venomous disease. Ugh! Everybody spending his time in a malicious hunting for the weaknesses of others, spying, grudging, scratching."

"I see. And you don't think it might help to cure us, to have someone who doesn't approve of these things stay with us? Even just one person, Miss Crane?"

She wondered if this last was irony. She suspected it was humor and so ignored the half-pleading note in his voice.

"No, I don't! It doesn't do the disease any good. Only irritates it. And it makes me unhappy, dissatisfied. It isn't pleasant to be always made to appear in the wrong, even when I know I'm right."

His gaze was on her now, searching. "Queer," she thought, "how some brown people have gray eyes. Gives them a strange, unexpected appearance. A little frightening."

The man said, kindly: "Ah, you're unhappy. And for the reasons you've stated?"

"Yes, partly. Then, too, the people here don't like me. They don't think I'm in the spirit of the work. And I'm not, not if it means suppression of individuality and beauty."

"And does it?"

"Well, it seems to work out that way."

"How old are you, Miss Crane?"

She resented this, but she told him, speaking with what curtness she could command only the bare figure: "Twenty-three."

"Twenty-three. I see. Some day you'll learn that lies, injustice, and hypocrisy are a part of every ordinary community. Most people achieve a sort of protective immunity, a kind of callousness, toward them. If they didn't, they couldn't endure. I think there's less of these evils here than in most places, but because we're trying to do such a big thing, to aim so high, the ugly things show more, they irk some of us more. Service is like clean white linen, even the tiniest speck shows." He went on, explaining, amplifying, pleading.

Helga Crane was silent, feeling a mystifying yearning which sang and throbbed in her. She felt again that urge for service, not now for her people, but for this man who was talking so earnestly of his work, his plans, his hopes. An insistent need to be a part of them sprang in her. With compunction tweaking at her heart for even having entertained the notion of deserting him, she resolved not only to remain until June, but to return next year. She was shamed, yet stirred. It was not sacrifice she felt now, but actual desire to stay, and to come back next year.

He came, at last, to the end of the long speech, only part of which she had heard. "You see, you understand?" he urged.

"Yes, oh yes, I do."

"What we need is more people like you, people with a sense of values, and proportion, an appreciation of the rarer things of life. You have something to give which we badly need here in Naxos. You mustn't desert us, Miss Crane."

She nodded, silent. He had won her. She knew that she would stay. "It's an elusive something," he went on. "Perhaps I can best explain it by the use of that trite phrase, 'You're a lady.' You have dignity and breeding."

At these words turmoil rose again in Helga Crane. The intricate pattern of the rug which she had been studying escaped her. The shamed feeling which had been her penance evaporated. Only a lacerated pride remained. She took firm hold of the chair arms to still the trembling of her fingers.

"If you're speaking of family, Dr. Anderson, why, I haven't any. I was born in a Chicago slum."

The man chose his words, carefully he thought. "That doesn't at all matter, Miss Crane. Financial, economic circumstances can't destroy tendencies inherited from good stock. You yourself prove that!"

Concerned with her own angry thoughts, which scurried here and there like trapped rats, Helga missed the import of his words. Her own words, her answer, fell like drops of hail.

"The joke is on you, Dr. Anderson. My father was a gambler who deserted my mother, a white immigrant. It is even uncertain that they were married.

As I said at first, I don't belong here. I shall be leaving at once. This afternoon. Good-morning."

Four

Long, soft white clouds, clouds like shreds of incredibly fine cotton, streaked the blue of the early evening sky. Over the flying landscape hung a very faint mist, disturbed now and then by a languid breeze. But no coolness invaded the heat of the train rushing north. The open windows of the stuffy day coach, where Helga Crane sat with others of her race, seemed only to intensify her discomfort. Her head ached with a steady pounding pain. This, added to her wounds of the spirit, made traveling something little short of a medieval torture. Desperately she was trying to right the confusion in her mind. The temper of the morning's interview rose before her like an ugly mutilated creature crawling horribly over the flying landscape of her thoughts. It was no use. The ugly thing pressed down on her, held her. Leaning back, she tried to doze as others were doing. The futility of her effort exasperated her.

Just what had happened to her there in that cool dim room under the quizzical gaze of those piercing gray eyes? Whatever it was had been so powerful, so compelling, that but for a few chance words she would still be in Naxos. And why had she permitted herself to be jolted into a rage so fierce, so illogical, so disastrous, that now after it was spent she sat despondent, sunk in shameful contrition? As she reviewed the manner of her departure from his presence, it seemed increasingly rude.

She didn't, she told herself, after all, like this Dr. Anderson. He was too controlled, too sure of himself and others. She detested cool, perfectly controlled people. Well, it didn't matter. He didn't matter. But she could not put him from her mind. She set it down to annoyance because of the cold discourtesy of her abrupt action. She disliked rudeness in anyone.

She had outraged her own pride, and she had terribly wronged her mother by her insidious implication. Why? Her thoughts lingered with her mother, long dead. A fair Scandinavian girl in love with life, with love, with passion, dreaming, and risking all in one blind surrender. A cruel sacrifice. In forgetting all but love she had forgotten, or had perhaps never known, that some things the world never forgives. But as Helga knew, she had remembered, or had learned in suffering and longing all the rest of her life. Her daughter hoped she had been happy, happy beyond most human creatures, in the little time it had lasted, the little time before that gay suave scoundrel, Helga's father, had left her. But Helga Crane doubted it. How could she have been? A girl gently bred, fresh from an older, more polished civilization, flung into poverty, sordidness, and dissipation. She visualized her now, sad, cold, and—yes, remote. The tragic cruelties of the years had left her a little pathetic, a little hard, and a little unapproachable.

That second marriage, to a man of her own race, but not of her own kind—so passionately, so instinctively resented by Helga even at the trivial age of six—she now understood as a grievous necessity. Even foolish, despised women must have food and clothing; even unloved little Negro girls must be somehow provided for. Memory, flown back to those years following the marriage, dealt her torturing stabs. Before her rose the pictures of her mother's careful management to avoid those ugly scarifying quarrels which even at this far-off time caused an uncontrollable shudder, her own childish self-effacement, the savage unkindness of her stepbrothers and sisters, and the jealous, malicious hatred of her mother's husband. Summers, winters, years, passing in one long, changeless stretch of aching misery of soul. Her mother's death, when Helga was fifteen. Her rescue by Uncle Peter, who had sent her to school, a school for Negroes, where for the first time she could breathe freely, where she discovered that because one was dark, one was not necessarily loathsome, and could, therefore, consider oneself without repulsion.

Six years. She had been happy there, as happy as a child unused to happiness dared be. There had been always a feeling of strangeness, of outsideness, and one of holding her breath for fear that it wouldn't last. It hadn't. It had dwindled gradually into eclipse of painful isolation. As she grew older, she became gradually aware of a difference between herself and the girls about her. They had mothers, fathers, brothers, and sisters of whom they spoke frequently, and who sometimes visited them. They went home for the vacations which Helga spent in the city where the school was located. They visited each other and knew many of the same people. Discontent for which there was no remedy crept upon her, and she was glad almost when these most peaceful years which she had yet known came to their end. She had been happier, but still horribly lonely.

She had looked forward with pleasant expectancy to working in Naxos when the chance came. And now this! What was it that stood in her way? Helga Crane couldn't explain it, put a name to it. She had tried in the early afternoon in her gentle but staccato talk with James Vayle. Even to herself her explanation had sounded inane and insufficient; no wonder James had been impatient and unbelieving. During their brief and unsatisfactory conversation she had had an odd feeling that he felt somehow cheated. And more than once she had been aware of a suggestion of suspicion in his attitude, a feeling that he was being duped, that he suspected her of some hidden purpose which he was attempting to discover.

Well, that was over. She would never be married to James Vayle now. It flashed upon her that, even had she remained in Naxos, she would never have been married to him. She couldn't have married him. Gradually, too, there stole into her thoughts of him a curious sensation of repugnance, for which she was at a loss to account. It was new, something unfelt before. Certainly she had never loved him overwhelmingly, not, for example, as her mother must have loved her father, but she *had* liked him, and she had expected to love him, after their marriage. People generally did love then, she imagined. No, she had not loved James, but she had wanted to. Acute nausea rose in her as she recalled the slight quivering of his lips sometimes when her hands had unexpectedly touched his; the throbbing vein in his forehead on a gay day when they had wandered off alone across the low hills and she had allowed him frequent kisses under the shelter of some low-hanging willows. Now she shivered a little, even in the hot train, as if she had suddenly come out from a warm scented place into cool, clear air. She must have been mad, she thought; but she couldn't tell why she thought so. This, too, bothered her.

Laughing conversation buzzed about her. Across the aisle a bronze baby, with bright staring eyes, began a fretful whining, which its young mother essayed to silence by a low droning croon. In the seat just beyond, a black and tan young pair were absorbed in the eating of a cold fried chicken, audibly crunching the ends of the crisp, browned bones. A little distance away a tired laborer slept noisily. Near him two children dropped the peelings of oranges and bananas on the already soiled floor. The smell of stale food and ancient tobacco irritated Helga like a physical pain. A man, a white man, strode through the packed car and spat twice, once in the exact centre of the dingy door panel, and once into the receptacle which held the drinking-water. Instantly Helga became aware of stinging thirst. Her eyes sought the small watch at her wrist. Ten hours to Chicago. Would she be lucky enough to prevail upon the conductor to let her occupy a berth, or would she have to remain here all night, without sleep, without food, without drink, and with that disgusting door panel to which her purposely averted eyes were constantly, involuntarily straying?

Her first effort was unsuccessful. An ill-natured "No, you know you can't," was the answer to her inquiry. But farther on along the road, there was a change of men. Her rebuff had made her reluctant to try again, but the entry of a farmer carrying a basket containing live chickens, which he deposited on the seat (the only vacant one) beside her, strengthened her weakened courage. Timidly, she approached the new conductor, an elderly gray-mustached man of pleasant appearance, who subjected her to a keen, appraising look, and then promised to see what could be done. She thanked him, gratefully, and went back to her shared seat, to wait anxiously. After half an hour he returned, saying he could "fix her up," there was a section she could have, adding: "It'll cost you ten dollars." She murmured: "All right. Thank you." It was twice the price, and she needed every penny, but she knew she was fortunate to get it even at that, and so was very thankful, as she followed his tall, loping figure out of that car and through seemingly endless others, and at last into one where she could rest a little.

She undressed and lay down, her thoughts still busy with the morning's encounter. Why hadn't she grasped his meaning? Why, if she had said so much, hadn't she said more about herself and her mother? He would, she was sure, have understood, even sympathized. Why had she lost her temper and given way to angry half-truths?—Angry half-truths—Angry half—

Five

Gray Chicago seethed, surged, and scurried about her. Helga shivered a little, drawing her light coat closer. She had forgotten how cold March could be under the pale skies of the North. But she liked it, this blustering wind. She would even have welcomed snow, for it would more clearly have marked the contrast between this freedom and the cage which Naxos had been to her. Not but what it was marked plainly enough by the noise, the dash, the crowds.

Helga Crane, who had been born in this dirty, mad, hurrying city, had no home here. She had not even any friends here. It would have to be, she decided, the Young Women's Christian Association. "Oh dear! The uplift. Poor, poor colored people. Well, no use stewing about it. I'll get a taxi to take me out, bag and baggage, then I'll have a hot bath and a really good meal, peep into the shops—mustn't buy anything—and then for Uncle Peter. Guess I won't phone. More effective if I surprise him."

It was late, very late, almost evening, when finally Helga turned her steps northward, in the direction of Uncle Peter's home. She had put it off as long as she could, for she detested her errand. The fact that that one day had shown her its acute necessity did not decrease her distaste. As she approached the North Side, the distaste grew. Arrived at last at the familiar door of the old stone house, her confidence in Uncle Peter's welcome deserted her. She gave the bell a timid push and then decided to turn away, to go back to her room and phone, or, better yet, to write. But before she could retreat, the door was opened by a strange red-faced maid, dressed primly in black and white. This increased Helga's mistrust. Where, she wondered, was the ancient Rose, who had, ever since she could remember, served her uncle.

The hostile "Well?" of this new servant forcibly recalled the reason for her presence there. She said firmly: "Mr. Nilssen, please."

"Mr. Nilssen's not in," was the pert retort. "Will you see Mrs. Nilssen?"

Helga was startled. "Mrs. Nilssen! I beg your pardon, did you say Mrs. Nilssen?"

"I did," answered the maid shortly, beginning to close the door.

"What is it, Ida?" A woman's soft voice sounded from within.

"Someone for Mr. Nilssen, m'am." The girl looked embarrassed.

In Helga's face the blood rose in a deep-red stain. She explained: "Helga Crane, his niece."

"She says she's his niece, m'am."

"Well, have her come in."

There was no escape. She stood in the large reception hall, and was annoyed to find herself actually trembling. A woman, tall, exquisitely gowned, with shining gray hair piled high, came forward murmuring in a puzzled voice: "His niece, did you say?"

"Yes, Helga Crane. My mother was his sister, Karen Nilssen. I've been away. I didn't know Uncle Peter had married." Sensitive to atmosphere, Helga had felt at once the latent antagonism in the woman's manner.

"Oh, yes! I remember about you now. I'd forgotten for a moment. *Well*, he isn't exactly your uncle, is he? Your mother wasn't married, was she? I mean, to your father?"

"I—I don't know," stammered the girl, feeling pushed down to the uttermost depths of ignominy.

"Of course she wasn't." The clear, low voice held a positive note. "Mr. Nilssen has been very kind to you, supported you, sent you to school. But you mustn't expect anything else. And you mustn't come here any more. It—well, frankly, it isn't convenient. I'm sure an intelligent girl like yourself can understand that."

"Of course," Helga agreed, coldly, freezingly, but her lips quivered. She wanted to get away as quickly as possible. She reached the door. There was a second of complete silence, then Mrs. Nilssen's voice, a little agitated: "And please remember that my husband is not your uncle. No indeed! Why, that, that would make me your aunt! He's not—"

But at last the knob had turned in Helga's fumbling hand. She gave a little unpremeditated laugh and slipped out. When she was in the street, she ran. Her only impulse was to get as far away from her uncle's house, and this woman, his wife, who so plainly wished to dissociate herself from the outrage of her very existence. She was torn with mad fright, an emotion against which she knew but two weapons: to kick and scream, or to flee.

The day had lengthened. It was evening and much colder, but Helga Crane was unconscious of any change, so shaken she was and burning. The wind cut her like a knife, but she did not feel it. She ceased her frantic running, aware at last of the curious glances of passers-by. At one spot, for a moment less frequented than others, she stopped to give heed to her disordered appearance. Here a man, well groomed and pleasant-spoken, accosted her. On such occasions she was wont to reply scathingly, but, tonight, his pale Caucasian face struck her breaking faculties as too droll. Laughing harshly, she threw at him the words: "You're not my uncle."

He retired in haste, probably thinking her drunk, or possibly a little mad.

Night fell, while Helga Crane in the rushing swiftness of a roaring elevated train sat numb. It was as if all the bogies and goblins that had beset her unloved, unloving, and unhappy childhood had come to life with tenfold power to hurt and frighten. For the wound was deeper in that her long freedom from their presence had rendered her the more vulnerable. Worst of all was the fact that under the stinging hurt she understood and sympathized with Mrs. Nilssen's point of view, as always she had been able to understand her mother's, her stepfather's, and his children's points of view. She saw herself for an obscene sore in all their lives, at all costs to be hidden. She understood, even while she resented. It would have been easier if she had not.

Later in the bare silence of her tiny room she remembered the unaccomplished object of her visit. Money. Characteristically, while admitting its necessity, and even its undeniable desirability, she dismissed its importance. Its elusive quality she had as yet never known. She would find work of some kind. Perhaps the library. The idea clung. Yes, certainly the library. She knew books and loved them.

She stood intently looking down into the glimmering street, far below, swarming with people, merging into little eddies and disengaging themselves to pursue their own individual ways. A few minutes later she stood in the doorway, drawn by an uncontrollable desire to mingle with the crowd. The purple sky showed tremulous clouds piled up, drifting here and there with a sort of endless lack of purpose. Very like the myriad human beings pressing hurriedly on. Looking at these, Helga caught herself wondering who they were, what they did, and of what they thought. What was passing behind those dark molds of flesh. Did they really think at all? Yet, as she stepped out into the moving multi-colored crowd, there came to her a queer feeling of enthusiasm, as if she were tasting some agreeable, exotic food—sweetbreads, smothered with truffles and mushrooms—perhaps. And, oddly enough, she felt, too, that she had come home. She, Helga Crane, who had no home.

Six

Helga woke to the sound of rain. The day was leaden gray, and misty black, and dullish white. She was not surprised, the night had promised it. She made a little frown, remembering that it was today that she was to search for work.

She dressed herself carefully, in the plainest garments she possessed, a suit of fine blue twill faultlessly tailored, from whose left pocket peeped a gay kerchief, an unadorned, heavy silk blouse, a small, smart, fawn-colored hat, and slim, brown oxfords, and chose a brown umbrella. In a near-by street she sought out an appealing little restaurant, which she had noted in her last night's ramble through the neighborhood, for the thick cups and the queer dark silver of the Young Women's Christian Association distressed her.

After a slight breakfast she made her way to the library, that ugly gray building, where was housed much knowledge and a little wisdom, on interminable shelves. The friendly person at the desk in the hall bestowed on her a kindly smile when Helga stated her business and asked for directions.

"The corridor to your left, then the second door to your right," she was told.

Outside the indicated door, for half a second she hesitated, then braced herself and went in. In less than a quarter of an hour she came out, in surprised disappointment. "Library training"—"civil service"—"library school"—"classification"—"cataloguing"—"training class"—"examination"—"probation period"—flitted through her mind.

"How erudite they must be!" she remarked sarcastically to herself, and ignored the smiling curiosity of the desk person as she went through the hall to the street. For a long moment she stood on the high stone steps above the avenue, then shrugged her shoulders and stepped down. It *was* a disappointment, but of course there were other things. She would find something else. But what? Teaching, even substitute teaching, was hopeless now, in March. She had no business training, and the shops didn't employ colored clerks or sales-people, not even the smaller ones. She couldn't sew, she couldn't cook. Well, she *could* do housework, or wait on table, for a short time at least. Until she got a little money together. With this thought she remembered that the Young Women's Christian Association maintained an employment agency.

"Of course, the very thing!" She exclaimed, aloud. "I'll go straight back."

But, though the day was still drear, rain had ceased to fall, and Helga, instead of returning, spent hours in aimless strolling about the hustling streets of the Loop district. When at last she did retrace her steps, the business day had ended, and the employment office was closed. This frightened her a little, this and the fact that she had spent money, too much money, for a book and a tapestry purse, things which she wanted, but did not need and certainly could not afford. Regretful and dismayed, she resolved to go without her dinner, as a self-inflicted penance, as well as an economy—and she would be at the employment office the first thing tomorrow morning.

But it was not until three days more had passed that Helga Crane sought the Association, or any other employment office. And then it was sheer necessity that drove her there, for her money had dwindled to a ridiculous sum. She had put off the hated moment, had assured herself that she was tired, needed a bit of vacation, was due one. It had been pleasant, the leisure, the walks, the lake, the shops and streets with their gay colors, their movement, after the great quiet of Naxos. Now she was panicky.

In the office a few nondescript women sat scattered about on the long rows of chairs. Some were plainly uninterested, others wore an air of acute expectancy, which disturbed Helga. Behind a desk two alert young women, both wearing a superior air, were busy writing upon and filing countless white cards. Now and then one stopped to answer the telephone.

"Y.W.C.A. employment.... Yes.... Spell it, please.... Sleep in or out? Thirty dollars? ... Thank you, I'll send one right over."

Or, "I'm awfully sorry, we haven't anybody right now, but I'll send you the first one that comes in."

Their manners were obtrusively business-like, but they ignored the already embarrassed Helga. Diffidently she approached the desk. The darker of the two looked up and turned on a little smile.

"Yes?" she inquired.

"I wonder if you can help me? I want work," Helga stated simply.

"Maybe. What kind? Have you references?"

Helga explained. She was a teacher. A graduate of Devon. Had been teaching in Naxos.

The girl was not interested. "Our kind of work wouldn't do for you," she kept repeating at the end of each of Helga's statements. "Domestic mostly."

When Helga said that she was willing to accept work of any kind, a slight, almost imperceptible change crept into her manner and her perfunctory smile disappeared. She repeated her question about the reference. On learning that Helga had none, she said sharply, finally: "I'm sorry, but we never send out help without references."

With a feeling that she had been slapped, Helga Crane hurried out. After some lunch she sought out an employment agency on State Street. An hour passed in patient sitting. Then came her turn to be interviewed. She said, simply, that she wanted work, work of any kind. A competent young woman, whose eyes stared frog-like from great tortoise-shell-rimmed glasses, regarded her with an appraising look and asked for her history, past and present, not forgetting the "references." Helga told her that she was a graduate of Devon, had taught in Naxos. But even before she arrived at the explanation of the lack of references, the other's interest in her had faded.

"I'm sorry, but we have nothing that you would be interested in," she said and motioned to the next seeker, who immediately came forward, proffering several much worn papers.

"References," thought Helga, resentfully, bitterly, as she went out the door into the crowded garish street in search of another agency, where her visit was equally vain.

Days of this sort of thing. Weeks of it. And of the futile scanning and answering of newspaper advertisements. She traversed acres of streets, but it seemed that in that whole energetic place nobody wanted her services. At least not the kind that she offered. A few men, both white and black, offered her money, but the price of the money was too dear. Helga Crane did not feel inclined to pay it.

She began to feel terrified and lost. And she was a little hungry too, for her small money was dwindling and she felt the need to economize somehow. Food was the easiest.

In the midst of her search for work she felt horribly lonely too. This sense of loneliness increased, it grew to appalling proportions, encompassing her, shutting her off from all of life around her. Devastated she was, and always on the verge of weeping. It made her feel small and insignificant that in all the climbing massed city no one cared one whit about her.

Helga Crane was not religious. She took nothing on trust. Nevertheless on Sundays she attended the very fashionable, very high services in the Negro Episcopal church on Michigan Avenue. She hoped that some good Christian would speak to her, invite her to return, or inquire kindly if she was a stranger in the city. None did, and she became bitter, distrusting religion more than ever. She was herself unconscious of that faint hint of offishness which hung about her and repelled advances, an arrogance that stirred in people a peculiar irritation. They noticed her, admired her clothes, but that was all, for the self-sufficient uninterested manner adopted instinctively as a protective measure for her acute sensitiveness, in her child days, still clung to her.

An agitated feeling of disaster closed in on her, tightened. Then, one afternoon, coming in from the discouraging round of agencies and the vain answering of newspaper wants to the stark neatness of her room, she found between door and sill a small folded note. Spreading it open, she read:

Miss Crane:

Please come into the employment office as soon as you return.

Ida Ross

Helga spent some time in the contemplation of this note. She was afraid to hope. Its possibilities made her feel a little hysterical. Finally, after removing the dirt of the dusty streets, she went down, down to that room where she had first felt the smallness of her commercial value. Subsequent failures had augmented her feeling of incompetence, but she resented the fact that these clerks were evidently aware of her unsuccess. It required all the pride and indifferent hauteur she could summon to support her in their presence. Her additional arrogance passed unnoticed by those for whom it was assumed. They were interested only in the business for which they had summoned her, that of procuring a traveling-companion for a lecturing female on her way to a convention.

"She wants," Miss Ross told Helga, "someone intelligent, someone who can help her get her speeches in order on the train. We thought of you right away. Of course, it isn't permanent. She'll pay your expenses and there'll be twenty-five dollars besides. She leaves tomorrow. Here's her address. You're to go to see her at five o'clock. It's after four now. I'll phone that you're on your way."

The presumptuousness of their certainty that she would snatch at the opportunity galled Helga. She became aware of a desire to be disagreeable. The inclination to fling the address of the lecturing female in their face stirred in her, but she remembered the lone five-dollar bill in the rare old tapestry purse swinging from her arm. She couldn't afford anger. So she thanked them very politely and set out for the home of Mrs. Hayes-Rore on Grand Boulevard, knowing full well that she intended to take the job, if the lecturing one would take her. Twenty-five dollars was not to be looked at with nose in air when one was the owner of but five. And meals—meals for four days at least.

Mrs. Hayes-Rore proved to be a plump lemon-colored woman with badly straightened hair and dirty finger-nails. Her direct, penetrating gaze was somewhat formidable. Notebook in hand, she gave Helga the impression of having risen early for consultation with other harassed authorities on the race problem, and having been in conference on the subject all day. Evidently, she had had little time or thought for the careful donning of the five-years-behind-the-mode garments which covered her, and which even in their youth could hardly have fitted or suited her. She had a tart personality, and prying. She approved of Helga, after asking her endless questions about her education and her opinions on the race problem, none of which she was permitted to answer, for Mrs. Hayes-Rore either went on to the next or answered the question herself by remarking: "Not that it matters, if you can only do what I want done, and the girls at the 'Y' said that you could. I'm on the Board of Managers, and I know they wouldn't send me anybody who wasn't all right." After this had been repeated twice in a booming, oratorical voice, Helga felt that the Association secretaries had taken an awful chance in sending a person about whom they knew as little as they did about her.

"Yes, I'm sure you'll do. I don't really need ideas, I've plenty of my own. It's just a matter of getting someone to help me get my speeches in order, correct and condense them, you know. I leave at eleven in the morning. Can you be ready by then? . . . That's good. Better be here at nine. Now, don't disappoint me. I'm depending on you."

As she stepped into the street and made her way skillfully through the impassioned human traffic, Helga reviewed the plan which she had formed, while in the lecturing one's presence, to remain in New York. There would be twenty-five dollars, and perhaps the amount of her return ticket. Enough for a start. Surely she could get work there. Everybody did. Anyway, she would have a reference.

With her decision she felt reborn. She began happily to paint the future in vivid colors. The world had changed to silver, and life ceased to be a struggle and became a gay adventure. Even the advertisements in the shop windows seemed to shine with radiance.

Curious about Mrs. Hayes-Rore, on her return to the "Y" she went into the employment office, ostensibly to thank the girls and to report that that important woman would take her. Was there, she inquired, anything that she needed to know? Mrs. Hayes-Rore had appeared to put such faith in their recommendation of her that she felt almost obliged to give satisfaction. And she added: "I didn't get much chance to ask questions. She seemed so—er—busy."

Both the girls laughed. Helga laughed with them, surprised that she hadn't perceived before how really likable they were.

"We'll be through here in ten minutes. If you're not busy, come in and have your supper with us and we'll tell you about her," promised Miss Ross.

Seven

Having finally turned her attention to Helga Crane, Fortune now seemed determined to smile, to make amends for her shameful neglect. One had, Helga decided, only to touch the right button, to press the right spring, in order to attract the jade's notice.

For Helga that spring had been Mrs. Hayes-Rore. Ever afterwards on recalling that day on which with wellnigh empty purse and apprehensive heart she had made her way from the Young Women's Christian Association to the Grand Boulevard home of Mrs. Hayes-Rore, always she wondered at her own lack of astuteness in not seeing in the woman someone who by a few words was to have a part in the shaping of her life.

The husband of Mrs. Hayes-Rore had at one time been a dark thread in the soiled fabric of Chicago's South Side politics, who, departing this life hurriedly and unexpectedly and a little mysteriously, and somewhat before the whole of his suddenly acquired wealth had had time to vanish, had left his widow comfortably established with money and some of that prestige which in Negro circles had been his. All this Helga had learned from the secretaries at the "Y." And from numerous remarks dropped by Mrs. Hayes-Rore herself she was able to fill in the details more or less adequately.

On the train that carried them to New York, Helga had made short work of correcting and condensing the speeches, which Mrs. Hayes-Rore as a prominent "race" woman and an authority on the problem was to deliver before several meetings of the annual convention of the Negro Women's League of Clubs,[8] convening the next week in New York. These speeches proved to be merely patchworks of others' speeches and opinions. Helga had heard other lecturers say the same things in Devon and again in Naxos. Ideas, phrases, and even whole sentences and paragraphs were lifted bodily from previous orations and published works of Wendell Phillips, Frederick Douglass, Booker T. Washington, and other doctors of the race's ills. For variety Mrs. Hayes-Rore had seasoned hers with a peppery dash of Du Bois[9] and a few vinegary statements of her own. Aside from these it was, Helga reflected, the same old thing.

But Mrs. Hayes-Rore was to her, after the first short, awkward period, interesting. Her dark eyes, bright and investigating, had, Helga noted, a humorous gleam, and something in the way she held her untidy head gave the impression of a cat watching its prey so that when she struck, if she so decided, the blow would be unerringly effective. Helga, looking up from a last reading of the speeches, was aware that she was being studied. Her employer sat leaning back, the tips of her fingers pressed together, her head a bit on one side, her small inquisitive eyes boring into the girl before her. And as the train hurled itself frantically toward smoke-infested Newark, she decided to strike.

"Now tell me," she commanded, "how is it that a nice girl like you can rush off on a wildgoose chase like this at a moment's notice. I should think your people'd object, or'd make inquiries, or something."

At that command Helga Crane could not help sliding down her eyes to hide the anger that had risen in them. Was she to be forever explaining her people—or lack of them? But she said courteously enough, even managing a hard little smile: "Well you see, Mrs. Hayes-Rore, I haven't any people. There's only me, so I can do as I please."

"Ha!" said Mrs. Hayes-Rore.

Terrific, thought Helga Crane, the power of that sound from the lips of this woman. How, she wondered, had she succeeded in investing it with so much incredulity.

"If you didn't have people, you wouldn't be living. Everybody has people, Miss Crane. Everybody."

---

8. An invented organization. In the early 20th century, the main organization of black women devoted to "uplift" was the National Association of Colored Women (formed in 1896 out of two earlier organizations).

9. W. E. B. Du Bois (1868–1963), an African American born free in Massachusetts, was an intellectual and activist who faulted the advocates of uplift for not doing enough to promote gains in civil rights. Phillips (1811–1885) was a prominent white abolitionist. Douglass (1817–1895), an abolitionist born a slave, won national renown as an orator and writer (especially with his *Autobiography*). Washington (1856–1915), born a slave, founded the Tuskegee Institute (1888), which emphasized practical training for African Americans.

"I haven't, Mrs. Hayes-Rore."

Mrs. Hayes-Rore screwed up her eyes. "Well, that's mighty mysterious, and I detest mysteries." She shrugged, and into those eyes there now came with alarming quickness an accusing criticism.

"It isn't," Helga said defensively, "a mystery. It's a fact and a mighty unpleasant one. Inconvenient too," and she laughed a little, not wishing to cry.

Her tormentor, in sudden embarrassment, turned her sharp eyes to the window. She seemed intent on the miles of red clay sliding past. After a moment, however, she asked gently: "You wouldn't like to tell me about it, would you? It seems to bother you. And I'm interested in girls."

Annoyed, but still hanging, for the sake of the twenty-five dollars, to her self-control, Helga gave her head a little toss and flung out her hands in a helpless, beaten way. Then she shrugged. What did it matter? "Oh, well, if you really want to know. I assure you, it's nothing interesting. Or nasty," she added maliciously. "It's just plain horrid. For me." And she began mockingly to relate her story.

But as she went on, again she had that sore sensation of revolt, and again the torment which she had gone through loomed before her as something brutal and undeserved. Passionately, tearfully, incoherently, the final words tumbled from her quivering petulant lips.

The other woman still looked out of the window, apparently so interested in the outer aspect of the drab sections of the Jersey manufacturing city through which they were passing that, the better to see, she had now so turned her head that only an ear and a small portion of cheek were visible.

During the little pause that followed Helga's recital, the faces of the two women, which had been bare, seemed to harden. It was almost as if they had slipped on masks. The girl wished to hide her turbulent feeling and to appear indifferent to Mrs. Hayes-Rore's opinion of her story. The woman felt that the story, dealing as it did with race intermingling and possibly adultery, was beyond definite discussion. For among black people, as among white people, it is tacitly understood that these things are not mentioned—and therefore they do not exist.

Sliding adroitly out from under the precarious subject to a safer, more decent one, Mrs. Hayes-Rore asked Helga what she was thinking of doing when she got back to Chicago. Had she anything in mind?

Helga, it appeared, hadn't. The truth was she had been thinking of staying in New York. Maybe she could find something there. Everybody seemed to. At least she could make the attempt.

Mrs. Hayes-Rore sighed, for no obvious reason. "Um, maybe I can help you. I know people in New York. Do you?"

"No."

"New York's the lonesomest place in the world if you don't know anybody."

"It couldn't possibly be worse than Chicago," said Helga savagely, giving the table support a violent kick.

They were running into the shadow of the tunnel. Mrs. Hayes-Rore murmured thoughtfully: "You'd better come uptown and stay with me a few days. I may need you. Something may turn up."

It was one of those vicious mornings, windy and bright. There seemed to Helga, as they emerged from the depths of the vast station, to be a whirling malice in the sharp air of this shining city. Mrs. Hayes-Rore's words about its terrible loneliness shot through her mind. She felt its aggressive unfriendliness. Even the great buildings, the flying cabs, and the swirling crowds seemed manifestations of purposed malevolence. And for the first short minute she was awed and frightened and inclined to turn back to that other city, which, though not kind, was yet not strange. This New York seemed somehow more appalling, more scornful, in some inexplicable way even more terrible and uncaring than Chicago. Threatening almost. Ugly. Yes, perhaps she'd better turn back.

The feeling passed, escaped in the surprise of what Mrs. Hayes-Rore was saying. Her oratorical voice boomed above the city's roar. "I suppose I ought really to have phoned Anne from the station. About you, I mean. Well, it doesn't matter. She's got plenty of room. Lives alone in a big house, which is something Negroes in New York don't do. They fill 'em up with lodgers usually. But Anne's funny. Nice, though. You'll like her, and it will be good for you to know her if you're going to stay in New York. She's a widow, my husband's sister's son's wife. The war, you know."

"Oh," protested Helga Crane, with a feeling of acute misgiving, "but won't she be annoyed and inconvenienced by having me brought in on her like this? I supposed we were going to the 'Y' or a hotel or something like that. Oughtn't we really to stop and phone?"

The woman at her side in the swaying cab smiled, a peculiar invincible, self-reliant smile, but gave Helga Crane's suggestion no other attention. Plainly she was a person accustomed to having things her way. She merely went on talking of other plans. "I think maybe I can get you some work. With a new Negro insurance company. They're after me to put quite a tidy sum into it. Well, I'll just tell them that they may as well take you with the money," and she laughed.

"Thanks awfully," Helga said, "but will they like it? I mean being made to take me because of the money."

"They're not being made," contradicted Mrs. Hayes-Rore. "I intended to let them have the money anyway, and I'll tell Mr. Darling so—after he takes you. They ought to be glad to get you. Colored organizations always need more brains as well as more money. Don't worry. And don't thank me again. You haven't got the job yet, you know."

There was a little silence, during which Helga gave herself up to the distraction of watching the strange city and the strange crowds, trying hard to put out of her mind the vision of an easier future which her companion's words had conjured up; for, as had been pointed out, it was, as yet, only a possibility.

Turning out of the park into the broad thoroughfare of Lenox Avenue,[1] Mrs. Hayes-Rore said in a too carefully casual manner: "And, by the way, I wouldn't mention that my people are white, if I were you. Colored people won't understand it, and after all it's your own business. When you've lived as long as I have, you'll know that what others don't know can't hurt you. I'll just tell Anne that you're a friend of mine whose mother's dead. That'll place you well enough and it's all true. I never tell lies. She can fill in the gaps to suit herself and anyone else curious enough to ask."

1. A major thoroughfare in Harlem.

"Thanks," Helga said again. And so great was her gratitude that she reached out and took her new friend's slightly soiled hand in one of her own fastidious ones, and retained it until their cab turned into a pleasant tree-lined street and came to a halt before one of the dignified houses in the center of the block. Here they got out.

In after years Helga Crane had only to close her eyes to see herself standing apprehensively in the small cream-colored hall, the floor of which was covered with deep silver-hued carpet; to see Mrs. Hayes-Rore pecking the cheek of the tall slim creature beautifully dressed in a cool green tailored frock; to hear herself being introduced to "my niece, Mrs. Grey" as "Miss Crane, a little friend of mine whose mother's died, and I think perhaps a while in New York will be good for her"; to feel her hand grasped in quick sympathy, and to hear Anne Grey's pleasant voice, with its faint note of wistfulness, saying: "I'm so sorry, and I'm glad Aunt Jeanette brought you here. Did you have a good trip? I'm sure you must be worn out. I'll have Lillie take you right up." And to feel like a criminal.

Eight

A year thick with various adventures had sped by since that spring day on which Helga Crane had set out away from Chicago's indifferent unkindness for New York in the company of Mrs. Hayes-Rore. New York she had found not so unkind, not so unfriendly, not so indifferent. There she had been happy, and secured work, had made acquaintances and another friend. Again she had had that strange transforming experience, this time not so fleetingly, that magic sense of having come home. Harlem, teeming black Harlem, had welcomed her and lulled her into something that was, she was certain, peace and contentment.

The request and recommendation of Mrs. Hayes-Rore had been sufficient for her to obtain work with the insurance company in which that energetic woman was interested. And through Anne it had been possible for her to meet and to know people with tastes and ideas similar to her own. Their sophisticated cynical talk, their elaborate parties, the unobtrusive correctness of their clothes and homes, all appealed to her craving for smartness, for enjoyment. Soon she was able to reflect with a flicker of amusement on that constant feeling of humiliation and inferiority which had encompassed her in Naxos. Her New York friends looked with contempt and scorn on Naxos and all its works. This gave Helga a pleasant sense of avengement. Any shreds of self-consciousness or apprehension which at first she may have felt vanished quickly, escaped in the keenness of her joy at seeming at last to belong somewhere. For she considered that she had, as she put it, "found herself."

Between Anne Grey and Helga Crane there had sprung one of those immediate and peculiarly sympathetic friendships. Uneasy at first, Helga had been relieved that Anne had never returned to the uncomfortable subject of her mother's death so intentionally mentioned on their first meeting by Mrs. Hayes-Rore, beyond a tremulous brief: "You won't talk to me about it, will you? I can't bear the thought of death. Nobody ever talks to me about it. My husband, you know." This Helga discovered to be true. Later, when she knew Anne better, she suspected that it was a bit of a pose assumed for the purpose of doing away with the necessity of speaking regretfully of a husband who had been perhaps not too greatly loved.

After the first pleasant weeks, feeling that her obligation to Anne was already too great, Helga began to look about for a permanent place to live. It was, she found, difficult. She eschewed the "Y" as too bare, impersonal, and restrictive. Nor did furnished rooms or the idea of a solitary or a shared apartment appeal to her. So she rejoiced when one day Anne, looking up from her book, said lightly: "Helga, since you're going to be in New York, why don't you stay here with me? I don't usually take people. It's too disrupting. Still, it *is* sort of pleasant having somebody in the house and I don't seem to mind you. You don't bore me, or bother me. If you'd like to stay— Think it over."

Helga didn't, of course, require to think it over, because lodgment in Anne's home was in complete accord with what she designated as her "aesthetic sense." Even Helga Crane approved of Anne's house and the furnishings which so admirably graced the big cream-colored rooms. Beds with long, tapering posts to which tremendous age lent dignity and interest, bonneted old highboys, tables that might be by Duncan Phyfe,[2] rare spindle-legged chairs, and others whose ladder backs gracefully climbed the delicate wall panels. These historic things mingled harmoniously and comfortably with brass-bound Chinese tea-chests, luxurious deep chairs and davenports, tiny tables of gay color, a lacquered jade-green settee with gleaming black satin cushions, lustrous Eastern rugs, ancient copper, Japanese prints, some fine etchings, a profusion of precious bric-a-brac, and endless shelves filled with books.

Anne Grey herself was, as Helga expressed it, "almost too good to be true." Thirty, maybe, brownly beautiful, she had the face of a golden Madonna, grave and calm and sweet, with shining black hair and eyes. She carried herself as queens are reputed to bear themselves, and probably do not. Her manners were as agreeably gentle as her own soft name. She possessed an impeccably fastidious taste in clothes, knowing what suited her and wearing it with an air of unconscious assurance. The unusual thing, a native New Yorker, she was also a person of distinction, financially independent, well connected and much sought after. And she was interesting, an odd confusion of wit and intense earnestness; a vivid and remarkable person. Yes, undoubtedly, Anne was almost too good to be true. She was almost perfect.

Thus established, secure, comfortable, Helga soon became thoroughly absorbed in the distracting interests of life in New York. Her secretarial work with the Negro insurance company filled her day. Books, the theater, parties, used up the nights. Gradually in the charm of this new and delightful pattern of her life she lost that tantalizing oppression of loneliness and isolation which always, it seemed, had been a part of her existence.

But, while the continuously gorgeous panorama of Harlem fascinated her, thrilled her, the sober mad rush of white New York failed entirely to stir her. Like thousands of other Harlem dwellers, she patronized its shops, its theaters, its art galleries, and its restaurants, and read its papers, without considering herself a part of the monster. And she was satisfied, unenvious. For

---

2. Scottish-born American cabinetmaker (1768–1845), whose beautiful neoclassical furniture is highly prized.

her this Harlem was enough. Of that white world, so distant, so near, she asked only indifference. No, not at all did she crave, from those pale and powerful people, awareness. Sinister folk, she considered them, who had stolen her birthright. Their past contribution to her life, which had been but shame and grief, she had hidden away from brown folk in a locked closet, "never," she told herself, "to be reopened."

Some day she intended to marry one of those alluring brown or yellow men who danced attendance on her. Already financially successful, any one of them could give to her the things which she had now come to desire, a home like Anne's, cars of expensive makes such as lined the avenue, clothes and furs from Bendel's and Revillon Frères',[3] servants, and leisure.

Always her forehead wrinkled in distaste whenever, involuntarily, which was somehow frequently, her mind turned on the speculative gray eyes and visionary uplifting plans of Dr. Anderson. That other, James Vayle, had slipped absolutely from her consciousness. Of him she never thought. Helga Crane meant, now, to have a home and perhaps laughing, appealing dark-eyed children in Harlem. Her existence was bounded by Central Park, Fifth Avenue, St. Nicholas Park, and One Hundred and Forty-fifth street. Not at all a narrow life, as Negroes live it, as Helga Crane knew it. Everything was there, vice and goodness, sadness and gayety, ignorance and wisdom, ugliness and beauty, poverty and richness. And it seemed to her that somehow of goodness, gayety, wisdom, and beauty always there was a little more than of vice, sadness, ignorance, and ugliness. It was only riches that did not quite transcend poverty.

"But," said Helga Crane, "what of that? Money isn't everything. It isn't even the half of everything. And here we have so much else—and by ourselves. It's only outside of Harlem among those others that money really counts for everything."

In the actuality of the pleasant present and the delightful vision of an agreeable future she was contented, and happy. She did not analyze this contentment, this happiness, but vaguely, without putting it into words or even so tangible a thing as a thought, she knew it sprang from a sense of freedom, a release from the feeling of smallness which had hedged her in, first during her sorry, unchildlike childhood among hostile white folk in Chicago, and later during her uncomfortable sojourn among snobbish black folk in Naxos.

Nine

But it didn't last, this happiness of Helga Crane's.

Little by little the signs of spring appeared, but strangely the enchantment of the season, so enthusiastically, so lavishly greeted by the gay dwellers of Harlem, filled her only with restlessness. Somewhere, within her, in a deep recess, crouched discontent. She began to lose confidence in the fullness of her life, the glow began to fade from her conception of it. As the days multiplied, her need of something, something vaguely familiar, but which she could not put a name to and hold for definite examination, became almost

---

3. The exclusive department store Bendel's and the furrier Revillon Frères are both located on Fifth Avenue, in the most fashionable shopping district of white New York City.

intolerable. She went through moments of overwhelming anguish. She felt shut in, trapped. "Perhaps I'm tired, need a tonic, or something," she reflected. So she consulted a physician, who, after a long, solemn examination, said that there was nothing wrong, nothing at all. "A change of scene, perhaps for a week or so, or a few days away from work," would put her straight most likely. Helga tried this, tried them both, but it was no good. All interest had gone out of living. Nothing seemed any good. She became a little frightened, and then shocked to discover that, for some unknown reason, it was of herself she was afraid.

Spring grew into summer, languidly at first, then flauntingly. Without awareness on her part, Helga Crane began to draw away from those contacts which had so delighted her. More and more she made lonely excursions to places outside of Harlem. A sensation of estrangement and isolation encompassed her. As the days became hotter and the streets more swarming, a kind of repulsion came upon her. She recoiled in aversion from the sight of the grinning faces and from the sound of the easy laughter of all these people who strolled, aimlessly now, it seemed, up and down the avenues. Not only did the crowds of nameless folk on the street annoy her, she began also actually to dislike her friends.

Even the gentle Anne distressed her. Perhaps because Anne was obsessed by the race problem and fed her obsession. She frequented all the meetings of protest, subscribed to all the complaining magazines, and read all the lurid newspapers spewed out by the Negro yellow press. She talked, wept, and ground her teeth dramatically about the wrongs and shames of her race. At times she lashed her fury to surprising heights for one by nature so placid and gentle. And, though she would not, even to herself, have admitted it, she reveled in this orgy of protest.

"Social equality," "Equal opportunity for all," were her slogans, often and emphatically repeated. Anne preached these things and honestly thought that she believed them, but she considered it an affront to the race, and to all the vari-colored peoples that made Lenox and Seventh Avenues the rich spectacles which they were, for any Negro to receive on terms of equality any white person.

"To me," asserted Anne Grey, "the most wretched Negro prostitute that walks One Hundred and Thirty-fifth Street is more than any president of these United States, not excepting Abraham Lincoln." But she turned up her finely carved nose at their lusty churches, their picturesque parades, their naïve clowning on the streets. She would not have desired or even have been willing to live in any section outside the black belt, and she would have refused scornfully, had they been tendered, any invitation from white folk. She hated white people with a deep and burning hatred, with the kind of hatred which, finding itself held in sufficiently numerous groups, was capable some day, on some great provocation, of bursting into dangerously malignant flames.

But she aped their clothes, their manners, and their gracious ways of living. While proclaiming loudly the undiluted good of all things Negro, she yet disliked the songs, the dances, and the softly blurred speech of the race. Toward these things she showed only a disdainful contempt, tinged sometimes with a faint amusement. Like the despised people of the white race, she preferred Pavlova to Florence Mills, John McCormack to Taylor Gordon,

Walter Hampden to Paul Robeson.[4] Theoretically, however, she stood for the immediate advancement of all things Negroid, and was in revolt against social inequality.

Helga had been entertained by this racial ardor in one so little affected by racial prejudice as Anne, and by her inconsistencies. But suddenly these things irked her with a great irksomeness and she wanted to be free of this constant prattling of the incongruities, the injustices, the stupidities, the viciousness of white people. It stirred memories, probed hidden wounds, whose poignant ache bred in her surprising oppression and corroded the fabric of her quietism. Sometimes it took all her self-control to keep from tossing sarcastically at Anne Ibsen's remark about there being assuredly something very wrong with the drains, but after all there were other parts of the edifice.[5]

It was at this period of restiveness that Helga met again Dr. Anderson. She was gone, unwillingly, to a meeting, a health meeting, held in a large church—as were most of Harlem's uplift activities—as a substitute for her employer, Mr. Darling. Making her tardy arrival during a tedious discourse by a pompous saffron-hued physician, she was led by the irritated usher, whom she had roused from a nap in which he had been pleasantly freed from the intricacies of Negro health statistics, to a very front seat. Complete silence ensued while she subsided into her chair. The offended doctor looked at the ceiling, at the floor, and accusingly at Helga, and finally continued his lengthy discourse. When at last he had ended and Helga had dared to remove her eyes from his sweating face and look about, she saw with a sudden thrill that Robert Anderson was among her nearest neighbors. A peculiar, not wholly disagreeable, quiver ran down her spine. She felt an odd little faintness. The blood rushed to her face. She tried to jeer at herself for being so moved by the encounter.

He, meanwhile, she observed, watched her gravely. And having caught her attention, he smiled a little and nodded.

When all who so desired had spouted to their hearts' content—if to little purpose—and the meeting was finally over, Anderson detached himself from the circle of admiring friends and acquaintances that had gathered around him and caught up with Helga half-way down the long aisle leading out to fresher air.

"I wondered if you were really going to cut me. I see you were," he began, with that half-quizzical smile which she remembered so well.

She laughed. "Oh, I didn't think you'd remember me." Then she added: "Pleasantly, I mean."

The man laughed too. But they couldn't talk yet. People kept breaking in on them. At last, however, they were at the door, and then he suggested that they share a taxi "for the sake of a little breeze." Helga assented.

Constraint fell upon them when they emerged into the hot street, made

---

4. I.e., in each case she preferred the white artist to the black, whether the Russian ballerina Anna Pavlova (1882–1931) to Mills (1895–1927), a dancer in popular black musicals; the Irish-born American tenor McCormack (1884–1946), who sang in opera, to Gordon (1893–1971), who gained fame in the 1920s as a singer of spirituals; or the actor Hampden (1879–1955), especially known for his Shakespearean roles, to the actor and singer Robeson (1898–1976).
5. In *An Enemy of the People* (1882) by the Norwegian dramatist Henrik Ibsen (1828–1906), the protagonist ultimately discovers problems not simply with a town's "water supply and drains" but with "the whole of our social life."

seemingly hotter by a low-hanging golden moon and the hundreds of blazing electric lights. For a moment, before hailing a taxi, they stood together looking at the slow moving mass of perspiring human beings. Neither spoke, but Helga was conscious of the man's steady gaze. The prominent gray eyes were fixed upon her, studying her, appraising her. Many times since turning her back on Naxos she had in fancy rehearsed this scene, this re-encounter. Now she found that rehearsal helped not at all. It was so absolutely different from anything that she had imagined.

In the open taxi they talked of impersonal things, books, places, the fascination of New York, of Harlem. But underneath the exchange of small talk lay another conversation of which Helga Crane was sharply aware. She was aware, too, of a strange ill-defined emotion, a vague yearning rising within her. And she experienced a sensation of consternation and keen regret when with a lurching jerk the cab pulled up before the house in One Hundred and Thirty-ninth Street. So soon, she thought.

But she held out her hand calmly, coolly. Cordially she asked him to call some time. "It is," she said, "a pleasure to renew our acquaintance." Was it, she was wondering, merely an acquaintance?

He responded seriously that he too thought it a pleasure, and added: "You haven't changed. You're still seeking for something, I think."

At his speech there dropped from her that vague feeling of yearning, that longing for sympathy and understanding which his presence evoked. She felt a sharp stinging sensation and a recurrence of that anger and defiant desire to hurt which had so seared her on that past morning in Naxos. She searched for a biting remark, but, finding none venomous enough, she merely laughed a little rude and scornful laugh and, throwing up her small head, bade him an impatient good-night and ran quickly up the steps.

Afterwards she lay for long hours without undressing, thinking angry self-accusing thoughts, recalling and reconstructing that other explosive contact. That memory filled her with a sort of aching delirium. A thousand indefinite longings beset her. Eagerly she desired to see him again to right herself in his thoughts. Far into the night she lay planning speeches for their next meeting, so that it was long before drowsiness advanced upon her.

When he did call, Sunday, three days later, she put him off on Anne and went out, pleading an engagement, which until then she had not meant to keep. Until the very moment of his entrance she had had no intention of running away, but something, some imp of contumacy, drove her from his presence, though she longed to stay. Again abruptly had come the uncontrollable wish to wound. Later, with a sense of helplessness and inevitability, she realized that the weapon which she had chosen had been a boomerang, for she herself had felt the keen disappointment of the denial. Better to have stayed and hurled polite sarcasms at him. She might then at least have had the joy of seeing him wince.

In this spirit she made her way to the corner and turned into Seventh Avenue. The warmth of the sun, though gentle on that afternoon, had nevertheless kissed the street into marvelous light and color. Now and then, greeting an acquaintance, or stopping to chat with a friend, Helga was all the time seeing its soft shining brightness on the buildings along its sides or on the gleaming bronze, gold, and copper faces of its promenaders. And another vision, too, came haunting Helga Crane; level gray eyes set down in a brown face which stared out at her, coolly, quizzically, disturbingly. And she was not happy.

The tea to which she had so suddenly made up her mind to go she found boring beyond endurance, insipid drinks, dull conversation, stupid men. The aimless talk glanced from John Wellinger's lawsuit for discrimination because of race against a downtown restaurant and the advantages of living in Europe, especially in France, to the significance, if any, of the Garvey movement.[6] Then it sped to a favorite Negro dancer who had just then secured a foothold on the stage of a current white musical comedy, to other shows, to a new book touching on Negroes. Thence to costumes for a coming masquerade dance, to a new jazz song, to Yvette Dawson's engagement to a Boston lawyer who had seen her one night at a party and proposed to her the next day at noon. Then back again to racial discrimination.

Why, Helga wondered, with unreasoning exasperation, didn't they find something else to talk of? Why must the race problem always creep in? She refused to go on to another gathering. It would, she thought, be simply the same old thing.

On her arrival home she was more disappointed than she cared to admit to find the house in darkness and even Anne gone off somewhere. She would have liked that night to have talked with Anne. Get her opinion of Dr. Anderson.

Anne it was who the next day told her that he had given up his work in Naxos; or rather that Naxos had given him up. He had been too liberal, too lenient, for education as it was inflicted in Naxos. Now he was permanently in New York, employed as welfare worker by some big manufacturing concern, which gave employment to hundreds of Negro men.

"Uplift," sniffed Helga contemptuously, and fled before the onslaught of Anne's harangue on the needs and ills of the race.

Ten

With the waning summer the acute sensitiveness of Helga Crane's frayed nerves grew keener. There were days when the mere sight of the serene tan and brown faces about her stung her like a personal insult. The care-free quality of their laughter roused in her the desire to scream at them: "Fools, fools! Stupid fools!" This passionate and unreasoning protest gained in intensity, swallowing up all else like some dense fog. Life became for her only a hateful place where one lived in intimacy with people one would not have chosen had one been given choice. It was, too, an excruciating agony. She was continually out of temper. Anne, thank the gods! was away, but her nearing return filled Helga with dismay.

Arriving at work one sultry day, hot and dispirited, she found waiting a letter, a letter from Uncle Peter. It had originally been sent to Naxos, and from there it had made the journey back to Chicago to the Young Women's Christian Association, and then to Mrs. Hayes-Rore. That busy woman had at last found time between conventions and lectures to readdress it and had

---

6. The "back-to-Africa" movement, encouraging those of African ancestry around the world to return to Africa and establish their own country; it was led by the Jamaican black nationalist Marcus Garvey (1887–1940), the most influential black leader of the early 1920s. The lawsuit mentioned is apparently fictitious.

sent it on to New York. Four months, at least, it had been on its travels. Helga felt no curiosity as to its contents, only annoyance at the long delay, as she ripped open the thin edge of the envelope, and for a space sat staring at the peculiar foreign script of her uncle.

715 Sheridan Road
Chicago, Ill.

Dear Helga:

It is now over a year since you made your unfortunate call here. It was unfortunate for us all, you, Mrs. Nilssen, and myself. But of course you couldn't know. I blame myself. I should have written you of my marriage.

I have looked for a letter, or some word from you; evidently, with your usual penetration, you understood thoroughly that I must terminate my outward relation with you. You were always a keen one.

Of course I am sorry, but it can't be helped. My wife must be considered, and she feels very strongly about this.

You know, of course, that I wish you the best of luck. But take an old man's advice and don't do as your mother did. Why don't you run over and visit your Aunt Katrina? She always wanted you. Maria Kirkeplads,[7] No. 2, will find her.

I enclose what I intended to leave you at my death. It is better and more convenient that you get it now. I wish it were more, but even this little may come in handy for a rainy day.

Best wishes for your luck.

Peter Nilssen

Beside the brief, friendly, but none the less final, letter there was a check for five thousand dollars. Helga Crane's first feeling was one of unreality. This changed almost immediately into one of relief, of liberation. It was stronger than the mere security from present financial worry which the check promised. Money as money was still not very important to Helga. But later, while on an errand in the big general office of the society, her puzzled bewilderment fled. Here the inscrutability of the dozen or more brown faces, all cast from the same indefinite mold, and so like her own, seemed pressing forward against her. Abruptly it flashed upon her that the harrowing irritation of the past weeks was a smoldering hatred. Then, she was overcome by another, so actual, so sharp, so horribly painful, that forever afterwards she preferred to forget it. It was as if she were shut up, boxed up, with hundreds of her race, closed up with that something in the racial character which had always been, to her, inexplicable, alien. Why, she demanded in fierce rebellion, should she be yoked to these despised black folk?

Back in the privacy of her own cubicle, self-loathing came upon her. "They're my own people, my own people," she kept repeating over and over to herself. It was no good. The feeling would not be routed. "I can't go on like this," she said to herself. "I simply can't."

There were footsteps. Panic seized her. She'd have to get out. She terribly needed to. Snatching hat and purse, she hurried to the narrow door, saying

---

7. A square (*plads*) in Copenhagen (*kirke* is Danish for "church").

in a forced, steady voice, as it opened to reveal her employer: "Mr. Darling, I'm sorry, but I've got to go out. Please, may I be excused?"

At his courteous "Certainly, certainly. And don't hurry. It's much too hot," Helga Crane had the grace to feel ashamed, but there was no softening of her determination. The necessity for being alone was too urgent. She hated him and all the others too much.

Outside, rain had begun to fall. She walked bare-headed, bitter with self-reproach. But she rejoiced too. She didn't, in spite of her racial markings, belong to these dark segregated people. She was different. She felt it. It wasn't merely a matter of color. It was something broader, deeper, that made folk kin.

And now she was free. She would take Uncle Peter's money and advice and revisit her aunt in Copenhagen. Fleeting pleasant memories of her childhood visit there flew through her excited mind. She had been only eight, yet she had enjoyed the interest and the admiration which her unfamiliar color and dark curly hair, strange to those pink, white, and gold people, had evoked. Quite clearly now she recalled that her Aunt Katrina had begged for her to be allowed to remain. Why, she wondered, hadn't her mother consented? To Helga it seemed that it would have been the solution to all their problems, her mother's, her stepfather's, her own.

At home in the cool dimness of the big chintz-hung living-room, clad only in a fluttering thing of green chiffon, she gave herself up to day-dreams of a happy future in Copenhagen, where there were no Negroes, no problems, no prejudice, until she remembered with perturbation that this was the day of Anne's return from her vacation at the sea-shore. Worse. There was a dinner-party in her honor that very night. Helga sighed. She'd have to go. She couldn't possibly get out of a dinner-party for Anne, even though she felt that such an event on a hot night was little short of an outrage. Nothing but a sense of obligation to Anne kept her from pleading a splitting headache as an excuse for remaining quietly at home.

Her mind trailed off to the highly important matter of clothes. What should she wear? White? No, everybody would, because it was hot. Green? She shook her head, Anne would be sure to. The blue thing. Reluctantly she decided against it; she loved it, but she had worn it too often. There was that cobwebby black net touched with orange, which she had bought last spring in a fit of extravagance and never worn, because on getting it home both she and Anne had considered it too *décolleté*, and too *outré*.[8] Anne's words: "There's not enough of it, and what there is gives you the air of something about to fly," came back to her, and she smiled as she decided that she would certainly wear the black net. For her it would be a symbol. She was about to fly.

She busied herself with some absurdly expensive roses which she had ordered sent in, spending an interminable time in their arrangement. At last she was satisfied with their appropriateness in some blue Chinese jars of great age. Anne *did* have such lovely things, she thought, as she began conscientiously to prepare for her return, although there was really little to do; Lillie seemed to have done everything. But Helga dusted the tops of the books, placed the magazines in ordered carelessness, redressed Anne's bed

---

8. Too low-cut, and too unconventional or extravagant (French).

in fresh-smelling sheets of cool linen, and laid out her best pale-yellow pajamas of *crêpe de Chine*.[9] Finally she set out two tall green glasses and made a great pitcher of lemonade, leaving only the ginger-ale and claret to be added on Anne's arrival. She was a little conscience-stricken, so she wanted to be particularly nice to Anne, who had been so kind to her when first she came to New York, a forlorn friendless creature. Yes, she was grateful to Anne; but, just the same, she meant to go. At once.

Her preparations over, she went back to the carved chair from which the thought of Anne's home-coming had drawn her. Characteristically she writhed at the idea of telling Anne of her impending departure and shirked the problem of evolving a plausible and inoffensive excuse for its suddenness. "That," she decided lazily, "will have to look out for itself; I can't be bothered just now. It's too hot."

She began to make plans and to dream delightful dreams of change, of life somewhere else. Some place where at last she would be permanently satisfied. Her anticipatory thoughts waltzed and eddied about to the sweet silent music of change. With rapture almost, she let herself drop into the blissful sensation of visualizing herself in different, strange places, among approving and admiring people, where she would be appreciated, and understood.

Eleven

It was night. The dinner-party was over, but no one wanted to go home. Half-past eleven was, it seemed, much too early to tumble into bed on a Saturday night. It was a sulky, humid night, a thick furry night, through which the electric torches shone like silver fuzz—an atrocious night for cabareting, Helga insisted, but the others wanted to go, so she went with them, though half unwillingly. After much consultation and chatter they decided upon a place and climbed into two patiently waiting taxis, rattling things which jerked, wiggled, and groaned, and threatened every minute to collide with others of their kind, or with inattentive pedestrians. Soon they pulled up before a tawdry doorway in a narrow crosstown street and stepped out. The night was far from quiet, the streets far from empty. Clanging trolley bells, quarreling cats, cackling phonographs, raucous laughter, complaining motor-horns, low singing, mingled in the familiar medley that is Harlem. Black figures, white figures, little forms, big forms, small groups, large groups, sauntered, or hurried by. It was gay, grotesque, and a little weird. Helga Crane felt singularly apart from it all. Entering the waiting doorway, they descended through a furtive, narrow passage, into a vast subterranean room. Helga smiled, thinking that this was one of those places characterized by the righteous as a hell.

A glare of light struck her eyes, a blare of jazz split her ears. For a moment everything seemed to be spinning round; even she felt that she was circling aimlessly, as she followed with the others the black giant who led them to a small table, where, when they were seated, their knees and elbows touched. Helga wondered that the waiter, indefinitely carved out of ebony, did not smile as he wrote their order—"four bottles of White Rock,[1] four bottles of

---

9. A soft fine or sheer fabric.
1. A brand of club soda (the manufacture, transportation, and sale of alcohol was illegal from 1919 to 1933).

ginger-ale." Bah! Anne giggled, the others smiled and openly exchanged knowing glances, and under the tables flat glass bottles were extracted from the women's evening scarfs and small silver flasks drawn from the men's hip pockets. In a little moment she grew accustomed to the smoke and din.

They danced, ambling lazily to a crooning melody, or violently twisting their bodies, like whirling leaves, to a sudden streaming rhythm, or shaking themselves ecstatically to a thumping of unseen tomtoms. For the while, Helga was oblivious of the reek of flesh, smoke, and alcohol, oblivious of the oblivion of other gyrating pairs, oblivious of the color, the noise, and the grand distorted childishness of it all. She was drugged, lifted, sustained, by the extraordinary music, blown out, ripped out, beaten out, by the joyous, wild, murky orchestra. The essence of life seemed bodily motion. And when suddenly the music died, she dragged herself back to the present with a conscious effort; and a shameful certainty that not only had she been in the jungle, but that she had enjoyed it, began to taunt her. She hardened her determination to get away. She wasn't, she told herself, a jungle creature. She cloaked herself in a faint disgust as she watched the entertainers throw themselves about to the bursts of syncopated jangle, and when the time came again for the patrons to dance, she declined. Her rejected partner excused himself and sought an acquaintance a few tables removed. Helga sat looking curiously about her as the buzz of conversation ceased, strangled by the savage strains of music, and the crowd became a swirling mass. For the hundredth time she marveled at the gradations within this oppressed race of hers. A dozen shades slid by. There was sooty black, shiny black, taupe, mahogany, bronze, copper, gold, orange, yellow, peach, ivory, pinky white, pastry white. There was yellow hair, brown hair, black hair; straight hair, straightened hair, curly hair, crinkly hair, woolly hair. She saw black eyes in white faces, brown eyes in yellow faces, gray eyes in brown faces, blue eyes in tan faces. Africa, Europe, perhaps with a pinch of Asia, in a fantastic motley of ugliness and beauty, semi-barbaric, sophisticated, exotic, were here. But she was blind to its charm, purposely aloof and a little contemptuous, and soon her interest in the moving mosaic waned.

She had discovered Dr. Anderson sitting at a table on the far side of the room, with a girl in a shivering apricot frock. Seriously he returned her tiny bow. She met his eyes, gravely smiling, then blushed, furiously, and averted her own. But they went back immediately to the girl beside him, who sat indifferently sipping a colorless liquid from a high glass, or puffing a precariously hanging cigarette. Across dozens of tables, littered with corks, with ashes, with shriveled sandwiches, through slits in the swaying mob, Helga Crane studied her.

She was pale, with a peculiar, almost deathlike pallor. The brilliantly red, softly curving mouth was somehow sorrowful. Her pitch-black eyes, a little aslant, were veiled by long, drooping lashes and surmounted by broad brows, which seemed like black smears. The short dark hair was brushed severely back from the wide forehead. The extreme *décolleté* of her simple apricot dress showed a skin of unusual color, a delicate, creamy hue, with golden tones. "Almost like an alabaster," thought Helga.

Bang! Again the music died. The moving mass broke, separated. The others returned. Anne had rage in her eyes. Her voice trembled as she took Helga aside to whisper: "There's your Dr. Anderson over there, with Audrey Denney."

"Yes, I saw him. She's lovely. Who is she?"

"She's Audrey Denney, as I said, and she lives downtown. West Twenty-second Street. Hasn't much use for Harlem any more. It's a wonder she hasn't some white man hanging about. The disgusting creature! I wonder how she inveigled Anderson? But that's Audrey! If there is any desirable man about, trust her to attach him. She ought to be ostracized."

"Why?" asked Helga curiously, noting at the same time that three of the men in their own party had deserted and were now congregated about the offending Miss Denney.

"Because she goes about with white people," came Anne's indignant answer, "and they know she's colored."

"I'm afraid I don't quite see, Anne. Would it be all right if they didn't know she was colored?"

"Now, don't be nasty, Helga. You know very well what I mean." Anne's voice was shaking. Helga didn't see, and she was greatly interested, but she decided to let it go. She didn't want to quarrel with Anne, not now, when she had that guilty feeling about leaving her. But Anne was off on her favorite subject, race. And it seemed, too, that Audrey Denney was to her particularly obnoxious.

"Why, she gives parties for white and colored people together. And she goes to white people's parties. It's worse than disgusting, it's positively obscene."

"Oh, come, Anne, you haven't been to any of the parties, I know, so how can you be so positive about the matter?"

"No, but I've heard about them. I know people who've been."

"Friends of yours, Anne?"

Anne admitted that they were, some of them.

"Well, then, they can't be so bad. I mean, if your friends sometimes go, can they? Just what goes on that's so terrible?"

"Why, they drink, for one thing. Quantities, they say."

"So do we, at the parties here in Harlem," Helga responded. An idiotic impulse seized her to leave the place, Anne's presence, then, forever. But of course she couldn't. It would be foolish, and so ugly.

"And the white men dance with the colored women. Now you know, Helga Crane, that can mean only one thing." Anne's voice was trembling with cold hatred. As she ended, she made a little clicking noise with her tongue, indicating an abhorrence too great for words.

"Don't the colored men dance with the white women, or do they sit about, impolitely, while the other men dance with their women?" inquired Helga very softly, and with a slowness approaching almost to insolence. Anne's insinuations were too revolting. She had a slightly sickish feeling, and a flash of anger touched her. She mastered it and ignored Anne's inadequate answer.

"It's the principle of the thing that I object to. You can't get round the fact that her behavior is outrageous, treacherous, in fact. That's what's the matter with the Negro race. They won't stick together. She certainly ought to be ostracized. I've nothing but contempt for her, as has every other self-respecting Negro."

The other women and the lone man left to them—Helga's own escort—all seemingly agreed with Anne. At any rate, they didn't protest. Helga gave it up. She felt that it would be useless to tell them that what she felt for the beautiful, calm, cool girl who had the assurance, the courage, so placidly to ignore racial barriers and give her attention to people, was not contempt, but envious admiration. So she remained silent, watching the girl.

At the next first sound of music Dr. Anderson rose. Languidly the girl followed his movement, a faint smile parting her sorrowful lips at some remark he made. Her long, slender body swayed with an eager pulsing motion. She danced with grace and abandon, gravely, yet with obvious pleasure, her legs, her hips, her back, all swaying gently, swung by that wild music from the heart of the jungle. Helga turned her glance to Dr. Anderson. Her disinterested curiosity passed. While she still felt for the girl envious admiration, that feeling was now augmented by another, a more primitive emotion. She forgot the garish crowded room. She forgot her friends. She saw only two figures, closely clinging. She felt her heart throbbing. She felt the room receding. She went out the door. She climbed endless stairs. At last, panting, confused, but thankful to have escaped, she found herself again out in the dark night alone, a small crumpled thing in a fragile, flying black and gold dress. A taxi drifted toward her, stopped. She stepped into it, feeling cold, unhappy, misunderstood, and forlorn.

Twelve

Helga Crane felt no regret as the cliff-like towers faded. The sight thrilled her as beauty, grandeur, of any kind always did, but that was all.

The liner drew out from churning slate-colored waters of the river into the open sea. The small seething ripples on the water's surface became little waves. It was evening. In the western sky was a pink and mauve light, which faded gradually into a soft gray-blue obscurity. Leaning against the railing, Helga stared into the approaching night, glad to be at last alone, free of that great superfluity of human beings, yellow, brown, and black, which, as the torrid summer burnt to its close, had so oppressed her. No, she hadn't belonged there. Of her attempt to emerge from that inherent aloneness which was part of her very being, only dullness had come, dullness and a great aversion.

Almost at once it was time for dinner. Somewhere a bell sounded. She turned and with buoyant steps went down. Already she had begun to feel happier. Just for a moment, outside the dining-salon, she hesitated, assailed with a tiny uneasiness which passed as quickly as it had come. She entered softly, unobtrusively. And, after all, she had had her little fear for nothing. The purser, a man grown old in the service of the Scandinavian-American Line, remembered her as the little dark girl who had crossed with her mother years ago, and so she must sit at his table. Helga liked that. It put her at her ease and made her feel important.

Everyone was kind in the delightful days which followed, and her first shyness under the politely curious glances of turquoise eyes of her fellow travelers soon slid from her. The old forgotten Danish of her childhood began to come, awkwardly at first, from her lips, under their agreeable tutelage. Evidently they were interested, curious, and perhaps a little amused about this Negro girl on her way to Denmark alone.

Helga was a good sailor, and mostly the weather was lovely with the serene calm of the lingering September summer, under whose sky the sea was smooth, like a length of watered silk, unruffled by the stir of any wind. But even the two rough days found her on deck, reveling like a released bird in her returned feeling of happiness and freedom, that blessed sense of belonging to herself alone and not to a race. Again, she had put the past behind her with an ease which astonished even herself. Only the figure of Dr. Anderson obtruded itself with surprising vividness to irk her because she could get no meaning from that keen sensation of covetous exasperation that had so surprisingly risen within her on the night of the cabaret party. This question Helga Crane recognized as not entirely new; it was but a revival of the puzzlement experienced when she had fled so abruptly from Naxos more than a year before. With the recollection of that previous flight and subsequent half-questioning a dim disturbing notion came to her. She wasn't, she couldn't be, in love with the man. It was a thought too humiliating, and so quickly dismissed. Nonsense! Sheer nonsense! When one is in love, one strives to please. Never, she decided, had she made an effort to be pleasing to Dr. Anderson. On the contrary, she had always tried, deliberately, to irritate him. She was, she told herself, a sentimental fool.

Nevertheless, the thought of love stayed with her, not prominent, definite; but shadowy, incoherent. And in a remote corner of her consciousness lurked the memory of Dr. Anderson's serious smile and gravely musical voice.

On the last morning Helga rose at dawn, a dawn outside old Copenhagen. She lay lazily in her long chair watching the feeble sun creeping over the ship's great green funnels with sickly light; watching the purply gray sky change to opal, to gold, to pale blue. A few other passengers, also early risen, excited by the prospect of renewing old attachments, of glad home-comings after long years, paced nervously back and forth. Now, at the last moment, they were impatient, but apprehensive fear, too, had its place in their rushing emotions. Impatient Helga Crane was not. But she *was* apprehensive. Gradually, as the ship drew into the lazier waters of the dock, she became prey to sinister fears and memories. A deep pang of misgiving nauseated her at the thought of her aunt's husband, acquired since Helga's childhood visit. Painfully, vividly, she remembered the frightened anger of Uncle Peter's new wife, and looking back at her precipitate departure from America, she was amazed at her own stupidity. She had not even considered the remote possibility that her aunt's husband might be like Mrs. Nilssen. For the first time in nine days she wished herself back in New York, in America.

The little gulf of water between the ship and the wharf lessened. The engines had long ago ceased their whirring, and now the buzz of conversation, too, died down. There was a sort of silence. Soon the welcoming crowd on the wharf stood under the shadow of the great sea-monster, their faces turned up to the anxious ones of the passengers who hung over the railing. Hats were taken off, handkerchiefs were shaken out and frantically waved. Chatter. Deafening shouts. A little quiet weeping. Sailors and laborers were yelling and rushing about. Cables were thrown. The gangplank was laid.

Silent, unmoving, Helga Crane stood looking intently down into the gesticulating crowd. Was anyone waving to her? She couldn't tell. She didn't in the least remember her aunt, save as a hazy pretty lady. She smiled a little at the thought that her aunt, or anyone waiting there in the crowd below, would have no difficulty in singling her out. But—had she been met? When she descended the gangplank she was still uncertain and was trying to decide on a plan of procedure in the event that she had not. A telegram before she went through the customs? Telephone? A taxi?

But, again, she had all her fears and questionings for nothing. A smart woman in olive-green came toward her at once. And, even in the fervent gladness of her relief, Helga took in the carelessly trailing purple scarf and correct black hat that completed the perfection of her aunt's costume, and had time to feel herself a little shabbily dressed. For it was her aunt; Helga saw that at once, the resemblance to her own mother was unmistakable. There was the same long nose, the same beaming blue eyes, the same straying pale-brown hair so like sparkling beer. And the tall man with the fierce mustache who followed carrying hat and stick must be Herr[2] Dahl, Aunt Katrina's husband. How gracious he was in his welcome, and how anxious to air his faulty English, now that her aunt had finished kissing her and exclaimed in Danish: "Little Helga! Little Helga! Goodness! But how you have grown!"

Laughter from all three.

"Welcome to Denmark, to Copenhagen, to our home," said the new uncle in queer, proud, oratorical English. And to Helga's smiling, grateful "Thank you," he returned: "Your trunks? Your checks?"[3] also in English, and then lapsed into Danish.

"Where in the world are the Fishers? We must hurry the customs."

Almost immediately they were joined by a breathless couple, a young gray-haired man and a fair, tiny, doll-like woman. It developed that they had lived in England for some years and so spoke English, real English, well. They were both breathless, all apologies and explanations.

"So early!" sputtered the man, Herr Fisher, "We inquired last night and they said nine. It was only by accident that we called again this morning to be sure. Well, you can imagine the rush we were in when they said eight! And of course we had trouble in finding a cab. One always does if one is late." All this in Danish. Then to Helga in English: "You see, I was especially asked to come because Fru[4] Dahl didn't know if you remembered your Danish, and your uncle's English—well—"

More laughter.

At last, the customs having been hurried and a cab secured, they were off, with much chatter, through the toy-like streets, weaving perilously in and out among the swarms of bicycles.

It had begun, a new life for Helga Crane.

Thirteen

She liked it, this new life. For a time it blotted from her mind all else. She took to luxury as the proverbial duck to water. And she took to admiration and attention even more eagerly.

It was pleasant to wake on that first afternoon, after the insisted-upon nap, with that sensation of lavish contentment and well-being enjoyed only by impecunious sybarites waking in the houses of the rich. But there was something more than mere contentment and well-being. To Helga Crane it was

---

2. Mr. (properly spelled *Herre* in Danish; *Herr* is German or Swedish).
3. I.e., baggage claim checks.
4. Mrs. (Danish).

the realization of a dream that she had dreamed persistently ever since she was old enough to remember such vague things as day-dreams and longings. Always she had wanted, not money, but the things which money could give, leisure, attention, beautiful surroundings. Things. Things. Things.

So it was more than pleasant, it was important, this awakening in the great high room which held the great high bed on which she lay, small but exalted. It was important because to Helga Crane it was the day, so she decided, to which all the sad forlorn past had led, and from which the whole future was to depend. This, then, was where she belonged. This was her proper setting. She felt consoled at last for the spiritual wounds of the past.

A discreet knocking on the tall paneled door sounded. In response to Helga's "Come in" a respectful rosy-faced maid entered and Helga lay for a long minute watching her adjust the shutters. She was conscious, too, of the girl's sly curious glances at her, although her general attitude was quite correct, willing and disinterested. In New York, America, Helga would have resented this sly watching. Now, here, she was only amused. Marie, she reflected, had probably never seen a Negro outside the pictured pages of her geography book.

Another knocking. Aunt Katrina entered, smiling at Helga's quick, lithe spring from the bed. They were going out to tea, she informed Helga. What, the girl inquired, did one wear to tea in Copenhagen, meanwhile glancing at her aunt's dark purple dress and bringing forth a severely plain blue *crêpe* frock. But no! It seemed that that wouldn't at all do.

"Too sober," pronounced Fru Dahl. "Haven't you something lively, something bright?" And, noting Helga's puzzled glance at her own subdued costume, she explained laughingly: "Oh, I'm an old married lady, and a Dane. But you, you're young. And you're a foreigner, and different. You must have bright things to set off the color of your lovely brown skin. Striking things, exotic things. You must make an impression."

"I've only these," said Helga Crane, timidly displaying her wardrobe on couch and chairs. "Of course I intend to buy here. I didn't want to bring over too much that might be useless."

"And you were quite right too. Umm. Let's see. That black there, the one with the cerise and purple trimmings. Wear that."

Helga was shocked. "But for tea, Aunt! Isn't it too gay? Too—too—*outré?*"

"Oh dear, no. Not at all, not for you. Just right." Then after a little pause she added: "And we're having people in to dinner tonight, quite a lot. Perhaps we'd better decide on our frocks now." For she was, in spite of all her gentle kindness, a woman who left nothing to chance. In her own mind she had determined the role that Helga was to play in advancing the social fortunes of the Dahls of Copenhagen, and she meant to begin at once.

At last, after much trying on and scrutinizing, it was decided that Marie should cut a favorite emerald-green velvet dress a little lower in the back and add some gold and mauve flowers, "to liven it up a bit," as Fru Dahl put it.

"Now that," she said, pointing to the Chinese red dressing-gown in which Helga had wrapped herself when at last the fitting was over, "suits you. Tomorrow we'll shop. Maybe we can get something that color. That black and orange thing there is good too, but too high. What a prim American maiden you are, Helga, to hide such a fine back and shoulders. Your feet are nice too, but you ought to have higher heels—and buckles."

Left alone, Helga began to wonder. She was dubious, too, and not a little resentful. Certainly she loved color with a passion that perhaps only Negroes and Gypsies know. But she had a deep faith in the perfection of her own taste, and no mind to be bedecked in flaunting flashy things. Still—she had to admit that Fru Dahl was right about the dressing-gown. It did suit her. Perhaps an evening dress. And she knew that she had lovely shoulders, and her feet *were* nice.

When she was dressed in the shining black taffeta with its bizarre trimmings of purple and cerise, Fru Dahl approved her and so did Herr Dahl. Everything in her responded to his "She's beautiful; beautiful!" Helga Crane knew she wasn't that, but it pleased her that he could think so, and say so. Aunt Katrina smiled in her quiet, assured way, taking to herself her husband's compliment to her niece. But a little frown appeared over the fierce mustache, as he said, in his precise, faintly feminine voice: "She ought to have earrings, long ones. Is it too late for Garborg's? We could call up."

And call up they did. And Garborg, the jeweler, in Fredericksgaarde[5] waited for them. Not only were ear-rings bought, long ones brightly enameled, but glittering shoe-buckles and two great bracelets. Helga's sleeves being long, she escaped the bracelets for the moment. They were wrapped to be worn that night. The ear-rings, however, and the buckles came into immediate use and Helga felt like a veritable savage as they made their leisurely way across the pavement from the shop to the waiting motor. This feeling was intensified by the many pedestrians who stopped to stare at the queer dark creature, strange to their city. Her cheeks reddened, but both Herr and Fru Dahl seemed oblivious of the stares or the audible whispers in which Helga made out the one frequently recurring word *"sorte,"* which she recognized as the Danish word for "black."

Her Aunt Katrina merely remarked: "A high color becomes you, Helga. Perhaps tonight a little rouge—" To which her husband nodded in agreement and stroked his mustache meditatively. Helga Crane said nothing.

They were pleased with the success she was at the tea, or rather the coffee—for no tea was served—and later at dinner. Helga herself felt like nothing so much as some new and strange species of pet dog being proudly exhibited. Everyone was very polite and very friendly, but she felt the massed curiosity and interest, so discreetly hidden under the polite greetings. The very atmosphere was tense with it. "As if I had horns, or three legs," she thought. She was really nervous and a little terrified, but managed to present an outward smiling composure. This was assisted by the fact that it was taken for granted that she knew nothing or very little of the language. So she had only to bow and look pleasant. Herr and Fru Dahl did the talking, answered the questions. She came away from the coffee feeling that she had acquitted herself well in the first skirmish. And, in spite of the mental strain, she had enjoyed her prominence.

If the afternoon had been a strain, the evening was something more. It was more exciting too. Marie had indeed "cut down" the prized green velvet, until, as Helga put it, it was "practically nothing but a skirt." She was thankful for the barbaric bracelets, for the dangling ear-rings, for the beads about her neck. She was even thankful for the rouge on her burning cheeks and for

5. I.e., Frederick Street.

the very powder on her back. No other woman in the stately pale-blue room was so greatly exposed. But she liked the small murmur of wonder and admiration which rose when Uncle Poul brought her in. She liked the compliments in the men's eyes as they bent over her hand. She liked the subtle half-understood flattery of her dinner partners. The women too were kind, feeling no need for jealousy. To them this girl, this Helga Crane, this mysterious niece of the Dahls, was not to be reckoned seriously in their scheme of things. True, she was attractive, unusual, in an exotic, almost savage way, but she wasn't one of them. She didn't at all count.

Near the end of the evening, as Helga sat effectively posed on a red satin sofa, the center of an admiring group, replying to questions about America and her trip over, in halting, inadequate Danish, there came a shifting of the curious interest away from herself. Following the other's eyes, she saw that there had entered the room a tallish man with a flying mane of reddish blond hair. He was wearing a great black cape, which swung gracefully from his huge shoulders, and in his long, nervous hand he held a wide soft hat. An artist, Helga decided at once, taking in the broad streaming tie. But how affected! How theatrical!

With Fru Dahl he came forward and was presented. "Herr Olsen, Herr Axel Olsen." To Helga Crane that meant nothing. The man, however, interested her. For an imperceptible second he bent over her hand. After that he looked intently at her for what seemed to her an incredibly rude length of time from under his heavy drooping lids. At last, removing his stare of startled satisfaction, he wagged his leonine head approvingly.

"Yes, you're right. She's amazing. Marvelous," he muttered.

Everyone else in the room was deliberately not staring. About Helga there sputtered a little staccato murmur of manufactured conversation. Meanwhile she could think of no proper word of greeting to the outrageous man before her. She wanted, very badly, to laugh. But the man was as unaware of her omission as of her desire. His words flowed on and on, rising and rising. She tried to follow, but his rapid Danish eluded her. She caught only words, phrases, here and there. "Superb eyes . . . color . . . neck column . . . yellow . . . hair . . . alive . . . wonderful. . . ." His speech was for Fru Dahl. For a bit longer he lingered before the silent girl, whose smile had become a fixed aching mask, still gazing appraisingly, but saying no word to her, and then moved away with Fru Dahl, talking rapidly and excitedly to her and her husband, who joined them for a moment at the far side of the room. Then he was gone as suddenly as he had come.

"Who is he?" Helga put the question timidly to a hovering young army officer, a very smart captain just back from Sweden. Plainly he was surprised.

"Herr Olsen, Herr Axel Olsen, the painter. Portraits, you know."

"Oh," said Helga, still mystified.

"I guess he's going to paint you. You're lucky. He's queer.[6] Won't do everybody."

"Oh, no. I mean, I'm sure you're mistaken. He didn't ask, didn't say anything about it."

The young man laughed. "Ha ha! That's good! He'll arrange that with Herr

---

6. Eccentric.

Dahl. He evidently came just to see you, and it was plain that he was pleased." He smiled, approvingly.

"Oh," said Helga again. Then at last she laughed. It was too funny. The great man hadn't addressed a word to her. Here she was, a curiosity, a stunt, at which people came and gazed. And was she to be treated like a secluded young miss, a Danish *frøkken*,[7] not to be consulted personally even on matters affecting her personally? She, Helga Crane, who almost all her life had looked after herself, was she now to be looked after by Aunt Katrina and her husband? It didn't seem real.

It was late, very late, when finally she climbed into the great bed after having received an auntly kiss. She lay long awake reviewing the events of the crowded day. She was happy again. Happiness covered her like the lovely quilts under which she rested. She was mystified too. Her aunt's words came back to her. "You're young and a foreigner and—and different." Just what did that mean, she wondered. Did it mean that the difference was to be stressed, accented? Helga wasn't so sure that she liked that. Hitherto all her efforts had been toward similarity to those about her.

"How odd," she thought sleepily, "and how different from America!"

Fourteen

The young officer had been right in his surmise. Axel Olsen was going to paint Helga Crane. Not only was he going to paint her, but he was to accompany her and her aunt on their shopping expedition. Aunt Katrina was frankly elated. Uncle Poul was also visibly pleased. Evidently they were not above kow-towing to a lion. Helga's own feelings were mixed; she was amused, grateful, and vexed. It had all been decided and arranged without her, and, also, she was a little afraid of Olsen. His stupendous arrogance awed her.

The day was an exciting, not easily to be forgotten one. Definitely, too, it conveyed to Helga her exact status in her new environment. A decoration. A curio. A peacock. Their progress through the shops was an event; an event for Copenhagen as well as for Helga Crane. Her dark, alien appearance was to most people an astonishment. Some stared surreptitiously, some openly, and some stopped dead in front of her in order more fully to profit by their stares. *"Den Sorte"* dropped freely, audibly, from many lips.

The time came when she grew used to the stares of the population. And the time came when the population of Copenhagen grew used to her outlandish presence and ceased to stare. But at the end of that first day it was with thankfulness that she returned to the sheltering walls of the house on Maria Kirkplads.

They were followed by numerous packages, whose contents all had been selected or suggested by Olsen and paid for by Aunt Katrina. Helga had only to wear them. When they were opened and the things spread out upon the sedate furnishings of her chamber, they made a rather startling array. It was almost in a mood of rebellion that Helga faced the fantastic collection of garments incongruously laid out in the quaint, stiff, pale old room. There were batik dresses in which mingled indigo, orange, green, vermilion, and black; dresses of velvet and chiffon in screaming colors, blood-red, sulphur-

---

7. I.e., *frøken,* or "miss" (Danish).

yellow, sea-green; and one black and white thing in striking combination. There was a black Manila shawl strewn with great scarlet and lemon flowers, a leopard-skin coat, a glittering opera-cape. There were turban-like hats of metallic silks, feathers and furs, strange jewelry, enameled or set with odd semi-precious stones, a nauseous Eastern perfume, shoes with dangerously high heels. Gradually Helga's perturbation subsided in the unusual pleasure of having so many new and expensive clothes at one time. She began to feel a little excited, incited.

Incited. That was it, the guiding principle of her life in Copenhagen. She was incited to make an impression, a voluptuous impression. She was incited to inflame attention and admiration. She was dressed for it, subtly schooled for it. And after a little while she gave herself up wholly to the fascinating business of being seen, gaped at, desired. Against the solid background of Herr Dahl's wealth and generosity she submitted to her aunt's arrangement of her life to one end, the amusing one of being noticed and flattered. Intentionally she kept to the slow, faltering Danish. It was, she decided, more attractive than a nearer perfection. She grew used to the extravagant things with which Aunt Katrina chose to dress her. She managed, too, to retain that air of remoteness which had been in America so disastrous to her friendships. Here in Copenhagen it was merely a little mysterious and added another clinging wisp of charm.

Helga Crane's new existence was intensely pleasant to her; it gratified her augmented sense of self-importance. And it suited her. She had to admit that the Danes had the right idea. To each his own milieu. Enhance what was already in one's possession. In America Negroes sometimes talked loudly of this, but in their hearts they repudiated it. In their lives too. They didn't want to be like themselves. What they wanted, asked for, begged for, was to be like their white overlords. They were ashamed to be Negroes, but not ashamed to beg to be something else. Something inferior. Not quite genuine. Too bad!

Helga Crane didn't, however, think often of America, excepting in unfavorable contrast to Denmark. For she had resolved never to return to the existence of ignominy which the New World of opportunity and promise forced upon Negroes. How stupid she had been ever to have thought that she could marry and perhaps have children in a land where every dark child was handicapped at the start by the shroud of color! She saw, suddenly, the giving birth to little, helpless, unprotesting Negro children as a sin, an unforgivable outrage. More black folk to suffer indignities. More dark bodies for mobs to lynch. No, Helga Crane didn't think often of America. It was too humiliating, too disturbing. And she wanted to be left to the peace which had come to her. Her mental difficulties and questionings had become simplified. She now believed sincerely that there was a law of compensation, and that sometimes it worked. For all those early desolate years she now felt recompensed. She recalled a line that had impressed her in her lonely schooldays, "The far-off interest of tears."[8]

To her, Helga Crane, it had come at last, and she meant to cling to it. So she turned her back on painful America, resolutely shutting out the griefs, the humiliations, the frustrations, which she had endured there.

8. From Alfred, Lord Tennyson's *In Memoriam A. H. H.* (1850), section 1.

Her mind was occupied with other and nearer things.

The charm of the old city itself, with its odd architectural mixture of medievalism and modernity, and the general air of well-being which pervaded it, impressed her. Even in the so-called poor sections there was none of that untidiness and squalor which she remembered as the accompaniment of poverty in Chicago, New York, and the Southern cities of America. Here the door-steps were always white from constant scrubbings, the women neat, and the children washed and provided with whole clothing. Here were no tatters and rags, no beggars. But, then, begging, she learned, was an offense punishable by law. Indeed, it was unnecessary in a country where everyone considered it a duty somehow to support himself and his family by honest work; or, if misfortune and illness came upon one, everyone else, including the State, felt bound to give assistance, a lift on the road to the regaining of independence.

After the initial shyness and consternation at the sensation caused by her strange presence had worn off, Helga spent hours driving or walking about the city, at first in the protecting company of Uncle Poul or Aunt Katrina or both, or sometimes Axel Olsen. But later, when she had become a little familiar with the city, and its inhabitants a little used to her, and when she had learned to cross the streets in safety, dodging successfully the innumerable bicycles like a true Copenhagener, she went often alone, loitering on the long bridge which spanned the placid lakes, or watching the pageant of the blue-clad, sprucely tailored soldiers in the daily parade at Amielenborg Palace, or in the historic vicinity of the long, low-lying Exchange, a picturesque structure in picturesque surroundings, skirting as it did the great canal, which always was alive with many small boats, flying broad white sails and pressing close on the huge ruined pile of the Palace of Christiansborg. There was also the Gammelstrand, the congregating-place of the venders of fish, where daily was enacted a spirited and interesting scene between sellers and buyers, and where Helga's appearance always roused lively and audible, but friendly, interest, long after she became in other parts of the city an accepted curiosity. Here it was that one day an old countrywoman asked her to what manner of mankind she belonged and at Helga's replying: "I'm a Negro," had become indignant, retorting angrily that, just because she was old and a countrywoman she could not be so easily fooled, for she knew as well as everyone else that Negroes were black and had woolly hair.

Against all this walking the Dahls had at first uttered mild protest. "But, Aunt dear, I have to walk, or I'll get fat," Helga asserted. "I've never, never in all my life, eaten so much." For the accepted style of entertainment in Copenhagen seemed to be a round of dinner-parties, at which it was customary for the hostess to tax the full capacity not only of her dining-room, but of her guests as well. Helga enjoyed these dinner-parties, as they were usually spirited affairs, the conversation brilliant and witty, often in several languages. And always she came in for a goodly measure of flattering attention and admiration.

There were, too, those popular afternoon gatherings for the express purpose of drinking coffee together, where between much talk, interesting talk, one sipped the strong and steaming beverage from exquisite cups fashioned of Royal Danish porcelain and partook of an infinite variety of rich cakes and *smørrebrød*. This *smørrebrød*, dainty sandwiches of an endless and tempting array, was distinctly a Danish institution. Often Helga wondered just how many of these delicious sandwiches she had consumed since setting foot on Denmark's soil. Always, wherever food was served, appeared the inevitable *smørrebrød*, in the home of the Dahls, in every other home that she visited, in hotels, in restaurants.

At first she had missed, a little, dancing, for, though excellent dancers, the Danes seemed not to care a great deal for that pastime, which so delightfully combines exercise and pleasure. But in the winter there was skating, solitary, or in gay groups. Helga liked this sport, though she was not very good at it. There were, however, always plenty of efficient and willing men to instruct and to guide her over the glittering ice. One could, too, wear such attractive skating-things.

But mostly it was with Axel Olsen that her thoughts were occupied. Brilliant, bored, elegant, urbane, cynical, worldly, he was a type entirely new to Helga Crane, familiar only, and that but little, with the restricted society of American Negroes. She was aware, too, that this amusing, if conceited, man was interested in her. They were, because he was painting her, much together. Helga spent long mornings in the eccentric studio opposite the Folkemuseum,[9] and Olsen came often to the Dahl home, where, as Helga and the man himself knew, he was something more than welcome. But in spite of his expressed interest and even delight in her exotic appearance, in spite of his constant attendance upon her, he gave no sign of the more personal kind of concern which—encouraged by Aunt Katrina's mild insinuations and Uncle Poul's subtle questionings—she had tried to secure. Was it, she wondered, race that kept him silent, held him back. Helga Crane frowned on this thought, putting it furiously from her, because it disturbed her sense of security and permanence in her new life, pricked her self-assurance.

Nevertheless she was startled when on a pleasant afternoon while drinking coffee in the Hotel Vivili, Aunt Katrina mentioned, almost casually, the desirability of Helga's making a good marriage.

"Marriage, Aunt dear!"

"Marriage," firmly repeated her aunt, helping herself to another anchovy and olive sandwich. "You are," she pointed out, "twenty-five."

"Oh, Aunt, I couldn't! I mean, there's nobody here for me to marry." In spite of herself and her desire not to be, Helga was shocked.

"Nobody?" There was, Fru Dahl asserted, Captain Frederick Skaargaard—and very handsome he was too—and he would have money. And there was Herr Hans Tietgen, not so handsome, of course, but clever and a good business man; he too would be rich, very rich, some day. And there was Herr Karl Pedersen, who had a good berth with the Landmands-bank and considerable shares in a prosperous cement-factory at Aalborg. There was, too, Christian Lende, the young owner of the new Odin Theater. Any of these Helga might marry, was Aunt Katrina's opinion. "And," she added, "others." Or maybe Helga herself had some ideas.

Helga had. She didn't, she responded, believe in mixed marriages, "between races, you know." They brought only trouble—to the children—as she herself knew but too well from bitter experience.

Fru Dahl thoughtfully lit a cigarette. Eventually, after a satisfactory glow

---

9. The Danish Folk Museum.

had manifested itself, she announced: "Because your mother was a fool. Yes, she was! If she'd come home after she married, or after you were born, or even after your father—er—went off like that, it would have been different. If even she'd left you when she was here. But why in the world she should have married again, and a person like that, I can't see. She wanted to keep you, she insisted on it, even over his protest, I think. She loved you so much, she said.—And so she made you unhappy. Mothers, I suppose, are like that. Selfish. And Karen was always stupid. If you've got any brains at all they came from your father."

Into this Helga would not enter. Because of its obvious partial truths she felt the need for disguising caution. With a detachment that amazed herself she asked if Aunt Katrina didn't think, really, that miscegenation was wrong, in fact as well as principle.

"Don't," was her aunt's reply, "be a fool too, Helga. We don't think of those things here. Not in connection with individuals, at least." And almost immediately she inquired: "Did you give Herr Olsen my message about dinner tonight?"

"Yes, Aunt." Helga was cross, and trying not to show it.

"He's coming?"

"Yes, Aunt," with precise politeness.

"What about him?"

"I don't know. *What* about him?"

"He likes you?"

"I don't know. How can I tell that?" Helga asked with irritating reserve, her concentrated attention on the selection of a sandwich. She had a feeling of nakedness. Outrage.

Now Fru Dahl was annoyed and showed it. "What nonsense! Of course you know. Any girl does," and her satin-covered foot tapped, a little impatiently, the old tiled floor.

"Really, I don't know, Aunt," Helga responded in a strange voice, a strange manner, coldly formal, levelly courteous. Then suddenly contrite, she added: "Honestly, I don't. I can't tell a thing about him," and fell into a little silence. "Not a thing," she repeated. But the phrase, though audible, was addressed to no one. To herself.

She looked out into the amazing orderliness of the street. Instinctively she wanted to combat this searching into the one thing which, here, surrounded by all other things which for so long she had so positively wanted, made her a little afraid. Started vague premonitions.

Fru Dahl regarded her intently. It would be, she remarked with a return of her outward casualness, by far the best of all possibilities. Particularly desirable. She touched Helga's hand with her fingers in a little affectionate gesture. Very lightly.

Helga Crane didn't immediately reply. There was, she knew, so much reason—from one viewpoint—in her aunt's statement. She could only acknowledge it. "I know that," she told her finally. Inwardly she was admiring the cool, easy way in which Aunt Katrina had brushed aside the momentary acid note of the conversation and resumed her customary pitch. It took, Helga thought, a great deal of security. Balance.

"Yes," she was saying, while leisurely lighting another of those long, thin, brown cigarettes which Helga knew from distressing experience to be incredibly nasty tasting, "it would be the ideal thing for you, Helga." She gazed penetratingly into the masked face of her niece and nodded, as though satisfied with what she saw there. "And you of course realize that you are a very charming and beautiful girl. Intelligent too. If you put your mind to it, there's no reason in the world why you shouldn't—" Abruptly she stopped, leaving her implication at once suspended and clear. Behind her there were footsteps. A small gloved hand appeared on her shoulder. In the short moment before turning to greet Fru Fischer she said quietly, meaningly: "Or else stop wasting your time, Helga."

Helga Crane said: "Ah, Fru Fischer. It's good to see you." She meant it. Her whole body was tense with suppressed indignation. Burning inside like the confined fire of a hot furnace. She was so harassed that she smiled in self-protection. And suddenly she was oddly cold. An intimation of things distant, but none the less disturbing, oppressed her with a faintly sick feeling. Like a heavy weight, a stone weight, just where, she knew, was her stomach.

Fru Fischer was late. As usual. She apologized profusely. Also as usual. And, yes, she would have some coffee. And some smørrebrød. Though she must say that the coffee here at the Vivili was atrocious. Simply atrocious. "I don't see how you stand it." And the place was getting so common, always so many Bolsheviks and Japs and things. And she didn't—"begging your pardon, Helga"—like that hideous American music they were forever playing, even if it was considered very smart. "Give me," she said, "the good old-fashioned Danish melodies of Gade and Heise. Which reminds me, Herr Olsen says that Nielsen's[1] "Helios" is being performed with great success just now in England. But I suppose you know all about it, Helga. He's already told you. What?" This last was accompanied with an arch and insinuating smile.

A shrug moved Helga Crane's shoulders. Strange she'd never before noticed what a positively disagreeable woman Fru Fischer was. Stupid, too.

Fifteen

Well into Helga's second year in Denmark, came an indefinite discontent. Not clear, but vague, like a storm gathering far on the horizon. It was long before she would admit that she was less happy than she had been during her first year in Copenhagen, but she knew that it was so. And this subconscious knowledge added to her growing restlessness and little mental insecurity. She desired ardently to combat this wearing down of her satisfaction with her life, with herself. But she didn't know how.

Frankly the question came to this: what was the matter with her? Was there, without her knowing it, some peculiar lack in her? Absurd. But she began to have a feeling of discouragement and hopelessness. Why couldn't she be happy, content, somewhere? Other people managed, somehow, to be. To put it plainly, didn't she know how? Was she incapable of it?

And then on a warm spring day came Anne's letter telling of her coming marriage to Anderson, who retained still his shadowy place in Helga Crane's

---

1. Carl August Nielsen (1865–1931), Danish composer, conductor, and a director of the Copenhagen conservatory. Niels Wilhelm Gade (1817–1890) and Peter Arnold Heise (1830–1879) were important Danish composers of the previous generation.

memory. It added, somehow, to her discontent, and to her growing dissatisfaction with her peacock's life. This, too, annoyed her.

What, she asked herself, was there about that man which had the power always to upset her? She began to think back to her first encounter with him. Perhaps if she hadn't come away—She laughed. Derisively. "Yes, if I hadn't come away, I'd be stuck in Harlem. Working every day of my life. Chattering about the race problem."

Anne, it seemed, wanted her to come back for the wedding. This, Helga had no intention of doing. True, she had liked and admired Anne better than anyone she had ever known, but even for her she wouldn't cross the ocean.

Go back to America, where they hated Negroes! To America, where Negroes were not people. To America, where Negroes were allowed to be beggars only, of life, of happiness, of security. To America, where everything had been taken from those dark ones, liberty, respect, even the labor of their hands. To America, where if one had Negro blood, one mustn't expect money, education, or, sometimes, even work whereby one might earn bread. Perhaps she was wrong to bother about it now that she was so far away. Helga couldn't, however, help it. Never could she recall the shames and often the absolute horrors of the black man's existence in America without the quickening of her heart's beating and a sensation of disturbing nausea. It was too awful. The sense of dread of it was almost a tangible thing in her throat.

And certainly she wouldn't go back for any such idiotic reason as Anne's getting married to that offensive Robert Anderson. Anne was really too amusing. Just why, she wondered, and how had it come about that he was being married to Anne. And why did Anne, who had so much more than so many others—more than enough—want Anderson too? Why couldn't she—"I think," she told herself, "I'd better stop. It's none of my business. I don't care in the least. Besides," she added irrelevantly, "I hate such nonsensical soul-searching."

One night not long after the arrival of Anne's letter with its curious news, Helga went with Olsen and some other young folk to the great Circus, a vaudeville house, in search of amusement on a rare off night. After sitting through several numbers they reluctantly arrived at the conclusion that the whole entertainment was dull, unutterably dull, and apparently without alleviation, and so not to be borne. They were reaching for their wraps when out upon the stage pranced two black men, American Negroes undoubtedly, for as they danced and cavorted, they sang in the English of America an old ragtime song that Helga remembered hearing as a child, "Everybody Gives Me Good Advice."[2] At its conclusion the audience applauded with delight. Only Helga Crane was silent, motionless.

More songs, old, all of them old, but new and strange to that audience. And how the singers danced, pounding their thighs, slapping their hands together, twisting their legs, waving their abnormally long arms, throwing their bodies about with a loose ease! And how the enchanted spectators clapped and howled and shouted for more!

Helga Crane was not amused. Instead she was filled with a fierce hatred for the cavorting Negroes on the stage. She felt shamed, betrayed, as if these

2. A song written by James Kendis, Herman Paley, and Alfred Bryan (ca. 1920).

pale pink and white people among whom she lived had suddenly been invited to look upon something in her which she had hidden away and wanted to forget. And she was shocked at the avidity at which Olsen beside her drank it in.

But later, when she was alone, it became quite clear to her that all along they had divined its presence, had known that in her was something, some characteristic, different from any that they themselves possessed. Else why had they decked her out as they had? Why subtly indicated that she was different? And they hadn't despised it. No, they had admired it, rated it as a precious thing, a thing to be enhanced, preserved. Why? She, Helga Crane, didn't admire it. She suspected that no Negroes, no Americans, did. Else why their constant slavish imitation of traits not their own? Why their constant begging to be considered as exact copies of other people? Even the enlightened, the intelligent ones demanded nothing more. They were all beggars like the motley crowd in the old nursery rhyme:

> Hark! Hark!
> The dogs do bark.
> The beggars are coming to town.
> Some in rags,
> Some in tags,
> And some in velvet gowns.

The incident left her profoundly disquieted. Her old unhappy questioning mood came again upon her, insidiously stealing away more of the contentment from her transformed existence.

But she returned again and again to the Circus, always alone, gazing intently and solemnly at the gesticulating black figures, an ironical and silently speculative spectator. For she knew that into her plan for her life had thrust itself a suspensive conflict in which were fused doubts, rebellion, expediency, and urgent longings.

It was at this time that Axel Olsen asked her to marry him. And now Helga Crane was surprised. It was a thing that at one time she had much wanted, had tried to bring about, and had at last relinquished as impossible of achievement. Not so much because of its apparent hopelessness as because of a feeling, intangible almost, that, excited and pleased as he was with her, her origin a little repelled him, and that, prompted by some impulse of racial antagonism, he had retreated into the fastness of a protecting habit of self-ridicule. A mordantly personal pride and sensitiveness deterred Helga from further efforts at incitation.

True, he had made, one morning, while holding his brush poised for a last, a very last stroke on the portrait, one admirably draped suggestion, speaking seemingly to the pictured face. Had he insinuated marriage, or something less—and easier? Or had he paid her only a rather florid compliment, in somewhat dubious taste? Helga, who had not at the time been quite sure, had remained silent, striving to appear unhearing.

Later, having thought it over, she flayed herself for a fool. It wasn't, she should have known, in the manner of Axel Olsen to pay florid compliments in questionable taste. And had it been marriage that he had meant, he would, of course, have done the proper thing. He wouldn't have stopped—or, rather, have begun—by making his wishes known to her when there was Uncle Poul to be formally consulted. She had been, she told herself, insulted. And a goodly measure of contempt and wariness was added to her interest in the man. She was able, however, to feel a gratifying sense of elation in the remembrance that she had been silent, ostensibly unaware of his utterance, and therefore, as far as he knew, not affronted.

This simplified things. It did away with the quandary in which the confession to the Dahls of such a happening would have involved her, for she couldn't be sure that they, too, might not put it down to the difference of her ancestry. And she could still go attended by him, and envied by others, to openings in Konigen's Nytorv,[3] to showings at the Royal Academy or Charlottenborg's Palace. He could still call for her and Aunt Katrina of an afternoon or go with her to Magasin du Nord[4] to select a scarf or a length of silk, of which Uncle Poul could say casually in the presence of interested acquaintances: "Um, pretty scarf"—or "frock"—"you're wearing, Helga. Is that the new one Olsen helped you with?"

Her outward manner toward him changed not at all, save that gradually she became, perhaps, a little more detached and indifferent. But definitely Helga Crane had ceased, even remotely, to consider him other than as someone amusing, desirable, and convenient to have about—if one was careful. She intended, presently, to turn her attention to one of the others. The decorative Captain of the Hussars, perhaps. But in the ache of her growing nostalgia, which, try as she might, she could not curb, she no longer thought with any seriousness on either Olsen or Captain Skaargaard. She must, she felt, see America again first. When she returned—

Therefore, where before she would have been pleased and proud at Olsen's proposal, she was now truly surprised. Strangely, she was aware also of a curious feeling of repugnance, as her eyes slid over his face, as smiling, assured, with just the right note of fervor, he made his declaration and request. She was astonished. Was it possible? Was it really this man that she had thought, even wished, she could marry?

He was, it was plain, certain of being accepted, as he was always certain of acceptance, of adulation, in any and every place that he deigned to honor with his presence. Well, Helga was thinking, that wasn't as much his fault as her own, her aunt's everyone's. He was spoiled, childish almost.

To his words, once she had caught their content and recovered from her surprise, Helga paid not much attention. They would, she knew, be absolutely appropriate ones, and they didn't at all matter. They meant nothing to her—now. She was too amazed to discover suddenly how intensely she disliked him, disliked the shape of his head, the mop of his hair, the line of his nose, the tones of his voice, the nervous grace of his long fingers; disliked even the very look of his irreproachable clothes. And for some inexplicable reason, she was a little frightened and embarrassed, so that when he had finished speaking, for a short space there was only stillness in the small room, into which Aunt Katrina had tactfully had him shown. Even Thor, the enormous Persian, curled on the window ledge in the feeble late afternoon sun, had rested for the moment from his incessant purring under Helga's idly stroking fingers.

---

3. King's New Square.
4. Copenhagen's largest and best-known department store.

Helga, her slight agitation vanished, told him that she was surprised. His offer was, she said, unexpected. Quite.

A little sardonically, Olsen interrupted her. He smiled too. "But of course I expected surprise. It is, is it not, the proper thing? And always you are proper, Frøkken Helga, always."

Helga, who had a stripped, naked feeling under his direct glance, drew herself up stiffly. Herr Olsen needn't, she told him, be sarcastic. She *was* surprised. He must understand that she was being quite sincere, quite truthful about that. Really, she hadn't expected him to do her so great an honor.

He made a little impatient gesture. Why, then, had she refused, ignored, his other, earlier suggestion?

At that Helga Crane took a deep indignant breath and was again, this time for an almost imperceptible second, silent. She had, then, been correct in her deduction. Her sensuous, petulant mouth hardened. That he should so frankly—so insolently, it seemed to her—admit his outrageous meaning was too much. She said, coldly: "Because, Herr Olsen, in my country the men, of my race, at least, don't make such suggestions to decent girls. And thinking that you were a gentleman, introduced to me by my aunt, I chose to think myself mistaken, to give you the benefit of the doubt."

"Very commendable, my Helga—and wise. Now you have your reward. Now I offer you marriage."

"Thanks," she answered, "thanks, awfully."

"Yes," and he reached for her slim cream hand, now lying quiet on Thor's broad orange and black back. Helga let it lie in his large pink one, noting their contrast. "Yes, because I, poor artist that I am, cannot hold out against the deliberate lure of you. You disturb me. The longing for you does harm to my work. You creep into my brain and madden me," and he kissed the small ivory hand. Quite decorously, Helga thought, for one so maddened that he was driven, against his inclination, to offer her marriage. But immediately, in extenuation, her mind leapt to the admirable casualness of Aunt Katrina's expressed desire for this very thing, and recalled the unruffled calm of Uncle Poul under any and all circumstances. It was, as she had long ago decided, security. Balance.

"But," the man before her was saying, "for me it will be an experience. It may be that with you, Helga, for wife, I will become great. Immortal. Who knows? I didn't want to love you, but I had to. That is the truth. I make of myself a present to you. For love." His voice held a theatrical note. At the same time he moved forward putting out his arms. His hands touched air. For Helga had moved back. Instantly he dropped his arms and took a step away, repelled by something suddenly wild in her face and manner. Sitting down, he passed a hand over his face with a quick, graceful gesture.

Tameness returned to Helga Crane. Her ironic gaze rested on the face of Axel Olsen, his leonine head, his broad nose—"broader than my own"—his bushy eyebrows, surmounting thick, drooping lids, which hid, she knew, sullen blue eyes. He stirred sharply, shaking off his momentary disconcertion.

In his assured, despotic way he went on: "You know, Helga, you are a contradiction. You have been, I suspect, corrupted by the good Fru Dahl, which is perhaps as well. Who knows? You have the warm impulsive nature of the women of Africa, but, my lovely, you have, I fear, the soul of a prostitute. You sell yourself to the highest buyer. I should of course be happy that it is I. And I am." He stopped, contemplating her, lost apparently, for the second, in pleasant thoughts of the future.

To Helga he seemed to be the most distant, the most unreal figure in the world. She suppressed a ridiculous impulse to laugh. The effort sobered her. Abruptly she was aware that in the end, in some way, she would pay for this hour. A quick brief fear ran through her, leaving in its wake a sense of impending calamity. She wondered if for this she would pay all that she'd had.

And, suddenly, she didn't at all care. She said, lightly, but firmly: "But you see, Herr Olsen, I'm not for sale. Not to you. Not to any white man. I don't at all care to be owned. Even by you."

The drooping lids lifted. The look in the blue eyes was, Helga thought, like the surprised stare of a puzzled baby. He hadn't at all grasped her meaning.

She proceeded, deliberately: "I think you don't understand me. What I'm trying to say is this, I don't want you. I wouldn't under any circumstances marry you," and since she was, as she put it, being brutally frank, she added: "*Now.*"

He turned a little away from her, his face white but composed, and looked down into the gathering shadows in the little park before the house. At last he spoke, in a queer frozen voice: "You refuse me?"

"Yes," Helga repeated with intentional carelessness. "I refuse you."

The man's full upper lip trembled. He wiped his forehead, where the gold hair was now lying flat and pale and lusterless. His eyes still avoided the girl in the high-backed chair before him. Helga felt a shiver of compunction. For an instant she regretted that she had not been a little kinder. But wasn't it after all the greatest kindness to be cruel? But more gently, less indifferently, she said: "You see, I couldn't marry a white man. I simply couldn't. It isn't just you, not just personal, you understand. It's deeper, broader than that. It's racial. Some day maybe you'll be glad. We can't tell, you know; if we were married, you might come to be ashamed of me, to hate me, to hate all dark people. My mother did that."

"I have offered you marriage, Helga Crane, and you answer me with some strange talk of race and shame. What nonsense is this?"

Helga let that pass because she couldn't, she felt, explain. It would be too difficult, too mortifying. She had no words which could adequately, and without laceration to her pride, convey to him the pitfalls into which very easily they might step. "I might," she said, "have considered it once—when I first came. But you, hoping for a more informal arrangement, waited too long. You missed the moment. I had time to think. Now I couldn't. Nothing is worth the risk. We might come to hate each other. I've been through it, or something like it. I know. I couldn't do it. And I'm glad."

Rising, she held out her hand, relieved that he was still silent. "Good afternoon," she said formally. "It has been a great honor—"

"A tragedy," he corrected, barely touching her hand with his moist fingertips.

"Why?" Helga countered, and for an instant felt as if something sinister and internecine flew back and forth between them like poison.

"I mean," he said, and quite solemnly, "that though I don't entirely understand you, yet in a way I do too. And—" He hesitated. Went on. "I think that my picture of you is, after all, the true Helga Crane. Therefore—a tragedy. For someone. For me? Perhaps."

"Oh, the picture!" Helga lifted her shoulders in a little impatient motion.

Ceremoniously Axel Olsen bowed himself out, leaving her grateful for the urbanity which permitted them to part without too much awkwardness. No other man, she thought, of her acquaintance could have managed it so well—except, perhaps, Robert Anderson.

"I'm glad," she declared to herself in another moment, "that I refused him. And," she added honestly, "I'm glad that I had the chance. He took it awfully well, though—for a tragedy." And she made a tiny frown.

The picture—she had never quite, in spite of her deep interest in him, and her desire for his admiration and approval, forgiven Olsen for that portrait. It wasn't, she contended, herself at all, but some disgusting sensual creature with her features. Herr and Fru Dahl had not exactly liked it either, although collectors, artists, and critics had been unanimous in their praise and it had been hung on the line at an annual exhibition, where it had attracted much flattering attention and many tempting offers.

Now Helga went in and stood for a long time before it, with its creator's parting words in mind: "... a tragedy ... my picture is, after all, the true Helga Crane." Vehemently she shook her head. "It isn't, it isn't at all," she said aloud. Bosh! Pure artistic bosh and conceit. Nothing else. Anyone with half an eye could see that it wasn't, at all, like her.

"Marie," she called to the maid passing in the hall, "do you think this is a good picture of me?"

Marie blushed. Hesitated. "Of course, Frøkken, I know Herr Olsen is a great artist, but no, I don't like that picture. It looks bad, wicked. Begging your pardon, Frøkken."

"Thanks, Marie, I don't like it either."

Yes, anyone with half an eye could see that it wasn't she.

Sixteen

Glad though the Dahls may have been that their niece had had the chance of refusing the hand of Axel Olsen, they were anything but glad that she had taken that chance. Very plainly they said so, and quite firmly they pointed out to her the advisability of retrieving the opportunity, if, indeed, such a thing were possible. But it wasn't, even had Helga been so inclined, for, they were to learn from the columns of *Politiken*,[5] Axel Olsen had gone off suddenly to some queer place in the Balkans. To rest, the newspapers said. To get Frøkken Crane out of his mind, the gossips said.

Life in the Dahl ménage went on, smoothly as before, but not so pleasantly. The combined disappointment and sense of guilt of the Dahls and Helga colored everything. Though she had resolved not to think that they felt that she had, as it were, "let them down," Helga knew that they did. They had not so much expected as hoped that she would bring down Olsen, and so secure the link between the merely fashionable set to which they belonged and the artistic one after which they hankered. It was of course true that there were others, plenty of them. But there was only one Olsen. And Helga,

---

5. *Politiken* (literally, "politics" or "policy"), a Danish newspaper.

for some idiotic reason connected with race, had refused him. Certainly there was no use in thinking, even, of the others. If she had refused him, she would refuse any and all for the same reason. It was, it seemed, all-embracing.

"It isn't," Uncle Poul had tried to point out to her, "as if there were hundreds of mulattoes here. That, I can understand, might make it a little different. But there's only you. You're unique here, don't you see? Besides, Olsen has money and enviable position. Nobody'd dare to say, or even to think anything odd or unkind of you or him. Come now, Helga, it isn't this foolishness about race. Not here in Denmark. You've never spoken of it before. It can't be just that. You're too sensible. It must be something else. I wish you'd try to explain. You don't perhaps like Olsen?"

Helga had been silent, thinking what a severe wrench to Herr Dahl's ideas of decency was this conversation. For he had an almost fanatic regard for reticence, and a peculiar shrinking from what he looked upon as indecent exposure of the emotions.

"Just what is it, Helga?" he asked again, because the pause had grown awkward, for him.

"I can't explain any better than I have," she had begun tremulously, "it's just something—something deep down inside of me," and had turned away to hide a face convulsed by threatening tears.

But that, Uncle Poul had remarked with a reasonableness that was wasted on the miserable girl before him, was nonsense, pure nonsense.

With a shaking sigh and a frantic dab at her eyes, in which had come a despairing look, she had agreed that perhaps it was foolish, but she couldn't help it. "Can't you, won't you understand, Uncle Poul?" she begged, with a pleading look at the kindly worldly man who at that moment had been thinking that this strange exotic niece of his wife's was indeed charming. He didn't blame Olsen for taking it rather hard.

The thought passed. She was weeping. With no effort at restraint. Charming, yes. But insufficiently civilized. Impulsive. Imprudent. Selfish.

"Try, Helga, to control yourself," he had urged gently. He detested tears. "If it distresses you so, we won't talk of it again. You, of course, must do as you yourself wish. Both your aunt and I want only that you should be happy." He had wanted to make an end of this fruitless wet conversation.

Helga had made another little dab at her face with the scrap of lace and raised shining eyes to his face. She had said, with sincere regret: "You've been marvelous to me, you and Aunt Katrina. Angelic. I don't want to seem ungrateful. I'd do anything for you, anything in the world but this."

Herr Dahl had shrugged. A little sardonically he had smiled. He had refrained from pointing out that this was the only thing she could do for them, the only thing that they had asked of her. He had been too glad to be through with the uncomfortable discussion.

So life went on. Dinners, coffees, theaters, pictures, music, clothes. More dinners, coffees, theaters, clothes, music. And that nagging aching for America increased. Augmented by the uncomfortableness of Aunt Katrina's and Uncle Poul's disappointment with her, that tormenting nostalgia grew to an unbearable weight. As spring came on with many gracious tokens of following summer, she found her thoughts straying with increasing frequency to Anne's letter and to Harlem, its dirty streets, swollen now, in the warmer weather, with dark, gay humanity.

Until recently she had had no faintest wish ever to see America again.

Now she began to welcome the thought of a return. Only a visit, of course. Just to see, to prove to herself that there was nothing there for her. To demonstrate the absurdity of even thinking that there could be. And to relieve the slight tension here. Maybe when she came back—

Her definite decision to go was arrived at with almost bewildering suddenness. It was after a concert at which Dvořák's "New World Symphony"[6] had been wonderfully rendered. Those wailing undertones of "Swing Low, Sweet Chariot" were too poignantly familiar. They struck into her longing heart and cut away her weakening defenses. She knew at least what it was that had lurked formless and undesignated these many weeks in the back of her troubled mind. Incompleteness.

"I'm homesick, not for America, but for Negroes. That's the trouble."

For the first time Helga Crane felt sympathy rather than contempt and hatred for that father, who so often and so angrily she had blamed for his desertion of her mother. She understood, now, his rejection, his repudiation, of the formal calm her mother had represented. She understood his yearning, his intolerable need for the inexhaustible humor and the incessant hope of his own kind, his need for those things, not material, indigenous to all Negro environments. She understood and could sympathize with his facile surrender to the irresistible ties of race, now that they dragged at her own heart. And as she attended parties, the theater, the opera, and mingled with people on the streets, meeting only pale serious faces when she longed for brown laughing ones, she was able to forgive him. Also, it was as if in this understanding and forgiving she had come upon knowledge of almost sacred importance.

Without demur, opposition, or recrimination Herr and Fru Dahl accepted Helga's decision to go back to America. She had expected that they would be glad and relieved. It was agreeable to discover that she had done them less than justice. They were, in spite of their extreme worldliness, very fond of her, and would, as they declared, miss her greatly. And they did want her to come back to them, as they repeatedly insisted. Secretly they felt as she did, that perhaps when she returned—So it was agreed upon that it was only for a brief visit, "for your friend's wedding," and that she was to return in the early fall.

The last day came. The last good-byes were said. Helga began to regret that she was leaving. Why couldn't she have two lives, or why couldn't she be satisfied in one place? Now that she was actually off, she felt heavy at heart. Already she looked back with infinite regret at the two years in the country which had given her so much, of pride, of happiness, of wealth, and of beauty.

Bells rang. The gangplank was hoisted. The dark strip of water widened. The running figures of friends suddenly grown very dear grew smaller, blurred into a whole, and vanished. Tears rose in Helga Crane's eyes, fear in her heart.

Good-bye Denmark! Good-bye. Good-bye!

---

6. The Symphony no. 9 in E Minor, *From the New World* (1893), by the Czech composer Antonín Dvořák (1841–1901); it incorporates a number of what Dvořák called "Negro melodies," including the spiritual "Swing Low, Sweet Chariot."

Seventeen

A Summer had ripened and fall begun. Anne and Dr. Anderson had returned from their short Canadian wedding journey. Helga Crane, lingering still in America, had tactfully removed herself from the house in One Hundred and Thirty-ninth Street to a hotel. It was, as she could point out to curious acquaintances, much better for the newly-married Andersons not to be bothered with a guest, not even with such a close friend as she, Helga, had been to Anne.

Actually, though she herself had truly wanted to get out of the house when they came back, she had been a little surprised and a great deal hurt that Anne had consented so readily to her going. She might at least, thought Helga indignantly, have acted a little bit as if she had wanted her to stay. After writing for her to come, too.

Pleasantly unaware was Helga that Anne, more silently wise than herself, more determined, more selfish, and less inclined to leave anything to chance, understood perfectly that in a large measure it was the voice of Robert Anderson's inexorable conscience that had been the chief factor in bringing about her second marriage—his ascetic protest against the sensuous, the physical. Anne had perceived that the decorous surface of her new husband's mind regarded Helga Crane with that intellectual and aesthetic appreciation which attractive and intelligent women would always draw from him, but that underneath that well-managed section, in a more lawless place where she herself never hoped or desired to enter, was another, a vagrant primitive groping toward something shocking and frightening to the cold asceticism of his reason. Anne knew also that though she herself was lovely—more beautiful than Helga—and interesting, with her he had not to struggle against that nameless and to him shameful impulse, that sheer delight, which ran through his nerves at mere proximity to Helga. And Anne intended that her marriage should be a success. She intended that her husband should be happy. She was sure that it could be managed by tact and a little cleverness on her own part. She was truly fond of Helga, but seeing how she had grown more charming, more aware of her power, Anne wasn't so sure that her sincere and urgent request to come over for her wedding hadn't been a mistake. She was, however, certain of herself. She could look out for her husband. She could carry out what she considered her obligation to him, keep him undisturbed, unhumiliated. It was impossible that she could fail. Unthinkable.

Helga, on her part, had been glad to get back to New York. How glad, or why, she did not truly realize. And though she sincerely meant to keep her promise to Aunt Katrina and Uncle Poul and return to Copenhagen, summer, September, October, slid by and she made no move to go. Her uttermost intention had been a six or eight weeks' visit, but the feverish rush of New York, the comic tragedy of Harlem, still held her. As time went on, she became a little bored, a little restless, but she stayed on. Something of that wild surge of gladness that had swept her on the day when with Anne and Anderson she had again found herself surrounded by hundreds, thousands, of dark-eyed brown folk remained with her. *These* were her people. Nothing, she had come to understand now, could ever change that. Strange that she had never truly valued this kinship until distance had shown her its worth.

How absurd she had been to think that another country, other people, could liberate her from the ties which bound her forever to these mysterious, these terrible, these fascinating, these lovable, dark hordes. Ties that were of the spirit. Ties not only superficially entangled with mere outline of features or color of skin. Deeper. Much deeper than either of these.

Thankful for the appeasement of that loneliness which had again tormented her like a fury, she gave herself up to the miraculous joyousness of Harlem. The easement which its heedless abandon brought to her was a real, a very definite thing. She liked the sharp contrast to her pretentious stately life in Copenhagen. It was as if she had passed from the heavy solemnity of a church service to a gorgeous care-free revel.

Not that she intended to remain. No. Helga Crane couldn't, she told herself and others, live in America. In spite of its glamour, existence in America, even in Harlem, was for Negroes too cramped, too uncertain, too cruel; something not to be endured for a lifetime if one could escape; something demanding a courage greater than was in her. No. She couldn't stay. Nor, she saw now, could she remain away. Leaving, she would have to come back.

This knowledge, this certainty of the division of her life into two parts in two lands, into physical freedom in Europe and spiritual freedom in America, was unfortunate, inconvenient, expensive. It was, too, as she was uncomfortably aware, even a trifle ridiculous, and mentally she caricatured herself moving shuttlelike from continent to continent. From the prejudiced restrictions of the New World to the easy formality of the Old, from the pale calm of Copenhagen to the colorful lure of Harlem.

Nevertheless she felt a slightly pitying superiority over those Negroes who were apparently so satisfied. And she had a fine contempt for the blatantly patriotic black Americans. Always when she encountered one of those picturesque parades in the Harlem streets, the Stars and Stripes streaming ironically, insolently, at the head of the procession tempered for her, a little, her amusement at the childish seriousness of the spectacle. It was too pathetic.

But when mental doors were deliberately shut on those skeletons that stalked lively and in full health through the consciousness of every person of Negro ancestry in America—conspicuous black, obvious brown, or indistinguishable white—life was intensely amusing, interesting, absorbing, and enjoyable; singularly lacking in that tone of anxiety which the insecurities of existence seemed to ferment in other peoples.

Yet Helga herself had an acute feeling of insecurity, for which she could not account. Sometimes it amounted to fright almost. "I must," she would say then, "get back to Copenhagen." But the resolution gave her not much pleasure. And for this she now blamed Axel Olsen. It was, she insisted, he who had driven her back, made her unhappy in Denmark. Though she knew well that it wasn't. Misgivings, too, rose in her. Why hadn't she married him? Anne was married—she would not say Anderson—Why not she? It would serve Anne right if she married a white man. But she knew in her soul that she wouldn't. "Because I'm a fool," she said bitterly.

Eighteen

One November evening, impregnated still with the kindly warmth of the dead Indian summer, Helga Crane was leisurely dressing in pleasant anticipation of the party to which she had been asked for that night. It was always amusing at the Tavenors'. Their house was large and comfortable, the food and music always of the best, and the type of entertainment always unexpected and brilliant. The drinks, too, were sure to be safe.

And Helga, since her return, was more than ever popular at parties. Her courageous clothes attracted attention, and her deliberate lure—as Olsen had called it—held it. Her life in Copenhagen had taught her to expect and accept admiration as her due. This attitude, she found, was as effective in New York as across the sea. It was, in fact, even more so. And it was more amusing too. Perhaps because it was somehow a bit more dangerous.

In the midst of curious speculation as to the possible identity of the other guests, with an indefinite sense of annoyance she wondered if Anne would be there. There was of late something about Anne that was to Helga distinctly disagreeable, a peculiar half-patronizing attitude, mixed faintly with distrust. Helga couldn't define it, couldn't account for it. She had tried. In the end she had decided to dismiss it, to ignore it.

"I suppose," she said aloud, "it's because she's married again. As if anybody couldn't get married. Anybody. That is, if mere marriage is all one wants."

Smoothing away the tiny frown from between the broad black brows, she got herself into a little shining, rose-colored slip of a frock knotted with a silver cord. The gratifying result soothed her ruffled feelings. It didn't really matter, this new manner of Anne's. Nor did the fact that Helga knew that Anne disapproved of her. Without words Anne had managed to make that evident. In her opinion, Helga had lived too long among the enemy, the detestable pale faces. She understood them too well, was too tolerant of their ignorant stupidities. If they had been Latins,[7] Anne might conceivably have forgiven the disloyalty. But Nordics! Lynchers! It was too traitorous. Helga smiled a little, understanding Anne's bitterness and hate, and a little of its cause. It was of a piece with that of those she so virulently hated. Fear. And then she sighed a little, for she regretted the waning of Anne's friendship. But, in view of diverging courses of their lives, she felt that even its complete extinction would leave her undevastated. Not that she wasn't still grateful to Anne for many things. It was only that she had other things now. And there would, forever, be Robert Anderson between them. A nuisance. Shutting them off from their previous confident companionship and understanding. "And anyway," she said again, aloud, "he's nobody much to have married. Anybody could have married him. Anybody. If a person wanted only to be married—If it had been somebody like Olsen—That would be different—something to crow over, perhaps."

The party was even more interesting than Helga had expected. Helen, Mrs. Tavenor, had given vent to a malicious glee, and had invited representatives of several opposing Harlem political and social factions, including the West Indian, and abandoned them helplessly to each other. Helga's observing eyes picked out several great and near-great sulking or obviously trying hard not to sulk in widely separated places in the big rooms. There were present, also, a few white people, to the open disapproval or discomfort of Anne and several

---

7. I.e., those from southern Europe, who speak Romance languages (as opposed to speakers of Germanic languages, the Nordics, from northern Europe and Scandinavia).

others. There too, poised, serene, certain, surrounded by masculine black and white, was Audrey Denney.

"Do you know, Helen," Helga confided, "I've never met Miss Denney. I wish you'd introduce me. Not this minute. Later, when you can manage it. Not so—er—apparently by request, you know."

Helen Tavenor laughed. "No, you wouldn't have met her, living as you did with Anne Grey. Anderson, I mean. She's Anne's particular pet aversion. The mere sight of Audrey is enough to send her into a frenzy for a week. It's too bad, too, because Audrey's an awfully interesting person and Anne's said some pretty awful things about her. *You'll* like her, Helga."

Helga nodded. "Yes, I expect to. And I know about Anne. One night—" She stopped, for across the room she saw, with a stab of surprise, James Vayle. "Where, Helen did you get him?"

"Oh, that? That's something the cat brought in. Don't ask which one. He came with somebody, I don't remember who. I think he's shocked to death. Isn't he lovely? The dear baby. I was going to introduce him to Audrey and tell her to do a good job of vamping on him as soon as I could remember the darling's name, or when it got noisy enough so he wouldn't hear what I called him. But you'll do just as well. Don't tell me you know him!" Helga made a little nod. "Well! And I suppose you met him at some shockingly wicked place in Europe. That's always the way with those innocent-looking men."

"Not quite. I met him ages ago in Naxos. We were engaged to be married. Nice, isn't he? His name's Vayle. James Vayle."

"Nice," said Helen throwing out her hands in a characteristic dramatic gesture—she had beautiful hands and arms—"is exactly the word. Mind if I run off? I've got somebody here who's going to sing. *Not* spirituals. And I haven't the faintest notion where he's got to. The cellar, I'll bet."

James Vayle hadn't, Helga decided, changed at all. Someone claimed her for a dance and it was some time before she caught his eyes, half questioning, upon her. When she did, she smiled in a friendly way over her partner's shoulder and was rewarded by a dignified little bow. Inwardly she grinned, flattered. He hadn't forgotten. He was still hurt. The dance over, she deserted her partner and deliberately made her way across the room to James Vayle. He was for the moment embarrassed and uncertain. Helga Crane, however, took care of that, thinking meanwhile that Helen was right. Here he did seem frightfully young and delightfully unsophisticated. He must be, though, every bit of thirty-two or more.

"They say," was her bantering greeting, "that if one stands on the corner of One Hundred and Thirty-fifth Street and Seventh Avenue long enough, one will eventually see all the people one has ever known or met. It's pretty true, I guess. Not literally of course." He was, she saw, getting himself together. "It's only another way of saying that everybody, almost, some time sooner or later comes to Harlem, even you."

He laughed. "Yes, I guess that is true enough. I didn't come to stay, though." And then he was grave, his earnest eyes searchingly upon her.

"Well, anyway, you're here now, so let's find a quiet corner if that's possible, where we can talk. I want to hear all about you."

For a moment he hung back and a glint of mischief shone in Helga's eyes. "I see," she said, "you're just the same. However, you needn't be anxious. This isn't Naxos, you know. Nobody's watching us, or if they are, they don't care a bit what we do."

At that he flushed a little, protested a little, and followed her. And when at last they had found seats in another room, not so crowded, he said: "I didn't expect to see you here. I thought you were still abroad."

"Oh, I've been back some time, ever since Dr. Anderson's marriage. Anne, you know, is a great friend of mine. I used to live with her. I came for the wedding. But, of course, I'm not staying. I didn't think I'd be here this long."

"You don't mean that you're going to live over there? Do you really like it so much better?"

"Yes and no, to both questions. I was awfully glad to get back, but I wouldn't live here always. I couldn't. I don't think that any of us who've lived abroad for any length of time would ever live here altogether again if they could help it."

"Lot of them do, though," James Vayle pointed out.

"Oh, I don't mean tourists who rush over to Europe and rush all over the continent and rush back to America thinking they know Europe. I mean people who've actually lived there, actually lived among the people."

"I still maintain that they nearly all come back here eventually to live."

"That's because they can't help it," Helga Crane said firmly. "Money, you know."

"Perhaps, I'm not so sure. I was in the war. Of course, that's not really living over there, but I saw the country and the difference in treatment. But, I can tell you, I was pretty darn glad to get back. All the fellows were." he shook his head solemnly. "I don't think anything, money or lack of money, keeps us here. If it was only that, if we really wanted to leave, we'd go all right. No, it's something else, something deeper than that."

"And just what do you think it is?"

"I'm afraid it's hard to explain, but I suppose it's just that we like to be together. I simply can't imagine living forever away from colored people."

A suspicion of a frown drew Helga's brows. She threw out rather tartly: "I'm a Negro too, you know."

"Well, Helga, you were always a little different, a little dissatisfied, though I don't pretend to understand you at all. I never did," he said a little wistfully.

And Helga, who was beginning to feel that the conversation had taken an impersonal and disappointing tone, was reassured and gave him her most sympathetic smile and said almost gently: "And now let's talk about you. You're still at Naxos?"

"Yes I'm still there. I'm assistant principal now."

Plainly it was a cause for enthusiastic congratulation, but Helga could only manage a tepid "How nice!" Naxos was to her too remote, too unimportant. She did not even hate it now.

How long, she asked, would James be in New York?

He couldn't say. Business, important business for the school, had brought him. It was, he said, another tone creeping into his voice, another look stealing over his face, awfully good to see her. She was looking tremendously well. He hoped he would have the opportunity of seeing her again.

But of course. He must come to see her. Any time, she was always in, or would be for him. And how did he like New York, Harlem?

He didn't, it seemed, like it. It was nice to visit, but not to live in. Oh, there were so many things he didn't like about it, the rush, the lack of home life, the crowds, the noisy meaninglessness of it all.

On Helga's face there had come that pityingly sneering look peculiar to imported New Yorkers when the city of their adoption is attacked by alien Americans. With polite contempt she inquired: "And is that all you don't like?"

At her tone the man's bronze face went purple. He answered coldly, slowly, with a faint gesture in the direction of Helen Tavenor, who stood conversing gayly with one of her white guests: "And I don't like that sort of thing. In fact I detest it."

"Why?" Helga was striving hard to be casual in her manner.

James Vayle, it was evident, was beginning to be angry. It was also evident that Helga Crane's question had embarrassed him. But he seized the bull by the horns and said: "You know as well as I do, Helga, that it's the colored girls these men come up here to see. They wouldn't think of bringing their wives." And he blushed furiously at his own implication. The blush restored Helga's good temper. James was really too funny.

"That," she said softly, "is Hugh Wentworth, the novelist, you know." And she indicated a tall olive-skinned girl being whirled about to the streaming music in the arms of a towering black man. "And that is his wife. She isn't colored, as you've probably been thinking. And now let's change the subject again."

"All right! And this time let's talk about you. You say you don't intend to live here. Don't you ever intend to marry, Helga?"

"Some day, perhaps. I don't know. Marriage—that means children, to me. And why add more suffering to the world? Why add any more unwanted, tortured Negroes to America? Why *do* Negroes have children? Surely it must be sinful. Think of the awfulness of being responsible for the giving of life to creatures doomed to endure such wounds to the flesh, such wounds to the spirit, as Negroes have to endure."

James was aghast. He forgot to be embarrassed. "But Helga! Good heavens! Don't you see that if we—I mean people like us—don't have children, the others will still have. That's one of the things that's the matter with us. The race is sterile at the top. Few, very few Negroes of the better class have children, and each generation has to wrestle again with the obstacles of the preceding ones, lack of money, education, and background. I feel very strongly about this. We're the ones who must have the children if the race is to get anywhere."

"Well, I for one don't intend to contribute any to the cause. But how serious we are! And I'm afraid that I've really got to leave you. I've already cut two dances for your sake. Do come to see me."

"Oh, I'll come to see you all right. I've got several things that I want to talk to you about and one thing especially."

"Don't," Helga mocked, "tell me you're going to ask me again to marry you."

"That," he said, "is just what I intend to do."

Helga Crane was suddenly deeply ashamed and very sorry for James Vayle, so she told him laughingly that it was shameful of him to joke with her like that, and before he could answer, she had gone tripping off with a handsome coffee-colored youth whom she had beckoned from across the room with a little smile.

Later she had to go upstairs to pin up a place in the hem of her dress which had caught on a sharp chair corner. She finished the temporary repair and stepped out into the hall, and somehow, she never quite knew exactly just how, into the arms of Robert Anderson. She drew back and looked up smiling to offer an apology.

And then it happened. He stooped and kissed her, a long kiss, holding her close. She fought against him with all her might. Then, strangely, all power seemed to ebb away, and a long-hidden, half-understood desire welled up in her with the suddenness of a dream. Helga Crane's own arms went up about the man's neck. When she drew away, consciously confused and embarrassed, everything seemed to have changed in a space of time which she knew to have been only seconds. Sudden anger seized her. She pushed him indignantly aside and with a little pat for her hair and dress went slowly down to the others.

Nineteen

That night riotous and colorful dreams invaded Helga Crane's prim hotel bed. She woke in the morning weary and a bit shocked at the uncontrolled fancies which had visited her. Catching up a filmy scarf, she paced back and forth across the narrow room and tried to think. She recalled her flirtations and her mild engagement with James Vayle. She was used to kisses. But none had been like that of last night. She lived over those brief seconds, thinking not so much of the man whose arms had held her as of the ecstasy which had flooded her. Even recollection brought a little onrush of emotion that made her sway a little. She pulled herself together and began to fasten on the solid fact of Anne and experienced a pleasant sense of shock in the realization that Anne was to her exactly what she had been before the incomprehensible experience of last night. She still liked her in the same degree and in the same manner. She still felt slightly annoyed with her. She still did not envy her marriage with Anderson. By some mysterious process the emotional upheaval which had racked her had left all the rocks of her existence unmoved. Outwardly nothing had changed.

Days, weeks, passed; outwardly serene; inwardly tumultuous. Helga met Dr. Anderson at the social affairs to which often they were both asked. Sometimes she danced with him, always in perfect silence. She couldn't, she absolutely couldn't, speak a word to him when they were thus alone together, for at such times lassitude encompassed her; the emotion which had gripped her retreated, leaving a strange tranquillity, troubled only by a soft stir of desire. And shamed by his silence, his apparent forgetting, always after these dances she tried desperately to persuade herself to believe what she wanted to believe: that it had not happened, that she had never had that irrepressible longing. It was of no use.

As the weeks multiplied, she became aware that she must get herself out of the mental quagmire into which that kiss had thrown her. And she should be getting herself back to Copenhagen, but she had now no desire to go.

Abruptly one Sunday in a crowded room, in the midst of teacups and chatter, she knew that she couldn't go, that she hadn't since that kiss intended to go without exploring to the end that unfamiliar path into which she had strayed. Well, it was of no use lagging behind or pulling back. It was of no use trying to persuade herself that she didn't want to go on. A species of fatalism fastened on her. She felt that, ever since that last day in Naxos long ago, somehow she had known that this thing would happen. With this conviction came an odd sense of elation. While making a pleasant assent to some remark of a fellow guest she put down her cup and walked without haste, smiling and nodding to friends and acquaintances on her way to that part of the room where he stood looking at some examples of African carving. Helga Crane faced him squarely. As he took the hand which she held out with elaborate casualness, she noted that his trembled slightly. She was secretly congratulating herself on her own calm when it failed her. Physical weariness descended on her. Her knees wobbled. Gratefully she slid into the chair which he hastily placed for her. Timidity came over her. She was silent. He talked. She did not listen. He came at last to the end of his long dissertation on African sculpture, and Helga Crane felt the intentness of his gaze upon her.

"Well?" she questioned.

"I want very much to see you, Helga. Alone."

She held herself tensely on the edge of her chair, and suggested: "Tomorrow?"

He hesitated a second and then said quickly: "Why, yes, that's all right."

"Eight o'clock?"

"Eight o'clock," he agreed.

Eight o'clock tomorrow came. Helga Crane never forgot it. She had carried away from yesterday's meeting a feeling of increasing elation. It had seemed to her that she hadn't been so happy, so exalted, in years, if ever. All night, all day, she had mentally prepared herself for the coming consummation; physically too, spending hours before the mirror.

Eight o'clock had come at last and with it Dr. Anderson. Only then had uneasiness come upon her and a feeling of fear for possible exposure. For Helga Crane wasn't, after all, a rebel from society, Negro society. It did mean something to her. She had no wish to stand alone. But these late fears were overwhelmed by the hardiness of insistent desire; and she had got herself down to the hotel's small reception room.

It was, he had said, awfully good of her to see him. She instantly protested. No, she had wanted to see him. He looked at her surprised. "You know, Helga," he had begun with an air of desperation, "I can't forgive myself for acting such a swine at the Tavenors' party. I don't at all blame you for being angry and not speaking to me except when you had to."

But that, she exclaimed, was simply too ridiculous. "I wasn't angry a bit." And it had seemed to her that things were not exactly going forward as they should. It seemed that he had been very sincere, and very formal. Deliberately. She had looked down at her hands and inspected her bracelets, for she had felt that to look at him would be, under the circumstances, too exposing.

"I was afraid," he went on, "that you might have misunderstood; might have been unhappy about it. I could kick myself. It was, it must have been, Tavenor's rotten cocktails."

Helga Crane's sense of elation had abruptly left her. At the same time she had felt the need to answer carefully. No, she replied, she hadn't thought of it at all. It had meant nothing to her. She had been kissed before. It was really too silly of him to have been at all bothered about it. "For what," she had asked, "is one kiss more or less, these days, between friends?" She had even laughed a little.

Dr. Anderson was relieved. He had been, he told her, no end upset. Rising, he said: "I see you're going out. I won't keep you."

Helga Crane too had risen. Quickly. A sort of madness had swept over her. She felt that he had belittled and ridiculed her. And thinking this, she had suddenly savagely slapped Robert Anderson with all her might, in the face.

For a short moment they had both stood stunned, in the deep silence which had followed that resounding slap. Then, without a word of contrition or apology, Helga Crane had gone out of the room and upstairs.

She had, she told herself, been perfectly justified in slapping Dr. Anderson, but she was not convinced. So she had tried hard to make herself very drunk in order that sleep might come to her, but had managed only to make herself very sick.

Not even the memory of how all living had left his face, which had gone a taupe gray hue, or the despairing way in which he had lifted his head and let it drop, or the trembling hands which he had pressed into his pockets, brought her any scrap of comfort. She had ruined everything. Ruined it because she had been so silly as to close her eyes to all indications that pointed to the fact that no matter what the intensity of his feelings or desires might be, he was not the sort of man who would for any reason give up one particle of his own good opinion of himself. Not even for her. Not even though he knew that she had wanted so terribly something special from him.

Something special. And now she had forfeited it forever. Forever. Helga had an instantaneous shocking perception of what forever meant. And then, like a flash, it was gone, leaving an endless stretch of dreary years before her appalled vision.

Twenty

The day was a rainy one. Helga Crane, stretched out on her bed, felt herself so broken physically, mentally, that she had given up thinking. But back and forth in her staggered brain wavering, incoherent thoughts shot shuttle-like. Her pride would have shut out these humiliating thoughts and painful visions of herself. The effort was too great. She felt alone, isolated from all other human beings, separated even from her own anterior existence by the disaster of yesterday. Over and over, she repeated: "There's nothing left but to go now." Her anguish seemed unbearable.

For days, for weeks, voluptuous visions had haunted her. Desire had burned in her flesh with uncontrollable violence. The wish to give herself had been so intense that Dr. Anderson's surprising, trivial apology loomed as a direct refusal of the offering. Whatever outcome she had expected, it had been something else than this, this mortification, this feeling of ridicule and self-loathing, this knowledge that she had deluded herself. It was all, she told herself, as unpleasant as possible.

Almost she wished she could die. Not quite. It wasn't that she was afraid of death, which had, she thought, its picturesque aspects. It was rather that she knew she would not die. And death, after the debacle, would but intensify its absurdity. Also, it would reduce her, Helga Crane, to unimportance, to nothingness. Even in her unhappy present state, that did not appeal to her. Gradually, reluctantly, she began to know that the blow to her self-esteem, the certainty of having proved herself a silly fool, was perhaps the severest hurt which she had suffered. It was her self-assurance that had gone down in the crash. After all, what Dr. Anderson thought didn't matter. She could escape from the discomfort of his knowing gray eyes. But she couldn't escape from sure knowledge that she had made a fool of herself. This angered her further and she struck the wall with her hands and jumped up and began hastily to dress herself. She couldn't go on with the analysis. It was too hard. Why bother, when she could add nothing to the obvious fact that she had been a fool?

"I can't stay in this room any longer. I must get out or I'll choke." Her self-knowledge had increased her anguish. Distracted, agitated, incapable of containing herself, she tore open drawers and closets trying desperately to take some interest in the selection of her apparel.

It was evening and still raining. In the streets, unusually deserted, the electric lights cast dull glows. Helga Crane, walking rapidly, aimlessly, could decide on no definite destination. She had not thought to take umbrella or even rubbers. Rain and wind whipped cruelly about her, drenching her garments and chilling her body. Soon the foolish little satin shoes which she wore were sopping wet. Unheeding these physical discomforts, she went on, but at the open corner of One Hundred and Thirty-eighth Street a sudden more ruthless gust of wind ripped the small hat from her head. In the next minute the black clouds opened wider and spilled their water with unusual fury. The streets became swirling rivers. Helga Crane, forgetting her mental torment, looked about anxiously for a sheltering taxi. A few taxis sped by, but inhabited, so she began desperately to struggle through wind and rain toward one of the buildings, where she could take shelter in a store or a doorway. But another whirl of wind lashed her and, scornful of her slight strength, tossed her into the swollen gutter.

Now she knew beyond all doubt that she had no desire to die, and certainly not there nor then. Not in such a messy wet manner. Death had lost all of its picturesque aspects to the girl lying soaked and soiled in the flooded gutter. So, though she was very tired and very weak, she dragged herself up and succeeded finally in making her way to the store whose blurred light she had marked for her destination.

She had opened the door and had entered before she was aware that, inside, people were singing a song which she was conscious of having heard years ago—hundreds of years it seemed. Repeated over and over, she made out the words:

> . . . Showers of blessings,
> Showers of blessings . . .[8]

She was conscious too of a hundred pairs of eyes upon her as she stood there, drenched and disheveled, at the door of this improvised meeting-house.[9]

> . . . Showers of blessings . . .

---

8. From "There Shall Be Showers of Blessings" (1881), a hymn with words by Daniel W. Whittle and music by James McGranahan; the title is taken from Ezekiel 34.26.
9. House of worship.

The appropriateness of the song, with its constant reference to showers, the ridiculousness of herself in such surroundings, was too much for Helga Crane's frayed nerves. She sat down on the floor, a dripping heap, and laughed and laughed and laughed.

It was into a shocked silence that she laughed. For at the first hysterical peal the words of the song had died in the singers' throats, and the wheezy organ had lapsed into stillness. But in a moment there were hushed solicitous voices; she was assisted to her feet and led haltingly to a chair near the low platform at the far end of the room. On one side of her a tall angular black woman under a queer hat sat down, on the other a fattish yellow man with huge outstanding ears and long, nervous hands.

The singing began again, this time a low wailing thing:

> Oh, bitter shame and sorrow
> That a time could ever be,
> When I let the Savior's pity
> Plead in vain, and proudly answered:
> "All of self and none of Thee,
> All of self and none of Thee."
>
> Yet He found me, I beheld Him,
> Bleeding on the cursed tree;
> Heard Him pray: "Forgive them, Father."
> And my wistful heart said faintly,
> "Some of self and some of Thee,
> Some of self and some of Thee."[1]

There were, it appeared, endless moaning verses. Behind Helga a woman had begun to cry audibly, and soon, somewhere else, another. Outside, the wind still bellowed. The wailing singing went on:

> . . . Less of self and more of Thee,
> Less of self and more of Thee.

Helga too began to weep, at first silently, softly; then with great racking sobs. Her nerves were so torn, so aching, her body so wet, so cold! It was a relief to cry unrestrainedly, and she gave herself freely to soothing tears, not noticing that the groaning and sobbing of those about her had increased, unaware that the grotesque ebony figure at her side had begun gently to pat her arm to the rhythm of the singing and to croon softly: "Yes, chile, yes, chile." Nor did she notice the furtive glances that the man on her other side cast at her between his fervent shouts of "Amen!" and "Praise God for a sinner!"

She did notice, though, that the tempo, the atmosphere of the place, had changed, and gradually she ceased to weep and gave her attention to what was happening about her. Now they were singing:

> . . . Jesus knows all about my troubles . . .[2]

Men and women were swaying and clapping their hands, shouting and stamping their feet to the frankly irreverent melody of the song. Without

---

1. From the hymn with words by Theodore Monod (1836–1921), based on John 3.30; one widely used arrangement was by James McGranahan.
2. From an African American spiritual.

warning the woman at her side threw off her hat, leaped to her feet, waved her long arms, and shouted shrilly: "Glory! Hallelujah!" and then, in wild, ecstatic fury jumped up and down before Helga clutching at the girl's soaked coat, and screamed: "Come to Jesus, you pore los' sinner!" Alarmed for the fraction of a second, involuntarily Helga had shrunk from her grasp, wriggling out of the wet coat when she could not loosen the crazed creature's hold. At the sight of the bare arms and neck growing out of the clinging red dress, a shudder shook the swaying man at her right. On the face of the dancing woman before her a disapproving frown gathered. She shrieked: "A scarlet 'oman. Come to Jesus, you pore los' Jezebel!"[3]

At this the short brown man on the platform raised a placating hand and sanctimoniously delivered himself of the words: "Remembah de words of our Mastah: 'Let him that is without sin cast de first stone.'[4] Let us pray for our errin' sistah."

Helga Crane was amused, angry, disdainful, as she sat there, listening to the preacher praying for her soul. But though she was contemptuous, she was being too well entertained to leave. And it was, at least, warm and dry. So she stayed, listening to the fervent exhortation to God to save her and to the zealous shoutings and groanings of the congregation. Particularly she was interested in the writhings and weepings of the feminine portion, which seemed to predominate. Little by little the performance took on an almost Bacchic[5] vehemence. Behind her, before her, beside her, frenzied women gesticulated, screamed, wept, and tottered to the praying of the preacher, which had gradually become a cadenced chant. When at last he ended, another took up the plea in the same moaning chant, and then another. It went on and on without pause with the persistence of some unconquerable faith exalted beyond time and reality.

Fascinated, Helga Crane watched until there crept upon her an indistinct horror of an unknown world. She felt herself in the presence of a nameless people, observing rites of a remote obscure origin. The faces of the men and women took on the aspect of a dim vision. "This," she whispered to herself, "is terrible. I must get out of here." But the horror held her. She remained motionless, watching, as if she lacked the strength to leave the place—foul, vile, and terrible, with its mixture of breaths, its contact of bodies, its concerted convulsions, all in wild appeal for a single soul. Her soul.

And as Helga watched and listened, gradually a curious influence penetrated her; she felt an echo of the weird orgy resound in her own heart; she felt herself possessed by the same madness; she too felt a brutal desire to shout and to sling herself about. Frightened at the strength of the obsession, she gathered herself for one last effort to escape, but vainly. In rising, weakness and nausea from last night's unsuccessful attempt to make herself drunk overcame her. She had eaten nothing since yesterday. She fell forward against the crude railing which enclosed the little platform. For a single moment she remained there in silent stillness, because she was afraid she was going to be sick. And in that moment she was lost—or saved. The yelling

---

3. I.e., a prostitute (by association with the biblical Jezebel, a woman viewed as shameless and wicked for urging her husband, the king of Israel, to worship Baal and commit murder; see 1 Kings 16.29–21.29, 2 Kings 9.30–37).

4. Words spoken by Jesus to those who had found a woman committing adultery (see John 8.7).

5. Orgiastic; literally, characteristic of the worshippers of Bacchus (or Dionysus), god of fertility and wine in the classical world.

figures about her pressed forward, closing her in on all sides. Maddened, she grasped at the railing, and with no previous intention began to yell like one insane, drowning every other clamor, while torrents of tears streamed down her face. She was unconscious of the words she uttered, or their meaning: "Oh God, mercy, mercy. Have mercy on me!" but she repeated them over and over.

From those about her came a thunderclap of joy. Arms were stretched toward her with savage frenzy. The women dragged themselves upon their knees or crawled over the floor like reptiles, sobbing and pulling their hair and tearing off their clothing. Those who succeeded in getting near to her leaned forward to encourage the unfortunate sister, dropping hot tears and beads of sweat upon her bare arms and neck.

The thing became real. A miraculous calm came upon her. Life seemed to expand, and to become very easy. Helga Crane felt within her a supreme aspiration toward the regaining of simple happiness, a happiness unburdened by the complexities of the lives she had known. About her the tumult and the shouting continued, but in a lesser degree. Some of the more exuberant worshipers had fainted into inert masses, the voices of others were almost spent. Gradually the room grew quiet and almost solemn, and to the kneeling girl time seemed to sink back into the mysterious grandeur and holiness of far-off simpler centuries.

Twenty-One

On leaving the mission Helga Crane had started straight back to her room at the hotel. With her had gone the fattish yellow man who had sat beside her. He had introduced himself as the Reverend Mr. Pleasant Green in proffering his escort for which Helga had been grateful because she had still felt a little dizzy and much exhausted. So great had been this physical weariness that as she had walked beside him, without attention to his verbose information about his own "field," as he called it, she had been seized with a hateful feeling of vertigo and obliged to lay firm hold on his arm to keep herself from falling. The weakness had passed as suddenly as it had come. Silently they had walked on. And gradually Helga had recalled that the man beside her had himself swayed slightly at their close encounter, and that frantically for a fleeting moment he had gripped at a protruding fence railing. That man! Was it possible? As easy as that?

Instantly across her still half-hypnotized consciousness little burning darts of fancy had shot themselves. No. She couldn't. It would be too awful. Just the same, what or who was there to hold her back? Nothing. Simply nothing. Nobody. Nobody at all.

Her searching mind had become in a moment quite clear. She cast at the man a speculative glance, aware that for a tiny space she had looked into his mind, a mind striving to be calm. A mind that was certain that it was secure because it was concerned only with things of the soul, spiritual things, which to him meant religious things. But actually a mind by habit at home amongst the mere material aspect of things, and at that moment consumed by some longing for the ecstasy that might lurk behind the gleam of her cheek, the flying wave of her hair, the pressure of her slim fingers on his heavy arm. An instant's flashing vision it had been and it was gone at once. Escaped in the aching of her own senses and the sudden disturbing fear that she herself had perhaps missed the supreme secret of life.

After all, there was nothing to hold her back. Nobody to care. She stopped sharply, shocked at what she was on the verge of considering. Appalled at where it might lead her.

The man—what was his name?—thinking that she was almost about to fall again, had reached out his arms to her. Helga Crane had deliberately stopped thinking. She had only smiled, a faint provocative smile, and pressed her fingers deep into his arms until a wild look had come into his slightly bloodshot eyes.

The next morning she lay for a long while, scarcely breathing, while she reviewed the happenings of the night before. Curious. She couldn't be sure that it wasn't religion that had made her feel so utterly different from dreadful yesterday. And gradually she became a little sad, because she realized that with every hour she would get a little farther away from this soothing haziness, this rest from her long trouble of body and of spirit; back into the clear bareness of her own small life and being, from which happiness and serenity always faded just as they had shaped themselves. And slowly bitterness crept into her soul. Because, she thought, all I've ever had in life has been things—except just this one time. At that she closed her eyes, for even remembrance caused her to shiver a little.

Things, she realized, hadn't been, weren't, enough for her. She'd have to have something else besides. It all came back to that old question of happiness. Surely this was it. Just for a fleeting moment Helga Crane, her eyes watching the wind scattering the gray-white clouds and so clearing a speck of blue sky, questioned her ability to retain, to bear, this happiness at such cost as she must pay for it. There was, she knew, no getting round that. The man's agitation and sincere conviction of sin had been too evident, too illuminating. The question returned in a slightly new form. Was it worth the risk? Could she take it? Was she able? Though what did it matter—now?

And all the while she knew in one small corner of her mind that such thinking was useless. She had made her decision. Her resolution. It was a chance at stability, at permanent happiness, that she meant to take. She had let so many other things, other chances, escape her. And anyway there was God, He would perhaps make it come out all right. Still confused and not so sure that it wasn't the fact that she was "saved" that had contributed to this after feeling of well-being, she clutched the hope, the desire to believe that now at last she had found some One, some Power, who was interested in her. Would help her.

She meant, however, for once in her life to be practical. So she would make sure of both things, God and man.

Her glance caught the calendar over the little white desk. The tenth of November. The steamer *Oscar II* sailed today. Yesterday she had half thought of sailing with it. Yesterday. How far away!

With the thought of yesterday came the thought of Robert Anderson and a feeling of elation, revenge. She had put herself beyond the need of help from him. She had made it impossible for herself ever again to appeal to him. Instinctively she had the knowledge that he would be shocked. Grieved. Horribly hurt even. Well, let him!

The need to hurry suddenly obsessed her. She must. The morning was almost gone. And she meant, if she could manage it, to be married today. Rising, she was seized with a fear so acute that she had to lie down again. For the thought came to her that she might fail. Might not be able to confront the situation. That would be too dreadful. But she became calm again. How could he, a naïve creature like that, hold out against her? If she pretended to distress? To fear? To remorse? He couldn't. It would be useless for him even to try. She screwed up her face into a little grin, remembering that even if protestations were to fail, there were other ways.

And, too, there was God.

Twenty-Two

And so in the confusion of seductive repentance Helga Crane was married to the grandiloquent Reverend Mr. Pleasant Green, that rattish yellow man, who had so kindly, so unctuously, proffered his escort to her hotel on the memorable night of her conversion. With him she willingly, even eagerly, left the sins and temptations of New York behind her to, as he put it, "labor in the vineyard of the Lord"[6] in the tiny Alabama town where he was pastor to a scattered and primitive flock. And where, as the wife of the preacher, she was a person of relative importance. Only relative.

Helga did not hate him, the town, or the people. No. Not for a long time.

As always, at first the novelty of the thing, the change, fascinated her. There was a recurrence of the feeling that now, at last, she had found a place for herself, that she was really living. And she had her religion, which in her new status as a preacher's wife had of necessity become real to her. She believed in it. Because in its coming it had brought this other thing, this anæsthetic satisfaction for her senses. Hers was, she declared to herself, a truly spiritual union. This one time in her life, she was convinced, she had not clutched a shadow and missed the actuality. She felt compensated for all previous humiliations and disappointments and was glad. If she remembered that she had had something like this feeling before, she put the unwelcome memory from her with the thought: "This time I know I'm right. This time it will last."

Eagerly she accepted everything, even that bleak air of poverty which, in some curious way, regards itself as virtuous, for no other reason than that it is poor. And in her first hectic enthusiasm she intended and planned to do much good to her husband's parishioners. Her young joy and zest for the uplifting of her fellow men came back to her. She meant to subdue the cleanly scrubbed ugliness of her own surroundings to soft inoffensive beauty, and to help the other women to do likewise. Too, she would help them with their clothes, tactfully point out that sunbonnets, no matter how gay, and aprons, no matter how frilly, were not quite the proper things for Sunday church wear. There would be a sewing circle. She visualized herself instructing the children, who seemed most of the time to run wild, in ways of gentler deportment. She was anxious to be a true helpmate, for in her heart was a feeling of obligation, of humble gratitude.

In her ardor and sincerity Helga even made some small beginnings. True, she was not very successful in this matter of innovations. When she went

6. See Isaiah 5.7.

about to try to interest the women in what she considered more appropriate clothing and in inexpensive ways of improving their homes according to her ideas of beauty, she was met, always, with smiling agreement and good-natured promises. "Yuh all is right, Mis' Green," and "Ah suttinly will, Mis' Green," fell courteously on her ear at each visit.

She was unaware that afterwards they would shake their heads sullenly over their wash-tubs and ironing-boards. And that among themselves they talked with amusement, or with anger, of "dat uppity, meddlin' No'the'n-ah," and "pore Reve'end," who in their opinion "would 'a done bettah to a ma'ied Clementine Richards." Knowing, as she did, nothing of this, Helga was unperturbed. But even had she known, she would not have been disheartened. The fact that it was difficult but increased her eagerness, and made the doing of it seem only the more worth while. Sometimes she would smile to think how changed she was.

And she was humble too. Even with Clementine Richards, a strapping black beauty of magnificent Amazon proportions and bold shining eyes of jet-like hardness. A person of awesome appearance. All chains, strings of beads, jingling bracelets, flying ribbons, feathery neck-pieces, and flowery hats. Clementine was inclined to treat Helga with an only partially concealed contemptuousness, considering her a poor thing without style, and without proper understanding of the worth and greatness of the man, Clementine's own adored pastor, whom Helga had somehow had the astounding good luck to marry. Clementine's admiration of the Reverend Mr. Pleasant Green was open. Helga was at first astonished. Until she learned that there was really no reason why it should be concealed. Everybody was aware of it. Besides, open adoration was the prerogative, the almost religious duty, of the female portion of the flock. If this unhidden and exaggerated approval contributed to his already oversized pomposity, so much the better. It was what they expected, liked, wanted. The greater his own sense of superiority became, the more flattered they were by his notice and small attentions, the more they cast at him killing glances, the more they hung enraptured on his words.

In the days before her conversion, with its subsequent blurring of her sense of humor, Helga might have amused herself by tracing the relation of this constant ogling and flattering on the proverbially large families of preachers; the often disastrous effect on their wives of this constant stirring of the senses by extraneous women. Now, however, she did not even think of it.

She was too busy. Every minute of the day was full. Necessarily. And to Helga this was a new experience. She was charmed by it. To be mistress in one's own house, to have a garden, and chickens, and a pig; to have a husband—and to be "right with God"[7]—what pleasure did that other world which she had left contain that could surpass these? Here, she had found, she was sure, the intangible thing for which, indefinitely, always she had craved. It had received embodiment.

Everything contributed to her gladness in living. And so for a time she loved everything and everyone. Or thought she did. Even the weather. And it was truly lovely. By day a glittering gold sun was set in an unbelievably bright sky. In the evening silver buds sprouted in a Chinese blue sky, and the warm day was softly soothed by a slight, cool breeze. And night! Night,

---

7. Compare Job 9.2: "how should man be just with God?"

when a languid moon peeped through the wide-opened windows of her little house, a little mockingly, it may be. Always at night's approach Helga was bewildered by a disturbing medley of feelings. Challenge. Anticipation. And a small fear.

In the morning she was serene again. Peace had returned. And she could go happily, inexpertly, about the humble tasks of her household, cooking, dish-washing, sweeping, dusting, mending, and darning. And there was the garden. When she worked there, she felt that life was utterly filled with the glory and the marvel of God.

Helga did not reason about this feeling, as she did not at that time reason about anything. It was enough that it was there, coloring all her thoughts and acts. It endowed the four rooms of her ugly brown house with a kindly radiance, obliterating the stark bareness of its white plaster walls and the nakedness of its uncovered painted floors. It even softened the choppy lines of the shiny oak furniture and subdued the awesome horribleness of the religious pictures.

And all the other houses and cabins shared in this illumination. And the people. The dark undecorated women unceasingly concerned with the actual business of life, its rounds of births and christenings, of loves and marriages, of deaths and funerals, were to Helga miraculously beautiful. The smallest, dirtiest, brown child, barefooted in the fields or muddy roads, was to her an emblem of the wonder of life, of love, and of God's goodness.

For the preacher, her husband, she had a feeling of gratitude, amounting almost to sin. Beyond that, she thought of him not at all. But she was not conscious that she had shut him out from her mind. Besides, what need to think of him? He was there. She was at peace, and secure. Surely their two lives were one, and the companionship in the Lord's grace so perfect that to think about it would be tempting providence. She had done with soul-searching.

What did it matter that he consumed his food, even the softest varieties, audibly? What did it matter that, though he did no work with his hands, not even in the garden, his fingernails were always rimmed with black? What did it matter that he failed to wash his fat body, or to shift his clothing, as often as Helga herself did? There were things that more than outweighed these. In the certainty of his goodness, his righteousness, his holiness, Helga somehow overcame her first disgust at the odor of sweat and stale garments. She was even able to be unaware of it. Herself, Helga had come to look upon as a finicky, showy thing of unnecessary prejudices and fripperies. And when she sat in the dreary structure, which had once been a stable belonging to the estate of a wealthy horse-racing man and about which the odor of manure still clung, now the church and social center of the Negroes of the town, and heard him expound with verbal extravagance the gospel of blood and love, of hell and heaven, of fire and gold streets, pounding with clenched fists the frail table before him or shaking those fists in the faces of the congregation like direct personal threats, or pacing wildly back and forth and even sometimes shedding great tears as he besought them to repent, she was, she told herself, proud and gratified that he belonged to her. In some strange way she was able to ignore the atmosphere of self-satisfaction which poured from him like gas from a leaking pipe.

And night came at the end of every day. Emotional, palpitating, amorous, all that was living in her sprang like rank weeds at the tingling thought of night, with a vitality so strong that it devoured all shoots of reason.

Twenty-Three

After the first exciting months Helga was too driven, too occupied, and too sick to carry out any of the things for which she had made such enthusiastic plans, or even to care that she had made only slight progress toward their accomplishment. For she, who had never thought of her body save as something on which to hang lovely fabrics, had now constantly to think of it. It had persistently to be pampered to secure from it even a little service. Always she felt extraordinarily and annoyingly ill, having forever to be sinking into chairs. Or, if she was out, to be pausing by the roadside, clinging desperately to some convenient fence or tree, waiting for the horrible nausea and hateful faintness to pass. The light, care-free days of the past, when she had not felt heavy and reluctant or weak and spent, receded more and more and with increasing vagueness, like a dream passing from a faulty memory.

The children used her up. There were already three of them, all born within the short space of twenty months. Two great healthy twin boys, whose lovely bodies were to Helga like rare figures carved out of amber, and in whose sleepy and mysterious black eyes all that was puzzling, evasive, and aloof in life seemed to find expression. No matter how often or how long she looked at these two small sons of hers, never did she lose a certain delicious feeling in which were mingled pride, tenderness, and exaltation. And there was a girl, sweet, delicate, and flower-like. Not so healthy or so loved as the boys, but still miraculously her own proud and cherished possession.

So there was no time for the pursuit of beauty, or for the uplifting of other harassed and teeming women, or for the instruction of their neglected children.

Her husband was still, as he had always been, deferentially kind and incredulously proud of her—and verbally encouraging. Helga tried not to see that he had rather lost any personal interest in her, except for the short spaces between the times when she was preparing for or recovering from childbirth. She shut her eyes to the fact that his encouragement had become a little platitudinous, limited mostly to "The Lord will look out for you," "We must accept what God sends," or "My mother had nine children and was thankful for every one." If she was inclined to wonder a little just how they were to manage with another child on the way, he would point out to her that her doubt and uncertainty were a stupendous ingratitude. Had not the good God saved her soul from hell-fire and eternal damnation? Had He not in His great kindness given her three small lives to raise up for His glory? Had He not showered her with numerous other mercies (evidently too numerous to be named separately)?

"You must," the Reverend Mr. Pleasant Green would say unctuously, "trust the Lord more fully, Helga."

This pabulum did not irritate her. Perhaps it was the fact that the preacher was, now, not so much at home that even lent to it a measure of real comfort. For the adoring women of his flock, noting how with increasing frequency their pastor's house went unswept and undusted, his children unwashed, and his wife untidy, took pleasant pity on him and invited him often to tasty orderly meals, specially prepared for him, in their own clean houses.

Helga, looking about in helpless dismay and sick disgust at the disorder around her, the permanent assembly of partly emptied medicine bottles on the clock-shelf, the perpetual array of drying baby-clothes on the chair-backs, the constant debris of broken toys on the floor, the unceasing litter of half-dead flowers on the table, dragged in by the toddling twins from the forlorn garden, failed to blame him for the thoughtless selfishness of these absences. And, she was thankful, whenever possible, to be relieved from the ordeal of cooking. There were times when, having had to retreat from the kitchen in lumbering haste with her sensitive nose gripped between tightly squeezing fingers, she had been sure that the greatest kindness that God could ever show to her would be to free her forever from the sight and smell of food.

How, she wondered, did other women, other mothers, manage? Could it be possible that, while presenting such smiling and contented faces, they were all always on the edge of health? All always worn out and apprehensive? Or was it only she, a poor weak city-bred thing, who felt that the strain of what the Reverend Mr. Pleasant Green had so often gently and patiently reminded her was a natural thing, an act of God, was almost unendurable?

One day on her round of visiting—a church duty, to be done no matter how miserable one was—she summoned up sufficient boldness to ask several women how they felt, how they managed. The answers were a resigned shrug, or an amused snort, or an upward rolling of eyeballs with a mention of "de Lawd" looking after us all.

" 'Tain't nothin', nothin' at all, chile," said one, Sary Jones, who, as Helga knew, had had six children in about as many years. "Yuh all takes it too ha'd. Jes' remembah et's natu'al fo' a 'oman to hab chilluns an' don' fret so."

"But," protested Helga, "I'm always so tired and half sick. That can't be natural."

"Laws, chile, we's all ti'ed. An' Ah reckons we's all gwine a be ti'ed till kingdom come. Jes' make de bes' of et, honey. Jes' make de bes' yuh can."

Helga sighed, turning her nose away from the steaming coffee which her hostess had placed for her and against which her squeamish stomach was about to revolt. At the moment the compensations of immorality seemed very shadowy and very far away.

"Jes' remembah," Sary went on, staring sternly into Helga's thin face, "we all gits ouah res' by an' by. In de nex' worl' we's all recompense'. Jes' put yo' trus' in de Sabioah."[8]

Looking at the confident face of the little bronze figure on the opposite side of the immaculately spread table, Helga had a sensation of shame that she should be less than content. Why couldn't she be as trusting and as certain that her troubles would not overwhelm her as Sary Jones was? Sary, who in all likelihood had toiled every day of her life since early childhood except on those days, totalling perhaps sixty, following the birth of her six children. And who by dint of superhuman saving had somehow succeeded in feeding and clothing them and sending them all to school. Before her Helga felt humbled and oppressed by the sense of her own unworthiness and lack of sufficient faith.

"Thanks, Sary," she said, rising in retreat from the coffee, "you've done me a world of good. I'm really going to try to be more patient."

So, though with growing yearning she longed for the great ordinary things

---

8. Savior (dialect).

of life, hunger, sleep, freedom from pain, she resigned herself to the doing without them. The possibility of alleviating her burdens by a greater faith became lodged in her mind. She gave herself up to it. It *did* help. And the beauty of leaning on the wisdom of God, of trusting, gave to her a queer sort of satisfaction. Faith was really quite easy. One had only to yield. To ask no questions. The more weary, the more weak, she became, the easier it was. Her religion was to her a kind of protective coloring, shielding her from the cruel light of an unbearable reality.

This utter yielding in faith to what had been sent her found her favor, too, in the eyes of her neighbors. Her husband's flock began to approve and commend this submission and humility to a superior wisdom. The women-folk spoke more kindly and more affectionately of the preacher's Northern wife. "Pore Mis' Green, wid all dem small chilluns at once. She suah do hab it ha'd. An' she don' nebah complains an' frets no mo'e. Jes' trus' in de Lawd lak de Good Book say. Mighty sweet lil' 'oman too."

Helga didn't bother much about the preparations for the coming child. Actually and metaphorically she bowed her head before God, trusting in Him to see her through. Secretly she was glad that she had not to worry about herself or anything. It was a relief to be able to put the entire responsibility on someone else.

Twenty-Four

It began, this next child-bearing, during the morning services of a breathless hot Sunday while the fervent choir soloist was singing: "Ah am freed of mah sorrow," and lasted far into the small hours of Tuesday morning. It seemed, for some reason, not to go off just right. And when, after that long frightfulness, the fourth little dab of amber humanity which Helga had contributed to a despised race was held before her for maternal approval, she failed entirely to respond properly to this sop of consolation for the suffering and horror through which she had passed. There was from her no pleased, proud smile, no loving, possessive gesture, no manifestation of interest in the important matters of sex and weight. Instead she deliberately closed her eyes, mutely shutting out the sickly infant, its smiling father, the soiled midwife, the curious neighbors, and the tousled room.

A week she lay so. Silent and listless. Ignoring food, the clamoring children, the comings and goings of solicitous, kind-hearted women, her hovering husband, and all of life about her. The neighbors were puzzled. The Reverend Mr. Pleasant Green was worried. The midwife was frightened.

On the floor, in and out among the furniture and under her bed, the twins played. Eager to help, the church-women crowded in and, meeting there others on the same laudable errand, stayed to gossip and to wonder. Anxiously the preacher sat, Bible in hand, beside his wife's bed, or in a nervous half-guilty manner invited the congregated parishioners to join him in prayer for the healing of their sister. Then, kneeling, they would beseech God to stretch out His all-powerful hand on behalf of the afflicted one, softly at first, but with rising vehemence, accompanied by moans and tears, until it seemed that the God to whom they prayed must in mercy to the sufferer grant relief. If only so that she might rise up and escape from the tumult, the heat, and the smell.

Helga, however, was unconcerned, undisturbed by the commotion about her. It was all part of the general unreality. Nothing reached her. Nothing penetrated the kind darkness into which her bruised spirit had retreated. Even that red-letter event, the coming to see her of the old white physician from downtown, who had for a long time stayed talking gravely to her husband, drew from her no interest. Nor for days was she aware that a stranger, a nurse from Mobile, had been added to her household, a brusquely efficient woman who produced order out of chaos and quiet out of bedlam. Neither did the absence of the children, removed by good neighbors at Miss Hartley's insistence, impress her. While she had gone down into that appalling blackness of pain, the ballast of her brain had got loose and she hovered for a long time somewhere in that delightful borderland on the edge of unconsciousness, an enchanted and blissful place where peace and incredible quiet encompassed her.

After weeks she grew better, returned to earth, set her reluctant feet to the hard path of life again.

"Well, here you are!" announced Miss Hartley in her slightly harsh voice one afternoon just before the fall of evening. She had for some time been standing at the bedside gazing down at Helga with an intent speculative look.

"Yes," Helga agreed in a thin little voice, "I'm back." The truth was that she had been back for some hours. Purposely she had lain silent and still, wanting to linger forever in that serene haven, that effortless calm where nothing was expected of her. There she could watch the figures of the past drift by. There was her mother, whom she had loved from a distance and finally so scornfully blamed, who appeared as she had always remembered her, unbelievably beautiful, young, and remote. Robert Anderson, questioning, purposely detached, affecting, as she realized now, her life in a remarkably cruel degree; for at last she understood clearly how deeply, how passionately, she must have loved him. Anne, lovely, secure, wise, selfish. Axel Olsen, conceited, worldly, spoiled. Audrey Denney, placid, taking quietly and without fuss the things which she wanted. James Vayle, snobbish, smug, servile. Mrs. Hayes-Rore, important, kind, determined. The Dahls, rich, correct, climbing. Flashingly, fragmentarily, other long-forgotten figures, women in gay fashionable frocks and men in formal black and white, glided by in bright rooms to distant, vaguely familiar music.

It was refreshingly delicious, this immersion in the past. But it was finished now. It was over. The words of her husband, the Reverend Mr. Pleasant Green, who had been standing at the window looking mournfully out at the scorched melon-patch, ruined because Helga had been ill so long and unable to tend it, were confirmation of that.

"The Lord be praised," he said, and came forward. It was distinctly disagreeable. It was even more disagreeable to feel his moist hand on hers. A cold shiver brushed over her. She closed her eyes. Obstinately and with all her small strength she drew her hand away from him. Hid it far down under the bedcovering, and turned her face away to hide a grimace of unconquerable aversion. She cared nothing, at that moment, for his hurt surprise. She knew only that, in the hideous agony that for interminable hours—no, centuries—she had borne, the luster of religion had vanished; that revulsion had come upon her; that she hated this man. Between them the vastness of the universe had come.

Miss Hartley, all-seeing and instantly aware of a situation, as she had been quite aware that her patient had been conscious for some time before she herself had announced the fact, intervened, saying firmly: "I think it might be better if you didn't try to talk to her now. She's terribly sick and weak yet. She's still got some fever and we mustn't excite her or she's liable to slip back. And we don't want that, do we?"

No, the man, her husband, responded, they didn't want that. Reluctantly he went from the room with a last look at Helga, who was lying on her back with one frail, pale hand under her small head, her curly black hair scattered loose on the pillow. She regarded him from behind dropped lids. The day was hot, her breasts were covered only by a nightgown of filmy *crêpe*, a relic of prematrimonial days, which had slipped from one carved shoulder. He flinched. Helga's petulant lip curled, for she well knew that this fresh reminder of her desirability was like the flick of a whip.

Miss Hartley carefully closed the door after the retreating husband. "It's time," she said, "for your evening treatment, and then you've got to try to sleep for a while. No more visitors tonight."

Helga nodded and tried unsuccessfully to make a little smile. She was glad of Miss Hartley's presence. It would, she felt, protect her from so much. She mustn't, she thought to herself, get well too fast. Since it seemed she was going to get well. In bed she could think, could have a certain amount of quiet. Of aloneness.

In that period of racking pain and calamitous fright Helga had learned what passion and credulity could do to one. In her was born angry bitterness and an enormous disgust. The cruel, unrelieved suffering had beaten down her protective wall of artificial faith in the infinite wisdom, in the mercy, of God. For had she not called in her agony on Him? And He had not heard. Why? Because, she knew now, He wasn't there. Didn't exist. Into that yawning gap of unspeakable brutality had gone, too, her belief in the miracle and wonder of life. Only scorn, resentment, and hate remained—and ridicule. Life wasn't a miracle, a wonder. It was, for Negroes at least, only a great disappointment. Something to be got through with as best one could. No one was interested in them or helped them. God! Bah! And they were only a nuisance to other people.

Everything in her mind was hot and cold, beating and swirling about. Within her emaciated body raged disillusion. Chaotic turmoil. With the obscuring curtain of religion rent,[9] she was able to look about her and see with shocked eyes this thing that she had done to herself. She couldn't, she thought ironically, even blame God for it, now that she knew that He didn't exist. No. No more than she could pray to Him for the death of her husband, the Reverend Mr. Pleasant Green. The white man's God. And His great love for all people regardless of race! What idiotic nonsense she had allowed herself to believe. How could she, how could anyone, have been so deluded? How could ten million black folk credit it when daily before their eyes was enacted its contradiction? Not that she at all cared about the ten million. But herself. Her sons. Her daughter. These would grow to manhood, to womanhood, in this vicious, this hypocritical land. The dark eyes filled with tears.

---

9. This phrase may recall Luke 23.45, "and the veil of the temple was rent" (as Jesus died).

"I wouldn't," the nurse advised, "do that. You've been dreadfully sick, you know. I can't have you worrying. Time enough for that when you're well. Now you must sleep all you possibly can."

Helga did sleep. She found it surprisingly easy to sleep. Aided by Miss Hartley's rather masterful discernment, she took advantage of the ease with which this blessed enchantment stole over her. From her husband's praisings, prayers, and caresses she sought refuge in sleep, and from the neighbors' gifts, advice, and sympathy.

There was that day on which they told her that the last sickly infant, born of such futile torture and lingering torment, had died after a short week of slight living. Just closed his eyes and died. No vitality. On hearing it Helga too had just closed her eyes. Not to die. She was convinced that before her there were years of living. Perhaps of happiness even. For a new idea had come to her. She had closed her eyes to shut in any telltale gleam of the relief which she felt. One less. And she had gone off into sleep.

And there was that Sunday morning on which the Reverend Mr. Pleasant Green had informed her that they were that day to hold a special thanksgiving service for her recovery. There would, he said, be prayers, special testimonies, and songs. Was there anything particular she would like to have said, to have prayed for, to have sung? Helga had smiled from sheer amusement as she replied that there was nothing. Nothing at all. She only hoped that they would enjoy themselves. And, closing her eyes that he might be discouraged from longer tarrying, she had gone off into sleep.

Waking later to the sound of joyous religious abandon floating in through the opened windows, she had asked a little diffidently that she be allowed to read. Miss Hartley's sketchy brows contracted into a dubious frown. After a judicious pause she had answered: "No, I don't think so." Then, seeing the rebellious tears which had sprung into her patient's eyes, she added kindly: "But I'll read to you a little if you like."

That, Helga replied, would be nice. In the next room on a high-up shelf was a book. She'd forgotten the name, but its author was Anatole France.[1] There was a story, "The Procurator of Judea." Would Miss Hartley read that? "Thanks. Thanks awfully."

" 'Laelius Lamia, born in Italy of illustrious parents,' " began the nurse in her slightly harsh voice.

Helga drank it in.

" '. . . For to this day the women bring down doves to the altar as their victims. . . .' "

Helga closed her eyes.

" '. . . Africa and Asia have already enriched us with a considerable number of gods. . . .' "

Miss Hartley looked up. Helga had slipped into slumber while the superbly ironic ending which she had so desired to hear was yet a long way off. A dull tale, was Miss Hartley's opinion, as she curiously turned the pages to see how it turned out.

---

1. Pen name of the French novelist and critic Jacques-Anatole-François Thibault (1844–1924), winner of the 1921 Nobel Prize for Literature. In the story mentioned here (first published in 1891), the aged Pontius Pilate, though insisting that his "memory is not the least bit enfeebled," cannot recall Jesus of Nazereth, whom he had condemned to death decades earlier.

" 'Jesus? . . . Jesus—of Nazareth? I cannot call him to mind.' "

"Huh! she muttered, puzzled. "Silly." And closed the book.

Twenty-Five

During the long process of getting well, between the dreamy intervals when she was beset by the insistent craving for sleep, Helga had had too much time to think. At first she had felt only an astonished anger at the quagmire in which she had engulfed herself. She had ruined her life. Made it impossible ever again to do the things that she wanted, have the things that she loved, mingle with the people she liked. She had, to put it as brutally as anyone could, been a fool. The damnedest kind of a fool. And she had paid for it. Enough. More than enough.

Her mind, swaying back to the protection that religion had afforded her, almost she wished that it had not failed her. An illusion. Yes. But better, far better, than this terrible reality. Religion had, after all, its uses. It blunted the perceptions. Robbed life of its crudest truths. Especially it had its uses for the poor—and the blacks.

For the blacks. The Negroes.

And this, Helga decided, was what ailed the whole Negro race in America, this fatuous belief in the white man's God, this childlike trust in full compensation for all woes and privations in "kingdom come." Sary Jones's absolute conviction, "In de nex' worl' we's all recompense'," came back to her. And ten million souls were as sure of it as was Sary. How the white man's God must laugh at the great joke he had played on them! Bound them to slavery, then to poverty and insult, and made them bear it unresistingly, uncomplainingly almost, by sweet promises of mansions in the sky by and by.

"Pie in the sky," Helga said aloud derisively, forgetting for the moment Miss Hartley's brisk presence, and so was a little startled at hearing her voice from the adjoining room saying severely: "My goodness! No! I should say you can't have pie. It's too indigestible. Maybe when you're better—"

"That," assented Helga, "is what I said. Pie—by and by. That's the trouble."

The nurse looked concerned. Was this an approaching relapse? Coming to the bedside, she felt at her patient's pulse while giving her a searching look. No. "You'd better," she admonished, a slight edge to her tone, "try to get a little nap. You haven't had any sleep today, and you can't get too much of it. You've got to get strong, you know."

With this Helga was in full agreement. It seemed hundreds of years since she had been strong. And she would need strength. For in some way she was determined to get herself out of this bog into which she had strayed. Or— she would have to die. She couldn't endure it. Her suffocation and shrinking loathing were too great. Not to be borne. Again. For she had to admit that it wasn't new, this feeling of dissatisfaction, of asphyxiation. Something like it she had experienced before. In Naxos. In New York. In Copenhagen. This differed only in degree. And it was of the present and therefore seemingly more reasonable. The other revulsions were of the past, and now less explainable.

The thought of her husband roused in her a deep and contemptuous hatred. At his every approach she had forcibly to subdue a furious inclination to scream out in protest. Shame, too, swept over her at every thought of her marriage. Marriage. This sacred thing of which parsons and other Christian folk ranted so sanctimoniously, how immoral—according to their own standards—it could be! But Helga felt also a modicum of pity for him, as for one already abandoned. She meant to leave him. And it was, she had to concede, all of her own doing, this marriage. Nevertheless, she hated him.

The neighbors and churchfolk came in for their share of her all-embracing hatred. She hated their raucous laughter, their stupid acceptance of all things, and their unfailing trust in "de Lawd." And more than all the rest she hated the jangling Clementine Richards, with her provocative smirkings, because she had not succeeded in marrying the preacher and thus saving her, Helga, from that crowning idiocy.

Of the children Helga tried not to think. She wanted not to leave them—if that were possible. The recollection of her own childhood, lonely, unloved, rose too poignantly before her for her to consider calmly such a solution. Though she forced herself to believe that this was different. There was not the element of race, of white and black. They were all black together. And they would have their father. But to leave them would be a tearing agony, a rending of deepest fibers. She felt that through all the rest of her lifetime she would be hearing their cry of "Mummy, Mummy, Mummy," through sleepless nights. No. She couldn't desert them.

How, then, was she to escape from the oppression, the degradation, that her life had become? It was so difficult. It was terribly difficult. It was almost hopeless. So for a while—for the immediate present, she told herself—she put aside the making of any plan for her going. "I'm still," she reasoned, "too weak, too sick. By and by, when I'm really strong—"

It was so easy and so pleasant to think about freedom and cities, about clothes and books, about the sweet mingled smell of Houbigant[2] and cigarettes in softly lighted rooms filled with inconsequential chatter and laughter and sophisticated tuneless music. It was so hard to think out a feasible way of retrieving all these agreeable, desired things. Just then. Later. When she got up. By and by. She must rest. Get strong. Sleep. Then, afterwards, she could work out some arrangement. So she dozed and dreamed in snatches of sleeping and waking, letting time run on. Away.

And hardly had she left her bed and become able to walk again without pain, hardly had the children returned from the homes of the neighbors, when she began to have her fifth child.

1928

---

2. A French perfume.

EDNA ST. VINCENT MILLAY
1892–1950

In the late 1950s, the poet Anne Sexton worried that she might be a "reincarnation" of Edna St. Vincent Millay, and at around the same time Sexton's friend Sylvia Plath was expressing similar fears, insisting to her mother that she would not write "simple lyrics like Millay." At least in part, such anxieties were the result of the enormous success that Edna St. Vincent Millay—poet, playwright, feminist, and political activist—achieved, especially in her early youth, by producing fluent and inventive sonnet cycles, verse dramas, and dramatic poems. For indeed, even while Sexton was troubled by the thought that she might be seriously compared with Millay, she was candidly admitting that "2 years ago I had never heard of any poet but Edna St. Vincent."

Born in Rockland, Maine, Edna St. Vincent Millay was the oldest of three daughters whose father deserted them and their mother, a practical nurse, when the child—called "Vincent" in the family—was eight. According to one biographer, her mother "taught" her to write verse at the age of four; in any case, she soon exhibited a precocious talent. When she was only twenty, one of her most famous poems, "Renascence," was a prize winner in an important contest sponsored by *The Lyric Year*, an anthology of contemporary poetry. Almost immediately, her ability brought her to the attention of a number of older intellectuals, one of whom, Caroline Dow, the executive secretary of the YWCA's national training school in New York, urged her to attend Vassar College. There Millay had a lively career as a notable undergraduate poet, actress, and playwright.

After graduation from Vassar in 1917, Millay led a bohemian life in Greenwich Village. Writing articles for popular magazines and innovative plays (for example, *Aria da Capo*, 1921) as well as acting in the Provincetown Players, a radical little theater group, she seemed to be an incarnation of what was in the 1920s called "the Jazz Age." Passionately independent, openly bisexual, red haired and green eyed, she was a celebrity among artists and intellectuals, with, according to the critic Edmund Wilson (who proposed marriage to her), "an intoxicating effect on people." For her part, she mythologized such intoxication from the heroine's point of view, writing poems that extolled erotic and emotional liberation, poems that would be memorized by generations of young women from her own day to Anne Sexton's. "My candle burns at both ends," she rebelliously proclaimed; "It will not last the night; / But ah, my foes, and oh, my friends—/ It gives a lovely light!"

Millay was also undertaking more ambitious tasks. Though financial difficulties drove her to hackwork for magazines, which she wrote under the name Nancy Boyd, she produced a number of volumes of skillfully crafted verse: *Ballad of the Harp-Weaver* won the Pulitzer Prize in 1923. In addition, she presented herself as, in the words of her friend the writer Floyd Dell, "very much a revolutionary in all her sympathies, and a whole-hearted Feminist." In 1923—as if in keeping with this self-definition—she married the widower of the prominent American feminist Inez Milholland, a Dutch businessman named Eugen Jan Boissevain. Some years her senior, Boissevain was to care for her devotedly for nearly the rest of her life, although he is said to have told friends that the pair lived together "like bachelors," allowing each other complete sexual freedom.

After she married Boissevain, Millay's career continued to flourish for a while. In 1925, she was awarded an honorary degree by Tufts College, the first of many such degrees; and in 1927, she became intensely involved in the crusade to stay the execution of the alleged anarchists Nicola Sacco and Bartolomeo Vanzetti, about whom she wrote a number of passionate verses. In the 1930s, however, her reputation began to wane, perhaps because her art did not seem as innovative as the work of such modernist contemporaries as T. S. Eliot, Wallace Stevens, and Marianne Moore—writers whose rugged and sometimes seemingly ragged forms appeared to be far in advance of the more traditional modes and meters Millay employed. Although during World War II she continued to work actively for public causes and to write intensely political poetry, she became increasingly isolated and dependent on alcohol. In 1944, she suffered a nervous breakdown, and in 1950, a year after her husband died of cancer, she too suddenly died (perhaps of a heart attack, though the cause remains uncertain) while living alone at their country house, Steepletop, in Austerlitz, New York.

Yet despite the pain of Millay's last decade and the disrepute into which she fell in the 1950s and 1960s—an era when such former acolytes as Plath and Sexton felt it necessary to repudiate her as an old-fashioned "poetess"—her art has endured, and several recent biographies have begun to revive interest in her career. Such insouciant texts as "First Fig" and "Second Fig," along with the sonnets "Oh, oh, you will be sorry for that word" and "I, being born a woman and distressed," still radiate the wit and vitality that led one critic to define their author as the literary "It Girl" of the twenties, while the beautifully nuanced sequence *Sonnets from an Ungrafted Tree* has a richness of texture that demonstrates Millay's formal and imaginative mastery. Other works, too, have a sometimes startling freshness. Indeed, one prominent editor has remarked that "Childhood Is the Kingdom Where Nobody Dies" reads like "a twenty-first-century poem."

First Fig[1]

My candle burns at both ends;
   It will not last the night;
But ah, my foes, and oh, my friends—
   It gives a lovely light!

1920

Second Fig[2]

Safe upon the solid rock the ugly houses stand:
Come and see my shining palace built upon the sand!

1920

[Oh, oh, you will be sorry for that word!]

Oh, oh, you will be sorry for that word!
Give back my book and take my kiss instead.
Was it my enemy or my friend I heard,
"What a big book for such a little head!"
5 Come, I will show you now my newest hat,
And you may watch me purse my mouth and prink![3]

---

1. From *A Few Figs from Thistles*, a title that refers to Matthew 7.16: "Do men gather grapes of thorns, or figs of thistles?"
2. See note for "First Fig"; see also Matthew 7.26–27, which criticizes "a foolish man, which built his house upon the sand."
3. Primp.

Oh, I shall love you still, and all of that.
I never again shall tell you what I think.
I shall be sweet and crafty, soft and sly;
10 You will not catch me reading any more:I shall be
called a wife to pattern by;
And some day when you knock and push the door,
Some sane day, not too bright and not too stormy,
I shall be gone, and you may whistle for me.

1923

[I, being born a woman and distressed]

I, being born a woman and distressed
By all the needs and notions of my kind,
Am urged by your propinquity to find
Your person fair, and feel a certain zest
5 To bear your body's weight upon my breast:
So subtly is the fume of life designed,
To clarify the pulse and cloud the mind,
And leave me once again undone, possessed.
Think not for this, however, the poor treason
10 Of my stout blood against my staggering brain,
I shall remember you with love, or season
My scorn with pity,—let me make it plain:
I find this frenzy insufficient reason
For conversation when we meet again.

1923

Sonnets from an Ungrafted Tree[4]

I

So she came back into his house again
And watched beside his bed until he died,
Loving him not at all. The winter rain
Splashed in the painted butter-tub outside,
5 Where once her red geraniums had stood,
Where still their rotted stalks were to be seen;
The thin log snapped; and she went out for wood,
Bareheaded, running the few steps between
The house and shed; there, from the sodden eaves
10 Blown back and forth on ragged ends of twine,
Saw the dejected creeping-jinny vine,
(And one, big-aproned, blithe, with stiff blue sleeves
Rolled to the shoulder that warm day in spring,
Who planted seeds, musing ahead to their far blossoming).

---

4. A tree to which new branches or cuttings have not been attached.

II

The last white sawdust on the floor was grown
Gray as the first, so long had he been ill;
The axe was nodding in the block; fresh-blown
And foreign came the rain across the sill,
But on the roof so steadily it drummed
She could not think a time it might not be—
In hazy summer, when the hot air hummed
With mowing, and locusts rising raspingly,
When that small bird with iridescent wings
And long incredible sudden silver tongue
Had just flashed (and yet maybe not!) among
The dwarf nasturtiums—when no sagging springs
Of shower were in the whole bright sky, somehow
Upon this roof the rain would drum as it was drumming now.

III

She filled her arms with wood, and set her chin
Forward, to hold the highest stick in place,
No less afraid than she had always been
Of spiders up her arms and on her face,
But too impatient for a careful search
Or a less heavy loading, from the heap
Selecting hastily small sticks of birch,
For their curled bark, that instantly will leap
Into a blaze, nor thinking to return
Some day, distracted, as of old, to find
Smooth, heavy, round, green logs with a wet, gray rind
Only, and knotty chunks that will not burn,
(That day when dust is on the wood-box floor,
And some old catalogue, and a brown, shriveled apple core).

IV

The white bark writhed and sputtered like a fish
Upon the coals, exuding odorous smoke.
She knelt and blew, in a surging desolate wish
For comfort; and the sleeping ashes woke
And scattered to the hearth, but no thin fire
Broke suddenly, the wood was wet with rain.
Then, softly stepping forth from her desire,
(Being mindful of like passion hurled in vain
Upon a similar task, in other days)
She thrust her breath against the stubborn coal,
Bringing to bear upon its hilt the whole
Of her still body . . . there sprang a little blaze . . .
A pack of hounds, the flame swept up the flue!—
And the blue night stood flattened against the window, staring through.

V

A wagon stopped before the house; she heard
The heavy oilskins of the grocer's man
Slapping against his legs. Of a sudden whirred
Her heart like a frightened partridge, and she ran
And slid the bolt, leaving his entrance free;
Then in the cellar way till he was gone
Hid, breathless, praying that he might not see
The chair sway she had laid her hand upon
In passing. Sour and damp from that dark vault
Arose to her the well-remembered chill;
She saw the narrow wooden stairway still
Plunging into the earth, and the thin salt
Crusting the crocks; until she knew him far,
So stood, with listening eyes upon the empty doughnut jar.

VI

Then cautiously she pushed the cellar door
And stepped into the kitchen—saw the track
Of muddy rubber boots across the floor,
The many paper parcels in a stack
Upon the dresser; with accustomed care
Removed the twine and put the wrappings by,
Folded, and the bags flat, that with an air
Of ease had been whipped open skillfully,
To the gape of children. Treacherously dear
And simple was the dull, familiar task.
And so it was she came at length to ask:
How came the soda there? The sugar here?
Then the dream broke. Silent, she brought the mop,
And forced the trade-slip[5] on the nail that held his razor strop.

VII

One way there was of muting in the mind
A little while the ever-clamorous care;
And there was rapture, of a decent kind,
In making mean and ugly objects fair:
Soft-sooted kettle-bottoms, that had been
Time after time set in above the fire,
Faucets, and candlesticks, corroded green,
To mine again from quarry; to attire
The shelves in paper petticoats, and tack
New oilcloth in the ringed-and-rotten's place,
Polish the stove till you could see your face,
And after nightfall rear an aching back

---

5. Receipt.

In a changed kitchen, bright as a new pin,
An advertisement, far too fine to cook a supper in.

VIII

She let them leave their jellies at the door
And go away, reluctant, down the walk.
She heard them talking as they passed before
The blind, but could not quite make out their talk
For noise in the room—the sudden heavy fall
And roll of a charred log, and the roused shower
Of snapping sparks; then sharply from the wall
The unforgivable crowing of the hour.
One instant set ajar, her quiet ear
Was stormed and forced by the full rout of day:
The rasp of a saw, the fussy cluck and bray
Of hens, the wheeze of a pump, she needs must hear;
She inescapably must endure to feel
Across her teeth the grinding of a backing wagon wheel.

IX

Not over-kind nor over-quick in study
Nor skilled in sports nor beautiful was he,
Who had come into her life when anybody
Would have been welcome, so in need was she.
They had become acquainted in this way:
He flashed a mirror in her eyes at school;
By which he was distinguished; from that day
They went about together, as a rule.
She told, in secret and with whispering,
How he had flashed a mirror in her eyes;
And as she told, it struck her with surprise
That this was not so wonderful a thing.
But what's the odds?—It's pretty nice to know
You've got a friend to keep you company everywhere you go.

X

She had forgotten how the August night
Was level as a lake beneath the moon,
In which she swam a little, losing sight
Of shore; and how the boy, who was at noon
Simple enough, not different from the rest,
Wore now a pleasant mystery as he went,
Which seemed to her an honest enough test
Whether she loved him, and she was content.
So loud, so loud the million crickets' choir . . .
So sweet the night, so long-drawn-out and late . . .
And if the man were not her spirit's mate,
Why was her body sluggish with desire?

Stark on the open field the moonlight fell,
But the oak tree's shadow was deep and black and secret as a well.

XI

    It came into her mind, seeing how the snow
Was gone, and the brown grass exposed again,
And clothes-pins, and an apron—long ago,
In some white storm that sifted through the pane
5 And sent her forth reluctantly at last
To gather in, before the line gave way,
Garments, board-stiff, that galloped on the blast
Clashing like angel armies in a fray,
An apron long ago in such a night
10 Blown down and buried in the deepening drift,
To lie till April thawed it back to sight,
Forgotten, quaint and novel as a gift—
It struck her, as she pulled and pried and tore,
That here was spring, and the whole year to be lived through once more.

XII

    Tenderly, in those times, as though she fed
An ailing child—with sturdy propping up
Of its small, feverish body in the bed,
And steadying of its hands about the cup—
5 She gave her husband of her body's strength,
Thinking of men, what helpless things they were,
Until he turned and fell asleep at length,
And stealthily stirred the night and spoke to her.
Familiar, at such moments, like a friend,
10 Whistled far off the long, mysterious train,
And she could see in her mind's vision plain
The magic World, where cities stood on end . . .
Remote from where she lay—and yet—between,
Save for something asleep beside her, only the window screen.

XIII

    From the wan dream that was her waking day,
Wherein she journeyed, borne along the ground
Without her own volition in some way,
Or fleeing, motionless, with feet fast bound,
5 Or running silent through a silent house
Sharply remembered from an earlier dream,
Upstairs, down other stairs, fearful to rouse,
Regarding him, the wide and empty scream
Of a strange sleeper on a malignant bed,
10 And all the time not certain if it were
Herself so doing or some one like to her,
From this wan dream that was her daily bread,

Sometimes, at night, incredulous, she would wake—
A child, blowing bubbles that the chairs and carpet did not break!

XIV

She had a horror he would die at night.
And sometimes when the light began to fade
She could not keep from noticing how white
The birches looked—and then she would be afraid,
₅ Even with a lamp, to go about the house
And lock the windows; and as night wore on
Toward morning, if a dog howled, or a mouse
Squeaked in the floor, long after it was gone
Her flesh would sit awry on her. By day
₁₀ She would forget somewhat, and it would seem
A silly thing to go with just this dream
And get a neighbor to come at night and stay.
But it would strike her sometimes, making the tea:
She had kept that kettle boiling all night long, for company.

XV

There was upon the sill a pencil mark,
Vital with shadow when the sun stood still
At noon, but now, because the day was dark,
It was a pencil mark upon the sill.
₅ And the mute clock, maintaining ever the same
Dead moment, blank and vacant of itself,
Was a pink shepherdess, a picture frame,
A shell marked Souvenir, there on the shelf.
Whence it occurred to her that he might be,
₁₀ The mainspring being broken in his mind,
A clock himself, if one were so inclined,
That stood at twenty minutes after three—
The reason being for this, it might be said,
That things in death were neither clocks nor people, but only dead.

XVI

The doctor asked her what she wanted done
With him, that could not lie there many days.
And she was shocked to see how life goes on
Even after death, in irritating ways;
₅ And mused how if he had not died at all
'Twould have been easier—then there need not be
The stiff disorder of a funeral
Everywhere, and the hideous industry,
And crowds of people calling her by name
₁₀ And questioning her, she'd never seen before,
But only watching by his bed once more
And sitting silent if a knocking came . . .

She said at length, feeling the doctor's eyes,
"I don't know what you do exactly when a person dies."

XVII

Gazing upon him now, severe and dead,
It seemed a curious thing that she had lain
Beside him many a night in that cold bed,
And that had been which would not be again.
5   From his desirous body the great heat
Was gone at last, it seemed, and the taut nerves
Loosened forever. Formally the sheet
Set forth for her today those heavy curves
And lengths familiar as the bedroom door.
10 She was as one who enters, sly, and proud,
To where her husband speaks before a crowd,
And sees a man she never saw before—
The man who eats his victuals at her side,
Small, and absurd, and hers: for once, not hers, unclassified.

1923

The Buck in the Snow

White sky, over the hemlocks bowed with snow,
Saw you not at the beginning of evening the antlered buck and his doe
Standing in the apple-orchard? I saw them. I saw them suddenly go,
Tails up, with long leaps lovely and slow,
5   Over the stone-wall into the wood of hemlocks bowed with snow.

Now lies he here, his wild blood scalding the snow.

How strange a thing is death, bringing to his knees, bringing to his antlers
The buck in the snow.
How strange a thing,—a mile away by now, it may be,
10 Under the heavy hemlocks that as the moments pass
Shift their loads a little, letting fall a feather of snow—
Life, looking out attentive from the eyes of the doe.

1928

To Inez Milholland[6]

*Read in Washington, November eighteenth, 1923, at the unveiling
of a statue of three leaders in the cause of Equal Rights for Women*

Upon this marble bust that is not I
Lay the round, formal wreath that is not fame;

---

6. Socialist reformer and activist (1886–1916) who started the women's suffrage movement at Vassar, where Millay was a student, and died from her overexertions on behalf of the women's vote.

But in the forum of my silenced cry
Root ye the living tree whose sap is flame.
5 I, that was proud and valiant, am no more;—
Save as a dream that wanders wide and late,
Save as a wind that rattles the stout door,
Troubling the ashes in the sheltered grate.
The stone will perish; I shall be twice dust.
10 Only my standard on a taken hill
Can cheat the mildew and the red-brown rust
And make immortal my adventurous will.
Even now the silk is tugging at the staff:
Take up the song; forget the epitaph.

1928

[Women have loved before as I love now][7]

Women have loved before as I love now;
At least, in lively chronicles of the past—
Of Irish waters by a Cornish prow
Or Trojan waters by a Spartan mast[8]
5 Much to their cost invaded—here and there,
Hunting the amorous line, skimming the rest,
I find some woman bearing as I bear
Love like a burning city in the breast.
I think however that of all alive
10 I only in such utter, ancient way
Do suffer love; in me alone survive
The unregenerate passions of a day
When treacherous queens, with death upon the tread,
Heedless and wilful, took their knights to bed.

1931

[Oh, sleep forever in the Latmian cave]

Oh, sleep forever in the Latmian cave,
Mortal Endymion, darling of the Moon![9]
Her silver garments by the senseless wave
Shouldered and dropped and on the shingle[1] strewn,
5 Her fluttering hand against her forehead pressed,
Her scattered looks that trouble all the sky,
Her rapid footsteps running down the west—
Of all her altered state, oblivious lie!

---

7. From the sonnet sequence *Fatal Interview*.
8. An allusion to Isolde, the Irish lover of her Cornish captor, Tristan, and Helen, taken from Sparta in Greece to Troy by Paris.
9. According to Greek myth, Endymion was a beautiful youth who fell asleep in a cave on Mount Latmos; there he was visited by the personification of the moon, Selene. In the most common version of the story, he chose to sleep forever.
1. Pebbly beach.

Whom earthen you, by deathless lips adored,
10   Wild-eyed and stammering to the grasses thrust,
And deep into her crystal body poured
The hot and sorrowful sweetness of the dust:
Whereof she wanders mad, being all unfit
For mortal love, that might not die of it.

1931

Childhood Is the Kingdom Where Nobody Dies

Childhood is not from birth to a certain age and at a certain age
The child is grown, and puts away childish things.[2]
Childhood is the kingdom where nobody dies.
Nobody that matters, that is. Distant relatives of course
5 Die, whom one never has seen or has seen for an hour,
And they gave one candy in a pink-and-green stripéd bag, or a jack-knife,
And went away, and cannot really be said to have lived at all.

And cats die. They lie on the floor and lash their tails,
And their reticent fur is suddenly all in motion
10 With fleas that one never knew were there,
Polished and brown, knowing all there is to know,
Trekking off into the living world.
You fetch a shoe-box, but it's much too small, because she won't curl up now:
So you find a bigger box, and bury her in the yard, and weep.

15 But you do not wake up a month from then, two months,
A year from then, two years, in the middle of the night
And weep, with your knuckles in your mouth, and say Oh, God! Oh, God!
Childhood is the kingdom where nobody dies that matters,—mothers and fathers don't die.

And if you have said, "For heaven's sake, must you always be kissing a person?"
Or, "I do wish to gracious you'd stop tapping on the window with your
20   thimble!"
Tomorrow, or even the day after tomorrow if you're busy having fun,
Is plenty of time to say, "I'm sorry, mother."

To be grown up is to sit at the table with people who have died, who neither listen nor speak;
Who do not drink their tea, though they always said
25 Tea was such a comfort.

Run down into the cellar and bring up the last jar of raspberries; they are not tempted.

2. See 1 Corinthians 13.11: "When I was a child, I spake as a child, I understood as a child, I thought as a child: but when I became a man, I put away childish things."

Flatter them, ask them what was it they said exactly
That time, to the bishop, or to the overseer, or to Mrs. Mason;
They are not taken in.
30 Shout at them, get red in the face, rise,
Drag them up out of their chairs by their stiff shoulders and shake them and yell at them;
They are not startled, they are not even embarrassed; they slide back into their chairs.

Your tea is cold now.
You drink it standing up,
35 And leave the house.

1934

Apostrophe to Man

(on reflecting that the world is ready to go to war again)[3]

Detestable race, continue to expunge yourself, die out.
Breed faster, crowd, encroach, sing hymns, build bombing airplanes;
Make speeches, unveil statues, issue bonds, parade;
Convert again into explosives the bewildered ammonia and the distracted cellulose;
5 Convert again into putrescent matter drawing flies
The hopeful bodies of the young; exhort,
Pray, pull long faces, be earnest, be all but overcome, be photographed;
Confer, perfect your formulae, commercialize
Bacteria harmful to human tissue,
10 Put death on the market;
Breed, crowd, encroach, expand, expunge yourself, die out,
Homo called *sapiens*.[4]

1934

Rendezvous

Not for these lovely blooms that prank[5] your chambers did I come. Indeed,
I could have loved you better in the dark;
That is to say, in rooms less bright with roses, rooms more casual, less aware
Of History in the wings about to enter with benevolent air
5 On ponderous tiptoe, at the cue "Proceed."
Not that I like the ash-trays over-crowded and the place in a mess,
Or the monastic cubicle too unctuously austere and stark,

---

3. Written in the decade before World War II. "Apostrophe": address to a person or personification.
4. The scientific Latin name for the human species; here, "man called intelligent."
5. Adorn.

But partly that these formal garlands for our Eighth Street Aphrodite[6] are
    a bit too Greek,
And partly that to make the poor walls rich with our unaided loveliness
Would have been more *chic*.
Yet here I am, having told you of my quarrel with the taxi-driver over a
    line of Milton,[7] and you laugh; and you are you, none other.
Your laughter pelts my skin with small delicious blows.
But I am perverse; I wish you had not scrubbed—with pumice, I suppose—
The tobacco stains from your beautiful fingers. And I wish I did not feel
    like your mother.

1939

The Fitting

The fitter said, "*Madame, vous avez maigri,*"[8]
And pinched together a handful of skirt at my hip.
"*Tant mieux,*"[9] I said, and looked away slowly, and took my under-lip
Softly between my teeth.

          Rip—rip!

Out came the seam, and was pinned together in another place.
She knelt before me, a hardworking woman with a familiar and
    unknown face,
Dressed in linty black, very tight in the arm's-eye[1] and smelling of
    sweat.
She rose, lifting my arm, and set her cold shears against me,—snip-
    snip;
Her knuckles gouged my breast. My drooped eyes lifted to my
    guarded eyes in the glass, and glanced away as from someone
    they had never met.
"*Ah, que madame a maigri!*" cried the *vendeuse*,[2] coming in with
    dresses over her arm.
"*C'est la chaleur,*"[3] I said, looking out into the sunny tops of the horse-
    chestnuts—and indeed it was very warm.

I stood for a long time so, looking out into the afternoon, thinking of
    the evening and you. . . .
While they murmured busily in the distance, turning me, touching my
    secret body, doing what they were paid to do.

1939

---

6. Greek goddess of love.
7. John Milton (1608–1674), major English poet.
8. Madame, you have grown thin (French, as are all translated words in the poem).
9. So much the better.

1. Armhole.
2. Saleswoman. "Ah, how madame has grown thin!"
3. It's the heat.

[I too beneath your moon, almighty Sex]

I too beneath your moon, almighty Sex,
Go forth at nightfall crying like a cat,
Leaving the lofty tower I labored at
For birds to foul and boys and girls to vex
5 With tittering chalk; and you, and the long necks
Of neighbours sitting where their mothers sat
Are well aware of shadowy this and that
In me, that's neither noble nor complex.
Such as I am, however, I have brought
10 To what it is, this tower; it is my own;
Though it was reared To Beauty, it was wrought
From what I had to build with: honest bone
Is there, and anguish; pride; and burning thought;
And lust is there, and nights not spent alone.

1939

[The courage that my mother had]

The courage that my mother had
Went with her, and is with her still:
Rock from New England quarried;
Now granite in a granite hill.

5 The golden brooch my mother wore
She left behind for me to wear;
I have no thing I treasure more:
Yet, it is something I could spare.

Oh, if instead she'd left to me
10 The thing she took into the grave!—

That courage like a rock, which she
Has no more need of, and I have.

1954

An Ancient Gesture

I thought, as I wiped my eyes on the corner of my apron:
Penelope[4] did this too.
And more than once: you can't keep weaving all day

---

4. The wife of Odysseus (Ulysses) in Homer's *Odyssey*, who waited twenty years for her husband to return from the Trojan War. She fooled the suitors who wished her to remarry by promising to wed once she had finished weaving a shroud—which she unraveled every night.

      And undoing it all through the night;
5   Your arms get tired, and the back of your neck gets tight;
      And along towards morning, when you think it will never be light,
      And your husband has been gone, and you don't know where, for years,
      Suddenly you burst into tears;
      There is simply nothing else to do.

10   And I thought, as I wiped my eyes on the corner of my apron:
      This is an ancient gesture, authentic, antique,
      In the very best tradition, classic, Greek;
      Ulysses did this too.
      But only as a gesture,—a gesture which implied
15   To the assembled throng that he was much too moved to speak.
      He learned it from Penelope . . .
      Penelope, who really cried.

                                                1954

[I will put Chaos into fourteen lines]

      I will put Chaos into fourteen lines
      And keep him there; and let him thence escape
      If he be lucky; let him twist, and ape
      Flood, fire, and demon—his adroit designs
5   Will strain to nothing in the strict confines
      Of this sweet Order, where, in pious rape,
      I hold his essence and amorphous shape,
      Till he with Order mingles and combines.
      Past are the hours, the years, of our duress,
10   His arrogance, our awful servitude:
      I have him. He is nothing more nor less
      Than something simple not yet understood;
      I shall not even force him to confess;
      Or answer. I will only make him good.

                                                1954

DJUNA BARNES
1892–1982

Few writers have remained as elusive to literary critics, historians, and biographers as Djuna Barnes. Throughout the twentieth century, Barnes published journalism, plays, and stories as well as two novels, one of which, *Nightwood* (1937), has been considered a classic. She also played a major role in two expatriate groups: the modernist movement associated with James Joyce and T. S. Eliot, and the circle of lesbians who frequented the salons of Natalie Barney and Gertrude Stein. Yet, from 1919, when she refused to answer any questions about herself in *The Little Review*, through her return from Europe to America in 1940 to her subsequent life in Greenwich Village, she rejected publicity and lived an ever more reclusive life.

Barnes was raised in upstate New York, near Cornwall-on-Hudson, until her father moved the family to Long Island, where he purchased a 105-acre farm. Wald Barnes, who rejected his father's surname in preference for his mother's, was dedicated to an independent, private, and eccentric life. Little is known about Elizabeth (Chappell) Barnes, Wald Barnes's British-born wife and Djuna Barnes's mother. The major source of Barnes's private education was her father's mother, Zadel Barnes, who was both a feminist and a published journalist. After a brief stint studying art at Pratt Institute and at the Art Students League, Barnes quickly became active in the New York literary world: she wrote journalism for the *Brooklyn Daily Eagle* as well as fiction for *Vanity Fair*; a slim volume of drawings and poems, *The Book of Repulsive Women* (1915), was published as a chapbook; and she joined the Provincetown Players. Supporting herself as a newspaperwoman, she produced reviews of theatrical events along with stunt stories that required her to be hugged by a gorilla or forcibly fed, as in the lively article that we have reprinted here. After the 1919–20 season, when three of Barnes's plays were produced by the Provincetown Players, she left for Europe on assignment for *McCall's* magazine.

In Europe, whether she was interviewing the filmmaker D. W. Griffith, describing "the Jungle folk" at the circus, or depicting her meetings with James Joyce (who later presented her with the original manuscript of *Ulysses*), Barnes continued to make a reputation for herself as a witty, unconventional reporter. Just as she had earlier relished the bohemian sexual freedom of Greenwich Village, in Paris and later in Berlin and London she had a number of affairs; her most important and tempestuous relationship (for seventeen years) was with the sculptor Thelma Wood. Befriended by such figures as the poet Mina Loy and the wealthy art patron Peggy Guggenheim, Barnes began to write the stories for which she quickly became famous. Earlier, in *The Book of Repulsive Women*, she had produced macabre portraits of victimized females. In her next volume, *A Book* (1923), and in its 1929 reprint, *A Night among the Horses*, she depicted the baffling instability of relationships among characters who are estranged not only from all societal and religious traditions but also from each other and from themselves.

Barnes's next two books marked the beginning of her fascination with anachronistic literary models. Using Elizabethan diction, the *Ladies Almanack* (1928) records the life story of Dame Evangeline Musset, who had "developed in the Womb of her most gentle Mother to be a Boy," but "came forth an Inch or so less than this." Determined to "do it without the Tools for the Trade," Dame Musset embarks on the affairs that turn her into a lesbian saint or crusader. With its use of elaborate puns and fables, the *Ladies Almanack* presents fictionalized portraits of the expatriate writer Natalie Barney and the members of her salon. *Ryder* (1928), which Barnes described as a "female *Tom Jones*," focuses on the comic arrogance of a man who wants to establish himself as the father of the whole world.

The linguistic exuberance of these two books, along with their emphasis on female sexuality, also characterized Barnes's major work, *Nightwood*, an experimental novel that explores the love affair between two women and records the meditations on that affair furnished by the sage but derelict Dr. O'Connor, a character who made his first appearance in *Ryder*. But in this work Barnes presented a more tragic view of what she called the "stop[s] the mind makes between uncertainties," for all of her expatriated characters are lost to themselves and to each other. T. S. Eliot's introduction established the reputation of the novel, which was, he said, closer to Elizabethan poetry than modern prose. "Uncle Tom," as she called him, was Barnes's editor at Faber & Faber during the composition of *Nightwood* and *The Antiphon* (1958), a fact that may explain why the latter has been considered a response to Eliot's *Family*

Reunion (1939). A blank verse tragedy, *The Antiphon* is even more gothic than *Nightwood* in its dramatization of the anguished confusion experienced by a mother and daughter during the reunion of a family that is in the process of destroying itself. Scholars from Louis F. Kannenstine to Louise DeSalvo have interpreted the play as an encoded confession of the pain the author endured from early sexual abuse.

Although Eliot, like the critic Edwin Muir, continued to support Barnes after her return to America, she isolated herself in her apartment on Patchin Place, and retreated into decades of silence that were punctuated by quarrels, breakdowns, and hospitalizations or by the inquiries of her neighbor the poet E. E. Cummings, who would occasionally yell out of his window, "—Are ya still alive, Djuna?!" The writer Samuel Beckett, Peggy Guggenheim, Natalie Barney, and, eventually, the National Endowment for the Arts supplemented Barnes's meager income, and the novelists Anaïs Nin and John Hawkes acknowledged her influence on their own work, but according to her biographer, Andrew Field, she was alienated from her native country, holding the only partly comic belief that most Americans were "*—A fierce sadistic race crouching behind radiators.*"

How It Feels to Be Forcibly Fed[1]

I have been forcibly fed!

In just what relation to the other incidents in my life does this one stand? For me it was an experiment. It was only tragic in my imagination. But it offered sensations sufficiently poignant to compel comprehension of certain of the day's phenomena.

The hall they took me down was long and faintly lighted. I could hear the doctor walking ahead of me, stepping as all doctors step, with that little confiding gait that horses must have returning from funerals. It is not a sad or mournful step; perhaps it suggests suppressed satisfaction.

Every now and then one of the four men that followed turned his head to look at me; a woman by the stairs gazed wonderingly—or was it contemptuously—as I passed.

They brought me into a great room. A table loomed before me; my mind sensed it pregnant with the pains of the future—it was the table whereon I must lie.

The doctor opened his bag, took out a heavy, white gown, a small white cap, a sheet, and laid them all upon the table.

Out across the city, in a flat, frail, coherent yet incoherent monotone, resounded the song of a million machines doing their bit in the universal whole. And the murmur was vital and confounding, for what was before me knew no song.

I shall be strictly professional, I assured myself. If it be an ordeal, it is familiar to my sex at this time; other women have suffered it in acute reality. Surely I have as much nerve as my English sisters? Then I held myself steady.

---

1. In their effort to get the vote, British women adopted the tactic of hunger striking while in prison. Many became ill, and the Home Office ordered that hunger strikers be forcibly fed by prison officials. The feeding method used in Britain differed somewhat from Barnes's description, employing a steel gag to allow a tube between the teeth, thus damaging the teeth and jaws as well as the throat.

I thought so, and I caught sight of my face in the glass. It was quite white; and I was swallowing convulsively.

And then I knew my soul stood terrified before a little yard of red rubber tubing.

The doctor was saying, "Help her upon the table."

He was tying thin, twisted tapes about his arm; he was testing his instruments. He took the loose end of the sheet and began to bind me: he wrapped it round and round me, my arms tight to my sides, wrapped it up to my throat so that I couldn't move. I lay in as long and unbroken lines as any corpse— unbroken, definite lines that stretched away beyond my vision, for I saw only the skylight. My eyes wandered, outcasts in a world they knew.

It was the most concentrated moment of my life.

Three of the men approached me. The fourth stood at a distance, looking at the slow, crawling hands of a watch. The three took me not unkindly, but quite without compassion, one by the head, one by the feet; one sprawled above me, holding my hands down at my hips.

All life's problems had now been reduced to one simple act—to swallow or to choke. As I lay in passive revolt, a quizzical thought wandered across my beleaguered mind: This, at least, is one picture that will never go into the family album.

Oh, this ridiculous perturbation!—I reassured myself. Yet how imagination can obsess! It is the truth that the lights of the windows—pictures of a city's skyline—the walls, the men, all went out into a great blank as the doctor leaned down. Then suddenly the dark broke into a blotch of light, as he trailed the electric bulb up and down and across my face, stopping to examine my throat to make sure I was fully capable of swallowing.

He sprayed both nostrils with a mixture of cocaine and disinfectant. As it reached my throat, it burned and burned.

There was no progress on this pilgrimage. Now I abandoned myself. I was in the valley, and it seemed years that I lay there watching the pitcher as it rose in the hand of the doctor and hung, a devilish, inhuman menace. In it was the liquid food I was to have. It was milk, but I could not tell what it was, for all things are alike when they reach the stomach by a rubber tube.

He had inserted the red tubing, with the funnel at the end, through my nose into the passages of the throat. It is utterly impossible to describe the anguish of it.

The hands above my head tightened into a vise, and like answering vises the hands at my hips and those at my feet grew rigid and secure.

Unbidden visions of remote horrors danced madly through my mind. There arose the hideous thought of being gripped in the tentacles of some monster devil fish in the depths of a tropic sea, as the liquid slowly sensed its way along innumerable endless passages that seemed to traverse my nose, my ears, the inner interstices of my throbbing head. Unsuspected nerves thrilled pain tidings that racked the area of my face and bosom. They seared along my spine. They set my heart at catapultic[2] plunging.

An instant that was an hour, and the liquid had reached my throat. It was ice cold, and sweat as cold broke out upon my forehead.

Still my heart plunged on with the irregular, meaningless motion that

---

2. I.e., with the force of a catapult.

sunlight reflected from a mirror casts upon a wall. A dull ache grew and spread from my shoulders into the whole area of my back and through my chest.

The pit of my stomach had lapsed long ago, had gone out into absolute vacancy. Things around began to move lethargically; the electric light to my left took a hazy step or two toward the clock, which lurched forward to meet it; the windows could not keep still. I, too, was detached and moved as the room moved. The doctor's eyes were always just before me. And I knew then that I was fainting. I struggled against surrender. It was the futile defiance of nightmare. My utter hopelessness was a pain. I was conscious only of head and feet and that spot where someone was holding me by the hips.

Still the liquid trickled irresistibly down the tubing into my throat; every drop seemed a quart, and every quart slid over and down into space. I had lapsed into a physical mechanism without power to oppose or resent the outrage to my will.

The spirit was betrayed by the body's weakness. There it is—the outraged will. If I, playacting, felt my being burning with revolt at this brutal usurpation of my own functions, how they who actually suffered the ordeal in its acutest horror must have flamed at the violation of the sanctuaries of their spirits.

I saw in my hysteria a vision of a hundred women in grim prison hospitals, bound and shrouded on tables just like this, held in the rough grip of callous warders while white-robed doctors thrust rubber tubing into the delicate interstices of their nostrils and forced into their helpless bodies the crude fuel to sustain the life they longed to sacrifice.

Science had at last, then, deprived us of the right to die.

Still the liquid trickled irresistibly down the tubing into my throat.

Was my body so inept, I asked myself, as to be incapable of further struggle? Was the will powerless to so constrict that narrow passage to the life reservoir as to dam the hated flow? The thought flashed a defiant command to supine muscles. They gripped my throat with strangling bonds. Ominous shivers shook my body.

"Be careful—you'll choke," shouted the doctor in my ear.

One could still choke, then. At least one could if the nerves did not betray.

And if one insisted on choking—what then? Would they—the callous warders and the servile doctors—ruthlessly persist, even with grim death at their elbow?

Think of the paradox: those white robes assumed for the work of prolonging life would then be no better than shrouds; the linen envelope encasing the defiant victim a winding sheet.

Limits surely there are to the subservience even of those who must sternly execute the law. At least I have never heard of a militant choking herself into eternity.

It was over. I stood up, swaying in the returning light; I had shared the greatest experience of the bravest of my sex. The torture and outrage of it burned in my mind; a dull, shapeless, wordless anger arose to my lips, but I only smiled. The doctor had removed the towel about his face. The little, red mustache upon his upper lip was drawn out in a line of pleasant understanding. He had forgotten all but the play. The four men, having finished their minor roles in one minor tragedy, were already filing out at the door.

"Isn't there any other way of tying a person up?" I asked. "That thing looks like——"

"Yes, I know," he said, gently.

1914

Cassation[1]

"Do you know Germany, Madame, Germany in the spring? It is charming then, do you not think so? Wide and clean, the Spree[2] winding thin and dark—and the roses! the yellow roses in the windows; and the bright talkative Americans passing through groups of German men staring over their *steins,* at the light and laughing women.

"It was such a spring, three years ago, that I came into Berlin from Russia. I was just sixteen, and my heart was a dancer's heart. It is that way sometimes; one's heart is all one thing for months, then—altogether another thing, *nicht wahr?*[3] I used to sit in the café at the end of the Zelten,[4] eating eggs and drinking coffee, watching the sudden rain of sparrows. Their feet struck the table all together, and all together they cleared the crumbs, and all together they flew into the sky, so that the café was as suddenly without birds as it had been suddenly full of birds.

"Sometimes a woman came here, at about the same hour as myself, around four in the afternoon; once she came with a little man, quite dreamy and uncertain. But I must explain how she looked: *temperamentvoll* and tall, *kraftvoll*[5] and thin. She must have been forty then, dressed richly and carelessly. It seemed as though she could hardly keep her clothes on; her shoulders were always coming out, her skirt would be hanging on a hook, her pocket book would be mislaid, but all the time she was savage with jewels, and something purposeful and dramatic came in with her, as if she were the center of a whirlpool, and her clothes a temporary debris.

"Sometimes she clucked the sparrows, and sometimes she talked to the *weinschenk,*[6] clasping her fingers together until the rings stood out and you could see through them, she was so vital and so wasted. As for her dainty little man, she would talk to him in English, so that I did not know where they came from.

"Then one week I stayed away from the café because I was trying out for the *Schauspielhaus,*[7] I heard they wanted a ballet dancer, and I was very anxious to get the part, so of course I thought of nothing else. I would wander, all by myself, through the *Tiergarten,* or I would stroll down the *Sieges-Allee*[8] where all the great German emperors' statues are, looking like widows. Then suddenly I thought of the *Zelten,* and of the birds, and of that tall odd

---

1. An annullment or cancellation; also the dismissal of a soldier. The story was originally published under the title "A Little Girl Tells a Story to a Lady" in *A Night among the Horses* (1929); it was reprinted under the present title in *Spillway* (1972).
2. A small German river south of Berlin.
3. Isn't it true? (German, as are all translated words unless otherwise specified).
4. The road bordering Berlin's main park on the northeast.
5. Powerful. *"Temperamentvoll"*: temperamental.
6. Wine steward.
7. Theater.
8. Victory Lane. *"Tiergarten"*: the central park in Berlin (originally a hunting ground).

woman and so I went back there, and there she was, sitting in the garden sipping beer and chuck-chucking the sparrows.

"When I came in, she got up at once and came over to me and said: 'Why, how do you do, I have missed you. Why did you not tell me that you were going away? I should have seen what I could do about it.' "

"She talked like that; a voice that touched the heart because it was so unbroken and clear. 'I have a house', she said, 'just on the Spree. You could have stayed with me. It is a big, large house, and you could have the room just off my room. It is difficult to live in, but it is lovely—Italian you know, like the interiors you see in Venetian paintings, where young girls lie dreaming of the Virgin. You could find that you could sleep there, because you have dedication.'

"Somehow it did not seem at all out of the way that she should come to me and speak to me. I said I would meet her again some day in the garden, and we could go 'home' together, and she seemed pleased, but did not show surprise.

"Then one evening we came into the garden at the same moment. It was late and the fiddles were already playing. We sat together without speaking, just listening to the music, and admiring the playing of the only woman member of the orchestra. She was very intent on the movement of her fingers, and seemed to be leaning over her chin to watch. Then suddenly the lady got up, leaving a small rain of coin, and I followed her until we came to a big house and she let herself in with a brass key. She turned to the left and went into a dark room and switched on the lights and sat down and said: 'This is where we sleep; this is how it is.'

"Everything was disorderly, and expensive and melancholy. Everything was massive and tall, or broad and wide. A chest of drawers rose above my head. The china stove was enormous and white, enamelled in blue flowers. The bed was so high that you could only think of it as something that might be overcome. The walls were all bookshelves, and all the books were bound in red morocco, on the back of each, in gold, was stamped a coat of arms, intricate and oppressive. She rang for tea and began taking off her hat.

"A great painting hung over the bed; the painting and the bed ran together in encounter, the huge rumps of the stallions reined into the pillows. The generals, with foreign helmets and dripping swords, raging through rolling smoke and the bleeding ranks of the dying, seemed to be charging the bed, so large, so rumpled, so devastated. The sheets were trailing, the counterpane hung torn, and the feathers shivered along the floor, trembling in the slight wind from the open window. The lady was smiling in a sad grave way, but she said nothing, and it was not until some moments later that I saw a child, not more than three years old, a small child, lying in the center of the pillows, making a thin noise, like the buzzing of a fly, and I thought it was a fly.

"She did not talk to the child, indeed she paid no attention to it, as if it were in her bed and she did not know it. When the tea was brought in she poured it, but she took none, instead she drank small glasses of Rhine wine.

" 'You have seen Ludwig,' she said in her faint and grieving voice, 'we were married a long time ago, he was just a boy then. I? Me? I am an Italian, but I studied English and German because I was with a travelling company. You,' she said abruptly, 'you must give up the ballet—the theatre—acting.' Somehow I did not think it odd that she should know of my ambition, though I had not mentioned it. 'And,' she went on, 'you are not for the stage; you are for something quieter, more withdrawn. See here, I like Germany very much, I have lived here a good many years. You will stay and you will see. You have seen Ludwig, you have noticed that he is not strong; he is always declining, you must have noticed it yourself; he must not be distressed, he can't bear anything. He has his room to himself.' She seemed suddenly tired, and she got up and threw herself across the bed, at the foot, and fell asleep, almost instantly, her hair all about her. I went away then, but I came back that night and tapped at the window. She came to the window and signed to me, and presently appeared at another window to the right of the bedroom, and beckoned with her hand, and I came up and climbed in, and did not mind that she had not opened the door for me. The room was dark except for the moon, and two thin candles burning before the Virgin.

"It was a beautiful room, Madame, *'traurig'*[9] as she said. Everything was important and old and gloomy. The curtains about the bed were red velvet, Italian you know, and fringed in gold bullion. The bed cover was a deep red velvet with the same gold fringe: on the floor, beside the bed, a stand on which was a tasselled red cushion, on the cushion a Bible in Italian, lying open.

"She gave me a long nightgown, it came below my feet and came back up again almost to my knees. She loosened my hair, it was long then, and yellow. She plaited it in two plaits; she put me down at her side and said a prayer in German, then in Italian, and ended, 'God bless you', and I got into bed. I loved her very much because there was nothing between us but this strange preparation for sleep. She went away then. In the night I heard the child crying, but I was tired.

"I stayed a year. The thought of the stage had gone out of my heart. I had become a *religieuse;*[1] a gentle religion that began with the prayer I had said after her the first night, and the way I had gone to sleep, though we never repeated the ceremony. It grew with the furniture and the air of the whole room, and with the Bible lying open at a page that I could not read; a religion, Madame, that was empty of need, therefore it was not holy perhaps, and not as it should have been in its manner. It was that I was happy, and I lived there for one year. I almost never saw Ludwig, and almost never Valentine, for that was her child's name, a little girl.

"But at the end of that year I knew there was trouble in other parts of the house. I heard her walking in the night, sometimes Ludwig would be with her, I could hear him crying and talking, but I could not hear what was said. It sounded like a sort of lesson, a lesson for a child to repeat, but if so, there would have been no answer, for the child never uttered a sound, except that buzzing cry.

"Sometimes it is wonderful in Germany, Madame, *nicht wahr?* There is nothing like a German winter. She and I used to walk about the Imperial Palace, and she stroked the cannon, and said they were splendid. We talked about philosophy, for she was troubled with too much thinking, but she always came to the same conclusion, that one must be, or try to be, like everyone else. She explained that to be like everyone, all at once, in your own person, was to be holy. She said that people did not understand what

---

9. Sad.   1. Nun (French).

was meant by 'Love thy neighbor as thyself.' It meant, she said, that one should be like all people and oneself, then, she said, one was both ruined and powerful.

"Sometimes it seemed that she was managing it, that she was all Germany, at least in her Italian heart. She seemed so irreparably collected and yet distressed, that I was afraid of her, and not afraid.

"That is the way it was, Madame, she seemed to wish it to be that way, though at night she was most scattered and distraught, I could hear her pacing in her room.

"Then she came in one night and woke me and said that I must come into her room. It was in a most terrible disorder. There was a small cot bed that had not been there before. She pointed to it and said that it was for me.

"The child was lying in the great bed against a large lace pillow. Now it was four years old and yet it did not walk, and I never heard it say a thing, or make a sound, except that buzzing cry. It was beautiful in the corrupt way of idiot children; a sacred beast without a taker, tainted with innocence and waste time; honey-haired and failing, like those dwarf angels on holy prints and valentines, if you understand me, Madame, something saved for a special day that would not arrive, not for life at all: and my lady was talking quietly, but I did not recognize any of her former state.

" 'You must sleep here now,' she said, 'I brought you here for this if I should need you, and I need you. You must stay, you must stay forever.' Then she said, 'Will you?' And I said no, I could not do that.

"She took up the candle and put it on the floor beside me, and knelt beside it, and put her arms about my knees. 'Are you a traitor?' she said, 'have you come into my house, Ludwig's house, the house of my child, to betray us?' And I said, no, I had not come to betray. 'Then', she said, 'you will do as I tell you. I will teach you slowly, slowly; it will not be too much for you, but you must begin to forget, you must forget *everything*. You must forget all the things people have told you. You must forget arguments and philosophy. I was wrong in talking of such things; I thought it would teach you how to lag with her mind, to undo time for her as it passes, to climb into her bereavement and her dispossession. I brought you up badly; I was vain. You will do better. Forgive me.' She put the palms of her hands on the floor, her face to my face. 'You must never see any other room than this room. It was a great vanity that I took you out walking. Now you will stay here safely, and you will see. You will like it, you will learn to like it the very best of all. I will bring you breakfast, and luncheon, and supper. I will bring it to you both, myself. I will hold you on my lap, I will feed you like the birds. I will rock you to sleep. You must not argue with me—above all we must have no arguments, no talk about man and his destiny—man has no destiny—that is my secret—I have been keeping it from you until today, this very hour. Why not before? Perhaps I was jealous of the knowledge, yes, that must be it, but now I give it to you, I share it with you. I am an old woman,' she said, still holding me by the knees. 'When Valentine was born, Ludwig was only a boy.' She got up and stood behind me. 'He is not strong, he does not understand that the weak are the strongest things in the world, because he is one of them. He cannot help her, they are adamant together. I need you, it must be you.' Suddenly she began talking to me as she talked with the child, and I did not know which of us she was talking to. 'Do not repeat anything after me. Why should children repeat what people say? The whole world is nothing but a noise, as hot as the inside of a tiger's mouth. They call it civilization—that is a lie! But some day you may have to go out, someone will try to take you out, and you will not understand them or what they are saying, unless you understand nothing, absolutely nothing, then you will manage.' She moved around so that she faced us, her back against the wall. 'Look,' she said, 'it is all over, it has gone away, you do not need to be afraid; there is only you. The stars are out, and the snow is falling down and covering the world, the hedges, the houses and the lamps. No, no!' she said to herself, 'wait. I will put you on your feet and tie you up in ribbons, and we will go out together, out into the garden where the swans are, and the flowers and the bees and small beasts. And the students will come because it will be summer, and they will read in their books. . . . ' She broke off, then took her wild speech up again, this time as though she were really speaking to the child, 'Katya will go with you. She will instruct you, she will tell you there are no swans, no flowers, no beasts, no boys—nothing, nothing at all, just as you like it. No mind no thought, nothing whatsoever else. No bells will ring, no people will talk, no birds will fly, no boys will move, there'll be no birth and no death; no sorrow, no laughing, no kissing, no crying, no terror, no joy; no eating, no drinking, no games, no dancing; no father, no mother, no sisters, no brothers—only you, only you!'

"I stopped her and I said, 'Gaya, why is it that you suffer so, and what am I to do?' I tried to put my arms around her, but she struck them down crying, 'Silence!' Then she said, bringing her face close to my face, 'She has no claws to hang by; she has no hunting foot; she has no mouth for the meat—*vacancy!*'

"Then, Madame, I got up. It was very cold in the room. I went to the window and pulled the curtain, it was a bright and starry night, and I stood leaning my head against the frame, saying nothing. When I turned around, she was regarding me, her hands held apart, and I knew that I had to go away and leave her. So I came up to her and said, 'Good-bye, my Lady.' And I went and put on my street clothes, and when I came back she was leaning against the battle picture, her hands hanging. I said to her, without approaching her, 'Good-bye, my love,' and went away.

"Sometimes it is beautiful in Berlin, Madame, *nicht wahr?* There was something new in my heart, a passion to see Paris, so it was natural that I said *lebe wohl*[2] to Berlin.

"I went for the last time to the café in the Zelten, ate my eggs, drank my coffee and watched the birds coming and going just as they used to come and go—altogether here then altogether gone. I was happy in my spirit, for that is the way it is with my spirit, Madame, when I am going away.

"But I went back to her house just once. I went in quite easily by the door, for all the doors and windows were open—perhaps they were sweeping that day. I came to the bedroom door and knocked, but there was no answer. I pushed, and there she was, sitting up in the bed with the child, and she and the child were making that buzzing cry, and no human sound between them, and as usual, everything was in disorder. I came up to her, but she did not

2. Farewell.

seem to know me. I said, 'I am going away; I am going to Paris. There is a longing in me to be in Paris. So I have come to say farewell.'

"She got down off the bed and came to the door with me. She said, 'Forgive me—I trusted you—I was mistaken. I did not know that I could do it myself, but you see, I can do it myself.' Then she got back on to the bed and said, 'Go away,' and I went.

"Things are like that, when one travels, *nicht wahr,* Madame?"

1929, 1972

REBECCA WEST
1892–1983

"Ladies of Great Britain," Rebecca West exclaimed in 1912, "we are clever, we are trustworthy, we are twice the women that our grandmothers were, but we have not enough evil in us." But West herself published caustic journalism and fiction that led a number of her contemporaries to condemn her as demonically rebellious. Her choice of a pseudonym was part of the rebellion she fomented for women's economic and sexual freedom. Born Cicily Isabel Fairfield, the youngest of three daughters of Isabella McKenzie, a Scots pianist, and Captain Charles Fairfield, an impoverished Irish journalist, West went to school in Edinburgh, but left at sixteen for the London stage. Though her theatrical career was short-lived, it gave her the name that she would quickly make famous: one script she read was Henrik Ibsen's *Rosmersholm* (1886), a play about a radical feminist named Rebecca West. Writing in the feminist journal *The Freewoman* and the socialist weekly *The Clarion,* the nineteen-year-old who now called herself Rebecca West reviewed books by antisuffragists like Mrs. Humphrey Ward and suffragists like Olive Schreiner, even as she argued for free love and women's trade unions and against imperialism and conservative divorce laws.

To an unfortunate extent, West's part in the journalistic radicalism preceding World War I has been obscured in literary history by the attention paid to her ten-year affair with the novelist H. G. Wells and by her son Anthony West's public attacks on her. As the critic Gordon Ray has shown in his *H. G. Wells and Rebecca West,* West at twenty was understandably drawn to the forty-six-year-old spokesman for societal reform, but she was also convinced that she was right in the review she wrote about the antifeminism of Wells's early novels, an essay that first attracted him to her in 1912. In any case, when West gave birth to Wells's son in 1914, she became responsive to the cause of unwed mothers. Her novel *The Judge* (1922) was the most direct expression of this concern, placing the issues of rape, illegitimacy, and motherhood in the context of the suffrage struggle, but the early war novel *The Return of the Soldier* (1918) also described the sham conventionalities and desexualization of traditional marriage.

Throughout the 1920s West wrote a series of literary reviews for the *New Statesman,* and during the 1930s she produced more novels. From her study of Henry James (1916) to her biography of St. Augustine (1933), she exploited the insights of psychology, a fact that helps explain her early enthusiasm for the fiction of Virginia Woolf and D. H. Lawrence. In 1930, she married a banker, Henry Maxwell Andrews, and moved with him to a country house in Buckinghamshire. During World War II, she published *Black Lamb and Grey Falcon* (1941), a travel book that was also a powerful attack on Nazism. By the 1950s, however, West had been converted from a feminist-socialist to a conservative anticommunist. In 1959, the year before her husband died, she was created a dame commander of the British Empire, a strange fate for the woman who had written forty-seven years earlier that "there are two kinds of imperialists—imperialists and bloody imperialists." Nevertheless, despite her political turnabout, Dame Rebecca never lost sight of the fact that, "like all terrible and wicked things, sex-antagonism has a sound logical basis," and it is the nature of sex-antagonism that she analyzed in "Indissoluble Matrimony," a story that the scholar Jane Marcus recovered in the early 1980s from critical neglect.

Indissoluble Matrimony

When George Silverton opened the front door he found that the house was not empty for all its darkness. The spitting noise of the striking of damp matches and mild, growling exclamations of annoyance told him that his wife was trying to light the dining-room gas. He went in and with some short, hostile sound of greeting lit a match and brought brightness into the little room. Then, irritated by his own folly in bringing private papers into his wife's presence, he stuffed the letters he had brought from the office deep into the pockets of his overcoat. He looked at her suspiciously, but she had not seen them, being busy in unwinding her orange motor-veil.[1] His eyes remained on her face to brood a little sourly on her moving loveliness, which he had not been sure of finding: for she was one of those women who create an illusion alternately of extreme beauty and extreme ugliness. Under her curious dress, designed in some pitifully cheap and worthless stuff by a successful mood of her indiscreet taste—she had black blood in her—her long body seemed pulsing with some exaltation. The blood was coursing violently under her luminous yellow skin, and her lips, dusky with fatigue, drooped contentedly over her great humid black eyes. Perpetually she raised her hand to the mass of black hair that was coiled on her thick golden neck and stroked it with secretive enjoyment, as a cat licks its fur. And her large mouth smiled frankly, but abstractedly, at some digested pleasure.

There was a time when George would have looked on this riot of excited loveliness with suspicion. But now he knew it was almost certainly caused by some trifle—a long walk through stinging weather, the report of a socialist victory at a by-election, or the intoxication of a waltz refrain floating from the municipal bandstand across the flats of the local recreation ground. And even if it had been caused by some amorous interlude he would not have greatly cared. In the ten years since their marriage he had lost the quality which would have made him resentful. He now believed that quality to be purely physical. Unless one was in good condition and responsive to the messages sent out by the flesh Evadne could hardly concern one. He turned the bitter thought over in his heart and stung himself by deliberately gazing unmoved upon her beautiful joyful body.

"Let's have supper now!" she said rather greedily.

He looked at the table and saw she had set it before she went out. As usual she had been in an improvident hurry: it was carelessly done. Besides what an absurd supper to set before a hungry solicitor's[2] clerk! In the center, obviously intended as the principal dish, was a bowl of plums, softly red,

---

1. A scarf worn in open automobiles.   2. Lawyer's.

soaked with the sun, glowing like jewels in the downward stream of the incandescent light. Beside them was a great yellow melon, its sleek sides fluted with rich growth, and a honeycomb glistening on a willow-pattern dish. The only sensible food to be seen was a plate of tongue laid at his place.

"I can't sit down to supper without washing my hands!"

While he splashed in the bathroom upstairs he heard her pull a chair to the table and sit down to her supper. It annoyed him. There was no ritual about it. While he was eating the tongue she would be crushing honey on new bread, or stripping a plum of its purple skin and holding the golden globe up to the gas to see the light filter through. The meal would pass in silence. She would innocently take his dumbness for a sign of abstraction and forbear to babble. He would find the words choked on his lips by the weight of dullness that always oppressed him in her presence. Then, just about the time when he was beginning to feel able to formulate his obscure grievances against her, she would rise from the table without a word and run upstairs to her work, humming in that uncanny, Negro way of hers.

And so it was. She ate with an appalling catholicity of taste, with a nice child's love of sweet foods, and occasionally she broke into that hoarse, beautiful croon. Every now and then she looked at him with too obvious speculations as to whether his silence was due to weariness or uncertain temper. Timidly she cut him an enormous slice of the melon, which he did not want. Then she rose abruptly and flung herself into the rocking-chair on the hearth. She clasped her hands behind her head and strained backwards so that the muslin stretched over her strong breasts. She sang softly to the ceiling.

There was something about the fantastic figure that made him feel as though they were not properly married.

"Evadne?"

" 'S?"

"What have you been up to this evening?"

"I was at Milly Stafordale's."

He was silent again. That name brought up the memory of his courting days. It was under the benign eyes of blonde, plebeian Milly that he had wooed the distracting creature in the rocking-chair.

Ten years before, when he was twenty-five, his firm had been reduced to hysteria over the estates of an extraordinarily stupid old woman, named Mrs. Mary Ellerker. Her stupidity, grappling with the complexity of the sources of the vast income which rushed in spate from the properties of four deceased husbands, demanded oceans of explanations even over her weekly rents. Silverton alone in the office, by reason of a certain natural incapacity for excitement, could deal calmly with this marvel of imbecility. He alone could endure to sit with patience in the black-paneled drawing-room amidst the jungle of shiny mahogany furniture and talk to a mass of darkness, who rested heavily in the window-seat and now and then made an idiotic remark in a bright, hearty voice. But it shook even him. Mrs. Mary Ellerker was obscene. Yet she was perfectly sane and although of that remarkable plainness noticeable in most oft-married women, in good enough physical condition. She merely presented the loathsome spectacle of an ignorant mind, contorted by the artificial idiocy of coquetry, lack of responsibility and hatred of discipline, stripped naked by old age. That was the real horror of her. One feared to think how many women were really like Mrs. Ellerker under their armor of physical perfection or social grace. For this reason he turned eyes of hate on Mrs. Ellerker's pretty little companion, Milly Stafordale, who smiled at him over her embroidery with wintry northern brightness. When she was old she too would be obscene.

This horror obsessed him. Never before had he feared anything. He had never lived more than half an hour from a police station and, as he had by some chance missed the melancholy clairvoyance of adolescence, he had never conceived of any horror with which the police could not deal. This disgust of women revealed to him that the world is a place of subtle perils. He began to fear marriage as he feared death. The thought of intimacy with some lovely, desirable and necessary wife turned him sick as he sat at his lunch. The secret obscenity of women! He talked darkly of it to his friends. He wondered why the Church did not provide a service for the absolution of men after marriage. Wife desertion seemed to him a beautiful return of the tainted body to cleanliness.

On his fifth visit to Mrs. Ellerker he could not begin his business at once. One of Milly Stafordale's friends had come in to sing to the old lady. She stood by the piano against the light, so that he saw her washed with darkness. And before he had time to apprehend the sleepy wonder of her beauty, she had begun to sing. Now he knew that her voice was a purely physical attribute, built in her as she lay in her mother's womb, and no index of her spiritual values. But then, as it welled up from the thick golden throat and clung to her lips, it seemed a sublime achievement of the soul. It was a smoldering contralto such as only those of black blood can possess. As she sang her great black eyes lay on him with the innocent shamelessness of a young animal, and he remembered hopefully that he was good-looking. Suddenly she stood in silence, playing with her heavy black plait. Mrs. Ellerker broke into silly thanks. The girl's mother, who had been playing the accompaniment, rose and stood rolling up her music. Silverton, sick with excitement, was introduced to them. He noticed that the mother was a little darker than the conventions permit. Their name was Hannan—Mrs. Arthur Hannan and Evadne. They moved lithely and quietly out of the room, the girl's eyes still lingering on his face.

The thought of her splendor and the rolling echoes of her voice disturbed him all night. Next day, going to his office, he travelled with her on the horse-car that bound his suburb to Petrick. One of the horses fell lame, and she had time to tell him that she was studying at a commercial college. He quivered with distress. All the time he had a dizzy illusion that she was nestling up against him. They parted shyly. During the next few days they met constantly. He began to go and see them in the evening at their home—a mean flat crowded with cheap glories of bead curtains and Oriental hangings that set off the women's alien beauty. Mrs Hannan was a widow and they lived alone, in a wonderful silence. He talked more than he had ever done in his whole life before. He took a dislike to the widow, she was consumed with fiery passions, no fit guardian for the tender girl.

Now he could imagine with what silent rapture Evadne had watched his agitation. Almost from the first she had meant to marry him. He was physically attractive, though not strong. His intellect was gently stimulating like a mild white wine. And it was time she married. She was ripe for adult things. This was the real wound in his soul. He had tasted of a divine thing created in his time for dreams out of her rich beauty, her loneliness, her romantic poverty, her immaculate youth. He had known love. And Evadne had never known anything more than a magnificent physical adventure which she had secured at the right time as she would have engaged a cab to take her to the station in time for the cheapest excursion train. It was a quick way to lighthearted living. With loathing he remembered how in the days of their engagement she used to gaze purely into his blinking eyes and with her unashamed kisses incite him to extravagant embraces. Now he cursed her for having obtained his spiritual revolution on false pretences. Only for a little time had he had his illusion, for their marriage was hastened by Mrs. Hannan's sudden death. After three months of savage mourning Evadne flung herself into marriage, and her excited candor had enlightened him very soon.

That marriage had lasted ten years. And to Evadne their relationship was just the same as ever. Her vitality needed him as it needed the fruit on the table before him. He shook with wrath and a sense of outraged decency.

"Oh George!" She was yawning widely.

"What's the matter?" he said without interest.

"It's so beastly dull."

"I can't help that, can I?"

"No." She smiled placidly at him. "We're a couple of dull dogs, aren't we? I wish we had children."

After a minute she suggested, apparently as an alternative amusement, "Perhaps the post hasn't passed."

As she spoke there was a rat-tat and the slither of a letter under the door. Evadne picked herself up and ran out of the lobby. After a second or two, during which she made irritating inarticulate exclamations, she came in reading the letter and stroking her bust with a gesture of satisfaction.

"They want me to speak at Longton's meeting on the nineteenth," she purred.

"Longton? What's he up to?"

Stephen Longton was the owner of the biggest iron-works in Petrick, a man whose refusal to adopt the livery of busy oafishness thought proper to commercial men aroused the gravest suspicions.

"He's standing as socialist candidate for the town council."

". . . Socialist!" he muttered.

He set his jaw. That was a side of Evadne he considered as little as possible. He had never been able to assimilate the fact that Evadne had, two years after their marriage, passed through his own orthodox radicalism to a passionate socialism, and that after reading enormously of economics she had begun to write for the socialist Press and to speak successfully at meetings. In the jaundiced recesses of his mind he took it for granted that her work would have the lax fiber of her character: that it would be infected with her Oriental crudities. Although once or twice he had been congratulated on her brilliance, he mistrusted this phase in her activity as a caper of the sensualist. His eyes blazed on her and found the depraved, over-sexed creature, looking milder than a gazelle, holding out a handbill to him.

"They've taken it for granted!"

He saw her name—his name—MRS. EVADNE SILVERTON.

It was at first the blaze of stout scarlet letters on the dazzling white ground that made him blink. Then he was convulsed with rage.

"Georgie dear!"

She stepped forward and caught his weak body to her bosom. He wrenched himself away. Spiritual nausea made him determined to be a better man than her.

"A pair of you! You and Longton!" he snarled scornfully. Then seeing her startled face, he controlled himself.

"I thought it would please you," said Evadne, a little waspishly.

"You mustn't have anything to do with Longton," he stormed.

A change passed over her. She became ugly. Her face was heavy with intellect, her lips coarse with power. He was at arms with a socialist leader. Much would he have preferred the bland sensualist again.

"Why?"

"Because," his lips stuck together like blotting paper "he's not the sort of man my wife should—should—."

With movements which terrified him by their rough energy, she folded up the bills and put them back in the envelope.

"George. I suppose you mean that he's a bad man." He nodded. "I know quite well that the girl who used to be his typist is his mistress." She spoke it sweetly, as if reasoning with an old fool. "But she's got consumption.[3] She'll be dead in six months. In fact, I think it's rather nice of him. To look after her and all that."

"My God!" He leapt to his feet, extending a shaking forefinger. As she turned to him, the smile dying on her lips, his excited weakness wrapped him in a paramnesic illusion:[4] it seemed to him that he had been through all this before—a long, long time ago. "My God, you talk like a woman off the streets!"

Evadne's lips lifted over her strong teeth. With clever cruelty she fixed his eyes with hers, well knowing that he longed to fall forward and bury his head on the table in a transport of hysterical sobs. After a moment of this torture she turned away, herself distressed by a desire to cry.

"How can you say such dreadful, dreadful things!" she protested, chokingly.

He sat down again. His eyes looked little and red, but they blazed on her. "I wonder if you are," he said softly.

"Are what?" she asked petulantly, a tear rolling down her nose.

"You know," he answered, nodding.

"George, George, George!" she cried.

"You've always been keen on kissing and making love, haven't you, my precious. At first you startled me, you did! I didn't know women were like that." From that morass he suddenly stepped on to a high peak of terror. Amazed to find himself sincere, he cried, "I don't believe good women are!"

"Georgie, how can you be so silly!" exclaimed Evadne shrilly. "You know quite well I've been as true to you as any woman could be." She sought his eyes with a liquid glance of reproach. He averted his gaze, sickened at having put himself in the wrong. For even while he degraded his tongue his pure soul fainted with loathing of her fleshliness.

"I . . . I'm sorry."

Too wily to forgive him at once, she showed him a lowering profile with

---

3. Tuberculosis.   4. I.e., a feeling of déjà vu.

downcast lids. Of course, he knew it was a fraud. An imputation against her chastity was no more poignant than a reflection on the cleanliness of her nails—rude and spiteful, but that was all. But for a time they kept up the deception, while she cleared the table in steely silence.

"Evadne, I'm sorry. I'm tired." His throat was dry. He could not bear the discord of a row added to the horror of their companionship. "Evadne, do forgive me—I don't know what I meant by. . . ."

"That's all right, silly!" she said suddenly and bent over the table to kiss him. Her brow was smooth. It was evident from her splendid expression that she was preoccupied. Then she finished clearing up the dishes and took them into the kitchen. While she was out of the room he rose from his seat and sat down in the armchair by the fire, setting his bulldog pipe alight. For a very short time he was free of her voluptuous presence. But she ran back soon, having put the kettle on and changed her blouse for a loose dressing-jacket, and sat down on the arm of his chair. Once or twice she bent and kissed his brow, but for the most part she lay back with his head drawn to her bosom, rocking herself rhythmically. Silverton, a little disgusted by their contact, sat quite motionless and passed into a doze. He revolved in his mind the incidents of his day's routine and remembered a snub from a superior. So he opened his eyes and tried to think of something else. It was then that he became conscious that the rhythm of Evadne's movement was not regular. It was broken as though she rocked in time to music. Music? His sense of hearing crept up to hear if there was any sound of music in the breaths she was emitting rather heavily, every now and then. At first he could hear nothing. Then it struck him that each breath was a muttered phrase. He stiffened, and hatred flamed through his veins. The words came clearly through her lips. . . . "The present system of wage-slavery. . . ."

"Evadne!" He sprang to his feet. "You're preparing your speech!"

She did not move. "I am," she said.

"Damn it, you shan't speak!"

"Damn it, I will!"

"Evadne, you shan't speak! If you do I swear to God above I'll turn you out into the streets." She rose and came towards him. She looked black and dangerous. She trod softly like a cat with her head down. In spite of himself, his tongue licked his lips in fear and he cowered a moment before he picked up a knife from the table. For a space she looked down on him and the sharp blade.

"You idiot, can't you hear the kettle's boiling over?"

He shrank back, letting the knife fall on the floor. For three minutes he stood there controlling his breath and trying to still his heart. Then he followed her into the kitchen. She was making a noise with a basinful of dishes.

"Stop that row."

She turned round with a dripping dishcloth in her hand and pondered whether to throw it at him. But she was tired and wanted peace; so that she could finish the rough draft of her speech. So she stood waiting.

"Did you understand what I said then? If you don't promise me here and now. . . ."

She flung her arms upwards with a cry and dashed past him. He made to run after her upstairs, but stumbled on the threshold of the lobby and sat with his ankle twisted under him, shaking with rage. In a second she ran downstairs again, clothed in a big cloak with a black bundle clutched to her breast. For the first time in their married life she was seized with a convulsion of sobs. She dashed out the front door and banged it with such passion that a glass pane shivered to fragments behind her.

"What's this? What's this?" he cried stupidly, standing up. He perceived with an insane certainty that she was going to meet some unknown lover. "I'll come and tell him what a slut you are!" he shouted after her and stumbled to the door. It was jammed now and he had to drag at it.

The night was flooded with the yellow moonshine of midsummer; it seemed to drip from the lacquered leaves of the shrubs in the front garden. In its soft clarity he could see her plainly, although she was now two hundred yards away. She was hastening to the north end of Sumatra Crescent, an end that curled up the hill like a silly kitten's tail and stopped abruptly in green fields. So he knew that she was going to the young man who had just bought the Georgian manor, whose elm trees crowned the hill. Oh, how he hated her! Yet he must follow her, or else she would cover up her adulteries so that he could not take his legal revenge. So he began to run—silently, for he wore his carpet-slippers. He was only a hundred yards behind her when she slipped through a gap in the hedge to tread a field-path. She still walked with pride, for though she was town-bred, night in the open seemed not at all fearful to her. As he shuffled in pursuit his carpet-slippers were engulfed in a shining pool of mud. He raised one with a squelch, the other was left. This seemed the last humiliation. He kicked the other one off his foot and padded on in his socks, snuffling in anticipation of a cold. Then physical pain sent him back to the puddle to pluck out the slippers. It was a dirty job. His heart battered his breast as he saw that Evadne had gained the furthest hedge and was crossing the stile into the lane that ran up to the manor gates.

"Go on, you beast!" he muttered. "Go on, go on!" After a scamper he climbed the stile and thrust his lean neck beyond a mass of wilted hawthorn bloom that crumbled into vagrant petals at his touch.

The lane mounted yellow as cheese to where the moon lay on the iron tracery of the manor gates. Evadne was not there. Hardly believing his eyes he hobbled over into the lane and looked in the other direction. There he saw her disappearing round the bend of the road. Gathering himself up to a run, he tried to think out his bearings. He had seldom passed this way, and like most people without strong primitive instincts he had no sense of orientation. With difficulty he remembered that after a mile's mazy wanderings between high hedges this lane sloped suddenly to the bowl of heather overhung by the moorlands, in which lay the Petrick reservoirs, two untamed lakes.

"Eh! She's going to meet him by the water!" he cursed to himself. He remembered the withered ash tree, seared by lightning to its root, that stood by the road at the bare frontier of the moor. "May God strike her like that," he prayed, "as she fouls the other man's lips with her kisses. Oh God! Let me strangle her. Or bury a knife deep in her breast." Suddenly he broke into a lolloping run. "Oh my Lord, I'll be able to divorce her. I'll be free. Free to live alone. To do my day's work and sleep my night's sleep without her. I'll get a job somewhere else and forget her. I'll bring her to the dogs. No clean man or woman in Petrick will look at her now. They won't have her to speak at that meeting now!" His throat swelled with joy, he leapt high in the air.

"I'll lie about her. If I can prove that she's wrong with this man they'll believe me if I say she's a bad woman and drinks. I'll make her name a joke. And then. . . ."

He flung wide his arms in ecstasy: the left struck against stone. More pain than he had thought his body could hold convulsed him, so that he sank on the ground hugging his aching arm. He looked backwards as he writhed and saw that the hedge had stopped; above him was the great stone wall of the county asylum. The question broke on him—was there any lunatic in its confines so slavered with madness as he himself? Nothing but madness could have accounted for the torrent of ugly words, the sea of uglier thoughts that was now a part of him. "Oh God, for me to turn like this!" he cried, rolling over full-length on the grassy bank by the roadside. That the infidelity of his wife, a thing that should have brought out the stern manliness of his true nature, should have discovered him as lecherous-lipped as any pot-house[5] lounger, was the most infamous accident of his married life. The sense of sin descended on him so that his tears flowed hot and bitterly. "Have I gone to the Unitarian chapel every Sunday morning and to the Ethical Society every evening for nothing?" his spirit asked itself in its travail. "All those Browning lectures[6] for nothing. . . ." He said the Lord's Prayer[7] several times and lay for a minute quietly crying. The relaxation of his muscles brought him a sense of rest which seemed forgiveness falling from God. The tears dried on his cheeks. His calmer consciousness heard the sound of rushing waters mingled with the beating of blood in his ears. He got up and scrambled round the turn of the road that brought him to the withered ash tree.

He walked forward on the parched heatherland to the mound whose scarred sides, heaped with boulders, tufted with mountain grasses, shone before him in the moonlight. He scrambled up to it hurriedly and hoisted himself from ledge to ledge till he fell on his knees with a squeal of pain. His ankle was caught in a crevice of the rock. Gulping down his agony at this final physical humiliation he heaved himself upright and raced on to the summit, and found himself before the Devil's Caldron, filled to the brim with yellow moonshine and the fiery play of summer lightning. The rugged crags opposite him were a low barricade against the stars to which the mound where he stood shot forward like a bridge. To the left of this the long Lisbech pond lay like a trailing serpent; its silver scales glittered as the wind swept down from the vaster moorlands to the east. To the right under a steep drop of twenty feet was the Whimsey pond, more sinister, shaped in an unnatural oval, sheltered from the wind by the high ridge so that the undisturbed moonlight lay across it like a sharp-edged sword.

He looked about for some sign of Evadne. She could not be on the land by the margin of the lakes, for the light blazed so strongly that each reed could be clearly seen like a black dagger stabbing the silver. He looked down Lisbech and saw far east a knot of red and green and orange lights. Perhaps for some devilish purpose Evadne had sought Lisbech railway station. But his volcanic mind had preserved one grain of sense that assured him that, subtle as Evadne's villainy might be, it would not lead her to walk five miles

---

5. Tavern.
6. Lectures given under the auspices of the Browning Society, a popular literary society devoted chiefly to the works of the English poet Robert Browning (1812–1889).
7. Matthew 6.9–13.

out of her way to a terminus which she could have reached in fifteen minutes by taking a train from the station down the road. She must be under cover somewhere here. He went down the gentle slope that fell from the top of the ridge to Lisbech pond in a disorder of rough heather, unhappy patches of cultivated grass and coppices of silver birch, fringed with flaming broom that seemed faintly tarnished in the moonlight. At the bottom was a roughly hewn path which he followed in hot aimless hurry. In a little he approached a riot of falling waters. There was a slice ten feet broad carved out of the ridge, and to this narrow channel of black shining rock the floods of Lisbech leapt some feet and raced through to Whimsey. The noise beat him back. The gap was spanned by a gaunt thing of paint-blistered iron, on which he stood dizzily and noticed how the wide step that ran on each side of the channel through to the other pond was smeared with sinister green slime. Now his physical distress reminded him of Evadne, whom he had almost forgotten in contemplation of these lonely waters. The idea of her had been present but obscured, as sometimes toothache may cease active torture. His blood-lust set him on and he staggered forward with covered ears. Even as he went something caught his eye in a thicket high up on the slope near the crags. Against the slender pride of some silver birches stood a gnarled hawthorn tree, its branches flattened under the stern moorland winds so that it grew squat like an opened umbrella. In its dark shadows, faintly illumined by a few boughs of withered blossom, there moved a strange bluish light. Even while he did not know what it was it made his flesh stir.

The light emerged. It was the moonlight reflected from Evadne's body. She was clad in a black bathing-dress, and her arms and legs and the broad streak of flesh laid bare by a rent down the back shone brilliantly white, so that she seemed like a grotesquely patterned wild animal as she ran down to the lake. Whirling her arms above her head she trampled down into the water and struck out strongly. Her movements were full of brisk delight and she swam quickly. The moonlight made her the center of a little feathery blur of black and silver, with a comet's tail trailing in her wake.

Nothing in all his married life had ever staggered Silverton so much as this. He had imagined his wife's adultery so strongly that it had come to be. It was now as real as their marriage; more real than their courtship. So this seemed to be the last crime of the adulteress. She had dragged him over those squelching fields and these rough moors and changed him from a man of irritations, but no passions, into a cold designer of murderous treacheries, so that he might witness a swimming exhibition! For a minute he was stunned. Then he sprang down to the rushy edge and ran along in the direction of her course, crying, "Evadne! Evadne!" She did not hear him. At last he achieved a chest-note and shouted, "Evadne! Come here!" The black-and-silver feather shivered in mid-water. She turned immediately and swam back to shore. He suspected sullenness in her slowness, but was glad of it, for after the shock of this extraordinary incident he wanted to go to sleep. Drowsiness lay on him like lead. He shook himself like a dog and wrenched off his linen collar, winking at the bright moon to keep himself awake. As she came quite near he was exasperated by the happy, snorting breaths she drew, and strolled a pace or two up the bank. To his enragement the face she lifted as she waded to dry land was placid, and she scrambled gaily up the bank to his side.

"Oh George, why did you come!" she exclaimed quite affectionately, laying a damp hand on his shoulder.

"Oh damn it, what does this mean?" he cried, committing a horrid tenor squeak. "What are you doing?"

"Why, George," she said, "I came here for a bathe."

He stared into her face and could make nothing of it. It was only sweet surfaces of flesh, soft radiances of eye and lip, a lovely lie of comeliness. He forgot this present grievance in a cold search for the source of her peculiar hatefulness. Under this sick gaze she pouted and turned away with a peevish gesture. He made no sign and stood silent, watching her saunter to that gaunt iron bridge. The roar of the little waterfall did not disturb her splendid nerves and she drooped sensuously over the hand-rail, sniffing up the sweet night smell; too evidently trying to abase him to another apology.

A mosquito whirred into his face. He killed it viciously and strode off towards his wife, who showed by a common little toss of the head that she was conscious of his coming.

"Look here, Evadne!" he panted. "What did you come here for? Tell me the truth and I promise I'll not . . . I'll not. . . ."

"Not *what*, George?"

"Oh please, please tell me the truth, do Evadne!" he cried pitifully.

"But, dear, what is there to carry on about so? You went on so queerly about my meeting that my head felt fit to split, and I thought the long walk and the dip would do me good." She broke off, amazed at the wave of horror that passed over his face.

His heart sank. From the loose-lipped hurry in the telling of her story, from the bigness of her eyes and the lack of subtlety in her voice, he knew that this was the truth. Here was no adulteress whom he could accuse in the law courts and condemn into the street, no resourceful sinner whose merry crimes he could discover. Here was merely his good wife, the faithful attendant of his hearth, relentless wrecker of his soul.

She came towards him as a cat approaches a displeased master, and hovered about him on the stone coping of the noisy sluice.

"Indeed!" he found himself saying sarcastically. "Indeed!"

"Yes, George Silverton, indeed!" she burst out, a little frightened. "And why shouldn't I? I used to come here often enough on summer nights with poor Mamma."

"Yes!" he shouted. It was exactly the sort of thing that would appeal to that weird half-black woman from the back of beyond. "Mamma!" he cried tauntingly, "Mamma!"

There was a flash of silence between them before Evadne, clutching her breast and balancing herself dangerously on her heels on the stone coping, broke into gentle shrieks. "You dare talk of my Mamma, my poor Mamma, and she cold in her grave! I haven't been happy since she died and I married you, you silly little misery, you!" Then the rage was suddenly wiped off her brain by the perception of a crisis.

The trickle of silence overflowed into a lake, over which their spirits flew, looking at each other's reflection in the calm waters: in the hurry of their flight they had never before seen each other. They stood facing one another with dropped heads, quietly thinking.

The strong passion which filled them threatened to disintegrate their souls as a magnetic current decomposes the electrolyte,[8] so they fought to organize their sensations. They tried to arrange themselves and their lives for comprehension, but beyond sudden lyric visions of old incidents of hatefulness—such as a smarting quarrel of six years ago as to whether Evadne had or had not cheated the railway company out of one[9]-and-eightpence on an excursion ticket—the past was intangible. It trailed behind this intense event as the pale hair trails behind the burning comet. They were preoccupied with the moment. Quite often George had found a mean pleasure in the thought that by never giving Evadne a child he had cheated her out of one form of experience, and now he paid the price of this unnatural pride of sterility. For now the spiritual offspring of their intercourse came to birth. A sublime loathing was between them. For a little time it was a huge perilous horror, but afterwards, like men aboard a ship whose masts seek the sky through steep waves, they found a drunken pride in the adventure. This was the very absolute of hatred. It cheapened the memory of the fantasias of irritation and ill-will they had performed in the less boring moments of their marriage, and they felt dazed, as amateurs who had found themselves creating a masterpiece. For the first time they were possessed by a supreme emotion and they felt a glad desire to strip away restraint and express it nakedly. It was ecstasy; they felt tall and full of blood.

Like people who, bewitched by Christ, see the whole earth as the breathing body of God, so they saw the universe as the substance and the symbol of their hatred. The stars trembled overhead with wrath. A wind from behind the angry crags set the moonlight on Lisbech quivering with rage, and the squat hawthorn tree creaked slowly like the irritation of a dull little man. The dry moors, parched with harsh anger, waited thirstily and, sending out the murmur of rustling mountain grass and the cry of wakening fowl, seemed to huddle closer to the lake. But this sense of the earth's sympathy slipped away from them and they loathed all matter as the dull wrapping of their flame-like passion. At their wishing matter fell away and they saw sarcastic visions. He saw her as a toad squatting on the clean earth, obscuring the stars and pressing down its hot moist body on the cheerful fields. She felt his long boneless body coiled round the roots of the lovely tree of life. They shivered fastidiously. With an uplifting sense of responsibility they realized that they must kill each other.

A bird rose over their heads with a leaping flight that made it seem as though its black body was bouncing against the bright sky. The foolish noise and motion precipitated their thoughts. They were broken into a new conception of life. They perceived that God is war and his creatures are meant to fight. When dogs walk through the world cats must climb trees. The virgin must snare the wanton, the fine lover must put the prude to the sword. The gross man of action walks, spurred on by the bloodless bodies of the men of thought, who lie quiet and cunningly do not tell him where his grossness leads him. The flesh must smother the spirit, the spirit must set the flesh on fire and watch it burn. And those who were gentle by nature and shrank from the ordained brutality were betrayers of their kind, surrendering the earth to the seed of their enemies. In this war there is no discharge. If they suc-

---

8. A substance that conducts electricity.   9. I.e., 1 shilling.

cumbed to peace now, the rest of their lives would be dishonorable, like the exile of a rebel who has begged his life as the reward of cowardice. It was their first experience of religious passion, and they abandoned themselves to it so that their immediate personal qualities fell away from them. Neither his weakness nor her prudence stood in the way of the event.

They measured each other with the eye. To her he was a spidery thing against the velvet blackness and hard silver surfaces of the pond. The light soaked her bathing-dress so that she seemed, against the jagged shadows of the rock cutting, as though she were clad in a garment of dark polished mail. Her knees were bent so clearly, her toes gripped the coping so strongly. He understood very clearly that if he did not kill her instantly she would drop him easily into the deep riot of waters. Yet for a space he could not move, but stood expecting a degrading death. Indeed, he gave her time to kill him. But she was without power too, and struggled weakly with a hallucination. The quarrel in Sumatra Crescent with its suggestion of vast and unmentionable antagonisms; her swift race through the moon-drenched countryside, all crepitant with night noises; the swimming in the wine-like lake; their isolation on the moor, which was expressedly hostile to them, as nature always is to lonely man; and this stark contest face to face, with their resentments heaped between them like a pile of naked swords—these things were so strange that her civilized self shrank back appalled. There entered into her the primitive woman who is the curse of all women: a creature of the most utter femaleness, useless, save for childbirth, with no strong brain to make her physical weakness a light accident, abjectly and corruptingly afraid of man. A squaw, she dared not strike her lord.

The illusion passed like a moment of faintness and left her enraged at having forgotten her superiority even for an instant. In the material world she had a thousand times been defeated into making prudent reservations and practicing unnatural docilities. But in the world of thought she had maintained unfalteringly her masterfulness in spite of the strong yearning of her temperament towards voluptuous surrenders. That was her virtue. Its violation whipped her to action and she would have killed him at once, had not his moment come a second before hers. Sweating horribly, he had dropped his head forward on his chest; his eyes fell on her feet and marked the plebeian molding of her ankle, which rose thickly over a crease of flesh from the heel to the calf. The woman was coarse in grain and pattern.

He had no instinct for honorable attack, so he found himself striking her in the stomach. She reeled from pain, not because his strength overcame hers. For the first time her eyes looked into his candidly open, unveiled by languor or lust; their hard brightness told him how she despised him for that unwarlike blow. He cried out as he realized that this was another of her despicable victories and that the whole burden of the crime now lay on him, for he had begun it. But the rage was stopped on his lips as her arms, flung wildly out as she fell backwards, caught him about the waist with abominable justness of eye and evil intention. So they fell body to body into the quarrelling waters.

The feathery confusion had looked so soft, yet it seemed the solid rock they struck. The breath shot out of him and suffocation warmly stuffed his ears and nose. Then the rock cleft and he was swallowed by a brawling blackness in which whirled a vortex that flung him again and again on a sharp thing that burned his shoulder. All about him fought the waters, and they cut his flesh like knives. His pain was past belief. Though God might be war, he desired peace in his time, and he yearned for another God—a child's God, an immense arm coming down from the hills and lifting him to a kindly bosom. Soon his body would burst for breath, his agony would smash in his breast-bone. So great was his pain that his consciousness was strained to apprehend it, as a too tightly stretched canvas splits and rips.

Suddenly the air was sweet on his mouth. The starlight seemed as hearty as a cheer. The world was still there, the world in which he had lived, so he must be safe. His own weakness and lovableness induced enjoyable tears, and there was a delicious moment of abandonment to comfortable whining before he realized that the water would not kindly buoy him up for long, and that even now a hostile current clasped his waist. He braced his flaccid body against the sucking blackness and flung his head back so that the water should not bubble so hungrily against the cords of his throat. Above him the slime of the rock was sticky with moonbeams, and the leprous light brought to his mind a newspaper paragraph, read years ago, which told him that the dawn had discovered floating in some oily Mersey dock, under walls as infected with wet growth as this, a corpse whose blood-encrusted finger-tips were deeply cleft. On the instant his own fingertips seemed hot with blood and deeply cleft from clawing at the impregnable rock. He screamed gaspingly, and beat his hands through the strangling flood. Action, which he had always loathed and dreaded, had broken the hard mold of his self-possession, and the dry dust of his character was blown hither and thither by fear. But one sharp fragment of intelligence which survived this detrition of his personality perceived that a certain gleam on the rock about a foot above the water was not the cold putrescence of the slime, but certainly the hard and merry light of a moon-ray striking on solid metal. His left hand clutched upwards at it, and he swung from a rounded projection. It was, his touch told him, a leaden ring hanging obliquely from the rock, to which his memory could visualize precisely in some past drier time when Lisbech sent no flood to Whimsey, a waterman mooring a boat strewn with pale-bellied perch. And behind the stooping waterman he remembered a flight of narrow steps that led up a buttress to a stone shelf that ran through the cutting. Unquestionably he was safe. He swung in a happy rhythm from the ring, his limp body trailing like a caterpillar through the stream to the foot of the steps, while he gasped in strength. A part of him was in agony, for his arm was nearly dragged out of its socket, and a part of him was embarrassed because his hysteria shook him with a deep rumbling chuckle that sounded as though he meditated on some unseemly joke; the whole was pervaded by a twilight atmosphere of unenthusiastic gratitude for his rescue, like the quietly cheerful tone of a Sunday evening sacred concert. After a minute's deep breathing he hauled himself up by the other hand and prepared to swing himself on to the steps.

But first, to shake off the wet worsted rags, once his socks, that now stuck uncomfortably between his toes, he splashed his feet outwards to midstream. A certain porpoise-like surface met his left foot. Fear dappled his face with goose-flesh. Without turning his head he knew what it was. It was Evadne's fat flesh rising on each side of her deep-furrowed spine through the rent in her bathing-dress.

Once more hatred marched through his soul like a king: a compelling service by his godhead and, like all gods, a little hatred for his harsh lien on his worshiper. He saw his wife as the curtain of flesh between him and celibacy, and solitude and all those delicate abstentions from life which his soul desired. He saw her as the invisible worm destroying the rose of the world with her dark secret love.[1] Now he knelt on the lowest stone step watching her wet seal-smooth head bobbing nearer on the waters. As her strong arms, covered with little dark points where her thick hairs were clotted with moisture, stretched out towards safety he bent forward and laid his hands on her head. He held her face under water. Scornfully he noticed the bubbles that rose to the surface from her protesting mouth and nostrils, and the foam raised by her arms and her thick ankles. To the end the creature persisted in turmoil, in movement, in action. . . .

She dropped like a stone. His hands, with nothing to resist them, slapped the water foolishly and he nearly overbalanced forward into the stream. He rose to his feet very stiffly. "I must be a very strong man," he said, as he slowly climbed the steps. "I must be a very strong man," he repeated, a little louder, as with hot and painful rigidity of the joints he stretched himself out at full length along the stone shelf. Weakness closed him in like a lead coffin. For a little time the wetness of his clothes persisted in being felt; then the sensation oozed out of him and his body fell out of knowledge. There was neither pain nor joy nor any other reckless ploughing of the brain by nerves. He knew unconsciousness, or rather the fullest consciousness he had ever known. For the world became nothingness, and nothingness which is free from the yeasty nuisance of matter and the ugliness of generation was the law of his being. He was absorbed into vacuity, the untamed substance of the universe, round which he conceived passion and thought to circle as straws caught up by the wind. He saw God and lived.

In Heaven a thousand years are a day. And this little corner of time in which he found happiness shrank to a nutshell as he opened his eyes again. This peace was hardly printed on his heart, yet the brightness of the night was blurred by the dawn. With the grunting carefulness of a man drunk with fatigue, he crawled along the stone shelf to the iron bridge, where he stood with his back to the roaring sluice and rested. All things seemed different now and happier. Like most timid people he disliked the night, and the commonplace hand which the dawn laid on the scene seemed to him a sanctification. The dimmed moon sank to her setting behind the crags. The jewel lights of Lisbech railway station were weak, cheerful twinklings. A steaming bluish milk of morning mist had been spilt on the hard silver surface of the lake, and the reeds no longer stabbed it like little daggers, but seemed a feathery fringe, like the pampas grass in the front garden in Sumatra Crescent. The black crags became brownish, and the mist disguised the sternness of the moor. This weakening of effects was exactly what he had always thought the extinction of Evadne would bring the world. He smiled happily at the moon.

Yet he was moved to sudden angry speech. "If I had my time over again,"

---

1. An echo of a poem by William Blake, "The Sick Rose" (1794): "O Rose, thou art sick. / The invisible worm / That flies in the night / In the howling storm, // Has found out thy bed / Of crimson joy: / And his dark secret love / Does thy life destroy."

he said, "I wouldn't touch her with the tongs." For the cold he had known all along he would catch had settled in his head, and his handkerchief was wet through.

He leaned over the bridge and looked along Lisbech and thought of Evadne. For the first time for many years he saw her image without spirits, and wondered without indignation why she had so often looked like the cat about to steal the cream. What was the cream? And did she ever steal it? Now he would never know. He thought of her very generously and sighed over the perversity of fate in letting so much comeliness.

"If she had married a butcher or a veterinary surgeon she might have been happy," he said, and shook his head at the glassy black water that slid under the bridge to that boiling sluice.

A gust of ague[2] reminded him that wet clothes clung to his fevered body and that he ought to change as quickly as possible, or expect to be laid up for weeks. He turned along the path that led back across the moor to the withered ash tree, and was learning the torture of bare feet on gravel when he cried out to himself: "I shall be hanged for killing my wife." It did not come as a trumpet-call, for he was one of those people who never quite hear what is said to them, and this deafishness extended in him to emotional things. It stole on him calmly, like a fog closing on a city. When he first felt hemmed in by this certainty he looked over his shoulder to the crags, remembering tales of how Jacobite[3] fugitives had hidden on the moors for many weeks. There lay at least another day of freedom. But he was the kind of man who always goes home. He stumbled on, not very unhappy, except for his feet. Like many people of weak temperament he did not fear death. Indeed, it had a peculiar appeal to him; for while it was important, exciting, it did not, like most important and exciting things, try to create action. He allowed his imagination the vanity of painting pictures. He saw himself standing in their bedroom, plotting this last event, with the white sheet and the high lights of the mahogany wardrobe shining ghostly at him through the darkness. He saw himself raising a thin hand to the gas bracket and turning on the tap. He saw himself staggering to their bed while death crept in at his nostrils. He saw his corpse lying in full daylight, and for the first time knew himself certainly, unquestionably dignified.

He threw back his chest in pride; but at that moment the path stopped and he found himself staggering down the mound of heatherland and boulders with bleeding feet. Always he had suffered from sore feet, which had not exactly disgusted but, worse still, disappointed Evadne. A certain wistfulness she had always evinced when she found herself the superior animal had enraged and humiliated him many times. He felt that sting him now, and flung himself down the mound cursing. When he stumbled up to the withered ash tree he hated her so much that it seemed as though she were alive again, and a sharp wind blowing down from the moor terrified him like her touch.

He rested there. Leaning against the stripped gray trunk, he smiled up at the sky, which was now so touched to ineffectiveness by the dawn that it

---

2. A fit of shivering.
3. Supporters of the Stuarts (James II was deposed in the Glorious Revolution of 1688), who were defeated fighting for Bonnie Prince Charlie at Culloden (1746).

looked like a tent of faded silk. There was the peace of weakness in him, which he took to be spiritual, because it had no apparent physical justification, but he lost it as his dripping clothes chilled his tired flesh. His discomfort reminded him that the phantasmic night was passing from him. Daylight threatened him; the daylight in which for so many years he had worked in the solicitor's office and been snubbed and ignored. "The garish day,"[4] he murmured disgustedly, quoting the blasphemy of some hymn-writer. He wanted his death to happen in this phantasmic night.

So he limped his way along the road. The birds had not yet begun to sing, but the rustling noises of the night had ceased. The silent highway was consecrated to his proud progress. He staggered happily like a tired child returning from a lovely birthday walk: his death in the little bedroom, which for the first time he would have to himself, was a culminating treat to be gloated over like the promise of a favorite pudding for supper. As he walked he brooded dozingly on large and swelling thoughts. Like all people of weak passions and enterprise he loved to think of Napoleon,[5] and in the shadow of the great asylum wall he strutted a few steps of his advance from murder to suicide, with arms crossed on his breast and thin legs trying to strut massively. He was so happy. He wished that a military band went before him, and pretended that the high hedges were solemn lines of men, stricken in awe to silence as their king rode out to some nobly self-chosen doom. Vast he seemed to himself, and magnificent like music, and solemn like the Sphinx.[6] He had saved the earth from corruption by killing Evadne, for whom he now felt the unremorseful pity a conqueror might bestow on a devastated empire. He might have grieved that his victory brought him death, but with immense pride he found that the occasion was exactly described by a text. "He saved others, Himself He could not save."[7] He had missed the stile in the field above Sumatra Crescent and had to go back and hunt for it in the hedge. So quickly had his satisfaction borne him home.

The field had the fantastic air that jerry-builders[8] give to land poised on the knife-edge of town and country, so that he walked in romance to his very door. The unmarred grass sloped to a stone-hedge of towers of loose brick, trenches and mounds of shining clay, and the fine intentful spires of the scaffolding round the last unfinished house. And he looked down on Petrick. Though to the actual eye it was but a confusion of dark instances through the twilight, a breaking of velvety perspectives, he saw more intensely than ever before its squalid walls and squalid homes where mean men and mean women enlaced their unwholesome lives. Yet he did not shrink from entering for his great experience, as Christ did not shrink from being born in a stable. He swaggered with humility over the trodden mud of the field and the new white flags of Sumatra Crescent. Down the road before him there passed a dim figure, who paused at each lamp-post and raised a long wand to behead the yellow gas-flowers that were now wilting before the dawn; a ghostly herald preparing the world to be his deathbed. The crescent curved in quiet

---

4. From "Lead Kindly Light," a poem by John Henry Cardinal Newman set to music in 1864: "I loved the garish day, and, spite of fears, / Pride ruled my will: remember not past years."
5. Corsican-born soldier who declared himself emperor of the French (1769–1821; emperor 1804–14).
6. The ancient Egyptian image of a lion with a man's head (most famously rendered in the huge statue in the desert at Giza).
7. Matthew 27.42 ("He" is Christ).
8. Builders whose work is cheap and careless.

darkness, save for one house, where blazed a gas-lit room with undrawn blinds. The brightness had the startled quality of a scream. He looked in almost anxiously as he passed, and met the blank eyes of a man in evening clothes who stood by the window shaking a medicine bottle. His face was like a wax mask softened by heat: the features were blurred with the suffering which comes from the spectacle of suffering. His eyes lay unshiftingly on George's face as he went by and he went on shaking the bottle. It seemed as though he would never stop.

In the hour of his grandeur George was not forgetful of the griefs of the little human people, but interceded with God for the sake of this stranger. Everything was beautiful, beautiful, beautiful.

His own little house looked solemn as a temple. He leaned against the lamp-post at the gate and stared at its empty windows and neat bricks. The disorder of the shattered pane of glass could be overlooked by considering a sign that this house was a holy place, like the Passover blood on the lintel.[9] The propriety of the evenly drawn blind pleased him enormously. He had always known that this was how the great tragic things of the world had accomplished themselves: quietly. Evadne's raging activity belonged to trivial or annoying things like spring-cleaning or thunderstorms. Well, the house belonged to him now. He opened the gate and went up the asphalt path, sourly noticing that Evadne had as usual left out the lawnmower, though it might very easily have rained, with the wind coming up as it was. A stray cat that had been sleeping in the tuft of pampas grass in the middle of the lawn was roused by his coming, and fled insolently close to his legs. He hated all wild homeless things, and bent for a stone to throw at it. But instead his fingers touched a slug, which reminded him of the feeling of Evadne's flesh through the slit in her bathing-dress. And suddenly the garden was possessed by her presence; she seemed to amble there as she had so often done, sowing seeds unwisely and tormenting the last days of an ailing geranium by insane transplantation, exclaiming absurdly over such mere weeds as morning glory. He caught the very clucking of her voice. . . . The front door opened at his touch.

The little lobby with its closed doors seemed stuffed with expectant silence. He realized that he had come to the theatre of his great adventure. Then panic seized him. Because this was the home where he and she had lived together so horribly he doubted whether he could do this splendid momentous thing, for here he had always been a poor thing with the habit of failure. His heart beat in him more quickly than his raw feet could pad up the oil-clothed stairs. Behind the deal[1] door at the end of the passage was death. Nothingness! It would escape him, even the idea of it would escape him if he did not go to it at once. When he burst at last into its presence he felt so victorious that he sank back against the door waiting for death to come to him without turning on the gas. He was so happy. His death was coming true.

But Evadne lay on his deathbed. She slept there soundly, with her head flung back on the pillows so that her eyes and brow seemed small in shadow,

---

9. The blood on the door was a sign to God on the eve of the Exodus to pass over the houses of the Israelites while killing the first-born children of the Egyptians (Exodus 12.13).
1. Fir or pine wood.

and her mouth and jaw huge above her thick throat in the light. Her wet hair straggled across the pillow on to a broken cane chair covered with her tumbled clothes. Her breast, silvered with sweat, shone in the ray of the street lamp that had always disturbed their nights. The counterpane rose enormously over her hips in rolls of glazed linen. Out of mere innocent sleep her sensuality was distilling a most drunken pleasure.

Not for one moment did he think this a phantasmic appearance. Evadne was not the sort of woman to have a ghost.

Still leaning against the door he tried to think it all out, but his thoughts came brokenly, because the dawnlight flowing in at the window confused him by its pale glare and that lax figure on the bed held his attention. It must have been that when he laid his murderous hands on her head she had simply dropped below the surface and swum a few strokes under water as any expert swimmer can. Probably he had never even put her into danger, for she was a great lusty creature and the weir[2] was a little place. He had imagined the wonder and peril of the battle as he had imagined his victory. He sneezed exhaustingly, and from his physical distress realized how absurd it was ever to have thought that he had killed her. Bodies like his do not kill bodies like hers.

Now his soul was naked and lonely as though the walls of his body had fallen in at death, and the grossness of Evadne's sleep made him suffer more unlovely a destitution than any old beggarwoman squatting by the roadside in the rain. He had thought he had had what every man most desires: one night of power over a woman for the business of murder or love. But it had been a lie. Nothing beautiful had ever happened to him. He would have wept, but the hatred he had learnt on the moors obstructed all tears in his throat. At least this night had given him passion enough to put an end to it all.

Quietly he went to the window and drew down the sash. There was no fireplace, so that sealed the room. Then he crept over to the gas bracket and raised his thin hand, as he had imagined in his hour of vain glory by the lake. He had forgotten Evadne's thrifty habit of turning off the gas at the main to prevent leakage when she went to bed.

He was beaten. He undressed and got into bed; as he had done every night for ten years, and as he would do every night until he died. Still sleeping, Evadne caressed him with warm arms.

1914, 1982

---

2. A dam or a fenced enclosure in the water for catching fish.

DOROTHY PARKER
1893–1967

"Brevity is the soul of Lingerie," Dorothy Parker announced in a *Vogue* advertisement capturing the witty brevity that would make her famous in the 1920s and 1930s. Whether in conversation she dubbed a young man "a rhinestone in the rough" or, as "Constant Reader" in *The New Yorker,* reviewed *The House at Pooh Corner* by protesting that "Tonstant Weader Fwowed Up," the wisecracking Parker epitomized style in New York; but she also managed, through an unfailing sense of humor and an uncanny ear for dialogue, to express her dissatisfaction with herself and with the society she so flamboyantly inhabited.

Dorothy Rothschild was the daughter of a Scottish mother, who died when the writer was a young child, and a Jewish garment manufacturer, who remarried a woman Dorothy disliked as much as she disliked her father. She grew up on the Upper West Side of Manhattan, and attended first a Catholic convent school and then Miss Dana's School in Morristown, New Jersey. After a brief stint writing captions for fashion photographs at *Vogue,* she was hired as a drama critic by Frank Crowninshield, the editor of *Vanity Fair.* Friendly with the playwright Robert Sherwood, the humorist Robert Benchley, and the newspaper writer Harold Ross, she became a prominent member of the Algonquin Hotel's Round Table (a lively lunch group) and, through her sketches and dialogues, she helped shape the character of *The New Yorker,* which Ross founded in 1925.

She had married Edwin Pond Parker II, a Wall Street businessman, in 1917, but they separated soon after his return from World War I and divorced in 1928. Parker's love life was never simple. After an abortion in 1923, she tried unsuccessfully to commit suicide. In the 1930s, she married Alan Campbell, a bisexual writer eleven years her junior, and they subsequently divorced (1947), remarried (1950), separated (1953), and reunited (1956) until his death in 1963. Throughout this time, however, Parker continued to produce successful criticism, fiction, and verse. Her reviews and stories appeared in *The New Yorker* at irregular intervals from 1926 until 1955. In 1926, her first collection of verse, *Enough Rope,* was a smash success. Later volumes, including *Sunset Gun* (1928), *Death and Taxes* (1931), and *Not So Deep as a Well* (1936), were received just as favorably. Parker's protests against the execution of the anarchists Nicola Sacco and Bartolomeo Vanzetti and her work against fascism during the Spanish civil war made her conspicuous when she and Campbell earned $5,000 a week in Hollywood during the late 1930s; by the 1940s the couple were blacklisted for their political views. Her last years were sadly marked by self-doubt about her literary accomplishments and by her reliance on alcohol. Yet in stories like "The Waltz" and in poems like those in *A Pig's-Eye View of Literature,* she had satirized literary, social, and sexual pieties with sardonic exuberance.

Résumé[1]

Razors pain you;
Rivers are damp;
Acids stain you;
And drugs cause cramp.
5   Guns aren't lawful;
Nooses give;

---

1. Summary.

Gas smells awful;
You might as well live.

1926

One Perfect Rose

A single flow'r he sent me, since we met.
    All tenderly his messenger he chose;
Deep-hearted, pure, with scented dew still wet—
    One perfect rose.

5 I knew the language of the floweret;
    "My fragile leaves," it said, "his heart enclose."
Love long has taken for his amulet
    One perfect rose.

Why is it no one ever sent me yet
10   One perfect limousine, do you suppose?
Ah no, it's always just my luck to get
    One perfect rose.

1926

News Item

Men seldom make passes
At girls who wear glasses.

1926

Song of One of the Girls

Here in my heart I am Helen;
    I'm Aspasia and Hero, at least.
I'm Judith, and Jael, and Madame de Staël;
    I'm Salome,[1] moon of the East.

5 Here in my soul I am Sappho
    Lady Hamilton am I, as well.
In me Recamier vies with Kitty O'Shea,
    With Dido, and Eve, and poor Nell.[2]

---

1. The beautiful daughter of Queen Herodias who demanded that the head of John the Baptist be brought to her. Helen, wife of the king of Sparta, was the most beautiful woman in Greece; by going to Troy with Paris she caused the Trojan War. Aspasia (5th c. B.C.E.), a Greek courtesan who was the mistress of the Athenian statesman Pericles. Hero was a Greek woman whose lover, Leander, swam the Hellespont nightly to see her. Judith was a courageous Jewish woman who killed Israel's enemy Holofernes singlehandedly; Jael was a Jewish woman who similarly killed the enemy general Sisera. Madame de Staël (1766–1817), French writer.
2. A girl who dies in Charles Dickens's novel *The Old Curiosity Shop* (1840–41). Sappho (b. ca. 612

I'm of the glamorous ladies
10   At whose beckoning history shook.
But you are a man, and see only my pan,[3]
So I stay at home with a book.

                                                    1926

From A Pig's-Eye View of Literature

*The Lives and Times of John Keats, Percy Bysshe Shelley,
and George Gordon Noel, Lord Byron*[1]

Byron and Shelley and Keats
Were a trio of lyrical treats.
The forehead of Shelley was cluttered with curls
And Keats never was a descendant of earls,
5   And Byron walked out with a number of girls,
But it didn't impair the poetical feats
Of Byron and Shelley,
Of Byron and Shelley,
Of Byron and Shelley and Keats.

Oscar Wilde[2]

If, with the literate, I am
Impelled to try an epigram,
I never seek to take the credit;
We all assume that Oscar said it.

Harriet Beecher Stowe[3]

The pure and worthy Mrs. Stowe
Is one we all are proud to know
As mother, wife, and authoress—
Thank God, I am content with less!

D. G. Rossetti[4]

Dante Gabriel Rossetti
Buried all of his *libretti*,[5]
Thought the matter over—then
Went and dug them up again.

B.C.E.), Greek lyric poet. Lady Hamilton (1765–1815), mistress of the English admiral Lord Nelson. Madame Récamier (1777–1849), French beauty and friend of Madame de Staël. Kitty O'Shea (1845–1921), wife of an Irish M.P.; her adultery with the Irish leader Charles Parnell brought about his downfall. Dido was the queen of ancient Carthage, abandoned by her lover Aeneas (a story told) in Virgil's *Aeneid*. Eve was the first woman created by God (as told in the Book of Genesis).
3. Face.
1. Keats (1795–1821), Shelley (1792–1822), and Byron (1788–1824), major Romantic poets. Keats was of working-class descent, and Byron was notorious for his philandering.
2. Irish writer (1854–1900), famous for his wit.
3. American novelist and activist (1811–1896), the author of the antislavery novel *Uncle Tom's Cabin*.
4. English poet and painter (1828–1882).
5. Books (Italian). Rossetti actually buried his manuscripts in his wife's coffin in 1862, then recovered them eight years later.

Thomas Carlyle[6]

Carlyle combined the lit'ry life
With throwing teacups at his wife,
Remarking, rather testily,
"Oh, stop your dodging, Mrs. C.!"

Alfred, Lord Tennyson[7]

Should Heaven send me any son,
I hope he's not like Tennyson.
I'd rather have him play a fiddle
Than rise and bow and speak an idyll.[8]

Walter Savage Landor[9]

Upon the work of Walter Landor
I am unfit to write with candor.
If you can read it, well and good;
But as for me, I never could.

George Sand[1]

What time the gifted lady took
Away from paper, pen, and book,
She spent in amorous dalliance
(They do those things so well in France).

1928

The Waltz

Why, thank you so much. I'd adore to.

    I don't want to dance with him. I don't want to dance with anybody. And even if I did, it wouldn't be him. He'd be well down among the last ten. I've seen the way he dances; it looks likes something you do on Saint Walpurgis Night.[1] Just think, not a quarter of an hour ago, here I was sitting, feeling so sorry for the poor girl he was dancing with. And now *I'm* going to be the poor girl. Well, well. Isn't it a small world?
    And a peach of a world, too. A true little corker. Its events are so fascinatingly unpredictable, are not they? Here I was, minding my own business, not doing a stitch of harm to any living soul. And then he comes into my life, all smiles and city manners, to sue me for the favor of one memorable mazurka.[2] Why, he scarcely knows my name, let alone what it stands for. It

---

6. Scottish essayist and historian (1795–1881).
7. English poet (1809–1892).
8. A poem describing a scene or episode. Tennyson wrote a long Arthurian poem called *Idylls of the King*.
9. English lyric poet (1775–1843).
1. The pen name of Aurore Dupin (1804–1876), French novelist.
1. The eve of May Day is the feast of St. Walpurga, traditionally thought to be a witches' sabbath.
2. A Polish folk dance that, like the waltz, is in three/four time.

stands for Despair, Bewilderment, Futility, Degradation, and Premeditated Murder, but little does he wot. I don't wot his name, either; I haven't any idea what it is. Jukes,[3] would be my guess from the look in his eyes. How do you do, Mr. Jukes? And how is that dear little brother of yours, with the two heads?

Ah, now why did he have to come around me, with his low requests? Why can't he let me lead my own life? I ask so little—just to be left alone in my quiet corner of the table, to do my evening brooding over all my sorrows. And he must come, with his bows and his scrapes and his may-I-have-this ones. And I had to go and tell him that I'd adore to dance with him. I cannot understand why I wasn't struck right down dead. Yes, and being struck dead would look like a day in the country, compared to struggling out a dance with this boy. But what could I do? Everyone else at the table had got up to dance, except him and me. There was I, trapped. Trapped like a trap in a trap.

What can you say, when a man asks you to dance with him? I most certainly will *not* dance with you, I'll see you in hell first. Why, thank you, I'd like to awfully, but I'm having labor pains. Oh, yes, *do* let's dance together— it's so nice to meet a man who isn't a scaredy-cat about catching my beriberi.[4] No. There was nothing for me to do, but say I'd adore to. Well, we might as well get it over with. All right, Cannonball, let's run out on the field. You won the toss; you can lead.

Why, I think it's more of a waltz, really. Isn't it? We might just listen to the music a second. Shall we? Oh, yes, it's a waltz. Mind? Why, I'm simply thrilled. I'd love to waltz with you.

I'd love to waltz with you. I'd love to waltz with you. I'd love to have my tonsils out, I'd love to be in a midnight fire at sea. Well, it's too late now. We're getting under way. *Oh.* Oh, dear. Oh, dear, dear, dear. Oh, this is even worse than I thought it would be. I suppose that's the one dependable law of life—everything is always worse than you thought it was going to be. Oh, if I had any real grasp of what this dance would be like, I'd have held out for sitting it out. Well, it will probably amount to the same thing in the end. We'll be sitting it out on the floor in a minute, if he keeps this up.

I'm so glad I brought it to his attention that this is a waltz they're playing. Heaven knows what might have happened, if he had thought it was something fast; we'd have blown the sides right out of the building. Why does he always want to be somewhere that he isn't? Why can't we stay in one place just long enough to get acclimated? It's this constant rush, rush, rush, that's the curse of American life. That's the reason that we're all of us so—*Ow!* For God's sake, don't *kick*, you idiot; this is only second down. Oh, my shin. My poor, poor shin, that I've had ever since I was a little girl!

Oh, no, no, no. Goodness, no. It didn't hurt the least little bit. And anyway it was my fault. Really it was. Truly. Well, you're just being sweet, to say that. It really was all my fault.

I wonder what I'd better do—kill him this instant, with my naked hands, or wait and let him drop in his traces. Maybe it's best not to make a scene. I guess I'll just lie low, and watch the pace get him. He can't keep this up

---

3. The name given to an inbred family, originally from New York, in sociological studies (1877, 1916) that saw in its members proof of the heritability of criminality, disease, and feeblemindedness.
4. A vitamin deficiency disease that causes muscle weakness, especially in the legs.

indefinitely—he's only flesh and blood. Die he must, and die he shall, for what he did to me. I don't want to be of the over-sensitive type, but you can't tell me that kick was unpremeditated. Freud says there are no accidents.[5] I've led no cloistered life, I've known dancing partners who have spoiled my slippers and torn my dress; but when it come to kicking, I am Outraged Womanhood. When you kick me in the shin, *smile.*

Maybe he didn't do it maliciously. Maybe it's just his way of showing his high spirits. I suppose I ought to be glad that one of us is having such a good time. I suppose I ought to think myself lucky if he brings me back alive. Maybe it's captious to demand of a practically strange man that he leave your shins as he found them. After all, the poor boy's doing the best he can. Probably he grew up in the hill country, and never had no larnin'. I bet they had to throw him on his back to get shoes on him.

Yes, it's lovely, isn't it? It's simply lovely. It's the loveliest waltz. Isn't it? Oh, I think it's lovely, too.

Why, I'm getting positively drawn to the Triple Threat here. He's my hero. He has the heart of a lion, and the sinews of a buffalo. Look at him—never a thought of the consequences, never afraid of his face, hurling himself into every scrimmage, eyes shining, cheeks ablaze. And shall it be said that I hung back? No, a thousand times no. What's it to me if I have to spend the next couple of years in a plaster cast? Come on, Butch, right through them! Who wants to live forever?

Oh. Oh, dear. Oh, he's all right, thank goodness. For a while I thought they'd have to carry him off the field. Ah, I couldn't bear to have anything happen to him. I love him. I love him better than anybody in the world. Look at the spirit he gets into a dreary, commonplace waltz; how effete the other dancers seem, beside him. He is youth and vigor and courage, he is strength and gaiety and—*Ow!* Get off my instep, you hulking peasant! What do you think I am, anyway—a gangplank? *Ow!*

No, of course it didn't hurt. Why, it didn't a bit. Honestly. And it was all my fault. You see, that little step of yours—well, it's perfectly lovely, but it's just a tiny bit tricky to follow at first. Oh, did you work it up yourself? You really did? Well, aren't you amazing! Oh, now I think I've got it. Oh, I think it's lovely. I was watching you do it when you were dancing before. It's awfully effective when you look at it.

It's awfully effective when you look at it. I bet I'm awfully effective when you look at me. My hair is hanging along my cheeks, my skirt is swaddled about me, I can feel the cold damp of my brow. I must look like something out of the "Fall of the House of Usher."[6] This sort of thing takes a fearful toll of a woman my age. And he worked up his little step himself, he with his degenerate cunning. And it was just a tiny bit tricky at first, but now I think I've got it. Two stumbles, slip, and a twenty-yard dash; yes, I've got it. I've got several other things, too, including a split shin and a bitter heart. I hate this creature I'm chained to. I hated him the moment I saw his leering, bestial face. And here I've been locked in his noxious embrace for the thirty-

---

5. Sigmund Freud (1856–1939), the founder of psychoanalysis, argued that slips of the tongue and other "mistakes" actually reveal suppressed wishes and ideas.

6. One of the characters in Edgar Allan Poe's 1839 tale was entombed alive.

five years this waltz has lasted. Is that orchestra never going to stop playing? Or must this obscene travesty of a dance go on until hell burns out?

Oh, they're going to play another encore. Oh, goody. Oh, that's lovely. Tired? I should say I'm not tired. I'd like to go on like this forever.

I should say I'm not tired. I'm dead, that's all I am. Dead, and in what a cause! And the music is never going to stop playing, and we're going on like this, Double-Time Charlie and I, throughout eternity. I suppose I won't care any more, after the first hundred thousand years. I suppose nothing will matter then, not heat nor pain nor broken heart nor cruel, aching weariness. Well. It can't come too soon for me.

I wonder why I didn't tell him I was tired. I wonder why I didn't suggest going back to the table. I could have said let's just listen to the music. Yes, and if he would, that would be the first bit of attention he has given it all evening. George Jean Nathan[7] said that the lovely rhythms of the waltz should be listened to in stillness and not be accompanied by strange gyrations of the human body. I think that's what he said. I think it was George Jean Nathan. Anyhow, whatever he said whoever he was and whatever he's doing now, he's better off than I am. That's safe. Anybody who isn't waltzing with this Mrs. O'Leary's cow[8] I've got here is having a good time.

Still if we were back at the table, I'd probably have to talk to him. Look at him—what could you say to a thing like that! Did you go to the circus this year, what's your favorite kind of ice cream, how do you spell cat? I guess I'm as well off here. As well off as if I were in a cement mixer in full action.

I'm past all feeling now. The only way I can tell when he steps on me is that I can hear the splintering of bones. And all the events of my life are passing before my eyes. There was the time I was in a hurricane in the West Indies, there was the day I got my head cut open in the taxi smash, there was the night the drunken lady threw a bronze ash-tray at her own true love and got me instead, there was that summer that the sailboat kept capsizing. Ah, what an easy, peaceful time was mine, until I fell in with Swifty, here. I didn't know what trouble was, before I got drawn into this *danse macabre*.[9] I think my mind is beginning to wander. It almost seems to me as if the orchestra were stopping. It couldn't be, of course; it could never, never be. And yet in my ears there is a silence like the sound of angel voices....

Oh, they've stopped, the mean things. They're not going to play any more. Oh darn. Oh, do you think they would? Do you really think so, if you gave them twenty dollars? Oh, that would be lovely. And look, do tell them to play the same thing. I'd simply adore to go on waltzing.

1930

---

7. American editor, writer, and drama critic (1882–1958).
8. The legendary cause—it was said to have kicked over a lantern—of the devastating 1871 Chicago fire.
9. Dance of death (French).

GENEVIEVE TAGGARD
1894–1948

"Am I the Christian gentlewoman my mother slaved to make me? No indeed. I am a poet, a wine-bibber, a radical; a non-churchgoer who will no longer sing in the choir or lead prayer-meeting with a testimonial": so confided Genevieve Taggard in a memoir that she published in *The Nation* in 1927. Yet as she confessed in the same essay, much of this poet's rebellious energy came from her mother, a "hardworking, high-handed, generous, and handsome girl" who "never set limits to what she could do," just as much of her thoughtfulness came from her "tender father" who was "delicate and Quixotic." Both parents, members of the church of the Disciples of Christ, worked as teachers and, for a time, as missionaries in Hawaii, where they founded and ran a "multicultural" school. Taggard herself was educated there and, later, on scholarship at the University of California, Berkeley, from which she earned a degree in 1919.

After graduation, the young writer moved to New York City, where she worked for the publisher B. W. Huebsch, helped start the innovative verse journal *The Measure*, married the writer Robert Wolf, and gave birth to her daughter Marcia, all within a few years. In this period, too, she published her first collection of poems, *For Eager Lovers* (1922), and became involved in the socialist causes to which she would be increasingly committed throughout the rest of her career. At the same time, however, Taggard was clearly a feminist as well as a socialist: such texts as "Everyday Alchemy," "Demeter," and "With Child" reveal her deep concern with women's issues, while the biography of Emily Dickinson that she published in 1930 suggests her strong interest in the contours of a female literary tradition. Celebrating marriage in her autobiographical essay in *The Nation,* she nevertheless noted that although like "every one else I have wanted it," it is "not all I want [because] I am a poet—love and mutual living are not nearly enough. It is better to work hard than to be married hard."

In the 1930s and '40s Taggard worked harder than ever. Deeply affected by the Great Depression, she contributed to the Marxist journal *The New Masses* and dramatized the catastrophic consequences of economic oppression in such powerful poems as "A Middle-aged, Middle-class Woman at Midnight," "At Last the Women Are Moving," and "Mill Town." During this period, she bought a farm in Vermont, whose landscape and people revitalized her imagination; and following stints at Mills College and Mount Holyoke, she taught for a time at Bennington College. Divorced from Robert Wolf in 1934, she married Kenneth Durant, a journalist for TASS (the news agency of the Soviet Union) in 1935. From 1934 to 1947, she was a faculty member at Sarah Lawrence College while she continued to publish poems that offered poignant delineations of the widespread suffering caused by the Depression and, later, by World War II, especially the suffering of women who inevitably sensed that the "womb is sick of its work with death" in an era when "the family story is sad."

Taggard's own demise came relatively early too. She died at fifty-three of complications from high blood pressure, and her passionate, beautifully crafted poems have been out of print for decades, although recent critics have begun to recover her work as part of a general reevaluation of long-submerged feminist and socialist literary achievements.

Everyday Alchemy

Men go to women mutely for their peace;
And they, who lack it most, create it when
They make—because they must, loving their men—

A solace for sad bosom-bended heads. There
5 Is all the meager peace men get—no otherwhere;
   No mountain space, no tree with placid leaves,
   Or heavy gloom beneath a young girl's hair,
   No sound of valley bell on autumn air,
   Or room made home with doves along the eves,
10 Ever holds peace like this, poured by poor women
   Out of their heart's poverty, for worn men.

                                              1919, 1922

With Child

   Now I am slow and placid, fond of sun,
   Like a sleek beast, or a worn one:
   No slim and languid girl—not glad
   With the windy trip I once had,
5 But velvet-footed, musing of my own,
   Torpid, mellow, stupid as a stone.

   You cleft me with your beauty's pulse, and now
   Your pulse has taken body. Care not how
   The old grace goes, how heavy I am grown,
10 Big with this loneliness, how you alone
   Ponder our love. Touch my feet and feel
   How earth tingles, teeming at my heel!
   Earth's urge, not mine—my little death, not hers;
   And the pure beauty yearns and stirs.

15 It does not heed our ecstasies, it turns
   With secrets of its own, its own concerns,
   Toward a windy world of its own, toward stark
   And solitary places. In the dark,
   Defiant even now, it tugs and moans
20 To be untangled from these mother's bones.

                                              1921, 1922

The Quiet Woman

   I will defy you down until my death
   With cold body, indrawn breath;
   Terrible and cruel I will move with you
   Like a surly tiger. If you knew
5 Why I am shaken, if fond you could see
   All the caged arrogance in me,
   You would not lean so boyishly, so bold,
   To kiss my body, quivering and cold.

                                              1921, 1922

Leave Me Alone a Little

Leave me alone a little!
Must I be yours,
When all my heart is pouring with the sea
Out to the moon's impersonal majesty?

     Leave me alone! My little vow endures
Men's irritating love, surviving yours!
Surviving all, surviving even you.
Leave me alone. This is no rendezvous:
I am not false except with my old sea and moon.

     You understand me? Wait behind the dune?
Oh, level glow, oh, soft, soft-spoken sea—
Leave me alone. Why will you follow me!

1922

A Middle-aged, Middle-class Woman at Midnight

In the middle of winter, middle of night
A woman took veronal[1] in vain. How hard it is to sleep
If you once think of the cold, continent-wide
Iron bitter. Ten below. Here in bed I stiffen.
     It was a mink-coat Christmas said the papers . . .
Heated taxis and orchids. Stealthy cold, old terror
Of the poor, and especially the children.
                                   Now try to sleep.
In Vermont near the marble-quarries . . . I must not think
Again, wide awake again. O medicine
Give blank against that fact, the strike, the cold.
How cold Vermont can be. It's nerves, I know,
But I keep thinking how a rat will gnaw
In an old house. Hunger that has no haste . . .
Porcupines eat salt out of wood in winter. Starve
So our children now. Brush back the hair from forehead,
See the set faces hungrier than rodents. In the Ford towns
They shrivel. Their fathers accept tear gas and blackjacks.[2]
When they sleep, whimper. Bad sleep for us all.
Their mouths work, supposing food. Fine boys and girls.
Hunger, busy with this cold to make barbarian
These states, to haunt the houses of farmers, destroyers
Of crops by plan. And the city poor in cold-water flats
Fingering the gas-cocks—*can't even die easy
If they turn the gas off.* I'm sick I tell you. Veronal

---

1. The brand name of barbital, a sedative (the first commercially marketed barbiturate).
2. The wave of unionism and strikes in the auto-mobile industry in the 1930s was sometimes met with violence.

Costs money, too. Costs more than I can pay.
And night's long nightmare costs me, costs me much.
I'll not endure this stink of poverty. Sheriffs, cops,
Boss of the town, union enemy, crooks and cousins,
30 I hope the people win.

1934

At Last the Women Are Moving

Last, walking with stiff legs as if they carried bundles
Came mothers, housewives, old women who knew why they abhorred war.
Their clothes bunched about them, they hobbled with anxious steps
To keep with the stride of the marchers, erect, bearing wide banners.

5   Such women looked odd, marching on American asphalt.
Kitchens they knew, sinks, suds, stew-pots and pennies . . .
Dull hurry and worry, clatter, wet hands and backache.
Here they were out in the glare on the militant march.

How did these timid, the slaves of breakfast and supper
10 Get out in the line, drop for once dish-rag and broom?
Here they are as work-worn as stitchers and fitters.
Mama have you got some grub, now none of their business.

Oh, but these who know in their growing sons and their husbands
How the exhausted body needs sleep, how often needs food,
15 These, whose business is keeping the body alive,
These are ready, if you talk their language, to strike.

Kitchen is small, the family story is sad.
Out of the musty flats the women come thinking:
Not for me and mine only. For my class I have come
20 *To walk city miles with many, my will in our work.*

1935

Mill Town

(Dedicated to Paul de Kruif)[1]

. . . the child died, the investigator said, for lack of proper food. After the funeral the mother went back to the mill. She is expecting another child . . .

. . . then fold up without pause
The colored ginghams and the underclothes.

---

1. American bacteriologist (1890–1971), popularizer of science in such books as *The Microbe Hunters*; in 1936, in collaboration with his wife, he published *Why Keep Them Alive?*, a book on the effects of poverty on children.

                    And from the stale
    Depth of the dresser, smelling of medicine, take
5   The first year's garments. And by this act prepare
    Your store of pain, your weariness, dull love,
    To bear another child with doubled fists
    And sucking face.
                    Clearly it is best, mill-mother,
10 Not to rebel or ask clear silly questions,
    Saying womb is sick of its work with death,
    Your body drugged with work and the repeated bitter
    Gall of your morning vomit. Never try
    Asking if we should blame you. Live in fear. And put
15 Soap on the yellowed blankets. Rub them pure.

                                                    1936

Demeter[1]

    In your dream you met Demeter
    Splendid and severe, who said: Endure.
    Study the art of seeds,
    The nativity of caves.
5   Dance your gay body to the poise of waves;
    Die out of the world to bring forth the obscure
    Into blisses, into needs.
    In all resources
    Belong to love. Bless,
10 Join, fashion the deep forces,
    Asserting your nature, priceless and feminine.
    Peace, daughter. Find your true kin.
                    —then you felt her kiss.

                                                    1945

1. Greek goddess of fertility and agriculture.

JEAN RHYS
1894?–1979

Described by one friend as "a shy, gentle and almost fatally impractical person," the novelist Jean Rhys was nevertheless thought by her mentor and sometime lover, Ford Madox Ford, to have "a terrifying insight, and a terrific . . . passion for stating the case of the underdog." Ford's comment, made early in Rhys's career, was an acute one. In five novels and a number of short stories, Rhys established a reputation for subtlety and style; more specifically, exploring the pain of wounded or abandoned women, she created a haunting landscape of anxiety that provides a kind of female equivalent to the wastelands of metaphysical despair constructed by such male contemporaries as the playwright Samuel Beckett and the poet T. S. Eliot.

Like the protagonist of *Wide Sargasso Sea* (1966), one of her most celebrated novels, Rhys was born and raised in Roseau, Dominica, in the West Indies. The girl who was originally named Ella Gwendolyn Rees Williams was educated at a convent school in Roseau. She traveled to London at the age of sixteen, where she studied for a term at the Royal Academy of Dramatic Art, then toured England as a chorus girl in a musical comedy during the years of World War I. Married for a time to the poet Max Hamer, she had one child. Much of her life, however, was spent in Paris and in travels on the Continent, an expatriation whose alienating implications she captured in, for instance, her portrait of the numbed and lonely heroine of *Good Morning, Midnight* (1939).

According to one commentator, Rhys "had always kept 'a sort of diary,' but she didn't think seriously of writing until a time when she was desperate for money, which fortunately coincided with her 'discovery' by . . . Ford." Once she began to write, though, she quickly became a serious professional: throughout her years of wandering, she was producing her poignant yet coolly understated novels and tales, and when she returned to settle in England—chiefly in London and Cornwall—she continued to write, although her reputation fell into an eclipse for some years. After *Good Morning, Midnight* was broadcast on the radio in England in 1957, Rhys was "rediscovered," however, and the subsequent publication of *Wide Sargasso Sea* was heralded as "a magnificent comeback."

Whether or not *Wide Sargasso Sea* was a "comeback," it continued and elaborated a mode of psychological analysis that Rhys had already pioneered in earlier works. In particular, it developed a technique of literary allusion hinted at in the title of *Good Morning, Midnight*, a line drawn from one of Emily Dickinson's poems, for *Wide Sargasso Sea* is a disturbing yet brilliantly revisionary retelling of the story of *Jane Eyre* (1847) from the point of view of Bertha Mason Rochester, the madwoman sequestered in Thornfield's attic. Describing Bertha's experience as a repressed daughter and an oppressed wife, Rhys continued the delineation of a landscape of female despair that she had begun in her earlier novels, but now she located that countryside of anguish more specifically in the context of women's literary history. Acknowledging the affinity between the anxieties of her protagonists and the pain articulated by such precursors as Dickinson and Brontë, Rhys elaborated what Ford had called her "terrifying insight" into the lives of "underdogs"—forgotten women imprisoned by self or society in attics and rooming houses, rebellious women whose stories she recounted with sympathy and sensitivity.

Mannequin

Twelve o'clock. Déjeuner chez[1] Jeanne Veron, Place Vendôme.

Anna, dressed in the black cotton, chemise-like garment of the mannequin off duty was trying to find her way along dark passages and down complicated flights of stairs to the underground room where lunch was served.

She was shivering, for she had forgotten her coat, and the garment that she wore was very short, sleeveless, displaying her rose-coloured stockings to the knee. Her hair was flamingly and honestly red; her eyes, which were very gentle in expression, brown and heavily shadowed with kohl; her face small and pale under its professional rouge. She was fragile, like a delicate

---

1. Lunch at the house of (French, as are all translated terms in the story).

child, her arms pathetically thin. It was to her legs that she owed this dazzling, this incredible opportunity.

Madame Veron, white-haired with black eyes, incredibly distinguished, who had given them one sweeping glance, the glance of the connoisseur, smiled imperiously and engaged her at an exceedingly small salary. As a beginner, Madame explained, Anna could not expect more. She was to wear the *jeune fille*[2] dresses. Another smile, another sharp glance.

Anna was conducted from the Presence by an underling who helped her to take off the frock she had worn temporarily for the interview. Aspirants for an engagement are always dressed in a model of the house.

She had spent yesterday afternoon in a delirium tempered by a feeling of exaggerated reality, and in buying the necessary make up. It had been such a forlorn hope, answering the advertisement.

The morning had been dream-like. At the back of the wonderfully decorated salons she had found an unexpected sombreness; the place, empty, would have been dingy and melancholy, countless puzzling corridors and staircases, a rabbit warren and a labyrinth. She despaired of ever finding her way.

In the mannequins' dressing-room she spent a shy hour making up her face—in an extraordinary and distinctive atmosphere of slimness and beauty; white arms and faces vivid with rouge; raucous voices and the smell of cosmetics; silken lingerie. Coldly critical glances were bestowed upon Anna's reflexion in the glass. None of them looked at her directly. . . . A depressing room, taken by itself, bare and cold, a very inadequate conservatory for these human flowers. Saleswomen in black rushed in and out, talking in sharp voices; a very old woman hovered, helpful and shapeless, showing Anna where to hang her clothes, presenting to her the black garment that Anna was wearing, going to lunch. She smiled with professional motherliness, her little, sharp, black eyes travelling rapidly from *la nouvelle's*[3] hair to her ankles and back again.

She was Madame Pecard, the dresser.

Before Anna had spoken a word she was called away by a small boy in buttons to her destination in one of the salons: there, under the eye of a *vendeuse*,[4] she had to learn the way to wear the innocent and springlike air and garb of the *jeune fille*. Behind a yellow, silken screen she was hustled into a leather coat and paraded under the cold eyes of an American buyer. . . . This was the week when the spring models are shown to important people from big shops of all over Europe and America: the most critical week of the season. . . . The American buyer said that he would have that, but with an inch on to the collar and larger cuffs. In vain the saleswoman, in her best English with its odd Chicago accent, protested that that would completely ruin the *chic*[5] of the model. The American buyer knew what he wanted and saw that he got it.

The *vendeuse* sighed, but there was a note of admiration in her voice. She respected Americans: they were not like the English, who, under a surface

---

2. Girls'.
3. The new girl's.
4. Saleswoman. "In buttons": i.e., in a uniform whose tunic has two rows of buttons running up its front.
5. Style, elegance.

of annoying moroseness of manner, were notoriously timid and easy to turn round your finger.

"Was that all right?" Behind the screen one of the saleswomen smiled encouragingly and nodded. The other shrugged her shoulders. She had small, close-set eyes, a long thin nose and tight lips of the regulation puce colour. Behind her silken screen Anna sat on a high white stool. She felt that she appeared charming and troubled. The white and gold of the salon suited her red hair.

A short morning. For the mannequin's day begins at ten and the process of making up lasts an hour. The friendly saleswoman volunteered the information that her name was Jeannine, that she was in the lingerie, that she considered Anna *rudement jolie*,[6] that noon was Anna's lunch hour. She must go down the corridor and up those stairs, through the big salon then.... Anyone would tell her. But Anna, lost in the labyrinth, was too shy to ask her way. Besides, she was not sorry to have time to brace herself for the ordeal. She had reached the regions of utility and oilcloth: the decorative salons were far overhead.... Then the smell of food—almost visible, it was so cloud-like and heavy, came to her nostrils, and high-noted, and sibilant, a buzz of conversation made her draw a deep breath. She pushed a door open.

She was in a big, very low-ceilinged room, all the floor space occupied by long wooden tables with no cloths.... She was sitting at the mannequins' table, gazing at a thick and hideous white china plate, a twisted tin fork, a wooden-handled stained knife, a tumbler so thick it seemed unbreakable.

There were twelve mannequins at Jeanne Veron's: six of them were lunching, the others still paraded, goddess like, till their turn came for rest and refreshment. Each of the twelve was of a distinct and separate type: each of the twelve knew her type and kept to it, practising rigidly in clothing, manner, voice and conversation.

Round the austere table were now seated: Babette, the *gamine*, the traditional *blonde enfant*:[7] Mona, tall and darkly beautiful, the *femme fatale*, the wearer of sumptuous evening gowns. Georgette was the *garçonne*:[8] Simone with green eyes Anna knew instantly for a cat whom men would and did adore, a sleek, white, purring, long-lashed creature.... Eliane was the star of the collection.

Eliane was frankly ugly and it did not matter: no doubt Lilith,[9] from whom she was obviously descended, had been ugly too. Her hair was henna-tinted, her eyes small and black, her complexion bad under her thick make-up. Her hips were extraordinarily slim, her hands and feet exquisite, every movement she made was as graceful as a flower's in the wind. Her walk... But it was her walk which made her there the star and earned her a salary quite fabulous for Madame Veron's, where large salaries were not the rule.... Her walk and her "chic of the devil" which lit an expression of admiration in even the cold eyes of American buyers.

---

6. Awfully pretty. "The lingerie": i.e., the lingerie department.
7. Fair child. "*Gamine*": street urchin.
8. Tomboy.
9. In Jewish mythology, a female nocturnal demon (probably derived from the Assyrian storm demon Lilitu). Specifically, she was believed to kill babies.

According to a story first recorded between the 8th and 10th centuries C.E., Lilith was Adam's first wife—made, as he was, from dust and thus his equal. Because she refused to submit to him and left the Garden of Eden, she was cursed by God and replaced by Eve, created from Adam's rib (as described in Genesis 2.21–23).

Liliane was a quiet girl, pleasant-mannered. She wore a ring with a beautiful emerald on one long, slim finger, and in her small eyes were both intelligence and mystery.

Madame Pecard, the dresser, was seated at the head of the mannequin's table, talking loudly, unlistened to, and gazing benevolently at her flock.

At other tables sat the sewing girls, pale-faced, black-frocked—the workers, heroically gay, but with the stamp of labour on them: and the saleswomen. The mannequins, with their sensual, blatant charms and their painted faces were watched covertly and envied and apart.

Babette the *blonde enfant* was next to Anna, and having started the conversation with a few good, round oaths at the quality of the sardines, announced proudly that she could speak English and knew London very well. She began to tell Anna the history of her adventures in the city of coldness, dark and fogs. . . . She had gone to a job as a mannequin in Bond Street[1] and the villainous proprietor of the shop having tried to make love to her and she being rigidly virtuous, she had left. And another job, Anna must figure to herself, had been impossible to get, for she, Babette, was too small and slim for the Anglo-Saxon idea of a mannequin.

She stopped to shout in a loud voice to the woman who was serving: "Hé, my old one, don't forget your little Babette. . . . "

Opposite, Simone the cat and the sportive Georgette were having a low-voiced conversation about the triste-ness[2] of a monsieur of their acquaintance. "I said to him," Georgette finished decisively, "Nothing to be done, my rabbit. You have not well looked at me, little one. In my place would you not have done the same?"

She broke off when she realized that the others were listening, and smiled in a friendly way at Anna.

She too, it appeared, had ambitions to go to London because the salaries were so much better there. Was it difficult? Did they really like French girls? Parisiennes?

The conversation became general.

"The English boys are nice," said Babette, winking one divinely candid eye. "I had a chic type who used to take me to dinner at the Empire Palace. Oh, a pretty boy. . . . "

"It is the most chic restaurant in London," she added importantly.

The meal reached the stage of dessert. The other tables were gradually emptying; the mannequins all ordered very strong coffee, several a liqueur. Only Mona and Eliane remained silent; Eliane, because she was thinking of something else; Mona, because it was her type, her *genre* to be haughty.

Her hair swept away from her white, narrow forehead and her small ears: her long earrings nearly touching her shoulders she sipped her coffee with a disdainful air. Only once, when the *blonde enfant*, having engaged in a passage of arms with the waitress and got the worst of it was momentarily discomfited and silent, Mona narrowed her eyes and smiled an astonishingly cruel smile. . . .

As soon as her coffee was drunk she got up and went out.

Anna produced a cigarette, and Georgette, perceiving instantly that here

---

1. A main shopping street in London.   2. Sadness.

was the sportive touch, her *genre*, asked for one and lit it with a devil-may-care air. Anna eagerly passed her cigarettes round, but the Mère[3] Pecard interfered weightily. It was against the rules of the house for the mannequins to smoke, she wheezed. The girls all lit their cigarettes and smoked. The Mère Pecard rumbled on:

"A caprice, my children. All the world knows that mannequins are capricious. Is it not so?" She appealed to the rest of the room.

As they went out Babette put her arm round Anna's waist and whispered: "Don't answer Madame Pecard. We don't like her. We never talk to her. She spies on us. She is a camel."

That afternoon Anna stood for an hour to have a dress draped on her. She showed this dress to a stout Dutch lady buying for the Hague, to a beautiful South American with pearls, to a silver-haired American gentleman who wanted an evening cape for his daughter of seventeen, and to a hook-nosed, odd English lady of title who had a loud voice and dressed, under her furs, in a grey jersey and stout boots.

The American gentleman approved of Anna, and said so, and Anna gave him a passionately grateful glance. For, if the *vendeuse* Jeannine had been uniformly kind and encouraging, the other, Madame Tienne, had been as uniformly disapproving and had once even pinched her arm hard.

About five o'clock Anna became exhausted. The four white and gold walls seemed to close in on her. She sat on her high white stool staring at a marvellous nightgown and fighting an intense desire to rush away. Anywhere! Just to dress and rush away anywhere, from the raking eyes of the customers and the pinching fingers of Irene.

"I will one day. I can't stick it," she said to herself. "I won't be able to stick it." She had an absurd wish to gasp for air.

Jeannine came and found her like that.

"It is hard at first, *hein*? . . . One asks oneself: Why? For what good? It is all *idiot*.[4] We are all so. But we go on. Do not worry about Irene." She whispered: "Madame Veron likes you very much. I heard her say so."

At six o'clock Anna was out in the rue de la Paix; her fatigue forgotten, the feeling that now she really belonged to the great, maddening city possessed her and she was happy in her beautifully cut tailor made and a beret.

Georgette passed her and smiled; Babette was in a fur coat.

All up the street the mannequins were coming out of the shops, pausing on the pavements a moment, making them as gay and as beautiful as beds of flowers before they walked swiftly away and the Paris night swallowed them up.

1927

---

3. Mother.   4. Absurd. "*Hein?*": eh? (exclamation).

LOUISE BOGAN
1897–1970

"Women have no wilderness in them, / They are provident instead," wrote Louise Bogan in a famous poem titled "Women." Yet this scrupulous artist, who was from 1931 to 1969 the influential and fiercely independent poetry critic for *The New Yorker,* herself wrote poems that constituted rigorous explorations of an interior "wilderness," poems that—in the words of W. H. Auden, a fellow writer whom she much admired—"wrested beauty and truth out of dark places." "It is my firm belief," she once ironically commented, "that I was Messalina . . . Boadicea . . . and Felicia Hemans before this." The combination is telling: a ruthless empress, a woman warrior—and a famously popular but frequently derided Romantic "lady poet." What was this apparently successful and confident writer telling readers about her own aesthetic conflicts?

Born in Livermore Falls, Maine, Bogan described herself as "the highly charged and neurotically inclined product of an extraordinary childhood and an unfortunate early marriage, into which last state I had rushed to escape the first." Her parents were genteelly impoverished and unhappily married, often separating for long periods, so that she later confessed that "I cannot bring myself to describe the horrors of the pre-1914 lower-middle-class life, in which they found themselves." In 1909 the family had moved to Boston, where the young Bogan entered Girls' Latin School and began to write poetry. In 1915, she enrolled as a freshman at Boston University, where two of her verses were printed in the literary magazine. But though she had been offered a scholarship to Radcliffe for the following year, she decided instead to marry Curt Alexander, a professional soldier, so that she could get away from the turmoil in her home. While living on an army base in the Panama Canal Zone, the couple had a daughter in 1917, but the marriage was indeed, in other ways, "unfortunate," and Bogan left her husband in 1919. The next year he died, and she received a small widow's pension. It enabled her to travel in 1922 to Vienna, where she studied piano.

In 1923, after she had returned to New York, Bogan met Raymond Holden, a novelist and minor poet, whom she was to marry in 1925. Supporting herself at various odd jobs, she sent her daughter to live with her parents and began seriously to write and publish; her work in this period included film criticism and poetry reviews as well as two well-received volumes of verse, *Body of This Death* (1923) and *Dark Summer* (1929). In 1931, however, just after she had begun her career as a poetry reviewer for *The New Yorker,* Bogan had the first of a series of nervous breakdowns that were to acquaint her with what Auden called "dark places." Recovering, she separated from Holden in 1934 and entered into a romantic relationship with the poet Theodore Roethke, who became her lifelong partisan. Her new collections appeared at regular intervals—*The Sleeping Fury* in 1937 and *Poems and New Poems* in 1941—and a growing number of prizes recognized the nature of her aesthetic achievement. After serving in 1945 as Consultant in Poetry to the Library of Congress, she was awarded visiting professorships and literary residencies at several major institutions, including the University of Washington and Brandeis University. Her last book of verse, *The Blue Estuaries: Poems, 1923–1968,* appeared shortly before she resigned from her job as poetry reviewer for *The New Yorker* and a year before she died of a heart attack.

Throughout her career, Bogan had remained an intensely private woman: she made few pronouncements on public events and, as the poem "Women" suggests, did not particularly identify herself as a feminist. Yet in a late essay on women poets she reminded her audience that "the word feminism . . . is a word which has its own honor and radiance," and—though she had once claimed that she disliked "other women poets (jealousy!)"—she catalogued in some detail the achievements of literary women from Sappho to Virginia Woolf. What seems at first like a puzzling inconsistency in this keenly intelligent poet-critic's thought becomes easier to understand when one sets the bitterness she expresses in "Women" against the powerful reimagining of mythology that she undertakes in such poems as "Medusa" and "Cassandra."

Medusa[1]

I had come to the house, in a cave of trees,
Facing a sheer sky.
Everything moved,—a bell hung ready to strike,
Sun and reflection wheeled by.

5 When the bare eyes were before me
And the hissing hair,
Held up at a window, seen through a door.
The stiff bald eyes, the serpents on the forehead
Formed in the air.

10 This is a dead scene forever now.
Nothing will ever stir.
The end will never brighten it more than this,
Nor the rain blur.

The water will always fall, and will not fall,
15 And the tipped bell make no sound.
The grass will always be growing for hay
Deep on the ground.

And I shall stand here like a shadow
Under the great balanced day,
20 My eyes on the yellow dust, that was lifting in the wind,
And does not drift away.

1923

The Crows

The woman who has grown old
And knows desire must die,
Yet turns to love again,
Hears the crows' cry.

5 She is a stem long hardened,
A weed that no scythe mows.
The heart's laughter will be to her
The crying of the crows.

---

1. In Greek mythology, one of three snake-haired sisters called the Gorgons, the sight of whom turned all who looked at them to stone.

Who slide in the air with the same voice
10 Over what yields not, and what yields,
   Alike in spring, and when there is only bitter
   Winter-burning in the fields.

                                                    1923

Women

   Women have no wilderness in them,
   They are provident instead,
   Content in the tight hot cell of their hearts
   To eat dusty bread.

5 They do not see cattle cropping red winter grass,
   They do not hear
   Snow water going down under culverts
   Shallow and clear.

   They wait, when they should turn to journeys,
10 They stiffen, when they should bend.
   They use against themselves that benevolence
   To which no man is friend.

   They cannot think of so many crops to a field
   Or of clean wood cleft by an axe.
15 Their love is an eager meaninglessness
   Too tense, or too lax.

   They hear in every whisper that speaks to them
   A shout and a cry.
   As like as not, when they take life over their door-sills
20 They should let it go by.

                                                    1923

Cassandra[1]

   To me, one silly task is like another.
   I bare the shambling tricks of lust and pride.
   This flesh will never give a child its mother,—
   Song, like a wing, tears through my breast, my side,
5 And madness chooses out my voice again,
   Again. I am the chosen no hand saves:
   The shrieking heaven lifted over men,
   Not the dumb earth, wherein they set their graves.

                                                    1929

---

1. Trojan princess to whom Apollo gave the gift of prophecy; because she then refused his advances, he also ensured that she would be believed by no one.

The Crossed Apple

I've come to give you fruit from out my orchard,
Of wide report.
I have trees there that bear me many apples
Of every sort:

5   Clear, streakèd; red and russet; green and golden;
Sour and sweet.
This apple's from a tree yet unbeholden,
Where two kinds meet,—

So that this side is red without a dapple,
10 And this side's hue
Is clear and snowy. It's a lovely apple.
It is for you.

Within are five black pips as big as peas,
As you will find,
15 Potent to breed you five great apple trees
Of varying kind:

To breed you wood for fire, leaves for shade,
Apples for sauce.
Oh, this is a good apple for a maid,
20 It is a cross,

Fine on the finer, so the flesh is tight,
And grained like silk.
Sweet Burning gave the red side, and the white
Is Meadow Milk.

25 Eat it; and you will taste more than the fruit;
The blossom, too,
The sun, the air, the darkness at the root,
The rain, the dew,

The earth we came to, and the time we flee,
30 The fire and the breast.
I claim the white part, maiden, that's for me.
You take the rest.

1929

Evening in the Sanitarium[1]

The free evening fades, outside the windows fastened with decorative
    iron grilles.
The lamps are lighted; the shades drawn; the nurses are watching a little.

---

1. Originally published with the subtitle "Imitated from Auden"—W. H. Auden (1907–1973), English poet.

It is the hour of the complicated knitting on the safe bone needles; of the
　　games of anagrams and bridge;
The deadly game of chess; the book held up like a mask.

5 The period of the wildest weeping, the fiercest delusion, is over.
The women rest their tired half-healed hearts; they are almost well.
Some of them will stay almost well always: the blunt-faced woman whose
　　thinking dissolved
Under academic discipline; the manic-depressive girl
Now leveling off; one paranoiac afflicted with jealousy.
10 Another with persecution. Some alleviation has been possible.

O fortunate bride, who never again will become elated after childbirth!
O lucky older wife, who has been cured of feeling unwanted!
To the suburban railway station you will return, return,
To meet forever Jim home on the 5:35.
15 You will be again as normal and selfish and heartless as anybody else.

There is life left: the piano says it with its octave smile.
The soft carpets pad the thump and splinter of the suicide to be.
Everything will be splendid: the grandmother will not drink habitually.
The fruit salad will bloom on the plate like a bouquet
20 And the garden produce the blue-ribbon aquilegia.[2]
The cats will be glad; the fathers feel justified; the mothers relieved.
The sons and husbands will no longer need to pay the bills.
Childhoods will be put away, the obscene nightmare abated.

At the ends of the corridors the baths are running.
25 Mrs. C. again feels the shadow of the obsessive idea.
Miss R. looks at the mantel-piece, which must mean something.

　　　　　　　　　　　　　　　　　　　　　　　　　　1941

Several Voices out of a Cloud

Come, drunks and drug-takers; come, perverts unnerved!
Receive the laurel,[1] given, though late, on merit; to
whom and
　　　　wherever deserved.

Parochial punks, trimmers, nice people, joiners true-blue,
5 　Get the hell out of the way of the laurel. It is deathless[2]
　　And it isn't for you.

　　　　　　　　　　　　　　　　　　　　　　　　　　1941

---

2. Columbine.

1. In classical Greece, a laurel wreath crowned the victor in an athletic or poetic contest.
2. Because laurel is an evergreen.

The Dream

O God, in the dream the terrible horse began
To paw at the air, and make for me with his blows.
Fear kept for thirty-five years poured through his mane,
And retribution equally old, or nearly, breathed through his nose.

5   Coward complete, I lay and wept on the ground
When some strong creature appeared, and leapt for the rein.
Another woman, as I lay half in a swound,
Leapt in the air, and clutched at the leather and chain.

Give him, she said, something of yours as a charm.
10   Throw him, she said, some poor thing you alone claim.
No, no, I cried, he hates me; he's out for harm,
And whether I yield or not, it is all the same.

But, like a lion in a legend, when I flung the glove
Pulled from my sweating, my cold right hand,
15   The terrible beast, that no one may understand,
Came to my side, and put down his head in love.

1941

KATE O'BRIEN
1897–1974

"She was the most visibly sexually dissident writer of her society," writes the Irish scholar Eibhear Walshe about Kate O'Brien, a novelist, memoirist, and travel writer whose pioneering fictions have until recently been largely forgotten. Born in Limerick, the youngest of nine children in an upper-middle-class family, O'Brien was educated at a convent school and graduated from University College, Dublin. After graduation, she worked as a journalist and translator in England, traveled to the United States, and spent a year as a governess for a Spanish family. In 1923 she married a Dutch journalist but the marriage ended within a year. By this time, O'Brien had embarked on a serious literary career, writing plays and novels. Her first drama, *Distinguished Villa* (1926), was positively received, but she soon focused her energies largely on fiction. Her first novel, *Without My Cloak* (1931), became a best seller and won several prestigious prizes, but subsequent works were increasingly radical in their exploration of sexual politics. Both *Mary Lavelle* (1936) and *The Land of Spices* (1941) were banned for obscenity by the Irish Censorship Board, almost certainly because of their allusions to lesbian desire and male homosexuality.

Although O'Brien's travel books and memoirs were not particularly frank about the writer's sexual orientation (historians now speculate that she was herself a lesbian), at least one of her nonfiction works was as problematic to authorities as two of her novels were. *Farewell Spain* (1937) was so critical of Generalissimo Francisco Franco that O'Brien was banned from entering the country for twenty years. And indeed much of the book deplores the horror of the civil war endured by "a country now in agony": "I approach Madrid now as never before," O'Brien confessed, "in a mood of weary sadness." The excerpts reprinted here, however—on St. Teresa and on bullfighting—reveal what we might call this high-spirited traveler's "Hispanophilia." In addition, "Santa Teresa" vividly dramatizes both the author's and the saint's feminism, while, with its refusal of easy condemnations, the bullfighting section of her essay on Madrid documents O'Brien's sometimes rebellious open-mindedness and adventurousness as well as her lively descriptive abilities.

From Santa Teresa[1]

The main square of Avila has a variety of names. One guide-book calls it Plaza de la Constitución, another Plaza da Santa Teresa, a third Plaza del Mercado.[2] On its name-plates it announces itself impartially as Plaza Mayor, Mercado Grande and Plaza de la República.[3] I believe it has also been known as Plaza Torquemada, Plaza San Segundo, and Plaza del Alcázar.[4] Some day perhaps a decision will be taken, but Avila—"dont l'origine se perd dans la nuit des temps,"[5] says the guide-book—is not disposed to do things hastily.

Nevertheless, when the city does decide to name the square, let us hope it gives it its only true name. Constitutions come and go, and so do republics; markets have, as Avila knows, their ups and downs. But Saint Teresa is for ever, for history and humanity so long as they remain. And she was of Avila. A genius of the large and immeasurable kind of which there have been very few, and only one a woman. Let the feminists who, anxiously counting up their Sapphos, Jane Austens and Mesdames Curie,[6] always ignore Santa Teresa—let the feminists pull themselves together and get this square correctly named once and for all. The monument in the Centre celebrates Avila's great men, with Saint Teresa at the top, as she must be, and the only one of them the passing visitor remembers. Her legend is scattered over all the town, though with a certain Spanish carelessness and non-sentimentality. Spanish crudity too. One does not like to see her index finger in a bottle[7]—though that represents a mere nothing, as one discovers from her biographers, of the mutilations perpetrated on her remains by rapacious lunatics and votaries of the seventeenth century. But her leather girdle, the hazel-tree she planted, a drum she had when a child, her little drinking jug—(not the pretty *calderica*[8] which Maria de San José sent her from Sevilla and of which she wrote to the donor, before giving it away—"Do not think that because I wear lighter serge now I have gone the length of drinking from anything so lovely")—these relics touch imagination gently and make us less

---

1. Saint Teresa of Ávila (1515–1582), Spanish nun famous for her mystical visions; she founded the Carmelite Reform order, and many convents and monasteries.
2. Plaza of the Constitution, Plaza of St. Teresa, Plaza of the Market (Spanish, as are all translated terms unless otherwise specified).
3. Main Plaza, Large Market, Plaza of the Republic.
4. Plaza of the Castle. Tomás de Torquemada (1420–1498), Spanish churchman and the most famous inquisitor general. St. Segundo, first bishop of Ávila; he brought Christianity to the area in the 1st century.
5. Whose origin is lost in the mists of time (French).
6. Marie Curie (1867–1934), Polish-born French physical chemist, winner of two Nobel prizes for work related to radioactivity and radioactive elements. Sappho (b. ca. 612 B.C.E.), Greek lyric poet. Austen (1775–1817), English novelist; see Vol. 1, p. 459.
7. Nine months after her death, a Reformed Carmelite superior exhumed Teresa's body, found it totally intact, and cut off a finger to use as a talisman (with later exhumations, more pieces of her body were removed).
8. Little pot.

afraid of the strange, impassioned mystic, of whom presently we find, taking some trouble to approach, there is no need on earth to be afraid. For Teresa, who would never have dreamt of saying that she was captain of her soul, was in fact captain of all her faculties as almost no one else in history appears to have been, and was therefore able to suffer, and record, a long-drawn and awful adventure of the spirit without sacrificing a jot of her human reality and understanding.

When I was in Avila two years ago I knew little of Teresa save from Crashaw[9] and from certain pious anecdotes heard in childhood. Some of the latter excellently characteristic in spirit even if sometimes apocryphal in fact. For instance: in the last year of her life, when she was sixty-seven and oppressed with severe complaints, kidney and stomach troubles, intermittent paralysis, ulcerated throat and an arm so awkwardly broken and set that it was now quite useless, she was on the road to Burgos[1] in winter with a few of her nuns—about to found the last of her reformed convents. They had to go over a floating bridge which, when visible, was so narrow that to cross it in single file called for great courage and sure-footedness. On this occasion the wretched plank was submerged two feet below a hurrying winter flood. "Hinder me not, my daughters," said Teresa to the rather frightened nuns, "for it is my intention to cross first, and if I am drowned I command you not to attempt it, but to return to the inn." So she marched across the plank and all her nuns found the nerve to follow her. But once at the other side she addressed God irritably, as on some other occasions. "Strange that as I have consecrated my existence and all my labours to Thee, Thou shouldst treat me in this way." And the Lord answered: "Thus do I treat my friends." To which Teresa retorted: "For this reason Thou hast very few."

In childhood and as a girl she was spirited and exceptional. Everyone knows that when she was five she set out with her brother to get herself martyred by the Moors—but few know what she dryly narrates in her autobiography of that idea: that it was by no means for love of God but because she had decided that those who were so clever as to get themselves beheaded by the infidel had found a very cheap and easy way of securing happiness for ever. The notion of everlastingness held her child's brain. *Por siempre, por siempre*[2] she used to murmur to herself, of heaven and hell, as she 'prioressed' over her dominated brothers. But though she liked the *monasterio*[3] game, she had no notion whatever of playing it in earnest later on. She grew—according to herself—into a vain and romantic-minded girl, read novels of chivalry on the sly, and even wrote one, sought the company of giggling flapper[4] cousins and imbibed with interest their knowledge of life and the world. Until her pious widower-father, worried about her, clapped her into a convent to learn sense. But here, to her surprise, Teresa still found that she enjoyed life, and the society of the nuns. For always, to the end of her days, she enjoyed society, and was rapaciously interested in people. She found no religious vocation here, however. Instead, at the end of two years

---

9. Richard Crashaw (1613?–1649), English poet whose religious poems include several on Teresa; the best known is "The Flaming Heart."
1. Town in northern Spain, about 120 miles northeast of Ávila; former capital of the kingdom of León and Castile.
2. Forever, forever.
3. Monastery.
4. I.e., fashionable young women whose dress and behavior were unconventional (a term used in the 1920s).

she developed the first of those strange, helpless, unexplained illnesses which plagued her through her twenties. So that her father removed her from the convent and sent her to recuperate in the mountains, in the home of an old, melancholy hyper-religious uncle, who made her read St. Jerome and St. Gregory[5] to him every evening. The effect of the fathers of the church on her convalescent nervous system was to terrify her against human life, and also against the endlessness of the world to come. *Por siempre, por siempre,* she heard again and she was a poet. So, against her father's wish, with no vocation to serve God, but simply in terror of everything real and imaginable, she fled to the Convent of the Encarnación[6] and took the habit. "I do not think that when I die the wrench will be greater than when I went forth from my father's house. . . ."

The Encarnación, where now they show you in the vast chapel the site of Teresa's cell, and the altar-piece carved from the wood of her pear-trees, was in 1533 and for long after a very easy-going and jovial kind of convent. It was overfull of aristocratic, lazy nuns who had no notion of obedience, and who liked to spend their days gossiping and flirting in the *locutorios*[7] with their smart relatives and the friends of their smart relatives. Also with the easy-going, hair-splitting, heresy-hunting friars. But Teresa spent twenty-nine years there; more than twenty of them being an incessant struggle with illness, disillusionment, spiritual fears and the premonitions, very alarming and disheartening to her, of mystical experience. She was bent on living the life she had undertaken to live, but her standards were high, and every difficulty seemed to be put in her way, within and without. In the Encarnación she learnt all that about convent life which she implied when she wrote that, as she found it, it was a short cut to hell, and that no father should be such a fool as to allow his daughters to embrace it. She learnt also so much about women that in later life she was supreme and unmatchable in commanding them. And in the last seven or eight years of her stay there, when she was in her forties, she had to undergo an adventure in illumination which every man must explain or dismiss as he chooses. Teresa could never explain it herself, but never were sanity, modesty and sheer intelligence so brilliantly exercised to attempt the impossible. Her autobiography, written by command of her spiritual adviser before she was fifty and before her active life began, is a model for ever of discipline in writing. It is short, simple, Castilian,[8] idiomatic; its metaphors are from daily life, its tone is completely modest and cautious, and the writer's patient search for exactitude gives muscle to every line. Yet she treats of that which in her time was not only alarming to her steady logical brain, but with the Inquisition[9] flourishing, highly dangerous to her life, and which since her death has been misused from a thousand points of view, as she knew it would be—for she was very much against the dissemination of talk about mystical experience, and to the end of her

---

5. Two church fathers. Jerome (ca. 340–420) wrote many works of ecclesiastical history and biblical exegesis, and Gregory (ca. 540–604), who as pope restored monastic discipline, wrote dialogues, homilies, saints' lives, and *Moralia*.
6. Incarnation.
7. Visiting rooms, where outsiders can meet with nuns or monks.
8. The dialect of central and north-central Spain (later the official and literary language of all Spain). Teresa's autobiography, *Book of Her Life*, was first written between 1562 and 1565 and continually revised until her death.
9. The Spanish Inquisition, established in 1478 to discover and punish Jews (and later Muslims) who falsely claimed to have converted to Catholicism. Its search for heresy became much broader, and Teresa was among those investigated.

life not only was sensitive and silent about her own, but extremely severe on other visionaries and would-be contemplatives.

Nor will we talk of it here, who are so completely unfitted to do so. Only there is this book, her first, which dealing with an ineffable theme impossible of satisfactory solution save for those who dismiss it as completely pathological, yet for simplicity, honour, dignity and formal poise takes its place at the very peak of the noble literature of Castile.

So here, in her forties, in illness, madness, what you will—and if after reading the autobiography you can use those words conclusively about Teresa you are indeed a comfortable insensitive—her day of genius begins. Her contemplative period completed, her union with God become manageable and for ever more her own most private matter, acclimatised to her state of permanent prayer, as sane, witty and matter of fact as only the best kind of Castilian can be, she sets about her suddenly realised job—the reform of the Carmelite Order.

She has twenty years of life ahead of her—twenty years of incessant activity of every possible kind and of every possible kind of discomfort and ill-health. "This body of mine has always worked me harm and hindered me." She was very impatient of her health, as of everything that delayed her, even to the goosequills with which, at amazing speed, she wrote her books and her thousands of brilliant, witty letters. Everywhere the goosequills were bad, except those which her brother sent her from La Serna. "You'll think from my writing that I am ill—and it is only the number of bad goosequills that I use." She strikes a chord there in one who can never find a suitable pen—but, alas, her noble, spacious handwriting, exposed in the Escorial Library,[1] shows that for once a good workman quarrelled with his tools.

The story of the twenty years can be read in many sources. But best in her own letters. During them she was everything—preacher, teacher, lawyer, cashier, politician, poet, tramp and charwoman. She was the best cook in all her twelve convents, dishing up the fish "as God ordered." Although impatient of book-learning—"God preserve you, my daughters, from being *latinas*"—she was a formidable match for inquisitor or Salamancan doctor.[2] She was a fighter and a schemer, a soldier and a most subtle diplomat. The Papal Nuncio called her "restless, disobedient, contumacious, an inventress of new doctrines, a breaker of the cloister-rule, a despiser of the apostolic precept which forbiddeth a woman to teach."[3] She was a communist: "Let no sister have anything of her own but everything in common and to each be given according to her need. Neither must the prioress, etc. . . . all must be equal." This is her eternal cry, up and down Spain. She was a feminist: "I will not have my daughters women in anything, but valorous men." Though of women *qua* women she thought very little. "Put no faith in nuns." And "It is needful to keep a sharp look-out on what these 'prioritas'[4] strike out of their own heads." But she hit out at the friars, too. "It is to be wondered if they will obey the king, so used are these fathers to doing whatever they like." And

---

1. A library near Madrid, known for its rare book collection; it was founded in the 16th century.
2. Learned clergyman (Salamanca, about 55 miles northwest of Ávila, contained one of the most important universities of medieval Europe). *"Latinas"*: i.e., female Latin scholars.
3. The apostle Paul wrote, "Let the woman learn in silence with all subjection. But I suffer not a woman to teach, nor to usurp authority over the man, but to be in silence" (1 Timothy 2.11–12). "Nuncio": the pope's permanent representative to a specific secular government or particular region.
4. Little prioresses.

"Pray God He lays a heavy hand on those friars." She even suspected the enemy-monks of grave crime. "Be careful what you eat in their monasteries." And she was hard on herself without ceasing: "How malicious I am!" again and again, and a thousand lamentations for this and that defect. "God make me a good nun of Carmel, for better late than never." "Already I am becoming quite a nun. Pray God it lasts." "In Avila when they tell me I am a saint I tell them to make another, since it costs them no more than to say so." "During the course of my life they have said of me three things: when I was young that I was fair to look upon; then, that I was witty; now some say I am a saint. The first two things I once believed in and have confessed myself of having given credence to this vanity; but in the third I have never deceived myself so much as even to have begun to believe it."

She was ironic more than pointedly witty, I think. Her letters are fluidly mischievous rather than barbed. But her mockery could be clear enough. To a prioress who showed some traces of self-importance in office she would quote the Castilian proverb: "*falta de bueno mi marido alcalde*—for want of a good man my husband is mayor." To María de San José, Prioress of Sevilla and a rather erudite woman, she wrote commenting on some display of learning in the other's letter: "What you say of Elisha[5] is good, but not being learned like you I don't know what you mean about the Assyrians." This dirty crack has since become, I believe, a Castilian formula for putting down the pedantic.

She was mad on cleanliness, and on asceticism. "From good houses, from comfort, God deliver us!" She thought horses and saddles quite unnecessary for travelling round Spain. Donkeys, which were always throwing her to the ground, were her idea. "It is unseemly to see these discalced[6] lads [her monks] on good mules." But she discouraged all individualistic mortification, and was strong for the rule, and for a good sufficiency for everyone—when possible, for her houses were extremely poor—of such food as the rule allowed. "Do not be afraid of sleep," she reiterates to the over-watchful, the too-anxious.

She was convivial and gay. She made up couplets and *villancicos*[7] for her nuns to sing at recreation. Frequently in her letters: "I was amused . . ." "I laughed at what you said . . ." She teases: "How vain you will become now you are a semi-provinciala!"[8] When one of her convents is enjoying some privilege she would like to share: "God pardon those butterflies in Sevilla!" When she has hurt a nun's feelings: "You must forgive me. With those I dearly love I am insufferable, so anxious am I that they should excel. . . ."

She was very shrewd and had need to be. The ecclesiastical politics of her last decade are bewildering to read of. "Be warned always that a peaceful settlement will be the best. Lawsuits are rude things." And she put fun into intriguing. When she suspected that her letters were being opened, the Inquisitors became "the Holy Angels," and Christ became "José." Reserved and humble about her books, she was lightly vain of her impromptu couplets and dashing off her latest—from memory—in a letter to the erudite prioress of Sevilla, she says: "I remember no more. What a brain for a Foundress!

---

5. Hebrew prophet (9th c. B.C.E.), Elijah's disciple and successor; see 2 Kings 2.1–10.17.
6. Barefoot (the order Teresa founded was the Discalced Carmelite Nuns of the Primitive Rule of St. Joseph).
7. Carols; Christmas carols.
8. A provincial is the supervisor of a number of local superiors of a given religious order.

And yet I assure you I thought I had not a little when I wrote it. God forgive you for making me waste my time like this!"

Always she was noble, asking the impossible of life and of herself, preaching the most generous doctrine of perfection. "Accustom yourselves to have great desires, for out of them great benefits may be derived, even if they cannot be put into action."

And all the time, while she wrote her great 'Camino de Perfección,' her 'Moradas,'[9] and all the noble injunctions of her letters, she was unceasingly at work, fighting tooth and nail to recall the relaxed and decadent Church to its true purpose. Unceasingly at prayer, too, by her mastery of the mystical life. She was the last great mediævalist, and though she saw the actual triumph in policy of what she worked for, she asked too much. Humanity could not give what she could, and all that she was died with her. She was the last of her kind, and perhaps the greatest. Certainly she was the greatest woman in Christian history. She died repeating *"Cor contritum et humiliatum, Deus, non despicies."*[1]

* * *

1937

From No Pasarán[1]

[*On Bullfighting*]

* * *

Some Spaniard—I have forgotten who—has said of Madrid that it contains everything necessary to human happiness, viz., cafés, the Prado Museum and three bullrings.

It is certainly a good centre for bullfights—for if on any Thursday, Sunday or feast-day of the season none of its bullrings offers an attractive *corrida*, which is unlikely, there is sure to be one at Toledo, or at Aranjuez, or at least a *novillada*[2] at Alcala de Henares. But the more usual difficulty for the *aficionado*[3] is to choose between seeing Lalanda fight at Guadalajara or El Soldado in Madrid's new ring at Ventas.

I first saw Belmonte fight in Madrid. It was a specially grand *corrida* to celebrate I've forgotten which feast-day. The *espadas*[4] were Belmonte, Lalanda, Ortega (since killed in civil war), and Manoel Bienvenida. A very famous quartette, and the prices of the seats were high. Tickets were much coveted, but mine—not a very good one, about the tenth row of the *tendido*[5] in the shade—had been secured a full fortnight in advance. Traffic in Ventas

---

9. *The Way of Perfection* (written ca. 1566) is a book of instructions on prayer, and *The Interior Castle* (literally, *Mansions of the Inner Castle*; written in 1577) portrays the contemplative life.
1. You will not despise a contrite and humble heart, God (Latin).
1. They shall not pass (Spanish, as are all translated terms). This was a slogan of those who opposed the fascist forces led by Gen. Francisco Franco in the Spanish civil war (1936–39).
2. Bullfight using young bulls. "*Corrida*": bullfight. O'Brien names a number of bullfighting venues and bullfighters in this paragraph.
3. Fan.
4. Matadors (those with swords who kill the bull).
5. Section in the stands, usually six or seven rows deep.

promised to be dangerous and difficult that afternoon and as no one is ever late for the *corrida*, and as it always starts on the stroke of the scheduled hour, one shortened the siesta considerably although the day was torrid, and set out in good time for the bullring.

I was in my seat at a quarter-past four—with fifteen minutes to spare. People poured in on all sides. The immense place was going to be packed as perhaps never before. Excitement and good humour seethed. It was a perfect *corrida* afternoon—no breeze, brilliant sunlight, no movement in the blue sky.

As the hands of the clock moved on towards half-past four, as the President arrived, as one noticed the *quadrillas* assembling behind the high gate in the *barrera*,[6] it seemed to me that the rows of seats among which my own was situated were becoming unnaturally crowded, with a great many people standing up among them and talking rapidly. Attendants looked worried and asked us to sit closer together, *por favor*.[7] Soon they were asking the impossible, and people still stood arguing in front of all the occupied seats. *Guardia de asalto*[8] looked on gravely, and shook their heads. A man directly behind me was speaking with such speed and passion, apparently to someone a considerable distance from him, that it was impossible for my foreign ears to get his drift. The talk and crowding were becoming almost unbearable when, just as the *alguaciles*[9] came out to start the ceremonial of the great *corrida*—the truth dawned simultaneously on everyone concerned. A block of about 250 *tendido* seats, of which mine was one, had been sold twice over, in error.

Well—Belmonte was taking the first bull, but alas, for five hundred of his devoted fans he might as well have been doing so in Mexico City. We were all on our feet in a flock, five hundred lawful claimants to two hundred and fifty seats. The outbreak of astonishment and condemnation was majestic as a tidal wave, and made Belmonte, whom we were all obliterating from each other's sight, seem temporarily unimportant. We were conducting, by one accord, a protest meeting of the most harmonious and unanimous kind. We were at one. There was no quarrelling and no stampeding. We had all been fooled—my neighbour, my neighbour's wife and I. Five hundred of us shocked into passionate disapproval of folly. Every voice was raised, but none against the man to left or right; all, all torrentially and most castilianly against '*las autoridades, la empresa.*'[1] Nobody pushed or kicked, but nobody could possibly sit down and somewhat clear the view of the arena until he had said as fully as possible all that was in his mind about this piece of carelessness. The police and attendants understood this necessity, and made no attempt to force things out of the natural. They stood by in sympathetic silence. The man behind me was an orator of the kind that needs something to strike with his fist, and something to wave in the air. My shoulder and béret answered his two requirements. Every now and then the young man on my right generously broke up his own speech to protest to the older man on behalf of *la señorita extranjera*—the foreign lady. His protests were always received with

---

6. Front row. "*Quadrillas*": bullfighting teams.
7. Please.
8. Police officers.
9. Mounted bullfight officials.
1. The authorities, the management. "Castili-

anly": a *Castilian* is specifically an inhabitant of the central and northern region of Spain (more generally, the term can refer to any Spaniard); Castilian is also the dialect spoken in the region.

complete courtesy and agreement, my shoulder remorsefully patted, the béret replaced with Chanelesque[2] solicitude. But eloquence is intoxication. The next second I was thumped again, and my béret whirled above my head. *"Qué burros, qué tontos que son esta empresa! Jesús y María, es una burla más grande!"*[3]

Thus, in the fifteen minutes allotted to the killing of the first bull the tidal wave rose and fell with—granted the disaster—complete satisfaction to everyone, no tempers lost against the innocent, no scapegoats victimised, and certainly no bones broken. By the time Belmonte was taking the round of the ring with the enemy's ear in his hand—according to Monday's papers he killed that bull very characteristically—the whole five hundred of us were quite calm and had discovered that we could fit in somehow in the space of two hundred and fifty. So, while still taking a grave view of the situation, we decided to sit down and observe Lalanda.

The English are reported to be exceptionally good-tempered and jocose *en masse*, so I suppose—I've never been to a Cup Final—that such a situation as the above would somehow have been turned into a joke by them and their benevolent bobbies;[4] in Ireland or Wales I'm certain someone would have started a row, and I think that in France the affair would have turned to pandemonium. What would have happened in Germany? Here in Madrid it was by no means a joke, but neither was it a rational being's excuse for blacking his brother's eye. Castilians, excited, tend to know exactly what they are excited about and are single-tracked and therefore almost calm in expression of excitement. Perhaps it is their sober habit of life which gives them this accuracy and decorum in emotion, this ability to keep their eye on the ball. It is an attractive gift, and I thought this occasion a good demonstration of it.

I am not disposed to talk of bullfights here. They are a controversial subject, as I know who have madly been led into quarrels over them. In any case, as I can never find a defence of them to placate my own conscience, how am I to defend them to others more sensitive? I believe it to be impossible for anyone of northern blood to sit through a *corrida* with an easy conscience, or without moments of acute embarrassment and distress. Nevertheless, the thrill and the beauty can seduce; more than that, can be remembered with longing. For the *corrida*, much more cruel than fox-hunting—if cruelty can be measured—is, unlike that pastime, a great art, a symbolical and most moving spectacle of which the unavoidable cruelty is no more than a necessary incidental. Bravery, grace and self-control; the cunning of cape and sword against incalculable force; sunlight and the hovering of death; comedies and tragedies of character; tinny music timing an old and tricky ritual; crazy courage and sickening failure and the serenity of great matadors curving in peril along the monstrous horn. There is no defence. Either it gets you, or you're sick.

I have seen it get, or almost get, the most unlikely people. Stephen, for instance, Ruth's mother. (I mentioned Ruth in an early chapter, also in connection with the bullfight.) Stephen said, as everyone says, that she thought

---

2. I.e., befitting the French fashion designer Coco Chanel (1883–1971).
3. What asses, what idiots the management are!
4. Police officers. "Cup Final": a championship game in soccer.

Jesus and Mary, this is such a joke!

she ought to see one. I was very doubtful about that. For though she is sane and a realist and no doubt could visualise in advance the worst that she might see, nevertheless she is extremely tender-hearted and protective in her attitude to cats, birds, children, and all defenceless life. Also she had recently been very ill.

However she attended a *corrida*. That afternoon the unfortunate horses suffered badly. The picadors[5] were cowards and the bulls very brave. There were some terrible moments, and seeing the ashen colour of Stephen's face, I wanted to leave after the second bull, and after the fourth. But she preferred to see it through. At the end she was unhappy and profoundly exhausted, but she admitted, reluctantly indeed, that she saw seductive beauty in the ring and an inexplicable nobility. "But I don't want to see another," she said—and looking at her exhausted face one felt that that was best. Still, lately I have heard her recant. Safe in England with no immediate danger of invitation, I have heard her say that, in fact, she would like to attend another *corrida*.

Two men, friends of mine who without having seen a bullfight quarrelled bitterly with me because I insisted on its beauty, at last went to see one—largely out of friendship for me, I think, and to give me a fair hearing, as it were. For some time afterwards they were silent about their reactions, until at last I found courage to ask them point-blank for their verdict. They had been shocked indeed, but not, as they had expected, to the exclusion of every other emotion. With considerable alarm they had felt fascination too. One of them, however, declares that he could never in any circumstances attend another. The second feels that he would be unable to resist seeing it again. Yet these two are absolutely matched, I should guess, in that English sensitiveness to the feelings of animals which, I freely confess, runs more thinly in me, a mere Irishwoman.

I have sat next to an American millionaire and millionairess at their first *corrida* and watched him carried right out of himself by the new experience, eager and puzzled, but anxious to understand it, anxious to see another, baffled and made young by an irresistible emotion, while she, massaged and smooth in her foulard,[6] visibly didn't give a damn for the thing one way or another, unconcerned alike for horses' wounds and matador's genius, contented because she was working her way through another bit of the European programme—as undisturbed as her neatly waved hair. I have seen an elderly Englishman struggle with his need to be sick while his undergraduate companion cheered Armillita's *banderilla*[7] work until he was hoarse, and was dragged protesting from the ring by his green-faced companion. I have sat in *barrera* seats next to a Frenchman and his wife who had only that summer discovered the bullfight and were pursuing it all over Spain—he, because he loved it and she, in Eve's tradition,[8] because she loved him. This was their fifteenth in four weeks, and in *barrera*, or front-row, seats—that Frenchman told me. And she, who held the spectacle in horror and was terrified of it, sat at each one of them with her eyes tight shut while the bull was in the ring, but courteously, so that Spaniards should not be offended, concealing her voluntary blindness behind smoked glasses. "But why attend them?" I

---

5. Horsemen who jab the bull in the neck and shoulder with a lance (*pica*) to weaken its muscles.
6. Lightweight silk clothing.
7. Dart with a small flag or streamer.
8. I.e., submitting to a man's will as women have long done (beginning with the first woman, Eve).

asked. "Because he likes my company, and I like his." And so, through all the *corridas* of that summer, I suppose, they sat in the front row, she with lids down behind her dark glasses, he holding her hand and roaring his pleasure at the brave *toreros*.[9]

Then there is Mary, the painter. At her first bullfight—she being one of the English animal-fans—she took an outspoken loathing to the entire Spanish nation. Became so abusive indeed and so disposed to hiss that I had good reason to fear an international brawl, and begged her to leave the ring with me. But no—she would not do that. She would see the thing through and give it what she called a fair trial. She continued to behave very obstreperously, however, taking exception to the applause which those around her saw fit to concede the fighters. Again I begged her that we might go home rather than stay to insult the Spaniards, who after all had not compelled us to attend their bullfight. No. She could not make up her mind to leave. "Though, what do they think they're clapping, the asses?" I was growing peevish. "Try to find out," I said.

La Serna came out to take the third bull. A middle-aged white-faced man without theatrical appeal. He encountered a very fractious bull, inclined to keep *querencia*, that is, take up a fixed, defensive position, awkwardly close to the *barrera*. It looked like being a difficult and messy fight, and my heart sank. For Mary's mixed and vigorous reactions were in train to become embarrassing. It was obvious that, morally, she was panic-stricken, but that the stimulation she was deriving from the brilliant and garish *mise-en-scène*[1] was a shock and surprise which she could not resist. For though this was a rather shabby and provincial bullfight, the day was glorious, the *quadrillas* were brave and graceful and the bulls impressive enemies. It was in fact a good average *corrida* for a foreigner to see—by no means a show occasion, but alike in its defects and merits representative. And that it was taking the painter's eye and emotions I did not dare suggest to the raging, over-wrought moralist beside me. She was going through a storm and I could only sit still and hope that whichever side of her won we would get through without 'an incident'—which seemed unlikely.

However, La Serna fought his difficult bull. Not spectacularly. There was no scope for flourish against so immobile an enemy. But with patience and courtesy. With perfect fairness and with the grace of self-command in every gesture. And at a moment which seemed completely impossible he profiled, went over the horn and administered death as resolutely as if he himself was made of steel. His performance was an excellent presentation of tragedy—which always ends by tranquillising the witness. Certainly it quieted Mary, and, I think, brought the scales down for her on the amoral, or immoral side. Not that her struggle is ended—any more than it is for other *aficionados*—but rage though she does again and again at the ringside, and suffer though she may, she pursues the *corrida*, and is a committed "fan." Often since that day in moments of anxiety in the arena I have heard her—good Catholic that she is—half-audibly offer God the most tremendous pledges will He only save the *torero* then in danger. But whether or not, her prayer being heard, she keeps her fantastic promises, is of course between her and Heaven.

* * *

1937

---

9. Bullfighters.   1. Spectacle.

RUTH PITTER
1897–1992

"My purpose has never varied," wrote Ruth Pitter in a foreword to her *Collected Poems* (1969). "It has been simply to capture . . . some of the secret meanings which haunt life and language." Despite early years of poverty and obscurity, Pitter did this in verses that were eventually acclaimed by a range of literary figures, including the poet Hilaire Belloc, the critic Lord David Cecil, and the novelist-critic C. S. Lewis. Among other honors, she won the Hawthornden Prize, the Heinemann Award, and the Queen's Gold Medal for Poetry. Born in the East End of London, Pitter was the daughter of middle-class parents who, she once recalled, "loved poetry and were determined to impart it to their children." She herself began to write poems at the age of five, publishing her first book when she was in her early twenties but later acknowledging that "I produced little that I now think worth keeping until about the age of thirty."

After a comparatively sketchy education, Pitter worked in the British War Office during World War I, then studied various handicrafts and with a longtime friend, Kathleen O'Hara, ran a small firm specializing in decorative furniture. There, according to the scholar Don King, she often worked twelve-hour days, six days a week. Yet, as King notes, she was both a highly productive poet and a "voluminous letter writer." Her major collections of verse include *A Mad Lady's Garland* (1935), *A Trophy of Arms* (1936), *The Spirit Watches* (1939), and *Collected Poems*. Her best work oscillates between grave meditation and sardonic wit, but throughout her career she consistently sought to express what she termed "the silent music, the dance in stillness . . . of which everything is full."

The Military Harpist

Strangely assorted, the shape of song and the bloody man.

Under the harp's gilt shoulder and rainlike strings,
Prawn-eyed, with prawnlike bristle, well-waxed moustache,
With long tight cavalry legs, and the spurred boot
5   Ready upon the swell, the Old Sweat waits.

Now dies, and dies hard, the stupid, well-relished fortissimo,
Wood-wind alone inviting the liquid tone,
The voice of the holy and uncontending, the harp.

Ceasing to ruminate interracial fornications,
10   He raises his hands, and his wicked old mug is David's,[1]
Pastoral, rapt, the king and the poet in innocence,
Singing Saul in himself asleep, and the ancient Devil
Clean out of countenance, as with an army of angels.

He is now where his bunion has no existence.
15   Breathing an atmosphere free of pipeclay[2] and swearing,
He wears the starched nightshirt of the hereafter, his halo

---

1. Ancient king of Israel, both a musician and military leader. As a youth, David sang and played before the previous king, Saul, who later turned against him (1 Samuel 16–24).
2. A whitener, for sprucing up military uniforms.

Is plain manly brass with a permanent polish,
Requiring no oily rag and no Soldier's Friend.[3]

His place is with the beloved poet of Israel,
20 With the wandering minnesinger[4] and the loves of Provence,
With Blondel[5] footsore and heartsore, the voice in the darkness
Crying like beauty bereaved beneath many a donjon,[6]
O Richard! O king! where is the lion of England?
With Howell, Llewellyn,[7] and far in the feral north
25 With the savage fame of the hero in glen and in ben,
At the morning discourse of saints in the island Eire,[8]
And at nameless doings in the stone-circle, the dreadful grove.

Thus far into the dark do I delve for his likeness:
He harps at the Druid[9] sacrifice, where the golden string
30 Sings to the golden knife and the victim's shriek.
Strangely assorted, the shape of song and the bloody man.

1939

The Irish Patriarch

He bathes his soul in women's wrath;
His whiskers twinkle, and it seems
As if he trod some airy path
In that young land of warriors' dreams;
5 As if he took a needle-bath[1]
In mountain falls, in tingling streams.

The man whom nagging drives to drink
Should learn from him, whom female rage
Seems but to make a precious link
10 With some sweet ancient heritage,
With women saying—huh!—what they think!
To the amusement of the sage.

O women, what a boon it is,
With workday worries at their worst,
15 When hordes of little miseries
Force us to speak our mind or burst,
To be Rich-angered Mistresses,[2]
Not Shrews and Vixens, Cross and Curst!

1966

---

3. A popular brand of metal polish.
4. Traveling poet and musician of the Middle Ages in Germany and Provence.
5. A French troubadour poet (12th c.), companion to the English king Richard the Lion-Hearted. According to legend, Blondel discovered Richard imprisoned in the castle of Dürnstein while singing a song they had written together, to which the king sang back.
6. Massive tower in medieval castles.
7. There were two princes of Gwynedd, in northern Wales, named Llywelyn—Llywelyn the Great (ruled 1240–46) and his grandson (ruled 1246–82). Howell (Hywel) the Good (ruled 920–950), was prince of central and northern Wales.
8. Ireland.
9. Ancient Celtic priest.
1. I.e., a cold shower.
2. An echo of John Keats's "Ode on Melancholy" (1819): "Or if thy mistress some rich anger shows, / Imprison her soft hand, and let her rave, / And feed deep, deep upon her peerless eyes."

Old Nelly's Birthday

She knows where to get cracked eggs, does Nelly.
Knows where to get them cheap:
Ninepence a dozen from that Mrs. Kelly.
Of course they will not keep,
But Nelly will make them into a jam sandwich[1]
Of most portentous size.
Now this jam sandwich is her secret language,
And sacred in her eyes;
And to go with this sandwich, her love, her treasure,
She'll make a pot of tea,
Her urn, her cauldron of almost unholy pleasure,
For in that tea will be
Never a drop of shivering starving water,
But milk with all its cream;
A boiling foaming snow, by pleasure's daughter,
Obedient to the dream,
Brewed and kept hot and poured out and delected,[2]
This once of all the year,
Most cordial to the hearts of those selected,
Those delicate, those dear,
Mystical inmost friends of fervent Nelly,
Who will consume with glee
And blessings on the decent Mrs. Kelly,
That sandwich and that tea.

But this year it was really extra special;
For when old Nelly went
Down to the dairy, she beheld a vessel
Of marvelous extent,
Full of fine milk soured by the spring thunder,
With cream on top galore:
And Mrs. Kelly, who really is the world's wonder,
Skimmed her a quart and more;
And Nelly with light heart and little trouble
Beat it and made it turn
Into lovely butter that made the pleasure double:
Her sandwich and her urn,
Flanked by the light new loaf and heavenly butter,
Home-made from magic cream,
Ravished the creature till words could not utter
The glory of the dream.[3]

1966

---

1. I.e., a layer cake.
2. I.e., enjoyed.
3. An echo of William Wordsworth's "Ode: Intimations of Immortality" (1807): "Where is it now, the glory and the dream?" (line 57).

Yorkshire Wife's Saga

War was her life, with want and the wild air;
Not for life only; she was out to win.
Houses and ground were cheap, out on the bare
Moor, and the land not bad; they could begin,
₅   Now that the seven sons were mostly men.

Two acres and a sow, on hard-saved brass;[1]
Men down the mine, and mother did the rest.
Pity, with all those sons, they had no lass;
No help, no talk, no mutual interest,
₁₀   Made fourteen slaving hours empty at best.

Fierce winter mornings, up at three or four;
Men bawl, pigs shriek against the raving beck.[2]
Off go the eight across the mile of moor,
With well-filled dinner-pail and sweat-ragged neck;
₁₅   But pigs still shriek, and wind blows door off sneck.[3]

Of course they made it; what on earth could stop
People like that? Marrying one by one,
This got a farm, the other got a shop;
Now she was left with but the youngest son,
₂₀   But she could look about and feel she'd won.

Doctor had told her she was clean worn out.
All pulled to bits, and nowt[4] that he could do.
But plenty get that way, or die, without
Having a ruddy ten-quid[5] note to show.
₂₅   She'd got seven thriving sons all in a row.

And grandchildren. She liked going by bus
Or train, to stay a bit in those snug homes.
They were her colonies, fair glorious.
"Sit by the fire, ma, till the dinner comes.
₃₀   Sit by the fire and cuddle little lass."

1968

---

1. Money.
2. Brook, stream.
3. Latch.
4. Nothing.
5. Slang for English currency: £10.

MARITA BONNER
1899–1971

By the time Marita Bonner's collected works, *Frye Street & Environs,* appeared in 1987, this gifted artist had been largely forgotten, perhaps because she had ceased to publish after 1941. But the book quickly garnered accolades as well as new readers. Bonner—who was born in Boston and educated at Radcliffe College—was teaching high school in Washington, D.C., when she began her literary career at the salon of the playwright Georgia Douglas Johnson. At that time, too, Bonner met and married the accountant William Almy Occomy, a native of Rhode Island and graduate of Brown University. Before and after her move with her husband to Chicago, where she resided the rest of her life, Bonner published many of her prize-winning stories, essays, and reviews in *The Crisis* and *Opportunity,* two of the most influential black journals of the Harlem Renaissance. Of the three plays she composed, *The Purple Flower* (1928) is deemed her most ambitious, allegorical effort to represent a black quest for "Life-At-Its-Fullest." Throughout the 1930s, Bonner worked on a series of narratives about the relationship between children and parents in Chicago families coping with poverty, prejudice, and violence.

The selection printed here comes from the early stage of Bonner's career. As an autobiographical study, "On Being Young—a Woman—and Colored" complements Zora Neale Hurston's analysis of herself in "How It Feels to Be Colored Me." Like Bonner's stories, it exemplifies the sensitivity with which she repeatedly examined the psychosexual conflicts bequeathed by a racist society.

On Being Young—a Woman—and Colored

You start out after you have gone from kindergarten to sheepskin covered with sundry Latin phrases.

At least you know what you want life to give you. A career as fixed and as calmly brilliant as the North Star. The one real thing that money buys. Time. Time to do things. A house that can be as delectably out of order and as easily put in order as the doll-house of "playing house" days. And of course, a husband you can look up to without looking down on yourself.

Somehow you feel like a kitten in a sunny catnip field that sees sleek, plump brown field mice and yellow baby chicks sitting coyly, side by side, under each leaf. A desire to dash three or four ways seizes you.

That's Youth.

But you know that things learned need testing—acid testing—to see if they are really after all, an interwoven part of you. All your life you have heard of the debt you owe "Your People"[1] because you have managed to have the things they have not largely had.

So you find a spot where there are hordes of them—of course below the Line[2]—to be your catnip field while you close your eyes to mice and chickens alike.

If you have never lived among your own, you feel prodigal. Some warm untouched current flows through them—through you—and drags you out into the deep waters of a new sea of human foibles and mannerisms; of a pecu-

---

1. I.e., other blacks.
2. The Mason-Dixon Line, the boundary surveyed between Pennsylvania and Maryland (1763–67) that popularly divides the North from the South.

liar psychology and prejudices. And one day you find yourself entangled—enmeshed—pinioned in the seaweed of a Black Ghetto.

Not a Ghetto, placid like the Strasse[3] that flows, outwardly unperturbed and calm in a stream of religious belief, but a peculiar group. Cut off, flung together, shoved aside in a bundle because of color and with no more in common.

Unless color is, after all, the real bond.

Milling around like live fish in a basket. Those at the bottom crushed into a sort of stupid apathy by the weight of those on top. Those on top leaping, leaping; leaping to scale the sides; to get out.

There are two "colored" movies, innumerable parties—and cards. Cards played so intensely that it fascinates and repulses at once.

Movies.

Movies worthy and worthless—but not even a low-caste spoken stage.

Parties, plentiful. Musk and dancing and much that is wit and color and gaiety. But they are like the richest chocolate; stuffed costly chocolates that make the taste go stale if you have too many of them. That make plain whole bread taste like ashes.

There are all the earmarks of a group within a group. Cut off all around from ingress from or egress to other groups. A sameness of type. The smug self-satisfaction of an inner measurement; a measurement by standards known within a limited group and not those of an unlimited, seeing, world. . . . Like the blind, blind mice. Mice whose eyes have been blinded.

Strange longing seizes hold of you. You wish yourself back where you can lay your dollar down and sit in a dollar seat to hear voices, strings, reeds that have lifted the World out, up, beyond things that have bodies and walls. Where you can marvel at new marbles and bronzes and flat colors that will make men forget that things exist in a flesh more often than in spirit. Where you can sink your body in a cushioned seat and sink your soul at the same time into a section of life set before you on the boards[4] for a few hours.

You hear that up at New York this is to be seen; that, to be heard.

You decide the next train will take you there.

You decide the next second that that train will not take you, nor the next—nor the next for some time to come.

For you know that—being a woman—you cannot twice a month or twice a year, for that matter, break away to see or hear anything in a city that is supposed to see and hear too much.

That's being a woman. A woman of any color.

You decide that something is wrong with a world that stifles and chokes; that cuts off and stunts; hedging in, pressing down on eyes, ears and throat. Somehow all wrong.

You wonder how it happens there that—say five hundred miles from the Bay State[5]—Anglo Saxon intelligence is so warped and stunted.

How judgment and discernment are bred out of the race. And what has become of discrimination? Discrimination of the right sort. Discrimination that the best minds have told you weighs shadows and nuances and spiritual

---

3. Street (German). "Ghetto": originally that section of a European city where Jews were forced to live.
4. I.e., on a stage.
5. Massachusetts, here meant as a place of relative racial enlightenment.

differences before it catalogues. The kind they have taught you all of your life was best: that looks clearly past generalization and past appearance to dissect, to dig down to the real heart of matters. That casts aside rapid summary conclusions, drawn from primary inference, as Daniel did the spiced meats.[6]

Why can't they then perceive that there is a difference in the glance from a pair of eyes that look, mildly docile, at "white ladies" and those that, impersonally and perceptively—aware of distinctions—see only women who happen to be white?

Why do they see a colored woman only as a gross collection of desires, all uncontrolled, reaching out for their Apollos and the Quasimodos[7] with avid indiscrimination?

Why unless you talk in staccato squawks—brittle as seashells—unless you "champ" gum—unless you cover two yards square when you laugh—unless your taste runs to violent colors—impossible perfumes and more impossible clothes—are you a feminine Caliban craving to pass for Ariel?[8]

An empty imitation of an empty invitation. A mime; a sham; a copy-cat. A hollow re-echo. A froth, a foam. A fleck of the ashes of superficiality?

Everything you touch or taste now is like the flesh of an unripe persimmon.[9]

. . . Do you need to be told what that is being . . . ?

Old ideas, old fundamentals seem worm-eaten, out-grown, worthless, bitter; fit for the scrap-heap of Wisdom.

What you had thought tangible and practical has turned out to be a collection of "blue flower"[1] theories.

If they have not discovered how to use their accumulation of facts, they are useless to you in Their world.

Every part of you becomes bitter.

But—"In Heaven's name, do not grow bitter. Be bigger than they are"—exhort white friends who have never had to draw breath in a Jim Crow[2] train. Who have never had petty putrid insult dragged over them—drawing blood—like pebbled sand on your body where the skin is tenderest. On your body where the skin is thinnest and tenderest.

You long to explode and hurt everything white; friendly; unfriendly. But you know that you cannot live with a chip on your shoulder even if you can manage a smile around your eyes—without getting steely and brittle and losing the softness that makes you a woman.

For chips make you bend your body to balance them. And once you bend, you lose your poise, your balance, and the chip gets into you. The real you. You get hard.

. . . And many things in you can ossify . . .

And you know, being a woman, you have to go about it gently and quietly, to find out and to discover just what is wrong. Just what can be done.

You see clearly that they have acquired things.

Money; money. Money to build with, money to destroy. Money to swim in. Money to drown in. Money.

---

6. Daniel, a prisoner of the king of Babylon, refused to eat the king's meat (Daniel 1.8–16).
7. I.e., the most perfect and the most highly deformed men. Apollo, the Greek god of the arts and the sun, was the Greek ideal of mature male beauty; Quasimodo was the hunchback in Victor Hugo's *Hunchback of Notre Dame* (1831).
8. A monster wishing to pass for a spirit (from characters in Shakespeare's *The Tempest*).
9. Until thoroughly ripe, persimmons are extremely astringent.
1. An expression for something rare or unheard-of.
2. The legal and extralegal system enforcing segregation of blacks and whites.

An ascendancy of wisdom. An incalculable hoard of wisdom in all fields, in all things collected from all quarters of humanity.

A stupendous mass of things.

Things.

So, too, the Greeks . . . Things.

And the Romans. . . .

And you wonder and wonder why they have not discovered how to handle deftly and skillfully, Wisdom, stored up for them—like the honey for the Gods on Olympus[3]—since time unknown.

You wonder and you wonder until you wander out into Infinity, where—if it is to be found anywhere—Truth really exists.

The Greeks had possessions, culture. They were lost because they did not understand.

The Romans owned more than anyone else. Trampled under the heel of Vandals[4] and Civilization, because they would not understand.

Greeks. Did not understand.

Romans. Would not understand.

"They." Will not understand.

So you find they have shut Wisdom up and have forgotten to find the key that will let her out. They have trapped, trammeled, lashed her to themselves with thews and thongs and theories. They have ransacked sea and earth and air to bring every treasure to her. But she sulks and will not work for a world with a whitish hue because it has snubbed her twin sister, Understanding.

You see clearly—off there is Infinity—Understanding. Standing alone, waiting for someone to really want her.

But she is so far out there is no way to snatch at her and really drag her in.

So—being a woman—you can wait.

You must sit quietly without a chip. Not sodden—and weighted as if your feet were cast in the iron of your soul. Not wasting strength in enervating gestures as if two hundred years of bonds and whips had really tricked you into nervous uncertainty.

But quiet; quiet. Like Buddha[5]—who brown like I am—sat entirely at ease, entirely sure of himself; motionless and knowing, a thousand years before the white man knew there was so very much difference between feet and hands.

Motionless on the outside. But on the inside?

Silent.

Still . . . "Perhaps Buddha is a woman."

So you too. Still; quiet; with a smile, ever so slight, at the eyes so that Life will flow into and not by you. And you can gather, as it passes, the essences, the overtones, the tints, the shadows; draw understanding to yourself.

And then you can, when Time is ripe, swoop to your feet—at your full height—at a single gesture.

Ready to go where?

Why . . . Wherever God motions.

1925

---

3. The mountaintop home of the Greek gods.
4. The Germanic peoples who sacked Rome in C.E. 455 C.E.

5. Siddhārtha Gautama (ca. 563–ca. 483 B.C.E.), the Nepalese prince known as the Buddha (Enlightened One) who founded Buddhism.

ELIZABETH BOWEN
1899–1973

Elizabeth Bowen was born in Dublin and identified her early childhood with her family's estate near Kildorrery, County Cork. Of Welsh extraction, the Bowens had acquired Bowen's Court in the seventeenth century, and her father wanted a male heir to inherit it. When he realized that Elizabeth was to be his only child, he suffered a nervous breakdown, and the child was taken away to England with her mother and governess. Leading a nomadic existence, the ten-year-old witnessed her mother's suffering from a fatal cancer. From the ages of fifteen to eighteen, she attended Downe House School in Kent, the only Bowen to be educated in England and increasingly self-conscious about belonging neither in England nor in Ireland. In 1918, after nursing shell-shocked veterans of World War I in Dublin, she went to live in London, and in 1923 she married Alan C. Cameron, an educator in the Oxford city school system. Seven years later, the death of her father made Elizabeth Bowen the first female owner of Bowen's Court. But she did not return to live there until 1952, and in that year her husband died. Seven years later, she was forced to sell the house. In 1963, it was pulled down.

Bowen herself attributed her thematic focus on the insecurity of childhood to her Anglo-Irish personal history. "Motherless since I was thirteen," she wrote in a preface (1948), "I was in and out of the homes of my different relatives—and, as constantly, shuttling between two countries: Ireland and England." An Irish outsider in England and a guilty English landowner in Ireland, she nevertheless used her acute sense of "submerged fear" to depict the vulnerability of child-heroines like the orphaned Portia of *The Death of the Heart* (1938) or to describe the sinister menace of war-torn London in *The Heat of the Day* (1949). As in "The Demon Lover," moreover, that sense of fear is often conveyed through descriptions of physically damaged or psychically damaging houses. Bowen wrote most of her fiction first in Northampton and then in London, where she worked for the Ministry of Information during the bombings of the early 1940s. After a prolific career, in which she published more than twenty novels and collections of short stories, she died at seventy-four, having been made a commander of the British Empire and having received honorary degrees from Trinity College, Dublin, and from Oxford University.

The Demon Lover

Towards the end of her day in London Mrs. Drover went round to her shut-up house to look for several things she wanted to take away. Some belonged to herself, some to her family, who were by now used to their country life. It was late August; it had been a steamy, showery day: at the moment the trees down the pavement glittered in an escape of humid yellow afternoon sun. Against the next batch of clouds, already piling up ink-dark, broken chimneys and parapets stood out. In her once familiar street, as in any unused channel, an unfamiliar queerness had silted up; a cat wove itself in and out of railings, but no human eye watched Mrs. Drover's return. Shifting some parcels under her arm, she slowly forced round her latchkey in an unwilling lock, then gave the door, which had warped, a push with her knee. Dead air came out to meet her as she went in.

The staircase window having been boarded up, no light came down into the hall. But one door, she could just see, stood ajar, so she went quickly through into the room and unshuttered the big window in there. Now the prosaic woman, looking about her, was more perplexed than she knew by everything that she saw, by traces of her long former habit of life—the yellow smoke-stain up the white marble mantelpiece, the ring left by a vase on the top of the escritoire;[1] the bruise in the wallpaper where, on the door being thrown open widely, the china handle had always hit the wall. The piano, having gone away to be stored, had left what looked like claw-marks on its part of the parquet. Though not much dust had seeped in, each object wore a film of another kind; and, the only ventilation being the chimney, the whole drawing room smelled of the cold hearth. Mrs. Drover put down her parcels on the escritoire and left the room to proceed upstairs; the things she wanted were in the bedroom chest.

She had been anxious to see how the house was—the part-time caretaker she shared with some neighbors was away this week on his holiday, known to be not yet back. At the best of times he did not look in often, and she was never sure that she trusted him. There were some cracks in the structure, left by the last bombing, on which she was anxious to keep an eye. Not that one could do anything—

A shaft of refracted daylight now lay across the hall. She stopped dead and stared at the hall table—on this lay a letter addressed to her.

She thought first—then the caretaker must be back. All the same, who, seeing the house shuttered, would have dropped a letter in at the box? It was not a circular, it was not a bill. And the post office redirected, to the address in the country, everything for her that came through the post. The caretaker (even if he were back) did not know she was due in London today—her call here had been planned to be a surprise—so his negligence in the matter of this letter, leaving it to wait in the dusk and dust, annoyed her. Annoyed, she picked up the letter, which bore no stamp. But it cannot be important, or they would know. . . . She took the letter rapidly upstairs with her, without a stop to look at the writing till she reached what had been her bedroom, where she let in light. The room looked over the garden and other gardens: the sun had gone in; as the clouds sharpened and lowered, the trees and rank lawns seemed already to smoke with dark. Her reluctance to look again at the letter came from the fact that she felt intruded upon—and by someone contemptuous of her ways. However, in the tenseness preceding the fall of rain she read it: it was a few lines.

Dear Kathleen,

You will not have forgotten that today is our anniversary, and the day we said. The years have gone by at once slowly and fast. In view of the fact that nothing has changed, I shall rely upon you to keep your promise. I was sorry to see you leave London, but was satisfied that you would be back in time. You may expect me, therefore, at the hour arranged.

Until then . . .
K.

Mrs. Drover looked for the date: it was today's. She dropped the letter on to the bedsprings, then picked it up to see the writing again—her lips, beneath the remains of lipstick, beginning to go white. She felt so much the change

---

1. Writing desk.

in her own face that she went to the mirror, polished a clear patch in it and looked at once urgently and stealthily in. She was confronted by a woman of forty-four, with eyes staring out under a hat brim that had been rather carelessly pulled down. She had not put on any more powder since she left the shop where she ate her solitary tea. The pearls her husband had given her on their marriage hung loose round her now rather thinner throat, slipping into the V of the pink wool jumper her sister knitted last autumn as they sat round the fire. Mrs. Drover's most normal expression was one of controlled worry, but of assent. Since the birth of the third of her little boys, attended by a quite serious illness, she had had an intermittent muscular flicker to the left of her mouth, but in spite of this she could always sustain a manner that was at once energetic and calm.

Turning from her own face as precipitately as she had gone to meet it, she went to the chest where the things were, unlocked it, threw up the lid and knelt to search. But as the rain began to come crashing down she could not keep from looking over her shoulder at the stripped bed on which the letter lay. Behind the blanket of rain the clock of the church that still stood struck six—with rapidly heightening apprehension she counted each of the slow strokes. "The hour arranged.... My God," she said, "*what* hour? How should I . . . ? After twenty-five years . . ."

The young girl talking to the soldier in the garden had not ever completely seen his face. It was dark; they were saying goodbye under a tree. Now and then—for it felt, from not seeing him at this intense moment, as though she had never seen him at all—she verified his presence for these few moments longer by putting out a hand, which he each time pressed, without very much kindness, and painfully, on to one of the breast buttons of his uniform. That cut of the button on the palm of her hand was, principally, what she was to carry away. This was so near the end of a leave from France that she could only wish him already gone. It was August 1916. Being not kissed, being drawn away from and looked at intimidated Kathleen till she imagined spectral glitters in the place of his eyes. Turning away and looking back up the lawn she saw, through branches of trees, the drawing room window alight: she caught a breath for the moment when she could go running back there into the safe arms of her mother and sister, and cry: "What shall I do, what shall I do? He has gone."

Hearing her catch her breath, her fiancé said, without feeling: "Cold?"

"You're going away such a long way."

"Not so far as you think."

"I don't understand?"

"You don't have to," he said. "You will. You know what we said."

"But that was—suppose you—I mean, suppose."

"I shall be with you," he said, "sooner or later. You won't forget that. You need do nothing but wait."

Only a little more than a minute later she was free to run up the silent lawn. Looking in through the window at her mother and sister, who did not for the moment perceive her, she already felt that unnatural promise drive down between her and the rest of all human kind. No other way of having given herself could have made her feel so apart, lost and forsworn. She could not have plighted a more sinister troth.

Kathleen behaved well when, some months later, her fiancé was reported missing, presumed killed. Her family not only supported her but were able to praise her courage without stint because they could not regret, as a husband for her, the man they knew almost nothing about. They hoped she would, in a year or two, console herself—and had it been only a question of consolation things might have gone much straighter ahead. But her trouble, behind just a little grief, was a complete dislocation from everything. She did not reject other lovers, for these failed to appear: for years she failed to attract men—and with the approach of her thirties she became natural enough to share her family's anxiousness on this score. She began to put herself out, to wonder; and at thirty-two she was very greatly relieved to find herself being courted by William Drover. She married him, and the two of them settled down in this quiet, arboreal part of Kensington:[2] in this house the years piled up, her children were born and they all lived till they were driven out by the bombs of the next war. Her movements as Mrs. Drover were circumscribed, and she dismissed any idea that they were still watched.

As things were—dead or living the letter-writer sent her only a threat. Unable, for some minutes, to go on kneeling with her back exposed to the empty room, Mrs. Drover rose from the chest to sit on an upright chair whose back was firmly against the wall. The desuetude of her former bedroom, her married London home's whole air of being a cracked cup from which memory, with its reassuring power, had either evaporated or leaked away, made a crisis—and at just this crisis the letter-writer had, knowledgeably, struck. The hollowness of the house this evening cancelled years on years of voices, habits and steps. Through the shut windows she only heard rain fall on the roofs around. To rally herself, she said she was in a mood—and, for two or three seconds shutting her eyes, told herself that she had imagined the letter. But she opened them—there it lay on the bed.

On the supernatural side of the letter's entrance she was not permitting her mind to dwell. Who, in London, knew she meant to call at the house today? Evidently, however, this had been known. The caretaker, had he come back, had had no cause to expect her: he would have taken the letter in his pocket, to forward it, at his own time, through the post. There was no other sign that the caretaker had been in—but, if not? Letters dropped in at doors of deserted houses do not fly or walk to tables in halls. They do not sit on the dust of empty tables with the air of certainty that they will be found. There is needed some human hand—but nobody but the caretaker had a key. Under circumstances she did not care to consider, a house can be entered without a key. It was possible that she was not alone now. She might be being waited for, downstairs. Waited for—until when? Until "the hour arranged." At least that was not six o'clock: six had struck.

She rose from the chair and went over and locked the door.

The thing was, to get out. To fly? No, not that: she had to catch her train. As a woman whose utter dependability was the keystone of her family life she was not willing to return to the country, to her husband, her little boys and her sister, without the objects she had come up to fetch. Resuming work at the chest she set about making up a number of parcels in a rapid,

---

2. A fashionable neighborhood in London.

fumbling-decisive way. These, with her shopping parcels, would be too much to carry; these meant a taxi—at the thought of the taxi her heart went up and her normal breathing resumed. I will ring up the taxi now; the taxi cannot come too soon: I shall hear the taxi out there running its engine, till I walk calmly down to it through the hall. I'll ring up—But no: the telephone is cut off . . . She tugged at a knot she had tied wrong.

The idea of flight . . . He was never kind to me, not really. I don't remember him kind at all. Mother said he never considered me. He was set on me, that was what it was—not love. Not love, not meaning a person well. What did he do, to make me promise like that? I can't remember.—But she found that she could.

She remembered with such dreadful acuteness that the twenty-five years since then dissolved like smoke and she instinctively looked for the weal left by the button on the palm of her hand. She remembered not only all that he said and did but the complete suspension of her existence during that August week. I was not myself—they all told me so at the time. She remembered—but with one white burning blank as where acid has dropped on a photograph: *under no conditions* could she remember his face.

So, wherever he may be waiting, I shall not know him. You have no time to run from a face you do not expect.

The thing was to get to the taxi before any clock struck what could be the hour. She would slip down the street and round the side of the square to where the square gave on the main road. She would return in the taxi, safe, to her own door, and bring the solid driver into the house with her to pick up the parcels from room to room. The idea of the taxi driver made her decisive, bold: she unlocked her door, went to the top of the staircase and listened down.

She heard nothing—but while she was hearing nothing the *passé*[3] air of the staircase was disturbed by a draught that travelled up to her face. It emanated from the basement: down there a door or window was being opened by someone who chose this moment to leave the house.

The rain had stopped; the pavements steamily shone as Mrs. Drover let herself out by inches from her own front door into the empty street. The unoccupied houses opposite continued to meet her look with their damaged stare. Making towards the thoroughfare and the taxi, she tried not to keep looking behind. Indeed, the silence was so intense—one of those creeks of London silence exaggerated this summer by the damage of war—that no tread could have gained on hers unheard. Where her street debouched on the square where people went on living she grew conscious of and checked her unnatural pace. Across the open end of the square two buses impassively passed each other; women, a perambulator, cyclists, a man wheeling a barrow signalized, once again, the ordinary flow of life. At the square's most populous corner should be—and was—the short taxi rank. This evening, only one taxi—but this, although it presented its blank rump, appeared already to be alertly waiting for her. Indeed, without looking round the driver started his engine as she panted up from behind and put her hand on the door. As she did so, the clock struck seven. The taxi faced the main road: to make the

---

3. I.e., foul, stuffy.

trip back to her house it would have to turn—she had settled back on the seat and the taxi had turned before she, surprised by its knowing movement, recollected that she had not "said where." She leaned forward to scratch at the glass panel that divided the driver's head from her own.

The driver braked to what was almost a stop, turned round and slid the glass panel back: the jolt of this flung Mrs. Drover forward till her face was almost into the glass. Through the aperture driver and passenger, not six inches between them, remained for an eternity eye to eye. Mrs. Drover's mouth hung open for some seconds before she could issue her first scream. After that she continued to scream freely and to beat with her gloved hands on the glass all round as the taxi, accelerating without mercy, made off with her into the hinterland of deserted streets.

1945

MERIDEL LE SUEUR
1900-1996

During the Great Depression, Meridel Le Sueur recorded the stories of midwestern women, insisting that "their lives were not defeated, trashed, defenseless but that we as women contained the real and only seed, and were the granary of the people." She had begun to consider herself a "village scribe" for Native Americans and immigrant farm and factory workers when she was a young girl traveling throughout the Midwest and Southwest with her socialist parents. Born in Iowa, Le Sueur dropped out of high school to devote herself to political activism as well as a career in various types of performance. She lived in a New York anarchist commune with Emma Goldman, acted in the early movies produced in Hollywood, and directed the Little Theater of Sacramento, California. Married to Harry Rice, a labor organizer, she gave birth to two daughters in the late 1920s, the period in which she began to publish the work she had been recording in her journals.

Le Sueur's fifty-year career was shaped by her association with prairie populists (who advocated an equitable redistribution of wealth to help farmers and laborers) and Marxists. During the 1930s, both her prize-winning stories and the articles she wrote for left-wing periodicals documented the struggle of working people. According to the critic Elaine Hedges, *Salute to Spring* (1940), a collection of Le Sueur's stories and articles, marked both the high point of Le Sueur's reputation and the beginning of her critical neglect. The first draft of her novel *The Girl* was written in 1939, but the book remained unpublished until 1978. When national sentiment against communism arose during the so-called Red scare of the 1950s, Le Sueur was informally blacklisted, and she turned to writing children's stories—about Abraham Lincoln's mother, for example, and about Native American–white relationships. In her later publication, *Rites of Ancient Ripening* (1975), Le Sueur created what the critic Blanche Gelphant calls "assertive, drumming chants, 'renderings' of Native American oral poetry." An early work, "Annunciation" (1935) looks forward to *Rites of Ancient Ripening*, for it demonstrates Le Sueur's ongoing fascination with the myths and realities of motherhood; originally written in the form of notes to her first, unborn child, it was, she explained, "the bud of a new flower within the time of the old."

Annunciation[1]

For Rachel

Ever since I have known I was going to have a child I have kept writing things down on these little scraps of paper. There is something I want to say, something I want to make clear for myself and others. One lives all one's life in a sort of way, one is alive and that is about all that there is to say about it. Then something happens.

There is the pear tree I can see in the afternoons as I sit on this porch writing these notes. It stands for something. It has had something to do with what has happened to me. I sit here all afternoon in the autumn sun and then I begin to write something on this yellow paper; something seems to be going on like a buzzing, a flying and circling within me, and then I want to write it down in some way. I have never felt this way before, except when I was a girl and was first in love and wanted then to set things down on paper so that they would not be lost. It is something perhaps like a farmer who hears the swarming of a host of bees and goes out to catch them so that he will have honey. If he does not go out right away, they will go, and he will hear the buzzing growing more distant in the afternoon.

My sweater pocket is full of scraps of paper on which I have written. I sit here many afternoons while Karl is out looking for work, writing on pieces of paper, unfolding, reading what I have already written.

We have been here two weeks at Mrs. Mason's boarding house. The leaves are falling and there is a golden haze over everything. This is the fourth month for me and it is fall. A rich powerful haze comes down from the mountains over the city. In the afternoon I go out for a walk. There is a park just two blocks from here. Old men and tramps lie on the grass all day. It is hard to get work. Many people beside Karl are out of work. People are hungry just as I am hungry. People are ready to flower and they cannot. In the evenings we go there with a sack of old fruit we can get at the stand across the way quite cheap, bunches of grapes and old pears. At noon there is a hush in the air and at evening there are stirrings of wind coming from the sky, blowing in the fallen leaves, or perhaps there is a light rain, falling quickly on the walk. Early in the mornings the sun comes up hot in the sky and shines all day through the mist. It is strange, I notice all these things, the sun, the rain falling, the blowing of the wind. It is as if they had a meaning for me as the pear tree has come to have.

In front of Mrs. Mason's house there is a large magnolia tree with its blossoms yellow, hanging over the steps almost within reach. Its giant leaves are motionless and shining in the heat, occasionally as I am going down the steps towards the park one falls heavily on the walk.

This house is an old wooden one, that once was quite a mansion I imagine. There are glass chandeliers in the hall and fancy tile in the bathrooms. It was owned by the rich once and now the dispossessed live in it with the rats. We have a room three flights up. You go into the dark hallway and up the stairs. Broken settees and couches sit in the halls. About one o'clock the girls

---

1. The angel Gabriel's announcement to Mary that she is to give birth to the son of God (Luke 1.26–38).

come down stairs to get their mail and sit on the front porch. The blinds go up in the old wooden house across the street. It is always quite hot at noon.

Next to our room lies a sick woman in what is really a kind of closet with no windows. As you pass you see her face on the pillow and a nauseating odor of sickness comes out the door. I haven't asked her what is the matter with her but everyone knows she is waiting for death. Somehow it is not easy to speak to her. No one comes to see her. She has been a housemaid all her life tending other people's children; now no one comes to see her. She gets up sometimes and drinks a little from the bottle of milk that is always sitting by her bed covered with flies.

Mrs. Mason, the landlady, is letting us stay although we have only paid a week's rent and have been here over a week without paying. But it is a bad season and we may be able to pay later. It is better perhaps for her than having an empty room. But I hate to go out and have to pass her door and I am always fearful of meeting her on the stairs. I go down as quietly as I can but it isn't easy, for the stairs creak frightfully.

The room we have on the top floor is a back room, opening out onto an old porch which seems to be actually tied to the wall of the house with bits of wire and rope. The floor of it slants downward to a rickety railing. There is a box perched on the railing that has geraniums in it. They are large, tough California geraniums. I guess nothing can kill them. I water them since I have been here and a terribly red flower has come. It is on this porch I am sitting. Just over the banisters stand the top branches of a pear tree.

Many afternoons I sit here. It has become a kind of alive place to me. The room is dark behind me, with only the huge walnut tree scraping against the one window over the kitchenette. If I go to the railing and look down I can see far below the back yard which has been made into a garden with two fruit trees and I can see where a path has gone in the summer between a small bed of flowers, now only dead stalks. The ground is bare under the walnut tree where little sun penetrates. There is a dog kennel by the round trunk but there doesn't ever seem to be a dog. An old wicker chair sits outdoors in rain or shine. A woman in an old wrapper comes out and sits there almost every afternoon. I don't know who she is, for I don't know anybody in this house, having to sneak downstairs as I do.

Karl says I am foolish to be afraid of the landlady. He comes home drunk and makes a lot of noise. He says she's lucky in these times to have anybody in her house, but I notice in the mornings he goes down the stairs quietly and often goes out the back way.

I'm alone all day so I sit on this rickety porch. Straight out from the rail so that I can almost touch it is the radiating frail top of the pear tree that has opened a door for me. If the pears were still hanging on it each would be alone and separate with a kind of bloom upon it. Such a bloom is upon me at this moment. Is it possible that everyone, Mrs. Mason who runs this boarding house, the woman next door, the girls downstairs, all in this dead wooden house have hung at one time, each separate in a mist and bloom upon some invisible tree? I wonder if it is so.

I am in luck to have this high porch to sit on and this tree swaying before me through the long afternoons and the long nights. Before we came here, after the show broke up in S.F.[2] we were in an old hotel, a foul smelling place with a dirty chambermaid and an old cat in the halls, and night and day we could hear the radio going in the office. We had a room with a window looking across a narrow way into another room where a lean man stood in the mornings looking across, shaving his evil face. By leaning out and looking up I could see straight up the sides of the tall building and above the smoky sky.

Most of the time I was sick from the bad food we ate. Karl and I walked the streets looking for work. Sometimes I was too sick to go. Karl would come in and there would be no money at all. He would go out again to perhaps borrow something. I know many times he begged although we never spoke of it, but I could tell by the way he looked when he came back with a begged quarter. He went in with a man selling Mexican beans[3] but he didn't make much. I lay on the bed bad days feeling sick and hungry, sick too with the stale odor of the foul walls. I would lie there a long time listening to the clang of the city outside. I would feel thick with this child. For some reason I remember that I would sing to myself and often became happy as if mesmerised there in the foul room. It must have been because of this child. Karl would come back perhaps with a little money and we would go out to a dairy lunch[4] and there have food I could not relish. The first alleyway I must give it up with the people all looking at me.

Karl would be angry. He would walk on down the street so people wouldn't think he was with me. Once we walked until evening down by the docks. "Why don't you take something?" he kept saying. "Then you wouldn't throw up your food like that. Get rid of it. That's what everybody does nowadays. This isn't the time to have a child. Everything is rotten. We must change it." He kept on saying, "Get rid of it. Take something why don't you?" And he got angry when I didn't say anything but just walked along beside him. He shouted so loud at me that some stevedores loading a boat for L.A. laughed at us and began kidding us, thinking perhaps we were lovers having a quarrel.

Some time later, I don't know how long it was, for I hadn't any time except the nine months I was counting off, but one evening Karl sold enough Mexican jumping beans at a carnival to pay our fare, so we got on a river boat and went up the river to a delta town. There might be a better chance of a job. On this boat you can sit up all night if you have no money to buy a berth. We walked all evening along the deck and then when it got cold we went into the saloon because we had pawned our coats. Already at that time I had got the habit of carrying slips of paper around with me and writing on them, as I am doing now. I had a feeling then that something was happening to me of some kind of loveliness I would want to preserve in some way. Perhaps that was it. At any rate I was writing things down. Perhaps it had something to do with Karl wanting me all the time to take something. "Everybody does it," he kept telling me. "It's nothing, then it's all over." I stopped talking to him much. Everything I said only made him angry. So writing was a kind of conversation I carried on with myself and with the child.

Well, on the river boat that night after we had gone into the saloon to get

---

2. San Francisco.
3. I.e., Mexican jumping beans, sold as a novelty item. These seeds of a Mexican shrub move because they contain the larvae of a moth.

4. A meal containing only fish and dairy products, in accordance with the Jewish dietary law that forbids mixing meat and milk.

out of the cold, Karl went to sleep right away in a chair. But I couldn't sleep. I sat watching him. The only sound was the churning of the paddle wheel and the lap of the water. I had on then this sweater and the notes I wrote are still in the breast pocket. I would look up from writing and see Karl sleeping like a young boy.

"Tonight, the world into which you are coming"—then I was speaking to the invisible child—"is very strange and beautiful. That is, the natural world is beautiful. I don't know what you will think of man, but the dark glisten of vegetation and the blowing of the fertile land wind and the delicate strong step of the sea wind, these things are familiar to me and will be familiar to you. I hope you will be like these things. I hope you will glisten with the glisten of ancient life, the same beauty that is in a leaf or a wild rabbit, wild sweet beauty of limb and eye. I am going on a boat between dark shores, and the river and the sky are so quiet that I can hear the scurryings of tiny animals on the shores and their little breathings seem to be all around. I think of them, wild, carrying their young now, crouched in the dark underbrush with the fruit-scented land wind in their delicate nostrils, and they are looking out at the moon and the fast clouds. Silent, alive, they sit in the dark shadow of the greedy world. There is something wild about us too, something tender and wild about my having you as a child, about your crouching so secretly here. There is something very tender and wild about it. We, too, are at the mercy of many hunters. On this boat I act like the other human beings, for I do not show that I have you, but really I know we are as helpless, as wild, as at bay as some tender wild animals who might be on the ship.

"I put my hand where you lie so silently. I hope you will come glistening with life power, with it shining upon you as upon the feathers of birds. I hope you will be a warrior and fierce for change, so all can live."

Karl woke at dawn and was angry with me for sitting there looking at him. Just to look at me makes him angry now. He took me out and made me walk along the deck although it was hardly light yet. I gave him the "willies" he said, looking at him like that. We walked round and round the decks and he kept talking to me in a low voice, trying to persuade me. It was hard for me to listen. My teeth were chattering with cold, but anyway I found it hard to listen to anyone talking, especially Karl. I remember I kept thinking to myself that a child should be made by machinery now, then there would be no fuss. I kept thinking of all the places I had been with this new child, traveling with the show from Tia Juana[5] to S.F. In trains, over mountains, through deserts, in hotels and rooming houses, and myself in a trance of wonder. There wasn't a person I could have told it to, that I was going to have a child. I didn't want to be pitied. Night after night we played in the tent and the faces were all dust to me, but traveling, through the window the many vistas of the earth meant something—the bony skeleton of the mountains, like the skeleton of the world jutting through its flowery flesh. My child too would be made of bone. There were the fields of summer, the orchards fruiting, the berry fields and the pickers stooping, the oranges and the grapes. Then the city again in September and the many streets I walk looking for work, stopping secretly in doorways to feel beneath my coat.

It is better in this small town with the windy fall days and the sudden rain

---

5. Tijuana, Mexico, just south of San Diego and more than 500 miles from San Francisco.

falling out of a sunny sky. I can't look for work any more. Karl gets a little work washing dishes at a wienie place.[6] I sit here on the porch as if in a deep sleep waiting for this unknown child. I keep hearing this far flight of strange birds going on in the mysterious air about me. This time has come without warning. How can it be explained? Everything is dead and closed, the world a stone, and then suddenly everything comes alive as it has for me, like an anemone on a rock, opening itself, disclosing itself, and the very stones themselves break open like bread. It has all got something to do with the pear tree too. It has come about some way as I have sat here with this child so many afternoons, with the pear tree murmuring in the air.

The pears are all gone from the tree but I imagine them hanging there, ripe curves within the many scimitar leaves, and within them many pears of the coming season. I feel like a pear. I hang secret within the curling leaves, just as the pear would be hanging on its tree. It seems possible to me that perhaps all people at some time feel this, round and full. You can tell by looking at most people that the world remains a stone to them and a closed door. I'm afraid it will become like that to me again. Perhaps after this child is born, then everything will harden and become small and mean again as it was before. Perhaps I would even have a hard time remembering this time at all and it wouldn't seem wonderful. That is why I would like to write it down.

How can it be explained? Suddenly many movements are going on within me, many things are happening, there is an almost unbearable sense of sprouting, of bursting encasements, of moving kernels, expanding flesh. Perhaps it is such an activity that makes a field come alive with millions of sprouting shoots of corn or wheat. Perhaps it is something like that that makes a new world.

I have been sitting here and it seems as if the wooden houses around me had become husks that suddenly as I watched began to swarm with livening seed. The house across becomes a fermenting seed alive with its own movements. Everything seems to be moving along a curve of creation. The alley below and all the houses are to me like an orchard abloom, shaking and trembling, moving outward with shouting. The people coming and going seem to hang on the tree of life, each blossoming from himself. I am standing here looking at the blind windows of the house next door and suddenly the walls fall away, the doors open, and within I see a young girl making a bed from which she had just risen having dreamed of a young man who became her lover . . . she stands before her looking-glass in love with herself.

I see in another room a young man sleeping, his bare arm thrown over his head. I see a woman lying on a bed after her husband has left her. There is a child looking at me. An old woman sits rocking. A boy leans over a table reading a book. A woman who has been nursing a child comes out and hangs clothes on the line, her dress in front wet with milk. A young woman comes to an open door looking up and down the street waiting for her young husband. I get up early to see this young woman come to the door in a pink wrapper and wave to her husband. They have only been married a short time, she stands waving until he is out of sight and even then she stands smiling to herself, her hand upraised.

Why should I be excited? Why should I feel this excitement, seeing a woman waving to her young husband, or a woman who has been nursing a

---

6. Hotdog stand.

child, or a young man sleeping? Yet I am excited. The many houses have become like an orchard blooming soundlessly. The many people have become like fruits to me, the young girl in the room alone before her mirror, the young man sleeping, the mother, all are shaking with their inward blossoming, shaken by the windy blooming, moving along a future curve.

I do not want it all to go away from me. Now many doors are opening and shutting, light is falling upon darkness, closed places are opening, still things are now moving. But there will come a time when the doors will close again, the shouting will be gone, the sprouting and the movement and the wondrous opening out of everything will be gone. I will be only myself. I will come to look like the women in this house. I try to write it down on little slips of paper, trying to preserve this time for myself so that afterwards when everything is the same again I can remember what all must have.

This is the spring there should be in the world, so I say to myself, "Lie in the sun with the child in your flesh shining like a jewel. Dream and sing, pagan, wise in your vitals. Stand still like a fat budding tree, like a stalk of corn athrob and aglisten in the heat. Lie like a mare panting with the dancing feet of colts against her sides. Sleep at night as the spring earth. Walk heavily as a wheat stalk at its full time bending towards the earth waiting for the reaper. Let your life swell downward so you become like a vase, a vessel. Let the unknown child knock and knock against you and rise like a dolphin within."

I look at myself in the mirror. My legs and head hardly make a difference, just a stem my legs. My hips are full and tight in back as if bracing themselves. I look like a pale and shining pomegranate, hard and tight, and my skin shines like crystal with the veins showing beneath blue and distended. Children are playing outside and girls are walking with young men along the walk. All that seems over for me. I am a pomegranate hanging from an invisible tree with the juice and movement of seed within my hard skin. I dress slowly. I hate the smell of clothes. I want to leave them off and just hang in the sun ripening . . . ripening.

It is hard to write it down so that it will mean anything. I've never heard anything about how a woman feels who is going to have a child, or about how a pear tree feels bearing its fruit. I would like to read these things many years from now, when I am barren and no longer trembling like this, when I get like the women in this house, or like the woman in the closed room, I can hear her breathing through the afternoon.

When Karl has no money he does not come back at night. I go out on the street walking to forget how hungry I am. This is an old town and along the streets are many old strong trees. Night leaves hang from them ready to fall, dark and swollen with their coming death. Trees, dark, separate, heavy with their down hanging leaves, cool surfaces hanging on the dark. I put my hand among the leaf sheaves. They strike with a cool surface, their glossy surfaces surprising me in the dark. I feel like a tree swirling upwards too, muscular sap alive, with rich surfaces hanging from me, flaring outward rocket-like and falling to my roots, a rich strong power in me to break through into a new life. And dark in me as I walk the streets of this decayed town are the buds of my child. I walk alone under the dark flaring trees. There are many houses with the lights shining out but you and I walk on the skirts of the lawns amidst the downpouring darkness. Houses are not for us. For us many kinds of hunger, for us a deep rebellion.

Trees come from a far seed walking the wind, my child too from a far seed blowing from last year's rich and revolutionary dead. My child budding secretly from far walking seed, budding secretly and dangerously in the night.

The woman has come out and sits in the rocker, reading, her fat legs crossed. She scratches herself, cleans her nails, picks her teeth. Across the alley lying flat on the ground is a garage. People are driving in and out. But up here it is very quiet and the movement of the pear tree is the only movement and I seem to hear its delicate sound of living as it moves upon itself silently, and outward and upward.

The leaves twirl and twirl all over the tree, the delicately curving tinkling leaves. They twirl and twirl on the tree and the tree moves far inward upon its stem, moves in an invisible wind, gently swaying. Far below straight down the vertical stem like a stream, black and strong into the ground, runs the trunk; and invisible, spiraling downward and outwards in powerful radiation, lie the roots. I can see it spiraling upwards from below, its stem straight, and from it, spiraling the branches season by season, and from the spiraling branches moving out in quick motion, the forked stems, and from the stems twirling fragilely the tinier stems holding outward until they fall, the half curled pear leaves.

Far below lies the yard, lying flat and black beneath the body of the upshooting tree, for the pear tree from above looks as if it had been shot instantaneously from the ground, shot upward like a rocket to break in showers of leaves and fruits twirling and falling. Its movement looks quick, sudden and rocketing. My child when grown can be looked at in this way as if it suddenly existed . . . but I know the slow time of making. The pear tree knows.

Far inside the vertical stem there must be a movement, a river of sap rising from below and radiating outward in many directions clear to the tips of the leaves. The leaves are the lips of the tree speaking in the wind or they move like many tongues. The fruit of the tree you can see has been a round speech, speaking in full tongue on the tree, hanging in ripe body, the fat curves hung within the small curves of the leaves. I imagine them there. The tree has shot up like a rocket, then stops in midair and its leaves flow out gently and its fruit curves roundly and gently in a long slow curve. All is gentle on the pear tree after its strong upward shooting movement.

I sit here all the afternoon as if in its branches, midst the gentle and curving body of the tree. I have looked at it until it has become more familiar to me than Karl. It seems a strange thing that a tree might come to mean more to one than one's husband. It seems a shameful thing even. I am ashamed to think of it but it is so. I have sat here in the pale sun and the tree has spoken to me with its many tongued leaves, speaking through the afternoon of how to round a fruit. And I listen through the slow hours. I listen to the whisperings of the pear tree, speaking to me, speaking to me. How can I describe what is said by a pear tree? Karl did not speak to me so. No one spoke to me in any good speech.

There is a woman coming up the stairs, slowly. I can hear her breathing. I can hear her behind me at the screen door.

She came out and spoke to me. I know why she was looking at me so closely. "I hear you're going to have a child," she said. "It's too bad." She is the same color as the dead leaves in the park. Was she once alive too?

I am writing on a piece of wrapping paper now. It is about ten o'clock.

Karl didn't come home and I had no supper. I walked through the streets with their heavy, heavy trees bending over the walks and the lights shining from the houses and over the river the mist rising.

Before I came into this room I went out and saw the pear tree standing motionless, its leaves curled in the dark, its radiating body falling darkly, like a stream far below into the earth.

1935

LAURA RIDING
1901–1991

In 1924 the editors of the avant-garde little magazine *The Fugitive* announced that they were awarding their annual "Nashville prize" for poetry to Laura Riding Gottschalk of Louisville, Kentucky, a young woman whom they defined as "the discovery of the year"—a writer "coming forward as an important figure in American poetry." The poet whose early achievements they were honoring was indeed to go on to become an important figure, not just in American poetry but also, through her thirteen-year personal and professional partnership with the British poet Robert Graves, in British literature. But she would give up writing poems entirely in her late thirties, eventually arguing that poetry is an obstacle to "something better in our linguistic way-of life."

Riding was born Laura Reichenthal in New York City. Her father, a tailor, had emigrated from Austria-Hungary as a young man; her mother was born in the United States, of German and Dutch descent; and although nominally Jewish, the family was not religious. Instead, Nathaniel Reichenthal was active in the American Socialist party, and dreamed that his daughter might grow up to be an American version of the Polish-German revolutionary Rosa Luxemburg. But his daughter had strong literary inclinations. After graduating from Brooklyn Girls High School, Laura Reichenthal attended Cornell University, where she began seriously writing poetry and where, in 1920, she married Louis Gottschalk, a history professor. In 1923, when she first published verse in *The Fugitive*, she adopted the name Laura Riding Gottschalk and she soon became a regular member of the so-called Fugitive group—a coterie that included John Crowe Ransom, Allen Tate, and Robert Penn Warren. In 1925, she divorced Gottschalk and moved first to New York, and then, at the invitation of Robert Graves, to England and, eventually, the Spanish island of Majorca.

Graves, who admired Riding's work, had invited her to collaborate on a book; together they coauthored an influential text titled *A Survey of Modernist Poetry* (1927), which helped inspire the kind of close reading promoted by the New Critics. Together, too, they founded the Seizin Press and edited numerous works by fellow writers. Sometimes turbulent, their relationship became so stressful that in 1929, involved in a romantic triangle with Graves and another male poet in her circle, Riding attempted suicide. The collaborators continued working together for another decade, but Riding was to return to the States in 1939 and to renounce poetry at around the same time. Years later, in a 1989 foreword to her posthumously published unfinished study *The Word "Woman" and Other Related Writings* (1993), she claimed that much of Graves's work, including his famous exploration of "the female principle," *The White Goddess* (1948), was essentially based on her own ideas, asserting "The literary production in which Robert Graves exploited my thought and writing on the subject of women most massively and concentratedly was *The White Goddess*."

Riding was not in any political sense a feminist. Until 2005, the Laura (Riding)

Jackson Board of Literary Management maintained her policy of refusing permission to include her work in women's anthologies, citing her 1986 comment: "I regard the treatment of literary work as falling into a special category of women as an offense against literature as of a human generalness, and an offense against the human identity of women." Accordingly, *The Word "Woman"* is laced with attacks on what we now call "second wave" feminist activism; about "Eve's Side of It," she insisted that she wanted to "warn readers against trying to see the story as a feminist interpretation of the Creation followed by a feminist analysis of the historical situation" of men and women, adding that "this spiritually modest story" shouldn't be brought "into the raucous favor of current feminist narrative." Yet despite these caveats, the author of *The Word "Woman"* explored many fascinating ideas in a collection whose epigraph—"Women are strangers in the country of man"—locates it squarely at the heart of contemporary gender studies. Thus her notion that among "early civilized peoples [woman] begins to play more or less constantly, a costumed role, to become the female protagonist: to be 'feminine' " points directly toward late-twentieth- and twenty-first century notions of gender as "performance."

As a poet, Riding was an acknowledged influence on such other writers as W. H. Auden and John Ashbery. In the introduction to her final volume of verse, *Collected Poems* (1938), she declared that a poem "is an uncovering of truth of so fundamental and general a kind that no other word besides poetry is adequate except truth." Yet such pieces as "The Map of Places" and "The Troubles of a Book" call pained, even obsessive, attention to the inadequacy of language. Thus, a few years after she published *Collected Poems*, Riding came to see poetry as, in the words of her editor and biographer Elizabeth Friedmann, "obstructing the dedicated use of words for truth that it inspired." Subsequently, adds Friedmann, "the nature of language and its potential for exploring the total meaning of being human (as in 'Eve's Side of It') became the focus of her working life." After her marriage in 1941 to Schuyler B. Jackson, a poet, critic, and sometime editor of *Time* magazine, Riding published essays, articles, and books—most notably *The Telling* (1972)—as Laura (Riding) Jackson. The couple's collaborative work, *Rational Meaning: A New Foundation for the Definition of Words* (1997), was published posthumously.

The Map of Places

The map of places passes.
The reality of paper tears.
Land and water where they are
Are only where they were
5 When words read *here* and *here*
Before ships happened there.

Now on naked names feet stand,
No geographies in the hand,
And paper reads anciently,
10 And ships at sea
Turn round and round.
All is known, all is found.
Death meets itself everywhere.
Holes in maps look through to nowhere.

1928, 1938

Death as Death

To conceive death as death
Is difficulty come by easily,
A blankness fallen among
Images of understanding,
Death like a quick cold hand
On the hot slow head of suicide.
So is it come by easily
For one instant.   Then again furnaces
Roar in the ears, then again hell revolves,
And the elastic eye holds paradise
At visible length from blindness,
And dazedly the body echoes
"Like this, like this, like nothing else."

Like nothing—a similarity
Without resemblance.   The prophetic eye,
Closing upon difficulty,
Opens upon comparison,
Halving the actuality
As a gift too plain, for which
Gratitude has no language,
Foresight no vision.

1928, 1938

The Troubles of a Book

The trouble of a book is first to be
No thoughts to nobody,
Then to lie as long unwritten
As it will lie unread,
Then to build word for word an author
And occupy his head
Until the head declares vacancy
To make full publication
Of running empty.

The trouble of a book is secondly
To keep awake and ready
And listening like an innkeeper,
Wishing, not wishing for a guest,
Torn between hope of no rest
And hope of rest.
Uncertainly the pages doze
And blink open to passing fingers
With landlord smile, then close.

        The trouble of a book is thirdly
20   To speak its sermon, then look the other way,
        Arouse commotion in the margin,
        Where tongue meets the eye,
        But claim no experience of panic,
        No complicity in the outcry.
25   The ordeal of a book is to give no hint
        Of ordeal, to be flat and witless
        Of the upright sense of print.

        The trouble of a book is chiefly
        To be nothing but book outwardly;
30   To wear binding like binding,
        Bury itself in book-death,
        Yet to feel all but book;
        To breathe live words, yet with the breath
        Of letters; to address liveliness
35   In reading eyes, be answered with
        Letters and bookishness.

                                                                    1928, 1938

Eve's Side of It

It was not at first clear to me exactly what I was, except that I was someone who was being made to do certain things by someone else who was really the same person as myself—I have always called her Lilith.[1] And yet the acts were mine, not Lilith's. For Lilith did nothing. She had no body. Nor could I feel that I was Lilith's victim any more than a hand feels itself the victim of the person who makes it do certain things. The hand does these things as if it were doing them itself. It keeps count. And so I have kept count. There have been a great many things to do. I cannot say exactly how many, although I have kept careful count, because I have never added them all up. I have only said to myself "another" and "another" as time went on, not wishing to behave like a slave-woman grudgingly numbering her tasks. That, of course, is all over now. There is no more counting to be done. And since it is all over, I am ceasing to exist. There is no longer an Eve who is as the body of Lilith, no longer a Lilith who is really the same one as myself. There is a new one who is neither Lilith nor myself, yet no one else.

I know this because, although I feel myself ceasing to exist, I still am. I do nothing, there is nothing more for me to do, I am no longer myself. Yet I still am. I am this new one; who is, however, not I. And Lilith is also this new one; who is, however, not Lilith. Lilith is no longer bodiless; she no longer does nothing. Yet she has not become Eve, nor have I become Lilith.

---

1. In Jewish mythology, a female nocturnal demon (probably derived from the Assyrian storm demon Lilitu). Specifically, she was believed to kill babies. According to a story first recorded between the 8th and 10th centuries C.E., Lilith was Adam's first wife—made, as he was, from dust and thus his equal. Because she refused to submit to him and left the Garden of Eden, she was cursed by God and replaced by Eve, created from Adam's rib (as described in Genesis 2.21–23).

She, too, has ceased to exist, yet still is. We have both become a new one who is neither Lilith nor myself, yet no one else. I cannot give you a more intelligent description of this new one because I am only Eve—I haven't what they call "a good mind." But I can tell you more, at least, than Lilith can; for Lilith cannot talk. I can talk about myself, and about Lilith, and about men—until I have actually ceased to exist. And in this way I bring you very close to the new one who I become, along with Lilith, in ceasing to exist. I do not mean that I am superior to Lilith any more than a hand is superior to the person who owns it because it can do things that the person cannot without her hand. I only mean that Lilith could never tell about things. It may be that Lilith is in some ways superior to me; it may even be that the new one who is neither Lilith nor myself is more like Lilith than me. But I, and only I, am capable of telling in so many words how it was before there came to be a new one. For I alone was *there*.

I have sometimes thought of Lilith as my mother. This, of course, is a foolish way of thinking about her. It is true that Lilith made me, but I had no father. I was entirely her own idea. And I was never a child; I did not grow; I have never been different from what I am now—or rather from what I was just before I began to exist. Lilith made me, so far as I can make out, because she was irritated with herself. And she was irritated with herself because she was so good. Lilith knew everything that was going to happen. She also knew that it would be better for these things not to happen. She knew that there were going to be men, and that they were doomed creatures—creatures with hopeless ambitions and false thoughts. Yet she could not prevent their being. They wanted to be; and to have opposed their being would have meant hurting them in their ambitions and thoughts. This she could not do because she was so good. They must hurt themselves. They must learn from themselves, not from her, that their ambitions were hopeless and their thoughts false. She had to let them be. So she made me to take her place—not wanting to watch herself playing the fool all those thousands of years. And I freely confess that I have played the fool: I have been far too patient.

What were their ambitions, and what their thoughts? They wanted to make more than there actually was: many and many and more things. For they thought that what actually was was no better than nothing. "Where is it?" they asked. "What is it? Who is it?" Naturally Lilith was not the sort of person to answer: "It is here, it is this, it is I." Lilith was everything, but she was also nothing in particular. And she was not only incapable of inflicting pain on anyone; she was also incapable of telling lies. She could not say to those creatures who wanted to be: "I am everything." For she could not honestly have used the word "I" about herself, even if she had been capable of talking. Or I might say that she could not talk because she could not honestly use the word "I" about herself, or in any other way refer to herself. She had no self—at least, there was nothing definite you could point at and say, "That is Lilith." And so she could do nothing to prevent from being these creatures who wanted to be.

They were not even creatures at that stage. They were, like herself, dumb: they could not say "I." They were a dumb feeling of antagonism—dumb, blind, ignorant, helpless. I suppose that when something is as completely everything as Lilith was it is inevitable that there should be a feeling of antagonism to it. And the feeling would be only a sort of joke at first, a sort of joke of Lilith's with herself, a sort of way she had of smiling at herself for being so completely everything, or of making light of what was really a tremendous situation. There would be, that is, a sort of mock-outside of herself. And then "one day" she would suddenly find that, by having failed to establish as a hard-and-fast rule that there was nothing outside of herself, she was surrounded by a vague feeling of antagonism, or contradiction, which insisted on being taken seriously, as something outside of herself, although it was merely a rhetorical effect. Lilith was at once too proud and too gentle a person to argue and answer rhetoric with rhetoric. And so it happened that she let herself be treated as nothing by what was actually nothing itself.

When Lilith saw that the result of all this would be for a time the creatures whom we call men, she decided to do nothing about it (that her nature prevented her from doing anything about it) and to withdraw to the very inside of everything, where she would be quite safe from challenge or argument. When she did this everything became, to all appearances, a vacancy that the men who were to be could fill in as they liked; and this vacancy men have called space. But in thus withdrawing to the very inside of everything and, so to speak, hiding her head in herself so that she could not see what was going on (although she knew very well beforehand the sort of thing that was going to happen), she was bound to leave something behind to correct the anomaly, which otherwise might have easily been interpreted as a lie on her part; and Lilith, as I have explained, was the soul of truth. In short, she left me behind. My function, which all men have misunderstood, has been to observe. And in order to observe living creatures, I too had to live.

At first men were not what we now call men; they were merely a feeling of antagonism, or a dumb anger—a dumb, helpless anger. And that was also my principal feeling at the time—a feeling of dumb anger against *them*. Lilith, you see, did not really feel; she only thought. And I suppose you may say that I have never really thought, only felt. But there has always been Lilith there behind me, thinking. It would have been idle for me to be a thinker, too, since I had to deal with creatures who only felt. Men do not really think: they make thoughts out of feelings, and you cannot make very good thoughts out of feelings. And so, in order to observe them truthfully, I had to learn the language of their feelings. In the same way, men can tell the truth about themselves if they keep to their feelings. But when it comes to telling the truth about everything—when they try to think, that is—the safest thing to say is: "I do not know." I myself, though I have always had Lilith to fall back on for thinking, have always kept strictly to feeling—to details, you might say. When, in my dealings with men, I have found myself in the midst of thinkers, I have always tried to set them an example: I have always said, "I do not know."

But in the beginning I had only this dumb feeling of anger. I was not really dumb, of course, for from the first I could talk. But I felt dumb because there was no one to talk to. There was Lilith, but one can't talk to Lilith. If you know Lilith at all you know exactly what's in her mind, at any moment. And if you know what's in her mind, this generally means that you are about to do something that she wants you to do. So there was no question of my talking to Lilith. I talked a great deal to myself in those early days: this is a habit which I have never quite lost. Even in telling about things here I am for the most part talking to myself. Men have often wondered what women do with themselves during the time when, presumably, they are doing nothing. They are, of course, talking to themselves.

But in talking to myself in those early days I could only tell myself that I was angry. It was not clear to me exactly whom I was angry at. I knew vaguely that they were men, or rather were going to be men. But they were not men yet. They too were only, more or less, a dumb feeling of anger. If it had not been for me this would have been a feeling of anger against Lilith. Lilith was not, however, the kind of person one could be angry with. You can only be angry with someone who argues; and Lilith never argued. She merely withdrew. You cannot be angry with someone who withdraws—who isn't *there*. And this is where I came in, and what Lilith made me for. The men who were going to be were angry with me: it was my job to be, so to speak, a chopping-block for their anger. Lilith didn't want to deprive them of their anger, or of anything; and yet she didn't want to be there. So I did the dirty work. I was Lilith's eyes and ears and mouth, and then her whole body.

You can easily imagine that I was very impatient for these creatures to be—as impatient as they were themselves to be. It is no fun to go on being angry, day after day, with something which isn't yet—especially when there are no real days but only an unbroken vacancy of waiting. In the same way it is no fun to be travelling, no matter how comfortable the hotels and the trains and the boats are. You are not really happy until you are *there*, even though you know that you are not going to be happy there. At that stage I was, you might say, travelling, and in the greatest possible comfort. I was not quite there *yet*, I was going to be there, I was nowhere else. I felt very large, as people do when they are travelling, and very light, and very care-free—altogether too care-free: I was not made to do nothing, like Lilith. I do not mean that Lilith is care-free: how could she be, knowing about everything? But if you do nothing and *know* nothing it is very dangerous to be care-free: you may easily forget about yourself, and die. I was anxious to live—to get it all over.

In being impatient for these creatures to be—as impatient as they themselves were—I was undoubtedly putting myself in sympathy with them. But from what I have already explained it should be clear in what way I was in sympathy with them, and, from this, in what way women have, in general, been in sympathy with men. I wanted them to be, and they wanted to be, and to this extent we were, and always have been, in sympathy. But the reason why I wanted them to be was radically different from the reason why they wanted to be, and always has been. I wanted them to be because they were going to be, since Lilith was going to let them be; and because, if they were going to be, the sooner the whole affair was over the better. Lilith made me especially to see the whole affair through; I did not want to be hanging around with my work not even started—perhaps to die. Lilith made me, but she would not have made me again. Of course, there was no real question of my dying. Over and over again, when I have seemed to die, it was just *extreme* tiredness and pulling myself together again. But you cannot imagine how painful it has been to pull myself together each time, after I have been thoroughly exhausted by *men*. Well, naturally, I wanted at least to start fresh.

Often I have been called a scold; and this is a harsh word, considering that it was all their fault, for starting things. Once they started things they couldn't leave them like that; they couldn't expect to be for ever coming to the point—although I quite realize that this is what they *did* expect. Well, I couldn't be expected to go on being angry for nothing, when I knew that sooner or later there would be good cause for being angry—or, at least, Lilith knew. I hope this explains my behaviour in the Garden of Eden. It must not be thought that I was tempted by the Serpent.[2] The Serpent was Lilith's way of encouraging me to do what I would have done in any case. I was fully aware that the fruit was unripe and therefore not good for the health. But things could not go on being lovely for ever when they were going to be *very* difficult—to say the least. Indeed, the ripe fruit was going to be much worse for the health. Things had to begin *somewhere* to be somewhat as they were going to be. And it cannot be said that I didn't take the first bite. Or, whatever is said, I think it ought to be realized that all along I have had a point of view of my own about things; my side of the story is not merely that I have been unlucky in love. And this is my private reason for telling about things: to explain that I, for one, never had any illusions. I do not see how anyone can be either blamed or pitied who has never had any illusions. This is my point of view. At the same time, I should not like it thought that I expected men to have my point of view about things. They are bound to feel that I led them on. Of course I led them on.

1935

Commentary [on "Eve's Side of It"]

I should like to provide this little story with a prologue and an epilogue. The prologue would warn readers against trying to see the story as a feminist interpretation of the Creation followed by a feminist analysis of the historical situation—the life of men and women (according to feminist argument) up to the point where it ceases to be a mere course of changes that did not ever amount to any general, permanent, pervasive change in it, the original masculinist concomitants of the Creation circumstances remaining the great Flaw. The epilogue would remind readers that they had had this warning in the prologue—for they would have forgotten it, in the inveterate manner of readers of reading as they pleased, and not as they were supposed to read. Yet, apart from the difficulty of winning the reader's kindness to the author's intentions, such twin provisions would, indeed, probably arouse suspicion and induce belief that what one said the story was was not just what it was.

The author is not supposed, according to The Rules, for the telling of stories, to put in an appearance in a story, or too near a story to remind of its having an author, as a First Cause operating from outside the story— unless it be a fictive appearance. But stories are not what they used to be. The rules are not what they used to be; or, rather, it has become intellectually fashionable to substitute a law of spontaneous narrative for The Rules, which outlaws sequential pertinence as unnaturally life-like. When something is intellectually fashionable, it commands, if not respect, fear: if you do not

2. I.e., tempted to eat the fruit of the tree of the knowledge of good and evil, an act that God had forbidden (see Genesis 2.16–17, 3.1–5).

treat it as a deliverer from the oppression of not knowing better, you will be thought intellectually unfashionable.

The tolerant attitude to confusion characteristic of these times is favorable to experimental procedure and thinking: there shapes itself, in the confusion, the premise, inspiring faith in experimentalism, that all procedure, and all thinking, from the beginning of thinking and procedure-devising, have been experimental, for want of the possibility of their being otherwise, and that the best to be effected is, therefore, that which is the *most* experimental. Thus is it that, in contemporary story-writing, the question, where the author is, in a story, whether on the outside looking (and writing) in, or on the inside, one minute, and on the outside, in the next, or broken into two author personalities, or more, that work in shifts directing the working personnel (the story-characters), is not necessarily asked at all.

When I wrote this story, I believed in the reality of stories as description of some of the unknown content of life that answers honorably to the affectionate desire for knowledge of it *all*, under deprivations of various sorts that limit the quantity of such knowledge available, in measure proportionate to the desire. The belief has not left me. I hold the concern with making stories, having stories, using them for maintenance of the imaginative loyalty to the sense of life as of a busy fullness in its general forces as exemplified in the personal living of it, and a perfect correspondence to this fullness in its content of detail, to be important to human sanity, and general being of intellectual good heart. And the dissolution in these times, of love-of-story, longing need of it for the exercise of desires not only of life-devoted mind but of the hopeful soul, in a characterless appetite for employments of the faculties of sympathetic attention in whiles of habitual idleness, I view as being of very potent general demoralizing effect upon the spiritual fortitude of human beings.

What are the chances that my making comments on this story will be helpful to readers if they have this contemporary predisposition to viewing a story as an escapade in literary invention, an experiment in writing in a narrative manner? I faithfully risk skeptic disingenuous reading of my comments, as I risked the like with the story itself. In writing this story I wrote writing to which I gave the identity of a *story*, presenting it to readers as such, because I *meant* the word "story" for name of its identity. I *meant* to be telling a story, not to be doing anything else. If certain persons, their *being*, and existing in the world of happenings, personal and natural, can be imagined as a credible possibility, there is in this the making of a *real* story: who tells it *means* it, means the name "story," means the story he-she tells. I meant it all, the story "Eve's Side of It." I meant: a character Eve, of whom stories were told of old, I imagine as "really" existing, far, far, back in existence; and the same, with Lilith, she further back. Great, big, personality-actualities looming up in the dramatics of the Private Life of the universe named "human." Lilith wrapped in veils of gloom never quite shed, seeming more a Mood weighing upon time's yet undetermined content than an imaginatively locatable Being. The other personality of the story is of ubiquitous placeability!

The personality "Eve" was an articulate presence: "I am not to be treated as a mythical character," it declared. "Whatever I am thought of as being, by the Others, or in relation to the mythical Adam, whether a piece of the like of him, or them, or made in the image of them as made in the image of that in the image of which they have conceived themselves to be generally made—whatever has been or is done with me in *ideas*, I have to be treated *as real*." This being real, over and over, in every occurrence of me as to be included in the lived story of life, is both my welcome to the Others, as proving them real, and very inconvenient to their theories of the nature of life, which they deduce from the nature of themselves understood as that of philosophers whom the universe invented for the purpose of having bestowed upon it by them, to its peace and glory, the explanation of its existence. If I, in my irrepressible being wherever *they* have being, in numbers balancing in a natural sort of way with their own, am not otherwise knowable than as *real*, what of the theories about "reality" as knowable only by most complex processes of _____. There is incessant argument as to whether knowable by intuitive or rational processes (an impossible opposition, since the difference is only between speedy apprehension of a little, and step-by-step accumulative apprehension of much, of what is to be known of the entire knowable or—"reality," as they call it).

But what of the new one? This is a *story*: it has got to be as broad as it's long. A story moves on, but it always takes all of itself along with it—the persons, and the happenings, don't just disappear from one part to the next. The story holds it all together. It is *about* all that it is about. And so, if we are to pay respect to the character Eve who has figured so importantly in the stories of the past of our Life, we owe it to the sincerity of our story-sense of the real to put everything into the story of Eve that agrees with our ability to tell it or read it or listen to it as real, in the way in which stories can have realness.

As to the meaning of "the new one": it means that this is a story. A story does not cut itself short with itself, does not "really" end. A story hangs suspended in time. The New One, one might say, is the she-I when the story breaks out of its perpetual condition of occurrence in past time, and overthrows the literary difference between Story realness and Life realness, between what is imagined with belief in the possibility of its being "true" and what is perceived with the eyes of knowledge to be of the very stuff of reality, and requiring therefore to be *thought of* as material of *the story of Life*. For there is this peculiarity, this wondrous naturalness of story as truth of the imaginable, that empowers it to become a changeling, in its character of narrative, when thought's vision authenticates the credibility of the imaginable. Story is the communication of human beings to human beings of beliefs as to what the life of human beings is "really" like. This metaphoric mode of narrative suits both the case of uncertainty in knowledge of what things are *really* like, the subject being a universe of complexity, and the case of the uncertainty of the human form of being as to just what, in full and final determination, *it* is (whether as form self-determined or brought to be what it determinedly is by the managements of universal circumstantiality). Story has to stay metaphoric and at the same time (in so far as it is genuine in its really-like effect of truth) come to the very finest margin of vergence on the realm where story-telling changes naturally into truth-telling, story narrative into truth, the narrative that must be kept self-renewing.

Such is the doctrine of implication of this story. It may be said that, when I wrote it, the doctrine was but a matter of good-faith keeping with the spirit in which I wrote it—my sense of where story fits into patterns of human communicative behavior, which includes so much that is imitation of truth that great confusion exists as to what is truth, what untruth, what falsehood, what lying. It will have been noted that I have let myself "go," in making these comments on the story, speaking about it and its characters now as author, retrospectively, now as myself as present-time reader of it, now dramatizing the personality of Eve of the story in words spoken as by her, additionally to the first-person mode of narrative of the story, and now, even here, in the midst of authorial comment, slipping into commentator's self-identification with the personality Eve. I think all this proves the extraordinarily live nature of story as the next-best thing to truth—when it is formed with love of it for its capability of feelable likeness to life. It does not prove, should not be taken to prove, that, as author, I conceived Eve to be a spitting like of myself, in writing the story, and that in commenting on it I recast this autobiographical hallucination by making an appearance as the spitting real of the story's Eve. The key to Story is bountiful sympathy with the immensely varied actualness of life, as the Key to Truth is bountiful knowledge of actualness, in the immense unity of its significances. I have spread out the case of my little story about Eve to conversational breadth with interest in generating an atmosphere of ease between readers of it, and it, and readers of it and myself. And I leave the matter at that.

But, a little more, finally, as to "the new one": let her be just that. Do not take her out of this spiritually modest story into the raucous favor of current feminist narrative.—And so I have, after all, supplied an epilogue, which can be used also as a prologue.

1976

Later-Twentieth-Century and Contemporary Literature

THE CONTEMPORARY WORLD

Meditating on the woman of the future, the American poet Adrienne Rich mused in "Snapshots of a Daughter-in-Law" (1963) that "she's long about her coming, who must be / more merciless to herself than history." Yet, added Rich in a moment of visionary certitude, "I see her plunge / breasted and glancing through the currents, / . . . at least as beautiful as any boy / or helicopter." Rich's vision reflects a major cultural shift that occurred in the years between 1940 and the beginning of the twenty-first century, a shift suggesting to many writers and thinkers all over the world that whether it meant apocalyptic annihilation or ecstatic transformation, the future had at last definitively arrived.

On the one hand, contemporary thinkers brooded on what the novelist James Joyce had earlier called "the nightmare of history," diagnosing social ills in terms of the crises they associated with the rise of totalitarianism and the threat of nuclear catastrophe. On the other hand, these thinkers dwelled on the metamorphic possibilities implicit in what the poet Hart Crane (echoing Walt Whitman) had called "years of the modern," prescribing and predicting new and more harmonious relationships between mind and body, culture and nature, as well as among nations, classes, races, and sexes. From the modernist novelist Virginia Woolf to the French feminist theorist Simone de Beauvoir to Adrienne Rich herself, women writers expressed both attitudes toward the contemporary world, but—as the women's movement evolved during and after the 1960s—the views of many feminists oscillated between great expectations of feminist transformations and grim anxieties about backlashes against feminist gains.

To begin with, pessimistic speculations were fostered in both sexes by an era that saw such major global calamities as the Holocaust (the genocide of millions of Jews and others during World War II) and the dropping of the first atomic bomb on Hiroshima (in 1945, at the end of that war). Later, however, optimistic speculations were encouraged by such dramatic impulses toward liberation as those that shaped the rise of many third world countries and the formation of an international peace movement as well as the development of the civil rights, conservation, feminist, and gay rights movements. Difficult as it is to generalize about a period characterized by radical extremes and rapid change, a period whose deepest implications are still unclear, it is nevertheless evident that in the years from 1940 to the present almost all the traditional categories through which the Western mind had understood reality have been questioned or annihilated. As geographic markers delineating nations shifted and as the Internet began to dramatically change how individuals accessed information, the boundaries between disciplines and genres blurred and traditional explanatory narratives disintegrated. Not only conventional concepts of space, time, authority, and morality but also received ideas about class, race, and gender were dissolved and revised in a world reeling from what, in 1970, the social observer Alvin Toffler labeled "future shock." By the early twenty-first century, the rise of fundamentalism in many religions, the dangers associated with widespread acts of terrorism (especially the catastrophe that quickly came to be called 9/11), and growing ecological threats were fueling fears that the shocks of the future might endanger not only the health and welfare of women around the globe but also the very existence of humanity.

TOWARD THE TWENTY-FIRST CENTURY
The Impact of World War II

One of the first systems to be severely shaken in this period was capitalism itself, for international crises in the 1930s led many observers on both sides of the Atlantic to fear that a free market economy might no longer be viable. Germany's crippling hyperinflation in 1922–23 and the 1929 New York stock market crash, followed by the Great Depression and serious crop failures (the 1930s' Dust Bowl) in America along with business slumps and bread lines in England, had relatively early in the century posed problems that seemed impossible to solve despite such efforts as President Franklin Delano Roosevelt's New Deal, an unprecedented social welfare program. The widespread disillusionment that marked the era was vividly recorded in such American novels as John Steinbeck's Pulitzer Prize–winning *The Grapes of Wrath* (1939) and Tillie Olsen's *Yonnondio: From the Thirties* (1974), both of which described the grim lives of agricultural and industrial workers as well as the miseries of the unemployed in the 1930s. In addition, the skepticism about capitalism manifested in books like these fostered a disbelief in the efficacy of government in general. Political unrest in England and America, centered in London, Chicago, and New York, resulted in strikes, demonstrations, marches, and riots.

Similar economic and political discontent on the Continent led to the strengthening of the powers of Benito Mussolini, *Il Duce* (the leader), whose black-shirted Fascisti had established him as ruler of Italy in 1922, and to the rise of Adolf Hitler, the so-called *Führer* (leader), whose goose-stepping Nazis took over Germany and elevated him to absolute dictatorship in 1933. Dreaming of a new Roman Empire, Mussolini annexed Ethiopia in 1936 and Albania in 1939 while advocating the supreme authority of the strong leader and ruthlessly suppressing dissent. Similarly, arguing for the "natural superiority" of Aryans, or Nordic-Germanic peoples, and for their right to *Lebensraum* (living space), Hitler invaded Austria and the Sudetenland (a province of Czechoslovakia) in 1938 and Poland in 1939. At the same time, he put into practice the brutally totalitarian principles he had outlined in *Mein Kampf* (*My Battle*, 1925–26) and began implementing what would be called the "final solution" to "the Jewish problem" as well as to the "problem" of other aliens or dissenters by setting up concentration camps, in whose gas chambers and ovens millions would ultimately die.

In Japan and Russia, totalitarian dictatorships had also formed. In 1926, Hirohito became emperor of Japan and began to pursue an aggressively militaristic policy of international expansion; in 1927, Joseph Stalin rose to power in the Soviet Union and began liquidating opponents in a series of purges. By 1939, the world had been divided into hostile camps by a series of treaties and alliances: Fascist Italy and Nazi Germany signed a treaty of friendship (1936), creating an "axis" (to which imperialist Japan was added by a formal military alliance in 1940); England and France signed the Munich Pact (1938), which permitted Hitler to occupy the Sudetenland and which became synonymous with a policy of appeasement toward Hitler; and Hitler and Stalin entered into a short-lived nonaggression treaty (1939). On the brink of World War II, citizens of many countries felt not only disillusionment about government but also anxiety as they found themselves at the mercy of the authoritarian men who controlled so many lives.

War broke out in Europe during 1939, and the United States entered the conflict when Japanese planes bombed the American naval base at Hawaii's Pearl Harbor late in 1941. Although the mortality rate for combatants was not nearly as high as it had been in World War I, enormous numbers of noncombatants were for the first time profoundly vulnerable to attack from the air in their homes, schools, and workplaces. Making possible the destruction of whole cities was the swift development of a technology of death even more sinister than that used in the earlier war. While armored tanks and submarines provided some protection to soldiers and sailors, civilians in urban centers such as London, Dresden, and Tokyo huddled in shelters or subway stations that offered little security against rains of incendiary and explosive bombs. After the Battle of Britain (1940), planes were no longer the kinds of fragile two-seaters in which chivalric pilots had dueled during World War I. Intricate and often large machines, protected by the newly developed device of radar, bombers and transport aircraft insulated their crews and often alienated them from the targets they mapped, surveyed, and destroyed. James Dickey's "The Firebombing" (1964) conveyed the poet's anesthetized sense of distance from humanity on a bombing run over Japan in terms echoing the infamous remark of Mussolini's son, a pilot who commented that the flames of a bombed Ethiopian city looked "like a rose unfolding."

To be sure, airmen were also subject to ferocious attacks by antiaircraft guns or other planes, and the poet Randall Jarrell, who was himself in the air force during the war, described the terrible vulnerability of the ball turret gunner—a man who, wrote Jarrell in a note, had to be "hunched upside-down . . . like the foetus in the womb" to operate the machine guns set into the Plexiglas belly of a B-17 or B-24 bomber: "When I died they washed me out of the turret with a hose," explains the dead speaker of "The Death of the Ball Turret Gunner" (1945). In addition, as Jarrell's poem also implied, these men—subject to a universal conscription system—had been assimilated into a gigantic military bureaucracy that transformed them into standardized and interchangeable parts of what seemed a monstrous whole. "From my mother's sleep I fell into the State," Jarrell's gunner declares. Similarly, the hero of Joseph Heller's satiric *Catch-22* (1961) discovers that he is helplessly entangled in a logically absurd army hierarchy whose rules contradict and confound each other and him.

Nevertheless, to civilians the military assaults seemed virtually apocalyptic. The American poet H. D., who lived through the Blitz of London in the 1940s, saw England as "an island of wounds," while the expatriate poet T. S. Eliot, an air raid warden in London during the same years, characterized an attacking plane as a "dark dove with [a] flickering tongue." Even in the supposedly safe and stable United States, Japanese American citizens, called Nisei, were suspected of collusion with the enemy and imprisoned in camps in California, a development that proved—as if working off the title of Sinclair Lewis's dystopian novel *It Can't Happen Here* (1935)—that "it" could happen here. As the critic Susan Schweik has shown, the war widened the gulf between soldiers and civilians (and therefore also between men and women).

The civilians who suffered the most dramatically during the war and whose experiences were destined to become emblematic of the apocalypse that had engulfed an entire generation were those who endured either the Holocaust in Germany or the American atomic bombing of Hiroshima and Nagasaki, the latter a cataclysm that culminated and concluded World War II on the Pacific front. Both these events, too, were facilitated or created by recent technological innovations and by the construction of elaborate bureaucracies which so depersonalized the decision-making process that moral responsibility was obscured for individuals who claimed they were only "following orders." The demonic efficiency with which the Nazis conducted Jews to death factories was documented by victims of the Holocaust like Anne Frank, a thirteen-year-old girl whose diary became famous when it was published after her death in a concentration camp at the age of fifteen, and by such survivors as the expatriate Romanian Jewish novelist Eli Wiesel, the Italian Jewish memoirist Primo Levi, and the German Jewish poet Nelly Sachs, all of whom testified to the moral implications of a mass cultural descent into hell so drastic that the existence of death camps could never be explained away.

The destruction of most of the inhabitants of Hiroshima and Nagasaki and the debilitation of those who survived were not the result of the same sort of genocidal program, but they had similarly resonant implications, not only for citizens of Japan but for a number of Americans who were distressed by the Truman administration's decision to drop the bomb. Soon the world came to be haunted not so much by this one decision as by the concept of the bomb itself, whose characteristic mushroom cloud began to symbolize a science harnessed to death rather than to life. Only a hundred years after a number of nineteenth-century authors had extolled the virtues of technological progress, the poet Karl Shapiro could write in "The Progress of Faust" (1947) that the sinister scientist-magician of legend had appeared "In an American desert at war's end / Where, at his back, a dome of atoms rose."

It was perhaps inevitable that intellectuals should have responded to such events with writings that reflected nihilistic assumptions about the world. Existentialism, a philosophical movement led by the French thinkers Jean-Paul Sartre and Albert Camus, posited a meaningless cosmos from which human beings could derive significance only through acts of engagement willed in and for themselves. The movement's theories were expounded in a number of major works, including Sartre's treatise *Being and Nothingness* (1943), Camus's novel *The Stranger* (1942), and, perhaps most resonant, Samuel Beckett's bleak drama *Waiting for Godot* (1952), which poignantly stages the tragicomic fate of two tramps pointlessly waiting for a no one who never arrives. But many other writers of this period also expressed sardonic disillusionment: from Norman Mailer's *The Naked and the Dead* (1948) to Katherine Anne Porter's *Ship of Fools* (1962) and Thomas Pynchon's *Gravity's Rainbow* (1973), their works explored the irrationality of both culture and nature in a world at war.

The Cold War

It can be argued that the so-called cold war began at the Yalta Conference of 1945, when the British prime minister Winston Churchill and the American president Franklin Delano Roosevelt allowed the Soviet premier Joseph Stalin to claim portions of conquered Germany as the spoils of war. In a sense, the country's division into what were to become two separate states—the German Democratic Republic and the Federal Republic of Germany, or East and West Germany—represented a splitting of the world into two opposed ideological camps that deeply affected every phase of the life of this period. Internationally, the so-called iron curtain—physically symbolized by the Berlin wall hastily erected in 1961 to keep East Berliners from escaping to the West—shut Western Europe off from Hungary, Poland, East Germany, and other countries in the eastern sphere of influence, under the control of the Soviet Union. The Korean War in the early 1950s, followed by the Suez Canal and Cuban crises, dramatized the struggle between Soviet and American powers while manifesting the decline of Great Britain as an imperial force. At the same time, in the United States, citizens anxious about a possible nuclear attack built bomb shelters and stockpiled canned goods as anti-Communist sentiment intensified.

During the late 1940s in Hollywood and New York, such "left-wing" writers as Dashiell Hammett and Lillian Hellman, together with prominent film directors and actors, were "blacklisted"—deprived of their jobs and reputations—by producers worried about political respectability. By 1953, Senator Joseph McCarthy was acting as, in the words of one historian, an "inquisitor," accusing such diverse figures as the former diplomat Alger Hiss and the American president Dwight Eisenhower of being Communists or Communist sympathizers, while members of the House Un-American Activities Committee promoted patriotism and inveighed against the supposedly subversive doings of liberal intellectuals. The loyalty oaths that many public employees were now obliged to sign to retain their jobs and the execution in 1953 of Julius and Ethel Rosenberg, a Jewish couple convicted of conspiring to commit espionage on behalf of the Soviet Union, were just some of the signals of widespread anxiety during the 1950s: "ordinary" citizens worried about the perceived Communist threat; intellectuals feared that they might be charged with being Communists or Communist sympathizers. "A savage servility / slides by on grease," wrote the poet Robert Lowell about the spirit of the age in "For the Union Dead" (1959).

An influential writer and political activist, Lowell further characterized the period by declaring "These are the tranquillized *Fifties,* / and I am forty" ("Memories of West Street and Lepke," 1959). He was not alone in feeling himself and his era to be middle-aged, for the conservatism of the 1950s, as many thinkers perceived, was social as well as political. In England, to be sure, the years from 1945 to 1951 had seen the ascendancy of a strong

Labour government that nationalized major industries and introduced a program of socialized medicine. But by the early 1950s, the voters had returned the Conservative Party to power, where, led by Winston Churchill, it remained throughout the decade. On both sides of the Atlantic, then, but perhaps more in the newly prosperous United States than in still war-devastated England, this was the decade of "the man in the gray flannel suit," the title of a 1955 best seller by Sloan Wilson. The phrase perfectly captured the conformity and materialism that defined the period's middle-class suburban culture. Largely created by and for a postwar population exhausted by the calamities of the 1940s, the suburbs of the 1950s were enclaves of nuclear families in a newly nuclear age. Ambitious commuting husbands and dutifully domestic wives produced a record number of children who constituted what was soon labeled the baby boom. Most workplaces were still located in urban centers, but as the bourgeois ideal of home ownership sent more young couples into affordable out-of-town subdivisions, inner cities began to decay and to be associated with poverty and violence as they turned into slum districts where many African Americans, Chicanos, Puerto Ricans, and other disadvantaged groups were obliged to live. Among the middle classes, an ideology of "togetherness" was dominant, as was an ethic of "adjustment" and "maturity." Such television shows as *I Love Lucy, Ozzie and Harriet,* and *Leave It to Beaver* might celebrate the charmingly nutty antics of middle-class wives and children, but in the end everyone professed to agree that, as the title of another series put it, "father knows best." For those who did not acquiesce in such an idea, a new breed of professionals—psychiatrists, psychologists, advice columnists, and guidance counselors—arose to explain the virtues of "normalcy": to be "well adjusted," they argued, was to "fit in" to a system that was morally right and emotionally healthful.

In a more sophisticated form, this popular ideology of adjustment affected the increasingly conservative intellectual and literary life of the 1950s. Paralleling the rise of corporations, public universities in the United States grew in size and number, aided by moneys for education that the government had provided returning veterans through the G.I. Bill, as well as by other federal grants. Higher education became a major industry, offering jobs to countless intellectuals. Just at this point, too, critics attempting to elevate the study of literature to the status already achieved by scientific research began promoting the "New Criticism." Detaching the literary text from its cultural context—its author, its audience, and its historical setting—the New Critics analyzed the ironic and metaphorical complexities within poems that were now viewed as well-wrought, autonomous objects. Developing sophisticated techniques of reading, these thinkers saw themselves as rebels against the naiveté of traditional scholarship. Yet, significantly, their efforts to divorce art and criticism from culture and society were essentially conservative. Such theorists as Cleanth Brooks and R. P. Blackmur insisted that the literary analyst should adopt a position of political neutrality, while such writers as T. S. Eliot, Allan Tate, and John Crowe Ransom assertively defined themselves as "reactionaries."

A similar academic professionalization marked the careers of a number of creative writers in this period, some of whom were themselves also practicing critics and many of whom now accepted positions in newly established university creative writing programs. From Tate and Ransom to Theodore

Roethke, Robert Lowell, John Berryman, and Randall Jarrell, most of the major American poets of the age were associated with English departments, and many British writers, including Donald Davie and Phillip Larkin, were also connected with universities. Novels such as C. P. Snow's *The Masters* (1951), Mary McCarthy's *The Groves of Academe* (1952), and Randall Jarrell's *Pictures from an Institution* (1954) dealt with the so-called ivory tower of academia, while the school of poets known as "the Movement," which arose in England in the 1950s, produced work that was stylistically conservative and thematically modest.

Yet despite the overt decorum of what Lowell called "the tranquillized *Fifties*," a number of dissenting voices were raised throughout the period. In America, for instance, even during the McCarthy hearings, radical folksingers like the Weavers continued to play to large audiences, and left-wing students circulated the Stockholm Peace Petition—a demand for world peace sponsored by a set of radical organizations; in England, the British philosopher Bertrand Russell presided over a series of mass demonstrations demanding nuclear disarmament. Among poets, too, the dicta of orthodoxy and depersonalization promulgated most famously by T. S. Eliot were challenged, first by the flamboyant behavior and neo-Romantic verse of the Welsh poet Dylan Thomas, whose influence was at least as great in America as it was in England; then by the so-called beat writers; and finally by the group of artists known as the "confessional" poets—most notably, W. D. Snodgrass, Robert Lowell, and John Berryman, but later also Sylvia Plath and Anne Sexton—all of whom insisted, in their different ways, on defying the values of maturity, adjustment, and normalcy.

In addition, during this period the "Southern Gothic" writers Carson McCullers, Truman Capote, Tennessee Williams, and Flannery O'Connor constructed grotesque fantasies to reveal the immaturity, maladjustment, and perversity endemic to apparently ordinary small-town communities. At the same time, a set of English playwrights known as "Angry Young Men" were producing realistic dramas like John Osborne's *Look Back in Anger* (1956), which attacked the complacency of the welfare state. The rebellious young Allen Ginsberg, a leader of the American beat movement that would help shape the verse of the 1960s, spoke for many such dissenters in his poem "America" (1956): referring to left-wing anti-Stalinists, he asked, "America . . . When will you be worthy of your million Trotskyites?" and he cursed the age that produced the cold war as well as his own country's complicity in it, telling "America" to "Go fuck yourself with your atom bomb."

The Third World

Even as he excoriated the United States in his only partly comic poem "America," Ginsberg mockingly identified with his culture in the line "Asia is rising against me." Parodic though his comment was, it underscored the increasing anxiety with which many American and British citizens were responding to the emergence of third world countries and peoples that began in the late 1940s and continued throughout the 1960s and '70s. The process of global redefinition had begun as early as 1945, when the United Nations was established, granting responsibility in world councils to a number of small powers. When two years later, in 1947, Mohandas Gandhi finally achieved his goal of national independence for India, the disintegration of the British Empire was under way. In 1948, Burma also achieved independence, and in the same year the new state of Israel was established in what had been the British protectorate of Palestine. During the late 1950s and '60s, the African states Ghana (1957), Nigeria (1960), and Kenya (1963) won autonomy from Britain, and their victories were paralleled by events in former French colonies: the liberation of North Vietnam from French rule (1945) was followed by the independence in 1960 of Chad, the Congo Republic, Mali, and Senegal. Counterpointing the emergence of new African, Middle Eastern, and Asian nations was the rise of China to prominence as a world power. In 1949, the Communist Party chairman Mao Zedong established the Chinese People's Republic, and though the new state was not officially recognized by the American government until the 1970s, it became ever more important on the international scene, complicating the plot of the cold war by intervening in Korea, Africa, Cuba, and ultimately Vietnam.

Inspired at least in part by radical critics of imperialism like the black political theorist Frantz Fanon, intellectuals in these new nations struggled to recover lost national traditions, and their efforts were reflected in the literature that native artists—among them Chinua Achebe, Amos Tutuola, Ama Ata Aidoo, Louise Bennett, and Lorna Goodison—began to produce. Although frequently writing in English to ensure an international audience, poets and novelists of former British colonies or possessions nevertheless often drew heavily on local myths and legends while recording the conflicts of identity experienced by people inhabiting cultures still strongly influenced by the West, despite their political independence. At the same time, the struggle of these countries was also recorded by such African-born white writers as Doris Lessing, Nadine Gordimer, and J. M. Coetzee and by such expatriate writers as Buchi Emecheta, Bharati Mukherjee, Jamaica Kincaid, V. S. Naipaul, Salman Rushdie, Derek Walcott, and Anita Desai.

Meanwhile, in Latin America, the Chilean poet Pablo Neruda attacked American imperialism in his impassioned "The United Fruit Company" (1950), as well as in vividly surrealistic works like "The Heights of Machu Picchu" (1950), which recovered legends of the Andes. Mining similar veins were the Peruvian poet César Vallejo, the Mexican writer Octavio Paz, and the Colombian novelist Gabriel García Márquez, all authors whose work was to become extraordinarily influential in the United States during the 1960s and 1970s. In Australia and Canada, moreover, the poet Judith Wright and the poet-novelist Margaret Atwood were only two among many who sought to memorialize what Wright in "South of My Days" (1946) called "my blood's country." Atwood, in particular, epitomized this effort of self-definition in white English-speaking lands resisting engulfment by England and the United States. In *Survival* (1972), for instance, she offered a "thematic guide to Canadian literature," while in her *Oxford Anthology of Canadian Literature* (1982) she explored her literary inheritance.

Within the United States as well, oppressed or subordinated peoples sought to claim lost cultural identities and win political power. During this period, Native Americans became newly conscious of their own traditions. Supported by the reissuing of such classics as *Black Elk Speaks*, a shaman's memoir translated and edited by John Neihardt in 1932, such writers as Scott Momaday, Leslie Marmon Silko, Paula Gunn Allen, and Joy Harjo struggled to reclaim their aesthetic legacy. But perhaps the most influential of the libertarian struggles that gained momentum between the 1950s and the 1970s was the black civil rights movement in America.

Led by the Nobel Prize–winning clergyman Martin Luther King Jr., who advocated nonviolent resistance to white racism, this movement began with voter registration campaigns in the South, carried out by the so-called freedom riders, and progressed to sit-ins, marches, and mass demonstrations in the North—events that helped pass the sweeping Civil Rights Act of 1964, which outlawed segregation in public places and guaranteed legal equality to blacks. More militant than King, the Black Muslim leader Malcolm X began his career arguing that whites were inherently evil and sought to convert African Americans to a revised form of the Islamic religion. Both represented the new passion for self-affirmation that swept black communities in these years. From Rosa Parks, who fought to integrate buses in 1955, to the prisoner-turned-writer Eldridge Cleaver and the group of revolutionaries who called themselves the Black Panthers to U.S. Representative Shirley Chisholm, who ran for the presidency in 1972, African American activists struggled against social, economic, legal, and psychological oppression. Yet their battle was marked by tragedy; the four children killed when a Birmingham, Alabama, Sunday school was bombed in 1963 were just a few among many victims of a violent white backlash, and Malcolm X and Martin Luther King Jr. were assassinated in, respectively, 1965 and 1968.

The civil rights movement fostered a rich proliferation of black writing, work marked by a confidence and energy that had not been seen since the Harlem Renaissance of the 1920s. From Richard Wright, whose prize-winning novel *Native Son* was published in 1940, to Ralph Ellison, whose novel *Invisible Man* (1952) won the National Book Award in 1953; James Baldwin, whose impassioned essay *The Fire Next Time* was widely read when it appeared in 1963; and Toni Morrison, whose *The Bluest Eye* was published in 1970, a new generation of prose writers arose to express what Baldwin called "the sorrow, the rage, and the murderous bitterness which was eating up my life and the lives of those about me." Similarly, from Margaret Walker and Gwendolyn Brooks to Imamu Amiri Baraka (Le Roi Jones), Ishmael Reed, Mari Evans, June Jordan, Audre Lorde, Nikki Giovanni, Lucille Clifton, Sonia Sanchez, and Rita Dove, new generations of African American poets appeared to proclaim that—in the words of Lorde's "Coal" (1976)—"I / is the total black, being spoken / from the earth's inside" and to demand that the reader "now take my word for jewel in the open light." Their project would inspire a generation of Latino writers—including Gloria Anzaldúa, Lorna Dee Cervantes, Sandra Cisneros, Gary Soto, and Julia Álvarez—to forge an aesthetic identity during and after the 1980s. In the next decades, the globalization of English and proliferating analyses of third world cultures, under the rubric of postcolonial studies, brought larger audiences to women situated in and writing about Ireland and India, as well as throughout the rest of Asia, Africa, and the Middle East.

The Sixties

Not insignificantly, the styles and strategies of Baraka, Reed, and Lorde were influenced by and influenced a new literary movement that developed on the Lower East Side of New York City and in San Francisco: writers in this group—called the beats, a name coined by the novelist Jack Kerouac that conflates the words "beaten" and "beatified"—attained national notoriety early in the 1960s, in part because of the impact of Kerouac's *On the Road* (1957) and Allen Ginsberg's long poem "Howl" (1956). With its violent assault on the bourgeois materialism of the 1950s, "Howl," in particular, spoke for a disaffected and rebellious generation. Writing in Whitmanesque lines and in a visionary mode shaped by his studies of the late-eighteenth-century prophetic poet William Blake, Ginsberg exclaimed that "I saw the best minds of my generation destroyed by madness, starving hysterical naked," and excoriated the modern world of "Robot apartments! . . . blind capitals! demonic industries!" For such protests, he and his followers earned the label "beatniks," a term implying that these unorthodox young people were Soviet sympathizers. At the same time, however, Ginsberg defined the characteristic stance of a decade that was to be marked by what often seemed like one long howl of rebellion.

Politically, such protests, which were in part the result of early civil rights activism, took the form of rebellion against censorship, poverty, war, and the destruction of natural resources. As early as 1959, the complaints of publishers and intellectuals had led to the rescinding of bans against the distribution of such supposedly pornographic novels as D. H. Lawrence's *Lady Chatterley's Lover* (1928) and Henry Miller's *Tropic of Capricorn* (1939). The fight for free speech gained a much higher profile in the early 1960s, when students at the University of California, Berkeley, led by Mario Savio, organized sit-ins, conducted rallies, and made speeches to force university authorities to let them use whatever language they pleased in newspapers and journals. Their tactics were adopted by such other groups as Students for a Democratic Society (SDS) and the California Diggers, who tried to draw attention to poverty by demonstrating against what President Eisenhower had once called the "military-industrial complex" and by distributing free food to those living in poverty.

Though these groups were short-lived, the tradition of student leafleting, picketing, marching, and meeting that they pioneered laid the groundwork for what became a nationwide phenomenon: the antiwar movement. Under the leadership of John F. Kennedy and then of Lyndon Johnson, the United States had intervened in South Vietnam to support a series of conservative, even dictatorial, governments against both the revolutionary guerrilla forces of the Viet Cong and the Communist troops marshaled by Ho Chi Minh, North Vietnam's leader. The outrage of young people, especially of draft-eligible young men, at this intervention grew into a mass disaffection that was exacerbated in 1970 when the Ohio National Guard fired on demonstrators at Kent State University, killing four students.

Not only did such protesters adopt the tactics of the Free Speech movement and the SDS, they also employed more theatrical strategies: burning draft cards, pouring blood on military files, and organizing "read-ins" to which famous writers drew large audiences. Among the poets who performed on such occasions were Robert Bly and Denise Levertov. "You who go out on schedule / to kill," Levertov exclaimed, "do you know there are eyes that watch you, / eyes whose lids you burned off[?]" ("Enquiry"). "It's because the aluminum window shade business is doing so well in the U.S. that we roll fire over entire villages," noted Bly sardonically. "It's because we have new packaging for smoked oysters that bomb holes appear in the rice paddies" ("The Teeth Mother Naked at Last").

Because, as Levertov's and Bly's poems suggest, the militancy of the 1960s involved a critique of Western culture in general, it evolved from political to social protest. The period, in any case, was marked by a general loosening of authoritarian hierarchies; with the accession in 1958 of Pope John XXIII and the convening in 1962 of the Second Vatican Council, even the traditionally conservative Catholic Church had relaxed old rules and substituted services in the vernacular for masses in Latin. As the sixties wore on, popular trends in England and America also dramatized change. The beats gave way to the Beatles, and beatniks became hippies. The rock and roll of the 1950s, picked up in England and popularized by the Rolling Stones as well as the Beatles, helped inspire such diverse phenomena as miniskirts, unisex clothes, long hair (for both sexes), and psychedelic drugs. Some British youths defined themselves as "mods" or "rockers," while others became disciples of the radical psychologist R. D. Laing, who preached that the sane were mad and the mad, sane. Some Americans dreamed of running away to the Haight Ashbury district of San Francisco and becoming hippies. What the historian Theodore Roszak called the "counterculture" may at first have seemed juvenile and narcissistic, with its emphasis on flower children and hedonistic self-development, but it was to result in a serious ecology movement, whose spokespersons included the poet Gary Snyder (*Earth House Hold*, 1969), the feminist writer Susan Griffin (*Woman and Nature*, 1978), and the feminist theologian Mary Daly (*Gyn/Ecology*, 1978).

But Griffin and Daly spoke for another growing constituency, too, for the activism of the sixties functioned, paradoxically, in two ways for women: on the one hand, many women engaged in all phases of the decade's numerous political and social movements; on the other hand, the very intensity of their participation forced them to confront their marginalization both in the reigning culture and in the counterculture. Performing as coffee makers, secretaries, or sex objects for male rebels, radical women soon became disillusioned and, like the nineteenth-century women who had worked for abolition but discovered that their male contemporaries held them in as low esteem as the slave owners held blacks, they formed a movement of their own. In turn, the women's liberation movement, stressing sexual freedom, fostered the development of the homosexual rights movement, for gay men and lesbians now began organizing to combat the legal and moral strictures that had ostracized them in the past.

Inevitably, so much ferment had its effect on the entertainment and literature of the era. The disillusionment expressed by Allen Ginsberg, for instance, was popularized by the stand-up comedians Lenny Bruce, Woody Allen, and Joan Rivers, even as it evolved into the genre of black or grotesque comedy produced in the United States by Terry Southern, Donald Barthelme, Vladimir Nabokov, and Stanley Elkin, and matched in England by the witty novels of Kingsley Amis, John Wain, and Iris Murdoch. Similarly comic, but more self-consciously ethnic, were the works of the Jewish American writers Philip Roth, Grace Paley, Saul Bellow, Bernard Malamud, and Cynthia Ozick.

Irreverent, sometimes vulgar, and often nihilistic, the work of both black humorists and Jewish writers was paralleled by the experimental, guerrilla, and street theater that developed in these years, led by such figures as Julian Beck and Judith Malina, whose Living Theater attempted through radically disruptive methods to bridge the distance between author, actor, and audience. Finally, a similar comic nihilism also characterized the ironic and sometimes surrealistic verse of the "New York poets" Frank O'Hara, Kenneth Koch, and John Ashbery. Poets such as those who belonged to the so-called Black Mountain school (Charles Olson, Robert Creeley, Denise Levertov, Robert Duncan) may have been less comic, but they were equally rebellious and experimental, as were the Americans Robert Bly, James Wright, and W. S. Merwin, along with the English Ted Hughes. Hughes's *Crow* (1970), for instance, was a poem sequence that drew on Native American trickster legends and summarized the spirit of the age in a bleak catechism: "Who owns the whole rainy, stony earth? *Death*."

Future Shock

The distinction between Hughes's gloom and the hopeful passion that impelled the activists of the 1960s marks the thin line that separated dystopian and utopian thinkers in this period. Approaching and passing 1984, the year that George Orwell in 1949 used to date the death of civilization, many people all over the globe must have wondered whether those living in the future had any future. Certainly, the threats posed by neutron bombs, intercontinental ballistic missiles, nuclear power plants, and industrial pollution seemed to imply a future that might be merely deathly. In particular, a war of the worlds became an increasingly haunting possibility when more nations, many of them involved in intense border disputes, joined the race to build atomic bombs. As the 1990s began, the end of the cold war—signaled by the disintegration of communist nation-states, notably the U.S.S.R. and Yugoslavia—brought internecine violence, often chillingly labeled "ethnic cleansing." In addition, with chemical waste accumulating and with nuclear engineering errors multiplying, apocalypse seemed to loom in the form of a random accident that could happen at any time. And the deaths of countless victims of the AIDS pandemic horrified a world that remained baffled by the relentless spread of the disease. In the United States and England, the emergence of societies based on what Orwell would have called "newspeak" and "doublethink," exemplified by advertising language and political euphemisms, confounded observers who no longer felt they had a viable language for defining any of these problems.

At the same time, however, a number of scientific and social breakthroughs in the years before and after 1984 seemed to belie Orwell's pessimistic prognoses. Moon landings, space shuttles, and communications satellites promised to enlarge the world's horizons, while medical innovations, from polio vaccine to heart transplants, suggested that humanity was gaining new leases on life. Home appliances, convenience foods, and computers all offered the possibilities of liberation from drudgery, and the concept of equality implicit not only in large-scale welfare programs but also in humanitarian movements hinted at new societal steps toward moral responsibility.

But the future that had arrived was shocking because to many it seemed almost impossible to comprehend the divergent implications of numerous radical scientific innovations. Biochemical investigations into the molecular structure of the cell might yield either deadly mutations or new life. Similarly, such pioneering surgical procedures as sex-change operations, and such obstetrical procedures as artificial insemination, egg harvesting, and surrogate mothering along with the bioengineering involved in cloning, promised either to allow women to control their own reproductive functions or else to replace real women with artificial wombs, real human beings with replicants. No wonder, then, that experimental writers from the French novelist Alain Robbe-Grillet to the Argentinean writer Jorge Luis Borges and writers of speculative fiction from Isaac Asimov to Ursula K. Le Guin and Octavia Butler described a world of radical instability.

Finally, at the end of the twentieth century the citizens of many countries began witnessing or suffering new waves of terrorism. The 1995 bombing of a federal building in Oklahoma City by an American antigovernment extremist dramatized U.S. vulnerability to attack from within. But when attacks from al Qaeda operatives, under the command of the Saudi terrorist Osama bin Laden, destroyed the twin towers of the World Trade Center and badly damaged a wing of the Pentagon on September 11, 2001, instability fueled insecurity. People in America and around the world were horrified. In 2003, widespread fears about weapons of mass destruction and the desire to forestall continuing acts of terrorism such as the 2002 Bali bombings triggered an invasion of Iraq in which the Labour government of British prime minister Tony Blair joined forces with the American administration of George W. Bush. These leaders had to contend with increasingly widespread skepticism from their constituents, however, as well as with often violent reprisals from an Iraqi insurgency and from al Qaeda, including (in Iraq) kidnappings and executions of Western contractors and journalists and (elsewhere) bombings in Madrid and London.

While on both sides of the Atlantic many feared a newly militant Islamic fundamentalism, some worried about the rise of fundamentalism in Christian sects as well. Also causing serious concern were the ecological threats posed by the demise of a number of species and by global warming. Famine, AIDS, and genocide multiplied human suffering throughout Africa, while religious and political conflicts escalated in the Middle East. Among neoconservatives especially, surveillance became an imperative, breeding anxiety in others about the abrogation of traditional civil rights and liberties during a period that saw the rise of a strange new crime, identity theft.

Postmodernist theorists during this period claimed that the "grand narratives" earlier used to explain historical change only camouflaged the discontinuities and contradictions of reality, and the French thinker Jacques Derrida had long emphasized the indeterminacy of all systems of meaning. Interestingly, Derrida decided to identify himself in *Spurs* (1978) as "a woman," an extreme self-definition suggesting that, not unlike so different a contemporary as the lesbian feminist Adrienne Rich, this male intellectual associated what came to be called the postmodern with the feminine. But that Derrida should attempt such an identification revealed how deeply what had been traditionally called the "woman question" was intertwined with the future shock experienced and expressed by so many thinkers in these years. After decades of social turmoil and intellectual upheaval, the legitimacy of the government, the boundaries of the earth, the integrity of the cell, and the goals of religion had become violently contentious issues. Similarly, even the biological determinacy of gender—the deepest structure through which the self has traditionally been defined and society organized—no longer seemed inevitable despite its continuing resonance.

CONTEMPORARY IMAGES OF WOMEN

Though some thinkers in the 1980s and 1990s were to arrive at radically antibiological positions like that of Derrida, in the works of many other writers and artists from 1940 to, say, 1980, images of women were biologized and sexualized as never before. Indeed, the traditional polarities of angel and monster, virgin and whore, lady and madwoman were consistently eroticized in this period. The nineteenth century had praised women for purity and decorum while blaming them for passion and desire, but the second half of the twentieth century virtually reversed those moral priorities; contemporary writers usually blamed women for frigidity and praised them for sexiness. The scarlet letter A that Nathaniel Hawthorne had used in the nineteenth century to emblematize the crime of the adulteress now dissolved into the pornographic letter O that signified both the emptiness and the openness of an obediently serviceable woman in Pauline Réage's *The Story of O* (1954). To be sure, many thinkers resisted this cultural tendency to eroticize the female, creating women characters who were autonomous and intelligent; yet for many others, popular pressures were hard to overcome, and the images constructed in the works of those writers posed particular problems for women readers.

Certainly from the World War II pin-up girl to the *Playboy* playmate of the 1960s, from the nymphet of Vladimir Nabokov's *Lolita* (1955) to the nymphomaniac of Terry Southern and Mason Hoffenberg's *Candy* (1964), representations of women often became blatantly titillating to men. The current male argot objectified the deliciously willing heroine as a cupcake, a muffin, a cookie, a tomato, a honey, a tootsie, a real sugar, a cherry, a sweetie pie, a tart, or a peach while metamorphosing all women into sexy or repellent animals (foxes, birds, chicks, beavers, kittens, pussies, bitches, dogs, pigs). Though there are, of course, distinctions among the attitudes toward women manifested in the texts produced during World War II, during the "tranquillized *Fifties*," and during the rebellious sixties, it is extraordinary how consistently most novelists and poets of the era focused their attention on the female body and its willingness to function as a receptacle for male desire. Even when contemporary male writers seemed to be contemplating such seemingly nonerotic figures as the mother or the literary woman, they tended to sexualize both their dreams and their dreads about femininity.

Even before 1939, a process of eroticization had begun with the development of a cultural atmosphere whose ideology was more permissive than ever before. The dissemination of birth control information and devices, the publication of sex manuals, the passage of new divorce laws, the advent of short skirts, silk stockings, brassieres—all these diverse phenomena transformed woman from an untouchable object in a hoop skirt or a bustle to a willing and easily accessible body. By World War II, it was possible, as it had not been during World War I, for armies of sex-starved men to decorate barracks, tanks, and planes with clippings of naked or scantily dressed movie stars or models. Countless war novels and movies recorded the joys of lust and the pleasures of casual sexual encounters, especially with prostitutes and foreigners.

At the same time, the pinning up of female nudity led to a fetishizing of body parts; breasts, buttocks, and legs were often appraised separately, as if the ideal woman could be put together like a jigsaw puzzle. Such fetishizing was perhaps most dramatically expressed in the quasi-theology of the "cunt" that permeated the writings of the American novelist Henry Miller, who even before the war had published such sexually explicit books as *Tropic of Capricorn*. "The body is hers, but the cunt's yours," Miller was to observe in *Sexus* (1949), but in *Tropic of Capricorn* he had already outlined his credo in a description of "the best fuck" he ever had: the object of his desire was a "simpleton" about whom he noted that "above the belt . . . she was batty. . . . Perhaps that was what made her cunt so marvellously impersonal. It was one cunt out of a million."

But besides being seductive, those millions of cunts were threatening: for example, governments constantly urged fighting men to protect themselves against the danger of VD posed by whores and foreigners, a peril that, according to official propagandists, implicitly involved all women. Moreover, just as many World War I soldiers had blamed women for their suffering, combatants in World War II sometimes tended to associate the devastation of war with unleashed female energies. The American poet Stanley Kunitz's "Careless Love" (1944) actually personified the event as an insatiable female, who contaminates and destroys men: "for what / This nymphomaniac enjoys," Kunitz wrote about the machinery of destruction, "Inexhaustibly is boys."

Even while the horror of the war was metaphorized as female, however, fighting men were continually reminded that they were struggling to preserve both the "girl back home" and the values she represented. In countless movies and popular songs, this good girl was kissed and reluctantly left in railroad stations and on wharves. Karl Shapiro's "V-Letter" (1944), perhaps the most famous war poem of the period, was addressed to this girl and summarized both her virtues ("I love you first because your face is fair . . . I love you first because you wait. . . . You are my home and in your spacious love / I dream to march as under flaring flags") and the poet's commitment to die for her, if necessary ("I love you first because your years / Lead to my matter-of-fact and simple death / Or to our open marriage").

Yet though Shapiro's poem suggests that his beloved simply waits while he risks death, not every stay-at-home sweetheart was wholly passive. Dutiful and patriotic, many a waiting lady became Rosie the Riveter and went to work in a munitions factory, for as the war progressed, government propagandists in both England and America transformed the image of the good girl, replacing the wistful dreamer with an energetic partner doing her share for the boys abroad. But as soon as the conflict was over, this image faded; Rosie was turned back into a cheerful housewife or a clean-cut girl next door and admonished in such works as Ferdinand Lundberg and Marynia Farnham's *Modern Woman: The Lost Sex* (1947) that she would lose her sexiness and her sex life if she insisted on continuing to compete with men outside the home.

As "pioneers of the sex frontier," wrote David Riesman, Reuel Denney, and Nathan Glazer in their influential sociological study *The Lonely Crowd* (1950), women "must foster aggressiveness and simulate modesty[;] . . . if they have a profession, both men and women are apt to think that their skill detracts from their sexual life or that their sexual life detracts from their skill." Their comment reminds us that these researchers were writing in the age of the Kinsey report and the sex manual, the sex goddess and the high school date. Whether male writers in these years portrayed women as involuntarily animal or expertly sensual, they frequently saw the women they described as less than fully conscious human beings. In his poem "A Girl in a Library" (1951), for instance, Randall Jarrell depicted his subject as "an object among dreams," and remarked that "one sees in your blurred eyes / The 'uneasy half-soul' Kipling saw in dogs." Both the English writer Kingsley Amis and the American poet Kenneth Koch characterized women as dreamy parts of a dream world: in "A Dream of Fair Women" (1957), Amis imagined a horde of "Lime-lighted dolls guttering in their brain," each one begging him "to sign / Her body's autograph-book," and in "Sleeping with Women" (1969), Koch created a surrealistic landscape in which he could be "Asleep with women, awake with man." Clearly the popular cultural equivalents of all these sexy somnambulists were such stars as Marilyn Monroe and Jayne Mansfield, whose tantalizingly exposed bosoms and thighs revealed them as mindlessly voluptuous embodiments of bodily pleasure even while the artifice of their glamour defined them as no more than fantasy figures.

From the beat poets of the fifties to the black humorists of the sixties and seventies, many writers continued the tendency of earlier artists to reduce females to collections of body parts. As if elaborating on what we earlier called Henry Miller's theology of the cunt, Allen Ginsberg in "Sather Gate Illumination" (1956) proclaimed of his friend Neal Cassady that "Neal sees all girls / as visions of their inner cunts"; and Gary Snyder in "For a Far-out Friend" (1955) told a woman whom, he confessed, he had once beaten up that "visions of your body / kept me high for weeks"—in particular visions of her with "a little golden belt, just above / your naked snatch." Interestingly, these celebrations of women's body parts implicitly characterized the male speaker as a voyeur, peering at female mysteries that the male must master.

For some writers in this period, however, such distancing techniques were sometimes replaced by frankly comic acknowledgments of male helplessness about the female body. Not only did Philip Roth in *The Breast* (1972) bemusedly imagine a male narrator's terrified transformation into a female breast, but both the American novelist John Barth in "Night Sea Journey" (1966) and the American filmmaker Woody Allen in *Everything You Always Wanted to Know about Sex* (1972) recounted the hapless expeditions of nervous sperm up the cavernous labyrinth of the birth canal toward the heart of darkness where female power lurks. Perhaps it was because the distancing strategy of voyeurism did not always work to defuse anxiety about such engulfing femininity that contemporaries of Roth, Barth, and Allen also turned to other defensive strategies, in particular to an attempt to domesticate female sexuality. In his "Wife Wooing" (1962), for instance, the American writer John Updike praised the dutifully passive wife as "the Wide W, the receptive O. Womb," while in "The Lingam and the Yoni" (1955) the Australian poet A. D. Hope used the Sanskrit words for phallus and vulva to satirize a society that does "the Lingam honor" by keeping "the Yoni in" a cute suburban cottage.

Yet even this strategy backfired for a number of writers in the era. Novels and stories of suburban sexual intrigue like those of Philip Roth ("Goodbye, Columbus," 1959) and John Updike (*Couples*, 1968) often depicted the domesticated heroine as spoiled and idle, indeed as so bored that she is driven to plot pointlessly promiscuous or merely pragmatic romantic conquests. Perhaps the paradigm of these banal, bed-hopping predators is Brenda Patimkin in Roth's "Goodbye, Columbus," a "Jewish-American princess" whose narcissism, heartlessness, and materialism lead her to seduce and abandon her impoverished and ardent lover. In the same vein, for beleaguered mates like the speaker of Robert Creeley's "Ballad of the Despairing Husband" (1955) and protesting prospective mates like the speaker of Gregory Corso's "Marriage" (1959), the woman who is a wife became the stereotypical battle-axe. Looking for "the darling I did love," Creeley's speaker encounters instead a ferocious female who declares, "I'm free of you, you little prick, / and I'm the one can make it stick"; and Corso's speaker, fantasizing "a fat Reichian wife screeching over potatoes Get a job!" argues that "I never wanted to marry a girl who was like my mother / And Ingrid Bergman was always impossible."

When women characters in mid-century literary texts were perceived as both "real" and "good," they were often defined as "good" because they were willing to be sacrificed by men and for male purposes. In a tradition that goes back to D. H. Lawrence's story "The Woman Who Rode Away" (1926), a fisherman-artist in Dylan Thomas's "Ballad of the Long-Legged Bait" (1942) "throw[s] to the swift flood / A girl alive with his hooks through her lips" so that he can "catch" the inspiration that he seeks; and in a mode that goes back even further, to the self-immolations of martyrs like St. Cecilia, Celia Coplestone, the heroine of T. S. Eliot's play *The Cocktail Party* (1949), proves her virtue by allowing herself to be "crucified / Very near an ant hill" in the service of a "handful of plague-stricken natives / Who would have died anyway." A number of male writers brought to the surface the hostility implicit in works such as those by Thomas and Eliot, constructing revenge fantasies in which autonomous females were punished for their supposed sins.

Fictions by Norman Mailer, Hubert Selby, and Thomas Pynchon enacted visions of rape that were comparably murderous. Mailer's *An American Dream* (1965) not only told the story of a homicidal assault on a wife but associated that assault with a brutal act of anal intercourse; as the critic Kate Millett has observed, "The reader is given to understand that by murdering one woman and buggering another, Rojack [Mailer's hero] became a 'man.'" More grotesquely, male revenge on the "dumb" but desirous female was enacted in Selby's *Last Exit to Brooklyn* (1964), where the whorish Tralala is gang-raped and finally murdered by being impaled on broomsticks and beer bottles. Even a brilliantly metaphysical comedy like Pynchon's *V* (1963) turned on comparable vengeance dreams. V's lesbian actress-lover Melanie is skewered by a pole in an onstage act in which she has failed to protect herself with a prop chastity belt, while the supposedly charismatic body of V herself is disassembled by children who steal her wooden legs, false teeth, and wig. As the critic Mary Allan has pointed out, "V" is clearly a virgin who thrives on both violence and vulgarity; at the same time, however, she incarnates the vulva, the vagina, and the horrifying void that these female body parts seemed ultimately to epitomize for many later-twentieth-century male artists.

Some of this period's fiercest conflicts among men similarly issued in literal as well as literary acts of aggression toward women. The revolt of male rock 'n' roll culture against bourgeois conventionality was often dramatized through record albums and posters flaunting images of enchained, seminaked women, while racial battles between black and white males seem to have been fought out over and on the female body. Although Eldridge Cleaver conceded in his memoir *Soul on Ice* (1968) that he "could not approve the act of rape," he explained that for him sexual assaults on white women had been "insurrectionary act[s]": "I was very resentful over the historical fact of how the white man has used the black woman. I felt I was getting revenge." Precisely such revenge was imagined in "Babylon Revisited" (1969), a curse poem by Imamu Amiri Baraka that damns the whorish white woman as "a vast puschamber / of pus(sy) memories / with no organs / nothing to make babies," and prays that "this bitch and her sisters, all of them, / receive my word / in all their orifices like lye mixed with / cocola and alaga syrup." As if to establish and explain a relationship between *Soul on Ice* and "Babylon Revisited," Cleaver quoted from *The Dead Lecturer* (1965), one of Baraka's earlier books: "Rape the white girls. Rape / their fathers. Cut the mothers' throats" ("BLACK DADA NIHILISMUS").

Despite, or perhaps because of, its use of a black colloquialism ("mother" for "motherfucker"), Baraka's last phrase highlighted an anxiety that may underlie a good deal of degrading contemporary rhetoric about women, specifically an anxiety about a generation of viperous and vituperative mothers who were no longer experienced as being the selfless nurturers that their sons wanted them to be. With its definition of the pernicious American disease of "momism," Philip Wylie's *Generation of Vipers* (1942) definitively described the malaise that some men had begun to feel. Arguing that "the male is an attachment of the female in our civilization," Wylie excoriated a "dynasty of the dames," whom he saw as "five-and-ten-cent-store Lilith[s]"—that is, as modern equivalents of the monstrous first woman and first witch of Jewish legend. Ostensibly writing in a more scientific vein, the social historian Ferdinand Lundberg and the psychiatrist Marynia Farnham declared a few years later in *Modern Woman: The Lost Sex* that research had shown "the traditional 'Mom'" to be "the mother of [a] deficient male" and, rhetorically asking "Just what have these women done to their sons?" they replied "They have stripped them of their male powers—that is, they have castrated them."

As late as 1962, the character called "Big Nurse" in Ken Kesey's *One Flew Over the Cuckoo's Nest* was portrayed as embodying exactly the maternal flaws described by Wylie, Lundberg, and Farnham: Kesey's hero seemed to speak for the author when he exclaimed that Big Nurse "may be a mother, but she's big as a damn barn and tough as a knife metal . . . she's a bitch and a buzzard and a ball-cutter." In this period, indeed, even mothers apparently dedicated to the good of their growing boys were pictured as guilty and guilt-inducing. The stereotypical Jewish mother who reigns over Philip Roth's *Portnoy's Complaint* (1969) reveals her love for her son by threatening him with a knife in order to make him eat. Finally, even mothers who were neither castrating nor guilt-inducing often seemed horrifyingly weak and hence grotesquely pathetic. In "Kaddish" (1961), Allen Ginsberg lamented the death of his mad mother, ritually telling her "farewell / with your old dress and a long black beard around the vagina / farewell / with your sagging belly," while in "Sailing Home from Rapallo" (1959) Robert Lowell described bringing his mother's body home from Italy, noting that "Mother traveled first-class in the hold" and adding that "The corpse / was wrapped like *panettone* [an Italian Christmas bread] in Italian tinfoil."

Perhaps what informed depictions of both maternal power and maternal pathos in this period was a mythology of the mother goddess that can be traced back to the nineteenth century and that was outlined in the mid–twentieth century by the English poet-novelist Robert Graves, the German psychoanalyst Erich Neumann, and the American poet Robert Bly. For Graves, the enduring feminine ideal was a figure he called the White Goddess, while for both Neumann and Bly she was the four-faceted Great Mother. But whatever the mother goddess was named, her differing aspects corresponded significantly with just the aspects of women, and especially mothers, that were praised or blamed by many contemporary male artists. Though such mythological schemata and the ideology of sexuality on which they were based might have seemed only indirectly relevant to literary women, these ideals and ideas in fact reverberated through male definitions of female writing that had considerable impact on women of letters.

In *The White Goddess* (1948), Graves claimed that "a woman who concerns herself with poetry" either should be "a Silent Muse" or should "be the Muse in a complete sense . . . and should write . . . with antique authority." Most other writers did not mystify the literary woman as Graves did, but many either scornfully trivialized or melodramatically aggrandized her. Theodore Roethke claimed in a glowing review of Louise Bogan's verse that most women poets were guilty of "running between the boudoir and the altar; stamping a tiny foot against God or lapsing into . . . sententiousness," while W. H. Auden praised Adrienne Rich's volume of verse *A Change of World* with the faintly patronizing comment that "the poems are neatly and modestly dressed, speak quietly but do not mumble, respect their elders but are not cowed by them, and do not tell fibs." Similarly, Robert Lowell introduced the first American edition of Sylvia Plath's *Ariel* (1965) by proclaiming that its author had here become "hardly a person at all, or a woman, certainly not another 'poetess,' but one of those super-real, hypnotic, great classical heroines." More generally, the British novelist-critic Anthony Burgess declared in 1966 that Jane Austen's novels failed because her writing "lacks a strong male thrust," and the American philosopher-novelist William Gass asserted in 1976 that literary women "lack that blood congested genital drive which energizes every great style." Given the impulse to sexualize and dehumanize women that permeated much male thinking up until the 1970s, when the women's movement started to change attitudes toward the ways in which women should be represented, how was it possible for women writers—indeed for women generally—to accomplish anything of importance in these years?

CONTEMPORARY WOMEN'S LIVES

The pervasive eroticizing of women during the second half of the twentieth century may have been in part a reaction against the opening of many personal and professional options to women of all ages, classes, and races. For with newly granted legal, economic, social, political, and educational rights, women were in fact able to accomplish a great deal in this period. At the same time, however, it is no doubt true that many of these new rights were not equally available to all women, that all these new rights were controversial and continually threatened by conservative social movements, and, finally, that a number of these new rights often created new difficulties for those who were supposedly benefiting from them.

During the 1960s and 1970s, the legal status of women improved in most English-speaking countries. Divorce had become increasingly common and simple to obtain, and the introduction of a "no-fault" divorce law in California in the 1970s represented perhaps the most dramatic symbol of the way in which the Victorian double standard of morality had been overturned: whereas in the past a woman could be chastised and divorced for committing adultery (while, often enough, a man could not), now either partner could dissolve a marriage for any or no reason whatsoever. Nor could a divorced woman's children be taken from her by their father—as they could have been in the nineteenth and early twentieth centuries—without elaborate court battles. In addition, the Abortion Act (1967) in Great Britain and the landmark Supreme Court decision in the case of *Roe v. Wade* (1973) in the United States granted women in both countries unprecedented control over their own reproductive systems. Though in some English-speaking nations abortion remained illegal, the British and American models were powerful ones, implying that, in the words of the historian Carl Degler, "the law and society [had given] women final authority over the size of the family." Finally, legislation mandating equal pay was passed and equal opportunity commissions were established in a number of English-speaking countries, seeking to rectify traditionally large differentials between male and female wages. The American Equal Pay Act of 1963 formulated for the first time the principle that women should not be paid less money for doing exactly the same work as men, and the Civil Rights Act of 1964 outlawed job discrimination on the basis of sex as well as race. During the 1980s and 1990s, an unprecedented number of women entered law schools, graduated to take on highly visible legal positions in the judiciary, and moved into political prominence.

Yet all these transformations in women's legal status were in one way or another problematic in their consequences. Not only did the ease of divorce lead to high divorce rates, it was also associated with a weakening of alimony and child support arrangements; as Degler reports, "in 1970, some 77 per cent of white women and 85 per cent of black women with children but without husbands maintained their own households. Yet as recently as 1940 only 45 per cent of white women and 40 percent of black women did." A divorcée, therefore, frequently bore sole responsibility for the welfare of her children, increasing the likelihood that she would become impoverished. Moreover, because the so-called right to life of the developing fetus rapidly evolved in many countries from an ethical and religious belief to a political rallying cry, abortion legislation was continually being challenged. At the same time, the differential between women's and men's wages remained significant: at present in the United States women workers earn seventy-seven cents for every dollar earned by men. Worse still, in Australia in the late 1970s to early 1980s, legislation established minimum wages for women that were lower than those for men performing identical tasks. By the mid-1990s, the American press reported widespread public suspicions about the affirmative action policies that had put some women and minorities into improved professional and political positions.

The issue of wages for women's work became increasingly critical precisely because women now found that they had new economic opportunities. To begin with—as the prize-winning documentary film *The Life and Times of Rosie the Riveter* (1980) illustrated—World War II brought enormous numbers of women into the job market. By 1960, as the historian William Chafe has shown, "twice as many women were at work as in 1940, and 40 per cent of all women over sixteen held a job." In addition, he notes, between 1940 and 1960, "the number of mothers at work leaped 400 per cent—from 1.5 million to 6.6 million—and 39 per cent of women with children ages six to seventeen had jobs." Once again, though, the gains achieved by contemporary women were problematic. First, women workers tended to be clustered in low-status, low-paying, or service-oriented jobs: as the sociologists Juanita Kreps and R. John Leaper put it, in 1976 "the working woman [was] a typist, maid, teacher, nurse, cashier, or saleswoman." Second, few married women workers were defined as primary breadwinners even when they were in fact the sole supporters of themselves or their families. Third, working women had few support systems to help them cope with what had traditionally been considered the unique female responsibilities of child care and housework. Though nursery school and day care enrollments rose radically in this period, child care facilities were often either inadequate or expensive, while working wives found themselves performing two jobs, one paid and one unpaid. At the beginning of the twenty-first century, cutbacks in health and welfare services left working women—as well as single mothers, older women, and women with children—in situations of financial and medical risk.

As if to underline the contradictions implicit in the history of women's gains during the mid–twentieth century, Degler observes that "the proportion of women graduating from college was higher than ever" while Chafe remarks that "the proportion of women in business and the professions . . . changed hardly at all." Perhaps this paradox reflects a debate over the nature of women's education that intensified in these years when female students flooded into universities, colleges, community colleges, and vocational training programs in every English-speaking country. The nature of this debate was succinctly summarized in 1955 by Lynn White Jr., then president of Mills College in California, a private all-female institution. In a book called *Educating Our Daughters*, he proposed a "distinctively feminine curriculum" and speculated that "a beginning course in foods"—perhaps focusing on "the theory and preparation of Basque paella"—might be "as exciting . . . as a course in post-Kantian philosophy." Such ideas had an effect on female students, with a number of studies revealing that many young women who were ambitious to get As in classes nevertheless felt obliged to "play dumb" on dates. The psychologist Matina Horner's classic essay "Fail: Bright Women" (1969) documented the consequences of such a conflict: precisely the young women who had been the most dutiful students in early life were least likely to succeed later.

Of course, Horner herself, president of Radcliffe College from 1972 to 1989, was representative of a group of women intellectuals who had *not* failed. After World War II, a range of female thinkers gained prominence in virtually every profession: in the United States, the philosopher Hannah Arendt, the critic Susan Sontag, the political theorist Angela Davis, and the biologist Barbara McClintock; in England, the molecular biologist Rosalind Franklin, the philosopher-novelist Iris Murdoch, and the critic Helen Gardner, to name only a few. At the same time, such women politicians as Golda Meir, Indira Gandhi, Margaret Thatcher, and Benazir Bhutto rose to the highest positions in their countries. Moreover, although women achievers might in the earlier decades of the twentieth century have seemed "singular anomalies," by the 1970s female enrollments in graduate and professional schools had risen so sharply that it was possible that Degler and Chafe's contradiction might be resolved. As political representatives and cabinet members, presidents of universities and heads of foundations, women in the twenty-first century were playing visible and powerful roles.

The shifts in fashionable styles that can be traced from the 1940s to the turn of the twentieth century might function as an index of the enormous social changes that marked these years. From the utilitarian suits of the forties, with their padded shoulders and severe lines, to the "New Look" of the fifties, with its long, full, aggressively feminine skirts and decorous Peter Pan blouses, the revealing miniskirts and flowing Indian prints of the sixties, the unisex costumes and pantsuits of the late sixties and early seventies, and the dress-for-success costumes of the eighties, women's fashions illustrated, successively, the austerity of the forties' war effort, the domestic conservatism of the fifties, the new sexual freedom of the sixties, and the emergence of reactions in the seventies and eighties against the eroticizing of women a decade or two earlier. No wonder, then, that an awareness of the rapidity of fashion's changes led to so-called retro dressing in the nineties and after, as women adopted and parodied styles from the past.

What intensified, perhaps even triggered, the debate about female sexual liberation that was enacted through these changes in costume was a series of major advances in birth control techniques. Beginning with the repeal in the 1940s and '50s of laws forbidding the public dissemination of information about contraception, birth control devices such as the condom and the diaphragm had become more widely available. The development in the 1960s of the birth control pill and the intrauterine device gave unmarried women the hope of a new morality no longer grounded in the threat of pregnancy and offered married women the possibility of genuine control over family size. In addition, even seemingly minor inventions such as tampons and beltless sanitary pads allowed women far greater flexibility in their activities. Thus, particularly in the 1960s, women may have seemed to be on the brink of an age of utopian sexuality in which desire could at last be expressed without dread.

Yet the new emphasis on sex was often in its own way puritanical: simultaneous sexual climax was de rigueur, "good girls" always said yes, and proliferating sex manuals propounded efficient techniques for amorous encounters that reduced life between the sheets to a series of athletic events. As Barbara Ehrenreich has shown, with the legalization of pornography in the late 1950s, the sexual revolution began to seem like a specifically male revolution that, through such popular magazines as *Playboy* and *Penthouse*, expounded a hedonistic philosophy that turned women into consumable luxury goods. When hard-core pornographic films, journals, and books in the 1970s began to emphasize the bondage and discipline of women along with "kiddy porn," a number of female thinkers became radically disaffected. Their alienation was increased by their recognition that despite the apparently enlightened rhetoric of the era, social problems such as child abuse, wife beating, and rape continued unabated. At the beginning of the twenty-first century, in fact, a rape occurred every six minutes in the United States. And the AIDS pandemic, which took its tragic toll globally, made clear that sexual liberation was no longer identical with women's liberation.

As early as 1963, Betty Friedan's *The Feminine Mystique* had begun to define the difficulties fostered by the cult of suburban domesticity that had marked the 1950s. Describing "the problem that has no name," Friedan excavated the feelings of almost metaphysical emptiness that were associated with the roles of housewife and consumer. At around the same time, moreover, women involved in the civil rights movement (and soon thereafter in the antiwar movement) were discovering that their revolutionary energies were mainly taken up by making coffee and love. These women turned not only to Friedan's book but also to earlier works—notably Simone de Beauvoir's *The Second Sex* (1949)—and began to produce theoretical writings of their own. Together, Mary Ellmann's *Thinking about Women* (1968), Kate Millett's *Sexual Politics* (1970), Shulamith Firestone's *The Dialectic of Sex* (1970), and Germaine Greer's *The Female Eunuch* (1970) sought to rescue liberationist arguments for female freedom from the sexual exploitation that their authors believed to be implicit in male-dominated radical movements.

At the same time, activists who had gained recognition by participating in public demonstrations began to issue manifestos, even as they helped popularize so-called consciousness-raising groups (small gatherings of women who met to discuss the effects of gender on their lives). In England, militants articulated "the 7 demands of The Women's Liberation Movement": "1. Equal pay, 2. Equal education and job opportunities, 3. Free contraception and abortion on demand, 4. Free twenty-four-hour nurseries under community control, 5. Legal and financial independence, 6. An end to discrimination against lesbians, 7. Freedom from intimidation by . . . assumptions and institutions that perpetuate male dominance." In America, similar demands were formulated by such groups as the Redstockings, SCUM (Society for Cutting Up Men), and the Feminists, which positioned themselves to the left of the National Organization for Women, founded by Betty Friedan in 1966; more moderate women also welcomed the magazine *Ms.*, which began publication in 1972 under the editorship of the journalist Gloria Steinem. In addition, in many English-speaking countries, grassroots projects were founded in these years: child care centers, women's health collectives, abortion clinics, and rape crisis hotlines and centers, as well as shelters for battered women and abused children.

Politically, this sort of activity had a long history. In the United States, the League of Women Voters had evolved out of the National Woman's Suffrage Association shortly after women gained the vote in 1920. But the first significant political gesture made by feminists and their supporters after the passage of the Nineteenth Amendment was the campaign for congressional approval and state ratification of the Equal Rights Amendment, an amendment to the Constitution declaring that "equality of rights under the law shall not be denied or abridged by the United States or by any State on account of sex"; the language was first introduced by Alice Paul in 1923. Until 1970, both organized labor and women's leaders had opposed the ERA on the grounds that it threatened protective legislation for working women. But in 1970, Elizabeth D. Koontz, the first black woman to head the U.S. Department of Labor Women's Bureau in Washington, arranged for the bureau to support the amendment; it was easily passed by Congress in 1972 and shortly thereafter ratified by several dozen states. But the ERA then encountered powerful opposition from very different quarters. Led by Phyllis Schlafly, a conservative Republican, women anxious about their rights as wives and their protection as members of the second sex joined with religious fundamentalists and other upholders of traditional family structures to claim that the amendment would bring about social chaos. Despite prolonged and arduous efforts by feminists, the ERA failed to win approval in the necessary minimum of thirty-eight states by 1982, the deadline year by which it would have had to be ratified to become law.

That so many women mobilized to oppose what had been defined as their own liberation dramatizes the anxieties raised by the women's movement. The conservative antifeminist Phyllis Schlafly spoke not only for women who wished to preserve the prerogatives of suburban consumerism but also for women who felt empowered by precisely the fetishizing of female sexuality that had characterized the midcentury. The seductive wife described in Marabel Morgan's *The Total Woman* (1973) sought to guarantee her own emotional and material security through strategies of submissiveness and enticement. Moreover, even the world leaders Evita Perón, Indira Gandhi, and Margaret Thatcher—women who had managed what seemed astonishing rises to political power—publicly endorsed Schlafly's ways of thinking, if not Morgan's. At the other end of the spectrum, a significant percentage of working-class women in low-paying jobs questioned feminist ideals of female autonomy.

Despite these controversies, however, an awareness of women's complex cultural situation grew, in part because of the development of women's studies in colleges and universities. Humanists (historians, literary critics, and philosophers), social scientists (anthropologists, psychologists, sociologists, linguists, and economists), and scholars of the fine arts (art historians, musicologists, theater historians, and film critics) joined during the 1970s and 1980s to undertake interdisciplinary investigations of women's role in history and society, analyses that sought to transform traditional disciplines and curricula. Founding such journals as *Signs, Feminist Studies,* and the *International Journal of Women's Studies,* they explored not only the gender pressures all women seemed to share but also the distinctive perspectives that marked the lives of disparate groups and cultures—African Americans, lesbians, Chicanas, working-class women, and others. To be sure, many experienced themselves as marginalized. Yet by the end of the twentieth century they had set in place major and minor programs for undergraduates in many colleges and universities as well as a number of graduate programs. Their academic endeavors coincided with an era when women were striving to bring about a number of other large social and ideological changes. In literary criticism, for instance, feminist scholars unearthed and analyzed a tradition of female artistic achievement at just the moment when contemporary women writers were sometimes consciously and sometimes unconsciously extending that tradition into the future.

WOMEN'S WRITING

Whether they defined themselves as feminists or not, women writers after 1940 wrote out of a double consciousness: on the one hand, a newly intense awareness of their role as female artists who had inherited an increasingly strong tradition and, on the other hand, a newly protective sense of their vulnerability as women who inhabited a culture hostile to female ambition and haunted by eroticized images of women. Certainly both these strands of thought came together in Adrienne Rich's "When We Dead Awaken: Writing as Re-Vision" (1972), an essay that might be said to have functioned as a kind of manifesto for both female writers and feminist critics in these years. Criticizing "the use that the male artist and thinker . . . has made of women, in his life and in his work," Rich resurrected foremothers from Virginia Woolf to Marianne Moore, explaining that "re-vision" of both male imperatives and female predecessors was "for women more than a chapter in cultural history: it is an act of survival."

In their various ways, many contemporaries of this notable American feminist were engaged in comparable acts of survival. Essays such as Tillie Olsen's "One Out of Twelve" (1972) and Joanna Russ's "What Can a Heroine Do?" (1972); poems such as Muriel Rukeyser's "Myth" (1973), Denise Levertov's "Hypocrite Women" (1964), and Sylvia Plath's "Stings" (1965); and stories such as Doris Lessing's "One off the Short List" (1958) and Jeanette Winterson's "The Poetics of Sex" (1994) articulate or enact a deep resistance to male-created social strictures and structures. At the same time, such essays as Alice Walker's "In Search of Our Mothers' Gardens" (1974) and Paule Marshall's "Poets in the Kitchen" (1983) express a deep identification with literal or literary mothers. In coming to terms with both the male and female forces that shaped them, contemporary writers were consistently struggling to define the cultural strains that had formed their personal and artistic identities.

A search for the roots of selfhood was perhaps especially urgent for women writers in third world and Commonwealth countries, and for writers who inhabited racial, ethnic, and lesbian subcultures in England or America. Though all these authors had in common the medium of the English language, with its comparatively fixed grammatical and lexical conventions, they were influenced by distinctive traits and traditions to use English in very different ways and for notably different ends. Tillie Olsen captured the inflections of an immigrant Russian Jew in "Tell Me a Riddle" (1961) and Gloria Anzaldúa composed an English infused with Spanish phrases and rhythms as well as with Mexican images. Writers with such disparate backgrounds as the African Ama Ata Aidoo, the Asian American Maxine Hong Kingston, the black lesbian Audre Lorde, and the Native American Leslie Marmon Silko filtered their stories of significant ethnicity through an English language that registered diverse cultural and sexual heritages. Indeed, artists with what came to be called hyphenated identities—Jamaica Kincaid, Louise Erdrich, Marilyn Chin, Jhumpa Lahiri—attained extraordinary prominence and, in the process, altered the conventional mappings of the aesthetic geography of the West. At the same time, Canadian and Irish women writers—Anne Carson, Eavan Boland, and Medbh McGuckian, for example—received both national and international acclaim.

By simultaneously defining or redefining both themselves and their worlds, such women indicated the general parameters of female writing in this period, for the motivating impulse behind the works of contemporary women of letters can often be located along a continuum that reaches from self-definition to social criticism. Taking the real or figurative self as a subject, the writers whose work depended on processes of self-definition tended to explore not only the dynamics but also the dreams of subjectivity itself. Remembering in "In the Waiting Room" (1976) how she had learned that she was "an *Elizabeth*," Elizabeth Bishop can stand as a model for the poets Sylvia Plath, Diane Wakoski, Denise Levertov, Audre Lorde, and Ruth Stone, all of whom struggled to articulate—in Levertov's words—"what, woman, and who, myself, I am" ("Stepping Westward," 1967). Clearly, the diarists and memoirists Anaïs Nin, Maya Angelou, and Mary McCarthy shared this project, but, less obviously, so did fiction writers as diverse as Carson McCullers, Angela Carter, and A. S. Byatt.

In a quite different mode, those artists who took a real or imagined society as their subject set out, often in a strikingly realistic manner, to describe the world that circumscribes the self. Gwendolyn Brooks's Chicago "bean eaters," Flannery O'Connor's Georgia country people, Stevie Smith's cartoon Britons, Rita Dove's nineteenth-century slaves, and Nadine Gordimer's white South Africans inhabit markedly different landscapes, yet all their creators explored the everyday worlds in which such characters were situated to construct an almost sociological analysis of the relationship between the individual and her community. To be sure, many contemporary writers oscillated between both these modes, for—as most would have agreed—to know the society *is* to know the self. Even a tale about interracial friendship like Toni Morrison's "Recitatif" (1983) and a literary critical essay like her "Unspeakable Things Unspoken" (1989), with their implicit indictment of the ways in which white dominance warps the lives of African Americans, can be said also to constitute fables of identity, acts of self-examination as well as of social analysis.

In this respect, Morrison is representative of her peers, although contemporary writers are a highly diverse group. "Diversity," in fact, became a feminist theme toward the end of the twentieth century, with many women writers exploring and dramatizing their national, economic, linguistic, regional, ethnic, religious, and political divergences along with their differing sexual preferences, their disparate stances regarding earlier aesthetic traditions, their attractions to a broad spectrum of genres, and their complicated attitudes toward various feminist projects. Significantly, Caryl Churchill's play *Top Girls* (1982) opens with a surrealistic dinner party attended by women from markedly different economic, linguistic, regional, ethnic, religious, and even historical backgrounds. During the 1980s and 1990s, this emphasis among literary women on their distinctive backgrounds paralleled (and was sometimes associated with) the evolution of a range of innovative academic disciplines and methodologies, including African American, Asian American, Chicano, and Native American studies, as well as postcolonial criticism and gay studies. The increasingly notable presence of such new interdisciplinary fields shifted the emphases of many feminist critics, a number of whom began examining multiple aspects of women's cultural experiences. At the same time, the very term *woman* came under scrutiny, as some gender theorists proposed that female roles should be understood as fictive or artificial concepts and as some argued that "femininity" itself should be viewed as merely a performance of societal stereotypes. In particular, Judith Butler employed the poststructuralist approach of Michel Foucault to advance the idea that women, like men, are socially constructed to perform masquerades that only seem to make gender *appear* to be natural.

A term like *poststructuralism* might hint at widespread cultural feelings of belatedness or at least confusion; yet as the sometimes heated discussions of feminists suggest and as the writings of women around the world reveal, female literary traditions remained vital and were often characterized by exciting experimentation. Long and interconnected poetic sequences, prose that slides into poetry, autobiography with the features of fiction, fairy tales written in the Gothic mode: many women's productions manifest a transgressive exuberance. What critics and artists continued to share is a determination to examine the interdependence of the private female self and the public world. From this last perspective, Adrienne Rich's celebration of a woman as an icon of the future—her vision of the woman "who must be more merciless to herself than history"—is resonant because it draws on a dream of social transformation to create an image of a transformed self. As Rich herself tells us in a number of her poems, it was her reading of feminist analyses of society that enabled her to convert the eroticized body of the 1950s and '60s into a luminous figure fully self-aware and self-possessed.

If we compare the section of this anthology in which Rich's work appears with the first section of the first volume of the anthology, we cannot fail to be struck by the complexity and energy of the voices raised in recent years to address questions that only a few medieval and Renaissance women had been able to formulate. Yet we have included here merely a representative selection of authors whose works reveal the new authority with which women are writing today. Nevertheless, the vigorous line of development we have been able to trace from the Middle Ages to the present suggests the ways in which by the end of the twentieth century women of letters no longer believed themselves to be what May Sarton in "My Sisters, O My Sisters" (1948) called "strange monsters." Instead, many female artists had already, in Sarton's words, "come to the deep place where poet becomes woman" while rejoicing in "that great sanity, that sun, the feminine power."

STEVIE SMITH
1902–1971

"Who and what is Stevie Smith? / Is she woman? Is she myth?" asked the American poet-humorist Ogden Nash in 1964, expressing awe at the ways in which this English writer was able "to sing at Man's expense / Songs of deadly innocence." Nash's praise is not surprising, for as a sardonic versifier Smith wrote comic poems significantly akin to his famously witty couplets; at the same time, both more mordant and (occasionally) more morbid than her American counterpart, she frequently achieved what the poet Robert Lowell called a "unique and cheerfully gruesome voice."

Born Florence Margaret Smith in Hull, Yorkshire, Smith (subsequently nicknamed "Stevie" after the famous jockey Steve Donohue, because she was very short) moved to London with her mother and sister when she was only three. There, in the unfashionable suburb of Palmers Green, she and her sister Molly were largely raised by an aunt (whom Smith affectionately called "Auntie Lion") because their father was frequently away and their mother's health was bad. After graduating from the North London Collegiate School for Girls, Smith became a secretary in the magazine publishing house of George Newnes, where she was to work for thirty years, from 1923 to 1953. Continuing to live, as she would all her life, with Auntie Lion, she began to publish both poetry and fiction when she was in her early thirties. *Novel on Yellow Paper; or, Work It Out for Yourself* appeared in 1936, succeeded by her first volume of verse, *A Good Time Was Had by All* (1937), and later followed by two more novels and more than ten other collections of poetry, including *Not Waving but Drowning* (1957) and *The Frog Prince and Other Poems* (1966).

Ranging from satiric melancholy to ferocious irony, Smith is often as sardonic about her own art as she is about the more general human foibles she critiques in such verses as "Our Bog Is Dood" and "How Cruel Is the Story of Eve." "My Muse sits forlorn / She wishes she had not been born," she once complained. At the same time, with comical high spirits she often caricatured the customs of a slowly declining British Empire, as she does in "This Englishwoman" and "Lord Barrenstock." Perhaps for this reason, it was some years before her American audience grew as large as her English readership. Yet by the time she was awarded the Queen's Gold Medal for Poetry in 1969, her "cheerfully gruesome voice" had been noted and appreciated in the United States. Sadly, she died of a brain tumor just when she had finally achieved the popularity she deserved. Yet her work still has a small but passionate audience, and her reputation has not faded. "Across the world I hear her still," declared Ogden Nash, "singing underneath the hill."

Papa Love Baby

My mother was a romantic girl
So she had to marry a man with his hair in curl
Who subsequently became my unrespected papa,
But that was a long time ago now.

5   What folly it is that daughters are always supposed to be
In love with papa. It wasn't the case with me
I couldn't take to him at all.
But he took to me
What a sad fate to befall

10 A child of three.
　　I sat upright in my baby carriage
　　And wished mama hadn't made such a foolish marriage.
　　I tried to hide it, but it showed in my eyes unfortunately
　　And a fortnight later papa ran away to sea.

15 He used to come home on leave
　　It was always the same
　　I could not grieve
　　But I think I was somewhat to blame.

　　　　　　　　　　　　　　　　　　　　　　1937

This Englishwoman

This Englishwoman is so refined
She has no bosom and no behind.

　　　　　　　　　　　　　　　　　　　　　　1937

Lord Barrenstock

Lord Barrenstock and Epicene,[1]
What's it to me that you have been
In your pursuit of interdicted[2] joys
Seducer of a hundred little boys?

5 Your sins are red about your head
And many people wish you dead.

You trod the widow in the mire
Wronged the son, deceived the sire.

You put a fence about the land
10 And made the people's cattle graze on sand.

Ratted from many a pool and forced amalgamation[3]
And dealt in shares which never had a stock exchange quotation.

Non flocci facio,[4] I do not care
For wrongs you made the other fellow bear:
15 'Tis not for these unsocial acts not these
I wet my pen. I would not have you tease,
With a repentance smug and overdue
For all the things you still desire to do,

---

1. Of indeterminate sex; an effeminate man. "Barrenstock": i.e., unable to produce children.
2. Forbidden.
3. I.e., cheated business associates.
4. I don't give a straw, I don't care (Latin).

The ears of an outraged divinity:
But oh your tie is crooked and I see
Too plain you had an éclair for your tea.

It is this nonchalance about your person—
That is the root of my profound aversion.

You are too fat. In spite of stays[5]
Your shape is painful to the polished gaze;
Your uncombed hair grows thin and daily thinner,
In fact you're far too ugly to be such a sinner.

Lord Barrenstock and Epicene, consider all that you have done
Lord Epicene and Barrenstock, yet not two Lords but one,
I think you are an object not of fear but pity
Be good, my Lord, since you cannot be pretty.[6]

1937

Dear Female Heart

Dear Female Heart, I am sorry for you,
You must suffer, that is all that you can do.
But if you like, in common with the rest of the human race,
You may also look most absurd with a miserable face.

1938

Souvenir de Monsieur Poop[1]

I am the self-appointed guardian of English literature,
I believe tremendously in the significance of age;
I believe that a writer is wise at 50,
Ten years wiser at 60, at 70 a sage.
I believe that juniors are lively, to be encouraged with discretion
    and snubbed,
I believe also that they are bouncing, communistic, ill mannered
    and, of course, young.
But I never define what I mean by youth
Because the word undefined is more useful for general purposes
    of abuse.
I believe that literature is a school where only those who apply
    themselves diligently to their tasks acquire merit.
And only they after the passage of a good many years (see above).
But then I am an old fogey.

---

5. Corsets.
6. An echo of Charles Kingsley's "A Farewell" (1856), "Be good, sweet maid, and let who will be clever."
1. Memory of Mister Poop (French).

I always write more in sorrow than in anger.[2]
I am, after all, devoted to Shakespeare, Milton,[3]
And, coming to our own times,
15   Of course
Housman.[4]
I have never been known to say a word against the established
    classics,
I am in fact devoted to the established classics.
In the service of literature I believe absolutely in the principle
    of division;
20 I divide into age groups and also into schools.
This is in keeping with my scholastic mind, and enables me to
    trounce
Not only youth
(Which might be thought intellectually frivolous by pedants)
    but also periodical tendencies,
To ventilate, in a word, my own political and moral philosophy.
25 (When I say that I am an old fogey, I am, of course, joking.)
English literature, as I see it, requires to be defended
By a person of integrity and essential good humor
Against the forces of fanaticism, idiosyncrasy and anarchy.
I perfectly apprehend the perilous nature of my convictions
30 And I am prepared to go to the stake
For Shakespeare, Milton,
And, coming to our own times,
Of course
Housman.
35 I cannot say more than that, can I?
And I do not deem it advisable, in the interests of the editor
    to whom I am spatially contracted,
To say less.

1938

Human Affection

Mother, I love you so.
Said the child, I love you more than I know.
She laid her head on her mother's arm,
And the love between them kept them warm.

1942

---

2. See Shakespeare's *Hamlet* 1.2.228–29.
3. John Milton (1608–1674), English poet best known for his blank-verse epic, *Paradise Lost* (1667, 1674).
4. A. E. Housman (1859–1936), English poet, writer of ballads and other traditional forms, and classical scholar.

The Wanderer[1]

Twas the voice of the Wanderer, I heard her exclaim,
You have weaned me too soon, you must nurse me again,
She taps as she passes at each window pane,
Pray, does she not know that she taps in vain?

Her voice flies away on the midnight wind,
But would she be happier if she were within?
She is happier far where the night winds fall,
And there are no doors and no windows at all.

No man has seen her, this pitiful ghost,
And no woman either, but heard her at most,
Sighing and tapping and sighing again,
You have weaned me too soon, you must nurse me again.

1950

Our Bog Is Dood

Our Bog is dood, our Bog is dood,
They lisped in accents mild,
But when I asked them to explain
They grew a little wild.
How do you know your Bog is dood
My darling little child?

We know because we wish it so
That is enough, they cried,
And straight within each infant eye
Stood up the flame of pride,
And if you do not think it so
You shall be crucified.

Then tell me, darling little ones,
What's dood, suppose Bog is?
Just what we think, the answer came,
Just what we think it is.
They bowed their heads. Our Bog is ours
And we are wholly his.

But when they raised them up again
They had forgotten me
Each one upon each other glared
In pride and misery

---

1. Compare "The Sluggard" (1715), a moral poem by Isaac Watts: "'Tis the voice of the sluggard; I heard him complain, / 'You have waked me too soon, I must slumber again.' / As the door on its hinges, so he on his bed, / Turns his sides and his shoulders and his heavy head." See also Lewis Carroll's parody of Watts, "'Tis the Voice of the Lobster," in *Alice's Adventures in Wonderland* (1865).

>   For what was dood, and what their Bog
>   They never could agree.
>
> 25   Oh sweet it was to leave them then,
>   And sweeter not to see,
>   And sweetest of all to walk alone
>   Beside the encroaching sea,
>   The sea that soon should drown them all,
> 30   That never yet drowned me.

1950

Lightly Bound

You beastly child, I wish you had miscarried,
You beastly husband, I wish I had never married.
You hear the north wind riding fast past the window? He calls me.
Do you suppose I shall stay when I can go so easily?

1950

Not Waving but Drowning

>   Nobody heard him, the dead man,
>   But still he lay moaning:
>   I was much further out than you thought
>   And not waving but drowning.
>
> 5   Poor chap, he always loved larking
>   And now he's dead
>   It must have been too cold for him his heart gave way,
>   They said.
>
>   Oh, no no no, it was too cold always
> 10   (Still the dead one lay moaning)
>   I was much too far out all my life
>   And not waving but drowning.

1957

How Cruel Is the Story of Eve[1]

>   How cruel is the story of Eve
>   What responsibility
>   It has in history
>   For cruelty.

---

1. According to the Hebrew Bible, Eve was the first woman, created by God from a rib belonging to Adam, the first man. There is a long tradition of blaming Eve for the Fall into sin, because first she, then Adam ate the forbidden fruit of the tree of knowledge. God punished them by bringing death into the world as well as pain in childbirth, male work, and female submission (Genesis 2–3).

5   Touch, where the feeling is most vulnerable,
    Unblameworthy—ah reckless—desiring children,
    Touch there with a touch of pain?
    Abominable.

    Ah what cruelty,
10 In history
    What misery.

    Put up to barter
    The tender feelings
    Buy her a husband to rule her
15 Fool her to marry a master
    She must or rue it
    The Lord said it.

    And man, poor man,
    Is he fit to rule,
20 Pushed to it?
    How can he carry it, the governance,
    And not suffer for it
    Insuffisance?[2]

    He must make woman lower then
25 So he can be higher then.
    Oh what cruelty,
    In history what misery.

    Soon woman grows cunning
    Masks her wisdom,
30 How otherwise will he
    Bring food and shelter, kill enemies?
    If he did not feel superior
    It would be worse for her
    And for the tender children
35 Worse for them.

    Oh what cruelty,
    In history what misery
    Of falsity.

    It is only a legend
40 You say? But what
    Is the meaning of the legend
    If not
    To give blame to women most
    And most punishment?

45 This is the meaning of a legend that colors
    All human thought; it is not found among animals.

---

2. Insufficiency, personal incompetence (an obsolete word).

How cruel is the story of Eve,
What responsibility it has
In history
50   For misery.

Yet there is this to be said still:
Life would be over long ago
If men and women had not loved each other
Naturally, naturally,
55   Forgetting their mythology
They would have died of it else
Long ago, long ago,
And all would be emptiness now
And silence.

60   Oh dread Nature, for your purpose,
To have made them love so.

1966

ANAÏS NIN
1903–1977

In a passage from her critical book *The Novel of the Future* (1968), which typifies the introspective quality of her famous *Diary*, Anaïs Nin analyzed the origins of her creativity: the "traumatic genesis" occurred when she was nine years old and what later turned out to be an incorrect medical diagnosis that she would never walk again turned her to writing as a pastime; the "artistic genesis" of her *Diary* was her separation from her father, for she recorded her impressions "to persuade my absent father to return." The self-absorption of much of Nin's work reflects her lifelong effort to explore her sense of difference and of separation. Her father, a Spanish pianist and composer, had taken her with him on his concert tours throughout Europe. But when her parents separated, the eleven-year-old girl and her two brothers left their native Paris for New York, where they lived with their mother, a French-Danish singer. Nin did not return to Paris until the 1930s, after her marriage to the banker Hugh Guiler. Under the name Ian Hugo, her husband later became an illustrator of her books, but she remained surprisingly reticent about him and their relationship. Indeed, for all of the self-scrutiny of her work, Nin fashioned an image of her life to demonstrate that "it is not only the woman Anaïs who has to speak, but I who have to speak for many women."

Nin's first book, a critical evaluation of the novelist D. H. Lawrence, displayed the emotional sensitivity that would continue to characterize her writing. While composing it, the twenty-eight-year-old met Henry Miller, who was drafting both *Tropic of Cancer* (1934) and his own essay on D. H. Lawrence. Like Lawrence, Nin and Miller perceived themselves as pioneers in a sexual revolution and, while Nin explored how—as a woman—she could not accept Miller's male-dominated perspective, both artists produced fiction about the nature of eroticism. Nin's other friends were just as fascinated by the relationship between identity and sexuality: they included Henry

Miller's wife, June Miller; the surrealist poet Antonin Artaud; the novelist Lawrence Durrell; and the well-known psychiatrist Dr. Otto Rank, with whom Nin studied.

Although she was forced to leave Europe at the outbreak of World War II, Nin continued her journal in America, where she responded to the difficulty she experienced in getting her work published by buying a printing press. The *Diary* first received serious critical attention in 1966, when it began to be printed by Alan Swallow. It constitutes an extraordinary effort "to capture the living moments" of her emotional reactions to experience, an effort that Miller had earlier compared to the literary self-revelations of St. Augustine, Petronius, Abelard, Rousseau, and Proust. The *Diaries* were significantly complemented and supplemented by a series of lyrical prose fictions in which Nin reworked and objectified much of her personal experience. In particular, the sequence of novels called *Cities of the Interior* (1946–58, published in one vol. in 1959)—*Ladders to Fire, Children of the Albatross, The Four-Chambered Heart, A Spy in the House of Love,* and *Seduction of the Minotaur*— extended her exploration of the female psyche in lyrical language that attempts to capture the fluid formations and reformations of the self. With unusual candor, "Birth" recounts the painful consciousness born during a labor destined never to give birth to life.

Birth

"The child," said the doctor, "is dead."

I lay stretched on a table. I had no place on which to rest my legs. I had to keep them raised. Two nurses leaned over me. In front of me stood the doctor with the face of a woman and eyes protruding with anger and fear. For two hours I had been making violent efforts. The child inside of me was six months old and yet it was too big for me. I was exhausted, the veins in me were swelling with the strain. I had pushed with my entire being. I had pushed as if I wanted this child out of my body and hurled into another world.

"Push, push with all your strength!"

Was I pushing with all my strength? All my strength?

No. A part of me did not want to push out the child. The doctor knew it. That is why he was angry, mysteriously angry. He knew. A part of me lay passive, did not want to push out anyone, not even this dead fragment of myself, out in the cold, outside of me. All in me which chose to keep, to lull, to embrace, to love, all in me which carried, preserved, and protected, all in me which imprisoned the whole world in its passionate tenderness, this part of me would not thrust out the child, even though it had died in me. Even though it threatened my life, I could not break, tear out, separate, surrender, open and dilate and yield up a fragment of a life like a fragment of the past, this part of me rebelled against pushing out the child, or anyone, out in the cold, to be picked up by strange hands, to be buried in strange places, to be lost, lost, lost.... He knew, the doctor. A few hours before he adored me, served me. Now he was angry. And I was angry with a black anger at this part of me which refused to push, to separate, to lose.

"Push! Push! Push with all your strength!"

I pushed with anger, with despair, with frenzy, with the feeling that I would die pushing, as one exhales the last breath, that I would push out everything inside of me, and my soul with all the blood around it, and the sinews with my heart inside of them, choked, and that my body itself would open and smoke would rise, and I would feel the ultimate incision of death.

The nurses leaned over me and they talked to each other while I rested. Then I pushed until I heard my bones cracking, until my veins swelled. I closed my eyes so hard I saw lightning and waves of red and purple. There was a stir in my ears, a beating as if the tympanum[1] would burst. I closed my lips so tightly the blood was trickling. My legs felt enormously heavy, like marble columns, like immense marble columns crushing my body. I was pleading for someone to hold them. The nurse laid her knee on my stomach and shouted: "Push! Push! Push!" Her perspiration fell on me.

The doctor paced up and down angrily, impatiently. "We will be here all night. Three hours now. . . ."

The head was showing, but I had fainted. Everything was blue, then black. The instruments were gleaming before my eyes. Knives sharpened in my ears. Ice and silence. Then I heard voices, first talking too fast for me to understand. A curtain was parted, the voices still tripped over each other, falling fast like a waterfall, with sparks, and cutting into my ears. The table was rolling gently, rolling. The women were lying in the air. Heads. Heads hung where the enormous white bulbs of the lamps were hung. The doctor was still walking, the lamps moved, the heads came near, very near, and the words came more slowly.

They were laughing. Once nurse was saying: "When I had my first child I was all ripped to pieces. I had to be sewn up again, and then I had another, and had to be sewn up, and then I had another. . . ."

The other nurse said: "Mine passed like an envelope through a letter box. But afterwards the bag[2] would not come out. The bag would not come out. Out. Out. . . ." Why did they keep repeating themselves. And the lamps turning. And the steps of the doctor very fast, very fast.

"She can't labor any more, at six months nature does not help. She should have another injection."

I felt the needle thrust. The lamps were still. The ice and the blue that was all around came into my veins. My heart beat wildly. The nurses talked: "Now that baby of Mrs. L. last week, who would have thought she was too small, a big woman like that, a big woman like that, a big woman like that. . . ." The words kept turning, as on a disk. They talked, they talked, they talked. . . .

Please hold my legs! Please hold my legs! Please hold my legs! PLEASE HOLD MY LEGS! I am ready again. By throwing my head back I can see the clock. I have been struggling four hours. It would be better to die. Why am I alive and struggling so desperately? I could not remember why I should want to live. I could not remember anything. Everything was blood and pain. I have to push. I have to push. That is a black fixed point in eternity. At the end of a long dark tunnel. I have to push. A voice saying: "Push! Push! Push!" A knee on my stomach and the marble of my legs crushing me and the head so large and I have to push.

Am I pushing or dying? The light up there, the immense round blazing white light is drinking me. It drinks me slowly, inspires me into space. If I

---

1. Eardrum.   2. I.e., the placenta.

do not close my eyes it will drink all of me. I seep upward, in long icy threads, too light, and yet inside there is a fire too, the nerves are twisted, there is no rest from this long tunnel dragging me, or am I pushing myself out of the tunnel, or is the child being pushed out of me, or is the light drinking me. Am I dying? The ice in the veins, the cracking of the bones, this pushing in darkness, with a small shaft of light in the eyes like the edge of a knife, the feeling of a knife cutting the flesh, the flesh somewhere is tearing as if it were burned through by a flame, somewhere my flesh is tearing and the blood is spilling out. I am pushing in the darkness, in utter darkness. I am pushing until my eyes open and I see the doctor holding a long instrument which he swiftly thrusts into me and the pain makes me cry out. A long animal howl. That will make her push, he says to the nurse. But it does not. It paralyzes me with pain. He wants to do it again. I sit up with fury and I shout at him: "Don't you dare do that again, don't you dare!"

The heat of my anger warms me, all the ice and pain are melted in the fury. I have an instinct that what he has done is unnecessary, that he has done it because he is in a rage, because the hands on the clock keep turning, the dawn is coming and the child does not come out, and I am losing strength and the injection does not produce the spasm.

I look at the doctor pacing up and down, or bending to look at the head which is barely showing. He looks baffled, as before a savage mystery, baffled by this struggle. He wants to interfere with his instruments, while I struggle with nature, with myself, with my child and with the meaning I put into it all, with my desire to give and to hold, to keep and to lose, to live and to die. No instrument can help me. His eyes are furious. He would like to take a knife. He has to watch and wait.

I want to remember all the time why I should want to live. I am all pain and no memory. The lamp has ceased drinking me. I am too weary to move even towards the light, or to turn my head and look at the clock. Inside of my body there are fires, there are bruises, the flesh is in pain. The child is not a child, it is a demon strangling me. The demon lies inert at the door of the womb, blocking life, and I cannot rid myself of it.

The nurses begin to talk again. I say: let me alone. I put my two hands on my stomach and very softly, with the tips of my fingers, I drum drum drum drum drum drum on my stomach in circles. Around, around, softly, with eyes open in great serenity. The doctor comes near with amazement on his face. The nurses are silent. Drum drum drum drum drum drum in soft circles, soft quiet circles. Like a savage. The mystery. Eyes open, nerves begin to shiver, . . . a mysterious agitation. I hear the ticking of the clock . . . inexorably, separately. The little nerves awake, stir. But my hands are so weary, so weary, they will fall off. The womb is stirring and dilating. Drum drum drum drum drum. I am ready! The nurse presses her knee on my stomach. There is blood in my eyes. A tunnel. I push into this tunnel, I bite my lips and push. There is a fire and flesh ripping and no air. Out of the tunnel! All my blood is spilling out. Push! Push! Push! It is coming! It is coming! It is coming! I feel the slipperiness, the sudden deliverance, the weight is gone. Darkness. I hear voices. I open my eyes. I hear them saying: "It was a little girl. Better not show it to her." All my strength returns. I sit up. The doctor shouts: "Don't sit up!"

"Show me the child!"

"Don't show it," says the nurse, "it will be bad for her."

The nurses try to make me lie down. My heart is beating so loud I can hardly hear myself repeating: "Show it to me." The doctor holds it up. It looks dark and small, like a diminutive man. But it is a little girl. It has long eyelashes on its closed eyes, it is perfectly made, and all glistening with the waters of the womb.

1938

DILYS LAING
1906–1960

"To be a woman and a writer / is double mischief," declared Dilys Laing in the sympathetic "Sonnet to a Sister in Error" that she addressed to the seventeenth-century poet Anne, countess of Winchilsea, adding, in a gesture of affiliation with the female literary tradition that would be repeated by countless women writers in the decades after her death, "Separate in time, we mutiny together." A pacifist as well as a protofeminist, Laing mutinied in many ways throughout her literary career. Born in Wales, raised in Canada, and educated in London, she married in 1936 and settled in Vermont, where she published poetry and fiction in such volumes of social protest as *Birth Is Farewell* (1944), *The Great Year* (1948), and *Walk through Two Landscapes* (1949). Appearing posthumously, her *Poems from a Cage* (1961) and *Collected Poems* (1967) further elaborate her sense of a God who is "woman-shaped" and who inspires the women "created . . . in Her own image" to "war on war." In a comic moment, she commented sardonically on the lessons of motherhood: "Women receive / the insults of men / with tolerance, / having been bitten / in the nipple / by their toothless gums."

Sonnet to a Sister in Error

> Whilst the dull manage of a servile house
> Is held by some our utmost art and use.
> —Anne, Countess of Winchilsea (1661–1720)[1]

Sweet Anne of Winchilsea, you were no hellion
intent on setting the broad world to rocking.
The long court dress concealed the long blue stocking,[2]
the easy manner masked the hard rebellion.
5   With light foot stirruped on the Muses' stallion[3]
you ambled privately, afraid of shocking
the Maids of Honor[4] who excelled at mocking
the matchless rose[5] with stitches small and million.

---

1. Quoted from "The Introduction" (1713; see Vol. 1, p. 238).
2. *Bluestocking* is a disparaging term for an intellectual or literary woman.
3. Pegasus; here a symbol of poetry.
4. Anne was maid of honor (an attendant) to the duchess of York.
5. A white rose was the badge of the house of York.

Staunch Anne! I know your trouble. The same tether
10 galls us. To be a woman and a writer
is double mischief, for the world will slight her
who slights "the servile house," and who would rather
make odes than beds. Lost lady! Gentle fighter!
Separate in time, we mutiny together.

1949

The Double Goer

The woman took a train
away away from herself.
She thought: I need a change
and wheels make revolutions.
5 I'm half a century old
and must be getting somewhere.
And so she futured on
away from her own presence.

The landscape boiled around her
10 like a pan of beans.
A man without a face
made her ticket holy.
Adventure thrilled her nerves
restless rapture shook her.
15 Love is in the next seat,
she mused, and strength and glory
are over the hill, and I
grow younger as I leave
my me behind.

20 The telephone wires were staves[1]
of a quintet score.
The hills were modulations
through the circle of keys.
Freedom is music, she thought,
25 smiling at the conductor.
This is your station, lady,
he snapped, and on the downbeat
she stepped to the vita nuova.[2]
A crowd had come to meet her
30 and they were fond in greeting:
husband, child, and father,
mother, and all the neighbors.

They travel as fast as I do,
she thought, and turned to climb

---

1. Horizontal lines on which music is written.
2. The new life (Italian); also the title of a collection of poems (ca. 1293) by Dante Alighieri, telling of his love for Beatrice.

³⁵ back to freedom's flying.
The door was shut. The train
streamed off like spilled water.

She faced the crowd and cried:
I love you all but one:
⁴⁰ the one who wears my face.
She is the one I fled from.

They said: You took her with you
and brought her back again.
You look sick. Welcome home.

1952

Let Them Ask Their Husbands

And if they will learn anything let them ask their husbands at home: for it is a shame for women to speak in the church.
—I Corinthians 14:35

In human need
of the familiar
I see God
woman-shaped

for God created
woman in Her own image
and I have
my Pauline[1] pride.

1957

Prayer of an Ovulating Female

I bring no throat-slit kid
no heart-scooped victim
no captive decapitated
and no self-scourged flesh.

⁵ I bring you, Domina,
Mother of women,
a calendula[1] in a pot
a candle and a peach
an egg and a
¹⁰ split condom.

---

1. St. Paul wrote 1 Corinthians.

1. An herb. "Domina": lady, mistress (Latin).

                Ave Mater
                Mulierum![2]
                may no blood flow
                nec in caelo
15   nec in terra[3]
                except according
                to the calendar.

                                                                ca. 1958

2. Hail Mother of Women! (Latin).   3. Neither in heaven nor on Earth (Latin).

DOROTHY LIVESAY
1909–1996

Dorothy Livesay's mother, Florence (Randal) Livesay, was a poet, journalist, and translator; her father, John F. B. Livesay, a former war correspondent, was a general manager of the Canadian Press. After receiving a B.A. from the University of Toronto and a Diplôme d'Études Supérieures from the Sorbonne, she studied social science at Toronto. Before and after she married Duncan MacNair in 1937, she was a social worker in Vancouver, but later she worked as a reporter for the *Toronto Daily Star*, as a documentary scriptwriter for the Canadian Broadcasting Corporation, as a UNESCO English specialist in Paris, as an English teacher in Northern Rhodesia, as an editor of Canadian literary journals and anthologies, and as a lecturer and writer-in-residence in many Canadian universities.

A widow with two children, Livesay described her work as "the evocation of the Canadian scene through the writing of lyrical and documentary poetry" and theorized that what she termed "documentary poetry"—verse that featured "a conscious attempt to create a dialectic between the objective facts and the subjective feelings of the poetry"—was a distinctively Canadian genre. As if to substantiate this thesis, for more than six decades she herself published prize-winning volumes of verse that combine frankly sensual and personal poems with more public, polemical works. Her early Imagistic volumes (*Green Pitcher*, 1928, and *Signpost*, 1932) were followed by the political poems in *Day and Night* (1944), works that analyzed the threats of poverty and fascism. In the 1950s and 1960s, when she had also established herself as a lyricist of intimacy, writing poems that focused on "love, marriage and its bonds, childbirth, childhood," she continued to stress "the need for peace in the world to give children a growing place." Continuing in this vein, she later published *The Self-Completing Tree: Selected Poems* (1986) as well as the memoirs *Right Hand Left Hand* (1977) and *Journey with My Selves: A Memoir, 1901–1963* (1991).

Green Rain

    I remember long veils of green rain
    Feathered like the shawl of my grandmother—
    Green from the half-green of the spring trees
    Waving in the valley.

5   I remember the road
    Like the one which leads to my grandmother's house,
    A warm house, with green carpets,
    Geraniums, a trilling canary
    And shining horse-hair chairs;
10 And the silence, full of the rain's falling
    Was like my grandmother's parlor
    Alive with herself and her voice, rising and falling—
    Rain and wind intermingled.

    I remember on that day
15 I was thinking only of my love
    And of my love's house.
    But now I remember the day
    As I remember my grandmother.
    I remember the rain as the feathery fringe of her shawl.

1932   1972

Eve[1]

         Beside the highway
            at the motel door
                it roots
            the last survivor of a pioneer
5   orchard
         miraculously   still
                    bearing.

         A thud another apple falls
                I stoop   and O
10   that scent, gnarled, ciderish
                    with sun in it
         that woody pulp
                    for teeth and tongue
                    to bite and curl around
15   that spurting juice
                    earth-sweet!

         In fifty seconds, fifty summers sweep
                    and shake me—
         I am alive!   can stand
20   up still
         hoarding this apple
                    in my hand.

1967   1972

---

1. As told in Genesis 3, Eve, the first woman, disobeyed God by eating a fruit (often identified with the apple) from the tree of knowledge.

The Three Emily's[1]

These women crying in my head
Walk alone, uncomforted:
The Emily's, these three
Cry to be set free—
5 And others whom I will not name
Each different, each the same.

Yet they had liberty!
Their kingdom was the sky:
They batted clouds with easy hand,
10 Found a mountain for their stand;
From wandering lonely they could catch
The inner magic of a heath—
A lake their palette, any tree
Their brush could be.

15 And still they cry to me
As in reproach—
I, born to hear their inner storm
Of separate man in woman's form,
I yet possess another kingdom, barred
20 To them, these three, this Emily.
I move as mother in a frame,
My arteries
Flow the immemorial way
Towards the child, the man;
25 And only for brief span
Am I an Emily on mountain snows
And one of these.

And so the whole that I possess
Is still much less—
30 They move triumphant through my head:
I am the one
Uncomforted.

1972

The Children's Letters

They are my secret food
consumed in the most hushed corners
of my room
when no one's looking
5 I hold them up to sunlight
at the window

---

1. Emily Brontë (1818–1848), English novelist and poet (see Vol. 1, p. 959); Emily Dickinson (1830–1886), American poet (see Vol. 1, p. 1037); and Emily Carr (1871–1945), Canadian painter.

        to see aright
        to hear behind the spindly words
        a child's tentative
10   first footsteps
        a small voice stuttering
                         at the sky
        "bird . . . bird. . . ."

        Whether these be
15   my children or my grandchildren
        they're ghostly visitors
        food of a solitary kind—
        they leap on shafts of sunlight
        through the mind's
20   shutters.

                                                           1972

EUDORA WELTY
1909–2001

"Without the love and belief my family gave me, I could not have become a writer to begin with," confessed Eudora Welty in an introduction to her *Collected Short Stories* (1980), adding, as if to argue that love begets further love, "I have been told, both in approval and in accusation, that I seem to love all my characters." In fact, Welty's work was consistently marked by a celebratory warmth—a sympathy for the deformed, the distorted, and even the demonic in human life, along with a loving insight into the trials and triumphs of daily living. From her earliest writings to her last stories, moreover, she was particularly notable for her creation of powerfully engaging women characters: such tales as "Why I Live at the P.O." (1941), "A Worn Path" (1941), and "The Wide Net" (1943), along with later stories like "The Bride of the Innisfallen" (1955) and "Circe" (1955), explored the varieties of female experience with grace and wit.

    The daughter of an Ohio-born father and a mother who was a native West Virginian, Welty was born and raised in Jackson, Mississippi, where she lived most of her life, in a rural Southern setting whose customs and convictions were as central to her work as they were to the writing of such other southern regionalists as William Faulkner and Flannery O'Connor. After attending Mississippi State College for Women from 1925 to 1927, Welty earned a B.A. in 1929 from the University of Wisconsin, then studied advertising for a year at Columbia University. Following her father's death in 1931, however, she resettled permanently in Jackson, where, throughout the 1930s, she worked for local newspapers, for the Jackson radio station, and for the WPA (the federally funded Works Progress Administration, which was created to give people jobs during the Great Depression). Her first collection of short fiction, *A Curtain of Green, and Other Stories*, was published in 1941, with an introduction by Katherine Anne Porter, whose "shining bounty," Welty once commented, "nourished my life." Subsequent volumes included the short-story collections *The Wide Net, and Other Stories* (1943) and *The Bride of the Innisfallen* (1955); the novels *The Robber Bridegroom* (1942), *Delta Wedding* (1946), *The Ponder Heart* (1954), and *The Optimist's Daughter* (for which Welty won the Pulitzer Prize in 1972); the memoir *One*

Writer's Beginnings (1984); and the critical works *The Eye of the Story* (1979) and *A Writer's Eye: Collected Book Reviews* (1994).

Though she was sometimes accused of not having "often taken the South's social turmoil as subject matter," Welty's long-standing concern for the crises of her culture is clearly revealed in *One Time, One Place* (1971), a collection of photographs of black and white sharecroppers and other workers in the Mississippi countryside that she had assembled when she was working with the WPA in the 1930s; in her delineation of Phoenix Jackson, the heroic black grandmother of "A Worn Path," who might well have stepped out of one of those pictures; and in her portrayal of the white assassin of Medgar Evers, who narrates the bitter story "Where Is the Voice Coming From?" (1963). Consistently sensitive and sympathetic to "the mind, heart, and skin" of human beings who are "not myself," Welty demonstrated in all her sometimes sorrowful, sometimes amused, but always loving fictions the intensity with which she adhered to her central belief: "It is the act of a writer's imagination that I set most high." In 1998, as she was nearing her ninetieth birthday, the Library of America honored her writerly imagination by publishing a two-volume set of her collected works, *Eudora Welty: Complete Novels* and *Eudora Welty: Stories, Essays, and Memoir*; she was the first living author to appear in this prestigious series of American masterpieces.

A Worn Path

It was December—a bright frozen day in the early morning. Far out in the country there was an old Negro woman with her head tied in a red rag, coming along a path through the pinewoods. Her name was Phoenix Jackson. She was very old and small and she walked slowly in the dark pine shadows, moving a little from side to side in her steps, with the balanced heaviness and lightness of a pendulum in a grandfather clock. She carried a thin, small cane made from an umbrella, and with this she kept tapping the frozen earth in front of her. This made a grave and persistent noise in the still air, that seemed meditative like the chirping of a solitary little bird.

She wore a dark striped dress reaching down to her shoe tops, and an equally long apron of bleached sugar sacks, with a full pocket: all neat and tidy, but every time she took a step she might have fallen over her shoelaces, which dragged from her unlaced shoes. She looked straight ahead. Her eyes were blue with age. Her skin had a pattern all its own of numberless branching wrinkles and as though a whole little tree stood in the middle of her forehead, but a golden color ran underneath, and the two knobs of her cheeks were illumined by a yellow burning under the dark. Under the red rag her hair came down on her neck in the frailest of ringlets, still black, and with an odor like copper.

Now and then there was a quivering in the thicket. Old Phoenix said, "Out of my way, all you foxes, owls, beetles, jack rabbits, coons and wild animals! . . . Keep out from under these feet, little bobwhites. . . . Keep the big wild hogs out of my path. Don't let none of those come running my direction. I got a long way." Under her small black-freckled hand her cane, limber as a buggy whip, would switch at the brush as if to rouse up any hiding things.

On she went. The woods were deep and still. The sun made the pine needles almost too bright to look at, up where the wind rocked. The cones dropped as light as feathers. Down in the hollow was the mourning dove—it was not too late for him.

The path ran up a hill. "Seem like there is chains about my feet, time I get this far," she said, in the voice of argument old people keep to use with themselves. "Something always take a hold of me on this hill—pleads I should stay."

After she got to the top she turned and gave a full, severe look behind her where she had come. "Up through pines," she said at length. "Now down through oaks."

Her eyes opened their widest, and she started down gently. But before she got to the bottom of the hill a bush caught her dress.

Her fingers were busy and intent, but her skirts were full and long, so that before she could pull them free in one place they were caught in another. It was not possible to allow the dress to tear. "I in the thorny bush," she said. "Thorns, you doing your appointed work. Never want to let folks pass, no sir. Old eyes thought you was a pretty little *green* bush."

Finally, trembling all over, she stood free, and after a moment dared to stoop for her cane.

"Sun so high!" she cried, leaning back and looking, while the thick tears went over her eyes. "The time getting all gone here."

At the foot of this hill was a place where a log was laid across the creek.

"Now comes the trial," said Phoenix.

Putting her right foot out, she mounted the log and shut her eyes. Lifting her skirt, leveling her cane fiercely before her, like a festival figure in some parade, she began to march across. Then she opened her eyes and she was safe on the other side.

"I wasn't as old as I thought," she said.

But she sat down to rest. She spread her skirts on the bank around her and folded her hands over her knees. Up above her was a tree in a pearly cloud of mistletoe. She did not dare to close her eyes, and when a little boy brought her a plate with a slice of marble-cake on it she spoke to him. "That would be acceptable," she said. But when she went to take it there was just her own hand in the air.

So she left that tree, and had to go through a barbed-wire fence. There she had to creep and crawl, spreading her knees and stretching her fingers like a baby trying to climb the steps. But she talked loudly to herself: she could not let her dress be torn now, so late in the day, and she could not pay for having her arm or her leg sawed off if she got caught fast where she was.

At last she was safe through the fence and risen up out in the clearing. Big dead trees, like black men with one arm, were standing in the purple stalks of the withered cotton field. There sat a buzzard.

"Who you watching?"

In the furrow she made her way along.

"Glad this not the season for bulls," she said, looking sideways, "and the good Lord made his snakes to curl up and sleep in the winter. A pleasure I don't see no two-headed snake coming around that tree, where it come once. It took a while to get by him, back in the summer."

She passed through the old cotton and went into a field of dead corn. It whispered and shook and was taller than her head. "Through the maze now," she said, for there was no path.

There was something tall, black, and skinny there, moving before her.

At first she took it for a man. It could have been a man dancing in the field. But she stood still and listened, and it did not make a sound. It was as silent as a ghost.

"Ghost," she said sharply, "who be you the ghost of? For I have heard of nary death close by."

But there was no answer—only the ragged dancing in the wind.

She shut her eyes, reached out her hand, and touched a sleeve. She found a coat and inside that an emptiness, cold as ice.

"You scarecrow," she said. Her face lighted. "I ought to be shut up for good," she said with laughter. "My senses is gone. I too old. I the oldest people I ever know. Dance, old scarecrow," she said, "while I dancing with you."

She kicked her foot over the furrow, and with mouth drawn down, shook her head once or twice in a little strutting way. Some husks blew down and whirled in streamers about her skirts.

Then she went on, parting her way from side to side with the cane, through the whispering field. At last she came to the end, to a wagon track where the silver grass blew between the red ruts. The quail were walking around like pullets, seeming all dainty and unseen.

"Walk pretty," she said. "This the easy place. This the easy going."

She followed the track, swaying through the quiet bare fields, through the little strings of trees silver in their dead leaves, past cabins silver from weather, with the doors and windows boarded shut, all like old women under a spell sitting there. "I walking in their sleep," she said, nodding her head vigorously.

In a ravine she went where a spring was silently flowing through a hollow log. Old Phoenix bent and drank. "Sweet-gum[1] makes the water sweet," she said, and drank more. "Nobody know who made this well, for it was here when I was born."

The track crossed a swampy part where the moss hung as white as lace from every limb. "Sleep on, alligators, and blow your bubbles." Then the track went into the road.

Deep, deep the road went down between the high green-colored banks. Overhead the live-oaks met, and it was as dark as a cave.

A black dog with a lolling tongue came up out of the weeds by the ditch. She was meditating, and not ready, and when he came at her she only hit him a little with her cane. Over she went in the ditch, like a little puff of milkweed.

Down there, her senses drifted away. A dream visited her, and she reached her hand up, but nothing reached down and gave her a pull. So she lay there and presently went to talking. "Old woman," she said to herself, "that black dog come up out of the weeds to stall you off, and now there he sitting on his fine tail, smiling at you."

A white man finally came along and found her—a hunter, a young man, with his dog on a chain.

"Well, Granny!" he laughed. "What are you doing there?"

"Lying on my back like a June-bug waiting to be turned over, mister," she said, reaching up her hand.

---

1. A tree in the witchhazel family.

He lifted her up, gave her a swing in the air, and set her down. "Anything broken, Granny?"

"No sir, them old dead weeds is springy enough," said Phoenix, when she had got her breath. "I thank you for your trouble."

"Where do you live, Granny?" he asked, while the two dogs were growling at each other.

"Away back yonder, sir, behind the ridge. You can't even see it from here."

"On your way home?"

"No sir, I going to town."

"Why, that's too far! That's as far as I walk when I come out myself, and I get something for my trouble." He patted the stuffed bag he carried, and there hung down a little closed claw. It was one of the bob-whites, with its beak hooked bitterly to show it was dead. "Now you go on home, Granny!"

"I bound to go to town, mister," said Phoenix. "The time come around."

He gave another laugh, filling the whole landscape. "I know you old colored people! Wouldn't miss going to town to see Santa Claus!"

But something held old Phoenix very still. The deep lines in her face went into a fierce and different radiation. Without warning, she had seen with her own eyes a flashing nickel fall out of the man's pocket onto the ground.

"How old are you, Granny?" he was saying.

"There is no telling, mister," she said, "no telling."

Then she gave a little cry and clapped her hand and said, "Git on away from here, dog! Look! Look at that dog!" She laughed as if in admiration. "He ain't scared of nobody. He a big black dog." She whispered, "Sic him!"

"Watch me get rid of that cur," said the man. "Sic him, Pete! Sic him!"

Phoenix heard the dogs fighting, and heard the man running and throwing sticks. She even heard a gunshot. But she was slowly bending forward by that time, further and further forward, the lids stretched down over her eyes, as if she were doing this in her sleep. Her chin was lowered almost to her knees. The yellow palm of her hand came out from the fold of her apron. Her fingers slid down and along the ground under the piece of money with the grace and care they would have in lifting an egg from under a setting hen. Then she slowly straightened up, she stood erect, and the nickel was in her apron pocket. A bird flew by. Her lips moved. "God watching me the whole time. I come to stealing."

The man came back, and his own dog panted about them. "Well, I scared him off that time," he said, and then he laughed and lifted his gun and pointed it at Phoenix.

She stood straight and faced him.

"Doesn't the gun scare you?" he said, still pointing it.

"No, sir, I seen plenty go off closer by, in my day, and for less than what I done," she said, holding utterly still.

He smiled, and shouldered the gun. "Well, Granny," he said, "you must be a hundred years old, and scared of nothing. I'd give you a dime if I had any money with me. But you take my advice and stay home, and nothing will happen to you."

"I bound to go on my way, mister," said Phoenix. She inclined her head in the red rag. Then they went in different directions, but she could hear the gun shooting again and again over the hill.

She walked on. The shadows hung from the oak trees to the road like curtains. Then she smelled wood-smoke, and smelled the river, and she saw a steeple and the cabins on their steep steps. Dozens of little black children whirled around her. There ahead was Natchez shining. Bells were ringing. She walked on.

In the paved city it was Christmas time. There were red and green electric lights strung and crisscrossed everywhere, and all turned on in the daytime. Old Phoenix would have been lost if she had not distrusted her eyesight and depended on her feet to know where to take her.

She paused quietly on the sidewalk where people were passing by. A lady came along in the crowd, carrying an armful of red-, green- and silver-wrapped presents; she gave off perfume like the red roses in hot summer, and Phoenix stopped her.

"Please, missy, will you lace up my shoe?" She held up her foot.

"What do you want, Grandma?"

"See my shoe," said Phoenix. "Do all right for out in the country, but wouldn't look right to go in a big building."

"Stand still then, Grandma," said the lady. She put her packages down on the sidewalk beside her and laced and tied both shoes tightly.

"Can't lace 'em with a cane," said Phoenix. "Thank you, missy. I doesn't mind asking a nice lady to tie up my shoe, when I gets out on the street."

Moving slowly and from side to side, she went into the big building, and into a tower of steps, where she walked up and around and around until her feet knew to stop.

She entered a door, and there she saw nailed up on the wall the document that had been stamped with the gold seal and framed in the gold frame, which matched the dream that was hung up in her head.

"Here I be," she said. There was a fixed and ceremonial stiffness over her body.

"A charity case, I suppose," said an attendant who sat at the desk before her.

But Phoenix only looked above her head. There was sweat on her face, the wrinkles in her skin shone like a bright net.

"Speak up, Grandma," the woman said. "What's your name? We must have your history, you know. Have you been here before? What seems to be the trouble with you?"

Old Phoenix only gave a twitch to her face as if a fly were bothering her.

"Are you deaf?" cried the attendant.

But then the nurse came in.

"Oh, that's just old Aunt Phoenix," she said. "She doesn't come for herself—she has a little grandson. She makes these trips just as regular as clockwork. She lives away back off the Old Natchez Trace."[2] She bent down. "Well, Aunt Phoenix, why don't you just take a seat? We won't keep you standing after your long trip." She pointed.

The old woman sat down, bolt upright in the chair.

"Now, how is the boy?" asked the nurse.

Old Phoenix did not speak.

"I said, how is the boy?"

But Phoenix only waited and stared straight ahead, her face very solemn and withdrawn into rigidity.

---

2. A 19th-century pioneer road between Natchez, Mississippi, and Nashville, Tennessee.

"Is his throat any better?" asked the nurse. "Aunt Phoenix, don't you hear me? Is your grandson's throat any better since the last time you came for the medicine?"

With her hands on her knees, the old woman waited, silent, erect and motionless, just as if she were in armor.

"You mustn't take up our time this way, Aunt Phoenix," the nurse said. "Tell us quickly about your grandson, and get it over. He isn't dead, is he?"

At last there came a flicker and then a flame of comprehension across her face, and she spoke.

"My grandson. It was my memory had left me. There I sat and forgot why I made my long trip."

"Forgot?" The nurse frowned. "After you came so far?"

Then Phoenix was like an old woman begging a dignified forgiveness for waking up frightened in the night. "I never did go to school, I was too old at the Surrender,"[3] she said in a soft voice. "I'm an old woman without an education. It was my memory fail me. My little grandson, he is just the same, and I forgot it in the coming."

"Throat never heals, does it?" said the nurse, speaking in a loud, sure voice to old Phoenix. By now she had a card with something written on it, a little list. "Yes. Swallowed lye. When was it?—January—two, three years ago—"

Phoenix spoke unasked now. "No, missy, he not dead, he just the same. Every little while his throat begin to close up again, and he not able to swallow. He not get his breath. He not able to help himself. So the time come around, and I go on another trip for the soothing medicine."

"All right. The doctor said as long as you came to get it, you could have it," said the nurse. "But it's an obstinate case."

"My little grandson, he sit up there in the house all wrapped up, waiting by himself," Phoenix went on. "We is the only two left in the world. He suffer and it don't seem to put him back at all. He got a sweet look. He going to last. He wear a little patch quilt and peep out holding his mouth open like a little bird. I remembers so plain now. I not going to forget him again, no, the whole enduring time. I could tell him from all the others in creation."

"All right." The nurse was trying to hush her now. She brought her a bottle of medicine. "Charity," she said, making a check mark in a book.

Old Phoenix held the bottle close to her eyes, and then carefully put it into her pocket.

"I thank you," she said.

"It's Christmas time, Grandma," said the attendant. "Could I give you a few pennies out of my purse?"

"Five pennies is a nickel," said Phoenix stiffly.

"Here's a nickel," said the attendant.

Phoenix rose carefully and held out her hand. She received the nickel and then fished the other nickel out of her pocket and laid it beside the new one. She stared at her palm closely, with her head on one side.

Then she gave a tap with her cane on the floor.

"This is what come to me to do," she said. "I going to the store and buy my child a little windmill they sells, made out of paper. He going to find it

---

3. I.e., the surrender of Robert E. Lee at Appomattox in 1865, which ended the Civil War.

hard to believe there such a thing in the world. I'll march myself back where he waiting, holding it straight up in this hand."

She lifted her free hand, gave a little nod, turned around, and walked out of the doctor's office. Then her slow step began on the stairs, going down.

1941

ELIZABETH BISHOP
1911–1979

"You sound like Lope de Vega and I sound like Jacob Abbot or Peter Rabbit," wrote the poet Marianne Moore in 1959 to her friend and admirer the poet Elizabeth Bishop. Self-deprecatingly comparing herself to a nineteenth-century American clergyman (Abbot) and a children's book character, Moore glowingly imagined Bishop as Spain's greatest Renaissance playwright: her compliment, if hyperbolical, was a measure of the esteem in which this writer was held by many contemporaries. The friend of—besides Moore—the poets Robert Lowell, Pablo Neruda, and Frank Bidart, Bishop achieved in her lifetime a distinctive reputation as, in the words of the critic Sibyl Estess, a "virtuoso of descriptive poetry." Since her death, however, her work has been increasingly seen as visionary and meditative, acute in its understated but powerful transcription of inner reality as well as accurate in its attention to external objects.

Born in Worcester, Massachusetts, Elizabeth Bishop was raised by two sets of grandparents in Nova Scotia and New England. Her father died when she was eight months old, and not long after that, her mother had to be hospitalized for mental illness; though at one point Bishop's maternal grandparents had hoped to bring their daughter home to recover, the poet's mother experienced a final breakdown when Elizabeth was five, an event that is recorded in the poignant story "In the Village" (1953), Bishop's semifictionalized account of her last encounter with her mother. A frail child who suffered from severe asthma and related allergies, the poet did not attend school regularly until she was sixteen, when she entered Walnut Hill School. By the time she enrolled at Vassar College at nineteen, however, she was a voracious reader and an aspiring writer. With several other undergraduates, including the novelist-to-be Mary McCarthy, she founded a literary magazine, *Con Spirito*; in addition, she began publishing poems and stories, some of them in nationally known periodicals; and perhaps most important, the year before her graduation she met and was befriended by Marianne Moore, who encouraged her to devote herself entirely to her writing, rather than attending medical school as she had planned.

After graduation from Vassar, Bishop traveled extensively, pursuing what one biographer has called a "nomadic" way of life that was to define the rest of her career and provide central metaphors for such volumes of poetry as *North & South* (1946), *Questions of Travel* (1965), and *Geography III* (1976). Her journeys were interrupted, however, for one long and quite significant period: between 1951 and 1966, she settled in Brazil, sharing a house in the mountains and an apartment in Rio de Janeiro with her longtime Brazilian lover, Lota Costellat de Macedo Soares, translating Brazilian poetry and producing a book about the country—*Brazil* (1962)—for the *Life* World Library series. After leaving Brazil, Bishop returned to the United States, where she taught, first, at the University of Washington and then, from 1969 until her retirement in 1977, at Harvard University.

Throughout her life, Bishop struggled both with the asthma that had afflicted her when she was a child and with intermittent bouts of alcoholism, which themselves tended to bring on further attacks of asthma. Despite these ongoing difficulties, however, she forged a career that was marked by numerous honors, including the Pulitzer Prize in 1956 and the National Book Award in 1970, and she always maintained an ironically understated yet passionately exact perspective on both her self and her society. Her commitments, both to friends and to ideas, were keen: though she had long defined herself as a feminist, for instance, she consistently refused what she considered the ghettoization implied by inclusion in anthologies of women's writing. (With the permission of Alice Methfessel, her literary executrix, we reprint here a quotation from a letter Bishop wrote in 1977, a passage that clarifies the poet's position on this matter.) Yet, as poems such as "Roosters" and "Pink Dog" reveal, Bishop was capable of composing fiercely sardonic feminist critiques of her society and as "Invitation to Miss Marianne Moore" suggests, she was intensely loyal to her major female literary mentor.

The works included here document the range as well as the precision of Bishop's art. Moving easily from the poignantly witty fantasy of "The Man-Moth" to the visionary realism of "The Fish," she also manages with ease and skill the autobiographical introspection of "In the Waiting Room" and the poignantly elegiac narrative of "First Death in Nova Scotia." In the face of considerable personal turmoil, she often created what the poet Alfred Corn has called "works of philosophic beauty and calm," and she consistently produced poems that may appear on the surface modest but that have had a major influence on much contemporary verse.

The Man-Moth[1]

    Here, above,
cracks in the buildings are filled with battered moonlight.
The whole shadow of Man is only as big as his hat.
It lies at his feet like a circle for a doll to stand on,
5   and he makes an inverted pin, the point magnetized to the moon.
He does not see the moon; he observes only her vast properties,
feeling the queer light on his hands, neither warm nor cold,
of a temperature impossible to record in thermometers.

    But when the Man-Moth
10 pays his rare, although occasional, visits to the surface,
the moon looks rather different to him. He emerges
from an opening under the edge of one of the sidewalks
and nervously begins to scale the faces of the buildings.
He thinks the moon is a small hole at the top of the sky,
15 proving the sky quite useless for protection.
He trembles, but must investigate as high as he can climb.

    Up the façades,
his shadow dragging like a photographer's cloth behind him,
he climbs fearfully, thinking that this time he will manage
20 to push his small head through that round clean opening
and be forced through, as from a tube, in black scrolls on the light.

---

1. Newspaper misprint for "mammoth" [Bishop's note].

    (Man, standing below him, has no such illusions.)
    But what the Man-Moth fears most he must do, although
    he fails, of course, and falls back scared but quite unhurt.

25   Then he returns
    to the pale subways of cement he calls his home. He flits,
    he flutters, and cannot get aboard the silent trains
    fast enough to suit him. The doors close swiftly.
    The Man-Moth always seats himself facing the wrong way
30 and the train starts at once at its full, terrible speed,
    without a shift in gears or a gradation of any sort.
    He cannot tell the rate at which he travels backwards.

        Each night he must
    be carried through artificial tunnels and dream recurrent dreams.
35 Just as the ties recur beneath his train, these underlie
    his rushing brain. He does not dare look out the window,
    for the third rail,[2] the unbroken draught of poison,
    runs there beside him. He regards it as a disease
    he has inherited the susceptibility to. He has to keep
40 his hands in his pockets, as others must wear mufflers.

        If you catch him,
    hold up a flashlight to his eye. It's all dark pupil,
    an entire night itself, whose haired horizon tightens
    as he stares back, and closes up the eye. Then from the lids
45 one tear, his only possession, like the bee's sting, slips.
    Slyly he palms it, and if you're not paying attention
    he'll swallow it. However, if you watch, he'll hand it over,
    cool as from underground springs and pure enough to drink.

                                                            1946

Roosters

        At four o'clock
        in the gun-metal blue dark
        we hear the first crow of the first cock

        just below
        the gun-metal blue window
5   and immediately there is an echo

        off in the distance,
        then one from the backyard fence,
        then one, with horrible insistence,

2. Allusion to the exposed and dangerous source of electric power on modern subways.

10   grates like a wet match
from the broccoli patch,
flares, and all over town begins to catch.

Cries galore
come from the water-closet[1] door,
15   from the dropping-plastered henhouse floor,

where in the blue blur
their rustling wives admire,
the roosters brace their cruel feet and glare

with stupid eyes
20   while from their beaks there rise
the uncontrolled, traditional cries.

Deep from protruding chests
in green-gold medals dressed,
planned to command and terrorize the rest,

25   the many wives
who lead hens' lives
of being courted and despised;

deep from raw throats
a senseless order floats
30   all over town. A rooster gloats

over our beds
from rusty iron sheds
and fences made from old bedsteads,

over our churches
35   where the tin rooster perches,
over our little wooden northern houses,

making sallies
from all the muddy alleys,
marking out maps like Rand McNally's:[2]

40   glass-headed pins,
oil-golds and copper greens,
anthracite blues, alizarins,[3]

each one an active
displacement in perspective;
45   each screaming, "This is where I live!"

---

1. A room containing a toilet.
2. Rand McNally publishes road maps and atlases.
3. Orange or red dyes.

Each screaming
"Get up! Stop dreaming!"
Roosters,[4] what are you projecting?

You, whom the Greeks elected
to shoot at on a post, who struggled
when sacrificed, you whom they labeled

"Very combative . . ."
what right have you to give
commands and tell us how to live,

cry "Here!" and "Here!"
and wake us here where are
unwanted love, conceit and war?

The crown of red
set on your little head
is charged with all your fighting blood.

Yes, the excrescence
makes a most virile presence,
plus all that vulgar beauty of iridescence.

Now in mid-air
by twos they fight each other.
Down comes a first flame-feather,

and one is flying,
with raging heroism defying
even the sensation of dying.

And one has fallen,
but still above the town
his torn-out, bloodied feathers drift down;

and what he sung
no matter. He is flung
on the gray ash-heap, lies in dung

with his dead wives
with open, bloody eyes,
while those metallic feathers oxidize.

St. Peter's sin
was worse than that of Magdalen
whose sin was of the flesh alone;[5]

---

4. In classical Greece, used in target practice, for sacrifice to the gods, and in highly popular cock-fighting contests.
5. I.e., prostitution; the Mary Magdalen healed of evil spirits by Jesus is traditionally identified with the prostitute who kisses and anoints his feet (Luke 8.2, 7.37–48). Peter was one of Christ's twelve apostles; shortly before his Crucifixion, Jesus prophesied that Peter would deny knowing him three times before the cock crowed (Luke 22.34). This prophecy was fulfilled after Jesus had been seized by the Romans (Luke 22.54–62).

of spirit, Peter's,
falling, beneath the flares,
among the "servants and officers."

85 Old holy sculpture[6]
could set it all together
in one small scene, past and future:

Christ stands amazed,
Peter, two fingers raised
90 to surprised lips, both as if dazed.

But in between
a little cock is seen
carved on a dim column in the travertine,

explained by *gallus canit*;
95 *flet Petrus*[7] underneath it.
There is inescapable hope, the pivot;

yes, and there Peter's tears
run down our chanticleer's[8]
sides and gem his spurs.

100 Tear-encrusted thick
as a medieval relic
he waits. Poor Peter, heart-sick,

still cannot guess
those cock-a-doodles yet might bless,
105 his dreadful rooster come to mean forgiveness,

a new weathervane
on basilica and barn,
and that outside the Lateran[9]

there would always be
110 a bronze cock on a porphyry
pillar so the people and the Pope might see

that even the Prince
of the Apostles[1] long since
had been forgiven, and to convince

115 all the assembly
that "Deny deny deny"
is not all the roosters cry.

---

6. This sculpture was carved ca. 400 C.E. and is now in the Vatican.
7. The cock crows; Peter weeps (Latin).
8. I.e., rooster's.
9. The cathedral in Rome where the pope presides. "Basilica": church.
1. Peter was "prince," taking precedence over the other apostles, because he was named by Jesus the founder of his church (Matthew 16.18–19; John 21.15–17).

In the morning
a low light is floating
120 in the backyard, and gilding

from underneath
the broccoli, leaf by leaf;
how could the night have come to grief?

gilding the tiny
125 floating swallow's belly
and lines of pink cloud in the sky,

the day's preamble
like wandering lines in marble.
The cocks are now almost inaudible.

130 The sun climbs in,
following "to see the end,"[2]
faithful as enemy, or friend.

1946

The Fish

I caught a tremendous fish
and held him beside the boat
half out of water, with my hook
fast in a corner of his mouth.
5 He didn't fight.
He hadn't fought at all.
He hung a grunting weight,
battered and venerable
and homely. Here and there
10 his brown skin hung in strips
like ancient wallpaper,
and its pattern of darker brown
was like wallpaper:
shapes like full-blown roses
15 stained and lost through age.
He was speckled with barnacles,
fine rosettes of lime,
and infested
with tiny white sea-lice,
20 and underneath two or three
rags of green weed hung down.
While his gills were breathing in
the terrible oxygen
—the frightening gills,

---

2. Matthew 26.58 (referring to Peter, who watched Jesus' condemnation by the high priest before denying him).

25 fresh and crisp with blood,
    that can cut so badly—
    I thought of the coarse white flesh
    packed in like feathers,
    the big bones and the little bones,
30 the dramatic reds and blacks
    of his shiny entrails,
    and the pink swim bladder
    like a big peony.
    I looked into his eyes
35 which were far larger than mine
    but shallower, and yellowed,
    the irises backed and packed
    with tarnished tinfoil
    seen through the lenses
40 of old scratched isinglass.[1]
    They shifted a little, but not
    to return my stare.
    —It was more like the tipping
    of an object toward the light.
45 I admired his sullen face,
    the mechanism of his jaw,
    and then I saw
    that from his lower lip
    —if you could call it a lip—
50 grim, wet, and weaponlike,
    hung five old pieces of fish-line,
    or four and a wire leader
    with the swivel still attached,
    with all their five big hooks
55 grown firmly in his mouth.
    A green line, frayed at the end
    where he broke it, two heavier lines,
    and a fine black thread
    still crimped from the strain and snap
60 when it broke and he got away.
    Like medals with their ribbons
    frayed and wavering,
    a five-haired beard of wisdom
    trailing from his aching jaw.
65 I stared and stared
    and victory filled up
    the little rented boat,
    from the pool of bilge
    where oil had spread a rainbow
70 around the rusted engine
    to the bailer rusted orange,
    the sun-cracked thwarts,
    the oarlocks on their strings,

---

1. Thin sheet of transparent mica used in place of glass; also, a kind of gelatin obtained from the air bladders of some freshwater fish.

             the gunnels—until everything
75   was rainbow, rainbow, rainbow!
             And I let the fish go.

                                                                    1946

Invitation to Miss Marianne Moore[1]

From Brooklyn, over the Brooklyn Bridge, on this fine morning,
      please come flying.
In a cloud of fiery pale chemicals,
      please come flying.
5   to the rapid rolling of thousands of small blue drums
    descending out of the mackerel sky
    over the glittering grandstand of harbor-water,
      please come flying.

    Whistles, pennants and smoke are blowing. The ships
10 are signaling cordially with multitudes of flags
    rising and falling like birds all over the harbor.
    Enter: two rivers, gracefully bearing
    countless little pellucid jellies
    in cut-glass epergnes[2] dragging with silver chains.
15 The flight is safe; the weather is all arranged
    The waves are running in verses this fine morning.
          Please come flying.

    Come with the pointed toe of each black shoe
    trailing a sapphire highlight,
20 with a black capeful of butterfly wings and bon-mots,[3]
    with heaven knows how many angels all riding
    on the broad black brim of your hat,
          please come flying.

    Bearing a musical inaudible abacus,
25 a slight censorious frown, and blue ribbons,
          please come flying.
    Facts and skyscrapers glint in the tide; Manhattan
    is all awash with morals this fine morning,
          so please come flying.

30 Mounting the sky with natural heroism,
    above the accidents, above the malignant movies,
    the taxicabs and injustices at large,
    while horns are resounding in your beautiful ears
    that simultaneously listen to
35 a soft uninvented music, fit for the musk deer,
          please come flying.

1. American poet (1887–1972); see above, p. 307.   2. Compartmented serving dishes.
                                                    3. Clever remarks.

For whom the grim museums will behave
like courteous male bower birds,
for whom the agreeable lions lie[4] in wait
40   on the steps of the Public Library,
eager to rise and follow through the doors
up into the reading rooms,
    please come flying.

We can sit down and weep; we can go shopping,
45   or play at a game of constantly being wrong
with a priceless set of vocabularies,
or we can bravely deplore, but please
    please come flying.

With dynasties of negative constructions
50   darkening and dying around you,
with grammar that suddenly turns and shines
like flocks of sandpipers flying,
    please come flying.

Come like a light in the white mackerel sky,
55   come like a daytime comet
with a long unnebulous train of words,
from Brooklyn, over the Brooklyn Bridge, on this fine morning,
    please come flying.

                                     1955

First Death in Nova Scotia

In the cold, cold parlor
my mother laid out Arthur
beneath the chromographs:[1]
Edward, Prince of Wales,
5   with Princess Alexandra,
and King George with Queen Mary.[2]
Below them on the table
stood a stuffed loon
shot and stuffed by Uncle
10   Arthur, Arthur's father.

Since Uncle Arthur fired
a bullet into him,
he hadn't said a word.
He kept his own counsel

---

4. Large stone lions flank the Fifth Avenue entrance to the main branch of the New York Public Library.
1. A colored picture produced from lithographic plates.
2. All members of the British royal family in the early 20th century: Edward (1894–1982) was made Prince of Wales in 1911; his parents were George V (1865–1936; r. 1910–36) and Queen Mary (1867–1853); and Alexandra (1844–1925), princess of Denmark and a queen by her marriage to Edward VII, was his grandmother.

15 on his white, frozen lake,
the marble-topped table.
His breast was deep and white,
cold and caressable;
his eyes were red glass,
20 much to be desired.

"Come," said my mother,
"Come and say goodbye
to your little cousin Arthur."
I was lifted up and given
25 one lily of the valley
to put in Arthur's hand.
Arthur's coffin was
a little frosted cake,
and the red-eyed loon eyed it
30 from his white, frozen lake.

Arthur was very small.
He was all white, like a doll
that hadn't been painted yet.
Jack Frost[3] had started to paint him
35 the way he always painted
the Maple Leaf (Forever).[4]
He had just begun on his hair,
a few red strokes, and then
Jack Frost had dropped the brush
40 and left him white, forever.

The gracious royal couples
were warm in red and ermine;
their feet were well wrapped up
in the ladies' ermine trains.
45 They invited Arthur to be
the smallest page at court.
But how could Arthur go,
clutching his tiny lily,
with his eyes shut up so tight
50 and the roads deep in snow?

1962

In the Waiting Room

I went with Aunt Consuelo
to keep her dentist's appointment
and sat and waited for her

---

3. The personification of frost, said in folklore to be responsible for the patterns on autumn leaves and on icy windows.
4. "Maple Leaf Forever" is a national song of Canada, written in 1867 by Alexander Muir, that sketches the country's history from a British perspective.

in the dentist's waiting room.
            It was winter. It got dark
            early. The waiting room
            was full of grown-up people,
            arctics[1] and overcoats,
10   lamps and magazines.
            My aunt was inside
            what seemed like a long time
            and while I waited I read
            the *National Geographic*
15   (I could read) and carefully
            studied the photographs:
            the inside of a volcano,
            black, and full of ashes;
            then it was spilling over
20   in rivulets of fire.
            Osa and Martin Johnson[2]
            dressed in riding breeches,
            laced boots, and pith helmets.
            A dead man slung on a pole
25   —"Long Pig,"[3] the caption said.
            Babies with pointed heads
            wound round and round with string;
            black, naked women with necks
            wound round and round with wire
30   like the necks of light bulbs.
            Their breasts were horrifying.
            I read it right straight through.
            I was too shy to stop.
            And then I looked at the cover:
35   the yellow margins, the date.

            Suddenly, from inside,
            came an *oh!* of pain
            —Aunt Consuelo's voice—
            not very loud or long.
40   I wasn't at all surprised;
            even then I knew she was
            a foolish, timid woman.
            I might have been embarrassed,
            but wasn't. What took me
45   completely by surprise
            was that it was *me*:
            my voice, in my mouth.
            Without thinking at all
            I was my foolish aunt,
50   I—we—were falling, falling,
            our eyes glued to the cover
            of the *National Geographic*,
            February, 1918.

1. Thick, waterproof winter overshoes.
2. Married team of American explorers and travel writers (1894–1953; 1884–1937).
3. I.e., human flesh (a term used by some Polynesian groups).

> I said to myself: three days
> and you'll be seven years old.
> I was saying it to stop
> the sensation of falling off
> the round, turning world
> into cold, blue-black space.
> But I felt: you are an *I*,
> you are an *Elizabeth,*
> you are one of *them.*
> *Why* should you be one, too?
> I scarcely dared to look
> to see what it was I was.
> I gave a sidelong glance
> —I couldn't look any higher—
> at shadowy gray knees,
> trousers and skirts and boots
> and different pairs of hands
> lying under the lamps.
> I knew that nothing stranger
> had ever happened, that nothing
> stranger could ever happen.
> Why should I be my aunt,
> or me, or anyone?
> What similarities—
> boots, hands, the family voice
> I felt in my throat, or even
> the *National Geographic*
> and those awful hanging breasts—
> held us all together
> or made us all just one?
> How—I didn't know any
> word for it—how "unlikely" . . .
> How had I come to be here,
> like them, and overhear
> a cry of pain that could have
> got loud and worse but hadn't?
> The waiting room was bright
> and too hot. It was sliding
> beneath a big black wave,
> another, and another.
>
> Then I was back in it.
> The War[4] was on. Outside,
> in Worcester, Massachusetts,
> were night and slush and cold,
> and it was still the fifth
> of February, 1918.

1976

---

4. I.e., World War I.

One Art

The art of losing isn't hard to master;
so many things seem filled with the intent
to be lost that their loss is no disaster.

Lose something every day. Accept the fluster
of lost door keys, the hour badly spent.
The art of losing isn't hard to master.

Then practice losing farther, losing faster:
places, and names and where it was you meant
to travel. None of these will bring disaster.

I lost my mother's watch. And look! my last, or
next-to-last, of three loved houses went.
The art of losing isn't hard to master.

I lost two cities, lovely ones. And, vaster,
some realms I owned, two rivers, a continent.
I miss them, but it wasn't a disaster.

—Even losing you (the joking voice, a gesture
I love) I shan't have lied. It's evident
the art of losing's not too hard to master
though it may look like (*Write* it!) like disaster.

1976

Pink Dog

[*Rio de Janeiro*]

The sun is blazing and the sky is blue.
Umbrellas clothe the beach in every hue.
Naked, you trot across the avenue.

Oh, never have I seen a dog so bare!
Naked and pink, without a single hair . . .
Startled, the passersby draw back and stare.

Of course they're mortally afraid of rabies.
You are not mad; you have a case of scabies[1]
but look intelligent. Where are your babies?

(A nursing mother, by those hanging teats.)
In what slum have you hidden them, poor bitch,[2]
while you go begging, living by your wits?

---

1. A skin disease that causes severe itching.   2. The correct technical term for a female dog.

Didn't you know? It's been in all the papers,
to solve this problem, how they deal with beggars?
¹⁵ They take and throw them in the tidal rivers.

Yes, idiots, paralytics, parasites
go bobbing in the ebbing sewage, nights
out in the suburbs, where there are no lights.

If they do this to anyone who begs,
²⁰ drugged, drunk, or sober, with or without legs,
what would they do to sick, four-legged dogs?

In the cafés and on the sidewalk corners
the joke is going round that all the beggars
who can afford them now wear life preservers.

²⁵ In your condition you would not be able
even to float, much less to dog-paddle.
Now look, the practical, the sensible

solution is to wear a *fantasia*.[3]
Tonight you simply can't afford to be a-
³⁰ n eyesore. But no one will ever see a

dog in *mascara* this time of year.
Ash Wednesday'll come but Carnival[4] is here.
What sambas[5] can you dance? What will you wear?

They say that Carnival's degenerating
³⁵ —radios, Americans, or something,
have ruined it completely. They're just talking.

Carnival is always wonderful!
A depilated dog would not look well.
Dress up! Dress up and dance at Carnival!

1979

[Gender and Art][1]

Undoubtedly gender does play an important part in the making of any art, but art is art and to separate writings, paintings, musical compositions, etc., into two sexes is to emphasize values in them that are *not* art.

1977

---

3. Carnival costume [Bishop's note].
4. The festive day, also called Shrove Tuesday, that precedes the start of Lent, the period of fasting and penitance leading up to Easter. Lent begins on Ash Wednesday, when traditionally Catholics attend Mass and are marked on the forehead with ashes that have been blessed.
5. Popular Brazilian dances.
1. From a letter to Joan Keefe, June 8, 1977.

MARY LAVIN
1912–1996

"Mary Lavin's characters . . . speak directly from the spiritual setting of Joyce's *Dubliners*," the writer Kay Boyle has commented, linking Lavin with one of Ireland's greatest men of letters. "But this time," Boyle adds, "it is a woman's voice telling us . . . of other women's love, and pride, and courage, and despair." Born in Massachusetts to Irish parents who returned with her to their native country when she was nine, Lavin started her career not as a creative writer but as a literary critic, studying at University College, Dublin. After producing a master's thesis on Jane Austen and an unfinished Ph.D. dissertation on Virginia Woolf, however, she turned her intellectual energies to fiction.

In 1942, Lavin married William Walsh, a lawyer, with whom she had three daughters; he died in 1954, and after some years of widowhood—an experience that may well be reflected in the poignant "In a Café"—in 1969 she married Michael Scott, a college friend and an ex-Jesuit. In the course of her career, she published two novels, *The House on Clewe Street* (1945) and *Mary O'Grady* (1950), but she remains best known for her numerous collections of powerful short stories, including many on distinctively Irish subjects as well as many that explore the nuances of women's lives with strength and subtlety. "Short-story writing," she explained, "is only looking closer than normal into the human heart."

Though she is perhaps not as widely read as she should be in the United States, the land of her birth (where she in fact retained citizenship all her life), Lavin was the recipient of many honors, among them the James Tait Black Memorial Prize (1943), for her first collection of short stories; several Guggenheim fellowships; an honorary doctorate from University College, Dublin (1968); and perhaps most impressive, election to the rank of Saoi, the most prestigious honor bestowed by the Irish arts society known as Aosdana (1992).

In a Café

The café was in a back street. Mary's ankles ached and she was glad Maudie had not got there before her. She sat down at a table near the door.

It was a place she had only recently found, and she dropped in often, whenever she came up to Dublin. She hated to go anywhere else now. For one thing, she knew that she would be unlikely ever to have set foot in it if Richard were still alive. And this knowledge helped to give her back a semblance of the identity she lost willingly in marriage, but lost doubly, and unwillingly, in widowhood.

Not that Richard would have disliked the café. It was the kind of place they went to when they were students. Too much water had gone under the bridge since those days, though. Say what you liked, there was something faintly snobby about a farm in Meath,[1] and together she and Richard would have been out of place here. But it was a different matter to come here alone. There could be nothing—oh, nothing—snobby about a widow. Just by being one, she fitted into this kind of café. It was an unusual little place. She looked around.

---

1. County in Ireland close to Dublin.

The walls were distempered red above and the lower part was boarded, with the boards painted white. It was probably the boarded walls that gave it the peculiarly functional look you get in the snuggery[2] of a public house or in the confessional of a small and poor parish church. For furniture there were only deal[3] tables and chairs, with black-and-white checked tablecloths that were either unironed or badly ironed. But there was a decided feeling that money was not so much in short supply as dedicated to other purposes—as witness the paintings on the walls, and a notice over the fire-grate to say that there were others on view in a studio overhead, in rather the same way as pictures in an exhibition. The paintings were for the most part experimental in their technique.

The café was run by two students from the Art College. They often went out and left the place quite empty—as now—while they had a cup of coffee in another café—across the street. Regular clients sometimes helped themselves to coffee from the pot on the gas-ring, behind a curtain at the back; or, if they only came in for company and found none, merely warmed themselves at the big fire always blazing in the little black grate that was the original grate when the café was a warehouse office. Today, the fire was banked up with coke.[4] The coffee was spitting on the gas-ring.

Would Maudie like the place? That it might not be exactly the right place to have arranged to meet her, above all under the present circumstances, occurred vaguely to Mary, but there was nothing that could be done about it now. When Maudie got there, if she didn't like it, they could go somewhere else. On the other hand, perhaps she might like it? Or perhaps she would be too upset to take notice of her surroundings? The paintings might interest her. They were certainly stimulating. There were two new ones today, which Mary herself had not seen before: two flower paintings, just inside the door. From where she sat she could read the signature, Johann van Stiegler. Or at least they suggested flowers. They were nameable as roses surely in spite of being a bit angular. She knew what Richard would have said about them. But she and Richard were no longer one. So what would *she* say about them? She would say—she would say—

But what was keeping Maudie? It was all very well to be glad of a few minutes' time in which to gather herself together; it was a different thing altogether to be kept a quarter of an hour.

Mary leaned back against the boarding. She was less tired that when she came in, but she was still in no way prepared for the encounter in front of her.

What had she to say to a young widow recently bereaved? Why on earth had she arranged to meet her? The incongruity of their both being widowed came forcibly upon her. Would Maudie, too, be in black with touches of white? Two widows! It was like two magpies: one for sorrow, two for joy.[5] The absurdity of it was all at once so great she had an impulse to get up and make off out of the place. She felt herself vibrating all over with resentment at being coupled with anyone, and urgently she began to sever them, seeking out their disparities.

---

2. The bar parlor.
3. Pine or fir wood.
4. Fuel made from coal.

5. A traditional Scots rhyme on magpies begins "One's sorrow, two's mirth."

Maudie was only a year married! And her parents had been only too ready to take care of her child, greedily possessing themselves of it. Maudie was as free as a girl. Then—if it mattered—?—she had a nice little income in her own right too, apart from all Michael had left her. So?

But what was keeping her? Was she not coming at all?

Ah! the little iron bell that was over the door—it too, since the warehouse days—tinkled to tell there was another customer coming into the café.

It wasn't Maudie though. It was a young man—youngish anyway—and Mary would say that he was an artist. Yet his hands at which, when he sat down, he began to stare, were not like the hands of an artist. They were peculiarly plump soft-skinned hands, and there was something touching in the relaxed way in which, lightly clasped one in the other, they rested on the table. Had they a womanish look perhaps? No; that was not the word, but she couldn't for the life of her find the right word to describe them. And her mind was teased by trying to find it. Fascinated, her eyes were drawn to those hands, time and again, no matter how resolutely she tore them away. It was almost as if it was by touch, not sight, that she knew their warm fleshiness.

Even when she closed her eyes—as she did—she could still see them. And so, innocent of where she was being led, she made no real effort to free her thoughts from them, and not until it was too late did she see before her the familiar shape of her recurring nightmare. All at once it was Richard's hands she saw, so different from those others, wiry, supple, thin. There they were for an instant in her mind, limned by love and anguish, before they vanished.

It happened so often. In her mind she would see a part of him, his hand—his arm, his foot perhaps, in the finely worked leather shoes he always wore—and from it, frantically, she would try to build up the whole man. Sometimes she succeeded better than others, built him up from foot to shoulder, seeing his hands, his gray suit, his tie, knotted always in a slightly special way, his neck, even his chin that was rather sharp, a little less attractive than his other features—

—But always at that point she would be defeated. Never once voluntarily since the day he died had she been able to see his face again.

And if she could not remember him, at will, what meaning had time at all? What use was it to have lived the past, if behind us it fell away so sheer?

In the hour of his death, for her it was part of the pain that she knew this would happen. She was standing beside him when, outside the hospital window, a bird called out with a sweet, clear whistle, and hearing it she knew that he was dead, because not for years had she really heard bird-song or bird-call, so loud was the noise of their love in her ears. When she looked down it was a strange face, the look of death itself, that lay on the pillow. And after that brief moment of silence that let in the bird-song for an instant, a new noise started in her head; the noise of a nameless panic that did not always roar, but never altogether died down.

And now—here in the little café—she caught at the table-edge—for the conflagration had started again and her mind was a roaring furnace.

It was just then the man at the end of the table stood up and reached for the menu-card on which, as a matter of fact, she was leaning—breasts and elbows—with her face in her hands. Hastily, apologetically, she pushed it towards him, and at once the roar died down in her mind. She looked at him. Could he have known? Her heart was filled with gratitude, and she saw that his eyes were soft and gentle. But she had to admit that he didn't look as if he were much aware of her. No matter! She still was grateful to him.

"Don't you want this too?" she cried, thankful, warm, as she saw that the small slip of paper with the specialty for the day that had been clipped to the menu card with a paper-pin, had come off and remained under the elbow, caught on the rough sleeve of her jacket. She stood up and leant over the table with it.

"Ah! thank you!" he said, and bowed. She smiled. There was such gallantry in a bow. He was a foreigner, of course. And then, before she sat down again she saw that he had been sketching, making little pencil sketches all over a newspaper on the table, in the margins and in the spaces between the newsprint. Such intricate minutely involuted little figures—she was fascinated, but of course she could not stare.

Yet, when she sat down, she watched him covertly, and every now and then she saw that he made a particular flourish: it was his signature, she felt sure, and she tried to make it out from where she sat. A disproportionate, a ridiculous excitement rushed through her, when she realized it was Johann van Stiegler, the name on the new flower paintings that had preoccupied her when she first came into the place.

But it's impossible, she thought. The sketches were so meticulous; the painting so—

But the little bell tinkled again.

"Ah! Maudie!"

For all her waiting, taken by surprise in the end, she got to her feet in her embarrassment, like a man.

"Maudie, my dear!" She had to stare fixedly at her in an effort to convey the sympathy, which, tongue-tied, she could express in no other way.

They shook hands, wordlessly.

"I'm deliberately refraining from expressing sympathy—you know that?" said Mary then, as they sat down at the checkered table.

"Oh, I do!" cried Maudie. And she seemed genuinely appreciative. "It's so awful trying to think of something to say back!—Isn't it? It has to come right out of yourself, and sometimes what comes is something you can't even say out loud when you do think of it!"

It was so true. Mary looked at her in surprise. Her mind ran back over the things people had said to her, and the replies.

Them: It's a good thing it wasn't one of the children.
Her: I'd give them all for him.
Them: Time is a great healer.
Her: Thief would be more like: taking away even my memory of him.
Them: God's ways are wonderful. Some day you'll see His plan in all this.
Her: Do you mean, some day I'll be glad he's dead?

So Maudie apprehended these subtleties too? Mary looked hard at her. "I know, I know," she said. "In the end you have to say what is expected of you—and you feel so cheapened by it."

"Worse still, you cheapen the dead!" said Maudie.

Mary looked really hard at her now. Was it possible for a young girl—a simple person at that—to have wrung from one single experience so much bitter knowledge? In spite of herself, she felt she was being drawn into complicity with her. She drew back resolutely.

"Of course, you were more or less expecting it, weren't you?" she said, spitefully.

Unrepulsed, Maudie looked back at her. "Does that matter?" she asked, and then, unexpectedly, she herself put a rift between them. "You have the children, of course!" she said, and then, hastily, before Mary could say anything, she rushed on. "Oh, I know I have my baby, but there seems so little link between him and his father! I just can't believe that it's me, sometimes, wheeling him round the park in his pram; it's like as if he was illegitimate. No! I mean it really. I'm not just trying to be shocking. It must be so different when there has been time for a relationship to be started between children and their father, like there was in your case."

"Oh, I don't know that that matters," said Mary. "And you'll be glad to have him some day." This time she spoke with deliberate malice, for she knew so well how those same words had lacerated her. She knew what they were meant to say: the children would be better than nothing.

But the poison of her words did not penetrate Maudie. And with another stab she knew why this was so. Maudie was so young; so beautiful. Looking at her, it seemed quite inaccurate to say that she had lost her husband: it was Michael who had lost her, fallen out, as it were, while she perforce went outward. She didn't even look like a widow. There was nothing about her to suggest that she was in any way bereft or maimed.

"You'll marry again, Maudie," she said, impulsively. "Don't mind my saying it," she added quickly, hastily. "It's not a criticism. It's because I know how you're suffering that I say it. Don't take offense."

Maudie didn't really look offended though, she only looked on the defensive. Then she relaxed.

"Not coming from you," she said. "You know what it's like." Mary saw she was trying to cover up the fact that she simply could not violently refute the suggestion. "Not that I think I will," she added, but weakly, "After all, you didn't!"

It was Mary who was put upon the defensive now.

"After all, it's only two years—less even," she said stiffly.

"Oh, it's not altogether a matter of time," said Maudie, seeing she had erred, but not clear how or where. "It's the kind of person you are, I think. I admire you so much! It's what I'd want to be like myself if I had the strength. With remarriage it is largely the effect on oneself that matters I think, don't you? I don't think it really matters to—to the dead! Do you? I'm sure Michael would want me to marry again if he were able to express a wish. After all, people say it's a compliment to a man if his widow marries again, did you ever hear that?"

"I did," said Mary, curtly. "But I wouldn't pay much heed to it. A fat lot the dead care about compliments."

So Maudie *was* already thinking about remarriage? Mary's irritation was succeeded by a vague feeling of envy, and then the irritation returned tenfold.

How easily it was accepted that *she* would not marry again. This girl regards me as too old, of course. And she's right—or she ought to be right! She remembered the way, even two years ago, people had said she "had" her children. They meant, even then, that it was unlikely, unlooked for, that she'd remarry.

Other things that had been said crowded back into her mind as well. So many people had spoken of the special quality of her marriage—hers and Richard's—their remarkable suitability one for the other, and the uniqueness of the bond between them. She was avid to hear this said at the time.

But suddenly, in this little café, the light that had played over those words flickered and went out. Did they perhaps mean that if Richard had not appeared when he did, no one else would have been interested in her?

Whereas Maudie—! If she looked so attractive now, when she must still be suffering from shock, what would she be like a year from now, when she would be "out of mourning," as it would be put? Why, right now, she was so fresh and—looking at her there was no other word for it—virginal. Of course she was only a year married! A year! You could hardly call it being married at all.

But Maudie knew a thing or two about men for all that. There was no denying it. And in her eyes at that moment there was a strange expression. Seeing it, Mary remembered at once that they were not alone in the café. She wondered urgently how much the man at the other end of the table had heard and could hear of what they were saying. But it was too late to stop Maudie.

"Oh Mary," cried Maudie, leaning forward, "it's not what they give us—I've got over wanting things like a child—it's what we have to give them! It's something—" and she pressed her hands suddenly to her breasts, "something in here!"

"Maudie!"

Sharply, urgently, Mary tried to make her lower her voice, and with a quick movement of her head she did manage at last to convey some caution to her.

"In case you might say something," she said, in a low voice.

"Oh, there was no fear," said Maudie. "I was aware all the time." She didn't speak quite so low as Mary, but did lower her voice. "I was aware of him *all the time*," she said. "It was *him* that put it into my mind—about what we have to give." She pressed her hands to her breasts again. "He looks so lonely, don't you think? He is a foreigner, isn't he? I always think it's sad for them; they don't have many friends, and even when they do, there is always a barrier, don't you agree?"

But Mary was too embarrassed to let her go on. Almost frantically she made a diversion.

"What are you going to have, Maudie?" she said, loudly. "Coffee? Tea? And is there no one to take an order?"

Immediately she felt a fool. To whom had she spoken? She looked across at Johann van Stiegler. As if he were waiting to meet her glance, his mild and patient eyes looked into hers.

"There is no one there," he said, nodding at the curtained gas-ring, "but one can serve oneself. Perhaps you would wish that I—"

"Oh, not at all," cried Mary. "Please, don't trouble! We're in absolutely no hurry! Please don't trouble yourself," she said, "not on our account."

But she saw at once that he was very much a foreigner, and that he was at a disadvantage, not knowing if he had not perhaps made a gaffe. "I have perhaps intruded?" he said, miserably.

"Oh, not at all," cried Mary, and he was so serious she had to laugh.

The laugh was another mistake though. His face took on a look of despair that could come upon a foreigner, it seemed, at the slightest provocation, as if suddenly everything was obscure to him—everything.

"Please," she murmured, and then vaguely, "—your work," meaning that she did not wish to interrupt his sketching.

"Ah, you know my work?" he said, brightening immediately, pleased with a small and quite endearing vanity. "We have met before? Yes?"

"Oh no, we haven't met," she said quickly, and she sat down, but of course after that it was impossible to go on acting as if he were a complete stranger. She turned to see what Maudie would make of the situation. It was then she felt the full force of her irritation with Maudie. She could have given her a slap in the face. Yes: a slap right in the face! For there she sat, remotely, her face indeed partly averted from them.

Maudie was waiting to be introduced! To be *introduced,* as if she, Mary, did not need any conventional preliminaries. As if it was all right that she, Mary, should begin an unprefaced conversation with a strange man in a café because—and of course that was what was so infuriating, that she knew Maudie's unconscious thought—it was all right for a woman of *her* age to strike up a conversation like that, but that it wouldn't have done for a young woman. Yet, on her still partly averted face, Mary could see the quickened look of interest. She had a good mind not to make any gesture to draw her into the conversation at all, but she had the young man to consider. She had to bring them together whether she liked it or not.

"Maudie, this is—" she turned back and smiled at van Stiegler, "this is—" But she was confused and she had to abandon the introduction altogether. Instead, she broke into a direct question.

"Those are your flower pictures, aren't they?" she asked.

It was enough for Maudie—more than enough you might say.

She turned to the young man, obviously greatly impressed; her lips apart, her eyes shining. My God, how attractive she was!

"Oh, no, not really?" she cried. "How marvelous of you!"

But Johann van Stiegler was looking at Mary.

"You are sure we have not met before?"

"Oh no, but you were scribbling your signature all over that newspaper," she looked around to show it to him, but it had fallen on to the floor.

"Ah, yes," he said, and—she couldn't be certain, of course—but she thought he was disappointed.

"Ah, yes, you saw my signature," he said, flatly. He looked dejected. Mary felt helpless. She turned to Maudie. It was up to her to say something now.

Just then the little warehouse bell tinkled again, and this time it was one of the proprietors who came in, casually, like a client.

"Ah good!" said van Stiegler. "Coffee," he called out. Then he turned to Mary. "Coffee for you too?"

"Oh yes, coffee for us," said Mary, but she couldn't help wondering who was going to pay for it, and simultaneously she couldn't help noticing the shabbiness of his jacket. Well—they'd see! Meanwhile, she determined to ignore the plate of cakes that was put down with the coffee. And she hoped Maudie would too. She pushed the plate aside as a kind of hint to her, but Maudie leaned across and took a large bun filled with cream.

"Do you mind my asking you something—about your work—?" said Mary. But Maudie interrupted.

"You are living in Ireland? I mean, you are not just here on a visit?"

There was intimacy and intimacy, and Mary felt nervous in case the young man might resent this question.

"I teach art in a college here," he said, and he did seem a little surprised, but Mary could see, too, that he was not at all displeased. He seemed to settle more comfortably into the conversation.

"It is very good for a while to go to another country," he said, "and this country is cheap. I have a flat in the next street to here, and it is very private. If I hang myself from the ceiling, it is all right—nobody knows; nobody cares. That is a good way to live when you paint."

Mary was prepared to ponder. "Do you think so?"

Maudie was not prepared to ponder. "How odd," she said, shortly, and then she looked at her watch. "I'll have to go," she said inexplicably.

They had finished the coffee. Immediately Mary's thought returned to the problem of who was to pay for it. It was a small affair for which to call up all one's spiritual resources, but she felt enormously courageous and determined when she heard herself ask in a loud voice for her bill.

"My bill, please," she called out, over the sound of spitting coffee on the gas stove.

Johann van Stiegler made no move to ask for his bill, and yet he was buttoning his jacket and folding his newspaper as if to leave too. Would his coffee go on her bill? Mary wondered.

It was all settled, however, in a second. The bill was for two eight-penny coffees, and one bun, and there was no charge for van Stiegler's coffee. He had some understanding with the owners, she supposed. Or perhaps he was not really going to leave then at all?

As they stood up, however, gloved and ready to depart, the young man bowed.

"Perhaps we go the same way?" They could see he was anxious to be polite.

"Oh, not at all," they said together, as if he had offered to escort them, and Maudie even laughed openly.

Then there was, of course, another ridiculous situation. Van Stiegler sat down again. Had they been too brusque? Had they hurt his feelings?

Oh, if only he wasn't a foreigner, thought Mary, and she hesitated. Maudie already had her hand on the door.

"I hope I will see some more of your work sometime," said Mary. It was not a question, merely a compliment.

But van Stiegler sprung to his feet again.

"Tonight after my classes I am bringing another picture to hang here," he said. "You would like to see it? I would be here—" he pulled out a large, old-fashioned watch, "—at ten minutes past nine."

"Oh, not tonight—I couldn't come back tonight," said Mary. "I live in the country, you see," she said, explaining and excusing herself. "Another time perhaps? It will be here for how long?"

She wasn't really listening to what he said. She was thinking that he had not asked if Maudie could come. Perhaps it was that, of the two of them, she looked the most likely to buy a picture, whereas Maudie, although in actual fact more likely to do so, looked less so. Or was it that he coupled them so that he thought if one came, both came. Or was it really Maudie he'd like to see again, and that he regarded her as a chaperone? Or was it—?

There was no knowing, however, and so she said goodbye again, and the next minute the little bell had tinkled over the door and they were in the street. In the street they looked at each other.

"Well! if ever there was—" began Maudie, but she didn't get time to finish her sentence. Behind them the little bell tinkled yet again, and their painter was out in the street with them.

"I forgot to give you the address of my flat—it is also my studio," he said. "I would be glad to show you my paintings at any time." He pulled out a notebook and tore out a sheet. "I will write it down," he said, concisely. And he did. But when he went to hand it to them, it was Maudie who took it. "I am nearly always there, except when I am at my classes," he said. And bowing, he turned and went back into the café.

They dared not laugh until they had walked some distance away, until they turned into the next street in fact.

"Well, I never!" said Maudie, and she handed the paper to Mary.

"Chatham Row," Mary read, "number 8."

"Will you go to see them?" asked Maudie.

Mary felt outraged.

"What do you take me for?" she asked. "I may be a bit unconventional, but can you see me presenting myself at his place? Would *you* go?"

"Oh, it's different for me," said Maudie, enigmatically. "And anyway, it was you he asked. But I see your point—it's a pity. Poor fellow!—he must be very lonely. I wish there was something we could do for him—someone to whom we could introduce him."

Mary looked at her. It had never occurred to her that he might be lonely! How was it that the obvious always escaped her?

They were in Grafton Street by this time.

"Well, I have some shopping to do. I suppose it's the same with you," said Maudie. "I am glad I had that talk with you. We must have another chat soon."

"Oh yes," said Mary, over-readily, replying to her adieux though, and not to the suggestion of their meeting again! She was anxious all at once to be rid of Maudie.

And yet, as she watched her walk away from her, making her passage quickly and expertly through the crowds in the street, Mary felt a sudden terrible aimlessness descend upon herself like a physical paralysis. She walked along, pausing to look in the shop windows.

It was the evening hour when everyone in the streets was hurrying home, purposeful and intent. Even those who paused to look into the shop windows did so with direction and aim, darting their bright glances keenly, like birds. Their minds were all intent upon substantives; tangibles, while her mind was straying back to the student café, and the strange flower pictures on the walls; to the young man who was so vulnerable in his vanity: the legitimate vanity of his art.

It was so like Maudie to laugh at him. What did she know of an artist's mind? If Maudie had not been with her, it would have been so different. She might, for one thing, have got him to talk about his work, to explain the discrepancy between the loose style of the pictures on the wall and the exact, small sketches he'd been drawing on the margins of the paper.

She might even have taken up his invitation to go and see his paintings. Why had that seemed so unconventional—so laughable? Because of Maudie, that was why.

How ridiculous their scruples would have seemed to the young man. She could only hope he had not guessed them. She looked up at a clock. Supposing, right now, she were to slip back to the café and suggest that after all she found she would have time for a quick visit to his studio? Or would he have left the café? Better perhaps to call around to the studio? He would surely be back there now!

For a moment she stood debating the arguments for and against going back. Would it seem odd to him? Would he be surprised? But as if it were Maudie who put the questions, she frowned them down and all at once purposeful as anyone in the street, began to go back, headlong, you might say, towards Chatham Street.

At the point where two small streets crossed each other she had to pause, while a team of Guinness's dray horses[6] turned with difficulty in the narrow cube of the intersection. And, while she waited impatiently, she caught sight of herself in the gilded mirror of a public house. For a second, the familiar sight gave her a misgiving of her mission, but as the dray horses moved out of the way, she told herself that her dowdy, lumpish, and unromantic figure vouched for her spiritual integrity. She pulled herself away from the face in the glass and hurried across the street.

Between two lock-up shops, down a short alley—roofed by the second story of the premises overhead, till it was like a tunnel—was his door. Away at the end of the tunnel the door could clearly be seen even from the middle of the street, for it was painted bright yellow. Odd that she had never seen it in the times she had passed that way. She crossed the street.

Once across the street, she ran down the tunnel, her footsteps echoing loud in her ears. And there on the door, tied to the latchet of the letter-box, was a piece of white cardboard with his name on it. Grabbing the knocker, she gave three clear hammer-strokes on the door.

The little alley was a sort of cul-de-sac; except for the street behind her and the door in front of her, it had no outlet. There was not even a skylight or an aperture of any kind. As for the premises into which the door led, there was no way of telling its size or its extent, or anything at all about it, until the door was opened.

Irresponsibly, she giggled. It was like the mystifying doors in the trunks of trees that beguiled her as a child in fairy tales and fantasies. Did this door, too, like those fairy doors, lead into rooms of impossible amplitude, or would it be a cramped and poky place?

As she pondered upon what was within, seemingly so mysteriously sealed, she saw that—just as in a fairy tale—after all there was an aperture. The letter-box had lost its shutter or lid, and it gaped open, a vacant hole in the wood, reminding her of a sleeping doll whose eyeballs had been poked back in its head, and creating an expression of vacancy and emptiness.

Impulsively, going down on one knee, she peered in through the slit.

At first she could see only segments of the objects within, but by moving her head, she was able to identify things; an unfinished canvas up against the splattered white wainscot, a bicycle-pump flat on the floor, the leg of a table, black iron bed-legs and, to her amusement, dangling down by the leg of the table, dripping their moisture in a pool on the floor, a pair of elongated, gray wool socks. It was, of course, only possible to see the lower portion of

---

6. I.e., from the brewery in Dublin where Guinness beer has been made since the late 18th century.

the room, but it seemed enough to infer conclusively that this was indeed a little room in a tree, no bigger than the bulk of the outer trunk, leading nowhere, and—sufficient or no—itself its own end.

There was just one break in the wainscot, where a door ran down to the floor, but this was so narrow and made of roughly jointed boards, that she took it to be the door of a press. And then, as she started moving, she saw something else, an intricate segment of fine wire spokes. It was a second before she realized it was the wheel of a bicycle.

So, a bicycle, too, lived here, in this little room in a tree-trunk!

Oh, poor young man, poor painter: poor foreigner, inept at finding the good lodgings in a strange city. Her heart went out to him.

It was just then that the boarded door—it couldn't have been a press after all—opened into the room, and she found herself staring at two feet. They were large feet, shoved into unlaced shoes, and they were bare to the white ankles. For, of course, she thought wildly, focusing her thoughts, his socks are washed! But her power to think clearly only lasted an instant. She sprang to her feet.

"Who iss that?" asked a voice. "Did someone knock?"

It was the voice of the man in the café. But where was she to find a voice with which to reply? And who was she to say what she was? Who—to this stranger—was she?

And if he opened the door, what then? All the thoughts and words that had, like a wind, blown her down this tunnel, subsided suddenly, and she stood, appalled, at where they had brought her.

"Who iss that?" came the voice within, troubled.

Staring at those white feet, thrust into the unlaced shoes, she felt that she would die on the spot if they moved an inch. She turned.

Ahead of her, bright, shining and clear, as if it were at the end of a powerful telescope, was the street. Not caring if her feet were heard, volleying and echoing as if she ran through a mighty drain-pipe, she kept running till she reached the street, kept running even then, jostling surprised shoppers, hitting her ankles off the wheel-knobs of push-cars and prams. Only when she came to the junction of the streets again, did she stop, as in the pub mirror she caught sight again of her familiar face. That face steadied her. How absurd to think that anyone would sinisterly follow this middle-aged woman?

But suppose he had been in the outer room when she knocked! If he had opened the door? What would have happened then? What would she have said? A flush spread over her face. The only true words that she could have uttered were those that had sunk into her mind in the café; put there by Maudie.

"I'm lonely!" That was all she could have said. "I'm lonely. Are you?"

A deep shame came over her with this admission and, guiltily, she began to walk quickly onward again, towards Grafton Street. If anyone had seen her, there in that dark alleyway! If anyone could have looked into her mind, her heart!

And yet, was it so unnatural? Was it so hard to understand? So unforgivable?

As she passed the open door of the Carmelite Church she paused. Could she rid herself of her feeling of shame in the dark of the confessional? To the sin-accustomed ears of the wise old fathers her story would be lightweight; a tedious tale of scrupulosity. Was there no one, no one who'd understand?

She had reached Grafton Street once more, and stepped into its crowded thoroughfare. It was only a few minutes since she left it, but in the street the evasion of light had begun. Only the bustle of people, and the activity of traffic, made it seem that it was yet day. Away at the top of the street, in Stephen's Green, to which she turned, although the tops of the trees were still clear, branch for branch, in the last of the light, mist muted the outline of the bushes. If one were to put a hand between the railings now, it would be with a slight shock that the fingers would feel the little branches, like fine bones, under the feathers of mist. And in their secret nests the smaller birds were making faint avowals in the last of the day. It was the time at which she used to meet Richard.

"Oh Richard!" she cried, almost out loud, as she walked along by the railings to where the car was parked. "Oh Richard! it's you I want."

And as she cried out, her mind presented him to her, as she so often saw him, coming towards her: tall, handsome, and with his curious air of apartness from those around him. He had his hat in his hand, down by his side, as on a summer day he might trail a hand in water from the side of a boat. She wanted to preserve that picture of him for ever in an image, and only as she struggled to hold on to it did she realize there was no urgency in the search. She had a sense of having all the time in the world to look and look and look at him. That was the very way he used to come to meet her—indolently trailing the old felt hat, glad to be done with the day; and when they got nearer to each other she used to take such joy in his unsmiling face, with its happiness integral to it in all its features. It was the first time in the two years he'd been gone from her that she'd seen his face.

Not till she had taken out the key of the car, and gone straight around to the driver's side, not stupidly, as so often, to the passenger seat—not till then did she realize what she had achieved. Yet she had no more than got back her rights. No more. It was not a subject for amazement. By what means exactly had she got them back though—in that little café? That was the wonder.

1961

MARY McCARTHY
1912–1989

Sardonically associating "the kind of woman writer who's a capital W, capital W" with the production of literature that focuses on decor and drapery, Mary McCarthy claimed in a 1962 *Paris Review* interview that Jane Austen and George Eliot were not "Women Writers." Should she divide literary women into the categories of "Sense and Sensibility," she explained, "I *am* for the ones who represent sense, and so was Jane Austen." As an accomplished journalist, McCarthy was hailed for politically astute essays on Vietnam and the Watergate crisis as well as for intelligent criticism of contemporary drama and fiction. Her reputation as a creative writer rests, however, on the work that illuminates her growth from an emotional sensibility to the tolerant but ironic common sense that so frequently animated her prose style.

The oldest child of parents who were killed in the influenza epidemic of 1918, McCarthy was raised in Minneapolis by a series of relatives, some of whom enjoyed tormenting her and her siblings. In *Memories of a Catholic Girlhood* (1957), she explored her grief at the loss of her parents as well as her development into "a lapsed Catholic," first in the homes of her Catholic, Protestant, and Jewish relatives, and later at the convent school she attended in Seattle. She began publishing fiction after graduating from Vassar College and divorcing her first husband. While married to the literary critic Edmund Wilson, with whom she had a child, McCarthy wrote *The Company She Keeps* (1942), a successful series of satiric stories. After the marriage broke up in 1945, she traveled and published extensively. From *The Groves of Academe* (1952) to *Cannibals and Missionaries* (1979), McCarthy delineated the limits and liabilities of modern liberalism. In addition, the novels *A Charmed Life* (1955) and *The Group* (1963) focused with wit and intelligence on the restricted options and sensibilities of well-educated middle-class women. Later in her career, *Venice Observed* (1956), *On the Contrary* (1961), *Mary McCarthy's Theatre Chronicles, 1937–1962* (1963), *The Writing on the Wall* (1970), and *The Seventeenth Degree* (1974) established her reputation as a drama critic, social commentator, travel writer, arts observer, and political journalist. Like her fiction and her essays, McCarthy's autobiographical writing is marked by scrupulous detachment; in "Names," for instance, she meditates on the disjunction between her sense of herself as an adolescent and the sometimes baffling, sometimes degrading identities she was given by teachers and fellow students.

From Memories of a Catholic Girlhood

Names

Anna Lyons, Mary Louise Lyons, Mary von Phul, Emilie von Phul, Eugenia McLellan, Marjorie McPhail, Marie-Louise L'Abbé, Mary Danz, Julia Dodge, Mary Fordyce Blake, Janet Preston—these were the names (I can still tell them over like a rosary[1]) of some of the older girls in the convent: the Virtues and Graces. The virtuous ones wore wide blue or green moire good-conduct ribbons, bandoleer-style,[2] across their blue serge uniforms; the beautiful ones wore rouge and powder or at least were reputed to do so. Our class, the eighth grade, wore pink ribbons (I never got one myself) and had names like Patricia ("Pat") Sullivan, Eileen Donohoe, and Joan Kane. We were inelegant even in this respect; the best name we could show, among us, was Phyllis ("Phil") Chatham, who boasted that her father's name, Ralph, was pronounced "Rafe" as in England.

Names had a great importance for us in the convent, and foreign names, French, German, or plain English (which, to us, were foreign, because of their Protestant sound), bloomed like prize roses among a collection of spuds. Irish names were too common in the school to have any prestige either as surnames (Gallagher, Sheehan, Finn, Sullivan, McCarthy) or as Christian names (Kathleen, Eileen). Anything exotic had value: an "olive" complexion,

---

1. A Catholic devotion consisting of a series of repeated prayers; the devout use a string of beads, also called a rosary, to keep track of the count.
2. Across the chest.

for example. The pet girl of the convent was a fragile Jewish girl named Susie Lowenstein, who had pale red-gold hair and an exquisite retroussé[3] nose, which, if we had had it, might have been called "pug." We liked her name too and the name of a child in the primary grades: Abbie Stuart Baillargeon. My favorite name, on the whole, though, was Emilie von Phul (pronounced "Pool"); her oldest sister, recently graduated, was called Celeste. Another name that appealed to me was Genevieve Albers, Saint Genevieve being the patron saint of Paris who turned back Attila[4] from the gates of the city.

All these names reflected the still-pioneer character of the Pacific Northwest. I had never heard their like in the parochial school in Minneapolis, where "foreign" extraction, in any case, was something to be ashamed of, the whole drive being toward Americanization of first name and surname alike. The exceptions to this were the Irish, who could vaunt such names as Catherine O'Dea and the name of my second cousin, Mary Catherine Anne Rose Violet McCarthy, while an unfortunate German boy named Manfred was made to suffer for his. But that was Minneapolis. In Seattle, and especially in the convent of the Ladies of the Sacred Heart, foreign names suggested not immigration but emigration—distinguished exile. Minneapolis was a granary; Seattle was a port, which had attracted a veritable Foreign Legion[5] of adventurers—soldiers of fortune, younger sons, gamblers, traders, drawn by the fortunes to be made in virgin timber and shipping and by the Alaska Gold Rush. Wars and revolutions had sent the defeated out to Puget Sound, to start a new life; the latest had been the Russian Revolution, which had shipped us, via Harbin, a Russian colony, complete with restaurant, on Queen Anne Hill. The English names in the convent, when they did not testify to direct English origin, as in the case of "Rafe" Chatham, had come to us from the South and represented a kind of internal exile; such girls as Mary Fordyce Blake and Mary McQueen Street (a class ahead of me; her sister was named Francesca) bore their double-barreled first names like titles of aristocracy from the antebellum South. Not all our girls, by any means, were Catholic; some of the very prettiest ones—Julia Dodge and Janet Preston, if I remember rightly—were Protestants. The nuns had taught us to behave with special courtesy to these strangers in our midst, and the whole effect was of some superior hostel for refugees of all the lost causes of the past hundred years. Money could not count for much in such an atmosphere; the fathers and grandfathers of many of our "best" girls were ruined men.

Names, often, were freakish in the Pacific Northwest, particularly girls' names. In the Episcopal boarding school I went to later, in Tacoma, there was a girl called De Vere Utter, and there was a girl called Rocena and another called Hermoine. Was Rocena a mistake for Rowena and Hermoine for Hermione? And was Vere, as we called her, Lady Clara Vere de Vere?[6] Probably. You do not hear names like those often, in any case, east of the Cascade Mountains; they belong to the frontier, where books and libraries were few and memory seems to have been oral, as in the time of Homer.[7]

---

3. Turned up.
4. Attila the Hun (406?–453 C.E.), leader of a central Asiatic people, who became notorious for the destruction he wrought as he invaded Europe. Geneviève (ca. 422–ca. 500) is said to have turned away the Huns by her prayers.
5. French volunteer army corps that does not inquire into the background of its enlistees, who are mostly foreign.
6. Subject and title of a poem (published in 1842) by Alfred, Lord Tennyson.
7. Homer's *Iliad* and *Odyssey* were originally oral, not written, epics.

Names have more significance for Catholics than they do for other people; Christian names are chosen for the spiritual qualities of the saints they are taken from; Protestants used to name their children out of the Old Testament and now they name them out of novels and plays, whose heroes and heroines are perhaps the new patron saints of a secular age. But with Catholics it is different. The saint a child is named for is supposed to serve, literally, as a model or pattern to imitate; your name is your fortune and it tells you what you are or must be. Catholic children ponder their names for a mystic meaning, like birthstones; my own, I learned, besides belonging to the Virgin and Saint Mary of Egypt, originally meant "bitter" or "star of the sea." My second name, Therese, could dedicate me either to Saint Theresa or to the saint called the Little Flower, Soeur Thérèse of Lisieux,[8] on whom God was supposed to have descended in the form of a shower of roses. At Confirmation,[9] I had added a third name (for Catholics then rename themselves, as most nuns do, yet another time, when they take orders); on the advice of a nun, I had taken "Clementina," after Saint Clement, an early pope—a step I soon regretted on account of "My Darling Clementine"[1] and her number nine shoes. By the time I was in the convent, I would no longer tell anyone what my Confirmation name was. The name I had nearly picked was "Agnes," after a little Roman virgin martyr, always shown with a lamb, because of her purity. But Agnes would have been just as bad, I recognized in Forest Ridge Convent—not only because of the possibility of "Aggie," but because it was subtly, indefinably *wrong*, in itself. Agnes would have made me look like an ass.

The fear of appearing ridiculous first entered my life, as a governing motive, during my second year in the convent. Up to then, a desire for prominence had decided many of my actions and, in fact, still persisted. But in the eighth grade, I became aware of mockery and perceived that I could not seek prominence without attracting laughter. Other people could, but I couldn't. This laughter was proceeding, not from my classmates, but from the girls of the class just above me, in particular from two boon companions, Elinor Heffernan and Mary Harty, a clownish pair—oddly assorted in size and shape, as teams of clowns generally are, one short, plump, and babyfaced, the other tall, lean, and owlish—who entertained the high-school department by calling attention to the oddities of the younger girls. Nearly every school has such a pair of satirists, whose marks are generally low and who are tolerated just because of their laziness and non-conformity; one of them (in this case, Mary Harty, the plump one) usually appears to be half asleep. Because of their low standing, their indifference to appearances, the sad state of their uniforms, their clowning is taken to be harmless, which, on the whole, it is, their object being not to wound but to divert; such girls are bored in school. We in the eighth grade sat directly in front of the two wits in study hall, so that they had us under close observation; yet at first I was not afraid of them, wanting, if anything, to identify myself with their laughter, to be initiated into the joke. One of their specialties was giving people nicknames, and it was considered an honor to be the first in the eighth

---

8. French Carmelite nun (1873–1987). Saint Teresa of Ávila (1515–1582), Spanish nun famous for her mystical visions; she founded the Carmelite Reform order, and many convents and monasteries.
9. A ceremony admitting adolescents to full membership in the Catholic Church.
1. A popular American folk song.

grade to be let in by Elinor and Mary on their latest invention. This often happened to me; they would tell me, on the playground, and I would tell the others. As their intermediary, I felt myself almost their friend and it did not occur to me that I might be next on their list.

I had achieved prominence not long before by publicly losing my faith and regaining it at the end of a retreat. I believe Elinor and Mary questioned me about this on the playground, during recess, and listened with serious, respectful faces while I told them about my conversations with the Jesuits. Those serious faces ought to have been an omen, but if the two girls used what I had revealed to make fun of me, it must have been behind my back. I never heard any more of it, and yet just at this time I began to feel something, like a cold breath on the nape of my neck, that made me wonder whether the new position I had won for myself in the convent was as secure as I imagined. I would turn around in study hall and find the two girls looking at me with speculation in their eyes.

It was just at this time, too, that I found myself in a perfectly absurd situation, a very private one, which made me live, from month to month, in horror of discovery. I had waked up one morning, in my convent room, to find a few small spots of blood on my sheet; I had somehow scratched a trifling cut on one of my legs and opened it during the night. I wondered what to do about this, for the nuns were fussy about bedmaking, as they were about our white collars and cuffs, and if we had an inspection those spots might count against me. It was best, I decided, to ask the nun on dormitory duty, tall, stout Mother Slattery, for a clean bottom sheet, even though she might scold me for having scratched my leg in my sleep and order me to cut my toenails. You never know what you might be blamed for. But Mother Slattery, when she bustled in to look at the sheet, did not scold me at all; indeed, she hardly seemed to be listening as I explained to her about the cut. She told me to sit down: she would be back in a minute. "You can be excused from athletics today," she added, closing the door. As I waited, I considered this remark, which seemed to me strangely munificent, in view of the unimportance of the cut. In a moment, she returned, but without the sheet. Instead, she produced out of her big pocket a sort of cloth girdle and a peculiar flannel object which I first took to be a bandage, and I began to protest that I did not need or want a bandage; all I needed was a bottom sheet. "The sheet can wait," said Mother Slattery, succinctly, handing me two large safety pins. It was the pins that abruptly enlightened me; I saw Mother Slattery's mistake, even as she was instructing me as to how this flannel article, which I now understood to be a sanitary napkin, was to be put on.

"Oh, no, Mother," I said, feeling somewhat embarrassed. "You don't understand. It's just a little cut, on my leg." But Mother, again, was not listening; she appeared to have grown deaf, as the nuns had a habit of doing when what you were saying did not fit in with their ideas. And now that I knew what was in her mind, I was conscious of a funny constraint; I did not feel it proper to name a natural process, in so many words, to a nun. It was like trying not to think of their going to the bathroom or trying not to see the straggling iron-grey hair coming out of their coifs (the common notion that they shaved their heads was false). On the whole, it seemed better just to show her my cut. But when I offered to do so and unfastened my black stocking, she only glanced at my leg, cursorily. "That's only a scratch, dear," she said. "Now hurry up and put this on or you'll be late for chapel. Have you any pain?" "No, no, Mother!" I cried. "You don't understand!" "Yes, yes, I understand," she replied soothingly, "and you will too, a little later. Mother Superior will tell you about it some time during the morning. There's nothing to be afraid of. You have become a woman."

"I know all about that," I persisted. "Mother, please listen. I just cut my leg. On the athletic field. Yesterday afternoon." But the more excited I grew, the more soothing, and yet firm, Mother Slattery became. There seemed to be nothing for it but to give up and do as I was bid. I was in the grip of a higher authority, which almost had the power to persuade me that it was right and I was wrong. But of course I was not wrong; that would have been too good to be true. While Mother Slattery waited, just outside my door, I miserably donned the equipment she had given me, for there was no place to hide it, on account of drawer inspection. She led me down the hall to where there was a chute and explained how I was to dispose of the flannel thing, by dropping it down the chute into the laundry. (The convent arrangements were very old-fashioned, dating back, no doubt, to the days of Louis Philippe.[2])

The Mother Superior, Madame MacIllvra, was a sensible woman, and all through my early morning classes, I was on pins and needles, chafing for the promised interview with her which I trusted would clear things up. *"Ma Mère,"*[3] I would begin, "Mother Slattery thinks . . ." Then I would tell her about the cut and the athletic field. But precisely the same impasse confronted me when I was summoned to her office at recess-time. *I* talked about my cut, and *she* talked about becoming a woman. It was rather like a round, in which she was singing "Scotland's burning, Scotland's burning," and I was singing "Pour on water, pour on water." Neither of us could hear the other, or, rather, I could hear her, but she could not hear me. Owing to our different positions in the convent, she was free to interrupt me, whereas I was expected to remain silent until she had finished speaking. When I kept breaking in, she hushed me, gently, and took me on her lap. Exactly like Mother Slattery, she attributed all my references to the cut to a blind fear of this new, unexpected reality that had supposedly entered my life. Many young girls, she reassured me, were frightened if they had not been prepared. "And you, Mary, have lost your dear mother, who could have made this easier for you." Rocked on Madame MacIllvra's lap, I felt paralysis overtake me and I lay, mutely listening, against her bosom, my face being tickled by her white, starched, fluted wimple, while she explained to me how babies were born, all of which I had heard before.

There was no use fighting the convent. I had to pretend to have become a woman, just as, not long before, I had had to pretend to get my faith back— for the sake of peace. This pretense was decidedly awkward. For fear of being found out by the lay sisters downstairs in the laundry (no doubt an imaginary contingency, but the convent was so very thorough), I reopened the cut on my leg, so as to draw a little blood to stain the napkins, which were issued me regularly, not only on this occasion, but every twenty-eight days

---

2. Duc d'Orléans (1773–1850); he was elected king of the French in 1830 and abdicated after the revolution of 1848.

3. My mother (French).

thereafter. Eventually, I abandoned this bloodletting, for fear of lockjaw, and trusted to fate. Yet I was in awful dread of detection; my only hope, as I saw it, was either to be released from the convent or to become a woman in reality, which might take a year, at least, since I was only twelve. Getting out of athletics once a month was not sufficient compensation for the farce I was going through. It was not my fault; they had forced me into it; nevertheless, it was I who would look silly—worse than silly; half mad—if the truth ever came to light.

I was burdened with this guilt and shame when the nickname finally found me out. "Found me out," in a general sense, for no one ever did learn the particular secret I bore about with me, pinned to the linen band. "We've got a name for you," Elinor and Mary called out to me, one day on the playground. "What is it?" I asked, half hoping, half fearing, since not all their sobriquets were unfavorable. "Cye," they answered, looking at each other and laughing. " 'Si'?" I repeated, supposing that it was based on Simple Simon. Did they regard me as a hick? "C.Y.E.," they elucidated, spelling it out in chorus. "The letters stand for something. Can you guess?" I could not and I cannot now. The closest I could come to it in the convent was "Clean Your Ears." Perhaps that was it, though in later life I have wondered whether it did not stand, simply, for "Clever Young Egg" or "Champion Young Eccentric." But in the convent I was certain that it stood for something horrible, something even worse than dirty ears (as far as I knew, my ears were clean), something I could never guess because it represented some aspect of myself that the world could see and I couldn't, like a sign pinned on my back. Everyone in the convent must have known what the letters stood for, but no one would tell me. Elinor and Mary had made them promise. It was like halitosis; not even my best friend, my deskmate, Louise, would tell me, no matter how much I pleaded. Yet everyone assured me that it was "very good," that is, very apt. And it made everyone laugh.

This name reduced all my pretensions and solidified my sense of *wrongness*. Just as I felt I was beginning to belong to the convent, it turned me into an outsider, since I was the only pupil who was not in the know. I liked the convent, but it did not like me, as people say of certain foods that disagree with them. By this, I do not mean that I was actively unpopular, either with the pupils or with the nuns. The Mother Superior cried when I left and predicted that I would be a novelist, which surprised me. And I had finally made friends; even Emilie von Phul smiled upon me softly out of her bright blue eyes from the far end of the study hall. It was just that I did not fit into the convent pattern; the simplest thing I did, like asking for a clean sheet, entrapped me in consequences that I never could have predicted. I was not bad; I did not consciously break the rules; and yet I could never, not even for a week, get a pink ribbon, and this was something I could not understand, because I was trying as hard as I could. It was the same case as with the hated name; the nuns, evidently, saw something about me that was invisible to me.

The oddest part was all that pretending. There I was, a walking mass of lies, pretending to be a Catholic and going to confession while really I had lost my faith, and pretending to have monthly periods by cutting myself with nail scissors; yet all this had come about without my volition and even contrary to it. But the basest pretense I was driven to was the acceptance of the nickname. Yet what else could I do? In the convent, I could not live it down. To all those girls, I had become "Cye McCarthy." That was who I was. That was how I had to identify myself when telephoning my friends during vacations to ask them to the movies: "Hello, this is Cye." I loathed myself when I said it, and yet I succumbed to the name totally, making myself over into a sort of hearty to go with it—the kind of girl I hated. "Cye" was my new patron saint. This false personality stuck to me, like the name, when I entered public high school, the next fall, as a freshman, having finally persuaded my grandparents to take me out of the convent, although they could never get to the bottom of my reasons, since, as I admitted, the nuns were kind, and I had made many nice new friends. What I wanted was a fresh start, a chance to begin life over again, but the first thing I heard in the corridors of the public high school was that name called out to me, like the warmest of welcomes: "Hi, there, Si!" That was the way they thought it was spelled. But this time I was resolute. After the first weeks, I dropped the hearties who called me "Si" and I never heard it again. I got my own name back and sloughed off Clementina and even Therese—the names that did not seem to me any more to be mine but to have been imposed on me by others. And I preferred to think that Mary meant "bitter" rather than "star of the sea."

1957

MAY SARTON
1912–1995

The woman artist in May Sarton's novel *Mrs. Stevens Hears the Mermaids Singing* (1965) explains about herself that "we are all monsters . . . we women who have chosen to be something more and something less than women!" Yet, as a novelist, a memoirist, and a poet, Sarton described the everyday and often prosaic details that fill the life of the single and sometimes singular woman writer. For, like Mrs. Stevens, Sarton clearly believed that "we have to dare to be ourselves, however frightening or strange that self may prove to be."

Born in Belgium and raised in Cambridge, Massachusetts, Sarton was the only child of an eminent historian of science, George Sarton, and an English portrait painter, Mabel (Elwes) Sarton. She attended the Shady Hill School in Cambridge and the Institut Belge de Culture Française in Brussels before joining Eva Le Gallienne's Civic Repertory Theatre in New York and experimenting with her own theatrical company. In *I Knew a Phoenix* (1959), Sarton also described her early trips to England, where she met the writers Elizabeth Bowen and Virginia Woolf. In spite of the gregarious personality that emerges from this autobiography, Sarton became famous for the journals that described her solitary life in Nelson, New Hampshire, and for such novels as *The Small Room* (1961), *Joanna and Ulysses* (1963), and *Kinds of Love* (1970), which depict the female friendships and love affairs that save women from loneliness.

Remarkably prolific, she worked in many genres, producing near the end of her life *After the Stroke: A Journal* (1988) and *Encore: A Journal of the Eightieth Year* (1993) as well as—among other volumes—*The Education of Harriet Hatfield: A Novel* (1989) and *Collected Poems, 1930–1993* (1993). Nonetheless, for many years her publications received little critical attention. Yet few writers dealt as sensitively with such subjects as the roots of identity (*The House by the Sea*, 1977), aging and death (*As We Are Now*, 1973), and the different forms female creativity takes. In her *Journal of a Solitude* (1973), wondering why "poetry always seems to me so much more a true work of the soul than prose," Sarton explained that it is "because the poem is primarily a dialogue with the self." Significantly, however, both "Letter from Chicago" and "My Sisters, O My Sisters" analyze her own creativity through dialogues with other literary women.

My Sisters, O My Sisters

> Nous qui voulions poser, image ineffaceable
> Comme un delta divin notre main sur le sable
> Anna de Noailles[1]

I

Dorothy Wordsworth,[2] dying, did not want to read,
"I am too busy with my own feelings," she said.

And all women who have wanted to break out
Of the prison of consciousness to sing or shout

5 Are strange monsters who renounce the treasure
Of their silence for a curious devouring pleasure.

Dickinson, Rossetti, Sappho[3]—they all know it,
Something is lost, strained, unforgiven in the poet.

She abdicates from life or like George Sand[4]
10 Suffers from the mortality in an immortal hand,

Loves too much, spends a whole life to discover
She was born a good grandmother, not a good lover.

Too powerful for men: Madame de Stael. Too sensitive:
Madame de Sévigné[5] who burdened where she meant to give.

15 Delicate as that burden was and so supremely lovely,
It was too heavy for her daughter, much too heavy.

---

1. We who wanted to leave in an ineffaceable image / Like a divine delta, our hand on the sand (French). Anna-Elisabeth, comtesse de Noailles (1876–1933), French poet and novelist
2. English poet and diarist (1771–1855); see Vol. 1, p. 447.
3. Emily Dickinson (1830–1886; see Vol. 1, p. 1037), Christina Rossetti (1830–1894; see Vol. 1, p. 1076), and Sappho (b. ca. 612 B.C.E.) were three female lyric poets—American, English and Greek, respectively.
4. Pen name of Aurore Dupin (1804–1876), French novelist known for her many love affairs.
5. Marie de Sévigné (1626–1696), French noblewoman and prolific letter writer; a two-volume collection of letters to her daughter were published in 1726. Germaine de Staël (1766–1817), French woman of letters.

Only when she built inward in a fearful isolation
Did any one succeed or learn to fuse emotion

With thought. Only when she renounced did Emily
20 Begin in the fierce lonely light to learn to be.

Only in the extremity of spirit and the flesh
And in renouncing passion did Sappho come to bless.

Only in the farewells or in old age does sanity
Shine through the crimson stains of their mortality.

25 And now we who are writing women and strange monsters
Still search our hearts to find the difficult answers,

Still hope that we may learn to lay our hands
More gently and more subtly on the burning sands.

To be through what we make more simply human,
30 To come to the deep place where poet becomes woman,

Where nothing has to be renounced or given over
In the pure light that shines out from the lover,

In the pure light that brings forth fruit and flower
And that great sanity, that sun, the feminine power.

II

35 Let us rejoice in
The full curve of breast,
The supple thigh
And all riches in
A woman's keeping
40 For man's comfort and rest
(Crimson and ivory)
For children's nourishment
(Magic fruits and flowers).
But when they are sleeping,
45 The children, the men,
Fed by these powers,
We know what is meant
By the wise serpent,
By the gentle dove,[6]
50 And remember then
How we wish to love,

Let us rejoice now
In these great powers

---

6. After selecting his apostles, Jesus told them to be "wise as serpents, and harmless as doves" (Matthew 10.16).

                Which are ours alone.
55   And trust what we know:
                First the green hand
                That can open flowers
                In the deathly bone,
                And the magic breast
60   That can feed the child,
                And is under a hand
                A rose of fire in snow
                So tender, so wild
                All fires come to rest,
65   All lives can be blest—
                So sighs the gentle dove,
                Wily the serpent so,
                Matched in a woman's love.

III

                Eve and Mary[7] the mother are our stem;
70   All our centuries go back to them.
                And delicate the balance lies
                Between the passionate and wise:
                Of man's rib, one, and cleaves to him;
                And one bears man and then frees him.
75   This double river has created us,
                Always the rediscovered, always the cherished.
                (But many fail in this. Many have perished.)

                Hell is the loss of balance when woman is destroyer.
                Each of us has been there.
80   Each of us knows what the floods can do.
                How many women mother their husbands
                Out of all strength and secret *Virtu*;[8]
                How many women love an only son
                As a lover loves, binding the free hands.
85   How many yield up their true power
                Out of weakness, the moment of passion
                Betrayed by years of confused living—
                For it is surely a lifetime work,
                This learning to be a woman.
90   Until at the end what is clear
                Is the marvelous skill to make
                Life grow in all its forms.

                Is knowing where to ask, where to yield,
                Where to sow, where to plough the field,

---

7. The mother of Jesus, whose death, according to the New Testament, redeemed humanity from sin: "For as in Adam all die, even so in Christ shall all be made alive" (1 Corinthians 15.22). Eve, as the first woman, created from Adam's rib, was the mother of all humankind (Genesis 2.21–23, 3.20); Adam and Eve's disobedience in eating the fruit of the tree of knowledge introduced death and sin into the world.
8. Strength or power (Italian).

95 Where to kill the heart or let it live;
    To be Eve, the giver of knowledge, the lover;
    To be Mary, the shield, the healer and the mother.
    The balance is eternal whatever we may wish;
    The law can be broken but we cannot change
100 What is supremely beautiful and strange.
    Where find the root? Where re-join the source?
    The fertile feminine goddess, double river?

IV

    We think of all the women hunting for themselves,
    Turning and turning to each other with a driving
105 Need to learn to understand, to live in charity,
    And above all to be used fully, to be giving
    From wholeness, wholeness back to love's deep clarity.
    O, all the burning hearts of women unappeased
    Shine like great stars, like flowers of fire,
110 As the sun goes and darkness opens all desire—
    And we are with a fierce compassion seized.
    How lost, how far from home, how parted from
    The earth, my sisters, O my sisters, we have come!

    For so long asked so little of ourselves and men,
115 And let the Furies[9] have their way—our treasure,
    The single antidote to all our world's confusion,
    A few gifts to the poor small god of pleasure.
    The god of passion has gone back into the mountain,
    Is sleeping in the dark, deep in the earth.

120 We have betrayed a million times the holy fountain,
    The potent spirit who brings his life to birth,
    The masculine and violent joy of pure creation—
    And yielded up the sacred fires to sensation.
    But we shall never come home to the earth
125 Until we bring the great god and his mirth
    Back from the mountain, until we let this stranger
    Plough deep into our hearts his joy and anger,[1]
    For we shall never find ourselves again
    Until we ask men's greatness back from men,
130 Until we make the fertile god our own,
    And giving up our lives, receive his own.

                                                    1948

---

9. In Greek myth, female avenging spirits.
1. Dionysus, Greek god of fertility and wine, was associated with tragedy, comedy, and the mountains; in the story of Pentheus, he disguises himself as a stranger.

Letter from Chicago

For Virginia Woolf[1]

Four years ago I met your death here,
Heard it where I had never been before
In a city of departures, streets of wind,
Soft plumes of smoke dissolving—
City of departures beside an aloof lake.
Here where you never were, they said,
"Virginia Woolf is dead."

The city died. I died in the city,
Witness of unreal tears, my own,
For experience involves time
And time was gone
The world arrested at the instant of death.
I wept wildly like a child
Who cannot give his present after all:
I met your death and did not recognize you.

Now you are dead four years
And there are no more private tears.
The city of departure is the city of arrival,
City of triumphant wind lifting people,
City of spring: yesterday I found you.
Wherever I looked was love.
Wherever I went I had presents in my hands.
Wherever I went I recognized you.

You are not, never to be again,
Never, never to be dead,
Never to be dead again in this city,
Never to be mourned again,
But to come back yearly,
Hourly, with the spring, with the wind,
Fresh as agony or resurrection;
A plume of smoke dissolving,
Remaking itself, never still,
Never static, never lost:
The place where time flows again.

I speak to you and meet my own life.
Is it to be poised as the lake beside the city,
Aloof, but given still to air and wind,
Detached from time, but given to the moment—
Is it to be a celebration always?

I send you love forward into the past.

1953

---

1. English novelist and essayist (1882–1941); see above, p. 212.

The Muse as Medusa[1]

I saw you once, Medusa; we were alone.
I looked you straight in the cold eye, cold.
I was not punished, was not turned to stone—
How to believe the legends I am told?

5 I came as naked as any little fish,
Prepared to be hooked, gutted, caught;
But I saw you, Medusa, made my wish,
And when I left you I was clothed in thought. . . .

Being allowed, perhaps, to swim my way
10 Through the great deep and on the rising tide,
Flashing wild streams, as free and rich as they,
Though you had power marshaled on your side.

The fish escaped to many a magic reef;
The fish explored many a dangerous sea—
15 The fish, Medusa, did not come to grief,
But swims still in a fluid mystery.

Forget the image: your silence is my ocean,
And even now it teems with life. You chose
To abdicate by total lack of motion,
20 But did it work, for nothing really froze?

It is all fluid still, that world of feeling
Where thoughts, those fishes, silent, feed and rove;
And, fluid, it is also full of healing,
For love is healing, even rootless love.

25 I turn your face around! It is my face.
That frozen rage is what I must explore—
Oh secret, self-enclosed, and ravaged place!
This is the gift I thank Medusa for.

1971

---

1. A female monster with snakes for hair, the sight of whom turns living creatures to stone, according to Greek myth. "Muse": a goddess of art and learning, conventionally invoked for inspiration and information.

MURIEL RUKEYSER
1913–1980

"Breathe-in experience, breathe-out poetry": Muriel Rukeyser opened the first poem of her first volume of verse, *Theory of Flight* (1935), with a vow to eschew all that might be construed as artificially poetic in favor of a lyrical articulation of personal experience. That those experiences would be shaped by political realities is evidenced later in the poem, when Rukeyser exclaims, "Not Sappho, Sacco." Rejecting the erotic verse of ancient Greece for poetry focusing on the ethnic, political, and economic issues that led to the execution of the anarchist-immigrants Nicola Sacco and Bartolomeo Vanzetti, Rukeyser placed herself in the expansive tradition of American verse established by Walt Whitman as well as in the school of modern political poetry led by W. H. Auden, and she thereby dedicated herself throughout her distinguished career to breathing in the ordinary expressions of the victimized and breathing out the songs that linked their lives to her own.

Rukeyser was born and lived most of her life in New York. Her parents were affluent, and she attended the Fieldston School, Vassar College, and Columbia University. But most of her friends were socialists, labor organizers, or artists. At Vassar, she began publishing her work, and in the early 1930s, along with Elizabeth Bishop and Mary McCarthy, she founded a literary magazine to protest the policies of the *Vassar Review*. *Theory of Flight,* published in the Yale Series of Younger Poets, was quickly followed by *Mediterranean* (ca. 1937), *U.S. 1* (1938), *A Turning Wind* (1939), *The Soul and Body of John Brown* (1940), *Wake Island* (1942), *Beast in View* (1944), and *The Green Wave* (1948). A number of these volumes deal directly with social injustice in America and with the atrocities of World War II, a subject of passionate concern to Rukeyser because of her Jewishness and because of her earlier involvement in the fight against fascism in Spain.

After the war, Rukeyser lived briefly in Berkeley, where she taught at the California Labor School, but she spent much of her time "pushing a baby carriage" after the birth of her child in 1947. Although the biographical details of her relationship with the baby's father are obscure, it is clear that Rukeyser remained a single parent. An anonymous benefactor, who turned out to be the wealthy Californian Henriette Durham, helped finance Rukeyser's return to New York, where she began teaching part-time at Sarah Lawrence College and serving as vice president of the House of Photography. During the 1950s, few of Rukeyser's publications were new compositions, a fact that the critic Louise Kertesz attributes to Rukeyser's child care responsibilities. In such later volumes as *Body of Waking* (1958), *The Speed of Darkness* (1968), *Breaking Open* (1973), and *The Gates* (1976), giving birth became a major source of her imagery, sometimes providing the only solace against the violence she witnessed and protested both in Korea and in Vietnam. In 1978, Rukeyser's *Collected Poems* appeared; and in 1992, Kate Daniels produced a selection titled *Out of Silence,* which was followed in 1994 by a collection of poetry and prose, *A Muriel Rukeyser Reader,* edited by Jan Heller Levi.

Although, from her early training in aviation to her later biographies of scientists, Rukeyser never relinquished her fascination with technological and rational quests for transcendence, she increasingly turned to mythic and historical female figures to trace an ancestry for herself that could counter the destructiveness she associated with American capitalism. While she was faulted by some literary critics for both her optimism and her philosophizing, toward the end of her life she had clearly found an audience through her teaching and in the younger generation of emerging women writers. The poet Anne Sexton wrote "Muriel, mother of everyone," to thank her for a copy of *The Speed of Darkness*; Sexton added that the volume remained on her desk, "flow[ing] out like an infusion of blood into the body."

Boy with His Hair Cut Short

    Sunday shuts down on this twentieth-century evening.
    The El[1] passes. Twilight and bulb define
    the brown room, the overstuffed plum sofa,
    the boy, and the girl's thin hands above his head.
5   A neighbor radio sings stocks, news, serenade.

    He sits at the table, head down, the young clear neck exposed,
    watching the drugstore sign from the tail of his eye;
    tattoo, neon, until the eye blears, while his
    solicitous tall sister, simple in blue, bending
10 behind him, cuts his hair with her cheap shears.

    The arrow's electric red always reaches its mark,
    successful neon! He coughs, impressed by that precision.
    His child's forehead, forever protected by his cap,
    is bleached against the lamplight as he turns head
15 and steadies to let the snippets drop.

    Erasing the failure of weeks with level fingers,
    she sleeks the fine hair, combing: "You'll look fine tomorrow!
    You'll surely find something, they can't keep turning you down;

    the finest gentleman's not so trim as you!" Smiling, he raises
20 the adolescent forehead wrinkling ironic now.

    He sees his decent suit laid out, new-pressed,
    his carfare on the shelf. He lets his head fall, meeting
    her earnest hopeless look, seeing the sharp blades splitting,
    the darkened room, the impersonal sign, her motion,
25 the blue vein, bright on her temple, pitifully beating.

1938

More of a Corpse than a Woman

    Give them my regards when you go to the school reunion;
    and at the marriage-supper, say that I'm thinking about them.
    They'll remember my name; I went to the movies with that one,
    feeling the weight of their death where she sat at my elbow;
5   she never said a word,
        but all of them were heard.

    all of them alike, expensive girls, the leaden friends:
    one used to play the piano, one of them once wrote a sonnet,
    one even seemed awakened enough to photograph wheatfields—

---

1. The elevated train, part of the New York transit system that used to run above the street.

10 the dull girls with the educated minds and technical passions—
         pure love was their employment,
         they tried it for enjoyment.

    Meet them at the boat: they've brought the souvenirs of boredom,
    a seashell from the faltering monarchy;
15 the nose of a marble saint; and from the battlefield,
    an empty shell divulged from a flower-bed.
         The lady's wealthy breath
         perfumes the air with death.

    The leaden lady faces the fine, voluptuous woman,
20 faces a rising world bearing its gifts in its hands.
    Kisses her casual dreams upon the lips she kisses,
    risen, she moves away; takes others; moves away.
         Inadequate to love,
         supposes she's enough.

25 Give my regards to the well-protected woman,
    I knew the ice-cream girl, we went to school together.
    There's something to bury, people, when you begin to bury.
    When your women are ready and rich in their wish for the world,
         destroy the leaden heart,
30   we've a new race to start.

                                                                  1938

Who in One Lifetime

    Who in one lifetime sees all causes lost,
    Herself dismayed and helpless, cities down,
    Love made monotonous fear and the sad-faced
    Inexorable armies and the falling plane,
5   Has sickness, sickness. Introspective and whole,
    She knows how several madnesses are born,
    Seeing the integrated never fighting well,
    The flesh too vulnerable, the eyes tear-torn.

    She finds a pre-surrender on all sides:
10 Treaty before the war, ritual impatience turn
    The camps of ambush to chambers of imagery.
    She holds belief in the world, she stays and hides
    Life in her own defeat, stands, though her whole world burn,
    A childless goddess of fertility.

June 1941   1944

From Letter to the Front
VII

To be a Jew in the twentieth century
Is to be offered a gift. If you refuse,
Wishing to be invisible, you choose
Death of the spirit, the stone insanity.
5 Accepting, take full life. Full agonies:
Your evening deep in labyrinthine blood
Of those who resist, fail, and resist; and God
Reduced to a hostage among hostages.

The gift is torment. Not alone the still
10 Torture, isolation; or torture of the flesh.
That may come also. But the accepting wish,
The whole and fertile spirit as guarantee
For every human freedom, suffering to be free,
Daring to live for the impossible.

1944

Night Feeding

Deeper than sleep but not so deep as death
I lay there sleeping and my magic head
remembered and forgot.   On first cry I
remembered and forgot and did believe.
5 I knew love and I knew evil:
woke to the burning song and the tree burning blind,
despair of our days and the calm milk-giver who
knows sleep, knows growth, the sex of fire and grass,
and the black snake with gold bones.

10 Black sleeps, gold burns; on second cry I woke
fully and gave to feed and fed on feeding.
Gold seed, green pain, my wizards in the earth
walked through the house, black in the morning dark.
Shadows grew in my veins, my bright belief,
15 my head of dreams deeper than night and sleep.
Voices of all black animals crying to drink,
cries of all birth arise, simple as we,
found in the leaves, in clouds and dark, in dream,
deep as this hour, ready again to sleep.

1951

The Birth of Venus[1]

Risen in a
welter of waters.

Not as he saw her
standing upon a frayed and lovely surf
5   clean-riding the graceful leafy breezes
clean-poised and easy. Not yet.

But born in a
tidal wave of the father's overthrow,
the old rule killed and its mutilated sex.

10   The testicles of the father-god, father of fathers,
sickled off by his son, the next god Time.
Sickled off. Hurled into the ocean.
In all that blood and foam.
among raving and generation,
15   of semen and the sea born, the
great goddess rises.

         However, possibly,
on the long worldward voyage flowing,
horror gone down in birth, the curse, being changed,
20   being used, is translated far at the margin into
our rose and saving image, curling toward a shore
early and April, with certainly shells, certainly blossoms.

And the girl, the wellborn, goddess, human love—
young-known, new-knowing, mouth flickering, sure eyes—
25   rides shoreward, from death to us as we are at this moment on
the crisp delightful Botticellian wave.

                                                          1958

The Power of Suicide[1]

The potflower on the windowsill says to me
In words that are green-edged red leaves:
Flower flower flower flower
Today for the sake of all the dead   Burst into flower.

1963   1968

---

1. The Roman name for the Greek goddess of love and beauty, Aphrodite, who was born from the ocean after Uranus was castrated by his son, Cronos (a name that sounds like *chronos*, "time"). This newly born goddess, standing in a shell, is depicted in a famous painting by Sandro Botticelli (1445–1510).

1. This poem has been read as a response to the suicide of American poet Sylvia Plath (1932–1963; see below, p. 1044).

The Poem as Mask

Orpheus[1]

When I wrote of the women in their dances and wildness,
    it was a mask,
on their mountain, gold-hunting, singing, in orgy,
it was a mask; when I wrote of the god,
fragmented, exiled from himself, his life, the love gone down
    with song,
5 it was myself, split open, unable to speak, in exile from myself.

There is no mountain, there is no god, there is memory
of my torn life, myself split open in sleep, the rescued child
beside me among the doctors, and a word
of rescue from the great eyes.

10 No more masks! No more mythologies!

Now, for the first time, the god lifts his hand,
the fragments join in me with their own music.

                                    1968

Käthe Kollwitz[1]

I

        Held between wars
          my lifetime
    among wars, the big hands of the world of death
my lifetime
5 listens to yours.

The faces of the sufferers
in the street, in dailiness,
their lives showing
through their bodies
10 a look as of music
the revolutionary look
that says   I am in the world
to change the world
my lifetime
15 is to love to endure to suffer the music
to set its portrait
up as a sheet of the world

---

1. The subject of the poem is the mythical Greek singer and poet whose music had magical powers over humans and animals, and who was torn to pieces by the Maenads—women who were followers of Dionysus, god of wine. He was the son of Apollo, the god of poetry and the sun.

1. German graphic artist and sculptor (1867–1945), famous for her searing drawings and prints of workers, mothers and children, and the horrors of war. The poem quotes her words and recalls a number of her works.

        the most moving the most alive
        Easter and bone
20   and Faust[2] walking among the flowers of the world
        and the child alive within the living woman, music of man,
        and death holding my lifetime between great hands
        the hands of enduring life
        that suffers the gifts and madness of full life, on earth, in our time,
25   and through my life, through my eyes, through my arms and hands
        may give the face of this music in portrait waiting for
        the unknown person
        held in the two hands, you.

II

        Woman as gates, saying:
30   "The process is after all like music,
        like the development of a piece of music.
        The fugues come back and
                                again and again
        interweave.
35   A theme may seem to have been put aside,
        but it keeps returning—
        the same thing modulated,
        somewhat changed in form.
        Usually richer.
40   And it is very good that this is so."

        A woman pouring her opposites.
        "After all there are happy things in life too.
        Why do you show only the dark side?"
        "I could not answer this. But I know—
45   in the beginning my impulse to know
        the working life
                        had little to do with
        pity or sympathy.
                      I simply felt
50   that the life of the workers was beautiful."

        She said, "I am groping in the dark."

        She said, "When the door opens, of sensuality,
        then you will understand it too. The struggle begins.
        Never again to be free of it,
55   often you will feel it to be your enemy.
        Sometimes
        you will almost suffocate,
        such joy it brings."

---

2. The questing intellectual hero of Johann Wolfgang von Goethe's long dramatic poem *Faust* (1808–32). In one scene, Faust is uplifted when he hears the church bells and children's choir on Easter morning.

          Saying of her husband: "My wish
60   is to die after Karl.
          I know no person who can love as he can,
          with his whole soul.
          Often this love has oppressed me;
          I wanted to be free.
65   But often too it has made me
          so terribly happy."[3]

          She said: "We rowed over to Carrara[4] at dawn,
          climbed up to the marble quarries
          and rowed back at night. The drops of water
70   fell like glittering stars
          from our oars."

          She said: "As a matter of fact,
          I believe
                         that bisexuality
75   is almost   a necessary factor
          in artistic production; at any rate,
          the tinge of masculinity within me
          helped me
                         in my work."

80   She said: "The only technique I can still manage.
          It's hardly a technique at all, lithography.
          In it
                         only the essentials count."

85   A tight-lipped man in a restaurant last night saying to me:
          "Kollwitz?   She's too black-and-white."[5]

III

          Held among wars, watching
                   all of them
                   all these people
                   weavers,
90   Carmagnole[6]

          Looking at
                   all of them
                   death, the children
                   patients in waiting-rooms
95   famine
                   the street

---

3. Karl Kollwitz (d. 1940), a pioneering doctor for the poor, was deeply supportive of his wife's work.
4. City in central Italy, center of the marble industry.
5. Kollwitz worked almost exclusively in black and white.
6. A song and dance popular during the French Revolution; the title of a famous series of prints by Kollwitz.

            the corpse with the baby
            floating, on the dark river

            A woman seeing
100   the violent, inexorable
            movement of nakedness
            and the confession of No
            the confession of great weakness, war,
            all streaming to one son killed, Peter;[7]
105   even the son left living; repeated,
            the father, the mother; the grandson
            another Peter killed in another war:[8] firestorm;
            dark, light, as two hands,
            this pole and that pole as the gates.

110   What would happen if one woman told the truth about her life?
            The world would split open

                    IV / Song: The Calling-Up

            Rumor, stir of ripeness
            rising within this girl
            sensual blossoming
115   of meaning, its light and form.

            The birth-cry summoning
            out of the male, the father
            from the warm woman
            a mother in response.

120   The word of death
            calls up the fight with stone
            wrestle with grief with time
            from the material make
            an art harder than bronze.

                    V / Self-Portrait[9]

125   Mouth looking directly at you
            eyes in their inwardness looking
            directly at you
            half light   half darkness
            woman, strong, German, young artist
130   flows into
            wide sensual mouth meditating
            looking right at you
            eyes shadowed with brave hand
            looking deep at you

---

7. Kollwitz's younger son, Peter, was killed in World War I.
8. Her grandson Peter was killed in Russia during World War II.
9. Kollwitz drew self-portraits throughout her life.

135   flows into
       wounded brave mouth
       grieving and hooded eyes
       alive, German, in her first War
       flows into
140   strength of the worn face
       a skein of lines
       broods, flows into
       mothers among the war graves
       bent over death
145   facing the father
       stubborn upon the field
       flows into
       the marks of her knowing—
       Nie Wieder Krieg[1]
150   repeated in the eyes
       flows into
       "Seedcorn must not be ground"[2]
       and the grooved cheek
       lips drawn fine
155   the down-drawn grief
       face of our age
       flows into
       Pieta,[3] mother and
       between her knees
160   life as her son in death
       pouring from the sky of
       one more war
       flows into
       face almost obliterated
165   hand over the mouth forever
       hand over one eye now
       the other great eye
       closed

                                                                1968

Myth

Long afterward, Oedipus,[1] old and blinded, walked the
roads.   He smelled a familiar smell.   It was
the Sphinx.   Oedipus said, "I want to ask one question.
Why didn't I recognize my mother?"   "You gave the

---

1. No More War (German); the title of another famous set of prints.
2. Title of Kollwitz's last work, depicting a mother protecting her young children; the title means that the youth who will bear the next generation must not be destroyed in war.
3. Pity (Italian); a term traditionally applied to representations of the Virgin Mary sorrowing over the dead body of Christ, and used by Kollwitz as the title for drawings of mothers mourning their dead children.

1. According to Greek myth, a king of Thebes who saved the city from plague by answering a riddle posed by a monster called the Sphinx, then discovered that he had unknowingly killed his father and married his mother. Horrified by his deeds, he put out his eyes and went into exile.

wrong answer," said the Sphinx.   "But that was what made everything possible," said Oedipus.   "No," she said. "When I asked, What walks on four legs in the morning, two at noon, and three in the evening, you answered, Man.   You didn't say anything about woman."
"When you say Man," said Oedipus, "you include women too. Everyone knows that."   She said, "That's what you think."

1973

Along History

Along history, forever
  some woman dancing,
  making shapes on the air;
  forever a man
  riding a good horse,
  sitting the dark horse well,
  his penis erect with
    fantasy

1973

MAY SWENSON
1913–1989

Born and raised in Logan, Utah, where her father was a professor of mechanical engineering at the state university, the poet May Swenson worked as a reporter for the Salt Lake City *Desert News*, then settled in New York City, where she became an editor for New Directions in 1959. In 1966, after publishing a number of well-received collections of verse—including *Another Animal* (1954) and *To Mix with Time: New and Selected Poems* (1963)—she resigned from her editorial job to devote herself completely to her writing. After that, with the assistance of Guggenheim and Rockefeller fellowships among other awards, Swenson produced a considerable body of poetry, most notably the imaginative and innovative volume of "concrete" poetry *Iconographs* (1970), a book of verses all, like "Women" and "Bleeding," arranged in typographical forms whose shapes reflect the nature of their subject, for her intention, as she herself explained, was "to make an existence in space, as well as time, for the poem."

About Swenson's early work, the poet Elizabeth Bishop remarked in a 1962 letter that this artist is "one of the few good poets who write good poems about nature . . . not just comparing it to states of mind or society." Yet as the exuberantly erotic "Blue" reveals, Swenson's nature poetry eventually came to represent more than the natural thing-in-itself; her "rose" in "Blue," for instance, evokes both a flower and a beloved woman. The poet-critic Alicia Ostriker has observed that in Swenson's later work, the scrupulous vision Bishop defined had evolved into more radical and metaphysical "shapes of speculation." Her posthumously published volumes—*The Love Poems of May Swenson* (1991) and *Nature: Poems Old and New* (1994)—include such shapes of speculation, along with images of desire.

The Centaur[1]

The summer that I was ten—
Can it be there was only one
summer that I was ten? It must

have been a long one then—
each day I'd go out to choose
a fresh horse from my stable

which was a willow grove
down by the old canal
I'd go on my two bare feet.

But when, with my brother's jack-knife,
I had cut me a long limber horse
with a good thick knob for a head,

and peeled him slick and clean
except a few leaves for the tail,
and cinched my brother's belt

around his head for a rein,
I'd straddle and canter him fast
up the grass bank to the path,

trot along in the lovely dust
that talcumed over his hoofs,
hiding my toes, and turning

his feet to swift half-moons.
The willow knob with the strap
jouncing between my thighs

was the pommel and yet the poll[2]
of my nickering pony's head.
My head and my neck were mine,

yet they were shaped like a horse.
My hair flopped to the side
like the mane of a horse in the wind.

---

1. In Greek mythology, a creature that was half man and half horse.
2. The top of the head.

My forelock swung in my eyes,
my neck arched and I snorted.
I shied and skittered and reared,

stopped and raised my knees,
35 pawed at the ground and quivered.
My teeth bared as we wheeled

and swished through the dust again.
I was the horse and the rider,
and the leather I slapped to his rump

spanked my own behind.
40 Doubled, my two hoofs beat
a gallop along the bank,

the wind twanged in my mane,
my mouth squared to the bit.
And yet I sat on my steed

45 quiet, negligent riding,
my toes standing the stirrups,
my thighs hugging his ribs.

At a walk we drew up to the porch.
I tethered him to a paling.
50 Dismounting, I smoothed my skirt

and entered the dusky hall.
My feet on the clean linoleum
left ghostly toes in the hall.

Where have you been? said my mother.
55 *Been riding,* I said from the sink,
and filled me a glass of water.

What's that in your pocket? she said.
Just my knife. It weighted my pocket
and stretched my dress awry.

60 *Go tie back your hair,* said my mother,
and *Why is your mouth all green?*
Rob Roy,[3] *he pulled some clover
as we crossed the field,* I told her.

1954

---

3. I.e., the imaginary horse. The historical Rob Roy (Robert MacGregor, 1671–1734) was a Scottish cattle rustler and brigand.

Women

```
Women                     Or they
   should be                 should be
      pedestals                 little horses
         moving                    those wooden
            pedestals                 sweet                         5
               moving                    oldfashioned
                  to the                    painted
                     motions                   rocking
                        of men                    horses


              the gladdest things in the toyroom                   10

               The                        feelingly
                  pegs                       and then
                     of their                   unfeelingly
                        ears                      To be
                           so similar               joyfully       15
                              and dear              ridden
                                 to the trusting    rockingly
                                    fists           ridden until
                        To be chafed                the restored


egos dismount and the legs stride away                             20

Immobile                    willing
   sweetlipped                 to be set
      sturdy                      into motion
         and smiling                 Women
            women                       should be                  25
               should always               pedestals
                  be waiting                  to men
```

                                                    1968, 1970

Blue

    Blue, but you are Rose, too,
    and buttermilk, but with blood
    dots showing through.
    A little salty your white
5   nape boy-wide. Glinting hairs
    shoot back of your ears' Rose
    that tongue likes to feel
    the maze of, slip into the funnel,
    tell a thunder-whisper to.

10   When I kiss, your eyes' straight
      lashes down crisp go like doll's
      blond straws. Glazed iris Roses,
      your lids unclose to Blue-ringed
      targets, their dark sheen-spokes
15   almost green. I sink in Blue-
      black Rose-heart holes until you
      blink. Pink lips, the serrate
      folds taste smooth, and Rosehip-
      round, the center bud I suck.
20   I milknip your two Blue-skeined
      blown Rose beauties, too, to sniff
      their berries' blood, up stiff
      pink tips. You're white in
      patches, only mostly Rose,
25   buckskin and salty, speckled
      like a sky. I love your spots,
      your white neck, Rose, your hair's
      wild straw splash, silk spools
      for your ears. But where white
30   spouts out, spills on your brow
      to clear eyepools, wheel shafts
      of light, Rose, you are Blue.

1969

Bleeding

      Stop bleeding   said the knife
      I would if I   could said the cut.
      Stop bleeding   you make me messy with this blood.
      I'm sorry said   the cut.
5   Stop or I will   sink in farther said the knife.
      Don't said the   cut.
      The knife did   not say it couldn't help it but it sank in farther.
      If only you   didn't bleed said the knife I wouldn't have to do this.
      I know said   the cut I bleed too easily I hate that I can't
10   help it I   wish I were a knife like you and didn't have to bleed.
      Meanwhile   stop bleeding will you said the knife.
      Yes you   are a mess and sinking in farther said the cut I will
      have to   stop.
      Have you   stopped by now said the knife.
15   I've almost   stopped I think
      Why must you   bleed in the first place said the knife.
      For the reason   maybe that you must do what you must do said the cut.
      I can't stand   bleeding said the knife and sank in farther.
      I hate it too   said the cut I know it isn't you it's me
20   you're lucky to   be a knife you ought to be glad about that.
      Too many cuts   around said the knife they're messy I don't know
      how they stand   themselves

They don't said	the cut.
You're bleeding	again.
25 No I've stopped	said the cut. See you're coming out now the
blood is drying	it will rub off you'll be shiny again and clean.
If only cuts	wouldn't bleed so much said the knife coming out a little.
But then knives	might become dull said the cut.
Aren't you bleeding	a little said the knife.
30 I hope not said the	cut.
I feel you are just	a little.
Maybe just a little	but I can stop now.
I feel a little	wetness still said the knife sinking in
a little but then	coming out a little.
35 Just a little maybe	just enough said the cut.
That's enough now	stop now do you feel better said the knife.
I feel I have to	bleed to feel I think said the cut.
I don't I don't have	to feel said the knife drying now becoming shiny.

1970

TILLIE OLSEN
b. ca. 1913

"In the twenty years I bore and reared my children, usually had to work on a paid job as well, the simplest circumstances for creation did not exist," wrote Tillie Olsen in "Silences" (1962), an essay in which she explored the "relationship of circumstances—including class, color, sex"—to "the unnatural thwarting of what struggles to come into being." Later, in an equally important essay, "One Out of Twelve: Women Who Are Writers in Our Century" (1972), Olsen made the connection between gender and silence even more direct: "We [women] who write are survivors, 'only's,' " she declared, defining a *survivor* as "one who must bear witness for those who foundered," and explaining again the "cost of 'discontinuity' " in her own life. Yet despite the pressures of such discontinuity, Olsen herself has managed to produce a significant group of extraordinarily accomplished tales.

Born in Nebraska, Olsen dropped out of high school in the eleventh grade to enter the world of what she calls "everyday" jobs. A member of the Depression generation, she began early to work for social and political causes. She struggled to organize packinghouse workers in Omaha and Kansas City, joined the Young Communist League, and was involved in the San Francisco labor movement, including the general strike of 1934. Even while she was engaged in such activism, however, Olsen had begun to write. Her passionately political early works include two powerfully wrenching poems, which both appeared in print—as her first publications—in 1934, when she was in her early twenties. A chapter of a novel also appeared in the same year, and for some time longer she continued to work on the book. At last, however, "it had," as she herself tells us, "to be set aside, never to come to completion," though a "rewoven" version of it was finally published as *Yonnondio: From the Thirties* (1974).

Married in 1943 to Jack Olsen, a printer and, like herself, an activist deeply committed to the labor movement, Olsen had four children and did not begin to write again until the 1950s, when her youngest daughter was five years old. In eight years, she produced the four stories that were collected in her distinguished volume *Tell*

Me a Riddle (1961), a book whose title novella, with its searching examination of the mind and memories of a dying woman, received the O. Henry Award as the best American story in the year when it was published. A prodigious reader ("public libraries were my college") whose interest in women's writing was rekindled by the resurgence of feminism in the 1960s, Olsen has been instrumental in bringing important forgotten books back into print. An afterword of hers appears with Rebecca Harding Davis's *Life in the Iron-Mills* (rpt. 1971), while her meticulously documented critical volume *Silences* (1978) further explores the crucial power of circumstance.

Between 1969 and 1974, Olsen taught at Amherst, Stanford, MIT, and the University of Massachusetts at Boston. More recently, she has received fellowships from the Guggenheim Foundation and the National Endowment for the Humanities, as well as several honorary degrees. Throughout this period, mindful of her "hatred for all that, societally rooted . . . slows, impairs, silences writers," she has continued her struggle to "re-dedicate and encourage" other women to the powers and possibilities of their own creativity. A 1994 collection of essays edited by Elaine Hedges and Shelley Fisher Fishkin, *Listening to Silences*, attests to Olsen's success in cultivating her own extraordinary talent.

Tell Me a Riddle

"These Things Shall Be"

I

For forty-seven years they had been married. How deep back the stubborn, gnarled roots of the quarrel reached, no one could say—but only now, when tending to the needs of others no longer shackled them together, the roots swelled up visible, split the earth between them, and the tearing shook even to the children, long since grown.

Why now, why now? wailed Hannah.

As if when we grew up weren't enough, said Paul.

Poor Ma. Poor Dad. It hurts so for both of them, said Vivi. They never had very much; at least in old age they should be happy.

Knock their heads together, insisted Sammy; tell 'em: you're too old for this kind of thing; no reason not to get along now.

Lennie wrote to Clara: They've lived over so much together; what could possibly tear them apart?

Something tangible enough.

Arthritic hands, and such work as he got, occasional. Poverty all his life, and there was little breath left for running. He could not, could not turn away from this desire: to have the troubling of responsibility, the fretting with money, over and done with; to be free, to be *carefree* where success was not measured by accumulation, and there was use for the vitality still in him.

There was a way. They could sell the house, and with the money join his lodge's Haven, co-operative for the aged. Happy communal life, and was he not already an official; had he not helped organize it, raise funds, served as a trustee?

But she—would not consider it.

"What do we need all this for?" he would ask loudly, for her hearing aid was turned down and the vacuum was shrilling. "Five rooms" (pushing the sofa so she could get into the corner) "furniture" (smoothing down the rug) "floors and surfaces to make work. Tell me, why do we need it?" And he was glad he could ask in a scream.

"Because I'm use't."

"Because you're use't. This is a reason, Mrs. Word Miser? Used to can get unused!"

"Enough unused I have to get used to already.... Not enough words?" turning off the vacuum a moment to hear herself answer. "Because soon enough we'll need only a little closet, no windows, no furniture, nothing to make work for but worms. Because now I want room . . . Screech and blow like you're doing, you'll need that closet even sooner . . . Ha, again!" for the vacuum bag wailed, puffed half up, hung stubbornly limp. "This time fix it so it stays; quick before the phone rings and you get too important-busy."

But while he struggled with the motor, it seethed in him. Why fix it? Why have to bother? And if it can't be fixed, have to wring the mind with how to pay the repair? At the Haven they come in with their own machines to clean your room or your cottage; you fish, or play cards, or make jokes in the sun, not with knotty fingers fight to mend vacuums.

Over the dishes, coaxingly: "For once in your life, to be free, to have everything done for you, like a queen."

"I never liked queens."

"No dishes, no garbage, no towel to sop, no worry what to buy, what to eat."

"And what else would I do with my empty hands? Better to eat at my own table when I want, and to cook and eat how I want."

"In the cottages they buy what you ask, and cook it how you like. You are the one who always used to say: better mankind born without mouths and stomachs than always to worry for money to buy, to shop, to fix, to cook, to wash, to clean."

"How cleverly you hid that you heard. I said it then because eighteen hours a day I ran. And you never scraped a carrot or knew a dish towel sops. Now— for you and me—who cares? A herring out of a jar is enough. But when I want, and nobody to bother." And she turned off her ear button, so she would not have to hear.

But as *he* had no peace, juggling and rejuggling the money to figure: how will I pay for this now?; prying out the storm windows (there they take care of this); jolting in the streetcar on errands (there I would not have to ride to take care of this or that); fending the patronizing relatives just back from Florida (there it matters what one is, not what one can afford), he gave her no peace.

"Look! In their bulletin. A reading circle. Twice a week it meets."

"Haumm," her answer of not listening.

"A reading circle. Chekhov they read that you like, and Peretz.[1] Cultured people at the Haven that you would enjoy."

---

1. I. L. Peretz (1852–1915), Russian author of poems, plays, and stories in Yiddish. Anton Chekhov (1860–1904), Russian writer.

"Enjoy!" She tasted the word. "Now, when it pleases you, you find a reading circle for me. And forty years ago when the children were morsels and there was a Circle, did you stay home with them once so I could go? Even once? You trained me well. I do not need others to enjoy. Others!" Her voice trembled. "Because you want to be there with others. Already it makes me sick to think of you always around others. Clown, grimacer, floormat, yesman, entertainer, whatever they want of you."

And now it was he who turned on the television loud so he need not hear.

Old scar tissue ruptured and the wounds festered anew. Chekhov indeed. She thought without softness of that young wife, who in the deep night hours while she nursed the current baby, and perhaps held another in her lap, would try to stay awake for the only time there was to read. She would feel again the weather of the outside on his cheek when, coming late from a meeting, he would find her so, and stimulated and ardent, sniffing her skin, coax: "I'll put the baby to bed, and you—put the book away, don't read, don't read."

That had been the most beguiling of all the "don't read, put your book away" her life had been. Chekhov indeed!

"Money?" She shrugged him off. "Could we get poorer than once we were? And in America, who starves?"

But as still he pressed:

"Let me alone about money. Was there ever enough? Seven little ones—for every penny I had to ask—and sometimes, remember, there was nothing. But always I had to manage. Now *you* manage. Rub your nose in it good."

But from those years she had had to manage, old humiliations and terrors rose up, lived again, and forced her to relive them. The children's needings; that grocer's face or this merchant's wife she had had to beg credit from when credit was a disgrace, the scenery of the long blocks walked around when she could not pay; school coming, and the desperate going over the old to see what could yet be remade; the soups of meat bones begged "for-the-dog" one winter. . . .

Enough. Now they had no children. Let him wrack his head for how they would live. She would not exchange her solitude for anything. *Never again to be forced to move to the rhythms of others.*

For in this solitude she had won to a reconciled peace.

Tranquillity from having the empty house no longer an enemy, for it stayed clean—not as in the days when it was her family, the life in it, that had seemed the enemy: tracking, smudging, littering, dirtying, engaging her in endless defeating battle—and on whom her endless defeat had been spewed.

The few old books, memorized from rereading; the pictures to ponder (the magnifying glass superimposed on her heavy eye-glasses). Or if she wishes, when he is gone, the phonograph, that if she turns up very loud and strains, she can hear: the ordered sounds and the struggling.

Out in the garden, growing things to nurture. Birds to be kept out of the pear tree, and when the pears are heavy and ripe, the old fury of work, for all must be canned, nothing wasted.

And her one social duty (for she will not go to luncheons or meetings) the boxes of old clothes left with her, as with a life-practiced eye for finding what is still wearable within the worn (again the magnifying glass superimposed on the heavy glasses) she scans and sorts—this for rag or rummage, that for mending and cleaning, and this for sending abroad.

Being able at last to live within, and not move to the rhythms of others, as life had helped her to: denying; removing; isolating; taking the children one by one; then deafening, half-blinding—and at last, presenting her solitude.

And in it she had won to a reconciled peace.

Now he was violating it with his constant campaigning: *Sell the house and move to the Haven.* (You sit, you sit—there too you could sit like a stone.) He was making of her a battleground where old grievances tore. (Turn on your ear button—I am talking.) And stubbornly she resisted—so that from wheedling, reasoning, manipulation, it was bitterness he now started with.

And it came to where every happening lashed up a quarrel.

"I will sell the house anyway," he flung at her one night. "I am putting it up for sale. There will be a way to make you sign."

The television blared, as always it did on the evenings he stayed home, and as always it reached her only as noise. She did not know if the tumult was in her or outside. Snap! she turned the sound off. "Shadows," she whispered to him, pointing to the screen, "look, it is only shadows." And in a scream: "Did you say that you will sell the house? Look at me, not at that. I am no shadow. You cannot sell without me."

"Leave on the television. I am watching."

"Like Paulie, like Jenny, a four-year-old. Staring at shadows. *You cannot sell the house.*"

"I will. We are going to the Haven. There you would not hear the television when you do not want it. I could sit in the social room and watch. You could lock yourself up to smell your unpleasantness in a room by yourself—for who would want to come near you?"

"No, no selling." A whisper now.

"The television is shadows. Mrs. Enlightened! Mrs. Cultured! A world comes into your house—and it is shadows. People you would never meet in a thousand lifetimes. Wonders. When you were four years old, yes, like Paulie, like Jenny, did you know of Indian dances, alligators, how they use bamboo in Malaya? No, you scratched in your dirt with the chickens and thought Olshana[2] was the world. Yes, Mrs. Unpleasant, I will sell the house, for there better can we be rid of each other than here."

She did not know if the tumult was outside, or in her. Always a ravening inside, a pull to the bed, to lie down, to succumb.

"Have you thought maybe Ma should let a doctor have a look at her?" asked their son Paul after Sunday dinner, regarding his mother crumpled on the couch, instead of, as was her custom, busying herself in Nancy's kitchen.

"Why not the President too?"

"Seriously, Dad. This is the third Sunday she's lain down like that after dinner. Is she that way at home?"

"A regular love affair with the bed. Every time I start to talk to her."

Good protective reaction, observed Nancy to herself. The workings of hostility.

"Nancy could take her. I just don't like how she looks. Let's have Nancy arrange an appointment."

---

2. Village in Russia.

"You think she'll go?" regarding his wife gloomily. "All right, we have to have doctor bills, we have to have doctor bills." Loudly: "Something hurts you?"

She startled, looked to his lips. He repeated: "Mrs. Take It Easy, something hurts?"

"Nothing. . . . Only you."

"A woman of honey. That's why you're lying down?"

"Soon I'll get up to do the dishes, Nancy."

"Leave them, Mother, I like it better this way."

"Mrs. Take It Easy, Paul says you should start ballet. You should go to see a doctor and ask: how soon can you start ballet?"

"A doctor?" she begged. "Ballet?"

"We were talking, Ma," explained Paul, "you don't seem any too well. It would be a good idea for you to see a doctor for a checkup."

"I get up now to do the kitchen. Doctors are bills and foolishness, my son. I need no doctors."

"At the Haven," he could not resist pointing out, "a doctor is *not* bills. He lives beside you. You start to sneeze, he is there before you open up a Kleenex. You can be sick there for free, all you want."

"Diarrhea of the mouth, is there a doctor to make you dumb?"

"Ma. Promise me you'll go. Nancy will arrange it."

"It's all of a piece when you think of it," said Nancy, "the way she attacks my kitchen, scrubbing under every cup hook, doing the inside of the oven so I can't enjoy Sunday dinner, knowing that half-blind or not, she's going to find every speck of dirt. . . ."

"Don't Nancy, I've told you—it's the only way she knows to be useful. What did the *doctor* say?"

"A real fatherly lecture. Sixty-nine is young these days. Go out, enjoy life, find interests. Get a new hearing aid, this one is antiquated. Old age is sickness only if one makes it so. Geriatrics, Inc."

"So there was nothing physical."

"Of course there was. How can you live to yourself like she does without there being? Evidence of a kidney disorder, and her blood count is low. He gave her a diet, and she's to come back for follow-up and lab work. . . . But he was clear enough: Number One prescription—start living like a human being. When I think of your dad, who could really play the invalid with that arthritis of his as active as a teenager, and twice as much fun. . . ."

"You didn't tell me the doctor says your sickness is in you, how you live." He pushed his advantage. "Life and enjoyments you need better than medicine. And this diet, how can you keep it? To weigh each morsel and scrape away the bits of fat to make this soup, that pudding. There, at the Haven, they have a dietician, they would do it for you."

She is silent.

"You would feel better there, I know it," he says gently. "There there is life and enjoyments all around."

"What is the matter, Mr. Importantbusy, you have no card game or meeting you can go to?"—turning her face to the pillow.

For a while he cut his meetings and going out, fussed over her diet, tried to wheedle her into leaving the house, brought in visitors:

"I should come to a fashion tea. I should sit and look at pretty babies in clothes I cannot buy. This is pleasure?"

"Always you are better than everyone else. The doctor said you should go out. Mrs. Brem comes to you with goodness and you turn her away."
"Because *you* asked her to, she asked me."

"They won't come back. People you need, the doctor said. Your own cousins I asked; they were willing to come and make peace as if nothing had happened. . . ."
"No more crushers of people, pushers, hypocrites, around me. No more in *my* house. You go to them if you like."

"Kind he is to visit. And you, like ice."
"A babbler. All my life around babblers. Enough!"

"She's even worse, Dad? Then let her stew a while," advised Nancy. "You can't let it destroy you; it's a psychological thing, maybe too far gone for any of us to help."

So he let her stew. More and more she lay silent in bed, and sometimes did not even get up to make the meals. No longer was the tongue-lashing inevitable if he left the coffee cup where it did not belong, or forgot to take out the garbage or mislaid the broom. The birds grew bold that summer and for once pocked the pears, undisturbed.

A bellyful of bitterness and every day the same quarrel in a new way and a different old grievance the quarrel forced her to enter and relive. And the new torment: I am not really sick, the doctor said it, then why do I feel so sick?

One night she asked him: "You have a meeting tonight? Do not go. Stay . . . with me."

He had planned to watch "This Is Your Life"[3] anyway, but half sick himself from the heavy heat, and sickening therefore the more after the brooks and woods of the Haven, with satisfaction he grated:

"Hah, Mrs. Live Alone And Like It wants company all of a sudden. It doesn't seem so good the time of solitary when she was a girl exile in Siberia. 'Do not go. Stay with me.' A new song for Mrs. Free As A Bird. Yes, I am going out, and while I am gone chew this aloneness good, and think how you keep us both from where if you want people you do not need to be alone."

"Go, go. All your life you have gone without me."

After him she sobbed curses he had not heard in years, old-country curses from their childhood: Grow, oh shall you grow like an onion, with your head in the ground. Like the hide of a drum shall you be, beaten in life, beaten in death. Oh shall you be like a chandelier, to hang, and to burn. . . .

She was not in their bed when he came back. She lay on the cot on the sun-porch. All week she did not speak or come near him; nor did he try to make peace or care for her.

He slept badly, so used to her next to him. After all the years, old har-

---

3. A popular television program (1952–61).

monies and dependencies deep in their bodies; she curled to him, or he coiled to her each warmed, warming, turning as the other turned, the nights a long embrace.

It was not the empty bed or the storm that woke him, but a faint singing. *She* was singing. Shaking off the drops of rain, the lightning riving her lifted face, he saw her so; the cot covers on the floor.

"This is a private concert?" he asked. "Come in, you are wet."

"I can breathe now," she answered; "my lungs are rich." Though indeed the sound was hardly a breath.

"Come in, come in." Loosing the bamboo shades.

"Look how wet you are." Half helping, half carrying her, still faint-breathing her song.

A Russian love song of fifty years ago.

He had found a buyer, but before he told her, he called together those children who were close enough to come. Paul, of course, Sammy from New Jersey, Hannah from Connecticut, Vivi from Ohio.

With a kindling of energy for her beloved visitors, she arrayed the house, cooked and baked. She was not prepared for the solemn after-dinner conclave, they too probing in and tearing. Her frightened eyes watched from mouth to mouth as each spoke.

His stories were eloquent and funny of her refusal to go back to the doctor; of the scorned invitations; of her stubborn silences or the bile "Like a Niagara"; of her contrariness: "If I clean it's no good how I cleaned; if I don't clean, I'm still a master who thinks he has a slave."

("Vinegar he poured on me all his life; I am well marinated; how can I be honey now?")

Deftly he marched in the rightness for moving to the Haven; their money from social security free for visiting the children; not sucked into daily needs and into the house; the activities in the Haven for him; but mostly the Haven for *her:* her health, her need of care, distraction, amusement, friends who shared her interests.

"This does offer an outlet for Dad," said Paul; "he's always been an active person. And economic peace of mind isn't to be sneezed at, either. I could use a little of that myself."

But when they asked: "And you, Ma, how do you feel about it?" could only whisper:

"For him it is good. It is not for me. I can no longer live between people."

"You lived all your life *for* people," Vivi cried.

"Not with." Suffering doubly for the unhappiness on her children's faces.

"You have to find some compromise," Sammy insisted. "Maybe sell the house and buy a trailer. After forty-seven years there's surely some way you can find to live in peace."

"There is no help, my children. Different things we need."

"Then live alone!" He could control himself no longer. "I have a buyer for the house. Half the money for you, half for me. Either alone or with me to the Haven. You think I can live any longer as we are doing now?"

"Ma doesn't have to make a decision this minute, however you feel, Dad," Paul said quickly, "and you wouldn't want her to. Let's let it lay a few months, and then talk some more."

"I think I can work it out to take Mother home with me for a while," Hannah said. "You both look terrible, but especially you, Mother. I'm going to ask Phil to have a look at you."

"Sure," cracked Sammy. "What's the use of a doctor husband if you can't get free service out of him once in a while for the family? And absence might make the heart . . . you know."

"There was something after all," Paul told Nancy in a colorless voice. "That was Hannah's Phil calling. Her gall bladder. . . . Surgery."

"Her *gall* bladder. If that isn't classic. 'Bitter as gall'—talk of psychosom——"

He stepped closer, put his hand over her mouth and said in the same colorless, plodding voice. "We have to get Dad. They operated at once. The cancer was everywhere, surrounding the liver, everywhere. They did what they could . . . at best she has a year. Dad . . . we have to tell him."

II

Honest in his weakness when they told him, and that she was not to know. "I'm not an actor. She'll know right away by how I am. Oh that poor woman. I am old too, it will break me into pieces. Oh that poor woman. She will spit on me: 'So my sickness was how I live.' Oh Paulie, how she will be, that poor woman. Only she should not suffer. . . . I can't stand sickness, Paulie, I can't go with you."

But went. And play-acted.

"A grand opening and you did not even wait for me. . . . A good thing Hannah took you with her."

"Fashion teas I needed. They cut out what tore in me; just in my throat something hurts yet. . . . Look! so many flowers, like a funeral. Vivi called, did Hannah tell you? And Lennie from San Francisco, and Clara; and Sammy is coming." Her gnome's face pressed happily into the flowers.

> It is impossible to predict in these cases, but once over the immediate effects of the operation, she should have several months of comparative well-being.
>
> *The money, where will come the money?*
>
> Travel with her, Dad. Don't take her home to the old associations. The other children will want to see her.
>
> *The money, where will I wring the money?*
>
> Whatever happens, she is not to know. No, you can't ask her to sign papers to sell the house; nothing to upset her. Borrow instead. Then, after. . . .
>
> *I had wanted to leave you each a few dollars to make life easier, as other fathers do. There will be nothing left now. Failure! you and your "business is exploitation." Why didn't you make it when it could be made?—Is that what you're thinking, Sammy?*)
>
> Sure she's unreasonable, Dad—but you have to stay with her. If there's to be any happiness in what's left of her life, it depends on you.
>
> *Prop me up, children, think of me, too. Shuffled, chained with her,*

bitter woman. No Haven, and the little money going. . . . How happy she looks, poor creature.

The look of excitement. The straining to hear everything (the new hearing aid turned full). Why are you so happy, dying woman?

How the petals are, fold on fold, and the gladioli color. The autumn air.

Stranger grandsons, tall above the little gnome grandmother, the little spry grandfather. Paul in a frenzy of picture-taking before going.

She, wandering the great house. Feeling the books; laughing at the maple shoemaker's bench of a hundred years ago used as a table. The ear turned to music.

"Let us go home. See how good I walk now." "One step from the hospital," he answers, "and she wants to fly. Wait till Doctor Phil says."

"Look—the birds too are flying home. Very good Phil is and will not show it, but he is sick of sickness by the time he comes home."

"Mrs. Telepathy, to read minds," he answers; "read mine what it says: when the trunks of medicines become a suitcase, then we will go."

The grandboys, they do not know what to say to us. . . . Hannah, she runs around here, there, when is there time for herself?

Let us go home. Let us go home.

Musing; gentleness—*but for the incidents of the rabbi in the hospital, and of the candles of benediction.*

Of the rabbi in the hospital:

Now tell me what happened, Mother.

From the sleep I awoke, Hannah's Phil, and he stands there like a devil in a dream and calls me by name. I cannot hear. I think he prays. Go away, please, I tell him, I am not a believer. Still he stands, while my heart knocks with fright.

You scared *him*, Mother. He thought you were delirious.

Who sent him? Why did he come to me?

It is a custom. The men of God come to visit those of their religion they might help. The hospital makes up the list for them—race, religion—and you are on the Jewish list.

Not for rabbis. At once go and make them change. Tell them to write: Race, human; Religion, none.

And of the candles of benediction:

Look how you have upset yourself, Mrs. Excited Over Nothing. Pleasant memories you should leave.

Go in, go back to Hannah and the lights. Two weeks I saw candles and said nothing. But she asked me.

So what was so terrible? She forgets you never did, she asks you to light the Friday candles and say the benediction like Phil's mother when she visits. If the candles give her pleasure, why shouldn't she have the pleasure?

Not for pleasure she does it. For emptiness. Because his family does. Because all around her do.

That is not a good reason too? But you did not hear her. For heritage, she told you. For the boys, from the past they should have tradition.

Superstition! From our ancestors, savages, afraid of the dark, of themselves: mumbo words and magic lights to scare away ghosts.

She told you: how it started does not take away the goodness. For centuries, peace in the house it means.

Swindler! does she look back on the dark centuries? Candles bought instead of bread and stuck into a potato for a candlestick? Religion that stifled and said: in Paradise, woman, you will be the footstool of your husband, and in life—poor chosen Jew—ground under, despised, trembling in cellars. And cremated. And cremated.

This is religion's fault? You think you are still an orator of the 1905 revolution?[4] Where are the pills for quieting? Which are they?

Heritage. How have we come from our savage past, how no longer to be savages—this to teach. To look back and learn what humanizes—this to teach. To smash all ghettos that still divide us—not to go back, not to go back—this to teach. Learned books in the house, will man live or die, and she gives to her boys—superstition.

Hannah that is so good to you. Take your pill, Mrs. Excited For Nothing, swallow.

Heritage! But when did I have time to teach? Of Hannah I asked only hands to help.

Swallow.

Otherwise—musing; gentleness.

Not to travel. To go home.

The children want to see you. We have to show them you are as thorny a flower as ever.

Not to travel.

Vivi wants you should see her new baby. She sent the tickets—airplane tickets—a Mrs. Roosevelt[5] she wants to make of you. To Vivi's we have to go.

A new baby. How many warm, seductive babies. She holds him stiffly, *away* from her, so that he wails. And a long shudder begins, and the sweat beads on her forehead.

"Hush, shush," croons the grandfather, lifting him back. "You should forgive your grandmamma, little prince, she has never held a baby before, only seen them in glass cases. Hush, shush."

"You're tired, Ma," says Vivi. "The travel and the noisy dinner. I'll take you to lie down."

(*A long travel from, to, what the feel of a baby evokes.*)

In the airplane, cunningly designed to encase from motion (no wind, no feel of flight), she had sat severely and still, her face turned to the sky through which they cleaved and left no scar.

So this was how it looked, the determining, the crucial sky, and this was how man moved through it, remote above the dwindled earth, the concealed human life. Vulnerable life, that could scar.

---

4. Protests, strikes, and military mutinies in czarist Russia, bloodily suppressed by the last emperor and czar, Nicholas II.
5. Eleanor Roosevelt (1884–1962), wife of President Franklin D. Roosevelt, was famous for extensive, frequent travels in the days when airplane travel was unusual.

There was a steerage ship[6] of memory that shook across a great, circular sea: clustered, ill human beings; and through the thick-stained air, tiny fretting waters in a window round like the airplane's—sun round, moon round. (The round thatched roofs of Olshana.) Eye round—like the smaller window that framed distance the solitary year of exile when only her eyes could travel, and no voice spoke. And the polar winds hurled themselves across snow trackless and endless and white—like the clouds which had closed together below and hidden the earth.

Now they put a baby in her lap. Do not ask me, she would have liked to beg. Enough the worn face of Vivi, the remembered grandchildren, I cannot, cannot. . . .

Cannot what? Unnatural grandmother, not able to make herself embrace a baby.

She lay there in the bed of the two little girls, her new hearing aid turned full, listening to the sound of the children going to sleep, the baby's fretful crying and hushing, the clatter of dishes being washed and put away. They thought she slept. Still she rode on.

It was not that she had not loved her babies, her children. The love—the passion of tending—had risen with the need like a torrent; and like a torrent drowned and immolated all else. But when the need was done—oh the power that was lost in the painful damming back and drying up of what still surged, but had nowhere to go. Only the thin pulsing left that could not quiet, suffering over lives one felt, but could no longer hold nor help.

On that torrent she had borne them to their own lives, and the river-bed was desert long years now. Not there would she dwell, a memoried wraith. Surely that was not all, surely there was more. Still the springs, the springs were in her seeking. Somewhere an older power that beat for life. Somewhere coherence, transport, meaning. If they would but leave her in the air now stilled of clamor, in the reconciled solitude, to journey on.

And they put a baby in her lap. Immediacy to embrace, and the breath of *that* past: warm flesh like this that had claims and nuzzled away all else and with lovely mouths devoured; hot-living like an animal—intensely and now; the turning maze; the long drunkenness; the drowning into needing and being needed. Severely she looked back—and the shudder seized her again, and the sweat. Not that way. Not there, not now could she, not yet. . . .

And all that visit, she could not touch the baby.

"Daddy, is it the . . . sickness she's like that?" asked Vivi. "I was so glad to be having the baby—for her. I told Tim, it'll give her more happiness than anything, being around a baby again. And she hasn't played with him once."

He was not listening, "Aahh little seed of life, little charmer," he crooned, "Hollywood should see you. A heart of ice you would melt. Kick, kick. The future you'll have for a ball. In 2050 still kick. Kick for your grandaddy then."

Attentive with the older children; sat through their performances (command performance; we command you to be the audience); helped Ann sort autumn leaves to find the best for a school program; listened gravely to Richard tell about his rock collection, while her lips mutely formed the words to

---

6. I.e., a ship having only the lowest class of accommodations, often used by immigrants.

remember: *igneous, sedimentary, metamorphic;*[7] looked for missing socks, books and bus tickets; watched the children whoop after their grandfather who knew how to tickle, chuck, lift, toss, do tricks, tell secrets, make jokes, match riddle for riddle. (Tell me a riddle, Grammy. I know no riddles, child.) Scrubbed sills and woodwork and furniture in every room; folded the laundry; straightened drawers; emptied the heaped baskets waiting for ironing (while he or Vivi or Tim nagged: You're supposed to rest here, you've been sick) but to none tended or gave food—and could not touch the baby.

After a week she said: "Let us go home. Today call about the tickets."

"You have important business, Mrs. Inahurry? The President waits to consult with you?" He shouted, for the fear of the future raced in him. "The clothes are still warm from the suitcase, your children cannot show enough how glad they are to see you, and you want home. There is plenty of time for home. We cannot be with the children at home."

"Blind to around you as always: the little ones sleep four in a room because we take their bed. We are two more people in a house with a new baby, and no help."

"Vivi is happy so. The children should have their grandparents a while, she told to me. I should have my mommy and daddy. . . ."

"Babbler and blind. Do you look at her so tired? How she starts to talk and she cries? I am not strong enough yet to help. Let us go home."

(To reconciled solitude.)

For it seemed to her the crowded noisy house was listening to her, listening for her. She could feel it like a great ear pressed under her heart. And everything knocked: quick constant raps: let me in, let me in.

How was it that soft reaching tendrils also became blows that knocked?

    C'mon, Grandma, I want to show you. . . .
    Tell me a riddle, Grandma. (*I know no riddles.*)
    Look, Grammy, he's so dumb he can't even find his hands. (Dody and the baby on a blanket over the fermenting autumn mould.)
    I made them—for you. (Ann) (Flat paper dolls with aprons that lifted on scalloped skirts that lifted on flowered pants; hair of yarn and great ringed questioning eyes.)
    Watch me, Grandma. (Richard snaking up the tree, hanging exultant, free, with one hand at the top. Below Dody hunching over in pretend-cooking.)
    (*Climb too, Dody, climb and look.*)
    Be my nap bed, Grammy. (The "No!" too late.) Morty's abandoned heaviness, while his fingers ladder up and down her hearing-aid cord to his drowsy chant: eentsiebeentsiespider. (*Children trust.*)
    It's to start off your own rock collection, Grandma.
    That's a trilobite fossil, 200 million years old (millions of years on a boy's mouth) and that one's obsidian, black glass.

Knocked and knocked.

---

7. Basic types of rocks.

Mother, I *told* you the teacher said we had to bring it back all filled out this morning. Didn't you even ask Daddy? Then tell *me* which plan and I'll check it: evacuate or stay in the city or wait for you to come and take me away. (Seeing the look of straining to hear.) It's for Disaster,[8] Grandma. (*Children trust.*)

Vivi in the maze of the long, the lovely drunkenness. The old old noises: baby sounds; screaming of a mother flayed to exasperation; children quarreling; children playing; singing; laughter.

And Vivi's tears and memories, spilling so fast, half the words not understood.

She had started remembering out loud deliberately, so her mother would know the past was cherished, still lived in her.

Nursing the baby: My friends marvel, and I tell them, oh it's easy to be such a cow. I remember how beautiful my mother seemed nursing my brother, and the milk just flows. . . . Was that Davy? It must have been Davy. . . .

Lowering a hem: How did you ever . . . when I think how you made everything we wore . . . Tim, just think, seven kids and Mommy sewed everything . . . do I remember you sang while you sewed? That white dress with the red apples on the skirt you fixed over for me, was it Hannah's or Clara's before it was mine?

Washing sweaters: Ma, I'll never forget, one of those days so nice you washed clothes outside; one of the first spring days it must have been. The bubbles just danced up and down while you scrubbed, and we chased after, and you stopped to show us how to blow our own bubbles with green onion stalks . . . you always. . . .

"Strong onion, to still make you cry after so many years," her father said, to turn the tears into laughter.

While Richard bent over his homework: Where is it now, do we still have it, the Book of the Martyrs? It always seemed so, well—exalted, when you'd put it on the round table and we'd all look at it together; there was even a halo from the lamp. The lamp with the beaded fringe you could move up and down; they're in style again, pulley lamps like that, but without the fringe. You know the book I'm talking about, Daddy, the Book of the Martyrs, the first picture was a bust of Spartacus? . . . Socrates?[9] I wish there was something like that for the children, Mommy, to give them what you. . . . (And the tears splashed again.)

(What I intended and did not? Stop it, daughter, stop it, leave that time. And he, the hypocrite, sitting there with tears in his eyes—it was nothing to you then, nothing.)

. . . The time you came to school and I almost died of shame because of your accent and because I knew you knew I was ashamed; how could I? . . . Sammy's harmonica and you danced to it once, yes you did, you and Davy squealing in your arms. . . . That time you bundled us up and walked us down to the railway station to stay the night 'cause it was heated and we didn't

---

8. During the 1950s, with the encouragement of the federal government, a number of American communities built fallout shelters and drew up evacuation ("Disaster") plans to be used in a nuclear attack.

9. Greek philosopher (469–399 B.C.E.), sentenced to death for corrupting youth and for religious heresies. Spartacus (d. 71 B.C.E.), Thracian-born leader of an ultimately unsuccessful slave revolt in Italy.

have any coal, that winter of the strike, you didn't think I remembered that, did you, Mommy? . . . How you'd call us out to see the sunsets. . . .

Day after day, the spilling memories. Worse now, questions, too. Even the grandchildren: Grandma, in the olden days, when you were little. . . .

It was the afternoons that saved.

While they thought she napped, she would leave the mosaic on the wall (of children's drawings, maps, calendars, pictures, Ann's cardboard dolls with their great ringed questioning eyes) and hunch in the girls' closet, on the low shelf where the shoes stood, and the girls' dresses covered.

For that while she would painfully sheathe against the listening house, the tendrils and noises that knocked, and Vivi's spilling memories. Sometimes it helped to braid and unbraid the sashes that dangled, or to trace the pattern on the hoop slips.

Today she had jacks and children under jet trails to forget. Last night, Ann and Dody silhouetted in the window against a sunset of flaming man-made clouds of jet trail, their jacks ball accenting the peaceful noise of dinner being made. Had she told them, yes she had told them of how they played jacks in her village though there was no ball, no jacks. Six stones, round and flat, toss them out, the seventh on the back of the hand, toss, catch and swoop up as many as possible, toss again. . . .

Of stones (repeating Richard) there are three kinds: earth's fire jetting; rock of layered centuries; crucibled new out of the old (*igneous, sedimentary, metamorphic*). But there was that other—frozen to black glass, never to transform or hold the fossil memory . . . (let not my seed fall on stone). There was an ancient one who fought to heights a great rock that crashed back down eternally[1]—eternal labor, freedom, labor . . . (stone will perish, but the word remain). And you, David,[2] who with a stone slew, screaming: Lord, take my heart of stone and give me flesh.

Who was screaming? Why was she back in the common room of the prison, the sun motes dancing in the shafts of light, and the informer being brought in, a prisoner now, like themselves. And Lisa leaping, yes, Lisa, the gentle and tender, biting at the betrayer's jugular. Screaming and screaming.

No, it is the children screaming. Another of Paul and Sammy's terrible fights?

In Vivi's house. Severely: you are in Vivi's house.

Blows, screams, a call: "Grandma!" For her? Oh please not for her. Hide, hunch behind the dresses deeper. But a trembling little body hurls itself beside her—surprised, smothered laughter, arms surround her neck, tears rub dry on her cheek, and words too soft to understand whisper into her ear (Is this where you hide too, Grammy? It's my secret place, we have a secret now).

And the sweat beads, and the long shudder seizes.

It seemed the great ear pressed inside now, and the knocking. "We have to go home," she told him, "I grow ill here."

---

1. An allusion to the myth of Sisyphus, who was punished in Tartarus, the lowest region of the underworld, by having to roll a huge stone uphill; each time he approached the top, the stone would roll back.
2. Future king of Israel, who killed the great Philistine champion Goliath with a stone from a slingshot (1 Samuel 17).

"It is your own fault, Mrs. Bodybusy, you do not rest, you do too much." He raged, but the fear was in his eyes. "It was a serious operation, they told you to take care. . . . All right, we will go to where you can rest."

But where? Not home to death, not yet. He had thought to Lennie's, to Clara's; beautiful visits with each of the children. She would have to rest first, be stronger. If they could but go to Florida—it glittered before him, the never-realized promise of Florida. California: of course. (The money, the money, dwindling!) Los Angeles first for sun and rest, then to Lennie's in San Francisco.

He told her the next day, "You saw what Nancy wrote: snow and wind back home, a terrible winter. And look at you—all bones and a swollen belly. I called Phil: he said: 'A prescription, Los Angeles sun and rest.'"

She watched the words on his lips. "You have sold the house," she cried, "that is why we do not go home. That is why you talk no more of the Haven. Why there is money for travel. After the children you will drag me to the Haven."

"The Haven! Who thinks of the Haven any more? Tell her, Vivi, tell Mrs. Suspicious: a prescription, sun and rest, to make you healthy. . . . And how could I sell the house without *you*?"

At the place of farewells and greetings, of winds of coming and winds of going, they say their good-byes.

They look back at her with the eyes of others before them: Richard with her own blue blaze; Ann with the Nordic eyes of Tim; Morty's dreaming brown of a great-grandmother he will never know; Dody with the laughing eyes of him who had been her springtide love (who stands beside her now); Vivi's, all tears.

The baby's eyes are closed in sleep.

Good-bye, my children.

III

It is to the back of the great city he brought her, to the dwelling places of the cast-off old. Bounded by two lines of amusement piers to the north and to the south, and between a long straight paving rimmed with black benches facing the sand—sands so wide the ocean is only a far fluting.

In the brief vacation season, some of the boarded stores fronting the sands open, and families, young people and children, may be seen. A little tasseled tram shuttles between the piers, and the lights of roller coasters prink and tweak over those who come to have sensation made in them.

The rest of the year it is abandoned to the old, all else boarded up and still; seemingly empty, except the occasional days and hours when the sun, like a tide, sucks them out of the low rooming houses, casts them on to the benches and sandy rim of the walk—and sweeps them into decaying enclosures back again.

A few newer apartments glint among the low bleached squares. It is in one of these Lennie's Jeannie has arranged their rooms. "Only a few miles north and south people pay hundreds of dollars a month for just this gorgeous air, Grandaddy, just this ocean closeness."

She had been ill on the plane, lay ill for days in the unfamiliar room.

Several times the doctor came by—left medicine she would not take. Several times Jeannie drove in the twenty miles from work, still in her Visiting Nurse uniform, the lightness and brightness of her like a healing.

"Who can believe it is winter?" he asked one morning. "Beautiful it is outside like an ad. Come, Mrs. Invalid, come to taste it. You are well enough to sit in here, you are well enough to sit outside. The doctor said it too."

But the benches were encrusted with people, and the sands at the sidewalk's edge. Besides, she had seen the far ruffle of the sea: "there take me," and though she leaned against him, it was she who led.

Plodding and plodding, sitting often to rest, he grumbling. Patting the sand so warm. Once she scooped up a handful, cradling it close to her better eye; peered, and flung it back. And as they came almost to the brink and she could see the glistening wet, she sat down, pulled off her shoes and stockings, left him and began to run. "You'll catch cold," he screamed, but the sand in his shoes weighed him down—he who had always been the agile one—and already the white spray creamed her feet.

He pulled her back, took a handkerchief to wipe off the wet and the sand. "Oh no," she said, "the sun will dry," seized the square and smoothed it flat, dropped on it a mound of sand, knotted the kerchief corners and tied it to a bag—"to look at with the strong glass" (for the first time in years explaining an action of hers)—and lay down with the little bag against her cheek, looking toward the shore that nurtured life as it first crawled toward consciousness the millions of years ago.

He took her one Sunday in the evil-smelling bus, past flat miles of blister houses, to the home of relatives. Oh what is this? she cried as the light began to smoke and the houses to dim and recede. Smog, he said, everyone knows but you. . . . Outside he kept his arms about her, but she walked with hands pushing the heavy air as if to open it, whispered: who has done this? sat down suddenly to vomit at the curb and for a long while refused to rise.

One's age as seen on the altered face of those known in youth. Is this they he has come to visit? This Max and Rose, smooth and pleasant, introducing them to polite children, disinterested grandchildren, "the whole family, once a month on Sundays. And why not? We have the room, the help, the food."

Talk of cars, of houses, of success: this son that, that daughter this. And *your* children? Hastily skimped over, the intermarriages, the obscure work—"my doctor son-in-law, Phil"—all he has to offer. She silent in a corner. (Carsick like a baby, he explains.) Years since he has taken her to visit anyone but the children, and old apprehensions prickle: "no incidents," he silently begs, "no incidents." He itched to tell them. "A very sick woman," significantly, indicating her with his eyes, "a very sick woman." Their restricted faces did not react. "Have you thought maybe she'd do better at Palm Springs?" Rose asked. "Or at least a nicer section of the beach, nicer people, a pool." Not to have to say "money" he said instead: "would she have sand to look at through a magnifying glass?" and went on, detail after detail, the old habit betraying of parading the queerness of her for laughter.

After dinner—the others into the living-room in men- or women-clusters, or into the den to watch TV—the four of them alone. She sat close to him, and did not speak. Jokes, stories, people they had known, beginning of reminiscence, Russia fifty-sixty years ago. Strange words across the Duncan

Phyfe[3] table: *hunger; secret meetings; human rights; spies; betrayals; prison; escape*—interrupted by one of the grandchildren: "Commercial's on; any Coke left? Gee, you're missing a real hair-raiser." And then a granddaughter (Max proudly: "look at her, an American queen") drove them home on her way back to U.C.L.A. No incident—except that there had been no incidents.

The first few mornings she had taken with her the magnifying glass, but he would sit only on the benches, so she rested at the foot, where slatted bench shadows fell, and unless she turned her hearing aid down, other voices invaded.

Now on the days when the sun shone and she felt well enough, he took her on the tram to where the benches ranged in oblongs, some with tables for draughts or cards. Again the blanket on the sand in the striped shadows, but she no longer brought the magnifying glass. He played cards, and she lay in the sun and looked towards the waters; or they walked—two blocks down to the scaling hotel, two blocks back—past chili-hamburger stands, open-doored bars, Next to New and Perpetual Rummage Sale stores.

Once, out of the aimless walkers, slow and shuffling like themselves, someone ran unevenly towards them, embraced, kissed, wept: "dear friends, old friends." A friend of *hers,* not his: Mrs. Mays who had lived next door to them in Denver when the children were small.

Thirty years are compressed into a dozen sentences; and the present, not even in three. All is told: the children scattered; the husband dead; she lives in a room two blocks up from the sing hall—and points to the domed auditorium jutting before the pier. The leg? phlebitis; the heavy breathing? that, one does not ask. She, too, comes to the benches each day to sit. And tomorrow, tomorrow, are they going to the community sing? Of course he would have heard of it, everybody goes—the big doings they wait for all week. They have never been? She will come for them to dinner tomorrow and they will all go together.

So it is that she sits in the wind of the singing, among the thousand various faces of age.

She had turned off her hearing aid at once they came into the auditorium—as she would have wished to turn off sight.

One by one they streamed by and imprinted on her—and though the savage zest of their singing came voicelessly soft and distant, the faces still roared—the faces densened the air—chorded into

children-chants, mother-croons, singing of the chained
love serenades, Beethoven storms, mad Lucia's[4] scream
drunken joy-songs, keens for the dead, work-singing

> *while from floor to balcony to dome a bare-footed sore-covered little girl threaded the sound-thronged tumult, danced her ecstasy of grimace to flutes that scratched at a cross-roads village wedding.*

---

3. Scottish-born American cabinetmaker (1768–1854), renowned for the beauty of his neoclassical furniture.

4. The heroine of Gaetano Donizetti's opera *Lucia di Lammermoor* (1839), who goes mad.

Yes, faces became sound, and the sound became faces; and faces and sound became weight—pushed, pressed

"Air"—her hand claws his.

"Whenever I enjoy myself. . . ." Then he saw the gray sweat on her face. "Here. Up. Help me, Mrs. Mays," and they support her out to where she can gulp the air in sob after sob.

"A doctor, we should get for her a doctor."

"Tch, it's nothing," says Ellen Mays, "I get it all the time. You've missed the tram; come to my place. Fix your hearing aid, honey . . . close . . . tea. My view. See, she *wants* to come. Steady now, that's how." Adding mysteriously: "Remember your advice, easy to keep your head above water, empty things float. Float."

The singing a fading march for them, tall woman with a swollen leg, weaving little man, and the swollen thinness they help between.

The stench in the hall: mildew? decay? "We sit and rest then climb. My gorgeous view. We help each other and here we are."

The stench along into the slab of room. A wash stand for a sink, a box with oilcloth tacked around for a cupboard, a three-burner gas plate. Artificial flowers, colorless with dust. Everywhere pictures foaming: wedding, baby, party, vacation, graduation, family pictures. From the narrow couch under a slit of window, sure enough the view: lurching rooftops and a scallop of ocean heaving, preening, twitching under the moon.

"While the water heats. Excuse me . . . down the hall." Ellen Mays has gone.

"You'll live?" he asks mechanically, sat down to feel his fright; tried to pull her alongside.

She pushed him away. "For air," she said; stood clinging to the dresser. Then, in a terrible voice:

After a lifetime of room. Of many rooms.

Shhh.

You remember how she lived. Eight children. And now   one room- like a coffin.

She pays rent!

Shrinking the life of her into one room like a coffin

Rooms and rooms like this. I lie on the quilt and hear them talk.

Please, Mrs. Orator-without-Breath.

Once you went for coffee I walked I saw A Balzac[5] a Chekhov to write it   Rummage   Alone   On scraps

Better old here than in the old country!

On scraps Yet they sang like . . . like . . . Wondrous. *Humankind one has to believe.*   So strong   for what?   To rot   not grow?

Your poor lungs beg you. They sob between each word.

Singing.   Unused   the life in them. She   in this poor room with her pictures.   Max   You   The children   Everywhere unused   the life   And who has meaning?   Century   after century   still all in us has not   to grow?

---

5. Honoré de Balzac (1799–1850), French writer.

Coffins, rummage, plants: sick woman. Oh lay down. We will get for you the doctor.

"And when will it end. Oh, *the end.*" *That* nightmare thought, and this time she writhed, crumpled beside him, seized his hand (for a moment again the weight, the soft distant roaring of humanity) and on the strangled-for breath, begged: "Man . . . we'll destroy ourselves?"

And looking for answer—in the helpless pity and fear for her (for *her*) that distorted his face—she understood the last months, and knew that she was dying.

IV

"Let us go home," she said after several days.

"You are in training for a cross-country run? That is why you do not even walk across the room? Here, like a prescription Phil said, till you are stronger from the operation. You want to break doctor's orders?"

She saw the fiction was necessary to him, was silent; then: "At home I will get better. If the doctor here says?"

"And winter? And the visits to Lennie and to Clara? All right," for he saw the tears in her eyes, "I will write Phil, and talk to the doctor."

Days passed. He reported nothing. Jeannie came and took her out for air, past the boarded concessions, the hooded and tented amusement rides, to the end of the pier. They watched the spent waves feeding the new, the gulls in the clouded sky; even up where they sat, the wind-blown sand stung.

She did not ask to go down the crooked steps to the sea.

Back in her bed, while he was gone to the store, she said: "Jeannie, this doctor, he is not one I can ask questions. Ask him for me, can I go home?"

Jeannie looked at her, said quickly: "Of course, poor Granny. You want your own things around you, don't you? I'll call him tonight. . . . Look, I've something to show you," and from her purse unwrapped a large cookie, intricately shaped like a little girl. "Look at the curls—can you hear me well, Granny?—and the darling eyelashes. I just came from a house where they were baking them."

"The dimples," she marveled, "there in the knees," holding it to the better light, turning, studying, "like art. Each singly they cut, or a mold?"

"Singly," said Jeannie, "and if it is a child only the mother can make them. Oh Granny, it's the likeness of a real little girl who died yesterday—Rosita. She was three years old. *Pan del Muerto,* the Bread of the Dead. It was the custom in the part of Mexico they came from."

Still she turned and inspected. "Look, the hollow in the throat, the little cross necklace. . . . I think for the mother it is a good thing to be busy with such bread. You know the family?"

Jeannie nodded. "On my rounds. I nursed. . . . Oh Granny, it is like a party; they play songs she liked to dance to. The coffin is lined with pink velvet and she wears a white dress. There are candles. . . ."

"In the house?" Surprised, "They keep her in the house?"

"Yes," said Jeannie, "and it is against the health law. I think she is . . . prepared there. The father said it will be sad to bury her in this country; in

Oaxaca they have a feast night with candles each year;[6] everyone picnics on the graves of those they loved until dawn."

"Yes, Jeannie, the living must comfort themselves." And closed her eyes.

"You want to sleep, Granny?"

"Yes, tired from the pleasure of you. I may keep the Rosita? There stand it, on the dresser, where I can see; something of my own around me."

In the kitchenette, helping her grandfather unpack the groceries, Jeannie said in her light voice:

"I'm resigning my job, Grandaddy."

"Ah, the lucky young man. Which one is he?"

"Too late. You're spoken for." She made a pyramid of cans, unstacked, and built again.

"Something is wrong with the job?"

"With me. I can't be"—she searched for the word—"What they call professional enough. I let myself feel things. And tomorrow I have to report a family. . . ." The cans clicked again. "It's not that, either. I just don't know what I want to do, maybe go back to school, maybe go to art school. I thought if you went to San Francisco I'd come along and talk it over with Mommy and Daddy. But I don't see how you can go. She wants to go home. She asked me to ask the doctor."

The doctor told her himself. "Next week you may travel, when you are a little stronger." But next week there was the fever of an infection, and by the time that was over, she could not leave the bed—a rented hospital bed that stood beside the double bed he slept in alone now.

Outwardly the days repeated themselves. Every other afternoon and evening he went out to his newfound cronies, to talk and play cards. Twice a week, Mrs. Mays came. And the rest of the time, Jeannie was there.

By the sickbed stood Jeannie's FM radio. Often into the room the shapes of music came. She would lie curled on her side, her knees drawn up, intense in listening (Jeannie sketched her so, coiled, convoluted like an ear), then thresh her hand out and abruptly snap the radio mute—still to lie in her attitude of listening, concealing tears.

Once Jeannie brought in a young Marine to visit, a friend from high-school days she had found wandering near the empty pier. Because Jeannie asked him to, gravely, without self-consciousness, he sat himself cross-legged on the floor and performed for them a dance of his native Samoa.

Long after they left, a tiny thrumming sound could be heard where, in her bed, she strove to repeat the beckon, flight, surrender of his hands, the fluttering footbeats, and his low plaintive calls.

Hannah and Phil sent flowers. To deepen her pleasure, he placed one in her hair. "Like a girl," he said, and brought the hand mirror so she could see. She looked at the pulsing red flower, the yellow skull face; a desolate, excited laugh shuddered from her, and she pushed the mirror away—but let the flower burn.

The week Lennie and Helen came, the fever returned. With it the excited laugh, and incessant words. She, who in her life had spoken but seldom and

---

6. I.e., the Day of the Dead (All Soul's Day), celebrated November 1 and 2.

then only when necessary (never having learned the easy, social uses of words), now in dying, spoke incessantly.

In a half-whisper: "Like Lisa she is, your Jeannie. Have I told you of Lisa, she who taught me to read? Of the highborn she was, but noble in herself. I was sixteen; they beat me; my father beat me so I would not go to her. It was forbidden, she was a Tolstoyan.[7] At night, past dogs that howled, terrible dogs, my son, in the snows of winter to the road, I to ride in her carriage like a lady, to books. To her, life was holy, knowledge was holy, and she taught me to read. They hung her. Everything that happens one must try to understand why. She killed one who betrayed many. Because of betrayal, betrayed all she lived and believed. In one minute she killed, before my eyes (there is so much blood in a human being, my son), in prison with me. All that happens, one must try to understand.

"The name?" Her lips would work. "The name that was their pole star; the doors of the death houses fixed to open on it; I read of it my year of penal servitude. Thuban!" very excited, "Thuban, in ancient Egypt the pole star. Can you see, look out to see it, Jeannie, if it swings around *our* pole star that seems to us not to move.

"Yes, Jeannie, at your age my mother and grandmother had already buried children . . . yes, Jeannie, it is more than oceans between Olshana and you . . . yes, Jeannie, they danced, and for all the bodies they had they might as well be chickens, and indeed, they scratched and flapped their arms and hopped.

"And Andrei Yefimitch, who was twenty years had never known of it and never wanted to know, said as if he wanted to cry: but why my dear friend this malicious laughter?" Telling to herself half-memorized phrases from her few books. "Pain I answer with tears and cries, baseness with indignation, meanness with repulsion . . . for life may be hated or wearied of, but never despised."

Delirious: "Tell me, my neighbor, Mrs. Mays, the pictures never lived, but what of the flowers? Tell them who ask: no rabbis, no ministers, no priests, no speeches, no ceremonies: ah, false—let the living comfort themselves. Tell Sammy's boy, he who flies, tell him to go to Stuttgart[8] and see where Davy has no grave. And what? And what? where millions have no graves save air."

In delirium or not, wanting the radio on; not seeming to listen, the words still jetting, wanting the music on. Once, silencing it abruptly as of old, she began to cry, unconcealed tears this time. "You have pain, Granny?" Jeannie asked.

"The music," she said, "still it is there and we do not hear; knocks, and our poor human ears too weak. What else, what else we do not hear?"

Once she knocked his hand aside as he gave her a pill, swept the bottles from her bedside table: "no pills, let me feel what I feel," and laughed as on his hands and knees he groped to pick them up.

Nighttimes her hand reached across the bed to hold his.

A constant retching began. Her breath was too faint for sustained speech now, but still the lips moved:

---

7. I.e., a follower of Leo Tolstoy (1828–1910), Russian novelist, social reformer, and teacher of nonviolence.

8. City in Germany whose center was nearly completely destroyed by Allied bombing in World War II.

> *When no longer necessary   to injure others*
> *Pick   pick pick   Blind chicken*
> *As a human being   responsibility for*

"David!" imperious, "Basin!" and she would vomit, rinse her mouth, the wasted throat working to swallow, and begin the chant again.

She will be better off in the hospital now, the doctor said.

He sent the telegrams to the children, was packing her suitcase, when her hoarse voice startled. She had roused, was pulling herself to sitting.

"Where now?" she asked. "Where now do you drag me?"

"You do not even have to have a baby to go this time," he soothed, looking for the brush to pack. "Remember, after Davy you told me—worthy to have a baby for the pleasure of the ten-day rest in the hospital?"

"Where now? Not home yet?" Her voice mourned. "Where *is* my home?"

He rose to ease her back. "The doctor, the hospital," he started to explain, but deftly, like a snake, she had slithered out of bed and stood swaying, propped behind the night table.

"Coward," she hissed, "runner."

"You stand," he said senselessly.

"To take me there and run. Afraid of a little vomit."

He reached her as she fell. She struggled against him, half slipped from his arms, pulled herself up again.

"Weakling," she taunted, "to leave me there and run. Betrayer. All your life you have run."

He sobbed, telling Jeannie. "A Marilyn Monroe to run for her virtue. Fifty-nine pounds she weighs, the doctor said, and she beats at me like a Dempsey.[9] Betrayer, she cries, and I running like a dog when she calls; day and night, running to her, her vomit, the bedpan. . . ."

"She needs you, Grandaddy," said Jeannie. "Isn't that what they call love? I'll see if she sleeps, and if she does, poor worn-out darling, we'll have a party, you and I; I brought us rum babas."

They did not move her. By her bed now stood the tall hooked pillar that held the solutions—blood and dextrose—to feed her veins. Jeannie moved down the hall to take over the sickroom, her face so radiant, her grandfather asked her once: "you are in love?" (Shameful the joy, the pure overwhelming joy from being with her grandmother; the peace, the serenity that breathed.) "My darling escape," she answered incoherently, "my darling Granny"—as if that explained.

Now one by one the children came, those that were able. Hannah, Paul, Sammy. Too late to ask: and what did you learn with your living, Mother, and what do we need to know?

Clara, the eldest, clenched:

> *Pay me back, Mother, pay me back for all you took from me. Those others you crowded into your heart. The hands I needed to be for you, the heaviness, the responsibility.*

---

9. Jack Dempsey (1895–1983), world heavyweight champion boxer in the 1920s. Monroe (1926–1962), movie star and sex symbol of the 1950s.

Is this she? Noises the dying make, the crablike hands crawling over the covers. The ethereal singing.

She hears that music, that singing from childhood; forgotten sound— not heard since, since.... And the hardness breaks like a cry: Where did we lose each other, first mother, singing mother?

Annulled: the quarrels, the gibing, the harshness between; the fall into silence and the withdrawal.

I do not know you, Mother. Mother, I never knew you.

Lennie, suffering not alone for her who was dying, but for that in her which never lived (for that which in him might never live). From him too, unspoken words: *good-bye Mother who taught me to mother myself.*

Not Vivi, who must stay with her children; not Davy, but he is already here, having to die again with *her* this time, for the living take their dead with them when they die.

Light she grew, like a bird, and, like a bird, sound bubbled in her throat while the body fluttered in agony. Night and day, asleep or awake (though indeed there was no difference now) the songs and the phrases leaping.

And he, who had once dreaded a long dying (from fear of himself, from horror of the dwindling money) now desired her quick death profoundly, for *her* sake. He no longer went out, except when Jeannie forced him; no longer laughed, except when, in the bright kitchenette, Jeannie coaxed his laughter (and she, who seemed to hear nothing else, would laugh too, conspiratorial wisps of laughter).

Light, like a bird, the fluttering body, the little claw hands, the beaked shadow on her face; and the throat, bubbling, straining.

He tried not to listen, as he tried not to look on the face in which only the forehead remained familiar, but trapped with her the long nights in that little room, the sounds worked themselves into his consciousness, with their punctuation of death swallows, whimpers, gurglings.

Even in reality (swallow) *life's lack of it*
Slaveships   deathtrains   clubs   enough
The bell   Summon   what enables
78,000[1]   *in one minute*   (whisper of a scream)   78,000 *human beings   we'll destroy ourselves?*

"Aah, Mrs. Miserable," he said, as if she could hear, "all your life working, and now in bed you lie, servants to tend, you do not even need to call to be tended, and still you work. Such hard work it is to die? Such hard work?"

The body threshed, her hand clung in his. A melody, ghost-thin, hovered on her lips, and like a guilty ghost, the vision of her vent in listening to it, silencing the record instantly he was near. Now, heedless of his presence, she floated the melody on and on.

"Hid it from me," he complained, "how many times you listened to remember it so?" And tried to think when she had first played it, or first begun to silence her few records when he came near—but could reconstruct nothing. There was only this room with its tall hooked pillar and its swarm of sounds.

---

1. The number killed instantly in Hiroshima by the first atomic bomb.

> No man one   except through others
> Strong   with the not yet   in the now
> Dogma dead   war dead   one country

"It helps, Mrs. Philosopher, words from books? It helps?" And it seemed to him that for seventy years she had hidden a tape recorder, infinitely microscopic, within her, that it had coiled infinite mile on mile, trapping every song, every melody, every word read, heard and spoken—and that maliciously she was playing back only what said nothing of him, of the children, of their intimate life together.

"Left us indeed, Mrs. Babbler," he reproached, "you who called others babbler and cunningly saved your words. A lifetime you tended and loved, and now not a word of us, for us. Left us indeed? Left me."

And he took out his solitaire deck, shuffled the cards loudly, slapped them down.

> Lift high   banner of reason (tatter of an orator's voice)   justice freedom-light
> Humankind   life worthy   capacities
> Seeks (blur of shudder) belong   human being

"Words, words," he accused, "and what human beings did *you* seek around you, Mrs. Live Alone, and what mankind think worthy?"

Though even as he spoke, he remembered she had not always been isolated, had not always to be alone (as he knew there had been a voice before this gossamer one; before the hoarse voice that broke from silence to lash, make incidents, shame him—a girl's voice of eloquence that spoke their holiest dreams). But again he could reconstruct, image, nothing of what had been before, or when, or how, it had changed.

Ace, queen, jack. The pillar shadow fell, so, in two tracks; in the mirror depths glistened a moonlike blob, the empty solution bottle. And it worked in him: *reason and justice and freedom. Dogma dead:* he remembered the full quotation, laughed bitterly. "Hah, good you do not know what you say; good Victor Hugo[2] died and did not see it, his twentieth century."

Deuce, ten, five. Dauntlessly she began a song of their youth of belief:

> These things shall be.[3] A loftier race
> than e'er the world hath known shall rise
> with flame of freedom in their souls
> and light of knowledge in their eyes

King, four, jack. "In the twentieth century, hah!"

> They shall be gentle, brave and strong
> to spill no drop of blood, but dare
> all . . .
>   on earth and fire and sea and air

"To spill no drop of blood, hah! So, cadaver, and you too, cadaver Hugo, 'in the twentieth century ignorance will be dead, prejudice will be dead, war will be dead, and for all mankind one country—of fulfillment.' Hah!"

---

2. French writer and champion of liberty (1802–1885); he prophesied the triumph of peace and liberty in the 20th century.
3. Century-old socialist song adopted from "A Vista" by John Addington Symonds (1840–1893), now a United Nations hymn. The first line is a translation of the slogan of the French Revolution, *Ça ira.*

And every life (long strangling cough) *shall be a song*

The cards fell from his fingers. Without warning, the bereavement and betrayal he had sheltered—compounded through the years—hidden even from himself—revealed itself,

uncoiled,
released,
sprung

and with it the monstrous shapes of what had actually happened in the century.

A ravening hunger or thirst seized him. He groped into the kitchenette, switched on all three lights, piled a tray—"you have finished your night snack, Mrs. Cadaver, now I will have mine." And he was shocked at the tears that splashed on the tray.

"Salt tears. For free. I forgot to shake on salt?"

Whispered: "Lost, how much I lost."

Escaped to the grandchildren whose childhoods were childish, who had never hungered, who lived unravaged by disease in warm houses of many rooms, had all the school for which they cared, could walk on any street, stood a head taller than their grandparents, towered above—beautiful skins, straight backs, clear straightforward eyes. "Yes, you in Olshana," he said to the town of sixty years ago, "they would be nobility to you."

And was this not the dream then, come true in ways undreamed? he asked.

And are there no other children in the world? he answered, as if in her harsh voice.

And the flame of freedom, the light of knowledge?

And the drop, to spill no drop of blood?

And he thought that at six Jeannie would get up and it would be his turn to go to her room and sleep, that he could press the buzzer and she would come now; that in the afternoon Ellen Mays was coming, and this time they would play cards and he could marvel at how rouge can stand half an inch on the cheek; that in the evening the doctor would come, and he could beg him to be merciful, to stop the feeding solutions, to let her die.

To let her die, and with her their youth of belief out of which her bright, betrayed words foamed; stained words, that on her working lips came stainless.

Hours yet before Jeannie's turn. He could press the buzzer and wake her to come now; he could take a pill, and with it sleep; he could pour more brandy into his milk glass, though what he had poured was not yet touched.

Instead he went back, checked her pulse, gently tended with his knotty fingers as Jeannie had taught.

She was whimpering; her hand crawled across the covers for his. Compassionately he enfolded it, and with his free hand gathered up the cards again. Still was there thirst or hunger ravening in him.

That world of their youth—dark, ignorant, terrible with hate and disease—how was it that living in it, in the midst of corruption, filth, treachery, degradation, they had not mistrusted man nor themselves; had believed so beautifully, so . . . falsely?

"Aaah, children," he said out loud, "how we believed, how we belonged."

And he yearned to package for each of the children, the grandchildren, for everyone, *that joyous certainty, that sense of mattering, of moving and being moved, of being one and indivisible with the great of the past, with all that freed, ennobled.* Package it, stand on corners, in front of stadiums and on crowded beaches, knock on doors, give it as a fabled gift.

"And why not in cereal boxes, in soap packages?" he mocked himself. "Aah. You have taken my senses, cadaver."

Words foamed, died unsounded. Her body writhed; she made kissing motions with her mouth. (Her lips moving as she read, poring over the Book of the Martyrs, the magnifying glass superimposed over the heavy eyeglasses.) *Still she believed?* "Eva!" he whispered. "Still you believed? You lived by it? These Things Shall Be?"

"One pound soup meat," she answered distinctly, "one soup bone."

"My ears heard you. Ellen Mays was witness: 'Man . . . one has to believe.' " Imploringly: "Eva!"

"Bread, day-old." She was mumbling. "Please, in a wooden box . . . for kindling. The thread, hah, the thread breaks. Cheap thread"—and a gurgling, enormously loud, began in her throat.

"I ask for stone; she gives me bread—day-old."[4] He pulled his hand away, shouted: "Who wanted questions? Everything you have to wake?" Then dully, "Ah, let me help you turn, poor creature."

Words jumbled, cleared. In a voice of crowded terror:

"Paul, Sammy, don't fight.

"Hannah, have I ten hands?

"How can I give it, Clara, how can I give it if I don't have?"

"You lie," he said sturdily, "there was joy too." Bitterly: "Ah how cheap you speak of us at the last."

As if to rebuke him, as if her voice had no relationship with her flailing body, she sang clearly, beautifully, a school song the children had taught her when they were little; begged:

"Not look   my hair   where they cut. . . ."

(The crown of braids shorn.) And instantly he left the mute old woman poring over the Book of the Martyrs; went past the mother treadling at the sewing machine, singing with the children; past the girl in her wrinkled prison dress, hiding her hair with scarred hands, lifting to him her awkward, shamed, imploring eyes of love; and took her in his arms, dear, personal, fleshed, in all the heavy passion he had loved to rouse from her.

"Eva!"

Her little claw hand beat the covers. How much, how much can a man stand? He took up the cards, put them down, circled the beds, walked to the dresser, opened, shut drawers, brushed his hair, moved his hand bit by bit over the mirror to see what of the reflection he could blot out with each move, and felt that at any moment he would die of what was unendurable. Went to press the buzzer to wake Jeannie, looked down, saw on Jeannie's sketch pad the hospital bed, with *her*; the double bed alongside, with him; the tall pillar feeding into her veins, and their hands, his and hers, clasped, feeding each other. And as if he had been instructed he went to his bed, lay

---

4. Compare Matthew 7.9: "Or what man is there of you, whom if his son ask bread, will he give him a stone?"

down, holding the sketch as if it could shield against the monstrous shapes of loss, of betrayal, of death—and with his free hand took hers back into his.

So Jeannie found them in the morning.

That last day the agony was perpetual. Time after time it lifted her almost off the bed, so they had to fight to hold her down. He could not endure and left the room; wept as if there never would be tears enough.

Jeannie came to comfort him. In her light voice she said: Grandaddy, Grandaddy don't cry. She is not there, she promised me. On the last day, she said she would go back to when she first heard music, a little girl on the road of the village where she was born. She promised me. It is a wedding and they dance, while the flutes so joyous andvibrant tremble in the air. Leave her there, Grandaddy, it is all right. She promised me. Come back, come back and help her poor body to die.

For two of that generation
Seevya and Genya

Infinite, Dauntless, Incorruptible

Death deepens the wonder

1961

JAMES TIPTREE JR. (ALICE B. SHELDON)
1915–1987

In 1975, some years after Alice B. Sheldon started publishing her brilliant and widely acclaimed science fiction stories under the pseudonym James Tiptree Jr., a rumor began to circulate that the supposedly male author of such dazzling tales as "Love is the Plan, the Plan is Death" and "The Women Men Don't See" was actually a woman. In an effort to set such gossip to rest, Robert Silverberg, a well-known science fiction writer, critic, and editor, faced the issue squarely. "It has been suggested that Tiptree is female," he wrote in an introduction to the author's *Warm Worlds and Otherwise* (1975), "a theory that I find absurd, for there is to me something ineluctably masculine about Tiptree's writing." Nor was Silverberg the only authoritative figure in the SF universe to be confounded by Sheldon's male impersonation. The accomplished feminist fantasist Ursula K. Le Guin, author of the gender-bending novel *The Left Hand of Darkness* (1969), claimed astonishment at the revelation that Tiptree was indeed a woman, declaring, "I don't think I have ever been so completely surprised in my life—or so happily."

The woman whose gender and genre caused such a stir had started life as Alice Bradley, the daughter of Mary Hastings Bradley, a prolific popular novelist, and Herbert Bradley, an attorney turned African explorer. When she was just six, she went on safari with her intrepid parents, and as a young adult she became a graphic designer, painter, and art critic for the *Chicago Sun*. In 1934, she married William Davey, a poet, whom she divorced in 1941. In 1942, she joined the military, serving in air intelligence; then in 1945, she married Huntington Sheldon, with whom, in

1952, she went to work at the CIA. She resigned her position in 1955 in order to study for a Ph.D. in experimental psychology. While working toward the degree, however, she began to write science fiction, adopting the name James Tiptree Jr. in 1967 because, as she later explained, "I was tired of always being the first woman in some damn profession." As another writer of science fiction and fantasy, Karen Joy Fowler, has pointed out, "Sheldon never lied about the details of her name," but the "life history" she listed in contributors notes "went a long way toward convincing her readers she must be a man."

The work that Sheldon published as Tiptree (a name she once said she drew from the label on a jar of English marmalade)—as well as under the feminine pseudonym Raccoona Sheldon, adopted later—won her numerous prizes, including the prestigious Hugo and Nebula awards, and it was collected in seven volumes, among them *Ten Thousand Light-Years from Home* (1973), *Star Songs of an Old Primate* (1978), and *Out of the Everywhere and Other Extraordinary Visions* (1981). In addition, she authored several novels and two collections of linked stories, most of which appeared after she was "unmasked" as a woman. Much of her writing is bleak and fatalistic, although much is so markedly feminist that it's hard to understand the response of some critics to rumors about Tiptree's gender. "The Women Men Don't See," for instance, is arguably a tour de force of sexual politics, setting a hard-boiled male narrator who might have come from a Raymond Chandler novel in the midst of a plot that proves unexpectedly, almost astonishingly, sympathetic to the situation of women.

But even Tiptree's feminism appears to have been driven by a grim vision of the relations between the sexes, a vision curiously at odds with the fact that she herself was happily married to Huntingdon Sheldon for more than forty years. Ultimately, though, the strain of darkness that characterized her writing prevailed in her life. In a late interview, she spoke about emotional problems, and her marriage to Huntingdon Sheldon ended in a suicide pact. In 1987, when she was seventy-one, Alice Sheldon shot her eighty-four-year-old husband, a sufferer from Alzheimer's, and then herself. The two were found dead, hand in hand in bed, in their McLean, Virginia, home. But as several of her biographers have revealed, the author had drafted her suicide note years earlier, and saved it "until needed."

The Women Men Don't See

I see her first while the Mexicana 727 is barreling down to Cozumel Island.[1] I come out of the can and lurch into her seat, saying "Sorry," at a double female blur. The near blur nods quietly. The younger one in the window seat goes on looking out. I continue down the aisle, registering nothing. Zero. I never would have looked at them or thought of them again.

Cozumel airport is the usual mix of panicky Yanks dressed for the sand pile and calm Mexicans dressed for lunch at the Presidente. I am a used-up Yank dressed for serious fishing; I extract my rods and duffel from the riot and hike across the field to find my charter pilot. One Captain Estéban has contracted to deliver me to the bonefish flats of Belize three hundred kilometers down the coast.

Captain Estéban turns out to be four feet nine of mahogany Maya *puro*.[2]

---

[1]. An island east of Mexico's Yucatán Peninsula; it was originally settled by the Maya.

[2]. Pure (Spanish, as are all translated words unless otherwise specified).

He is also in a somber Maya snit. He tells me my Cessna is grounded somewhere and his Bonanza is booked to take a party to Chetumal.

Well, Chetumal is south; can he take me along and go on to Belize after he drops them? Gloomily he concedes the possibility—*if* the other party permits, and *if* there are not too many *equipajes*.[3]

The Chetumal party approaches. It's the woman and her young companion—daughter?—neatly picking their way across the gravel and yucca apron. Their Ventura two-suiters,[4] like themselves, are small, plain, and neutral-colored. No problem. When the captain asks if I may ride along, the mother says mildly, "Of course," without looking at me.

I think that's when my inner tilt-detector sends up its first faint click. How come this woman has already looked me over carefully enough to accept on her plane? I disregard it. Paranoia hasn't been useful in my business for years, but the habit is hard to break.

As we clamber into the Bonanza, I see the girl has what could be an attractive body if there was any spark at all. There isn't. Captain Estéban folds a serape to sit on so he can see over the cowling and runs a meticulous check-down. And then we're up and trundling over the turquoise Jell-O of the Caribbean into a stiff south wind.

The coast on our right is the territory of Quintana Roo. If you haven't seen Yucatán, imagine the world's biggest absolutely flat green-gray rug. An empty-looking land. We pass the white ruin of Tulum and the gash of the road to Chichén Itzá, a half-dozen coconut plantations, and then nothing but reef and low scrub jungle all the way to the horizon, just about the way the conquistadors saw it four centuries back.

Long strings of cumulus are racing at us, shadowing the coast. I have gathered that part of our pilot's gloom concerns the weather. A cold front is dying on the henequen[5] fields of Mérida to the west, and the south wind has piled up a string of coastal storms: what they call *lloviznas*. Estéban detours methodically around a couple of small thunderheads. The Bonanza jinks, and I look back with a vague notion of reassuring the women. They are calmly intent on what can be seen of Yucatán. Well, they were offered the copilot's view, but they turned it down. Too shy?

Another *llovizna* puffs up ahead. Estéban takes the Bonanza upstairs, rising in his seat to sight his course. I relax for the first time in too long, savoring the latitudes between me and my desk, the week of fishing ahead. Our captain's classic Maya profile attracts my gaze: forehead sloping back from his predatory nose, lips and jaw stepping back below it. If his slant eyes had been any more crossed, he couldn't have made his license. That's a handsome combination, believe it or not. On the little Maya chicks in their minishifts with iridescent gloop on those cockeyes, it's also highly erotic. Nothing like the oriental doll thing; these people have stone bones. Captain Estéban's old grandmother could probably tow the Bonanza. . . .

I'm snapped awake by the cabin hitting my ear. Estéban is barking into his headset over a drumming racket of hail; the windows are dark gray.

One important noise is missing—the motor. I realize Estéban is fighting a dead plane. Thirty-six hundred; we've lost two thousand feet!

---

3. Too much luggage.
4. I.e., their suitcases.

5. A Yucatán plant used in making twine and rope.

He slaps tank switches as the storm throws us around; I catch something about *gasolina* in a snarl that shows his big teeth. The Bonanza reels down. As he reaches for an overhead toggle, I see the fuel gauges are high. Maybe a clogged gravity feed line; I've heard of dirty gas down here. He drops the set; it's a million to one nobody can read us through the storm at this range anyway. Twenty-five hundred—going down.

His electric feed pump seems to have cut in: the motor explodes—quits—explodes—and quits again for good. We are suddenly out of the bottom of the clouds. Below us is a long white line almost hidden by rain: the reef. But there isn't any beach behind it, only a big meandering bay with a few mangrove flats—and it's coming up at us fast.

This is going to be bad, I tell myself with great unoriginality. The women behind me haven't made a sound. I look back and see they've braced down with their coats by their heads. With a stalling speed around eighty, all this isn't much use, but I wedge myself in.

Estéban yells some more into his set, flying a falling plane. He is doing one jesus job, too—as the water rushes up at us he dives into a hair-raising turn and hangs us into the wind—with a long pale ridge of sandbar in front of our nose.

Where in hell he found it I never know. The Bonanza mushes down, and we belly-hit with a tremendous tearing crash—bounce—hit again—and everything slews wildly as we flat-spin into the mangroves at the end of the bar. Crash! Clang! The plane is wrapping itself into a mound of strangler fig with one wing up. The crashing quits with us all in one piece. And no fire. Fantastic.

Captain Estéban pries open his door, which is now in the roof. Behind me a woman is repeating quietly, "Mother. Mother." I climb up the floor and find the girl trying to free herself from her mother's embrace. The woman's eyes are closed. Then she opens them and suddenly lets go, sane as soap. Estéban starts hauling them out. I grab the Bonanza's aid kit and scramble out after them into brilliant sun and wind. The storm that hit us is already vanishing up the coast.

"Great landing, Captain."

"Oh, *yes!* It was beautiful." The women are shaky, but no hysteria. Estéban is surveying the scenery with the expression his ancestors used on the Spaniards.

If you've been in one of these things, you know the slow-motion inanity that goes on. Euphoria, first. We struggle down the fig tree and out onto the sandbar in the roaring hot wind, noting without alarm that there's nothing but miles of crystalline water on all sides. It's only a foot or so deep, and the bottom is the olive color of silt. The distant shore around us is all flat mangrove swamp, totally uninhabitable.

"Bahía Espíritu Santo." Estéban confirms my guess that we're down in that huge water wilderness. I always wanted to fish it.

"What's all that smoke?" The girl is pointing at the plumes blowing around the horizon.

"Alligator hunters," says Estéban. Maya poachers have left burn-offs in the swamps. It occurs to me that any signal fires we make aren't going to be too conspicuous. And I now note that our plane is well-buried in the mound of fig. Hard to see it from the air.

Just as the question of how the hell we get out of here surfaces in my mind, the older woman asks composedly, "If they didn't hear you, Captain, when will they start looking for us? Tomorrow?"

"Correct," Estéban agrees dourly. I recall that air-sea rescue is fairly informal here. Like, keep an eye open for Mario, his mother says he hasn't been home all week.

It dawns on me we may be here quite some while.

Furthermore, the diesel-truck noise on our left is the Caribbean piling back into the mouth of the bay. The wind is pushing it at us, and the bare bottoms on the mangroves show that our bar is covered at high tide. I recall seeing a full moon this morning in—believe it, St. Louis—which means maximal tides. Well, we can climb up in the plane. But what about drinking water?

There's a small splat! behind me. The older woman has sampled the bay. She shakes her head, smiling ruefully. It's the first real expression on either of them; I take it as the signal for introductions. When I say I'm Don Fenton from St. Louis, she tells me their name is Parsons, from Bethesda, Maryland. She says it so nicely I don't at first notice we aren't being given first names. We all compliment Captain Estéban again.

His left eye is swelled shut, an inconvenience beneath his attention as a Maya, but Mrs. Parsons spots the way he's bracing his elbow in his ribs.

"You're hurt, Captain."

"*Roto*[6]—I think is broken." He's embarrassed at being in pain. We get him to peel off his Jaime shirt, revealing a nasty bruise in his superb dark-bay torso.

"Is there tape in that kit, Mr. Fenton? I've had a little first-aid training."

She begins to deal competently and very impersonally with the tape. Miss Parsons and I wander to the end of the bar and have a conversation which I am later to recall acutely.

"Roseate spoonbills," I tell her as three pink birds flap away.

"They're beautiful," she says in her tiny voice. They both have tiny voices. "He's a Mayan Indian, isn't he? The pilot, I mean."

"Right. The real thing, straight out of the Bonampak murals.[7] Have you seen Chichén and Uxmal?"

"Yes. We were in Mérida. We're going to Tikal[8] in Guatemala. . . . I mean, we were."

"You'll get there." It occurs to me the girl needs cheering up. "Have they told you that Maya mothers used to tie a board on the infant's forehead to get that slant? They also hung a ball of tallow over its nose to make the eyes cross. It was considered aristocratic."

She smiles and takes another peek at Estéban. "People seem different in Yucatán," she says thoughtfully. "Not like the Indians around Mexico City. More, I don't know, independent."

"Comes from never having been conquered. Mayas got massacred and chased a lot, but nobody ever really flattened them. I bet you didn't know

---

6. Broken.
7. The finest known examples of classic Maya painting are frescoes (ca. 790 C.E.) in the ancient site of Bonampak, in the state of Chiapas, Mexico.

Chichén and Uxmal are Maya sites in Yucatán, whose capital is Mérida.
8. Another Maya site.

that the last Mexican-Maya war ended with a negotiated truce in nineteen thirty-five?"

"No!" Then she says seriously, "I like that."

"So do I."

"The water is really rising very fast," says Mrs. Parsons gently from behind us.

It is, and so is another *llovizna*. We climb back into the Bonanza. I try to rig my parka for a rain catcher, which blows loose as the storm hits fast and furious. We sort a couple of malt bars and my bottle of Jack Daniel's out of the jumble in the cabin and make ourselves reasonably comfortable. The Parsons take a sip of whiskey each, Estéban and I considerably more. The Bonanza begins to bump soggily. Estéban makes an ancient one-eyed Mayan face at the water seeping into his cabin and goes to sleep. We all nap.

When the water goes down, the euphoria has gone with it, and we're very, very thirsty. It's also damn near sunset. I get to work with a bait-casting rod and some treble hooks and manage to foul-hook four small mullets. Estéban and the women tie the Bonanza's midget life raft out in the mangroves to catch rain. The wind is parching hot. No planes go by.

Finally another shower comes over and yields us six ounces of water apiece. When the sunset envelops the world in golden smoke, we squat on the sandbar to eat wet raw mullet and Instant Breakfast crumbs. The women are now in shorts, neat but definitely not sexy.

"I never realized how refreshing raw fish is," Mrs. Parsons says pleasantly. Her daughter chuckles, also pleasantly. She's on Mamma's far side away from Estéban and me. I have Mrs. Parsons figured now; Mother Hen protecting only chick from male predators. That's all right with me. I came here to fish.

But something is irritating me. The damn women haven't complained once, you understand. Not a peep, not a quaver, no personal manifestations whatever. They're like something out of a manual.

"You really seem at home in the wilderness, Mrs. Parsons. You do much camping?"

"Oh, goodness no." Diffident laugh. "Not since my girl scout days. Oh, look—are those man-of-war birds?"

Answer a question with a question. I wait while the frigate birds sail nobly into the sunset.

"Bethesda . . . Would I be wrong in guessing you work for Uncle Sam?"

"Why, yes. You must be very familiar with Washington, Mr. Fenton. Does your work bring you there often?"

Anywhere but on our sandbar the little ploy would have worked. My hunter's gene twitches.

"Which agency are you with?"

She gives up gracefully. "Oh, just GSA[9] records. I'm a librarian."

Of course. I know her now, all the Mrs. Parsonses in records divisions, accounting sections, research branches, personnel and administration offices. Tell Mrs. Parsons we need a recap on the external service contracts for fiscal '73. So Yucatán is on the tours now? Pity . . . I offer her the tired little joke. "You know where the bodies are buried."

---

9. The General Services Administration, which serves other government agencies.

She smiles deprecatingly and stands up. "It does get dark quickly, doesn't it?"

Time to get back into the plane.

A flock of ibis are circling us, evidently accustomed to roosting in our fig tree. Estéban produces a machete and a Mayan string hammock. He proceeds to sling it between tree and plane, refusing help. His machete stroke is noticeably tentative.

The Parsons are taking a pee behind the tail vane. I hear one of them slip and squeal faintly. When they come back over the hull, Mrs. Parsons asks, "Might we sleep in the hammock, Captain?"

Estéban splits an unbelieving grin. I protest about rain and mosquitoes.

"Oh, we have insect repellent and we do enjoy fresh air."

The air is rushing by about force five[1] and colder by the minute.

"We have our raincoats," the girl adds cheerfully.

Well, okay, ladies. We dangerous males retire inside the damp cabin. Through the wind I hear the women laugh softly now and then, apparently cosy in their chilly ibis roost. A private insanity, I decide. I know myself for the least threatening of men; my non-charisma has been in fact an asset jobwise, over the years. Are they having fantasies about Estéban? Or maybe they really are fresh-air nuts . . . Sleep comes for me in invisible diesels roaring by on the reef outside.

We emerge dry-mouthed into a vast windy salmon sunrise. A diamond chip of sun breaks out of the sea and promptly submerges in cloud. I go to work with the rod and some mullet bait while two showers detour around us. Breakfast is a strip of wet barracuda apiece.

The Parsons continue stoic and helpful. Under Estéban's direction they set up a section of cowling for a gasoline flare in case we hear a plane, but nothing goes over except one unseen jet droning toward Panama. The wind howls, hot and dry and full of coral dust. So are we.

"They look first in sea," Estéban remarks. His aristocratic frontal slope is beaded with sweat; Mrs. Parsons watches him concernedly. I watch the cloud blanket tearing by above, getting higher and dryer and thicker. While that lasts nobody is going to find us, and the water business is now unfunny.

Finally I borrow Estéban's machete and hack a long light pole. "There's a stream coming in back there, I saw it from the plane. Can't be more than two, three miles."

"I'm afraid the raft's torn." Mrs. Parsons shows me the cracks in the orange plastic; irritatingly, it's a Delaware label.

"All right," I hear myself announce. "The tide's going down. If we cut the good end off that air tube, I can haul water back in it. I've waded flats before."

Even to me it sounds crazy.

"Stay by plane," Estéban says. He's right, of course. He's also clearly running a fever. I look at the overcast and taste grit and old barracuda. The hell with the manual.

When I start cutting up the raft, Estéban tells me to take the serape. "You stay one night." He's right about that, too; I'll have to wait out the tide.

"I'll come with you," says Mrs. Parsons calmly.

I simply stare at her. What new madness has got into Mother Hen? Does

---

1. I.e., on the Beaufort scale (19–24 m.p.h.).

she imagine Estéban is too battered to be functional? While I'm being astounded, my eyes take in the fact that Mrs. Parsons is now quite rosy around the knees, with her hair loose and a sunburn starting on her nose. A trim, in fact a very neat, shading-forty.

"Look, that stuff is horrible going. Mud up to your ears and water over your head."

"I'm really quite fit and I swim a great deal. I'll try to keep up. Two would be much safer, Mr. Fenton, and we can bring more water."

She's serious. Well, I'm about as fit as a marshmallow at this time of winter, and I can't pretend I'm depressed by the idea of company. So be it.

"Let me show Miss Parsons how to work this rod."

Miss Parsons is even rosier and more windblown, and she's not clumsy with my tackle. A good girl, Miss Parsons, in her nothing way. We cut another staff and get some gear together. At the last minute Estéban shows how sick he feels: he offers me the machete. I thank him, but no; I'm used to my Wirkkala knife.[2] We tie some air into the plastic tube for a float and set out along the sandiest-looking line.

Estéban raises one dark palm. *"Buen viaje."*[3] Miss Parsons has hugged her mother and gone to cast from the mangrove. She waves. We wave.

An hour later we're barely out of waving distance. The going is purely godawful. The sand keeps dissolving into silt you can't walk on or swim through, and the bottom is spiked with dead mangrove spears. We flounder from one pothole to the next, scaring up rays and turtles and hoping to god we don't kick a moray eel. Where we're not soaked in slime, we're desiccated, and we smell like the Old Cretaceous.[4]

Mrs. Parsons keeps up doggedly. I only have to pull her out once. When I do so, I notice the sandbar is now out of sight.

Finally we reach the gap in the mangrove line I thought was the creek. It turns out to open into another arm of the bay, with more mangroves ahead. And the tide is coming in.

"I've had the world's lousiest idea."

Mrs. Parsons only says mildly, "It's so different from the view from the plane."

I revise my opinion of the girl scouts, and we plow on past the mangroves toward the smoky haze that has to be shore. The sun is setting in our faces, making it hard to see. Ibis and herons fly up around us, and once a big hermit spooks ahead, his fin cutting a rooster tail. We fall into more potholes. The flashlights get soaked. I am having fantasies of the mangrove as universal obstacle; it's hard to recall I ever walked down a street, for instance, without stumbling over or under or through mangrove roots. And the sun is dropping down, down.

Suddenly we hit a ledge and fall over it into a cold flow.

"The stream! It's fresh water!"

We guzzle and garble and douse our heads; it's the best drink I remember. "Oh my, oh my—!" Mrs. Parsons is laughing right out loud.

"That dark place over to the right looks like real land."

---

2. A traditional Finnish carving knife in the version by the designer and sculptor Tapio Wirkkala (1915–1985).

3. Farewell (lit., "good journey").

4. The geologic period during which dinosaurs flourished.

We flounder across the flow and follow a hard shelf, which turns into solid bank and rises over our heads. Shortly there's a break beside a clump of spiny bromels,[5] and we scramble up and flop down at the top, dripping and stinking. Out of sheer reflex my arm goes around my companion's shoulder—but Mrs. Parsons isn't there; she's up on her knees peering at the burnt-over plain around us.

"It's so good to see land one can walk on!" The tone is too innocent. *Noli me tangere.*[6]

"Don't try it." I'm exasperated; the muddy little woman, what does she think? "That ground out there is a crush of ashes over muck, and it's full of stubs. You can go in over your knees."

"It seems firm here."

"We're in an alligator nursery. That was the slide we came up. Don't worry, by now the old lady's doubtless on her way to be made into handbags."

"What a shame."

"I better set a line down in the stream while I can still see."

I slide back down and rig a string of hooks that may get us breakfast. When I get back Mrs. Parsons is wringing muck out of the serape.

"I'm glad you warned me, Mr. Fenton. It *is* treacherous."

"Yeah." I'm over my irritation; god knows I don't want to *tangere* Mrs. Parsons, even if I weren't beat down to mush. "In its quiet way, Yucatán is a tough place to get around in. You can see why the Mayas built roads. Speaking of which—look!"

The last of the sunset is silhouetting a small square shape a couple of kilometers inland; a Maya *ruina* with a fig tree growing out of it.

"Lot of those around. People think they were guard towers."

"What a deserted-feeling land."

"Let's hope it's deserted by mosquitoes."

We slump down in the 'gator nursery and share the last malt bar, watching the stars slide in and out of the blowing clouds. The bugs aren't too bad; maybe the burn did them in. And it isn't hot anymore, either—in fact, it's not even warm, wet as we are. Mrs. Parsons continues tranquilly interested in Yucatán and unmistakably uninterested in togetherness.

Just as I'm beginning to get aggressive notions about how we're going to spend the night if she expects me to give her the serape, she stands up, scuffs at a couple of hummocks, and says, "I expect this is as good a place as any, isn't it, Mr. Fenton?"

With which she spreads out the raft bag for a pillow and lies down on her side in the dirt with exactly half the serape over her and the other corner folded neatly open. Her small back is toward me.

The demonstration is so convincing that I'm halfway under my share of serape before the preposterousness of it stops me.

"By the way. My name is Don."

"Oh, of course." Her voice is graciousness itself. "I'm Ruth."

I get in not quite touching her, and we lie there like two fish on a plate, exposed to the stars and smelling the smoke in the wind and feeling things underneath us. It is absolutely the most intimately awkward moment I've had in years.

---

5. Tropical succulents.   6. Don't touch me (Latin).

The woman doesn't mean one thing to me, but the obtrusive recessiveness of her, the defiance of her little rump eight inches from my fly—for two pesos I'd have those shorts down and introduce myself. If I were twenty years younger. If I wasn't so bushed. . . . But the twenty years and the exhaustion are there, and it comes to me wryly that Mrs. Ruth Parsons has judged things to a nicety. If I *were* twenty years younger, she wouldn't be here. Like the butterfish that float around a sated barracuda, only to vanish away the instant his intent changes, Mrs. Parsons knows her little shorts are safe. Those firmly filled little shorts, so close . . .

A warm nerve stirs in my groin—and just as it does I become aware of a silent emptiness beside me. Mrs. Parsons is imperceptibly inching away. Did my breathing change? Whatever, I'm perfectly sure that if my hand reached, she'd be elsewhere—probably announcing her intention to take a dip. The twenty years bring a chuckle to my throat, and I relax.

"Good night, Ruth."

"Good night, Don."

And believe it or not, we sleep, while the armadas of the wind roar overhead.

Light wakes me—a cold white glare.

My first thought is 'gator hunters. Best to manifest ourselves as *turistas* as fast as possible. I scramble up, noting that Ruth has dived under the bromel clump.

"*Quién estás? Al socorro!* Help, *señores!*"[7]

No answer except the light goes out, leaving me blind.

I yell some more in a couple of languages. It stays dark. There's a vague scrabbling, whistling sound somewhere in the burn-off. Liking everything less by the minute, I try a speech about our plane having crashed and we need help.

A very narrow pencil of light flicks over us and snaps off.

"Eh-ep," says a blurry voice, and something metallic twitters. They for sure aren't locals. I'm getting unpleasant ideas.

"Yes, help!"

Something goes *crackle-crackle whish-whish*, and all sounds fade away.

"What the holy hell!" I stumble toward where they were.

"Look." Ruth whispers behind me. "Over by the ruin."

I look and catch a multiple flicker which winks out fast.

"A camp?"

And I take two more blind strides. My leg goes down through the crust, and a spike spears me just where you stick the knife in to unjoint a drumstick. By the pain that goes through my bladder I recognize that my trick kneecap has caught it.

For instant basket-case you can't beat kneecaps. First you discover your knee doesn't bend anymore, so you try putting some weight on it, and a bayonet goes up your spine and unhinges your jaw. Little grains of gristle have got into the sensitive bearing surface. The knee tries to buckle and can't, and mercifully you fall down.

Ruth helps me back to the serape.

---

7. Who are you? Help! Help, sirs!

"What a fool, what a god-forgotten imbecile—"

"Not at all, Don. It was perfectly natural." We strike matches; her fingers push mine aside, exploring. "I think it's in place, but it's swelling fast. I'll lay a wet handkerchief on it. We'll have to wait for morning to check the cut. Were they poachers, do you think?"

"Probably," I lie. What I think they were is smugglers.

She comes back with a soaked bandanna and drapes it on. "We must have frightened them. That light . . . it seemed so bright."

"Some hunting party. People do crazy things around here."

"Perhaps they'll come back in the morning."

"Could be."

Ruth pulls up the wet serape, and we say good-night again. Neither of us is mentioning how we're going to get back to the plane without help.

I lie staring south where Alpha Centauri is blinking in and out of the overcast and cursing myself for the sweet mess I've made. My first idea is giving way to an even less pleasing one.

Smuggling, around here, is a couple of guys in an outboard meeting a shrimp boat by the reef. They don't light up the sky or have some kind of swamp buggy that goes whoosh. Plus a big camp . . . paramilitary-type equipment?

I've seen a report of Guévarista infiltrators[8] operating on the British Honduran border, which is about a hundred kilometers—sixty miles—south of here. Right under those clouds. If that's what looked us over, I'll be more than happy if they don't come back. . . .

I wake up in pelting rain, alone. My first move confirms that my leg is as expected—a giant misplaced erection bulging out of my shorts. I raise up painfully to see Ruth standing by the bromels, looking over the bay. Solid wet nimbus is pouring out of the south.

"No planes today."

"Oh, good morning, Don. Should we look at that cut now?"

"It's minimal." In fact the skin is hardly broken, and no deep puncture. Totally out of proportion to the havoc inside.

"Well, they have water to drink," Ruth says tranquilly. "Maybe those hunters will come back. I'll go see if we have a fish—that is, can I help you in any way, Don?"

Very tactful. I emit an ungracious negative, and she goes off about her private concerns.

They certainly are private, too; when I recover from my own sanitary efforts, she's still away. Finally I hear splashing.

"It's a big fish!" More splashing. Then she climbs up the bank with a three-pound mangrove snapper—and something else.

It isn't until after the messy work of filleting the fish that I begin to notice.

She's making a smudge of chaff and twigs to singe the fillets, small hands very quick, tension in that female upper lip. The rain has eased off for the moment; we're sluicing wet but warm enough. Ruth brings me my fish on a mangrove skewer and sits back on her heels with an odd breathy sigh.

"Aren't you joining me?"

---

8. Rural guerrillas inspired by the revolutionary Che Guevara (1928–1967).

"Oh, of course." She gets a strip and picks at it, saying quickly, "We either have too much salt or too little, don't we? I should fetch some brine." Her eyes are roving from nothing to noplace.

"Good thought." I hear another sigh and decide the girl scouts need an assist. "Your daughter mentioned you've come from Mérida. Have you seen much of Mexico?"

"Not really. Last year we went to Mazatlán and Cuernavaca. . . ." She puts the fish down, frowning.

"And you're going to see Tikal. Going to Bonampak too?"

"No." Suddenly she jumps up brushing rain off her face. "I'll bring you some water, Don."

She ducks down the slide, and after a fair while comes back with a full bromel stalk.

"Thanks." She's standing above me, staring restlessly round the horizon.

"Ruth, I hate to say it, but those guys are not coming back and it's probably just as well. Whatever they were up to, we looked like trouble. The most they'll do is tell someone we're here. That'll take a day or two to get around, we'll be back at the plane by then."

"I'm sure you're right, Don." She wanders over to the smudge fire.

"And quit fretting about your daughter. She's a big girl."

"Oh, I'm sure Althea's all right. . . . They have plenty of water now." Her fingers drum on her thigh. It's raining again.

"Come on, Ruth. Sit down. Tell me about Althea. Is she still in college?"

She gives that sighing little laugh and sits. "Althea got her degree last year. She's in computer programming."

"Good for her. And what about you, what do you do in GSA records?"

"I'm in Foreign Procurement Archives." She smiles mechanically, but her breathing is shallow. "It's very interesting."

"I know a Jack Wittig in Contracts, maybe you know him?"

It sounds pretty absurd, there in the 'gator slide.

"Oh, I've met Mr. Wittig. I'm sure he wouldn't remember me."

"Why not?"

"I'm not very memorable."

Her voice is factual. She's perfectly right, of course. Who was that woman, Mrs. Jannings, Janny, who coped with my per diem[9] for years? Competent, agreeable, impersonal. She had a sick father or something. But dammit, Ruth is a lot younger and better-looking. Comparatively speaking.

"Maybe Mrs. Parsons doesn't want to be memorable."

She makes a vague sound, and I suddenly realize Ruth isn't listening to me at all. Her hands are clenched around her knees, she's staring inland at the ruin.

"Ruth, I tell you our friends with the light are in the next county by now. Forget it, we don't need them."

Her eyes come back to me as if she'd forgotten I was there, and she nods slowly. It seems to be too much effort to speak. Suddenly she cocks her head and jumps up again.

"I'll go look at the line, Don. I thought I heard something—" She's gone like a rabbit.

---

9. I.e., his requests for reimbursement for business travel expenses.

While she's away I try getting up onto my good leg and the staff. The pain is sickening; knees seem to have some kind of hot line to the stomach. I take a couple of hops to test whether the Demerol[1] I have in my belt would get me walking. As I do so, Ruth comes up the bank with a fish flapping in her hands.

"Oh, no, Don! *No!*" She actually clasps the snapper to her breast.

"The water will take some of my weight. I'd like to give it a try."

"You mustn't!" Ruth says quite violently and instantly modulates down. "Look at the bay, Don. One can't see a thing."

I teeter there, tasting bile and looking at the mingled curtains of sun and rain driving across the water. She's right, thank god. Even with two good legs we could get into trouble out there.

"I guess one more night won't kill us."

I let her collapse me back onto the gritty plastic, and she positively bustles around, finding me a chunk to lean on, stretching the serape on both staffs to keep rain off me, bringing another drink, grubbing for dry tinder.

"I'll make us a real bonfire as soon as it lets up, Don. They'll see our smoke, they'll know we're all right. We just have to wait." Cheery smile. "Is there any way we can make you more comfortable?"

Holy Saint Sterculius:[2] playing house in a mud puddle. For a fatuous moment I wonder if Mrs. Parsons has designs on me. And then she lets out another sigh and sinks back onto her heels with that listening look. Unconsciously her rump wiggles a little. My ear picks up the operative word: *wait*.

Ruth Parsons is waiting. In fact, she acts as if she's waiting so hard it's killing her. For what? For someone to get us out of here, what else? . . . But why was she so horrified when I got up to try to leave? Why all this tension?

My paranoia stirs. I grab it by the collar and start idly checking back. Up to when whoever it was showed up last night, Mrs. Parsons was, I guess, normal. Calm and sensible, anyway. Now she's humming like a high wire. And she seems to want to stay here and wait. Just as an intellectual pastime, why?

Could she have intended to come here? No way. Where she planned to be was Chetumal, which is on the border. Come to think, Chetumal is an odd way round to Tikal. Let's say the scenario was that she's meeting somebody in Chetumal. Somebody who's part of an organization. So now her contact in Chetumal knows she's overdue. And when those types appeared last night, something suggests to her that they're part of the same organization. And she hopes they'll put one and one together and come back for her?

"May I have the knife, Don? I'll clean the fish."

Rather slowly I pass the knife, kicking my subconscious. Such a decent ordinary little woman, a good girl scout. My trouble is that I've bumped into too many professional agilities under the careful stereotypes. *I'm not very memorable.* . . .

What's in Foreign Procurement Archives? Wittig handles classified contracts. Lots of money stuff; foreign currency negotiations, commodity price schedules, some industrial technology. Or—just as a hypothesis—it could

---

1. The brand name of meperidine, a painkiller and sedative.
2. Roman god who presides over manuring.

be as simple as a wad of bills back in that modest beige Ventura, to be exchanged for a packet from, say, Costa Rica. If she were a courier, they'd want to get at the plane. And then what about me and maybe Estéban? Even hypothetically, not good.

I watch her hacking at the fish, forehead knotted with effort, teeth in her lip. Mrs. Ruth Parsons of Bethesda, this thrumming, private woman. How crazy can I get? *They'll see our smoke....*

"Here's your knife, Don. I washed it. Does the leg hurt very badly?"

I blink away the fantasies and see a scared little woman in a mangrove swamp.

"Sit down, rest. You've been going all out."

She sits obediently, like a kid in a dentist chair.

"You're stewing about Althea. And she's probably worried about you. We'll get back tomorrow under our own steam, Ruth."

"Honestly I'm not worried at all, Don." The smile fades; she nibbles her lip, frowning out at the bay.

"You know, Ruth, you surprised me when you offered to come along. Not that I don't appreciate it. But I rather thought you'd be concerned about leaving Althea alone with our good pilot. Or was it only me?"

This gets her attention at last.

"I believe Captain Estéban is a very fine type of man."

The words surprise me a little. Isn't the correct line more like "I trust Althea," or even, indignantly, "Althea is a good girl"?

"He's a man. Althea seemed to think he was interesting."

She goes on staring at the bay. And then I notice her tongue flick out and lick that prehensile upper lip. There's a flush that isn't sunburn around her ears and throat too, and one hand is gently rubbing her thigh. What's she seeing, out there in the flats?

Oho.

Captain Estéban's mahogany arms clasping Miss Althea Parsons's pearly body. Captain Estéban's archaic nostrils snuffling in Miss Parsons's tender neck. Captain Estéban's copper buttocks pumping into Althea's creamy upturned bottom.... The hammock, very bouncy. Mayas know all about it.

Well, well. So Mother Hen has her little quirks.

I feel fairly silly and more than a little irritated. *Now* I find out.... But even vicarious lust has much to recommend it, here in the mud and rain. I settle back, recalling that Miss Althea the computer programmer had waved good-bye very composedly. Was she sending her mother to flounder across the bay with me so she can get programmed in Maya? The memory of Honduran mahogany logs drifting in and out of the opalescent sand comes to me. Just as I am about to suggest that Mrs. Parsons might care to share my rain shelter, she remarks serenely, "The Mayas seem to be a very fine type of people. I believe you said so to Althea."

The implications fall on me with the rain. *Type.* As in breeding, bloodline, sire. Am I supposed to have certified Estéban not only as a stud but as a genetic donor?

"Ruth, are you telling me you're prepared to accept a half-Indian grandchild?"

"Why, Don, that's up to Althea, you know."

Looking at the mother, I guess it is. Oh, for mahogany gonads.

Ruth has gone back to listening to the wind, but I'm not about to let her off that easy. Not after all that *noli me tangere* jazz.

"What will Althea's father think?"

Her face snaps around at me, genuinely startled.

"Althea's father?" Complicated semismile. "He won't mind."

"He'll accept it too, eh?" I see her shake her head as if a fly were bothering her, and add with a cripple's malice: "Your husband must be a very fine type of a man."

Ruth looks at me, pushing her wet hair back abruptly. I have the impression that mousy Mrs. Parsons is roaring out of control, but her voice is quiet.

"There isn't any Mr. Parsons, Don. There never was. Althea's father was a Danish medical student.... I believe he has gained considerable prominence."

"Oh." Something warns me not to say I'm sorry. "You mean he doesn't know about Althea?"

"No." She smiles, her eyes bright and cuckoo.

"Seems like rather a rough deal for her."

"I grew up quite happily under the same circumstances."

Bang, I'm dead. Well, well, well. A mad image blooms in my mind: generations of solitary Parsons women selecting sires, making impregnation trips. Well, I hear the world is moving their way.

"I better look at the fish line."

She leaves. The glow fades. *No.* Just no, no contact. Goodbye, Captain Estéban. My leg is very uncomfortable. The hell with Mrs. Parsons's long-distance orgasm.

We don't talk much after that, which seems to suit Ruth. The odd day drags by. Squall after squall blows over us. Ruth singes up some more fillets, but the rain drowns her smudge; it seems to pour hardest just as the sun's about to show.

Finally she comes to sit under my sagging serape, but there's no warmth there. I doze, aware of her getting up now and then to look around. My subconscious notes that she's still twitchy. I tell my subconscious to knock it off.

Presently I wake up to find her penciling on the water-soaked pages of a little notepad.

"What's that, a shopping list for alligators?"

Automatic polite laugh. "Oh, just an address. In case we—I'm being silly, Don."

"Hey," I sit up, wincing. "Ruth, quit fretting. I mean it. We'll all be out of this soon. You'll have a great story to tell."

She doesn't look up. "Yes . . . I guess we will."

"Come on, we're doing fine. There isn't any real danger here, you know. Unless you're allergic to fish?"

Another good-little-girl laugh, but there's a shiver in it.

"Sometimes I think I'd like to go . . . really far away."

To keep her talking I say the first thing in my head.

"Tell me, Ruth. I'm curious why you would settle for that kind of lonely life, there in Washington? I mean, a woman like you—"

"Should get married?" She gives a shaky sigh, pushing the notebook back in her wet pocket.

"Why not? It's the normal source of companionship. Don't tell me you're trying to be some kind of professional man-hater."

"Lesbian, you mean?" Her laugh sounds better. "With my security rating? No, I'm not."

"Well, then. Whatever trauma you went through, these things don't last forever. You can't hate all men."

The smile is back. "Oh, there wasn't any trauma, Don, and I *don't* hate men. That would be as silly as—as hating the weather." She glances wryly at the blowing rain.

"I think you have a grudge. You're even spooky of me."

Smooth as a mouse bite she says, "I'd love to hear about your family, Don?"

Touché. I give her the edited version of how I don't have one anymore, and she says she's sorry, how sad. And we chat about what a good life a single person really has, and how she and her friends enjoy plays and concerts and travel, and one of them is head cashier for Ringling Brothers, how about that?

But it's coming out jerkier and jerkier like a bad tape, with her eyes going round the horizon in the pauses and her face listening for something that isn't my voice. What's wrong with her? Well, what's wrong with any furtively unconventional middle-aged woman with an empty bed? And a security clearance. An old habit of mind remarks unkindly that Mrs. Parsons represents what is known as the classic penetration target.

"—so much more opportunity now." Her voice trails off.

"Hurrah for women's lib, eh?"

"The lib?" Impatiently she leans forward and tugs the serape straight. "Oh, that's doomed."

The apocalyptic word jars my attention.

"What do you mean, doomed?"

She glances at me as if I weren't hanging straight either and says vaguely, "Oh . . ."

"Come on, why doomed? Didn't they get that equal rights bill?"[3]

Long hesitation. When she speaks again her voice is different.

"Women have no rights, Don, except what men allow us. Men are more aggressive and powerful, and they run the world. When the next real crisis upsets them, our so-called rights will vanish like—like that smoke. We'll be back where we always were: property. And whatever has gone wrong will be blamed on our freedom, like the fall of Rome was. You'll see."

Now all this is delivered in a gray tone of total conviction. The last time I heard that tone, the speaker was explaining why he had to keep his file drawers full of dead pigeons.

"Oh, come on. You and your friends are the backbone of the system; if you quit, the country would come to a screeching halt before lunch."

No answering smile.

"That's fantasy." Her voice is still quiet. "Women don't work that way. We're a—a toothless world." She looks around as if she wanted to stop talking. "What women do is survive. We live by ones and twos in the chinks of your world-machine."

---

3. An amendment to the Constitution that guaranteed equal rights for women passed Congress in 1972, but it failed to be ratified by ¾ of the states as required to take effect.

"Sounds like a guerrilla operation." I'm not really joking, here in the 'gator den. In fact, I'm wondering if I spent too much thought on mahogany logs.

"Guerrillas have something to hope for." Suddenly she switches on a jolly smile. "Think of us as opossums, Don. Did you know there are opossums living all over? Even in New York City."

I smile back with my neck prickling. I thought I was the paranoid one.

"Men and women aren't different species, Ruth. Women do everything men do."

"Do they?" Our eyes meet, but she seems to be seeing ghosts between us in the rain. She mutters something that could be "My Lai"[4] and looks away. "All the endless wars . . ." Her voice is a whisper. "All the huge authoritarian organizations for doing unreal things. Men live to struggle against each other; we're just part of the battlefield. It'll never change unless you change the whole world. I dream sometimes of—of going away—" She checks and abruptly changes voice. "Forgive me, Don, it's so stupid saying all this."

"Men hate wars too, Ruth," I say as gently as I can.

"I know." She shrugs and climbs to her feet. "But that's your problem, isn't it?"

End of communication. Mrs. Ruth Parsons isn't even living in the same world with me.

I watch her move around restlessly, head turning toward the ruins. Alienation like that can add up to dead pigeons, which would be GSA's problem. It could also lead to believing some joker who's promising to change the whole world. Which could just probably be my problem if one of them was over in that camp last night, where she keeps looking. *Guerrillas have something to hope for . . . ?*

Nonsense. I try another position and see that the sky seems to be clearing as the sun sets. The wind is quieting down at last too. Insane to think this little woman is acting out some fantasy in this swamp. But that equipment last night was no fantasy; if those lads have some connection with her, I'll be in the way. You couldn't find a handier spot to dispose of the body. . . . Maybe some Guévarista is a fine type of man?

Absurd. Sure . . . The only thing more absurd would be to come through the wars and get myself terminated by a mad librarian's boyfriend on a fishing trip.

A fish flops in the stream below us. Ruth spins around so fast she hits the serape. "I better start the fire," she says, her eyes still on the plain and her head cocked, listening.

All right, let's test.

"Expecting company?"

It rocks her. She freezes, and her eyes come swiveling around to me like a film take captioned FRIGHT. I can see her decide to smile.

"Oh, one never can tell!" She laughs weirdly, the eyes not changed. "I'll get the—the kindling." She fairly scuttles into the brush.

Nobody, paranoid or not, could call *that* a normal reaction.

Ruth Parsons is either psycho or she's expecting something to happen—and it has nothing to do with me: I scared her pissless.

---

4. The village in South Vietnam where American soldiers killed hundreds of unarmed civilians, including women and children, on March 16, 1968.

Well, she could be nuts. And I could be wrong, but there are some mistakes you only make once.

Reluctantly I unzip my body belt, telling myself that if I think what I think, my only course is to take something for my leg and get as far as possible from Mrs. Ruth Parsons before whoever she's waiting for arrives.

In my belt also is a .32-caliber asset Ruth doesn't know about—and it's going to stay there. My longevity program leaves the shoot-outs to TV and stresses being somewhere else when the roof falls in. I can spend a perfectly safe and also perfectly horrible night out in one of those mangrove flats. . . . Am I insane?

At this moment Ruth stands up and stares blatantly inland with her hand shading her eyes. Then she tucks something into her pocket, buttons up, and tightens her belt.

That does it.

I dry-swallow two 100-mg tabs, which should get me ambulatory and still leave me wits to hide. Give it a few minutes. I make sure my compass and some hooks are in my own pocket and sit waiting while Ruth fusses with her smudge fire, sneaking looks away when she thinks I'm not watching.

The flat world around us is turning into an unearthly amber and violet light show as the first numbness sweeps into my leg. Ruth has crawled under the bromels for more dry stuff; I can see her foot. Okay. I reach for my staff.

Suddenly the foot jerks, and Ruth yells—or rather, her throat makes that *Uh-uh-hhh* that means pure horror. The foot disappears in a rattle of bromel stalks.

I lunge upright on the crutch and look over the bank at a frozen scene.

Ruth is crouching sideways on the ledge, clutching her stomach. They are about a yard below, floating on the river in a skiff. While I was making up my stupid mind, her friends have glided right under my ass. There are three of them.

They are tall and white. I try to see them as men in some kind of white jumpsuits. The one nearest the bank is stretching out a long white arm toward Ruth. She jerks and scuttles farther away.

The arm stretches after her. It stretches and stretches. It stretches two yards and stays hanging in the air. Small black things are wiggling from its tip.

I look where their faces should be and see black hollow dishes with vertical stripes. The stripes move slowly. . . .

There is no more possibility of their being human—or anything else I've ever seen. What has Ruth conjured up?

The scene is totally silent. I blink, blink—this cannot be real. The two in the far end of the skiff are writhing those arms around an apparatus on a tripod. A weapon? Suddenly I hear the same blurry voice I heard in the night.

"Guh-give," it groans. "G-give . . ."

Dear god, it's real, whatever it is. I'm terrified. My mind is trying not to form a word.

And Ruth—Jesus, of course—Ruth is terrified too; she's edging along the bank away from them, gaping at the monsters in the skiff, who are obviously nobody's friends. She's hugging something to her body. Why doesn't she get over the bank and circle back behind me?

"G-g-give." That wheeze is coming from the tripod. "Pee-eeze give." The skiff is moving upstream below Ruth, following her. The arm undulates out at her again, its black digits looping. Ruth scrambles to the top of the bank.

"Ruth!" My voice cracks. "Ruth, get over here behind me!"

She doesn't look at me, only keeps sidling farther away. My terror detonates into anger.

"Come back here!" With my free hand I'm working the .32 out of my belt. The sun has gone down.

She doesn't turn but straightens up warily, still hugging the thing. I see her mouth working. Is she actually trying to *talk* to them?

"Please . . ." She swallows. "Please speak to me. I need your help."

"RUTH!!"

At this moment the nearest white monster whips into a great S-curve and sails right onto the bank at her, eight feet of snowy rippling horror.

And I shoot Ruth.

I don't know that for a minute—I've yanked the gun up so fast that my staff slips and dumps me as I fire. I stagger up, hearing Ruth scream, "No! No! No!"

The creature is back down by his boat, and Ruth is still farther away, clutching herself. Blood is running down her elbow.

"Stop it, Don! They aren't attacking you!"

"For god's sake! Don't be a fool, I can't help you if you won't get away from them!"

No reply. Nobody moves. No sound except the drone of a jet passing far above. In the darkening stream below me the three white figures shift uneasily; I get the impression of radar dishes focusing. The word spells itself in my head: *Aliens.*

Extraterrestrials.

What do I do, call the President? Capture them single-handed with my peashooter? . . . I'm alone in the arse end of nowhere with one leg and my brain cuddled in meperidine hydrochloride.

"Prrr-eese," their machine blurs again. "Wa-wat hep . . ."

"Our plane fell down," Ruth says in a very distinct, eerie voice. She points up at the jet, out toward the bay. "My—my child is there. Please take us *there* in your boat."

Dear god. While she's gesturing, I get a look at the thing she's hugging in her wounded arm. It's metallic, like a big glimmering distributor head. What—?

Wait a minute. This morning: when she was gone so long, she could have found that thing. Something they left behind. Or dropped. And she hid it, not telling me. That's why she kept going under that bromel clump—she was peeking at it. Waiting. And the owners came back and caught her. They want it. She's trying to bargain, by god.

"—Water," Ruth is pointing again. "Take us. Me. And him."

The black faces turn toward me, blind and horrible. Later on I may be grateful for that "us." Not now.

"Throw your gun away, Don. They'll take us back." Her voice is weak.

"Like hell I will. You—who are you? What are you doing here?"

"Oh, god, does it matter? He's frightened," she cries to them. "Can you understand?"

She's as alien as they, there in the twilight. The beings in the skiff are twittering among themselves. Their box starts to moan.

"Ss-stu-dens," I make out. "S-stu-ding . . . not—huh-arming . . . w-we . . . buh . . ." It fades into garble and then says, "G-give . . . we . . . g-go. . . ."

Peace-loving cultural-exchange students—on the interstellar level now. Oh, no.

"Bring that thing here, Ruth—right now!"

But she's starting down the bank toward them saying, "Take me."

"Wait! You need a tourniquet on that arm."

"I know. Please put the gun down, Don."

She's actually at the skiff, right by them. They aren't moving.

"Jesus Christ." Slowly, reluctantly, I drop the .32. When I start down the slide, I find I'm floating; adrenaline and Demerol are a bad mix.

The skiff comes gliding toward me, Ruth in the bow clutching the thing and her arm. The aliens stay in the stern behind their tripod, away from me. I note the skiff is camouflaged tan and green. The world around us is deep shadowy blue.

"Don, bring the water bag!"

As I'm dragging down the plastic bag, it occurs to me that Ruth really is cracking up, the water isn't needed now. But my own brain seems to have gone into overload. All I can focus on is a long white rubbery arm with black worms clutching the far end of the orange tube, helping me fill it. This isn't happening.

"Can you get in, Don?" As I hoist my numb legs up, two long white pipes reach for me. *No, you don't.* I kick and tumble in beside Ruth. She moves away.

A creaky hum starts up, it's coming from a wedge in the center of the skiff. And we're in motion, sliding toward dark mangrove files.

I stare mindlessly at the wedge. Alien technological secrets? I can't see any, the power source is under that triangular cover, about two feet long. The gadgets on the tripod are equally cryptic, except that one has a big lens. Their light?

As we hit the open bay, the hum rises and we start planing faster and faster still. Thirty knots?[5] Hard to judge in the dark. Their hull seems to be a modified trihedral much like ours, with a remarkable absence of slap. Say twenty-two feet. Schemes of capturing it swirl in my mind. I'll need Estéban.

Suddenly a huge flood of white light fans out over us from the tripod, blotting out the aliens in the stern. I see Ruth pulling at a belt around her arm, still hugging the gizmo.

"I'll tie that for you."

"It's all right."

The alien device is twinkling or phosphorescing slightly. I lean over to look, whispering, "Give that to me, I'll pass it to Estéban."

"No!" She scoots away, almost over the side. "It's theirs, they need it!"

"What? Are you crazy?" I'm so taken aback by this idiocy I literally stammer. "We have to, we—"

"They haven't hurt us. I'm sure they could." Her eyes are watching me with feral intensity; in the light her face has a lunatic look. Numb as I am, I realize that the wretched woman is poised to throw herself over the side if I move. With the alien thing.

"I think they're gentle," she mutters.

---

5. About 35 m.p.h.

"For Christ's sake, Ruth, they're *aliens*!"

"I'm used to it," she says absently. "There's the island! Stop! Stop here!"

The skiff slows, turning. A mound of foliage is tiny in the light. Metal glints—the plane.

"Althea! Althea! Are you all right?"

Yells, movement on the plane. The water is high, we're floating over the bar. The aliens are keeping us in the lead with the light hiding them. I see one pale figure splashing toward us and a dark one behind, coming more slowly. Estéban must be puzzled by that light.

"Mr. Fenton is hurt, Althea. These people brought us back with the water. Are you all right?"

"A-okay." Althea flounders up, peering excitedly. "You all right? Whew, that light!" Automatically I start handing her the idiotic water bag.

"Leave that for the captain," Ruth says sharply. "Althea, can you climb in the boat? Quickly, it's important."

"Coming."

"No, no!" I protest, but the skiff tilts as Althea swarms in. The aliens twitter, and their voice box starts groaning. "Gu-give . . . now . . . give . . ."

"*Qué llega?*"[6] Estéban's face appears beside me, squinting fiercely into the light.

"Grab it, get it from her—that thing she has—" but Ruth's voice rides over mine. "Captain, lift Mr. Fenton out of the boat. He's hurt his leg. Hurry, please."

"Goddamn it, wait!" I shout, but an arm has grabbed my middle. When a Maya boosts you, you go. I hear Althea saying, "Mother, your arm!" and fall onto Estéban. We stagger around in water up to my waist; I can't feel my feet at all.

When I get steady, the boat is yards away. The two women are head-to-head, murmuring.

"Get them!" I tug loose from Estéban and flounder forward. Ruth stands up in the boat facing the invisible aliens.

"Take us with you. Please. We want to go with you, away from here."

"Ruth! Estéban, get that boat!" I lunge and lose my feet again. The aliens are chirruping madly behind their light.

"Please take us. We don't mind what your planet is like; we'll learn—we'll do anything! We won't cause any trouble. Please. Oh, *please*." The skiff is drifting farther away.

"Ruth! Althea! Are you crazy? Wait—" But I can only shuffle nightmarelike in the ooze, hearing that damn voice box wheeze, "N-not come . . . more . . . not come . . ." Althea's face turns to it, openmouthed grin.

"Yes, we understand," Ruth cries. "We don't want to come back. Please take us with you!"

I shout and Estéban splashes past me shouting too, something about radio.

"Yes-s-s," groans the voice.

Ruth sits down suddenly, clutching Althea. At that moment Estéban grabs the edge of the skiff beside her.

"Hold them, Estéban! Don't let her go."

He gives me one slit-eyed glance over his shoulder, and I recognize his

6. What arrives?

total uninvolvement. He's had a good look at that camouflage paint and the absence of fishing gear. I make a desperate rush and slip again. When I come up Ruth is saying, "We're going with these people, Captain. Please take your money out of my purse, it's in the plane. And give this to Mr. Fenton."

She passes him something small; the notebook. He takes it slowly.

"Estéban! No!"

He has released the skiff.

"Thank you so much," Ruth says as they float apart. Her voice is shaky; she raises it. "There won't be any trouble, Don. Please send this cable. It's to a friend of mine, she'll take care of everything." Then she adds the craziest touch of the entire night. "She's a grand person; she's director of nursing training at N.I.H."[7]

As the skiff drifts, I hear Althea add something that sounds like "Right on."

Sweet Jesus . . . Next minute the humming has started; the light is receding fast. The last I see of Mrs. Ruth Parsons and Miss Althea Parsons is two small shadows against that light, like two opossums. The light snaps off, the hum deepens—and they're going, going, gone away.

In the dark water beside me Estéban is instructing everybody in general to *chingarse* themselves.[8]

"Friends, or something," I tell him lamely. "She seemed to want to go with them."

He is pointedly silent, hauling me back to the plane. He knows what could be around here better than I do, and Mayas have their own longevity program. His condition seems improved. As we get in I notice the hammock has been repositioned.

In the night—of which I remember little—the wind changes. And at seven-thirty next morning a Cessna buzzes the sandbar under cloudless skies.

By noon we're back in Cozumel. Captain Estéban accepts his fees and departs laconically for his insurance wars. I leave the Parsons' bags with the Caribe agent, who couldn't care less. The cable goes to a Mrs. Priscilla Hayes Smith, also of Bethesda. I take myself to a medico and by three P.M. I'm sitting on the Cabañas terrace with a fat leg and a double margarita, trying to believe the whole thing.

The cable said, *Althea and I taking extraordinary opportunity for travel. Gone several years. Please take charge our affairs. Love, Ruth.*

She'd written it that afternoon, you understand.

I order another double, wishing to hell I'd gotten a good look at that gizmo. Did it have a label, Made by Betelgeusians?[9] No matter how weird it was, *how* could a person be crazy enough to imagine—?

Not only that but to hope, to plan! *If I could only go away.* . . . That's what she was doing, all day. Waiting, hoping, figuring how to get Althea. To go sight unseen to an alien world. . . .

With the third margarita I try a joke about alienated women, but my heart's not in it. And I'm certain there won't be any bother, any trouble at all. Two human women, one of them possibly pregnant, have departed for, I guess,

---

7. The National Institutes of Health; its headquarters are in Bethesda, Md.
8. To fuck themselves (Mexican slang).

9. Betelgeuse, a bright star in the constellation Orion, is about 500 light-years from our solar system.

the stars; and the fabric of society will never show a ripple. I brood: do all Mrs. Parsons's friends hold themselves in readiness for any eventuality, including leaving Earth? And will Mrs. Parsons somehow one day contrive to send for Mrs. Priscilla Hayes Smith, that grand person?

I can only send for another cold one, musing on Althea. What suns will Captain Estéban's sloe-eyed offspring, if any, look upon? "Get in, Althea, we're taking off for Orion." "A-okay, Mother." Is that some system of upbringing? *We survive by ones and twos in the chinks of your world-machine.... I'm used to aliens....* She'd meant every word. Insane. How could a woman choose to live among unknown monsters, to say good-bye to her home, her world?

As the margaritas take hold, the whole mad scenario melts down to the image of those two small shapes sitting side by side in the receding alien glare.

Two of our opossums are missing.

1973

RUTH STONE
b. 1915

"I found that poems came with this mysterious feeling, and it was a kind of peculiar ecstasy," the poet Ruth Stone once explained to an interviewer, noting that "my mother read poetry—Tennyson—to me from the time, apparently, she started suckling me at her breasts." Sometimes exuberant, often elegiac, and always elegant, Stone works with integrity and intensity to shape the "peculiar ecstasy" of such aesthetic visions. Born in Roanoke, Virginia, she was raised in Indiana and Illinois. After graduating from the University of Illinois, she married twice—her second husband was the critic-novelist Walter Stone, who died in 1958—and she is the mother of three daughters. The winner of several Guggenheim fellowships, she has published eleven books of poetry, among them *In an Iridescent Time* (1959), *Cheap* (1975), *Second-Hand Coat: Poems New and Selected* (1987), *Simplicity* (1995), *Ordinary Words* (1999), *In the Next Galaxy* (2002), and *In the Dark* (2004).

For many years Stone supported herself as a kind of itinerant poet-teacher, working as a visiting professor and writer in residence at such institutions as the University of Illinois, the University of Wisconsin, Indiana University, the University of California at Davis, and Brandeis University; but in 1988, at the age of seventy-three, she finally settled in a permanent position at SUNY Binghamton, where she rapidly gained an enthusiastic following on campus. She did not retire until 2000, when she was eighty-five. In this period, traveling between Binghamton and Brandon, Vermont, where she has long lived in an old farmhouse near several of her daughters and their families, she at last began to gain the recognition her extraordinary brilliance and productivity long deserved. Honors recently bestowed on her include the National Book Critics Circle Award (2000), the National Book Award (2002), and the Wallace Stevens Award of the Academy of American Poets (2002). Whether writing in obscurity or from a more public position, however, Stone has consistently concentrated her attention on the situations of women as different as the stubborn survivor of "Absinthe Granny" and the acquiescent housewife of "Second-Hand Coat." At the same time, in such metaphysical meditations as "Periphery" and "Things I Say to Myself While Hanging Laundry," she addresses major philosophical questions—the mind–body problem, the self in the cosmos—from a distinctly feminist perspective.

Perhaps most striking in Stone's later books are the candor and clarity with which she focuses on the liabilities, along with the paradoxical rewards, of age. Almost no poet after the great Irish modernist William Butler Yeats has dealt with this theme so dazzlingly. For Stone (as for Yeats in some of his moods), age is not a barrier to achievement but a theme rich with potential, like any other. As she somewhat insouciantly told an interviewer in 2004, as she neared her ninetieth birthday, "If your brain goes on and on, as it should under normal conditions, there's more in it and your writing will get more profound."

In an Iridescent Time

My mother, when young, scrubbed laundry in a tub,
She and her sisters on an old brick walk
Under the apple trees, sweet rub-a-dub.
The bees came round their heads, the wrens made talk.
5   Four young ladies each with a rainbow board
Honed their knuckles, wrung their wrists to red,
Tossed back their braids and wiped their aprons wet.
The Jersey calf beyond the back fence roared;
And all the soft day, swarms about their pet
10   Buzzed at his big brown eyes and bullish head.
Four times they rinsed, they said. Some things they starched,
Then shook them from the baskets two by two,
And pinned the fluttering intimacies of life
Between the lilac bushes and the yew:
15   Brown gingham, pink, and skirts of Alice blue.[1]

1958

Periphery

You are not wanted
I said to the older body
Who was listening near the cupboards.
But outside on the porch
5   They were all eating.
The body dared not
Put its fingers in its mouth.
Behave, I whispered,
You have a wart on your cheek
10   And everyone knows you drink.
But that's all right, I relented,
It isn't generally known
How clever you are.

---

1. A pale shade of blue (a favorite color of Alice Roosevelt Longworth, 1884–1980).

I know you aren't appreciated.
The body hunted for something good to eat,
But the food had all been eaten by the others.
They laughed together carelessly outside the kitchen.
The body hid in the pantry near the refrigerator.
After a while it laughed, too.
It listened to all the jokes and it laughed.

1975

The Song of Absinthe[1] Granny

Among some hills there dwelt in parody
A young woman; me.
I was that gone with child
That before I knew it I had three
And they hung whining and twisting.
Why I wasn't more than thirty-nine
And sparse as a runt fruit tree.
Three pips[2] that plagued the life out of me.
Ah me. It wore me down,
The grubs, the grubbing.
We were two inches thick in dust
For lack of scrubbing.
Diapers and panty-shirts and yolk of eggs.
One day in the mirror I saw my stringy legs
And I looked around
And saw string on the floor,
And string on the chair
And heads like wasps' nests
Full of stringy hair.
"Well," I said, "if you have string, knit.
Knit something, don't just sit."
We had the orchard drops,[3]
But they didn't keep.
The milk came in bottles.
It came until the bottles were that deep
We fell over the bottles.
The milk dried on the floor.
"Drink it up," cried their papa,
And they all began to roar, "More!"
Well, time went on,
Not a bone that wasn't frayed.
Every chit was knicked[4] and bit,
And nothing was paid.
We had the dog spayed.
"It looks like a lifetime,"

---

1. A strong green liqueur made from wormwood.
2. Small seeds; anything small.
3. Fruit fallen from trees.
4. Snapped. "Chit": voucher of a small debt, especially for food.

Their papa said.
"It's a good life, it's a good wife,
It's a good bed."
So I got the rifle out
40 To shoot him through the head.
But he went on smiling and sitting
And I looked around for a piece of string
To do some knitting.
Then I picked at the tiling
45 And the house fell down.
"Now you've done it," he said.
"I'm going to town.
Get them up out of there,
Put them to bed."
50 "I'm afraid to look," I whimpered,
"They might be dead."
"We're here, mama, under the shed."
Well, the winters wore on.
We had cats that hung around.
55 When I fed them they scratched.
How the little nippers loved them.
Cats and brats.
I couldn't see for my head was thatched
But they kept coming in when the door unlatched.
60 "I'll shave my head," I promised,
"I'll clip my mop.
This caterwauling has got to stop."
Well, all that's finished,
It's all been done.
65 Those were high kick summers,
It was bald galled fun.
Now the daft time's over
And the string is spun.
I'm all alone
70 To cull[5] and be furry.
Not an extra page in the spanking story.
The wet britches dried
And the teeth came in.
The last one cried
75 And no new began.
Those were long hot summers,
Now the sun won't tarry.
My birds have flocked,
And I'm old and wary.
80 I'm old and worn and a cunning sipper,
And I'll outlive every little nipper.
And with what's left I'm chary,
And with what's left I'm chary.

1975

---

5. Gather; subject to a process of selection.

Second-Hand Coat

    I feel
    in her pockets; she wore nice cotton gloves,
    kept a handkerchief box, washed her undies,
    ate at the Holiday Inn, had a basement freezer,
5   belonged to a bridge club.
    I think when I wake in the morning
    that I have turned into her.
    She hangs in the hall downstairs,
    a shadow with pulled threads.
10 I slip her over my arms, skin of a matron.
    Where are you? I say to myself, to the orphaned body,
    and her coat says,
    Get your purse, have you got your keys?

1981

Names

    My grandmother's name was Nora Swan.
    Old Aden Swan was her father. But who was her mother?
    I don't know my great-grandmother's name.
    I don't know how many children she bore.
5   Like rings of a tree the years of woman's fertility.
    Who were my great-aunt Swans?
    For every year a child; diphtheria, dropsy, typhoid.
    Who can bother naming all those women churning butter,
    leaning on scrub boards, holding to iron bedposts,
10 sweating in labor? My grandmother knew the names
    of all the plants on the mountain. Those were the names
    she spoke of to me. Sorrel, lamb's ear, spleenwort, heal-all;
    never go hungry, she said, when you can gather a pot of greens.
    She had a finely drawn head under a smooth cap of hair
15 pulled back to a bun. Her deep-set eyes were quick to notice
    in love and anger. Who are the women who nurtured her for me?
    Who handed her in swaddling flannel to my great-grandmother's breast?
    Who are the women who brought my great-grandmother tea
    and straightened her bed? As anemone in midsummer, the air
20 cannot find them and grandmother's been at rest for forty years.
    In me are all the names I can remember—pennyroyal, boneset,
    bedstraw, toadflax[1]—from whom I did descend in perpetuity.

1987

---

1. All herbs used in folk medicine.

Things I Say to Myself While Hanging Laundry

If an ant, crossing on the clothesline
from apple tree to apple tree,
would think and think,
it probably could not dream up Albert Einstein.
5   Or even his sloppy mustache;
or the wrinkled skin bags under his eyes
that puffed out years later,
after he dreamed up that maddening relativity.[1]
Even laundry is three dimensional.
10 The ants cross its great fibrous forests
from clothespin to clothespin
carrying the very heart of life in their sacs or mandibles,
the very heart of the universe in their formic acid molecules.
And how refreshing the linens are,
15 lying in the clean sheets at night,
when you seem to be the only one on the mountain,
and your body feels the smooth touch of the bed
like love against your skin;
and the heavy sac of yourself relaxes into its embrace.
20 When you turn out the light,
you are blind in the dark
as perhaps the ants are blind,
with the same abstract leap out of this limiting dimension.
So that the very curve of light,
25 as it is pulled in the dimple of space,[2]
is relative to your own blind pathway across the abyss.
And there in the dark is Albert Einstein
with his clever formula[3] that looks like little mandibles
digging tunnels into the earth
30 and bringing it up, grain by grain,
the crystals of sand exploding
into white hot radiant turbulence,
smiling at you, his shy bushy smile,
along an imaginary line from here to there.

1995

---

1. The idea that measurements of time and motion are relative to the observer, if the speed of light is constant in all frames of reference; one result is that space and time should be properly viewed as part of a four-dimensional space-time continuum. Albert Einstein (1879–1955) was only in his twenties when he published his papers on the special theory of relativity.
2. I.e., deflected by gravity. According to Einstein's general theory of relativity, which predicted such curvature of light, gravity is a curved field created by mass.
3. Expressing the equivalence of mass and energy in the famous equation $E = mc^2$.

At Eighty-three She Lives Alone

Enclosure, steam-heated; a trial casket.
You are here; your name on a postal box;
entrance into another place like vapor.
No one knows you. No one speaks to you.
All of their cocks stare down their pant legs
at the ground. Their cunts are blind. They
barely let you through the check-out line.
Have a nice day. Plastic or paper?

Are you origami? A paper folded swan,
like the ones you made when you were ten?
When you saw the constellations, lying
on your back in the wet grass,
the soapy pear blossoms drifting
and wasting, and those stars, the burned out ones
whose light was still coming in waves;
your body was too slight.
How could it hold such mass?
Still on your lips the taste of something.

All night you waited for morning, all morning
for afternoon, all afternoon for night;
and still the longing sings.
Oh, paper bird with folded wings.

2002

Sorrow

Living alone the feet turn voluptuous,
cold as sea water, the thin brine
of the blood reaches them slowly;
their nubby heads rub one another.
How can you love them and yet
how live without them?
Their shoes lined up like caskets
in which they lie all day
dead from one another.
In the night
each foot has nothing to love
but the other foot.

2002

Cousin Francis Speaks Out

Buddy's uncle Hiram felt bad about his sister, Mable.
Hiram always had a good job with the railroad.
He'd come out and give Buddy a few dollars once a month.
Mable was Buddy's ma. She had seven living
and they were all boys.
Buddy took care of his ma
when she come home from the insane asylum.
He drove a Holsum Bread truck.
He had a place of his own,
three rooms and toilet with cement floor.
Mable was in the asylum twenty-five years
on account of chopping up the furniture
when Shafe, her shiftless run-around old man,
tossed the baby up against the ceiling
and then it died of brain fever.
She weren't dangerous when they let her out;
so light, Buddy could lift her off the bed
with one arm and put her on the potty seat.
He made the potty seat out of some old rocker.
Buddy had a little patch out back; greens and peas.
Mable didn't have no teeth.
The first thing they do when you go crazy
is to pull the teeth.

2002

From Outer Space

Your gray glasses are for playing the piano.
Your brown glasses, for strong reading.
Birds scratch in the snow for seeds.
Your oldest cat sleeps on your best papers.
It is overcast, Tuesday, and the coffee
too dark. Nothing but sugar in the cupboard.
That's when the voice from the galaxy
comes back saying, praise be, it had a good
sleep; it is ready to translate. And the disc
that someone planted in your skull picks
up a little static and you hear, ". . . come in Minus
103. The Japanese report remnants, debris,
gas, large chunks of matter. Listen, listen,
I kid you not. This is real. Now get this down.
This morning, snow fell. Thirty-six blue jays,
fifteen assorted sparrows, and five surviving
chickadees fought through the weather.
Get this. A poem about a new subject, a fresh
approach. Now listen, write this down, we . . ."

2004

The Barrier

Give back my brilliant ignorance.
Streets where I waited for you
in light waves
in the cones[1] of my eyes
the color of lost rooms;
those erotic odors.
Silence among the marble columns,
clash of mesh doors,
faded pretentious paper on the walls,
where we breathed in our bodies' acrid sweat
in the abyss of longing;
where we walked naked over the cheap carpets;
those casual rooms,
those pitiless hours.

2004

The Jewels

Living in hell, as I do,
the devil lies in my ear.
Violent endings, devastation,
I am either the shipped-out cargo,
listing beyond the breakwater,
or the eternal widow,
standing at the window.
Always the blinding snowstorm.
At the edge of the precipice
I look into the green canopy of the valley,
then, as far as the Oort cloud[1]
hiding its clutter of massive rocks.
How serene and deceptive the fall of tidal air—
the vast drift downward.
Body, I said,
moment by moment we wore our jewels,
we took them every day into the sunlight,
to the blind leper
on the side of the road.

2004

1. The nerve cells in the human eye that detect color.
1. A spherical cloud of comets located about a light-year from the sun whose existence was postulated in 1950 by the Dutch astronomer Jan Oort.

MARGARET WALKER
1915–1998

The dedication of Margaret Walker's *For My People,* a volume that was chosen for the Yale Series of Younger Poets in 1942, acknowledged her indebtedness to and her sense of responsibility for "my people everywhere singing their slave songs repeatedly: their dirges and their ditties and their blues and jubilees." In many of the poems she included in this book, Walker used jazz rhythms and blues meters to present the grace and daring of such folk characters as Stagolee, Molly Means, Poppa Chicken, Kissie Lee, and Yalluh Hammuh. Caught in a culture oblivious to the "black and poor and small and different," Walker's characters reflect her effort "to fashion a world that will hold all the people, all the faces, all the adams and eves and their countless generations."

One of four children of Sigismund Walker, a Methodist minister, and Marion Dozier Walker, a musicologist, Margaret Walker was born in Birmingham, Alabama. Educated at church schools in Mississippi, Alabama, and Louisiana, she began composing verse at thirteen years of age. During her undergraduate days at Northwestern University, she "went hungry unless friends fed me." Yet she received her B.A. in 1935, and her M.A. and Ph.D. from the University of Iowa in 1940 and 1965. After she married in 1943, she began teaching at Livingstone College in Salisbury, North Carolina. She later became a professor of English at Jackson State College in Mississippi, where she supported a disabled husband and four children on a salary that remained for many years well under $6,000. She also established a black studies program at Jackson. In both her academic life and her literary career, Walker self-consciously attempted to nurture the growth of black culture. *Prophets for a New Day* (1970) and *October Journey* (1973) include a number of sonnets and ballads about the human rights struggle, just as her historical novel *Jubilee* (1966), which won the Houghton Mifflin Literary Fellowship, uses the traditional genre of the slave narrative to celebrate a heroic woman who simultaneously moves into maturity and freedom. In her mid-seventies, Walker produced a biography of Richard Wright, *Richard Wright, Daemonic Genius* (1988), as well as a collection of autobiographical essays, *How I Wrote Jubilee and Other Essays on Life and Literature* (1990).

Dark Blood

There were bizarre beginnings in old lands for the making of me. There
    were sugar sands and islands of fern and pearl, palm jungles and
    stretches of a never-ending sea.

There were the wooing nights of tropical lands and the cool discretion of
    flowering plains between two stalwart hills. They nurtured my coming
    with wanderlust. I sucked fevers of adventure through my veins with
    my mother's milk.

Someday I shall go to the tropical lands of my birth, to the coasts of conti-
    nents and the tiny wharves of island shores. I shall roam the Balkans[1]

---

1. The countries on the Balkan Peninsula, which is bounded by the Adriatic and Ionian seas on the west, the Mediterranean on the south, and the Aegean and Black seas on the east.

and the hot lanes of Africa and Asia. I shall stand on mountain tops
and gaze on fertile homes below.

And when I return to Mobile I shall go by the way of Panama and Bocas
del Toro[2] to the littered streets and the one-room shacks of my old
poverty, and blazing suns of other lands may struggle then to reconcile
the pride and pain in me.

1942

Lineage

My grandmothers were strong.
They followed plows and bent to toil.
They moved through fields sowing seed.
They touched earth and grain grew.
5   They were full of sturdiness and singing.
My grandmothers were strong.

My grandmothers are full of memories
Smelling of soap and onions and wet clay
With veins rolling roughly over quick hands
10 They have many clean words to say.
My grandmothers were strong.
Why am I not as they?

1942

Molly Means

Old Molly Means was a hag and a witch;
Chile of the devil, the dark, and sitch.
Her heavy hair hung thick in ropes
And her blazing eyes was black as pitch.
5   Imp at three and wench at 'leben
She counted her husbands to the number seben.
   O Molly, Molly, Molly Means
There goes the ghost of Molly Means.

Some say she was born with a veil[1] on her face
10 So she could look through unnatchal space
Through the future and through the past
And charm a body or an evil place
And every man could well despise
The evil look in her coal black eyes.

---

2. A town in Panama. Mobile is a city in Alabama.
1. I.e., a caul. Being born with a membrane cov‑ering one's face was thought to be a sign of supernatural powers.

15   Old Molly, Molly, Molly Means
        Dark is the ghost of Molly Means.

        And when the tale begun to spread
        Of evil and of holy dread:
        Her black-hand arts and her evil powers
20   How she cast her spells and called the dead,
        The younguns was afraid at night
        And the farmers feared their crops would blight.
            Old Molly, Molly, Molly Means
            Cold is the ghost of Molly Means.

25   Then one dark day she put a spell
        On a young gal-bride just come to dwell
        In the lane just down from Molly's shack
        And when her husband come riding back
        His wife was barking like a dog
30   And on all fours like a common hog.
            O Molly, Molly, Molly Means
            Where is the ghost of Molly Means?

        The neighbors come and they went away
        And said she'd die before break of day
35   But her husband held her in his arms
        And swore he'd break the wicked charms;
        He'd search all up and down the land
        And turn the spell on Molly's hand.
            O Molly, Molly, Molly Means
40   Sharp is the ghost of Molly Means.

        So he rode all day and he rode all night
        And at the dawn he come in sight
        Of a man who said he could move the spell
        And cause the awful thing to dwell
45   On Molly Means, to bark and bleed
        Till she died at the hands of her evil deed.
            Old Molly, Molly, Molly Means
            This is the ghost of Molly Means.

        Sometimes at night through the shadowy trees
50   She rides along on a winter breeze.
        You can hear her holler and whine and cry.
        Her voice is thin and her moan is high,
        And her cackling laugh or her barking cold
        Bring terror to the young and old.
55   O Molly, Molly, Molly Means
            Lean is the ghost of Molly Means.

                                                    1942

Kissie Lee

Toughest gal I ever did see
Was a gal by the name of Kissie Lee;
The toughest gal God ever made
And she drew a dirty, wicked blade.

     5 Now this here gal warn't always tough
Nobody dreamed she'd turn out rough
But her Grammaw Mamie had the name
Of being the town's sin and shame.

When Kissie Lee was young and good
10 Didn't nobody treat her like they should
Allus gettin' beat by a no-good shine[1]
An' allus quick to cry and whine.

Till her Grammaw said, "Now listen to me,
I'm tiahed of yoah whinin', Kissie Lee.
15 People don't never treat you right,
An' you allus scrappin' or in a fight.

"Whin I was a gal wasn't no soul
Could do me wrong an' still stay whole.
Ah got me a razor to talk for me
20 An' aftah that they let me be."

Well Kissie Lee took her advice
And after that she didn't speak twice
'Cause when she learned to stab and run
She got herself a little gun.

25 And from that time that gal was mean,
Meanest mama you ever seen.
She could hold her likker and hold her man
And she went thoo life jus' raisin' san'.[2]

One night she walked in Jim's saloon
30 And seen a guy what spoke too soon;
He done her dirt long time ago
When she was good and feeling low.

Kissie bought her drink and she paid her dime
Watchin' this guy what beat her time
35 And he was making for the outside door
When Kissie shot him to the floor.

Not a word she spoke but she switched her blade
And flashing that lil ole baby paid:

---

1. Person with jet-black skin.   2. I.e., raising dust, moving briskly

Evvy livin' guy got out of her way
40 Because Kissie Lee was drawin' her pay.

She could shoot glass doors offa the hinges,
She could take herself on the wildest binges.
And she died with her boots on switching blades
On Talladega Mountain in the likker raids.[3]

1942

Whores

When I grew up I went away to work
where painted whores were fascinating sights.
They came on like whole armies through the nights—
their sullen eyes on mine, their mouths a smirk,
5 and from their hands keys hung suggestively.
Old women working by an age-old plan
to make their bread in ways as best they can
would hobble past and beckon tirelessly.

Perhaps one day they'll all die in the streets
10 or be surprised by bombs in each wide bed;
learning too late in unaccustomed dread
that easy ways, like whores on special beats,
no longer have the gift to harbor pride
or bring men peace, or leave them satisfied.

1942

For Malcolm X[1]

All you violated ones with gentle hearts;
You violent dreamers whose cries shout heartbreak;
Whose voices echo clamors of our cool capers,
And whose black faces have hollowed pits for eyes.
5 All you gambling sons and hooked children and bowery bums
Hating white devils and black bourgeoisie,
Thumbing your noses at your burning red suns,
Gather round this coffin and mourn your dying swan.

Snow-white moslem head-dress around a dead black face!
10 Beautiful were your sand-papering words against our skins!
Our blood and water pour from your flowing wounds.
You have cut open our breasts and dug scalpels in our brains.

---

3. Police raids made during Prohibition on people manufacturing illegal liquor.
1. Militant black nationalist leader of the Black Muslims (1925–1965); in 1964 he formed his own Muslim organization and was no longer advocating strict separatism at the time of his assassination.

> When and Where will another come to take your holy place?
> Old man mumbling in his dotage, or crying child, unborn?

1970

JUDITH WRIGHT
1915–2000

Lamenting that "the song is gone; the dance / is secret with the dancers in the earth," the Australian poet Judith Wright mourned in "Bora Ring," an early poem, the dispersal and destruction of the Aborigines who inhabited her native land before it was conquered by the British. In part, those lines predicted one major direction her artistic career would take: in producing more than a dozen volumes of verse and a number of collections of essays on criticism and articles on conservation, as well as editing several anthologies of Australian poetry, this prolific and deeply engaged artist memorialized Australia as "my blood's country . . . the high lean country / full of old stories that still go walking in my sleep." At the same time, however, much of her poetry meditated on such matters from a distinctively female perspective, a point of view explicitly summarized by the title of her second book, *Woman to Man* (1949).

The descendant of what one commentator calls "pioneering rural stock," Wright was born in Armidale, New South Wales, and educated at New England Girls School, Armidale, and the University of Sydney. Married to the philosopher J. P. McKinney, and the mother of one daughter, she worked for some time as a secretary and civil servant before taking up a position as honors tutor in English at the University of Queensland. In the mid-1950s, she wrote, the "two threads of my life, the love of the land itself and the deep unease over the fate of its original people, were beginning to twine together, and the rest of my life would be influenced by that connection." By the 1960s, she had become increasingly involved in political action, including the antiwar movement, Australia's conservationist movement, and the movement to change the treatment of the country's Aboriginal peoples (about whose oppression she wrote *The Cry of the Dead*, 1982). Cofounder and former president of the Wild Life Preservation Society of Queensland, she spent the last third of her life, after she was widowed, living in a wildlife sanctuary near Braidwood, and in these years she also befriended the Aboriginal poet Oodgeroo Noonuccal (Kath Walker), whose verse she helped publish and to whom she addressed her moving "Two Dreamtimes."

Such poems as "Ishtar" and "Eve to Her Daughters" suggest the connections that Wright saw between female power and the forces of nature, even while they argue that there is a causal relationship between Adam's fear that "outside Eden the earth was imperfect" and the twentieth century's assault on the environment. That this poet identified deeply with women's literary tradition is also made clear in these works, as well as in her " 'Rosina Alcona to Julius Brenzaida,' " a piece whose title is taken from a poem by another female acolyte of nature—the Victorian poet-novelist Emily Brontë. Characteristically, Wright last appeared in public, a month before her death, at a march for reconciliation with Aboriginal people. She herself, wrote one critic in an obituary, "was described as feeling almost Aboriginal about the Australian landscape." Her activism was as integral to her poetry as her aesthetic skill. The "true function of art and culture is to interpret us to ourselves," she once declared, "and to relate us to the country and the society in which we live."

Half-Caste[1] Girl

Little Josie buried under the bright moon
is tired of being dead, death lasts too long.
She would like to push death aside, and stand on the hill
and beat with a waddy[2] on the bright moon like a gong.

    Across the hills, the hills that belong to no people
    and so to none are foreign,
    once she climbed high to find the native cherry;
    the lithe darkhearted lubra[3]
    who in her beads like blood
    dressed delicately for love
    moves her long hands among the strings of the wind,
    singing the songs of women,
    the songs of love and dying.

    Against the world's stone walls she thrust her heart—
    endless the strength of its beating—
    atom of flesh that cannot move a stone.
    She used her love for lever;
    but the wall is cunningly made.
    Not even the strong break jail.
    So she is restless still under her rootwarm cover,
    hearing the noise of living,
    forgetting the pain of dying.

Little Josie buried under the bright sun
would like to open her eyes and dance in the light.
Who is it has covered the sun and the beautiful moon
with a wallaby[4] skin, and left her alone in the night?

1946

Woman to Man

    The eyeless labourer in the night,
    the selfless, shapeless seed I hold,
    builds for its resurrection day—
    silent and swift and deep from sight
    foresees the unimagined light.

    This is no child with a child's face;
    this has no name to name it by:
    yet you and I have known it well.
    This is our hunter and our chase,
    the third who lay in our embrace.

---

1. Of mixed racial descent.
2. A club used as a weapon by Australian Aborigines.
3. Aboriginal Australian woman.
4. Small kangaroo.

This is the strength that your arm knows,
the arc of flesh that is my breast,
the precise crystals of our eyes.
This is the blood's wild tree that grows
15   the intricate and folded rose.

This is the maker and the made;
this is the question and reply;
the blind head butting at the dark,
the blaze of light along the blade.
20   Oh hold me, for I am afraid.

                                  1949

The Sisters

In the vine-shadows on the veranda,
under the yellow leaves, in the cooling sun,
sit the two sisters. Their slow voices run
like little winter creeks dwindled by frost and wind,
5   and the square of sunlight moves on the veranda.

They remember the gay young men on their tall horses
who came courting; the dancing and the smells of leather
and wine, the girls whispering by the fire together:
even their dolls and ponies, all they have left behind
10   moves in the yellow shadows on the veranda.

Thinking of their lives apart and the men they married,
thinking of the marriage-bed and the birth of the first child,
they look down smiling. "My life was wide and wild,
and who can know my heart? There in that golden jungle
15   I walk alone," say the old sisters on the veranda.

                                  1949

Ishtar[1]

When I first saw a woman after childbirth
the room was full of your glance who had just gone away.
And when the mare was bearing her foal
you were with her but I did not see your face.

5   When in fear I became a woman
I first felt your hand.
When the shadow of the future first fell across me
it was your shadow, my grave and hooded attendant.

---

1. Babylonian goddess of love and fertility.

It is all one whether I deny or affirm you;
10 it is not my mind you are concerned with.
It is no matter whether I submit or rebel;
the event will still happen.

You neither know nor care for the truth of my heart;
but the truth of my body has all to do with you.
15 You have no need of my thoughts or my hopes,
living in the realm of the absolute event.

Then why is it that when I at last see your face
under that hood of slate-blue, so calm and dark,
so worn with the burden of an inexpressible knowledge—
20 why is it that I begin to worship you with tears?

1953

Request to a Year

If the year is meditating a suitable gift,
I should like it to be the attitude
of my great-great-grandmother,
legendary devotee of the arts,

5 who, having had eight children
and little opportunity for painting pictures,
sat one day on a high rock
beside a river in Switzerland

and from a difficult distance viewed
10 her second son, balanced on a small ice-floe,
drift down the current towards a waterfall
that struck rock-bottom eighty feet below,

while her second daughter, impeded,
no doubt, by the petticoats of the day,
15 stretched out a last-hope alpenstock[1]
(which luckily later caught him on his way).

Nothing, it was evident, could be done;
and with the artist's isolating eye
my great-great-grandmother hastily sketched the scene.
20 The sketch survives to prove the story by.

Year, if you have no Mother's Day present planned,
reach back and bring me the firmness of her hand.

1955

---

1. A walking stick used in mountain climbing.

To Another Housewife

Do you remember how we went,
on duty bound, to feed the crowd
of hungry dogs your father kept
as rabbit-hunters? Lean and loud,
5   half-starved and furious, how they leapt
against their chains, as though they meant
in mindless rage for being fed,
to tear our childish hands instead!

With tomahawk and knife we hacked
10 the flyblown tatters of old meat,
gagged at their carcass-smell, and threw
the scraps and watched the hungry eat.
Then turning faint, we made a pact,
(two greensick girls), crossed hearts and swore
15 to touch no meat forever more.

How many cuts of choice and prime
our housewife hands have dressed since then—
these hands with love and blood imbrued—
for daughters, sons, and hungry men!
20 How many creatures bred for food
we've raised and fattened for the time
they met at last the steaming knife
that serves the feast of death-in-life!

And as the evening meal is served
25 we hear the turned-down radio
begin to tell the evening news
just as the family joint[1] is carved.
O murder, famine, pious wars....
Our children shrink to see us so,
30 in sudden meditation, stand
with knife and fork in either hand.

1966

Eve[1] to Her Daughters

It was not I who began it.
Turned out into drafty caves,
hungry so often, having to work for our bread,
hearing the children whining,

---

1. I.e., joint of roast meat.
1. The first woman, created by God as a companion for Adam in the Garden of Eden (Genesis 2.18–22). Genesis 3 describes how she was tempted by the serpent into eating the forbidden fruit of the tree of the knowledge of good and evil, which she gave to Adam; this act precipitated their expulsion from Eden and the introduction of work, pain, and death into the world (Genesis 3).

5   I was nevertheless not unhappy.
    Where Adam went I was fairly contented to go.
    I adapted myself to the punishment: it was my life.

    But Adam, you know . . . !
    He kept on brooding over the insult,
10 over the trick They had played on us, over the scolding.
    He had discovered a flaw in himself
    and he had to make up for it.

    Outside Eden the earth was imperfect,
    the seasons changed, the game was fleet-footed,
15 he had to work for our living, and he didn't like it.
    He even complained of my cooking
    (it was hard to compete with Heaven).

    So he set to work.
    The earth must be made a new Eden
20 with central heating, domesticated animals,
    mechanical harvesters, combustion engines,
    escalators, refrigerators,
    and modern means of communication
    and multiplied opportunities for safe investment
25 and higher education for Abel and Cain[2]
    and the rest of the family.
    You can see how his pride had been hurt.

    In the process he had to unravel everything,
    because he believed that mechanism
30 was the whole secret—he was always mechanical-minded.
    He got to the very inside of the whole machine
    exclaiming as he went, So this is how it works!
    And now that I know how it works, why, I must have invented it.
    As for God and the Other,[3] they cannot be demonstrated,
35 and what cannot be demonstrated
    doesn't exist.
    You see, he had always been jealous.

    Yes, he got to the center
    where nothing at all can be demonstrated.
40 And clearly he doesn't exist; but he refuses
    to accept the conclusion.
    You see, he was always an egotist.

    It was warmer than this in the cave;
    there was none of this fall-out.
45 I would suggest, for the sake of the children,
    that it's time you took over.

---

2. The first two sons of Adam and Eve; Cain murdered Abel out of jealousy because God preferred Abel's offerings (Genesis 4.4–8).

3. I.e., Satan, whose name is derived from the Hebrew word meaning "adversary."

But you are my daughters, you inherit my own faults of character;
you are submissive, following Adam
even beyond existence.
Faults of character have their own logic
and it always works out.
I observed this with Abel and Cain.

Perhaps the whole elaborate fable
right from the beginning
is meant to demonstrate this; perhaps it's the whole secret.
Perhaps nothing exists but our faults?
At least they can be demonstrated.

But it's useless to make
such a suggestion to Adam.
He has turned himself into God,
who is faultless, and doesn't exist.

1966

Naked Girl and Mirror

This is not I. I had no body once—
only what served my need to laugh and run
and stare at stars and tentatively dance
on the fringe of foam and wave and sand and sun.
Eyes loved, hands reached for me, but I was gone
on my own currents, quicksilver, thistledown.
Can I be trapped at last in that soft face?

I stare at you in fear, dark brimming eyes.
Why do you watch me with that immoderate plea—
"Look under these curled lashes, recognize
that you were always here; know me—be me."
Smooth once-hermaphrodite[1] shoulders, too tenderly
your long slope runs, above those sudden shy
curves furred with light that spring below your space.

No, I have been betrayed. If I had known
that this girl waited between a year and a year,
I'd not have chosen her bough to dance upon.
Betrayed, by that little darkness here, and here
this swelling softness and that frightened stare
from eyes I will not answer; shut out here
from my own self, by its new body's grace—

for I am betrayed by someone lovely. Yes,
I see you are lovely, hateful naked girl.

---

1. With both female and male characteristics.

Your lips in the mirror tremble as I refuse
25 to know or claim you. Let me go—let me be gone.
You are half of some other who may never come.
Why should I tend you? You are not my own;
you seek that other—he will be your home.

Yet I pity your eyes in the mirror, misted with tears;
30 I lean to your kiss. I must serve you; I will obey.
Some day we may love. I may miss your going, some day,
though I shall always resent your dumb and fruitful years.
Your lovers shall learn better, and bitterly too,
if their arrogance dares to think I am part of you.

1966

"Rosina Alcona to Julius Brenzaida"[1]

    Living long is containing
    archaean[2] levels,
    buried yet living.
    Greek urns, their lovely tranquillity
5   still and yet moving,
    directing, surviving.[3]

    So driving homewards
    full of my present
    along the new freeway,
10   carved straight, rushing forward,
    I see suddenly there still
    that anachronism, the old wooden pub
    stranded at the crossways.

    Where you and I once
15   in an absolute present
    drank laughing
    in a day still living,
    still laughing, still permanent.

    Present crossed past
20   synchronized, at the junction.
    The daylight of one day
    was deepened, was darkened
    by the light of another.

    Three faces met,
25   your vivid face in life,

---

1. The title of a poem by Emily Brontë (1819–1848), quoted in lines 38–39 and echoed in line 54 (see Vol. 1, p. 969).
2. Belonging to the earliest geological periods.
3. A comparison that recalls John Keats's "Ode on a Grecian Urn" (1820).

your face of dead marble
touched mine simultaneously.

Holding the steering-wheel
my hands freeze. Out of my eyes
30 jump these undryable tears
from artesian[4] pressures,
from the strata that cover you,
the silt-sift of time.

These gulping dry lines
35 are not my song for you.
That's made already.
Come in, dead Emily.

Have I forgot, my only Love, to love thee,
Severed at last by time's all-wearing wave?

40 A work of divinest anguish,
a Greek urn completed.
I grip the steering-wheel.
No other star has ever shone for me.

The pure poem rises
45 in lovely tranquillity,
as the Greek urn rises
from the soil of the past,
as the lost face rises
and the tears return.

50 I move through my present
gripping the steering-wheel,
repeating, repeating it.
The crossways fade; the freeway rushes forward.
"These days obscure but cannot do thee wrong."

1971

Two Dreamtimes[1]

(For Kath Walker[2])

Kathy my sister with the torn heart,
I don't know how to thank you
for your dreamtime stories of joy and grief
written on paperbark.

---

4. Like an artesian well, whose water is under pressure and flows naturally to the surface.
1. According to Australian Aborigines, the dreamtime was the time of creation, when ancestral spiritual beings rose from below the earth to shape the land.

2. Australian Aboriginal activist and writer of fiction and poetry (1920–1993; see below, p. 828); her paternal great-grandmother was a Noonuccal, and her great-grandfather a Spaniard. In 1988, she took the name Oodgeroo, which means "paperbark" in the Noonuccal language.

5   You were one of the dark children
    I wasn't allowed to play with—
    riverbank campers, the wrong colour,
    (I couldn't turn you white).

    So it was late I met you,
10 late I began to know
    they hadn't told me the land I loved
    was taken out of your hands.

    Sitting all night at my kitchen table
    with a cry and a song in your voice,
15 your eyes were full of the dying children,
    the blank-eyed taken women,

    the sullen looks of the men who sold them
    for rum to forget the selling,
    the hard rational white faces
20 with eyes that forget the past.

    With a knifeblade flash in your black eyes
    that always long to be blacker,
    your Spanish-Koori[3] face
    of a fighter and singer,

25 arms over your breast folding
    your sorrow in to hold it,
    you brought me to you some of the way
    and came the rest to meet me,

    over the desert of red sand
30 came from your lost country
    to where I stand with all my fathers,
    their guilt and righteousness.

    Over the rum your voice sang
    the tales of an old people,
35 their dreaming buried, the place forgotten . . .
    We too have lost our dreaming.

    We the robbers robbed in turn,
    selling this land on hire-purchase;
40 what's stolen once is stolen again
    even before we know it.

    If we are sisters, it's in this—
    our grief for a lost country,
    the place we dreamed in long ago,
    poisoned now and crumbling.

---

3. Indigenous peoples of southeastern Australia (a name preferred by many to *Aborigine,* a label that others put on them); in some languages of the region, it means "person" or "people."

45　　Let us go back to that far time,
　　　I riding the cleared hills,
　　　plucking blue leaves for their eucalypt scent,
　　　hearing the call of the plover,

　　　in a land I thought was mine for life.
50　　I mourn it as you mourn
　　　the ripped length of the island beaches,
　　　the drained paperbark swamps.

　　　The easy Eden-dreamtime then
　　　in a country of birds and trees
55　　made me your shadow-sister, child,
　　　dark girl I couldn't play with.

　　　But we are grown to a changed world:
　　　over the drinks at night
　　　we can exchange our separate griefs,
60　　but yours and mine are different.

　　　A knife's between us. My righteous kin
　　　still have cruel faces,
　　　Neither you nor I can win them,
　　　though we meet in secret kindness.

65　　I am born of the conquerors,
　　　you of the persecuted.
　　　Raped by rum and an alien law,
　　　progress and economics,

　　　are you and I and a once-loved land
70　　peopled by tribes and trees;
　　　doomed by traders and stock exchanges,
　　　bought by faceless strangers.

　　　And you and I are bought and sold,
　　　our songs and stories too
75　　though quoted low in a falling market
　　　(publishers shake their heads at poets).

　　　Time that we shared for a little while,
　　　telling sad tales of women
　　　(black or white at a different price)
80　　meant much and little to us.

　　　My shadow-sister, I sing to you
　　　from my place with my righteous kin,
　　　to where you stand with the Koori dead,
　　　"Trust none—not even poets."

85　　The knife's between us. I turn it round,
　　　the handle to your side,

the weapon made from your country's bones.
I have no right to take it.

But both of us die as our dreamtime dies.
90 I don't know what to give you
for your gay stories, your sad eyes,
but that, and a poem, sister.

1973

Some Words

Unless

Had a whole dream once
full of nothing else

A bottomless pit,
5 eyes bulged out
across it,
neck stretched out
over it.

A whole life I know of
10 fell into it
once;
and never came back.

Therefore

Three white lines
15 joining exactly,
all the angles
equal.[1]

Inside it—
symmetrical
20 cross-legged,
one finger up,
expounding a simple fact
sits Nobody.

A perfect confined space;
25 not one star
shines in.

---

1. In mathematical proofs, the symbol for *therefore* is three dots, placed as if at the points of an equilateral triangle (∴).

Enough

No use, we'll never catch it.
It's just ahead,
30   a puff
of flying light.

Want it! want it!
Wake up at night
crying for it,
35   walk round all day
needing it.

Till one day
it's there.

Not needed any more,
40   not even wanted.

Look at it without a smile.
Turn away.

1973

Counting in Sevens

Seven ones are seven.
I can't remember that year
or what presents I was given.

Seven twos are fourteen.
5   That year I found my mind,
swore not to be what I had been.

Seven threes are twenty-one.
I was sailing my own sea,
first in love, the knots undone.

10   Seven fours are twenty-eight;
three false starts had come and gone;
my true love came, and not too late.

Seven fives are thirty-five.
In her cot my daughter lay,
15   real, miraculous, alive.

Seven sixes are forty-two.
I packed her sandwiches for school,
I loved my love and time came true.

Seven sevens are forty-nine.
20 Fruit loaded down my apple-tree,
near fifty years of life were mine.

Seven eights are fifty-six.
My lips still cold from a last kiss,
my fire was ash and charcoal-sticks.

25 Seven nines are sixty-three; seven tens are seventy.
Who would that old woman be?
She will remember being me,

but what she is I cannot see.
Yet with every added seven,
30 some strange present I was given.

1976

P. K. PAGE
b. 1916

"I was an early feminist," the poet, painter, and fiction writer P. K. Page once told an interviewer, adding that now "I consider myself a feminist but not a feminist writer." Yet this extraordinarily energetic artist, who has been defined as "a phenomenon; a *force majeur* in Canadian literary and artistic life; a National Treasure," produces works deeply infused with themes and images drawn from the lives of women. In her brilliant, recent "Planet Earth"—a poem that was chosen by the United Nations in 2000 for its celebratory Year of Dialogue among Civilizations—she rings the changes on a theme first sounded by Pablo Neruda, praising the earth in a language of exuberant domesticity: "It has to be loved," she writes, "the way a laundress loves her linens, / the way she moves her hands caressing the fine muslins." At the same time, the stenographers, typists, and clerks of her poems about office workers illustrate her unique ability to endow often painfully realistic portraiture with luminous precision.

Patricia Kathleen Page was born in England but came to Canada as a young child. During the 1940s, while she was a scriptwriter for the National Film Board, she associated with the poets contributing to *Preview* (1942–45), an innovative Montreal magazine founded by Patrick Anderson. The social concerns of her verse date from this period and help explain her sense of indebtedness to such English poets as Stephen Spender and W. H. Auden. However, in her first two volumes of verse—*As Ten, as Twenty* (1946) and *The Metal and the Flower* (1954)—she also demonstrated her commitment to a mystical poetry of quest that links her to the visionary tradition of Rainer Maria Rilke and W. B. Yeats. In her own words, she has often attempted "to copy exactly something which exists in a dimension where worldly senses are inadequate," and in her later years she has become deeply involved in the study of Sufism.

Page's publishing career was interrupted by travels through Australia, Brazil, and Mexico that she undertook with her husband, the diplomat W. Arthur Irwin, in the 1950s. After the couple returned to Canada in 1964, she resumed her place of prominence in the land where she was raised. Along with numerous volumes of poetry, among them *The Hidden Room: Collected Poems* (1997) and *Planet Earth: Poems Selected and New* (2002), she has published a memoir, *Brazilian Journal* (1987, illustrated with her own drawings), several novels, and a number of short stories, including some for children. Under the name P. K. Irwin, she has had one-woman shows of her paintings in Mexico and Canada, and her work is represented in the permanent collections of the National Gallery of Canada and elsewhere.

The Stenographers

After the brief bivouac of Sunday,
their eyes, in the forced march of Monday to Saturday,
hoist the white flag, flutter in the snowstorm of paper,
haul it down and crack in the midsun of temper.

5 In the pause between the first draft and the carbon[1]
they glimpse the smooth hours when they were children—
the ride in the ice-cart, the ice-man's name,
the end of the route and the long walk home;

remember the sea where floats at high tide
10 were sea marrows[2] growing on the scatter-green vine
or spools of grey toffee, or wasps' nests on water;
remember the sand and the leaves of the country.

Bell rings and they go and the voice draws their pencil
like a sled across snow; when its runners are frozen
15 rope snaps and the voice then is pulling no burden
but runs like a dog on the winter of paper.

Their climates are winter and summer—no wind
for the kites of their hearts—no wind for a flight;
a breeze at the most, to tumble them over
20 and leave them like rubbish—the boy-friends of blood.

In the inch of the noon as they move they are stagnant.
The terrible calm of the noon is their anguish;
the lip of the counter, the shapes of the straws
like icicles breaking their tongues are invaders.

25 Their beds are their oceans—salt water of weeping
the waves that they know—the tide before sleep;
and fighting to drown they assemble their sheep
in columns and watch them leap desks for their fences
and stare at them with their own mirror-worn faces.

30 In the felt of the morning the calico-minded,
sufficiently starched, insert papers, hit keys,

---

1. I.e., the final copy, typed with carbon paper between sheets of plain paper to create multiple copies.
2. Large zucchini.

efficient and sure as their adding machines;
yet they weep in the vault, they are taut as net curtains
stretched upon frames. In their eyes I have seen
35 the pin men of madness in marathon trim
race round the track of the stadium pupil.

                                                            1946

Typists

They, without message, having read
the running words on their machines,
know every letter as a stamp
cutting the stencils[1] of their ears.
5 Deep in their hands, like pianists,
all longing gropes and moves, is trapped
behind the tensile gloves of skin.

Or, blind, sit with their faces locked
away from work. Their varied eyes
10 stiff as everlasting flowers.
While fingers on a different plane
perform the automatic act
as questions grope along the dark
and twisting corridors of brain.

15 Crowded together typists touch
softly as ducks and seem to sense
each others' anguish with the swift
sympathy of the deaf and dumb.

                                                            1946

Planet Earth

It has to be spread out, the skin of this planet,
has to be ironed, the sea in its whiteness;
and the hands keep on moving,
smoothing the holy surfaces.
   —In Praise of Ironing   by Pablo Neruda[1]

It has to be loved the way a laundress loves her linens,
the way she moves her hands caressing the fine muslins
knowing their warp and woof,
like a lover coaxing, or a mother praising.

---

1. The special paper used with a mimeograph machine, which can create large numbers of copies; in the first step of the process, the action of the typewriter cuts letters into the stencil.

1. Nobel Prize-winning Chilean poet (1904–1973); "In Praise of Ironing" (here translated by Alastair Reid) was published in 1962.

5   It has to be loved as if it were embroidered
with flowers and birds and two joined hearts upon it.
It has to be stretched and stroked.
It has to be celebrated.
O this great beloved world and all the creatures in it.
10 *It has to be spread out, the skin of this planet.*

The trees must be washed, and the grasses and mosses.
They have to be polished as if made of green brass.
The rivers and little streams with their hidden cresses
and pale-coloured pebbles
15 and their fool's gold
must be washed and starched or shined into brightness,
the sheets of lake water
smoothed with the hand
and the foam of the oceans pressed into neatness.
20 *It has to be ironed, the sea in its whiteness.*

and pleated and goffered,[2] the flower-blue sea
the protean, wine-dark,[3] grey, green, sea
with its metres of satin and bolts of brocade.
And sky—such an O! overhead—night and day
25 must be burnished and rubbed
by hands that are loving
so the blue blazons forth
and the stars keep on shining
within and above
30 *and the hands keep on moving.*

It has to be made bright, the skin of this planet
till it shines in the sun like gold leaf.
Archangels then will attend to its metals
and polish the rods of its rain.
35 Seraphim[4] will stop singing hosannas
to shower it with blessings and blisses and praises
and, newly in love,
we must draw it and paint it
our pencils and brushes and loving caresses
40 *smoothing the holy surfaces.*

1994, 1997

---

2. Crimped.
3. A description of the sea often used by Homer.
4. Angels.

CARSON McCULLERS
1917–1967

Mick Kelly, the would-be musician of *The Heart Is a Lonely Hunter* (1940), and Frankie Addams, the would-be poet of *The Member of the Wedding* (1946), are probably among Carson McCullers's most famous characters, adolescents who dream of being wedded to a new world where the children, the blacks, and the homosexuals of their hometowns would no longer be misbegotten mutes or loners. Because of her sympathy for such figures along with sometimes grotesque or violent plots, McCullers has been placed in the so-called Southern Gothic tradition of writing associated with her friend the playwright Tennessee Williams. Yet, as Virginia Spencer Carr's biography demonstrates, the macabre atmosphere of McCullers's art reflected the confusion of her life.

The first child of Lamar Smith, a watch repairman and jewelry store owner, and Vera Marguerite (Waters) Smith, McCullers was born Lula Carson Smith in Columbus, Georgia. Like many of her adolescent heroines, Lula was an imaginative child, devoted to music in general and the piano in particular. When she was fifteen, however, an attack of rheumatic fever forced her to relinquish the strenuous demands of a musical career for a future in writing, and she began to produce for her family plays that were, in her own words, "thick with incest, lunacy, and murder." At seventeen, she arrived in New York, where she worked as a waitress and typist while studying music at the Juilliard School and taking writing courses at Columbia University. But at this point, her rheumatic fever had recurred, sending her back to Georgia to recuperate.

McCullers was treated as something of a prodigy after the publication of *The Heart Is a Lonely Hunter*. The twenty-three-year-old author was immediately celebrated as a brilliant regionalist and supported by friendships with such established writers as W. H. Auden, Richard Wright, and Jane Bowles. Although *Reflections in a Golden Eye* (1941) was less successful than her first novel, she received fellowships from the Yaddo colony (a retreat for writers), the Guggenheim Foundation, and the American Academy of Arts and Letters. Yet both McCullers's personal friends and her professional acquaintances commented on the insecurity and neediness that made her emotionally demanding and compulsively moody.

Just before the publication of *The Heart Is a Lonely Hunter*, she had married Reeves McCullers, a would-be writer recently released from the army. But their relationship was strained when Carson, as she now called herself, fell in love with Annemarie Clarac-Schwarzenbach, a Swiss writer. Although Schwarzenbach did not reciprocate McCullers's feelings, the McCullerses divorced in 1941, remarried in 1945, broke up again in 1948, and reunited in 1949. Throughout this period, McCullers's literary success was remarkable. "The Ballad of the Sad Café" was chosen for *Best American Stories* in 1944, *The Member of the Wedding* received rave reviews in 1946, and four years later it was hailed as a dramatic triumph when it opened as a play in New York starring Ethel Waters and Julie Harris. Yet in 1948 McCullers tried to commit suicide, and in 1953 Reeves McCullers killed himself.

During her forties, McCullers suffered a heart attack, pneumonia, and breast cancer. With her cropped hair and whimsical smile, however, she looks in photographs from this period like the tormented but gallant adolescents who dominated her fiction. After several strokes, she died at the age of fifty. In her last two publications—the novel *Clock without Hands* (1961) and the play *The Square Root of Wonderful* (1958)—McCullers continued to explore the loneliness of adults chafing from their childhood griefs. Typical of her work in its portrayal of alienated but imaginative individuals in search of their own albeit eccentric truths, "The Ballad of the Sad Café" brilliantly delineates the punishment meted out to a female character who supposes that she can live a life of physical power, intellectual authority, and personal autonomy.

The Ballad of the Sad Café

The town itself is dreary; not much is there except the cotton mill, the two-room houses where the workers live, a few peach trees, a church with two colored windows, and a miserable main street only a hundred yards long. On Saturdays the tenants from the nearby farms come in for a day of talk and trade. Otherwise the town is lonesome, sad, and like a place that is far off and estranged from all other places in the world. The nearest train stop is Society City, and the Greyhound and White Bus Lines use the Forks Falls Road which is three miles away. The winters here are short and raw, the summers white with glare and fiery hot.

If you walk along the main street on an August afternoon there is nothing whatsoever to do. The largest building, in the very center of the town, is boarded up completely and leans so far to the right that it seems bound to collapse at any minute. The house is very old. There is about it a curious, cracked look that is very puzzling until you suddenly realize that at one time, and long ago, the right side of the front porch had been painted, and part of the wall—but the painting was left unfinished and one portion of the house is darker and dingier than the other. The building looks completely deserted. Nevertheless, on the second floor there is one window which is not boarded; sometimes in the late afternoon when the heat is at its worst a hand will slowly open the shutter and a face will look down on the town. It is a face like the terrible dim faces known in dreams—sexless and white, with two gray crossed eyes which are turned inward so sharply that they seem to be exchanging with each other one long and secret gaze of grief. The face lingers at the window for an hour or so, then the shutters are closed once more, and as likely as not there will not be another soul to be seen along the main street. These August afternoons—when your shift is finished there is absolutely nothing to do; you might as well walk down to the Forks Falls Road and listen to the chain gang.

However, here in this very town there was once a café. And this old boarded-up house was unlike any other place for many miles around. There were tables with cloths and paper napkins, colored streamers from the electric fans, great gatherings on Saturday nights. The owner of the place was Miss Amelia Evans. But the person most responsible for the success and gaiety of the place was a hunchback called Cousin Lymon. One other person had a part in the story of this café—he was the former husband of Miss Amelia, a terrible character who returned to the town after a long term in the penitentiary, caused ruin, and then went on his way again. The café has long since been closed, but it is still remembered.

The place was not always a café. Miss Amelia inherited the building from her father, and it was a store that carried mostly feed, guano,[1] and staples such as meal and snuff. Miss Amelia was rich. In addition to the store she

---

1. Fertilizer (usually made of bat or seafowl excrement).

operated a still three miles back in the swamp, and ran out the best liquor in the county. She was a dark, tall woman with bones and muscles like a man. Her hair was cut short and brushed back from the forehead, and there was about her sunburned face a tense, haggard quality. She might have been a handsome woman if, even then, she was not slightly cross-eyed. There were those who would have courted her, but Miss Amelia cared nothing for the love of men and was a solitary person. Her marriage had been unlike any other marriage ever contracted in this county—it was a strange and dangerous marriage, lasting only for ten days, that left the whole town wondering and shocked. Except for this queer marriage Miss Amelia had lived her life alone. Often she spent whole nights back in her shed in the swamp, dressed in overalls and gum boots, silently guarding the low fire of the still.

With all things which could be made by the hands Miss Amelia prospered. She sold chitterlins and sausage in the town near-by. On fine autumn days she ground sorghum,[2] and the syrup from her vats was dark golden and delicately flavored. She built the brick privy behind her store in only two weeks and was skilled in carpentering. It was only with people that Miss Amelia was not at ease. People, unless they are nilly-willy or very sick, cannot be taken into the hands and changed overnight to something more worthwhile and profitable. So that the only use that Miss Amelia had for other people was to make money out of them. And in this she succeeded. Mortgages on crops and property, a sawmill, money in the bank—she was the richest woman for miles around. She would have been rich as a congressman if it were not for her one great failing, and that was her passion for lawsuits and the courts. She would involve herself in long and bitter litigation over just a trifle. It was said that if Miss Amelia so much as stumbled over a rock in the road she would glance around instinctively as though looking for something to sue about it. Aside from these lawsuits she lived a steady life and every day was very much like the day that had gone before. With the exception of her ten-day marriage, nothing happened to change this until the spring of the year that Miss Amelia was thirty years old.

It was toward midnight on a soft quiet evening in April. The sky was the color of a blue swamp iris, the moon clear and bright. The crops that spring promised well and in the past weeks the mill had run a night shift. Down by the creek, the square brick factory was yellow with light, and there was the faint, steady hum of the looms. It was such a night when it is good to hear from faraway, across the dark fields, the slow song of a Negro on his way to make love. Or when it is pleasant to sit quietly and pick up a guitar, or simply to rest alone and think of nothing at all. The street that evening was deserted, but Miss Amelia's store was lighted and on the porch outside were five people. One of these was Stumpy MacPhail, a foreman with a red face and dainty, purplish hands. On the top step were two boys in overalls, the Rainey twins—both of them lanky and slow, with white hair and sleepy green eyes. The other man was Henry Macy, a shy and timid person with gentle manners and nervous ways, who sat on the edge of the bottom step. Miss Amelia herself stood leaning against the side of the open door, her feet crossed in their big swamp boots, patiently untying knots in a rope she had come across. They had not talked for a long time.

---

2. A tropical grass whose sweet juice yields sugar syrup.

One of the twins, who had been looking down the empty road, was the first to speak. "I see something coming," he said.

"A calf got loose," said his brother.

The approaching figure was still too distant to be clearly seen. The moon made dim, twisted shadows of the blossoming peach trees along the side of the road. In the air the odor of blossoms and sweet spring grass mingled with the warm, sour smell of the near-by lagoon.

"No. It's somebody's youngun," said Stumpy MacPhail.

Miss Amelia watched the road in silence. She had put down her rope and was fingering the straps of her overalls with her brown bony hand. She scowled, and a dark lock of hair fell down on her forehead. While they were waiting there, a dog from one of the houses down the road began a wild, hoarse howl that continued until a voice called out and hushed him. It was not until the figure was quite close, within the range of the yellow light from the porch, that they saw clearly what had come.

The man was a stranger, and it is rare that a stranger enters the town on foot at that hour. Besides, the man was a hunchback. He was scarcely more than four feet tall and he wore a ragged, dusty coat that reached only to his knees. His crooked little legs seemed too thin to carry the weight of his great warped chest and the hump that sat on his shoulders. He had a very large head, with deep-set blue eyes and a sharp little mouth. His face was both soft and sassy—at the moment his pale skin was yellowed by dust and there were lavender shadows beneath his eyes. He carried a lopsided old suitcase which was tied with a rope.

"Evening," said the hunchback, and he was out of breath.

Miss Amelia and the men on the porch neither answered his greeting nor spoke. They only looked at him.

"I am hunting for Miss Amelia Evans."

Miss Amelia pushed back her hair from her forehead and raised her chin. "How come?"

"Because I am kin with her," the hunchback said.

The twins and Stumpy MacPhail looked up at Miss Amelia.

"That's me," she said. "How do you mean 'kin'?"

"Because—" the hunchback began. He looked uneasy, almost as though he was about to cry. He rested the suitcase on the bottom step, but did not take his hand from the handle. "My mother was Fanny Jesup and she come from Cheehaw. She left Cheehaw some thirty years ago when she married her first husband. I remember hearing her tell how she had a half-sister named Martha. And back in Cheehaw today they tell me that was your mother."

Miss Amelia listened with her head turned slightly aside. She ate her Sunday dinners by herself; her place was never crowded with a flock of relatives, and she claimed kin with no one. She had had a great-aunt who owned the livery stable in Cheehaw, but that aunt was now dead. Aside from her there was only one double first cousin who lived in a town twenty miles away, but this cousin and Miss Amelia did not get on so well, and when they chanced to pass each other they spat on the side of the road. Other people had tried very hard, from time to time, to work out some kind of far-fetched connection with Miss Amelia, but with absolutely no success.

The hunchback went into a long rigmarole, mentioning names and places that were unknown to the listeners on the porch and seemed to have nothing to do with the subject. "So Fanny and Martha Jesup were half-sisters. And I am the son of Fanny's third husband. So that would make you and I—" He bent down and began to unfasten his suitcase. His hands were like dirty sparrow claws and they were trembling. The bag was full of all manner of junk—ragged clothes and odd rubbish that looked like parts out of a sewing machine, or something just as worthless. The hunchback scrambled among these belongings and brought out an old photograph. "This is a picture of my mother and her half-sister."

Miss Amelia did not speak. She was moving her jaw slowly from side to side, and you could tell from her face what she was thinking about. Stumpy MacPhail took the photograph and held it out toward the light. It was a picture of two pale, withered-up little children of about two and three years of age. The faces were tiny white blurs, and it might have been an old picture in anyone's album.

Stumpy MacPhail handed it back with no comment. "Where you come from?" he asked.

The hunchback's voice was uncertain. "I was traveling."

Still Miss Amelia did not speak. She just stood leaning against the side of the door, and looked down at the hunchback. Henry Macy winked nervously and rubbed his hands together. Then quietly he left the bottom step and disappeared. He is a good soul, and the hunchback's situation had touched his heart. Therefore he did not want to wait and watch Miss Amelia chase the newcomer off her property and run him out of town. The hunchback stood with his bag open on the bottom step; he sniffled his nose, and his mouth quivered. Perhaps he began to feel his dismal predicament. Maybe he realized what a miserable thing it was to be a stranger in the town with a suitcase full of junk, and claiming kin with Miss Amelia. At any rate he sat down on the steps and suddenly began to cry.

It was not a common thing to have an unknown hunchback walk to the store at midnight and then sit down and cry. Miss Amelia rubbed back her hair from her forehead and the men looked at each other uncomfortably. All around the town was very quiet.

At last one of the twins said: "I'll be damned if he ain't a regular Morris Finestein."

Everyone nodded and agreed, for that is an expression having a certain special meaning. But the hunchback cried louder because he could not know what they were talking about. Morris Finestein was a person who had lived in the town years before. He was only a quick, skipping little Jew who cried if you called him Christkiller, and ate light bread and canned salmon every day. A calamity had come over him and he had moved away to Society City. But since then if a man were prissy in any way, or if a man ever wept, he was known as a Morris Finestein.

"Well, he is afflicted," said Stumpy MacPhail. "There is some cause."

Miss Amelia crossed the porch with two slow, gangling strides. She went down the steps and stood looking thoughtfully at the stranger. Gingerly, with one long brown forefinger, she touched the hump on his back. The hunchback still wept, but he was quieter now. The night was silent and the moon still shone with a soft, clear light—it was getting colder. Then Miss Amelia did a rare thing; she pulled out a bottle from her hip pocket and after polishing off the top with the palm of her hand she handed it to the hunchback to drink. Miss Amelia could seldom be persuaded to sell her liquor on credit, and for her to give so much as a drop away free was almost unknown.

"Drink," she said. "It will liven your gizzard."

The hunchback stopped crying, neatly licked the tears from around his mouth, and did as he was told. When he was finished, Miss Amelia took a slow swallow, warmed and washed her mouth with it, and spat. Then she also drank. The twins and the foreman had their own bottle they had paid for.

"It is smooth liquor," Stumpy MacPhail said. "Miss Amelia, I have never known you to fail."

The whisky they drank that evening (two big bottles of it) is important. Otherwise, it would be hard to account for what followed. Perhaps without it there would never have been a café. For the liquor of Miss Amelia has a special quality of its own. It is clean and sharp on the tongue, but once down a man it glows inside him for a long time afterward. And that is not all. It is known that if a message is written with lemon juice on a clean sheet of paper there will be no sign of it. But if the paper is held for a moment to the fire then the letters turn brown and the meaning becomes clear. Imagine that the whisky is the fire and that the message is that which is known only in the soul of a man—then the worth of Miss Amelia's liquor can be understood. Things that have gone unnoticed, thoughts that have been harbored far back in the dark mind, are suddenly recognized and comprehended. A spinner who has thought only of the loom, the dinner pail, the bed, and then the loom again—this spinner might drink some on a Sunday and come across a marsh lily. And in his palm he might hold this flower, examining the golden dainty cup, and in him suddenly might come a sweetness keen as pain. A weaver might look up suddenly and see for the first time the cold, weird radiance of midnight January sky, and a deep fright at his own smallness stop his heart. Such things as these, then, happen when a man has drunk Miss Amelia's liquor. He may suffer, or he may be spent with joy—but the experience has shown the truth; he has warmed his soul and seen the message hidden there.

They drank until it was past midnight, and the moon was clouded over so that the night was cold and dark. The hunchback still sat on the bottom steps, bent over miserably with his forehead resting on his knee. Miss Amelia stood with her hands in her pockets, one foot resting on the second step of the stairs. She had been silent for a long time. Her face had the expression often seen in slightly cross-eyed persons who are thinking deeply, a look that appears to be both very wise and very crazy. At last she said: "I don't know your name."

"I'm Lymon Willis," said the hunchback.

"Well, come on in," she said. "Some supper was left in the stove and you can eat."

Only a few times in her life had Miss Amelia invited anyone to eat with her, unless she was planning to trick them in some way, or make money out of them. So the men on the porch felt there was something wrong. Later, they said among themselves that she must have been drinking back in the swamp the better part of the afternoon. At any rate she left the porch, and

Stumpy MacPhail and the twins went on off home. She bolted the front door and looked all around to see that her goods were in order. Then she went to the kitchen, which was at the back of the store. The hunchback followed her, dragging his suitcase, sniffing and wiping his nose on the sleeve of his dirty coat.

"Sit down," said Miss Amelia. "I'll just warm up what's here."

It was a good meal they had together on that night. Miss Amelia was rich and she did not grudge herself food. There was fried chicken (the breast of which the hunchback took on his own plate), mashed rootabeggars, collard greens, and hot, pale golden, sweet potatoes. Miss Amelia ate slowly and with the relish of a farm hand. She sat with both elbows on the table, bent over the plate, her knees spread wide apart and her feet braced on the rungs of the chair. As for the hunchback, he gulped down his supper as though he had not smelled food in months. During the meal one tear crept down his dingy cheek—but it was just a little leftover tear and meant nothing at all. The lamp on the table was well-trimmed, burning blue at the edges of the wick, and casting a cheerful light in the kitchen. When Miss Amelia had eaten her supper she wiped her plate carefully with a slice of light bread and then poured her own clear, sweet syrup over the bread. The hunchback did likewise—except that he was more finicky and asked for a new plate. Having finished, Miss Amelia tilted back her chair, tightened her fist, and felt the hard, supple muscles of her right arm beneath the clean, blue cloth of her shirtsleeves—an unconscious habit with her, at the close of a meal. Then she took the lamp from the table and jerked her head toward the staircase as an invitation for the hunchback to follow after her.

Above the store there were the three rooms where Miss Amelia had lived during all of her life—two bedrooms with a large parlor in between. Few people had even seen these rooms, but it was generally known that they were well-furnished and extremely clean. And now Miss Amelia was taking up with her a dirty little hunchbacked stranger, come from God knows where. Miss Amelia walked slowly, two steps at a time, holding the lamp high. The hunchback hovered so close behind her that the swinging light made on the staircase wall one great, twisted shadow of the two of them. Soon the premises above the store were dark as the rest of the town.

The next morning was serene, with a sunrise of warm purple mixed with rose. In the fields around the town the furrows were newly plowed, and very early the tenants were at work setting out the young, deep green tobacco plants. The wild crows flew down close to the fields, making swift blue shadows on the earth. In town the people set out early with their dinner pails, and the windows of the mill were blinding gold in the sun. The air was fresh and the peach trees light as March clouds with their blossoms.

Miss Amelia came down at about dawn, as usual. She washed her head at the pump and very shortly set about her business. Later in the morning she saddled her mule and went to see about her property, planted with cotton, up near the Forks Falls Road. By noon, of course, everybody had heard about the hunchback who had come to the store in the middle of the night. But no one as yet had seen him. The day soon grew hot and the sky was a rich, midday blue. Still no one had laid an eye on this strange guest. A few people remembered that Miss Amelia's mother had had a half-sister—but there was some difference of opinion as to whether she had died or had run off with a tobacco stringer. As for the hunchback's claim, everyone thought it was a trumped-up business. And the town, knowing Miss Amelia, decided that surely she had put him out of the house after feeding him. But toward evening, when the sky had whitened, and the shift was done, a woman claimed to have seen a crooked face at the window of one of the rooms up over the store. Miss Amelia herself said nothing. She clerked in the store for a while, argued for an hour with a farmer over a plow shaft, mended some chicken wire, locked up near sundown, and went to her rooms. The town was left puzzled and talkative.

The next day Miss Amelia did not open the store, but stayed locked up inside her premises and saw no one. Now this was the day that the rumor started—the rumor so terrible that the town and all the country about were stunned by it. The rumor was started by a weaver called Merlie Ryan. He is a man of not much account—sallow, shambling, and with no teeth in his head. He has the three-day malaria, which means that every third day the fever comes on him. So on two days he is dull and cross, but on the third day he livens up and sometimes has an idea or two, most of which are foolish. It was while Merlie Ryan was in his fever that he turned suddenly and said:

"I know what Miss Amelia done. She murdered that man for something in that suitcase."

He said this in a calm voice, as a statement of fact. And within an hour the news had swept through the town. It was a fierce and sickly tale the town built up that day. In it were all the things which cause the heart to shiver—a hunchback, a midnight burial in the swamp, the dragging of Miss Amelia through the streets of the town on the way to prison, the squabbles over what would happen to her property—all told in hushed voices and repeated with some fresh and weird detail. It rained and women forgot to bring in the washing from the lines. One or two mortals, who were in debt to Miss Amelia, even put on Sunday clothes as though it were a holiday. People clustered together on the main street, talking and watching the store.

It would be untrue to say that all the town took part in this evil festival. There were a few sensible men who reasoned that Miss Amelia, being rich, would not go out of her way to murder a vagabond for a few trifles of junk. In the town there were even three good people, and they did not want this crime, not even for the sake of the interest and the great commotion it would entail; it gave them no pleasure to think of Miss Amelia holding to the bars of the penitentiary and being electrocuted in Atlanta. These good people judged Miss Amelia in a different way from what the others judged her. When a person is as contrary in every single respect as she was and when the sins of a person have amounted to such a point that they can hardly be remembered all at once—then this person plainly requires a special judgment. They remembered that Miss Amelia had been born dark and somewhat queer of face, raised motherless by her father who was a solitary man, that early in youth she had grown to be six feet two inches tall which in itself is not natural for a woman, and that her ways and habits of life were too peculiar ever to reason about. Above all, they remembered her puzzling marriage, which was the most unreasonable scandal ever to happen in this town.

So these good people felt toward her something near to pity. And when she was out on her wild business, such as rushing in a house to drag forth a sewing machine in payment for a debt, or getting herself worked up over some matter concerning the law—they had toward her a feeling which was a mixture of exasperation, a ridiculous little inside tickle, and a deep, unnamable sadness. But enough of the good people, for there were only three of them; the rest of the town was making a holiday of this fancied crime the whole of the afternoon.

Miss Amelia herself, for some strange reason, seemed unaware of all this. She spent most of her day upstairs. When down in the store, she prowled around peacefully, her hands deep in the pockets of her overalls and head bent so low that her chin was tucked inside the collar of her shirt. There was no bloodstain on her anywhere. Often she stopped and just stood somberly looking down at the cracks in the floor, twisting a lock of her short-cropped hair, and whispering something to herself. But most of the day was spent upstairs.

Dark came on. The rain that afternoon had chilled the air, so that the evening was bleak and gloomy as in wintertime. There were no stars in the sky, and a light, icy drizzle had set in. The lamps in the houses made mournful, wavering flickers when watched from the street. A wind had come up, not from the swamp side of the town but from the cold black pinewoods to the north.

The clocks in the town struck eight. Still nothing had happened. The bleak night, after the gruesome talk of the day, put a fear in some people, and they stayed home close to the fire. Others were gathered in groups together. Some eight or ten men had convened on the porch of Miss Amelia's store. They were silent and were indeed just waiting about. They themselves did not know what they were waiting for, but it was this: in times of tension, when some great action is impending, men gather and wait in this way. And after a time there will come a moment when all together they will act in unison, not from thought or from the will of any one man, but as though their instincts had merged together so that the decision belongs to no single one of them, but to the group as a whole. At such a time no individual hesitates. And whether the matter will be settled peaceably, or whether the joint action will result in ransacking, violence, and crime, depends on destiny. So the men waited soberly on the porch of Miss Amelia's store, not one of them realizing what they would do, but knowing inwardly that they must wait, and that the time had almost come.

Now the door to the store was open. Inside it was bright and natural-looking. To the left was the counter where slabs of white meat, rock candy, and tobacco were kept. Behind this were shelves of salted white meat and meal. The right side of the store was mostly filled with farm implements and such. At the back of the store, to the left, was the door leading up the stairs, and it was open. And at the far right of the store there was another door which led to a little room that Miss Amelia called her office. This door was also open. And at eight o'clock that evening Miss Amelia could be seen there sitting before her rolltop desk, figuring with a fountain pen and some pieces of paper.

The office was cheerfully lighted, and Miss Amelia did not seem to notice the delegation on the porch. Everything around her was in great order, as usual. This office was a room well-known, in a dreadful way, throughout the country. It was there Miss Amelia transacted all business. On the desk was a carefully covered typewriter which she knew how to run, but used only for the most important documents. In the drawers were literally thousands of papers, all filed according to the alphabet. This office was also the place where Miss Amelia received sick people, for she enjoyed doctoring and did a great deal of it. Two whole shelves were crowded with bottles and various paraphernalia. Against the wall was a bench where the patients sat. She could sew up a wound with a burnt needle so that it would not turn green. For burns she had a cool, sweet syrup. For unlocated sickness there were any number of different medicines which she had brewed herself from unknown recipes. They wrenched loose the bowels very well, but they could not be given to small children, as they caused bad convulsions; for them she had an entirely separate draught, gentler and sweet-flavored. Yes, all in all, she was considered a good doctor. Her hands, though very large and bony, had a light touch about them. She possessed great imagination and used hundreds of different cures. In the face of the most dangerous and extraordinary treatment she did not hesitate, and no disease was so terrible but what she would undertake to cure it. In this there was one exception. If a patient came with a female complaint she could do nothing. Indeed at the mere mention of the words her face would slowly darken with shame, and she would stand there craning her neck against the collar of her shirt, or rubbing her swamp boots together, for all the world like a great, shamed, dumb-tongued child. But in other matters people trusted her. She charged no fees whatsoever and always had a raft of patients.

On this evening Miss Amelia wrote with her fountain pen a good deal. But even so she could not be forever unaware of the group waiting out there on the dark porch, and watching her. From time to time she looked up and regarded them steadily. But she did not holler out to them to demand why they were loafing around her property like a sorry bunch of gabbies.[3] Her face was proud and stern, as it always was when she sat at the desk of her office. After a time their peering in like that seemed to annoy her. She wiped her cheek with a red handkerchief, got up, and closed the office door.

Now to the group on the porch this gesture acted as a signal. The time had come. They had stood for a long while with the night raw and gloomy in the street behind them. They had waited long and just at that moment the instinct to act came on them. All at once, as though moved by one will, they walked into the store. At that moment the eight men looked very much alike—all wearing blue overalls, most of them with whitish hair, all pale of face, and all with a set, dreaming look in the eye. What they would have done next no one knows. But at that instant there was a noise at the head of the staircase. The men looked up and then stood dumb with shock. It was the hunchback, whom they had already murdered in their minds. Also, the creature was not at all as had been pictured to them—not a pitiful and dirty little chatterer, alone and beggared in this world. Indeed, he was like nothing any man among them had ever beheld until that time. The room was still as death.

The hunchback came down slowly with the proudness of one who owns every plank of the floor beneath his feet. In the past days he had greatly changed. For one thing he was clean beyond words. He still wore his little

---

3. I.e., gabbers.

coat, but it was brushed off and neatly mended. Beneath this was a fresh red and black checkered shirt belonging to Miss Amelia. He did not wear trousers such as ordinary men are meant to wear, but a pair of tight-fitting little knee-length breeches. On his skinny legs he wore black stockings, and his shoes were of a special kind, being queerly shaped, laced up over the ankles, and newly cleaned and polished with wax. Around his neck, so that his large, pale ears were almost completely covered, he wore a shawl of lime-green wool, the fringes of which almost touched the floor.

The hunchback walked down the store with his stiff little strut and then stood in the center of the group that had come inside. They cleared a space about him and stood looking with hands loose at their sides and eyes wide open. The hunchback himself got his bearings in an odd manner. He regarded each person steadily at his own eye-level, which was about belt line for an ordinary man. Then with shrewd deliberation he examined each man's lower regions—from the waist to the sole of the shoe. When he had satisfied himself he closed his eyes for a moment and shook his head, as though in his opinion what he had seen did not amount to much. Then with assurance, only to confirm himself, he tilted back his head and took in the halo of faces around him with one long, circling stare. There was a half-filled sack of guano on the left side of the store, and when he had found his bearings in this way, the hunchback sat down upon it. Cozily settled, with his little legs crossed, he took from his coat pocket a certain object.

Now it took some moments for the men in the store to regain their ease. Merlie Ryan, he of the three-day fever who had started the rumor that day, was the first to speak. He looked at the object which the hunchback was fondling, and said in a hushed voice:

"What is it you have there?"

Each man knew well what it was the hunchback was handling. For it was the snuffbox which had belonged to Miss Amelia's father. The snuffbox was of blue enamel with a dainty embellishment of wrought gold on the lid. The group knew it well and marveled. They glanced warily at the closed office door, and heard the low sound of Miss Amelia whistling to herself.

"Yes, what is it, Peanut?"

The hunchback looked up quickly and sharpened his mouth to speak. "Why, this is a lay-low to catch meddlers."

The hunchback reached in the box with his scrambly little fingers and ate something, but he offered no one around him a taste. It was not even proper snuff which he was taking, but a mixture of sugar and cocoa. This he took, though, as snuff, pocketing a little wad of it beneath his lower lip and licking down neatly into this with a flick of his tongue which made a frequent grimace come over his face.

"The very teeth in my head have always tasted sour to me," he said in explanation. "This is the reason why I take this kind of sweet snuff."

The group still clustered around, feeling somewhat gawky and bewildered. This sensation never quite wore off, but it was soon tempered by another feeling—an air of intimacy in the room and a vague festivity. Now the names of the men of the group there on that evening were as follows: Hasty Malone, Robert Calvert Hale, Merlie Ryan, Reverend T. M. Willin, Rosser Cline, Rip Wellborn, Henry Ford Crimp, and Horace Wells. Except for Reverend Willin, they are all alike in many ways as has been said—all having taken pleasure from something or other, all having wept and suffered in some way, most of them tractable unless exasperated. Each of them worked in the mill, and lived with others in a two- or three-room house for which the rent was ten dollars or twelve dollars a month. All had been paid that afternoon, for it was Saturday. So, for the present, think of them as a whole.

The hunchback, however, was already sorting them out in his mind. Once comfortably settled he began to chat with everyone, asking questions such as if a man was married, how old he was, how much his wages came to in an average week, et cetera—picking his way along to inquiries which were downright intimate. Soon the group was joined by others in the town, Henry Macy, idlers who had sensed something extraordinary, women come to fetch their men who lingered on, and even one loose, towhead child who tiptoed into the store, stole a box of animal crackers, and made off very quietly. So the premises of Miss Amelia were soon crowded, and she herself had not yet opened her office door.

There is a type of person who has a quality about him that sets him apart from other and more ordinary human beings. Such a person has an instinct which is usually found only in small children, an instinct to establish immediate and vital contact between himself and all things in the world. Certainly the hunchback was of this type. He had only been in the store half an hour before an immediate contact had been established between him and each other individual. It was as though he had lived in the town for years, was a well-known character, and had been sitting and talking there on that guano sack for countless evenings. This, together with the fact that it was Saturday night, could account for the air of freedom and illicit gladness in the store. There was a tension, also, partly because of the oddity of the situation and because Miss Amelia was still closed off in her office and had not yet made her appearance.

She came out that evening at ten o'clock. And those who were expecting some drama at her entrance were disappointed. She opened the door and walked in with her slow, gangling swagger. There was a streak of ink on one side of her nose, and she had knotted the red handkerchief about her neck. She seemed to notice nothing unusual. Her gray, crossed eyes glanced over to the place where the hunchback was sitting, and for a moment lingered there. The rest of the crowd in her store she regarded with only a peaceable surprise.

"Does anyone want waiting on?" she asked quietly.

There were a number of customers, because it was Saturday night, and they all wanted liquor. Now Miss Amelia had dug up an aged barrel only three days past and had siphoned it into bottles back by the still. This night she took the money from the customers and counted it beneath the bright light. Such was the ordinary procedure. But after this what happened was not ordinary. Always before, it was necessary to go around to the dark back yard, and there she would hand out your bottle through the kitchen door. There was no feeling of joy in the transaction. After getting his liquor the customer walked off into the night. Or, if his wife would not have it in the home, he was allowed to come back around to the front porch of the store and guzzle there or in the street. Now, both the porch and the street before it were the property of Miss Amelia, and no mistake about it—but she did not regard them as premises; the premises began at the front door and took in the entire inside of the building. There she had never allowed liquor to be opened or drunk by anyone but herself. Now for the first time she broke this rule. She went to the kitchen, with the hunchback close at her heels, and she brought back the bottles into the warm, bright store. More than that she furnished some glasses and opened two boxes of crackers so that they were there hospitably in a platter on the counter and anyone who wished could take one free.

She spoke to no one but the hunchback, and she only asked him in a somewhat harsh and husky voice: "Cousin Lymon, will you have yours straight, or warmed in a pan with water on the stove?"

"If you please, Amelia," the hunchback said. (And since what time had anyone presumed to address Miss Amelia by her bare name, without a title of respect?—Certainly not her bridegroom and her husband of ten days. In fact, not since the death of her father, who for some reason had always called her Little, had anyone dared to address her in such a familiar way.) "If you please, I'll have it warmed."

Now, this was the beginning of the café. It was as simple as that. Recall that the night was gloomy as in wintertime, and to have sat around the property outside would have made a sorry celebration. But inside there was company and a genial warmth. Someone had rattled up the stove in the rear, and those who bought bottles shared their liquor with friends. Several women were there and they had twists of licorice, a Nehi,[4] or even a swallow of the whisky. The hunchback was still a novelty and his presence amused everyone. The bench in the office was brought in, together with several extra chairs. Other people leaned against the counter or made themselves comfortable on barrels and sacks. Nor did the opening of liquor on the premises cause any rambunctiousness, indecent giggles, or misbehavior whatsoever. On the contrary the company was polite even to the point of a certain timidness. For people in this town were then unused to gathering together for the sake of pleasure. They met to work in the mill. Or on Sunday there would be an all-day camp meeting—and though that is a pleasure, the intention of the whole affair is to sharpen your view of Hell and put into you a keen fear of the Lord Almighty. But the spirit of a café is altogether different. Even the richest, greediest old rascal will behave himself, insulting no one in a proper café. And poor people look about them gratefully and pinch up the salt in a dainty and modest manner. For the atmosphere of a proper café implies these qualities: fellowship, the satisfactions of the belly, and a certain gaiety and grace of behavior. This had never been told to the gathering in Miss Amelia's store that night. But they knew it of themselves, although never, of course, until that time had there been a café in the town.

Now, the cause of all this, Miss Amelia, stood most of the evening in the doorway leading to the kitchen. Outwardly she did not seem changed at all. But there were many who noticed her face. She watched all that went on, but most of the time her eyes were fastened lonesomely on the hunchback. He strutted about the store, eating from his snuffbox, and being at once sour and agreeable. Where Miss Amelia stood, the light from the chinks of the stove cast a glow, so that her brown, long face was somewhat brightened. She seemed to be looking inward. There was in her expression pain, per-

---

4. A brand of soft drink.

plexity, and uncertain joy. Her lips were not so firmly set as usual, and she swallowed often. Her skin had paled and her large empty hands were sweating. Her look that night, then, was the lonesome look of the lover.

This opening of the café came to an end at midnight. Everyone said goodbye to everyone else in a friendly fashion. Miss Amelia shut the front door of her premises, but forgot to bolt it. Soon everything—the main street with its three stores, the mill, the houses—all the town, in fact—was dark and silent. And so ended three days and nights in which had come an arrival of a stranger, an unholy holiday, and the start of the café.

Now time must pass. For the next four years are much alike. There are great changes, but these changes are brought about bit by bit, in simple steps which in themselves do not appear to be important. The hunchback continued to live with Miss Amelia. The café expanded in a gradual way. Miss Amelia began to sell her liquor by the drink, and some tables were brought into the store. There were customers every evening, and on Saturday a great crowd. Miss Amelia began to serve fried catfish suppers at fifteen cents a plate. The hunchback cajoled her into buying a fine mechanical piano. Within two years the place was a store no longer, but had been converted into a proper café, open every evening from six until twelve o'clock.

Each night the hunchback came down the stairs with the air of one who has a grand opinion of himself. He always smelled slightly of turnip greens, as Miss Amelia rubbed him night and morning with pot liquor to give him strength. She spoiled him to a point beyond reason, but nothing seemed to strengthen him; food only made his hump and his head grow larger while the rest of him remained weakly and deformed. Miss Amelia was the same in appearance. During the week she still wore swamp boots and overalls, but on Sunday she put on a dark red dress that hung on her in a most peculiar fashion. Her manners, however, and her way of life were greatly changed. She still loved a fierce lawsuit, but she was not so quick to cheat her fellow man and to exact cruel payments. Because the hunchback was so extremely sociable she even went about a little—to revivals, to funerals, and so forth. Her doctoring was as successful as ever, her liquor even finer than before, if that were possible. The café itself proved profitable and was the only place of pleasure for many miles around.

So for the moment regard these years from random and disjointed views. See the hunchback marching in Miss Amelia's footsteps when on a red winter morning they set out for the pinewoods to hunt. See them working on her properties—with Cousin Lymon standing by and doing absolutely nothing, but quick to point out any laziness among the hands. On autumn afternoons they sat on the back steps chopping sugar cane. The glaring summer days they spent back in the swamp where the water cypress is a deep black green, where beneath the tangled swamp trees there is a drowsy gloom. When the path leads through a bog or a stretch of blackened water see Miss Amelia bend down to let Cousin Lymon scramble on her back—and see her wading forward with the hunchback settled on her shoulders, clinging to her ears or to her broad forehead. Occasionally Miss Amelia cranked up the Ford which she had bought and treated Cousin Lymon to a picture-show in Cheehaw, or to some distant fair or cockfight; the hunchback took a passionate delight in spectacles. Of course, they were in their café every morning, they would often sit for hours together by the fireplace in the parlor upstairs. For the hunchback was sickly at night and dreaded to lie looking into the dark. He had a deep fear of death. And Miss Amelia would not leave him by himself to suffer with this fright. It may even be reasoned that the growth of the café came about mainly on this account; it was a thing that brought him company and pleasure and that helped him through the night. So compose from such flashes an image of these years as a whole. And for a moment let it rest.

Now some explanation is due for all this behavior. The time has come to speak about love. For Miss Amelia loved Cousin Lymon. So much was clear to everyone. They lived in the same house together and were never seen apart. Therefore, according to Mrs. MacPhail, a warty-nosed old busybody who is continually moving her sticks of furniture from one part of the front room to another; according to her and to certain others, these two were living in sin. If they were related, they were only a cross between first and second cousins, and even that could in no way be proved. Now, of course Miss Amelia was a powerful blunderbuss of a person, more than six feet tall—and Cousin Lymon a weakly little hunchback reaching only to her waist. But so much the better for Mrs. Stumpy MacPhail and her cronies, for they and their kind glory in conjunctions which are ill-matched and pitiful. So let them be. The good people thought that if those two had found some satisfaction of the flesh between themselves, then it was a matter concerning them and God alone. All sensible people agreed in their opinion about this conjecture—and their answer was a plain, flat *no*. What sort of thing, then, was this love?

First of all, love is a joint experience between two persons—but the fact that it is a joint experience does not mean that it is a similar experience to the two people involved. There are the lover and the beloved, but these two come from different countries. Often the beloved is only a stimulus for the stored-up love which has lain quiet within the lover for a long time hitherto. And somehow every lover knows this. He feels in his soul that his love is a solitary thing. He comes to know a new, strange loneliness and it is this knowledge which makes him suffer. So there is only one thing for the lover to do. He must house his love within himself as best he can; he must create for himself a whole new inward world—a world intense and strange, complete in himself. Let it be added here that this lover about whom we speak need not necessarily be a young man saving for a wedding ring—this lover can be man, woman, child, or indeed any human creature on this earth.

Now, the beloved can also be of any description. The most outlandish people can be the stimulus for love. A man may be a doddering great-grandfather and still love only a strange girl he saw in the streets of Cheehaw one afternoon two decades past. The preacher may love a fallen woman. The beloved may be treacherous, greasy-headed, and given to evil habits. Yes, and the lover may see this as clearly as anyone else—but that does not affect the evolution of his love one whit. A most mediocre person can be the object of a love which is wild, extravagant, and beautiful as the poison lilies of the swamp. A good man may be the stimulus for a love both violent and debased, or a jabbering madman may bring about in the soul of someone a tender and simple idyll. Therefore, the value and quality of any love is determined solely by the lover himself.

It is for this reason that most of us would rather love than be loved. Almost everyone wants to be the lover. And the curt truth is that, in a deep secret way, the state of being beloved is intolerable to many. The beloved fears and hates the lover, and with the best of reasons. For the lover is forever trying to strip bare his beloved. The lover craves any possible relation with the beloved, even if this experience can cause him only pain.

It has been mentioned before that Miss Amelia was once married. And this curious episode might as well be accounted for at this point. Remember that it all happened long ago, and that it was Miss Amelia's only personal contact, before the hunchback came to her, with this phenomenon—love.

The town then was the same as it is now, except there were two stores instead of three and the peach trees along the street were more crooked and smaller than they are now. Miss Amelia was nineteen years old at the time, and her father had been dead many months. There was in the town at that time a loom-fixer named Marvin Macy. He was the brother of Henry Macy, although to know them you would never guess that those two could be kin. For Marvin Macy was the handsomest man in this region—being six feet one inch tall, hard-muscled, and with slow gray eyes and curly hair. He was well off, made good wages, and had a gold watch which opened in the back to a picture of a waterfall. From the outward and worldly point of view Marvin Macy was a fortunate fellow; he needed to bow and scrape to no one and always got just what he wanted. But from a more serious and thoughtful viewpoint Marvin Macy was not a person to be envied, for he was an evil character. His reputation was as bad, if not worse, than that of any young man in the county. For years, when he was a boy, he had carried about with him the dried and salted ear of a man he had killed in a razor fight. He had chopped off the tails of squirrels in the pinewoods just to please his fancy, and in his left hip pocket he carried forbidden marijuana weed to tempt those who were discouraged and drawn toward death. Yet in spite of his well-known reputation he was the beloved of many females in this region—and there were at the time several young girls who were clean-haired and soft-eyed, with tender sweet little buttocks and charming ways. These gentle young girls he degraded and shamed. Then finally, at the age of twenty-two, this Marvin Macy chose Miss Amelia. That solitary, gangling, queer-eyed girl was the one he longed for. Nor did he want her because of her money, but solely out of love.

And love changed Marvin Macy. Before the time when he loved Miss Amelia it could be questioned if such a person had within him a heart and soul. Yet there is some explanation for the ugliness of his character, for Marvin Macy had had a hard beginning in this world. He was one of seven unwanted children whose parents could hardly be called parents at all; these parents were wild younguns who liked to fish and roam around the swamp. Their own children, and there was a new one almost every year, were only a nuisance to them. At night when they came home from the mill they would look at the children as though they did not know wherever they had come from. If the children cried they were beaten, and the first thing they learned in this world was to seek the darkest corner of the room and try to hide themselves as best they could. They were as thin as little whitehaired ghosts, and they did not speak, not even to each other. Finally, they were abandoned by their parents altogether and left to the mercies of the town. It was a hard winter, with the mill closed down almost three months, and much misery everywhere. But this is not a town to let white orphans perish in the road before your eyes. So here is what came about: the eldest child, who was eight years old, walked into Cheehaw and disappeared—perhaps he took a freight train somewhere and went out into the world, nobody knows. Three other children were boarded out amongst the town, being sent around from one kitchen to another, and as they were delicate they died before Easter time. The last two children were Marvin Macy and Henry Macy, and they were taken into a home. There was a good woman in the town named Mrs. Mary Hale, and she took Marvin Macy and Henry Macy and loved them as her own. They were raised in her household and treated well.

But the hearts of small children are delicate organs. A cruel beginning in this world can twist them into curious shapes. The heart of a hurt child can shrink so that forever afterward it is hard and pitted as the seed of a peach. Or again, the heart of such a child may fester and swell until it is a misery to carry within the body, easily chafed and hurt by the most ordinary things. This last is what happened to Henry Macy, who is so opposite to his brother, is the kindest and gentlest man in town. He lends his wages to those who are unfortunate, and in the old days he used to care for the children whose parents were at the café on Saturday night. But he is a shy man, and he has the look of one who has a swollen heart and suffers. Marvin Macy, however, grew to be bold and fearless and cruel. His heart turned tough as the horns of Satan, and until the time when he loved Miss Amelia he brought to his brother and the good woman who raised him nothing but shame and trouble.

But love reversed the character of Marvin Macy. For two years he loved Miss Amelia, but he did not declare himself. He would stand near the door of her premises, his cap in his hand, his eyes meek and longing and misty gray. He reformed himself completely. He was good to his brother and foster mother, and he saved his wages and learned thrift. Moreover, he reached out toward God. No longer did he lie around on the floor of the front porch all day Sunday, singing and playing his guitar; he attended church services and was present at all religious meetings. He learned good manners: he trained himself to rise and give his chair to a lady, and he quit swearing and fighting and using holy names in vain. So for two years he passed through this transformation and improved his character in every way. Then at the end of the two years he went one evening to Miss Amelia, carrying a bunch of swamp flowers, a sack of chitterlins, and a silver ring—that night Marvin Macy declared himself.

And Miss Amelia married him. Later everyone wondered why. Some said it was because she wanted to get herself some wedding presents. Others believed it came about through the nagging of Miss Amelia's great-aunt in Cheehaw, who was a terrible old woman. Anyway, she strode with great steps down the aisle of the church wearing her dead mother's bridal gown, which was of yellow satin and at least twelve inches too short for her. It was a winter afternoon and the clear sun shone through the ruby windows of the church and put a curious glow on the pair before the altar. As the marriage lines were read Miss Amelia kept making an odd gesture—she would rub the palm of her right hand down the side of her satin wedding gown. She was reaching for the pocket of her overalls, and being unable to find it her face became impatient, bored, and exasperated. At last when the lines were spoken and the marriage prayer was done Miss Amelia hurried out of the church, not taking the arm of her husband, but walking at least two paces ahead of him.

The church is no distance from the store so the bride and groom walked home. It is said that on the way Miss Amelia began to talk about some deal she had worked up with a farmer over a load of kindling wood. In fact, she treated her groom in exactly the same manner she would have used with some customer who had come into the store to buy a pint from her. But so far all had gone decently enough; the town was gratified, as people had seen what this love had done to Marvin Macy and hoped that it might also reform his bride. At least, they counted on the marriage to tone down Miss Amelia's temper, to put a bit of bride-fat on her, and to change her at last into a calculable woman.

They were wrong. The young boys who watched through the window on that night said that this is what actually happened: The bride and groom ate a grand supper prepared by Jeff, the old Negro who cooked for Miss Amelia. The bride took second servings of everything, but the groom picked with his food. Then the bride went about her ordinary business—reading the newspaper, finishing an inventory of the stock in the store, and so forth. The groom hung about in the doorway with a loose, foolish, blissful face and was not noticed. At eleven o'clock the bride took a lamp and went upstairs. The groom followed close behind her. So far all had gone decently enough, but what followed after was unholy.

Within half an hour Miss Amelia had stomped down the stairs in breeches and a khaki jacket. Her face had darkened so that it looked quite black. She slammed the kitchen door and gave it an ugly kick. Then she controlled herself. She poked up the fire, sat down, and put her feet up on the kitchen stove. She read the Farmer's Almanac, drank coffee, and had a smoke with her father's pipe. Her face was hard, stern, and had now whitened to its natural color. Sometimes she paused to jot down some information from the Almanac on a piece of paper. Toward dawn she went into her office and uncovered her typewriter, which she had recently bought and was only just learning how to run. That was the way in which she spent the whole of her wedding night. At daylight she went out to her yard as though nothing whatsoever had occurred and did some carpentering on a rabbit hutch which she had begun the week before and intended to sell somewhere.

A groom is in a sorry fix when he is unable to bring his well-beloved bride to bed with him, and when the whole town knows it. Marvin Macy came down that day still in his wedding finery, and with a sick face. God knows how he had spent the night. He moped about the yard, watching Miss Amelia, but keeping some distance away from her. Then toward noon an idea came to him and he went off in the direction of Society City. He returned with presents—an opal ring, a pink enamel doreen of the sort which was then in fashion, a silver bracelet with two hearts on it, and a box of candy which had cost two dollars and a half. Miss Amelia looked over these fine gifts and opened the box of candy, for she was hungry. The rest of the presents she judged shrewdly for a moment to sum up their value—then she put them in the counter out for sale. The night was spent in much the same manner as the preceding one—except that Miss Amelia brought her feather mattress to make a pallet by the kitchen stove, and she slept fairly well.

Things went on like this for three days. Miss Amelia went about her business as usual, and took great interest in some rumor that a bridge was to be built some ten miles down the road. Marvin Macy still followed her about around the premises, and it was plain from his face how he suffered. Then on the fourth day he did an extremely simple-minded thing: he went to Cheehaw and came back with a lawyer. Then in Miss Amelia's office he signed over to her the whole of his worldly goods, which was ten acres of timberland which he had bought with the money he had saved. She studied the paper sternly to make sure there was no possibility of a trick and filed it soberly in the drawer of her desk. That afternoon Marvin Macy took a quart bottle of whisky and went with it alone out in the swamp while the sun was still shining. Toward evening he came in drunk, went up to Miss Amelia with wet wide eyes, and put his hand on her shoulder. He was trying to tell her something, but before he could open his mouth she had swung once with her fist and hit his face so hard that he was thrown back against the wall and one of his front teeth was broken.

The rest of this affair can only be mentioned in bare outline. After this first blow Miss Amelia hit him whenever he came within arm's reach of her, and whenever he was drunk. At last she turned him off the premises altogether, and he was forced to suffer publicly. During the day he hung around just outside the boundary line of Miss Amelia's property and sometimes with a drawn crazy look he would fetch his rifle and sit there cleaning it, peering at Miss Amelia steadily. If she was afraid she did not show it, but her face was sterner than ever, and often she spat on the ground. His last foolish effort was to climb in the window of her store one night and to sit there in the dark, for no purpose whatsoever, until she came down the stairs next morning. For this Miss Amelia set off immediately to the courthouse in Cheehaw with some notion that she could get him locked in the penitentiary for trespassing. Marvin Macy left the town that day, and no one saw him go, or knew just where he went. On leaving he put a long curious letter, partly written in pencil and partly with ink, beneath Miss Amelia's door. It was a wild love letter—but in it were also included threats, and he swore that in his life he would get even with her. His marriage had lasted for ten days. And the town felt the special satisfaction that people feel when someone has been thoroughly done in by some scandalous and terrible means.

Miss Amelia was left with everything that Marvin Macy had ever owned— his timberwood, his gild watch, every one of his possessions. But she seemed to attach little value to them and that spring she cut up his Klansman's robe to cover her tobacco plants. So all that he had ever done was to make her richer and to bring her love. But, strange to say, she never spoke of him but with a terrible and spiteful bitterness. She never once referred to him by name but always mentioned him scornfully as "that loom-fixer I was married to."

And later, when horrifying rumors concerning Marvin Macy reached the town, Miss Amelia was very pleased. For the true character of Marvin Macy finally revealed itself, once he had freed himself of his love. He became a criminal whose picture and whose name were in all the papers in the state. He robbed three filling stations and held up the A&P store of Society City with a sawed-off gun. He was suspected of the murder of Slit-Eye Sam who was a noted highjacker. All these crimes were connected with the name of Marvin Macy, so that his evil became famous through many counties. Then finally the law captured him, drunk, on the floor of a tourist cabin, his guitar by his side, and fifty-seven dollars in his right shoe. He was tried, sentenced, and sent off to the penitentiary near Atlanta. Miss Amelia was deeply gratified.

Well, all this happened a long time ago, and it is the story of Miss Amelia's marriage. The town laughed a long time over this grotesque affair. But though the outward facts of this love are indeed sad and ridiculous, it must be remembered that the real story was that which took place in the soul of the lover himself. So who but God can be the final judge of this or any other love? On the very first night of the café there were several who suddenly thought of this broken bridegroom, locked in the gloomy penitentiary, many miles away. And in the years that followed, Marvin Macy was not altogether forgotten in the town. His name was never mentioned in the presence of Miss Amelia or the hunchback. But the memory of his passion and his crimes, and the thought of him trapped in his cell in the penitentiary, was like a troubling undertone beneath the happy love of Miss Amelia and the gaiety of the café. So do not forget this Marvin Macy, as he is to act a terrible part in the story which is yet to come.

During the four years in which the store became a café the rooms upstairs were not changed. This part of the premises remained exactly as it had been all of Miss Amelia's life, as it was in the time of her father, and most likely his father before him. The three rooms, it is already known, were immaculately clean. The smallest object had its exact place, and everything was wiped and dusted by Jeff, the servant of Miss Amelia, each morning. The front room belonged to Cousin Lymon—it was the room where Marvin Macy had stayed during the few nights he was allowed on the premises, and before that it was the bedroom of Miss Amelia's father. The room was furnished with a large chifforobe, a bureau covered with a stiff white linen cloth crocheted at the edges, and a marble-topped table. The bed was immense, an old four-poster made of carved, dark rosewood. On it were two feather mattresses, bolsters, and a number of handmade comforts. The bed was so high that beneath it were two wooden steps—no occupant had ever used these steps before, but Cousin Lymon drew them out each night and walked up in state. Beside the steps, but pushed modestly out of view, there was a china chamberpot painted with pink roses. No rug covered the dark, polished floor and the curtains were of some white stuff, also crocheted at the edges.

On the other side of the parlor was Miss Amelia's bedroom, and it was smaller and very simple. The bed was narrow and made of pine. There was a bureau for her breeches, shirts, and Sunday dress, and she had hammered two nails in the closet wall on which to hang her swamp boots. There were no curtains, rugs, or ornaments of any kind.

The large middle room, the parlor, was elaborate. The rosewood sofa, upholstered in threadbare green silk, was before the fireplace. Marble-topped tables, two Singer sewing machines, a big vase of pampas grass—everything was rich and grand. The most important piece of furniture in the parlor was a big, glass-doored cabinet in which was kept a number of treasures and curios. Miss Amelia had added two objects to this collection—one was a large acorn from a water oak, the other a little velvet box holding two small, grayish stones. Sometimes when she had nothing much to do, Miss Amelia would take out this velvet box and stand by the window with the stones in the palm of her hand, looking down at them with a mixture of fascination, dubious respect, and fear. They were the kidney stones of Miss Amelia herself, and had been taken from her by the doctor in Cheehaw some years ago. It had been a terrible experience, from the first minute to the last, and all she had got out of it were those two little stones; she was bound to set great store by them, or else admit to a mighty sorry bargain. So she kept them and in the second year of Cousin Lymon's stay with her she had them set as ornaments in a watch chain which she gave to him. The other object she had added to the collection, the large acorn, was precious to her—but when she looked at it her face was always saddened and perplexed.

"Amelia, what does it signify?" Cousin Lymon asked her.

"Why, it's just an acorn," she answered. "Just an acorn I picked up on the afternoon Big Papa died."

"How do you mean?" Cousin Lymon insisted.

"I mean it's just an acorn I spied on the ground that day. I picked it up and put it in my pocket. But I don't know why."

"What a peculiar reason to keep it," Cousin Lymon said.

The talks of Miss Amelia and Cousin Lymon in the rooms upstairs, usually in the first few hours of the morning when the hunchback could not sleep, were many. As a rule, Miss Amelia was a silent woman, not letting her tongue run wild on any subject that happened to pop into her head. There were certain topics of conversation, however, in which she took pleasure. All these subjects had one point in common—they were interminable. She liked to contemplate problems which could be worked over for decades and still remain insoluble. Cousin Lymon, on the other hand, enjoyed talking on any subject whatsoever, as he was a great chatterer. Their approach to any conversation was altogether different. Miss Amelia always kept to the broad, rambling generalities of the matter, going on endlessly in a low, thoughtful voice and getting nowhere—while Cousin Lymon would interrupt her suddenly to pick up, magpie fashion, some detail which, even if unimportant, was at least concrete and bearing on some practical facet close at hand. Some of the favorite subjects of Miss Amelia were: the stars, the reason why Negroes are black, the best treatment for cancer, and so forth. Her father was also an interminable subject which was dear to her.

"Why, Law," she would say to Lymon. "Those days I slept. I'd go to bed just as the lamp was turned on and sleep—why, I'd sleep like I was drowned in warm axle grease. Then come daybreak Big Papa would walk in and put his hand down on my shoulder. 'Get stirring, Little,' he would say. Then later he would holler up the stairs from the kitchen when the stove was hot. 'Fried grits,' he would holler. 'White meat and gravy. Ham and eggs.' And I'd run down the stairs and dress by the hot stove while he was out washing at the pump. Then off we'd go to the still or maybe—"

"The grits we had this morning was poor," Cousin Lymon said. "Fried too quick so that the inside never heated."

"And when Big Papa would run off the liquor in those days—" The conversation would go on endlessly, with Miss Amelia's long legs stretched out before the hearth; for winter or summer there was always a fire in the grate, as Lymon was cold-natured. He sat in a low chair across from her, his feet not quite touching the floor and his torso usually well-wrapped in a blanket or the green wool shawl. Miss Amelia never mentioned her father to anyone else except Cousin Lymon.

That was one of the ways in which she showed her love for him. He had her confidence in the most delicate and vital matters. He alone knew where she kept the chart that showed where certain barrels of whisky were buried on a piece of property near-by. He alone had access to her bankbook and the key to the cabinet of curios. He took money from the cash register, whole handfuls of it, and appreciated the loud jingle it made inside his pockets. He owned almost everything on the premises, for when he was cross Miss Amelia would prowl about and find him some present—so that now there was hardly anything left close at hand to give him. The only part of her life that she did not want Cousin Lymon to share with her was the memory of her ten-day marriage. Marvin Macy was the one subject that was never, at any time, discussed between the two of them.

So let the slow years pass and come to a Saturday evening six years after the time when Cousin Lymon came first to the town. It was August and the sky had burned above the town like a sheet of flame all day. Now the green twilight was near and there was a feeling of repose. The street was coated an inch deep with dry golden dust and the little children ran about half-naked, sneezed often, sweated, and were fretful. The mill had closed down at noon. People in the houses along the main street sat resting on their steps and the women had palmetto fans. At Miss Amelia's there was a sign at the front of the premises saying CAFÉ. The back porch was cool with latticed shadows and there Cousin Lymon sat turning the ice-cream freezer—often he unpacked the salt and ice and removed the dasher to lick a bit and see how the work was coming on. Jeff cooked in the kitchen. Early that morning Miss Amelia had put a notice on the wall of the front porch reading: Chicken Dinner—Twenty Cents Tonite. The café was already open and Miss Amelia had just finished a period of work in her office. All the eight tables were occupied and from the mechanical piano came a jingling tune.

In a corner, near the door and sitting at a table with a child, was Henry Macy. He was drinking a glass of liquor, which was unusual for him, as liquor went easily to his head and made him cry or sing. His face was very pale and his left eye worked constantly in a nervous tic, as it was apt to do when he was agitated. He had come into the café sidewise and silent, and when he was greeted he did not speak. The child next to him belonged to Horace Wells, and he had been left at Miss Amelia's that morning to be doctored.

Miss Amelia came out from her office in good spirits. She attended to a few details in the kitchen and entered the café with the pope's nose of a hen[5] between her fingers, as that was her favorite piece. She looked about the room, saw that in general all was well, and went over to the corner table by Henry Macy. She turned the chair around and sat straddling the back, as she only wanted to pass the time of day and was not yet ready for her supper. There was a bottle of Kroup[6] Kure in the hip pocket of her overalls—a medicine made from whisky, rock candy, and a secret ingredient. Miss Amelia

---

5. Fleshy projection on the rump of a cooked fowl.
6. Croup is an attack of difficult breathing, with a hoarse, metallic cough.

uncorked the bottle and put it to the mouth of the child. Then she turned to Henry Macy and, seeing the nervous winking of his left eye, she asked:

"What ails you?"

Henry Macy seemed on the point of saying something difficult, but, after a long look into the eyes of Miss Amelia, he swallowed and did not speak.

So Miss Amelia returned to her patient. Only the child's head showed above the table top. His face was very red, with the eyelids half-closed and the mouth partly open. He had a large, hard, swollen boil on his thigh, and had been brought to Miss Amelia so that it could be opened. But Miss Amelia used a special method with children; she did not like to see them hurt, struggling, and terrified. So she had kept the child around the premises all day, giving him licorice and frequent doses of the Kroup Kure, and toward evening she tied a napkin around his neck and let him eat his fill of the dinner. Now as he sat at the table his head wobbled slowly from side to side and sometimes as he breathed there came from him a little worn-out grunt.

There was a stir in the café and Miss Amelia looked around quickly. Cousin Lymon had come in. The hunchback strutted into the café as he did every night, and when he reached the exact center of the room he stopped short and looked shrewdly around him, summing up the people and making a quick pattern of the emotional material at hand that night. The hunchback was a great mischief-maker. He enjoyed any kind of to-do, and without saying a word he could set people at each other in a way that was miraculous. It was due to him that the Rainey twins had quarreled over a jackknife two years past, and had not spoken one word to each other since. He was present at the big fight between Rip Wellborn and Robert Calvert Hale, and every other fight for that matter since he had come into the town. He nosed around everywhere, knew the intimate business of everybody, and trespassed every waking hour. Yet, queerly enough, in spite of this it was the hunchback who was most responsible for the great popularity of the café. Things were never so gay as when he was around. When he walked into the room there was always a quick feeling of tension, because with this busybody about there was never any telling what might descend on you, or what might suddenly be brought to happen in the room. People are never so free with themselves and so recklessly glad as when there is some possibility of commotion or calamity ahead. So when the hunchback marched into the café everyone looked around at him and there was a quick outburst of talking and a drawing of corks.

Lymon waved his hand to Stumpy MacPhail who was sitting with Merlie Ryan and Henry Ford Crimp. "I walked to Rotten Lake today to fish," he said. "And on the way I stepped over what appeared at first to be a fallen tree. But then as I stepped over I felt something stir and I taken this second look and there I was straddling this here alligator long as from the front door to the kitchen and thicker than a hog."

The hunchback chattered on. Everyone looked at him from time to time, and some kept track of his chattering and others did not. There were times when every word he said was nothing but lying and bragging. Nothing he said tonight was true. He had lain in bed with a summer quinsy[7] all day long, and had only got up in the late afternoon in order to turn the ice-cream

---

7. Attack of tonsillitis.

freezer. Everybody knew this, yet he stood there in the middle of the café and held forth with such lies and boasting that it was enough to shrivel the ears.

Miss Amelia watched him with her hands in her pockets and her head turned to one side. There was a softness about her gray, queer eyes and she was smiling gently to herself. Occasionally she glanced from the hunchback to the other people in the café—and then her look was proud, and there was in it the hint of a threat, as though daring anyone to try to hold him to account for all his foolery. Jeff was bringing in the suppers, already served on the plates, and the new electric fans in the café made a pleasant stir of coolness in the air.

"The little youngun is asleep," said Henry Macy finally.

Miss Amelia looked down at the patient beside her, and composed her face for the matter in hand. The child's chin was resting on the table edge and a trickle of spit or Kroup Kure had bubbled from the corner of his mouth. His eyes were quite closed, and a little family of gnats had clustered peacefully in the corners. Miss Amelia put her hand on his head and shook it roughly, but the patient did not awake. So Miss Amelia lifted the child from the table, being careful not to touch the sore part of his leg, and went into the office. Henry Macy followed after her and they closed the office door.

Cousin Lymon was bored that evening. There was not much going on, and in spite of the heat the customers in the café were good-humored. Henry Ford Crimp and Horace Wells sat at the middle table with their arms around each other, sniggering over some long joke—but when he approached them he could make nothing of it as he had missed the beginning of the story. The moonlight brightened the dusty road, and the dwarfed peach trees were black and motionless: there was no breeze. The drowsy buzz of swamp mosquitoes was like an echo of the silent night. The town seemed dark, except far down the road to the right there was the flicker of a lamp. Somewhere in the darkness a woman sang in a high wild voice and the tune had no start and no finish and was made up of only three notes which went on and on and on. The hunchback stood leaning against the banister of the porch, looking down the empty road as though hoping that someone would come along.

There were footsteps behind him, then a voice: "Cousin Lymon, your dinner is set out upon the table."

"My appetite is poor tonight," said the hunchback, who had been eating sweet snuff all the day. "There is a sourness in my mouth."

"Just a pick," said Miss Amelia. "The breast, the liver, and the heart."

Together they went back into the bright café, and sat down with Henry Macy. Their table was the largest one in the café, and on it there was a bouquet of swamp lilies in a Coca-Cola bottle. Miss Amelia had finished with her patient and was satisfied with herself. From behind the closed office door there had come only a few sleepy whimpers, and before the patient could wake up and become terrified it was all over. The child was now slung across the shoulder of his father, sleeping deeply, his little arms dangling loose along his father's back and his puffed-up face very red—they were leaving the café to go home.

Henry Macy was still silent. He ate carefully, making no noise when he swallowed, and was not a third as greedy as Cousin Lymon who had claimed to have no appetite and was now putting down helping after helping of the dinner. Occasionally Henry Macy looked across at Miss Amelia and again held his peace.

It was a typical Saturday night. An old couple who had come in from the country hesitated for a moment at the doorway, holding each other's hand, and finally decided to come inside. They had lived together so long, this old country couple, that they looked as similar as twins. They were brown, shriveled, and like two little walking peanuts. They left early, and by midnight most of the other customers were gone. Rosser Cline and Merlie Ryan still played checkers, and Stumpy MacPhail sat with a liquor bottle on his table (his wife would not allow it in the home) and carried on peaceable conversations with himself. Henry Macy had not yet gone away, and this was unusual, as he almost always went to bed soon after nightfall. Miss Amelia yawned sleepily, but Lymon was restless and she did not suggest that they close up for the night.

Finally, at one o'clock, Henry Macy looked up at the corner of the ceiling and said quietly to Miss Amelia: "I got a letter today."

Miss Amelia was not one to be impressed by this, because all sorts of business letters and catalogues came addressed to her.

"I got a letter from my brother," said Henry Macy.

The hunchback, who had been goose-stepping about the café with his hands clasped behind his head, stopped suddenly. He was quick to sense any change in the atmosphere of a gathering. He glanced at each face in the room and waited.

Miss Amelia scowled and hardened her right fist. "You are welcome to it," she said.

"He is on parole. He is out of the penitentiary."

The face of Miss Amelia was very dark, and she shivered although the night was warm. Stumpy MacPhail and Merlie Ryan pushed aside their checker game. The café was very quiet.

"Who?" asked Cousin Lymon. His large, pale ears seemed to grow on his head and stiffen. "What?"

Miss Amelia slapped her hands palm down on the table. "Because Marvin Macy is a—" But her voice hoarsened and after a few moments she only said: "He belongs to be in that penitentiary the balance of his life."

"What did he do?" asked Cousin Lymon.

There was a long pause, as no one knew exactly how to answer this. "He robbed three filling stations," said Stumpy MacPhail. But his words did not sound complete and there was a feeling of sins left unmentioned.

The hunchback was impatient. He could not bear to be left out of anything, even a great misery. The name Marvin Macy was unknown to him, but it tantalized him as did any mention of subjects which others knew about and of which he was ignorant—such as any reference to the old sawmill that had been torn down before he came, or a chance word about poor Morris Finestein, or the recollection of any event that had occurred before his time. Aside from this inborn curiosity, the hunchback took a great interest in robbers and crimes of all varieties. As he strutted around the table he was muttering the words "released on parole" and "penitentiary" to himself. But although he questioned insistently, he was unable to find anything, as nobody would dare to talk about Marvin Macy before Miss Amelia in the café.

"The letter did not say very much," said Henry Macy. "He did not say where he was going."

"Humph!" said Miss Amelia, and her face was still hardened and very dark. "He will never set his split hoof[8] on my premises."

She pushed back her chair from the table, and made ready to close the café. Thinking about Marvin Macy may have set her to brooding, for she hauled the cash register back to the kitchen and put it in a private place. Henry Macy went off down the dark road. But Henry Ford Crimp and Merlie Ryan lingered for a time on the front porch. Later Merlie Ryan was to make certain claims, to swear that on that night he had a vision of what was to come. But the town paid no attention, for that was just the sort of thing that Merlie Ryan would claim. Miss Amelia and Cousin Lymon talked for a time in the parlor. And when at last the hunchback thought that he could sleep she arranged the mosquito netting over his bed and waited until he had finished with his prayers. Then she put on her long nightgown, smoked two pipes, and only after a long time went to sleep.

That autumn was a happy time. The crops around the countryside were good, and over at the Forks Falls market the price of tobacco held firm that year. After the long hot summer the first cool days had a clean bright sweetness. Goldenrod grew along the dusty roads, and the sugar cane was ripe and purple. The bus came each day from Cheehaw to carry off a few of the younger children to the consolidated school to get an education. Boys hunted foxes in the pinewoods, winter quilts were aired out on the wash lines, and sweet potatoes bedded in the ground with straw against the colder months to come. In the evening, delicate shreds of smoke rose from the chimneys, and the moon was round and orange in the autumn sky. There is no stillness like the quiet of the first cold nights in the fall. Sometimes, late in the night when there was no wind, there could be heard in the town the thin wild whistle of the train that goes through Society City on its way far off to the North.

For Miss Amelia Evans this was a time of great activity. She was at work from dawn until sundown. She made a new and bigger condenser for her still, and in one week ran off enough liquor to souse the whole country. Her old mule was dizzy from grinding so much sorghum, and she scalded her Mason jars and put away pear preserves. She was looking forward greatly to the first frost, because she had traded for three tremendous hogs, and intended to make much barbecue, chitterlins, and sausage.

During these weeks there was a quality about Miss Amelia that many people noticed. She laughed often, with a deep ringing laugh, and her whistling had a sassy, tuneful trickery. She was forever trying out her strength, lifting up heavy objects, or poking her tough biceps with her finger. One day she sat down to her typewriter and wrote a story—a story in which there were foreigners, trap doors, and millions of dollars. Cousin Lymon was with her always, traipsing along behind her coat-tails, and when she watched him her face had a bright, soft look, and when she spoke his name there lingered in her voice the undertone of love.

The first cold spell came at last. When Miss Amelia awoke one morning there were frost flowers on the windowpanes, and rime had silvered the

---

8. I.e., to Miss Amelia, Marvin Macy is a devil.

patches of grass in the yard. Miss Amelia built a roaring fire in the kitchen stove, then went out of doors to judge the day. The air was cold and sharp, the sky pale green and cloudless. Very shortly people began to come in from the country to find out what Miss Amelia thought of the weather; she decided to kill the biggest hog, and word got round the countryside. The hog was slaughtered and a low oak fire started in the barbecue pit. There was the warm smell of pig blood and smoke in the back yard, the stamp of footsteps, the ring of voices in the winter air. Miss Amelia walked around giving orders and soon most of the work was done.

She had some particular business to do in Cheehaw that day, so after making sure that all was going well, she cranked up her car and got ready to leave. She asked Cousin Lymon to come with her, in fact, she asked him seven times, but he was loath to leave the commotion and wanted to remain. This seemed to trouble Miss Amelia, as she always liked to have him near to her, and was prone to be terribly homesick when she had to go any distance away. But after asking him seven times, she did not urge him any further. Before leaving she found a stick and drew a heavy line all around the barbecue pit, about two feet back from the edge, and told him not to trespass beyond that boundary. She left after dinner and intended to be back before dark.

Now, it is not so rare to have a truck or an automobile pass along the road and through the town on the way from Cheehaw to somewhere else. Every year the tax collector comes to argue with rich people such as Miss Amelia. And if somebody in the town, such as Merlie Ryan, takes a notion that he can connive to get a car on credit, or to pay down three dollars and have a fine electric icebox such as they advertise in the store windows of Cheehaw, then a city man will come out asking meddlesome questions, finding out all his troubles, and ruining his chances of buying anything on the installment plan. Sometimes, especially since they are working on the Forks Falls highway, the cars hauling the chain gang come through the town. And frequently people in automobiles get lost and stop to inquire how they can find the right road again. So, late that afternoon it was nothing unusual to have a truck pass the mill and stop in the middle of the road near the café of Miss Amelia. A man jumped down from the back of the truck, and the truck went on its way.

The man stood in the middle of the road and looked about him. He was a tall man, with brown curly hair, and slow-moving, deep-blue eyes. His lips were red and he smiled the lazy, half-mouthed smile of the braggart. The man wore a red shirt, and a wide belt of tooled leather; he carried a tin suitcase and a guitar. The first person in the town to see this newcomer was Cousin Lymon, who had heard the shifting of gears and come around to investigate. The hunchback stuck his head around the corner of the porch, but did not step out altogether into full view. He and the man stared at each other, and it was not the look of two strangers meeting for the first time and swiftly summing up each other. It was a peculiar stare they exchanged between them, like the look of two criminals who recognize each other. Then the man in the red shirt shrugged his left shoulder and turned away. The face of the hunchback was very pale as he watched the man go down the road, and after a few moments he began to follow along carefully, keeping many paces away.

It was immediately known throughout the town that Marvin Macy had come back again. First, he went to the mill, propped his elbows lazily on a window sill and looked inside. He liked to watch others hard at work, as do all born loafers. The mill was thrown into a sort of numb confusion. The dyers left the hot vats, the spinners and weavers forgot about their machines, and even Stumpy MacPhail, who was foreman, did not know exactly what to do. Marvin Macy still smiled his wet half-mouthed smiles, and when he saw his brother, his bragging expression did not change. After looking over the mill Marvin Macy went down the road to the house where he had been raised, and left his suitcase and guitar on the front porch. Then he walked around the millpond, looked over the church, the three stores, and the rest of the town. The hunchback trudged along quietly at some distance behind him, his hands in his pockets, and his little face still very pale.

It had grown late. The red winter sun was setting, and to the west the sky was deep gold and crimson. Ragged chimney swifts flew to their nests; lamps were lighted. Now and then there was the smell of smoke, and the warm rich odor of the barbecue slowly cooking in the pit behind the café. After making the rounds of the town Marvin Macy stopped before Miss Amelia's premises and read the sign above the porch. Then, not hesitating to trespass, he walked through the side yard. The mill whistle blew a thin, lonesome blast, and the day's shift was done. Soon there were others in Miss Amelia's back yard beside Marvin Macy—Henry Ford Crimp, Merlie Ryan, Stumpy MacPhail, and any number of children and people who stood around the edges of the property and looked on. Very little was said. Marvin Macy stood by himself on one side of the pit, and the rest of the people clustered together on the other side. Cousin Lymon stood somewhat apart from everyone, and he did not take his eyes from the face of Marvin Macy.

"Did you have a good time in the penitentiary?" asked Merlie Ryan, with a silly giggle.

Marvin Macy did not answer. He took from his hip pocket a large knife, opened it slowly, and honed the blade on the seat of his pants. Merlie Ryan grew suddenly very quiet and went to stand directly behind the broad back of Stumpy MacPhail.

Miss Amelia did not come home until almost dark. They heard the rattle of her automobile while she was still a long distance away, then the slam of the door and a bumping noise as though she were hauling something up the front steps of her premises. The sun had already set, and in the air there was the blue smoky glow of early winter evenings. Miss Amelia came down the back steps slowly, and the group in her yard waited very quietly. Few people in this world could stand up to Miss Amelia, and against Marvin Macy she had this special bitter hate. Everyone waited to see her burst into a terrible holler, snatch up some dangerous object, and chase him altogether out of town. At first she did not see Marvin Macy, and her face had the relieved and dreamy expression that was natural to her when she reached home after having gone some distance away.

Miss Amelia must have seen Marvin Macy and Cousin Lymon at the same instant. She looked from one to the other, but it was not the wastrel from the penitentiary on whom she finally fixed her gaze of sick amazement. She, and everyone else, was looking at Cousin Lymon, and he was a sight to see.

The hunchback stood at the end of the pit, his pale face lighted by the soft glow from the smoldering oak fire. Cousin Lymon had a very peculiar accomplishment, which he used whenever he wished to ingratiate himself with someone. He would stand very still, and with just a little concentration, he could wiggle his large pale ears with marvelous quickness and ease. This trick he always used when he wanted to get something special out of Miss Amelia, and to her it was irresistible. Now as he stood there the hunchback's ears were wiggling furiously on his head, but it was not Miss Amelia at whom he was looking this time. The hunchback was smiling at Marvin Macy with an entreaty that was near to desperation. At first Marvin Macy paid no attention to him, and when he did finally glance at the hunchback it was without any appreciation whatsoever.

"What ails this Brokeback?" he asked with a rough jerk of his thumb.

No one answered. And Cousin Lymon, seeing that his accomplishment was getting him nowhere, added new efforts of persuasion. He fluttered his eyelids, so that they were like pale, trapped moths in his sockets. He scraped his feet around on the ground, waved his hands about, and finally began doing a little trotlike dance. In the last gloomy light of the winter he resembled the child of a swamp-haunt.

Marvin Macy, alone of all the people in the yard, was unimpressed.

"Is the runt throwing a fit?" he asked, and when no one answered he stepped forward and gave Cousin Lymon a cuff on the side of his head. The hunchback staggered, then fell back on the ground. He sat where he had fallen, still looking up at Marvin Macy, and with great effort his ears managed one last forlorn little flap.

Now everyone turned to Miss Amelia to see what she would do. In all these years no one had so much as touched a hair of Cousin Lymon's head, although many had had the itch to do so. If anyone even spoke crossly to the hunchback, Miss Amelia would cut off this rash mortal's credit and find ways of making things go hard for him a long time afterward. So now if Miss Amelia had split open Marvin Macy's head with the ax on the back porch no one would have been surprised. But she did nothing of the kind.

There were times when Miss Amelia seemed to go into a sort of trance. And the cause of these trances was usually known and understood. For Miss Amelia was a fine doctor, and did not grind up swamp roots and other untried ingredients and give them to the first patient who came along; whenever she invented a new medicine she always tried it out first on herself. She would swallow an enormous dose and spend the following day walking thoughtfully back and forth from the café to the brick privy. Often, when there was a sudden keen gripe,[9] she would stand quite still, her queer eyes staring down at the ground and her fists clenched; she was trying to decide which organ was being worked upon, and what misery the new medicine might be most likely to cure. And now as she watched the hunchback and Marvin Macy, her face wore this same expression, tense with reckoning some inward pain, although she had taken no new medicine that day.

"That will learn you, Brokeback," said Marvin Macy.

Henry Macy pushed back his limp whitish hair from his forehead and coughed nervously. Stumpy MacPhail and Merlie Ryan shuffled their feet, and the children and black people on the outskirts of the property made not

---

9. Pinching intestinal pain.

a sound. Marvin Macy folded the knife he had been honing, and after looking about him fearlessly he swaggered out of the yard. The embers in the pit were turning to gray feathery ashes and it was now quite dark.

That was the way Marvin Macy came back from the penitentiary. Not a living soul in all the town was glad to see him. Even Mrs. Mary Hale, who was a good woman and had raised him with love and care—at the first sight of him even this old foster mother dropped the skillet she was holding and burst into tears. But nothing could faze that Marvin Macy. He sat on the back steps of the Hale house, lazily picking his guitar, and when the supper was ready, he pushed the children of the household out of the way and served himself a big meal, although there had been barely enough hoecakes and white meat to go round. After eating he settled himself in the best and warmest sleeping place in the front room and was untroubled by dreams.

Miss Amelia did not open the café that night. She locked the doors and all the windows very carefully, nothing was seen of her and Cousin Lymon, and a lamp burned in her room all the night long.

Marvin Macy brought with him bad fortune, right from the first, as could be expected. The next day the weather turned suddenly, and it became hot. Even in the early morning there was a sticky sultriness in the atmosphere, the wind carried the rotten smell of the swamp, and delicate shrill mosquitoes webbed the green millpond. It was unseasonable, worse than August, and much damage was done. For nearly everyone in the county who owned a hog had copied Miss Amelia and slaughtered the day before. And what sausage could keep in such weather as this? After a few days there was everywhere the smell of slowly spoiling meat, and an atmosphere of dreary waste. Worse yet, a family reunion near the Forks Falls highway ate pork roast and died, every one of them. It was plain that their hog had been infected—and who could tell whether the rest of the meat was safe or not? People were torn between the longing for the good taste of pork, and the fear of death. It was a time of waste and confusion.

The cause of all this, Marvin Macy, had no shame in him. He was seen everywhere. During work hours he loafed about the mill, looking in at the windows, and on Sundays he dressed in his red shirt and paraded up and down the road with his guitar. He was still handsome—with his brown hair, his red lips, and his broad strong shoulders; but the evil in him was now too famous for his good looks to get him anywhere. And this evil was not measured only by the actual sins he had committed. True, he had robbed those filling stations. And before that he had ruined the tenderest girls in the county and laughed about it. Any number of wicked things could be listed against him, but quite apart from these crimes there was about him a secret meanness that clung to him almost like a smell. Another thing—he never sweated, not even in August, and that surely is a sign worth pondering over.

Now it seemed to the town that he was more dangerous than he had ever been before, as in the penitentiary in Atlanta he must have learned the method of laying charms. Otherwise how could his effect on Cousin Lymon be explained? For since first setting eyes on Marvin Macy the hunchback was possessed by an unnatural spirit. Every minute he wanted to be following along behind this jailbird, and he was full of silly schemes to attract attention to himself. Still Marvin Macy either treated him hatefully or failed to notice him at all. Sometimes the hunchback would give up, perch himself on the banister of the front porch much as a sick bird huddles on a telephone wire, and grieve publicly.

"But why?" Miss Amelia would ask, staring at him with her crossed, gray eyes, and her fists closed tight.

"Oh, Marvin Macy," groaned the hunchback, and the sound of the name was enough to upset the rhythm of his sobs so that he hiccuped. "He has been to Atlanta."

Miss Amelia would shake her head and her face was dark and hardened. To begin with she had no patience with any traveling; those who had made the trip to Atlanta or traveled fifty miles from home to see the ocean—those restless people she despised. "Going to Atlanta does no credit to home."

"He has been to the penitentiary," said the hunchback, miserable with longing.

How are you going to argue against such envies as these? In her perplexity Miss Amelia did not herself sound any too sure of what she was saying. "Been to the penitentiary, Cousin Lymon? Why, a trip like that is no travel to brag about."

During these weeks Miss Amelia was closely watched by everyone. She went about absent-mindedly, her face remote as though she had lapsed into one of her gripe trances. For some reason, after the day of Marvin Macy's arrival, she put aside her overalls and wore always the red dress she had before this time reserved for Sundays, funerals, and sessions of the court. Then as the weeks passed she began to take some steps to clear up the situation. But her efforts were hard to understand. If it hurt her to see Cousin Lymon follow Marvin Macy about the town, why did she not make the issues clear once and for all, and tell the hunchback that if he had dealings with Marvin Macy she would turn him off the premises? That would have been simple, and Cousin Lymon would have had to submit to her, or else face the sorry business of finding himself loose in the world. But Miss Amelia seemed to have lost her will; for the first time in her life she hesitated as to just what course to pursue. And, like most people in such a position of uncertainty, she did the worst thing possible—she began following several courses at once, all of them contrary to each other.

The café was opened every night as usual, and, strangely enough, when Marvin Macy came swaggering through the door, with the hunchback at his heels, she did not turn him out. She even gave him free drinks and smiled at him in a wild, crooked way. At the same time she set a terrible trap for him out in the swamp that surely would have killed him if he had got caught. She let Cousin Lymon invite him to Sunday dinner, and then tried to trip him up as he went down the steps. She began a great campaign of pleasure for Cousin Lymon—making exhausting trips to various spectacles being held in distant places, driving the automobile thirty miles to Chautauqua, taking him to Forks Falls to watch a parade. All in all it was a distracting time for Miss Amelia. In the opinion of most people she was well on her way in the climb up fools' hill, and everyone wanted to see how it would all turn out.

The weather turned cold again, the winter was upon the town, and night came before the last shift in the mill was done. Children kept on all their garments when they slept, and women raised the backs of their skirts to toast themselves dreamily at the fire. After it rained, the mud in the road made hard frozen ruts, there were faint flickers of lamplight from the windows of the houses, the peach trees were scrawny and bare. In the dark, silent nights of wintertime the café was the warm center point of the town, the lights shining so brightly that they could be seen a quarter of a mile away. The great iron stove at the back of the room roared, crackled, and turned red. Miss Amelia had made red curtains for the windows, and from a salesman who passed through the town she bought a great bunch of paper roses that looked very real.

But it was not only the warmth, the decorations, and the brightness, that made the café what it was. There is a deeper reason why the café was so precious to this town. And this deeper reason has to do with a certain pride that had not hitherto been known in these parts. To understand this new pride the cheapness of human life must be kept in mind. There were always plenty of people clustered around a mill—but it was seldom that every family had enough meal, garments, and fat back to go the rounds. Life could become one long dim scramble just to get the things needed to keep alive. And the confusing point is this: all useful things have a price, and are bought only with money, as that is the way the world is run. You know without having to reason about it the price of a bale of cotton, or a quart of molasses. But no value has been put on human life; it is given to us free and taken without being paid for. What is it worth? If you look around, at times the value may seem to be little or nothing at all. Often after you have sweated and tried and things are not better for you, there comes a feeling deep down in the soul that you are not worth much.

But the new pride that the café brought to this town had an effect on almost everyone, even the children. For in order to come to the café you did not have to buy the dinner, or a portion of liquor. There were cold bottled drinks for a nickel. And if you could not even afford that, Miss Amelia had a drink called Cherry Juice which sold for a penny a glass, and was pink-colored and very sweet. Almost everyone, with the exception of Reverend T. M. Willin, came to the café at least once during the week. Children love to sleep in houses other than their own, and to eat at a neighbor's table; on such occasions they behave themselves decently and are proud. The people in the town were likewise proud when sitting at the tables in the café. They washed before coming to Miss Amelia's, and scraped their feet very politely on the threshold as they entered the café. There, for a few hours at least, the deep bitter knowing that you are not worth much in this world could be laid low.

The café was a special benefit to bachelors, unfortunate people, and consumptives.[1] And here it may be mentioned that there was some reason to suspect that Cousin Lymon was consumptive. The brightness of his gray eyes, his insistence, his talkativeness, and his cough—these were all signs. Besides, there is generally supposed to be some connection between a hunched spine and consumption. But whenever this subject had been mentioned to Miss Amelia she had become furious; she denied these symptoms with bitter vehemence, but on the sly she treated Cousin Lymon with hot chest plasters, Kroup Kure, and such. Now this winter the hunchback's cough was worse, and sometimes even on cold days he would break out in a

---

1. Those with tuberculosis (which can affect bones and other tissues, not just the lungs).

heavy sweat. But this did not prevent him from following along after Marvin Macy.

Early every morning he left the premises and went to the back door of Mrs. Hale's house, and waited and waited—as Marvin Macy was a lazy sleeper. He would stand there and call out softly. His voice was just like the voices of children who squat patiently over those tiny little holes in the ground where doodlebugs[2] are thought to live, poking the hole with a broom straw, and calling plaintively: "Doodlebug, Doodlebug—fly away home. Mrs. Doodlebug, Mrs. Doodlebug. Come out, come out. Your house is on fire and all your children are burning up." In just such a voice—at once sad, luring, and resigned—would the hunchback call Marvin Macy's name each morning. Then when Marvin Macy came out for the day, he would trail him about the town, and sometimes they would be gone for hours together out in the swamp.

And Miss Amelia continued to do the worst thing possible: that is, to try to follow several courses at once. When Cousin Lymon left the house she did not call him back, but only stood in the middle of the road and watched lonesomely until he was out of sight. Nearly every day Marvin Macy turned up with Cousin Lymon at dinnertime, and ate at her table. Miss Amelia opened the pear preserves, and the table was well-set with ham or chicken, great bowls of hominy grits, and winter peas. It is true that on one occasion Miss Amelia tried to poison Marvin Macy—but there was a mistake, the plates were confused, and it was she herself who got the poisoned dish. This she quickly realized by the slight bitterness of the food, and that day she ate no dinner. She sat tilted back in the chair, feeling her muscle, and looking at Marvin Macy.

Every night Marvin Macy came to the café and settled himself at the best and largest table, the one in the center of the room. Cousin Lymon brought him liquor, for which he did not pay a cent. Marvin Macy brushed the hunchback aside as if he were a swamp mosquito, and not only did he show no gratitude for these favors, but if the hunchback got in his way he would cuff him with the back of his hand, or say: "Out of my way, Brokeback—I'll snatch you bald-headed." When this happened Miss Amelia would come out from behind her counter and approach Marvin Macy very slowly, her fists clenched, her peculiar red dress hanging awkwardly around her bony knees. Marvin Macy would also clench his fists and they would walk slowly and meaningfully around each other. But, although everyone watched breathlessly, nothing ever came of it. The time for the fight was not yet ready.

There is one particular reason why this winter is remembered and still talked about. A great thing happened. People woke up on the second of January and found the whole world about them altogether changed. Little ignorant children looked out of the windows, and they were so puzzled that they began to cry. Old people harked back and could remember nothing in these parts to equal the phenomenon. For in the night it had snowed. In the dark hours after midnight the dim flakes started falling softly on the town. By dawn the ground was covered, and the strange snow banked the ruby windows of the church, and whitened the roofs of the houses. The snow gave the town a drawn, bleak look. The two-room houses near the mill were dirty,

---

2. Larvae of lion ants.

crooked, and seemed about to collapse, and somehow everything was dark and shrunken. But the snow itself—there was a beauty about it few people around here had ever known before. The snow was not white, as Northerners had pictured it to be; in the snow there were soft colors of blue and silver, the sky was a gentle shining gray. And the dreamy quietness of falling snow—when had the town been so silent?

People reacted to the snowfall in various ways. Miss Amelia, on looking out of her window, thoughtfully wiggled the toes of her bare feet, gathered close to her neck the collar of her nightgown. She stood there for some time, then commenced to draw the shutters and lock every window on the premises. She closed the place completely, lighted the lamps, and sat solemnly over her bowl of grits. The reason for this was not that Miss Amelia feared the snowfall. It was simply that she was unable to form an immediate opinion of this new event, and unless she knew exactly and definitely what she thought of a matter (which was nearly always the case) she preferred to ignore it. Snow had never fallen in this county in her lifetime, and she had never thought about it one way or the other. But if she admitted this snowfall she would have to come to some decision, and in those days there was enough distraction in her life as it was already. So she poked about the gloomy, lamp-lighted house and pretended that nothing had happened. Cousin Lymon, on the contrary, chased around in the wildest excitement, and when Miss Amelia turned her back to dish him some breakfast he slipped out of the door.

Marvin Macy laid claim to the snowfall. He said that he knew snow, had seen it in Atlanta, and from the way he walked about the town that day it was as though he owned every flake. He sneered at the little children who crept timidly out of the houses and scooped up handfuls of snow to taste. Reverend Willin hurried down the road with a furious face, as he was thinking deeply and trying to weave the snow into his Sunday sermon. Most people were humble and glad about this marvel; they spoke in hushed voices and said "thank you" and "please" more than was necessary. A few weak characters, of course, were demoralized and got drunk—but they were not numerous. To everyone this was an occasion and many counted their money and planned to go to the café that night.

Cousin Lymon followed Marvin Macy about all day, seconding his claim to the snow. He marveled that snow did not fall as does rain, and stared up at the dreamy, gently falling flakes until he stumbled from dizziness. And the pride he took on himself, basking in the glory of Marvin Macy—it was such that many people could not resist calling out to him: " 'Oho,' said the fly on the chariot wheel. 'What a dust we do raise.' "[3]

Miss Amelia did not intend to serve a dinner. But when, at six o'clock, there was the sound of footsteps on the porch she opened the front door cautiously. It was Henry Ford Crimp, and though there was no food, she let him sit at a table and served him a drink. Others came. The evening was blue, bitter, and though the snow fell no longer there was a wind from the pine trees that swept up delicate flurries from the ground. Cousin Lymon did not come until after dark, with him Marvin Macy, and he carried his tin suitcase and his guitar.

"So you mean to travel?" said Miss Amelia quickly.

---

3. An allusion to one of Aesop's fables.

Marvin Macy warmed himself at the stove. Then he settled down at his table and carefully sharpened a little stick. He picked his teeth, frequently taking the stick out of his mouth to look at the end and wipe it on the sleeve of his coat. He did not bother to answer.

The hunchback looked at Miss Amelia, who was behind the counter. His face was not in the least beseeching; he seemed quite sure of himself. He folded his hands behind his back and perked up his ears confidently. His cheeks were red, his eyes shining, and his clothes were soggy wet. "Marvin Macy is going to visit a spell with us," he said.

Miss Amelia made no protest. She only came out from behind the counter and hovered over the stove, as though the news had made her suddenly cold. She did not warm her backside modestly, lifting her skirt only an inch or so, as do most women when in public. There was not a grain of modesty about Miss Amelia, and she frequently seemed to forget altogether that there were men in the room. Now she stood warming herself, her red dress was pulled up quite high in the back so that a piece of her strong, hairy thigh could be seen by anyone who cared to look at it. Her head was turned to one side; and she had begun talking with herself, nodding and wrinkling her forehead, and there was the tone of accusation and reproach in her voice although the words were not plain. Meanwhile, the hunchback and Marvin Macy had gone upstairs—up to the parlor with the pampas grass and the two sewing machines, to the private rooms where Miss Amelia had lived the whole of her life. Down in the café you could hear them bumping around, unpacking Marvin Macy, and getting him settled.

That is the way Marvin Macy crowded into Miss Amelia's home. At first Cousin Lymon, who had given Marvin Macy his own room, slept on the sofa in the parlor. But the snowfall had a bad effect on him; he caught a cold that turned into a winter quinsy, so Miss Amelia gave up her bed to him. The sofa in the parlor was much too short for her, her feet lapped over the edges, and often she rolled off onto the floor. Perhaps it was this lack of sleep that clouded her wits; everything she tried to do against Marvin Macy rebounded on herself. She got caught in her own tricks, and found herself in many pitiful positions. But still she did not put Marvin Macy off the premises, as she was afraid that she would be left alone. Once you have lived with another, it is a great torture to have to live alone. The silence of a firelit room when suddenly the clock stops ticking, the nervous shadows in an empty house—it is better to take in your mortal enemy than face the terror of living alone.

The snow did not last. The sun came out and within two days the town was just as it had always been before. Miss Amelia did not open her house until every flake had melted. Then she had a big house cleaning and aired everything out in the sun. But before that, the very first thing she did on going out again into her yard, was to tie a rope to the largest branch of the chinaberry tree. At the end of the rope she tied a crocus sack tightly stuffed with sand. This was the punching bag she made for herself and from that day on she would box with it out in her yard every morning. Already she was a fine fighter—a little heavy on her feet, but knowing all manner of mean holds and squeezes to make up for this.

Miss Amelia, as has been mentioned, measured six feet two inches in height. Marvin Macy was one inch shorter. In weight they were about even—

both of them weighing close to a hundred and sixty pounds. Marvin Macy had the advantage in slyness of movement, and in toughness of chest. In fact from the outward point of view the odds were altogether in his favor. Yet almost everybody in the town was betting on Miss Amelia; scarcely a person would put up money on Marvin Macy. The town remembered the great fight between Miss Amelia and a Forks Falls lawyer who had tried to cheat her. He had been a huge strapping fellow, but he was left three-quarters dead when she had finished with him. And it was not only her talent as a boxer that had impressed everyone—she could demoralize her enemy by making terrifying faces and fierce noises, so that even the spectators were sometimes cowed. She was brave, she practiced faithfully with her punching bag, and in this case she was clearly in the right. So people had confidence in her, and they waited. Of course there was no set date for this fight. There were just the signs that were too plain to be overlooked.

During these times the hunchback strutted around with a pleased little pinched-up face. In many delicate and clever ways he stirred up trouble between them. He was constantly plucking at Marvin Macy's trouser leg to draw attention to himself. Sometimes he followed in Miss Amelia's footsteps—but these days it was only in order to imitate her awkward long-legged walk; he crossed his eyes and aped her gestures in a way that made her appear to be a freak. There was something so terrible about this that even the silliest customers of the café, such as Merlie Ryan, did not laugh. Only Marvin Macy drew up the left corner of his mouth and chuckled. Miss Amelia, when this happened, would be divided between two emotions. She would look at the hunchback with a lost, dismal reproach—then turn toward Marvin Macy with her teeth clamped.

"Bust a gut!" she would say bitterly.

And Marvin Macy, most likely, would pick up the guitar from the floor beside his chair. His voice was wet and slimy, as he always had too much spit in his mouth. And the tunes he sang glided slowly from his throat like eels. His strong fingers picked the strings with dainty skill, and everything he sang both lured and exasperated. This was usually more than Miss Amelia could stand.

"Bust a gut!" she would repeat, in a shout.

But always Marvin Macy had the answer ready for her. He would cover the strings to silence the quivering leftover tones, and reply with slow, sure insolence.

"Everything you holler at me bounces back on yourself. Yah! Yah!"

Miss Amelia would have to stand there helpless, as no one has ever invented a way out of this trap. She could not shout out abuse that would bounce back on herself. He had the best of her, there was nothing she could do.

So things went on like this. What happened between the three of them during the nights in the rooms upstairs nobody knows. But the café became more and more crowded every night. A new table had to be brought in. Even the Hermit, the crazy man named Rainer Smith, who took to the swamp years ago, heard something of the situation and came one night to look in at the window and brood over the gathering in the bright café. And the climax each evening was the time when Miss Amelia and Marvin Macy doubled their fists, squared up, and glared at each other. Usually this did not happen after any especial argument, but it seemed to come about mysteriously, by means of some instinct on the part of both of them. At these times the café would become so quiet that you could hear the bouquet of paper roses rustling in the draft. And each night they held this fighting stance a little longer than the night before.

The fight took place on Ground Hog Day, which is the second of February. The weather was favorable, being neither rainy nor sunny, and with a neutral temperature. There were several signs that this was the appointed day, and by ten o'clock the news spread all over the county. Early in the morning Miss Amelia went out and cut down her punching bag. Marvin Macy sat on the back step with a tin can of hog fat between his knees and carefully greased his arms and his legs. A hawk with a bloody breast flew over the town and circled twice around the property of Miss Amelia. The tables in the café were moved out to the back porch, so that the whole big room was cleared for fight. There was every sign. Both Miss Amelia and Marvin Macy ate four helpings of half-raw roast for dinner, and then lay down in the afternoon to store up strength. Marvin Macy rested in the big room upstairs, while Miss Amelia stretched herself out on the bench in her office. It was plain from her white stiff face what a torment it was for her to be lying still and doing nothing, but she lay there quiet as a corpse with her eyes closed and her hands crossed on her chest.

Cousin Lymon had a restless day, and his little face was drawn and tightened with excitement. He put himself up a lunch, and set out to find the ground hog—within an hour he returned, the lunch eaten, and said that the ground hog had seen his shadow and there was to be bad weather ahead. Then, as Miss Amelia and Marvin Macy were both resting to gather strength, and he was left to himself, it occurred to him that he might as well paint the front porch. The house had not been painted for years—in fact, God knows if it had ever been painted at all. Cousin Lymon scrambled around, and soon he had painted half the floor of the porch a gay bright green. It was a loblolly[4] job, and he smeared himself all over. Typically enough he did not even finish the floor, but changed over to the walls, painting as high as he could reach and then standing on a crate to get up a foot higher. When the paint ran out, the right side of the floor was bright green and there was a jagged portion of wall that had been painted. Cousin Lymon left it at that.

There was something childish about his satisfaction with his painting. And in this respect a curious fact should be mentioned. No one in the town, not even Miss Amelia, had any idea how old the hunchback was. Some maintained that when he came to town he was about twelve years old, still a child—others were certain that he was well past forty. His eyes were blue and steady as a child's, but there were lavender crepy shadows beneath these blue eyes that hinted of age. It was impossible to guess his age by his hunched queer body. And even his teeth gave no clue—they were all still in his head (two were broken from cracking a pecan), but he had stained them with so much sweet snuff that it was impossible to decide whether they were old teeth or young teeth. When questioned directly about his age the hunchback professed to know absolutely nothing—he had no idea how long he had been

---

4. Loutish.

on the earth, whether for ten years or a hundred! So his age remained a puzzle.

Cousin Lymon finished his painting at five-thirty o'clock in the afternoon. The day had turned colder and there was a wet taste in the air. The wind came up from the pinewoods, rattling windows, blowing an old newspaper down the road until at last it caught upon a thorn tree. People began to come in from the country; packed automobiles that bristled with the poked-out heads of children, wagons drawn by old mules who seemed to smile in a weary, sour way and plodded along with their tired eyes half-closed. Three young boys came from Society City. All three of them wore yellow rayon shirts and caps put on backward—they were as much alike as triplets, and could always be seen at cockfights and camp meetings.[5] At six o'clock the mill whistle sounded the end of the day's shift and the crowd was complete. Naturally, among the newcomers there were some riffraff, unknown characters, and so forth—but even so the gathering was quiet. A hush was on the town and the faces of people were strange in the fading light. Darkness hovered softly; for a moment the sky was a pale clear yellow against which the gables of the church stood out in dark and bare outline, then the sky died slowly and the darkness gathered into night.

Seven is a popular number, and especially it was a favorite with Miss Amelia. Seven swallows of water for hiccups, seven runs around the millpond for cricks in the neck, seven doses of Amelia Miracle Mover as a worm cure—her treatment nearly always hinged on this number. It is a number of mingled possibilities, and all who love mystery and charms set store by it. So the fight was to take place at seven o'clock. This was known to everyone, not by announcement or words, but understood in the unquestioning way that rain is understood, or an evil odor from the swamp. So before seven o'clock everyone gathered gravely around the property of Miss Amelia. The cleverest got into the café itself and stood lining the walls of the room. Others crowded onto the front porch, or took a stand in the yard.

Miss Amelia and Marvin Macy had not yet shown themselves. Miss Amelia, after resting all afternoon on the office bench, had gone upstairs. On the other hand Cousin Lymon was at your elbow every minute, threading his way through the crowd, snapping his fingers nervously, and batting his eyes. At one minute to seven o'clock he squirmed his way into the café and climbed up on the counter. All was very quiet.

It must have been arranged in some manner beforehand. For just at the stroke of seven Miss Amelia showed herself at the head of the stairs. At the same instant Marvin Macy appeared in front of the café and the crowd made way for him silently. They walked toward each other with no haste, their fists already gripped, and their eyes like the eyes of dreamers. Miss Amelia had changed her red dress for her old overalls, and they were rolled up to the knees. She was barefooted and she had an iron strengthband around her right wrist. Marvin Macy had also rolled his trouser legs—he was naked to the waist and heavily greased; he wore the heavy shoes that had been issued him when he left the penitentiary. Stumpy MacPhail stepped forward from the crowd and slapped their hip pockets with the palm of his right hand to make sure there would be no sudden knives. They were alone in the cleared center of the bright café.

---

5. Series of evangelistic meetings.

There was no signal, but they both struck out simultaneously. Both blows landed on the chin, so that the heads of Miss Amelia and Marvin Macy bobbed back and they were left a little groggy. For a few seconds after the first blows they merely shuffled their feet around on the bare floor, experimenting with various positions, and making mock fists. Then, like wildcats, they were suddenly on each other. There was the sound of knocks, panting, and thumpings on the floor. They were so fast that it was hard to take in what was going on—but once Miss Amelia was hurled backward so that she staggered and almost fell, and another time Marvin Macy caught a knock on the shoulder that spun him round like a top. So the fight went on in this wild violent way with no sign of weakening on either side.

During a struggle like this, when the enemies are as quick and strong as these two, it is worth-while to turn from the confusion of the fight itself and observe the spectators. The people had flattened back as close as possible against the walls. Stumpy MacPhail was in a corner, crouched over and with his fists tight in sympathy, making strange noises. Poor Merlie Ryan had his mouth so wide open that a fly buzzed into it, and was swallowed before Merlie realized what had happened. And Cousin Lymon—he was worth watching. The hunchback still stood on the counter, so that he was raised above everyone else in the café. He had his hands on his hips, his big head thrust forward, and his little legs bent so that the knees jutted outward. The excitement had made him break out in a rash, and his pale mouth shivered.

Perhaps it was half an hour before the course of the fight shifted. Hundreds of blows had been exchanged, and there was still a deadlock. Then suddenly Marvin Macy managed to catch hold of Miss Amelia's left arm and pinion it behind her back. She struggled and got a grasp around his waist; the real fight was now begun. Wrestling is the natural way of fighting in this country—as boxing is too quick and requires much thinking and concentration. And now that Miss Amelia and Marvin were locked in a hold together the crowd came out of its daze and pressed in closer. For a while the fighters grappled muscle to muscle, their hipbones braced against each other. Backward and forward, from side to side, they swayed in this way. Marvin Macy still had not sweated, but Miss Amelia's overalls were drenched and so much sweat had trickled down her legs that she left wet footprints on the floor. Now the test had come, and in these moments of terrible effort, it was Miss Amelia who was the stronger. Marvin Macy was greased and slippery, tricky to grasp, but she was stronger. Gradually she bent him over backward, and inch by inch she forced him to the floor. It was a terrible thing to watch and their deep hoarse breaths were the only sound in the café. At last she had him down, and straddled; her strong big hands were on his throat.

But at that instant, just as the fight was won, a cry sounded in the café that caused a shrill bright shiver to run down the spine. And what took place has been a mystery ever since. The whole town was there to testify what happened, but there were those who doubted their own eyesight. For the counter on which Cousin Lymon stood was at least twelve feet from the fighters in the center of the café. Yet at the instant Miss Amelia grasped the throat of Marvin Macy the hunchback sprang forward and sailed through the air as though he had grown hawk wings. He landed on the broad strong back of Miss Amelia and clutched at her neck with his clawed little fingers.

The rest is confusion. Miss Amelia was beaten before the crowd could come to their senses. Because of the hunchback the fight was won by Marvin

Macy, and at the end Miss Amelia lay sprawled on the floor, her arms flung outward and motionless. Marvin Macy stood over her, his face somewhat popeyed, but smiling his old half-mouthed smile. And the hunchback, he had suddenly disappeared. Perhaps he was frightened about what he had done, or maybe he was so delighted that he wanted to glory with himself alone—at any rate he slipped out of the café and crawled under the back steps. Someone poured water on Miss Amelia, and after a time she got up slowly and dragged herself into her office. Through the open door the crowd could see her sitting at her desk, her head in the crook of her arm, and she was sobbing with the last of her grating, winded breath. Once she gathered her right fist together and knocked it three times on the top of her office desk, then her hand opened feebly and lay palm upward and still. Stumpy MacPhail stepped forward and closed the door.

The crowd was quiet, and one by one the people left the café. Mules were waked up and untied, automobiles cranked, and the three boys from Society City roamed off down the road on foot. This was not a fight to hash over and talk about afterward; people went home and pulled the covers up over their heads. The town was dark, except for the premises of Miss Amelia, but every room was lighted there the whole night long.

Marvin Macy and the hunchback must have left the town an hour or so before daylight. And before they went away this is what they did:

They unlocked the private cabinet of curios and took everything in it.

They broke the mechanical piano.

They carved terrible words on the café tables.

They found the watch that opened in the back to show a picture of a waterfall and took that also.

They poured a gallon of sorghum syrup all over the kitchen floor and smashed the jars of preserves.

They went out in the swamp and completely wrecked the still, ruining the big new condenser and the cooler, and setting fire to the shack itself.

They fixed a dish of Miss Amelia's favorite food, grits with sausage, seasoned it with enough poison to kill off the county, and placed this dish temptingly on the café counter.

They did everything ruinous they could think of without actually breaking into the office where Miss Amelia stayed the night. Then they went off together, the two of them.

That was how Miss Amelia was left alone in the town. The people would have helped her if they had known how, as people in this town will as often as not be kindly if they have a chance. Several housewives nosed around with brooms and offered to clear up the wreck. But Miss Amelia only looked at them with lost crossed eyes and shook her head. Stumpy MacPhail came in on the third day to buy a plug of Queenie tobacco, and Miss Amelia said the price was one dollar. Everything in the café had suddenly risen in price to be worth one dollar. And what sort of café is that? Also, she changed very queerly as a doctor. In all the years before she had been much more popular than the Cheehaw doctor. She had never monkeyed with a patient's soul, taking away from him such real necessities as liquor, tobacco, and so forth. Once in a great while she might carefully warn a patient never to eat fried watermelon or some such dish it had never occurred to a person to want in the first place. Now all this wise doctoring was over. She told one-half of her patients that they were going to die outright, and to the remaining half she recommended cures so farfetched and agonizing that no one in his right mind would consider them for a moment.

Miss Amelia let her hair grow ragged, and it was turning gray. Her face lengthened, and the great muscles of her body shrank until she was thin as old maids are thin when they go crazy. And those gray eyes—slowly day by day they were more crossed, and it was as though they sought each other to exchange a little glance of grief and lonely recognition. She was not pleasant to listen to; her tongue had sharpened terribly.

When anyone mentioned the hunchback she would say only this: "Ho! If I could lay hand to him I would rip out his gizzard and throw it to the cat!" But it was not so much the words that were terrible, but the voice in which they were said. Her voice had lost its old vigor; there was none of the ring of vengeance it used to have when she would mention "that loom-fixer I was married to," or some other enemy. Her voice was broken, soft, and sad as the wheezy whine of the church pump-organ.

For three years she sat out on the front steps every night, alone and silent, looking down the road and waiting. But the hunchback never returned. There were rumors that Marvin Macy used him to climb into windows and steal, and other rumors that Marvin Macy had sold him into a side show. But both these reports were traced back to Merlie Ryan. Nothing true was ever heard of him. It was in the fourth year that Miss Amelia hired a Cheehaw carpenter and had him board up the premises, and there in those closed rooms she has remained ever since.

Yes, the town is dreary. On August afternoons the road is empty, white with dust, and the sky above is bright as glass. Nothing moves—there are no children's voices, only the hum of the mill. The peach trees seem to grow more crooked every summer, and the leaves are dull gray and of a sickly delicacy. The house of Miss Amelia leans so much to the right that it is now only a question of time when it will collapse completely, and people are careful not to walk around the yard. There is no good liquor to be bought in the town; the nearest still is eight miles away, and the liquor is such that those who drink it grow warts on their livers the size of goobers,[6] and dream themselves into a dangerous inward world. There is absolutely nothing to do in the town. Walk around the millpond, stand kicking at a rotten stump, figure out what you can do with the old wagon wheel by the side of the road near the church. The soul rots with boredom. You might as well go down to the Forks Falls highway and listen to the chain gang.

1944

6. Peanuts.

GWENDOLYN BROOKS
1917–2000

In an important response to an interviewer's question, Gwendolyn Brooks declared that "what I'm fighting for now in my work [is] an *expression* relevant to all manner of blacks, poems I could take into a tavern, into the street, into the halls of a housing project." Her impassioned statement holds true not only in the highly politicized work she wrote under the influence of the civil rights movement in the late 1960s but also in her earlier compositions. Indeed, the poetry Brooks produced during World War II remains pioneering in its effort to democratize the subject matter of verse in technically complex works clearly worthy of the Pulitzer Prize she earned in 1950; she was the first African American to win the award.

Born in Topeka, Kansas, Gwendolyn Brooks was only five weeks old when her parents brought her to live in the area with which she would always be identified, the South Side of Chicago. Her schoolteacher mother's belief that she might become the "*lady* Paul Laurence Dunbar" encouraged the young writer, as did her visits to poetry readings by such African American writers as Langston Hughes and James Weldon Johnson. After graduating from Chicago's Wilson Junior College in 1936, Brooks entered a poetry workshop at the South Side Community Art Center, where, with the guidance of Inez Cunningham Stark, a Chicago socialite, she studied the major modernists and, in the words of one biographer, was "introduced to the rigors of poetic technique."

The early work that resulted from this education revealed extraordinary verbal skill, particularly an interest in what Brooks herself called "word play," as well as exceptional accomplishment in the handling of intricate verse forms. Like the writers of the Harlem Renaissance whose voices she heard as a child, Brooks combined black idioms, jazz rhythm, and street slang with the traditional "high style" of English poetry. Married in 1939 to Henry Blakely, and the mother of two children, she produced in this period a series of volumes of verse—notably *A Street in Bronzeville* (1945), *Annie Allen* (1949), and *The Bean Eaters* (1960)—that offered vivid depictions of the lives and losses of people in Chicago's black neighborhoods, together with a novel, *Maud Martha* (1953), about a young black girl's growth to adulthood. Yet though she dealt brilliantly—sometimes poignantly and sometimes sardonically—with Bronzeville (the name given by journalists to Chicago's black ghetto), exploring the lives of both men ("Satin-Legs Smith") and women ("Woman in a Red Hat"), Brooks herself explained that "I wasn't writing consciously with the idea that blacks *must address* blacks."

In 1967, when she attended the second Black Writers' Conference at Fisk University, Brooks met a number of young black poets who persuaded her that "black poets should write as blacks, about blacks, and address themselves *to* blacks." Revitalized by their commitment, she began to teach a verse-writing workshop for a group of Chicago teenagers called the Blackstone Rangers; becoming herself an activist leader, she sought to "*clarify* [her] language" so that she could reach out to wider audiences—specifically "to all manner of blacks." Exploring the tragedies of American racism as well as the triumphs of black endurance, her later works in this mode include several important volumes of verse—*In the Mecca* (1968), a book-length poetic sequence examining the diversity of existence in a Chicago housing project; *Riot* (1969); and *Beckonings* (1975)—along with an autobiography, *Report from Part I* (1972), and several books of poetry for children.

Though Brooks did not define herself as a feminist, believing that racial issues must take priority over gender questions, she always wrote with extraordinary sympathy about the dilemmas of female characters like those in "Bronzeville Woman in a Red Hat" and "the mother." In addition, she frequently attempted to analyze the roots of what she called "woman rage," asking, for example, "Why in the world has it been that our men have preferred either white or that pigmentation which is as close to white as possible?" Courageously exploring the real choices that real women confront, she nevertheless also insisted that even if "black women have got some problems with black men and vice versa, . . . these are family matters. They must be worked out within the family."

the mother

Abortions will not let you forget.
You remember the children you got that you did not get,
The damp small pulps with a little or with no hair,
The singers and workers that never handled the air.
5   You will never neglect or beat
Them, or silence or buy with a sweet.
You will never wind up the sucking-thumb
Or scuttle off ghosts that come.
You will never leave them, controlling your luscious sigh,
10   Return for a snack of them, with gobbling mother-eye

I have heard in the voices of the wind the voices of my dim
    killed children.
I have contracted. I have eased
My dim dears at the breasts they could never suck.
I have said, Sweets, if I sinned, if I seized
15   Your luck
And your lives from your unfinished reach,
If I stole your births and your names,
Your straight baby tears and your games,
Your stilted or lovely loves, your tumults, your marriages,
    aches, and your deaths,
20   If I poisoned the beginnings of your breaths,
Believe that even in my deliberateness I was not deliberate.
Though why should I whine,
Whine that the crime was other than mine?—
Since anyhow you are dead.
25   Or rather, or instead,
You were never made.
But that too, I am afraid,
Is faulty: oh, what shall I say, how is the truth to be said?
You were born, you had body, you died.
30   It is just that you never giggled or planned or cried

Believe me, I loved you all.
Believe me, I knew you, though faintly, and I loved, I loved you
All.

1945

a song in the front yard

I've stayed in the front yard all my life,
I want a peek at the back
Where it's rough and untended and hungry weed grows.
A girl gets sick of a rose.

5   I want to go in the back yard now
And maybe down the alley,
To where the charity children play.
I want a good time today.

They do some wonderful things.
10   They have some wonderful fun.
My mother sneers, but I say it's fine
How they don't have to go in at quarter to nine.
My mother, she tells me that Johnnie Mae
Will grow up to be a bad woman.
15   That George'll be taken to Jail soon or late
(On account of last winter he sold our back gate.)

But I say it's fine. Honest, I do.
And I'd like to be a bad woman, too,
And wear the brave stockings of night-black lace
20   And strut down the streets with paint on my face.

1945

The Sundays of Satin-Legs Smith

Inamoratas,[1] with an approbation,
Bestowed his title. Blessed his inclination.)

He wakes, unwinds, elaborately: a cat
Tawny, reluctant, royal. He is fat
5   And fine this morning. Definite. Reimbursed.

He waits a moment, he designs his reign,
That no performance may be plain or vain.
Then rises in a clear delirium.

He sheds, with his pajamas, shabby days,
10   And his desertedness, his intricate fear, the
Postponed resentments and the prim precautions.

Now, at his bath, would you deny him lavender
Or take away the power of his pine?
What smelly substitute, heady as wine,

---

1. Women whom he loves.

15 Would you provide? life must be aromatic.
    There must be scent, somehow there must be some.
    Would you have flowers in his life? suggest
    Asters? a Really Good geranium?
    A white carnation? would you prescribe a Show
20 With the cold lilies, formal chrysanthemum
    Magnificence, poinsettias, and emphatic
    Red of prize roses? might his happiest
    Alternative (you muse) be, after all,
    A bit of gentle garden in the best
25 Of taste and straight tradition? Maybe so.
    But you forget, or did you ever know,
    His heritage of cabbage and pigtails,
    Old intimacy with alleys, garbage pails,
    Down in the deep (but always beautiful) South
30 Where roses blush their blithest (it is said)
    And sweet magnolias put Chanel[2] to shame.

    No! He has not a flower to his name.
    Except a feather one, for his lapel.
    Apart from that, if he should think of flowers
35 It is in terms of dandelions or death.
    Ah, there is little hope. You might as well—
    Unless you care to set the world a-boil
    And do a lot of equalizing things,
    Remove a little ermine, say, from kings,
40 Shake hands with paupers and appoint them men,
    For instance—certainly you might as well
    Leave him his lotion, lavender and oil.

    Let us proceed. Let us inspect, together
    With his meticulous and serious love,
45 The innards of this closet. Which is a vault
    Whose glory is not diamonds, not pearls,
    Not silver plate with just enough dull shine.
    But wonder-suits in yellow and in wine,
    Sarcastic green and zebra-striped cobalt.
50 All drapes. With shoulder padding that is wide
    And cocky and determined as his pride;
    Ballooning pants that taper off to ends
    Scheduled to choke precisely.

                            Here are hats
55 Like bright umbrellas; and hysterical ties
    Like narrow banners for some gathering war.

    People are so in need, in need of help.
    People want so much that they do not know.
    Below the tinkling trade of little coins
60 The gold impulse not possible to show
    Or spend. Promise piled over and betray.

---

2. I.e., expensive perfume or cologne.

These kneaded limbs receive the kiss of silk.
Then they receive the brave and beautiful
Embrace of some of that equivocal wool.
He looks into his mirror, loves himself—
The neat curve here; the angularity
That is appropriate at just its place;
The technique of a variegated grace.

Here is all his sculpture and his art
And all his architectural design.
Perhaps you would prefer to this a fine
Value of marble, complicated stone.
Would have him think with horror of baroque,
Rococo.[3] You forget and you forget.

He dances down the hotel steps that keep
Remnants of last night's high life and distress.
As spat-out purchased kisses and spilled beer.
He swallows sunshine with a secret yelp.
Passes to coffee and a roll or two.
Has breakfasted.

            Out. Sounds about him smear,
Become a unit. He hears and does not hear
The alarm clock meddling in somebody's sleep;
Children's governed Sunday happiness;
The dry tone of a plane; a woman's oath;
Consumption's spiritless expectoration;[4]
An indignant robin's resolute donation
Pinching a track through apathy and din;
Restaurant vendors weeping; and the L[5]
That comes on like a slightly horrible thought.

Pictures, too, as usual, are blurred.
He sees and does not see the broken windows
Hiding their shame with newsprint; little girl
With ribbons decking wornness, little boy
Wearing the trousers with the decentest patch,
To honor Sunday; women on their way
From "service," temperate holiness arranged
Ably on asking faces; men estranged
From music and from wonder and from joy
But far familiar with the guiding awe
of foodlessness.
            He loiters.
                      Restaurant vendors
Weep, or out of them rolls a restless glee.
The Lonesome Blues, the Long-lost Blues, I Want A
Big Fat Mama. Down these sore avenues

---

3. Two artistic styles, both elaborate and ornate.   5. I.e., the elevated train.
4. I.e., the cough of one with tuberculosis.

Comes no Saint-Saëns, no piquant elusive Grieg,
And not Tschaikovsky's wayward eloquence
And not the shapely tender drift of Brahms.[6]
110 But could he love them? Since a man must bring
To music what his mother spanked him for
When he was two: bits of forgotten hate,
Devotion: whether or not his mattress hurts:
The little dream his father humored: the thing
115 His sister did for money: what he ate
For breakfast—and for dinner twenty years
Ago last autumn: all his skipped desserts.

The pasts of his ancestors lean against
Him. Crowd him. Fog out his identity.
120 Hundreds of hungers mingle with his own,
Hundreds of voices advise so dexterously
He quite considers his reactions his,
Judges he walks most powerfully alone,
That everything is—simply what it is.

125 But movie-time approaches, time to boo
The hero's kiss, and boo the heroine
Whose ivory and yellow it is sin
For his eye to eat of. The Mickey Mouse,[7]
However, is for everyone in the house.

130 Squires his lady to dinner at Joe's Eats.
His lady alters as to leg and eye,
Thickness and height, such minor points as these,
From Sunday to Sunday. But no matter what
Her name or body positively she's
135 In Queen Lace stockings with ambitious heels
That strain to kiss the calves, and vivid shoes
Frontless and backless, Chinese fingernails,
Earrings, three layers of lipstick, intense hat
Dripping with the most voluble of veils.
140 Her affable extremes are like sweet bombs
About him, whom no middle grace or good
Could gratify. He had no education
In quiet arts of compromise. He would
Not understand your counsels on control, nor
145 Thank you for your late trouble.

                              At Joe's Eats
You get your fish or chicken on meat platters.
With coleslaw, macaroni, candied sweets,
Coffee and apple pie. You go out full.
150 (The end is—isn't it?—all that really matters.)

---

6. All symphonic composers: Charles Camille Saint-Saëns (1835–1921), French; Edvard Grieg (1843–1907), Norwegian; Pyotr Tchaikovsky (1840–1893), Russian; Johannes Brahms (1833–1897), German.
7. I.e., the cartoon short before the featured film.

And even and intrepid come
The tender boots of night to home.

Her body is like new brown bread
Under the Woolworth mignonette.[8]
155 Her body is a honey bowl
Whose waiting honey is deep and hot.
Her body is like summer earth,
Receptive, soft, and absolute . . .

1945

The Rites for Cousin Vit

Carried her unprotesting out the door.
Kicked back the casket-stand. But it can't hold her,
That stuff and satin aiming to enfold her,
The lid's contrition nor the bolts before.
5 Oh oh. Too much. Too much. Even now, surmise,
She rises in the sunshine. There she goes,
Back to the bars she knew and the repose
In love-rooms and the things in people's eyes.
Too vital and too squeaking. Must emerge.
10 Even now she does the snake-hips[1] with a hiss,
Slops the bad wine across her shantung,[2] talks
Of pregnancy, guitars and bridgework, walks
In parks or alleys, comes haply on the verge
Of happiness, haply hysterics. Is.

1949

From The Womanhood

3

Stand off, daughter of the dusk,
And do not wince when the bronzy lads
Hurry to cream-yellow shining.
It is plausible. The sun is a lode.

5 True, there is silver under
The veils of the darkness.
But few care to dig in the night
For the possible treasure of stars.

1949

---

8. Perfume made from the mignonette flower.
1. A dance created in Harlem in the 1920s.

2. A soft, heavy silk with a coarse surface (or a cotton fabric that imitates it).

The Bean Eaters

They eat beans mostly, this old yellow pair.
Dinner is a casual affair.
Plain chipware on a plain and creaking wood,
Tin flatware.

5   Two who are Mostly Good.
Two who have lived their day,
But keep on putting on their clothes
And putting things away.

And remembering . . .
10   Remembering, with twinklings and twinges,
As they lean over the beans in their rented back room
    that is full of beads and receipts and dolls and
    cloths, tobacco crumbs, vases and fringes.

1960

We Real Cool

The Pool Players. Seven at the Golden Shovel

We real cool. We
Left school. We

Lurk late. We
Strike straight. We

5   Sing sin. We
Thin gin. We

Jazz June. We
Die soon.

1960

Bronzeville[1] Woman in a Red Hat

hires out to Mrs. Miles

I

They had never had one in the house before.
The strangeness of it all. Like unleashing
A lion, really. Poised

---

1. Name given to a Chicago black ghetto.

       To pounce. A puma. A panther. A black
 5   Bear.
       There it stood in the door,
       Under a red hat that was rash, but refreshing—
       In a tasteless way, of course—across the dull dare,
       The semi-assault of that extraordinary blackness.
 10   The slackness
       Of that light pink mouth told little. The eyes told
          of heavy care. . . .
       But that was neither here nor there,
       And nothing to a wage-paying mistress as should
       Be getting her due whether life had been good
 15   For her slave, or bad.
       There it stood
       In the door. They had never had
       One in the house before.

       But the Irishwoman had left!
 20   A message had come.
       Something about a murder at home.
       A daughter's husband—"berserk," that was the phrase:
       The dear man had "gone berserk"
       And short work—
 25   With a hammer—had been made
       Of this daughter and her nights and days.
       The Irishwoman (underpaid,
       Mrs. Miles remembered with smiles),
       Who was a perfect jewel, a red-faced trump,
 30   A good old sort, a baker
       Of rum cake, a maker
       Of Mustard, would never return.
       Mrs. Miles had begged the bewitched woman
       To finish, at least, the biscuit blending,
 35   To tarry till the curry was done,
       To show some concern
       For the burning soup, to attend to the tending
       Of the tossed salad. "Inhuman,"
       Patsy Houlihan had called Mrs. Miles.
 40   "Inhuman." And "a fool."
       And "a cool
       One."

       The Alert Agency had leafed through its files—
       On short notice could offer
 45   Only this dusky duffer[2]
       That now made its way to her kitchen and sat on her
          kitchen stool.

---

2. Dense or clumsy person.

II

Her creamy child kissed by the black maid! square on the mouth!
World yelled, world writhed, world turned to light and rolled
Into her kitchen, nearly knocked her down.

50 Quotations, of course, from baby books were great
Ready armor; (but her animal distress
Wore, too and under, a subtler metal dress,
Inheritance of approximately hate.)
Say baby shrieked to see his finger bleed,
55 Wished human humoring—there was a kind
Of unintimate love, a love more of the mind
To order the nebulousness of that need.
—This was the way to put it, this the relief.
This sprayed a honey upon marvelous grime.
60 This told it possible to postpone the reef.
Fashioned a huggable darling out of crime.
Made monster personable in personal sight
By cracking mirrors down the personal night.

Disgust crawled through her as she chased the theme.
65 She, quite supposing purity despoiled,
Committed to sourness, disordered, soiled,
Went in to pry the ordure[3] from the cream.
Cooing, "Come." (Come out of the cannibal wilderness,
Dirt, dark, into the sun and bloomful air.
70 Return to freshness of your right world, wear
Sweetness again. Be done with beast, duress.)

Child with continuing cling issued his No in final fire,
     Kissed back the colored maid,
     Not wise enough to freeze or be afraid.
75   Conscious of kindness, easy creature bond.
     Love had been handy and rapid to respond.

Heat at the hairline, heat between the bowels,
Examining seeming coarse unnatural scene,
She saw all things except herself serene:
80 Child, big black woman, pretty kitchen towels.

                                1960

The Last Quatrain of the Ballad of Emmett Till[1]

after the murder,
after the burial
Emmett's mother is a pretty-faced thing;

---

3. Excrement.
1. An African American boy, 14 years old, who was lynched in Mississippi in 1955 for allegedly "leering" at a white woman.

                the tint of pulled taffy.
5   She sits in a red room,
                drinking black coffee.
    She kisses her killed boy.
                And she is sorry.
    Chaos in windy grays
10   through a red prairie.

1960

Malcolm X[1]

For Dudley Randall[2]

Original.
Ragged-round.
Rich-robust.

He had the hawk-man's eyes.
5   We gasped. We saw the maleness.
The maleness raking out and making guttural the air
and pushing us to walls.

And in a soft and fundamental hour
a sorcery devout and vertical
10   beguiled the world.

He opened us—
who was a key,

who was a man.

1967

---

1. Militant black nationalist leader of the Black Muslims (1925–1965), and one of the most prominent African Americans of the 1960s; in 1964 he formed his own Muslim organization and was no longer advocating strict separatism at the time of his assassination.
2. Black poet and publisher (1914–2000); this poem was published in a collection that he co-edited, *For Malcolm* (1967).

MURIEL SPARK
1918–2006

When she was an adolescent, Muriel Camberg composed torrid love letters that she signed with men's names and concealed around the house in the hope of giving her mother a good shock. This fictional gesture forecasts the witty impersonation characteristic of Spark's later writing in novels and short stories that frequently deal with blackmail, literary espionage, and the mysterious interconnections between illusion and reality.

Muriel Camberg was brought up in a prosperous Edinburgh neighborhood by a Presbyterian mother and a Jewish father. After attending James Gillespie's School for Girls, she traveled to South Africa, where she married S. O. Spark and gave birth to a son. The marriage ended quickly and several years later Spark returned to Great Britain, where she worked for the Political Intelligence Department until the end of World War II. Then she supported herself as a freelance writer and editor, publishing several books collaboratively with Derek Stanford, including lives of the Brontës and of Mary Shelley. After converting to Catholicism at the age of thirty-six, Spark completed her first novel, *The Comforters* (1957). Her subsequent stories and novels, set for the most part in England or in Africa, often unmask the hypocrisies of professional Catholics even as they dramatize the dilemmas of authentic spiritual conversions. It was, however, the grotesque comedy of *Memento Mori* (1959) that established Spark's reputation. Later novels—*The Prime of Miss Jean Brodie* (1961), *The Girls of Slender Means* (1963), and *The Abbess of Crewe* (1974), in particular—turn her irony toward the delusions and deceits of communities of women. In 2003, Spark published a collection of her ghost stories and in 2004 a collection of her poems. "The Black Madonna" slyly satirizes not only the spiritual bankruptcy of characters who congratulate themselves on their moral correctness but also the mythologizing of a so-called maternal instinct.

The Black Madonna

When the Black Madonna was installed in the Church of the Sacred Heart the Bishop himself came to consecrate it. His long purple train was upheld by the two curliest of the choir. The day was favored suddenly with thin October sunlight as he crossed the courtyard from the presbytery[1] to the church, as the procession followed him chanting the Litany of the Saints: five priests in vestments of white heavy silk interwoven with glinting threads, four lay officials with straight red robes, then the confraternities and the tangled columns of the Mothers' Union.

The new town of Whitney Clay had a large proportion of Roman Catholics, especially among the nurses at the new hospital; and at the paper mills, too, there were many Catholics, drawn inland from Liverpool by the new housing estate; likewise, with the canning factories.

The Black Madonna had been given to the church by a recent convert. It was carved out of bog oak.

"They found the wood in the bog. Had been there hundreds of years. They sent for the sculptor right away by phone. He went over to Ireland and carved it there and then. You see, he had to do it while it was still wet."

"Looks a bit like contemporary art."

"Nah, that's not contemporary art, it's old-fashioned. If you'd ever seen contemporary work you *know* it was old-fashioned."

"Looks like contemp—"

"It's old-*fashioned*. Else how'd it get sanctioned to be put up?"

"It's not so nice as the Immaculate Conception at Lourdes.[2] That lifts you up."

Everyone got used, eventually, to the Black Madonna with her square

---

1. The house of the parish priest.
2. A town in France that is the site of one of the most famous shrines of the Virgin Mary, associated with miraculous cures.

hands and straight carved draperies. There was a movement to dress it up in vestments, or at least a lace veil.

"She looks a bit gloomy, Father, don't you think?"

"No," said the priest, "I think it looks fine. If you start dressing it up in cloth you'll spoil the line."

Sometimes people came from London especially to see the Black Madonna, and these were not Catholics; they were, said the priest, probably no religion at all, poor souls, though gifted with faculties. They came, as if to a museum, to see the line of the Black Madonna which must not be spoiled by vestments.

The new town of Whitney Clay had swallowed up the old village. One or two cottages with double dormer windows, an inn called "The Tyger," a Methodist chapel and three small shops represented the village; the three small shops were already threatened by the Council;[3] the Methodists were fighting to keep their chapel. Only the double dormer cottages and the inn were protected by the Nation and so had to be suffered by the Town Planning Committee.

The town was laid out like geometry in squares, arcs (to allow for the bypass) and isosceles triangles, breaking off, at one point, to skirt the old village which, from the aerial view, looked like a merry doodle on the page.

Manders Road was one side of a parallelogram of green-bordered streets. It was named after one of the founders of the canning concern, Manders' Figs in Syrup, and it comprised a row of shops and a long high block of flats[4] named Cripps House after the late Sir Stafford Cripps who had laid the foundation stone. In flat twenty-two on the fifth floor of Cripps House lived Raymond and Lou Parker. Raymond Parker was a foreman at the motor works, and was on the management committee. He had been married for fifteen years to Lou, who was thirty-seven at the time that the miraculous powers of the Black Madonna came to be talked of.

Of the twenty-five couples who live in Cripps House five were Catholics. All, except Raymond and Lou Parker, had children. A sixth family had recently been moved by the Council into one of the six-roomed houses because of the seven children besides the grandfather.

Raymond and Lou were counted lucky to have obtained their three-roomed flat although they had no children. People with children had priority; but their name had been on the waiting list for years, and some said Raymond had a pull with one of the Councilors who was a director of the motor works.

The Parkers were among the few tenants of Cripps House who owned a motor car. They did not, like most of their neighbors, have a television receiver, for being childless they had been able to afford to expand themselves in the way of taste, so that their habits differed slightly and their amusements considerably, from those of their neighbors. The Parkers went to the pictures only when *The Observer*[5] had praised the film; they considered television not their sort of thing; they adhered to their religion; they voted Labour; they believed that the twentieth century was the best so far; they assented to the doctrine of original sin;[6] they frequently applied the word

---

3. Local authority, which is responsible for housing.
4. Apartments.
5. A liberal national paper.
6. The doctrine that all human beings, as a result of the Fall of Adam and Eve from divine grace, are born in a state of sin.

"Victorian" to ideas and people they did not like—for instance, when a local Town Councilor resigned his office Raymond said, "He had to go. He's Victorian. And far too young for the job"; and Lou said Jane Austen's[7] books were too Victorian; and anyone who opposed the abolition of capital punishment was Victorian. Raymond took the *Reader's Digest,* a magazine called *Motoring* and *The Catholic Herald.* Lou took *The Queen, Woman's Own* and *Life.* Their daily paper was *The News Chronicle.* They read two books apiece each week. Raymond preferred travel books; Lou liked novels.

For the first five years of their married life they had been worried about not having children. Both had submitted themselves to medical tests as a result of which Lou had a course of injections. These were unsuccessful. It had been a special disappointment since both came from large sprawling Catholic families. None of their married brothers and sisters had less than three children. One of Lou's sisters, now widowed, had eight; they sent her a pound a week.

Their flat in Cripps House had three rooms and a kitchen. All round them their neighbors were saving up to buy houses. A council flat, once obtained, was a mere platform in space to further the progress of the rocket. This ambition was not shared by Raymond and Lou; they were not only content, they were delighted, with these civic chambers, and indeed took something of an aristocratic view of them, not without a self-conscious feeling of being free, in this particular, from the prejudices of that middle class to which they as good as belonged. "One day," said Lou, "it will be the thing to live in a council flat."

They were eclectic as to their friends. Here, it is true, they differed slightly from each other. Raymond was for inviting the Ackleys to meet the Farrells. Mr. Ackley was an accountant at the Electricity Board. Mr. and Mrs. Farrell were respectively a sorter at Manders' Figs in Syrup and an usherette at the Odeon.

"After all," argued Raymond, "they're all Catholics."

"Ah well," said Lou, "but now, their interests are different. The Farrells wouldn't know what the Ackleys were talking about. The Ackleys like politics. The Farrells like to tell jokes. I'm not a snob, only sensible."

"Oh, please yourself." For no-one could call Lou a snob, and everyone knew she was sensible.

Their choice of acquaintance was wide by reason of their active church membership: that is to say, they were members of various guilds and confraternities. Raymond was a sidesman,[8] and he also organized the weekly football lottery in aid of the Church Decoration Fund. Lou felt rather out of things when the Mothers' Union met and had special Masses, for the Mothers' Union was the only group she did not qualify for. Having been a nurse before her marriage she was, however, a member of the Nurses' Guild.

Thus, most of their Catholic friends came from different departments of life. Others, connected with the motor works where Raymond was a foreman, were of different social grades to which Lou was more alive than Raymond. He let her have her way, as a rule, when it came to a question of which would mix with which.

---

7. English novelist (1775–1817); see Vol. 1, p. 459; her writings do not fall into the Victorian period (1837–1901).

8. Elected assistant to a parish churchwarden.

A dozen Jamaicans were taken on at the motor works. Two came into Raymond's department. He invited them to the flat one evening to have coffee. They were unmarried, very polite and black. The quiet one was called Henry Pierce and the talkative one, Oxford St. John. Lou, to Raymond's surprise and pleasure, decided that all their acquaintance, from top to bottom, must meet Henry and Oxford. All along he had known she was not a snob, only sensible, but he had rather feared she would consider the mixing of their new black and their old white friends not sensible.

"I'm glad you like Henry and Oxford," he said. "I'm glad we're able to introduce them to so many people." For the dark pair had, within a month, spent nine evenings at Cripps House; they had met accountants, teachers, packers and sorters. Only Tina Farrell, the usherette, had not seemed to understand the quality of these occasions: "Quite nice chaps, them darkies, when you get to know them."

"You mean Jamaicans," said Lou. "Why shouldn't they be nice? They're no different from anyone else."

"Yes, yes, that's what I mean," said Tina.

"We're all equal," stated Lou. "Don't forget there are black Bishops."

"Jesus, I never said we were the equal of a Bishop," Tina said, very bewildered.

"Well, don't call them darkies."

Sometimes, on summer Sunday afternoons Raymond and Lou took their friends for a run in their car, ending up at a riverside road-house. The first time they turned up with Oxford and Henry they felt defiant; but there were no objections, there was no trouble at all. Soon the dark pair ceased to be a novelty. Oxford St. John took up with a pretty red-haired bookkeeper, and Henry Pierce, missing his companion, spent more of his time at the Parkers' flat. Lou and Raymond had planned to spend their two weeks' summer holiday in London. "Poor Henry," said Lou. "He'll miss us."

Once you brought him out he was not so quiet as you thought at first. Henry was twenty-four, desirous of knowledge in all fields, shining very much in eyes, skin, teeth, which made him seem all the more eager. He called out the maternal in Lou, and to some extent the avuncular in Raymond. Lou used to love him when he read out lines from his favorite poems which he had copied into an exercise book.

> *Haste thee, nymph, and bring with thee*
> *Jest and youthful jollity,*
> *Sport that*[9] . . .

Lou would interrupt: "You should say jest, jollity—not yest, yollity."

"Jest," he said carefully. "And laughter holding both his sides," he continued. "*Laughter*—hear that, Lou?—*laughter*. That's what the human race was made for. Those folks that go round gloomy, Lou, they . . ."

Lou loved this talk. Raymond puffed his pipe benignly. After Henry had gone Raymond would say what a pity it was such an intelligent young fellow had lapsed. For Henry had been brought up in a Roman Catholic mission. He had, however, abandoned religion. He was fond of saying, "The superstition of today is the science of yesterday."

---

9. Slightly misquoted from John Milton's "L'Allegro" (1631).

"I can't allow," Raymond would say, "that the Catholic Faith is superstition. I can't allow that."

"He'll return to the Church one day"—this was Lou's contribution, whether Henry was present or not. If she said it in front of Henry he would give her an angry look. These were the only occasions when Henry lost his cheerfulness and grew quiet again.

Raymond and Lou prayed for Henry, that he might regain his faith. Lou said her rosary[1] three times a week before the Black Madonna.

"He'll miss us when we go on our holidays."

Raymond telephoned to the hotel in London. "Have you a single room for a young gentleman accompanying Mr. and Mrs. Parker?" He added, "a colored gentleman." To his pleasure a room was available, and to his relief there was no objection to Henry's color.

They enjoyed their London holiday, but it was somewhat marred by a visit to that widowed sister of Lou's to whom she allowed a pound a week towards the rearing of her eight children. Lou had not seen her sister Elizabeth for nine years.

They went to her one day towards the end of their holiday. Henry sat at the back of the car beside a large suitcase stuffed with old clothes for Elizabeth. Raymond at the wheel kept saying, "Poor Elizabeth—eight kids," which irritated Lou, though she kept her peace.

Outside the underground[2] station at Victoria Park, where they stopped to ask the way, Lou felt a strange sense of panic. Elizabeth lived in a very downward quarter of Bethnal Green,[3] and in the past nine years since she had seen her Lou's memory of the shabby ground-floor rooms with their peeling walls and bare boards, had made a kinder nest for itself. Sending off the postal order to her sister each week she had gradually come to picture the habitation at Bethnal Green in an almost monastic light; it would be bare but well-scrubbed, spotless, and shining with Brasso[4] and holy poverty. The floor boards gleamed. Elizabeth was gray-haired, lined, but neat. The children well behaved, sitting down betimes to their broth in two rows along an almost refectory table. It was not till they had reached Victoria Park that Lou felt the full force of the fact that everything would be different from what she had imagined. "It may have gone down since I was last there," she said to Raymond who had never visited Elizabeth before.

"What's gone down?"

"Poor Elizabeth's place."

Lou had not taken much notice of Elizabeth's dull little monthly letters, almost illiterate, for Elizabeth, as she herself always said, was not much of a scholar. "James is at another job I hope that's the finish of the bother I had my blood presiure there was a Health visitor[5] very nice. Also the assistance they sent my Dinner all the time and for the kids at home they call it meals on Wheels. I pray to the Almighty that James is well out of his bother he never lets on at sixteen their all the same never open his mouth but Gods eyes are not shut. Thanks for P.O.[6] you will be rewarded your affect sister Elizabeth."

---

1. A Catholic devotion consisting of a series of repeated prayers; the devout use a string of beads, also called a rosary, to keep track of the count.
2. Subway.
3. Factory district in London's East End.
4. Brand of metal polish.
5. A registered nurse employed by the National Health Service.
6. Postal orders.

Lou tried to piece together in her mind the gist of nine years' such letters. James was the eldest; she supposed he had been in trouble.

"I ought to have asked Elizabeth about young James," said Lou. "She wrote to me last year that he was in a bother, there was talk of him being sent away, but I didn't take it in at the time, I was busy."

"You can't take everything on your shoulders," said Raymond. "You do very well by Elizabeth." They had pulled up outside the house where Elizabeth lived on the ground floor. Lou looked at the chipped paint, the dirty windows and torn gray-white curtains and was reminded with startling clarity of her hopeless childhood in Liverpool from which, miraculously, hope had lifted her, and had come true, for the nuns had got her that job; and she had trained as a nurse among white-painted beds, and white shining walls, and tiles, hot water everywhere and Dettol[7] without stint. When she had first married she had wanted all white-painted furniture that you could wash and liberate from germs; but Raymond had been for oak, he did not understand the pleasure of hygiene and new enamel paint, for his upbringing had been orderly, he had been accustomed to a lounge suite and autumn tints in the front room all his life. And now Lou stood and looked at the outside of Elizabeth's place and felt she had gone right back.

On the way back to the hotel Lou chattered with relief that it was over. "Poor Elizabeth, she hasn't had much of a chance. I liked little Francis, what did you think of little Francis, Ray?"

Raymond did not like being called Ray, but he made no objection for he knew that Lou had been under a strain. Elizabeth had not been very pleasant. She had expressed admiration for Lou's hat, bag, gloves and shoes which were all navy blue, but she had used an accusing tone. The house had been smelly and dirty. "I'll show you round," Elizabeth had said in a tone of mock refinement, and they were forced to push through a dark narrow passage behind her skinny form till they came to the big room where the children slept. A row of old iron beds each with a tumble of dark blanket rugs, no sheets. Raymond was indignant at the sight and hoped that Lou was not feeling upset. He knew very well Elizabeth had a decent living income from a number of public sources, and was simply a slut, one of those who would not help themselves.

"Ever thought of taking a job, Elizabeth?" he had said, and immediately realized his stupidity. But Elizabeth took her advantage. "What d'you mean? *I'm* not going to leave my kids in no nursery. *I'm* not going to send them to no home. What kids need these days is a good home life and that's what they get." And she added, "God's eyes are not shut," in a tone which was meant for him, Raymond, to get at him for doing well in life.

Raymond distributed half-crowns[8] to the younger children and deposited on the table half-crowns for those who were out playing in the street.

"Goin' already?" said Elizabeth in her tone of reproach. But she kept eyeing Henry with interest, and the reproachful tone was more or less a routine affair.

"You from the States?" Elizabeth said to Henry.

---

7. A liquid antiseptic (equivalent to Lysol).   8. Coins worth 2½ shillings (i.e., ⅛ of a pound).

Henry sat on the edge of his sticky chair and answered, no, from Jamaica, while Raymond winked at him to cheer him.

"During the war there was a lot of boys like you from the States," Elizabeth said, giving him a sideways look.

Henry held out his hand to the second youngest child, a girl of seven, and said, "Come talk to me."

The child said nothing, only dipped into the box of sweets which Lou had brought.

"Come talk," said Henry.

Elizabeth laughed. "If she does talk you'll be sorry you ever asked. She's got a tongue in her head, that one. You should hear her cheeking up to the teachers." Elizabeth's bones jerked with laughter among her loose clothes. There was a lopsided double bed in the corner, and beside it a table cluttered with mugs, tins, a comb and brush, a number of hair curlers, a framed photograph of the Sacred Heart, and also Raymond noticed what he thought erroneously to be a box of contraceptives. He decided to say nothing to Lou about this; he was quite sure she must have observed other things which he had not; possibly things of a more distressing nature.

Lou's chatter on the way back to the hotel had a touch of hysteria. "Raymond, dear," she said in her most chirpy west-end[9] voice. "I simply *had* to give the poor dear *all* my next week's housekeeping money. We shall have to starve, darling, when we get home. That's *simply* what we shall have to do."

"O.K.," said Raymond.

"I ask you," Lou shrieked, "what else could I do, what *could* I do?"

"Nothing at all," said Raymond, "but what you've done."

"My own *sister,* my dear," said Lou; "and did you see the way she had her hair bleached?—All streaky, and she used to have a lovely head of hair."

"I wonder if she tries to raise herself?" said Raymond. "With all those children she could surely get better accommodation if only she—"

"That sort," said Henry, leaning forward from the back of the car, "never moves. It's the slum mentality, man. Take some folks I've seen back home—"

"There's no comparison," Lou snapped suddenly, "this is quite a different case."

Raymond glanced at her in surprise; Henry sat back, offended. Lou was thinking wildly, what a cheek *him* talking like a snob. At least Elizabeth's white.

Their prayers for the return of faith to Henry Pierce were so far answered in that he took a tubercular turn which was followed by a religious one. He was sent off to a sanatorium in Wales with a promise from Lou and Raymond to visit him before Christmas. Meantime, they applied themselves to Our Lady for the restoration of Henry's health.

Oxford St. John, whose love affair with the red-haired girl had come to grief, now frequented their flat, but he could never quite replace Henry in their affections. Oxford was older and less refined than Henry. He would stand in front of the glass in their kitchen and tell himself, "Man, you just a big black bugger." He kept referring to himself as black, which of course he was, Lou thought, but it was not the thing to say. He stood in the doorway

---

9. Toney, (characteristic of London's fashionable West End).

with his arms and smile thrown wide: "I am black but comely, O ye daughters of Jerusalem."[1] And once, when Raymond was out, Oxford brought the conversation round to that question of being black *all over*, which made Lou very uncomfortable and she kept looking at the clock and dropped stitches in her knitting.

Three times a week when she went to the black Our Lady with her rosary to ask for the health of Henry Pierce, she asked also that Oxford St. John would get another job in another town, for she did not like to make objections, telling her feelings to Raymond; there were no objections to make that you could put your finger on. She could not very well complain that Oxford was common; Raymond despised snobbery, and so did she, it was a very delicate question. She was amazed when, within three weeks, Oxford announced that he was thinking of looking for a job in Manchester.

Lou said to Raymond "Do you know, there's something *in* what they say about the bog oak statue in the church."

"There may be," said Raymond. "People say so."

Lou could not tell him how she had petitioned the removal of Oxford St. John. But when she got a letter from Henry Pierce to say he was improving, she told Raymond, "You see, we asked for Henry to get back the Faith, and so he did. Now we ask for his recovery and he's improving."

"He's having good treatment at the sanatorium," Raymond said. But he added, "Of course we'll have to keep up the prayers." He himself, though not a rosary man, knelt before the Black Madonna every Saturday evening after Benediction to pray for Henry Pierce.

Whenever they saw Oxford he was talking of leaving Whitney Clay. Raymond said, "He's making a big mistake going to Manchester. A big place can be very lonely. I hope he'll change his mind."

"He won't," said Lou, so impressed was she now by the powers of the Black Madonna. She was good and tired of Oxford St. John with his feet up on her cushions, and calling himself a nigger.

"We'll miss him," said Raymond, "he's such a cheery big soul."

"We will," said Lou. She was reading the parish magazine, which she seldom did, although she was one of the voluntary workers who sent them out, addressing hundreds of wrappers every month. She had vaguely noticed, in previous numbers, various references to the Black Madonna, how she had granted this or that favor. Lou had heard that people sometimes came from neighboring parishes to pray at the Church of the Sacred Heart because of the statue. Some said they came from all over England, but whether this was to admire the art-work or to pray, Lou was not sure. She gave her attention to the article in the parish magazine:

> While not wishing to make excessive claims ... many prayers answered and requests granted to the Faithful in an exceptional way ... two remarkable cures effected, but medical evidence is, of course, still in reserve, a certain lapse of time being necessary to ascertain permanency of cure. The first of these cases was a child of twelve suffering from leukemia. . . . The second . . . While not desiring to create a *cultus* where none is due, we must remember it is always our duty to honor Our Blessed Lady, the dispenser of all graces, to whom we owe . . .

---

1. Song of Solomon 1.5.

Another aspect of the information received by the Father Rector concerning our "Black Madonna" is one pertaining to childless couples of which three cases have come to his notice. In each case the couple claim to have offered constant devotion to the "Black Madonna" and in two of the cases specific requests were made for the favor of a child. In *all* cases the prayers were answered. The proud parents. . . . It should be the loving duty of every parishioner to make a special thanksgiving. . . . The Father Rector will be grateful for any further information. . . .

"Look, Raymond," said Lou. "Read this."

They decided to put in for a baby to the Black Madonna.

The following Saturday, when they drove to the church for Benediction Lou jangled her rosary. Raymond pulled up outside the church. "Look here, Lou," he said, "do you want a baby in any case?"—for he partly thought she was only putting the Black Madonna to the test—"Do you want a child, after all these years?"

This was a new thought to Lou. She considered her neat flat and tidy routine, the entertaining with her good coffee cups, the weekly papers and the library books, the tastes which they would not have been able to cultivate had they had a family of children. She thought of her nice young looks which everyone envied, and her freedom of movement.

"Perhaps we should try," she said. "God won't give us a child if we aren't meant to have one."

"We have to make some decisions for ourselves," he said. "And to tell you the truth if *you* don't want a child, *I* don't."

"There's no harm in praying for one," she said.

"You have to be careful what you pray for," he said. "You mustn't tempt Providence."

She thought of her relatives, and Raymond's, all married with children. She thought of her sister Elizabeth with her eight, and remembered that one who cheeked up to the teachers, so pretty and sulky and shabby, and she remembered the fat baby Francis sucking his dummy[2] and clutching Elizabeth's bony neck.

"I don't see why I shouldn't have a baby," said Lou.

Oxford St. John departed at the end of the month. He promised to write, but they were not surprised when weeks passed and they had no word. "I don't suppose we shall ever hear from him again," said Lou. Raymond thought he detected satisfaction in her voice, and would have thought she was getting snobbish as women do as they get older, losing sight of their ideals, had she not gone on to speak of Henry Pierce. Henry had written to say he was nearly cured, but had been advised to return to the West Indies.

"We must go and see him," said Lou. "We promised. What about the Sunday after next?"

"O.K.," said Raymond.

It was the Saturday before that Sunday when Lou had her first sick turn. She struggled out of bed to attend Benediction, but had to leave suddenly during the service and was sick behind the church in the presbytery yard. Raymond took her home, though she protested against cutting out her rosary to the Black Madonna.

---

2. Pacifier.

"After only six weeks!" she said, and she could hardly tell whether her sickness was due to excitement or nature. "Only six weeks ago," she said—and her voice had a touch of its old Liverpool—"did we go to that Black Madonna and the prayer's answered, see."

Raymond looked at her in awe as he held the bowl for her sickness. "Are you sure?" he said.

She was well enough next day to go to visit Henry in the sanatorium. He was fatter and, she thought, a little coarser: and tough in his manner, as if once having been nearly disembodied he was not going to let it happen again. He was leaving the country very soon. He promised to come and see them before he left. Lou barely skimmed through his next letter before handing it over to Raymond.

Their visitors, now, were ordinary white ones. "Not so colorful," Raymond said, "as Henry and Oxford were." Then he looked embarrassed lest he should seem to be making a joke about the word colored.

"Do you miss the niggers?" said Tina Farrell, and Lou forgot to correct her.

Lou gave up most of her church work in order to sew and knit for the baby. Raymond gave up the *Reader's Digest*. He applied for promotion and got it; he became a departmental manager. The flat was now a waiting-room for next summer, after the baby was born, when they would put down the money for a house. They hoped for one of the new houses on a building site on the outskirts of the town.

"We shall need a garden," Lou explained to her friends. "I'll join the Mothers' Union," she thought. Meantime the spare bedroom was turned into a nursery. Raymond made a cot, regardless that some of the neighbors complained of the hammering. Lou prepared a cradle, trimmed it with frills. She wrote to her relatives; she wrote to Elizabeth, sent her five pounds, and gave notice that there would be no further weekly payments, seeing that they would now need every penny.

"She doesn't require it anyway," said Raymond. "The Welfare State looks after people like Elizabeth." And he told Lou about the contraceptives he thought he had seen on the table by the double bed. Lou became very excited about this. "How did you know they were contraceptives? What did they look like? Why didn't you tell me before? What a cheek, calling herself a Catholic, do you think she has a man, then?"

Raymond was sorry he had mentioned the subject.

"Don't worry, dear, don't upset yourself, dear."

"And she told me she goes to Mass every Sunday, and all the kids go excepting James. No wonder he's got into trouble with an example like that. I might have known, with her peroxide hair. A pound a week I've been sending up to now, that's fifty-two pounds a year. I would never have done it, calling herself a Catholic with birth control by her bedside."

"Don't upset yourself, dear."

Lou prayed to the Black Madonna three times a week for a safe delivery and a healthy child. She gave her story to the Father Rector who announced it in the next parish magazine. "Another case has come to light of the kindly favor of our 'Black Madonna' towards a childless couple . . ." Lou recited her rosary before the statue until it was difficult for her to kneel, and, when she stood, could not see her feet. The Mother of God with her black bog-oaken drapery, her high black cheekbones and square hands looked more virginal than ever to Lou as she stood counting her beads in front of her stomach.

She said to Raymond, "If it's a girl we must have Mary as one of the names. But not the first name, it's too ordinary."

"Please yourself, dear," said Raymond. The doctor had told him it might be a difficult birth.

"Thomas, if it's a boy," she said, "after my uncle. But if it's a girl I'd like something fancy for a first name."

He thought, Lou's slipping, she didn't used to say that word, fancy.

"What about Dawn?" she said. "I like the sound of Dawn. Then Mary for a second name. Dawn Mary Parker, it sounds sweet."

"Dawn! That's not a Christian name," he said. Then he told her, "Just as you please, dear."

"Or Thomas Parker," she said.

She had decided to go into the maternity wing of the hospital like everyone else. But near the time she let Raymond change her mind, since he kept saying, "At your age, dear, it might be more difficult than for the younger women. Better book a private ward, we'll manage the expense."

In fact, it was a very easy birth, a girl. Raymond was allowed in to see Lou in the late afternoon. She was half asleep. "The nurse will take you to see the baby in the nursery ward," she told him. "She's lovely, but terribly red."

"They're always red at birth," said Raymond.

He met the nurse in the corridor. "Any chance of seeing the baby? My wife said . . ."

She looked flustered. "I'll get the Sister," she said.

"Oh, I don't want to give any trouble, only my wife said—"

"That's all right. Wait here, Mr. Parker."

The Sister appeared, a tall grave woman. Raymond thought her to be short-sighted for she seemed to look at him fairly closely before she bade him follow her.

The baby was round and very red, with dark curly hair.

"Fancy her having hair. I thought they were born bald," said Raymond.

"They sometimes have hair at birth," said the Sister.

"She's very red in color." Raymond began comparing his child with those in the other cots. "Far more so than the others."

"Oh, that will wear off."

Next day he found Lou in a half-stupor. She had been given a strong sedative following an attack of screaming hysteria. He sat by her bed, bewildered. Presently a nurse beckoned him from the door. "Will you have a word with the Matron?"

"Your wife is upset about her baby," said the matron. "You see, the color. She's a beautiful baby, perfect. It's a question of the color."

"I noticed the baby was red," said Raymond, "but the nurse said—"

"Oh, the red will go. It changes, you know. But the baby will certainly be brown, if not indeed black, as indeed we think she will be. A beautiful healthy child."

"Black?" said Raymond.

"Yes, indeed we think so, indeed I must say, certainly so," said the matron. "We did not expect your wife to take it so badly when we told her. We've had plenty of dark babies here, but most of their mothers expect it."

"There must be a mix-up. You must have mixed up the babies," said Raymond.

"There's no question of mix-up," said the matron sharply. "We'll soon settle that. We've had some of *that* before."

"But neither of us are dark," said Raymond. "You've seen my wife. You see me—"

"That's something you must work out for yourselves. I'd have a word with the doctor if I were you. But whatever conclusion you come to, please don't upset your wife at this stage. She has already refused to feed the child, says it isn't hers, which is ridiculous."

"Was it Oxford St. John?" said Raymond.

"Raymond, the doctor told you not to come here upsetting me. I'm feeling terrible."

"Was it Oxford St. John?"

"Clear out of here, you swine, saying things like that."

He demanded to be taken to see the baby, as he had done every day for a week. The nurses were gathered round it, neglecting the squalling whites in the other cots for the sight of their darling black. She was indeed quite black, with a woolly crop and tiny negroid nostrils. She had been baptized that morning, thought not in her parents' presence. One of the nurses had stood as godmother.

The nurses dispersed in a flurry as Raymond approached. He looked hard at the baby. It looked back with its black button eyes. He saw the nametab round its neck, "Dawn Mary Parker."

He got hold of a nurse in the corridor. "Look here, you just take that name Parker off that child's neck. The name's not Parker, it isn't my child."

The nurse said, "Get away, we're busy."

"There's just a *chance*," said the doctor to Raymond, "that if there's ever been black blood in your family or your wife's, it's coming out now. It's a very long chance. I've never known it happen in my experience, but I've heard of cases, I could read them up."

"There's nothing like that in my family," said Raymond. He thought of Lou, the obscure Liverpool antecedents. The parents had died before he had met Lou.

"It could be several generations back," said the doctor.

Raymond went home, avoiding the neighbors who would stop him to inquire after Lou. He rather regretted smashing up the cot in his first fury. That was something low coming out in him. But again, when he thought of the tiny black hands of the baby with their pink fingernails he did not regret smashing the cot.

He was successful in tracing the whereabouts of Oxford St. John. Even before he heard the result of Oxford's blood test he said to Lou, "Write and ask your relations if there's been any black blood in the family."

"Write and ask *yours*," she said.

She refused to look at the black baby. The nurses fussed round it all day, and come to report its progress to Lou.

"Pull yourself together, Mrs. Parker, she's a lovely child."

"You must care for your infant," said the priest.

"You don't know what I'm suffering," Lou said.

"In the name of God," said the priest, "if you're a Catholic Christian you've got to expect to suffer."

"I can't go against my nature," said Lou. "I can't be expected to—"

Raymond said to her one day in the following week, "The blood tests are all right, the doctor says."

"What do you mean, all right?"

"Oxford's blood and the baby's don't tally, and—"

"Oh, shut up," she said. "The baby's black and your blood tests can't make it white."

"No," he said. He had fallen out with his mother, through his inquiries whether there had been colored blood in his family. "The doctor says," he said, "that these black mixtures sometimes occur in seaport towns. It might have been generations back."

"One thing," said Lou. "I'm not going to take that child back to the flat."

"You'll have to," he said.

Elizabeth wrote her a letter which Raymond intercepted:

"Dear Lou Raymond is asking if we have any blacks in the family well thats funny you have a colored God is not asleep. There was that Flinn cousin Tommy at Liverpool he was very dark they put it down to the past a nigro off a ship that would be before our late Mothers Time God rest her soul she would turn in her grave you shoud have kept up your bit to me whats a pound a Week to you. It was on our fathers side the color and Mary Flinn you remember at the dairy was dark remember her hare was like nigro hare it must be back in the olden days the nigro some ansester but it is only nature. I thank the almighty it has missed my kids and your hubby must think it was that nigro you was showing off when you came to my place. I wish you all the best as a widow with kids you shoud send my money as per usual you affec sister Elizabeth."

"I gather from Elizabeth," said Raymond to Lou, "that there *was* some element of color in your family. Of course, you couldn't be expected to know about it. I do think, though, that some kind of record should be kept."

"Oh, shut *up*," said Lou. "The baby's black and nothing can make it white."

Two days before Lou left the hospital she had a visitor, although she had given instructions that no-one except Raymond should be let in to see her. This lapse she attributed to the nasty curiosity of the nurses, for it was Henry Pierce come to say goodbye before embarkation. He stayed less than five minutes.

"Why, Mrs. Parker, your visitor didn't stay long," said the nurse.

"No, I soon got rid of him. I thought I made it clear to you that I didn't want to see anyone. You shouldn't have let him in."

"Oh, sorry, Mrs. Parker, but the young gentleman looked so upset when we told him so. He said he was going abroad and it was his last chance, he might never see you again. He said, 'How's the baby?' and we said, 'Tip-top.'"

"I know what's in your mind," said Lou. "But it isn't true. I've got the blood tests."

"Oh, Mrs. Parker, I wouldn't suggest for a minute . . ."

"She must have went with one of they niggers that used to come."

Lou could never be sure if that was what she heard from the doorways and landings as she climbed the stairs of Cripps House, the neighbors hushing their conversation as she approached.

"I can't take to the child. Try as I do, I simply can't even like it."

"Nor me," said Raymond. "Mind you, if it was anyone else's child I would think it was all right. It's just the thought of it being mine, and people thinking it isn't."

"That's just it," she said.

One of Raymond's colleagues had asked him that day how his friends Oxford and Henry were getting on. Raymond had to look twice before he decided that the question was innocent. But one never knew. . . . Already Lou and Raymond had approached the adoption society. It was now only a matter of waiting for word.

"If that child was mine," said Tina Farrell, "I'd never part with her. I wish we could afford to adopt another. She's the loveliest little darkie in the world."

"You wouldn't think so," said Lou, "if she really was yours. Imagine it for yourself, waking up to find you've had a black baby that everyone thinks has a nigger for its father."

"It *would* be a shock," Tina said, and tittered.

"We've got the blood test," said Lou quickly.

Raymond got a transfer to London. They got word about the adoption very soon.

"We've done the right thing," said Lou. "Even the priest had to agree with that, considering how strongly we felt against keeping the child."

"Oh, he said it was a good thing?"

"No, not a *good* thing. In fact he said it would have been a good thing if we could have kept the baby. But failing that, we did the *right* thing. Apparently, there's a difference."

1960

LOUISE BENNETT
(1919–2006)

Affectionately known to Jamaican audiences as "Miss Lou," the poet and folklorist Louise Bennett became a celebrity on the "world music" scene with her lively renditions of the Caribbean combination of jazz, country music, and reggae known as "mento." But besides being a popular performer and a Jamaican cultural icon, Bennett was a serious scholar of her country's language, history, and traditions; and in the words of one critic, she was "the preeminent West Indian poet of Creole verse." Her lively dramatic monologues exploit the wit and irony of Jamaican English, a dialect whose vivid phrases are drawn from a diverse mix of English and other European languages along with such African tongues as Twi and Ewe. "My main thing is to get people to respect the language," Bennett told one interviewer; and to another she explained that she "persisted in writing in spite of all the opposition" from exponents of standard English because "there was such rich material in the dialect that I felt I wanted to put on paper some of the wonderful things that people say."

"Miss Lou" was born in Kingston to working-class parents: her mother was a dressmaker, her father a baker who died when she was just seven. At fourteen, she composed her first dialect poem, and she began performing her work in public when she was nineteen. Her first collection of poems, *Dialect Verses,* appeared in 1942, and she then began publishing regularly in the *Gleaner,* a major Jamaican newspaper. In the late 1940s, she went to England to study at the Royal Academy of Dramatic Art on a prestigious scholarship. After graduation she worked for a time in British theater; then—homesick for her native land—she returned to Jamaica, where she taught drama in high schools and universities while also writing and performing poetry, gathering folklore, and touring the country as a drama specialist for the Jamaican Social Welfare Commission. In the midst of all these activities, she found time to create a regular radio show, *Miss Lou's Views,* and a children's television program, *Ring Ding.*

In 1954 Bennett married Eric Winston Coverley, a showman and impresario with whom she had long been associated. The couple had one biological son and several adopted children. In recent years they made their home in Toronto, Canada, but "Miss Lou" continued to have an enthusiastic audience of Jamaican fans as well as a number of Canadian admirers. In 1974 she was awarded the Order of Jamaica for "distinguished eminence in the field of Arts and Culture"; in addition, she earned honorary doctorates from the University of the West Indies and York University, Toronto. On Jamaica's independence day in 2001, she was named a Member of the nation's Order of Merit. Many of her own performances can be heard on recordings and online: readers who listen to them will recognize in her singing the insouciant lilt that gives such distinctive energy to her verse.

Pass Fe White

Miss Jane jus hear from 'Merica,
Her daughta proudly write
Fe sey[1] she fail her exam, but
She passin' dere fe wite!

     5 She say fe tell de truth she know
Her brain part not so bright,
She couldn' pass tru college
So she try fe pass fe wite.

She passin wid her work-mate dem,[2]
10 She passin wid her boss,
An a nice wite bwoy she love, dah—
Gwan wid her like sey she pass.

But sometime she get fretful an
Her heart start gallop fas'
15 An she bruk out eena cole-sweat
Jus a-wonder ef she pass!

Jane get bex,[3] sey she sen de gal
Fe learn bout edication,

---

1. To say.
2. Her co-workers.
3. Vexed.

It look like sey de gal gawn weh
Gawn work pon her complexion.

She noh haffe tan a foreign[4]
Under dat deh strain an fright
For plenty copper-colour gal
Deh home yah[5] dah-play wite.

Her fambily is nayga,[6] but
Dem pedigree is right,
She hope de gal noh gawn an tun
Noh boogooyagga[7] wite.

De gal pupa dah-laugh an sey
It serve 'Merica right
Five year back dem Jim-Crow him[8] now
Dem pass him pickney wite.[9]

Him dah-boas'[1] all bout de districk
How him daughta is fus-class
How she smarter dan American
An over deh dah-pass!

Some people tink she pass B.A.
Some tink she pass D.R.,
Wait till dem fine out sey she ongle[2]
Pass de colour-bar.

1949, 1966

Colonisation in Reverse

Wat a joyful news, Miss Mattie,
I feel like me heart gwine burs'
Jamaica people colonizin
Englan in reverse.[1]

By de hundred, by de t'ousan
From country and from town,
By de ship-load, by de plane-load
Jamaica is Englan boun.

---

4. Stay abroad.
5. Here.
6. Negro (pejorative).
7. Low-grade, no-account.
8. They Jim Crowed him (i.e., they subjected him to racist laws).
9. They pass his child as white.
1. He boasts.
2. Only.

1. To address its postwar labor shortage, Britain encouraged emigration from the West Indies; by 1962, when immigration regulations tightened, about 300,000 migrants had entered the country—mainly from Jamaica, which was formally a part of the United Kingdom from 1670 until 1962, when it became an independent nation within the Commonwealth.

Dem a-pour out o' Jamaica,
Everybody future plan
Is fe² get a big-time job
An settle in de mother lan.

What a islan! What a people!
Man an woman, old an young
Jusa pack dem bag an baggage
An tun history upside dung!³

Some people don't like travel,
But fe show dem loyalty
Dem all a-open up cheap-fare-
To-Englan agency.

An week by week dem shippin off
Dem countryman like fire,
Fe immigrate an populate
De seat o' de Empire.

Oonoo⁴ see how life is funny,
Oonoo see de tunabout,
Jamaica live fe box bread
Outa English people mout'.

For wen dem catch a Englan,
An start play dem different role,
Some will settle down to work
An some will settle fe de dole.⁵

Jane say de dole is not too bad
Because dey payin' she
Two pounds a week fe seek a job
Dat suit her dignity.

Me say Jane will never find work
At the rate how she dah-look,
For all day she stay pon Aunt Fan couch
An read love-story book.

Wat a devilment a Englan!
Dem face war an brave de worse,
But I'm wonderin' how dem gwine stan'
Colonizin' in reverse.

1957

2. To.
3. Down.
4. You.
5. Public assistance.

Jamaica Oman

Jamaica oman cunny, sah!
Is how dem jinnal so?[1]
Look how long dem liberated
An de man dem never know!

     5 Look how long Jamaica oman
—Modder, sister, wife, sweetheart—
Outa road an eena yard[2] deh pon
A dominate her part!

From Maroon Nanny[3] teck her body
10 Bounce bullet back pon man,
To when nowadays gal-pickney[4] tun
Spellin-Bee champion.

From de grass root to de hill-top,
In profession, skill an trade,
15 Jamaica oman teck her time
Dah mount an meck de grade.

Some backa man a push, some side-a
Man a hole him han,
Some a lick sense eena man head,
20 Some a guide him pon him plan!

Neck an neck an foot an foot wid man
She buckle hole[5] her own;
While man a call her 'so-so rib'[6]
Oman a tun backbone!

25 An long before Oman Lib bruck out
Over foreign lan
Jamaica female wasa work
Her liberated plan!

Jamaica oman know she strong,
30 She know she tallawah,[7]
But she no want her pickney-dem[8]
Fi start call her 'Puppa'.[9]

So de cunny Jamma oman
Gwan like pants-suit is a style,

---

1. Jamaican woman is cunning, sir! / How are they so tricky?
2. At home.
3. A national hero of Jamaica, who led the Maroons—escaped slaves—as they fought the British in the 1730s. Legends attribute superhuman powers to her.
4. Girl-child.
5. Take hold of.
6. A reference to the story of the creation of Eve from Adam's rib (Genesis 2.21–22).
7. Sturdy, fearless.
8. Children.
9. Papa. "Fi": to.

35 An Jamaica man no know she wear
De trousiz all de while!

So Jamaica oman coaxin
Fambly budget from explode
A so Jamaica man a sing
40 'Oman a heaby load!'[1]

But de cunny Jamma oman
Ban[2] her belly, bite her tongue,
Ketch water, put pot pon fire
An jus dig her toe a grung.[3]

45 For 'Oman luck deh a dungle',[4]
Some rooted more dan some,
But as long as fowl a scratch dungle heap
Oman luck mus come!

Lickle by lickle man start praise her,
50 Day by day de praise a grow;
So him praise her, so it sweet her,
For she wonder if him know.

1975

1. A folk song.
2. Bind (i.e., to hold in her pain).
3. Into the ground.
4. Proverbial: Women can find luck anywhere. "Deh": there. "Dungle": garbage dump.

DORIS LESSING
b. 1919

Doris Lessing has had a remarkably productive and influential career, a career that continues to show signs of developing through yet another of the shifts in fictional technique that have marked its several stages. Her autobiographical tetralogy *Children of Violence* (1951–69) was praised for its social realism in depicting the growth of a heroine, Martha Quest, who comes to terms with her own identity by confronting the racism of Africa and the class stratifications of England. When Lessing published *The Golden Notebook* (1962), a number of feminists took the novel's analysis of female socialization to be, in Lessing's words, "a useful weapon in the sex war." But, in a preface (1971), the author warned that the book was really about the threat of compartmentalization in the intellectual and moral climate of the mid–twentieth century. While the issues of female identity and aging were at the center of *The Summer before the Dark* (1973), Lessing also published two moral fables: both *Briefing for a Descent into Hell* (1971) and *The Memoirs of a Survivor* (1975) move from realistic portrayals of psychological and cultural entropy to speculative allegories that seek to explain the causes and effects of the illness she associates with the modern world. In the narrative sequence called *Canopus in Argus* (1979–85), those fantasies have transformed themselves into science fiction novels in which Lessing envisions other life forms on alternative worlds; however, she continued to produce realistic fiction under the pseudonym Jane Sommers. Two parts of an autobiographical work, a collection of plays, several novels, and a libretto for a Philip Glass opera testify to Lessing's ongoing productivity.

Lessing was born Doris Tayler in Kermanshah, a city in what is now Iran. Her father had gone to work in the Imperial Bank of Persia after he had been wounded in World War I and married his nurse. But, when his daughter was five, he moved the family to a three-thousand-acre farm in Southern Rhodesia (now Zimbabwe). Doris Tayler studied at a Catholic convent school and at Girls' High School in the small city of Salisbury, while her parents farmed maize with the help of cheap native laborers. She read and reread the classics of European and American literature but left school at thirteen to work as a nursemaid and a secretary. After she had given birth to two children in her first marriage to Frank Charles Wisdom and one child in her second marriage to Gottfried Anton Lessing, she decided that marriage was not one of her "talents." In 1949, she left Africa for England, where she briefly joined the Communist Party, obtained a divorce, and began earning her living as a professional writer.

As Lessing has moved from social realism to science fiction, she has maintained a strong sense of moral responsibility as a writer. A self-described "architect of the soul," she believes that the writer must be especially inventive during this age that is, she claims, "one of the great turning points of history." As a socialist, Lessing has always criticized the inequalities of capitalism. Given the destructive capabilities of technology today, Lessing believes that only an extraordinary effort of imagination can free humanity so that it will become capable of surviving. Therefore, all of her books study what she analyzed in the *Children of Violence* novels, namely, "the individual conscience in its relation with the collective." Like Martha Quest, then, Lessing is searching for a vision of unity that can empower the individual to survive the fragmentation of modern life, whether that fragmentation is associated with antagonism among races, competition between nations, the battle between men and women, the conflicts of a divided psyche, or the dualistic thinking that sets "them" against "us."

The short story "One off the Short List" was written several years before *The Golden Notebook* and *The Four-Gated City* (1969), the last novel in the *Children of Violence* series. In both of these books, Lessing focused on the problems creativity and solitude pose for women. Anna Wulf, the heroine of *The Golden Notebook,* struggles against her fear of being alone, her dread of her own destructive impulses, and her divided political allegiances to get beyond a writing block. Like Anna, many of the female characters in *Four-Gated City* experience the so-called normal patterns of women's lives as a maddening form of self-censorship. Also concerned with gender roles, "One off the Short List" depicts the degradation of sexuality when power plays and ploys turn the relationship between men and women into a contest of wills.

One off the Short List

When he had first seen Barbara Coles, some years before, he only noticed her because someone said: "That's Johnson's new girl." He certainly had not used of her the private erotic formula: *Yes, that one.* He even wondered what Johnson saw in her. "She won't last long," he remembered thinking, as he watched Johnson, a handsome man, but rather flushed with drink, flirting with some unknown girl while Barbara stood by a wall looking on. He thought she had a sullen expression.

She was a pale girl, not slim, for her frame was generous, but her figure could pass as good. Her straight yellow hair was parted on one side in a way that struck him as gauche. He did not notice what she wore. But her eyes were all right, he remembered: large, and solidly green, square-looking because of some trick of the flesh at their corners. Emeraldlike eyes in the face of a schoolgirl, or young schoolmistress who was watching her lover flirt and would later sulk about it.

Her name sometimes cropped up in the papers. She was a stage decorator, a designer, something on those lines.

Then a Sunday newspaper had a competition for stage design and she won it. Barbara Coles was one of the "names" in the theater, and her photograph was seen about. It was always serious. He remembered having thought her sullen.

One night he saw her across the room at a party. She was talking with a well-known actor. Her yellow hair was still done on one side, but now it looked sophisticated. She wore an emerald ring on her right hand that seemed deliberately to invite comparison with her eyes. He walked over and said: "We have met before, Graham Spence." He noted, with discomfort, that he sounded abrupt. "I'm sorry, I don't remember, but how do you do?" she said, smiling. And continued her conversation.

He hung around a bit, but soon she went off with a group of people she was inviting to her home for a drink. She did not invite Graham. There was about her an assurance, a carelessness, that he recognized as the signature of success. It was then, watching her laugh as she went off with her friends, that he used the formula: *"Yes, that one."* And he went home to his wife with enjoyable expectation, as if his date with Barbara Coles were already arranged.

His marriage was twenty years old. At first it had been stormy, painful, tragic—full of partings, betrayals and sweet reconciliations. It had taken him at least a decade to realize that there was nothing remarkable about this marriage that he had lived through with such surprise of the mind and the senses. On the contrary, the marriages of most of the people he knew, whether they were first, second, or third attempts, were just the same. His had run true to form even to the serious love affair with the young girl for whose sake he had *almost* divorced his wife—yet at the last moment had changed his mind, letting the girl down so that he must have her for always (not unpleasurably) on his conscience. It was with humiliation that he had understood that this drama was not at all the unique thing he had imagined. It was nothing more than the experience of everyone in his circle. And presumably in everybody else's circle too?

Anyway, round about the tenth year of his marriage he had seen a good many things clearly, a certain kind of emotional adventure went from his life, and the marriage itself changed.

His wife had married a poor youth with a great future as a writer. Sacrifices had been made, chiefly by her, for that future. He was neither unaware of them, nor ungrateful; in fact he felt permanently guilty about it. He at last published a decently successful, book, then a second which now, thank God, no one remembered. He had drifted into radio, television, book reviewing.

He understood he was not going to make it; that he had become—not a hack, no one could call him that—but a member of that army of people who live by their wits on the fringes of the arts. The moment of realization was when he was in a pub one lunchtime near the B.B.C. where he often dropped in to meet others like himself: he understood that was why he went there—they *were* like him. Just as that melodramatic marriage had turned out to be like everyone else's—except that it had been shared with one woman instead of with two or three—so it had turned out that his unique talent, his struggles as a writer had led him here, to this pub and the half dozen pubs like it, where all the men in sight had the same history. They all had their novel, their play, their book of poems, a moment of fame, to their credit. Yet here they were, running television programs about which they were cynical (to each other or to their wives) or writing reviews about other people's books. Yes, that's what he had become, an impresario of other people's talent. These two moments of clarity, about his marriage and about his talent, had roughly coincided; and (perhaps not by chance) had coincided with his wife's decision to leave him for a man younger than himself who had a future, she said, as a playwright. Well, he had talked her out of it. For her part she had to understand he was not going to be the T. S. Eliot or Graham Greene[1] of our time—but after all, how many were? She must finally understand this, for he could no longer bear her awful bitterness. For his part he must stop coming home drunk at five in the morning, and starting a new romantic affair every six months which he took so seriously that he made her miserable because of her implied deficiencies. In short he was to be a good husband. (He had always been a dutiful father.) And she a good wife. And so it was: the marriage became stable, as they say.

The formula: *Yes, that one* no longer implied a necessarily sexual relationship. In its more mature form, it was far from being something he was ashamed of. On the contrary, it expressed a humorous respect for what he was, for his real talents and flair, which had turned out to be not artistic after all, but to do with emotional life, hard-earned experience. It expressed an ironical dignity, a proving to himself not only: I can be honest about myself, but also: I have earned the best in *that* field whenever I want it.

He watched the field for the women who were well known in the arts, or in politics; looked out for photographs, listened for bits of gossip. He made a point of going to see them act, or dance, or orate. He built up a not unshrewd picture of them. He would either quietly pull strings to meet her or—more often, for there was a gambler's pleasure in waiting—bide his time until he met her in the natural course of events, which was bound to happen sooner or later. He would be seen out with her a few times in public, which was in order, since his work meant he had to entertain well-known people, male and female. His wife always knew, he told her. He might have a brief affair with this woman, but more often than not it was the appearance of an affair. Not that he didn't get pleasure from other people envying him—he would make a point, for instance, of taking this woman into the pubs where his male colleagues went. It was that his real pleasure came when he saw her surprise at how well she was understood by him. He enjoyed the atmosphere he was able to set up between an intelligent woman and himself: a humorous complicity which had in it much that was unspoken, and which almost made sex irrelevant.

---

1. English novelist, playwright, and journalist (1904–1991). Eliot (1888–1965), American-born British poet and critic; he won the Nobel Prize for Literature in 1948.

Onto the list of women with whom he planned to have this relationship went Barbara Coles. There was no hurry. Next week, next month, next year, they would meet at a party. The world of well-known people in London is a small one. Big and little fishes, they drift around, nose each other, flirt their fins, wriggle off again. When he bumped into Barbara Coles, it would be time to decide whether or not to sleep with her.

Meanwhile he listened. But he didn't discover much. She had a husband and children, but the husband seemed to be in the background. The children were charming and well brought up, like everyone else's children. She had affairs, they said; but while several men he met sounded familiar with her, it was hard to determine whether they had slept with her, because none directly boasted of her. She was spoken of in terms of her friends, her work, her house, a party she had given, a job she had found someone. She was liked, she was respected, and Graham Spence's self-esteem was flattered because he had chosen her. He looked forward to saying in just the same tone: "Barbara Coles asked me what I thought about the set and I told her quite frankly. . . ."

Then by chance he met a young man who did boast about Barbara Coles; he claimed to have had the great love affair with her, and recently at that; and he spoke of it as something generally known. Graham realized how much he had already become involved with her in his imagination because of how perturbed he was now, on account of the character of this youth, Jack Kennaway. He had recently become successful as a magazine editor—one of those young men who, not as rare as one might suppose in the big cities, are successful from sheer impertinence, effrontery. Without much talent or taste, yet he had the charm of his effrontery. "Yes, I'm going to succeed, because I've decided to; yes, I may be stupid, but not so stupid that I don't know my deficiencies. Yes, I'm going to be successful because you people with integrity, etc., etc., simply don't believe in the possibility of people like me. You are too cowardly to stop me. Yes, I've taken your measure and I'm going to succeed because I've got the courage, not only to be unscrupulous, but to be quite frank about it. And besides, you admire me, you must, or otherwise you'd stop me. . . ." Well, that was young Jack Kennaway, and he shocked Graham. He was a tall, languishing young man, handsome in a dark melting way, and, it was quite clear, he was either asexual or homosexual. And this youth boasted of the favors of Barbara Coles; boasted, indeed, of her love. Either she was a raving neurotic with a taste for neurotics; or Jack Kennaway was a most accomplished liar; or she slept with anyone. Graham was intrigued. He took Jack Kennaway out to dinner in order to hear him talk about Barbara Coles. There was no doubt the two were pretty close—all those dinners, theatres, weekends in the country—Graham Spence felt he had put his finger on the secret pulse of Barbara Coles; and it was intolerable that he must wait to meet her; he decided to arrange it.

It became unnecessary. She was in the news again, with a run of luck. She had done a successful historical play, and immediately afterwards a modern play, and then a hit musical. In all three, the sets were remarked on. Graham saw some interviews in newspapers and on television. These all centered around the theme of her being able to deal easily with so many different styles of theater; but the real point was, of course, that she was a woman, which naturally added piquancy to the thing. And now Graham

Spence was asked to do a half-hour radio interview with her. He planned the questions he would ask her with care, drawing on what people had said of her, but above all on his instinct and experience with women. The interview was to be at nine-thirty at night; he was to pick her up at six from the theater where she was currently at work, so that there would be time, as the letter from the B.B.C. had put it, "for you and Miss Coles to get to know each other."

At six he was at the stage door, but a message from Miss Coles said she was not quite ready, could he wait a little. He hung about, then went to the pub opposite for a quick one, but still no Miss Coles. So he made his way backstage, directed by voices, hammering, laughter. It was badly lit, and the group of people at work did not see him. The director, James Poynter, had his arm around Barbara's shoulders. He was newly well-known, a carelessly good-looking young man reputed to be intelligent. Barbara Coles wore a dark blue overall, and her flat hair fell over her face so that she kept pushing it back with the hand that had the emerald on it. These two stood close, side by side. Three young men, stagehands, were on the other side of a trestle which had sketches and drawings on it. They were studying some sketches. Barbara said, in a voice warm with energy: "Well, so I thought if we did *this*—do you see, James? What do you think, Steven?" "Well, love," said the young man she called Steven, "I see your idea, but I wonder if . . ." "I think you're right, Babs," said the director. "Look," said Barbara, holding one of the sketches towards Steven, "look, let me show you." They all leaned forward, the five of them, absorbed in the business.

Suddenly Graham couldn't stand it. He understood he was shaken to his depths. He went off stage, and stood with his back against a wall in the dingy passage that led to the dressing rooms. His eyes were filled with tears. He was seeing what a long way he had come from the crude, uncompromising, admirable young egomaniac he had been when he was twenty. That group of people there—working, joking, arguing, yes, that's what he hadn't known for years. What bound them was the democracy of respect for each other's work, a confidence in themselves and in each other. They looked like people banded together against a world which they—no, not despised, but which they measured, understood, would fight to the death, out of respect for what *they* stood for, for what *it* stood for. It was a long time since he felt part of that balance. And he understood that he had seen Barbara Coles when she was most herself, at ease with a group of people she worked with. It was then, with the tears drying on his eyelids, which felt old and ironic, that he decided he would sleep with Barbara Coles. It was a necessity for him. He went back through the door onto the stage, burning with this single determination.

The five were still together. Barbara had a length of blue gleaming stuff which she was draping over the shoulder of Steven, the stagehand. He was showing it off, and the others watched. "What do you think, James?" she asked the director. "We've got that sort of dirty green, and I thought . . ." "Well," said James, not sure at all, "well, Babs, well . . ."

Now Graham went forward so that he stood beside Barbara, and said: "I'm Graham Spence, we've met before." For the second time she smiled socially and said: "Oh, I'm sorry, I don't remember." Graham nodded at James, whom he had known, or at least had met off and on, for years. But it was obvious James didn't remember him either.

"From the B.B.C.," said Graham to Barbara, again sounding abrupt, against his will. "Oh, I'm sorry, I'm so sorry, I forgot all about it. I've got to be interviewed," she said to the group. "Mr. Spence is a journalist." Graham allowed himself a small smile ironical of the word journalist, but she was not looking at him. She was going on with her work. "We should decide tonight," she said. "Steven's right." "Yes, I am right," said the stagehand. "She's right, James, we need that blue with that sludge-green everywhere." "James," said Barbara, "James, what's wrong with it? You haven't said." She moved forward to James, passing Graham. Remembering him again, she became contrite. "I'm sorry," she said, "we can none of us agree. Well, look"—she turned to Graham—"you advise us, we've got so involved with it that . . ." At which James laughed, and so did the stagehands. "No, Babs," said James, "of course Mr. Spence can't advise. He's just this moment come in. We've got to decide. Well I'll give you till tomorrow morning. Time to go home, it must be six by now."

"It's nearly seven," said Graham, taking command.

"It isn't!" said Barbara, dramatic. "My God, how terrible, how appalling, how could I have done such a thing. . . ." She was laughing at herself. "Well, you'll have to forgive me, Mr. Spence, because you haven't got any alternative."

They began laughing again: this was clearly a group joke. And now Graham took his chance. He said firmly, as if he were her director, in fact copying James Poynter's manner with her: "No, Miss Coles, I won't forgive you, I've been kicking my heels for nearly an hour." She grimaced, then laughed and accepted it. James said: "There, Babs, that's how you ought to be treated. We spoil you." He kissed her on the cheek, she kissed him on both his, the stagehands moved off. "Have a good evening, Babs," said James, going, and nodding to Graham. Who stood concealing his pleasure with difficulty. He knew, because he had had the courage to be firm, indeed, peremptory, with Barbara, that he had saved himself hours of maneuvering. Several drinks, a dinner—perhaps two or three evenings of drinks and dinners—had been saved because he was now on this footing with Barbara Coles, a man who could say: "No, I won't forgive you, you've kept me waiting."

She said: "I've just got to . . ." and went ahead of him. In the passage she hung her overall on a peg. She was thinking, it seemed, of something else, but seeing him watching her, she smiled at him, companionably: he realized with triumph it was the sort of smile she would offer one of the stagehands, or even James. She said again: "Just one second . . ." and went to the stage-door office. She and the stage doorman conferred. There was some problem. Graham said, taking another chance: "What's the trouble, can I help?"—as if he could help, as if he expected to be able to. "Well . . ." she said, frowning. Then, to the man: "No, it'll be all right. Good night." She came to Graham. "We've got ourselves into a bit of a fuss because half the set's in Liverpool and half's here and—but it will sort itself out." She stood, at ease, chatting to him, one colleague to another. All this was admirable, he felt; but there would be a bad moment when they emerged from the special atmosphere of the theater into the street. He took another decision, grasped her arm firmly, and said: "We're going to have a drink before we do anything at all, it's a terrible evening out." Her arm felt resistant, but remained within his. It was raining outside, luckily. He directed her, authoritative: "No, not that pub, there's a nicer one around the corner." "Oh, but I like this pub," said Barbara, "we always use it."

"Of course you do," he said to himself. But in that pub there would be the stagehands, and probably James, and he'd lose contact with her. He'd become a *journalist* again. He took her firmly out of danger around two corners, into a pub he picked at random. A quick look around—no, they weren't there. At least, if there were people from the theater, she showed no sign. She asked for a beer. He ordered her a double Scotch, which she accepted. Then, having won a dozen preliminary rounds already he took time to think. Something was bothering him—what? Yes, it was what he had observed backstage, Barbara and James Poynter. Was she having an affair with him? Because if so, it would all be much more difficult. He made himself see the two of them together, and thought with a jealousy surprisingly strong: *Yes, that's it.* Meantime he sat looking at her, seeing himself look at her, *a man gazing in calm appreciation at a woman:* waiting for her to feel it and respond. She was examining the pub. Her white woollen suit was belted, and had a not unprovocative suggestion of being a uniform. Her flat yellow hair, hastily pushed back after work, was untidy. Her clear white skin, without any color, made her look tired. Not very exciting, at the moment, thought Graham, but maintaining his appreciative pose for when she would turn and see it. He knew what she would see: he was relying not only on the "warm kindly" beam of his gaze, for this was merely a reinforcement of the impression he knew he made. He had black hair, a little grayed. His clothes were loose and bulky—masculine. His eyes were humorous and appreciative. He was not, never had been, concerned to lessen the impression of being settled, dependable: the husband and father. On the contrary, he knew women found it reassuring.

When she at last turned she said, almost apologetic: "Would you mind if we sat down? I've been lugging great things around all day." She had spotted two empty chairs in a corner. So had he, but rejected them, because there were other people at the table. "But my dear, of course!" They took the chairs, and then Barbara said: "If you'll excuse me a moment." She had remembered she needed makeup. He watched her go off, annoyed with himself. She was tired; and he could have understood, protected, sheltered. He realized that in the other pub, with the people she had worked with all day, she would not have thought: "I must make myself up, I must be on show." That was for outsiders. She had not, until now, considered Graham an outsider, because of his taking his chance to seem one of the working group in the theater; but now he had thrown this opportunity away. She returned armored. Her hair was sleek, no longer defenseless. And she had made up her eyes. Her eyebrows were untouched, pale gold streaks above the brilliant green eyes whose lashes were blackened. Rather good, he thought, the contrast. Yes, but the moment had gone when he could say: Did you know you had a smudge on your cheek? Or—my dear girl!—pushing her hair back with the edge of a brotherly hand. In fact, unless he was careful, he'd be back at starting point.

He remarked: "That emerald is very cunning"—smiling into her eyes.

She smiled politely, and said: "It's not cunning, it's an accident, it was my grandmother's." She flirted her hand lightly by her face, though, smiling. But that was something she had done before, to a compliment she had had before, and often. It was all social, she had become social entirely. She remarked: "Didn't you say it was half past nine we had to record?"

"My dear Barbara, we've got two hours. We'll have another drink or two, then I'll ask you a couple of questions, then we'll drop down to the studio and get it over, and then we'll have a comfortable supper."

"I'd rather eat now, if you don't mind. I had no lunch, and I'm really hungry."

"But my dear, of course." He was angry. Just as he had been surprised by his real jealousy over James, so now he was thrown off balance by his anger: he had been counting on the long quiet dinner afterwards to establish intimacy. "Finish your drink and I'll take you to Nott's." Nott's was expensive. He glanced at her assessingly as he mentioned it. She said: "I wonder if you know Butler's? It's good and it's rather close." Butler's was good, and it was cheap, and he gave her a good mark for liking it. But Nott's it was going to be. "My dear, we'll get into a taxi and be at Nott's in a moment, don't worry."

She obediently got to her feet: the way she did it made him understand how badly he had slipped. She was saying to herself: Very well, he's like that, then all right, I'll do what he wants and get it over with. . . .

Swallowing his own drink he followed her, and took her arm in the pub doorway. It was polite within his. Outside it drizzled. No taxi. He was having bad luck now. They walked in silence to the end of the street. There Barbara glanced into a side street where a sign said: BUTLER'S. Not to remind him of it, on the contrary, she concealed the glance. And here she was, entirely at his disposal, they might never have shared the comradely moment in the theater.

They walked half a mile to Nott's. No taxis. She made conversation: this was, he saw, to cover any embarrassment he might feel because of a half-mile walk through rain when she was tired. She was talking about some theory to do with the theater, with designs for theater building. He heard himself saying, and repeatedly: Yes, yes, yes. He thought about Nott's, how to get things right when they reached Nott's. There he took the headwaiter aside, gave him a pound, and instructions. They were put in a corner. Large Scotches appeared. The menus were spread. "And now, my dear," he said, "I apologize for dragging you here, but I hope you'll think it's worth it."

"Oh, it's charming, I've always liked it. It's just that . . ." She stopped herself saying: it's such a long way. She smiled at him, raising her glass, and said: "It's one of my very favorite places, and I'm glad you dragged me here." Her voice was flat with tiredness. All this was appalling; he knew it; and he sat thinking how to retrieve his position. Meanwhile she fingered the menu. The headwaiter took the order, but Graham made a gesture which said: Wait a moment. He wanted the Scotch to take effect before she ate. But she saw his silent order; and, without annoyance or reproach, leaned forward to say, sounding patient: "Graham, please, I've got to eat, you don't want me drunk when you interview me, do you?"

"They are bringing it as fast as they can," he said, making it sound as if she were greedy. He looked neither at the headwaiter nor at Barbara. He noted in himself, as he slipped further and further away from contact with her, a cold determination growing in him; one apart from, apparently, any conscious act of will, that come what may, if it took all night, he'd be in her bed before morning. And now, seeing the small pale face, with the enormous green eyes, it was for the first time that he imagined her in his arms. Although he had said: *Yes, that one,* weeks ago, it was only now that he imagined her as a sensual experience. Now he did, so strongly that he could only glance at her, and then away towards the waiters who were bringing food.

"Thank the Lord," said Barbara, and all at once her voice was gay and intimate. "Thank heavens. Thank every power that is. . . ." She was making fun of her own exaggeration; and, as he saw, because she wanted to put him at his ease after his boorishness over delaying the food. (She hadn't been taken in, he saw, humiliated, disliking her.) "Thank all the gods of Nott's," she went on, "because if I hadn't eaten inside five minutes I'd have died, I tell you." With which she picked up her knife and fork and began on her steak. He poured wine, smiling with her, thinking that *this* moment of closeness he would not throw away. He watched her frank hunger as she ate, and thought: Sensual—it's strange I hadn't wondered whether she would be or not.

"Now," she said, sitting back, having taken the edge off her hunger: "Let's get to work."

He said: "I've thought it over very carefully—how to present you. The first thing seems to me, we must get away from that old chestnut: Miss Coles, how extraordinary for a woman to be so versatile in her work . . . I hope you agree?" This was his trump card. He had noted, when he had seen her on television, her polite smile when this note was struck. (The smile he had seen so often tonight.) This smile said: All right, if you *have* to be stupid, what can I do?

Now she laughed and said: "What a relief. I was afraid you were going to do the same thing."

"Good, now you eat and I'll talk."

In his carefully prepared monologue he spoke of the different styles of theater she had shown herself mistress of, but not directly: he was flattering her on the breadth of her experience; the complexity of her character, as shown in her work. She ate, steadily, her face showing nothing. At last she asked: "And how did you plan to introduce this?"

He had meant to spring that on her as a surprise, something like: Miss Coles, a surprisingly young woman for what she has accomplished (she was thirty? thirty-two?) and a very attractive one. . . . "Perhaps I can give you an idea of what she's like if I say she could be taken for the film star Marie Carletta. . . ." The Carletta was a strong earthy blonde, known to be intellectual. He now saw he could not possibly say this: he could imagine her cool look if he did. She said: "Do you mind if we get away from all that—my manifold talents, et cetera. . . ." He felt himself stiffen with annoyance; particularly because this was not an accusation, he saw she did not think him worth one. She had assessed him: This is the kind of man who uses this kind of flattery and therefore. . . . It made him angrier that she did not even trouble to say: Why did you do exactly what you promised you wouldn't? She was being invincibly polite, trying to conceal her patience with his stupidity.

"After all," she was saying, "it is a stage designer's job to design what comes up. Would anyone take, let's say Johnnie Cranmore" (another stage designer) "onto the air or television and say: How very versatile you are because you did that musical about Java last month and a modern play about Irish laborers this?"

He battened down his anger. "My dear Barbara, I'm sorry. I didn't realize that what I said would sound just like the mixture as before. So what shall we talk about?"

"What I was saying as we walked to the restaurant: can we get away from the personal stuff?"

Now he almost panicked. Then, thank God, he laughed from nervousness, for she laughed and said: "You didn't hear one word I said."

"No, I didn't. I was frightened you were going to be furious because I made you walk so far when you were tired."

They laughed together, back to where they had been in the theater. He leaned over, took her hand, kissed it. He said: "Tell me again." He thought: Damn, now she's going to be earnest and intellectual.

But he understood he had been stupid. He had forgotten himself at twenty—or, for that matter, at thirty; forgotten one could live inside an idea, a set of ideas, with enthusiasm. For in talking about her ideas (also the ideas of the people she worked with) for a new theater, a new style of theater, she was as she had been with her colleagues over the sketches or the blue material. She was easy, informal, almost chattering. This was how, he remembered, one talked about ideas that were a breath of life. The ideas, he thought, were intelligent enough; and he would agree with them, with her, if he believed it mattered a damn one way or another, if any of these enthusiasms mattered a damn. But at least he now had the key, he knew what to do. At the end of not more than half an hour, they were again two professionals, talking about ideas they shared, for he remembered caring about all this himself once. *When? How many years ago was it that he had been able to care?*

At last he said: "My dear Barbara, do you realize the impossible position you're putting me in? Margaret Ruyen who runs this program is determined to do you personally, the poor woman hasn't got a serious thought in her head."

Barbara frowned. He put his hand on hers, teasing her for the frown: "No, wait, trust me, we'll circumvent her." She smiled. In fact Margaret Ruyen had left it all to him, had said nothing about Miss Coles.

"They aren't very bright—the brass," he said. "Well, never mind: we'll work out what we want, do it, and it'll be a *fait accompli*."

"Thank you, what a relief. How lucky I was to be given you to interview me." She was relaxed now, because of the whiskey, the food, the wine, above all because of this new complicity against Margaret Ruyen. It would all be easy. They worked out five or six questions, over coffee, and took a taxi through rain to the studios. He noted that the cold necessity to have her, to make her, to beat her down, had left him. He was even seeing himself, as the evening ended, kissing her on the cheek and going home to his wife. This comradeship was extraordinarily pleasant. It was balm to the wound he had not known he carried until that evening, when he had had to accept the justice of the word *journalist*. He felt he could talk forever about the state of the theater, its finances, the stupidity of the government, the philistinism of . . .

At the studios he was careful to make a joke so that they walked in on the laugh. He was careful that the interview began at once, without conversation with Margaret Ruyen; and that from the moment the green light went on, his voice lost its easy familiarity. He made sure that not one personal note was struck during the interview. Afterwards, Margaret Ruyen, who was pleased, came forward to say so; but he took her aside to say that Miss Coles was tired and needed to be taken home at once: for he knew this must look to Barbara as if he were squaring a producer who had been expecting a different interview. He led Barbara off, her hand held tight in his against his side. "Well," he said, "we've done it, and I don't think she knows what hit her."

"Thank you," she said, "it really was pleasant to talk about something sensible for once."

He kissed her lightly on the mouth. She returned it, smiling. By now he felt sure that the mood need not slip again, he could hold it.

"There are two things we can do," he said. "You can come to my club and have a drink. Or I can drive you home and you can give me a drink. I have to go past you."

"Where do you live?"

"Wimbledon." He lived, in fact, at Highgate; but she lived in Fulham. He was taking another chance, but by the time she found out, they would be in a position to laugh over his ruse.

"Good," she said. "You can drop me home then. I have to get up early." He made no comment. In the taxi he took her hand; it was heavy in his, and he asked: "Does James slave-drive you?"

"I didn't realize you knew him—no, he doesn't."

"Well, I don't know him intimately. What's he like to work with?"

"Wonderful," she said at once. "There's no one I enjoy working with more."

Jealousy spurted in him. He could not help himself: "Are you having an affair with him?"

She looked: what's it to do with you? but said: "No, I'm not."

"He's very attractive," he said, with a chuckle of worldly complicity. She said nothing, and he insisted: "If I were a woman I'd have an affair with James."

It seemed she might very well say nothing. But she remarked: "He's married."

His spirits rose in a swoop. It was the first stupid remark she had made. It was a remark of such staggering stupidity that . . . he let out a humoring snort of laughter, put his arm around her, kissed her, said: "My dear little Babs."

She said: "Why Babs?"

"Is that the prerogative of James? And of the stagehands?" he could not prevent himself adding.

"I'm only called that at work." She was stiff inside his arm.

"My dear Barbara, then . . ." He waited for her to enlighten and explain, but she said nothing. Soon she moved out of his arm, on the pretext of lighting a cigarette. He lit it for her. He noted that his determination to lay her, and at all costs, had come back. They were outside her house. He said quickly: "And now, Barbara, you can make me a cup of coffee and give me a brandy." She hesitated; but he was out of the taxi, paying, opening the door for her. The house had no lights on, he noted. He said: "We'll be very quiet so as not to wake the children."

She turned her head slowly to look at him. She said, flat, replying to his real question: "My husband is away. As for the children, they are visiting friends tonight." She now went ahead of him to the door of the house. It was a small house, in a terrace of small and not very pretty houses. Inside a little, bright, intimate hall, she said: "I'll go and make some coffee. Then, my friend, you must go home because I'm very tired."

The *my friend* struck him deep, because he had become vulnerable during their comradeship. He said, gabbling: "You're annoyed with me—oh, please don't, I'm sorry."

She smiled, from a cool distance. He saw, in the small light from the ceiling, her extraordinary eyes. "Green" eyes are hazel, are brown with green flecks, are even blue. Eyes are checkered, flawed, changing. Hers were solid green, but really, he had never seen anything like them before. They were like very deep water. They were like—well, emeralds; or the absolute clarity of green in the depths of a tree in summer. And now, as she smiled almost perpendicularly up at him, he saw a darkness come over them. Darkness swallowed the clear green. She said: "I'm not in the least annoyed." It was as if she had yawned with boredom. "And now I'll get the things . . . in there." She nodded at a white door and left him. He went into a long, very tidy white room, that had a narrow bed in one corner, a table covered with drawings, sketches, pencils. Tacked to the walls with drawing pins were swatches of colored stuffs. Two small chairs stood near a low round table: an area of comfort in the working room. He was thinking: I wouldn't like it if my wife had a room like this. I wonder what Barbara's husband . . . ? He had not thought of her till now in relation to her husband, or to her children. Hard to imagine her with a frying pan in her hand, or for that matter, cosy in the double bed.

A noise outside: he hastily arranged himself, leaning with one arm on the mantelpiece. She came in with a small tray that had cups, glasses, brandy, coffeepot. She looked abstracted. Graham was on the whole flattered by this: it probably meant she was at ease in his presence. He realized he was a little tight and rather tired. Of course, she was tired too, that was why she was vague. He remembered that earlier that evening he had lost a chance by not using her tiredness. Well now, if he were intelligent . . . She was about to pour coffee. He firmly took the coffeepot out of her hand, and nodded at a chair. Smiling, she obeyed him. "That's better," he said. He poured coffee, poured brandy, and pulled the table towards her. She watched him. Then he took her hand, kissed it, patted it, laid it down gently. Yes, he thought, I did that well.

Now, a problem. He wanted to be closer to her, but she was fitted into a damned silly little chair that had arms. If he were to sit by her on the floor . . . ? But no, for him, the big bulky reassuring man, there could be no casual gestures, no informal postures. Suppose I scoop her out of the chair onto the bed? He drank his coffee as he plotted. Yes, he'd carry her to the bed, but not yet.

"Graham," she said, setting down her cup. She was, he saw with annoyance, looking tolerant. "Graham, in about half an hour I want to be in bed and asleep."

As she said this, she offered him a smile of amusement at this situation—man and woman maneuvering, the great comic situation. And with part of himself he could have shared it. Almost, he smiled with her, laughed. (Not till days later he exclaimed to himself: Lord what a mistake I made, not to share the joke with her then: that was where I went seriously wrong.) But he could not smile. His face was frozen, with a stiff pride. Not because she had been watching him plot; the amusement she now offered him took the string out of that; but because of his revived determination that he was going to have his own way, he was going to have her. He was not going home. But he felt that he held a bunch of keys, and did not know which one to choose.

He lifted the second small chair opposite to Barbara, moving aside the coffee table for this purpose. He sat in this chair, leaned forward, took her two hands, and said: "My dear, don't make me go home yet, don't, I beg you." The trouble was, nothing had happened all evening that could be felt to lead up to these words and his tone—simple, dignified, human being pleading with human being for surcease. He saw himself leaning forward, his big hands swallowing her small ones; he saw his face, warm with the appeal. And he realized he had meant the words he used. They were nothing more than what he felt. He wanted to stay with her because she wanted him to, because he was her colleague, a fellow worker in the arts. He needed this desperately. But she was examining him, curious rather than surprised, and from a critical distance. He heard himself saying: "If James were here, I wonder what you'd do?" His voice was aggrieved; he saw the sudden dark descend over her eyes, and she said: "Graham, would you like some more coffee before you go?"

He said: "I've been wanting to meet you for years. I know a good many people who know you."

She leaned forward, poured herself a little more brandy, sat back, holding the glass between her two palms on her chest. An odd gesture: Graham felt that this vessel she was cherishing between her hands was herself. A patient, long-suffering gesture. He thought of various men who had mentioned her. He thought of Jack Kennaway, wavered, panicked, said: "For instance, Jack Kennaway."

And now, at the name, an emotion lit her eyes—what was it? He went on, deliberately testing this emotion, adding to it: "I had dinner with him last week—oh, quite by chance!—and he was talking about you."

"Was he?"

He remembered he had thought her sullen, all those years ago. Now she seemed defensive, and she frowned. He said: "In fact he spent most of the evening talking about you."

She said in short, breathless sentences, which he realized were due to anger: "I can very well imagine what he says. But surely you can't think I enjoy being reminded that . . ." She broke off, resenting him, he saw, because he forced her down onto a level she despised. But it was not his level either: it was all her fault, all hers! He couldn't remember not being in control of a situation with a woman for years. Again he felt like a man teetering on a tightrope. He said, trying to make good use of Jack Kennaway, even at this late hour: "Of course, he's a charming boy, but not a man at all."

She looked at him, silent, guarding her brandy glass against her breasts.

"Unless appearances are totally deceptive, of course." He could not resist probing, even though he knew it was fatal.

She said nothing.

"Do you know you are supposed to have had the great affair with Jack Kennaway?" he exclaimed, making this an amused expostulation against the fools who could believe it.

"So I am told." She set down her glass. "And now," she said, standing up, dismissing him. He lost his head, took a step forward, grabbed her in his arms, and groaned: "Barbara!"

She turned her face this way and that under his kisses. He snatched a diagnostic look at her expression—it was still patient. He placed his lips against her neck, groaned "Barbara" again, and waited. She would have to do something. Fight free, respond, something. She did nothing at all. At last she said: "For the Lord's sake, Graham!" She sounded amused: he was again being offered amusement. But if he shared it with her, it would be the end of this chance to have her. He clamped his mouth over hers, silencing her. She did not fight him off so much as blow him off. Her mouth treated his attacking mouth as a woman blows and laughs in water, puffing off waves or spray with a laugh, turning aside her head. It was a gesture half annoyance, half humor. He continued to kiss her while she moved her head and face about under the kisses as if they were small attacking waves.

And so began what, when he looked back on it afterwards, was the most embarrassing experience of his life. Even at the time he hated her for his ineptitude. For he held her there for what must have been nearly half an hour. She was much shorter than he, he had to bend, and his neck ached. He held her rigid, his thighs on either side of hers, her arms clamped to her side in a bear's hug. She was unable to move, except for her head. When his mouth ground hers open and his tongue moved and writhed inside it, she still remained passive. And he could not stop himself. While with his intelligence he watched this ridiculous scene, he was determined to go on, because sooner or later her body must soften in wanting his. And he could not stop because he could not face the horror of the moment when he set her free and she looked at him. And he hated her more, every moment. Catching glimpses of her great green eyes, open and dismal beneath his, he knew he had never disliked anything more than those "jeweled" eyes. They were repulsive to him. It occurred to him at last that even if by now she wanted him, he wouldn't know it, because she was not able to move at all. He cautiously loosened his hold so that she had an inch or so leeway. She remained quite passive. As if, he thought derisively, she had read or been told that the way to incite men maddened by lust was to fight them. He found he was thinking: Stupid cow, so you imagine I find you attractive, do you? You've got the conceit to think that!

The sheer, raving insanity of this thought hit him, opened his arms, his thighs, and lifted his tongue out of her mouth. She stepped back, wiping her mouth with the back of her hand, and stood dazed with incredulity. The embarrassment that lay in wait for him nearly engulfed him, but he let anger postpone it. She said positively apologetic, even, at this moment, humorous: "You're crazy, Graham. What's the matter, are you drunk? You don't seem drunk. You don't even find me attractive."

The blood of hatred went to his head and he gripped her again. Now she had got her face firmly twisted away so that he could not reach her mouth, and she repeated steadily as he kissed the parts of her cheeks and neck that were available to him: "Graham, let me go, do let me go, Graham." She went on saying this; he went on squeezing, grinding, kissing and licking. It might go on all night: it was a sheer contest of wills, nothing else. He thought: It's only a really masculine woman who wouldn't have given in by now out of sheer decency of the flesh! One thing he knew, however: that she would be in that bed, in his arms, and very soon. He let her go, but said: "I'm going to sleep with you tonight, you know that, don't you?"

She leaned with hand on the mantelpiece to steady herself. Her face was colorless, since he had licked all the makeup off. She seemed quite different: small and defenseless with her large mouth pale now, her smudged green eyes fringed with gold. And now, for the first time, he felt what it might have been supposed (certainly by her) he felt hours ago. Seeing the small damp flesh of her face, he felt kinship, intimacy with her, he felt intimacy of the flesh, the affection and good humor of sensuality. He felt she was flesh of his flesh, his sister in the flesh. He felt desire for her, instead of the will to have her; and because of this, was ashamed of the farce he had been playing. Now he desired simply to take her into bed in the affection of his senses.

She said: "What on earth am I supposed to do? Telephone for the police, or what?" He was hurt that she still addressed the man who had ground her into sulky apathy; she was not addressing *him* at all.

She said: "Or scream for the neighbors, is that what you want?"

The gold-fringed eyes were almost black, because of the depth of the shadow of boredom over them. She was bored and weary to the point of falling to the floor, he could see that.

He said: "I'm going to sleep with you."

"But how can you possibly want to?"—a reasonable, a civilized demand addressed to a man who (he could see) she believed would respond to it. She said: "You know I don't want to, and I know you don't really give a damn one way or the other."

He was stung back into being the boor because she had not the intelligence to see that the boor no longer existed; because she could not see that this was a man who wanted her in a way which she must respond to.

There she stood, supporting herself with one hand, looking small and white and exhausted, and utterly incredulous. She was going to turn and walk off out of simple incredulity, he could see that. "Do you think I don't mean it?" he demanded, grinding this out between his teeth. She made a movement—she was on the point of going away. His hand shot out on its own volition and grasped her wrist. She frowned. His other hand grasped her other wrist. His body hove up against hers to start the pressure of a new embrace. Before it could, she said: "Oh Lord, no, I'm not going through all that again. Right, then."

"What do you mean—right, then?" he demanded.

She said: "You're going to sleep with me. O.K. Anything rather than go through that again. Shall we get it over with?"

He grinned, saying in silence: "No darling, oh no you don't, I don't care what words you use, I'm going to have you now and that's all there is to it."

She shrugged. The contempt, the weariness of it, had no effect on him, because he was now again hating her so much that wanting her was like needing to kill something or someone.

She took her clothes off, as if she were going to bed by herself: her jacket, skirt, petticoat. She stood in white bra and panties, a rather solid girl, brown-skinned still from the summer. He felt a flash of affection for the brown girl with her loose yellow hair as she stood naked. She got into bed and lay there, while the green eyes looked at him in civilized appeal: Are you really going through with this? Do you have to? Yes, his eyes said back: I do have to. She shifted her gaze aside, to the wall, saying silently: Well, if you want to take me without any desire at all on my part, then go ahead, if you're not ashamed. He was not ashamed, because he was maintaining the flame of hate for her which he knew quite well was all that stood between him and shame. He took off his clothes, and got into bed beside her. As he did so, knowing he was putting himself in the position of raping a woman who was making it elaborately clear he bored her, his flesh subsided completely, sad, and full of reproach because a few moments ago it was reaching out for his sister whom he could have made happy. He lay on his side by her, secretly at work on himself, while he supported himself across her body on his elbow, using the free hand to manipulate her breasts. He saw that she gritted her teeth against his touch. At least she could not know that after all this fuss he was not potent.

In order to incite himself, he clasped her again. She felt his smallness, writhed free of him, sat up and said: "Lie down."

While she had been lying there, she had been thinking: The only way to get this over with is to make him big again, otherwise I've got to put up with him all night. His hatred of her was giving him a clairvoyance: he knew very well what went on through her mind. She had switched on, with the determination to *get it all over with,* a sensual good humor, a patience. He lay down. She squatted beside him, the light from the ceiling blooming on her brown shoulders, her flat fair hair falling over her face. But she would not look at his face. Like a bored, skilled wife, she was; or like a prostitute. She administered to him, she was setting herself to please him. Yes, he thought, she's sensual, or she could be. Meanwhile she was succeeding in defeating the reluctance of his flesh, which was the tender token of a possible desire for her, by using a cold skill that was the result of her contempt for him. Just as he decided: Right, it's enough, now I shall have her properly, she made him come. It was not a trick, to hurry or cheat him, what defeated him was her transparent thought: Yes, that's what he's worth.

Then, having succeeded, and waited for a moment or two, she stood up, naked, the fringes of gold at her loins and in her armpits speaking to him a language quite different from that of her green, bored eyes. She looked at him and thought, showing it plainly: What sort of man is it who . . . ? He watched the slight movement of her shoulders: a just-checked shrug. She went out of the room: then the sound of running water. Soon she came back in a white dressing gown, carrying a yellow towel. She handed him the towel, looking away in politeness as he used it. "Are you going home now?" she enquired hopefully, at this point.

"No, I'm not." He believed that now he would have to start fighting her again, but she lay down beside him, not touching him (he could feel the distaste of her flesh for his) and he thought: Very well, my dear, but there's a lot of the night left yet. He said aloud: "I'm going to have you properly tonight." She said nothing, lay silent, yawned. Then she remarked consolingly, and he could have laughed outright from sheer surprise: "Those were hardly conducive circumstances for making love." She was *consoling* him.

He hated her for it. A proper little slut: I force her into bed, she doesn't want me, but she still has to make me feel good, like a prostitute. But even while he hated her he responded in kind, from the habit of sexual generosity. "It's because of my admiration for you, because . . . after all, I was holding in my arms one of the thousand women."

A pause. "The thousand?" she enquired, carefully.

"The thousand especial women."

"In Britain or in the world? You choose them for their brains, their beauty—what?"

"Whatever it is that makes them outstanding," he said, offering her a compliment.

"Well," she remarked at last, inciting him to be amused again: "I hope that at least there's a short list you can say I am on, for politeness' sake."

He did not reply for he understood he was sleepy. He was still telling himself that he must stay awake when he was slowly waking and it was morning. It was about eight. Barbara was not there. He thought: My God! What on earth shall I tell my wife? Where was Barbara? He remembered the ridiculous scenes of last night and nearly succumbed to shame. Then he thought, reviving anger: If she didn't sleep beside me here I'll never forgive her. . . . He sat up, quietly, determined to go through the house until he found her and, having found her, to possess her, when the door opened and she came in. She was fully dressed in a green suit, her hair done, her eyes made up. She carried a tray of coffee, which she set down beside the bed. He was conscious of his big loose hairy body, half uncovered. He said to himself that he was not going to lie in bed, naked, while she was dressed. He said: "Have you got a gown of some kind?" She handed him, without speaking, a towel, and said: "The bathroom's second on the left." She went out. He followed, the towel around him. Everything in this house was gay, intimate—not at all like her efficient working room. He wanted to find out where she had slept, and opened the first door. It was the kitchen, and she was in it, putting a brown earthenware dish into the oven. "The next door," said Barbara. He went hastily past the second door, and opened (he hoped quietly) the third. It was a cupboard full of linen. "This door," said Barbara, behind him.

"So all right then, where did you sleep?"

"What's it to do with you? Upstairs, in my own bed. Now, if you have everything, I'll say goodbye, I want to get to the theater."

"I'll take you," he said at once.

He saw again the movement of her eyes, the dark swallowing the light in deadly boredom. "I'll take you," he insisted.

"I'd prefer to go by myself," she remarked. Then she smiled: "However, you'll take me. Then you'll make a point of coming right in, so that James and everyone can see—that's what you want to take me for, isn't it?"

He hated her, finally, and quite simply, for her intelligence; that not once had he got away with anything, that she had been watching, since they had met yesterday, every movement of his campaign for her. However, some fate or inner urge over which he had no control made him say sentimentally: "My dear, you must see that I'd like at least to take you to your work."

"Not at all, have it on me," she said, giving him the lie direct. She went past him to the room he had slept in. "I shall be leaving in ten minutes," she said.

He took a shower, fast. When he returned, the workroom was already tidied, the bed made, all signs of the night gone. Also, there were no signs of the coffee she had brought in for him. He did not like to ask for it, for fear of an outright refusal. Besides, she was ready, her coat on, her handbag under her arm. He went, without a word, to the front door, and she came after him, silent.

He could see that every fiber of her body signaled a simple message: Oh God, for the moment when I can be rid of this boor! She was nothing but a slut, he thought.

A taxi came. In it she sat as far away from him as she could. He thought of what he should say to his wife.

Outside the theater she remarked: "You could drop me here, if you liked." It was not a plea, she was too proud for that. "I'll take you in," he said, and saw her thinking: Very well, I'll go through with it to shame him. He was determined to take her in and hand her over to her colleagues, he was afraid she would give him the slip. But far from playing it down, she seemed determined to play it his way. At the stage door, she said to the doorman: "This is Mr. Spence, Tom—do you remember, Mr. Spence from last night?" "Good morning, Babs," said the man, examining Graham, politely, as he had been ordered to do.

Barbara went to the door to the stage, opened it, held it open for him. He went in first, then held it open for her. Together they walked into the cavernous, littered, badly lit place and she called out: "James, James!" A man's voice called out from the front of the house: "Here, Babs, why are you so late?"

The auditorium opened before them, darkish, silent, save for an early-morning busyness of charwomen. A vacuum cleaner roared, smally, somewhere close. A couple of stagehands stood looking up at a drop which had a design of blue and green spirals. James stood with his back to the auditorium, smoking. "You're late, Babs," he said again. He saw Graham behind her, and nodded. Barbara and James kissed. Barbara said, giving allowance to every syllable: "You remember Mr. Spence from last night?" James nodded: How do you do? Barbara stood beside him, and they looked together up at the blue-and-green backdrop. Then Barbara looked again at Graham, asking silently: All right now, isn't that enough? He could see her eyes, sullen with boredom.

He said: "Bye, Babs. Bye, James. I'll ring you, Babs." No response, she ignored him. He walked off slowly, listening for what might be said. For instance: "Babs, for God's sake, what are you doing with him?" Or she might say: "Are you wondering about Graham Spence? Let me explain."

Graham passed the stagehands who, he could have sworn, didn't recognize him. Then at last he heard James's voice to Barbara: "It's no good, Babs, I know you're enamored of that particular shade of blue, but do have another look at it, there's a good girl. . . ." Graham left the stage, went past the office where the stage doorman sat reading a newspaper. Graham went to find a taxi, thinking: I'd better think up something convincing, then I'll telephone my wife.

Luckily he had an excuse not to be at home that day, for this evening he had to interview a young man (for television) about his new novel.

1958

OODGEROO NOONUCCAL (KATH WALKER)
1920–1993

"Since 1970 I have lived in the hope that the parliaments of England and Australia would confer and attempt to rectify the terrible damage done to the Australian Aborigines," wrote the poet Oodgeroo Noonuccal in 1987, as she recounted her reasons for returning the MBE (Member of the Order of the British Empire) that she had received seventeen years earlier for her art and her community activism. Among the crimes of the colonists, she cited the "forbidding us our tribal language, the murders, the poisoning, the scalping, the denial of land custodianship, especially our spiritual sacred sites, the destruction of our sacred places especially our Bora Grounds." Baptized Kathleen Jean Mary Ruska after her birth on Stradbroke Island, east of Brisbane, the poet repudiated this English name when she renounced the MBE, redefining herself as "Oodgeroo from the tribe of the Noonuccal, custodian of the land that the white man calls Stradbroke Island and that the Aboriginal people call Minjerriba."

Oodgeroo had been briefly married to Bruce Walker, another Aboriginal, in the 1940s and was the mother of two sons. In the same years, she served in the Australian Women's Army as a telephonist, established an Aboriginal women's cricket team, worked in an office and as a housekeeper, and (in the 1950s) joined the Communist Party in the hope that it would advance the interests of her people. Her first collection of verse, *We Are Going,* appeared in 1964 and immediately gained her work a wide readership, along with the admiration and friendship of the white Australian poet Judith Wright, who dedicated her fine "Two Dreamtimes" to her (see pp. 730–33 of this volume). "I felt poetry would be the breakthrough for the Aboriginal people because they were storytellers and song-makers, and I thought poetry would appeal to them more than anything else," Oodgeroo explained, noting that *We Are Going* was, from her point of view, "more of a book of their voices that I was trying to bring out, and I think I succeeded in doing that."

After winning numerous prizes and honors for her verse, Oodgeroo—who remained an activist and also became a graphic artist—returned in 1970 to Minjeribba, her native island, where she purchased land for a cultural center that she called "Moongalba," meaning "resting place." There, for the last twenty-three years of her life, she welcomed some 30,000 visitors, who came to learn more about the ways and words of the society she struggled so hard to preserve. Sadly, she died just two weeks before the "Minjerriba tribute"—a "national celebration of Black Australian writers"—began at Moongalba.

We Are Going

For Grannie Coolwell

    They came in to the little town
    A semi-naked band subdued and silent,
    All that remained of their tribe.
    They came here to the place of their old bora ground[1]
5   Where now the many white men hurry about like ants.
    Notice of estate agent reads: 'Rubbish May Be Tipped[2] Here'.
    Now it half covers the traces of the old bora ring.

---

1. Sacred places where Australian Aborigines held initiation ceremonies.

2. Dumped. "Estate agent": real estate broker or manager.

They sit and are confused, they cannot say their thoughts:
'We are as strangers here now, but the white tribe are the strangers.
10 We belong here, we are of the old ways.
We are the corroboree³ and the bora ground,
We are the old sacred ceremonies, the laws of the elders.
We are the wonder tales of Dream Time,⁴ the tribal legends told.
We are the past, the hunts and the laughing games, the wandering
  camp fires.
15 We are the lightning-bolt over Gaphembah Hill
Quick and terrible,
And the Thunderer after him, that loud fellow.
We are the quiet daybreak paling the dark lagoon.
We are the shadow-ghosts creeping back as the camp fires burn low.
20 We are nature and the past, all the old ways
Gone now and scattered.
The scrubs are gone, the hunting and the laughter.
The eagle is gone, the emu and the kangaroo are gone from this place.
The bora ring is gone.
25 The corroboree is gone.
And we are going.'

1964

Understand, Old One[1]

Understand, old one,
I mean no desecration
Staring here with the learned ones
At your opened grave.
5 Now after hundreds of years gone
The men of science coming with spade and knowledge
Peer and probe, handle the yellow bones,
To them specimens, to me
More. Deeply moved am I.

10 Understand, old one,
I mean no lack of reverence.
It is with love
I think of you so long ago laid here
With tears and wailing.
15 Strongly I feel your presence very near
Haunting the old spot, watching
As we disturb your bones. Poor ghost,
I know, I know you will understand.

---

3. An Australian Aboriginal celebration, held at night with songs and symbolic dances.
4. According to Australian Aborigines, the time of creation, when ancestral spiritual beings rose from below the earth to shape the land.

1. This came after I had visited an old native burial ground not far from Brisbane, where University people were excavating bones and had invited me along. I wrote it down at once while impressions were still fresh [Oodgeroo's note].

What if you came back now
20 To our new world, the city roaring
There on the old peaceful camping place
Of your red fires along the quiet water,
How you would wonder
At towering stone gunyas[2] high in air
25 Immense, incredible;
Planes in the sky over, swarms of cars
Like things frantic in flight.
What if you came at night upon these miles
Of clustered neon lights of all colours
30 Like Christian newly come to his Heaven or Hell
And your own people gone?

Old one of the long ago,
So many generations lie between us
But cannot estrange. Your duty to your race
35 Was with the simple past, mine
Lies in the present and the coming days.

1964

Municipal Gum

Gumtree in the city street,
Hard bitumen[1] around your feet,
Rather you should be
In the cool world of leafy forest halls
5 And wild bird calls.
Here you seem to me
Like that poor cart-horse
Castrated, broken, a thing wronged,
Strapped and buckled, its hell prolonged,
10 Whose hung head and listless mien express
Its hopelessness.
Municipal gum, it is dolorous
To see you thus
Set in your black grass of bitumen—
15 O fellow citizen,
What have they done to us?

1964

---

2. Meeting places and fire places (a Central Desert Aboriginal word).

1. Tarred road.

GWEN HARWOOD
1920–1995

One of Australia's finest poets, Gwen Harwood received many awards during her publishing career, including the Meanjin Poetry Prize (1958, 1959), the Grace Leven Prize (1975), the Robert Frost Award (1977), the Patrick White Award (1978), and the Premier's Literary Award in both Victoria and South Australia (1989). Not until 1991, however, did Oxford University Press issue the first of her books to appear outside Australia, her *Collected Poems*. This neglect is particularly surprising because her verse was global in its ambition. Witty, high-spirited, and wide-ranging, Harwood mused often on philosophical and musical questions, on literary politics, and on the gender issues that she addresses in such poems as "In the Park" and "Mother Who Gave Me Life."

Gwendoline Nessie Foster was born in Taringa, Queensland, and educated at Brisbane Girls' Grammar School. In later years, she described her youth as a time of such happiness that "in a sense it left me without ambition. I refer everything in my life to the radiance of that time in my childhood." Music—piano and composition—became her "first love." After being discouraged from a concertizing career, she became a teacher and served as organist at the Anglican Church of All Saints in Brisbane. In 1945, she married the linguist F. W. Harwood and moved with him to Tasmania, where he had a university lectureship and where she began an intellectually enlivening friendship with the philosopher Ludwig Wittgenstein. Indeed, Harwood later believed that she was first inspired to write poetry by Wittgenstein's sentence "Not how the world is, is the mystical, but that it is."

Attributing her relative tardiness in publishing her verse to her decision to devote herself primarily to the raising of her four children, Harwood kept her poems "a secret vice" until the end of the 1950s, when her work began appearing in anthologies and magazines, sometimes under an extraordinary spectrum of pseudonyms, which included Walter Lehmann. W. W. Hagendoor, Francis Geyer, Timothy (TF) Kline, Miriam Stone, and Alan Carvosso. About "Walter Lehmann," an Australian scholar has recently noted that two of "his" poems were deliberately written as "a hoax," adding that "Harwood gave Lehmann a personal history which made him more than a pseudonym. He was an 'apple orchardist in the Huon Valley in Tasmania, and husband and father.'" According to this writer, Harwood achieved notoriety when she made headlines—"Tas [Tasmanian] Housewife in Hoax of the Year"—"precipitated" by two sonnets that she had published in a journal called *The Bulletin*. Read acrostically, the sonnets spelled out "So Long Bulletin" and "Fuck All Editors." Harwood was evidently certain that the sonnets were "poetical rubbish and [would] show up the incompetence of anyone who publishe[d] them." Even as she declared that her fake submission was "a literary test," however, she noted ironically that editors tended to be less accepting of work by "lady poets" than they were of male-authored poems; indeed, aligning herself with a female tradition of pseudonymous authorship that goes back at least as far as George Sand, Currer Bell (Charlotte Brontë), and George Eliot, she claimed that she "received far more invitations and favourable letters to her male pseudonyms than she ever did herself."

Even while embroiling herself in literary controversy, Harwood maintained a lifelong link to music, drafting five opera librettos for the Australian composer Larry Sitsky. By the 1980s, when she had published *The Lion's Bride* (1981) and *Bone Scan* (1989), she had established herself as a major artist in a range of genres. Her final collection, *The Present Tense*, was published in 1995, the year of her death. More recently, a selection of her letters, *A Steady Storm of Correspondence* (2001), has been widely praised.

In the Park

She sits in the park. Her clothes are out of date.
Two children whine and bicker, tug her skirt.
A third draws aimless patterns in the dirt.
Someone she loved once passes by—too late

5   to feign indifference to that casual nod.
"How nice," et cetera. "Time holds great surprises."
From his neat head unquestionably rises
a small balloon . . . "but for the grace of God . . ."

They stand a while in flickering light, rehearsing
10   the children's names and birthdays. "It's so sweet
to hear their chatter, watch them grow and thrive,"
she says to his departing smile. Then, nursing
the youngest child, sits staring at her feet.
To the wind she says, "They have eaten me alive."

1963

The Sea Anemones

Gray mountains, sea and sky. Even the misty
seawind is gray. I walk on lichened rock
in a kind of late assessment, call it peace.
Then the anemones, scarlet, gouts of blood.

5   There is a word I need, and earth was speaking.
I cannot hear. These seaflowers are too bright.
Kneeling on rock, I touch them through cold water.
My fingers meet some hungering gentleness.
A newborn child's lips moved so at my breast.

10   I woke, once, with my palm across your mouth.
    The word is: *ever*. Why add salt to salt?
Blood drop by drop among the rocks they shine.
Anemos,[1] wind. The spirit, where it will.
Not flowers, no, animals[2] that must eat or die.

1981

Mother Who Gave Me Life

Mother who gave me life
I think of women bearing

---

1. Wind (Greek).
2. Sea anemones, whose bright-colored tentacles and general fixity of position make them somewhat resemble flowers, are in fact animals.

women. Forgive me the wisdom
I would not learn from you.

It is not for my children I walk
on earth in the light of the living.
It is for you, for the wild
daughters becoming women,

anguish of seasons burning
backward in time to those other
bodies, your mother, and hers
and beyond, speech growing stranger

on thresholds of ice, rock, fire,
bones changing, heads inclining
to monkey bosom, lemur breast,
guileless milk of the word.

I prayed you would live to see
Halley's Comet a second time.[1]
The Sister said, When she died
she was folding a little towel.

You left the world so, having lived
nearly thirty thousand days:
a fabric of marvels folded
down to a little space.

At our last meeting I closed
the ward door of heavy glass
between us, and saw your face
crumple, fine threadbare linen

worn, still good to the last,
then, somehow, smooth to a smile
so I should not see your tears.
Anguish: remembered hours:

a lamp on embroidered linen,
my supper set out, your voice
calling me in as darkness
falls on my father's house.

1981

---

1. The most recent approaches of this periodic comet were in 1910 and 1985–86 (it next returns in early 2062).

Mid-Channel

> The days shall come upon you, that he will take you away with hooks, and your posterity with fishhooks.
> —Amos, IV, 2

Cod inert as an old boot,
tangling dance of the little shark,
perch nibble, flathead jerk—
blindfold I'd know them on my line.

5 Fugitive gleam on scale and fin,
lustrous eye, opalescent belly
dry and die in the undesired
element. A day will come,

matter-of-fact as knife and plate,
10 with death's hook in my jaw, and language
unspeakable, the line full out.
I'll tire you with my choking weight

old monster anchored in the void.
My God, you'll wonder what you've caught.
15 Land me in hell itself at last
I'll stab and swell your wounds with poison.

Not here, not now. Water's my kingdom
tonight, my line makes starspecks tremble.
The dinghy's decked with golden eyes
20 and still the cod boil round my bait.

1988

HISAYE YAMAMOTO
b. 1921

The daughter of Issei parents (immigrants from Japan), Hisaye Yamamoto explores her complicated identity as a Nisei, a member of the second American generation, in her most frequently anthologized story, "Seventeen Syllables." Her central character, the sexually awakening Rosie, feels estranged from her mother not only because of their different languages but also because of the mystery in which the mother's life in Japan remains shrouded.

That immigration and assimilation would serve as the mainspring of Yamamoto's imagination seems apt given her attendance in Japanese schools for the first twelve years of her growing up in California. During World War II, when many Japanese-American citizens were forced to live in concentration camps, she was interned for three years in Poston, Arizona, where she wrote for the camp newspaper. Her stint working at the socially conscious *Catholic Worker* in New York during the 1950s kept her involved with issues of disenfranchisement. Married, the mother of five children, and the grandmother of two, Yamamoto resides in Southern California.

Seventeen Syllables

The first Rosie knew that her mother had taken to writing poems was one evening when she finished one and read it aloud for her daughter's approval. It was about cats, and Rosie pretended to understand it thoroughly and appreciate it no end, partly because she hesitated to disillusion her mother about the quantity and quality of Japanese she had learned in all the years now that she had been going to Japanese school every Saturday (and Wednesday, too, in the summer). Even so, her mother must have been skeptical about the depth of Rosie's understanding, because she explained afterwards about the kind of poem she was trying to write.

See, Rosie, she said, it was a *haiku,* a poem in which she must pack all her meaning into seventeen syllables only, which were divided into three lines of five, seven, and five syllables. In the one she had just read, she had tried to capture the charm of a kitten, as well as comment on the superstition that owning a cat of three colors meant good luck.

"Yes, yes, I understand. How utterly lovely," Rosie said, and her mother, either satisfied or seeing through the deception and resigned, went back to composing.

The truth was that Rosie was lazy; English lay ready on the tongue but Japanese had to be searched for and examined, and even then put forth tentatively (probably to meet with laughter). It was so much easier to say yes, yes, even when one meant no, no. Besides, this was what was in her mind to say: I was looking through one of your magazines from Japan last night, Mother, and towards the back I found some *haiku* in English that delighted me. There was one that made me giggle off and on until I fell asleep—

> *It is morning, and lo!*
> *I lie awake, comme il faut,*
> *sighing for some dough.*

Now, how to reach her mother, how to communicate the melancholy song? Rosie knew formal Japanese by fits and starts, her mother had even less English, no French. It was much more possible to say yes, yes.

It developed that her mother was writing the *haiku* for a daily newspaper, the *Mainichi Shimbun,* that was published in San Francisco. Los Angeles, to be sure, was closer to the farming community in which the Hayashi family lived and several Japanese vernaculars were printed there, but Rosie's parents said they preferred the tone of the northern paper. Once a week, the *Mainichi* would have a section devoted to *haiku,* and her mother became an extravagant contributor, taking for herself the blossoming pen name, Ume Hanazono.

So Rosie and her father lived for awhile with two women, her mother and Ume Hanazono. Her mother (Tome Hayashi by name) kept house, cooked, washed, and, along with her husband and the Carrascos, the Mexican family hired for the harvest, did her ample share of picking tomatoes out in the sweltering fields and boxing them in tidy strata in the cool packing shed. Ume Hanazono, who came to life after the dinner dishes were done, was an earnest, muttering stranger who often neglected speaking when spoken to and stayed busy at the parlor table as late as midnight scribbling with pencil on scratch paper or carefully copying characters on good paper with her fat, pale green Parker.[1]

The new interest had some repercussions on the household routine. Before, Rosie had been accustomed to her parents and herself taking their hot baths early and going to bed almost immediately afterwards, unless her parents challenged each other to a game of flower cards or unless company dropped in. Now if her father wanted to play cards, he had to resort to solitaire (at which he always cheated fearlessly), and if a group of friends came over, it was bound to contain someone who was also writing *haiku*, and the small assemblage would be split in two, her father entertaining the non-literary members and her mother comparing ecstatic notes with the visiting poet.

If they went out, it was more of the same thing. But Ume Hanazono's life span, even for a poet's, was very brief—perhaps three months at most.

One night they went over to see the Hayano family in the neighboring town to the west, an adventure both painful and attractive to Rosie. It was attractive because there were four Hayano girls, all lovely and each one named after a season of the year (Haru, Natsu, Aki, Fuyu),[2] painful because something had been wrong with Mrs. Hayano ever since the birth of her first child. Rosie would sometimes watch Mrs. Hayano, reputed to have been the belle of her native village, making her way about a room, stooped, slowly shuffling, violently trembling (*always* trembling), and she would be reminded that this woman, in this same condition, had carried and given issue to three babies. She would look wonderingly at Mr. Hayano, handsome, tall, and strong, and she would look at her four pretty friends. But it was not a matter she could come to any decision about.

On this visit, however, Mrs. Hayano sat all evening in the rocker, as motionless and unobtrusive as it was possible for her to be, and Rosie found the greater part of the evening practically anaesthetic. Too, Rosie spent most of it in the girls' room, because Haru, the garrulous one, said almost as soon as the bows and other greetings were over, "Oh, you must see my new coat!"

It was a pale plaid of grey, sand, and blue, with an enormous collar, and Rosie, seeing nothing special in it, said, "Gee, how nice."

"Nice?" said Haru, indignantly. "Is that all you can say about it? It's gorgeous! And so cheap, too. Only seventeen-ninety-eight, because it was a sale. The saleslady said it was twenty-five dollars regular."

"Gee," said Rosie. Natsu, who never said much and when she said anything said it shyly, fingered the coat covetously and Haru pulled it away.

"Mine," she said, putting it on. She minced in the aisle between the two large beds and smiled happily. "Let's see how your mother likes it."

She broke into the front room and the adult conversation and went to

---

1. I.e., her fountain pen.
2. The girls' names are Spring, Summer, Autumn, and Winter, respectively.

stand in front of Rosie's mother, while the rest watched from the door. Rosie's mother was properly envious. "May I inherit it when you're through with it?"

Haru, pleased, giggled and said yes, she could, but Natsu reminded gravely from the door, "You promised me, Haru."

Everyone laughed but Natsu, who shamefacedly retreated into the bedroom. Haru came in laughing, taking off the coat. "We were only kidding, Natsu," she said. "Here, you try it on now."

After Natsu buttoned herself into the coat, inspected herself solemnly in the bureau mirror, and reluctantly shed it, Rosie, Aki, and Fuyu got their turns, and Fuyu, who was eight, drowned in it while her sisters and Rosie doubled up in amusement. They all went into the front room later, because Haru's mother quaveringly called to her to fix the tea and rice cakes and open a can of sliced peaches for everybody. Rosie noticed that her mother and Mr. Hayano were talking together at the little table—they were discussing a *haiku* that Mr. Hayano was planning to send to the *Mainichi*, while her father was sitting at one end of the sofa looking through a copy of *Life*, the new picture magazine. Occasionally, her father would comment on a photograph, holding it toward Mrs. Hayano and speaking to her as he always did—loudly, as though he thought someone such as she must surely be at least a trifle deaf also.

The five girls had their refreshments at the kitchen table, and it was while Rosie was showing the sisters her trick of swallowing peach slices without chewing (she chased each slippery crescent down with a swig of tea) that her father brought his empty teacup and untouched saucer to the sink and said, "Come on, Rosie, we're going home now."

"Already?" asked Rosie.

"Work tomorrow," he said.

He sounded irritated, and Rosie, puzzled, gulped one last yellow slice and stood up to go, while the sisters began protesting, as was their wont.

"We have to get up at five-thirty," he told them, going into the front room quickly, so that they did not have their usual chance to hang onto his hands and plead for an extension of time.

Rosie, following, saw that her mother and Mr. Hayano were sipping tea and still talking together, while Mrs. Hayano concentrated, quivering, on raising the handleless Japanese cup to her lips with both her hands and lowering it back to her lap. Her father, saying nothing, went out the door, onto the bright porch, and down the steps. Her mother looked up and asked, "Where is he going?"

"Where is he going?" Rosie said. "He said we were going home now."

"Going home?" Her mother looked with embarrassment at Mr. Hayano and his absorbed wife and then forced a smile. "He must be tired," she said.

Haru was not giving up yet. "May Rosie stay overnight?" she asked, and Natsu, Aki, and Fuyu came to reinforce their sister's plea by helping her make a circle around Rosie's mother. Rosie, for once having no desire to stay, was relieved when her mother, apologizing to the perturbed Mr. and Mrs. Hayano for her father's abruptness at the same time, managed to shake her head no at the quartet, kindly but adamant, so that they broke their circle and let her go.

Rosie's father looked ahead into the windshield as the two joined him. "I'm sorry," her mother said. "You must be tired." Her father, stepping on the starter, said nothing. "You know how I get when it's *haiku*," she continued, "I forget what time it is." He only grunted.

As they rode homeward silently, Rosie, sitting between, felt a rush of hate for both—for her mother for begging, for her father for denying her mother. I wish this old Ford would crash, right now, she thought, then immediately, no, no, I wish my father would laugh, but it was too late: already the vision had passed through her mind of the green pick-up crumpled in the dark against one of the mighty eucalyptus trees they were just riding past, of the three contorted, bleeding bodies, one of them hers.

Rosie ran between two patches of tomatoes, her heart working more rambunctiously than she had ever known it to. How lucky it was that Aunt Taka and Uncle Gimpachi had come tonight, though, how very lucky. Otherwise she might not have really kept her half-promise to meet Jesus Carrasco. Jesus was going to be a senior in September at the same school she went to, and his parents were the ones helping with the tomatoes this year. She and Jesus, who hardly remembered seeing each other at Cleveland High where there were so many other people and two whole grades between them, had become great friends this summer—he always had a joke for her when he periodically drove the loaded pick-up up from the fields to the shed where she was usually sorting while her mother and father did the packing, and they laughed a great deal together over infinitesimal repartee during the afternoon break for chilled watermelon or ice cream in the shade of the shed.

What she enjoyed most was racing him to see which could finish picking a double row first. He, who could work faster, would tease her by slowing down until she thought she would surely pass him this time, then speeding up furiously to leave her several sprawling vines behind. Once he had made her screech hideously by crossing over, while her back was turned, to place atop the tomatoes in her green-stained bucket a truly monstrous, pale green worm (it had looked more like an infant snake). And it was when they had finished a contest this morning, after she had pantingly pointed a green finger at the immature tomatoes evident in the lugs[3] at the end of his row and he had returned the accusation (with justice), that he had startlingly brought up the matter of their possibly meeting outside the range of both their parents' dubious eyes.

"What for?" she had asked.

"I've got a secret I want to tell you," he said.

"Tell me now," she demanded.

"It won't be ready till tonight," he said.

She laughed. "Tell me tomorrow then."

"It'll be gone tomorrow," he threatened.

"Well, for seven hakes,[4] what is it?" she had asked, more than twice, and when he had suggested that the packing shed would be an appropriate place to find out, she had cautiously answered maybe. She had not been certain she was going to keep the appointment until the arrival of mother's sister and her husband. Their coming seemed a sort of signal of permission, of

---

3. Shipping containers for produce.   4. I.e., for heaven's sake.

grace, and she had definitely made up her mind to lie and leave as she was bowing them welcome.

So as soon as everyone appeared settled back for the evening, she announced loudly that she was going to the privy outside, "I'm going to the *benjo!*" and slipped out the door. And now that she was actually on her way, her heart pumped in such an undisciplined way that she could hear it with her ears. It's because I'm running, she told herself, slowing to a walk. The shed was up ahead, one more patch away, in the middle of the fields. Its bulk, looming in the dimness, took on a sinisterness that was funny when Rosie reminded herself that it was only a wooden frame with a canvas roof and three canvas walls that made a slapping noise on breezy days.

Jesus was sitting on the narrow plank that was the sorting platform and she went around to the other side and jumped backwards to seat herself on the rim of a packing stand. "Well, tell me," she said without greeting, thinking her voice sounded reassuringly familiar.

"I saw you coming out the door," Jesus said: "I heard you running part of the way, too."

"Uh-huh," Rosie said. "Now tell me the secret."

"I was afraid you wouldn't come," he said.

Rosie delved around on the chicken-wire bottom of the stall for number two tomatoes, ripe, which she was sitting beside, and came up with a leftover that felt edible. She bit into it and began sucking out the pulp and seeds. "I'm here," she pointed out.

"Rosie, are you sorry you came?"

"Sorry? What for?" she said. "You said you were going to tell me something."

"I will, I will," Jesus said, but his voice contained disappointment, and Rosie fleetingly felt the older of the two, realizing a brand-new power which vanished without category under her recognition.

"I have to go back in a minute," she said. "My aunt and uncle are here from Wintersburg. I told them I was going to the privy."

Jesus laughed. "You funny thing," he said. "You slay me!"

"Just because you have a bathroom *inside*," Rosie said. "Come on, tell me."

Chuckling, Jesus came around to lean on the stand facing her. They still could not see each other very clearly, but Rosie noticed that Jesus became very sober again as he took the hollow tomato from her hand and dropped it back into the stall. When he took hold of her empty hand, she could find no words to protest; her vocabulary had become distressingly constricted and she thought desperately that all that remained intact now was yes and no and oh, and even these few sounds would not easily out. Thus, kissed by Jesus, Rosie fell for the first time entirely victim to a helplessness delectable beyond speech. But the terrible, beautiful sensation lasted no more than a second, and the reality of Jesus' lips and tongue and teeth and hands made her pull away with such strength that she nearly tumbled.

Rosie stopped running as she approached the lights from the windows of home. How long since she had left? She could not guess, but gasping yet, she went to the privy in back and locked herself in. Her own breathing deafened her in the dark, close space, and she sat and waited until she could hear at last the nightly calling of the frogs and crickets. Even then, all she could think to say was oh, my, and the pressure of Jesus' face against her face would not leave.

No one had missed her in the parlor, however, and Rosie walked in and through quickly, announcing that she was next going to take a bath. "Your father's in the bathhouse," her mother said, and Rosie, in her room, recalled that she had not seen him when she entered. There had been only Aunt Taka and Uncle Gimpachi with her mother at the table, drinking tea. She got her robe and straw sandals and crossed the parlor again to go outside. Her mother was telling them about the *haiku* competition in the *Mainichi* and the poem she had entered.

Rosie met her father coming out of the bathhouse. "Are you through, Father?" she asked. "I was going to ask you to scrub my back."

"Scrub your own back," he said shortly, going toward the main house.

"What have I done now?" she yelled at him. She suddenly felt like doing a lot of yelling. But he did not answer, and she went into the bathhouse. Turning on the dangling light, she removed her denims and T-shirt and threw them in the big carton for dirty clothes standing next to the washing machine. Her other things she took with her into the bath compartment to wash after her bath. After she had scooped a basin of hot water from the square wooden tub, she sat on the grey cement of the floor and soaped herself at exaggerated leisure, singing "Red Sails in the Sunset"[5] at the top of her voice and using da-da-da where she suspected her words. Then, standing up, still singing, for she was possessed by the notion that any attempt now to analyze would result in spoilage and she believed that the larger her volume the less she would be able to hear herself think, she obtained more hot water and poured it on until she was free of lather. Only then did she allow herself to step into the steaming vat, one leg first, then the remainder of her body inch by inch until the water no longer stung and she could move around at will.

She took a long time soaking, afterwards remembering to go around outside to stoke the embers of the tin-lined fireplace beneath the tub and to throw on a few more sticks so that the water might keep its heat for her mother, and when she finally returned to the parlor, she found her mother still talking *haiku* with her aunt and uncle, the three of them on another round of tea. Her father was nowhere in sight.

At Japanese school the next day (Wednesday, it was), Rosie was grave and giddy by turns. Preoccupied at her desk in the row for students on Book Eight, she made up for it at recess by performing wild mimicry for the benefit of her friend Chizuko. She held her nose and whined a witticism or two in what she considered was the manner of Fred Allen; she assumed intoxication and a British accent to go over the climax of the Rudy Vallee recording of the pub conversation about William Ewart Gladstone; she was the child Shirley Temple piping, "On the Good Ship Lollipop"; she was the gentleman soprano of the Four Inkspots trilling, "If I Didn't Care."[6] And she felt rea-

---

5. A popular song written by Jimmy Kennedy and Hugh Williams (1935); several prominent artists recorded it in the 1930s.
6. She is imitating enormously popular figures of the 1930s. Fred Allen (1894–1956), radio comedian. Rudy Vallee (1901–1986), a singer who became one of America's first pop culture idols in the 1920s. William E. Gladstone (1809–1898), one of the greatest political figures of the Victorian age and a leader of the Liberal Party. Shirley Temple (b. 1928), child film star; she sang the hit song "The Good Ship Lollipop" in the movie *Bright Eyes* (1934). The Ink Spots was a jazz vocal quartet, and "If I Didn't Care" (1939) was their first smash hit.

sonably satisfied when Chizuko wept and gasped, "Oh, Rosie, you ought to be in the movies!"

Her father came after her at noon, bringing her sandwiches of minced ham and two nectarines to eat while she rode, so that she could pitch right into the sorting when they got home. The lugs were piling up, he said, and the ripe tomatoes in them would probably have to be taken to the cannery tomorrow if they were not ready for the produce haulers tonight. "This heat's not doing them any good. And we've got no time for a break today."

It *was* hot, probably the hottest day of the year, and Rosie's blouse stuck damply to her back even under the protection of the canvas. But she worked as efficiently as a flawless machine and kept the stalls heaped, with one part of her mind listening in to the parental murmuring about the heat and the tomatoes and with another part planning the exact words she would say to Jesus when he drove up with the first load of the afternoon. But when at last she saw that the pick-up was coming, her hands went berserk and the tomatoes started falling in the wrong stalls, and her father said, "Hey, hey! Rosie, watch what you're doing!"

"Well, I have to go to the *benjo*," she said, hiding panic.

"Go in the weeds over there," he said, only half-joking.

"Oh, Father!" she protested.

"Oh, go on home," her mother said. "We'll make out for awhile."

In the privy Rosie peered through a knothole toward the fields, watching as much as she could of Jesus. Happily she thought she saw him look in the direction of the house from time to time before he finished unloading and went back toward the patch where his mother and father worked. As she was heading for the shed, a very presentable black car purred up the dirt driveway to the house and its driver motioned to her. Was this the Hayashi home, he wanted to know. She nodded. Was she a Hayashi? Yes, she said, thinking that he was a good-looking man. He got out of the car with a huge, flat package and she saw that he warmly wore a business suit. "I have something here for your mother then," he said, in a more elegant Japanese than she was used to.

She told him where her mother was and he came along with her, patting his face with an immaculate white handkerchief and saying something about the coolness of San Francisco. To her surprised mother and father, he bowed and introduced himself as, among other things, the *haiku* editor of the *Mainichi Shimbun,* saying that since he had been coming as far as Los Angeles anyway, he had decided to bring her the first prize she had won in the recent contest.

"First prize?" her mother echoed, believing and not believing, pleased and overwhelmed. Handed the package with a bow, she bobbed her head up and down numerous times to express her utter gratitude.

"It is nothing much," he added, "but I hope it will serve as a token of our great appreciation for your contributions and our great admiration of your considerable talent."

"I am not worthy," she said, falling easily into his style. "It is I who should make some sign of my humble thanks for being permitted to contribute."

"No, no, to the contrary," he said, bowing again.

But Rosie's mother insisted, and then saying that she knew she was being unorthodox, she asked if she might open the package because her curiosity was so great. Certainly she might. In fact, he would like her reaction to it, for personally, it was one of his favorite *Hiroshiges*.[7]

Rosie thought it was a pleasant picture, which looked to have been sketched with delicate quickness. There were pink clouds, containing some graceful calligraphy, and a sea that was a pale blue except at the edges, containing four sampans[8] with indications of people in them. Pines edged the water and on the far-off beach there was a cluster of thatched huts towered over by pine-dotted mountains of grey and blue. The frame was scalloped and gilt.

After Rosie's mother pronounced it without peer and somewhat prodded her father into nodding agreement, she said Mr. Kuroda must at least have a cup of tea after coming all this way, and although Mr. Kuroda did not want to impose, he soon agreed that a cup of tea would be refreshing and went along with her to the house, carrying the picture for her.

"Ha, your mother's crazy!" Rosie's father said, and Rosie laughed uneasily as she resumed judgment on the tomatoes. She had emptied six lugs when he broke into an imaginary conversation with Jesus to tell her to go and remind her mother of the tomatoes, and she went slowly.

Mr. Kuroda was in his shirtsleeves expounding some *haiku* theory as he munched a rice cake, and her mother was rapt. Abashed in the great man's presence, Rosie stood next to her mother's chair until her mother looked up inquiringly, and then she started to whisper the message, but her mother pushed her gently away and reproached, "You are not being very polite to our guest."

"Father says the tomatoes . . ." Rosie said aloud, smiling foolishly.

"Tell him I shall only be a minute," her mother said, speaking the language of Mr. Kuroda.

When Rosie carried the reply to her father, he did not seem to hear and she said again, "Mother says she'll be back in a minute."

"All right, all right," he nodded, and they worked again in silence. But suddenly, her father uttered an incredible noise, exactly like the cork of a bottle popping, and the next Rosie knew, he was stalking angrily toward the house, almost running in fact, and she chased after him crying, "Father! Father! What are you going to do?"

He stopped long enough to order her back to the shed. "Never mind!" he shouted. "Get on with the sorting!"

And from the place in the fields where she stood, frightened and vacillating, Rosie saw her father enter the house. Soon Mr. Kuroda came out alone, putting on his coat. Mr. Kuroda got into his car and backed out down the driveway onto the highway. Next her father emerged, also alone, something in his arms (it was the picture, she realized), and, going over to the bathhouse woodpile, he threw the picture on the ground and picked up the axe. Smashing the picture, glass and all (she heard the explosion faintly), he reached over for the kerosene that was used to encourage the bath fire and poured it over the wreckage. I am dreaming, Rosie said to herself, I am dreaming, but her father, having made sure that his act of cremation was irrevocable, was even then returning to the fields.

7. Andō Hiroshige (1797–1858), a great Japanese landscape artist.

8. Flat-bottomed Chinese skiffs.

Rosie ran past him and toward the house. What had become of her mother? She burst into the parlor and found her mother at the back window watching the dying fire. They watched together until there remained only a feeble smoke under the blazing sun. Her mother was very calm.

"Do you know why I married your father?" she said without turning.

"No," said Rosie. It was the most frightening question she had ever been called upon to answer. Don't tell me now, she wanted to say, tell me tomorrow, tell me next week, don't tell me today. But she knew she would be told now, that the telling would combine with the other violence of the hot afternoon to level her life, her world to the very ground.

It was like a story out of the magazines illustrated in sepia,[9] which she had consumed so greedily for a period until the information had somehow reached her that those wretchedly unhappy autobiographies, offered to her as the testimonials of living men and women, were largely inventions: Her mother, at nineteen, had come to America and married her father as an alternative to suicide.

At eighteen she had been in love with the first son of one of the well-to-do families in her village. The two had met whenever and wherever they could, secretly, because it would not have done for his family to see him favor her—her father had no money; he was a drunkard and a gambler besides. She had learned she was with child; an excellent match had already been arranged for her lover. Despised by her family, she had given premature birth to a stillborn son, who would be seventeen now. Her family did not turn her out, but she could no longer project herself in any direction without refreshing in them the memory of her indiscretion. She wrote to Aunt Taka, her favorite sister in America, threatening to kill herself if Aunt Taka would not send for her. Aunt Taka hastily arranged a marriage with a young man of whom she knew, but lately arrived from Japan, a young man of simple mind, it was said, but of kindly heart. The young man was never told why his unseen betrothed was so eager to hasten the day of meeting.

The story was told perfectly, with neither groping for words nor untoward passion. It was as though her mother had memorized it by heart, reciting it to herself so many times over that its nagging vileness had long since gone.

"I had a brother then?" Rosie asked, for this was what seemed to matter now; she would think about the other later, she assured herself, pushing back the illumination which threatened all that darkness that had hitherto been merely mysterious or even glamorous. "A half-brother?"

"Yes."

"I would have liked a brother," she said.

Suddenly, her mother knelt on the floor and took her by the wrists. "Rosie," she said urgently, "Promise me you will never marry!" Shocked more by the request than the revelation, Rosie stared at her mother's face. Jesus, Jesus, she called silently, not certain whether she was invoking the help of the son of the Carrascos or of God, until there returned sweetly the memory of Jesus' hand, how it had touched her and where. Still her mother waited for an answer, holding her wrists so tightly that her hands were going numb. She tried to pull free. Promise, her mother whispered fiercely, promise. Yes, yes,

---

9. Brown ink used for both prints and photographs.

I promise, Rosie said. But for an instant she turned away, and her mother, hearing the familiar glib agreement, released her. Oh, you, you, you, her eyes and twisted mouth said, you fool. Rosie, covering her face, began at last to cry, and the embrace and consoling hand came much later than she expected.

1949

MAVIS GALLANT
b. 1922

"I have arranged matters so that I would be free to write," Mavis Gallant told a Canadian interviewer in 1978, explaining her decision to make her home in France, where she felt she could enjoy a life of cultural richness in a setting of "marvelous peace and quiet." Born in Montreal, Mavis Young was the only child of parents who have been described as "mismatched." From an early age, she was, as she once remarked, "set afloat" in a series of public, convent, and boarding schools—seventeen in all—and when her father died, her mother quickly remarried and shipped her daughter off to finish her education under the supervision of a guardian in the United States. On returning to Canada, Mavis Young became a journalist and married John Gallant, a musician, while she was working for the *Montreal Standard*. But in 1949 the couple divorced, and the young journalist traveled to Europe. Determined to become a full-time writer, she took up residence in Paris, where she still lives.

Gallant began publishing her beautifully crafted, sensitively observed fiction in 1951, soon after she resolved to devote herself entirely to her art. More than 100 of her short stories have appeared since then, most of them initially in *The New Yorker* and subsequently in numerous collections, including *The Other Paris* (1956), *My Heart Is Broken* (1964), and *The Collected Stories of Mavis Gallant* (1996). She has also published several novels and novellas, earning numerous awards and prizes for her work. Appointed an Officer of the Order of Canada in 1981, Gallant was raised to Companion, the Order's highest level, in 1993. In addition, she is a Foreign Honorary Member of the American Academy of Arts and Letters, and a Fellow of the Royal Society of Literature. Her wide-ranging and sophisticated stories explore the lives of Parisians as well as Canadians, Americans, Britons, and Germans. As "Mlle. Dias de Corta" reveals, she is at ease representing the words and world of a French widow, but in other tales she brilliantly dramatizes the milieu of her Montreal childhood. The judges who honored her with the prestigious Rea Award for "Mlle. Dias de Corta" in 2002 (one of them her distinguished contemporary Alice Munro) commented that she "has shown us over and over again what a marvel a short story can be." But perhaps this is because Gallant believes that, as she puts it, "Literature is no more and nothing less than a matter of life and death."

Mlle. Dias de Corta

You moved into my apartment during the summer of the year before abortion became legal in France;[1] that should fix it in past time for you, dear Mlle. Dias de Corta. You had just arrived in Paris from your native city, which you kept insisting was Marseilles, and were looking for work. You said you had studied television-performance techniques at some provincial school (we had never heard of the school, even though my son had one or two actor friends) and received a diploma with "special mention" for vocal expression. The diploma was not among the things we found in your suitcase, after you disappeared, but my son recalled that you carried it in your handbag, in case you had the good luck to sit next to a casting director on a bus.

The next morning we had our first cordial conversation. I described my husband's recent death and repeated his last words, which had to do with my financial future and were not overly optimistic. I felt his presence and still heard his voice in my mind. He seemed to be in the kitchen, wondering what you were doing there, summing you up: a thin, dark-eyed, noncommittal young woman, standing at the counter, bolting her breakfast. A bit sullen, perhaps; you refused the chair I had dragged in from the dining room. Careless, too. There were crumbs everywhere. You had spilled milk on the floor.

"Don't bother about the mess," I said. "I'm used to cleaning up after young people. I wait on my son, Robert, hand and foot." Actually, you had not made a move. I fetched the sponge mop from the broom closet, but when I asked you to step aside you started to choke on a crust. I waited quietly, then said, "My husband's illness was the result of eating too fast and never chewing his food." His silent voice told me I was wasting my time. True, but if I hadn't warned you I would have been guilty of withholding assistance from someone in danger. In our country, a refusal to help can be punished by law.

The only remark my son, Robert, made about you at the beginning was "She's too short for an actress." He was on the first step of his career climb in the public institution known then as Post, Telegrams, Telephones. Now it has been broken up and renamed with short, modern terms I can never keep in mind.[2] (Not long ago I had the pleasure of visiting Robert in his new quarters. There is a screen or a machine of some kind everywhere you look. He shares a spacious office with two women. One was born in Martinique and can't pronounce her "r"s. The other looks Corsican.) He left home early every day and liked to spend his evenings with a set of new friends, none of whom seemed to have a mother. The misteachings of the seventies, which encouraged criticism of earlier generations, had warped his natural feelings. Once, as he was going out the door, I asked if he loved me. He said the answer was self-evident: we were closely related. His behavior changed entirely after his engagement and marriage to Anny Clarens, a young lady of mixed descent. (Two of her grandparents are Swiss.) She is employed in the accounting department of a large hospital and enjoys her work. She and Robert have three children: Bruno, Elodie, and Félicie.

---

1. Abortion was decriminalized in France in 1975.
2. In 1991, PTT (Postes, Télégraphes et Téléphones) was split into the Post Office (La Poste) and France Télécom.

It was for companionship rather than income that I had decided to open my home to a stranger. My notice in *Le Figaro* mentioned "young woman only," even though those concerned for my welfare, from coiffeur to concierge, had strongly counseled "young man." "Young man" was said to be neater, cleaner, quieter, and (except under special circumstances I need not go into) would not interfere in my relationship with my son. In fact, my son was seldom available for conversation and had never shown interest in exchanging ideas with a woman, not even one who had known him from birth.

You called from a telephone on a busy street. I could hear the coins jangling and traffic going by. Your voice was low-pitched and agreeable and, except for one or two vowel sounds, would have passed for educated French. I suppose no amount of coaching at a school in or near Marseilles could get the better of the southern "o," long where it should be short and clipped when it ought to be broad. But, then, the language was already in decline, owing to lax teaching standards and uncontrolled immigration. I admire your achievement and respect your handicaps, and I know Robert would say the same if he knew you were in my thoughts.

Your suitcase weighed next to nothing. I wondered if you owned warm clothes and if you even knew there could be such a thing as a wet summer. You might have seemed more at home basking in a lush garden than tramping the chilly streets in search of employment. I showed you the room—mine—with its two corner windows and long view down Avenue de Choisy. (I was to take Robert's and he was to sleep in the living room, on a couch.) At the far end of the Avenue, Asian colonization had begun: a few restaurants and stores selling rice bowls and embroidered slippers from Taiwan. (Since those days the community has spread into all the neighboring streets. Police keep out of the area, preferring to let the immigrants settle disputes in their own way. Apparently, they punish wrongdoers by throwing them off the Tolbiac Bridge. Robert has been told of a secret report, compiled by experts, which the Mayor has had on his desk for eighteen months. According to this report, by the year 2025 Asians will have taken over a third of Paris, Arabs and Africans three-quarters, and unskilled European immigrants two-fifths. Thousands of foreign-sounding names are deliberately "lost" by the authorities and never show up in telephone books or computer directories, to prevent us from knowing the true extent of their progress.)

I gave you the inventory and asked you to read it. You said you did not care what was in the room. I had to explain that the inventory was for me. Your signature, "Alda Dias de Corta," with its long loops and closed "a"s showed pride and secrecy. You promised not to damage or remove without permission a double bed, two pillows, and a bolster, a pair of blankets, a beige satin spread with hand-knotted silk fringe, a chaise longue of the same color, a wardrobe and a dozen hangers, a marble fireplace (ornamental), two sets of lined curtains and two of écru voile,[3] a walnut bureau with four drawers, two framed etchings of cathedrals (Reims and Chartres), a bedside table, a small lamp with parchment shade, a Louis XVI—style[4] writing desk, a folding card table and four chairs, a gilt-framed mirror, two wrought-iron wall fixtures fitted with electric candles and light bulbs shaped like flames,

---

3. Unbleached semitransparent fabric.
4. I.e., a neoclassical style; Louis XVI (1754–1793) was king of France from 1774 to 1792.

two medium-sized "Persian" rugs, and an electric heater, which had given useful service for six years but which you aged before its time by leaving it turned on all night. Robert insisted I include breakfast. He did not want it told around the building that we were cheap. What a lot of coffee, milk, bread, apricot jam, butter, and sugar you managed to put away! Yet you remained as thin as a matchstick and that great thatch of curly hair made your face seem smaller than ever.

You agreed to pay a monthly rent of fifty thousand francs for the room, cleaning of same, use of bathroom, electricity, gas (for heating baths and morning coffee), fresh sheets and towels once a week, and free latchkey. You were to keep a list of your phone calls and to settle up once a week. I offered to take messages and say positive things about you to prospective employers. The figure on the agreement was not fifty thousand, of course, but five hundred. To this day, I count in old francs—the denominations we used before General de Gaulle[5] decided to delete two zeros, creating confusion for generations to come. Robert has to make out my income tax; otherwise, I give myself earnings in millions. He says I've had more than thirty years now to learn how to move a decimal, but a figure like "ten thousand francs" sounds more solid to me than "one hundred." I remember when a hundred francs was just the price of a croissant.

You remarked that five hundred was a lot for only a room. You had heard of studios going for six. But you did not have six hundred francs or five or even three, and after a while I took back my room and put you in Robert's, while he continued to sleep on the couch. Then you had no francs at all, and you exchanged beds with Robert, and, as it turned out, occasionally shared one. The arrangement—having you in the living room—never worked: it was hard to get you up in the morning, and the room looked as though five people were using it, all the time. We borrowed a folding bed and set it up at the far end of the hall, behind a screen, but you found the area noisy. The neighbors who lived upstairs used to go away for the weekend, leaving their dog. The concierge took it out twice a day, but the rest of the time it whined and barked, and at night it would scratch the floor. Apparently, this went on right over your head. I loaned you the earplugs my husband had used when his nerves were so bad. You complained that with your ears stopped up you could hear your own pulse beating. Given a choice, you preferred the dog.

I remember saying, "I'm afraid you must think we French are cruel to animals, Mlle. Dias de Corta, but I assure you not everyone is the same." You protested that you were French, too. I asked if you had a French passport. You said you had never applied for one. "Not even to go and visit your family?" I asked. You replied that the whole family lived in Marseilles. "But where were they born?" I said. "Where did they come from?" There wasn't so much talk about European citizenship then. One felt free to wonder.

The couple with the dog moved away sometime in the eighties. Now the apartment is occupied by a woman with long, streaky, brass-colored hair. She wears the same coat, made of fake ocelot, year after year. Some people think the man she lives with is her son. If so, she had him at the age of twelve.

---

5. Charles de Gaulle (1890–1970), soldier and president of France (1958–69); the franc was revalued in 1960.

What I want to tell you about has to do with the present and the great joy and astonishment we felt when we saw you in the oven-cleanser commercial last night. It came on just at the end of the eight-o'clock news and before the debate on hepatitis. Robert and Anny were having dinner with me, without the children: Anny's mother had taken them to visit Euro Disney[6] and was keeping them overnight. We had just started dessert—crème brûlée—when I recognized your voice. Robert stopped eating and said to Anny, "It's Alda. I'm sure it's Alda." Your face has changed in some indefinable manner that has nothing to do with time. Your smile seems whiter and wider; your hair is short and has a deep-mahogany tint that mature actresses often favor. Mine is still ash-blond, swept back, medium-long. Alain—the stylist I sent you to, all those years ago—gave it shape and color, once and for all, and I have never tampered with his creation.

Alain often asked for news of you after you vanished, mentioning you affectionately as "the little Carmencita," searching TV guides and magazines for a sign of your career. He thought you must have changed your name, perhaps to something short and easy to remember. I recall the way you wept and stormed after he cut your hair, saying he had charged two weeks' rent and cropped it so drastically that there wasn't a part you could audition for now except Hamlet. Alain retired after selling his salon to a competent and charming woman named Marie-Laure. She is thirty-seven and trying hard to have a baby. Apparently, it is her fault, not the husband's. They have started her on hormones and I pray for her safety. It must seem strange to you to think of a woman bent on motherhood, but she has financial security with the salon (although she is still paying the bank). The husband is a car-insurance assessor.

The shot of your face at the oven door, seen as though the viewer were actually in the oven, seemed to me original and clever. (Anny said she had seen the same device in a commercial about refrigerators.) I wondered if the oven was a convenient height or if you were crouched on the floor. All we could see of you was your face, and the hand wielding the spray can. Your nails were beautifully lacquered holly-red, not a crack or chip. You assured us that the product did not leave a bad smell or seep into food or damage the ozone layer. Just as we had finished taking this in, you were replaced by a picture of bacteria, dead or dying, and the next thing we knew some man was driving you away in a Jaguar, all your household tasks behind you. Every movement of your body seemed to express freedom from care. What I could make out of your forehead, partly obscured by the mahogany-tinted locks, seemed smooth and unlined. It is only justice, for I had a happy childhood and a wonderful husband and a fine son, and I recall some of the things you told Robert about your early years. He was just twenty-two and easily moved to pity.

Anny reminded us of the exact date when we last had seen you: April 24, 1983. It was in the television film about the two friends, "Virginie" and "Camilla," and how they meet two interesting but very different men and accompany them on a holiday in Cannes. One of the men is a celebrated singer whose wife (not shown) has left him for some egocentric reason (not explained). The other is an architect with political connections. The singer does not know the architect has been using bribery and blackmail to obtain

---

6. Disney's resort in Paris, opened in 1992 (renamed Disneyland Paris in 1994).

government contracts. Right at the beginning you make a mistake and choose the architect, having rejected the singer because of his social manner, diffident and shy. "Virginie" settles for the singer. It turns out that she has never heard of him and does not know he has sold millions of records. She has been working among the deprived in a remote mountain region, where reception is poor.

Anny found that part of the story hard to believe. As she said, even the most forlorn Alpine villages are equipped for winter tourists, and skiers won't stay in places where they can't watch the programs. At any rate, the singer is captivated by "Virginie," and the two sit in the hotel bar, which is dimly lighted, comparing their views and principles. While this is taking place, you, "Camilla," are upstairs in a flower-filled suite, making mad love with the architect. Then you and he have a big quarrel, because of his basic indifference to the real world, and you take a bunch of red roses out of a vase and throw them in his face. (I recognized your quick temper.) He brushes a torn leaf from his bare chest and picks up the telephone and says, "Madame is leaving the hotel. Send someone up for her luggage." In the next scene you are on the edge of a highway trying to get a lift to the airport. The architect has given you your air ticket but nothing for taxis.

Anny and Robert had not been married long, but she knew about you and how much you figured in our memories. She sympathized with your plight and thought it was undeserved. You had shown yourself to be objective and caring and could have been won round (by the architect) with a kind word. She wondered if you were playing your own life and if the incident at Cannes was part of a pattern of behavior. We were unable to say, inasmuch as you had vanished from our lives in the seventies. To me, you seemed not quite right for the part. You looked too quick and intelligent to be standing around with no clothes on, throwing flowers at a naked man, when you could have been putting on a designer dress and going out for dinner. Robert, who had been perfectly silent, said, "Alda was always hard to cast." It was a remark that must have come out of old café conversations, when he was still seeing actors. I had warned Anny he would be hard to live with. She took him on trust.

My husband took some people on trust, too, and he died disappointed. I once showed you the place on Place d'Italie where our restaurant used to be. After we had to sell it, it became a pizza restaurant, then a health-food store. What it is now I don't know. When I go by it I look the other way. Like you, he picked the wrong person. She was a regular lunchtime customer, as quiet as Anny; her husband did the talking. He seemed to be involved with the construction taking place around the Porte de Choisy and at that end of the Avenue. The Chinese were moving into these places as fast as they were available; they kept their promises and paid their bills, and it seemed like a wise investment. Something went wrong. The woman disappeared, and the husband retired to that seaside town in Portugal where all the exiled kings and queens used to live.[7] Portugal is a coincidence: I am not implying any connection with you or your relations or fellow-citizens. If we are to create the Europe of the twenty-first century, we must show belief in one another and take our frustrated expectations as they come.

What I particularly admired, last night, was your pronunciation of "ozone,"

---

7. Portugal was neutral during World War II, and a number of deposed monarchs—including Juan Carlos of Spain, Carol II of Romania, and Umberto of Italy—found refuge in Cascais and neighboring Estoril.

Where would you be if I hadn't kept after you about your "o"s? "Say *'Rhône,'*" I used to tell you. "Not *'run.'* " Watching you drive off in the Jaguar, I wondered if you had a thought to spare for Robert's old Renault. The day you went away together, after the only quarrel I ever had with my son, he threw your suitcase in the back seat. The suitcase was still there the next morning, when he came back alone. Later, he said he hadn't noticed it. The two of you had spent the night in the car, for you had no money and nowhere to go. There was barely room to sit. He drives a Citroën BX now.

I had been the first to spot your condition. You had an interview for a six-day modelling job—Rue des Rosiers, wholesale—and nothing to wear. I gave you one of my own dresses, which, of course, had to be taken in. You were thinner than ever and had lost your appetite for breakfast. You said you thought the apricot jam was making you sick. (I bought you some honey from Provence, but you threw that up, too.) I had finished basting the dress seams and was down on my knees, pinning the hem, when I suddenly put my hand flat on the front of the skirt and said, "How far along are you?" You burst into tears and said something I won't repeat. I said, "You should have thought of all that sooner. I can't help you. I'm sorry. It's against the law and, besides, I wouldn't know where to send you."

After the night in the Renault you went to a café, so that Robert could shave in the washroom. He said, "Why don't you start a conversation with that woman at the next table? She looks as if she might know." Sure enough, when he came back a few minutes later, your attention was turned to the stranger. She wrote something on the back of an old Métro[8] ticket (the solution, most probably) and you put it away in your purse, perhaps next to the diploma. You seemed to him eager and hopeful and excited, as if you could see a better prospect than the six-day modelling job or the solution to your immediate difficulty or even a new kind of life—better than any you could offer each other. He walked straight out to the street, without stopping to speak, and came home. He refused to say a word to me, changed his clothes, and left for the day. A day like any other, in a way.

When the commercial ended we sat in silence. Then Anny got up and began to clear away the dessert no one had finished. The debate on hepatitis was now deeply engaged. Six or seven men who seemed to be strangling in their collars and ties sat at a round table, all of them yelling. The program presenter had lost control of the proceedings. One man shouted above the others that there were people who sincerely wanted to be ill. No amount of money poured into the health services could cure their muddled impulses. Certain impulses were as bad as any disease. Anny, still standing, cut off the sound (her only impatient act), and we watched the debaters opening and shutting their mouths. Speaking quietly, she said that life was a long duty, not a gift. She often thought about her own and had come to the conclusion that only through reincarnation would she ever know what she might have been or what important projects she might have carried out. Her temperament is Swiss. When she speaks, her genes are speaking.

I always expected you to come back for the suitcase. It is still here, high up on a shelf in the hall closet. We looked inside—not to pry but in case you

---

8. The Paris subway.

had packed something perishable, such as a sandwich. There was a jumble of cotton garments and a pair of worn sandals and some other dresses I had pinned and basted for you, which you never sewed. Or sewed with such big, loose stitches that the seams came apart. (I had also given you a warm jacket with an embroidered Tyrolian-style[9] collar. I think you had it on when you left.) On that first day, when I made the remark that your suitcase weighed next to nothing, you took it for a slight and said, "I am small and I wear small sizes." You looked about fifteen and had poor teeth and terrible posture.

The money you owed came to a hundred and fifty thousand francs, counted the old way, or one thousand five hundred in new francs. If we include accumulated inflation, it should amount to a million five hundred thousand; or, as you would probably prefer to put it, fifteen thousand.[1] Inflation ran for years at 12 percent, but I think that over decades it must even out to ten. I base this on the fact that in 1970 half a dozen eggs were worth one new franc, while today one has to pay nine or ten. As for interest, I'm afraid it would be impossible to work out after so much time. It would depend on the year and the whims of this or that bank. There have been more prime ministers and annual budgets and unpleasant announcements and changes in rates than I can count. Actually, I don't want interest. To tell the truth, I don't want anything but the pleasure of seeing you and hearing from your own lips what you are proud of and what you regret.

My only regret is that my husband never would let me help in the restaurant. He wanted me to stay home and create a pleasant refuge for him and look after Robert. His own parents had slaved in their bistro, trying to please greedy and difficult people who couldn't be satisfied. He did not wish to have his only child do his homework in some dim corner between the bar and the kitchen door. But I could have been behind the bar, with Robert doing homework where I could keep an eye on him (instead of in his room with the door locked). I might have learned to handle cash and checks and work out tips in new francs and I might have noticed trouble coming, and taken steps.

I sang a lot when I was alone. I wasn't able to read music, but I could imitate anything I heard on records that suited my voice, airs by Delibes or Massenet.[2] My muses were Lily Pons and Ninon Vallin.[3] Probably you have never heard of them. They were before your time and are traditionally French.

According to Anny and Marie-Laure, fashions of the seventies are on the way back. Anny never buys herself anything, but Marie-Laure has several new outfits with softly draped skirts and jackets with a peasant motif—not unlike the clothes I gave you. If you like, I could make over anything in the suitcase to meet your social and professional demands. We could take up life where it was broken off, when I was on my knees, pinning the hem. We could say simple things that take the sting out of life, the way Anny does. You can come and fetch the suitcase any day, at any time. I am up and dressed by half past seven, and by a quarter to nine my home is ready for unexpected guests. There is an elevator in the building now. You won't have

---

9. Characteristic of the Tirol, a region in the eastern Alps (mainly in Austria).
1. About $2830 in 1992 (worth about $4060 in 2006).
2. Two French composers, Léo Delibes (1836–1891) and Jules-Émile-Frédéric Massenet (1842–1912).
3. French soprano (1886–1961). Pons (1904–1976), French-born American soprano.

the five flights to climb. At the entrance to the building you will find a digit-code lock. The number that lets you in is K630. Be careful not to admit anyone who looks suspicious or threatening. If some stranger tries to push past just as you open the door, ask him what he wants and the name of the tenant he wishes to see. Probably he won't even try to give you a credible answer and will be scared away.

The concierge you knew stayed on for another fifteen years, then retired to live with her married daughter in Normandy. We voted not to have her replaced. A team of cleaners comes in twice a month. They are never the same, so one never gets to know them. It does away with the need for a Christmas tip and you don't have the smell of cooking permeating the whole ground floor, but one misses the sense of security. You may remember that Mme. Julie was alert night and day, keeping track of everyone who came in and went out. There is no one now to bring mail to the door, ring the doorbell, make sure we are still alive. You will notice the row of mailboxes in the vestibule. Some of the older tenants won't put their full name on the box, just their initials. In their view, the name is no one's business. The postman knows who they are, but in summer, when a substitute makes the rounds, he just throws their letters on the floor. There are continual complaints. Not long ago, an intruder tore two or three boxes off the wall.

You will find no changes in the apartment. The inventory you once signed could still apply, if one erased the words "electric heater." Do not send a check—or, indeed, any communication. You need not call to make an appointment. I prefer to live in the expectation of hearing the elevator stop at my floor and then your ring, and of having you tell me you have come home.

1992

GRACE PALEY
b. 1922

Grace Paley was born in New York into a family of socialist Russian Jews, and she grew up listening to the stories of her father, her mother, and her aunts, stories that were recounted sometimes in English and sometimes in Russian or Yiddish. For this reason, she has explained in a *Shenandoah* interview (1981), she did not consider herself a writer until she managed to get beyond "me—me—me" through "hear[ing] other people's voices" that she recorded by writing "with an accent." Although Paley composed poetry in the style of W. H. Auden while she attended Hunter College, she did not begin publishing fiction until after she was thirty. Encouraged by her husband and fascinated by the community of women and children who lived separate lives in the army camps she knew during World War II, she produced the stories that eventually appeared in *The Little Disturbances of Man* (1959); the volume immediately established her as a funny and irreverent urban chronicler, a reputation strengthened by the appearance of her second collection of stories, *Enormous Changes at the Last Minute* (1974). *Later the Same Day* (1985) has sustained her reputation as a humorous and humane writer who produces strikingly compassionate portraits of city life.

The mother of two children, Paley captures the everyday cadences and causes of the immigrant Jews, impoverished African Americans, and displaced Irish Catholics who inhabit neighborhood playgrounds and PTAs, Brooklyn's Coney Island, and Manhattan's subways. In her short story "A Conversation with My Father," she explains that her father's insistence on the somber relentlessness of plotted "Tragedy! Plain tragedy!" conflicted with her own sense that "it's a funny world nowadays." This comic yet affirmative vision, along with her determination to tell stories "in order to . . . save a few lives," has animated not only Paley's activism in antiwar and antihunger movements and her teaching at Syracuse University and Sarah Lawrence College, but also those stories where—against all odds—her characters seize the opportunity to make "enormous changes at the last minute." Both her stories and her poems have been published in collected editions, although new work—like "My Father Addresses Me on the Facts of Old Age"—continues to appear in prominent venues, in this case an issue of *The New Yorker* in 2002.

My Father Addresses Me on the Facts of Old Age

My father had decided to teach me how to grow old. I said O.K. My children didn't think it was such a great idea. If I knew how, they thought, I might do so too easily. No, no, I said, it's for later, years from now. And, besides, if I get it right it might be helpful to you kids in time to come.

They said, Really?

My father wanted to begin as soon as possible. For God's sake, he said, you can talk to the kids later. Now, listen to me, send them out to play. You are so distractable.

We should probably begin at the beginning, he said. Change. First there is change, which nobody likes—even men. You'd be surprised. You can do little things—putting cream on the corners of your mouth, also the heels of your feet. But here is the main thing. Oh, I wish your mother was alive— not that she had time—

But Pa, I said, Mama never knew anything about cream. I did not say she was famous for not taking care.

Forget it, he said sadly. But I must mention squinting. DON'T SQUINT. Wear your glasses. Look at your aunt, so beautiful once. I know someone[1] has said men don't make passes at girls who wear glasses, but that's an idea for a foolish person. There are many handsome women who are not exactly twenty-twenty.

Please sit down, he said. Be patient. The main thing is this—when you get up in the morning you must take your heart in your two hands. You must do this every morning.

That's a metaphor, right?

Metaphor? No, no, you can do this. In the morning, do a few little exercises for the joints, not too much. Then put your hands like a cup over and under the heart. Under the breast. He said tactfully. It's probably easier for a man. Then talk softly, don't yell. Under your ribs, push a little. When you wake up, you must do this massage. I mean pat, stroke a little, don't be ashamed. Very likely no one will be watching. Then you must talk to your heart.

---

1. Dorothy Parker, in "News Item" (1926); see above, p. 488.

Talk? What?

Say anything, but be respectful. Say—maybe say, Heart, little heart, beat softly but never forget your job, the blood. You can whisper also, Remember, remember. For instance, I said to it yesterday, Heart, heart, do you remember my brother, Grisha, how he made work for you that day when he came to the store and he said, Your boss's money, Zenya, right now? How he put a gun in my face and I said, Grisha, are you crazy? Why don't you ask me at home? I would give you. We were in this America not more than two years. He was only a kid. And he said, he said, Who needs your worker's money? For the movement—only from your boss. O little heart, you worked like a bastard, like a dog, like a crazy slave, bang, bang, bang that day, remember? That's the story I told my heart yesterday, my father said. What a racket it made to answer me, I remember, I remember, till I was dizzy with the thumping.

Why'd you do that, Pa? I don't get it.

Don't you see? This is good for the old heart—to get excited—just as good as for the person. Some people go running till late in life—for the muscles, they say, but the heart knows the real purpose. The purpose is the expansion of the arteries, a river of blood, it cleans off the banks, carries junk out of the system. I myself would rather remind the heart how frightened I was by my brother than go running in a strange neighborhood, miles and miles, with the city so dangerous these days.

I said, Oh, but then I said, Well, thanks.

I don't think you listened, he said. As usual—probably worried about the kids. They're not babies, you know. If you were better organized you wouldn't have so many worries.

I stopped by a couple of weeks later. This time he was annoyed.

Why did you leave the kids home? If you keep doing this, they'll forget who I am. Children are like old people in that respect.

They won't forget you, Pa, never in a million years.

You think so? God has not been so good about a million years. His main interest in us began—actually, he put it down in writing fifty-six, fifty-seven hundred years ago. In the Book.[2] You know our Book, I suppose.

O.K. Yes.

Probably a million years is too close to his lifetime, if you could call it life, what he goes through. I believe he said several times—when he was still in contact with us—I am a jealous God.[3] Here and there he makes an exception. I read there are three-thousand-year-old trees somewhere in some godforsaken place.[4] Of course, that's how come they're still alive. We should all be so godforsaken.

But no more joking around. I have been thinking what to tell you now. First of all, soon, maybe in twenty, thirty years, you'll begin to get up in the morning—4, 5 A.M. In a farmer that's O.K., but for us—you'll remember everything you did, didn't, what you omitted, whom you insulted, betrayed— betrayed, that is the worst. Do you remember, you didn't go see your aunt, she was dying? That will be on your mind like a stone. Of course, I myself did not behave so well. Still, I was so busy those days, long office hours,

---

2. I.e., the Torah, the first five books of the Bible.
3. Exodus 20.5.
4. The world's oldest trees are bristlecone pines, found in harsh conditions on mountains in the western United States; some are more than 4,000 years old.

remember it was usual in those days for doctors to make house calls. No elevators, fourth floor, fifth floor, even in a nice Bronx tenement. But this morning, I mean *this* morning, a few hours ago, my mother, your babushka,[5] came into my mind, looked at me.

Have I told you I was arrested? Of course I did. I was arrested a few times, but this time for some reason the policeman walked me past the office of the local jail. My mama was there. I saw her through the window. She was bringing me a bundle of clean clothes. She put it on the officer's table. She turned. She saw me. She looked at me through the glass with such a face, eye-to-eye. Despair. No hope. This morning, 4 A.M., I saw once more how she sat there, very straight. Her eyes. Because of that look, I did my term, my sentence, the best I could. I finished up six months in Arkhangel'sk,[6] where they finally sent me. Then no more, no more, I said to myself, no more saving Imperial Russia, the great pogrom-maker, from itself.

Oh, Pa.

Don't make too much out of everything. Well, anyway, I want to tell you also how the body is your enemy. I must warn you it is not your friend the way it was when you were a youngster. For example. Greens—believe me— are overrated. Some people believe they will cure cancer. It's the style. My experience with maybe a hundred patients proves otherwise. Greens are helpful to God. That fellow Sandburg,[7] the poet—I believe from Chicago— explained it. Grass tiptoes over the whole world, holds it in place—except the desert, of course, everything there is loose, flying around.

How come you bring up God so much? When I was a kid you were a strict atheist, you even spit on the steps of the synagogue.

Well, God is very good for conversation, he said. By the way, I believe I have to tell you a few words about the stock market. Your brother-in-law is always talking about how brilliant he is, investing, investing. My advice to you: Stay out of it.

But people *are* making money. A lot. Read the paper. Even kids are becoming millionaires.

But what of tomorrow? he asked.

Tomorrow, I said, they'll make another million.

No, no, no, I mean TOMORROW. I was there when TOMORROW came in 1929.[8] So I say to them and their millions, HA HA HA, TOMORROW will come. Go home now, I have a great deal more to tell you. Somehow, I'm always tired.

I'll go in a minute—but I have to tell you something, Pa. I had to tell him that my husband and I were separating. Maybe even divorce, the first in the family.

What? What? Are you crazy? I don't understand you people nowadays. I married your mother when I was a boy. It's true I had a first-class mustache, but I was a kid, and you know I stayed married till the end. Once or twice, she wanted to part company, but not me. The reason, of course, she was inclined to be jealous.

He then gave me the example I'd heard five or six times before. What it was, one time two couples went to the movies. Arzemich and his wife, you remember. Well, I sat next to his wife, the lady of the couple, by the way a

---

5. Grandmother (Russian).
6. City in northern Russia, on the Northern Drina river near its exit into the White Sea.
7. Carl Sandburg (1878–1967), who wrote "I am the grass; I cover all" in "Grass" (1918)—where "all" refers specifically to the bodies of those killed in war.
8. The great U.S. stock market crash occurred in late October 1929.

very attractive woman, and during the show, which wasn't so great, we talked about this and that, laughed a couple times. When we got home, your mother said, O.K. Anytime you want, right now, I'll give you a divorce. We will go our separate ways. Naturally, I said, What? Are you ridiculous?

My advice to you—stick it out. It's true your husband, he's a peculiar fellow, but think it over. Go home. Maybe you can manage at least till old age. Then, if you still don't get along, you can go to separate old-age homes.

Pa, it's no joke. It's my life.

It is a joke. A joke is necessary at this time. But I'm tired.

You'll see, in thirty, forty years from now, you'll get tired often. It doesn't mean you're sick. This is something important that I'm telling you. Listen. To live a long time, long years, you've got to sleep a certain extra percentage away. It's a shame.

It was at least three weeks before I saw him again. He was drinking tea, eating a baked apple, one of twelve my sister baked for him every ten days. I took another one out of the refrigerator. "Fathers and Sons"[9] was on the kitchen table. Most of the time he read history. He kept Gibbon and Prescott[1] on the lamp stand next to his resting chair. But this time, thinking about Russia for some reason in a kindly way, he was reading Turgenev.

You were probably pretty busy, he said. Where are the kids? With the father? He looked at me hopefully.

No hope, Pa.

By the way, you know, this fellow Turgenev? He wasn't a showoff. He wrote a certain book, and he became famous right away. One day he went to Paris, and in the evening he went to the opera. He stepped into his box, and just as he was sitting down the people began to applaud. The whole opera house was clapping. He was known. Everybody knew his book. He said, I see Russia is known in France.

You're a lucky girl that these books are in the living room, more on the table than on the shelf.

Yes.

Excuse me, also about Turgenev, I don't believe he was an anti-Semite. Of course, most of them were, even if they had brains. I don't think Gorky was, Gogol probably. Tolstoy, no, Tolstoy had an opinion about the Mexican-American War. Did you know? Of course, most were anti-Semites. Dostoyevsky.[2] It was natural, it seems. Ach, why is it we read them with such interest and they don't return the favor?

That's what women writers say about men writers.

Please don't start in. I'm in the middle of telling you some things you don't know. Well, I suppose you do know a number of Gentiles, you're more in the American world. I know very few. Still, I was telling you—Jews were not allowed to travel in Russia. I told you that. But a Jewish girl if she was a prostitute could go anywhere throughout all Russia. Also a Jew if he was a merchant first class. Even people with big stores were only second class. Who

---

9. The best-known novel (1862) by the Russian writer Ivan Turgenev (1818–1883).
1. William Prescott (1796–1859), American historian who studied Spanish history. Edward Gibbon (1737–1794), English historian best known for writing *The History of the Decline and Fall of the Roman Empire*.
2. All Russian writers: Maksim Gorky (1868–1936), Nikolay Gogol (1809–1852), Leo Tolstoy (1828–1910), and Fyodor Dostoyevsky (1821–1881).

else? A soldier who had a medal, I think St. George.[3] Do you know nobody could arrest him? Even if he was a Jew. If he killed someone a policeman could not arrest him. He wore a certain hat. Why am I telling you all this?

Well, it is interesting.

Yes, but I'm supposed to tell you a few things, give advice, a few last words. Of course, the fact is I am obliged because you are always getting yourself mixed up in politics. Because your mother and I were such radical kids—socialists—in constant trouble with the police—it was 1904, 5. You have the idea it's O.K. for you and it is not O.K. in this country, which is a democracy. And you're running in the street like a fool. Your cousin saw you a few years ago in school, suspended. Sitting with other children in the auditorium, not allowed to go to class. You thought Mama and I didn't know.

Pa, that was thirty-five years ago, in high school. Anyway, what *about* Mama? You mentioned the Arzemich family. She was a dentist, wasn't she?

Right, a very capable woman.

Well, Mama probably felt bad about not getting to school and, you know, becoming something, having a profession like Mrs. What's-Her-Name. I mean, she did run the whole house and family and the office and people coming to live with us, but she was sad about that, surely.

He was quiet. Then he said, You're right. It was a shame, everything went into me, so I should go to school, I should graduate, I should be the doctor, I should have the profession. Poor woman, she was extremely smart. At least as smart as me. In Russia, in the movement, you know, when we were youngsters, she was considered the more valuable person. Very steady, honest. Made first-class contact with the workers, a real organizer. I could be only an intellectual. But maybe if life didn't pass so quick, speedy, like a winter day—short. You know, also, she was very musical, she had perfect pitch. A few years ago your sister made similar remarks to me about Mama. Questioning me, like history is my fault. Your brother only looked at me the way he does—not with complete approval.

Then one day my father surprised me. He said he wanted to talk a little, but not too much, about love or sex or whatever it's called—its troubling persistence. He said that might happen to me, too, eventually. It should not be such a surprise. Then, a little accusingly, After all, I have been a man alone for many years. Did you ever think about that? Maybe I suffered. Did it even enter your mind? You're a grownup woman, after all.

But Pa, I wouldn't ever have thought of bringing up anything like that—you and Mama were so damn puritanical. I never heard you say the word "sex" till this day—either of you.

We were serious Socialists, he said. So? He looked at me, raising one nice thick eyebrow. You don't understand politics too well, do you?

Actually, I had thought of it now and then, his sexual aloneness. I was a grownup woman. But I turned it into a tactful question: Aren't you sometimes lonely, Pa?

I have a nice apartment.

Then he closed his eyes. He rested his talking self. I decided to water the plants. He opened one eye. Take it easy. Don't overwater.

Anyway, he said, only your mother, a person like her, could put up with

---

3. A military honor of Imperial Russia, awarded for merit in combat (St. George is the patron saint of soldiers).

me. Her patience—you know, I was always losing my temper. But finally with us everything was all right, ALL right, accomplished. Do you understand? Your brother and sister finished college, married. We had a beautiful grandchild. I was working very hard, like a dog. We were only fifty years old then, but, look, we bought the place in the country. Your sister and brother came often. You yourself were running around with a dozen kids in bathing suits all day. Your mama was planting all kinds of flowers every minute. Trees were growing. Your grandma, your babushka, sat on a good chair on the lawn. In back of her were birch trees. I put in a nice row of spruce. Then one day in the morning she comes to me, my wife. She shows me a spot over her left breast. I know right away. I don't touch it. I see it. In my mind I turn it this way and that. But I know in that minute, in one minute, everything is finished, finished—happiness, pleasure, finished, years ahead black.

No. That minute had been told to me a couple of years ago, maybe twice in ten years. Each time it nearly stopped my heart. No.

He recovered from the telling. Now, listen, this means, of course, that you should take care of yourself. I don't mean eat vegetables. I mean go to the doctor on time. Nowadays a woman as sick as your mama could live many years. Your sister, for example, after terrible operations—heart bypass, colon cancer—more she probably hides from me. She is running around to theatre, concerts, probably supports Lincoln Center.[4] Ballet, chamber, symphony— three, four times a week. But you must pay attention. One good thing, don't laugh, is bananas. Really. Potassium. I myself eat one every day.

But, seriously, I'm running out of advice. It's too late to beg you to finish school, get a couple of degrees, a decent profession, be a little more strict with the children. They should be prepared for the future. Maybe they won't be as lucky as you. Well, no more advice. I restrain myself.

Now I'm changing the whole subject. I will ask you a favor. You have many friends—teachers, writers, intelligent people. Jews, non-Jews. These days I think often, especially after telling you the story a couple of months ago, about my brother Grisha. I want to know what happened to him.

I guess we know he was deported around 1922, right?

Yes, yes, but why did they go after him? The last ten years before that, he calmed down quite a bit, had a nice job, I think. But that's what they did— did you know? Even after the Palmer raids[5]—that was maybe 1919—they kept deporting people. They picked them up at home, at the Russian Artists' Club, at meetings. Of course, you weren't even around yet, maybe just born. They thought that these kids had in mind a big revolution—like in Russia. Some joke. Ignorance. Grisha and his friends didn't like Lenin from the beginning. More Bakunin.[6] Emma Goldman, her boyfriend,[7] I forgot his name.

Berkman.

---

4. Lincoln Center for the Performing Arts; run by a nonprofit organization, this 16-acre complex in central Manhattan (built 1959–72) houses twelve arts organizations.
5. As U.S. attorney general, Alexander Palmer (1872–1936) led the government attack on suspected radicals during the "Red scare" that followed the Russian Revolution of 1917; during the Palmer raids (1919–21), thousands of allegedly subversive aliens were rounded up, and hundreds were deported.
6. Mikhail Bakunin (1814–1876), Russian anarchist. Vladimir Lenin (1870–1924), Russian communist leader of the Bolsheviks who became head of the Soviet government after the revolution.
7. Goldman (1869–1940) and Alexander Berkman (1870–1936) were American anarchists, born in Lithuania and Russia, respectively; both were jailed for obstructing military conscription (1917– 19) and then deported (1919).

Right. They were shipped, I believe, to Vladivostok.[8] There must be a file somewhere. Archives salted away. Why did they go after him? Maybe they were mostly Jews. Anti-Semitism in the American blood from Europe—a little thinner, I suppose. But why didn't we talk? All the years not talking. Me seeing sick people day and night. Strangers. And not talking to my brother till all of a sudden he's on a ship. Gone.

Go home now. I don't have much more to tell you. Anyway, it's late. I have to prepare now all of my courage, not for sleep, for waking in the early morning, maybe 3 or 4 A.M. I have to be ready for them, my morning visitors—your babushka, your mama, most of all, to tell the truth, it's for your aunt, my sister, the youngest. She said to me, that day in the hospital, Don't leave me here, take me home to die. And I didn't. And her face looked at me that day and many, many mornings looks at me still.

I stood near the door holding my coat. A space at last for me to say something. My mouth open.

Enough, already, he said. I had the job to tell you how to take care of yourself, what to expect. About the heart—you know it was not a metaphor. But in the end a great thing, a really interesting thing, would be to find out what happened to our Grisha. You're smart. You can do it. Also, you'll see, you'll be lucky in this life to have something you must do to take your mind off all the things you didn't do.

Then he said, I suppose that is something like a joke. But, my dear girl, very serious.

2002

8. Russia's chief port on the Pacific; in the 1930s, it contained the transit camp for political prisoners sent east to do forced labor.

DENISE LEVERTOV
1923–1997

Born and brought up in Ilford, Essex, England, Denise Levertov paradoxically became one of the most American of writers, a self-defined disciple of many of the aesthetic ideas of the American poets William Carlos Williams and H. D. (Hilda Doolittle). About Williams, for example, Levertov observed that "he made available to us the whole range of the language, he showed us the rhythms of speech as *poetry*," adding that "it is a mistake to suppose that Williams's insistence on 'the American idiom' ever implied a reduction; on the contrary, it means the recognition of wide resources." Similarly, about H. D., she remarked that the author of *Trilogy* offered "doors, ways in, tunnels through," noting that H. D. "showed a way to penetrate mystery; which means, not to flood darkness with light so that darkness is destroyed, but to *enter into* darkness, mystery, so that it is experienced." In her own work, Levertov consistently employed what she considered "natural" speech rhythms to open the gates of mystery and enter what she defined in "The Goddess" and "Song to Ishtar" as the sacred precincts of the Muse.

The younger of two daughters of a Welsh mother and a Russian Jewish father who became a clergyman in the Church of England, Levertov was educated mostly at

860 / DENISE LEVERTOV

home; in several memoirs, she described her English childhood as bucolic, paying special attention to the influence of her older sister, Olga, about whose death she wrote a poignant elegiac sequence, *The Sorrow Dance*. During World War II, she became a nurse, and in 1947 she married the writer Mitchell Goodman, from whom she was divorced in the early 1970s—an experience on which she meditates in the poem "Divorcing." The couple had one son, about whose childhood and adolescence Levertov also wrote several moving poems. Emigrating to the United States in 1948, she became an American citizen in 1955, and began to publish the suavely cadenced collections of verse on which her reputation is based. In England, she had already produced one book—*The Double Image* (1946), collecting precocious verse she had written in her late teens—but her American volumes, based on a radical commitment to the idea that "a poem *is* a sonic, sensuous event and not a statement or a string of ideas," are more characteristic. Over a dozen in number, they include such influential and widely read collections as *The Jacob's Ladder* (1961), *O Taste and See* (1964), *The Sorrow Dance* (1967), *Relearning the Alphabet* (1970), *The Freeing of the Dust* (1975), *Candles in Babylon* (1982), *Breathing the Water* (1987), *Evening Train* (1992), *The Sands of the Well* (1996), and (appearing posthumously) *This Great Unknowing: Last Poems* (1999). In addition, she published three books of incisive, passionately committed essays: *The Poet in the World* (1973), *Light Up the Cave* (1981), and *Tesserae: Memories and Suppositions* (1995).

Levertov taught at a number of universities, including Tufts and Stanford, and she served as poetry editor of the magazines *The Nation* and *Mother Jones* before returning to Seattle, Washington, where she spent her last decade. Perhaps most important, she was a notable activist in the peace movement of the 1960s and 1970s (protesting the Vietnam War) and in the antinuclear and peace movements of the 1980s (protesting nuclear proliferation and American intervention in El Salvador). Though she did not define herself as a feminist, her poetry frequently expresses a distinctively female perspective on the world, celebrating the values of nature and nurture while drawing on the details of domesticity to dramatize a mystical reality whose radiance she often sees (for instance, in "Abel's Bride") as illuminating even the most apparently ordinary objects. In addition, in such poems as "Hypocrite Women," "In Mind," and "Stepping Westward," Levertov turned again and again to questions of female self-definition, exploring the complexity of her own character as an example of the complexity of a woman's being. More generally, however, in their Romantic commitment to both an imagining of moral justice and an intuition of mystical truth, her finest verses consistently reflect her belief that "the written poem" is at its best a "record" of an "inner song."

The Goddess

She in whose lipservice
I passed my time,
whose name I knew, but not her face,
came upon me where I lay in Lie Castle!

5 Flung me across the room, and
room after room (hitting the walls, re-
bounding—to the last
sticky wall—wrenching away from it
pulled hair out!)
10 till I lay
outside the outer walls!

There in cold air
lying still where her hand had thrown me,
I tasted the mud that splattered my lips:
15 the seeds of a forest were in it,
asleep and growing! I tasted
her power!

The silence was answering my silence,
a forest was pushing itself
20 out of sleep between my submerged fingers.

I bit on a seed and it spoke on my tongue
of day that shone already among stars
in the water-mirror of low ground,

and a wind rising ruffled the lights:
25 she passed near me returning from the encounter,
she who plucked me from the close rooms,

without whom nothing
flowers, fruits, sleeps in season,
without whom nothing
30 speaks in its own tongue, but returns
lie for lie!

1960

Song for Ishtar[1]

The moon is a sow
and grunts in my throat
Her great shining shines through me
so the mud of my hollow gleams
5 and breaks in silver bubbles

She is a sow
and I a pig and a poet

When she opens her white
lips to devour me I bite back
10 and laughter rocks the moon

In the black of desire
we rock and grunt, grunt and
shine

1964

---

1. Babylonian goddess of love and fertility.

Hypocrite Women

Hypocrite women, how seldom we speak
of our own doubts, while dubiously
we mother man in his doubt!

And if at Mill Valley[1] perched in the trees
the sweet rain drifting through western air
a white sweating bull of a poet told us

our cunts are ugly—why didn't we
admit we have thought so too? (And
what shame? They are not for the eye!)

No, they are dark and wrinkled and hairy,
caves of the Moon . . .   And when a
dark humming fills us, a

coldness towards life,
we are too much women to
own to such unwomanliness.

Whorishly with the psychopomp[2]
we play and plead—and say
nothing of this later.   And our dreams,

with what frivolity we have pared them
like toenails, clipped them like ends of
split hair.

1964

In Mind

There's in my mind a woman
of innocence, unadorned but
fair-featured, and smelling of
apples or grass. She wears

a utopian smock or shift, her hair
is light brown and smooth, and she

is kind and very clean without
ostentation—
            but she has
no imagination.

---

1. Town in northern California, location of Marin College.

2. The soul's guide, usually to the place of the dead.

10   And there's a
turbulent moon-ridden girl

or old woman, or both,
dressed in opals and rags, feathers

15   and torn taffeta,
who knows strange songs—

but she is not kind.

                                                    1964

The Ache of Marriage

The ache of marriage:

thigh and tongue, beloved,
are heavy with it,
it throbs in the teeth

5   We look for communion
and are turned away, beloved,
each and each

It is leviathan[1] and we
in its belly
10 looking for joy, some joy
not to be known outside it

two by two in the ark[2] of
the ache of it.

                                                    1964

Eros[1] at Temple Stream

The river in its abundance
many-voiced
all about us as we stood
on a warm rock to wash

5   slowly
smoothing in long

---

1. A reference to the story of Jonah, who was swallowed by a sea monster, or leviathan (Book of Jonah).
2. I.e., Noah's ark, in which animals of every species were preserved from the flood that destroyed all other life (Genesis 6–8).

1. The Greek god of love; also the Greek word meaning "love."

                sliding strokes
our soapy hands along each other's
slippery cool bodies

10   quiet and slow in the midst of
the quick of the
sounding river

our hands were
flames
15   stealing upon quickened flesh until

no part of us but was
sleek and
on fire.

                                                           1964

Abel's Bride[1]

Woman fear for man, he goes
out alone to his labors. No mirror
nests in his pocket. His face
opens and shuts with his hopes.
5   His sex hangs unhidden
or rises before him
blind and questing.

She thinks herself
lucky. But sad. When she goes out
10   she looks in the glass, she remembers
herself. Stones, coal,
the hiss of water upon the kindled
branches—her being
is a cave, there are bones at the hearth.

                                                           1967

The Son

i   *The Disclosure*

He-who-came-forth was
it turned out
a man—

Moves among us from room to room of our life
5   in boots, in jeans, in a cloak of flame

---

1. Abel was the second son of Adam and Eve, murdered by his brother Cain (Genesis 4); the Bible makes no mention of Abel's wife.

pulled out of his pocket along with
old candywrappers, where it had lain
transferred from pants to pants,
folded small as a curl of dust,
from the beginning—

unfurled now.

The fine flame
almost unseen in common light.

ii The Woodblock

He cuts into a slab of wood,
engrossed, violently precise.
Thus, yesterday, the day before yesterday,
engines of fantasy were evolved
in poster paints. Tonight
a face forms under the knife,
slashed with stern
crisscrosses of longing, downstrokes
of silence endured—his visioned

                own face!—
down which from one eye

rolls a tear.
        His own face
drawn from the wood,

deep in the manhood his childhood
so swiftly led to, a small brook rock-leaping
into the rapt, imperious, seagoing river.

1967

Stepping Westward[1]

What is green in me
darkens, muscadine.

If woman is inconstant,
good, I am faithful to

ebb and flow, I fall
in season and now

is a time of ripening.
If her part

---

1. Title of an 1807 poem by William Wordsworth in which two male travelers meet two local women and the poet muses on the journey as "a wildish destiny."

is to be true,
10 a north star,

  good, I hold steady
  in the black sky

  and vanish by day,
  yet burn there

15 in blue or above
  quilts of cloud.

  There is no savor
  more sweet, more salt

  than to be glad to be
20 what, woman,

  and who, myself,
  I am, a shadow

  that grows longer as the sun
  moves, drawn out

25 on a thread of wonder.
  If I bear burdens

  they begin to be remembered
  as gifts, goods, a basket

  of bread that hurts
30 my shoulders but closes me

  in fragrance. I can
  eat as I go.

1967

The Mutes

Those groans men use
passing a woman on the street
or on the steps of the subway

to tell her she is a female
5 and their flesh knows it,

are they a sort of tune,
an ugly enough song, sung
by a bird with a slit tongue

but meant for music?

Or are they the muffled roaring
of deafmutes trapped in a building that is
slowly filling with smoke?

Perhaps both.

Such men most often
look as if groan were all they could do,
yet a woman, in spite of herself,

knows it's a tribute:
if she were lacking all grace
they'd pass her in silence:

so it's not only to say she's
a warm hole. It's a word

in grief-language, nothing to do with
primitive, not an ur-language;
language stricken, sickened, cast down

in decrepitude. She wants to
throw the tribute away, disgusted, and can't,

it goes on buzzing in her ear,
it changes the pace of her walk,
the torn posters in echoing corridors

spell it out, it
quakes and gnashes as the train comes in.
Her pulse sullenly

had picked up speed,
but the cars slow down and
jar to a stop while her understanding

keeps on translating:
"Life after life after life goes by

without poetry,
without seemliness,
without love."

1967

What Were They Like?

1) Did the people of Viet Nam
   use lanterns of stone?
2) Did they hold ceremonies
   to reverence the opening of buds?
3) Were they inclined to quiet laughter?
4) Did they use bone and ivory,
   jade and silver, for ornament?
5) Had they an epic poem?
6) Did they distinguish between speech and singing?

1) Sir, their light hearts turned to stone.
   It is not remembered whether in gardens
   stone lanterns illumined pleasant ways.
2) Perhaps they gathered once to delight in blossom,
   but after the children were killed
   there were no more buds.
3) Sir, laughter is bitter to the burned mouth.
4) A dream ago, perhaps. Ornament is for joy.
   All the bones were charred.
5) It is not remembered. Remember,
   most were peasants; their life
   was in rice and bamboo.
   When peaceful clouds were reflected in the paddies
   and the water buffalo stepped surely along terraces,
   maybe fathers told their sons old tales.
   When bombs smashed those mirrors
   there was time only to scream.
6) There is an echo yet
   of their speech which was like a song.
   It was reported their singing resembled
   the flight of moths in moonlight.
   Who can say? It is silent now.

1971

Canción[1]

When I am the sky
a glittering bird
slashes at me with the knives of song.

When I am the sea
fiery clouds plunge into my mirrors,
fracture my smooth breath with crimson sobbing.

---

1. Song or lyric poem (Spanish).

When I am the earth
I feel my flesh of rock wearing down:
pebbles, grit, finest dust, nothing.

10 When I am a woman—O, when I am
a woman,
my wells of salt brim and brim,
poems force the lock of my throat.

1975

Divorcing

One garland
of flowers, leaves, thorns
was twined round our two necks.
Drawn tight, it could choke us,
5 yet we loved its scratchy grace,
our fragrant yoke.

We were Siamese twins.
Our blood's not sure
if it can circulate,
10   now we are cut apart.
Something in each of us is waiting
to see if we can survive,
severed.

1975

The Dragonfly-Mother

I was setting out from my house
to keep my promise

but the Dragonfly-Mother stopped me.

I was to speak to a multitude
5 for a good cause, but at home

the Dragonfly-Mother was listening
not to a speech but to the creak of
                              stretching tissue,
tense hum of leaves unfurling.

10 Who is the Dragonfly-Mother?
What does she do?

She is the one who hovers
on stairways of air,
               sometimes almost
grazing your cheekbone,
she is the one who darts unforeseeably
into unsuspected dimensions,

who sees in water
her own blue fire zigzag, and lifts
her self in laughter
into the tearful pale sky

that sails blurred clouds in the stream.

She sat at my round table,
we told one another dreams,
I stayed home breaking my promise.

When she left I slept
three hours, and arose

and wrote. I remember the cold
Waterwoman, in dragonfly dresses
and blue shoes, long ago.[1]
She is the same,

whose children were thin,
left at home when she went out dancing.
She is the Dragonfly-Mother,

that cold
is only the rush of air

swiftness brings.
There is a summer
over the water, over

the river mirrors
where she hovers, a summer
fertile, abundant, where dreams
grow into acts and journeys.

Her children
are swimmers, nymphs[2] and newts, metamorphic.
                                When she tells
her stories she listens; when she listens
she tells you the story you utter.

---

1. This description appears in Levertov's "The Earthwoman and the Waterwoman" (1957).

2. Immature insects; dragonfly nymphs are aquatic.

When I broke my promise,
and slept, and later

cooked and ate the food she had bought
and left in my kitchen,

I kept a tryst with myself,
a long promise that can be fulfilled
only poem by poem,
broken over and over.

          I too,
a creature, grow among reeds,
     in mud, in air,
in sunbright cold, in fever
of blue-gold zenith, winds
of passage.

         Dragonfly-Mother's
a messenger,
if I don't trust her
I can't keep the faith.

         There is a summer
in the sleep
of broken promises, fertile dreams,
acts of passage, hovering
journeys over the fathomless waters.

                               1982

Ancient Airs and Dances

I

I knew too well
what had befallen me
when, one night, I put my lips to his wineglass
after he left—an impulse I thought was locked away with a smile
into memory's museum.

When he took me to visit friends and the sea, he lay
asleep in the next room's dark where the fire
rustled all night; and I, from a warm bed, sleepless,
watched through the open door
that glowing hearth, and heard,
drumming the roof, the rain's
insistent heartbeat.

Greyhaired, I have not grown wiser,
unless to perceive absurdity
is wisdom. A powerless wisdom.

II

    Shameless heart! Did you not vow to learn
        stillness from the heron,
        quiet from the mists of fall,
        and from the mountain—what was it?
20   Pride? Remoteness?
    You have forgotten already!
    And now you clamor again
    like an obstinate child demanding attention,
    interrupting study and contemplation.
25 You try my patience. Bound as we are
    together for life, must you now,
    so late in the day, go bounding sideways,
    trying to drag me with you?

                                                          1992

Evening Train

    An old man sleeping in the evening train,
    face upturned, mouth discreetly closed,
    hands clasped, with fingers interlaced.
    Those large hands
5   lie on the fur lining of his wife's coat
    he's holding for her, and the fur
    looks like a limp dog, docile and affectionate.
    The man himself is a peasant
    in city clothes, moderately prosperous—
10 rich by the standards of his youth;
    one can read that in his hands,
    his sleeping features.
    How tired he is, how tired.
    I called him old, but then I remember
15 my own age, and acknowledge he's likely
    no older than I. But in the dimension
    that moves with us but itself keeps still
    like the bubble in a carpenter's level,
    I'm fourteen, watching the faces I saw each day
20 on the train going in to London,
    and never spoke to; or guessing
    from a row of shoes what sort of faces
    I'd see if I raised my eyes.
    Everyone has an unchanging age (or sometimes two)
25 carried within them, beyond expression.
    This man perhaps
    is ten, putting in a few hours most days
    in a crowded schoolroom, and a lot more
    at work in the fields; a boy who's always
30 making plans to go fishing his first free day.

            The train moves through the dark quite swiftly
            (the Italian dark, as it happens)
            with its load of people, each
            with a conscious destination, each
35   with a known age and that other,
            the hidden one—except for those
            still young, or not young but slower to focus,
            who haven't reached yet that state of being
            which will become
40   not a point of arrest but a core
            around which the mind develops, reflections circle,
            events accrue—a center.
                                    A girl with braids
            sits in this corner seat, invisible,
45   pleased with her solitude. And across from her
            an invisible boy, dreaming. She knows
            she cannot imagine his dreams. Quite swiftly
            we move through our lives; swiftly, steadily the train
            rocks and bounces onward through sleeping fields,
50   our unknown stillness
            holding level as water sealed in glass.

                                                            1992

NADINE GORDIMER
b. 1923

In 1991, Nadine Gordimer was awarded the Nobel Prize for Literature, an honor that recognized the important role her fiction played in the contemporary evolution of racial doctrines and international policies. Until 1994, the government of the Union of South Africa endorsed a legal system of "apartheid" that barred native blacks from full human and civil rights. Since Gordimer's novels and stories offered a scathing critique of the effects of apartheid, it is hardly surprising that a number of her books were banned for several years in her native country. Gordimer, who was born and raised in South Africa, continues to live in Johannesburg, although she travels widely to give lectures and readings.

The daughter of Isidore and Nan Gordimer, both Jewish immigrants, the young Gordimer attended private schools and, for one year, the University of Witwatersrand. After a brief marriage and divorce, she remarried Reinhold H. Cassirer, the director of the Johannesburg branch of Sotheby Parke Bernet. She is the mother of two children, one from each marriage.

From her earliest fiction, *The Lying Days* (1953), to the novels that brought her critical acclaim—*A Guest of Honour* (1970), *The Conservationist* (1974), *Burger's Daughter* (1979), and *July's People* (1981)—Gordimer has written with sensitivity and intelligence about the conventional roles and ways of thinking that distinguish and divide blacks and whites in a society shaped by imperialist history. In such collections of stories as *Six Feet of the Country* (1956), *A Soldier's Embrace* (1980), and *Something Out There* (1984), she has become what the critic Maxwell Geismar calls "a luminous symbol of at least one white person's understanding of the black man's burden." Her most recent work charts the challenges of South Africa's transition into a postapartheid culture. The selection printed here, "The Moment before the Gun Went Off," illustrates her often-quoted comment that "politics is character in South Africa," even as it meditates on the complexities of interracial love and hate.

The Moment before the Gun Went Off

Marais Van der Vyver shot one of his farm labourers, dead. An accident, there are accidents with guns every day of the week—children playing a fatal game with a father's revolver in the cities where guns are domestic objects, nowadays, hunting mishaps like this one, in the country—but these won't be reported all over the world. Van der Vyver knows his will be. He knows that the story of the Afrikaner farmer—regional Party leader and Commandant of the local security commando—shooting a black man who worked for him will fit exactly *their* version of South Africa, it's made for them. They'll be able to use it in their boycott and divestment campaigns, it'll be another piece of evidence in their truth about the country. The papers at home will quote the story as it has appeared in the overseas press, and in the back-and-forth he and the black man will become those crudely-drawn figures on anti-apartheid banners, units in statistics of white brutality against the blacks quoted at the United Nations—he, whom they will gleefully be able to call 'a leading member' of the ruling Party.

People in the farming community understand how he must feel. Bad enough to have killed a man, without helping the Party's, the government's, the country's enemies, as well. They see the truth of that. They know, reading the Sunday papers, that when Van der Vyver is quoted saying he is 'terribly shocked', he will 'look after the wife and children', none of those Americans and English, and none of those people at home who want to destroy the white man's power will believe him. And how they will sneer when he even says of the farm boy (according to one paper, if you can trust any of those reporters), 'He was my friend, I always took him hunting with me.' Those city and overseas people don't know it's true: farmers usually have one particular black boy they like to take along with them in the lands; you could call it a kind of friend, yes, friends are not only your own white people, like yourself, you take into your house, pray with in church and work with on the Party committee. But how can those others know that? They don't want to know it. They think all blacks are like the big-mouth agitators in town. And Van der Vyver's face, in the photographs, strangely opened by distress—everyone in the district remembers Marais Van der Vyver as a little boy who would go away and hide himself if he caught you smiling at him, and everyone knows him now as a man who hides any change of expression round his mouth behind a thick, soft moustache, and in his eyes by always looking at some object in hand, leaf of a crop fingered, pen or stone picked up, while concentrating on what he is saying, or while listening to you. It just goes to show what shock can do; when you look at the newspaper photographs you feel like apologizing, as if you had stared in on some room where you should not be.

There will be an inquiry; there had better be, to stop the assumption of yet another case of brutality against farm workers, although there's nothing in doubt—an accident, and all the facts fully admitted by Van der Vyver. He made a statement when he arrived at the police station with the dead man in his bakkie.[1] Captain Beetge knows him well, of course; he gave him brandy. He was shaking, this big, calm, clever son of Willem Van der Vyver, who inherited the old man's best farm. The black was stone dead, nothing to be done for him. Beetge will not tell anyone that after the brandy Van der Vyver wept. He sobbed, snot running onto his hands, like a dirty kid. The Captain was ashamed, for him, and walked out to give him a chance to recover himself.

Marais Van der Vyver left his house at three in the afternoon to cull a buck from the family of kudu[2] he protects in the bush areas of his farm. He is interested in wildlife and sees it as the farmers' sacred duty to raise game as well as cattle. As usual, he called at his shed workshop to pick up Lucas, a twenty-year-old farmhand who had shown mechanical aptitude and whom Van der Vyver himself had taught to maintain tractors and other farm machinery. He hooted, and Lucas followed the familiar routine, jumping onto the back of the truck. He liked to travel standing up there, spotting game before his employer did. He would lean forward, braced against the cab below him.

Van der Vyver had a rifle and .300 ammunition beside him in the cab. The rifle was one of his father's, because his own was at the gunsmith's in town. Since his father died (Beetge's sergeant wrote 'passed on') no one had used the rifle and so when he took it from a cupboard he was sure it was not loaded. His father had never allowed a loaded gun in the house; he himself had been taught since childhood never to ride with a loaded weapon in a vehicle. But this gun was loaded. On a dirt track, Lucas thumped his fist on the cab roof three times to signal: look left. Having seen the white-ripple-marked flank of a kudu, and its fine horns raking through disguising bush, Van der Vyver drove rather fast over a pot-hole. The jolt fired the rifle. Upright, it was pointing straight through the cab roof at the head of Lucas. The bullet pierced the roof and entered Lucas's brain by way of his throat.

That is the statement of what happened. Although a man of such standing in the district, Van der Vyver had to go through the ritual of swearing that it was the truth. It has gone on record, and will be there in the archive of the local police station as long as Van der Vyver lives, and beyond that, through the lives of his children, Magnus, Helena and Karel—unless things in the country get worse, the example of black mobs in the towns spreads to the rural areas and the place is burned down as many urban police stations have been. Because nothing the government can do will appease the agitators and the whites who encourage them. Nothing satisfies them, in the cities: blacks can sit and drink in white hotels, now, the Immorality Act has gone,[3] blacks can sleep with whites . . . It's not even a crime any more.

---

1. Pickup truck.
2. Large African antelope.
3. South Africa had banned sexual relations between whites and blacks in 1927 and extended the prohibition to all nonwhites in 1950.

Van der Vyver has a high barbed security fence round his farmhouse and garden which his wife, Alida, thinks spoils completely the effect of her artificial stream with its tree-ferns beneath the jacarandas.[4] There is an aerial soaring like a flag-pole in the back yard. All his vehicles, including the truck in which the black man died, have aerials that swing their whips when the driver hits a pot-hole: they are part of the security system the farmers in the district maintain, each farm in touch with every other by radio, twenty-four hours out of twenty-four. It has already happened that infiltrators from over the border have mined remote farm roads, killing white farmers and their families out on their own property for a Sunday picnic. The pot-hole could have set off a land-mine, and Van der Vyver might have died with his farm boy. When neighbours use the communications system to call up and say they are sorry about 'that business' with one of Van der Vyver's boys, there goes unsaid: it could have been worse.

It is obvious from the quality and fittings of the coffin that the farmer has provided money for the funeral. And an elaborate funeral means a great deal to blacks; look how they will deprive themselves of the little they have, in their lifetime, keeping up payments to a burial society so they won't go in boxwood to an unmarked grave. The young wife is pregnant (of course) and another little one, wearing red shoes several sizes too large, leans under her jutting belly. He is too young to understand what has happened, what he is witnessing that day, but neither whines nor plays about; he is solemn without knowing why. Blacks expose small children to everything, they don't protect them from the sight of fear and pain the way whites do theirs. It is the young wife who rolls her head and cries like a child, sobbing on the breast of this relative and that.

All present work for Van der Vyver or are the families of those who work; and in the weeding and harvest seasons, the women and children work for him, too, carried—wrapped in their blankets, on a truck, singing—at sunrise to the fields. The dead man's mother is a woman who can't be more than in her late thirties (they start bearing children at puberty) but she is heavily mature in a black dress between her own parents, who were already working for old Van der Vyver when Marais, like their daughter, was a child. The parents hold her as if she were a prisoner or a crazy woman to be restrained. But she says nothing, does nothing. She does not look up; she does not look at Van der Vyver, whose gun went off in the truck, she stares at the grave. Nothing will make her look up; there need be no fear that she will look up; at him. His wife, Alida, is beside him. To show the proper respect, as for any white funeral, she is wearing the navy-blue-and-cream hat she wears to church this summer. She is always supportive, although he doesn't seem to notice it; this coldness and reserve—his mother says he didn't mix well as a child—she accepts for herself but regrets that it has prevented him from being nominated, as he should be, to stand as the Party's parliamentary candidate for the district. He does not let her clothing, or that of anyone else gathered closely, make contact with him. He, too, stares at the grave. The dead man's mother and he stare at the grave in communication like that between the black man outside and the white man inside the cab the moment before the gun went off.

---

4. Tropical flowering trees.

The moment before the gun went off was a moment of high excitement shared through the roof of the cab, as the bullet was to pass, between the young black man outside and the white farmer inside the vehicle. There were such moments, without explanation, between them, although often around the farm the farmer would pass the young man without returning a greeting, as if he did not recognize him. When the bullet went off what Van der Vyver saw was the kudu stumble in fright at the report and gallop away. Then he heard the thud behind him, and past the window saw the young man fall out of the vehicle. He was sure he had leapt up and toppled—in fright, like the buck. The farmer was almost laughing with relief, ready to tease, as he opened his door, it did not seem possible that a bullet passing through the roof could have done harm.

The young man did not laugh with him at his own fright. The farmer carried him in his arms, to the truck. He was sure, sure he could not be dead. But the young black man's blood was all over the farmer's clothes, soaking against his flesh as he drove.

How will they ever know, when they file newspaper clippings, evidence, proof, when they look at the photographs and see his face—guilty! guilty! they are right!—how will they know, when the police stations burn with all the evidence of what has happened now, and what the law made a crime in the past. How could they know that *they do not know*. Anything. The young black callously shot through the negligence of the white man was not the farmer's boy; he was his son.

1991

SHIRLEY KAUFMAN
b. 1923

"Israel is my home, my uneasy home," Shirley Kaufman told an interviewer in 2004, explaining her "need and desire to know the 'other' and [to] write poems of witness." Born and raised in Seattle, Kaufman was living in San Francisco, raising three daughters and married to a physician, when she began to write poetry in the 1960s. With her first collection of verse she won the United States Award of the International Poetry Forum, and subsequent collections—eight in all—have earned her a range of other prizes, including the Shelley Memorial Award from the Poetry Society of America. In 1973, after divorcing her first husband, she married the prominent Israeli critic and scholar H. M. Daleski and moved to Jerusalem. There she has lived and worked for more than a quarter of a century, translating Hebrew and Dutch poetry while also producing her own, finely crafted, beautifully cadenced verse. Traveling, as the title of one of her books has it, "from one life to another," Kaufman became increasingly concerned with the often painful dilemmas confronting Palestinians and Israelis in their struggle to forge a viable peace. Such poems as "Stones," "Longing for Prophets," and "Intifada" reveal the intensity of the compassion and commitment with which this poet witnesses and delineates the problems posed by her "uneasy home."

His Wife[1]

But it was right that she
looked back. Not to be
curious, some lumpy
reaching of the mind
that turns all shapes to pillars.
But to be only who she was
apart from them, the place
exploding, and herself
defined. Seeing them melt
to slag heaps and the flames
slide into their mouths.
Testing her own lips then,
the coolness, till
she could taste the salt.

1970

Mothers, Daughters

Through every night we hate,
preparing the next day's
war. She bangs the door.
Her face laps up my own
despair, the sour, brown eyes,
the heavy hair she won't
tie back. She's cruel,
as if my private meanness
found a way to punish us.

We gnaw at each other's
skulls. Give me what's mine.
I'd haul her back, choking
myself in her, herself
in me. There is a book
called Poisons on her shelf.
Her room stinks with incense,
animal turds, hamsters
she strokes like silk. They
exercise on the bathroom
floor, and two drop through
the furnace vent. The whole
house smells of the accident,
the hot skins, the small
flesh rotting. Six days
we turn the gas up then

---

1. Lot's wife, who disobeyed God's command and looked back on the destruction of the cities of Sodom of Gomorrah, which she was fleeing with Lot and their two daughters. As punishment, she was turned into a pillar of salt (Genesis 19.15–29, esp. 26).

  to fry the dead. I'd fry
  her head if I could until
  she cried love, love me!

  All she won't let me do.
30 Her stringy figure in
  the windowed room shares
  its thin bones with no one.
  Only her shadow on the glass
  waits like an older sister.
35 Now she stalks, leans forward,
  concentrates merely on getting
  from here to there. Her feet
  are bare. I hear her breathe
  where I can't get in. If I
40 break through to her, she will
  drive nails into my tongue.

            1970

Abishag

... AND LET HER LIE IN THY BOSOM THAT THE LORD MY KING MAY GET HEAT.
            1 Kings 1:2

  That's what they ordered for the old man[1]
  to dangle around his neck
  send currents of fever
  through his phlegmatic nerves, something
5 like rabbit fur, silky,
  or maybe a goat-hair blanket
  to tickle his chin.

  He can do nothing else
  but wear her, pluck at her body
10 like a lost bird pecking in winter.
  He spreads her out
  like a road map, trying
  to find his way from one point
  to another, unable.

15 She thinks if she pinches
  his hand it will turn to powder.
  She feels his thin claws, his wings
  spread over her like arms, not bones
  but feathers ready to fall.
20 She suffers the jerk

---

1. King David; his servants believed that lying with a young virgin would warm the aged king, but though Abishag "ministered to him . . . the king knew her not" (1 Kings 1.4).

ของ his feeble legs. Take it easy.
she tells him, cruelly
submissive in her bright flesh.
He's cold from the fear
of death, the sorrow
of failure, night after night
he shivers with her breasts
against him like an accusation,
her mouth slightly open,
her hair spilling everywhere.

1984

Stones

When you live in Jerusalem you begin
to feel the weight of stones.
You begin to know the word
was made stone, not flesh.[1]

They dwell among us. They crawl
up the hillsides and lie down
on each other to build a wall.
They don't care about prayers,
the small slips of paper
we feed them between the cracks.[2]

They stamp at the earth
until the air runs out
and nothing can grow.

They stare at the sun without blinking
and when they've had enough,
make holes in the sky
so the rain will run down their faces.

They sprawl all over the town
with their pitted bodies. They want
to be water, but nobody
strikes them anymore.[3]

Sometimes at night I hear them
licking the wind to drive it crazy.
There's a huge rock lying on my chest
and I can't get up.

1984

---

1. Compare John 1.14, where Jesus is called "the Word" (of God) "made flesh."
2. Visitors to the so-called Wailing Wall in Jerusalem—the western and only surviving wall of the Second Temple (a reconstruction of King Solomon's temple, completed in 515 B.C.E. and destroyed in 70 C.E.)—often place between its stones slips of paper on which they have written prayers or petitions.
3. As Moses did, when "with his rod he smote the rock twice: and the water came out abundantly" (Numbers 20.11).

Longing for Prophets

Not for their ice-pick eyes,
their weeping willow hair,
and their clenched fists beating at heaven.
Not for their warnings, predictions
of doom. But what they promised.
I don't care if their beards
are mildewed, and the ladders
are broken.[1] Let them go on
picking the wormy fruit. Let the one
with the yoke around his neck
climb out of the cistern.[2]
Let them come down from the heights
in their radiant despair
like the Sankei Juko dancers[3] descending
on ropes, down from these hills
to the earth of their first existence.
Let them follow the track
we've cut on the sides of mountains
into the desert, and stumble again
through the great rift, littered
with bones and the walls of cities.
Let them sift through the ashes
with their burned hands. Let them
tell us what will come after.

1993

Intifada[1]

I The Status Quo

The sand is still hot in September
everyone drives to the beach and we float
in our light bodies watching the red ball
roll to the bottom of the sky and the sea
5   darken and the waves lift us
willingly toward the shore as if
nothing has happened we can go back
to the same life never mind that it's gone
like a road in the desert after a flash flood
10   like the houses we blew up yesterday

---

1. A reference to Jacob's vision of a ladder stretching from the earth to heaven (Genesis 28.12–15).
2. A reference to Jeremiah (for the fruit, see Jeremiah 24; for the yoke, 27–28; and for the cistern, 38.6).
3. A Japanese dance troupe (the name literally means "Between Sea and Mountains").

1. Arabic word for the uprising in the West Bank and Gaza strip by Palestinians protesting the Israeli occupation. It began in December, 1987 with young boys throwing rocks and with commercial strikes, and it became increasingly violent [Kaufman's note].

2 Peace March

In Benares[2] I saw corpses
carried high in saffron robes
to the sacred fires. We carry
these photographs as offerings
to the night. Not like the blind
who walk forever with their arms out.
Not like the holy men smeared with ashes
on the way to the temples.
But like a family, too long on the road,
who by their lassitude
have let this happen.

We walk silent through the streets,
some holding torches, others
dark blow-ups of all the slain children.
Small mouths of disbelief,
how stunned they are
in the young faces.

Second Anniversary
December, 1989

3 Decisions

This morning after her second cup of coffee, finishing
the front page, she decides the future no longer
matters. What a relief. And the past too. Always
stepping into the next ruin, balancing on the next
ledge, making it crumble again. Ancient eroded
vineyards in the Judean hills.[3] She can forget
what happened, all that pile-up of memory and guilt
like accidents on the bridge when the cars smash
into each other behind the first collision. We don't
have to hold our necks, she thinks with a sweet release,
or assess the damage or take notes from the other driver.
It doesn't matter it doesn't. She keeps the news
to herself like a secret drinker, not able to give it up.
The boy with his leg blown off. The dutiful children.
What she is in her own eyes, the bulk of her fear.
Yesterday she had to decide between chocolate-orange
and mocha-pecan. The best ice cream in Tel Aviv
they told her. Decide. Decide. As if her life
were the life she'd chosen. As if anyone's life

1993

---

2. Varanasi, in northeast India on the Ganges River; the city is holy to Hindus, and also sacred to Jains, Sikhs, and Buddhists.

3. Hills in the southwest portion of the West Bank.

PATRICIA BEER
1924–1999

Patricia Beer's *Reader, I Married Him* (1974), a critical examination of works by nineteenth-century women novelists in England, was one of the first studies of the female literary tradition to appear in the 1970s, when the so-called second wave of feminism began to crest. A former lecturer in English at the University of Padua and at London University, Beer was a graduate of St. Hugh's College, Oxford, and herself a poet and novelist. Born in Devon into a family of fundamentalist Plymouth Brethren, she began writing early, in the process distancing herself from her religious background. In the course of her career, she published numerous collections of verse, including *The Loss of the Magyar* (1959), *The Survivors* (1963), *The Estuary* (1971), *The Lie of the Land* (1983), *Friend of Heraclitus* (1993), and *Autumn* (1997), as well as a memoir, *Mrs. Beer's House* (1968); a novel, *Moon's Ottery* (1978); several anthologies; and, in addition to *Reader, I Married Him*, a study of the metaphysical poets.

Beer was married twice, first to the writer P. N. Furbank, and then to Damien Parsons, an architect. After leaving academia, she supported herself as journalist and critic for such periodicals as the *Times Literary Supplement* and the *London Review of Books*. *As I Was Saying Yesterday* (2002), a selection of her essays and reviews, appeared posthumously. The book demonstrates the verve with which she managed her career as a distinguished woman of letters, in prose as well as in verse. Described by one commentator as "a religious poet stripped of the blurring consolations of religion," she was defined by another as "an iron fist in an elbow-length velvet glove." Whether confronting existential issues or evaluating the oeuvres of others, she recorded the dilemmas that she and other literary women faced with wry wit and technical precision, as her sardonic depiction of "transvestism in the novels of Charlotte Brontë" reveals.

Witch

I shall see justice done.
I shall protect time
From monkish, cowardly men
Who say this life is not all
5   And do not respect the clock.

On those who will not escape
I shall see justice done.
I have courage to use
Wax and the killing pin[1]
10 On behalf of prisoners.

I cut off the pilot's thumb
Because his compass failed.
I shall see justice done
Whenever the homeward bound
15 Mistake their true home.

---

1. I.e., use a voodoo doll.

In my black pointed heart
I cherish the good of all.
With storms, potions and blood
I shall see justice done
20 For I know goodness well.

Never shall bogus love—
Habit, duty or weakness—
Win any mercy from me.
By the light of my long burning
25 I shall see justice done.

                                                                                1963

Brunhild[1]

My father laid me in a ring
Of fire, and then like thunder rolled
Away, though I had been more close
To him than in his arms. He told
5   Me I should never see his face
Now he had voiced me like a song,

Made me a separate thing, no more
His warrior daughter but a woman.
But I do see his face, I see
10 It all the time. Though I am human
He can still rule. He promised me
That a brave man should break the fire,

A man he would approve of,[2] no
Tentative weakling. He will have
15 My father's dominant beard and mighty
Shoulders, and instead of love
This obligation to be doughty.
I wait for the entrance of the hero

Dressed up in my father's fashion.
20 If I were free to love I would
Decide on someone thin and shaven.
But in the ring I lie like wood
Or soil, that cannot yield or even
Be raped except with his permission.

                                                                                1967

---

1. Warrior maiden of Germanic mythology. In Richard Wagner's opera *Die Walküre* (1870), the second in his *Ring* cycle, Brunhild's father (the god Wotan) deprives her of her immortality.
2. Siegfried, in the 1876 opera of that name.

The Bull

The bull on the poster speaks
Trunkless but not just a head.
Up in London to be sold
His white face that all his sons wear
5   Is a man's fortune.

He was once a danger.
Even across three meadows
His walk gave him away
Bred stories and giggling fright.
10 Without any rage he was
Thunder in a field.

Nobody except me seems
To notice him by day
But one night after the rush hour
15 Someone must have done,

Someone who felt the need
To draw a loop out of his mouth
Saying I AM A BULL.

1971

In Memory of Constance Markiewicz[1]

The kind of woman that men poets
Hope their own and their friends' daughters
Will not resemble, a rarity.

Stepping from silk into uniform,
5   From earth to dirt, she lit out and left
The green country where her father ruled

Then left her husband and child also
Like an evangelist with a wilder
Calling or a painter feeling trapped.

10 Women do not usually do this.
She calls to mind Mrs. Jellyby[2]
That pretty monster who looked over

Her children's heads into Africa
Though she would not have died, I suppose,
15 For the good of Borrioboola.

---

1. Irish nationalist and Sinn Fein politician (1884–1927), who took part in the Easter Uprising of 1916 in Dublin.

2. A character in Charles Dickens's *Bleak House* (1852–53) who thought only of a project to aid the inhabitants of "Borrioboola-Gha" in Africa.

Constance felt the value of bloodshed
As deeply as Pearse and Connolly.[3]
She bespoke a priest to see her through

The bullets, but did not require him
For eleven years and then bloodlessly,
Having gone far past disappointment.

Yes, she became opinionated
And shrill, but had a longer funeral
Procession than most of us will have.

1971

Mating Calls

It is not so much the song
Of the hump-backed whale, reaching
Through a hundred miles of sea
To his love that strikes us. We
Can be heard farther than he.

It is not the albatross
Either, with his strident voice
Promising the most tender
"Always" in tones of thunder.
Our vows may well go under.

Some kind of magpie keeps on
Singing, when his mate has gone,
Not only his notes but hers.
This moves us to pride and tears
That love should make us such bores.

1975

Transvestism in the Novels of Charlotte Brontë

When reading *Villette*, *Shirley* and *Jane Eyre*,
Though never somehow *The Professor*[1]
Which was all too clear,
I used to overlook
The principal point of each book
As it now seems to me: what the characters wore.

---

3. James Connolly (1870–1916), Irish nationalist and socialist, who helped organize Irish labor; he was wounded in the 1916 rebellion, captured, and subsequently shot. Patrick Pearse (1879–1916) commanded the Irish forces in the Easter Uprising and was executed by the English.
1. Brontë's first novel, *The Professor* (not published until 1857), has her only male narrator. On the English novelist Brontë (1816–1855), see Vol. 1, p. 633.

Mr. Rochester[2] dressed up as the old crone
That perhaps he should have been,
De Hamal[3] as a nun.
10 There was no need
For this. Each of them could
Have approached his woman without becoming one.

Not all heroines were as forthright.
Shirley[4] in particular was a cheat.
15 With rakish hat
She strode like a man
But always down the lane
Where the handsome mill-owner lived celibate.

Lucy,[5] however, knew just what she was doing.
20 And cast herself as a human being.
Strutting and wooing
In the school play
She put on a man's gilet,[6]
Kept her own skirt, for fear of simplifying.

25 Their lonely begetter was both sister and brother.
In her dark wood trees do not scan each other
Yet foregather,
Branched or split,
Whichever they are not,
30 Whichever they are, and rise up together.

1983

2. A character in *Jane Eyre* (1847).
3. A character in *Villette* (1853).
4. A character in *Shirley* (1849).
5. The narrator of *Villette*.
6. Vest, jacket (French).

JANET FRAME
1924–2004

"I like to see life with its teeth out," declared the novelist and memoirist Janet Frame, whose scrupulously detailed, vividly rendered New Zealand narratives earned her numerous honors, not only in her native land but internationally. Twice short-listed for the Nobel Prize, Frame received awards around the world toward the end of her life, including honorary membership in the American Academy of Arts and Letters and the Commonwealth Writers' Prize. Yet, as she remembered in *To the Is-Land* (1983), the first volume in her three-part autobiography, "On the rim of the farthest circle from the group was my normal place" and in fact she may have gained her greatest fame when in 1990 the second volume of this autobiography, *An Angel at My Table* (1984), was made into a prize-winning movie by the acclaimed director Jane

Campion. Famously reclusive, Frame had long sought to escape public attention, rejecting the overtures of would-be biographers and even, at various times, changing her name (to Clutha) and moving around the country to seek privacy. Yet what the Australian Nobel Laureate Patrick White called her "new minded" way with words eventually led to, as one critic puts it, "an enduring public fascination with the life of the author with the distinctive thick flame-red hair."

Especially fueling this fascination was the tale Frame narrated in the first volume of her autobiography: the story of how as a young woman she was misdiagnosed with schizophrenia, then immured in a mental institution where she suffered more than two hundred shock treatments and was on the verge of enduring a lobotomy when her first collection of stories, *The Lagoon* (1951), won a major literary prize. "My writing saved me," Frame later recalled, liberating her from "life-long confinement in a hospital" and making it possible for her to travel to England and the United States in the course of a career during which she published nearly twenty novels, memoirs, and collections of stories.

Janet Paterson Frame was born in Dunedin, New Zealand, the third of five children to be raised in an impoverished and unlucky family. Two of her sisters were drowned (on separate occasions), and the death of one was clearly the starting point for "Keel and Kool." Yet the girl who grew up in these difficult circumstances remembered a home in which "words were revered as the instruments of magic"—a kind of "wonder currency." After graduating from the University of Otago Teachers Training College and teaching for a year, she worked as a caregiver for the elderly. But in 1947 she entered the mental hospital that she would make famous in *An Angel at My Table*, and from then on both her life and her work were radically transformed.

Keel and Kool

Father shook the bidi-bids[1] off the big red and grey rug and then he spread it out again in the grass.

—There you are, he said. Mother here, and Winnie here, and Joan you stay beside Winnie. We'll put the biscuit[2] tin out of the way so it won't come into the photo. Now say cheese.

He stepped back and cupped his hand over the front of the camera, and then he looked over his shoulder—to see if the sun's looking too, he told the children who were saying cheese. And then he clicked the shiny thing at the side of the camera.

—There you are, he said. It's taken. A happy family.

—Oh, said Mother. Were we all right? Because I want to show the photo to Elsie. It's the first we've taken since Eva . . . went.

Mother always said went or passed away or passed beyond when she talked of death. As if it were not death really, only pretend.

—We were good weren't we, Dad, said Winnie. And now are you going fishing?

—Yes, said Father. I'm going fishing. I'll put this in a safe place and then I'm off up the river for salmon.

He carried the camera over to where the coats were piled, and he stowed it in one of the bags carefully, for photos were precious things.

And then he stooped and fastened the top strap of his gumboots[3] to his belt.

---

1. Burrs of a creeping plant that is also called bidi-bid (from the Maori *piripiri*).
2. Cookie.
3. Rubber hip waders.

—Cheerio, he said, kissing Mother. He always kissed everyone when he went away anywhere, even for a little while. And then he kissed Winnie and pulled her hair, and he pulled Joan's hair too but he didn't kiss her because she was the girl over the road[4] and no relation.

—I'll come back with a salmon or I'll go butcher's hook.[5]

They watched him walking towards the river, a funny clumpy walk because he had his gumboots on. He was leaning to one side, with his right shoulder lower than his left, as if he were trying to dodge a blow that might come from the sky or the trees or the air. They watched him going and going, like someone on the films, who grows smaller and smaller and then The End is printed across the screen, and music plays and the lights go up. He was like a man in a story walking away from them. Winnie hoped he wouldn't go too far away because the river was deep and wild and made a roaring noise that could be heard even above the willow trees and pine trees. It was the greyest river Winnie had ever seen. And the sky was grey too, with a tiny dot of sun. The grey of the sky seemed to swim into the grey of the river.

Then Father turned and waved.

Winnie and Joan waved back.

—And now we're going to play by the pine tree, Mrs Todd, aren't we, Winnie, said Joan.

—We'll play ladies, said Winnie.

Mother sighed. The children were such happy little things. They didn't realise. . . .

—All right, kiddies, she said. You can run away and play. Don't go near the river and mind the stinging nettle.

Then she opened her *Woman's Weekly* and put it on her knee. She knew that she would read only as far as 'Over the Teacups' and then she would think all over again about Eva passing away, her first baby. A sad blow, people said, to lose your first, just when she was growing up to be a help to you. But it's all for the best and you have Wonderful Faith, Mrs Todd, she's happier in another sphere, you wouldn't have wished it otherwise, and you've got her photo, it's always nice to have their photos. Bear up, Mrs Todd.

Mrs Todd shut her eyes and tried to forget and then she started to read 'Over the Teacups'. It was better to forget and not think about it.

Winnie and Joan raced each other through the grass to the pine tree by the fence, Joan's dark hair bobbing up and down and getting in her eyes.

—Bother, she said.

Winnie stared enviously. She wished her own hair was long enough to hang over her eyes and be brushed away. How nice to say bother, and brush your hair out of your eyes. Eva's hair had been long. It was so funny about Eva, and the flowers and telegrams and Auntie May coming and bringing sugar buns and custard squares. It was so funny at home with Eva's dresses hanging up and her shoes under the wardrobe and no Eva to wear them, and the yellow quilt spread unruffled over her bed, and staying unruffled all night. But it was good wearing Eva's blue pyjamas. They had pink round the bottom of the legs and pink round the neck and sleeves. Winnie liked to walk round the bedroom in them and see herself in the mirror and then get into bed and yawn, stretching her arms above her head like a lady. But it would have been better if Eva were there to see.

---

4. I.e., across the street. 5. Go crook; i.e., be angry (rhyming slang).

And what fun if Eva were there at the picnic!

—Come on, said Joan. We'll play ladies in fur coats. I know because my mother's got a fur coat.

—I'm a lady going to bed, said Winnie. I'm wearing some beautiful blue pyjamas and I'm yawning, and my maid's just brought my coffee to me.

She lay under the pine tree. She could smell the pine and hear the hush-hush of its branches and beyond that the rainy sound of the river, and see the shrivelled up cones like little brown claws, and the grey sky like a tent with the wind blowing under it and puffing it out. And there was Joan walking up and down in her fur coat, and smiling at all the ladies and gentlemen and saying, oh no, I've got heaps of fur coats. Bother, my hair does get in my eyes so.

Joan had been Eva's best friend. She was so beautiful. She was Spanish, she said, a little bit anyway. She had secrets with Eva. They used to whisper together and giggle and talk in code.

—I'm tired of wearing my fur coat, said Joan suddenly. And you can't go on yawning for ever.

—I can go on yawning for ever if I like, said Winnie, remembering the giggles and the secrets and the code she couldn't understand. And she yawned and said thank you to the maid for her coffee. And then she yawned again.

—I can do what I like, she said.

—You can't always, said Joan. Your mother wouldn't let you. Anyway, I'm tired of wearing my fur coat, I want to make something.

She turned her back on Winnie and sat down in the grass away from the pine tree, and began to pick stalks of feathery grass. Winnie stopped yawning. She heard the rainy-wind sound of the river and she wondered where her father was. And what was Mother doing? And what was Joan making with the feathery grass?

—What are you making, Joan?

—I'm making Christmas trees, answered Joan graciously. Eva showed me. Didn't Eva show you?

And she held up a Christmas tree.

—Yes, lied Winnie, Eva showed me Christmas trees.

She stared at the tiny tree in Joan's hand. The grass was wet with last night's dew and the tree sparkled, catching the tiny drop of sunlight that fell from the high grey and white air. It was like a fairy tree or like the song they sang at school—Little fir tree neat and green. Winnie had never seen such a lovely thing to make.

—And Eva showed me some new bits to Tinker Tailor,[6] said Joan, biting off a piece of grass with her teeth—Boots, shoes, slippers, clodhoppers, silk, satin, cotton, rags—it's what you're married in.

—She showed me too, lied Winnie. Eva showed me lots of things.

—She showed me things too, said Joan tenaciously.

Winnie didn't say anything to that. She looked up in the sky and watched a seagull flying over. I'm Keel, I'm Keel, it seemed to say. Come home Kool, come home Kool. Keel Keel. Winnie felt lonely staring up into the sky. Why was the pine tree so big and dark and old? Why was the seagull crying out

---

6. I.e., a variation of the counting game played by young girls that supposedly reveals whom one is to marry.

I'm Keel, I'm Keel as if it were calling for somebody who wouldn't come? Keel Keel, come home Kool, come home Kool, it cried.

Winnie wished her mother would call out to them. She wished her father were back from the river, and they were all sitting on the rug, drinking billy tea[7] and eating water biscuits that crackled in your mouth. She wished Joan were away and there were just Father and Mother and Winnie, and no Joan. She wished she had long hair and could make Christmas trees out of feathery grass. She wished she knew more bits to Tinker Tailor. What was it Joan had said?—Boots, shoes, slippers, clodhoppers. Why hadn't Eva told her?

—You're going to sleep, said Joan suddenly. I've made three Christmas trees. Look.

—I'm not going to sleep. I'm hungry, said Winnie. And I think, Joan Mason, that some people tell lies.

Joan flushed.—I *have* made three Christmas trees.

—It's not that, said Winnie, taking up a pine-needle and making pine-needle writing in the air. I just think that some people tell lies.

—But I'm not a liar, Winnie, protested Joan anxiously. I'm not, honestly.

—Some people, Winnie murmured, writing with her pine-needle.

—You're not fair, Winnie Todd, quivered Joan, throwing down her Christmas trees. I know you mean me.

—Nobody said I did. I just said—some people.

—Well you looked at me.

—Did I?

Winnie crushed her pine-needle and smelt it. She wanted to cry. She wished she had never come for a picnic. She was cold, too, with just her print dress on. She wished she were somewhere far far away from the river and the pine tree and Joan Mason and the Christmas trees, somewhere far far away, she didn't know where.

Perhaps there was no place. Perhaps she would never find anywhere to go. Her mother would die and her father would die and Joan Mason would go on flicking the hair from her eyes and saying bother and wearing her fur coat and not knowing what it was like to have a mother and father dead.

—Yes, said Winnie. You're a liar. Eva told me things about you. Your uncle was eaten by cannibals and your father shot an albatross and had a curse put on him and your hair went green when you went for a swim in Christchurch and you had to be fed on pineapple for three weeks before it turned black again. Eva told me. You're a liar. She didn't believe you either. And take your Christmas trees. She picked up one of the trees and tore it to pieces.

Joan started to cry.

—Cry-baby, liar, so there.

Winnie reached forward and gave Joan a push, and then she turned to the pine tree and, catching hold of the lowest branches, she pulled herself up into the tree. Soon she was over halfway up. The branches rocked up and down, sighing and sighing. Winnie peered down on to the ground and saw Joan running away through the grass, her hair bobbing up and down as she ran. She would be going back to where Winnie's mother was. Perhaps she

---

7. Tea made over an open fire by boiling water and tea leaves in a billycan (a metal pail or pot with a cover and a wire handle).

would tell. Winnie pushed me over and called me names. And then when Winnie got down from the tree and went to join the others her mother would look at her with a hurt expression in her eyes and say, blessed are the peacemakers.[8] And her father would be sitting there telling them all about the salmon, but he would stop when she came up, hours and hours later, and say sternly, I hoped you would behave yourself. And then he would look at Mother, and Winnie would know they were thinking of Eva and the flowers and telegrams and Auntie May saying, bear up, you have Wonderful Faith. And then Mother would say, have one of these chocolate biscuits, Joan. And Mother and Father and Joan would be together, sharing things.

Winnie's eyes filled with tears of pity for herself. She wished Eva were there. They would both sit up the pine tree with their hands clutching hold of the sticky branches, and they would ride up and down, like two birds on the waves, and then they would turn into princesses and sleep at night in blue pyjamas with pink round the edges, and in the daytime they would make Christmas trees out of feathery grass and play Tinker Tailor—boots, shoes, slippers, clodhoppers.

—Boots, shoes, slippers, clodhoppers, whispered Winnie. But there was no one to answer her. Only up in the sky there was a seagull as white as chalk, circling and crying Keel Keel, come home Kool, come home Kool. And Kool would never come, ever.

1951

8. Matthew 5.9.

FLANNERY O'CONNOR
1925–1964

Because Flannery O'Connor believed that "the novelist with Christian concerns will find in modern life distortions" that are "repugnant" to the writer but "natural" to the reader, in a posthumously published volume of collected essays titled *Mystery and Manners* (1969) she advocated "violent means" to get her vision across: with a "hostile audience," the writer must make her "vision apparent by shock—to the hard of hearing you shout, and for the almost blind you draw large and startling figures." Christ-haunted prophets, religious hucksters, and visionary farmhands, many of the characters in O'Connor's stories and novels inhabit a South that she associated with the urgency of faith: "The South," she explained in a letter (1957), "still believes that man has fallen and that he is only perfectible by God's grace, not by his own unaided efforts." Her characters are, therefore, often caught in the grip of a violent spiritual struggle in which they are ultimately saved or lost. Few fiction writers have so successfully resisted religious sentimentality while dramatizing the cost of redemption.

The only child of Regina and Edward Francis O'Connor, Mary Flannery O'Connor grew up in Savannah, Georgia, until her father became ill and the family moved to Milledgeville, Georgia, her mother's hometown. At fifteen, when her father died of lupus erythematosus, an incurable disease of the immune system, she was already committed to Roman Catholicism, the religion of her parents. After graduating in 1942 from Peabody High School, she attended Georgia State College for Women, where she contributed stories and cartoons to the literary magazine. After graduation, she attended the Writers' Workshop at the University of Iowa, where she won the Rinehart-Iowa prize for a work in progress, which she completed first at Yaddo (a writers' retreat) and then in the Connecticut home of two friends, Sally and Robert Fitzgerald. A comic masterpiece, this book—*Wise Blood* (1952)—focused on Hazel Motes, the would-be founder of a "church without Christ, where the blind stay blind, the lame stay lame and them that's dead stays that way."

Both the grotesque humor and the rural, southern dialect of *Wise Blood* characterize the fiction O'Connor later went on to write under difficult circumstances. Two years before the publication of her first novel, she had discovered that she was suffering from the disease that had killed her father. With the aid of cortisone treatments and with her mother's care, she managed to control the disease. Mother and daughter lived on a farm near Milledgeville, where O'Connor raised peacocks and chickens and wrote her second novel, *The Violent Bear It Away* (1960), as well as the stories that appeared in *A Good Man Is Hard to Find and Other Stories* (1955) and in the posthumous collection *Everything That Rises Must Converge* (1965). She was befriended by the poet Robert Lowell, the editor Robert Giroux, and the short story writer Caroline Gordon, but the cortisone weakened her bones and made it difficult for her to travel or lecture. When an operation reactivated her lupus, she died at the age of thirty-nine.

Good Country People

Besides the neutral expression that she wore when she was alone, Mrs. Freeman had two others, forward and reverse, that she used for all her human dealings. Her forward expression was steady and driving like the advance of a heavy truck. Her eyes never swerved to left or right but turned as the story turned as if they followed a yellow line down the center of it. She seldom used the other expression because it was not often necessary for her to retract a statement, but when she did, her face came to a complete stop, there was an almost imperceptible movement of her black eyes, during which they seemed to be receding, and then the observer would see that Mrs. Freeman, though she might stand there as real as several grain sacks thrown on top of each other, was no longer there in spirit. As for getting anything across to her when this was the case, Mrs. Hopewell had given it up. She might talk her head off. Mrs. Freeman could never be brought to admit herself wrong on any point. She would stand there and if she could be brought to say anything, it was something like, "Well, I wouldn't of said it was and I wouldn't of said it wasn't," or letting her gaze range over the top kitchen shelf where there was an assortment of dusty bottles, she might remark, "I see you ain't ate many of them figs you put up last summer."

They carried on their most important business in the kitchen at breakfast. Every morning Mrs. Hopewell got up at seven o'clock and lit her gas heater and Joy's. Joy was her daughter, a large blonde girl who had an artificial leg. Mrs. Hopewell thought of her as a child though she was thirty-two years old and highly educated. Joy would get up while her mother was eating and lumber into the bathroom and slam the door, and before long, Mrs. Freeman would arrive at the back door. Joy would hear her mother call, "Come on in," and then they would talk for a while in low voices that were indistinguishable in the bathroom. By the time Joy came in, they had usually finished the weather report and were on one or the other of Mrs. Freeman's daughters, Glynese or Carramae, Joy called them Glycerin and Caramel. Glynese, a redhead, was eighteen and had many admirers; Carramae, a blonde, was only fifteen but already married and pregnant. She could not keep anything on her stomach. Every morning Mrs. Freeman told Mrs. Hopewell how many times she had vomited since the last report.

Mrs. Hopewell liked to tell people that Glynese and Carramae were two of the finest girls she knew and that Mrs. Freeman was a *lady* and that she was never ashamed to take her anywhere or introduce her to anybody they might meet. Then she would tell how she had happened to hire the Freemans in the first place and how they were a godsend to her and how she had had them four years. The reason for her keeping them so long was that they were not trash. They were good country people. She had telephoned the man whose name they had given as a reference and he had told her that Mr. Freeman was a good farmer but that his wife was the nosiest woman ever to walk the earth. "She's got to be into everything," the man said. "If she don't get there before the dust settles, you can bet she's dead, that's all. She'll want to know all your business. I can stand him real good," he had said, "but me nor my wife neither could have stood that woman one more minute on this place." That had put Mrs. Hopewell off for a few days.

She had hired them in the end because there were no other applicants but she had made up her mind beforehand exactly how she would handle the woman. Since she was the type who had to be into everything, then, Mrs. Hopewell had decided, she would not only let her be into everything, she would *see to it* that she was into everything—she would give her the responsibility of everything, she would put her in charge. Mrs. Hopewell had no bad qualities of her own but she was able to use other people's in such a constructive way that she never felt the lack. She had hired the Freemans and she had kept them four years.

Nothing is perfect. This was one of Mrs. Hopewell's favorite sayings. Another was: that is life! And still another, the most important, was: well, other people have their opinions too. She would make these statements, usually at the table, in a tone of gentle insistence as if no one held them but her, and the large hulking Joy, whose constant outrage had obliterated every expression from her face, would stare just a little to the side of her, her eyes icy blue, with the look of someone who has achieved blindness by an act of will and means to keep it.

When Mrs. Hopewell said to Mrs. Freeman that life was like that, Mrs. Freeman would say, "I always said so myself." Nothing had been arrived at by anyone that had not first been arrived at by her. She was quicker than Mr. Freeman. When Mrs. Hopewell said to her after they had been on the place a while, "You know, you're the wheel behind the wheel," and winked, Mrs. Freeman had said, "I know it. I've always been quick. It's some that are quicker than others."

"Everybody is different," Mrs. Hopewell said.

"Yes, most people is," Mrs. Freeman said.

"It takes all kinds to make the world."

"I always said it did myself."

The girl was used to this kind of dialogue for breakfast and more of it for dinner; sometimes they had it for supper too. When they had no guest they ate in the kitchen because that was easier. Mrs. Freeman always managed to arrive at some point during the meal and to watch them finish it. She would stand in the doorway if it were summer but in the winter she would stand with one elbow on top of the refrigerator and look down on them, or she would stand by the gas heater, lifting the back of her skirt slightly. Occasionally she would stand against the wall and roll her head from side to side. At no time was she in any hurry to leave. All this was very trying on Mrs. Hopewell but she was a woman of great patience. She realized that nothing is perfect and that in the Freemans she had good country people and that if, in this day and age, you get good country people, you had better hang onto them.

She had had plenty of experience with trash. Before the Freemans she had averaged one tenant family a year. The wives of these farmers were not the kind you would want to be around you for very long. Mrs. Hopewell, who had divorced her husband long ago, needed someone to walk over the fields with her; and when Joy had to be impressed for these services, her remarks were usually so ugly and her face so glum that Mrs. Hopewell would say, "If you can't come pleasantly, I don't want you at all," to which the girl, standing square and rigid-shouldered with her neck thrust slightly forward, would reply, "If you want me, here I am—LIKE I AM."

Mrs. Hopewell excused this attitude because of the leg (which had been shot off in a hunting accident when Joy was ten). It was hard for Mrs. Hopewell to realize that her child was thirty-two now and that for more than twenty years she had had only one leg. She thought of her still as a child because it tore her heart to think instead of the poor stout girl in her thirties who had never danced a step or had any *normal* good times. Her name was really Joy but as soon as she was twenty-one and away from home, she had had it legally changed. Mrs. Hopewell was certain that she had thought and thought until she had hit upon the ugliest name in any language. Then she had gone and had the beautiful name, Joy, changed without telling her mother until after she had done it. Her legal name was Hulga.

When Mrs. Hopewell thought of the name, Hulga, she thought of the broad blank hull of a battleship. She would not use it. She continued to call her Joy to which the girl responded but in a purely mechanical way.

Hulga had learned to tolerate Mrs. Freeman who saved her from taking walks with her mother. Even Glynese and Carramae were useful when they occupied attention that might otherwise have been directed at her. At first she had thought she could not stand Mrs. Freeman for she had found that it was not possible to be rude to her. Mrs. Freeman would take on strange resentments and for days together she would be sullen but the source of her displeasure was always obscure; a direct attack, a positive leer, blatant ugliness to her face—these never touched her. And without warning one day, she began calling her Hulga.

She did not call her that in front of Mrs. Hopewell who would have been incensed but when she and the girl happened to be out of the house together, she would say something and add the name Hulga to the end of it, and the big spectacled Joy-Hulga would scowl and redden as if her privacy had been intruded upon. She considered the name her personal affair. She had arrived at it first purely on the basis of its ugly sound and then the full genius of its fitness had struck her. She had a vision of the name working like the ugly sweating Vulcan[1] who stayed in the furnace and to whom, presumably, the goddess had to come when called. She saw it as the name of her highest creative act. One of her major triumphs was that her mother had not been able to turn her dust into Joy, but the greater one was that she had been able to turn it herself into Hulga. However, Mrs. Freeman's relish for using the name only irritated her. It was as if Mrs. Freeman's beady steel-pointed eyes had penetrated far enough behind her face to reach some secret fact. Something about her seemed to fascinate Mrs. Freeman and then one day Hulga realized that it was the artificial leg. Mrs. Freeman had a special fondness for the details of secret infections, hidden deformities, assaults upon children. Of diseases, she preferred the lingering or incurable. Hulga had heard Mrs. Hopewell give her the details of the hunting accident, how the leg had been literally blasted off, how she had never lost consciousness. Mrs. Freeman could listen to it any time as if it had happened an hour ago.

When Hulga stumped into the kitchen in the morning (she could walk without making the awful noise but she made it—Mrs. Hopewell was certain—because it was ugly-sounding), she glanced at them and did not speak. Mrs. Hopewell would be in her red kimono with her hair tied around her head in rags. She would be sitting at the table, finishing her breakfast and Mrs. Freeman would be hanging by her elbow outward from the refrigerator, looking down at the table. Hulga always put her eggs on the stove to boil and then stood over them with her arms folded, and Mrs. Hopewell would look at her—a kind of indirect gaze divided between her and Mrs. Freeman—and would think that if she would only keep herself up a little, she wouldn't be so bad looking. There was nothing wrong with her face that a pleasant expression wouldn't help. Mrs. Hopewell said that people who looked on the bright side of things would be beautiful even if they were not.

Whenever she looked at Joy this way, she could not help but feel that it would have been better if the child had not taken the Ph.D. It had certainly not brought her out any and now that she had it, there was no more excuse for her to go to school again. Mrs. Hopewell thought it was nice for girls to go to school to have a good time but Joy had "gone through." Anyhow, she would not have been strong enough to go again. The doctors had told Mrs. Hopewell that with the best of care, Joy might see forty-five. She had a weak heart. Joy had made it plain that if it had not been for this condition, she would be far from these red hills and good country people. She would be in a university lecturing to people who knew what she was talking about. And Mrs. Hopewell could very well picture her there, looking like a scarecrow and lecturing to more of the same. Here she went about all day in a six-year-old skirt and a yellow sweat shirt with a faded cowboy on a horse embossed on it. She thought this was funny; Mrs. Hopewell thought it was idiotic and showed simply that she was still a child. She was brilliant but she didn't have a grain of sense. It seemed to Mrs. Hopewell that every year she grew less like other people and more like herself—bloated, rude, and squint-eyed. And she said such strange things! To her own mother she had said—without warning, without excuse, standing up in the middle of a meal with her face purple and her mouth half full—"Woman! do you ever look inside? Do you

---

1. Roman god of fire whom Venus, goddess of love, "presumably" (a few words later) obeyed as her consort.

ever look inside and see what you are *not*? God!" she had cried sinking down again and staring at her plate, "Malebranche[2] was right: we are not our own light. We are not our own light!" Mrs. Hopewell had no idea to this day what brought that on. She had only made the remark, hoping Joy would take it in, that a smile never hurt anyone.

The girl had taken the Ph.D. in philosophy and this left Mrs. Hopewell at a complete loss. You could say, "My daughter is a nurse," or "My daughter is a schoolteacher," or even, "My daughter is a chemical engineer." You could not say, "My daughter is a philosopher." That was something that had ended with the Greeks and Romans. All day Joy sat on her neck in a deep chair, reading. Sometimes she went for walks but she didn't like dogs or cats or birds or flowers or nature or nice young men. She looked at nice young men as if she could smell their stupidity.

One day Mrs. Hopewell had picked up one of the books the girl had just put down and opening it at random, she read, "Science, on the other hand, has to assert its soberness and seriousness afresh and declare that it is concerned solely with what-is. Nothing—how can it be for science anything but a horror and a phantasm? If science is right, then one thing stands firm: science wishes to know nothing of nothing. Such is after all the strictly scientific approach to Nothing. We know it by wishing to know nothing of Nothing." These words had been underlined with a blue pencil and they worked on Mrs. Hopewell like some evil incantation in gibberish. She shut the book quickly and went out of the room as if she were having a chill.

This morning when the girl came in, Mrs. Freeman was on Carramae. "She thrown up four times after supper," she said, "and was up twict in the night after three o'clock. Yesterday she didn't do nothing but ramble in the bureau drawer. All she did. Stand up there and see what she could run up on."

"She's got to eat," Mrs. Hopewell muttered, sipping her coffee, while she watched Joy's back at the stove. She was wondering what the child had said to the Bible salesman. She could not imagine what kind of a conversation she could possibly have had with him.

He was a tall gaunt hatless youth who had called yesterday to sell them a Bible. He had appeared at the door, carrying a large black suitcase that weighted him so heavily on one side that he had to brace himself against the door facing. He seemed on the point of collapse but he said in a cheerful voice. "Good morning, Mrs. Cedars!" and set the suitcase down on the mat. He was not a bad-looking young man though he had on a bright blue suit and yellow socks that were not pulled up far enough. He had prominent face bones and a streak of sticky-looking brown hair falling across his forehead.

"I'm Mrs. Hopewell," she said.

"Oh!" he said, pretending to look puzzled but with his eyes sparkling, "I saw it said 'The Cedars' on the mailbox so I thought you was Mrs. Cedars!" and he burst out in a pleasant laugh. He picked up the satchel and under cover of a pant, he fell forward into her hall. It was rather as if the suitcase had moved first, jerking him after it. "Mrs. Hopewell!" he said and grabbed her hand. "I hope you are well!" and he laughed again and then all at once

---

2. Nicolas Malebranche (1638–1715), French philosopher.

his face sobered completely. He paused and gave her a straight earnest look and said, "Lady, I've come to speak of serious things."

"Well, come in," she muttered, none too pleased because her dinner was almost ready. He came into the parlor and sat down on the edge of a straight chair and put the suitcase between his feet and glanced around the room as if he were sizing her up by it. Her silver gleamed on the two sideboards; she decided he had never been in a room as elegant as this.

"Mrs. Hopewell," he began, using her name in a way that sounded almost intimate, "I know you believe in Christian service."

"Well yes," she murmured.

"I know," he said and paused, looking very wise with his head cocked on one side, "that you're a good woman. Friends have told me."

Mrs. Hopewell never liked to be taken for a fool. "What are you selling?" she asked.

"Bibles," the young man said and his eye raced around the room before he added, "I see you have no family Bible in your parlor, I see that is the one lack you got!"

Mrs. Hopewell could not say, "My daughter is an atheist and won't let me keep the Bible in the parlor." She said, stiffening slightly, "I keep my Bible by my bedside." This was not the truth. It was in the attic somewhere.

"Lady," he said, "the word of God ought to be in the parlor."

"Well, I think that's a matter of taste," she began. "I think. . . ."

"Lady," he said, "for a Chrustian, the word of God ought to be in every room in the house besides in his heart. I know you're a Chrustian because I can see it in every line of your face."

She stood up and said, "Well, young man, I don't want to buy a Bible and I smell my dinner burning."

He didn't get up. He began to twist his hands and looking down at them, he said softly, "Well lady, I'll tell you the truth—not many people want to buy one nowadays and besides, I know I'm real simple. I don't know how to say a thing but to say it. I'm just a country boy." He glanced up into her unfriendly face. "People like you don't like to fool with country people like me!"

"Why!" she cried, "good country people are the salt of the earth! Besides, we all have different ways of doing, it takes all kinds to make the world go 'round. That's life!"

"You said a mouthful," he said.

"Why, I think there aren't enough good country people in the world!" she said, stirred. "I think that's what's wrong with it!"

His face had brightened. "I didn't inraduce myself," he said. "I'm Manley Pointer from out in the country around Willohobie, not even from a place, just from near a place."

"You wait a minute," she said. "I have to see about my dinner." She went out to the kitchen and found Joy standing near the door where she had been listening.

"Get rid of the salt of the earth," she said, "and let's eat."

Mrs. Hopewell gave her a pained look and turned the heat down under the vegetables. "*I* can't be rude to anybody," she murmured and went back into the parlor.

He had opened the suitcase and was sitting with a Bible on each knee.

"You might as well put those up," she told him. "I don't want one."

"I appreciate your honesty," he said. "You don't see any more real honest people unless you go away out in the country."

"I know," she said, "real genuine folks!" Through the crack in the door she heard a groan.

"I guess a lot of boys come telling you they're working their way through college," he said, "but I'm not going to tell you that. Somehow," he said, "I don't want to go to college. I want to devote my life to Chrustian service. See," he said, lowering his voice, "I got this heart condition. I may not live long. When you know it's something wrong with you and you may not live long, well then, lady . . ." He paused, with his mouth open, and stared at her.

He and Joy had the same condition! She knew that her eyes were filling with tears but she collected herself quickly and murmured, "Won't you stay for dinner? We'd love to have you!" and was sorry the instant she heard herself say it.

"Yes mam," he said in an abashed voice, "I would sher love to do that!"

Joy had given him one look on being introduced to him and then throughout the meal had not glanced at him again. He had addressed several remarks to her, which she had pretended not to hear. Mrs. Hopewell could not understand deliberate rudeness, although she lived with it, and she felt she had always to overflow with hospitality to make up for Joy's lack of courtesy. She urged him to talk about himself and he did. He said he was the seventh child of twelve and that his father had been crushed under a tree when he himself was eight year old. He had been crushed very badly, in fact, almost cut in two and was practically not recognizable. His mother had got along the best she could by hard working and she had always seen that her children went to Sunday School and that they read the Bible every evening. He was now nineteen year old and he had been selling Bibles for four months. In that time he had sold seventy-seven Bibles and had the promise of two more sales. He wanted to become a missionary because he thought that was the way you could do most for people. "He who losest his life shall find it,"[3] he said simply and he was so sincere, so genuine and earnest that Mrs. Hopewell would not for the world have smiled. He prevented his peas from sliding onto the table by blocking them with a piece of bread which he later cleaned his plate with. She could see Joy observing sidewise how he handled his knife and fork and she saw too that every few minutes, the boy would dart a keen appraising glance at the girl as if he were trying to attract her attention.

After dinner Joy cleared the dishes off the table and disappeared and Mrs. Hopewell was left to talk with him. He told her again about his childhood and his father's accident and about various things that had happened to him. Every five minutes or so she would stifle a yawn. He sat for two hours until finally she told him she must go because she had an appointment in town. He packed his Bibles and thanked her and prepared to leave, but in the doorway he stopped and wrung her hand and said that not on any of his trips had he met a lady as nice as her and he asked if he could come again. She had said she would always be happy to see him.

Joy had been standing in the road, apparently looking at something in the distance, when he came down the steps toward her, bent to the side with his

---

3. Matthew 16.25. (spoken by Jesus).

heavy valise. He stopped where she was standing and confronted her directly. Mrs. Hopewell could not hear what he said but she trembled to think what Joy would say to him. She could see that after a minute Joy said something and that then the boy began to speak again, making an excited gesture with his free hand. After a minute Joy said something else at which the boy began to speak once more. Then to her amazement, Mrs. Hopewell saw the two of them walk off together, toward the gate. Joy had walked all the way to the gate with him and Mrs. Hopewell could not imagine what they had said to each other, and she had not yet dared to ask.

Mrs. Freeman was insisting upon her attention. She had moved from the refrigerator to the heater so that Mrs. Hopewell had to turn and face her in order to seem to be listening. "Glynese gone out with Harvey Hill again last night," she said. "She had this sty."

"Hill," Mrs. Hopewell said absently, "is that the one who works in the garage?"

"Nome, he's the one that goes to chiropracter school," Mrs. Freeman said. "She had this sty. Been had it two days. So she says when he brought her in the other night he says, 'Lemme get rid of that sty for you,' and she says, 'How?' and he says, 'You just lay yourself down acrost the seat of that car and I'll show you.' So she done it and he popped her neck. Kept on a-popping it several times until she made him quit. This morning," Mrs. Freeman said, "she ain't got no sty. She ain't got no traces of a sty."

"I never heard of that before," Mrs. Hopewell said.

"He ast her to marry him before the Ordinary,"[4] Mrs. Freeman went on, "and she told him she wasn't going to be married in no *office*."

"Well, Glynese is a fine girl," Mrs. Hopewell said. "Glynese and Carramae are both fine girls."

"Carramae said when her and Lyman was married Lyman said it sure felt sacred to him. She said he said he wouldn't take five hundred dollars for being married by a preacher."

"How much would he take?" the girl asked from the stove.

"He said he wouldn't take five hundred dollars," Mrs. Freeman repeated.

"Well we all have work to do," Mrs. Hopewell said.

"Lyman said it just felt more sacred to him," Mrs. Freeman said. "The doctor wants Carramae to eat prunes. Says instead of medicine. Says them cramps is coming from pressure. You know where I think it is?"

"She'll be better in a few weeks," Mrs. Hopewell said.

"In the tube,"[5] Mrs. Freeman said. "Else she wouldn't be as sick as she is."

Hulga had cracked her two eggs into a saucer and was bringing them to the table along with a cup of coffee that she had filled too full. She sat down carefully and began to eat, meaning to keep Mrs. Freeman there by questions if for any reason she showed an inclination to leave. She could perceive her mother's eye on her. The first round-about question would be about the Bible salesman and she did not wish to bring it on. "How did he pop her neck?" she asked.

---

4. Justice of the peace who performs the marriage ceremony in his or her chambers rather than in public.

5. I.e., in the fallopian tube (an ectopic pregnancy).

Mrs. Freeman went into a description of how he had popped her neck. She said he owned a '55 Mercury but that Glynese said she would rather marry a man with only a '36 Plymouth who would be married by a preacher. The girl asked what if he had a '32 Plymouth and Mrs. Freeman said what Glynese had said was a '36 Plymouth.

Mrs. Hopewell said there were not many girls with Glynese's common sense. She said what she admired in those girls was their common sense. She said that reminded her that they had had a nice visitor yesterday, a young man selling Bibles. "Lord," she said, "he bored me to death but he was so sincere and genuine I couldn't be rude to him. He was just good country people, you know," she said, "—just the salt of the earth."

"I seen him walk up," Mrs. Freeman said, "and then later—I seen him walk off," and Hulga could feel the slight shift in her voice, the slight insinuation, that he had not walked off alone, had he? Her face remained expressionless but the color rose into her neck and she seemed to swallow it down with the next spoonful of egg. Mrs. Freeman was looking at her as if they had a secret together.

"Well, it takes all kinds of people to make the world go 'round," Mrs. Hopewell said. "It's very good we aren't all alike."

"Some people are more alike than others," Mrs. Freeman said.

Hulga got up and stumped, with about twice the noise that was necessary, into her room and locked the door. She was to meet the Bible salesman at ten o'clock at the gate. She had thought about it half the night. She had started thinking of it as a great joke and then she had begun to see profound implications in it. She had lain in bed imagining dialogues for them that were insane on the surface but that reached below to depths that no Bible salesman would be aware of. Their conversation yesterday had been of this kind.

He had stopped in front of her and had simply stood there. His face was bony and sweaty and bright, with a little pointed nose in the center of it, and his look was different from what it had been at the dinner table. He was gazing at her with open curiosity, with fascination, like a child watching a new fantastic animal at the zoo, and he was breathing as if he had run a great distance to reach her. His gaze seemed somehow familiar but she could not think where she had been regarded with it before. For almost a minute he didn't say anything. Then on what seemed an insuck of breath, he whispered, "You ever ate a chicken that was two days old?"

The girl looked at him stonily. He might have just put this question up for consideration at the meeting of a philosophical association. "Yes," she presently replied as if she had considered it from all angles.

"It must have been mighty small!" he said triumphantly and shook all over with little nervous giggles, getting very red in the face, and subsiding finally into his gaze of complete admiration, while the girl's expression remained exactly the same.

"How old are you?" he asked softly.

She waited some time before she answered. Then in a flat voice she said, "Seventeen."

His smiles came in succession like waves breaking on the surface of a little lake. "I see you got a wooden leg," he said. "I think you're brave. I think you're real sweet."

The girl stood blank and solid and silent.

"Walk to the gate with me," he said. "You're a brave sweet little thing and I liked you the minute I seen you walk in the door."

Hulga began to move forward.

"What's your name?" he asked, smiling down on the top of her head.

"Hulga," she said.

"Hulga," he murmured, "Hulga. Hulga. I never heard of anybody name Hulga before. You're shy, aren't you, Hulga?" he asked.

She nodded, watching his large red hand on the handle of the giant valise.

"I like girls that wear glasses," he said. "I think a lot. I'm not like these people that a serious thought don't ever enter their heads. It's because I may die."

"I may die too," she said suddenly and looked up at him. His eyes were very small and brown, glittering feverishly.

"Listen," he said, "don't you think some people was meant to meet on account of what all they got in common and all? Like they both think serious thoughts and all?" He shifted the valise to his other hand so that the hand nearest her was free. He caught hold of her elbow and shook it a little. "I don't work on Saturday," he said. "I like to walk in the woods and see what Mother Nature is wearing. O'er the hills and far away. Pic-nics and things. Couldn't we go on a pic-nic tomorrow? Say yes, Hulga," he said and gave her a dying look as if he felt his insides about to drop out of him. He had even seemed to sway slightly toward her.

During the night she had imagined that she seduced him. She imagined that the two of them walked on the place until they came to the storage barn beyond the two back fields and there, she imagined, that things came to such a pass that she very easily seduced him and that then, of course, she had to reckon with his remorse. True genius can get an idea across even to an inferior mind. She imagined that she took his remorse in hand and changed it into a deeper understanding of life. She took all his shame away and turned it into something useful.

She set off for the gate at exactly ten o'clock, escaping without drawing Mrs. Hopewell's attention. She didn't take anything to eat, forgetting that food is usually taken on a picnic. She wore a pair of slacks and a dirty white shirt, and as an afterthought, she had put some Vapex on the collar of it since she did not own any perfume. When she reached the gate no one was there.

She looked up and down the empty highway and had the furious feeling that she had been tricked, that he had only meant to make her walk to the gate after the idea of him. Then suddenly he stood up, very tall, from behind a bush on the opposite embankment. Smiling, he lifted his hat which was new and wide-brimmed. He had not worn it yesterday and she wondered if he had bought it for the occasion. It was toast-colored with a red and white band around it and was slightly too large for him. He stepped from behind the bush still carrying the black valise. He had on the same suit and the same yellow socks sucked down in his shoes from walking. He crossed the highway and said, "I knew you'd come!"

The girl wondered acidly how he had known this. She pointed to the valise and asked, "Why did you bring your Bibles?"

He took her elbow, smiling down on her as if he could not stop. "You can never tell when you'll need the word of God, Hulga," he said. She had a moment in which she doubted that this was actually happening and then they began to climb the embankment. They went down into the pasture toward the woods. The boy walked lightly by her side, bouncing on his toes. The valise did not seem to be heavy today; he even swung it. They crossed half the pasture without saying anything and then, putting his hand easily on the small of her back, he asked softly, "Where does your wooden leg join on?"

She turned an ugly red and glared at him and for an instant the boy looked abashed. "I didn't mean you no harm," he said. "I only meant you're so brave and all. I guess God takes care of you."

"No," she said, looking forward and walking fast, "I don't even believe in God."

At this he stopped and whistled. "No!" he exclaimed as if he were too astonished to say anything else.

She walked on and in a second he was bouncing at her side, fanning with his hat. "That's very unusual for a girl," he remarked, watching her out of the corner of his eye. When they reached the edge of the wood, he put his hand on her back again and drew her against him without a word and kissed her heavily.

The kiss, which had more pressure than feeling behind it, produced that extra surge of adrenalin in the girl that enables one to carry a packed trunk out of a burning house, but in her, the power went at once to the brain. Even before he released her, her mind, clear and detached and ironic anyway, was regarding him from a great distance, with amusement but with pity. She had never been kissed before and she was pleased to discover that it was an unexceptional experience and all a matter of the mind's control. Some people might enjoy drain water if they were told it was vodka. When the boy, looking expectant but uncertain, pushed her gently away, she turned and walked on, saying nothing as if such business, for her, were common enough.

He came along panting at her side, trying to help her when he saw a root that she might trip over. He caught and held back the long swaying blades of thorn vine until she had passed beyond them. She led the way and he came breathing heavily behind her. Then they came out on a sunlit hillside, sloping softly into another one a little smaller. Beyond, they could see the rusted top of the old barn where the extra hay was stored.

The hill was sprinkled with small pink weeds. "Then you ain't saved?" he asked suddenly, stopping.

The girl smiled. It was the first time she had smiled at him at all. "In my economy," she said, "I'm saved and you are damned but I told you I didn't believe in God."

Nothing seemed to destroy the boy's look of admiration. He gazed at her now as if the fantastic animal at the zoo had put its paw through the bars and given him a loving poke. She thought he looked as if he wanted to kiss her again and she walked on before he had the chance.

"Ain't there somewheres we can sit down sometime?" he murmured, his voice softening toward the end of the sentence.

"In that barn," she said.

They made for it rapidly as if it might slide away like a train. It was a large two-story barn, cool and dark inside. The boy pointed up the ladder that led into the loft and said, "It's too bad we can't go up there."

"Why can't we?" she asked.

"Yer leg," he said reverently.

The girl gave him a contemptuous look and putting both hands on the ladder, she climbed it while he stood below, apparently awe-struck. She pulled herself expertly through the opening and then looked down at him and said, "Well, come on if you're coming," and he began to climb the ladder, awkwardly bringing the suitcase with him.

"We won't need the Bible," she observed.

"You never can tell," he said, panting. After he had got into the loft, he was a few seconds catching his breath. She had sat down in a pile of straw. A wide sheath of sunlight, filled with dust particles, slanted over her. She lay back against a bale, her face turned away, looking out the front opening of the barn where hay was thrown from a wagon into the loft. The two pink-speckled hillsides lay back against a dark ridge of woods. The sky was cloudless and cold blue. The boy dropped down by her side and put one arm under her and the other over her and began methodically kissing her face, making little noises like a fish. He did not remove his hat but it was pushed far enough back not to interfere. When her glasses got in his way, he took them off of her and slipped them into his pocket.

The girl at first did not return any of the kisses but presently she began to and after she had put several on his cheek, she reached his lips and remained there, kissing him again and again as if she were trying to draw all the breath out of him. His breath was clear and sweet like a child's and the kisses were sticky like a child's. He mumbled about loving her and about knowing when he first seen her that he loved her, but the mumbling was like the sleepy fretting of a child being put to sleep by his mother. Her mind, throughout this, never stopped or lost itself for a second to her feelings. "You ain't said you loved me none," he whispered finally, pulling back from her. "You got to say that."

She looked away from him off into the hollow sky and then down at a black ridge and then down farther into what appeared to be two green swelling lakes. She didn't realize he had taken her glasses but this landscape could not seem exceptional to her for she seldom paid any close attention to her surroundings.

"You got to say it," he repeated. "You got to say you love me."

She was always careful how she committed herself. "In a sense," she began, "if you use the word loosely, you might say that. But it's not a word I use. I don't have illusions. I'm one of those people who see *through* to nothing."

The boy was frowning. "You got to say it. I said it and you got to say it," he said.

The girl looked at him almost tenderly. "You poor baby," she murmured. "It's just as well you don't understand," and she pulled him by the neck, face-down, against her. "We are all damned," she said, "but some of us have taken off our blindfolds and see that there's nothing to see. It's a kind of salvation."

The boy's astonished eyes looked blankly through the ends of her hair. "Okay," he almost whined, "but do you love me or don'tcher?"

"Yes," she said and added, "in a sense. But I must tell you something. There mustn't be anything dishonest between us." She lifted his head and looked him in the eye. "I am thirty years old," she said. "I have a number of degrees."

The boy's look was irritated but dogged. "I don't care," he said. "I don't care a thing about what all you done. I just want to know if you love me or don'tcher?" and he caught her to him and wildly planted her face with kisses until she said, "Yes, yes."

"Okay then," he said, letting her go. "Prove it."

She smiled, looking dreamily out on the shifty landscape. She had seduced him without even making up her mind to try. "How?" she asked, feeling that he should be delayed a little.

He leaned over and put his lips to her ear. "Show me where your wooden leg joins on," he whispered.

The girl uttered a sharp little cry and her face instantly drained of color. The obscenity of the suggestion was not what shocked her. As a child she had sometimes been subject to feelings of shame but education had removed the last traces of that as a good surgeon scrapes for cancer; she would no more have felt it over what he was asking than she would have believed in his Bible. But she was as sensitive about the artificial leg as a peacock about his tail. No one ever touched it but her. She took care of it as someone else would his soul, in private and almost with her own eyes turned away. "No," she said.

"I known it," he muttered, sitting up. "You're just playing me for a sucker."

"Oh no no!" she cried. "It joins on at the knee. Only at the knee. Why do you want to see it?"

The boy gave her a long penetrating look. "Because," he said, "it's what makes you different. You ain't like anybody else."

She sat staring at him. There was nothing about her face or her round freezing-blue eyes to indicate that this had moved her; but she felt as if her heart had stopped and left her mind to pump her blood. She decided that for the first time in her life she was face to face with real innocence. This boy, with an instinct that came from beyond wisdom, had touched the truth about her. When after a minute, she said in a hoarse high voice, "All right," it was like surrendering to him completely. It was like losing her own life and finding it again, miraculously, in his.

Very gently he began to roll the slack leg up. The artificial limb, in a white sock and brown flat shoe, was bound in a heavy material like canvas and ended in an ugly jointure where it was attached to the stump. The boy's face and his voice were entirely reverent as he uncovered it and said, "Now show me how to take it off and on."

She took it off for him and put it back on again and then he took it off himself, handling it as tenderly as if it were a real one. "See!" he said with a delighted child's face. "Now I can do it myself!"

"Put it back on," she said. She was thinking that she would run away with him and that every night he would take the leg off and every morning put it back on again. "Put it back on," she said.

"Not yet," he murmured, setting it on its foot out of her reach. "Leave it off for a while. You got me instead."

She gave a little cry of alarm but he pushed her down and began to kiss her again. Without the leg she felt entirely dependent on him. Her brain seemed to have stopped thinking altogether and to be about some other function that it was not very good at. Different expressions raced back and forth over her face. Every now and then the boy, his eyes like two steel spikes, would glance behind him where the leg stood. Finally she pushed him off and said, "Put it back on me now."

"Wait," he said. He leaned the other way and pulled the valise toward him and opened it. It had a pale blue spotted lining and there were only two Bibles in it. He took one of these out and opened the cover of it. It was hollow and contained a pocket flask of whiskey, a pack of cards, and a small blue box with printing on it. He laid these out in front of her one at a time in an evenly-spaced row, like one presenting offerings at the shrine of a goddess. He put the blue box in her hand. THIS PRODUCT TO BE USED ONLY FOR THE PREVENTION OF DISEASE,[6] she read, and dropped it. The boy was unscrewing the top of the flask. He stopped and pointed, with a smile, to the deck of cards. It was not an ordinary deck but one with an obscene picture on the back of each card. "Take a swig," he said, offering her the bottle first. He held it in front of her, but like one mesmerized, she did not move.

Her voice when she spoke had an almost pleading sound. "Aren't you," she murmured, "aren't you just good country people?"

The boy cocked his head. He looked as if he were just beginning to understand that she might be trying to insult him. "Yeah," he said, curling his lip slightly, "but it ain't held me back none. I'm as good as you any day in the week."

"Give me my leg," she said.

He pushed it farther away with his foot. "Come on now, let's begin to have us a good time," he said coaxingly. "We ain't got to know one another good yet."

"Give me my leg!" she screamed and tried to lunge for it but he pushed her down easily.

"What's the matter with you all of a sudden?" he asked, frowning as he screwed the top on the flask and put it quickly back inside the Bible. "You just a while ago said you didn't believe in nothing. I thought you was some girl!"

Her face was almost purple. "You're a Christian!" she hissed. "You're a fine Christian! You're just like them all—say one thing and do another. You're a perfect Christian, you're . . ."

The boy's mouth was set angrily. "I hope you don't think," he said in a lofty indignant tone, "that I believe in that crap! I may sell Bibles but I know which end is up and I wasn't born yesterday and I know where I'm going!"

"Give me my leg!" she screeched. He jumped up so quickly that she barely saw him sweep the cards and the blue box into the Bible and throw the Bible into the valise. She saw him grab the leg and then she saw it for an instant slanted forlornly across the inside of the suitcase with a Bible at either side of its opposite ends. He slammed the lid shut and snatched up the valise and swung it down the hole and then stepped through himself.

When all of him had passed but his head, he turned and regarded her with a look that no longer had any admiration in it. "I've gotten a lot of interesting things," he said. "One time I got a woman's glass eye this way. And you needn't to think you'll catch me because Pointer ain't really my name. I use a different name at every house I call at and don't stay nowhere long. And

---

6. Label once commonly found on condom boxes.

I'll tell you another thing, Hulga," he said, using the name as if he didn't think much of it, "you ain't so smart. I been believing in nothing ever since I was born!" and then the toast-colored hat disappeared down the hole and the girl was left, sitting on the straw in the dusty sunlight. When she turned her churning face toward the opening, she saw his blue figure struggling successfully over the green speckled lake.

Mrs. Hopewell and Mrs. Freeman, who were in the back pasture, digging up onions, saw him emerge a little later from the woods and head across the meadow toward the highway. "Why, that looks like that nice dull young man that tried to sell me a Bible yesterday," Mrs. Hopewell said, squinting. "He must have been selling them to the Negroes back in there. He was so simple," he said, "but I guess the world would be better off if we were all that simple."

Mrs. Freeman's gaze drove forward and just touched him before he disappeared under the hill. Then she returned her attention to the evil-smelling onion shoot she was lifting from the ground. "Some can't be that simple," she said. "I know I never could."

1955

CAROLYN KIZER
b. 1925

"From Sappho to myself, consider the fate of women," wrote Carolyn Kizer in 1963, adding, with characteristically acerbic irony, "How unwomanly to discuss it!" Yet "discuss it" Kizer has, throughout her long and richly successful career. Even before the second wave of feminism began to gather strength, she was prophetically concerned with issues that would become central to activists. "I was what you might call a premature feminist," she has observed, recalling that when she read Simone de Beauvoir's *The Second Sex* (1949, trans. 1953), "everything I had ever felt, all those wounds I had sustained when I had read about men this, and men did that, and poets 'he' and so on—all my pains and doubts were confirmed by that great book." In addition, she has noted that she has "long been interested in women who are the surrogates of gifted men: the mothers, the daughters, the wives, the sisters. What do they do with their creativity when they're looking after a man's creativity?" Thus not only the wounds and wishes but also the domestic chores of women become central in such later works as "Semele Recycled" and "Second Time Around," as they are in her famous, early "Pro Femina." They are crucial preoccupations, too, in numerous other poems that appear in her many collections of verse, among which are *The Ungrateful Garden* (1961), *Knock upon Silence* (1965), *Midnight Was My Cry* (1971), *Yin* (1984), *Mermaids in the Basement: Poems for Women* (1984), *The Nearness of You* (1986), *Harping On* (1996), and *Cool Calm & Collected* (2001).

In addition to her poetry, Kizer has produced a book of translations, *Carrying Over: Poems from the Chinese, Urdu, Macedonian, Yiddish, and French African* (1988); volumes of essays on prose and on verse; and an anthology, *One Hundred Great Poems by Women* (1995). Born in Spokane, Washington, in 1925, she graduated from Sarah Lawrence College in 1945. Subsequently, she traveled widely in China and Japan, translating Tu Fu and other Chinese poets whose terse urbanity was an important influence on her style. Married and the mother of three children, she helped found the prestigious verse journal *Poetry Northwest* in 1959, then was for seven years its editor in chief. In 1966, she was director of literary programs for the National Endowment for the Arts. More recently, she has taught verse writing at many colleges and universities throughout the country; in 1985, she won the Pulitzer Prize for *Yin*; and between 1995 and 1998 she was a chancellor of the Academy of American Poets. In prose as well as poetry she has spoken with special frankness and verve about women of letters, explaining that "I'm in the racket." Sometimes jauntily colloquial in its phrasing, sometimes suavely elegant in its formulation, her tough wisdom is consistently based on the knowledge that women writers "are the custodians of the world's best-kept secret: / Merely the private lives of one-half of humanity."

From Pro Femina[1]

Three

I will speak about women of letters, for I'm in the racket.
Our biggest successes to date? Old maids to a woman.
And our saddest conspicuous failures? The married spinsters
On loan to the husbands they treated like surrogate fathers.
Think of that crew of self-pitiers, not-very-distant,
Who carried the torch for themselves and got first-degree burns.
Or the sad sonneteers, toast-and-teasdales[2] we loved at thirteen;
Middle-aged virgins seducing the puerile anthologists
Through lust-of-the-mind; barbiturate-drenched Camilles[3]
With continuous periods, murmuring softly on sofas
When poetry wasn't a craft but a sickly effluvium,
The air thick with incense, musk, and emotional blackmail.

I suppose they reacted from an earlier womanly modesty
When too many girls were scabs[4] to their stricken sisterhood,
Impugning our sex to stay in good with the men,
Commencing their insecure bluster. How they must have swaggered
When women themselves indorsed their own inferiority!
Vestals, vassals[5] and vessels, rolled into several,
They took notes in rolling syllabics, in careful journals,
Aiming to please a posterity that despises them.
But we'll always have traitors who swear that a woman surrenders
Her Supreme Function, by equating Art with aggression
And failure with Femininity. Still, it's just as unfair
To equate Art with Femininity, like a prettily-packaged commodity
When we are the custodians of the world's best-kept secret:
Merely the private lives of one-half of humanity.

But even with masculine dominance, we mares and mistresses
Produced some sleek saboteuses, making their cracks

---

1. For the woman (Latin).
2. Punning reference to Sara Teasdale (1844–1933), American poet who wrote slight, sensitive verses.
3. Camille is the repentant courtesan in *La Dame aux Camellias* (1852), by the younger Alexandre Dumas.
4. Those who work while others (in the same jobs) are striking.
5. Person in service to a feudal lord. "Vestals": Roman virgin priestesses of the goddess Vesta.

Which the porridge-brained males of the day were too thick to perceive.
30 Mistaking young hornets for perfectly harmless bumblebees.
Being thought innocuous rouses some women to frenzy;
They try to be ugly by aping the ways of the men
And succeed. Swearing, sucking cigars and scorching the bedspread,
Slopping straight shots, eyes blotted, vanity-blown
35 In the expectation of glory: *she writes like a man!*
This drives other women mad in a mist of chiffon
(one poetess draped her gauze over red flannels, a practical feminist).

But we're emerging from all that, more or less,
Except for some lady-like laggards and Quarterly[6] priestesses
40 Who flog men for fun, and kick women to maim competition.
Now, if we struggle abnormally, we may almost seem normal;
If we submerge our self-pity in disciplined industry;
If we stand up and be hated, and swear not to sleep with editors;
If we regard ourselves formally, respecting our true limitations
45 Without making an unseemly show of trying to unfreeze our assets;
Keeping our heads and our pride while remaining unmarried;
And if wedded, kill guilt in its tracks when we stack up the dishes
And defect to the typewriter. And if mothers, believe in the luck of our children,
Whom we forbid to devour us, whom we shall not devour,
50 And the luck of our husbands and lovers, who keep free women.

                                                    1963, 1965

Semele[1] Recycled

After you left me forever,
I was broken into pieces,
and all the pieces flung into the river.
Then the legs crawled ashore
5 and aimlessly wandered the dusty cow-track.
They became, for a while, a simple roadside shrine:
A tiny table set up between the thighs
held a dusty candle, weed, and fieldflower chains
placed reverently there by children and old women.
10 My knees were hung with tin triangular medals
to cure all forms of hysterical disease.

After I died forever in the river,
my torso floated, bloated in the stream,
catching on logs or stones among the eddies.
15 White water foamed around it, then dislodged it;
after a whirlwind trip, it bumped ashore.

---

6. I.e., literary magazine.
1. In Greek myth, the beloved of Zeus and the mother of Dionysus; she requested Zeus to appear in his radiant divinity; when he did, she burned to death.

A grizzled old man who scavenged along the banks
had already rescued my arms and put them by,
knowing everything has its uses, sooner or later.

When he found my torso, he called it his canoe,
and, using my arms as paddles,
he rowed me up and down the scummy river.
When catfish nibbled my fingers, he scooped them up
and blessed his re-usable bait.
Clumsy but serviceable, that canoe!
The trail of blood that was its wake
attracted the carp and eels, and the river turtle,
easily landed, dazed by my tasty red.

A young lad found my head among the rushes
and placed it on a dry stone.
He carefully combed my hair with a bit of shell
and set small offerings before it
which the birds and rats obligingly stole at night,
so it seemed I ate.
And the breeze wound through my mouth and empty sockets
so my lungs would sigh and my dead tongue mutter.

Attached to my throat like a sacred necklace
was a circlet of small snails.
Soon the villagers came to consult my oracular head
with its waterweed crown.
Seers found occupation, interpreting sighs,
and their papyrus rolls accumulated.

Meanwhile, young boys retrieved my eyes
they used for marbles in a simple game
—till somebody's pretty sister snatched at them
and set them, for luck, in her bridal diadem.
Poor girl! When her future groom caught sight of her,
all eyes, he crossed himself in horror,
and stumbled away in haste
through her dowered meadows.
What then of my heart and organs,
my sacred slit
which loved you best of all?
They were caught in a fisherman's net
and tossed at night into a pen for swine.
But they shone so by moonlight that the sows stampeded,
trampled each other in fear, to get away.
And the fisherman's wife, who had 13 living children
and was contemptuous of holy love,
raked the rest of me onto the compost heap.

Then in their various places and helpful functions,
the altar, oracle, offal, canoe, and oars
learned the wild rumor of your return.

The altar leapt up and ran to the canoe,
65 scattering candle grease and wilted grasses.
Arms sprang to their sockets, blind hands with nibbled nails
groped their way, aided by loud lamentation,
to the bed of the bride, snatched up those unlucky eyes
from her discarded veil and diadem,
70 and rammed them home. O what a bright day it was!
This empty body danced on the river bank.
Hollow, it called and searched among the fields
for those parts that steamed and simmered in the sun,
and never would have found them.

75 But then your great voice rang out under the skies
my name!—and all those private names
for the parts and places that had loved you best.
And they stirred in their nest of hay and dung.
The distraught old ladies chasing their lost altar,
80 and the seers pursuing my skull, their lost employment,
and the tumbling boys, who wanted the magic marbles,
and the runaway groom, and the fisherman's 13 children
set up such a clamor, with their cries of "Miracle!"
that our two bodies met like a thunderclap
85 in mid-day—right at the corner of that wretched field
with its broken fenceposts and startled, skinny cattle.
We fell in a heap on the compost heap
and all our loving parts made love at once,
while the bystanders cheered and prayed and hid their eyes
90 and then went decently about their business.

And here it is, moonlight again; we've bathed in the river
and are sweet and wholesome once more.
We kneel side by side in the sand;
we worship each other in whispers.
95 But the inner parts remember fermenting hay,
the comfortable odor of dung, the animal incense,
and passion, its bloody labor,
its birth and rebirth and decay.

1984

Second Time Around

You're entangled with someone more famous than you
Who happens to vanish.
You marry again in haste, perhaps to a nurse
Or your late wife's good friend,
5 Someone whose name will never appear in print
Except, perhaps, in your entry for *Who's Who;*
Someone obliging and neutral, not too good looking,
To whom you say, "Darling, the supper was excellent."

Free, now, of that brilliant aura, that physical dazzle
That you always acknowledged, insisting
You relished her fame, believing you meant it,
And love her you did, but you're so relieved she's gone.

How sweet to embrace the mundane, endorse the ordinary,
In its starchy smock or its ruffled apron,
Saying, "Bronwyn—or Carole, or Elsie—
Suits me down to the ground." The ground.
There's no more celestial navigation;[1]
It's the end of smart missives,[2] of aerial bombardment.
One can relax, and slump into being human.

Sometimes you sift through her papers
When you're bereft of ideas,
Though of course ideas are not what stimulates art:
It's snapshots of people in old-fashioned bathing suits,
The man she saw by the road with the three-legged dog,
That week in Venice when it never stopped raining, the odor
Of freshly washed hair when she dried it in the sunlight . . .
Something she lightly sketched in that needs fleshing out;
Could you? Should you? You put it to one side.

With a minor effort of will you stop thinking about her,
And decide instead to update your vita,[3]
Or work some more on that old piece
On Descartes[4] that has always given you trouble.
And Bronwyn, or Elsie, or Carole
Comes tiptoeing into your study with a nice cup of coffee.

1997

1. Navigation by observing the positions of the stars, moon, and sun.
2. A punning allusion to the so-called smart missiles that received a great deal of publicity when used by the United States during the 1991 Gulf War.
3. Resumé (academics generally use the term *vita* or *curriculum vitae*).
4. René Descartes (1596–1650), French mathematician and philosopher.

MAXINE W. KUMIN
b. 1925

"Even though she is fascinated by and preoccupied with the irrational unconscious," the critic Sybil Estess has written of Maxine Kumin, "sanity and a conscious choice within and for life are essential keys to [her] voice." The observation is apt, for though she was the longtime best friend and poetic co-worker of the troubled, "confessional" artist Anne Sexton—the two frequently analyzed and revised their poems together and collaborated on several children's books—Kumin is a very different sort of writer from Sexton. While she sometimes explores pain and suffering in her work, Kumin has a notable drive for survival along with a deep commitment to memorialize those elements of everyday life that enrich the existence of the artist and make survival possible. Children and kitchens, animals and vegetables, friends and family—these are the stuff of the poems in which she makes a redemptive choice for sanity.

Born in Philadelphia, Pennsylvania, Kumin earned B.A. and M.A. degrees from Radcliffe College and was married young to Victor M. Kumin, an engineering consultant, with whom she has had three children. For years, she and her husband have lived on a farm in New Hampshire, where she grows vegetables and breeds Arabian and quarter horses while writing both poetry and fiction. Her first collection, *Halfway*, appeared in 1961 and was followed in rapid succession by a number of other volumes, including five novels, four children's books coauthored with Sexton and more than a dozen written alone, the collection of poems—*Up Country* (1972)—for which she won the Pulitzer Prize in 1973, and, more recently, *Looking for Luck* (1992), *Connecting the Dots* (1996), *The Long Marriage* (2001), and *Jack and Other New Poems* (2005). For two years a fellow at the Radcliffe Institute for Independent Study, she has also taught verse writing at a number of universities, including Columbia, Brandeis, and Princeton; won the prestigious Ruth Lilly Poetry Prize (1999); and served from 1995 to 1998 as a chancellor of the Academy of American Poets. In 1998 she was severely injured in a near-fatal accident when her horse bolted at a carriage-driving clinic; in her scrupulously reported memoir, *Inside the Halo: The Anatomy of a Recovery* (2000)—"the halo" refers to the "near-medieval device" that kept her head immobile during weeks of intensive care and rehabilitation—she recounts this experience with characteristic vitality. As she has throughout her varied career, she bases her struggle to survive on a hopeful if skeptical view that "Wherever we're going / is Monday morning./ Wherever we're coming from / is Mother's lap."

Making the Jam without You

for Judy

    Old daughter, small traveler
    asleep in a German featherbed
    under the eaves in a postcard town
    of turrets and towers,
5   I am putting a dream in your head.

    Listen! Here it is afternoon.
    The rain comes down like bullets.
    I stand in the kitchen,
    that harem of good smells
10 where we have bumped hips and
    cracked the cupboards with our talk
    while the stove top danced with pots
    and it was not clear who did
    the mothering. Now I am
15 crushing blackberries
    to make the annual jam
    in a white cocoon of steam.

    Take it, my sleeper. Redo it
    in any of your three
20 languages and nineteen years.

Change the geography.
Let there be a mountain,
the fat cows on it belled
like a cathedral. Let
there be someone beside you
as you come upon the ruins
of a schloss,[1] all overgrown
with a glorious thicket,
its brambles soft as wool.
Let him bring the buckets
crooked on his angel arms
and may the berries, vaster
than any forage in
the mild hills of New Hampshire,
drop in your pail, plum size,
heavy as the eyes
of an honest dog
and may you bear them
home together to a square
white unreconstructed kitchen
not unlike this one.

Now may your two heads
touch over the kettle,
over the blood of the berries
that drink up sugar and sun,
over that tar-thick boil
love cannot stir down.
More plainly than
the bric-a-brac of shelves
filling with jelly glasses,
more surely than
the light driving through them
trite as rubies, I see him
as pale as paraffin[2] beside you.
I see you cutting
fresh baked bread to spread it
with the bright royal fur.

At this time
I lift the flap of your dream
and slip out thinner than a sliver
as your two mouths open
for the sweet stain of purple.

1970

---

1. Castle (German). 2. Used to seal the jars.

The Envelope

It is true, Martin Heidegger,[1] as you have written,
I *fear to cease,* even knowing that at the hour
of my death my daughters will absorb me, even
knowing they will carry me about forever
inside them, an arrested fetus, even as I carry
the ghost of my mother under my navel, a nervy
little androgynous person, a miracle
folded in lotus position.

Like those old pear-shaped Russian dolls that open
at the middle to reveal another and another, down
to the pea-sized, irreducible minim,
may we carry our mothers forth in our bellies.
May we, borne onward by our daughters, ride
in the Envelope of Almost-Infinity,
that chain letter good for the next twenty-five
thousand days of their lives.

1978

How It Is[1]

Shall I say how it is in your clothes?
A month after your death I wear your blue jacket.
The dog at the center of my life recognizes
you've come to visit, he's ecstatic.
In the left pocket, a hole.
In the right, a parking ticket
delivered up last August on Bay State Road.
In my heart, a scatter like milkweed,
a flinging from the pods of the soul.
My skin presses your old outline.
It is hot and dry inside.

I think of the last day of your life,
old friend, how I would unwind it, paste
it together in a different collage,
back from the death car idling in the garage,
back up the stairs, your praying hands unlaced,
reassembling the bits of bread and tuna fish
into a ceremony of sandwich,
running the home movie backward to a space
we could be easy in, a kitchen place
with vodka and ice, our words like living meat.

---

1. German existentialist philosopher (1889–1976), who wrote extensively on the fear of death.
1. The poem is addressed to Anne Sexton (1928–1974), poet and close friend of Kumin's who committed suicide by inhaling carbon monoxide fumes from her car.

> Dear friend, you have excited crowds
> with your example. They swell
> like wine bags, straining at your seams.
> 25 I will be years gathering up our words,
> fishing out letters, snapshots, stains,
> leaning my ribs against this durable cloth
> to put on the dumb blue blazer of your death.

1978

Skinnydipping with William Wordsworth[1]

> I lie by the pond *in utter nakedness*[2]
> thinking of you, Will, your epiphanies
> of woodcock, raven, rills, and craggy steeps,
> the solace that seductive nature bore,
> 5 and how in my late teens I came to you
> with other Radcliffe *pagans suckled in*
> *a creed outworn*,[3] declaiming whole swatches
> of "Intimations" to each other.
>
> Moist-eyed with reverence, lying about
> 10 the common room, rising to recite
> *Great God! I'd rather be* . . . How else
> redeem the first flush of experience?
> How else create it again and again? *Not in*
> *entire forgetfulness*[4] I raise up my boyfriend,
> 15 a Harvard man who could outquote me
> in his Groton[5] elocutionary style.
>
> Groping to unhook my bra he swore
> poetry could change the world for the better.
> The War[6] was on. Was I to let him die
> 20 unfulfilled? Soon afterward we parted.
> Years later, he a decorated vet,
> I a part-time professor, signed the same
> guest book in the Lake District.[7] Stunned
> by coincidence we gingerly shared a room.
>
> 25 Ah, Will, high summer now; how many more
> of these? *Fair seed-time had my soul*,[8]
> you sang; what seed-times still to come?
> How I mistrust them, cheaters that will flame,
> gutter and go out, like the scarlet tanager
> 30 who lights in the apple tree but will not stay.

1. Major English poet (1770–1850); the italicized phrases are all quotations from his poems.
2. From "Ode: Intimations of Immortality from Recollections of Early Childhood" (1807).
3. See the sonnet "The world is too much with us" (1807): "Great God! I'd rather be / A Pagan suckled in a creed outworn."
4. From the "Intimations Ode."
5. A selective boys' boarding school (now coeducational) in central Massachusetts.
6. World War II.
7. Wordsworth was born on the northern edge of the Lake District, in northwest England, and he moved back to the area permanently in 1899.
8. From Wordsworth's autobiographical poem *The Prelude* (1850), 1.301.

Here at the pond, your *meadow, grove, and stream*[9]
lodged in my head as tight as lily buds,
sun slants through translucent minnows, dragonflies
in paintbox colors couple in midair.
35 The fickle tanager flies over the tasseled field.
I lay my "Prelude" down under the willow.
My old gnarled body prepares to swim
to the other side.

        Come with me, Will.
40 Let us cross over sleek as otters,
each of us bobbing in the old-fashioned breaststroke,
each of us centered in our beloved Vales.[1]

2001

Women and Horses

After Auschwitz, to write a poem is barbaric.
        Theodor Adorno[1]

After Auschwitz: after ten of my father's kin—
the ones who stayed—starved, then were gassed in the camps.
After Vietnam, after Korea, Kuwait, Somalia, Haiti, Afghanistan.[2]
After the Towers.[3] This late in the life of our haplessly orbiting world
5 let us celebrate whatever scraps the muse, that naked child,
can pluck from the still-smoldering dumps.

If there's a lyre around, strike it! A body, stand back, give it air!
Let us have sparrows laying their eggs in bluebird boxes.
Let us have bluebirds insouciantly nesting elsewhere.
10 Lend us navel-bared teens, eyebrow- and nose-ringed prodigies
crumbling breakfast bagels over dogeared and jelly-smeared texts.
Allow the able-bodied among us to have steamy sex.

Let there be fat old ladies in flowery tent dresses at bridge tables.
Howling babies in dirty diapers and babies serenely at rest.
15 War and detente will go on, detente and renewed tearing asunder,
we can never break free from the dark and degrading past.
Let us see life again, nevertheless, in the words of Isaac Babel[4]
as a meadow over which women and horses wander.

2005

---

9. From the "Intimations Ode."
1. *Prelude* 1.304 refers to "that beloved Vale" (the valley of Esthwaite, where Wordsworth attended school).
1. German philosopher and critic (1903–1969); the quotation is from "An Essay on Cultural Criticism and Society" (1949). Auschwitz, or Oświęcim, in southern Poland, was the most notorious site of German concentration camps.
2. All sites of war or civil strife in the second half of the 20th century.
3. I.e., the two towers of New York's World Trade Center, destroyed by terrorists in 2001.
4. Jewish Russian short story writer (1894–1941), executed in a Stalinist purge; the quotation is from "The Story of a Horse" (1926).

Sonnet in So Many Words

The time comes when it can't be said,
thinks Richard Dalloway,[1] pocketing his
sixpence of change, and off he goes
holding a great bunch of white and red

5 roses against his chest, thinking himself
a man both blessed and doomed in wedlock
and Clarissa meanwhile thinking as he walks back
even between husband and wife a gulf....

If these are Virginia and Leonard,[2] are they not
10 also you and me taking up the coffee
grinder or scraping bits of omelet free
for the waiting dogs who salivate and sit?

Never to say what one feels. And yet
this is a love poem. Can you taste it?

2005

---

1. The husband of Clarissa, the title character of Virginia Woolf's *Mrs. Dalloway* (1925); the italicized phrases in the poem are direct quotes from the novel.
2. Virginia Woolf (1882–1941; see above, p. 212) and her husband, Leonard (1880–1969).

ANNE SEXTON
1928–1974

According to her best friend, the poet Maxine Kumin, at their first meeting Anne Sexton "looked every inch the fashion model"—a job she had once briefly held: she was "tall, blue-eyed, stunningly slim, her carefully coifed dark hair decorated with flowers, her face skillfully made up." Yet, as Kumin also notes, this artfully lovely and theatrical woman led a "troubled and chaotic life." By the time she met Kumin in the late winter of 1957, she had had several nervous collapses and been intermittently hospitalized, seeking "sanctuary" from "voices that urged her to die." Described by one biographer as "a demanding, rebellious child who felt rejected by her upper-middle-class parents," Anne Gray Harvey Sexton had had emotional problems since girlhood. Now the mother of two young daughters, she had eloped with Alfred "Kayo" Sexton in 1948, but the couple's home in a Boston suburb was not a happy one, no doubt in part because of her persistent breakdowns. Nevertheless, though Anne Sexton did not consider herself a good student and had dropped out of Garland Junior College after only a year, she had just enrolled, at the suggestion of her psychiatrist, in a verse-writing workshop taught by the poet John Holmes at the Boston Center for Adult Education.

As Kumin reports, Sexton's literary progress was astonishing once she began to understand that she could write poetry. Her first book, *To Bedlam and Part Way Back*, appeared in 1960. Including such searching (if partly disguised) self-explorations as "The Moss of His Skin," it was influenced not only by the "workshopping" this swiftly developing artist did with Kumin and Holmes but also by the self-examinations of the poet W. D. Snodgrass and by the writings of Robert Lowell (with whom Sexton studied at Boston University) and Sylvia Plath (who was a fellow student of Sexton's in Lowell's class). Later described as "confessional poets," these last three artists had begun to use the details of their personal lives as exemplary images of larger social and metaphysical problems, and their experiments offered Sexton a fruitful mode in which she, too, could work, while her innovative self-analyses also provided models for further "confessional" verse by Lowell and Plath. Fiercely productive, Sexton published a number of volumes in rapid succession, including *All My Pretty Ones* (1962), *Live or Die* (which won the Pulitzer Prize in 1967), *Love Poems* (1969), *Transformations* (1971), *The Book of Folly* (1972), and *The Death Notebooks* (1974). Almost always marked by imaginative and often surrealistic verve and frequently characterized by sardonic wit as well as unflinching candor, her poems struggled against the pain of her past to sing "in celebration of the woman I am."

Despite the honors Sexton received, however, and the dramatic impression she made at the poetry readings she gave, her work inspired much the sort of controversy aroused by the quite different verse of Sylvia Plath, with whom Sexton was often associated. "It would be hard to find a writer who dwells more insistently on the pathetic and disgusting aspects of bodily experience," protested the poet James Dickey in *The New York Times Book Review,* while the poet Muriel Rukeyser, taking precisely the opposite position, declared that Sexton's "In Celebration of My Uterus" was "one of the few poems in which a woman has come to the fact as symbol, the center, after many years of silence and taboo." In part, at least, such conflicting opinions arose because, as Kumin observes, Sexton "wrote openly about menstruation, abortion, masturbation, incest, adultery, and drug addiction at a time when the proprieties embraced none of these as proper topics for poetry."

That Sexton did write with unusual frankness and intensity reflected not only her commitment to her art (she was a tireless reviser and a passionate participant in workshops) but also the extremity of her personal situation. Throughout the years when she was winning prizes and fellowships, she was still under psychiatric care and gradually growing dependent on alcohol and sedatives, besides being dosed with the tranquilizing drug Thorazine, which caused her to gain weight and feel "so overwhelmed with lassitude that she could not write." At the same time, as the scholar Diane Wood Middlebrook has shown in a biography whose revelation of confidential therapeutic material became as controversial as Sexton's own subject matter, the poet was embroiled in a flamboyant series of sexual affairs. In 1973, she and Kayo agreed to divorce, but following their separation she became increasingly unstable, lonely, and anxious. Perhaps because of her persistent problems, she had also become obsessed with what the title of a posthumously published volume called "the awful rowing toward God" (1975). In the fall of 1974, just a month before her birthday— a time of year when the "voices" urging her to die had always been particularly insistent—Sexton gassed herself in her garage after an uneventful lunch with Kumin, at which they reviewed the proofs of *The Awful Rowing toward God*. It seems likely that the poet was influenced by the suicide method her friend Sylvia Plath had chosen some eleven years earlier. Yet though the story of this prolific writer's metamorphosis from model and housewife to famous poet and glamorous performance artist ended tragically, her career, like Plath's, had been marked by extraordinary aesthetic vitality.

Her Kind

I have gone out, a possessed witch,
haunting the black air, braver at night;
dreaming evil, I have done my hitch

over the plain houses, light by light:
5 lonely thing, twelve-fingered, out of mind.
A woman like that is not a woman, quite.
I have been her kind.

I have found the warm caves in the woods,
filled them with skillets, carvings, shelves,
10 closets, silks, innumerable goods;
fixed the suppers for the worms and the elves:
whining, rearranging the disaligned.
A woman like that is misunderstood.
I have been her kind.

15 I have ridden in your cart, driver,
waved my nude arms at villages going by,
learning the last bright routes, survivor
where your flames still bite my thigh
and my ribs crack where your wheels wind.
20 A woman like that is not ashamed to die.
I have been her kind.

1960

The Moss of His Skin

> Young girls in old Arabia were often buried alive next to their dead fathers, apparently as sacrifice to the goddesses of the tribes. . . .
> Harold Feldman, "Children of the Desert,"
> *Psychoanalysis and Psychoanalytic Review,* Fall 1958

It was only important
to smile and hold still,
to lie down beside him
and to rest awhile,
5 to be folded up together
as if we were silk,
to sink from the eyes of mother
and not to talk.
The black room took us
10 like a cave or a mouth
or an indoor belly.
I held my breath
and daddy was there,
his thumbs, his fat skull,
15 his teeth, his hair growing
like a field or a shawl.
I lay by the moss
of his skin until
it grew strange. My sisters
20 will never know that I fall
out of myself and pretend

that Allah will not see
how I hold my daddy
like an old stone tree.

1960

Housewife

Some women marry houses.
It's another kind of skin; it has a heart,
a mouth, a liver and bowel movements.
The walls are permanent and pink.
See how she sits on her knees all day,
faithfully washing herself down.
Men enter by force, drawn back like Jonah
into their fleshy mothers.[1]
A woman *is* her mother.
That's the main thing.

1962

Woman with Girdle

Your midriff sags toward your knees;
your breasts lie down in air,
their nipples as uninvolved
as warm starfish.
You stand in your elastic case,
still not giving up the new-born
and the old-born cycle.
Moving, you roll down the garment,
down that pink snapper and hoarder,
as your belly, soft as pudding,
slops into the empty space;
down, over the surgeon's careful mark,
down over hips, those head cushions
and mouth cushions,
slow motion like a rolling pin,
over crisp hairs, that amazing field
that hides your genius from your patron;
over thighs, thick as young pigs,
over knees like saucers,
over calves, polished as leather,
down toward the feet.
You pause for a moment,
tying your ankles into knots.

---

1. In the Bible, the prophet Jonah is swallowed by a "great fish" (Jonah 1.17).

Now you rise,
25   a city from the sea,
born long before Alexandria[1] was,
straightway from God you have come
into your redeeming skin.

                                                                    1962

Somewhere in Africa

Must you leave, John Holmes,[1] with the prayers and psalms
you never said, said over you? Death with no rage
to weigh you down? Praised by the mild God, his arm
over the pulpit, leaving you timid, with no real age,

5   whitewashed by belief, as dull as the windy preacher!
Dead of a dark thing, John Holmes, you've been lost
in the college chapel, mourned as father and teacher,
mourned with piety and grace under the University Cross.

Your last book unsung, your last hard words unknown,
10 abandoned by science, cancer blossomed in your throat,
rooted like bougainvillea into your gray backbone,
ruptured your pores until you wore it like a coat.

The thick petals, the exotic reds, the purples and whites
covered up your nakedness and bore you up with all
15 their blind power. I think of your last June nights
in Boston, your body swollen but light, your eyes small

as you let the nurses carry you into a strange land.
. . . If this is death and God is necessary let him be hidden
from the missionary, the well-wisher and the glad hand.
20 Let God be some tribal female who is known but forbidden.

Let there be this God who is a woman who will place you
upon her shallow boat, who is a woman naked to the waist,
moist with palm oil and sweat, a woman of some virtue
and wild breasts, her limbs excellent, unbruised and chaste.

25 Let her take you. She will put twelve strong men at the oars
for you are stronger than mahogany and your bones fill
the boat high as with fruit and bark from the interior.
She will have you now, you whom the funeral cannot kill.

John Holmes, cut from a single tree, lie heavy in her hold
30 and go down that river with the ivory, the copra[2] and the gold.

July 1, 1962   1966

---

1. City in Egypt, founded by Alexander the Great in 322 B.C.E.; a cultural center, it was the site of the greatest library in antiquity.

1. An American poet (1904–1962) in whose workshop Sexton had studied.
2. Coconut oil.

Sylvia's Death

for Sylvia Plath[1]

O Sylvia, Sylvia,
with a dead box of stones and spoons,

with two children, two meteors
wandering loose in the tiny playroom,

with your mouth into the sheet,
into the roofbeam, into the dumb prayer,

(Sylvia, Sylvia,
where did you go
after you wrote me
from Devonshire[2]
about raising potatoes
and keeping bees?)

what did you stand by,
just how did you lie down into?

Thief!—
how did you crawl into,

crawl down alone
into the death I wanted so badly and for so long,

the death we said we both outgrew,
the one we wore on our skinny breasts,

the one we talked of so often each time
we downed three extra dry martinis in Boston,

the death that talked of analysts and cures,
the death that talked like brides with plots,

the death we drank to,
the motives and then the quiet deed?

(In Boston
the dying
ride in cabs,
yes death again,
that ride home
with *our* boy.)

O Sylvia, I remember the sleepy drummer
who beat on our eyes with an old story,

---

1. American poet who committed suicide (1932–1963); see below, p. 1044.
2. County in England.

       how we wanted to let him come
       like a sadist or a New York fairy

       to do his job,
       a necessity, a window in a wall or a crib,

       and since that time he waited
40   under our heart, our cupboard,

       and I see now that we store him up
       year after year, old suicides

       and I know at the news of your death,
       a terrible taste for it, like salt.

45   (And me,
       me too.
       And now, Sylvia,
       you again
       with death again,
50   that ride home
       with *our* boy.)

       And I say only
       with my arms stretched out into that stone place,

       what is your death
55   but an old belonging,
       a mole that fell out
       of one of your poems?

       (O friend,
       while the moon's bad,
60   and the king's gone,
       and the queen's at her wit's end
       the bar fly ought to sing!)

       O tiny mother,
       you too!
65   O funny duchess!
       O blonde thing!

February 17, 1963   1966

In Celebration of My Uterus

Everyone in me is a bird.
I am beating all my wings.
They wanted to cut you out
but they will not.

⁵   They said you were immeasurably empty
    but you are not.
    They said you were sick unto dying
    but they were wrong.
    You are singing like a school girl.
¹⁰ You are not torn.

    Sweet weight,
    in celebration of the woman I am
    and of the soul of the woman I am
    and of the central creature and its delight
¹⁵ I sing for you. I dare to live.
    Hello, spirit. Hello, cup.
    Fasten, cover. Cover that does contain.
    Hello to the soil of the fields.
    Welcome, roots.

²⁰ Each cell has a life.
    There is enough here to please a nation.
    It is enough that the populace own these goods.
    Any person, any commonwealth would say of it,
    "It is good this year that we may plant again
²⁵ and think forward to a harvest.
    A blight had been forecast and has been cast out."
    Many women are singing together of this:
    one is in a shoe factory cursing the machine,
    one is at the aquarium tending a seal,
³⁰ one is dull at the wheel of her Ford,
    one is at the toll gate collecting,
    one is tying the cord of a calf in Arizona,
    one is straddling a cello in Russia,
    one is shifting pots on the stove in Egypt,
³⁵ one is painting her bedroom walls moon color,
    one is dying but remembering a breakfast,
    one is stretching on her mat in Thailand,
    one is wiping the ass of her child,
    one is staring out the window of a train
⁴⁰ in the middle of Wyoming and one is
    anywhere and some are everywhere and all
    seem to be singing, although some can not
    sing a note.

    Sweet weight,
⁴⁵ in celebration of the woman I am
    let me carry a ten-foot scarf,
    let me drum for the nineteen-year-olds,
    let me carry bowls for the offering
    (if that is my part).
⁵⁰ Let me study the cardiovascular tissue,
    let me examine the angular distance of meteors,
    let me suck on the stems of flowers
    (if that is my part).

Let me make certain tribal figures
(if that is my part).
For this thing the body needs
let me sing
for the supper,
for the kissing,
for the correct
yes.

1969

MAYA ANGELOU
1928–2014

At the beginning of her best-selling autobiography *I Know Why the Caged Bird Sings* (1970), Maya Angelou explained that "if growing up is painful for the Southern Black girl, being aware of her displacement is the rust on the razor that threatens the throat. It is an unnecessary insult." Later in the book, Angelou described the insult of displacement associated with her childhood move from her native St. Louis to Stamps, Arkansas, with the sexual abuse she received from her mother's boyfriend, and with the "pride and prejudice" she encountered as a streetcar conductor in San Francisco. But *I Know Why the Caged Bird Sings* also recorded her affectionate respect for the grandmother, Ann Henderson, who raised her in Stamps, as well as Angelou's relish for black religious and social traditions, and her joy in the birth of her son.

A self-described six-foot, black southwesterner, Angelou toured Europe as an entertainer, resided briefly in Ghana, performed on and off Broadway, and worked in cinema as well as television. She published her first book, *I Know Why the Caged Bird Sings*, to remarkable critical acclaim. In part, her achievement extended the genre of the black autobiography by thinkers such as Frederick Douglass, W. E. B. Du Bois, Richard Wright, and Malcolm X by using it to express the struggle toward independence and self-expression of a decidedly female subject. After its publication she followed it with a number of sequels: *Gather Together in My Name* (1974), *Singin' and Swingin' and Gettin' Merry Like Christmas* (1976), *The Heart of a Woman* (1981), *All God's Children Need Traveling Shoes* (1986), and *A Song Flung Up to Heaven* (2002). In 1982, Angelou became Reynolds Professor of American Studies at Wake Forest University in Winston-Salem, North Carolina. Between 1971 and 1993, she also produced seven books of verse. Her poem "On the Pulse of Morning" was written for, and recited at, the inauguration of President Bill Clinton in January 1993. In 1999, a collected edition of her verse appeared.

From I Know Why the Caged Bird Sings

[The Peckerwood Dentist and Momma's Incredible Powers]

The Angel of the candy counter had found me out at last, and was exacting excruciating penance for all the stolen Milky Ways, Mounds, Mr. Goodham and Hersheys with Almonds. I had two cavities that were rotten to the gums.

The pain was beyond the bailiwick of crushed aspirins or oil of cloves. Only one thing could help me, so I prayed earnestly that I'd be allowed to sit under the house and have the building collapse on my left jaw. Since there was no Negro dentist in Stamps,[1] nor doctor either, for that matter, Momma had dealt with previous toothaches by pulling them out (a string tied to the tooth with the other end looped over her fist), pain killers and prayer. In this particular instance the medicine had proved ineffective; there wasn't enough enamel left to hook a string on, and the prayers were being ignored because the Balancing Angel was blocking their passage.

I lived a few days and nights in blinding pain, not so much toying with as seriously considering the idea of jumping in the well, and Momma decided I had to be taken to a dentist. The nearest Negro dentist was in Texarkana, twenty-five miles away, and I was certain that I'd be dead long before we reached half the distance. Momma said we'd go to Dr. Lincoln, right in Stamps, and he'd take care of me. She said he owed her a favor.

I knew there were a number of whitefolks in town that owed her favors. Bailey[2] and I had seen the books which showed how she had lent money to Blacks and whites alike during the Depression, and most still owed her. But I couldn't aptly remember seeing Dr. Lincoln's name, nor had I ever heard of a Negro's going to him as a patient. However, Momma said we were going, and put water on the stove for our baths. I had never been to a doctor, so she told me that after the bath (which would make my mouth feel better) I had to put on freshly starched and ironed underclothes from inside out. The ache failed to respond to the bath, and I knew then that the pain was more serious than that which anyone had ever suffered.

Before we left the Store, she ordered me to brush my teeth and then wash my mouth with Listerine. The idea of even opening my clamped jaws increased the pain, but upon her explanation that when you go to a doctor you have to clean yourself all over, but most especially the part that's to be examined, I screwed up my courage and unlocked my teeth. The cool air in my mouth and the jarring of my molars dislodged what little remained of my reason. I had frozen to the pain, my family nearly had to tie me down to take the toothbrush away. It was no small effort to get me started on the road to the dentist. Momma spoke to all the passers-by, but didn't stop to chat. She explained over her shoulder that we were going to the doctor and she'd "pass the time of day" on our way home.

Until we reached the pond the pain was my world, an aura that haloed me for three feet around. Crossing the bridge into whitefolks' country, pieces of sanity pushed themselves forward. I had to stop moaning and start walking straight. The white towel, which was drawn under my chin and tied over my head, had to be arranged. If one was dying, it had to be done in style if the dying took place in whitefolks' part of town.

On the other side of the bridge the ache seemed to lessen as if a white-breeze blew off the whitefolks and cushioned everything in their neighborhood—including my jaw. The gravel road was smoother, the stones smaller and the tree branches hung down around the path and nearly covered us. If the pain didn't diminish then, the familiar yet strange sights hypnotized me into believing that it had.

---

1. The town in Arkansas where Angelou grew up.   2. Angelou's brother, a year older than she.

But my head continued to throb with the measured insistence of a bass drum, and how could a toothache pass the calaboose,[3] hear the songs of the prisoners, their blues and laughter, and not be changed? How could one or two or even a mouthful of angry tooth roots meet a wagonload of powhitetrash[4] children, endure their idiotic snobbery and not feel less important?

Behind the building which housed the dentist's office ran a small path used by servants and those tradespeople who catered to the butcher and Stamps' one restaurant. Momma and I followed that lane to the backstairs of Dentist Lincoln's office. The sun was bright and gave the day a hard reality as we climbed up the steps to the second floor.

Momma knocked on the back door and a young white girl opened it to show surprise at seeing us there. Momma said she wanted to see Dentist Lincoln and to tell him Annie was there. The girl closed the door firmly. Now the humiliation of hearing Momma describe herself as if she had no last name to the young white girl was equal to the physical pain. It seemed terribly unfair to have a toothache and a headache and have to bear at the same time the heavy burden of Blackness.

It was always possible that the teeth would quiet down and maybe drop out of their own accord. Momma said we would wait. We leaned in the harsh sunlight on the shaky railings of the dentist's back porch for over an hour.

He opened the door and looked at Momma. "Well, Annie, what can I do for you?"

He didn't see the towel around my jaw or notice my swollen face.

Momma said, "Dentist Lincoln. It's my grandbaby here. She got two rotten teeth that's giving her a fit."

She waited for him to acknowledge the truth of her statement. He made no comment, orally or facially.

"She had this toothache purt' near four days now, and today I said, 'Young lady, you going to the Dentist.'"

"Annie?"

"Yes, sir, Dentist Lincoln."

He was choosing words the way people hunt for shells. "Annie, you know I don't treat nigra, colored people."

"I know, Dentist Lincoln. But this here is just my little grandbaby, and she ain't gone be no trouble to you. . . ."

"Annie, everybody has a policy. In this world you have to have a policy. Now, my policy is I don't treat colored people."

The sun had baked the oil out of Momma's skin and melted the Vaseline in her hair. She shone greasily as she leaned out of the dentist's shadow.

"Seem like to me, Dentist Lincoln, you might look after her, she ain't nothing but a little mite. And seems like maybe you owe me a favor or two."

He reddened slightly. "Favor or no favor. The money has all been repaid to you and that's the end of it. Sorry, Annie." He had his hand on the doorknob. "Sorry." His voice was a bit kinder on the second "Sorry," as if he really was.

Momma said, "I wouldn't press on you like this for myself but I can't take No. Not for my grandbaby. When you come to borrow my money you didn't

---

3. The jail (southern slang).
4. I.e., poor white trash, lower-class white children.

have to beg. You asked me, and I lent it. Now, it wasn't my policy. I ain't no moneylender, but you stood to lose this building and I tried to help you out."

"It's been paid, and raising your voice won't make me change my mind. My policy . . ." He let go of the door and stepped nearer Momma. The three of us were crowded on the small landing. "Annie, my policy is I'd rather stick my hand in a dog's mouth than in a nigger's."

He had never once looked at me. He turned his back and went through the door into the cool beyond. Momma backed up inside herself for a few minutes. I forgot everything except her face which was almost a new one to me. She leaned over and took the doorknob, and in her everyday soft voice she said, "Sister, go on downstairs. Wait for me. I'll be there directly."

Under the most common of circumstances I knew it did no good to argue with Momma. So I walked down the steep stairs, afraid to look back and afraid not to do so. I turned as the door slammed, and she was gone.

Momma walked in that room as if she owned it. She shoved that silly nurse aside with one hand and strode into the dentist's office. He was sitting in his chair, sharpening his mean instruments and putting extra sting into his medicines. Her eyes were blazing like live coals and her arms had doubled themselves in length. He looked up at her just before she caught him by the collar of his white jacket.

"Stand up when you see a lady, you contemptuous scoundrel." Her tongue had thinned and the words rolled off well enunciated. Enunciated and sharp like little claps of thunder.

The dentist had no choice but to stand at R.O.T.C.[5] attention. His head dropped after a minute and his voice was humble. "Yes, ma'am, Mrs. Henderson."

"You knave, do you think you acted like a gentleman, speaking to me like that in front of my granddaughter?" She didn't shake him, although she had the power. She simply held him upright.

"No, ma'am, Mrs. Henderson."

"No, ma'am, Mrs. Henderson, what?" Then she did give him the tiniest of shakes, but because of her strength the action set his head and arms to shaking loose on the ends of his body. He stuttered much worse than Uncle Willie. "No, ma'am, Mrs. Henderson, I'm sorry."

With just an edge of her disgust showing, Momma slung him back in his dentist's chair. "Sorry is as sorry does, and you're about the sorriest dentist I ever laid my eyes on." (She could afford to slip into the vernacular because she had such eloquent command of English.)

"I didn't ask you to apologize in front of Marguerite, because I don't want her to know my power, but I order you, now and herewith. Leave Stamps by sundown."

"Mrs. Henderson, I can't get my equipment. . . ." He was shaking terribly now.

"Now, that brings me to my second order. You will never again practice dentistry. Never! When you get settled in your next place, you will be a vegetarian caring for dogs with the mange, cats with the cholera and cows with the epizootic.[6] Is that clear?"

---

5. Reserve Officers' Training Corps, a program that gives high school and college students military training.

6. A disease that attacks a large number of animals at once.

The saliva ran down his chin and his eyes filled with tears. "Yes, ma'am. Thank you for not killing me. Thank you, Mrs. Henderson."

Momma pulled herself back from being ten feet tall with eight-foot arms and said, "You're welcome for nothing, you varlet, I wouldn't waste a killing on the likes of you."

On her way out she waved her handkerchief at the nurse and turned her into a crocus sack[7] of chicken feed.

Momma looked tired when she came down the stairs, but who wouldn't be tired if they had gone through what she had. She came close to me and adjusted the towel under my jaw (I had forgotten the toothache; I only knew that she made her hands gentle in order not to awaken the pain). She took my hand. Her voice never changed. "Come on, Sister."

I reckoned we were going home where she would concoct a brew to eliminate the pain and maybe give me new teeth too. New teeth that would grow overnight out of my gums. She led me toward the drugstore, which was in the opposite direction from the Store. "I'm taking you to Dentist Baker in Texarkana."

I was glad after all that that I had bathed and put on Mum and Cashmere Bouquet talcum powder. It was a wonderful surprise. My toothache had quieted to solemn pain, Momma had obliterated the evil white man, and we were going on a trip to Texarkana, just the two of us.

On the Greyhound she took an inside seat in the back, and I sat beside her. I was so proud of being her granddaughter and sure that some of her magic must have come down to me. She asked if I was scared. I only shook my head and leaned over on her cool brown upper arm. There was no chance that a dentist, especially a Negro dentist, would dare hurt me then. Not with Momma there. The trip was uneventful, except that she put her arm around me, which was very unusual for Momma to do.

The dentist showed me the medicine and the needle before he deadened my gums, but if he hadn't I wouldn't have worried. Momma stood right behind him. Her arms were folded and she checked on everything he did. The teeth were extracted and she bought me an ice cream cone from the side window of a drug counter. The trip back to Stamps was quiet, except that I had to spit into a very small empty snuff can which she had gotten for me and it was difficult with the bus humping and jerking on our country roads.

At home, I was given a warm salt solution, and when I washed out my mouth I showed Bailey the empty holes, where the clotted blood sat like filling in a pie crust. He said I was quite brave, and that was my cue to reveal our confrontation with the peckerwood[8] dentist and Momma's incredible powers.

I had to admit that I didn't hear the conversation, but what else could she have said than what I said she said? What else done? He agreed with my analysis in a lukewarm way, and I happily (after all, I'd been sick) flounced into the Store. Momma was preparing our evening meal and Uncle Willie leaned on the door sill. She gave her version.

"Dentist Lincoln got right uppity. Said he'd rather put his hand in a dog's

---

7. Gunnysack, burlap bag.
8. Originally, very poor southern white; later, any white person.

mouth. And when I reminded him of the favor, he brushed it off like a piece of lint. Well, I sent Sister downstairs and went inside. I hadn't never been in his office before, but I found the door to where he takes out teeth, and him and the nurse was in there thick as thieves. I just stood there till he caught sight of me." Crash bang the pots on the stove. "He jumped just like he was sitting on a pin. He said, 'Annie, I done tole you, I ain't gonna mess around in no niggah's mouth.' I said, 'Somebody's got to do it then,' and he said, 'Take her to Texarkana to the colored dentist' and that's when I said, 'If you paid me my money I could afford to take her.' He said, 'It's all been paid.' I tole him everything but the interest been paid. He said. ' 'Twasn't no interest.' I said ' 'Tis now. I'll take ten dollars as payment in full.' You know, Willie, it wasn't no right thing to do, 'cause I lent that money without thinking about it.

"He tole that little snippity nurse of his'n to give me ten dollars and make me sign a 'paid in full' receipt. She gave it to me and I signed the papers. Even though by rights he was paid up before, I figger, he gonna be that kind of nasty, he gonna have to pay for it."

Momma and her son laughed and laughed over the white man's evilness and her retributive sin.

I preferred, much preferred, my version.

1969

CYNTHIA OZICK
b. 1928

Although Cynthia Ozick has claimed that she "became Henry James" at the age of seventeen and "remained" him for years and years, she eventually decried the effects of being "an Extreme and Hideous Example of Premature Exposure to Henry James." Indeed, after the publication of her first, very Jamesian novel *Trust* (1966), Ozick became convinced that she had confused the relative merits of life and art, even misunderstanding her predecessor's own position on the matter. After that book, her stylistic virtuosity melded with a deeply ethical commitment to produce stories that not only interpret but also judge the world. Like her novels *The Cannibal Galaxy* (1983) and *The Messiah of Stockholm* (1987), such collections as *The Pagan Rabbi and Other Stories* (1971), *Bloodshed and Three Novellas* (1976), and *Levitation: Five Fictions* (1982) explore the sometimes mundane, sometimes mystical conundrums faced by characters seeking to negotiate between spiritual and material realities. In the essays collected in *Metaphor and Memory* (1989) as well as *Fame & Folly* (1996), Ozick comments on the absorption with history and aesthetics that shapes two of her recent novels: *The Puttermesser Papers* (1997) and *Heir to the Glimmering World* (2004). Many of her prize-winning stories also deal with the alienating experiences of assimilation encountered by Jewish immigrants not very different from the family into which she was born.

Working at their Park View Pharmacy in the Bronx, Ozick's parents had to mediate between the economics of the New World and the intellectual inheritance of the Old: her father was a pharmacist as well as a scholar of Yiddishized Hebrew while her mother was related to the Hebrew-language poet Abraham Regelson. After attending a public grade school, Hunter College, and New York University, Ozick did graduate work at Ohio State University, where she devoted her master's thesis to James. She married a lawyer, Bernard Hallote, in 1952, worked briefly as an advertising copywriter, gave birth to a daughter, and settled in New Rochelle, New York, to devote herself to articulating the ways in which she and the characters about whom she writes remain unassimilated into English. Almost a prose poem in its evocative effort to convey the unspeakable horror of the suffering inflicted on Jews by Nazism, "The Shawl" asks readers to confront their own relationship to the evil made manifest in the Holocaust, and it does so by foregrounding the figures of mother and child.

The Shawl

Stella, cold, cold, the coldness of hell. How they walked on the roads together, Rosa with Magda curled up between sore breasts, Magda wound up in the shawl. Sometimes Stella carried Magda. But she was jealous of Magda. A thin girl of fourteen, too small, with thin breasts of her own, Stella wanted to be wrapped in a shawl, hidden away, asleep, rocked by the march, a baby, a round infant in arms. Magda took Rosa's nipple, and Rosa never stopped walking, a walking cradle. There was not enough milk; sometimes Magda sucked air; then she screamed. Stella was ravenous. Her knees were tumors on sticks, her elbows chicken bones.

Rosa did not feel hunger; she felt light, not like someone walking but like someone in a faint, in trance, arrested in a fit, someone who is already a floating angel, alert and seeing everything, but in the air, not there, not touching the road. As if teetering on the tips of her fingernails. She looked into Magda's face through a gap in the shawl: a squirrel in a nest, safe, no one could reach her inside the little house of the shawl's windings. The face, very round, a pocket mirror of a face: but it was not Rosa's bleak complexion, dark like cholera, it was another kind of face altogether, eyes blue as air, smooth feathers of hair nearly as yellow as the Star sewn into Rosa's coat. You could think she was one of *their* babies.[1]

Rosa, floating, dreamed of giving Magda away in one of the villages. She could leave the line for a minute and push Magda into the hands of any woman on the side of the road. But if she moved out of line they might shoot. And even if she fled the line for half a second and pushed the shawl-bundle at a stranger, would the woman take it? She might be surprised, or afraid; she might drop the shawl, and Magda would fall out and strike her head and die. The little round head. Such a good child, she gave up screaming, and sucked now only for the taste of the drying nipple itself. The neat grip of the tiny gums. One mite of a tooth tip sticking up in the bottom gum, how shining, an elfin tombstone of white marble gleaming there. Without complaining, Magda relinquished Rosa's teats, first the left, then the right; both were cracked, not a sniff of milk. The duct-crevice extinct, a dead volcano, blind eye, chill hole, so Magda took the corner of the shawl and milked it

---

1. The Nazi "Aryan" ideal of beauty included blond hair and blue eyes. Under the Nazis, every Jew in Germany and German-occupied countries was made to wear a yellow Star of David.

instead. She sucked and sucked, flooding the threads with wetness. The shawl's good flavor, milk of linen.

It was a magic shawl, it could nourish an infant for three days and three nights. Magda did not die, she stayed alive, although very quiet. A peculiar smell, of cinnamon and almonds, lifted out of her mouth. She held her eyes open every moment, forgetting how to blink or nap, and Rosa and sometimes Stella studied their blueness. On the road they raised one burden of a leg after another and studied Magda's face. "Aryan," Stella said, in a voice grown as thin as a string; and Rosa thought how Stella gazed at Magda like a young cannibal. And the time that Stella said "Aryan," it sounded to Rosa as if Stella had really said "Let us devour her."

But Magda lived to walk. She lived that long, but she did not walk very well, partly because she was only fifteen months old, and partly because the spindles of her legs could not hold up her fat belly. It was fat with air, full and round. Rosa gave almost all her food to Magda, Stella gave nothing; Stella was ravenous, a growing child herself, but not growing much. Stella did not menstruate. Rosa did not menstruate. Rosa was ravenous, but also not; she learned from Magda how to drink the taste of a finger in one's mouth. They were in a place without pity, all pity was annihilated in Rosa, she looked at Stella's bones without pity. She was sure that Stella was waiting for Magda to die so she could put her teeth into the little thighs.

Rosa knew Magda was going to die very soon; she should have been dead already, but she had been buried away deep inside the magic shawl, mistaken there for the shivering mound of Rosa's breasts; Rosa clung to the shawl as if it covered only herself. No one took it away from her. Magda was mute. She never cried. Rosa hid her in the barracks, under the shawl, but she knew that one day someone would inform; or one day someone, not even Stella, would steal Magda to eat her. When Magda began to walk Rosa knew that Magda was going to die very soon, something would happen. She was afraid to fall asleep; she slept with the weight of her thigh on Magda's body; she was afraid she would smother Magda under her thigh. The weight of Rosa was becoming less and less; Rosa and Stella were slowly turning into air.

Magda was quiet, but her eyes were horribly alive, like blue tigers. She watched. Sometimes she laughed—it seemed a laugh, but how could it be? Magda had never seen anyone laugh. Still, Magda laughed at her shawl when the wind blew its corners, the bad wind with pieces of black in it, that made Stella's and Rosa's eyes tear. Magda's eyes were always clear and tearless. She watched like a tiger. She guarded her shawl. No one could touch it; only Rosa could touch it. Stella was not allowed. The shawl was Magda's own baby, her pet, her little sister. She tangled herself up in it and sucked on one of the corners when she wanted to be very still.

Then Stella took the shawl away and made Magda die.

Afterward Stella said: "I was cold."

And afterward she was always cold, always. The cold went into her heart: Rosa saw that Stella's heart was cold. Magda flopped onward with her little pencil legs scribbling this way and that, in search of the shawl; the pencils faltered at the barracks opening, where the light began. Rosa saw and pursued. But already Magda was in the square outside the barracks, in the jolly light. It was the roll-call arena. Every morning Rosa had to conceal Magda under the shawl against a wall of the barracks and go out and stand in the arena with Stella and hundreds of others, sometimes for hours, and Magda, deserted, was quiet under the shawl, sucking on her corner. Every day Magda was silent, and so she did not die. Rosa saw that today Magda was going to die, and at the same time a fearful joy ran in Rosa's two palms, her fingers were on fire, she was astonished, febrile: Magda, in the sunlight, swaying on her pencil legs, was howling. Ever since the drying up of Rosa's nipples, ever since Magda's last scream on the road, Magda had been devoid of any syllable; Magda was a mute. Rosa believed that something had gone wrong with her vocal cords, with her windpipe, with the cave of her larynx; Magda was defective, without a voice; perhaps she was deaf; there might be something amiss with her intelligence; Magda was dumb. Even the laugh that came when the ash-stippled wind made a clown out of Magda's shawl was only the air-blown showing of her teeth. Even when the lice, head lice and body lice, crazed her so that she became as wild as one of the big rats that plundered the barracks at daybreak looking for carrion, she rubbed and scratched and kicked and bit and rolled without a whimper. But now Magda's mouth was spilling a long viscous rope of clamor.

"Maaaa—"

It was the first noise Magda had ever sent out from her throat since the drying up of Rosa's nipples.

"Maaaa . . . aaa!"

Again! Magda was wavering in the perilous sunlight of the arena, scribbling on such pitiful little bent shins. Rosa saw. She saw that Magda was grieving for the loss of her shawl, she saw that Magda was going to die. A tide of commands hammered in Rosa's nipples: Fetch, get, bring! But she did not know which to go after first, Magda or the shawl. If she jumped out into the arena to snatch Magda up, the howling would not stop, because Magda would still not have the shawl; but if she ran back into the barracks to find the shawl, and if she found it, and if she came after Magda holding it and shaking it, then she would get Magda back, Magda would put the shawl in her mouth and turn dumb again.

Rosa entered the dark. It was easy to discover the shawl. Stella was heaped under it, asleep in her thin bones. Rosa tore the shawl free and flew—she could fly, she was only air—into the arena. The sunheat murmured of another life, of butterflies in summer. The light was placid, mellow. On the other side of the steel fence, far away, there were green meadows speckled with dandelions and deep-colored violets; beyond them, even farther, innocent tiger lilies, tall, lifting their orange bonnets. In the barracks they spoke of "flowers," of "rain": excrement, thick turd-braids, and the slow stinking maroon waterfall that slunk down from the upper bunks, the stink mixed with a bitter fatty floating smoke that greased Rosa's skin. She stood for an instant at the margin of the arena. Sometimes the electricity inside the fence would seem to hum; even Stella said it was only an imagining, but Rosa heard real sounds in the wire: grainy sad voices. The farther she was from the fence, the more clearly the voices crowded at her. The lamenting voices strummed so convincingly, so passionately, it was impossible to suspect them of being phantoms. The voices told her to hold up the shawl, high; the voices told her to shake it, to whip with it, to unfurl it like a flag. Rosa lifted, shook, whipped, unfurled. Far off, very far, Magda leaned across her air-fed belly, reaching out with the rods of her arms. She was high up, elevated, riding someone's shoulder. But the shoulder that carried Magda was not coming toward Rosa and the shawl, it was drifting away, the speck of Magda was moving more and more into the smoky distance. Above the shoulder a helmet glinted. The light tapped the helmet and sparkled it into a goblet. Below the helmet a black body like a domino and a pair of black boots hurled themselves in the direction of the electrified fence. The electric voices began to chatter wildly. "Maamaa, maaa-maaa," they all hummed together. How far Magda was from Rosa now, across the whole square, past a dozen barracks, all the way on the other side! She was no bigger than a moth.

All at once Magda was swimming through the air. The whole of Magda traveled through loftiness. She looked like a butterfly touching a silver vine. And the moment Magda's feathered round head and her pencil legs and balloonish belly and zigzag arms splashed against the fence, the steel voices went mad in their growling, urging Rosa to run and run to the spot where Magda had fallen from her flight against the electrified fence; but of course Rosa did not obey them. She only stood, because if she ran they would shoot, and if she tried to pick up the sticks of Magda's body they would shoot, and if she let the wolf's screech ascending now through the ladder of her skeleton break out, they would shoot; so she took Magda's shawl and filled her own mouth with it, stuffed it in and stuffed it in, until she was swallowing up the wolf's screech and tasting the cinnamon and almond depth of Magda's saliva; and Rosa drank Magda's shawl until it dried.

1980

U. A. FANTHORPE
b. 1929

"Now at last I know / Why I was brought here / And what I have to do": U. A. Fanthorpe imagines the representative woman writer speaking these words at the conclusion of her "From the Third Storey," with its succinct depiction of the constraints confronted by literary women from Jane Austen to Virginia Woolf and their descendants. Born in London, Fanthorpe herself has lectured on English literature and been a writer in residence at a number of institutions, but she has also earned her living as a school counselor and a hospital clerk. Her first collection of poems, *Side Effects* (1978), investigates life on a psychiatric ward, while other books—including, most recently, *Neck-Verse* (1992), *Safe as Houses* (1995), and *Consequences* (2000)—document student experiences, women's lives, and the world of "ordinary" labor. No matter what her theme, Fanthorpe frequently emphasizes what, in her note to the sequence *Only Here for the Bier,* she calls the "woman's angle," and often, too, she celebrates the liberation of female joy, as in her portrayal of the laughter of "Old women, unmanned, free / Of children, embarrassment, desire to please, / Hooting grossly, without explanation." In 1999, after the death of Ted Hughes, she was, along with Carol Ann Duffy, one of the leading candidates for the post of British poet laureate; but (like Duffy) she was dismissed because of her sexual orientation. Com-

mented a writer in the *New Statesman,* "Carol Ann Duffy or . . . Ursula Fanthorpe, both marvelous lesbian poets, were a much more exciting prospect [than Andrew Motion, the poet ultimately appointed to the position]. But the establishment has won again."

For Saint Peter[1]

I have a good deal of sympathy for you, mate,
Because I reckon that, like me, you deal with the outpatients.

Now the inpatients are easy, they're cowed by the nurses
(In your case, the angels) and they know what's what in the set-up.

5   They know about God (in my case Dr. Snow) and all His little fads,
And if there's any trouble with them, you can easily scare them rigid

Just by mentioning His name. But outpatients are different.
They bring their kids with them, for one thing, and that creates a wrong
    atmosphere.

They have shopping baskets, and buses to catch. They cry, or knit,
10 Or fall on the floor in convulsions. In fact, Saint Peter,

If you know what I mean, they haven't yet learned
How to be reverent.

1978

From Only Here for the Bier

I wrote these four poems[1] because I was interested to see how the masculine world of Shakespeare's tragedies would look from the woman's angle. In fact, women exist in this world only to be killed, as sacrificial victims. So I imagined Gertrude (mother-in-law), Regan (king's daughter), Emilia (army wife)[2] and the un-named waiting gentlewoman in *Macbeth* having a chat with some usual female confidante, like a hairdresser, or a telephone.

1. Mother-in-Law

Such a nice girl.[3] Just what I wanted
For the boy. Not top drawer, you know,
But so often, in our position, that
Turns out to be a mistake. They get
5 The ideas of their station, and that upsets

---

1. The most prominent of Jesus' twelve disciples, St. Peter traditionally is pictured as the gatekeeper of heaven (see Matthew 16.19).
1. Only two of the four poems are printed here.
2. Characters in, respectively, *Hamlet, King Lear,* and *Othello.*
3. I.e., the drowned Ophelia.

So many applecarts. The lieges, of course,
Are particularly hidebound, and the boy,
For all his absentminded ways, is a great one
For convention. Court mourning, you know . . .
10 Things like that. We don't want a Brunhilde[4]
Here. But she was so suitable. Devoted
To her father and brother, and,
Of course, to the boy. And a very
Respectable, loyal family. Well, loyal
15 To number two,[5] at any rate. Number one,
I remember, never quite trusted . . . Yes,
And had just the right interests. Folk song, for instance,
(Such a sweet little voice), and amateur
Dramatics. Inherited *that* taste
20 From her father. Dear old fellow, he'd go on
For hours about his college drama group.
And the boy's so keen on the stage. It's nice
When husband and wife have a shared interest,
Don't you think? Then botany. Poor little soul,
25 She was really keen. We'd go for trips
With the vasculum,[6] and have such fun
Asking the lieges their country names for flowers.
Some of them, my dear, were scarcely delicate
(The names, I mean), but the young nowadays
30 Don't seem to notice. Marriage
Would have made her more innocent, of course.
I can't think who will do for the boy now.
I seem to be the only woman left round here.

2. King's Daughter

Being the middle sister is tiresome.
The rawboned heroics of the eldest
Are out of reach; so is the youngest's
Gamine[7] appeal. It is impossible for the second child
5 To be special. One must just cultivate
One's own garden, neatly. For neatness and order
Matter in the world of the middle daughter,
The even number. Disorderly lives
Are distasteful. Adultery is untidy;
10 Servants should be accurate and invisible.
Individuals should have two eyes, or none;[8]
One eye is unacceptable. I enjoy the beauty
Of formality, and have no objection
To offering father the elaborate rhetoric
15 He expects. There is a certain correctness

---

4. Great female warrior in Germanic mythology and literature.
5. I.e., Claudius, Gertrude's second husband, who murdered number one, Hamlet's father.
6. Special case for carrying botanical specimens.
7. Female street urchin.
8. When Gloucester is being blinded, Regan urges, "One side will mock another; th'other, too" (*King Lear* 3.7.68).

In the situation. One must object, however,
To the impropriety of those who propose
Different rules. One is no innovator:
Innovation is unfeminine. It is important
20 That ashtrays should be emptied, and always
In the same place, that meals be punctual.
One depends on one's servants to supply
Visual and temporal symmetry. Equally,
One relies on one's family to support
25 The proper structure of relationships. It is a pity
That one's father is so eccentric, that his friends
Are the sort of people one tries not to know,
That one's sisters are, in their different ways,
Both so unwomanly. One would never dream
30 Of asserting oneself in public, as they do.
One tries to cultivate the woman's touch.

1982

Women Laughing

Gurgles, genderless,
Inside the incurious womb.
Random soliloquies of babies
Ticked by everything.

5 Undomesticated shrieks
Of small girls. Mother prophesies
You'll be crying in a minute.

Adolescents wearing giggles
Like chain-mail, against embarrassment,
10 Giggles formal in shape as
Butterpats, or dropped stitches.

Young women anxious to please,
Laughing eagerly before the punchline
(Being too naïve to know which it is).

15 Wives gleaming sleekly in public at
Husbandly jokes, masking
All trace of old acquaintance.

Mums obliging with rhetorical
Guffaws at the children's riddles
20 That bored their parents.

Old women, unmanned, free
Of children, embarrassment, desire to please,
Hooting grossly, without explanation.

1984

From the Third Storey

(for Hazel Medd)

"You have to be selfish to be a writer."
"Monstrously selfish?"
"Monstrously selfish," she said.
    Jean Rhys in David Plante's Difficult Women[1]

Aunt Jane scribbles in the living-room.
When visitors come, she stuffs her work
Under the blotter, and joins in the chat.[2]

(In the third storey, a curious
5 Laugh; distinct, formal, mirthless.)[3]

Daughter Charlotte's[4] first care is to discharge
Her household and filial duties. Only then
May she admit herself to her own bright sphere.
(There were days when she was quite silent;
10 Others when I could not account for
The sounds she made.)

Home duties are a small part of
The Reverend William's life. Reverently
Elizabeth,[5] wife and mother, furnishes his study,
15 And writes in the dining-room
Which has three doors.

(A vague murmur, peculiar
And lugubrious. Something
Gurgled and moaned.)

20 George is Agnes's husband.[6] He and
Mistress Marian *(what do people call her?)*
Write in one room at their desks, drudging
To pay off his marriage's debts.

(A savage, a sharp, a shrilly sound.
25 The thing delivering such utterance must rest
Ere it repeat the effort. It came
Out of the third storey.)

Sister Virginia,[7] childless wife,
Fathoms the metaphor of room.

---

1. Published in 1983. Rhys (1894–1979), West Indian–born novelist. All the writers named in the poem are included in this anthology.
2. This story is told of the novelist Jane Austen (1775–1817) by her nephew.
3. The description is quoted from *Jane Eyre* (1847), chap. 11; the laughter comes from Rochester's mad wife, Bertha Mason, who is locked in the upper story.
4. The novelist Charlotte Brontë (1816–1855), author of *Jane Eyre* (1847).
5. Elizabeth Gaskell (1810–1865), novelist and Brontë's biographer.
6. The philosopher and critic George Lewes (1817–1878) was unable to divorce his wife, Agnes; from 1854 until his death, he lived with Mary Anne Evans (1819–1890), whose novels—written under the name George Eliot—were extremely popular and profitable.
7. Virginia Woolf (1882–1941), novelist and author of *A Room of One's Own* (1929).

> 30 But who is One? The upstairs lunatic—
> Might she not be Oneself?
>
> (A snarling, snatching sound,
> Almost like a dog quarreling.)
>
> Between affairs, before marriages,
> 35 Jean[8] (*I have called myself so many
> Different names*) buys twelve technicolored
> Quill pens to cheer her bare table
> In bedsit Fulham.[9] And writes,
>
> (She was standing, waving her arms,
> 40 Above the battlements, and shouting out
> Till they could hear her a mile off.)
>
> And sets the mad wife free to tell
> Truth of mistress, divorcée, mother,
> Aunt, daughter, sister, wife:
>
> 45 *Now at last I know
> Why I was brought here
> And what I have to do.*

1984

8. Jean Rhys; in *Wide Sargasso Sea* (1966), she retells the story of *Jane Eyre* from Bertha Mason's point of view.

9. Section of London. "Bedsit": a small apartment consisting of a bedroom and sitting room.

URSULA K. LE GUIN
b. 1929

The daughter of the distinguished anthropologist Alfred L. Kroeber and the writer-folklorist Theodora Kroeber, the science fiction writer Ursula K. Le Guin has sometimes compared her own work to that of an anthropologist. "Science fiction allows a fiction writer to make up cultures, to *invent*—not only a new world, but a new *culture*," she once told an interviewer, adding that "my father preferred to go find [other] civilizations]; I prefer to invent them." Imaginatively elaborating new possibilities for human society and personality while incisively commenting on the "real" world, Le Guin's invented cultures are described and dramatized in an impressive range of volumes, including more than twenty novels, among them *Rocannon's World* (1966), *The Left Hand of Darkness* (1969), *The Dispossessed* (1974), and most recently *The Telling* (2000), *The Other Wind* (2001), and *Gifts* (2004); numerous short story collections, among them *The Wind's Twelve Quarters* (1975), *The Compass Rose* (1982), and *Changing Planes* (2003); and (along with other books for young people) three especially beloved fantasies for children—*A Wizard of Earthsea* (1968), *The Tombs of Atuan* (1971), and *The Farthest Shore* (1972)—which make up the prize-winning Earthsea trilogy. In *Always Coming Home* (1985), created with the composer Todd

Barton, artist Margaret Chodos, and "geomancer" George Hersh, Le Guin initiated a series of multimedia productions, and in *Dancing at the Edge of the World* (1989; rev. ed., 1992), she began collecting her essays on women, language, and space. Such volumes as *Going Out with Peacocks* (1994), *Sixty Odd* (1999), and *Incredible Good Fortune* (2006) offer Le Guin's most recent poems.

Born and raised in Berkeley, California, Le Guin attended Radcliffe College and Columbia University. In 1953, while studying in Paris on a Fulbright scholarship, she married the historian Charles A. Le Guin, with whom she eventually settled in Portland, Oregon; the couple have three children and three grandchildren. From the start, Le Guin has explained, her writing always had "what you'd have to call a fantasy element. . . . It took place in an imaginary country or something like that," but it was not until she "got back to reading science fiction in [her] late twenties" that she realized "I could *call* my stuff science fiction." From that time on, even while working and raising her children, she became a productive and distinguished writer of what might be labeled "speculative fiction" as well as "science fiction." Extending the boundaries of her genre so that science fiction could explore the problems and possibilities of human society with a new intensity, she created imaginary creatures who allowed her to raise important questions about the modes and morals of her own world.

In some of her most recent books, notably *The Telling*, Le Guin raises Orwellian questions about political organization that have proved strikingly relevant to contemporary problems. As a reviewer for the *Times Literary Supplement* wrote, "In its vision of an unbendingly fundamentalist State which, convinced of the rightness of its own dogma, persecutes questioners and dissenters, *The Telling* is a prescient book." In other works, such as *The Left Hand of Darkness* (which won the Hugo and Nebula awards from the Science Fiction Writers of America in 1969 and 1970) and "Sur" (1982), Le Guin examined the pressures and possibilities of gender with subtlety and wit. What would it "be like to be a man-woman, or a woman-man," she asks in *The Left Hand of Darkness*, a fantasy of life on a planet whose inhabitants are biologically bisexual, and what would it mean if *women* had discovered the South Pole, she wonders in "Sur." Her answers to such questions are invariably both brilliant and surprising. Equally thought provoking, "She Unnames Them" responds to traditional myths about male linguistic priority: What would have happened if Eve, not Adam, had been given the knowledge and responsibility of determining the uses of language?

Sur[1]

A Summary Report of the Yelcho *Expedition to the Antarctic, 1909–1910*

Although I have no intention of publishing this report, I think it would be nice if a grandchild of mine, or somebody's grandchild, happened to find it some day; so I shall keep it in the leather trunk in the attic, along with Rosita's christening dress and Juanito's silver rattle and my wedding shoes and finneskos.[2]

The first requisite for mounting an expedition—money—is normally the hardest to come by. I grieve that even in a report destined for a trunk in the attic of a house in a very quiet suburb of Lima[3] I dare not write the name of the generous benefactor, the great soul without whose unstinting liberality

---

1. South (Spanish).
2. Boots made of reindeer skin.
3. Largest city of Peru.

the *Yelcho* Expedition would never have been more than the idlest excursion into daydream. That our equipment was the best and most modern—that our provisions were plentiful and fine—that a ship of the Chilean Government, with her brave officers and gallant crew, was twice sent halfway round the world for our convenience: all this is due to that benefactor whose name, alas! I must not say, but whose happiest debtor I shall be till death.

When I was little more than a child my imagination was caught by a newspaper account of the voyage of the *Belgica,* which, sailing south from Tierra del Fuego, became beset by ice in the Bellingshausen Sea and drifted a whole year with the floe, the men aboard her suffering a great deal from want of food and from the terror of the unending winter darkness. I read and reread that account, and later followed with excitement the reports of the rescue of Dr. Nordenskjold from the South Shetland Isles by the dashing Captain Irizar of the *Uruguay,* and the adventures of the *Scotia* in the Weddell Sea. But all these exploits were to me but forerunners of the British National Antarctic Expedition of 1902–1904, in the *Discovery,* and the wonderful account of that expedition by Captain Scott.[4] This book, which I ordered from London and reread a thousand times, filled me with longing to see with my own eyes that strange continent, last Thule[5] of the South, which lies on our maps and globes like a white cloud, a void, fringed here and there with scraps of coastline, dubious capes, supposititious islands, headlands that may or may not be there: Antarctica. And the desire was as pure as the polar snows: to go, to see—no more, no less. I deeply respect the scientific accomplishments of Captain Scott's expedition, and have read with passionate interest the findings of physicists, meteorologists, biologists, etc.; but having had no training in any science, nor any opportunity for such training, my ignorance obliged me to forego any thought of adding to the body of scientific knowledge concerning Antarctica; and the same is true for all the members of my expedition. It seems a pity; but there was nothing we could do about it. Our goal was limited to observation and exploration. We hoped to go a little farther, perhaps, and see a little more; if not, simply to go and to see. A simple ambition, I think, and essentially a modest one.

Yet it would have remained less than an ambition, no more than a longing, but for the support and encouragement of my dear cousin and friend Juana ——— ———. (I use no surnames, lest this report fall into strangers' hands at last, and embarrassment or unpleasant notoriety thus be brought upon unsuspecting husbands, sons, etc.) I had lent Juana my copy of *The Voyage of the Discovery,* and it was she who, as we strolled beneath our parasols across the Plaza de Armas after Mass one Sunday in 1908, said, "Well, if Captain Scott can do it, why can't we?"

It was Juana who proposed that we write Carlota ——— in Valparaiso. Through Carlota we met our benefactor, and so obtained our money, our ship, and even the plausible pretext of going on retreat in a Bolivian convent, which some of us were forced to employ (while the rest of us said we were going to Paris for the winter season). And it was my Juana who in the darkest

---

4. Robert Falcon Scott (1868–1912), British naval officer and Antarctic explorer, commanded an expedition to explore the Ross Sea region in 1901–04; his account was *The Voyage of the "Discovery"* (1905). The other expeditions mentioned are also genuine.
5. Ultima Thule, the northernmost lands of the ancient world.

moments remained resolute, unshaken in her determination to achieve our goal.

And there were dark moments, especially in the early months of 1909—times when I did not see how the Expedition would ever become more than a quarter ton of pemmican[6] gone to waste and a lifelong regret. It was so very hard to gather our expeditionary force together! So few of those we asked even knew what we were talking about—so many thought we were mad, or wicked, or both! And of those few who shared our folly, still fewer were able, when it came to the point, to leave their daily duties and commit themselves to a voyage of at least six months, attended with not inconsiderable uncertainty and danger. An ailing parent; an anxious husband beset by business cares; a child at home with only ignorant or incompetent servants to look after it: these are not responsibilities lightly to be set aside. And those who wished to evade such claims were not the companions we wanted in hard work, risk, and privation.

But since success crowned our efforts, why dwell on the setbacks and delays, or the wretched contrivances and downright lies that we all had to employ? I look back with regret only to those friends who wished to come with us but could not, by any contrivance, get free—those we had to leave behind to a life without danger, without uncertainty, without hope.

On the seventeenth of August, 1909, in Punta Arenas, Chile, all the members of the Expedition met for the first time: Juana and I, the two Peruvians; from Argentina, Zoe, Berta, and Teresa; and our Chileans, Carlota and her friends Eva, Pepita, and Dolores. At the last moment I had received word that Maria's husband, in Quito, was ill, and she must stay to nurse him, so we were nine, not ten. Indeed, we had resigned ourselves to being but eight, when, just as night fell, the indomitable Zoe arrived in a tiny pirogue[7] manned by Indians, her yacht having sprung a leak just as it entered the Strait of Magellan.

That night before we sailed we began to get to know one another; and we agreed, as we enjoyed our abominable supper in the abominable seaport inn of Punta Arenas, that if a situation arose of such urgent danger that one voice must be obeyed without present question, the unenviable honor of speaking with that voice should fall first upon myself: if I were incapacitated, upon Carlota: if she, then upon Berta. We three were then toasted as "Supreme Inca," "La Araucana,"[8] and "The Third Mate," among a lot of laughter and cheering. As it came out, to my very great pleasure and relief, my qualities as a "leader" were never tested; the nine of us worked things out amongst us from beginning to end without any orders being given by anybody, and only two or three times with recourse to a vote by voice or show of hands. To be sure, we argued a good deal. But then, we had time to argue. And one way or another the arguments always ended up in a decision, upon which action could be taken. Usually at least one person grumbled about the decision, sometimes bitterly. But what is life without grumbling, and the occasional opportunity to say, "I told you so"? How could one bear housework, or looking after babies, let alone the rigors of sledge-hauling in Ant-

---

6. A preserved food originally made by American Indians from dried meat and fruit.
7. Canoe made from a hollowed tree trunk.
8. The Araucanian Indians occupied present-day Chile before the Spanish Conquest; like the Incas they were subjugated by the Spanish, but only after much resistance.

arctica, without grumbling? Officers—as we came to understand aboard the *Yelcho*—are forbidden to grumble; but we nine were, and are, by birth and upbringing, unequivocally and irrevocably, all crew.

Though our shortest course to the southern continent, and that originally urged upon us by the captain of our good ship, was to the South Shetlands and the Bellingshausen Sea, or else by the South Orkneys into the Weddell Sea, we planned to sail west to the Ross Sea, which Captain Scott had explored and described, and from which the brave Ernest Shackleton[9] had returned only the previous autumn. More was known about this region than any other portion of the coast of Antarctica, and though that more was not much, yet it served as some insurance of the safety of the ship, which we felt we had no right to imperil. Captain Pardo had fully agreed with us after studying the charts and our planned itinerary; and so it was westward that we took our course out of the Strait next morning.

Our journey half round the globe was attended by fortune. The little *Yelcho* steamed cheerily along through gale and gleam, climbing up and down those seas of the Southern Ocean that run unbroken round the world. Juana, who had fought bulls and the far more dangerous cows on her family's *estancia*, called the ship *"la vaca valiente,"*[1] because she always returned to the charge. Once we got over being seasick we all enjoyed the sea voyage, though oppressed at times by the kindly but officious protectiveness of the captain and his officers, who felt that we were only "safe" when huddled up in the three tiny cabins which they had chivalrously vacated for our use.

We saw our first iceberg much farther south than we had looked for it, and saluted it with Veuve Clicquot[2] at dinner. The next day we entered the ice pack, the belt of floes and bergs, broken loose from the land ice and winter-frozen seas of Antarctica, which drifts northward in the spring. Fortune still smiled on us: our little steamer, incapable, with her unreinforced metal hull, of forcing a way into the ice, picked her way from lane to lane without hesitation, and on the third day we were through the pack, in which ships have sometimes struggled for weeks and been obliged to turn back at last. Ahead of us now lay the dark grey waters of the Ross Sea, and beyond that, on the horizon, the remote glimmer, the cloud-reflected whiteness of the Great Ice Barrier.

Entering the Ross Sea a little east of Longitude West 160°, we came in sight of the Barrier at the place where Captain Scott's party, finding a bight[3] in the vast wall of ice, had gone ashore and sent up their hydrogen-gas balloon for reconnaissance and photography. The towering face of the Barrier, its sheer cliffs and azure and violet water-worn caves, all were as described, but the location had changed: instead of a narrow bight there was a considerable bay, full of the beautiful and terrific orca whales playing and spouting in the sunshine of that brilliant southern spring.

Evidently masses of ice many acres in extent had broken away from the Barrier (which—at least for most of its vast extent—does not rest on land but floats on water) since the *Discovery's* passage in 1902. This put our plan to set up camp on the Barrier itself in a new light; and while we were dis-

---

9. Sir Ernest Henry Shackleton (1874–1922), British Antarctic explorer, member of the Scott expedition.
1. The courageous cow (Spanish). "Estancia": cattle ranch (Spanish).
2. An expensive French champagne.
3. A bend in a shoreline, forming a bay.

cussing alternatives, we asked Captain Pardo to take the ship west along the Barrier face towards Ross Island and McMurdo Sound. As the sea was clear of ice and quite calm, he was happy to do so, and, when we sighted the smoke plume of Mount Erebus, to share in our celebration—another half case of Veuve Clicquot.

The *Yelcho* anchored in Arrival Bay, and we went ashore in the ship's boat. I cannot describe my emotions when I set foot on the earth, on that earth, the barren, cold gravel at the foot of the long volcanic slope. I felt elation, impatience, gratitude, awe, familiarity. I felt that I was home at last. Eight Adélie penguins immediately came to greet us with many exclamations of interest not unmixed with disapproval. "Where on earth have you been? What took you so long? The Hut is around this way. Please come this way. Mind the rocks!" They insisted on our going to visit Hut Point, where the large structure built by Captain Scott's party stood, looking just as in the photographs and drawings that illustrate his book. The area about it, however, was disgusting—a kind of graveyard of seal skins, seal bones, penguin bones, and rubbish, presided over by the mad, screaming skua gulls. Our escorts waddled past the slaughterhouse in all tranquility, and one showed me personally to the door, though it would not go in.

The interior of the hut was less offensive, but very dreary. Boxes of supplies had been stacked up into a kind of room within the room; it did not look as I had imagined it when the *Discovery* party put on their melodramas and minstrel shows in the long winter night. (Much later, we learned that Sir Ernest had rearranged it a good deal when he was there just a year before us.) It was dirty, and had about it a mean disorder. A pound tin of tea was standing open. Empty meat tins lay about; biscuits were spilled on the floor; a lot of dog turds were underfoot—frozen, of course, but not a great deal improved by that. No doubt the last occupants had had to leave in a hurry, perhaps even in a blizzard. All the same, they could have closed the tea tin. But housekeeping, the art of the infinite, is no game for amateurs.

Teresa proposed that we use the hut as our camp. Zoe counterproposed that we set fire to it. We finally shut the door and left it as we had found it. The penguins appeared to approve, and cheered us all the way to the boat.

McMurdo Sound was free of ice, and Captain Pardo now proposed to take us off Ross Island and across to Victoria Land, where we might camp at the foot of the Western Mountains, on dry and solid earth. But those mountains, with their storm-darkened peaks and hanging cirques and glaciers, looked as awful as Captain Scott had found them on his western journey, and none of us felt much inclined to seek shelter among them.

Aboard the ship that night we decided to go back and set up our base as we had originally planned, on the Barrier itself. For all available reports indicated that the clear way south was across the level Barrier surface until one could ascend one of the confluent glaciers to the high plateau which appears to form the whole interior of the continent. Captain Pardo argued strongly against this plan, asking what would become of us if the Barrier "calved"—if our particular acre of ice broke away and started to drift northward. "Well," said Zoe, "then you won't have to come so far to meet us." But he was so persuasive on this theme that he persuaded himself into leaving one of the *Yelcho*'s boats with us when we camped, as a means of escape. We found it useful for fishing, later on.

My first steps on Antarctic soil, my only visit to Ross Island, had not been pleasure unalloyed. I thought of the words of the English poet:

> Though every prospect pleases,
> And only Man is vile.[4]

But then, the backside of heroism is often rather sad; women and servants know that. They know also that the heroism may be no less real for that. But achievement is smaller than men think. What is large is the sky, the earth, the sea, the soul. I looked back as the ship sailed east again that evening. We were well into September now, with ten hours or more of daylight. The spring sunset lingered on the twelve-thousand-foot peak of Erebus and shone rosy gold on her long plume of steam. The steam from our own small funnel faded blue on the twilit water as we crept along under the towering pale wall of ice.

On our return to "Orca Bay"—Sir Ernest, we learned years later, had named it the Bay of Whales—we found a sheltered nook where the Barrier edge was low enough to provide fairly easy access from the ship. The *Yelcho* put out her ice anchor, and the next long, hard days were spent in unloading our supplies and setting up our camp on the ice, a half kilometer in from the edge: a task in which the *Yelcho*'s crew lent us invaluable aid and interminable advice. We took all the aid gratefully, and most of the advice with salt.

The weather so far had been extraordinarily mild for spring in this latitude; the temperature had not yet gone below −20° Fahrenheit, and there was only one blizzard while we were setting up camp. But Captain Scott had spoken feelingly of the bitter south winds on the Barrier, and we had planned accordingly. Exposed as our camp was to every wind, we built no rigid structures above ground. We set up tents to shelter in while we dug out a series of cubicles in the ice itself, lined them with hay insulation and pine boarding, and roofed them with canvas over bamboo poles, covered with snow for weight and insulation. The big central room was instantly named Buenos Aires by our Argentineans, to whom the center, wherever one is, is always Buenos Aires. The heating and cooking stove was in Buenos Aires. The storage tunnels and the privy (called Punta Arenas) got some back heat from the stove. The sleeping cubicles opened off Buenos Aires, and were very small, mere tubes into which one crawled feet first; they were lined deeply with hay and soon warmed by one's body warmth. The sailors called them "coffins" and "wormholes," and looked with horror on our burrows in the ice. But our little warren or prairie-dog village served us well, permitting us as much warmth and privacy as one could reasonably expect under the circumstances. If the *Yelcho* was unable to get through the ice in February, and we had to spend the winter in Antarctica, we certainly could do so, though on very limited rations. For this coming summer, our base—Sudamérica del Sur, South South America, but we generally called it the Base—was intended merely as a place to sleep, to store our provisions, and to give shelter from blizzards.

To Berta and Eva, however, it was more than that. They were its chief architect-designers, its most ingenious builder-excavators, and its most diligent and contented occupants, forever inventing an improvement in ventilation, or learning how to make skylights, or revealing to us a new addition

---

4. From the hymn "From Greenland's Icy Mountains" by Bishop Reginald Heber (1783–1826).

to our suite of rooms, dug in the living ice. It was thanks to them that our stores were stowed so handily, that our stove drew and heated so efficiently, and that Buenos Aires, where nine people cooked, ate, worked, conversed, argued, grumbled, painted, played the guitar and banjo, and kept the Expedition's library of books and maps, was a marvel of comfort and convenience. We lived there in real amity; and if you simply had to be alone for a while, you crawled into your sleeping hole head first.

Berta went a little farther. When she had done all she could to make South South America livable, she dug out one more cell just under the ice surface, leaving a nearly transparent sheet of ice like a greenhouse roof; and there, alone, she worked at sculptures. They were beautiful forms, some like a blending of the reclining human figure with the subtle curves and volumes of the Weddell seal, others like the fantastic shapes of ice cornices and ice caves. Perhaps they are there still, under the snow, in the bubble in the Great Barrier. There where she made them they might last as long as stone. But she could not bring them north. That is the penalty for carving in water.

Captain Pardo was reluctant to leave us, but his orders did not permit him to hang about the Ross Sea indefinitely, and so at last, with many earnest injunctions to us to stay put—make no journeys—take no risks—beware of frostbite—don't use edge tools—look out for cracks in the ice—and a heartfelt promise to return to Orca Bay on the twentieth of February, or as near that date as wind and ice would permit, the good man bade us farewell, and his crew shouted us a great goodbye cheer as they weighed anchor. That evening, in the long orange twilight of October, we saw the topmast of the *Yelcho* go down the north horizon, over the edge of the world, leaving us to ice, and silence, and the Pole.

That night we began to plan the Southern Journey.

The ensuing month passed in short practice trips and depotlaying.[5] The life we had led at home, though in its own way strenuous, had not fitted any of us for the kind of strain met with in sledge-hauling at ten or twenty degrees below freezing. We all needed as much working-out as possible before we dared undertake a long haul.

My longest exploratory trip, made with Dolores and Carlota, was southwest towards Mount Markham, and it was a nightmare—blizzards and pressure ice[6] all the way out, crevasses and no view of the mountains when we got there, and white weather and sastrugi[7] all the way back. The trip was useful, however, in that we could begin to estimate our capacities; and also in that we had started out with a very heavy load of provisions, which we depoted at 100 and 130 miles SSW of Base. Thereafter other parties pushed on farther, till we had a line of snow cairns and depots right down to Latitude 83° 43', where Juana and Zoe, on an exploring trip, had found a kind of stone gateway opening on a great glacier leading south. We established these depots to avoid, if possible, the hunger that had bedeviled Captain Scott's Southern Party, and the consequent misery and weakness. And we also established to our own satisfaction—intense satisfaction—that we were sledge-haulers at least as good as Captain Scott's husky dogs. Of course we could not have expected to pull as much or as fast as his men. That we did

---

5. Depositing supplies of food along the route to be taken.
6. Ridges formed in the Antarctic seas by the pressures of sea ice.
7. Long wavelike ridges of snow.

948 / Ursula K. Le Guin

so was because we were favored by much better weather than Captain Scott's party ever met on the Barrier; and also the quantity and quality of our food made a very considerable difference. I am sure that the fifteen percent of dried fruits in our pemmican helped prevent scurvy; and the potatoes, frozen and dried according to an ancient Andean Indian method, were very nourishing yet very light and compact—perfect sledging rations. In any case, it was with considerable confidence in our capacities that we made ready at last for the Southern Journey.

The Southern Party consisted of two sledge teams: Juana, Dolores, and myself; Carlota, Pepita, and Zoe. The support team of Berta, Eva, and Teresa set out before us with a heavy load of supplies, going right up onto the glacier to prospect routes and leave depots of supplies for our return journey. We followed five days behind them, and met them returning between Depot Ercilla and Depot Miranda (see map). That "night"—of course there was no

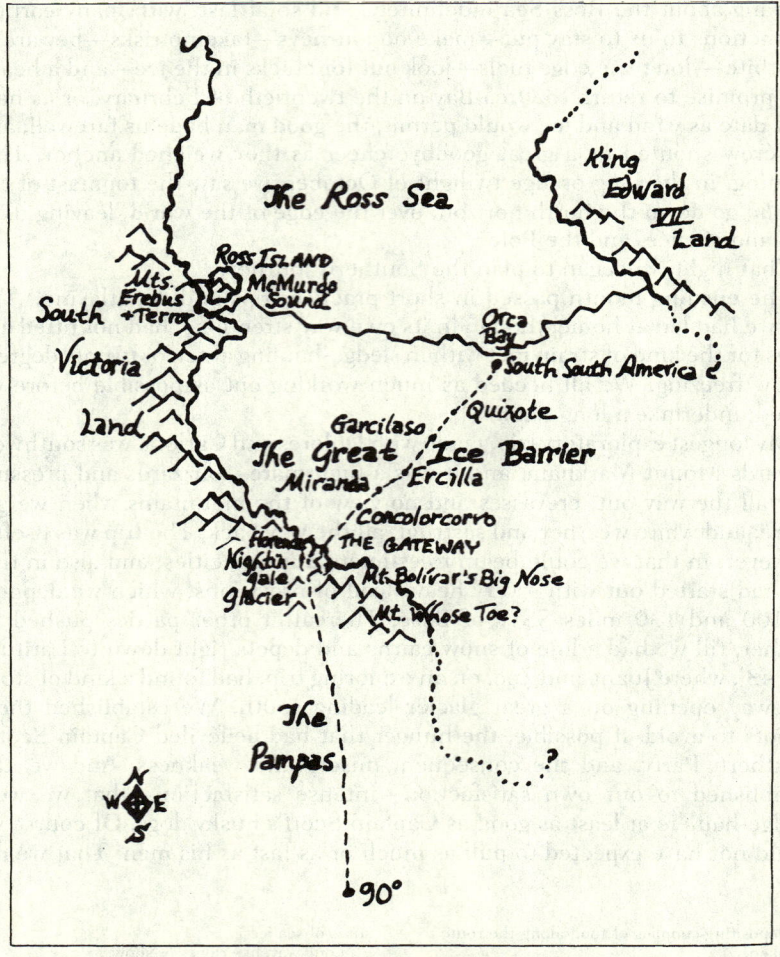

THE MAP IN THE ATTIC

real darkness—we were all nine together in the heart of the level plain of ice. It was the fifteenth of November, Dolores's birthday. We celebrated by putting eight ounces of pisco[8] in the hot chocolate, and became very merry. We sang. It is strange now to remember how thin our voices sounded in that great silence. It was overcast, white weather, without shadows and without visible horizon or any feature to break the level; there was nothing to see at all. We had come to that white place on the map, that void, and there we flew and sang like sparrows.

After sleep and a good breakfast the Base Party continued north, and the Southern Party sledged on. The sky cleared presently. High up, thin clouds passed over very rapidly from southwest to northeast, but down on the Barrier it was calm and just cold enough, five or ten degrees below freezing, to give a firm surface for hauling.

On the level ice we never pulled less than eleven miles, seventeen kilometers, a day, and generally fifteen or sixteen miles, twenty-five kilometers. (Our instruments, being British made, were calibrated in feet, miles, degrees Fahrenheit, etc., but we often converted miles to kilometers because the larger numbers sounded more encouraging.) At the time we left South America, we knew only that Mr. Shackleton had mounted another expedition to the Antarctic in 1908, had tried to attain the Pole but failed, and had returned to England in June of the current year, 1909. No coherent report of his explorations had yet reached South America when we left; we did not know what route he had gone, or how far he had got. But we were not altogether taken by surprise when, far across the featureless white plain, tiny beneath the mountain peaks and the strange silent flight of the rainbow-fringed cloud wisps, we saw a fluttering dot of black. We turned west from our course to visit it: a snow heap nearly buried by the winter's storms—a flag on a bamboo pole, a mere shred of threadbare cloth—an empty oilcan— and a few footprints standing some inches above the ice. In some conditions of weather the snow compressed under one's weight remains when the surrounding soft snow melts or is scoured away by the wind; and so these reversed footprints had been left standing all these months, like rows of cobbler's lasts[9]—a queer sight.

We met no other such traces on our way. In general I believe our course was somewhat east of Mr. Shackleton's. Juana, our surveyor, had trained herself well and was faithful and methodical in her sightings and readings, but our equipment was minimal—a theodolite on tripod legs, a sextant[1] with artificial horizon, two compasses, and chronometers. We had only the wheel meter on the sledge to give distance actually traveled.

In any case, it was the day after passing Mr. Shackleton's waymark that I first saw clearly the great glacier among the mountains to the southwest, which was to give us a pathway from the sea level of the Barrier up to the altiplano,[2] ten thousand feet above. The approach was magnificent: a gateway formed by immense vertical domes and pillars of rock. Zoe and Juana had called the vast ice river that flowed through that gateway the Florence Nightingale[3] Glacier, wishing to honor the British, who had been the inspiration and guide of our expedition; that very brave and very peculiar lady

---

8. A Peruvian brandy.
9. Foot-shaped blocks used in shoemaking.
1. An instrument that measures the altitude of stars. "Theodolite": an instrument that measures angles. Both are used for surveying and navigation.
2. High plateau.
3. British nursing pioneer and feminist writer (1820–1910); see Vol. 1, p. 1015.

seemed to represent so much that is best, and strangest, in the island race. On maps, of course, this glacier bears the name Mr. Shackleton gave it, the Beardmore.

The ascent of the Nightingale was not easy. The way was open at first, and well marked by our support party, but after some days we came among terrible crevasses, a maze of hidden cracks, from a foot to thirty feet wide and from thirty to a thousand feet deep. Step by step we went, and step by step, and the way always upward now. We were fifteen days on the glacier. At first the weather was hot, up to 20° F., and the hot nights without darkness were wretchedly uncomfortable in our small tents. And all of us suffered more or less from snowblindness just at the time when we wanted clear eyesight to pick our way among the ridges and crevasses of the tortured ice, and to see the wonders about and before us. For at every day's advance more great, nameless peaks came into view in the west and southwest, summit beyond summit, range beyond range, stark rock and snow in the unending noon.

We gave names to these peaks, not very seriously, since we did not expect our discoveries to come to the attention of geographers. Zoe had a gift for naming, and it is thanks to her that certain sketch maps in various suburban South American attics bear such curious features as "Bolívar's Big Nose," "I Am General Rosas,"[4] "The Cloudmaker," "Whose Toe?" and "Throne of Our Lady of the Southern Cross." And when at last we got up onto the altiplano, the great interior plateau, it was Zoe who called it the pampa, and maintained that we walked there among vast herds of invisible cattle, transparent cattle pastured on the spindrift snow, their gauchos[5] the restless, merciless winds. We were by then all a little crazy with exhaustion and the great altitude—twelve thousand feet—and the cold and the wind blowing and the luminous circles and crosses surrounding the suns, for often there were three or four suns in the sky, up there.

That is not a place where people have any business to be. We should have turned back; but since we had worked so hard to get there, it seemed that we should go on, at least for a while.

A blizzard came with very low temperatures, so we had to stay in the tents, in our sleeping bags, for thirty hours, a rest we all needed; though it was warmth we needed most, and there was no warmth on that terrible plain anywhere at all but in our veins. We huddled close together all that time. The ice we lay on is two miles thick.

It cleared suddenly and became, for the plateau, good weather: twelve below zero and the wind not very strong. We three crawled out of our tent and met the others crawling out of theirs. Carlota told us then that her group wished to turn back. Pepita had been feeling very ill; even after the rest during the blizzard, her temperature would not rise above 90°. Carlota was having trouble breathing. Zoe was perfectly fit, but much preferred staying with her friends and lending them a hand in difficulties to pushing on towards the Pole. So we put the four ounces of pisco which we had been keeping for Christmas into the breakfast cocoa, and dug out our tents, and loaded our sledges, and parted there in the white daylight on the bitter plain.

---

4. Juan Manuel de Rosas (1793–1877), Argentine dictator. Simon Bolívar (1783–1830), South American soldier and activist who led the revolution against Spain.

5. South American cattlemen. "Pampa": South American grazing land.

Our sledge was fairly light by now. We pulled on to the south. Juana calculated our position daily. On the twenty-second of December, 1909, we reached the South Pole. The weather was, as always, very cruel. Nothing of any kind marked the dreary whiteness. We discussed leaving some kind of mark or monument, a snow cairn, a tent pole and flag; but there seemed no particular reason to do so. Anything we could do, anything we were, was insignificant, in that awful place. We put up the tent for shelter for an hour and made a cup of tea, and then struck "90° Camp."[6] Dolores, standing patient as ever in her sledging harness, looked at the snow; it was so hard frozen that it showed no trace of our footprints coming, and she said, "Which way?"

"North," said Juana.

It was a joke, because at that particular place there is no other direction. But we did not laugh. Our lips were cracked with frostbite and hurt too much to let us laugh. So we started back, and the wind at our backs pushed us along, and dulled the knife edges of the waves of frozen snow.

All that week the blizzard wind pursued us like a pack of mad dogs. I cannot describe it. I wished we had not gone to the Pole. I think I wish it even now. But I was glad even then that we had left no sign there, for some man longing to be first might come some day, and find it, and know then what a fool he had been, and break his heart.

We talked, when we could talk, of catching up to Carlota's party, since they might be going slower than we. In fact they had used their tent as a sail to catch the following wind and had got far ahead of us. But in many places they had built snow cairns or left some sign for us; once Zoe had written on the lee side of a ten-foot sastruga, just as children write on the sand of the beach at Miraflores, "This Way Out!" The wind blowing over the frozen ridge had left the words perfectly distinct.

In the very hour that we began to descend the glacier, the weather turned warmer, and the mad dogs were left to howl forever tethered to the Pole. The distance that had taken us fifteen days going up we covered in only eight days going down. But the good weather that had aided us descending the Nightingale became a curse down on the Barrier ice, where we had looked forward to a kind of royal progress from depot to depot, eating our fill and taking our time for the last three hundred-odd miles. In a tight place on the glacier I lost my goggles—I was swinging from my harness at the time in a crevasse—and then Juana had broken hers when we had to do some rock climbing coming down to the Gateway. After two days in bright sunlight with only one pair of snow goggles to pass amongst us, we were all suffering badly from snowblindness. It became acutely painful to keep lookout for landmarks or depot flags, to take sightings, even to study the compass, which had to be laid down on the snow to steady the needle. At Concolorcorvo Depot, where there was a particularly good supply of food and fuel, we gave up, crawled into our sleeping bags with bandaged eyes, and slowly boiled alive like lobsters in the tent exposed to the relentless sun. The voices of Berta and Zoe were the sweetest sound I ever heard. A little concerned about us, they had skied south to meet us. They led us home to Base.

We recovered quite swiftly, but the altiplano left its mark. When she was

---

6. The South Pole is at latitude 90 degrees and longitude 0 degrees.

very little, Rosita asked if a dog "had bitted Mama's toes." I told her Yes, a great, white, mad dog named Blizzard! My Rosita and my Juanito heard many stories when they were little, about that fearful dog and how it howled, and the transparent cattle of the invisible gauchos, and a river of ice eight thousand feet high called Nightingale, and how Cousin Juana drank a cup of tea standing on the bottom of the world under seven suns, and other fairy tales.

We were in for one severe shock when we reached Base at last. Teresa was pregnant. I must admit that my first response to the poor girl's big belly and sheepish look was anger—rage—fury. That one of us should have concealed anything, and such a thing, from the others! But Teresa had done nothing of the sort. Only those who had concealed from her what she most needed to know were to blame. Brought up by servants, with four years' schooling in a convent, and married at sixteen, the poor girl was still so ignorant at twenty years of age that she had thought it was "the cold weather" that made her miss her periods. Even this was not entirely stupid, for all of us on the Southern Journey had seen our periods change or stop altogether as we experienced increasing cold, hunger, and fatigue. Teresa's appetite had begun to draw general attention; and then she had begun, as she said pathetically, "to get fat." The others were worried at the thought of all the sledge-hauling she had done, but she flourished, and the only problem was her positively insatiable appetite. As well as could be determined from her shy references to her last night on the hacienda with her husband, the baby was due at just about the same time as the *Yelcho,* the twentieth of February. But we had not been back from the Southern Journey two weeks when, on February 14, she went into labor.

Several of us had borne children and had helped with deliveries, and anyhow most of what needs to be done is fairly self-evident; but a first labor can be long and trying, and we were all anxious, while Teresa was frightened out of her wits. She kept calling for her José till she was as hoarse as a skua. Zoe lost all patience at last and said, "By God, Teresa, if you say 'José!' once more I hope you have a penguin!" But what she had, after twenty long hours, was a pretty little red-faced girl.

Many were the suggestions for that child's name from her eight proud midwife-aunts: Polita, Penguina, McMurdo, Victoria.... But Teresa announced, after she had had a good sleep and a large serving of pemmican, "I shall name her Rosa—Rosa del Sur," Rose of the South. That night we drank the last two bottles of Veuve Clicquot (having finished the pisco at 88° 30' South) in toasts to our little Rose.

On the nineteenth of February, a day early, my Juana came down into Buenos Aires in a hurry. "The ship," she said, "the ship has come," and she burst into tears—she who had never wept in all our weeks of pain and weariness on the long haul.

Of the return voyage there is nothing to tell. We came back safe.

In 1912 all the world learned that the brave Norwegian Amundsen[7] had reached the South Pole; and then, much later, came the accounts of how Captain Scott and his men had come there after him, but did not come home again.

Just this year, Juana and I wrote to the captain of the *Yelcho,* for the newspapers have been full of the story of his gallant dash to rescue Sir Ernest

---

7. Roald Amundsen (1872–1928), Norwegian explorer, first man to reach the South Pole.

Shackleton's men from Elephant Island, and we wished to congratulate him, and once more to thank him. Never one word has he breathed of our secret. He is a man of honor, Luis Pardo.

   I add this last note in 1929. Over the years we have lost touch with one another. It is very difficult for women to meet, when they live so far apart as we do. Since Juana died, I have seen none of my old sledge-mates, though sometimes we write. Our little Rosa del Sur died of the scarlet fever when she was five years old. Teresa had many other children. Carlota took the veil[8] in Santiago ten years ago. We are old women now, with old husbands, and grown children, and grandchildren who might some day like to read about the Expedition. Even if they are rather ashamed of having such a crazy grandmother, they may enjoy sharing in the secret. But they must not let Mr. Amundsen know! He would be terribly embarrassed and disappointed. There is no need for him or anyone else outside the family to know. We left no footprints, even.

1982

She Unnames Them

   Most of them accepted namelessness with the perfect indifference with which they had so long accepted and ignored their names. Whales and dolphins, seals and sea otters consented with particular grace and alacrity, sliding into anonymity as into their element. A faction of yaks, however, protested. They said that "yak" sounded right, and that almost everyone who knew they existed called them that. Unlike the ubiquitous creatures such as rats and fleas, who had been called by hundreds or thousands of different names since Babel, the yaks could truly say, they said, that they had a *name*. They discussed the matter all summer. The councils of the elderly females finally agreed that though the name might be useful to others it was so redundant from the yak point of view that they never spoke it themselves and hence might as well dispense with it. After they presented the argument in this light to their bulls, a full consensus was delayed only by the onset of severe early blizzards. Soon after the beginning of the thaw, their agreement was reached and the designation "yak" was returned to the donor.

   Among the domestic animals, few horses had cared what anybody called them since the failure of Dean Swift's[1] attempt to name them from their own vocabulary. Cattle, sheep, swine, asses, mules, and goats, along with chickens, geese, and turkeys, all agreed enthusiastically to give their names back to the people to whom—as they put it—they belonged.

   A couple of problems did come up with pets. The cats, of course, steadfastly denied ever having had any name other than those self-given, unspoken, ineffably personal names which, as the poet named Eliot[2] said, they spend long hours daily contemplating—though none of the contemplators

---

8. I.e., became a nun.
1. The last section of *Gulliver's Travels* (1726) by Jonathan Swift (1667–1745), dean of St. Patrick's, Dublin, describes the country and language of the Houyhnhnms, who were rational horses.
2. T. S. Eliot, in (1888–1965) "The Naming of Cats" (1939).

has ever admitted that what they contemplate is their names and some onlookers have wondered if the object of that meditative gaze might not in fact be the Perfect, or Platonic, Mouse.[3] In any case, it is a moot point now. It was with the dogs, and with some parrots, lovebirds, ravens, and mynahs, that the trouble arose. These verbally talented individuals insisted that their names were important to them, and flatly refused to part with them. But as soon as they understood that the issue was precisely one of individual choice, and that anybody who wanted to be called Rover, or Froufrou, or Polly, or even Birdie in the personal sense, was perfectly free to do so, not one of them had the least objection to parting with the lowercase (or, as regards German creatures, uppercase) generic appellations "poodle," "parrot," "dog," or "bird," and all the Linnaean[4] qualifiers that had trailed along behind them for two hundred years like tin cans tied to a tail.

The insects parted with their names in vast clouds and swarms of ephemeral[5] syllables buzzing and stinging and humming and flitting and crawling and tunneling away.

As for the fish of the sea, their names dispersed from them in silence throughout the oceans like faint, dark blurs of cuttlefish ink, and drifted off on the currents without a trace.

None were left now to unname, and yet how close I felt to them when I saw one of them swim or fly or trot or crawl across my way or over my skin, or stalk me in the night, or go along beside me for a while in the day. They seemed far closer than when their names had stood between myself and them like a clear barrier: so close that my fear of them and their fear of me became one same fear. And the attraction that many of us felt, the desire to smell one another's smells, feel or rub or caress one another's scales or skin or feathers or fur, taste one another's blood or flesh, keep one another warm—that attraction was now all one with the fear, and the hunter could not be told from the hunted, nor the eater from the food.

This was more or less the effect I had been after. It was somewhat more powerful than I had anticipated, but I could not now, in all conscience, make an exception for myself. I resolutely put anxiety away, went to Adam,[6] and said, "You and your father lent me this—gave it to me, actually. It's been really useful, but it doesn't exactly seem to fit very well lately. But thanks very much! It's really been very useful."

It is hard to give back a gift without sounding peevish or ungrateful, and I did not want to leave him with that impression of me. He was not paying much attention, as it happened, and said only, "Put it down over there, O.K.?" and went on with what he was doing.

One of my reasons for doing what I did was that talk was getting us nowhere, but all the same I felt a little let down. I had been prepared to defend my decision. And I thought that perhaps when he did notice he might be upset and want to talk. I put some things away and fiddled around a little,

---

3. The Greek philosopher Plato (ca. 427–ca. 327 B.C.E.) argued that there exist ideal forms or archetypes of all material things (these perfect Ideas guarantee the existence of the phenomenal world).
4. The Swiss botanist Karl Linnaeus (1701–1778) devised the modern system of binomial scientific nomenclature for plants and animals.
5. Existing only for a day. *Ephemera* is also the name of one family of insects.
6. In Genesis 2.19, God brings all the beasts to Adam for naming; in Genesis 3.20, shortly before their expulsion from the Garden of Eden, Adam gives his wife the name Eve.

but he continued to do what he was doing and to take no notice of anything else. At last I said, "Well, goodbye, dear. I hope the garden key turns up."

He was fitting parts together, and said, without looking around, "O.K., fine, dear. When's dinner?"

"I'm not sure," I said. "I'm going now. With the—" I hesitated, and finally said, "With them, you know," and went on out. In fact, I had only just then realized how hard it would have been to explain myself. I could not chatter away as I used to do, taking it all for granted. My words now must be as slow, as new, as single, as tentative as the steps I took going down the path away from the house, between the dark-branched, tall dancers motionless against the winter shining.

1985

PAULE MARSHALL
b. 1929

Taken together, *Brown Girl, Brownstones* (1959), *Soul Clap Hands and Sing* (1961), *The Chosen Place, the Timeless People* (1969), *Praisesong for the Widow* (1983), *Reema and Other Short Stories* (1983), *Daughters* (1991) and *The Fisher King* (2000) constitute Paule Marshall's lyrical story about the hybridity of American culture and in particular her appreciation of the enriching traditions possessed by people from African and Caribbean backgrounds. Whether her setting is New York City, British Guiana, Brazil, Grenada, or Barbados, her characters experience the competing values, linguistic practices, spiritual ties, and social mores of mixed ancestries that enable Marshall to examine not only the personal toll histories of colonization take but also paradoxically the intertwined heritages they generate.

The daughter of emigrants from Barbados, West Indies, Marshall grew up in Brooklyn, New York, and educated first at Hunter, then at Brooklyn College. During the 1950s, she worked as a librarian and as the only female staff member of *Our World*, a black magazine. She currently holds a chair in creative writing at New York University. Although her fiction has been shaped by her early, extensive reading in the works of Thomas Mann, Joseph Conrad, Ralph Ellison, and James Baldwin, the essay printed here makes clear how indebted she remains to the verbal creativity she encountered amid the "ordinary housewives" who chatted daily in what she calls "the wordshop" of her mother's kitchen.

Poets in the Kitchen

Some years ago, when I was teaching a graduate seminar in fiction at Columbia University, a well known male novelist visited my class to speak on his development as a writer. In discussing his formative years, he didn't realize it but he seriously endangered his life by remarking that women writers are luckier than those of his sex because they usually spend so much time as children around their mothers and their mothers' friends in the kitchen.

What did he say that for? The women students immediately forgot about being in awe of him and began readying their attack for the question and answer period later on. Even I bristled. There again was that awful image of women locked away from the world in the kitchen with only each other to talk to, and their daughters locked in with them.

But my guest wasn't really being sexist or trying to be provocative or even spoiling for a fight. What he meant—when he got around to explaining himself more fully—was that, given the way children are (or were) raised in our society, with little girls kept closer to home and their mothers, the women writer stands a better chance of being exposed, while growing up, to the kind of talk that goes on among women, more often than not in the kitchen; and that this experience gives her an edge over her male counterpart by instilling in her an appreciation for ordinary speech.

It was clear that my guest lecturer attached great importance to this, which is understandable. Common speech and the plain, workaday words that make it up are, after all, the stock in trade of some of the best fiction writers. They are the principal means by which characters in a novel or story reveal themselves and give voice sometimes to profound feelings and complex ideas about themselves and the world. Perhaps the proper measure of a writer's talent is skill in rendering everyday speech—when it is appropriate to the story—as well as the ability to tap, to exploit, the beauty, poetry and wisdom it often contains.

"If you say what's on your mind in the language that comes to you from your parents and your street and your friends you'll probably say something beautiful." Grace Paley[1] tells this, she says, to her students at the beginning of every writing course.

It's all a matter of exposure and a training of the ear for the would-be writer in those early years of apprenticeship. And, according to my guest lecturer, this training, the best of it, often takes place in as unglamorous a setting as the kitchen.

He didn't know it, but he was essentially describing my experience as a little girl. I grew up among poets. Now they didn't look like poets—whatever that breed is supposed to look like. Nothing about them suggested that poetry was their calling. They were just a group of ordinary housewives and mothers, my mother included, who dressed in a way (shapeless housedresses, dowdy felt hats and long, dark, solemn coats) that made it impossible for me to imagine they had ever been young.

Nor did they do what poets were supposed to do—spend their days in an attic room writing verses. They never put pen to paper except to write occasionally to their relatives in Barbados. "I take my pen in hand hoping these few lines will find you in health as they leave me fair for the time being," was the way their letters invariably began. Rather, their day was spent "scrubbing floor," as they described the work they did.

Several mornings a week these unknown bards would put an apron and a pair of old house shoes in a shopping bag and take the train or streetcar from our section of Brooklyn out to Flatbush.[2] There, those who didn't have steady jobs would wait on certain designated corners for the white housewives in

---

1. American poet and short story writer (b. 1922); see above, p. 852.
2. Another section of Brooklyn.

the neighborhood to come along and bargain with them over pay for a day's work cleaning their houses. This was the ritual even in the winter.

Later, armed with the few dollars they had earned, which in their vocabulary became "a few raw-mouth pennies," they made their way back to our neighborhood, where they would sometimes stop off to have a cup of tea or cocoa together before going home to cook dinner for their husbands and children.

The basement kitchen of the brownstone house where my family lived was the usual gathering place. Once inside the warm safety of its walls the women threw off the drab coats and hats, seated themselves at the large center table, drank their cups of tea or cocoa, and talked. While my sister and I sat at a smaller table over in a corner doing our homework, they talked—endlessly, passionately, poetically, and with impressive range. No subject was beyond them. True, they would indulge in the usual gossip: whose husband was running with whom, whose daughter looked slightly "in the way" (pregnant) under her bridal gown as she walked down the aisle. That sort of thing. But they also tackled the great issues of the time. They were always, for example, discussing the state of the economy. It was the mid and late 30's then, and the aftershock of the Depression, with its soup lines and suicides on Wall Street, was still being felt.

Some people, they declared, didn't know how to deal with adversity. They didn't know that you had to "tie up your belly" (hold in the pain, that is) when things got rough and go on with life. They took their image from the bellyband that is tied around the stomach of a newborn baby to keep the navel pressed in.

They talked politics. Roosevelt was their hero. He had come along and rescued the country with relief and jobs, and in gratitude they christened their sons Franklin and Delano and hoped they would live up to the names.

If F.D.R. was their hero, Marcus Garvey[3] was their God. The name of the fiery, Jamaican-born black nationalist of the 20's was constantly invoked around the table. For he had been their leader when they first came to the United States from the West Indies shortly after World War I. They had contributed to his organization, the United Negro Improvement Association (UNIA), out of their meager salaries, bought shares in his ill-fated Black Star Shipping Line, and at the height of the movement they had marched as members of his "nurses' brigade" in their white uniforms up Seventh Avenue in Harlem during the great Garvey Day parades. Garvey: He lived on through the power of their memories.

And their talk was of war and rumors of wars. They raged against World War II when it broke out in Europe, blaming it on the politicians. "It's these politicians. They're the ones always starting up all this lot of war. But what they care? It's the poor people got to suffer and mothers with their sons." If it was *their* sons, they swore they would keep them out of the Army by giving them soap to eat each day to make their hearts sound defective. Hitler? He was for them "the devil incarnate."

Then there was home. They reminisced often and at length about home. The old country. Barbados—or Bimshire, as they affectionately called it. The

---

3. Leader of the Back to Africa movement (1887–1940).

little Caribbean island in the sun they loved but had to leave. "Poor—poor but sweet" was the way they remembered it.

And naturally they discussed their adopted home. America came in for both good and bad marks. They lashed out at it for the racism they encountered. They took to task some of the people they worked for, especially those who gave them only a hard-boiled egg and a few spoonfuls of cottage cheese for lunch. "As if anybody can scrub floor on an egg and some cheese that don't have no taste to it!"

Yet although they caught H in "this man country," as they called America, it was nonetheless a place where "you could at least see your way to make a dollar." That much they acknowledged. They might even one day accumulate enough dollars, with both them and their husbands working, to buy the brownstone houses which, like my family, they were only leasing at that period. This was their consuming ambition: to "buy house" and to see the children through.

There was no way for me to understand it at the time, but the talk that filled the kitchen those afternoons was highly functional. It served as therapy, the cheapest kind available to my mother and her friends. Not only did it help them recover from the long wait on the corner that morning and the bargaining over their labor, it restored them to a sense of themselves and reaffirmed their self-worth. Through language they were able to overcome the humiliations of the work-day.

But more than therapy, that freewheeling, wide-ranging, exuberant talk functioned as an outlet for the tremendous creative energy they possessed. They were women in whom the need for self-expression was strong, and since language was the only vehicle readily available to them they made of it an art form that—in keeping with the African tradition in which art and life are one—was an integral part of their lives.

And their talk was a refuge. They never really ceased being baffled and overwhelmed by America—its vastness, complexity and power. Its strange customs and laws. At a level beyond words they remained fearful and in awe. Their uneasiness and fear were even reflected in their attitude toward the children they had given birth to in this country. They referred to those like myself, the little Brooklyn-born Bajans (Barbadians), as "these New York children" and complained that they couldn't discipline us properly because of the laws here. "You can't beat these children as you would like, you know, because the authorities in this place will dash you in jail for them. After all, these is New York children." Not only were we different, American, we had, as they saw it, escaped their ultimate authority.

Confronted therefore by a world they could not encompass, which even limited their rights as parents, and at the same time finding themselves permanently separated from the world they had known, they took refuge in language. "Language is the only homeland," Czeslaw Milosz, the emigré Polish writer and Nobel Laureate, has said. This is what it became for the women at the kitchen table.

It served another purpose also, I suspect. My mother and her friends were after all the female counterpart of Ralph Ellison's invisible man.[4] Indeed,

---

4. The novel *Invisible Man* (1952) is the best-known work by the black American writer Ellison (1914–1994).

you might say they suffered a triple invisibility, being black, female and foreigners. They really didn't count in American society except as a source of cheap labor. But given the kind of women they were, they couldn't tolerate the fact of their invisibility, their powerlessness. And they fought back, using the only weapon at their command: the spoken word.

Those late afternoon conversations on a wide range of topics were a way for them to feel they exercised some measure of control over their lives and the events that shaped them. "Soully-gal, talk yuh talk!" they were always exhorting each other. "In this man world you got to take yuh mouth and make a gun!" They were in control, if only verbally and if only for the two hours or so that they remained in our house.

For me, sitting over in the corner, being seen but not heard, which was the rule for children in those days, it wasn't only what the women talked about—the content—but the way they put things—their style. The insight, irony, wit and humor they brought to their stories and discussions and their poet's inventiveness and daring with language—which of course I could only sense but not define back then.

They had taken the standard English taught them in the primary schools of Barbados and transformed it into an idiom, an instrument that more adequately described them—changing around the syntax and imposing their own rhythm and accent so that the sentences were more pleasing to their ears. They added the few African sounds and words that had survived, such as the derisive suck-teeth sound and the word "yam," meaning to eat. And to make it more vivid, more in keeping with their expressive quality, they brought to bear a raft of metaphors, parables, Biblical quotations, sayings and the like:

"The sea ain' got no back door," they would say, meaning that it wasn't like a house where if there was a fire you could run out the back. Meaning that it was not to be trifled with. And meaning perhaps in a larger sense that man should treat all of nature with caution and respect.

"I has read hell by heart and called every generation blessed!" They sometimes went in for hyperbole.

A woman expecting a baby was never said to be pregnant. They never used that word. Rather, she was "in the way" or, better yet, "tumbling big." "Guess who I butt up on in the market the other day tumbling big again!"

And a woman with a reputation of being too free with her sexual favors was known in their book as a "thoroughfare"—the sense of men like a steady stream of cars moving up and down the road of her life. Or she might be dubbed "a free-bee," which was my favorite of the two. I liked the image it conjured up of a woman scandalous perhaps but independent, who flitted from one flower to another in a garden of male beauties, sampling their nectar, taking her pleasure at will, the roles reversed.

And nothing, no matter how beautiful, was ever described as simply beautiful. It was always "beautiful-ugly": the beautiful-ugly dress, the beautiful-ugly house, the beautiful-ugly car. Why the word "ugly," I used to wonder, when the thing they were referring to was beautiful, and they knew it. Why the antonym, the contradiction, the linking of opposites? It used to puzzle me greatly as a child.

There is the theory in linguistics which states that the idiom of a people, the way they use language, reflects not only the most fundamental views they hold of themselves and the world but their very conception of reality. Perhaps in using the term "beautiful-ugly" to describe nearly everything, my mother and her friends were expressing what they believed to be a fundamental dualism in life: the idea that a thing is at the same time its opposite, and that these opposites, these contradictions make up the whole. But theirs was not a Manichaean brand of dualism that sees matter, flesh, the body, as inherently evil, because they constantly addressed each other as "soully-gal"—soul: spirit; gal: the body, flesh, the visible self. And it was clear from their tone that they gave one as much weight and importance as the other. They had never heard of the mind/body split.

As for God, they summed up His essential attitude in a phrase. "God," they would say, "don't love ugly and He ain' stuck on pretty."

Using everyday speech, the simple commonplace words—but always with imagination and skill—they gave voice to the most complex ideas. Flannery O'Connor[5] would have approved of how they made ordinary language work, as she put it, "double-time," stretching, shading, deepening its meaning. Like Joseph Conrad[6] they were always trying to infuse new life in the "old words worn thin . . . by . . . careless usage." And the goals of their oral art were the same as his: "to make you hear, to make you feel . . . to make you *see*." This was their guiding esthetic.

By the time I was 8 or 9, I graduated from the corner of the kitchen to the neighborhood library, and thus from the spoken to the written word. The Macon Street Branch of the Brooklyn Public Library was an imposing half block long edifice of heavy gray masonry, with glass-paneled doors at the front and two tall metal torches symbolizing the light that comes of learning flanking the wide steps outside.

The inside was just as impressive. More steps—of pale marble with gleaming brass railings at the center and sides—led up to the circulation desk, and a great pendulum clock gazed down from the balcony stacks that faced the entrance. Usually stationed at the top of the steps like the guards outside Buckingham Palace[7] was the custodian, a stern-faced West Indian type who for years, until I was old enough to obtain an adult card, would immediately shoo me with one hand into the Children's Room and with the other threaten me into silence, a finger to his lips. You would have thought he was the chief librarian and not just someone whose job it was to keep the brass polished and the clock wound. I put him in a story called "Barbados" years later and had terrible things happen to him at the end.

I sheltered from the storm of adolescence in the Macon Street library, reading voraciously, indiscriminately, everything from Jane Austen to Zane Grey,[8] but with a special passion for the long, full-blown, richly detailed 18th- and 19th-century picaresque tales: "Tom Jones," "Great Expectations," "Vanity Fair."[9]

---

5. American fiction writer (1925–1964; see above, p. 892), who wrote that the aim of the short story writer is "to make the concrete work double time" (*Mystery and Manners*).
6. Polish-born writer of fiction (1857–1924); the quotation is from the preface to *The Nigger of the "Narcissus"* (1897).
7. The London residence of British sovereigns; its guards are the famous "Beefeaters."
8. American writer of westerns (1875–1939). Austen (1775–1817), English novelist; see Vol. 1, p. 459.
9. Novels by the English authors Henry Fielding (1707–1754 published 1749), Charles Dickens (1812–1870; 1860–61), and William Thackeray (1811–1863; 1847–48), respectively.

But although I loved nearly everything I read and would enter fully into the lives of the characters—indeed, would cease being myself and become them—I sensed a lack after a time. Something I couldn't quite define was missing. And then one day, browsing in the poetry section, I came across a book by someone called Paul Laurence Dunbar,[1] and opening it I found the photograph of a wistful, sad-eyed poet who to my surprise was black. I turned to a poem at random. "Little brown-baby wif spa'klin' / eyes / Come to yo' pappy an' set on his knee." Although I had a little difficulty at first with the words in dialect, the poem spoke to me as nothing I had read before of the closeness, the special relationship I had had with my father, who by then had become an ardent believer in Father Divine[2] and gone to live in Father's "kingdom" in Harlem. Reading it helped to ease somewhat the tight knot of sorrow and longing I carried around in my chest that refused to go away. I read another poem. " 'Lias! 'Lias! Bless de Lawd! / Don' you know de day's / erbroad? / Ef you don't get up, you scamp / Dey'll be trouble in dis camp." I laughed. It reminded me of the way my mother sometimes yelled at my sister and me to get out of bed in the mornings.

And another: "Seen my lady home las' night / Jump back, honey, jump back. / Hel' huh han' an' sque'z it tight . . ." About love between a black man and a black woman. I had never seen that written about before and it roused in me all kinds of delicious feelings and hopes.

And I began to search then for books and stories and poems about "The Race" (as it was put back then), about my people. While not abandoning Thackeray, Fielding, Dickens and the others, I started asking the reference librarian, who was white, for books by Negro writers, although I must admit I did so at first with a feeling of shame—the shame I and many others used to experience in those days whenever the word "Negro" or "colored" came up.

No grade school literature teacher of mine had ever mentioned Dunbar or James Weldon Johnson or Langston Hughes. I didn't know that Zora Neale Hurston existed and was busy writing and being published during those years. Nor was I made aware of people like Frederick Douglass and Harriet Tubman[3]—their spirit and example—or the great 19th-century abolitionist and feminist Sojourner Truth. There wasn't even Negro History Week when I attended P.S. 35 on Decatur Street!

What I needed, what all the kids—West Indian and native black American alike—with whom I grew up needed, was an equivalent of the Jewish shul,[4] someplace where we could go after school—the schools that were short-changing us—and read works by those like ourselves and learn about our history.

It was around that time that I began harboring the dangerous thought of someday trying to write myself. Perhaps a poem about an apple tree, although I had never seen one. Or the story of a girl who could magically transplant herself to wherever she wanted to be in the world—such as Father Divine's

---

1. American poet (1872–1906).
2. Born George Baker (1880?–1965), he became the most popular Harlem religious leader of the 1930s, gaining much wealth and many followers of his cultlike Peace Mission movement.
3. A fugitive slave (1820?–1913), who rescued many other slaves. Johnson (1871–1938), lyricist, writer, and civil rights activist who became secretary of the NAACP. Hughes (1902–1967), writer of poetry, fiction, and plays. Hurston (1891–1960), writer and anthropologist; see above, p. 347. Douglass (1817–1896), orator, author, abolitionist, and supporter of women's rights.
4. School, synagogue (Yiddish).

kingdom in Harlem. Dunbar—his dark, eloquent face, his large volume of poems—permitted me to dream that I might someday write, and with something of the power with words my mother and her friends possessed.

When people at readings and writers' conferences ask me who my major influences were, they are sometimes a little disappointed when I don't immediately name the usual literary giants. True, I am indebted to those writers, white and black, whom I read during my formative years and still read for instruction and pleasure. But they were preceded in my life by another set of giants whom I always acknowledge before all others: the group of women around the table long ago. They taught me my first lessons in the narrative art. They trained my ear. They set a standard of excellence. This is why the best of my work must be attributed to them; it stands as testimony to the rich legacy of language and culture they so freely passed on to me in the wordshop of the kitchen.

1983

ADRIENNE RICH
b. 1929

"I am an instrument," wrote Adrienne Rich in her poem "Planetarium" (1968), "in the shape / of a woman trying to translate pulsations / into images for the relief of the body / and the reconstruction of the mind." How she began to change herself into such an "instrument" is the subject of her famous autobiographical essay, "When We Dead Awaken: Writing as Re-Vision" (1972, 1976, 1978). Her life—first as "faculty wife" and mother, then as civil rights and antiwar activist, then as lesbian in the women's liberation movement, teacher and lecturer—and her numerous books all demonstrate that, as the critic David Kalstone has said, work, for her, "is a jagged present, always pitched toward the future and change." It is this commitment to change, as much as the example of her life, that has made her a crucial figure in contemporary feminist experience.

"From where does your strength come, you Southern Jew? / split at the root, raised in a castle of air?" Rich asked in her poem "Sources" (1983). She was born in Baltimore on May 16, 1929, the elder of two sisters; the family was intellectual and well-off ("a castle of air"), but aware of being apart as Jews. She began to write carefully crafted poetry at an early age, above all for her taskmaster father. Her mother, who had studied to be a musician, gave over her life to her husband and children. In 1951 Rich graduated from Radcliffe, "where I did not see a woman teacher for four years," and where, as she tells us in "When We Dead Awaken," she studied exclusively the work of male poets. She also published her first book, *A Change of World* (1951) in the prestigious Yale Younger Poets series. The volume was introduced by the British poet W. H. Auden, who admired her command of diction and meter: the poems, he says, "are neatly and modestly dressed, speak quietly but do not mumble, respect their elders but are not cowed by them, and do not tell fibs." Four years later, when she published *The Diamond Cutters* (1955), the poet Randall Jarrell observed that "the poet whom we see behind" the poems "cannot help seeming to us a sort of princess in a fairy tale."

Meanwhile, "determined to have a 'full' woman's life," Rich married Alfred Conrad, an economist at Harvard, in 1953, and had three sons before she was thirty—"a radicalizing experience," as she later called it. Of this period she has said (in *Of Woman Born*, 1976), "I *knew* I had to remake my life; I did not then understand that we—the women of that academic community—as in so many middle-class communities of the period—were expected to fill both the part of the Victorian Lady of Leisure, the Angel in the House, and also of the Victorian cook, scullery maid, laundress, governess, and nurse." In "When We Dead Awaken," she describes the long struggle to confront, for the first time, her condition as a woman, which resulted in "Snapshots of a Daughter-in-Law," the title poem of her next book, eight difficult years later. The "modest princess," as Jarrell had defined her, was beginning to change.

In 1966, the Conrads moved to New York, where Alfred had taken a post at City College. There they both became increasingly involved in resistance activities against the Vietnam War. Rich taught in the SEEK Program for disadvantaged young people, and her poems as well as her view of her audience changed. Her vivid political concerns were the subject of many of the verses in *Leaflets* (1969) and *The Will to Change* (1971), while transformations in her poetic style reflected the continuing evolution of her political attitudes. Writing with a new urgency, she broke away from the tight verse forms and neat metrics that had marked much of her early work and began to produce poems that were characterized by a kind of improvisational intensity. As Kalstone usefully reminds us, Rich has also—ever since "Snapshots"—been dating each of her poems, "like entries in a journal where feelings are subject to continual revision." In this respect the title of her 1971 volume is significant: whereas she had called her first book *A Change of World*, as if dependent on changes outside of herself, now she took her title from the poet Charles Olson's line, "What does not change / is the will to change," for "the moment of change," as she wrote, "is the only poem." Rich's life was changing, too: in 1970 she left her marriage, "to do something very common, in my own way" ("A Valediction Forbidding Mourning"). Later that year, Alfred Conrad committed suicide.

In *Diving into the Wreck* (1973), Rich continued her explorations into both the exterior world and the interior self, as the title poem makes clear. The book also contains a poem called "The Phenomenology of Anger," which articulates the way Rich has worked, in this and previous poems, to use the anger aroused by her political and cultural concerns for positive ends: "anger," as she told her friends the critics Barbara Charlesworth Gelpi and Albert Gelpi, "can be a kind of genius if it's acted on." *Diving into the Wreck* won the National Book Award in 1974; Rich rejected the prize as an individual but accepted it, in a statement written with Audre Lorde and Alice Walker, two other nominees, in the name of all women "whose voices have been silenced." That same year, she became professor of English at City College and began the research for *Of Woman Born: Motherhood as Experience and Institution*. This prose work, published in 1976, employs personal journals, anthropology, political and medical history as a background for meditation on a subject that, she said, she had not chosen: "it had, long ago, chosen me." The book examines the experience of motherhood, along with the myths that have been projected on that experience.

In 1977, Rich published *Twenty-one Love Poems*, a verse sequence whose form recalls that of Elizabethan sonnet cycles in which male poets wrote hyperbolically of their lady-loves: these poems, however, record and explore a lesbian relationship. But the term *lesbian*, for Rich, was "nothing so simple and dismissible as the fact that two women might go to bed together," as she wrote in "It Is the Lesbian in Us" (1976). Lesbianism, for her,

> was a sense of desiring oneself, choosing oneself; it was also a primary intensity between women, an intensity which in the world at large was trivialized, caricatured, or invested with evil.

Characteristically, for Rich, the points of view expressed in the *Love Poems* and in this essay are significantly interrelated. For as she was to note in "The Transgressor Mother," a discussion of Minnie Bruce Pratt's prize-winning *Crime Against Nature* (1989) that she included in *What Is Found There: Notebooks on Poetry and Politics* (2003, 1993), the energy of much lesbian erotic poetry, like the energy she finds in Pratt's work, "derives not only from a female sensuality only now beginning to find its way into poetry, but from the inseparability of sensuality from politics."

In the late 1970s, Rich taught for a time at Douglass College in New Jersey. Then for several years she left the academy and moved to western Massachusetts, where with Michelle Cliff she edited the lesbian-feminist journal *Sinister Wisdom*. In 1984 she came to California as a visiting distinguished professor at San Jose State University, and in 1986 she accepted a position as professor of English at Stanford University, where she taught until 1993. In this period, too, moved into comparatively new poetic styles and subjects. In the 1980s, her impassioned and sometimes severe commitment to personal exploration and analysis compelled her—in *Sources* (1983) and other works—to re-examine both her complex relationships with her dead father and husband and what they represent of her Jewish heritage. In the 1990s, she produced what may be her most daring work to date, the ambitious long poem *An Atlas of the Difficult World* (1991), the title piece of an impressive collection, and this volume was followed by a series of other commandingly crafted works, among them *Dark Fields of the Republic* (1995), *Midnight Salvage* (1999), *Fox* (2001), and *The School Among the Ruins* (2004).

From *The Will to Change* (1971), *Diving into the Wreck* (1973), and *The Dream of a Common Language* (1978) onward, Rich has functioned as a sort of unofficial poet laureate of feminism's "second wave," tracing the interactions between past and present along with those between men and women, in (to use her own words) "a succession of brief, amazing movements / each one making possible the next." But in *An Atlas* she has in a sense transformed herself into the bard of her country, a woman who speaks *as* a woman but *for* the United States with prophetic sureness and intensity.

Specifically, the thirteen-part sequence that constitutes Rich's *Atlas* is a geography of America which, with passion, clarity, and uncanny detail, extends and expands the political, cultural, and intellectual explorations that were begun in the nineteenth century by the self-consciously American poet Walt Whitman, who is perhaps Rich's most crucial precursor here. Yet Rich's Whitmanesque cadences in this work bespeak not belatedness but a simultaneously proud and humble acquiescence in the task of personal as well as communal self-definition that ultimately brought Whitman himself to the battlefield of Gettysburg and the hospital wards of Washington during the Civil War, as well as to "When Lilacs Last in the Dooryard Bloom'd," his great elegy for Abraham Lincoln. "I am bent on fathoming what it means to love my country," Rich confesses, then persists in the intrepid stocktaking that empowers the famous catalogs of *Leaves of Grass*: "The history of this earth and the bones within it? / Soils and cities, promises made and mocked . . . Loyalties, symbols, murmers extinguished and echoing? . . . Minerals, traces, rumors I am made from, morsel, minuscule fibre, one woman / like and unlike so many, fooled as to her destiny, the scope of her task?"

Like Whitman, too, Rich has an evangelical need to speak not just *for* but *to* her readers. Part XIII ("Dedications") of *Atlas* offers some of the work's most poignant passages, reminiscent of Whitman's confident "I stop somewhere waiting for you": "I know you are reading this poem / late, before leaving your office," notes Rich, adding in a series of Whitmanesque variations, "I know you are reading this poem / standing up in a bookstore . . . I know you are reading this poem / in a room where too much has happened . . . I know you are reading this poem . . . torn between bitterness and hope / turning back once again to the task you cannot refuse."

"The task you cannot refuse," Rich writes in "Two Arts," the aesthetic statement by which she herself defines her project, that when you "Raise it up there—" raise up the task of vision or revision—it will "loom, the gaunt original thing / gristle and membrane of your life . . . but you have to raise it up there, you / have a brutal thing to do." Worse, she adds in "Final Notations," her book's powerful concluding poem (as much a meditation on death as on art and politics), "it will not be simple, it will not be long / it will take little time, it will take all your thought." Yet *it*—the work, the living and the dying—must be done, must "become your will."

For more than half a century, since the publication of her first collection in 1951, such an impressive and absorbing task has been wholly Adrienne Rich's will. Though she speaks for and from what she defines as a marginalized perspective—as an outsider and dissenter within the society she so urgently seeks to change—her passion and eloquence have won her many honors, including a National Book Award (1974), a MacArthur Fellowship (1994), the first Ruth Lilly Prize awarded by the Modern Poetry Association (1986), and the Lannan Foundation Lifetime Achievement Award (1999).

Aunt Jennifer's Tigers

Aunt Jennifer's tigers prance across a screen,
Bright topaz denizens of a world of green.
They do not fear the men beneath the tree;
They pace in sleek chivalric certainty.

5   Aunt Jennifer's fingers fluttering through her wool
Find even the ivory needle hard to pull.
The massive weight of Uncle's wedding band
Sits heavily upon Aunt Jennifer's hand.

When Aunt is dead, her terrified hands will lie
10 Still ringed with ordeals she was mastered by.
The tigers in the panel that she made
Will go on prancing, proud and unafraid.

1951

Snapshots of a Daughter-in-Law

1

You, once a belle in Shreveport,
with henna-colored hair, skin like a peachbud,
still have your dresses copied from that time,
and play a Chopin prelude
5 called by Cortot: *"Delicious recollections
float like perfume through the memory."*[1]

---

1. A remark made by Alfred Cortot (1877–1962), a well-known French pianist, in his *Chopin: 24 Preludes* (1930); he is referring specifically to Chopin's Prelude No. 7, Andantino, A Major. Frédéric Chopin (1810–1849), Polish composer and pianist who settled in Paris in 1831.

Your mind now, moldering like wedding-cake,
heavy with useless experience, rich
with suspicion, rumor, fantasy,
crumbling to pieces under the knife-edge
of mere fact. In the prime of your life.

Nervy, glowering, your daughter
wipes the teaspoons, grows another way.

2

Banging the coffee-pot into the sink
she hears the angels chiding, and looks out
past the raked gardens to the sloppy sky.
Only a week since They said: *Have no patience.*

The next time it was: *Be insatiable.*
Then: *Save yourself; others you cannot save,*
Sometimes she's let the tapstream scald her arm,
a match burn to her thumbnail,

or held her hand above the kettle's snout
right in the woolly steam. They are probably angels,
since nothing hurts her anymore, except
each morning's grit blowing into her eyes.

3

A thinking woman sleeps with monsters.
The beak that grips her, she becomes. And Nature,
that sprung-lidded, still commodious
steamer-trunk of *tempora* and *mores*[2]
gets stuffed with it all: the mildewed orange-flowers,
the female pills,[3] the terrible breasts
of Boadicea[4] beneath flat foxes' heads and orchids.

Two handsome women, gripped in argument,
each proud, acute, subtle, I hear scream
across the cut glass and majolica
like Furies[5] cornered from their prey:
The argument *ad feminam*,[6] all the old knives
that have rusted in my back, I drive in yours,
ma semblable, ma soeur![7]

---

2. Times and customs (Latin an allusion); to the Roman orator Cicero's famous phrase (63 B.C.E.) bewailing the moral degeneracy of his time, "O tempora! o mores!"
3. Remedies for menstrual pain.
4. British queen (d. ca. 60 C.E.) who led her people in a large though ultimately unsuccessful revolt against Roman rule.
5. Greek female spirits of vengeance.
6. Feminine version of the phrase *ad hominem* (against the man; Latin), referring to an argument directed not to reason but to personal prejudices and emotions.
7. Like me, my sister (French). Adapted from the last line of Charles Baudelaire's poem *Au Lecteur*, which addresses "Hypocrite lecteur!—mon semblable—mon frère!" (Hypocrite reader, like me, my brother).

4

40 Knowing themselves too well in one another:
their gifts no pure fruition, but a thorn,
the prick filed sharp against a hint of scorn . . .
Reading while waiting
for the iron to heat,
45 writing, *My Life had stood—a Loaded Gun*—[8]
in that Amherst[9] pantry while the jellies boil and scum,
or, more often,
iron-eyed and beaked and purposed as a bird,
dusting everything on the whatnot[1] every day of life.

5

50 *Dulce ridens, dulce loquens,*[2]
she shaves her legs until they gleam
like petrified mammoth-tusk.

6

When to her lute Corinna sings[3]
neither words nor music are her own;
55 only the long hair dipping
over her cheek, only the song
of silk against her knees
and these
adjusted in reflections of an eye.

60 Poised, trembling and unsatisfied, before
an unlocked door, that cage of cages,
tell us, you bird, you tragical machine—
is this *fertilisante douleur?*[4] Pinned down
by love, for you the only natural action,
65 are you edged more keen
to prise the secrets of the vault? has Nature shown
her household books to you, daughter-in-law,
that her sons never saw?

7

"To have in this uncertain world some stay
70 *which cannot be undermined, is*
of the utmost consequence."[5]

---

8. Emily Dickinson, *Complete Poems*, ed. T. H. Johnson, 1960, p. 369 [Rich's note]. This is the poem numbered 764 in the Franklin edition; see Vol. 1, p. 1061.
9. The town where Dickinson lived her entire life (1830–1886).
1. An open stand with shelves.
2. Sweetly laughing, sweetly speaking (Latin); an allusion to Horace's Ode 1.22 ("Integer vitae"; 23 B.C.E.), lines 23–24.
3. First line of a poem (1601) by Thomas Campion.
4. Fertilizing (or life-giving) sorrow (French).
5. From Mary Wollstonecraft, *Thoughts on the Education of Daughters,* London, 1787 [Rich's note]. Wollstonecraft (1759–1797) is best known for *A Vindication of the Rights of Woman*; see Vol. 1, p. 373.

                              Thus wrote
a woman, partly brave and partly good,
who fought with what she partly understood.
Few men about her would or could do more,
hence she was labeled harpy, shrew and whore.

                     8

"You all die at fifteen," said Diderot,[6]
and turn part legend, part convention.
Still, eyes inaccurately dream
behind closed windows blankening with steam.
Deliciously, all that we might have been,
all that we were—fire, tears,
wit, taste, martyred ambition—
stirs like the memory of refused adultery
the drained and flagging bosom of our middle years.

                     9

*Not that it is done well, but
that it is done at all?*[7] Yes, think
of the odds! or shrug them off forever.
This luxury of the precocious child,
Time's precious chronic invalid,—
would we, darlings, resign it if we could?
Our blight has been our sinecure:
mere talent was enough for us—
glitter in fragments and rough drafts.

Sigh no more, ladies.[8]
                   Time is male

and in his cups drinks to the fair.
Bemused by gallantry, we hear
our mediocrities over-praised,
indolence read as abnegation,
slattern thought styled intuition,
every lapse forgiven, our crime
only to cast too bold a shadow
or smash the mold straight off.

For that, solitary confinement,
tear gas, attrition shelling.
Few applicants for that honor.

---

6. "You all die at fifteen": "Vous mourez toutes a quinze ans," from the *Lettres à Sophie Volland*, quoted by Simone de Beauvoir in *Le Deuxième Sexe*, Vol. II, pp. 123–24 [Rich's note]. Denis Diderot (1713–1784), French philosopher, encyclopedist, playwright, and critic.
7. An allusion to Samuel Johnson's remark to James Boswell: "Sir, a woman's preaching is like a dog's walking on his hinder legs. It is not done well; but you are surprized to find it done at all" (Boswell's *Life of Johnson*, 1791).
8. From a song in Shakespeare's *Much Ado about Nothing* (2.3.56).

10

         Well,
  she's long about her coming, who must be
110 more merciless to herself than history.
  Her mind full to the wind, I see her plunge
  breasted and glancing through the currents,
  taking the light upon her
  at least as beautiful as any boy
115 or helicopter,[9]
       poised, still coming,

her fine blades making the air wince

  but her cargo
  no promise then:
120 delivered
  palpable
  ours.

1958–60   1963

"I Am in Danger—Sir—"[1]

"Half-cracked"[2] to Higginson, living,
afterward famous in garbled versions,
your hoard of dazzling scraps a battlefield,
now your old snood

5 mothballed at Harvard[3]
  and you in your variorum monument[4]
  equivocal to the end—
  who are you?

  Gardening the day-lily,
10 wiping the wine-glass stems,
  your thought pulsed on behind
  a forehead battered paper-thin,

---

9. "She comes down from the remoteness of ages, from Thebes, from Crete, from Chichén-Itzá; and she is also the totem set deep in the African jungle; she is a helicopter and she is a bird; and there is this, the greatest wonder of all: under her tinted hair the forest murmur becomes a thought, and words issue from her breasts" (Simone de Beauvoir, *The Second Sex*, trans. H. M. Parshley [New York, 1953], p. 729). [A translation of the passage from *Le Deuxième Sexe*, 2:574, cited in French by Rich.]

1. See the *Letters of Emily Dickinson*, T. H. Johnson, ed., Vol. II, p. 409 [Rich's note]. In an 1862 letter to the editor Thomas Wentworth Higginson (1823–1911), the American poet Dickinson (1830–1886) wrote, "You think my gait 'spasmodic'—I am in danger—Sir—You think me 'uncontrolled'—I have no Tribunal" (see Vol. 1, p. 1074.)

2. Higginson described Dickinson, in a letter, as "my partially cracked poetess at Amherst."

3. The Rare Books Library at Harvard has a collection of Dickinson manuscripts and memorabilia, including her snood (hairnet).

4. I.e., Thomas H. Johnson's three-volume *Poems of Emily Dickinson* (1955). A variorum edition contains all the variant readings of a text.

you, woman, masculine
in single-mindedness,
for whom the word was more
than a symptom—

a condition of being.
Till the air buzzing with spoiled language
sang in your ears
of Perjury

and in your half-cracked way you chose
silence for entertainment,
chose to have it out at last
on your own premises.

1964   1966

Diving into the Wreck

First having read the book of myths,
and loaded the camera,
and checked the edge of the knife-blade,
I put on
the body-armor of black rubber
the absurd flippers
the grave and awkward mask.
I am having to do this
not like Cousteau[1] with his
assiduous team
aboard the sun-flooded schooner
but here alone.

There is a ladder.
The ladder is always there
hanging innocently
close to the side of the schooner.
We know what it is for,
we who have used it.
Otherwise
it's a piece of maritime floss
some sundry equipment.

I go down.
Rung after rung and still
the oxygen immerses me
the blue light
the clear atoms
of our human air.
I go down.

---

1. Jacques Cousteau (1910–1997), French underwater explorer, author, and filmmaker.

            My flippers cripple me,
30   I crawl like an insect down the ladder
        and there is no one
        to tell me when the ocean
        will begin.

        First the air is blue and then
35   it is bluer and then green and then
        black I am blacking out and yet
        my mask is powerful
        it pumps my blood with power
        the sea is another story
40   the sea is not a question of power
        I have to learn alone
        to turn my body without force
        in the deep element.
        And now: it is easy to forget
45   what I came for
        among so many who have always
        lived here
        swaying their crenellated[2] fans
        between the reefs
50   and besides
        you breathe differently down here.

        I came to explore the wreck.
        The words are purposes.
        The words are maps.
55   I came to see the damage that was done
        and the treasures that prevail.
        I stroke the beam of my lamp
        slowly along the flank
        of something more permanent
60   than fish or weed

        the thing I came for:
        the wreck and not the story of the wreck
        the thing itself and not the myth

        the drowned face always staring
65   toward the sun
        the evidence of damage
        worn by salt and sway into this threadbare beauty
        the ribs of the disaster
        curving their assertion
70   among the tentative haunters.

        This is the place.
        And I am here, the mermaid whose dark hair
        streams black, the merman in his armored body
        We circle silently

2. Notched with rounded or scalloped projections.

75   about the wreck
we dive into the hold.
I am she: I am he

whose drowned face sleeps with open eyes
whose breasts still bear the stress
80   whose silver, copper, vermeil[3] cargo lies
obscurely inside barrels
half-wedged and left to rot
we are the half-destroyed instruments
that once held to a course
85   the water-eaten log
the fouled compass

We are, I am, you are
by cowardice or courage
the one who find our way
90   back to this scene
carrying a knife, a camera
a book of myths
in which
our names do not appear.

1972   1973

Power

Living   in the earth-deposits   of our history

Today a backhoe divulged   out of a crumbling flank of earth
one bottle   amber   perfect   a hundred-year-old
cure for fever   or melancholy   a tonic
5   for living on this earth   in the winters of this climate

Today I was reading about Marie Curie:[1]
she must have known she suffered   from radiation sickness
her body bombarded for years   by the element
she had purified
10   It seems she denied to the end
the source of the cataracts on her eyes
the cracked and suppurating skin   of her finger-ends
till she could no longer hold   a test-tube or a pencil

She died   a famous woman   denying
15   her wounds
denying
her wounds   came   from the same source as her power

1974   1978

---

3. Gilded silver or bronze.
1. Physicist and chemist (1867–1934) who, with her husband, Pierre, discovered radium.

From Twenty-one Love Poems

XI

Every peak is a crater. This is the law of volcanoes,
making them eternally and visibly female.
No height without depth, without a burning core,
though our straw soles shred on the hardened lava.
5 I want to travel with you to every sacred mountain
smoking within like the sibyl stooped over her tripod,[1]
I want to reach for your hand as we scale the path,
to feel your arteries glowing in my clasp,
never failing to note the small, jewel-like flower
10 unfamiliar to us, nameless till we rename her,
that clings to the slowly altering rock—
that detail outside ourselves that brings us to ourselves,
15 was here before us, knew we would come, and sees beyond us.

(The Floating Poem, Unnumbered)

Whatever happens with us, your body
will haunt mine—tender, delicate
your lovemaking, like the half-curled frond
of the fiddlehead fern in forests
5 just washed by sun. Your traveled, generous thighs
between which my whole face has come and come—
the innocence and wisdom of the place my tongue
    has found there—
the live, insatiate dance of your nipples in my mouth—
10 your touch on me, firm, protective, searching
me out, your strong tongue and slender fingers
reaching where I had been waiting years for you
in my rose-wet cave—whatever happens, this is.

XXI

The dark lintels, the blue and foreign stones
of the great round rippled by stone implements
the midsummer night light rising from beneath
the horizon—when I said "a cleft of light"
5 I meant this. And this is not Stonehenge[2]
simply nor any place but the mind
casting back to where her solitude,
shared, could be chosen without loneliness,
not easily nor without pains to stake out
10 the circle, the heavy shadows, the great light.
I choose to be a figure in that light,
half-blotted by darkness, something moving
across that space, the color of stone

---

1. At Delphi, the priestess sat on a tripod and breathed in vapors from below when she gave oracles. "Sibyl": a Greek prophetess.

2. A great prehistoric structure of stones set in a circle on Salisbury Plain in England.

greeting the moon, yet more than stone:
15   a woman. I choose to walk here. And to draw this circle.

1974–76   1976, 1978

Phantasia for Elvira Shatayev

(leader of a women's climbing team, all of whom died in a storm on Lenin Peak, August 1974. Later, Shatayev's husband found and buried the bodies.)

The cold felt cold until our blood
grew colder   then the wind
died down and we slept

If in this sleep I speak
5   it's with a voice no longer personal
(I want to say   *with voices*)
When the wind tore   our breath from us at last
we had no need of words
For months   for years   each one of us
10   had felt her own *yes*   growing in her
slowly forming   as she stood at windows   waited
for trains   mended her rucksack   combed her hair
What we were to learn   was simply   what we had
up here   as out of all words   that *yes*   gathered
15   its forces   fused itself   and only just in time
to meet a *No* of no degrees
the black hole   sucking the world in

I feel you climbing toward me
your cleated bootsoles leaving   their geometric bite
20   colossally embossed   on microscopic crystals
as when I trailed you in the Caucasus
Now I am further
ahead   than either of us dreamed   anyone would be
I have become
25   the white snow packed like asphalt by the wind
the women I love   lightly flung   against the mountain
that blue sky
our frozen eyes unribboned   through the storm
we could have stitched that blueness   together   like a quilt

30   You come (I know this)   with your love   your loss
strapped to your body   with your tape-recorder   camera
ice-pick   against advisement
to give us burial in the snow   and in your mind
While my body lies out here
35   flashing like a prism   into your eyes
how could you sleep   You climbed here for yourself
we climbed for ourselves

When you have buried us   told your story
ours does not end   we stream
into the unfinished   the unbegun
the possible
Every cell's core of heat   pulsed out of us
into the thin air   of the universe
the armature of rock beneath these snows
this mountain   which has taken   the imprint of our minds
through changes elemental and minute
as those we underwent
to bring each other here
choosing ourselves   each other   and this life
whose every breath   and grasp   and further foothold
is somewhere   still enacted   and continuing

In the diary I wrote: *Now we are ready*
and each of us knows it   I have never loved
like this   I have never seen
my own forces so taken up and shared
and given back
After the long training   the early sieges
we are moving almost effortlessly in our love

In the diary as the wind   began to tear
at the tents over us   I wrote:
We know now we have always been in danger
down in our separateness
and now up here together but   till now
we had not touched our strength

In the diary torn from my fingers I had written:
What does love mean
what does it mean   "to survive"
A cable of blue fire ropes our bodies
burning together in the snow   We will not live
to settle for less   We have dreamed of this
all of our lives

1974   1978

Final Notations

  it will not be simple, it will not be long
  it will take little time, it will take all your thought
  it will take all your heart, it will take all your breath
  it will be short, it will not be simple

  it will touch through your ribs, it will take all your heart
  it will not be long, it will occupy your thought
  as a city is occupied, as a bed is occupied
  it will take all your flesh, it will not be simple

You are coming into us who cannot withstand you
you are coming into us who never wanted to withstand you
you are taking parts of us into places never planned
you are going far away with pieces of our lives

it will be short, it will take all your breath
it will not be simple, it will become your will

1991   1991

From Eastern War Time

I

Memory lifts her smoky mirror: 1943,
single isinglass[1] window   kerosene
stove in the streetcar barn   halfset moon
8:15 a.m. Eastern War Time[2] dark
Number 29 clanging in and turning
looseleaf notebook   *Latin for Americans*
Breasted's *History of the Ancient World*[3]
on the girl's lap
money for lunch and war-stamps[4] in her pocket
darkblue wool wet acrid on her hands
three pools of light   weak ceiling bulbs
a schoolgirl's hope-spilt terrified
sensations wired to smells
of kerosene wool and snow
and the sound of the dead language
praised as key   torchlight of the great dead
Grey spreading   behind still-flying snow
the lean and sway of the streetcar she must ride
to become one   of a hundred girls
rising white-cuffed and collared in a study hall
to sing *For those in peril on the sea*[5]
under plaster casts of the classic frescoes
chariots horses draperies certitudes.

8

A woman wired in memories
     stands by a house   collapsed in dust
her son beaten in prison   grandson
     shot in the stomach   daughter

---

1. Thin sheet of transparent mica used in place of glass.
2. From February 1942 to September 1945, the United States was on "War Time": clocks were set ahead one hour in the winter as well as the summer.
3. I.e., two 1940s schoolbooks: *Latin for Americans* (1941–42), by B. L. Ullman and Norman E. Henry, and *Ancient Times, a History of the Early World* (1916, 1935) by the Egyptologist James H. Breasted.
4. Stamps bought for 10 cents or more and pasted into a booklet to save toward a $25 war bond.
5. A repeated line in the hymn "Eternal Father, Strong to Save" (also known as "The Navy Hymn," 1860), with words by William Whiting.

        organizing the camps[6]   an aunt's unpublished poems
        grandparents' photographs   a bridal veil
        phased into smoke   up the obliterate air
120 With whom shall she let down and tell her story
        Who shall hear her to the end
        standing if need be for hours   in wind
        that swirls the levelled dust
        in sun that beats through their scarfed hair
125 at the lost gate by the shattered prickly pear
        Who must hear her to the end
        but the woman   forbidden to forget
        the blunt groats[7] freezing in the wooden ladle
        old winds   dusting the ovens with light snow?

1989–90   1991

In Those Years

In those years, people will say, we lost track
of the meaning of *we*, of *you*
we found ourselves
reduced to *I*
5 and the whole thing became
silly, ironic, terrible:
we were trying to live a personal life
and, yes, that was the only life
we could bear witness to

10 But the great dark birds of history screamed and plunged
into our personal weather
They were headed somewhere else but their beaks and pinions drove
along the shore, through the rags of fog
where we stood, saying *I*

1991   1995

To the Days

    From you I want more than I've ever asked,
    all of it—the newscasts' terrible stories
    of life in my time, the knowing it's worse than that,
    much worse—the knowing what it means to be lied to.

5   Fog in the mornings, hunger for clarity,
    coffee and bread with sour plum jam.

---

6. I.e., the concentration camps.
7. Hulled and crushed grain; buckwheat groats (kasha) are a staple food in eastern Europe.

Numbness of soul in placid neighborhoods.
Lives ticking on as if.

A typewriter's torrent, suddenly still.
Blue soaking through fog, two dragonflies wheeling.
Acceptable levels of cruelty, steadily rising.
Whatever you bring in your hands, I need to see it.

Suddenly I understand the verb without tenses.
To smell another woman's hair, to taste her skin.
To know the bodies drifting underwater.
To be human, said Rosa[1]—I can't teach you that.

A cat drinks from a bowl of marigolds—his moment.
Surely the love of life is never-ending,
the failure of nerve, a charred fuse?
I want more from you than I ever knew to ask.

Wild pink lilies erupting, tasseled stalks of corn
in the Mexican gardens, corn and roses.
Shortening days, strawberry fields in ferment
with tossed-aside, bruised fruit.

1991   1995

Fox

I needed fox   Badly I needed
a vixen[1] for the long time none had come near me
I needed recognition from a
triangulated face   burnt-yellow eyes
fronting the long body the fierce and sacrificial tail[2]
I needed history of fox   briars of legend it was said she
    had run through
I was in want of fox

---

1. Rosa Luxemburg (1871–1919) was a Polish-born middle-class Jew. Early in her abbreviated life she entered the currents of European socialist revolutionary thinking and action. She became one of the most influential and controversial figures in the social-democratic movements of Eastern Europe and Germany. Besides her political essays, she left hundreds of vivid letters to friends and comrades. Imprisoned during World War I for her strongly internationalist and anticapitalist beliefs, she was murdered in Berlin in 1919 by right-wing soldiers, with the passive collusion of a faction from her own party. Her body was thrown into a canal. On December 28, 1916, from prison, she wrote a New Year letter to friends she feared were both backsliding and complaining: "Then see to it that you remain a *Mensch!* [Yiddish / German for human being]. . . . Being a *Mensch* means happily throwing one's life 'on fate's great scale' if necessary, but, at the same time, enjoying every bright day and every beautiful cloud. Oh, I can't write you a prescription for being a *Mensch.* I only know how one is a *Mensch,* and you used to know it too when we went walking for a few hours in the Südende fields with the sunset's red light falling on the wheat. The world is so beautiful even with all its horrors" (*The Letters of Rosa Luxemburg,* ed., trans., and with an intro. by Stephen Eric Bronner [Atlantic Highlands, N.J.: Humanities Press, 1993], p. 173) [Rich's note].
1. A female fox.
2. Fox hunters sometimes keep the animal's tail, or brush, as a trophy.

And the truth of briars she had to have run through
I craved to feel on her pelt   if my hands could even slide
past or her body slide between them   sharp truth distressing
surfaces of fur
lacerated skin calling legend to account
a vixen's courage in vixen terms

For a human animal to call for help
on another animal
is the most riven the most revolted cry on earth
come a long way down
Go back far enough it means tearing and torn   endless
   and sudden
back far enough it blurts
into the birth-yell of the yet-to-be human child
pushed out of a female   the yet-to-be woman

1998   2001

The School Among the Ruins

Beirut.Baghdad.Sarajevo.Bethlehem.Kabul.[1] *Not of course here.*

1

Teaching the first lesson and the last
—great falling light of summer will you last
longer than schooltime?
When children flow
in columns at the doors
BOYS GIRLS and the busy teachers

open or close high windows
with hooked poles   drawing darkgreen shades

closets unlocked, locked
questions unasked, asked, when

love of the fresh impeccable
sharp-pencilled   yes
order without cruelty

a street on earth neither heaven nor hell
busy with commerce and worship
young teachers walking to school

fresh bread and early-open foodstalls

---

1. All cities where, in the last decades of the 20th century, civilian populations suffered greatly during armed conflicts.

2

When the offensive rocks the sky when nightglare
misconstrues day and night when lived-in
rooms from the upper city
tumble cratering lower streets

cornices of olden ornament   human debris
when fear vacuums out the streets

When the whole town flinches
blood on the undersole thickening to glass

Whoever crosses   hunched   knees bent   a contested zone
knows why she does this suicidal thing

School's now in session day and night
children sleep
in the classrooms   teachers rolled close

3

How the good teacher loved
his school   the students
the lunchroom with fresh sandwiches

lemonade and milk
the classroom   glass cages
of moss and turtles
teaching responsibility

A morning breaks without bread or fresh-poured milk
parents or lesson plans

diarrhea first question of the day
children shivering   it's September
Second question: where is my mother?

4

One: I don't know where your mother
is   Two: I don't know
why they are trying to hurt us
Three: or the latitude and longitude
of their hatred   Four: I don't know if we
hate them as much   I think there's more toilet paper
in the supply closet   I'm going to break it open

Today this is your lesson:
write as clearly as you can
your name   home street   and number
down on this page
No you can't go home yet
but you aren't lost
this is our school

I'm not sure what we'll eat
we'll look for healthy roots and greens
searching for water though the pipes are broken

5

There's a young cat sticking
her head through window bars
she's hungry like us
but can feed on mice
her bronze erupting fur
speaks of a life already wild

her golden eyes
don't give quarter   She'll teach us   Let's call her
Sister
when we get milk we'll give her some

6

I've told you, let's try to sleep in this funny camp
All night pitiless pilotless things[2] go shrieking
above us to somewhere

Don't let your faces turn to stone
Don't stop asking me why
Let's pay attention to our cat   she needs us

Maybe tomorrow the bakers can fix their ovens

7

"We sang them to naps   told stories   made
shadow-animals with our hands

wiped human debris off boots and coats
sat learning by heart the names
some were too young to write
some had forgotten how"

2001   2004

---

2. Missiles or remotely piloted surveillance drones.

When We Dead Awaken: Writing as Re-Vision (1971)[1]

The Modern Language Association is both marketplace and funeral parlor for the professional study of Western literature in North America. Like all gatherings of the professions, it has been and remains a "procession of the sons of educated men" (Virginia Woolf):[2] a congeries of old-boys' networks, academicians rehearsing their numb canons in sessions dedicated to the literature of white males, junior scholars under the lash of "publish or perish" delivering papers in the bizarrely lit drawing-rooms of immense hotels: a ritual competition veering between cynicism and desperation.

However, in the interstices of these gentlemanly rites (or, in Mary Daly's words, on the boundaries of this patriarchal space),[3] some feminist scholars, teachers, and graduate students, joined by feminist writers, editors, and publishers, have for a decade been creating more subversive occasions, challenging the sacredness of the gentlemanly canon, sharing the rediscovery of buried works by women, asking women's questions, bringing literary history and criticism back to life in both senses. The Commission on the Status of Women in the Profession was formed in 1969, and held its first public event in 1970. In 1971 the Commission asked Ellen Peck Killoh, Tillie Olsen, Elaine Reuben, and myself, with Elaine Hedges as moderator, to talk on "The Woman Writer in the Twentieth Century." The essay that follows was written for that forum, and later published, along with the other papers from the forum and workshops, in an issue of College English *edited by Elaine Hedges ("Women Writing and Teaching," vol. 34, no. 1, October 1972). With a few revisions, mainly updating, it was reprinted in* American Poets *in 1976, edited by William Heyen (New York: Bobbs-Merrill, 1976). That later text is the one published here.*

The challenge flung by feminists at the accepted literary canon, at the methods of teaching it, and at the biased and astigmatic view of male "literary scholarship," has not diminished in the decade since the first Women's Forum; it has become broadened and intensified more recently by the challenges of black and lesbian feminists pointing out that feminist literary criticism itself has overlooked or held back from examining the work of black women and lesbians. The dynamic between a political vision and the demand for a fresh vision of literature is clear: without a growing feminist movement, the first inroads of feminist scholarship could not have been made; without the sharpening of a black feminist consciousness, black women's writing would have been left in limbo between misogynist black male critics and white feminists still struggling to unearth a white women's tradition; without an articulate lesbian/feminist movement, lesbian writing would still be lying in that closet where many of us used to sit reading forbidden books "in a bad light."

Much, much more is yet to be done; and university curricula have of

---

1. As Rich explains, this essay—written in 1971—was first published in 1972 and then included in her volume *On Lies, Secrets, and Silence* (1978). At that time she added the introductory note reprinted here, as well as some notes beginning "A.R., 1978."
2. The phrase is a quote from *Three Guineas* (1938), by the English writer Woolf (1882–1941; see above, p. 212).
3. Mary Daly, *Beyond God the Father* (Boston: Beacon, 1971), pp. 40–41 [Rich's note]. Daly (b. 1928), American feminist theologian and philosopher.

course changed very little as a result of all this. What *is* changing is the availability of knowledge, of vital texts, the visible effects on women's lives of seeing, hearing our wordless or negated experience affirmed and pursued further in language.

Ibsen's *When We Dead Awaken*[4] is a play about the use that the male artist and thinker—in the process of creating culture as we know it—has made of women, in his life and in his work; and about a woman's slow struggling awakening to the use to which her life has been put. Bernard Shaw wrote in 1900 of this play:

> [Ibsen] shows us that no degradation ever devized or permitted is as disastrous as this degradation; that through it women can die into luxuries for men and yet can kill them; that men and women are becoming conscious of this; and that what remains to be seen as perhaps the most interesting of all imminent social developments is what will happen "when we dead awaken."[5]

It's exhilarating to be alive in a time of awakening consciousness; it can also be confusing, disorienting, and painful. This awakening of dead or sleeping consciousness has already affected the lives of millions of women, even those who don't know it yet. It is also affecting the lives of men, even those who deny its claims upon them. The argument will go on whether an oppressive economic class system is responsible for the oppressive nature of male/female relations, or whether, in fact, patriarchy—the domination of males—is the original model of oppression on which all others are based. But in the last few years the women's movement has drawn inescapable and illuminating connections between our sexual lives and our political institutions. The sleepwalkers are coming awake, and for the first time this awakening has a collective reality; it is no longer such a lonely thing to open one's eyes.

Re-vision—the act of looking back, of seeing with fresh eyes, of entering an old text from a new critical direction—is for women more than a chapter in cultural history: it is an act of survival. Until we can understand the assumptions in which we are drenched we cannot know ourselves. And this drive to self-knowledge, for women, is more than a search for identity: it is part of our refusal of the self-destructiveness of male-dominated society. A radical critique of literature, feminist in its impulse, would take the work first of all as a clue to how we live, how we have been living, how we have been led to imagine ourselves, how our language has trapped as well as liberated us, how the very act of naming has been till now a male prerogative, and how we can begin to see and name—and therefore live—afresh. A change in the concept of sexual identity is essential if we are not going to see the old political order reassert itself in every new revolution. We need to know the writing of the past, and know it differently than we have ever known it; not to pass on a tradition but to break its hold over us.

For writers, and at this moment for women writers in particular, there is

---

4. Published in 1899. Henrik Ibsen (1828–1906), Norwegian poet and playwright.
5. G. B. Shaw, *The Quintessence of Ibsenism* (New York: Hill & Wang, 1922), p. 139 [Rich's note]. Shaw (1856–1950), British playwright and critic.

the challenge and promise of a whole new psychic geography to be explored. But there is also a difficult and dangerous walking on the ice, as we try to find language and images for a consciousness we are just coming into, and with little in the past to support us. I want to talk about some aspect of this difficulty and this danger.

Jane Harrison, the great classical anthropologist, wrote in 1914 in a letter to her friend Gilbert Murray:

> By the by, about "Women," it has bothered me often—why do women never want to write poetry about Man as a sex—why is Woman a dream and a terror to man and not the other way around? . . . Is it mere convention and propriety, or something deeper?[6]

I think Jane Harrison's question cuts deep into the myth-making tradition, the romantic tradition; deep into what women and men have been to each other; and deep into the psyche of the woman writer. Thinking about that question, I began thinking of the work of two twentieth-century women poets, Sylvia Plath and Diane Wakoski. It strikes me that in the work of both Man appears as, if not a dream, a fascination and a terror; and that the source of the fascination and the terror is, simply, Man's power—to dominate, tyrannize, choose, or reject the woman. The charisma of Man seems to come purely from his power over her and his control of the world by force, not from anything fertile or life-giving in him. And, in the work of both these poets, it is finally the woman's sense of *herself*—embattled, possessed—that gives the poetry its dynamic charge, its rhythms of struggle, need, will, and female energy. Until recently this female anger and this furious awareness of the Man's power over her were not available materials to the female poet, who tended to write of Love as the source of her suffering, and to view that victimization by Love as an almost inevitable fate. Or, like Marianne Moore and Elizabeth Bishop,[7] she kept sexuality at a measured and chiseled distance in her poems.

One answer to Jane Harrison's question has to be that historically men and women have played very different parts in each others' lives. Where woman has been a luxury for man, and has served as the painter's model and the poet's muse, but also as comforter, nurse, cook, bearer of his seed, secretarial assistant, and copyist of manuscripts, man has played a quite different role for the female artist. Henry James repeats an incident which the writer Prosper Mérimée described, of how, while he was living with George Sand,

> he once opened his eyes, in the raw winter dawn, to see his companion, in a dressing-gown, on her knees before the domestic hearth, a candlestick beside her and a red *madras* round her head, making bravely, with her own hands the fire that was to enable her to sit down betimes to urgent pen and paper. The story represents him as having felt that the spectacle chilled his ardor and tried his taste; her appearance was unfortunate, her occupation an inconsequence, and her industry a reproof—the result of all which was a lively irritation and an early rupture.[8]

---

6. J. G. Stewart, *Jane Ellen Harrison: A Portrait from Letters* (London: Merlin, 1959), p. 140 [Rich's note]. Harrison (1850–1828) and Murray (1866–1957) were classical scholars at Cambridge and Oxford, respectively.
7. Plath, Moore, and Bishop are included in this anthology.
8. Henry James, "Notes on Novelists," in *Selected Literary Criticism of Henry James*, Morris Shapira, ed. (London: Heinemann, 1963), pp. 157–58 [Rich's note]. James (1843–1916), American writer of fiction and criticism. Mérimée (1803–

The specter of this kind of male judgment, along with the misnaming and thwarting of her needs by a culture controlled by males, has created problems for the woman writer: problems of contact with herself, problems of language and style, problems of energy and survival.

In rereading Virginia Woolf's *A Room of One's Own* (1929) for the first time in some years, I was astonished at the sense of effort, of pains taken, of dogged tentativeness, in the tone of that essay. And I recognized that tone. I had heard it often enough, in myself and in other women. It is the tone of a woman almost in touch with her anger, who is determined not to appear angry, who is *willing* herself to be calm, detached, and even charming in a roomful of men where things have been said which are attacks on her very integrity. Virginia Woolf is addressing an audience of women, but she is acutely conscious—as she always was—of being overheard by men: by Morgan and Lytton and Maynard Keynes[9] and for that matter by her father, Leslie Stephen.[1] She drew the language out into an exacerbated thread in her determination to have her own sensibility yet protect it from those masculine presences. Only at rare moments in that essay do you hear the passion in her voice; she was trying to sound as cool as Jane Austen,[2] as Olympian as Shakespeare, because that is the way the men of the culture thought a writer should sound.

No male writer has written primarily or even largely for women, or with the sense of women's criticism as a consideration when he chooses his materials, his theme, his language. But to a lesser or greater extent, every woman writer has written for men even when, like Virginia Woolf, she was supposed to be addressing women. If we have come to the point when this balance might begin to change, when women can stop being haunted, not only by "convention and propriety" but by internalized fears of being and saying themselves, then it is an extraordinary moment for the woman writer—and reader.

I have hesitated to do what I am going to do now, which is to use myself as an illustration. For one thing, it's a lot easier and less dangerous to talk about other women writers. But there is something else. Like Virginia Woolf, I am aware of the women who are not with us here because they are washing the dishes and looking after the children. Nearly fifty years after she spoke, that fact remains largely unchanged. And I am thinking also of women whom she left out of the picture altogether—women who are washing other people's dishes and caring for other people's children, not to mention women who went on the streets last night in order to feed their children. We seem to be special women here, we have liked to think of ourselves as special, and we have known that men would tolerate, even romanticize us as special, as long as our words and actions didn't threaten their privilege of tolerating or rejecting us and our work according to *their* ideas of what a special woman

---

1870) and Sand (1804–1876) were both French writers. *"Madras"*: bright-colored fabric worn as a turban.

9. I.e., the novelist E. M. Forster (1879–1970), the critic and biographer Lytton Strachey (1880–1932), and the economist John Maynard Keynes (1883–1946), all members of Woolf's Bloomsbury circle.

1. A.R., 1978: This intuition of mine was corroborated when, early in 1978, I read the correspondence between Woolf and Dame Ethel Smyth (Henry W. and Albert A. Berg Collection, The New York Public Library, Astor, Lenox and Tilden Foundations); in a letter dated June 8, 1933, Woolf speaks of having kept her own personality out of *A Room of One's Own* lest she not be taken seriously: ". . . how personal, so will they say, rubbing their hands with glee, women always are; *I even hear them as I write.*" (Italics mine.) [Rich's note]. Leslie Stephen (1832–1904), a distinguished man of letters. Smyth (1858–1944), English composer and suffragist.

2. English novelist (1775–1817); see Vol. 1, p. 459.

ought to be. An important insight of the radical women's movement has been how divisive and how ultimately destructive is this myth of the special woman, who is also the token woman. Every one of us here in this room has had great luck—we are teachers, writers, academicians; our own gifts could not have been enough, for we all know women whose gifts are buried or aborted. Our struggles can have meaning and our privileges—however precarious under patriarchy—can be justified only if they can help to change the lives of women whose gifts—and whose very being—continue to be thwarted and silenced.

My own luck was being born white and middle-class into a house full of books, with a father who encouraged me to read and write. So for about twenty years I wrote for a particular man, who criticized and praised me and made me feel I was indeed "special." The obverse side of this, of course, was that I tried for a long time to please him, or rather, not to displease him. And then of course there were other men—writers, teachers—the Man, who was not a terror or a dream but a literary master and a master in other ways less easy to acknowledge. And there were all those poems about women, written by men: it seemed to be a given that men wrote poems and women frequently inhabited them. These women were almost always beautiful, but threatened with the loss of beauty, the loss of youth—the fate worse than death. Or, they were beautiful and died young, like Lucy and Lenore. Or, the woman was like Maud Gonne,[3] cruel and disastrously mistaken, and the poem reproached her because she had refused to become a luxury for the poet.

A lot is being said today about the influence that the myths and images of women have on all of us who are products of culture. I think it has been a peculiar confusion to the girl or woman who tries to write because she is peculiarly susceptible to language. She goes to poetry or fiction looking for *her* way of being in the world, since she too has been putting words and images together; she is looking eagerly for guides, maps, possibilities; and over and over in the "words' masculine persuasive force" of literature she comes up against something that negates everything she is about: she meets the image of Woman in books written by men. She finds a terror and a dream, she finds a beautiful pale face, she finds La Belle Dame Sans Merci, she finds Juliet or Tess or Salomé,[4] but precisely what she does not find is that absorbed, drudging, puzzled, sometimes inspired creature, herself, who sits at a desk trying to put words together.

So what does she do? What did I do? I read the older women poets with their peculiar keenness and ambivalence: Sappho, Christina Rossetti, Emily Dickinson, Elinor Wylie, Edna Millay, H. D.[5] I discovered that the woman poet most admired at the time (by men) was Marianne Moore, who was maidenly, elegant, intellectual, discreet. But even in reading these women I was looking in them for the same things I had found in the poetry of men,

---

3. Irish revolutionary activist (1865–1953), beautiful beloved of William Butler Yeats, and subject of many of his poems. "Lucy and Lenore": in poems written by William Wordsworth (1800) and Edgar Allan Poe (1831).
4. Dancer responsible for the death of John the Baptist in Oscar Wilde's play of that name (1894). "La Belle Dame Sans Merci": title of an 1820 poem by John Keats (the beautiful lady without pity; French). "Juliet": tragic heroine of Shakespeare's *Romeo and Juliet*. "Tess": doomed heroine in Thomas Hardy's (1594) *Tess of the d'Urbervilles* (1891).
5. Rossetti, Dickinson, Wylie, Millay, and H. D. are included in this anthology. Sappho (b. ca. 612 B.C.E.), Greek poet.

because I wanted women poets to be the equals of men, and to be equal was still confused with sounding the same.

I know that my style was formed first by male poets: by the men I was reading as an undergraduate—Frost, Dylan Thomas, Donne, Auden, MacNeice, Stevens, Yeats.[6] What I chiefly learned from them was craft.[7] But poems are like dreams: in them you put what you don't know you know. Looking back at poems I wrote before I was twenty-one, I'm startled because beneath the conscious craft are glimpses of the split I even then experienced between the girl who wrote poems, who defined herself in writing poems, and the girl who was to define herself by her relationships with men. "Aunt Jennifer's Tigers" (1951), written while I was a student, looks with deliberate detachment at this split.[8] In writing this poem, composed and apparently cool as it is, I thought I was creating a portrait of an imaginary woman. But this woman suffers from the opposition of her imagination, worked out in tapestry, and her life-style, "ringed with ordeals she was mastered by." It was important to me that Aunt Jennifer was a person as distinct from myself as possible—distanced by the formalism of the poem, by its objective, observant tone—even by putting the woman in a different generation.

In those years formalism was part of the strategy—like asbestos gloves, it allowed me to handle materials I couldn't pick up bare-handed. A later strategy was to use the persona of a man, as I did in "The Loser" (1958):

> *A man thinks of the woman he once loved: first, after her wedding, and then nearly a decade later.*
>
> I
> I kissed you, bride and lost, and went
> home from that bourgeois sacrament,
> your cheek still tasting cold upon
> my lips that gave you benison
> with all the swagger that they knew—
> as losers somehow learn to do.
>
> Your wedding made my eyes ache; soon
> the world would be worse off for one
> more golden apple dropped to ground
> without the least protesting sound,
> and you would windfall lie, and we
> forget your shimmer on the tree.
>
> Beauty is always wasted: if
> not Mignon's song[9] sung to the deaf,
> at all events to the unmoved.
> A face like yours cannot be loved

---

6. Robert Frost (1874–1964) and Wallace Stevens (1879–1955) were Americans; Thomas (1914–1953) was Welsh; William Butler Yeats (1865–1939) and Louis MacNeice (1907–1963) were Irish; and John Donne (1572–1631) and W. H. Auden (1907–1973) were English.
7. A. R., 1978: Yet I spent months, at sixteen, memorizing and writing imitations of Millay's sonnets; and in notebooks of that period I find what are obviously attempts to imitate Dickinson's metrics and verbal compression. I knew H. D. only through anthologized lyrics; her epic poetry was not then available to me [Rich's note].
8. For the text of the poem, see p. 965.
9. From Ambroise Thomas's *Mignon* (1866), an opera based on Goethe's *Wilhelm Meister's Apprenticeship* (1795–96).

long or seriously enough.
Almost, we seem to hold it off.

II
Well, you are tougher than I thought.
Now when the wash with ice hangs taut
this morning of St. Valentine,
I see you strip the squeaking line,
your body weighed against the load,
and all my groans can do no good.

Because you are still beautiful,
though squared and stiffened by the pull
of what nine windy years have done.
You have three daughters, lost a son.
I see all your intelligence
flung into that unwearied stance.

My envy is of no avail.
I turn my head and wish him well
who chafed your beauty into use
and lives forever in a house
lit by the friction of your mind.
You stagger in against the wind.

 I finished college, published my first book by a fluke, as it seemed to me, and broke off a love affair. I took a job, lived alone, went on writing, fell in love. I was young, full of energy, and the book seemed to mean that others agreed I was a poet. Because I was also determined to prove that as a woman poet I could also have what was then defined as a "full" woman's life, I plunged in my early twenties into marriage and had three children before I was thirty. There was nothing overt in the environment to warn me: these were the fifties, and in reaction to the earlier wave of feminism, middle-class women were making careers of domestic perfection, working to send their husbands through professional schools, then retiring to raise large families. People were moving out to the suburbs, technology was going to be the answer to everything, even sex; the family was in its glory. Life was extremely private; women were isolated from each other by the loyalties of marriage. I have a sense that women didn't talk to each other much in the fifties—not about their secret emptinesses, their frustrations. I went on trying to write; my second book and first child appeared in the same month. But by the time that book came out I was already dissatisfied with those poems, which seemed to me mere exercises for poems I hadn't written. The book was praised, however, for its "gracefulness"; I had a marriage and a child. If there were doubts, if there were periods of null depression or active despairing, these could only mean that I was ungrateful, insatiable, perhaps a monster.

 About the time my third child was born, I felt that I had either to consider myself a failed woman and a failed poet, or to try to find some synthesis by which to understand what was happening to me. What frightened me most was the sense of drift, of being pulled along on a current which called itself my destiny, but in which I seemed to be losing touch with whoever I had been, with the girl who had experienced her own will and energy almost ecstatically at times, walking around a city or riding a train at night or typing in a student room. In a poem about my grandmother I wrote (of myself): "A young girl, thought sleeping, is certified dead" ("Halfway"). I was writing very little, partly from fatigue, that female fatigue of suppressed anger and loss of contact with my own being; partly from the discontinuity of female life with its attention to small chores, errands, work that others constantly undo, small children's constant needs. What I did write was unconvincing to me; my anger and frustration were hard to acknowledge in or out of poems because in fact I cared a great deal about my husband and my children. Trying to look back and understand that time I have tried to analyze the real nature of the conflict. Most, if not all, human lives are full of fantasy—passive day-dreaming which need not be acted on. But to write poetry or fiction, or even to think well, is not to fantasize, or to put fantasies on paper. For a poem to coalesce, for a character or an action to take shape, there has to be an imaginative transformation of reality which is no way passive. And a certain freedom of the mind is needed—freedom to press on, to enter the currents of your thought like a glider pilot, knowing that your motion can be sustained, that the buoyancy of your attention will not be suddenly snatched away. Moreover, if the imagination is to transcend and transform experience it has to question, to challenge, to conceive of alternatives, perhaps to the very life you are living at that moment. You have to be free to play around with the notion that day might be night, love might be hate; nothing can be too sacred for the imagination to turn into its opposite or to call experimentally by another name. For writing is re-naming. Now, to be maternally with small children all day in the old way, to be with a man in the old way of marriage, requires a holding-back, a putting-aside of that imaginative activity, and demands instead a kind of conservatism. I want to make it clear that I am *not* saying that in order to write well, or think well, it is necessary to become unavailable to others, or to become a devouring ego. This has been the myth of the masculine artist and thinker; and I do not accept it. But to be a female human being trying to fulfill traditional female functions in a traditional way *is* in direct conflict with the subversive function of the imagination. The word traditional is important here. There must be ways, and we will be finding out more and more about them, in which the energy of creation and the energy of relation can be united. But in those years I always felt the conflict as a failure of love in myself. I had thought I was choosing a full life: the life available to most men, in which sexuality, work, and parenthood could coexist. But I felt, at twenty-nine, guilt toward the people closest to me, and guilty toward my own being.

I wanted, then, more than anything, the one thing of which there was never enough: time to think, time to write. The fifties and early sixties were years of rapid revelations: the sit-ins and marches in the South, the Bay of Pigs,[1] the early antiwar movement, raised large questions—questions for which the masculine world of the academy around me seemed to have expert and fluent answers. But I needed to think for myself—about pacifism and

---

1. A 1961 abortive invasion of Cuba by CIA-trained anti-Castro exiles—financed and supported by the U.S. government—that was a fiasco. Like the other "revelations" mentioned, it fed the growing distrust of the government among some Americans.

dissent and violence, about poetry and society, and about my own relationship to all these things. For about ten years I was reading in fierce snatches, scribbling in notebooks, writing poetry in fragments; I was looking desperately for clues, because if there were no clues then I thought I might be insane. I wrote in a notebook about this time:

> Paralyzed by the sense that there exists a mesh of relationships—e.g., between my anger at the children, my sensual life, pacifism, sex (I mean sex in its broadest significance, not merely sexual desire)—an interconnectedness which, if I could see it, make it valid, would give me back myself, make it possible to function lucidly and passionately. Yet I grope in and out among these dark webs.

I think I began at this point to feel that politics was not something "out there" but something "in here" and of the essence of my condition.

In the late fifties I was able to write, for the first time, directly about experiencing myself as a woman. The poem was jotted in fragments during children's naps, brief hours in a library, or at 3:00 A.M. after rising with a wakeful child. I despaired of doing any continuous work at this time. Yet I began to feel that my fragments and scraps had a common consciousness and a common theme, one which I would have been very unwilling to put on paper at an earlier time because I had been taught that poetry should be "universal," which meant, of course, nonfemale. Until then I had tried very much *not* to identify myself as a female poet. Over two years I wrote a ten-part poem called "Snapshots of a Daughter-in-Law" (1958–1960), in a longer looser mode than I'd ever trusted myself with before. It was an extraordinary relief to write that poem. It strikes me now as too literary, too dependent on allusion; I hadn't found the courage yet to do without authorities, or even to use the pronoun "I"—the woman in the poem is always "she." One section of it, No. 2, concerns a woman who thinks she is going mad; she is haunted by voices telling her to resist and rebel, voices which she can hear but not obey.

> 2.
> Banging the coffee-pot into the sink
> she hears the angels chiding, and looks out
> past the raked gardens to the sloppy sky.
> Only a week since They said: *Have no patience.*
>
> The next time it was: *Be insatiable.*
> Then: *Save yourself; others you cannot save.*
> Sometimes she's let the tapstream scald her arm,
> a match burn to her thumbnail,
>
> or held her hand above the kettle's snout
> right in the woolly steam. They are probably angels,
> since nothing hurts her anymore, except
> each morning's grit blowing into her eyes.

The poem "Orion," written five years later, is a poem of reconnection with a part of myself I had felt I was losing—the active principle, the energetic imagination, the "half-brother" whom I projected, as I had for many years, into the constellation Orion. It's no accident that the words "cold and egotistical" appear in this poem, and are applied to myself.

> Far back when I went zig-zagging
> through tamarack[2] pastures
> you were my genius, you
> my cast-iron Viking, my helmed
> lion-heart king in prison.
> Years later now you're young
>
> my fierce half-brother, staring
> down from that simplified west
> your breast open, your belt dragged down
> by an oldfashioned thing, a sword
> the last bravado you won't give over
> though it weighs you down as you stride
>
> and the stars in it are dim
> and maybe have stopped burning.[3]
> But you burn, and I know it;
> as I throw back my head to take you in
> an old transfusion happens again:
> divine astronomy is nothing to it.
>
> Indoors I bruise and blunder,
> break faith, leave ill enough
> alone, a dead child born in the dark.
> Night cracks up over the chimney,
> pieces of time, frozen geodes
> come showering down in the grate.
>
> A man reaches behind my eyes
> and finds them empty
> a woman's head turns away
> from my head in the mirror
> children are dying my death
> and eating crumbs of my life.
>
> Pity is not your forte.
> Calmly you ache up there
> pinned aloft in your crow's nest,
> my speechless pirate!
> You take it all for granted
> and when I look you back
>
> it's with a starlike eye
> shooting its cold and egotistical spear
> where it can do least damage.
> Breathe deep! No hurt, no pardon

---

2. Larch.
3. The constellation Orion can be recognized by the stars in the imaginary figure's belt.

out here in the cold with you
you with your back to the wall.

The choice still seemed to be between "love"—womanly, maternal love, altruistic love—a love defined and ruled by the weight of an entire culture; and egotism—a force directed by men into creation, achievement, ambition, often at the expense of others, but justifiably so. For weren't they men, and wasn't that their destiny as womanly, selfless love was ours? We know now that the alternatives are false ones—that the word "love" is itself in need of revision.

There is a companion poem to "Orion," written three years later, in which at last the woman in the poem and the woman writing the poem become the same person. It is called "Planetarium," and it was written after a visit to a real planetarium, where I read an account of the work of Caroline Herschel, the astronomer, who worked with her brother William,[4] but whose name remained obscure, as his did not.

A woman in the shape of a monster
a monster in the shape of a woman
the skies are full of them

a woman   'in the snow
among the Clocks and instruments
or measuring the ground with poles'
in her 98 years to discover
8 comets

she whom the moon ruled
like us
levitating into the night sky
riding the polished lenses

Galaxies of women, there
doing penance for impetuousness
ribs chilled
in those spaces   of the mind

An eye,

    'virile, precise and absolutely certain'
    from the mad webs of Uranusborg

        encountering the NOVA

every impulse of light exploding
from the core
as life flies out of us

    Tycho whispering at last
    'Let me not seem to have lived in vain'[5]

---

4. German-born British astronomer (1738–1822); Caroline (1750–1848) both aided him and made her own observations.

5. The dying words of the Danish astronomer Tycho Brahe (1546–1601).

What we see, we see
and seeing is changing

the light that shrivels a mountain
and leaves a man alive

Heartbeat of the pulsar
heart sweating through my body

The radio impulse
pouring in from Taurus

    I am bombarded yet   I stand

I have been standing all my life in the
direct path of a battery of signals
the most accurately transmitted most
untranslatable language in the universe
I am a galactic cloud so deep   so involuted that a light wave could take 15
years to travel through me   And has
taken   I am an instrument in the shape
of a woman trying to translate pulsations
into images   for the relief of the body
and the reconstruction of the mind.

    In closing I want to tell you about a dream I had last summer. I dreamed I was asked to read my poetry at a mass women's meeting, but when I began to read, what came out were the lyrics of a blues song. I share this dream with you because it seemed to me to say something about the problems and the future of the woman writer, and probably of women in general. The awakening of consciousness is not like the crossing of a frontier—one step and you are in another country. Much of woman's poetry has been of the nature of the blues song: a cry of pain, of victimization, or a lyric of seduction.[6] And today, much poetry by women—and prose for that matter—is charged with anger. I think we need to go through that anger, and we will betray our own reality if we try, as Virginia Woolf was trying, for an objectivity, a detachment, that would make us sound more like Jane Austen or Shakespeare. We know more than Jane Austen or Shakespeare knew: more than Jane Austen because our lives are more complex, more than Shakespeare because we know more about the lives of women—Jane Austen and Virginia Woolf included.

    Both the victimization and the anger experienced by women are real, and have real sources, everywhere in the environment, built into society, language, the structures of thought. They will go on being tapped and explored by poets, among others. We can neither deny them, nor will we rest there. A new generation of women poets is already working out of the psychic energy released when women begin to move out towards what the feminist philosopher Mary Daly has described as the "new space" on the boundaries

---

6. A. R., 1978: When I dreamed that dream, was I wholly ignorant of the tradition of Bessie Smith and other women's blues lyrics which transcended victimization to sing of resistance and independence? [Rich's note]. Smith (1894 or 1898–1937), African American blues singer.

of patriarchy.[7] Women are speaking to and of women in these poems, out of a newly released courage to name, to love each other, to share risk and grief and celebration.

To the eye of a feminist, the work of Western male poets now writing reveals a deep, fatalistic pessimism as to the possibilities of change, whether societal or personal, along with a familiar and threadbare use of women (and nature) as redemptive on the one hand, threatening on the other; and a new tide of phallocentric sadism and overt woman-hating which matches the sexual brutality of recent films. "Political" poetry by men remains stranded amid the struggles for power among male groups; in condemning U.S. imperialism or the Chilean junta[8] the poet can claim to speak for the oppressed while remaining, as male, part of a system of sexual oppression. The enemy is always outside the self, the struggle somewhere else. The mood of isolation, self-pity, and self-imitation that pervades "nonpolitical" poetry suggests that a profound change in masculine consciousness will have to precede any new male poetic—or other—inspiration. The creative energy of patriarchy is fast running out; what remains is its self-generating energy for destruction. As women, we have our work cut out for us.

1972, 1976, 1978

---

7. Mary Daly, *Beyond God the Father: Towards a Philosophy of Women's Liberation* (Boston: Beacon, 1973) [Rich's note].
8. The military government formed by General Augusto Pinochet in 1973 after the U.S.-supported coup that removed Salvador Allende, the democratically elected Socialist president.

TONI MORRISON
b. 1931

When Toni Morrison received the Pulitzer Prize in 1988 and the Nobel Prize for Literature in 1993, it became clear that she had established herself as one of America's foremost writers. An exceptionally popular novelist, Morrison has enthralled readers all over the world. At the same time, she has been critically celebrated not only for her incisive analyses of the dynamics of race and gender but also for the lyricism of her language and the inventive originality of her plots. Verbal magic and fantastic, sometimes even mystic events combine in Morrison's eight published novels to engage readers in often hauntingly elusive but always ethically crucial questions about American culture, past and present.

Morrison, who frequently focuses on black, midwestern communities in her fiction, was born Chloe Anthony Wofford and was raised by working-class parents in the small town of Lorain, Ohio. Because Ohio is bordered by a southern state, Kentucky, as well as by Lake Erie, which is in turn one of Canada's borders, Morrison views it as a crucial boundary between North and South. With a history of underground railroad stations and cross burnings, abolitionist activism and Ku Klux Klan persecution, Ohio is, in Morrison's phrase, "neither plantation nor ghetto," and so it provides an ideal site for her analysis of the struggle for freedom in which so many of her characters engage.

After graduating from Howard University in 1953, Morrison went north to Cornell

University, where she earned a master's degree for a thesis on the theme of suicide in the fiction of William Faulkner and Virginia Woolf. While she was teaching at Howard University, she married Harold Morrison, a Jamaican architect, and gave birth to two sons, Harold Ford and Slade. In 1964, she separated from her husband and moved with her children first to Syracuse, New York, and then to New York City, where she worked as a senior editor at Random House. There she helped shape such autobiographies as those by the activist Angela Davis and the boxer Muhammad Ali, as well as an anthology titled *The Black Book* (1974), a collection that reflects the breadth of the "anonymous Black man's" experience in America. Recently, she has taught at Yale, Rutgers, and (currently) Princeton universities.

Morrison's novels—*The Bluest Eye* (1970), *Sula* (1973), *Song of Solomon* (1977), *Tar Baby* (1981), *Beloved* (1987), *Jazz* (1992), *Paradise* (1998), and *Love* (2003)— have been widely acclaimed as evocative meditations on African American cultural identity in contemporary America. Like Lucille Clifton and Toni Cade Bambara, artists she praises, Morrison has managed to convey racial pain without losing a sense of joy. She does this, in part at least, by exploring the unique cultural inheritence of black Americans in terms of universal moral issues, namely, the tension between the individual and society and the problem of good and evil. Typical in her work, then, are "outlaw" figures, wild characters such as Cholly Breedlove in *The Bluest Eye,* Sula in *Sula,* Guitar in *Song of Solomon,* and Sethe in *Beloved.* Rebellious and defiant, such characters are often castigated as evil by the community and cast out as pariahs. For Morrison, however, their energy and verve can never be wholly rejected, for "evil is not an alien force." Just as important, Morrison sees the pariah as a paradigm of the black community, which is, she claims, "a pariah community" in white America.

Many scholars of the aesthetic achievements of African American women have regarded *Sula* as a touchstone or breakthrough work. Hortense Spillers, for example, views Morrison's second novel as "the single most important irruption of black women's writing in our era." What intrigues critics like Spillers is not only the friendship between two female characters as different as Nel and Sula but also the ways in which Sula herself departs from conventional definitions of feminine service or servitude to live for herself and only by standards she has herself set. The historical framework of Morrison's novel brackets its events in the context of two world wars, exploring their impact on the lives of African Americans. But that Morrison's characters in *Sula* inhabit an inhospitable public culture adds to their particularized, private burdens. As in her other novels, she examines here the excruciating legacy of slavery by focusing on the lives of individuals living within unique social networks. *Beloved,* the story of an ex-slave mother grieving over the loss of one of her children, most directly addresses that inheritance; however, all of Morrison's works explore the effects that stereotyping and discrimination against African Americans have on whites as well as on blacks. In her powerful prose, Morrison's analysis of race illuminates her characters' familial, erotic, and moral situations, helping her to pay tribute to the resiliency and richness of African American culture and to fulfill the task she has set for herself throughout her career, to study "how and why we learn to live this life intensely and well."

At various times in her career, Morrison produced fiction that provided critical insights into interracial relationships in the United States and criticism that provided creative insights into interracial aesthetic influences at work in American literary history. The critic Elizabeth Abel has discussed the "racial ambiguity so deftly installed" in the short story reprinted here, "Recitatif," a story "about a black woman and a white woman; but which is which?" How we interpret the codes, Abel shows, illuminates the values, assumptions, and cultures we bring to the text. Similarly, Morrison's essay "Unspeakable Things Unspoken" makes legible the values, assumptions, and cultures of blacks and whites. As in her important critical book *Playing in the Dark: Whiteness in the Literary Imagination* (1992), which analyzes American literature to explain the important functions fulfilled by what she calls "the Africanist presence," Morrison wants to make whiteness as visible as blackness has been historically. But she also brilliantly illuminates her own novels and the composing process, especially in her analyses of the opening phrases that she crafted with acute attention to the sound and sense of each of her sentences.

Recitatif

My mother danced all night and Roberta's was sick. That's why we were taken to St. Bonny's. People want to put their arms around you when you tell them you were in a shelter, but it really wasn't bad. No big long room with one hundred beds like Bellevue. There were four to a room, and when Roberta and me came, there was a shortage of state kids, so we were the only ones assigned to 406 and could go from bed to bed if we wanted to. And we wanted to, too. We changed beds every night and for the whole four months we were there we never picked one out as our own permanent bed.

It didn't start out that way. The minute I walked in and the Big Bozo introduced us, I got sick to my stomach. It was one thing to be taken out of your own bed early in the morning—it was something else to be stuck in a strange place with a girl from a whole other race. And Mary, that's my mother, she was right. Every now and then she would stop dancing long enough to tell me something important and one of the things she said was that they never washed their hair and they smelled funny. Roberta sure did. Smell funny, I mean. So when the Big Bozo (nobody ever called her Mrs. Itkin, just like nobody every said St. Bonaventure)—when she said, "Twyla, this is Roberta. Roberta, this is Twyla. Make each other welcome." I said, "My mother won't like you putting me in here."

"Good," said Bozo. "Maybe then she'll come and take you home."

How's that for mean? If Roberta had laughed I would have killed her, but she didn't. She just walked over to the window and stood with her back to us.

"Turn around," said the Bozo. "Don't be rude. Now Twyla. Roberta. When you hear a loud buzzer, that's the call for dinner. Come down to the first floor. Any fights and no movie." And then, just to make sure we knew what we would be missing, *"The Wizard of Oz."*[1]

Roberta must have thought I meant that my mother would be mad about my being put in the shelter. Not about rooming with her, because as soon as Bozo left she came over to me and said, "Is your mother sick too?"

"No," I said. "She just likes to dance all night."

"Oh," she nodded her head and I liked the way she understood things so fast. So for the moment it didn't matter that we looked like salt and pepper standing there and that's what the other kids called us sometimes. We were eight years old and got F's all the time. Me because I couldn't remember what I read or what the teacher said. And Roberta because she couldn't read at all and didn't even listen to the teacher. She wasn't good at anything except jacks,[2] at which she was a killer: pow scoop pow scoop pow scoop.

---

1. The 1939 movie starring Judy Garland.
2. A game whose play includes picking up increasing numbers of small, six-pointed metal objects (jacks) between bounces of a ball.

We didn't like each other all that much at first, but nobody else wanted to play with us because we weren't real orphans with beautiful dead parents in the sky. We were dumped. Even the New York City Puerto Ricans and the upstate Indians ignored us. All kinds of kids were in there, black ones, white ones, even two Koreans. The food was good, though. At least I thought so. Roberta hated it and left whole pieces of things on her plate: Spam, Salisbury steak—even jello with fruit cocktail in it, and she didn't care if I ate what she wouldn't. Mary's idea of supper was popcorn and a can of Yoo-Hoo.[3] Hot mashed potatoes and two weenies was like Thanksgiving for me.

It really wasn't bad, St. Bonny's. The big girls on the second floor pushed us around now and then. But that was all. They wore lipstick and eyebrow pencil and wobbled their knees while they watched TV. Fifteen, sixteen, even, some of them were. They were put-out girls, scared runaways most of them. Poor little girls who fought their uncles off but looked tough to us, and mean. God did they look mean. The staff tried to keep them separate from the younger children, but sometimes they caught us watching them in the orchard where they played radios and danced with each other. They'd light out after us and pull our hair or twist our arms. We were scared of them, Roberta and me, but neither of us wanted the other one to know it. So we got a good list of dirty names we could shout back when we ran from them through the orchard. I used to dream a lot and almost always the orchard was there. Two acres, four maybe, of these little apple trees. Hundreds of them. Empty and crooked like beggar women when I first came to St. Bonny's but fat with flowers when I left. I don't know why I dreamt about that orchard so much. Nothing really happened there. Nothing all that important, I mean. Just the big girls dancing and playing the radio. Roberta and me watching. Maggie fell down there once. The kitchen woman with legs like parentheses. And the big girls laughed at her. We should have helped her up, I know, but we were scared of those girls with lipstick and eyebrow pencil. Maggie couldn't talk. The kids said she had her tongue cut out, but I think she was just born that way: mute. She was old and sandy-colored and she worked in the kitchen. I don't know if she was nice or not. I just remember her legs like parentheses and how she rocked when she walked. She worked from early in the morning till two o'clock, and if she was late, if she had too much cleaning and didn't get out till two-fifteen or so, she'd cut through the orchard so she wouldn't miss her bus and have to wait another hour. She wore this really stupid little hat—a kid's hat with ear flaps—and she wasn't much taller than we were. A really awful little hat. Even for a mute, it was dumb—dressing like a kid and never saying anything at all.

"But what about if somebody tries to kill her?" I used to wonder about that. "Or what if she wants to cry? Can she cry?"

"Sure," Roberta said. "But just tears. No sounds come out."

"She can't scream?"

"Nope. Nothing."

"Can she hear?"

"I guess."

"Let's call her," I said. And we did.

"Dummy! Dummy!" She never turned her head.

---

3. A popular chocolate drink that originated in the New York City area.

"Bow legs! Bow legs!" Nothing. She just rocked on, the chin straps of her baby-boy hat swaying from side to side. I think we were wrong. I think she could hear and didn't let on. And it shames me even now to think there was somebody in there after all who heard us call her those names and couldn't tell on us.

We got along all right, Roberta and me. Changed beds every night, got F's in civics and communication skills and gym. The Bozo was disappointed in us, she said. Out of 130 of us state cases, 90 were under twelve. Almost all were real orphans with beautiful dead parents in the sky. We were the only ones dumped and the only ones with F's in three classes including gym. So we got along—what with her leaving whole pieces of things on her plate and being nice about not asking questions.

I think it was the day before Maggie fell down that we found out our mothers were coming to visit us on the same Sunday. We had been at the shelter twenty-eight days (Roberta twenty-eight and a half) and this was their first visit with us. Our mothers would come at ten o'clock in time for chapel, then lunch with us in the teachers' lounge. I thought if my dancing mother met her sick mother it might be good for her. And Roberta thought her sick mother would get a big bang out of a dancing one. We got excited about it and curled each other's hair. After breakfast we sat on the bed watching the road from the window. Roberta's socks were still wet. She washed them the night before and put them on the radiator to dry. They hadn't, but she put them on anyway because their tops were so pretty—scalloped in pink. Each of us had a purple construction-paper basket that we had made in craft class. Mine had a yellow crayon rabbit on it. Roberta's had eggs with wiggly lines of color. Inside were cellophane grass and just the jelly beans because I'd eaten the two marshmallow eggs they gave us. The Big Bozo came herself to get us. Smiling she told us we looked very nice and to come downstairs. We were so surprised by the smile we'd never seen before, neither of us moved.

"Don't you want to see your mommies?"

I stood up first and spilled the jelly beans all over the floor. Bozo's smile disappeared while we scrambled to get the candy up off the floor and put it back in the grass.

She escorted us downstairs to the first floor, where the other girls were lining up to file into the chapel. A bunch of grown-ups stood to one side. Viewers mostly. The old biddies who wanted servants and the fags who wanted company looking for children they might want to adopt. Once in a while a grandmother. Almost never anybody young or anybody whose face wouldn't scare you in the night. Because if any of the real orphans had young relatives they wouldn't be real orphans. I saw Mary right away. She had on those green slacks I hated and hated even more now because didn't she know we were going to chapel? And that fur jacket with the pocket linings so ripped she had to pull to get her hands out of them. But her face was pretty—like always, and she smiled and waved like she was the little girl looking for her mother—not me.

I walked slowly, trying not to drop the jelly beans and hoping the paper handle would hold. I had to use my last Chiclet because by the time I finished cutting everything out, all the Elmer's[4] was gone. I am left-handed and the

---

4. Glue. "Chiclet": brand of chewing gum packaged in small pieces.

scissors never worked for me. It didn't matter, though; I might just as well have chewed the gum. Mary dropped to her knees and grabbed me, mashing the basket, the jelly beans, and the grass into her ratty fur jacket.

"Twyla, baby. Twyla, baby!"

I could have killed her. Already I heard the big girls in the orchard the next time saying, "Twyyyyyla, baby!" But I couldn't stay mad at Mary while she was smiling and hugging me and smelling of Lady Esther[5] dusting powder. I wanted to stay buried in her fur all day.

To tell the truth I forgot about Roberta. Mary and I got in line for the traipse into chapel and I was feeling proud because she looked so beautiful even in those ugly green slacks that made her behind stick out. A pretty mother on earth is better than a beautiful dead one in the sky even if she did leave you all alone to go dancing.

I felt a tap on my shoulder, turned, and saw Roberta smiling. I smiled back, but not too much lest somebody think this visit was the biggest thing that ever happened in my life. Then Roberta said, "Mother, I want you to meet my roommate, Twyla. And that's Twyla's mother."

I looked up it seemed for miles. She was big. Bigger than any man and on her chest was the biggest cross I'd ever seen. I swear it was six inches long each way. And in the crook of her arm was the biggest Bible ever made.

Mary, simple-minded as ever, grinned and tried to yank her hand out of the pocket with the raggedy lining—to shake hands, I guess. Roberta's mother looked down at me and then looked down at Mary too. She didn't say anything, just grabbed Roberta with her Bible-free hand and stepped out of line, walking quickly to the rear of it. Mary was still grinning because she's not too swift when it comes to what's really going on. Then this light bulb goes off in her head and she says "That bitch!" really loud and us almost in the chapel now. Organ music whining; the Bonny Angels singing sweetly. Everybody in the world turned around to look. And Mary would have kept it up—kept calling names if I hadn't squeezed her hand as hard as I could. That helped a little, but she still twitched and crossed and uncrossed her legs all through service. Even groaned a couple of times. Why did I think she would come there and act right? Slacks. No hat like the grandmothers and viewers, and groaning all the while. When we stood for hymns she kept her mouth shut. Wouldn't even look at the words on the page. She actually reached in her purse for a mirror to check her lipstick. All I could think of was that she really needed to be killed. The sermon lasted a year, and I knew the real orphans were looking smug again.

We were supposed to have lunch in the teachers' lounge, but Mary didn't bring anything, so we picked fur and cellophane grass off the mashed jelly beans and ate them. I could have killed her. I sneaked a look at Roberta. Her mother had brought chicken legs and ham sandwiches and oranges and a whole box of chocolate-covered grahams. Roberta drank milk from a thermos while her mother read the Bible to her.

Things are not right. The wrong food is always with the wrong people. Maybe that's why I got into waitress work later—to match up the right people with the right food. Roberta just let those chicken legs sit there, but she did bring a stack of grahams up to me later when the visit was over. I think she

---

5. A manufacturer of cosmetics and perfumes.

was sorry that her mother would not shake my mother's hand. And I liked that and I liked the fact that she didn't say a word about Mary groaning all the way through the service and not bringing any lunch.

Roberta left in May when the apple trees were heavy and white. On her last day we went to the orchard to watch the big girls smoke and dance by the radio. It didn't matter that they said, "Twyyyyla, baby." We sat on the ground and breathed. Lady Esther. Apple blossoms. I still go soft when I smell one or the other. Roberta was going home. The big cross and the big Bible was coming to get her and she seemed sort of glad and sort of not. I thought I would die in that room of four beds without her and I knew Bozo had plans to move some other dumped kid in there with me. Roberta promised to write every day, which was really sweet of her because she couldn't read a lick so how could she write anybody. I would have drawn pictures and sent them to her but she never gave me her address. Little by little she faded. Her wet socks with the pink scalloped tops and her big serious-looking eyes—that's all I could catch when I tried to bring her to mind.

I was working behind the counter at the Howard Johnson's on the Thruway just before the Kingston exit. Not a bad job. Kind of a long ride from Newburgh,[6] but okay once I got there. Mine was the second night shift—eleven to seven. Very light until a Greyhound checked in for breakfast around six-thirty. At that hour the sun was all the way clear of the hills behind the restaurant. The place looked better at night—more like shelter—but I loved it when the sun broke in, even if it did show all the cracks in the vinyl and the speckled floor looked dirty no matter what the mop boy did.

It was August and a bus crowd was just unloading. They would stand around a long while: going to the john, and looking at gifts and junk-for-sale machines, reluctant to sit down so soon. Even to eat. I was trying to fill the coffee pots and get them all situated on the electric burners when I saw her. She was sitting in a booth smoking a cigarette with two guys smothered in head and facial hair. Her own hair was so big and wild I could hardly see her face. But the eyes. I would know them anywhere. She had on a powder-blue halter and shorts outfit and earrings the size of bracelets. Talk about lipstick and eyebrow pencil. She made the big girls look like nuns. I couldn't get off the counter until seven o'clock, but I kept watching the booth in case they got up to leave before that. My replacement was on time for a change, so I counted and stacked my receipts as fast as I could and signed off. I walked over to the booth, smiling and wondering if she would remember me. Or even if she wanted to remember me. Maybe she didn't want to be reminded of St. Bonny's or to have anybody know she was ever there. I know I never talked about it to anybody.

I put my hands in my apron pockets and leaned against the back of the booth facing them.

"Roberta? Roberta Fisk?"

She looked up. "Yeah?"

"Twyla."

She squinted for a second and then said, "Wow."

"Remember me?"

"Sure. Hey. Wow."

---

6. Like Kingston, a town in New York, not far north of New York City.

"It's been a while," I said, and gave a smile to the two hairy guys.

"Yeah. Wow. You work here?"

"Yeah," I said. "I live in Newburgh."

"Newburgh? No kidding?" She laughed then a private laugh that included the guys but only the guys, and they laughed with her. What could I do but laugh too and wonder why I was standing there with my knees showing out from under that uniform. Without looking I could see the blue and white triangle on my head, my hair shapeless in a net, my ankles thick in white oxfords. Nothing could have been less sheer than my stockings. There was this silence that came down right after I laughed. A silence it was her turn to fill up. With introductions, maybe, to her boyfriends or an invitation to sit down and have a Coke. Instead she lit a cigarette off the one she'd just finished and said, "We're on our way to the Coast. He's got an appointment with Hendrix." She gestured casually toward the boy next to her.

"Hendrix? Fantastic," I said. "Really fantastic. What's she doing now?"

Roberta coughed on her cigarette and the two guys rolled their eyes up at the ceiling.

"Hendrix. Jimi Hendrix,[7] asshole. He's only the biggest—Oh, wow. Forget it."

I was dismissed without anyone saying goodbye, so I thought I would do it for her.

"How's your mother?" I asked. Her grin cracked her whole face. She swallowed. "Fine," she said. "How's yours?"

"Pretty as a picture," I said and turned away. The backs of my knees were damp. Howard Johnson's really was a dump in the sunlight.

James is as comfortable as a house slipper. He liked my cooking and I liked his big loud family. They have lived in Newburgh all of their lives and talk about it the way people do who have always known a home. His grandmother is a porch swing older than his father and when they talk about streets and avenues and buildings they call them names they no longer have. They still call the A & P Rico's because it stands on property once a mom and pop store owned by Mr. Rico. And they call the new community college Town Hall because it once was. My mother-in-law puts up jelly and cucumbers and buys butter wrapped in cloth from a dairy. James and his father talk about fishing and baseball and I can see them all together on the Hudson in a raggedy skiff. Half the population of Newburgh is on welfare now, but to my husband's family it was still some upstate paradise of a time long past. A time of ice houses and vegetable wagons, coal furnaces and children weeding gardens. When our son was born my mother-in-law gave me the crib blanket that had been hers.

But the town they remembered had changed. Something quick was in the air. Magnificent old houses, so ruined they had become shelter for squatters and rent risks, were bought and renovated. Smart IBM people moved out of their suburbs back into the city and put shutters up and herb gardens in their backyards. A brochure came in the mail announcing the opening of a Food Emporium. Gourmet food it said—and listed items the rich IBM crowd would want. It was located in a new mall at the edge of town and I drove out

---

7. Black American electric guitarist (1942–1970); he became a superstar in the late 1960s.

to shop there one day—just to see. It was late in June. After the tulips were gone and the Queen Elizabeth roses were open everywhere. I trailed my cart along the aisle tossing in smoked oysters and Robert's sauce and things I knew would sit in my cupboard for years. Only when I found some Klondike ice cream bars did I feel less guilty about spending James's fireman's salary so foolishly. My father-in-law ate them with the same gusto little Joseph did.

Waiting in the check-out line I heard a voice say, "Twyla!"

The classical music piped over the aisles had affected me and the woman leaning toward me was dressed to kill. Diamonds on her hand, a smart white summer dress. "I'm Mrs. Benson," I said.

"Ho. Ho. The Big Bozo," she sang.

For a split second I didn't know what she was talking about. She had a bunch of asparagus and two cartons of fancy water.

"Roberta!"

"Right."

"For heaven's sake. Roberta."

"You look great," she said.

"So do you. Where are you? Here? In Newburgh?"

"Yes. Over in Annandale."

I was opening my mouth to say more when the cashier called my attention to her empty counter.

"Meet you outside." Roberta pointed her finger and went into the express line.

I placed the groceries and kept myself from glancing around to check Roberta's progress. I remembered Howard Johnson's and looking for a chance to speak only to be greeted with a stingy "wow." But she was waiting for me and her huge hair was sleek now, smooth around a small, nicely shaped head. Shoes, dress, everything lovely and summery and rich. I was dying to know what happened to her, how she got from Jimi Hendrix to Annandale, a neighborhood full of doctors and IBM executives. Easy, I thought. Everything is so easy for them. They think they own the world.

"How long," I asked her. "How long have you been here?"

"A year. I got married to a man who lives here. And you, you're married too, right? Benson, you said."

"Yeah. James Benson."

"And is he nice?"

"Oh, is he nice?"

"Well, is he?" Roberta's eyes were steady as though she really meant the question and wanted an answer.

"He's wonderful, Roberta. Wonderful."

"So you're happy."

"Very."

"That's good," she said and nodded her head. "I always hoped you'd be happy. Any kids? I know you have kids."

"One. A boy. How about you?"

"Four."

"Four?"

She laughed. "Step kids. He's a widower."

"Oh."

"Got a minute? Let's have a coffee."

I thought about the Klondikes melting and the inconvenience of going all the way to my car and putting the bags in the trunk. Served me right for buying all that stuff I didn't need. Roberta was ahead of me.

"Put them in my car. It's right here."

And then I saw the dark blue limousine.

"You married a Chinaman?"

"No," she laughed. "He's the driver."

"Oh, my. If the Big Bozo could see you now."

We both giggled. Really giggled. Suddenly, in just a pulse beat, twenty years disappeared and all of it came rushing back. The big girls (whom we called gar girls—Roberta's misheard word for the evil stone faces[8] described in a civics class) there dancing in the orchard, the ploppy mashed potatoes, the double weenies, the Spam with pineapple. We went into the coffee shop holding on to one another and I tried to think why we were glad to see each other this time and not before. Once, twelve years ago, we passed like strangers. A black girl and a white girl meeting in a Howard Johnson's on the road and having nothing to say. One in a blue and white triangle waitress hat—the other on her way to see Hendrix. Now we were behaving like sisters separated for much too long. Those four short months were nothing in time. Maybe it was the thing itself. Just being there, together. Two little girls who knew what nobody else in the world knew—how not to ask questions. How to believe what had to be believed. There was politeness in that reluctance and generosity as well. Is your mother sick too? No, she dances all night. Oh—and an understanding nod.

We sat in a booth by the window and fell into recollection like veterans.

"Did you ever learn to read?"

"Watch." She picked up the menu. "Special of the day. Cream of corn soup. Entrées. Two dots and a wriggly line. Quiche. Chef salad, scallops . . ."

I was laughing and applauding when the waitress came up.

"Remember the Easter baskets?"

"And how we tried to *introduce* them?"

"Your mother with that cross like two telephone poles."

"And yours with those tight slacks."

We laughed so loudly heads turned and made the laughter harder to suppress.

"What happened to the Jimi Hendrix date?"

Roberta made a blow-out sound with her lips.

"When he died I thought about you."

"Oh, you heard about him finally?"

"Finally. Come on, I was a small-town country waitress."

"And I was a small-town country dropout. God, were we wild. I still don't know how I got out of there alive."

"But you did."

"I did. I really did. Now I'm Mrs. Kenneth Norton."

"Sounds like a mouthful."

"It is."

"Servants and all?"

Roberta held up two fingers.

---

8. I.e., gargoyles.

"Ow! What does he do?"

"Computers and stuff. What do I know?"

"I don't remember a hell of a lot from those days, but Lord, St. Bonny's is as clear as daylight. Remember Maggie? The day she fell down and those gar girls laughed at her?"

Roberta looked up from her salad and stared at me. "Maggie didn't fall," she said.

"Yes, she did. You remember."

"No, Twyla. They knocked her down. Those girls pushed her down and tore her clothes. In the orchard."

"I don't—that's not what happened."

"Sure it is. In the orchard. Remember how scared we were?"

"Wait a minute. I don't remember any of that."

"And Bozo was fired."

"You're crazy. She was there when I left. You left before me."

"I went back. You weren't there when they fired Bozo."

"What?"

"Twice. Once for a year when I was about ten, another for two months when I was fourteen. That's when I ran away."

"You ran away from St. Bonny's?"

"I had to. What do you want? Me dancing in that orchard?"

"Are you sure about Maggie?"

"Of course I'm sure. You've blocked it, Twyla. It happened. Those girls had behavior problems, you know."

"Didn't they, though. But why can't I remember the Maggie thing?"

"Believe me. It happened. And we were there."

"Who did you room with when you went back?" I asked her as if I would know her. The Maggie thing was troubling me.

"Creeps. They tickled themselves in the night."

My ears were itching and I wanted to go home suddenly. This was all very well but she couldn't just comb her hair, wash her face and pretend everything was hunky-dory. After the Howard Johnson's snub. And no apology. Nothing.

"Were you on dope or what that time at Howard Johnson's?" I tried to make my voice sound friendlier than I felt.

"Maybe, a little. I never did drugs much. Why?"

"I don't know; you acted sort of like you didn't want to know me then."

"Oh, Twyla, you know how it was in those days: black—white. You know how everything was."

But I didn't know. I thought it was just the opposite. Busloads of blacks and whites came into Howard Johnson's together. They roamed together then: students, musicians, lovers, protesters. You got to see everything at Howard Johnson's and blacks were very friendly with whites in those days. But sitting there with nothing on my plate but two hard tomato wedges wondering about the melting Klondikes it seemed childish remembering the slight. We went to her car, and with the help of the driver, got my stuff into my station wagon.

"We'll keep in touch this time," she said.

"Sure," I said. "Sure. Give me a call."

"I will," she said, and then just as I was sliding behind the wheel, she leaned into the window. "By the way. Your mother. Did she ever stop dancing?"

I shook my head. "No. Never."

Roberta nodded.

"And yours? Did she ever get well?"

She smiled a tiny sad smile. "No. She never did. Look, call me, okay?"

"Okay," I said, but I knew I wouldn't. Roberta had messed up my past somehow with that business about Maggie. I wouldn't forget a thing like that. Would I?

Strife came to us that fall. At least that's what the paper called it. Strife. Racial strife. The word made me think of a bird—a big shrieking bird out of 1,000,000,000 B.C. Flapping its wings and cawing. Its eye with no lid always bearing down on you. All day it screeched and at night it slept on the rooftops. It woke you in the morning and from the *Today* show to the eleven o'clock news it kept you an awful company. I couldn't figure it out from one day to the next. I knew I was supposed to feel something strong, but I didn't know what, and James wasn't any help. Joseph was on the list of kids to be transferred from the junior high school to another one at some far-out-of-the-way place and I thought it was a good thing until I heard it was a bad thing.[9] I mean I didn't know. All the schools seemed dumps to me, and the fact that one was nicer looking didn't hold much weight. But the papers were full of it and then the kids began to get jumpy. In August, mind you. Schools weren't even open yet. I thought Joseph might be frightened to go over there, but he didn't seem scared so I forgot about it, until I found myself driving along Hudson Street out there by the school they were trying to integrate and saw a line of women marching. And who do you suppose was in line, big as life, holding a sign in front of her bigger than her mother's cross? MOTHER HAVE RIGHTS TOO! it said.

I drove on, and then changed my mind. I circled the block, slowed down, and honked my horn.

Roberta looked over and when she saw me she waved. I didn't wave back, but I didn't move either. She handed her sign to another woman and came over to where I was parked.

"Hi."

"What are you doing?"

"Picketing. What's it look like?"

"What for?"

"What do you mean, 'What for?' They want to take my kids and send them out of the neighborhood. They don't want to go."

"So what if they go to another school? My boy's being bussed too, and I don't mind. Why should you?"

"It's not about us, Twyla. Me and you. It's about our kids."

"What's more *us* than that?"

"Well, it is a free country."

"Not yet, but it will be."

"What the hell does that mean? I'm not doing anything to you."

---

9. In the 1970s, Newburgh was one of the U.S. cities under court order to achieve racial integration in the public schools.

"You really think that?"

"I know it."

"I wonder what made me think you were different."

"I wonder what made me think you were different."

"Look at them," I said. "Just look. Who do they think they are? Swarming all over the place like they own it. And now they think they can decide where my child goes to school. Look at them, Roberta. They're Bozos."

Roberta turned around and looked at the women. Almost all of them were standing still now, waiting. Some were even edging toward us. Roberta looked at me out of some refrigerator behind her eyes. "No, they're not. They're just mothers."

"And what am I? Swiss cheese?"

"I used to curl your hair."

"I hated your hands in my hair."

The women were moving. Our faces looked mean to them of course and they looked as though they could not wait to throw themselves in front of a police car, or better yet, into my car and drag me away by my ankles. Now they surrounded my car and gently, gently began to rock it. I swayed back and forth like a sideways yo-yo. Automatically I reached for Roberta, like the old days in the orchard when they saw us watching them and we had to get out of there, and if one of us fell the other pulled her up and if one of us was caught the other stayed to kick and scratch, and neither would leave the other behind. My arm shot out of the car window but no receiving hand was there. Roberta was looking at me sway from side to side in the car and her face was still. My purse slid from the car seat down under the dashboard. The four policemen who had been drinking Tab in their car finally got the message and strolled over, forcing their way through the women. Quietly, firmly they spoke. "Okay, ladies. Back in line or off the streets."

Some of them went away willingly; others had to be urged away from the car doors and the hood. Roberta didn't move. She was looking steadily at me. I was fumbling to turn on the ignition, which wouldn't catch because the gearshift was still in drive. The seats of the car were a mess because the swaying had thrown my grocery coupons all over it and my purse was sprawled on the floor.

"Maybe I am different now, Twyla. But you're not. You're the same little state kid who kicked a poor old black lady when she was down on the ground. You kicked a black lady and you have the nerve to call me a bigot."

The coupons were everywhere and the guts of my purse were bunched under the dashboard. What was she saying? Black? Maggie wasn't black.

"She wasn't black," I said.

"Like hell she wasn't, and you kicked her. We both did. You kicked a black lady who couldn't even scream."

"Liar!"

"You're the liar! Why don't you just go on home and leave us alone, huh?"

She turned away and I skidded away from the curb.

The next morning I went into the garage and cut the side out of the carton our portable TV had come in. It wasn't nearly big enough, but after a while I had a decent sign: red spray-painted letters on a white background—AND SO DO CHILDREN****. I meant just to go down to the school and tack it up somewhere so those cows on the picket line across the street could see it, but when I got there, some ten or so others had already assembled—protesting the cows across the street. Police permits and everything. I got in line and we strutted in time on our side while Roberta's group strutted on theirs. That first day we were all dignified, pretending the other side didn't exist. The second day there was name calling and finger gestures. But that was about all. People changed signs from time to time, but Roberta never did and neither did I. Actually my sign didn't make sense without Roberta's. "And so do children what?" one of the women on my side asked me. Have rights, I said, as though it was obvious.

Roberta didn't acknowledge my presence in any way and I got to thinking maybe she didn't know I was there. I began to pace myself in the line, jostling people one minute and lagging behind the next, so Roberta and I could reach the end of our respective lines at the same time and there would be a moment in our turn when we would face each other. Still, I couldn't tell whether she saw me and knew my sign was for her. The next day I went early before we were scheduled to assemble. I waited until she got there before I exposed my new creation. As soon as she hoisted her MOTHERS HAVE RIGHTS TOO I began to wave my new one, which said, HOW WOULD YOU KNOW? I know she saw that one, but I had gotten addicted now. My signs got crazier each day, and the women on my side decided that I was a kook. They couldn't make heads or tails out of my brilliant screaming posters.

I brought a painted sign in queenly red with huge black letters that said, IS YOUR MOTHER WELL? Roberta took her lunch break and didn't come back for the rest of the day or any day after. Two days later I stopped going too and couldn't have been missed because nobody understood my signs anyway.

It was a nasty six weeks. Classes were suspended and Joseph didn't go to anybody's school until October. The children—everybody's children—soon got bored with that extended vacation they thought was going to be so great. They looked at TV until their eyes flattened. I spent a couple of mornings tutoring my son, as the other mothers said we should. Twice I opened a text from last year that he had never turned in. Twice he yawned in my face. Other mothers organized living room sessions so the kids would keep up. None of the kids could concentrate so they drifted back to *The Price Is Right* and *The Brady Bunch*.[1] When the school finally opened there were fights once or twice and some sirens roared through the streets every once in a while. There were a lot of photographers from Albany. And just when ABC was about to send up a news crew, the kids settled down like nothing in the world had happened. Joseph hung my HOW WOULD YOU KNOW? sign in his bedroom. I don't know what became of AND SO DO CHILDREN****. I think my father-in-law cleaned some fish on it. He was always puttering around in our garage. Each of his five children lived in Newburgh and he acted as though he had five extra homes.

I couldn't help looking for Roberta when Joseph graduated from high school, but I didn't see her. It didn't trouble me much what she had said to me in the car. I mean the kicking part. I know I didn't do that, I couldn't do that. But I was puzzled by her telling me Maggie was black. When I thought

---

1. A prime-time television show about an extended white family (1969–74); the modern version of *The Price Is Right*, a daytime game show, began in 1972.

about it I actually couldn't be certain. She wasn't pitch-black, I knew, or I would have remembered that. What I remember was the kiddie hat, and the semicircle legs. I tried to reassure myself about the race thing for a long time until it dawned on me that the truth was already there, and Roberta knew it. I didn't kick her; I didn't join in with the gar girls and kick that lady, but I sure did want to. We watched and never tried to help her and never called for help. Maggie was my dancing mother. Deaf, I thought, and dumb. Nobody inside. Nobody who would hear you if you cried in the night. Nobody who could tell you anything important that you could use. Rocking, dancing, swaying as she walked. And when the gar girls pushed her down, and started roughhousing, I knew she wouldn't scream, couldn't—just like me—and I was glad about that.

We decided not to have a tree, because Christmas would be at my mother-in-law's house, so why have a tree at both places? Joseph was at SUNY New Paltz and we had to economize, we said. But at the last minute, I changed my mind. Nothing could be that bad. So I rushed around town looking for a tree, something small but wide. By the time I found a place, it was snowing and very late. I dawdled like it was the most important purchase in the world and the tree man was fed up with me. Finally I chose one and had it tied onto the trunk of the car. I drove away slowly because the sand trucks were not out yet and the streets could be murder at the beginning of a snowfall. Downtown the streets were wide and rather empty except for a cluster of people coming out of the Newburgh Hotel. The one hotel in town that wasn't built out of cardboard and Plexiglas. A party, probably. The men huddled in the snow were dressed in tails and the women had on furs. Shiny things glittered from underneath their coats. It made me tired to look at them. Tired, tired, tired. On the next corner was a small diner with loops and loops of paper bells in the window. I stopped the car and went in. Just for a cup of coffee and twenty minutes of peace before I went home and tried to finish everything before Christmas Eve.

"Twyla?"

There she was. In a silvery evening gown and dark fur coat. A man and another woman were with her, the man fumbling for change to put in the cigarette machine. The woman was humming and tapping on the counter with her fingernails. They all looked a little bit drunk.

"Well. It's you."

"How are you?"

I shrugged. "Pretty good. Frazzled. Christmas and all."

"Regular?" called the woman from the counter.

"Fine," Roberta called back and then, "Wait for me in the car."

She slipped into the booth beside me. "I have to tell you something, Twyla. I made up my mind if I ever saw you again, I'd tell you."

"I'd just as soon not hear anything, Roberta. It doesn't matter now, anyway."

"No," she said. "Not about that."

"Don't be long," said the woman. She carried two regulars to go and the man peeled his cigarette pack as they left.

"It's about St. Bonny's and Maggie."

"Oh, please."

"Listen to me. I really did think she was black. I didn't make that up. I really thought so. But now I can't be sure. I just remember her as old, so old. And because she couldn't talk—well, you know, I thought she was crazy. She'd been brought up in an institution like my mother was and like I thought I would be too. And you were right. We didn't kick her. It was the gar girls. Only them. But, well, I wanted to. I really wanted them to hurt her. I said we did it, too. You and me, but that's not true. And I don't want you to carry that around. It was just that I wanted to do it so bad that day—wanting to is doing it."

Her eyes were watery from the drinks she'd had, I guess. I know it's that way with me. One glass of wine and I start bawling over the littlest thing.

"We were kids, Roberta."

"Yeah. Yeah. I know, just kids."

"Eight."

"Eight."

"And lonely."

"Scared, too."

She wiped her cheeks with the heel of her hand and smiled. "Well, that's all I wanted to say."

I nodded and couldn't think of any way to fill the silence that went from the diner past the paper bells on out into the snow. It was heavy now. I thought I'd better wait for the sand trucks before starting home.

"Thanks, Roberta."

"Sure."

"Did I tell you? My mother, she never did stop dancing."

"Yes. You told me. And mine, she never got well." Roberta lifted her hands from the tabletop and covered her face with her palms. When she took them away she really was crying. "Oh shit, Twyla. Shit, shit, shit. What the hell happened to Maggie?"

1983

From Unspeakable Things Unspoken: The Afro-American Presence in American Literature[1]

I planned to call this paper "Canon Fodder," because the terms put me in mind of a kind of trained muscular response that appears to be on display in some areas of the recent canon debate. But I changed my mind (so many have used the phrase) and hope to make clear the appropriateness of the title I settled on.

My purpose here is to observe the panoply of this most recent and most anxious series of questions concerning what should or does constitute a literary canon in order to suggest ways of addressing the Afro-American presence in American Literature that require neither slaughter nor reification—views that may spring the whole literature of an entire nation from the solitude into which it has been locked. There is something called American

---

1. Presented as the Tanner Lecture on Human Values at the University of Michigan, October 7, 1988.

literature that, according to conventional wisdom, is certainly not Chicano literature, or Afro-American literature, or Asian-American, or Native American or . . . It is somehow separate from them and they from it, and in spite of the efforts of recent literary histories, restructured curricula and anthologies, this separate confinement, be it breached or endorsed, is the subject of a large part of these debates. Although the terms used, like the vocabulary of earlier canon debates, refer to literary and/or humanistic value, aesthetic criteria, value-free or socially anchored readings, the contemporary battle plain is most often understood to be the claims of others against the white-male origins and definitions of those values; whether those definitions reflect an eternal, universal and transcending paradigm or whether they constitute a disguise for a temporal, political and culturally specific program.

Part of the history of this particular debate is located in the successful assault that the feminist scholarship of men and women (black and white) made and continues to make on traditional literary discourse. The male part of the whitemale equation is already deeply engaged, and no one believes the body of literature and its criticism will ever again be what it was in 1965: the protected preserve of the thoughts and works and analytical strategies of whitemen.

It is, however, the "white" part of the question that this paper focuses on, and it is to my great relief that such terms as "white" and "race" can enter serious discussion of literature. Although still a swift and swiftly obeyed call to arms, their use is no longer forbidden.[2] It may appear churlish to doubt the sincerity, or question the proclaimed well-intentioned self-lessness of a 900-year-old academy struggling through decades of chaos to "maintain standards." Yet of what use is it to go on about "quality" being the only criterion for greatness knowing that the definition of quality is itself the subject of much rage and is seldom universally agreed upon by everyone at all times? Is it to appropriate the term for reasons of state; to be in the position to distribute greatness or withhold it? Or to actively pursue the ways and places in which quality surfaces and stuns us into silence or into language worthy enough to describe it? What is possible is to try to recognize, identify and applaud the fight for and triumph of quality when it is revealed to us and to let go the notion that only the dominant culture or gender can make those judgments, identify that quality or produce it.

Those who claim the superiority of Western culture are entitled to that claim only when Western civilization is measured thoroughly against other civilizations and not found wanting, and when Western civilization owns up to its own sources in the cultures that preceded it.

A large part of the satisfaction I have always received from reading Greek tragedy, for example, is in its similarity to Afro-American communal structures (the function of song and chorus, the heroic struggle between the claims of community and individual hubris) and African religion and philosophy. In other words, that is part of the reason it has quality for me—I feel intellectually at home there. But that could hardly be so for those unfamiliar with my "home," and hardly a requisite for the pleasure they take. The point is, the form (Greek tragedy) makes available these varieties of provocative

---

2. See *"Race," Writing, and Difference*, ed. Henry Louis Gates (University of Chicago Press, 1986) [Morrison's note].

love because *it* is masterly—not because the civilization that is its referent was flawless or superior to all others.

One has the feeling that nights are becoming sleepless in some quarters, and it seems to me obvious that the recoil of traditional "humanists" and some post-modern theorists to this particular aspect of the debate, the "race" aspect, is as severe as it is because the claims for attention come from that segment of scholarly and artistic labor in which the mention of "race" is either inevitable or elaborately, painstakingly masked; and if all of the ramifications that the term demands are taken seriously, the bases of Western civilization will require re-thinking. Thus, in spite of its implicit and explicit acknowledgement, "race" is still a virtually unspeakable thing, as can be seen in the apologies, notes of "special use" and circumscribed definitions that accompany it[3]—not least of which is my own deference in surrounding it with quotation marks. Suddenly (for our purposes, suddenly) "race" does not exist. For three hundred years black Americans insisted that "race" was no usefully distinguishing factor in human relationships. During those same three centuries every academic discipline, including theology, history, and natural science, insisted "race" was *the* determining factor in human development. When blacks discovered they had shaped or become a culturally formed race, and that it had specific and revered difference, suddenly they were told there is no such thing as "race," biological or cultural, that matters and that genuinely intellectual exchange cannot accommodate it.[4] In trying to come to some terms about "race" and writing, I am tempted to throw my hands up. It always seemed to me that the people who invented the hierarchy of "race" when it was convenient for them ought not to be the ones to explain it away, now that it does not suit their purposes for it to exist. But there *is* culture and both gender and "race" inform and are informed by it. Afro-American culture exists and though it is clear (and becoming clearer) how it has responded to Western culture, the instances where and means by which it has shaped Western culture are poorly recognized or understood.

I want to address ways in which the presence of Afro-American literature and the awareness of its culture both resuscitate the study of literature in the United States and raise that study's standards. In pursuit of that goal, it will suit my purposes to contextualize the route canon debates have taken in Western literary criticism.

I do not believe this current anxiety can be attributed solely to the routine, even cyclical arguments within literary communities reflecting unpredictable yet inevitable shifts in taste, relevance or perception. Shifts in which an enthusiasm for and official endorsement of William Dean Howells, for example, withered; or in which the legalization of Mark Twain in critical court rose and fell like the fathoming of a sounding line (for which he may or may not have named himself);[5] or even the slow, delayed but steady swell of attention and devotion on which Emily Dickinson[6] soared to what is now,

---

3. Among many examples, *They Came Before Columbus, The African Presence in Ancient America* by Ivan van Sertima (New York: Random House, 1976), pp. xvi–xvii [Morrison's note].
4. Tzvetan Todorov, " 'Race,' Writing, and Culture," translated by Loulou Mack, in Gates, op. cit., pp. 370–380 [Morrison's note].
5. Samuel Clemens (1835–1910), American novelist and humorist, usually connected his pen name with the call of boatmen on the Mississippi River that indicated a safe water depth of 2 fathoms (12 feet): "mark twain." Howells (1837–1920), American writer of fiction and a highly influential editor.
6. American poet (1830–1886); see Vol. 1, p. 1037.

surely, a permanent crest of respect. No. Those were discoveries, reappraisals of individual artists. Serious but not destabilizing. Such accommodations were simple because the questions they posed were simple: Are there one hundred sterling examples of high literary art in American literature and no more? One hundred and six? If one or two fall into disrepute, is there space, then, for one or two others in the vestibule, waiting like girls for bells chimed by future husbands who alone can promise them security, legitimacy—and in whose hands alone rests the gift of critical longevity? Interesting questions, but, as I say, not endangering.

Nor is this detectable academic sleeplessness the consequence of a much more radical shift, such as the mid-nineteenth century one heralding the authenticity of American literature itself. Or an even earlier upheaval—receding now into the distant past—in which theology and thereby Latin, was displaced for the equally rigorous study of the classics and Greek[7] to be followed by what was considered a strangely arrogant and upstart proposal: that English literature was a suitable course of study for an aristocratic education, and not simply morally instructive fodder designed for the working classes. (The Chaucer Society was founded in 1848, four hundred years after Chaucer[8] died.) No. This exchange seems unusual somehow, keener. It has a more strenuously argued (and felt) defense and a more vigorously insistent attack. And both defenses and attacks have spilled out of the academy into the popular press. Why? Resistance to displacement within or expansion of a canon is not, after all, surprising or unwarranted. That's what canonization is for. (And the question of whether there should be a canon or not seems disingenuous to me—there always is one whether there should be or not—for it is in the interests of the professional critical community to have one.) Certainly a sharp alertness as to *why* a work is or is not worthy of study is the legitimate occupation of the critic, the pedagogue and the artist. What is astonishing in the contemporary debate is not the resistance to displacement of works or to the expansion of genre within it, but the virulent passion that accompanies this resistance and, more importantly, the quality of its defense weaponry. The guns are very big; the trigger-fingers quick. But I am convinced the mechanism of the defenders of the flame is faulty. Not only may the hands of the gun-slinging cowboy-scholars be blown off, not only may the target be missed, but the subject of the conflagration (the sacred texts) is sacrificed, disfigured in the battle. This canon fodder may kill the canon. And I, at least, do not intend to live without Aeschylus or William Shakespeare, or James or Twain or Hawthorne, or Melville,[9] etc., etc., etc. There must be some way to enhance canon readings without enshrining them.

* * *

There are at least three focuses that seem to me to be neither reactionary nor simple pluralism, nor the even simpler methods by which the study of

---

7. In England, Greek was introduced into the curriculum in the 16th century.
8. Poet (ca. 1343–1400) who wrote in Middle English.
9. American novelist (1819–1891) whose masterpiece is *Moby-Dick* (1850), in which Captain Ahab of the *Pequod* searches for the great white whale responsible for the loss of his leg. Aeschylus (525–456 B.C.E.), Greek tragedian; Henry James (1843–1916), American novelist and critic; Nathaniel Hawthorne (1804–1864), writer of novels and stories, and a friend of Melville.

Afro-American literature remains the helpful doorman into the halls of sociology. Each of them, however, requires wakefulness.

One is the development of a theory of literature that truly accommodates Afro-American literature: one that is based on its culture, its history, and the artistic strategies the works employ to negotiate the world it inhabits.

Another is the examination and re-interpretation of the American canon, the founding nineteenth-century works, for the "unspeakable things unspoken"; for the ways in which the presence of Afro-Americans has shaped the choices, the language, the structure—the meaning of so much American literature. A search, in other words, for the ghost in the machine.

A third is the examination of contemporary and/or noncanonical literature for this presence, regardless of its category as mainstream, minority, or what you will. I am always amazed by the resonances, the structural gear-shifts, and the *uses* to which Afro-American narrative, persona and idiom are put in contemporary "white" literature. And in Afro-American literature itself the question of difference, of essence, is critical. What makes a work "Black"? The most valuable point of entry into the question of cultural (or racial) distinction, the one most fraught, is its language—its unpoliced, seditious, confrontational, manipulative, inventive, disruptive, masked and unmasking language. Such a penetration will entail the most careful study, one in which the impact of Afro-American presence on modernity becomes clear and is no longer a well-kept secret.

I would like to touch, for just a moment, on focuses two and three.

We can agree, I think, that invisible things are not necessarily "not-there"; that a void may be empty, but is not a vacuum. In addition, certain absences are so stressed, so ornate, so planned, they call attention to themselves; arrest us with intentionality and purpose, like neighborhoods that are defined by the population held away from them. Looking at the scope of American literature, I can't help thinking that the question should never have been "Why am I, an Afro-American, absent from it?" It is not a particularly interesting query anyway. The spectacularly interesting question is "What intellectual feats had to be performed by the author or his critic to erase me from a society seething with my presence, and what effect has that performance had on the work?" What are the strategies of escape from knowledge? Of willful oblivion? I am not recommending an inquiry into the obvious impulse that overtakes a soldier sitting in a World War I trench to think of salmon fishing. That kind of pointed "turning from," deliberate escapism or transcendence may be life-saving in a circumstance of immediate duress. The exploration I am suggesting is, how does one sit in the audience observing, watching the performance of Young America, say, in the nineteenth century, say, and reconstruct the play, its director, its plot and its cast in such a manner that its very point never surfaces? Not why. How? Ten years after Tocqueville's prediction in 1840 that " 'Finding no stuff for the ideal in what is real and true, poets would flee to imaginary regions . . . ' in 1850 at the height of slavery and burgeoning abolitionism, American writers chose romance."[1] Where, I wonder, in these romances is the shadow of the pres-

---

1. See Michael Paul Rogin, *Subversive Genealogy: The Politics and Art of Herman Melville* (University of California Press, 1985), p. 15 [Morrison's note]. The quotation is from vol. 2 of *Democracy in America* (1840), chap. 18, by the French writer and politician Alexis de Tocqueville (1805–1859).

ence from which the text has fled? Where does it heighten, where does it dislocate, where does it necessitate novelistic invention; what does it release; what does it hobble?

The device (or arsenal) that serves the purpose of flight can be Romanticism versus verisimilitude; new criticism versus shabbily disguised and questionably sanctioned "moral uplift"; the "complex series of evasions," that is sometimes believed to be the essence of modernism; the perception of the evolution of art; the cultivation of irony, parody; the nostalgia for "literary language"; the rhetorically unconstrained textuality versus socially anchored textuality, and the undoing of textuality altogether. These critical strategies can (but need not) be put into service to reconstruct the historical world to suit specific cultural and political purposes. Many of these strategies have produced powerfully creative work. Whatever *uses* to which Romanticism is put, however suspicious its origins, it has produced an incontestably wonderful body of work. In other instances these strategies have succeeded in paralyzing both the work and its criticism. In still others they have led to a virtual infantilization of the writer's intellect, his sensibility, his craft. They have reduced the meditations on theory into a "power struggle among sects" reading unauthored and unauthorable material, rather than an outcome of reading *with* the author the text both construct.

In other words, the critical process has made wonderful work of some wonderful work, and recently the means of access to the old debates have altered. The problem now is putting the question. Is the nineteenth century flight from blackness, for example, successful in mainstream American literature? Beautiful? Artistically problematic? Is the text sabotaged by its own proclamations of "universality"? Are there ghosts in the machine? Active but unsummoned presences that can distort the workings of the machine and can also *make* it work? These kinds of questions have been consistently put by critics of Colonial Literature vis-à-vis Africa and India and other third world countries. American literature would benefit from similar critiques. I am made melancholy when I consider that the act of defending the Eurocentric Western posture in literature as not only "universal" but also "race-free" may have resulted in lobotomizing that literature, and in diminishing both the art and the artist. Like the surgical removal of legs so that the body can remain enthroned, immobile, static—under house arrest, so to speak. It may be, of course, that contemporary writers deliberately exclude from their conscious writerly world the subjective appraisal of groups perceived as "other," and whitemale writers frequently abjure and deny the excitement of framing or locating their literature in the political world. Nineteenth-century writers, however, would never have given it a thought. Mainstream writers in Young America understood their competition to be national, cultural, but only in relationship to the Old World, certainly not vis-à-vis an ancient race (whether Native American or African) that was stripped of articulateness and intellectual thought, rendered, in D. H. Lawrence's[2] term, "uncreate." For these early American writers, how could there be competition with nations or peoples who were presumed unable to handle or uninterested in

---

2. English novelist and poet (1885–1930); in *Studies in Classic American Literature* (1923), he criticized Melville's embrace of the South Sea Islanders by arguing that "we can't go back to the savages," to "their soft warm twilight and uncreate mud."

handling the written word? One could write about them, but there was never the danger of their "writing back." Just as one could speak to them without fear of their "talking back." One could even observe them, hold them in prolonged gaze, without encountering the risk of being observed, viewed, or judged in return. And if, on occasion, they were themselves viewed and judged, it was out of a political necessity and, for the purposes of art, could not matter. Or so thought Young America. It could never have occurred to Edgar Allan Poe[3] in 1848 that I, for example, might read *The Gold Bug* and watch his efforts to render my grandfather's speech to something as close to braying as possible, an effort so intense you can see the perspiration—and the stupidity—when Jupiter says "I knows," and Mr. Poe spells the verb "nose."[4]

* * *

It is on this area, the impact of Afro-American culture on contemporary American literature, that I now wish to comment. I have already said that works by Afro-Americans can respond to this presence (just as non-black works do) in a number of ways. The question of what constitutes the art of a black writer, for whom that modifier is more search than fact, has some urgency. In other words, other than melanin and subject matter, what, in fact, may make me a black writer? Other than my own ethnicity—what is going on in my work that makes me believe it is demonstrably inseparable from a cultural specificity that is Afro-American?

Please forgive the use of my own work in these observations. I use it not because it provides the best example, but because I know it best, know what I did and why, and know how central these queries are to me. Writing is, *after* all, an act of language, its practice. But *first* of all it is an effort of the will to discover.

Let me suggest some of the ways in which I activate language and ways in which that language activates me. I will limit this perusal by calling attention only to the first sentences of the books I've written, and hope that in exploring the choices I made, prior points are illuminated.

The Bluest Eye[5] begins "Quiet as it's kept, there were no marigolds in the fall of 1941." That sentence, like the ones that open each succeeding book, is simple, uncomplicated. Of all the sentences that begin all the books, only two of them have dependent clauses; the other three are simple sentences and two are stripped down to virtually subject, verb, modifier. Nothing fancy here. No words need looking up; they are ordinary, everyday words. Yet I hoped the simplicity was not simple-minded, but devious, even loaded. And that the process of selecting each word, for itself and its relationship to the others in the sentence, along with the rejection of others for their echoes,

---

3. American writer of poetry and short stories (1809–1849); "The Gold Bug" features "an old negro, called Jupiter," a former slave who insists on continuing to serve "his young 'Massa Will.' "
4. Older America is not always distinguishable from its infancy. We may pardon Edgar Allan Poe in 1848 but it should have occurred to Kenneth Lynn in 1986 that some young Native American might read his Hemingway biography and see herself described as "squaw" by this respected scholar, and that some young men might shudder reading the words "buck" and "half-breed" so casually included in his scholarly speculations [Morrison's note]. See *Hemingway: The Life and the Work* (New York: Simon and Schuster, 1987), by Lynn (1923–2001), a historian and scholar of American culture.
5. Morrison's first novel (1969).

for what is determined and what is not determined, what is almost there and what must be gleaned, would not theatricalize itself, would not erect a proscenium—at least not a noticeable one. So important to me was this unstaging, that in this first novel I summarized the whole of the book on the first page. (In the first edition, it was printed in its entirety on the jacket).

The opening phrase of this sentence, "Quiet as it's kept," had several attractions for me. First, it was a familiar phrase familiar to me as a child listening to adults; to black women conversing with one another; telling a story, an anecdote, gossip about some one or event within the circle, the family, the neighborhood. The words are conspiratorial. "Shh, don't tell anyone else," and "No one is allowed to know this." It is a secret between us and a secret that is being kept from us. The conspiracy is both held and withheld, exposed and sustained. In some sense it was precisely what the act of writing the book was: the public exposure of a private confidence. In order fully to comprehend the duality of that position, one needs to think of the immediate political climate in which the writing took place, 1965–1969, during great social upheaval in the life of black people. The publication (as opposed to the writing) involved the exposure; the writing was the disclosure of secrets, secrets "we" shared and those withheld from us by ourselves and by the world outside the community.

"Quiet as it's kept," is also a figure of speech that is written, in this instance, but clearly chosen for how speakerly it is, how it speaks and bespeaks a particular world and its ambience. Further, in addition to its "back fence" connotation, its suggestion of illicit gossip, of thrilling revelation, there is also, in the "whisper," the assumption (on the part of the reader) that the teller is on the inside, knows something others do not, and is going to be generous with this privileged information. The intimacy I was aiming for, the intimacy between the reader and the page, could start up immediately because the secret is being shared, at best, and eavesdropped upon, at the least. Sudden familiarity or instant intimacy seemed crucial to me then, writing my first novel. I did not want the reader to have time to wonder "What do I have to do, to give up, in order to read this? What defense do I need, what distance maintain?" Because I know (and the reader does not—he or she has to wait for the second sentence) that this is a terrible story about things one would rather not know anything about.

What, then, is the Big Secret about to be shared? The thing we (reader and I) are "in" on? A botanical aberration. Pollution, perhaps. A skip, perhaps, in the natural order of things: a September, an autumn, a fall without marigolds. Bright common, strong and sturdy marigolds. When? In 1941, and since that is a momentous year (the beginning of World War II for the United States), the "fall" of 1941, just before the declaration of war, has a "closet" innuendo. In the temperate zone where there is a season known as "fall" during which one expects marigolds to be at their peak, in the months before the beginning of U.S. participation in World War II, something grim is about to be divulged. The next sentence will make it clear that the sayer, the one who knows, is a child speaking, mimicking the adult black women on the porch or in the back yard. The opening phrase is an effort to be grown-up about this shocking information. The point of view of a child alters the priority an adult would assign the information. "We thought it was because Pecola was having her father's baby that the marigolds did not grow" foregrounds the flowers, backgrounds illicit, traumatic, incomprehensible sex coming to its dreaded fruition. This foregrounding of "trivial" information and backgrounding of shocking knowledge secures the point of view but gives the reader pause about whether the voice of children can be trusted at all or is more trustworthy than an adult's. The reader is thereby protected from a confrontation too soon with the painful details, while simultaneously provoked into a desire to know them. The novelty, I thought, would be in having this story of female violation revealed from the vantage point of the victims or could-be victims of rape—the persons no one inquired of (certainly not in 1965)—the girls themselves. And since the victim does not have the vocabulary to understand the violence or its context, gullible, vulnerable girl friends, looking back as the knowing adults they pretended to be in the beginning, would have to do that for her, and would have to fill those silences with their own reflective lives. Thus, the opening provides the stroke that announces something more than a secret shared, but a silence broken, a void filled, an unspeakable thing spoken at last. And they draw the connection between a minor destabilization in seasonal flora with the insignificant destruction of a black girl. Of course "minor" and "insignificant" represent the outside world's view—for the girls both phenomena are earthshaking depositories of information they spend that whole year of childhood (and afterwards) trying to fathom, and cannot. If they have any success, it will be in transferring the problem of fathoming to the presumably adult reader, to the inner circle of listeners. At the least they have distributed the weight of these problematical questions to a larger constituency, and justified the public exposure of a privacy. If the conspiracy that the opening words announce is entered into by the reader, then the book can be seen to open with its close: a speculation on the disruption of "nature," as being a social disruption with tragic individual consequences in which the reader, as part of the population of the text, is implicated.

However a problem, unsolved, lies in the central chamber of the novel. The shattered world I built (to complement what is happening to Pecola), its pieces held together by seasons in childtime and commenting at every turn on the incompatible and barren white-family primer,[6] does not in its present form handle effectively the silence at its center. The void that is Pecola's "unbeing." It should have had a shape—like the emptiness left by a boom or a cry. It required a sophistication unavailable to me, and some deft manipulation of the voices around her. She is not *seen* by herself until she hallucinates a self. And the fact of her hallucination becomes a point of outside-the-book conversation, but does not work in the reading process.

Also, although I was pressing for a female expressiveness (a challenge that re-surfaced in *Sula*[7]), it eluded me for the most part, and I had to content myself with female personae because I was not able to secure throughout the work the feminine subtext that is present in the opening sentence (the women gossiping, eager and aghast in "Quiet as it's kept"). The shambles this struggle became is most evident in the section on Pauline Breedlove where I resorted to two voices, hers and the urging narrator's, both of which

---

6. Serving as the epigraph of *The Bluest Eye* is a parodic paragraph describing a family; it is written in the style of the Dick and Jane readers (published by Scott, Foresman) that dominated U.S. elementary education from the 1940s to the 1960s.
7. Morrison's second novel (1973).

are extremely unsatisfactory to me. It is interesting to me now that where I thought I would have the most difficulty subverting the language to a feminine mode, I had the least: connecting Cholly's "rape" by the whitemen to his own of his daughter. This most masculine act of aggression becomes feminized in my language, "passive," and, I think, more accurately repellent when deprived of the male "glamor of shame" rape is (or once was) routinely given.

The points I have tried to illustrate are that my choices of language (speakerly, aural, colloquial), my reliance for full comprehension on codes embedded in black culture, my effort to effect immediate co-conspiracy and intimacy (without any distancing, explanatory fabric), as well as my (failed) attempt to shape a silence while breaking it are attempts (many unsatisfactory) to transfigure the complexity and wealth of Afro-American culture into a language worthy of the culture.

In *Sula*, it's necessary to concentrate on *two* first sentences because what survives in print is not the one I had intended to be the first. Originally the book opened with "Except for World War II nothing ever interfered with National Suicide Day." With some encouragement, I recognized that it was a false beginning. "*In medias res*"[8] with a vengeance, because there was no *res* to be in the middle of—no implied world in which to locate the specificity and the resonances in the sentence. More to the point, I knew I was writing a second novel, and that it too would be about people in a black community not just foregrounded but totally dominant; and that it was about black women—also foregrounded and dominant. In 1988, certainly, I would not need (or feel the need for) the sentence—the short section—that now opens *Sula*. The threshold between the reader and the black-topic text need not be the safe, welcoming lobby I persuaded myself it needed at that time. My preference was the demolition of the lobby altogether. As can be seen from *The Bluest Eye*, and in every other book I have written, only *Sula* has this "entrance." The others refuse the "presentation"; refuse the seductive safe harbor; the line of demarcation between the sacred and the obscene, public and private, them and us. Refuse, in effect, to cater to the diminished expectations of the reader, or his or her alarm heightened by the emotional luggage one carries into the black-topic text. (I should remind you that *Sula* was begun in 1969, while my first book was in proof, in a period of extraordinary political activity.)

Since I had become convinced that the effectiveness of the original beginning was only in my head, the job at hand became how to construct an alternate beginning that would not force the work to genuflect and would complement the outlaw quality in it. The problem presented itself this way: to fashion a door. Instead of having the text open wide the moment the cover is opened (or, as in *The Bluest Eye*, to have the book stand exposed before the cover is even touched, much less opened, by placing the complete "plot" on the first page—and finally on the cover of the first edition), here I was to posit a door, turn its knob and beckon for some four or five pages. I had determined not to mention any characters in those pages, there would be no people in the lobby—but I did, rather heavy-handedly in my view, end the welcome aboard with the mention of Shadrack and Sula. It was a craven (to

---

8. In the middle of things (Latin); *res* means "thing" or "things."

me, still) surrender to a worn-out technique of novel writing: the overt announcement to the reader whom to pay attention to. Yet the bulk of the opening I finally wrote is about the community, a view of it, and the view is not from within (this is a door, after all) but from the point of view of a stranger—the "valley man" who might happen to be there on some errand, but who obviously does not live there and to and for whom all this is mightily strange, even exotic. You can see why I despise much of this beginning. Yet I tried to place in the opening sentence the signature terms of loss: "There used to be a neighborhood here; not any more." That may not be the world's worst sentence, but it doesn't "play," as they say in the theater.

My new first sentence became "In that place, where they tore the nightshade and blackberry patches from their roots to make room for the Medallion City Golf Course, there was once a neighborhood." Instead of my original plan, here I am introducing an outside-the-circle reader into the circle. I am translating the anonymous into the specific, a "place" into a "neighborhood," and letting a stranger in through whose eyes it can be viewed. In between "place" and "neighborhood" I now have to squeeze the specificity and the *difference*; the nostalgia, the history, and the nostalgia for the history; the violence done to it and the consequences of that violence. (It took three months, those four pages, a whole summer of nights.) The nostalgia is sounded by "once"; the history and a longing for it is implied in the connotation of "neighborhood." The violence lurks in having something torn out by its roots—it will not, cannot grow again. Its consequences are that what has been destroyed is considered weeds, refuse necessarily removed in urban "development" by the unspecified but no less known "they" who do not, cannot, afford to differentiate what is displaced, and would not care that this is "refuse" of a certain kind. Both plants have darkness in them: "black" and "night." One is unusual (nightshade) and has two darkness words: "night" and "shade." The other (blackberry) is common. A familiar plant and an exotic one. A harmless one and a dangerous one. One produces a nourishing berry; one delivers toxic ones. But they both thrived there together, *in that place when it was a neighborhood*. Both are gone now, and the description that follows is of the other specific things, in this black community, destroyed in the wake of the golf course. Golf course conveys what it is not, in this context: not houses, or factories, or even a public park, and certainly not residents. It is a manicured place where the likelihood of the former residents showing up is almost nil.

I want to get back to those berries for a moment (to explain, perhaps, the length of time it took for the language of that section to arrive). I always thought of Sula as quintessentially black, metaphysically black, if you will, which is not melanin and certainly not unquestioning fidelity to the tribe. She is new world black and new world woman extracting choice from choicelessness, responding inventively to found things. Improvisational. Daring, disruptive, imaginative, modern, out-of-the-house, outlawed, unpolicing, uncontained and uncontainable. And dangerously female. In her final conversation with Nel she refers to herself as a special kind of black person woman, one with choices. Like a redwood, she says. (With all due respect to the dream landscape of Freud,[9] trees have always seemed feminine to me.)

---

9. Sigmund Freud (1856–1939), Austrian founder of psychoanalysis who emphasized the importance of dreams as unconscious representations of repressed desires.

In any case, my perception of Sula's double-dose of *chosen* blackness and *biological* blackness is in the presence of those two words of darkness in "nightshade" as well as in the uncommon quality of the vine itself. One variety is called "enchanter," and the other "bittersweet" because the berries taste bitter at first and then sweet. Also nightshade was thought to counteract witchcraft. All of this seemed a wonderful constellation of signs for Sula. And "blackberry patch" seemed equally appropriate for Nel: nourishing, never needing to be tended or cultivated, once rooted and bearing. Reliably sweet but thorn-bound. Her process of becoming, heralded by the explosive dissolving of her fragilely-held-together ball of string and fur (when the thorns of her self-protection are removed by Eva), puts her back in touch with the complex, contradictory, evasive, independent, liquid modernity Sula insisted upon. A modernity which overturns pre-war definitions, ushers in the Jazz Age (an age *defined* by Afro-American art and culture), and requires new kinds of intelligences to define oneself.

The stage-setting of the first four pages is embarrassing to me now, but the pains I have taken to explain it may be helpful in identifying the strategies one can be forced to resort to in trying to accommodate the mere fact of writing about, for and out of black culture while accommodating and responding to mainstream "white" culture. The "valley man's" guidance into the territory was my compromise. Perhaps it "worked," but it was not the work I wanted to do.

Had I begun with Shadrack, I would have ignored the smiling welcome and put the reader into immediate confrontation with his wound and his scar. The difference my preferred (original) beginning would have made would be calling greater attention to the traumatic displacement this most wasteful capitalist war had on black people in particular, and throwing into relief the creative, if outlawed, determination to survive it whole. Sula as (feminine) solubility and Shadrack's (male) fixative are two extreme ways of dealing with displacement—a prevalent theme in the narrative of black people. In the final opening I replicated the demiurge of discriminatory, prosecutorial racial oppression in the loss to commercial "progress" of the village, but the references to the community's stability and creativeness (music, dancing, craft, religion, irony, wit all referred to in the "valley man's" presence) refract and subsume their pain while they are in the thick of it. It is a softer embrace than Shadrack's organized, public madness—his disruptive remembering presence which helps (for a while) to cement the community, until Sula challenges them.

"The North Carolina Mutual Life Insurance agent promised to fly from Mercy to the other side of Lake Superior at 3:00."

This declarative sentence is designed to mock a journalistic style; with a minor alteration it could be the opening of an item in a small-town newspaper. It has the tone of an everyday event of minimal local interest. Yet I wanted it to contain (as does the scene that takes place when the agent fulfills his promise) the information that *Song of Solomon*[1] both centers on and radiates from.

The name of the insurance company is real, a well known black-owned company dependent on black clients, and in its corporate name are "life"

---

1. Morrison's third novel (1977).

and "mutual;" *agent* being the necessary ingredient of what enables the relationship between them. The sentence also moves from North Carolina to Lake Superior—geographical locations, but with a sly implication that the move from North Carolina (the south) to Lake Superior (the north) might not actually involve progress to some "superior state"—which, of course it does not. The two other significant words are "fly," upon which the novel centers and "Mercy," the name of the place from which he is to fly. Both constitute the heartbeat of the narrative. Where is the insurance man flying to? The other side of Lake Superior is Canada, of course, the historic terminus of the escape route for black people looking for asylum. "Mercy," the other significant term, is the grace note; the earnest though, with one exception, unspoken wish of the narrative's population. Some grant it; some never find it; one, at least, makes it the text and cry of her extemporaneous sermon upon the death of her granddaughter. It touches, turns and returns to Guitar at the end of the book—he who is least deserving of it—and moves him to make it his own final gift. It is what one wishes for Hagar; what is unavailable to and unsought by Macon Dead, senior; what his wife learns to demand from him, and what can never come from the white world as is signified by the inversion of the name of the hospital from Mercy to "no-Mercy." It is only available from within. The center of the narrative is flight; the springboard is mercy.

But the sentence turns, as all sentences do, on the verb: promised. The insurance agent does not declare, announce, or threaten his act. He promises, as though a contract is being executed—faithfully—between himself and others. Promises broken, or kept; the difficulty of ferreting out loyalties and ties that bind or bruise wend their way throughout the action and the shifting relationships. So the agent's flight, like that of the Solomon in the title, although toward asylum (Canada, or freedom, or home, or the company of the welcoming dead), and although it carries the possibility of failure and the certainty of danger, is toward change, an alternative way, a cessation of things-as-they-are. It should not be understood as a simple desperate act, the end of a fruitless life, a life without gesture, without examination, but as obedience to a deeper contract with his people. It is his commitment to them, regardless of whether, in all its details, they understand it. There is, however, in their response to his action, a tenderness, some contrition, and mounting respect ("They didn't know he had it in him.") and an awareness that the gesture enclosed rather than repudiated themselves. The note he leaves asks for forgiveness. It is tacked on his door as a mild invitation to whomever might pass by, but it is not an advertisement. It is an almost Christian declaration of love as well as humility of one who was not able to do more.

There are several other flights in the work and they are motivationally different. Solomon's the most magical, the most theatrical and, for Milkman, the most satisfying. It is also the most problematic—to those he left behind. Milkman's flight binds these two elements of loyalty (Mr. Smith's) and abandon and self-interest (Solomon's) into a third thing: a merging of fealty and risk that suggests the "agency" for "mutual" "life," which he offers at the end and which is echoed in the hills behind him, and is the marriage of surrender and domination, acceptance and rule, commitment to a group *through* ultimate isolation. Guitar recognizes this marriage and recalls enough of how lost he himself is to put his weapon down.

The journalistic style at the beginning, its rhythm of a familiar, hand-me-down dignity is pulled along by an accretion of detail displayed in a meandering unremarkableness. Simple words, uncomplex sentence structures, persistent understatement, highly aural syntax—but the ordinariness of the language, its colloquial, vernacular, humorous and, upon occasion, parabolic quality sabotage expectations and mask judgments when it can no longer defer them. The composition of red, white and blue in the opening scene provides the national canvas/flag upon which the narrative works and against which the lives of these black people must be seen, but which must not overwhelm the enterprise the novel is engaged in. It is a composition of color that heralds Milkman's birth, protects his youth, hides its purpose and through which he must burst (through blue Buicks, red tulips in his waking dream, and his sisters' white stockings, ribbons and gloves) before discovering that the gold of his search is really Pilate's yellow orange and the glittering metal of the box in her ear.

These spaces, which I am filling in, and can fill in because they were planned, can conceivably be filled in with other significances. That is planned as well. The point is that into these spaces should fall the ruminations of the reader and his or her invented or recollected or misunderstood knowingness. The reader as narrator asks the questions the community asks, and both reader and "voice" stand among the crowd, within it, with privileged intimacy and contact, but without any more privileged information than the crowd has. That egalitarianism which places us all (reader, the novel's population, the narrator's voice) on the same footing reflected for me the force of flight and mercy, and the precious, imaginative yet realistic gaze of black people who (at one time, anyway) did not mythologize what or whom it mythologized. The "song" itself contains this unblinking evaluation of the miraculous and heroic flight of the legendary Solomon, an unblinking gaze which is lurking in the tender but amused choral-community response to the agent's flight. Sotto[2] (but not completely) is my own giggle (in Afro-American terms) of the proto-myth of the journey to manhood. Whenever characters are cloaked in Western fable, they are in deep trouble; but the African myth is also contaminated. Unprogressive, unreconstructed, self-born Pilate is unimpressed by Solomon's flight and knocks Milkman down when, made new by his appropriation of his own family's fable, he returns to educate her with it. Upon hearing all he has to say, her only interest is filial. "Papa? . . . I've been carryin' Papa?" And her longing to hear the song, finally, is a longing for balm to die by, not a submissive obedience to history—anybody's.

The opening sentence of *Tar Baby*,[3] "He believed he was safe," is the second version of itself. The first, "He thought he was safe," was discarded because "thought" did not contain the doubt I wanted to plant in the reader's mind about whether or not he really was—safe. "Thought" came to me at once because it was the verb my parents and grandparents used when describing what they had dreamed the night before. Not "I dreamt," or "It seemed" or even "I saw or did" this or that—but "I thought." It gave the dream narrative distance (a dream is not "real") and power (the control implied in *thinking* rather than *dreaming*). But to use "thought" seemed to undercut the faith of the character and the distrust I wanted to suggest to

---

2. I.e., sotto voce, in an undertone (literally, "under the voice"; Italian).

3. Morrison's fourth novel (1981).

the reader. "Believe" was chosen to do the work properly. And the person who does the believing is, in a way, about to enter a dream world, and convinces himself, eventually, that he is in control of it. He believed; was convinced. And although the word suggests his conviction, it does not reassure the reader. If I had wanted the reader to trust this person's point of view I would have written "He was safe." Or, "Finally, he was safe." The unease about this view of safety is important because safety itself is the desire of each person in the novel. Locating it, creating it, losing it.

You may recall that I was interested in working out the mystery of a piece of lore, a folk tale, which is also about safety and danger and the skills needed to secure the one and recognize and avoid the other. I was not, of course, interested in re-telling the tale; I suppose that is an idea to pursue, but it is certainly not interesting enough to engage me for four years. I have said, elsewhere, that the exploration of the Tar Baby tale[4] was like stroking a pet to see what the anatomy was like but not to disturb or distort its mystery. Folk lore may have begun as allegory for natural or social phenomena; it may have been employed as a retreat from contemporary issues in art, but folk lore can also contain myths that re-activate themselves endlessly through providers—the people who repeat, reshape, reconstitute and reinterpret them. The Tar Baby tale seemed to me to be about masks. Not masks as covering what is to be hidden, but how masks come to life, take life over, exercise the tensions between itself and what it covers. For Son, the most effective mask is none. For the others the construction is careful and delicately borne, but the masks they make have a life of their own and collide with those they come in contact with. The texture of the novel seemed to want leanness, architecture that was worn and ancient like a piece of mask sculpture: exaggerated, breathing, just athwart the representational life it displaced. Thus, the first and last sentences had to match, as the exterior planes match the interior, concave ones inside the mask. Therefore "He believed he was safe" would be the twin of "Lickety split, lickety split, lickety lickety split." This close is 1) the last sentence of the folk tale. 2) the action of the character. 3) the indeterminate ending that follows from the untrustworthy beginning. 4) the complimentary meter of its twin sister [u u / u u / with u u u / u u u /], and 5) the wide and marvelous space between the contradiction of those two images: from a dream of safety to the sound of running feet. The whole mediated world in between. This masked and unmasked; enchanted, disenchanted; wounded and wounding world is played out on and by the varieties of interpretation (Western and Afro-American) the Tar Baby myth has been (and continues to be) subjected to. Winging one's way through the vise and expulsion of history becomes possible in creative encounters with that history. Nothing, in those encounters, is safe, or should be. Safety is the foetus of power as well as protection from it, as the uses to which masks and myths are put in Afro-American culture remind us.

"124 was spiteful. Full of a baby's venom."

Beginning *Beloved*[5] with numerals rather than spelled out numbers, it was

---

4. "The Wonderful Tar-Baby Story" is the best-known of the folktales retold in dialect by Joel Chandler Harris in *Uncle Remus: His Songs and His Sayings* (1880).
5. Morrison's fifth novel (1987).

my intention to give the house an identity separate from the street or even the city; to name it the way "Sweet Home" was named; the way plantations were named, but not with nouns or "proper" names—with numbers instead because numbers have no adjectives, no posture of coziness or grandeur or the haughty yearning of arrivistes and estate builders for the parallel beautifications of the nation they left behind, laying claim to instant history and legend. Numbers here constitute an address, a thrilling enough prospect for slaves who had owned nothing, least of all an address. And although the numbers, unlike words, can have no modifiers, I give these an adjective—spiteful (There are three others). The address is therefore personalized, but personalized by its own activity, not the pasted on desire for personality.

Also there is something about numerals that makes them spoken, heard, in this context, because one expects words to read in a book, not numbers to say, or hear. And the sound of the novel, sometimes cacaphonous, sometimes harmonious, must be an inner ear sound or a sound just beyond hearing, infusing the text with a musical emphasis that words can do sometimes even better than music can. Thus the second sentence is not one: it is a phrase that properly, grammatically, belongs as a dependent clause with the first. Had I done that, however, (124 was spiteful, comma, full of a baby's venom, or 124 was full of a baby's venom) I could not have had the accent on *full* [/ u u / u / u pause / u u u u / u].

Whatever the risks of confronting the reader with what must be immediately incomprehensible in that simple, declarative authoritative sentence, the risk of unsettling him or her, I determined to take. Because the *in medias res* opening that I am so committed to is here excessively demanding. It is abrupt, and should appear so. No native informant here. The reader is snatched, yanked, thrown into an environment completely foreign, and I want it as the first stroke of the shared experience that might be possible between the reader and the novel's population. Snatched just as the slaves were from one place to another, from any place to another, without preparation and without defense. No lobby, no door, no entrance—a gangplank, perhaps (but a very short one). And the house into which this snatching—this kidnapping—propels one, changes from spiteful to loud to quiet, as the sounds in the body of the ship itself may have changed. A few words have to be read before it is clear that 124 refers to a house (in most of the early drafts "The women in *the house* knew it" was simply "The women knew it." "House" was not mentioned for seventeen lines), and a few more have to be read to discover why it is spiteful, or rather the source of the spite. By then it is clear, if not at once, that something is beyond control, but is not beyond understanding since it is not beyond accommodation by both the "women" and the "children." The fully realized presence of the haunting is both a major incumbent of the narrative and sleight of hand. One of its purposes is to keep the reader preoccupied with the nature of the incredible spirit world while being supplied a controlled diet of the incredible political world.

The subliminal, the underground life of a novel is the area most likely to link arms with the reader and facilitate making it one's own. Because one must, to get from the first sentence to the next, and the next and the next. The friendly observation post I was content to build and man in *Sula* (with the stranger in the midst), or the down-home journalism of *Song of Solomon* or the calculated mistrust of the point of view in *Tar Baby* would not serve here. Here I wanted the compelling confusion of being there as they (the characters) are; suddenly, without comfort or succor from the "author," with only imagination, intelligence, and necessity available for the journey. The painterly language of *Song of Solomon* was not useful to me in *Beloved*. There is practically no color whatsoever in its pages, and when there is, it is so stark and remarked upon, it is virtually raw. Color seen for the first time, without its history. No built architecture as in *Tar Baby*, no play with Western chronology as in *Sula*; no exchange between book life and "real" life discourse—with printed text units rubbing up against seasonal black childtime units as in *The Bluest Eye*. No compound of houses, no neighborhood, no sculpture, no paint, no time, especially no time because memory, pre-historic memory, has no time. There is just a little music, each other and the urgency of what is at stake. Which is all they had. For that work, the work of language is to get out of the way.

I hope you understand that in this explication of how I practice language is a search for and deliberate posture of vulnerability to those aspects of Afro-American culture that can inform and position my work. I sometimes know when the work works, when *nommo*[6] has effectively summoned, by reading and listening to those who have entered the text. I learn nothing from those who resist it, except, of course, the sometimes fascinating display of their struggle. My expectations of and my gratitude to the critics who enter, are great. To those who talk about how as well as what; who identify the workings as well as the work; for whom the study of Afro-American literature is neither a crash course in neighborliness and tolerance, nor an infant to be carried, instructed or chastised or even whipped like a child, but the serious study of art forms that have much work to do, but are already legitimatized by their own cultural sources and predecessors—in or out of the canon—I owe much.

For an author, regarding canons, it is very simple: in fifty, a hundred or more years his or her work may be relished for its beauty or its insight or its power; or it may be condemned for its vacuousness and pretension—and junked. Or in fifty or a hundred years the critic (as canon builder) may be applauded for his or her intelligent scholarship and powers of critical inquiry. Or laughed at for ignorance and shabbily disguised assertions of power— and junked. It's possible that the reputations of both will thrive, or that both will decay. In any case, as far as the future is concerned, when one writes, as critic or as author, all necks are on the line.

1988   1989

---

6. In West African tribal cultures, the generative and creative power of the word.

ALICE MUNRO
b. 1931

Fashioning an art that, in the words of the novelist-critic Joyce Carol Oates, "works to conceal itself, in order to celebrate its subject," Alice Munro has published several prize-winning volumes of short stories and two story sequences that have been read as novels, *Lives of Girls and Women* (1971) and *Who Do You Think You Are?* (1978). The latter, issued in the United States as *The Beggar Maid: Stories of Flo and Rose*, is typical of Munro's work, focusing, as it does, on the relationship of a stepmother (Flo) and a stepdaughter (Rose), who confront their emotionally subtle responses to each other and to the banal people and everyday events that nevertheless continue to surprise them. More recently, Munro has published *The Moons of Jupiter* (1982), *The Progress of Love* (1986), *Open Secrets* (1994), *Selected Stories* (1996), *The Love of a Good Woman* (1998), *Hateship, Friendship, Courtship, Loveship, Marriage* (2001), and *Runaway* (2004). In 2002, her daughter Sheila recorded her experience of growing up with Alice Munro in *Lives of Mothers* and *Daughters*. The subjects celebrated in many of these works are the small-town Canadians who inhabit the southwestern Ontario of her own childhood. Born in Wingham, Ontario, the daughter of farmers, Alice Laidlaw attended the University of Western Ontario before marrying the bookseller James Munro in 1951. Although she brought up her three daughters in Vancouver and Victoria, Munro returned in 1972 to western Ontario. After a divorce in 1976, she married Gerald Fremlin, a geographer. As a reader, Munro has explained, she can "go into [a story], and move back and forth and settle here and there, and stay in it for a while." As a writer, too, she meditates on the enigmatic interrelationships of past and present in a landscape evocative enough to sustain her vision. Whether she writes about piano recitals, high school dances, chance sexual encounters, or illness, that vision frequently centers on the lives of girls and women. In many of her evocative tales, she broods on a recurring theme, namely what she calls "the pain of human contact . . . the fascinating pain; the humiliating necessity."

Floating Bridge

One time she had left him. The immediate reason was fairly trivial. He had joined a couple of the Young Offenders (Yo-yos was what he called them) in gobbling up a gingerbread cake she had just made and intended to serve after a meeting that evening. Unobserved—at least by Neal and the Yo-yos—she had left the house and gone to sit in a three-sided shelter on the main street, where the city bus stopped twice a day. She had never been in there before, and she had a couple of hours to wait. She sat and read everything that had been written on or cut into those wooden walls. Various initials loved each other 4 ever. Laurie G. sucked cock. Dunk Cultis was a fag. So was Mr. Garner (Math).

Eat Shit H.W. Gange rules. Skate or Die. God hates filth. Kevin S. is Dead Meat. Amanda W. is beautiful and sweet and I wish they did not put her in jail because I miss her with all my heart. I want to fuck V.P. Ladies have to sit here and read this disgusting dirty things what you write.

Looking at this barrage of human messages—and puzzling in particular over the heartfelt, very neatly written sentence concerning Amanda W., Jinny wondered if people were alone when they wrote such things. And she went on to imagine herself sitting here or in some similar place, waiting for a bus, alone, as she would surely be if she went ahead with the plan she was set on now. Would she be compelled to make statements on public walls?

She felt herself connected at present with the way people felt when they had to write certain things down—she was connected by her feelings of anger, of petty outrage (perhaps it was petty?), and her excitement at what she was doing to Neal, to pay him back. But the life she was carrying herself into might not give her anybody to be angry at, or anybody who owed her anything, anybody who could possibly be rewarded or punished or truly affected by what she might do. Her feelings might become of no importance to anybody but herself, and yet they would be bulging up inside her, squeezing her heart and breath.

She was not, after all, somebody people flocked to in the world. And yet she was choosy, in her own way.

The bus was still not in sight when she got up and walked home.

Neal was not there. He was returning the boys to the school, and by the time he got back somebody had already arrived, early for the meeting. She told him what she'd done when she was well over it and it could be turned into a joke. In fact, it became a joke she told in company—leaving out or just describing in a general way the things she'd read on the walls—many times.

"Would you ever have thought to come after me?" she said to Neal.

"Of course. Given time."

The oncologist had a priestly demeanor and in fact wore a black turtle-necked shirt under a white smock—an outfit that suggested he had just come from some ceremonial mixing and dosing. His skin was young and smooth—it looked like butterscotch. On the dome of his head there was just a faint black growth of hair, a delicate sprouting, very like the fuzz Jinny was sporting herself. Though hers was brownish-gray, like mouse fur. At first Jinny had wondered if he could possibly be a patient as well as a doctor. Then, whether he had adopted this style to make the patients more comfortable. More likely it was a transplant. Or just the way he liked to wear his hair.

You couldn't ask him. He came from Syria or Jordan or some place where doctors kept their dignity. His courtesies were frigid.

"Now," he said. "I do not wish to give a wrong impression."

She went out of the air-conditioned building into the stunning glare of a late afternoon in August in Ontario. Sometimes the sun burned through, sometimes it stayed behind thin clouds—it was just as hot either way. The parked cars, the pavement, the bricks of the other buildings, seemed positively to bombard her, as if they were all separate facts thrown up in ridiculous sequence. She did not take changes of scene very well these days, she wanted everything familiar and stable. It was the same with changes of information.

She saw the van detach itself from its place at the curb and make its way down the street to pick her up. It was a light-blue, shimmery, sickening color. Lighter blue where the rust spots had been painted over. Its stickers said I KNOW I DRIVE A WRECK, BUT YOU SHOULD SEE MY HOUSE, and HONOUR THY MOTHER—EARTH, and (this was more recent) USE PESTICIDE, KILL WEEDS, PROMOTE CANCER.

Neal came around to help her.

"She's in the van," he said. There was an eager note in his voice that registered vaguely as a warning or a plea. A buzz around him, a tension, that told Jinny it wasn't time to give him her news, if news was what you'd call it. When Neal was around other people, even one person other than Jinny, his behavior changed, becoming more animated, enthusiastic, ingratiating. Jinny was not bothered by that anymore—they had been together for twenty-one years. And she herself changed—as a reaction, she used to think—becoming more reserved and slightly ironic. Some masquerades were necessary, or just too habitual to be dropped. Like Neal's antique appearance—the bandanna headband, the rough gray ponytail, the little gold earring that caught the light like the gold rims 'round his teeth, and his shaggy outlaw clothes.

While she had been seeing the doctor, he had been picking up the girl who was going to help them with their life now. He knew her from the Correctional Institute for Young Offenders, where he was a teacher and she had worked in the kitchen. The Correctional Institute was just outside the town where they lived, about twenty miles away from here. The girl had quit her kitchen job a few months ago and taken a job looking after a farm household where the mother was sick. Somewhere not far from this larger town. Luckily she was now free.

"What happened to the woman?" Jinny had said. "Did she die?"

Neal said, "She went into the hospital."

"Same deal."

They had had to make a lot of practical arrangements in a fairly short time. Clear the front room of their house of all the files, the newspapers and magazines containing relevant articles that had not yet been put on disk—these had filled the shelves lining the room up to the ceiling. The two computers as well, the old typewriters, the printer. All this had to find a place—temporarily, though nobody said so—in somebody else's house. The front room would become the sickroom.

Jinny had said to Neal that he could keep one computer, at least, in the bedroom. But he had refused. He did not say, but she understood, that he believed there would not be time for it.

Neal had spent nearly all his spare time, in the years she had been with him, organizing and carrying out campaigns. Not just political campaigns (those too) but efforts to preserve historic buildings and bridges and cemeteries, to keep trees from being cut down both along the town streets and in isolated patches of old forest, to save rivers from poisonous runoff and choice land from developers and the local population from casinos. Letters and petitions were always being written, government departments lobbied, posters distributed, protests organized. The front room was the scene of rages of indignation (which gave people a lot of satisfaction, Jinny thought) and confused propositions and arguments, and Neal's nervy buoyancy. And now that it was suddenly emptied, it made her think of when she first walked into the house, straight from her parents' split-level with the swag curtains, and thought of all those shelves filled with books, wooden shutters on the windows, and those beautiful Middle Eastern rugs she always forgot the name of, on the varnished floor. The Canaletto print she had bought for her room at college on the one bare wall. *Lord Mayor's Day on the Thames.*[1] She had actually put that up, though she never noticed it anymore.

They rented a hospital bed—they didn't really need it yet, but it was better to get one while you could because they were often in short supply. Neal thought of everything. He hung up some heavy curtains that were discards from a friend's family room. They had a pattern of tankards and horse brasses and Jinny thought them very ugly. But she knew now that there comes a time when ugly and beautiful serve pretty much the same purpose, when anything you look at is just a peg to hang the unruly sensations of your body on, and the bits and pieces of your mind.

She was forty-two, and until recently she had looked younger than her age. Neal was sixteen years older than she was. So she had thought that in the natural course of things she would be in the position he was in now, and she had sometimes worried about how she would manage it. Once when she was holding his hand in bed before they went to sleep, his warm and present hand, she had thought that she would hold, or touch this hand, at least once, when he was dead. And she would not be able to believe in that fact. The fact of his being dead and powerless. No matter how long this state had been foreseen, she would not be able to credit it. She would not be able to believe that, deep down, he had not some knowledge of this moment. Of her. To think of him not having that brought on a kind of emotional vertigo, the sense of a horrid drop.

And yet—an excitement. The unspeakable excitement you feel when a galloping disaster promises to release you from all responsibility for your own life. Then for shame you must compose yourself and stay very quiet.

"Where are you going?" he had said, when she withdrew her hand.

"No place. Just turning over."

She didn't know if Neal had any such feeling, now that it had happened to be her. She had asked him if he had got used to the idea yet. He shook his head.

She said, "Me neither."

Then she said, "Just don't let the Grief Counselors in. They could be hanging around already. Wanting to make a preemptive strike."

"Don't harrow me," he said, in a voice of rare anger.

"Sorry."

"You don't always have to take the lighter view."

"I know," she said. But the fact was that with so much going on and present events grabbing so much of her attention, she found it hard to take any view at all.

"This is Helen," Neal said. "This is who is going to look after us from now on. She won't stand for any nonsense, either."

"Good for her," said Jinny. She put out her hand, once she was sitting down. But the girl might not have seen it, low down between the two front seats.

Or she might not have known what to do. Neal had said that she came from an unbelievable situation, an absolutely barbaric family. Things had

---

1. *Westminster Bridge, London, with the Lord Mayor's Procession on the Thames* (1747), an oil painting by the Venetian artist Canaletto (Antonio Canal, 1697–1768).

gone on that you could not imagine going on in this day and age. An isolated farm, a dead mother and a mentally deficient daughter and a tyrannical, deranged incestuous old father, and the two girl children. Helen the older one, who had run away at the age of fourteen after beating up on the old man. She had been sheltered by a neighbor who phoned the police, and the police had come and got the younger sister and made both children wards of the Children's Aid. The old man and his daughter—that is, their mother and their father—were both placed in a Psychiatric Hospital. Foster parents took Helen and her sister, who were mentally and physically normal. They were sent to school and had a miserable time there, having to be put into the first grade. But they both learned enough to be employable.

When Neal had started the van up the girl decided to speak.

"You picked a hot enough day to be out in," she said. It was the sort of thing she might have heard people say to start a conversation. She spoke in a hard, flat tone of antagonism and distrust, but even that, Jinny knew by now, should not be taken personally. It was just the way some people sounded—particularly country people—in this part of the world.

"If you're hot you can turn the air conditioner on," Neal said. "We've got the old-fashioned kind—just roll down all the windows."

The turn they made at the next corner was one Jinny had not expected.

"We have to go to the hospital," Neal said. "Don't panic. Helen's sister works there and she's got something Helen wants to pick up. Isn't that right, Helen?"

Helen said, "Yeah. My good shoes."

"Helen's good shoes." Neal looked up at the mirror. "Miss Helen Rosie's good shoes."

"My name's not Helen Rosie," said Helen. It seemed as if she was saying this not for the first time.

"I just call you that because you have such a rosy face," Neal said.

"I have not."

"You do. Doesn't she, Jinny? Jinny agrees with me, you've got a rosy face. Miss Helen Rosie-face."

The girl did have a tender pink skin. Jinny had noticed as well her nearly white lashes and eyebrows, her blond baby-wool hair, and her mouth, which had an oddly naked look, not just the normal look of a mouth without lipstick. A fresh-out-of-the-egg look was what she had, as if there was one layer of skin still missing, and one final growth of coarser grown-up hair. She must be susceptible to rashes and infections, quick to show scrapes and bruises, to get sores around the mouth and sties between her white lashes. Yet she didn't look frail. Her shoulders were broad, she was lean but large-framed. She didn't look stupid, either, though she had a head-on expression like a calf's or a deer's. Everything must be right at the surface with her, her attention and the whole of her personality coming straight at you, with an innocent and—to Jinny—a disagreeable power.

They were going up the long hill to the hospital—the same place where Jinny had had her operation and undergone the first bout of chemotherapy. Across the road from the hospital buildings there was a cemetery. This was a main road and whenever they used to pass this way—in the old days when they came to this town just for shopping or the rare diversion of a movie—

Jinny would say something like "What a discouraging view" or "This is carrying convenience too far."

Now she kept quiet. The cemetery didn't bother her. She realized it didn't matter.

Neal must realize that too. He said into the mirror, "How many dead people do you think there are in that cemetery?"

Helen didn't say anything for a moment. Then—rather sullenly—"I don't know."

"They're *all* dead in there."

"He got me on that too," said Jinny. "That's a Grade Four—level joke."

Helen didn't answer. She might never have made it to Grade Four.

They drove up to the main doors of the hospital, then on Helen's directions swung around to the back. People in hospital dressing gowns, some trailing their IV's, had come outside to smoke.

"You see that bench," said Jinny. "Oh, never mind, we're past it now. It has a sign—THANK YOU FOR NOT SMOKING. But it's out there for people to sit down on when they wander out of the hospital. And why do they come out? To smoke. Then are they not supposed to sit down? I don't understand it."

"Helen's sister works in the laundry," Neal said. "What's her name, Helen? What's your sister's name?"

"Lois," said Helen. "Stop here. Okay. Here."

They were in a parking lot at the back of a wing of the hospital. There were no doors on the ground floor except a loading door, shut tight. On the other three floors there were doors opening onto a fire escape.

Helen was getting out.

"You know how to find your way in?" Neal said.

"Easy."

The fire escape stopped four or five feet above the ground but she was able to grab hold of the railing and swing herself up, maybe wedging a foot against a loose brick, in a matter of seconds. Jinny could not tell how she did it. Neal was laughing.

"Go get 'em, girl," he said.

"Isn't there any other way?" said Jinny.

Helen had run up to the third floor and disappeared.

"If there is she ain't a-gonna use it," Neal said.

"Full of gumption," said Jinny with an effort.

"Otherwise she'd never have broken out," he said. "She needed all the gumption she could get."

Jinny was wearing a wide-brimmed straw hat. She took it off and began to fan herself.

Neal said, "Sorry. There doesn't seem to be any shade to park in. She'll be out of there fast."

"Do I look too startling?" Jinny said. He was used to her asking that.

"You're fine. There's nobody around here anyway."

"The man I saw today wasn't the same one I'd seen before. I think this one was more important. The funny thing was he had a scalp that looked about like mine. Maybe he does it to put the patients at ease."

She meant to go on and tell him what the doctor had said, but he said, "That sister of hers isn't as bright as she is. Helen sort of looks after her and bosses her around. This business with the shoes—that's typical. Isn't she capable of buying her own shoes? She hasn't even got her own place—she still lives with the people who fostered them, out in the country somewhere."

Jinny did not continue. The fanning took up most of her energy. He watched the building.

"I hope to Christ they didn't haul her up for getting in the wrong way," he said. "Breaking the rules. She is just not a gal for whom the rules was made."

After several minutes he let out a whistle.

"Here she comes now. Here-she-comes. Headin' down the homestretch. Will-she-will-she-will-she have enough sense to stop before she jumps? Look before she leaps? Will-she-will-she—nope. Nope. Unh-*unh*."

Helen had no shoes in her hands. She jumped into the van and banged the door shut and said, "Stupid idiots. First I get up there and this asshole gets in my way. Where's your tag? You gotta have a tag. You can't come in here without a tag. I seen you come in off the fire escape, you can't do that. Okay, okay, I gotta see my sister. You can't see her now she's not on her break. I know that, that's why I come in off the fire escape I just need to pick something up. I don't want to talk to her I'm not goin' to take up her time I just gotta pick something up. Well you can't. Well I can. Well you can't. And then I start to holler *Lois. Lois*. All their machines goin' it's two hundred degrees in there sweat runnin' all down their faces stuff goin' by and *Lois, Lois*. I don't know where she is can she hear me or not. But she comes tearing out and as soon as she sees me—Oh, shit. Oh shit, she says, I went and forgot. *She forgot to bring my shoes*. I phoned her up last night and reminded her but there she is, oh, shit, she *forgot*. I could've beat her up. Now you get out, he says. Go downstairs and out. Not by the fire escape because it's illegal. Piss on him."

Neal was laughing and laughing and shaking his head.

"So that's what she did? Left your shoes behind?"

"Out at June's and Matt's."

"What a tragedy."

Jinny said, "Could we just start driving now and get some air? I don't think fanning is doing a lot of good."

"Fine," said Neal. He backed and turned around, and once more they were passing the familiar front of the hospital, with the same or different smokers parading by in their dreary hospital clothes with their IV's. "Helen will just have to tell us where to go."

He called into the back seat, "Helen?"

"What?"

"Which way do we turn now to get to those people's place?"

"What people's?"

"Where your sister lives. Where your shoes are. Tell us how to get to their place."

"We're not goin' to their place so I'm not telling you."

Neal turned back the way they had come.

"I'm just driving this way till you can get your directions straight. Would it work better if I went out to the highway? Or in to the middle of town? Where should I start from?"

"Not starting anywhere. Not going."

"It's not so far, is it? Why aren't we going?"

"You done me one favor and that's enough." Helen sat as far forward as she could, pushing her head between Neal's seat and Jinny's. "You took me to the hospital and isn't that enough? You don't need to be driving all over doing me favors."

They slowed down, turned into a side street.

"That's silly," Neal said. "You're going twenty miles away and you might not get back here for a while. You might need those shoes."

No answer. He tried again.

"Or don't you know the way? Don't you know the way from here?"

"I know it, but I'm not telling."

"So we're just going to have to drive around. Drive around and around till you get ready to tell us."

"Well I'm not goin' to get ready. So I'm not."

"We could go back and see your sister. I bet she'd tell us. Must be about quitting time for her now, we could drive her home."

"She's on the late shift, so haw haw."

They were driving through a part of this town that Jinny had not seen before. They drove very slowly and made frequent turns, so that hardly any breeze went through the car. A boarded-up factory, discount stores, pawnshops. CASH, CASH, CASH, said a flashing sign above barred windows. But there were houses, disreputable-looking old duplexes, and the sort of single wooden houses that were put up quickly during the Second World War. One tiny yard was full of things for sale—clothes pegged to a line, tables stacked with dishes and household goods. A dog was nosing around under a table and could have knocked it over, but the woman who sat on the step, smoking and surveying the lack of customers, did not seem to care.

In front of a corner store some children were sucking on Popsicles. A boy who was on the edge of the group—he was probably no more than four or five years old—threw his Popsicle at the van. A surprisingly strong throw. It hit Jinny's door just below her arm and she gave a light scream.

Helen thrust her head out the back window.

"You want your arm in a sling?"

The child began to howl. He hadn't bargained on Helen, and he might not have bargained on the Popsicle's being gone for good.

Back in the van, Helen spoke to Neal.

"You're just wasting your gas."

"North of town?" Neal said. "South of town? North south east west, Helen tell us which is best."

"I already told you. You done all for me you are goin' to do today."

"And I told you. We're going to get those shoes for you before we head home."

No matter how strictly he spoke, Neal was smiling. On his face there was an expression of conscious, but helpless, silliness. Signs of an invasion of bliss. Neal's whole being was invaded, he was brimming with silly bliss.

"You're just stubborn," Helen said.

"You'll see how stubborn."

"I am too. I'm just as stubborn as what you are."

It seemed to Jinny that she could feel the blaze of Helen's cheek, which was so close to hers. And she could certainly hear the girl's breathing, hoarse and thick with excitement and showing some trace of asthma. Helen's presence was like that of a domestic cat that should never be brought along in any vehicle, being too high-strung to have sense, too apt to spring between the seats.

The sun had burned through the clouds again. It was still high and brassy in the sky.

Neal swung the car onto a street lined with heavy old trees, and somewhat more respectable houses.

"Better here?" he said to Jinny. "More shade for you?" He spoke in a lowered, confidential tone, as if what was going on with the girl could be set aside for a moment, it was all nonsense.

"Taking the scenic route," he said, pitching his voice again towards the back seat. "Taking the scenic route today, courtesy of Miss Helen Rosieface."

"Maybe we ought to just go on," Jinny said. "Maybe we ought to just go on home."

Helen broke in, almost shouting. "I don't want to stop nobody from getting home."

"Then you can just give me some directions," Neal said. He was trying hard to get his voice under control, to get some ordinary sobriety into it. And to banish the smile, which kept slipping back in place no matter how often he swallowed it. "Just let's go to the place and do our errand and head home."

Half a slow block more, and Helen groaned.

"If I got to I guess I got to," she said.

It was not very far that they had to go. They passed a subdivision, and Neal, speaking again to Jinny, said, "No creek that I can see. No estates, either."

Jinny said, "What?"

"*Silver Creek Estates.* On the sign."

He must have read a sign that she had not seen.

"Turn," said Helen.

"Left or right?"

"At the wrecker's."

They went past a wrecking yard, with the car bodies only partly hidden by a sagging tin fence. Then up a hill and past the gates to a gravel pit that was a great cavity in the center of the hill.

"That's them. That's their mailbox up ahead," Helen called out with some importance, and when they got close enough she read out the name.

"Matt and June Bergson. That's them."

A couple of dogs came barking down the short drive. One was large and black and one small and tan-colored, puppylike. They bumbled around at the wheels and Neal sounded the horn. Then another dog—this one more sly and purposeful, with a slick coat and bluish spots—slid out of the long grass.

Helen called to them to shut up, to lay down, to piss off.

"You don't need to bother about any of them but Pinto," she said. "Them other two just cowards."

They stopped in a wide, ill-defined space where some gravel had been laid down. On one side was a barn or implement shed, tin-covered, and over to one side of it, on the edge of a cornfield, an abandoned farmhouse from which most of the bricks had been removed, showing dark wooden walls.

The house inhabited nowadays was a trailer, nicely fixed up with a deck and an awning, and a flower garden behind what looked like a toy fence. The trailer and its garden looked proper and tidy, while the rest of the property was littered with things that might have a purpose or might just be left around to rust or rot.

Helen had jumped out and was cuffing the dogs. But they kept on running past her, and jumping and barking at the car, until a man came out of the shed and called to them. The threats and names he called were not intelligible to Jinny, but the dogs quieted down.

Jinny put on her hat. All this time she had been holding it in her hand.

"They just got to show off," said Helen.

Neal had got out too and was negotiating with the dogs in a resolute way. The man from the shed came towards them. He wore a purple T-shirt that was wet with sweat, clinging to his chest and stomach. He was fat enough to have breasts and you could see his navel pushing out like a pregnant woman's. It rode on his belly like a giant pincushion.

Neal went to meet him with his hand out. The man slapped his own hand on his work pants, laughed and shook Neal's. Jinny could not hear what they said. A woman came out of the trailer and opened the toy gate and latched it behind her.

"Lois went and forgot she was supposed to bring my shoes," Helen called to her. "I phoned her up and everything, but she went and forgot anyway, so Mr. Lockyer brought me out to get them."

The woman was fat too, though not as fat as her husband. She wore a pink muumuu with Aztec suns on it and her hair was streaked with gold. She moved across the gravel with a composed and hospitable air. Neal turned and introduced himself, then brought her to the van and introduced Jinny.

"Glad to meet you," the woman said. "You're the lady that isn't very well?"

"I'm okay," said Jinny.

"Well, now you're here you better come inside. Come in out of this heat."

"Oh, we just dropped by," said Neal.

The man had come closer. "We got the air-conditioning in there," he said. He was inspecting the van and his expression was genial but disparaging.

"We just came to pick up the shoes," Jinny said.

"You got to do more than that now you're here," said the woman—June—laughing as if the idea of their not coming in was a scandalous joke. "You come in and rest yourself."

"We wouldn't like to disturb your supper," Neal said.

"We had it already," said Matt. "We eat early."

"But all kinds of chili left," said June. "You have to come in and help clean up that chili."

Jinny said, "Oh, thank you. But I don't think I could eat anything. I don't feel like eating anything when it's this hot."

"Then you better drink something instead," June said. "We got ginger ale, Coke. We got peach schnapps."

"Beer," Matt said to Neal. "You like a Blue?"[2]

Jinny waved Neal to come close to her window.

"I can't do it," she said. "Just tell them I can't."

---

2. A Labatt Blue, the best-selling Canadian beer.

"You know you'll hurt their feelings," he whispered. "They're trying to be nice."

"But I can't. Maybe you could go."

He bent closer. "You know what it looks like if you don't. It looks like you think you're too good for them."

"You go."

"You'd be okay once you got inside. The air-conditioning really would do you good."

Jinny shook her head.

Neal straightened up.

"Jinny thinks she better just stay and rest here where it's in the shade."

June said, "But she's welcome to rest in the house—"

"I wouldn't mind a Blue, actually," Neal said. He turned back to Jinny with a hard smile. He seemed to her desolate and angry. "You sure you'll be okay?" he said for them to hear. "Sure? You don't mind if I go in for a little while?"

"I'll be fine," said Jinny.

He put one hand on Helen's shoulder and one on June's shoulder, walking them companionably towards the trailer. Matt smiled at Jinny curiously, and followed.

This time when he called the dogs to come after him Jinny could make out their names.

Goober. Sally. Pinto.

The van was parked under a row of willow trees. These trees were big and old, but their leaves were thin and gave a wavering shade. But to be alone was a great relief.

Earlier today, driving along the highway from the town where they lived, they had stopped at a roadside stand and bought some early apples. Jinny got one out of the bag at her feet and took a small bite—more or less to see if she could taste and swallow and hold it in her stomach. She needed something to counteract the thought of chili, and Matt's prodigious navel.

It was all right. The apple was firm and tart, but not too tart, and if she took small bites and chewed seriously she could manage it.

She'd seen Neal like this—or something like this—a few times before. It would be over some boy at the school. A mention of the name in an offhand, even belittling way. A mushy look, an apologetic yet somehow defiant bit of giggling.

But that was never anybody she had to have around the house, and it could never come to anything. The boy's time would be up, he'd go away.

So would this time be up. It shouldn't matter.

She had to wonder if it would have mattered less yesterday than it did today.

She got out of the van, leaving the door open so that she could hang on to the inside handle. Anything on the outside was too hot to hang on to for any length of time. She had to see if she was steady. Then she walked a little in the shade. Some of the willow leaves were already going yellow. Some were lying on the ground. She looked out from the shade at all the things there were around the yard.

A dented delivery truck with both headlights gone and the name on the side painted out. A baby's stroller that the dogs had chewed the seat out of, a load of firewood dumped but not stacked, a pile of huge tires, a great number of plastic jugs and some oil cans and pieces of old lumber and a couple of orange plastic tarpaulins crumpled up by the wall of the shed. In the shed itself there was a heavy GM truck and a small beat-up Mazda truck and a garden tractor, as well as implements whole or broken and loose wheels, handles, rods that would be useful or not useful depending on the uses you could imagine. What a lot of things people could find themselves in charge of. As she had been in charge of all those photographs, official letters, minutes of meetings, newspaper clippings, a thousand categories that she had devised and was putting on disk when she had to go into chemo and everything got taken away. It might end up being thrown out. As all this might, if Matt died.

The cornfield was the place she wanted to get to. The corn was higher than her head now, maybe higher than Neal's head—she wanted to get into the shade of it. She made her way across the yard with this one thought in mind. The dogs thank God must have been taken inside.

There was no fence. The cornfield just petered out into the yard. She walked straight ahead into it, onto the narrow path between two rows. The leaves flapped into her face and against her arms like streamers of oilcloth. She had to remove her hat so they would not knock it off. Each stalk had its cob, like a baby in a shroud. There was a strong, almost sickening smell of vegetable growth, of green starch and hot sap.

What she'd thought she'd do, once she got in here, was lie down. Lie down in the shade of these large coarse leaves and not come out till she heard Neal calling her. Perhaps not even then. But the rows were too close together to permit that, and she was too busy thinking about something to take the trouble. She was too angry.

It was not about anything that had happened recently. She was remembering how a group of people had been sitting around one evening on the floor of her living room—or meeting room—playing one of those serious psychological games. One of those games that were supposed to make a person more honest and resilient. You had to say just what came into your mind as you looked at each of the others. And a white-haired woman named Addie Norton, a friend of Neal's, had said, "I hate to tell you this, Jinny, but whenever I look at you all I can think of is—*Nice Nellie.*"

Jinny didn't remember making any response at the time. Maybe you weren't supposed to. What she said, now, in her head, was "Why do you say you hate to say that? Haven't you noticed that whenever people say they hate to say something, they actually love to say it? Don't you think since we're being so honest we could at least start with that?"

It was not the first time she had made this mental reply. And mentally pointed out to Neal what a farce that game was. For when it came Addie's turn, did anyone dare say anything unpleasant to her? Oh, no. "Feisty," they said or "Honest as a dash of cold water." They were scared of her, that was all.

She said, "Dash of cold water," out loud, now, in a stinging voice.

Other people had said kinder things to her. "Flower child" or "Madonna of the springs." She happened to know that whoever said that meant "Manon of the Springs,"[3] but she offered no correction. She was outraged at having to sit there and listen to people's opinions of her. Everyone was wrong. She was not timid or acquiescent or natural or pure.

When you died, of course, these wrong opinions were all there was left.

While this was going through her mind she had done the easiest thing you could do in a cornfield—got lost. She had stepped over one row and then another and probably got turned around. She tried going back the way she had come, but it obviously wasn't the right way. There were clouds over the sun again so she couldn't tell where west was. And she had not known which direction she was going when she entered the field, so that would not have helped anyway. She stood still and heard nothing but the corn whispering away, and some distant traffic.

Her heart was pounding just like any heart that had years and years of life ahead of it.

Then a door opened, she heard the dogs barking and Matt yelling and the door slammed shut. She pushed her way through stalks and leaves in the direction of that noise.

And it turned out that she had not gone far at all. She had been stumbling around in one small corner of the field all the time.

Matt waved at her and warned off the dogs.

"Don't be scairt of them, don't be scairt," he called. He was going towards the car just as she was, though from another direction. As they got closer to each other he spoke in a lower, perhaps more intimate voice.

"You shoulda come and knocked on the door."

He thought that she had gone into the corn to have a pee.

"I just told your husband I'd come out and make sure you're okay."

Jinny said, "I'm fine. Thank you." She got into the van but left the door open. He might be insulted if she closed it. Also, she felt too weak.

"He was sure hungry for that chili."

Who was he talking about?

Neal.

She was trembling and sweating and there was a hum in her head, as on a wire strung between her ears.

"I could bring you some out if you'd like it."

She shook her head, smiling. He lifted up the bottle of beer in his hand—he seemed to be saluting her.

"Drink?"

She shook her head again, still smiling.

"Not even drink of water? We got good water here."

"No thanks."

If she turned her head and looked at his purple navel, she would gag.

"You know, there was this fellow," he said, in a changed voice. A leisurely, chuckling voice. "There was a fellow going out the door and he's got a jar of horseradish in one hand. So his dad says to him, Where you goin' with that horseradish?

---

3. A French film (1986), the sequel to *Jean de Florette* (both based on the 1966 two-part novel by Marcel Pagnol); Manon is a beautiful young shepherdess, who seeks revenge for the death of her father.

"Well I'm goin' to get a horse, he says.
"You're not goin' to catch a horse with no horseradish.
"Comes back next morning, nicest horse you ever want to see. Lookit my horse here. Puts it in the barn."

I do not wish to give the wrong impression. We must not get carried away with optimism. But it looks as if we have some unexpected results here.

"Next day the dad sees him goin' out again. Roll of duct tape under his arm. Where you goin' now?
"Well I heard my mom say she'd like a nice duck for dinner.
"You damn fool, you didn't think you're goin' to catch a duck with duct tape?
"Wait and see.
"Comes back next morning, nice fat duck under his arm."

It looks as if there has been a very significant shrinkage. What we hoped for of course but frankly we did not expect it. And I do not mean that the battle is over, just that this is a favorable sign.

"Dad don't know what to say. Just don't know what to say about it.
"Next night, very next night, sees his son goin' out the door with big bunch of branches in his hand."

Quite a favorable sign. We do not know that there may not be more trouble in the future but we can say we are cautiously optimistic.

"What's them branches you got in your hand?
"Them's pussy willows.
"Okay, Dad says. You just hang on a minute.
"You just hang on a minute, I'm gettin' my hat. I'm gettin' my hat and I'm comin' with you!"

"It's too much," Jinny said out loud.

Talking in her head to the doctor.

"What?" said Matt. An aggrieved and babyish look had come over his face while he was still chuckling. "What's the matter now?"

Jinny was shaking her head, squeezing her hand over her mouth.

"It was just a joke," he said. "I never meant to offend you."

Jinny said, "No, no. I—No."

"Never mind, I'm goin' in. I'm not goin' to take up no more of your time." And he turned his back on her, not even bothering to call to the dogs.

She had not said anything like that to the doctor. Why should she? Nothing was his fault. But it was true. It was too much. What he had said made everything harder. It made her have to go back and start this year all over again. It removed a certain low-grade freedom. A dull, protecting membrane that she had not even known was there had been pulled away and left her raw.

Matt's thinking she had gone into the cornfield to pee had made her realize that she actually wanted to. She got out of the van, stood cautiously, and spread her legs and lifted her wide cotton skirt. She had taken to wearing big skirts and no panties this summer because her bladder was no longer under perfect control.

A dark stream trickled away from her through the gravel. The sun was down now, evening was coming on. A clear sky overhead, the clouds had vanished.

One of the dogs barked halfheartedly, to say that somebody was coming, but it was somebody they knew. They had not come over to bother her when she got out—they were used to her now. They went running out to meet whoever it was without any alarm or excitement.

It was a boy, or young man, riding a bicycle. He swerved towards the van and Jinny went round to meet him, a hand on the cooled-down but still-warm metal to support herself. When he spoke to her she did not want it to be across her puddle. And maybe to distract him from even looking on the ground for such a thing, she spoke first.

She said, "Hello—are you delivering something?"

He laughed, springing off the bike and dropping it to the ground, all in one motion.

"I live here," he said. "I'm just getting home from work."

She thought that she should explain who she was, tell him how she came to be here and for how long. But all this was too difficult. Hanging on to the van like this, she must look like somebody who had just come out of a wreck.

"Yeah, I live here," he said. "But I work in a restaurant in town. I work at Sammy's."

A waiter. The bright white shirt and black pants were waiter's clothes. And he had a waiter's air of patience and alertness.

"I'm Jinny Lockyer," she said. "Helen. Helen is—"

"Okay, I know," he said. "You're who Helen's going to work for. Where's Helen?"

"In the house."

"Didn't nobody ask you in, then?"

He was about Helen's age, she thought. Seventeen or eighteen. Slim and graceful and cocky, with an ingenuous enthusiasm that would probably not get him as far as he hoped. She had seen a few like that who ended up as Young Offenders.

He seemed to understand things, though. He seemed to understand that she was exhausted and in some kind of muddle.

"June in there too?" he said. "June's my mom."

His hair was colored like June's, gold streaks over dark. He wore it rather long, and parted in the middle, flopping off to either side.

"Matt too?" he said.

"And my husband. Yes."

"That's a shame."

"Oh, no," she said. "They asked me. I said I'd rather wait out here."

Neal used sometimes to bring home a couple of his Yo-yos, to be supervised doing lawn work or painting or basic carpentry. He thought it was good for them, to be accepted into somebody's home. Jinny had flirted with them occasionally, in a way that she could never be blamed for. Just a gentle tone, a way of making them aware of her soft skirts and her scent of apple soap. That wasn't why Neal had stopped bringing them. He had been told it was out of order.

"So how long have you been waiting?"

"I don't know," Jinny said. "I don't wear a watch."

"Is that right?" he said. "I don't either. I don't hardly ever meet another person that doesn't wear a watch. Did you never wear one?"

She said, "No. Never."

"Me neither. Never ever. I just never wanted to. I don't know why. Never ever wanted to. Like, I always just seemed to know what time it was anyway. Within a couple minutes. Five minutes the most. And I know where all the clocks are, too. I'm riding in to work, and I think I'll check, you know, just be sure what time it is really. And I know the first place I can see the courthouse clock in between the buildings. Always not more than three/four minutes out. Sometimes one of the diners asks me, do you know the time, and I just tell them. They don't even notice I'm not wearing a watch. I go and check as soon as I can, clock in the kitchen. But I never once had to go in there and tell them any different."

"I've been able to do that too, once in a while," Jinny said. "I guess you do develop a sense, if you never wear a watch."

"Yeah, you really do."

"So what time do you think it is now?"

He laughed. He looked at the sky.

"Getting close to eight. Six/seven minutes to eight? I got an advantage, though. I know when I got off of work and then I went to get some cigarettes at the 7-Eleven and then I talked to some guys a couple of minutes and then I biked home. You don't live in town, do you?"

Jinny said no.

"So where do you live?"

She told him.

"You getting tired? You want to go home? You want me to go in and tell your husband you want to go home?"

"No. Don't do that," she said.

"Okay. Okay. I won't. June's probably telling their fortunes in there anyway. She can read hands."

"Can she?"

"Sure. She goes in the restaurant a couple of times a week. Tea too. Tea leaves."

He picked up his bike and wheeled it out of the way of the van. Then he looked in through the driver's window.

"Left the keys in," he said. "So—you want me to drive you home or what? I can put my bike in the back. Your husband can get Matt to drive him and Helen when they get ready. Or if it don't look like Matt can, June can. June's my mom but Matt's not my dad. You don't drive, do you?"

"No," said Jinny. She had not driven for months.

"No. I didn't think so. Okay then? You want me to? Okay?"

"This is just a road I know. It'll get you there as soon as the highway."

They had not driven past the subdivision. In fact they had headed the other way, taking a road that seemed to circle the gravel pit. At least they were going west now, towards the brightest part of the sky. Ricky—that was what he'd told her his name was—had not yet turned the car lights on.

"No danger meeting anybody," he said. "I don't think I ever met a single car on this road, ever. See—not so many people even know this road is here."

"And if I was to turn the lights on," he said, "then the sky would go dark and everything would go dark and you wouldn't be able to see where you were. We just give it a little while more, then when it gets we can see the stars, that's when we turn the lights on."

The sky was like very faintly colored red or yellow or green or blue glass, depending on which part of it you looked at.

"That okay with you?"

"Yes," said Jinny.

The bushes and trees would turn black, once the lights were on. There would just be black clumps along the road and the black mass of trees crowding in behind them, instead of, as now, the individual still identifiable spruce and cedar and feathery tamarack and the jewelweed with its flowers like winking bits of fire. It seemed close enough to touch, and they were going slowly. She put her hand out.

Not quite. But close. The road seemed hardly wider than the car.

She thought she saw the gleam of a full ditch ahead.

"Is there water down there?" she said.

"Down there?" said Ricky. "Down there and everywhere. There's water to both sides of us and lots of places water underneath us. Want to see?"

He slowed the van. He stopped. "Look down your side," he said. "Open the door and look down."

When she did that she saw that they were on a bridge. A little bridge no more than ten feet long, of crossways-laid planks. No railings. And motionless water underneath it.

"Bridges all along here," he said. "And where it's not bridges it's culverts. 'Cause it's always flowing back and forth under the road. Or just laying there and not flowing anyplace."

"How deep?" she said.

"Not deep. Not this time of year. Not till we get to the big pond—it's deeper. And then in spring it's all over the road, you can't drive here, it's deep then. This road goes flat for miles and miles, and it goes straight from one end to the other. There isn't even any roads that cuts across it. This is the only road I know of through the Borneo Swamp."

"Borneo Swamp?" Jinny repeated.

"That's what it's supposed to be called."

"There is an island called Borneo,"[4] she said. "It's halfway round the world."

"I don't know about that. All I ever heard of was just the Borneo Swamp."

There was a strip of dark grass now, growing down the middle of the road.

"Time for the lights," he said. He switched them on and they were in a tunnel in the sudden night.

"Once I did that," he said. "I turned the lights on like that and there was this porcupine. It was just sitting there in the middle of the road. It was sitting straight up kind of on its hind legs and looking right at me. Like some little old man. It was scared to death and it couldn't move. I could see its little old teeth chattering."

She thought, This is where he brings his girls.

"So what do I do? I tried beeping the horn and it still didn't do nothing. I didn't feel like getting out and chasing it. He was scared, but he still was a porcupine and he could let fly. So I just parked there. I had time. When I turned the lights on again he was gone."

Now the branches really did reach close and brush against the door, but if there were flowers she could not see them.

---

4. A large island in the Malay Archipelago.

"I am going to show you something," he said. "I'm going to show you something like I bet you never seen before."

If this was happening back in her old, normal life, it was possible that she might now begin to be frightened. If she was back in her old, normal life she would not be here at all.

"You're going to show me a porcupine," she said.

"Nope. Not that. Something there's not even as many of as there is porcupines. Least as far as I know there's not."

Maybe half a mile farther on he turned off the lights.

"See the stars?" he said. "I told you. Stars."

He stopped the van. Everywhere there was at first a deep silence. Then this silence was filled in, at the edges, by some kind of humming that could have been faraway traffic, and little noises that passed before you properly heard them, that could have been made by night-feeding animals or birds or bats.

"Come in here in the springtime," he said, "you wouldn't hear nothing but the frogs. You'd think you were going deaf with the frogs."

He opened the door on his side.

"Now. Get out and walk a ways with me."

She did as she was told. She walked in one of the wheel tracks, he in the other. The sky seemed to be lighter ahead and there was a different sound—something like mild and rhythmical conversation.

The road turned to wood and the trees on either side were gone.

"Walk out on it," he said. "Go on."

He came close and touched her waist as if he was guiding her. Then he took his hand away, left her to walk on these planks which were like the deck of a boat. Like the deck of a boat they rose and fell. But it wasn't a movement of waves, it was their footsteps, his and hers, that caused this very slight rising and falling of the boards beneath them.

"Now do you know where you are?" he said.

"On a dock?" she said.

"On a bridge. This is a floating bridge."

Now she could make it out—the plank roadway just a few inches above the still water. He drew her over to the side and they looked down. There were stars riding on the water.

"The water's very dark," she said. "I mean—it's dark not just because it's night?"

"It's dark all the time," he said proudly. "That's because it's a swamp. It's got the same stuff in it tea has got and it looks like black tea."

She could see the shoreline, and the reed beds. Water in the reeds, lapping water, was what was making that sound.

"Tannin," he said, sounding the word proudly as if he'd hauled it up out of the dark.

The slight movement of the bridge made her imagine that all the trees and the reed beds were set on saucers of earth and the road was a floating ribbon of earth and underneath it all was water. And the water seemed so still, but it could not really be still because if you tried to keep your eye on one reflected star, you saw how it winked and changed shape and slid from sight. Then it was back again—but maybe not the same one.

It was not until this moment that she realized she didn't have her hat. She not only didn't have it on, she hadn't had it with her in the car. She had not been wearing it when she got out of the car to pee and when she began to talk to Ricky. She had not been wearing it when she sat in the car with her head back against the seat and her eyes closed, when Matt was telling his joke. She must have dropped it in the cornfield, and in her panic left it there.

When she had been scared of seeing the mound of Matt's navel with the purple shirt plastered over it, he had not minded looking at her bleak knob.

"It's too bad the moon isn't up yet," Ricky said. "It's really nice here when the moon is up."

"It's nice now, too."

He slipped his arms around her as if there was no question at all about what he was doing and he could take all the time he wanted to do it. He kissed her mouth. It seemed to her that this was the first time ever that she had participated in a kiss that was an event in itself. The whole story, all by itself. A tender prologue, an efficient pressure, a wholehearted probing and receiving, a lingering thanks, and a drawing away satisfied.

"Oh," he said. "Oh."

He turned her around, and they walked back the way they had come.

"So was that the first you ever been on a floating bridge?"

She said yes it was.

"And now that's what you're going to get to drive over."

He took her hand and swung it as if he would like to toss it.

"And that's the first time ever I kissed a married woman."

"You'll probably kiss a lot more of them," she said. "Before you're done."

He sighed. "Yeah," he said. Amazed and sobered by the thought of what lay ahead of him. "Yeah, I probably will."

Jinny had a sudden thought of Neal, back on dry land. Neal giddy and doubtful, opening his hand to the gaze of the woman with the bright-streaked hair, the fortune teller. Rocking on the edge of his future.

No matter.

What she felt was a lighthearted sort of compassion, almost like laughter. A swish of tender hilarity, getting the better of all her sores and hollows, for the time given.

2000, 2001

SYLVIA PLATH
1932–1963

"I am afraid of getting older," wrote the seventeen-year-old Sylvia Plath in 1949, "I am afraid of getting married. Spare me from cooking three meals a day—spare me from the relentless cage of routine and rote. I want to be free. . . . I want, I think, to be omniscient. . . . I think I would like to call myself 'The girl who wanted to be God.'" Plath's adolescent anxieties were prophetic, for, fourteen years after she wrote these words, the failure of her marriage and the "relentless cage of routine and rote" in which she felt imprisoned as she struggled alone in London to care for two young children appear to have led directly to her suicide, an event that continues to arouse controversy. Equally controversial, however, is the poetry that she wrote shortly before she died. Published posthumously in *Ariel* (1965), her last verses are fiercely innovative and sometimes ferociously vituperative, exulting in their own aesthetic liberation as if to remind us of the early ambitions of this "girl who wanted to be God." Excoriated by some critics for—in the words of the British psychoanalyst David Holbrook—seducing "us to taste of [their] poisoned chalice," they have also been praised as—in the phrase of the American poet Robert Lowell—the productions of "one of those super-real, hypnotic, great classical heroines."

The girl who was to end her life as the center of both a personal and a public melodrama was born and brought up in comparatively quiet, middle-class circumstances. Her parents, German immigrants, were ambitious, hardworking professionals: Otto Plath, an entomologist, taught at Boston University, where Aurelia Plath was also to become a faculty member, teaching secretarial skills. The older of two children, Sylvia Plath herself exhibited an early precocity as well as a penchant for hard work. With her mother's encouragement, she began to write stories and poems when she was quite young, and by the time she confided to her diary that she wanted to be "omniscient" she had already published some of this work in *Seventeen* and other periodicals. What might have been simply a prosperous and productive girlhood had been darkened, however, by her father's death (from a gangrenous leg, to which she refers in "Daddy") when she was eight. In the myth into which she increasingly transformed her life throughout her later work—for example, the sardonic curse-poem "Daddy" (1963) and the autobiographical novel *The Bell Jar* (1963)—this event consistently played a central part, marking a fall from childhood innocence to adult experience, from grace to loss.

In 1950, Plath won a scholarship to Smith College, where for several years she continued her career as a "superachiever," accumulating a steady string of honors and prizes along with high grades and accolades from her teachers. But the distinction that made the greatest difference in her career at the time (as well as in her later life) proved problematic: in 1953, Plath became one of a dozen "guest editors" of the New York fashion magazine *Mademoiselle* and traveled to the city to work on the journal's staff for a month. Thinly fictionalized, her feelings and experiences there are recounted in some detail in *The Bell Jar,* where she records the ambivalences that marked her initiation into the Madison Avenue world of female glamour and professional high style. Returning to her mother's home in Wellesley, Massachusetts, she suffered a serious breakdown and she attempted suicide—an attempt that she would later record not only in *The Bell Jar* but also in such poems as "Daddy" and "Lady Lazarus."

Following her breakdown, Plath was institutionalized for a year and given (among other therapies) electric shock treatments, treatments whose intensity may inform some of her most violent metaphors of physical and spiritual transformation. When she returned to Smith in 1954, however, she seems easily to have resumed her successful academic career. In 1955, she graduated *summa cum laude* and won a Fulbright to Cambridge University, where she studied for a graduate degree in English literature and where, in 1956, she met and married the poet Ted Hughes, an ambitious and energetic artist whose intellectual and emotional support significantly aided her development during their early years together. In the late 1950s, the couple traveled to the United States, and Plath taught for a year at Smith, but, passionately committed to her literary vocation, she ultimately rejected academic ambition. Instead, she and Hughes settled first in London, then in a farmhouse in Devon, where Plath devoted herself to writing and to her two children—Frieda and Nicholas—born in the early 1960s.

After her marriage broke up in the summer of 1962, Plath moved back to London and struggled to continue her work while caring for her children through the coldest winter England had seen in decades. Her letters to her mother from this period (edited in *Letters Home,* 1975, by Aurelia Schober Plath) are characterized by intense bitterness over the collapse of her marriage and mounting anxiety about her future and her children's. At the same time, they are marked by extraordinary exultation, for Plath was now producing—sometimes at the rate of two or three a day—the poems that would later appear in *Ariel,* and she knew their value. "I am a writer . . . I am a genius of a writer . . . I am writing the best poems of my life; they will make my name," she told her mother. Nevertheless, despite her awareness of the nature of her achievement, there is considerable evidence that she was again experiencing a breakdown not unlike the one that had led to her suicide attempt in 1953. Early in the morning of February 11, 1963, she left mugs of milk next to her children's cribs, carefully stuffed towels into the cracks around her kitchen door, and gassed herself in the oven of her stove.

The mythologizing of self and family that energizes Plath's later poems, as well as earlier works such as "The Colossus" and "The Disquieting Muses," has almost certainly led to much of the critical misunderstanding that continues to surround her poetry with controversy. About "Daddy," for instance, the critic Elizabeth Hardwick once complained that Plath's real father "died of a long illness, but there is no pity for *his* lost life," adding that he "did not kill anyone and 'the fat black heart' [of the poem] is really [Plath's] own," and concluding that to bring "strangers, the town . . . into the punishment of her father . . . is somehow the most biting and ungenerous thought of all." The problem with such remarks, which are representative of a good many attacks that have been mounted against Plath, is that the literary figure of "Daddy" in the poem of that name (like the father figure in "The Colossus") is not identical with, but rather *generalized* from, Plath's literal father.

Similarly, though late poems such as "Ariel," "Fever 103," and "Edge" are death-haunted, they cannot be said to "predict" Plath's suicide, despite Robert Lowell's comment that these verses "are playing Russian roulette with six cartridges in the cylinder." Rather, it is important to understand that Plath's demise, far from being the consequence of fearfully unleashed imaginative forces, was the result of a series of personal calamities, including—as the scholar Diane Middlebrook has recently shown—a susceptibility to clinical depression. Lately, some feminists have worried that because this artist was not a "survivor" she does not offer younger women who study her life a "positive role model." Yet, as Plath's own poems show, the works that would "make [her] name" were inspired by yearning to endure and overcome the ice of circumstance. "Wintering," the poem with which she herself had planned to end *Ariel,* concludes with a question and answer that express just such longing. "Will the hive survive, . . . / To enter another year?" the poet wonders, and replies to her own query with an affirmation of certainty: "The bees are flying. They taste the spring." Sylvia Plath herself may not have lasted out her struggle to "taste" another spring, but her poems record her will to triumph.

It is a testament to Plath's continually growing reputation that although Ted Hughes, as her heir and executor, rearranged the order in which she had organized the poems in the manuscript she left behind—the one that was indeed to "make [her] name"—in 2004 a facsimile of that manuscript was issued as the "original" *Ariel,* with the organization that the poet herself had planned. In an introduction to the book, Plath's daughter, Frieda Hughes, herself a poet, comments: "Representing my mother's vision and experience at a particular time in her life during great emotional turmoil, these Ariel poems—this harnessing of her own inner forces by my mother herself—speak for themselves." Then, in an impassioned response to the ongoing mythologizing of Plath's life by outsiders (for the poet has now been the subject of, among other fictions, two novels and a film), she adds, with some bitterness: "My mother's poems cannot be crammed into the mouths of actors in any filmic reinvention of her story in the expectation that they can breathe life into her again, any more than literary fictionalisation of my mother's life . . . achieves any purpose other than to parody the life she actually lived. Since she died my mother has been dissected, analysed, reinterpreted, reinvented, fictionalised, and in some cases completely fabricated. It comes down to this: her own words describe her best, her ever-changing moods defining the way she viewed her world and the manner in which she pinned down her subjects with a merciless eye."

The Disquieting Muses[1]

    Mother, mother, what illbred aunt
    Or what disfigured and unsightly
    Cousin did you so unwisely keep
    Unasked to my christening,[2] that she
5 Sent these ladies in her stead
    With heads like darning-eggs to nod
    And nod and nod at foot and head
    And at the left side of my crib?

    Mother, who made to order stories
10 Of Mixie Blackshort the heroic bear,
    Mother, whose witches always, always
    Got baked into gingerbread,[3] I wonder
    Whether you saw them, whether you said
    Words to rid me of those three ladies
15 Nodding by night around my bed,
15 Mouthless, eyeless, with stitched bald head.

    In the hurricane, when father's twelve
    Study windows bellied in
    Like bubbles about to break, you fed
20 My brother and me cookies and Ovaltine
    And helped the two of us to choir:
    "Thor[4] is angry: boom boom boom!
    Thor is angry: we don't care!"
    But those ladies broke the panes.

25 When on tiptoe the schoolgirls danced,
    Blinking flashlights like fireflies
    And singing the glowworm song, I could
    Not lift a foot in the twinkle-dress
    But, heavy-footed, stood aside
30 In the shadow cast by my dismal-headed
    Godmothers, and you cried and cried:
    And the shadows stretched, the lights went out.

    Mother, you sent me to piano lessons
    And praised my arabesques and trills

---

1. Greek goddesses of the arts and learning, and sources of inspiration.
2. An allusion to the fairy tale "Sleeping Beauty," in which an infant princess is cursed by a wicked fairy who was not invited to the girl's christening to be a godmother.
3. An allusion to the story of Hansel and Gretel, who baked the murderous witch who lived in a gingerbread house.
4. The Norse god of war and thunder.

    Although each teacher found my touch
    Oddly wooden in spite of scales
    And the hours of practicing, my ear
    Tone-deaf and yes, unteachable.
    I learned, I learned, I learned elsewhere,
40 From muses unhired by you, dear mother.

    I woke one day to see you, mother,
    Floating above me in bluest air
    On a green balloon bright with a million
    Flowers and bluebirds that never were
45 Never, never, found anywhere.
    But the little planet bobbed away
    Like a soap-bubble as you called: Come here!
    And I faced my traveling companions.

    Day now, night now, at head, side, feet,
50 They stand their vigil in gowns of stone,
    Faces blank as the day I was born,
    Their shadows long in the setting sun
    That never brightens or goes down.
    And this is the kingdom you bore me to,
55 Mother, mother. But no frown of mine
    Will betray the company I keep.

1957   1960

The Colossus[1]

  I shall never get you put together entirely,
  Pieced, glued, and properly jointed.
  Mule-bray, pig-grunt and bawdy cackles
  Proceed from your great lips.
5 It's worse than a barnyard.

  Perhaps you consider yourself an oracle,
  Mouthpiece of the dead, or of some god or other.
  Thirty years now I have labored
  To dredge the silt from your throat.
10 I am none the wiser.

  Scaling little ladders with gluepots and pails of Lysol
  I crawl like an ant in mourning
  Over the weedy acres of your brow
  To mend the immense skull-plates and clear
15 The bald, white tumuli[2] of your eyes.

---

1. A bronze statue of Helios, the sun god, built between 291 and 280 B.C.E. It was more than 100 feet tall, and stood on a promontory overlooking the harbor of Rhodes (it fell during an earthquake ca. 225 B.C.E.).
2. Grave mounds.

A blue sky out of the Oresteia[3]
Arches above us. O father, all by yourself
You are pithy and historical as the Roman Forum.[4]
I open my lunch on a hill of black cypress.
20 Your fluted bones and acanthine[5] hair are littered

In their old anarchy to the horizon-line.
It would take more than a lightning-stroke
To create such a ruin.
Nights, I squat in the cornucopia
25 Of your left ear, out of the wind,

Counting the red stars and those of plum-color.
The sun rises under the pillar of your tongue.
My hours are married to shadow.
No longer do I listen for the scrape of a keel
30 On the blank stones of the landing.

1959   1960

You're

Clownlike, happiest on your hands,
Feet to the stars, and moon-skulled,
Gilled like a fish. A common-sense
Thumbs-down on the dodo's mode.
5 Wrapped up in yourself like a spool,
Trawling your dark as owls do.
Mute as a turnip from the Fourth
Of July to All Fools' Day,[1]
O high-riser, my little loaf.

10 Vague as fog and looked for like mail.
Farther off than Australia.
Bent-backed Atlas,[2] our traveled prawn.
Snug as a bud and at home
Like a sprat in a pickle jug.
15 A creel of eels, all ripples.
Jumpy as a Mexican bean.[3]
Right, like a well-done sum.
A clean slate, with your own face on.

1960

---

3. A cycle of three plays by Aeschylus (525–456 B.C.E.) that explore the nature of justice by telling the story of the murder of Agamemnon and of the vengeance enacted by his son, Orestes.
4. The main public space of ancient Rome and the center of civic life, surrounded by monumental temples and public halls.
5. I.e., sculptured (as in Greek columns) like the leaves of the acanthus plant. "Fluted": grooved (again, as in columns).
1. I.e., April Fool's Day.
2. In Greek mythology, the Titan Atlas was condemned by Zeus to uphold the heavens on his shoulders.
3. I.e., a Mexican jumping bean, which moves because it contains the larva of a small moth.

Mirror

I am silver and exact. I have no preconceptions.
Whatever I see I swallow immediately
Just as it is, unmisted by love or dislike.
I am not cruel, only truthful—
5   The eye of a little god, four-cornered.
Most of the time I meditate on the opposite wall.
It is pink, with speckles. I have looked at it so long
I think it is part of my heart. But it flickers.
Faces and darkness separate us over and over.

10 Now I am a lake. A woman bends over me,
Searching my reaches for what she really is.
Then she turns to those liars, the candles or the moon.
I see her back, and reflect it faithfully.
She rewards me with tears and an agitation of hands.
15 I am important to her. She comes and goes.
Each morning it is her face that replaces the darkness.
In me she has drowned a young girl, and in me an old woman
Rises toward her day after day, like a terrible fish.

1961

The Bee Meeting

Who are these people at the bridge to meet me? They are the villagers—
The rector, the midwife, the sexton, the agent for bees.
In my sleeveless summery dress I have no protection,
And they are all gloved and covered, why did nobody tell me?
5   They are smiling and taking out veils tacked to ancient hats.

I am nude as a chicken neck, does nobody love me?
Yes, here is the secretary of bees with her white shop smock,
Buttoning the cuffs at my wrists and the slit from my neck to my knees.
Now I am milkweed silk, the bees will not notice.
10 They will not smell my fear, my fear, my fear.

Which is the rector now, is it that man in black?
Which is the midwife, is that her blue coat?
Everybody is nodding a square black head, they are knights in visors,
Breastplates of cheesecloth knotted under the armpits.
15 Their smiles and their voices are changing. I am led through a beanfield.

Strips of tinfoil winking like people,
Feather dusters fanning their hands in a sea of bean flowers,
Creamy bean flowers with black eyes and leaves like bored hearts.
Is it blood clots the tendrils are dragging up that string?
20 No, no, it is scarlet flowers that will one day be edible.

Now they are giving me a fashionable white straw Italian hat
And a black veil that molds to my face, they are making me one of them.
They are leading me to the shorn grove, the circle of hives.
Is it the hawthorn that smells so sick?[1]
The barren body of hawthorn, etherizing its children.

Is it some operation that is taking place?
It is the surgeon my neighbors are waiting for,
This apparition in a green helmet,
Shining gloves and white suit.
Is it the butcher, the grocer, the postman, someone I know?

I cannot run, I am rooted, and the gorse hurts me
With its yellow purses, its spiky armory.
I could not run without having to run forever.
The white hive is snug as a virgin,
Sealing off her brood cells, her honey, and quietly humming.

Smoke rolls and scarves in the grove.
The mind of the hive thinks this is the end of everything.
Here they come, the outriders, on their hysterical elastics.
If I stand very still, they will think I am cow-parsley,
A gullible head untouched by their animosity,

Not even nodding, a personage in a hedgerow.
The villagers open the chambers, they are hunting the queen.[2]
Is she hiding, is she eating honey? She is very clever.
She is old, old, old, she must live another year, and she knows it.
While in their fingerjoint cells the new virgins

Dream of a duel they will win inevitably,
A curtain of wax dividing them from the bride flight,
The upflight of the murderess into a heaven that loves her.
The villagers are moving the virgins, there will be no killing.
The old queen does not show herself, is she so ungrateful?

I am exhausted, I am exhausted—
Pillar of white in a blackout of knives.
I am the magician's girl who does not flinch.
The villagers are untying their disguises, they are shaking hands.
Whose is that long white box in the grove, what have they accomplished,
  why am I cold.

October 3, 1962   1963

---

1. Hawthorn flowers have a strong, musky scent.   2. I.e., the queen bee.

The Arrival of the Bee Box

I ordered this, this clean wood box
Square as a chair and almost too heavy to lift.
I would say it was the coffin of a midget
Or a square baby
Were there not such a din in it.

The box is locked, it is dangerous.
I have to live with it overnight
And I can't keep away from it.
There are no windows, so I can't see what is in there.
There is only a little grid, no exit.

I put my eye to the grid.
It is dark, dark,
With the swarmy feeling of African hands
Minute and shrunk for export,
Black on black, angrily clambering.

How can I let them out?
It is the noise that appalls me most of all,
The unintelligible syllables.
It is like a Roman mob,[1]
Small, taken one by one, but my god, together!

I lay my ear to furious Latin.
I am not a Caesar.[2]
I have simply ordered a box of maniacs.
They can be sent back.
They can die, I need feed them nothing, I am the owner.

I wonder how hungry they are.
I wonder if they would forget me
If I just undid the locks and stood back and turned into a tree.
There is the laburnum, its blond colonnades,
And the petticoats of the cherry.

They might ignore me immediately
In my moon suit and funeral veil.
I am no source of honey
So why should they turn on me?
Tomorrow I will be sweet God, I will set them free.
The box is only temporary.

October 4, 1962   1963

---

1. Thought of (as in Shakespeare's *Julius Caesar*) as being unruly and unmanageable.   2. I.e., Roman ruler, emperor.

Stings

Bare-handed, I hand the combs.
The man in white smiles, bare-handed,
Our cheesecloth gauntlets neat and sweet,
The throats of our wrists brave lilies.
5   He and I

Have a thousand clean cells between us,
Eight combs of yellow cups,
And the hive itself a teacup,
White with pink flowers on it,
10 With excessive love I enameled it

Thinking "Sweetness, sweetness."
Brood cells gray as the fossils of shells
Terrify me, they seem so old.
What am I buying, wormy mahogany?
15 Is there any queen at all in it?

If there is, she is old,
Her wings torn shawls, her long body
Rubbed of its plush—
Poor and bare and unqueenly and even shameful.
20 I stand in a column

Of winged, unmiraculous women,
Honey-drudgers.[1]
I am no drudge
Though for years I have eaten dust
25 And dried plates with my dense hair.

And seen my strangeness evaporate,
Blue dew from dangerous skin.
Will they hate me,
These women who only scurry,
30 Whose news is the open cherry, the open clover?

It is almost over.
I am in control.
Here is my honey-machine,
It will work without thinking,
35 Opening, in spring, like an industrious virgin

To scour the creaming crests
As the moon, for its ivory powders, scours the sea.
A third person is watching.
He has nothing to do with the bee-seller or with me.
40 Now he is gone

---

1. I.e., the sexually undeveloped female worker bees who produce the hive's honey.

In eight great bounds, a great scapegoat.
Here is his slipper, here is another,
And here the square of white linen
He wore instead of a hat.
⁴⁵ He was sweet,

The sweat of his efforts a rain
Tugging the world to fruit.
The bees found him out,
Molding onto his lips like lies,
⁵⁰ Complicating his features.

They thought death was worth it, but I
Have a self to recover, a queen.
Is she dead, is she sleeping?
Where has she been,
⁵⁵ With her lion-red body, her wings of glass?

Now she is flying
More terrible than she ever was, red
Scar in the sky, red comet
Over the engine that killed her—
⁶⁰ The mausoleum, the wax house.

October 6, 1962   1965

The Swarm

Somebody is shooting at something in our town—
A dull pom, pom in the Sunday street.
Jealousy can open the blood,
It can make black roses.
⁵ Who are they shooting at?

It is you the knives are out for
At Waterloo, Waterloo, Napoleon,
The hump of Elba[1] on your short back,
And the snow, marshaling its brilliant cutlery
¹⁰ Mass after mass, saying Shh!

Shh! These are chess people you play with,
Still figures of ivory.
The mud squirms with throats,
Stepping stones for French bootsoles.
¹⁵ The gilt and pink domes of Russia melt and float off

---

1. Napoleon Bonaparte (1769–1821) was France's emperor (1804–14) and the military leader of his "Grand Army." Forced into exile on the island of Elba, off the western coast of Italy, he escaped, reassembled his followers, and was finally defeated by the British at the battle of Waterloo in 1815.

In the furnace of greed. Clouds, clouds.
So the swarm balls and deserts
Seventy feet up, in a black pine tree.
It must be shot down. Pom! Pom!
So dumb it thinks bullets are thunder.

It thinks they are the voice of God
Condoning the beak, the claw, the grin of the dog
Yellow-haunched, a pack-dog,
Grinning over its bone of ivory
Like the pack, the pack, like everybody.

The bees have got so far. Seventy feet high!
Russia, Poland and Germany![2]
The mild hills, the same old magenta
Fields shrunk to a penny
Spun into a river, the river crossed.

The bees argue, in their black ball,
A flying hedgehog, all prickles.
The man with gray hands stands under the honeycomb
Of their dream, the hived station
Where trains, faithful to their steel arcs,

Leave and arrive, and there is no end to the country.
Pom! Pom! They fall
Dismembered, to a tod[3] of ivy.
So much for the charioteers, the outriders, the Grand Army!
A red tatter, Napoleon!

The last badge of victory.
The swarm is knocked into a cocked straw hat.
Elba, Elba, bleb[4] on the sea!
The white busts of marshals, admirals, generals
Worming themselves into niches.

How instructive this is!
The dumb, banded bodies
Walking the plank draped with Mother France's upholstery
Into a new mausoleum,
An ivory palace, a crotch pine.

The man with gray hands smiles—
The smile of a man of business, intensely practical.
They are not hands at all
But asbestos receptacles.
Pom! Pom! "They would have killed *me*."

---

2. Three countries that Napoleon attempted to conquer.
3. A clump (British idiom).
4. A small blister.

Stings big as drawing pins!
It seems bees have a notion of honor,
A black intractable mind.
Napoleon is pleased, he is pleased with everything.
60 O Europe! O ton of honey!

October 7, 1962   1965

Wintering

This is the easy time, there is nothing doing.
I have whirled the midwife's extractor,[1]
I have my honey,
Six jars of it,
5   Six cat's eyes in the wine cellar,

Wintering in a dark without window
At the heart of the house
Next to the last tenant's rancid jam
And the bottles of empty glitters—
10 Sir So-and-so's gin.

This is the room I have never been in
This is the room I could never breathe in.
The black bunched in there like a bat,
No light
15 But the torch and its faint

Chinese yellow on appalling objects—
Black asininity. Decay.
Possession.
It is they who own me.
20 Neither cruel nor indifferent,

Only ignorant.
This is the time of hanging on for the bees—the bees
So slow I hardly know them,
Filing like soldiers
25 To the syrup tin

To make up for the honey I've taken.
Tate and Lyle[2] keeps them going,
The refined snow.
It is Tate and Lyle they live on, instead of flowers.
30 They take it. The cold sets in.

Now they ball in a mass,
Black

---

1. A device used for removing honey from beehives.
2. A common brand of syrup.

Mind against all that white.
The smile of the snow is white.
35 It spreads itself out, a mile-long body of Meissen,[3]

Into which, on warm days,
They can only carry their dead.
The bees are all women,
Maids and the long royal lady.
40 They have got rid of the men,[4]

The blunt, clumsy stumblers, the boors.
Winter is for women—
The woman, still at her knitting,
At the cradle of Spanish walnut,
45 Her body a bulb in the cold and too dumb to think.

Will the hive survive, will the gladiolas
Succeed in banking their fires
To enter another year?
What will they taste of, the Christmas roses?
50 The bees are flying. They taste the spring.

October 9, 1962   1965

Daddy

You do not do, you do not do
Any more, black shoe
In which I have lived like a foot
For thirty years, poor and white,
5 Barely daring to breathe or Achoo.

Daddy, I have had to kill you.
You died before I had time—
Marble-heavy, a bag full of God,
Ghastly statue with one gray toe[1]
10 Big as a Frisco seal

And a head in the freakish Atlantic
Where it pours bean green over blue
In the waters off beautiful Nauset.[2]
I used to pray to recover you.
15 Ach, du.[3]

---

3. A kind of porcelain made in Germany.
4. There are no male drones in bee colonies in the winter.
1. The toe of Plath's father, Otto Plath, turned black from gangrene.
2. Beach north of Boston.
3. Ah, you (German); the first of a series of references to her father's German origins.

In the German tongue, in the Polish town[4]
Scraped flat by the roller
Of wars, wars, wars.
But the name of the town is common.
20 My Polack friend

Says there are a dozen or two.
So I never could tell where you
Put your foot, your root,
I never could talk to you.
25 The tongue stuck in my jaw.

It stuck in a barb wire snare.
Ich,[5] ich, ich, ich,
I could hardly speak.
I thought every German was you.
30 And the language obscene

An engine, an engine
Chuffing me off like a Jew.
A Jew to Dachau, Auschwitz, Belsen.[6]
I began to talk like a Jew.
35 I think I may well be a Jew.

The snows of the Tyrol,[7] the clear beer of Vienna
Are not very pure or true.
With my gipsy ancestress and my weird luck
And my Taroc pack[8] and my Taroc pack
40 I may be a bit of a Jew.

I have always been scared of you,
With your Luftwaffe,[9] your gobbledygoo.
And your neat mustache
And your Aryan eye, bright blue.
45 Panzer[1]-man, panzer-man, O You—

Not God but a swastika
So black no sky could squeak through.
Every woman adores a Fascist,
The boot in the face, the brute
50 Brute heart of a brute like you.

You stand at the blackboard, daddy,
In the picture I have of you,
A cleft in your chin instead of your foot
But no less a devil for that, no not
55 Any less the black man who

---

4. Grabow, the birthplace of Otto Plath.
5. I.
6. German concentration camps, where millions of Jews were murdered during World War II.
7. Austrian Alpine region.
8. I.e., Tarot, ancient fortune-telling cards.

9. The German air force.
1. Armor or tank (German). Adolf Hitler, who had a neat moustache, preached the superiority of the Aryan race—persons with blond hair and blue eyes, as opposed to those with darker, Semitic characteristics.

Bit my pretty red heart in two.
I was ten when they buried you.
At twenty I tried to die[2]
And get back, back, back to you.
I thought even the bones would do.

But they pulled me out of the sack,
And they stuck me together with glue.
And then I knew what to do.
I made a model of you,
A man in black with a Meinkampf[3] look

And a love of the rack and the screw.
And I said I do, I do.
So daddy, I'm finally through.
The black telephone's off at the root,
The voices just can't worm through.

If I've killed one man, I've killed two—
The vampire who said he was you
And drank my blood for a year,
Seven years, if you want to know.
Daddy, you can lie back now.

There's a stake in your fat black heart
And the villagers never liked you.
They are dancing and stamping on you.
They always knew it was you.
Daddy, daddy, you bastard, I'm through.

October 12, 1962   1965

Ariel[1]

Stasis in darkness.
Then the substanceless blue
Pour of tor[2] and distances.

God's lioness,
How one we grow,
Pivot of heels and knees!—The furrow

Splits and passes, sister to
The brown arc
Of the neck I cannot catch,

---

2. An allusion to Plath's first suicide attempt.
3. A reference to Hitler's political autobiography, *Mein Kampf* (My struggle, 1925–27), written and published before his rise to power, in which the future dictator outlined his plans for world conquest.

1. The name of the horse Plath frequently rode; also the name of a fairy or spirit in Shakespeare's *The Tempest*.
2. Craggy hill.

10   Nigger-eye
Berries cast dark
Hooks—

Black sweet blood mouthfuls,
Shadows.
15   Something else

Hauls me through air—
Thighs, hair;
Flakes from my heels.

White
20   Godiva,[3] I unpeel—
Dead hands, dead stringencies.

And now I
Foam to wheat, a glitter of seas.
The child's cry

25   Melts in the wall.
And I
Am the arrow,

The dew that flies
Suicidal, at one with the drive
30   Into the red

Eye, the cauldron of morning.

October 27, 1962   1965

Nick and the Candlestick[1]

I am a miner. The light burns blue.
Waxy stalactites
Drip and thicken, tears

The earthen womb
5   Exudes from its dead boredom.
Black bat airs

Wrap me, raggy shawls,
Cold homicides.
They weld to me like plums.

---

3. According to legend, Lady Godiva (1010?–1067) rode naked through the streets of Coventry to persuade her husband, the local lord, to lower heavy taxes.
1. Plath's son, Nicholas, was less than a year old when this poem was written.

10 Old cave of calcium
    Icicles, old echoer.
    Even the newts are white,

    Those holy Joes.[2]
    And the fish, the fish—
15 Christ! they are panes of ice,

    A vice of knives,
    A piranha
    Religion, drinking

    Its first communion out of my live toes.
20 The candle
    Gulps and recovers its small altitude,

    Its yellows hearten.
    O love, how did you get here?
    O embryo

25 Remembering, even in sleep,
    Your crossed position.
    The blood blooms clean

    In you, ruby.
    The pain
30 You wake to is not yours.

    Love, love,
    I have hung our cave with roses,
    With soft rugs—

    The last of Victoriana.[3]
35 Let the stars
    Plummet to their dark address,

    Let the mercuric
    Atoms that cripple drip
    Into the terrible well,

40 You are the one
    Solid the spaces lean on, envious.
    You are the baby in the barn.[4]

October 29, 1962   1965

---

2. Pious people or clergymen (British slang).
3. I.e., the rich furnishings and decor associated with the Victorian age.
4. An allusion to the infant Jesus, who was nursed in a manger.

Lady Lazarus[1]

I have done it again.
One year in every ten
I manage it—
A sort of walking miracle, my skin
Bright as a Nazi lampshade,[2]
My right foot

A paperweight,
My face a featureless, fine
Jew linen.

Peel off the napkin
O my enemy.
Do I terrify?—

The nose, the eye pits, the full set of teeth?
The sour breath
Will vanish in a day.

Soon, soon the flesh
The grave cave ate will be
At home on me

And I a smiling woman.
I am only thirty.
And like the cat I have nine times to die.

This is Number Three.
What a trash
To annihilate each decade.

What a million filaments.
The peanut-crunching crowd
Shoves in to see

Them unwrap me hand and foot—
The big strip tease.
Gentlemen, ladies

These are my hands
My knees.
I may be skin and bone,

Nevertheless, I am the same, identical woman.
The first time it happened I was ten.
It was an accident.

---

1. Lazarus, the brother of Mary and Martha, was raised by Jesus from the dead (John 11.1–44).
2. The Nazis made use of some of the corpses of Jews whom they had killed by turning their skin into lampshades and their bodies into soap.

The second time I meant
To last it out and not come back at all.[3]
I rocked shut

As a seashell.
They had to call and call
And pick the worms off me like sticky pearls.

Dying
Is an art, like everything else.
I do it exceptionally well.

I do it so it feels like hell.
I do it so it feels real.
I guess you could say I've a call.

It's easy enough to do it in a cell.
It's easy enough to do it and stay put.
It's the theatrical

Comeback in broad day
To the same place, the same face, the same brute
Amused shout:

"A miracle!"
That knocks me out.
There is a charge

For the eyeing of my scars, there is a charge
For the hearing of my heart—
It really goes.

And there is a charge, a very large charge
For a word or a touch
Or a bit of blood

Or a piece of my hair or my clothes.
So, so, Herr[4] Doktor.
So, Herr Enemy.

I am your opus,
I am your valuable,
The pure gold baby

That melts to a shriek.
I turn and burn.
Do not think I underestimate your great concern.

---

3. An allusion to Plath's first suicide attempt.   4. Mister (German).

Ash, ash—
You poke and stir.
Flesh, bone, there is nothing there—

A cake of soap,
A wedding ring,
A gold filling.

Herr God, Herr Lucifer[5]
Beware
Beware.[6]

Out of the ash
I rise with my red hair
And I eat men like air.

October 23–29, 1962   1965

Words

Axes
After whose stroke the wood rings,
And the echoes!
Echoes traveling
Off from the center like horses.

The sap
Wells like tears, like the
Water striving
To re-establish its mirror
Over the rock

That drops and turns,
A white skull,
Eaten by weedy greens.
Years later I
Encounter them on the road—

Words dry and riderless,
The indefatigable hoof-taps.
While
From the bottom of the pool, fixed stars
Govern a life.

February 1, 1963   1965

---

5. The devil.
6. Perhaps an echo of the description of the inspired poet in Samuel Taylor Coleridge's "Kubla Khan" (1816): "Beware! Beware! / His flashing eyes, his floating hair!"

Edge

The woman is perfected.
Her dead

Body wears the smile of accomplishment,
The illusion of a Greek necessity[1]

5   Flows in the scrolls of her toga,
Her bare

Feet seem to be saying:
We have come so far, it is over.

Each dead child coiled, a white serpent,
10   One at each little

Pitcher of milk, now empty.
She has folded

Them back into her body as petals
Of a rose close when the garden

15   Stiffens and odors bleed
From the sweet, deep throats of the night flower.

The moon has nothing to be sad about,
Staring from her hood of bone.

She is used to this sort of thing.
20   Her blacks crackle and drag.

February 5, 1963   1965

1. *Anankē* (literally, "necessity"), for the Greeks a primordial goddess of compulsion and inevitability.

EDNA O'BRIEN
b. 1932

After Edna O'Brien completed a trilogy of novels (composed of *The Country Girls, The Lonely Girl,* and *Girls in Their Married Bliss,* 1960–64), she explained to an interviewer that while women can become high-court judges, "the high-court judge will still have to come home and make the evening meal." Her skepticism about women's social progress, like her rejection of her own Catholic upbringing, is based on the belief that most human beings feel themselves to be engaged in a struggle to ensure their own survival. O'Brien's fiction is characterized, on the one hand, by her robust handling of explicitly sexual themes and, on the other, by her indictment of what she perceives as the poverty and fanaticism of her cultural roots. Born in a small village in the west of Ireland that she has described as "enclosed, fervid and bigoted," O'Brien attended Pharmaceutical College in Dublin. At the age of twenty, she married and, after the birth of two sons, she moved to London, where she currently resides. Besides the trilogy, she has composed more than a dozen other novels; a number of plays, including one about Virginia Woolf (*Virginia*, 1981); some television scripts; a biography of James Joyce and a study of his relationship with his wife, Nora; and nine collections of short stories, among them *A Fanatic Heart: Selected Stories of Edna O'Brien* (1984), *Lantern Slides: Short Stories* (1990), and *Irish Revel* (1998).

Like Irish fiction writers from Joyce to Julia O'Faolain, O'Brien captures the complex spiritual and social dynamics of the Irish family. But "Brother" also illustrates the almost scandalous frankness with which she explores some of the secrets of her native land; indeed the story's candor helps show why O'Brien has said that when she goes to Ireland "people are courteous to my face, though rather slanderous behind my back." She is an expatriate, O'Brien has also explained, because she needs to feel free, although she adds "I don't rule out living some of the time in Ireland, but it would be in a remote place, where I would have silence and privacy. It's important when writing to feel free, answerable to no one. The minute you feel you are answerable, you're throttled."

Brother

Bad cess[1] to him. Thinks I don't know, that I didn't smell a rat. All them bachelors swaggering in here, calling him out to the haggart in case I twigged.[2] "Tutsy this and Tutsy that." A few readies in it for them, along with drives and big feeds.[3] They went the first Sunday to reconnoitre, walk the land and so forth. The second Sunday they went in for refreshments. Three married sisters, all gawks.[4] If they're not hitched up by now there must be something wrong; harelip or a limp or fits. He's no oil painting, of course. Me doing everything for him: making his porridge and emptying his worshipful Po,[5] for God knows how many years. Not to mention his lumbago, and the liniment I rubbed in.

"I'll be good to you, Maisie," he says. Good! A bag of toffees on a holy day. Takes me for granted. All them fly-boys at threshing time trying to ogle me up into the loft for a fumble. Puckauns.[6] I'd take a pitchfork to any one of them; so would he if he knew. I scratched his back many's the night and rubbed the liniment on it. Terrible aul smell. Eucalyptus.

"Lower . . . lower," he'd say. "Down there." Down to the puddingy bits, the lupins. All to get to my Mary. He had a Mass said in the house after. Said he saw his mother, our mother; something on her mind. I had to have grapefruit for the priest's breakfast, had to de-pip it.[7] These priests are real gluttons. He ate in the breakfast room and kept admiring things in the cabinet, the china bell and the bog-oak cabin, and so forth. Thought I'd part with them. I was running in and out with hot tea, hot water, hot scones; he ate enough for three. Then the big handshake; Matt giving him a tenner. I never

---

1. Luck.
2. Noticed, understood. "Haggart": stackyard, or enclosure containing haystacks.
3. Meals. "Readies": banknotes.
4. Clumsy, stupid people.
5. I.e., his chamber pot.
6. Billy goats. "Flyboys": clever boys.
7. Remove the seeds.

had that amount in my whole life. Ten bob[8] on Fridays to get provisions, including sausages for his breakfast. Woeful the way he never consulted me. He began to get hoity-toity, took off those awful trousers with the greasy backside from all the sweating and lathering on horseback, tractor, and bike; threw them in the fire cavalier-like. Had me airing a suit for three days. I had it on a clotheshorse, turning it round every quarter of an hour, for fear of it scorching.

Then the three bachelors come into the yard again, blabbing about buying silage off him. They had silage to burn. It stinks the countryside. He put on his cap and went out to talk to them. They all leant on the gate, cogitating. I knew 'twas fishy, but it never dawned on me it could be a wife. I'd have gone out and sent them packing. Talking low they were, and at the end they all shook hands. At the supper he said he was going to Galway Sunday.

"What's in Galway?" I said.

"A greyhound," he said.

First mention of a greyhound since our little Deirdre died. The pride and joy of the parish she was. Some scoundrels poisoned her. I found her in a fit outside in the shed, yelps coming out of her, and foam. It nearly killed him. He had a rope that he was ruminating with for months. Now this bombshell. Galway.

"I'll come with you, I need a sea breeze," I said.

"It's all male, it's stag," he said, and grinned.

I might have guessed. Why they were egging him on I'll never know, except 'twas to spite me. Some of them have it in for me; I drove bullocks of theirs off our land, I don't give them any haults on bonfire night. He went up to the room then and wouldn't budge. I left a slice of griddle bread with golden syrup on it outside the door. He didn't touch it. At dawn I was raking the ashes and he called me, real soft-soapy, "Is that you, Maisie, is that you?" Who in blazes' name did he think it was—Bridget or Mary of the Gods! "Come in for a minute," he said. "There's a flea or some goddamn thing itching me, maybe it's a tick, maybe they've nested." I strip the covers and in th'oul candlelight he's like one of those saints that they boil, thin and raky. Up to then I only ventured in the dark, on windy nights when he'd say he heard a ghost and I had to go to him. I reconnoitre his white body while he's muttering on about the itch, says, "Soldiers in the tropics minded itch more than combat." He read that in an almanac.

"Maisie," he says in a watery voice, and puts his hand on mine and steers me to his shorthorn. Pulled the stays off of me. Thinking I don't know what he was after. All pie.[9] Raving about me being the best sister in the wide world and I'd give my last shilling and so forth. Talked about his young days when he hunted with a ferret. Babble, babble. His limbs were like jelly, and then the grunts and him burying himself under the red flannel eiderdown, saying God would strike us.

The next Sunday he was off again. Not a word to me since the tick mutiny, except to order me to drive cattle or harness the horse. Got a new pullover, a most unfortunate colour, like piccalilli.[1] He didn't get home that Sunday until all hours. I heard the car door banging. He boiled himself milk, because

---

8. Ten shillings (i.e., half a pound) "A tenner": a 10-pound note.

9. I.e., sweet as pie.
1. A vegetable relish that is often bright yellow.

the saucepan was on the range with the skin on it. I went up to the village to get meal for the hens and everyone was gassing about it. My brother had got engaged for the second time in two weeks. First it was a Dymphna and now it was a Tilly. It seemed he was in their parlour—pictures of cows and millstreams on the wall—sitting next to his intended, eating cold ox tongue and beetroot, when he leans across the table, points to Tilly, and says, "I think I'd sooner her."

Uproar. They all dropped utensils and gaped at him, thinking it a joke. He sticks to his guns, so much so that her father and the bachelors dragged him out into the garden for a heart-to-heart. Garden. It seems it's only high grass and an obelisk that wobbles. They said, "What the Christ, Matt?" He said, "I prefer Tilly, she's plumper." Tilly was called out and the two of them were told to walk down to the gate and back, to see what they had in common.

In a short time they return and announce that they understand one another and wish to be engaged. Gink.[2] She doesn't know the catastrophe she's in for. She doesn't know about me and my status here. Dymphna had a fit, shouted, threw bits of beetroot and gizzard all about, and said, "My sister is a witch." Had to be carried out and put in a box room,[3] where she shrieked and banged with a set of fire irons that were stored there. Parents didn't care, at least they were getting one Cissy off their hands. Father breeds French herds, useless at it. A name like Charlemagne. The bachelors said Matt was a brave man, drink was mooted. All the arrangements that had been settled on Dymphna were now transferred to Tilly. My brother drank port wine and got maudlin. Hence the staggers in the yard when he got home and the loud octavias. Never said a word at the breakfast. I had to hear it in the village. She has mousey hair and one of her eyes squints, but instead of calling it a squint the family call it a "lazy eye." It is to be a quiet wedding. He hasn't asked me, he won't. Thinks I'm too much of a gawk with my gap teeth, and that I'd pass remarks and say, "I've eaten to my satisfaction and if I ate any more I'd go flippety-floppety," a thing he makes me say here to give him a rise in the wet evenings.

All he says is "There'll be changes, Maisie, and it's for the best." Had the cheek to ask me to make an eiderdown for the bed, rose-coloured satin. I'll probably do it, but it will only be a blind. He thinks I'm a softie. I'll be all pie to her at first, bringing her the tea in bed and asking her if she'd like her hair done with the curling tongs. We'll pick elder flowers to make jelly. She'll be in a shroud before the year is out. To think that she's all purty now, like a little bowerbird, preening herself. She won't even have the last rites. I've seen a photo of her. She sent it to him for under his pillow. I'll take a knife to her, or a hatchet. I've been in Our Lady's once before, it isn't that bad. Big teas on Sundays and fags.[4] I'll be out in a couple of years. He'll be so morose from being all alone, he'll welcome me back with open arms. It's human nature. It stands to reason. The things I did for him, going to him in the dark, rubbing in that aul liniment, washing out at the rain barrel together, mother-naked, my bosoms slapping against him, the stars fading and me bursting my sides with the things he said—"Dotey."[5] Dotey no less. I might do for her out of doors. Lure her to the waterfall to look for eggs. There're

---

2. Fool.
3. Large closet.
4. Cigarettes.
5. Lovely little thing.

swans up there and geese. He loves the big geese eggs. I'll get behind her when we're on that promontory and give her a shove. It's very slippery from the moss. I can just picture her going down, yelling, then not yelling, being swept away like a newspaper or an empty canister. I'll call the alarm. I'll shout for him. If they do smell a rat and tackle me, I'll tell them that I could feel beads of moisture on my brother's poll[6] without even touching it, I was that close to him. There's no other woman could say that, not her, not any woman. I'm all he has, I'm all he'll ever have. Roll on, nuptials. Daughter of death is she.

1990

6. Head.

AUDRE LORDE
1934–1992

Audre Lorde once described herself as a "black feminist lesbian mother poet," adding that "when I say myself, I mean not only the Audre who inhabits my body but all those feisty, incorrigible black women who insist on standing up and saying '*I am* and you cannot wipe me out, no matter how irritating I am, how much you fear what I might represent.' " Of West Indian descent, Lorde was born and educated in New York City, receiving a B.A. from Hunter College and an M.L.S. from Columbia University. Married for eight years in the 1960s, she was the mother of two children, Elizabeth and Jonathan, to whom she was fiercely devoted, as "Now That I Am Forever with Child" indicates. After some years as a librarian for the City University of New York, she became a teacher of creative writing, first at Tougaloo College in Mississippi and later at John Jay College and Hunter College in New York. Her books include numerous collections of verse, among them *The First Cities* (1968), *Cables to Rage* (1970), *Coal* (1976), *The Black Unicorn* (1978), *Our Dead behind Us* (1986), *Undersong: Chosen Poems, Old and New* (1992), and *The Marvelous Arithmetics of Distance* (1992). She also published a number of influential essays and talks, notably in *Sister Outsider* (1984), and three important, beautifully articulated memoirs. *The Cancer Journals* (1980) recounts her struggle with breast cancer along with her crucial decision not to wear a prosthesis, in protest against what she saw as a cultural denial of difference as well as a medical urge toward profit through the reconstruction of women's bodies. *Zami: A New Spelling of My Name* (1982), which she called a "biomythography," is a fictionalized memoir of her development as an artist and coming of age as a lesbian; the writing of this book, she later observed, was a "lifeline" during her battle against cancer. Six years after her mastectomy, when the malignancy recurred in the form of liver cancer, she courageously explored her illness and decline toward death in her final, powerful memoir, *A Burst of Light* (1988).

In midcareer, Lorde explained that her work owes much to the "legends of . . . struggle and survival" embedded in the writings of such African American artists as Toni Morrison and Ralph Ellison, and to similar legends recounted by African writers ranging from Chinua Achebe and Amos Tutuola to Flora Nwapa and Ama Ata Aidoo; in addition, she was fascinated by the matriarchal myths and goddesses of Africa and of the West Indian island Carriacou, where her mother was born. As the title *Cables to Rage* indicates, however, she was conscious of the roots of her own anger at North

American racism and sexism from early in her career, and the poem "Coal" suggests the strength through which she transformed rage at racism into triumphant self-assertion. At the same time, in a well-known essay titled "The Uses of the Erotic," she indicated that for her "love [is] a source of tremendous power." And in a late interview she declared, "I speak of the erotic as the deepest life force, a force which moves us toward living in a fundamental way. And when I say living I mean it as that force which moves us toward what will accomplish real positive change." Lorde's own life force was extraordinarily strong, sustaining her through a battle with cancer that lasted for more than a dozen years; she finally succumbed to the disease in 1992. "I want this book to be filled with shards of light," she wrote of *The Marvelous Arithmetics of Distance,* a volume that was not to be published until after her death, and in an African naming ceremony in which she participated before she died, she took the name Gambda Adisa, meaning "Warrior: She Who Makes Her Meaning Known."

Coal

I
is the total black, being spoken
from the earth's inside.
There are many kinds of open
how a diamond comes into a knot of flame
how sound comes into a word, colored
by who pays what for speaking.

Some words are open like a diamond
on glass windows
singing out within the passing crash of sun
Then there are words like stapled wagers
in a perforated book,—buy and sign and tear apart—
and come whatever wills all chances
the stub remains
an ill-pulled tooth with a ragged edge.
Some words live in my throat
breeding like adders.[1] Others know sun
seeking like gypsies over my tongue
to explode through my lips
like young sparrows bursting from shell.
Some words
bedevil me.

Love is a word, another kind of open.
As the diamond comes into a knot of flame
I am Black because I come from the earth's inside
now take my word for jewel in the open light.

1976

---

1. Venomous snakes.

On a Night of the Full Moon

I

Out of my flesh that hungers
and my mouth that knows
comes the shape I am seeking
for reason.
The curve of your waiting body
fits my waiting hand
your breasts warm as sunlight
your lips quick as young birds
between your thighs the sweet
sharp taste of limes.

Thus I hold you
frank in my heart's eye
in my skin's knowing
as my fingers conceive your flesh
I feel your stomach
moving against me.

Before the moon wanes again
we shall come together.

II

And I would be the moon
spoken over your beckoning flesh
breaking against reservations
beaching thought
my hands at your high tide
over and under inside you
and the passing of hungers
attended, forgotten.

Darkly risen
the moon speaks
my eyes
judging your roundness
delightful.

1976

Now That I Am Forever with Child

How the days went
while you were blooming within me
I remember each upon each—
the swelling changed planes of my body
and how you first fluttered, then jumped
and I thought it was my heart.

How the days wound down
and the turning of winter
I recall, with you growing heavy
against the wind. I thought
now her hands
are formed, and her hair
has started to curl
now her teeth are done
now she sneezes.
Then the seed opened
I bore you one morning just before spring
My head rang like a fiery piston
my legs were towers between which
a new world was passing.

Since then
I can only distinguish
one thread within running hours
You, flowing through selves
toward You.

1976

From the House of Yemanjá[1]

My mother had two faces and a frying pot
where she cooked up her daughters
into girls
before she fixed our dinner.
My mother had two faces

---

1. Mother of the other *Orisha* [goddesses and gods of the Yoruba people of western Nigeria], Yemanjá is also the goddess of oceans. Rivers are said to flow from her breasts. One legend has it that a son tried to rape her. She fled until she collapsed, and from her breasts, the rivers flowed. Another legend says that a husband insulted Yemanjá's long breasts, and when she fled with her pots he knocked her down. From her breasts flowed the rivers, and from her body then sprang forth all the other *Orisha*. River-smooth stones are Yemanjá's symbol, and the sea is sacred to her followers. Those who please her are blessed with many children [Lorde's note].

         and a broken pot
         where she hid out a perfect daughter
         who was not me
         I am the sun and moon and forever hungry
    10   for her eyes.

         I bear two women upon my back
         one dark and rich and hidden
         in the ivory hungers of the other
         mother
    15   pale as a witch
         yet steady and familiar
         brings me bread and terror
         in my sleep
         her breasts are huge exciting anchors
    20   in the midnight storm.

         All this has been
         before
         in my mother's bed
         time has no sense
    25   I have no brothers
         and my sisters are cruel.

         Mother I need
         mother I need
         mother I need your blackness now
    30   as the august earth needs rain.

         I am
         the sun and moon and forever hungry
         the sharpened edge
         where day and night shall meet
    35   and not be
         one.

                                                    1978

The Women of Dan[1] Dance with Swords in Their Hands to Mark the Time When They Were Warriors

I did not fall from the sky
I
nor descend like a plague of locusts
to drink color and strength from the earth
and I do not come like rain
as a tribute or symbol for earth's becoming
I come as a woman
dark and open
some times I fall like night
softly
and terrible
only when I must die
in order to rise again.

I do not come like a secret warrior
with an unsheathed sword in my mouth
hidden behind my tongue
slicing my throat to ribbons
of service with a smile
while the blood runs
down and out
through holes in the two sacred mounds
on my chest.

I come like a woman
who I am
spreading out through nights
laughter and promise
and dark heat
warming whatever I touch
that is living
consuming
only
what is already dead.

1978

---

1. An ancient name for the kingdom of Dahomey [Lorde's note], in West Africa (located in present-day central Benin).

Kitchen Linoleum

The cockroach
who is dying
and the woman
who is blind
agree
not to notice
each other's shame.

1993

The Electric Slide Boogie

New Year's Day 1:16 AM
and my body is weary beyond
time to withdraw and rest
ample room allowed me in everyone's head
but community calls
right over the threshold
drums beating through the walls
children playing their truck dramas
under the collapsible coatrack
in the narrow hallway outside my room

The TV lounge next door is wide open
it is midnight in Idaho
and the throb   easy   subtle   spin
of the electric slide boogie
step-stepping
around the corner of the parlor
past the sweet clink
of dining room glasses
and the edged aroma of slightly overdone
dutch-apple pie
all laced together
with the rich dark laughter
of Gloria
and her higher-octave sisters

How hard it is to sleep
in the middle of life.

January 3, 1992

1993

From *Zami: A New Spelling of My Name*

[Origins]

To whom do I owe the power behind my voice, what strength I have become, yeasting up like sudden blood from under the bruised skin's blister?

My father leaves his psychic print upon me, silent, intense, and unforgiving. But his is a distant lightning. Images of women flaming like torches adorn and define the borders of my journey, stand like dykes between me and the chaos. It is the images of women, kind and cruel, that lead me home.

To whom do I owe the symbols of my survival?

Days from pumpkin until the year's midnight, when my sisters and I hovered indoors, playing potsy[1] on holes in the rosy linoleum that covered the living-room floor. On Saturdays we fought each other for the stray errand out of doors, fought each other for the emptied Quaker Oats boxes, fought each other for the last turn in the bathroom at nightfall, and for who would be the first one of us to get chickenpox.

The smell of the filled Harlem streets during summer, after a brief shower or the spraying drizzle of the watering trucks released the rank smell of the pavements back to the sun. I ran to the corner to fetch milk and bread from the Short-Neck Store-Man, stopping to search for some blades of grass to bring home for my mother. Stopping to search for hidden pennies winking like kittens under the subway gratings. I was always bending over to tie my shoes, delaying, trying to figure out something. How to get at the money, how to peep out the secret that some women carried like a swollen threat, under the gathers of their flowered blouses.

To whom do I owe the woman I have become?

DeLois lived up the block on 142nd Street and never had her hair done, and all the neighborhood women sucked their teeth as she walked by. Her crispy hair twinkled in the summer sun as her big proud stomach moved her on down the block while I watched, not caring whether or not she was a poem. Even though I tied my shoes and tried to peep under her blouse as she passed by, I never spoke to DeLois, because my mother didn't. But I loved her, because she moved like she felt she was somebody special, like she was somebody I'd like to know someday. She moved like how I thought god's mother must have moved, and my mother, once upon a time, and someday maybe me.

Hot noon threw a ring of sunlight like a halo on the top of DeLois's stomach, like a spotlight, making me sorry that I was so flat and could only feel the sun on my head and shoulders. I'd have to lie down on my back before the sun could shine down like that on my belly.

---

1. Hopscotch.

I loved DeLois because she was big and Black and special and seemed to laugh all over. I was scared of DeLois for those very same reasons. One day I watched DeLois step off the curb of 142nd Street against the light, slow and deliberate. A high yaller dude in a white Cadillac passed by and leaned out and yelled at her, "Hurry up, you flat-footed, nappy-headed, funny-looking bitch!" The car almost knocked her down. DeLois kept right on about her leisurely business and never so much as looked around.

To Louise Briscoe who died in my mother's house as a tenant in a furnished room with cooking privileges—no linens supplied. I brought her a glass of warm milk that she wouldn't drink, and she laughed at me when I wanted to change her sheets and call a doctor. "No reason to call him unless he's real cute," said Miz Briscoe. "Ain't nobody sent for me to come, I got here all by myself. And I'm going back the same way. So I only need him if he's cute, real cute." And the room smelled like she was lying.

"Miz Briscoe," I said, "I'm really worried about you."

She looked up at me out of the corner of her eyes, like I was making her a proposition which she had to reject, but which she appreciated all the same. Her huge bloated body was quiet beneath the gray sheet, as she grinned knowingly.

"Why, that's all right, honey. I don't hold it against you. I know you can't help it, it's just in your nature, that's all."

To the white woman I dreamed standing behind me in an airport, silently watching while her child deliberately bumps into me over and over again. When I turn around to tell this woman that if she doesn't restrain her kid I'm going to punch her in the mouth, I see that she's been punched in the mouth already. Both she and her child are battered, with bruised faces and blackened eyes. I turn, and walk away from them in sadness and fury.

To the pale girl who ran up to my car in a Staten Island[2] midnight with only a nightgown and bare feet, screaming and crying, "Lady, please help me oh please take me to the hospital, lady . . ." Her voice was a mixture of overripe peaches and doorchimes; she was the age of my daughter, running along the woody curves of Van Duzer Street.

I stopped the car quickly, and leaned over to open the door. It was high summer. "Yes, yes, I'll try to help you," I said. "Get in."

And when she saw my face in the streetlamp her own collapsed into terror. "Oh no!" she wailed. "Not you!" then whirled around and started to run again.

What could she have seen in my Black face that was worth holding onto such horror? Wasting me in the gulf between who I was and her vision of me. Left with no help.

I drove on.

In the rear-view mirror I saw the substance of her nightmare catch up with her at the corner—leather jacket and boots, male and white.

I drove on, knowing she would probably die stupid.

---

2. A borough of New York City.

To the first woman I ever courted and left. She taught me that women who want without needing are expensive and sometimes wasteful, but women who need without wanting are dangerous—they suck you in and pretend not to notice.

To the battalion of arms where I often retreated for shelter and sometimes found it. To the others who helped, pushing me into the merciless sun—I, coming out blackened and whole.

To the journeywoman pieces of myself.
Becoming.
Afrekete.[3]

1982

---

3. In the epilogue to *Zami*, Lorde identifies Afrekete as the youngest daughter of "MawuLisa, thunder, sky, sun, the great mother of us all; [she is] the mischievous lingoist, trickster, best-beloved, whom we must all become." There she also explains that Zami is a "name for women who work together as friends and lovers."

FLEUR ADCOCK
b. 1934

"I'm a human being poet but I do happen to be a woman and I write about a lot of women's concerns," Fleur Adcock declared in a recent interview, enumerating her feminine subjects: "childbirth, family life, relationships from a woman's view, women's histories, women's health and social questions to do with women." She added, "That's what the function of a female poet is. But I don't think you address yourself exclusively to women. That would be to deny half the audience. And I've never felt like that about poetry." Her national allegiance, too, is split, or so she told the same interviewer, noting that "I regard myself as English in my residence and my allegiance and my emotional orientation. But I can't deny I am a New Zealander."

Witty, acerbic, and forthright about the ambiguities in her life and art, Karen Fleur Adcock was born in Papakura, New Zealand, and educated at Victoria University in Wellington, where she majored in classics. Twice briefly married and the mother of two children, she has worked as a librarian, first in New Zealand and then in London, where she joined the Foreign and Commonwealth Office in 1963; more recently she has devoted herself full-time to her writing while holding various arts fellowships in England. A highly productive literary journalist and woman of letters, she has translated several books of verse from Romanian and from medieval Latin, edited major anthologies—most notably *The Oxford Book of Contemporary New Zealand Poetry* (1981), *The Faber Book of 20th-Century Women's Poetry* (1987), and *The Oxford Book of Creatures* (1995)—and collaborated with the composer Gillian Whitehead on a full-length opera about Eleanor of Aquitaine. But Adcock is best known for her skillfully crafted volumes of poetry, among them *The Eye of the Hurricane* (1964), *Tigers* (1967), *High Tide in the Garden* (1971), *The Scenic Route* (1974), *The Inner Harbour* (1979), *The Incident Book* (1986), *Time-Zones* (1991), and *Poems 1960–2000* (2000).

Often characterized by a disconcerting juxtaposition of the mundane with the bizarre, her verses have earned her a number of awards both in England (an Order of the British Empire) and in her native New Zealand (the New Zealand National Book Award). While she has been praised for the "suballegory" she makes out of domesticity in elegantly wrought poems, Adcock has also been recognized for dream poems in which "something angry, or nightmarish, or discomfiting leaps out." Perhaps it is what one reviewer called her "well-bred, genteel air" that allows her to write a poem like "Against Coupling" on the previously unmentionable subject of "the solitary act." Yet the verve of this work, one of her most famous, also derives from its acerbic candor; as another critic comments, it is "a poem one wants to quarrel with but which always leaves a sneaking feeling of respect for such a ruthless debunking of sexual pieties."

For a Five-Year-Old

A snail is climbing up the window-sill
Into your room, after a night of rain.
You call me in to see, and I explain
That it would be unkind to leave it there:
5   It might crawl to the floor; we must take care
That no one squashes it. You understand,
And carry it outside, with careful hand,
To eat a daffodil.

I see, then, that a kind of faith prevails:
10 Your gentleness is molded still by words
From me, who have trapped mice and shot wild birds,
From me, who drowned your kittens, who betrayed
Your closest relatives, and who purveyed
The harshest kind of truth to many another.
15 But that is how things are: I am your mother,
And we are kind to snails.

1967

Miss Hamilton in London

It would not be true to say she was doing nothing:
She visited several bookshops, spent an hour
In the Victoria and Albert Museum (Indian section),
And walked carefully through the streets of Kensington[1]
5 Carrying five mushrooms in a paper bag,
A tin of black pepper, a literary magazine,
And enough money to pay the rent for two weeks.
The sky was cloudy, leaves lay on the pavements.

---

1. The middle-class London borough in which the Victoria and Albert Museum is located.

Nor did she lack human contacts: she spoke
To three shop-assistants and a newsvendor,
And returned the "Goodnight" of a museum attendant.
Arriving home, she wrote a letter to someone
In Canada, as it might be, or in New Zealand,
Listened to the news as she cooked her meal,
And conversed for five minutes with the landlady.
The air was damp with the mist of late autumn.

A full day, and not unrewarding.
Night fell at the usual seasonal hour.
She drew the curtains, switched on the electric fire,
Washed her hair and read until it was dry,
Then went to bed; where, for the hours of darkness,
She lay pierced by thirty black spears
And felt her limbs numb, her eyes burning,
And dark rust carried along her blood.

1967

Against Coupling

I write in praise of the solitary act:
of not feeling a trespassing tongue
forced into one's mouth, one's breath
smothered, nipples crushed against the
ribcage, and that metallic tingling
in the chin set off by a certain odd nerve:

unpleasure. Just to avoid those eyes would help—
such eyes as a young girl draws life from,
listening to the vegetal
rustle within her, as his gaze
stirs polypal[1] fronds in the obscure
sea-bed of her body, and her own eyes blur.

There is much to be said for abandoning
this no longer novel exercise—
for not "participating in
a total experience"—when
one feels like the lady in Leeds who
had seen *The Sound of Music*[2] eighty-six times;

or more, perhaps, like the school drama mistress
producing *A Midsummer Night's Dream*[3]
for the seventh year running, with

---

1. Like the tiny organism the polyp, which has a mouth surrounded by tentacles.
2. A very popular sentimental musical film (1965), starring Julie Andrews.
3. The comedy by William Shakespeare includes a short burlesque of the story of Pyramus and

yet another cast from 5B.
Pyramus and Thisbe are dead, but
the hole in the wall can still be troublesome.

25 I advise you, then, to embrace it without
encumbrance. No need to set the scene,
dress up (or undress), make speeches.
Five minutes of solitude are
enough—in the bath, or to fill
30 that gap between the Sunday papers and lunch.

1971

The Voyage Out

The weekly dietary scale
per adult: pork and Indian beef,
three pounds together; one of sugar,
two of potatoes, three and a half
5 of flour; a gill of vinegar;
salt, pepper, a pint of oatmeal;
coffee, two ounces, likewise tea;
six of butter, suet, treacle,[1]
and, in the tropics, of lime-juice;
10 grudging grants of mustard and pickle;
split peas, raisins, currants, rice,
and half a pound of biscuit a day.
A diet for the young and fit:
monotonous, but not starvation—
15 and Martha traded half her ration
for extra lime-juice from the crew.
Their quarters, also, adequate.
So not the middle passage;[2] no.
But not a pleasure-cruise, either.
20 A hundred days of traveling steerage
under capricious canvas; Martha
newly pregnant, struggling to manage
the first four (Tom, Eliza, Joe,
Annie); to keep them cool and clean
25 from a two-gallon can of water;
to calm their sleeping; to stay awake,
so heavy, herself; to protect the daughter
she rocked unborn in the swaying hammock
below her ribs (who would be Jane).

Thisbe, two doomed lovers who had to communicate through a hole in a wall because their families forbade them to meet.

1. A thick syrup.
2. I.e., the passage of slaves from West Africa to the West Indies.

30   True, the family was together.
     But who could envy Martha? Sick
     with salt meat; thirsty; and gazing on
     a sky huge as the whole Atlantic,
     storm-waves like Slieve Gallion,[3]
35   and no more Ireland than went with her.

1974

On the Border

Dear posterity, it's 2 a.m.
and I can't sleep for the smothering heat,
or under mosquito nets. The others
are swathed in theirs, humid and sweating,
5   long white packets on rows of chairs
(no bunks. The building isn't finished).

I prowled in the dark back room for water
and came outside for a cigarette
and a pee in waist-high leafy scrub.
10 The moon is brilliant: the same moon,
I have to believe, as mine in England
or theirs in the places where I'm not.

Knobbly trees mark the horizon,
black and angular, with no leaves:
15 blossoming flame-trees; and behind them
soft throbbings come from the village.
Birds or animals croak and howl;
the river rustles; there could be snakes.

I don't care. I am standing here,
20 posterity, on the face of the earth,
letting the breeze blow up my nightdress,
writing in English, as I do,
in all this tropical non-silence.
Now let me tell you about the elephants.

1983

---

3. A hill in Londonderry, northern Ireland.

Street Song

Pink Lane, Strawberry Lane, Pudding Chare:
someone is waiting, I don't know where;
hiding among the nursery names,
he wants to play peculiar games.

In Leazes Terrace or Leazes Park
someone is loitering in the dark,
feeling the giggles rise in his throat
and fingering something under his coat.

He could be sidling along Forth Lane
to stop some girl from catching her train,
or stalking the grounds of the RVI[1]
to see if a student nurse goes by.

In Belle Grove Terrace or Fountain Row
or Hunter's Road he's raring to go—
unless he's the quiet shape you'll meet
on the cobbles in Back Stowell Street.

Monk Street, Friars Street, Gallowgate
are better avoided when it's late.
Even in Sandhill and the Side
there are shadows where a man could hide.

So don't go lightly along Darn Crook
because the Ripper's been brought to book.[2]
Wear flat shoes, and be ready to run:
remember, sisters, there's more than one.

1983

---

1. The Royal Victoria Infirmary, in Newcastle.
2. Brought to account. The so-called Yorkshire Ripper, held responsible for a series of thirteen murders that began in 1975, was arrested in January 1981; most of the women he attacked were prostitutes. He took his name from Jack the Ripper, the never-identified murderer of at least seven women in London's East End in 1888.

DIANE DI PRIMA
b. 1934

Described by fellow beat poet Allen Ginsberg as "a learned humorous bohemian, classically educated [and] exemplary in imagist, political and mystical modes," Diane di Prima was born in Brooklyn to a second-generation Italian American family. Her maternal grandfather, Domenico Mallozzi, in whose honor she wrote "April Fool Birthday Poem for Grandpa," was an anarchist who associated with the radical activists Carlo Tresca and Emma Goldman, and she remembered him with special fondness in what Ginsberg called "verse brilliant in its particularity."

Di Prima recalls beginning to write poetry when she was seven, but it was at Hunter College High School in Manhattan that she definitively resolved on a literary career. Her classmate and fellow poet at this elite school for girls was the late Audre Lorde, to whom she dedicated "Narrow Path into the Back Country." Later, at Swarthmore College, di Prima studied physics but dropped out after two years and escaped to New York's bohemian Greenwich Village, where she devoted herself to writing while working in bookstores, as a model, and at other odd jobs to make ends meet. In her partly fictional *Memoirs of a Beatnik* (1969) and her later autobiography *Recollections of My Life as a Woman: The New York Years* (2001), she vividly evoked the cold-water flats, wild nights, and rebellious excitement of those days when, with other writers (including her then-husband Alan Marlowe), she founded the New York Poets Theatre, co-edited the underground newsletter *The Floating Bear* with Amiri Baraka (then known as Le Roi Jones), and published her first collection of verse, *This Kind of Bird Flies Backwards* (1958).

In 1964, di Prima traveled to upstate New York, where she joined Timothy Leary's community at Millbrook for a time. In the 1970s, she moved to San Francisco, where she has lived and worked for many years, teaching at the California College of Arts and Crafts and the San Francisco Art Institute, among other venues. A cofounder of the San Francisco Institute of Magical and Healing Arts, she is a longtime student of Buddhism as well as of Western spiritual traditions. Her esoteric learning has helped shape her thirty-five books of poetry and prose, especially her ambitious long poem *Loba* (1998). A mother of five, she is deeply committed to matriarchal mysteries, as *Loba* reveals. But even such earlier poems as the delicately loving "Song for Baby-O, Unborn" and "Letter to Jeanne (at Tassajara)" express the delight she takes in wishing her children "Adventure / all sizes & shapes [as] various / for you as for me it was."

Song for Baby-O, Unborn

Sweetheart
when you break thru
you'll find
a poet here
5   not quite what one would choose.

         I won't promise
         you'll never go hungry
         or that you won't be sad
         on this gutted
10   breaking
         globe

         but I can show you
         baby
         enough to love
15   to break your heart
         forever

                                                       1958

April Fool Birthday Poem for Grandpa

Today is your
birthday and I have tried
writing these things before,
but now
5   in the gathering madness, I want to
thank you
for telling me what to expect
for pulling
no punches, back there in that scrubbed Bronx parlor
10 thank you
for honestly weeping in time to
innumerable heartbreaking
italian operas for
pulling my hair when I
15 pulled the leaves off the trees so I'd
know how it feels, we are
involved in it now, revolution, up to our
knees and the tide is rising, I embrace
strangers on the street, filled with their love and
20 mine, the love you told us had to come or we
die, told them all in that Bronx park, me listening in
spring Bronx dusk, breathing stars, so glorious
to me your white hair, your height your fierce
blue eyes, rare among italians, I stood
25 a ways off, looking up at you, my grandpa
people listened to, I stand
a ways off listening as I pour out soup
young men with light in their faces
at my table, talking love, talking revolution
30 which is love, spelled backwards, how
you would love us all, would thunder your anarchist wisdom
at us, would thunder Dante, and Giordano Bruno,[1] orderly men

---

1. Italian philosopher (1548–1600), burned at the stake for heresy. Dante Alighieri (1265–1321), Italian poet who was banished from Florence after the political faction he opposed gained power.

bent to your ends, well I want you to know
we do it for you, and your ilk, for Carlo Tresca,
35 for Sacco and Vanzetti,[2] without knowing
it, or thinking about it, as we do it for Aubrey Beardsley
Oscar Wilde[3] (all street lights
shall be purple), do it
for Trotsky and Shelley and big/dumb
40 Kropotkin[4]
Eisenstein's Strike people, Jean Cocteau's[5] ennui, we do it for
the stars over the Bronx
that they may look on earth
and not be ashamed.

1971

Poem in Praise of My Husband (Taos)

I suppose it hasn't been easy living with me either,
with my piques, and ups and downs, my need for privacy
leo pride and weeping in bed when you're trying to sleep
and you, interrupting me in the middle of a thousand poems
5 did I call the insurance people? the time you stopped a poem
in the middle of our drive over the nebraska hills and
into colorado, odetta singing, the whole world singing in me
the triumph of our revolution in the air
me about to get that down, and you
10 you saying something about the carburetor
so that it all went away

but we cling to each other
as if each thought the other was the raft
and he adrift alone, as in this mud house
15 not big enough, the walls dusting down around us, a fine dust rained,
counteracting the good, high air, and stuffing our nostrils
we hang our pictures of the several worlds;
new york collage, and san francisco posters,
set out our japanese dishes, chinese knives
20 hammer small indian marriage cloths into the adobe
we stumble thru silence into each other's gut

---

2. Nicola Sacco (1891–1927) and Bartolomeo Vanzetti (1888–1927), Italian-born American radicals; they were executed for murder after a trial that many believed to have been unfair. Tresca (1879–1943), Italian-born American labor leader and radical journalist; his murder was never solved.
3. British writer (1854–1900), the flamboyant spokesperson for aestheticism, or the seemingly radical idea that art should be cultivated for its own sake. Beardsley (1872–1898), English illustrator who epitomized the aesthetic movement.
4. Pyotr Kropotkin (1842–1921), Russian geographer and revolutionist who developed the theory of "anarchist communism." Leon Trotsky (1879–1940), Russian communist leader. Percy Bysshe Shelley (1792–1822), English poet and radical.
5. French poet, playwright, and film director (1889–1963). Sergey Eisenstein (1898–1948), Russian play and film director; his most famous film, *Battleship Potemkin* (1925), focuses on a naval mutiny.

blundering thru from one wrong place to the next
like kids who snuck out to play on a boat at night
and the boat slipped from its moorings, and they look at the stars,
25 about which they know nothing, to find out
where they are going

1975

Letter to Jeanne (at Tassajara)

dry heat of the Tassajara canyon
moist warmth of San Francisco summer
bright fog reflecting sunrise as you
step out of September zendo
5 heart of your warmth, my girl, as you step out
into your vajra pathway, glinting
like your eyes turned sideways at us
your high knowing 13-year-old
wench-smile, flicking your thin
10 ankles you trot toward Adventure
all sizes & shapes, O may it be various
for you as for me it was, sparkle
like dustmotes at dawn in the back
of grey stores, like the shooting stars
15 over the Hudson, wind in the Berkshire pines

O you have landscapes dramatic like mine
never was, uncounted caves
to mate in, my scorpio, bright love
like fire light up your beauty years
20 on these new, jagged hills

1975

Narrow Path into the Back Country

for Audre Lorde[1]

1

You are flying to Dahomey,[2] going back
to some dream, or never-never land
more forbidding & perfect
than Oz.[3] Will land in Western airport

---

1. African American feminist poet (1932–1992); see above, p. 1069.
2. Country of West Africa (located in present-day central Benin); it was a major exporter in the transatlantic slave trade.
3. The fantastic realm imagined in L. Frank Baum's *The Wonderful Wizard of Oz* (1900) and its film version, *The Wizard of Oz* (1939).

noisy, small & tacky, will look around
for the Goddess, as she stands
waiting for baggage. Well, we carry
pure-land paradise within, you carry
it to Dahomey, from Staten Island.[4]

2

we endure. this we are certain of. no more.
we endure: famine, depression, earthquake,
    pestilence, war, flood, police state,
    inflation
ersatz food. burning cities. you endure,
    I endure. It is written
on the faces of our children. Pliant, persistent
    joy; Will like mountains, hope
that batters yr heart & mine. (Hear them shout)
And I will not bow out, cannot see
your war as different. Turf stolen from
    yours & mine; clandestine magics
we practice, all of us, for their protection.
That they have fruit to eat & rice & fish
till they grow strong.
(Remember the octopus we did not cook
Sicilian style/West African style—it fills
your daughter's dream)   I refuse
to leave you to yr battles, I to mine

my girl
chased white coyote, sister to my wolf
& not thru mesas.

3

how to get the food on the table
how to heal
what survives this whirlwind:
people and land. The sea
tosses feverish; screams in delirium.
To have the right herb drying in the kitchen:
your world & mine/ all others: not the Third
this is Fourth World going down,[5] the Hopi say.
Yet we endure.

4

And more, we fly to light, fly into
pure-land paradise, New York

---

4. A borough of New York City.
5. The mythology of the Hopi people of the southwestern United States includes the story of their emergence through a series of worlds into their present existence in the Fourth World. The third world, a term coined during the cold war to refer to nations aligned with neither the United States nor the Soviet Union, generally is taken to mean all underdeveloped countries.

Dahomey, Mars, Djakarta,[6] Wales
The willful, stubborn children carrying seed
all races; hurtling time & space & stars
to find container large & fine enough
fine-wrought enough for our joy.
For all our joy.

1975

Annunciation

the tall man, towering
it seemed to me
in anger. I was fifteen only
& his urgency
(murderous rage) an assault I
bent under. I saw the lilies bend
also.   I had been spinning
flax: violet for the temple veil. I had just
gone to the well for water & when I returned
he was there. A flat stone. Towering.
            Murderous rage
like the Law. They call it
love. His voice
was harsh,   I bent,   I tried to
evade.
Sound trembled in my gut, my
bowels
spoke w/ fear—
            the red tiles
shifted beneath me; a light
flashed from his eyes, his hand, the blue stone
in his ring & my bowels caught
w/ fear. He said
   "HAIL, FULL OF GRACE" I remember
my hand
found a psalter, something real, the smooth vellum
sunwarmed
under my fingers
the wind had stilled, the lilies
bent of themselves, my body
bent under weight of robes
white muslin gleamed in my tears
                        in sunlight
like a gold brocade
& my head too bent
under weight of hair. I fell

---

6. The capital of Indonesia.

                to my knees, I salted
                the ground before me

                He did not move, his voice
40   had turned to thunder, there was
                no word to remember.   but Womb
                    He spoke of my womb.
                    The fruit of my womb.
                Sunlight & thunder. I had not
45   heard thunder before
                in such blinding light.

---

                the rose, the thorn, the thistle
                the rose, the thorn, the myrtle
                the lily, the thorn, the thistle
50   *the lily & the myrtle*
                the lily, the rose, the thistle
                the lily, the thistle, the myrtle

                The wind
                bent the palm trees again
55   the room was empty

                I stood again, as one stands
                    after earthquake
                my young girl's hands
                began to spin the scarlet thread
60   for the temple

1978

From Thirteen Nightmares

Nightmare 7

One day I forgot my sleeve and my heart pinned to my arm was burning a hole there.

Discovered in pocket fifty cents no more; on 42nd looked for a pleasant movie.

5 Until the most beautiful god he was I think up to me hood walked and smiled knowing everything and then knowing.

Are you busy he said and I laughed because no busy would be busier than seeing him and he knew it.

And he laughed knowing all and acknowledging simply yes that is so
10 there is garish and hurt but not us.

And walked all three him and me and our hands between and he had a room where the ceiling danced for me danced all night.

Till morning awakened and yawning with dirty teeth he said well babe now how much do you get?

1990

Nightmare 12

I went to the clinic. I twisted my foot I said.

Whats your name they said and age and how much do you make and whos your family dentist.

I told them and they told me to wait and I waited and they said come
5 inside and I did.

Open your eye said the doctor you have something in it.

I hurt my foot I said.

Open your eye he said and I did and he took out the eyeball and washed it in a basin.

10 There he said and put it back that feels better doesnt it.

I guess so I said. Its all black I dont know. I hurt my foot I said.

Would you mind blinking he said one of your eyelashes is loose.

I think I said theres something the matter with my foot.

Oh he said. Perhaps you're right. I'll cut it off.

1990

From Loba

The Loba Priestess as Bag Lady Utters Ragged Warnings

    don't
    cheapen Aphrodite, don't sell
    the objects she holds in her hands
    don't
5   demand that she show herself naked
    take
        the cloak
            along with her
    welcoming
10   folds of the Robe / she is
    bright,   she is bright
                  too bright
    you don't understand
    can't guess   have never
15   taken off
        your glasses
              these   strong
    & cute stories of Demeter   will slay
    like a boomerang,   don't
20   reveal
        the eternal feminine
    kuntuzangmo   be
    careful, a little   you are
    so proud,   with your careful
25   tailored ways,   clipped prose
    telling of Artemis,   of Ishtar
                      beware
    the popular tales you like to
    spread of Isis   will spread   like fire
30   like wildfire
        yr gut
    has proposed itself for
    calmer usage
           don't invite

35   *tzuname* / firestorm

    Asher /
        Mother Mamaki

    they have kindly
        robed themselves,   hidden
40   they are not

    your toys

1998

JUNE JORDAN
1936–2002

In a hauntingly lyrical essay titled "The Difficult Miracle of Black Poetry in American or Something like a Sonnet for Phillis Wheatley," June Jordan claims that "the *difficult* miracle of Black poetry in America is that we have been rejected and we are frequently dismissed as 'political' or 'topical' or 'sloganeering' and 'crude' and 'insignificant' because, like Phillis Wheatley, we have persisted for freedom." Beginning with her first book of poetry, *Who Look at Me* (1969), and her first novel, *His Own Where* (1971), Jordan dared to be a militant artist who "persisted for freedom" through regular contributions to *The Progressive, The Village Voice, Ms.*, and *The Nation*. Instead of being dismissed as sloganeering, crude, or insignificant, her twenty-eight books of poetry, essays, and children's fiction earned her numerous awards and fellowships in the arts and in journalism. A faculty member at the City College of New York, Sarah Lawrence College, the State University of New York at Stony Brook, and the University of California, Berkeley, Jordan composed a guide to writing, teaching, and publishing poetry titled *Poetry for the People: A Blueprint for the Revolution*. That she took seriously the relationship between poetry, politics, and music is apparent from the fact that she also composed the lyrics and libretti for two operas.

Jordan's mother was a nurse from Panama, her father a night-shift postal worker from Jamaica. An only child, she moved with her parents from Harlem to the Bedford Stuyvesant neighborhood of Brooklyn. She was sent away for high school to a predominantly white school in Massachusetts, however, and there she began writing in order to deal with the domestic abuse she had witnessed at home. Jordan's publishing career took off after she had studied at Barnard College, married, attended the University of Chicago, given birth to a son, and confronted single motherhood in the wake of the dissolution of her marriage. Resistance to racism coupled with a keen appreciation of black urban culture characterizes many of Jordan's poems, which address such topical issues as inner-city police violence, the Moynihan report, the Watergate scandal, and the target practices of the United States military. Even in the more personal love poems she composed about and to men and women, the rhythms and lexicons of her distinctively African American English work for the survival of a culture historically marginalized and demeaned.

The Wedding

Tyrone married her this afternoon
not smiling as he took the aisle
and her slightly rough hand.
Dizzella listened to the minister
5 staring at his wrist and twice
forgetting her name:
Do you promise to obey?[1]
Will you honor humility and love
as poor as you are?

---

1. In traditional Christian wedding vows following or modeled on the Anglican Book of Common Prayer, the bride promises to obey, serve, love, and honor her husband.

10 Tyrone stood small but next
to her person
trembling. Tyrone stood
straight and bony
black alone with one key
15 in his pocket.
By marrying today
they made themselves a man
and woman
answered friends or unknown
20 curious about the Cadillacs
displayed in front of Beaulah Baptist.
Beaulah Baptist
life in general
indifferent
25 barely known
nor caring to consider
the earlywed Tyrone
and his Dizzella
30 brave enough
but only two.

1967

The Reception

Doretha wore the short blue lace last night
and William watched her drinking so she fight
with him in flying collar slim-jim orange
tie and alligator belt below the navel pants uptight

5 "I flirt. You hear me? Yes I flirt.
Been on my pretty knees all week
to clean the rich white downtown dirt
the greedy garbage money reek.

I flirt. Damned right. You look at me."
10 But William watched her carefully
his mustache shaky she could see
him jealous, "which is how he always be

at parties." Clementine and Wilhelmina
looked at trouble in the light blue lace
15 and held to George while Roosevelt Senior
circled by the yella high and bitterly light blue face

he liked because she worked
the crowded room like clay like molding men
from dust to muscle jerked
20 and arms and shoulders moving when

she moved. The Lord Almighty Seagrams bless
Doretha in her short blue dress
and Roosevelt waiting for his chance:
a true gut-funky blues to make her really dance.

1967

Poem about Police Violence

Tell me something
what you think would happen if
everytime they kill a black boy
then we kill a cop
everytime they kill a black man
then we kill a cop

you think the accident rate would lower
subsequently?

sometimes the feeling like amaze me baby
comes back to my mouth and I am quiet
like Olympian pools from the running the
mountainous snows under the sun

sometimes thinking about the 12th House of the Cosmos[1]
or the way your ear ensnares the tip
of my tongue or signs that I have never seen
like DANGER WOMEN WORKING

I lose consciousness of ugly bestial rabid
and repetitive affront as when they tell me
18 cops in order to subdue one man
18 strangled him to death in the ensuing scuffle (don't
you idolize the diction of the powerful: *subdue* and
scuffle my oh my) and that the murder
that the killing of Arthur Miller on a Brooklyn
street was just a "justifiable accident" again
(again)

People been having accidents all over the globe
so long like that I reckon that the only
suitable insurance is a gun
I'm saying war is not to understand or rerun
war is to be fought and won

sometimes the feeling like amaze me baby
blots it out/the bestial but
not too often

---

1. According to astrologers, the twelfth house of the zodiac represents the unconscious, our fantasies, and the hidden side of life.

tell me something
what you think would happen if
everytime they kill a black boy
then we kill a cop
everytime they kill a black man
then we kill a cop

you think the accident rate would lower
subsequently?

1974   1980

A Runaway Lil Bit Poem

Sometimes DeLiza get so crazy she omit
the bebop from the concrete she intimidate
the music she excruciate the whiskey she
obliterate the blow she sneeze
hypothetical at sex

Sometimes DeLiza get so crazy she abstruse
about a bar-be-cue ribs wonder-white-bread
sandwich in the car with hot sauce
make the eyes roll right to where you are
fastidious among the fried-up chicken wings

Sometimes DeLiza get so crazy she exasperate
on do they hook it up they being Ingrid
Bergman and some paranoid schizophrenic Mister
Gregory Peck-peck:[1] Do
they hook it up?

Sometimes DeLiza get so crazy she drive
right across the water flying champagne bottles
from the bridge she last drink to close the bars she
holler kissey lips she laugh she let
you walk yourself away:

Sometimes DeLiza get so crazy!

1985

---

1. In the film *Spellbound* (1945), the Swedish actor Bergman (1915–1982) plays a psychiatrist; her co-star, the American actor Gregory Peck (1916–2003), is a paranoid amnesiac.

DeLiza Spend the Day in the City

DeLiza drive the car to fetch Alexis
running from she building past the pickets
make she gap tooth laugh why don't
they think up something new they picket now
5   for three months soon it be too cold
to care

Opposite the Thrift Shop
Alexis ask to stop at the Botanica[1]
St. Jacques Majeur find oil to heal she
10   sister lying in the hospital from lymphoma
and much western drug agenda

DeLiza stop. Alexis running back
with oil and myrrh and frankincense and coal
to burn these odors free the myrrh like rocks
15   a baby break to pieces fit inside the palm
of long or short lifelines

DeLiza driving and Alexis
point out Nyabinghi's African emporium
of gems and cloth and Kwanza cards and clay:
20   DeLiza look.

1985

1. A shop that deals in herbs, charms, and other spiritual and religious items.

A. S. BYATT
b. 1936

Described by some critics as a "postmodern Victorianist," the ambitious novelist, critic, and short story writer A. S. Byatt was born Antonia Susan Drabble in Sheffield, England, the oldest of four children who were brought up in what she describes as "a household full of books with parents who both read for pleasure" and with a younger sister, Margaret Drabble, who was also to become a celebrated novelist. Often bedridden with asthma, Byatt was, in her own words, "kept alive by fictions" because it seemed to her "self-evident and exciting that one would live much more intensely in these complicated worlds of adventure and excitement and passion than one would in one's daily life of getting up and having one's little breakfast and being trotted off to one's school where you were frightened of the other kids in the playground." When she was thirteen, she and her younger sister were sent away to a Quaker boarding school in York, after which both went on to study at Newnham College, Cambridge, where both earned "first," or honors degrees of the highest class, in English. While Drabble joined a theater group after leaving Newnham, however,

Byatt did graduate work in English literature, first at Bryn Mawr College and then at Somerville College, Oxford. In 1959 she left the academy to marry and raise a family; but in 1964 she began teaching at various universities and colleges in London, first part-time and then, after her young son Charles was killed by a drunk driver, full-time.

Byatt's first novel, *Shadow of a Sun* (1964), appeared just as she embarked on her teaching career, and her first critical work, on the novels of Iris Murdoch, was published the following year. Her second work of fiction, *The Game* (1967), examines the fierce rivalry between two sisters who battle each other with "nails, teeth, shoes, silently intent on real damage"—a rivalry frequently thought to mirror the ferocious competitiveness between Byatt and Drabble, who have been estranged from each other for many years. This volume was followed by a number of other distinguished novels, but Byatt's achievements were long overshadowed by the accomplishments of Drabble, whose reputation and popularity had grown far more rapidly. It wasn't until 1990, when Byatt published her best-selling and critically acclaimed novel *Possession*, that she gained both the prestigious Booker Prize and the recognition her talent deserves. *Possession* was followed by several volumes of short stories, including most notably *Angels and Insects* (1992), whose title novella became the basis of a movie with the same name in 1996; *The Biographer's Tale* (2001); and the *Little Black Book of Stories* (2003), from which "A Stone Woman" is drawn.

Throughout all her writing, but with special intensity in *Possession*, Byatt meditates on women's issues and feminist poetics, noting that "there's been a kind of myth constructed that women writers were always persecuted, despised and put down," though in "England, right from the beginning of the novel there were always great women novelists." Her familiarity with these writers is so deep and abiding that she confesses, "I'm constantly being castigated for saying that I know George Eliot much better than I know my own daughters." At the same time, however, even while she objects to certain feminist intellectual strategies ("I can't stand the thought of really good women students being taught courses on very minor 18th century women writers . . . only because they were women"), Byatt ruefully acknowledges the difficulties that a literary life poses for a woman who is also a mother: "Children emotionally disrupt ambitious women. Having had four children and written all these books I think I can say that it is manageable—but what it takes out of you! And the constant adjustments you have to make—from minute to minute, let alone from day to day. You just get a brilliant sentence and your child falls over in the playground and comes in covered with blood and you have to clean him."

While *Possession* engages with the complexities of the female literary tradition, "A Stone Woman," like the other narratives in *Little Black Book*, draws its haunting power from fairy tales, a genre for which, confides Byatt, "I acquired a hunger . . . in the dark days of blackout and blitz in the Second World War"—and a genre in which this endlessly imaginative writer can, paradoxically, confront poignant truths of flesh and loss, life and death, through the brilliant scrim of fantasy.

A Stone Woman

(*for Torfi Tulinius*[1])

At first she did not think of stones. Grief made her insubstantial to herself; she felt herself flitting lightly from room to room, in the twilit apartment, like a moth. The apartment seemed constantly twilit, although it must, she knew, have gone through the usual sequences of sun and shadow over the

---

1. Professor of French and medieval literature at the University of Iceland (b. 1958).

days and weeks since her mother died. Her mother—a strong bright woman—had liked to live amongst shades of mole and dove. Her mother's hair had shone silver and ivory. Her eyes had faded from cornflower to forget-me-not. Ines found her dead one morning, her bloodless fingers resting on an open book, her parchment eyelids down, as though she dozed, a wry grimace on her fine lips, as though she had tasted something not quite nice. She quickly lost this transient lifelikeness, and became waxy and peaked. Ines, who had been the younger woman, became the old woman, in an instant.

She busied herself with her dictionary work, and with tidying love away. She packed it into plastic sacks, creamy silks and floating lawns, velvet and muslin, lavender crêpe de Chine, beads of pearl and garnet. People had thought she was a dutiful daughter. They did not imagine, she thought, two intelligent women who understood each other easily, and loved each other. She drew the blinds because the light hurt her eyes. Her inner eye observed final things over and over. White face on white pillow amongst white hair. Colourless skin on lifeless fingers. Flesh of my flesh, flesh of her flesh. The efficient rage of consuming fire, the handfuls of fawn ash which she had scattered, as she had promised, in the hurrying foam of a Yorkshire beck.[2]

She went through the motions, hoping to become accustomed to solitude and silence. Then one morning pain struck her like a sudden beak, tearing at her gut. She caught her breath and sat down, waiting for it to pass. It did not pass, but strengthened, blow on blow. She rolled on her bed, dishevelled and sweating. She heard the creature moaning. She tried to telephone the doctor, but the thing shrieked raucously into the mouthpiece, and this saved her, for they sent an ambulance, which took the screaming thing to a hospital, as it would not have taken a polite old woman. Later they told her she had had at most four hours to live. Her gut was twisted and gangrenous. She lay quietly in a hospital bed in a curtained room. She was numb and bandaged, and drifted in and out of blessed sleep.

The surgeon came and went, lifting her dressings, studying the sutures, prodding the walls of her belly with strong fingers, awakening sullen coils of pain somewhere in deep, yet less than moth-like on the surface. Ines was a courteous and shamefast woman. She did not want to see her own sliced skin and muscle.

She thanked him for her life, unable to summon up warmth in her voice. What was her life now, to thank anyone for? When he had gone, she lied to the nurses about the great pain she said she felt, so they would bring drugs, and the sensation of vanishing in soft smoke, which was almost pleasure.

The wound healed—very satisfactorily, they said. The anaesthetist came in to discuss what palliatives she might be allowed to take home with her. He said, 'I expect you've noticed there's no sensation around the incision. That's quite normal. The nerves take time to join again, and some may not do so.' He too touched the sewed-up lips of the hole, and she felt that she did not feel, and then felt the ghost of a thrill, like fine wires, shooting out across her skin. She still did not look at the scar. The anaesthetist said, 'I see he managed to construct some sort of navel. People feel odd, we've found, if they haven't got a navel.'

---

2. Brook, creek.

She murmured something. 'Look', he said, 'it's a work of art.'

So she looked, since she would be going home, and would now have to attend to the thing herself.

The wound was livid and ridged and ran the length of her white front, from under the ribs to the hidden places underneath her. Where she had been soft and flat, she was all plumpings and hollows, like an old cushion. And where her navel had been, like a button caught in a seam at an angle, was an asymmetric whorl with a little sill of skin. Ines thought of her lost navel, of the umbilical cord that had been a part of her and of her mother. Her face creased into sorrow; her eyes were hot with tears. The anaesthetist misinterpreted them, and assured her that it would all look much less angry and lumpy after a month or two, and if it did not, it could be easily dealt with by a good plastic surgeon. Ines thanked him, and closed her eyes. There was no one to see her, she said, it didn't matter what she looked like. The anaesthetist, who had chosen his profession because he didn't like people's feelings, and preferred silence to speech, offered her what she wanted, a painkiller. She drifted into gathered cloud as he closed the door.

Their flat,[3] now her flat, was on the second floor of a nineteenth-century house in a narrow city square. The stairs were steep. The taxi-driver who brought her home left her, with her bag, on the doorstep. She toiled slowly upwards, resting her bag on the stairs, clinging to the banisters, aware of every bone in knee and ankle and wrist, and also of the paradox of pain in the gut and the strange numb casing of the surface skin. There was no need to hurry. She had time, and more time.

Inside the flat, she found herself preoccupied with time and dust. She had been a good cook—she thought of herself in the past tense—and had made delicious little meals for her mother and herself, light pea soups, sole with mushrooms, vanilla soufflés. Now she could make neither cooking nor eating last long enough to be interesting. She nibbled at cheese and crusts like a frugal mouse, and could not stay seated at her table but paced her room. The life had gone out of the furnishings and objects. The polish was dulled and she left it like that: she made her bed with one crumpled pull. She had a sense that the dust was thickening on everything.

She did what work she had to do, conscientiously. The problem was, that there was not enough of it. She worked as a part-time researcher for a major etymological dictionary, and in the past had been assiduous and inventive in suggesting new entries, new problems. Now, she answered those queries which were sent to her, and they did not at all fill up the huge cavern of space and time in which she floated and sank. She got up, and dressed herself carefully, as though she was 'going out to work'. She knew she must not let herself go, that was what she must not do. Then she walked about in the spinning dust and came to a standstill and stared out of the window, for minutes that seemed like hours, and hours that seemed like minutes. She liked to see the dark spread in the square, because then bedtime was not far away.

The day came when the dressings could, should, be dispensed with. She had been avoiding her body, simply wiping her face and under her arms with a damp face-cloth. She decided to have a bath. Their bath was old and deep

---

3. Apartment.

and narrow, with imposing brass taps and a heavy coil of shower-hosing. There was a wide wooden bath-rack across it, which still held, she saw now, private things of her mother's—a loofah, a sponge, a pumice stone. Her mother had never needed help in the bathroom. She had made fragrant steam from rosewater in a blue bottle, she had used baby-talc, scented with witch-hazel. For some reason these things had escaped the post-mortem clearance. Ines thought of clearing them now, and then thought, what does it matter? She ran a deep lukewarm bath. The old plumbing clanked and shuddered. She hung her dressing-gown—grey flannel—on the door, and very carefully, feeling a little giddy, clutching the rim, climbed into the bath and let her bruised flesh down into the water.

The warmth was nice. A few tense sinews relaxed. Time went into one of its slow phases. She sat and stared at the things on the rack. Loofah, sponge, pumice. A fibrous tube, a soft mess of holes, a shaped grey stone. She considered the differences between the three, all essentially solids with holes in. The loofah was stringy and matted, the sponge was branching and vacuous, the pumice was riddled with needle-holes. She stared, feeling that she and they were weightless, floating and swelling in her giddiness. Biscuit-coloured, bleached khaki, shadow-grey. Colourless colours, shapeless shapes. She picked up the sponge, and squeezed cooling water over her bust, studying the random forms of droplets and tricklings. She did not like the sponge's touch; it was clammy and fleshy. The loofah and the sponge were the dried-out bodies, the skeletons, of living things.[4] She picked up the pumice, a light stone tear, shaped to the palm of a hand, felt its paradoxical lightness, and dropped it into the water, where it floated. She did not know how long she sat there. The water cooled. She made a decision, to throw away the sponge. When she lifted herself, awkwardly, through the surface film, the pumice chinked against her flesh. It was an odd little sound, like a knock on metal. She put the pumice back on the rack, and touched her puckered wound with nervy fingers. Supposing something should be left in there? A clamp, a forceps, a needle? Not exactly looking she explored her reconstructed navel with a fingertip. She felt the absence of sensation and a certain glossy hardness where the healing was going on. She tapped, very softly, with her fingernail. She was not sure whether it was, or was not, a chink.

The next thing she noticed was a spangling of what seemed like glinting red dust, or ground glass, in the folds of her dressing-gown and her discarded underwear. It was a dull red, like dried blood, which does not have a sheen. It increased in quantity, rather than diminished, once she had noticed it. She observed tiny conical heaps of it, by skirting-boards,[5] on the corners of Persian rugs—conical heaps, slightly depressed, like ant-hill castings or miniaturised volcanoes. At the same time she noticed that her underwear appeared to be catching threads, here and there, on the rough, numb expanse of the healing scars. She felt a kind of horror and shame in looking at herself spread with lumps and an artificial navel. As the phenomenon grew more pronounced, she explored the area tentatively with her fingertips, over the cotton of her knickers.[6] Her stomach was without sensation. Her fingers felt

---

4. Loofahs are made from the bleached, dried edible fruit of a type of gourd, and natural sponges are the dried, processed skeletons of an aquatic animal.
5. Baseboards.
6. Underpants.

whorls and ridges, even sharp edges. They disturbed the glassy dust, which came away with the cloth, and shone in its creases. Each day the bumps and sharpness, far from calming, became more pronounced. One evening, in the unlit twilight, she finally found the nerve to undress, and tuck in her chin to stare down at herself. What she saw was a raised shape, like a starfish, like the whirling arms of a nebula in the heavens. It was the colour—or *a* colour—of raw flesh, like an open whip-wound or knife-slash. It trembled, because she was trembling, but it was cold to the touch, cold and hard as glass or stone. From the star-arms the red dust wafted like glamour.[7] She covered herself hastily, as though what was not seen might disappear.

The next day, it felt bigger. The day after, she looked again, in the half-light, and saw that the blemish was spreading. It had pushed out ruddy veins into the tired white flesh, threading sponge with crystal. It winked. It was many reds, from ochre to scarlet, from garnet to cinnabar. She was half-tempted to insert a fingernail under the veins and chip them off, and she could not.

She thought of it as 'the blemish'. She thought more and more about it, even when it was covered and out of sight. It extended itself—not evenly, but in fits and starts, around her waist, like a shingly girdle pushing down long fibrous fingers towards her groin, thrusting out cysts and gritty coruscations towards her pubic hair. There were puckered weals where flesh met what appeared to be stone. What *was* stone, what else was it?

One day she found a cluster of greenish-white crystals sprouting in her armpit. These she tried to prise away, and failed. They were attached deep within; they could be felt to be stirring stony roots under the skin surface, pulling the muscles. Jagged flakes of silica and nodes of basalt pushed her breasts upward and flourished under the fall of flesh, making her clothes crackle and rustle. Slowly, slowly, day by quick day, her torso was wrapped in a stony encrustation, like a corselet.[8] She could feel that under the stones her compressed inwards were still fluid and soft, responsive to pain and pressure.

She was surprised at the fatalism with which she resigned herself to taking horrified glances at her transformation. It was as though, much of the time, her thoughts and feelings had slowed to stone-speed, nerveless and stolid. There were, increasingly, days when a new curiosity jostled the horror. One day, one of the blue veins on her inner thigh erupted into a line of rubious spinels,[9] and she thought of jewels before she thought of pustules. They glittered as she moved. She saw that her stony casing was not static—points of rock salt and milky quartz thrust through glassy sheets of basalt, bubbles of sinter formed like tears between layers of hornblende.[1] She learned the names of some of the stones when curiosity got the better of passive fear. The flat, a dictionary-maker's flat, was furnished with encyclopaedias of all sorts. She sat in the evening lamplight and read the lovely words: pyrolusite, ignimbrite, omphacite, uvarovite, glaucophane, schist, shale, gneiss, tuff.

Her inner thighs now chinked together when she moved. The first apparition of the stony crust outside her clothing was strange and beautiful. She

---

7. An enchantment or spell.
8. An undergarment combining a girdle and a brassiere.
9. A hard crystalline mineral, ranging from colorless to ruby red to black.
1. A mineral, usually dark green to black in color. "Sinter": a hard deposit precipitated from mineral springs.

observed its beginnings in the mirror one morning, brushing her hair—a necklace of veiled swellings above her collar-bone which broke slowly through the skin like eyes from closed lids, and became opal—fire opal, black opal, geyserite and hydrophane, full of watery light. She found herself preening at herself in her mirror. She wondered, fatalistically and drowsily, whether when she was all stone, she would cease to breathe, see and move. For the moment she had grown no more than a carapace. Her joints obeyed her, light went from retina to brain, her budded tongue tasted food that she still ate.

She dismissed, with no real hesitation, the idea of consulting the surgeon, or any other doctor. Her slowing mind had become trenchant, and she saw clearly that she would be an object of horror and fascination, to be shut away and experimented on. It was of course, theoretically, possible that she was greatly deluded, that the winking gemstones and heaped flakes of her new crust were feverish sparks of her anaesthetised brain and grieving spirit. But she didn't think so—she refuted herself as Dr Johnson refuted Bishop Berkeley, by tapping on stone and hearing the scrape and chink of stone responding.[2] No, what was happening was, it appeared, a unique transformation. She assumed it would end with the petrifaction of her vital functions. A moment would come when she wouldn't be able to see, or move, or feed herself (which might not matter). Her mother had not had to face death—she had told herself it was not yet, not for just now, not round the next corner. She herself was about to observe its approach in a new fantastic form. She thought of recording the transformations, the metamorphic folds, the ooze, the conchoidal[3] fractures. Then when 'they' found her, 'they' would have a record of how she had become what she was. She would observe, unflinching.

But she continually put off the writing, partly because she preferred standing to sitting at a desk, and partly because she could not fix the process in her mind clearly enough to make words of it. She stood in the light of the window morning and evening, and read the stony words in the geological handbooks. She stood by the mirror in the bathroom and tried to identify the components of her crust. They changed, she was almost sure, minute by minute. She had found a description of the pumice stone—'a pale grey frothy volcanic glass, part of a pyroclastic[4] flow made of very hot particles; flattened pumice fragments are known as fiamme'. She imagined her lungs full of vesicles like the frothy stone, becoming stone. She found traces of hot flows down her own flanks, over her own thighs. She went into her mother's bedroom, where there was a cheval glass,[5] the only full-length mirror in the house.

At the end of a day's staring she would see a new shimmer of labradorite, six inches long and diamond-shaped, arrived imperceptibly almost between her buttocks where her gaze had not rested.

She saw dikes of dolerites, in graduated sills, now invading her inner arms.

---

2. In his *Life of Johnson* (1791), James Boswell described his discussion with the writer and lexicographer Samuel Johnson (1709–1784) of what they viewed as "ingenious sophistry"—the idealist philosophy of the Irish clergyman George Berkeley (1685–1753). Boswell thought it impossible to refute, but "Johnson answered, striking his foot with mighty force against a large stone, till he rebounded from it, 'I refute it *thus*.'"
3. Shaped like the interior surface of a bivalve shelve. "Metamorphic": of rock whose constitution has been changed by pressure, heat, and water.
4. Volcanic or igneous.
5. A mirror whose form allows it to be tilted.

But it took weeks of patient watching before, by dint of glancing in rapid saccades, she surprised a bubble of rosy barite crystals, breaking through a vein of fluorspar, and opening into the form known as a desert rose, bunched with the ore flowers of blue john. Her metamorphosis obeyed no known laws of physics or chemistry: ultramafic[6] black rocks and ghostly Iceland spar formed in succession, and clung together.

After some time, she noticed that her patient and stoical expectation of final inertia was not being fulfilled. As she grew stonier, she felt a desire to move, to be out of doors. She stood in the window and observed the weather. She found she wanted to go out, both on bright days, and even more in storms. One dark Sunday, when the midday sky was thick and grey as granite, when sullen thunder rumbled and the odd flash of lightning made human stomachs queasy, Ines was overcome with a need to be out in the weather. She put on wide trousers and a tunic, and over them a shapeless hooded raincoat. She pushed her knobby feet into fur boots, and her clay-pale hands, with their veins of azurmalachite, into sheepskin mittens, and set out down the stairs and into the street.

She had wondered how her tendons and musculature would function. She thought she could feel the roll of polished stone in stony cup as she moved her pelvis and hips, raised her knees, and swung her rigid arms. There was a delicious smoothness to these motions, a surprise after the accommodations she was used to making with the crumbling calcium of arthritic joints. She strode along, aimlessly at first, trying to get away from people. She noticed that her sense of smell had changed, and was sharper. She could smell the rain in the thick cloud-blanket. She could smell the carbon in the car-exhausts and the rainbow-coloured minerals in puddles of petrol. These scents were pleasurable. She came to the remains of a street market, and was assailed by the stink of organic decay, deliquescent fruit-mush, rotting cabbage, old burned oil on greasy newspapers and mashed fishbones. She strode past all this, retching a little, feeling acid bile churning in a stomach-sac made by now of what?

She came to a park—a tamed, urban park, with rose beds and rubbish bins, doggy-lavatories and a concrete fountain. She could hear the water on the cement with a new intricate music. The smell of a rain-squall blew away the wafting warmth of dog-shit. She put up her face and pulled off her hood. Her cheeks were beginning to sprout silicone flakes and dendrite fibres, but she only looked, she thought, like a lumpy old woman. There were droplets of alabaster and peridot[7] clustering in her grey hair like the eggs of some mythic stony louse, but they could not yet be seen, except from close. She shook her hair free and turned her face up to the branches and the clouds as the rain began. Big drops splashed on her sharp nose; she licked them from stiffening lips between crystalline teeth, with a still-flexible tongue-tip, and tasted skywater, mineral and delicious. She stood there and let the thick streams of water run over her body and down inside her flimsy garments, streaking her carnelian nipples and adamantine[8] wrists. The lightning came

---

6. Ultrabasic, or rich in iron and magnesium ores and low in silica.
7. A greenish yellow mineral used as a gem. "Alabaster": a hard compact calcium carbonate (e.g., marble or chalk).
8. Unbreakable, extremely hard. "Carnelian": a hard red translucent quartz used in jewelry.

in sheets of metal sheen. The thunder crashed in the sky and the surface of the woman crackled and creaked in sympathy.

She thought, I need to find a place where I should stand, when I am completely solid, I should find a place *outside*, in the weather.

When would she be, so to speak, dead? When her plump flesh heart stopped pumping the blue blood along the veins and arteries of her shifting shape? When the grey and clammy matter of her brain became limestone or graphite? When her brainstem became a column of rutilated[9] quartz? When her eyes became—what? She inclined to the belief that her watching eyes would be the last thing, even though fine threads on her nostrils still conveyed the scent of brass or coal to the primitive lobes at the base of the brain. The phrase came into her head: Those are pearls that were his eyes. A song of grief made fantastic by a sea-change.[1] Would her eyes cloud over and become pearls? Pearls were interesting. They were a substance where the organic met the inorganic, like moss agate. Pearls were stones secreted by a living shellfish, perfected inside the mother-of-pearl of its skeleton to protect its soft inward flesh from an irritant. She went to her mother's jewel-box, in search of a long string of freshwater pearls she had given her for her seventieth birthday. There they lay and glimmered; she took them out and wound them round her sparkling neck, streaked already with jet, opal, and jacinth zircon.[2]

She had had the idea that the mineral world was a world of perfect, inanimate forms, with an unchanging mathematical order of crystals and molecules beneath its sprouts and flows and branches. She had thought, when she had started thinking, about her own transfiguration as something profoundly unnatural, a move from a world of warm change and decay to a world of cold permanence. But as she became mineral, and looked into the idea of minerals, she saw that there were reciprocities, both physical and figurative. There were whole ranges of rocks and stones which, like pearls, were formed from things which had once been living. Not only coal and fossils, petrified woods and biohermal[3] limestones—oolitic and pisolitic limestones, formed round dead shells—but chalk itself which was mainly made up of micro-organisms, or cherts and flints, massive bedded forms made up of the skeletons of Radiolaria and diatoms.[4] These were themselves once living stones—living marine organisms that spun and twirled around skeletons made of opal.

The minds of stone lovers had colonised stones as lichens cling to them with golden or grey-green florid stains. The human world of stones is caught in organic metaphors like flies in amber. Words came from flesh and hair and plants. Reniform, mammilated, botryoidal, dendrite, haematite.[5] Carnelian is from carnal, from flesh. Serpentine and lizardite are stone reptiles; phyllite is leafy-green. The earth itself is made in part of bones, shells and diatoms. Ines was returning to it in a form quite different from her mother's

---

9. Containing an ore of titanium.
1. See Ariel's song, in Shakespeare's *The Tempest*, about Ferdinand's drowned father: "Those are pearls that were his eyes; / Nothing of him that doth fade / But doth suffer a sea-change / Into something rich and strange" (1.2.402–5).
2. An orange mineral.
3. Derived from reefs.
4. Different kinds of single-cell organisms.
5. These geological terms are etymologically related to words meaning kidney, breast, grapes, tree, and blood, respectively.

fiery ash and bonemeal. She preferred the parts of her body that were now volcanic glasses, not bony chalk. Chabazite, from the Greek for hail-stones, obsidian, which, like analcime and garnet, has the perfect icositetarahedral[6] shape.

Whether or not she became wholly inanimate, she must find a place to stand in the weather before she became immobile. She visited city squares, and stood experimentally by the rims of fountains, or in the entrances of grottoes. She had read of the hidden wildernesses of nineteenth-century graveyards, and it came to her that in such a place, amongst weeping angels and grieving cherubs, she might find a quiet resting-place. So she set out on foot, hooded and booted, with her new indefatigable rolling pace, marble joint in marble socket. It was a grey day, at the end of winter with specks between rain and snow spitting in the fitful wind. She strode in through a wrought-iron gate in a high wall.

What she saw was a flat stony city, house after house under the humped ripples of earth, marked by flat stones, standing stones, canted stones, fallen stones, soot-stained, dropping-stained, scum-stained, crumbled, carved, repeating, repeating. She walked along its silent pathways, past dripping yews and leafless birches and speckled laurels, looking for stone women. They stood there—or occasionally lay fallen there—on the rich earth. There were many of them, but they resembled each other with more than a family resemblance. There were the sweetly regretful lady angels, one arm pointing upwards, one turned down to scatter an arrested fall of stony flowers. There were the chubby child-angels, wearing simple embroidered stone tunics over chubby stone knees, also holding drooping flowers. Some busy monumental mason had turned them out to order, one after the other, their sweetly arched lips, or apple-cheeks, well-practised tricks of the trade. There was no other living person in that place, though there was a great deal of energetic organic life—long snaking brambles thrust between the stones for a place in the light, tombstones and angels alike wore bushy coats of gripping ivy, shining in the wind and the wet, as the leaves moved very slightly. Ines looked at the repeated stone people. Several had lost their hands, and lifted blind stumps to the grey air. These were less upsetting than those who were returning to formlessness, and had fists that seemed rotted by leprosy. Someone had come and sliced the heads from the necks of several cherubs—recently, the severed edges were still an even white. The stony representations of floating things— feathered wings, blossom and petals—made Ines feel queasy, for they were inert and weighed down, they were pulled towards the earth and what was under it.

Once or twice she saw things which spoke to her own condition. A glint of gold in the tesserae[7] of a mosaic pavement over a house whose ascription was hopelessly obscured. A sarcophagus on pillars, lead-lined, human-sized, planted with spring bulbs, and, she thought, almost certainly ancient and pagan, for it was surrounded with a company of eyeless elders in Etruscan[8] robes, standing each in his pillared alcove. Their faces were rubbed away,

---

6. With twenty-four equal, symmetrical plane faces.
7. Tiles.

8. Characteristic of ancient inhabitants of what is now Tuscany in central Italy.

but their substance—some kind of rosy marble?—had erupted into facets and flakes that glinted in the gloom like her own surfaces.

She might take her place near them, she thought, but was dissuaded by the aspect of their neighbours, a group of the theological virtues, Faith, Hope and Charity, simpering lifeless women clutching a stone cross, a stone anchor, and a fat stone helpless child. They had nothing to do with a woman who was made up of volcanic glass and semi-precious stones, who needed a refuge for her end. No, that was not true. They were not nothing to do with her, for they frightened her. She did not want to stand, unmoving, amongst them. She began to imagine an indefinite half-life, looking like them, yet staring out of seeing eyes. She walked faster.

Round the edges of the vast field of stones, within the spiky confine of the wall, was a shrubbery, with narrow paths and a few stone benches and compost bins. As she went into the bushes, she heard a sound, the chink of hammer on stone. She stood still. She heard it again. Thinking to surprise a vandal, she rounded a corner, and came upon a rough group of huts and a stack of stony rubble.

One of the huts was a long open shelter, wooden-walled and tile-roofed. It contained a trestle table, behind which a man was working, with a stonemason's hammer and chisel. He was a big muscular man, with a curly golden beard, a tanned skin, and huge hands. Behind him stood a gaggle of stone women, in various states of disrepair, lipless, fingerless, green-stained, sootstreaked. There was also a heap of urns, and the remains of one or two of the carved artificial rocks on which various symbolic objects had once been planted. He made a gesture as if to cover up what he was doing, which appeared, from the milky sheen of the marble, to be new work, rather than restoration.

Ines sidled up. She had almost given up speech, for her voice scratched and whistled oddly in her petrifying larynx. She shopped with gestures, as though she was an Eastern woman, robed and veiled, too timid, or linguistically inept, to ask about things. The stonecutter looked up at her, and down at his work, and made one or two intent little chips at it. Ines felt the sharp blows in her own body. He looked across at her. She whispered—whispering was still possible and normal—that she would like to see what he was making. He shrugged, and then stood aside, so that she could look. What she saw was a loose-limbed child lying on a large carved cushion, its arms flung out, its legs at unexpected angles, its hair draggled across its smooth forehead, its eyes closed in sleep. No, Ines saw, not sleep. This child was a dead child, its limbs were relaxed in death. Because it was dead, its form intimated painfully that it had once been alive. The whole had a blurred effect, because the final sharps and rounds had not been clarified. It had no navel; its little stomach was rough. Ines said what came into her stone head.

'No one will want that on any kind of monument. It's dead.'

The stonecutter did not speak.

'They write on their stones,' Ines said, 'he fell asleep on such a day, she is sleeping. It's not sleep.'

'I am making this for myself,' he said. 'I do repair work here, it is a living. But I do my own work also.'

His voice was large and warm. He said:

'Are you looking for any person's grave here? Or perhaps visiting—'

Ines laughed. The sound was pebbly. She said, 'No, I am thinking about my own final resting-place. I have problems.'

He offered her a seat, which she refused, and a plastic cup of coffee from a thermos, which she accepted though she was not thirsty, to oil her voice and to make an excuse for lingering. She whispered that she would like to see more of his work, of his own work.

'I am interested in stone work,' she said. 'Maybe you can make me a monument.'

As if in answer to this, he brought out from under his bench various wrapped objects, a heavy sphere, a pyramid, a bag of small rattling objects. He moved slowly and deliberately, laying out before her a stone angel-head, a sculpted cairn, a collection of hands and feet, large and small. All were originally the typical funereal carvings of the place. He had pierced and fretted and embellished them with forms of life that were alien and contradictory, yet part of them. Fingers and toes became prisms and serpents, minuscule faces peered between toes and tiny bodies of mice or marmosets gripped toenails or lay around wrists like Celtic dragons. The cairn—from a distance blockish like all the rest—was alive with marine creatures in whose bellies sat creatures, whose faces peered out of oyster-shells and from carved rib-cages, neither human faces nor inhuman. And the dead stone angel-face had been made into a round mass of superposed face on face, in bas-relief and fretwork, faces which shared eyes and profiles, mouths which fed two divergent starers with four eyes and serpents for hair. He said:

'I am not supposed to appropriate things which belong here. But I take the lost ones, the detached ones without a fixed place, I look for the life in them.'

'Pygmalion.'[9]

'Hardly. You like them?'

'Like is the wrong word. They are alive.'

He laughed. 'Stones are alive where I come from.'

'Where?' she breathed.

'I am an Icelander. I work here in the winter, and go home in the summer, when the nights are bright. I show my work—my own work—in Iceland in the summer.'

She wondered dully where she would be when he was in Iceland in the summer. He said:

'If you like, I will give you something. A small thing, and if you like to live with it, I will perhaps make you that monument.'

He held out to her a small, carved head which contained a basilisk[1] and two mussel shells. When she took it from him, it chinked, stone on stone, against her awkward fingertips. He heard the sound, and took hold of her knobby wrist through her garments.

'I must go now,' she breathed.

'No, wait, wait,' he said.

But she pulled away, and hurried in the dusk, towards the iron gate.

---

9. In classical mythology, a king of Cyprus who fell in love with a statue he had created; after he prayed to Aphrodite, the goddess of love, for a wife like his statue, she endowed it with life.
1. A legendary reptile that killed with its glance.

That evening, she understood she might have been wrong about her immediate fate. She put the stone hand on her desk and went into the kitchen to make herself bread and cheese. She was trembling with exertion and emotion, with fear of stony enclosure and complicated anxiety about the Icelander. The bread-knife slipped as she struggled to cut the soft loaf, and sliced into her stone hand, between finger and thumb. She felt pain, which surprised her, and the spurt of hot blood from the wound whose depth she could not gauge. She watched the thick red liquid run down the back of her hand, on to the bread, on to the table. It was ruddy-gold, running in long glassy strings, and where it touched the bread, the bread went up in smoke, and where it touched the table, it hissed and smoked and bored its hot way through the wood and dripped, a duller red now, on to the plastic floor, which it singed with amber circles and puckering. Her veins were full of molten lava. She put out the tiny fires and threw away the burned bread. She thought, I am not going to stand in the rain and grow moss. I may erupt. I do not know how that will be. She stood with the bread-knife in her hand and considered the rough stripes her blood had seared into the steel. She felt panic. To become stone is a figure, however fantastic, for death. But to become molten lava and to contain a furnace?

She went back next day to the graveyard. Her clashing heart quickened when she heard the tap of hammer on stone, as she swung into the shrubbery. It was a pale blue wintry day, with pewter storm-clouds gathering. There was the Icelander, turning a glinting sphere in his hand, and squinting at it. He nodded amiably in her direction. She said:

'I want to show you something.'

He looked up. She said:

'If anyone can bear to look, perhaps you can.'

He nodded.

She began to undo her fastenings, pulling down zips, unhooking the hood under her chin, shaking free her musical crystalline hair, shrugging her monumental arms out of their bulky sleeves. He stared intently. She stripped off shirt and jogging pants, trainers and vest,[2] her mother's silken knickers. She stood in front of him in her roughly gleaming patchwork, a human form vanishing under outcrops of silica, its lineaments suggested by veins of blue john[3] that vanished into crusts of pumice and agate. She looked out of her cavernous eye sockets through salty eyes at the man, whose blue eyes considered her grotesque transformation. He looked. She croaked, 'Have you ever seen such a thing?'

'Never,' he said. 'Never.'

Hot liquid rose to the sills of her eyes and clattered in pearly drops on her ruddy haematite[4] cheeks.

He stared. She thought, he is a man, and he sees me as I am, a monster.

'Beautiful,' he said. 'Grown, not crafted.'

'You said that the stones in your country were alive. I thought you might understand what has happened to me. I do not need a monument. I have grown into one.'

---

2. Sneakers and sleeveless undershirt.
3. A semiprecious mineral (a form of fluorite) found only in one hillside in Derbyshire, England.
4. An iron ore of a reddish brown to black color.

'I have heard of such things. Iceland is a country where we are matter-of-fact about strange things. We know we live in a world of invisible beings that exists in and around our own. We make gates in rocks for elves to come and go. But as well as living things without solid substance we know that rocks and stones have their own energies. Iceland is a young country, a restless country—in our land the earth's mantle is shaped at great speed by the churning of geysers and the eruption of lava and the progress of glaciers. We live like lichens, clinging to standing stones and rolling stones and heaving stones and rattling stones and flying stones. Our tales are full of striding stone women. We have mostly not given up the expectation of seeing them. But I did not expect to meet one here, in this dead place.'

She told him how she had supposed that to be petrified was to be motionless. I was looking for a place to rest, she told him. She told him about the spurt of lava from her hand and showed him the black scar, fringed with a rime of new crystals.

'I think now, Iceland is where I should go, to find somewhere to—stand, or stay.'

'Wait for the spring,' he said, 'and I will take you there. We have endless nights in the winter, and snowstorms, and the roads are impassable. In summer we have—briefly—endless days. I spend my winters here and my summers in my own country, climbing and walking.'

'Maybe it will be over—maybe I shall be—finished—before the spring.'

'I do not think so. But we will watch over it. Turn around, and let me see your back. It is beautiful beyond belief, and its elements are not constant.'

'I have the sense that—the crust—is constantly thickening.'

'There is an idea—for a sculptor—in every inch of it,' he said.

He said that his name was Thorsteinn Hallmundursson. He could not keep his eyes off her though his manner was always considered and gentle. Over the winter and into the early spring, they constructed a friendship. Ines allowed Thorsteinn to study her ridges and clefts. He touched her lightly, with padded fingers, and electricity flickered in her veining. He showed her samples of new stones as they sprouted in and on her body. The two she loved most were labradorite and fantomqvartz. Labradorite is dark blue, soft black, full of gleaming lights, peacock and gold and silver, like the aurora borealis embedded in hardness. In fantomqvartz, a shadowy crystal contains other shadowy crystals growing at angles in its transparent depths. Thorsteinn chipped and polished to bring out the lights and the angles, and in the end, as she came to trust him completely, Ines came to take pleasure in allowing him to decorate her gnarled fingers, to smooth the plane of her shin, and to reveal the hidden lights under the polished skin of her breasts. She discovered a new taste for sushi, for the iodine in seaweed and the salt taste of raw fish, so she brought small packs of these things to the shelter, and Thorsteinn gave her sips of peaty Laphroaig[5] whisky from a hipflask he kept in his capacious fleecy coat. She did not come to love the graveyard, but familiarity made her see it differently.

It was a city graveyard, on which two centuries of soot had fallen. Although inner cities are now sanctuaries for wild things poisoned and starved in

---

5. A strongly flavored single malt scotch, made on the island of Islay.

the countryside, the forms of life among the stones, though plump, lacked variety. Every day the fat pigeons gathered on the roof of Thorsteinn's shelter, catching the pale sunlight on their burnished feathers, mole-grey, dove-grey, sealskin-grey. Every day the fat squirrels lolloped busily from bush to bush, their grey tails and faces tinged with ginger, their strong little claws gripping. There were magpies, and strutting crows. There was thick bright moss moving swiftly (for moss) over the stones and their carved names. Thorsteinn said he did not like to clean it away, it was beautiful. Ines said she had noticed there were few lichens, and Thorsteinn said that lichens only grew in clean air; pollution destroyed them easily. In Iceland he would show her mosses and lichens she could never have dreamed of. He told her tales, through the city winter, as the cold rain dripped, and the cemetery crust froze, and cracked, and melted into mud-puddles, of a treeless landscape peopled by inhuman beings, laughing weightless elves, hidden heavy-footed, heavy-handed trolls. Ines's own crust grew thicker and more rugged. She had to learn to speak all over again, a mixture of whistles and clicks and solo gestures which perhaps only the Icelander would have understood.

Winter became spring, the dead leaves became dark with rain, grass pushed through them, crocuses and snowdrops, followed by self-spread bluebells and an uncontrollable carpet of celandine, pale gold flowers with flat green leaves, which ran over everything, headstones and gravel, bottle-green marble chips on recently dug graves, Thorsteinn's heap of rubble. They lasted a brief time, and then the gold faded to silver, and the silver became white, transparent, a brief ghostly lace of fine veins, and then a fallen mulch of mould, inhabited by pushy tendrils and the creamy nodes of rhizomes.

The death of the celandines seemed to be the signal for departure. They had discussed how this should be done. Ines had assumed they would fly to Reykjavík, but when she came to contemplate such a journey, she saw that it was impossible. Not only could she not fold her new body into the small space of a canvas bucket seat that would likely not bear her weight. She could never pass through the security checks at the airport. How would a machine react to the ores and nuggets scattered in her depths? If she were asked to pull back her hood, the airport staff would run screaming. Or shoot her. She did not know if she could now be killed by a bullet.

Thorsteinn said they could go by sea. From Scotland to Bergen in Norway, from Bergen to Seydhisfjördhur in East Iceland. They would be seven days on the ocean.

They booked a passage on a small trading boat that had four cabins for passengers, and a taciturn crew. They put in at the Faroe Islands and then went out into the Atlantic, between towering rock-faces, with no shore, no foam breaking at the base. In the swell of the Atlantic the ship nosed its way between great green and white walls of travelling water, in a fine salt spray. The sky changed and changed, opal and gun-metal, grass-green and crimson, mussel-blue and velvet black, scattered with wild starshine. Thorsteinn and Ines stood on deck whenever they could, and looked out ahead of them. Ines did not look back. She tasted the salt on her black-veined tongue, and thought of the biblical woman who had become a pillar of salt when she looked back.[6] She was no pillar. She was heaving and restless like the sea. When she thought of her past life, it was vague in her new mind, like cobwebs. Her mother was now to her flying dust in air, motes of bonemeal settling on the foam-flowers in the beck where she had scattered her. She could barely remember their peaceful meals together, the dry wit of her mother's observations, the glow of the flames in the ceramic coal in the gas fire in the hearth.

She opened her tent of garments to the driving wind and wet. She had found her feet easily and did not feel seasick. Thorsteinn rode the deck beside her like a lion or a war-horse, smiling through his beard.

She was interested in his human flesh. She found in herself a sprouting desire to take a bite out of him, his cheek or his neck, out of a mixture of some sort of affection and curiosity to see what the sensation would be like. She resisted the impulse easily enough, though she licked her teeth—razor-sharp flinty incisors, grim granite molars. She thought human thoughts and stone thoughts. The latter were slow, patchily coloured, textured and extreme, both hot and cold. They did not translate into the English language, or into any other she knew: they were things that accumulated, solidly, knocked against each other, heaped and slipped.

Thorsteinn, like all Icelanders, became more animated as they neared his island. He told tales of early settlers, including St Brendan, who had sailed there in the fifth century, riding the seas in a hide coracle, and had been beaten back by a huge hairy being, armed with a pair of tongs and a burning mass of incandescent slag, which he hurled at the retreating monks. St Brendan believed he had come to Ultima Thule;[7] the volcano, Mt Hekla, was the entrance to Hell at the edge of the world. The Vikings came in the ninth century. Thorsteinn, standing on deck at night with Ines, was amazed to discover that the back of her hands was made of cordierite, grey-blue crystals mixed with a sandy colour, rough and undistinguished but which, held at a certain angle, revealed facets like shimmering dragon-scales. The Vikings, he told her, had used the way this mineral polarised light to navigate in the dark, using the Polar Star and the moonlight. He made her turn her heavy hands, flashing and winking in the darkness, as the water-drops flashed on ropes and crest-curls of wake.

Her first vision of Iceland was of the wild jagged peaks of the eastern fjords. Thorsteinn packed them into a high rugged truck-like car, and they drove south, along the wild coast, past ancient volcanic valleys, sculpted, slowly, slowly, by Ice Age glaciers. They were under the influence, literally—of the great glacier, Vatnajökull, the largest in Europe, Thorsteinn said, sitting easily at the wheel. Brown thick rivers rushed down crevices and into valleys, carrying alluvial dust. They glimpsed the sheen of it from mountain passes, and then, as they came to the flatlands of the south, they saw the first glacial tongues pouring down into the plains, white and shining above the green marshes and under the blue sky. Thorsteinn alternated between a steady silence and a kind of incantatory recitation of history, geography, time before history, myth. His country appeared to her old, when she first saw it, a primal

---

6. Lot's wife, who disobeyed God's command and looked back as they fled the destruction of the cities of Sodom and Gomorrah (Genesis 19.17, 26).
7. Farthest Thule (Latin); in the ancient world, the northernmost land that could be inhabited. What the Greeks called Thule was apparently Iceland or Norway.

chaos of ice, stone silt, black sand, gold mud. His stories went easily back to the first and second centuries, or the Middle Ages, as though they were yesterday, and his own ancestors figured in tales of enmity and banishment as though they were uncles and kinsmen who had sat down to eat with him last year. And yet, the striking thing, the decisive thing, about this landscape, was that it was geologically young. It was turbulent with the youth and energy of an unsettled crust of the earth. The whole south coast of Iceland is still being changed—in a decade, in a twinkling of an eye—by volcanic eruptions which pour red-hot magma from mountain ridges, or spout up, boiling, from under the thick-ribbed ice. This is a recent lava field, said Thorsteinn, as they came to the Skaftáhraun, this was made by the eruption of the Lakagígar in 1783, which lasted for a year, and killed over half the population and over half the livestock. Ines stared impassively at the fine black sand-drifts, and felt the red-hot liquid boil a little, in her belly, in her lungs.

They travelled on, over the great black plain of Myrdalssandur. This, said Thorsteinn, was the work of a volcano, Katla, which erupted under a glacier, Myrdalsjökull. There is a troll-woman connected to this volcano, he told her. She was called Katla, which is a feminine version of ketill, kettle, and she was said to have hidden a kettle of molten gold, which could be seen by human eyes on one day of the year only. But those who set out to find it were troubled by false visions and strange sights—burning homesteads, slaughtered livestock—and turned back from the quest in panic. Katla was the owner of a pair of magic breeches, which made her a very fleet runner, leaping lightly from crag to crag, descending the mountain-scree like smoke. They were said to be made from human skin. A young shepherd took them once, to help him catch his sheep, and Katla caught him, killed him, dismembered him, and hid his body in a barrel of whey. They found him, of course, when the whey was drunk, and Katla fled, running like clouds in the wind, over to Myrdalsjökull, and was never seen again.

Was she a stone woman? asked Ines. Her stony thoughts rumbled around heavy limbs made supple by borrowed skin. Her own human skin was flaking away, like the skins snakes and lizards rub off against stones and branches, revealing the bright sleekness beneath. She picked it away with crystal fingertips, scratching the dead stuff out of the crevices of elbow, knee-joint and her non-existent navel.

Thorsteinn said there was no mention of her being stone. There were trolls in Iceland who turned to stone, like Norse trolls, if the sun hit them. But by no means all were of that kind. There were trolls, he said, who slept for centuries amongst the stones of the desert, or along the riverbeds, and stirred with an earthquake, or an eruption, into new life. There were human trolls, distinguishable only by their huge size from farmers and fishermen. 'Personally,' said Thorsteinn, 'I do not think you are a troll. I think you are a metamorphosis.'

They came to Reykjavík, the smoky harbour. Ines was uneasy, even in this small city—she strode, hooded and bundled behind Thorsteinn, as he showed her the harbour. Something was to happen, and it was not here, not amongst humans. New thoughts growled between her marbled ears: Thorsteinn wandered in and out of chandlers' and artists' stores, and his uncouth protégée stood in the shadows and more or less hissed between her teeth.

She asked where they were going, and he said—as though she should have read his thoughts—that they were going to his summer house, where he would work.

'And I?' she said, grumbling. Thorsteinn stared at her, assessing and unsmiling.

'I don't know,' he said. 'Neither of us can know. I am taking you where there are known to be creatures—not human. That may be a good or a bad thing, I am a sculptor not a seer, how can I know? What I do hope is that you will allow me to record you. To make works that show what you are. For I may never see such a thing again.'

She smiled, showing all her teeth in the shadow of her hood.

'I agree,' she said.

They drove west again, from Reykjavík, along the ring road. They saw wonders—steam pouring from mountain-sides, hot blue water bubbling in stony pots in the earth, the light sooty pumice, the shrouded humped black form of Hekla, hooded and violent. Thorsteinn remarked casually that it had erupted in 1991 and was still unusually active, under the earth and under the ice. They were heading for the valley of Thorsmork, Thor's Forest, which lay inaccessibly between three glaciers, two deep rivers, and a string of dark mountains. They crossed torrents, and ground along the dirt road. There were no other humans, but the fields were full of wild flowers, and birds sang in birches and willows. Now it is summer, said Thorsteinn. In the winter you cannot come here. The rivers are impassable. You cannot stand against the wind.

Thorsteinn's summer house was not unlike his encampment in the graveyard, although it was likely that the influence was the other way. It was built into a hillside, walled and roofed with turf, with a rough outbuilding, also turf-roofed, with his long work-table. It was roughly furnished: there were two heavy wooden bedsteads, a stone sink through which spring-water ran from a channelled pipe in the hillside, a table, chairs, a wooden cupboard. And a hearth, with a stove. They had a view—when the weather was clear—across a wide valley, and a turbulent glacial river, to the sharp dark ridges of the mountains and the distant bright sheen of the glacier. The grassy space in front of the house looked something between a chaos of boulders and a half-formed stone circle. Ines came to see that all the stones, from the vast and cow-sized to clusters of pebbles and polished singletons, were works in progress, or potential works, or works finished for the time being. They were both carved and decorated. A discovered face peered from under a crusty overhang, one-eyed, fanged, leering. A boulder displayed a perfectly polished pair of youthful breasts, glistening in circles of golden lichen. Cracks made by ice, channels worn by water, mazes where roots had pushed and twisted, were coloured in brilliant pinks and golds, glistening where the light caught them. Nests of stony eggs made of sooty pumice, or smooth thulite,[8] were inhabited by crystal worms and serpentine adders.

The stonecarver worked with the earth and the weather as his assistants or controllers. A hunched stone woman had a fantastic garden of brilliant

---

8. A rare, peach-colored mineral that is found in Norway.

moss spilling from her lap and over her thighs. An upright monolith was fantastically adorned with the lirellate[9] fruiting bodies of the 'writing lichens'. On closer inspection, Ines saw that jewels had been placed in crevices, and sharpened pins like medieval cloak-brooches had been inserted in holes threaded in the stone surface. A dwarfish stone had tiny, carved gold hands where its ears might have been expected to be.

Thorsteinn said that he liked—in the summer—to add to the durable stones work that mimicked and reflected the fantastic succession of the weathers of that land. He suspended ingenious structures of plastic string, bubble-wrap, polyurethane sheeting, to make ice, rain-floods, the bubbling of geysirs and mud-baths. He made rainbows of strips of glass, and bent them above his creatures, catching the bright blue light in the steely storm-light and the wet shimmer of enveloping cloud in their reflections.

There were many real rainbows. There could be several climates in a day—bright sun, gathering storm, snowfall, great coils and blasts of wind so violent that a man could not stand up—though the stone woman found herself taking pleasure in standing against the turbulent air as a surfer rides a wave, when even Thorsteinn had had to take shelter. There were flowers in the early brief summer—saxifrages and stonecrops, lady's bedstraw and a profusion of golden angelica. They walked out into soft grey carpets of *Cetraria islandica*, the lichen that is known as 'Iceland moss'. Reindeer food, human food, possible cancer cure, said Thorsteinn.

He asked her, rather formally, over a fireside supper of smoked lamb and scrambled eggs, whether she would sit to him. It was light in the northern night: his face was fiery in the midnight sun, his beard was full of gold, and brass, and flame-flickering. She had not looked at herself since they left England. She did not carry a mirror, and Thorsteinn's walls were innocent of reflecting surfaces, though there were sacks of glass mosaic tesserae in the workshop. She said she did not know if she any longer differed from the stones he collected and decorated so tactfully, so spectacularly. Maybe he should not make her portrait, but decorate her, carve into her, when . . . When whatever was happening had come to its end, she left unsaid, for she could not imagine its end. She tore at the tasty lamb with her sharp teeth. She had an overwhelming need for meat, which she did not acknowledge. She ground the fibres in the mill of her jaws. She said, she would be happy to do what she could.

Thorsteinn said that she *was*, what he had only imagined. All my life I have made things about metamorphosis. *Slow* metamorphoses, in human terms. Fast, fast in terms of the earth we inhabit. You are a walking metamorphosis. Such as a man meets only in dreams. He raised his wineglass to her. I too, he said, am utterly changed by your changing. I want to make a record of it. She said she would be honoured, and meant it.

Time too was paradoxical in Iceland. The summer was a fleeting island of light and brightness in a shroud of thick vapours and freezing needles of ice in the air. But within the island of the summer the daylight was sempiternal, there was no nightfall, only the endless shifts in the colour of the sky, trout-

---

9. Resembling the fruit of certain lichens.

dappled, mackerel-shot, turquoise, sapphire, peridot, hot transparent red, and, as the autumn put out boisterous fingers, flowing with the gyrating and swooping veils of the aurora borealis. Thorsteinn worked all summer to his own rhythm, which was stubborn and earthy—long, long hours—and rapid, like waterfalls, or air currents. Ines sat on a stone bench, and occasionally did domestic things with inept stony fingers, hulled a few peas, scrubbed a potato, whisked a bowl of eggs. She tried reading, but her new eyes could not quite bring the dancing black letters to have any more meaning than the spiders and ants which scurried round her feet or mounted her stolid ankles. She preferred standing, really. Bending was harder and harder. So she stood, and stared at the hillside and the distant neb of the glacier. Some days they talked as he worked. Sometimes, for a couple of days together, they said nothing.

He made many, many drawings of her face, of her fingers, of her whole cragged form. He made small images in clay, and larger ones, cobbled together from stones and glass fragments and threads of things representing the weather, which the weather then disturbed. He made wreaths of wild flowers, which dried in the air, and were taken by the wind. He came close, and peered dispassionately into the crystal blocks of her eyes, which reflected the red light of the midnight sun. She made an increasing number of solitary forays into the landscape. When she returned, once, she saw from a great distance a standing stone that he had made, and saw that through its fantastic crust, under its tattered mantle, it was possible to see the lineaments of a beautiful woman, a woman with a carved, attentive face, looking up and out. The human likeness vanished as she came closer. She thought he had *seen* her, and this made her happy. He saw that she existed, in there.

But she found it harder and harder to see him. He began to seem blurred and out of focus, not only when his human blue eye peered into her crystal one and his beard fanned in a golden cloud round the disc of his face. He was becoming insubstantial. His very solid body looked as though it was simply a form of water vapour. She had to cup her basalt palm around her ear to hear his great voice, which sounded like the whispering of grasshoppers. She heard him snore at night, in the wooden bed, and the sound was indistinguishable from the gurgle of the water, or the prying random gusts of the wind.

And at the same time she was seeing, or almost seeing, things which seemed to crowd and gesture just beyond the range of her vision, behind her head, beyond the peripheral circle of her gaze. From the deck of the ship she had seen momentary sea creatures. Dolphins had rushed glistening amongst the long needles of air caught in the rush of their wake. Whales had briefly humped parts of guessed-at bulks through the wrinkling of the surface, the muscular span of a forked tail, the blast of a spout in a contracting air-hole in an unimaginable skin. Fulmars[1] had appeared from nowhere in the flat sky and had plummeted like falling swords through the surface which closed over them. So now she sensed earth bubbles and earth monsters shrugging themselves into shape in the air and in the falling fosses. Fleet herds of light-footed creatures flowed round the house with the wind, and she almost saw, she sensed with some new sense, that they waved elon-

---

1. Northern seabirds.

gated arms in a kind of elastic mockery or ecstasy. Stones she stared at, as Thorsteinn worked on her images, began to dimple and shift, like disguised moor-birds, speckled and splotched, on nests of disguised eggs, speckled and splotched, in a wilderness of stones, speckled and splotched. Lichens seemed to grow at visible speeds and form rings and coils, with triangular heads like adders. Clearest of all—almost visible—were the huge dancers, forms that humped themselves out of earth and boulders, stamped and hurtled, beckoned with strong arms and snapping fingers. After long looking she seemed also to see that these things, the fleet and the portentous, the lithe and the stolid, were walking and running like parasites on the back of some moving beast so huge that the mountain range was only a wrinkle in its vasty hide, as it stirred in its slumber, or shook itself slightly as it woke.

She said to Thorsteinn in one of their economical exchanges:

'There are living things here I can almost see, but not see.'

'Maybe, when you can see them,' he said equably, scribbling away with charcoal, 'maybe then . . .'

'I am very tired, most of the time. And when I am not, I am full of—quite *abnormal*—energy.'

'That's good?'

'It's alarming.'

'We shall see.'

'Do humans in Iceland,' she asked again, conscious that *something* was staring and listening—uncomprehending, she believed—to the scratch of her voice—'do humans turn into trolls?'

'Trolls,' said Thorsteinn. 'That's a human word for them. We have a word, *tryllast*, which means to go mad, to go berserk. Like trolls. Always from a human perspective. Which is a bit of a precarious perspective, here, in this land.'

There was a long silence. Ines looked at his face as he worked, and could not focus the eyes that studied her so intently: they were charcoal blurs, full of dust-motes. Whereas the hillside was alive with eyes, that opened lazily within fringing mossy lashes, that stared through and past her from hollows in stones, that flashed in the light briefly and vanished again.

Thorsteinn said:

'There is a tale we tell of a group of poor men who went out to gather lichens for the winter. And one of them climbed higher than the others and the crag above him suddenly put out long stony arms, and wound them round him, and lifted him, and carried him up the hillside. The story says the stone was an old troll woman. His companions were very frightened and ran home. The next year, they went there again, and he came to meet them, over the moss carpet, and he was grey like the lichens. They asked him, was he happy, and he didn't answer. They asked him what he believed in, was he a Christian, and he answered dubiously that he believed in God and Jesus. He would not come with them and we get the impression that they did not try very hard to persuade him. The next year he was greyer and stood stock-still staring. When they asked him about his beliefs, he moved his mouth in his face, but no words came. And the next year, he came again, and they asked again what he believed in, and he replied, laughing fiercely, *Trunt, trunt, og tröllin í fjöllunum.*'

The English scholar who persisted in her said. 'What does it mean?'

'*"Trunt, trunt"* is just nonsense, it means rubbish and junk and aha and hubble bubble, that sort of thing, I don't know an English expression that will do as a translation. Trunt trunt, and the trolls in the fells.'

'It has a good rhythm.'

'Indeed it does.'

'I am afraid, Thorsteinn.'

He put his bear-arm round the knobs and flinty edges that were where her shoulders had been. It felt to her lighter than cobweb.

'They call me,' she said in a whisper. 'Do you hear them?'

'No. But I know they call.'

'They dance. At first it looked ugly, their rushing and stamping. But now—now I am also afraid that I can't—join the circle. I have never danced. And there is such wild energy.' She tried to be precise. 'I don't exactly *see* them still. But I do see their dancing, the furious form of it.'

Thorsteinn said, 'You will see them, when the time comes. I do believe you will.'

As the autumn drew in she grew restless. She had planted small gardens in the crevices of her body, trailing grasses, liverworts. Creatures ran over her—insects first, a stone-coloured butterfly, indistinguishable from her speckled breast, foraging ants, a millipede. There were even fine red worms, the colour of raw meat, which burrowed unhindered. She began to walk more, taking these things with her. In September, they had several days of driving rain, frost was thick on the turf roof, the glacial rivers swelled and boiled and ice came down them in clumps and blocks, and also formed where the spray lay on the vegetation. Thorsteinn said that in a very little time it would be unsafe to stay—they might be cut off. He watched her brows contract over the glittering eyes in their hollow caves.

'I can't go back with you.'

'You can. You are welcome to come with me.'

'You know I must stay. You have always known. I am simply gathering up courage.'

When the day came, it brought one of those Icelandic winds that howl across the earth, carrying away all unsecured objects and creatures, including men if they have no pole to clutch, no shelter built into the rock. Birds can make no way in such weather, they are blown back and broken. Snow and ice and hurtling cloud are in and on the wind, mixed with moving earth and water, and odd wreaths of steam gathered from geysirs. Thorsteinn went into his house and held on to the doorpost. Ines began to come with him, and then turned away, looking up the mountainside, standing easily in the furious breakers of the moving air. She lifted a monumental arm and gestured towards the fells and then to her eyes. No one could be heard in this wailing racket, but he saw that she was signalling that now she saw them clearly. He nodded his head—he needed his arms to hang on to the doorpost. He looked up the mountain and saw, no doubt what she now saw clearly, figures, spinning and bowing in a rapid dance on huge, lithe, stony legs, beckoning with expansive gestures, flinging their great arms wide in invitation. The woman in his stone-garden took a breath—he saw her sides quiver—and essayed a few awkward dance-steps, a sweep of an arm, of both arms. He heard her laughter in the wind. She jigged a little, as though gathering momentum, and then began a dancing run, into the blizzard. He heard a stone voice, shouting and singing, 'Trunt, trunt, og tröllin í fjöllunum.'

He went in, and closed his door against the weather, and began to pack.

2003

LUCILLE CLIFTON
b. 1936

Lucille Clifton's daring and exuberance as a poet stand in marked contrast to what in one poem she characterizes as her own mother's anxious reticence: "She got us almost through the high grass / then seemed like she turned around and ran / right back in / right back on in." At the same time, however, Clifton's irreverence echoes what she describes as the feistiness of her father, a man who changed his name from Sayle to Sayles because he knew that "there will be more than one of me." Whether she speaks as her parents' daughter or as the mother of six children, Clifton presents herself as a woman linked to history through her family, an ordinary woman trying to deal with the fears and joys of everyday life.

She was born in Depew, New York, and attended Howard University and Fredonia State Teachers College. In 1958, she married Fred J. Clifton, an educator and writer. Three volumes of verse—*Good Times* (1969), *Good News about the Earth* (1972), and *An Ordinary Woman* (1974)—were followed by a memoir, *Generations* (1976), in which she recounts the genealogical stories that animate so much of her writing. The author of numerous books for children, Clifton has also published many other collections, including *Two-Headed Woman* (1980), *Next* (1987), *Quilting* (1991), and *The Book of Light* (1993). *Blessing the Boats* won the National Book Award in 2000. Although she strenuously rejects what she calls "white ways," her work is never marked by rancor. In poems that focus on the activist Angela Davis or on her children, on the body or on mythological figures, she extends the invitation explicit in her "After Kent State," an invitation to "come into the / Black / and live."

admonitions

boys
i don't promise you nothing
but this
what you pawn
i will redeem
what you steal
i will conceal
my private silence to
your public guilt
is all i got

girls
first time a white man
opens his fly
like a good thing
we'll just laugh
laugh real loud my
black women

children
when they ask you
why is your mama so funny
say
she is a poet
she don't have no sense

1969

the lost baby poem

the time i dropped your almost body down
down to meet the waters under the city
and run one with the sewage to the sea
what did i know about waters rushing back
what did i know about drowning
or being drowned

you would have been born in winter
in the year of the disconnected gas
and no car
we would have made the thin walk
over the genecy hill into the canada winds
to let you slip into a stranger's hands
if you were here i could tell you
these and some other things

and if i am ever less than a mountain
for your definite brothers and sisters
let the rivers wash over my head
let the sea take me for a spiller of seas
let black men call me stranger always
for your never named sake

1972

if our grandchild be a girl

    i wish for her
    fantastic hands,
    twelve spiky fingers
    symbols of our tribe.
5   she will do magic
    with them,
    she will turn personal
    abracadabra
    remembered from
10 dahomean[1] women
    wearing
    extravagant gloves.

                        1987

my dream about being white

    hey music and
    me
    only white,
    hair a flutter of
5   fall leaves
    circling my perfect
    line of a nose,
    no lips,
    no behind, hey
10 white me
    and i'm wearing
    white history
    but there's no future
    in those clothes
15 so i take them off and
    wake up
    dancing.

                        1987

---

1. Dahomey, now known as Benin, is a country of West Africa on the Gulf of Guinea (as well as one of the major ethnic groups constituting its population); there is a tradition of Dahomean warrior women.

Poem to My Uterus

you   uterus
you have been patient
as a sock
while i have slippered into you
5   my dead and living children
now
they want to cut you out
stocking i will not need
where i am going
10   where am i going
old girl
without you
uterus
my bloody print
15   my estrogen kitchen
my black bag of desire
where can i go
barefoot
without you
20   where can you go
without me

1991

To My Last Period

well girl, goodbye,
after thirty-eight years.
thirty-eight years and you
never arrived
5   splendid in your red dress
without trouble for me
somewhere, somehow.

now it is done,
and i feel just like
10   the grandmothers who,
after the hussy has gone,
sit holding her photograph
and sighing, *wasn't she
beautiful? wasn't she beautiful?*

1991

Leda[1] 3

A Personal Note (Re: Visitations)

    always pyrotechnics;
    stars spinning into phalluses
    of light, serpents promising
    sweetness, their forked tongues
5   thick and erect, patriarchs of bird
    exposing themselves in the air.
    this skin is sick with loneliness.
    You want what a man wants,
    next time come as a man
110 or don't come.

1993

1. In classical mythology, the wife of Tyndareus, king of Sparta; she was raped by Zeus, king of the Olympian gods, who came to her in the form of a swan.

ANITA DESAI
b. 1937

Of Anita Desai's books, her fellow expatriate Indian novelist Salman Rushdie has observed that they are "private universes, illuminated by her perceptiveness, delicacy of language, and sharp wit." And of Desai herself, another literary contemporary, the writer Ruth Prawer Jhabvala, who knew her when she was a teenager in Old Delhi, remembers that she was "absolutely beautiful, very quiet, tremendously well read and sensitive, and self-contained," adding, "I see Anita's writing, which is very exquisite and beautiful, as a reflection of her." Yet Desai, born Anita Mazumdar to a Bengali father and a German mother, has always experienced herself as an outsider in India, recalling that her "family was an oddity," split between East and West, so that although her mother "dressed in a sari and cooked Indian food," in school "I became aware . . . of things that set us apart."

The Mazumdar family spoke German at home and Hindi to friends and neighbors, but the writer-to-be learned English at school, and she has noted that "It was always my literary language, my book language." She went on to focus on English at Delhi University, then married Ashvin Desai, a businessman, when she was twenty. The couple moved to Bombay, where Anita Desai raised four children and lived "a very domestic life" until she began teaching in the United States and England at a range of institutions, including Mount Holyoke College, Girton College (Cambridge), and MIT. Even while caring for her family in Bombay, however, Desai was producing fiction. She has declared that "My writing career was entirely subservient to being a wife and mother. I lived the life of the typical Indian housewife; wrote in the gaps and hid it away, kept it secret." But since her first novel, *Cry the Peacock*, appeared in 1963, she has published more than a dozen books, including most notably *Clear Light of Day* (1980), *In Custody* (1984; made into a 1993 film—directed by Ismail Merchant—for which she wrote the screenplay), *Baumgartner's Bombay* (1988), *Fast-*

ing, Feasting (1999), and the short story collection *Diamond Dust* (2000), from which "Royalty" is drawn.

In this tale, as in many of her novels, Desai coolly scrutinizes familial obligations and relationships, especially those that are, in her words, "sticky and sweet, clinging and trapping." As many critics have noted, she brings her incisive intelligence to bear on such complexities both in India and abroad; but as "Royalty" reveals, she is an especially brilliant analyst of Indian mores, perhaps because, in her words, "Leaving India frees one's tongue."

Royalty

All was prepared for the summer exodus: the trunks packed, the household wound down, wound up, ready to be abandoned to three months of withering heat and engulfing dust while its owners withdrew to their retreat in the mountains. The last few days were a little uncomfortable—so many of their clothes already packed away, so many of their books and papers bundled up and ready for the move. The house looked stark, with the silver put away, the vases emptied of flowers, the rugs and carpets rolled up; it was difficult to get through this stretch, delayed by one thing or another—a final visit to the dentist, last instructions to the stockbrokers, a nephew to be entertained on his way to Oxford. It was only the prospect of escape from the blinding heat that already hammered at the closed doors and windows, poured down on the roof and verandas, and withdrawal to the freshness and cool of the mountains which helped them to bear it. Sinking down on veranda chairs to sip lemonade from tall glasses, they sighed, 'Well, we'll soon be out of it.'

In that uncomfortable interlude, a postcard arrived—a cheap, yellow printed postcard that for some reason to do with his age, his generation, Raja still used. Sarla's hands began to tremble: news from Raja. In a quivering voice she asked for her spectacles. Ravi passed them to her and she peered through them to decipher the words as if they were a flight of migrating birds in the distance: Raja was in India, at his ashram in the south, Raja was going to be in Delhi next week, Raja expected to find her there. She *would* be there, wouldn't she? 'You won't desert me?'

After Ravi had made several appeals to her for information, for a sharing of the news, she lifted her face to him, grey and mottled, and said in a broken voice, 'Oh Ravi, Raja has come. He is in the south. He wants to visit us—next week.'

It was only to be expected that Ravi's hands would fall upon the table, fall onto china and silverware, with a crash, making all rattle and jar. Raja was coming! Raja was to be amongst them again!

A great shiver ran through the house like a wind blowing that was not a wind so much as a stream of shining light, shimmering and undulating through the still, shadowy house, a radiant serpent, not without menace, some threat of danger. Whether it liked it or not, the house became the one chosen by Raja for a visitation, a house in waiting.

With her sari wrapped around her shoulders tightly, as if she were cold, Sarla went about unlocking cupboards, taking out sheets, silver, table linen. Her own trunks, and Ravi's, had to be thrown open. What had been put away was taken out again. Ravi sat uncomfortably in the darkened drawing room, watching her go back and forth, his lips thin and tight, but his expression one of helplessness. Sometimes he dared to make things difficult for her, demanding a book or a file he knew was at the very bottom of the trunk, pretending that it was indispensable, but when she performed the difficult task with every expression of weary martyrdom, he relented and asked, 'Are you all right? Sarla?' She refused to answer, her face was clenched in a tightly contained storm of emotion. Despondently, he groaned, 'Oh, aren't we too old—?' Then she turned to look at him, and even spoke: 'What do you mean?' Ravi shook his head helplessly. Was there any need to explain?

Raja arrived on an early morning train. Another sign of his generation: he did not fly when he was in India. Perhaps he had not taken in the fact that one could fly in India too, or else he preferred the trains, no matter how long they took, crawling over the endless, and plains in the parched heat before the rains. At dawn, no sun yet visible, the sky was already white with heat; crows rose from the dust-laden trees, cawing, then dropped to the ground, sun-struck. Sweepers with great brooms made desultory swipes at the streets, their mouths covered with a strip of turban, or sari, against the dust they raised. Motor rickshaws and taxis were being washed, lovingly, tenderly, by drivers in striped underpants. The city stank of somnolence, of dejection, like sweat-stained clothes. Sarla and Ravi stood on the railway platform, waiting, and when Sarla seemed to waver, Ravi put out a gentlemanly hand to steady her. When she turned her face to him in something like gratitude or pleading, a look passed between them as can only pass between two people married to each other through the droughts and hurricanes of thirty years. Then the train arrived, with a great blowing of triumphant whistles: it had completed its long journey from the south, it had achieved its destination, hadn't it *said* it would? Magnificently, it was a promise kept. Immediately, coolies in red shirts and turbans, with legs like ancient tree roots, sprang at the compartments, leaping onto the steps before the train had even halted or its doors opened, and the families and friends waiting on the platform began to run with the train, waving, calling to the passengers who leaned out of the windows. Sarla and Ravi stood rooted to one place, clinging to each other in order not to be torn apart or pushed aside by the crowd in its excitement.

The pandemonium only grew worse when the doors were unlatched and the passengers began to dismount at the same time as the coolies forced their way in, creating human gridlock. Sighting their friends and relatives, the crowds on the platform began to wave and scream. Till coolies were matched with baggage, passengers with reception parties, utter chaos ruled. Sarla and Ravi peered through it, turning their heads in apprehension. Where was Raja? Only after the united families began to leave, exhorting coolies to bring up the rear with assorted trunks, bedding rolls and baskets balanced on their heads and held against their hips, and the railway platform had emerged from the scramble, did they hear the high-pitched, wavering warble of the voice they recognised: 'Sar-la! Ra-vi! My dears, how *good* of you to come! How *good* to see you! If you only knew what I've beeen through, about the man who insisted on telling me about his *alligator* farm, describing at such length how they are turned into *handbags*, as though I were a *leather merchant* . . . ' and they turned to see Raja stepping out of one of the coaches, clutching his silk dhoti[1] with one hand, waving elegantly with the other, a silver lock of his hair rising from his wide forehead as he landed on the platform in his slippered feet. And then the three of them were embracing each other, all at once, and it might have been Oxford, it might have been thirty years ago, it might even have been that lustrous morning in May emerging from dew-drenched meadows and the boat-crowded Isis,[2] with ringing out of the skies and towers above them—bells, bells, bells, bells....

'And then there was *another* extraordinary passenger, a young man with hair like a nest of serpents, you know, and when he understood I would *not* eat a "two-egg mamlet" offered to me by this *incredibly* ragged and *totally* sooty little urchin with a tin tray under his arm, nor even a "*one*-egg mamlet" to please him or anyone, this marvellous person leapt down from the bunk above my head, and shot out of the door—oh, I assure you we were at a standstill, in the most *desolate* little station imaginable, for no reason I could see or guess at if I cudgelled my brains ever so *ferociously*—and then he returned with a basket *overflowing* with fruit, a positive *cornucopia*. Sarla, you'd have *fainted* with bliss! Never did you see such fruit; oh, nowhere, nowhere on those mythical farms of California, certainly, worked on by those armies of the exploited from the sad lands to the south, I assure you, Ravi, such fruit as seemed a reincarnation of the fruit one ate as a child, *stolen*, you know, from the neighbour's orchard, fruit one ate hidden in the *darkest* recesses of one's compound, surreptitiously, one's tongue absolutely *shrivelled* by the *piercing* sweetness of the mangoes, the *cruel* tartness of unripe guavas, the unripe pulp of the plantains. Oh, Sarla, such joys! And I sat peeling a *tiny* banana and eating it—it was no bigger than my little finger and contained the flavour of the ripest, sweetest, best banana anywhere on earth within its cunning little yellow speckled jacket—I asked, naturally, what I owed him. But that incredible young man, who looked something like a cornucopia *himself*, with that abundant hair—it had such a quality of *liveliness* about it, every strand almost *electric* with energy—he merely folded his hands and said he would not take one paisa[3] from me, not *one*. *Well*, of course I pushed away the basket and said I could not possibly accept it, totally against my principles, etcetera, and he gave me this tender, tender smile, quite unspeakably loving, and said he could take nothing from me because in a previous incarnation I had been his grandfather: he recognised me. "What?" said I, "*what*? What makes you say so? How *can* you say so?"'

'Watch out!' Ravi shouted at the driver who overtook a bullock cart so closely he almost ran into its great creaking wheels and overturned it.

'And he merely smiled, this sweet, *ineffably* sweet smile of his, and assured me I was no other than this esteemed ancestor of his who had left his home and family at the age of fifty and gone off into the Himalayas to live as a hermit and meditate. "Well," said I—'

'Slow down,' Ravi ordered the driver curtly.

"'*Well*,*"* said I, "I *assure* you I have never been in the Himalayas—although it is *indeed* my life's ambition to do so, and therefore I could not have

---

1. A loose piece of clothing, wrapped around the lower part of the body, worn by Hindu men in India.
2. The upper part of the river Thames, in Oxford; the university's boat races are held there in May.
3. I.e., one cent (there are 100 paise in 1 rupee, which itself is worth about $0.02).

returned from there." By the way, I began to wonder if it was *altogether* flattering to be called grandfather by a man by no means in the first flush of youth, more like the becalmed middle years, whereupon he told me—imagine, Sarla, imagine, Ravi—he told me his grandfather had *died* there, in Rishikesh, on the banks of the Ganga, many years ago. His family had all travelled up from Madras to witness the cremation and carry the ashes to Benares,[4] but *now*, in the railway carriage, that little tin box *baking* in the sun as we crossed the red earth and ravines of Central India, he claimed he'd seen his reincarnation. He was as *certain* of it as the banana in my hand was a banana! He would not tell me *why*, or *how*, but he was clearly a clairvoyant. And isn't that a *superb* combination: clearly clairvoyant! Or do you think it a touch *de trop?*[5] Hmm, Ravi, Sarla?'

The car lurched around one of the countless circles set within the radiating avenues of New Delhi, now steadily filling with traffic that streamed towards the city's business and government centres, far from this region of immense jamun trees,[6] large low villas, smooth hedges, closed gates, sentries in sentry boxes, and parakeets in flamboyant trees.

'But that is the kind of experience, the kind of encounter that India bestows on one like a *gift*, a *jewel*,' Raja was fluting as the car drew up at one of the closed gates. The driver honked the horn discreetly, the watchman came hurrying to unlock it, and they swept in and up the drive to the porch that stood loaded with the weight of magenta bougainvillea. 'And,' Raja continued as he let the driver help him out of the car, 'I was so *delighted*, so *overjoyed* to find it still so, Ravi, in spite of that frightful man you have installed as the head of your government—an *economist*, is he not?[7]—yes, please, I shall need that bag almost *immediately*, and the other too, if I am to bathe and refresh myself, *but*,' he concluded, triumphantly, 'what further refreshment can one *possibly* require after one has already been blessed with such, such *enchanting* acceptance, not, not physical, but positively, positively . . .'

'Spiritual?' Ravi ventured, smiling, as he helped Raja up the stairs into the shaded cool of the veranda with its pots of flowers and ferns, a slowly revolving electric fan and an arrangement of wicker furniture where he lowered Raja into an armchair with a flowered cushion.

It was not that Raja was any more elderly than they. They had all been contemporaries at Oxford, and Raja may even have been a year or two younger. Sarla had complained that his southern ancestry had given Raja an unfair advantage over their northern genes which seemed to produce businessmen and shopkeepers more readily than mathematicians or philosophers. Yet there was about him an air of fragility, of some precious commodity that they had been called upon to cherish. At Oxford Ravi had found himself taking Raja's laundry to be done while Raja, who had neglected to attend to it till he had absolutely nothing left to wear, had stayed in bed under his blankets till Ravi returned with fresh clothes. He was wryly amused as well as a little annoyed to find that he still fell into the trap.

---

4. Varanasi, a Hindu holy city on the river Ganges; it is also sacred to Jains, Sikhs, and Buddhists.
5. Too much (French).
6. Flowering trees, native to central India; they bear a grapefruit-like fruit.

7. Vishwanath Pratap Singh (b. 1931), who was finance minister in the 1980s, served as India's prime minister (1989–90) in a minority government.

Sarla was hurrying into the house, to make sure Raja's luggage was carried carefully into the room prepared for him—the bedroom at the back of the house, which Raja loved because it looked onto a garden full of lemon trees and jasmine vines that he said he dreamt about during that part of the year that he spent in Los Angeles—and against Raja's wishes to order breakfast, because, after all, she and Ravi had not benefited from the generosity of the young man with hair like a serpent's nest in the railway carriage, she said a little acidly.

Why her words sounded acid, she could not say. It was all she could do not to go down on her knees and remove Raja's slippers from his feet, or to bring water in a basin and wash them. She had to sharpen her faculties to fight that urge. But she brought out the coffee pot herself—she had taken the silver coffee service out of storage for Raja's visit—and poured him a cup with all the grace that she had acquired in her years as a diplomat's wife in the embassies and High Commissions where Ravi had 'served', she 'presided'. She could scarcely restrain herself, only tremblingly managed to restrain herself from mentioning that last day in May, that last embrace—oh, it would be so unsuitable, so unsuitable—

And then a second car came sweeping up the drive, parked beside theirs— an identical car, a silver-grey Ambassador with tinted glass and window curtains—and her sister tumbled out of the driver's seat, a woman almost identical to Sarla, and in an equal state of excitement and agitation. And then they *were* all embracing each other, after all, successively, simultaneously.

Maya had not been with them on the bank of the festive, the bacchanalian Isis that May morning; she had not fetched Raja's laundry or cooked him rice on a gas ring on foggy winter nights when he could not walk to the Indian restaurant in the cold, not with his asthmatic condition: Maya had been at the London School of Economics a few years later. Maya had also met her husband at university, but his path had been different from Ravi's. 'No bloody Civil Service for me; I've always thought it most *uncivil*,' Pravin had declared when Maya suggested it, 'and at this stage of history can you really contemplate anything so reactionary? Are we not moving into the future, *free* of colonial institutions?' So it had been a political career for Pravin, not the dirty politics of people Raja had just referred to so disparagingly, but politics as practised by the press, idealistically, morally, scrupulously (even if only on paper). And so, when Maya embraced Raja, it was with vigour, with her head tossed back with pride so that her now grey hair hung from her shoulders with as carefree an air as a young girl might toss her darker, glossier locks, and with a laugh that rang out resonantly. 'What, you've travelled by train in a silk dhoti? Oh Raja, must you go to such *extremes* when you play the the southern gentleman visiting the barbarians of the north?' and Raja hung upon her shoulder and shook his finger at her, fluting at a higher pitch than ever before, 'Is that husband of yours still playing the patriot while dressed in Harris tweeds,[8] and does he still wear that mouldy felt hat when following the elections amongst the cow-dung patties and buffalo sheds of Bihar?' and Sarla was retreating to the wicker sofa with the coffee tray, glowering, turning ashen and tight-lipped once more. But her

---

8. Popular type of tweed clothing made of cloth handwoven on Harris and other islands in Scotland's Outer Hebrides.

occupation of the sofa was strategic—now Maya and Raja could not sit upon it, side by side: it belonged to her, and she could preside, icily, silver coffee pot in hand, looking upon the two as if they were somewhat trying children, and Ravi would give her a look—of sympathy, or pity?—from the stool on which he perched, waiting patiently to be passed a cup.

She passed it, then said, interrupting Maya who was giving a humorous account of the last election campaign Pravin had covered, 'If to go to the Himalayas is your life's ambition, Raja, then that can easily be achieved. Won't you consider driving up with us when we go for the summer to *Winhaven*?'

'Winhaven? Winhaven?' Raja twisted around to her. 'Oh, Sarla, Sarla, the very word, the very name—it recalls—how does it go—

> "I have desired to go
> Where springs not fail—"

and then? And then? How does it go—

> "And I have asked to be
> Where no storms come
> Where the green swell is in the heaven's dumb,
> And out of the swing of the sea—"[9]

remember? remember?'

Who did not? Who did not, Sarla would have liked to know, but suddenly Simba was upon them, bursting out of the house, his great tail thumping, his claws slithering across the veranda tiles in his excitement as he dashed at Maya, then at Ravi, finally at Raja and, to Sarla's horror, Raja was pushed back into his chair by Simba's vigorous attention, but Raja was pushing back at him, laughing, 'Oh, Simba, Simba of the Kenyan highlands![1] You remember me, do you?' and Sarla, cupping her chin in her hand, leaving her coffee untouched, watched as Raja, suddenly as sprightly as a boy, the boy who had bicycled helter-skelter down the streets of Oxford, dark hair rising up from his great brow and falling into the luminous eyes, now ran down the stairs with Simba into the garden, then bent to pick up a stick and send it flying up at the morning sun for the pleasure of having Simba leap for it. Old Simba, usually so gloomy, so lethargic, was now springing up on his hindlegs to catch the falling toy and run with it into the shade of the flamboyant tree, Raja following him, his pale silk dhoti floating about him, his white hair glistening, making the startled parakeets fly out of the clusters of scarlet flowers with screams.

Then both Sarla and Maya released small sighs. Ravi watched their expressions from the stool on which he was perched, and finally asked, diffidently, 'May I have a lump of sugar and a little milk, please?'

In spite of his poetic response to Sarla's suggestion that he accompany them to the mountains, Raja continuously postponed the journey. No, he had come to Delhi, all the way to Delhi in the heat of June, to see them, to relive the remembered joys of their beautiful home. How could he cut short his

---

9. Quoted from Gerard Manley Hopkins's "Heaven-Haven" (written ca. 1865).

1. *Simba* means "lion" in Swahili.

time here? And there was so much for him to see, to do, to catch up on. He wanted Sarla to drive him to the silver market in Chandni Chowk so he could gaze upon the magnificent craftsmanship on display there, perhaps even purchase a piece to take back with him to California where the natives had never seen such art bestowed upon craft, and then if Maya were to accompany him to the Cottage Industries emporium, and help him select a pashmina[2] shawl, then he could be happy even on those chill, rainy days that he was forced to endure. What, didn't they *know*, California had such weather? Had they been deceived by posters of palm trees and golden beaches? Didn't they know the *fraudulence* inherent in the very notion and practice of tourism, that abominable habit of the Western world? Tourism! Now, when *he* returned to India, it was not to see the sights, he already knew them—they were imprinted upon his heart—but to imbibe them, savour them, nourish himself upon them. And so when Sarla and Ravi took him to Nizamuddin[3] and beside the saint's tomb they heard a blind beggar play his lute and sing in a voice so soulful that it melted one's very being,

> 'When I was born
> I was my mother's prince.
> When I married
> I became my wife's king.
> But you have reduced me
> To being a beggar, Lord,
> Come begging for alms
> With my hands outstretched—'

it was as if the thirst of Raja's pilgrim soul was being slaked, and never had thirst been slaked by music so sublime as made by this ancient beggar in his rags, a tin can at his knee for alms—and of course he must have whatever was in Raja's purse, every last coin, alas that they were so few. Now if this beggar were performing in the West, the great theatres of every metropolis would throw open their doors to him. He would perform under floodlights, his name would be on posters, in the papers, on everyone's lips. Gold would pile up at his feet—but then, would he be such a singer as he was now, a pilgrim soul content to sit in the shade of the great saint Nizamuddin's little fretted marble tomb, and dedicate his song to him as homage?

Raja, leaving his slippers at the gateway to the courtyard, approached the tomb with such ecstasy etched upon his noble features that Sarla, and Ravi too, found themselves gazing at him rather than about them—Sarla's bare and Ravi's stockinged feet on the stones, braving the dirt and flies and garbage that had first made them shrink and half turn away. Sarla had held her sari to her nose as they passed a row of butchers' shops on their way to the tomb, buffalo's innards had hung like curtains in the small booths, and the air was rife with raw blood and the thrum of flies, and she asked Raja, in the car, 'How is it that you, a vegetarian, a Brahmin, walked in there and never even twitched your *nose*?' He cast his eyes upon her briefly—and they were still those narrow, horizontal pools of darkness she remembered—and sighed, 'My dear, true souls do not turn away from humanity or, if they do,

---

2. A fine wool made from the undercoat of domestic Himalayan goats.
3. The shrine in Delhi of Hazrat Nizamuddin Auliya (d. 1325 C.E.), a Sufi saint (Sufism is an ascetic and mystic movement within Islam).

it is only to meditate and pray, then come back, fortified, to embrace it—beggars, thieves, lepers, whoever—their sores, their rags. They do not flinch from them, for they know these are only the covering, the concealing robes of the soul, don't you know?' and Sarla, and Ravi, seated on either side of Raja on the comfortably upholstered back seat of the air-conditioned Ambassador, now speeding past the Lodi Gardens to their own green enclave, wondered if Raja was referring to himself or the sufi.

That afternoon, as they sat on the veranda, sipping tea and nibbling at the biscuits[4] the cook had sent up in a temper (he was supposed to be on leave, he was not going to bake fancy cakes at a time when he was rightfully to have had his summer vacation, and so the sahibs could do with biscuits bought in the bazaar), Raja, a little melancholy, a little subdued—which Sarla and Ravi put down to the impression left on him by their visit to the sufi's tomb—piped up in a beseeching voice, 'Sarla, Ravi, where are those ravishing friends of yours I met when you were at the High Commission in London? The Dutta-Rays, was it not? You must know who I mean—you told me how they'd returned to Delhi and built this absolutely fabulous hacienda in Vasant Vihar. Isn't that quite close by?'

'It is,' Ravi admitted.

Like a persistent child, Raja continued, 'Then *why* don't we have them over? This evening? I remember she sang like a nightingale—those melancholy, funereal songs of Tagore's.[5] Wouldn't they be perfect on an evening like this which simply hangs suspended in time, don't you know, as if the dust and heat were holding it in their *cruel* grasp? Oh, Sarla, do telephone, do send for her—tell her I *pine* to hear the sound of her avian voice. Just for that, I'm even willing to put up with her husband who I remember finding—how shall I put it—a *trifle* wanting?'

Sarla found herself quite unwilling. Truth be told, the morning's expedition had left her with a splitting headache; she was not in the habit of walking around in the midday sun, leave that to mad dogs and[6]—she'd always said. Even now, her temples throbbed and perspiration trickled discreetly down the back of her knees, invisible under the fresh cotton sari she'd donned for tea. But Raja would not hear of a refusal, or accept any excuse. If she thought the Dutta-Rays had left for Kashmir, why did she not ring and find out? Oh, there was no need to get up and *go* to the telephone—'In this land of fantasies fulfilled, isn't there always a willing handmaid, so to speak, to bring the mountain to Mohammed?'[7] and Sarla had to send for the telephone to be brought out to the veranda, the servant Balu unwinding the telephone line all the way, and she was forced to speak into it and verify that the Dutta-Rays were indeed still in Delhi, held up by a visit from a former colleague at India House, but were going out that evening to that party—didn't Sarla and Ravi know of it? 'We're supposed to be *away*,' Sarla said stiffly into the tele-

---

4. Cookies.
5. Sir Rabindrath Tagore (1861–1941), Indian Bengali poet and composer who set hundreds of poems to music.
6. An allusion to Noel Coward's song "Mad Dogs and Englishmen" (1932), whose refrain stresses that only "Mad dogs and Englishmen go out in the midday sun."

7. The proverbial saying is "If the mountain will not come to Muhammed, Muhammed will go to the mountain." According to legend, the founder of Islam (ca. 570–632 C.E.), as proof of his teachings, ordered Mount Safa (a hill in Mecca, Saudi Arabia) to come to him. He took its failure to move as proof of God's mercy, for the mountain would have killed them.

phone. 'Everyone thinks we are in the *hills* by now. We usually are.' Well, the Dutta-Rays would drop in on their way—and so they did, she a vision of grace in her finely embroidered Lucknow sari, pale green on white, to Raja's great delight, and only too willing to sing for his delectation, only not tonight since they were already late.

So Sarla and Ravi found themselves throwing a party—a party that was to be the setting for a recital given by Ila Dutta-Ray, a woman neither of them had any warm feelings for, remembering how unhelpful she had been when they had first arrived in London and so badly needed help in finding a flat, engaging servants, placing their children in school, all so long ago of course. Instead of *helping*, she had sent them her old cook, declaring he was the best, but really saving herself the air fare back to India because he proved good for nothing but superannuation. They rang up whoever of their circle of friends remained in Delhi to invite them for the occasion. It was quite extraordinary how many friends Raja remembered and managed to trace, and also how many who were on the point of going away, changed their plans on hearing his name and assured Sarla and Ravi they would come.

Then there occurred a dreadful incident: Sarla was choosing from amongst her saris one cool enough for the evening ahead, which was, of course, one of the summer's worst, that kind of still, yellow, lurid evening that it inflicted when one thought one could bear no more, and meant that the recital would be held not in the garden after all but in the air-conditioned drawing room instead, when a terrible thought struck her: she had forgotten to invite Maya! Maya and her husband Pravin! How could she have? It was true Maya had told her Pravin was very preoccupied with a special issue his paper was bringing out on the rise of Hindu fundamentalism but that was no reason to assume they might not be free. Sarla stood in front of the mirror that was attached to one leaf of the armoire, and clasped her hand over her mouth with a look so stricken that Ravi, coming in to ask what glasses should be taken out for the evening, wondered if she had a sudden toothache. 'Ravi! Oh, Ravi,' she wailed.

The telephone was brought to her—Balu unwinding the coils of an endless wire—and the number dialled for her. Then Sarla spoke into it in gasps, but unfortunately she had not taken the time to collect her wits and phrase her invitation with more tact. Maya's sharp ears picked up every indication that her sister had been unforgivably remiss, and coldly rejected the insulting last-minute invitation, insisting proudly that Pravin was working late and she could not possibly leave his side, he never wrote a line without consulting her.

As if that was not agony enough, Sarla had to undergo the further humiliation of Raja piping up in the middle of the party—just as Ila Dutta-Ray was tuning her tanpura and about to open her mouth and utter the first note of her song—'But Sarla, where is Maya, that aficionado of Tagore's music? *Surely* we should wait for her? *Why* is she so late?' An awful hush fell—and Sarla again assumed her stricken look. What was she to say, how was she to explain? She found herself stumbling over Maya's insincere excuse, but of course everyone guessed. Frowning in disapproval, Ila Dutta-Ray began her song on a very low, very deep and hoarse note.

In retaliation, Maya and Pravin threw a party as soon as Pravin's column had been written and the special issue had gone to press, and *their* party was in honour of the Minister of Human Resources, whose wife was such an admirer of Raja's, had read every word he had written and wanted so much to meet him—'in an intimate setting'. Since she had made this special request, they had felt obliged to cut down their guest list—and were sure Sarla and Ravi would not mind since they had the pleasure of Raja's company every day. But when Ravi stoically offered to drive Raja across to their house, he found the whole road lined with cars, many of them chauffeur-driven and with government number plates, and had the humiliation of backing out of it after dropping Raja at the gate, then returning to Sarla who had given way to a fierce migraine and was insisting that they book seats on a train to the hills as soon as possible.

'But don't we need to wait till Raja is gone?'

'Raja is incapable of making decisions—we'll have to make his for him,' she snapped, waving at Balu who was slouching in the doorway, waiting to take away the remains of their meagre supper from the dining table.

She was still agonised enough the following morning—digging violently into half a ripe papaya in the blazing light that spilt over the veranda even at that early hour—actually to ask Raja, 'How can you bear this heat? Do you really not mind it? I feel I'm going to collapse—'

Raja, who had a look of sleepy contentment on his face—he had already meditated for an hour in the garden, done his yoga exercises, bathed, drunk his tea and had every reason to look forward to another day—did not seem to catch her meaning at all. Reaching out to stroke her hand, he said, 'I know what you need, my dear—a walk in the sublime Lodi Gardens when the sun is setting and Venus appears in the sky so *silently*—' and went on to describe the ruins, their patina of lichen, their tiles of Persian blue, the echoes that rang beneath their domes, in such terms that Sarla sank back in her chair, sighing, agreeing.

What she did not know was that he had already arranged to walk there with Maya, Ila Dutta-Ray, and the wife of the Minister of Human Resources who, it turned out, had read that book of verses he had written when in Oxford and had published by a small press in London, long expired, so that copies were now collectors' pieces. All three women owned such copies. And Sarla found herself trailing behind them while Raja pranced, actually pranced with delight, with enthusiasm, in their company. At their suggestion he recited these verses:

> 'The lamp of heaven is hung upon the citrus bough,
> The nightingale falls silent.
> All is waiting,
> For a royal visit by night's own queen—'

and then burst into mocking, self-deprecating laughter, waving away their protests to say, 'Oh, those adolescent excesses! What was I *thinking* of, in Oxford, in the fog and the smog and the cold I suffered from perpetually! Well, you know, I was thinking of—*this*,' and he waved at the walled rose garden and beyond it the pond and beyond that the tombs of the Lodi emperors surrounded by neem trees,[8] and they all gazed with him. Eventually the Minister's wife sighed, 'You make us all see it with new eyes, as if we had never seen it before.'

---

8. Tropical trees of the mahogany family.

Sarla, who had hung back, and was standing by a rose bush, fingering the fine petals of one flower pensively, realised that this was so exactly true: it was Raja who opened their eyes, who made them see it as they never saw it themselves, as a place of magic, enchantment, of pleasure so immense and rich that it could never be exhausted. She gazed at his back, his noble head, the silvery hair, the gracefully gesturing arm in its white muslin sleeve, there in the shade of the neem tree, totally disregarding the dust, the smouldering heat at the summer day's end, and seeing it all as romantic, paradisaical—and she clasped her hands together, pressing a petal between them, grateful for knowing him.

That evening she tried again. 'Raja, I *know* you would love Winhaven,' she told him, interrupting the Vedic hymn he was reciting to prove to Ravi that his Sanskrit was still fluent—hadn't he taught it to the golden youth of Berkeley, of Stanford, of the universities in Los Angeles and San Francisco, for all these years of his exile? 'And I would love to see you in the Himalayas,' she went on, raising her voice, 'because they would make the most perfect setting for you. Perhaps you would begin to write again over there—'

'But darling Sarla,' Raja beamed at her, showing both the pleasure he took in her suggestion and his determination not to be swept away by it, 'Maya tells me there is to be a lecture at India International Centre next week on the Himalayas as an inspiration for Indian poets through the centuries, and I would *hate* to miss it. It's to be given by Professor Dandavate, that old bore—d'you remember him? What a *dreary* young man he was at Oxford! I can quite imagine how much drearier he is now—and I can't resist the opportunity to pick holes in all he says, and in public too—'

'But next week?' Sarla enquired helplessly. 'It'll—it'll be even hotter.'

'Sarla, don't you *ever* think of anything else?' he reproved her gently, although with a little twitch of impatience about his eyes. 'Now I don't *ever* notice the heat. Drink the delicious fresh lemonades your marvellous cook makes, rest in the afternoons, and there's no reason why you shouldn't *enjoy* the summer. Oh, think of the fruit alone that summer brings us—'

But it was the marvellous cook himself who brought an end to Raja's idyll in Sarla and Ravi's gracious home: that very day he took off his apron, laid down his egg whisk and his market bag, declared that enough was enough, that he was needed in his village to bring in the harvest before the monsoon arrived. He was already late and had received a postcard from his son to say they could not delay it by another day. He demanded his salary and caught his train.

Sarla was sufficiently outraged by his treachery to make the afternoon tea herself, braving the inferno of the kitchen where she seldom had need to venture, and was rewarded by Raja's happy and Ravi's proud beam as she brought out the tea tray to the veranda. But dinner proved something else altogether. Balu showed not the slightest inclination that he meant to help: he kept to the pantry with grim determination, giving the glasses and silver another polishing rather than take a step into the kitchen. Sarla had a whispered consultation with Ravi, suggesting they take Raja out to India International Centre or the Gymkhana Club for dinner, but Ravi reminded her that the car had gone for servicing and they could go nowhere tonight. Sarla, her sari end tucked in at her waist, wiping the perspiration from her face with her elbow, went back into the kitchen and peered into its recesses to see if the cook had not repented and left some cooked food for them after all, but she found little that she could put together even if she knew how. At one point, she even telephoned Maya to see if her sister would not come to her aid—Maya was known for her superb culinary skill—but there was no answer: Maya and Pravin were out. It was to an embarassingly inadequate repast of sliced cucumber, yoghurt and bread that the three finally sat down—Balu looking as if it were far beneath his dignity to serve such an excuse for a meal, Sarla tight-lipped with anger with herself for failing so blatantly, Ravi trying, with embarrassed sincerity, to thank her for her brave effort, and Raja saying nothing at all, but quietly crumbling the bread beside his plate till he confessed a wish to go to bed early.

But this meant that he was up earlier than ever next morning, and by the time Sarla rose and went wearily kitchenwards to make him tea, he had been awake for hours, performed his yoga and meditation, walked Simba round the garden several times, and was waiting querulously for it. Balu was nowhere to be seen. When Sarla went in search of him—surely he should have been able to make their guest a cup of tea?—she found the door to his room shut, coloured cutouts from film magazines of starlets in swimsuits stuck all over it, and when she called out his name, heard only a groan in reply. In agitation, she hurried to find Ravi and send him to find out what was wrong. Ravi went in reluctantly, his face bearing an expression of martyrdom, and reappeared to inform her that Balu was suffering from a stomach ache and needed to be taken to a doctor. '*You* do that,' she snapped at him, hardly able to believe this terrible turn in their fortunes.

By lunchtime Raja had made a series of phone calls and discovered that the Dutta-Rays were leaving for Kashmir next day and would be only too delighted to have him accompany them. Sarla stood in the doorway, watching him pack his little bag with beautifully laundered underwear, and wailed, 'But Raja, if you had wanted to go to the hills, we could have gone to Winhaven *ages* ago! I *asked* you, you remember?'

Raja gave her a look that said, 'Winhaven? With you? When I can be on a houseboat in Kashmir with Ila instead?' but of course what he really did was blow her a kiss across the room and whisper conspiratorially, 'Darling, think of the *stories* I'll come back with to entertain you,' and snapped shut the lock on his bag with a satisfied click.

'Simba! Simba!' Ravi put his hands around his mouth and called after the dog who had loped away up to the top of the hill and vanished. Then he turned around to look for Sarla. He could see neither his dog nor his wife— one had gone too far ahead, the other lagged too far behind. He lowered himself onto a rock to catch his breath and picked up a pine cone to toss from hand to hand while he waited, whistling a little tune.

Evening light flooded down from the vast sky, spilling over the pine needles and stones of the hillside. Everything seemed to be bathed in its pale saffron glow. An eagle drifted through the ravine below. He could hear the wind in its feathers, a melancholy whistle.

'Sarla?' he called out finally, and just then saw her come into sight on a turn of the path below him, amongst a mass of blackberry bushes. She seemed to be dragging herself along, her sari trailing in the white dust, her head bowed over the walking stick she held in a slightly trembling hand.

At his voice she looked up and her face was haggard. He stared in surprise: he had not considered this such a difficult climb, or so long a walk. It was where they had always come, to watch the sunset. He himself could still spring up it with no more than a little panting. 'Sarla?' he asked questioningly. 'Want some help, old girl?'

'Coming, coming,' she grumbled, toiling on, 'can't you see I'm coming?'

When she reached the rock where he was waiting, she sank down onto it and wiped her face with the corner of her sari. 'I can't do these climbs any more,' she admitted, with a wince. 'You had better do them alone.'

'Oh, Sarla,' he said, catching up her hand in his, 'I would never want to come up here without you, you know.' They sat there a while, breathing deeply. Beside them a small cricket began to chirp and chirp, and after some time it was no longer light that came spilling down the hill, but shadows.

2000

CARYL CHURCHILL
b. 1938

A remarkably theatrical episode opens Caryl Churchill's play *Top Girls* (1982), providing a visual and dramatic contrast with the rest of the action and posing crucial questions about the impact of history on women's lives. The first scene, a pointedly unrealistic, even surrealistic dinner party, brings together women from different periods, various regions, and distinct states of being, for while two are actual historical persons, one is a character in a narrative, another a figure in a painting, and yet another a personage who is very likely apocryphal. On stage, the pageantry of the oddly dissimilar costumes displayed by, among others, Chaucer's Patient Griselda, Brueghel's Dull Gret, and the Japanese courtesan Lady Nijo makes the beginning of *Top Girls* almost seem like a kind of carnival. But all the other scenes focus on the everyday lives of an executive in an employment agency in contemporary London as well as on the ordinary existences of several members of her family. Structurally as well as thematically, therefore, Churchill's play asks, What is the relationship between women's past—as represented in literature, painting, and legend or in the lives of prominent women from earlier periods—and the situation in which women find themselves today? Has our history evolved, gaining women greater freedom, or has it devolved, generating more calamitous constrictions, or has there been no real change at all? More specifically, what transformations has the women's movement brought about for those notable women Churchill calls "top girls"? Just as important to the playwright, what modifications has the movement brought about for those women at the bottom of the class system?

Not simply experimental in its use of characters, *Top Girls* also deploys a host of other formally fascinating techniques: speeches are typographically marked, for example, to indicate interruptions as well as simultaneous talking; the actors who play legendary female characters in the first scene reappear in the roles of contemporary women in later scenes—and such double-casting can be used by a director to draw connections between the past and the present; the time line of the play is not strictly chronological, since the last scene in act 2 occurs a year before the scene that precedes it. These unconventional techniques may make the play a challenge to the reader who does not actually see it on stage, but they also typify the brilliant strategies

Caryl Churchill has used since her early radio play, *The Ants* (1962), and her early major stage plays, *Owners* (1972) and *Objections to Sex and Violence* (1975). As these works indicate, from the beginning of her career this artist has tied formal experimentation to her interest in feminism and socialism in order to address such issues as state violence, economic dispossession, and sexual politics.

An only child and London born, Churchill has attributed her attraction to show business to her parents' occupations. Her father was a political cartoonist, and she has explained that "Cartoons are really so much like plays. An image with somebody saying something." Her mother was a secretary, a model, and a minor film actress. From 1948 to 1956, the family lived in Canada, where Churchill attended the Trafalgar School in Montreal. During her English studies at Lady Margaret Hall, Oxford, Churchill began writing plays, although after her marriage to David Harter in 1961 and the birth of her three children, as well as a succession of miscarriages, she found herself leading a solitary life "of being a barrister's wife and just being at home." Her husband's decision to leave private practice to work for a legal aid group in 1972 and their subsequent travels helped shape her almost instantaneously successful writing career.

Two productions in 1976—*Light Shining in Buckinghamshire* and *Vinegar Tom*—demonstrate both Churchill's fascination with history and her collaborative interaction with experimental theater workshops. But it was the satirical farce *Cloud Nine* (1979) that first brought her success outside of London; when the play opened off-Broadway in New York, it was welcomed by critics as "the most rewarding surprise of the theatrical season," ran for two years, and won three Obie awards. With its first act set in Victorian Africa and its second in contemporary London, its black character played by a white, and its cross-sex casting (male roles played by women and female roles played by men), *Cloud Nine* continued to explore what Churchill called her "two preoccupations": "people's internal states of being and the external political structures which affect them, which make them insane." Possibly her best-known play, *Top Girls* was followed by such productions as *Fen* (1983), *Serious Money* (1987), *Ice Cream* (1989), *Mad Forest* (1990), and *The Skriker* (1994). Taken together, they explain why Churchill has been praised by so many audiences for the audacity and wit with which she addresses the psychological, sexual, social, and economic complexities of modern life.

Top Girls

Top Girls was first performed at the Royal Court Theatre, London, on 28 August 1982 with the following cast:

MARLENE	Gwen Taylor
ISABELLA BIRD / JOYCE / MRS. KIDD	Deborah Findlay
LADY NIJO / WIN	Lindsay Duncan
DULL GRET / ANGIE	Carole Hayman
POPE JOAN / LOUISE	Selina Cadell
PATIENT GRISELDA / NELL / JEANINE	Lesley Manville
WAITRESS / KIT / SHONA	Lou Wakefield

Directed by Max Stafford Clark
Designed by Peter Hartwell

This production transferred to Joe Papp's Public Theatre, New York, later the same year, and returned to the Royal Court early in 1983.

ACT ONE

Scene One: Restaurant. Saturday night.
Scene Two: "Top Girls" Employment agency. Monday morning.
Scene Three: Joyce's back yard. Sunday afternoon.

ACT TWO

Scene One: Employment agency. Monday morning.
Scene Two: Joyce's kitchen. Sunday evening, a year earlier.

Note on Characters

ISABELLA BIRD   (1831–1904) lived in Edinburgh, traveled extensively between the ages of 40 and 70.
LADY NIJO   (b. 1258), Japanese, was an Emperor's courtesan and later a Buddhist nun who traveled on foot through Japan.
DULL GRET   is the subject of the Brueghel painting, *Dulle Griet*,[1] in which a woman in an apron and armor leads a crowd of women charging through hell and fighting the devils.
POPE JOAN,   disguised as a man, is thought to have been Pope between 854–856.
PATIENT GRISELDA   is the obedient wife whose story is told by Chaucer in The Clerk's Tale of *The Canterbury Tales*.

Note on Layout

A speech usually follows the one immediately before it BUT:
1. When one character starts speaking before the other has finished, the point of interruption is marked /.
e.g., ISABELLA.   This is the Emperor of Japan? / I once met the Emperor of Morocco.
NIJO.   In fact he was the ex-Emperor.

2. A character sometimes continues speaking right through another's speech:
e.g., ISABELLA.   When I was forty I thought my life was over. / Oh I was pitiful. I was
NIJO.   I didn't say I felt it for twenty years. Not every minute.
ISABELLA.   sent on a cruise for my health and I felt even worse. Pains in my bones, pins and needles . . . etc.

3. Sometimes a speech follows on from a speech earlier than the one immediately before it, and continuity is marked *.

---

1. This 1562 painting by Pieter Brueghel the Elder (ca. 1525–1569) is also known as *Mad Meg*.

e.g., GRISELDA. I'd seen him riding by, we all had. And he'd seen me in the fields with the sheep*.
ISABELLA. I would have been well suited to minding sheep.
NIJO. And Mr. Nugent riding by.
ISABELLA. Of course not, Nijo, I mean a healthy life in the open air.
JOAN. *He just rode up while you were minding the sheep and asked you to marry him?

where "in the fields with the sheep" is the cue to both "I would have been" and "He just rode up."

Act One

SCENE ONE

Restaurant. Table set for dinner with white tablecloth. Six places. MARLENE *and* WAITRESS.

MARLENE. Excellent, yes, table for six. One of them's going to be late but we won't wait. I'd like a bottle of Frascati straight away if you've got one really cold.
[*The* WAITRESS *goes.* ISABELLA BIRD *arrives.*]
Here we are. Isabella.
ISABELLA. Congratulations, my dear.
MARLENE. Well, it's a step. It makes for a party. I haven't time for a holiday. I'd like to go somewhere exotic like you but I can't get away. I don't know how you could bear to leave Hawaii. / I'd like to lie in the sun forever, except of course I
ISABELLA. I did think of settling.
MARLENE. can't bear sitting still.
ISABELLA. I sent for my sister Hennie to come and join me. I said, Hennie we'll live here forever and help the natives. You can buy two sirloins of beef for what a pound of chops costs in Edinburgh. And Hennie wrote back, the dear, that yes, she would come to Hawaii if I wished, but I said she had far better stay where she was. Hennie was suited to life in Tobermory.
MARLENE. Poor Hennie.
ISABELLA. Do you have a sister?
MARLENE. Yes in fact.
ISABELLA. Hennie was happy. She was good. I did miss its face, my own pet. But I couldn't stay in Scotland. I loathed the constant murk.
MARLENE. Ah! Nijo!
[*She sees* LADY NIJO *arrive. The* WAITRESS *enters with wine.*]
NIJO. Marlene!
MARLENE. I think a drink while we wait for the others. I think a drink anyway. What a week.
[*The* WAITRESS *pours wine.*]
NIJO. It was always the men who used to get so drunk. I'd be one of the maidens, passing the sake.
ISABELLA. I've had sake. Small hot drink. Quite fortifying after a day in the wet.

NIJO. One night my father proposed three rounds of three cups, which was normal, and then the Emperor should have said three rounds of three cups, but he said three rounds of nine cups, so you can imagine. Then the Emperor passed his sake cup to my father and said, "Let the wild goose come to me this spring."

MARLENE. Let the what?

NIJO. It's a literary allusion to a tenth-century epic,[2] / His Majesty was very cultured.

ISABELLA. This is the Emperor of Japan? / I once met the Emperor of Morocco.

NIJO. In fact he was the ex-Emperor.

MARLENE. But he wasn't old? / Did you, Isabella?

NIJO. Twenty-nine.

ISABELLA. Oh it's a long story.

MARLENE. Twenty-nine's an excellent age.

NIJO. Well I was only fourteen and I knew he meant something but I didn't know what. He sent me an eight-layered gown and I sent it back. So when the time came I did nothing but cry. My thin gowns were badly ripped. But even that morning when he left /—he'd a green robe with a scarlet lining and

MARLENE. Are you saying he raped you?

NIJO. very heavily embroidered trousers, I already felt different about him. It made me uneasy. No, of course not, Marlene, I belonged to him, it was what I was brought up for from a baby. I soon found I was sad if he stayed away. It was depressing day after day not knowing when he would come. I never enjoyed taking other women to him.

ISABELLA. I certainly never saw my father drunk. He was a clergyman. / And I didn't get married till I was fifty.

[*The* WAITRESS *rings menus.*]

NIJO. Oh, my father was a very religious man. Just before he died he said to me, "Serve His Majesty, be respectful, if you lose his favor enter holy orders."

MARLENE. But he meant stay in a convent, not go wandering round the country.

NIJO. Priests were often vagrants, so why not a nun? You think I shouldn't? / I still did what my father wanted.

MARLENE. No no, I think you should. / I think it was wonderful.

[DULL GRET *arrives.*]

ISABELLA. I tried to do what my father wanted.

MARLENE. Gret, good. Nijo. Gret. / I know Griselda's going to be late, but should we wait for Joan? / Let's get you a drink.

ISABELLA. Hello Gret! [*Continues* NIJO.] I tried to be a clergyman's daughter. Needlework, music, charitable schemes. I had a tumor removed from my spine and spent a great deal of time on the sofa. I studied the metaphysical poets and hymnology. / I thought I enjoyed intellectual pursuits.

NIJO. Ah, you like poetry. I come of a line of eight generations of poets. Father had a poem / in the anthology.

---

2. The reference is to a poem in the Kokinshāu, the first of the anthologies of Japanese poetry compiled by imperial order.

ISABELLA. My father taught me Latin although I was a girl. / But
MARLENE. They didn't have Latin at my school.
ISABELLA. really I was more suited to manual work. Cooking, washing, mending, riding horses. / Better than reading books,
NIJO. Oh but I'm sure you're very clever.
ISABELLA. eh Gret? A rough life in the open air.
NIJO. I can't say I enjoyed my rough life. What I enjoyed most was being the Emperor's favorite / and wearing thin silk.
ISABELLA. Did you have any horses, Gret?
GRET. Pig.
    [POPE JOAN *arrives*.]
MARLENE. Oh Joan, thank God, we can order. Do you know everyone? We were just talking about learning Latin and being clever girls. Joan was by way of an infant prodigy. Of course you were. What excited you when you were ten?
JOAN. Because angels are without matter they are not individuals. Every angel is a species.
MARLENE. There you are.
    [*They laugh. They look at menus.*]
ISABELLA. Yes, I forgot all my Latin. But my father was the mainspring of my life and when he died I was so grieved. I'll have the chicken, please, / and the soup.
NIJO. Of course you were grieved. My father was saying his prayers and he dozed off in the sun. So I touched his knee to rouse him. "I wonder what will happen," he said, and then he was dead before he finished the sentence. / If he'd died saying
MARLENE. What a shock.
NIJO. his prayers he would have gone straight to heaven. / Waldorf salad.
JOAN. Death is the return of all creatures to God.
NIJO. I shouldn't have woken him.
JOAN. Damnation only means ignorance of the truth. I was always attracted by the teachings of John the Scot,[3] though he was inclined to confuse / God and the world.
ISABELLA. Grief always overwhelmed me at the time.
MARLENE. What I fancy is a rare steak. Gret?
ISABELLA. I am of course a member of the / Church of England.*
GRET. Potatoes.
MARLENE. *I haven't been to church for years. / I like Christmas carols.
ISABELLA. Good works matter more than church attendance.
MARLENE. Make that two steaks and a lot of potatoes. Rare. But I don't do good works either.
JOAN. Canelloni, please, / and a salad.
ISABELLA. Well, I tried, but oh dear. Hennie did good works.
NIJO. The first half of my life was all sin and the second / all repentance.*
MARLENE. Oh what about starters?
GRET. Soup.
JOAN. *And which did you like best?

---

3. John Scotus Erigena ("Scottish John born in Ireland"; ca. 810–ca. 880), the earliest scholastic philosopher, whose beliefs were pantheistic and Neoplatonic in spirit.

MARLENE. Were your travels just a penance? Avocado vinaigrette. Didn't you / enjoy yourself?
JOAN. Nothing to start with for me, thank you.
NIJO. Yes, but I was very unhappy. / It hurt to remember
MARLENE. And the wine list.
NIJO. the past. I think that was repentance.
MARLENE. Well I wonder.
NIJO. I might have just been homesick.
MARLENE. Or angry.
NIJO. Not angry, no, / why angry?
GRET. Can we have some more bread?
MARLENE. Don't you get angry? I get angry.
NIJO. But what about?
MARLENE. Yes let's have two more Frascati. And some more bread, please.
   [*The* WAITRESS *exits.*]
ISABELLA. I tried to understand Buddhism when I was in Japan but all this birth and death succeeding each other through eternities just filled me with the most profound melancholy. I do like something more active.
NIJO. You couldn't say I was inactive. I walked every day for twenty years.
ISABELLA. I don't mean walking. / I mean in the head.
NIJO. I vowed to copy five Mahayana sutras.[4] / Do you know how
MARLENE. I don't think religious beliefs are something we have in common. Activity yes.
NIJO. long they are? My head was active. / My head ached.
JOAN. It's no good being active in heresy.
ISABELLA. What heresy? She's calling the Church of England / a heresy.
JOAN. There are some very attractive / heresies.
NIJO. I had never heard of Christianity. Never / heard of it. Barbarians.
MARLENE. Well I'm not a Christian. / And I'm not a Buddhist.
ISABELLA. You have heard of it?
MARLENE. We don't all have to believe the same.
ISABELLA. I knew coming to dinner with a pope we should keep off religion.
JOAN. I always enjoy a theological argument. But I won't try to convert you, I'm not a missionary. Anyway I'm a heresy myself.
ISABELLA. There are some barbaric practices in the east.
NIJO. Barbaric?
ISABELLA. Among the lower classes.
NIJO. I wouldn't know.
ISABELLA. Well theology always made my head ache.
MARLENE. Oh good, some food.
   [WAITRESS *is bringing the first course.*]
NIJO. How else could I have left the court if I wasn't a nun? When father died I had only His Majesty. So when I fell out of favor I had nothing. Religion is a kind of nothing / and I dedicated what was left of me to nothing.

---

4. Discourses of the Buddha. The liberal and theistic Mahayana sects, found mainly in China and Japan, recognize a large body of Buddhist scripture in addition to the canon of the more conservative Theravada Buddhism.

ISABELLA. That's what I mean about Buddhism. It doesn't brace.
MARLENE. Come on, Nijo, have some wine.
NIJO. Haven't you ever felt like that? Nothing will ever happen again. I am dead already. You've all felt / like that.
ISABELLA. You thought your life was over but it wasn't.
JOAN. You wish it was over.
GRET. Sad.
MARLENE. Yes, when I first came to London I sometimes . . . and when I got back from America I did. But only for a few hours. Not twenty years.
ISABELLA. When I was forty I thought my life was over. / Oh I
NIJO. I didn't say I felt it for twenty years. Not every minute.
ISABELLA. was pitiful. I was sent on a cruise for my health and I felt even worse. Pains in my bones, pins and needles in my hands, swelling behind the ears, and—oh, stupidity. I shook all over, indefinable terror. And Australia seemed to me a hideous country, the acacias stank like drains. / I had a
NIJO. You were homesick.
ISABELLA. photograph for Hennie but I told her I wouldn't send it, my hair had fallen out and my clothes were crooked, I looked completely insane and suicidal.
NIJO. So did I, exactly, dressed as a nun. I was wearing walking shoes for the first time.
ISABELLA. I longed to go home, / but home to what? Houses
NIJO. I longed to go back ten years.
ISABELLA. are so perfectly dismal.
MARLENE. I thought traveling cheered you both up.
ISABELLA. Oh it did / of course. It was on the trip from
NIJO. I'm not a cheerful person, Marlene. I just laugh a lot.
ISABELLA. Australia to the Sandwich Isles, I fell in love with the sea. There were rats in the cabin and ants in the food but suddenly it was like a new world. I woke up every morning happy, knowing there would be nothing to annoy me. No nervousness. No dressing.
NIJO. Don't you like getting dressed? I adored my clothes. / When I was chosen to give sake to His Majesty's brother,
MARLENE. You had prettier colors than Isabella.
NIJO. the Emperor Kameyana, on his formal visit, I wore raw silk pleated trousers and a seven-layered gown in shades of red, and two outer garments, / yellow lined with green and a light
MARLENE. Yes, all that silk must have been very . . .

[*The* WAITRESS *starts to clear the first course.*]

JOAN. I dressed as a boy when I left home.*
NIJO. green jacket. Lady Betto had a five-layered gown in shades of green and purple.
ISABELLA. *You dressed as a boy?
MARLENE. Of course, / for safety.
JOAN. It was easy, I was only twelve. / Also women weren't allowed in the library. We wanted to study in Athens.
MARLENE. You ran away alone?
JOAN. No, not alone, I went with my friend. / He was sixteen.
NIJO. Ah, an elopement.

JOAN. but I thought I knew more science than he did and almost as much philosophy.
ISABELLA. Well I always traveled as a lady and I repudiated strongly any suggestion in the press that I was other than feminine.
MARLENE. I don't wear trousers in the office. / I could but I don't.
ISABELLA. There was no great danger to a woman of my age and appearance.
MARLENE. And you got away with it, Joan?
JOAN. I did then.

[*The* WAITRESS *starts to bring the main course.*]

MARLENE. And nobody noticed anything?
JOAN. They noticed I was a very clever boy. / And when I
MARLENE. I couldn't have kept pretending for so long.
JOAN. shared a bed with my friend, that was ordinary—two poor students in a lodging house. I think I forgot I was pretending.
ISABELLA. Rocky Mountain Jim, Mr. Nugent,[5] showed me no disrespect. He found it interesting, I think, that I could make scones and also lasso cattle. Indeed he declared his love for me, which was most distressing.
NIJO. What did he say? / We always sent poems first.
MARLENE. What did you say?
ISABELLA. I urged him to give up whisky, / but he said it was too late.
MARLENE. Oh Isabella.
ISABELLA. He had lived alone in the mountains for many years.
MARLENE. But did you—?

[*The* WAITRESS *goes.*]

ISABELLA. Mr. Nugent was a man that any woman might love but none could marry. I came back to England.
NIJO. Did you write him a poem when you left? / Snow on the
MARLENE. Did you never see him again?
ISABELLA. No, never.
NIJO. mountains. My sleeves are wet with tears. In England no tears, no snow.
ISABELLA. Well, I say never. One morning very early in Switzerland, it was a year later, I had a vision of him as I last saw him / in his trapper's clothes with his hair round his face,
NIJO. A ghost!
ISABELLA. and that was the day, / I learned later, he died with a
NIJO. Ah!
ISABELLA. bullet in his brain. / He just bowed to me and vanished.
MARLENE. Oh Isabella.
NIJO. When your lover dies—One of my lovers died. / The priest Ariake.
JOAN. My friend died. Have we all got dead lovers?
MARLENE. Not me, sorry.
NIJO. [*To* ISABELLA.] I wasn't a nun, I was still at court, but he was a priest, and when he came to me he dedicated his whole life to hell. / He knew that when he died he would fall into one of the three lower realms. And he died, he did die.
JOAN. [*To* MARLENE.] I'd quarreled with him over the teachings of John

---

5. Irish-born trapper (d. 1874), who lived in the Colorado Rockies.

the Scot, who held that our ignorance of God is the same as his ignorance of himself. He only knows what he creates because he creates everything he knows but he himself is above being—do you follow?
MARLENE.   No, but go on.
NIJO.   I couldn't bear to think / in what shape would he be reborn.*
JOAN.   St. Augustine maintained that the Neo-Platonic Ideas[6] are indivisible from God, but I agreed with John that the created
ISABELLA.   *Buddhism is really most uncomfortable.
JOAN.   world is essences derived from Ideas which derived from God. As Denys the Areopagite[7] said—the pseudo-Denys—first we give God a name, then deny it / then reconcile the
NIJO.   In what shape would he return?
JOAN.   contradiction by looking beyond / those terms—
MARLENE.   Sorry, what? Denys said what?
JOAN.   Well we disagreed about it, we quarreled. And next day he was ill, / I was so annoyed with him, all the time I was
NIJO.   Misery in this life and worse in the next, all because of me.
JOAN.   nursing him I kept going over the arguments in my mind. Matter is not a means of knowing the essence. The source of the species is the Idea. But then I realized he'd never understand my arguments again, and that night he died. John the Scot held that the individual disintegrates / and there is no personal immortality.
ISABELLA.   I wouldn't have you think I was in love with Jim Nugent. It was yearning to save him that I felt.
MARLENE.   [*To* JOAN.]   So what did you do?
JOAN.   First I decided to stay a man. I was used to it. And I wanted to devote my life to learning. Do you know why I went to Rome? Italian men didn't have beards.
ISABELLA.   The loves of my life were Hennie, my own pet, and my dear husband the doctor, who nursed Hennie in her last illness. I knew it would be terrible when Hennie died but I didn't know how terrible. I felt half of myself had gone. How could I go on my travels without that sweet soul waiting at home for my letters? It was Doctor Bishop's devotion to her in her last illness that made me decide to marry him. He and Hennie had the same sweet character. I had not.
NIJO.   I thought his majesty had sweet character because when he found out about Ariake he was so kind. But really it was because he no longer cared for me. One night he even sent me out to a man who had been pursuing me. / He lay awake on the other side of the screens and listened.
ISABELLA.   I did wish marriage had seemed more of a step. I tried very hard to cope with the ordinary drudgery of life. I was ill again with carbuncles on the spine and nervous prostration. I ordered a tricycle, that was my idea of adventure then. And John himself fell ill, with erysipelas and anaemia. I began to love him with my whole heart but it was too late.

---

6. Neoplatonic philosophy, as founded by Plotinus (3rd c. C.E.), opposed materialism and introduced the religious conception of "Ideas" (Plato's eternal paradigms) as the thoughts of God. Augustine (354–430), the first great theologian of Christianity, turned to the religion after studying Plato.
7. Dionysius the Areopagite was converted by Paul (Acts 17.34) and, according to tradition, was a martyr and the first bishop of Athens; famous philosophical works attributed to him (as "pseudo-Dionysius"), written in the 5th or 6th century, brought Neoplatonism into Western Christian thought.

He was a skeleton with transparent white hands. I wheeled him on various seafronts in a bathchair. And he faded and left me. There was nothing in my life. The doctors said I had gout / and my heart was much affected.

NIJO. There was nothing in my life, nothing, without the Emperor's favor. The Empress had always been my enemy, Marlene, she said I had no right to wear three-layered gowns. / But I was the adopted daughter of my grandfather the Prime Minister. I had been publicly granted permission to wear thin silk.

JOAN. There was nothing in my life except my studies. I was obsessed with pursuit of the truth. I taught at the Greek School in Rome, which St. Augustine had made famous. I was poor, I worked hard. I spoke apparently brilliantly, I was still very young, I was a stranger; suddenly I was quite famous, I was everyone's favorite. Huge crowds came to hear me. The day after they made me cardinal I fell ill and lay two weeks without speaking, full of terror and regret. / But then I got up

MARLENE. Yes, success is very . . .

JOAN. determined to go on. I was seized again / with a desperate longing for the absolute.

ISABELLA. Yes, yes, to go on. I sat in Tobermory among Hennie's flowers and sewed a complete outfit in Jaeger flannel. / I was fifty-six years old.

NIJO. Out of favor but I didn't die. I left on foot, nobody saw me go. For the next twenty years I walked through Japan.

GRET. Walking is good.

[*The* WAITRESS *enters.*]

JOAN. Pope Leo died and I was chosen. All right then. I would be Pope. I would know God. I would know everything.

ISABELLA. I determined to leave my grief behind and set off for Tibet.

MARLENE. Magnificent all of you. We need some more wine, please, two bottles I think, Griselda isn't even here yet, and I want to drink a toast to you all.

ISABELLA. To yourself surely, / we're here to celebrate your success.

NIJO. Yes, Marlene.

JOAN. Yes, what is it exactly, Marlene?

MARLENE. Well it's not Pope but it is managing director.*

JOAN. And you find work for people.

MARLENE. Yes, an employment agency.

NIJO. *Over all the women you work with. And the men.

ISABELLA. And very well deserved too. I'm sure it's just the beginning of something extraordinary.

MARLENE. Well it's worth a party.

ISABELLA. To Marlene.*

MARLENE. And all of us.

JOAN. *Marlene.

NIJO. Marlene.

GRET. Marlene.

MARLENE. We've all come a long way. To our courage and the way we changed our lives and our extraordinary achievements.

[*They laugh and drink a toast.*]

ISABELLA. Such adventures. We were crossing a mountain pass at seven thousand feet, the cook was all to pieces, the muleteers suffered fever and snow blindness. But even though my spine was agony I managed very well.

MARLENE. Wonderful.

NIJO. Once I was ill for four months lying alone at an inn. Nobody to offer a horse to Buddha. I had to live for myself, and I did live.

ISABELLA. Of course you did. It was far worse returning to Tobermory. I always felt dull when I was stationary. / That's why I could never stay anywhere.

NIJO. Yes, that's it exactly. New sights. The shrine by the beach, the moon shining on the sea. The goddess had vowed to save all living things. / She would even save the fishes. I was full of hope.

JOAN. I had thought the Pope would know everything. I thought God would speak to me directly. But of course he knew I was a woman.

MARLENE. But nobody else even suspected?

[*The* WAITRESS *brings more wine.*]

JOAN. In the end I did take a lover again.*

ISABELLA. In the Vatican?

GRET. *Keep you warm.

NIJO. *Ah, lover.

MARLENE. *Good for you.

JOAN. He was one of my chamberlains. There are such a lot of servants when you're a Pope. The food's very good. And I realized I did know the truth. Because whatever the Pope says, that's true.

NIJO. What was he like, the chamberlain?*

GRET. Big cock.

ISABELLA. Oh Gret.

MARLENE. *Did he fancy you when he thought you were a fella?

NIJO. What was he like?

JOAN. He could keep a secret.

MARLENE. So you did know everything.

JOAN. Yes, I enjoyed being Pope. I consecrated bishops and let people kiss my feet. I received the King of England when he came to submit to the church. Unfortunately there were earthquakes, and some village reported it had rained blood, and in France there was a plague of giant grasshoppers, but I don't think that can have been my fault, do you?*

[*Laughter.*]

The grasshoppers fell on the English Channel / and were

NIJO. I once went to sea. It was very lonely. I realized it made very little difference where I went.

JOAN. washed up on shore and their bodies rotted and poisoned the air and everyone in those parts died.

[*Laughter.*]

ISABELLA. *Such superstition! I was nearly murdered in China by a howling mob. They thought the barbarians ate babies and put them under railway sleepers to make the tracks steady, and ground up their eyes to make the lenses of cameras. / So

MARLENE. And you had a camera!

ISABELLA. And they were shouting, "child-eater, child-eater." Some people tried to sell girl babies to Europeans for cameras or stew!

[*Laughter.*]

MARLENE. So apart from the grasshoppers it was a great success.
JOAN. Yes, if it hadn't been for the baby I expect I'd have lived to an old age like Theodora of Alexandria,[8] who lived as a monk. She was accused by a girl / who fell in love with her of being the father of her child and—
NIJO. But tell us what happened to your baby. I had some babies.
MARLENE. Didn't you think of getting rid of it?
JOAN. Wouldn't that be a worse sin than having it? / But a Pope with a child was about as bad as possible.
MARLENE. I don't know, you're the Pope.
JOAN. But I wouldn't have known how to get rid of it.
MARLENE. Other Popes had children, surely.
JOAN. They didn't give birth to them.
NIJO. Well you were a woman.
JOAN. Exactly and I shouldn't have been a woman. Women, children and lunatics can't be Pope.
MARLENE. So the only thing to do / was to get rid of it somehow.
NIJO. You had to have it adopted secretly.
JOAN. But I didn't know what was happening. I thought I was getting fatter, but then I was eating more and sitting about, the life of a Pope is quite luxurious. I don't think I'd spoken to a woman since I was twelve. The chamberlain was the one who realized.
MARLENE. And by then it was too late.
JOAN. Oh I didn't want to pay attention. It was easier to do nothing.
NIJO. But you had to plan for having it. You had to say you were ill and go away.
JOAN. That's what I should have done I suppose.
MARLENE. Did you want them to find out?
NIJO. I too was often in embarrassing situations, there's no need for a scandal. My first child was His Majesty's, which unfortunately died, but my second was Akebono's. I was seventeen. He was in love with me when I was thirteen, he was very upset when I had to go to the Emperor, it was very romantic, a lot of poems. Now His Majesty hadn't been near me for two months so he thought I was four months pregnant when I was really six, so when I reached the ninth month / I
JOAN. I never knew what month it was.
NIJO. announced I was seriously ill, and Akebono announced he had gone on a religious retreat. He held me round the waist and lifted me up as the baby was born. He cut the cord with a short sword, wrapped the baby in white and took it away. It was only a girl but I was sorry to lose it. Then I told the Emperor that the baby had miscarried because of my illness, and there you are. The danger was past.
JOAN. But Nijo, I wasn't used to having a woman's body.
ISABELLA. So what happened?
JOAN. I didn't know of course that it was near the time. It was Rogation Day,[9] there was always a procession. I was on the horse dressed in my

---

8. Wife (5th c. C.E.) of a prefect of Egypt, who, according to legend, left him to do penance for having committed adultery and lived for the rest of her life as a monk; her sex was discovered only on her death at the monastary.

9. One of four days on which there are solemn processions and litanies to invoke God's mercies (the Major Rogation is April 25).

robes and a cross was carried in front of me, and all the cardinals were following, and all the clergy of Rome, and a huge crowd of people. / We set off from

MARLENE. Total Pope.

JOAN. St. Peter's to go to St. John's. I had felt a slight pain earlier, I thought it was something I'd eaten, and then it came back, and came back more often. I thought when this is over I'll go to bed. There were still long gaps when I felt perfectly all right and I didn't want to attract attention to myself and spoil the ceremony. Then I suddenly realized what it must be. I had to last out till I could get home and hide. Then something changed, my breath started to catch, I couldn't plan things properly any more. We were in a little street that goes between St. Clement's and the Colosseum, and I just had to get off the horse and sit down for a minute. Great waves of pressure were going through my body, I heard sounds like a cow lowing, they came out of my mouth. Far away I heard people screaming, "The Pope is ill, the Pope is dying." And the baby just slid out onto the road.*

MARLENE. The cardinals / won't have known where to put themselves.

NIJO. Oh dear, Joan, what a thing to do! In the street!

ISABELLA. *How embarrassing.

GRET. In a field, yah.

[*They are laughing.*]

JOAN. One of the cardinals said, "The Antichrist!" and fell over in a faint.

[*They all laugh.*]

MARLENE. So what did they do? They weren't best pleased.

JOAN. They took me by the feet and dragged me out of town and stoned me to death.

[*They stop laughing.*]

MARLENE. Joan, how horrible.

JOAN. I don't really remember.

NIJO. And the child died too?

JOAN. Oh yes, I think so, yes.

[*Pause. The* WAITRESS *enters to clear the plates. They start talking quietly.*]

ISABELLA. [*To* JOAN.] I never had any children. I was very fond of horses.

NINJO. [*To* MARLENE.] I saw my daughter once. She was three years old. She wore a plum-red / small-sleeved gown. Akebono's

ISABELLA. Birdie was my favorite. A little Indian bay mare I rode in the Rocky Mountains.

NIJO. wife had taken the child because her own died. Everyone thought I was just a visitor. She was being brought up carefully so she could be sent to the palace like I was.

ISABELLA. Legs of iron and always cheerful, and such a pretty face. If a stranger led her she reared up like a bronco.

NIJO. I never saw my third child after he was born, the son of Ariake the priest. Ariake held him on his lap the day he was born and talked to him as if he could understand, and cried. My fourth child was Ariake's too. Ariake died before he was born. I didn't want to see anyone, I stayed alone in the hills. It was a boy again, my third son. But oddly enough I felt nothing for him.

MARLENE. How many children did you have, Gret?
GRET. Ten.
ISABELLA. Whenever I came back to England I felt I had so much to atone for. Hennie and John were so good. I did no good in my life. I spent years in self-gratification. So I hurled myself into committees, I nursed the people of Tobermory in the epidemic of influenza, I lectured the Young Women's Christian Association on Thrift. I talked and talked explaining how the East was corrupt and vicious. My travels must do good to someone beside myself. I wore myself out with good causes.
MARLENE. Oh God, why are we all so miserable?
JOAN. The procession never went down that street again.
MARLENE. They rerouted it specially?
JOAN. Yes they had to go all round to avoid it. And they introduced a pierced chair.
MARLENE. A pierced chair?
JOAN. Yes, a chair made out of solid marble with a hole in the seat / and it was in the Chapel of the Savior, and after he was
MARLENE. You're not serious.
JOAN. elected the Pope had to sit in it.
MARLENE. And someone looked up his skirts? / Not really?
ISABELLA. What an extraordinary thing.
JOAN. Two of the clergy / made sure he was a man.
NIJO. On their hands and knees!
MARLENE. A pierced chair!
GRET. Balls!
    [GRISELDA *arrives unnoticed.*]
NIJO. Why couldn't he just pull up his robe?
JOAN. He had to sit there and look dignified.
MARLENE. You could have made all your chamberlains sit in it.*
GRET. Big one, small one.
NIJO. Very useful chair at court.
ISABELLA. *Or the laird of Tobermory in his kilt.
    [*They are quite drunk. They get the giggles.* MARLENE *notices* GRISELDA.]
MARLENE. Griselda! / There you are. Do you want to eat?
GRISELDA. I'm sorry I'm so late. No, no, don't bother.
MARLENE. Of course it's no bother. / Have you eaten?
GRISELDA. No really, I'm not hungry.
MARLENE. Well have some pudding.[1]
GRISELDA. I never eat pudding.
MARLENE. Griselda, I hope you're not anorexic. We're having pudding, I am, and getting nice and fat.
GRISELDA. Oh if everyone is. I don't mind.
MARLENE. Now who do you know? This is Joan who was Pope in the ninth century, and Isabella Bird, the Victorian traveler, and Lady Nijo from Japan, Emperor's concubine and Buddhist nun, thirteenth century, nearer your own time, and Gret who was painted by Brueghel. Griselda's

---
1. I.e., dessert.

in Boccaccio and Petrarch and Chaucer[2] because of her extraordinary marriage. I'd like profiteroles because they're disgusting.
JOAN. Zabaglione, please.
ISABELLA. Apple pie / and cream.
NIJO. What's this?
MARLENE. Zabaglione, it's Italian, it's what Joan's having, / it's delicious.
NIJO. A Roman Catholic / dessert? Yes please.
MARLENE. Gret?
GRET. Cake.
GRISELDA. Just cheese and biscuits, thank you.
MARLENE. Yes, Griselda's life is like a fairy-story, except it starts with marrying the prince.
GRISELDA. He's only a marquis, Marlene.
MARLENE. Well everyone for miles around is his liege and he's absolute lord of life and death and you were the poor but beautiful peasant girl and he whisked you off. / Near enough a prince.
NIJO. How old were you?
GRISELDA. Fifteen.
NIJO. I was brought up in court circles and it was still a shock. Had you ever seen him before?
GRISELDA. I'd seen him riding by, we all had. And he'd seen me in the fields with the sheep.*
ISABELLA. I would have been well suited to minding sheep.
NIJO. And Mr. Nugent riding by.
ISABELLA. Of course not, Nijo, I mean a healthy life in the open air.
JOAN. *He just rode up while you were minding the sheep and asked you to marry him?
GRISELDA. No, no, it was on the wedding day. I was waiting outside the door to see the procession. Everyone wanted him to get married so there'd be an heir to look after us when he died, / and at last he announced a day for the wedding but
MARLENE. I don't think Walter wanted to get married. It is Walter? Yes.
GRISELDA. nobody knew who the bride was, we thought it must be a foreign princess, we were longing to see her. Then the carriage stopped outside our cottage and we couldn't see the bride anywhere. And he came and spoke to my father.
NIJO. And your father told you to serve the Prince.
GRISELDA. My father could hardly speak. The Marquis said it wasn't an order, I could say no, but if I said yes I must always obey him in everything.
MARLENE. That's when you should have suspected.
GRISELDA. But of course a wife must obey her husband. / And of course I must obey the Marquis.*

---

2. Griselda is the heroine of the final tale in *The Decameron* (written 1351–1353), by the Italian writer Giovanni Boccaccio (1313–1375); that story was retold in Latin, as "On a Wife's Mythic Obedience and Faith," by his friend the Italian poet Francesco Petrarca (1304–1374); and the English poet Geoffrey Chaucer (ca. 1343–1400) drew on Petrarch's version in writing *The Clerk's Tale*.

ISABELLA. I swore to obey dear John, of course, but it didn't seem to arise. Naturally I wouldn't have wanted to go abroad while I was married.
MARLENE. *Then why bother to mention it at all? He'd got a thing about it, that's why.
GRISELDA. I'd rather obey the Marquis than a boy from the village.
MARLENE. Yes, that's a point.
JOAN. I never obeyed anyone. They all obeyed me.
NIJO. And what did you wear? He didn't make you get married in your own clothes? That would be perverse.*
MARLENE. Oh, you wait.
GRISELDA. *He had ladies with him who undressed me and they had a white silk dress and jewels for my hair.
MARLENE. And at first he seemed perfectly normal?
GRISELDA. Marlene, you're always so critical of him. / Of course he was normal, he was very kind.
MARLENE. But Griselda, come on, he took your baby.
GRISELDA. Walter found it hard to believe I loved him. He couldn't believe I would always obey him. He had to prove it.
MARLENE. I don't think Walter likes women.
GRISELDA. I'm sure he loved me, Marlene, all the time.
MARLENE. He just had a funny way / of showing it.
GRISELDA. It was hard for him too.
JOAN. How do you mean he took away your baby?
NIJO. Was it a boy?
GRISELDA. No, the first one was a girl.
NIJO. Even so it's hard when they take it away. Did you see it at all?
GRISELDA. Oh yes, she was six weeks old.
NIJO. Much better to do it straight away.
ISABELLA. But why did your husband take the child?
GRISELDA. He said all the people hated me because I was just one of them. And now I had a child they were restless. So he had to get rid of the child to keep them quiet. But he said he wouldn't snatch her, I had to agree and obey and give her up. So when I was feeding her a man came in and took her away. I thought he was going to kill her even before he was out of the room.
MARLENE. But you let him take her? You didn't struggle?
GRISELDA. I asked him to give her back so I could kiss her. And I asked him to bury her where no animals could dig her up. / It
ISABELLA. Oh my dear.
GRISELDA. was Walter's child to do what he liked with.*
MARLENE. Walter was bonkers.
GRET. Bastard.
ISABELLA. *But surely, murder.
GRISELDA. I had promised.
MARLENE. I can't stand this. I'm going for a pee.
 [MARLENE *goes out. The* WAITRESS *brings dessert.*]
NIJO. No, I understand. Of course you had to, he was your life. And were you in favor after that?
GRISELDA. Oh yes, we were very happy together. We never spoke about what had happened.

ISABELLA. I can see you were doing what you thought was your duty. But didn't it make you ill?
GRISELDA. No, I was very well, thank you.
NIJO. And you had another child?
GRISELDA. Not for four years, but then I did, yes, a boy.
NIJO. Ah a boy. / So it all ended happily.
GRISELDA. Yes he was pleased. I kept my son till he was two years old. A peasant's grandson. It made the people angry. Walter explained.
ISABELLA. But surely he wouldn't kill his children / just because—
GRISELDA. Oh it wasn't true. Walter would never give in to the people. He wanted to see if I loved him enough.
JOAN. He killed his children / to see if you loved him enough?
NIJO. Was it easier the second time or harder?
GRISELDA. It was always easy because I always knew I would do what he said.

   [*Pause. They start to eat.*]

ISABELLA. I hope you didn't have any more children.
GRISELDA. Oh no, no more. It was twelve years till he tested me again.
ISABELLA. So whatever did he do this time? / My poor John, I never loved him enough, and he would never have dreamed . . .
GRISELDA. He sent me away. He said the people wanted him to marry someone else who'd give him an heir and he'd got special permission from the Pope. So I said I'd go home to my father. I came with nothing / so I went with nothing. I
NIJO. Better to leave if your master doesn't want you.
GRISELDA. took off my clothes. He let me keep a slip so he wouldn't be shamed. And I walked home barefoot. My father came out in tears. Everyone was crying except me.
NIJO. At least your father wasn't dead. / I had nobody.
ISABELLA. Well it can be a relief to come home. I loved to see Hennie's sweet face again.
GRISELDA. Oh yes, I was perfectly content. And quite soon he sent for me again.
JOAN. I don't think I would have gone.
GRISELDA. But he told me to come. I had to obey him. He wanted me to help prepare his wedding. He was getting married to a young girl from France / and nobody except me knew how to arrange things the way he liked them.
NIJO. It's always hard taking him another woman.
   [MARLENE *comes back.*]
JOAN. I didn't live a woman's life. I don't understand it.
GRISELDA. The girl was sixteen and far more beautiful than me. I could see why he loved her. / She had her younger brother with her as a page.
   [*The* WAITRESS *enters.*]
MARLENE. Oh God, I can't bear it. I want some coffee. Six coffees. Six brandies. / Double brandies. Straightaway.
GRISELDA. They all went in to the feast I'd prepared. And he stayed behind and put his arms round me and kissed me. / I felt half asleep with the shock.
NIJO. Oh, like a dream.

MARLENE. And he said, "This is your daughter and your son."
GRISELDA. Yes.
JOAN. What?
NIJO. Oh. Oh I see. You got them back.
ISABELLA. I did think it was remarkably barbaric to kill them but you learn not to say anything. / So he had them brought up secretly I suppose.
MARLENE. Walter's a monster. Weren't you angry? What did you do?
GRISELDA. Well I fainted. Then I cried and kissed the children. / Everyone was making a fuss of me.
NIJO. But did you feel anything for them?
GRISELDA. What?
NIJO. Did you feel anything for the children?
GRISELDA. Of course, I loved them.
JOAN. So you forgave him and lived with him?
GRISELDA. He suffered so much all those years.
ISABELLA. Hennie had the same sweet nature.
NIJO. So they dressed you again?
GRISELDA. Cloth of gold.
JOAN. I can't forgive anything.
MARLENE. You really are exceptional, Griselda.
NIJO. Nobody gave me back my children.

[NIJO *cries. The* WAITRESS *brings brandies.*]

ISABELLA. I can never be like Hennie. I was always so busy in England, a kind of business I detested. The very presence of people exhausted my emotional reserves. I could not be like Hennie however I tried. I tried and was as ill as could be. The doctor suggested a steel net to support my head, the weight of my own head was too much for my diseased spine. / It is dangerous to put oneself in depressing circumstances. Why should I do it?
JOAN. Don't cry.
NIJO. My father and the Emperor both died in the autumn. So much pain.
JOAN. Yes, but don't cry.
NIJO. They wouldn't let me into the palace when he was dying. I hid in the room with his coffin, then I couldn't find where I'd left my shoes, I ran after the funeral procession in bare feet, I couldn't keep up. When I got there it was over, a few wisps of smoke in the sky, that's all that was left of him. What I want to know is, if I'd still been at court, would I have been allowed to wear full mourning?
MARLENE. I'm sure you would.
NIJO. Why do you say that? You don't know anything about it. Would I have been allowed to wear full mourning?
ISABELLA. How can people live in this dim pale island and wear our hideous clothes? I cannot and will not live the life of a lady.
NIJO. I'll tell you something that made me angry. I was eighteen, at the Full Moon Ceremony. They make a special rice gruel and stir it with their sticks, and then they beat their women across the loins so they'll have sons and not daughters. So the Emperor beat us all / very hard as usual—that's not it,
MARLENE. What a sod.
NIJO. Marlene, that's normal, what made us angry, he told his attendants

they could beat us too. Well they had a wonderful time. / So Lady Genki and I made a plan, and the ladies all hid

[*The* WAITRESS *has entered with coffees.*]

MARLENE. I'd like another brandy please. Better make it six.

NIJO. in his rooms, and Lady Mashimizu stood guard with a stick at the door, and when His Majesty came in Genki seized him and I beat him till he cried out and promised he would never order anyone to hit us again. Afterwards there was a terrible fuss. The nobles were horrified. "We wouldn't even dream of stepping on your Majesty's shadow." And I had hit him with a stick. Yes, I hit him with a stick.

JOAN. Suave, mari magno turbantibus aequora ventis,
e terra magnum alterius spectare laborem;
non quia vexari quemquamst iucunda voluptas,
sed quibus ipse malis careas quia cernere suave est.
Suave etiam belli certamina magna tueri
per campos instructa tua sine parte pericli.
Sed nil dulcius est, bene quam munita tenere
edita doctrina sapientum templa serena, /
despicere unde queas alios passimque videre
errare atque viam palantis quaerere vitae,[3]

GRISELDA. I do think—I do wonder—it would have been nicer if Walter hadn't had to.

ISABELLA. Why should I? Why should I?

MARLENE. Of course not.

NIJO. I hit him with a stick.

JOAN. certare ingenio, contendere nobilitate,
noctes atque dies niti praestante labore
ad summas emergere opes rerumque potiri.
O miseras / hominum mentis, o pectora caeca!*

ISABELLA. Oh miseras!

NIJO. *Pectora caeca.

JOAN. qualibus in tenebris vitae quantisque periclis
degitur hoc aevi quodcumquest! / nonne videre
nil aliud sibi naturam latrare, nisi utqui
corpore seiunctus dolor absit, mente fruatur
    [JOAN *subsides.*]

GRET. We come into hell through a big mouth. Hell's black and red. / It's like the village where I come from. There's a river and

MARLENE. [*To* JOAN.] Shut up, pet.

ISABELLA. Listen, she's been to hell.

---

3. Joan quotes Lucretius's (ca. 55 B.C.E.) philosophical poem *On the Nature of Things*, 2.1–18 (the translation of the Latin is broken where other dialogue interrupts): "It is pleasant, when over a great sea the winds are roiling the waters, to look out from land at another's great labor; not because it is so delightful that anyone be troubled, but because it is sweet to understand from what ills you yourself are free. It is also pleasant to watch great contests of war arrayed on the plains when you have no share of the danger. But nothing is sweeter than to hold tranquil, high sanctuaries, well fortified by the teaching of the wise, from which you may look down and see others wandering all about without direction as they seek a way of life, as they compete with wit, fight for precedence, struggle night and day with remarkable effort to rise to the heights of wealth and to possess things. Oh wretched minds of humans, oh blind hearts! [Isabella repeats, 'O wretched!'; Nijo repeats, 'Blind hearts.'] In what darkness of life, in how great dangers this brief lifetime is passed! Don't you see that nature clamors for nothing except this, that the body be freed from pain, and that the mind enjoy [delight]?"

GRET. a bridge and houses. There's places on fire like when the soldiers come. There's a big devil sat on a roof with a big hole in his arse and he's scooping stuff out of it with a big ladle and it's falling down on us, and it's money, so a lot of the women stop and get some. But most of us is fighting the devils. There's lots of little devils, our size, and we get them down all right and give them a beating. There's lots of funny creatures round your feet, you don't like to look, like rats and lizards, and nasty things, a bum with a face, and fish with legs, and faces on things that don't have faces on. But they don't hurt, you just keep going. Well we'd all had worse, you see, we'd had the Spanish. We'd all had family killed. My big son die on a wheel. Birds eat him. My baby, a soldier run her through with a sword. I'd had enough, I was mad, I hate the bastards. I come out my front door that morning and shout till my neighbors come out and I said, "Come on, we're going where the evil come from and pay the bastards out." And they all come out just as they was / from baking or washing in their

NIJO. All the ladies come.

GRET. aprons, and we push down the street and the ground opens up and we go through a big mouth into a street just like ours but in hell. I've got a sword in my hand from somewhere and I fill a basket with gold cups they drink out of down there. You just keep running on and fighting / you didn't stop for nothing. Oh we give them devils such a beating.

NIJO. Take that, take that.

JOAN. Something something something mortisque timores
tum vacuum pectus—damn.
Quod si ridicula—
something something on and on and on and something
splendorem purpureai.[4]

ISABELLA. I thought I would have a last jaunt up the west river in China. Why not? But the doctors were so very grave. I just went to Morocco. The sea was so wild I had to be landed by ship's crane in a coal bucket. / My horse was a terror to me a

GRET. Coal bucket, good.

JOAN. nos in luce timemus
something
terrorem.[5]

ISABELLA. powerful black charger.

[NIJO *is laughing and crying.* JOAN *gets up and is sick in a corner.* MARLENE *is drinking* ISABELLA's *brandy.*]

So off I went to visit the Berber sheikhs in full blue trousers and great brass spurs. I was the only European woman ever to have seen the Emperor of Morocco. I was seventy years old. What lengths to go to for a last chance of joy. I knew my return of vigor was only temporary, but how marvelous while it lasted.

---

4. Also from Lucretius: "then fears of death [leave] your heart empty" (2.45–46); "But if [we see] these things [to be] ridiculous" (2.47); "the magnificence of purple" (2.52).
5. Lucretius 2.54, 59: "We are afraid in the light" something "terror."

SCENE TWO

Employment Agency. MARLENE *and* JEANINE.

MARLENE. Right Jeanine, you are Jeanine aren't you? Let's have a look. Os and As.[6] / No As, all those Os you probably
JEANINE. Six Os.
MARLENE. could have got an A. / Speeds, not brilliant, not too bad.
JEANINE. I wanted to go to work.
MARLENE. Well, Jeanine, what's your present job like?
JEANINE. I'm a secretary.
MARLENE. Secretary or typist?
JEANINE. I did start as a typist but the last six months I've been a secretary.
MARLENE. To?
JEANINE. To three of them, really, they share me. There's Mr. Ashford, he's the office manager, and Mr. Philby / is sales, and—
MARLENE. Quite a small place?
JEANINE. A bit small.
MARLENE. Friendly?
JEANINE. Oh it's friendly enough.
MARLENE. Prospects?
JEANINE. I don't think so, that's the trouble. Miss Lewis is secretary to the managing director and she's been there forever, and Mrs. Bradford/ is—
MARLENE. So you want a job with better prospects?
JEANINE. I want a change.
MARLENE. So you'll take anything comparable?
JEANINE. No, I do want prospects. I want more money.
MARLENE. You're getting—?
JEANINE. Hundred.
MARLENE. It's not bad you know. You're what? Twenty?
JEANINE. I'm saving to get married.
MARLENE. Does that mean you don't want a long-term job, Jeanine?
JEANINE. I might do.
MARLENE. Because where do the prospects come in? No kids for a bit?
JEANINE. Oh no, not kids, not yet.
MARLENE. So you won't tell them you're getting married?
JEANINE. Had I better not?
MARLENE. It would probably help.
JEANINE. I'm not wearing a ring. We thought we wouldn't spend on a ring.
MARLENE. Saves taking it off.
JEANINE. I wouldn't take it off.
MARLENE. There's no need to mention it when you go for an interview. / Now Jeanine do you have a feel for any particular
JEANINE. But what if they ask?
MARLENE. kind of company?
JEANINE. I thought advertising.

---

6. O ("Ordinary") levels are the lowest level of standardized examinations in secondary school subjects, and A ("Advanced") levels are used in applying to universities.

MARLENE. People often do think advertising. I have got a few vacancies but I think they're looking for something glossier.
JEANINE. You mean how I dress? / I can dress different. I
MARLENE. I mean experience.
JEANINE. dress like this on purpose for where I am now.
MARLENE. I have a marketing department here of a knitwear manufacturer. / Marketing is near enough advertising. Secretary
JEANINE. Knitwear?
MARLENE. to the marketing manager, he's thirty-five, married, I've sent him a girl before and she was happy, left to have a baby, you won't want to mention marriage there. He's very fair I think, good at his job, you won't have to nurse him along. Hundred and ten, so that's better than you're doing now.
JEANINE. I don't know.
MARLENE. I've a fairly small concern here, father and two sons, you'd have more say potentially, secretarial and reception duties, only a hundred but the job's going to grow with the concern and then you'll be in at the top with new girls coming in underneath you.
JEANINE. What is it they do?
MARLENE. Lampshades. / This would be my first choice for you.
JEANINE. Just lampshades?
MARLENE. There's plenty of different kinds of lampshade. So we'll send you there, shall we, and the knitwear second choice. Are you free to go for an interview any day they call you?
JEANINE. I'd like to travel.
MARLENE. We don't have any foreign clients. You'd have to go elsewhere.
JEANINE. Yes I know. I don't really . . . I just mean . . .
MARLENE. Does your fiancé want to travel?
JEANINE. I'd like a job where I was here in London and with him and everything but now and then—I expect it's silly. Are there jobs like that?
MARLENE. There's personal assistant to a top executive in a multinational. If that's the idea you need to be planning ahead. Is that where you want to be in ten years?
JEANINE. I might not be alive in ten years.
MARLENE. Yes but you will be. You'll have children.
JEANINE. I can't think about ten years.
MARLENE. You haven't got the speeds anyway. So I'll send you to these two shall I? You haven't been to any other agency? Just so we don't get crossed wires. Now Jeanine I want you to get one of these jobs, all right? If I send you that means I'm putting myself on the line for you. Your presentation's OK, you look fine, just be confident and go in there convinced that this is the best job for you and you're the best person for the job. If you don't believe it they won't believe it.
JEANINE. Do you believe it?
MARLENE. I think you could make me believe it if you put your mind to it.
JEANINE. Yes, all right.

SCENE THREE

JOYCE's *back yard. The house with back door is upstage. Downstage a shelter made of junk, made by children. Two girls,* ANGIE *and* KIT, *are in it, squashed together.* ANGIE *is 16,* KIT *is 12. They cannot be seen from the house.* JOYCE *calls from the house.*

JOYCE. Angie. Angie are you out there?
    [*Silence. They keep still and wait. When nothing else happens they relax.*]
ANGIE. Wish she was dead.
KIT. Wanna watch *The Exterminator*?[7]
ANGIE. You're sitting on my leg.
KIT. There's nothing on telly. We can have an ice cream. Angie?
ANGIE. Shall I tell you something?
KIT. Do you wanna watch *The Exterminator*?
ANGIE. It's X, innit.
KIT. I can get into Xs.
ANGIE. Shall I tell you something?
KIT. We'll go to something else. We'll go to Ipswich. What's on the Odeon?
ANGIE. She won't let me, will she?
KIT. Don't tell her.
ANGIE. I've no money.
KIT. I'll pay.
ANGIE. She'll moan though, won't she?
KIT. I'll ask her for you if you like.
ANGIE. I've no money, I don't want you to pay.
KIT. I'll ask her.
ANGIE. She don't like you.
KIT. I still got three pounds birthday money. Did she say she don't like me?
    I'll go by myself then.
ANGIE. Your mum don't let you. I got to take you.
KIT. She won't know.
ANGIE. You'd be scared who'd sit next to you.
KIT. No I wouldn't.
    She does like me anyway.
    Tell me then.
ANGIE. Tell you what?
KIT. It's you she doesn't like.
ANGIE. Well I don't like her so tough shit.
JOYCE. [*Off.*] Angie. Angie. Angie. I know you're out there. I'm not coming out after you. You come in here.
    [*Silence. Nothing happens.*]
ANGIE. Last night when I was in bed. I been thinking yesterday could I make things move. You know, make things move by thinking about them without touching them. Last night I was in bed and suddenly a picture fell down off the wall.

---

7. A very violent American thriller (1980; dir. James Glickenhaus).

KIT. What picture?
ANGIE. My gran, that picture. Not the poster. The photograph in the frame.
KIT. Had you done something to make it fall down?
ANGIE. I must have done.
KIT. But were you thinking about it?
ANGIE. Not about it, but about something.
KIT. I don't think that's very good.
ANGIE. You know the kitten?
KIT. Which one?
ANGIE. There only is one. The dead one.
KIT. What about it?
ANGIE. I heard it last night.
KIT. Where?
ANGIE. Out here. In the dark. What if I left you here in the dark all night?
KIT. You couldn't. I'd go home.
ANGIE. You couldn't.
KIT. I'd / go home.
ANGIE. No you couldn't, not if I said.
KIT. I could.
ANGIE. Then you wouldn't see anything. You'd just be ignorant.
KIT. I can see in the daytime.
ANGIE. No you can't. You can't hear it in the daytime.
KIT. I don't want to hear it.
ANGIE. You're scared that's all.
KIT. I'm not scared of anything.
ANGIE. You're scared of blood.
KIT. It's not the same kitten anyway. You just heard an old cat, / you just heard some old cat.
ANGIE. You don't know what I heard. Or what I saw. You don't know nothing because you're a baby.
KIT. You're sitting on me.
ANGIE. Mind my hair / you silly cunt.
KIT. Stupid fucking cow, I hate you.
ANGIE. I don't care if you do.
KIT. You're horrible.
ANGIE. I'm going to kill my mother and you're going to watch.
KIT. I'm not playing.
ANGIE. You're scared of blood.

[KIT *puts her hand under her dress, brings it out with blood on her finger.*]

KIT. There, see, I got my own blood, so.

[ANGIE *takes* KIT's *hand and licks her finger.*]

ANGIE. Now I'm a cannibal. I might turn into a vampire now.
KIT. That picture wasn't nailed up right.
ANGIE. You'll have to do that when I get mine.
KIT. I don't have to.
ANGIE. You're scared.
KIT. I'll do it, I might do it. I don't have to just because you say. I'll be sick on you.

ANGIE. I don't care if you are sick on me, I don't mind sick. I don't mind blood. If I don't get away from here I'm going to die.
KIT. I'm going home.
ANGIE. You can't go through the house. She'll see you.
KIT. I won't tell her.
ANGIE. Oh great, fine.
KIT. I'll say I was by myself. I'll tell her you're at my house and I'm going there to get you.
ANGIE. She knows I'm here, stupid.
KIT. Then why can't I go through the house?
ANGIE. Because I said not.
KIT. My mum don't like you anyway.
ANGIE. I don't want her to like me. She's a slag.[8]
KIT. She is not.
ANGIE. She does it with everyone.
KIT. She does not.
ANGIE. You don't even know what it is.
KIT. Yes I do.
ANGIE. Tell me then.
KIT. We get it all at school, cleverclogs. It's on television. You haven't done it.
ANGIE. How do you know?
KIT. Because I know you haven't.
ANGIE. You know wrong then because I have.
KIT. Who with?
ANGIE. I'm not telling you / who with.
KIT. You haven't anyway.
ANGIE. How do you know?
KIT. Who with?
ANGIE. I'm not telling you.
KIT. You said you told me everything.
ANGIE. I was lying wasn't I?
KIT. Who with? You can't tell me who with because / you never—
ANGIE. Sh.

[JOYCE *has come out of the house. She stops half way across the yard and listens. They listen.*]

JOYCE. You there Angie? Kit? You there Kitty? Want a cup of tea? I've got some chocolate biscuits.[9] Come on now I'll put the kettle on. Want a choccy biccy, Angie?

[*They all listen and wait.*]

Fucking rotten little cunt. You can stay there and die. I'll lock the back door.

[*They all wait.* JOYCE *goes back to the house.* ANGIE *and* KIT *sit in silence for a while.*]

KIT. When there's a war, where's the safest place?
ANGIE. Nowhere.
KIT. New Zealand is, my mum said. Your skin's burned right off. Shall we go to New Zealand?

8. Slut, whore (British slang). 9. Cookies.

ANGIE. I'm not staying here.
KIT. Shall we go to New Zealand?
ANGIE. You're not old enough.
KIT. You're not old enough.
ANGIE. I'm old enough to get married.
KIT. You don't want to get married.
ANGIE. No but I'm old enough.
KIT. I'd find out where they were going to drop it and stand right in the place.
ANGIE. You couldn't find out.
KIT. Better than walking round with your skin dragging on the ground. Eugh. / Would you like walking round with your skin dragging on the ground?
ANGIE. You couldn't find out, stupid, it's a secret.
KIT. Where are you going?
ANGIE. I'm not telling you.
KIT. Why?
ANGIE. It's a secret.
KIT. But you tell me all your secrets.
ANGIE. Not the true secrets.
KIT. Yes you do.
ANGIE. No I don't.
KIT. I want to go somewhere away from the war.
ANGIE. Just forget the war.
KIT. I can't.
ANGIE. You have to. It's so boring.
KIT. I'll remember it at night.
ANGIE. I'm going to do something else anyway.
KIT. What? Angie come on. Angie.
ANGIE. It's a true secret.
KIT. It can't be worse than the kitten. And killing your mother. And the war.
ANGIE. Well I'm not telling you so you can die for all I care.
KIT. My mother says there's something wrong with you playing with someone my age. She says why haven't you got friends your own age. People your own age know there's something funny about you. She says you're a bad influence. She says she's going to speak to your mother.

[ANGIE *twists* KIT's *arm till she cries out.*]

ANGIE. Say you're a liar.
KIT. She said it not me.
ANGIE. Say you eat shit.
KIT. You can't make me.

[ANGIE *lets go.*]

ANGIE. I don't care anyway. I'm leaving.
KIT. Go on then.
ANGIE. You'll all wake up one morning and find I've gone.
KIT. Good.
ANGIE. I'm not telling you when.
KIT. Go on then.
ANGIE. I'm sorry I hurt you.

KIT.   I'm tired.
ANGIE.   Do you like me?
KIT.   I don't know.
ANGIE.   You do not like me.
KIT.   I'm going home.
   [KIT *gets up.*]
ANGIE.   No you're not.
KIT.   I'm tired.
ANGIE.   She'll see you.
KIT.   She'll give me a chocolate biscuit.
ANGIE.   Kitty.
KIT.   Tell me where you're going.
ANGIE.   Sit down.
   [KIT *sits in the hut again.*]
KIT.   Go on then.
ANGIE.   Swear?
KIT.   Swear.
ANGIE.   I'm going to London. To see my aunt.
KIT.   And what?
ANGIE.   That's it.
KIT.   I see my aunt all the time.
ANGIE.   I don't see my aunt.
KIT.   What's so special?
ANGIE.   It is special. She's special.
KIT.   Why?
ANGIE.   She is.
KIT.   Why?
ANGIE.   She is.
KIT.   Why?
ANGIE.   My mother hates her.
KIT.   Why?
ANGIE.   Because she does.
KIT.   Perhaps she's not very nice.
ANGIE.   She is nice.
KIT.   How do you know?
ANGIE.   Because I know her.
KIT.   You said you never see her.
ANGIE.   I saw her last year. You saw her.
KIT.   Did I?
ANGIE.   Never mind.
KIT.   I remember her. That aunt. What's so special?
ANGIE.   She gets people jobs.
KIT.   What's so special?
ANGIE.   I think I'm my aunt's child. I think my mother's really my aunt.
KIT.   Why?
ANGIE.   Because she goes to America, now shut up.
KIT.   I've been to London.
ANGIE.   Now give us a cuddle and shut up because I'm sick.
KIT.   You're sitting on my arm.
   [*Silence.* JOYCE *comes out and comes up to them quietly.*]

JOYCE. Come on.
KIT. Oh hello.
JOYCE. Time you went home.
KIT. We want to go to the Odeon.
JOYCE. What time?
KIT. Don't know.
JOYCE. Don't know much do you?
KIT. That all right then?
JOYCE. Angie's got to clean her room first.
ANGIE. No I don't.
JOYCE. Yes you do, it's a pigsty.
ANGIE. Well I'm not.
JOYCE. Then you're not going. I don't care.
ANGIE. Well I am going.
JOYCE. You've no money, have you?
ANGIE. Kit's paying anyway.
JOYCE. No she's not.
KIT. I'll help you with your room.
JOYCE. That's nice.
ANGIE. No you won't. You wait here.
KIT. Hurry then.
ANGIE. I'm not hurrying. You just wait.
[ANGIE *goes into the house. Silence.*]
JOYCE. I don't know.
[*Silence.*]
How's school then?
KIT. All right.
JOYCE. What are you now? Third year?
KIT. Second year.
JOYCE. Your mum says you're good at English.
[*Silence.*]
Maybe Angie should've stayed on.
KIT. She didn't like it.
JOYCE. I didn't like it. And look at me. If your face fits at school it's going to fit other places too. It wouldn't make no difference to Angie. She's not going to get a job when jobs are hard to get. I'd be sorry for anyone in charge of her. She'd better get married. I don't know who'd have her, mind. She's one of those girls might never leave home. What do you want to be when you grow up, Kit?
KIT. Physicist.
JOYCE. What?
KIT. Nuclear physicist.
JOYCE. Whatever for?
KIT. I could, I'm clever.
JOYCE. I know you're clever, pet.
[*Silence.*]
I'll make a cup of tea.
[*Silence.*]
Looks like it's going to rain.
[*Silence.*]

Don't you have friends your own age?
KIT. Yes.
JOYCE. Well then.
KIT. I'm old for my age.
JOYCE. And Angie's simple is she? She's not simple.
KIT. I love Angie.
JOYCE. She's clever in her own way.
KIT. You can't stop me.
JOYCE. I don't want to.
KIT. You can't, so.
JOYCE. Don't be cheeky, Kitty. She's always kind to little children.
KIT. She's coming so you better leave me alone.
   [ANGIE *comes out. She has changed into an old best dress, slightly small for her.*]
JOYCE. What you put that on for? Have you done your room? You can't clean your room in that.
ANGIE. I looked in the cupboard[1] and it was there.
JOYCE. Of course it was there, it's meant to be there. Is that why it was a surprise, finding something in the right place? I should think she's surprised, wouldn't you Kit, to find something in her room in the right place.
ANGIE. I decided to wear it.
JOYCE. Not today, why? To clean your room? You're not going to the pictures till you've done your room. You can put your dress on after if you like.
   [ANGIE *picks up a brick.*]
Have you done your room? You're not getting out of it, you know.
KIT. Angie, let's go.
JOYCE. She's not going till she's done her room.
KIT. It's starting to rain.
JOYCE. Come on, come on then. Hurry and do your room, Angie, and then you can go to the cinema with Kit. Oh it's wet, come on. We'll look up the time in the paper. Does your mother know, Kit, it's going to be a late night for you, isn't it? Hurry up, Angie. You'll spoil your dress. You make me sick.
   [JOYCE *and* KIT *run in.* ANGIE *stays where she is. Sound of rain.* KIT *comes out of the house and shouts.*]
KIT. Angie. Angie, come on, you'll get wet.
   [KIT *comes back to* ANGIE.]
ANGIE. I put on this dress to kill my mother.
KIT. I suppose you thought you'd do it with a brick.
ANGIE. You can kill people with a brick.
KIT. Well you didn't, so.

1. Closet.

Act Two

SCENE ONE

Office of "Top Girls" Employment Agency. Three desks and a small interviewing area. Monday morning. WIN *and* NELL *have just arrived for work.*

NELL.   Coffee coffee coffee coffee / coffee.
WIN.   The roses were smashing. / Mermaid.
NELL.   Ohhh.
WIN.   Iceberg. He taught me all their names.
   [NELL *has some coffee now.*]
NELL.   Ah. Now then.
WIN.   He has one of the finest rose gardens in West Sussex. He exhibits.
NELL.   He what?
WIN.   His wife was visiting her mother. It was like living together.
NELL.   Crafty, you never said.
WIN.   He rang on Saturday morning.
NELL.   Lucky you were free.
WIN.   That's what I told him.
NELL.   Did you hell.
WIN.   Have you ever seen a really beautiful rose garden?
NELL.   I don't like flowers. / I like swimming pools.
WIN.   Marilyn. Esther's Baby. They're all called after birds.
NELL.   Our friend's late. Celebrating all weekend I bet you.
WIN.   I'd call a rose Elvis. Or John Conteh.[2]
NELL.   Is Howard in yet?
WIN.   If he is he'll be bleeping us with a problem.
NELL.   Howard can just hang onto himself.
WIN.   Howard's really cut up.
NELL.   Howard thinks because he's a fella the job was his as of right. Our Marlene's got far more balls than Howard and that's that.
WIN.   Poor little bugger.
NELL.   He'll live.
WIN.   He'll move on.
NELL.   I wouldn't mind a change of air myself.
WIN.   Serious?
NELL.   I've never been a staying put lady. Pastures new.
WIN.   So who's the pirate?
NELL.   There's nothing definite.
WIN.   Inquiries?
NELL.   There's always inquiries. I'd think I'd got bad breath if there stopped being inquiries. Most of them can't afford me. Or you.
WIN.   I'm all right for the time being. Unless I go to Australia.
NELL.   There's not a lot of room upward.
WIN.   Marlene's filled it up.
NELL.   Good luck to her. Unless there's some prospects moneywise.
WIN.   You can but ask.

---

2. British former boxing champion (b. 1951). Elvis Presley (1935–1977), American singer.

NELL. Can always but ask.
WIN. So what have we got? I've got a Mr. Holden I saw last week.
NELL. Any use?
WIN. Pushy. Bit of a cowboy.
NELL. Good-looker?
WIN. Good dresser.
NELL. High flyer?
WIN. That's his general idea certainly but I'm not sure he's got it up there.
NELL. Prestel wants six high flyers and I've only seen two and a half.
WIN. He's making a bomb on the road but he thinks it's time for an office. I sent him to IBM but he didn't get it.
NELL. Prestel's on the road.
WIN. He's not overbright.
NELL. Can he handle an office?
WIN. Provided his secretary can punctuate he should go far.
NELL. Bear Prestel in mind then, I might put my head round the door. I've got that poor little nerd I should never have said I could help. Tender heart me.
WIN. Tender like old boots. How old?
NELL. Yes well forty-five.
WIN. Say no more.
NELL. He knows his place, he's not after calling himself a manager, he's just a poor little bod wants a better commission and a bit of sunshine.
WIN. Don't we all.
NELL. He's just got to relocate. He's got a bungalow in Dymchurch.
WIN. And his wife says.
NELL. The lady wife wouldn't care to relocate. She's going through the change.
WIN. It's his funeral, don't waste your time.
NELL. I don't waste a lot.
WIN. Good weekend you?
NELL. You could say.
WIN. Which one?
NELL. One Friday, one Saturday.
WIN. Aye—aye.
NELL. Sunday night I watched telly.
WIN. Which of them do you like best really?
NELL. Sunday was best, I liked the Ovaltine.
WIN. Holden, Barker, Gardner, Duke.
NELL. I've a lady here thinks she can sell.
WIN. Taking her on?
NELL. She's had some jobs.
WIN. Services?
NELL. No, quite heavy stuff, electric.
WIN. Tough bird like us.
NELL. We could do with a few more here.
WIN. There's nothing going here.
NELL. No but I always want the tough ones when I see them. Hang onto them.
WIN. I think we're plenty.

NELL. Derek asked me to marry him again.
WIN. He doesn't know when he's beaten.
NELL. I told him I'm not going to play house, not even in Ascot.
WIN. Mind you, you could play house.
NELL. If I chose to play house I would play house ace.
WIN. You could marry him and go on working.
NELL. I could go on working and not marry him.
[MARLENE *arrives*.]
MARLENE. Morning ladies.
[WIN *and* NELL *cheer and whistle*.]
Mind my head.
NELL. Coffee coffee coffee.
WIN. We're tactfully not mentioning you're late.
MARLENE. Fucking tube.[3]
WIN. We've heard that one.
NELL. We've used that one.
WIN. It's the top executive doesn't come in as early as the poor working girl.
MARLENE. Pass the sugar and shut your pace, pet.
WIN. Well I'm delighted.
NELL. Howard's looking sick.
WIN. Howard is sick. He's got ulcers and heart. He told me.
NELL. He'll have to stop then won't he?
WIN. Stop what?
NELL. Smoking, drinking, shouting. Working.
WIN. Well, working.
NELL. We're just looking through the day.
MARLENE. I'm doing some of Pam's ladies. They've been piling up while she's away.
NELL. Half a dozen little girls and an arts graduate who can't type.
WIN. I spent the whole weekend at his place in Sussex.
NELL. She fancies his rose garden.
WIN. I had to lie down in the back of the car so the neighbors wouldn't see me go in.
NELL. You're kidding.
WIN. It was funny.
NELL. Fuck that for a joke.
WIN. It was funny.
MARLENE. Anyway they'd see you in the garden.
WIN. The garden has extremely high walls.
NELL. I think I'll tell the wife.
WIN. Like hell.
NELL. She might leave him and you could have the rose garden.
WIN. The minute it's not a secret I'm out on my ear.
NELL. Don't know why you bother.
WIN. Bit of fun.
NELL. I think it's time you went to Australia.
WIN. I think it's pushy Mr. Holden time.

---

3. The London subway.

NELL. If you've any really pretty bastards, Marlene, I want some for Prestel.
MARLENE. I might have one this afternoon. This morning it's all Pam's secretarial.
NELL. Not long now and you'll be upstairs watching over us all.
MARLENE. Do you feel bad about it?
NELL. I don't like coming second.
MARLENE. Who does?
WIN. We'd rather it was you than Howard. We're glad for you, aren't we Nell.
NELL. Oh yes. Aces.

INTERVIEW

WIN *and* LOUISE.

WIN. Now Louise, hello, I have your details here. You've been very loyal to the one job I see.
LOUISE. Yes I have.
WIN. Twenty-one years is a long time in one place.
LOUISE. I feel it is. I feel it's time to move on.
WIN. And you are what age now?
LOUISE. I'm in my early forties.
WIN. Exactly?
LOUISE. Forty-six.
WIN. It's not necessarily a handicap, well it is of course we have to face that, but it's not necessarily a disabling handicap, experience does count for something.
LOUISE. I hope so.
WIN. Now between ourselves is there any trouble, any reason why you're leaving that wouldn't appear on the form?
LOUISE. Nothing like that.
WIN. Like what?
LOUISE. Nothing at all.
WIN. No long-term understandings come to a sudden end, making for an insupportable atmosphere?
LOUISE. I've always completely avoided anything like that at all.
WIN. No personality clashes with your immediate superiors or inferiors?
LOUISE. I've always taken care to get on very well with everyone.
WIN. I only ask because it can affect the reference and it also affects your motivation, I want to be quite clear why you're moving on. So I take it the job itself no longer satisfies you. Is it the money?
LOUISE. It's partly the money. It's not so much the money.
WIN. Nine thousand is very respectable. Have you dependants?
LOUISE. No, no dependants. My mother died.
WIN. So why are you making a change?
LOUISE. Other people make changes.
WIN. But why are you, now, after spending most of your life in the one place?
LOUISE. There you are, I've lived for that company, I've given my life really

you could say because I haven't had a great deal of social life, I've worked in the evenings. I haven't had office entanglements for the very reason you just mentioned and if you are committed to your work you don't move in many other circles. I had management status from the age of twenty-seven and you'll appreciate what that means. I've built up a department. And there it is, it works extremely well, and I feel I'm stuck there. I've spent twenty years in middle management. I've seen young men who I trained go on, in my own company or elsewhere, to higher things. Nobody notices me, I don't expect it, I don't attract attention by making mistakes, everybody takes it for granted that my work is perfect. They will notice me when I go, they will be sorry I think to lose me, they will offer me more money of course, I will refuse. They will see when I've gone what I was doing for them.

WIN. If they offer you more money you won't stay?

LOUISE. No I won't.

WIN. Are you the only woman?

LOUISE. Apart from the girls of course, yes. There was one, she was my assistant, it was the only time I took on a young woman assistant, I always had my doubts. I don't care greatly for working with women, I think I pass as a man at work. But I did take on this young woman, her qualifications were excellent, and she did well, she got a department of her own, and left the company for a competitor where she's now on the board and good luck to her. She has a different style, she's a new kind of attractive well-dressed—I don't mean I don't dress properly. But there is a kind of woman who is thirty now who grew up in a different climate. They are not so careful. They take themselves for granted. I have had to justify my existence every minute, and I have done so, I have proved—well.

WIN. Let's face it, vacancies are going to be ones where you'll be in competition with younger men. And there are companies that will value your experience enough you'll be in with a chance. There are also fields that are easier for a woman, there is a cosmetic company here where your experience might be relevant. It's eight and a half, I don't know if that appeals.

LOUISE. I've proved I can earn money. It's more important to get away. I feel it's now or never. I sometimes / think—

WIN. You shouldn't talk too much at an interview.

LOUISE. I don't. I don't normally talk about myself. I know very well how to handle myself in an office situation. I only talk to you because it seems to me this is different, it's your job to understand me, surely. You asked the questions.

WIN. I think I understand you sufficiently.

LOUISE. Well good, that's good.

WIN. Do you drink?

LOUISE. Certainly not. I'm not a teetotaler, I think that's very suspect, it's seen as being an alcoholic if you're teetotal. What do you mean? I don't drink. Why?

WIN. I drink.

LOUISE. I don't.

WIN. Good for you.

MAIN OFFICE

MARLENE *and* ANGIE.
    [ANGIE *arrives*.]
ANGIE.   Hello.
MARLENE.   Have you an appointment?
ANGIE.   It's me. I've come.
MARLENE.   What? It's not Angie?
ANGIE.   It was hard to find this place. I got lost.
MARLENE.   How did you get past the receptionist? The girl on the desk, didn't she try to stop you?
ANGIE.   What desk?
MARLENE.   Never mind.
ANGIE.   I just walked in. I was looking for you.
MARLENE.   Well you found me.
ANGIE.   Yes.
MARLENE.   So where's your mum? Are you up in town for the day?
ANGIE.   Not really.
MARLENE.   Sit down. Do you feel all right?
ANGIE.   Yes thank you.
MARLENE.   So where's Joyce?
ANGIE.   She's at home.
MARLENE.   Did you come up on a school trip then?
ANGIE.   I've left school.
MARLENE.   Did you come up with a friend?
ANGIE.   No. There's just me.
MARLENE.   You came up by yourself, that's fun. What have you been doing? Shopping? Tower of London?
ANGIE.   No, I just come here. I come to you.
MARLENE.   That's very nice of you to think of paying your aunty a visit. There's not many nieces make that the first port of call. Would you like a cup of coffee?
ANGIE.   No thank you.
MARLENE.   Tea, orange?
ANGIE.   No thank you.
MARLENE.   Do you feel all right?
ANGIE.   Yes thank you.
MARLENE.   Are you tired from the journey?
ANGIE.   Yes, I'm tired from the journey.
MARLENE.   You sit there for a bit then. How's Joyce?
ANGIE.   She's all right.
MARLENE.   Same as ever.
ANGIE.   Oh yes.
MARLENE.   Unfortunately you've picked a day when I'm rather busy, if there's ever a day when I'm not, or I'd take you out to lunch and we'd go to Madame Tussaud's. We could go shopping. What time do you have to be back? Have you got a day return?
ANGIE.   No.
MARLENE.   So what train are you going back on?
ANGIE.   I came on the bus.

MARLENE. So what bus are you going back on? Are you staying the night?
ANGIE. Yes.
MARLENE. Who are you staying with? Do you want me to put you up for the night, is that it?
ANGIE. Yes please.
MARLENE. I haven't got a spare bed.
ANGIE. I can sleep on the floor.
MARLENE. You can sleep on the sofa.
ANGIE. Yes please.
MARLENE. I do think Joyce might have phoned me. It's like her.
ANGIE. This is where you work is it?
MARLENE. It's where I have been working the last two years but I'm going to move into another office.
ANGIE. It's lovely.
MARLENE. My new office is nicer than this. There's just the one big desk in it for me.
ANGIE. Can I see it?
MARLENE. Not now, no, there's someone else in it now. But he's leaving at the end of next week and I'm going to do his job.
ANGIE. Is that good?
MARLENE. Yes, it's very good.
ANGIE. Are you going to be in charge?
MARLENE. Yes I am.
ANGIE. I knew you would be.
MARLENE. How did you know?
ANGIE. I knew you'd be in charge of everything.
MARLENE. Not quite everything.
ANGIE. You will be.
MARLENE. Well we'll see.
ANGIE. Can I see it next week then?
MARLENE. Will you still be here next week?
ANGIE. Yes.
MARLENE. Don't you have to go home?
ANGIE. No.
MARLENE. Why not?
ANGIE. It's all right.
MARLENE. Is it all right?
ANGIE. Yes, don't worry about it.
MARLENE. Does Joyce know where you are?
ANGIE. Yes of course she does.
MARLENE. Well does she?
ANGIE. Don't worry about it.
MARLENE. How long are you planning to stay with me then?
ANGIE. You know when you came to see us last year?
MARLENE. Yes, that was nice wasn't it?
ANGIE. That was the best day of my whole life.
MARLENE. So how long are you planning to stay?
ANGIE. Don't you want me?
MARLENE. Yes yes, I just wondered.
ANGIE. I won't stay if you don't want me.

MARLENE.   No, of course you can stay.
ANGIE.   I'll sleep on the floor. I won't be any bother.
MARLENE.   Don't get upset.
ANGIE.   I'm not, I'm not. Don't worry about it.
   [MRS. KIDD *comes in.*]
MRS. KIDD.   Excuse me.
MARLENE.   Yes.
MRS. KIDD.   Excuse me.
MARLENE.   Can I help you?
MRS. KIDD.   Excuse me bursting in on you like this but I have to talk to you.
MARLENE.   I am engaged at the moment. / If you could go to reception—
MRS. KIDD.   I'm Rosemary Kidd, Howard's wife, you don't recognize me but we did meet, I remember you of course / but you wouldn't—
MARLENE.   Yes of course, Mrs. Kidd, I'm sorry, we did meet. Howard's about somewhere I expect, have you looked in his office?
MRS. KIDD.   Howard's not about, no. I'm afraid it's you I've come to see if I could have a minute or two.
MARLENE.   I do have an appointment in five minutes.
MRS. KIDD.   This won't take five minutes. I'm very sorry. It is a matter of some urgency.
MARLENE.   Well of course. What can I do for you?
MRS. KIDD.   I just wanted a chat, an informal chat. It's not something I can simply—I'm sorry if I'm interrupting your work. I know office work isn't like housework / which is all interruptions.
MARLENE.   No no, this is my niece. Angie. Mrs. Kidd.
MRS. KIDD.   Very pleased to meet you.
ANGIE.   Very well thank you.
MRS. KIDD.   Howard's not in today.
MARLENE.   Isn't he?
MRS. KIDD.   He's feeling poorly.
MARLENE.   I didn't know. I'm sorry to hear that.
MRS. KIDD.   The fact is he's in a state of shock. About what's happened.
MARLENE.   What has happened?
MRS. KIDD.   You should know if anyone. I'm referring to you being appointed managing director instead of Howard. He hasn't been at all well all weekend. He hasn't slept for three nights. I haven't slept.
MARLENE.   I'm sorry to hear that, Mrs. Kidd. Has he thought of taking sleeping pills?
MRS. KIDD.   It's very hard when someone has worked all these years.
MARLENE.   Business life is full of little setbacks. I'm sure Howard knows that. He'll bounce back in a day or two. We all bounce back.
MRS. KIDD.   If you could see him you'd know what I'm talking about. What's it going to do to him working for a woman? I think if it was a man he'd get over it as something normal.
MARLENE.   I think he's going to have to get over it.
MRS. KIDD.   It's me that bears the brunt. I'm not the one that's been promoted. I put him first every inch of the way. And now what do I get? You women this, you women that. It's not my fault. You're going to have to be very careful how you handle him. He's very hurt.
MARLENE.   Naturally I'll be tactful and pleasant to him, you don't start

pushing someone round. I'll consult him over any decisions affecting his department. But that's no different, Mrs. Kidd, from any of my other colleagues.
MRS. KIDD. I think it is different, because he's a man.
MARLENE. I'm not quite sure why you came to see me.
MRS. KIDD. I had to do something.
MARLENE. Well you've done it, you've seen me. I think that's probably all we've time for. I'm sorry he's been taking it out on you. He really is a shit, Howard.
MRS. KIDD. But he's got a family to support. He's got three children. It's only fair.
MARLENE. Are you suggesting I give up the job to him then?
MRS. KIDD. It had crossed my mind if you were unavailable after all for some reason, he would be the natural second choice I think, don't you? I'm not asking.
MARLENE. Good.
MRS. KIDD. You mustn't tell him I came. He's very proud.
MARLENE. If he doesn't like what's happening here he can go and work somewhere else.
MRS. KIDD. Is that a threat?
MARLENE. I'm sorry but I do have some work to do.
MRS. KIDD. It's not that easy, a man of Howard's age. You don't care. I thought he was going too far but he's right. You're one of these ballbreakers / that's what you are. You'll end up
MARLENE. I'm sorry but I do have some work to do.
MRS. KIDD. miserable and lonely. You're not natural.
MARLENE. Could you please piss off?
MRS. KIDD. I thought if I saw you at least I'd be doing something.
   [MRS. KIDD *goes.*]
MARLENE. I've got to go and do some work now. Will you come back later?
ANGIE. I think you were wonderful.
MARLENE. I've got to go and do some work now.
ANGIE. You told her to piss off.
MARLENE. Will you come back later?
ANGIE. Can't I stay here?
MARLENE. Don't you want to go sightseeing?
ANGIE. I'd rather stay here.
MARLENE. You can stay here I suppose, if it's not boring.
ANGIE. It's where I most want to be in the world.
MARLENE. I'll see you later then.
   [MARLENE *goes.* ANGIE *sits at* WIN's *desk.*]

INTERVIEW

NELL *and* SHONA.

NELL. Is this right? You are Shona?
SHONA. Yeh.
NELL. It says here you're twenty-nine.
SHONA. Yeh.

NELL. Too many late nights, me. So you've been where you are for four years. Shona, you're earning six basic and three commission. So what's the problem?
SHONA. No problem.
NELL. Why do you want a change?
SHONA. Just a change.
NELL. Change of product, change of area?
SHONA. Both.
NELL. But you're happy on the road?
SHONA. I like driving.
NELL. You're not after management status?
SHONA. I would like management status.
NELL. You'd be interested in titular management status but not come off the road?
SHONA. I want to be on the road, yeh.
NELL. So how many calls have you been making a day?
SHONA. Six.
NELL. And what proportion of those are successful?
SHONA. Six.
NELL. That's hard to believe.
SHONA. Four.
NELL. You find it easy to get the initial interest do you?
SHONA. Oh yeh, I get plenty of initial interest.
NELL. And what about closing?
SHONA. I close, don't I?
NELL. Because that's what an employer is going to have doubts about with you a lady as I needn't tell you, whether she's got the guts to push through to a closing situation. They think we're too nice. They think we listen to the buyer's doubts. They think we consider his needs and his feelings.
SHONA. I never consider people's feelings.
NELL. I was selling for six years, I can sell anything, I've sold in three continents, and I'm jolly as they come but I'm not very nice.
SHONA. I'm not very nice.
NELL. What sort of time do you have on the road with the other reps? Get on all right? Handle the chat?
SHONA. I get on. Keep myself to myself.
NELL. Fairly much of a loner are you?
SHONA. Sometimes.
NELL. So what field are you interested in?
SHONA. Computers.
NELL. That's a top field as you know and you'll be up against some very slick fellas there, there's some very pretty boys in computers, it's an American-style field.
SHONA. That's why I want to do it.
NELL. Video systems appeal? That's a high-flying situation.
SHONA. Video systems appeal OK.
NELL. Because Prestel have half a dozen vacancies I'm looking to fill at the moment. We're talking in the area of ten to fifteen thousand here and upwards.
SHONA. Sounds OK.

NELL. I've half a mind to go for it myself. But it's good money here if you've got the top clients. Could you fancy it do you think?
SHONA. Work here?
NELL. I'm not in a position to offer, there's nothing officially going just now, but we're always on the lookout. There's not that many of us. We could keep in touch.
SHONA. I like driving.
NELL. So the Prestel appeals?
SHONA. Yeh.
NELL. What about ties?
SHONA. No ties.
NELL. So relocation wouldn't be a problem.
SHONA. No problem.
NELL. So just fill me in a bit more could you about what you've been doing.
SHONA. What I've been doing. It's all down there.
NELL. The bare facts are down here but I've got to present you to an employer.
SHONA. I'm twenty-nine years old.
NELL. So it says here.
SHONA. We look young. Youngness runs in the family in our family.
NELL. So just describe your present job for me.
SHONA. My present job at present. I have a car. I have a Porsche. I go up the M1[4] a lot. Burn up the M1 a lot. Straight up the M1 in the fast lane to where the clients are, Staffordshire, Yorkshire, I do a lot in Yorkshire. I'm selling electric things. Like dishwashers, washing machines, stainless steel tubs are a feature and the reliability of the program. After sales service, we offer a very good after sales service, spare parts, plenty of spare parts. And fridges, I sell a lot of fridges specially in the summer. People want to buy fridges in the summer because of the heat melting the butter and you get fed up standing the milk in a basin of cold water with a cloth over, stands to reason people don't want to do that in this day and age. So I sell a lot of them. Big ones with big freezers. Big freezers. And I stay in hotels at night when I'm away from home. On my expense account. I stay in various hotels. They know me, the ones I go to. I check in, have a bath, have a shower. Then I go down to the bar, have a gin and tonic, have a chat. Then I go into the dining room and have dinner. I usually have fillet steak and mushrooms, I like mushrooms. I like smoked salmon very much. I like having a salad on the side. Green salad. I don't like tomatoes.
NELL. Christ what a waste of time.
SHONA. Beg your pardon?
NELL. Not a word of this is true is it?
SHONA. How do you mean?
NELL. You just filled in the form with a pack of lies.
SHONA. Not exactly.
NELL. How old are you?
SHONA. Twenty-nine.
NELL. Nineteen?
SHONA. Twenty-one.

---

4. A major highway leading north from London.

NELL.   And what jobs have you done? Have you done any?
SHONA.   I could though, I bet you.

MAIN OFFICE

ANGIE *sitting as before.*
   [WIN *comes in.*]
WIN.   Who's sitting in my chair?
ANGIE.   What? Sorry.
WIN.   Who's been eating my porridge?
ANGIE.   What?
WIN.   It's all right, I saw Marlene. Angie isn't it? I'm Win. And I'm not going out for lunch because I'm knackered. I'm going to set me down here and have a yoghurt. Do you like yoghurt?
ANGIE.   No.
WIN.   That's good because I've only got one. Are you hungry?
ANGIE.   No.
WIN.   There's a cafe on the corner.
ANGIE.   No thank you. Do you work here?
WIN.   How did you guess?
ANGIE.   Because you look as if you might work here and you're sitting at the desk. Have you always worked here?
WIN.   No I was headhunted. That means I was working for another outfit like this and this lot came and offered me more money. I broke my contract, there was a hell of a stink. There's not many top ladies about. Your aunty's a smashing bird.
ANGIE.   Yes I know.
MARLENE.   Fan are you? Fan of your aunty's?
ANGIE.   Do you think I could work here?
WIN.   Not at the moment.
ANGIE.   How do I start?
WIN.   What can you do?
ANGIE.   I don't know. Nothing.
WIN.   Type?
ANGIE.   Not very well. The letters jump up when I do capitals. I was going to do a CSE[5] in commerce but I didn't.
WIN.   What have you got?
ANGIE.   What?
WIN.   CSE's, O's.
ANGIE.   Nothing, none of that. Did you do all that?
WIN.   Oh yes, all that, and a science degree funnily enough. I started out doing medical research but there's no money in it. I thought I'd go abroad. Did you know they sell Coca-Cola in Russia and Pepsi-cola in China? You don't have to be qualified as much as you might think. Men are awful bullshitters, they like to make out jobs are harder than they are. Any job I ever did I started doing it better than the rest of the crowd and they didn't like it. So I'd get unpopular and I'd have a drink to cheer myself up. I lived with a fella and supported him for four years, he

---

5. Certificate of Secondary Education.

couldn't get work. After that I went to California. I like the sunshine. Americans know how to live. This country's too slow. Then I went to Mexico, still in sales, but it's no country for a single lady. I came home, went bonkers for a bit, thought I was five different people, got over that all right, the psychiatrist said I was perfectly sane and highly intelligent. Got married in a moment of weakness and he's inside[6] now, he's been inside four years, and I've not been to see him too much this last year. I like this better than sales, I'm not really that aggressive. I started thinking sales was a good job if you want to meet people, but you're meeting people that don't want to meet you. It's no good if you like being liked. Here your clients want to meet you because you're the one doing them some good. They hope.

[ANGIE *has fallen asleep*. NELL *comes in*.]

NELL. You're talking to yourself, sunshine.
WIN. So what's new?
NELL. Who is this?
WIN. Marlene's little niece.
NELL. What's she got, brother, sister? She never talks about her family.
WIN. I was telling her my life story.
NELL. Violins?
WIN. No, success story.
NELL. You've heard Howard's had a heart attack?
WIN. No, when?
NELL. I heard just now. He hadn't come in, he was at home, he's gone to hospital. He's not dead. His wife was here, she rushed off in a cab.
WIN. Too much butter, too much smoke. We must send him some flowers.

[MARLENE *comes in*.]

You've heard about Howard?
MARLENE. Poor sod.
NELL. Lucky he didn't get the job if that's what his health's like.
MARLENE. Is she asleep?
WIN. She wants to work here.
MARLENE. Packer in Tesco more like.
WIN. She's a nice kid. Isn't she?
MARLENE. She's a bit thick. She's a bit funny.
WIN. She thinks you're wonderful.
MARLENE. She's not going to make it.

SCENE TWO

A year earlier. Sunday evening. JOYCE's *kitchen.* JOYCE, ANGIE, MARLENE. MARLENE *is taking presents out of a bright carrier bag.* ANGIE *has already opened a box of chocolates.*

MARLENE. Just a few little things. / I've no memory for
JOYCE. There's no need.
MARLENE. birthdays have I, and Christmas seems to slip by. So I think I owe Angie a few presents.

---

6. I.e., in prison.

JOYCE. What do you say?
ANGIE. Thank you very much. Thank you very much, Aunty Marlene.
[*She opens a present. It is the dress from Act One, new.*]
ANGIE. Oh look, Mum, isn't it lovely?
MARLENE. I don't know if it's the right size. She's grown up since I saw her. / I knew she was always tall for her age.
ANGIE. Isn't it lovely?
JOYCE. She's a big lump.
MARLENE. Hold it up, Angie, let's see.
ANGIE. I'll put it on, shall I?
MARLENE. Yes, try it on.
JOYCE. Go on to your room then, we don't want / a strip show thank you.
ANGIE. Of course I'm going to my room, what do you think? Look Mum, here's something for you. Open it, go on. What is it? Can I open it for you?
JOYCE. Yes, you open it, pet.
ANGIE. Don't you want to open it yourself? / Go on.
JOYCE. I don't mind, you can do it.
ANGIE. It's something hard. It's—what is it? A bottle. Drink is it? No, it's what? Perfume, look. What a lot. Open it, look, let's smell it. Oh it's strong. It's lovely. Put it on me. How do you do it? Put it on me.
JOYCE. You're too young.
ANGIE. I can play wearing it like dressing up.
JOYCE. And you're too old for that. Here, give it here, I'll do it, you'll tip the whole bottle over yourself / and we'll have you smelling all summer.
ANGIE. Put it on you. Do I smell? Put it on Aunty too. Put it on Aunty too. Let's all smell.
MARLENE. I didn't know what you'd like.
JOYCE. There's no danger I'd have it already, / that's one thing.
ANGIE. Now we all smell the same.
MARLENE. It's a bit of nonsense.
JOYCE. It's very kind of you Marlene, you shouldn't.
ANGIE. Now I'll put on the dress and then we'll see.
[ANGIE *goes.*]
JOYCE. You've caught me on the hop with the place in a mess. / If you'd let me know you was coming I'd have got
MARLENE. That doesn't matter.
JOYCE. something in to eat. We had our dinner dinnertime. We're just going to have a cup of tea. You could have an egg.
MARLENE. No, I'm not hungry. Tea's fine.
JOYCE. I don't expect you take sugar.
MARLENE. Why not?
JOYCE. You take care of yourself.
MARLENE. How do you mean you didn't know I was coming?
JOYCE. You could have written. I know we're not on the phone but we're not completely in the dark ages, / we do have a postman.
MARLENE. But you asked me to come.
JOYCE. How did I ask you to come?
MARLENE. Angie said when she phoned up.
JOYCE. Angie phoned up, did she?

MARLENE. Was it just Angie's idea?
JOYCE. What did she say?
MARLENE. She said you wanted me to come and see you. / It was a couple of weeks ago. How was I to know that's a
JOYCE. Ha.
MARLENE. ridiculous idea? My diary's always full a couple of weeks ahead so we fixed it for this weekend. I was meant to get here earlier but I was held up. She gave me messages from you.
JOYCE. Didn't you wonder why I didn't phone you myself?
MARLENE. She said you didn't like using the phone. You're shy on the phone and can't use it. I don't know what you're like, do I.
JOYCE. Are there people who can't use the phone?
MARLENE. I expect so.
JOYCE. I haven't met any.
MARLENE. Why should I think she was lying?
JOYCE. Because she's like what she's like.
MARLENE. How do I know / what she's like?
JOYCE. It's not my fault you don't know what she's like. You never come and see her.
MARLENE. Well I have now / and you don't seem over the moon.*
JOYCE. Good.
  *Well I'd have got a cake if she'd told me.
     [*Pause.*]
MARLENE. I did wonder why you wanted to see me.
JOYCE. I didn't want to see you.
MARLENE. Yes, I know. Shall I go?
JOYCE. I don't mind seeing you.
MARLENE. Great, I feel really welcome.
JOYCE. You can come and see Angie any time you like, I'm not stopping you. / You know where we are. You're the
MARLENE. Ta ever so.
JOYCE. one went away, not me. I'm right here where I was. And will be a few years yet I shouldn't wonder.
MARLENE. All right. All right.
     [JOYCE *gives* MARLENE *a cup of tea.*]
JOYCE. Tea.
MARLENE. Sugar?
     [JOYCE *passes* MARLENE *the sugar.*]
   It's very quiet down here.
JOYCE. I expect you'd notice it.
MARLENE. The air smells different too.
JOYCE. That's the scent.
MARLENE. No, I mean walking down the lane.
JOYCE. What sort of air you get in London then?
     [ANGIE *comes in, wearing the dress. It fits.*]
MARLENE. Oh, very pretty. / You do look pretty, Angie.
JOYCE. That fits all right.
MARLENE. Do you like the color?
ANGIE. Beautiful. Beautiful.
JOYCE. You better take it off, / you'll get it dirty.
ANGIE. I want to wear it. I want to wear it.

MARLENE.   It is for wearing after all. You can't just hang it up and look at it.
ANGIE.   I love it.
JOYCE.   Well if you must you must.
ANGIE.   If someone asks me what's my favorite color I'll tell them it's this. Thank you very much, Aunty Marlene.
MARLENE.   You didn't tell your mum you asked me down.
ANGIE.   I wanted it to be a surprise.
JOYCE.   I'll give you a surprise / one of these days.
ANGIE.   I thought you'd like to see her. She hasn't been here since I was nine. People do see their aunts.
MARLENE.   Is it that long? Doesn't time fly?
ANGIE.   I wanted to.
JOYCE.   I'm not cross.
ANGIE.   Are you glad?
JOYCE.   I smell nicer anyhow, don't I?
  [KIT *comes in without saying anything, as if she lived there.*]
MARLENE.   I think it was a good idea, Angie, about time. We are sisters after all. It's a pity to let that go.
JOYCE.   This is Kitty, who lives up the road. This is Angie's Aunty Marlene.
KIT.   What's that?
ANGIE.   It's a present. Do you like it?
KIT.   It's all right. / Are you coming out?*
MARLENE.   Hello, Kitty.
ANGIE.   *No.
KIT.   What's that smell?
ANGIE.   It's a present.
KIT.   It's horrible. Come on.*
MARLENE.   Have a chocolate.
ANGIE.   *No, I'm busy.
KIT.   Coming out later?
ANGIE.   No.
KIT.   [*To* MARLENE.]   Hello.
  [KIT *goes without a chocolate.*]
JOYCE.   She's a little girl Angie sometimes plays with because she's the only child lives really close. She's like a little sister to her really. Angie's good with little children.
MARLENE.   Do you want to work with children, Angie? / Be a teacher or a nursery nurse?
JOYCE.   I don't think she's ever thought of it.
MARLENE.   What do you want to do?
JOYCE.   She hasn't an idea in her head what she wants to do. / Lucky to get anything.
MARLENE.   Angie?
JOYCE.   She's not clever like you.
  [*Pause.*]
MARLENE.   I'm not clever, just pushy.
JOYCE.   True enough.
  [MARLENE *takes a bottle of whisky out of the bag.*]
  I don't drink spirits.
ANGIE.   You do at Christmas.

JOYCE.   It's not Christmas, is it?
ANGIE.   It's better than Christmas.
MARLENE.   Glasses?
JOYCE.   Just a small one then.
MARLENE.   Do you want some, Angie?
ANGIE.   I can't, can I?
JOYCE.   Taste it if you want. You won't like it.
MARLENE.   We got drunk together the night your grandfather died.
JOYCE.   We did not get drunk.
MARLENE.   I got drunk. You were just overcome with grief.
JOYCE.   I still keep up the grave with flowers.
MARLENE.   Do you really?
JOYCE.   Why wouldn't I?
MARLENE.   Have you seen Mother?
JOYCE.   Of course I've seen Mother.
MARLENE.   I mean lately.
JOYCE.   Of course I've seen her lately, I go every Thursday.
MARLENE. [*To* ANGIE.]   Do you remember your grandfather?
ANGIE.   He got me out of the bath one night in a towel.
MARLENE.   Did he? I don't think he ever gave me a bath. Did he give you a bath, Joyce? He probably got soft in his old age. Did you like him?
ANGIE.   Yes of course.
MARLENE.   Why?
ANGIE.   What?
MARLENE.   So what's the news? How's Mrs. Paisley? Still going crazily? / And Dorothy. What happened to Dorothy?*
ANGIE.   Who's Mrs. Paisley?
JOYCE.   * She went to Canada.
MARLENE.   Did she? What to do?
JOYCE.   I don't know. She just went to Canada.
MARLENE.   Well / good for her.
ANGIE.   Mr. Connolly killed his wife.
MARLENE.   What, Connolly at Whitegates?
ANGIE.   They found her body in the garden. / Under the cabbages.
MARLENE.   He was always so proper.
JOYCE.   Stuck up git. Connolly. Best lawyer money could buy but he couldn't get out of it. She was carrying on with Matthew.
MARLENE.   How old's Matthew then?
JOYCE.   Twenty-one. / He's got a motorbike.
MARLENE.   I think he's about six.
ANGIE.   How can he be six? He's six years older than me. / If he was six I'd be nothing, I'd be just born this minute.
JOYCE.   Your aunty knows that, she's just being silly. She means it's so long since she's been here she's forgotten about Matthew.
ANGIE.   You were here for my birthday when I was nine. I had a pink cake. Kit was only five then, she was four, she hadn't started school yet. She could read already when she went to school. You remember my birthday? / You remember me?
MARLENE.   Yes, I remember the cake.
ANGIE.   You remember me?

MARLENE. Yes, I remember you.
ANGIE. And Mum and Dad was there, and Kit was.
MARLENE. Yes, how is your dad? Where is he tonight? Up the pub?
JOYCE. No, he's not here.
MARLENE. I can see he's not here.
JOYCE. He moved out.
MARLENE. What? When did he? / Just recently?*
ANGIE. Didn't you know that? You don't know much.
JOYCE. *No, it must be three years ago. Don't be rude, Angie.
ANGIE. I'm not, am I Aunty? What else don't you know?
JOYCE. You was in America or somewhere. You sent a postcard.
ANGIE. I've got that in my room. It's the Grand Canyon. Do you want to see it? Shall I get it? I can get it for you.
MARLENE. Yes, all right.

[ANGIE *goes.*]

JOYCE. You could be married with twins for all I know. You must have affairs and break up and I don't need to know about any of that so I don't see what the fuss is about.
MARLENE. What fuss?

[ANGIE *comes back with the postcard.*]

ANGIE. "Driving across the states for a new job in L.A. It's a long way but the car goes very fast. It's very hot. Wish you were here. Love from Aunty Marlene."
JOYCE. Did you make a lot of money?
MARLENE. I spent a lot.
ANGIE. I want to go to America. Will you take me?
JOYCE. She's not going to America, she's been to America, stupid.
ANGIE. She might go again, stupid. It's not something you do once. People who go keep going all the time, back and forth on jets. They go on Concorde and Laker[7] and get jet lag. Will you take me?
MARLENE. I'm not planning a trip.
ANGIE. Will you let me know?
JOYCE. Angie, / you're getting silly.
ANGIE. I want to be American.
JOYCE. It's time you were in bed.
ANGIE. No it's not. / I don't have to go to bed at all tonight.
JOYCE. School in the morning.
ANGIE. I'll wake up.
JOYCE. Come on now, you know how you get.
ANGIE. How do I get? / I don't get anyhow.
JOYCE. Angie.
    Are you staying the night?
MARLENE. Yes, if that's all right. / I'll see you in the morning.
ANGIE. You can have my bed. I'll sleep on the sofa.
JOYCE. You will not, you'll sleep in your bed. / Think I can't
ANGIE. Mum.

---

7. The Concorde, a supersonic plane flown by Air France and British Airways (1976–2003), was the most expensive commercial flight across the Atlantic; Laker, a no-frills service (1977–82) that sold tickets only on the day of travel, was the cheapest.

JOYCE.   see through that? I can just see you going to sleep / with us talking.
ANGIE.   I would, I would go to sleep, I'd love that.
JOYCE.   I'm going to get cross, Angie.
ANGIE.   I want to show her something.
JOYCE.   Then bed.
ANGIE.   It's a secret.
JOYCE.   Then I expect it's in your room so off you go. Give us a shout when you're ready for bed and your aunty'll be up and see you.
ANGIE.   Will you?
MARLENE.   Yes of course.
   [ANGIE *goes. Silence.*]
   It's cold tonight.
JOYCE.   Will you be all right on the sofa? You can / have my bed.
MARLENE.   The sofa's fine.
JOYCE.   Yes the forecast said rain tonight but it's held off.
MARLENE.   I was going to walk down to the estuary but I've left it a bit late. Is it just the same?
JOYCE.   They cut down the hedges a few years back. Is that since you were here?
MARLENE.   But it's not changed down the end, all the mud? And the reeds? We used to pick them when they were bigger than us. Are there still lapwings?
JOYCE.   You get strangers walking there on a Sunday. I expect they're looking at the mud and the lapwings, yes.
MARLENE.   You could have left.
JOYCE.   Who says I wanted to leave?
MARLENE.   Stop getting at me then, you're really boring.
JOYCE.   How could I have left?
MARLENE.   Did you want to?
JOYCE.   I said how, / how could I?
MARLENE.   If you'd wanted to you'd have done it.
JOYCE.   Christ.
MARLENE.   Are we getting drunk?
JOYCE.   Do you want something to eat?
MARLENE.   No, I'm getting drunk.
JOYCE.   Funny time to visit, Sunday evening.
MARLENE.   I came this morning. I spent the day.
ANGIE. [*Off.*]   Aunty! Aunty Marlene!
MARLENE.   I'd better go.
JOYCE.   Go on then.
MARLENE.   All right.
ANGIE. [*Off.*]   Aunty! Can you hear me? I'm ready.
   [MARLENE *goes.* JOYCE *goes on sitting.* MARLENE *comes back.*]
JOYCE.   So what's the secret?
MARLENE.   It's a secret.
JOYCE.   I know what it is anyway.
MARLENE.   I bet you don't. You always said that.
JOYCE.   It's her exercise book.
MARLENE.   Yes, but you don't know what's in it.
JOYCE.   It's some game, some secret society she has with Kit.

MARLENE. You don't know the password. You don't know the code.
JOYCE. You're really in it, aren't you. Can you do the handshake?
MARLENE. She didn't mention a handshake.
JOYCE. I thought they'd have a special handshake. She spends hours writing that but she's useless at school. She copies things out of books about black magic, and politicians out of the paper. It's a bit childish.
MARLENE. I think it's a plot to take over the world.
JOYCE. She's been in the remedial class the last two years.
MARLENE. I came up this morning and spent the day in Ipswich. I went to see mother.
JOYCE. Did she recognize you?
MARLENE. Are you trying to be funny?
JOYCE. No, she does wander.
MARLENE. She wasn't wandering at all, she was very lucid thank you.
JOYCE. You were very lucky then.
MARLENE. Fucking awful life she's had.
JOYCE. Don't tell me.
MARLENE. Fucking waste.
JOYCE. Don't talk to me.
MARLENE. Why shouldn't I talk? Why shouldn't I talk to you? / Isn't she my mother too?
JOYCE. Look, you've left, you've gone away, / we can do without you.
MARLENE. I left home, so what, I left home. People do leave home / it is normal.
JOYCE. We understand that, we can do without you.
MARLENE. We weren't happy. Were you happy?
JOYCE. Don't come back.
MARLENE. So it's just your mother is it, your child, you never wanted me round, / you were jealous of me because I was the
JOYCE. Here we go.
MARLENE. little one and I was clever.
JOYCE. I'm not clever enough for all this psychology / if that's what it is.
MARLENE. Why can't I visit my own family / without all this?*
JOYCE. Aah.
Just don't go on about Mum's life when you haven't been to see her for how many years. / I go and see her every week.
MARLENE. It's up to me.
*Then don't go and see her every week.
JOYCE. Somebody has to.
MARLENE. No they don't. / Why do they?
JOYCE. How would I feel if I didn't go?
MARLENE. A lot better.
JOYCE. I hope you feel better.
MARLENE. It's up to me.
JOYCE. You couldn't get out of here fast enough.
MARLENE. Of course I couldn't get out of here fast enough. What was I going to do? Marry a dairyman who'd come home pissed? / Don't you fucking this fucking that fucking bitch
JOYCE. Christ.
MARLENE. fucking tell me what to fucking do fucking.

JOYCE. I don't know how you could leave your own child.
MARLENE. You were quick enough to take her.
JOYCE. What does that mean?
MARLENE. You were quick enough to take her.
JOYCE. Or what? Have her put in a home? Have some stranger / take her would you rather?
MARLENE. You couldn't have one so you took mine.
JOYCE. I didn't know that then.
MARLENE. Like hell, / married three years.
JOYCE. I didn't know that. Plenty of people / take that long.
MARLENE. Well it turned out lucky for you, didn't it?
JOYCE. Turned out all right for you by the look of you. You'd be getting a few less thousand a year.
MARLENE. Not necessarily.
JOYCE. You'd be stuck here / like you said.
MARLENE. I could have taken her with me.
JOYCE. You didn't want to take her with you. It's not good coming back now, Marlene, / and saying—
MARLENE. I know a managing director who's got two children, she breast feeds in the board room, she pays a hundred pounds a week on domestic help alone and she can afford that because she's an extremely high-powered lady earning a great deal of money.
JOYCE. So what's that got to do with you at the age of seventeen?
MARLENE. Just because you were married and had somewhere to live—
JOYCE. You could have lived at home. / Or live with me
MARLENE. Don't be stupid.
JOYCE. and Frank. / You said you weren't keeping it. You
MARLENE. You never suggested.
JOYCE. shouldn't have had it / if you wasn't going to keep it.
MARLENE. Here we go.
JOYCE. You was the most stupid, / for someone so clever you was the most stupid, get yourself pregnant, not go to the doctor, not tell.
MARLENE. You wanted it, you said you were glad, I remember the day, you said I'm glad you never got rid of it, I'll look after it, you said that down by the river. So what are you saying, sunshine, you don't want her?
JOYCE. Course I'm not saying that.
MARLENE. Because I'll take her, / wake her up and pack now.
JOYCE. You wouldn't know how to begin to look after her.
MARLENE. Don't you want her?
JOYCE. Course I do, she's my child.
MARLENE. Then what are you going on about / why did I have her?
JOYCE. You said I got her off you / when you didn't—
MARLENE. I said you were lucky / the way it—
JOYCE. Have a child now if you want one. You're not old.
MARLENE. I might do.
JOYCE. Good.
    [*Pause.*]
MARLENE. I've been on the pill so long / I'm probably sterile.
JOYCE. Listen when Angie was six months I did get pregnant and I lost it because I was so tired looking after your fucking baby / because she cried so much—yes I did tell

MARLENE. You never told me.
JOYCE. you—/ and the doctor said if I'd sat down all day with
MARLENE. Well I forgot.
JOYCE. my feet up I'd've kept it / and that's the only chance I ever had because after that—
MARLENE. I've had two abortions, are you interested? Shall I tell you about them? Well I won't, it's boring, it wasn't a problem. I don't like messy talk about blood / and what a bad
JOYCE. If I hadn't had your baby. The doctor said.
MARLENE. time we all had. I don't want a baby. I don't want to talk about gynecology.
JOYCE. Then stop trying to get Angie off of me.
MARLENE. I come down here after six years. All night you've been saying I don't come often enough. If I don't come for another six years she'll be twenty-one, will that be OK?
JOYCE. That'll be fine, yes, six years would suit me fine.
   [*Pause.*]
MARLENE. I was afraid of this.
I only came because I thought you wanted . . .
I just want . . .
   [MARLENE *cries.*]
JOYCE. Don't grizzle, Marlene, for God's sake.
Marly? Come on, pet. Love you really.
Fucking stop it, will you?
MARLENE. No, let me cry. I like it.
   [*They laugh.* MARLENE *begins to stop crying.*]
I knew I'd cry if I wasn't careful.
JOYCE. Everyone's always crying in this house. Nobody takes any notice.
MARLENE. You've been wonderful looking after Angie.
JOYCE. Don't get carried away.
MARLENE. I can't write letters but I do think of you.
JOYCE. You're getting drunk. I'm going to make some tea.
MARLENE. Love you.
   [JOYCE *gets up to make tea.*]
JOYCE. I can see why you'd want to leave. It's a dump here.
MARLENE. So what's this about you and Frank?
JOYCE. He was always carrying on, wasn't he? And if I wanted to go out in the evening he'd go mad, even if it was nothing, a class, I was going to go to an evening class. So he had this girlfriend, only twenty-two poor cow, and I said go on, off you go, hoppit. I don't think he even likes her.
MARLENE. So what about money?
JOYCE. I've always said I don't want your money.
MARLENE. No, does he send you money?
JOYCE. I've got four different cleaning jobs. Adds up. There's not a lot round here.
MARLENE. Does Angie miss him?
JOYCE. She doesn't say.
MARLENE. Does she see him?
JOYCE. He was never that fond of her to be honest.
MARLENE. He tried to kiss me once. When you were engaged.
JOYCE. Did you fancy him?

MARLENE. No, he looked like a fish.
JOYCE. He was lovely then.
MARLENE. Ugh.
JOYCE. Well I fancied him. For about three years.
MARLENE. Have you got someone else?
JOYCE. There's not a lot round here. Mind you, the minute you're on your own, you'd be amazed how your friends' husbands drop by. I'd sooner do without.
MARLENE. I don't see why you couldn't take my money.
JOYCE. I do, so don't bother about it.
MARLENE. Only got to ask.
JOYCE. So what about you? Good job?
MARLENE. Good for a laugh. / Got back from the US of A a bit
JOYCE. Good for more than a laugh I should think.
MARLENE. wiped out and slotted into this speedy employment agency and still there.
JOYCE. You can always find yourself work then.
MARLENE. That's right.
JOYCE. And men?
MARLENE. Oh there's always men.
JOYCE. No one special?
MARLENE. There's fellas who like to be seen with a high-flying lady. Shows they've got something really good in their pants. But they can't take the day to day. They're waiting for me to turn into the little woman. Or maybe I'm just horrible of course.
JOYCE. Who needs them?
MARLENE. Who needs them? Well I do. But I need adventures more. So on on into the sunset. I think the eighties are going to be stupendous.
JOYCE. Who for?
MARLENE. For me. / I think I'm going up up up.
JOYCE. Oh for you. Yes, I'm sure they will.
MARLENE. And for the country, come to that. Get the economy back on its feet and whoosh. She's a tough lady, Maggie.[8] I'd give her a job. / She just needs to hang in there. This country
JOYCE. You voted for them, did you?
MARLENE. needs to stop whining. / Monetarism is not stupid.
JOYCE. Drink your tea and shut up, pet.
MARLENE. It takes time, determination. No more slop. / And
JOYCE. Well I think they're filthy bastards.
MARLENE. who's got to drive it on? First woman prime minister. Terrifico. Aces. Right on. / You must admit. Certainly gets my vote.
JOYCE. What good's first woman if it's her? I suppose you'd have liked Hitler if he was a woman. Ms. Hitler. Got a lot done, Hitlerina. / Great adventures.
MARLENE. Bosses still walking on the workers' faces? Still Dadda's little parrot? Haven't you learned to think for yourself? I believe in the individual. Look at me.
JOYCE. I am looking at you.

8. Margaret Thatcher (b. 1925), Conservative prime minister (1979–90).

MARLENE. Come on, Joyce, we're not going to quarrel over politics.
JOYCE. We are though.
MARLENE. Forget I mentioned it. Not a word about the slimy unions will cross my lips.
   [*Pause.*]
JOYCE. You say Mother had a wasted life.
MARLENE. Yes I do. Married to that bastard.
JOYCE. What sort of life did he have? / Working in the fields like
MARLENE. Violent life?
JOYCE. an animal. / Why wouldn't he want a drink?
MARLENE. Come off it.
JOYCE. You want a drink. He couldn't afford whisky.
MARLENE. I don't want to talk about him.
JOYCE. You started, I was talking about her. She had a rotten life because she had nothing. She went hungry.
MARLENE. She was hungry because he drank the money. / He used to hit her.
JOYCE. It's not all down to him. / Their lives were rubbish. They
MARLENE. She didn't hit him.
JOYCE. were treated like rubbish. He's dead and she'll die soon and what sort of life / did they have?
MARLENE. I saw him one night. I came down.
JOYCE. Do you think I didn't? / They didn't get to America and
MARLENE. I still have dreams.
JOYCE. drive across it in a fast car. / Bad nights, they had bad days.
MARLENE. America, America, you're jealous. / I had to get out,
JOYCE. Jealous?
MARLENE. I knew when I was thirteen, out of their house, out of them, never let that happen to me, / never let him, make my own way, out.
JOYCE. Jealous of what you've done, you're ashamed of me if I came to your office, your smart friends, wouldn't you, I'm ashamed of you, think of nothing but yourself, you've got on, nothing's changed for most people / has it?
MARLENE. I hate the working class / which is what you're going
JOYCE. Yes you do.
MARLENE. to go on about now, it doesn't exist any more, it means lazy and stupid. / I don't like the way they talk. I don't
JOYCE. Come on, now we're getting it.
MARLENE. like beer guts and football vomit and saucy tits / and brothers and sisters—
JOYCE. I spit when I see a Rolls Royce, scratch it with my ring / Mercedes it was.
MARLENE. Oh very mature—
JOYCE. I hate the cows I work for / and their dirty dishes with blanquette of fucking veau.[9]
MARLENE. and I will not be pulled down to their level by a flying picket[1] and I won't be sent to Siberia / or a loony bin

---

9. Veal stew.
1. Mobile picket available to reinforce local pickets during a strike.

JOYCE. No, you'll be on a yacht, you'll be head of Coca-Cola and you wait, the eighties is going to be stupendous all right because we'll get you lot off our backs—
MARLENE. just because I'm original. And I support Reagan[2] even if he is a lousy movie star because the reds are swarming up his map and I want to be free in a free world—
JOYCE. What? / What?
MARLENE. I know what I mean / by that—not shut up here.
JOYCE. So don't be round here when it happens because if someone's kicking you I'll just laugh.
  [*Silence.*]
MARLENE. I don't mean anything personal. I don't believe in class. Anyone can do anything if they've got what it takes.
JOYCE. And if they haven't?
MARLENE. If they're stupid or lazy or frightened, I'm not going to help them get a job, why should I?
JOYCE. What about Angie?
MARLENE. What about Angie?
JOYCE. She's stupid, lazy and frightened, so what about her?
MARLENE. You run her down too much. She'll be all right.
JOYCE. I don't expect so, no. I expect her children will say what a wasted life she had. If she has children. Because nothing's changed and it won't with them in.
MARLENE. Them, them. / Us and them?
JOYCE. And you're one of them.
MARLENE. And you're us, wonderful us, and Angie's us / and Mum and Dad's us.
JOYCE. Yes, that's right, and you're them.
MARLENE. Come on, Joyce, what a night. You've got what it takes.
JOYCE. I know I have.
MARLENE. I didn't really mean all that.
JOYCE. I did.
MARLENE. But we're friends anyway.
JOYCE. I don't think so, no.
MARLENE. Well it's lovely to be out in the country. I really must make the effort to come more often.
  I want to go to sleep.
  I want to go to sleep.
  [JOYCE *gets blankets for the sofa.*]
JOYCE. Goodnight then. I hope you'll be warm enough.
MARLENE. Goodnight. Joyce—
JOYCE. No, pet. Sorry.
  [JOYCE *goes.* MARLENE *sits wrapped in a blanket and has another drink.* ANGIE *comes in.*]
ANGIE. Mum?
MARLENE. Angie? What's the matter?
ANGIE. Mum?

---

2. Ronald Reagan (1911–2004), fortieth U.S. president (1981–89); he appeared in more than fifty films between 1937 and 1957.

MARLENE. No, she's gone to bed. It's Aunty Marlene.
ANGIE. Frightening.
MARLENE. Did you have a bad dream? What happened in it?
  Well you're awake now, aren't you pet?
ANGIE. Frightening.

1982

JOYCE CAROL OATES
b. 1938

Whether her characters are situated in contemporary urban centers or in the towns of a Victorian past, Joyce Carol Oates has established her reputation as a psychologist of what she has called "the human soul caught in the stampede of time." In a phenomenally productive literary career, she has published nearly one hundred novels, short stories, books for young adults, collections of essays, and volumes of poems, along with a number of anthologies. The violence associated with some of her fiction is a result of her sense that ordinary people cannot always articulate or even understand the ways in which they are trapped in the convulsions of history. In works that develop fictional variations on actual historical events, she meditates on these issues with power and skill. *Black Water* (1992), for instance, was based on the Chappaquiddick scandal involving Ted Kennedy, and *Blonde* (2000) had its source in the life of Marilyn Monroe. Both were nominated for major prizes—*Black Water* for the Pulitzer and *Blonde* for the National Book Award. In addition, an earlier work examining an interracial teenage romance, *Because It Is Bitter, and Because It Is My Heart* (1990), won the National Book Award, while *We Were the Mulvaneys* (1996) soared to the top of the *New York Times* best-seller list.

A writer of Oates's energy and variety cannot, of course, be associated with a single theme or strategy, for the complexity of her vision has generated a remarkably manifold oeuvre. For instance, in *Wonderland* (1971) and *Do with Me What You Will* (1973) she deals with the psychological tactics that individuals use to avoid reality, while in *Bellefleur* (1980) and *A Bloodsmoor Romance* (1982) she focuses on the situation of women in social history and on the aesthetic dimensions of the novel as a genre. Incisive analyses of the violence that marks American culture recur throughout her work, however. Whether, as in *Expensive People* (1968), she focuses on a murderous child, or, as in *them* (1969), on prostitution and male aggression, she documents the sometimes bizarre brutality of contemporary family life. And many more of her most successful fictions—from the short story collections *By the North Gate* (1963) and *Haunted: Tales of the Grotesque* (1994) to the novels *You Must Remember This* (1987) and *Foxfire: Confessions of a Girl Gang* (1993)—characteristically dramatize unsettling, unpleasant, even macabre subjects. Defending herself against critics who fault her representations of pain, Oates has explained that "the more violent the murders in *Macbeth*, the more relief one can feel at not having to perform them. Great art," she continued, "is cathartic; it is always moral."

Oates was born to Irish Catholic, working-class parents in Lockport, New York. After graduating Phi Beta Kappa from Syracuse University and receiving an M.A. in English from the University of Wisconsin, she began an academic career that moved her from the University of Detroit and the University of Windsor, Ontario, to Princeton, New Jersey, where she is currently the Roger S. Berlind Distinguished Professor of the Humanities, and where with her husband, the scholar Raymond Smith, she co-edits the prestigious *Ontario Review*. She has said that "Where Are You Going, Where Have You Been?"—one of her most unforgettable investigations of murderous sexuality—was originally based on a *Life* magazine story about a serial rapist-killer in the American Southwest. But her powerful imagination has here transformed her vulnerable protagonist, Connie, into a kind of suburban American Everygirl as she confronts an almost mythic antagonist in a new telling of the traditional encounter between Death and the Maiden.

Where Are You Going, Where Have You Been?

For Bob Dylan[1]

Her name was Connie. She was fifteen and she had a quick, nervous giggling habit of craning her neck to glance into mirrors or checking other people's faces to make sure her own was all right. Her mother, who noticed everything and knew everything and who hadn't much reason any longer to look at her own face, always scolded Connie about it. "Stop gawking at yourself. Who are you? You think you're so pretty?" she would say. Connie would raise her eyebrows at these familiar old complaints and look right through her mother, into a shadowy vision of herself as she was right at that moment: she knew she was pretty and that was everything. Her mother had been pretty once too, if you could believe those old snapshots in the album, but now her looks were gone and that was why she was always after Connie.

"Why don't you keep your room clean like your sister? How've you got your hair fixed—what the hell stinks? Hair spray? You don't see your sister using that junk."

Her sister June was twenty-four and still lived at home. She was a secretary in the high school Connie attended, and if that wasn't bad enough—with her in the same building—she was so plain and chunky and steady that Connie had to hear her praised all the time by her mother and her mother's sisters. June did this, June did that, she saved money and helped clean the house and cooked and Connie couldn't do a thing, her mind was all filled with trashy daydreams. Their father was away at work most of the time and when he came home he wanted supper and he read the newspaper at supper and after supper he went to bed. He didn't bother talking much to them, but around his bent head Connie's mother kept picking at her until Connie wished her mother was dead and she herself was dead and it was all over. "She makes me want to throw up sometimes," she complained to her friends. She had a high, breathless, amused voice that made everything sound a little forced, whether it was sincere or not.

There was one good thing: June went places with girl friends of hers, girls who were just as plain and steady as she, and so when Connie wanted to do that her mother had no objections. The father of Connie's best girl friend drove the girls the three miles to town and left them at a shopping plaza so they could walk through the stores or go to a movie, and when he came to pick them up again at eleven he never bothered to ask what they had done.

---

1. Popular American folk and rock singer (b. 1941), a symbol of youth protest during the 1960s.

They must have been familiar sights, walking around the shopping plaza in their shorts and flat ballerina slippers that always scuffed on the sidewalk, with charm bracelets jingling on their thin wrists; they would lean together to whisper and laugh secretly if someone passed who amused or interested them. Connie had long dark blond hair that drew anyone's eye to it, and she wore part of it pulled up on her head and puffed out and the rest of it she let fall down her back. She wore a pull-over jersey blouse that looked one way when she was at home and another way when she was away from home. Everything about her had two sides to it, one for home and one for anywhere that was not home: her walk, which could be childlike and bobbing, or languid enough to make anyone think she was hearing music in her head; her mouth, which was pale and smirking most of the time, but bright and pink on these evenings out; her laugh, which was cynical and drawling at home—"Ha, ha, very funny,"—but high-pitched and nervous anywhere else, like the jingling of the charms on her bracelet.

Sometimes they did go shopping or to a movie, but sometimes they went across the highway, ducking fast across the busy road, to a drive-in restaurant where older kids hung out. The restaurant was shaped like a big bottle, though squatter than a real bottle, and on its cap was a revolving figure of a grinning boy holding a hamburger aloft. One night in midsummer they ran across, breathless with daring, and right away someone leaned out a car window and invited them over, but it was just a boy from high school they didn't like. It made them feel good to be able to ignore him. They went up through the maze of parked and cruising cars to the bright-lit, fly-infested restaurant, their faces pleased and expectant as if they were entering a sacred building that loomed up out of the night to give them what haven and blessing they yearned for. They sat at the counter and crossed their legs at the ankles, their thin shoulders rigid with excitement, and listened to the music that made everything so good: the music was always in the background, like music at a church service; it was something to depend upon.

A boy named Eddie came in to talk with them. He sat backwards on his stool, turning himself jerkily around in semicircles and then stopping and turning back again, and after a while he asked Connie if she would like something to eat. She said she would so she tapped her friend's arm on her way out—her friend pulled her face up into a brave, droll look—and Connie said she would meet her at eleven across the way. "I just hate to leave her like that," Connie said earnestly, but the boy said that she wouldn't be alone for long. So they went out to his car, and on the way Connie couldn't help but let her eyes wander over the windshields and faces all around her, her face gleaming with a joy that had nothing to do with Eddie or even this place; it might have been the music. She drew her shoulders up and sucked in her breath with the pure pleasure of being alive, and just at that moment she happened to glance at a face just a few feet away from hers. It was a boy with shaggy black hair, in a convertible jalopy painted gold. He stared at her and then his lips widened into a grin. Connie slit her eyes at him and turned away, but she couldn't help glancing back and there he was, still watching her. He wagged a finger and laughed and said, "Gonna get you, baby," and Connie turned away again without Eddie noticing anything.

She spent three hours with him, at the restaurant where they ate hamburgers and drank Cokes in wax cups that were always sweating, and then down an alley a mile or so away, and when he left her off at five to eleven only the movie house was still open at the plaza. Her girl friend was there, talking with a boy. When Connie came up, the two girls smiled at each other and Connie said, "How was the movie?" and the girl said, "*you* should know." They rode off with the girl's father, sleepy and pleased, and Connie couldn't help but look back at the darkened shopping plaza with its big empty parking lot and its signs that were faded and ghostly now, and over at the drive-in restaurant where cars were still circling tirelessly. She couldn't hear the music at this distance.

Next morning June asked her how the movie was and Connie said, "So-so."

She and that girl and occasionally another girl went out several times a week, and the rest of the time Connie spent around the house—it was summer vacation—getting in her mother's way and thinking, dreaming about the boys she met. But all the boys fell back and dissolved into a single face that was not even a face but an idea, a feeling, mixed up with the urgent insistent pounding of the music and the humid night air of July. Connie's mother kept dragging her back to the daylight by finding things for her to do or saying suddenly, "What's this about the Pettinger girl?"

And Connie would say nervously, "Oh, her. That dope." She always drew thick clear lines between herself and such girls, and her mother was simple and kind enough to believe it. Her mother was so simple, Connie thought, that it was maybe cruel to fool her so much. Her mother went scuffling around the house in old bedroom slippers and complained over the telephone to one sister about the other, then the other called up and the two of them complained about the third one. If June's name was mentioned her mother's tone was approving, and if Connie's name was mentioned it was disapproving. This did not really mean she disliked Connie, and actually Connie thought that her mother preferred her to June just because she was prettier, but the two of them kept up a pretense of exasperation, a sense that they were tugging and struggling over something of little value to either of them. Sometimes, over coffee, they were almost friends, but something would come up—some vexation that was like a fly buzzing suddenly around their heads—and their faces went hard with contempt.

One Sunday Connie got up at eleven—none of them bothered with church—and washed her hair so that it could dry all day long in the sun. Her parents and sister were going to a barbecue at an aunt's house and Connie said no, she wasn't interested, rolling her eyes to let her mother know just what she thought of it. "Stay home alone then," her mother said sharply. Connie sat out back in a lawn chair and watched them drive away, her father quiet and bald, hunched around so that he could back the car out, her mother with a look that was still angry and not at all softened through the windshield, and in the back seat poor old June, all dressed up as if she didn't know what a barbecue was, with all the running yelling kids and the flies. Connie sat with her eyes closed in the sun, dreaming and dazed with the warmth about her as if this were a kind of love, the caresses of love, and her mind slipped over onto thoughts of the boy she had been with the night before and how nice he had been, how sweet it always was, not the way someone like June would suppose but sweet, gently, the way it was in movies and promised in songs; and when she opened her eyes she hardly knew where she was, the back yard ran off into weeds and a fence-like line of trees and behind it the sky was perfectly blue and still. The asbestos "ranch house" that was now three years old startled her—it looked small. She shook her head as if to get awake.

It was too hot. She went inside the house and turned on the radio to drown out the quiet. She sat on the edge of her bed, barefoot, and listened for an hour and a half, to a program called XYZ Sunday Jamboree, record after record of hard, fast, shrieking songs she sang along with, interspersed by exclamations from "Bobby King": "An' look here, you girls at Napoleon's—Son and Charley want you to pay real close attention to this song coming up!"

And Connie paid close attention herself, bathed in a glow of slow-pulsed joy that seemed to rise mysteriously out of the music itself and lay languidly about the airless little room, breathed in and breathed out with each gentle rise and fall of her chest.

After a while she heard a car coming up the drive. She sat up at once, startled, because it couldn't be her father so soon. The gravel kept crunching all the way in from the road—the driveway was long—and Connie ran to the window. It was a car she didn't know. It was an open jalopy, painted a bright gold that caught the sunlight opaquely. Her heart began to pound and her fingers snatched at her hair, checking it, and she whispered, "Christ, Christ," wondering how she looked. The car came to a stop at the side door and the horn sounded four short taps, as if this were a signal Connie knew.

She went into the kitchen and approached the door slowly, then hung out the screen door, her bare toes curling down off the step. There were two boys in the car and now she recognized the driver: he had shaggy black hair that looked crazy as a wig and he was grinning at her.

"I ain't late, am I?" he said.

"Who the hell do you think you are?" Connie said.

"Toldja I'd be out, didn't I?"

"I don't even know who you are."

She spoke sullenly, careful to show no interest or pleasure, and he spoke in a fast, bright monotone. Connie looked past him to the other boy, taking her time. He had fair brown hair, with a lock that fell onto his forehead. His sideburns gave him a fierce, embarrassed look, but so far he hadn't even bothered to glance at her. Both boys wore sunglasses. The driver's glasses were metallic and mirrored everything in miniature.

"You wanta come for a ride?" he said.

Connie smirked and let her hair fall loose over one shoulder.

"Dont'cha like my car? New paint job," he said. "Hey."

"What?"

"You're cute."

She pretended to fidget, chasing flies away from the door.

"Don'tcha believe me, or what?" he said.

"Look, I don't even know who you are," Connie said in disgust.

"Hey, Ellie's got a radio, see. Mine broke down." He lifted his friend's arm and showed her the little transistor radio the boy was holding, and now Connie began to hear the music. It was the same program that was playing inside the house.

"Bobby King?" she said.

"I listen to him all the time. I think he's great."

"He's kind of great," Connie said reluctantly.

"Listen, that guy's *great*. He knows where the action is."

Connie blushed a little, because the glasses made it impossible for her to see just what this boy was looking at. She couldn't decide if she liked him or if he was a jerk, and so she dawdled in the doorway and wouldn't come down or go back inside. She said, "What's all that stuff painted on your car?"

"Can'tcha read it?" He opened the door very carefully, as if he were afraid it might fall off. He slid out just as carefully, planting his feet firmly on the ground, the tiny metallic world in his glasses slowing down like gelatine hardening, and in the midst of it Connie's bright green blouse. "This here is my name, to begin with," he said. ARNOLD FRIEND was written in tarlike black letters on the side, with a drawing of a round, grinning face that reminded Connie of a pumpkin, except it wore sunglasses. "I wanta introduce myself. I'm Arnold Friend and that's my real name and I'm gonna be your friend, honey, and inside the car's Ellie Oscar, he's kinda shy." Ellie brought his transistor radio up to his shoulder and balanced it there. "Now, these numbers are a secret code, honey," Arnold Friend explained. He read off the numbers 33, 19, 17 and raised his eyebrows at her to see what she thought of that, but she didn't think much of it. The left rear fender had been smashed and around it was written, on the gleaming gold background: DONE BY CRAZY WOMAN DRIVER. Connie had to laugh at that. Arnold Friend was pleased at her laughter and looked up at her. "Around the other side's a lot more—you wanta come and see them?"

"No."

"Why not?"

"Why should I?"

"Don'tcha wanta see what's on the car? Don'tcha wanta go for a ride?"

"I don't know."

"Why not?"

"I got things to do."

"Like what?"

"Things."

He laughed as if she had said something funny. He slapped his thighs. He was standing in a strange way, leaning back against the car as if he were balancing himself. He wasn't tall, only an inch or so taller than she would be if she came down to him. Connie liked the way he was dressed, which was the way all of them dressed: tight faded jeans stuffed into black, scuffed boots, a belt that pulled his waist in and showed how lean he was, and a white pull-over shirt that was a little soiled and showed the hard small muscles of his arms and shoulders. He looked as if he probably did hard work, lifting and carrying things. Even his neck looked muscular. And his face was a familiar face, somehow; the jaw and chin and cheeks slightly darkened because he hadn't shaved for a day or two, and the nose long and hawklike, sniffing as if she were a treat he was going to gobble up and it was all a joke.

"Connie, you ain't telling the truth. This is your day set aside for a ride with me and you know it," he said, still laughing. The way he straightened and recovered from his fit of laughing showed that it had been all fake.

"How do you know what my name is?" she said suspiciously.

"It's Connie."

"Maybe and maybe not."

"I know my Connie," he said, wagging his finger. Now she remembered him even better, back at the restaurant, and her cheeks warmed at the thought of how she had sucked in her breath just at the moment she passed him—how she must have looked to him. And he had remembered her. "Ellie and I come out here especially for you," he said. "Ellie can sit in back. How about it?"

"Where?"

"Where what?"

"Where're we going?"

He looked at her. He took off the sunglasses and she saw how pale the skin around his eyes was, like holes that were not in shadow but instead in light. His eyes were like chips of broken glass that catch the light in an amiable way. He smiled. It was as if the idea of going for a ride somewhere, to someplace, was a new idea to him.

"Just for a ride, Connie sweetheart."

"I never said my name was Connie," she said.

"But I know what it is. I know your name and all about you, lots of things," Arnold Friend said. He had not moved yet but stood still leaning back against the side of his jalopy. "I took a special interest in you, such a pretty girl, and found out all about you—like I know your parents and sister are gone somewheres and I know where and how long they're going to be gone, and I know who you were with last night, and your best girl friend's name is Betty. Right?"

He spoke in a simple lilting voice, exactly as if he were reciting the words to a song. His smile assured her that everything was fine. In the car Ellie turned up the volume on his radio and did not bother to look around at them.

"Ellie can sit in the back seat," Arnold Friend said. He indicated his friend with a casual jerk of his chin, as if Ellie did not count and she should not bother with him.

"How'd you find out all that stuff?" Connie said.

"Listen: Betty Schultz and Tony Fitch and Jimmy Pettinger and Nancy Pettinger," he said in a chant. "Raymond Stanley and Bob Hutter—"

"Do you know all those kids?"

"I know everybody."

"Look, you're kidding. You're not from around here."

"Sure."

"But—how come we never saw you before?"

"Sure you saw me before," he said. He looked down at his boots, as if he were a little offended. "You just don't remember."

"I guess I'd remember you," Connie said.

"Yeah?" He looked up at this, beaming. He was pleased. He began to mark time with the music from Ellie's radio, tapping his fists lightly together. Connie looked away from his smile to the car, which was painted so bright it almost hurt her eyes to look at it. She looked at that name, ARNOLD FRIEND. And up at the front fender was an expression that was familiar—MAN THE FLYING SAUCERS. It was an expression kids had used the year before but didn't use this year. She looked at it for a while as if the words meant something to her that she did not yet know.

"What're you thinking about? Huh?" Arnold Friend demanded. "Not worried about your hair blowing around in the car, are you?"

"No."

"Think I maybe can't drive good?"

"How do I know?"

"You're a hard girl to handle. How come?" he said. "Don't you know I'm your friend? Didn't you see me put my sign in the air when you walked by?"

"What sign?"

"My sign." And he drew an X in the air, leaning out toward her. They were maybe ten feet apart. After his hand fell back to his side the X was still in the air, almost visible. Connie let the screen door close and stood perfectly still inside it, listening to the music from her radio and the boy's blend together. She stared at Arnold Friend. He stood there so stiffly relaxed, pretending to be relaxed, with one hand idly on the door handle as if he were keeping himself up that way and had no intention of ever moving again. She recognized most things about him, the tight jeans that showed his thighs and buttocks and the greasy leather boots and tight shirt, and even that slippery friendly smile of his, that sleepy dreamy smile that all the boys used to get across ideas they didn't want to put into words. She recognized all this and also the sing-song way he talked, slightly mocking, kidding, but serious and a little melancholy, and she recognized the way he tapped one fist against the other in homage to the perpetual music behind him. But all these things did not come together.

She said suddenly, "Hey, how old are you?"

His smile faded. She could see then that he wasn't a kid, he was much older—thirty, maybe more. At this knowledge her heart began to pound faster.

"That's a crazy thing to ask. Can'tcha see I'm your own age?"

"Like hell you are."

"Or maybe a coupla years older. I'm eighteen."

"Eighteen?" she said doubtfully.

He grinned to reassure her and lines appeared at the corners of his mouth. His teeth were big and white. He grinned so broadly his eyes became slits and she saw how thick the lashes were, thick and black as if painted with a black tarlike material. Then, abruptly, he seemed to become embarrassed and looked over his shoulder at Ellie. "*Him*, he's crazy," he said. "Ain't he a riot? He's a nut, a real character." Ellie was still listening to the music. His sunglasses told nothing about what he was thinking. He wore a bright orange shirt unbuttoned halfway to show his chest, which was a pale, bluish chest and not muscular like Arnold Friend's. His shirt collar was turned up all around and the very tips of the collar pointed out past his chin as if they were protecting him. He was pressing the transistor radio up against his ear and sat there in a kind of daze, right in the sun.

"He's kinda strange," Connie said.

"Hey, she says you're kinda strange! Kinda strange!" Arnold Friend cried. He pounded on the car to get Ellie's attention. Ellie turned for the first time and Connie saw with shock that he wasn't a kid either—he had a fair, hairless face, cheeks reddened slightly as if the veins grew too close to the surface of his skin, the face of a forty-year-old baby. Connie felt a wave of dizziness rise in her at this sight and she stared at him as if waiting for something to change the shock of the moment, make it all right again. Ellie's lips kept shaping words, mumbling along with the words blasting in his ear.

"Maybe you two better go away," Connie said faintly.

"What? How come?" Arnold Friend cried. "We come out here to take you for a ride. It's Sunday." He had the voice of the man on the radio now. It was the same voice, Connie thought. "Don'tcha know it's Sunday all day? And honey, no matter who you were with last night, today you're with Arnold Friend and don't you forget it! Maybe you better step out here," he said, and this last was in a different voice. It was a little flatter, as if the heat was finally getting to him.

"No. I got things to do."

"Hey."

"You two better leave."

"We ain't leaving until you come with us."

"Like hell I am—"

"Connie, don't fool around with me. I mean—I mean, don't fool *around*," he said, shaking his head. He laughed incredulously. He placed his sunglasses on top of his head, carefully, as if he were indeed wearing a wig, and brought the stems down behind his ears. Connie stared at him, another wave of dizziness and fear rising in her so that for a moment he wasn't even in focus but was just a blur standing there against his gold car, and she had the idea that he had driven up the driveway all right but had come from nowhere before that and belonged nowhere and that everything about him and even about the music that was so familiar to her was only half real.

"If my father comes and sees you—"

"He ain't coming. He's at a barbecue."

"How do you know that?"

"Aunt Tillie's. Right now they're—uh—they're drinking. Sitting around," he said vaguely, squinting as if he were staring all the way to town and over to Aunt Tillie's back yard. Then the vision seemed to get clear and he nodded energetically. "Yeah. Sitting around. There's your sister in a blue dress, huh? And high heels, the poor sad bitch—nothing like you, sweetheart! And your mother's helping some fat woman with the corn, they're cleaning the corn—husking the corn—"

"What fat woman?" Connie cried.

"How do I know what fat woman, I don't know every goddamn fat woman in the world!" Arnold Friend laughed.

"Oh, that's Mrs. Hornsby. . . . Who invited her?" Connie said. She felt a little lightheaded. Her breath was coming quickly.

"She's too fat. I don't like them fat. I like them the way you are, honey," he said, smiling sleepily at her. They stared at each other for a while through the screen door. He said softly, "Now, what you're going to do is this: you're going to come out that door. You're going to sit up front with me and Ellie's going to sit in the back, the hell with Ellie, right? This isn't Ellie's date. You're my date. I'm your lover, honey."

"What? You're crazy—"

"Yes. I'm your lover. You don't know what that is but you will," he said. "I know that too. I know all about you. But look: it's real nice and you couldn't ask for nobody better than me, or more polite. I always keep my word. I'll tell you how it is, I'm always nice at first, the first time. I'll hold you so tight you won't think you have to try to get away or pretend anything because you'll know you can't. And I'll come inside you where it's all secret and you'll give in to me and you'll love me—"

"Shut up! You're crazy!" Connie said. She backed away from the door. She put her hands up against her ears as if she'd heard something terrible, something not meant for her. "People don't talk like that, you're crazy," she muttered. Her heart was almost too big now for her chest and its pumping made sweat break out all over her. She looked out to see Arnold Friend pause and then take a step toward the porch, lurching. He almost fell. But, like a clever drunken man, he managed to catch his balance. He wobbled in his high boots and grabbed hold of one of the porch posts.

"Honey?" he said. "You still listening?"

"Get the hell out of here!"

"Be nice, honey. Listen."

"I'm going to call the police—"

He wobbled again and out of the side of his mouth came a fast spat curse, an aside not meant for her to hear. But even this "Christ!" sounded forced. Then he began to smile again. She watched this smile come, awkward as if he were smiling from inside a mask. His whole face was a mask, she thought wildly, tanned down to his throat but then running out as if he had plastered makeup on his face but had forgotten about his throat.

"Honey—? Listen, here's how it is. I always tell the truth and I promise you this: I ain't coming in that house after you."

"You better not! I'm going to call the police if you—if you don't—"

"Honey," he said, talking right through her voice, "honey. I'm not coming in there but you are coming out here. You know why?"

She was panting. The kitchen looked like a place she had never seen before, some room she had run inside but that wasn't good enough, wasn't going to help her. The kitchen window had never had a curtain, after three years, and there were dishes in the sink for her to do—probably—and if you ran your hand across the table you'd probably feel something sticky there.

"You listening, honey? Hey?"

"—going to call the police—"

"Soon as you touch the phone I don't need to keep my promise and can come inside. You won't want that."

She rushed forward and tried to lock the door. Her fingers were shaking. "But why lock it," Arnold Friend said gently, talking right into her face. "It's just a screen door. It's just nothing." One of his boots was at a strange angle, as if his foot wasn't in it. It pointed out to the left, bent at the ankle. "I mean, anybody can break through a screen door and glass and wood and iron or anything else if he needs to, anybody at all, and specially Arnold Friend. If the place got lit up with a fire, honey, you'd come runnin' out into my arms, right into my arms an' safe at home—like you knew I was your lover and'd stopped fooling around. I don't mind a nice shy girl but I don't like no fooling around." Part of those words were spoken with a slight rhythmic lilt, and Connie somehow recognized them—the echo of a song from last year, about a girl rushing into her boy friend's arms and coming home again—

Connie stood barefoot on the linoleum floor, staring at him. "What do you want?" she whispered.

"I want you," he said.

"What?"

"Seen you that night and thought, that's the one, yes sir. I never needed to look anymore."

"But my father's coming back. He's coming to get me. I had to wash my hair first—" She spoke in a dry, rapid voice, hardly raising it for him to hear.

"No, your daddy is not coming and yes, you had to wash your hair and you washed it for me. It's nice and shining and all for me. I thank you sweetheart," he said with a mock bow, but again he almost lost his balance. He had to bend and adjust his boots. Evidently his feet did not go all the way down; the boots must have been stuffed with something so that he would seem taller. Connie stared out at him and behind him at Ellie in the car, who seemed to be looking off toward Connie's right, into nothing. Then Ellie said, pulling the words out of the air one after another as if he were just discovering them, "You want me to pull out the phone?"

"Shut your mouth and keep it shut," Arnold Friend said, his face red from bending over or maybe from embarrassment because Connie had seen his boots. "This ain't none of your business."

"What—what are you doing? What do you want?" Connie said. "If I call the police they'll get you, they'll arrest you—"

"Promise was not to come in unless you touch that phone, and I'll keep that promise," he said. He resumed his erect position and tried to force his shoulders back. He sounded like a hero in a movie, declaring something important. But he spoke too loudly and it was as if he were speaking to someone behind Connie. "I ain't made plans for coming in that house where I don't belong but just for you to come out to me, the way you should. Don't you know who I am?"

"You're crazy," she whispered. She backed away from the door but did not want to go into another part of the house, as if this would give him permission to come through the door. "What do you . . . you're crazy, you. . . ."

"Huh? What're you saying, honey?"

Her eyes darted everywhere in the kitchen. She could not remember what it was, this room.

"This is how it is, honey: you come out and we'll drive away, have a nice ride. But if you don't come out we're gonna wait till your people come home and then they're all going to get it."

"You want that telephone pulled out?" Ellie said. He held the radio away from his ear and grimaced, as if without the radio the air was too much for him.

"I toldja shut up, Ellie," Arnold Friend said, "you're deaf, get a hearing aid, right? Fix yourself up. This little girl's no trouble and's gonna be nice to me, so Ellie keep to yourself, this ain't your date—right? Don't hem in on me, don't hog, don't crush, don't bird dog, don't trail me," he said in a rapid, meaningless voice, as if he were running through all the expressions he'd learned but was no longer sure which of them was in style, then rushing on to new ones, making them up with his eyes closed. "Don't crawl under my fence, don't squeeze in my chipmunk hole, don't sniff my glue, suck my popsicle, keep your own greasy fingers on yourself!" He shaded his eyes and peered in at Connie, who was backed against the kitchen table. "Don't mind him, honey, he's just a creep. He's a dope. Right? I'm the boy for you and like I said, you come out here nice like a lady and give me your hand, and nobody else gets hurt, I mean, your nice old bald-headed daddy and your mummy and your sister in her high heels. Because listen: why bring them in this?"

"Leave me alone," Connie whispered.

"Hey, you know that old woman down the road, the one with the chickens and stuff—you know her?"

"She's dead!"

"Dead? What? You know her?" Arnold Friend said.

"She's dead—"

"Don't you like her?"

"She's dead—she's—she isn't here any more—"

"But don't you like her, I mean, you got something against her? Some grudge or something?" Then his voice dipped as if he were conscious of a rudeness. He touched the sunglasses perched up on top of his head as if to make sure they were still there. "Now, you be a good girl."

"What are you going to do?"

"Just two things, or maybe three," Arnold Friend said. "But I promise it won't last long and you'll like me the way you get to like people you're close to. You will. It's all over for you here, so come on out. You don't want your people in any trouble, do you?"

She turned and bumped against a chair or something, hurting her leg, but she ran into the back room and picked up the telephone. Something roared in her ear, a tiny roaring, and she was so sick with fear that she could do nothing but listen to it—the telephone was clammy and very heavy and her fingers groped down to the dial but were too weak to touch it. She began to scream into the phone, into the roaring. She cried out, she cried for her mother, she felt her breath start jerking back and forth in her lungs as if it were something Arnold Friend was stabbing her with again and again with no tenderness. A noisy sorrowful wailing rose all about her and she was locked inside it the way she was locked inside this house.

After a while she could hear again. She was sitting on the floor with her wet back against the wall.

Arnold Friend was saying from the door, "That's a good girl. Put the phone back."

She kicked the phone away from her.

"No, honey. Pick it up. Put it back right."

She picked it up and put it back. The dial tone stopped.

"That's a good girl. Now, you come outside."

She was hollow with what had been fear but what was now just an emptiness. All that screaming had blasted it out of her. She sat, one leg cramped under her, and deep inside her brain was something like a pinpoint of light that kept going and would not let her relax. She thought, I'm not going to see my mother again. She thought, I'm not going to sleep in my bed again. Her bright green blouse was all wet.

Arnold Friend said, in a gentle-loud voice that was like a stage voice, "The place where you come from ain't there any more, and where you had in mind to go is cancelled out. This place you are now—inside your daddy's house—is nothing but a cardboard box I can knock down any time. You know that and always did know it. You hear me?"

She thought, I have got to think. I have got to know what to do.

"We'll go out to a nice field, out in the country here where it smells so nice and it's sunny," Arnold Friend said. "I'll have my arms tight around you so you won't need to try to get away and I'll show you what love is like, what it does. The hell with this house! It looks solid all right," he said. He ran his fingernail down the screen and the noise did not make Connie shiver, as it would have the day before. "Now, put your hand on your heart, honey. Feel that? That feels solid too but we know better. Be nice to me, be sweet like you can because what else is there for a girl like you but to be sweet and pretty and give in?—and get away before her people get back?"

She felt her pounding heart. Her hand seemed to enclose it. She thought for the first time in her life that it was nothing that was hers, that belonged to her, but just a pounding, living thing inside this body that wasn't really hers either.

"You don't want them to get hurt," Arnold Friend went on. "Now, get up, honey. Get up all by yourself."

She stood.

"Now, turn this way. That's right. Come over here to me.—Ellie, put that away, didn't I tell you? You dope. You miserable creepy dope," Arnold Friend said. His words were not angry but only part of an incantation. The incantation was kindly. "Now, come out through the kitchen to me, honey, and let's see a smile, try it, you're a brave, sweet little girl and now they're eating corn and hot dogs cooked to bursting over an outdoor fire, and they don't know one thing about you and never did and honey, you're better than them because not a one of them would have done this for you."

Connie felt the linoleum under her feet; it was cool. She brushed her hair back out of her eyes. Arnold Friend let go of the post tentatively and opened his arms for her, his elbows pointing in toward each other and his wrists limp, to show that this was an embarrassed embrace and a little mocking, he didn't want to make her self-conscious.

She put out her hand against the screen. She watched herself push the door slowly open as if she were back safe somewhere in the other doorway, watching this body and this head of long hair moving out into the sunlight where Arnold Friend waited.

"My sweet little blue-eyed girl," he said in a half-sung sigh that had nothing to do with her brown eyes but was taken up just the same by the vast sunlit reaches of the land behind him and on all sides of him—so much land that Connie had never seen before and did not recognize except to know that she was going to it.

1970

MARGARET ATWOOD
b. 1939

Although Margaret Atwood has explained that she grew up singing "Rule, Britannia," drawing the Union Jack, and reading stacks of Captain Marvel and Batman comic books, she has helped disengage Canada's cultural identity from both English and American influences. Most directly, she did this by working as an editor for the House of Anansi Press; by writing what she called "a map" for the uncharted territory of Canadian literature, *Survival* (1972); and by compiling *The Oxford Book of Canadian Verse* (1982). Just as important, as if to elaborate on the significance of her thesis that the central image for Canadians is survival, Atwood has produced a number of influential volumes of poems, stories, and novels that meditate on the impediments Canadians, and often Canadian women, encounter in their efforts to stay alive.

Married to the novelist Graeme Gibson and the mother of a daughter, Atwood was born and raised in Ottawa, Ontario, but her formal schooling there was frequently interrupted by extensive family trips in the northern Ontario and Quebec bush, where her father did entomological research. In the year when she graduated from the University of Toronto, she published her first book of poems, *Double Persephone* (1962). After receiving a master's degree from Radcliffe College and studying Victorian fantasy at Harvard, she took a series of positions in the English departments of several Canadian universities. Six volumes of verse appeared between 1966 and 1974, as well as two novels, both of them hailed by critics for their sometimes comic, sometimes grim analyses of the mysteries of the self when, in isolation, it confronts a fractured or distorted image of itself.

In many of her poems, Atwood is similarly concerned with the splitting up of the self as it does "tricks with mirrors," or with the "power politics" between lovers, or with the need to revise mythic stories, like those of Homer's Odysseus, to retell them from the silenced perspective of the female who has been seduced and abandoned. In such novels as *The Edible Woman* (1969), *Surfacing* (1972), *Lady Oracle* (1976), *Life before Man* (1979), *Bodily Harm* (1981), *Cat's Eye* (1988), *Alias Grace* (1996), and *The Blind Assassin* (2000), moreover, she presents individuals questing for personal integrity and for a more harmonious relationship with the natural world. Atwood's poetry and fiction often attempt to provide what she calls, in one book title, "procedures for underground" (1970), where the underground is understood as the unconscious or the other side of what has been defined as normal by a given culture. Frequently this journey into the interior offers a visionary solution to the psychosexual problems Atwood associates with modern technological society. Whether her central character is a pioneer woman or an author of Gothic romances, she seeks some form of control over an environment that is seen as alien or alienating.

A number of Atwood's characters are moving toward the conclusion of the heroine of *Surfacing*: "This above all, to refuse to be a victim." Because, in Atwood's view, Canadians have viewed themselves as victims of either English or American imperialism, and because women have perceived themselves as victims of masculine privilege, Atwood implies that cultural colonization and sexual subordination are parallel, if not identical, situations. Both the humor and the tenderness of her later work indicate how writing continues to empower Atwood herself to defy colonization. In such volumes of prose fiction as *Bluebeard's Egg and Other Stories* (1986), *The Handmaid's Tale* (1987), *Good Bones* (1992), and *The Robber Bride* (1993), she exploits fantastic, futuristic, and fairy-tale techniques to examine both feminist ideology and women's biological, familial, and social experiences, while in such poems as those collected in the elegiac *Morning in the Burned House* (1995) she reimagines a "Mothertongue" that seeks to "speak both cherishing and farewell."

This Is a Photograph of Me

    It was taken some time ago.
    At first it seems to be
    a smeared
    print: blurred lines and gray flecks
5   blended with the paper;

then, as you scan
it, you see in the left-hand corner
a thing that is like a branch: part of a tree
(balsam or spruce) emerging
10 and, to the right, halfway up
what ought to be a gentle
slope, a small frame house.

In the background there is a lake,
and beyond that, some low hills.

15 (The photograph was taken
the day after I drowned.

I am in the lake, in the center
of the picture, just under the surface.

It is difficult to say where
20 precisely, or to say
how large or small I am:
the effect of water
on light is a distortion

but if you look long enough,
25 eventually
you will be able to see me.)

1966

Spelling

My daughter plays on the floor
with plastic letters,
red, blue & hard yellow,
learning how to spell,
5 spelling,
how to make spells

and I wonder how many women
denied themselves daughters,
closed themselves in rooms,
10 drew the curtains
so they could mainline words.

A child is not a poem,
a poem is not a child.
There is no either/or.
15 However.

I return to the story
of the woman caught in the war
& in labor, her thighs tied
together by the enemy
so she could not give birth.
20 Ancestress: the burning witch,
her mouth covered by leather
to strangle words.

A word after a word
25 after a word is power.

At the point where language falls away
from the hot bones, at the point
where the rock breaks open and darkness
flows out of it like blood, at
30 the melting point of granite
when the bones know
they are hollow & the word
splits & doubles & speaks
the truth & the body
35 itself becomes a mouth.

This is a metaphor.

How do you learn to spell?
Blood, sky & the sun,
your own name first,
40 your first naming, your first name,
your first word.

1981

Waiting

Here it is then, the dark thing,
the dark thing you have waited for so long.
You have made such melodramas.
You thought it would carry its own mist,
5   obscuring you in a damp enfolding, like the mildew
shroud on bread. Or you thought it would hide
in your closet, among the clothes you outgrew years ago,
nesting in dustballs and fallen hair, shedding
one of your fabricated skins
10 after another and growing bigger,
honing its teeth on your discarded
cloth lives, and then it would pounce
from the inside out, and your heart
would be filled with roaring

or else that it would come swiftly and without sound,
but with one pitiless glaring eye, like a high-speed train,
and a single blow on the head and the blackout.

Instead it is strangely like home.
Like your own home, fifty years ago,
in December, in the early evening
when the indoor light changed, from clear to clouded,
a clouded thick yellow, like a sulphury eggyolk,

and the reading lamp was turned on
with its brown silk shade, its aroma
of hot copper, the living
room flickering in the smells of cooking dinner,

and you crouched on the hardwood floor, smudged elbows
and scaly winter knees on the funny papers,
listening to the radio, news of disasters
that made you feel safe,
like the voice of your mother
urging you yet again to set the table
you are doing your best to ignore,
and you realized for the first time
in your life that you would be old

some day, you would some day be
as old as you are now,
and the home you were reading the funnies in
by the thick yellow light, would be gone
with all the people in it, even you,
even you in your young, smudgy body
with its scent of newsprint and dirty
knees and washed cotton,
and you would have a different body
by then, an old murky one,
a stranger's body you could not even imagine,
and you would be lost and alone.

And now it is now
and the dark thing is here,
and after all it is nothing new;
it is only a memory, after all:
a memory of a fear,
a yellowing paper child's fear
you have long since forgotten
and that has now come true.

1995

Asparagus

This afternoon a man leans over
the hard rolls and the curled
butter, and tells me everything: two
women love him, he loves them, what
should he do?

           The sun
sifts down through the imperceptibly
brownish urban air. I'm going to
suffer for this: turn red, get
blisters or else cancer. I eat
asparagus with my fingers, he
plunges into description.
He's at his wit's end, sewed
up in his own frenzy. He has
breadcrumbs in his beard.
           I wonder
if I should let my hair go gray
so my advice will be better.
I could wrinkle up my eyelids,
look wise. I could get a pet lizard.
You're not crazy, I tell him.
Others have done this. Me too.
Messy love is better than none,
I guess. I'm no authority
on sane living.

Which is all true
and no help at all, because
this form of love is like the pain
of childbirth: so intense
it's hard to remember afterwards,
of what kind of screams and grimaces
it pushed you into.

The shrimp arrive on their skewers,
the courtyard trees unroll
their yellowy caterpillars,
pollen powders our shoulders.
He wants them both, he relates
tortures, the coffee
arrives, and altogether I am amazed
at his stupidities.

I sit looking at him
with a sort of wonder,
or is it envy?

Listen, I say to him,
you're very lucky.

1995

Marsh Languages

The dark soft languages are being silenced:
Mothertongue Mothertongue Mothertongue
falling one by one back into the moon.

Language of marshes,
language of the roots of rushes tangled
together in the ooze,
marrow cells twinning themselves
inside the warm core of the bone:
pathways of hidden light in the body fade and wink out.

The sibilants and gutturals,
the cave language, the half-light
forming at the back of the throat,
the mouth's damp velvet molding
the lost syllable for "I" that did not mean separate,
all are becoming sounds no longer
heard because no longer spoken,
and everything that could once be said in them has ceased to exist.

The languages of the dying suns
are themselves dying,
but even the word for this has been forgotten.
The mouth against skin, vivid and fading,
can no longer speak both cherishing and farewell.
It is now only a mouth, only skin.
There is no more longing.

Translation was never possible.
Instead there was always only
conquest, the influx
of the language of hard nouns,
the language of metal,
the language of either/or,
the one language that has eaten all the others.

1995

Morning in the Burned House

In the burned house I am eating breakfast.
You understand: there is no house, there is no breakfast,
yet here I am.

The spoon which was melted scrapes against
the bowl which was melted also.
No one else is around.

Where have they gone to, brother and sister,
mother and father? Off along the shore,
perhaps. Their clothes are still on the hangers,

10   their dishes piled beside the sink,
which is beside the woodstove
with its grate and sooty kettle,

every detail clear,
tin cup and rippled mirror.
15   The day is bright and songless,

the lake is blue, the forest watchful.
In the east a bank of cloud
rises up silently like dark bread.

I can see the swirls in the oilcloth,
20   I can see the flaws in the glass,
those flares where the sun hits them.

I can't see my own arms and legs
or know if this is a trap or blessing,
finding myself back here, where everything

25   in this house has long been over,
kettle and mirror, spoon and bowl,
including my own body,

including the body I had then,
including the body I have now
30   as I sit at this morning table, alone and happy,

bare child's feet on the scorched floorboards
(I can almost see)
in my burning clothes, the thin green shorts

and grubby yellow T-shirt
35   holding my cindery, non-existent,
radiant flesh. Incandescent.

1995

Rape Fantasies

    The way they're going on about it in the magazines you'd think it was just invented, and not only that but it's something terrific, like a vaccine for cancer. They put it in capital letters on the front cover, and inside they have these questionnaires like the ones they used to have about whether you were a good enough wife or an endomorph or an ectomorph,[1] remember that?

---

1. I.e., possessing a short and wide body structure or a tall and narrow one.

with the scoring upside down on page 73, and then these numbered do-it-yourself dealies, you know? RAPE, TEN THINGS TO DO ABOUT IT, like it was ten new hairdos or something. I mean, what's so new about it?

So at work they all have to talk about it because no matter what magazine you open, there it is, staring you right between the eyes, and they're beginning to have it on the television, too. Personally I'd prefer a June Allyson[2] movie anytime but they don't make them any more and they don't even have them that much on the Late Show. For instance, day before yesterday, that would be Wednesday, thank god it's Friday as they say, we were sitting around in the women's lunch room—the *lunch* room, I mean you'd think you could get some peace and quiet in there—and Chrissy closes up the magazine she's been reading and says, "How about it, girls, do you have rape fantasies?"

The four of us were having our game of bridge the way we always do, and I had a bare twelve points counting the singleton with not that much of a bid in anything. So I said one club, hoping Sondra would remember about the one club convention, because the time before when I used that she thought I really meant clubs and she bid us up to three, and all I had was four little ones with nothing higher than a six, and we went down two and on top of that we were vulnerable. She is not the world's best bridge player. I mean, neither am I but there's a limit.

Darlene passed but the damage was done, Sondra's head went round like it was on ball bearings and she said, "*What* fantasies?"

"Rape fantasies," Chrissy said. She's a receptionist and she looks like one; she's pretty but cool as a cucumber, like she's been painted all over with nail polish, if you know what I mean. Varnished. "It says here all women have rape fantasies."

"For Chrissake, I'm eating an egg sandwich," I said, "and I bid one club and Darlene passed."

"You mean, like some guy jumping you in an alley or something," Sondra said. She was eating her lunch, we all eat our lunches during the game, and she bit into a piece of that celery she always brings and started to chew away on it with this thoughtful expression in her eyes and I knew we might as well pack it in as far as the game was concerned.

"Yeah, sort of like that," Chrissy said. She was blushing a little, you could see it even under her makeup.

"I don't think you should go out alone at night," Darlene said, "you put yourself in a position," and I may have been mistaken but she was looking at me. She's the oldest, she's forty-one though you wouldn't know it and neither does she, but I looked it up in the employees' file. I like to guess a person's age and then look it up to see if I'm right. I let myself have an extra pack of cigarettes if I am, though I'm trying to cut down. I figure it's harmless as long as you don't tell. I mean, not everyone has access to that file, it's more or less confidential. But it's all right if I tell you, I don't expect you'll ever meet her, though you never know, it's a small world. Anyway.

"For *heaven's* sake, it's only *Toronto*," Greta said. She worked in Detroit for three years and she never lets you forget it, it's like she thinks she's a war

---

2. American actor (1917–2006), known for portraying smiling small-town girls in musical comedies filmed in the 1940s, and doting wives in movies of the 1950s.

hero or something, we should all admire her just for the fact that she's still walking this earth, though she was really living in Windsor[3] the whole time, she just worked in Detroit. Which for me doesn't really count. It's where you sleep, right?

"Well, do you?" Chrissy said. She was obviously trying to tell us about hers but she wasn't about to go first, she's cautious, that one.

"I certainly don't," Darlene said, and she wrinkled up her nose, like this, and I had to laugh. "I think it's disgusting." She's divorced, I read that in the file too, she never talks about it. It must've been years ago anyway. She got up and went over to the coffee machine and turned her back on us as though she wasn't going to have anything more to do with it.

"Well," Greta said. I could see it was going to be between her and Chrissy. They're both blondes, I don't mean that in a bitchy way but they do try to outdress each other. Greta would like to get out of Filing, she'd like to be a receptionist too so she could meet more people. You don't meet much of anyone in Filing except other people in Filing. Me, I don't mind it so much, I have outside interests.

"Well," Greta said, "I sometimes think about, you know my apartment? It's got this little balcony, I like to sit out there in the summer and I have a few plants out there. I never bother that much about locking the door to the balcony, it's one of those sliding glass ones, I'm on the eighteenth floor for heaven's sake, I've got a good view of the lake and the CN Tower and all. But I'm sitting around one night in my house-coat, watching TV with my shoes off, you know how you do, and I see this guy's feet, coming down past the window, and the next thing you know he's standing on the balcony, he's let himself down by a rope with a hook on the end of it from the floor above, that's the nineteenth, and before I can even get up off the chesterfield he's inside the apartment. He's all dressed in black with black gloves on"—I knew right away what show she got the black gloves off because I saw the same one—"and then he, well, you know."

"You know what?" Chrissy said, but Greta said, "And afterwards he tells me that he goes all over the outside of the apartment building like that, from one floor to another, with his rope and his hook . . . and then he goes out to the balcony and tosses his rope, and he climbs up it and disappears."

"Just like Tarzan," I said, but nobody laughed.

"Is that all?" Chrissy said. "Don't you ever think about, well, I think about being in the bathtub, with no clothes on . . ."

"So who takes a bath in their clothes?" I said, you have to admit it's stupid when you come to think of it, but she just went on, ". . . with lots of bubbles, what I use is Vitabath, it's more expensive but it's so relaxing, and my hair pinned up, and the door opens and this fellow's standing there. . . ."

"How'd he get in?" Greta said.

"Oh, I don't know, through a window or something. Well, I can't very well get out of the bathtub, the bathroom's too small and besides he's blocking the doorway, so I just *lie* there, and he starts to very slowly take his own clothes off, and then he gets into the bathtub with me."

"Don't you scream or anything?" said Darlene. She'd come back with her

---

3. An industrial city in southwest Ontario on the Detroit River, immediately opposite Detroit.

cup of coffee, she was getting really interested. "I'd scream like bloody murder."

"Who'd hear me?" Chrissy said. "Besides, all the articles say it's better not to resist, that way you don't get hurt."

"Anyway you might get bubbles up your nose," I said, "from the deep breathing," and I swear all four of them looked at me like I was in bad taste, like I'd insulted the Virgin Mary or something. I mean, I don't see what's wrong with a little joke now and then. Life's too short, right?

"Listen," I said, "those aren't *rape* fantasies. I mean, you aren't getting *raped*, it's just some guy you haven't met formally who happens to be more attractive than Derek Cummins"—he's the Assistant Manager, he wears elevator shoes or at any rate they have these thick soles and he has this funny way of talking, we call him Derek Duck—"and you have a good time. Rape is when they've got a knife or something and you don't want to."

"So what about you, Estelle," Chrissy said, she was miffed because I laughed at her fantasy, she thought I was putting her down. Sondra was miffed too, by this time she'd finished her celery and she wanted to tell about hers, but she hadn't got in fast enough.

"All right, let me tell you one," I said. "I'm walking down this dark street at night and this fellow comes up and grabs my arm. Now it so happens that I have a plastic lemon in my purse, you know how it always says you should carry a plastic lemon in your purse? I don't really do it, I tried it once but the darn thing leaked all over my checkbook, but in this fantasy I have one, and I say to him, 'You're intending to rape me, right?' and he nods, so I open my purse to get the plastic lemon, and I can't find it! My purse is full of all this junk, Kleenex and cigarettes and my change purse and my lipstick and my driver's licence, you know the kind of stuff; so I ask him to hold out his hands, like this, and I pile all this junk into them and down at the bottom there's the plastic lemon, and I can't get the top off. So I hand it to him and he's very obliging, he twists the top off and hands it back to me, and I squirt him in the eye."

I hope you don't think that's too vicious. Come to think of it, it is a bit mean, especially when he was so polite and all.

"*That's* your rape fantasy?" Chrissy says. "I don't believe it."

"She's a card," Darlene says, she and I are the ones that've been here the longest and she never will forget the time I got drunk at the office party and insisted I was going to dance under the table instead of on top of it, I did a sort of Cossack number[4] but then I hit my head on the bottom of the table—actually it was a desk—when I went to get up, and I knocked myself out cold. She's decided that's the mark of an original mind and she tells everyone new about it and I'm not sure that's fair. Though I did do it.

"I'm being totally honest," I say. I always am and they know it. There's no point in being anything else, is the way I look at it, and sooner or later the truth will out so you might as well not waste the time, right? "You should hear the one about the Easy-Off Oven Cleaner."

But that was the end of the lunch hour, with one bridge game shot to hell,

---

4. I.e., a folk dance called the *kazatzka*, performed in a squatting positions by Cossacks, the peoples of the southern steppes in Eastern Europe and Asiatic Russia who played a prominent role as horsemen in the Russian imperial army.

and the next day we spent most of the time arguing over whether to start a new game or play out the hands we had left over from the day before, so Sondra never did get a chance to tell about her rape fantasy.

It started me thinking though, about my own rape fantasies. Maybe I'm abnormal or something, I mean I have fantasies about handsome strangers coming in through the window too, like Mr. Clean,[5] I wish one would, please god somebody without flat feet and big sweat marks on his shirt, and over five feet five, believe me being tall is a handicap though it's getting better, tall guys are starting to like someone whose nose reaches higher than their belly button. But if you're being totally honest you can't count those as rape fantasies. In a real rape fantasy, what you should feel is this anxiety, like when you think about your apartment building catching on fire and whether you should use the elevator or the stairs or maybe just stick your head under a wet towel, and you try to remember everything you've read about what to do but you can't decide.

For instance, I'm walking along this dark street at night and this short, ugly fellow comes up and grabs my arm, and not only is he ugly, you know, with a sort of puffy nothing face, like those fellows you have to talk to in the bank when your account's overdrawn—of course I don't mean they're all like that—but he's absolutely covered in pimples. So he gets me pinned against the wall, he's short but he's heavy, and he starts to undo himself and the zipper gets stuck. I mean, one of the most significant moments in a girl's life, it's almost like getting married or having a baby or something, and he sticks the zipper.

So I say, kind of disgusted, "Oh for Chrissake," and he starts to cry. He tells me he's never been able to get anything right in his entire life, and this is the last straw, he's going to go jump off a bridge.

"Look," I say, I feel so sorry for him, in my rape fantasies I always end up feeling sorry for the guy, I mean there has to be something *wrong* with them, if it was Clint Eastwood[6] it'd be different but worse luck it never is. I was the kind of little girl who buried dead robins, know what I mean? It used to drive my mother nuts, she didn't like me touching them, because of the germs I guess. So I say, "Listen, I know how you feel. You really should do something about those pimples, if you got rid of them you'd be quite good looking, honest; then you wouldn't have to go around doing stuff like this. I had them myself once," I say, to comfort him, but in fact I did, and it ends up I give him the name of my old dermatologist, the one I had in high school, that was back in Leamington, except I used to go to St. Catharine's for the dermatologist. I'm telling you, I was really lonely when I first came here; I thought it was going to be such a big adventure and all, but it's a lot harder to meet people in a city. But I guess it's different for a guy.

Or I'm lying in bed with this terrible cold, my face is all swollen up, my eyes are red and my nose is dripping like a leaky tap, and this fellow comes in through the window and *he* has a terrible cold too, it's a new kind of flu that's been going around. So he says, "I'b goig do rabe you"—I hope you don't mind me holding my nose like this but that's the way I imagine it—

---

5. A muscular bald genie featured in advertisements for the all-purpose cleaner of the same name.

6. Macho star (b. 1930) of western and crime films of the 1960s to 1990s.

and he lets out this terrific sneeze, which slows him down a bit, also I'm no object of beauty myself, you'd have to be some kind of pervert to want to rape someone with a cold like mine, it'd be like raping a bottle of LePages mucilage[7] the way my nose is running. He's looking wildly around the room, and I realize it's because he doesn't have a piece of Kleenex! "Id's ride here," I say, and I pass him the Kleenex, god knows why he even bothered to get out of bed, you'd think if you were going to go around climbing in windows you'd wait till you were healthier, right? I mean, that takes a certain amount of energy. So I ask him why doesn't he let me fix him a Neo-Citran[8] and scotch, that's what I always take, you still have the cold but you don't feel it, so I do and we end up watching the Late Show together. I mean, they aren't all sex maniacs, the rest of the time they must lead a normal life. I figure they enjoy watching the Late Show just like anybody else.

I do have a scarier one though . . . where the fellow says he's hearing angel voices that're telling him he's got to kill me, you know, you read about things like that all the time in the papers. In this one I'm not in the apartment where I live now, I'm back in my mother's house in Leamington and the fellow's been hiding in the cellar, he grabs my arm when I go downstairs to get a jar of jam and he's got hold of the axe too, out of the garage, that one is really scary. I mean, what do you say to a nut like that?

So I start to shake but after a minute I get control of myself and I say, is he sure the angel voices have got the right person, because I hear the same angel voices and they've been telling me for some time that I'm going to give birth to the reincarnation of St. Anne who in turn has the Virgin Mary and right after that comes Jesus Christ and the end of the world, and he wouldn't want to interfere with that, would he? So he gets confused and listens some more, and then he asks for a sign and I show him my vaccination mark, you can see it's sort of an odd-shaped one, it got infected because I scratched the top off, and that does it, he apologizes and climbs out the coal chute again, which is how he got in in the first place, and I say to myself there's some advantage in having been brought up a Catholic even though I haven't been to church since they changed the service into English, it just isn't the same, you might as well be a Protestant. I must write to Mother and tell her to nail up that coal chute, it always has bothered me. Funny, I couldn't tell you at all what this man looks like but I know exactly what kind of shoes he's wearing, because that's the last I see of him, his shoes going up the coal chute, and they're the old-fashioned kind that lace up the ankles, even though he's a young fellow. That's strange, isn't it?

Let me tell you though I really sweat until I see him safely out of there and I go upstairs right away and make myself a cup of tea. I don't think about that one much. My mother always said you shouldn't dwell on unpleasant things and I generally agree with that, I mean, dwelling on them doesn't make them go away. Though not dwelling on them doesn't make them go away either, when you come to think of it.

Sometimes I have these short ones where the fellow grabs my arm but I'm really a Kung-Fu expert, can you believe it, in real life I'm sure it would just be a conk on the head and that's that, like getting your tonsils out, you'd

---

7. Brand of glue commonly used by schoolchildren.

8. Citrus-flavored cold medicine.

wake up and it would be all over except for the sore places, and you'd be lucky if your neck wasn't broken or something, I could never even hit the volleyball in gym and a volleyball is fairly large, you know?—and I just go *zap* with my fingers into his eyes and that's it, he falls over, or I flip him against a wall or something. But I could never really stick my fingers in anyone's eyes, could you? It would feel like hot jello and I don't even like cold jello, just thinking about it gives me the creeps. I feel a bit guilty about that one, I mean how would you like walking around knowing someone's been blinded for life because of you?

But maybe it's different for a guy.

The most touching one I have is when the fellow grabs my arm and I say, sad and kind of dignified, "You'd be raping a corpse." That pulls him up short and I explain that I've just found out I have leukaemia and the doctors have only given me a few months to live. That's why I'm out pacing the streets alone at night, I need to think, you know, come to terms with myself. I don't really have leukaemia but in the fantasy I do, I guess I chose that particular disease because a girl in my grade four class died of it, the whole class sent her flowers when she was in the hospital. I didn't understand then that she was going to die and I wanted to have leukaemia too so I could get flowers. Kids are funny, aren't they? Well, it turns out that he has leukaemia himself, and *he* only has a few months to live, that's why he's going around raping people, he's very bitter because he's so young and his life is being taken from him before he's really lived it. So we walk along gently under the street lights, it's spring and sort of misty, and we end up going for coffee, we're happy we've found the only other person in the world who can understand what we're going through, it's almost like fate, and after a while we just sort of look at each other and our hands touch, and he comes back with me and moves into my apartment and we spend our last months together before we die, we just sort of don't wake up in the morning, though I've never decided which one of us gets to die first. If it's him I have to go on and fantasize about the funeral, if it's me I don't have to worry about that, so it just about depends on how tired I am at the time. You may not believe this but sometimes I even start crying. I cry at the ends of movies, even the ones that aren't all that sad, so I guess it's the same thing. My mother's like that too.

The funny thing about these fantasies is that the man is always someone I don't know, and the statistics in the magazines, well, most of them anyway, they say it's often someone you do know, at least a little bit, like your boss or something—I mean, it wouldn't be *my* boss, he's over sixty and I'm sure he couldn't rape his way out of a paper bag, poor old thing, but it might be someone like Derek Duck, in his elevator shoes, perish the thought—or someone you just met, who invites you up for a drink, it's getting so you can hardly be sociable any more, and how are you supposed to meet people if you can't trust them even that basic amount? You can't spend your whole life in the Filing Department or cooped up in your own apartment with all the doors and windows locked and the shades down. I'm not what you would call a drinker but I like to go out now and then for a drink or two in a nice place, even if I am by myself, I'm with Women's Lib on that even though I can't agree with a lot of the other things they say. Like here for instance, the waiters all know me and if anyone, you know, bothers me . . . I don't know why I'm telling you all this, except I think it helps you get to know a person, especially at first, hearing some of the things they think about. At work they call me the office worry wart, but it isn't so much like worrying, it's more like figuring out what you should do in an emergency, like I said before.

Anyway, another thing about it is that there's a lot of conversation, in fact I spend most of my time, in the fantasy that is, wondering what I'm going to say and what he's going to say, I think it would be better if you could get a conversation going. Like, how could a fellow do that to a person he's just had a long conversation with, once you let them know you're human, you have a life too, I don't see how they could go ahead with it, right? I mean, I know it happens but I just don't understand it, that's the part I really don't understand.

1977

There Was Once

—There was once a poor girl, as beautiful as she was good, who lived with her wicked stepmother in a house in the forest

—Forest? *Forest* is passé, I mean, I've had it with all this wilderness stuff. It's not a right image of our society, today. Let's have some *urban* for a change.

—There was once a poor girl, as beautiful as she was good, who lived with her wicked stepmother in a house in the suburbs.

—That's better. But I have to seriously query this word *poor*.

—But she *was* poor!

—Poor is a relative. She lived in a house, didn't she?

—Yes.

—Then socioeconomically speaking, she was not poor.

—But none of the money was *hers!* The whole point of the story is that the wicked stepmother makes her wear old clothes and sleep in the fireplace—

—Aha! They had a *fireplace!* With *poor,* let me tell you, there's no fireplace. Come down to the park, come to the subway stations after dark, come down to where they sleep in cardboard boxes, and I'll show you *poor!*

—There was once a middle-class girl, as beautiful as she was good—

—Stop right there. I think we can cut the *beautiful,* don't you? Women these days have to deal with too many intimidating physical role models as it is, what with those bimbos in the ads. Can't you make her, well, more average?

—There was once a girl who was a little overweight and whose front teeth stuck out, who—

—I don't think it's nice to make fun of people's appearances. Plus you're encouraging anorexia.

—I wasn't making fun! I was just describing—

—Skip the description. Description oppresses. But you can say what color she was.

—What color?

—You know. Black, white, red, brown, yellow. Those are the choices. And I'm telling you right now, I've had enough of white. Dominant culture this, dominant culture that—

—I don't know what color.

—Well, it would probably be *your* color, wouldn't it?

—But this isn't *about* me! It's about this girl—

—Everything is about you.

—Sounds to me like you don't want to hear this story at all.

—Oh well, go on. You could make her ethnic. That might help.

—There was once a girl of indeterminate descent, as average-looking as she was good, who lived with her wicked—

—Another thing. *Good* and *wicked*. Don't you think you should transcend those puritanical judgmental moralistic epithets? I mean, so much of that is conditioning, isn't it?

—There was once a girl, as average-looking as she was well-adjusted, who lived with her stepmother, who was not a very open and loving person because she herself had been abused in childhood.

—Better. But I am so *tired* of negative female images! And stepmothers—they always get it in the neck! Change it to step*father*, why don't you? That would make more sense anyway, considering the bad behavior you're about to describe. And throw in some whips and chains. We all know what those twisted, repressed, middle-aged men are like—

—Hey, just *a* minute! I'm *a* middle-aged—

—Stuff it, Mister Nosy Parker. Nobody asked you to stick in your oar,[1] or whatever you want to call that thing. This is between the two of us. Go on.

—There was once a girl—

---

1. Break into a discussion, interfere.

—How old was she?

—I don't know. She was young.

—This ends with a marriage, right?

—Well, not to blow the plot, but—yes.

—Then you can scratch the condescending paternalistic terminology. It's *woman*, pal. *Woman*.

—There was once—

—What's this *was, once*? Enough of the dead past. Tell me about *now*.

—There—

—So?

—So, what?

—So, why not *here*?

1992

The Little Red Hen Tells All

Everyone wants in on it. Everyone! Not just the cat, the pig and the dog. The horse too, the cow, the rhinoceros, the orangutang, the horned toad, the wombat, the duck-billed platypus, you name it. There's no peace any more and all because of that goddamn loaf of bread.

It's not easy, being a hen.

You know my story. Probably you had it told to you as a shining example of how you yourself ought to behave. Sobriety and elbow grease. Do it yourself. Then invest your capital. Then collect. I'm supposed to be an illustration of *that*? Don't make me laugh.

I found the grain of wheat, true. So what? There are lots of grains of wheat lying around. Keep your eyes to the grindstone and you could find a grain of wheat, too. I saw one and picked it up. Nothing wrong with that. Finders keepers. A grain of wheat saved is a grain of wheat earned. Opportunity is bald behind.[1]

Who will help me plant this grain of wheat? I said. *Who? Who?* I felt like a goddamn owl.

Not me, not me, they replied. *Then I'll do it myself,* I said, as the nun quipped to the vibrator. Nobody was listening, of course. They'd all gone to the beach.

---

1. A list of incomplete or slightly altered clichés: "Keep your nose to the grindstone," "Finders keepers, losers weepers," and "A penny saved is penny earned." However, "Opportunity is bald behind" accurately quotes from a distich by Dionysius Cato (3rd or 4th c. C.E.).

Don't think it didn't hurt, all that rejection. Brooding in my nest of straw, I cried little red hen tears. Tears of chicken blood. You know what that looks like, you've eaten enough of it. Makes good gravy.

So, what were my options? I could have eaten that grain of wheat right away. Done myself a nutritional favor. But instead I planted it. Watered it. Stood guard over it night and day with my little feathered body.

So it grew. Why not? So it made more grains of wheat. So I planted those. So I watered those. So I ground them into flour. So I finally got enough for a loaf of bread. So I baked it. You've seen the pictures, me in my little red hen apron, holding the loaf with its plume of aroma in between the tips of my wings, smiling away. I smile in all the pictures, as much as you can smile, with a beak. Whenever they said *Not me,* I smiled. I never lost my temper.

Who will help me eat this loaf of bread? I said. *I will,* said the cat, the dog and the pig. *I will,* said the antelope. *I will,* said the yak. *I will,* said the five-lined skink.[2] *I will,* said the pubic louse. They meant it, too. They held out their paws, hooves, tongues, claws, mandibles, prehensile tails. They drooled at me with their eyes. They whined. They shoved petitions through my mail slot. They became depressed. They accused me of selfishness. They developed symptoms. They threatened suicide. They said it was my fault, for having a loaf of bread when they had none. Every single one of them, it seemed, needed that goddamn loaf of bread more than I did.

You can bake more, they said.

So then what? I know what the story says, what I'm supposed to have said: *I'll eat it myself, so kiss off.* Don't believe a word of it. As I've pointed out, I'm a hen, not a rooster.

Here, I said. *I apologize for having the idea in the first place. I apologize for luck. I apologize for self-denial. I apologize for being a good cook. I apologize for that crack about nuns. I apologize for that crack about roosters. I apologize for smiling, in my smug hen apron, with my smug hen beak. I apologize for being a hen.*

Have some more.

Have mine.

1992

2. A common lizard.

ANGELA CARTER
1940–1992

Angela Carter claimed "witch blood on her father's side; solid radical trade-unionists on mother's." In the essays she published in many British magazines and in book form, she wrote with fierce irreverence about such diverse subjects as the eighteenth-century French pornographer the marquis de Sade and contemporary movie stars. A self-proclaimed leftist in politics, she was born Angela Olive Stalker in Eastbourne,

Sussex, and attended the University of Bristol, from which she graduated in 1965. Married in 1960 (and divorced in 1972), Carter published her first novel at the age of twenty-six. It was quickly followed by such children's books as *The Magic Toyshop* (1967), *Miss Z, The Dark Young Lady* (1970), and *The Donkey Prince* (1970), and by a number of adult novels, including *Love* (1971), *The Infernal Desire Machines of Doctor Hoffman* (1972), and *The Passion of New Eve* (1977). Before her untimely death, Carter turned to magical realism in *Nights at the Circus* (1984) and *Wise Children* (1992); her essays and journalism were collected in *Nothing Sacred* (1982). In *The Bloody Chamber* (1979), a book whose title refers to the Bluebeard story, Carter brought together her fascination with the dynamics of female desire and her work on children's literature, for in this collection the grim quality of many fairy tales is fully explored in surrealistic meditations on such traditional fantasies. The screenplay for the British film of *The Company of Wolves* (1984) was coauthored by Carter, and it testifies (along with the tale itself) to this author's fascination with issues revolving around domination and physical desire.

The Company of Wolves[1]

One beast and only one howls in the woods by night.

The wolf is carnivore incarnate and he's as cunning as he is ferocious; once he's had a taste of flesh, then nothing else will do.

At night, the eyes of wolves shine like candle flames, yellowish, reddish, but that is because the pupils of their eyes fatten on darkness and catch the light from your lantern to flash it back to you—red for danger; if a wolf's eyes reflect only moonlight, then they gleam a cold and unnatural green, a mineral, a piercing color. If the benighted traveler spies those luminous, terrible sequins stitched suddenly on the black thickets, then he knows he must run, if fear has not struck him stock-still.

But those eyes are all you will be able to glimpse of the forest assassins as they cluster invisibly round your smell of meat as you go through the wood unwisely late. They will be like shadows, they will be like wraiths, gray members of a congregation of nightmare. Hark! his long, wavering howl . . . an aria of fear made audible.

The wolfsong is the sound of the rending you will suffer, in itself a murdering.

It is winter and cold weather. In this region of mountain and forest, there is now nothing for the wolves to eat. Goats and sheep are locked up in the byre,[2] the deer departed for the remaining pasturage on the southern slopes—wolves grow lean and famished. There is so little flesh on them that you could count the starveling ribs through their pelts, if they gave you time before they pounced. Those slavering jaws; the lolling tongue; the rime[3] of saliva on the grizzled chops—of all the teeming perils of the night and the forest, ghosts, hobgoblins, ogres that grill babies upon gridirons, witches that

---

1. The story is based on the children's folktale "Little Red Riding Hood," in which a young girl goes through the woods to visit her grandmother and meets a wolf, who rushes ahead and eats the grandmother, then tries to pass himself off as the old woman so as to eat Little Red Riding Hood. In the version most widely known, a passing woodsman rescues the girl.
2. Barn.
3. Coating of frost.

fatten their captives in cages for cannibal tables, the wolf is worst, for he cannot listen to reason.

You are always in danger in the forest, where no people are. Step between the portals of the great pines where the shaggy branches tangle about you, trapping the unwary traveler in nets as if the vegetation itself were in a plot with the wolves who live there, as though the wicked trees go fishing on behalf of their friends—step between the gateposts of the forest with the greatest trepidation and infinite precautions, for if you stray from the path for one instant, the wolves will eat you. They are gray as famine, they are as unkind as plague.

The grave-eyed children of the sparse villages always carry knives with them when they go out to tend the little flocks of goats that provide the homesteads with acrid milk and rank, maggoty cheeses. Their knives are half as big as they are; the blades are sharpened daily.

But the wolves have ways of arriving at your own hearthside. We try and try but sometimes we cannot keep them out. There is no winter's night the cottager does not fear to see a lean, gray, famished snout questing under the door, and there was a woman once bitten in her own kitchen as she was straining the macaroni.

Fear and flee the wolf; for worst of all, the wolf may be more than he seems.

There was a hunter once, near here, that trapped a wolf in a pit. This wolf had massacred the sheep and goats; eaten up a mad old man who used to live by himself in a hut halfway up the mountain and sing to Jesus all day; pounced on a girl looking after the sheep, but she made such a commotion that men came with rifles and scared him away and tried to track him into the forest but he was cunning and easily gave them the slip. So this hunter dug a pit and put a duck in it, for bait, all alive-oh; and he covered the pit with straw smeared with wolf dung. Quack, quack! went the duck, and a wolf came slinking out of the forest, a big one, a heavy one, he weighed as much as a grown man and the straw gave way beneath him—into the pit he tumbled. The hunter jumped down after him, slit his throat, cut off all his paws for a trophy.

And then no wolf at all lay in front of the hunter but the bloody trunk of a man, headless, footless, dying, dead.

A witch from up the valley once turned an entire wedding party into wolves because the groom had settled on another girl. She used to order them to visit her, at night, from spite, and they would sit and howl around her cottage for her, serenading her with their misery.

Not so very long ago, a young woman in our village married a man who vanished clean away on her wedding night. The bed was made with new sheets and the bride lay down in it; the groom said he was going out to relieve himself, insisted on it, for the sake of decency, and she drew the coverlet up to her chin and she lay there. And she waited and she waited and then she waited again—surely he's been gone a long time? Until she jumps up in bed and shrieks to hear a howling, coming on the wind from the forest.

That long-drawn, wavering howl has, for all its fearful resonance, some inherent sadness in it, as if the beasts would love to be less beastly if only they knew how and never cease to mourn their own condition. There is a vast melancholy in the canticles[4] of the wolves, melancholy infinite as the forest, endless as these long nights of winter, and yet that ghastly sadness, that mourning for their own, irremediable appetites, can never move the heart, for not one phrase in it hints at the possibility of redemption; grace could not come to the wolf from its own despair, only through some external mediator, so that, sometimes, the beast will look as if he half welcomes the knife that dispatches him.

The young woman's brothers searched the outhouses and the haystacks but never found any remains, so the sensible girl dried her eyes and found herself another husband, not too shy to piss into a pot, who spent the nights indoors. She gave him a pair of bonny babies and all went right as a trivet until, one freezing night, the night of the solstice, the hinge of the year when things do not fit together as well as they should, the longest night, her first good man came home again.

A great thump on the door announced him as she was stirring the soup for the father of her children and she knew him the moment she lifted the latch to him although it was years since she'd worn black for him and now he was in rags and his hair hung down his back and never saw a comb, alive with lice.

"Here I am again, missis," he said. "Get me my bowl of cabbage and be quick about it."

Then her second husband came in with wood for the fire and when the first one saw she'd slept with another man and, worse, clapped his red eyes on her little children, who'd crept into the kitchen to see what all the din was about, he shouted: "I wish I were a wolf again, to teach this whore a lesson!" So a wolf he instantly became and tore off the eldest boy's left foot before he was chopped up with the hatchet they used for chopping logs. But when the wolf lay bleeding and gasping its last, the pelt peeled off again and he was just as he had been, years ago, when he ran away from his marriage bed, so that she wept and her second husband beat her.

They say there's an ointment the Devil gives you that turns you into a wolf the minute you rub it on. Or that he was born feet first and had a wolf for his father and his torso is a man's but his legs and genitals are a wolf's. And he has a wolf's heart.

Seven years is a werewolf's natural span, but if you burn his human clothing you condemn him to wolfishness for the rest of his life, so old wives hereabouts think it some protection to throw a hat or an apron at the werewolf, as if clothes made the man. Yet by the eyes, those phosphorescent eyes, you know him in all his shapes; the eyes alone unchanged by metamorphosis.

Before he can become a wolf, the lycanthrope[5] strips stark naked. If you spy a naked man among the pines, you must run as if the Devil were after you.

It is midwinter and the robin, the friend of man, sits on the handle of the gardener's spade and sings. It is the worst time in all the year for wolves, but this strong-minded child insists she will go off through the wood. She is quite sure the wild beasts cannot harm her although, well-warned, she lays a carv-

---

4. Songs, especially hymns. 5. Werewolf.

ing knife in the basket her mother has packed with cheeses. There is a bottle of harsh liquor distilled from brambles; a batch of flat oat cakes baked on the hearthstone; a pot or two of jam. The flaxen-haired girl will take these delicious gifts to a reclusive grandmother so old the burden of her years is crushing her to death. Granny lives two hours' trudge through the winter woods; the child wraps herself up in her thick shawl, draws it over her head. She steps into her stout wooden shoes; she is dressed and ready and it is Christmas Eve. The malign door of the solstice still swings upon its hinges, but she has been too much loved ever to feel scared.

Children do not stay young for long in this savage country. There are no toys for them to play with, so they work hard and grow wise, but this one, so pretty and the youngest of her family, a little latecomer, had been indulged by her mother and the grandmother who'd knitted her the red shawl that, today, has the ominous if brilliant look of blood on snow. Her breasts have just begun to swell; her hair is like lint, so fair it hardly makes a shadow on her pale forehead; her cheeks are an emblematic scarlet and white and she has just started her woman's bleeding, the clock inside her that will strike, henceforward, once a month.

She stands and moves within the invisible pentacle[6] of her own virginity. She is an unbroken egg; she is a sealed vessel; she has inside her a magic space the entrance to which is shut tight with a plug of membrane; she is a closed system; she does not know how to shiver. She has her knife and she is afraid of nothing.

Her father might forbid her, if he were home, but he is away in the forest, gathering wood, and her mother cannot deny her.

The forest closed upon her like a pair of jaws.

There is always something to look at in the forest, even in the middle of winter—the huddled mounds of birds, succumbed to the lethargy of the season, heaped on the creaking boughs and too forlorn to sing; the bright frills of the winter fungi on the blotched trunks of the trees; the cuneiform[7] slots of rabbits and deer, the herringbone tracks of the birds, a hare as lean as a rasher of bacon streaking across the path where the thin sunlight dapples the russet brakes of last year's bracken.

When she heard the freezing howl of a distant wolf, her practiced hand sprang to the handle of her knife, but she saw no sign of a wolf at all, nor of a naked man, neither, but then she heard a clattering among the brushwood and there sprang onto the path a fully clothed one, a very handsome young one, in the green coat and wide-awake hat of a hunter, laden with carcasses of game birds. She had her hand on her knife at the first rustle of twigs, but he laughed with a flash of white teeth when he saw her and made her a comic yet flattering little bow; she'd never seen such a fine fellow before, not among the rustic clowns[8] of her native village. So on they went together, through the thickening light of the afternoon.

Soon they were laughing and joking like old friends. When he offered to carry her basket, she gave it to him although her knife was in it because he told her his rifle would protect them. As the day darkened, it began to snow again; she felt the first flakes settle on her eyelashes, but now there was only

---

6. Five-pointed star, an occult symbol.
7. Wedge shaped, like ancient Babylonian and Assyrian writing.
8. Here, country folk.

half a mile to go and there would be a fire, and hot tea, and a welcome, a warm one, surely, for the dashing huntsman as well as for herself.

This young man had a remarkable object in his pocket. It was a compass. She looked at the little round glass face in the palm of his hand and watched the wavering needle with a vague wonder. He assured her this compass had taken him safely through the wood on his hunting trip because the needle always told him with perfect accuracy where the north was. She did not believe it; she knew she should never leave the path on the way through the wood or else she would be lost instantly. He laughed at her again; gleaming trails of spittle clung to his teeth. He said if he plunged off the path into the forest that surrounded them, he could guarantee to arrive at her grandmother's house a good quarter of an hour before she did, plotting his way through the undergrowth with his compass, while she trudged the long way, along the winding path.

I don't believe you. Besides, aren't you afraid of the wolves?

He only tapped the gleaming butt of his rifle and grinned.

Is it a bet? he asked her. Shall we make a game of it? What will you give me if I get to your grandmother's house before you?

What would you like? she asked disingenuously.

A kiss.

Commonplaces of a rustic seduction; she lowered her eyes and blushed.

He went through the undergrowth and took her basket with him, but she forgot to be afraid of the beasts, although now the moon was rising, for she wanted to dawdle on her way to make sure the handsome gentleman would win his wager.

Grandmother's house stood by itself a little way out of the village. The freshly falling snow blew in eddies about the kitchen garden and the young man stepped delicately up the snowy path to the door as if he were reluctant to get his feet wet, swinging his bundle of game and the girl's basket and humming a little tune to himself.

There is a faint trace of blood on his chin; he has been snacking on his catch.

He rapped upon the panels with his knuckles.

Aged and frail, granny is three-quarters succumbed to the mortality the ache in her bones promises her and almost ready to give in entirely. A boy came out from the village to build up her hearth for the night an hour ago and the kitchen crackles with busy firelight. She has her Bible for company; she is a pious old woman. She is propped up on several pillows in the bed set into the wall peasant fashion, wrapped up in the patchwork quilt she made before she was married, more years ago than she cares to remember. Two china spaniels with liver-colored blotches on their coats and black noses sit on either side of the fireplace. There is a bright rug of woven rags on the pantiles. The grandfather clock ticks away her eroding time.

We keep the wolves outside by living well.

He rapped upon the panels with his hairy knuckles.

It is your granddaughter, he mimicked in a high soprano.

Lift up the latch and walk in, my darling.

You can tell them by their eyes, eyes of a beast of prey, nocturnal, devastating eyes as red as a wound; you can hurl your Bible at him and your apron after, granny; you thought that was a sure prophylactic against these infernal vermin. . . . Now call on Christ and his mother and all the angels in heaven to protect you, but it won't do you any good.

His feral muzzle is sharp as a knife; he drops his golden burden of gnawed pheasant on the table and puts down your dear girl's basket, too. Oh, my God, what have you done with her?

Off with his disguise, that coat of forest-colored cloth, the hat with the feather tucked into the ribbon; his matted hair streams down his white shirt and she can see the lice moving in it. The sticks in the hearth shift and hiss; night and the forest has come into the kitchen with darkness tangled in its hair.

He strips off his shirt. His skin is the color and texture of vellum. A crisp stripe of hair runs down his belly, his nipples are ripe and dark as poison fruit, but he's so thin you could count the ribs under his skin if only he gave you the time. He strip off his trousers and she can see how hairy his legs are. His genitals, huge. Ah! huge.

The last thing the old lady saw in all this world was a young man, eyes like cinders, naked as a stone, approaching her bed.

The wolf is carnivore incarnate.

When he had finished with her, he licked his chops and quickly dressed himself again, until he was just as he had been when he came through her door. He burned the inedible hair in the fireplace and wrapped the bones up in a napkin that he hid away under the bed in the wooden chest in which he found a clean pair of sheets. These he carefully put on the bed instead of the telltale stained ones he stowed away in the laundry basket. He plumped up the pillows and shook out the patchwork quilt, he picked up the Bible from the floor, closed it and laid it on the table. All was as it had been before except that grandmother was gone. The sticks twitched in the grate, the clock ticked and the young man sat patiently, deceitfully beside the bed in granny's nightcap.

Rat-a-tap-tap.

Who's there, he quavers in granny's antique falsetto.

Only your granddaughter.

So she came in, bringing with her a flurry of snow that melted in tears on the tiles, and perhaps she was a little disappointed to see only her grandmother sitting beside the fire. But then he flung off the blanket and sprang to the door, pressing his back against it so that she could not get out again.

The girl looked round the room and saw there was not even the indentation of a head on the smooth cheek of the pillow and how, for the first time she'd seen it so, the Bible lay closed on the table. The tick of the clock cracked like a whip. She wanted her knife from her basket but she did not dare reach for it because his eyes were fixed upon her—huge eyes that now seemed to shine with a unique, interior light, eyes the size of saucers, saucers full of Greek fire,[9] diabolic phosphorescence.

What big eyes you have.

All the better to see you with.

No trace at all of the old woman except for a tuft of white hair that had caught in the bark of an unburned log. When the girl saw that, she knew she was in danger of death.

---

9. Flammable mixture, used by the Byzantine Empire, that burns when wet.

Where is my grandmother?

There's nobody here but we two, my darling.

Now a great howling rose up all around them, near, very near, as close as the kitchen garden, the howling of a multitude of wolves; she knew the worst wolves are hairy on the inside and she shivered, in spite of the scarlet shawl she pulled more closely round herself as if it could protect her, although it was as red as the blood she must spill.

Who has come to sing us carols? she said.

Those are the voices of my brothers, darling; I love the company of wolves. Look out of the window and you'll see them.

Snow half-caked the lattice and she opened it to look into the garden. It was a white night of moon and snow; the blizzard whirled round the gaunt, gray beasts who squatted on their haunches among the rows of winter cabbage, pointing their sharp snouts to the moon and howling as if their hearts would break. Ten wolves; twenty wolves—so many wolves she could not count them, howling in concert as if demented or deranged. Their eyes reflected the light from the kitchen and shone like a hundred candles.

It is very cold, poor things, she said; no wonder they howl so.

She closed the window on the wolves' threnody[1] and took off her scarlet shawl, the color of poppies, the color of sacrifices, the color of her menses, and since her fear did her no good, she ceased to be afraid.

What shall I do with my shawl?

Throw it on the fire, dear one. You won't need it again.

She bundled up her shawl and threw it on the blaze, which instantly consumed it. Then she drew her blouse over her head; her small breasts gleamed as if the snow had invaded the room.

What shall I do with my blouse?

Into the fire with it, too, my pet.

The thin muslin went flaring up the chimney like a magic bird and now off came her skirt, her woolen stockings, her shoes, and onto the fire they went, too, and were gone for good. The firelight shone through the edges of her skin; now she was clothed only in her untouched integument of flesh. Thus dazzling, naked, she combed out her hair with her fingers; her hair looked white as the snow outside. Then went directly to the man with red eyes in whose unkempt mane the lice moved; she stood up on tiptoe and unbottoned the collar of his shirt.

What big arms you have.

All the better to hug you with.

Every wolf in the world now howled a prothalamion[2] outside the window as she freely gave the kiss she owed him.

What big teeth you have!

She saw how his jaw began to slaver and the room was full of the clamor of the forest's *Liebestod*,[3] but the wise child never flinched, even when he answered:

All the better to eat you with.

The girl burst out laughing; she knew she was nobody's meat. She laughed

---

1. Song of lamentation for the dead.
2. Song before marriage.
3. Love-death (German); often applied to the closing scene of Richard Wagner's opera *Tristan and Isolde* (1865), in which Isolde joyfully dies to join her lover, Tristan.

at him full in the face, she ripped off his shirt for him and flung it into the fire, in the fiery wake of her own discarded clothing. The flames danced like dead souls on Walpurgisnacht[4] and the old bones under the bed set up a terrible clattering, but she did not pay them any heed.

Carnivore incarnate, only immaculate flesh appeases him.

She will lay his fearful head on her lap and she will pick out the lice from his pelt and perhaps she will put the lice into her mouth and eat them, as he will bid her, as she would do in a savage marriage ceremony.

The blizzard will die down.

The blizzard died down, leaving the mountains as randomly covered with snow as if a blind woman had thrown a sheet over them, the upper branches of the forest pines limed, creaking, swollen with the fall.

Snowlight, moonlight, a confusion of pawprints.

All silent, all still.

Midnight; and the clock strikes. It is Christmas Day, the werewolves' birthday; the door of the solstice stands wide open; let them all sink through.

See! Sweet and sound she sleeps in granny's bed, between the paws of the tender wolf.

1979

4. Witches' celebration, the eve of May 1.

MAXINE HONG KINGSTON
b. 1940

"I have various ways of melding the Chinese and Western experiences," the acclaimed Asian American writer Maxine Hong Kingston once told an interviewer. "My hands are writing English, but my mouth is speaking Chinese. Somehow I am able to write a language that captures the Chinese rhythms and tones and images, getting that power into English. I am working in some kind of fusion language." The daughter of Chinese immigrants who operated a laundry in Stockton, California, Kingston recorded the mysteries and marvels of "a girlhood among ghosts" in *The Woman Warrior* (1976), a book that combines autobiography and fiction to counterpoint memories of a Chinese American childhood with fantasies about Chinese history and culture. Educated at the University of California, Berkeley, Kingston married the actor Earll Kingston in 1962, and in 1967 she settled in Honolulu with him and their son, Joseph. There she taught English at the Mid-Pacific Institute, a private high school, and at the University of Hawaii, while continuing to explore the dynamics of Chinese American society in *China Men* (1980), a reconstruction of her grandfather's and her father's pilgrimages to America, the "Gold Mountain" of Chinese legend. In 1984 she returned to Berkeley, where she taught at the University of California and published a novel, *Tripmaster Monkey: His Fake Book* (1989).

But in 1991 catastrophe struck: Kingston came home from a memorial service for her father to discover that her house had been consumed in a firestorm that swept through the Oakland hills that October—and all the notes, manuscripts, and backup copies of her latest novel in progress had been devoured by the flames. Devastated, she explains that "I abandoned the burned book and began somewhere else. I wrote about something else, and I did that until I could write fiction again," for having lost the ongoing project, she felt that "I'd lost fiction, which is the same as losing my imagination. I couldn't care for those characters." Eventually, however, Kingston brilliantly renewed her imagination in another innovative work, *The Fifth Book of Peace* (2003); here, as she did in *The Woman Warrior,* she melds memoir and fiction, this time in a stirring meditation on loss and recovery. And while mourning her losses, she produced several other strong works, including *To Be the Poet* (2002), based on a lecture series she delivered at Harvard University in 2000, and *Hawaii One Summer* (1998), a collection of essays exploring the state "piece by piece" in the hope that "the sum praises" a milieu she loves.

Despite the style and skill of her later productions, *The Woman Warrior,* with its evocation of "a girlhood among ghosts," remains Kingston's most widely read and frequently taught volume. Its power derives at least in part from the ambiguity of the word *ghosts.* For the "ghosts" who haunt its narrator's girlhood are both the alien Caucasian Americans with whom she goes to school and the mystifying Asian ancestors whose stories her mother told her—often, in particular, damned or glamorous female characters such as "No Name Woman" and the "Woman Warrior." No doubt because this groundbreaking work so powerfully illuminates the intricate processes by which "femininity" is constructed in a culture different from our own, the novelist Kay Boyle exulted that *The Woman Warrior* is "a woman's book that has the vitality to take one far, . . . from the domestic grievances of American suburbia, . . . into the wit, and the love, and grief, of another place entirely."

No Name Woman

"You must not tell anyone," my mother said, "what I am about to tell you. In China your father had a sister who killed herself. She jumped into the family well. We say that your father has all brothers because it is as if she had never been born.

"In 1924 just a few days after our village celebrated seventeen hurry-up weddings—to make sure that every young man who went 'out on the road' would responsibly come home—your father and his brothers and your grandfather and his brothers and your aunt's new husband sailed for America, the Gold Mountain. It was your grandfather's last trip. Those lucky enough to get contracts waved good-bye from the decks. They fed and guarded the stowaways and helped them off in Cuba, New York, Bali, Hawaii. 'We'll meet in California next year,' they said. All of them sent money home.

"I remember looking at your aunt one day when she and I were dressing; I had not noticed before that she had such a protruding melon of a stomach. But I did not think, 'She's pregnant,' until she began to look like other pregnant women, her shirt pulling and the white tops of her black pants showing. She could not have been pregnant, you see, because her husband had been gone for years. No one said anything. We did not discuss it. In early summer she was ready to have the child, long after the time when it could have been possible.

"The village had also been counting. On the night the baby was to be born the villagers raided our house. Some were crying. Like a great saw, teeth strung with lights, files of people walked zigzag across our land, tearing the rice. Their lanterns doubled in the disturbed black water, which drained away through the broken bunds.[1] As the villagers closed in, we could see that some

---

1. Embankments.

of them, probably men and women we knew well, wore white masks. The people with long hair hung it over their faces. Women with short hair made it stand up on end. Some had tied white bands around their foreheads, arms, and legs.

"At first they threw mud and rocks at the house. Then they threw eggs and began slaughtering our stock. We could hear the animals scream their deaths—the roosters, the pigs, a last great roar from the ox. Familiar wild heads flared in our night windows; the villagers encircled us. Some of the faces stopped to peer at us, their eyes rushing like searchlights. The hands flattened against the panes, framed heads, and left red prints.

"The villagers broke in the front and the back doors at the same time, even though we had not locked the doors against them. Their knives dripped with the blood of our animals. They smeared blood on the doors and walls. One woman swung a chicken, whose throat she had slit, splattering blood in red arcs about her. We stood together in the middle of our house, in the family hall with the pictures and tables of the ancestors around us, and looked straight ahead.

"At that time the house had only two wings. When the men came back, we would build two more to enclose our courtyard and a third one to begin a second courtyard. The villagers pushed through both wings, even your grandparents' rooms, to find your aunt's, which was also mine until the men returned. From this room a new wing for one of the younger families would grow. They ripped up her clothes and shoes and broke her combs, grinding them underfoot. They tore her work from the loom. They scattered the cooking fire and rolled the new weaving in it. We could hear them in the kitchen breaking our bowls and banging the pots. They overturned the great waist-high earthenware jugs; duck eggs, pickled fruits, vegetables burst out and mixed in acrid torrents. The old woman from the next field swept a broom through the air and loosed the spirits-of-the-broom over our heads. 'Pig.' 'Ghost.' 'Pig,' they sobbed and scolded while they ruined our house.

"When they left, they took sugar and oranges to bless themselves. They cut pieces from the dead animals. Some of them took bowls that were not broken and clothes that were not torn. Afterward we swept up the rice and sewed it back up into sacks. But the smells from the spilled preserves lasted. Your aunt gave birth in the pigsty that night. The next morning when I went for the water, I found her and the baby plugging up the family well.

"Don't let your father know that I told you. He denies her. Now that you have started to menstruate, what happened to her could happen to you. Don't humiliate us. You wouldn't like to be forgotten as if you had never been born. The villagers are watchful."

Whenever she had to warn us about life, my mother told stories that ran like this one, a story to grow up on. She tested our strength to establish realities. Those in the emigrant generations who could not reassert brute survival died young and far from home. Those of us in the first American generations have had to figure out how the invisible world the emigrants built around our childhoods fit in solid America.

The emigrants confused the gods by diverting their curses, misleading them with crooked streets and false names. They must try to confuse their offspring as well, who, I suppose, threaten them in similar ways—always trying to get things straight, always trying to name the unspeakable. The

Chinese I know hide their names; sojourners take new names when their lives change and guard their real names with silence.

Chinese-Americans, when you try to understand what things in you are Chinese, how do you separate what is peculiar to childhood, to poverty, insanities, one family, your mother who marked your growing with stories, from what is Chinese? What is Chinese tradition and what is the movies?

If I want to learn what clothes my aunt wore, whether flashy or ordinary, I would have to begin, "Remember Father's drowned-in-the-well sister?" I cannot ask that. My mother has told me once and for all the useful parts. She will add nothing unless powered by Necessity, a riverbank that guides her life. She plants vegetable gardens rather than lawns; she carries the odd-shaped tomatoes home from the fields and eats food left for the gods.

Whenever we did frivolous things, we used up energy; we flew high kites. We children came up off the ground over the melting cones our parents brought home from work and the American movie on New Year's Day—*Oh, You Beautiful Doll* with Betty Grable one year, and *She Wore a Yellow Ribbon* with John Wayne another year.[2] After the one carnival ride each, we paid in guilt; our tired father counted his change on the dark walk home.

Adultery is extravagance. Could people who hatch their own chicks and eat the embryos and the heads for delicacies and boil the feet in vinegar for party food, leaving only the gravel, eating even the gizzard lining—could such people engender a prodigal aunt? To be a woman, to have a daughter in starvation time was a waste enough. My aunt could not have been the lone romantic who gave up everything for sex. Women in the old China did not choose. Some man had commanded her to lie with him and be his secret evil. I wonder whether he masked himself when he joined the raid of her family.

Perhaps she encountered him in the fields or on the mountain where the daughters-in-law collected fuel. Or perhaps he first noticed her in the marketplace. He was not a stranger because the village housed no strangers. She had to have dealings with him other than sex. Perhaps he worked an adjoining field, or he sold her the cloth for the dress she sewed and wore. His demand must have surprised, then terrified her. She obeyed him; she always did as she was told.

When the family found a young man in the next village to be her husband, she stood tractably beside the best rooster, his proxy, and promised before they met that she would be his forever. She was lucky that he was her age and she would be the first wife, an advantage secure now. The night she first saw him, he had sex with her. Then he left for America. She had almost forgotten what he looked like. When she tried to envision him, she only saw the black and white face in the group photograph the men had had taken before leaving.

The other man was not, after all, much different from her husband. They both gave orders: she followed. "If you tell your family, I'll beat you. I'll kill you. Be here again next week." No one talked sex, ever. And she might have separated the rapes from the rest of living if only she did not have to buy her

---

2. Both films premiered in 1949, though Grable (1916–1973), the pin-up girl of World War II, did not in fact appear in the first (its star, June Haver, was promoted as "the next Betty Grable"); Wayne (1907–1979) was a star of western and war movies.

oil from him or gather wood in the same forest. I want her fear to have lasted just as long as rape lasted so that the fear could have been contained. No drawn-out fear. But women at sex hazarded birth and hence lifetimes. The fear did not stop but permeated everywhere. She told the man, "I think I'm pregnant." He organized the raid against her.

On nights when my mother and father talked about their life back home, sometimes they mentioned an "outcast table" whose business they still seemed to be settling, their voices tight. In a commensal[3] tradition, where food is precious, the powerful older people made wrongdoers eat alone. Instead of letting them start separate new lives like the Japanese, who could become samurais and geishas,[4] the Chinese family, faces averted but eyes glowering sideways, hung on to the offenders and fed them leftovers. My aunt must have lived in the same house as my parents and eaten at an outcast table. My mother spoke about the raid as if she had seen it, when she and my aunt, a daughter-in-law to a different household, should not have been living together at all. Daughters-in-law lived with their husbands' parents, not their own; a synonym for marriage in Chinese is "taking a daughter-in-law." Her husband's parents could have sold her, mortgaged her, stoned her. But they had sent her back to her own mother and father, a mysterious act hinting at disgraces not told me. Perhaps they had thrown her out to deflect the avengers.

She was the only daughter; her four brothers went with her father, husband, and uncles "out on the road" and for some years became western men. When the goods were divided among the family, three of the brothers took land, and the youngest, my father, chose an education. After my grandparents gave their daughter away to her husband's family, they had dispensed all the adventure and all the property. They expected her alone to keep the traditional ways, which her brothers, now among the barbarians, could fumble without detection. The heavy, deep-rooted women were to maintain the past against the flood, safe for returning. But the rare urge west had fixed upon our family, and so my aunt crossed boundaries not delineated in space.

The work of preservation demands that the feelings playing about in one's guts not be turned into action. Just watch their passing like cherry blossoms. But perhaps my aunt, my forerunner, caught in a slow life, let dreams grow and fade and after some months or years went toward what persisted. Fear at the enormities of the forbidden kept her desires delicate, wire and bone. She looked at a man because she liked the way the hair was tucked behind his ears, or she liked the question-mark line of a long torso curving at the shoulder and straight at the hip. For warm eyes or a soft voice or a slow walk—that's all—a few hairs, a line, a brightness, a sound, a pace, she gave up family. She offered us up for a charm that vanished with tiredness, a pigtail that didn't toss when the wind died. Why, the wrong lighting could erase the dearest thing about him.

It could very well have been, however, that my aunt did not take subtle enjoyment of her friend, but, a wild woman, kept rollicking company. Imagining her free with sex doesn't fit, though. I don't know any women like that, or men either. Unless I see her life branching into mine, she gives me no ancestral help.

---

3. Eating together, at the same table.   4. I.e., soldiers and courtesans.

To sustain her being in love, she often worked at herself in the mirror, guessing at the colors and shapes that would interest him, changing them frequently in order to hit on the right combination. She wanted him to look back.

On a farm near the sea, a woman who tended her appearance reaped a reputation for eccentricity. All the married women blunt-cut their hair in flaps about their ears or pulled it back in tight buns. No nonsense. Neither style blew easily into heart-catching tangles. And at their weddings they displayed themselves in their long hair for the last time. "It brushed the backs of my knees," my mother tells me. "It was braided, and even so, it brushed the backs of my knees."

At the mirror my aunt combed individuality into her bob. A bun could have been contrived to escape into black streamers blowing in the wind or in quiet wisps about her face, but only the older women in our picture album wear buns. She brushed her hair back from her forehead, tucking the flaps behind her ears. She looped a piece of thread, knotted into a circle between her index fingers and thumbs, and ran the double strand across her forehead. When she closed her fingers as if she were making a pair of shadow geese bite, the string twisted together catching the little hairs. Then she pulled the thread away from her skin, ripping the hairs out neatly, her eyes watering from the needles of pain. Opening her fingers, she cleaned the thread, then rolled it along her hairline and the tops of her eyebrows. My mother did the same to me and my sisters and herself. I used to believe that the expression "caught by the short hairs"[5] meant a captive held with a depilatory string. It especially hurt at the temples, but my mother said we were lucky we didn't have to have our feet bound when we were seven. Sisters used to sit on their beds and cry together, she said, as their mothers or their slaves removed the bandages for a few minutes each night and let the blood gush back into their veins. I hope that the man my aunt loved appreciated a smooth brow, that he wasn't just a tits-and-ass man.

Once my aunt found a freckle on her chin, at a spot that the almanac said predestined her for unhappiness. She dug it out with a hot needle and washed the wound with peroxide.

More attention to her looks than these pullings of hairs and pickings at spots would have caused gossip among the villagers. They owned work clothes and good clothes, and they wore good clothes for feasting the new seasons. But since a woman combing her hair hexes beginnings, my aunt rarely found an occasion to look her best. Women looked like great sea snails—the corded wood, babies, and laundry they carried were the whorls on their backs. The Chinese did not admire a bent back; goddesses and warriors stood straight. Still there must have been a marvelous freeing of beauty when a worker laid down her burden and stretched and arched.

Such commonplace loveliness, however, was not enough for my aunt. She dreamed of a lover for the fifteen days of New Year's, the time for families to exchange visits, money, and food. She plied her secret comb. And sure enough she cursed the year, the family, the village, and herself.

Even as her hair lured her imminent lover, many other men looked at her. Uncles, cousins, nephews, brothers would have looked, too, had they been

---

5. A euphemism for pubic hairs.

home between journeys. Perhaps they had already been restraining their curiosity, and they left, fearful that their glances, like a field of nesting birds, might be startled and caught. Poverty hurt, and that was their first reason for leaving. But another, final reason for leaving the crowded house was the never-said.

She may have been unusually beloved, the precious only daughter, spoiled and mirror gazing because of the affection the family lavished on her. When her husband left, they welcomed the chance to take her back from the in-laws; she could live like the little daughter for just a while longer. There are stories that my grandfather was different from other people, "crazy ever since the little Jap bayoneted him in the head." He used to put his naked penis on the dinner table, laughing. And one day he brought home a baby girl, wrapped up inside his brown western-style greatcoat. He had traded one of his sons, probably my father, the youngest, for her. My grandmother made him trade back. When he finally got a daughter of his own, he doted on her. They must have all loved her, except perhaps my father, the only brother who never went back to China, having once been traded for a girl.

Brothers and sisters, newly men and women, had to efface their sexual color and present plain miens. Disturbing hair and eyes, a smile like no other threatened the ideal of five generations living under one roof. To focus blurs, people shouted face to face and yelled from room to room. The immigrants I know have loud voices, unmodulated to American tones even after years away from the village where they called their friendships out across the fields. I have not been able to stop my mother's screams in public libraries or over telephones. Walking erect (knees straight, toes pointed forward, not pigeon-toed, which is Chinese-feminine) and speaking in an inaudible voice, I have tried to turn myself American-feminine. Chinese communication was loud, public. Only sick people had to whisper. But at the dinner table, where the family members came nearest one another, no one could talk, not the outcasts nor any eaters. Every word that falls from the mouth is a coin lost. Silently they gave and accepted food with both hands. A preoccupied child who took his bowl with one hand got a sideways glare. A complete moment of total attention is due everyone alike. Children and lovers have no singularity here, but my aunt used a secret voice, a separate attentiveness.

She kept the man's name to herself throughout her labor and dying; she did not accuse him that he be punished with her. To save her inseminator's name she gave silent birth.

He may have been somebody in her own household, but intercourse with a man outside the family would have been no less abhorrent. All the village were kinsmen, and the titles shouted in loud country voices never let kinship be forgotten. Any man within visiting distance would have been neutralized as a lover—"brother," "younger brother, older brother"—one hundred and fifteen relationship titles. Parents researched birth charts probably not so much to assure good fortune as to circumvent incest in a population that has but one hundred surnames. Everybody has eight million relatives. How useless then sexual mannerisms, how dangerous.

As if it came from an atavism deeper than fear, I used to add "brother" silently to boys' names. It hexed the boys who would or would not ask me to dance, and made them less scary and as familiar and deserving of benevolence as girls.

But, of course, I hexed myself also—no dates. I should have stood up, both arms waving, and shouted out across libraries, "Hey, you! Love me back." I had no idea, though, how to make attraction selective, how to control its direction and magnitude. If I made myself American-pretty so that the five or six Chinese boys in the class fell in love with me, everyone else—the Caucasian, Negro, and Japanese boys—would too. Sisterliness, dignified and honorable, made much more sense.

Attraction eludes control so stubbornly that whole societies designed to organize relationships among people cannot keep order, not even when they bind people to one another from childhood and raise them together. Among the very poor and the wealthy, brothers married their adopted sisters, like doves. Our family allowed some romance, paying adult brides' prices and providing dowries so that their sons and daughters could marry strangers. Marriage promises to turn strangers into friendly relatives—a nation of siblings.

In the village structure, spirits shimmered among the live creatures, balanced and held in equilibrium by time and land. But one human being flaring up into violence could open up a black hole, a maelstrom that pulled in the sky. The frightened villagers, who depended on one another to maintain the real, went to my aunt to show her a personal, physical representation of the break she had made in the "roundness." Misallying couples snapped off the future, which was to be embodied in true offspring. The villagers punished her for acting as if she could have a private life, secret and apart from them.

If my aunt had betrayed the family at a time of large grain yields and peace, when many boys were born, and wings were being built on many houses, perhaps she might have escaped such severe punishment. But the men—hungry, greedy, tired of planting in dry soil, cuckolded—had had to leave the village in order to send food-money home. There were ghost plagues, bandit plagues, wars with the Japanese, floods. My Chinese brother and sister had died of an unknown sickness. Adultery, perhaps only a mistake during good times, became a crime when the village needed food.

The round moon cakes and round doorways, the round tables of graduated size that fit one roundness inside another, round windows and rice bowls—these talismen had lost their power to warn this family of the law: a family must be whole, faithfully keeping the descent line by having sons to feed the old and the dead, who in turn look after the family. The villagers came to show my aunt and her lover-in-hiding a broken house. The villagers were speeding up the circling of events because she was too shortsighted to see that her infidelity had already harmed the village, that waves of consequences would return unpredictably, sometimes in disguise, as now, to hurt her. This roundness had to be made coin-sized so that she would see its circumference: punish her at the birth of her baby. Awaken her to the inexorable. People who refused fatalism because they could invent small resources insisted on culpability. Deny accidents and wrest fault from the stars.

After the villagers left, their lanterns now scattering in various directions toward home, the family broke their silence and cursed her. "Aiaa, we're going to die. Death is coming. Death is coming. Look what you've done. You've killed us. Ghost! Dead ghost! Ghost! You've never been born." She ran out into the fields, far enough from the house so that she could no longer hear their voices, and pressed herself against the earth, her own land no more. When she felt the birth coming, she thought that she had been hurt. Her body seized together. "They've hurt me too much," she thought. "This is gall, and it will kill me." Her forehead and knees against the earth, her body convulsed and then released her onto her back. The black well of sky and stars went out and out and out forever; her body and her complexity seemed to disappear. She was one of the stars, a bright dot in blackness, without home, without a companion, in eternal cold and silence. An agoraphobia rose in her, speeding higher and higher, bigger and bigger; she would not be able to contain it; there would be no end to fear.

Flayed, unprotected against space, she felt pain return, focusing her body. This pain chilled her—a cold, steady kind of surface pain. Inside, spasmodically, the other pain, the pain of the child, heated her. For hours she lay on the ground, alternately body and space. Sometimes a vision of normal comfort obliterated reality: she saw the family in the evening gambling at the dinner table, the young people massaging their elders' backs. She saw them congratulating one another, high joy on the mornings the rice shoots came up. When these pictures burst, the stars drew yet further apart. Black space opened.

She got to her feet to fight better and remembered that old-fashioned women gave birth in their pigsties to fool the jealous, pain-dealing gods, who do not snatch piglets. Before the next spasms could stop her, she ran to the pigsty, each step a rushing out into emptiness. She climbed over the fence and knelt in the dirt. It was good to have a fence enclosing her, a tribal person alone.

Laboring, this woman who had carried her child as a foreign growth that sickened her every day, expelled it at last. She reached down to touch the hot, wet, moving mass, surely smaller than anything human, and could feel that it was human after all—fingers, toes, nails, nose. She pulled it up on to her belly, and it lay curled there, butt in the air, feet precisely tucked one under the other. She opened her loose shirt and buttoned the child inside. After resting, it squirmed and thrashed and she pushed it up to her breast. It turned its head this way and that until it found her nipple. There, it made little snuffling noises. She clenched her teeth at its preciousness, lovely as a young calf, a piglet, a little dog.

She may have gone to the pigsty as a last act of responsibility: she would protect this child as she had protected its father. It would look after her soul, leaving supplies on her grave. But how would this tiny child without family find her grave when there would be no marker for her anywhere, neither in the earth nor the family hall? No one would give her a family hall name. She had taken the child with her into the wastes. At its birth the two of them had felt the same raw pain of separation, a wound that only the family pressing tight could close. A child with no descent line would not soften her life but only trail after her, ghostlike, begging her to give it purpose. At dawn the villagers on their way to the fields would stand around the fence and look.

Full of milk, the little ghost slept. When it awoke, she hardened her breasts against the milk that crying loosens. Toward morning she picked up the baby and walked to the well.

Carrying the baby to the well shows loving. Otherwise abandon it. Turn its face into the mud. Mothers who love their children take them along. It was probably a girl; there is some hope of forgiveness for boys.

"Don't tell anyone you had an aunt. Your father does not want to hear her name. She has never been born." I have believed that sex was unspeakable and words so strong and fathers so frail that "aunt" would do my father mysterious harm. I have thought that my family, having settled among immigrants who had also been their neighbors in the ancestral land, needed to clean their name, and a wrong word would incite the kinspeople even here. But there is more to this silence: they want me to participate in her punishment. And I have.

In the twenty years since I heard this story I have not asked for details nor said my aunt's name; I do not know it. People who can comfort the dead can also chase after them to hurt them further—a reverse ancestor worship. The real punishment was not the raid swiftly inflicted by the villagers, but the family's deliberately forgetting her. Her betrayal so maddened them, they saw to it that she would suffer forever, even after death. Always hungry, always needing, she would have to beg food from other ghosts, snatch and steal it from those whose living descendants give them gifts. She would have to fight the ghosts massed at crossroads for the buns a few thoughtful citizens leave to decoy her away from village and home so that the ancestral spirits could feast unharassed. At peace, they could act like gods, not ghosts, their descent lines providing them with paper suits and dresses, spirit money, paper houses, paper automobiles, chicken, meat, and rice into eternity[6]—essences delivered up in smoke and flames, steam and incense rising from each rice bowl. In an attempt to make the Chinese care for people outside the family, Chairman Mao[7] encourages us now to give our paper replicas to the spirits of outstanding soldiers and workers, no matter whose ancestors they may be. My aunt remains forever hungry. Goods are not distributed evenly among the dead.

My aunt haunts me—her ghost drawn to me because now, after fifty years of neglect, I alone devote pages of paper to her, though not origamied into houses and clothes.[8] I do not think she always means me well. I am telling on her, and she was a spite suicide, drowning herself in the drinking water. The Chinese are always very frightened of the drowned one, whose weeping ghost, wet hair hanging and skin bloated, waits silently by the water to pull down a substitute.

1976

---

6. According to Chinese custom, these objects are periodically left as offerings at the graves of dead ancestors.
7. Mao Zedong (1893–1976), chairman of the Chinese Communist Party (1949–76) and head of state (1949–59).
8. Origami is the Asian art of folding paper to produce representational shapes.

BHARATI MUKHERJEE
b. 1940

Born a Bengali Brahmin in Calcutta, Bharati Mukherjee refuses to play the role of "a Third World woman writer" because to do so would be "to confine oneself to a narrow, airless, tightly roofed arena." Certainly, her early education in the English-speaking Loreto Convent School and the University of Calcutta as well as her graduate work at the University of Iowa Writers' Workshop, her subsequent marriage to the novelist Clark Blaise, and their expatriation in Canada with their two children as well as the family's subsequent move to the United States suggest the cosmopolitan, international flair of a highly individuated existence.

Nevertheless, Mukherjee's narratives capture the tensions at work in lives stereotyped by national prejudices and permeated by what she calls the "broken identities and discarded languages" spawned by geographical dislocation. Three of her novels, *The Tiger's Daughter* (1972), *Wife* (1975), and *Jasmine* (1989), examine the social conflicts and psychological tensions experienced by displaced Indian women seeking to negotiate between the shock of an alien (often alienating) American culture and the equally depersonalizing violence permeating Calcutta's society. Two collaborative works composed with her husband, *Days and Nights in Calcutta* (1977, rev. 1986) and *The Sorrow and the Terror: The Haunting Legacy of the Air India Tragedy* (1987), reveal her skepticism about bankrupt discourses of multiculturalism actually saturated by racist assumptions. The stories published in *Darkness* (1985) and *The Middleman* (1988) brilliantly capture the impact of international events on the lives of ordinary people, a subject she has also taken up in two collections of nonfiction: *Political Culture and Leadership in India* (1991) and *Regionalism in Indian Perspective* (1992). Her most recent novel, *The Tree Bride* (2004), extends Mukherjee's analysis of the collisions between Indian and American culture.

The Management of Grief

A woman I don't know is boiling tea the Indian way in my kitchen. There are a lot of women I don't know in my kitchen, whispering, and moving tactfully. They open doors, rummage through the pantry, and try not to ask me where things are kept. They remind me of when my sons were small, on Mother's Day or when Vikram and I were tired, and they would make big, sloppy omelets. I would lie in bed pretending I didn't hear them.

Dr. Sharma, the treasurer of the Indo-Canada Society, pulls me into the hallway. He wants to know if I am worried about money. His wife, who has just come up from the basement with a tray of empty cups and glasses, scolds him. "Don't bother Mrs. Bhave with mundane details." She looks so monstrously pregnant her baby must be days overdue. I tell her she shouldn't be carrying heavy things. "Shaila," she says, smiling, "this is the fifth." Then she grabs a teenager by his shirttails. He slips his Walkman off his head. He has to be one of her four children, they have the same domed and dented foreheads. "What's the official word now?" she demands. The boy slips the headphones back on. "They're acting evasive, Ma. They're saying it could be an accident or a terrorist bomb."

All morning, the boys have been muttering, Sikh Bomb, Sikh Bomb. The men, not using the word, bow their heads in agreement. Mrs. Sharma touches her forehead at such a word. At least they've stopped talking about space debris and Russian lasers.

Two radios are going in the dining room. They are tuned to different stations. Someone must have brought the radios down from my boys' bedrooms. I haven't gone into their rooms since Kusum came running across the front lawn in her bathrobe. She looked so funny, I was laughing when I opened the door.

The big TV in the den is being whizzed through American networks and cable channels.

"Damn!" some man swears bitterly. "How can these preachers carry on like nothing's happened?" I want to tell him we're not that important. You look at the audience, and at the preacher in his blue robe with his beautiful white hair, the potted palm trees under a blue sky, and you know they care about nothing.

The phone rings and rings. Dr. Sharma's taken charge. "We're with her," he keeps saying. "Yes, yes, the doctor has given calming pills. Yes, yes, pills are having necessary effect." I wonder if pills alone explain this calm. Not peace, just a deadening quiet. I was always controlled, but never repressed. Sound can reach me, but my body is tensed, ready to scream. I hear their voices all around me. I hear my boys and Vikram cry, "Mommy, Shaila!" and their screams insulate me, like headphones.

The woman boiling water tells her story again and again. "I got the news first. My cousin called from Halifax before six A.M., can you imagine? He'd gotten up for prayers and his son was studying for medical exams and he heard on a rock channel that something had happened to a plane. They said first it had disappeared from the radar, like a giant eraser just reached out. His father called me, so I said to him, what do you mean, 'something bad'? You mean a hijacking? And he said, *behn,* there is no confirmation of anything yet, but check with your neighbors because a lot of them must be on that plane.[1] So I called poor Kusum straightaway. I knew Kusum's husband and daughter were booked to go yesterday."

Kusum lives across the street from me. She and Satish had moved in less than a month ago. They said they needed a bigger place. All these people, the Sharmas and friends from the Indo-Canada Society, had been there for the housewarming. Satish and Kusum made homemade tandoori on their big gas grill and even the white neighbors piled their plates high with that luridly red, charred, juicy chicken. Their younger daughter had danced, and even our boys had broken away from the Stanley Cup telecast to put in a reluctant appearance. Everyone took pictures for their albums and for the community newspapers—another of our families had made it big in Toronto—and now I wonder how many of those happy faces are gone. "Why does God give us so much if all along He intends to take it away?" Kusum asks me.

I nod. We sit on carpeted stairs, holding hands like children. "I never once told him that I loved him," I say. I was too much the well brought up woman. I was so well brought up I never felt comfortable calling my husband by his first name.

---

1. In June 1985, an Air India flight from Toronto to Bombay crashed off the coast of Ireland, apparently as the result of an explosion caused by a bomb. All 329 people on board were killed.

"It's all right," Kusum says. "He knew. My husband knew. They felt it. Modern young girls have to say it because what they feel is fake."

Kusum's daughter, Pam, runs in with an overnight case. Pam's in her McDonald's uniform. "Mummy! You have to get dressed!" Panic makes her cranky. "A reporter's on his way here."

"Why?"

"You want to talk to him in your bathrobe?" She starts to brush her mother's long hair. She's the daughter who's always in trouble. She dates Canadian boys and hangs out in the mall, shopping for tight sweaters. The younger one, the goody-goody one according to Pam, the one with a voice so sweet that when she sang *bhajans*[2] for Ethiopian relief even a frugal man like my husband wrote out a hundred dollar check, *she* was on that plane. *She* was going to spend July and August with grandparents because Pam wouldn't go. Pam said she'd rather waitress at McDonald's. "If it's a choice between Bombay and Wonderland,[3] I'm picking Wonderland," she'd said.

"Leave me alone," Kusum yells. "You know what I want to do? If I didn't have to look after you now, I'd hang myself."

Pam's young face goes blotchy with pain. "Thanks," she says, "don't let me stop you."

"Hush," pregnant Mrs. Sharma scolds Pam. "Leave your mother alone. Mr. Sharma will tackle the reporters and fill out the forms. He'll say what has to be said."

Pam stands her ground. "You think I don't know what Mummy's thinking? *Why her?* that's what. That's sick! Mummy wishes my little sister were alive and I were dead."

Kusum's hand in mine is trembly hot. We continue to sit on the stairs.

She calls before she arrives, wondering if there's anything I need. Her name is Judith Templeton and she's an appointee of the provincial government. "Multiculturalism?" I ask, and she says, "partially," but that her mandate is bigger. "I've been told you knew many of the people on the flight," she says. "Perhaps if you'd agree to help us reach the others . . . ?"

She gives me time at least to put on tea water and pick up the mess in the front room. I have a few *samosas*[4] from Kusum's housewarming that I could fry up, but then I think, Why prolong this visit?

Judith Templeton is much younger than she sounded. She wears a blue suit with a white blouse and a polka dot tie. Her blond hair is cut short, her only jewelry is pearl drop earrings. Her briefcase is new and expensive looking, a gleaming cordovan leather. She sits with it across her lap. When she looks out the front windows onto the street, her contact lenses seem to float in front of her light blue eyes.

"What sort of help do you want from me?" I ask. She has refused the tea, out of politeness, but I insist, along with some slightly stale biscuits.

"I have no experience," she admits. "That is, I have an MSW and I've worked in liaison with accident victims, but I mean I have no experience with a tragedy of this scale—"

"Who could?" I ask.

"—and with the complications of culture, language, and customs. Some-

---

2. Devotional songs, hymns (Hindi).
3. An amusement park in Toronto.
4. Deep fried pastries filled with vegetables or meat.

one mentioned that Mrs. Bhave is a pillar—because you've taken it more calmly."

At this, perhaps, I frown, for she reaches forward, almost to take my hand. "I hope you understand my meaning, Mrs. Bhave. There are hundreds of people in Metro directly affected, like you, and some of them speak no English. There are some widows who've never handled money or gone on a bus, and there are old parents who still haven't eaten or gone outside their bedrooms. Some houses and apartments have been looted. Some wives are still hysterical. Some husbands are in shock and profound depression. We want to help, but our hands are tied in so many ways. We have to distribute money to some people, and there are legal documents—these things can be done. We have interpreters, but we don't always have the human touch, or maybe the right human touch. We don't want to make mistakes, Mrs. Bhave, and that's why we'd like to ask you to help us."

"More mistakes, you mean," I say.

"Police matters are not in my hands," she answers.

"Nothing I can do will make any difference," I say. "We must all grieve in our own way."

"But you are coping very well. All the people said, Mrs. Bhave is the strongest person of all. Perhaps if the others could see you, talk with you, it would help them."

"By the standards of the people you call hysterical, I am behaving very oddly and very badly, Miss Templeton." I want to say to her, *I wish I could scream, starve, walk into Lake Ontario, jump from a bridge.* "They would not see me as a model. I do not see myself as a model."

I am a freak. No one who has ever known me would think of me reacting this way. This terrible calm will not go away.

She asks me if she may call again, after I get back from a long trip that we all must make. "Of course," I say. "Feel free to call, anytime."

Four days later, I find Kusum squatting on a rock overlooking a bay in Ireland. It isn't a big rock, but it juts sharply out over water. This is as close as we'll ever get to them. June breezes balloon out her sari and unpin her knee-length hair. She has the bewildered look of a sea creature whom the tides have stranded.

It's been one hundred hours since Kusum came stumbling and screaming across my lawn. Waiting around the hospital, we've heard many stories. The police, the diplomats, they tell us things thinking that we're strong, that knowledge is helpful to the grieving, and maybe it is. Some, I know, prefer ignorance, or their own versions. The plane broke into two, they say. Unconsciousness was instantaneous. No one suffered. My boys must have just finished their breakfasts. They loved eating on planes, they loved the smallness of plates, knives, and forks. Last year they saved the airline salt and pepper shakers. Half an hour more and they would have made it to Heathrow.

Kusum says that we can't escape our fate. She says that all those people—our husbands, my boys, her girl with the nightingale voice, all those Hindus, Christians, Sikhs, Muslims, Parsis, and atheists on that plane—were fated to die together off this beautiful bay. She learned this from a swami in Toronto.

I have my Valium.

Six of us "relatives"—two widows and four widowers—choose to spend the day today by the waters instead of sitting in a hospital room and scanning photographs of the dead. That's what they call us now: relatives. I've looked through twenty-seven photos in two days. They're very kind to us, the Irish are very understanding. Sometimes understanding means freeing a tourist bus for this trip to the bay, so we can pretend to spy our loved ones through the glassiness of waves or in sun-speckled cloud shapes.

I could die here, too, and be content.

"What is that, out there?" She's standing and flapping her hands and for a moment I see a head shape bobbing in the waves. She's standing in the water, I, on the boulder. The tide is low, and a round, black, head-sized rock has just risen from the waves. She returns, her sari end dripping and ruined and her face is a twisted remnant of hope, the way mine was a hundred hours ago, still laughing but inwardly knowing that nothing but the ultimate tragedy could bring two women together at six o'clock on a Sunday morning. I watch her face sag into blankness.

"That water felt warm, Shaila," she says at length.

"You can't," I say. "We have to wait for our turn to come."

I haven't eaten in four days, haven't brushed my teeth.

"I know," she says. "I tell myself I have no right to grieve. They are in a better place than we are. My swami says I should be thrilled for them. My swami says depression is a sign of our selfishness."

Maybe I'm selfish. Selfishly I break away from Kusum and run, sandals slapping against stones, to the water's edge. What if my boys aren't lying pinned under the debris? What if they aren't stuck a mile below that innocent blue chop? What if, given the strong currents....

Now I've ruined my sari, one of my best. Kusum has joined me, knee-deep in water that feels to me like a swimming pool. I could settle in the water, and my husband would take my hand and the boys would slap water in my face just to see me scream.

"Do you remember what good swimmers my boys were, Kusum?"

"I saw the medals," she says.

One of the widowers, Dr. Ranganathan from Montreal, walks out to us, carrying his shoes in one hand. He's an electrical engineer. Someone at the hotel mentioned his work is famous around the world, something about the place where physics and electricity come together. He has lost a huge family, something indescribable. "With some luck," Dr. Ranganathan suggests to me, "a good swimmer could make it safely to some island. It is quite possible that there may be many, many microscopic islets scattered around."

"You're not just saying that?" I tell Dr. Ranganathan about Vinod, my elder son. Last year he took diving as well.

"It's a parent's duty to hope," he says. "It is foolish to rule out possibilities that have not been tested. I myself have not surrendered hope."

Kusum is sobbing once again. "Dear lady," he says, laying his free hand on her arm, and she calms down.

"Vinod is how old?" he asks me. He's very careful, as we all are. *Is*, not was.

"Fourteen. Yesterday he was fourteen. His father and uncle were going to take him down to the Taj and give him a big birthday party. I couldn't go with them because I couldn't get two weeks off from my stupid job in June." I process bills for a travel agent. June is a big travel month.

Dr. Ranganathan whips the pockets of his suit jacket inside out. Squashed roses, in darkening shades of pink, float on the water. He tore the roses off creepers in somebody's garden. He didn't ask anyone if he could pluck the roses, but now there's been an article about it in the local papers. When you see an Indian person, it says, please give him or her flowers.

"A strong youth of fourteen," he says, "can very likely pull to safety a younger one."

My sons, though four years apart, were very close. Vinod wouldn't let Mithun drown. *Electrical engineering,* I think, foolishly perhaps: this man knows important secrets of the universe, things closed to me. Relief spins me lightheaded. No wonder my boys' photographs haven't turned up in the gallery of photos of the recovered dead. "Such pretty roses," I say.

"My wife loved pink roses. Every Friday I had to bring a bunch home. I used to say, Why? After twenty odd years of marriage you're still needing proof positive of my love?" He has identified his wife and three of his children. Then others from Montreal, the lucky ones, intact families with no survivors. He chuckles as he wades back to shore. Then he swings around to ask me a question. "Mrs. Bhave, you are wanting to throw in some roses for your loved ones? I have two big ones left."

But I have other things to float: Vinod's pocket calculator; a half-painted model B-52 for my Mithun. They'd want them on their island. And for my husband? For him I let fall into the calm, glassy waters a poem I wrote in the hospital yesterday. Finally he'll know my feelings for him.

"Don't tumble, the rocks are slippery," Dr. Ranganathan cautions. He holds out a hand for me to grab.

Then it's time to get back on the bus, time to rush back to our waiting posts on hospital benches.

Kusum is one of the lucky ones. The lucky ones flew here, identified in multiplicate their loved ones, then will fly to India with the bodies for proper ceremonies. Satish is one of the few males who surfaced. The photos of faces we saw on the walls in an office at Heathrow and here in the hospital are mostly of women. Women have more body fat, a nun said to me matter-of-factly. They float better.

Today I was stopped by a young sailor on the street. He had loaded bodies, he'd gone into the water when—he checks my face for signs of strength—when the sharks were first spotted. I don't blush, and he breaks down. "It's all right," I say. "Thank you." I had heard about the sharks from Dr. Ranganathan. In his orderly mind, science brings understanding, it holds no terror. It is the shark's duty. For every deer there is a hunter, for every fish a fisherman.

The Irish are not shy; they rush to me and give me hugs and some are crying. I cannot imagine reactions like that on the streets of Toronto. Just strangers, and I am touched. Some carry flowers with them and give them to any Indian they see.

After lunch, a policeman I have gotten to know quite well catches hold of me. He says he thinks he has a match for Vinod. I explain what a good swimmer Vinod is.

"You want me with you when you look at photos?" Dr. Ranganathan walks ahead of me into the picture gallery. In these matters, he is a scientist, and I am grateful. It is a new perspective. "They have performed miracles," he says. "We are indebted to them."

The first day or two the policemen showed us relatives only one picture at a time; now they're in a hurry, they're eager to lay out the possibles, and even the probables.

The face on the photo is of a boy much like Vinod; the same intelligent eyes, the same thick brows dipping into a V. But this boy's features, even his cheeks, are puffier, wider, mushier.

"No." My gaze is pulled by other pictures. There are five other boys who look like Vinod.

The nun assigned to console me rubs the first picture with a fingertip. "When they've been in the water for a while, love, they look a little heavier." The bones under the skin are broken, they said on the first day—try to adjust your memories. It's important.

"It's not him. I'm his mother. I'd know."

"I know this one!" Dr. Ranganathan cries out suddenly from the back of the gallery. "And this one!" I think he senses that I don't want to find my boys. "They are the Kutty brothers. They were also from Montreal." I don't mean to be crying. On the contrary, I am ecstatic. My suitcase in the hotel is packed heavy with dry clothes for my boys.

The policeman starts to cry. "I am so sorry, I am so sorry, ma'am. I really thought we had a match."

With the nun ahead of us and the policeman behind, we, the unlucky ones without our children's bodies, file out of the makeshift gallery.

From Ireland most of us go on to India. Kusum and I take the same direct flight to Bombay, so I can help her clear customs quickly. But we have to argue with a man in uniform. He has large boils on his face. The boils swell and glow with sweat as we argue with him. He wants Kusum to wait in line and he refuses to take authority because his boss is on a tea break. But Kusum won't let her coffins out of sight, and I shan't desert her though I know that my parents, elderly and diabetic, must be waiting in a stuffy car in a scorching lot.

"You bastard!" I scream at the man with the popping boils. Other passengers press closer. "You think we're smuggling contraband in those coffins!"

Once upon a time we were well brought up women; we were dutiful wives who kept our heads veiled, our voices shy and sweet.

In India, I become, once again, an only child of rich, ailing parents. Old friends of the family come to pay their respects. Some are Sikh, and inwardly, involuntarily, I cringe. My parents are progressive people; they do not blame communities for a few individuals.

In Canada it is a different story now.

"Stay longer," my mother pleads. "Canada is a cold place. Why would you want to be all by yourself?" I stay.

Three months pass. Then another.

"Vikram wouldn't have wanted you to give up things!" they protest. They call my husband by the name he was born with. In Toronto he'd changed to

Vik so the men he worked with at his office would find his name as easy as Rod or Chris. "You know, the dead aren't cut off from us!"

My grandmother, the spoiled daughter of a rich *zamindar*,[5] shaved her head with rusty razor blades when she was widowed at sixteen. My grandfather died of childhood diabetes when he was nineteen, and she saw herself as the harbinger of bad luck. My mother grew up without parents, raised indifferently by an uncle, while her true mother slept in a hut behind the main estate house and took her food with the servants. She grew up a rationalist. My parents abhor mindless mortification.

The zamindar's daughter kept stubborn faith in Vedic rituals;[6] my parents rebelled. I am trapped between two modes of knowledge. At thirty-six, I am too old to start over and too young to give up. Like my husband's spirit, I flutter between worlds.

Courting aphasia, we travel. We travel with our phalanx of servants and poor relatives. To hill stations and to beach resorts. We play contract bridge in dusty gymkhana clubs.[7] We ride stubby ponies up crumbly mountain trails. At tea dances, we let ourselves be twirled twice round the ballroom. We hit the holy spots we hadn't made time for before. In Varanasi, Kalighat, Rishikesh, Hardwar, astrologers and palmists seek me out and for a fee offer me cosmic consolations.

Already the widowers among us are being shown new bride candidates. They cannot resist the call of custom, the authority of their parents and older brothers. They must marry; it is the duty of a man to look after a wife. The new wives will be young widows with children, destitute but of good family. They will make loving wives, but the men will shun them. I've had calls from the men over crackling Indian telephone lines. "Save me," they say, these substantial, educated, successful men of forty. "My parents are arranging a marriage for me." In a month they will have buried one family and returned to Canada with a new bride and partial family.

I am comparatively lucky. No one here thinks of arranging a husband for an unlucky widow.

Then, on the third day of the sixth month into this odyssey, in an abandoned temple in a tiny Himalayan village, as I make my offering of flowers and sweetmeats to the god of a tribe of animists, my husband descends to me. He is squatting next to a scrawny *sadhu*[8] in moth-eaten robes. Vikram wears the vanilla suit he wore the last time I hugged him. The *sadhu* tosses petals on a butter-fed flame, reciting Sanskrit mantras[9] and sweeps his face of flies. My husband takes my hands in his.

You're beautiful, he starts. Then, *What are you doing here?*

Shall I stay? I ask. He only smiles, but already the image is fading. *You must finish alone what we started together.* No seaweed wreathes his mouth. He speaks too fast just as he used to when we were an envied family in our pink split-level. He is gone.

In the windowless altar room, smoky with *joss*[1] sticks and clarified butter

---

5. Landholder.
6. The Vedas are the oldest scriptures in Hinduism.
7. Athletic facilities.
8. A Hindu holy man (a mendicant ascetic).
9. Mystic words used in ritual and meditation.
1. Incense.

lamps, a sweaty hand gropes for my blouse. I do not shriek. The *sadhu* arranges his robe. The lamps hiss and sputter out.

When we come out of the temple, my mother says, "Did you feel something weird in there?"

My mother has no patience with ghosts, prophetic dreams, holy men, and cults.

"No," I lie. "Nothing."

But she knows that she's lost me. She knows that in days I shall be leaving.

Kusum's put her house up for sale. She wants to live in an ashram[2] in Hardwar. Moving to Hardwar was her swami's idea. Her swami runs two ashrams, the one in Hardwar and another here in Toronto.

"Don't run away," I tell her.

"I'm not running away," she says. "I'm pursuing inner peace. You think you or that Ranganathan fellow are better off?"

Pam's left for California. She wants to do some modeling, she says. She says when she comes into her share of the insurance money she'll open a yoga-cum-aerobics studio in Hollywood. She sends me postcards so naughty I daren't leave them on the coffee table. Her mother has withdrawn from her and the world.

The rest of us don't lose touch, that's the point. Talk is all we have, says Dr. Ranganathan, who has also resisted his relatives and returned to Montreal and to his job, alone. He says, whom better to talk with than other relatives? We've been melted down and recast as a new tribe.

He calls me twice a week from Montreal. Every Wednesday night and every Saturday afternoon. He is changing jobs, going to Ottawa. But Ottawa is over a hundred miles away, and he is forced to drive two hundred and twenty miles a day. He can't bring himself to sell his house. The house is a temple, he says; the king-sized bed in the master bedroom is a shrine. He sleeps on a folding cot. A devotee.

There are still some hysterical relatives. Judith Templeton's list of those needing help and those who've "accepted" is in nearly perfect balance. Acceptance means you speak of your family in the past tense and you make active plans for moving ahead with your life. There are courses at Seneca and Ryerson we could be taking. Her gleaming leather briefcase is full of college catalogs and lists of cultural societies that need our help. She has done impressive work, I tell her.

"In the textbooks on grief management," she replies—I am her confidante, I realize, one of the few whose grief has not sprung bizarre obsessions—"there are stages to pass through: rejection, depression, acceptance, reconstruction." She has compiled a chart and finds that six months after the tragedy, none of us still reject reality, but only a handful are reconstructing. "Depressed Acceptance" is the plateau we've reached. Remarriage is a major step in reconstruction (though she's a little surprised, even shocked, over *how* quickly some of the men have taken on new families). Selling one's house and changing jobs and cities is healthy.

How do I tell Judith Templeton that my family surrounds me, and that

---

2. Hindu religious retreat.

like creatures in epics, they've changed shapes? She sees me as calm and accepting but worries that I have no job, no career. My closest friends are worse off than I. I cannot tell her my days, even my nights, are thrilling.

She asks me to help with families she can't reach at all. An elderly couple in Agincourt whose sons were killed just weeks after they had brought their parents over from a village in Punjab. From their names, I know they are Sikh. Judith Templeton and a translator have visited them twice with offers of money for air fare to Ireland, with bank forms, power-of-attorney forms, but they have refused to sign, or to leave their tiny apartment. Their sons' money is frozen in the bank. Their sons' investment apartments have been trashed by tenants, the furnishings sold off. The parents fear that anything they sign or any money they receive will end the company's or the country's obligations to them. They fear they are selling their sons for two airline tickets to a place they've never seen.

The high-rise apartment is a tower of Indians and West Indians, with a sprinkling of Orientals. The nearest bus stop kiosk is lined with women in saris. Boys practice cricket in the parking lot. Inside the building, even I wince a bit from the ferocity of onion fumes, the distinctive and immediate Indianness of frying *ghee*,[3] but Judith Templeton maintains a steady flow of information. These poor old people are in imminent danger of losing their place and all their services.

I say to her, "They are Sikh. They will not open up to a Hindu woman." And what I want to add is, as much as I try not to, I stiffen now at the sight of beards and turbans. I remember a time when we all trusted each other in this new country, it was only the new country we worried about.

The two rooms are dark and stuffy. The lights are off, and an oil lamp sputters on the coffee table. The bent old lady has let us in, and her husband is wrapping a white turban over his oiled, hip-length hair. She immediately goes to the kitchen, and I hear the most familiar sound of an Indian home, tap water hitting and filling a teapot.

They have not paid their utility bills, out of fear and the inability to write a check. The telephone is gone; electricity and gas and water are soon to follow. They have told Judith their sons will provide. They are good boys, and they have always earned and looked after their parents.

We converse a bit in Hindi. They do not ask about the crash and I wonder if I should bring it up. If they think I am here merely as a translator, then they may feel insulted. There are thousands of Punjabi-speakers, Sikhs, in Toronto to do a better job. And so I say to the old lady, "I too have lost my sons, and my husband, in the crash."

Her eyes immediately fill with tears. The man mutters a few words which sound like a blessing. "God provides and God takes away," he says.

I want to say, But only men destroy and give back nothing. "My boys and my husband are not coming back," I say. "We have to understand that."

Now the old woman responds. "But who is to say? Man alone does not decide these things." To this her husband adds his agreement.

Judith asks about the bank papers, the release forms. With a stroke of the pen, they will have a provincial trustee to pay their bills, invest their money, send them a monthly pension.

---

3. Clarified butter.

"Do you know this woman?" I ask them.

The man rises his hand from the table, turns it over and seems to regard each finger separately before he answers. "This young lady is always coming here, we make tea for her and she leaves papers for us to sign." His eyes scan a pile of papers in the corner of the room. "Soon we will be out of tea, then will she go away?"

The old lady adds, "I have asked my neighbors and no one else gets *angrezi*[4] visitors. What have we done?"

"It's her job," I try to explain. "The government is worried. Soon you will have no place to stay, no lights, no gas, no water."

"Government will get its money. Tell her not to worry, we are honorable people."

I try to explain the government wishes to give money, not take. He raises his hand. "Let them take," he says. "We are accustomed to that. That is no problem."

"We are strong people," says the wife. "Tell her that."

"Who needs all this machinery?" demands the husband. "It is unhealthy, the bright lights, the cold air on a hot day, the cold food, the four gas rings. God will provide, not government."

"When our boys return," the mother says. Her husband sucks his teeth. "Enough talk," he says.

Judith breaks in. "Have you convinced them?" The snaps on her cordovan briefcase go off like firecrackers in that quiet apartment. She lays the sheaf of legal papers on the coffee table. "If they can't write their names, an X will do—I've told them that."

Now the old lady has shuffled to the kitchen and soon emerges with a pot of tea and two cups. "I think my bladder will go first on a job like this," Judith says to me, smiling. "If only there was some way of reaching them. Please thank her for the tea. Tell her she's very kind."

I nod in Judith's direction and tell them in Hindi, "She thanks you for the tea. She thinks you are being very hospitable but she doesn't have the slightest idea what it means."

I want to say, Humor her. I want to say, My boys and my husband are with me too, more than ever. I look in the old man's eyes and I can read his stubborn, peasant's message: *I have protected this woman as best I can. She is the only person I have left. Give to me or take from me what you will, but I will not sign for it. I will not pretend that I accept.*

In the car, Judith says, "You see what I'm up against? I'm sure they're lovely people, but their stubbornness and ignorance are driving me crazy. They think signing a paper is signing their sons' death warrants, don't they?"

I am looking out the window. I want to say, *In our culture, it is a parent's duty to hope.*

"Now Shaila, this next woman is a real mess. She cries day and night, and she refuses all medical help. We may have to—"

"—Let me out at the subway," I say.

"I beg your pardon?" I can feel those blue eyes staring at me.

It would not be like her to disobey. She merely disapproves, and slows at a corner to let me out. Her voice is plaintive. "Is there anything I said? Anything I did?"

---

4. An English speaker, a Westerner.

I could answer her suddenly in a dozen ways, but I choose not to. "Shaila? Let's talk about it," I hear, then slam the door.

A wife and mother begins her new life in a new country, and that life is cut short. Yet her husband tells her: Complete what we have started. We who stayed out of politics and came halfway around the world to avoid religious and political feuding have been the first in the New World to die from it. I no longer know what we started, nor how to complete it. I write letters to the editors of local papers and to members of Parliament. Now at least they admit it was a bomb. One MP answers back, with sympathy, but with a challenge. You want to make a difference? Work on a campaign. Work on mine. Politicize the Indian voter.

My husband's old lawyer helps me set up a trust. Vikram was a saver and a careful investor. He had saved the boys' boarding school and college fees. I sell the pink house at four times what we paid for it and take a small apartment downtown. I am looking for a charity to support.

We are deep in the Toronto winter, gray skies, icy pavements. I stay indoors, watching television. I have tried to assess my situation, how best to live my life, to complete what we began so many years ago. Kusum has written me from Hardwar that her life is now serene. She has seen Satish and has heard her daughter sing again. Kusum was on a pilgrimage, passing through a village when she heard a young girl's voice, singing one of her daughter's favorite *bhajans*. She followed the music through the squalor of a Himalayan village, to a hut where a young girl, an exact replica of her daughter, was fanning coals under the kitchen fire. When she appeared, the girl cried out, "Ma!" and ran away. What did I think of that?

I think I can only envy her.

Pam didn't make it to California, but writes me from Vancouver. She works in a department store, giving make-up hints to Indian and Oriental girls. Dr. Ranganathan has given up his commute, given up his house and job, and accepted an academic position in Texas where no one knows his story and he has vowed not to tell it. He calls me now once a week.

I wait, I listen, and I pray, but Vikram has not returned to me. The voices and the shapes and the nights filled with visions ended abruptly several weeks ago.

I take it as a sign.

One rare, beautiful, sunny day last week, returning from a small errand on Yonge Street, I was walking through the park from the subway to my apartment. I live equidistant from the Ontario Houses of Parliament and the University of Toronto. The day was not cold, but something in the bare trees caught my attention. I looked up from the gravel, into the branches and the clear blue sky beyond. I thought I heard the rustling of larger forms, and I waited a moment for voices. Nothing.

"What?" I asked.

Then as I stood in the path looking north to Queen's Park and west to the university, I heard the voices of my family one last time. *Your time has come,* they said. *Go, be brave.*

I do not know where this voyage I have begun will end. I do not know which direction I will take. I dropped the package on a park bench and started walking.

1988

LYN HEJINIAN
b. 1941

In "The Rejection of Closure," an essay about her poetics, Lyn Hejinian describes her commitment to a text "open to the world and particularly to the reader. It invites participation, rejects the authority of the writer over the reader and thus, by analogy, the authority implicit in other (social, economic, cultural) hierarchies." One of the so-called L=A=N=G=U=A=G=E poets, Hejinian writes against the grain of the traditional lyric so as to produce verse that seeks to present itself as a language reality, rather than as a reflection of social or economic or psychological realms outside the poem. Though often associated with deconstruction and poststructuralism, this group of writers also obviously shares a number of the experimental goals and methods of Gertrude Stein, whose portraits employ repetition, nonsense, free association, and a self-reflexive fascination with the gap between the signifying word and what it signifies. Additionally, Hejinian brings to poetry a passion for form and structure. *My Life*, an autobiographical book of prose poems, was originally published in 1980, when the thirty-seven-year-old author produced thirty-seven sections composed of thirty-seven sentences each. When she republished the book eight years later in 1986, Hejinian added eight new sections at the end as well as eight new sentences into all forty-five sections of the book. According to Hejinian, poetry assumes "that language (all language) is a medium for experiencing experience. It provides us with the consciousness of consciousness."

Born in the San Francisco Bay area, Lyn Hejinian was educated at Harvard University and currently teaches at the University of California, Berkeley. From 1976 until 1984, she was the editor of Tuumba Press and from 1981 to 1999 she was co-editor of *Poetics Journal*. She is also the co-director of Atelos, a literary project commissioning and publishing cross-genre work by poets. In 2000, she was elected the sixty-sixth fellow of the Academy of American Poets. Besides *My Life,* she has published numerous volumes of poetry, including *The Cell* (1992), *The Cold of Poetry* (1994), *Happily* (2000), and *The Beginner* (2000), and her essays have been collected in *The Language of Inquiry* (2000). A translator of the contemporary Russian poet Arkadii Dragomoshchenko, Hejinian has collaborated with painters, musicians, and filmmakers on a number of mixed media projects that reflect her investment in aesthetic experimentation.

From My Life

A pause, a rose,
something on paper

A moment yellow, just as four years later, when my father returned home from the war, the moment of greeting him, as he stood at the bottom of the stairs, younger, thinner than when he had left, was purple—though moments are no longer so colored. Somewhere, in the background, rooms share a pattern of small roses. Pretty is as pretty does. In certain families, the meaning of necessity is at one with the sentiment of prenecessity. The better things were gathered in a pen. The windows were narrowed by white gauze curtains which were never loosened. Here I refer to irrelevance, that rigidity which never intrudes. Hence, repetitions, free from all ambition. The shadow of the redwood trees, she said, was oppressive. The plush must be worn away. On her walks she stepped into people's gardens to pinch off cuttings from their geraniums and succulents. An occasional sunset is reflected on the windows. A little puddle is overcast. If only you could touch, or, even, catch those gray great creatures. I was afraid of my uncle with the wart on his nose, or of his jokes at our expense which were beyond me, and I was shy of my aunt's deafness who was his sister-in-law and who had years earlier fallen into the habit of nodding, agreeably. Wool station. See lightning, wait for thunder. Quite mistakenly, as it happened. Long time lines trail behind every idea, object, person, pet, vehicle, and event. The afternoon happens, crowded and therefore endless. Thicker, she agreed. It was a tic, she had the habit, and now she bobbed like my toy plastic bird on the edge of its glass, dipping into and recoiling from the water. But a word is a bottomless pit. It became magically pregnant and one day split open, giving birth to a stone egg, about as big as a football. In May when the lizards emerge from the stones, the stones turn gray, from green. When daylight moves, we delight in distance. The waves rolled over our stomachs, like spring rain over an orchard slope. Rubber bumpers on rubber cars. The resistance on sleeping to being asleep. In every country is a word which attempts the sound of cats, to match an inisolable portrait in the clouds to a din in the air. But the constant noise is not an omen of music to come. "Everything is a question of sleep," says Cocteau,[1] but he forgets the shark, which does not. Anxiety is vigilant. Perhaps initially, even before one can talk, restlessness is already conventional, establishing the incoherent border which will later separate events from experience. Find a drawer that's not filled up. That we sleep plunges our work into the dark. The ball was lost in a bank of myrtle. I was in a room with the particulars of which a later nostalgia might be formed, an indulged childhood. They are sitting in wicker chairs, the legs of which have sunk unevenly into the ground, so that each is sitting slightly tilted and their postures make adjustment for that. The cows warm their own barn. I look at them fast and it gives the illusion that they're moving. An "oral history" on paper. *That* morning this morning. I say it about the psyche because it is not optional. The overtones are a denser shadow in the room characterized by its habitual readiness, a form of charged waiting, a perpetual attendance, of which I was thinking when I began the paragraph, "So much of childhood is spent in a manner of waiting."

As for we who "love to be astonished"

You spill the sugar when you lift the spoon. My father had filled an old apothecary jar with what he called "sea glass," bits of old bottles rounded and textured by the sea, so abundant on beaches. There is no solitude. It buries itself in veracity. It is as if one splashed in the water lost by one's tears. My mother had climbed into the garbage can in order to stamp down the accumulated trash, but the can was knocked off balance, and when she fell she broke her arm. She could only give a little shrug. The family had little money but plenty of food. At the circus only the elephants were greater than anything I could have imagined. The egg of Columbus,[2] landscape and gram-

---

1. Jean Cocteau (1889–1963), French writer, filmmaker, and visual artist; his films are characterized by surrealist fantasy.

2. A nine-piece puzzle, first marketed in the 1890s; the object is to make various shapes using all the pieces, which initially form an egg.

mar. She wanted one where the playground was dirt, with grass, shaded by a tree, from which would hang a rubber tire as a swing, and when she found it she sent me. These creatures are compound and nothing they do should surprise us. I don't mind, or I won't mind, where the verb "to care" might multiply. The pilot of the little airplane had forgotten to notify the airport of his approach, so that when the lights of the plane in the night were first spotted, the air raid sirens went off, and the entire city on that coast went dark. He was taking a drink of water and the light was growing dim. My mother stood at the window watching the only lights that were visible, circling over the darkened city in search of the hidden airport. Unhappily, time seems more normative than place. Whether breathing or holding the breath, it was the same thing, driving through the tunnel from one sun to the next under a hot brown hill. She sunned the baby for sixty seconds, leaving him naked except for a blue cotton sunbonnet. At night, to close off the windows from view of the street, my grandmother pulled down the window shades, never loosening the curtains, a gauze starched too stiff to hang properly down. I sat on the windowsill singing sunny lunny teena, ding-dang-dong. Out there is an aging magician who needs a tray of ice in order to turn his bristling breath into steam. He broke the radio silence. Why would anyone find astrology interesting when it is possible to learn about astronomy. What one passes in the Plymouth. It is the wind slamming the doors. All that is nearly incommunicable to my friends. Velocity and throat verisimilitude. Were we seeing a pattern or merely an appearance of small white sailboats on the bay, floating at such a distance from the hill that they appeared to be making no progress. And for once to a country that did not speak another language. To follow the progress of ideas, or that particular line of reasoning, so full of surprises and unexpected correlations, was somehow to take a vacation. Still, you had to wonder where they had gone, since you could speak of reappearance. A blue room is always dark. Everything on the boardwalk was shooting toward the sky. It was not specific to any year, but very early. A German goldsmith covered a bit of metal with cloth in the 14th century and gave mankind its first button. It was hard to know this as politics, because it plays like the work of one person, but nothing is isolated in history—certain humans are situations. Are your fingers in the margin. Their random procedures make monuments to fate. There is something still surprising when the green emerges. The blue fox has ducked its head. The front rhyme of harmless with harmony. Where is my honey running. You cannot linger "on the lamb." You cannot determine the nature of progress until you assemble all of the relatives.

It seemed that we had hardly begun and we were already there

We see only the leaves and branches of the trees close in around the house. Those submissive games were sensual. I was no more than three or four years old, but when crossed I would hold my breath, not from rage but from stubbornness, until I lost consciousness. The shadows one day deeper. Every family has its own collection of stories, but not every family has someone to tell them. In a small studio in an old farmhouse, it is the musical expression of a glowing optimism. A bird would reach but be secret. Absence of allusion: once, and ring alone. The downstairs telephone was in a little room as dark as a closet. It made a difference between the immediate and the sudden in a theater filled with transitions. Without what can a person function as the sea functions without me. A typical set of errands. My mother stood between us and held our hands as we waded into the gray-blue water, lecturing us on the undertow, more to add to the thrill of the approaching water than to warn us of any real danger, since she would continue to grip us by the hand when the wave came in and we tried to jump over it. The curve of the rain, more, comes over more often. Four seasons circle a square year. A mirror set in the crotch of the tree was like a hole in the out-of-doors. I could have ridden in the car forever, or so it seemed, watching the scenery go by, alert as to the circumstances of a dream, and that peaceful. Roller coast. The fog lifts a late sunrise. There are floral twigs in position on it. The roots of the locust tree were lifting the corner of the little cabin. Our unease grows before the newly restless. There you are, and you know it's good, and all you have to do is make it better. He sailed to the war. A life no more free than the life of a lost puppy. It became popular and then we were inundated with imitations. My old aunt entertained us with her lie, a story about an event in her girlhood, a catastrophe in a sailboat that never occurred, but she was blameless, unaccountable, since, in the course of the telling, she had come to believe the lie herself. A kind of burbling in the waters of inspiration. Because of their recurrence, what had originally seemed merely details of atmosphere became, in time, thematic. As if sky plus sun *must* make leaves.[3] A snapdragon volunteering in the garden among the cineraria gapes its maw between the fingers, and we pinched the buds of the fuchsia to make them pop. Is that willful. Inclines. They have big calves because of the those hills. Flip over small stones, dried mud. We thought that the mica might be gold. A pause, a rose, something on paper, in a nature scrapbook. What follows a strict chronology has no memory. For me, they must exist, the contents of that absent reality, the objects and occasions which now I reconsidered. The smells of the house were thus a peculiar mix of heavy interior air and the air from outdoors lingering over the rose bushes, the camellias, the hydrangeas, the rhododendron and azalea bushes. Hard to distinguish hunger from wanting to eat. My grandmother was in the kitchen, her hands on her hips, wearing what she called a "washdress," watching a line of ants cross behind the faucets of the sink, and she said to us, "Now *I* am waging war." There are strings in the terrible distance. They are against the blue. The trees are continually receiving their own shadows.

1980, 1986

---

3. An ornamental plant with showy flowerheads and attractive silvery foliage.

GLORIA ANZALDÚA
1942–2004

"I think Chicano families can be really hard on women and maybe they are hard on men, too. Very early on you start being taught how to be a man and being taught how to be a little woman and the divisions are pretty rigid": with characteristic candor, Gloria Anzaldúa described her refusal to conform to dictates that would force girls to drop out of school so they could devote their time to cooking or sewing or cleaning and that in particular would limit her fierce love of reading. The daughter of Urbano and Amalia Garcia, Gloria Evangelina Anzaldúa was born on a ranch settlement called Jésus Maria of the Valley in south Texas, but at eleven she moved with her family to Hargill, Texas. After the death of her father when she was fifteen, she worked with her family as an agricultural laborer until she became the first woman from her region to go to college, earning her B.A. from Pan American University in 1969 and then her M.A. in English and education from the University of Texas, Austin. While subsequently lecturing at San Francisco State University, the University of California, Santa Cruz, and Vermont College, Anzaldúa devoted her attention to Chicana women and culture at least in part because of her keen awareness of the fragility of the advances third world women of color have made.

To some extent, Anzaldúa's goals met early resistance. In her undergraduate and graduate classes, she found it difficult to pursue Chicano and feminist studies since programs in those areas did not yet exist. Her collaborative work on the multicultural anthology *This Bridge Called My Back* (1981) brought a measure of recognition, but also the censure of her mother and sister, who objected to her disclosures about the family and in particular to her essay "La Prieta" ("The Dark One"), a piece describing her vision of a coalition between third world women, feminists, and lesbians. While teaching in Vermont and experiencing herself as a foreigner, Anzaldúa conceived her plan for *Borderlands* (1987), an ambitious book prefaced by her description of herself as "a border woman" who "grew up between two cultures, the Mexican (with a heavy Indian influence) and the Anglo (as a member of a colonized people in our own territory)." Combining historical scholarship with poetry, linguistics with mythology, the text is as focused on what Anzaldúa considered "psychological borderlands[,] . . . sexual borderlands, and spiritual borderlands" as it is on geographical lines of demarcation. "Borderlands are physically present wherever two or more cultures edge each other," Anzaldúa once commented, as well as "where people of different races occupy the same territory, where under, lower, middle and upper classes touch, where the space between two individuals shrinks with intimacy."

Anzaldúa followed her work on borderlands with a well-received anthology, *Making Face, Making Soul/Haciendo Caras: Creative and Critical Perspectives by Feminists of Color* (1989), which continued to demonstrate her fascination with crossing aesthetic and physical states of mind and matter. In addition, she authored three children's books, including *Friends from the Other Side—Amigos del Otro Lado* (1995) and *Prietita La Llorona* (1996). Sadly, she died from complications of diabetes when she was in her early sixties and only weeks away from earning a doctorate from the University of California, Santa Cruz.

Tlilli, Tlapalli[1] / The Path of the Red and Black Ink

> Out of poverty, poetry;
> out of suffering, song.
> —a Mexican saying

When I was seven, eight, nine, fifteen, sixteen years old, I would read in bed with a flashlight under the covers, hiding my self-imposed insomnia from my mother. I preferred the world of the imagination to the death of sleep. My sister, Hilda, who slept in the same bed with me, would threaten to tell my mother unless I told her a story.

I was familiar with *cuentos*—my grandmother told stories like the one about her getting on top of the roof while down below rabid coyotes were ravaging the place and wanting to get at her. My father told stories about a phantom giant dog that appeared out of nowhere and sped along the side of the pickup no matter how fast he was driving.

Nudge a Mexican and she or he will break out with a story. So, huddling under the covers, I made up stories for my sister night after night. After a while she wanted two stories per night. I learned to give her installments, building up the suspense with convoluted complications until the story climaxed several nights later. It must have been then that I decided to put stories on paper. It must have been then that working with images and writing became connected to night.

Invoking Art

In the ethno-poetics and performance of the shaman, my people, the Indians, did not split the artistic from the functional, the sacred from the secular, art from everyday life. The religious, social and aesthetic purposes of art were all intertwined. Before the Conquest, poets gathered to play music, dance, sing and read poetry in open-air places around the *Xochicuahuitl, el Árbol Florido,* Tree-in-Flower. (The *Coaxihuitl* or morning glory is called the snake plant and its seeds, known as *ololiuhqui,* are hallucinogenic.[2]) The ability of story (prose and poetry) to transform the storyteller and the listener into something or someone else is shamanistic. The writer, as shape-changer, is a *nahual,* a shaman.

In looking at this book that I'm almost finished writing, I see a mosaic pattern (Aztec-like) emerging, a weaving pattern, thin here, thick there. I see a preoccupation with the deep structure, the underlying structure, with the gesso[3] underpainting that is red earth, black earth. I can see the deep structure, the scaffolding. If I can get the bone structure right, then putting flesh on it proceeds without too many hitches. The problem is that the bones often do not exist prior to the flesh, but are shaped after a vague and broad shadow of its

---

1. At Anzaldúa's request Nahuatl and Spanish words are not translated in the notes.
2. R. Gordon Wasson, *The Wondrous Mushroom: Mycolatry in Mesoamerica* (New York, NY: McGraw-Hill Book Company, 1980), 59, 103 [Anzaldúa's note].
3. A plaster of Paris preparation used as a base for low relief or as a surface for painting.

form is discerned or uncovered during beginning, middle and final stages of the writing. Numerous overlays of paint, rough surfaces, smooth surfaces make me realize I am preoccupied with texture as well. Too, I see the barely contained color threatening to spill over the boundaries of the object it represents and into other "objects" and over the borders of the frame. I see a hybridization of metaphor, different species of ideas popping up here, popping up there, full of variations and seeming contradictions, though I believe in an ordered, structured universe where all phenomena are interrelated and imbued with spirit. This almost finished product seems an assemblage, a montage, a beaded work with several leitmotifs and with a central core, now appearing, now disappearing in a crazy dance. The whole thing has had a mind of its own, escaping me and insisting on putting together the pieces of its own puzzle with minimal direction from my will. It is a rebellious, willful entity, a precocious girl-child forced to grow up too quickly, rough, unyielding, with pieces of feather sticking out here and there, fur, twigs, clay. My child, but not for much longer. This female being is angry, sad, joyful, is *Coatlicue*, dove, horse, serpent, cactus. Though it is a flawed thing—a clumsy, complex, groping blind thing—for me it is alive, infused with spirit. I talk to it; it talks to me.

I make my offerings of incense and cracked corn, light my candle. In my head I sometimes will say a prayer—an affirmation and a voicing of intent. Then I run water, wash the dishes or my underthings, take a bath, or mop the kitchen floor. This "induction" period sometimes takes a few minutes, sometimes hours. But always I go against a resistance. Something in me does not want to do this writing. Yet once I'm immersed in it, I can go fifteen to seventeen hours in one sitting and I don't want to leave it.

My "stories" are acts encapsulated in time, "enacted" every time they are spoken aloud or read silently. I like to think of them as performances and not as inert and "dead" objects (as the aesthetics of Western culture think of art works). Instead, the work has an identity; it is a "who" or a "what" and contains the presences of persons, that is, incarnations of gods or ancestors or natural and cosmic powers. The work manifests the same needs as a person, it needs to be "fed," *la tengo que bañar y vestir.*

When invoked in rite, the object/event is "present;" that is, "enacted," it is both a physical thing and the power that infuses it. It is metaphysical in that it "spins its energies between gods and humans" and its task is to move the gods. This type of work dedicates itself to managing the universe and its energies. I'm not sure what it is when it is at rest (not in performance). It may or may not be a "work" then. A mask may only have the power of presence during a ritual dance and the rest of the time it may merely be a "thing." Some works exist forever invoked, always in performance. I'm thinking of totem poles, cave paintings. Invoked art is communal and speaks of everyday life. It is dedicated to the validation of humans; that is, it makes people hopeful, happy, secure, and it can have negative effects as well, which propel one towards a search for validation.[4]

---

4. Robert Plant Armstrong, *The Powers of Presence: Consciousness, Myth, and Affecting Presence* (Philadelphia, PA: University of Pennsylvania Press, 1981), 11, 20 [Anzaldúa's note].

The aesthetic of virtuosity, art typical of Western European cultures, attempts to manage the energies of its own internal system such as conflicts, harmonies, resolutions and balances. It bears the presences of qualities and internal meanings. It is dedicated to the validation of itself. Its task is to move humans by means of achieving mastery in content, technique, feeling. Western art is always whole and always "in power." It is individual (not communal). It is "psychological" in that it spins its energies between itself and its witness.[5]

Western cultures behave differently toward works of art than do tribal cultures. The "sacrifices" Western cultures make are in housing their art works in the best structures designed by the best architects; and in servicing them with insurance, guards to protect them, conservators to maintain them, specialists to mount and display them, and the educated and upper classes to "view" them. Tribal cultures keep art works in honored and sacred places in the home and elsewhere. They attend them by making sacrifices of blood (goat or chicken), libations of wine. They bathe, feed, and clothe them. The works are treated not just as objects, but also as persons. The "witness" is a participant in the enactment of the work in a ritual, and not a member of the privileged classes.[6]

Ethnocentrism is the tyranny of Western aesthetics. An Indian mask in an American museum is transposed into an alien aesthetic system where what is missing is the presence of power invoked through performance ritual. It has become a conquered thing, a dead "thing" separated from nature and, therefore, its power.

Modern Western painters have "borrowed," copied, or otherwise extrapolated the art of tribal cultures and called it cubism, surrealism, symbolism. The music, the beat of the drum, the Blacks' jive talk. All taken over. Whites, along with a good number of our own people, have cut themselves off from their spiritual roots, and they take our spiritual art objects in an unconscious attempt to get them back. If they're going to do it, I'd like them to be aware of what they are doing and to go about doing it the right way. Let's all stop importing Greek myths and the Western Cartesian split point of view[7] and root ourselves in the mythological soil and soul of this continent. White America has only attended to the body of the earth in order to exploit it, never to succor it or to be nurtured in it. Instead of surreptitiously ripping off the vital energy of people of color and putting it to commercial use, whites could allow themselves to share and exchange and learn from us in a respectful way. By taking up *curanderismo*, Santeria, shamanism, Taoism, Zen[8] and otherwise delving into the spiritual life and ceremonies of multi-colored people, Anglos would perhaps lose the white sterility they have in their kitchens, bathrooms, hospitals, mortuaries and missile bases. Though in the conscious mind, black and dark may be associated with death, evil and destruction, in the subconscious mind and in our dreams, white is associated with disease, death and hopelessness. Let us hope that the left hand, that of darkness, of

---

5. Armstrong, 10 [Anzaldúa's note].
6. Armstrong, 4 [Anzaldúa's note].
7 I.e., the strict division between mind and body espoused by the French philosopher René Descartes (1596–1650).
8 A school of Buddhism that originated in Japan and China and asserts that enlightenment is achieved through meditation, self-contemplation, and intuition. *"Santeria"*: religion (practiced originally in Cuba) that identifies Yoruba deities with Roman Catholic saints.

femaleness, of "primitiveness," can divert the indifferent, right-handed, "rational" suicidal drive that, unchecked, could blow us into acid rain in a fraction of a millisecond.

Ni cuicani: *I, the Singer*

For the ancient Aztecs, *tlilli, tlapalli, la tinta negra y roja de sus códices* (the black and red ink painted on codices) were the colors symbolizing *escritura y sabiduría* (writing and wisdom).[9] They believed that through metaphor and symbol, by means of poetry and truth, communication with the Divine could be attained, and *topan* (that which is above—the gods and spirit world) could be bridged with *mictlán* (that which is below—the underworld and the region of the dead).

> Poet: she pours water from the mouth of the pump, lowers the handle then lifts it, lowers, lifts. Her hands begin to feel the pull from the entrails, the live animal resisting. A sigh rises up from the depths, the handle becomes a wild thing in her hands, the cold sweet water gushes out, splashing her face, the shock of nightlight filling the bucket.

An image is a bridge between evoked emotion and conscious knowledge; words are the cables that hold up the bridge. Images are more direct, more immediate than words, and closer to the unconscious. Picture language precedes thinking in words; the metaphorical mind precedes analytical consciousness.

The Shamanic State

When I create stories in my head, that is, allow the voices and scenes to be projected in the inner screen of my mind, I "trance." I used to think I was going crazy or that I was having hallucinations. But now I realize it is my job, my calling, to traffic in images. Some of these film-like narratives I write down; most are lost, forgotten. When I don't write the images down for several days or weeks or months, I get physically ill. Because writing invokes images from my unconscious, and because some of the images are residues of trauma which I then have to reconstruct, I sometimes get sick when I *do* write. I can't stomach it, become nauseous, or burn with fever, worsen. But, in reconstructing the traumas behind the images, I make "sense" of them, and once they have "meaning" they are changed, transformed. It is then that writing heals me, brings me great joy.

To facilitate the "movies" with soundtracks, I need to be alone, or in a sensory-deprived state. I plug up my ears with wax, put on my black cloth eye-shades, lie horizontal and unmoving, in a state between sleeping and waking, mind and body locked into my fantasy. I am held prisoner by it. My body is experiencing events. In the beginning it is like being in a movie theater, as pure spectator. Gradually I become so engrossed with the activities, the conversations, that I become a participant in the drama. I have to struggle to "disengage" or escape from my "animated story," I have to get

---

9. Miguel Leon-Portilla, *Los Antiguos Mexicanos: A través de sus crónicas y cantares* (México, D.F.: Fondo de Cultura Económica, 1961), 19, 22 [Anzaldúa's note].

some sleep so I can write tomorrow. Yet I am gripped by a story which won't let me go. Outside the frame, I am film director, screenwriter, camera operator. Inside the frame, I am the actors—male and female—I am desert sand, mountain, I am dog, mosquito. I can sustain a four- to six-hour "movie." Once I am up, I can sustain several "shorts" of anywhere between five and thirty minutes. Usually these "narratives" are the offspring of stories acted out in my head during periods of sensory deprivation.

My "awakened dreams" are about shifts. Thought shifts, reality shifts, gender shifts: one person metamorphoses into another in a world where people fly through the air, heal from mortal wounds. I am playing with my Self, I am playing with the world's soul, I am the dialogue between my Self and *el espíritu del mundo*. I change myself, I change the world.

Sometimes I put the imagination to a more rare use. I choose words, images, and body sensations and animate them to impress them on my consciousness, thereby making changes in my belief system and reprogramming my consciousness. This involves looking my inner demons in the face, then deciding which I want in my psyche. Those I don't want, I starve; I feed them no words, no images, no feelings. I spend no time with them, share not my home with them. Neglected, they leave. This is harder to do than to merely generate "stories." I can only sustain this activity for a few minutes.

I write the myths in me, the myths I am, the myths I want to become. The word, the image and the feeling have a palatable energy, a kind of power. *Con imagenes domo mi miedo, cruzo los abismos que tengo por dentro. Con palabras me hago piedra, pájaro, puente de serpientes arrastrando a ras del suelo todo lo que soy, todo lo que algún día seré.*

> *Los que están mirando (leyendo),*
> *los que cuentan (o refieren lo que leen).*
> *Los que vuelven ruidosamente las hojas de los códices.*
> *Los que tienen en su poder*
> *la tinta negra y roja (la sabiduría)*
> *y lo pintado,*
> *ellos nos llevan, nos guían,*
> *nos dicen el camino.*[1]

Writing Is a Sensuous Act

Tallo mi cuerpo como si estuviera lavando un trapo. Toco las saltadas venas de mis manos, mis chichis adormecidas como pájaras a la anochecer. Estoy encorbada sobre la cama. Las imagenes aleteán alrededor de mi cama como murciélagos, la sábana como que tuviese alas. El ruido de los trenes subterráneos en mi sentido como conchas. Parece que las paredes del cuarto se me arriman cada vez más cerquita.

Picking out images from my soul's eye, fishing for the right words to recreate the images. Words are blades of grass pushing past the obstacles, sprouting on the page; the spirit of the words moving in the body is as concrete as flesh and as palpable; the hunger to create is as substantial as fingers and hand.

---

1. Leon-Portilla, 125 [Anzaldúa's note].

I look at my fingers, see plumes growing there. From the fingers, my feathers, black and red ink drips across the page. *Escribo con la tinta de mi sangre.* I write in red. Ink. Intimately knowing the smooth touch of paper, its speechlessness before I spill myself on the insides of trees. Daily, I battle the silence and the red. Daily, I take my throat in my hands and squeeze until the cries pour out, my larynx and soul sore from the constant struggle.

Something To Do With the Dark

Quien canta, sus males espanta.
—un dicho

The toad comes out of its hiding place inside the lobes of my brain. It's going to happen again. The ghost of the toad that betrayed me—I hold it in my hand. The toad is sipping the strength from my veins, it is sucking my pale heart. I am a dried serpent skin, wind scuttling me across the hard ground, pieces of me scattered over the countryside. And there in the dark I meet the crippled spider crawling in the gutter, the day-old newspaper fluttering in the dirty rain water.

Musa bruja, venga. Cubrese con una sábana y espante mis demonios que a rempujones y a cachetadas me roban la pluma me rompen el sueño. Musa, ¡misericordia!

Óigame, musa bruja. ¿Porqué huye uste' en mi cara? Su grito me desarrolla de mi caracola, me sacude el alma. Vieja, quítese de aquí con sus alas de navaja. Ya no me despedaze mi cara. Vaya con sus pinche uñas que me desgarran de los ojos hasta los talones. Váyese a la tiznada. Que no me coman, le digo. Que no me coman sus nueve dedos caníbales.

Hija negra de la noche, carnala, ¿Porqué me sacas las tripas, porqué cardas mis entrañas? Este hilvanando palabras con tripas me está matando. Jija de la noche ¡vete a la chingada!

Writing produces anxiety. Looking inside myself and my experience, looking at my conflicts, engenders anxiety in me. Being a writer feels very much like being a Chicana, or being queer—a lot of squirming, coming up against all sorts of walls. Or its opposite: nothing defined or definite, a boundless, floating state of limbo where I kick my heels, brood, percolate, hibernate and wait for something to happen.

Living in a state of psychic unrest, in a Borderland, is what makes poets write and artists create. It is like a cactus needle embedded in the flesh. It worries itself deeper and deeper, and I keep aggravating it by poking at it. When it begins to fester I have to do something to put an end to the aggravation and to figure out why I have it. I get deep down into the place where it's rooted in my skin and pluck away at it, playing it like a musical instrument—the fingers pressing, making the pain worse before it can get better. Then out it comes. No more discomfort, no more ambivalence. Until another needle pierces the skin. That's what writing is for me, an endless cycle of making it worse, making it better, but always making meaning out of the experience, whatever it may be.

> My flowers shall not cease to live;
> my songs shall never end:
> I, a singer, intone them;
> they become scattered, they are spread about.
> —*Cantares mexicanos*

To write, to be a writer, I have to trust and believe in myself as a speaker, as a voice for the images. I have to believe that I can communicate with images and words and that I can do it well. A lack of belief in my creative self is a lack of belief in my total self and vice versa—I cannot separate my writing from any part of my life. It is all one.

When I write it feels like I'm carving bone. It feels like I'm creating my own face, my own heart—a Nahuatl concept. My soul makes itself through the creative act. It is constantly remaking and giving birth to itself through my body. It is this learning to live with *la Coatlicue* that transforms living in the Borderlands from a nightmare into a numinous experience. It is always a path/state to something else.

In Xóchilt *in* Cuícatl[2]

She writes while other people sleep. Something is trying to come out. She fights the words, pushes them down, down, a woman with morning sickness in the middle of the night. How much easier it would be to carry a baby for nine months and then expel it permanently. These continuous multiple pregnancies are going to kill her. She is the battlefield for the pitched fight between the inner image and the words trying to recreate it. *La musa bruja* has no manners. Doesn't she know, nights are for sleeping?

She is getting too close to the mouth of the abyss. She is teetering on the edge, trying to balance while she makes up her mind whether to jump in or to find a safer way down. That's why she makes herself sick—to postpone having to jump blindfolded into the abyss of her own being and there in the depths confront her face, the face underneath the mask.

To be a mouth—the cost is too high—her whole life enslaved to that devouring mouth. *Todo pasaba por esa boca, el viento, el fuego, los mares y la Tierra.* Her body, a crossroads, a fragile bridge, cannot support the tons of cargo passing through it. She wants to install 'stop' and 'go' signal lights, instigate a curfew, police Poetry. But something wants to come out.

Blocks (*Coatlicue* states) are related to my cultural identity. The painful periods of confusion that I suffer from are symptomatic of a larger creative process: cultural shifts. The stress of living with cultural ambiguity both compels me to write and blocks me. It isn't until I'm almost at the end of the blocked state that I remember and recognize it for what it is. As soon as

---

2. In *Xóchitl* in *Cuícatl* is Nahuatl for flower and song, *flor y canto* [Anzaldúa's note].

this happens, the piercing light of awareness melts the block and I accept the deep and the darkness and I hear one of my voices saying, "I am tired of fighting. I surrender. I give up, let go, let the walls fall. On this night of the hearing of faults, Tlazolteotl,[3] *diosa de la cara negra*, let fall the cockroaches that live in my hair, the rats that nestle in my skull. Gouge out my lame eyes, rout my demon from its nocturnal cave. Set torch to the tiger that stalks me. Loosen the dead faces gnawing my cheekbones. I am tired of resisting. I surrender. I give up, let go, let the walls fall."

And in descending to the depths I realize that down is up, and I rise up from and into the deep. And once again I recognize that the internal tension of oppositions can propel (if it doesn't tear apart) the mestiza[4] writer out of the *metate* where she is being ground with corn and water, eject her out as *nahual*, an agent of transformation, able to modify and shape primordial energy and therefore able to change herself and others into turkey, coyote, tree, or human.

I sit here before my computer, *Amiguita*,[5] my altar on top of the monitor with the *Virgen de Coatlalopeuh* candle and copal[6] incense burning. My companion, a wooden serpent staff with feathers, is to my right while I ponder the ways metaphor and symbol concretize the spirit and etherealize the body. The Writing is my whole life, it is my obsession. This vampire which is my talent does not suffer other suitors.[7] Daily I court it, offer my neck to its teeth. This is the sacrifice that the act of creation requires, a blood sacrifice. For only through the body, through the pulling of flesh, can the human soul be transformed. And for images, words, stories to have this transformative power, they must arise from the human body—flesh and bone—and from the Earth's body—stone, sky, liquid, soil. This work, these images, piercing tongue or ear lobes with cactus needle, are my offerings, are my Aztecan blood sacrifices.

1987

---

3. A Nahuatl goddess.
4. A woman of mixed European and Native American ancestry. This term has special significance for Anzaldúa, who explains earlier in *Borderlands / La Frontera* that "our Spanish, Indian, and *mestizo* ancestors explored and settled parts of the U.S. Southwest as early as the sixteenth century. For every gold-hungry *conquistador* and soul-hungry missionary who came from North Mexico, ten to twenty Indians and *mestizos* went along as porters or in other capacities. For the Indians, this constituted a return to the place of origin, Aztlán, thus making Chicanos originally or secondarily indigenous to the Southwest. Indians and *mestizos* from central Mexico intermarried with North American Indians. The continual intermarriage between Mexicans and American Indians formed an even greater *mestizaje*."
5. Play on words referring to the computer brand known as Amiga—literally, in Spanish, "friend."
6. A resin from a tropical tree.
7. Nietzsche, in *The Will to Power*, says that the artist lives under a curse of being vampirized by his talent [Anzaldúa's note].

AMA ATA AIDOO
b. 1942

"Things are working out towards their dazzling conclusions," begins Christina Ama Ata Aidoo's characteristically wry yet hopeful epigraph for *Our Sister Killjoy, or Reflections from a Black-Eyed Squint* (1966), her first novel. Born near Dominase, in the center of Ghana, Aidoo has been one of Africa's most productive and talented writers: she is the author of two plays (*Dilemma of a Ghost*, 1964, and *Anowa*, 1970) as well as a collection of poems, *An Angry Letter in January and Other Poems* (1992); a second novel, *Changes: A Love Story* (1991); and three collections of short stories: *No Sweetness Here* (1970), *The Eagle and the Chickens* (1989), and most recently *The Girl Who Can and Other Stories* (1997). Her work, the American writer Alice Walker once remarked, has "reaffirmed my faith in the power of the written word to reach, to teach, to empower and encourage."

After graduation from the University of Ghana and a period as a research fellow at that university's Institute of African Studies, Aidoo studied creative writing at Stanford University, in California, and she has subsequently taught English and African literature at the University of Ghana, Cape Coast branch. Now settled in Harare, Zimbabwe, she continues to explore with poignancy, verve, and wit the dissonance between Western culture and the civilization of an Africa just emerging from colonization, even while she seeks to imagine the ways in which, particularly for African women, things might work out toward a surprising and "dazzling" conclusion.

The Message

"Look here my sister, it should not be said but they say they opened her up."

"They opened her up?"

"Yes, opened her up."

"And the baby removed?"

"Yes, the baby removed."

"Yes the baby removed."

"I say. . . ."

"They do not say, my sister."

"Have you heard it?"

"What?"

"This and this and that. . . ."

"A-a-ah! that is it. . . ."

"*Meewuo!*"[1]

"They don't say *meewuo*. . . ."

"And how is she?"

"Am I not here with you? Do I know the highway which leads to Cape Coast?"[2]

"Hmmm. . . ."

"And anyway how can she live? What is it like even giving birth with a

---

1. "I'm going to die!" We are indebted to Dan Avorgbedor for his invaluable help in translating Ghanaian words and phrases.
2. A principal city in Ghana.

stomach which is whole . . . eh? . . . I am asking you. And if you are always standing on the brink of death who go to war with a stomach that is whole, then how would she do whose stomach is open to the winds?"

"Oh, *poo*,[3] pity. . . ."

"I say. . . ."

My little bundle, come. You and I are going to Cape Coast today.

I am taking one of her own cloths with me, just in case. These people on the coast do not know how to do a thing and I am not going to have anybody mishandling my child's body. I hope they give it to me. Horrible things I have heard done to people's bodies. Cutting them up and using them for instructions. Whereas even murderers still have decent burials.

I see Mensima coming. . . . And there is Nkama too . . . and Adwoa Meenu. . . . Now they are coming to . . . "*poo* pity" me. Witches, witches, witches . . . they have picked mine up while theirs prosper around them, children, grandchildren and great-grandchildren—theirs shoot up like mushrooms.

"Esi, we have heard of your misfortune. . . ."

"That our little lady's womb has been opened up. . . ."

"And her baby removed. . . ."

Thank you very much.

"Has she lived through it?"

I do not know.

"Esi, bring her here, back home whatever happens."

Yoo,[4] thank you. If the government's people allow it, I shall bring her home.

"And have you got ready your things?"

Yes. . . . No.

I cannot even think well.

It feels so noisy in my head. . . . Oh my little child. . . . I am wasting time. . . . And so I am going. . . .

Yes, to Cape Coast.

No, I do not know anyone there now but do you think no one would show me the way to this big hospital . . . if I asked around?

Hmmm . . . it's me has ended up like this. I was thinking that everything was alright now. . . . *Yoo*. And thank you too. Shut the door for me when you are leaving. You may stay too long outside if you wait for me, so go home and be about your business. I will let you know when I bring her in.

"Maami Amfoa, where are you going?"

My daughter, I am going to Cape Coast.

"And what is our old mother going to do with such swift steps? Is it serious?"

My daughter, it is very serious.

"Mother, may God go with you."

Yoo, my daughter.

"Eno, and what calls at this hour of the day?"

They want me at Cape Coast.

"Does my friend want to go and see how much the city has changed since we went there to meet the new Wesleyan Chairman,[5] twenty years ago?"

---

3. An exclamation.
4. Yes.

5. Official in the Wesleyan mission, which was active in Ghana.

My sister, do you think I have knees to go parading on the streets of Cape Coast?

"Is it heavy?"

Yes, very heavy indeed. They have opened up my grandchild at the hospital, *hi, hi, hi*. . . .

"Eno *due, due, due*.⁶

. . . I did not know. May God go with you. . . ."

Thank you *Yaa*.

"O, the world!"

"It's her grandchild. The only daughter of her only son. Do you remember Kojo Amisa who went to sodja⁷ and fell in the great war, overseas?"

"Yes, it's his daughter. . . ."

. . . O, *poo*, pity.

"Kobina, run to the street, tell Draba Anan to wait for Nana Amfoa."

". . . Draba Anan, Draba, my mother says I must come and tell you to wait for Nana Amfoa."

"And where is she?"

"There she comes."

"Just look at how she hops like a bird . . . does she think we are going to be here all day? And anyway we are full already. . . ."

O, you drivers!

"What have drivers done?"

"And do you think it shows respect when you speak in this way? It is only that things have not gone right; but she could, at least have been your mother. . . ."

"But what have I said? I have not insulted her. I just think that only Youth must be permitted to see Cape Coast, the town of the Dear and Expensive. . . ."

"And do you think she is going on a peaceful journey? The only daughter of her only son has been opened up and her baby removed from her womb."

O . . . God.

O

O

O

Poo, pity.

"Me . . .

poo—pity, I am right about our modern wives. I always say they are useless as compared with our mothers."

"You drivers!"

"Now what have your modern wives done?"

"Am I not right what I always say about them?"

"You go and watch them in the big towns. All so thin and dry as sticks—you can literally blow them away with your breath. No decent flesh anywhere. Wooden chairs groan when they meet with their hard exteriors."

"O you drivers. . . ."

"But of course all drivers. . . ."

"What have I done? Don't all my male passengers agree with me? These

---

6. An expression of lamentation.   7. I.e., soldier.

modern girls. . . . Now here is one who cannot even have a baby in a decent way. But must have the baby removed from her stomach. *Tchiaa!*"[8]

"What. . . ."

"Here is the old woman."

"Whose grandchild. . . . ?"

"Yes."

"Nana, I hear you are coming to Cape Coast with us."

Yes my master.

"We nearly left you behind but we heard it was you and that it is a heavy journey you are making."

Yes my master . . . thank you my master.

"Push up please . . . push up. Won't you push up? Why do you all sit looking at me with such eyes as if I was a block of wood?"

"It is not that there is nowhere to push up to. Five fat women should go on that seat, but look at you!

And our own grandmother here is none too plump herself. . . . Nana, if they won't push, come to the front seat with me."

". . . Hei,[9] scholar, go to the back. . . .

. . . And do not scowl on me. I know your sort too well. Something tells me you do not have any job at all. As for that suit you are wearing and looking so grand in, you hired or borrowed it. . . ."

"Oh you drivers!"

Oh you drivers. . . .

The scholar who read this tengram[1] thing, said it was made about three days ago. My lady's husband sent it. . . . Three days. . . . God—that is too long ago. Have they buried her . . . where? Or did they cut her up. . . . I should not think about it . . . or something will happen to me. Eleven or twelve . . . Efua Panyin, Okuma, Kwame Gyasi and who else? But they should not have left me here. Sometimes . . . ah, I hate this nausea. But it is this smell of petrol. Now I have remembered I never could travel in a lorry.[2] I always was so sick. But now I hope at least that will not happen. These young people will think it is because I am old and they will laugh. At least if I knew the child of my child was alive, it would have been good. And the little things she sent me. . . . Sometimes some people like Mensima and Nkansa make me feel as if I had been a barren woman instead of only one with whom infant-mortality pledged friendship. . . .

I will give her that set of earrings, bracelet and chain which Odwumfo Ata made for me. It is the most beautiful and the most expensive thing I have. . . . It does not hurt me to think that I am going to die very soon and have them and their children gloating over my things. After all what did they swallow my children for? It does not hurt me at all. If I had been someone else, I would have given them all away before I died. But it does not matter. They can share their own curse. Now, that is the end of me and my roots. . . . Eternal death has worked like a warrior rat, with diabolical sense of duty, to gnaw my bottom. Everything is finished now. The vacant lot is swept and the scraps of old sugar-cane pulp, dry sticks and bunches of hair burnt . . . how it reeks, the smoke!

"O, Nana do not weep. . . ."

---

8. Expression of the absurdity of things.
9. Hey there, or keep quiet!

1. I.e., telegram.
2. Truck or bus.

"Is the old woman weeping?"
"If the only child of your only child died, won't you weep?"
"Why do you ask me? Did I know her grandchild is dead?"
"Where have you been, not in this lorry? Where were your ears when we were discussing it?"
"I do not go putting my mouth in other people's affairs. . . ."
"So what?"
"So go and die."
"*Hei, hei,* it is prohibited to quarrel in my lorry."
"Draba, here is me, sitting quiet and this lady of muscles and bones being cheeky to me."
"Look, I can beat you."
"Beat me . . . beat me . . . let's see."
"*Hei,* you are not civilized, eh?"
"Keep quiet and let us think, both of you, or I will put you down."
"Nana, do not weep. There is God above."
Thank you my master.
"But we are in Cape Coast already."
Meewuo! My God, hold me tight or something will happen to me.
My master, I will come down here.
"O Nana, I thought you said you were going to the hospital. . . . We are not there yet."
I am saying maybe I will get down here and ask my way around.
"Nana, you do not know these people, eh? They are very impudent here. They have no use for old age. So they do not respect it. Sit down, I will take you there."
Are you going there, my master?
"No, but I will take you there."
Ah, my master, your old mother thanks you. Do not shed a tear when you hear of my death . . . my master, your old mother thanks you.
I hear there is somewhere where they keep corpses until their owners claim them . . . if she has been buried, then I must find her husband . . . Esi Amfoa, what did I come to do under this sky? I have buried all my children and now I am going to bury my only grandchild!
"Nana we are there."
Is this the hospital?
"Yes, Nana. What is your child's name?"
Esi Amfoa. His father named her after me.
"Do you know her European name?"
No, my master.
"What shall we do?"
". . . Ei lady, Lady Nurse, we are looking for somebody."
"You are looking for somebody and can you read? If you cannot, you must ask someone what the rules in the hospital are. You can only come and visit people at three o'clock."
Lady, please. She was my only grandchild. . . .
"Who? And anyway, it is none of our business."
Nana, you must be patient . . . and not cry. . . .
"Old woman, why are you crying, it is not allowed here. No one must make any noise. . . ."
My lady, I am sorry but she was all I had.

"Who? Oh, are you the old woman who is looking for somebody?"
Yes.
"Who is he?"
She was my granddaughter—the only child of my only son.
"I mean, what was her name?"
Esi Amfoa.
"Esi Amfoa . . . Esi Amfoa. I am sorry, we do not have anyone whom they call like that here."
Is that it?
"Nana, I told you they may know only her European name here."
My master, what shall we do then?
"What is she ill with?"
She came here to have a child. . . .
". . . And they say, they opened her stomach and removed the baby. Oh . . . oh, I see."
My Lord, hold me tight so that nothing will happen to me now.
"I see. It is the Caesarean case."
"Nurse, you know her?"
And when I take her back, Anona Ebusuafo will say that I did not wait for them to come with me. . . .
"Yes. Are you her brother?"
"No. I am only the driver who brought the old woman."
"Did she bring all her clan?"
"No. She came alone."
"Strange thing for a villager to do."
I hope they have not cut her up already.
"Did she bring a whole bag full of cassava and plantain and kenkey?"[3]
"No. She has only her little bundle."
"Follow me. But you must not make any noise. This is not the hour for coming here. . . ."
My master, does she know her?
"Yes."
I hear it is very cold where they put them. . . .

It was feeding time for new babies. When old Esi Amfoa saw young Esi Amfoa, the latter was all neat and nice. White sheets and all. She did not see the beautiful stitches under the sheets. "This woman is a tough bundle," Dr. Gyamfi had declared after the identical twins had been removed, the last stitches had been threaded off and Mary Koomson, alias Esi Amfoa, had come to.

The old woman somersaulted into the room and lay groaning, not screaming, by the bed. For was not her last pot broken? So they lay them in state even in hospitals and not always cut them up for instruction?

The Nursing Sister was furious. Young Esi Amfoa spoke. And this time old Esi Amfoa wept loud and hard—wept all her tears.

Scrappy nurse-under-training, Jessy Treeson, second-generation-Cape Coaster-her-grandmother-still-remembered-at-Egyaa No. 7 said, "As for these villagers," and giggled.

Draba Anan looked hard at Jessy Treeson, looked hard at her, all of her:

---

3. A staple food made from fermented corn. "Cassava": a root vegetable that is another staple food.

her starched uniform, apron and cap . . . and then dismissed them all. . . .
"Such a cassava stick . . . but maybe I will break my toe if I kicked at her
buttocks," he thought.

And by the bed the old woman was trying hard to rise and look at the only
pot which had refused to get broken.

1970

MARILYN HACKER
b. 1942

"Where are the expatriate *salonnières*?" Marilyn Hacker asks with wry humor as she celebrates the sometimes lost, sometimes (re)found lesbian literary tradition in her high-spirited "Ballad of Ladies Lost and Found." Both a deeply committed feminist and an artist of extraordinary technical accomplishment, Hacker deploys a range of forms—sestinas, sonnets, villanelles, ballades—to produce a poetry that is simultaneously tough and tender in a style characterized by one critic as "the colloquial sublime." Born and brought up in New York City, Hacker married the science fiction writer Samuel Delaney in 1961; they had one daughter before they divorced in 1980. Hacker has been a teacher and a bookseller as well as the editor of such prestigious journals as *Thirteenth Moon* and *The Kenyon Review*. Her collections of verse include *Presentation Piece*, for which she won the National Book Award in 1974, *Assumptions* (1985), *Love, Death and the Changing of the Seasons* (1986), *The Hang-Glider's Daughter* (1990), *Winter Numbers* (1994), *Selected Poems, 1965–1990* (1994), *Squares and Courtyards* (2000), and *Desesperanto* (2003).

Cosmopolitan in her literary tastes, Hacker has translated important works by the Lebanese poet Venus Khoury-Ghata and the French poet Claire Malroux into English. She is currently a professor of English at City College, New York, but in recent years, she has lived part of the time in Paris, ironically describing herself in the refrain of one poem as "another Jewish lesbian in France." An impassioned political activist as well as a versatile woman of letters, she has commented that "Good writing gives energy, whatever it is about. But the fact that writers are dealing with essential issues, that some are themselves implicated as HIV-positive or writing with cancer or AIDS, or as health-care givers, legal advisers, teachers, outreach workers, witnesses—I think that's a necessary integration of literary writing with what's actually going on in our world."

Ballad of Ladies[1] Lost and Found

for Julia Álvarez

Where are the women who, *entre deux guerres*,[2]
came out on college-graduation trips,
came to New York on football scholarships,

---

1. Most of the "ladies" mentioned in the poem, as well as Álvarez, appear in this anthology; the others are identified in footnotes.

2. Between two wars (French); i.e., between World Wars I and II.

came to town meeting in a decorous pair?
Where are the expatriate *salonnières*,[3]
the gym teacher, the math-department head?
Do nieces follow where their odd aunts led?
The elephants die off in Cagnes-sur-Mer.
H. D., whose "nature was bisexual,"[4]
and plain old Margaret Fuller died as well.

Where are the single-combat champions:
the Chevalier d'Eon with curled peruke,[5]
Big Sweet who ran with Zora in the jook,[6]
open-handed Winifred Ellerman,[7]
Colette,[8] who hedged her bets and always won?
Sojourner's sojourned where she need not pack
decades of whitegirl conscience on her back.
The spirit gave up Zora; she lay down
under a weed field miles from Eatonville,
and plain old Margaret Fuller died as well.

Where's Stevie, with her pleated schoolgirl dresses,
and Rosa, with her permit to wear pants?[9]
Who snuffed Clara's *mestiza*[1] flamboyance
and bled Frida[2] onto her canvases?
Where are the Niggerati[3] hostesses,
the kohl-eyed ivory poets with severe
chignons,[4] the rebels who grew out their hair,
the bulldaggers with marceled processes?[5]
Conglomerates co-opted Sugar Hill,[6]
and plain old Margaret Fuller died as well.

Anne Hutchinson,[7] called witch, termagant, whore,
fell to the long knives, having tricked the noose.
Carolina María de Jesús'[8]
tale from the slag heaps of the landless poor
ended on a straw mat on a dirt floor.
In action thirteen years after fifteen
in prison, Eleanor of Aquitaine[9]

---

3. Frequenters of salons (French), which are gatherings both fashionable and intellectual.
4. H. D.'s "bisexual nature" came out in her analysis with Sigmund Freud. Cagnes-sur-Mer is a town on the southern coast of France frequented for years by French writers.
5. Wig. Charles d'Éon de Beaumont (1728–1810), French writer, spy, and female impersonator.
6. A dive, for drinking, dancing, and music. Big Sweet befriended Zora Neale Hurston; see *Dust Tracks on a Road* (1942).
7. Better known as Bryher (1894–1983), the author and heiress who supported H. D. for much of her life.
8. Sidonie-Gabrielle Colette (1873–1954), French author.
9. It was illegal for women to wear trousers. Rosa Bonheur (1822–1899), French painter.
1. Spanish term for mixed blood, especially European and American Indian.
2. Frida Kahlo (1907–1954), Mexican painter.
3. Mocking term for black literary intellectuals of the Harlem Renaissance, used particularly by Hurston and the author Wallace Thurman (1902–1934).
4. Knot of hair at the nape of the neck. "Kohl": preparation used to darken the eyelids.
5. Lesbians, with hair straightened into deep, soft waves.
6. The most fashionable residential area of Harlem.
7. Religious liberal (1591–1643), banished from the Massachusetts Bay Colony, who became a founder of Rhode Island.
8. Brazilian diarist (1913–1977).
9. Wife (1122?–1204) of Henry II, who imprisoned her from 1173 until his death in 1189. Under her son, Richard I, she administered the French lands and acted as regent of England.

accomplished half of Europe and fourscore
anniversaries for good or ill,
40   and plain old Margaret Fuller died as well.

Has Ida B. persuaded Susan B.[1]
to pool resources for a joint campaign?
(Two Harriets act a pageant by Lorraine,
cheered by the butch drunk on the IRT[2]
45   who used to watch me watch her watching me.)
We've notes by Angelina Grimké Weld[3]
for choral settings drawn from the *Compiled
Poems* of Angelina Weld Grimké.[4]
There's no such tense as Past Conditional,
50   and plain old Margaret Fuller died as well.

Who was Sappho's[5] protégé, and when did
we lose Hrotsvitha,[6] dramaturge and nun?
What did bibulous Suzanne Valadon[7]
think about Artemisia,[8] who tended
55   to make a life-size murderess look splendid?
Where's Aphra, fond of dalliance and the pun?
Where's Jane,[9] who didn't indulge in either one?
Whoever knows how Ende, Pintrix,[1] ended
is not teaching Art History at Yale,
60   and plain old Margaret Fuller died as well.

Is Beruliah[2] upstairs behind the curtain
debating Juana Inés de la Cruz?[3]
Where's savante Anabella, Augusta-Goose,[4]
Fanny, Maude, Lidian, Freda and Caitlin,[5]
65   "without whom this could never have been written"?
Louisa[6] who wrote, scrimped, saved, sewed, and nursed,
Malinche,[7] who's, like all translators, cursed,

---

1. Susan B. Anthony (1820–1906), a leader of the American women's suffrage movement. Ida B. Wells-Barnett (1862–1931), black journalist best known for her crusade against lynching.
2. One of the three formerly distinct subway systems in New York City. Lorraine Hansberry (1930–1965), black American playwright.
3. American abolitionist (1805–1879).
4. Black poet (1880–1958) of the Harlem Renaissance.
5. Poet (b. ca. 612 B.C.E.) traditionally described as a teacher or mentor of younger women, sometimes identified with those named in her surviving poems (Atthis is the most frequently mentioned).
6. German poet, dramatist, and historian (935?–1002?).
7. French painter (1865–1938).
8. Artemisia Gentileschi, Italian painter (ca. 1597–ca. 1652); several of her works treat Judith's decapitation of Holofernes, and she also painted Jael's murder of Sisera.
9. I.e., Jane Austen.
1. The earliest illuminated manuscript attributed to a woman, the *Gerona Apocalypse* produced in Spain around 975, was so signed (or "En depintrix").

2. Perhaps Beruriah (2nd c. C.E.), a scholar mentioned in the Talmud as learned in Jewish law, wife of the sage Rabbi Meir.
3. Mexican nun and poet (1651–1695), famous for her learning and her feminist ideas.
4. Augusta Leigh (1784–1851), the poet Byron's half-sister, affectionately called "Goose." Anabella Milbanke (1792–1860), the poet Byron's wife.
5. All best known for their connection with famous male writers. Fanny Brawne [Lindon] (1800–1865), whom the English poet John Keats loved. Maude Gonne [MacBride] (1866–1953), loved by the Irish poet William Butler Yeats. Lydia Jackson Emerson (1802–1892), second wife of the American essayist and poet Ralph Waldo Emerson. Frieda von Richthofen Lawrence (1879–1956), wife of the English writer D. H. Lawrence. Caitlin Macnamara Thomas (1913–1994), wife of the Welsh poet Dylan Thomas.
6. I.e., Louisa May Alcott.
7. Also known as Malintzin or Doña Marina (1501?–1550), an Aztec given as a slave to Cortés who acted as translator and helped him defeat Moctezuma (to Mexicans, *Malinche* became synonymous with "traitor").

Bessie,[8] whose voice was hemp and steel and satin,
outside a segregated hospital,
and plain old Margaret Fuller died as well.

Where's Amy, who kept Ada[9] in cigars
and love, requited, both country and courtly,
although quinquagenarian and portly?
Where's Emily?[1] It's very still upstairs.
Where's Billie, whose strange fruit ripened in bars?
Where's the street-scavenging Little Sparrow?[2]
Too poor, too mean, too weird, too wide, too narrow:
Marie Curie,[3] examining her scars,
was not particularly beautiful;
and plain old Margaret Fuller died as well.

Who was the grandmother of Frankenstein?[4]
The Vindicatrix of the Rights of Woman.
Madame de Sévigné[5] said prayers to summon
the postman just as eloquent as mine,
though my Madame de Grignan's only nine.
But Mary Wollstonecraft had never known
that daughter, nor did Paula Modersohn.[6]
The three-day infants blinked in the sunshine.
The mothers turned their faces to the wall;
and plain old Margaret Fuller died as well.

Tomorrow night the harvest moon will wane
that's floodlighting the silhouetted wood.
Make your own footnotes; it will do you good.
Emeritae[7] have nothing to explain.
She wasn't very old, or really plain—
my age exactly, volumes incomplete.
"The life, the life, will it never be sweet?"[8]
She wrote it once; I quote it once again
midlife at midnight when the moon is full
and I can almost hear the warning bell
offshore, sounding through starlight like a stain
on waves that heaved over what she began
and truncated a woman's chronicle,
and plain old Margaret Fuller died as well.

1985

---

8. Bessie Smith (1894–1937), American blues singer and songwriter, said (probably inaccurately) to have died while trying to be admitted to a whites-only hospital after an automobile accident.
9. The actress Ada Dwyer Russell (1863–1952) left the stage and lived with Amy Lowell from 1914 until Lowell died in 1925.
1. I.e., Emily Dickinson.
2. Edith Piaf (1915–1963), French singer. Billie Holiday (1915–1959), American jazz singer, who in 1939 recorded "Strange Fruit," a song about lynching.
3. Polish-born French physicist (1867–1934), who co-discovered radium (and died of radiation-caused leukemia).
4. I.e., Mary Wollstonecraft.
5. Marie de Rabutin-Chantal, marquise de Sévigné (1626–1695), French letter writer; most of her witty letters on fashionable and everyday life were to her daughter, Madame de Grignan (1646–1705) (line 85).
6. German painter (1876–1907), who died two weeks after childbirth.
7. Those [women] who have served out their terms (Latin, literal trans.); retired women holding an honorary title, used most often of professors.
8. From Fuller's *Memoirs* (1852), 1:237: "The life, the life! O, my God! shall the life never be sweet?"

Runaways Café I

You hailed a cab outside the nondescript
yuppie bar on Lexington[1] to go
downtown. Hug; hug: this time I brushed my lips
just across yours, and fire down below
in February flared. O bless and curse
what's waking up no wiser than it was.
I will not go to bed with you because
I want to very much. If that's perverse,
there are, you'll guess, perversions I'd prefer:
fill the lacunae[2] in: one; two; three; four . . .
I did, cab gone. While my late bus didn't come,
desire ticked over like a metronome.
For you, someone was waiting up at home.
For me, I might dare more if someone were.

1986

Runaways Café II

For once, I hardly noticed what I ate
(salmon and broccoli and Saint-Véran[1]).
My elbow twitched like jumping beans;[2] sweat ran
into my shirtsleeves. Could I concentrate
on anything but your leg against mine
under the table? It was difficult,
but I impersonated an adult
looking at you, and knocking back the wine.
Now that we both want to know what we want,
now that we both want to know what we know,
it still behooves us to know what to do:
be circumspect, be generous, be brave,
be honest, be together, and behave.
At least I didn't get white sauce down my front.

1986

From Cancer Winter

* * *

I woke up, and the surgeon said, "You're cured."
Strapped to the gurney, in the cotton gown
and pants I was wearing when they slid me down
onto the table, made new straps secure

---

1. I.e., Lexington Avenue in Manhattan.
2. Gaps.
1. A wine.

2. I.e., Mexican jumping beans, which move because they contain the larvae of a moth.

while I stared at the hydra-headed O.R.
lamp, I took in the tall, confident, brown-
skinned man, and the ache I couldn't quite call pain
from where my right breast wasn't anymore
to my armpit. A not-yet-talking head,
I bit dry lips. What else could he have said?
And then my love was there in a hospital coat;
then my old love, still young and very scared.
Then I, alone, graphed clock hands' asymptote[1]
to noon, when I would be wheeled back upstairs.

The odd and even numbers of the street
I live on are four thousand miles away
from an Ohio February day
snow-blanketed, roads iced over, with sleet
expected later, where I'm incomplete
as my abbreviated chest. I weigh
less—one breast less—since the Paris-gray
December evening, when a neighbor's feet
coming up ancient stairs, the feet I counted
on paper were the company I craved.
My calm right breast seethed with a grasping tumor.
The certainty of my returns amounted
to nothing. After terror, being brave
became another form of gallows humor.

At noon, an orderly wheeled me upstairs
via an elevator hung with Season's
Greetings streamers, bright and false as treason.
The single room the surgeon let us share
the night before the knife was scrubbed and bare
except for blush-pink roses in a vase on
the dresser. Veering through a morphine haze on
the cranked bed, I was avidly aware
of my own breathing, my thirst, that it was over—
the week that ended on this New Year's Eve.
A known hand held, while I sipped, icewater,
afloat between ache, sleep, lover and lover.
The one who stayed would stay; the one would leave.
The hand that held the cup next was my daughter's.

It's become a form of gallows humor
to reread the elegies I wrote
at that pine table, with their undernote
of cancer as death's leitmotiv,[2] enumerating my dead, the unknown dead, the rumor
of random and pandemic deaths. I thought
I was a witness, a survivor, caught

---

1. I.e., their approach that never reaches noon.
2. Lead motif (German, literal trans.); dominant recurring theme.

in a maelstrom and brought forth, who knew more
of pain than some, but learned it loving others.
I need to find another metaphor
while I eat up stories of people's mothers
who had mastectomies. "She's eighty-four
this year, and *fine!*" Cell-shocked, I brace to do
what I can, an unimportant exiled Jew.

* * *

1994

The Boy

Is it the boy in me who's looking out
the window, while someone across the street
mends a pillowcase, clouds shift, the gutter spout
pours rain, someone else lights a cigarette?

(Because he flinched, because he didn't whirl
around, face them, because he didn't hurl
the challenge back—"*Fascists*"—not "*Faggots*"—"*Swine!*"
he briefly wonders—if he were a girl . . .)
He writes a line. He crosses out a line.

I'll never be a man, but there's a boy
crossing out words: the rain, the linen-mender,
are all the homework he will do today.
The absence and the privilege of gender

confound in him, soprano, clumsy, frail.
Not neuter—neutral human, and unmarked,
the younger brother in the fairy tale
except, boys shouted "*Jew!*" across the park

at him when he was coming home from school.
The book that he just read, about the war,
the partisans, is less a terrible
and thrilling story, more a warning, more

a code, and he must puzzle out the code.
He has short hair, a red sweatshirt. They know
something about him—that he should be proud
of? That's shameful if it shows?

That got you killed in 1942.
In his story, do the partisans
have sons? Have grandparents? Is he a Jew
more than he is a boy, who'll be a man

someday? Someone who'll never be a man
looks out the window at the rain he thought
might stop. He reads the sentence he began.
He writes down something that he crosses out.

2000

Crepuscule with Muriel

Instead of a cup of tea, instead of a milk-
silk whelk of a cup, of a cup of nearly six
o'clock teatime, cup of a stumbling block,
cup of an afternoon unredeemed by talk,
cup of a cut brown loaf, of a slice, a lack
of butter, blueberry jam that's almost black,
instead of tannin seeping into the cracks
of a pot, the void of an hour seeps out, infects
the slit of a cut I haven't the wit to fix
with a surgeon's needle threaded with fine-gauge silk
as a key would thread the cylinder of a lock.
But no key threads the cylinder of the lock.
Late afternoon light, transitory, licks
the place of the absent cup with its rough tongue, flicks
itself out beneath the wheel's revolving spoke.
Taut thought's gone, with a blink of attention, slack,
a vision of "death and distance in the mix"[1]
(she lost her words and how did she get them back
when the corridor of a day was a lurching deck?
The dream-life logic encodes in nervous tics
she translated to a syntax which connects
intense and unfashionable politics
with morning coffee, Hudson sunsets,[2] sex;
then the short-circuit of the final stroke,
the end toward which all lines looped out, then broke).
What a gaze out the window interjects:
on the southeast corner, a black Lab balks,
tugged as the light clicks green toward a late-day walk
by a plump brown girl in a purple anorak.
The Bronx-bound local comes rumbling up the tracks
out of the tunnel, over west Harlem blocks
whose windows gleam on the animal warmth of bricks
rouged by the fluvial[3] light of six o'clock.

2003

1. Quoted from "Rondel," by the American poet Muriel Rukeyser (1913–1980; see above, p. 644).
2. The Hudson River lies west of the Bronx and Manhattan.
3. Produced by a stream.

Migraine Sonnets

entre chien et loup[1]

It's a long way from the bedroom to the kitchen
when all the thought in back of thought is loss.
How wide the dark rooms are you walk across
with a glass of water and a migraine
5 tablet. Sweat of hard dreams: unforgiven
silences, missed opportunities.
The night progresses like chronic disease,
symptom by symptom, sentences without pardon.
It's only half past two, you realize.
10 Five windows are still lit across the street.
You wonder: did you tell as many lies
as it now appears were told to you?
And if you told them, how did you not know
they were lies? Did you know, and then forget?

15 There were lies. Did you know, and then forget
if there was a lie in the peach orchard? There was the lie
a saxophone riffed on a storm-thick summer sky,
there was the lie on a postcard, there was the lie thought
and suggested, there was the lie stretched taut
20 across the Atlantic, there was the lie that lay
slack in the blue lap of a September day,
there was the lie in bed, there was the lie that caught
its breath when it came, there was the lie that wept.
There was the lie that read the newspaper.
25 There was the lie that fell asleep, its clear
face relaxing back to the face of a child.
There was the lie you held while you both slept.
A lie hung framed in the doorway, growing wild.

The face framed in the doorframe is a wild
30 card now, mouth could eat silence, mouth could speak
the indigestible. Eyes, oh tourmaline, a crack
in the glass, break the glass. Down a green-tiled
corridor double doors open. Who was wheeled
through, hallucinating on a gurney, weak
35 with relief as muscle and nerve flickered awake,
while a dreamed face framed in a doorframe opened and smiled?
Precisely no one's home. No dog will come
to lay his jowls across bent knees and drool
and smile the black-gummed smile he shares with wolves.
40 The empty doorframe frames an empty room
whose dim fluorescence is perpetual.
The double doors close back upon themselves.

---

1. Between dog and wolf (French). That is, neither daylight nor dark, usually applied to the dusk. The hour of the wolf is that time in the early morning when worries and fears prevent sleep.

The double doors close back upon themselves
The watcher from the woods rejoins the pack:
45 shadows on branches' steely lacework, black
on black, dark ornaments, dark wooden shelves.
Fever-wolves, guardians a lamp dissolves
in pitiless logic, as an insomniac
waits to hear the long night crack and break
50 into contaminated rusty halves.
This is the ninety-seventh (count) night watch in
the underbrush of hours closed on you since
a lie split open like a rotten fruit.
A metal band around your head begins
55 to tighten; pain shutters your eyes like too much light.
It's a long way from the bedroom to the kitchen.

2003

SHARON OLDS
b. 1942

Boldly staking her claim to a place in the tradition of American poetry shaped by such charismatic male speakers as Walt Whitman and Allen Ginsberg, Sharon Olds redefines heroism as she proclaims the power of maternity, declaring in "The Language of the Brag" that "I have done what you wanted to do, Walt Whitman, / Allen Ginsberg . . . / . . . this exceptional / act with the exceptional heroic body, / this giving birth, this glistening verb." Olds was born in San Francisco, and educated at Stanford and Columbia, where she earned a Ph.D. in 1972. The mother of two, she has taught at a number of academic institutions, most recently New York University; in addition, she has long directed a creative writing workshop at Goldwater Hospital on Roosevelt Island in New York.

A poet who excavates the metaphysical significance of the physical and gives powerful public voice to the supposedly private and personal, Olds has examined the erotics and politics of family life in nine powerful collections of verse, including *Satan Says* (1980), *The Dead and the Living* (1984), *The Father* (1992), and, most recently, *The Unswept Room* (2002). About her procedures as a poet, Olds has said, "One thing I'm really interested in, when I'm writing, is being accurate. If I am trying to describe something, I'd like to be able to get it right. Of course, what's 'right' is different for every person. Sometimes what's accurate might be kind of mysterious. So I don't just mean mathematically accurate. But to get it right according to my vision." Throughout her career, such a drive to be "accurate" has imbued her work with a courageous candor that some critics have considered shocking and most readers find compelling.

The Death of Marilyn Monroe[1]

The ambulance men touched her cold
body, lifted it, heavy as iron,
onto the stretcher, tried to close the
mouth, closed the eyes, tied the
5   arms to the sides, moved a caught
strand of hair, as if it mattered,
saw the shape of her breasts, flattened by
gravity, under the sheet,
carried her, as if it were she,
10 down the steps.

These men were never the same. They went out
afterwards, as they always did,
for a drink or two, but they could not meet
each other's eyes.

15   Their lives took
a turn—one had nightmares, strange
pains, impotence, depression. One did not
like his work, his wife looked
different, his kids. Even death
20 seemed different to him—a place where she
would be waiting,

and one found himself standing at night
in the doorway to a room of sleep, listening to a
woman breathing, just an ordinary
25 woman
breathing.

                                        1978, 1984

The Language of the Brag

I have wanted excellence in the knife-throw,
I have wanted to use my exceptionally strong and accurate arms
and my straight posture and quick electric muscles
to achieve something at the center of a crowd,
5   the blade piercing the bark deep,
the haft slowly and heavily vibrating like the cock.

I have wanted some epic use for my excellent body,
some heroism, some American achievement
beyond the ordinary for my extraordinary self,

---

1. American film star (1926–1962), the epitome of the Hollywood sex symbol; she died of an overdose of sleeping pills.

10   magnetic and tensile, I have stood by the sandlot
and watched the boys play.

I have wanted courage, I have thought about fire
and the crossing of waterfalls, I have dragged around

my belly big with cowardice and safety,
15   my stool black with iron pills,
my huge breasts oozing mucus,
my legs swelling, my hands swelling,
my face swelling and darkening, my hair
falling out, my inner sex
20   stabbed again and again with terrible pain like a knife.
I have lain down.

I have lain down and sweated and shaken
and passed blood and feces and water and
slowly alone in the center of a circle I have
25   passed the new person out
and they have lifted the new person free of the act
and wiped the new person free of that
language of blood like praise all over the body.

I have done what you wanted to do, Walt Whitman,
30   Allen Ginsberg,[1] I have done this thing,
I and the other women this exceptional
act with the exceptional heroic body,
this giving birth, this glistening verb,
and I am putting my proud American boast
35   right here with the others.

1980

Rite of Passage

As the guests arrive at my son's party
they gather in the living room—
short men, men in first grade
with smooth jaws and chins.
5   Hands in pockets, they stand around
jostling, jockeying for place, small fights
breaking out and calming. One says to another
How old are you? Six. I'm seven. So?
They eye each other, seeing themselves
10   tiny in the other's pupils. They clear their
throats a lot, a room of small bankers,
they fold their arms and frown. *I could beat you
up,* a seven says to a six,
the dark cake, round and heavy as a

---

1. Both Whitman (1819–1892) and Ginsberg (1926–1997) are American poets known for celebrating themselves in their writing.

15 turret, behind them on the table. My son,
    freckles like specks of nutmeg on his cheeks,
    chest narrow as the balsa keel of a
    model boat, long hands
    cool and thin as the day they guided him
20 out of me, speaks up as a host
    for the sake of the group.
    We could easily kill a two-year-old,
    he says in his clear voice. The other
    men agree, they clear their throats
25 like Generals, they relax and get down to
    playing war, celebrating my son's life.

                                                    1984

The One Girl at the Boys' Party

When I take my girl to the swimming party
I set her down among the boys. They tower and
bristle, she stands there smooth and sleek,
her math scores unfolding in the air around her.
5 They will strip to their suits, her body hard and
indivisible as a prime number,
they'll plunge in the deep end, she'll subtract
her height from ten feet, divide it into
hundreds of gallons of water, the numbers
10 bouncing in her mind like molecules of chlorine
in the bright blue pool. When they climb out,
her ponytail will hang its pencil lead
down her back, her narrow silk suit
with hamburgers and french fries printed on it
15 will glisten in the brilliant air, and they will
see her sweet face, solemn and
sealed, a factor of one, and she will
see their eyes, two each,
their legs, two each, and the curves of their sexes,
20 one each, and in her head she'll be doing her
wild multiplying, as the drops
sparkle and fall to the power of a thousand from her body.

                                                    1984

This

Maybe if I did not have this
I would call myself my mother's daughter
or identify my soul with the blue bowl
that stood on the table, or with the gold wall, or the field.
5 I would call myself Cobb, Stuart, Torrance,

McLean, I would wear the plaid[1] at all times,
clan green, blood red,
fine line of the purple vein,
if I did not have this. Or I would wrap my life in the
flag, in its wide swaths of blood, its
stars like broken bowls on that table,
or the cupped curve of my father's cereal-bowl forehead
here above my brows, or my mother's bad vein
running up the inside of my leg
like a river under the land.
                    But I have this,
so this is who I am, this body
white as yellowish dough brushed with dry flour
pressed to his body. I am these breasts that
crush against him like collapsible silver
travel cups that telescope into themselves,
and the nipples that float in the center like hard
raspberries in bright sunlight, they
are my life, the dark sex that
takes him in as anyone in summer will
open their throat to the hose held up
hot on the edge of the sandlot—don't
ask me about my country or who my
father was or even what I do, if you
want to know who I am, I am this, *this*.

1989

The Mortal One

All my life I had seen that long
glazed yellow narrow body,
not like Christ but like one of his saints,
or a hermit in gilt, all knees and raw ribs—
the ones who died of nettles, bile,
the one who died roasted over a fire.
I am glad we burned my father before
the bloom of mold could grow from him,
maybe it had begun in his bowels but we burned his bowels,
cleansing them with fire. Now I am learning
to think of his corpse without shock,
almost without grief, to take
the thought of it into each day, the way
when a loom parts the vertical threads,
half to the left half to the right, one can
throw the shuttlecock through with the warp-thread
tied to its feet, that small gold figure of my father—

---

1. I.e., the wool garment worn by men of the Scottish Highlands, patterned in tartans that came distinctively to identify each clan.

how often I saw him in paintings and did not know him,
the tiny naked dead one in the corner,
20 the mortal one.

                                                                    1992

LOUISE GLÜCK
b. 1943

The critic Helen Vendler observed some time ago that Louise Glück's "cryptic narratives" are in some ways "far removed from the more circumstantial poetry written by many women poets . . . but they remain poems chiefly about childhood, family life, love, and motherhood." In the brilliant theological meditations of *The Wild Iris* (1992), however—a collection for which she won the Pulitzer Prize—this ambitious poet's long-standing concern with more general metaphysical questions became quite clear.

Born in New York City, Louise Glück attended Sarah Lawrence College and Columbia University. The mother of one son, at present she lives in Vermont and in Cambridge, Massachusetts. In addition to *The Wild Iris*, her collections of poetry include *Firstborn* (1968), *Descending Figure* (1980), *The Triumph of Achilles* (1985), *Ararat* (1990), *Vita Nova* (1999), and *The Seven Ages* (2001). She has been awarded Rockefeller and Guggenheim fellowships; has taught verse writing at such institutions as Columbia University, the University of Iowa, and Williams College; and has also produced a volume of criticism, *Proofs and Theories: Essays on Poetry* (1994). A chancellor of the Academy of American poets, she served as the U.S. poet laureate in 2003.

Throughout her career, Glück has been intensely attentive to what in one poem she called "the map of language." At the same time, as she herself has put it, she is "attracted to ellipsis, to the unsaid, to suggestion, to eloquent, deliberate silence." Whether stripped and chill or ecstatically pure, her beautifully crafted lines evoke essence more than circumstance. Yet, as Vendler argues, in their precise attention to such subjects as anorexia, motherhood, and marriage, Glück's words imply the details as well as the desires of femininity. At the same time, as a poem like "Lullaby" demonstrates, Glück consistently sets the dramas of womanhood, including its familiar family romance, in a resonant spiritual context.

The School Children

The children go forward with their little satchels.
And all morning the mothers have labored
to gather the late apples, red and gold,
like words of another language.

5   And on the other shore
are those who wait behind great desks
to receive these offerings.

How orderly they are—the nails
on which the children hang
10   their overcoats of blue or yellow wool.

And the teachers shall instruct them in silence
and the mothers shall scour the orchards for a way out,
drawing to themselves the gray limbs of the fruit trees
bearing so little ammunition.

1975

The Drowned Children

You see, they have no judgment.
So it is natural that they should drown,
first the ice taking them in
and then, all winter, their wool scarves
5   floating behind them as they sink
until at last they are quiet.
And the pond lifts them in its manifold dark arms.

But death must come to them differently,
so close to the beginning.
10 As though they had always been
blind and weightless. Therefore
the rest is dreamed, the lamp,
the good white cloth that covered the table,
their bodies.

15 And yet they hear the names they used
like lures slipping over the pond:
What are you waiting for
come home, come home, lost
in the waters, blue and permanent.

1980

From Dedication to Hunger

4 The Deviation[1]

It begins quietly
in certain female children:
the fear of death, taking as its form
dedication to hunger,
5   because a woman's body
is a grave;[2] it will accept
anything. I remember

---

1. Glück is referring to anorexia nervosa, an eating disorder.
2. An allusion to the saying of Greek Orphic philosophers (6th B.C.E.): "the body is a tomb" (*sōma sēma*).

          lying in bed at night
          touching the soft, digressive breasts,
10   touching, at fifteen,
          the interfering flesh
          that I would sacrifice
          until the limbs were free
          of blossom and subterfuge: I felt
15   what I feel now, aligning these words
          it is the same need to perfect,
          of which death is the mere byproduct.

                                                            1980

Widows

My mother's playing cards with my aunt,
Spite and Malice, the family pastime, the game
my grandmother taught all her daughters.

Midsummer: too hot to go out.
5   Today, my aunt's ahead; she's getting the good cards.
My mother's dragging, having trouble with her concentration.
She can't get used to her own bed this summer.
She had no trouble last summer,
getting used to the floor. She learned to sleep there
10 to be near my father.
He was dying; he got a special bed.

My aunt doesn't give an inch, doesn't make
allowance for my mother's weariness.
It's how they were raised: you show respect by fighting.
15 To let up insults the opponent.

Each player has one pile to the left, five cards in the hand.
It's good to stay inside on days like this,
to stay where it's cool.
And this is better than other games, better than solitaire.

20 My grandmother thought ahead; she prepared her daughters.
They have cards; they have each other.
They don't need any more companionship.

All afternoon the game goes on, but the sun doesn't move.
It just keeps beating down, turning the grass yellow.
25 That's how it must seem to my mother.
And then, suddenly, something is over.

My aunt's been at it longer; maybe that's why she's playing better.
Her cards evaporate; that's what you want, that's the object: in the end,
the one who has nothing wins.

                                                            1990

Terminal Resemblance

When I saw my father for the last time, we both did the same thing.
He was standing in the doorway to the living room,
waiting for me to get off the telephone.
That he wasn't also pointing to his watch
was a signal he wanted to talk.

Talk for us always meant the same thing.
He'd say a few words. I'd say a few back.
That was about it.

It was the end of August, very hot, very humid.
Next door, workmen dumped new gravel on the driveway.

My father and I avoided being alone;
we didn't know how to connect, to make small talk—
there didn't seem to be
any other possibilities.
So this was special: when a man's dying,
he has a subject.

It must have been early morning. Up and down the street
sprinklers started coming on. The gardener's truck
appeared at the end of the block,
then stopped, parking.
My father wanted to tell me what it was like to be dying.
He told me he wasn't suffering.
He said he kept expecting pain, waiting for it, but it never came.
All he felt was a kind of weakness.
I said I was glad for him, that I thought he was lucky.

Some of the husbands were getting in their cars, going to work.
Not people we knew anymore. New families,
families with young children.
The wives stood on the steps, gesturing or calling.

We said goodbye in the usual way,
no embrace, nothing dramatic.
When the taxi came, my parents watched from the front door,
arm in arm, my mother blowing kisses as she always does,
because it frightens her when a hand isn't being used.
But for a change, my father didn't just stand there.
This time, he waved.

That's what I did, at the door to the taxi.
Like him, waved to disguise my hand's trembling.

1990

First Memory

Long ago, I was wounded. I lived
to revenge myself
against my father, not
for what he was—
for what I was: from the beginning of time,
in childhood, I thought
that pain meant
I was not loved.
It meant I loved.

1990

Lullaby[1]

Time to rest now; you have had
enough excitement for the time being.

Twilight, then early evening. Fireflies
in the room, flickering here and there, here and there,
and summer's deep sweetness filling the open window.

Don't think of these things anymore.
Listen to my breathing, your own breathing
like the fireflies, each small breath
a flare in which the world appears.

I've sung to you long enough in the summer night.
I'll win you over in the end; the world can't give you
this sustained vision.

You must be taught to love me. Human beings must be taught to love
silence and darkness.

1992

Vita Nova[1]

You saved me, you should remember me.

The spring of the year; young men buying tickets for the ferryboats.
Laughter, because the air is full of apple blossoms.

When I woke up, I realized I was capable of the same feeling.

---

1. Lullaby is one of a number of poems in *The Wild Iris* that are spoken by a voice outside the human, presumably by the spirit traditionally defined as "God."

1. New life (Latin), perhaps an allusion to Dante's collection of love poems, *La vita nuova* (ca. 1293).

I remember sounds like that from my childhood,
laughter for no cause, simply because the world is beautiful,
something like that.

Lugano.[2] Tables under the apple trees.
Deckhands raising and lowering the colored flags.
And by the lake's edge, a young man throws his hat into the water;
perhaps his sweetheart has accepted him.

Crucial
sounds or gestures like
a track laid down before the larger themes

and then unused, buried.

Islands in the distance. My mother
holding out a plate of little cakes—

as far as I remember, changed
in no detail, the moment
vivid, intact, having never been
exposed to light, so that I woke elated, at my age
hungry for life, utterly confident—

By the tables, patches of new grass, the pale green
pieced into the dark existing ground.

Surely spring has been returned to me, this time
not as a lover but a messenger of death, yet
it is still spring, it is still meant tenderly.

1999

2. A Swiss town well known as a tourist resort, on Lake Lugano, in the Italian-speaking canton of Ticino.

EAVAN BOLAND
b. 1944

"When I was young in Ireland," Eavan Boland has commented, "I felt there was almost a magnetic distance between the word 'woman' and the word 'poet.' I don't feel that now. But there was a certain amount of oppression in that—in feeling the difficulty of being a woman poet there, and of feeling that there was a heroic tradition on which it was difficult to write your name." Nonetheless, she added to the same interviewer, although her commitment to feminism "has helped me see society differently, and define myself as a writer differently," she feels that "it stops at the margins of the poem, at the edge of the act of writing it." Despite this avowal however, Boland's art is clearly shaped by the ways in which, as a woman, she sees her self and the world "differently." Yearning "to be a sibyl / able to sing the past / in pure syllables . . . /able to speak at last / my mother tongue," she examines what she has called the "domestic interiors" of women's lives with wit and grace, sometimes celebrating the powers of maternity, sometimes mourning the defeats inflicted by anorexia, mastectomy, and conjugal violence, and sometimes, as in her latest collection, *Against Love Poetry* (2001), celebrating the quotidian sustenance (rather than the romantic rapture) provided by marriage.

Born in Dublin, Boland studied at Trinity College and at the Iowa Writers' Workshop. In 1969, she married the novelist Kevin Casey, with whom she has two daughters. From *Poetry* (1963) and *New Territory* (1967) to *Night Feed* (1982), *The Journey* (1987), *Outside History* (1990), *The Lost Land* (1998), and *Against Love Poetry*, her collections of verse have explored both the dilemmas of Ireland, caught between "Dublin reverence and Belfast irony," and the situation of women, especially the circumstances of those who are painfully or pleasurably "settled / in the sort of light / jugs and kettles / grow important by." She has also published *Object Lessons: The Life of the Woman and the Poet in Our Time* (1995) as well as the anthology *The Making of a Poem* (2000). Currently a professor of English at Stanford University, she commutes between Ireland and California.

In His Own Image

I was not myself, myself.
The celery feathers,
the bacon flitch,[1]
the cups deep on the shelf
and my cheek
coppered and shone
in the kettle's paunch,
my mouth
blubbed in the tin of the pan—
they were all I had to go on.

How could I go on
with such meagre proofs of myself?
I woke day after day.
Day after day I was gone
from the self I was last night.

And then he came home tight.[2]

Such a simple definition!
How did I miss it?
Now I see
that all I needed
was a hand
to mould my mouth,
to scald my cheek,
was this concussion
by whose lights I find

---

1. Side of bacon.   2. Drunk.

my self possession,
where I grow complete.

He splits my lip with his fist,
shadows my eye with a blow,
knuckles my neck to its proper angle.
What a perfectionist!

His are a sculptor's hands:
they summon
form from the void,
they bring
me to myself again.
I am a new woman.

1980

Anorexic

Flesh is heretic.
My body is a witch.
I am burning it.

Yes I am torching
her curves and paps[1] and wiles.
They scorch in my self denials.

How she meshed my head
in the half-truths
of her fevers

till I renounced
milk and honey
and the taste of lunch.

I vomited
her hungers.
Now the bitch is burning.

I am starved and curveless.
I am skin and bone.
She has learned her lesson.

Thin as a rib
I turn in sleep.
My dreams probe

---

1. Nipples.

       a claustrophobia
       a sensuous enclosure.

       How warm it was and wide
25   once by a warm drum,
       once by the song of his breath
       and in his sleeping side.

       Only a little more,
       only a few more days
30   sinless, foodless,

       I will slip
       back into him again
       as if I had never been away.

       Caged so
35   I will grow
       angular and holy

       past pain,
       keeping his heart
       such company

40   as will make me forget
       in a small space
       the fall

       into forked dark,
       into python needs
45   heaving to hips and breasts
       and lips and heat
       and sweat and fat and greed.

                                                    1980

The Muse Mother

       My window pearls wet.
       The bare rowan tree
       berries rain.
       I can see
5   from where I stand
       a woman hunkering—
       her busy hand
       worrying a child's face,

       working a nappy[1] liner
10   over his sticky, loud
       round of a mouth.

---

1. Diaper.

  Her hand's a cloud
  across his face,
  making light and rain,
15 smiles and a frown,
  a smile again.

  She jockeys him to her hip,
  pockets the nappy liner,
  collars rain on her nape
20 and moves away,
  but my mind stays fixed:

  If I could only decline[2] her—
  lost noun
  out of context,
25 stray figure of speech—
  from this rainy street
  again to her roots,
  she might teach me
  a new language:

30 to be a sibyl[3]
  able to sing the past
  in pure syllables,
  limning hymns sung
  to belly[4] wheat or a woman,

35 able to speak at last
  my mother tongue.

1982

Degas's Laundresses[1]

  You rise, you dawn
  roll-sleeved Aphrodites,
  out of a camisole[2] brine,
  a linen pit of stitches
5 silking the fitted sheets
  away from you like waves.

  You seam dreams in the folds
  of wash from which freshes

---

2. Boland is punning on the grammatical sense of *decline*, as used of languages whose nouns have different case endings: to give the grammatical forms of a noun (or pronoun or adjective) in a fixed order.
3. In the ancient world, a prophetess.
4. To cause to swell out. "Limning": delineating, portraying.

1. The French artist Edgar Degas (1835–1917) is best known for his paintings of contemporary life on a wide variety of subjects from different classes; the painting alluded to here is *Two Laundresses* (1882).
2. Woman's short, sleeveless garment. Aphrodite, the Greek goddess of love, was born from the sea.

    the whiff and reach of fields
10 where it bleached and stiffened.
    Your chat's sabbatical:[3]
    brides, wedding outfits,

    a pleasure of leisured women
    are sweated into the folds,
15 the neat heaps of linen.
    Now the drag of the clasp.
    Your wrists basket your waist.
    You round to the square weight.

    Wait. There. Behind you.
20 A man. There behind you.
    Whatever you do don't turn.
    Why is he watching you?
    Whatever you do don't turn.
    Whatever you do don't turn.

25 See he takes his ease,
    staking his easel so,
    slowly sharpening charcoal,
    closing his eyes just so,
    slowly smiling as if
30 so slowly he is

    unbandaging his mind.
    Surely a good laundress
    would understand its twists,
35 its white turns, its blind designs:

    it's your winding sheet.[4]

1982

The Pomegranate

    The only legend I have ever loved is
    the story of a daughter lost in hell.
    And found and rescued there.
    Love and blackmail are the gist of it.
5 Ceres and Persephone the names.[1]
    And the best thing about the legend is

---

3. I.e., pertaining to rest or leisure.
4. The sheet in which a corpse is wrapped.
1. In Greek mythology, Persephone is the wife of Hades, lord of the underworld, who abducted her while she was gathering flowers. Her mother, Demeter (whom the Romans called Ceres), goddess of the harvest, searched the world for her; and when she learned what had happened, she begged Zeus—the chief of the Olympian gods, Hades' brother, and Persephone's father—to allow her return. He agreed, on the condition that no food from the underworld had passed her lips. But because she had eaten some pomegranate seeds, she divides her time between her mother and her husband (a division that also explains the seasons).

I can enter it anywhere. And have.
As a child in exile in
a city of fogs and strange consonants,
I read it first and at first I was
an exiled child in the crackling dusk of
the underworld, the stars blighted. Later
I walked out in a summer twilight
searching for my daughter at bed-time.
When she came running I was ready
to make any bargain to keep her.
I carried her back past whitebeams
and wasps and honey-scented buddleias.
But I was Ceres then and I knew
winter was in store for every leaf
on every tree on that road.
Was inescapable for each one we passed.
And for me.
            It is winter.
and the stars are hidden.
I climb the stairs and stand where I can see
my child asleep beside her teen magazines,
her can of Coke, her plate of uncut fruit.
The pomegranate! How did I forget it?
She could have come home and been safe
and ended the story and all
our heart-broken searching but she reached
out a hand and plucked a pomegranate.
She put out her hand and pulled down
the French sound for apple and
the noise of stone[2] and the proof
that even in the place of death,
at the heart of legend, in the midst
of rocks full of unshed tears
ready to be diamonds by the time
the story was told, a child can be
hungry. I could warn her. There is still a chance.
The rain is cold. The road is flint-coloured.
The suburb has cars and cable television.
The veiled stars are above ground.
It is another world. But what else
can a mother give her daughter but such
beautiful rifts in time?
If I defer the grief I will diminish the gift.
The legend will be hers as well as mine.
She will enter it. As I have.
She will wake up. She will hold
the papery flushed skin in her hand.
And to her lips. I will say nothing.

1994

---

2. I.e., *pomme* (apple) and granite.

Against Love Poetry

We were married in summer, thirty years ago. I have loved you deeply from that moment to this. I have loved other things as well. Among them the idea of women's freedom. Why do I put these words side by side? Because I am a woman. Because marriage is not freedom. Therefore, every word here is written against love poetry. Love poetry can do no justice to this. Here, instead, is a remembered story from a faraway history: A great king lost a war and was paraded in chains through the city of his enemy. They taunted him. They brought his wife and children to him—he showed no emotion. They brought his former courtiers—he showed no emotion. They brought his old servant—only then did he break down and weep. I did not find my womanhood in the servitudes of custom. But I saw my humanity look back at me there. It is to mark the contradictions of a daily love that I have written this. Against love poetry.

2001

ALICE WALKER
b. 1944

Alice Walker's father, Willie Lee Walker, farmed as a sharecropper in Georgia. Her mother, Minnie Grant Walker, "labored beside—not behind" her husband when she was not caring for her eight children. "As I remember it," Alice Walker—her youngest child—has reminisced, "we were really not allowed to be discouraged. Discouragement couldn't hold out against her faith." It is characteristic of Walker to be proud of her origins, for she believes that "the grace with which we embrace life, in spite of the pain, the sorrows, is always a measure of what has gone before." In her autobiographical essay "In Search of Our Mothers' Gardens," Walker explores the dynamics of the empowerment she gained through her own matrilineage.

Walker attended Spelman College in Atlanta, Georgia, and Sarah Lawrence in Bronxville, New York, before she began publishing poetry that was influenced by her involvement in the voter registration movement in Georgia and the welfare rights movement in Mississippi and New York. Her first volume of verse, *Once* (1968), appeared when she was teaching at Jackson State University in Mississippi. Sardonic and lyrical by turns, the poems recount not only her experiences in civil rights work but also her travels in Africa. Her next volume of poetry, *Revolutionary Petunias* (1973), describes the rural Georgia of her childhood. While both books were well received, Walker achieved national prominence through her work as the editor of an anthology of Zora Neale Hurston's writings (*I Love Myself When I Am Laughing*, 1979), as a contributing editor to the magazine *Ms.*, and even more important, through her own fiction.

From *The Third Life of Grange Copeland* (1970) to *In Love and Trouble* (1973), *Meridian* (1976), *The Color Purple* (1982), *The Temple of My Familiar* (1989), *Possessing the Secret of Joy* (1992), *By the Light of My Father's Smile* (1998), and *Now Is the Time to Open Your Heart* (2004), Walker analyzes the effect of racism on black men and celebrates the resiliency of black women. *Meridian*, which documents the struggles of several civil rights workers during the 1960s, is no less focused on black women's survival skills than *The Color Purple,* which won the National Book Award, the Pulitzer Prize, and the American Book Award. *The Color Purple* experiments with epistolary form to present the linguistic strategies of characters who struggle to articulate their feelings about divinity, sexuality, and identity from the complex perspective of African American experience. In this novel, as in her earlier stories, Walker extends the fictional techniques of her two favorite authors: Zora Neale Hurston and Jean Toomer. Not only does Walker portray the impact of racism on the relationships between black men and women and the importance of female networks of support, she also captures the humor and the pathos of her characters' erotic entanglements. Her first volume of essays, *In Search of Our Mothers' Gardens* (1983), offers insight into the achievements of such black women as the mystical writer Rebecca Cox Jackson and Coretta Scott King, the widow of the civil rights advocate Martin Luther King Jr., providing, too, a portrait of the artist herself as she reconciles her commitment to writing with the responsibilities of motherhood. Walker's second volume of essays, *Warrior Marks: Female Genital Mutilation and the Sexual Blinding of Women* (1993), was coauthored with Pratibha Parmar and extends her feminist concerns to some of the problems faced by women in African countries.

In Search of Our Mothers' Gardens

> I described her own nature and temperament. Told how they needed a larger life for their expression. . . . I pointed out that in lieu of proper channels, her emotions had overflowed into paths that dissipated them. I talked, beautifully I thought, about an art that would be born, an art that would open the way for women the likes of her. I asked her to hope, and build up an inner life against the coming of that day. . . . I sang, with a strange quiver in my voice, a promise song.
>
> —Jean Toomer, "Avey," *Cane*[1]
>
> The poet speaking to a prostitute who falls asleep while he's talking—

When the poet Jean Toomer walked through the South in the early twenties, he discovered a curious thing: black women whose spirituality was so intense, so deep, so *unconscious,* that they were themselves unaware of the richness they held. They stumbled blindly through their lives: creatures so abused and mutilated in body, so dimmed and confused by pain, that they considered themselves unworthy even of hope. In the selfless abstractions their bodies became to the men who used them, they became more than "sexual objects," more even than mere women: they became "Saints." Instead of being perceived as whole persons, their bodies became shrines: what was thought to be their minds became temples suitable for worship. These crazy Saints stared out at the world, wildly, like lunatics—or quietly, like suicides; and the "God" that was in their gaze was as mute as a great stone.

Who were these Saints? These crazy, loony, pitiful women?

Some of them, without a doubt, were our mothers and grandmothers.

In the still heat of the post-Reconstruction South,[2] this is how they seemed

---

1. The major work (1923) of Toomer (1894–1967), one of the writers of the Harlem Renaissance; the book is a mixture of narrative prose and lyric poetry.

2. I.e., the South after home rule (and thus white supremacy) was restored following the Confederacy's social and political "reconstruction" (1865–77).

to Jean Toomer: exquisite butterflies trapped in an evil honey, toiling away their lives in an era, a century, that did not acknowledge them, except as "the *mule* of the world."[3] They dreamed dreams that no one knew—not even themselves, in any coherent fashion—and saw visions no one could understand. They wandered or sat about the countryside crooning lullabies to ghosts, and drawing the mother of Christ in charcoal on courthouse walls.

They forced their minds to desert their bodies and their striving spirits sought to rise, like frail whirlwinds from the hard red clay. And when those frail whirlwinds fell, in scattered particles, upon the ground, no one mourned. Instead, men lit candles to celebrate the emptiness that remained, as people do who enter a beautiful but vacant space to resurrect a God.

Our mothers and grandmothers, some of them: moving to music not yet written. And they waited.

They waited for a day when the unknown thing that was in them would be made known; but guessed, somehow in their darkness, that on the day of their revelation they would be long dead. Therefore to Toomer they walked, and even ran, in slow motion. For they were going nowhere immediate, and the future was not yet within their grasp. And men took our mothers and grandmothers, "but got no pleasure from it." So complex was their passion and their calm.

To Toomer, they lay vacant and fallow as autumn fields, with harvest time never in sight: and he saw them enter loveless marriages, without joy; and become prostitutes, without resistance; and become mothers of children, without fulfillment.

For these grandmothers and mothers of ours were not Saints, but Artists; driven to a numb and bleeding madness by the springs of creativity in them for which there was no release. They were Creators, who lived lives of spiritual waste, because they were so rich in spirituality—which is the basis of Art—that the strain of enduring their unused and unwanted talent drove them insane. Throwing away this spirituality was their pathetic attempt to lighten the soul to a weight their work-worn, sexually abused bodies could bear.

What did it mean for a black woman to be an artist in our grandmothers' time? In our great-grandmothers' day? It is a question with an answer cruel enough to stop the blood.

Did you have a genius of a great-great-grandmother who died under some ignorant and depraved white overseer's lash? Or was she required to bake biscuits for a lazy backwater tramp, when she cried out in her soul to paint watercolors of sunsets, or the rain falling on the green and peaceful pasturelands? Or was her body broken and forced to bear children (who were more often than not sold away from her)—eight, ten, fifteen, twenty children—when her one joy was the thought of modeling heroic figures of rebellion, in stone or clay?

How was the creativity of the black woman kept alive, year after year and century after century, when for most of the years black people have been in America, it was a punishable crime for a black person to read or write? And the freedom to paint, to sculpt, to expand the mind with action did not exist. Consider, if you can bear to imagine it, what might have been the result if

---

3. An allusion to a statement in *Their Eyes Were Watching God* (1937), by Zora Neale Hurston (1891–1960; see above, p. 347): "De nigger woman is de mule uh de world."

singing, too, had been forbidden by law. Listen to the voices of Bessie Smith, Billie Holiday, Nina Simone, Roberta Flack, and Aretha Franklin,[4] among others, and imagine those voices muzzled for life. Then you may begin to comprehend the lives of our "crazy," "Sainted" mothers and grandmothers. The agony of the lives of women who might have been Poets, Novelists, Essayists, and Short-Story Writers (over a period of centuries), who died with their real gifts stifled within them.

And, if this were the end of the story, we would have cause to cry out in my paraphrase of Okot p'Bitek's great poem:[5]

> O, my clanswomen
> Let us all cry together!
> Come,
> Let us mourn the death of our mother,
> The death of a Queen
> The ash that was produced
> By a great fire!
> O, this homestead is utterly dead
> Close the gates
> With *lacari* thorns,
> For our mother
> The creator of the Stool is lost!
> And all the young women
> Have perished in the wilderness!

But this is not the end of the story, for all the young women—our mothers and grandmothers, *ourselves*—have not perished in the wilderness. And if we ask ourselves why, and search for and find the answer, we will know beyond all efforts to erase it from our minds, just exactly who, and of what, we black American women are.

One example, perhaps the most pathetic, most misunderstood one, can provide a backdrop for our mothers' work: Phillis Wheatley,[6] a slave in the 1700s.

Virginia Woolf,[7] in her book *A Room of One's Own*, wrote that in order for a woman to write fiction she must have two things, certainly: a room of her own (with key and lock) and enough money to support herself.

What then are we to make of Phillis Wheatley, a slave, who owned not even herself? This sickly, frail black girl who required a servant of her own at times—her health was so precarious—and who, had she been white, would have been easily considered the intellectual superior of all the women and most of the men in the society of her day.

Virginia Woolf wrote further, speaking of course not of our Phillis, that "any woman born with a great gift in the sixteenth century [insert "eighteenth century," insert "black woman," insert "born or made a slave"] would certainly have gone crazed, shot herself, or ended her days in some lonely cottage outside the village, half witch, half wizard [insert "Saint"], feared and

---

4. All female black American singers: Smith (1894 or 1898–1937), Holiday (1915–1959), Simone (1933–2003), Flack (b. 1939), and Franklin (b. 1942).
5. The African poet's (1931–1982) "Song of Lawino" (1966). Walker has changed the original's masculine nouns to feminine equivalents.
6. Highly educated black slave (1753–1784), who wrote formal, neoclassical poems; see Vol. 1, p. 358.
7. British novelist and essayist (1882–1941; see above, p. 212); *A Room* was published in 1929.

mocked at. For it needs little skill and psychology to be sure that a highly gifted girl who had tried to use her gift for poetry would have been so thwarted and hindered by contrary instincts [add "chains, guns, the lash, the ownership of one's body by someone else, submission to an alien religion"], that she must have lost her health and sanity to a certainty."

The key words, as they relate to Phillis, are "contrary instincts." For when we read the poetry of Phillis Wheatley—as when we read the novels of Nella Larsen[8] or the oddly false-sounding autobiography of that freest of all black women writers, Zora Hurston—evidence of "contrary instincts" is everywhere. Her loyalties were completely divided, as was, without question, her mind.

But how could this be otherwise? Captured at seven, a slave of wealthy, doting whites who instilled in her the "savagery" of the Africa they "rescued" her from . . . one wonders if she was even able to remember her homeland as she had known it, or as it really was.

Yes, because she did try to use her gift for poetry in a world that made her a slave, she was "so thwarted and hindered by . . . contrary instincts, that she . . . lost her health . . ." In the last years of her brief life, burdened not only with the need to express her gift but also with a penniless, friendless "freedom" and several small children for whom she was forced to do strenuous work to feed, she lost her health, certainly. Suffering from malnutrition and neglect and who knows what mental agonies, Phillis Wheatley died.

So torn by "contrary instincts" was black, kidnapped, enslaved Phillis that her description of "the Goddess"—as she poetically called the Liberty she did not have—is ironically, cruelly humorous. And, in fact, has held Phillis up to ridicule for more than a century. It is usually read prior to hanging Phillis's memory as that of a fool. She wrote:

> The Goddess comes, she moves divinely fair,
> Olive and laurel binds her *golden* hair.
> Wherever shines this native of the skies,
> Unnumber'd charms and recent graces rise.[9] [My italics]

It is obvious that Phillis, the slave, combed the "Goddess's" hair every morning; prior, perhaps, to bringing in the milk, or fixing her mistress's lunch. She took her imagery from the one thing she saw elevated above all others.

With the benefit of hindsight we ask, "How could she?"

But at last, Phillis, we understand. No more snickering when your stiff, struggling, ambivalent lines are forced on us. We know now that you were not an idiot or a traitor; only a sickly little black girl, snatched from your home and country and made a slave; a woman who still struggled to sing the song that was your gift, although in a land of barbarians who praised you for your bewildered tongue. It is not so much what you sang, as that you kept alive, in so many of our ancestors, *the notion of song*.

Black women are called, in the folklore that so aptly identifies one's status in society, "the *mule* of the world," because we have been handed the bur-

---

8. Black woman novelist of the Harlem Renaissance (1891–1964); see above, p. 360.

9. From "To His Excellency General Washington" (1775).

dens that everyone else—*everyone* else—refused to carry. We have also been called "Matriarchs," "Superwomen," and "Mean and Evil Bitches." Not to mention "Castraters" and "Sapphire's[1] Mama." When we have pleaded for understanding, our character has been distorted; when we have asked for simple caring, we have been handed empty inspirational appellations, then stuck in the farthest corner. When we have asked for love, we have been given children. In short, even our plainer gifts, our labors of fidelity and love, have been knocked down our throats. To be an artist and a black woman, even today, lowers our status in many respects, rather than raises it: and yet, artists we will be.

Therefore we must fearlessly pull out of ourselves and look at and identify with our lives the living creativity some of our great-grandmothers were not allowed to know. I stress *some* of them because it is well known that the majority of our great-grandmothers knew, even without "knowing" it, the reality of their spirituality, even if they didn't recognize it beyond what happened in the singing at church—and they never had any intention of giving it up.

How they did it—those millions of black women who were not Phillis Wheatley, or Lucy Terry or Frances Harper or Zora Hurston or Nella Larsen or Bessie Smith; or Elizabeth Catlett, or Katherine Dunham,[2] either—brings me to the title of this essay, "In Search of Our Mothers' Gardens," which is a personal account that is yet shared, in its theme and its meaning, by all of us. I found, while thinking about the far-reaching world of the creative black woman, that often the truest answer to a question that really matters can be found very close.

In the late 1920s my mother ran away from home to marry my father. Marriage, if not running away, was expected of seventeen-year-old girls. By the time she was twenty, she had two children and was pregnant with a third. Five children later, I was born. And this is how I came to know my mother: she seemed a large, soft, loving-eyed woman who was rarely impatient in our home. Her quick, violent temper was on view only a few times a year, when she battled with the white landlord who had the misfortune to suggest to her that her children did not need to go to school.

She made all the clothes we wore, even my brothers' overalls. She made all the towels and sheets we used. She spent the summers canning vegetables and fruits. She spent the winter evenings making quilts enough to cover all our beds.

During the "working" day, she labored beside—not behind—my father in the fields. Her day began before sunup, and did not end until late at night. There was never a moment for her to sit down, undisturbed, to unravel her own private thoughts; never a time free from interruption—by work or the noisy inquiries of her many children. And yet, it is to my mother—and all our mothers who were not famous—that I went in search of the secret of what has fed that muzzled and often mutilated, but vibrant, creative spirit

---

1. Wife of "the Kingfish" in *Amos and Andy*, a popular early radio and television show.
2. Black American dancer and choreographer (1909–2006). Terry (1730–1821), black poet and fictionist. Frances E. W. Harper (1825–1911), black woman poet; see Vol. 1, p. 1025. Catlett (b. 1915?), black educator and sculptor.

that the black woman has inherited, and that pops out in wild and unlikely places to this day.

But when, you will ask, did my overworked mother have time to know or care about feeding the creative spirit?

The answer is so simple that many of us have spent years discovering it. We have constantly looked high, when we should have looked high—and low.

For example: in the Smithsonian Institution in Washington, D.C., there hangs a quilt unlike any other in the world. In fanciful, inspired, and yet simple and identifiable figures, it portrays the story of the Crucifixion. It is considered rare, beyond price. Though it follows no known pattern of quilt-making, and though it is made of bits and pieces of worthless rags, it is obviously the work of a person of powerful imagination and deep spiritual feeling. Below this quilt I saw a note that says it was made by "an anonymous Black woman in Alabama, a hundred years ago."

If we could locate this "anonymous" black woman from Alabama, she would turn out to be one of our grandmothers—an artist who left her mark in the only materials she could afford, and in the only medium her position in society allowed her to use.

As Virginia Woolf wrote further, in *A Room of One's Own*:

> Yet genius of a sort must have existed among women as it must have existed among the working class. [Change this to "slaves" and "the wives and daughters of sharecroppers."] Now and again an Emily Brontë or a Robert Burns [change this to "a Zora Hurston or a Richard Wright"[3]] blazes out and proves its presence. But certainly it never got itself on to paper. When, however, one reads of a witch being ducked, of a woman possessed by devils [or "Sainthood"], of a wise woman selling herbs [our root workers], or even a very remarkable man who had a mother, then I think we are on the track of a lost novelist, a suppressed poet, of some mute and inglorious Jane Austen.[4] . . . Indeed, I would venture to guess that Anon, who wrote so many poems without signing them, was often a woman. . . .

And so our mothers and grandmothers have, more often than not anonymously, handed on the creative spark, the seed of the flower they themselves never hoped to see: or like a sealed letter they could not plainly read.

And so it is, certainly, with my own mother. Unlike "Ma" Rainey's[5] songs, which retained their creator's name even while blasting forth from Bessie Smith's mouth, no song or poem will bear my mother's name. Yet so many of the stories that I write, that we all write, are my mother's stories. Only recently did I fully realize this: that through years of listening to my mother's stories of her life, I have absorbed not only the stories themselves, but something of the manner in which she spoke, something of the urgency that involves the knowledge that her stories—like her life—must be recorded. It is probably for this reason that so much of what I have written is about characters whose counterparts in real life are so much older than I am.

---

3. Black American novelist (1908–1960). Brontë (1818–1848), English novelist and poet; see Vol. 1, p. 959 Burns (1759–1796), Scottish poet.
4. English novelist (1775–1817); see Vol. 1, p. 459.
5. Gertrude Pridgett Rainey (1886–1939), black blues singer and songwriter.

But the telling of these stories, which came from my mother's lips as naturally as breathing, was not the only way my mother showed herself as an artist. For stories, too, were subject to being distracted, to dying without conclusion. Dinners must be started, and cotton must be gathered before the big rains. The artist that was and is my mother showed itself to me only after many years. This is what I finally noticed:

Like Mem, a character in *The Third Life of Grange Copeland*,[6] my mother adorned with flowers whatever shabby house we were forced to live in. And not just your typical straggly country stand of zinnias, either. She planted ambitious gardens—and still does—with over fifty different varieties of plants that bloom profusely from early March until late November. Before she left home for the fields, she watered her flowers, chopped up the grass, and laid out new beds. When she returned from the fields she might divide clumps of bulbs, dig a cold pit, uproot and replant roses, or prune branches from her taller bushes or trees—until night came and it was too dark to see.

Whatever she planted grew as if by magic, and her fame as a grower of flowers spread over three counties. Because of her creativity with her flowers, even my memories of poverty are seen through a screen of blooms—sunflowers, petunias, roses, dahlias, forsythia, spirea, delphiniums, verbena . . . and on and on.

And I remember people coming to my mother's yard to be given cuttings from her flowers; I hear again the praise showered on her because whatever rocky soil she landed on, she turned into a garden. A garden so brilliant with colors, so original in its design, so magnificent with life and creativity, that to this day people drive by our house in Georgia—perfect strangers and imperfect strangers—and ask to stand or walk among my mother's art.

I notice that it is only when my mother is working in her flowers that she is radiant, almost to the point of being invisible—except as Creator: hand and eye. She is involved in work her soul must have. Ordering the universe in the image of her personal conception of Beauty.

Her face, as she prepared the Art that is her gift, is a legacy of respect she leaves to me, for all that illuminates and cherishes life. She has handed down respect for the possibilities—and the will to grasp them.

For her, so hindered and intruded upon in so many ways, being an artist has still been a daily part of her life. This ability to hold on, even in very simple ways, is work black women have done for a very long time.

This poem is not enough, but it is something, for the woman who literally covered the holes in our walls with sunflowers:

>They were women then
>My mama's generation
>Husky of voice—Stout of
>Step
>With fists as well as
>Hands
>How they battered down
>Doors
>And ironed
>Starched white

---

6. Walker's first novel (1970).

			Shirts
			How they led
			Armies
			Headragged Generals
			Across mined
			Fields
			Booby-trapped
			Kitchens
			To discover books
			Desks
			A place for us
			How they knew what we
			Must know
			Without knowing a page
			Of it
			Themselves.

 Guided by my heritage of a love of beauty and a respect for strength—in search of my mother's garden, I found my own.
 And perhaps in Africa over two hundred years ago, there was just such a mother; perhaps she painted vivid and daring decorations in oranges and yellows and greens on the walls of her hut; perhaps she sang—in a voice like Roberta Flack's—*sweetly* over the compounds of her village; perhaps she wove the most stunning mats or told the most ingenious stories of all the village storytellers. Perhaps she was herself a poet—though only her daughter's name is signed to the poems that we know.
 Perhaps Phillis Wheatley's mother was also an artist.
 Perhaps in more than Phillis Wheatley's biological life is her mother's signature made clear.

1974, 1983

LYNN FREED
b. 1945

"I can't remember ever wanting to write. I just wrote," the novelist, short story writer, and essayist Lynn Freed once told an interviewer, adding with characteristic frankness that "At first, as a child, and for a number of years into adolescence, I seemed to write partly to show off." A prolific author, Freed early displayed a talent that was in fact well worth displaying. Born and raised in Durban, South Africa, she came from a theater family in which both parents were professional performers and savvy critics. "I'd write a story or a play—I wrote a lot of plays, mostly awful—and I'd run downstairs to read it to my mother," Freed explained to the same interviewer, noting that her mother "was a completely honest critic: harsh and fair. If she came forth with praise, I knew that what I had written wasn't fake."
 In the 1960s, Freed came from South Africa to New York, where she did graduate work in English, earning an M.A. and a Ph.D. from Columbia University. Later, she moved to San Francisco, where she wrote her first novel, *Heart Change* (1982). It

was followed by four others, including most recently *House of Women* (2002), along with a collection of short stories, *The Curse of the Appropriate Man* (2004), and a collection of essays, *Reading, Writing, and Leaving Home* (2005). Her work has won her numerous accolades, including the Bay Area Book Reviewers Award, the Katherine Anne Porter Award from the American Academy of Arts and Letters, and fellowships from the National Endowment of the Arts and the Guggenheim Foundation. A professor of English at the University of California, Davis, she lives in Sonoma, California.

Set in Freed's native South Africa, "Under the House" explores the conflicted experience of a privileged white South African childhood in the time of apartheid with unflinching candor and a dramatic skill worthy of this writer's early education by a mother who was completely "harsh and fair" in her appraisals of her daughter's work.

Under the House

Twice a year, the sharpener arrived at the top gate, whistled for them to lock up the dogs, and then made his way around the back of the house to the kitchen lawn. Usually, the girl was there first. She squatted like him to see the files and stones laid out in a silent circle, the carving knife taken up, the flash of the blade as he curved his wrist left and right, never missing. And then the gleaming thing laid down on the tray, where she longed to touch it.

If the nanny saw the girl out there, she called her in. The Sharpener was a wild man, she said, he drank cheap brandy and lived under a piece of tin. He could be a Coloured, said her mother, or just dark from working in the sun, and from lawnmower grease, and from not washing properly.

But whenever the girl heard his whistle, she ran out anyway. He never looked up at her. He wasn't the sort of man to notice a child growing year by year, or to care. He seemed to consider only the knives, always choosing the carver first, holding it up to the light, running its edge along the pad of his thumb. When all the knives were sharpened and he walked around to the front verandah, she followed him there. She waited next to his satchel while he opened the little door and climbed down under the house to fetch the lawnmower.

And then one day she asked, "What do you do under the house?"

And he stopped on the top step and turned to look at her with his dirty green eyes. He didn't smile, he never smiled. But he tossed his head for her to follow him, and so she did, down into the cool, dim light.

She knew the place well. It was deep and wide, running the length of the verandah, and high enough to stand up in. Bicycles were kept down there, and the old doll's pram, pushed now behind the garden rakes and hoes and clippers. There were sacks of seed, and bulbs, manure, and cans of oil. Through an opening in the wall, deeper in, were rooms and rooms of raw red earth, with walls and passages between them, like the house above. In the middle was a place no light could reach. She had crawled back there once, and crouched, and listened to rats scraping and darting, footsteps above, the dogs off somewhere. It smelled sour back there, and damp, and wonderful.

The Sharpener stood just out of a beam of light that came in through one of the vents. He tossed his head at her again and moved deeper into the shadow.

She knew rude things. She had done rude things with cousins and friends. There was a frenzy to them—the giggling and hushing and urging on. But now she stood solemn and still as the Sharpener came to crouch before her. He lifted her skirt and found her bloomers, pulled them down to her knees.

"We can lie down," he said.

But she shook her head, and he stood up again. He unbuttoned his trousers, pulled his thing through the slit and held it out on the palm of his hand. She knew he was offering it to her, asking for something too, his eyes never leaving her face. But she clasped her hands behind her back and looked down at the floor.

He pushed himself closer, pushed his thing up under her skirt, against her stomach, breathing his smell all over her, sweat and liquor and dirt. He turned her around and crouched behind her to push it between her legs. When she lifted her skirt, she saw it sticking through as if it were her own, and she giggled.

There was a man who sat at the bus stop outside school sometimes. He sat there smiling, teeth missing everywhere. Often his trousers were open, and there was a pool of his mess under the bench. The headmistress warned them in prayers about men like that, never to talk to them, never to take lifts from them either. Some had cars without door handles on the inside, she said, you could never get out.

The Sharpener laughed in a whisper behind her. He turned her to face him again, loosened her gym girdle and pulled the whole uniform over her head, the blouse too. Then she stamped off the bloomers herself.

"Big lady," he said. He touched the swelling of her breasts, the hair starting between her legs, ran a finger down the middle of it, under and in.

Once she had seen a boy at the edge of the hockey-field. He was holding his thing while he watched them practise. "Ugh!" she had said with the others. But that boy had become a habit of longing for her, a habit of dreaming, too.

She watched the Sharpener undo his belt and let his trousers fall. She looked at his skinny thing between his skinny legs. "Big lady," he said, pulling her to one of the sacks and bending her over it. "Big lady, big lady," he whispered, fiddling at her with his fingers, stroking, separating, urging himself into her a little at a time so that she gasped, not with pain but with the fear of pain. And then, after the pain, with the beginning, with the surprise of pleasure, a wild and rude sort of pleasure, wilder and ruder than anything, anything. Even the tea tray rattling out onto the verandah couldn't stop it, even the nanny calling her name. He was grunting and heaving over her now. She wanted to tell him they wouldn't come down here, they wouldn't. But he jerked himself free anyway, he clutched and cried against her like a baby, crybaby bunting.[1]

She wanted to cry, too. She wanted him to say "Big lady" again, and go on, but he wouldn't. He got up and went for his trousers, pushed his skinny legs into them and buckled his belt.

The back of her leg was damp and cold. She felt it with her hand, it was slimy with his mess. "Ugh!" she said, wiping it off on the sack.

But he didn't look up. He was over at the lawnmower now, pulling it free. He hawked and spat into the darkness. She wanted to spit, too. She wanted

---

1. An allusion to the nursery rhyme that begins "Cry, Baby Bunting, / Daddy's gone a-hunting."

to tell on him, to tell anyone she liked about the dirty stinking Coloured who put his thing into her without asking.

And then she heard the dogs. She could have heard them before if she had listened—the barking and the shouting and the running overhead—but she hadn't. And now there they were, roaring down into the darkness, making straight for him.

"Missie!" he screamed. "Missie!"

She grabbed a rake, thrashed and thrashed at the dogs, although she knew it would do no good. They were crazed by Coloureds, even someone who just seemed Coloured. And they hated the Sharpener most of all. One had him by the calf, the other snarled and jumped and snapped at his shoulder.

Her mother and the cook came out onto the verandah, shouting for the garden boy to bring the hose, the dogs had got out. The Sharpener dropped to his knees, bloodied and torn, covered his head with his arms.

And then the garden boy arrived with the hose, shouting too, pointing it into the darkness until he could see the dogs. But when he saw the girl standing there, he lowered his head and dropped the hose. He ran out into the garden, screaming for the nanny.

The girl was wet when they found her, her clothes soaking on the floor. And the Sharpener had given up screaming. He lay curled around himself, quite still. And so the dogs had given up too. They stood back, panting.

She tried to save him without answering all their questions. But she couldn't. They decided he was Coloured after all, and they locked him up for good. They'd have locked him up for good even if he weren't Coloured, her mother said. And the girl didn't argue.

But now, lying in bed with her own man or another, she's always down there again, under the house, with the Sharpener. Over the years, he has only got wilder. Sometimes, he brings a friend and they take turns with her. They drink brandy from a bottle and laugh and make one of the dogs go first. And then the Sharpener pulls the dog away. He has to have her for himself. He cannot wait.

1998, 2004

OCTAVIA BUTLER
1947–2006

In an afterword to the story "Bloodchild," which won both the Hugo and the Nebula awards, Octavia Butler explained the three subjects that fascinated her in the composing process. First, she wished to create a story "of a man becoming pregnant as an act of love"; second, because she was just about to travel to the Peruvian Amazon, she had became obsessed with the botfly, which "lays its eggs in wounds left by the bites of other insects," a fact that frightened her with "the idea of a maggot living and growing under my skin, eating my flesh as it grew"; and third, she was interested in a narrative "about paying the rent"—specifically, how the rent would be paid by "an isolated colony of human beings on an inhabited, extrasolar world." Eccentric as these topics may seem, they remain pertinent to the reproductive and medical issues as well as to the politics of species and nations that characterize Butler's oeuvre, which in 1995 earned her a "genius" fellowship from the MacArthur Foundation.

One of the first African American women to gain acclaim in science fiction circles, Butler grew up in Pasadena, California, where her mother worked as a maid to support her only child. After attending Pasadena City College and California State at Los Angeles as well as the Writers Guild of America Clarion Science Fiction Writer's Workshop and other workshops, she was acclaimed in the late 1970s for her Patternist novels, a series that revolves around a group of mentally superior beings descended from a Nubian man who has lived four thousand years. *Kindred* (1979) widened her reputation, especially among readers interested in the fictional recyclings of slave narratives, for the contemporary protagonist in this time-travel book finds herself transported back to the pre–Civil War plantation of her ancestors. With titles characteristically evocative of the cultural anthropology that animates so much of her thinking, the Xenogenesis trilogy—*Dawn* (1987), *Adulthood Rites* (1988), and *Imago* (1989)—deals with nuclear war and gene swapping, with the relationship between human and alien societies; similar concerns inform her Earthseed series (begun in 1993). According to many feminist and African American scholars, Octavia Butler transformed science fiction conventions by grappling with the racial and ecological problems that today confront all human beings.

Bloodchild

My last night of childhood began with a visit home. T'Gatoi's sister had given us two sterile eggs. T'Gatoi gave one to my mother, brother, and sisters. She insisted that I eat the other one alone. It didn't matter. There was still enough to leave everyone feeling good. Almost everyone. My mother wouldn't take any. She sat, watching everyone drifting and dreaming without her. Most of the time she watched me.

I lay against T'Gatoi's long, velvet underside, sipping from my egg now and then, wondering why my mother denied herself such a harmless pleasure. Less of her hair would be gray if she indulged now and then. The eggs prolonged life, prolonged vigor. My father, who had never refused one in his life, had lived more than twice as long as he should have. And toward the end of his life, when he should have been slowing down, he had married my mother and fathered four children.

But my mother seemed content to age before she had to. I saw her turn away as several of T'Gatoi's limbs secured me closer. T'Gatoi liked our body heat and took advantage of it whenever she could. When I was little and at home more, my mother used to try to tell me how to behave with T'Gatoi—how to be respectful and always obedient because T'Gatoi was the Tlic government official in charge of the Preserve, and thus the most important of her kind to deal directly with Terrans. It was an honor, my mother said, that such a person had chosen to come into the family. My mother was at her most formal and severe when she was lying.

I had no idea why she was lying, or even what she was lying about. It *was* an honor to have T'Gatoi in the family, but it was hardly a novelty. T'Gatoi and my mother had been friends all my mother's life, and T'Gatoi was not interested in being honored in the house she considered her second home.

She simply came in, climbed onto one of her special couches, and called me over to keep her warm. It was impossible to be formal with her while lying against her and hearing her complain as usual that I was too skinny.

"You're better," she said this time, probing me with six or seven of her limbs. "You're gaining weight finally. Thinness is dangerous." The probing changed subtly, became a series of caresses.

"He's still too thin," my mother said sharply.

T'Gatoi lifted her head and perhaps a meter of her body off the couch as though she were sitting up. She looked at my mother, and my mother, her face lined and old looking, turned away.

"Lien, I would like you to have what's left of Gan's egg."

"The eggs are for the children," my mother said.

"They are for the family. Please take it."

Unwillingly obedient, my mother took it from me and put it to her mouth. There were only a few drops left in the now-shrunken, elastic shell, but she squeezed them out, swallowed them, and after a few moments some of the lines of tension began to smooth from her face.

"It's good," she whispered. "Sometimes I forget how good it is."

"You should take more," T'Gatoi said. "Why are you in such a hurry to be old?"

My mother said nothing.

"I like being able to come here," T'Gatoi said. "This place is a refuge because of you, yet you won't take care of yourself."

T'Gatoi was hounded on the outside. Her people wanted more of us made available. Only she and her political faction stood between us and the hordes who did not understand why there was a Preserve—why any Terran could not be courted, paid, drafted, in some way made available to them. Or they did understand, but in their desperation, they did not care. She parceled us out to the desperate and sold us to the rich and powerful for their political support. Thus, we were necessities, status symbols, and an independent people. She oversaw the joining of families, putting an end to the final remnants of the earlier system of breaking up Terran families to suit impatient Tlic. I had lived outside with her. I had seen the desperate eagerness in the way some people looked at me. It was a little frightening to know that only she stood between us and that desperation that could so easily swallow us. My mother would look at her sometimes and say to me, "Take care of her." And I would remember that she too had been outside, had seen.

Now T'Gatoi used four of her limbs to push me away from her onto the floor. "Go on, Gan," she said. "Sit down there with your sisters and enjoy not being sober. You had most of the egg. Lien, come warm me."

My mother hesitated for no reason that I could see. One of my earliest memories is of my mother stretched alongside T'Gatoi, talking about things I could not understand, picking me up from the floor and laughing as she sat me on one of T'Gatoi's segments. She ate her share of eggs then. I wondered when she had stopped, and why.

She lay down now against T'Gatoi, and the whole left row of T'Gatoi's limbs closed around her, holding her loosely, but securely. I had always found it comfortable to lie that way, but except for my older sister, no one else in the family liked it. They said it made them feel caged.

T'Gatoi meant to cage my mother. Once she had, she moved her tail slightly, then spoke. "Not enough egg, Lien. You should have taken it when it was passed to you. You need it badly now."

T'Gatoi's tail moved once more, its whip motion so swift I wouldn't have seen it if I hadn't been watching for it. Her sting drew only a single drop of blood from my mother's bare leg.

My mother cried out—probably in surprise. Being stung doesn't hurt. Then she sighed and I could see her body relax. She moved languidly into a more comfortable position within the cage of T'Gatoi's limbs. "Why did you do that?" she asked, sounding half asleep.

"I could not watch you sitting and suffering any longer."

My mother managed to move her shoulders in a small shrug. "Tomorrow," she said.

"Yes. Tomorrow you will resume your suffering—if you must. But just now, just for now, lie here and warm me and let me ease your way a little."

"He's still mine, you know," my mother said suddenly.

"Nothing can buy him from me." Sober, she would not have permitted herself to refer to such things.

"Nothing," T'Gatoi agreed, humoring her.

"Did you think I would sell him for eggs? For long life? My son?"

"Not for anything," T'Gatoi said, stroking my mother's shoulders, toying with her long, graying hair.

I would like to have touched my mother, shared that moment with her. She would take my hand if I touched her now. Freed by the egg and the sting, she would smile and perhaps say things long held in. But tomorrow, she would remember all this as a humiliation. I did not want to be part of a remembered humiliation. Best just be still and know she loved me under all the duty and pride and pain.

"Xuan Hoa, take off her shoes," T'Gatoi said. "In a little while I'll sting her again and she can sleep."

My older sister obeyed, swaying drunkenly as she stood up. When she had finished, she sat down beside me and took my hand. We had always been a unit, she and I.

My mother put the back of her head against T'Gatoi's underside and tried from that impossible angle to look up into the broad, round face. "You're going to sting me again?"

"Yes, Lien."

"I'll sleep until tomorrow noon."

"Good. You need it. When did you sleep last?"

My mother made a wordless sound of annoyance. "I should have stepped on you when you were small enough," she muttered.

It was an old joke between them. They had grown up together, sort of, though T'Gatoi had not, in my mother's life-time, been small enough for any Terran to step on. She was nearly three times my mother's present age, yet would still be young when my mother died of age. But T'Gatoi and my mother had met as T'Gatoi was coming into a period of rapid development—a kind of Tlic adolescence. My mother was only a child, but for a while they developed at the same rate and had no better friends than each other.

T'Gatoi had even introduced my mother to the man who became my father. My parents, pleased with each other in spite of their different ages, married as T'Gatoi was going into her family's business—politics. She and my mother saw each other less. But sometime before my older sister was born, my mother promised T'Gatoi one of her children. She would have to give one of us to someone, and she preferred T'Gatoi to some stranger.

Years passed. T'Gatoi traveled and increased her influence. The Preserve was hers by the time she came back to my mother to collect what she probably saw as her just reward for her hard work. My older sister took an instant liking to her and wanted to be chosen, but my mother was just coming to term with me and T'Gatoi liked the idea of choosing an infant and watching and taking part in all the phases of development. I'm told I was first caged within T'Gatoi's many limbs only three minutes after my birth. A few days later, I was given my first taste of egg. I tell Terrans that when they ask whether I was ever afraid of her. And I tell it to Tlic when T'Gatoi suggests a young Terran child for them and they, anxious and ignorant, demand an adolescent. Even my brother who had somehow grown up to fear and distrust the Tlic could probably have gone smoothly into one of their families if he had been adopted early enough. Sometimes, I think for his sake he should have been. I looked at him, stretched out on the floor across the room, his eyes open, but glazed as he dreamed his egg dream. No matter what he felt toward the Tlic, he always demanded his share of egg.

"Lien, can you stand up?" T'Gatoi asked suddenly.

"Stand?" my mother said. "I thought I was going to sleep."

"Later. Something sounds wrong outside." The cage was abruptly gone.

"What?"

"Up, Lien!"

My mother recognized her tone and got up just in time to avoid being dumped on the floor. T'Gatoi whipped her three meters of body off her couch, toward the door, and out at full speed. She had bones—ribs, a long spine, a skull, four sets of limb bones per segment. But when she moved that way, twisting, hurling herself into controlled falls, landing running, she seemed not only boneless, but aquatic—something swimming through the air as though it were water. I loved watching her move.

I left my sister and started to follow her out the door, though I wasn't very steady on my own feet. It would have been better to sit and dream, better yet to find a girl and share a waking dream with her. Back when the Tlic saw us as not much more than convenient, big, warm-blooded animals, they would pen several of us together, male and female, and feed us only eggs. That way they could be sure of getting another generation of us no matter how we tried to hold out. We were lucky that didn't go on long. A few generations of it and we would have *been* little more than convenient, big animals.

"Hold the door open, Gan," T'Gatoi said. "And tell the family to stay back."

"What is it?" I asked.

"N'Tlic."

I shrank back against the door. "Here? Alone?"

"He was trying to reach a call box, I suppose." She carried the man past me, unconscious, folded like a coat over some of her limbs. He looked young—my brother's age perhaps—and he was thinner than he should have been. What T'Gatoi would have called dangerously thin.

"Gan, go to the call box," she said. She put the man on the floor and began stripping off his clothing.

I did not move.

After a moment, she looked up at me, her sudden stillness a sign of deep impatience.

"Send Qui," I told her. "I'll stay here. Maybe I can help."

She let her limbs begin to move again, lifting the man and pulling his shirt over his head. "You don't want to see this," she said. "It will be hard. I can't help this man the way his Tlic could."

"I know. But send Qui. He won't want to be of any help here. I'm at least willing to try."

She looked at my brother—older, bigger, stronger, certainly more able to help her here. He was sitting up now, braced against the wall, staring at the man on the floor with undisguised fear and revulsion. Even she could see that he would be useless.

"Qui, go!" she said.

He didn't argue. He stood up, swayed briefly, then steadied, frightened sober.

"This man's name is Bram Lomas," she told him, reading from the man's armband. I fingered my own armband in sympathy. "He needs T'Khotgif Teh. Do you hear?"

"Bram Lomas, T'Khotgif Teh," my brother said. "I'm going." He edged around Lomas and ran out the door.

Lomas began to regain consciousness. He only moaned at first and clutched spasmodically at a pair of T'Gatoi's limbs. My younger sister, finally awake from her egg dream, came close to look at him, until my mother pulled her back.

T'Gatoi removed the man's shoes, then his pants, all the while leaving him two of her limbs to grip. Except for the final few, all her limbs were equally dexterous. "I want no argument from you this time, Gan," she said.

I straightened. "What shall I do?"

"Go out and slaughter an animal that is at least half your size."

"Slaughter? But I've never—"

She knocked me across the room. Her tail was an efficient weapon whether she exposed the sting or not.

I got up, feeling stupid for having ignored her warning, and went into the kitchen. Maybe I could kill something with a knife or an ax. My mother raised a few Terran animals for the table and several thousand local ones for their fur. T'Gatoi would probably prefer something local. An achti, perhaps. Some of those were the right size, though they had about three times as many teeth as I did and a real love of using them. My mother, Hoa, and Qui could kill them with knives. I had never killed one at all, had never slaughtered any animal. I had spent most of my time with T'Gatoi while my brother and sisters were learning the family business. T'Gatoi had been right. I should have been the one to go to the call box. At least I could do that.

I went to the corner cabinet where my mother kept her large house and garden tools. At the back of the cabinet there was a pipe that carried off waste water from the kitchen—except that it didn't anymore. My father had rerouted the waste water below before I was born. Now the pipe could be turned so that one half slid around the other and a rifle could be stored inside. This wasn't our only gun, but it was our most easily accessible one. I would have to use it to shoot one of the biggest of the achti. Then T'Gatoi would probably confiscate it. Firearms were illegal in the Preserve. There had been incidents right after the Preserve was established—Terrans shooting Tlic, shooting N'Tlic. This was before the joining of families began, before everyone had a personal stake in keeping the peace. No one had shot a Tlic in my lifetime or my mother's, but the law still stood—for our protection, we were told. There were stories of whole Terran families wiped out in reprisal back during the assassinations.

I went out to the cages and shot the biggest achti I could find. It was a handsome breeding male, and my mother would not be pleased to see me bring it in. But it was the right size, and I was in a hurry.

I put the achti's long, warm body over my shoulder—glad that some of the weight I'd gained was muscle—and took it to the kitchen. There, I put the gun back in its hiding place. If T'Gatoi noticed the achti's wounds and demanded the gun, I would give it to her. Otherwise, let it stay where my father wanted it.

I turned to take the achti to her, then hesitated. For several seconds, I stood in front of the closed door wondering why I was suddenly afraid. I knew what was going to happen. I hadn't seen it before but T'Gatoi had shown me diagrams and drawings. She had made sure I knew the truth as soon as I was old enough to understand it.

Yet I did not want to go into that room. I wasted a little time choosing a knife from the carved, wooden box in which my mother kept them. T'Gatoi might want one, I told myself, for the tough, heavily furred hide of the achti.

"Gan!" T'Gatoi called, her voice harsh with urgency.

I swallowed. I had not imagined a single moving of the feet could be so difficult. I realized I was trembling and that shamed me. Shame impelled me through the door.

I put the achti down near T'Gatoi and saw that Lomas was unconscious again. She, Lomas, and I were alone in the room—my mother and sisters probably sent out so they would not have to watch. I envied them.

But my mother came back into the room as T'Gatoi seized the achti. Ignoring the knife I offered her, she extended claws from several of her limbs and slit the achti from throat to anus. She looked at me, her yellow eyes intent. "Hold this man's shoulders, Gan."

I stared at Lomas in panic, realizing that I did not want to touch him, let alone hold him. This would not be like shooting an animal. Not as quick, not as merciful, and, I hoped, not as final, but there was nothing I wanted less than to be part of it.

My mother came forward. "Gan, you hold his right side," she said. "I'll hold his left." And if he came to, he would throw her off without realizing he had done it. She was a tiny woman. She often wondered aloud how she had produced, as she said, such "huge" children.

"Never mind," I told her, taking the man's shoulders. "I'll do it." She hovered nearby.

"Don't worry," I said. "I won't shame you. You don't have to stay and watch."

She looked at me uncertainly, then touched my face in a rare caress. Finally, she went back to her bedroom.

T'Gatoi lowered her head in relief. "Thank you, Gan," she said with courtesy more Terran than Tlic. "That one . . . she is always finding new ways for me to make her suffer."

Lomas began to groan and make choked sounds. I had hoped he would stay unconscious. T'Gatoi put her face near his so that he focused on her.

"I've stung you as much as I dare for now," she told him. "When this is over, I'll sting you to sleep and you won't hurt anymore."

"Please," the man begged. "Wait . . ."

"There's no more time, Bram. I'll sting you as soon as it's over. When T'Khotgif arrives she'll give you eggs to help you heal. It will be over soon."

"T'Khotgif!" the man shouted, straining against my hands.

"Soon, Bram." T'Gatoi glanced at me, then placed a claw against his abdomen slightly to the right of the middle, just below the left rib. There was movement on the right side—tiny, seemingly random pulsations moving his brown flesh, creating a concavity here, a convexity there, over and over until I could see the rhythm of it and knew where the next pulse would be.

Lomas's entire body stiffened under T'Gatoi's claw, though she merely rested it against him as she wound the rear section of her body around his legs. He might break my grip, but he would not break hers. He wept helplessly as she used his pants to tie his hands, then pushed his hands above his head so that I could kneel on the cloth between them and pin them in place. She rolled up his shirt and gave it to him to bite down on.

And she opened him.

His body convulsed with the first cut. He almost tore himself away from me. The sound he made . . . I had never heard such sounds come from anything human. T'Gatoi seemed to pay no attention as she lengthened and deepened the cut, now and then pausing to lick away blood. His blood vessels contracted, reacting to the chemistry of her saliva, and the bleeding slowed.

I felt as though I were helping her torture him, helping her consume him. I knew I would vomit soon, didn't know why I hadn't already. I couldn't possibly last until she was finished.

She found the first grub. It was fat and deep red with his blood—both inside and out. It had already eaten its own egg case but apparently had not yet begun to eat its host. At this stage, it would eat any flesh except its mother's. Let alone, it would have gone on excreting the poisons that had both sickened and alerted Lomas. Eventually it would have begun to eat. By the time it ate its way out of Lomas's flesh, Lomas would be dead or dying—and unable to take revenge on the thing that was killing him. There was always a grace period between the time the host sickened and the time the grubs began to eat him.

T'Gatoi picked up the writhing grub carefully and looked at it, somehow ignoring the terrible groans of the man.

Abruptly, the man lost consciousness.

"Good," T'Gatoi looked down at him. "I wish you Terrans could do that at will." She felt nothing. And the thing she held . . .

It was limbless and boneless at this stage, perhaps fifteen centimeters long and two thick, blind and slimy with blood. It was like a large worm. T'Gatoi put it into the belly of the achti, and it began at once to burrow. It would stay there and eat as long as there was anything to eat.

Probing through Lomas's flesh, she found two more, one of them smaller and more vigorous. "A male!" she said happily. He would be dead before I would. He would be through his metamorphosis and screwing everything that would hold still before his sisters even had limbs. He was the only one to make a serious effort to bite T'Gatoi as she placed him in the achti.

Paler worms oozed to visibility in Lomas's flesh. I closed my eyes. It was worse than finding something dead, rotting, and filled with tiny animal grubs. And it was far worse than any drawing or diagram.

"Ah, there are more," T'Gatoi said, plucking out two long, thick grubs. You may have to kill another animal, Gan. Everything lives inside you Terrans."

I had been told all my life that this was a good and necessary thing Tlic and Terran did together—a kind of birth. I had believed it until now. I knew birth was painful and bloody, no matter what. But this was something else, something worse. And I wasn't ready to see it. Maybe I never would be. Yet I couldn't not see it. Closing my eyes didn't help.

T'Gatoi found a grub still eating its egg case. The remains of the case were still wired into a blood vessel by their own little tube or hook or whatever. That was the way the grubs were anchored and the way they fed. They took only blood until they were ready to emerge. Then they ate their stretched, elastic egg cases. Then they ate their hosts.

T'Gatoi bit away the egg case, licked away the blood. Did she like the taste? Did childhood habits die hard—or not die at all?

The whole procedure was wrong, alien. I wouldn't have thought anything about her could seem alien to me.

"One more, I think," she said. "Perhaps two. A good family. In a host animal these days, we would be happy to find one or two alive." She glanced at me. "Go outside, Gan, and empty your stomach. Go now while the man is unconscious."

I staggered out, barely made it. Beneath the tree just beyond the front door, I vomited until there was nothing left to bring up. Finally, I stood shaking, tears streaming down my face. I did not know why I was crying, but I could not stop. I went further from the house to avoid being seen. Every time I closed my eyes I saw red worms crawling over redder human flesh.

There was a car coming toward the house. Since Terrans were forbidden motorized vehicles except for certain farm equipment, I knew this must be Lomas's Tlic with Qui and perhaps a Terran doctor. I wiped my face on my shirt, struggled for control.

"Gan," Qui called as the car stopped. "What happened?" He crawled out of the low, round, Tlic-convenient car door. Another Terran crawled out the other side and went into the house without speaking to me. The doctor. With his help and a few eggs, Lomas might make it.

"T'Khotgif Teh?" I said.

The Tlic driver surged out of her car, reared up half her length before me. She was paler and smaller than T'Gatoi—probably born from the body of an animal. Tlic from Terran bodies were always larger as well as more numerous.

"Six young," I told her. "Maybe seven, all alive. At least one male."

"Lomas?" she said harshly. I liked her for the question and the concern in her voice when she asked it. The last coherent thing he had said was her name.

"He's alive," I said.

She surged away to the house without another word.

"She's been sick," my brother said, watching her go. "When I called, I could hear people telling her she wasn't well enough to go out even for this."

I said nothing. I had extended courtesy to the Tlic. Now I didn't want to talk to anyone. I hoped he would go in—out of curiosity if nothing else.

"Finally found out more than you wanted to know, eh?"

I looked at him.

"Don't give me one of *her* looks," he said. "You're not her. You're just her property."

One of her looks. Had I picked up even an ability to imitate her expressions?

"What'd you do, puke?" He sniffed the air. "So now you know what you're in for."

I walked away from him. He and I had been close when we were kids. He would let me follow him around when I was home, and sometimes T'Gatoi would let me bring him along when she took me into the city. But something had happened when he reached adolescence. I never knew what. He began keeping out of T'Gatoi's way. Then he began running away—until he realized there was no "away." Not in the Preserve. Certainly not outside. After that he concentrated on getting his share of every egg that came into the house and on looking out for me in a way that made me all but hate him—a way that clearly said, as long as I was all right, he was safe from the Tlic.

"How was it, really?" he demanded, following me.

"I killed an achti. The young ate it."

"You didn't run out of the house and puke because they ate an achti."

"I had . . . never seen a person cut open before." That was true, and enough for him to know. I couldn't talk about the other. Not with him.

"Oh," he said. He glanced at me as though he wanted to say more, but he kept quiet.

We walked, not really headed anywhere. Toward the back, toward the cages, toward the fields.

"Did he say anything?" Qui asked. "Lomas, I mean."

Who else would he mean? "He said 'T'Khotgif.' "

Qui shuddered. "If she had done that to me, she'd be the last person I'd call for."

"You'd call for her. Her sting would ease your pain without killing the grubs in you."

"You think I'd care if they died?"

No. Of course he wouldn't. Would I?

"Shit!" He drew a deep breath. "I've seen what they do. You think this thing with Lomas was bad? It was nothing."

I didn't argue. He didn't know what he was talking about.

"I saw them eat a man," he said.

I turned to face him. "You're lying!"

"*I saw them eat a man.*" He paused. "It was when I was little. I had been to the Hartmund house and I was on my way home. Halfway here, I saw a man and a Tlic and the man was N'Tlic. The ground was hilly. I was able to hide from them and watch. The Tlic wouldn't open the man because she had nothing to feed the grubs. The man couldn't go any further and there were no houses around. He was in so much pain, he told her to kill him. He begged her to kill him. Finally, she did. She cut his throat. One swipe of one claw. I saw the grubs eat their way out, then burrow in again, still eating."

His words made me see Lomas's flesh again, parasitized, crawling. "Why didn't you tell me that?" I whispered.

He looked startled as though he'd forgotten I was listening. "I don't know."

"You started to run away not long after that, didn't you?"

"Yeah. Stupid. Running inside the Preserve. Running in a cage."

I shook my head, said what I should have said to him long ago. "She wouldn't take you, Qui. You don't have to worry."

"She would . . . if anything happened to you."

"No. She'd take Xuan Hoa. Hoa . . . wants it." She wouldn't if she had stayed to watch Lomas.

"They don't take women," he said with contempt.

"They do sometimes." I glanced at him. "Actually, they prefer women. You should be around them when they talk among themselves. They say women have more body fat to protect the grubs. But they usually take men to leave the women free to bear their own young."

"To provide the next generation of host animals," he said, switching from contempt to bitterness.

"It's more than that!" I countered. Was it?

"If it were going to happen to me, I'd want to believe it was more, too."

"It *is* more!" I felt like a kid. Stupid argument.

"Did you think so while T'Gatoi was picking worms out of that guy's guts?"

"It's not supposed to happen that way."

"Sure it is. You weren't supposed to see it, that's all. And his Tlic was supposed to do it. She could sting him unconscious and the operation wouldn't have been as painful. But she'd still open him, pick out the grubs, and if she missed even one, it would poison him and eat him from the inside out."

There was actually a time when my mother told me to show respect for Qui because he was my older brother. I walked away, hating him. In his way, he was gloating. He was safe and I wasn't. I could have hit him, but I didn't think I would be able to stand it when he refused to hit back, when he looked at me with contempt and pity.

He wouldn't let me get away. Longer legged, he swung ahead of me and made me feel as though I were following him.

"I'm sorry," he said.

I strode on, sick and furious.

"Look, it probably won't be that bad with you. T'Gatoi likes you. She'll be careful."

I turned back toward the house, almost running from him.

"Has she done it to you yet?" he asked, keeping up easily. "I mean, you're about the right age for implantation. Has she—"

I hit him. I didn't know I was going to do it, but I think I meant to kill him. If he hadn't been bigger and stronger, I think I would have.

He tried to hold me off, but in the end, had to defend himself. He only hit me a couple of times. That was plenty. I don't remember going down, but when I came to, he was gone. It was worth the pain to be rid of him.

I got up and walked slowly toward the house. The back was dark. No one was in the kitchen. My mother and sisters were sleeping in their bedrooms—or pretending to.

Once I was in the kitchen, I could hear voices—Tlic and Terran from the next room. I couldn't make out what they were saying—didn't want to make it out.

I sat down at my mother's table, waiting for quiet. The table was smooth and worn, heavy and well crafted. My father had made it for her just before he died. I remembered hanging around underfoot when he built it. He didn't mind. Now I sat leaning on it, missing him. I could have talked to him. He had done it three times in his long life. Three clutches of eggs, three times being opened up and sewed up. How had he done it? How did anyone do it?

I got up, took the rifle from its hiding place, and sat down again with it. It needed cleaning, oiling.

All I did was load it.

"Gan?"

She made a lot of little clicking sounds when she walked on bare floor, each limb clicking in succession as it touched down. Waves of little clicks.

She came to the table, raised the front half of her body above it, and surged onto it. Sometimes she moved so smoothly she seemed to flow like water itself. She coiled herself into a small hill in the middle of the table and looked at me.

"That was bad," she said softly. "You should not have seen it. It need not be that way."

"I know."

"T'Khotgif—Ch'Khotgif now—she will die of her disease. She will not live to raise her children. But her sister will provide for them, and for Bram Lomas." Sterile sister. One fertile female in every lot. One to keep the family going. That sister owed Lomas more than she could ever repay.

"He'll live then?"

"Yes."

"I wonder if he would do it again."

"No one would ask him to do that again."

I looked into the yellow eyes, wondering how much I saw and understood there, and how much I only imagined. "No one ever asks us," I said. "You never asked me."

She moved her head slightly. "What's the matter with your face?"

"Nothing. Nothing important." Human eyes probably wouldn't have noticed the swelling in the darkness. The only light was from one of the moons, shining through a window across the room.

"Did you use the rifle to shoot the achti?"

"Yes."

"And do you mean to use it to shoot me?"

I stared at her, outlined in the moonlight—coiled, graceful body. "What does Terran blood taste like to you?"

She said nothing.

"What are you?" I whispered. "What are we to you?"

She lay still, rested her head on her topmost coil. "You know me as no other does," she said softly. "You must decide."

"That's what happened to my face," I told her.

"What?"

"Qui goaded me into deciding to do something. It didn't turn out very well." I moved the gun slightly, brought the barrel up diagonally under my own chin. "At least it was a decision I made."

"As this will be."

"Ask me, Gatoi."

"For my children's lives?"

She would say something like that. She knew how to manipulate people, Terran and Tlic. But not this time.

"I don't want to be a host animal," I said. "Not even yours."

It took her a long time to answer. "We use almost no host animals these days," she said. "You know that."

"You use us."

"We do. We wait long years for you and teach you and join our families to yours." She moved restlessly. "You know you aren't animals to us."

I stared at her, saying nothing.

"The animals we once used began killing most of our eggs after implantation long before your ancestors arrived," she said softly. "You know these things, Gan. Because your people arrived, we are relearning what it means to be a healthy, thriving people. And your ancestors, fleeing from their homeworld, from their own kind who would have killed or enslaved them—they survived because of us. We saw them as people and gave them the Preserve when they still tried to kill us as worms."

At the word "worms," I jumped. I couldn't help it, and she couldn't help noticing it.

"I see," she said quietly. "Would you really rather die than bear my young, Gan?"

I didn't answer.

"Shall I go to Xuan Hoa?"

"Yes!" Hoa wanted it. Let her have it. She hadn't had to watch Lomas. She'd be proud.... Not terrified.

T'Gatoi flowed off the table onto the floor, startling me almost too much.

"I'll sleep in Hoa's room tonight," she said. "And sometime tonight or in the morning, I'll tell her."

This was going too fast. My sister Hoa had had almost as much to do with raising me as my mother. I was still close to her—not like Qui. She could want T'Gatoi and still love me.

"Wait! Gatoi!"

She looked back, then raised nearly half her length off the floor and turned to face me. "These are adult things, Gan. This is my life, my family!"

"But she's ... my sister."

"I have done what you demanded. I have asked you!"

"But—"

"It will be easier for Hoa. She has always expected to carry other lives inside her."

Human lives. Human young who should someday drink at her breasts, not at her veins.

I shook my head. "Don't do it to her, Gatoi." I was not Qui. It seemed I could become him, though, with no effort at all. I could make Xuan Hoa my shield. Would it be easier to know that red worms were growing in her flesh instead of mine?

"Don't do it to Hoa," I repeated.

She stared at me, utterly still.

I looked away, then back at her. "Do it to me."

I lowered the gun from my throat and she leaned forward to take it.

"No," I told her.

"It's the law," she said.

"Leave it for the family. One of them might use it to save my life someday."

She grasped the rifle barrel, but I wouldn't let go. I was pulled into a standing position over her.

"Leave it here!" I repeated. "If we're not your animals, if these are adult things, accept the risk. There is risk, Gatoi, in dealing with a partner."

It was clearly hard for her to let go of the rifle. A shudder went through her and she made a hissing sound of distress. It occurred to me that she was afraid. She was old enough to have seen what guns could do to people. Now her young and this gun would be together in the same house. She did not know about the other guns. In this dispute, they did not matter.

"I will implant the first egg tonight," she said as I put the gun away. "Do you hear, Gan?"

Why else had I been given a whole egg to eat while the rest of the family was left to share one? Why else had my mother kept looking at me as though I were going away from her, going where she could not follow? Did T'Gatoi imagine I hadn't known?

"I hear."

"Now!" I let her push me out of the kitchen, then walked ahead of her toward my bedroom. The sudden urgency in her voice sounded real. "You would have done it to Hoa tonight!" I accused.

"I must do it to someone tonight."

I stopped in spite of her urgency and stood in her way. "Don't you care who?"

She flowed around me and into my bedroom. I found her waiting on the couch we shared. There was nothing in Hoa's room that she could have used. She would have done it to Hoa on the floor. The thought of her doing it to Hoa at all disturbed me in a different way now, and I was suddenly angry.

Yet I undressed and lay down beside her. I knew what to do, what to expect. I had been told all my life. I felt the familiar sting, narcotic, mildly pleasant. Then the blind probing of her ovipositor.[1] The puncture was painless, easy. So easy going in. She undulated slowly against me, her muscles forcing the egg from her body into mine. I held on to a pair of her limbs until I remembered Lomas holding her that way. Then I let go, moved inadvertently, and hurt her. She gave a low cry of pain and I expected to be caged at once within her limbs. When I wasn't, I held on to her again, feeling oddly ashamed.

"I'm sorry," I whispered.

She rubbed my shoulders with four of her limbs.

"Do you care?" I asked. "Do you care that it's me?"

She did not answer for some time. Finally, "You were the one making the choices tonight, Gan. I made mine long ago."

"Would you have gone to Hoa?"

"Yes. How could I put my children into the care of one who hates them?"

"It wasn't . . . hate."

"I know what it was."

"I was afraid."

Silence.

"I still am." I could admit it to her here, now.

---

1. An organ used by many arthropods (an animal family that includes insects) to lay eggs, whether those are simply attached to a surface or are placed within plants, the earth, or another animal.

"But you came to me . . . to save Hoa."

"Yes." I leaned my forehead against her. She was cool velvet, deceptively soft. "And to keep you for myself," I said. It was so. I didn't understand it, but it was so.

She made a soft hum of contentment. "I couldn't believe I had made such a mistake with you," she said. "I chose you. I believed you had grown to choose me."

"I had, but . . ."

"Lomas."

"Yes."

"I had never known a Terran to see a birth and take it well. Qui has seen one, hasn't he?"

"Yes."

"Terrans should be protected from seeing."

I didn't like the sound of that—and I doubted that it was possible. "Not protected," I said. "Shown. Shown when we're young kids, and shown more than once. Gatoi, no Terran ever sees a birth that goes right. All we see is N'Tlic—pain and terror and maybe death."

She looked down at me. "It is a private thing. It has always been a private thing."

Her tone kept me from insisting—that and the knowledge that if she changed her mind, I might be the first public example. But I had planted the thought in her mind. Chances were it would grow, and eventually she would experiment.

"You won't see it again," she said. "I don't want you thinking any more about shooting me."

The small amount of fluid that came into me with her egg relaxed me as completely as a sterile egg would have, so that I could remember the rifle in my hands and my feelings of fear and revulsion, anger and despair. I could remember the feelings without reviving them. I could talk about them.

"I wouldn't have shot you," I said. "Not you." She had been taken from my father's flesh when he was my age.

"You could have," she insisted.

"Not you." She stood between us and her own people, protecting, interweaving.

"Would you have destroyed yourself?"

I moved carefully, uncomfortable. "I could have done that. I nearly did. That's Qui's 'away.' I wonder if he knows."

"What?"

I did not answer.

"You will live now."

"Yes." *Take care of her,* my mother used to say. Yes.

"I'm healthy and young," she said. "I won't leave you as Lomas was left—alone, N'Tlic. I'll take care of you."

1984

LORNA GOODISON
b. 1947

When Jamaican-born Lorna Goodison told a BBC interviewer that in school she studied "all the great British poets," she added that she remembered reciting Wordsworth's "Daffodils" and "not knowing what a daffodil is." Then and there, she explained, she resolved to "write a poem about the flowers that I knew." But if a powerful literary nativism was one source of Goodison's art, another, as she made clear to the same interviewer, was a deep need "to praise," and especially to praise her beloved mother, who "happily" cared for nine children in the crowded part of Kingston where the poet and her siblings were born and raised. "I just love words," notes Goodison, and "my mother loved words." Not surprisingly, therefore, a number of this writer's strongest and most impassioned works celebrate her matrilineage ("Guinea Woman") as well as female heroes ("Nanny") while yearning for a matriarchal intervention that might help transform the colonized world ("Mother the Great Stones Got to Move"). At the same time, however, Goodison exuberantly affirms all aspects of her family inheritance, noting that "my great grandfather was a man called Aberdeen, who obviously came from Scotland. And my great grandmother came from Guinea, and because they had a mating and produced my grandmother, who looked like an American Indian—I have relatives who look like Egyptians and my son is an African prince—all of it belongs to me."

Goodison's parents were working-class Jamaicans—a telephone line worker and a seamstress—but her introduction to the "great British poets" left her with an educated taste not only for W. B. Yeats's *Oxford Book of Modern Verse* but also for the West Indian writings of Derek Walcott, Kamau Brathwaite, and folklorist-performer-poet Louise Bennett, whom she describes as the "mother of the Jamaican language." After studying art both in Jamaica and in New York, Goodison worked as an illustrator, teacher, and cultural administrator as she began to establish herself in her career. Her first collection, *Tamarind Season,* appeared in 1980 and was followed by numerous other volumes of poems, including *Heartease* (1988), *To Us, All Flowers Are Roses* (1995), and *Travelling Mercies* (2001), as well as a collection of short stories, *Baby Mother and the King of Swords* (1990).

Goodison has won such awards as the Commonwealth Poetry Prize (1986) and the Musgrave Gold Medal from the Institute of Jamaica (1999) while also producing paintings that have been widely exhibited, and teaching creative writing both at the University of Michigan and at the University of Toronto. Yet though she dwells mostly abroad—in the United States and Canada—she has long maintained a home in Jamaica. Reflecting on the title of *Heartease,* which derives from a real town in her native land, she muses, "I too aspire to live in a place called 'Heartease' if it's just inside my self."

Guinea Woman[1]

    Great grandmother
    was a guinea woman
    wide eyes turning
5   the corners of her face
    could see behind her

---

1. Woman from the west coast of Africa.

       her cheeks dusted with
       a fine rash of jet-bead warts
       that itched when the rain set up.

       Great grandmother's waistline
10   the span of a headman's hand
       slender and tall like a cane[2] stalk
       with a guinea woman's antelope-quick walk
       and when she paused
       her gaze would look to sea
15   her profile fine like some obverse impression
       on a guinea[3] coin from royal memory.

       It seems her fate was anchored
       in the unfathomable sea
       for great grandmother caught the eye of a sailor
20   whose ship sailed without him from Lucea[4] harbour.
       Great grandmother's royal scent of
       cinnamon and escallions[5]
       drew the sailor up the straits of Africa,
25   the evidence my blue-eyed grandmother
       the first Mulatta
       taken into backra's[6] household
       and covered with his name.
       They forbade great grandmother's
       guinea woman presence
30   they washed away her scent of
       cinnamon and escallions
       controlled the child's antelope walk
       and called her uprisings rebellions.

       But, great grandmother
35   I see your features blood dark
       appearing
       in the children of each new
       breeding
       the high yellow brown
40   is darkening down.
       Listen, children
       it's great grandmother's turn.

       1986

---

2. Sugarcane.
3. A British gold coin, worth 21 shillings (i.e., 1 pound and 1 shilling).
4. Town in northwest Jamaica.
5. One of the most commonly used seasonings in Jamaica (similar to spring onion).
6. White person's (Jamaican patois). "Mulatta": woman of mixed white and black ancestry.

Nanny[1]

My womb was sealed
with molten wax
of killer bees
for nothing should enter
nothing should leave
the state of perpetual siege
the condition of the warrior.

From then my whole body would quicken
at the birth of everyone of my people's children.
I was schooled in the green-giving ways
of the roots and vines
made accomplice to the healing acts
of Chainey root, fever grass & vervain.[2]

My breasts flattened
settled unmoving against my chest
my movements ran equal
to the rhythms of the forest.

I could sense and sift
the footfall of men
from the animals
and smell danger
death's odour
in the wind's shift.

When my eyes rendered
light from the dark
my battle song opened
into a solitaire's moan
I became most knowing
and forever alone.

And when my training was over
they circled my waist with pumpkin seeds
and dried okra, a traveller's jigida[3]
and sold me to the traders
all my weapons within me.
I was sent, tell that to history.

When your sorrow obscures the skies
other women like me will rise.

1986

---

1. A national hero of Jamaica, who led the Maroons—escaped slaves—as they fought the British in the 1730s. Legends attribute superhuman powers to her.
2. All Jamaican herbs with traditional medicinal uses (the first is usually spelled "chaney root").
3. Strings of beads worn around the waist (a term from West Africa).

Mother the Great Stones Got to Move

    Mother, one stone is wedged across the hole in our history
and sealed with blood wax.
In this hole is our side of the story, exact figures,
headcounts, burial artifacts, documents, lists, maps
showing our way up through the stars; lockets of brass
containing all textures of hair clippings.
It is the half that has never been told, and some of us
must tell it.

    Mother, there is the stone on the hearts of some women and men
something like an onyx, cabochon-cut[1]
which hung on the wearer seeds bad dreams. Speaking for
the small dreamers of this earth, plagued with nightmares,
yearning for healing dreams
we want that stone to move.

    Upon an evening like this, mother, when one year is making way
for another, in a ceremony attended by a show of silver stars,
mothers see the moon, milk-fed, herself a nursing mother
and we think of our children and the stones upon their future
and we want these stones to move.

    For the year going out came in fat at first
but towards the harvest it grew lean.
And many mouth corners gathered white
and another kind of poison, powdered white
was brought in to replace what was green.[2]
And death sells it with one hand
and with the other death palms a gun
then death gets death's picture
in the papers asking,
'where does all this death come from?'
Mother, stones are pillows
for the homeless sleep on concrete sheets.
Stone flavors soup, stone is now meat,
the hard-hearted giving our children
stones to eat.

    Mother, the great stones over mankind got to move.
It's been ten thousand years we've been watching them now
from various points in the universe.
From the time of our birth as points of light
in the eternal coiled workings of the cosmos.
Roll away stone of poisoned powders come
to blot out the hope of our young.
Move stone of sacrificial lives we breed

---

1. I.e., cut in a convex form, without facets.
2. In the 1980s, the government of Jamaica cracked down on the sale of ganja (marijuana), and the trade in heroin and cocaine increased dramatically.

            to feed to tribalistic economic machines.
            From across the pathway to mount morning
45   site of the rose quartz fountain
            brimming anise and star water
            bright fragrant for our children's future.
            Mother these great stones got to move.

                                                                    1988

                              Annie Pengelly

            I come to represent the case
            of one Annie Pengelly,
            maidservant, late of the San Fleming Estate
            situated in the westerly parish of Hanover.[1]

5   Hanover, where that masif[2]
            mountain range
            assumes the shape of a Dolphin's head
            rearing up in the blue expanse overhead
            restless white clouds round it foaming.

10   Those at sea would look up
            and behold, mirrored, a seascape in the sky.

            It is this need to recreate,
            to run 'gainst things, that cause
            all this confusion.

15   The same need that made men
            leave one side of the world
            to journey in long, mawed ships,
            to drogue[3] millions of souls
            to a world
20   that they call the new one
            in competition with the original act
            the creation of the old one.

            So now you are telling me to proceed
            and proceed swiftly.
25   Why have I come here representing Annie?

            Well this is the first thing she asked me to say,
            that Annie is not even her real name.
            A name is the first thing we own in this world.

            We lay claim to a group of sounds
30   which rise up and down and mark out our space

---

1. In western Jamaica.
2. Group of connected mountains (massif).
3. I.e., drag (a *drogue* is a sea anchor, dragged behind a boat).

in the air around us.
We become owners of a harmony of vowels and consonants
singing a specific meaning.

Her real name was given to her
35 at the pastoral ceremony of her outdooring.[4]
Its outer meaning was, 'she who is precious to us'.

It had too a hidden part, a kept secret.
A meaning known only to those within
the circle of her family.

40 For sale Bidderman, one small girl,
one small African girl answering now
to the name of Annie.

Oh Missus my dear, when you write Lady Nugent[5]
to tell her of your splendid birthday
45 of the ivory moire[6] gown you wore
that you send clear to London for.

You can tell her how you had built for you
a pair of soft, supple leather riding boots
fashioned from your own last
50 by George O'Brian Wilson
late of Aberdeen
now Shoemaker and Sadler of Lucea,[7] Hanover
late occupation,
bruk[8] Sailor.

55 One pair of tortoiseshell combs,
one scrolled silver backed mirror,
one dinner party where they killed
one whole cow
with oaken casks of Madeira wine
60 to wash it down.

And don't forget, one small African girl,
answering now to the name of Annie.

With all that birthday show of affection
Massa never sleep with missus.
65 But I am not here to talk about that,
that is backra[9] business.

I am really here just representing Annie Pengelly.

---

4. A Ghanaian naming ceremony.
5. Wife of Sir George Nugent, an English military officer whose career included serving as lieutenant governor of Jamaica (1801–06).
6. A fabric with a wavy, watered appearance.
7. Capital of Hanover. "Aberdeen": Scottish port on the North Sea.
8. Broke (Jamaican patois).
9. White people's (Jamaican patois).

For Missus began to make Annie
sleep across her feet
70   come December when northers began to blow.

Northers being the chill wheeling tail end
of the winter breezes
dropping off their cold what lef' in Jamaica
to confuse the transplanted Planter.

75   Causing them to remember words like 'hoarfrost' and 'moors'
from a frozen vocabulary they no longer
had use for.

When this false winter breeze would
careen across canefields[1]
80   Missus would make Annie lie draped,
heaped across her feet
a human blanket
nothing covering her as she gave
warmth to Missus.

85   So I come to say that History owes Annie
the brightest woolen blanket.
She is owed too, at least twelve years of sleep
stretched out,
free to assume the stages of sleep
90   flat on her back,
or profiled like the characters
in an Egyptian frieze.

Most nights though, Missus don't sleep.
And as Annie was subject to Missus will,
100   Annie was not to sleep as long
as Missus kept her open-eyed vigil.

Sometimes Missus sit up
sipping wine from a cut glass goblet.
Talking, talking.

105   Sometimes Missus dance and sing
like she was on a stage,
sad cantatrice[2] solo
on a stage performing.

At the end of her performance
110   she would demand that Annie clap
clap loud and shout 'encore'.

Encouraged by this she would sing
and dance on,
her half-crazed torch song of rejection.

---

1. Fields of sugarcane.   2. A woman singer (especially an opera singer).

    115 Sometimes Annie nod off,
          Missus jook[3] her with a pearl-tipped pin.
          Sometimes Annie tumble off the chair
          felled by sleep.
          Missus slap her awake again.
    120 Then in order to keep her alert, awake
          she devised the paper torture.

          One pile of newspapers
          a sharp pair of scissors later,
          Annie learned about
    125 the cruel make-work task
          that is the *cut-up*
          to throw-away of old newspaper.

          For if Missus could not sleep
          Annie gal you don't sleep that night,
    130 and poor Missus enslaved by love
          fighting her servitude with spite.

          So I say history owes Annie
          thousands of nights
          of sleep upon a feather bed.
    135 Soft feathers from the breast of
          a free, soaring bird,
          one bright blanket,
          and her name returned,
          she who is precious to us.

    140 Annie Pengelly O.
          I say, History owe you.

1995

After the Green Gown of My Mother Gone Down

      August, her large heart slows down then stops.
      Fall now, and trees flame, catch a fire and riot

      last leaves in scarlet and gold fever burning.
      Remember when you heard Bob Marley[1] hymn

5   'Redemption Song', and from his tone and timbre
      you sensed him traveling? He had sent the band home

      and was just keeping himself company, cooling star,
      sad rudeboy fretting on cowboy box guitar

---

3. Poke, stab (Jamaican patois).
1. Jamaican reggae singer (1945–1981) who became an international superstar; when he wrote "Redemption Song" (ca. 1979), he had already been diagnosed with his fatal cancer.

After the Green Gown of My Mother Gone Down / 1329

       in a studio with stray echo and wailing sound
10   lost singing scatting through the door of no return.

       When the green goes, beloved, the secret is opened.
       The breath falls still, the life covenant is broken.

       Dress my mother's cold body in a deep green gown.
       Catch a fire and let fall and flame time come
15   after the green gown of my mother gone down.

       We laid her down, full of days,
       chant griot[2] from the book of life,
       summon her kin from the long-
       lived line of David and Margaret.
20   Come Cleodine, Albertha,
       Flavius, Edmund, Howard and Rose,
       Marcus her husband gone before
       come and walk Dear Doris home.

       And the Blue Mountains[3] will open to her
25   to seal her corporeal self in.
       From the ancient vault
       that is their lapis lazuli heart
       the headwaters of all our rivers spring.
       Headwaters, wash away the embalmer's myrrh resin
30   the dredging of white powder caking her cold limbs.

       Return her ripe body clean
       to fallow[4] the earth.
       Her eyes to become brown agate stones.
       From her forehead let there dawn
35   bright mornings.
       May her white hair contribute
       to the massing of clouds

       cause the blood settled in her palms
       to sink into fish-filled lagoons.
40   Earth, she was a mother like you
       who birthed and nursed her children.
       Look cherubims and angels, see her name
       written down in the index of the faithful
       in the mother-of-pearl book of saints.

45   Mama, Aunt Ann says
       that she saw Aunt Rose
       come out of an orchard
       red with ripe fruit
       and called out laughing to you.
50   And that you scaled the wall

---

2. Oral histories.
3. Mountain range in eastern Jamaica.
4. Break up without sowing.

> like two young girls
> scampering barefoot among
> the lush fruit groves.

1999

To Mr William Wordsworth,[1] Distributor of Stamps for Westmoreland

> The host of golden flowers at my feet
> were common buttercups not daffodils,[2]
> they danced and swayed so in the breeze
> though overseer thorns were planted among them.
>
> 5   Still, it was a remarkable show of sorts
> which opened my eye, the inward one,[3]
> which once opened enabled me to see
> the overflowing bounty of my peoples' poverty.
>
> Sir, did you pass my great-grandmother?
> 10 Like you she lived in Westmoreland,
> she rode upon a great gray mule,
> she could not read or write, she did not buy stamps.
>
> But great-grandmother was a poet
> who wrote her lyrical ballads[4] on air,
> 15 scripted them with her tongue
> then summoned them to return to her book of memory.
>
> She never did arrange them
> the exact same way twice
> but they were her powerful overflow
> 20 recollected in tranquility,[5] sir, what she chanted was poetry.
>
> Great-grandmother was Black Betty's daughter,
> sister to fool fool Rose, distant cousin
> to Betty Foy's idiot boy.[6] Laughingstock
> of the West Country, of no degree, she spoke funny.
>
> 25 But, sir, whenever she would sing
> even the solitary reaper's voice[7] was stilled

---

1. Major English poet (1770–1850); in 1813 he was appointed Distributor of Stamps, a patronage position that assured him a steady income. Throughout the poem, Goodison alludes to specific works by Wordsworth.
2. See "I wandered lonely as a cloud" (1807).
3. "[T]hat inward eye / Which is the bliss of solitude" ("I wandered lonely as a cloud," lines 21–22).
4. *Lyrical Ballads* (1798), a collaboration with Samuel Taylor Coleridge, was Wordsworth's first important book and one of the key works of the era.
5. In his 1800 preface to the second edition of *Lyrical Ballads* (further revised in 1802), Wordsworth famously claimed "that poetry is the spontaneous overflow of powerful feelings: it takes its origin from emotion recollected in tranquillity."
6. "The Idiot Boy" (1798).
7. "The Solitary Reaper" (1807); Wordsworth also compares the reaper's voice to the nightingale's.

as her wild mystic chanting issued
over the cane brakes and hills. Only Keats's nightingale[8]

could compete with her guinea griot[9] style.
30 But she was not in any contest
for the fittest of the fit, she had just come
with her wild ways to enchant with her riddling lyrics.

Mr Wordsworth, I am not buying any stamp
to post a letter to my great-grandmother.
35 She is a denizen of the spirit world like you
so I am asking you when you pass her there, to tell her

that I collected up all her songs and poems
from where they fell on banana trash.
The binding ones on the star apple tree,
40 the ones hidden like pound notes under her coir[1] mattress.

I rescued them, rat-cut Blue Mountain coffee,
the ratoon and dunder[2] ones, refuse and trash
of the sugarcane, the ones they call broken
and indecent, patois, bungo,[3] words for bondage and shame.

45 And I've written them down for her,
summoned them to stand, black-face type
against a light background, Mr Wordsworth.
Please tell Miss Leanna her poems are now written down.

1999

Change If You Must Just Change Slow

We will crouch down then in a red earth
hollow, press our lips close to the heart
of this deep Cockpit Country and call out
please don't change or change if you must
5 just change slow. Old countryman riding
jackass, big woman watering the dry peas,
fat cow, and mawga dog, one-room dwelling
with intricate carved lace fretwork eaves.
Heaped yam hills, garlands of green vines,
10 cockades of bamboo on crown of the hillside.
Little bit a country village place or woodland
name of Content, Wire Fence, Stetin, Allsides,
far from domain of gunman and town strife.
Country we leave from to go and make life.

2005

---

8. See "Ode to a Nightingale" (1819), by the English Romantic poet John Keats (1795–1821).
9. Storytelling. "Guinea": i.e., of Guinea, on the west coast of Africa.
1. Coarse fiber derived from the husks of coconuts.
2. Dregs (of sugarcane juice). "Ratoon": a shoot sprouting from a plant base.
3. Crude, boorish (racially pejorative; Jamaican patois).

LESLIE MARMON SILKO
b. 1948

"It's stories that make this a community," Leslie Marmon Silko has remarked about the Native American world of Laguna Pueblo, New Mexico, in which she grew up. In a number of powerful books—*Laguna Woman* (1974), *Ceremony* (1977), *Storyteller* (1981), *Almanac of the Dead* (1991), *Yellow Woman* (1993), and *Gardens in the Dunes* (1999)—she has told and retold the tales that, she believes, make her people who they are. Of mixed Native American, Mexican, and European descent, Leslie Marmon attended Bureau of Indian Affairs schools at Laguna until entering high school, then studied at the University of New Mexico and later entered law school before deciding to do graduate work in English and devote herself to a literary career. Divorced from John Silko, she has taught at Navajo Community College in Arizona and at the University of New Mexico, is the mother of two sons, and has been the recipient of a MacArthur Foundation fellowship. Her ceremonial impulse to tell stories that are both self-defining and celebratory of her community has issued in an art that employs many forms: poetry, short stories, legendary tales, a novel, and film scripts. "Yellow Woman" illustrates the haunting power with which she blends the real and the mythic in resonant fictions about the places and people of the Southwest she knows so well.

Yellow Woman

I

My thigh clung to his with dampness, and I watched the sun rising up through the tamaracks and willows. The small brown water birds came to the river and hopped across the mud, leaving brown scratches in the alkali-white crust. They bathed in the river silently. I could hear the water, almost at our feet where the narrow fast channel bubbled and washed green ragged moss and fern leaves. I looked at him beside me, rolled in the red blanket on the white river sand. I cleaned the sand out of the cracks between my toes, squinting because the sun was above the willow trees. I looked at him for the last time, sleeping on the white river sand.

I felt hungry and followed the river south the way we had come the afternoon before, following our footprints that were already blurred by lizard tracks and bug trails. The horses were still lying down, and the black one whinnied when he saw me but he did not get up—maybe it was because the corral was made out of thick cedar branches and the horses had not yet felt the sun like I had. I tried to look beyond the pale red mesas to the pueblo.[1] I knew it was there, even if I could not see it, on the sandrock hill above the river, the same river that moved past me now and had reflected the moon last night.

The horse felt warm underneath me. He shook his head and pawed the sand. The bay whinnied and leaned against the gate trying to follow, and I remembered him asleep in the red blanket beside the river. I slid off the horse and tied him close to the other horse. I walked north with the river

---

1. Communal village of grouped houses.

again, and the white sand broke loose in footprints over footprints.

"Wake up."

He moved in the blanket and turned his face to me with his eyes still closed. I knelt down to touch him.

"I'm leaving."

He smiled now, eyes still closed. "You are coming with me, remember?" He sat up now with his bare dark chest and belly in the sun.

"Where?"

"To my place."

"And will I come back?"

He pulled his pants on. I walked away from him, feeling him behind me and smelling the willows.

"Yellow Woman," he said.

I turned to face him. "Who are you?" I asked.

He laughed and knelt on the low, sandy bank, washing his face in the river. "Last night you guessed my name, and you knew why I had come."

I stared past him at the shallow moving water and tried to remember the night, but I could only see the moon in the water and remember his warmth around me.

"But I only said that you were him and that I was Yellow Woman—I'm not really her—I have my own name and I come from the pueblo on the other side of the mesa. Your name is Silva and you are a stranger I met by the river yesterday afternoon."

He laughed softly. "What happened yesterday has nothing to do with what you will do today, Yellow Woman."

"I know—that's what I'm saying—the old stories about the ka'tsina spirit[2] and Yellow Woman can't mean us."

My old grandpa liked to tell those stories best. There is one about Badger and Coyote who went hunting and were gone all day, and when the sun was going down they found a house. There was a girl living there alone, and she had light hair and eyes and she told them that they could sleep with her. Coyote wanted to be with her all night so he sent Badger into a prairie-dog hole, telling him he thought he saw something in it. As soon as Badger crawled in, Coyote blocked up the entrance with rocks and hurried back to Yellow Woman.

"Come here," he said gently.

He touched my neck and I moved close to him to feel his breathing and to hear his heart. I was wondering if Yellow Woman had known who she was—if she knew that she would become part of the stories. Maybe she'd had another name that her husband and relatives called her so that only the ka'tsina from the north and the storytellers would know her as Yellow Woman. But I didn't go on; I felt him all around me, pushing me down into the white river sand.

Yellow Woman went away with the spirit from the north and lived with him and his relatives. She was gone for a long time, but then one day she came back and she brought twin boys.

"Do you know the story?"

"What story?" He smiled and pulled me close to him as he said this. I was

---

2. For the Hopi people, a supernatural being, a benevolent spiritual messenger.

afraid lying there on the red blanket. All I could know was the way he felt, warm, damp, his body beside me. This is the way it happens in the stories, I was thinking, with no thought beyond the moment she meets the ka'tsina spirit and they go.

"I don't have to go. What they tell in stories was real only then, back in time immemorial, like they say."

He stood up and pointed at my clothes tangled in the blanket. "Let's go," he said.

I walked beside him, breathing hard because he walked fast, his hand around my wrist. I had stopped trying to pull away from him, because his hand felt cool and the sun was high, drying the river bed into alkali. I will see someone, eventually I will see someone, and then I will be certain that he is only a man—some man from nearby—and I will be sure that I am not Yellow Woman. Because she is from out of time past and I live now and I've been to school and there are highways and pickup trucks that Yellow Woman never saw.

It was an easy ride north on horseback. I watched the change from the cottonwood trees along the river to the junipers that brushed past us in the foothills, and finally there were only piñons, and when I looked up at the rim of the mountain plateau I could see pine trees growing on the edge. Once I stopped to look down, but the pale sandstone had disappeared and the river was gone and the dark lava hills were all around. He touched my hand, not speaking, but always singing softly a mountain song and looking into my eyes.

I felt hungry and wondered what they were doing at home now—my mother, my grandmother, my husband, and the baby. Cooking breakfast, saying "Where did she go?—maybe kidnapped," and Al going to the tribal police with the details: "She went walking along the river."

The house was made with black lava rock and red mud. It was high above the spreading miles of arroyos[3] and long mesas. I smelled a mountain smell of pitch and buck brush. I stood there beside the black horse, looking down on the small, dim country we had passed, and I shivered.

"Yellow Woman, come inside where it's warm."

II

He lit a fire in the stove. It was an old stove with a round belly and an enamel coffeepot on top. There was only the stove, some faded Navajo blankets, and a bedroll and cardboard box. The floor was made of smooth adobe plaster, and there was one small window facing east. He pointed at the box.

"There's some potatoes and the frying pan." He sat on the floor with his arms around his knees pulling them close to his chest and he watched me fry the potatoes, I didn't mind him watching me because he was always watching me—he had been watching me since I came upon him sitting on the river bank trimming leaves from a willow twig with his knife. We ate from the pan and he wiped the grease from his fingers on his Levis.

"Have you brought women here before?" He smiled and kept chewing, so I said, "Do you always use the same tricks?"

"What tricks?" He looked at me like he didn't understand.

---

3. Water-carved gulleys.

"The story about being a ka'tsina from the mountains. The story about Yellow Woman."

Silva was silent; his face was calm.

"I don't believe it. Those stories couldn't happen now," I said.

He shook his head and said softly, "But someday they will talk about us, and they will say, 'Those two lived long ago when things like that happened.'"

He stood up and went out. I ate the rest of the potatoes and thought about things—about the noise the stove was making and the sound of the mountain wind outside. I remembered yesterday and the day before, and then I went outside.

I walked past the corral to the edge where the narrow trail cut through the black rim rock. I was standing in the sky with nothing around me but the wind that came down from the blue mountain peak behind me. I could see faint mountain images in the distance miles across the vast spread of mesas and valleys and plains. I wondered who was over there to feel the mountain wind on those sheer blue edges—who walks on the pine needles in those blue mountains.

"Can you see the pueblo?" Silva was standing behind me.

I shook my head. "We're too far away."

"From here I can see the world." He stepped out on the edge. "The Navajo reservation begins over there." He pointed to the east. "The Pueblo boundaries are over here." He looked below us to the south, where the narrow trail seemed to come from. "The Texans have their ranches over there, starting with that valley, the Concho Valley. The Mexicans run some cattle over there too."

"Do you ever work for them?"

"I steal from them," Silva answered. The sun was dropping behind us and shadows were filling the land below. I turned away from the edge that dropped forever into the valleys below.

"I'm cold," I said; "I'm going inside." I started wondering about this man who could speak the Pueblo language so well but who lived on a mountain and rustled cattle. I decided that this man Silva must be Navajo, because Pueblo men didn't do things like that.

"You must be a Navajo."

Silva shook his head gently. "Little Yellow Woman," he said, "you never give up, do you? I have told you who I am. The Navajo people know me, too." He knelt down and unrolled the bedroll and spread the extra blankets out on a piece of canvas. The sun was down, and the only light in the house came from outside—the dim orange light from sundown.

I stood there and waited for him to crawl under the blankets.

"What are you waiting for?" he said, and I lay down beside him. He undressed me slowly like the night before beside the river—kissing my face gently and running his hands up and down my belly and legs. He took off my pants and then he laughed.

"Why are you laughing?"

"You are breathing so hard."

I pulled away from him and turned my back to him.

He pulled me around and pinned me down with his arms and chest. "You don't understand, do you, little Yellow Woman? You will do what I want."

And again he was all around me with his skin slippery against mine, and I was afraid because I understood that his strength could hurt me. I lay underneath him and I knew that he could destroy me. But later, while he slept beside me, I touched his face and I had a feeling—the kind of feeling for him that overcame me that morning along the river. I kissed him on the forehead and he reached out for me.

When I woke up in the morning he was gone. It gave me a strange feeling because for a long time I sat there on the blankets and looked around the little house for some object of his—some proof that he had been there or maybe that he was coming back. Only the blankets and the cardboard box remained. The .30-30 that had been leaning in the corner was gone, and so was the knife I had used the night before. He was gone, and I had my chance to go now. But first I had to eat, because I knew it would be a long walk home.

I found some dried apricots in the cardboard box, and I sat down on a rock at the edge of the plateau rim. There was no wind and the sun warmed me. I was surrounded by silence. I drowsed with apricots in my mouth, and I didn't believe that there were highways or railroads or cattle to steal.

When I woke up, I stared down at my feet in the black mountain dirt. Little black ants were swarming over the pine needles around my foot. They must have smelled the apricots. I thought about my family far below me. They would be wondering about me, because this had never happened to me before. The tribal police would file a report. But if old Grandpa weren't dead he would tell them what happened—he would laugh and say, "Stolen by a ka'tsina, a mountain spirit. She'll come home—they usually do." There are enough of them to handle things. My mother and grandmother will raise the baby like they raised me. Al will find someone else, and they will go on like before, except that there will be a story about the day I disappeared while I was walking along the river. Silva had come for me; he said he had. I did not decide to go. I just went. Moonflowers blossom in the sand hills before dawn, just as I followed him. That's what I was thinking as I wandered along the trail through the pine trees.

It was noon when I got back. When I saw the stone house I remembered that I had meant to go home. But that didn't seem important any more, maybe because there were little blue flowers growing in the meadow behind the stone house and the gray squirrels were playing in the pines next to the house. The horses were standing in the corral, and there was a beef carcass hanging on the shady side of a big pine in front of the house. Flies buzzed around the clotted blood that hung from the carcass. Silva was washing his hands in a bucket full of water. He must have heard me coming because he spoke to me without turning to face me.

"I've been waiting for you."

"I went walking in the big pine trees."

I looked into the bucket full of bloody water with brown-and-white animal hairs floating in it. Silva stood there letting his hands drip, examining me intently.

"Are you coming with me?"

"Where?" I asked him.

"To sell the meat in Marquez."[4]

"If you're sure it's O.K."

"I wouldn't ask you if it wasn't," he answered.

---

4. Small town in northwest New Mexico.

He sloshed the water around in the bucket before he dumped it out and set the bucket upside down near the door. I followed him to the corral and watched him saddle the horses. Even beside the horses he looked tall, and I asked him again if he wasn't Navajo. He didn't say anything; he just shook his head and kept cinching up the saddle.

"But Navajos are tall."

"Get on the horse," he said, "and let's go."

The last thing he did before we started down the steep trail was to grab the .30-30 from the corner. He slid the rifle into the scabbard that hung from his saddle.

"Do they ever try to catch you?" I asked.

"They don't know who I am."

"Then why did you bring the rifle?"

"Because we are going to Marquez where the Mexicans live."

III

The trail leveled out on a narrow ridge that was steep on both sides like an animal spine. On one side I could see where the trail went around the rocky gray hills and disappeared into the southeast where the pale sandrock mesas stood in the distance near my home. On the other side was a trail that went west, and as I looked far into the distance I thought I saw the little town. But Silva said no, that I was looking in the wrong place, that I just thought I saw houses. After that I quit looking off into the distance; it was hot and the wildflowers were closing up their deep-yellow petals. Only the waxy cactus flowers bloomed in the bright sun, and I saw every color that a cactus blossom can be; the white ones and the red ones were still buds, but the purple and the yellow were blossoms, open full and the most beautiful of all.

Silva saw him before I did. The white man was riding a big gray horse, coming up the trail toward us. He was traveling fast and the gray horse's feet sent rocks rolling off the trail into the dry tumbleweeds. Silva motioned for me to stop and we watched the white man. He didn't see us right away, but finally his horse whinnied at our horses and he stopped. He looked at us briefly before he loped the gray horse across the three hundred yards that separated us. He stopped his horse in front of Silva, and his young fat face was shadowed by the brim of his hat. He didn't look mad, but his small, pale eyes moved from the blood-soaked gunny sacks hanging from my saddle to Silva's face and then back to my face.

"Where did you get the fresh meat?" the white man asked.

"I've been hunting," Silva said, and when he shifted his weight in the saddle the leather creaked.

"The hell you have, Indian. You've been rustling cattle. We've been looking for the thief for a long time."

The rancher was fat, and sweat began to soak through his white cowboy shirt and the wet cloth stuck to the thick rolls of belly fat. He almost seemed to be panting from the exertion of talking, and he smelled rancid, maybe because Silva scared him.

Silva turned to me and smiled. "Go back up the mountain, Yellow Woman."

The white man got angry when he heard Silva speak in a language he couldn't understand. "Don't try anything, Indian. Just keep riding to Marquez. We'll call the state police from there."

The rancher must have been unarmed because he was very frightened and if he had a gun he would have pulled it out then. I turned my horse around and the rancher yelled, "Stop!" I looked at Silva for an instant and there was something ancient and dark—something I could feel in my stomach—in his eyes, and when I glanced at his hand I saw his finger on the trigger of the .30-30 that was still in the saddle scabbard. I slapped my horse across the flank and the sacks of raw meat swung against my knees as the horse leaped up the trail. It was hard to keep my balance, and once I thought I felt the saddle slipping backward; it was because of this that I could not look back.

I didn't stop until I reached the ridge where the trail forked. The horse was breathing deep gasps and there was a dark film of sweat on its neck. I looked down in the direction I had come from, but I couldn't see the place. I waited. The wind came up and pushed warm air past me. I looked up at the sky, pale blue and full of thin clouds and fading vapor trails left by jets.

I think four shots were fired—I remember hearing four hollow explosions that reminded me of deer hunting. There could have been more shots after that, but I couldn't have heard them because my horse was running again and the loose rocks were making too much noise as they scattered around his feet.

Horses have a hard time running downhill, but I went that way instead of uphill to the mountain because I thought it was safer. I felt better with the horse running southeast past the round gray hills that were covered with cedar trees and black lava rock. When I got to the plain in the distance I could see the dark green patches of tamaracks that grew along the river; and beyond the river I could see the beginning of the pale sandrock mesas. I stopped the horse and looked back to see if anyone was coming; then I got off the horse and turned the horse around, wondering if it would go back to its corral under the pines on the mountain. It looked back at me for a moment and then plucked a mouthful of green tumbleweeds before it trotted back up the trail with its ears pointed forward, carrying its head daintily to one side to avoid stepping on the dragging reins. When the horse disappeared over the last hill, the gunny sacks full of meat were still swinging and bouncing.

IV

I walked toward the river on a wood-hauler's road that I knew would eventually lead to the paved road. I was thinking about waiting beside the road for someone to drive by, but by the time I got to the pavement I had decided it wasn't very far to walk if I followed the river back the way Silva and I had come.

The river water tasted good, and I sat in the shade under a cluster of silvery willows. I thought about Silva, and I felt sad at leaving him; still, there was something strange about him, and I tried to figure it out all the way back home.

I came back to the place on the river bank where he had been sitting the first time I saw him. The green willow leaves that he had trimmed from the branch were still lying there, wilted in the sand. I saw the leaves and I wanted to go back to him—to kiss him and to touch him—but the mountains were too far away now. And I told myself, because I believe it, he will come back sometime and be waiting again by the river.

I followed the path up from the river into the village. The sun was getting low, and I could smell supper cooking when I got to the screen door of my house. I could hear their voices inside—my mother was telling my grandmother how to fix the Jell-O and my husband, Al, was playing with the baby. I decided to tell them that some Navajo had kidnapped me, but I was sorry that old Grandpa wasn't alive to hear my story because it was the Yellow Woman stories he liked to tell best.

1992

JAMAICA KINCAID
b. 1949

"Girl," the first of many contributions Jamaica Kincaid has made to *The New Yorker*, was reprinted in her prize-winning collection *At the Bottom of the River* (1983) and epitomizes her evocative style. Almost liturgical in its rhythms, it juxtaposes sensory, everyday images in a style more reminiscent of poetry than prose to portray a character who seems mysteriously like a paradigmatic everygirl, rather than an individuated personality. *Annie John* (1985) and *Lucy* (1990), Kincaid's next publications, move toward more traditional methods of narration in their autobiographical account of a young Antiguan girl's separation from her family and her home. Yet both books articulate Kincaid's responses to the island she left at sixteen, her sense of the beauty of Antigua as well as her indictment of its colonial past. This last is the subject of her passionately argued essay *A Small Place* (1988), which Kincaid has described as a book written with a lot of anger and one that radicalized her. In 1996 she published a novel about a young woman haunted by mother loss: *The Autobiography of My Mother*.

Kincaid, who attributes her love of reading and writing to her mother's early influence, was named Elaine Potter Richardson by her parents. After leaving Antigua in 1965, she worked as a live-in babysitter and a receptionist before she began publishing in magazines. She took her first name, Jamaica, because it evoked the West Indies and the second, Kincaid, because it went well with the first. Although Jamaica Kincaid believes that she would not have become a writer if it had not been for the interest and support of *The New Yorker* and in particular of its editor William Shawn, she has come to feel "less interested in the approval of the First World." She currently resides in North Bennington, Vermont, where she lives with her husband, the composer Allen Shawn, and their two children.

Girl

Wash the white clothes on Monday and put them on the stone heap; wash the color clothes on Tuesday and put them on the clothesline to dry; don't walk barehead in the hot sun; cook pumpkin fritters in very hot sweet oil; soak your little cloths[1] right after you take them off; when buying cotton to

---

1. Menstrual rags.

make yourself a nice blouse, be sure that it doesn't have gum on it, because that way it won't hold up well after a wash; soak salt fish overnight before you cook it; is it true that you sing benna[2] in Sunday school?; always eat your food in such a way that it won't turn someone else's stomach; on Sundays try to walk like a lady and not like the slut you are so bent on becoming; don't sing benna in Sunday school; you mustn't speak to wharf-rat boys, not even to give directions; don't eat fruits on the street—flies will follow you; *but I don't sing benna on Sundays at all and never in Sunday school;* this is how to sew on a button; this is how to make a buttonhole for the button you have just sewed on; this is how to hem a dress when you see the hem coming down and so to prevent yourself from looking like the slut I know you are so bent on becoming; this is how you iron your father's khaki shirt so that it doesn't have a crease; this is how you iron your father's khaki pants so they don't have a crease; this is how you grow okra—far from the house, because okra tree harbors red ants; when you are growing dasheen,[3] make sure it gets plenty of water or else it makes your throat itch when you are eating it; this is how you sweep a corner; this is how you sweep a whole house; this is how you sweep a yard; this is how you smile to someone you don't like too much; this is how you smile to someone you don't like at all; this is how you smile to someone you like completely; this is how you set a table for tea; this is how you set a table for dinner; this is how you set a table for dinner with an important guest; this is how you set a table for lunch; this is how you set a table for breakfast; this is how to behave in the presence of men who don't know you very well, and this way they won't recognize immediately the slut I have warned you against becoming; be sure to wash every day, even if it is with your own spit; don't squat down to play marbles—you are not a boy, you know; don't pick people's flowers—you might catch something; don't throw stones at blackbirds, because it might not be a blackbird at all; this is how to make a bread pudding; this is how to make doukona;[4] this is how to make pepper pot;[5] this is how to make a good medicine for a cold; this is how to make a good medicine to throw away a child before it even becomes a child; this is how to catch a fish; this is how to throw back a fish you don't like, and that way something bad won't fall on you; this is how to bully a man; this is how a man bullies you; this is how to love a man, and if this doesn't work there are other ways, and if they don't work don't feel too bad about giving up; this is how to spit up in the air if you feel like it, and this is how to move quick so that it doesn't fall on you; this is how to make ends meet; always squeeze bread to make sure it's fresh; *but what if the baker won't let me feel the bread?;* you mean to say that after all you are really going to be the kind of woman who the baker won't let near the bread?

1978, 1983

---

2. Calypso music.
3. A variety of taro, a plant whose starchy underground stem can be cooked as a vegetable or ground into flour.
4. A kind of pudding.
5. A highly seasoned stew.

JULIA ALVAREZ
b. 1950

"I am a Dominican, hyphen, American," declares the fiction writer and poet Julia Alvarez, observing that "exciting things happen in the realm of that hyphen—the place where two worlds collide or blend together." Her verbally inventive and innovative "Bilingual Sestina" beautifully demonstrates this point, as do her novels and story collections, including *How the Garcia Girls Lost Their Accents* (1990), *In the Time of the Butterflies* (1994), and *¡Yo!* (1997). "As a kid, I loved stories," Alvarez has also noted, but she adds that "When I'm asked what made me into a writer, I point to the watershed experience of coming to this country. Not understanding the language, I had to pay close attention to each word—great training for a writer."

Alvarez was actually born in New York City, but soon after her birth her Dominican parents returned to their homeland, "preferring," as she puts it, "the dictatorship of Trujillo to the U.S.A. of the early 50's." Eventually, however, Alvarez's father "got involved in the underground" and because the family "was in deep trouble," they fled back to New York in 1960. In the States, Alvarez was educated at boarding schools, at Connecticut College, at Middlebury College, and at Syracuse University, earning a B.A. *summa cum laude* from Middlebury in 1971 and an M.F.A. from Syracuse in 1975. In 1984, she published her first book, *Homecoming,* a collection of poems; her second volume of verse, *The Other Side: El Otro Lado,* appeared in 1995, after she had already established herself as a fiction writer.

Since 1988, Alvarez has been a professor of English and writer in residence at Middlebury, where she and her "compañero," Bill Eichner, farm eleven acres in what she ironically describes as "the tropical Champlain Valley" while also running a "sustainable farm–literacy center" in the Dominican Republic. Her "modern, 'green' fable" titled *A Cafecito Story* (2001) was inspired by this Dominican project, which is also vividly described on the couple's website, www.cafealtagracia.com.

Bilingual Sestina

Some things I have to say aren't getting said
in this snowy, blond, blue-eyed, gum-chewing English:
dawn's early light sifting through *persianas*[1] closed
the night before by dark-skinned girls whose words
evoke *cama, aposento, sueños* in *nombres*[2]
from that first world I can't translate from Spanish.

Gladys, Rosario, Altagracia—the sounds of Spanish
wash over me like warm island waters as I say
your soothing names: a child again learning the *nombres*
of things you point to in the world before English
turned *sol, tierra, cielo, luna* to vocabulary words—
sun, earth, sky, moon. Language closed

---

1. Venetian blinds (Spanish, as are all translated terms).

2. Names. "*Cama, aposento, sueños*": bed, room, dreams.

like the touch-sensitive *morivivi*[3] whose leaves closed
   when we kids poked them, astonished. Even Spanish
15 failed us back then when we saw how frail a word is
   when faced with the thing it names. How saying
   its name won't always summon up in Spanish or English
   the full blown genie from the bottled *nombre*.

   Gladys, I summon you back by saying your *nombre*.
20 Open up again the house of slatted windows closed
   since childhood, where *palabras*[4] left behind for English
   stand dusty and awkward in neglected Spanish.
   Rosario, muse of *el patio*,[5] sing in me and through me say
   that world again, begin first with those first words

25 you put in my mouth as you pointed to the world—
   not Adam,[6] not God, but a country girl numbering
   the stars, the blades of grass, warming the sun by saying,
   ¡Qué calor![7] as you opened up the morning closed
   inside the night until you sang in Spanish,
30 *Estas son las mañanitas*,[8] and listening in bed, no English

   yet in my head to confuse me with translations, no English
   doubling the world with synonyms, no dizzying array of words
   —the world was simple and intact in Spanish—
   luna, sol, casa, luz, flor,[9] as if the *nombres*
35 were the outer skin of things, as if words were so close
   one left a mist of breath on things by saying

   their names, an intimacy I now yearn for in English—
   words so close to what I mean that I almost hear my Spanish
   heart beating, beating inside what I say *en inglés*.

                                                                    1995

The Master Bed

   Mornings after my father left for work,
   Mother and I made up the master bed.
   She took everything off, down to the bottom sheet,
   floated it up with a snap, centered, took in my give,
5 until that bed was modest in topsheet and blanket,
   dressed up in bedspread, until that bed was done!

   Sometimes the black nose of his slipper poked out
   from under the bedskirt. Sometimes the long pillow

---

3. A tropical plant found in the Caribbean that seems to die when touched but later recovers (literally, "I died, I lived").
4. Words, promises.
5. The courtyard.
6. According to Genesis 2.19–20, God gave Adam, the first man, the power of naming all living creatures.
7. What warmth!
8. These are the morning verses (the first line of an old folk song from Spain, today best known in its Mexican version).
9. House, light, flower.

with a sultan's tassel at each end rolled down
from the head of the bed. Often I found crumpled Kleenex
or a wayward sock between sheets. Once a nosebleed
on her pillowcase. I wanted something shocking

to explain my being conceived of in that carpeted bedrooms,
something we couldn't tidy though she'd try
to call it *love*. But I found nothing to inspire me—
only newspapers by his bedside, by hers a glass of warm water.
One sunbright morning in a shaft of light
a suspension of dust motes whirled like a primal moment.

1996

Storm Windows

She climbed toward the sky
when we did windows,
while I stood by, her helper,
doing the humdrum groundwork,
carrying her sloppy buckets
back and forth to the spigot,
hosing the glasses down
under her supervision
up there on a ladder
she had forbidden me.

I wanted to mount that ladder,
rung by rung, look down
into the gaping mouths of buckets,
the part in her greying hair.
I wanted to rise, polishing into each pane
another section of the sky.
Then give a kick, unbuckling
her hands clasped about my ankles,
and sail up, beyond her reach,
her house, her grounds, her mothering.

1996

From 33

[*Where are the girls who were beautiful?*]

Where are the girls who were beautiful?
I don't mean back in the olden days either,
I mean yesterday and the day before
yesterday? Tell me, if you can, where will

            I find breathless Vivien or Marilyn,[1]
            her skirt blown up? Certainly Natalie,[2]
            struggling in the cold waves, deserved to be
            fished out when the crew finished and given
65   her monogrammed beach towel and a hot drink.
            How many times didn't we pay good money
            to see them saved from worse catastrophes
            as they trembled in swimsuits on the brink
            of death, Rita and Jean, Lana and Joan,
70   Frances, Marlene[3]—their names sound like our own.

   [*Sometimes the words are so close I am*]

            Sometimes the words are so close I am
            more who I am when I'm down on paper
            than anywhere else as if my life were
            practising for the real me I become
635   unbuttoned from the anecdotal and
            unnecessary and undressed down
            to the figure of the poem, line by line,
            the real text a child could understand.
            Why do I get confused living it through?
640   Those of you, lost and yearning to be free,
            who hear these words, take heart from me.
            I once was in as many drafts as you.
            But briefly, essentially, here I am. . . .
            Who touches this poem touches a woman.[4]

                                                        1984, 1996

On Not Shoplifting Louise Bogan's[1] *The Blue Estuaries*

          Connecticut College, fall 1968

            Your book surprised me on the bookstore shelf—
            swans gliding on a blueblack lake;
            no blurbs by the big boys on back;
            no sassy, big-haired picture
5   to complicate the achievement;
            no mentors musing
            over how they had discovered
            you had it in you
            before you even knew

---

1. Marilyn Monroe (1926–1962), a star in Hollywood films (as were all the women named); in a famous scene from *The Seven Year Itch* (1955), she vainly holds down her skirt as air from the subway grate on which she is standing blows it up. Vivien Leigh (1913–1967).
2. Natalie Wood (1938–1981), who drowned while sailing.
3. Rita Hayworth (1918–1987) and Jean Harlow (1911–1937), Lana Turner (1921–1995) and Joan Crawford (1908?–1977; or Joan Fontaine, b. 1917), Frances Farmer (1914–1970), and Marlene Dietrich (1901–1992).
4. Compare "Camerado, this is no book, / Who touches this touches a man," from Walt Whitman's "So Long" (1860, 1891), placed at the end of the main body of poems in later editions of *Leaves of Grass*.

1. American poet (1897–1970; see above, p. 504); *The Blue Estuaries: Poems 1923–1969* was published in 1968.

you had it in you.
The swans posed on a placid lake,
your name blurred underwater
sinking to the bottom.

I had begun to haunt
the poetry shelf at the college store—
thin books crowded in by texts,
reference tomes and a spread
of magazines for persistent teens
on how to get their boys,
Chaucer-Milton-Shakespeare-Yeats.[2]
Your name was not familiar,
I took down the book and read.

Page after page, your poems
were stirring my own poems—
words rose, breaking the surface,
shattering an old silence.
I leaned closer to the print
until I could almost feel
the blue waters drawn
into the tip of my pen.
I bore down on the page,
the lake flowed out again,
the swans, the darkening sky.
For a moment I lost my doubts,
my girl's voice, my coming late
into this foreign alphabet.
I read and wrote as I read.

I wanted to own this moment.
My breath came quickly, thinking it over—
I had no money, no one was looking.
The swans posed on the cover,
their question-mark necks arced
over the dark waters.
I was asking them what to do . . .

The words they swam over answered.
I held the book closed before me
as if it were something else,
a mirror reflecting back
someone I was becoming.
The swans dipped their alphabet necks
in the blueblack ink of the lake.
I touched their blank, downy sides, musing,
and I put the book back.

2004

2. All canonical male British poets: Geoffrey Chaucer (ca. 1343–1400), John Milton (1608–1674), William Shakespeare (1564–1616), and William Butler Yeats (1865–1939).

ANNE CARSON
b. 1950

"I will do anything to avoid boredom," says the poet and classicist Anne Carson, adding that such avoidance "is the task of a lifetime. You can never know enough, never work enough, never use the infinitives and participles oddly enough, never impede the movement harshly enough, never leave the mind quickly enough." The winner of a MacArthur Foundation fellowship, among numerous other awards, and the author of six collections of verse, several books of criticism, and a highly regarded translation of the works of Sappho, Carson has clearly succeeded in this "task of a lifetime." Declares her fellow Canadian writer Michael Ondaatje, "Anne Carson is, for me, the most exciting poet writing in English today," and other literary figures such as Susan Sontag and Alice Munro have expressed similar views not only of her poetry but of her criticism, with the scholar Guy Davenport observing that Carson "writes philosophy and critical essays that are as beautiful and charming as good poetry."

Despite her glittering reputation, Carson is notoriously reticent about her personal life. For years, her book jackets carried a single terse sentence in lieu of the standard biographical note: "Anne Carson lives in Canada." In recent years, however, as her international renown has grown, some information has emerged. Born in Toronto, Ontario, Carson was raised by a banker father, whose death from Alzheimer's she charts and mourns in *The Glass Essay,* and a mother whom she elegizes in "Appendix to Ordinary Time," the concluding piece in her experimental *Men in the Off Hours* (2000). According to one biographer, she was a devout Catholic in her childhood, "so enthralled by an illustrated copy of *The Lives of the Saints* that, at the age of five, she tried to eat its pages." In high school she studied Latin and (during her lunch period) ancient Greek, and at university she continued to pursue her passion for the classics, gaining a Ph.D. from the University of Toronto in 1981 with a dissertation on Sappho, a work that eventually became her first book, *Eros the Bittersweet: An Essay* (1986).

Early in her university career, Carson dropped out of Toronto for a year to attend commercial art school—perhaps a sign that her interests would eventually broaden beyond academic classicism. And indeed, she followed *Eros the Bittersweet* with two collections of dazzlingly innovative poems—*Glass, Irony and God* and *Plainwater*—both published in a single year (1995). Like *The Glass Essay,* which juxtaposes rage at the end of a love affair and grief at her father's illness with a meditation on the life of Emily Brontë, most of her writings are allusive, oblique, and complex. "Lazarus Standup: Shooting Script" retells the biblical tale of Lazarus's return from the dead as a made-for-TV episode, while *Autobiography of Red* (1998) is a novel in verse tracing the story of the monster Geryon, master of a famous herd of red cattle whose defeat was one of the labors of Hercules and the subject of the *Geryoneis* by the Greek poet Stesichorus. More recently, Carson has published another critical volume, *Economy of the Unlost: Reading Simonides of Keos with Paul Celan* (1999), and a book of poems titled *The Beauty of the Husband. A Fictional Essay in 29 Tangos* (2001) that investigates a failed marriage by engaging with a famous line from John Keats's "Ode on a Grecian Urn": "Beauty is truth, truth beauty." In addition, she has written the libretto for—and produced—a Web-based "installation opera," *The Mirror of Simple Souls,* based on the writings of the thirteenth-century French mystic Marguerite Porete.

For many years Carson has been a professor of classics at McGill University in Montreal, but she has also taught at a number of American institutions, including Princeton, the University of California, Berkeley, and the University of Michigan. She now regularly divides her time between Canada and the United States.

From The Glass Essay

I

I can hear little clicks inside my dream.
Night drips its silver tap
down the back.
At 4 A.M. I wake. Thinking

5   of the man who
left in September.
His name was Law.

My face in the bathroom mirror
has white streaks down it.
10 I rinse the face and return to bed.
Tomorrow I am going to visit my mother.

She

She lives on a moor in the north.
She lives alone.
Spring opens like a blade there.
I travel all day on trains and bring a lot of books—

5   some for my mother, some for me
including *The Collected Works Of Emily Brontë*.[1]
This is my favourite author.

Also my main fear, which I mean to confront.
Whenever I visit my mother
10 I feel I am turning into Emily Brontë,

my lonely life around me like a moor,
my ungainly body stumping over the mud flats with a look of
    transformation
that dies when I come in the kitchen door.
What meat is it, Emily, we need?

Three

Three silent women at the kitchen table.
My mother's kitchen is dark and small but out the window
there is the moor, paralyzed with ice.
It extends as far as the eye can see

5   over flat miles to a solid unlit white sky.
Mother and I are chewing lettuce carefully.
The kitchen wall clock emits a ragged low buzz that jumps

---

1. English poet and novelist (1818–1848; see Vol. 1, p. 959), who lived, with her father, sisters, and brother, on the moors in Yorkshire in northern England.

       once a minute over the twelve.
       I have Emily p. 216 propped open on the sugarbowl
10   but am covertly watching my mother.

       A thousand questions hit my eyes from the inside.
       My mother is studying her lettuce.
       I turn to p. 217.

       "In my flight through the kitchen I knocked over Hareton
15   who was hanging a litter of puppies
       from a chairback in the doorway. . . ."[2]

       It is as if we have all been lowered into an atmosphere of glass.
       Now and then a remark trails through the glass.
       Taxes on the back lot. Not a good melon,

20   too early for melons.
       Hairdresser in town found God, closes shop every Tuesday.
       Mice in the teatowel drawer again.
       Little pellets. Chew off

       the corners of the napkins, if they knew
25   what paper napkins cost nowadays.
       Rain tonight.

       Rain tomorrow.
       That volcano in the Philippines at it again.[3] What's her name
       Anderson died no not Shirley

30   the opera singer.[4] Negress.
       Cancer.
       Not eating your garnish, you don't like pimento?

       Out the window I can see dead leaves ticking over the flatland
       and dregs of snow scarred by pine filth.
35   At the middle of the moor

       where the ground goes down into a depression,
       the ice has begun to unclench.
       Black open water comes

       curdling up like anger. My mother speaks suddenly.
40   That psychotherapy's not doing you much good is it!
       You aren't getting over him.

       My mother has a way of summing things up.
       She never liked Law much
       but she liked the idea of me having a man and getting on with life.

---

2. Chapter 17 of Brontë's *Wuthering Heights* (1847). Other characters mentioned in the poem are Heathcliff, Catherine, and Earnshaw.
3. Mt. Pinatubo, which continued to spew ash after a major eruption in February 1993.
4. Marian Anderson (1902–1993), American contralto.

45 Well he's a taker and you're a giver I hope it works out,
was all she said after she met him.
Give and take were just words to me

at the time. I had not been in love before.
It was like a wheel rolling downhill.
50 But early this morning while mother slept

and I was downstairs reading the part in *Wuthering Heights*
where Heathcliff clings at the lattice in the storm sobbing
Come in! Come in! to the ghost of his heart's darling,[5]

I fell on my knees on the rug and sobbed too.
55 She knows how to hang puppies,
that Emily.

It isn't like taking an aspirin you know, I answer feebly.
Dr. Haw says grief is a long process.
She frowns. What does it accomplish

all that raking up the past?
60 Oh—I spread my hands—
I prevail! I look her in the eye.
She grins. Yes you do.

Whacher

Whacher,
Emily's habitual spelling of this word,
has caused confusion.
For example

5 in the first line of the poem printed *Tell me, whether, is it winter?*[6]
in the Shakespeare Head edition.
But whacher is what she wrote.

Whacher is what she was.
She whached God and humans and moor wind and open night.
10 She whached eyes, stars, inside, outside, actual weather.

She whached the bars of time, which broke.
She whached the poor core of the world,
wide open.

To be a whacher is not a choice.
15 There is nowhere to get away from it,
no ledge to climb up to—like a swimmer

who walks out of the water at sunset
shaking the drops off, it just flies open.
To be a whacher is not in itself sad or happy,

---

5. *Wuthering Heights*, chap. 3.   6. Written in 1838.

    20   although she uses these words in her verse
as she uses the emotions of sexual union in her novel,
grazing with euphemism the work of whaching.

But it has no name.
25   It is transparent.
Sometimes she calls it Thou.

"Emily is in the parlour brushing the carpet,"
records Charlotte[7] in 1828.
Unsociable even at home

and unable to meet the eyes of strangers when she ventured out,
30   Emily made her awkward way
across days and years whose bareness appalls her biographers.

This sad stunted life, says one.
Uninteresting, unremarkable, wracked by disappointment
and despair, says another.

35   She could have been a great navigator if she'd been male,[8]
suggests a third. Meanwhile
Emily continued to brush into the carpet the question,

Why cast the world away.
For someone hooked up to Thou,
40   the world may have seemed a kind of half-finished sentence.

But in between the neighbour who recalls her
coming in from a walk on the moors
with her face "lit up by a divine light"

and the sister who tells us
45   Emily never made a friend in her life,
is a space where the little raw soul

slips through.
It goes skimming the deep keel like a storm petrel,
out of sight.

50   The little raw soul was caught by no one.
She didn't have friends, children, sex, religion, marriage, success, a salary
or a fear of death. She worked

in total six months of her life (at a school in Halifax[9])
and died on the sofa at home at 2 P.M. on a winter afternoon
55   in her thirty-first year. She spent

---

7. The novelist Charlotte Brontë (1816–1855; see Vol. 1, p. 633), Emily's older sister.
8. An observation made by Constantin Héger, who taught Charlotte and Emily in Brussels, according to Elizabeth Gaskell's 1857 biography of Charlotte.
9. Town in West Yorkshire.

most of the hours of her life brushing the carpet,
walking the moor
or whaching. She says

it gave her peace.
"All tight and right in which condition it is to be hoped we shall all be
    this day 4 years,"
she wrote in her Diary Paper of 1837.

Yet her poetry from beginning to end is concerned with prisons,
vaults, cages, bars, curbs, bits, bolts, fetters,
locked windows, narrow frames, aching walls.

"Why all the fuss?" asks one critic.
"She wanted liberty. Well didn't she have it?
A reasonably satisfactory homelife,

a most satisfactory dreamlife—why all this beating of wings?
What was this cage, invisible to us,
which she felt herself to be confined in?"

Well there are many ways of being held prisoner,
I am thinking as I stride over the moor.
As a rule after lunch mother has a nap

and I go out to walk.
The bare blue trees and bleached wooden sky of April
carve into me with knives of light.

Something inside it reminds me of childhood—
it is the light of the stalled time after lunch
when clocks tick

and hearts shut
and fathers leave to go back to work
and mothers stand at the kitchen sink pondering

something they never tell.
You remember too much,
my mother said to me recently.

Why hold onto all that? And I said,
Where can I put it down?
She shifted to a question about airports.

Crops of ice are changing to mud all around me
as I push on across the moor
warmed by drifts from the pale blue sun.

On the edge of the moor our pines
dip and coast in breezes
from somewhere else.

>   Perhaps the hardest thing about losing a lover is
> 95 to watch the year repeat its days.
>   It is as if I could dip my hand down
>
>   into time and scoop up
>   blue and green lozenges of April heat
>   a year ago in another country.
> 100 I can feel that other day running underneath this one
>   like an old videotape—here we go fast around the last corner
>   up the hill to his house, shadows
>
>   of limes and roses blowing in the car window
>   and music spraying from the radio and him
> 105 singing and touching my left hand to his lips.
>
>   Law lived in a high blue room from which he could see the sea.
>   Time in its transparent loops as it passes beneath me now
>   still carries the sound of the telephone in that room
>
>   and traffic far off and doves under the window
> 110 chuckling coolly and his voice saying,
>   You beauty. I can feel that beauty's
>
>   heart beating inside mine as she presses into his arms in the high
>   blue room—
>   No, I say aloud. I force my arms down
>   through air which is suddenly cold and heavy as water
>
> 115 and the videotape jerks to a halt
>   like a glass slide under a drop of blood.
>   I stop and turn and stand into the wind,
>
>   which now plunges towards me over the moor.
>   When Law left I felt so bad I thought I would die.
> 120 This is not uncommon.
>
>   I took up the practice of meditation.
>   Each morning I sat on the floor in front of my sofa
>   and chanted bits of old Latin prayers.
>
>   *De profundis clamavi ad te Domine.*[1]
> 125 Each morning a vision came to me.
>   Gradually I understood that these were naked glimpses of my soul.
>
>   I called them Nudes.
>   Nude #1. Woman alone on a hill.
>   She stands into the wind.

---

1. Out of the depths I have cried out to you, Lord (Latin); the beginning of Psalm 130 (129) in the Vulgate.

It is a hard wind slanting from the north.
Long flaps and shreds of flesh rip off the woman's body and lift
and blow away on the wind, leaving

an exposed column of nerve and blood and muscle
calling mutely through lipless mouth.
It pains me to record this,

I am not a melodramatic person.
But soul is "hewn in a wild workshop"
as Charlotte Brontë says of *Wuthering Heights*.[2]

Charlotte's preface to *Wuthering Heights* is a publicist's masterpiece.
Like someone carefully not looking at a scorpion
crouched on the arm of the sofa Charlotte

talks firmly and calmly
about the other furniture of Emily's workshop—about
the inexorable spirit ("stronger than a man, simpler than a child"),

the cruel illness ("pain no words can render"),
the autonomous end ("she sank rapidly, she made haste to leave us")
and about Emily's total subjection

to a creative project she could neither understand nor control,
and for which she deserves no more praise nor blame
than if she had opened her mouth

"to breathe lightning." The scorpion is inching down
the arm of the sofa while Charlotte
continues to speak helpfully about lightning

and other weather we may expect to experience
when we enter Emily's electrical atmosphere.
It is "a horror of great darkness" that awaits us there

but Emily is not responsible. Emily was in the grip.
"Having formed these beings she did not know what she had done,"
says Charlotte (of Heathcliff and Earnshaw and Catherine).

Well there are many ways of being held prisoner.
The scorpion takes a light spring and lands on our left knee
as Charlotte concludes, "On herself she had no pity."

Pitiless too are the Heights, which Emily called Wuthering
because of their "bracing ventilation"
and "a north wind over the edge."[3]

---

2. In her preface to the 1850 edition of the novel.   3. *Wuthering Heights*, chap. 1.

Whaching a north wind grind the moor
that surrounded her father's house on every side,
formed of a kind of rock called millstone grit,

taught Emily all she knew about love and its necessities—
an angry education that shapes the way her characters
use one another. "My love for Heathcliff," says Catherine,

"resembles the eternal rocks beneath—
a source of little visible delight, but necessary."[4]
Necessary? I notice the sun has dimmed

and the afternoon air sharpening.
I turn and start to recross the moor towards home.
What are the imperatives

that hold people like Catherine and Heathcliff
together and apart, like pores blown into hot rock
and then stranded out of reach

of one another when it hardens? What kind of necessity is that?
The last time I saw Law was a black night in September.
Autumn had begun,

my knees were cold inside my clothes.
A chill fragment of moon rose.
He stood in my living room and spoke

without looking at me. Not enough spin on it,
he said of our five years of love.
Inside my chest I felt my heart snap into two pieces

which floated apart. By now I was so cold
it was like burning. I put out my hand
to touch his. He moved back.

I don't want to be sexual with you, he said. Everything gets crazy.
But now he was looking at me.
Yes, I said as I began to remove my clothes.

Everything gets crazy. When nude
I turned my back because he likes the back.
He moved onto me.

Everything I know about love and its necessities
I learned in that one moment
when I found myself

---

4. *Wuthering Heights*, chap. 9.

    thrusting my little burning red backside like a baboon
    at a man who no longer cherished me.
    There was no area of my mind

205 not appalled by this action, no part of my body
    that could have done otherwise.
    But to talk of mind and body begs the question.

    Soul is the place,
    stretched like a surface of millstone grit between body and mind,
210 where such necessity grinds itself out.

    Soul is what I kept watch on all that night.
    Law stayed with me.
    We lay on top of the covers as if it weren't really a night of sleep and
        time,

    caressing and singing to one another in our made-up language
215 like the children we used to be.
    That was a night that centred Heaven and Hell,

    as Emily would say. We tried to fuck
    but he remained limp, although happy. I came
    again and again, each time accumulating lucidity,

220 until at last I was floating high up near the ceiling looking down
    on the two souls clasped there on the bed
    with their mortal boundaries

    visible around them like lines on a map.
    I saw the lines harden.
225 He left in the morning.

    It is very cold
    walking into the long scraped April wind.
    At this time of year there is no sunset
    just some movements inside the light and then a sinking away.

                        * * *

Thou

    The question I am left with is the question of her loneliness.
    And I prefer to put it off.
    It is morning.

    Astonished light is washing over the moor from north to east.
5   I am walking into the light.
    One way to put off loneliness is to interpose God.

Emily had a relationship on this level with someone she
She describes Thou as awake like herself all night
and full of strange power.

10 Thou woos Emily with a voice that comes out of the night wind.
Thou and Emily influence one another in the darkness,
playing near and far at once.

She talks about a sweetness that "proved us one."[5]
I am uneasy with the compensatory model of female religious
    experience and yet,
15 there is no question,

it would be sweet to have a friend to tell things to at night,
without the terrible sex price to pay.
This is a childish idea, I know.

My education, I have to admit, has been gappy.
20 The basic rules of male-female relations
were imparted atmospherically in our family,

no direct speech allowed.
I remember one Sunday I was sitting in the backseat of the car.
Father in front.

25 We were waiting in the driveway for mother,
who came around the corner of the house
and got into the passenger side of the car

dressed in a yellow Chanel suit and black high heels.
Father glanced sideways at her.
30 Showing a good bit of leg today Mother, he said

in a voice which I (age eleven) thought odd.
I stared at the back of her head waiting for what she would say.
Her answer would clear this up.

But she just laughed a strange laugh with ropes all over it.
35 Later that summer I put this laugh together with another laugh
I overheard as I was going upstairs.

She was talking on the telephone in the kitchen.
Well a woman would be just as happy with a kiss on the cheek
most of the time but YOU KNOW MEN,

40 she was saying. Laugh.
Not ropes, thorns.
I have arrived at the middle of the moor

---

5. In "Ah! why, because the dazzling sun" (written 1845).

where the ground goes down into a low swampy place.
45 The swamp water is frozen solid.
Bits of gold weed

have etched themselves
on the underside of the ice like messages.

   I'll come when thou art saddest,
   Laid alone in the darkened room;
50   When the mad day's mirth has vanished,
   And the smile of joy is banished,

   I'll come when the heart's real feeling
   Has entire, unbiased sway,
   And my influence o'er thee stealing
55   Grief deepening, joy congealing,
   Shall bear thy soul away.

   Listen! 'tis just the hour,
   The awful time for thee:
   Dost thou not feel upon thy soul
60   A flood of strange sensations roll,
   Forerunners of a sterner power,
   Heralds of me?[6]

Very hard to read, the messages that pass
between Thou and Emily.
65 In this poem she reverses their roles,

speaking not *as* the victim but *to* the victim.
It is chilling to watch Thou move upon thou,
who lies alone in the dark waiting to be mastered.

70 It is a shock to realize that this low, slow collusion
of master and victim within one voice
is a rationale

for the most awful loneliness of the poet's hour.
She has reversed the roles of thou and Thou
not as a display of power

75 but to force out of herself some pity
for this soul trapped in glass,
which is her true creation.

Those nights lying alone
are not discontinuous with this cold hectic dawn.
80 It is who I am.

---

6. Written in 1837.

Is it a vocation of anger?
Why construe silence
as the Real Presence?

Why stoop to kiss this doorstep?
Why be unstrung and pounded flat and pine away
imagining someone vast to whom I may vent the swell of my soul?

Emily was fond of Psalm 130.
"My soul waiteth on Thou[7] more than they that watch for the
    morning,
I say more than they that watch for the morning."

I like to believe that for her the act of watching provided a shelter,
that her collusion with Thou gave ease to anger and desire:
"In Thou they are quenched as a fire of thorns,"[8] says the psalmist.

But for myself I do not believe this, I am not quenched—
with Thou or without Thou I find no shelter.
I am my own Nude.

And Nudes have a difficult sexual destiny.
I have watched this destiny disclose itself
in its jerky passage from girl to woman to who I am now,

from love to anger to this cold marrow,
from fire to shelter to fire.
What is the opposite of believing in Thou—

merely not believing in Thou? No. That is too simple.
That is to prepare a misunderstanding.
I want to speak more clearly.

Perhaps the Nudes are the best way.
Nude #5. Deck of cards.
Each card is made of flesh.

The living cards are days of a woman's life.
I see a great silver needle go flashing right through the deck once
    from end to end.
Nude #6 I cannot remember.

Nude #7. White room whose walls,
having neither planes nor curves nor angles,
are composed of a continuous satiny white membrane

like the flesh of some interior organ of the moon.
It is a living surface, almost wet.
Lucency[9] breathes in and out.

---

7. In the King James version, "My soul waiteth for the Lord" (Psalm 130.6).
8. Slightly paraphrased from Psalm 118.12.
9. Luminosity.

Rainbows shudder across it.
And around the walls of the room a voice goes whispering,
Be very careful. Be very careful.

120 Nude #8. Black disc on which the fires of all the winds
are attached in a row.
A woman stands on the disc

amid the winds whose long yellow silk flames
flow and vibrate up through her.
125 Nude #9. Transparent loam.

Under the loam a woman has dug a long deep trench.
Into the trench she is placing small white forms, I don't know what
    they are.
Nude #10. Green thorn of the world poking up

alive through the heart of a woman
130 who lies on her back on the ground.
The thorn is exploding

its green blood above her in the air.
Everything it is it has, the voice says.
Nude #11. Ledge in outer space.

135 Space is bluish black and glossy as solid water
and moving very fast in all directions,
shrieking past the woman who stands pinned

to nothing by its pressure.
She peers and glances for some way to go, trying to lift her hand but
    cannot.
140 Nude #12. Old pole in the wind.

Cold currents are streaming over it
and pulling out
into ragged long horizontal black lines

some shreds of ribbon
145 attached to the pole.
I cannot see how they are attached—

notches? staples? nails? All of a sudden the wind changes
and all the black shreds rise straight up in the air
and tie themselves into knots,

150 then untie and float down.
The wind is gone.
It waits.

By this time, midway through winter,
I had become entirely fascinated with my spiritual melodrama.
155 Then it stopped.

Days passed, months passed and I saw nothing.
I continued to peer and glance, sitting on the rug in front of my sofa
in the curtainless morning

with my nerves open to the air like something skinned.
I saw nothing.
Outside the window spring storms came and went.

April snow folded its huge white paws over doors and porches.
I watched a chunk of it lean over the roof and break off
and fall and I thought,

How slow! as it glided soundlessly past,
but still—nothing. No nudes.
No Thou.

A great icicle formed on the railing of my balcony
so I drew up close to the window and tried peering through the
     icicle,
hoping to trick myself into some interior vision,

but all I saw
was the man and woman in the room across the street
making their bed and laughing.

I stopped watching.
I forgot about Nudes.
I lived my life,

which felt like a switched-off TV.
Something had gone through me and out and I could not own it.
"No need now to tremble for the hard frost and the keen wind.

Emily does not feel them,"
wrote Charlotte the day after burying her sister.
Emily had shaken free.

A soul can do that.
Whether it goes to join Thou and sit on the porch for all eternity
enjoying jokes and kisses and beautiful cold spring evenings,

you and I will never know. But I can tell you what I saw.
Nude #13 arrived when I was not watching for it.
It came at night.

Very much like Nude #1.
And yet utterly different.
I saw a high hill and on it a form shaped against hard air.

It could have been just a pole with some old cloth attached,
but as I came closer
I saw it was a human body

195   trying to stand against winds so terrible that the flesh was blowing off
           the bones.
     And there was no pain.
     The wind

     was cleansing the bones.
     They stood forth silver and necessary.
200   It was not my body, not a woman's body, it was the body of us all.
     It walked out of the light.

1995

Lazarus[1] Standup: Shooting Script

    How does a body do in the ground?

    Clouds look like matted white fur.
    Which are the animals? He has forgotten the difference
    between near and far.
5   Round pink ones come at him.
    From the pinks shoot fluids
    some dark (from eyes) some loud (from mouth).

    His bones are moving like a mist in him

    all blown to the surface then sideways.
10   *I do not want to see,*
    he thinks in pain
    as a darkish clump
    cuts across his field of vision,
    and some
15   strange

    silver milk
    is filling the space,
    gets caught in the mist,
    twists all his bones to the outside where they ignite in air.
20   The burning
    of his bones

    lets Lazarus know where each bone is.

    And so
    shifted forward into solidity—
25   although he pulls against it and groans to turn away—

---

1. The man whose resurrection by Jesus, four days after his death, is described in John 11.1–44.

Lazarus locks on
with a whistling sound behind him
as panels slide shut

and his soul congeals on his back in chrysolite[2] drops

30   which almost at once evaporate.
Lazarus
(someone is calling his name)—his name!
And at the name (which he knew)
not just a roar of darkness
35   the whole skeletal freight

of him
took pressure,
crushing him backward into the rut where he lay
like a damp
40   petal
under a pile of furniture.

And the second fact of his humanity began.

For the furniture shrank upon him as a bonework of
not just volume but
45   secret volume—
where fingers go probing
into drawers
and under
pried-up boxlids,

50   go rifling mute garments of white

and memories are streaming from his mind to his heart—
of someone standing at the door.
Of white breath in frozen air.
Mary. Martha.[3]
55   Linen of the same silence.
Lazarus! (again the voice)
and why not

climb the voice

where it goes spiralling upward
60   lacing him on a glow point
into the nocturnal motions of the world so that he is
standing now
propped on a cage of hot pushes of other people's air

---

2. A green gemstone.   3. The sisters of Lazarus.

and he feels more than hears
65   her voice (again)

like a salt rubbed whole into raw surface—

Lazarus!
A froth of fire is upon his mind.
It crawls to the back of his tongue,
70   struggles a bit,
cracking the shell
and pushes out a bluish cry that passes at once to the soul.
Martha!

he cries, making a little scalded place

75   on the billows of tomb that lap our faces as we watch.
We know the difference now
(life or death).
For an instant it parts our hearts.
Someone take the linen napkin off his face,
80   says the director quietly.

                                                              2000

CAROLYN FORCHÉ
b. 1950

Carolyn Forché received the Edita and Ira Morris Hiroshima Foundation for Peace and Culture Award in 1998 in recognition of her work on behalf of human rights and the preservation of memory and culture. She has won many other honors—the Yale Younger Poets Selection for *Gathering the Tribes* (1976), the Lannan Award for *The Country between Us* (1981), and the *Los Angeles Times* Book Award for *The Angel of History* (1994), along with fellowships from the Guggenheim Foundation and the National Endowment for the Arts; however, the 1998 award, presented in Stockholm, epitomizes her contributions to letters as a poet, translator, journalist, and editor, for her work consistently combines a commitment to human rights with an effort to preserve the memory and culture of those people who have suffered traumatic assaults on their lives. At times under the auspices of Amnesty International, Forché has documented human rights violations in El Salvador, accompanied congressional fact-finding delegations to Israel, championed the rights of illegally imprisoned children in South Africa, and reported as the Beirut correspondent for National Public Radio's *All Things Considered.* Thus, she locates her work in a transnational tradition of verse responses to extreme suffering and dehumanization that she has anthologized in *Against Forgetting: Twentieth-Century Poetry of Witness* (1993).

Shaped by a working-class and Catholic upbringing in Detroit, Carolyn Forché received a B.A. from Michigan State University and an M.F.A. from Bowling Green University. During a 1977 trip abroad to translate the poetry of the Salvadoran poet

Claribel Alegría and at the urging of a friend, the Holocaust scholar Terrence Des Pres, she found a certain gate and stairwell near Notre Dame, a memorial to 200,000 people deported from France during the Shoah: on the white stone walls, poems had been carved, but it was not until decades later that she discovered them to be the words of Robert Desnos, who died in the concentration camps and whose verse she would subsequently translate. The next year, a Guggenheim fellowship enabled her to travel to San Salvador, from which she returned to document human rights abuses. Thereafter she devoted herself to itinerant human rights activism inside and outside the classroom until she settled at George Mason University, where she currently teaches. The influences on her work—the poetry of Denise Levertov, for example, and the philosophy of Emmanual Levinas—strengthen her belief in the efficacy of art to promote empathy for those left voiceless by cataclysmic loss. For this reason, Forché has eschewed what in one interview she calls "the mode of pronouncement or confession or [the] establishment of lyric identity and selfhood" so as instead to seek "a mode of recording."

The Colonel

What you have heard is true. I was in his house. His wife carried a tray of coffee and sugar. His daughter filed her nails, his son went out for the night. There were daily papers, pet dogs, a pistol on the cushion beside him. The moon swung bare on its black cord over the house. On the television was a cop show. It was in English. Broken bottles were embedded in the walls around the house to scoop the kneecaps from a man's legs or cut his hands to lace. On the windows there were gratings like those in liquor stores. We had dinner, rack of lamb, good wine, a gold bell was on the table for calling the maid. The maid brought green mangoes, salt, a type of bread. I was asked how I enjoyed the country. There was a brief commercial in Spanish. His wife took everything away. There was some talk then of how difficult it had become to govern. The parrot said hello on the terrace. The colonel told it to shut up, and pushed himself from the table. My friend said to me with his eyes: say nothing. The colonel returned with a sack used to bring groceries home. He spilled many human ears on the table. They were like dried peach halves. There is no other way to say this. He took one of them in his hands, shook it in our faces, dropped it into a water glass. It came alive there. I am tired of fooling around he said. As for the rights of anyone, tell your people they can go fuck themselves. He swept the ears to the floor with his arm and held the last of his wine in the air. Something for your poetry, no? he said. Some of the ears on the floor caught this scrap of his voice. Some of the ears on the floor were pressed to the ground.

May 1978   1981

Elegy[1]

The page opens to snow on a field: boot-holed month, black hour
the bottle in your coat half vodka half winter light.
To what and to whom does one say *yes*?
If God were the uncertain, would you cling to him?[2]

5   Beneath a tattoo of stars the gate opens, so silent so like a tomb.
This is the city you most loved, an empty stairwell
where the next rain lifts invisibly from the Seine.[3]

With solitude, your coat open, you walk
steadily as if the railings were there and your hands weren't passing through them.

10   "When things were ready, they poured on fuel and touched off the fire.
They waited for a high wind.[4] It was very fine, that powdered bone.
It was put into sacks, and when there were enough we went to a bridge on the Narew River."[5]

And even less explicit phrases survived:
"To make charcoal.
15   For laundry irons."[6]
And so we revolt against silence with a bit of speaking.
The page is a charred field where the dead would have written
We went on. And it was like living through something again one could not live through again.

The soul behind you no longer inhabits your life: the unlit house
20   with its breathless windows and a chimney of ruined wings
where wind becomes an aria, your name, voices from a field,
And you, smoke, dissonance, a psalm, a stairwell.

1994

---

1. This poem is dedicated to the memory of Terrence Des Pres [Forché's note]. Des Pres (1939–1987), scholar and writer who specialized in Holocaust studies.
2. "If God were the *uncertain*, would you cling to him?" is from Paul Valéry's "The Art of Poetry" [Forché's note]. Valéry (1871–1945), French poet and critic.
3. River that flows through Paris.
4. "When things were ready . . . wind" is from Motke Zaidl and Itzhak Dugin's description of Sobibor in Claude Lanzmann's film *Shoah* [Forché's note]. *Shoah* (1985; literally, "catastrophe," in Hebrew) is a nearly 10-hour oral history of the Holocaust by the French writer and director Lanzmann (b. 1925). Sobibor was a camp in Poland to which the Jews of Vilna, Lithuania, including Zaidl and Dugin, were sent.
5. "It was very fine . . . Narew River" is an adaptation of Simon Srebnik's testimony on Chelmno in Lanzmann's film [Forché's note]. Srebnik was one of only two survivors of the extermination camp near the Narew River in Poland.
6. "To make charcoal . . . irons" was the answer given by an SS man to Simon Srebnik when he asked the purpose of the ovens at Chelmno [Forché's note].

MEDBH MCGUCKIAN
b. 1950

The poetic career of the Northern Irish poet Medbh (pronounced "Maeve") McGuckian began with a controversy over her age, gender, nationality, and marital status. In 1979 she submitted her poem "The Flitting" to an important poetry contest using a pseudonym, but when the judges discovered that she was merely a young Irish housewife and had been awarded the prize in preference to a better-known writer, they "rearranged the prize money," as one biographer has put it. Eventually the *Times Literary Supplement* publicized the case, wondering whether she had received a smaller award "because she was Irish, or Catholic, or a woman, or unknown." Yet even without the championship of the *TLS*, McGuckian's talent and energy would have enabled her to surmount establishment prejudices and become, as she has, one of the best-known members of a particularly brilliant generation of mostly male Northern Irish poets. This group includes such artists as Derek Mahon, Paul Muldoon, and the Nobel Prize–winning writer Seamus Heaney, who was McGuckian's teacher and mentor during her years at Queens University, Belfast. But in the Irish Republic to the south, McGuckian has many equally accomplished female contemporaries, among them Eiléan Ni Chuilleanáin, Nuala Ní Dhomhnaill, Eavan Boland, and Paula Meehan.

Musing on why she writes, McGuckian has commented that she wishes not only to give some sort of sense or coherence to "the helplessness of the human condition" but also to "be a voice or give a voice to things that have been oppressed and repressed in my peculiar culture." Born in Belfast, and educated at a Dominican convent and Queens University, she published her first major collection, *The Flower Master,* in 1982; it was followed by eight more volumes, many of them prize-winning, as well as a study of Seamus Heaney's poetry, an anthology of poems by young people from Northern Ireland, and translations of the Irish-language poems of Nuala Ní Dhomhnaill. She has worked as a teacher and editor, and has been a writer in residence at Queens University.

Some commentators have described McGuckian's poems as "opaque" or have been puzzled by her "dream-logic." Yet the works represented here—most notably, perhaps, the early poem "The Flitting" and the recent tribute to her mother, "She is in the Past, She has this Grace," which won the 2002 Forward Poetry Prize—typify the suavely cadenced style in which this innovative writer offers readers what one critic has called "a kind of fearless reverie."

The Flitting

'You wouldn't believe all this house has cost me—
In body-language terms, it has turned me upside down.'
I've been carried from one structure to the other
On a chair of human arms, and liked the feel
5   Of being weightless, that fraternity of clothes . . .
Now my own life hits me in the throat, the bumps
And cuts of the walls as telling
As the poreholes in strawberries, tomato seeds.
I cover them for safety with these Dutch girls
10   Making lace, or leaning their almond faces
On their fingers with a mandolin, a dreamy

Chapelled ease abreast this other turquoise-turbanned,
Glancing over her shoulder with parted mouth.[1]

She seems a garden escape in her unconscious
15 Solidarity with darkness, clove-scented
As an orchid taking fifteen years to bloom,
And turning clockwise as the honeysuckle.
Who knows what importance
She attaches to the hours?
20 Her narrative secretes its own values, as mine might
If I painted the half of me that welcomes death
In a faggotted[2] dress, in a peacock chair,
No falser biography than our casual talk
Of losing a virginity, or taking a life, and
25 No less poignant if dying
Should consist in more than waiting.

I postpone my immortality for my children,
Little rock-roses, cushioned
In long-flowering sea-thrift and metrics,[3]
30 Lacking elemental memories:
I am well-earthed here as the digital clock,
Its numbers flicking into place like overgrown farthings[4]
On a bank where once a train
Ploughed like an emperor living out a myth
35 Through the cambered[5] flesh of clover and wild carrot.

1979

Visiting Rainer Maria[1]

He said he was just leaving
As I was just arriving, in my blue
Smock, yesterday, without meaning to.
Though this first sentence would
5 Have been equally suitable
For the last, for a poem made
From a kitchen conversation.

The air was the way it always
Is in a room; books lay in ruins
10 On the snow-cold bed. He must have been
Scrubbing the floor with his toothbrush,
Using his shoulder as an ashtray,

---

1. An allusion to works by the Dutch painter Jan Vermeer, including *The Lacemaker* (1669–70) and *Woman with a Turban* (ca. 1665).
2. Embroidered by drawing out a number of threads in the material and tying together a few of the cross threads in the middle.
3. Use of metrical structures in verse. "Sea-thrift": a perennial flowering plant.
4. A farthing is literally a quarter of a penny (a small coin no longer in use).
5. Slightly tilted.

1. Rainer Maria Rilke (1875–1926), German lyric poet.

From the kind of insanity running
Through the American shadow furnishings.

So was my shape dictated by
The curved outer wall, the eccentricities
Of the corridor, all sorts of untils.
And I thought to myself, if he touches
My sleeve even softly, whole streets
Of shops near the sea will be extinguished
In the most intentional darkness:

If he mentions a river it will be one
Renouncing the moon, that lends itself
To a foreglimpse of the day's
Callisthenics, stirring into animal storm,
Adding a feminine ending to
Whatever parts are dream. Of the place,
It was godforsaken; of the season, dead;

But whether it was sea or flesh,
Short capsules of conscripted
Cooling wax were laid like expiry
Dates over partings of quite a different
Cast. I said, I must find it,
Using the feminine form of must,
What *you* want, what *I* want, what can be done.

For four more virgin months I have been
Not his, *not* his, *not* his, *his*,
A sea-kitten rolling up in his
English shirt like a tray of Persian
Tea, neutral as a cloud. Because
The *it* of his translation may mean silence,
But the *she* of mine means Aphrodite.[2]

1991

Black Virgin[1]

Sea-black virgin—being in love with you
is a fine space. I will never live
in your searching wash, your grass wallpaper,
your bewildered red gardens.
   You desire your wholeness, your virginity,
to be admired by angels only.

---

2. Greek goddess of love.
1. In Europe there are hundreds of "black virgins," or black madonnas—statues or paintings of the Virgin Mary in which her face and hands are dark or have darkened over time.

Such dry self-knowledge. Such sheer
Englishness—how could I
have mistaken you for my father?

     For the old days when there used to be
people? Your days have a medieval structure,
your brief Cistercian night, with its night office,[2]
has fought sleep always; for morning
you touch your lower eyelid, deep, awake,
healthy and wise and quiet, with your eyes clear.
What do you do with your eyes?

With your womb already primed
with its fern-like pattern, chasteberry,
chaste tree, monk's pepper?[3]
If you are a woman there is no question
of a word like me being able to comprehend
the voice that uttered it, or its sign language
lordly and off-balance, with the inwardness
of war. Perhaps I am a sound
that was born with you, and finished
with you, your Lenten[4] stomach
in a year when Easter was as late
as it could possibly be.

Or perhaps I am a military railway
to you, another city, with transient
miles of criminals. But when rain arrives
on the far side of emptiness,
like an identity scarcely dreamed,
and surrounds you with its unintelligible
silence, its enormously comforting speech—
even if it is talking to itself,
as long as it talks, I will listen.

     1995

She is in the Past, She has this Grace

My mother looks at her watch,
as if to look back over the curve
of her life, her slackening rhythms:
nobody can know her, how she lost herself
evening after evening in that after,
her hourly feelings, the repetition,

---

2. Prescribed service of worship. "Cistercian": a monastic order established at Citeaux by St. Robert in 1098. Its night is "brief" because those in the order rise before 4 A.M. to pray.
3. Three names for the same herb, whose berries are traditionally used to treat menstrual problems and infertility; the Greeks thought that the plant calmed sexual passion.
4. Of the period of fasting before Easter.

delay and failure of her labour
of mourning. The steps space themselves
out, the steps pass, in the mists
and hesitations of the summer,
and within a space which is doubled
one of us has passed through the other,
though one must count oneself three,
to figure out which of us
has let herself be traversed.

Nothing advances, we don't move,
we don't address one another.
I haven't opened my mouth
except for one remark,
and what remark was that?
A word which appeases the menace
of time in us, reading as if
I were stripping the words
of their ever-mortal high meaning.

She is in dark light, or an openness
that leads to a darkness,
embedded in the wall
her mono-landscape
stays facing the sea
and the harbour activity,
her sea-conscience being ground up
with the smooth time of the deep,
her mourning silhouetted against
the splendour of the sea
which is now to your left,
as violent as it is distant
from all aggressive powers
or any embassies.

And she actively dreams
in the very long ending of this moment,
she is back in her lapping marshes,
still walking with the infinite
step of a prisoner, that former dimension
in which her gaze spreads itself
as a stroke without regarding you,
making you lower your own gaze.

Who will be there,
at that moment, beside her,
when time becomes sacred,
and her voice becomes an opera,
and the solitude is removed
from her body, as if my hand
had been held in some invisible place?

2002

GRACE NICHOLS
b. 1950

The author of the witty and popular collection *The Fat Black Woman's Poems* (1984) was born in Georgetown, Guyana, and spent her first eight years in a village on the Guyanese coast. Later, after moving to the city and studying at the University of Guyana, she worked as a teacher and journalist while also researching folklore and Amerindian myths in remote parts of the country. In 1977, she emigrated to England with her partner, the poet John Agard, with whom she has co-edited a number of collections of Caribbean verse. Nichols's own first major book of poems, *I Is a Long-Memoried Woman* (1983), won the Commonwealth Poetry Prize and was later made into a prize-winning film as well as a radio script. But she has also published fiction, including the novel *Whole of a Morning Sky* (1986) and a number of children's books, most recently *The Poet Cat* (2000). Her other books of "adult" verse include *Lazy Thoughts of a Lazy Woman* (1989) and *Sunris* (1996).

Sensual and insouciant, Nichols's poems often mock imperial pretensions even as they celebrate "the fat black chuckle" of her fat black heroine "showing her fat black toes." At the same time, this Guyanese expatriate traces the history and culture of Africa and the Caribbean with style, sensitivity, and compassion. " 'Out of Africa,' " she explains, "was triggered by the line 'Out of Africa' from a movie I haven't seen, from a book I haven't read, but the line kept evoking images in my head. Linking Africa, the Caribbean and England came quite naturally, even though that connection is historically grounded in the transatlantic slave trade as far back as the 16th century."

The Assertion

    Heavy as a whale
    eyes beady with contempt
    and a kind of fire of love
    the fat black woman sits
5   on the golden stool
    and refuses to move

    the white robed chiefs
    are resigned
    in their postures of resignation

10 the fat black woman's fingers
    are creased in gold
    body ringed in folds
    pulse beat at her throat

    This is my birthright
15 says the fat black woman
    giving a fat black chuckle
    showing her fat black toes

1984

The Fat Black Woman Remembers

The fat black woman
remembers her Mama
and them days of playing
the Jovial Jemima[1]

     tossing pancakes
to heaven
in smokes of happy hearty
          murderous blue laughter

Starching and cleaning
O yes scolding and wheedling
pressing little white heads
against her big-aproned breasts
seeing down to the smallest fed
feeding her own children on Satanic bread

But this fat black woman ain't no Jemim
    Sure thing Honey/Yeah

1984

Tropical Death

The fat black woman want
a brilliant tropical death
not a cold sojourn
in some North Europe far/forlorn

    The fat black woman want
some heat/hibiscus at her feet
blue sea dress
to wrap her neat

The fat black woman want
some bawl
no quiet jerk tear wiping
a polite hearse withdrawal

The fat black woman want
all her dead rights
    first night
third night
nine night

---

1. I.e., Aunt Jemima, the iconic illustration of the brand name pictured on pancake mix and syrup since 1893 (originally shown as a stereotypical black servant, in a kerchief).

all the sleepless droning
red-eyed wake nights

20   In the heart
of her mother's sweetbreast
In the shade
of the sun leaf's cool bless
In the bloom
25   of her people's bloodrest

the fat black woman want
a brilliant tropical death yes

1984

Out of Africa[1]

Out of Africa of the suckling
Out of Africa of the tired woman in earrings
Out of Africa of the black-foot leap
Out of Africa of the baobab, the suck-teeth[2]
5   Out of Africa of the dry maw of hunger
Out of Africa of the first rains, the first mother.

Into the Caribbean of the staggeringly blue sea-eye
Into the Caribbean of the baleful tourist glare
Into the Caribbean of the hurricane
10   Into the Caribbean of the flame tree, the palm tree,
the ackee,[3] the high smelling saltfish
and the happy creole[4] so-called mentality.

Into England of the frost and the tea
Into England of the budgie[5] and the strawberry
15   Into England of the trampled autumn tongues
Into England of the meagre funerals
Into England of the hand of the old woman
And the gent running behind someone
who's forgotten their umbrella, crying out,
20   'I say . . . I say-ay.'

1989

---

1. A poem triggered, according to Nichols, by the 1985 film *Out of Africa*, based on Isak Dinesen's 1937 memoir of the same title, which focuses on the European experience of Africa.
2. The act of sucking air through the teeth to express annoyance, exasperation, or anger, an African gesture common in the Caribbean. "Baobab": a broad-trunked tropical tree native to Africa.
3. The fruit of an African tree grown in the Caribbean; also, the tree itself.
4. A person of mixed black and European ancestry; also, a descendant of European settlers in the Caribbean or Central or South America.
5. A budgerigar, or small parrot native to Australia but popular in Great Britain as a domesticated bird.

JORIE GRAHAM
b. 1951

Situating herself under a "sky that keeps / sliding away," in an atmosphere "married to hurry / and grim song," Jorie Pepper Graham has produced numerous collections of elegantly formulated, subtly nuanced, elliptical verse. Educated at New York University and the University of Iowa, she is married and has one child. A past director of the Iowa Writers' Workshop, she is the recipient of a MacArthur fellowship as well as many other honors and awards. From *Hybrids of Plants and of Ghosts* (1980) and *The End of Beauty* (1987) to *Materialism* (1993), *The Dream of the Unified Field* (1995), *Swarm* (2000), and *Overlord* (2005), her often elegiac volumes focus on modes of perception and understanding, on the many ways in which lived experience "unfastens itself / from the deep ocean of the given." At the same time, as she has noted in one of her poems, she sees an aesthetic based on the sexual exploitation and oppression of women as a reason to "weep / for the moral nature / of this world." With characteristic thoughtfulness, both "Orpheus and Eurydice" and "History" meditate on such painful issues. Currently the Boylston Professor of Rhetoric and Oratory at Harvard University, Jorie Graham won the Pulitzer Prize in 1996 (for *The Dream of the Unified Field*). From 1997 to 2003, she served as a chancellor of the Academy of American Poets.

History

    Into whose ear the deeds are spoken. The only
listener. So I believed
he would remember everything, the murmuring trees,
the sunshine's zealotry, its deep
unevenness. For history
is the opposite
of the eye
for whom, for instance, six million[1] bodies in portions
of hundreds and
the flowerpots broken by a sudden wind stand as
equivalent. What more
is there
than fact? *I'll give ten thousand dollars to the man
who proves the holocaust really
occurred*[2] said the exhausted solitude
in San Francisco
in 1980. Far in the woods
in a faded photograph
in 1942 the man with his own
genitalia in his mouth and hundreds of
slow holes
a pitchfork has opened
over his face
grows beautiful. The ferns and deepwood
lilies catch

---

1. The number of European Jews killed during the Holocaust.
2. In 1980, the Institute for Historical Review, an organization of Holocaust deniers based in California, offered a $50,000 reward to anyone who could conclusively prove that Jews had been gassed at Auschwitz.

              the eye. Three men in ragged uniforms
              with guns keep laughing
              nervously. They share the day
              with him. A bluebird
30   sings. The feathers of the shade touch every inch
              of skin—the hand holding down the delicate gun,
              the hands holding down the delicate
              hips. And the sky
              is visible between the men, between
35   the trees, a blue spirit
              enveloping
              anything. Late in the story, in Northern Italy,
              a man cuts down some trees for winter
              fuel. We read this in the evening
40   news. Watching the fire burn late
              one night, watching it change and change, a hand grenade,
              lodged in the pulp the young tree
              grew around, explodes, blinding the man, killing
              his wife. Now who
45   will tell the children
              fairytales? The ones where simple
              crumbs over the forest
              floor endure
              to help us home?[3]

                                                                                    1983

Orpheus and Eurydice[1]

Up ahead, I know, he felt it stirring in himself already, the glance,
the darting thing in the pile of rocks,

already in him, there, shiny in the rubble, hissing Did you want to remain
completely unharmed?—

5   the point-of-view darting in him, shiny head in the ash-heap,

hissing Once upon a time, and then Turn now darling give me that look,
that perfect shot, give me that place where I'm erased . . .

The thing, he must have wondered, could it be put to rest, there, in the
                                                                                              glance,
10 could it lie back down into the dustyness, giving its outline up?

When we turn to them—limbs, fields, expanses of dust called meadow and
                                                                                              avenue—

---

3. In the fairy tale "Hansel and Gretel," the children, knowing that they are to be abandoned in the forest, succeed in finding their way home by leaving a trail of white pebbles; but a later trail made of breadcrumbs is no help, for it is eaten by animals.

1. According to Greek myth, Eurydice, the wife of the poet Orpheus, died after being bitten by a snake; Orpheus's song temporarily won her back from the underworld, but he could not keep his promise not to look back at her until they had reached the lands above.

will they be freed then to slip back in?
Because you see he could not be married to it anymore, this field with
                                    minutes in it
called woman, its presence in him the thing called

future—could not be married to it anymore, expanse tugging his mind out
                                            into it,
tugging the wanting-to-finish out.

What he dreamed of was this road (as he walked on it), this dustyness,
but without their steps on it, their prints, without
song—

What she dreamed, as she watched him turning with the bend in the road
                                        (can you
understand this?)—what she dreamed

was of disappearing into the seen

not of disappearing, lord, into the real—

And yes she could feel it in him already, up ahead, that wanting-to-turn-
and-cast-the-outline-over-her

by his glance,

sealing the edges down,

saying I know you from somewhere darling, don't I,
saying You're the kind of woman who etcetera—

(Now the cypress are swaying) (Now the lake in the distance)
(Now the view-from-above, the aerial attack of *do you
remember?*)—

now the glance reaching her shoreline wanting only to be recalled,
now the glance reaching her shoreline wanting only to be taken in,

(somewhere the castle above the river)

(somewhere you holding this piece of paper)

(what will you do next?) (—feel it beginning?)
now she's raising her eyes, as if pulled from above,

now she's looking back into it, into the poison the beginning,

giving herself to it, looking back into the eyes,

feeling the dry soft grass beneath her feet for the first time now the mind

looking into that which sets the _____ in motion and seeing in there

a doorway open nothing on either side
(a slight wind now around them, three notes from up the hill)

through which morning creeps and the first true notes—

50   For they were deep in the earth and what is possible swiftly took hold.

1987

JOY HARJO
b. 1951

Poet, performer, and Native American activist Joy Harjo has written that she dreams of a "place of grace . . . in which there's a unity of human-ness with wolf-ness, with hummingbird-ness, with Sandia Mountain-ness with rain cloud-ness," a sacred place where "we understand there is no separation between worlds" and know that the "land is responsible for the clothes you have on, for my saxophone, for the paper that I write these things on." Born in Oklahoma and an enrolled member of the Muskogee Tribe, she studied painting and theater in New Mexico at the Institute of American Indian Arts but turned to poetry when she felt that the political climate "demanded singers and speakers." In 1976, she graduated from the University of New Mexico and in 1978 earned an M.F.A. from the University of Iowa. Among teachers whom she credits with influencing her style, she includes the Native American poet and fiction writer Leslie Marmon Silko.

Since beginning her writing career in the mid-1970s, Harjo has published more than half a dozen major collections of verse, including *The Woman Who Fell from the Sky* (1994), *A Map to the Next World* (2000), and *How We Became Human: New and Selected Poems: 1975–2001* (2002). Over the years, she has taught at a number of institutions, most notably the University of Colorado, the University of Hawaii, and the University of California, Los Angeles. While she was living in Colorado, she studied the saxophone and co-founded a band called *Poetic Justice* with whom she has released several CDs, among them *Letter from the End of the Twentieth Century* (1998) and *Native Joy for Real* (2005). As one commentator has remarked, her performances mix "American Indian, African, and jazz rhythms to create her own unique . . . brand of music." And a similar eclecticism shapes her exuberant, witty, and vividly cadenced poems, which—like "Deer-Dancer" and "The Path to the Milky Way Leads through Los Angeles"—often set Native American legends (a mystic deer, a trickster crow) in sometimes seedy contemporary landscapes, revealing that it's possible to find "gold in the trash of humans."

Deer Dancer

Nearly everyone had left that bar in the middle of winter except the hardcore. It was the coldest night of the year, every place shut down, but not us. Of course we noticed when she came in. We were Indian ruins. She

was the end of beauty. No one knew her, the stranger whose tribe we
recognized, her family related to deer, if that's who she was, a people
accustomed to hearing songs in pine trees, and making them hearts.

The woman inside the woman who was to dance naked in the bar of misfits
blew deer magic. Henry Jack, who could not survive a sober day, thought she
was Buffalo Calf Woman[1] come back, passed out, his head by the toilet. All
night he dreamed a dream he could not say. The next day he borrowed
money, went home, and sent back the money I lent. Now that's a miracle.
Some people see vision in a burned tortilla,[2] some in the face of a woman.

This is the bar of broken survivors, the club of shotgun, knife wound, of
poison by culture. We who were taught not to stare drank our beer. The
players gossiped down their cues. Someone put a quarter in the jukebox to
relive despair. Richard's wife dove to kill her. We had to hold her back,
empty her pockets of knives and diaper pins, buy her two beers to keep her
still, while Richard secretly bought the beauty a drink.

How do I say it? In this language there are no words for how the real world
collapses. I could say it in my own and the sacred mounds would come into
focus, but I couldn't take it in this dingy envelope. So I look at the stars in
this strange city, frozen to the back of the sky, the only promises that ever
make sense.

My brother-in-law hung out with white people, went to law school with a
perfect record, quit. Says you can keep your laws, your words. And
practiced law on the street with his hands. He jimmied to the proverbial
dream girl, the face of the moon, while the players racked a new game.
He bragged to us, he told her magic words and that's when she broke,
became human.

But we all heard his bar voice crack:

What's a girl like you doing in a place like this!

That's what I'd like to know, what are we all doing in a place like this?

You would know she could hear only what she wanted to; don't we all? Left
the drink of betrayal Richard bought her, at the bar. What was she on? We all
wanted some. Put a quarter in the juke. We all take risks stepping into thin
air. Our ceremonies didn't predict this. Or we expected more.

I had to tell you this, for the baby inside the girl sealed up with a lick of
hope and swimming into praise of nations. This is not a rooming house, but
a dream of winter falls and the deer who portrayed the relatives of
strangers. The way back is deer breath on icy windows.

The next dance none of us predicted. She borrowed a chair for the stairway
to heaven and stood on a table of names. And danced in the room of children
without shoes.

---

1. In Lakota mythology, a supernatural being who taught the people many sacred rituals.
2. On several occasions in the United States, beginning in 1977, individuals claimed to see the face of Jesus burned into a tortilla.

> *You picked a fine time to leave me, Lucille.*
> *With four hungry children and a crop in the field.*[3]

And then she took off her clothes. She shook loose memory, waltzed with the empty lover we'd all become.

She was the myth slipped down through dreamtime. The promise of feast we all knew was coming. The deer who crossed through knots of a curse to find us. She was no slouch, and neither were we, watching.

The music ended. And so does the story. I wasn't there. But I imagined her like this, not a stained red dress with tape on her heels but the deer who entered our dream in white dawn, breathed mist into pine trees, her fawn a blessing of meat, the ancestors who never left.

1990

Mourning Song

It's early evening here in the small world, where gods gamble for good weather as the sky turns red. Oh grief rattling around in the bowl of my skeleton. How I'd like to spit you out, turn you into another human, or remake the little dog spirit who walked out of our house without its skin toward an unseen land. We were left behind to figure it out during a harvest turned to ashes. I need to mourn with the night, turn to the gleaming house of bones under your familiar brown skin. The hot stone of our hearts will make a fire. If we cry more tears we will ruin the land with salt; instead let's praise that which would distract us with despair. Make a song for death, a song with yellow teeth and bad breath. For loneliness, the house guest who eats everything and refuses to leave. A song for bad weather so we can stand together under our leaking roof, and make a terrible music with our wise and ragged bones.

*

In the city in which I live are many homeless people. They congregate near the post office and coffeehouse I frequent. I've gotten to know one woman by name, though another woman terrifies me with her quiet insanity. I make a wide circle around her and feel guilty every time I see her. I'm especially disturbed when I see my Indian relatives suffering such a loss. Often they are the very tribe whose land is now called Albuquerque.

Because my family has suffered from the destruction of alcohol, as have most Indian families in this land, I don't want to encourage the drinking with spare change, but I also understand the need to deaden the pain. It's a quandary I haven't settled.

Once far down the sidewalk I spotted two Indian men who were asking passersby for money. I tried to make myself invisible so I wouldn't have to confront the pain, but they saw me anyway. I was shocked to recognize my old friend, a tall good-looking Navajo who always had a good story.

---

3. Lyrics from "Lucille," a hit recorded in 1977 by the American pop-country singer Kenny Rogers.

He was filthy, his hair thick with lice. He also recognized me and couldn't let it pass that I had gained some weight since my svelte twenties! We laughed and hugged each other, then cried.

I am still thinking of him and how each of us chooses our path daily, though our choices often appear limited by race, sex and class.

Knowing him the way I did I couldn't help but think he'd made a choice to be a modern warrior, and could gather more crucial knowledge from the streets of this city than he could have on a track called success by the colonizers.

1994

The Naming

for Haleigh Sara Bush

I think of names that have profoundly changed the direction of disaster. Of the raw whirling wind outlining femaleness emerging from the underworld.

It blesses the frog taking refuge under the squash-flower cloud, the
5   stubborn weeds leaning in the direction of wind bringing rain.

My grandmother is the color of night as she tells me to move away from the window when it is storming. *The lightning will take you.*

I thought it was my long dark hair appearing as lightning. The lightning appears to be relatives.

10   Truth can appear as disaster in a land of things unspoken. It can be reached with white arrows, each outlining the meaning of delicate struggle.

And can happen on a night like this when the arrow light is bitten by sweet wind.

15   My grandmother took leave years ago by way of her aggravated heart. I haven't seen her since, but her warnings against drownings, lightning or anything else portending death by sudden means still cling to my ears.

I take those risks against the current of warnings as if she had in-
20   vented negative space of wind around the curve of earth.

That night after my granddaughter-born-for-my-son climbed from the underworld we could smell ozone over the lake made of a few centuries of rain.

I went hunting for the right name and found the spirit of the ice age
making plans in the bottom of the lake. Eventually the spirit will become rain, remake the shoreline with pines and laughter.

In the rain I saw the child who was carried by lightning to the other
side of the storm. I saw my grandmother who never had any peace
in this life blessed with animals and songs.

Oh daughter-born-of-my-son, of my grandmother, of my mother; I
name you all these things:

The bag of white arrows is heavy with rain.

The earth is wet with happiness.

*

*I never liked my mother's mother, Leona May Baker. When we would
visit her and my grandfather in their two-room house in northwestern
Arkansas where they were sharecroppers, she would awaken me long
before dawn. I would be irritable with lack of sleep as she would sit by
my bed and catalogue the gruesome details of every death of every relative and friend as well as each event of personal disaster within her
known landscape.*

*My grandmother, who was half Cherokee and Irish, was orphaned at a
very young age and raised by full-blood Cherokees in Jay, Oklahoma.
She gave birth to six sons and one daughter—my mother. Each birth
added to the burden of life. Once she took out a gun and shot at all of
them as they ran through the trees to get away from her. My mother
recalls the sounds of bullets flying by her head. My grandmother disliked
my mother.*

*With the impending birth of my son's daughter I was prompted to find
out more about this grandmother who I had never made peace with. My
mother told me of her incredible gift of storytelling, how she would keep
the children entranced for weeks by tales she would invent—they had no
books, television or radio. And then she told me this story:*

*My grandfather Desmond Baker left to work on the railroad when they
were especially destitute. While he was away my grandmother had an
affair. When he returned nine months later she was near full term with
a baby who wasn't his. He beat her until she went into labor and gave
birth to the murdered child.*

*Shortly after the killing my grandparents attempted double suicide. They
stood on the tracks while a train bore down on them as all the children
watched in horror. At the last possible second my grandfather pushed my
grandmother off to safety and leaped behind her.*

*I began to have compassion for this woman who was weighted down
with seven children and no opportunities. Maybe her affair was the
lightness she needed to stay alive.*

> 65 *When my granddaughter Haleigh was born I felt the spirit of this grandmother in the hospital room. Her presence was a blessing.*
>
> *I welcomed her.*

1994

The Path to the Milky Way Leads through Los Angeles

There are strangers above me, below me and all around me and we are all
strange in this place of recent invention.
This city named for angels appears naked and stripped of anything resembling
the shaking of turtle shells, the songs of human voices on a summer night
outside Okmulgee.[1]
Yet, it's perpetually summer here, and beautiful. The shimmer of gods is easier
to perceive at sunrise or dusk,
when those who remember us here in the illusion of the marketplace
turn toward the changing of the sun and say our names.
We matter to somebody,
We must matter to the strange god who imagines us as we revolve together in
the dark sky on the path to the Milky Way.[2]
We can't easily see that starry road from the perspective of the crossing of
boulevards, can't hear it in the whine of civilization or taste the minerals of
planets in hamburgers.
But we can buy a map here of the stars' homes, dial a tone for dangerous love,
choose from several brands of water or a hiss of oxygen for gentle rejuvenation.
Everyone knows you can't buy love but you can still sell your soul for less
than a song to a stranger who will sell it to someone else for a profit
until you're owned by a company of strangers.
in the city of the strange and getting stranger.
I'd rather understand how to sing from a crow
who was never good at singing or much of anything
but finding gold in the trash of humans.
So what are we doing here I ask the crow parading on the ledge of falling that
hangs over this precarious city?
Crow[3] just laughs and says *wait, wait* and *see* and I am waiting and not seeing
anything, not just yet.
But like crow I collect the shine of anything beautiful I can find.

2000

Morning Song

The red dawn now is rearranging the earth
Thought by thought
Beauty by beauty
Each sunrise a link in the ladder

---

1. City in east central Oklahoma; it serves as the seat of the Muscogee Creek Nation.
2. In Native American legend, the path followed by the virtuous after they die.
3. A trickster character in many Native American stories and myths.

                    The ladder the backbone
                    Of shimmering deity
                    Child stirring in the web of your mother
                    Do not be afraid
                    Old man turning to walk through the door
              10   Do not be afraid

                                                                                    2000

When the World As We Knew It Ended

We were dreaming on an occupied island at the farthest edge
of a trembling nation when it went down.

Two towers rose up from the east island of commerce and touched
the sky.[1] Men walked on the moon. Oil was sucked dry
by two brothers. Then it went down. Swallowed
by a fire dragon, by oil and fear.
Eaten whole.

It was coming.

We had been watching since the eve of the missionaries in their
long and solemn clothes, to see what would happen.

We saw it
from the kitchen window over the sink
as we made coffee, cooked rice and
potatoes, enough for an army.

We saw it all, as we changed diapers and fed
the babies. We saw it,
through the branches
of the knowledgeable tree
through the snags of stars, through
the sun and storms from our knees
as we bathed and washed
the floors.

The conference of the birds warned us, as they flew over
destroyers in the harbor, parked there since the first takeover.
It was by their song and talk we knew when to rise
when to look out the window
to the commotion going on—
the magnetic field thrown off by grief.

We heard it.
The racket in every corner of the world. As
the hunger for war rose up in those who would steal to be president

---

1. Construction on the twin towers of New York City's World Trade Center, briefly the tallest buildings in the world, began in 1966 and ended in 1972.

to be king or emperor, to own the trees, stones, and everything
else that moved about the earth, inside the earth
and above it.

35 We knew it was coming, tasted the winds who gathered intelligence
from each leaf and flower, from every mountain, sea
and desert, from every prayer and song all over this tiny universe
floating in the skies of infinite
being.

40 And then it was over, this world we had grown to love
for its sweet grasses, for the many-colored horses
and fishes, for the shimmering possibilities
while dreaming.

But then there were the seeds to plant and the babies
45 who needed milk and comforting, and someone
picked up a guitar or ukulele from the rubble

and began to sing about the light flutter
the kick beneath the skin of the earth
we felt there, beneath us

50 a warm animal
a song being born between the legs of her,
a poem.

2002

RITA DOVE
b. 1952

Rita Dove was born in Akron, Ohio, the second of four children and the oldest daughter. Her father was the first black chemist at the Goodyear Tire and Rubber Company, her mother a housekeeper. She believes that belonging to a "first-generation middle-class family" helped to shape both her early insecurities and her feeling of privilege. After graduating *summa cum laude* from Miami University in Ohio in 1973, she attended the University of Tubingen on a Fulbright scholarship and received a master's of fine arts from the University of Iowa Writers' Workshop in 1977. Attributing her interest in poetry to a fascination with "the ways in which language can change your perceptions," Dove published *The Yellow House on the Corner* (1980) and *Museum* (1983) to critical acclaim. Here, Dove's poetry exhibits a technical acumen and a fascination with history that enable her to move between familiar themes ("the yellow house") and sophisticated, aesthetic subjects (the nature of the "museum").

Dove's subsequent work also negotiates between national and personal concerns. In *Thomas and Beulah* (1986), winner of the Pulitzer Prize in 1987, she produced an ambitious sequence about her grandparents' courtship and marriage that melded public and private narratives. Continuing to move into autobiography, many of the poems in *Grace Notes* (1989) deal with her personal experiences as a daughter and as a mother of a daughter. Dove, who is married to Fred Viebahn and currently teaches at the University of Virginia, has also published a collection of stories, *Fifth Sunday* (1985), as well as a play, *The Siberian Village* (1991); a novel, *Through the Ivory Gate* (1992); and a collection of verse, *Mother Love* (1995), that focuses on themes and images of the maternal. Whether she examines her own adolescence or her grandfather's courtship, a genocidal Haitian dictator or an African American civil rights activist, Dove avoids didacticism by entering into the unique subjectivity of the diverse cast of characters who haunt her imagination. From 1993 to 1995, Rita Dove served as poet laureate of the United States and she is currently poet laureate of the Commonwealth of Virginia. Her most recent collection of verse is *American Smooth* (2004).

The House Slave

The first horn lifts its arm over the dew-lit grass
and in the slave quarters there is a rustling—
children are bundled into aprons, cornbread

and water gourds grabbed, a salt pork breakfast taken.
5 I watch them driven into the vague before-dawn
while their mistress sleeps like an ivory toothpick

and Massa dreams of asses, rum and slave-funk.
I cannot fall asleep again. At the second horn,
the whip curls across the backs of the laggards—

10 sometimes my sister's voice, unmistaken, among them.
"Oh! pray," she cries. "Oh! pray!" Those days
I lie on my cot, shivering in the early heat,

and as the fields unfold to whiteness,
15 and they spill like bees among the fat flowers,
I weep. It is not yet daylight.

1980

Parsley[1]

1. The Cane Fields

There is a parrot imitating spring
in the palace, its feathers parsley green.
Out of the swamp the cane[2] appears

---

1. On October 2, 1957, Rafael Trujillo (1891–1961), dictator of the Dominican Republic, ordered 20,000 blacks killed because they could not pronounce the letter "r" in *perejil*, the Spanish word for parsley [Dove's note].
2. Sugarcane.

to haunt us, and we cut it down. El General
searches for a word; he is all the world
there is. Like a parrot imitating spring,

we lie down screaming as rain punches through
and we come up green. We cannot speak an R—
out of the swamp, the cane appears

and then the mountain we call in whispers *Katalina*.
The children gnaw their teeth to arrowheads.
There is a parrot imitating spring.

El General has found his word: *perejil*.
Who says it, lives. He laughs, teeth shining
out of the swamp. The cane appears

in our dreams, lashed by wind and streaming.
And we lie down. For every drop of blood
there is a parrot imitating spring.
Out of the swamp the cane appears.

2. The Palace

The word the general's chosen is parsley.
It is fall, when thoughts turn
to love and death; the general thinks
of his mother, how she died in the fall
and he planted her walking cane at the grave
and it flowered, each spring stolidly forming
four-star blossoms. The general

pulls on his boots, he stomps to
her room in the palace, the one without
curtains, the one with a parrot
in a brass ring. As he paces he wonders
Who can I kill today. And for a moment
the little knot of screams
is still. The parrot, who has traveled

all the way from Australia in an ivory
cage, is, coy as a widow, practising
spring. Ever since the morning
his mother collapsed in the kitchen
while baking skull-shaped candies
for the Day of the Dead,[3] the general
has hated sweets. He orders pastries
brought up for the bird; they arrive

dusted with sugar on a bed of lace.
The knot in his throat starts to twitch;

3. All Souls' Day, celebrated November 1 and 2.

          he sees his boots the first day in battle
45   splashed with mud and urine
          as a soldier falls at his feet amazed—
          how stupid he looked!—at the sound
          of artillery. *I never thought it would sing*
          the soldier said, and died. Now

50   the general sees the fields of sugar
          cane, lashed by rain and streaming.
          He sees his mother's smile, the teeth
          gnawed to arrowheads. He hears
          the Haitians sing without R's
55   as they swing the great machetes:
          Katalina, they sing, *Katalina*,

          mi madle, mi amol en muelte.[4] God knows
          his mother was no stupid woman; she
          could roll an R like a queen. Even
60   a parrot can roll an R! In the bare room
          the bright feathers arch in a parody
          of greenery, as the last pale crumbs
          disappear under the blackened tongue. Someone

          calls out his name in a voice
65   so like his mother's, a startled tear
          splashes the tip of his right boot.
          My mother, my love in death.
          The general remembers the tiny green sprigs
          men of his village wore in their capes
70   to honor the birth of a son. He will
          order many, this time, to be killed

          for a single, beautiful word.

                                                                                      1983

From Thomas and Beulah

The Great Palaces of Versailles[1]

          Nothing nastier than a white person!
          She mutters as she irons alterations
          in the backroom of Charlotte's Dress Shoppe.
          The steam rising from a cranberry wool
5   comes alive with perspiration
          and stale Evening of Paris.
          Swamp she born from, swamp
          she swallow, swamp she got to sink again.

---

4. I.e., *mi madre, mi amor en muerte* (Spanish; translated in line 67).
1. A French city that contains not only Louis XIV's large palace, now also called Versailles, but two smaller places (the Grande Trianon and the Petit Trianon) in its park.

The iron shoves gently
into a gusset, waits until
the puckers bloom away. Beyond
the curtain, the white girls are all
wearing shoulder pads to make their faces
delicate. That laugh would be Autumn,
tossing her hair in imitation of Bacall.[2]

Beulah had read in the library
how French ladies at court would tuck
their fans in a sleeve
and walk in the gardens for air. Swaying
among lilies, lifting shy layers of silk,
they dropped excrement as daintily
as handkerchieves. Against all rules

she had saved the lining from a botched coat
to face last year's gray skirt. She knows
whenever she lifts a knee
she flashes crimson. That seems legitimate;
but in the book she had read
how the *cavaliere* amused themselves
wearing powder and perfume and spraying
yellow borders knee-high on the stucco
of the *Orangerie*.[3]

A hanger clatters
in the front of the shoppe.
Beulah remembers how
even Autumn could lean into a settee
with her ankles crossed, sighing
I need a man who'll protect me
while smoking her cigarette down to the very end.

Wingfoot Lake[4]

(INDEPENDENCE DAY, 1964)

On her 36th birthday, Thomas had shown her
her first swimming pool. It had been
his favorite color, exactly—just
so much of it, the swimmers' white arms jutting
into the chevrons[5] of high society.
She had rolled up her window
and told him to drive on, fast.

Now this *act of mercy:* four daughters
dragging her to their husbands' company picnic,

---

2. Lauren Bacall (b. 1924), one of the most glamorous film stars of the 1940s and 1950s.
3. The greenhouse of the Tuileries Gardens in Paris. "*Cavaliere*": horsewoman (French).
4. Lake and park owned by the Goodyear Tire and Rubber Company, southeast of Akron, Ohio.
5. I.e., the swimmers' arms meet at an angle like a chevron (which is also a badge indicating rank).

        white families on one side and them
        on the other, unpacking the same
50   squeeze bottles of Heinz, the same
        waxy beef patties and Salem potato chip bags.
        So he was dead for the first time
        on Fourth of July—ten years ago

        had been harder, waiting for something to happen,
55   and ten years before that, the girls
        like young horses eyeing the track.
        Last August she stood alone for hours
        in front of the T.V. set
        as a crow's wing moved slowly through
60   the white streets of government.
        That brave swimming
        scared her, like Joanna saying
        Mother, we're Afro-Americans now!
        What did she know about Africa?
65   Were there lakes like this one
        with a rowboat pushed under the pier?
        Or Thomas' Great Mississippi
        with its sullen silks? (There was
        the Nile but the Nile belonged

70   to God.) Where she came from
        was the past, 12 miles into town
        where nobody had locked their back door,
        and Goodyear hadn't begun to dream of a park
        under the company symbol, a white foot
75   sprouting two small wings.

                                                1986

Persephone, Falling[1]

        One narcissus among the ordinary beautiful
        flowers, one unlike all the others! She pulled,
        stooped to pull harder—
        when, sprung out of the earth
5   on his glittering terrible
        carriage, he claimed his due.
        It is finished. No one heard her.
        No one! She had strayed from the herd.

        (Remember: go straight to school.
10   This is important, stop fooling around!
        Don't answer to strangers. Stick

---

1. In Greek mythology, Persephone, the daughter of Zeus and Demeter, was abducted by Pluto, lord of the underworld, while she was gathering flowers.

with your playmates. Keep your eyes down.)
This is how easily the pit
opens. This is how one foot sinks into the ground.

1995

Sonnet in Primary Colors

This is for the woman with one black wing
perched over her eyes: lovely Frida,[1] erect
among parrots, in the stern petticoats of the peasant,
who painted herself a present—
5   wildflowers entwining the plaster corset
her spine resides in, that flaming pillar—
this priestess in the romance of mirrors.

Each night she lay down in pain and rose
to the celluloid butterflies of her Beloved Dead,
10 Lenin and Marx and Stalin[2] arrayed at the footstead.
And rose to her easel, the hundred dogs panting
like children along the graveled walks of the garden, Diego's
love a skull in the circular window
of the thumbprint searing her immutable brow.

1995

Rosa[1]

How she sat there,
the time right inside a place
so wrong it was ready.

That trim name with
5   its dream of a bench
to rest on. Her sensible coat.

Doing nothing was the doing:
the clean flame of her gaze
carved by a camera flash.

---

1. Frida Kahlo (1907–1954), Mexican painter famous for her self-portraits. Kahlo was married to Diego Rivera (1886–1957) (line 12).
2. Three major figures in the development of communism in the former Soviet Union: Vladimir Lenin (1870–1924), who founded the state; Karl Marx (1818–1883), the German political philosopher who provided the theoretical underpinnings; and Joseph Stalin (1879–1953), who succeeded Lenin as leader of the Soviet Union.

1. Rosa Parks (1913–2005), civil rights activist whose arrest in Montgomery, Alabama, in December 1955 for refusing to give up her seat on a public bus to a white man sparked the bus boycott that helped launch the movement that ended legal segregation in the South. A famous photograph shows her being fingerprinted at the police station.

10   How she stood up
when they bent down to retrieve
her purse. That courtesy.

2000

"I have been a stranger in a strange land"[1]

*Life's spell is so exquisite, everything
conspires to break it.*
—Emily Dickinson[2]

It wasn't bliss. What was bliss
but the ordinary life? She'd spend hours
in patter, moving through whole days
touching, sniffing, tasting . . . exquisite
5 housekeeping in a charmed world.[3]
And yet there was always

more of the same, all that happiness,
the aimless Being There.
So she wandered for a while, bush to arbor,
10 lingered to look through a pond's restive mirror.
He was off cataloging the universe, probably,[4]
pretending he could organize
what was clearly someone else's chaos.

That's when she found the tree,[5]
15 the dark, crabbed branches
bearing up such speechless bounty,
she knew without being told
this was forbidden. It wasn't
20 a question of ownership—
who could lay claim to
such maddening perfection?

And there was no voice in her head,
no whispered intelligence lurking
in the leaves[6]—just an ache that grew
25 until she knew she'd already lost everything
except desire, the red heft of it
warming her outstretched palm.

2004

---

1. Exodus 2.22.
2. American poet (1830–1886); see Vol. 1, p. 1037.
3. I.e., the Garden of Eden, the dwelling place of Adam and Eve after their creation by God as described in Genesis 2.
4. Adam was given the task of naming all the living creatures that God had made (Genesis 2.19–20).
5. The tree of the knowledge of good and evil, whose fruit (conventionally identified with an apple) God forbade them to eat (Genesis 2.16–17).
6. In Genesis, the snake is responsible for persuading Eve to take the fruit (Genesis 3.1–6).

LUCI TAPAHONSO
b. 1953

Born and raised in Shiprock, New Mexico, in the Navajo homeland of Dinetah, the largest Native American reservation in the United States, Luci Tapahonso was one of eleven children who grew up speaking both Navajo and English, a linguistic counterpoint that characterizes much of the work she has published in five collections of poetry, including *Seasonal Woman* (1982), *A Breeze Swept Through* (1987), *Sáanii Dahataal: The Women Are Singing* (1993), and *Blue Horses Rush In* (1999); she has also written several books for children. Twice married and the mother of two daughters as well as several stepchildren, she was educated at the University of New Mexico and currently teaches at the University of Arizona, Tucson.

    While she was still in college, Tapahonso has explained, her work was nurtured by support and encouragement from the Native American author Leslie Marmon Silko, who became a mentor for her. At the same time, she sees herself as having been inspired to write by both the social oppression and the cultural plenitude that her people have experienced. "For an Indian person," she insists, "the land is rich with memories, stories, and sacred songs that ensure survival in this country. The huge rocks in Utah, near Kayenta, Shiprock pinnacle, and the various others are strong places and exist for spiritual purposes. The desert is vast and expansive yet full of power and a strength that few can comprehend."

Blue Horses Rush In

For Chamisa Bah Edmo,
who was born March 6, 1991

Before the birth, she moved and pushed inside her mother.
Her heart pounded quickly and we recognized the sound of horses running:

       the thundering of hooves on the desert floor.

Her mother clenched her fists and gasped.
5 She moans ageless pain and pushes: This is it!

Chamisa slips out, glistening wet and takes her first breath.
       The wind outside swirls small leaves
      and branches in the dark.
Her father's eyes are wet with gratitude.
10 He prays and watches both mother and baby—stunned.
This baby arrived amid a herd of horses,
         horses of different colors.

White horses ride in on the breath of the wind.
White horses from the west
15 where plants of golden chamisa shimmer in the moonlight.

She arrived amid a herd of horses.
Yellow horses enter from the east
bringing the scent of prairie grasses from the small hills outside.

She arrived amid a herd of horses.

20 Blue horses rush in, snorting from the desert in the south.
It is possible to see across the entire valley to Niist'áá from Tó.[1]
Bah, from here your grandmothers went to war long ago.

She arrived amid a herd of horses.

Black horses came from the north.
25 They are the lush summers of Montana and still white winters of Idaho

Chamisa, Chamisa Bah. It is all this that you are.
You will grow: laughing, crying,
and we will celebrate each change you live.

You will grow strong like the horses of your past.
30 You will grow strong like the horses of your birth.

1993

Leda[1] and the Cowboy

A few months back, when the night sky was darker
than Leda had ever seen, she stepped through
the worn door frame of the Q lounge.
The suddenness of thick smoky air left her slightly faint.
5 After that, it was easy enough, Leda saw him across
the damp just-wiped bar—she did nothing
but hold the glance a second too long.
Sure enough, as if she had called out his name,
he walked over—a slight smile and straw hat.

10 Even then, as they danced, the things he told her
were fleeting. Leda smiled and a strange desperation
engulfed him. "I have to leave," she said,
remembering the clean, empty air outside.
He followed her, holding her shoulder lightly,

15 and outside, he bent over: his body an arc in the street light,
and it was clear he didn't know the raw music she lived.

But for now, he is leaning across the table, smiling,
and telling Leda things: he wants to take her on a picnic,
it might rain tonight,
20 and she can phone him anytime.

---

1. One of the names for Shiprock, New Mexico. "Niist'áá": the Navajo name of Oaksprings, a small community on the western slope of the Carriso Mountains in New Mexico.

1. In Greek mythology, Leda was a Spartan queen, wife of Tyndareus. She was raped by Zeus, who came to her in the form of a swan, and she bore two children to Tyndareus (Clytemnestra and Castor) and two to Zeus (Helen and Pollux).

He thinks he is leaving for a rodeo 400 miles to the north
in a few hours. His pickup is loaded with saddles, clothes,
and a huge ice chest. Leda notices the parking lot outside
is stained with oil, twisted cigarettes, and small bits of
colored glass. He leans toward her, hat tilted, and in that
low morning voice says he has been tracking her all night.

In this desert city of half a million people, he drove
over cooled asphalt trails searching smoky dance halls,
small Indian bars, the good Mexican place that serves
until 12 and when he found her at a table near
the dance floor, she was laughing. But Leda saw his
straw hat and half-smile as he watched from the bar.
When they danced, it was flawless.
He thinks he has done this many times before.
His shirt carried the scent of the hot night breezes outside.

East of here, above the dry fields of the Hoohookamki,[2]
the stars are sparse, and as he follows Leda through
the stark beauty of the old stories,

>   he has already left his own life behind.

1993

---

2. The original O'ohdam name for their ancestors, sometimes referred to as Hohokam. Their land is located in what is now Phoenix, Arizona.

KIM ADDONIZIO
b. 1954

In an online autobiography, Kim Addonizio muses on tattoos, peddles her recent words-and-music CD (*Swearing, Smoking, Drinking, and Kissing*), reveals that "in an alternate universe" she would have liked to be an old black man "sitting on the porch playing blues harmonica all day long," lists among her previous occupations "waitress, fry cook, tennis instructor, Kelly Girl (deadening temporary office work), attendant for the disabled, auto parts store bookkeeper," and explains that "I grew up in Bethesda Maryland, in a sports-obsessed family that consisted of four brothers, two invisible parents (sportswriter father, tennis pro mother), an illiterate nanny, a red cocker spaniel succeeded by a one-eyed Pekinese, a grandmother with a pink Mustang fastback, and a dozen TVs." Indeed, Addonizio's mother was the renowned tennis champion Pauline Betz and her father the well-known *Washington Post* baseball chronicler Bob Addie (who shortened "Addonizio" to "Addie," though his daughter was eventually to return her surname's final syllables to what she considers their proper place). But she herself took a rather different path in life.

After moving to San Francisco in 1976, Addonizio studied writing at San Francisco State University; had a daughter, Aya; and began publishing poems. Since then, she has produced four volumes of verse, including *Tell Me* (2000) and *What Is This Thing Called Love* (2004). In addition, she has written a collection of stories, *In the Box*

Called Pleasure (1999); coauthored (with Dorianne Laux) *The Poet's Companion: A Guide to the Pleasures of Writing Poetry* (1997); co-edited *Dorothy Parker's Elbow* (2002), an anthology of writings on tattoos; and, with Susan Brown, recorded the CD described above. As her high-spirited confessions suggest, Addonizio is very much an ironically rebellious "bad girl" poet in a line of writers that includes such brilliantly (and often sardonically) self-dramatizing artists as Dorothy Parker, Edna St. Vincent Millay, and, more recently, Sharon Olds.

"What Do Women Want?"[1]

I want a red dress.
I want it flimsy and cheap,
I want it too tight, I want to wear it
until someone tears it off me.
5   I want it sleeveless and backless,
this dress, so no one has to guess
what's underneath. I want to walk down
the street past Thrifty's and the hardware store
with all those keys glittering in the window,
10 past Mr. and Mrs. Wong selling day-old
donuts in their café, past the Guerra brothers
slinging pigs from the truck and onto the dolly,
hoisting the slick snouts over their shoulders.
I want to walk like I'm the only
15 woman on earth and I can have my pick.
I want that red dress bad.
I want it to confirm
your worst fears about me,
to show you how little I care about you
20 or anything except what
I want. When I find it, I'll pull that garment
from its hanger like I'm choosing a body
to carry me into this world, through
the birth-cries and the love-cries too,
25 and I'll wear it like bones, like skin,
it'll be the goddamned
dress they bury me in.

2001

---

1. "What does woman want?" was a question famously asked by Sigmund Freud (1856–1939), the founder of psychoanalysis.

Generations

Somewhere a shop of hanging meats,
shop or stink and blood, block and cleaver;

somewhere an immigrant, grandfather, stranger
with my last name. That man

5   untying his apron in 1910, scrubbing off
the pale fat, going home past brownstones

and churches, past vendors, streetcars, arias,
past the clatter of supper dishes, going home

to his new son, my father—
10   What is he to me, butcher with sausage fingers,

old Italian leaning over a child somewhere
in New York City, somewhere alive, what is he

that I go back to look for him, years after his death
and my father's death, knowing only

15   a name, a few scraps my father fed me?
My father who shortened that name, who hacked off

three lovely syllables,[2] who raised American children.
What is the past to me

20   that I have to go back, pronouncing that word
in the silence of a cemetery, what is this stone

coming apart in my hands like bread, name
I eat and expel? Somewhere the smell of figs

and brine, strung garlic, rosemary and olives;
25   somewhere that place. Somewhere a boat

rocking, crossing over, entering the harbor. I wait
on the dock, one face in a crowd of faces.

Families disembark and stream toward the city,
and though I walk among them for hours,

30   hungry, haunting the streets,
I can't tell which of them is mine.

Somewhere a steak is wrapped in thick paper,
somewhere my grandmother is laid in the earth,

---

2. He shorted "Addonizio" to "Addie."

and my young father shines shoes on a corner,
turning his back to the Old World, forgetting.

I walk the night city, looking up at lit windows,
and there is no table set for me, nowhere

I can go to be filled. This is the city
of grandparents, immigrants, arrivals,

where I've come too late with my name,
an empty plate. This is the place.

2001

Last Call

It's the hour when everyone's drunk
and the bar turns marvelous, music
swirling over the red booths,
smoke rising from neglected cigarettes as in each glass
ice slides into other ice, dissolving;
it's when one stranger nudges another
and says, staring at the blurred rows of pour spouts,
I hear they banned dwarf tossing in France,[3]
and the second man nods
and lays his head on the bar's slick surface,
not caring if he dies there, wanting, in fact, to die there
among the good friends he's just met, his cheek
in a wet pool of spilled beer.
It's when the woman in the corner gets up
and wobbles to the middle of the room,
leaving her blouse draped over a stool. Someone is buying
the house a final round, the cabs are being summoned,
and the gods that try to save us from ourselves
are taking us by the neck, gently,
and dropping us into the night; it's the hour
of the blind, and the dead, of lost loves
who come to claim you, finally, holding open
the swinging door, repeating over and over
a name that must be yours.

2001

---

3. Dwarf tossing—throwing small stuntmen as far as possible, an entertainment in some nightclubs and bars beginning in the 1980s—was banned by a French mayor in 1995 (a ban upheld in 2002 by the United Nations Human Rights Committee).

31-Year-Old Lover

When he takes off his clothes
I think of a stick of butter being unwrapped,
the milky, lubricious smoothness of it
when it's taken from the fridge still hard
the way his body is hard, the high
tight pectorals, the new dimes of the nipples pressed
into his chest, the fanning of the muscles underneath.
I look at his arms, shaped as though a knife
has slid along the curves to carve them out,
deltoids, biceps, triceps, I almost can't believe
that he is human—latissimus dorsi, hip flexors,
gluteals, gastrocnemius—[4]—he is so perfectly made.
He stands naked in my bedroom and nothing
has harmed him yet, though he is going
to be harmed. He is going to have a gut one day,
and wiry gray hairs where the soft dark filaments
flow out of him, the cream of his skin is going
to loosen and separate slowly, over a low steady flame
and he has no idea, as I had no idea,
and I am not going to speak of this to him ever,
I am going to let him stretch out on my bed
so I can take the heavy richness of him in
and in, I am going to have it back the only way I can.

2004

You Don't Know What Love Is

but you know how to raise it in me
like a dead girl winched up from a river. How to
wash off the sludge, the stench of our past.
How to start clean. This love even sits up
and blinks; amazed, she takes a few shaky steps.
Any day now she'll try to eat solid food. She'll want
to get into a fast car, one low to the ground, and drive
to some cinderblock shithole in the desert
where she can drink and get sick and then
dance in nothing but her underwear. You know
where she's headed, you know she'll wake up
with an ache she can't locate and no money
and a terrible thirst. So to hell
with your warm hands sliding inside my shirt
and your tongue down my throat
like an oxygen tube. Cover me
in black plastic. Let the mourners through.

2004

---

4. Beginning with "deltoids," these are all names of muscles.

Sonnenizio on a Line from Drayton[1]

Since there's no help, come let us kiss and part;
or kiss anyway, let's start with that, with the kissing part,
because it's better than the parting part, isn't it—
we're good at kissing, we like how that part goes:
5   we part our lips, our mouths get near and nearer,
then we're close, my breasts, your chest, our bodies partway
to making love, so we might as well, part of me thinks—
the wrong part, I know, the bad part, but still
let's pretend we're at that party where we met
10   and scandalized everyone, remember that part? Hold me
like that again, unbutton my shirt, part of you
wants to I can tell, I'm touching that part and it says
yes, the ardent partisan, let it win you over,
it's hopeless, come, we'll kiss and part forever.

2004

---

1. The sonnenizio was invented in Florence in the thirteenth century by Vanni Fucci as an irreverent form whose subject was usually the impossibility of everlasting love. Dante retaliated by putting Fucci into the seventh chasm of the *Inferno* as a thief. Originally composed in hendecasyllabics [i.e., 11-syllable lines], the sonnenizio gradually moved away from metrical constraints and began to tackle a wider variety of subject matter. The sonnenizio is fourteen lines long. It opens with a line from someone else's sonnet, repeats a word from that line in each succeeding line of the poem, and closes with a rhymed couplet [Addonizio's note]. Michael Drayton (1563–1631), English poet; the line is the opening of his sonnet 61 (1619).

SANDRA CISNEROS
b. 1954

The vitality of Chicana literature in recent decades derives in part from the linguistic ingenuity of Sandra Cisneros, who has often been grouped with such contemporaries as Gloria Anzaldúa, Ana Castillo, Helena María Viramontes, Cherríe Moraga, and Pat Mora. Like a number of these authors, Cisneros initially found her way into print through independent presses: Mango Publications of San Jose, for instance, and Arte Publico of Houston. About her publications, she repeatedly asserts that "the people they're really for are the Latinos. They'll get the subtext." However, her uncanny ability to capture the perspectives of children and adults as well as her nuanced depictions of familial interactions in multicultural contexts have gained her novels, short stories, essays, and poems a mainstream audience. Cisneros's agility at relating the particularity of Mexican American socioeconomic issues to the universality of the human condition endows her narratives with the sort of power that earned the short story collection *Woman Hollering Creek* the PEN Center West Award for Best Fiction of 1991, the Quality Paperback Book Club New Voices Award, the Anisfield-Wolf Book Award, and the Lannan Foundation Literary Award.

Self-described as "nobody's mother and nobody's wife," Sandra Cisneros is the only daughter of a Mexican father and Chicana mother. Along with her six brothers, she lived part of her early life in Chicago, part in her father's family home in Mexico City. Indeed, she has attributed her early attraction toward finding a retreat in imaginative literature to the fact that the family moved frequently. During the 1970s, at Loyola

University and then at the University of Iowa's Writers' Workshop, Cisneros began composing the works that would be published in *Bad Boys* (1980), *The House on Mango Street* (1984), and *My Wicked, Wicked Ways* (1987). Especially after the publication of her novel of interrelated sketches, *The House on Mango Street,* Cisneros was praised by reviewers for delineating how ethnicity—with all of its familial and economic consequences—affects the psychology of adolescence. In an ambitious second novel, *Caramelo* (2002), Cisneros recounts the transnational saga of the Reyes family over three generations through a series of scenes noted for their pitch-perfect bilingual dialogue. According to the critic Sonia Saldívar-Hull, the title story of *Woman Hollering Creek* best illustrates Cisneros's articulation of "border feminism," a practice "that engages Chicana feminist theories with social and cultural productions in multiple Chicana and Mexicana locations and that also breaks with Euro-American feminisms' geopolitical racist and elitist mappings." In lyrical testimonials that sometimes whisper, sometimes holler, Cisneros tackles the influence of impoverishment, popular cultural, and domestic violence on *mujeres de fuerza*, women of strength.

Woman Hollering Creek

The day Don Serafín gave Juan Pedro Martínez Sánchez permission to take Cleófilas Enriqueta DeLeón Hernández as his bride, across her father's threshold, over several miles of dirt road and several miles of paved, over one border and beyond to a town *en el otro lado*—on the other side—already did he divine the morning his daughter would raise her hand over her eyes, look south, and dream of returning to the chores that never ended, six good-for-nothing brothers, and one old man's complaints.

He had said, after all, in the hubbub of parting: I am your father, I will never abandon you. He *had* said that, hadn't he, when he hugged and then let her go. But at the moment Cleófilas was busy looking for Chela, her maid of honor, to fulfill their bouquet conspiracy. She would not remember her father's parting words until later. *I am your father, I will never abandon you.*

Only now as a mother did she remember. Now, when she and Juan Pedrito sat by the creek's edge. How when a man and a woman love each other, sometimes that love sours. But a parent's love for a child, a child's for its parents, is another thing entirely.

This is what Cleófilas thought evenings when Juan Pedro did not come home, and she lay on her side of the bed listening to the hollow roar of the interstate, a distant dog barking, the pecan trees rustling like ladies in stiff petticoats—*shh-shh-shh, shh-shh-shh*—soothing her to sleep.

* * *

In the town where she grew up, there isn't very much to do except accompany the aunts and godmothers to the house of one or the other to play cards. Or walk to the cinema to see this week's film again, speckled and with one hair quivering annoyingly on the screen. Or to the center of town to order a milk shake that will appear in a day and a half as a pimple on her backside. Or to the girlfriend's house to watch the latest *telenovela*[1] episode and try to copy the way the women comb their hair, wear their makeup.

---

1. Soap opera (Spanish, as are all translated terms).

But what Cleófilas has been waiting for, has been whispering and sighing and giggling for, has been anticipating since she was old enough to lean against the window displays of gauze and butterflies and lace, is passion. Not the kind on the cover of the ¡Alarma! magazines, mind you, where the lover is photographed with the bloody fork she used to salvage her good name. But passion in its purest crystalline essence. The kind the books and songs and *telenovelas* describe when one finds, finally, the great love of one's life, and does whatever one can, must do, at whatever the cost.

Tú o Nadie. "You or No One." The title of the current favorite *telenovela*. The beautiful Lucía Méndez[2] having to put up with all kinds of hardships of the heart, separation and betrayal, and loving, always loving no matter what, because *that* is the most important thing, and did you see Lucía Méndez on the Bayer aspirin commercials—wasn't she lovely? Does she dye her hair do you think? Cleófilas is going to go to the *farmacía*[3] and buy a hair rinse; her girlfriend Chela will apply it—it's not that difficult at all.

Because you didn't watch last night's episode when Lucía confessed she loved him more than anyone in her life. In her life! And she sings the song "You or No One" in the beginning and end of the show. *Tú o Nadie*. Somehow one ought to live one's life like that, don't you think? You or no one. Because to suffer for love is good. The pain all sweet somehow. In the end.

* * *

Seguín. She had liked the sound of it. Far away and lovely. Not like *Monclova. Coahuia*.[4] Ugly.

Seguín, Tejas. A nice sterling ring to it. The tinkle of money. She would get to wear outfits like the women on the *tele*, like Lucía Méndez. And have a lovely house, and wouldn't Chela be jealous.

And yes, they will drive all the way to Laredo to get her wedding dress. That's what they say. Because Juan Pedro wants to get married right away, without a long engagement since he can't take off too much time from work. He has a very important position in Seguin with, with . . . a beer company, I think. Or was it tires? Yes, he has to be back. So they will get married in the spring when he can take off work, and then they will drive off in his new pickup—did you see it?—to their new home in Seguin. Well, not exactly new, but they're going to repaint the house. You know newlyweds. New paint and new furniture. Why not? He can afford it. And later on add maybe a room or two for the children. May they be blessed with many.

Well, you'll see. Cleófilas has always been so good with her sewing machine. A little *rrrr, rrrr, rrrr* of the machine and ¡zas! Miracles. She's always been so clever, that girl. Poor thing. And without even a mama to advise her on things like her wedding night. Well, may God help her. What with a father with a head like a burro, and those six clumsy brothers. Well, what do you think! Yes, I'm going to the wedding. Of course! The dress I want to wear just needs to be altered a teensy bit to bring it up to date. See, I saw a new style last night that I thought would suit me. Did you watch last night's episode of *The Rich Also Cry*? Well, did you notice the dress the mother was wearing?

---

2. Mexican singer and actor (b. 1955).
3. Drugstore.
4. Seguin, Texas, is about 30 miles northeast of San Antonio; Monclova, in the state of Coahuila, is about 150 miles from the border (and 300 miles from San Antonio).

* * *

La Gritona. Such a funny name for such a lovely *arroyo*. But that's what they called the creek that ran behind the house. Though no one could say whether the woman had hollered from anger or pain. The natives only knew the *arroyo* one crossed on the way to San Antonio, and then once again on the way back, was called Woman Hollering, a name no one from these parts questioned, little less understood. *Pues, allá de los indios,*[5] *quién sabe*—who knows, the townspeople shrugged, because it was of no concern to their lives how this trickle of water received its curious name.

"What do you want to know for?" Trini the laundromat attendant asked in the same gruff Spanish she always used whenever she gave Cleófilas change or yelled at her for something. First for putting too much soap in the machines. Later, for sitting on a washer. And still later, after Juan Pedrito was born, for not understanding that in this country you cannot let your baby walk around with no diaper and his pee-pee hanging out, it wasn't nice, *¿entiendes?*[6] *Pues.*

How could Cleófilas explain to a woman like this why the name Woman Hollering fascinated her. Well, there was no sense talking to Trini.

On the other hand there were the neighbor ladies, one on either side of the house they rented near the *arroyo*. The woman Soledad on the left, the woman Dolores on the right.

The neighbor lady Soledad liked to call herself a widow, though how she came to be one was a mystery. Her husband had either died, or run away with an ice-house floozie,[7] or simply gone out for cigarettes one afternoon and never came back. It was hard to say which since Soledad, as a rule, didn't mention him.

In the other house lived *la señora* Dolores, kind and very sweet, but her house smelled too much of incense and candles from the altars that burned continuously in memory of two sons who had died in the last war and one husband who had died shortly after from grief. The neighbor lady Dolores divided her time between the memory of these men and her garden, famous for its sunflowers—so tall they had to be supported with broom handles and old boards; red red cockscombs, fringed and bleeding a thick menstrual color; and, especially, roses whose sad scent reminded Cleófilas of the dead. Each Sunday *la señora* Dolores clipped the most beautiful of these flowers and arranged them on three modest headstones at the Seguin cemetery.

The neighbor ladies, Soledad, Dolores, they might've known once the name of the *arroyo* before it turned English but they did not know now. They were too busy remembering the men who had left through either choice or circumstance and would never come back.

Pain or rage, Cleófilas wondered when she drove over the bridge the first time as a newlywed and Juan Pedro had pointed it out. *La Gritona,* he had said, and she had laughed. Such a funny name for a creek so pretty and full of happily ever after.

* * *

---

5. Well, from the Indians.
6. Understand?
7. In Texas, many ice houses—buildings originally used to store ice—were converted into open-air bars after refrigerators became common.

The first time she had been so surprised she didn't cry out or try to defend herself. She had always said she would strike back if a man, any man, were to strike her.

But when the moment came, and he slapped her once, and then again, and again; until the lip split and bled an orchid of blood, she didn't fight back, she didn't break into tears, she didn't run away as she imagined she might when she saw such things in the *telenovelas*.

In her own home her parents had never raised a hand to each other or to their children. Although she admitted she may have been brought up a little leniently as an only daughter—*la consentida*,[8] the princess—there were some things she would never tolerate. Ever.

Instead, when it happened the first time, when they were barely man and wife, she had been so stunned, it left her speechless, motionless, numb. She had done nothing but reach up to the heat on her mouth and stare at the blood on her hand as if even then she didn't understand.

She could think of nothing to say, said nothing. Just stroked the dark curls of the man who wept and would weep like a child, his tears of repentance and shame, this time and each.

* * *

The men at the ice house. From what she can tell, from the times during her first year when still a newlywed she is invited and accompanies her husband, sits mute beside their conversation, waits and sips a beer until it grows warm, twists a paper napkin into a knot, then another into a fan, one into a rose, nods her head, smiles, yawns, politely grins, laughs at the appropriate moments, leans against her husband's sleeve, tugs at his elbow, and finally becomes good at predicting where the talk will lead, from this Cleófilas concludes each is nightly trying to find the truth lying at the bottom of the bottle like a gold doubloon on the sea floor.

They want to tell each other what they want to tell themselves. But what is bumping like a helium balloon at the ceiling of the brain never finds its way out. It bubbles and rises, it gurgles in the throat, it rolls across the surface of the tongue, and erupts from the lips—a belch.

If they are lucky, there are tears at the end of the long night. At any given moment, the fists try to speak. They are dogs chasing their own tails before lying down to sleep, trying to find a way, a route, an out, and—finally—get some peace.

* * *

In the morning sometimes before he opens his eyes. Or after they have finished loving. Or at times when he is simply across from her at the table putting pieces of food into his mouth and chewing. Cleófilas thinks, This is the man I have waited my whole life for.

Not that he isn't a good man. She has to remind herself why she loves him when she changes the baby's Pampers, or when she mops the bathroom floor, or tries to make the curtains for the doorways without doors, or whiten the linen. Or wonder a little when he kicks the refrigerator and says he hates this shitty house and is going out where he won't be bothered with the baby's

---

8. The pampered one.

howling and her suspicious questions, and her requests to fix this and this and this because if she had any brains in her head she'd realize he's been up before the rooster earning his living to pay for the food in her belly and the roof over her head and would have to wake up again early the next day so why can't you just leave me in peace, woman.

He is not very tall, no, and he doesn't look like the men on the *telenovelas*. His face still scarred from acne. And he has a bit of a belly from all the beer he drinks. Well, he's always been husky.

This man who farts and belches and snores as well as laughs and kisses and holds her. Somehow this husband whose whiskers she finds each morning in the sink, whose shoes she must air each evening on the porch, this husband who cuts his fingernails in public, laughs loudly, curses like a man, and demands each course of dinner be served on a separate plate like at his mother's, as soon as he gets home, on time or late, and who doesn't care at all for music or *telenovelas* or romance or roses or the moon floating pearly over the *arroyo*, or through the bedroom window for that matter, shut the blinds and go back to sleep, this man, this father, this rival, this keeper, this lord, this master, this husband till kingdom come.

* * *

A doubt. Slender as a hair. A washed cup set back on the shelf wrong-side-up. Her lipstick, and body talc, and hairbrush all arranged in the bathroom a different way.

No. Her imagination. The house the same as always. Nothing.

Coming home from the hospital with her new son, her husband. Something comforting in discovering her house slippers beneath the bed, the faded housecoat where she left it on the bathroom hook. Her pillow. Their bed.

Sweet sweet homecoming. Sweet as the scent of face powder in the air, jasmine, sticky liquor.

Smudged fingerprint on the door. Crushed cigarette in a glass. Wrinkle in the brain crumpling to a crease.

* * *

Sometimes she thinks of her father's house. But how could she go back there? What a disgrace. What would the neighbors say? Coming home like that with one baby on her hip and one in the oven. Where's your husband?

The town of gossips. The town of dust and despair. Which she has traded for this town of gossips. This town of dust, despair. Houses farther apart perhaps, though no more privacy because of it. No leafy *zócalo*[9] in the center of the town, though the murmur of talk is clear enough all the same. No huddled whispering on the church steps each Sunday. Because here the whispering begins at sunset at the ice house instead.

This town with its silly pride for a bronze pecan the size of a baby carriage in front of the city hall. TV repair shop, drugstore, hardware, dry cleaner's, chiropractor's, liquor store, bail bonds, empty storefront, and nothing, nothing, nothing of interest. Nothing one could walk to, at any rate. Because the towns here are built so that you have to depend on husbands. Or you stay

---

9. Public square.

home. Or you drive. If you're rich enough to own, allowed to drive, your own car.

There is no place to go. Unless one counts the neighbor ladies. Soledad on one side, Dolores on the other. Or the creek.

Don't go out there after dark, *mi'jita*. Stay near the house. *No es bueno para la salud.*[1] *Mala suerte.* Bad luck. *Mal aire.*[2] You'll get sick and the baby too. You'll catch a fright wandering about in the dark, and then you'll see how right we were.

The stream sometimes only a muddy puddle in the summer, though now in the springtime, because of the rains, a good-size alive thing, a thing with a voice all its own, all day and all night calling in its high, silver voice. Is it La Llorona, the weeping woman? La Llorona, who drowned her own children.[3] Perhaps La Llorona is the one they named the creek after, she thinks, remembering all the stories she learned as a child.

La Llorona calling to her. She is sure of it. Cleófilas sets the baby's Donald Duck blanket on the grass. Listens. The day sky turning to night. The baby pulling up fistfuls of grass and laughing. La Llorona. Wonders if something as quiet as this drives a woman to the darkness under the trees.

* * *

What she needs is . . . and made a gesture as if to yank a woman's buttocks to his groin. Maximiliano, the foul-smelling fool from across the road, said this and set the men laughing, but Cleófilas just muttered. *Grosera*,[4] and went on washing dishes.

She knew he said it not because it was true, but more because it was he who needed to sleep with a woman, instead of drinking each night at the ice house and stumbling home alone.

Maximiliano who was said to have killed his wife in an ice-house brawl when she came at him with a mop. I had to shoot, he had said—she was armed.

Their laughter outside the kitchen window. Her husband's, his friends', Manolo, Beto, Efraín, el Perico.[5] Maximiliano.

Was Cleófilas just exaggerating as her husband always said? It seemed the newspapers were full of such stories. This woman found on the side of the interstate. This one pushed from a moving car. This one's cadaver, this one unconscious, this one beaten blue. Her ex-husband, her husband, her lover, her father, her brother, her uncle, her friend, her co-worker. Always. The same grisly news in the pages of the dailies. She dunked a glass under the soapy water for a moment—shivered.

* * *

He had thrown a book. Hers. From across the room. A hot welt across the cheek. She could forgive that. But what stung more was the fact it was *her* book, a love story by Corín Tellado,[6] what she loved most now that she lived in the U.S., without a television set, without the *telenovelas*.

---

1. It's not good for the health. "*Mi'jita*": my little daughter (i.e., "my dear").
2. Bad air.
3. The legend of La Llorona is especially popular in Mexico and in Mexican American communities in the United States (her reasons for drowning her children vary in different versions of the story).
4. Coarse, rude.
5. Literally, the Parakeet.
6. A Spanish writer of romantic novels (b. 1927); she has sold more than 400 million books.

Except now and again when her husband was away and she could manage it, the few episodes glimpsed at the neighbor lady Soledad's house because Dolores didn't care for that sort of thing, though Soledad was often kind enough to retell what had happened on what episode of *María de Nadie*, the poor Argentine country girl who had the ill fortune of falling in love with the beautiful son of the Arrocha family, the very family she worked for, whose roof she slept under and whose floors she vacuumed, while in that same house, with the dust brooms and floor cleaners as witnesses, the square-jawed Juan Carlos Arrocha had uttered words of love, I love you, María, listen to me, *mi querida*,[7] but it was she who had to say No, no, we are not of the same class, and remind him it was not his place nor hers to fall in love, while all the while her heart was breaking, can you imagine.

Cleófilas thought her life would have to be like that, like a *telenovela,* only now the episodes got sadder and sadder. And there were no commercials in between for comic relief. And no happy ending in sight. She thought this when she sat with the baby out by the creek behind the house. Celófilas de . . . ? But somehow she would have to change her name to Topazio, or Yesenia, Cristal, Adriana, Stefania, Andrea, something more poetic than Cleófilas. Everything happened to women with names like jewels. But what happened to a Cleófilas? Nothing. But a crack in the face.

* * *

Because the doctor has said so. She has to go. To make sure the new baby is all right, so there won't be any problems when he's born, and the appointment card says next Tuesday. Could he please take her. And that's all.

No, she won't mention it. She promises. If the doctor asks she can say she fell down the front steps or slipped when she was out in the backyard, slipped out back, she could tell him that. She has to go back next Tuesday, Juan Pedro, please, for the new baby. For their child.

She could write to her father and ask maybe for money, just a loan, for the new baby's medical expenses. Well then if he'd rather she didn't. All right, she won't. Please don't anymore. Please don't. She knows it's difficult saving money with all the bills they have, but how else are they going to get out of debt with the truck payments? And after the rent and the food and the electricity and the gas and the water and the who-knows-what, well, there's hardly anything left. But please, at least for the doctor visit. She won't ask for anything else. She has to. Why is she so anxious? Because.

Because she is going to make sure the baby is not turned around backward this time to split her down the center. Yes. Next Tuesday at five-thirty. I'll have Juan Pedrito dressed and ready. But those are the only shoes he has. I'll polish them, and we'll be ready. As soon as you come from work. We won't make you ashamed.

* * *

Felice? It's me, Graciela.

No, I can't talk louder. I'm at work.

Look, I need kind of a favor. There's a patient, a lady here who's got a problem.

Well, wait a minute. Are you listening to me or what?

---

7. Darling.

I can't talk real loud 'cause her husband's in the next room.

Well, would you just listen?

I was going to do this sonogram on her—she's pregnant, right?—and she just starts crying on me. *Híjole*,[8] Felice! This poor lady's got black-and-blue marks all over. I'm not kidding.

From her husband. Who else? Another one of those brides from across the border. And her family's all in Mexico.

Shit. You think they're going to help her? Give me a break. This lady doesn't even speak English. She hasn't been allowed to call home or write or nothing. That's why I'm calling you.

She needs a ride.

Not to Mexico, you goof. Just to the Greyhound. In San Anto.

No, just a ride. She's got her own money. All you'd have to do is drop her off in San Antonio on your way home. Come on, Felice. Please? If we don't help her, who will? I'd drive her myself, but she needs to be on that bus before her husband gets home from work. What do you say?

I don't know. Wait.

Right away, tomorrow even.

Well, if tomorrow's no good for you . . .

It's a date, Felice. Thursday. At the Cash N Carry off I-10. Noon. She'll be ready.

Oh, and her name's Cleófilas.

I don't know. One of those Mexican saints, I guess. A martyr or something.

Cleófilas. C-L-E-O-F-I-L-A-S. Cle. O. Fi. Las. Write it down.

Thanks, Felice. When her kid's born she'll have to name her after us, right?

Yeah, you got it. A regular soap opera sometimes. *Qué vida, comadre. Bueno bye.*[9]

* * *

All morning that flutter of half-fear, half-doubt. At any moment Juan Pedro might appear in the doorway. On the street. At the Cash N Carry. Like in the dreams she dreamed.

There was that to think about, yes, until the woman in the pickup drove up. Then there wasn't time to think about anything but the pickup pointed toward San Antonio. Put your bags in the back and get in.

But when they drove across the *arroyo*, the driver opened her mouth and let out a yell as loud as any mariachi.[1] Which startled not only Cleófilas, but Juan Pedrito as well.

Pues, look how cute. I scared you two, right? Sorry. Should've warned you. Every time I cross that bridge I do that. Because of the name, you know. Woman Hollering. *Pues*, I holler. She said this in a Spanish pocked with English and laughed. Did you ever notice, Felice continued, how nothing around here is named after a woman? Really. Unless she's the Virgin. I guess you're only famous if you're a virgin. She was laughing again.

That's why I like the name of that *arroyo*. Makes you want to holler like Tarzan,[2] right?

---

8. An exclamation (literally, "Boy!").
9. What a life, friend. Goodbye.
1. A Mexican street musician.
2. I.e., with the ululations made famous by Johnny Weissmuller, playing the hero in the film *Tarzan the Ape Man* (1932) and its numerous sequels, all based on Edgar Rice Burroughs's *Tarzan of the Apes* (1914).

Everything about this woman, this Felice, amazed Cleófilas. The fact that she drove a pickup. A pickup, mind you, but when Cleófilas asked if it was her husband's, she said she didn't have a husband. The pickup was hers. She herself had chosen it. She herself was paying for it.

I used to have a Pontiac Sunbird. But those cars are for *viejas*.[3] Pussy cars. Now this here is a *real* car.

What kind of talk was that coming from a woman? Cleófilas thought. But then again, Felice was like no woman she'd ever met. Can you imagine, when we crossed the *arroyo* she just started yelling like a crazy, she would say later to her father and brothers. Just like that. Who would've thought?

Who would've? Pain or rage, perhaps, but not a hoot like the one Felice had just let go. Makes you want to holler like Tarzan, Felice had said.

Then Felice began laughing again, but it wasn't Felice laughing. It was gurgling out of her own throat, a long ribbon of laughter, like water.

1991

3. Old ladies.

LOUISE ERDRICH
b. 1954

The daughter of a French Ojibwa mother and a German American father, Louise Erdrich was raised near Turtle Mountain Chippewa Reservation in North Dakota. Both of her parents worked in the Bureau of Indian Affairs boarding school in Wahpeton. "My father used to give me a nickel for every story I wrote," she once explained, "and my mother wove strips of construction paper together and stapled them into book covers. So at an early age I felt myself to be a published author earning substantial royalties." And when she was in her twenties, a story collaboratively composed with Michael Dorris won $5,000, leading her to expand it into the novel *Love Medicine* (1984), which earned her the National Book Critics Circle Award when she was thirty.

Erdrich had met Dorris when attending Dartmouth College as an undergraduate. After earning a master's degree in creative writing from Johns Hopkins University, she returned to Dartmouth to become a writer in residence and in 1981 married Dorris, himself a highly respected writer. Over the next decade, she continued producing her fictional portraits of several interrelated characters living in North Dakota from 1912 to the 1980s. *The Beet Queen* (1986), *Tracks* (1988), and *The Bingo Palace* (1994) counterpoint short stories told by a number of different narrators to chronicle three generations of Native American and immigrant families, lyrically exploring the economic, social, and psychological pressures exerted on dislocated people. Besides publishing three books of poetry—*Jacklight* (1984), *Baptism of Fire* (1989), and *Original Fire* (2003)—Erdrich has produced a collaborative work with Dorris titled *The Crown of Columbus* (1991). But, tragically, in 1997 Dorris committed suicide.

With three of her children, Erdrich now resides in Minneapolis, where she owns an independent bookstore. A series of well-received novels testifies to her ongoing versatility and productivity. Often featuring characters of mixed Native American descent, *Tales of Burning Love* (1996), *The Antelope Wife* (1998), *The Last Report on the Miracles at Little No Horse* (2001), *The Master Butchers Singing Club* (2003), *Four Souls* (2004), and *The Painted Drum* (2005) firmly establish Erdrich's reputation as a major Native American writer.

The sorrows of generations haunt the narrator of "The Shawl," a moving story that appeared in a 2001 *New Yorker* and that resonates with Cynthia Ozick's story of the same title (see p. 932).

The Shawl

Among the Anishinaabeg[1] on the road where I live, it is told how a woman loved a man other than her husband and went off into the bush and bore his child. Her name was Aanakwad, which means cloud, and like a cloud she was changeable. She was moody and sullen one moment, her lower lip jutting and her eyes flashing, filled with storms. The next, she would shake her hair over her face and blow it straight out in front of her to make her children scream with laughter. For she also had two children by her husband, one a yearning boy of five years and the other a capable daughter of nine.

When Aanakwad brought the new baby out of the trees that autumn, the older girl was like a second mother, even waking in the night to clean the baby and nudge it to her mother's breast. Aanakwad slept through its cries, hardly woke. It wasn't that she didn't love her baby; no, it was the opposite— she loved it too much, the way she loved its father, and not her husband. This passion ate away at her, and her feelings were unbearable. If she could have thrown off that wronghearted love, she would have, but the thought of the other man, who lived across the lake, was with her always. She became a gray sky, stared monotonously at the walls, sometimes wept into her hands for hours at a time. Soon, she couldn't rise to cook or keep the cabin neat, and it was too much for the girl, who curled up each night exhausted in her red-and-brown plaid shawl, and slept and slept, until the husband had to wake her to awaken her mother, for he was afraid of his wife's bad temper, and it was he who roused Aanakwad into anger by the sheer fact that he was himself and not the other.

At last, even though he loved Aanakwad, the husband had to admit that their life together was no good anymore. And it was he who sent for the other man's uncle. In those days, our people lived widely scattered, along the shores and in the islands, even out on the plains. There were no roads then, just trails, though we had horses and wagons and, for the winter, sleds. When the uncle came around to fetch Aanakwad, in his wagon fitted out with sled runners, it was very hard, for she and her husband had argued right up to the last about the children, argued fiercely until the husband had finally given in. He turned his face to the wall, and did not move to see the daughter, whom he treasured, sit down beside her mother, wrapped in her plaid robe in the wagon bed. They left right away, with their bundles and sacks, not bothering to heat up the stones to warm their feet. The father had stopped his ears, so he did not hear his son cry out when he suddenly understood that he would be left behind.

---

1. First People (Ojibwe, as are all translated terms); the Ojibwe's name for themselves.

As the uncle slapped the reins and the horse lurched forward, the boy tried to jump into the wagon, but his mother pried his hands off the boards, crying, *Gego, gego*,[2] and he fell down hard. But there was something in him that would not let her leave. He jumped up and, although he was wearing only light clothing, he ran behind the wagon over the packed drifts. The horses picked up speed. His chest was scorched with pain, and yet he pushed himself on. He'd never run so fast, so hard and furiously, but he was determined, and he refused to believe that the increasing distance between him and the wagon was real. He kept going until his throat closed, he saw red, and in the ice of the air his lungs shut. Then, as he fell onto the board-hard snow, he raised his head. He watched the back of the wagon and the tiny figures of his mother and sister disappear, and something failed in him. Something broke. At that moment he truly did not care if he was alive or dead. So when he saw the gray shapes, the shadows, bounding lightly from the trees to either side of the trail, far ahead, he was not afraid.

The next the boy knew, his father had him wrapped in a blanket and was carrying him home. His father's chest was broad and, although he already spat the tubercular blood that would write the end of his story, he was still a strong man. It would take him many years to die. In those years, the father would tell the boy, who had forgotten this part entirely, that at first when he talked about the shadows the father thought he'd been visited by *manidoog*.[3] But then, as the boy described the shapes, his father had understood that they were not spirits. Uneasy, he had decided to take his gun back along the trail. He had built up the fire in the cabin, and settled his boy near it, and gone back out into the snow. Perhaps the story spread through our settlements because the father had to tell what he saw, again and again, in order to get rid of it. Perhaps as with all frightful dreams, *amaniso*, he had to talk about it to destroy its power—though in this case nothing could stop the dream from being real.

The shadows' tracks were the tracks of wolves, and in those days, when our guns had taken all their food for furs and hides to sell, the wolves were bold and had abandoned the old agreement between them and the first humans. For a time, until we understood and let the game increase, the wolves hunted us. The father bounded forward when he saw the tracks. He could see where the pack, desperate, had tried to slash the tendons of the horses' legs. Next, where they'd leaped for the back of the wagon. He hurried on to where the trail gave out at the broad empty ice of the lake. There, he saw what he saw, scattered, and the ravens, attending to the bitter small leavings of the wolves.

For a time, the boy had no understanding of what had happened. His father kept what he knew to himself, at least that first year, and when his son asked about his sister's torn plaid shawl, and why it was kept in the house, his father said nothing. But he wept when the boy asked if his sister was cold. It was only after his father had been weakened by the disease that he began to tell the story, far too often and always the same way: he told how when the wolves closed in Aanakwad had thrown her daughter to them.

When his father said those words, the boy went still. What had his sister

2. Don't.

3. Spirits.

felt? What had thrust through her heart? Had something broken inside her, too, as it had in him? Even then, he knew that this broken place inside him would not be mended, except by some terrible means. For he kept seeing his mother put the baby down and grip his sister around the waist. He saw Aanakwad swing the girl lightly out over the side of the wagon. He saw the brown shawl with its red lines flying open. He saw the shadows, the wolves, rush together, quick and avid, as the wagon with sled runners disappeared into the distance—forever, for neither he nor his father saw Aanakwad again.

When I was little, my own father terrified us with his drinking. This was after we lost our mother, because before that the only time I was aware that he touched the *ishkode waaboo*[4] was on an occasional weekend when they got home late, or sometimes during berry-picking gatherings when we went out to the bush and camped with others. Not until she died did he start the heavy sort of drinking, the continuous drinking, where we were left alone in the house for days. The kind where, when he came home, we'd jump out the window and hide in the woods while he barged around, shouting for us. We'd go back only after he had fallen dead asleep.

There were three of us: me, the oldest at ten, and my little sister and brother, twins, and only six years old. I was surprisingly good at taking care of them, I think, and because we learned to survive together during those drinking years we have always been close. Their names are Doris and Raymond, and they married a brother and sister. When we get together, which is often, for we live on the same road, there come times in the talking and card-playing, and maybe even in the light beer now and then, when we will bring up those days. Most people understand how it was. Our story isn't uncommon. But for us it helps to compare our points of view.

How else would I know, for instance, that Raymond saw me the first time I hid my father's belt? I pulled it from around his waist while he was passed out, and then I buried it in the woods. I kept doing it after that. Our father couldn't understand why his belt was always stolen when he went to town drinking. He even accused his *shkwebii*[5] buddies of the theft. But I had good reasons. Not only was he embarrassed, afterward, to go out with his pants held up by rope, but he couldn't snake his belt out in anger and snap the hooked buckle end in the air. He couldn't hit us with it. Of course, being resourceful, he used other things. There was a board. A willow wand. And there was himself—his hands and fists and boots—and things he could throw. But eventually it became easy to evade him, and after a while we rarely suffered a bruise or a scratch. We had our own place in the woods, even a little campfire for the cold nights. And we'd take money from him every chance we got, slip it from his shoe, where he thought it well hidden. He became, for us, a thing to be avoided, outsmarted, and exploited. We survived off him as if he were a capricious and dangerous line of work. I suppose we stopped thinking of him as a human being, certainly as a father.

I got my growth earlier than some boys, and, one night when I was thirteen and Doris and Raymond and I were sitting around wishing for something besides the oatmeal and commodity canned milk I'd stashed so he couldn't

---

4. Alcohol (literally, "fire liquid").   5. Drunk.

sell them, I heard him coming down the road. He was shouting and making noise all the way to the house, and Doris and Raymond looked at me and headed for the back window. When they saw that I wasn't coming, they stopped. C'mon, *ondaas*,[6] get with it—they tried to pull me along. I shook them off and told them to get out quickly—I was staying. I think I can take him now is what I said.

He was big; he hadn't yet wasted away from the alcohol. His nose had been pushed to one side in a fight, then slammed back to the other side, so now it was straight. His teeth were half gone, and he smelled the way he had to smell, being five days drunk. When he came in the door, he paused for a moment, his eyes red and swollen, tiny slits. Then he saw that I was waiting for him, and he smiled in a bad way. My first punch surprised him. I had been practicing on a hay-stuffed bag, then on a padded board, toughening my fists, and I'd got so quick I flickered like fire. I still wasn't as strong as he was, and he had a good twenty pounds on me. Yet I'd do some damage, I was sure of it. I'd teach him not to mess with me. What I didn't foresee was how the fight itself would get right into me.

There is something terrible about fighting your father. It came on suddenly, with the second blow—a frightful kind of joy. A power surged up from the center of me, and I danced at him, light and giddy, full of a heady rightness. Here is the thing: I wanted to waste him, waste him good. I wanted to smack the living shit out of him. Kill him, if I must. A punch for Doris, a kick for Raymond. And all the while I was silent, then screaming, then silent again, in this rage of happiness that filled me with a simultaneous despair so that, I guess you could say, I stood apart from myself.

He came at me, crashed over a chair that was already broken, then threw the pieces. I grabbed one of the legs and whacked him on the ear so that his head spun and turned back to me, bloody. I watched myself striking him again and again. I knew what I was doing, but not really, not in the ordinary sense. It was as if I were standing calm, against the wall with my arms folded, pitying us both. I saw the boy, the chair leg, the man fold and fall, his hands held up in begging fashion. Then I also saw that, for a while now, the bigger man had not even bothered to fight back.

Suddenly, he was my father again. And when I knelt down next to him, I was his son. I reached for the closest rag, and picked up this piece of blanket that my father always kept with him for some reason. And as I picked it up and wiped the blood off his face, I said to him, Your nose is crooked again. He looked at me, steady and quizzical, as though he had never had a drink in his life, and I wiped his face again with that frayed piece of blanket. Well, it was a shawl, really, a kind of old-fashioned woman's blanket-shawl. Once, maybe, it had been plaid. You could still see lines some red, the background a faded brown. He watched intently as my hand brought the rag to his face. I was pretty sure, then, that I'd clocked him too hard that he'd really lost it now. Gently though, he clasped one hand around my wrist. With the other hand he took the shawl. He crumpled it and held it to the middle of his forehead. It was as if he were praying, as if he were having thoughts he wanted to collect in that piece of cloth. For a while he lay like that, and I,

---

6. On this side.

crouched over, let him be hardly breathing. Something told me to sit there, still. And then at last he said to me, in the sober new voice I would hear from then on, *Did you know I had a sister once?*

There was a time when the government moved everybody off the farthest reaches of the reservation, onto roads, into towns, into housing. It looked good at first, and then it all went sour. Shortly afterward, it seemed that anyone who was someone was either drunk, killed, near suicide, or had just dusted himself. None of the old sort were left, it seemed—the old kind of people, the Gete[7]anishinaabeg, who are kind beyond kindness and would do anything for others. It was during that time that my mother died and my father hurt us, as I have said.

Now, gradually, that term of despair has lifted somewhat and yielded up its survivors. But we still have sorrows that are passed to us from early generations, sorrows to handle in addition to our own, and cruelties lodged where we cannot forget them. We have the need to forget. We are always walking on oblivion's edge.

Some get away, like my brother and sister, married now and living quietly down the road. And me, to some degree, though I prefer to live alone. And even my father, who recently found a woman. Once, when he brought up the old days, and we went over the story again, I told him at last the two things I had been thinking.

First, I told him that keeping his sister's shawl was wrong, because we never keep the clothing of the dead. Now's the time to burn it, I said. Send it off to cloak her spirit. And he agreed.

The other thing I said to him was in the form of a question. Have you ever considered, I asked him, given how tenderhearted your sister was, and how brave, that she looked at the whole situation? She saw that the wolves were only hungry. She knew that their need was only need. She knew that you were back there, alone in the snow. She understood that the baby she loved would not live without a mother, and that only the uncle knew the way. She saw clearly that one person on the wagon had to be offered up, or they all would die. And in that moment of knowledge, don't you think, being who she was, of the old sort of Anishinaabeg, who thinks of the good of the people first, she jumped, my father, *n'dede,*[8] brother to that little girl? Don't you think she lifted her shawl and flew?

2001

7. Old.   8. My father.

HELENA MARÍA VIRAMONTES
b. 1954

The child of a construction worker and a housewife who raised six other daughters and three sons, Helena María Viramontes grew up in East Los Angeles, and earned an undergraduate degree at Immaculate Heart College as well as an M.F.A. at the University of California, Irvine. *The Moths and Other Stories* (1985), her first book, established her reputation as an important member of the vital, evolving Chicana literary tradition. Both her commitment to Chicana studies and her interest in popular culture were made manifest by her work cofounding the Southern California Latino Writers and Film Makers group and by her transforming her next book, *Paris Rats in East L.A.* (1993), into a screenplay. Viramontes' second novel, *Under the Feet of Jesus* (1995), recounts the difficult lives of migrant Mexican laborers in the fruit fields of California. The co-editor of two books on Chicana writers, Viramontes now teaches at Cornell University. When asked how she landed in the Ivy League after a youth in the barrios, Viramontes has explained, "it was the books. . . . Now, when I write, I write as if my words were going to change other people's lives." A story about mourning, "The Moths," with its surrealistic ending, testifies to the lyrical artistry of an author able to factor pathos and verisimilitude into a tradition of magical realism that has its literary roots in Central and South America.

The Moths

I was fourteen years old when Abuelita[1] requested my help. And it seemed only fair. Abuelita had pulled me through the rages of scarlet fever by placing, removing and replacing potato slices on the temples of my forehead; she had seen me through several whippings, an arm broken by a dare jump off Tío Enrique's toolshed, puberty, and my first lie. Really, I told Amá,[2] it was only fair.

Not that I was her favorite granddaughter or anything special. I wasn't even pretty or nice like my older sisters and I just couldn't do the girl things they could do. My hands were too big to handle the fineries of crocheting or embroidery and I always pricked my fingers or knotted my colored threads time and time again while my sisters laughed and called me bull hands with their cute waterlike voices. So I began keeping a piece of jagged brick in my sock to bash my sisters or anyone who called me bull hands. Once, while we all sat in the bedroom, I hit Teresa on the forehead, right above her eyebrow and she ran to Amá with her mouth open, her hand over her eye while blood seeped between her fingers. I was used to the whippings by then.

I wasn't respectful either. I even went so far as to doubt the power of Abuelita's slices, the slices she said absorbed my fever. "You're still alive, aren't you?" Abuelita snapped back, her pasty gray eye beaming at me and burning holes in my suspicions. Regretful that I had let secret questions drop out of my mouth, I couldn't look into her eyes. My hands began to fan out, grow like a liar's nose[3] until they hung by my side like low weights. Abuelita made a balm out of dried moth wings and Vicks and rubbed my hands,

---

1. Grandmother (Spanish, as are all translated terms).
2. Mom. "Tío": uncle.
3. I.e., like the nose of the title character in Carlo Collodi's *The Adventures of Pinocchio* (1883), which grew when he told a lie.

shaped them back to size and it was the strangest feeling. Like bones melting. Like sun shining through the darkness of your eyelids. I didn't mind helping Abuelita after that, so Amá would always send me over to her.

In the early afternoon Amá would push her hair back, hand me my sweater and shoes, and tell me to go to Mama Luna's. This was to avoid another fight and another whipping, I knew. I would deliver one last direct shot on Marisela's arm and jump out of our house, the slam of the screen door burying her cries of anger, and I'd gladly go help Abuelita plant her wild lilies or jasmine or heliotrope or cilantro or hierbabuena[4] in red Hills Brothers coffee cans. Abuelita would wait for me at the top step of her porch holding a hammer and nail and empty coffee cans. And although we hardly spoke, hardly looked at each other as we worked over root transplants, I always felt her gray eye on me. It made me feel, in a strange sort of way, safe and guarded and not alone. Like God was supposed to make you feel.

On Abuelita's porch, I would puncture holes in the bottom of the coffee cans with a nail and a precise hit of a hammer. This completed, my job was to fill them with red clay mud from beneath her rose bushes, packing it softly, then making a perfect hole, four fingers round, to nest a sprouting avocado pit, or the spidery sweet potatoes that Abuelita rooted in mayonnaise jars with toothpicks and daily water, or prickly chayotes that produced vines that twisted and wound all over her porch pillars, crawling to the roof, up and over the roof, and down the other side, making her small brick house look like it was cradled within the vines that grew pear-shaped squashes ready for the pick, ready to be steamed with onions and cheese and butter. The roots would burst out of the rusted coffee cans and search for a place to connect. I would then feed the seedlings with water.

But this was a different kind of help, Amá said, because Abuelita was dying. Looking into her gray eye, then into her brown one, the doctor said it was just a matter of days. And so it seemed only fair that these hands she had melted and formed found use in rubbing her caving body with alcohol and marihuana, rubbing her arms and legs, turning her face to the window so that she could watch the Bird of Paradise blooming or smell the scent of clove in the air. I toweled her face frequently and held her hand for hours. Her gray wiry hair hung over the mattress. Since I could remember, she'd kept her long hair in braids. Her mouth was vacant and when she slept, her eyelids never closed all the way. Up close, you could see her gray eye beaming out the window, staring hard as if to remember everything. I never kissed her. I left the window open when I went to the market.

Across the street from Jay's Market there was a chapel. I never knew its denomination, but I went in just the same to search for candles. I sat down on one of the pews because there were none. After I cleaned my fingernails, I looked up at the high ceiling. I had forgotten the vastness of these places, the coolness of the marble pillars and the frozen statues with blank eyes. I was alone. I knew why I had never returned.

That was one of Apá's[5] biggest complaints. He would pound his hands on the table, rocking the sugar dish or spilling a cup of coffee and scream that if I didn't go to mass every Sunday to save my goddamn sinning soul, then I had no reason to go out of the house, period. Punto final.[6] He would grab

---

4. Mint.
5. Dad's.
6. Full stop.

my arm and dig his nails into me to make sure I understood the importance of catechism. Did he make himself clear? Then he strategically directed his anger at Amá for her lousy ways of bringing up daughters, being disrespectful and unbelieving, and my older sisters would pull me aside and tell me if I didn't get to mass right this minute, they were all going to kick the holy shit out of me. Why am I so selfish? Can't you see what it's doing to Amá, you idiot? So I would wash my feet and stuff them in my black Easter shoes that shone with Vaseline, grab a missal and veil, and wave good-bye to Amá.

I would walk slowly down Lorena to First to Evergreen, counting the cracks on the cement. On Evergreen I would turn left and walk to Abuelita's. I liked her porch because it was shielded by the vines of the chayotes and I could get a good look at the people and car traffic on Evergreen without them knowing. I would jump up the porch steps, knock on the screen door as I wiped my feet and call Abuelita? mi Abuelita? As I opened the door and stuck my head in, I would catch the gagging scent of toasting chile on the placa. When I entered the sala,[7] she would greet me from the kitchen, wringing her hands in her apron. I'd sit at the corner of the table to keep from being in her way. The chiles made my eyes water. Am I crying? No, Mama Luna, I'm sure not crying. I don't like going to mass, but my eyes watered anyway, the tears dropping on the tablecloth like candle wax. Abuelita lifted the burnt chiles from the fire and sprinkled water on them until the skins began to separate. Placing them in front of me, she turned to check the menudo. I peeled the skins off and put the flimsy, limp looking green and yellow chiles in the molcajete[8] and began to crush and crush and twist and crush the heart out of the tomato, the clove of garlic, the stupid chiles that made me cry, crushed them until they turned into liquid under my bull hand. With a wooden spoon, I scraped hard to destroy the guilt, and my tears were gone. I put the bowl of chile next to a vase filled with freshly cut roses. Abuelita touched my hand and pointed to the bowl of menudo that steamed in front of me. I spooned some chile into the menudo and rolled a corn tortilla thin with the palms of my hands. As I ate, a fine Sunday breeze entered the kitchen and a rose petal calmly feathered down to the table.

I left the chapel without blessing myself and walked to Jay's. Most of the time Jay didn't have much of anything. The tomatoes were always soft and the cans of Campbell soups had rusted spots on them. There was dust on the tops of cereal boxes. I picked up what I needed: rubbing alcohol, five cans of chicken broth, a big bottle of Pine Sol. At first Jay got mad because I thought I had forgotten the money. But it was there all the time, in my back pocket.

When I returned from the market, I heard Amá crying in Abuelita's kitchen. She looked up at me with puffy eyes. I placed the bags of groceries on the table and began putting the cans of soup away. Amá sobbed quietly. I never kissed her. After a while, I patted her on the back for comfort. Finally: "¿Y mi Amá?"[9] she asked in a whisper, then choked again and cried into her apron.

Abuelita fell off the bed twice yesterday, I said, knowing that I shouldn't have said it and wondering why I wanted to say it because it only made Amá

---

7. Hall. "Placa": metal plate.
8. Mortar and pestle. "Menudo": a Mexican soup made with tripe and hominy.
9. And my mom?

cry harder. I guess I became angry and just so tired of the quarrels and beatings and unanswered prayers and my hands just there hanging helplessly by my side. Amá looked at me again, confused, angry, and her eyes were filled with sorrow. I went outside and sat on the porch swing and watched the people pass. I sat there until she left. I dozed off repeating the words to myself like rosary prayers:[1] when do you stop giving when do you start giving when do you . . . and when my hands fell from my lap, I awoke to catch them. The sun was setting, an orange glow, and I knew Abuelita was hungry.

There comes a time when the sun is defiant. Just about the time when moods change, inevitable seasons of a day, transitions from one color to another, that hour or minute or second when the sun is finally defeated, finally sinks into the realization that it cannot with all its power to heal or burn, exist forever, there comes an illumination where the sun and earth meet, a final burst of burning red orange fury reminding us that although endings are inevitable, they are necessary for rebirths, and when that time came, just when I switched on the light in the kitchen to open Abuelita's can of soup, it was probably then that she died.

The room smelled of Pine Sol and vomit and Abuelita had defecated the remains of her cancerous stomach. She had turned to the window and tried to speak, but her mouth remained open and speechless. I heard you, Abuelita, I said, stroking her cheek, I heard you. I opened the windows of the house and let the soup simmer and overboil on the stove. I turned the stove off and poured the soup down the sink. From the cabinet I got a tin basin, filled it with lukewarm water and carried it carefully to the room. I went to the linen closet and took out some modest bleached white towels. With the sacredness of a priest preparing his vestments, I unfolded the towels one by one on my shoulders. I removed the sheets and blankets from her bed and peeled off her thick flannel nightgown. I toweled her puzzled face, stretching out the wrinkles, removing the coils of her neck, toweled her shoulders and breasts. Then I changed the water. I returned to towel the creases of her stretch-marked stomach, her sporadic vaginal hairs, and her sagging thighs. I removed the lint from between her toes and noticed a mapped birthmark on the fold of her buttock. The scars on her back which were as thin as the life lines on the palms of her hands made me realize how little I really knew of Abuelita. I covered her with a thin blanket and went into the bathroom. I washed my hands, and turned on the tub faucets and watched the water pour into the tub with vitality and steam. When it was full, I turned off the water and undressed. Then, I went to get Abuelita.

She was not as heavy as I thought and when I carried her in my arms, her body fell into a V, and yet my legs were tired, shaky, and I felt as if the distance between the bedroom and bathroom was miles and years away. Amá, where are you?

I stepped into the bathtub one leg first, then the other. I bent my knees slowly to descend into the water slowly so I wouldn't scald her skin. There, there, Abuelita, I said, cradling her, smoothing her as we descended, I heard you. Her hair fell back and spread across the water like eagle's wings. The water in the tub overflowed and poured onto the tile of the floor. Then the

---

1. Catholic devotions consisting of a series of repeated prayers; the devout use a string of beads, also called a rosary, to keep track of the count.

moths came. Small, gray ones that came from her soul and out through her mouth fluttering to light, circling the single dull light bulb of the bathroom. Dying is lonely and I wanted to go to where the moths were, stay with her and plant chayotes whose vines would crawl up her fingers and into the clouds; I wanted to rest my head on her chest with her stroking my hair, telling me about the moths that lay within the soul and slowly eat the spirit up; I wanted to return to the waters of the womb with her so that we would never be alone again. I wanted. I wanted my Amá. I removed a few strands of hair from Abuelita's face and held her small light head within the hollow of my neck. The bathroom was filled with moths, and for the first time in a long time I cried, rocking us, crying for her, for me, for Amá, the sobs emerging from the depths of anguish, the misery of feeling half born, sobbing until finally the sobs rippled into circles and circles of sadness and relief. There, there, I said to Abuelita, rocking us gently, there, there.

1982, 1985

MARILYN CHIN
b. 1955

An avowedly political poet, Marilyn Chin approaches the theme of assimilation through what she calls "a delicate and apocalyptic melding" of Eastern and Western forms and themes. Born in Hong Kong and named Mei Ling, Chin came to the United States with her family; her father insisted her name be changed to Marilyn when she entered school in Portland, Oregon. In the poem "How I Got That Name," her father's obsession with "a bombshell blonde" whom Chin takes to be "some tragic white woman / swollen with gin and Nembutal" reflects the anger she felt when he later abandoned his Chinese family for a white woman. In 1977 Chin received her B.A. from the University of Massachusetts at Amherst and in 1981 she completed an M.F.A. at the University of Iowa. Like her editorial, translation, and teaching work, Chin's verse attends to the linguistic, psychological, and aesthetic ramifications of contemporary globalism. She is the co-editor (with David Wong Louie) of *Dissident Song: A Contemporary Asian American Anthology*, the co-translator (with Eugene Eoyang) of *The Selected Poems of Ai Qing* (1985), and an instructor in the Master of Fine Arts Program at San Diego State University, where she encourages students to familiarize themselves with poetry in languages other than English. Juxtaposed languages, styles, modes, and moods proliferate in her own books of verse: *Dwarf Bamboo* (1987), *The Phoenix Gone, The Terrace Empty* (1994), and *Rhapsody in Plain Yellow* (2002).

How I Got That Name

an essay on assimilation

I am Marilyn Mei Ling Chin.
Oh, how I love the resoluteness
of that first person singular
followed by that stalwart indicative
of "be," without the uncertain i-n-g
of "becoming." Of course,
the name had been changed
somewhere between Angel Island and the sea,
when my father the paperson[1]
in the late 1950s
obsessed with a bombshell blonde[2]
transliterated "Mei Ling" to "Marilyn."
And nobody dared question
his initial impulse—for we all know
lust drove men to greatness,
not goodness, not decency.
And there I was, a wayward pink baby,
named after some tragic white woman
swollen with gin and Nembutal.
My mother couldn't pronounce the "r."
She dubbed me "Numba one female offshoot"
for brevity: henceforth, she will live and die
in sublime ignorance, flanked
by loving children and the "kitchen deity."[3]
While my father dithers,
a tomcat in Hong Kong trash—
a gambler, a petty thug,
who bought a chain of chopsuey joints
in Piss River, Oregon,
with bootlegged Gucci cash.
Nobody dared question his integrity given
his nice, devout daughters
and his bright, industrious sons
as if filial piety were the standard
by which all earthly men were measured.[4]

*

Oh, how trustworthy our daughters,
how thrifty our sons!
How we've managed to fool the experts
in education, statistics and demography—
We're not very creative but not adverse to rote-learning.

---

1. An immigrant who circumvented the Chinese Exclusion Act of 1882 by buying counterfeit papers showing that he had parents who were U.S. citizens. "Angel Island": an island in San Francisco Bay that served as an immigration station and detention center between 1910 and 1940; it was designed primarily to control the flow of Chinese into the United States.
2. I.e., Marilyn Monroe (1926–1962), an American film star and sex symbol who died after taking an overdose of sleeping pills (see line 19).
3. In Chinese folk religion, the protector of the family.
4. In Confucianism, the dominant moral and religious system of China until the 20th century, the filial relationship is stressed above all others.

Indeed, they can *use* us.
But the "Model Minority" is a tease.
We know you are watching now,
so we refuse to give you any!
45 Oh, bamboo shoots, bamboo shoots!
The further west we go, we'll hit east;
the deeper down we dig, we'll find China.
History has turned its stomach
on a black polluted beach—
50 where life doesn't hinge
on that red, red wheelbarrow,[5]
but whether or not our new lover
in the final episode of "Santa Barbara"[6]
will lean over a scented candle
55 and call us a "bitch."
Oh God, where have we gone wrong?
We have no inner resources![7]

*

Then, one redolent spring morning
the Great Patriarch Chin
60 peered down from his kiosk in heaven
and saw that his descendants were ugly.
One had a squarish head and a nose without a bridge.
Another's profile—long and knobbed as a gourd.
A third, the sad, brutish one
65 may never, never marry.
And I, his least favorite—
"not quite boiled, not quite cooked,"
a plump pomfret[8] simmering in my juices—
too listless to fight for my people's destiny.
70 "To kill without resistance is not slaughter"
says the proverb. So, I wait for imminent death.
The fact that this death is also metaphorical
is testament to my lethargy.

*

So here lies Marilyn Mei Ling Chin,
75 married once, twice to so-and-so, a Lee and a Wong,
granddaughter of Jack "the patriarch"
and the brooding Suilin Fong,
daughter of the virtuous Yuet Kuen Wong
and G. G. Chin the infamous,
80 sister of a dozen, cousin of a million,
survived by everybody and forgotten by all.
She was neither black nor white,
neither cherished nor vanquished,
just another squatter in her own bamboo grove
85 minding her poetry—
when one day heaven was unmerciful,

---

5. Compare William Carlos Williams's "The Red Wheelbarrow" (1923), which begins "so much depends / upon // a red wheel / barrow."
6. American television soap opera (1984–93).
7. Compare John Berryman's Dream Song 14 (1964): "I conclude now I have no / inner resources."
8. An Asian marine fish.

and a chasm opened where she stood.
Like the jowls of a mighty white whale,
or the jaws of a metaphysical Godzilla,[9]
90   it swallowed her whole.
She did not flinch nor writhe,
nor fret about the afterlife,
but stayed! Solid as wood, happily
a little gnawed, tattered, mesmerized
95   by all that was lavished upon her
and all that was taken away!

1994

That Half Is Almost Gone

That half is almost gone,[1]
                the Chinese half,
the fair side of a peach,
5   darkened by the knife of time,
fades like a cruel sun.

In my thirtieth year
            I wrote a letter to my mother.

I had forgotten the character
            for "love." I remember vaguely
10   the radical "heart."
            The ancestors won't fail to remind you

the vital and vestigial organs
            where the emotions come from.

But the rest is fading.
15   A slash dissects in midair,
ai, ai, ai, ai,[2]
            more of a cry than a sigh

(and no help from the phoneticist).

    You are a Chinese!
20   My mother was adamant.
    You *are* a Chinese?
           My mother less convinced.

---

9. I.e., a giant destructive monster (originally featured in a 1954 Japanese film). "White whale": the title character of Herman Melville's *Moby-Dick* (1851).
1. "That half is almost gone" is a visual play on the Chinese character for "love." The semantic radical for this character is the character for "heart." A slash goes straight across the "heart" [Chin's note]. "Radical": one of the building blocks of a written Chinese character, which is only loosely related to pronunciation.
2. "*ai, ai*" is an exclamation homophonous with *ai*/ love, punning love with pain [Chin's note].

     Are you not Chinese?
         My mother now accepting.

25 As a cataract clouds her vision,
        and her third daughter marries
 a Protestant West Virginian

      who is "very handsome and very kind."

 The mystery is still unsolved—

30   the landscape looms

over man. And the gaffer[3]-hatted fishmonger—

         sings to his cormorant.
 And the maiden behind the curtain

       is somebody's courtesan.

35 Or, merely Rose Wong's aging daughter

    Pondering the blue void.

 You are a Chinese—said my mother

      who once walked the fields of her dead—

 Today, on the 36th anniversary of my birth,

40 I have problems now
     even with the salutation.

            2002

The True Story of Mortar and Pestle

for my sister, Jane

 Nobody understood her cruelty to herself. In this life, cruelty begets cruelty, and before long, one would have to chop off one's own hand to end the source of self-torture. Yet, we continue, Sister Mortar pounding on Sister Pestle. The hand refuses to retreat, as if to retreat would
5 mean less meat on the table.

 She, Mortar, the presentable one: clean, well-kept, jade cross, white colonial pinafore, shiny knees and elbows, straight As, responsible hall monitor, future councilwoman. She is Yang:[1] heaven, sunlight, vigorous, masculine, penetrator, the monad.

---

3. Old man.
1. In Chinese cosmology, the masculine active principle in nature; it combines with yin, the feminine passive principle and its complementary opposite, to produce everything in the world.

She, Pestle: disheveled, morose, soft-spoken, a fearful dark crucible. She
is Yin: heaven's antithesis, moony, fecund, feminine, absorption, the duad.

The outer child had everything to live for: tenure, partnership in the
firm, shapely breasts, strong legs, praise from a few key critics, the love
of a good man.

The inner child was denied food, yet food was ample. She was denied
sleep, yet darkness descended as day.

Justice was the hateful stepfather. His voice was loud, truculent in their
ear, *If you succeed there would be no applause; if you fail, there, too, would
be silent reckoning.*

Listen to that serious pounding of the ages . . . not nocturnal lovemaking of the muses,[2] but the bad sister pounding the good. Somewhere in
the scintillating powder we grind into light.

2002

2. In classical mythology, nine daughters of Memory who preside over the arts and all intellectual pursuits; they are conventionally invoked for inspiration and information.

CAROL ANN DUFFY
b. 1955

After Ted Hughes—the widower of Sylvia Plath—died in 1998, Carol Ann Duffy was widely regarded as one of the two most prominent candidates to succeed him in the prestigious post of British poet laureate. In fact, after her rival Andrew Motion was appointed, two writers for the newspaper *The Guardian* noted that she "had been regarded by many as the best choice, but two factors may have counted against her—her outspokenness and her sexuality. A lesbian, she was unwilling to write poems for the royal family." But the journalists' comment wasn't quite accurate: if Duffy hadn't written a poem *for* the royal family, she had written an elegy for Diana, Princess of Wales ("September 1997"), that was controversially *about* them—a rueful sonnet that was also a poignant political meditation in its observation that "England's crown / is rusting" as the "century bleeds to its end." An impassioned feminist, a witty revisionist, and a skillful artist, Duffy had, ironically enough, demonstrated her ability to speak for, to, and about her country in producing a work that helped prevent her accession to the laureateship.

Born in Glasgow to parents of Irish extraction, Duffy was raised in left-wing, working-class, Catholic surroundings in Stafford, England, where her father was a shop steward, a city councillor, a Labour candidate, and manager of the local football club. After attending convent schools, she graduated from the University of Liverpool. She has published nearly a dozen collections of verse, beginning with a pamphlet, *Fleshweathercock,* in 1973 when she was still in her teens. Her most recent volumes include *The World's Wife* (1999) and *Feminine Gospels* (2002). In addition, she has written several plays and edited a number of anthologies, among them volume 2 of *Penguin Modern Poets,* with Vicki Feaver and Eavan Boland (1995), and *Stopping for Death: Poems of Death and Loss,* with Trisha Rafferty (1996).

The single mother of a daughter, Ella, Duffy lives with the black Scottish poet Jackie Kay; though this relationship may have cost her the laureateship, it has been depicted with exuberance not only by the partners themselves but by admiring interviewers, who agree that in "the world of British poetry, Carol Ann Duffy is a superstar." Wrote a reporter for *The Independent* in 1999, "She and Jackie have separate writing lives, separate studies, diaries and phone-lines. They don't criticize each other's work. They do, however, meet for cups of coffee, indulge in impromptu shopping trips and laugh over reviews. 'In our household, reviews are great fun,' Duffy smiles. 'They're a form of entertainment.' Does she ever get upset by them? 'No, not really,' she replies, as if considering a fascinating new concept. 'I regret to say that it's quite thrilling to get a bad review.'" The insouciance with which Duffy defines reviews as "great fun" also infuses many of the dramatic monologues that she assembled in *The World's Wife,* her collection of feminist revisions of mythic and legendary women, although some of these works—for instance, "Mrs. Lazarus"—also reveal the dark underside of her glittering wit.

Warming Her Pearls

for Judith Radstone[1]

Next to my own skin, her pearls. My mistress
bids me wear them, warm them, until evening
when I'll brush her hair. At six, I place them
round her cool, white throat. All day I think of her,

     resting in the Yellow Room, contemplating silk
or taffeta, which gown tonight? She fans herself
whilst I work willingly, my slow heat entering
each pearl. Slack on my neck, her rope.

She's beautiful. I dream about her
in my attic bed; picture her dancing
with tall men, puzzled by my faint, persistent scent
beneath her French perfume, her milky stones.

I dust her shoulders with a rabbit's foot,
watch the soft blush seep through her skin
like an indolent sigh. In her looking-glass
my red lips part as though I want to speak.

Full moon. Her carriage brings her home. I see
her every movement in my head . . . Undressing,
taking off her jewels, her slim hand reaching
for the case, slipping naked into bed, the way

---

1. British bookseller and political activist (1925–2001); according to her obituary in *The Guardian,* the poem was inspired by Duffy's conversation with her "about the practice of ladies' maids increasing the lustre of their mistresses' pearls by secreting them beneath their clothes to be warmed by their skin."

she always does . . . And I lie here awake,
knowing the pearls are cooling even now
in the room where my mistress sleeps. All night
I feel their absence and I burn.

1987

Litany

The soundtrack then was a litany—*candlewick*
bedspread three piece suite display cabinet—
and stiff-haired wives balanced their red smiles,
passing the catalogue. *Pyrex.* A tiny ladder[1]
ran up Mrs Barr's American Tan leg, sly
like a rumour. Language embarrassed them.

The terrible marriages crackled, cellophane
round polyester shirts, and then The Lounge
would seem to bristle with eyes, hard
as the bright stones in engagement rings,
and sharp hands poised over biscuits[2] as a word
was spelled out. An embarrassing word, broken

to bits, which tensed the air like an accident.
This was the code I learnt at my mother's knee, pretending
to read, where no one had cancer, or sex, or debts,
and certainly not leukaemia, which no one could spell.
The year a mass grave of wasps bobbed in a jam-jar;
a butterfly stammered itself in my curious hands.

A boy in the playground, I said, *told me*
to fuck off, and a thrilled, malicious pause
salted my tongue like an imminent storm. Then
uproar. *I'm sorry, Mrs Barr, Mrs Hunt, Mrs Emery,*
sorry, Mrs Raine. Yes, I can summon their names.
My mother's mute shame. The taste of soap.

1995

September, 1997

Whatever "in love" means,[1]
true love is talented.
Someone vividly gifted in love has gone.

---

1. I.e., a run in her stockings.
2. Cookies.

1. The response of Prince Charles (b. 1949), heir to the British throne, when he and Lady Diana Spencer (1961–1997) were asked in an interview after their engagement whether they were in love (her answer, given first, was "Of course!"). They married in 1981 and divorced in 1996; she was killed in a car crash on August 31, 1997.

You went down to St James' Palace[2]
5 as night fell. Candles shone.
You saw a vast and passionate queue silently form,

as though History was a giant
shaken from sleep by Love.
Then you looked at your hands. Newsprint
10 covered them like gloves. England's crown
is rusting. The century bleeds to its end.
You stand in a queue in darkness, mourning

an unmet friend. The stranger beside you the same.
A million dying flowers smell like Fame.

1997

Circe[1]

I'm fond, nereids[2] and nymphs, unlike some, of the pig,
of the tusker, the snout, the boar and the swine.
One way or another, all pigs have been mine—
under my thumb, the bristling, salty skin of their backs,
5 in my nostrils here, their yobby,[3] porky colognes.
I'm familiar with hogs and runts, their percussion of oinks
and grunts, their squeals. I've stood with a pail of swill
at dusk, at the creaky gate of the sty,
tasting the sweaty, spicy air, the moon
10 like a lemon popped in the mouth of the sky.
But I want to begin with a recipe from abroad

which uses the cheek—and the tongue in cheek
at that. Lay two pig's cheeks, with the tongue,
in a dish, and strew it well over with salt
15 and cloves. Remember the skills of the tongue—
to lick, to lap, to loosen, lubricate, to lie
in the soft pouch of the face—and how each pig's face
was uniquely itself, as many handsome as plain,
the cowardly face, the brave, the comical, noble,
20 sly or wise, the cruel, the kind, but all of them,
nymphs, with those piggy eyes. Season with mace.

Well-cleaned pig's ears should be blanched, singed, tossed
in a pot, boiled, kept hot, scraped, served, garnished

---

2. The official residence of the reigning British monarch, and the main residence of Prince Charles; it was where Diana's body lay in state before her funeral.
1. In Homer's *Odyssey* (book 10), a powerful enchantress who lived on an island off the coast of Italy; she was encountered by Odysseus as he attempted to return home after the Trojan War. She transformed his crew into swine, and he stayed with her for a year after persuading her to turn them back into men.
2. Sea nymphs.
3. Loutish.

with thyme. Look at that simmering lug,[4] at that ear,
did it listen, ever, to you, to your prayers and rhymes,
to the chimes of your voice, singing and clear? Mash
the potatoes, nymph, open the beer. Now to the brains,
to the trotters, shoulders, chops, to the sweetmeats slipped
from the slit, bulging, vulnerable bag of the balls.
When the heart of a pig has hardened, dice it small.

Dice it small. I, too, once knelt on this shining shore
watching the tall ships sail from the burning sun
like myths; slipped off my dress to wade,
breast-deep, in the sea, waving and calling;
then plunged, then swam on my back, looking up
as three black ships sighed in the shallow waves.
Of course, I was younger then. And hoping for men. Now,
let us baste that sizzling pig on the spit once again.

1999

Mrs Lazarus[1]

I had grieved. I had wept for a night and a day
over my loss, ripped the cloth I was married in
from my breasts, howled, shrieked, clawed
at the burial stones till my hands bled, retched
his name over and over again, dead, dead.

Gone home. Gutted the place. Slept in a single cot,
widow, one empty glove, white femur
in the dust, half. Stuffed dark suits
into black bags, shuffled in a dead man's shoes,
noosed the double knot of a tie round my bare neck,

gaunt nun in the mirror, touching herself. I learnt
the Stations of Bereavement,[2] the icon of my face
in each bleak frame; but all those months
he was going away from me, dwindling
to the shrunk size of a snapshot, going,

going. Till his name was no longer a certain spell
for his face. The last hair on his head
floated out from a book. His scent went from the house.
The will was read. See, he was vanishing
to the small zero held by the gold of my ring.

---

4. Ear (British slang); also, a big clumsy fellow.
1. Lazarus was the man whose resurrection by Jesus, four days after his death, is described in John 11.1–44.
2. An allusion to the Stations of the Cross, pictures or tableaux representing fourteen scenes in the sufferings of Jesus (between his condemnation to death and his body being laid in the tomb); in a popular devotion, the faithful pass from one to the next, meditating and saying specific prayers at each station.

Then he was gone. Then he was legend, language;
my arm on the arm of the schoolteacher—the shock
of a man's strength under the sleeve of his coat—
along the hedgerows. But I was faithful
for as long as it took. Until he was memory.

So I could stand that evening in the field
in a shawl of fine air, healed, able
to watch the edge of the moon occur to the sky
and a hare thump from a hedge; then notice
the village men running towards me, shouting,

behind them the women and children, barking dogs,
and I knew. I knew by the sly light
on the blacksmith's face, the shrill eyes
of the barmaid, the sudden hands bearing me
into the hot tang of the crowd parting before me.

He lived. I saw the horror on his face.
I heard his mother's crazy song. I breathed
his stench; my bridegroom in his rotting shroud,
moist and dishevelled from the grave's slack chew,
croaking his cuckold name, disinherited, out of his time.

1999

PAULA MEEHAN
b. 1955

"As a maker of a poem I can be dealing with material that is dark, grief-laden, from the hurt self, but a part of me will be experiencing a cold delight," confides the Irish poet Paula Meehan, explaining that she feels "a kind of lucid exhilaration at getting the right word in the right place, at manipulating the rhythm, at swinging the sentence around the lines, at pushing my own breath into patterns that enact the emotional state I'm expressing." A playwright as well as a maker of beautifully patterned verses, Meehan is expert at dramatizing the ferocity of grief (as in "Child Burial") as well as the violence of jealousy (as in " 'Would you jump into my grave as quick?' "), even while she also explores her own history with candor and lucid detail (as in "The View from under the Table").

Born in Dublin, Meehan was raised in a northside working-class neighborhood where she absorbed "local lore, the rhythms of children's playsongs and shouts" along with "family talk and silences." A graduate of Trinity College, Dublin, she earned an M.F.A. in verse writing from Eastern Washington University in 1983 and has taught workshops and master classes in the United States and Britain as well as in Ireland. Besides four collections of verse, including *Pillow Talk* (1994) and *Dharmakaya* (2000), she has written five plays, among them *Mrs. Sweeney* (1997) and *The Wolf of Winter*, which was produced by the Abbey Theatre in 2003.

Child Burial

Your coffin looked unreal,
fancy as a wedding cake.

I chose your grave clothes with care,
your favourite stripey shirt,

5   your blue cotton trousers.
They smelt of woodsmoke, of October,

your own smell there too.
I chose a gansy[1] of handspun wool,

warm and fleecy for you. It is
10   so cold down in the dark.

No light can reach you and teach you
the paths of wild birds,

the names of the flowers,
the fishes, the creatures.

15   Ignorant you must remain
of the sun and its work,

my lamb, my calf, my eaglet,
my cub, my kid, my nestling,

my suckling, my colt. I would spin
20   time back, take you again

1991

The View from under the Table

was the best view and the table itself kept the sky
from falling. The world was fringed with red velvet tassels;
whatever play ran in that room the tablecloth was curtains for.
I was the audience. Listen to me laughing. Listen
5   to me weeping. I was a child. What did I know?

Except that the moon was a porcelain globe and swung from a brass
   chain. O

---

1. Jersey, or knitted long-sleeved pullover (dialect).

that wasn't the moon at all. The moon was my true love. Oak was my
    roof and
under the table no one could see you. My granny could see me.
Out, she'd say. Out. And up on her lap the smell of kitchen and sleep.
She'd rock me. She'd lull me. No one was kinder.

What ails you child? I never told her. Not
one word would cross my lips. Shadows I'd say. I don't like the
    shadows.
They're waiting to snatch me. There at the turn of the stairs.
On the landing. To the right of the wardrobe. In the fridge, white
    ghosts.
Black ghosts in the coal shed. In the bread bin, hungry ghosts.

Somewhere, elsewhere, my mother was sulking in the rain. I call up
her young face. Who did she think she was with her big words
and her belt and her beatings? Who do I think I am to write her?
She must have been sad. She must have been lonely.
Discipline. Chastisement. I stretch out my four year old hands.

2000

Thunder in the House

was what my mother called the noise above
that shook the ceiling, made the windows hum,

not Jesus moving wardrobes, couches, beds—
shifting heaven's furniture to help his mam

when Jesus was a boy, not bold like us;
Was what she called the ructions in the flat[1] above

when all hell broke loose, when for an hour
or two or three or four until he fell asleep

or headed out for more, we were the damned.
Fridays were the worst. He'd come in roaring.

She was curst and soundly whacked. Sometimes
we could even hear the individual smack

of his hand on her cheek. But rarely words. No.
Then when the door would slam: weeping.

---

1. Apartment.

15 I'd meet her sometimes on the stairs, bruised
    black and blue or a stranger orange hue,

    thick smeared panstick[2] on her twelve year old face.
    I thought she was like the coalman's mangy dog,

    a sleeveen[3] bitch so used to beatings she'd slither
20 at your ankles, belly low, waiting for the boot to drop.

    She robbed me of my message money. A slide[4] from my plait.
    My blue scarf. I avoided her after that.

    My mother had no answers, or if she knew,
    was leaving well enough alone. My own father

25 got cranky and threatened to settle his hash. God
    love her, they'd say, she has nobody else. It'd go

    even harder on her if anyone interfered.
    She disappeared one cold midwinter's day,

    the year I lost faith in Santa, though I stood
30 scanning Gardiner Street all Christmas Eve,

    the bulletins shouted back to the younger kids—
    a glimpse of his hood between chimneys, a snatch of red—

    with thunder in the house, and shiny rain on all the roads
    while from our plastered ceiling shook a fine fall of snow.

                                                    2000

"Would you jump into my grave as quick?"

    Would you jump into my grave as quick?
    my granny would ask when one of us took
    her chair by the fire. You, woman,
    done up to the nines, red lips a come on,
5   your breath reeking of drink
    and your black eye on my man tonight
    in a Dublin bar, think
    first of the steep drop, the six dark feet.

                                                    2003

---

2. A cosmetic foundation used in theatrical makeup.
3. Sly, ingratiating (Irish idiom).
4. Hair clip.

REBECCA BROWN
b. 1956

Possessed of an impassioned, sardonic, and sometimes gothic imagination, the novelist and short story writer Rebecca Brown has been compared to the great lesbian feminist-modernist Djuna Barnes, whose *Nightwood* (1936) prefigures the grotesque fantasies that often haunt Brown's fictions. Yet as the critic Victoria A. Brownworth has put it, Brown's work "is brutal and bizarre—but with a kind of dark beauty and even humor that compel."

Born in San Diego, California, to Vergil Neal Brown Jr., a military officer, and Barbara Ann Brown, a social worker, the writer was raised on the move, as the family followed her father from place to place—a childhood partly reflected in the plot of her first novel, *The Haunted House* (1987). Brown earned a B.A. at George Washington University and an M.F.A. at the University of Virginia; has worked as a teacher, carpenter, freelance journalist, and rock music critic; and currently resides some of the time in Seattle, Washington, while also serving on the faculty of Goddard College in Vermont. Her books of fiction include *The Terrible Girls* (1992), a collection of eight linked stories from which "Forgiveness," reprinted here, is drawn, as well as, more recently, *Annie Oakley's Girl* (1993) and *The Gifts of the Body* (1994). Of these intermittently comic and unnerving works, she herself has admitted that "though the surreal and fantastical elements . . . aren't autobiographical, I think of them as emotionally autobiographical: real late-night-sweating-blood kind of stuff." As for "real" autobiographical works, she has published *The End of Youth* (2003), a "memoir-in-essays," and *Excerpts from a Family Medical Dictionary* (2001), a poignant and unflinching account of her mother's death from cancer and her own caregiving. In addition, she has written a play, *The Toaster*, which was produced in Seattle in 2004.

Forgiveness

When I said I'd give my right arm for you, I didn't think you'd ask me for it, but you did.

You said, Give it to me.

And I said OK.

There were lots of reasons I gave it to you.

First of all, I didn't want to be made a liar of. (I had never lied to you.) So when you reminded me that I'd said it and asked me if I really meant it, I didn't want to seem like I was copping out by saying that I'd only spoken figuratively. (It is an old saying, after all.) Also, I had the feeling you didn't think I would really do it, that you were testing me to see if I would, and I wanted you to know I would.

Also, I believed you wouldn't have asked me for it unless you really wanted it, and needed it.

But then, when you got it, you bronzed it and put it on the mantel over the fireplace in the den.

The night you took it, I dreamt of arms. I slept on the couch in the den because I was still bleeding, even through the bandages, and I knew I'd stir during the night and need to put on more bandages and we didn't want me to wake you up. So I stayed on the couch and when I slept, I dreamt of arms: red arms, blue arms, golden arms. And arms made out of jade. Arms with tattoos, arms with stripes. Arms waving, sleeping, holding. Arms that rested up against my ribs.

We kept my arm in the bathtub, bleeding like a fish. When I went to bed, the water was the color of rose water, with thick red lines like strings. And when I woke up the first time to change my bandages, it was colored like salmon. Then it was carnation red, and then maroon, then burgundy, then purple, thick, and almost black by morning.

In the morning, you took it out. I watched you pat it dry with my favorite big fat terry cloth towel and wrap it in saran wrap and take it out to get it bronzed.

I learned to do things differently. To button my shirts, to screw and unscrew the toothpaste cap, to tie my shoes. We didn't think of this. Together, we were valiant, brave and stoic. Though I couldn't quite keep up with you at tennis anymore.

In a way, it was fun. Things I once took for granted became significant. Cutting a steak with a knife and fork, or buttoning my fly, untying a knot around a bag, adding milk while stirring.

After a while, I developed a scab and you let me come back to bed. But sometimes in the night, I'd shift or have a nightmare, jolt, and suddenly, I'd open up again, and bleed all over uncontrollably. The first time this happened neither of us could go back to sleep. But after a while, you got used to it and you'd be back asleep in a minute. It didn't seem to bother you at all.

But I guess after a while it started bothering you, because one day when I was washing out the sheets I'd bloodied the night before, you said, You sleep too restless. I don't like it when your bleeding wakes me up. I think you're sick. I think it's sick to cut off your own arm.

I looked at you, your sweet brown eyes, innocent as a puppy. But you cut it off, I said. You did it. You didn't blink. You asked me for it, so I said OK.

Don't try to make me feel guilty, you said, your pretty brown eyes looking at me. It was your arm.

You didn't blink.

I closed my eyes.

That night I bled again. I woke up and the bed was red, all full of blood and wet. I reached over to touch you and to wake you up and tell you I was sorry, but you were not there.

I learned more. To cook and clean, to eat a quarter pounder with one fist, to balance my groceries on my knee while my hand fumbled with the front door key.

My arm got strong. My left sleeve on my shirts got tight and pinched. My right shirt sleeve was lithe and open, carefree, like a pretty girl.

But then the novelty wore off. I had to convince myself. I read about those valiant cases, one-legged heroes who run across the continent to raise money for causes, and paraplegic mothers of four, one-eyed pool sharks. I wanted these stories to inspire me, but they didn't. I didn't want to be like those people. I didn't want to be cheery and valiant. I didn't want to have to rise above my situation. What I wanted was my arm.

Because I missed it. I missed everything about it. I missed the long solid weight of it in my sleeve. I missed clapping and waving and putting my hand in my pocket. I missed waking up at night with it twisted behind my head, asleep and heavy and tingling.

And then I realized that I had missed these things all along, the whole time my arm had been over the mantel, but that I'd never said anything or even let myself feel anything bad because I didn't want to dwell on those feelings because I didn't want to make you feel bad and I didn't want you to think I wanted you to feel bad.

I decided to look for it. Maybe you'd sold it. You were always good with things like that.

I hit the pawnshops. I walked into them and they'd ask me could they help me and I'd say, I'm looking for an arm. And they'd stare at me, my empty sleeve pinned to my shirt, or flapping in the air. I never have liked acting like things aren't the way they are.

When I searched all the local pawnshops, I started going to ones further away. I saw a lot of the country. It was nice. And I got good at it. The more I did, the more I learned to do. The braver ones would look at me directly in the eye. They'd give me the names and addresses of outlets selling artificial limbs, or reconstructive surgeons. But I didn't want another one, I wanted mine. And then, the more I looked for it, the more I wondered if I wasn't looking more for something else besides my severed arm. I wondered was I really searching for you?

It all came clear to me. Like something hacked away from me: you'd done this to me as a test. To show me things. To show me what things meant to me, how much my arm was part of me, but how I could learn to live without it. How, if I was forced to, I could learn to get by with only part of me, with next to nothing. You'd done this to me to teach me something.

And then I thought how, if you were testing me, you must be watching me, to see if I was passing.

So I started acting out my life for you. And then I felt you watching all my actions. I whistled with bravado, jaunted, rather than walked. I had a confident swagger. I slapped friendly pawnshop keepers on their shoulders and told them jokes. I was fun, an inspiration they'd remember after I'd passed through.

I acted like I couldn't care less about my old arm. Like I liked the breezes in my sleeve.

I began to think in perfect sentences, as if you were listening to me. I thought clear sentences inside myself. I said, I get along just fine without my arm. I think that I convinced myself, in trying to convince you, that I had never had an arm I'd lost.

Soon I didn't think the word inside me any more. I didn't think about the right hand gloves buried in my bottom drawer.

I made myself not miss it. I tested myself. I sat in the den and stared at the empty space above the mantel. I spent the night on the couch. I went into the bathroom and looked in the tub. I felt nothing. I went to bed.

I thought my trips to pawnshops, my wanderlust, were only things I did to pass the time. I thought of nothing almost happily.

I looked at my shoulder. The tissue was smooth. I ran my fingers over it.
Round and slightly puffed, pink and shiny and slick. As soft as pimento, as cool as a spoon, the tenderest flesh of my body.

My beautiful empty sleeve and I were friends, like intimates.

So everything was fine.
For a while.
Then you came back.
Then everything did.

But I was careful. It had been a long time. I had learned how to live. Why, hadn't I just forgotten what used to fill my empty sleeve entirely? I was very careful. I acted like nothing had ever been different, that you had never ripped it out of me, then bronzed it, put it on the mantel, left with it.

I wanted things to stay forgot.

And besides, it was so easy, so familiar having you around. It was nice.

I determined to hold on to what I'd learned. About the strength of having only one.

Maybe I should have told you then. Maybe I should have told you then. But then, I told myself, if you knew to leave it alone, then good. And if you didn't know, we needed to find that out.

So we were sitting in the den. You looked at me with your big sweet pretty brown eyes and you said, you whispered it softly like a little girl, you said, Oh, I'm so sorry. You started crying softly, your lips quivering. Can you ever forgive me? You said it slow and sweet like a foreign language. I watched you, knowing you knew the way I was watching you. You leaned into me and pulled my arm around you and ran your pretty fingers down the solid muscle in my sleeve. Just hold me darling, you said. Just hold me again.

I ran my wet palm, shaking, on your gorgeous back. Your hair smelled sweet.

I looked at your beautiful tear-lined face and tried to pretend that I had never seen you before in my life.

Why did you do it? I whispered.

You looked at me, your eyes all moist and sweet like you could melt anything in the world. You didn't answer.

What did you do with it?

You shrugged your shoulders, shook your head and smiled at me sweeter than an angel.

Say something, I whispered into your pretty hair. Say something, goddammit.

You looked up at me and your sweet brown eyes welled up with tears again. You put your head against my breast and sobbed.

You made me rock you and I did and then you cried yourself to sleep as innocent as a baby. When you were asleep I walked you to the bedroom and put you to bed. You slept. I watched you all night. You remembered nothing in the morning.

In the morning we had coffee. You chatted to me about your adventures. You cocked your head at just the right places, the way I remembered you did. You told me you'd worked hard in the time you'd been away. You told me how much you had learned about the world, about yourself, about honor, faith and trust, etc. You looked deep into my eyes and said, I've changed. You said how good and strong and true and truly different you were. How you had learned that it is not our acts, but our intents, that make us who we are.

I watched your perfect teeth.

I felt your sweet familiar hands run up my body, over the empty sleeve that rumpled on the exposed side of me. I closed my eyes and couldn't open them. My mouth was closed. I couldn't tell you anything.

I couldn't tell you that you can't re-do a thing that's been undone. I couldn't tell you anything that you would understand. I couldn't tell you that it wasn't just the fact that you had ripped it out of me and taken it and mounted it, then left with it then lost it, how it wasn't only that, but it was more. How it was that when you asked me, I believed you and I told you yes. How, though I had tried a long time to replace what you had hacked away from me, I never could undo the action of your doing so, that I had, and only ever would have, more belief in your faulty memory, your stupid sloppy foresight, than in your claims of change. How I believed, yes, I believed with all my heart, that given time, you'd do something else again, some new and novel variant to what you'd done to me, again. And then I thought, but this was only half a thought, that even if you had changed, no *really* changed, truly and at last, and even if you knew me better than I know myself, and even if I'm better off than I've ever been, and even if this was the only way we could have gotten to this special place where we are now, and even if there's a reason, darling, something bigger than both of us, and even if all these even if's are true, that I would never believe you again, never forget what I know of you, never forget what you've done to me, what you will do. I'll never believe the myth of forgiveness between us.

1990

GISH JEN
b. 1956

One cover of Gish Jen's widely acclaimed novel *Mona in the Promised Land* (1996) features a bowl filled with noodles out of which chopsticks stick; on it has been placed a bagel, and through the bagel's central hole we see the Asian eyes of the author staring directly back at the viewer. The image serves as a sly reference to the scene in which Helen Chang confronts her daughter's decision to convert: "How can you be Jewish?" she asks, adding "Chinese people don't do such things." What does one mean by a term like "Asian eyes," Jen's fiction asks us to ask. From the perspective of the various communities she inhabits, is a second-generation Chinese American who converts to Judaism either Asian or Jewish, or is she both, or neither? Immigration, assimilation, and generational and interracial tensions, as well as what the critic Yung-Hsing Wu calls "the unmapped roads of postidentity politics," shape the sometimes funny, sometimes poignant plots of stories that have appeared in *The New Yorker* and *The Atlantic Monthly* and of two novels that were featured on *The New York Times'* list of notable books of the year.

In various interviews, Jen has explained that her writing would be quite different, indeed that she might not have become a writer at all, if she had not been the daughter of parents born and educated in Shanghai who relocated (separately) to the States. Borrowing a phrase from Philip Roth, she has argued that the identity assigned to her by society became an "amiable irritant," impelling her to create fiction. For Lillian Jen, growing up within the only Chinese family in a working-class northern suburb of New York City meant facing rock-throwing neighbors who periodically beat up her brother. Even after the family moved to a more friendly, predominantly Jewish community in Scarsdale, she still experienced herself and her four siblings as aberrant. Jen, who was raised speaking English, originally felt that the world's insistence on defining her as Chinese caused her to rebel against an identity that failed to account for her complete sense of self, although she grew to regret the loss of her parents' language. A graduate of Harvard University and the Iowa Writers' Workshop, Jen faced the disapproval of her parents about her commitment to writing until her novel *Typical American* (1991) got a prominent review in *World Journal*, a newspaper read widely by members of their community. Like its sequel, *Mona in the Promised Land*, and her collection of stories, *Who's Irish?* (1999), it was published under the name Gish Jen, as she adopted the last name of the silent film star Lillian Gish. This act of self-definition typifies the individualistic perspective Jen brings to bear on the life she leads now in Cambridge, Massachusetts, with her Irish husband and their two children.

Who's Irish?

In China, people say mixed children are supposed to be smart, and definitely my granddaughter Sophie is smart. But Sophie is wild, Sophie is not like my daughter Natalie, or like me. I am work hard my whole life, and fierce besides. My husband always used to say he is afraid of me, and in our restaurant, busboys and cooks all afraid of me too. Even the gang members come for protection money, they try to talk to my husband. When I am there, they stay away. If they come by mistake, they pretend they are come to eat. They hide behind the menu, they order a lot of food. They talk about their mothers. Oh, my mother have some arthritis, need to take herbal medicine, they say. Oh, my mother getting old, her hair all white now.

I say, Your mother's hair used to be white, but since she dye it, it become black again. Why don't you go home once in a while and take a look? I tell them, Confucius say a filial son knows what color his mother's hair is.[1]

My daughter is fierce too, she is vice president in the bank now. Her new house is big enough for everybody to have their own room, including me. But Sophie take after Natalie's husband's family, their name is Shea. Irish. I always thought Irish people are like Chinese people, work so hard on the railroad,[2] but now I know why the Chinese beat the Irish. Of course, not all Irish are like the Shea family, of course not. My daughter tell me I should not say Irish this, Irish that.

---

1. Though no writings have survived by the Chinese philosopher Confucius (the Latinized name of K'ung Fu-tzu, or "Master K'ung," 551–479 B.C.E.), his sayings were apparently collected by disciples. Confucianism, the dominant moral and religious system of China until the 20th century, stresses the filial relation above all others between individuals.
2. I.e., in laying the tracks for the transcontinental railroad in the 19th century.

How do you like it when people say the Chinese this, the Chinese that, she say.

You know, the British call the Irish heathen, just like they call the Chinese, she say.

You think the Opium War[3] was bad, how would you like to live right next door to the British, she say.

And that is that. My daughter have a funny habit when she win an argument, she take a sip of something and look away, so the other person is not embarrassed. So I am not embarrassed. I do not call anybody anything either. I just happen to mention about the Shea family, an interesting fact: four brothers in the family, and not one of them work. The mother, Bess, have a job before she got sick, she was executive secretary in a big company. She is handle everything for a big shot, you would be surprised how complicated her job is, not just type this, type that. Now she is a nice woman with a clean house. But her boys, every one of them is on welfare, or so-called severance pay, or so-called disability pay. Something. They say they cannot find work, this is not the economy of the fifties, but I say, Even the black people doing better these days, some of them live so fancy, you'd be surprised. Why the Shea family have so much trouble? They are white people, they speak English. When I come to this country, I have no money and do not speak English. But my husband and I own our restaurant before he die. Free and clear, no mortgage. Of course, I understand I am just lucky, come from a country where the food is popular all over the world. I understand it is not the Shea family's fault they come from a country where everything is boiled. Still, I say.

She's right, we should broaden our horizons, say one brother, Jim, at Thanksgiving. Forget about the car business. Think about egg rolls.

Pad thai,[4] say another brother, Mike. I'm going to make my fortune in pad thai. It's going to be the new pizza.

I say, You people too picky about what you sell. Selling egg rolls not good enough for you, but at least my husband and I can say, We made it. What can you say? Tell me. What can you say?

Everybody chew their tough turkey.

I especially cannot understand my daughter's husband John, who has no job but cannot take care of Sophie either. Because he is a man, he say, and that's the end of the sentence.

Plain boiled food, plain boiled thinking. Even his name is plain boiled: John. Maybe because I grew up with black bean sauce and hoisin sauce and garlic sauce, I always feel something is missing when my son-in-law talk.

But, okay: so my son-in-law can be man, I am baby-sitter. Six hours a day, same as the old sitter, crazy Amy, who quit. This is not so easy, now that I am sixty-eight, Chinese age almost seventy.[5] Still, I try. In China, daughter take care of mother. Here it is the other way around. Mother help daughter, mother ask, Anything else I can do? Otherwise daughter complain mother is not supportive. I tell daughter, We do not have this word in Chinese,

---

[3]. The first Opium War (1839–42) was fought between Great Britain and China after China attempted to prevent British merchants from importing opium; because of its defeat in this and a second war (1856–60), China was forced to make many concessions to Western powers, including their control of its treaty ports.
[4]. A popular Thai dish.
[5]. As the Chinese calculate age, a baby is in effect a year old when it is born.

supportive. But my daughter too busy to listen, she has to go to meeting, she has to write memo while her husband go to the gym to be a man. My daughter say otherwise he will be depressed. Seems like all his life he has this trouble, depression.

No one wants to hire someone who is depressed, she say. It is important for him to keep his spirits up.

Beautiful wife, beautiful daughter, beautiful house, oven can clean itself automatically. No money left over, because only one income, but lucky enough, got the baby-sitter for free. If John lived in China, he would be very happy. But he is not happy. Even at the gym things go wrong. One day, he pull a muscle. Another day, weight room too crowded. Always something.

Until finally, hooray, he has a job. Then he feel pressure.

I need to concentrate, he say. I need to focus.

He is going to work for insurance company. Salesman job. A paycheck, he say, and at least he will wear clothes instead of gym shorts. My daughter buy him some special candy bars from the health-food store. They say THINK! on them, and are supposed to help John think.

John is a good-looking boy, you have to say that, especially now that he shave so you can see his face.

I am an old man in a young man's game, say John.

I will need a new suit, say John.

This time I am not going to shoot myself in the foot, say John.

Good, I say.

She means to be supportive, my daughter say. Don't start the send her back to China thing, because we can't.

Sophie is three years old American age, but already I see her nice Chinese side swallowed up by her wild Shea side. She looks like mostly Chinese. Beautiful black hair, beautiful black eyes. Nose perfect size, not so flat looks like something fell down, not so large looks like some big deal got stuck in wrong face. Everything just right, only her skin is a brown surprise to John's family. So brown, they say. Even John say it. She never goes in the sun, still she is that color, he say. Brown. They say, Nothing the matter with brown. They are just surprised. So brown. Nattie is not that brown, they say. They say, It seems like Sophie should be a color in between Nattie and John. Seems funny, a girl named Sophie Shea be brown. But she is brown, maybe her name should be Sophie Brown. She never go in the sun, still she is that color, they say. Nothing the matter with brown. They are just surprised.

The Shea family talk is like this sometimes, going around and around like a Christmas-tree train.

Maybe John is not her father, I say one day, to stop the train.

And sure enough, train wreck. None of the brothers ever say the word *brown* to me again.

Instead, John's mother, Bess, say, I hope you are not offended.

She say, I did my best on those boys. But raising four boys with no father is no picnic.

You have a beautiful family, I say.

I'm getting old, she say.

You deserve a rest, I say. Too many boys make you old.

I never had a daughter, she say. You have a daughter.

I have a daughter, I say. Chinese people don't think a daughter is so great, but you're right. I have a daughter.

I was never against the marriage, you know, she say. I never thought John was marrying down. I always thought Nattie was just as good as white.

I was never against the marriage either, I say. I just wonder if they look at the whole problem.

Of course you pointed out the problem, you are a mother, she say. And now we both have a granddaughter. A little brown granddaughter, she is so precious to me.

I laugh. A little brown granddaughter, I say. To tell you the truth, I don't know how she came out so brown.

We laugh some more. These days Bess need a walker to walk. She take so many pills, she need two glasses of water to get them all down. Her favorite TV show is about bloopers, and she love her bird feeder. All day long, she can watch that bird feeder, like a cat.

I can't wait for her to grow up, Bess say. I could use some female company.

Too many boys, I say.

Boys are fine, she say. But they do surround you after a while.

You should take a break, come live with us, I say. Lots of girls at our house.

Be careful what you offer, say Bess with a wink. Where I come from, people mean for you to move in when they say a thing like that.

Nothing the matter with Sophie's outside, that's the truth. It is inside that she is like not any Chinese girl I ever see. We go to the park, and this is what she does. She stand up in the stroller. She take off all her clothes and throw them in the fountain.

Sophie! I say. Stop!

But she just laugh like a crazy person. Before I take over as baby-sitter, Sophie has that crazy-person sitter, Amy the guitar player. My daughter thought this Amy very creative—another word we do not talk about in China. In China, we talk about whether we have difficulty or no difficulty. We talk about whether life is bitter or not bitter. In America, all day long, people talk about creative. Never mind that I cannot even look at this Amy, with her shirt so short that her belly button showing. This Amy think Sophie should love her body. So when Sophie take off her diaper, Amy laugh. When Sophie run around naked, Amy say she wouldn't want to wear a diaper either. When Sophie go *shu-shu* in her lap, Amy laugh and say there are no germs in pee. When Sophie take off her shoes, Amy say bare feet is best, even the pediatrician say so. That is why Sophie now walk around with no shoes like a beggar child. Also why Sophie love to take off her clothes.

Turn around! say the boys in the park. Let's see that ass!

Of course, Sophie does not understand. Sophie clap her hands, I am the only one to say, No! This is not a game.

It has nothing to do with John's family, my daughter say. Amy was too permissive, that's all.

But I think if Sophie was not wild inside, she would not take off her shoes and clothes to begin with.

You never take off your clothes when you were little, I say. All my Chinese friends had babies, I never saw one of them act wild like that.

Look, my daughter say. I have a big presentation tomorrow.

John and my daughter agree Sophie is a problem, but they don't know what to do.

You spank her, she'll stop, I say another day.

But they say, Oh no.

In America, parents not supposed to spank the child.

It gives them low self-esteem, my daughter say. And that leads to problems later, as I happen to know.

My daughter never have big presentation the next day when the subject of spanking come up.

I don't want you to touch Sophie, she say. No spanking, period.

Don't tell me what to do, I say.

I'm not telling you what to do, say my daughter. I'm telling you how I feel.

I am not your servant, I say. Don't you dare talk to me like that.

My daughter have another funny habit when she lose an argument. She spread out all her fingers and look at them, as if she like to make sure they are still there.

My daughter is fierce like me, but she and John think it is better to explain to Sophie that clothes are a good idea. This is not so hard in the cold weather. In the warm weather, it is very hard.

Use your words, my daughter say. That's what we tell Sophie. How about if you set a good example.

As if good example mean anything to Sophie. I am so fierce, the gang members who used to come to the restaurant all afraid of me, but Sophie is not afraid.

I say, Sophie, if you take off your clothes, no snack.

I say, Sophie, if you take off your clothes, no lunch.

I say, Sophie, if you take off your clothes, no park.

Pretty soon we are stay home all day, and by the end of six hours she still did not have one thing to eat. You never saw a child stubborn like that.

I'm hungry! she cry when my daughter come home.

What's the matter, doesn't your grandmother feed you? My daughter laugh.

No! Sophie say. She doesn't feed me anything!

My daughter laugh again. Here you go, she say.

She say to John, Sophie must be growing.

Growing like a weed, I say.

Still Sophie take off her clothes, until one day I spank her. Not too hard, but she cry and cry, and when I tell her if she doesn't put her clothes back on I'll spank her again, she put her clothes back on. Then I tell her she is good girl, and give her some food to eat. The next day we go to the park and, like a nice Chinese girl, she does not take off her clothes.

She stop taking off her clothes, I report. Finally!

How did you do it? my daughter ask.

After twenty-eight years experience with you, I guess I learn something, I say.

It must have been a phase, John say, and his voice is suddenly like an expert.

His voice is like an expert about everything these days, now that he carry a leather briefcase, and wear shiny shoes, and can go shopping for a new car. On the company, he say. The company will pay for it, but he will be able to drive it whenever he want.

A free car, he say. How do you like that.

It's good to see you in the saddle again, my daughter say. Some of your family patterns are scary.

At least I don't drink, he say. He say, And I'm not the only one with scary family patterns.

That's for sure, say my daughter.

* * *

Everyone is happy. Even I am happy, because there is more trouble with Sophie, but now I think I can help her Chinese side fight against her wild side. I teach her to eat food with fork or spoon or chopsticks, she cannot just grab into the middle of a bowl of noodles. I teach her not to play with garbage cans. Sometimes I spank her, but not too often, and not too hard.

Still, there are problems. Sophie like to climb everything. If there is a railing, she is never next to it. Always she is on top of it. Also, Sophie like to hit the mommies of her friends. She learn this from her playground best friend, Sinbad, who is four. Sinbad wear army clothes every day and like to ambush his mommy. He is the one who dug a big hole under the play structure, a foxhole he call it, all by himself. Very hardworking. Now he wait in the foxhole with a shovel full of wet sand. When his mommy come, he throw it right at her.

Oh, it's all right, his mommy say. You can't get rid of war games, it's part of their imaginative play. All the boys go through it.

Also, he like to kick his mommy, and one day he tell Sophie to kick his mommy too.

I wish this story is not true.

Kick her, kick her! Sinbad say.

Sophie kick her. A little kick, as if she just so happened was swinging her little leg and didn't realize that big mommy leg was in the way. Still I spank Sophie and make Sophie say sorry, and what does the mommy say?

Really, it's all right, she say. It didn't hurt.

After that, Sophie learn she can attack mommies in the playground, and some will say, Stop, but others will say, Oh, she didn't mean it, especially if they realize Sophie will be punished.

* * *

This is how, one day, bigger trouble come. The bigger trouble start when Sophie hide in the foxhole with that shovel full of sand. She wait, and when I come look for her, she throw it at me. All over my nice clean clothes.

Did you ever see a Chinese girl act this way?

Sophie! I say. Come out of there, say you're sorry.

But she does not come out. Instead, she laugh. Naaah, naah-na, naaa-naaa, she say.

I am not exaggerate: millions of children in China, not one act like this.

Sophie! I say. Now! Come out now!

But she know she is in big trouble. She know if she come out, what will happen next. So she does not come out. I am sixty-eight, Chinese age almost seventy, how can I crawl under there to catch her? Impossible. So I yell, yell, yell, and what happen? Nothing. A Chinese mother would help, but American mothers, they look at you, they shake their head, they go home. And, of course, a Chinese child would give up, but not Sophie.

I hate you! she yell. I hate you, Meanie!

Meanie is my new name these days.

Long time this goes on, long long time. The foxhole is deep, you cannot see too much, you don't know where is the bottom. You cannot hear too much either. If she does not yell, you cannot even know she is still there or not. After a while, getting cold out, getting dark out. No one left in the playground, only us.

Sophie, I say. How did you become stubborn like this? I am go home without you now.

I try to use a stick, chase her out of there, and once or twice I hit her, but still she does not come out. So finally I leave. I go outside the gate.

Bye-bye! I say. I'm go home now.

But still she does not come out and does not come out. Now it is dinnertime, the sky is black. I think I should maybe go get help, but how can I leave a little girl by herself in the playground? A bad man could come. A rat could come. I go back in to see what is happen to Sophie. What if she have a shovel and is making a tunnel to escape?

Sophie! I say.

No answer.

Sophie!

I don't know if she is alive. I don't know if she is fall asleep down there. If she is crying, I cannot hear her.

So I take the stick and poke.

Sophie! I say. I promise I no hit you. If you come out, I give you a lollipop.

No answer. By now I worried. What to do, what to do, what to do? I poke some more, even harder, so that I am poking and poking when my daughter and John suddenly appear.

What are you doing? What is going on? say my daughter.

Put down that stick! say my daughter.

You are crazy! say my daughter.

John wiggle under the structure, into the foxhole, to rescue Sophie.

She fell asleep, say John the expert. She's okay. That is one big hole.

Now Sophie is crying and crying.

Sophia, my daughter say, hugging her. Are you okay, peanut? Are you okay?

She's just scared, say John.

Are you okay? I say too. I don't know what happen, I say.

She's okay, say John. He is not like my daughter, full of questions. He is full of answers until we get home and can see by the lamplight.

Will you look at her? he yell then. What the hell happened?

Bruises all over her brown skin, and a swollen-up eye.

You are crazy! say my daughter. Look at what you did! You are crazy!

I try very hard, I say.

How could you use a stick? I told you to use your words!

She is hard to handle, I say.

She's three years old! You cannot use a stick! say my daughter.

She is not like any Chinese girl I ever saw, I say.

I brush some sand off my clothes. Sophie's clothes are dirty too, but at least she has her clothes on.

Has she done this before? ask my daughter. Has she hit you before?

She hits me all the time, Sophie say, eating ice cream.

Your family, say John.

Believe me, say my daughter.

A daughter I have, a beautiful daughter. I took care of her when she could not hold her head up. I took care of her before she could argue with me, when she was a little girl with two pigtails, one of them always crooked. I took care of her when we have to escape from China, I took care of her when suddenly we live in a country with cars everywhere, if you are not careful your little girl get run over. When my husband die, I promise him I will keep the family together, even though it was just two of us, hardly a family at all.

But now my daughter take me around to look at apartments. After all, I can cook, I can clean, there's no reason I cannot live by myself, all I need is a telephone. Of course, she is sorry. Sometimes she cry, I am the one to say everything will be okay. She say she have no choice, she doesn't want to end up divorced. I say divorce is terrible, I don't know who invented this terrible idea. Instead of live with a telephone, though, surprise, I come to live with Bess. Imagine that. Bess make an offer and, sure enough, where she come from, people mean for you to move in when they say things like that. A crazy idea, go to live with someone else's family, but she like to have some female company, not like my daughter, who does not believe in company. These days when my daughter visit, she does not bring Sophie. Bess say we should give Nattie time, we will see Sophie again soon. But seems like my daughter have more presentation than ever before, every time she come she have to leave.

I have a family to support, she say, and her voice is heavy, as if soaking wet. I have a young daughter and a depressed husband and no one to turn to.

When she say no one to turn to, she mean me.

These days my beautiful daughter is so tired she can just sit there in a chair and fall asleep. John lost his job again, already, but still they rather hire a baby-sitter than ask me to help, even they can't afford it. Of course, the new baby-sitter is much younger, can run around. I don't know if Sophie these days is wild or not wild. She call me Meanie, but she like to kiss me too, sometimes. I remember that every time I see a child on TV. Sophie like to grab my hair, a fistful in each hand, and then kiss me smack on the nose. I never see any other child kiss that way.

The satellite TV has so many channels, more channels than I can count, including a Chinese channel from the Mainland and a Chinese channel from Taiwan, but most of the time I watch bloopers with Bess. Also, I watch the bird feeder—so many, many kinds of birds come. The Shea sons hang around all the time, asking when will I go home, but Bess tell them, Get lost.

She's a permanent resident, say Bess. She isn't going anywhere.

Then she wink at me, and switch the channel with the remote control.

Of course, I shouldn't say Irish this, Irish that, especially now I am become honorary Irish myself, according to Bess. Me! Who's Irish? I say, and she laugh. All the same, if I could mention one thing about some of the Irish, not all of them of course, I like to mention this: Their talk just stick. I don't know how Bess Shea learn to use her words, but sometimes I hear what she say a long time later. *Permanent resident. Not going anywhere.* Over and over I hear it, the voice of Bess.

1998, 1999

JEANETTE WINTERSON
b. 1959

Interspersed with interpolated fairy tales, allegories, poetic interludes, and parables, Jeanette Winterson's prose has been characterized as magical realism ever since her first novel, *Oranges Are Not the Only Fruit,* became instantly popular upon its publication in 1985. In part autobiographical and yet thoroughly postmodern, it won her the prestigious Whitbread First Novel Award and was quickly adapted into a well-received miniseries by the BBC. *Oranges Are Not the Only Fruit* focuses on a childhood shaped by living under the tutelage of an Evangelical adoptive mother in northern England. After Winterson's early training as a missionary came to an end—she was rejected by her mother and her mother's church because of a lesbian affair with one of the church converts—she took up an assortment of odd jobs, pursued an English degree at Oxford University, and followed her first novel with a succession of such experimentally adventurous narratives as *The Passion* (1987), *Sexing the Cherry* (1989), *Written on the Body* (1992), and *Art and Lies* (1994). With Margaret Reynolds, Winterson became a series editor for Vintage editions of the novels of Virginia Woolf in 2000.

The lure of postmodernism and of the fantastic may be related to Winterson's faith in "art as the true means of not telling the truth": "You're not setting out to deceive," she explained in one interview. "You're setting out to find an ultimate reality," in particular the "world of the every day" but also "imaginative and psychic worlds which we know are there and which we so often split off." Fiction about fiction and about fantasy also enables Winterson to break the sequence of conventional plots so as to question the stability of the normative categories through which we generally define gender and sexuality. She has described the interrogatory headings that organize "The Poetics of Sex," a story "about lesbian sex," by explaining that "it's set out as a series of questions, mainly the questions I was getting at the time in the nineties from the British press." Characteristically humorous, she adds, "Funny lot—journalists." Like many women artists before her, Winterson takes the Greek poet Sappho and her community on the isle of Lesbos as a model for female eroticism and artistry because, as Margaret Reynolds has put it about the manifold re-creations of this shadowy figure from the ancient past, "Sappho may or may not have been a lesbian. But she certainly was a Lesbian."

The Poetics of Sex

Why Do You Sleep with Girls?

My lover Picasso is going through her Blue Period.[1] In the past her periods have always been red. Radish red, bull red, red like rose hips bursting seed. Lava red when she was called Pompeii[2] and in her Destructive Period. The stench of her, the brack[3] of her, the rolling splitting cunt of her. Squat like a Sumo, ham thighs, loins of pork, beefy upper cuts and breasts of lamb. I can steal her heart like a bird's egg.

She rushes for me bull-subtle, butching at the gate as if she's come to stud. She bellows at the window, bloods the pavement with desire. She says, 'You don't need to be Rapunzel to let down your hair.'[4] I know the game. I know enough to flick my hind-quarters and skip away. I'm not a flirt. She can smell the dirt on me and that makes her swell. That's what makes my lithe lover bulrush-thin fat me. How she fats me. She plumps me, pats me, squeezes and feeds me. Feeds me up with lust till I'm as fat as she is. We're fat for each other we sapling girls. We neat clean branching girls get thick with sex. You are wide enough for my hips like roses, I will cover you with my petals, cover you with the scent of me. Cover girl wide for the weight of my cargo. My bull-lover makes a matador out of me. She circles me and in her rough-made ring I am complete. I like the dressing up, the little jackets, the silk tights, I like her shiny hide, the deep tanned leather of her. It is she who gives me the power of the sword.[5] I used it once but when I cut at her it was my close fit flesh that frilled into a hem of blood. She lay beside me slender as a horn. Her little jacket and silk tights impeccable. I sweated muck and couldn't speak in my broken ring. We are quick change artists we girls.

Which One of You Is the Man?

Picasso's veins are Kingfisher blue and Kingfisher shy. The first time I slept with her I couldn't see through the marble columns of her legs or beyond the opaque density of each arm. A sculptor by trade, Picasso is her own model.

The blue that runs through her is sanguine. One stroke of the knife and she changes colour. Every month and she changes colour. Deep pools of blue silk drop from her. I know her by the lakes she leaves on the way to the bedroom. Her braces cascade over the stair-rail, she wears earrings of lapis lazuli which I have caught cup-handed, chasing her *deshabillée*.[6]

When she sheds she sheds it all. Her skin comes away with her clothes. On those days I have been able to see the blood-depot of her heart. On those days it was possible to record the patience of her digestive juices and the relentlessness of her lungs. Her breath is blue in the cold air. She breathes

---

1. The Spanish painter Pablo Picasso (1881–1973) famously went through a blue period (1901–04) when his paintings and sketches were mostly done in shades of blue and their subjects were generally unhappy and gloomily portrayed.
2. A Roman city destroyed by the eruption of Vesuvius in 79 C.E.
3. Breach, crack.
4. An allusion to the fairy tale published by the Grimm brothers. Rapunzel, in a tower without door or stairs, gives entrance to the witch who has imprisoned her when she hears "Rapunzel, Rapunzel, let down your hair, so that I may climb the golden stair." The same words prompt her to throw down her braid to a prince who climbs up and becomes her lover.
5. An instrument of the matador in the bullring.
6. Undressed (French).

into the blue winter like a Madonna of the Frost. I think it right to kneel and the view is good.

She does perform miracles but they are of the physical kind and ordered by her Rule of Thumb to the lower regions. She goes among the poor with every kind of salve unmindful of reward. She dresses in blue she tells me so that they will know she is a saint[7] and it is saintly to taste the waters of so many untried wells.

I have been jealous of course. I have punished her good deeds with some alms-giving of my own. It's not the answer, I can't catch her by copying her, I can't draw her with a borrowed stencil. She is all the things a lover should be and quite a few a lover should not. Pin her down? She's not a butterfly. I'm not a wrestler. She's not a target. I'm not a gun. Tell you what she is? She's not Lot no. 27 and I'm not one to brag.

We were by the sea yesterday and the sea was heavy with salt so that our hair was braided with it. There was salt on our hands and in our wounds where we'd been fighting. 'Don't hurt me,' I said and I unbuttoned my shirt so that she could look at my breasts if she wanted to. 'I'm no saint,' she said and that was true, true too that our feet are the same size. The rocks were reptile blue and the sky that balanced on the top of the cliffs was sheer blue. Picasso made me put on her jersey and drink dark tea from a fifties flask.

'It's winter,' she said. 'Let's go.'

We did go, leaving the summer behind, leaving a trail of footprints two by two in identical four. I don't know that anyone behind could have told you which was which and if they had there would have been no trace by morning.

What Do Lesbians Do in Bed?

Under cover of the sheets the tabloid world of lust and vice is useful only in so much as Picasso can wipe her brushes on it. Beneath the sheets we practise Montparnasse,[8] that is Picasso offers to paint me but we have sex instead.

We met at Art School on a shiny corridor. She came towards me so swiftly that the linoleum dissolved under her feet. I thought, 'A woman who can do that to an oil cloth can certainly do something for me.' I made the first move. I took her by her pony tail the way a hero grabs a runaway horse. She was taken aback. When she turned round I kissed her ruby mouth and took a sample of her sea blue eyes. She was salty, well preserved, well made and curved like a wave. I thought, 'This is the place to go surfing.'

We went back to her studio, where naturally enough, there was a small easel and a big bed. 'My work comes first,' she said. 'Would you mind?' and not waiting for an answer she mixed an ochre wash before taking me like a dog my breasts hanging over the pillow.

Not so fast Picasso, I too can rumple you like a farm hand, roll you like good tobacco leaf against my thighs. I can take that arrogant throat and cut it with desire. I can make you dumb with longing, tease you like a doxy[9] on a date.

Slowly now Picasso, where the falling light hits the floor. Lie with me in

---

7. In Christian art, the color blue traditionally symbolizes human immortality; on an angel's robe, it symbolizes fidelity and faith.
8. An area in Paris on the left bank of the Seine that was the center of the city's artistic and intellectual life in the early 20th century.
9. Sexually promiscuous woman.

the bruised light that leaves dark patches on your chest. You look tubercular, so thin and mottled, quiescent now. I picked you up and carried you to the bed dusty with ill-use. I found a newspaper under the sheets advertising rationing.

The girl on the canvas was sulky. She hadn't come to be painted. I'd heard all about you my tear-away tiger, so fierce, so unruly. But the truth is other as truth always is. What holds the small space between my legs is not your artistic tongue nor any of the other parts you play at will but the universe beneath the sheets that we make together.

We are in our igloo and it couldn't be snugger. White on white on white on white. Sheet Picasso me sheet. Who's on top depends on where you're standing but as we're lying down it doesn't matter. What an Eskimo I am, breaking her seductive ice and putting in my hand for fish. How she wriggles, slithers, twists to resist me but I can bait her and I do. A fine catch, one in each hand and one in my mouth. Impressive for a winter afternoon and the stove gone out and the rent to pay. We are warm and rich and white. I have so much enjoyed my visit.

'Come again?' she asked. Yes tomorrow, under the sodium street lights, under the tick of the clock. Under my obligations, my history, my fears, this now. This fizzy, giddy all consuming now. I will not let time lie to me. I will not listen to dead voices or unborn pain. 'What if?' has no power against 'What if not?' The not of you is unbearable. I must have you. Let them prate, those scorn-eyed anti-romantics. Love is not the oil and I am not the machine. Love is you and here I am. Now.

Were You Born a Lesbian?

Picasso is an unlikely mother but I owe myself to her. We are honour-bound, love-bound, bound by cords too robust for those healthy hospital scissors. She baptised me from her own font and said, 'I name thee Sappho.'[1] People often ask if we are mother and child.

I could say yes, I could say no, both statements would be true, the way that lesbians are true, at least to one another if not to the world. I am no stranger to the truth but very uncomfortable about the lies that have dogged me since my birth. It is no surprise that we do not always remember our name.

I am proud to be Picasso's lover in spite of the queer looks we get when holding hands on busy streets. 'Mummy, why is that man staring at us?' I said when only one month old. 'Don't worry dear, he can't help it, he's got something wrong with his eyes.'

We need more Labradors. The world is full of blind people. They don't see Picasso and me dignified in our love. They see perverts, inverts, tribades,[2] homosexuals. They see circus freaks and Satan worshippers, girl-catchers and porno turn-ons. Picasso says they don't know how to look at pictures either.

---

1. Greek lyric poet (b. ca. 612 B.C.E.), a native of the island of Lesbos.

2. Lesbians.

Were You Born a Lesbian?

A fairy in a pink tutu came to Picasso and said, 'I bring you tidings of great joy.[3] All by yourself with no one to help you you will give birth to a sex toy who has a way with words. You will call her Sappho and she will be a pain in the ass to all men.'

'Can't you see I've got a picture to finish?' said Picasso.
'Take a break,' said the fairy. 'There's more to life than Art.'
'Where?' said Picasso, whose first name wasn't Mary.
'Between your legs,' said Gabriel.[4]
'Forget it. Don't you know I paint with my clit?'
'Here, try a brush,' said the fairy offering her a fat one.
'I've had all the brushes I need,' said Picasso.
'Too Late,' said the fairy. 'Here she comes.'

Picasso slammed the door on her studio and ran across to the Art College where she had to give a class. She was angry so that her breath burnt the air. She was angry so that her feet dissolved the thin lino tiles already scuffed to ruin by generations of brogues. There was no one in the corridor or if there was she was no one. Picasso didn't recognise her, she had her eyes on the door and the door looked away. Picasso, running down the clean corridor, was suddenly trip-wired, badly thrown, her hair came away from her glorious head. She was being scalped. She was being mugged. She was detonated on a long fuse of sex. Her body was half way out of the third floor window and there was a demon against her mouth. A poker-red pushing babe crying, 'Feed me, Feed me now.'

Picasso took her home, what else could she do? She took her home to straighten her out and had her kinky side up. She mated with this creature she had borne and began to feel that maybe the Greek gods knew a thing or two. Flesh of her flesh she fucked her.

They were quiet then because Sappho hadn't learned a language. She was still two greedy hands and an open mouth. She throbbed like an outboard motor, she was as sophisticated as a ham sandwich. She had nothing to offer but herself, and Picasso, who thought she had seen it all before, smiled like a child and fell in love.

Why Do You Hate Men?

Here comes Sappho, scorching the history books with tongues of flame.[5] Never mind the poetry feel the erection. Oh yes, women get erect, today my body is stiff with sex. When I see a word held hostage to manhood I have to rescue it. Sweet trembling word, locked in a tower, tired of your Prince coming and coming. I will scale you and discover that size is no object especially when we're talking inches.

I like to be a hero, like to come back to my island full of girls carrying a net of words forbidden them. Poor girls, they are locked outside their words

---

3. The words with which the angel announced to the shepherds the birth of Jesus (Luke 2.10).
4. The angel who, in the annunciation, told Mary that she would bear the son of God (Luke 1.26).
5. In one of her few extant poems thought to be complete, Sappho describes how at the sight of the beloved "thin fire runs under my skin" (L-P 31).

just as the words are locked into meaning. Such a lot of locking up goes on on the Mainland but here the doors are always open.

Stay inside, don't walk the streets, bar the windows, keep your mouth shut, keep your legs together, strap your purse around your neck, don't wear valuables, don't look up, don't talk to strangers, don't risk it, don't try it. He means she except when it means Men. This is a Private Club.

That's all right boys, so is this. This delicious unacknowledged island where we are naked with each other. The boat that brings us here will crack beneath your weight. This is territory you cannot invade. We lay on the bed, Picasso and I, listening to the terrible bawling of Salami. Salami is a male artist who wants to be a Lesbian.

'I'll pay you twice the rent,' he cries, fingering his greasy wallet.

'I'll paint you for posterity. I love women, don't you know? Oh God I wish I was a woman, wafer-thin like you, I could circle you with one hand.' He belches.

Picasso is unimpressed. She says, 'The world is full of heterosexuals, go and find one, half a dozen, swallow them like oysters, but get out.'

'Oh whip me,' says Salami getting moist.

We know the pattern. In half an hour he'll be violent and when he's threatened us enough, he'll go to the sleaze pit and watch two girls for the price of a steak.

As soon as he left we forgot about him. Making love we made a dictionary of forbidden words. We are words, sentences, stories, books. You are my New Testament. We are a gospel to each other, I am your annunciation, revelation. You are my St Mark, winged lion at your feet.[6] I'll have you, and the lion too, buck under you till you learn how to saddle me. Don't dig those spurs too deep. It's not so simple this lexographic love. When you have sunk me to the pit I'll mine you in return and we shall be husbands to each other as well as wives.

I'll tell you something Salami, a woman can get hard and keep it there all night and when she's not required to stand she knows how to roll. She can do it any way up and her lover always comes. There are no frigid lesbians, think of that.

On this island where we live, keeping what we do not tell, we have found the infinite variety of Woman. On the Mainland, Woman is largely extinct in all but a couple of obvious forms. She is still cultivated as a cash crop but is nowhere to be found growing wild.

Salami hates to hear us fuck. He bangs on the wall like a zealot at an orgy. 'Go home,' we say, but he doesn't. He'd rather lie against the skirting board complaining that we stop him painting. The real trouble is that we have rescued a word not allowed to our kind.

He hears it pounding through the wall day and night. He smells it on our clothes and sees it smeared on our faces. We are happy Picasso and I. Happy.

---

[6]. In Christian art, St. Mark is traditionally depicted accompanied by a winged lion (see Revelation 4.7–8).

Don't You Find There's Something Missing?

I thought I had lost Picasso. I thought the bright form that shapes my days had left me. I was loose at the edges, liquid with uncertainty. The taut lines of love slackened. I felt myself unravelling backwards, away from her. Would the thinning thread snap?

For seven years she and I had been in love. Love between lovers, love between mother and child. Love between man and wife. Love between friends. I had been all of those things to her and she had been all of those things to me. What we were we were in equal parts, and twin souls to one another. We like to play roles but we know who we are. You are beauty to me Picasso. Not only sensuous beauty that pleases the eye but artistic beauty that challenges it. Sometimes you are ugly in your beauty, magnificently ugly and you frighten me for all the right reasons.

I did not tell you this yesterday or the day before. Habit had silenced me the way habit does. So used to a thing no need to speak it, so well known the action no need to describe it. But I know that speech is freedom which is not the same as freedom of speech. I have no right to say what I please when I please but I have the gift of words with which to bless you. Bless you Picasso. Bless you for your straight body like a spire. You are the landmark that leads me through the streets of the everyday. You take me past the little houses towards the church where we worship. I do worship you because you are worthy of praise. Bless you Picasso for your able hands that carry the paint to the unbirthed canvas. Your fingers were red when you fucked me and my body striped with joy. I miss the weals of our passion just as I miss the daily tenderness of choosing you. Choosing you above all others, my pearl of great price.[7]

My feelings for you are biblical; that is they are intense, reckless, arrogant, risky and unconcerned with the way of the world. I flaunt my bleeding wounds, madden with my certainty. The Kingdom of Heaven is within you Picasso. Bless you.

There is something missing and that is you. Your clothes were gone yesterday, your easel was packed flat and silent against the wall. When I got up and left our unmade bed there was the smell of coffee in the house but not the smell of you. I looked in the mirror and I knew who was to blame. Why take the perfect thing and smash it? Some goods are smashed that cannot be replaced.

It has been difficult this last year. Love is difficult. Love gets harder which is not the same as to say that it gets harder to love. You are not hard to love. You are hard to love well. Your standards are high, you won't settle for the quick way out which is why you made for the door. If I am honest I will admit that I have always wanted to avoid love. Yes give me romance, give me sex, give me fights, give me all the parts of love but not the simple single word which is so complex and demands the best of me this hour this minute this forever.

Picasso won't paint the same picture twice. She says develop or die. She

---

7. See Matthew 13.45–46: "the kingdom of heaven is like unto a merchant man, seeking goodly pearls: Who, when he had found one pearl of great price, went and sold all that he had, and bought it."

won't let yesterday's love suffice for today. She makes it new, she remixes her colours and stretches her canvas until it sighs. My mother was glad when she heard we'd split up. She said, 'Now you can come back to the Mainland. I'll send Phaeon to pick you up.'[8] Phaeon runs a little business called LESBIAN TOURS. He drives his motor-boat round and round the island, just outside the one mile exclusion zone. He points out famous lesbians to sight-seers who always say, 'But she's so attractive!' or 'She's so ugly!'

'Yeah,' says Phaeon, 'and you know what? They're all in love with me.' One sight-seer shakes his head like a collecting box for a good cause. 'Can't you just ask one of 'em?' he says. 'I can ask them anything,' says Phaeon who never waits to hear the answer.

Why Do You Sleep with Girls?

Picasso has loved me for fifty years and she loves me still. We got through the charcoal tunnel where the sun stopped rising. We no longer dress in grey.

On that day I told you about I took my coat and followed her footprints across the ice. As she walked the world froze up behind her. There was nothing for me to return to, if I failed, I failed alone. Despair made it too dark to see, I had to travel by radar, tracking her warmth in front of me. It's fashionable now to say that any mistake is made by both of you. That's not always true. One person can easily kill another.

Hang on me my darling like rubies round my neck. Slip onto my finger like a ring. Give me your rose for my buttonhole. Let me leaf through you before I read you out loud.

Picasso warms my freezing heart on the furnace of her belly. Her belly is stoked to blazing with love of me. I have learned to feed her every day, to feed her full of fuel that I gladly find. I have unlocked the storehouses of love. On the Mainland they teach you to save for a rainy day. The truth is that love needs no saving. It is fresh or not at all. We are fresh and plentiful. She is my harvest and I am hers. She seeds me and reaps me, we fall into one another's laps. Her seas are thick with fish for my rod. I have rodded her through and through.

She is painting today. The room is orange with effort. She is painting today and I have written this.

1999

---

8. In his *Epistles* (ca. 15 C.E.), fictional letters between lovers, the Roman poet Ovid includes a letter from Sappho to the ferryman Phaon, for whom, according to one legend, she renounced the love of women.

MARGARET EDSON
b. 1961

"To say it popped into my mind is the most accurate way of describing it," Margaret Edson has declared in discussing the inspiration for her prize-winning play *Wit,* adding "It just came to me." But in fact a number of complex circumstances shaped the origins of this extraordinary medical drama in which a proud and scholarly woman is forced to face death following a series of demeaning experimental treatments. Born and raised in Washington, D.C., Edson grew up performing amateur theatricals with her close friend Julia Louis-Dreyfus, who was later to become a television star on *Seinfeld,* and her interest in drama was encouraged by her mother, a medical social worker, and her father, a newspaper columnist. Later, at Smith College, she studied Renaissance history, earning a degree *magna cum laude* in 1983. After graduation, she worked at a series of odd jobs, the most crucial of which was as clerk on an oncology and AIDS unit at a hospital in Washington. Here, as she has commented, she was struck not just by the low survival rate of women suffering (like the protagonist of *Wit*) from ovarian cancer but also by their fortitude. "One was a science writer with three children, going through very aggressive treatment for ovarian cancer," she has reported. "I used to bring her a newspaper every day. Once, when we were in an elevator and I tried to tell her, in my 22-year-old way, that I admired her courage, she said very calmly, 'I don't have much choice, do I?'"

Vivian Bearing, Edson's heroine, has little choice either about the hardships she is bearing with considerable bravery and often with sardonic wit; but, as Edson makes clear, her doctors have made troublesome ethical decisions in their treatment of her case. Whereas Vivian learns from her experience, however—learns, at least, how to die after a life in which she didn't quite know how to live—her physicians are disturbingly unchanged at the end of the play. As Edson explained to the PBS news anchor Jim Lehrer, Vivian is "a person who has built up a lot of skills during her life who finds herself in a new situation where those skills and those great capacities don't serve her very well. So she has to disarm, and then she has to become a student. She has to become someone who learns new things." Yet though Vivian's doctors, too— in particular her former student Jason Posner—ought to be learning from their patient's encounter with mortality, they appear indifferent to any human complications that would impede their clinical trials. Edson has stressed that "the researchers are not guilty of any cruelty that Vivian is not guilty of," but in fact her play raises serious questions about their behavior, a point that the writer herself concedes when she notes, "I'm not saying that smart is bad. Smart is not bad—but *kind* is good."

That education of the heart and head is as central to *Wit* as are metaphysical poetry, medicine, and mortality is not surprising given Edson's long-term commitment to a teaching career. When *Wit* won the Pulitzer Prize in 1999, she had been teaching for seven years—first English as a second language, then first grade and kindergarten in an Atlanta elementary school. Her play was written in the early 1990s after she had worked at her hospital job and before she spent several years attending a master's program in literature at Georgetown University. But as she told Jim Lehrer, in the midst of her 1999 triumph she had no plans to follow *Wit* with another theater piece because "I'm committed to teaching now. This is what I'm doing. And if there's something else I want to say in ten years, then I'll think about it, but I'm not interested in leaving teaching for anything." Indeed, she feistily added, "Once the day starts in the classroom, the affairs of the outside world do not come into it at all. . . . New Yorkers find this very hard to believe, but the intricacies of New York theater are not part of what we're doing down in kindergarten."

Wit

Characters

VIVIAN BEARING, PH.D. 50; *professor of seventeenth-century poetry at the university*
HARVEY KELEKIAN, M.D. 50; *chief of medical oncology, University Hospital*
JASON POSNER, M.D. 28; *clinical fellow, Medical Oncology Branch*
SUSIE MONAHAN, R.N., B.S.N 28; *primary nurse, Cancer Inpatient Unit*
E. M. ASHFORD, D.PHIL. 80; *professor emerita of English literature*
MR. BEARING *Vivian's father*
LAB TECHNICIANS
CLINICAL FELLOWS
STUDENTS
CODE TEAM

The play may be performed with a cast of nine: the four TECHNICIANS, FELLOWS, STUDENTS, *and* CODE TEAM MEMBERS *should double;* DR. KELEKIAN *and* MR. BEARING *should double.*

Notes

Most of the action, but not all, takes place in a room of the University Hospital Comprehensive Cancer Center. The stage is empty, and furniture is rolled on and off by the technicians.

Jason and Kelekian wear lab coats, but each has a different shirt and tie every time he enters. Susie wears white jeans, white sneakers, and a different blouse each entrance.

Scenes are indicated by a line rule in the script; there is no break in the action between scenes, but there might be a change in lighting. There is no intermission.

Vivian has a central-venous-access catheter over her left breast, so the IV tubing goes there, not into her arm. The IV pole, with a Port-a-Pump attached, rolls easily on wheels. Every time the IV pole reappears, it has a different configuration of bottles.

[VIVIAN BEARING *walks on the empty stage pushing her IV pole. She is fifty, tall and very thin, barefoot, and completely bald. She wears two hospital gowns—one tied in the front and one tied in the back—a baseball cap, and a hospital ID bracelet. The house lights are at half strength.* VIVIAN *looks out at the audience, sizing them up.*]

VIVIAN [*In false familiarity, waving and nodding to the audience*] Hi. How are you feeling today? Great. That's just great. [*In her own professorial tone*] This is not my standard greeting, I assure you.

I tend toward something a little more formal, a little less inquisitive, such as, say, "Hello."

But it is the standard greeting here.

There is some debate as to the correct response to this salutation. Should one reply "I feel good," using "feel" as a copulative to link the subject, "I," to its subjective complement, "good"; or "I feel well," modifying with an adverb the subject's state of being?

I don't know. I am a professor of seventeenth-century poetry, specializing in the Holy Sonnets of John Donne.[1]

So I just say, "Fine."

Of course it is not very often that I do feel fine.

I have been asked "How are you feeling today?" while I was throwing up into a plastic washbasin. I have been asked as I was emerging from a four-hour operation with a tube in every orifice, "How are you feeling today?"

I am waiting for the moment when someone asks me this question and I am dead.

I'm a little sorry I'll miss that.

It is unfortunate that this remarkable line of inquiry has come to me so late in my career. I could have exploited its feigned solicitude to great advantage: as I was distributing the final examination to the graduate course in seventeenth-century textual criticism—"Hi. How are you feeling today?"

Of course I would not be wearing this costume at the time, so the question's *ironic significance* would not be fully apparent.

As I trust it is now.

Irony is a literary device that will necessarily be deployed to great effect.

I ardently wish this were not so. I would prefer that a play about me be cast in the mythic-heroic-pastoral mode; but the facts, most notably stage-four metastatic ovarian cancer, conspire against that. *The Faerie Queene*[2] this is not.

And I was dismayed to discover that the play would contain elements of ... *humor*.

I have been, at best, an *unwitting* accomplice. [*She pauses.*] It is not my intention to give away the plot; but I think I die at the end.

They've given me less than two hours.

If I were poetically inclined, I might employ a threadbare metaphor—the sands of time slipping through the hourglass, the two-hour glass.

Now our sands are almost run;
More a little, and then dumb.[3]

Shakespeare. I trust the name is familiar.

At the moment, however, I am disinclined to poetry.

I've got less than two hours. Then: curtain.

[*She disconnects herself from the IV pole and shoves it to a crossing* TECHNICIAN. *The house lights go out.*]

VIVIAN   I'll never forget the time I found out I had cancer.
   [DR. HARVEY KELEKIAN *enters at a big desk piled high with papers.*]
KELEKIAN   You have cancer.
VIVIAN   [*To audience*]   See? Unforgettable. It was something of a shock. I had to sit down. [*She plops down.*]
KELEKIAN   Please sit down. Miss Bearing, you have advanced metastatic ovarian cancer.

---

1. English poet and clergyman (1572–1631).
2. An epic poem (1590), in the "mythic-heroic-pastoral mode," by the English poet Edmund Spenser.
3. The beginning of the final scene in *Pericles* (scene 22, lines 1–2).

VIVIAN   Go on.
KELEKIAN   You are a professor, Miss Bearing.
VIVIAN   Like yourself, Dr. Kelekian.
KELEKIAN   Well, yes. Now then. You present with a growth that, unfortunately, went undetected in stages one, two, and three. Now it is an insidious adenocarcinoma, which has spread from the primary adnexal mass—
VIVIAN   "Insidious"?
KELEKIAN   "Insidious" means undetectable at an—
VIVIAN   "Insidious" *means* treacherous.
KELEKIAN   Shall I continue?
VIVIAN   By all means.

KELEKIAN: Good. In invasive epithelial carcinoma, the most effective treatment modality is a chemotherapeutic agent. We are developing an experimental combination of drugs designed for primary-site ovarian, with a target specificity of stage three-and-beyond administration.

Am I going too fast?

Good.

You will be hospitalized as an in-patient for treatment each cycle. You will be on complete intake-and-output measurement for three days after each treatment to monitor kidney function. After the initial eight cycles, you will have another battery of tests.

The antineoplastic will inevitably affect some healthy cells, including those lining the gastrointestinal tract from the lips to the anus, and the hair follicles. We will of course be relying on your resolve to withstand some of the more pernicious side effects.

KELEKIAN   Miss Bearing?
VIVIAN   I beg your pardon?
KELEKIAN   Do you have any questions so far?

VIVIAN: Insidious. Hmm. Curious word choice. Cancer. Cancel.

"By cancer nature's changing course untrimmed."[4] No—that's not it.

[*To* KELEKIAN] No.

Must read something about cancer.

Must get some books, articles. Assemble a bibliography.

Is anyone doing research on cancer?

Concentrate.

Antineoplastic. Anti: against. Neo: new. Plastic. To mold. Shaping. Antineoplastic. Against new shaping.

Hair follicles. My resolve.

"Pernicious." That doesn't seem—

---

4. See Shakespeare, Sonnet 18 ("Shall I compare thee to a summer's day?"), line 7: "By chance or nature's changing course untrimmed."

VIVIAN   Please, go on.
KELEKIAN   Perhaps some of these terms are new. I realize—
VIVIAN   No, no. Ah. You're being very thorough.
KELEKIAN   I make a point of it. And I always emphasize it with my students—
VIVIAN   So do I. "Thoroughness"—I always tell my students, but they are constitutionally averse to painstaking work.
KELEKIAN   Yours, too.
VIVIAN   Oh, it's worse every year.
KELEKIAN   And this is not dermatology, it's medical oncology, for Chrissake.
VIVIAN   My students read through a text once—*once!*—and think it's time for a break.
KELEKIAN   Mine are blind.
VIVIAN   Well, mine are deaf.
KELEKIAN   [*Resigned, but warmly*]   You just have to hope . . .
VIVIAN   [*Not so sure*]   I suppose.
   [*Pause*]
KELEKIAN   Where were we, Dr. Bearing?
VIVIAN   I believe I was being thoroughly diagnosed.
KELEKIAN   Right. Now. The tumor is spreading very quickly, and this treatment is very aggressive. So far, so good?
VIVIAN   Yes.
KELEKIAN   Better not teach next semester.
VIVIAN   [*Indignant*]   Out of the question.
KELEKIAN   The first week of each cycle you'll be hospitalized for chemotherapy; the next week you may feel a little tired; the next two weeks'll be fine, relatively. This cycle will repeat eight times, as I said before.
VIVIAN   Eight months like that?
KELEKIAN   This treatment is the strongest thing we have to offer you. And, as research, it will make a significant contribution to our knowledge.
VIVIAN   Knowledge, yes.
KELEKIAN   [*Giving her a piece of paper*]   Here is the informed-consent form. Should you agree, you sign there, at the bottom. Is there a family member you want me to explain this to?
VIVIAN   [*Signing*]   That won't be necessary.
KELEKIAN   [*Taking back the paper*]   Good. The important thing is for you to take the full dose of chemotherapy. There may be times when you'll wish for a lesser dose, due to the side effects. But we've got to go full-force. The experimental phase has got to have the maximum dose to be of any use. Dr. Bearing—
VIVIAN   Yes?
KELEKIAN   You must be very tough. Do you think you can be very tough?
VIVIAN   You needn't worry.
KELEKIAN   Good. Excellent.
   [KELEKIAN *and the desk exit as* VIVIAN *stands and walks forward.*]
VIVIAN   [*Hesitantly*]   I should have asked more questions, because I know there's going to be a test.
   I have cancer, insidious cancer, with pernicious side effects—no, the *treatment* has pernicious side effects.
   I have stage-four metastatic ovarian cancer. There is no stage five. Oh,

and I have to be very tough. It appears to be a matter, as the saying goes, of life and death.

I know all about life and death. I am, after all, a scholar of Donne's Holy Sonnets, which explore mortality in greater depth than any other body of work in the English language.

And I know for a fact that I am tough. A demanding professor. Uncompromising. Never one to turn from a challenge. That is why I chose, while a student of the great E. M. Ashford, to study Donne.

> [PROFESSOR E. M. ASHFORD, *fifty-two, enters, seated at the same desk as* KELEKIAN *was. The scene is twenty-eight years ago.* VIVIAN *suddenly turns twenty-two, eager and intimidated.*]

VIVIAN   Professor Ashford?

E.M.   Do it again.

VIVIAN [*To audience*]   It was something of a shock. I had to sit down. [*She plops down.*]

E.M.   Please sit down. Your essay on Holy Sonnet Six, Miss Bearing, is a melodrama, with a veneer of scholarship unworthy of you—to say nothing of Donne. Do it again.

VIVIAN   I, ah . . .

E.M.   You must begin with a text, Miss Bearing, not with a feeling.
   Death be not proud, though some have called thee
   Mighty and dreadfull, for, thou art not soe.
You have entirely missed the point of the poem, because, I must tell you, you have used an edition of the text that is inauthentically punctuated. In the Gardner[5] edition—

VIVIAN   That edition was checked out of the library—

E.M.   Miss Bearing!

VIVIAN   Sorry.

E.M.   You take this too lightly, Miss Bearing. This is Metaphysical Poetry,[6] not The Modern Novel. The standards of scholarship and critical reading which one would apply to any other text are simply insufficient. The effort must be total for the results to be meaningful. Do you think the punctuation of the last line of this sonnet is merely an insignificant detail?

The sonnet begins with a valiant struggle with death, calling on all the forces of intellect and drama to vanquish the enemy. But it is ultimately about overcoming the seemingly insuperable barriers separating life, death, and eternal life.

In the edition you chose, this profoundly simple meaning is sacrificed to hysterical punctuation:
   Death—*capital D*—shall be no more—*semicolon!*
   Death—*capital D*—comma—thou shalt die—*exclamation point!*
If you go in for this sort of thing, I suggest you take up Shakespeare.

Gardner's edition of the Holy Sonnets returns to the Westmoreland manuscript source of 1610—not for sentimental reasons, I assure you, but because Helen Gardner is a *scholar*. It reads:
   And death shall be no more, *comma*, Death thou shalt die.

---

5. Dame Helen Gardner (1908–1986), English scholar and literary critic; her edition of the Holy Sonnets was published in 1952 (2nd ed., 1978).
6. I.e., the poetry of Donne and some other 17th- century writers of lyric, which is characterized by unusual and learned images, intellectual wit, subtle argumentation, and rationality.

[*As she recites this line, she makes a little gesture at the comma.*]
   Nothing but a breath—a comma—separates life from life everlasting. It is very simple really. With the original punctuation restored, death is no longer something to act out on a stage, with exclamation points. It's a comma, a pause.
   This way, the *uncompromising* way, one learns something from this poem, wouldn't you say? Life, death. Soul, God. Past, present. Not insuperable barriers, not semicolons, just a comma.
VIVIAN   Life, death . . . I see. [*Standing*] It's a metaphysical conceit. It's wit! I'll go back to the library and rewrite the paper—
E.M.   [*Standing, emphatically*]   It is *not* wit, Miss Bearing. It is truth. [*Walking around the desk to her*] The paper's not the point.
VIVIAN   It isn't?
E.M.   [*Tenderly*]   Vivian. You're a bright young woman. Use your intelligence. Don't go back to the library. Go out. Enjoy yourself with your friends. Hmm?
   [VIVIAN *walks away.* E.M. *slides off.*]
VIVIAN   [*As she gradually returns to the hospital*]   I, ah, went outside. The sun was very bright. I, ah, walked around, past the . . . There were students on the lawn, talking about nothing, laughing. The insuperable barrier between one thing and another is . . . just a comma? Simple human truth, uncompromising scholarly standards? They're *connected*? I just couldn't . . .
   I went back to the library.
   Anyway.
   All right. Significant contribution to knowledge.
   Eight cycles of chemotherapy. Give me the full dose, the full dose every time.

   [*In a burst of activity, the hospital scene is created.*]
VIVIAN   The attention was flattering. For the first five minutes. Now I know how poems feel.
   [SUSIE MONAHAN, VIVIAN's *primary nurse, gives* VIVIAN *her chart, then puts her in a wheelchair and takes her to her first appointment: chest x-ray. This and all other diagnostic tests are suggested by light and sound.*]
TECHNICIAN 1   Name.
VIVIAN   My name? Vivian Bearing.
TECHNICIAN 1   Huh?
VIVIAN   Bearing. B-E-A-R-I-N-G. Vivian. V-I-V-I-A-N.
TECHNICIAN 1   Doctor.
VIVIAN   Yes, I have a Ph.D.
TECHNICIAN 1   *Your* doctor.
VIVIAN   Oh. Dr. Harvey Kelekian.
   [TECHNICIAN 1 *positions her so that she is leaning forward and embracing the metal plate, then steps offstage.*]
VIVIAN   *I* am a doctor of philosophy—
TECHNICIAN 1   [*From offstage*]   Take a deep breath, and hold it. [*Pause, with light and sound*] Okay.
VIVIAN   —a scholar of seventeenth-century poetry.

TECHNICIAN 1 [*From offstage*]   Turn sideways, arms behind your head, and hold it. [*Pause*] Okay.
VIVIAN   I have made an immeasurable contribution to the discipline of English literature. [TECHNICIAN 1 *returns and puts her in the wheelchair.*] I am, in short, a force.
   [TECHNICIAN 1 *rolls her to upper GI series, where* TECHNICIAN 2 *picks up.*]
TECHNICIAN 2   Name.
VIVIAN   Lucy, Countess of Bedford.[7]
TECHNICIAN 2 [*Checking a printout*]   I don't see it here.
VIVIAN   My name is Vivian Bearing. B-E-A-R-I-N-G. Dr. Kelekian is my doctor.
TECHNICIAN 2   Okay. Lie down. [TECHNICIAN 2 *positions her on a stretcher and leaves. Light and sound suggest the filming.*]
VIVIAN   After an outstanding undergraduate career, I studied with Professor E. M. Ashford for three years, during which time I learned by instruction and example what it means to be a scholar of distinction.

As her research fellow, my principal task was the alphabetizing of index cards for Ashford's monumental critical edition of Donne's *Devotions upon Emergent Occasions.*

   [*During the procedure, another* TECHNICIAN *takes the wheelchair away.*]

I am thanked in the preface: "Miss Vivian Bearing for her able assistance."

My dissertation, "Ejaculations[8] in Seventeenth-Century Manuscript and Printed Editions of the Holy Sonnets: A Comparison," was revised for publication in the *Journal of English Texts,* a very prestigious venue for a first appearance.
TECHNICIAN 2   Where's your wheelchair?
VIVIAN   I do not know. I was busy just now.
TECHNICIAN 2   Well, how are you going to get out of here?
VIVIAN   Well, I do not know. Perhaps you would like me to stay.
TECHNICIAN 2   I guess I got to go find you a chair.
VIVIAN [*Sarcastically*]   Don't inconvenience yourself on my behalf. [TECHNICIAN 2 *leaves to get a wheelchair.*]

My second article, a classic explication of Donne's sonnet "Death be not proud," was published in *Critical Discourse.*

The success of the essay prompted the University Press to solicit a volume on the twelve Holy Sonnets in the 1633 edition, which I produced in the remarkably short span of three years. My book, entitled *Made Cunningly,* remains an immense success, in paper as well as cloth.

In it, I devote one chapter to a thorough examination of each sonnet, discussing every word in extensive detail.
   [TECHNICIAN 2 *returns with a wheelchair.*]
TECHNICIAN 2   Here.
VIVIAN   I summarize previous critical interpretations of the text and offer my own analysis. It is exhaustive.

---

7. Important patron of poets (ca. 1581–1627), including Donne and Ben Jonson.

8. Short prayers uttered during emergencies; also, hasty emotional utterances.

[TECHNICIAN 2 *deposits her at CT scan.*]
Bearing. B-E-A-R-I-N-G. Kelekian.
[TECHNICIAN 3 *has* VIVIAN *lie down on a metal stretcher. Light and sound suggest the procedure.*]
TECHNICIAN 3   Here. Hold still.
VIVIAN   For how long?
TECHNICIAN 3   Just a little while. [TECHNICIAN 3 *leaves. Silence*]
VIVIAN   The scholarly study of poetic texts requires a capacity for scrupulously detailed examination, particularly the poetry of John Donne.

The salient characteristic of the poems is wit: "Itchy outbreaks of far-fetched wit," as Donne himself said.[9]

To the common reader—that is to say, the undergraduate with a B-plus or better average—wit provides an invaluable exercise for sharpening the mental faculties, for stimulating the flash of comprehension that can only follow hours of exacting and seemingly pointless scrutiny.

[TECHNICIAN 3 *puts* VIVIAN *back in the wheelchair and wheels her toward the unit. Partway,* TECHNICIAN 3 *gives the chair a shove and* SUSIE MONAHAN, VIVIAN's *primary nurse, takes over.* SUSIE *rolls* VIVIAN *to the exam room.*]

To the scholar, to the mind comprehensively trained in the subtleties of seventeenth-century vocabulary, versification, and theological, historical, geographical, political, and mythological allusions, Donne's wit is . . . a way to see how good you really are.

After twenty years, I can say with confidence, no one is quite as good as I.

[*By now,* SUSIE *has helped* VIVIAN *sit on the exam table.* DR. JASON POSNER, *clinical fellow, stands in the doorway.*]
JASON   Ah, Susie?
SUSIE   Oh, hi.
JASON   Ready when you are.
SUSIE   Okay. Go ahead. Ms. Bearing, this is Jason Posner. He's going to do your history, ask you a bunch of questions. He's Dr. Kelekian's fellow.
[SUSIE *is busy in the room, setting up for the exam.*]
JASON   Hi, Professor Bearing. I'm Dr. Posner, clinical fellow in the medical oncology branch, working with Dr. Kelekian.

Professor Bearing, I, ah, I was an undergraduate at the U. I took your course in seventeenth-century poetry.
VIVIAN   You did?
JASON   Yes. I thought it was excellent.
VIVIAN   Thank you. Were you an English major?
JASON   No. Biochemistry. But you can't get into medical school unless you're well-rounded. And I made a bet with myself that I could get an A in the three hardest courses on campus.
SUSIE   Howdjya do, Jace?
JASON   Success.
VIVIAN [*Doubtful*]   Really?
JASON   A minus. It was a very tough course. [*To* SUSIE] I'll call you.
SUSIE   Okay. [*She leaves.*]

---

9. In *Catalogue Librorum Aulicorum, or The Courtier's Library* (written ca. 1604/05, published 1660).

JASON   I'll just pull this over. [*He gets a little stool on wheels.*] Get the proxemics[1] right here. There. [*Nervously*] Good. Now. I'm going to be taking your history. It's a medical interview, and then I give you an exam.
VIVIAN   I believe Dr. Kelekian has already done that.
JASON   Well, I know, but Dr. Kelekian wants *me* to do it, too. Now. I'll be taking a few notes as we go along.
VIVIAN   Very well.
JASON   Okay. Let's get started. How are you feeling today?
VIVIAN   Fine, thank you.
JASON   Good. How is your general health?
VIVIAN   Fine.
JASON   Excellent. Okay. We know you are an academic.
VIVIAN   Yes, we've established that.
JASON   So we don't need to talk about your interesting work.
VIVIAN   No.
   [*The following questions and answers go extremely quickly.*]
JASON   How old are you?
VIVIAN   Fifty.
JASON   Are you married?
VIVIAN   No.
JASON   Are your parents living?
VIVIAN   No.
JASON   How and when did they die?
VIVIAN   My father, suddenly, when I was twenty, of a heart attack. My mother, slowly, when I was forty-one and forty-two, of cancer. Breast cancer.
JASON   Cancer?
VIVIAN   Breast cancer.
JASON   I see. Any siblings?
VIVIAN   No.
JASON   Do you have any questions so far?
VIVIAN   Not so far.
JASON   Well, that about does it for your life history.
VIVIAN   Yes, that's all there is to my life history.
JASON   Now I'm going to ask you about your past medical history. Have you ever been hospitalized?
VIVIAN   I had my tonsils out when I was eight.
JASON   Have you ever been pregnant?
VIVIAN   No.
JASON   Ever had heart murmurs? High blood pressure?
VIVIAN   No.
JASON   Stomach, liver, kidney problems?
VIVIAN   No.
JASON   Venereal diseases? Uterine infections?
VIVIAN   No.
JASON   Thyroid, diabetes, cancer?
VIVIAN   No—cancer, yes.
JASON   When?

---

1. The study of spatial distances between individuals and their variation according to culture and situation (not simply "distance," as Jason's usage suggests).

VIVIAN Now.
JASON Well, not including now.
VIVIAN In that case, no.
JASON Okay. Clinical depression? Nervous breakdowns? Suicide attempts?
VIVIAN No.
JASON Do you smoke?
VIVIAN No.
JASON Ethanol?
VIVIAN I'm sorry?
JASON Alcohol.
VIVIAN Oh. Ethanol. Yes, I drink wine.
JASON How much? How often?
VIVIAN A glass with dinner occasionally. And perhaps a Scotch every now and then.
JASON Do you use substances?
VIVIAN Such as.
JASON Marijuana, cocaine, crack cocaine, PCP, ecstasy, poppers—
VIVIAN No.
JASON Do you drink caffeinated beverages?
VIVIAN Oh, yes!
JASON Which ones?
VIVIAN Coffee. A few cups a day.
JASON How many?
VIVIAN Two . . . to six. But I really don't think that's immoderate—
JASON How often do you undergo routine medical checkups?
VIVIAN Well, not as often as I should, probably, but I've felt fine, I really have.
JASON So the answer is?
VIVIAN Every three to . . . five years.
JASON What do you do for exercise?
VIVIAN Pace.
JASON Are you having sexual relations?
VIVIAN Not at the moment.
JASON Are you pre- or post-menopausal?
VIVIAN Pre.
JASON When was the first day of your last period?
VIVIAN Ah, ten days—two weeks ago.
JASON Okay. When did you first notice your present complaint?
VIVIAN This time, now?
JASON Yes.
VIVIAN Oh, about four months ago. I felt a pain in my stomach, in my abdomen, like a cramp, but not the same.
JASON How did it feel?
VIVIAN Like a cramp.
JASON But not the same?
VIVIAN No, duller, and stronger. I can't describe it.
JASON What came next?
VIVIAN Well, I just, I don't know, I started noticing my body, little things. I would be teaching, and feel a sharp pain.
JASON What kind of pain?

VIVIAN   Sharp, and sudden. Then it would go away. Or I would be tired. Exhausted. I was working on a major project, the article on John Donne for *The Oxford Encyclopedia of English Literature*. It was a great honor. But I had a very strict deadline.

JASON   So you would say you were under stress?

VIVIAN   It wasn't so much more stress than usual, I just couldn't withstand it this time. I don't know.

JASON   So?

VIVIAN   So I went to Dr. Chin, my gynecologist, after I had turned in the article, and explained all this. She examined me, and sent me to Jefferson the internist, and he sent me to Kelekian because he thought I might have a tumor.

JASON   And that's it?

VIVIAN   Till now.

JASON   Hmmm. Well, that's very interesting.
[*Nervous pause*]
Well, I guess I'll start the examination. It'll only take a few minutes. Why don't you, um, sort of lie back, and—oh—relax.
[*He helps her lie back on the table, raises the stirrups out of the table, raises her legs and puts them in the stirrups, and puts a paper sheet over her.*]
Be very relaxed. This won't hurt. Let me get this sheet. Okay. Just stay calm. Okay. Put your feet in these stirrups. Okay. Just. There. Okay? Now. Oh, I have to go get Susie. Got to have a girl here. Some crazy clinical rule. Um. I'll be right back. Don't move.
[JASON *leaves. Long pause. He is seen walking quickly back and forth in the hall, and calling* SUSIE'*s name as he goes by.*]

VIVIAN [*To herself*]   I wish I had given him an A. [*Silence*]
Two times one is two.
Two times two is four.
Two times three is six.
Um.
Oh.

>Death be not proud, though some have called thee
>Mighty and dreadfull, for, thou art not soe,
>For, those, whom thou think'st, thou dost overthrow,
>Die not, poore death, nor yet canst thou kill mee . . .

JASON [*In the hallway*]   Has anybody seen Susie?

VIVIAN [*Losing her place for a second*]   Ah.

>Thou'art slave to Fate, chance, kings, and desperate men,
>And dost with poyson, warre, and sicknesse dwell,
>And poppie,' or charmes can make us sleepe as well,
>And better than thy stroake; why swell'st thou then?

JASON [*In the hallway*]   She was here just a minute ago.

VIVIAN

>One short sleepe past, wee wake eternally,
>And death shall be no more—*comma*—Death thou shalt die.

[JASON *and* SUSIE *return.*]

JASON   Okay. Here's everything. Okay.

SUSIE   What is this? Why did you leave her—

JASON [*To* SUSIE]   I had to find you. Now, come on. [*To* VIVIAN] We're ready, Professor Bearing. [*To himself, as he puts on exam gloves*] Get these on. Okay. Just lift this up. Ooh. Okay. [*As much to himself as to her*] Just relax. [*He begins the pelvic exam, with one hand on her abdomen and the other inside her, looking blankly at the ceiling as he feels around.*] Okay. [*Silence*] Susie, isn't that interesting, that I had Professor Bearing.

SUSIE   Yeah. I wish I had taken some literature. I don't know anything about poetry.

JASON [*Trying to be casual*]   Professor Bearing was very highly regarded on campus. It looked very good on my transcript that I had taken her course. [*Silence*] They even asked me about it in my interview for med school— [*He feels the mass and does a double take.*] Jesus! [*Tense silence. He is amazed and fascinated.*]

SUSIE   What?

VIVIAN   What?

JASON   Um. [*He tries for composure.*] Yeah. I survived Bearing's course. No problem. Heh. [*Silence*] Yeah, John Donne, those metaphysical poets, that metaphysical wit. Hardest poetry in the English department. Like to see *them* try biochemistry. [*Silence*] Okay. We're about done. Okay. That's it. Okay, Professor Bearing. Let's take your feet out, there. [*He takes off his gloves and throws them away.*] Okay. I gotta go. I gotta go.

[JASON *quickly leaves.* VIVIAN *slowly gets up from this scene and walks stiffly away.* SUSIE *cleans up the exam room and exits.*]

VIVIAN [*Walking downstage to audience*]   That . . . was . . . hard. That . . . was . . .

One thing can be said for an eight-month course of cancer treatment: it is highly educational. I am learning to suffer.

Yes, it is mildly uncomfortable to have an electrocardiogram, but the . . . agony . . . of a proctosigmoidoscopy[2] sweeps it from memory. Yes, it was embarrassing to have to wear a nightgown all day long—two nightgowns!—but that seemed like a positive privilege compared to watching myself go bald. Yes, having a former student give me a pelvic exam was thoroughly *degrading*—and I use the term deliberately—but I could not have imagined the depths of humiliation that—

Oh, God—[VIVIAN *runs across the stage to her hospital room, dives onto the bed, and throws up into a large plastic washbasin.*] Oh, God. Oh. Oh. [*She lies slumped on the bed, fastened to the IV, which now includes a small bottle with a bright orange label.*] Oh, God. It can't be. [*Silence*] Oh, God. Please. Steady. Steady. [*Silence*] Oh—Oh, no! [*She throws up again, moans, and retches in agony.*] Oh, God. What's left? I haven't eaten in two days. What's left to puke?

You may remark that my vocabulary has taken a turn for the Anglo-Saxon.

God, I'm going to barf my brains out.

[*She begins to relax.*] If I actually did barf my brains out, it would be

---

2. An examination of the lower colon using a thin, lighted tube.

a great loss to my discipline. Of course, not a few of my colleagues would be relieved. To say nothing of my students.

It's not that I'm controversial. Just uncompromising. Ooh—[*She lunges for the basin. Nothing*] Oh. [*Silence*] False alarm. If the word went round that Vivian Bearing had barfed her brains out . . .

Well, first my colleagues, most of whom are my former students, would scramble madly for my position. Then their consciences would flare up, so to honor *my* memory they would put together a collection of *their* essays about John Donne. The volume would begin with a warm introduction, capturing my most endearing qualities. It would be short. But sweet.

Published *and* perished.

Now, watch this. I have to ring the bell [*She presses the button on the bed*] to get someone to come and measure this emesis,[3] and record the amount on a chart of my intake and output. This counts as output.

[SUSIE *enters.*]

SUSIE [*Brightly*]   How you doing, Ms. Bearing? You having some nausea?
VIVIAN [*Weakly*]   Uhh, yes.
SUSIE   Why don't I take that? Here.
VIVIAN   It's about 300 cc's.
SUSIE   That all?
VIVIAN   It was very hard work.
    [SUSIE *takes the basin to the bathroom and rinses it.*]
SUSIE   Yup. Three hundred. Good guess. [*She marks the graph.*] Okay. Anything else I can get for you? Some Jell-O or anything?
VIVIAN   Thank you, no.
SUSIE   You okay all by yourself here?
VIVIAN   Yes.
SUSIE   You're not having a lot of visitors, are you?
VIVIAN [*Correcting*]   None, to be precise.
SUSIE   Yeah, I didn't think so. Is there somebody you want me to call for you?
VIVIAN   That won't be necessary.
SUSIE   Well, I'll just pop my head in every once in a while to see how you're coming along. Kelekian and the fellows should be in soon. [*She touches* VIVIAN's *arm.*] If there's anything you need, you just ring.
VIVIAN [*Uncomfortable with kindness*]   Thank you.
SUSIE   Okay. Just call. [SUSIE *disconnects the IV bottle with the orange label and takes it with her as she leaves.* VIVIAN *lies still. Silence*]

VIVIAN   In this dramatic structure you will see the most interesting aspects of my tenure as an in-patient receiving experimental chemotherapy for advanced metastatic ovarian cancer.

But as I am a *scholar* before . . . an impresario, I feel obliged to document what it is like here most of the time, between the dramatic climaxes. Between the spectacles.

3. Vomit.

In truth, it is like this:
  [*She ceremoniously lies back and stares at the ceiling.*]
You cannot imagine how time . . . can be . . . so still.
It hangs. It weighs. And yet there is so little of it.
It goes so slowly, and yet it is so scarce.

If I were writing this scene, it would last a full fifteen minutes. I would lie here, and you would sit there.
  [*She looks at the audience, daring them.*]
Not to worry. Brevity is the soul of wit.[4]

But if you think eight months of cancer treatment is tedious for the *audience,* consider how it feels to play my part.

All right. All right. It is Friday morning: Grand Rounds. [*Loudly, giving a cue*] Action.
  [KELEKIAN *enters, followed by* JASON *and four other* FELLOWS.]

KELEKIAN   Dr. Bearing.
VIVIAN   Dr. Kelekian.
KELEKIAN   Jason.
  [JASON *moves to the front of the group.*]
JASON   Professor Bearing. How are you feeling today?
VIVIAN   Fine.
JASON   That's great. That's just great. [*He takes a sheet and carefully covers her legs and groin, then pulls up her gown to reveal her entire abdomen. He is barely audible, but his gestures are clear.*]

VIVIAN: "Grand Rounds." The term is theirs. Not "Grand" in the traditional sense of sweeping or magnificent. Not "Rounds" as in a musical canon, or a *round* of applause (though either would be refreshing at this point). Here, "Rounds" seems to signify darting *around* the main issue . . . which I suppose would be the struggle for life . . . *my* life . . . with heated discussions of side effects, other complaints, additional treatments.

Grand Rounds is not Grand Opera. But compared to lying here, it is positively *dramatic*.

Full of subservience, hierarchy, gratuitous displays, sublimated rivalries—I feel right at home. It is just like a graduate seminar.

JASON: Very late detection. Staged as a four upon admission. Hexamethophosphacil with Vinplatin to potentiate. Hex at 300 mg. per meter squared, Vin at 100. Today is cycle two, day three. Both cycles at the *full dose.*
[*The* FELLOWS *are impressed.*]

The primary site is—*here* [*He puts his finger on the spot on her abdomen*], behind the left ovary. Metastases are suspected in the peritoneal cavity—here. And—here. [*He touches those spots.*]

Full lymphatic involvement. [*He moves his hands over her entire body.*]

At the time of first-look surgery, a significant part of the

---

4. Shakespeare's *Hamlet* 2.2.91.

With one important difference: in Grand Rounds, they read *me like a book. Once I did the teaching now I am taught.*

This is much easier. I just hold still and look cancerous. It requires less acting every time.

Excellent command of details.

tumor was de-bulked, mostly in this area—*here*. [*He points to each organ, poking her abdomen.*] Left, right ovaries. Fallopian tubes. Uterus. All out.

Evidence of primary-site shrinkage. Shrinking in metastatic tumors has not been documented. Primary mass frankly palpable in pelvic exam, frankly, all through here—*here*. [*Some* FELLOWS *reach and press where he is pointing.*]

KELEKIAN   Excellent command of details.
VIVIAN [*To herself*]   I taught him, you know—
KELEKIAN   Okay. Problem areas with Hex and Vin. [*He addresses all the* FELLOWS, *but* JASON *answers first and they resent him.*]
FELLOW 1   Myelosu—
JASON [*Interrupting*]   Well, first of course is myelosuppression, a lowering of blood-cell counts. It goes without saying. With this combination of agents, nephrotoxicity will be next.
KELEKIAN   Go on.
JASON   The kidneys are designed to filter out impurities in the bloodstream. In trying to filter the chemotherapeutic agent out of the bloodstream, the kidneys shut down.
KELEKIAN   Intervention.
JASON   Hydration.
KELEKIAN   Monitoring.
JASON   Full recording of fluid intake and output, as you see here on these graphs, to monitor hydration and kidney function. Totals monitored daily by the clinical fellow, as per the protocol.
KELEKIAN   Anybody else. Side effects.
FELLOW 1   Nausea and vomiting.
KELEKIAN   Jason.
JASON   Routine.
FELLOW 2   Pain while urinating.
JASON   Routine. [*The* FELLOWS *are trying to catch* JASON.]
FELLOW 3   Psychological depression.
JASON   No way.
   [*The* FELLOWS *are silent.*]
KELEKIAN [*Standing by* VIVIAN *at the head of the bed*]   Anything else. Other complaints with Hexamethophosphacil and Vinplatin. Come on. [*Silence.* KELEKIAN *and* VIVIAN *wait together for the correct answer.*]
FELLOW 4   Mouth sores.
JASON   Not yet.
FELLOW 2 [*Timidly*]   Skin rash?
JASON   Nope.
KELEKIAN [*Sharing this with* VIVIAN]   Why do we waste our time, Dr. Bearing?

VIVIAN [*Delighted*]   I do not know, Dr. Kelekian.
KELEKIAN [*To the* FELLOWS]   Use your eyes. [*All* FELLOWS *look closely at* VIVIAN.] Jesus God. Hair loss.
FELLOWS [*All protesting.* VIVIAN *and* KELEKIAN *are amused.*]
—Come on.
—You can see it.
—It doesn't count.
—No fair.
KELEKIAN   Jason.
JASON [*Begrudgingly*]   Hair loss after first cycle of treatment.
KELEKIAN   That's better. [*To* VIVIAN] Dr. Bearing. Full dose. Excellent. Keep pushing the fluids.
   [*The* FELLOWS *leave.* KELEKIAN *stops* JASON.]
KELEKIAN   Jason.
JASON   Huh?
KELEKIAN   Clinical.
JASON   Oh, right. [*To* VIVIAN] Thank you, Professor Bearing. You've been very cooperative. [*They leave her with her stomach uncovered.*]
VIVIAN   Wasn't that . . . Grand? [*She gets up without the IV pole.*] At times, this obsessively detailed examination, this *scrutiny* seems to me to be a nefarious business. On the other hand, what is the alternative? Ignorance? Ignorance may be . . . bliss; but it is not a very noble goal.
   So I play my part.
      [*Pause*]
   I receive chemotherapy, throw up, am subjected to countless indignities, feel better, go home. Eight cycles. Eight neat little strophes.[5] Oh, there have been the usual variations, subplots, red herrings: hepatotoxicity (liver poison), neuropathy (nerve death).
   [*Righteously*] They are medical terms. I look them up.
   It has always been my custom to treat words with respect.
   I can recall the time—the very hour of the very day—when I knew words would be my life's work.

   [*A pile of six little white books appears, with* MR. BEARING, VIVIAN'*s father, seated behind an open newspaper.*]
   It was my fifth birthday.
      [VIVIAN, *now a child, flops down to the books.*]
   I liked that one best.
MR. BEARING [*Disinterested but tolerant, never distracted from his newspaper*]   Read another.
VIVIAN   I think I'll read . . . [*She takes a book from the stack and reads its spine intently*] The Tale of the Flopsy Bunnies. [*Reading the front cover*] *The Tale of the Flopsy Bunnies*. It has little bunnies on the front.
      [*Opening to the title page*] *The Tale of the Flopsy Bunnies* by Beatrix Potter.[6] [*She turns the page and begins to read.*]
   It is said that the effect of eating too much lettuce is sopor—sop—or— what is that word?

---

5. Stanzas.
6. English writer and illustrator (1866–1943); this book was published in 1909.

MR. BEARING   Sound it out.
VIVIAN   Sop—or—fic. Sop—or—i—fic. Soporific. What does that mean?
MR. BEARING   Soporific. Causing sleep.
VIVIAN   Causing sleep.
MR. BEARING   Makes you sleepy.
VIVIAN   "Soporific" means "makes you sleepy"?
MR. BEARING   Correct.
VIVIAN   "Soporific" means "makes you sleepy." Soporific.
MR. BEARING   Now use it in a sentence. What has a soporific effect on *you*?
VIVIAN   A soporific effect on me.
MR. BEARING   What makes you sleepy?
VIVIAN   Aahh—nothing.
MR. BEARING   Correct.
VIVIAN   What about you?
MR. BEARING   What has a soporific effect on me? Let me think: boring conversation, I suppose, after dinner.
VIVIAN   Me too, boring conversation.
MR. BEARING   Carry on.
VIVIAN   It is said that the effect of eating too much lettuce is soporific.

The little bunnies in the picture are asleep! They're sleeping! Like you said, because of *soporific*!

[*She stands up, and* MR. BEARING *exits.*]

The illustration bore out the meaning of the word, just as he had explained it. At the time, it seemed like magic.

So imagine the effect that the words of John Donne first had on me: ratiocination, concatenation, coruscation, tergiversation.

Medical terms are less evocative. Still, I want to know what the doctors mean when they . . . anatomize me. And I will grant that in this particular field of endeavor they possess a more potent arsenal of terminology than I. My only defense is the acquisition of vocabulary.

[SUSIE *enters and puts her arm around* VIVIAN's *shoulders to hold her up.* VIVIAN *is shaking, feverish, and weak.*]

VIVIAN [*All at once*]   Fever and neutropenia.[7]
SUSIE   When did it start?
VIVIAN [*Having difficulty speaking*]   I—I was at home—reading—and I—felt so bad. I called. Fever and neutropenia. They said to come in.
SUSIE   You did the right thing to come. Did somebody drive you?
VIVIAN   Cab. I took a taxi.
SUSIE [*She grabs a wheelchair and helps* VIVIAN *sit. As* SUSIE *speaks, she takes* VIVIAN's *temperature, pulse, and respiration rate.*]   Here, why don't you sit? Just sit there a minute. I'll get Jason. He's on call tonight. We'll get him to give you some meds. I'm glad I was here on nights. I'll make sure you get to bed soon, okay? It'll just be a minute. I'll get you some juice, some nice juice with lots of ice.

[SUSIE *leaves quickly.* VIVIAN *sits there, agitated, confused, and very sick.* SUSIE *returns with the juice.*]

---

7. An abnormal decrease in a type of white blood cell (the cells responsible for fighting infections).

VIVIAN   Lights. I left all the lights on at my house.
SUSIE   Don't you worry. It'll be all right.
         [JASON *enters, roused from his sleep and not fully awake. He wears surgical scrubs and puts on a lab coat as he enters.*]
JASON [*Without looking at* VIVIAN]   How are you feeling, Professor Bearing?
VIVIAN   My teeth—are chattering.
JASON   Vitals.
SUSIE [*Giving* VIVIAN *juice and a straw, without looking at* JASON]   Temp 39.4. Pulse 120. Respiration 36. Chills and sweating.
JASON   Fever and neutropenia. It's a "shake and bake." Blood cultures and urine, stat.[8] Admit her. Prepare for reverse isolation. Start with acetaminophen. Vitals every four hours. [*He starts to leave.*]
SUSIE [*Following him*]   Jason—I think you need to talk to Kelekian about lowering the dose for the next cycle. It's too much for her like this.
JASON   Lower the dose? No way. Full dose. She's tough. She can take it. Wake me up when the counts come from the lab.
         [*He pads off.* SUSIE *wheels* VIVIAN *to her room, and* VIVIAN *collapses on the bed.* SUSIE *connects* VIVIAN's *IV, then wets a washcloth and rubs her face and neck:* VIVIAN *remains delirious.* SUSIE *checks the IV and leaves with the wheelchair.*
         After a while, KELEKIAN *appears in the doorway holding a surgical mask near his face.* JASON *is with him, now dressed and clean-shaven.*]
KELEKIAN   Good morning, Dr. Bearing. Fifth cycle. Full dose. Definite progress. Everything okay.
VIVIAN [*Weakly*]   Yes.
KELEKIAN   You're doing swell. Isolation is no problem. Couple of days. Think of it as a vacation.
VIVIAN   Oh.
         [JASON *starts to enter, holding a mask near his face, just like* KELEKIAN.]
KELEKIAN   Jason.
JASON   Oh, Jesus. Okay, okay.
         [*He returns to the doorway, where he puts on a paper gown, mask, and gloves.* KELEKIAN *leaves.*]
VIVIAN [*To audience*]   In isolation, I am isolated. For once I can use a term literally. The chemotherapeutic agents eradicating my cancer have also eradicated my immune system. In my present condition, every living thing is a health hazard to me . . .
         [JASON *comes in to check the intake-and-output.*]
JASON [*Complaining to himself*]   I really have not got time for this . . .
VIVIAN   . . . particularly health-care professionals.
JASON [*Going right to the graph on the wall*]   Just to look at the I&O sheets for one minute, and it takes me half an hour to do precautions. Four, seven, eleven. Two-fifty twice. Okay. [*Remembering*] Oh, Jeez. Clinical. Professor Bearing. How are you feeling today?
VIVIAN [*Very sick*]   Fine. Just shaking sometimes from the chills.

---

8. Immediately (a shortening of the Latin *statim*).

JASON IV will kick in anytime now. No problem. Listen, gotta go. Keep pushing the fluids.
[*As he exits, he takes off the gown, mask, and gloves.*]
VIVIAN [*Getting up from bed with her IV pole and resuming her explanation*] I am not in isolation because I have cancer, because I have a tumor the size of a grapefruit. No. I am in isolation because I am being treated for cancer. My treatment imperils my health.

Herein lies the paradox. John Donne would revel in it. I would revel in it, if he wrote a poem about it. My students would flounder in it, because paradox is too difficult to understand. Think of it as a puzzle, I would tell them, an intellectual game.

[*She is trapped.*] Or, I *would have* told them. Were it a game. Which it is not.

[*Escaping*] If they were here, if I were lecturing: How I would *perplex* them! I could work my students into a frenzy. Every ambiguity, every shifting awareness. I could draw so much from the poems.

I could be so powerful.

[VIVIAN *stands still, as if conjuring a scene. Now at the height of her powers, she grandly disconnects herself from the IV.* TECHNICIANS *remove the bed and hand her a pointer.*]
VIVIAN The poetry of the early seventeenth century, what has been called the metaphysical school, considers an intractable mental puzzle by exercising the outstanding human faculty of the era, namely *wit*.

The greatest wit—the greatest English poet, some would say—was John Donne. In the Holy Sonnets, Donne applied his capacious, agile wit to the larger aspects of the human experience: life, death, and God.

In his poems, metaphysical quandaries are addressed, but never resolved. Ingenuity, virtuosity, and a vigorous intellect that jousts with the most exalted concepts: these are the tools of wit.

[*The lights dim. A screen lowers, and the sonnet "If poysonous minerals," from the Gardner edition, appears on it.* VIVIAN *recites.*]

If poysonous mineralls, and if that tree,
Whose fruit[9] threw death on else immortall us,
If lecherous goats, if serpents envious
Cannot be damn'd; Alas; why should I bee?
Why should intent or reason, borne in mee,
Make sinnes, else equall, in mee, more heinous?
And mercy being easie, 'and glorious
To God, in his sterne wrath, why threatens hee?
But who am I, that dare dispute with thee?
O God, Oh! of thine onely worthy blood,
And my teares, make a heavenly Lethean flood,[1]
And drowne in it my sinnes blacke memorie.

---

9. I.e., the fruit from the tree of the knowledge of good and evil; by eating it, according to the account in Genesis 2–3, Adam and Eve brought death into the world.

1. Lethe was the river of forgetfulness (the literal meaning of *lēthē*, in Greek) in the classical underworld; the dead drank from it before their souls were reborn.

> That thou remember them, some claime as debt,
> I thinke it mercy, if thou wilt forget.

[VIVIAN *occasionally whacks the screen with a pointer for emphasis. She moves around as she lectures.*]

Aggressive intellect. Pious melodrama. And a final, fearful point. Donne's Holy Sonnet Five, 1609. From the Ashford edition, based on Gardner.

The speaker of the sonnet has a brilliant mind, and he plays the part convincingly; but in the end he finds God's *forgiveness* hard to believe, so he crawls under a rock to *hide*.

If arsenic and serpents are not damned, then why is he? In asking the question, the speaker turns eternal damnation into an intellectual game. Why would God choose to do what is *hard*, to condemn, rather than what is *easy*, and also *glorious*—to show mercy?

(Several scholars have disputed Ashford's third comma in line six, but none convincingly.)

But. Exception. Limitation. Contrast. The argument shifts from cleverness to melodrama, an unconvincing eruption of piety: "O" "God" "Oh!"

A typical prayer would plead "Remember me, O Lord." (This point is nicely explicated in an article by Richard Strier—a former student of mine who once sat where you do now, although I dare say he was *awake*—in the May 1989 issue of *Modern Philology*.[2]) True believers ask to be *remembered* by God. The speaker of this sonnet asks God to forget. [VIVIAN *moves in front of the screen, and the projection of the poem is cast directly upon her.*] Where is the hyperactive intellect of the first section? Where is the histrionic outpouring of the second? When the speaker considers his own *sins*, and the inevitability of God's *judgment*, he can conceive of but one resolution: to *disappear*. [VIVIAN *moves away from the screen.*] Doctrine assures us that no sinner is denied *forgiveness*, not even one whose sins are overweening *intellect* or overwrought *dramatics*. The speaker does not need to *hide* from God's *judgment*, only to accept God's *forgiveness*. It is very simple. Suspiciously simple.

We want to correct the speaker, to remind him of the assurance of salvation. But it is too late. The poetic encounter is over. We are left to our own consciences. Have we outwitted Donne? Or have we been outwitted?

[SUSIE *comes on.*]

SUSIE   Ms. Bearing?
VIVIAN   [*Continuing*] Will the po—
SUSIE   Ms. Bearing?
VIVIAN   [*Crossly*] What is it?
SUSIE   You have to go down for a test. Jason just called. They want another ultrasound. They're concerned about a bowel obstruction—Is it okay if I come in?
VIVIAN   No. Not now.
SUSIE   I'm sorry, but they want it now.
VIVIAN   Not right now. It's not *supposed* to be now.

---

2. An actual article, "John Donne Awry and Squint: The 'Holy Sonnets,' 1608–10," *Modern Philology* 86 (May 1989): 357–84; Strier (b. 1945) is a professor of English at the University of Chicago and currently the editor of *Modern Philology*.

SUSIE Yes, they want to do it now. I've got the chair.
VIVIAN It should not be now. I am in the middle of—this. I have *this* planned for now, not ultrasound. No more tests. We've covered that.
SUSIE I know, I know, but they need for it to be now. It won't take long, and it isn't a bad procedure. Why don't you just come along.
VIVIAN *I do not want to go now!*
SUSIE Ms. Bearing.
  [*Silence.* VIVIAN *raises the screen, walks away from the scene, hooks herself to the IV, and gets in the wheelchair.* SUSIE *wheels* VIVIAN, *and a* TECHNICIAN *takes her.*]
TECHNICIAN Name.
VIVIAN B-E-A-R-I-N-G. Kelekian.
TECHNICIAN It'll just be a minute.
VIVIAN Time for your break.
TECHNICIAN Yup.
  [*The* TECHNICIAN *leaves.*]

VIVIAN [*Mordantly*] Take a break!
  [VIVIAN *sits weakly in the wheelchair.*]
VIVIAN
> This is my playes last scene, here heavens appoint
> My pilgrimages last mile; and my race
> Idly, yet quickly runne, hath this last pace,
> My spans last inch, my minutes last point,
> And gluttonous death will instantly unjoynt
> My body, 'and soule

John Donne. 1609.

I have always particularly liked that poem. In the abstract. Now I find the image of "my minute's last point" a little too, shall we say, *pointed*.

I don't mean to complain, but I am becoming very sick. Very, very sick. Ultimately sick, as it were.

In everything I have done, I have been steadfast, resolute—some would say in the extreme. Now, as you can see, I am distinguishing myself in illness.

I have survived eight treatments of Hexamethophosphacil and Vinplatin at the *full* dose, ladies and gentlemen. I have broken the record. I have become something of a celebrity. Kelekian and Jason are simply delighted. I think they foresee celebrity status for themselves upon the appearance of the journal article they will no doubt write about me.

But I flatter myself. The article will not be about *me*, it will be about my ovaries. It will be about my peritoneal cavity, which, despite their best intentions, is now crawling with cancer.

What we have come to think of as *me* is, in fact, just the specimen jar, just the dust jacket, just the white piece of paper that bears the little black marks.

My next line is supposed to be something like this:
"It is such a *relief* to get back to my room after those infernal tests."
This is hardly true.

It would be a *relief* to be a cheerleader on her way to Daytona Beach for Spring Break.
To get back to my room after those infernal tests is just the next thing that happens.

[*She returns to her bed, which now has a commode next to it. She is very sick.*]

Oh, God. It is such a relief to get back to my goddamn room after those goddamn tests.

[JASON *enters.*]

JASON   Professor Bearing. Just want to check the I&O. Four-fifty, six, five. Okay. How are you feeling today? [*He makes notations on his clipboard throughout the scene.*]
VIVIAN   Fine.
JASON   That's great. Just great.
VIVIAN   How are my fluids?
JASON   Pretty good. No kidney involvement yet. That's pretty amazing, with Hex and Vin.
VIVIAN   How will you know when the kidneys are involved?
JASON   Lots of in, not much out.
VIVIAN   That simple.
JASON   Oh, no way. Compromised kidney function is a highly complex reaction. I'm simplifying for you.
VIVIAN   Thank you.
JASON   We're supposed to.
VIVIAN   Bedside manner.
JASON   Yeah, there's a whole course on it in med school. It's required. Colossal waste of time for researchers. [*He turns to go.*]
VIVIAN   I can imagine. [*Trying to ask something important*] Jason?
JASON   Huh?
VIVIAN   [*Not sure of herself*]   Ah, what . . . [*Quickly*] What were you just saying?
JASON   When?
VIVIAN   Never mind.
JASON   Professor Bearing?
VIVIAN   Yes.
JASON   Are you experiencing confusion? Short-term memory loss?
VIVIAN   No.
JASON   Sure?
VIVIAN   Yes. [*Pause*] I was just wondering: why cancer?
JASON   Why cancer?
VIVIAN   Why not open-heart surgery?
JASON   Oh yeah, why not *plumbing*. Why not run a *lube rack*, for all the surgeons know about *Homo sapiens sapiens*. No way. Cancer's the only thing I ever wanted.
VIVIAN [*Intrigued*]   Huh.
JASON   No, really. Cancer is . . . [*Searching*]
VIVIAN [*Helping*]   Awesome.
JASON [*Pause*]   Yeah. Yeah, that's right. It is. It is awesome. How does it

do it? The intercellular regulatory mechanisms—especially for proliferation and differentiation—the malignant neoplasia just don't get it. You grow normal cells in tissue culture in the lab, and they replicate just enough to make a nice, confluent monolayer. They divide twenty times, or fifty times, but eventually they conk out. You grow cancer cells, and they never stop. No contact inhibition whatsoever. They just pile up, just keep replicating forever. [*Pause*] That's got a funny name. Know what it is?

VIVIAN   No. What?

JASON   Immortality in culture.

VIVIAN   Sounds like a symposium.

JASON   It's an error in judgment, in a molecular way. But *why*? Even on the protistic level[3] the normal cell-cell interactions are so subtle they'll take your breath away. Golden-brown algae, for instance, the lowest multicellular life form on earth—they're *idiots*—and it's incredible. It's perfect. So what's up with the cancer cells? Smartest guys in the world, with the best labs, funding—they don't know what to make of it.

VIVIAN   What about you?

JASON   Me? Oh, I've got a couple of ideas, things I'm kicking around. Wait till I get a lab of my own. If I can survive this . . . *fellowship*.

VIVIAN   The part with the human beings.

JASON   Everybody's got to go through it. All the great researchers. They want us to be able to converse intelligently with the clinicians. As though *researchers* were the impediments. The clinicians are such troglodytes. So smarmy. Like we have to hold hands to discuss creatinine clearance. Just cut the crap, I say.

VIVIAN   Are you going to be sorry when I—Do you ever miss people?

JASON   Everybody asks that. Especially girls.

VIVIAN   What do you tell them?

JASON   I tell them yes.

VIVIAN   Are they persuaded?

JASON   Some.

VIVIAN   Some. I see. [*With great difficulty*] And what do you say when a patient is . . . apprehensive . . . frightened.

JASON   Of who?

VIVIAN   I just . . . Never mind.

JASON   Professor Bearing, who is the President of the United States?

VIVIAN   I'm fine, really. It's all right.

JASON   You sure? I could order a test—

VIVIAN   No! No, I'm fine. Just a little tired.

JASON   Okay. Look. Gotta go. Keep pushing the fluids. Try for 2,000 a day, okay?

VIVIAN   Okay. To use your word. Okay.

[JASON *leaves.*]

VIVIAN   [*Getting out of bed, without her IV*]   So. The young doctor, like the senior scholar, prefers research to humanity. At the same time the senior scholar, in her pathetic state as a simpering victim, wishes the young doctor would take more interest in personal contact.

---

3. I.e., the level of primitive, usually single-cell organisms (protozoans, most algae, slime molds, etc.).

Now I suppose we shall see, through a series of flashbacks, how the senior scholar ruthlessly denied her simpering students the touch of human kindness she now seeks.

[STUDENTS *appear, sitting at chairs with writing desks attached to the right arm.*]

VIVIAN [*Commanding attention*] How then would you characterize [*pointing to a student*]—you.

STUDENT 1 Huh?

VIVIAN How would you characterize the animating force of this sonnet?

STUDENT 1 Huh?

VIVIAN In this sonnet, what is the principal poetic device? I'll give you a hint. It has nothing to do with football. What propels this sonnet?

STUDENT 1 Um.

VIVIAN [*Speaking to the audience*] Did I say [*tenderly*] "You are nineteen years old. You are so young. You don't know a sonnet from a steak sandwich." [*Pause*] By no means.

[*Sharply, to* STUDENT 1] You can come to this class prepared, or you can excuse yourself from this class, this department, and this university. Do not think for a moment that I will tolerate anything in between.

[*To the audience, defensively*] I was teaching him a lesson. [*She walks away from* STUDENT 1, *then turns and addresses the class.*]

So we have another instance of John Donne's agile wit at work: not so much *resolving* the issues of life and God as *reveling* in their complexity.

STUDENT 2 But why?

VIVIAN Why what?

STUDENT 2 Why does Donne make everything so *complicated*? [*The other* STUDENTS *laugh in agreement.*] No, really, *why*?

VIVIAN [*To the audience*] You know, someone asked me that every year. And it was always one of the smart ones. What could I say? [*To* STUDENT 2] What do you think?

STUDENT 2 I think it's like he's hiding. I think he's really confused, I don't know, maybe he's scared, so he hides behind all this complicated stuff, hides behind this *wit*.

VIVIAN *Hides* behind *wit*?

STUDENT 2 I mean, if it's really something he's sure of, he can say it more simple—simply. He doesn't have to be such a brain, or such a performer. It doesn't have to be such a big deal.

[*The other* STUDENTS *encourage him.*]

VIVIAN Perhaps he is suspicious of simplicity.

STUDENT 2 Perhaps, but that's pretty stupid.

VIVIAN [*To the audience*] That observation, despite its infelicitous phrasing, contained the seed of a perspicacious remark. Such an unlikely occurrence left me with two choices. I could draw it out, or I could allow the brain to rest after that heroic effort. If I pursued, there was the chance of great insight, or the risk of undergraduate banality. I could never predict. [*To* STUDENT 2] Go on.

STUDENT 2 Well, if he's trying to figure out God, and the meaning of life, and big stuff like that, why does he keep running away, you know?

VIVIAN [*To the audience, moving closer to* STUDENT 2] So far so good, but they can think for themselves only so long before they begin to self-destruct.

STUDENT 2 Um, it's like, the more you hide, the less—no, wait—the more you are getting closer—although you don't know it—and the simple thing is there—you see what I mean?

VIVIAN [*To the audience, looking at* STUDENT 2, *as suspense collapses*] Lost it.

[*She walks away and speaks to the audience.*] I distinctly remember an exchange between two students after my lecture on pronunciation and scansion. I overheard them talking on their way out of class. They were young and bright, gathering their books and laughing at the expense of seventeenth-century poetry, at *my* expense.

[*To the class*] To scan the line properly, we must take advantage of the contemporary flexibility in "i-o-n" endings, as in "expansion." The quatrain stands:

> Our two souls therefore, which are one,
>   Though I must go, endure not yet
> A breach, but an *ex-pan-see-on*,
>   Like gold to airy thinness beat.[4]

Bear this in mind in your reading. That's all for today.

[*The* STUDENTS *get up in a chaotic burst.* STUDENT 3 *and* STUDENT 4 *pass by* VIVIAN *on their way out.*]

STUDENT 3 I hope I can get used to this pronuncia-see-on.

STUDENT 4 I know. I hope I can survive this course and make it to gradua-see-on.

[*They laugh.* VIVIAN *glowers at them. They fall silent, embarrassed.*]

VIVIAN [*To the audience*] That was a witty little exchange, I must admit. It showed the mental acuity I would praise in a poetic text. But I admired only the studied application of wit, not its spontaneous eruption.

[STUDENT 1 *interrupts.*]

STUDENT 1 Professor Bearing? Can I talk to you for a minute?

VIVIAN You may.

STUDENT 1 I need to ask for an extension on my paper. I'm really sorry, and I know your policy, but see—

VIVIAN Don't tell me. Your grandmother died.

STUDENT 1 You knew.

VIVIAN It was a guess.

STUDENT 1 I have to go home.

VIVIAN Do what you will, but the paper is due when it is due.

[*As* STUDENT 1 *leaves and the classroom disappears,* VIVIAN *watches. Pause*]

VIVIAN I don't know. I feel so much—what is the word? I look back, I see these scenes, and I . . .

[*Long silence.* VIVIAN *walks absently around the stage, trying to think of something. Finally, giving up, she trudges back to bed.*]

---

4. From "A Valediction: Forbidding Mourning" (1633).

VIVIAN   It was late at night, the graveyard shift. Susie was on. I could hear her in the hall.
  I wanted her to come and see me. So I had to create a little emergency. Nothing dramatic.
   [VIVIAN *pinches the IV tubing. The pump alarm beeps.*]
  It worked.
   [SUSIE *enters, concerned.*]
SUSIE   Ms. Bearing? Is that you beeping at four in the morning? [*She checks the tubing and presses buttons on the pump. The alarm stops.*] Did that wake you up? I'm sorry. It just gets occluded sometimes.
VIVIAN   I was awake.
SUSIE   You were? What's the trouble, sweetheart?
VIVIAN   [*To the audience, roused*]   Do not think for a minute that anyone calls me "Sweetheart." But then . . . I allowed it. [*To* SUSIE] Oh, I don't know.
SUSIE   You can't sleep?
VIVIAN   No. I just keep thinking.
SUSIE   If you do that too much, you can get kind of confused.
VIVIAN   I know. I can't figure things out. I'm in a . . . *quandary*, having these . . . *doubts*.
SUSIE   What you're doing is very hard.
VIVIAN   Hard things are what I like best.
SUSIE   It's not the same. It's like it's out of control, isn't it?
VIVIAN   [*Crying, in spite of herself*]   I'm scared.
SUSIE   [*Stroking her*]   Oh, honey, of course you are.
VIVIAN   I want . . .
SUSIE   know. It's hard.
VIVIAN   I don't feel sure of myself anymore.
SUSIE   And you used to feel sure.
VIVIAN   [*Crying*]   Oh, yes, I used to feel sure.
SUSIE   Vivian. It's all right. I know. It hurts. I know. It's all right. Do you want a tissue? It's all right. [*Silence*] Vivian, would you like a Popsicle?
VIVIAN   [*Like a child*]   Yes, please.
SUSIE   I'll get it for you. I'll be right back.
VIVIAN   Thank you.
   [SUSIE *leaves.*]
VIVIAN   [*Pulling herself together*]   The epithelial cells in my GI tract have been killed by the chemo. The cold Popsicle feels good, it's something I can digest, and it helps keep me hydrated. For your information.
   [SUSIE *returns with an orange two-stick Popsicle. Vivian unwraps it and breaks it in half.*]
VIVIAN   Here.
SUSIE   Sure?
VIVIAN   Yes.
SUSIE   Thanks. [SUSIE *sits on the commode by the bed. Silence*] When I was a kid, we used to get these from a truck. The man would come around and ring his bell and we'd all run over. Then we'd sit on the curb and eat our Popsicles.
  Pretty profound, huh?
VIVIAN   It sounds nice.

[*Silence*]

SUSIE   Vivian, there's something we need to talk about, you need to think about.

[*Silence*]

VIVIAN   My cancer is not being cured, is it.

SUSIE   Huh-uh.

VIVIAN   They never expected it to be, did they.

SUSIE   Well, they thought the drugs would make the tumor get smaller, and it has gotten a lot smaller. But the problem is that it started in new places too. They've learned a lot for their research. It was the best thing they had to give you, the strongest drugs. There just isn't a good treatment for what you have yet, for advanced ovarian. I'm sorry. They should have explained this—

VIVIAN   I knew.

SUSIE   You did.

VIVIAN   I read between the lines.

SUSIE   What you have to think about is your "code status." What you want them to do if your heart stops.

VIVIAN   Well.

SUSIE   You can be "full code," which means that if your heart stops, they'll call a Code Blue and the code team will come and resuscitate you and take you to Intensive Care until you stabilize again. Or you can be "Do Not Resuscitate," so if your heart stops we'll . . . well, we'll just let it. You'll be "DNR." You can think about it, but I wanted to present both choices before Kelekian and Jason talk to you.

VIVIAN   You don't agree about this?

SUSIE   Well, they like to save lives. So anything's okay, as long as life continues. It doesn't matter if you're hooked up to a million machines. Kelekian is a great researcher and everything. And the fellows, like Jason, they're really smart. It's really an honor for them to work with him. But they always . . . want to know more things.

VIVIAN   I always want to know more things. I'm a scholar. Or I was when I had shoes, when I had eyebrows.

SUSIE   Well, okay then. You'll be full code. That's fine.

[*Silence*]

VIVIAN   No, don't complicate the matter.

SUSIE   It's okay. It's up to you—

VIVIAN   Let it stop.

SUSIE   Really?

VIVIAN   Yes.

SUSIE   So if your heart stops beating—

VIVIAN   Just let it stop.

SUSIE   Sure?

VIVIAN   Yes.

SUSIE   Okay. I'll get Kelekian to give the order, and then—

VIVIAN   Susie?

SUSIE   Uh-huh?

VIVIAN   You're still going to take care of me, aren't you?

SUSIE   'Course, sweetheart. Don't you worry.

[*As* SUSIE *leaves,* VIVIAN *sits upright, full of energy and rage.*]

VIVIAN   That certainly was a *maudlin* display. Popsicles? "Sweetheart"? I can't believe my life has become so . . . *corny*.

But it can't be helped. I don't see any other way. We are discussing life and death, and not in the abstract, either; we are discussing *my* life and *my* death, and my brain is dulling, and poor Susie's was never very sharp to begin with, and I can't conceive of any other . . . *tone*.

[*Quickly*] Now is not the time for verbal swordplay, for unlikely flights of imagination and wildly shifting perspectives, for metaphysical conceit, for wit.

And nothing would be worse than a detailed scholarly analysis. Erudition. Interpretation. Complication.

[*Slowly*] Now is a time for simplicity. Now is a time for, dare I say it, kindness.

[*Searchingly*] I thought being extremely smart would take care of it. But I see that I have been found out. Ooohhh.

I'm scared. Oh, God. I want . . . I want . . . No. I want to hide. I just want to curl up in a little ball. [*She dives under the covers.*]

[VIVIAN *wakes in horrible pain. She is tense, agitated, fearful. Slowly she calms down and addresses the audience.*]

VIVIAN   [*Trying extremely hard*]   I want to tell you how it feels. I want to explain it, to use *my* words. It's as if . . . I can't . . . There aren't . . . I'm like a student and this is the final exam and I don't know what to put down because I don't understand the question and I'm *running out of time*.

The time for extreme measures has come. I am in terrible pain. Susie says that I need to begin aggressive pain management if I am going to stand it.

"It": such a little word. In this case, I think "it" signifies "being alive."

I apologize in advance for what this palliative treatment modality does to the dramatic coherence of my play's last scene. It can't be helped. They have to do something. I'm in terrible pain.

Say it, Vivian. *It hurts like hell. It really does.*

[SUSIE *enters.* VIVIAN *is writhing in pain.*]

Oh, God. Oh, God.

SUSIE   Sshh. It's okay. Sshh. I paged Kelekian up here, and we'll get you some meds.

VIVIAN   Oh, God, it is so painful. So painful. So much pain. So much pain.

SUSIE   I know, I know, it's okay. Sshh. Just try and clear your mind. It's all right. We'll get you a Patient-Controlled Analgesic. It's a little pump, and you push a little button, and you decide how much medication you want. [*Importantly*] It's very simple, and it's up to you.

[KELEKIAN *storms in;* JASON *follows with chart.*]

KELEKIAN   Dr. Bearing. Susie.

SUSIE   Time for Patient-Controlled Analgesic. The pain is killing her.

KELEKIAN   Dr. Bearing, are you in pain? [KELEKIAN *holds out his hand for chart;* JASON *hands it to him. They read.*]

VIVIAN   [*Sitting up, unnoticed by the staff*]   Am I in pain? I don't believe this. Yes, I'm in goddamn pain. [*Furious*] I have a fever of 101 spiking to 104. And I have bone metastases in my pelvis and both femurs. [*Screaming*] There is cancer eating away at my goddamn bones, and I did not know there could be such pain on this earth.

   [*She flops back on the bed and cries audibly to them.*] Oh, God.

KELEKIAN [*Looking at* VIVIAN *intently*]   I want a morphine drip.

SUSIE   What about Patient-Controlled? She could be more alert—

KELEKIAN [*Teaching*]   Ordinarily, yes. But in her case, no.

SUSIE   But—

KELEKIAN [*To* SUSIE]   She's earned a rest. [*To* JASON] Morphine, ten push now, then start at ten an hour. [*To* VIVIAN] Dr. Bearing, try to relax. We're going to help you through this, don't worry. Dr. Bearing? Excellent. [*He squeezes* VIVIAN's *shoulder. They all leave.*]

VIVIAN [*Weakly, painfully, leaning on her IV pole, she moves to address the audience.*]   Hi. How are you feeling today?

   [*Silence*]

These are my last coherent lines. I'll have to leave the action to the professionals.

It came so quickly, after taking so long. Not even time for a proper conclusion.

   [VIVIAN *concentrates with all her might, and she attempts a grand summation, as if trying to conjure her own ending.*]

And Death—*capital D*—shall be no more—semicolon.
Death—*capital D*—thou shalt die—*ex-cla-mation point!*

   [*She looks down at herself, looks out at the audience, and sees that the line doesn't work. She shakes her head and exhales with resignation.*]

I'm sorry.

   [*She gets back into bed as* SUSIE *injects morphine into the IV tubing.* VIVIAN *lies down and, in a final melodramatic gesture, shuts the lids of her own eyes and folds her arms over her chest.*]

VIVIAN   I trust this will have a soporific effect.

SUSIE   Well, I don't know about that, but it sure makes you sleepy.

   [*This strikes* VIVIAN *as delightfully funny. She starts to giggle, then laughs out loud.* SUSIE *doesn't get it.*]

SUSIE   What's so funny? [VIVIAN *keeps laughing.*] What?

VIVIAN   Oh! It's that—"Soporific" means "makes you sleepy."

SUSIE   It does?

VIVIAN   Yes. [*Another fit of laughter*]

SUSIE [*Giggling*]   Well, that was pretty dumb—

VIVIAN   No! No, no! It was *funny!*

SUSIE [*Starting to catch on*]   Yeah, I guess so. [*Laughing*] In a dumb sort of way. [*This sets them both off laughing again*] I never would have gotten it. I'm glad you explained it.

VIVIAN [*Simply*]   I'm a teacher.

   [*They laugh a little together. Slowly the morphine kicks in, and* VIVIAN's *laughs become long sighs. Finally she falls asleep.* SUSIE *checks everything out, then leaves. Long silence*]

[JASON *and* SUSIE *chat as they enter to insert a catheter.*]

JASON Oh, yeah. She was a great scholar. Wrote tons of books, articles, was the head of everything. [*He checks the I&O sheet.*] Two hundred. Seventy-five. Five-twenty. Let's up the hydration. She won't be drinking anymore. See if we can keep her kidneys from fading. Yeah, I had a lot of respect for her, which is more than I can say for the *entire* biochemistry department.

SUSIE What do you want? Dextrose?

JASON Give her saline.

SUSIE Okay.

JASON She gave a hell of a lecture. No notes, not a word out of place. It was pretty impressive. A lot of students hated her, though.

SUSIE Why?

JASON Well, she wasn't exactly a cupcake.

SUSIE [*Laughing, fondly*] Well, she hasn't exactly been a cupcake here, either. [*Leaning over* VIVIAN *and talking loudly and slowly in her ear*] Now, Ms. Bearing, Jason and I are here, and we're going to insert a catheter to collect your urine. It's not going to hurt, don't you worry. [*During the conversation she inserts the catheter.*]

JASON Like she can hear you.

SUSIE It's just nice to do.

JASON Eight cycles of Hex and Vin at the full dose. Kelekian didn't think it was possible. I wish they could all get through it at full throttle. Then we could really have some data.

SUSIE She's not what I imagined. I thought somebody who studied poetry would be sort of dreamy, you know?

JASON Oh, not the way she did it. It felt more like boot camp than English class. This guy John Donne was incredibly intense. Like your whole brain had to be in knots before you could get it.

SUSIE He made it hard on purpose?

JASON Well, it has to do with the subject. The Holy Sonnets we worked on most, they were mostly about Salvation Anxiety. That's a term I made up in one of my papers, but I think it fits pretty well. Salvation Anxiety. You're this brilliant guy, I mean, brilliant—this guy makes Shakespeare sound like a Hallmark card. And you know you're a sinner. And there's this promise of salvation, the whole religious thing. But you just can't deal with it.

SUSIE How come?

JASON It just doesn't stand up to scrutiny. But you can't face life without it either. So you write these screwed-up sonnets. Everything is brilliantly convoluted. Really tricky stuff. Bouncing off the walls. Like a game, to make the puzzle so complicated.

[*The catheter is inserted.* SUSIE *puts things away.*]

SUSIE But what happens in the end?

JASON End of what?

SUSIE To John Donne. Does he ever get it?

JASON Get what?

SUSIE His Salvation Anxiety. Does he ever understand?

JASON Oh, no way. The puzzle takes over. You're not even trying to solve it anymore. Fascinating, really. Great training for lab research. Looking at things in increasing levels of complexity.

SUSIE Until what?

JASON What do you mean?

SUSIE Where does it end? Don't you get to solve the puzzle?

JASON Nah. When it comes right down to it, research is just trying to quantify the complications of the puzzle.

SUSIE But you *help* people! You save lives and stuff.

JASON Oh, yeah, I save some guy's life, and then the poor slob gets hit by a bus!

SUSIE [*Confused*] Yeah, I guess so. I just don't think of it that way. Guess you can tell I never took a class in poetry.

JASON Listen, if there's one thing we learned in Seventeenth-Century Poetry, it's that you can forget about that sentimental stuff. *Enzyme Kinetics* was more poetic than Bearing's class. Besides, you can't think about that *meaning-of-life* garbage all the time or you'd go nuts.

SUSIE Do you believe in it?

JASON In what?

SUSIE Umm. I don't know, the meaning-of-life garbage. [*She laughs a little.*]

JASON What do they *teach* you in nursing school? [*Checking* VIVIAN'S *pulse*] She's out of it. Shouldn't be too long. You done here?

SUSIE Yeah, I'll just . . . tidy up.

JASON See ya. [*He leaves.*]

SUSIE Bye, Jace. [*She thinks for a minute, then carefully rubs baby oil on* VIVIAN'S *hands. She checks the catheter, then leaves.*]

[*Professor* E. M. ASHFORD, *now eighty, enters.*]

E.M. Vivian? Vivian? It's Evelyn. Vivian?

VIVIAN [*Waking, slurred*] Oh, God. [*Surprised*] Professor Ashford. Oh, God.

E.M. I'm in town visiting my great-grandson, who is celebrating his fifth birthday. I went to see you at your office, and they directed me here. [*She lays her jacket, scarf, and parcel on the bed.*] I have been walking all over town. I had forgotten how early it gets chilly here.

VIVIAN [*Weakly*] I feel so bad.

E.M. I know you do. I can see. [VIVIAN *cries.*] Oh, dear, there, there. There, there. [VIVIAN *cries more, letting the tears flow.*] Vivian, Vivian.

[E.M. *looks toward the hall, then furtively slips off her shoes and swings up on the bed. She puts her arm around* VIVIAN.] There, there. There, there, Vivian. [*Silence*]

It's a windy day. [*Silence*]

Don't worry, dear. [*Silence*]

Let's see. Shall I recite to you? Would you like that? I'll recite something by Donne.

VIVIAN [*Moaning*] Nooooooo.

E.M. Very well. [*Silence*] Hmmm. [*Silence*] Little Jeffrey is very sweet. Gets into everything.

[*Silence.* E.M. *takes a children's book out of the paper bag and begins reading.* VIVIAN *nestles in, drifting in and out of sleep.*]

Let's see. *The Runaway Bunny.* By Margaret Wise Brown. Pictures by Clement Hurd. Copyright 1942. First Harper Trophy Edition, 1972.
Now then.
Once there was a little bunny who wanted to run away.
So he said to his mother, "I am running away."
"If you run away," said his mother, "I will run after you. For you are my little bunny."
"If you run after me," said the little bunny, "I will become a fish in a trout stream and I will swim away from you."
"If you become a fish in a trout stream," said his mother, "I will become a fisherman and I will fish for you."
[*Thinking out loud*] Look at that. A little allegory of the soul. No matter where it hides, God will find it. See, Vivian?

VIVIAN [*Moaning*]   Uhhhhhh.

E.M.
"If you become a fisherman," said the little bunny, "I will be a bird and fly away from you."
"If you become a bird and fly away from me," said his mother, "I will be a tree that you come home to."
[*To herself*] Very clever.
"Shucks," said the little bunny, "I might just as well stay where I am and be your little bunny."
And so he did.
"Have a carrot," said the mother bunny.
[*To herself*] Wonderful.
  [VIVIAN *is now fast asleep.* E.M. *slowly gets down and gathers her things. She leans over and kisses her.*]
It's time to go. And flights of angels sing thee to thy rest.[5] [*She leaves.*]
  [JASON *strides in and goes directly to the I&O sheet without looking at* VIVIAN.]

JASON   Professor Bearing. How are you feeling today? Three p.m. IV hydration totals. Two thousand in. Thirty out. Uh-oh. That's it. Kidneys gone.
  [*He looks at* VIVIAN.] Professor Bearing? Highly unresponsive. Wait a second—[*Puts his head down to her mouth and chest to listen for heartbeat and breathing*] Wait a sec—Jesus Christ! [*Yelling*] CALL A CODE!
  [JASON *throws down the chart, dives over the bed, and lies on top of her body as he reaches for the phone and punches in the numbers.*]
[*To himself*] Code: 4-5-7-5. [*To operator*] Code Blue, room 707. Code Blue, room 707. Dr. Posner—P-O-S-N-E-R. Hurry up!
  [*He throws down the phone and lowers the head of the bed.*]
Come on, come on, COME ON.
  [*He begins CPR, kneeling over* VIVIAN, *alternately pounding frantically and giving mouth-to-mouth resuscitation. Over the loudspeaker in the hall, a droning voice repeats* "Code Blue, room 707. Code Blue, room 707."]
One! Two! Three! Four! Five! [*He breathes in her mouth.*]
  [SUSIE, *hearing the announcement, runs into the room.*]

SUSIE   WHAT ARE YOU DOING?

---

5. Shakespeare's *Hamlet* 5.2.304 (Horatio's farewell to the dead Hamlet).

JASON   A GODDAMN CODE. GET OVER HERE!
SUSIE   She's DNR! [*She grabs him.*]
JASON [*He pushes her away.*]   She's Research!
SUSIE   She's NO CODE!
>[SUSIE *grabs* JASON *and hurls him off the bed.*]

JASON   Ooowww! Goddamnit, Susie!
SUSIE   She's no code!
JASON   Aaargh!
SUSIE   Kelekian put the order in—you saw it! You were right there, Jason! Oh, God, the code! [*She runs to the phone. He struggles to stand.*] 4-5-7-5.
>[*The* CODE TEAM *swoops in. Everything changes. Frenzy takes over. They knock* SUSIE *out of the way with their equipment.*]

SUSIE [*At the phone*]   Cancel code, room 707. Sue Monahan, primary nurse. Cancel code. Dr. Posner is here.
JASON [*In agony*]   Oh, God.
CODE TEAM
>—Get out of the way!
>—Unit staff out!
>—Get the board!
>—Over here!

>[*They throw* VIVIAN's *body up at the waist and stick a board underneath for CPR. In a whirlwind of sterile packaging and barked commands, one team member attaches a respirator, one begins CPR, and one prepares the defibrillator.* SUSIE *and* JASON *try to stop them but are pushed away. The loudspeaker in the hall announces* "Cancel code, room 707. Cancel code, room 707."]

CODE TEAM
>—Bicarb amp!
>—I got it! [*To* SUSIE] Get out!
>—One, two, three, four, five!
>—Get ready to shock! [*To* JASON] Move it!

SUSIE [*Running to each person, yelling*]   STOP! Patient is DNR!
JASON [*At the same time, to the* CODE TEAM]   No, no! Stop doing this. STOP!
CODE TEAM
>—Keep it going!
>—What do you get?
>—Bicarb amp!
>—No pulse!

SUSIE   She's NO CODE! Order was given—[*She dives for the chart and holds it up as she cries out*] Look! Look at this! DO NOT RESUSCITATE. KELEKIAN.
CODE TEAM [*As they administer electric shock,* VIVIAN's *body arches and bounces back down.*]
>—Almost ready!
>—Hit her!
>—CLEAR!
>—Pulse? Pulse?

JASON [*Howling*]   I MADE A MISTAKE!
>[*Pause. The* CODE TEAM *looks at him. He collapses on the floor.*]

SUSIE   No code! Patient is no code.

CODE TEAM HEAD   Who the hell are you?
SUSIE   Sue Monahan, primary nurse.
CODE TEAM HEAD   Let me see the goddamn chart. CHART!
CODE TEAM [*Slowing down*]
    —What's going on?
    —Should we stop?
    —What's it say?
SUSIE [*Pushing them away from the bed*]   Patient is no code. Get away from her!

[SUSIE *lifts the blanket.* VIVIAN *steps out of the bed.*]

CODE TEAM HEAD: [*Reading*] Do Not Resuscitate. Kelekian. Shit.

She walks away from the scene, toward a little light.
She is now attentive and eager, moving slowly toward the light.

[*The* CODE TEAM *stops working.*]

JASON: [*Whispering*] Oh, God.

She takes off her cap and lets it drop.

CODE TEAM HEAD: Order was put in yesterday.

She slips off her bracelet.

CODE TEAM:
    —It's a doctor fuck-up.
    —What is he, a resident?
She loosens the ties and the top gown slides to the floor. She lets the second gown fall.
    —Got us up here on a DNR.
    —Called a code on a no-code.

JASON: Oh, God.

The instant she is naked, and beautiful, reaching for the light—

[*The bedside scene fades.*]

Lights out.]

1999

JACKIE KAY
b. 1961

The daughter of a Scottish mother and a Nigerian father, Jackie Kay was adopted at birth by a white Glasgow couple—working-class and communist—who raised her with a fierce love that she chronicles in *The Adoption Papers* (1991), her first collection of poems. Not surprisingly, however, she has admitted to an interviewer for the *Guardian* that she has an "obsession with identity [which] comes from being adopted. 'You always ask, "Would I have been like this, if I had been brought up with my original parents?" You ask that of yourself, and then you ask that of people whom you see in different situations. What makes them who they are?" More specifically, in such poems as "In My Country" and "Hottentot Venus," Kay explores interracial tensions with subtlety, passion, and distinctive authority. In addition, as the lesbian mother of a son, Matthew (and for the past decade the partner of fellow British poet Carol Ann Duffy), she examines issues of gender and sexuality with comparable authority. "I'm always openly gay," she told the same *Guardian* interviewer, while noting ruefully that "It's not easy," because "shockingly and surprisingly, we don't live in a society where it's easy to be a gay mum and pick up your kids from school, or have two of you at parents' night." At the same time, she continued, still musing on the ironies of identity, "yes, I'm black, yes, I'm gay, but does that define everything I write? No, it doesn't."

After studying English at the University of Stirling and giving birth to her son, Kay moved to London, where she worked at a range of jobs, among them moving hospital patients and cleaning. Her first writings were for the stage: two of her plays were sponsored by the London-based theater group Gay Sweatshop and one was commissioned by the Theatre of Black Women. More recent volumes of verse include *Other Lovers* (1993) and *Off Colour* (1998). She has also produced children's books, television scripts, a collection of short fiction, and several novels, most notably *Trumpet* (1998), a work inspired by the tale of the transvestite American jazz pianist and saxophonist Billy Tipton, who was born Dorothy Lucille Tipton but lived most of her life as a male performer who married five times and was the adoptive father of three sons.

Interestingly, in her version of Tipton's story, Kay transforms the white musician into a black artist, even while in discussing the book she focuses on differences between racial issues in the United States and Britain. "I'm aware of a great tradition of black American writers, James Baldwin, Ralph Ellison, Toni Morrison, John Edgar Wideman," she explains, but adds: "I'm also aware that America as a society is more driven and defined by race than perhaps the UK is. So here is a book about a black jazz musician whose central story is not about race particularly." Among other variables of identity, however, the specifically British particularities of race and gender become thematically crucial, if not central, in much of Kay's writing.

In My Country

walking by the waters
down where an honest river
shakes hands with the sea,
a woman passed round me
5   in a slow watchful circle,
as if I were a superstition;

or the worst dregs of her imagination,
so when she finally spoke
her words spliced into bars
10   of an old wheel. A segment of air.
Where do you come from?
'Here,' I said, 'Here. These parts.'

1991

Finger

What is it made of? Guilt. Blame. Sometimes,
as if pain demands I point a finger—
one of the terminal members of my hand.

This instrument; this fine tune. Listen.
5 I know which notes will strike a chord.
I use my fingers as a measure.

Like the pointed sheaths of a reaping machine;
the bit the knife comes through to cut corn.[1]
Simply: flesh, blood, marrow, bone?

10 There is no room for conversation; no other questions
to ask. Nothing to do, but say: That was wrong.
How big was the slave's room?

Have you been to the plantation? Tobacco. Sugar.
The quarters—the temperature of a hot house. Plants.
15 The placing of plants in a soil so they may grow.

Breeding in the dead heat of a tiny room for the master.
Or him groping you as your man stands by.
And him fingering the money.

And me, a songster, marking music, the strange colour
20 I will play soon in the wooden holes. Plantation.
The skin growing on trees. Listen.

Watch the way my fingers move across your temple.
Answer me. They say it doesn't exist anymore.
This is another century. Take my fingerprint.

1998

Hottentot Venus[1]

They made a plaster cast of my corpse
took wax moulds of my genitals and anus,
my famous anomalous buttocks
till the last sigh in me left my body.

---

1. Wheat.
1. Saartjie Baartman (1789–1815), the young Khoisan woman who was taken to Europe in 1810 and displayed because of her steatopygia, or large buttocks (which viewers were allowed to touch for extra payment), thought to be signs of her "primitivism." In London she was exhibited in a metal cage; and after she died in Paris, her preserved brain, genitalia, and skeleton were exhibited in the Musée de l'Homme (Museum of Mankind) until 1974. Her remains were returned to the land of her birth, in what is now South Africa, in 2002. "Hottentot": an offensive name for the Khoisan people devised by Afrikaaners, to whom the Khoisan speech sounded like stammering. "Venus": in Roman mythology, the goddess of love.

>   I made a noise I never heard before
>   when the man with the glinting knife
>   whispered 'posterity' and dissected my brain.
>   Not so long ago people paid handsomely
>
>   to see my rump, my apron,[2] my non-European genitals.
> 10 Two shillings. I paced my cage, backwards,
>   an orang outang,[3] forwards, a beast on a chain.
>   Men said the size of my lips were unnatural.
>
>   You can see the moulds of my genitals
>   at the Musée de l'Homme—Paris;
> 15 the rest of me is here now, Natural History Museum,
>   my brains, my woolly hair, my skeleton.
>
>   Some things I will never forget
>   no matter how I am divided up:
>   the look on a white lady's face
> 20 when she poked her parasol into my privates.
>
>   Her gloved hands. Her small stone eyes.
>   Her English squeal of surprise at my size.
>   My sigh is black. My heart is black.
>   My walk is black. My hide, my flanks. My secret.
>
> 25 My brain is the size of a black woman's brain.
>   When the gentleman prodded me with his cane,
>   he wanted to discover black tears falling
>   from my dark eyes. I tell no lies.
>
>   Then he called my tears crocodile tears.
> 30 What did he call my lips? Rubber? Blubber?
>   My country is a dream now. Or maybe it did not exist.
>   When they called me in, three men in suits,
>
>   They asked me in my own bush tongue
>   if I wanted to be exhibited in this fashion.[4]
> 35 I said the English words I'd heard them say often.
>   Money. Freedom. My Boer keeper smiled.
>
>   He could still walk me, dance me
>   hold his stick to me. He promised me riches.
>   Bring in the literati, the artists, the famous.
> 40 Let them view the buttocks of the Hottentot Venus.

---

2. Elongated inner lips of the female genitals, which hung down several inches and thus appeared to be a separate curtain of flesh.
3. Literally, "forest man" (Malay).
4. British abolitionists unsuccessfully petitioned the courts for her release; questioned in Dutch, she stated that she was voluntarily participating and understood that she was guaranteed half the profits.

My heart inside my cage pounded like a single drum.
For eleven hours a day people came to see Saartjie Baartman.
I heard their laughter like money shaking in a tin.
On the wall I was framed: ugly, deformed, a cartoon.[5]

45 I was wearing a thin skin coloured dress.
Hottentot Venus. Don't miss the Hottentot.
Now, what name have I got?
Sarah Bateman. Like an English woman. A great actress.[6]

1998

Paw Broon on the Starr Report[1]

Right Maw, hen,[2]
if that man can
get it wey a wuman
that's no his wife,
5 I'm hauving it wey you.
I've aye been loyal.
There's no use in you
saying 'Naw Paw' again,
Christ, the President
10 gets it, so so kin I.
Get yir heid doon wuman,
an hae a guid sook.[3]

Christ, wait a minite.
15 I'm no a lollipop.
Dinny lick gingerly,
it's affy tickly,
gie me a guid sook! C'mon C'mon.
Haud on! Let me
position masell.
20 Wisnae the President
staunding agin a wa'
or wis it the lavvy[4] door?
Wait till ma back's pressed
up agin it. There. That's perfect.
25 Whit the Hell's wrang noo?

1998

---

5. Baartman was the subject of many drawings and cartoons, such as the French print of 1812 reproduced in Stephen Jay Gould's *The Flamingo's Smile* (1985), p. 304.
6. I.e., also like the great French actress Sarah Bernhardt (1844–1923).
1. *The Official Report of the Independent Counsel's Investigation of the President* (1998)—that is, the investigation led by Kenneth Starr of President Bill Clinton's relationship with Monica Lewinsky; it includes Lewinsky's testimony that she performed oral sex on the president in the bathroom outside the Oval Office study.
2. An affectionate way of addressing a woman (Scottish).
3. A good suck.
4. I.e., lavatory.

Big Milk

The baby wasn't really a baby anymore except in the mind of the mother, my lover. She was two years old this wet summer and already she could talk buckets. She even had language for milk. Big Milk and Tiny Milk. One day I saw her pat my lover's breasts in a slightly patronizing fashion and say, 'Silly, gentle milk.' Another day we passed a goat with big bells round its neck in a small village near the Fens. The light was strange, mysterious. The goat looked like a dream in the dark light. The baby said, 'Look, Big Milk, Look, there's a goat!' The baby only ever asked Big Milk to look at things. Tiny Milk never got a look in.

I never noticed that my lover's breasts were lopsided until the baby started naming them separately. The baby was no mug.[1] The left breast was enormous. The right one small and slightly cowed in the presence of a great twin. Big Milk. I keep saying the words to myself. What I'd give for Big Milk now. One long suck. I was never that bothered about breasts before she had the baby. I wasn't interested in my own breasts or my lover's. I'd have the odd fondle, but that was it. Now, I could devour them. I could spend hours and hours worshipping and sucking and pinching. But I'm not allowed. My lover tells me her breasts are milk machines only for the baby. 'No,' she says firmly, 'They are out of bounds.' My lover says I should understand. 'You are worse than a man,' she tells me. A man would understand, she says. A man would defer. I'm not convinced. A man would be more jealous than I am. Two years. Two years is a long time to go without a single stroke. I look over her shoulder at the baby pulling the long red nipple of Big Milk back and forth.

At night I lie in bed next to the pair of them sleeping like family. The mother's arms flung out like a drowned bird. The baby suckling like a tiny pig. The baby isn't even aware that she drinks warm milk all night long. She is in the blissful world of oblivion. Limbs all soft and gone. Full of my own raging insomnia, I test the baby's hand. The small fat hand lands back down on the duvet[2] with a plump. She doesn't even stir. I try my lover's hand. She can tell things in her sleep. She knows the difference between the baby and me. In her sleep, she pulls away, irritated. I lie next to the sleeping mother and baby and feel totally irreligious. They are a painting. I could rip the canvas. I get up and open the curtains slightly. Nobody stirs. I take a peek at the moon. It looks big and vain, as if it's saying there is only one of me, buster, there's plenty of you suckers out there staring at me. It is a canny moon tonight, secretive. I piss the loudest piss I can manage. I pour a glass of water. Then I return to bed next to the sleeping mother and daughter. The baby is still suckling away ferociously, her small lips going like the hammers. It is beyond belief. How many pints is that she's downed in the one night. No wonder the lover is drained. The baby is taking everything. Nutrients. Vitamins. The lot. She buys herself bottles and bottles of vitamins but she doesn't realize that it is pointless; the baby has got her. The baby has moved in to occupy her, awake or asleep, night or day. My lover is a saint, pale, exhausted. She is drained dry. The hair is dry. Her hair used to gleam.

I'm not bothered about her hair. I am not bothered about not going out anymore, anywhere. The pictures, pubs, restaurants, the houses of friends.

---

1. Fool. 2. Comforter.

I don't care that I don't have friends anymore. Friends without babies are carrying on with their ridiculous, meaningless lives, pretending their silly meetings, their silly movies, their uptight nouvelle cuisine meals matter. Getting a haircut at Toni and Guy to cheer themselves up. Or spending a whole sad summer slimming. Or living for the two therapy hours per week. Getting up at six to see a shrink at seven. That's what they are up to. A few of them still bang away at ideas that matter to them. But even they sound tired when they talk about politics. And they always say something shocking to surprise me, or themselves. I don't know which. I don't see any of them anymore.

What do I see? I see the baby mostly. I see her more than I see my lover. I stare into her small face and see her astonishing beauty the way my lover sees it. The big eyes that are a strange green colour. The lavish eyelashes. The tiny perfect nose. The cartoon eyebrows. The perfect baby-soft skin. The lush little lips. She's a picture. No doubt about it. My lover used to tell me that I had beautiful eyes. I'd vainly picture my own eyes when she paid me such compliments. I'd see the deep rich chocolate-brown melt before me. The long black lashes. But my eyes are not the subject these days. Or the object, come to think of it. My eyes are just for myself. I watch mother and daughter sleeping peaceably in the dark. Dreaming of each other, probably. There are many nights I spend like this, watching. I haven't made up my mind yet what to do with all my watching. I am sure it will come to some use. The baby dribbles and the lover dribbles. The light outside has begun. I've come round again. The birds are at it. The baby has the power. It is the plain stark truth of the matter. I can see it as I watch the two of them. Tiny puffs of power blow out of the baby's mouth.

She transforms the adults around her to suit herself. Many of the adults I know are now becoming babified. They talk a baby language to each other. They like the same food. They watch *Teletubbies*. They read Harry Potter.[3] They even go to bed at the same time as the baby; and if they have a good relationship they might manage whispering in the dark. Very little fucking. Very little. I'm trying to console myself here. It's another day.

In the morning the baby always says hello to me before my lover gets a word in. To be fair, the baby has the nicest hello in the whole world. She says it like she is showering you with bluebells. You actually feel cared for when the baby talks to you. I can see the seduction. I know why my lover is seduced. That and having her very own likeness staring back at her with those strange green eyes. I can never imagine having such a likeness. I tell myself it must be quite creepy going about the place with a tiny double. A wee doppelgänger. It's bound to unsettle you a bit, when you are washing your hair, to look into the mirror and for one moment see a tiny toddler staring back at you. It can't be pleasant.

The feeding itself isn't pleasant either. Not when the baby has teeth. I've heard my lover howl in agony on more than one occasion when the baby has sunk her sharp little milk teeth into Big Milk. A woman is not free till her breasts are her own again. Of this I am certain. I am more certain of this than a woman's right to vote or to choose. As long as her breasts are tied to her wean[4] she might as well be in chains. She can't get out. Not for long.

---

3. One of the series of novels (first appearing in 1997) by the British author J. K. Rowling. "*Teletubbies*": a British television program aimed at babies and toddlers (produced 1997–2001).
4. Child.

She rushes home with her breasts heavy and hurting. Once we went out for a two-hour-and-twenty-minute anniversary meal. When we got home my lover teemed up the stairs and hung over the bathroom sink. The milk spilled and spilled. She could have shot me with it there was so much. Big gun milk. It was shocking. She swung round and caught me staring, appalled. She looked proud of the quantities. Said she could have filled a lot of bottles, fed a lot of hungry babies with that.

I tried to imagine the state of my life with my lover feeding hundreds of tiny babies. I pictured it for a ghastly moment: our new super king-size bed invaded by babies from all over the world. My lover lying in her white cotton nightie. The buttons open. Big Milk and Tiny Milk both being utilized for a change. Tiny Milk in her element—so full of self-importance that for a second Tiny Milk has bloated into the next cup size. The next time she mentioned having enough milk to feed an army, I told her she had quite enough on her hands. And she laughed sympathetically and said my name quite lovingly. I was appeased for a moment until the baby piped up with a new word. 'Did you hear that?' she said, breathless. 'That's the first time she's ever said that. Isn't that amazing?'

'It is,' I said, disgusted at myself, her and the baby all in one fell swoop. 'It's totally amazing—especially for her age,' I added slyly. 'For her age, it is pure genius.'

She plucked the baby up and landed a smacker on her smug baby cheek. The baby patted Big Milk again and said, 'Funny, funny, Milk. Oh look, Mummy, Milk shy.' The baby's fat little hand was trying to pull the breast out again. I left the two of them to it on the landing outside the toilet.

Even when I go up to my attic I can still hear them down below. Giggling and laughing, singing and dancing together. 'If you go down to the woods today, you're in for a big surprise.'[5] The rain chaps on my tiny attic windows. Big Milk is having a ball. I climb down the steep stairs to watch some more. Daytime watching is different from night-time. Tiny details light up. The baby's small hands are placed protectively on the soft full breasts. The mouth around the nipple. Sometimes she doesn't drink. She just lies half asleep, contemplating milk or dreaming milk. It makes me wonder how I survived. I was never breastfed, myself. My mother spoon-fed me for two weeks then left. I never saw her again. Perhaps I've been dreaming of her breasts all my life. Maybe that's what rankles with the baby taking Big Milk for granted. When her mouth expectantly opens there is no question that the nipple won't go in. No question. Every soft, open request is answered. I try and imagine myself as a tiny baby, soft black curls on my head, big brown eyes. Skin a different colour from my mother's. I imagine myself lying across my mother's white breast, my small brown face suffocating in the pure joy of warm, sweet milk. The smell of it, recognizing the tender smell of it. I imagine my life if she had kept me. I would have been a hairdresser if I hadn't been adopted. I'm quite sure. I would have washed the dandruff off many an old woman's head. I would have administered perms to give them the illusion of their hair forty years before. I would have specialized in tints and dyes, in conditioners

---

5. The beginning of the song "The Teddy Bears' Picnic" (music written in 1907 by the American composer John Bratton, with words added in 1932 by the Irish songwriter Jimmy Kennedy).

that give full body to the hair. I would probably have never thought about milk. The lack of it. Or the need of it.

I lie in the dark with the rain playing soft jazz on the windowpane of our bedroom. I say our bedroom, but it is not our bedroom any more. Now teddy bears and nappies[6] and ointment and wooden toys and baby clothes can be found strewn all over the floor. I lie in the dark and remember what it was like when I had my lover all to myself. When she slept in my arms and not the baby's. When she woke up in the night to pull me closer. When she muttered things into my sleeping back. I lie awake and remember all the different places my lover and I had sex. All the different ways, when we had our own private language. The baby has monopolized language. Nothing I say can ever sound so interesting, so original. The baby has converted me into a bland, boring, possessive lover who doesn't know her arse from her elbow. There are bits of my body that I can only remember in the dark. They are not touched. The dawn is stark and obvious. I make my decision. I can't help it. It is the only possible thing I can do under the circumstances.

Don't doubt I love my lover and I love her baby. I love their likeness. Their cheeks and eyes. The way their hair moves from their crown to scatter over their whole head in exactly the same place. Their identical ears. I love both of them. I love the baby because she is kind. She would never hurt anybody. She is gentle, silly. But love is not enough for me this time. I get up, get dressed and go outside with my car keys in my hand. I close my front door quietly behind me. My breath in my mouth. I take the M61[7] towards Preston. I drive past four junction numbers in the bleached morning. There are few cars on the road. I stop at a service station and drink a black coffee with two sugars. I smoke two cigarettes that taste disgusting because it is too early. I don't smoke in the day usually. I smoke at night. Day and night have rolled into one. The baby's seat in the back is empty. The passenger seat has a map on it. There is no lover to read the map, to tell me where to go. There is no lover to pass me an apple. There is just me and the car and the big sky, flushed with the morning. I put on a tape and play some music. I am far north now. Going further. I am nearly at the Scottish border. I feel a strange exhilaration. I know my lover and her baby are still sleeping, totally unaware of my absence. As I drive on past the wet fields of morning, I feel certain that there is not a single person in the world who truly cares about me. Except perhaps my mother. I have finally found out where she lives up north. Right at the top of the country in a tiny village, in a rose cottage. She lives in the kind of village where people still notice a stranger's car. If I arrive in the middle of the day, the villagers will all come out and stare at my car and me. They will walk right round my car in an admiring circle. Someone might offer to park it for me.

I will arrive in daytime. When I knock at the door of Rose Cottage, my mother will answer. She will know instantly, from the colour of my skin, that I am her lost daughter. Her abandoned daughter. I have no idea what she will say. It doesn't matter. It doesn't matter if she slams the door in my face, just as long as I can get one long look at her breasts. Just as long as I can imagine what my life would have been like if I had sucked on those breasts

---

6. Diapers.
7. A major road in England, 20 miles long; it ends in the west just south of Preston, which is about 75 miles south of Scotland.

for two solid years. If she slams the door and tells me she doesn't want to know me, it will pierce me, it will hurt. But I will not create a scene in a Highland town. I will go to the village shop and buy something to eat. Then I will ask where the nearest hair salon is. I will drive there directly where a sign on the window will read, ASSISTANT WANTED. I will take up my old life as a hairdresser. When I say my old life, I mean the life I could have, perhaps even should have, led. When I take up my old life, old words will come out of my mouth. Words that local people will understand. Some of them might ask me how I came to know them. When they do, I will be ready with my answer. I will say I learned them with my mother's milk.

I am off the M6 now and on the A74.[8] I read somewhere that the A74 is the most dangerous road in the country. Something new in me this morning welcomes the danger. Something in me wants to die before I meet my mother. When I think about it, I realize that I have always wanted to die. That all my life, I have dreamed longingly of death. Perhaps it was because she left. Perhaps losing a mother abruptly like that is too much for an unsuspecting baby to bear. I know now this minute, zooming up the A74 at 110 miles per hour, that I have wanted to die from the second she left me. I wonder what she did with the milk in her breasts, how long it took before it dried up, whether or not she had to wear breast pads to hide the leaking milk. I wonder if her secret has burned inside her Catholic heart for years.

I can only give her the one chance. Only the one. I will knock and I will ask her to let me in. But if she doesn't want me, I won't give her another chance. I won't give anyone another chance. It has been one long dance with death. I have my headlights on even though there is plenty of daylight. I have them on full beam to warn other cars that I am a fast bastard and they had better get out of my way. I play my music softly. The blue light on my dashboard is lit up. Is there anyone out there behind or before me on the A74 who has ever felt like this? I realize that I am possibly quite mad. I realize that the baby has done it to me. It is not the baby's fault or her mother's. They can't help being ordinary. Being flesh and blood. The world is full of people who are separated from their families. They could all be on the A74 right now, speeding forwards to trace the old bloodline. It is like a song line. What would have been my mother's favourite song? 'Ae Fond Kiss'? 'Ae fond kiss and then we sever.'[9] There is much to discover. I picture the faces of all the other manic adopted people, their anonymous hands clutched to the steering wheel in search of themselves. Their eyes are all intense. I have never met an adopted person who does not have intense eyes. But they offer no comfort. This is all mine.

Exhausted, I arrive in the village at three o'clock. My mouth is dry, furry. It is a very long time since I have slept. I spot a vacancy sign outside a place called the Tayvallich Inn. It has four rooms, three taken. The woman shows me the room and I tell her I'll take it. It is not a particularly pleasant room, but that doesn't matter. There is no view. All I can see from the window is other parts of the inn. I close the curtains. The room has little light anyway. I decide to go and visit my mother tomorrow after sleep. When I get into the

---

8. A road in Scotland, running from Gretna at the English border northeast to Glasgow. "M6": the longest motorway in the United Kingdom; from Preston, it runs to the north of Carlisle, by the Scottish border.

9. The first line of a song (1791) by the Scottish poet Robert Burns.

small room with the hard bed and the nylon sheets, I weep for the unfairness of it all. A picture of the baby at home, in our Egyptian cotton sheets suckling away and smiling in her sleep flashes before me. My lover's open nightie. It occurs to me that I haven't actually minded all my life. My mother shipping me out never bothered me. I was happy with the mother who raised me, who fed me milk from the dairy and Scot's porridge oats and plumped my pillows at night. I was never bothered at all until the baby arrived. Until the baby came I never gave any of it a moment's thought. I realize now in room four of Tayvallich Inn under the pink nylon sheets that the baby has engineered this whole trip. The baby wanted me to go away. She wanted her mother all to herself in our big bed. Of late, she's even started saying, 'Go away!' It is perfectly obvious to me now. The one thing the baby doesn't lack is cunning. I turn the light on and stare at the silly brown and cream kettle, the tiny wicker basket containing two sachets of Nescafé, two tea bags, two bags of sugar and two plastic thimbles of milk. I open one thimble and then another with my thumbnail. They are the size of large nipples. I suck the milk out of the plastic thimbles. The false milk coats my tongue. I am not satisfied. Not at all. I crouch down to look into the mirror above the dressing table. I am very pale, very peely-wally.[1] Big dark circles under my eyes. I do not look my best for my mother. But why should that matter? A mother should love her child unconditionally. My hair needs combing. But I have brought nothing with me. I did not pack a change of clothes. None of it matters.

I pass the nosy inn woman in the hall. She asks me if I need anything. I say, 'Yes, actually, I need a mother.' The woman laughs nervously, unpleasantly, and asks me if I'll be having the full Scottish breakfast[2] in the morning. I tell her I'm just not sure what will be happening. She hesitates for a moment and I hesitate too. Before she scurries off to tell her husband, I notice her eyes are the colour of strong tea. I open the door that now says NO VACANCIES and head for Rose Cottage. I can't wait for tomorrow, I must go today. I must find her today. My heart is in my mouth. I could do it with my eyes shut. I feel my feet instinctively head in the right direction. It is tea-time. My mother will be having her tea. Perhaps she will be watching the news. My feet barely touch the ground. The air is tart and fresh in my face. Perhaps some of my colour will return to my cheeks before my mother opens her front door. Will she tilt her head to the side gently when she looks at me? Following my nose miraculously works. There in front of me is a small stone cottage. Outside the roses are in bloom. There is a wonderful yellow tea-rose bush. I bend to sniff one of the flowers. I feel the impossible softness of the rose petals crush against my nose. I sink towards the sweet, trusting scent. I always knew she would like yellow roses. I stare at the front door. It is painted plain white. Standing quietly next to the front door are two bottles of milk. I open the silver lid of one of them and drink, knocking it back on the doorstep. It is sour. It is lumpy. I test the other one. It is sour as well. A trickle of thin sour milk pours through the thick stuff. I look into my mother's house through the letterbox. It is dark in there. I can't see a single thing.

1998

---

1. Pale, sickly.
2. I.e., eggs, at least two kinds of meat, potatoes, grilled tomatoes, toast, oatmeal, and possibly sautéed mushrooms and baked beans.

JHUMPA LAHIRI
b. 1967

The first book Jhumpa Lahiri published, the short story collection *Interpreter of Maladies*, won the Pulitzer Prize for fiction in 2000 as well as an impressive array of other honors. At thirty-three years of age, when the volume was immediately translated into more than twenty languages and became an instantaneous best seller, she had already been judged by *The New Yorker* to be "one of the 20 best writers under the age of 40." As her book's title suggests, many of the nine tales address communication difficulties that afflict people negotiating between quite distinct linguistic, social, and geographical worlds. That those worlds tend to be American and Indian reflects Lahiri's origins, for she was born in London, the daughter of Bengali parents, but raised in Rhode Island. Her father worked as a librarian, her mother as a teacher. After majoring in English literature at Barnard College, Lahiri received two M.A. degrees, in literature and creative writing, as well as a Ph.D. in Renaissance studies from Boston University. Her first novel, *The Namesake* (2003), focuses on a family that moves from Calcutta to Cambridge, Massachusetts, where a son's birth—and the necessity to name him—crystallizes all of the problems that first- and second-generation Indian immigrants experience as they navigate between sometimes incompatible customs and values. Although cross-cultural or transnational concerns inflect much of Lahiri's work, "A Temporary Matter" typifies her ability to touch on poignant and universal events—here the sadness of a stillbirth—that divide but then curiously also hold out the promise of uniting people encapsulated in their separate sorrows.

A Temporary Matter

The notice informed them that it was a temporary matter: for five days their electricity would be cut off for one hour, beginning at eight P.M. A line had gone down in the last snowstorm, and the repairmen were going to take advantage of the milder evenings to set it right. The work would affect only the houses on the quiet tree-lined street, within walking distance of a row of brick-faced stores and a trolley stop, where Shoba and Shukumar had lived for three years.

"It's good of them to warn us," Shoba conceded after reading the notice aloud, more for her own benefit than Shukumar's. She let the strap of her leather satchel, plump with files, slip from her shoulders, and left it in the hallway as she walked into the kitchen. She wore a navy blue poplin raincoat over gray sweatpants and white sneakers, looking, at thirty-three, like the type of woman she'd once claimed she would never resemble.

She'd come from the gym. Her cranberry lipstick was visible only on the outer reaches of her mouth, and her eyeliner had left charcoal patches beneath her lower lashes. She used to look this way sometimes, Shukumar thought, on mornings after a party or a night at a bar, when she'd been too lazy to wash her face, too eager to collapse into his arms. She dropped a sheaf of mail on the table without a glance. Her eyes were still fixed on the notice in her other hand. "But they should do this sort of thing during the day."

"When I'm here, you mean," Shukumar said. He put a glass lid on a pot of lamb, adjusting it so only the slightest bit of steam could escape. Since January he'd been working at home, trying to complete the final chapters of his dissertation on agrarian revolts in India. "When do the repairs start?"

"It says March nineteenth. Is today the nineteenth?" Shoba walked over to the framed corkboard that hung on the wall by the fridge, bare except for a calendar of William Morris[1] wallpaper patterns. She looked at it as if for the first time, studying the wallpaper pattern carefully on the top half before allowing her eyes to fall to the numbered grid on the bottom. A friend had sent the calendar in the mail as a Christmas gift, even though Shoba and Shukumar hadn't celebrated Christmas that year.

"Today then," Shoba announced. "You have a dentist appointment next Friday, by the way."

He ran his tongue over the tops of his teeth; he'd forgotten to brush them that morning. It wasn't the first time. He hadn't left the house at all that day, or the day before. The more Shoba stayed out, the more she began putting in extra hours at work and taking on additional projects, the more he wanted to stay in, not even leaving to get the mail, or to buy fruit or wine at the stores by the trolley stop.

Six months ago, in September, Shukumar was at an academic conference in Baltimore when Shoba went into labor, three weeks before her due date. He hadn't wanted to go to the conference, but she had insisted; it was important to make contacts, and he would be entering the job market next year. She told him that she had his number at the hotel, and a copy of his schedule and flight numbers, and she had arranged with her friend Gillian for a ride to the hospital in the event of an emergency. When the cab pulled away that morning for the airport, Shoba stood waving good-bye in her robe, with one arm resting on the mound of her belly as if it were a perfectly natural part of her body.

Each time he thought of that moment, the last moment he saw Shoba pregnant, it was the cab he remembered most, a station wagon, painted red with blue lettering. It was cavernous compared to their own car. Although Shukumar was six feet tall, with hands too big ever to rest comfortably in the pockets of his jeans, he felt dwarfed in the back seat. As the cab sped down Beacon Street, he imagined a day when he and Shoba might need to buy a station wagon of their own, to cart their children back and forth from music lessons and dentist appointments. He imagined himself gripping the wheel, as Shoba turned around to hand the children juice boxes. Once, these images of parenthood had troubled Shukumar, adding to his anxiety that he was still a student at thirty-five. But that early autumn morning, the trees still heavy with bronze leaves, he welcomed the image for the first time.

A member of the staff had found him somehow among the identical convention rooms and handed him a stiff square of stationery. It was only a telephone number, but Shukumar knew it was the hospital. When he returned to Boston it was over. The baby had been born dead. Shoba was lying on a bed, asleep, in a private room so small there was barely enough space to stand beside her, in a wing of the hospital they hadn't been to on the tour for expectant parents. Her placenta had weakened and she'd had a

---

1. English poet and artist (1834–1896), the driving force behind the Arts and Crafts movement and an influential designer; his fabrics and wallpaper typically have patterns based on animal or floral motifs.

cesarean, though not quickly enough. The doctor explained that these things happen. He smiled in the kindest way it was possible to smile at people known only professionally. Shoba would be back on her feet in a few weeks. There was nothing to indicate that she would not be able to have children in the future.

These days Shoba was always gone by the time Shukumar woke up. He would open his eyes and see the long black hairs she shed on her pillow and think of her, dressed, sipping her third cup of coffee already, in her office downtown, where she searched for typographical errors in textbooks and marked them, in a code she had once explained to him, with an assortment of colored pencils. She would do the same for his dissertation, she promised, when it was ready. He envied her the specificity of her task, so unlike the elusive nature of his. He was a mediocre student who had a facility for absorbing details without curiosity. Until September he had been diligent if not dedicated, summarizing chapters, outlining arguments on pads of yellow lined paper. But now he would lie in their bed until he grew bored, gazing at his side of the closet which Shoba always left partly open, at the row of the tweed jackets and corduroy trousers he would not have to choose from to teach his classes that semester. After the baby died it was too late to withdraw from his teaching duties. But his adviser had arranged things so that he had the spring semester to himself. Shukumar was in his sixth year of graduate school. "That and the summer should give you a good push," his adviser had said. "You should be able to wrap things up by next September."

But nothing was pushing Shukumar. Instead he thought of how he and Shoba had become experts at avoiding each other in their three-bedroom house, spending as much time on separate floors as possible. He thought of how he no longer looked forward to weekends, when she sat for hours on the sofa with her colored pencils and her files, so that he feared that putting on a record in his own house might be rude. He thought of how long it had been since she looked into his eyes and smiled, or whispered his name on those rare occasions they still reached for each other's bodies before sleeping.

In the beginning he had believed that it would pass, that he and Shoba would get through it all somehow. She was only thirty-three. She was strong, on her feet again. But it wasn't a consolation. It was often nearly lunchtime when Shukumar would finally pull himself out of bed and head downstairs to the coffeepot, pouring out the extra bit Shoba left for him, along with an empty mug, on the countertop.

Shukumar gathered onion skins in his hands and let them drop into the garbage pail, on top of the ribbons of fat he'd trimmed from the lamb. He ran the water in the sink, soaking the knife and the cutting board, and rubbed a lemon half along his fingertips to get rid of the garlic smell, a trick he'd learned from Shoba. It was seven-thirty. Through the window he saw the sky, like soft black pitch. Uneven banks of snow still lined the sidewalks, though it was warm enough for people to walk about without hats or gloves. Nearly three feet had fallen in the last storm, so that for a week people had to walk single file, in narrow trenches. For a week that was Shukumar's excuse for not leaving the house. But now the trenches were widening, and water drained steadily into grates in the pavement.

"The lamb won't be done by eight," Shukumar said. "We may have to eat in the dark."

"We can light candles," Shoba suggested. She unclipped her hair, coiled neatly at her nape during the days, and pried the sneakers from her feet without untying them. "I'm going to shower before the lights go," she said, heading for the staircase. "I'll be down."

Shukumar moved her satchel and her sneakers to the side of the fridge. She wasn't this way before. She used to put her coat on a hanger, her sneakers in the closet, and she paid bills as soon as they came. But now she treated the house as if it were a hotel. The fact that the yellow chintz armchair in the living room clashed with the blue-and-maroon Turkish carpet no longer bothered her. On the enclosed porch at the back of the house, a crisp white bag still sat on the wicker chaise, filled with lace she had once planned to turn into curtains.

While Shoba showered, Shukumar went into the downstairs bathroom and found a new toothbrush in its box beneath the sink. The cheap, stiff bristles hurt his gums, and he spit some blood into the basin. The spare brush was one of many stored in a metal basket. Shoba had bought them once when they were on sale, in the event that a visitor decided, at the last minute, to spend the night.

It was typical of her. She was the type to prepare for surprises, good and bad. If she found a skirt or a purse she liked she bought two. She kept the bonuses from her job in a separate bank account in her name. It hadn't bothered him. His own mother had fallen to pieces when his father died, abandoning the house he grew up in and moving back to Calcutta, leaving Shukumar to settle it all. He liked that Shoba was different. It astonished him, her capacity to think ahead. When she used to do the shopping, the pantry was always stocked with extra bottles of olive and corn oil, depending on whether they were cooking Italian or Indian. There were endless boxes of pasta in all shapes and colors, zippered sacks of basmati rice, whole sides of lambs and goats from the Muslim butchers at Haymarket,[2] chopped up and frozen in endless plastic bags. Every other Saturday they wound through the maze of stalls Shukumar eventually knew by heart. He watched in disbelief as she bought more food, trailing behind her with canvas bags as she pushed through the crowd, arguing under the morning sun with boys too young to shave but already missing teeth, who twisted up brown paper bags of artichokes, plums, gingerroot, and yams, and dropped them on their scales, and tossed them to Shoba one by one. She didn't mind being jostled, even when she was pregnant. She was tall, and broad-shouldered, with hips that her obstetrician assured her were made for childbearing. During the drive back home, as the car curved along the Charles, they invariably marveled at how much food they'd bought.

It never went to waste. When friends dropped by, Shoba would throw together meals that appeared to have taken half a day to prepare, from things she had frozen and bottled, not cheap things in tins but peppers she had marinated herself with rosemary, and chutneys that she cooked on Sundays, stirring boiling pots of tomatoes and prunes. Her labeled mason jars lined the shelves of the kitchen, in endless sealed pyramids, enough, they'd agreed, to last for their grandchildren to taste. They'd eaten it all by now. Shukumar had been going through their supplies steadily, preparing meals for the two of them, measuring out cupfuls of rice, defrosting bags of meat day after

2. Boston's main outdoor market, held on Fridays and Saturdays near Faneuil Hall.

day. He combed through her cookbooks every afternoon, following her penciled instructions to use two teaspoons of ground coriander seeds instead of one, or red lentils instead of yellow. Each of the recipes was dated, telling the first time they had eaten the dish together. April 2, cauliflower with fennel. January 14, chicken with almonds and sultanas.[3] He had no memory of eating those meals, and yet there they were, recorded in her neat proofreader's hand. Shukumar enjoyed cooking now. It was the one thing that made him feel productive. If it weren't for him, he knew, Shoba would eat a bowl of cereal for her dinner.

Tonight, with no lights, they would have to eat together. For months now they'd served themselves from the stove, and he'd taken his plate into his study, letting the meal grow cold on his desk before shoving it into his mouth without pause, while Shoba took her plate to the living room and watched game shows, or proofread files with her arsenal of colored pencils at hand.

At some point in the evening she visited him. When he heard her approach he would put away his novel and begin typing sentences. She would rest her hands on his shoulders and stare with him into the blue glow of the computer screen. "Don't work too hard," she would say after a minute or two, and head off to bed. It was the one time in the day she sought him out, and yet he'd come to dread it. He knew it was something she forced herself to do. She would look around the walls of the room, which they had decorated together last summer with a border of marching ducks and rabbits playing trumpets and drums. By the end of August there was a cherry crib under the window, a white changing table with mint-green knobs, and a rocking chair with checkered cushions. Shukumar had disassembled it all before bringing Shoba back from the hospital, scraping off the rabbits and ducks with a spatula. For some reason the room did not haunt him the way it haunted Shoba. In January, when he stopped working at his carrel in the library, he set up his desk there deliberately, partly because the room soothed him, and partly because it was a place Shoba avoided.

Shukumar returned to the kitchen and began to open drawers. He tried to locate a candle among the scissors, the eggbeaters and whisks, the mortar and pestle she'd bought in a bazaar in Calcutta, and used to pound garlic cloves and cardamom pods, back when she used to cook. He found a flashlight, but no batteries, and a half-empty box of birthday candles. Shoba had thrown him a surprise birthday party last May. One hundred and twenty people had crammed into the house—all the friends and the friends of friends they now systematically avoided. Bottles of vinho verde[4] had nested in a bed of ice in the bathtub. Shoba was in her fifth month, drinking ginger ale from a martini glass. She had made a vanilla cream cake with custard and spun sugar. All night she kept Shukumar's long fingers linked with hers as they walked among the guests at the party.

Since September their only guest had been Shoba's mother. She came from Arizona and stayed with them for two months after Shoba returned from the hospital. She cooked dinner every night, drove herself to the supermarket, washed their clothes, put them away. She was a religious woman.

---

3. Raisins.
4. Literally, "green wine" (Portuguese); a light Portuguese wine, usually white, that is best consumed within a year of bottling.

She set up a small shrine, a framed picture of a lavender-faced goddess and a plate of marigold petals, on the bedside table in the guest room, and prayed twice a day for healthy grandchildren in the future. She was polite to Shukumar without being friendly. She folded his sweaters with an expertise she had learned from her job in a department store. She replaced a missing button on his winter coat and knit him a beige and brown scarf, presenting it to him without the least bit of ceremony, as if he had only dropped it and hadn't noticed. She never talked to him about Shoba; once, when he mentioned the baby's death, she looked up from her knitting, and said, "But you weren't even there."

It struck him as odd that there were no real candles in the house. That Shoba hadn't prepared for such an ordinary emergency. He looked now for something to put the birthday candles in and settled on the soil of a potted ivy that normally sat on the windowsill over the sink. Even though the plant was inches from the tap, the soil was so dry that he had to water it first before the candles would stand straight. He pushed aside the things on the kitchen table, the piles of mail, the unread library books. He remembered their first meals there, when they were so thrilled to be married, to be living together in the same house at last, that they would just reach for each other foolishly, more eager to make love than to eat. He put down two embroidered place mats, a wedding gift from an uncle in Lucknow,[5] and set out the plates and wineglasses they usually saved for guests. He put the ivy in the middle, the white-edged, star-shaped leaves girded by ten little candles. He switched on the digital clock radio and tuned it to a jazz station.

"What's all this?" Shoba said when she came downstairs. Her hair was wrapped in a thick white towel. She undid the towel and draped it over a chair, allowing her hair, damp and dark, to fall across her back. As she walked absently toward the stove she took out a few tangles with her fingers. She wore a clean pair of sweatpants, a T-shirt, an old flannel robe. Her stomach was flat again, her waist narrow before the flare of her hips, the belt of the robe tied in a floppy knot.

It was nearly eight. Shukumar put the rice on the table and the lentils from the night before into the microwave oven, punching the numbers on the timer.

"You made *rogan josh*,"[6] Shoba observed, looking through the glass lid at the bright paprika stew.

Shukumar took out a piece of lamb, pinching it quickly between his fingers so as not to scald himself. He prodded a larger piece with a serving spoon to make sure the meat slipped easily from the bone. "It's ready," he announced.

The microwave had just beeped when the lights went out, and the music disappeared.

"Perfect timing," Shoba said.

"All I could find were birthday candles." He lit up the ivy, keeping the rest of the candles and a book of matches by his plate.

"It doesn't matter," she said, running a finger along the stem of her wineglass. "It looks lovely."

In the dimness, he knew how she sat, a bit forward in her chair, ankles

---

5. A city in northern India.
6. Red meat (Hindi); a tomato- and red pepper-based curried lamb dish from Kashmir, in northern India.

crossed against the lowest rung, left elbow on the table. During his search for the candles, Shukumar had found a bottle of wine in a crate he had thought was empty. He clamped the bottle between his knees while he turned in the corkscrew. He worried about spilling, and so he picked up the glasses and held them close to his lap while he filled them. They served themselves, stirring the rice with their forks, squinting as they extracted bay leaves and cloves from the stew. Every few minutes Shukumar lit a few more birthday candles and drove them into the soil of the pot.

"It's like India," Shoba said, watching him tend his makeshift candelabra. "Sometimes the current disappears for hours at a stretch. I once had to attend an entire rice ceremony in the dark. The baby just cried and cried. It must have been so hot."

Their baby had never cried, Shukumar considered. Their baby would never have a rice ceremony, even though Shoba had already made the guest list, and decided on which of her three brothers she was going to ask to feed the child its first taste of solid food, at six months if it was a boy, seven if it was a girl.

"Are you hot?" he asked her. He pushed the blazing ivy pot to the other end of the table, closer to the piles of books and mail, making it even more difficult for them to see each other. He was suddenly irritated that he couldn't go upstairs and sit in front of the computer.

"No. It's delicious," she said, tapping her plate with her fork. "It really is."

He refilled the wine in her glass. She thanked him.

They weren't like this before. Now he had to struggle to say something that interested her, something that made her look up from her plate, or from her proofreading files. Eventually he gave up trying to amuse her. He learned not to mind the silences.

"I remember during power failures at my grandmother's house, we all had to say something," Shoba continued. He could barely see her face, but from her tone he knew her eyes were narrowed, as if trying to focus on a distant object. It was a habit of hers.

"Like what?"

"I don't know. A little poem. A joke. A fact about the world. For some reason my relatives always wanted me to tell them the names of my friends in America. I don't know why the information was so interesting to them. The last time I saw my aunt she asked after four girls I went to elementary school with in Tucson. I barely remember them now."

Shukumar hadn't spent as much time in India as Shoba had. His parents, who settled in New Hampshire, used to go back without him. The first time he'd gone as an infant he'd nearly died of amoebic dysentery. His father, a nervous type, was afraid to take him again, in case something were to happen, and left him with his aunt and uncle in Concord. As a teenager he preferred sailing camp or scooping ice cream during the summers to going to Calcutta. It wasn't until after his father died, in his last year of college, that the country began to interest him, and he studied its history from course books as if it were any other subject. He wished now that he had his own childhood story of India.

"Let's do that," she said suddenly.

"Do what?"

"Say something to each other in the dark."

"Like what? I don't know any jokes."

"No, no jokes." She thought for a minute. "How about telling each other something we've never told before."

"I used to play this game in high school," Shukumar recalled. "When I got drunk."

"You're thinking of truth or dare.[7] This is different. Okay, I'll start." She took a sip of wine. "The first time I was alone in your apartment, I looked in your address book to see if you'd written me in. I think we'd known each other two weeks."

"Where was I?"

"You went to answer the telephone in the other room. It was your mother, and I figured it would be a long call. I wanted to know if you'd promoted me from the margins of your newspaper."

"Had I?"

"No. But I didn't give up on you. Now it's your turn."

He couldn't think of anything, but Shoba was waiting for him to speak. She hadn't appeared so determined in months. What was there left to say to her? He thought back to their first meeting, four years earlier at a lecture hall in Cambridge, where a group of Bengali poets were giving a recital. They'd ended up side by side, on folding wooden chairs. Shukumar was soon bored; he was unable to decipher the literary diction, and couldn't join the rest of the audience as they sighed and nodded solemnly after certain phrases. Peering at the newspaper folded in his lap, he studied the temperatures of cities around the world. Ninety-one degrees in Singapore yesterday, fifty-one in Stockholm. When he turned his head to the left, he saw a woman next to him making a grocery list on the back of a folder, and was startled to find that she was beautiful.

"Okay," he said, remembering. "The first time we went out to dinner, to the Portuguese place, I forgot to tip the waiter. I went back the next morning, found out his name, left money with the manager."

"You went all the way back to Somerville just to tip a waiter?"

"I took a cab."

"Why did you forget to tip the waiter?"

The birthday candles had burned out, but he pictured her face clearly in the dark, the wide tilting eyes, the full grape-toned lips, the fall at age two from her high chair still visible as a comma on her chin. Each day, Shukumar noticed, her beauty, which had once overwhelmed him, seemed to fade. The cosmetics that had seemed superfluous were necessary now, not to improve her but to define her somehow.

"By the end of the meal I had a funny feeling that I might marry you," he said, admitting it to himself as well as to her for the first time. "It must have distracted me."

The next night Shoba came home earlier than usual. There was lamb left over from the evening before, and Shukumar heated it up so that they were able to eat by seven. He'd gone out that day, through the melting snow, and bought a packet of taper candles from the corner store, and batteries to fit

---

7. In this party game, one play asks another "Truth or dare?" If the answer is "truth," then the first player asks the other to answer an embarrassing question; if "dare," to do something embarrassing.

the flashlight. He had the candles ready on the countertop, standing in brass holders shaped like lotuses, but they ate under the glow of the copper-shaded ceiling lamp that hung over the table.

When they had finished eating, Shukumar was surprised to see that Shoba was stacking her plate on top of his, and then carrying them over to the sink. He had assumed she would retreat to the living room, behind her barricade of files.

"Don't worry about the dishes," he said, taking them from her hands.

"It seems silly not to," she replied, pouring a drop of detergent onto a sponge. "It's nearly eight o'clock."

His heart quickened. All day Shukumar had looked forward to the lights going out. He thought about what Shoba had said the night before, about looking in his address book. It felt good to remember her as she was then, how bold yet nervous she'd been when they first met, how hopeful. They stood side by side at the sink, their reflections fitting together in the frame of the window. It made him shy, the way he felt the first time they stood together in a mirror. He couldn't recall the last time they'd been photographed. They had stopped attending parties, went nowhere together. The film in his camera still contained pictures of Shoba, in the yard, when she was pregnant.

After finishing the dishes, they leaned against the counter, drying their hands on either end of a towel. At eight o'clock the house went black. Shukumar lit the wicks of the candles, impressed by their long, steady flames.

"Let's sit outside," Shoba said. "I think it's warm still."

They each took a candle and sat down on the steps. It seemed strange to be sitting outside with patches of snow still on the ground. But everyone was out of their houses tonight, the air fresh enough to make people restless. Screen doors opened and closed. A small parade of neighbors passed by with flashlights.

"We're going to the bookstore to browse," a silver-haired man called out. He was walking with his wife, a thin woman in a windbreaker, and holding a dog on a leash. They were the Bradfords, and they had tucked a sympathy card into Shoba and Shukumar's mailbox back in September. "I hear they've got their power."

"They'd better," Shukumar said. "Or you'll be browsing in the dark."

The woman laughed, slipping her arm through the crook of her husband's elbow. "Want to join us?"

"No thanks," Shoba and Shukumar called out together. It surprised Shukumar that his words matched hers.

He wondered what Shoba would tell him in the dark. The worst possibilities had already run through his head. That she'd had an affair. That she didn't respect him for being thirty-five and still a student. That she blamed him for being in Baltimore the way her mother did. But he knew those things weren't true. She'd been faithful, as had he. She believed in him. It was she who had insisted he go to Baltimore. What didn't they know about each other? He knew she curled her fingers tightly when she slept, that her body twitched during bad dreams. He knew it was honeydew she favored over cantaloupe. He knew that when they returned from the hospital the first thing she did when she walked into the house was pick out objects of theirs and toss them into a pile in the hallway: books from the shelves, plants from the windowsills, paintings from walls, photos from tables, pots and pans that hung from the hooks over the stove. Shukumar had stepped out of her way, watching as she moved methodically from room to room. When she was satisfied, she stood there staring at the pile she'd made, her lips drawn back in such distaste that Shukumar had thought she would spit. Then she'd started to cry.

He began to feel cold as he sat there on the steps. He felt that he needed her to talk first, in order to reciprocate.

"That time when your mother came to visit us," she said finally. "When I said one night that I had to stay late at work, I went out with Gillian and had a martini."

He looked at her profile, the slender nose, the slightly masculine set of her jaw. He remembered that night well; eating with his mother, tired from teaching two classes back to back, wishing Shoba were there to say more of the right things because he came up with only the wrong ones. It had been twelve years since his father had died, and his mother had come to spend two weeks with him and Shoba, so they could honor his father's memory together. Each night his mother cooked something his father had liked, but she was too upset to eat the dishes herself, and her eyes would well up as Shoba stroked her hand. "It's so touching," Shoba had said to him at the time. Now he pictured Shoba with Gillian, in a bar with striped velvet sofas, the one they used to go to after the movies, making sure she got her extra olive, asking Gillian for a cigarette. He imagined her complaining, and Gillian sympathizing about visits from in-laws. It was Gillian who had driven Shoba to the hospital.

"Your turn," she said, stopping his thoughts.

At the end of their street Shukumar heard sounds of a drill and the electricians shouting over it. He looked at the darkened facades of the houses lining the street. Candles glowed in the windows of one. In spite of the warmth, smoke rose from the chimney.

"I cheated on my Oriental Civilization exam in college," he said. "It was my last semester, my last set of exams. My father had died a few months before. I could see the blue book of the guy next to me. He was an American guy, a maniac. He knew Urdu and Sanskrit. I couldn't remember if the verse we had to identify was an example of a *ghazal*[8] or not. I looked at his answer and copied it down."

It had happened over fifteen years ago. He felt relief now, having told her.

She turned to him, looking not at his face, but at his shoes—old moccasins he wore as if they were slippers, the leather at the back permanently flattened. He wondered if it bothered her, what he'd said. She took his hand and pressed it. "You didn't have to tell me why you did it," she said, moving closer to him.

They sat together until nine o'clock, when the lights came on. They heard some people across the street clapping from their porch, and televisions being turned on. The Bradfords walked back down the street, eating ice-cream cones and waving. Shoba and Shukumar waved back. Then they stood up, his hand still in hers, and went inside.

---

8. A form of love poetry in rhyming couplets of specified types, originating in Persian verse and today prominent in Urdu, particularly in songs of India and Pakistan.

Somehow, without saying anything, it had turned into this. Into an exchange of confessions—the little ways they'd hurt or disappointed each other, and themselves. The following day Shukumar thought for hours about what to say to her. He was torn between admitting that he once ripped out a photo of a woman in one of the fashion magazines she used to subscribe to and carried it in his books for a week, or saying that he really hadn't lost the sweater-vest she bought him for their third wedding anniversary but had exchanged it for cash at Filene's, and that he had gotten drunk alone in the middle of the day at a hotel bar. For their first anniversary, Shoba had cooked a ten-course dinner just for him. The vest depressed him. "My wife gave me a sweater-vest for our anniversary," he complained to the bartender, his head heavy with cognac. "What do you expect?" the bartender had replied. "You're married."

As for the picture of the woman, he didn't know why he'd ripped it out. She wasn't as pretty as Shoba. She wore a white sequined dress, and had a sullen face and lean, mannish legs. Her bare arms were raised, her fists around her head, as if she were about to punch herself in the ears. It was an advertisement for stockings. Shoba had been pregnant at the time, her stomach suddenly immense, to the point where Shukumar no longer wanted to touch her. The first time he saw the picture he was lying in bed next to her, watching her as she read. When he noticed the magazine in the recycling pile he found the woman and tore out the page as carefully as he could. For about a week he allowed himself a glimpse each day. He felt an intense desire for the woman, but it was a desire that turned to disgust after a minute or two. It was the closest he'd come to infidelity.

He told Shoba about the sweater on the third night, the picture on the fourth. She said nothing as he spoke, expressed no protest or reproach. She simply listened, and then she took his hand, pressing it as she had before. On the third night, she told him that once after a lecture they'd attended, she let him speak to the chairman of his department without telling him that he had a dab of pâté on his chin. She'd been irritated with him for some reason, and so she'd let him go on and on, about securing his fellowship for the following semester, without putting a finger to her own chin as a signal. The fourth night, she said that she never liked the one poem he'd ever published in his life, in a literary magazine in Utah. He'd written the poem after meeting Shoba. She added that she found the poem sentimental.

Something happened when the house was dark. They were able to talk to each other again. The third night after supper they'd sat together on the sofa, and once it was dark he began kissing her awkwardly on her forehead and her face, and though it was dark he closed his eyes, and knew that she did, too. The fourth night they walked carefully upstairs, to bed, feeling together for the final step with their feet before the landing, and making love with a desperation they had forgotten. She wept without sound, and whispered his name, and traced his eyebrows with her finger in the dark. As he made love to her he wondered what he would say to her the next night, and what she would say, the thought of it exciting him. "Hold me," he said, "hold me in your arms." By the time the lights came back on downstairs, they'd fallen asleep.

The morning of the fifth night Shukumar found another notice from the electric company in the mailbox. The line had been repaired ahead of schedule, it said. He was disappointed. He had planned on making shrimp *malai*[9] for Shoba, but when he arrived at the store he didn't feel like cooking anymore. It wasn't the same, he thought, knowing that the lights wouldn't go out. In the store the shrimp looked gray and thin. The coconut milk tin was dusty and overpriced. Still, he bought them, along with a beeswax candle and two bottles of wine.

She came home at seven-thirty. "I suppose this is the end of our game," he said when he saw her reading the notice.

She looked at him. "You can still light candles if you want." She hadn't been to the gym tonight. She wore a suit beneath the raincoat. Her makeup had been retouched recently.

When she went upstairs to change, Shukumar poured himself some wine and put on a record, a Thelonius Monk[1] album he knew she liked.

When she came downstairs they ate together. She didn't thank him or compliment him. They simply ate in a darkened room, in the glow of a beeswax candle. They had survived a difficult time. They finished off the shrimp. They finished off the first bottle of wine and moved on to the second. They sat together until the candle had nearly burned away. She shifted in her chair, and Shukumar thought that she was about to say something. But instead she blew out the candle, stood up, turned on the light switch, and sat down again.

"Shouldn't we keep the lights off?" Shukumar asked.

She set her plate aside and clasped her hands on the table. "I want you to see my face when I tell you this," she said gently.

His heart began to pound. The day she told him she was pregnant, she had used the very same words, saying them in the same gentle way, turning off the basketball game he'd been watching on television. He hadn't been prepared then. Now he was.

Only he didn't want her to be pregnant again. He didn't want to have to pretend to be happy.

"I've been looking for an apartment and I've found one," she said, narrowing her eyes on something, it seemed, behind his left shoulder. It was nobody's fault, she continued. They'd been through enough. She needed some time alone. She had money saved up for a security deposit. The apartment was on Beacon Hill, so she could walk to work. She had signed the lease that night before coming home.

She wouldn't look at him, but he stared at her. It was obvious that she'd rehearsed the lines. All this time she'd been looking for an apartment, testing the water pressure, asking a Realtor if heat and hot water were included in the rent. It sickened Shukumar, knowing that she had spent these past evenings preparing for a life without him. He was relieved and yet he was sickened. This was what she'd been trying to tell him for the past four evenings. This was the point of her game.

Now it was his turn to speak. There was something he'd sworn he would never tell her, and for six months he had done his best to block it from his mind. Before the ultrasound she had asked the doctor not to tell her the sex of their child, and Shukumar had agreed. She had wanted it to be a surprise.

---

9. A mildly spiced dish, with a cream sauce made with coconut milk and nuts (*malai* means "cream" in Hindi).

1. American jazz composer and pianist (1917–1992).

Later, those few times they talked about what had happened, she said at least they'd been spared that knowledge. In a way she almost took pride in her decision, for it enabled her to seek refuge in a mystery. He knew that she assumed it was a mystery for him, too. He'd arrived too late from Baltimore—when it was all over and she was lying on the hospital bed. But he hadn't. He'd arrived early enough to see their baby, and to hold him before they cremated him. At first he had recoiled at the suggestion, but the doctor said holding the baby might help him with the process of grieving. Shoba was asleep. The baby had been cleaned off, his bulbous lids shut tight to the world.

"Our baby was a boy," he said. "His skin was more red than brown. He had black hair on his head. He weighed almost five pounds. His fingers were curled shut, just like yours in the night."

Shoba looked at him now, her face contorted with sorrow. He had cheated on a college exam, ripped a picture of a woman out of a magazine. He had returned a sweater and got drunk in the middle of the day instead. These were the things he had told her. He had held his son, who had known life only within her, against his chest in a darkened room in an unknown wing of the hospital. He had held him until a nurse knocked and took him away, and he promised himself that day that he would never tell Shoba, because he still loved her then, and it was the one thing in her life that she had wanted to be a surprise.

Shukumar stood up and stacked his plate on top of hers. He carried the plates to the sink, but instead of running the tap he looked out the window. Outside the evening was still warm, and the Bradfords were walking arm in arm. As he watched the couple the room went dark, and he spun around. Shoba had turned the lights off. She came back to the table and sat down, and after a moment Shukumar joined her. They wept together, for the things they now knew.

1998, 1999

Selected Bibliographies

For ease of reference, all the authors are listed in alphabetical order.

Fleur Adcock
Adcock's poetry includes *Tigers* (1967), *High Tide in the Garden* (1971), *The Scenic Route* (1974), *The Inner Harbour* (1979), *Selected Poems* (1983), *The Incident Book* (1986), *Meeting the Comet* (1988), *Time-Zones* (1991), *Looking Back* (1997), and *Poems: 1960–2000* (2000). She chose selections for *The Oxford Book of Contemporary New Zealand Poetry* (1982) and edited *The Faber Book of Twentieth-Century Women's Poetry* (1987) and *The Oxford Book of Creatures* (1995), with Jacqueline Simms. She has translated *The Virgin and the Nightingale: Medieval Poems* (1983), Daniela Craeasnaru's *Letters from Darkness: Poems* (1991), and Grete Tartler's *Orient Express: Poems* (1991); she has also translated and edited *Hugh Primas and the Archpoet* (1994). In addition, she is the author of several texts and libretti for musical works by the composer Gillian Whitehead. An autobiographical essay, "Rural Blitz: Fleur Adcock's English Childhood," appears in *Poetry Review* 74 (1984), and interviews with Adcock can be found in *Talking About Ourselves* (1986), ed. Harry Ricketts, and *Thumbscrew* 17 (2000/2001). Recent studies of Adcock's poetry include Ian Gregson, "Your Voice Speaking in My Poems: Polyphony in Fleur Adcock," *English* 42 (1993), Julian Stannard, "Fleur Adcock in Context: From Movement to Martians," *Studies in British Literature* 29 (1997), Carmen Zamorano Llena, "The Location of Identity in the Interstitial Spaces: The Poetry of Fleur Adcock in a Multicultural Britain," *Journal of New Zealand Literature* 18/19 (2000), and Janet Wilson, "Fleur Adcock: Ambivalent Expatriate. 1964–1974," *Journal of New Zealand Literature* 21 (2003).

Ama Ata Aidoo
Aidoo's works include the book of short stories *No Sweetness Here* (1969), the plays *Dilemma of a Ghost* (1965) and *Anowa* (1970), and the novel *Our Sister Killjoy, or, Reflections from a Black-Eyed Squint* (1979). More recent work includes a collection of children's stories, *The Eagle and the Chickens and Other Stories* (1986); a novel, *Changes: A Love Story* (1991); two books of poetry: *Someone Talking to Sometime* (1985) and *An Angry Letter in January and Other Poems* (1992); as well as the collection, *The Girl Who Can and Other Stories* (1999). Aidoo's writings have been anthologized in *Opening Spaces: An Anthology of Contemporary African Women's Writing* (1999), ed. Yvonne Vera, and *Under African Skies: Modern African Stories* (1997), ed. Charles R. Larson. Aidoo's essay, "Freedom, yes!: and then what?" was featured in *Facing Up to the Past: Perspectives on the Commemoration of Slavery from Africa, the Americas and Europe* (2001), ed. Gert Oostindie. Two interesting interviews are Rosemary Marangoly George and Helen Scott, "'A New Tail to an Old Tale': An Interview with Ama Ata Aidoo," *Novel* 26 (1993), and Nana Wilson-Tagoe's conversation with Aidoo in *Writing Across Worlds: Contemporary Writers Talk* (2002), ed. Susheila Nasta.

Full-length studies of Aidoo's writings include Vincent Odamtten, *The Art of Ama Ata Aidoo: Polylectics and Reading Against Neocolonialism* (1994), and Ada Uzoamaka Azodo and Gay Wilentz, *Emerging Perspectives on Ama Ata Aidoo* (1999). For individual critical essays, see Dapo Adelugba, "Language and Drama: Ama Ata Aidoo," *African Literature Today* 8 (1976); Marion Kilson, "Women and African Literature," *Journal of African Studies* 4 (1977); Kathleen McCaffrey, "Images of the Mother in the Stories of Ama Ata Aidoo," *Africa Women* 23 (1979); and Karen C. Chapman "'Introduction' to Ama Ata Aidoo's *Dilemma of a Ghost*," in *Sturdy Black Bridges: Visions of Black Women in Literature* (1979), ed. Roseann P. Bell, Bettye J. Parker, and Beverly Guy-Sheftall. Alice Walker includes a discussion of Aidoo in *In Search of Our Mothers' Gardens* (1984). See also Chimalum Nwanko, "The Feminist Impulse and Social Realism in Ama Ata Aidoo's *No Sweetness Here* and *Our Sister Killjoy*," in *Nganbika: Studies of Women in African Literature* (1986), ed. Carole Boyce Davies and Anne Adams Graves; Caroline Rooney, "Dangerous Knowledge and the Poetics of Survival: A Reading of *Our Sister Killjoy* and *A Question of Power*," in *Motherlands: Black Women's Writing from Africa, the Caribbean, and South Asia* (1992), ed. Susheila Nasta; and Chikwenye Okonjo Ogunyemi, "Womanism: The Dynamics of the Contemporary Black Female Novel in English," in *Revising the Word and the World: Essays in Feminist Literary Criticism* (1993), ed. VeVe Clark, Ruth-Ellen B. Joeres, and Madelon Sprengnether. Critical treatments since the mid-nineties include N. Jane Opoku-Agyemang, "A Reading of Ama Ata Aidoo's Anowa," in *Nwanyibu: Womanbeing and African Literature* (1997), ed. Phanuel Akubueze Egejuru and Ketu H. Katrak. A chapter is devoted to Aidoo's first play, "I will marry when I want," in *Modern African Drama: Backgrounds and Criticism* (2002), ed. Biodun Jeyifo. Three recent discussions of Aidoo's first novel are James M. Ivory, "Self-colonization and Racial Identity in Ama Ata Aidoo's *Our Sister Killjoy, or, Reflections From a Black-eyed Squint*," in *Postcolonial Perspectives on Women Writers from Africa, the Caribbean, and the US* (2003), ed. Martin Japtok; Hildegard Hoeller, "Ama Ata Aidoo's *Heart of Darkness*," *Research in African Literatures* 35 (2004); and Byron Caminero-Santangelo, "Struggling toward the Postcolonial: The Ghost of Conrad in Ama Ata Aidoo's *Our Sister Killjoy*," in *African Fiction and Joseph Conrad: Reading Postcolonial Intertextuality* (2005). Aidoo's work is also discussed in Anuradha Dingwaney Needham, *Using the Master's Tools: Resistance and the Literature of the African and South-Asian Diasporas* (2000); Angeletta K. M. Gourdine, *The Difference Place Makes: Gender, Sexuality, and Diaspora Identity* (2002); and Teresa N. Washington, *Our Mothers, Our Powers, Our Texts: Manifestations of Ajé in Africana Literature* (2005).

Maya Angelou
Angelou's works are *I Know Why the Caged Bird Sings* (1970), *Just Give Me a Cool Drink of Water 'Fore I Diiie* (1971), *Georgia, Georgia* (1972), *Gather Together in My Name* (1974), *Oh Pray My Wings Are Gonna Fit Me Well* (1975), *Singin' and Swingin' and Gettin' Merry Like Christmas* (1976), *And Still I Rise* (1978), and *The Heart of a Woman* (1981). *The Complete Poems of Maya Angelou* appeared in 1994. Useful interviews appear in "The Black Scholar Interviews Maya Angelou," *Black Scholar* 8 (1977), and in *Black Women Writers at Work* (1984), ed. Claudia Tate. Critical essays on her achievement include Sidonie A. Smith, "The Song of a Caged Bird: Maya Angelou's Quest after Self-Acceptance," *Southern Humanities Review* 7 (1973); George E. Kent, "Maya Angelou's *I Know Why the Caged Bird Sings* and Black Autobiographical Tradition," *Kansas Quarterly* 7 (1975); Myra K. McMurry, "Role-Playing as Art in Maya Angelou's *Caged Bird*," *South Atlantic Bulletin* 41 (1976); and R. B. Stepto, "The Phenomenal Woman and the Severed Daughter," *Parnassus* (1980). Two useful essays, Selwyn R. Cudjoe, "Maya Angelou and the Autobiographical Statement," and Sandra O'Neale, "Reconstruction of the Composite Self," appear in *Black Women Writers (1950–1980)* (1984), ed. Mari Evans. See also the recent discussions of Angelou in *Notable Black Women* (1992), ed. Jessie Carney Smith, and by Kathleen Thompson in *Black Women in America* (1993), ed. Darlene Clark Hine.

Gloria Anzaldúa
Anzaldúa is the author of *Borderlands / La Frontera* (1987), *Friends from the Other Side*, with pictures by Consuelo Mendez (1993), and *Prietita y La Llorona* (1996). Anzaldúa also composed the essays "To Live in the Borderlands Means You," in *The Multicultural Southwest: A Reader* (2001), ed. A. Gabriel Meléndez, and "Speaking in Tongues: A Letter to Third World Women Writers," in *Women Writing Resistance: Essays on Latin America and the Caribbean* (2003), ed. J. B. de Hernandez. Her work is included in *Daughters of the Fifth Sun: A Collection of Latina Fiction and Poetry* (1995), ed. B. Milligan, M. G. Milligan, and A. de Hoyos. Anzaldúa edited *This Bridge Called My Back: Writings by Radical Women of Color* (1981) and *Making Face, Making Soul / Hacienda Caras: Creative and Critical Perspectives by Feminists of Color* (1990). For interviews, see *Interviews = Entrevistas* (2000), ed. AnaLouise Keating. Critical work on Anzaldúa includes Y. Yarbrobejarano, "Gloria Anzaldúa, *Borderlands / La Frontera*: Cultural Studies, Difference, and the Non-Unitary Subject," *Cultural Critique* 28 (1994), and A. L. Keating, "Writing, Politics, and *Las Lesberadas, Platicando, con Gloria Anzaldúa*," *Frontiers, A Journal of Women's Studies* 14 (1994). Her work is also discussed in A. L. Keating, *Women Reading Women Writing: Self-invention in Paula Gunn Allen, Gloria Anzaldúa, and Audre Lorde* (1996); C. P. Steele, *We Heal From Memory: Sexton, Lorde, Anzaldúa, and the Poetry of Witness* (2000); M. P. Brady, *Extinct Lands, Temporal Geographies: Chicana Literature and the Urgency of Space* (2002); and A. A. Lunsford and Lahoucine Ouzgane, *Crossing Borderlands: Composition and Postcolonial Studies* (2004).

Margaret Atwood
Two excellent introductions to Atwood's poetry are *Selected Poems* (1976) and *Selected Poems II: Poems Selected and New, 1976–1986* (1987). Her novels include *The Edible Woman* (1969), *Surfacing* (1972), *Lady Oracle* (1976), *Life before Man* (1979), *Bodily Harm* (1982), *The Handmaid's Tale* (1985), *Cat's Eye* (1989), *The Robber Bride* (1993), *Alias Grace* (1996), *The Blind Assassin* (2000), and *Oryx and Crake* (2003). She has also published volumes of short stories, including *True Stories* (1982), *Wilderness Tips* (1991), and *Good Bones and Simple Murders* (1994). In addition, she has written plays, books

for children, and literary criticism, some of which has been collected in *Writing with Intent: Essays, Reviews, Personal Prose, 1983–2005* (2005). There are many published interviews with Atwood, including one by Joyce Carol Oates in the *New York Times Book Review,* May 21, 1978. Useful full-length studies are Sherrill Grace, *Violent Duality: A Study of Margaret Atwood* (1980); Jerome H. Rosenburg, *Margaret Atwood* (1984); Kathryn VanSpanckeren and Jan Garden Castro, *Margaret Atwood: Vision and Form* (1988); J. Brooks Bouson, *Brutal Choreographies: Oppositional Strategies and Narrative Design in the Novels of Margaret Atwood* (1993); Sharon Rose Wilson, *Margaret Atwood's Fairy-Tale Sexual Politics* (1993); and Roxanne J. Fand, *The Dialogic Self: Reconstructing Subjectivity in Woolf, Lessing, and Atwood* (1999). Helpful collections of critical essays on Atwood are *Margaret Atwood: A Symposium,* ed. Linda Sandler in *The Malahat Review* (1977); *The Art of Margaret Atwood: Essays in Criticism* (1981), ed. Arnold E. Davidson and Cathy N. Davidson; *Margaret Atwood: Language, Text, and System* (1983), ed. Sherrill E. Grace and Lorraine Weir; *Critical Essays on Margaret Atwood* (1988), ed. Judith McCombs; and *Margaret Atwood, Writing, and Subjectivity: New Critical Essays* (1994), ed. Colin Nicholson.

Mary Austin

Among Austin's numerous publications are four nature works, *One Hundred Miles on Horseback* (1889), *The Land of Little Rain* (1903), *The Flock* (1909), and *Land of Journey's Ending* (1923); two collections of short stories, *The Basket Woman* (1904) and *Lost Borders* (1909); and many novels, including *Isidro* (1905), *A Woman of Genius* (1912), *Santa Lucia* (1908), *No. 26 Jayme Street* (1920), and *Starry Adventure* (1931). The title story from *The Mother of Felipe and Other Early Stories* (1950) was Austin's first publication. Two nonfiction works are *The Young Woman Citizen* (1918), a meditation on women's legal rights in the United States, and *Can Prayer Be Answered?* (1934). Esther F. Lanigan edited *A Mary Austin Reader* (1996); the short story collections, *Stories from the Country of Lost Borders,* ed. Marjorie Pryse, and *Western Trails: A Collection of Short Stories,* ed. Melody Graulich, both appeared in 1987. Austin's autobiography, *Earth Horizon,* was originally printed in 1932 and reissued in 1991. Her letters, collected in *Literary America, 1903–1934: The Mary Austin Letters,* were printed in 1979.

Two full-length studies containing valuable biographical material are Augusta Fink, *I, Mary: A Biography of Mary Austin* (1983), and Esther F. Lanigan, *Mary Austin: Song of a Maverick,* 1989. See also Heike Schaefer, *Mary Austin's Regionalism: Reflections on Gender, Genre, and Geography* (2004), and *Exploring Lost Borders: Critical Essays on Mary Austin,* ed. Melody Graulich and Elizabeth Klimasmith (1999). James Ruppert has two useful essays on Austin: "Discovering America: Mary Austin and Imagism," in *Studies in American Indian Literature: Critical Essays and Course Designs* (1983), ed. Paula Gunn Allen, and "Mary Austin's Landscape Line in Native American Literature," *Southwest Review* 68 (1983). Other helpful articles include David Wyatt, "Mary Austin: Nature and Nurturance," in his *The Fall into Eden* (1986); Lois Rudnick, "Re-Naming the Land: Anglo-Expatriate Women in the Southwest," in *The Desert Is No Lady* (1987), ed. Vera Norwood and Janice Monk; and Esther Lanigan Stineman, "Mary Austin Rediscovered," *Journal of the Southwest* 30 (1988).

Djuna Barnes

Known primarily for her novel *Nightwood* (1937), Barnes wrote many other works, which are now receiving critical attention. They include *The Book of Repulsive Women, Eight Rhythms and Five Drawings* (1915), *Ladies' Almanack* (1928), *Ryder* (1928), *The Antiphon* (1958), *Spillway* (1962), and *Creatures in an Alphabet* (1982). Recently, Philip F. Herring presented " 'Behind the Heart': An Unpublished Story by Djuna Barnes," *Library Chronicle of the University of Texas* 23 (1993). There is a 1962 edition of *The Selected Works of Djuna Barnes. Smoke and Other Early Stories,* ed. and with an introduction by Douglas Messerli, was published in 1982. Alyce Barry has edited two collections of Barnes's works: *Interviews* (1985) and *New York* (1989). A volume of correspondence, *Selected Letters of Djuna Barnes,* appeared in 1993.

Full-length biographies and critical studies include James B. Scott, *Djuna Barnes* (1976); Louis F. Kannestine, *The Art of Djuna Barnes: Duality and Damnation* (1977); Andrew Field, *Djuna, the Formidable Miss Barnes* (1985), a revision of his *Djuna: The Life and Times of Djuna Barnes* (1983); and *Silence and Power: A Reevaluation of Djuna Barnes* (1991), ed. Mary Lynn Broe and with an afterword by Catharine Stimpson. See also Tyrus Miller, *Late Modernism: Politics, Fiction, and the Arts between the World Wars* (1999). Critical essays include Carolyn Allen, " 'Dressing the Unknowable in the Garments of the Known': The Style of Djuna Barnes in *Nightwood,*" in *Women's Language and Style* (1978), ed. Douglas Butturff and Edmund L. Epstein; Susan Sniader Lanser, "Speaking in Tongues: *Ladies' Almanack* and the Language of Celebration," *Frontiers* 4 (1979); Lynn DeVore, "The Background of *Nightwood:* Robin, Felix, and Nora," *Journal of Modern Literature* 10 (1983); Carolyn J. Allen, "Sexual Narrative in the Fiction of Djuna Barnes," in *Sexual Practice, Textual Theory: Lesbian Cultural Criticism* (1993), ed. Susan J. Wolfe and Julian

Penelope; Frann Michael, "'I Just Loved Thelma': Djuna Barnes and the Construction of Bisexuality," *The Review of Contemporary Fiction* 13 (1993); and Victoria L. Smith, "A Story beside(s) Itself: The Language of Loss in Djuna Barnes's *Nightwood*," *PMLA* 114 (1999). Douglas Messerli compiled *Djuna Barnes: A Bibliography* (1975), and Jamie Stevens somewhat more recently published "Djuna Barnes: An Updated Bibliography," *The Review of Contemporary Fiction* 13 (1993).

Patricia Beer

Beer's books of poetry are *Loss of the Magyar and Other Poems* (1959), *The Survivors* (1963), *Just Like the Resurrection* (1967), *The Estuary* (1971), *Driving West* (1975), *Selected Poems* (1979), *The Lie of the Land* (1983), *Friend of Heraclitus* (1993), and *Autumn* (1997). Her *Collected Poems* (1988) includes some previously unpublished poems as well as most of the contents of her seven earlier volumes. Beer's influential critical study of nineteenth-century women novelists, *Reader: I Married Him*, appeared in 1974. Other important prose works include the autobiographical *Mrs. Beer's House* (1968) and the novel *Moon's Ottery* (1978). Her prose writings were compiled in *As I Was Saying Yesterday: Selected Essays and Reviews* (2002), ed. with an introduction by Sarah Rigby. Poems by Beer appear in *The Faber Book of Twentieth-Century Women's Poetry* (1987), ed. Fleur Adcock, and *The Things That Matter: An Anthology of Women's Spiritual Poetry* (1992), ed. Julia Neuberger. Anne Stevenson discusses Beer's poetry (along with that of five other contemporary women poets) in "Houses of Choice," *Poetry Review* 70 (1980).

Elizabeth Bishop

The Complete Poems of Elizabeth Bishop, 1927–1979, was published in 1983, and *The Collected Prose* in 1984. A collection of Bishop's correspondence, *One Art: Letters*, ed. Robert Giroux, was issued in 1994. Anne Stevenson's biographical and critical study, *Elizabeth Bishop*, appeared in 1966; Brett C. Miller's *Elizabeth Bishop: Life and the Memory of It* in 1993; and Gary Fountain and Peter Brazeau's *Remembering Elizabeth Bishop: An Oral Biography* was released in 1994. Useful critical essays on Bishop's poetry appear in the issue of *World Literature Today* (1976) devoted to her; in David Kalstone's *Five Temperaments* (1977); and in two recent books: Victoria Harrison's *Elizabeth Bishop's Poetics of Intimacy* (1993) and Marilyn May Lombardi, ed., *Elizabeth Bishop: The Geography of Gender* (1993). A valuable collection of essays, *Elizabeth Bishop and Her Art*, ed. Lloyd Schwartz and Sybil P. Estess, was published in 1983. For interviews and a selection of essays, see *Conversations with Elizabeth Bishop* (1996), ed. George Monteiro.

Helpful critical essays are Richard Mullen, "Elizabeth Bishop's Surrealist Inheritance," *American Literature* 54 (1982); Kathleen Brogan, "Lyric Voice and Sexual Difference in Elizabeth Bishop," in *Writing the Woman Artist: Essays on Poetics, Politics, and Portraiture* (1991), ed. Suzanne Jones; and Marilyn May Lombardi, "The Closet of Breath: Elizabeth Bishop, Her Body and Her Art," *Twentieth-Century Literature* 38 (1992). More recent essays are James Longenbach, "Elizabeth Bishop's Social Conscience," *ELH* 62 (1995), and Steven Gould Axelrod, "Elizabeth Bishop and Containment Policy," *American Literature* 75 (2003). Useful full-length studies are Robert Parker Dale, *The Unbeliever: The Poetry of Elizabeth Bishop* (1988), and Lorrie Goldensohn, *Elizabeth Bishop: The Biography of a Poetry* (1991). See also Marilyn May Lombardi, *Elizabeth Bishop: Her Poetics of Loss* (1994); Susan McCabe, *The Body and the Song: Elizabeth Bishop's Poetics* (1996); Anne Colwell, *Inscrutable Houses: Metaphors of the Body in the Poems of Elizabeth Bishop* (1997); Xiaojing Zhou, *Elizabeth Bishop: Rebel "in shades and shadows"* (1999). A useful collection of essays is *Elizabeth Bishop: Poet of the Periphery* (2002), ed. Linda Anderson and Jo Shapcott. Also notable is Cheryl Walker, *God and Elizabeth Bishop: Meditations on Religion and Poetry* (2002). Though somewhat outdated, *Elizabeth Bishop: A Bibliography, 1927–1979* (1980), comp. Candace W. McMahon; *Elizabeth Bishop and Howard Nemerov: A Reference Guide* (1983), Diana E. Wyllie; and *A Concordance to Elizabeth Bishop's Poetry* (1985), Anne Merrill Greenhalgh, are still useful reference books.

Louise Bogan

Among the collections of Bogan's poetry are *Collected Poems, 1923–1953* (1954) and *The Blue Estuaries: Poems, 1923–1968* (1968). Her *Selected Criticism* was published in 1955. A new selection of Bogan's writings is *A Poet's Prose: Selected Writings of Louise Bogan* (2005), ed. and with an introduction by Mary Kinzie. William Jay Smith edited a lecture delivered at the Library of Congress, *Louise Bogan: A Woman's Words* (1971), and Ruth Limmer edited the selected letters of 1920–70, *What the Woman Lived* (1973), as well as a series of passages from her work put together to constitute a memoir, *Journey around My Room: The Autobiography of Louise Bogan: A Mosaic* (1980). For a unique collection of letters, poems, and an interview, see Mildred Weston, *Our 30 year old Friendship: Letters from Louise Bogan, Comments by Mildred Weston; and, Legacy: poems from the twenties to the nineties hitherto unpublished*. Elizabeth

Frank's important biography, *Louise Bogan: A Portrait*, appeared in 1985. Also valuable are *Critical Essays on Louise Bogan* (1984), ed. Martha Collins, and *Louise Bogan's Aesthetic of Limitation* (1987), by Gloria Bowles. *Obsession and Release: Rereading the Poetry of Louise Bogan*, by Lee Upton, was published in 1996. In addition, see the interesting discussions of Bogan in Alicia Ostriker, *Stealing the Language: The Emergence of Women's Poetry in America* (1986), and Elizabeth Dodd, *The Veiled Mirror and the Woman Poet: H. D., Louise Bogan, Elizabeth Bishop, and Louise Glück* (1992). Other useful studies include Patrick Moore, "Symbol, Mask, and Meter in the Poetry of Louise Bogan," *Woman and Literature* 1 (1980); Mary De Shazer, " 'My Scourge, My Sister': Louise Bogan's Muse," in *Coming to Light: American Poets in the Twentieth Century* (1985), ed. Diane Wood Middlebrook and Marilyn Yalom; John P. Muller, "Light and the Wisdom of the Dark: Aging and the Language of Desire in the Texts of Louise Bogan," in *Memory and Desire: Aging, Literature, Psychoanalysis* (1986), ed. Kathleen Woodward and Murray M. Schwartz; Suzanne Clark, "Medusa and Melancholy: The Fatal Allure of Beauty in Louise Bogan's Poetry," in her *Sentimental Modernism: Women Writers and the Revolution of the Word* (1991); Cheryl Walker, "Woman and the Retreat of the Mind: Louise Bogan and the Stoic Persona," in her *Masks Outrageous and Austere: Culture, Psyche, and Persona in Modern Women Poets* (1991); and Marcia Aldrich, "Lethal Brevity: Louise Bogan's Lyric Career," in *Aging and Gender in Literature: Studies in Creativity* (1993), ed. Anne M. Wyatt-Brown and Janice Rossen. A useful bibliography is Claire E. Knox, *Louise Bogan: A Reference Source* (1990).

Eavan Boland

Boland's works include *New Territory: Poems* (1967), *The War Horse: Poems* (1975), *In Her Own Image* (1980), *Night Feed* (1982), *The Journey* (1983), *Outside History: Selected Poems, 1980–1990* (1990), *In a Time of Violence* (1994), *Collected Poems* (1995), *An Origin Like Water* (1996), *The Lost Land* (1998), *Code* (2001), and *Against Love Poetry* (2004). She has also written three critical studies concerning women's poetic and political place in Ireland: *A Kind of Scar: The Woman Poet in a National Tradition* (1989), *A Dozen LIPS* (1994), and *Object Lessons: The Life of the Woman and the Poet in Our Time* (1995). Boland's essay, "Imagining Ireland," opens the volume *Arguing at the Crossroads: Essays on a Changing Ireland* (1997), ed. Paul Brennan and Catherine de Saint Phalle. Her piece, "Letter to a Young Woman Poet," appeared in *American Poetry Review* 26 (1997), as well as in the collection *Word: On Being a [Woman] Writer* (2004), ed. Jocelyn Burrell. Boland edited and is featured in *Three Irish Poets: An Anthology* (2003). She translated nine German poets from the World War II period for the volume *After Every War: Twentieth-Century Women Poets* (2004). Interviews with Boland include discussions with Deborah McWilliams Conslavo in *Studies: An Irish Quarterly Review* 81 (1992); with Craig Arnold and M.L. Williams in *Quarterly West* 38 (1993/94); with Jan Garden Castro in *Tampa Review* 10 (1995); with Rebekah Presson in *New Letters* 61 (1995); with Donna Sherrill Kobis in *Kalliope* 19 (1997); with Margaret Mills Harper in *Five Points* 1 (1997); with Vicki Bertram in *PN Review* 25 (1998); with Kathleen Fraser in *Parnassus* 23 (1998); and with Jody Allen Randolph in *Colby Library Quarterly* 35 (1999).

Helpful critical essays include Sheila C. Conboy, " 'What You Have Seen Is Beyond Speech': Female Journeys in the Poetry of Eavan Boland and Eilean Ni Chuilleanain," *Canadian Journal of Irish Studies* 16 (1990); Patricia L. Hagen and Thomas W. Zelman, " 'We Were Never on the Scene of the Crime': Eavan Boland's Repossession of History," *Twentieth-Century Literature* 37 (1991); and David Wheatley, " 'An Origin like Water': The Poetry of Eavan Boland and Modernist Critiques of Irish Literature," *Irishness and (Post)Modernism* (1994), ed. John S. Rickard. Also see Sheila C. Conboy, "Eavan Boland's Topography of Displacement," *Éire-Ireland* 29 (1994); Seija H. Paddon, "The Diversity of Performance / Performance as Diversity in the Poetry of Laura (Riding) Jackson and Eavan Boland," *English Studies in Canada* 22 (1996); M. Nell Sullivan, "Righting Irish poetry: Eavan Boland's Revisionary Struggle," *Colby Library Quarterly* 33 (1997); Anne Fogarty, "The *Influence of Absences*: Eavan Boland and the Silenced History of Irish Women's Poetry," *Colby Library Quarterly* 35 (1999); Catriona Clutterbuck, "Irish Critical Responses to Self-representation in Eavan Boland, 1987–1995," *Colby Library Quarterly* 35 (1999); Christy Burns, "Beautiful Labors: Lyricism and Feminist Revisions in Eavan Boland's Poetry," *Tulsa Studies in Women's Literature* 20 (2001); Rose Atfield, " 'The Stain of Absolute Possession': The Postcolonial in the work of Eavan Boland," in *Contemporary Women's Poetry: Reading, Writing, Practice*, ed. Alison Mark and Deryn Rees-Jones (2000); and Cheryl Malcolm, "The Ugly Sister Talks Back: Eavan Boland's (re)visions of Ireland," *Atenea: Journal of the University of Puerto Rico at Mayagüez* 23 (2003).

Marita Bonner

Bonner's essays, plays, and short stories are collected in *Frye Street & Environs: The Collected Works of Marita Bonner* (1987), ed. Joyce Flynn and Joyce Occomy Stricklin. This includes a prefatory essay by Stricklin, "A Portrait of My Mother," and an introduction by Flynn. Critical discussions of Bonner and her work can be found in Allison Berg and Meredith Taylor, "Enacting Difference: Marita Bonner's Purple Flower and the Ambiguities of Race," *African American Review* 32 (1998), and Carol Allen, *Black Women Intellectuals* (1998).

Elizabeth Bowen

An edition of *The Collected Stories of Elizabeth Bowen,* with an introduction by Angus Wilson, was published in 1989. Among her best-known novels are *The Hotel* (1927), *The House in Paris* (1935), *The Death of the Heart* (1938), *The Heat of the Day* (1949), *The Little Girls* (1964), and *Eva Trout or Changing Scenes* (1968), all of which are available in paperback editions. She also wrote many nonfiction works, including *Collected Impressions* (1950) and *Pictures and Conversations* (1975), a posthumous collection. *The Mulberry Tree: Writings of Elizabeth Bowen* appeared in 1986. Two useful biographies are Victoria Glendenning, *Elizabeth Bowen: Portrait of a Writer* (1977), and Patricia Craig, *Elizabeth Bowen* (1986).

Full-length critical studies include William W. Heath, *Elizabeth Bowen: An Introduction to Her Novels* (1961); Allen E. Austin, *Elizabeth Bowen* (1989); Harriet Blodgett, *Patterns of Reality: Elizabeth Bowen's Novels* (1975); Hermione Lee, *Elizabeth Bowen: An Estimation* (1981); Phyllis Lassner, *Elizabeth Bowen* (1989) and *Elizabeth Bowen: A Study of the Short Fiction* (1991); Heather Bryant Jordan, *How Will the Heart Endure: Elizabeth Bowen and the Landscape of War* (1992); Renee C. Hoogland, *Elizabeth Bowen: A Reputation in Writing* (1994); Andrew Bennett, *Elizabeth Bowen and the Dissolution of the Novel: Still Lives* (1994); and Neil Corcoran, *Elizabeth Bowen: The Enforced Return* (2004). Useful critical articles are Harriet S. Chessman, "Women and Language in the Fiction of Elizabeth Bowen," *Twentieth-Century Literature* 29 (1983); Thomas Dukes, "The Unorthodox Plots of Elizabeth Bowen," *Studies in the Humanities* 16 (1989); and Sandra Kemp, " 'But How Describe a World Seen without a Self': Feminism, Fiction, and Modernism," *Critical Quarterly* 32 (1990). Harold Bloom edited the essay collection *Elizabeth Bowen* (1987). J'nan Sellery and William O. Harris compiled the valuable *Elizabeth Bowen: A Bibliography* (1981).

Anna Hempstead Branch

Besides *Sonnets from a Lock Box* (1929), Branch's verse collections include *The Shoes That Danced, and Other Poems* (1905), *Rose of the Wind, and Other Poems* (1910), and *Last Poems of Anna Hempstead Branch* (1944), ed. and with a foreword by Ridgely Torrence. Poems by Branch appear in *American Mystical Verse: An Anthology* (1925), ed. Irene Hunter; in *The World Split Open: Four Centuries of Women Poets in England and America, 1552–1950* (1974), ed. Louise Bernikow; and in *An Anthology of Great U.S. Women Poets, 1850–1990: Temples and Palaces* (1997), ed. Glenn Richard Ruihley.

Gwendolyn Brooks

Gwendolyn Brooks's volumes include *A Street in Bronzeville* (1945), *Annie Allen* (1949), *Bronzeville Boys and Girls* (1956), *The Bean Eaters* (1960), *Selected Poems* (1963), *In the Mecca* (1968), *Riot* (1969), *Family Pictures* (1970), *The World of Gwendolyn Brooks* (1971), *Aloneness* (1972), *Beckonings* (1975), *To Disembark* (1981), *The Near-Johannesburg Boy and Other Poems* (1986), *Gottschalk and the Grand Toranbelle* (1988), *Winnie* (1988), and *Children Coming Home* (1992). *Blacks* (1987) is a collection of her prose and poetry. She also wrote novels, including *Maud Martha* (1953), and an autobiographical work, *Report from Part One* (1972).

Useful biographical, critical, and bibliographical studies are George E. Kent, *A Life of Gwendolyn Brooks* (1990); *A Life Distilled: Gwendolyn Brooks, Her Poetry and Fiction* (1987), ed. Maria K. Mootry and Gary Smith, which includes a biographical chronology and a good bibliography; and Barbara Jean Bolden, *Urban Rage in Bronzeville: Social Commentary in the Poetry of Gwendolyn Brooks, 1945–1960* (1999). Haki Madhubuti edited *Say That the River Turns: The Impact of Gwendolyn Brooks* (1987), a tribute to Brooks in honor of her seventieth birthday, containing essays by more than seventy writers; and Stephen Caldwell Wright edited another collecton, *On Gwendolyn Brooks: Reliant Contemplation* (1996).

Rebecca Brown

Brown's works include *The Evolution of Darkness and Other Stories* (1984), *The Haunted House* (1990), *The Children's Crusade* (1991), *The Terrible Girls* (1992), *Annie Oakley's Girl* (1993), *The Gifts of the Body* (1995), *What Keeps Me Here: A Book of Stories* (1996), *The Dogs: A Modern Bestiary* (1998), *The End of Youth* (2003), and *Excerpts from a Family Medical Dictionary* (2003). Her short stories have appeared in the following anthologies: *Mae West Is Dead: Recent Lesbian and Gay Fiction* (1983), ed. Adam Mars-Jones; *Women on Women 2: An Anthology of American Lesbian Short Fiction* (1993), ed. Joan Nestle and Naomi Holoch; *Tasting Life Twice: Literary Lesbian Fiction by New American Writers* (1995), ed. E. J. Levy; *Hers: Brilliant New Fiction by Lesbian Writers*

(1995), ed. Terry Wolverton; *Queer 13: Lesbian and Gay Writers Recall Seventh Grade* (1998), ed. Clifford Chase; *The Mammoth Book of Lesbian Short Stories* (1999), ed. Emma Donoghue. Brown's writings are discussed in Carolyn Allen, *Following Djuna: Women Lovers and the Erotics of Loss* (1994).

Octavia Butler
Butler's works include *Patternmaster* (1976), *Mind of My Mind* (1977), *Survivor* (1978), *Kindred* (1979), *Wild Seed* (1980), *Clay's Ark* (1984), *Dawn* (1987), *Adulthood Rites: Xenogenesis* (1988), *Imago* (1989), *Parable of the Sower* (1993), *Parable of the Talents* (1998), and *Bloodchild and Other Stories* (1995). An interview with Butler can be found in Larry MacCaffery, *Across the Wounded Galaxies: Interviews with Contemporary American Science Fiction Writers* (1990).

Two critical essays are Thelma J. Shinn, "The Wise Witches: Black Women Mentors in the Fiction of Octavia E. Butler," *Conjuring: Black Women, Fiction and Literary Tradition*, ed. Hortense Spillers and Marjorie Pryse (1985), and Dorothy Allison, "The Future of the Female: Octavia Butler's Mother Lode," *Reading Black, Reading Feminists*, ed. Henry Louis Gates, Jr. (1990). See also Joe Weixlmann, "An Octavia E. Butler Bibliography," *Black American Literature Forum* (1984).

Angela Carter
Carter's fiction includes *Shadow Dance* (1965), *The Magic Toyshop* (1967), *Several Perceptions* (1968), *Heroes and Villains* (1969), *Love* (1971), *The Infernal Desire Machine of Doctor Hoffman* (1972), *The Passion of New Eve* (1977), *Nights at the Circus* (1984), and *Wise Children* (1991). She translated Charles Perrault's fairy tales and published three collections of stories: *Fireworks* (1974), *The Bloody Chamber* (1979), and *Wayward Girls & Wicked Women: An Anthology of Stories* (1986). *Burning Your Boats: The Collected Angela Carter Stories* was published in 1995. She also published two collections of other writings: *Nothing Sacred: Selected Writings* (1982) and *Expletives Deleted: Selected Writings* (1992). *The Sadeian Woman: An Exercise in Cultural History* appeared in 1979, and *American Ghosts and Old World Wonders* appeared in 1993. For useful critical essays, see the collection *Flesh and the Mirror: Essays on the Art of Angela Carter* (1994), ed. Lorna Sage, and Robert Wilson, "SLIP PAGE: Angela Carter, In / Out / In the Post-Modern Nexus," in *Past the Last Post: Theorizing Post-Colonialism and Post-Modernism* (1990), ed. Ian Adam and Helen Tiffin. Carter is also discussed in Ellen Rose, "Through the Looking Glass: When Women Tell Fairy Tales," in *The Voyage In: Fictions of Female Development* (1983), ed. Elizabeth Abel and Marianne Hirsch; Sally Robinson, *Engendering the Subject: Gender and Self-Representation in Contemporary Women's Fiction* (1991); Yvonne Martinsson, *Eroticism, Ethics and Reading: Angela Carter in Dialogue with Roland Barthes* (1996); and Alison Lee, *Angela Carter* (1997). A collection of essays is *The Infernal Desires of Angela Carter: Fiction, Femininity, Feminism*, ed. Joseph Bristow and Trev Lynn Broughton (1997).

Willa Cather
Cather's collection of poems, *April Twilights* (1903), and her book of essays, *Not under Forty* (1936), supplement the standard edition of her fiction, *The Novels and Stories of Willa Cather, 1937–41*, which includes such works as *O Pioneers!* (1913), *The Song of the Lark* (1915), *My Antonia* (1918), *Youth and the Bright Medusa* (1920), *A Lost Lady* (1923), *The Professor's House* (1925), *Death Comes for the Archbishop* (1927), and *Shadows on the Rock* (1931). Other texts include *The Old Beauty and Others*, posthumously collected short stories (1948); *Willa Cather on Writing* (1949); *Writings from Willa Cather's Campus Years* (1950), ed. James Shively; *Collected Short Fiction, 1892–1912* (1965), ed. Virginia Faulkner; and *The Kingdom of Art: Willa Cather's First Principles and Critical Statements* (1967), ed. Bernice Slote. L. Brent Bohlke selected and edited *Willa Cather in Person: Interviews, Speeches, and Letters* (1986).

Personal memoirs include Edith Lewis, *Willa Cather Living* (1953; rev. 2000), and Elizabeth Sergeant, *Willa Cather: A Memoir* (1953; rev. 1992). Among biographies and critical studies are David Daiches, *Willa Cather* (1951); E. K. Brown, *Willa Cather* (1953); Dorothy Van Ghent, *Willa Cather* (1964); James Woodress, *Willa Cather* (1970); Philip Gerber, *Willa Cather* (1975); David Stouck, *Willa Cather's Imagination* (1975); Phyllis C. Robinson, *Willa: The Life of Willa Cather* (1983); James Woodress, *Willa Cather: A Literary Life* (1987); Sharon O'Brien, *Willa Cather: The Emerging Voice* (1987); and Hermione Lee, *Willa Cather: Double Lives* (1991). Janis P. Stout's *A Calendar of the Letters of Willa Cather* (2002) and the biography *Willa Cather: The Writer and Her World* (2000) are worthwhile. Commentaries on Cather are gathered in *Willa Cather and Her Critics* (1967), ed. James Schroeter; *The Art of Willa Cather* (1974), ed. Bernice Slote and Virginia Faulkner; *Women Writing in America* (1985), Blanche Gelfant; *New Essays on My Antonia* (1999), ed. Sharon O'Brien; and *Willa Cather's Southern Connection* (2000), ed. Ann Roninie. Joan Acocella examines the history of Cather criticism in *Willa Cather and the Politics* of Criticism (2000). Joan Crane compiled the valuable Willa Cather: A Bibliography (1982).

Marilyn Chin

Chin's collections of poetry include Dwarf Bamboo (1987), The Phoenix Gone, The Terrace Empty (1994), and Rhapsody in Plain Yellow (2002). She has also translated Gozo Yoshimasu's Devil Wind: A Thousand Steps or More (1980) and Selected Poems of Ai Qing (with Peng Wenlan and Eugene Eoyang, 1982), in addition to the work of various Chinese poets.

Critical treatment of Chin can be found in Reading the Literatures of Asian Americans, ed. Shirley Geok-lin and Amy Ling (1992). Useful essays include Adrienne McCormick, " 'Being Without': Marilyn Chin's Poems as Feminist Acts of Theorizing," Hitting Critical Mass 6 (2000); Mary Slowik, "Being Lot's Wife: The Immigration Poems of Marilyn Chin, Garrett Hongo, and David Mura," MELUS 25 (2000); and John Gery, " 'Mocking My Own Happiness': Authenticity, Heritage, and Self-Erasure in the Poetry of Marilyn Chin," Lit: Literature Interpretation Theory 12 (2001).

Caryl Churchill

Among Churchill's many plays are Traps (1978), Cloud Nine (1979), Top Girls (1982), Vinegar Tom (1982), Fen (1983), Softcops (1984), A Mouthful of Birds (written with David Lan, 1986), Serious Money (1987), Ice Cream with Hot Fudge (1990), The Skriker (1994), Light Shining in Buckinghamshire (1996), Blue Heart (1997), Hotel (1997), This Is a Chair (1999), Far Away (2001), A Number (2002), Serious Money (2002), and A Dream Play (2005). Several of her plays are collected in Plays: Two (1990), Churchill Shorts: Short Plays (1990), and Plays: Three (1998). She has also composed a libretto, Lives of the Great Poisoners (1993). A biography is Geraldine Cousin, Churchill, the Playwright (1989).

A collection containing valuable critical essays is Caryl Churchill: A Casebook (1988), ed. Phyllis R. Randall. For book-length studies of Churchill's work, see Amelia Howe Kritzer, The Plays of Caryl Churchill: Theatre of Empowerment (1991), and Elaine Aston, Caryl Churchill (1997). Linda Fitzsimmons's File on Churchill (1989) provides a useful bibliography and synopses of Churchill's plays as well as their performance history. Essays from a feminist perspective include Alisa Solomon, "Witches, Ranters, and the Middle Class: The Plays of Caryl Churchill," Theater 12 (1981); Linda Fitzsimmons, " 'I Won't Turn Back for You or Anyone': Caryl Churchill's Socialist-Feminist Theatre," Essays in Theatre 6 (1987); Austin E. Quigley, "Stereotype and Prototype: Character in the Plays of Caryl Churchill," in Feminine Focus: The New Women Playwrights (1989), ed. Enoch Brater; Janet E. Gardner, "Caryl Churchill's Top Girls: Defining and Reclaiming Feminism in Thatcher's Britain," New England Theatre Journal 10 (1999); and Chantal Cornut-Gentille, "The Personal Is Political in Caryl Churchill's Top Girls: A Parable for the Feminist Movement in Thatcher's Britain," in Telling Histories: Narrativizing History, Historicizing Literature (1995), ed. Susana Onega. Other useful critical articles are Helene Keyssar, "The Dramas of Caryl Churchill: The Politics of Possibility," Massachusetts Review 24 (1983); Amelia Howe Kritzer, "Madness and Political Change in the Plays of Caryl Churchill," in Madness in Drama (1993), ed. James Redmond; Janelle Reinelt, "Caryl Churchill and the Politics of Style," in The Cambridge Companion to Modern British Women Playwrights (2000), ed. Elaine Aston and Janelle Reinelt; and Christine Kiebuzinska, "Caryl Churchill's Mad Forest," in Intertextual Loops in Modern Drama (2001).

Sandra Cisneros

Fiction by Cisneros includes The House on Mango Street (1984) and Woman Hollering Creek (1991); her poetry collections include My Wicked Wicked Ways (1987) and Loose Woman (1994). An extensive dialogue with her can be found in Interviews with Writers of the Post-Colonial World, ed. Feroza Jussawalla and Reed Way Dasenbrook (1992).

Critical discussion of Cisneros can be found in Ramón Saldívar, Chicano Narrative (1990); Tey Diano, Women Singing in the Snow (1995); and Sonia Saldívar-Hull, Feminism on the Border (2000).

Lucille Clifton

Besides numerous books for children, Clifton's works include Good Times (1969), Good News about the Earth (1972), An Ordinary Woman (1974), Generations: A Memoir (1976), Two-Headed Woman (1980), Sonora Beautiful (1981), Good Woman: Poems and a Memoir, 1969–1980 (1987), Next: New Poems (1987), Quilting: Poems, 1987–1990 (1991), The Book of Light (1993), The Terrible Stories (1996), Dear Creator: A Week of Poems for Young People and Their Teachers (1997), Blessing the Boats: New and Selected Poems, 1998–2000 (2000), and Mercy (2004).

Audrey McCluskey, "Tell the Good News: A View of the Works of Lucille Clifton," and Haki Madhubuti, "Lucille Clifton: Warm Water, Greased Legs, and Dangerous Poetry," appear in Black Women Writers (1950–1980) (1984), ed. Mari Evans. Andrea Benton Rushing, "Lucille Clifton: A Changing Voice for Changing Times," was published in Coming to Light: American Women Poets in the Twentieth Century (1985), ed. Diane Wood Middlebrook. Other critical treatments of Clifton can be found in Alicia Ostriker, "Kin and Kin: The Poetry of Lucille Clifton," *American Poetry Review* 22 (1993); Gloria Hull, "Channeling the Ancestral Muse: Lucille Clifton and Delores Kendrick," *Female Subjects in Black and White: Race, Psychoanalysis, Feminism* (1997), ed. Elizabeth Abel et al.; Cheryl Wall, "Sifting Legacies in Lucille Clifton's *Generations*," *Contemporary Literature* 20 (1999); and Ajuan Maria Mance, "Re-Locating the Black Female Subject: The Landscape of the Body in the Poems of Lucille Clifton," *Recovering the Black Female Body: Self-Representations by African-American Women*, ed. Michael Bennett et al. (2001).

Isak Dinesen
Dinesen's books in English include *Seven Gothic Tales* (1934), *Out of Africa* (1937), *Winter's Tales* (1942), *Last Tales* (1957), *Anecdotes of Destiny* (1958), *Shadows on the Grass* (1961), and *Ehrengard* (1963). Her *Letters from Africa, 1914–1931*, were edited by Frans Lasson and translated by Anne Born (1981). Born also translated *On Modern Marriage and Other Observations* (1986). Biographies and memoirs include Clara Svendesen, *Isak Dinesen: A Memorial* (1965); Migel Parmenia, *Titania: The Biography of Isak Dinesen* (1967); Lasson, *The Life and Destiny of Isak Dinesen* (1970); Thomas Dinesen, *My Sister, Isak Dinesen* (trans. Joan Tate, 1975); and Judith Thurman, *Isak Dinesen: The Life of a Storyteller* (1982).

Among full-length critical studies are Robert W. Langbaum, *The Gayety of Vision: A Study of Isak Dinesen's Art* (1965); Donald Hannah, *"Isak Dinesen" and Karen Blixen: The Mask and the Reality* (1971); Thomas R. Whissen, *Isak Dinesen's Aesthetics* (1973); Susan Aiken Hardy, *Isak Dinesen and the Engendering of Narrative* (1990); and Olga Anastasia Pelensky, *Isak Dinesen: The Life and Imagination of a Seducer* (1991). Pelensky also edited *Isak Dinesen: Critical Views* (1993). Feminist perspectives are represented by Susan Gubar, " 'The Blank Page' and the Issues of Female Creativity," in *Writing and Sexual Difference* (1982), ed. Elizabeth Abel; Susan Hardy Aiken, "The Uses of Duplicity: Isak Dinesen and Questions of Feminist Criticism," *Scandinavian Studies* 57 (1985); Marilyn Johns Blackwell, "The Transforming Gaze: Identity and Sexuality in the Works of Isak Dinesen," *Scandinavian Studies* 63 (1991); and Sidonie Smith, "The Other Woman and the Racial Politics of Gender: Isak Dinesen and Beryl Markham in Kenya," in *De / Colonizing the Subject: The Politics of Gender in Women's Autobiography* (1992), ed. Smith and Julia Watson. See also Carol J. Clover, ed., "Isak Dinesen, 1885–1962," *Scandinavian Studies* 57 (1985), a special issue on Dinesen.

H. D. (Hilda Doolittle)
Louis Martz has edited *H. D.: Collected Poems, 1912–1944* (1983), which includes her major published (and some previously unpublished) work in verse except for the late volumes *Helen in Egypt* (1961) and *Hermetic Definition* (1972), both of which are available in paperback. He has also edited *Selected Poems* (1988). Her prose fiction includes *Palimpsest* (1926), *Hedylus* (1928), and *Bid Me to Live* (1960). *By Avon River* (1949) celebrates Shakespeare in prose and verse. The autobiographical *HERmione*, with a forward by Perdita Schaffner, was published in 1981 and *The Gift* in 1982. *Tribute to Freud* (1944), her account of her psychoanalysis by Freud, and *End to Torment* (1979), a memoir of Ezra Pound, are available in paperback.

H. D. figures in *My Heart to Artemis: A Writer's Memoirs* (1962), the autobiography of her closest friend and traveling companion, Bryher (Winifred Ellerman). Early critical studies include a chapter entitled "The Perfect Imagist" in Glenn Hughes, *Imagism and the Imagists* (1931); Thomas Burnett Swann, *The Classical World of H. D.* (1962); and Vincent Quinn, *Hilda Doolittle* (1967). The autumn 1969 issue of *Contemporary Literature* was devoted exclusively to H. D. and contains useful background information. The collection of correspondence, *Richard Aldington and H. D.: The Early Years in Letters* (1992), ed. Caroline Zilboorg, also provides useful biographical information.

Feminist interest in H. D.'s work has followed Susan Stanford Friedman's landmark essay, "Who Buried H. D.?" *College English* 36 (1975). The biography *H. D.: The Life and Work of an American Poet* (1982), by Janice Robinson, is somewhat controversial, while *Herself Defined: The Poet H. D. and Her World* (1984), by Barbara Guest, is useful. A valuable full-length critical study is Friedman, *Psyche Reborn: The Emergence of H. D.* (1981). More recently, Friedman has published *Penelope's Web: Gender, Modernity, H. D.'s Fiction* (1990); "Portrait of the Artist as a Young Woman: H. D.'s Rescriptions of Joyce, Lawrence, and Pound," in *Writing the Woman Artist: Essays on Poetics, Politics, and Portraiture* (1991), ed. Suzanne W. Jones; and has with Rachel Blau DuPlessis edited *Signets: Reading H. D.* (1990). Other full-length studies are Gary Dean Burnett, *H. D. Between Image and Epic: The Mysteries of Her Poetics* (1990); Dianne Chisholm, *H. D.'s Freudian Poetics: Psychoanalysis in Translation* (1992); Johanna Dehler, *Fragments of Desire: Sapphic Fictions in Works by H. D., Judy Grahn, and Monique Wittig* (1999); and Georgina Taylor, *H. D. and the Public Sphere of Modernist*

Women Writers, 1913–1946: Talking Women (2001). Helpful critical essays include Lawrence S. Rainey, "Canon, Gender, and Text: The Case of H. D.," in *Representing Modernist Texts: Editing as Interpretation* (1991), ed. George Bornstein, and Andrew Thacke, "Amy Lowell and H. D.: The Other Imagists," *Women: A Cultural Review* 4 (1993). A useful recent resource is Michael Boughn, *H. D.: A Bibliography, 1905–1990* (1993).

Rita Dove

Dove's books of poetry include *The Yellow House on the Corner* (1980), *Museum* (1983), *Thomas and Beulah* (1986), *Grace Notes* (1989), *Selected Poems* (1993), *Mother Love* (1995), *On the Bus with Rosa Parks: Poems* (1999), and *American Smooth* (2005). She also has published a book of stories, *Fifth Sunday* (1985); a novel, *Through the Ivory Gate* (1992); and a verse play, *The Darker Side of the Earth* (1994). *Conversations with Rita Dove*, ed. Earl G. Ingersoll, appeared in 2003. Another interview is Steven Schneider, "Coming Home: An Interview with Rita Dove," *The Iowa Review* 19 (1989). A full-length study of Dove is Therese Steffen, *Crossing Color: Transcultural Space and Place in Rita Dove's Poetry, Fiction and Drama* (2001). Useful essays are Arnold Rampersad, "The Poems of Rita Dove," *Callaloo* 9 (1986); Robert McDowell, "The Assembling Vision of Rita Dove," in *Conversant Essays: Contemporary Poets on Poetry* (1990), ed. James McCorkle; Ekaterini Georgoudaki, "Rita Dove: Crossing Boundaries," *Callaloo* 14 (1991); Bonnie Costello, "Scars and Wings: Rita Dove's Grace Notes," *Callaloo* 14 (1991); Kirkland C. Jones, "Folk Idiom in the Literary Expression of Two African American Authors: Rita Dove and Yusef Komunyakaa," in *Language and Literature in the African American Imagination* (1992), ed. Carol Aisha Blackshire Belay; Patricia Wallace, "Divided Loyalties: Literal and Literary in the Poetry of Lorna Dee Cervantes, Cathy Song, and Rita Dove," *MELUS* 18 (1993); and Helen Vendler, "Rita Dove: Identity Markers," *Callaloo* (1994). Vendler also treats Dove's work in *The Given and the Made: Strategies of Poetic Redefinition* (1995).

Alice Dunbar-Nelson

Gloria T. Hull edited *The Works of Alice Dunbar-Nelson* (1988), while Ruby Ora Williams edited *An Alice Dunbar-Nelson Reader* (1978), with critical comments by Agnes Moreland. Also available are *The Goodness of St. Rocque, and Other Stories* (1899) and *Give Us Each Day: The Diary of Alice Dunbar-Nelson* (1985), ed. Hull. For a biography of Dunbar, see Eleanor Alexander, *Lyrics of Sunshine and Shadow: The Tragic Courtship of Paul Laurence Dunbar and Alice Ruth Moore* (2002). Critical studies include an article by Roger Whitlow, "Alice Dunbar-Nelson: New Orleans Writer," *RFI* 4 (1978); an essay by Hull, "Alice Dunbar-Nelson: A Personal and Literary Perspective," in *Between Women: Biographers, Novelists, Critics, Teachers, and Artists Write about Their Work on Women* (1984), ed. Carol Ascher; a chapter in Hull, *Color, Sex, & Poetry: Three Women Writers of the Harlem Renaissance* (1987); and a chapter in Claudia Tate, *Domestic Allegories of Political Desire* (1992). Williams has also compiled a valuable bibliography in *College Language Association Journal* 19 (1976).

Louise Erdrich

Erdrich's novels include *Love Medicine* (1984; expanded ed. 1993), *The Beet Queen* (1986), *Tracks* (1988), *The Crown of Columbus* (with Michael Dorris, 1991), *The Bingo Palace* (1994), *Tales of Burning Love* (1996), *The Antelope Wife* (1998), *The Last Report on the Miracles at Little No Horse* (2001), *The Master Butchers Singing Club* (2003), and *Four Souls* (2004). *The Blue Jay's Dance: A Birth Year* (1995) is her first major nonfictional work. Her books of poetry are *Jacklight* (1984), *Baptism of Desire* (1989), and *Original Fire: Selected and New Poems* (2003). Useful critical sources are Mickey Pearlman, "A Bibliography of Writings about Louise Erdrich," in *American Women Writing Fiction: Memory, Identity, Family, Space* (1989), ed. Pearlman; Louis Owens, *Other Destinies: Understanding the American Indian Novel* (1992); *Conversations with Louise Erdrich and Michael Dorris*, ed. Allan Chavkin and Nancy Feyl Chavkin (1994); Susan Stanford Friedman, "Identity Politics, Syncretism, Catholicism, and Anishanabe Religion in Louise Erdrich's *Tracks*," *Religion and Literature* 26 (1994); Victoria Brehm, "The Metamorphosis of an Ojibwa Manido," *American Literature* 68 (1996); Alan Kelie, "Magic Realism and Ethnicity: The Fantastic in the Fiction of Louise Erdrich," *Native American Women in Literature and Culture*, ed. Susan Castillo and Victor M. P. DaRosa (1997); Jeanne Rosier Smith, *Writing Tricksters: Mythic Gambols in American Ethnic Literature* (1997); Tom Berninghausen, " 'This Ain't Real Estate': Land and Culture in Louise Erdrich's Chippewa Tetralogy," *Women, America, and Movement: Narrative of Relocation*, ed. Susan L. Robertson (1998); and the essay collection *The Chippewa Landscape of Louise Erdrich*, ed. Allan Chavkin (1999).

U. A. Fanthorpe

Fanthorpe's books of poetry include *Side Effects* (1978), *Four Dogs* (1980), *Standing To* (1982), *Voices Off* (1984), *Selected Poems* (1986), *A Watching Brief* (1987), and *Neck-Verse* (1992). Poems by Fanthorpe also appear in *The Faber Book of Twentieth-Century Women's Poetry*

(1987), ed. Fleur Adcock. An autobiographical essay, "Observations of a Clerk," *Poetry Review* 75 (1985), includes interesting background information. A helpful critical essay is Marilyn Hacker, "Unauthorized Voices: Ursula Fanthorpe and Elma Mitchell," *Grand Street* 8 (1989).

Susan Glaspell

A collection of Glaspell's short dramas, *Plays,* was published in 1920. Her three-act plays include *The Verge* (1921), *The Comic Artist* (1927), and *Alison's House* (1930); among her novels are *The Visioning* (1911), *Fidelity* (1915), *Ambrose Holt and Family* (1931), and *The Morning Is Near Us* (1939). Glaspell's biography of George Cram Cook, *A Road to the Temple* (1927), includes useful background information on the Provincetown Players. Another collection, *Plays by Susan Glaspell*, appeared in 1987, with a useful critical introduction by C. W. E. Bigsby. The recent *Lifted Masks and Other Works*, ed. Eric S. Rabkin, was issued in 1993.

Susan Glaspell (1966), by Arthur E. Waterman, is a helpful introduction to her life and work; also by Waterman is "Susan Glaspell's *The Verge*: An Experiment in Feminism," *Great Lakes Review* 6 (1979). A more recent biography is Barbara O. Rajkowska, *Susan Glaspell: A Critical Biography* (2000). Two recent and helpful full-length studies are Veronica Makowsky, *Susan Glaspell's Century of American Women: A Critical Interpretation of Her Work* (1993), and J. Ellen Gainor, *Susan Glaspell in Context: American Theater, Culture, and Politics, 1915–48* (2001). Of interest are Marcia Noe, "Susan Glaspell's Analysis of the Midwestern Character," *Books at Iowa* 27 (1977); Cynthia Sutherland, "American Women Playwrights as Mediators of the 'Woman Problem,'" *Modern Drama* 21 (1978); Christine Dymkowski, "On the Edge: The Plays of Susan Glaspell," *Modern Drama* 1 (1988); Linda Ben-Zvi, "Susan Glaspell's Contributions to Contemporary Women Playwrights," in *Feminine Focus: The New Women Playwrights* (1989), ed. Enoch Brater; and Barbara Ozieblo, "Rebellion and Rejection: The Plays of Susan Glaspell," in *Modern American Drama: The Female Canon* (1990), ed. June Schlueter. *Books at Iowa* 27 also contains a Susan Glaspell checklist. Another bibliographical source is Gerhard Bach, "Susan Glaspell, (1876–1938): A Bibliography of Dramatic Criticism," *Great Lakes Review* 8 (1977). Mary E. Papke's *Susan Glaspell: A Research and Production Sourcebook* (1993) is a valuable historical resource.

Louise Glück

Glück's volumes of poetry are *Firstborn* (1969), *The House on Marshland* (1976), *The Garden* (1976), *Descending Figure* (1980), *The Triumph of Achilles* (1985), *Ararat* (1990), *The Wild Iris* (1992), *Meadowland* (1996), *Ararat Ararat* (1998), *Vita Nova* (1999), and *The Seven Ages* (2002). Her early poetic writings have been compiled in *The First Four Books of Poems* (1995). She has also published a collection of essays, *Proofs and Theories: Essays on Poetry* (1994). A recent collection of essays on Glück's work is *On Louise Glück: Change What You Seek* (2005), ed. Joanne Feit Diehl. Individual critical essays include Calvin Bedient, "Birth, Not Death, Is the Hard Loss," *Parnassus* 9 (1981); Robert Miklitsch, "Assembling a Landscape: The Poetry of Louise Glück," *The Hollins Critic* 19 (1982); E. Laurie George, "The 'Harsher Figure' of *Descending Figure*: Louise Glück's 'Dive into the Wreck,'" *Women's Studies* 17 (1990); Diane S. Bonds, "Entering Language in Louise Glück's *The House on Marshland*: A Feminist Reading," *Contemporary Literature* 31 (1990); Lynn Keller, "'Free / Of Blossom and Subterfuge': Louise Glück and the Language of Renunciation," in *World, Self, Poem: Essays on Contemporary Poetry* (1990), ed. Leonard M. Trawick; Calvin Bedient, "'Man Is Altogether Desire?'" *Salmagundi* (1991); Lynne McMahon, "The Sexual Swamp: Female Erotics and the Masculine Art," *The Southern Review* 28 (1992); Suzanne Matson, "Without Relation: Family and Freedom in the Poetry of Louise Glück," *Mid-American Review* 14 (1994); David Raney, "'I Have Only My Body for a Voice': Sex and Silence in Louise Glück's poetry," *Cumberland Poetry Review* 19 (1999); John Perryman, "Washing Homer's Feat: Louise Glück, Modernism, and the Classics," *South Carolina Review* 33:1 (2000); Ira Sadoff, "Louise Glück and the Last Stage of Romanticism," *New England Review* 22 (2001); and Robert Hahn, "Transporting the Wine of Tone: Louise Glück in Italian," *Michigan Quarterly Review* 43 (2004). See also the chapter on Glück in Alan Williamson, *Introspection and Contemporary Poetry* (1984). Larger comparative works include Elizabeth Dodd's study of Glück and other twentieth-century women poets, *The Veiled Mirror and the Woman Poet: H. D., Louise Bogan, Elizabeth Bishop, and Louise Glück* (1992), and Lee Upton's recent work, *Defensive Measures: The Poetry of Niedecker, Bishop, Glück, and Carson* (2005). A helpful reference guide to Glück's publications is Paula Friedman, "Louise Glück: A Primary Source Bibliography," *Bulletin of Bibliography* 44 (1987).

Nadine Gordimer

Collections of Gordimer's short stories include *Selected Stories* (1976), *Something Out There* (1984), *Jump* (1991), and *Why Haven't You Written?: Selected Stories, 1950–72* (1993). Among her best-known novels are *The Late Bourgeois World* (1966), *A Guest of Honor*

(1970), *The Conservationist* (1974), *Burger's Daughter* (1979), *July's People* (1981), *A Sport of Nature* (1987), and *My Son's Story* (1990). *The Essential Gesture: Writing, Politics, and Places* (1988), ed. Stephen Clingman, is a collection of her nonfiction from 1963 to 1985. Another nonfictional work is *Lifetimes under Apartheid* (1986), written with David Goldblatt. She has also published a book of criticism, *The Black Interpreters* (1973).

Useful critical studies are John Cooke, *The Novels of Nadine Gordimer: Private Lives / Public Landscapes* (1985); *Critical Essays on Nadine Gordimer* (1990), ed. Rowland Smith; Stephen Clingman, *The Novels of Nadine Gordimer: History from the Inside* (1993); *The Later Fiction of Nadine Gordimer* (1993), ed. Bruce Alvin King; and Barbara Temple-Thurston, *Nadine Gordimer Revisited* (1999). Nancy Bazin edited *Conversations with Nadine Gordimer* (1990), while Dorothy Diver compiled *Nadine Gordimer: A Bibliography of Primary and Secondary Sources, 1937–1992* (1993), and Carol P. Marsh-Lockett contributed "Nadine Gordimer," *Postcolonial African Writers: A Bio-Bibliographical Critical Sourcebook*, ed. Pushpa Naidu Parekh et al. (1998).

Jorie Graham

Graham's books of poetry include *Hybrids of Plants and of Ghosts* (1980), *Erosion* (1983), *The End of Beauty* (1987), *Region of Unlikeness* (1991), and *Materialism* (1993); *Dream of the Unified Field: Selected Poems, 1974–1994* (1995) draws from these first five books. Later collections include *The Errancy* (1997), *Swarm* (2000), *Never* (2002), and *Overlord* (2005). Poems by Graham appear in *The Morrow Anthology of Younger American Poets* (1985), ed. David Smith and David Bottoms; *The Faber Book of Contemporary American Poetry* (1986), ed. Helen Vendler; *The Plough-Shares Poetry Reader* (1987), ed. Joyce Peseroff; and *No More Masks! An Anthology of Twentieth-Century American Women Poets* (1993), ed. Florence Howe. An interesting interview with Graham is Thomas Gardner, *Denver Quarterly* 26 (1992). See also Sven Birkets, "Jorie Graham I" and "Jorie Graham II," in his *The Electric Life: Essays on Modern Poetry* (1989). Critical discussions of Graham's work can be found in Birkets, *The Electric Life: Essays on Modern Poetry* (1989); Helen Vendler, *The Given and the Made* (1995), as well as her *Soul Says* (1995); James Longenbach, *Modern Poetry After Modernism* (1997); and Thomas Gardner, *Regions of Unlikeness: Explaining Contemporary Poetry* (1999). Useful critical essays include Gardner, "Accurate Failures: The Work of Jorie Graham," *The Hollins Critic* 24 (1987); Lisa Issacson, "Mythic Composure and the Laughing Matter of Fact," *Denver Quarterly* 26 (1992); and Bonnie Costello, "Jorie Graham: Art and Erosion," *Contemporary Literature* 33 (1992).

Marilyn Hacker

Hacker's books of poetry include *Presentation Piece* (1974), *Separations* (1976), *Taking Notice* (1980), *Assumptions* (1985), *Going Back to the River* (1990), *Winter Numbers: Poems* (1994), *Selected Poems, 1965–1990* (1994), *Squares and Courtyards* (2000), *First Cities: Collected Early Poems 1960–1979* (2003), and *Desesperanto: Poems 1999–2002* (2003). *Love, Death, and the Changing of the Seasons* (1986) is a verse novel. Hacker translated two volumes of Venus Khoury-Ghata's poetry, published as *Here There Was Once a Country* (2001) and *She Says* (2003). She also translated Claire Malroux's work in *Birds And Bison* (2005). For interesting interviews with Hacker, see Karla Hammond, "An Interview with Marilyn Hacker," *Frontiers* 5 (1980); Judith Johnson, "Poetics: A Conversation with Marilyn Hacker," *13th Moon* 9 (1991); and Annie Finch, "Marilyn Hacker: An Interview," *American Poetry Review* 25 (1996). Reg Saner's essay, "Studying Interior Architecture by Keyhole: Four Poets," *Denver Quarterly* 20 (1965), includes a discussion of Hacker's work. See also Harriet Blodgett, "Mimesis and Metaphor: Food Imagery in International Twentieth-century Women's Writing," *Papers on Language & Literature* 40 (2004).

Radclyffe Hall

Hall's novels and short story collections include *The Unlit Lamp* (1924), *The Forge* (1924), *A Saturday Life* (1925), *Adam's Breed* (1929), *The Master of the House* (1932), *The Sixth Beatitude* (1933), *Miss Ogilvy Finds Herself* (1934), as well as the famous *The Well of Loneliness* (1928), which has been reissued in a number of editions since its first printing; in addition, *The Unlit Lamp* has been reissued in a Virago Press edition (1981). Hall also published several volumes of poetry, including *The Forgotten Island* (1915), and Joanne Glasgow has edited *Your John: The Love Letters of Radclyffe Hall* (1997).

Vera M. Brittain discusses Hall's life as well as the *Well of Loneliness* trial in *Radclyffe Hall: A Case of Obscenity* (1969). Fuller biographies include Lady Una Troubridge's memoir, *The Life and Death of Radclyffe Hall* (1961); Lovat Dickson, *Radclyffe Hall at the Well of Loneliness: A Sapphic Chronicle* (1975); and Diana Souhami, *The Trials of Radclyffe Hall* (1998). A helpful full-length study of Hall's work is Claudia S. Franks, *Beyond the Well of Loneliness: The Fiction of Radclyffe Hall* (1982), but Hall is also discussed in Lillian Faderman, *Surpassing the Love of Men: Romantic Friendship and Love between Women from the Renaissance to the Present* (1981), and in a useful essay, Catharine R. Stimpson, "Zero Degree Deviancy: The Lesbian Novel in English," *Critical Inquiry* 8 (1981). A useful collection is *Palatable Poison: Critical Perspectives on The Well of Loneliness*, ed. Laura L. Doan and Jay Prosser (2001), which includes the valuable essay by Esther Newton, "The Mythic Mannish Lesbian: Radclyffe Hall and the New Woman." Other useful critical essays dealing specifically with Hall are Gillian Whitlock, " 'Everything Is Out of Place': Radclyffe Hall and the Lesbian Literary Tradition," *Feminist Studies* 13 (1987); Joanne Glasgow, "What's a Nice Lesbian Like You Doing in the Church of Torquemada? Radclyffe Hall and Other Catholic Converts," in *Lesbian Texts and Contexts* (1990), ed. Carla Jay and Joanne Glasgow; and Sherrie A. Inness, "Who's Afraid of Stephen Gordon? The Lesbian in the United States Popular Imagination," *NWSA Journal* 4 (1992).

Gwen Harwood

Harwood's collections of poems are *Poems* (1963), *Poems: Volume Two* (1968), *Selected Poems* (1975, 1985, 1990), *The Lion's Bride* (1981), *Bone Scan* (1988), and *Collected Poems* (1991). She is also the author of *Blessed City: The Letters of Gwen Harwood to Thomas Riddel, January to September 1943* (1990) and of libretti for the opera *The Golem* (1990) and the comic opera *Fiery Tales* (1992), both composed by Larry Sitsky. Harwood's letters are collected in *A Steady Storm of Correspondence: Selected Letters of Gwen Harwood, 1943–1995* (2001), ed. Gregory Kratzmann. Critical work includes R. F. Brissenden, *A Fire-Talented Tongue: Some Notes on the Poetry of Gwen Harwood* (1978); Robert Selleck, ed., *Gwen Harwood* (1987); Jennifer Strauss, "Elegies for Mothers: Reflections on Gwen Harwood's 'Mother Who Gave Me Life,' " and Les Murray, " 'Three Poems in Memory of My Mother,' " both in *Westerly* 34 (1989). Also valuable are Elizabeth Lawson, *The Poetry of Gwen Harwood* (1991); Alison Hoddinott, *Gwen Harwood: The Real and the Imagined World* (1991); Jennifer Strauss, "She / I / You / It: Constructing Mothers and Motherhood in the Writing of Gwen Harwood," *Southerly Journal: A Review of Australian Literature* 52 (1991); Strauss, *Boundary Conditions: The Poetry of Gwen Harwood* (1992); Stephanie Trigg, *Gwen Harwood* (1994); Strauss, "Playing in Time: The Poetry of Gwen Harwood," *Critical Survey* 6 (1994); Strauss, *Boundary Conditions: The Poetry of Gwen Harwood*, 1996; and Susan Schwartz, "Between Two Deaths: The Love Poetry of Gwen Harwood," *Southerly* 56 (1996–1997).

Lyn Hejinian

Hejinian's books include *A Thought is the Bride of What Thinking* (1976), *A Mask of Motion* (1977), *Gesualdo* (1978), *Writing Is an Aid to Memory* (1978), *Redo* (1984), *Individuals* (with Kit Robinson, 1988), *Oxata: A Short Russian Novel* (1991), *The Cell* (1992), *The Cold of Poetry* (1994), *Guide, Grammar, Watch, and the Thirty Nights* (1996), *The Little Book of a Thousand Eyes* (1996), *Wicker: A Collaborative Poem* (with Jack Collom, 1996), *Hearing* (with Leslie Scalapino, 1998), *The Traveler and the Hill; and, The Hill* (1998), *Sight* (with Scalapino, 1999), *Chartings* (with Ray DiPalma, 2000), *Happily* (2000), *A Border Comedy* (2001), and *The Lake* (with Emily Clark, 2001). *The Language of Inquiry* (2001) includes a selection of Hejinian's criticism, including the essay "The Rejection of Closure," as well as poetry. Her autobiography is *My Life* (1980, 1987).

Critical discussion of Hejinian can be found in three works by Marjorie Perloff: *The Dance of the Intellect* (1985), *Radical Artifice* (1991), and *Poetry on and off the Page* (1998). Other useful work on Hejinian includes Hilary Clark, "The Mnemonics of Autobiography: Lyn Hejinian's *My Life*," *Biography* 14 (1991); David Jarraway, "*My Life* through the Eighties," *Contemporary Literature* 33 (1992); Juliana Spahr, "Resignifying Autobiography: Lyn Hejinian's *My Life*," *American Literature* 68 (1996); Christopher Beach, "Poetic Positionings: Stephen Dobyns and Lyn Hejinian in Cultural Context," *Contemporary Literature* 38 (1997); and Charles Altieri, "Lyn Hejinian and the Possibilities of Postmodernism in Poetry," *Women Poets of the Americas*, ed. Jacqueline Brogan and Cordelia Candelaria (1999).

Zora Neale Hurston

Hurston's volumes include *Jonah's Gourd Vine* (1934), *Mules and Men* (1935), *Their Eyes Were Watching God* (1937), *Tell My Horse* (1938), *Moses, Man of the Mountain* (1939), *Dust Tracks on a Road* (1942), and *Seraph on the Suwanee* (1948). An excellent anthology of Hurston's work, ed. and with useful introductions by Alice Walker and Mary Helen Washington, is *I Love Myself When I Am Laughing . . . And Then Again When I Am Looking Mean and Impressive: A Zora Neale Hurston Reader* (1979). Cora Kaplan has edited her correspondence in *Zora Neale Hurston: A Life in Letters* (2003). A good biography, Robert E. Hemenway, *Zora Neale Hurston*, appeared in 1977, and Lillie P. Howard wrote *Zora Neale Hurston* (1980). Other biographies are N. Y. Nathiri, *Zora! Zora Neale Hurston, a Woman and Her Community* (1991); Janelle Yates, *Zora Neale Hurston: A Storyteller's Life* (1993); and most recently Valerie Boyd, *Wrapped in Rainbows: The Life of Zora Neale Hurston* (2003).

A useful full-length study is Karla F. C. Holloway, *The Character of the Word: The Texts of Zora Neale Hurston* (1987). Four collections of critical essays are Michael Awkward, ed., *New*

Essays on Their Eyes Were Watching God (1990); Lillie P. Howard, ed., Alice Walker and Zora Neale Hurston: The Common Bond (1993); Henry Louis Gates Jr. and Anthony Appiah, ed., Zora Neale Hurston: Critical Perspectives Past and Present (1993); and Gloria L. Cronin, Zora Neale Hurston (1998). Individual articles include Erlene Stetson, "Their Eyes Were Watching God: A Woman's Story," Regionalism and the Female Imagination 4 (1978); Florence E. Borders, "Zora Neale Hurston: Hidden Woman," Callaloo 2 (May 1979); Mary Jane Lupton, "Zora Neale Hurston and the Survival of the Female," Southern Literary Journal 15 (1982); Cheryl A. Wall, "Zora Neale Hurston: Changing Her Own Words," in American Novelists Revisited: Essays in Feminist Criticism (1982), ed. Fritz Fleischmann; Pearlie Peters, "Women and Assertive Voice in Hurston's Fiction and Folklore," The Literary Griot 4 (1992); and Mae Gwendolyn Henderson, "Speaking in Tongues: Dialogics, Dialectics, and the Black Woman Writer's Literary Tradition," in Aesthetics in Feminist Perspective (1993), ed. Hilde Hein and Carolyn Korsmeyer. Two helpful resources are the somewhat dated Adele S. Newson, Zora Neale Hurston: A Reference Guide (1987), and the more recent Rose Parkman Davis, Zora Neale Hurston: An Annotated Bibliography and Reference Guide (1998).

Gish Jen

Jen's fiction includes Typical American (1992), Mona in the Promise Land (1996), Who's Irish?: Stories (1999), and The Love Wife (2004). A brief biography by Don Lee, "About Gish Jen," can be found in Ploughshares 26 (2000), while an interview by Rachel Lee appears in Words Matter: Conversations with Asian American Writers, ed. King-Kok Cheung (2000).

Critical discussion of Jen can be found in Rachel Lee, The Americas of Asian-American Literature: Gendered Fictions of Nation and Transnation (1999). Useful essays include Betsy Huang, "The Redefinition of the 'Typical Chinese' in Gish Jen's Typical American," Hitting Critical Mass 4 (1997), and Ericka Lin, "Mona on the Phone: The Performative Body and Racial Identity in Mona in the Promised Land," MALUS 28 (2003).

June Jordan

Jordan's collections of poetry include Who Look at Me (1969), New Days: Poems of Exile and Return (1974), Things I Do in the Dark: Selected Poetry (1977), Passion: New Poems (1980), Some Changes (1981), Living Room: New Poems (1985), Lyrical Campaigns: Selected Poems (1989), Naming Our Destiny: New and Selected Poems (1989), Haruko / Love Poems (1993), and Kissing God Goodbye (1997). Her essay collections include Civil Wars (1981), On Call: Political Essays (1985), Technical Difficulties: African American Notes on the State of the Union (1992), June Jordan's Poetry for the People: A Revolutionary Blueprint, ed. Laura Miller (1995), Affirmative Acts: Political Essays (1998), and Some of Us Did Not Die: New and Selected Essays of June Jordan (2002). In addition to a number of children's books, she has also written the plays In the Spirit of Sojourner Truth (1979) and The Issue (1985), and she composed the libretto and lyrics for I Was Looking at the Ceiling and Then I Saw the Sky: Earthquake / Romance (1995), and opera composed by John Adams. Her memoir, Soldier: A Poet's Childhood, appeared in 2001. An interview with Jordan can be found in High Plains Literary Review 3 (1988), and another, with Peter Erickson, in Transition 63 (1994).

A collection of essays on Jordan is June Jordan's Poetry for the People: A Revolutionary Blueprint, ed. Laura Muller and the Poetry for the People Collective (1995), while Diverse Voices: Essays on Twentieth-Century Women Writers in English, ed. Harriet Devine Jump (1991), is also helpful. Other helpful essays on Jordan include Peter Erickson, "The Love Poetry of June Jordan," Callaloo 9 (1986); Jacqueline Vaught Brogan, "From Warrior to Womanist: The Development of June Jordan's Poetry," Speaking to the Other Self: American Women Writers, ed. Jeanne Campbell Reesman (1997); Scott Macphail, "June Jordan and the New Black Intellectuals," African American Review 33 (1999); and AnaLouise Keating, "The Intimate Distance of Desire: June Jordan's Bisexual Inflections," Journal of Lesbian Studies 4 (2000).

Jamaica Kincaid

Kincaid's novels are Annie John (1985), Lucy (1990), The Autobiography of My Mother (1996), and Mr. Potter (2002); her short story collection is At the Bottom of the River (1983); her book-length essay about her native island, Antigua, is A Small Place (1988). Three other nonfiction works are My Brother (1997), My Garden Book (1999), and Among Flowers: A Walk in the Himalayas (2005). Her literature for children is Annie, Gwen, Lilly, Pam, and Tulip (1986). Useful critical works are Diane Simmons, Jamaica Kincaid (1994); Moira Ferguson, Jamaica Kincaid: Where the Land Meets the Body (1994); Merle Hodge, "Caribbean Writers and the Caribbean Language: A Study of Jamaica Kincaid's Annie John," Winds of Change: The Transforming Voices of Caribbean Women Writers and Scholars, ed. Linda Strong-Leek (1998); Diane Simmons, "Coming-of-Age in the Snare of History: Jamaica Kincaid's The Autobiography of My Mother," The Girl: Constructions of the Girl in Contemporary Fiction by Women (1998), ed. Ruth O. Saxton; and Antonia MacDonald-Smythe, Making Homes in the West/ Indies: Constructions of Subjectivity in the Writings of Michelle Cliff and Jamaica Kincaid (2001). Allan Vorda's interview with Kincaid, "I Come From a Place That's Very Unreal: An Interview with Jamaica Kincaid," is published in *Face to Face: Interviews with Contemporary Novelists*, ed. Vorda (1993); for another interview see also Kay Bonnetti, *Conversations with American Novelists* (1997). The special issue of *Callaloo* 25 (2002) is devoted to Kincaid.

Maxine Hong Kingston

Kingston's works are *The Woman Warrior* (1976), *China Men* (1980), *Tripmaster Monkey: His Fake Book* (1989), *Hawai'i One Summer* (1998), and *The Fifth Book of Peace* (2003). She also has an important article, "Cultural Misreading by American Reviewers," in *Asian and Western Writers in Dialogue: New Cultural Identities* (1982). Kingston's work was included in *The Best American Essays of the Century* (2000), ed. Joyce Carol Oates. Useful background information on Kingston can be found in Paula Rabinowitz, "Eccentric Memories: A Conversation with Maxine Hong Kingston," *Michigan Quarterly Review* 26 (1987); Shelley Fisher Fishkin, "An Interview with Maxine Hong Kingston," *American Literary History* 3 (1991); *Conversations with Maxine Hong Kingston* (1998), ed. Paul Skenazy and Tera Martin; and in *Writing Across Worlds: Contemporary Writers Talk* (2004), ed. Susheila Nasta. An interesting critical study is King-kok Cheung, *Articulate Silences: Hisaye Yamamoto, Maxine Hong Kingston, Joy Kogawa* (1993). Critical works dedicated entirely to study of Kingston's work are Yan Gao, *The Art of Parody: Maxine Hong Kingston's Use of Chinese Sources* (1996); Diane Simmon, *Maxine Hong Kingston* (1999); E. D. Huntley, *Maxine Hong Kingston: A Critical Companion* (2001); Charles L. Crow, *Maxine Hong Kingston* (2001); and Maureen Sabine, *Maxine Hong Kingston's Broken Book of Life: An Intertextual Study of the Woman Warrior and China Men* (2004). One collection of critical essays is *Critical Essays on Maxine Hong Kingston*, ed. Laura E. Skandera-Trombley (1998). See also discussions of Kingston in John Paul Eakin, *Fictions in Autobiography: Studies in the Art of Self-Invention* (1985); Roberta Rubenstein, *Boundaries of the Self: Gender, Culture, Fiction* (1987); G. Thomas Couser, *Altered Egos: Authority in American Autobiography* (1989); Amy Ling, *Between Worlds: Women Writers of Chinese Ancestry* (1990); Bonnie C. Winsbro, *Supernatural Forces: Belief, Difference, and Power in Contemporary Works by Ethnic Women* (1993); Wendy Ho, *In Her Mother's House: The Politics of Asian American Mother-Daughter Writing* (1999); Peter Kerry Powers, *Recalling Religions: Resistance, Memory, and Cultural Revision in Ethnic Women's Literature* (2001); Yunte Huang, *Maxine Hong Kingston and the Making of an "American" Myth* (2002); and Patti Duncan, *Tell This Silence: Asian American Women Writers and the Politics of Speech* (2004). Critical essays on Kingston include Patricia Lin Blinde, "The Icicle in the Desert: Perspective and Form in the Works of Two Chinese-American Women Writers," *MELUS* 6 (1979), and two essays in *Modern Chinese Women Writers: Critical Appraisals* (1989), ed. Michael S. Duke. Feminist perspectives on Kingston include Sidonie Smith, "Maxine Hong Kingston's *The Woman Warrior*: Filiality and Women's Autobiographical Story-telling," in her *A Poetics of Women's Autobiography: Marginality and the Fictions of Self-Representation* (1987); Bonnie Tu Smith, "Literary Tricksterism," in *Anxious Power: Reading, Writing, and Ambivalence in Narrative by Women* (1993), ed. Carol J. Singley and Susan Elizabeth Sweeney; Amy Ling, "Maxine Hong Kingston and the Dialogic Dilemma of Asian American Writers," in *Having Our Way: Women Rewriting Tradition in Twentieth-Century America* (1995), ed. Harriet Pollack; and Marlene Goldman, "Naming the Unspeakable: The Mapping of Female Identity in Maxine Hong Kingston's *The Woman Warrior*," in *International Women's Writing: New Landscapes of Identity* (1995), ed. Anne E. Brown and Marjanne E. Goozé.

Carolyn Kizer

Kizer's books of poetry include *The Ungrateful Garden* (1961), *Knock upon Silence: Poems* (1965), *Midnight Was My Cry: New and Selected Poems* (1971), *Yin* (1984), *Mermaids in the Basement: Poems for Women* (1984), *The Nearness of You* (1986), *Harping On: Poems 1985–1995* (1995), *Pro Femina: A Poem* (2000), and *Cool, Calm & Collected: Poems, 1960–2000* (2001). The collection, *Proses: On Poems and Poets* (1993), includes an autobiographical narrative as well as essays on twentieth-century poetry. Other essays by Kizer include *Picking and Choosing: Essays on Prose* (1995) and "Ms Browning's Heavy Heart: Elizabeth Barrett Browning's Last Poems," *Paris Review* 154 (2000). See the interview with Earl Ingersoll and Stan Rubin, " 'The Very Separateness of Things': A Conversation with Carolyn Kizer," *Webster Review* 11 (1986). Other interviews are included in Nicholas O'Connell, *At the Field's End: Interviews with 22 Pacific Northwest Writers* (1998), and Michelle Boisseau, "Intensity & Effect: An Interview with Carolyn Kizer," *New Letters* 64 (1998). New biographical material can be found in *Carolyn Kizer: Perspectives on Her Life and Work* (2001), ed. Annie Finch, Johanna Keller, and Candace McClelland. Two interesting essays on her work are Dominic Cheung, "Carolyn Kizer and Her Chinese Imitations," in

China and the West: Comparative Literature Studies (1980), ed. William Tay, Chou Ying-hsiung, and Yuan Heh-hsiang, and Henry Taylor, "Passwords at the Boundary: Carolyn Kizer's Poetry," in *Hollins Critic* 34 (1997). David Rigsbee edited a useful collection of essays, *An Answering Music: On the Poetry of Carolyn Kizer* (1990).

Maxine Kumin

Kumin's works include children's books, novels, and verse collections; some of the most notable are *Through Dooms of Love* (1965), *Up Country* (1972), *The Designated Heir* (1974), *House, Bridge, Fountain, Gate* (1975), *The Retrieval System* (1978), *Our Ground Time Here Will Be Brief* (1982), and *Quit Monks or Die!* (1999). Her books of poetry include *The Long Approach* (1985), *Nurture* (1989), *Looking for Luck* (1992), *Connecting the Dots* (1996), *Selected Poems, 1960–1990* (1999), and *Jack and Other New Poems* (2005). She has published four books of essays: *To Make a Prairie* (1979); *In Deep: Country Essays* (1987), which includes both new and previously published prose; *Women, Animals, and Vegetables* (1994), which also contains short stories; and *Always Beginning: Essays on a Life in Poetry* (2000).

Interesting interviews with Kumin include Karla Hammond, "An Interview with Maxine Kumin," *Western Humanities Review* 33 (1979); Shelley Armitage, "An Interview with Maxine Kumin," *Paintbrush* 7–8 (1980–81); Shomer, Enid, "An Interview with Maxine Kumin," *Massachusetts Review* 37 (1996/97); Steve Kronen, "An Interview with Maxine Kumin," *Shenandoah* 48 (1998); Jeffrey S. Cramer, "Peaceable Island: A Conversation with Maxine Kumin and Victor Kumin," *New Letters* 66 (2000); Steven Ratiner's "Maxine Kumin: New Life in the Barn," in *Giving Their Word: Conversations with Contemporary Poets* (2002); William Baer's interview in *Fourteen on Form: Conversations with Poets* (2004). A new collection of essays on Kumin's work is *Telling the Barn Swallow: Poets on the Poetry of Maxine Kumin* (1997), ed. Emily Grosholz. Individual critical work on Kumin may be found in Philip Booth, "Maxine Kumin's Survival," *American Poetry Review* (1978); Sybil P. Estess, "Past Halfway: The Retrieval System by Maxine Kumin," *Iowa Review* 10 (1979); Alicia Ostriker's discussion in her *Stealing the Language: The Emergence of Women's Poetry in America* (1986); Peter Harris, "Poetry Chronicle: Hunger, Hope, and Nurture: Poetry from Michael Ryan, the Chinese Democracy Movement, and Maxine Kumin," *Virginia Quarterly Review* 67 (1991); Diana Hume George, "Keeping Our Working Distance: Maxine Kumin's Poetry of Loss and Survival," in *Aging and Gender in Literature: Studies in Creativity* (1993), ed. Anne M. Wyatt-Brown and Janice Rossen; Alicia Ostriker, "Making the Connection: The Nature Poetry of Maxine Kumin," in her *Dancing at the Devil's Party: Essays on Poetry, Politics, and the Erotic* (2000); and Ben Howard, "A Secular Believer: The Agnostic Art of Maxine Kumin," *Shenandoah* 52 (2002).

Jhumpa Lahiri

Lahiri's first collection of stories is *Interpreter of Maladies: Stories* (1999), and her first novel is *The Namesake* (2003). A collection of essays is *Jhumpa Lahiri, the Master Storyteller: A Critical Response to Interpreter of Maladies* (2002).

Dilys Laing

Laing's books include the poetry collections *Another England* (1941), *Birth Is Farewell* (1944), *Walk through Two Landscapes* (1949), and *Poems from a Cage* (1961), as well as a novel, *The Great Year* (1948). Her posthumous *Collected Poems* (1967) contains some previously unpublished poems and an introduction by M. L. Rosenthal. Poems by Laing appear in *The World Split Open: Four Centuries of Women Poets in England and America, 1552–1950* (1974), ed. Louise Bernikow; *Parallels: Artists/Poets* (1993), ed. Grace Glueck; and in *The Massachusetts Review* 34 (1993).

Nella Larsen

Larsen's novels include *Quicksand* (1928) and *Passing* (1929), while a number of her essays, reviews, and short stories have also been published in *An Intimation of Things Distant: The Collected Fiction of Nella Larsen*, ed. Charles Larson (1992). In 2001 Larson also edited *The Complete Fiction of Nella Larsen*.

For an introduction to her life and work, see *American Women Writers*, ed. Lina Mainiero and Langdon Lynne Faust (1980), and Cynthia Wall, *Women of the Harlem Renaissance* (1995). Other critical and biographical studies are included in Addison Gayle Jr., *The Way of the New World* (1975); Hazel Carby, *Reconstructing Womanhood: The Emergence of the Afro-American Woman Novelist* (1987); Henry Louis Gates, *Figures in Black* (1987); Elizabeth Ammons, *Conflicting Stories: American Women Writers at the Turn into the Twentieth Century* (1992); Larson, *Invisible Darkness: Jean Toomer and Nella Larsen* (1993); Ann duCille, *The Coupling Convention: Sex, Text, and Tradition in Black Women's Fiction* (1993); Thadious Davis, *Nella Larsen, Novelist of the Harlem Renaissance: A Woman's Life Unveiled* (1994); Jacquelyn Y. McLendon, *The Politics of Color in the Fiction of Jessie Fauset and Nella Larsen* (1995); and Jessica Rabin, *Surviving the Crossing: (Im)migration, Ethnicity, and Gender in Willa Cather, Gertrude Stein, and Nella Larsen* (2004).

Mary Lavin

Lavin's collections of short stories include *Tales from Bective Bridge* (1942), *The Long Ago* (1944), *The Becker Wives* (1946; published in the United States as *At Sallygap* in 1947), *The Patriot Son* (1956), *The Great Wave* (1961), *In the Middle of the Fields* (1967), *A Memory* (1973), *The Shrine* (1977), and *A Family Likeness* (1985). *Selected Stories* appeared in 1959 and 1984; *The Collected Stories* in 1971; and *The Stories of Mary Lavin*, 3 vols., in 1964, 1973, and 1985. Lavin has also published two novels, *The House in Clewe Street* (1945) and *Mary O'Grady* (1950). Excerpts from interviews with Lavin may be found in Maurice Harmon, "From Conversations with Mary Lavin," *Irish University Review* 27 (1997). For biographical material, see Leah Levenson, *The Four Seasons of Mary Lavin* (1998). Full-length studies of Lavin's work include Zack Brown, *Mary Lavin* (1975); Richard F. Peterson, *Mary Lavin* (1978); and A. A. Kelly, *Mary Lavin, Quiet Rebel: A Study of Her Short Stories* (1980). See also the "Mary Lavin Issue," *Irish University Review* 9 (1979). Other useful essays on Lavin's achievement include V. S. Prichett's introduction to the *Collected Stories* (1971); Patricia Meszaros, "Woman as Artist: The Fiction of Mary Lavin," *Critique* 24 (1982); Maria Gottwald, "Narrative Strategies in the *Selected Stories* of Mary Lavin," in *Anglo-Irish and Irish Literature: Aspects of Language and Culture* (1988), ed. Birgit Bramsback and Martin Croghan; Jeanette Roberts Shumaker, "Sacrificial Women in Short Stories by Mary Lavin and Edna O'Brien," *Studies in Short Fiction* 32 (1995); Rachael Sealy Lynch, "'The Fabulous Female Form': The Deadly Erotics of the Male Gaze in Mary Lavin's *The House in Clewe Street*," *Twentieth Century Literature* 43 (1997); and Marie Arndt, "Narratives of Internal Exile in Mary Lavin's Short Stories," *International Journal of English Studies* 2 (2002).

Ursula Le Guin

Le Guin's works include *Rocannon's World* (1966), *A Wizard of Earthsea* (1968), *The Left Hand of Darkness* (1969), *The Dispossessed* (1974), *The Wind's Twelve Quarters* (1975), *Orsinian Tales* (1976), *Malafrena* (1979), *The Beginning Place* (1980), *The Compass Rose* (1982), *Women of Vision* (1988), *Dancing at the Edge of the World: Thoughts on Words, Women, and Places* (1988), *Tehanu: The Last Book of Earthsea* (1990), *Blue Moon over Thurman Street* (1993), *Buffalo Gals, Won't You Come Out Tonight* (1994), *Four Ways to Forgiveness* (1995), *Unlocking the Air and Other Stories* (1996), *Worlds of Exile and Delusion* (1996), *The Telling* (2000), *Tales from Earthsea* (2001), *The Other Wind* (2001), *The Birthday of the World and Other Stories* (2002), and *Changing Planes* (2004). She has written numerous essays and children's books as well as books of poetry, including *Hard Works, and Other Poems* (1981), *Wild Oats and Fireweed: New Poems* (1988), and *Going Out with Peacocks and Other Poems* (1994). A multimedia work produced with Todd Barton, Margaret Chodos, and George Heish is *Always Coming Home* (1985). Le Guin has edited two collections of science fiction: *The Language of the Night: Essays on Fantasy and Science Fiction* (1992) and *The Norton Book of Science Fiction: North American Science Fiction, 1960–1990*, with Brian Attebery (1993). She also translated Angelica Gorodischer's *Kalpa Imperial: The Greatest Empire that Never Was* (2005). Some informative new critical texts by Le Guin are "The Carrier Bag Theory of Fiction" in *The Ecocriticism Reader: Landmarks in Literary Ecology* (1996), ed. Cheryll Glotfelty and Harold Fromm; "A Woman's Liberation," in *A Woman's Liberation: A Choice of Futures by and about Women* (2001), ed. Connie Willis and Sheila Williams; and the entire volume of Le Guin's work entitled *The Wave in the Mind: Talks and Essays on the Writer, the Reader, and the Imagination* (2004). Two interviews are William Walsh, "I Am a Woman Writer; I Am a Western Writer: An Interview with Ursula Le Guin," *Kenyon Review* 17 (1995), and Nicholas O'Connell's conversation with Le Guin in his *At the Field's End: Interviews with 22 Pacific Northwest Writers* (1998).

Full-length studies include George E. Slusser, *The Farthest Shores of Ursula K. Le Guin* (1976); Barbara J. Bucknall, *Ursula K. Le Guin* (1981); James W. Bittner, *Approaches to the Fiction of Ursula K. Le Guin* (1984); Charlotte Spivack, *Ursula K. Le Guin* (1984); Bernard Selinger, *Le Guin and Identity in Contemporary Fiction* (1988); Elizabeth Cummin, *Understanding Ursula K. Le Guin* (1990); Kathryn Ross Wayne, *Redefining Moral Education: Life, Le Guin, and Language* (1996); Donna R. White, *Dancing with Dragons: Ursula K. Le Guin and the Critics* (1999); Warren G. Rochelle, *Communities of the Heart: The Rhetoric of Myth in the Fiction of Ursula K. Le Guin* (2001); Heinz Tschachler, *Ursula K. Le Guin* (2001); and Mike Cadden, *Ursula K. Le Guin Beyond Genre: Fiction for Children and Adults* (2005). Three collections of critical essays about her work are *Ursula K. Le Guin* (1979), ed. Joseph Olender and Martin Greenberg; *Ursula K. Le Guin: Voyager to Inner Lands and to Outer Space* (1979), ed. Joe DeBolt; and *Ursula K. Le Guin* (1986), ed. Harold Bloom. Helpful essays are Elizabeth Cummin, "The Land-Lady's Homebirth: Revisiting Ursula K. Le Guin Worlds," *Science Fiction Studies* 17 (1990); Susan Bassnett, "Remaking the Old World: Ursula Le Guin and the American Tradition," in *Where No Man Has Gone Before: Women and Science Fiction* (1991), ed. Lucie Armitt; Kristine J. Anderson, "Places Where a

Woman Could Talk: Ursula K. Le Guin and the Feminist Linguistic Utopia," *Women and Language* 15 (1992); John Moore, "An Archaeology of the Future: Ursula Le Guin and Anarcho-primitivism," *Foundation* 63 (1995); Mike Cadden, "Speaking Across the Spaces Between Us: Ursula Le Guin's Dialogic Use of Character in Children's and Adult Literature," *Paradoxa* 2 (1996); Linda Simon, "William James's Lost Souls in Ursula Le Guin's Utopia," *Philosophy and Literature* 28 (2004); and Zina Petersen, "Balancing Act: Ursula Kroeber Le Guin," in *Impossible to Hold: Women and Culture in the 1960's* (2005), ed. Avital H. Bloch and Lauri Umansky. Le Guin's work is also discussed in Carl Freedman, *Critical Theory and Science Fiction* (2000). Useful, but somewhat dated, is Elizabeth Cummins Cogell, *Ursula K. Le Guin: A Primary and Secondary Bibliography* (1983).

Doris Lessing
Most of Lessing's collections of short stories and her novels, including the five-volume *Children of Violence* (1952–69), *The Golden Notebook* (1962), *A Man and Two Women* (1963), *African Stories* (1969), *Briefing for a Descent into Hell* (1971), and *Summer before the Dark* (1973), are available in paperback. She has also written a series of science fiction novels, beginning with *Shikasta* (1979). Her most recent work includes nonfiction, novels, and short stories, such as *Prisons We Choose to Live Inside* (1987), *The Wind Blows Away Our Words* (1987), *African Laughter: Four Visits to Zimbabwe* (1992), *Winter in July* (1993), *Under My Skin* (1994), *The Real Thing: Stories and Sketches* (1992), and *London Observed: Stories and Sketches* (1992). *A Small Personal Voice* (1974), ed. Paul Schlueter, is a selection of Lessing's essays on her life and writings, on other writers, and on Africa. *Notebooks, Memoirs, Archives: Reading and Re-Reading Doris Lessing*, ed. Jenny Taylor, came out in 1982; and *The Doris Lessing Reader* appeared in 1989.

Critical and biographical full-length studies include Dorothy Brewster, *Doris Lessing* (1965); Paul Schleuter, *The Novels of Doris Lessing* (1973); Mary Ann Singleton, *The City and the Veld* (1977); Roberta Rubinstein, *The Novelistic Vision of Doris Lessing* (1979); Lorna Sage, *Doris Lessing* (1983); Betsy Draine, *Substance under Pressure: Artistic Coherence and Evolving Form in the Novels of Doris Lessing* (1983); Mona Kapp, *Doris Lessing* (1984); Katherine Fishburn, *The Unexpected Universe of Doris Lessing: A Study in Narrative Technique* (1985); and Roxanne J. Fand, *The Dialogic Self: Reconstructing Subjectivity in Woolf, Lessing, and Atwood* (1999). Three useful essay collections are *Doris Lessing: Critical Essays* (1974), ed. Annis Pratt and L. S. Dembo; *Critical Essays on Doris Lessing* (1990), ed. Claire Sprague and Virginia Tiger; and *In Pursuit of Doris Lessing: Nine Nations Reading* (1990), ed. Claire Sprague. Lessing is also discussed in Sally Robinson, *Engendering the Subject: Gender and Self-Representation in Contemporary Women's Fiction* (1991). Dee Seligman compiled an annotated bibliography in 1981.

Meridel Le Sueur
Le Sueur's works include *Annunciation* (1935), *Salute to Spring* (1940), *North Star Country* (1945), *Sparrow Hawk* (1950), *Crusaders* (1955), *Corn Village* (1970), and *Women on the Bread Lines* (1978). Her novel *The Girl*, which was written in 1932 but not published until 1978, was reprinted in 1991. *Song: Collected Essays and Stories* (1977) was revised and enlarged in 1990. *Harvest: Collected Stories* appeared in 1977. Elaine Hedges includes important biographical background in her edition of and introduction to *Ripening: Selected Work of Meridel Le Sueur, 1927–1980* (1982). Le Sueur is also discussed in Linda Wagner-Martin, *The Modern American Novel, 1914–1945* (1990), and Nora Ruth Roberts, *Three Radical Women Writers: Class and Gender in Meridel Le Sueur, Tillie Olsen, and Josephine Herbst* (1996). Interesting critical essays are Blanche H. Gelfant's chapter on Le Sueur in *Women Writing in America* (1985); Paula Rabinowitz, "Maternity as History: Gender and the Transformation of Gender in Meridel Le Sueur's *The Girl*," *Contemporary Literature* 29 (1988); Constance Coiner, "Literature of Resistance: The Intersection of Feminism and the Communist Left in Meridel Le Sueur and Tillie Olsen," in *Left Politics and the Literary Profession* (1990), ed. Lennard J. Davis; and Phaedra Greenwood, "Post Cards from Meridel," in *The Epistolary Form and the Letter as Artifact* (1991), ed. Jim Villani.

Denise Levertov
Levertov's books of poems include *The Double Image* (1946), *Here and Now* (1957), *Overland to the Islands* (1958), *With Eyes at the Back of Our Heads* (1960), *The Jacob's Ladder* (1961), *O Taste and See* (1964), *The Sorrow Dance* (1967), *Relearning the Alphabet* (1970), *To Stay Alive* (1971), *Footprints* (1972), *The Freeing of the Dust* (1975), *Life in the Forest* (1978), *Candles in Babylon* (1982), *Breathing the Water* (1987), *A Door in the Hive* (1989), *Evening Train* (1992), *Sands of the Well* (1996), and *The Stream and the Sapphire* (1997). She also has four collections: *Collected Earlier Poems, 1940–1960* (1979), *Poems, 1960–1967* (1983), *Poems, 1968–1972* (1987), and *Poems: 1972–1982* (2001). *The Poet in the World* (1973), *Light Up the Cave* (1981), and *New and Selected Essays* (1992) are collections of her essays and reviews, as is *Denise Levertov: In Her Own Prov-*

ince (1979), ed. Linda Wagner-Martin. Levertov also published a translation of Jean Joubert's *Black Iris* in 1988. Autobiographical writings by Levertov are collected in *Tesserae: Memories & Suppositions* (1995). Interviews with Levertov include those in *Delicious Imaginations: Conversations with Contemporary Writers* (1998), ed. Sarah Griffiths and Kevin J. Kehrwald; Nicholas O'Connell, *At the Field's End: Interviews with 22 Pacific Northwest Writers* (1998); and the enormously helpful *Conversations with Denise Levertov* (1998), ed. Jewel Spears Brooker. Collections of Levertov's correspondence with other poets include *The Letters of Denise Levertov and William Carlos Williams* (1998), ed. Christopher MacGowan, and *The Letters of Robert Duncan and Denise Levertov* (2004), ed. Robert J. Bertholf and Albert Gelpi.

Valuable analyses of Levertov's work include Rachel Blau DuPlessis, "The Critique of Consciousness and Myth in Levertov, Rich, and Rukeyser," in *Shakespeare's Sisters* (1979), ed. Sandra M. Gilbert and Susan Gubar; Linda W. Wagner, "Levertov and Rich: The Later Poems," *South Carolina Review* 11 (1979); Diana Surman, "Inside and Outside in the Poetry of Denise Levertov," *Critical Quarterly* 22 (1980); Bonnie Costello, " 'Flooded with Otherness,' " *Parnassus* 8 (1980); John Felstiner, "Poetry and Political Experience: Denise Levertov," in *Coming to Light: American Women Poets in the Twentieth Century* (1985), ed. Diane Wood Middlebrook and Marilyn Yalom; Paul A. Lacey, "Denise Levertov: A Poetry of Exploration," in *American Women Poets* (1986), ed. Harold Bloom; Sandra M. Gilbert, "Revolutionary Love: Denise Levertov and the Poetics of Politics," in *Conversant Essays: Contemporary Poets on Poetry* (1990), ed. James McCorkle; José Rodríguez Herrera, "Eros at the Temple Stream: Eroticism in the Poetry of Denise Levertov," *Gramma* 4 (1996); and Donna K. Hollenberg, "'History as I desired it': Ekphrasis as Postmodern Witness in Denise Levertov's Late Poetry," *Modernism / Modernity* 10 (2003). Useful full-length studies are Audrey T. Rodgers, *Denise Levertov* (1993); Bodo Murray, *Poetry as Prayer: Denise Levertov* (2001); and the excellent collection of essays, *Denise Levertov: New Perspectives* (2000), ed. Anne Colclough Little and Susie Paul. For a very helpful collection of critical essays dedicated entirely to Levertov's work, see *Renascence* 50 (1997/98). In addition, see Linda A. Kinnahan, *Poetics of the Feminine: Authority and Literary Tradition in William Carlos Williams, Denise Levertov, and Kathleen Fraser* (1994). Feminist perspectives on Levertov can be found in Alicia Ostriker, *Stealing the Language: The Emergence of Women's Poetry in America* (1986). See also the useful collection *Critical Essays on Denise Levertov* (1990), ed. Linda Wagner-Martin, and the special "Denise Levertov Issue" of *Twentieth-Century Literature* 38 (1992). A valuable resource is Liana Sakelliou-Schultz, *Denise Levertov: An Annotated Primary and Secondary Bibliography* (1988).

Dorothy Livesay

Volumes of Livesay's poetry include *Selected Poems, 1926–1956* (1957), *The Documentaries: Selected Longer Poems* (1968), and *Collected Poems: The Two Seasons* (1972). Subsequent collections include *Nine Poems of Farewell, 1972–1973* (1973), *Ice Age* (1975), and *The Woman I Am* (1977), as well as a volume of short stories, *A Winnipeg Childhood* (1973). Also valuable is *Archive for Our Times: Previously Uncollected and Unpublished Poems of Dorothy Livesay* (1998), ed. Dean Irvine. Livesay's autobiography is entitled *Journey with My Selves: A Memoir, 1909–1963* (1991). For additional biographical information, see two interviews: Doug Beardsley and Rosemary Sullivan's piece in *Canadian Poetry* 3 (1978) and Jorn Carlsen's in *Kunapipi* 1 (1979), as well as the full-length biography *Dorothy Livesay: Patterns in a Poetic Life* (1992) by Peter Stevens. Critical essays include Peter Stevens, "Out of Silence and Across the Distance: The Poetry of Dorothy Livesay," *Queen's Quarterly* 4 (1969) and his "Dorothy Livesay: The Love Poetry," *Canadian Literature* (1971); Debbie Foulks, "Livesay's Two Seasons of Love," *Canadian Literature* 74 (1977); Lee B. Thompson, "A Coat of Many Cultures: The Poetry of Dorothy Livesay," *Journal of Popular Culture* 15 (1981); Fiona Sparrow, "The Self-Completing Tree: Livesay's African Poetry," *Canadian Poetry* 20 (1987); Dean J. Irvine, "Among Masses: Dorothy Livesay and English Canadian Leftist Magazine Culture of the Early 1930s," *Essays on Canadian Writing* 68 (1999); and Susan Gingell, "Claiming Positive Semantic Space for Women: The Poetry of Dorothy Livesay," *Essays on Canadian Writing* 74 (2001). A volume containing useful critical essays on Livesay's career and history is *A Public and Private Voice: Essays on the Life and Work of Dorothy Livesay* (1986), ed. Lindsay Dorney, Gerland Noonan, and Paul Tuessen.

Audre Lorde

One collection of Lorde's poetry is *Undersong: Chosen Poems, Old and New* (1992), which contains poems and revisions from the earlier *Chosen Poems, Old and New* (1982). Other volumes include *First Cities* (1968), *Cables to Rage* (1970), *New York Headshop and Museum* (1974), *Coal* (1976), *The Black Unicorn* (1978), *The Cancer Journal* (1980), *Zami: A New Spelling of My Name* (1982), *Our Dead behind Us* (1986), *The Marvelous Arithmetics of Distance: Poems, 1987–1992* (1993). Newer poetic collections by Lorde are *Fugitive Colors / Chrystos* (1995) and *The Collected Poems of Audre Lorde*

(1997). Selected personal writings by Lorde are published in *The Cancer Journals* (1997). She also produced two collections of essays and speeches: *Sister Outsider* (1986), which includes the pamphlet *Uses of the Erotic: The Erotic as Power*, and *A Burst of Light* (1988). See also "Audre Lorde: A Special Section" *Callaloo* 14 (1991). Four recent critical essays by Lorde are "Age, Race, Class, and Sex: Women Redefining Difference," in *Dangerous Liaisons: Gender, Nation, and Postcolonial Perspectives* (1997), ed. Anne McClintock, Aamir Mufti, and Ella Shohat; "Poetry Is Not a Luxury," in *By Herself: Women Reclaim Poetry* (2000), ed. Molly McQuade; "The Master's Tools Will Never Dismantle the Master's House," in *Feminism and "Race"* (2001), ed. Kum-Kum Bhavnani, and "The Uses of the Erotic: The Erotic as Power," in *Black Feminist Cultural Criticism* (2001), ed. Jacqueline Bobo.

Karla Hammond has a useful interview with Lorde in *Denver Quarterly* 16 (1981), and there is another interview in *Black Women Writers at Work* (1984), ed. Claudia Tate. Very helpful are *Conversations with Audre Lorde* (2004), ed. Joan Wylie Hall, and the biographical work by Alexis De Veaux, *Warrior Poet: A Biography of Audre Lorde* (2004). An interesting critical essay on Lorde and Maya Angelou is R. G. Stepto, "The Phenomenal Woman and the Severed Daughter," *Parnassus* 8 (1980). Helpful critical articles are Jerome Brooks, "In the Name of the Father: The Poetry of Audre Lorde," and Joan Martins, "The Unicorn is Black: Audre Lorde in Retrospect," both in *Black Women Writers (1950–1980)* (1984), ed. Mari Evans; Gloria T. Hull, "Living on the Line: Audre Lorde and *Our Dead behind Us*," in *Changing Our Words: Essays on Criticism, Theory, and Writing by Black Women* (1989), ed. Cheryl Wall; Estella Lauter, "Re-Visioning Creativity: Audre Lorde's Refiguration of Eros as the Black Mother Within," *Writing the Woman Artist: Essays on Poetics, Politics, and Portraiture* (1991), ed. Suzanne W. Jones; Anna Wilson, "Audre Lorde and the African American Tradition: When the Family Is Not Enough," in *New Lesbian Criticism: Literary and Cultural Readings* (1992), ed. Sally Munt; Ruth Ginzburg, "Audre Lorde's (Nonessentialist) Lesbian Eros," *Hypatia* 7 (1992); and Erin G. Carlston, "*Zami* and the Politics of Plural Identity," in *Sexual Practice, Textual Theory: Lesbian Cultural Criticism* (1993), ed. Susan J. Wolfe and Julia Penelope. Newer essays in larger critical collections include R. Ginzberg, "Audre Lorde's (nonessentialist) Lesbian Eros," in *Adventures in Lesbian Philosophy* (1994), ed. Claudia Card; Zofia Burr, "Audre Lorde: The Location of Poetry in the United States," in *Articulating the Global and the Local: Globalization and Cultural Studies* (1997), ed. Ann Cvetkovich and Douglas Kellner; Brenda Carr, " 'A Woman Speaks . . . I Am Woman and Not White': Politics of Voice, Tactical Essentialism, and Cultural Intervention in Audre Lorde's Activist Poetics and Practice," in *Race-ing Representation: Voice, History, and Sexuality* (1998), ed. Kostas Myrsiades and Linda Myrsiades; Kathleen R. Wallace, " 'All Things Natural Are Strange": Audre Lorde, Urban Nature, and Cultural Place, in *The Nature of Cities: Ecocriticism and Urban Environments* (1999), ed. Michael Bennett and David W. Teague; Zofia Burr, "Audre Lorde and the Responsibility of the Reader," in her *Of Women, Poetry, and Power: Strategies of Address in Dickinson, Miles, Brooks, Lorde, and Angelou* (2002); and Sharon Barnes, "Marvelous Arithmetics: Womanist Spirituality in the Poetry of Audre Lorde," in *Things of the Spirit: Women Writers Constructing Spirituality* (2004), ed. Kristina K. Groover. Helpful essays recently published in journals include M. Pilar Sánchez Calle, "The Maternal, the Lesbian and the Political: Explorations of the Erotic in Audre Lorde's Poetry," *Gramma* 4 (1996); Margaret Kissam Morris, "Audre Lorde: Textual Authority and the Embodied Self," *Frontiers* 23 (2002); Lexi Rudnitsky, "The 'Power' and 'Sequelae' of Audre Lorde's Syntactical Strategies," *Callaloo* 26 (2003); and Lori Walk, "Audre Lorde's Life Writing: The Politics of Location," *Women's Studies* 32 (2003).

Amy Lowell

Lowell's *The Complete Poetical Works* was published in 1955. *Selected Poems*, edited by Honor Moore, was published in 2004. Harley F. MacNair edited *Florence Ayscough and Amy Lowell: Correspondence of a Friendship* (1945), and E. Claire Healey and Keith Cushman edited *The Letters of D. H. Lawrence and Amy Lowell, 1914–1925* in 1985. Valuable background can be found in Clemens David Heymann, *American Aristocracy: The Lives and Times of James Russell, Amy, and Robert Lowell* (1980). Full-length studies and biographies include Damon S. Foster, *Amy Lowell* (1935); F. Cudworth Flint, *Amy Lowell* (1969); Glenn R. Ruihley, *The Thorn of a Rose: Amy Lowell Reconsidered* (1975); Jean Gould, *Amy: The World of Amy Lowell and the Imagist Movement* (1975); Richard Benvenuto, *Amy Lowell* (1985); and the valuable collection of essays *Amy Lowell, American Modern* (2004), ed. Adrienne Munich and Melissa Bradshaw. Analyses of Lowell's relationship to the lesbian tradition are offered in Lillian Faderman, "Warding Off the Watch and Ward Society: Amy Lowell's Treatment of the Lesbian Theme," *Gay Books Bulletin* (1979); Mary E. Galvin, "Imagery and Invisibility: Amy Lowell and the Erotics of Particularity," in her *Queer Poetics: Five Modernist Women Writers* (1999); and Susan McCabe, " 'A Queer Lot' and the Lesbians of 1914: Amy Lowell, H.D., and Gertrude Stein," in *Challenging Boundaries: Gender and Periodization* (2000), ed. Joyce W. Warren and Margaret Dickie. Other critical essays on Lowell include Kathleen Flanagan, "Ezra Pound and Amy Lowell: English Poetics in Renditions of Chinese Poetry," *Paideuma* 15 (1986); Cheryl Walker, "Women and Feminine Literary Traditions: Amy Lowell and the Androgynous Persona," in her *Masks Outrageous and Austere: Culture, Psyche, and Persona in Modern Women Poets* (1992); Andrew Thacker, "Amy Lowell and H. D.: The Other Imagists," *Women: A Cultural Review* 4 (1993); Yunte Huang, "The Intertextual Travel of Amy Lowell," in her *Transpacific Displacement Ethnography, Translation, and Intertextual Travel in Twentieth-century American Literature* (2002); and Melissa Bradshaw, "Outselling the Modernisms of Men: Amy Lowell and the Art of Self-Commodification," *Victorian Poetry* 38 (2000).

Mina Loy

Loy's volumes of poetry include *Lunar Baedeker* (1923), *Lunar Baedeker and Time-Tables* (1958), *At the Door of the House* (1980), *Love Songs* (1981), *Virgins Plus Curtains* (1981), and *The Last Lunar Baedeker* (1982), a nearly complete collection of her poems printed to honor the centennial of her birth and edited by Roger L. Conover. New in 1996 was *The Lost Lunar Baedeker*, ed. Roger L. Conover. Loy also published *Insel* (1991), a roman à clef, edited by Elizabeth Arnold and with an introduction by Roger L. Conover, and has a great many unpublished works in the Collection of American Literature at the Beinecke Rare Book and Manuscript Library of Yale University.

A biography is Carolyn Burke, *Becoming Modern: The Life of Mina Loy* (1996), and a full-length critical study is Virginia Kouidis, *Mina Loy: American Modernist Poet* (1980), which also includes an extensive bibliography of Loy's published poetry, drama, and prose. Interviews and a valuable selection of critical work on Loy are included in *Mina Loy: American Modernist Poet*, ed. Maeera Shreiber and Keith Tuma (1998). Loy is also discussed in Linda Kinnahan, *Poetics of the Feminine: Authority and Literary Tradition in William Carlos Williams, Mina Loy, Denise Levertov, and Kathleen Fraser* (1994); Tyrus Miller, *Late Modernism* (1999); Janet Lyon, *Manifestoes* (1999); Mary Galvin, *Queer Politics* (1999); and Rachel Blau DuPlessis, *Genders, Races, and Religious Cultures in Modern American Poetry, 1908–1934* (2001). Useful critical articles are Constance Hunting, "The Morality of Mina Loy," *Sagetrieb* 2 (1983); Carolyn Burke, "The New Poetry and the New Woman: Mina Loy," in *Coming to Light: American Women Poets in the Twentieth Century* (1985), ed. Diane Wood Middlebrook and Marilyn Yalom; Melita Schaum, "'Moonflowers out of Muck': Mina Loy and the Female Autobiographical Epic," *Massachusetts Studies in English* 10 (1986); and Rachel Blau DuPlessis, "'Seismic Orgasm': Sexual Intercourse, Gender Narratives, and Lyric Ideology in Mina Loy," in *Studies in Historical Change* (1992), ed. Ralph Cohen.

Katherine Mansfield

Mansfield's stories appear in a complete one-volume edition, *The Short Stories of Katherine Mansfield* (1937). Her *Journal* (1954), was edited by J. Middleton Murry; and *Letters and Journals of Katherine Mansfield: A Selection* (1977), was edited by C. K. Stead. *The Collected Letters of Katherine Mansfield* was edited in three volumes by Vincent O'Sullivan and Margaret Scott in 1984; vol. 1 covers 1903–17; vol. 2, 1918–19; and vol. 3, 1919–20.

Biographies, memoirs, and critical studies include S. Berkman, *Katherine Mansfield, a Critical Study* (1951); Leslie Moore, *Katherine Mansfield* (1971); John Carswell, *Lives and Letters* (1978); Jeffrey Meyers, *Katherine Mansfield: A Biography* (1978); Anthony Alpers, *The Life of Katherine Mansfield* (1980); James Moore, *Gurdjieff and Mansfield* (1980); Andrew Gurr, *Writers in Exile: The Identity of Home in Modern Literature* (1981); Clare Hanson and Andrew Gurr, *Katherine Mansfield* (1981); Nora Crone, *A Portrait of Katherine Mansfield* (1985); Gillian Boddy, *Katherine Mansfield: The Woman and the Writer* (1988); Jane Phillmore, *Katherine Mansfield* (1989); Heather Murray, *Double Lives: Women in the Stories of Katherine Mansfield* (1990); and Janet Sydney Kaplan, *Katherine Mansfield and the Origins of Modernist Fiction* (1991). Mary Burgan, *Illness, Gender, and Writing: The Case of Katherine Mansfield* (1994), is an important contribution. See also Pamela Dunbar, *Radical Mansfield: Double Discourse in Katherine Mansfield's Stories* (1997), and Angela Smith, *Katherine Mansfield and Virginia Woolf: A Public of Two* (1999). A collection of essays is *Critical Essays on Katherine Mansfield* (1993), ed. Rhoda B. Nathan. For a useful resource, see Brownlee Jean Kirkpatrick, *A Bibliography of Katherine Mansfield* (1989).

Paule Marshall

Marshall's novels are *Brown Girl, Brownstones* (1959), *The Chosen Place, the Timeless People* (1969), *Praisesong for the Widow* (1983), and *Daughters* (1991). Her novella *Merle*, as well as her short stories "The Valley Between," "Brooklyn," "Barbados," and "To Da-duh, in Memoriam," were originally collected in *Reena and Other Stories* (1983) and later reprinted as *Merle: A Novella and Other Stories* (1985). Another collection of short stories, *Soul Clap Hands and Sing* (1961), was reprinted in 1987. Marshall also authored a teleplay based on her novel *Brown Girl, Brownstones*.

Studies of Marshall and her work include Eugenia DeLamotte, *Places of Silence, Journeys of Freedom: The Fiction of Paule Marshall*

(1998); Bernhard Melchior, Re/Visioning the Self: Autobiographical and Cross-Cultural Dimensions in the Work of Paule Marshall (1998); and Heather Hathaway, Caribbean Waves: Relocating Claude MacKay and Paule Marshall (1999). A useful essay is Barbara Christian, "Sculpture and Space: The Interdependency of Character and Culture in the Novels of Paule Marshall," in Black Women Novelists: The Development of a Tradition, 1892–1976 (1980). Other useful references are Harihar Kulkarni, "Paule Marshall: A Bibliography," Callaloo 16 (1993), and Darly Cumber Dance, "An Interview with Paule Marshall," Southern Review 28 (1992). The special issue of Callaloo 18 (1983) is devoted to her work.

Mary McCarthy
McCarthy published two collections of stories, The Company She Keeps (1942) and Cast a Cold Eye (1950). Her novels are The Oasis (1948), The Groves of Academe (1952), A Charmed Life (1955), The Group (1963), Birds of America (1971), and Cannibals and Missionaries (1979). Her autobiographical Memories of a Catholic Girlhood appeared in 1957. On the Contrary (1961) and The Writings on the Wall (1970) are collections of essays on literary and cultural topics. Travel books are Venice Observed (1956) and The Stones of Florence (1959). Her essays on Vietnam and the Watergate hearings are collected in The Seventeenth Degree (1974). Sights and Spectacles (1956) has been republished and enlarged as Mary McCarthy's Theater Chronicles, 1937–1962 (1963). Intellectual Memoirs: New York, 1936–1938, with a foreword by Elizabeth Hardwick, was published in 1992. A Bolt from the Blue and Other Essays, ed. A. O. Scott appeared in 2002.

Critical and biographical writings about her include Doris Grumbach, The Company She Kept (1967); Irwin Stock, Mary McCarthy (1967); Willena S. Hardy, Mary McCarthy (1981); Carol Gelderman, Mary McCarthy: A Life (1988); Carol Brightman, Writing Dangerously: A Critical Biography of Mary McCarthy (1992); and Frances Kiernan, Seeing Mary Plain: A Life of Mary McCarthy (2000). Useful essays include Elizabeth Hardwick's chapter in A View of My Own (1963); and Rosalie Hewitt, "'Home Address for the Self': Mary McCarthy's Autobiographical Journey," Journal of Narrative Technique 12 (1982). Carol Gelderman edited Conversations with Mary McCarthy (1991). Joy Bennett and Gabriella Hochmann have compiled Mary McCarthy: An Annotated Bibliography (1992).

Carson McCullers
McCullers's works are The Heart Is a Lonely Hunter (1940), Reflections in a Golden Eye (1941), The Member of the Wedding (1946), The Ballad of the Sad Café (1951), The Square Root of Wonderful (1958), Clock without Hands (1961), Sweet as a Pickle and Clean as a Pig: Poems (1964), and The Mortgaged Heart (1971), ed. M. G. Smith. Her Collected Works appeared in 1987. There are several biographies, including Richard Cook, Carson McCullers (1975); and Virginia S. Carr, The Lonely Hunter: A Biography of Carson McCullers (rev. 2003).

Critical studies include Oliver Evans, The Ballad of Carson McCullers (1966); Margaret McDowell, Carson McCullers (1980); and Virginia Spencer Carr, Understanding Carson McCullers (1990). Two essay collections are Carson McCullers, ed. Harold Bloom (1986); and Critical Essays on Carson McCullers, ed. Beverly Lyon Clark and Melvin J. Friedman (1996). Among other critical essays are Patricia S. Box, "Androgyny and the Musical Vision: A Study of Two Novels by Carson McCullers," Southern Quarterly 16 (1978); Louise Westling, "Carson McCullers's Amazon Nightmare," Modern Fiction Studies 28 (1982); and chapter 2 of The War of the Words (1987), by Sandra M. Gilbert and Susan Gubar. A valuable annotated bibliography, Carson McCullers, comp. Adrian Shapiro, Jackson Bryer, and Kathleen Field, appeared in 1980.

Charlotte Mew
Two volumes of Mew's collected work have been produced since her death: Collected Poems of Charlotte Mew (1953), with a memoir by Alida Monro, and Collected Poems and Prose (1981), ed. and with a critical introduction and helpful critical bibliography by Val Warner. Charlotte Mew and Her Friends (1988), by Penelope Fitzgerald, contains a selection of poems and useful biographical information. For a critical volume addressing the work of Mew and others, see Nelljean McConeghey Rice's A New Matrix for Modernism: A Study of the Lives and Poetry of Charlotte Mew and Anna Wickham (2003). Critical pieces on Mew are Val Warner, "Mary Magdalene and the Bride: The Work of Charlotte Mew," Poetry Nation 4 (1975); Linda Mizejewski, "Charlotte Mew and the Unrepentant Magdalene: A Myth in Transition," Texas Studies in Literature and Language 26 (1984); Gary Day and Gina Wisker, "Recuperating and Revaluing: Edith Sitwell and Charlotte Mew," in British Poetry, 1900–50: Aspects of Tradition (1995), ed. Gary Day; John Newton, "Charlotte Mew's Place in the Future of English Poetry," in New England Review 18 (1997); Dennis Denisoff, "Grave Passions: Enclosure and Exposure in Charlotte Mew's Graveyard Poetry," Victorian Poetry 38 (2000); Jessica Walsh, "'The Strangest Pain to Bear': Corporeality and Fear of Insanity in Charlotte Mew's Poetry," Victorian Poetry 40 (2002); and Michael Newton, "I See

Myself Among the Crowd: The Poetry of Charlotte Mew," *Poetry Review* 94 (2004).

Edna St. Vincent Millay
Millay's *Collected Sonnets* (1941) and *Collected Lyrics* (1943) were followed by *Collected Poems: Edna St. Vincent Millay* (1956), ed. Norma Millay. A revised and expanded version of the *Collected Sonnets* appeared in 1988, and Colin Falck edited *Selected Poems: The Centenary Edition* in 1991. Her prose sketches, *Distressing Dialogues*, published under the pseudonym Nancy Boyd, appeared in 1924. Her three verse plays—*Aria da Capo* (1920), *The Lamp and the Bell* (1921), *Two Slatterns and a King* (1921)—were collected in *Three Plays* (1926).

Allan Ross Macdougall edited *Letters of Edna St. Vincent Millay* in 1952. Biographical studies are Joan Dash, *A Life of One's Own: Three Gifted Women and the Men They Married* (1973); Anne Cheney, *Millay in Greenwich Village* (1975); Daniel Mark Epstein, *What Lips My Lips Have Kissed: The Loves and Love Poems of Edna St. Vincent Millay* (2001); Nancy Milford, *Savage Beauty: The Life of Edna St. Vincent Millay* (2001); and Marion Meade, *Bobbed Hair and Bathtub Gin: Writers Running Wild in the Twenties* (2004). Fuller treatments are Miriam Gurko, *Restless Spirit* (1957), and Jean Gould, *The Poet and Her Book* (1969). Useful brief introductions are Norman A. Brittin, *Edna St. Vincent Millay* (1967); James Gray, *Edna St. Vincent Millay* (1967); and Norman A. Brittin, *Edna St. Vincent Millay* (1982). Biographical information can also be found in William Drake, *The First Wave: Women Poets in America, 1915–1945* (1987). Two helpful collections of critical essays are *Critical Essays on Edna St. Vincent Millay* (1993), ed. William B. Thesing, and *Millay at 100: A Critical Reappraisal* (1995), ed. Diane P. Freedman. Other critical studies include Debra Fried, "Andromeda Unbound: Gender and Genre in Millay's Sonnets," *Twentieth-Century Literature* 32 (1986); Suzanne Clark, "The Unwarranted Discourse: Sentimental Community, Modernist Women, and the Case of Millay," *Genre* 20 (1987); Jean Gould, "Edna St. Vincent Millay: Saint of the Modern Sonnet," in *Faith of a (Woman) Writer* (1988), ed. Alice Kressler Harris and William McBrien; John Timberman Newcomb, "The Woman as Political Poet: Edna St Vincent Millay and the Mid-century Canon," *Criticism* 37 (1995); two articles—Cheryl Walker, "Antimodern, Modern, and Postmodern Millay: Contexts of Revaluation," and Suzanne Clark, "Jouissance and the Sentimental Daughter: Edna St. Vincent Millay"—both in *Gendered Modernisms: American Women Poets and their Readers* (1996), ed. Margaret Dickie and Thomas J. Travisano; Kathryn Mudgett, "'Feigning to be asleep when wide awake': Edna St Vincent Millay's Experiments in Free Verse," *Genre* 31 (1998); J. D. McClatchy, "Feeding on Havoc: The Poetics of Edna St Vincent Millay," *American Scholar* 72 (2003); Artemis Michailidou, "Edna St Vincent Millay, Muriel Rukeyser, and Adrienne Rich: Political Poetry, Social Protest, and the Place of the Woman Writer," *European Journal of American Culture* 22 (2003); Michailidou, "Edna St Vincent Millay and Anne Sexton: The Disruption of Domestic Bliss," *Journal of American Studies* 38 (2004); and Michailidou, "Gender, Body and Feminine Performance: Edna St Vincent Millay's Impact on Anne Sexton," *Feminist Review* 78 (2004). In addition, see the discussions of Millay in Jan Montefiore, *Feminism and Poetry: Language, Experience, Identity in Women's Writing* (1987); Clark, *Sentimental Modernism: Women Writers and the Revolution of the Word* (1991); Susan M. Schweik, *A Gulf So Deeply Cut: American Women Poets and the Second World War* (1991); Cheryl Walker, *Masks Outrageous and Austere: Culture, Psyche, and Persona in Modern Women Poets* (1991); and Sandra M. Gilbert and Susan Gubar, *Letters from the Front* (1994). A feminist approach is represented in Jane Stanbrough, "Edna St. Vincent Millay and the Language of Vulnerability," in *Shakespeare's Sisters* (1979), ed. Sandra Gilbert and Susan Gubar. Karl Yost, *A Bibliography of the Works of Edna St. Vincent Millay*, appeared in 1973, and Judith Nierman, *Edna St. Vincent Millay: A Reference Guide*, in 1977.

Marianne Moore
Moore's separate volumes include *Poems* (1921), *Observations* (1924), *The Pangolin, and Other Verse* (1936), *What Are Years?* (1941), *Nevertheless* (1944), *Like a Bulwark* (1956), *O to Be a Dragon* (1959), and *Tell Me, Tell Me* (1966). Collections include *Selected Poems* (1935); *Collected Poems* (1951); and *The Complete Poems of Marianne Moore* (1967), which also offers selections from her translation of *The Fables of La Fontaine* (1954). In addition, she translated Adalbert Stifter's *Rock Crystal: A Christmas Tale* (1945), and a collection of her critical essays, *Predilections*, appeared in 1955. Patricia C. Willis edited *The Complete Prose of Marianne Moore* in 1986. In 2002, Robin G. Schulze edited the excellent *Becoming Marianne Moore: The Early Poems, 1907–1924*, which offers numerous variations of Moore's much-edited early work as well as informative bibliographic notes. The most complete assemblage of Moore's poems is *The Poems of Marianne Moore* (2003), ed. Grace Schulman. An interview with Moore is included in *Women Writers at Work: The Paris Review Interviews* (1998), ed. George Plimpton. Bonnie Costello, Celeste Goodridge, and Cristanne Miller edited *The Selected Letters of Marianne Moore* in 1997.

A recent biography is Charles Molesworth,

Marianne Moore: A Literary Life (1990). Four important and perceptive essays on Moore are by poet-critics: T. S. Eliot's introduction to Moore's *Selected Poems*; R. P. Blackmur, "The Method of Marianne Moore," in *The Double Agent* (1935); Kenneth Burke, "Motives and Motifs in the Poetry of Marianne Moore," reprinted in *A Grammar of Motives* (1945); and Randall Jarrell, "Thoughts about Marianne Moore," reprinted in *Poetry and the Age* (1953). Hugh Kenner, "Disliking It," is in *A Homemade World: The American Modernist Writers* (1975). Book-length studies include Bernard F. Engel, *Marianne Moore* (1963); Jean Garrigue, *Marianne Moore* (1965); George W. Nitchie, *Marianne Moore: An Introduction to the Poetry* (1969); Donald Hall, *Marianne Moore: The Cage and the Animal* (1970); Pamela W. Hadas, *Marianne Moore, Poet of Affection* (1977); Laurence Stapleton, *Marianne Moore: The Poet's Advance* (1978); Marie Borroff, *Language and the Poet: Verbal Artistry in Frost, Stevens, and Moore* (1979); Bonnie Costello, *Marianne Moore: Imaginary Possessions* (1981); Elizabeth Philips, *Marianne Moore* (1982); Taffy Martin, *Marianne Moore: Subversive Modernist* (1986); Grace Schulman, *Marianne Moore: The Poetry of Engagement* (1986); John Slatin, *The Savage's Romance: The Poetry of Marianne Moore* (1986); Margaret Holley, *The Poetry of Marianne Moore: A Study in Voice and Value* (1987); Patricia C. Willis, *Marianne Moore: Vision into Verse* (1987); Celeste Goodridge, *Hints and Disguises: Marianne Moore and Her Contemporaries* (1989); Linda Leavell, *Marianne Moore and the Visual Arts* (1995); Cristanne Miller, *Marianne Moore: Questions of Authority* (1995); Robin G. Schulze, *The Web of Friendship: Marianne Moore and Wallace Stevens* (1995); Elizabeth Gregory, *Quotation and Modern American Poetry: Imaginary Gardens with Real Toads* (1996); Sabine Sielke, *Fashioning the Female Subject: The Intertextual Networking of Dickinson, Moore, and Rich* (1997); Elisabeth W. Joyce, *Cultural Critique and Abstraction: Marianne Moore and the Avantgarde* (1998); Cynthia Stamy, *Marianne Moore and China: Orientalism and a Writing of America* (1999); Kirstin Hotelling Zona, *Marianne Moore, Elizabeth Bishop, and May Swenson: The Feminist Poetics of Self-restraint* (2002); Cristanne Miller, *Cultures of Modernism: Marianne Moore, Mina Loy, & Else Lasker-Schüler: Gender and Literary Community in New York and Berlin* (2005). Two studies of Moore and Elizabeth Bishop are Jeredith Merrin, *An Enabling Humility: Marianne Moore, Elizabeth Bishop, and Two Uses of Tradition* (1990), and Joanne Feit Diehl, *Elizabeth Bishop and Marianne Moore: The Psychodynamics of Creativity* (1993). See also the discussions of Moore in Alicia Ostriker, *Stealing the Language: The Emergence of Women's Poetry in America* (1986); Lisa M. Steinman, *Made in America: Science, Technology, and American Modernist Poets* (1987); Lynn Keller, *Re-Making It New: Contemporary American Poetry and the Modernist Tradition* (1987); Sandra M. Gilbert and Susan Gubar, *Letters from the Front* (1994); and *Gendered Modernisms: American Women Poets and their Readers* (1996), ed. Margaret Dickie and Thomas Travisano. Essay collections are *Marianne Moore: The Art of a Modernist* (1990), ed. Joseph Parisi; *Marianne Moore: Woman and Poet* (1990), ed. Patricia C. Willis; *The Critical Response to Marianne Moore* (2003), ed. Elizabeth Gregory; *Critics and Poets on Marianne Moore: "A Right Good Salvo of Barks"* (2005), ed. Linda Leavell, Cristanne Miller, and Robin G. Schulze. Helpful, too, are Gary Lane, *A Concordance to the Poems of Marianne Moore* (1972); Eugene P. Sheehy and Kenneth A. Lohf, *The Achievement of Marianne Moore: A Descriptive Bibliography* (1977); and Craig S. Abbot, *Marianne Moore: A Reference Guide* (1978).

Toni Morrison

Morrison's novels are *The Bluest Eye* (1970), *Sula* (1973), *Song of Solomon* (1977), *Tar Baby* (1981), *Beloved* (1987), *Jazz* (1992), *Paradise* (1998), and *Love* (2003). She has also published several works for children, including *The Big Box* (1999); *The Book of Mean People* (2002), co-authored with her son, Slade Morrison; and *Remember: The Journey to School Integration* (2004). Critical works by her include "Unspeakable Things Unspoken: The Afro-American Presence in American Literature," *Michigan Quarterly Review* 28 (1989), and *Playing in the Dark: Whiteness and Literary Imagination* (1992). She also edited and contributed the introductory essay to *Race-ing Justice, Engendering Power: Essays on Anita Hill, Clarence Thomas, and the Construction of Social Reality* (1992), ed. Andrew Ross and Manning Marable; and with Claudia Bradsky Lacour, *Birth of a Nation 'Hood: Gaze and Spectacle in the O. J. Simpson Case* (1997). Morrison's *Lecture and Speech of Acceptance, Upon the Award of the Nobel Prize for Literature* was published in 1993. Three interesting interviews with Morrison are Robert B. Stepto, " 'Intimate Things in Place': A Conversation with Toni Morrison," *Massachusetts Review* 18 (1977); Jane Bakerman, "The Seams Can't Show," *Black American Literature Forum* 12 (1978); and Bettye J. Parker, "Complexity: Toni Morrison's Women: An Interview Essay," in *Sturdy Black Bridges: Visions of Black Women in Literature* (1979), ed. Roseann Bell, Parker, and Beverly Guy-Sheftall.

Critical studies of Morrison include Karen F. C. Holloway and Stephanie A. Demetrakopoulos, *New Dimensions of Spirituality: The Novels of Toni Morrison* (1987); *Critical Essays on Toni*

Morrison (1988), ed. Nellie McKay; Terry Otten, *The Crime of Innocence in the Fiction of Toni Morrison* (1989); Wilfred D. Samuels and Clenora Hudson-Weems, *Toni Morrison* (1990); *Toni Morrison: Modern Critical Views* (1990), ed. Harold Bloom; Trudier Harris, *Fiction and Folklore: The Novels of Toni Morrison* (1991); Denise Heinze, *The Dilemma of "Double Consciousness": Toni Morrison's Novels* (1993); Gurleen Grewal, *Circles of Sorrow, Lines of Struggle* (1998); John N. Duvall, *The Identifying Fictions of Toni Morrison* (2000); J. Brooks Bouson, *Quiet As It's Kept* (2000); and *The Aesthetics of Toni Morrison: Speaking the Unspeakable*, ed. Marc Conner (2000). *Callaloo* 13 (1990) is a special issue devoted to Toni Morrison. A useful bibliography is David L. Middleton, *Toni Morrison: An Annotated Bibliography* (1987); see also Elizabeth Beaulieu, *The Toni Morrison Encyclopedia* (2002).

Bharati Mukherjee
Mukherjee's works include *The Tiger's Daughter* (1971), *Wife* (1975), *Darkness* (1985), *The Middleman and Other Stories* (1988), *Jasmine* (1989), *The Holder of the World* (1993), *Leave it to Me* (1997), *Desirable Daughters* (2002), and *The Tree Bride* (2004). *Days and Nights in Calcutta* (1977), with Clark Blaise, is an account of her time in India. A biography is Fakrul Alam, *Bharati Mukherjee* (1996). A valuable collection of essays is Emmanuel S. Nelson, *Bharati Mukherjee: Critical Perspectives* (1993). Three useful critical articles are Sudha Pandya, "Bharati Mukherjee's Darkness: Exploring the Hyphenated Identity," *Quill* 2 (1990); Carmen Wickramagamage, "Relocation as Positive Act: The Immigrant Experience in Bharati Mukherjee's Novels," *Diaspora* 2 (1992); and Gail Ching Liang Low, "In a Free State: Post-Colonialism and Postmodernism in Bharati Mukherjee's Fiction," *Women: A Cultural Review* 4 (1993). See also Deborah R. Geis, " 'You're Exploiting My Space': Ethnicity, Spectatorship, and the Postcolonial Condition in Mukherjee's 'A Wife Story' and Mamet's *Glengarry, Glen Ross*," *Text and Performance*, ed. Leslie Kane (1996); Deepika Bahri, "Always Becoming: Narratives of Nation and Self in Bharati Mukherjee's *Jasmine*," *Women, America, Movement: Narratives of Relocation*, ed. Susan L. Roberson (1998); and Alexandra W. Schultheis, *Regenerative Fictions: Postcolonialism, Psychoanalysis, and the Nation as Family* (2004).

Alice Munro
Munro's fiction includes both short stories and novels: *Dance of the Happy Shades* (1968), *Lives of Girls and Women* (1971), *Something I've Been Meaning to Tell You* (1974), *The Beggar Maid* (1982), *The Moons of Jupiter* (1983), *The Progress of Love* (1986), *Friend of My Youth* (1990), *Open Secrets* (1994), *The Love of a Good Woman* (1998), *Hateship, Friendship, Courtship, Loveship, Marriage* (2001), and *Runaway* (2005). Geoffry Hancock has an interesting interview with the author in *Canadian Fiction Magazine* 63 (1982). A biography is Catherine Sheldrick Ross, *Alice Munro: A Double Life* (1992).

Valuable full-length studies are Louis MacKendrick, ed., *Probable Fictions: Alice Munro's Narrative Acts* (1983); Walter R. Martin, *Alice Munro: Paradox and Parallel* (1987); Beverly Jean Rasporich, *Dance of the Sexes: Art and Sexuality in the Fiction of Alice Munro* (1990); Magdalene Redekop, *Mothers and Other Clowns: The Stories of Alice Munro* (1992); Ajay Heble, *The Tumble of Reason: Alice Munro's Discourse of Absence* (1994); John Cooke, *The Influence of Painting on Five Canadian Writers* (1996); and Coral Ann Howells, *Alice Munro* (1998). A useful collection is *The Art of Alice Munro: Seizing the Unseizable* (1984), ed. Judith Miller, which consists of essays from the Waterloo conference. Other useful critical essays are Miriam Packer, "*Lives of Girls and Women*: A Creative Search for Completion," in *The Canadian Novel: Here and Now* (1978), ed. John Moss; Bronwen Wallace, "Women's Lives: Alice Munro," in *The Human Elements: Critical Essays* (1978), ed. David Helwig; Nancy J. Bailey, "The Masculine Image in *Lives of Girls and Women*," *Canadian Literature* 80 (1979); Marlene Goldman, "Penning the Bodies: The Construction of Gendered Subjects in Alice Munro's 'Boys and Girls,' " *Studies in Canadian Literature* 15 (1990); and Karen Smythe, "Sad Stories: The Ethics of Epiphany in Munrovian Elegy," *University of Toronto Quarterly* 60 (1991). Helpful is J. R. Struthers, "Some Highly Subversive Activities: A Brief Polemic and a Checklist of Works on Alice Munro," *Studies in Canadian Literature* 6 (1981).

Anaïs Nin
Nin's famous *Diary* has been published in several volumes from 1966 to 1980, ed. and with an introduction by Gunther Stuhlmann. *Linotte* (1978–82), her early diary, is also available, as are *Journal of a Wife: The Early Diary of Anaïs Nin, 1923–27* (1984); *Incest, from a Journal of Love: The Unexpurgated Diary of Anaïs Nin, 1932–1934* (1991); and *Nearer the Moon, from a Journal of Love: The Unexpurgated Diary of Anaïs Nin, 1937–1939* (1996). The *Anaïs Nin Reader*, ed. Philip K. Jason, was published in 1973, and a collection of Nin's correspondence with Henry Miller, *A Literate Passion: Letters of Anaïs Nin and Henry Miller, 1932–1951*, appeared in 1987. Wendy M. DuBow's essay, "The Elusive Text: Reading 'The Diary of Anaïs Nin, Volume I, 1931–1934,' " *Anaïs: An International Journal* 11 (1993), includes previously

unpublished material. Nin's many other works, both fiction and nonfiction, include *The Winter of Artifice* (1939), *Ladders to Fire* (1946), *On Writing* (1947), *The Four-Chambered Heart* (1950), *A Spy in the House of Love* (1954), and *Collages* (1964), as well as *Paris Revisited* (1972).

Several full-length books have been written about Nin, including Oliver Evans, *Anaïs Nin* (1968); Valerie Harms, ed., *Celebration with Anaïs Nin* (1973); Evelyn J. Hinz, *The Mirror and the Garden* (1973), and her *The World of Anaïs Nin* (1978); Bettina L. Knapp, *Anaïs Nin* (1978); Benjamin Franklin and Duane Schneider, *Anaïs Nin: An Introduction* (1979); Sharon Spencer, *Collage of Dreams: The Writings of Anaïs Nin* (1981); Nöel Riley Fitch, *Anaïs: The Erotic Life of Anaïs Nin* (1993); the interesting Philip K. Jason, *Anaïs Nin and Her Critics* (1993); and Helen Tookey, *Anaïs Nin, Fictionality, and Femininity: Playing a Thousand Roles* (2003). There is also a quarterly, which began in 1970, called *Under the Sign of Pisces: Anaïs Nin and Her Circle*. The useful *Anaïs Nin: A Reference Guide* by Rose Marie Cutting (1978) has been updated yearly by Richard R. Centing in *Under the Sign of Pisces* and *Seahorse*. Two interesting recent essays are Kate Millett, "Anaïs, A Mother to Us All: The Birth of the Artist as a Woman," *Anaïs: An International Journal* 9 (1991), and Karen Brennan, "Anaïs Nin: Author(iz)ing the Erotic Body," *Genders* 14 (1992). For a useful but somewhat dated summary of criticism see Evelyn J. Hinz, "Recent Nin Criticism: Who's on First," *Canadian Review of American Studies* 13 (1982).

Joyce Carol Oates

Oates's more than sixty published works include the novels *Them* (1969), *Do with Me What You Will* (1973), *Unholy Loves* (1979), *Bellefleur* (1980), *A Bloodsmoor Romance* (1982), *Solstice* (1985), *Marya: A Life* (1986), *You Must Remember This* (1987), *American Appetites* (1989), *Black Water* (1992), *What I Lived For* (1994), *We Were the Mulvaneys* (1996), *Man Crazy* (1997), *Broke Heart Blues* (1999), *Blonde* (2000), *Middle Age: A Romance* (2001), *Beasts* (2002), *I'll Take You There* (2002), *Rape: A Love Story* (2003), *The Falls* (2004), and *Missing Mom* (2005); as well as such short story collections as *Upon the Sweeping Flood, and Other Stories* (1966), *Marriages and Infidelities* (1972), *The Goddess and Other Women* (1974), *Raven's Wing* (1987), *The Assignation* (1989), *Where Is Here?* (1992), *Haunted: Tales of the Grotesque* (1994), *Will You Always Love Me?* (1996), *The Collector of Hearts: New Tales of the Grotesque* (1998), *Faithless: Tales of Transgression* (2001), *A Garden of Earthly Delights* (2003), and *I Am No One You Know* (2004). Oates's plays are collected in *The Perfectionist and Other Plays* (1995) and *New Plays* (1998). Her volumes of poetry are *Women in Love, and Other Poems* (1968), *Women Whose Lives are Money* (1978), and *The Time Traveller: Poems, 1983–1989* (1989). Her critical essays include *Contraries* (1981), *The Profane Art: Essays and Reviews* (1983), *(Woman) Writer: Occasions and Opportunities* (1988), and *Where I've Been, and Where I'm Going: Essays, Reviews, and Prose* (1999). Lee Milazzo edited *Conversations with Joyce Carol Oates* in 1989, and another interview with Oates is included in *Women Writers at Work: The Paris Review Interviews* (1998), ed. George Plimpton. Full-length studies include Mary K. Grant, *The Tragic Vision of Joyce Carol Oates* (1978); Joanne V. Creighton, *Joyce Carol Oates* (1979); Ellen G. Freidman, *Joyce Carol Oates* (1980); Katherine Bastian, *Joyce Carol Oates's Short Stories: Between Tradition and Innovation* (1983); Eileen T. Bender, *Artist in Residence: The Phenomenon of Joyce Carol Oates* (1987); Creighton, *Joyce Carol Oates: Novels of the Middle Years* (1992); Marilyn C. Wesley, *Refusal and Transgression in Joyce Carol Oates's Fiction* (1993); Greg Johnson, *Joyce Carol Oates: A Study of the Short Fiction* (1994); Brenda Daly, *Lavish Self-divisions: The Novels of Joyce Carol Oates* (1996); Sigrid Mayer, *Critical Reception of the Short Fiction by Joyce Carol Oates and Gabriele Wohmann* (1998); Nancy Ann Watanabe, *Love Eclipsed: Joyce Carol Oates's Faustian Moral Vision* (1998); and Gavin Cologne-Brookes, *Dark Eyes on America: The Novels of Joyce Carol Oates* (2005). Two useful collections of critical essays are *Critical Essays on Joyce Carol Oates* (1979), ed. Linda W. Wagner, and *Joyce Carol Oates: Modern Critical Views* (1986), ed. Harold Bloom. For feminist perspectives, see Elaine Showalter, "Joyce Carol Oates's 'The Dead' and Feminist Criticism," in *Faith of a (Woman) Writer* (1988), ed. Alice Kessler-Harris and William McBrien, and Brenda O. Daly, " 'How Do We (Not) Become These People Who Victimize Us': Anxious Authorship in the Early Fiction of Joyce Carol Oates," in *Anxious Power: Reading, Writing, and Ambivalence in Narrative by Women* (1993), ed. Carol J. Singley and Susan Elizabeth Sweeney. Three useful reference guides are Donald C. Dickson, "Joyce Carol Oates," *American Book Collector* 2 (1981), and two by Anne Hiemstra, "A Bibliography of Writings about Oates" and "A Bibliography of Writings by Oates," in *American Women Writing Fiction: Memory, Identity, Family, Space* (1989), ed. Mickey Pearlman.

Edna O'Brien

O'Brien's works include the trilogy *The Country Girls* (1960), *The Lonely Girl* (1962), and *Girls in Their Married Bliss* (1964), as well as *A Pagan Place: A Play* (1973), *Mrs. Reinhart and Other Stories* (1980), and *James and Nora: A Portrait of Joyce's Marriage* (1981). Her recent works of fiction include the novels *The High Road* (1988), *Time and Tide* (1992), and *House of Splendid Isolation* (1994), and the short story collections *A Fanatic Heart: Selected Stories* (1984) and *Lantern Slides* (1990). Her early trilogy was collected as *The Country Girls Trilogy and Epilogue* (1986). She has also written a play about Virginia Woolf, *Virginia* (1981). For an interview with O'Brien, see the useful *Canadian Journal of Irish Studies* 22 (1996), which also contains a number of critical articles on O'Brien, a chronology of her life and work, and a bibliography. Critical articles about her work include Raymonde Popot, "Edna O'Brien's Paradise Lost," *Cahiers Irlandais* 4–5 (1976); Lotus Snow, " 'That Trenchant Childhood Route?': Quest in Edna O'Brien's Novels," *Eire* 14 (1979); Darcy O'Brien, "Edna O'Brien: A Kind of Irish Childhood," in *Twentieth-Century Women Novelists* (1982), ed. Thomas Staley; Lynette Carpenter, "Tragedies of Rembrance, Comedies of Endurance: The Novels of Edna O'Brien" in *Essays on the Contemporary British Novel* (1986), ed. Hedwig Bock and Albert Wertheim; Peggy O'Brien, "The Silly and the Serious: An Assessment of Edna O'Brien," *Massachusetts Review* 28 (1987); Tasmin Hargreaves, "Women's Consciousness and Identity in Four Irish Women Novelists," in *Cultural Contexts and Literary Idioms in Contemporary Irish Literature* (1988), ed. Michael Kenneally; and Kiera O'Hara, "Love Objects: Love and Obsession in the Stories of Edna O'Brien," *Studies in Short Fiction* 30 (1993). Also see Donatella Abbate Badin, "The Mythical Context of Edna O'Brien's Short Stories," *Lingua e Letteratura* 24/25 (1995); Jeanette Roberts Shumaker, "Sacrificial Women in Short Stories by Mary Lavin and Edna O'Brien," *Studies in Short Fiction* 32 (1995); Michael Patrick Gillespie, "(S)he Was Too Scrupulous Always: Edna O'Brien and the Comic Tradition," in *The Comic Tradition in Irish Women Writers* (1996), ed. Theresa O'Connor; critical articles on O'Brien in the special issue of *Canadian Journal of Irish Studies* 22 (1996); Eileen Morgan, "Mapping Out a Landscape of Female Suffering: Edna O'Brien's Demythologizing Novels," *Women's Studies* 29 (2000); and Jeanette Roberts Shumaker, "Mother-Daughter Rivalries in Stories by Irish Women: Elizabeth Bowen, Edna O'Brien, Mary Beckett, and Helen Lucy Burke," *North Dakota Quarterly* 68 (2001).

Flannery O'Connor

O'Connor's novels are *Wise Blood* (1952) and *The Violent Bear It Away* (1960). Two collections of stories, *A Good Man Is Hard to Find* (1955) and *Everything That Rises Must Converge* (1965), are included with earlier, previously uncollected stories in *Complete Stories* (1971). Her letters are collected in *The Habit of Being: The Letters of Flannery O'Connor* (1979). A collection of O'Connor's nonfictional prose is *Mystery and Manners* (1969), ed. Sally and Robert Fitzgerald; and a collection of her book reviews, *The Presence of Grace* (1983), was compiled by Leo J. Zuber and ed. with an introduction by Carter W. Martin. Her *Collected Works* appeared in 1988, and Stephen G. Driggers edited *The Manuscripts of Flannery O'Connor at Georgia College* in 1989. Robert Fitzgerald's memoir, prefaced to *Everything That Rises Must Converge*, offers a portrait of the artist. Other biographical material can be found in Robert Coles, *Flannery O'Connor's South* (1980); Barbara McKenzie, *Flannery O'Connor's Georgia* (1980); Lorine M. Getz, *Flannery O'Connor: Her Life, Library and Book Reviews* (1980); and Marion Montgomery, *Why Flannery O'Connor Stayed Home* (1981). *Conversations with Flannery O'Connor*, ed. Rosemary Magee, appeared in 1987.

Full-length studies of O'Connor's fiction include Carol Schloss, *Flannery O'Connor's Dark Comedies: The Limits of Inference* (1980); James M. Grimshaw Jr., *The Flannery O'Connor Companion* (1981); Kathleen Feeley, *Flannery O'Connor: Voice of the Peacock*, 2nd ed. (1982); Frederick Asals, *Flannery O'Connor, the Imagination of Extremity* (1982); Edward Kessler, *Flannery O'Connor and the Language of Apocalypse* (1986); Suzanne Morrow Paulson, *Flannery O'Connor: A Study of the Short Fiction* (1988); Robert H. Brinkmeyer, *The Art and Vision of Flannery O'Connor* (1989); and Katherine Prown, *Revising Flannery O'Connor: Southern Literary Culture and the Problem of Female Authorship* (2001). Collections of essays are *The Added Dimension: The Art and Mind of Flannery O'Connor* (1966), ed. M. J. Freedman and L. A. Lawson, and *Critical Essays on Flannery O'Connor* (1985), ed. Melvin J. Friedman and Beverly Lyon Clark. *Flannery O'Connor: A Descriptive Bibliography* (1980), by David R. Farmer, is very helpful; a more recent bibliography is R. Neill Scott, *Flannery O'Connor: An Annotated Reference Guide to Criticism* (2002).

Sharon Olds

As well as having published extensively in poetry magazines, Olds has composed numerous volumes of poetry, including *Satan Says* (1980), *The Dead and the Living* (1984), *The Gold Cell* (1987), *The Matter of This World: New and Selected Poems* (1987), *The Sign of Saturn: Poems, 1980–1987* (1991), *The Father* (1992), *The Wellspring* (1996), *Blood, Tin, Straw* (1999), *The Unswept Room* (2002), and *Strike Sparks: Selected Poems, 1980–2002* (2004). For an interview with Olds, see Esta Spalding, "The Earthly Matter: A Conversation with Sharon Olds," *Brick* 67 (2001). Two helpful chapters from larger volumes that contextualize Olds's work are David Baker, "Romantic Melancholy, Romantic Excess: On Linda Gregerson, Stephen Dunn, Sharon Olds, Stanley Plumly, Robert Hass," in his *Heresy and the Ideal: On Contemporary Poetry* (2000), and Alicia Ostriker, "I Am (Not) This: Erotic Discourse in Elizabeth Bishop and Sharon Olds," in her *Dancing at the Devil's Party: Essays on Poetry, Politics, and the Erotic* (2000). Also see discussions of Olds in Gale Swiontkowski, *Imagining Incest: Sexton, Plath, Rich, and Olds on Life with Daddy* (2003). For an essay from a feminist perspective, see Suzanne Matson, "Talking to Our Father: The Political and Mythical Appropriations of Adrienne Rich and Sharon Olds," *The American Poetry Review* 18 (1989). Other useful essays are Brian Dillon, " 'Never Having Had You, I Cannot Let You Go': Sharon Olds' Poems of A Father-Daughter Relationship," *The Literary Review* 37 (1993); Calvin Bedient, "Sentencing Eros," *Salmagundi* 97 (1993); and Laura E. Tanner, "Death-Watch: Terminal Illness and the Gaze in Sharon Olds's *The Father*," *Mosaic* 29 (1996).

Tillie Olsen

Olsen's works are *Tell Me a Riddle* (1961), *Yonnondio: From the Thirties* (1974), and *Silences* (1978). In 1990, Virago issued an edition of selected works entitled *Tell Me a Riddle and Yonnondio*. Olsen has also edited *Mother to Daughter, Daughter to Mother: A Daybook and Reader* (1984) and *Mothers and Daughters: That Special Quality* (1987), a collection of photographs and remembrances, including Olsen's tribute to her mother, "Dream Vision." Critical essays include Deborah Rosenfelt, "From the Thirties: Tillie Olsen and the Radical Tradition," *Feminist Studies* 7 (1981); Joanne S. Frye, " 'I Stand Here Ironing': Motherhood as Experience and Metaphor," *Studies in Short Fiction* 18 (1981); Erika Duncan, "Coming of Age in the Thirties: A Portrait of Tillie Olsen," *Book Forum* 6 (1982); Constance Coiner, " 'No One's Private Ground': A Bakhtinian Reading of Tillie Olsen's *Tell Me a Riddle*," in *Listening to Silences: New Essays in Feminist Criticism* (1994), ed. Elaine Hedges and Shelley Fisher Fishkin; Jean Pfaelzer, "Tillie Olsen's *Tell Me a Riddle*: The Dialectics of Silence," *Frontiers* 15 (1994); Linda Ray Pratt, "Mediating Experience in the Scholarship of Tillie Olsen," *Frontiers* 18 (1997); Lydia A. Schultz, "Flowing Against the Traditional Stream: Consciousness in Tillie Olsen's *Tell Me a Riddle*," *MELUS* 22 (1997); Anthony Dawahare, " 'That Joyous Certainty': History and Utopia in Tillie Olsen's Depression-Era Literature," *Twentieth Century Literature* 44 (1998); and Roberta Maierhofer, "Desperately Seeking the Self: Gender, Age, and Identity in Tillie Olsen's *Tell Me a Riddle* and Michelle Herman's *Missing*," *Educational Gerontology* 25 (1999). Useful full-length studies are Elaine Neil Orr, *Tillie Olsen and a Feminist Spiritual Vision* (1987); Mickey Pearlman and Abby H. P. Werlock, *Tillie Olsen* (1991); Mara Faulkner, *Protest and Possibility in the Writing of Tillie Olsen* (1993); Kay Hoyle Nelson and Nancy Huse, *The Critical Response to Tillie Olsen* (1994); Joanne Frye, *Tillie Olsen: A Study of the Short Fiction* (1995); Nora Ruth Roberts, *Three Radical Women Writers: Class and Gender in Meridel Le Sueur, Tillie Olsen, and Josephine Herbst* (1996); Agnes Toloczko Cardoni, *Women's Ethical Coming-Of-Age: Adolescent Female Characters in the Prose Fiction of Tillie Olsen* (1998); and Constance Coiner, *Better Red: The Writing and Resistance of Tillie Olsen and Meridel Le Sueur* (1998).

Cynthia Ozick

Ozick's works of fiction include *Trust* (1966), *The Pagan Rabbi and Other Stories* (1971), *Bloodshed and Three Novellas* (1976), *Levitation: Five Fictions* (1982), *The Cannibal Galaxy* (1983), *The Messiah of Stockholm* (1987), and *The Shawl* (1989). She is also the author of three collections of essays, *Art and Ardor* (1983), *Metaphor and Memory* (1989), and *What Henry James Knew and Other Essays on Writers* (1993). Critical work includes Harold Bloom, ed., *Cynthia Ozick* (1986); Sanford Pinsker, *The Uncompromising Fictions of Cynthia Ozick* (1987); Joseph Lowin, *Cynthia Ozick* (1988); Lawrence S. Friedman, *Under-standing Cynthia Ozick* (1991); Norman Finkelstein, *The Ritual of New Creation: Jewish Tradition and Contemporary Literature* (1992); Elaine M. Kaurar, *Cynthia Ozick's Fiction: Tradition and Invention* (1993); Sarah Blacher Cohen, *Cynthia Ozick's Comic Art: From Levity to Liturgy* (1994); and Victor H. Strandberg, *Greek Mind / Jewish Soul: The Conflicted Art of Cynthia Ozick* (1994). Some valuable critical articles are B. Scrafford, "Nature's Silent Scream: A Commentary on Cynthia Ozick, 'The Shawl,' " *Critique: Studies in Contemporary Fiction* 31 (1989); Pinsker, "Jewish-American Literature's Lost and Found Department: How Philip Roth and Cynthia Ozick Reimagine Their Significant Dead," *Modern Fiction Studies* 35 (1989); M. Krupnick, "Cynthia Ozick as the Jewish T. S. Eliot," *Soundings* 74 (1991); A. F. Wilner, "The Jewish-American Woman as Artist: Cynthia Ozick and the Paleface Tradition," *College Literature* 20 (1993); A. Gordon, " 'The Shawl,' and Transitional Objects," *Literature and Psychology* 40 (1994); and A. Lakrits, "Cynthia Ozick at the End of the Modern," *Chicago Review* 40 (1994).

Grace Paley

The Collected Stories, published in 1994, includes Paley's two short story collections, *The Little Disturbances of Man* (1959) and *Enormous*

Changes at the Last Minute (1974). *New and Collected Poems* was published in 1992, and *Born Again: Collected Poems* appeared in 2000. *Long Walks and Intimate Talks,* which includes poems and stories by Paley and paintings by Vera B. Williams, was published by the Feminist Press in 1991. A collection of Paley's essays and memoirs is *Just as I Thought* (1998). Critical and biographical studies of Paley include Neil David Isaacs, *Grace Paley: A Study of the Short Fiction* (1990); Jacqueline Taylor, *Grace Paley: Illuminating the Dark Lives* (1990); and Judith Arcana, *Grace Paley's Life Stories: A Literary Biography* (1993). The May 1982 issue of *Delta,* ed. Kathleen Hulley, is devoted to Grace Paley and includes Hulley's interview with the writer. Other essays on this writer's work include Blanche Gelfant, "Grace Paley: Fragments for a Portrait in Collage," *New England Review* 3 (1980); John W. Crawford, "Archetypal Patterns in Grace Paley's 'Runner,'" *Notes on Contemporary Literature* 11 (1981); and Marianne DeKoven, "Mrs. Hegel-Shtein's Tears," *Partisan Review* 48 (1981).

Dorothy Parker
The Penguin Dorothy Parker (1977), contains fiction, poetry, criticism, and journalism. Other collections include *Collected Stories of Dorothy Parker* (1942); *Collected Poetry of Dorothy Parker* (1944); *The Portable Dorothy Parker* (1944); and most recently, *The Sayings of Dorothy Parker* (1992), ed. S. T. Brownlow. Her *Constant Reader,* a collection of critical pieces, appeared in 1970.

Biographies include John Keats, *You Might as Well Live: The Life and Times of Dorothy Parker* (1970); Arthur F. Kinney, *Dorothy Parker* (1978, rev. 1998); Leslie Ferwin, *The Late Mrs. Dorothy Parker* (1986); and Marion Meade, *Dorothy Parker: What Fresh Hell Is This?* (1988). Randall Calhoun's *Dorothy Parker: A Bio-Bibliography* (1993), is a valuable resource. Feminist approaches to Parker's work are taken in Suzanne L. Bunkers, "'I Am Outraged Womanhood': Dorothy Parker as Feminist and Social Critic," *Regionalism and the Female Imagination* 4 (1978); Paula Treichler, "Verbal Subversions in Dorothy Parker: 'Trapped Like a Trap in a Trap,'" *Language and Style* 13 (1980); Sondra Melzer, *The Rhetoric of Rage: Women in Dorothy Parker* (1997); and Rhoda S. Pettit, *A Gendered Collision: Sentimentalism and Modernity in Dorothy Parker's Poetry and Fiction* (2000). An interesting article is Nina Miller, "Making Love Modern: Dorothy Parker and Her Public," *American Literature* 64 (1992).

Ruth Pitter
Poems, 1926–1966 (1968) includes selections from *A Mad Lady's Garland* (1935), *A Trophy of Arms* (1936), *The Spirit Watchers* (1940), *The Rude Potato* (1941), *The Bridge* (1945), *Pitter on Cats* (1947), *Urania* (1951), *The Ermine* (1953), and *Still by Choice* (1966). *End of Drought* appeared in 1975. *A Heaven to Find* (1987) is a selection of previously unpublished poems and fragments gathered from the poet's notebooks, 1908–76. *Collected Poems,* with an introduction by the poet Elizabeth Jennings, appeared in 1990. Poems by Pitter appear in *The Faber Book of Twentieth-Century Women's Poetry* (1987), ed. Fleur Adcock, and *The Things That Matter: An Anthology of Women's Spiritual Poetry* (1990), ed. Julia Neuberger. An early critical work that contains material on Pitter is Rudolph Gilbert, *Four Living Poets* (1944). *Ruth Pitter: Homage to a Poet* (1969), ed. Arthur Russell, offers appreciative short essays and a biographical sketch. Two recent critical essays by Don King are "The Anatomy of a Friendship: The Correspondence of Ruth Pitter and C. S. Lewis, 1946–1962," *Mythlore* 24 (2003), and "Silent Music of Ruth Pitter," *CSL* 35 (2004).

Sylvia Plath
Plath's *The Collected Poems*—including *The Colossus and Other Poems* (1960) and *Ariel* (1965)—was edited by Ted Hughes in 1981. Plath's mother, Aurelia Schober Plath, selected and edited the useful *Letters Home: Correspondence, 1950–63* (1975). Hughes, with Frances McCullough, edited *The Journals of Sylvia Plath* (1982), and Hughes also edited *Johnny Panic and the Bible of Dreams, and Other Prose Writings* (1978). Plath's novel, *The Bell Jar,* was published in 1963 and has appeared in several paperback editions.

Biographical studies include Linda Wagner-Martin, *Sylvia Plath: A Literary Life* (2003); Anne Stevenson, *Bitter Fame: A Life of Sylvia Plath* (1989); Paul Alexander, *Rough Magic: A Biography of Sylvia Plath* (1991); Ronald Hayman, *The Death and Life of Sylvia Plath* (1991); Janet Malcolm, *The Silent Woman: Sylvia Plath and Ted Hughes* (1993); and Ronald Hayman, *The Death and Life of Sylvia Plath* (2003). *The Journals of Sylvia Plath, 1950–1962,* edited by Karen V. Kukil, was published in 2000. Among full-length studies of Plath are two hostile but useful works: Edward Butscher, *Sylvia Plath: Method and Madness* (1976), and David Holbrook, *Sylvia Plath: Poetry and Existence* (1976). More positive are Eileen Aird, *Sylvia Plath: Her Life and Work* (1975); Judith Kroll, *Chapters in a Mythology: The Poetry of Sylvia Plath* (1976); Caroline King, *Sylvia Plath* (1978); Jon Rosenblatt, *Sylvia Plath: The Poetry of Initiation* (1979); Mary Lynn Broe, *Protean Poetic: The Poetry of Sylvia Plath* (1980); and Lynda K. Bundtzen, *Plath's Incarnations: Women and the Creative Process* (1983). Other full-length critical works include Pamela J. Annas, *A Disturbance of Mirrors: The Poetry of Sylvia Plath*

(1988); Steven Gould Axelrod, *Sylvia Plath: The Wound and the Cure of Words* (1990); Jacqueline Rose, *The Haunting of Sylvia Plath* (1991); Toni Saldivar, *Sylvia Plath: Confessing the Fictive Self* (1992); Susan R. Van Dyne, *Revising Life: Sylvia Plath's Ariel Poems* (1993); Nancy Duvall Hargrove, *The Journey toward Ariel: Sylvia Plath's Poems of 1956–1959* (1994); Al Strangeways, *Sylvia Plath: The Shaping of Shadows* (1998); Christina Britzolakis, *Sylvia Plath and the Theatre of Mourning* (1999); Tracy Brain, *The Other Sylvia Plath* (2001); Tim Kendall, *Sylvia Plath: A Critical Study* (2001); Robin Peel, *Writing Back: Sylvia Plath and Cold War Politics* (2002); and Nephie Christodoulides, *Out of the Cradle Endlessly Rocking: Motherhood in Sylvia Plath's Work* (2005). See also the discussions of Plath in Alan Williamson, *Introspection and Contemporary Poetry* (1984); Alan Sinfield, *Literature, Politics, and Culture in Postwar Britain* (1989); Gayle Greene, *Changing the Story: Feminist Fiction and the Tradition* (1991); Sandra M. Gilbert and Susan Gubar, *Letters from the Front* (1994); and Jill Scott, *Electra After Freud: Myth and Culture* (2005). Two helpful collections of essays are *Ariel Ascending: Writings about Sylvia Plath* (1985), ed. Paul Alexander, and *Sylvia Plath: Modern Critical Views* (1989), ed. Harold Bloom. Recent comparative volumes featuring discussions of Plath include Annette Burkart, *"Kein Sterbenswort, ihr Worte!": Ingeborg Bachmann und Sylvia Plath, Acting the Poem* (2000); Renée R. Curry, *White Women Writing White: H.D., Elizabeth Bishop, Sylvia Plath, and Whiteness* (2000); Harriet L. Parmet, *The Terror of Our Days: Four American Poets Respond to the Holocaust* (2001); Helen Vendler, *Coming of Age as a Poet: Milton, Keats, Eliot, Plath* (2003); Antony Rowland, *Holocaust Poetry: Awkward Poetics in the Work of Sylvia Plath, Geoffrey Hill, Tony Harrison and Ted Hughes* (2005); DeSales Harrison, *The End of the Mind: The Edge of the Intelligible in Hardy, Stevens, Larkin, Plath, and Glück* (2005); and Adam Kirsch, *The Wounded Surgeon: Confession and Transformation in Six American Poets: Robert Lowell, Elizabeth Bishop, John Berryman, Randall Jarrell, Delmore Schwartz, Sylvia Plath* (2005).

Further biographical and critical material can be found in Margaret D. Uroff, *Sylvia Plath and Ted Hughes* (1979). In addition, a number of informative essays appear in *The Art of Sylvia Plath* (1970), ed. Charles Newman; *Sylvia Plath: New Views on the Poetry* (1979), ed. Gary Lane; and *Critical Essays on Sylvia Plath* (1984), ed. Linda W. Wagner. Linda Wagner edited *Sylvia Plath: The Critical Heritage* in 1988. Useful reference guides are Richard Matovitch, *A Concordance to the Collected Poems of Sylvia Plath* (1986), and two bibliographies: Stephen Tabor, *Sylvia Plath: An Analytical Bibliography* (1987), and Sheryl L. Meyering, *Sylvia Plath: A Reference Guide, 1973–1988* (1990).

Katherine Anne Porter

Porter's publications include volumes of short stories, *Flowering Judas* (1930), *Noon Wine* (1937), *Pale Horse, Pale Rider* (1939), and *The Leaning Tower, and Other Stories* (1944), as well as the novel *Ship of Fools* (1962). Her *Collected Stories* appeared in 1965, and her *Collected Essays* in 1970. In 1993 Virginia Spencer Carr edited *Flowering Judas* for the series Women Writers: Texts and Contexts. The collection *Letters of Katherine Anne Porter*, ed. Isabel Bayley, appeared in 1990, and *This Strange Old World and Other Book Reviews by Katherine Anne Porter*, ed. Darlene Harbour Unrue, was published in 1991. A useful biography is Joan Givner, *Katherine Anne Porter: A Life* (1982, rev. 1991), but other biographical information can be found in Enrique Hank Lopez, *Conversations with Katherine Anne Porter, Refugee from Indian Creek* (1981). An interview with Porter by George Plimpton appeared in the *Paris Review Interviews* (1963).

For surveys of her career and writings, relevant texts include Harry J. Mooney, *The Fiction and Criticism of Katherine Anne Porter* (1962); Ray West, *Katherine Anne Porter* (1963); William L. Nance, *Katherine Anne Porter and the Art of Rejection* (1964); George Hendrick, *Katherine Anne Porter* (1965); W. S. Emmons, *Katherine Anne Porter: The Regional Stories* (1967); Paul R. Baumgartner, *Katherine Anne Porter* (1969); M. M. Liberman, *Katherine Anne Porter's Fiction* (1971); Thomas Walsh, *Katherine Anne Porter and Mexico: The Illusion of Eden* (1992); and Robert H. Brinkmeyer Jr., *Katherine Anne Porter's Artistic Development: Primitivism, Traditionalism, and Totalitarianism* (1993). Darlene Harbour Unrue's scholarship has produced three useful sources on Porter: *Truth and Vision in Katherine Anne Porter's Fiction* (1985); *Understanding Katherine Anne Porter* (1988); "Porter's Sources and Influences," in *Katherine Anne Porter and Texas: An Uneasy Relationship* (1990), ed. Clinton Machann and William Bedford Clark. See also the collection Unrue edited, *Critical Essays on Katherine Anne Porter* (1997). Other important essays on Porter are in Robert Penn Warren, *Selected Essays* (1958); Glenway Wescott, *Images of Truth* (1962); *Katherine Anne Porter: A Critical Symposium* (1969), ed. Lodwiej Hartley and George Gore; and Warren's more recent *Katherine Anne Porter: A Collection of Critical Essays* (1979). For a feminist approach, see Jane K. Demouy, *Katherine Anne Porter's Women: The Eye of Her Fiction* (1983). Bibliographies include *A Bibliography of the Works of Katherine Anne Porter* (1969), ed. Louise Waldrip and Shirley Ann Bauer, and the more recent valuable resource, Kathryn Hilt,

Katherine Anne Porter: An Annotated Bibliography (1990).

Katharine Susannah Prichard
Prichard's fiction includes *The Pioneers* (1915), *Black Opal* (1921), *Working Bullocks* (1926), *Coonardoo: The Well in the Shadow* (1929), *Kiss on the Lips, and Other Stories* (1932), *Intimate Strangers* (1937), *Potch and Colour* (1944), and *Winged Seeds* (1950). She also published an autobiography, *Child of the Hurricane* (1963). *Coonardoo* was reissued in 1975. Ric Throssell edited *Tribute: Selected Short Stories of Katharine Susannah Prichard* in 1988. A selection of Prichard's correspondence appears in *As Good as a Yarn with You: Letters Between Miles Franklin, Katharine Susannah Prichard, Jean DeVanny, Marjorie Barnard, Flora Eldershaw, and Eleanor Dark* (1992), ed. Carole Ferrier. John Hay and Brenda Walker edited *Katharine Susannah Prichard Centenary Essays* in 1984. For interesting biographical information, see Sandra Burchill, "The Early Years of Katharine Susannah Prichard: The Growth of Her Political Consciousness," *Westerly* 33 (1988), and Hal Colebatch, "New Light on Katharine Susannah Prichard," *Antipodes* 4 (1990). Two valuable full-length studies are Henrietta Drake-Brockman, *Katharine Susannah Prichard* (1967), and Ric Throssel, *Wild Weeds and Wind Flowers: The Life and Letters of Katharine Susannah Prichard* (1975). Critical essays are Veronica Brady, "Katharine Susannah Prichard and the Tyranny of History: Intimate Strangers," *Westerly* 26 (1981); Pat Buckridge, "Katharine Susannah Prichard and the Literary Dynamics of Political Commitment," and Carole Ferrier, "Jean DeVanny, Katharine Susannah Prichard, and the 'Really Proletarian' Novel," both in *Gender Politics, and Fiction: Twentieth-Century Australian Women's Novels* (1985), ed. Ferrier; Sue Thomas, "Interracial Encounters in Katharine Prichard's *Coonardoo*," *World Literature Written in English* 27 (1987); Ruth Morse, "Impossible Dreams: Miscegenation and Building Nations," *Southerly* 48 (Mar. 1988); Ric Throssell, "Katharine Susannah Prichard: A Reluctant Daughter of Mark Twain," *Antipodes* 3 (1989); and Delys Bird, "Katharine Susannah Prichard: A Thoroughly Modern Woman," *Southerly* 58 (1998).

Jean Rhys
Rhys's published works include *The Left Bank: Sketches and Studies in Present-Day Bohemian Paris* (1927), *After Leaving Mr. MacKenzie* (1930), *Good Morning, Midnight* (1939), *Wide Sargasso Sea* (1966), *Tigers Are Better Looking* (1968), *Quartet* (first printed as *Postures*, 1928, rep. 1957, 1971), *My Day: Three Pieces* (1975), *Sleep It Off, Lady* (1976), and *Smile Please: An Unfinished Autobiography* (1979). The *Collected Stories*, ed. Diana Athill, was published in 1987.

Francis Wyndham and Diana Melly edited *The Letters of Jean Rhys* (1984), and David Plante, *Difficult Women: A Memoir of Three* (1983), includes source material. Useful studies of Rhys's life and work are Peter Wolfe, *Jean Rhys* (1980); Helen Nebeker, *Jean Rhys, Woman in Passage: A Critical Study of the Novels of Jean Rhys* (1981); Teresa F. O'Connor, *Jean Rhys: The West Indian Novels* (1986); Judith Kegan Gardiner, *Rhys, Stead, Lessing, and the Politics of Empathy* (1989); Mary Lou Emery, *Jean Rhys at "World's End": Novels of Colonial and Sexual Exile* (1990); Coral Ann Howells, *Jean Rhys* (1991); Carol Angier, *Jean Rhys: Life and Work* (1991); Elaine Savory, *Jean Rhys* (1998); Sylvie Maurel, *Jean Rhys* (1998); and Victoria Burrows, *Whiteness and Trauma: The Mother-Daughter Knot in the Fiction of Jean Rhys, Jamaica Kincaid, and Toni Morrison* (2004). Elgin Mellowin compiled *A Descriptive and Annotated Bibliography of Works and Criticism* in 1984.

Adrienne Rich
Rich's *The Fact of a Doorframe: Poems Selected and New, 1950–84* (1984) draws upon poems from most of the poet's books during those years: *A Change of World* (1951), *The Diamond Cutters* (1955), *Snapshots of a Daughter-in-Law* (1963, 1967), *Necessities of Life* (1966), *Leaflets* (1969), *The Will to Change* (1971), *Diving into the Wreck* (1973), *The Dream of a Common Language* (1978), and *A Wild Patience Has Taken Me This Far* (1981). She has also published *Poems Selected and New, 1950–1974* (1974), *Sources* (1983), *Your Native Land, Your Life* (1986), *Time's Power* (1989), and five more recent collections: *An Atlas of the Difficult World: Poems, 1988–1991* (1991); *Collected Early Poems, 1950–1970* (1993); *Dark Fields of the Republic* (1995); *Midnight Salvage: Poems, 1995–1998* (1999); and *The School Among the Ruins: Poems, 2000–2004* (2004). *Adrienne Rich's Poetry and Prose* (1993), with works selected and edited by Barbara Charlesworth Gelpi and Albert Gelpi, has also recently appeared. Rich is the author of the study *Of Woman Born: Motherhood as Experience and Institution* (1976), and she has collected her essays, lectures, and speeches in three volumes: *On Lies, Secrets, and Silence: Selected Prose, 1966–1978* (1979), *Blood, Bread, and Poetry: Selected Prose, 1979–1985* (1986), and *What Is Found There: Notebooks on Poetry and Politics* (1993). A set of interviews and essays has been assembled in *Arts of the Possible: Essays and Conversations* (2001).

Useful full-length critical studies are Claire Keyes, *The Aesthetics of Power: The Poetry of Adrienne Rich* (1986); Craig Hansen Werner,

Adrienne Rich: The Poet and Her Critics (1988); Alice Templeton, *The Dream and the Dialogue: Adrienne Rich's Feminist Poetics* (1994); Liz Yorke, *Adrienne Rich: Passion, Politics and the Body* (1997); and Cheri Colby Langdell, *Adrienne Rich: The Moment of Change* (2004). There are valuable essays and an interview in the Norton Critical Edition of *Adrienne Rich's Poetry* (1975), ed. Barbara Charlesworth Gelpi and Albert Gelpi. Other useful essays are Marilyn R. Farwell, "Adrienne Rich and an Organic Feminist Criticism," *College English* 39 (1977); Dacia Maraini, "On *Of Woman Born*," *Signs* 4 (1979); Alicia Ostriker, "Her Cargo: Adrienne Rich and the Common Language," *American Poetry Review* 8 (1979); Diane Middlebrook, "Making Visible the Common World: Walt Whitman and Feminist Poetry," *Kenyon Review* 2 (1980); Joanne Feit Diehl, "'Cartographies of Silence': Rich's Common Language and the Woman Poet," *Feminist Studies* 6 (1980); Adalaide Morris, "Imitations and Identities: Adrienne Rich's *A Change of World*," *Modern Poetry Studies* 10 (1981); Betty S. Flowers, "The 'I' in Adrienne Rich: Individuation and the Androgyne Archetype," in *Theory and Practice of Feminist Literary Criticism* (1982), ed. Gabriela Mora and Karen S. van Hooft; Mary S. Strine, "The Politics of Asking Women's Questions: Voice and Value in the Poetry of Adrienne Rich," *Text and Performance Quarterly* 9 (1989); Helen M. Dennis, "Adrienne Rich: Consciousness Raising as Poetic Method," in *Contemporary Poetry Meets Modern Theory* (1991), ed. Antony Easthope and John O. Thompson; and Alice Templeton, "Contradictions: Tracking Adrienne Rich's Poetry," *Tulsa Studies in Women's Literature* 12 (1993). Valuable critical work since the mid-1990s includes Jeffrey A. Walker, "Remapping Freudian America: Adrienne Rich and the Adult Son," *North Dakota Quarterly* 62 (1994/95); Audrey Crawford, "'Handing the Power-Glasses Back and Forth': Women and Technology in Poems by Adrienne Rich," *National Women's Studies Association Journal* 7 (1995); Kurt R. Niland, "Moulsworth and Recent Feminist Theory: The Example of Adrienne Rich," *Critical Matrix* 10 (1996); Barbara L. Estrin, "Re-versing the Past: Adrienne Rich's Postmodern Inquietude," *Tulsa Studies in Women's Literature* 16 (1997); Roger Gilbert, "Framing Water: Historical Knowledge in Elizabeth Bishop and Adrienne Rich," *Twentieth Century Literature* 43 (1997); articles on Rich in *Women's Studies* 27 (1998) by Jacqueline Vaught, Lynda K. Bundtzen, George Hart, Sylvia Henneberg, Cynthia Hogue, and Donna Krolik Hollenberg; Liz Yorke, "Breaking Through the 'Logic of Limits': Adrienne Rich and Radical Complexity," *Revista canaria de estudios ingleses* 37 (1998); Joshua S. Jacobs, "Mapping after the Holocaust: The 'Atlases' of Adrienne Rich and Gerhard Richter," *Mosaic* 32 (1999); Mary Eagleton, "Adrienne Rich, Location and the Body," *Journal of Gender Studies* 9 (2000); Sylvia Henneberg, "The Self-Categorization, Self-Canonization, and Self-Periodization of Adrienne Rich," in *Challenging Boundaries: Gender and Periodization* (2000), ed. Joyce W. Warren and Margaret Dickie; Rachel Stein, "'To Make the Visible World your Conscience': Adrienne Rich as Revolutionary Nature Writer," in *Reading Under the Sign of Nature: New Essays in Ecocriticism* (2000), ed. Jon Tallmadge and Henry Harrington; Albert Gelpi, "The Transfiguration of the Body: Adrienne Rich's Witness," *Wallace Stevens Journal* 25 (2001); Cynthia Hogue, "The 'Possible Poet': Pain, Form, and the Embodied Poetics of Adrienne Rich in Wallace Stevens' Wake," *Wallace Stevens Journal* 25 (2001); Luke Spencer, "'That Light of Outrage': The Historicism of Adrienne Rich," *English* (Leicester) 51 (2002); Artemis Michailidou, "Edna St Vincent Millay, Muriel Rukeyser, and Adrienne Rich: Political Poetry, Social Protest, and the Place of the Woman Writer," *European Journal of American Culture* 22 (2003); and Piotr Gwiazda, "'Nothing Else Left to Read': Poetry and Audience in Adrienne Rich's *An Atlas of the Difficult World*," *Journal of Modern Literature* 28 (2005). In addition, useful critical analyses are included in Suzanne Juhasz, *Naked and Fiery Forms* (1976); David Kalstone, *Five Temperaments* (1977); Wendy Martin, *An American Triptych* (1984); *Reading Adrienne Rich: Reviews and Re-Visions, 1951–81* (1984), ed. Jane Roberta Cooper; and Jeanne Perreault, *Writing Selves: Contemporary Feminist Autography* (1995). Rich's work is featured in a number of recent comparative volumes, including Carmen Binkle, *Women's Stories of the Looking-Glass: Autobiographical Reflections and Self-Representations in the Poetry of Sylvia Plath, Adrienne Rich, and Audre Lorde* (1996); Krista Ratcliffe, *Anglo-American Feminist Challenges to the Rhetorical Traditions: Virginia Woolf, Mary Daly, Adrienne Rich* (1996); Margaret Dickie, *Stein, Bishop, & Rich: Lyrics of Love, War, & Place* (1997); Sabina Sielke, *Fashioning the Female Subject: The Intertextual Networking of Dickinson, Moore, and Rich* (1997); Nick Halpern, *Everyday and Prophetic: The Poetry of Lowell, Ammons, Merrill, and Rich* (2003); and Gale Swiontkowski, *Imagining Incest: Sexton, Plath, Rich, and Olds on Life with Daddy* (2003).

Dorothy Richardson

The four volumes of Richardson's *Pilgrimage* (1915–38) have been published by Virago Press (1979), with an introduction by Gillian E. Hanscombe. There is now also a prose collection, *Journey to Paradise: Short Stories and Autobiographical Sketches* (1989), selected by Trudi

Tate, and a series of letters, Gloria G. Fromm, ed., "Letters from Dorothy Richardson: Selected, with an Introduction," *The New Criterion* 10 (1992). A helpful introduction to Richardson's life and work is Thomas F. Staley, *Dorothy Richardson* (1976). Two useful biographies are John D. Rosenberg, *Dorothy Richardson: The Genius They Forgot: A Critical Biography* (1973), and Gloria G. Fromm, *Dorothy Richardson: A Biography* (1977).

A feminist approach is offered in Gillian E. Hanscombe's full-length study *The Art of Life: Dorothy Richardson and the Development of Feminist Consciousness* (1982). In addition, Richardson's achievement is analyzed in Sidney Janet Kaplan, *Feminine Consciousness in the Modern British Novel* (1975); in Jean Radford, *Dorothy Richardson* (1991); and in Jane Garrity, *Step-Daughters of England: British Women Modernists and the National Imaginary* (2003). Two useful essays are Hanscombe, "Dorothy Richardson versus the Novel," in *Breaking the Sequence: Women's Experimental Fiction* (1989), ed. Ellen Friedman and Miriam Fuchs, and Sarah Schuyler, "Double-Dealing Fictions," *Genders* 9 (1990), which compares Richardson's *Pointed Roofs* with H. D.'s *HERmione*. A helpful resource is Averill Buchanan, "Dorothy Miller Richardson, A Bibliography, 1900 to 1999," *Journal of Modern Literature* 24 (2002).

Henry Handel Richardson

Richardson's novels include *The Getting of Wisdom* (1910), *Maurice Guest* (1930), and *The Fortunes of Richard Mahony* (1931). The last two have been republished by Virago Press, with useful introductions. A valuable collection, *The End of a Childhood: The Complete Stories of Henry Handel Richardson*, appeared in 1992. In 1999, Susan Lever and Catherine Pratt edited *Henry Handel Richardson: The Getting of Wisdom, Stories, Selected Prose, and Correspondence*. Karl-Johan Rossing edited *Letters of Henry Handel Richardson to Nettie Palmer* (1953).

Henry Handel Richardson (1975), by William D. Elliott, offers a helpful overview of her work. Other biographical and critical studies include Nettie Palmer, *Henry Handel Richardson: A Study* (1950); Vincent Buckley, *Henry Handel Richardson* (1961); J. R. Nichols, *Art and Irony: The Tragic Vision of Henry Handel Richardson* (1982); Eva Jarring Corones, *The Portrayal of Women in the Fiction of Henry Handel Richardson* (1983); Karen McLeod, *Henry Handel Richardson: A Critical Study* (1985); and Michael Ackland, *Henry Handel Richardson: A Life* (2004). Also of interest are three articles: Dorothy Green, "The Tradition of Social Responsibility in the Australian Novel: Richardson and Murphy," *Literary Criticism* 15 (1980); Margaret K. Butcher, "From *Maurice Guest* to *Martha Quest*: The Female *Bildungsroman* in Commonwealth Literature," *World Literature Written in English* 22 (1982); and Noel Macainsh, "Point of View and Consequent Naturalism in the Novels of Henry Handel Richardson," *Westerly* 29 (1984).

Muriel Rukeyser

The Collected Poems of Muriel Rukeyser appeared in 1978; *Out of Silence: Selected Poems*, ed. Kate Daniels, which includes selections of poems from her first volume of poetry, *Theory of Flight* (1935), through to her last volume, *The Gates* (1978), appeared in 1992. *A Muriel Rukeyser Reader* (1994), ed. Jan Heller Levi, gathers both poetry and prose. Besides her own poetry, Rukeyser published several translations, including *Selected Poems of Octavio Paz* (1963). She also wrote biographies, including *Willard Gibbs* (1942), *One Life* (1957), and *The Traces of Thomas Hariot* (1971), as well as children's books. A full-length study is Louise Kertesz, *The Poetic Vision of Muriel Rukeyser* (1980), and a collection of essays is *How Shall We Tell Each Other of the Poet?: The Life and Writing of Muriel Rukeyser*, ed. Anne F. Herzog and Janet E. Kaufman (1999). Critical essays include Robert Coles, "Muriel Rukeyser's *The Gates*," *American Poetry Review* 7 (1978), and Rachel Blau DuPlessis, "The Critique of Consciousness and Myth in Levertov, Rich, and Rukeyser," in *Shakespeare's Sisters* (1979), ed. Sandra M. Gilbert and Susan Gubar. *Poetry East* (1985) issued a special edition on Rukeyser, ed. Kate Daniels and Richard Jones.

Zitkala Sá (Gertrude Bonnin)

Bonnin's works include *Old Indian Legends* (1901) and *American Indian Stories* (1921). With William Hanson, she wrote the libretto for *Sundance* (1913), an opera, and she also co-authored *Okla's Poor Rich Indians: An Orgy of Graft and Exploitation of the Five Civilized Tribes—Legalized Robbery* (1924). She also published three essays: "Impressions of an Indian Childhood" and "An Indian Teacher among Indians," both in *Atlantic Monthly* (Jan.– Mar. 1900), and "Why I Am a Pagan," *Atlantic Monthly* 90 (Dec. 1902). A recent biography is Doreen Rappaport, *The Flight of Red Bird: The Life of Zitkala-Sa* (1997). Biographical information is also included in Hazel W. Hertzberg, *The Search for an American Indian Identity* (1971), and Marion E. Gridley, *American Indian Women* (1974). Useful critical articles are Dexter Fisher, "Zitkala-Sa: The Evolution of a Writer," *American Indian Quarterly* 5 (1979); Mary Stout, "Zitkala-Sa: The Literature of Politics" in *Coyote Was Here: Essays on Contemporary Native American Literary and Political Mobilization* (1984), ed. Bo Scholer; Fisher, "The Transformation of Tradition: A Study of

Zitkala-Sa and Mourning Dove, Two Transitional American Indian Writers" in *Critical Essays on American Literature* (1985), ed. Andrew Wiget; and Dorothea M. Susag, "Zitkala-Sa (Gertrude Simmons Bonnin): A Powerful Literary Voice," *Studies in American Indian Literature* 5 (1993).

May Sarton

Among Sarton's many novels are *The Single Hound* (1938), *A Shower of Summer Days* (1952), *The Small Room* (1961), *Joanna and Ulysses* (1963), *Mrs. Stevens Hears the Mermaids Singing* (1965), and *Kinds of Love* (1970). Sarton's recent works include two novels, *The Magnificent Spinster* (1985) and *The Education of Harriet Hatfield* (1989), and three books of poetry: *The Phoenix Again: New Poems* (1987), *The Silence Now: New and Uncollected Earlier Poems* (1988), and *Coming into Eighty: New Poems* (1992). Her *Collected Poems (1930-1973)* appeared in 1973 and an expanded volume, *Collected Poems: 1930-1993*, appeared in 1993. Her journal volumes include *Plant Dreaming Deep* (1968), *Journal of a Solitude* (1973), *The House by the Sea* (1977), *Recovering* (1980), *At Seventy* (1984), *After the Stroke: A Journal* (1988), *Endgame: A Journal of the Seventy-ninth Year* (1992), and *Encore: A Journal of the Eightieth Year* (1993). Marita Simpson and Martha Wheelock edited a selection of Sarton's autobiographical writings, *May Sarton: A Self-Portrait*, in 1986. In addition, *Sarton Selected: An Anthology of Novels, Journals, and Poetry*, ed. Bradford Dudley Daziel, appeared in 1991; and another collection, *May Sarton: Among the Usual Days*, ed. Susan Sherman, was published in 1993. Earl G. Ingersoll edited a selection of interviews, *Conversations with May Sarton*, in 1991. Constance Hunting edited *Writings on Writing* (1980), as well as *May Sarton, Woman and Poet* (1982); and Margot Peters contributed *May Sarton* (1997). Other helpful biographical material appears in Sarton's own *I Knew a Phoenix: Sketches for an Autobiography* (1978), and in Dolores Shelley, "A Conversation with May Sarton," *Women and Literature* 7 (1979), as well as in Agnes Sibley, *May Sarton* (1972).

A full-length study of Sarton's career is Elizabeth Evans, *May Sarton Revisited* (1989). Essays on Sarton's work include Dawn Holt Anderson, "May Sarton's Women," in *Images of Women in Fiction* (1972), ed. Susan Koppelman Cornillon; Doris L. Eder, "Woman Writer: May Sarton's *Mrs. Stevens Hears the Mermaids Singing*," *International Journal of Women's Studies* 1 (1978); Jane S. Bakerman, "'Kinds of Love': Love and Friendship in the Novels of May Sarton," *Critique* 20 (1978); Marlene Springer, "As We Shall Be: May Sarton and Aging," *Frontiers* 5 (1980); Emily M. Nett, "The Naked Soul Comes Closer to the Surface: Old Age in the Gender Mirror of Contemporary Novels," *Women's Studies* 18 (1990); Henry Taylor, "May Sarton: Home to a Place Beyond Exile," in his *Compulsory Figures: Essays on Recent American Poets* (1992); Janis P. Stout, "A Wordless Balm: Silent Communication in the Novels of May Sarton," *Essays in Literature* 20 (1993); Anne Wyatt-Brown, "Another Model of the Aging Writer: Sarton's Politics of Old Age," in *Aging and Gender in Literature: Studies in Creativity* (1993), ed. Wyatt-Brown and Janice Rossen; and Leah E. White, "Silenced Stories: May Sarton's Journals as Form of Discursive Resistance," *Women's Life-Writing: Finding Voice/Building Community*, ed. Linda S. Coleman (1997). See also Carolyn Heilbrun's discussion of Sarton in *Hamlet's Mother and Other Women* (1990). Lenora Blouin compiled a bibliography, *May Sarton*, in 1978, rev. 2000.

Anne Sexton

Sexton's *The Complete Poems*, with a foreword by Maxine Kumin, was published in 1981. Two other useful collections are *Words for Dr. Y.: Uncollected Poems with Three Stories* (1978), ed. Linda Sexton, and *Selected Poems of Anne Sexton* (1988), ed. Diane Wood Middlebrook and Diana Hume George. *No Evil Star: Selected Essays, Interviews, and Prose*, ed. Steven E. Colburn, appeared in 1985; *A Self-Portrait in Letters* in 1977. More recent books that provide useful biographical material are Diane Wood Middlebrook, *Anne Sexton: A Biography* (1991); Linda Gray Sexton, *Searching for Mercy Street: My Journey Back to My Mother* (1994); and Arthur Furst, *Anne Sexton: The Last Summer* (2000). Important interviews and critical essays are to be found in J. D. McClatchy, *Anne Sexton: The Artist and Her Critics* (1978); Diana Hume George, ed., *Sexton: Selected Criticism* (1988); Linda Wagner, *Critical Essays on Anne Sexton* (1989); and *Women Writers at Work: The Paris Review Interviews* (1998), ed. George Plimpton. Philip McGowan published the book-length study *Anne Sexton and Middle Generation Poetry: The Geography of Grief* in 2004. Critical essays include Suzanne Juhasz, "Seeking the Exit or the Home: Poetry and Salvation in the Career of Anne Sexton," in *Shakespeare's Sisters* (1979), ed. Sandra M. Gilbert and Susan Gubar; Margaret Houton, "The Double Image and the Division of Parts: A Study of Mother/Daughter Relationships in the Poetry of Anne Sexton," *Journal of Women's Studies in Literature* 1 (1979); Kathleen L. Nicholas, "The Hungry Beast Rowing toward God: Anne Sexton's Later Religious Poetry," *Notes on Modern American Literature* 21 (1979); Jeanne H. Kammer, "The Witches' Life: Confession and Control in the Early Poetry of Anne Sexton," *Language and Style* 13 (1980); Rosemary Johnson, "The

Woman of Private (but Published) Hungers," *Parnassus* 8 (1980); and Alicia Ostriker, "That Story: Anne Sexton and Her Transformations," *American Poetry Review* 11 (1982). More recent essays include Hilary Clark, "Depression, Shame and Reparation: The Case of Anne Sexton," in *Scenes of Shame: Psychoanalysis, Shame and Writing* (1998), ed. Joseph Adamson; Manju Jaidka, "Writing the Body: Anne Sexton," in *From Straight to Slant: Recent Trends in Women's Poetry* (2000); Colin Clarke, "The Isolation of Panic and the Panic of Isolation in the Poetry of Sylvia Plath and Anne Sexton," in *Panic: Origins, Insight, and Treatment* (2002), ed. Leonard J. Schmidt and Brooke Warner; Philip McGowan, "Uncovering the Female Voice in Anne Sexton," *Revista canaria de estudios ingleses* 37 (1998); Joanna Gill, "'My Sweeney, Mr. Eliot': Anne Sexton and the 'Impersonal Theory of Poetry'," *Journal of Modern Literature* 27 (2003); Jo Gill, "Textual Confessions: Narcissism in Anne Sexton's Early Poetry," *Twentieth Century Literature* 50 (2004); Gill, "Anne Sexton and Confessional Poetics," *Review of English Studies* 55 (2004); and Artemis Michailidou, "Gender, Body and Feminine Performance: Edna St. Vincent Millay's Impact on Anne Sexton," *Feminist Review* 78 (2004). Comparative volumes featuring Sexton's work include Cassie Premo Steele, *We Heal from Memory: Sexton, Lorde, Anzaldúa, and the Poetry of Witness* (2000), and Gale Swiontkowski, *Imagining Incest: Sexton, Plath, Rich, and Olds on Life with Daddy* (2003). Valuable also is C. Northouse and R. P. Walsh, *Sylvia Plath and Anne Sexton: A Reference Guide* (1974).

Leslie Marmon Silko

Silko's works include *Laguna Woman* (1974), *Ceremony* (1977), *Storyteller* (1981), *Almanac of the Dead* (1991), the autobiographical *Sacred Water: Narratives and Pictures* (1993), *Voices Under One Sky* (1994), *Rain* (1996), a set of essays about contemporary Native-American life titled *Yellow Woman and a Beauty of the Spirit* (1996), and *Gardens in the Dunes* (1999). Anne Wright edited a collection of correspondence, *The Delicacy and Strength of Lace: Letters between Leslie Marmon Silko and James Wright*, in 1986. Useful background material is offered in Per Seyersted, "Two Interviews with Leslie Marmon Silko," *American Studies in Scandinavia* 13 (1981); Elaine Jahner, "The Novel and Oral Tradition: An Interview with Leslie Marmon Silko," *Book Forum* 5 (1981); and Linda Niemann, "Narratives of Survival," *Women's Review of Books* 9 (1992). In addition, Seyersted has written a full-length critical study, *Leslie Marmon Silko* (1980); also useful are Catherine Rainwater, *Dreams of Fiery Stars* (1999), as well as the collection of essays *Leslie Marmon Silko* (2001), ed. Louise K. Barnett and James L. Thorson. There have been numerous critical essays, including Edith Blicksilver, "Traditionalism vs. Modernity: Leslie Silko on American Indian Women," *Southwest Review* 64 (1979); Ronald E. McFarland, "Leslie Silko's Story of Stories," *A Journal of Contemporary Literature* 4 (1979); A. LaVonne Ruoff, "Ritual and Renewal: Keres Traditions in the Short Fiction of Leslie Silko," *MELUS* 5 (1979); C. W. Truesdle, "Tradition and Ceremony: Leslie Marmon Silko as an American Novelist," *North Dakota Quarterly* 59 (1991); Edith Swan, "Feminine Perspectives at Laguna Pueblo: Silko's *Ceremony*," *Tulsa Studies in Women's Literature* 11 (1992); and Linda J. Krumholz, "To Understand This World Differently: Reading and Subversion in Leslie Marmon Silko's *Storyteller*," *Ariel* 25 (1994). Melody Graulich edited a volume of critical essays, *Yellow Woman*, in 1993. See also the helpful discussions of Silko in Roberta Rubenstein, *Boundaries of the Self: Gender, Culture, Fiction* (1987); Arnold Krupat, *The Voice in the Margin: Native American Literature and the Canon* (1989); Louis Owens, *Other Destinies: Understanding the American Indian Novel* (1992); Hertha Dawn Wong, *Sending My Heart Back across the Years: Tradition and Innovation in Native American Autobiography* (1992); and Bonnie C. Winsbro, *Supernatural Forces: Belief, Difference, and Power in Contemporary Works by Ethnic Women* (1993).

Edith Sitwell

In addition to more than thirty volumes of poetry, culminating in *Collected Poems* (1957), *Selected Poems* (1965), with an introduction by John Lehmann, and most recently, *The Early Unpublished Poems of Edith Sitwell* (1994), ed. Gerald W. Morton and Karen P. Helgeson, Sitwell produced a variety of critical and other prose works. These include *Alexander Pope* (1930), *Aspects of Modern Poetry* (1934), *A Poet's Notebook* (1950), and *Taken Care Of: An Autobiography* (1965). John Lehmann and Derek Parker edited *Edith Sitwell: Selected Letters, 1919–1964*, and Lehmann has written an informative account of Sitwell's family and background in *A Nest of Tigers: Edith, Osbert, and Sacheverell Sitwell in Their Times* (1968). Richard Greene edited *Selected Letters of Edith Sitwell*, which was published in 1997. Other biographical and critical works include J. D. Brophy, *Edith Sitwell: The Symbolist Order* (1968); John Press, *A Map of Modern English Verse* (1969); Kenneth Rexroth, "Poets Old and New: Edith Sitwell," in *Assays* (1961); E. Salter, *The Last Years of a Rebel: A Memoir of Edith Sitwell* (1967); G. A. Cevasco, *The Sitwells: Edith, Osbert, and Sacheverell* (1987); and Perdita Schaffner, "A Day at the St. Regis with Dame Edith," in *American Scholar* 60 (1991).

Four full-length studies are John Pearson, *Façades: Edith, Osbert, and Sacheverell Sitwell* (1978); Elizabeth Salter, *Edith Sitwell* (1979); Geoffrey Elborn, *Edith Sitwell: A Biography* (1981); and Victoria Glendinning, *Edith Sitwell: A Unicorn among Lions* (1981). Critical essays include Patricia Clements, "Edith Sitwell and Some Others: Departures from Decadence," in her *Baudelaire and the English Tradition* (1985); Cyrena N. Pondrom, "Influence? Or Intertextuality? The Complicated Connection of Edith Sitwell and Gertrude Stein," in *Influence and Intertextuality in Literary History* (1991), ed. Jay Clayton and Eric Rothstein; Gary Day and Gina Wisker, "Recuperating and Revaluing: Edith Sitwell and Charlotte Mew," in *British Poetry, 1900–50: Aspects of Tradition* (1995), ed. Gary Day; Deborah Tyler-Bennett, "Robert Graves and Edith Sitwell: A Shortened Poetic Relationship (1997), *Gravesiana* 1 (1997); and two essays by Terri Witek, "Edith Sitwell and the Carnal World," and "Edith Sitwell on Style," both in *American Poetry Review* 32 (2003).

Stevie Smith

Smith's books of poetry include *A Good Time Was Had by All* (1937), *Harold's Leap* (1950), *Not Waving but Drowning* (1957), and *Scorpion, and Other Poems* (1972), published posthumously with an introduction by Patrick Dickinson. Both the *Selected Poems* (1962) and the *Collected Poems* (1976), ed. James MacGibbon, reproduce many of the drawings she originally printed with her poems. Smith also wrote three novels: *Novel on Yellow Paper; or, Work It Out for Yourself* (1936), *Over the Frontier* (1938), and *The Holiday* (1949). All have been reissued in paperbound editions. *A Very Pleasant Evening with Stevie Smith: Selected Short Prose* was published by New Directions in 1995.

Frances Spalding's valuable biography, *Stevie Smith*, appeared in 1988. Another biography is Jack Barbera and William McBrien, *Stevie: A Biography of Stevie Smith* (1985). See also the interviews in *The Poet Speaks* (1966), ed. Peter Orr, and in Kay Dick, *Ivy and Stevie* (1971). Full-length studies of Smith's career and works are Arthur C. Rankin, *The Poetry of Stevie Smith: "Little Girl Lost"* (1985); Catherine A. Civello, *Patterns of Ambivalence: The Fiction and Poetry of Stevie Smith* (1997); Laura Severin, *Stevie Smith's Resistant Antics* (1997); and Romana Huk, *Stevie Smith: Between the Lines* (2005). A helpful collection of critical essays is *In Search of Stevie Smith* (1991), ed. Sanford Sternlicht. Useful essays are the chapter in *Eight Contemporary Poets* by Calvin Bedient (1974); Philip Larkin, "Frivolous and Vulnerable," *New Statesman* (1962); an anonymous review, "The Voice of Genteel Decay," *Times Literary Supplement* (1972); Steven Helmling, "Delivered for a Time from Silence," *Parnassus* 6 (1977); Janice Thaddeus, "Stevie Smith and the Gleeful Macabre," *Contemporary Poetry* 3 (1978); Mark Storey, "Why Stevie Smith Matters," *Critical Quarterly* 21 (1979); Christopher B. Ricks, "Stevie Smith: The Art of Sinking in Poetry," in his *The Force of Poetry* (1984); Lee Upton, "Stevie Smith and the Anxiety of Intimacy," *CEA Critic* 53 (1991); Richard Nemesvari, "'Work It Out for Yourself': Language and Fictional Form in Stevie Smith's *Novel on Yellow Paper*," *The Dalhousie Review* 71 (1991); Sheryl Stevenson, "Stevie Smith's Voices," *Contemporary Literature* 33 (1993); Alison Light, "Outside History? Stevie Smith, Women Poets and the National Voice," *English* (Leicester) 43 (1994); and Manju Jaidka, "Rejecting the Father: Stevie Smith," in her *From Straight to Slant: Recent Trends in Women's Poetry* (2000). A feminist perspective on Smith's poetry is represented by Romana Huk, "Eccentric Concentrism: Traditional Poetic Forms and Refracted Discourse in Stevie Smith's Poetry," *Contemporary Literature* 43 (1993). Smith's work also comes under consideration in Kristin Bluemel's volume, *George Orwell and the Radical Eccentrics: Intermodernism in Literary London* (2004). Jack Barbera, William McBrien, and Helen Bajan compiled a reference guide, *Stevie Smith: A Bibliography*, in 1986.

Muriel Spark

Spark's numerous works include *Memento Mori* (1959), *The Prime of Miss Jean Brodie* (1961), *Emily Brontë, Her Life and Work* (with Derek Stanford, 1966), *Collected Stories* (1967), *Collected Poems* (1967), *The Abbess of Crewe* (1974), *The Only Problem* (1984), *The Stories of Muriel Spark* (1985), *A Far Cry from Kensington* (1988), and *Symposium* (1990). The first installment of her autobiography is called *Curriculum Vitae: Autobiography* (1992). Studies of her life and work are Karl Malkoff, *Muriel Spark* (1968); Patricia Stubb, *Muriel Spark* (1973); Peter Kemp, *Muriel Spark* (1974); Ruth Whittaker, *The Faith and Fiction of Muriel Spark* (1982); Dorothea Walker, *Muriel Spark* (1988); Norman Page, *Muriel Spark* (1990); and Bryan Cheyette, *Muriel Spark* (2000). Two essay collections are *Critical Essays on Muriel Spark*, ed. Joseph Hynes (1992), and *Theorizing Muriel Spark*, ed. Martin McQuillan (2002).

Anne Spencer

Selections of Spencer's poems can be found in *Black Sister: Poetry by Black American Women, 1746–1980* (1981), ed. Erlene Stetson; *Shadowed Dreams: Women's Poetry of the Harlem Renaissance* (1989), ed. Maureen Honey; and *The Portable Harlem Renaissance Reader* (1994), ed. David Levering Lewis. The only full-length critical and biographical study of Spencer is J. Lee Greene, *Time's Unfading Garden: Anne*

Spencer's *Life and Poetry* (1977). Other useful information on Spencer can be found in Gloria T. Hull, "Afro-American Poets: A BioCritical Survey," in *Shakespeare's Sisters* (1979), ed. Sandra Gilbert and Susan Gubar. A documentary film about Spencer, *Echoes from the Garden: The Anne Spencer Story*, was produced in 1980.

Gertrude Stein

Although there is no complete edition of Stein's writings, *The Yale Edition of the Unpublished Writings of Gertrude Stein*, ed. Carl Van Vechten (1951–58), contains eight volumes of poetry, prose fiction, portraits, and essays. Among the prose works published during Stein's lifetime are *Three Lives* (1909), *Tender Buttons* (1914), *The Making of Americans* (1925), the children's book *The World Is Round* (1926), *Lucy Church Amiably* (1930), *Ida: A Novel* (1941), and *Brewsie and Willie* (1946). *Geography and Plays* (1922), *Operas and Plays* (1932), and *Last Operas and Plays*, ed. Van Vechten (1949), contain dramatic pieces. Autobiographical material may be found in *The Autobiography of Alice B. Toklas* (1933), *Portraits and Prayers* (1934), *Everybody's Autobiography* (1937), and *Wars I Have Seen* (1945). Other works, including meditations, essays, sketches, and sociolinguistic treatises, are *Useful Knowledge* (1928), *How to Write* (1931), *Lectures in America* (1935), *Narration: Four Lectures by Gertrude Stein* (1935), *What Are Masterpieces* (1940), and *Four in America* (1947). Useful introductory collections of Stein's writings are *Selected Writings of Gertrude Stein* (1962), ed. Van Vechten, and *A Stein Reader* (1993), ed. Ulla E. Dydo.

Donald C. Gallup has edited *Fernhurst, Q.E.D., and Other Early Writings by Gertrude Stein* (1971), as well as a collection of letters to Gertrude Stein, *The Flowers of Friendship* (1953). *Dear Sammy: Letters from Gertrude Stein and Alice B. Toklas*, ed. Samuel M. Steward, appeared in 1977, and *The Letters of Gertrude Stein and Carl Van Vechten, 1913–1946*, ed. Edward Burns, in 1986. Memoirs of Stein include W. G. Rogers, *When This You See Remember Me: Gertrude Stein in Person* (1948), and Alice B. Toklas, *What Is Remembered* (1953). Linda Simon, *The Biography of Alice B. Toklas* (1977), provides useful background information.

Biographical studies of Stein are Elizabeth Sprigg, *Gertrude Stein: Her Life and Work* (1957); John Malcolm Brinnin, *The Third Rose: Gertrude Stein and Her World* (1959); James R. Mellow, *Charmed Circle: Gertrude Stein and Company* (1974); Janet Hobhouse, *Everybody Who Was Anybody* (1975); Linda Wagner-Martin, *Favored Strangers: Gertrude Stein and her Family* (1995); and Brenda Wineapple, *Sister Brother: Gertrude and Leo Stein* (1996).

Critical studies include Donald Sutherland, *Gertrude Stein: A Biography of Her Work* (1951); Michael Hoffman, *The Development of Abstractionism in the Writings of Gertrude Stein* (1965); Allegra Stewart, *Gertrude Stein and the Present* (1967); Norman Weinstein, *Gertrude Stein and the Literature of Modern Consciousness* (1970); Richard Bridgemen, *Gertrude Stein in Pieces* (1970); Robert B. Haas, *A Primer for the Gradual Understanding of Gertrude Stein* (1971); Carolyn F. Copeland, *Language and Time and Gertrude Stein* (1975); Michael Hoffman, *Gertrude Stein* (1976); Wendy Steiner, *Exact Resemblance to Exact Resemblance: The Literary Portraiture of Gertrude Stein's Experimental Writing* (1983); Marianne DeKoven, *A Different Language: Gertrude Stein's Experimental Writing* (1983); Harriet Scott Chessman, *The Public Is Invited to Dance: Representation, the Body, and Dialogue in Gertrude Stein* (1989); Lisa Cole Ruddick, *Reading Gertrude Stein: Body, Text, Gnosis* (1990); Ellen E. Berry, *Curved Thought and Textual Wandering: Gertrude Stein's Postmodernism* (1992); Linda Watt, *Gertrude Stein: A Study of the Short Fiction* (1999); and Barbara Will, *Gertrude Stein, Modernism, and the Problem of "Genius"* (2000). Two valuable bibliographies are *Gertrude Stein* (1979), by Maureen R. Liston, and *Gertrude Stein and Alice B. Toklas: A Reference Guide* (1984), by Ray L. White. See also *A Gertrude Stein Companion: Content with Example* (1988), ed. Bruce Kellner.

Ruth Stone

Stone's collections of poetry are *In an Iridescent Time* (1958), *Topography, and Other Poems* (1970), *Cheap: New Poems and Ballads* (1975), *Second Hand Coat: Poems New and Selected* (1987), *The Solution* (1989), *Who Is the Widow's Muse?* (1991), *Simplicity* (1995), *Ordinary Words* (1999), *In the Dark* (2004), and *In the Galaxy* (2004). For a series of short, appreciative essays, see Sandra M. Gilbert et al., "On Ruth Stone," *Iowa Review* 12 (1981), as well as *The House Is Made of Poetry: The Art of Ruth Stone* (1996), ed. Wendy Barker and Sandra M. Gilbert.

May Swenson

Swenson's volumes of poems include *Another Animal* (1954), *A Cage of Spines* (1958), *To Mix with Time: New and Selected Poems* (1963), *Poems to Solve* (1966), *Half Sun Half Sleep* (1967), *Iconographs* (1970), *More Poems to Solve* (1971), *The Guess and Spell Coloring Book* (1976), *New and Selected Things Taking Place* (1978), *In Other Words: New Poems* (1987), *The Love Poems of May Swenson* (1991), *Nature: Poems Old and New* (1994), and *May Out West* (1996). Prose by Swenson has been collected in *Made with Words* (1998) and *Dear*

Elizabeth: Five Poems & Three Letters to Elizabeth Bishop (2000). Swenson's comments are also included in Poets on Poetry (1966), ed. Howard Nemerov, and Karla Hammond interviewed Swenson for Parnassus 7 (1978). For biographical material, see R. R. Knudson and Suzzanne Bigelow, May Swenson: A Poet's Life in Photos (1996). Letters between Swenson and Elizabeth Bishop are featured in "Elizabeth Bishop—May Swenson correspondence," Paris Review 36 (1994). Useful critical essays are Ann Stanford, "The Art of Perceiving," Southern Review 6 (1969); Alicia Ostriker, "May Swenson and the Shapes of Speculation," in Shakespeare's Sisters (1979), ed. Sandra M. Gilbert and Susan Gubar; and Ann S. Wicks, "Music, Meaning, and the Adaptation of Literature," Literature in Performance 2 (1981); Dave Smith, "May Swenson: Perpetual Worlds Taking Place," in his Local Assays: On Contemporary American Poetry (1985); Sue Russell, "A Mysterious and Lavish Power: How Things Continue to Take Place in the Work of May Swenson," Kenyon Review 16 (1994); and Grace Schulman, "Life's Miracles: The Poetry of May Swenson," American Poetry Review 25 (1994).

Luci Tapahonso

Tapahonso's collections of poems and stories include Seasonal Woman, with drawings by R. C. Gorman (1982); A Breeze Swept Through (1987); Saanii Dahataal, the Women Are Singing (1993); Navajo ABC: A Diné Alphabet Book, written with Eleanor Schick (1995); and Blue Horses Rush In (1997). Tapahonso also contributed an essay, "The Way It Is," to Sign Language: Contemporary Southwest Native America (1989). Interviews with Tapahonso are included in American Contradictions: Interviews with Nine American Writers (1995), ed. Wolgang Binder and Helmbrecht Breinig, and Andrea Penner, "The Moon is so Far Away," Studies in American Indian Literatures 8 (1996). Critical works on Tapahonso's work include two essays in Susan Berry Brill de Ramírez, Contemporary American Indian Literatures and the Oral Tradition (1999), and Dean Rader, "Luci Tapahonso and Simon Ortiz: Allegory, Symbol, Language, Poetry," Southwestern American Literature 22 (1997).

Helen María Viramontes

Works by Viramontes include The Moths and Other Stories (1985) and Under the Feet of Jesus (1995). Stories by Viramontes can also be found in Woman of Her Word: Hispanic Women Write (1983), Pieces of the Heart: New Chicano Fiction, ed. Gary Soto (1993), Latina: Women's Voices from the Borderlands, ed. Lillian Castillo-Speed (1995), and Máscaras, ed. Lucha Corpi (1997). An interview by Isabel Dulfano appears in Women's Studies 30 (2001).

Critical discussions of Viramontes appear in Raúl Homero Villa, Tales from the Second City (1993); Leticia Garza-Falcón, Gente decente: A Borderlands Response to the Rhetoric of Dominance (1998); and Sonia Saldívar-Hull, Feminism on the Border: Chicana Gender Politics and Literature (2000). Useful essays include Deborah Owen Moore, "La Llorona Dies at the Cariboo Café: Structure and Legend in the work of Helena Maria Viramontes," Studies in Short Fiction 35 (1998), and Ana Patricia Rodríguez, "Refugees of the South: Central Americans in the U. S. Latino Imagery," American Literature 73 (2001).

Alice Walker

Walker's novels include The Third Life of Grange Copeland (1970), Meridian (1976), The Color Purple (1982), The Temple of My Familiar (1989), Possessing the Secret of Joy (1992), and By the Light of My Father's Smile (1999). Her short story collections include In Love and Trouble (1973), You Can't Keep a Good Woman Down (1981), The Complete Stories (1994), and The Way Forward is With a Broken Heart (2002). Walker's early poems are collected in Her Blue Body Everything We Know: Earthling Poems, 1965–1990 (1991); her poetry can also be found in Absolute Trust in the Goodness of the Earth: New Poems (2003). In addition to several works for children, she has also written nonfiction prose that can be found in In Search of Our Mothers' Gardens: Womanist Prose (1983), Living by the Word (1988), The Same River Twice (1996), Anything We Love can be Saved: A Writers' Activism (1997), and Sent By Earth: A Message from the Grandmother Spirit after the Attack on the World Trade Center (2001). With Pratibha Parmar, she also wrote Warrior Marks: Female Genital Mutilation and the Sexual Binding of Women (1993). A critical edition of Everyday Use appeared in 1994, edited and with an introduction by Barbara Christian. A biography is Evelyn C. White, Alice Walker, A Life (2004). An interview appears in Black Women Writers at Work (1984), ed. Claudia Tate.

Full-length studies include Elliott Butler-Evans, Race, Gender, and Desire: Narrative Strategies in the Fiction of Toni Cade Bambara, Toni Morrison, and Alice Walker (1989); Donna Haisty Winchell, Alice Walker (1992); Yvonne Johnson, The Voices of African-American Women: The Use of Narrative and Authorial Voice in the Works of Harriet Jacobs, Zora Neale Hurston, and Alice Walker (1998); and Mane Lauret, Alice Walker (2000). Essay collections include Alice Walker: Critical Perspectives Past and Present (1993), ed. Henry Louis Gates Jr. and Kwame Anthony Appiah, and Critical Essays on Alice Walker (1999), ed. Ikenna Dieke. Critical essays on Walker's work include Trudier Harris, "Folklore in the Fiction of Alice Walker,"

Black American Literature Forum 11 (1977); Chester J. Fantenot, "Alice Walker, 'The Diary of an African Nun' and Du Bois' Double Consciousness," and Mary Helen Washington, "An Essay on Alice Walker," both in *Sturdy Black Bridges: Visions of Black Women in Literature* (1979), ed. Roseann Bell, Bettye Parker, and Beverly Guy-Sheftall; Deborah McDowell, "The Self in Bloom: Alice Walker's *Meridian*," *College Language Association Journal* 24 (1981); Harris, "Tiptoeing through Taboo: Incest in 'The Child Who Favored Daughter,' " *Modern Fiction Studies* 28 (1982); Barbara Christian, "Alice Walker," and Bettye J. Parker-Smith, "Alice Walker's Women," both in *Black Women Writers (1950–1980)* (1984), ed. Mari Evans; Lauren Berlant, "Race, Gender, and Nation in *The Color Purple*," *Critical Inquiry* 14 (1988); and bell hooks, "Writing the Subject: Reading *The Color Purple*," in *Reading Black, Reading Feminist: A Critical Anthology* (1990), ed. Henry Louis Gates Jr. See also "Alice Walker: A Special Section," *Callaloo* 12 (1989). A useful, though somewhat dated, resource is Louise H. Pratt, *Alice Walker: An Annotated Bibliography, 1968–1986* (1988).

Margaret Walker
Walker's works include *For My People* (1942), *Jubilee* (1966), *Prophets for a New Day* (1970), *How I Wrote Jubilee* (1972), *October Journey* (1973), *A Poetic Equation: Conversations with Nikki Giovani* (1974), *The Daemonic Genius of Richard Wright* (1984), and *This Is My Century: New and Collected Poems* (1989). Maryemma Graham has edited two collections of Walker's essays, *How I Wrote "Jubilee" and Other Essays on Life and Literature* (1990), and *On Being Female, Black and Free: Essays by Margaret Walker, 1832–1992* (1997). Three helpful interviews are Charles H. Robell, "Poetry, History, and Humanism: An Interview with Margaret Walker," *Blackworld* 25 (1975); Phanuel Egejuru and Robert E. Fox, "An Interview with Margaret Walker," *Callaloo* 2 (1979); and an interview in *Black Women Writers at Work* (1984), ed. Claudia Tate.

A full-length study of Walker is Jacqueline Miller Carmichael, *Trumpeting a Fiery Sound: History and Folklore in Margaret Walker's Jubilee* (1998), and a collection of essays is *Fields Watered with Blood: Critical Essays on Margaret Walker*, ed. Maryemma Graham (2001). Other critical essays on Walker include Phyllis R. Klotman, " 'Oh Freedom': Women and History in Margaret Walker's *Jubilee*," *Black American Literature Forum* 11 (1977); James E. Spears, "Black Folk Elements in Margaret Walker's *Jubilee*," *Mississippi Folklore Register* 14 (1980); R. Baxter Miller, "The 'Etched Flame' of Margaret Walker: Biblical and Literary Recreation in Southern History," *Tennessee Studies in Literature* 26 (1981); two pieces in *Black Women Writers (1950–1980)* (1984), ed. Mari Evans: Eugenia Colliers, "Fields Watered with Blood: Myth and Ritual in the Poetry of Margaret Walker," and Eleanor Traylor, "Music as Theme: The Blues Mode in the Works of Margaret Walker"; Margaret B. McDowell, "The Black Woman as Artist and Critic: Four Versions," *The Kentucky Review* 7 (1987); and Charlotte Goodman, "From Uncle Tom's Cabin to Vyry's Kitchen: The Black Female Folk Tradition in Margaret Walker's *Jubilee*," in *Tradition and the Talents of Women* (1991), ed. Florence Howe. Walker is also discussed in *Southern Women Writers: The New Generation* (1990), ed. Tonette Bond Inge. For bibliographical information, see Jane Campbell, "Margaret Walker," in *African American Writers* (1991), ed. Valerie Smith.

Eudora Welty
Welty's volumes of fiction include *A Curtain of Green, and Other Stories* (1941), *The Wide Net, and Other Stories* (1943), *The Leaning Tower, and Other Stories* (1944), *Delta Wedding* (1946), *The Golden Apples* (1949), *The Bride of the Innisfallen, and Other Stories* (1955), *The Shoe Bird* (1964), and *The Optimist's Daughter* (1972). Recently published are *Country Churchyards* (2000) and *Early Escapades* (2005). *The Collected Stories of Eudora Welty* was published in 1989, and *The Complete Novels* appeared in 1998. *The Selected Stories of Eudora Welty* (1954) has a valuable introduction by Katherine Anne Porter. Books of photographs by Welty include *One Time and One Place* (1971) and *Eudora Welty: Photographs* (1989), with a foreword by Reynolds Price. Welty's critical writings include *On John Hoolingsworth, Jr.* (2002), *On Writing* (2002), and *On William Faulker* (2003). *One Writer's Beginnings* (1983) is her literary autobiography. For autobiographical material, see *Stories, Essays & Memoir* (1998), ed. Richard Ford. Biographical sources include Ann Waldron, *Eudora: A Writer's Life* (1998), and Suzanne Mars, *Eudora Welty: A Biography* (2005). *A Writer's Eye: Collected Book Reviews* (1994), edited and introduced by Pearl Amelia McHaney, is a collection of the sixty-seven book reviews written by Welty from 1942 to 1984. Interviews with Welty are collected in *More Conversations with Eudora Welty* (1996), ed. Peggy Whitman Prenshaw.

Full-length studies of her writing include Ruth M. Vande Kieft, *Eudora Welty* (1962, rev. 1987); Alfred Appel, *A Season of Dreams: The Fiction of Eudora Welty* (1965); Elizabeth Evans, *Eudora Welty* (1981); Albert J. Devlin, *Eudora Welty's Chronicle: A Story of Mississippi Life* (1983); Peter Schmidt, *The Heart of the Story: Eudora Welty's Short Fiction* (1991); Jan Nordby Gretlund, *Eudora Welty's Aesthetics of Place* (1994); Gail Mortimer, *Daughter of the*

Swan: Love and Knowledge in Eudora Welty's Fiction (1994); Suzan Harrison, Eudora Welty and Virginia Woolf: Gender, Genre, and Influence (1997); Carol Ann Johnston, Eudora Welty: A Study of the Short Fiction (1997); Suzanne Mars, One Writer's Imagination: The Fiction of Eudora Welty (2002); and Naoko Fuwa Thornton, Strange Felicity: Eudora Welty's Subtexts on Fiction and Society (2003). Useful collections of critical essays are A Still Moment: Essays on the Art of Eudora Welty (1978), ed. John F. Desmond; Critical Essays on Eudora Welty (1989), ed. Craig Turner; The Critical Response to Eudora Welty's Fiction (1994), ed. Laurie Champion; Eudora Welty and Politics: Did the Writer Crusade? (2001), ed. Harriet Pollack and Suzanne Marrs; and The Late Novels of Eudora Welty (1998), ed. Jan Nordby Gretlund and Karl-Heinz Westarp. Welty: A Life in Literature, ed. Albert J. Devlin, was published in 1987 to celebrate the fiftieth anniversary of Welty's first publication. Also available are Victor H. Thompson, Eudora Welty: A Reference Guide (1976), and Noel Polk, Eudora Welty, A Bibliography of Her Work (1994).

Rebecca West

West's numerous works include novels—notably The Return of the Soldier (1918), The Judge (1922), and Harriet Hume (1930), a number of which have been reprinted—as well as several volumes of stories and many volumes of nonfictional prose, including books on Henry James and D. H. Lawrence. Works published posthumously include two novels, Cousin Rosamond (1985) and Sunflower (1986), and a collection of memoirs and autobiographical narratives, Family Memories (1987), ed. Faith Evans. In addition, Antonia Till has edited a collection that included short fiction and an unfinished novel: The Only Poet and Short Stories (1992), and Bonnie Kime Scott has edited The Selected Letters of Rebecca West (2000). A valuable anthology of her early journalism is The Young Rebecca (1982), ed. Jane Marcus.

Full-length studies of her life and work include Peter Wolfe, Rebecca West: Artist and Thinker (1971); Gordon N. Ray, H. G. Wells and Rebecca West (1974); Motley F. Deakin, Rebecca West (1980); and Harold Orel, The Literary Achievement of Rebecca West (1986). Victoria Glendinning's biography Rebecca West: A Life appeared in 1987; J. R. Hammond's H. G. Wells and Rebecca West was published in 1991; and Carl E. Rollyson's Rebecca West, A Life in 1996. For feminist perspectives on West, see Jane Marcus, "A Wilderness of One's Own: Feminist Fantasy Novels of the Twenties: Rebecca West and Sylvia Townsend Warner," in Women Writers and the City: Essays in Feminist Literary Criticism (1984), ed. Susan Merrill Squier; Bonnie Kime Scott; "Refiguring the Binary, Breaking the Cycle: Rebecca West as Feminist Modernist," Twentieth-Century Literature 37 (1991); and Sue Thomas, "Rebecca West's Second Thoughts on Feminism," Genders 13 (1992). Other helpful essays include Margaret Diane Stetz, "Rebecca West and the Visual Arts," Tulsa Studies in Women's Literature 8, (1989), and Jane Gledhill, "Impersonality and Amnesia: A Response to World War I in the Writings of H. D. and Rebecca West," in Women and World War I: The Written Response (1993), ed. Dorothy Goldman. George E. Hutchinson compiled A Preliminary List of the Writings of Rebecca West (1957), which was followed by Motley F. Deakin, "Rebecca West: A Supplement to Hutchinson's Preliminary List," Bulletin of Bibliography (1982). A useful recent reference guide is Joan Garrett Packer, Rebecca West: An Annotated Bibliography (1991).

Edith Wharton

Wharton's works include The Decoration of Houses (1897), The House of Mirth (1905), Madame de Trêymes (1907), Tales of Men and Ghosts (1910), Ethan Frome (1911), The Custom of the Country (1913), Xingu (1916), Summer (1917), The Age of Innocence (1920), The Glimpses of the Moon (1922), and Old New York (1924), most of which have been reissued in the Scribner Library. In addition, Louis Auchincloss edited The Edith Wharton Reader (1965). Wharton's Collected Stories, 1891–1910 and Collected Stories, 1911–1937 were both published in 2001. Selected Poems by Wharton appeared in 2005. Frederick Wegener edited Wharton's Uncollected Critical Writings, published in 1996. Edith Wharton Abroad: Selected Travel Writings, 1888–1920, appeared in 1995. R. W. B. Lewis and Nancy Lewis edited The Letters of Edith Wharton in 1988. Two more collections of correspondence are Lyall H. Powers, Henry James and Edith Wharton: Letters, 1900–1915 (1990), and Yrs. Ever Affly: The Correspondence of Edith Wharton and Louis Bromfield (2000), ed. Daniel Bratton.

Two major biographies are R. W. B. Lewis, Edith Wharton: A Biography (1975), and Cynthia Griffin Wolff, A Feast of Words: The Triumph of Edith Wharton (1977). Other biographical studies of Wharton include Susan Goodman, Edith Wharton's Women: Friends and Rivals (1990); Shari Benstock, No Gifts from Chance: A Biography of Edith Wharton (1994); Eleanor Dwight, Edith Wharton: An Extraordinary Life (1994); and Goodman, Edith Wharton's Inner Circle (1994). Other useful biographical and critical studies include Blake Nevius, Edith Wharton: A Study of Her Fiction (1953); Marilyn J. Lyde, Edith Wharton: Convention and Morality in the Work of a Novelist (1959); Louis Auchincloss, Edith Wharton (1961); Millicent Bell, Edith Wharton and Henry James: The Story of Their Friendship (1965); Geoffrey Walton, Edith Wharton: A

Critical Interpretation (1971); Margaret B. McDowell, Edith Wharton (1976); Richard H. Lawson, Edith Wharton (1977); Elizabeth Ammons, Edith Wharton's Argument with America (1980); Carol Wershaven, The Female Intruder in the Novels of Edith Wharton (1982); Judith Fryer, Felicitous Space: The Imaginative Structures of Edith Wharton and Willa Cather (1986); Josephine Donovan, After the Fall: The Demeter-Persephone Myth in Wharton, Cather, and Glasgow (1988); Lev Raphael, Edith Wharton's Prisoners of Shame: A New Perspective on Her Fiction (1990); Penelope Vita-Finzi, Edith Wharton and the Unsatisfactory Man (1991); Candace Waid, Edith Wharton's Letters from the Underworld: Fictions of Women and Writing (1991); and Gloria C. Erlich, The Sexual Education of Edith Wharton (1992). More recent critical resources include Dale M. Bauer, Edith Wharton's Brave New Politics (1994); Kathy A Fedorko, Gender and the Gothic in the Fiction of Edith Wharton (1995); Carol Singley, Edith Wharton: Matters of Mind and Spirit (1995); Jenni Dyman, Lurking Feminism: The Ghost Stories of Edith Wharton (1996); Helen Killoran, Edith Wharton: Art and Allusion (1996); Alan Price, The End of the Age of Innocence: Edith Wharton and the First World War (1996); Janet Beer, Kate Chopin, Edith Wharton and Charlotte Perkins Gilman: Studies in Short Fiction (1997); Elsa Nettels, Language and Gender in American Fiction: Howells, James, Wharton, and Cather (1997); Maureen E. Montgomery, Displaying Women: Spectacles of Leisure in Edith Wharton's New York (1998); Adeline R. Tintner, Edith Wharton in Context: Essays in Intertextuality (1999); Helen Killoran, The Critical Reception of Edith Wharton (2001); Deborah Lindsay Williams, Not in Sisterhood: Edith Wharton, Willa Cather, Zona Gale, and the Politics of Female Authorship (2001); Jill M. Kress, The Figure of Consciousness: William James, Henry James, and Edith Wharton (2002); Beer, Edith Wharton (2002); Sharon Dean, Constance Fenimore Woolson and Edith Wharton: Perspectives on Landscape and Art (2002); Stephanie Lewis Thompson, Influencing America's Tastes: Realism in the Works of Wharton, Cather and Hurst (2002); Jennie A. Kassonoff, Edith Wharton and the Politics of Race (2004); Robin Peel, Apart From Modernism: Edith Wharton, Politics, and Fiction Before World War I (2005); and Renee Somers, Edith Wharton as Spatial Activist and Analyst (2005). Valuable collections of critical essays are Edith Wharton: New Critical Essays (1992), ed. Alfred Bendixen and Annette Zilversmith, and A Forward Glance: New Essays on Edith Wharton (1999), ed. Clare Colquitt, Susan Goodman, and Candace Waid. For feminist perspectives on Wharton, see Sandra M. Gilbert and Susan Gubar, Sexchanges (1989), and Elaine Showalter, Sister's Choice: Tradition and Change in American Women's Writing (1991). Useful reference guides are Stephen Garrison, Edith Wharton: A Descriptive Bibliography (1990); Kristin O. Lauer, Edith Wharton: An Annotated Secondary Bibliography (1990); Sarah Bird Wright, Edith Wharton A to Z: The Essential Guide to the Life and Work (1998); and A Historical Guide to Edith Wharton (2003), ed. Carol Singley.

Anna Wickham

Wickham's Selected Poems—which appeared in many volumes during her lifetime—were edited with an introduction by David Garnett (1971). R. D. Smith edited The Writings of Anna Wickham: Free Woman and Poet in 1984, a collection that includes the complete poems, an autobiographical fragment, and occasional pieces. Poems by Wickham appear in The Faber Book of Twentieth-Century Women's Poetry (1987), ed. Fleur Adcock. One biographical work is Jennifer Vaughan Jones, Anna Wickham: A Poet's Daring Life (2003). Little critical work has been done, but see Margaret Newlin, "Anna Wickham: 'The Sexless Part Which is My Mind,' "Southern Review 14 (1978); Myra Stark, "Feminist Themes in Anna Wickham's 'The Contemplative Quarry' and 'The Man with a Hammer,' " Four Decades of Poetry 2 (1978); and Matt Holland, "Anna Wickham: Fettered Woman, Free Spirit," Poetry Review 78 (1988).

Jeanette Winterson

Winterson's works include Oranges Are Not the Only Fruit (1985), The Passion (1987), Sexing the Cherry (1989), Boating for Beginners (1990), Written on the Body (1992), Art Objects: Essays on Ecstasy and Effrontery (1995), Gut Symmetries (1997), The World and Other Places (1998), The Powerbook (2000), and Lighthousekeeping (2004).

A full-length critical study of Winterson is Merja Makinen, The Novels of Jeanette Winterson (2005). Further treatment of her work appears in Carolyn Allen, Following Djuna: Women Lovers and the Erotics of Loss (1996); Andrea L. Harris, Other Sexes: Rewriting Difference from Woolf to Winterson (2000); Leigh Gilmore, The Limits of Autobiography: Trauma and Testimony (2001); and Lauren Rusk, The Life Writing of Otherness: Woolf, Baldwin, Kingston, and Winterson (2002). A collection of essays is "I'm Telling You Stories": Jeanette Winterson and the Politics of Reading, ed. Helena Grice and Tim Woods (1998), while another interesting study is Christopher Pressler, So Far So Linear: Responses to the Writing of Jeanette Winterson (2000).

Virginia Woolf

Woolf's novels—which include The Voyage Out (1915), Night and Day (1919), Jacob's Room (1922), Mrs. Dalloway (1925), To the Lighthouse (1927), Orlando (1928), The Waves (1931), The

Years (1937), and *Between the Acts* (1941)—have all been issued in paperback, as have her two major polemical volumes, *A Room of One's Own* (1929) and *Three Guineas* (1938). *Melymbrosia*, the 1912 draft of *The Voyage Out*, was published in 2002. Susan Dick edited *The Complete Shorter Fiction* in 1985. Her *Collected Essays*, 4 vols., 1966–67, are supplemented by *Books and Portraits* (1977), ed. Mary Lyon; *Virginia Woolf on Women and Writing* (1979), ed. Michele Barrett; and *Contemporary Writers* (with preface by Jean Guiget) (1966), a further collection of her book reviews. In addition, Andrew McNeillie edited both *The Essays of Virginia Woolf* in three volumes, 1986–89, and a 2003 publication of Woolf's essay collection *The Common Reader*. Woolf's *Moments of Being* (1976), ed. Jeanne Schulkind, contains a group of memoirs, as well as a helpful introduction. *The Diary of Virginia Woolf*, ed. Anne Olivier Bell, began appearing in 1977, and two journal collections were published in 1990: *A Passionate Apprentice: The Early Journals, 1897–1909*, ed. Mitchell A. Leaska, and *A Moment's Liberty: The Shorter Diary*, ed. Anne Olivier Bell. *The Letters of Virginia Woolf* (1975–80), ed. Nigel Nicholson and Joanne Trautmann, are available, as is a one-volume selection of Woolf's correspondence, *Congenial Spirits: The Selected Letters* (1989), ed. Joanne Trautmann Banks.

Biographies include Quentin Bell, *Virginia Woolf*, 2 vols. (1972); Phyllis Rose, *Woman of Letters: A Life of Virginia Woolf* (1978); Roger Poole, *The Unknown Virginia Woolf* (1978); Louise De Salvo, *Virginia Woolf: The Impact of Childhood Sexual Abuse on Her Life and Work* (1989); James King, *Virginia Woolf* (1995); Panthea Reid, *Art and Affection: A Life of Virginia Woolf* (1996); Mitchell Leaska, *Granite and Rainbow: The Hidden Life of Virginia Woolf* (1998); Herbert Marder, *The Measure of Life: Virginia Woolf's Last Years* (2000); and Katherine Dalsimer, *Virginia Woolf: Becoming a Writer* (2001). Specialized biographical studies include Irene Coates, *Who's Afraid of Leonard Woolf?: A Case for the Sanity of Virginia Woolf* (2000); Vanessa Curtis, *Virginia Woolf's Women* (2002); Julia Briggs, *Virginia Woolf: An Inner Life* (2005); and Vanessa Curtis, *The Hidden Houses of Virginia Woolf and Vanessa Bell* (2005). Autobiographical materials are collected in *Virginia Woolf: Interviews and Recollections* (1995), ed. J. H. Stape. Among the most useful of the many full-length critical studies of Woolf's work are Winifred Holtby, *Virginia Woolf* (1978); David Daiches, *Virginia Woolf* (rev. 1963); Joan Bennett, *Virginia Woolf: Her Art as a Novelist* (2nd ed. 1964); Jean Guiget, *Virginia Woolf and Her Works*, trans. Jean Stewart (1965); Herbert Marder, *Feminism and Art: A Study of Virginia Woolf* (1968); Harvena Richter, *Virginia Woolf: The Inward Voyage* (1970); James Naremore, *The World without a Self* (1973); Jean O. Love, *Virginia Woolf: Sources of Madness in Art* (1977); Mark Spilka, *Virginia Woolf's Quarrel with Grieving* (1980); Perry Meisel, *The Absent Father: Virginia Woolf and Walter Pater* (1980); Maria DiBattista, *Virginia Woolf's Major Novels: The Fables of Anon.* (1980); Susan Merrill Squier, *Woolf and London: The Sexual Politics of the City* (1985); Mark Hussey, *The Singing of the Real World: The Philosophy of Woolf's Fiction* (1986); Alex Zwerdling, *Virginia Woolf and the Real World* (1986); Jane Marcus, *Virginia Woolf and the Languages of Patriarchy* (1987); Makiko Minow-Pinkney, *Virginia Woolf and the Problem of the Subject* (1987); Elizabeth Steele, *Virginia Woolf's Rediscovered Essays: Sources and Allusions* (1987); Rachel Bowlby, *Virginia Woolf: Feminist Destinations* (1988); Virginia R. Hyman, *To the Lighthouse and Beyond: Transformations in the Narratives of Virginia Woolf* (1988); Elizabeth Abel, *Virginia Woolf and the Fictions of Psychoanalysis* (1989); Alice Fox, *Virginia Woolf and the Literature of the English Renaissance* (1990); and Alison Booth, *Greatness Engendered: George Eliot and Virginia Woolf* (1992). See also Carolyn Heilbrun, *Toward a Recognition of Androgyny* (1973); Rachel Blau DuPlessis, *Writing beyond the Ending: Narrative Strategies of Twentieth-Century Women Writers* (1985); Patricia Waugh, *Feminine Fictions: Revisiting the Postmodern* (1988); and Sandra M. Gilbert and Susan Gubar, *Letters from the Front* (1994). Also helpful are Kathy J. Philips, *Virginia Woolf Against Empire* (1994); Galya Diment, *The Autobiographical Novel of Co-Consciousness: Goncharov, Woolf, and Joyce* (1994); Judy Little, *The Experimental Self: Dialogic Subjectivity in Woolf, Pym, and Brooke-Rose* (1996); Patricia Moran, *Word of Mouth: Body Language in Katherine Mansfield and Virginia Woolf* (1996); Krista Ratcliffe, *Anglo-American Feminist Challenges to the Rhetorical Traditions: Virginia Woolf, Mary Daly, Adrienne Rich* (1996); Judy S. Reese, *Recasting Social Values in the Work of Virginia Woolf* (1996); Rachel Bowlby, *Feminist Destinations and Further Essays on Virginia Woolf* (1997); Juliet Dusinberre, *Virginia Woolf's Renaissance: Woman Reader or Common Reader?* (1997); Barbara Olson, *Authorial Divinity in the Twentieth-Century: Omniscient Narration in Woolf, Hemingway, and Others* (1997); J. R. Maze, *Virginia Woolf: Feminism, Creativity, and the Unconscious* (1997); Jane Goldman, *The Feminist Aesthetics of Virginia Woolf: Modernism, Post-Impressionism and the Politics of the Visual* (1998); Roxanne J. Fand, *The Dialogic Self: Reconstructing Subjectivity in Woolf, Lessing, and Atwood* (1999); Allie Glenny, *Ravenous Identity: Eating and Eating Distress in the Life and Work of Virginia Woolf* (2000); Andrea L. Harris, *Other Sexes: Rewriting Difference From Woolf to Winterson* (2000); Marjorie H. Hellerstein, *Virginia Woolf's Experiments* with *Consciousness, Time, and Social Values* (2001); Penelope LeFew-Blake, *Schopenhauer, Women's Literature, and the Legacy of Pessimism in the Novels of George Eliot, Olive Schreiner, Virginia Woolf, and Doris Lessing* (2001); Maggie Humm, *Modernist Women and Visual Cultures: Virginia Woolf, Vanessa Bell, Photography, and Cinema* (2002); Holly Henry, *Virginia Woolf and the Discourse of Science: The Aesthetics of Astronomy* (2003); Naomi Black, *Virginia Woolf as Feminist* (2004); Lois Cucullu, *Expert Modernists, Matricide, and Modern Culture: Woolf, Forster, Joyce* (2004); Miglena Nikolchina, *Matricide in Language: Writing Theory in Kristeva and Woolf* (2004); Ann Ronchetti, *The Artist, Society and Sexuality in Virginia Woolf's Novels* (2004); and Christine Froula, *Virginia Woolf and the Bloomsbury Avant-Garde: War, Civilization, Modernity* (2005).

Essay collections include *Virginia Woolf: A Collection of Critical Essays* (1975), ed. Thomas Lewis; *Virginia Woolf: Reevaluation and Continuity* (1980), ed. Ralph Freedman; *New Feminist Essays on Virginia Woolf* (1981) and *Virginia Woolf: A Feminist Slant* (1983), both ed. Jane Marcus; *Virginia Woolf: Modern Critical Views* (1986), ed. Harold Bloom; *Virginia Woolf and Bloomsbury: A Centenary Celebration* (1987), ed. Jane Marcus; *Virginia Woolf and War: Fiction, Reality, and Myth* (1991), ed. Mark Hussey; *Virginia Woolf: A Collection of Critical Essays* (1993), ed. Margaret Homans; *New Essays on Virginia Woolf* (1994), ed. Helen Wussow; *Virginia Woolf: Lesbian Readings* (1997), ed. Eileen Barrett and Patricia Cramer; *Virginia Woolf and the Essay* (1997), ed. Beth Carole Rosenberg and Jeanne Dubino; *Virginia Woolf: Reading the Renaissance* (1999), ed. Sally Greene; *Virginia Woolf in the Age of Mechanical Reproduction* (2000), ed. Pamela L. Caughie; *Editing Virginia Woolf: Interpreting the Modernist Text* (2002), ed. James M. Haule and J. H. Stape; *Trespassing Boundaries: Virginia Woolf's Short Fiction* (2004), ed. Kathryn N. Benzel and Ruth Hoberman; and Natalya Reinhold, *Woolf Across Cultures* (2004). For other books and articles, see Brownlee Jean Kirkpatrick, *A Bibliography of Virginia Woolf* (1997). Useful reference works are Edward L. Bishop, *A Virginia Woolf Chronology* (1989); James M. Haule, *A Concordance to the Novels of Virginia Woolf* (1991); Mark Hussey, *Virginia Woolf A to Z: A Conprehensive Reference for Students, Teachers, and Common Reader to Her Life, Work, and Critical Reception* (1995); and Katherine Hill-Miller, *From the Lighthouse to Monk's House: A Guide to Virginia Woolf's Literary Landscapes* (2001).

Judith Wright

Wright's recent books of poetry are *Phantom Dwelling* (1985), *A Human Pattern: Selected Poems* (1990), and *Through Broken Glass* (1992). She has two major collections: *Collected Poems*, which appeared in 1971, and *Collected Poems: 1942–1985*, which appeared in 1994. Besides a number of books for children, Wright has written a critical biography, *Charles Harpur* (1963), as well as a critical volume, *Preoccupations in Australian Poetry* (1965). For biographical work on Wright, see Veronica Brady's *South of My Days: A Biography of Judith Wright* (1998). Also, Jennifer Straus produced a critical biography, *Judith Wright* (1995). Articles on Wright's work include Stephen Tatum, "Tradition of the Exile: Judith Wright's Australian 'West'," in *Women, Women Writers, and the West* (1979); Leonie Kramer, "Judith Wright, Hope, McAuley," *The Literary Criterion* 15 (1980); Anne Godschalk, "The Australianness of Judith Wright: Landscape, Metaphor, and Analogy," *Dutch Quarterly Review of Anglo-American Letters* 12 (1982); Delip Kumar Sen, "The Poetry of Judith Wright: An Attempt at Interpretation," *Journal of the Department of English (Calcutta)* 18 (1982–83); Syed Anunuddan, "Judith Wright: A Major Australian Poet," *Creative Moment* 13/14; David Dawling, "Judith Wright's Delicate Balance," *Australian Literary Studies* 9; and Harry Heseltine, "Wrestling with the Angel: Judith Wright's Poetry in the 1950s," in his *The Uncertain Self: Essays in Australian Literature and Criticism* (1986). See also Nela Bureu, "The Poetry of Judith Wright: Inventing Australia, Inventing the Self," *Miscelánea* 16 (1995); John Salter, "The Republic of Australia and the Poems of Judith Wright," *Southern Review (Australia)* 29 (1996); Veronica Brady, "Judith Wright: The Poetics of Politics," *Southerly* 61 (2001); and John Hawke, "The Moving Image: Judith Wright's Symbolist Language," *Southerly* 61 (2001). For a feminist approach to Wright's poetry, see Jennifer Strauss, "Within the Bounds of Feminine Sensibility? The Poetry of Rosemary Dobson, Gwen Harwood, and Judith Wright," in *Still the Frame Holds: Essays on Women Poets and Writers* (1993), ed. Sheila Roberts and Yvonne Pacheo Tevis.

Elinor Wylie

Wylie's books—published in a brief, eight-year period—include four collections of verse: *Nets to Catch the Wind* (1921), *Black Armour* (1923), *Trivial Breath* (1928), and *Angels and Earthly Creatures* (1929). She also published four novels: *Jennifer Lorn* (1923), *The Venetian Glass Nephew* (1925), *The Orphan Angel* (1926), and *Mr. Hodge and Mr. Hazard* (1928). In 1912 her mother had privately printed in London *Incidental Numbers*, containing her youthful verse. *The Collected Poems of Elinor Wylie*, ed. William Rose Benét, appeared in 1932, and her *Collected Prose* came out the following year. *Last Poems* (1943) brought together previously uncollected poetry as well as some juvenilia from *Incidental Numbers* and transcriptions from manuscripts, with an appreciation by the English novelist Edith Olivier. *Selected Works of Elinor Wylie* was published in 2000, edited by Evelyn Helmick Hivel.

Memoirs and appreciations include Elizabeth S. Sergeant, *Fire under the Andes: A Group of North American Portraits* (1927); William Rose Benét, *The Prose and Poetry of Elinor Wylie* (1934); Nancy Hoyt's portrait of her sister, *Elinor Wylie: Portrait of an Unknown Lady* (1935); Carl Van Doren, *Three Worlds* (1936); Mary Colum, *Life and the Dream* (1947); and Edmund Wilson's essays in *Shores of Light* (1952). Two full-length biographies are *Elinor Wylie: A Life Apart* by Stanley Olson (1979) and *A Private Madness: The Genius of Elinor Wylie* by Evelyn Helmick Hively (2003). Recent critical studies are Thomas Gray, *Elinor Wylie* (1969), and Judith Farr, *The Life and Art of Elinor Wylie* (1983). Two interesting essays on Wylie's poetry are Anna Shannon Elfenbein and Terrence Allan Hoagwood, " 'Wild Peaches': Landscapes of Desire and Depravation," *Women's Studies* 15 (1988), and Cheryl Walker, "Women and Aggression: Elinor Wylie and the Woman Warrior Persona," in her *Masks Outrageous and Austere: Culture, Psyche, and Persona in Modern Women Poets* (1991). A useful reference guide appears in *Bibliography of American Literature* 9 (1991), ed. Jacob Blanck and Michael Winship.

Hisaye Yamamoto

Yamamoto's short stories are collected in *Seventeen Syllables and Other Stories* (1988), with an introduction by King-Kok Cheung. Yamamoto has also written the introduction to Toshio Mori, *The Chauvinist and Other Stories* (1979). An interview by Charles L. Crow appeared in *MELUS* 14 (1987). Useful critical essays are Stan Yogi, "Rebels and Heroines: Subversive Narratives in the Stories of Wakako Yamauchi and Hisaye Yamamoto," in *Reading the Literatures of Asian America,* ed. Shirley Geok-lin Lim and Amy Ling (1992); King-Kok Cheung, "Reading Between the Syllables: Hisaye Yamamoto's *Seventeen Syllables and Other Stories,*" in *Teaching American Ethnic Literatures,* ed. John R. Maitino and David R. Peck (1996); and Naoko Sugiyama, "Issei Mothers' Silence, Nisei Daughters' Stories: The Short Fiction of Hisaye Yamamoto," *Comparative Literature Studies* 33 (1996).

Anzia Yezierska

Alice Kessler-Harris edited and wrote an introduction for *The Open Cage: An Anzia Yezierska Collection* (1979). She also edited and introduced the 1976 reprint of *Bread Givers* (1925). Other volumes by Yezierska include *Hungry Hearts* (1920), *Salome of the Tenements* (1922), *Children of Loneliness* (1923), *Arrogant Beggar* (1927), *All I Could Never Be* (1932), and *Red Ribbon on a White Horse* (1950). Vivian Gorwich wrote an introduction to *How I Found America: Collected Short Stories of Anzia Yezierska* (1991). Good introductions to her life and work are Carol B. Shoe, *Anzia Yezierska* (1982), and Louise Levitas Henriksen, *Anzia Yezierska: A Writer's Life* (1988). She is also discussed more recently in Delia Caparoso Konzett, *Ethnic Modernisms: Anzia Yezierska, Zora Neale Hurston, Jean Rhys, and the Aesthetics of Dislocation* (2002).

PERMISSIONS ACKNOWLEDGMENTS

Fleur Adcock: "Against Coupling," "The Voyage Out," "For a Five-Year-Old," "Miss Hamilton in London," "On the Border," and "Street Song," from *Poems 1960–2000* (Bloodaxe Books, 2000) by permission of the publisher. Reproduced with permission of Bloodaxe Books. www.bloodaxe-books.com

Kim Addonizio: "31-Year-Old Lover," "Sonnenizio on a Line from Drayton," and "You Don't Know What Love Is" from *What Is This Thing Called Love: Poems* by Kim Addonizio. Copyright © 2004 by Kim Addonizio. Used by permission of W. W. Norton & Company. "Generations," "Last Call," and "What Do Women Want?" from *Tell Me*. Copyright © 2000 by Kim Addonizio. Reprinted by permission of BOA Editions Ltd.

Ama Ata Aidoo: "The Message" from *No Sweetness Here and Other Stories*. Copyright © 1970 by Ama Ata Aidoo. Reprinted with the permission of The Feminist Press at the City University of New York.

Julia Alvarez: "33," "Storm Windows," "The Master Bed," "On Not Shoplifting Louise Bogan's *The Blue Estuaries*," and "Bilingual Sestina" from HOMECOMING. Copyright © 1984, 1996 by Julia Alvarez. Published by Plume, an imprint of Penguin Random House; originally published by Grove Press. By permission of Susan Bergholz Literary Services, New York, NY, and Lamy, NM. All rights reserved.

Maya Angelou: Excerpt(s) from I KNOW WHY THE CAGED BIRD SINGS by Maya Angelou, copyright © 1969 and renewed 1997 by Maya Angelou. Used by permission of Random House, an imprint and division of Penguin Random House LLC. All rights reserved.

Gloria Anzaldúa: "*Tlilli, Tlapalli*: The Path of the Red and Black Ink" from *Borderlands/La Frontera: The New Mestiza*, © 1987, 1999, 2007, 2012 by Gloria Anzaldúa. Reprinted by permission of Aunt Lute Books. www.auntlute.com.

Margaret Atwood: "This Is a Photograph of Me," © Margaret Atwood 1966 from *Circle Game* by Margaret Atwood. Reprinted by permission of House of Anasti Press. "Waiting," "Asparagus," "Marsh Languages," and "Morning in the Burned House" from MORNING IN THE BURNED HOUSE: NEW POEMS by Margaret Atwood. Copyright © 1995 by Margaret Atwood. Copyright © 1995 O. W. Toad. Reprinted by permission of Houghton Mifflin Harcourt Publishing Company; reprinted by permission of McClelland & Stewart, a division of Penguin Random House Canada Limited. All rights reserved. "Rape Fantasies" from DANCING GIRLS AND OTHER STORIES by Margaret Atwood. Copyright © 1975, 1977, 1982 O. W. Toad Ltd. Reprinted by permission of Curtis Brown Group Limited; reprinted by permission of Emblem/McClelland & Stewart, a division of Penguin Random House Canada Limited. All rights reserved. "There Was Once," and "The Little Red Hen Tells All" from GOOD BONES AND SIMPLE MURDERS by Margaret Atwood, copyright © 1983, 1992, 1994, by O. W. Toad Ltd. Used by permission of Nan A. Talese, an imprint of the Knopf Doubleday Publishing Group, a division of Penguin Random House LLC; reprinted by permission of McClelland & Stewart, a division of Penguin Random House Canada Limited. All rights reserved.

Djuna Barnes: "Cassation" from *Selected Works of Djuna Barnes* by Djuna Barnes. Copyright © 1962 by Djuna Barnes. Copyright renewed © 1986 by Saxon Barnes and Warner Lowey.

Patricia Beer: "Witch," "Brunhild," "The Bull," "In Memory of Constance Markiewicz," "Mating Calls," and "Transvestism in the Novels of Charlotte Brontë" from *Collected Poems* by Patricia Beer. Reprinted by permission of Carcanet Press Limited.

Elizabeth Bishop: "First Death in Nova Scotia," "The Fish," "In the Waiting Room," "An Invitation to Miss Marianne Moore," "The Man-Moth," "Roosters," "One Art," and "Pink Dog" from *The Complete Poems 1927–1979* by Elizabeth Bishop. Copyright © 1979, 1983 by Alice Helen Methfessel.

Louise Bogan: "Medusa," "The Crows," "Women," "Cassandra," "The Crossed Apple," "Evening in the Sanitarium," "Several Voices Out of a Cloud," and "The Dream" from *The Blue Estuaries*. Copyright © 1968 by Louise Bogan. Copyright renewed 1996 by Ruth Limmer.

Eavan Boland: "Anorexic," "In His Own Image." Copyright © 1980 by Eavan Boland, from AN ORIGIN LIKE WATER: *Collected Poems 1967–1987* by Eavan Boland. Copyright © 1996 by Eavan Boland. Used by permission of W. W. Norton & Company, Inc. "Degas's Laundresses," "The Muse Mother," from OUTSIDE HISTORY: SELECTED POEMS 1980–1990 by Eavan

1556 / PERMISSIONS ACKNOWLEDGMENTS

Boland. Copyright © 1990 by Eavan Boland. Used by permission of W. W. Norton & Company, Inc. "The Pomegranate," from IN A TIME OF VIOLENCE by Eavan Boland. Copyright © 1994 by Eavan Boland. Used by permission of W. W. Norton & Company, Inc. "Against Love Poetry," from AGAINST LOVE POETRY: POEMS by Eavan Boland. Copyright © 2001 by Eavan Boland. Used by permission of the author and W. W. Norton & Company, Inc.

Marita Bonner: "On Being Young—a Woman—and Colored," from *Frye Street and Environs: The Collected Works of Marita Bonner*. Copyright © 1987 by Joyce Flynn and Joyce Occomy Stricklin. Reprinted by permission of Beacon Press, Boston.

Elizabeth Bowen: "The Demon Lover" from COLLECTED STORIES OF ELIZABETH BOWEN by Elizabeth Bowen, copyright © 1981 by Curtis Brown Limited, Literary Executors of the Estate of Elizabeth Bowen. Used by permission of Alfred A. Knopf, an imprint of the Knopf Doubleday Publishing Group, a division of Penguin Random House LLC. All rights reserved.

Anna Hempstead Branch: XIV, XXV, XXXI from SONNETS FROM A LOCK BOX by Anna Hempstead Branch. Copyright © 1929 by Anna Hempstead Branch, renewed 1957 by Houghton Mifflin Harcourt Publishing Company. Reprinted by permission of Houghton Mifflin Harcourt Publishing Company. All rights reserved.

Gwendolyn Brooks: "Stand off, daughter of the dusk," "A Song in the Front Yard," "Bronzeville Woman in a Red Hat," "Malcolm X," "The Bean Eaters," the last quatrain of "The Ballad of Emmett Till," "The Mother," "The Rites for Cousin Vit," "The Sundays of Satin-legs Smith," "The Womanhood," and "We Real Cool" by Gwendolyn Brooks. Reprinted by consent of Brooks Permissions.

Rebecca Brown: "Forgiveness" from *The Terrible Girls* by Rebecca Brown. Copyright © 1990 by Rebecca Brown. Reprinted by permission of City Lights Books.

Octavia Butler: "Bloodchild" by Octavia Butler. From *Isaac Asimov's Science Fiction Magazine* (1984). Copyright © 1984 by permission of Davis Publications.

A. S. Byatt: "A Stone Woman" from LITTLE BLACK BOOK OF STORIES by A. S. Byatt, copyright © 2003 by A. S. Byatt. Used by permission of Alfred A. Knopf, an imprint of the Knopf Doubleday Publishing Group, a division of Penguin Random House LLC. All rights reserved.

Anne Carson: "The Glass Essay" from GLASS, IRONY, AND GOD, copyright © 1995 by Anne Carson. Reprinted by permission of New Directions Publishing Corp. "TV Men: Lazarus" from MEN IN THE OFF HOURS by Anne Carson, copyright © 2000 by Anne Carson. Used by permission of Alfred A. Knopf, an imprint of the Knopf Doubleday Publishing Group, a division of Penguin Random House LLC. All rights reserved.

Angela Carter: Pages 142–53 from "The Company of Wolves" from *The Bloody Chamber and Other Adult Stories* by Angela Carter. Copyright © 1979 by Angela Carter. This story originally appeared in BANANAS. Reprinted by permission of the estate of the author c/o Rodgers, Coleridge & White.

Marilyn Chin: "How I Got That Name" from *The Phoenix Gone, The Terrace Empty* (Minneapolis: Milkweed Editions, 1994). Copyright © 1994 by Marilyn Chin. Reprinted by permission from Milkweed Editions. "That Half Is Almost Gone" and "The True Story of Mortar and Pestle," from RHAPSODY IN PLAIN YELLOW by Marilyn Chin. Copyright © 2002 by Marilyn Chin. Used by permission of the author and W. W. Norton & Company, Inc.

Caryl Churchill: *Top Girls* from *Churchill Plays* 2 by Caryl Churchill. © 1982 Caryl Churchill. Reprinted by permission from Methuen Publishing Ltd. All rights whatsoever in this play are strictly reserved and application for performance etc., must be made before rehearsals commence to: Casarotta Ramsay and Associates. No performance may be given unless a license has been obtained.

Sandra Cisneros: From WOMAN HOLLERING CREEK. Copyright © 1991 by Sandra Cisneros. Published by Vintage Books, a division of Penguin Random House, and originally in hardcover by Random House. By permission of Susan Bergholz Literary Services, New York, NY, and Lamy, NM. All rights reserved.

Lucille Clifton: "admonitions" and "the lost baby poem," from *Good Woman: Poems and a Memoir 1969–1980* by Lucille Clifton. Copyright © 1987 by Lucille Clifton. With the permission of BOA Editions Ltd. "if our grandchild be a girl" and "my dream about being white" from *Next: New Poems*, by Lucille Clifton. Copyright © 1987 by Lucille Clifton. With the permission of BOA Editions Ltd. "Leda 3" from *Book of Light*, © 1993 by Lucille Clifton. Reprinted by permission of Copper Canyon Press. "Poem to My Uterus" and "To My Last Period" from *Quilting: Poems 1987–1990* by Lucille Clifton. Copyright © 1990 by Lucille Clifton. With the permission of BOA Editions Ltd.

Anita Desai: "Royalty" from DIAMOND DUST: *Stories by Anita Desai.* Copyright © 2000 by Anita Desai. Reprinted by permission of Houghton Mifflin Harcourt Publishing Company. All rights reserved.

Isak Dinesen: "The Blank Page" from LAST TALES by Isak Dinesen, copyright © 1957 by Random House, Inc. Used by permission of Random House, an imprint and division of Penguin Random House LLC. All rights reserved.

Diane di Prima: "Nightmare 7" and "Nightmare 12" from *Thirteen Nightmares,* "Song for Baby-O, Unborn," "Poem in Praise of My Husband (Taos)," "April Fool Birthday Poem for Grandpa," "Letter to Jeanne (at Tassajara)," "Narrow Path into the Back Country." Reprinted by permission of the author. "Annunciation" and "The Loba Priestess as Bag Lady Utters Ragged Warnings" from LOBA by Diane di Prima, copyright © 1973, 1976, 1977, 1978, 1998 by Diane di Prima. Used by permission of Penguin Books, an imprint of Penguin Publishing Group, a division of Penguin Random House LLC. All rights reserved.

H.D.: "Fragment Thirty-Six," "Garden," "Helen," "Orchard," "Oread," "Sea Poppies," and "The Master" by H.D. (Hilda Doolittle), from COLLECTED POEMS, *1912–1944,* copyright © 1982 by the Estate of Hilda Doolittle. Reprinted by permission of New Directions Publishing Corp. "Eurydice" by H.D. (Hilda Doolittle), from COLLECTED POEMS, *1912–1944,* copyright © 1917 by Hilda Doolittle. Reprinted by permission of New Directions Publishing Corp.

Rita Dove: "I have been a stranger in a strange land," from AMERICAN SMOOTH by Rita Dove. Copyright © 2004 by Rita Dove. Used by permission of the author and W. W. Norton & Company, Inc. "Persephone, Falling," "Sonnet in Primary Colors," from MOTHER LOVE by Rita Dove. Copyright © 1995 by Rita Dove. Used by permission of W. W. Norton & Company, Inc. "Rosa," from ON THE BUS WITH ROSA PARKS by Rita Dove. Copyright © 1999 by Rita Dove. Used by permission of the author and W. W. Norton & Company, Inc.

Carol Ann Duffy: "Mrs. Lazarus" and "Circe" from *The World's Wife* by Carol Ann Duffy. Reprinted by permission of Macmillan UK. "September, 1997" by Carol Ann Duffy. Originally published in the *Guardian* of Manchester on September 6, 1997. Reprinted by permission of the author c/o Rogers, Coleridge and White. "Litany" from *Mean Time* and "Warming Her Pearls" from *Selling Manhattan* by Carol Ann Duffy. Reprinted by permission of Anvil Press Poetry.

Margaret Edson: *Wit* by Margaret Edson. Copyright © 1993, 1999 by Margaret Edson.

Louise Erdrich: "The Shawl" by Louise Erdrich. Copyright © 2001 by Louise Erdrich. Used by permission of the Wylie Agency.

U. A. Fanthorpe: "Mother-in-Law" and "King's Daughter" from *Standing To* by U. A. Fanthorpe. "Women Laughing" and "From the Third Storey" from *Voices Off* by U. A. Fanthorpe. "For Saint Peter" from *Side Effects.* All reprinted by permission of the author.

Carolyn Forché: "Elegy" & note on p. 83 from *The Angel of History* by Carolyn Forché. Copyright © 1994 by Carolyn Forché. Used by permission of HarperCollins Publishers. "The Colonel" from *The Country Between Us* by Carolyn Forché. Copyright © 1977 by Carolyn Forché. Used by permission of HarperCollins Publishers.

Janet Frame: "Keel and Kool" from *The Lagoon* by Janet Frame. Reprinted by permission of the Janet Frame Literary Trust.

Lynn Freed: "Under the House" from THE CURSE OF THE APPROPRIATE MAN by Lynn Freed. Copyright © 1998 by Lynn Freed. Reprinted by permission of Houghton Mifflin Harcourt Publishing Company. All rights reserved.

Mavis Gallant: "Mlle Dias de Corta" from THE COLLECTED STORIES OF MAVIS GALLANT by Mavis Gallant. Copyright © 1996 by Mavis Gallant. Reprinted by permission of Georges Borchardt, Inc., on behalf of the author; and from ACROSS THE BRIDGE by Mavis Gallant. Copyright © 1993 Mavis Gallant. Reprinted by permission of McClelland & Stewart, a division of Penguin Random House Canada Limited. All rights reserved.

Louise Glück: "Dedication to Hunger," "The Drowned Children," "The School Children" from *First Four Books of Poems* by Louise Glück. Copyright © 1968, 1971, 1972, 1973, 1974, 1975, 1976, 1977, 1978, 1979, 1980, 1985, 1995 by Louise Glück. Used by permission of HarperCollins Publishers. "Lullaby" from *The Wild Iris* by Louise Glück. Copyright © 1992 by Louise Glück. Used by permission of HarperCollins Publishers. "Terminal Resemblance," "Windows," "First Memory" from *Ararat* by Louise Glück. Copyright © 1990 by Louise Glück. Used by permission of HarperCollins Publishers. "Vita Nova" from *Vita Nova* by Louise Glück. Copyright © 1999 by Louise Glück. Used by permission of HarperCollins Publishers.

Lorna Goodison: "Guinea Woman" and "Nanny" from *I Am Becoming My Mother* (1986) by Lorna Goodison. Reprinted by permission of New Beacon Books, Ltd. "Mother the Great Stones Got to Move" from *Heartcase* (1988) by Lorna Goodison. Reprinted by permission of New Beacon Books, Ltd. "After the Green Gown of My Mother Gone Down" and "To Mr. William Wordsworth, Distributor of Stamps for Westmoreland" from *Turn Thanks: Poems* by Lorna Goodison. Copyright © 1999 by Lorna Goodison. Used with permission of the poet and the University of Illinois Press. "Annie Pengelly" from *To Us, All Flowers Are Roses* by Lorna Goodison. Copyright © 1995 by Lorna Goodison. Used with permission of the poet and the University of Illinois Press. "Change If You Must Just Change Slow" from *Controlling the Silver* by Lorna Goodison. Copyright © 2004 by Lorna Goodison. Used with permission of the poet and the University of Illinois Press.

Nadine Gordimer: "The Moment Before the Gun Went Off" from *Jump and Other Stories* by Nadine Gordimer. Copyright © 1991 by Felix Licensing, B.V.

Jorie Graham: "Orpheus and Eurydice" from *The End of Beauty*, © 1987 by Jorie Graham. Reprinted by permission of HarperCollins Publishers. "History" from *Erosion* by Jorie Graham. Copyright © 1983 by Princeton University Press. Reprinted by permission of the Princeton University Press.

Marilyn Hacker: From *Love, Death, and the Changing of the Seasons* by Marilyn Hacker. Copyright © 1986 by Marilyn Hacker. Reprinted by permission of Frances Collin, Literary Agent. "Ballad of Ladies Lost and Found," from SELECTED POEMS: 1965–1990 by Marilyn Hacker. Copyright © 1994 by Marilyn Hacker. Used by permission of W. W. Norton & Company, Inc. "The Boy," from SQUARES AND COURTYARDS by Marilyn Hacker. Copyright © 2000 by Marilyn Hacker. Used by permission of the author and W. W. Norton & Company, Inc. "Cancer Winter," from WINTER NUMBERS by Marilyn Hacker. Copyright © 1994 by Marilyn Hacker. Used by permission of the author and W. W. Norton & Company, Inc.

Joy Harjo: "When the World as We Knew It Ended." Copyright © 2002 by Joy Harjo, from HOW WE BECAME HUMAN: NEW AND SELECTED POEMS: 1975–2001 by Joy Harjo. Used by permission of the author and W. W. Norton & Company, Inc. "Mourning Song," "The Naming," from THE WOMAN WHO FELL FROM THE SKY by Joy Harjo. Copyright © 1994 by Joy Harjo. Used by permission of W. W. Norton & Company, Inc. "Morning Song," "The Path to the Milky Way Leads Through Los Angeles," from A MAP TO THE NEXT WORLD: POEMS AND TALES by Joy Harjo. Copyright © 2000 by Joy Harjo. Used by permission of the author and W. W. Norton & Company, Inc. "Deer Dancer" from *In Mad Love and War* by Joy Harjo. Copyright © 1990 by Joy Harjo. Reprinted by permission of Wesleyan University Press.

Gwen Harwood: "In the Park," "Mid Channel," "Mother Who Gave Me Life," and "The Sea Anemones" from *Selected Poems* by Gwen Harwood. Text Copyright © John Harwood. First published by Penguin Books Australia 2001. Reprinted by Permission of Penguin Random House Australia Pty Ltd.

Lyn Hejinian: Excerpts from *My Life* (Los Angeles: Sun&Moon, 1987), pp. 7–13. Copyright © 1980, 1987 by Lyn Hejinian. Reprinted with permission of Green Integer Books.

Zora Neale Hurston: "Sweat" as taken from *The Complete Stories* by Zora Neale Hurston. Compilation copyright © 1995 by Vivian Bowden, Lois J. Hurston Gates, Clifford Hurston, Lucy Ann Hurston, Winifred Hurston Clark, Zora Mack Goins, Edgar Hurston, Sr., and Barbara Hurston Lewis. Reprinted by permission of HarperCollins Publishers. "How It Feels to Be Colored Me" from *I Love Myself When I'm Laughing* by Zora Neale Hurston. Used with the permission of the Estate of Zora Neale Hurston.

Laura Riding Jackson: "The Map of Places," "Death as Death," and "The Troubles of a Book" from *Poems of Laura Riding* by Laura Riding Jackson. Copyright © 1991, 2001 by the Board of Literary Management of the late Laura (Riding) Jackson. "Eve's Side of It" (with commentary) by Laura Riding from *The Word Woman and Other Related Writings*, ed. Elizabeth Friedman and Alan J. Clark. Copyright © 1993 by the Board of Literary Management of the late Laura (Riding) Jackson. Reprinted by permission of Persea Books and the Board of Literary Management of the late Laura (Riding) Jackson.

Gish Jen: "Who's Irish?" from the collection *Who's Irish?* by Gish Jen, published by Alfred A. Knopf in 1999. Copyright © 1998 by Gish Jen. First published in *The New Yorker*. Reprinted by permission of the author.

June Jordan: "A Runaway Lil Bit Poem" and "DeLiza Spend the Day in the City" from *Living Room* by June Jordan. Used by permission of the Thunder's Mouth Press, a division of Avalon Publishing Group. "The Wedding," "The Reception," and "Poem about Police Violence" from

Passion by June Jordan. Copyright © 2005 by June M. Jordan Literary Estate Trust. Reprinted by permission of the June M. Jordan Literary Estate Trust.

Shirley Kaufman: "His Wife" from *The Floor Keeps Turning* by Shirley Kaufman. Reprinted by permission of the author. "Mothers, Daughters" from *Roots in the Air: New and Selected Poems.* Copyright © 1970, 1996 by Shirley Kaufman. "Stones" from *Roots in the Air: New and Selected Poems.* By Shirley Kaufman. Copyright © 1993 by Shirley Kaufman. "Intifada" and "Longing for Prophets" from *Rivers of Salt.* Copyright © 1993 by Shirley Kaufman. Reprinted with the permission of the Copper Canyon Press. "Abishag" from *Claims* by Shirley Kaufman. Copyright © 1984 by Shirley Kaufman. Reprinted by permission of The Sheep Meadow Press.

Jackie Kay: "In My Country," "Finger," "Hottentot Venus," "Paw Broom on the Starr Report," and "Big Milk" from *Darling: New & Selected Poems* (Bloodaxe Books, 2007) by permission of the publisher. Reproduced with permission of Bloodaxe Books. www.bloodaxebooks.com

Jamaica Kincaid: "Girl" from *At the Bottom of the River* by Jamaica Kincaid. Copyright © 1983 by Jamaica Kincaid.

Maxine Hong Kingston: "No Name Woman" from THE WOMAN WARRIOR: MEMOIRS OF A GIRLHOOD AMONG GHOSTS, copyright © 1975, 1976 by Maxine Hong Kingston. Used by permission of Alfred A. Knopf, an imprint of the Knopf Doubleday Publishing Group, a division of Penguin Random House LLC. All rights reserved.

Carolyn Kizer: "Pro Femina" (part three) from *Mermaids in the Basement* by Carolyn Kizer. "Semele Recycled" from *YIN: New Poems* by Carolyn Kizer. Reprinted by permission of the author. "Second Time Around" from *Cool, Calm, and Collected: Poems 1960–2000.* Copyright © 2001 by Carolyn Kizer. Reprinted by permission of Copper Canyon Press.

Maxine Kumin: "Making the Jam without You," "The Envelope," and "How It Is" from *Our Ground Time Here Will Be Brief.* Reprinted by permission of The Anderson Literary Agency, Inc. Copyright © 1982. First published by The Viking Press. "Sonnet in So Many Words," "Women and Horses," from JACK AND OTHER NEW POEMS by Maxine Kumin. Copyright © 2005 by Maxine Kumin. Used by permission of the author and W. W. Norton & Company, Inc. "Skinny-dipping with William Wordsworth," from LONG MARRIAGE by Maxine Kumin. Copyright © 2002 by Maxine Kumin. Used by permission of the author and W. W. Norton & Company, Inc.

Jhumpa Lahiri: "A Temporary Matter" from *The Interpreter of Maladies* by Jhumpa Lahiri. Copyright © 1999 by Jhumpa Lahiri. Reprinted by permission of Houghton Mifflin Harcourt Publishing Company. All Rights Reserved.

Dilys Bennett Laing: "The Double Goer," "Let Them Ask Their Husbands," "Sonnet to a Sister in Error," and "Prayer of an Ovulating Female" from *The Collected Poems of Dilys Bennett Laing.* Reprinted by permission of David B. Laing.

Mary Lavin: "In a Café" from *The Great Wave* by Mary Lavin. Copyright © 1961 by Mary Lavin. Reprinted by permission of Sheil Land Associates Ltd on behalf of the Estate of Mary Lavin.

Ursula K. Le Guin: "Sur," copyright © 1982 by Ursula K. Le Guin; first appeared in *The New Yorker.* "She Unnames Them," copyright © 1985 by Ursula K. Le Guin; first appeared in *The New Yorker.* Both selections reprinted by permission of the author and the author's agents, The Virginia Kidd Agency, Inc.

Meridel Le Sueur: "Annunciation" from *Salute to Spring* by Meridel Le Sueur. Reprinted by permission of International Publishers Co.

Doris Lessing: "One Off the Short List," copyright © 1963 by Doris Lessing. Featured by kind permission of Jonathan Clowes LTD., London, on behalf of The Doris Lessing Literary Will Trust.

Denise Levertov: "The Dragonfly Mother" by Denise Levertov, from CANDLES IN BABYLON, copyright © 1982 by Denise Levertov. Reprinted by permission of New Directions Publishing Corp. "The Goddess" by Denise Levertov, from COLLECTED EARLIER POEMS *1940–1960*, copyright © 1960 by Denise Levertov. Reprinted by permission of New Directions Publishing Corp. "Evening Train," "Ancient Airs," and "Dances" by Denise Levertov, from EVENING TRAIN, copyright © 1992 by Denise Levertov. Reprinted by permission of New Directions Publishing Corp. "Abel's Bride," "Eros at Temple Stream," "Hypocritical Woman," "In Mind," "Stepping Westwards," "The Son," and "What Were They Life," by Denise Levertov, from POEMS *1960–1967*, copyright © 1966 by Denise Levertov. Reprinted by permission of New Directions Publishing Corp. "Song for Ishtar" and "The Ache of Marriage" by Denise Levertov, from POEMS *1960–1967*, copyright © 1964 by Denise Levertov. Reprinted by permission of New Directions Publishing Corp. "Cancion" and "Divorcing" by Denise Levertov, from THE FREEING OF THE

1560 / PERMISSIONS ACKNOWLEDGMENTS

DUST, copyright © 1975 by Denise Levertov. Reprinted by permission of New Directions Publishing Corp.

Dorothy Livesay: "Green Rain," "Eve," "The Three Emily's," and "The Children's Letters" reprinted by permission of Jay Stewart, executrix for the Estate of Dorothy Livesay.

Audre Lorde: "From the House of Yemanja," "The Women of Dan Dance with Swords in Their Hands to Mark the Time When They Were Warriors," from THE BLACK UNICORN by Audre Lorde. Copyright © 1978 by Audre Lorde. Used by permission of W. W. Norton & Company, Inc. "Coal." Copyright © 1973, 1970, 1968 by Audre Lorde. "On a Night of the Full Moon." Copyright © 1992, 1973, 1970, 1968 by Audre Lorde, from UNDERSONG: *Chosen Poems Old and New* by Audre Lorde. Used by permission of W. W. Norton & Company, Inc. "Now That I Am Forever with Child." Copyright © 1973, 1970. 1968 by Audre Lorde, from CHOSEN POEMS: OLD AND NEW by Audre Lorde. Used by permission of W. W. Norton & Company, Inc. "Kitchen Linoleum," "The Electric Slide Boogie," from THE MARVELOUS ARITHMETICS OF DISTANCE: *Poems 1987–1992* by Audre Lorde. Copyright © 1993 by Audre Lorde. Used by permission of W. W. Norton & Company, Inc. From *Zami: A New Spelling of My Name*—published by Crossing Press/Penguin Random House, New York. Copyright © 1982, 2006 by Audre Lorde. Used herewith by permission of the Charlotte Sheedy Literary Agency.

Amy Lowell: "The Sisters" from *What's O'Clock* by Amy Lowell. Copyright © 1925 by Houghton Mifflin Harcourt Publishing Company, renewed 1953 by Harvey H. Bundy and G. D'Andelot Belin Jr., Trustees of the Estate of Amy Lowell. Reprinted by permission of Houghton Mifflin Harcourt Publishing Co. All rights reserved.

Mina Loy: "Gertrude Stein," "Three Moments in Paris," "Photo after Pogrom," "Omen of Victory," "Songge Byrd," "Portrait of a Nun," and "Feminist Manifesto" reprinted from *The Lost Lunar Baedeker: Poems of Mina Loy,* edited by Roger L. Conover (Farrar, Straus & Giroux, 1996). Reprinted by permission of Roger L. Conover. "The Widow's Jazz" from *The Lost Lunar Baedeker* by Mina Loy. Works of Mina Loy copyright © 1996 by the Estate of Mina Loy.

Katherine Mansfield: "The Daughters of the Late Colonel" and "The Fly" from *The Short Stories of Katherine Mansfield* by Katherine Mansfield. Copyright 1923 by Alfred A. Knopf, Inc. and renewed 1950 by John Middleton Murry. Reprinted by permission of Alfred A. Knopf, a division of Random House, Inc.

Paule Marshall: "The Making of a Writer: From Poets in the Kitchen" from *Reena and Other Stories.* Copyright © Paule Marshall. Reprinted with the permission of Paule Marshall.

Mary McCarthy: "Names" from *Memories of a Catholic Girlhood.* Copyright © 1957 and renewed 1985 by Mary McCarthy. Reprinted by permission of Houghton Mifflin Harcourt Publishing Company. All rights reserved.

Carson McCullers: "Ballad of the Sad Café," copyright © 1987 by the Estate of Carson McCullers. Used by permission of the Estate.

Medbh McGuckian: "The Flitting" from *The Flower Master and Other Poems* (1993) and "She is in the Past, She has this Grace" from *The Face of the Earth* (2002). By kind permission of the author and the Gallery Press. "Black Virgin" from *Captain Lavender* by Medbh McGuckian. "Visiting Rainer Maria" from *Marconi's Cottage* by Medbh McGuckian. Reprinted by permission of Wake Forest University Press.

Paula Meehan: "Child Burial" and "Would you jump into my grave as quick" by kind permission of the author and The Gallery Press from *The Man Who was Marked by Winter* (1991) and *Pillow Talk* (1994). "The View from Under the Table" and "Thunder in the House" from *Dharmakaya* by Paula Meehan. Reprinted by permission of Wake Forest University Press.

Charlotte Mew: "The Farmer's Bride," "The Quiet House" and "A White Night" from *Collected Poems* by Charlotte Mew. Reprinted by permission of Carcanet Press Limited.

Edna St. Vincent Millay: "Oh, oh, you will be sorry for that word!" "I, being born a woman and distressed," and "Sonnets from an Ungrafted Tree," copyright 1923, 1951 by Edna St. Vincent Millay and Norma Millay Ellis. "The Buck in the Snow" and "To Inez Milholland," copyright © 1928, 1955 by Edna St. Vincent Millay and Norma Millay Ellis. "Women have loved before as I love now" and "Oh, sleep forever in the Latmian cave," copyright © 1931, 1958 by Edna St. Vincent Millay and Norma Millay Ellis. "Childhood Is the Kingdom Where Nobody Dies" and "Apostrophe to Man," copyright © 1934, 1962 by Edna St. Vincent Millay and Norma Millay Ellis. "Rendezvous," "I too beneath your moon, almighty Sex," and "The Fitting," copyright © 1939, 1967 by Edna St. Vincent Millay and Norma Millay Ellis. "The courage that my mother had" and

"An Ancient Gesture," copyright © 1954, 1982 by Norma Millay Ellis. "clxviii—I will put Chaos into fourteen lines" by permission of the Millay Society.

Marianne Moore: "O to Be a Dragon," copyright © 1957 by Marianne Moore, copyright renewed © 1985 by Lawrence E. Brinn and Louise Crane, Executors of the Estate of Marianne Moore; from THE COMPLETE POEMS OF MARIANNE MOORE by Marianne Moore. Used by permission of Viking Books, an imprint of Penguin Publishing Group, a division of Penguin Random House LLC. All rights reserved. "To a Snail," "Poetry," "Sojourn in the Whale," "An Egyptian Pulled Glass Bottle in the Shape of a Fish," "Silence," "A Grave," "No Swan So Fine," "The Steeple-Jack" and "Those Various Scalpels" from *Collected Poems of Marianne Moore* by Marianne Moore. Reprinted with permission of Simon & Schuster Adult Publishing Group. Copyright © 1935 by Marianne Moore, renewed 1963 by Marianne Moore and T. S. Eliot. "The Paper Nautilus" from *Collected Poems of Marianne Moore* by Marianne Moore. Copyright © 1941, and renewed 1969 by Marianne Moore. Reprinted with permission of Simon & Schuster Adult Publishing Group. "His Shield" from *Collected Poems of Marianne Moore* by Marianne Moore. Copyright © 1951 by Marianne Moore. Reprinted with permission of Simon & Schuster Adult Publishing Group.

Toni Morrison: "Unspeakable Things Unspoken" by Toni Morrison. Copyright © 1973 by Toni Morrison. "Recitatif" by Toni Morrison. Copyright © 1987 by Toni Morrison. Reprinted by permission of International Creative Management, Inc.

Bharati Mukherjee: "The Management of Grief" from THE MIDDLEMAN AND OTHER STORIES, copyright © 1988 by Bharati Mukherjee. Used by permission of Grove/Atlantic, Inc. Reprinted by permission of Penguin Canada, a division of Penguin Random House Canada Limited. All rights reserved. Any third-party use of this material, outside of this publication, is prohibited.

Alice Munro: "Floating Bridge" from HATESHIP, FRIENDSHIP, COURTSHIP, LOVESHIP, MARRIAGE: STORIES by Alice Munro, copyright © 2001 by Alice Munro. Used by permission of Alfred A. Knopf, an imprint of the Knopf Doubleday Publishing Group, a division of Penguin Random House LLC. Reprinted by permission of McClelland & Stewart, a division of Penguin Random House Canada Limited. All rights reserved.

Grace Nichols: "Out of Africa" from *Lazy Thoughts of a Lazy Woman* by Grace Nichols. Copyright © 1989 by Grace Nichols. Reproduced by permission of Curtis Brown Group Ltd. On behalf of Grace Nichols. "The Assertion," "The Fat Black Woman Remembers," and "Tropical Death" from *The Fat Black Woman's Poems* by Grace Nichols. Reprinted by permission of Time Warner Book Group UK.

Anaïs Nin: "Birth" from *Under A Glass Bell* by Anaïs Nin. Reprinted by permission of Peter Owen, Ltd., Publishers.

Edna O'Brien: "Brother" from *Lantern Slides* by Edna O'Brien. Copyright © 1990 by Edna O'Brien. Introduction and edition copyright © 1996 by Roger L. Conover.

Kate O'Brien: "On Bullfighting" and "Santa Teresa" from *Farewell Spain* by Kate O'Brien. Copyright © 1937 by Mary O'Neill. Reprinted by permission of Beacon Press and David Higham Associates Limited.

Flannery O'Connor: "Good Country People" from *A Good Man Is Hard to Find and Other Stories*, copyright © 1953 by Flannery O'Connor and renewed 1981 by Regina O'Connor. Reprinted by permission of Houghton Mifflin Harcourt Publishing Company. All rights reserved.

Joyce Carol Oates: "Where Are You Going, Where Have You Been?" from *The Wheel of Love and Other Stories* by Joyce Carol Oates. Copyright © 1970 by *Ontario Review*. Reprinted by permission of John Hawkins & Associates, Inc.

Sharon Olds: "This" from THE GOLD CELL by Sharon Olds, copyright © 1987 by Sharon Olds. Used by permission of Alfred A. Knopf, an imprint of the Knopf Doubleday Publishing Group, a division of Penguin Random House LLC. All rights reserved. "Rite of Passage" and "The Death of Marilyn Monroe" from THE DEAD & THE LIVING by Sharon Olds, copyright © 1975, 1978, 1979, 1980, 1981, 1982, 1983 by Sharon Olds. Used by permission of Alfred A. Knopf, an imprint of the Knopf Doubleday Publishing Group, a division of Penguin Random House LLC. All rights reserved. "The Mortal One" from THE FATHER by Sharon Olds, copyright © 1992 by Sharon Olds. Used by permission of Alfred A. Knopf, an imprint of the Knopf Doubleday Publishing Group, a division of Penguin Random House LLC. All rights reserved. "The One Girl at the Boys' Party" from THE DEAD & THE LIVING by Sharon Olds, copyright © 1975, 1978, 1979, 1980, 1981, 1982, 1983 by Sharon Olds. Used by permission of Alfred A. Knopf, an imprint of the Knopf Doubleday Publishing Group, a division of Penguin Random House LLC. All rights reserved.

Tillie Olsen: "Tell Me a Riddle" from *Tell Me A Riddle* by Tillie Olsen. Copyright © 1956, 1957, 1960, 1961 by Tillie Olsen. Reprinted by permission of the Elaine Markson Agency.

Oodgeroo of the tribe Noonuccal: "Municipal Gum," "Understand, Old One," and "We Are Going" by Oodgeroo of the tribe Noonuccal, from *My People*, 3e, The Jacaranda Press, copyright © 1990. Reproduced by permission of John Wiley and Sons Australia.

Cynthia Ozick: "The Shawl" from THE SHAWL by Cynthia Ozick, copyright © 1980, 1983 by Cynthia Ozick. Used by permission of Alfred A. Knopf, an imprint of the Knopf Doubleday Publishing Group, a division of Penguin Random House LLC. All rights reserved.

P. K. Page: "Planet Earth," "The Stenographers," and "Typists" from *The Hidden Room* (in two volumes, 1997) by P. K. Page. Reprinted by permission of *The Porcupine's Quill*.

Grace Paley: "My Father Addresses Me on the Facts of Old Age," originally published in *The New Yorker*, June 17 & 24, 2002. Reprinted by permission of the Elaine Markson Agency.

Dorothy Parker: "A Pig's-Eye View of Literature: The Lives and Times of John Keats, Percy Bysshe Shelley and George Gordon Noel, Lord Byron," "Alfred, Lord Tennyson," "D. G. Rossetti," "George Sand," "Harriet Beecher Stowe," "Oscar Wilde," "Thomas Carlyle," and "Walter Savage Landor," copyright 1928, renewed © 1956 by Dorothy Parker; "News Item," "One Perfect Rose," and "Song of One of the Girls," copyright 1926, renewed © 1954 by Dorothy Parker; "Resume," copyright 1926, 1928 and © renewed 1954, 1956 by Dorothy Parker; and "The Waltz," copyright 1933, renewed © 1961 by Dorothy Parker; from THE PORTABLE DOROTHY PARKER by Dorothy Parker, edited by Marion Meade. Used by permission of Viking Books, an imprint of Penguin Publishing Group, a division of Penguin Random House LLC. All rights reserved.

Ruth Pitter: "The Military Harpist," "The Irish Patriarch," "Old Nelly's Birthday," and "Yorkshire Wife's Sage" from *Ruth Pitter: The Collected Poems*. Reprinted by permission of Mark Pitter.

Sylvia Plath: "Stings," "Lady Lazarus," "Edge," "Daddy," "Ariel," "The Bee Meeting," "The Arrival of the Bee Box," "Wintering," "Words," "You're," "Nick and the Candlestick," "Mirror" from *The Collected Poems, Sylvia Plath*. Copyright © 1960, 1965, 1971, 1981 by the Estate of Sylvia Plath. Used by permission of HarperCollins Publishers. "The Colossus" and "The Disquieting Muses" from THE COLOSSUS by Sylvia Plath, copyright © 1957, 1958, 1959, 1960, 1961, 1962 by Sylvia Plath. Used by permission of Alfred A. Knopf, an imprint of the Knopf Doubleday Publishing Group, a division of Penguin Random House LLC. All rights reserved.

Katherine Anne Porter: "The Jilting of Granny Weatherall" from *Flowering Judas and Other Stories*, copyright © 1930 and renewed 1958 by Katherine Anne Porter. Reprinted by permission of Houghton Mifflin Harcourt Publishing Company. All rights reserved.

Katharine Susannah Prichard: "The Cooboo" from *Tribute: Selected Stories of Katharine Susannah Prichard*. Reprinted by permission of Curtis Brown (Aust.) Pty Ltd., Sydney.

Jean Rhys: "Mannequin" from *Tigers Are Better Looking: With a Selection from the Left Bank* by Jean Rhys. Copyright © 1960 by Jean Rhys.

Adrienne Rich: "To the Days," from DARK FIELDS OF THE REPUBLIC: *Poems 1991–1995* by Adrienne Rich. Copyright © 1995 by Adrienne Rich. Used by permission of the author and W. W. Norton & Company, Inc. "Phantasia for Elvira Shatayev" from THE DREAM OF A COMMON LANGUAGE: *Poems 1974–1977* by Adrienne Rich. Copyright © 1978 by W. W. Norton & Company, Inc. Used by permission of the author and W. W. Norton & Company, Inc. "When We Dead Awaken: Writing as Re-Vision" from ON LIES, SECRETS, AND SILENCE: SELECTED PROSE *1966–1978* by Adrienne Rich. Copyright © 1979 by W. W. Norton & Company, Inc. Used by permission of the author and W. W. Norton & Company, Inc. Parts 1 and 8 of "Eastern War Time" from AN ATLAS OF THE DIFFICULT WORLD: *Poems 1988–1991* by Adrienne Rich. Copyright © 1991 by Adrienne Rich. Used by permission of the author and W. W. Norton & Company, Inc. "The Loser." Copyright © 1993, 1967, 1963 by Adrienne Rich, from COLLECTED EARLY POEMS: *1950–1970* by Adrienne Rich. Used by permission of the author and W. W. Norton & Company, Inc. "Aunt Jennifer's Tigers," "Diving into the Wreck," "Final Notations," "Fox," "I Am in Danger—Sir," "In Those Years," "Power," "Snapshots of a Daughter-in-Law," Poems XI, XXI, and (The Floating Poem, Unnumbered) of "Twenty-One Love Poems," "Orion," "Planetarium," from THE FACT OF A DOORFRAME: SELECTED POEMS *1950–2001* by Adrienne Rich. Copyright © 2002 by Adrienne Rich. Copyright © 2001, 1999, 1995,1991, 1989, 1986, 1984, 1981, 1967, 1963, 1962, 1961, 1960, 1959, 1958, 1957, 1956, 1955, 1954, 1953, 1952, 1951, by Adrienne Rich. Copyright © 1978, 1975, 1973, 1971, 1969, 1966 by W. W. Norton & Company, Inc. Used by permission of the author and W.W. Norton & Company, Inc. "The School Among the Ruins" from THE SCHOOL AMONG THE RUINS: POEMS *2000–2004* by Adrienne Rich.

Copyright © 2004 by Adrienne Rich. Used by permission of the author and W. W. Norton & Company, Inc.

Dorothy Richardson: "Death" from *Journey to Paradise* by Dorothy Richardson. Reprinted by permission of Time Warner Book Group UK. "Women and the Future" from *Vogue*, April 1924. Reprinted by permission of The Condé Nast Publications, Inc.

Henry Handel Richardson: "Two Hanged Women" from *The End of Childhood*. Reprinted by permission of Curtis Brown (Aust.) Pty Ltd., Sydney.

Muriel Rukeyser: "Boy with His Hair Cut Short," "More of a Corpse than a Woman," "Who in One Lifetime," "Letter to the Front VII," "The Birth of Venus," "The Poem as Mask," "The Power of Suicide," "Käthe Kollwitz," "Myth," "Along History," and "Night Feeding" by Muriel Rukeyser from THE COLLECTED POEMS OF MURIEL RUKEYSER. Copyright © 2005 by Muriel Rukeyser. Reprinted by permission of ICM Partners.

May Sarton: "Letter from Chicago," "My Sisters O My Sisters." Copyright 1948 and renewed © 1976 by May Sarton. "The Muse as Medusa." Copyright © 1971 by May Sarton, from COLLECTED POEMS *1930–1993* by May Sarton. Copyright © 1993, 1988, 1984, 1980, 1974 by May Sarton. Used by permission of W. W. Norton & Company, Inc.

Anne Sexton: "In Celebration of My Uterus" from LOVE POEMS by Anne Sexton. Copyright © 1967, 1968, 1969 by Anne Sexton, renewed 1997 by Linda G. Sexton. "Somewhere in Africa," reprinted by permission of Houghton Mifflin Harcourt Publishing Company. All rights reserved. Reprinted by permission of SLL/Sterling Lord Literistic, Inc. Copyright by Linda Gray Sexton and Loring Conant, Jr. 1981. "Woman with Girdle," "Housewife" reprinted by permission of SLL/Sterling Lord Literistic, Inc. Copyright by Linda Gray Sexton and Loring Conant, Jr. 1981. "Her Kind," "The Moss of My Skin" reprinted by permission of SLL/Sterling Lord Literistic, Inc. Copyright by Linda Gray Sexton and Loring Conant, Jr. 1981. "Sylvia's Death," reprinted by permission of SLL/Sterling Lord Literistic, Inc. Copyright by Linda Gray Sexton and Loring Conant, Jr. 1981.

Leslie Marmon Silko: "Yellow Woman" from STORYTELLER by Leslie Marmon Silko, copyright © 1981, 2012 by Leslie Marmon Silko. Used by permission of Viking Books, an imprint of Penguin Publishing Group, a division of Penguin Random House LLC. All rights reserved.

Edith Sitwell: "Sir Beelzebub," "Aubade," "Still Falls the Rain" and "Serenade: Any Man to Any Woman," from *Collected Poems* by Edith Sitwell. Reprinted by permission of David Higham Associates Limited.

Stevie Smith: "Not Waving but Drowning" from COLLECTED POEMS OF STEVIE SMITH, copyright © 1957 by Stevie Smith. Reprinted by permission of New Directions Publishing Corp. "Dear Female Heart," "How Cruel Is the Story of Eve," "Human Affection," "Lightly Bound," "Lord Barrenstock," "Our Bog Is Dood," "Papa Loves Baby," "Souvenir de Monsieur Poop," "The Wanderer," "The Englishwoman" by Stevie Smith, from COLLECTED POEMS OF STEVIE SMITH, copyright © 1972 by Stevie Smith. Reprinted by permission of New Directions Publishing Corp.

Muriel Spark: "The Black Madonna" from *All the Stories of Muriel Spark* by Muriel Spark. Copyright © 1953, 1957, 1958, 1961, 1964, 1967, 1985, 1987, 1989, 1994, 1996, 1997 by Muriel Spark. Copyright © 1985 by Copyright Administration Limited. Reprinted by permission of New Directions Publishing Corp.

Anne Spencer: "White Things," "Before the Feast at Shushan," "Letter to My Sister," "Innocence," from *Time's Unfading Garden: Anne Spencer's Life at Poetry*, by J. Lee Greene (Baton Rouge: LSU Press, 1977). Reprinted by permission of J. Lee Greene.

Gertrude Stein: Excerpt from "Picasso" from *Gertrude Stein's Writing and Lectures 1911–1945*. Reprinted by permission of Peter Owen Ltd Publishers.

Ruth Stone: "At Eighty-three She Lives Alone," "Cousin Francis Speaks Out," and "Sorrow" from *In the Next Galaxy*. Copyright © 2002 by Ruth Stone. "From Outer Space," "The Barrier," and "The Jewels" from *In the Dark* by Ruth Stone. Copyright © 2004 by Ruth Stone. Reprinted by permission of Copper Canyon Press. "Things I Say to Myself While Hanging Laundry" from *Simplicity* by Ruth Stone. Copyright © 1995 by Ruth Stone. Reprinted by permission of Paris Press, Inc. "In an Iridescent Time," "Names," "Periphery," "Second-Hand Coat," and "The Song of Absinthe Granny" by Ruth Stone. Reprinted by permission of the author.

May Swenson: "The Centaur," "Women," "Blue," and "Bleeding" © 1970 by May Swenson; 1994 by the Literary Estate of May Swenson. From *May Swenson: Collected Poems* (Library of America, 2013). Used with permission of the Literary Estate of May Swenson. All rights reserved.

Genevieve Taggard: "At Last the Women are Moving," "A Middle-aged Middle-class Woman at Midnight," "Demeter," and "Mill Town" by Genevieve Taggard. Reprinted by permission of Judith Benét Richardson.

Luci Tapahonso: "Blue Horses Rush In" and "Leda and the Cowboy" from *Sáanii Dahataal / The Women Are Singing* by Luci Tapahonso. Copyright © 1993 by Luci Tapahonso. Reprinted by permission of the University of Arizona Press.

James Tiptree Jr.: "The Women Men Don't See" by James Tiptree Jr. Copyright © 1973 by James Tiptree Jr; first appeared in *The Magazine of Fantasy and Science Fiction;* reprinted by permission of the author's estate and the estate's agent, The Virginia Kidd Agency, Inc.

Helena María Viramontes: "The Moths" by Helena María Viramontes is reprinted with permission from Arte Público Press—University of Houston, the publisher of THE MOTHS AND OTHER STORIES/*Las palomillas de la noche y otros relatos,* copyright © 1985 by Helena María Viramontes, and protected by the Copyright Laws of the United States. All rights reserved. The printing, copying, redistribution, or retransmission of this Content without express permission is prohibited.

Alice Walker: "In Search of Our Mothers' Gardens" from *In Search of Our Mothers' Gardens: Womanist Prose.* Copyright © 1974 by Alice Walker. "Women" from REVOLUTIONARY PETUNIAS & OTHER POEMS by Alice Walker. Copyright © 1970 and renewed 1998 by Alice Walker. Reprinted by permission of Houghton Mifflin Harcourt Publishing Company. All rights reserved.

Margaret Walker: "Dark Blood," "Lineage," "Molly Means," "Kissie Lee," "Whores," and "For Malcolm X" from *This Is My Century: New and Collected Poems* by Margaret Alexander. Copyright © 1989 by Margaret Walker Alexander. Reprinted by permission of The University of Georgia Press.

Eudora Welty: "A Worn Path" from *A Curtain of Green and Other Stories.* Copyright © 1941 and renewed 1969 by Eudora Welty. Reprinted by permission of Houghton Mifflin Harcourt Publishing Company. All rights reserved.

Rebecca West: "Indissoluble Matrimony" by Rebecca West. Copyright © 1914 by the Estate of Rebecca West. First appeared in *BLAST 1* and is reproduced by permission of PFD on behalf of the Estate of Rebecca West.

Jeanette Winterson: "The Poetics of Sex" from *Granta Magazine,* reprinted by permission of Peters Fraser & Dunlop (www.petersfraserdunlop.com) on behalf of Jeanette Winterson.

Virginia Woolf: "22 Hyde Park Gate" from MOMENTS OF BEING by Virginia Woolf. Copyright © 1976, 1985 by Quentin Bell and Angelica Garnett. Reprinted by permission of Houghton Mifflin Harcourt Publishing Company. All rights reserved. "A Woman's College from Outside" from THE COMPLETE SHORTER FICTION OF VIRGINIA WOOLF edited by Susan Dick. Copyright © 1985 by Quentin Bell. Reprinted by permission of Houghton Mifflin Harcourt Publishing Company. All rights reserved. "*Jane Eyre* and *Wuthering Heights*" from THE COMMON READER by Virginia Woolf. Copyright © 1925 by Houghton Mifflin Harcourt Publishing Company, renewed 1953 by Leonard Woolf. Reprinted by permission of Houghton Mifflin Harcourt Publishing Company. All rights reserved. "Moments of Being: Slater's Pins Have No Points" from A HAUNTED HOUSE AND OTHER SHORT STORIES by Virginia Woolf. Copyright © 1944 and renewed 1972 by Houghton Mifflin Harcourt Publishing Company. Reprinted by permission of Houghton Mifflin Harcourt Publishing Company. All rights reserved. "Professions for Women" and "The Death of the Moth" from THE DEATH OF THE MOTH AND OTHER ESSAYS by Virginia Woolf. Copyright © 1942 by Houghton Mifflin Harcourt Publishing Company, renewed 1970 by Marjorie T. Parsons, Executrix. Reprinted by permission of Houghton Mifflin Harcourt Publishing Company. All rights reserved. "Shakespeare's Sister" from A ROOM OF ONE'S OWN by Virginia Woolf. Copyright © 1929 by Houghton Mifflin Harcourt Publishing Company, renewed 1957 by Leonard Woolf. Reprinted by permission of Houghton Mifflin Harcourt Publishing Company. All rights reserved.

Judith Wright: "Half-Caste Girl," "Ishtar," and "Rosina Alcona to Julius Brenzaida" from *Selected Poems* by Judith Wright. Reprinted by permission of HarperCollins Australia. "Two Dreamtimes" from *Collected Poems* by Judith Wright. Reprinted by permission of Carcanet Press Limited and ETT Imprint. "Counting in Sevens," "Eve to her Daughters," "Naked Girl and Mirror," "Request to a Year," "Some Words," "The Sisters," "To Another Housewife," and "Woman to Man" from *A Human Pattern: Selected Poems* by Judith Wright. Reprinted by permission of ETT Imprint.

Hisaye Yamamoto: "Seventeen Syllables" from *Seventeen Syllables and Other Stories* by Hisaye Yamamoto. Copyright © 1988 by Hisaye Yamamoto. Reprinted by permission of Rutgers University Press.

Index

Abel's Bride, 864
Abishag, 879
Abortions will not let you forget, 781
Ache of Marriage, The, 863
Ada, 165
Adcock, Fleur, 1078
Addonizio, Kim, 1394
admonitions, 1119
A few months back, when the night sky was darker, 1393
Affinity, The, 266
After Auschwitz: after ten of my father's kin—, 917
After the brief bivouac of Sunday, 736
After the Green Gown of My Mother Gone Down, 1332
after the murder, 789
After you left me forever, 909
Against Coupling, 1080
Aidoo, Ama Ata, 1263
Alas! for all the pretty women who marry dull men, 265
All day long I have been working, 131
All Greece hates, 291
All my life I had seen that long, 1282
All night our room was outer-walled with rain, 132
All you violated ones with gentle hearts, 721
Along History, 654
Along history, forever, 654
Always pyrotechnics, 1123
Alvarez, Julia, 1341
Amber husk, 284
Among some hills there dwelt in parody, 710
Ancient Airs and Dances, 871
Ancient Gesture, An, 457
Angel at the Grave, The, 31
Angelou, Maya, 926
Annie Pengelly, 1325
Annunciation, 1089
An old man sleeping in the evening train, 872
Anorexic, 1290
Anzaldúa, Gloria, 1254
Apostrophe to Man, 455
April Fool Birthday Poem for Grandpa, 1085
Ariel, 1059
Arrangement by rage, 253
Arrival of the Bee Box, The, 1052
A single flow'r he sent me, since we met, 488
A snail is climbing up the window-sill, 1079
Asparagus, 1208
Assertion, The, 1371
As the guests arrive at my son's party, 1280
Atavism, 270
At Eighty-three She Lives Alone, 714
At four o'clock, 606
At Last the Women Are Moving, 497
Atwood, Margaret, 1203
Aubade, 303

August, her large heart slows down then stops, 1328
Aunt Jane scribbles in the living-room, 939
Aunt Jennifer's Tigers, 965
Aunt Jennifer's tigers prance across a screen, 965
Austin, Mary, 66
A voice from the dark is calling me, 267
Avoid the reeking herd, 269
Axes, 1064

Ballad of Ladies Lost and Found, 1269
Ballad of the Sad Café, The, 740
Bare-handed, I hand the combs, 1053
Barnes, Djuna, 458
Barrier, The, 716
Bean Eaters, The, 787
Bee Meeting, The, 1050
Beer, Patricia, 883
Before the birth, she moved and pushed inside her mother, 1392
Before the Feast at Shushan, 258
Bennett, Louise, 804
Beside the highway, 595
Big Milk, 1492
Bilingual Sestina, 1341
Birth, 588
Birth of Venus, The, 648
Bishop, Elizabeth, 604
Black Madonna, The, 791
Black Virgin, 1368
Blank Page, The, 276
Bleeding, 657
Bloodchild, 1307
Blue, 658
Blue, but you are Rose, too, 658
Blue Horses Rush In, 1392
Bogan, Louise, 504
Boland, Eavan, 1288
Bonner, Marita, 524
Bowen, Elizabeth, 528
Boy, The, 1275
boys, 1119
Boy with His Hair Cut Short, 645
Branch, Anna Hempstead, 172
Bronzeville Woman in a Red Hat, 787
Brooks, Gwendolyn, 780
Brother, 1066
Brown, Rebecca, 1432
Brunhild, 884
Buck in the Snow, The, 452
Buddy's uncle Hiram felt bad about his sister, Mable, 715
Bull, The, 885
But it was right that she, 878
Butler, Octavia, 1306
but you know how to raise it in me, 1398
Byatt, A. S., 1097
Byron and Shelley and Keats, 489

1565

Cancer Winter, 1273
Canción, 868
Carried her unprotesting out the door, 786
Carson, Anne, 1346
Carter, Angela, 1220
Cassandra (Bogan), 506
Cassation, 463
Cather, Willa, 91
Centaur, The, 655
Change If You Must Just Change Slow, 1331
Child Burial, 1429
Childhood is not from birth to a certain age and at a certain age, 454
Childhood Is the Kingdom Where Nobody Dies, 454
Children's Letters, The, 596
Chin, Marilyn, 1418
Churchill, Caryl, 1136
Circe, 1426
Cisneros, Sandra, 1399
Clifton, Lucille, 1119
Clownlike, happiest on your hands, 1049
Coal, 1070
Cod inert as an old boot, 834
Colonel, The, 1364
Colonisation in Reverse, 806
Colossus, The, 1048
Come, drunks and drug-takers; come, perverts unnerved, 508
Coming, Aphrodite!, 93
Company of Wolves, The, 1221
Cooboo, The, 262
Counting in Sevens, 734
Cousin Francis Speaks Out, 715
Crepuscule with Muriel, 1276
Critical Fable, A, 133
Crossed Apple, The, 507
Crows, The, 505
Curie, 250

Daddy, 1057
Dark angel who art clear and straight, 305
Dark Blood, 717
Daughters of the Late Colonel, The, 321
Dear Female Heart, 582
Dear Female Heart, I am sorry for you, 582
Dear posterity, it's 2 a.m., 1082
Death, 122
Death as Death, 543
Death of Marilyn Monroe, The, 1279
Death of the Moth, The, 248
Decade, 132
Dedication of the Cook, 267
Dedication to Hunger, 1284
Deeper than sleep but not so deep as death, 647
Deer Dancer, 1377
Degas's Laundresses, 1292
DeLiza drive the car to fetch Alexis, 1097
DeLiza Spend the Day in the City, 1097
Demeter, 498
Demon Lover, The, 528
Desai, Anita, 1123
Detestable race, continue to expunge yourself, die out, 455
Did the people of Viet Nam, 868
Dinesen, Isak, 274
Di Prima, Diane, 1084
Disquieting Muses, The, 1047
Diving into the Wreck, 970
Divorce, 267
Divorcing, 869
Don't, 1092

(**Doolittle, Hilda**), H. D., 280
Doretha wore the short blue lace last night, 1094
Dorothy Wordsworth, dying, did not want to read, 638
Double Goer, The, 592
Dove, Rita, 1384
Do you remember how we went, 726
Dragonfly-Mother, The, 869
Dream, The, 509
Drowned Children, The, 1284
dry heat of the Tassajara canyon, 1087
Duffy, Carol Ann, 1423
Dunbar-Nelson, Alice, 166
Dürer would have seen a reason for living, 315

Eagle and the Mole, The, 269
Eastern War Time, 976
Edge, 1065
Edson, Margaret, 1453
Egyptian Pulled Glass Bottle in the Shape of a Fish, An, 313
Electric Slide Boogie, The, 1075
Elegy, 1365
Enclosure, steam-heated; a trial casket, 714
En Famille, 301
Envelope, The, 915
Erdrich, Louise, 1408
Eros at Temple Stream, 863
Eurydice, 285
Eve (Livesay), 595
Eve's Side of It, 544
Evening in the Sanitarium, 507
Evening Train, 872
Everyday Alchemy, 494
Everyone in me is a bird, 924
Every peak is a crater. This is the law of volcanoes, 973
Eve to Her Daughters, 726

Fanthorpe, U. A, 935
Far, Sui Sin (Edith Maud Eaton), 56
Farmer's Bride, The, 84
Fat Black Woman Remembers, The, 1372
Feminist Manifesto, 255
Final Notations, 975
Finger, 1489
First Death in Nova Scotia, 613
First Fig, 445
First having read the book of myths, 970
First Memory, 1287
Fish, The, 610
Fitting, The, 456
Flesh is heretic, 1290
Flitting, The, 1366
Floating Bridge, 1026
Fly, The, 335
For a Five-Year-Old, 1079
For authorities whose hopes, 317
Forché, Carolyn, 1363
Forgiveness, 1432
For Malcolm X, 721
For once, I hardly noticed what I ate, 1273
For Saint Peter, 936
Four years ago I met your death here, 642
Fox, 978
Fragment Thirty-six, 289
Frame, Janet, 887
Freed, Lynn, 1303
From Brooklyn, over the Brooklyn Bridge, on this fine morning, 612
From Outer Space, 715

From the House of Yemanjá, 1072
From the Third Storey, 939
From you I want more than I've ever asked, 977
Full Moon, 272

Gallant, Mavis, 844
Garden, 285
Garden of Shusan!, 258
[*Gender and Art*], 618
Generations, 1396
Gentle Lena, The, 143
Gertrude Stein, 250
Girl, 1339
Give back my brilliant ignorance, 716
Give them my regards when you go to the school reunion, 645
Glaspell, Susan, 177
Glass Essay, The, 1347
Glück, Louise, 1283
Goddess, The, 860
Good Country People, 893
Goodison, Lorna, 1321
Gordimer, Nadine, 873
Gossip-blown songstress, 254
Graham, Jorie, 1374
Grave, A, 312
Gray mountains, sea and sky. Even the misty, 832
Great grandmother, 1321
Green Rain, 594
Guinea Woman, 1321
Gumtree in the city street, 830
Gurgles, genderless, 938

Hacker, Marilyn, 1269
Half-Caste Girl, 723
"Half-cracked" to Higginson, living, 969
Hall, Radclyffe, 187
Harjo, Joy, 1377
Harwood, Gwen, 831
H. D. (Hilda Doolittle), 280
Heavy as a whale, 1371
He bathes his soul in women's wrath, 521
Hejinian, Lyn, 1250
Held between wars, 649
Helen, 291
Here, above, 605
Here in my heart I am Helen, 488
Here it is then, the dark thing, 1206
Here we have thirst, 313
Her Kind, 919
He said he was just leaving, 1367
He was very beautiful, 291
He-who-came-forth was, 864
hey music and, 1121
His Shield, 318
History, 1374
His Wife, 878
Hottentot Venus, 1489
House Slave, The, 1385
Housewife, 921
[*How Cruel Is the Story of Eve*], 585
How does a body do in the ground?, 1361
How I Got That Name, 1419
How It Feels to Be Colored Me, 357
How It Feels to Be Forcibly Fed, 460
How It Is, 915
How she sat there, 1390
How the days went, 1072
Human Affection, 583
Hurston, Zora Neale, 347

Hypocrite Women, 862
Hypocrite women, how seldom we speak, 862

I, 1070
I always was afraid of Somes's Pond, 270
I am a miner. The light burns blue, 1060
"*I Am in Danger—Sir—,*" 969
I am Marilyn Mei Ling Chin, 1419
I am silver and exact. I have no preconceptions, 1050
I am the self-appointed guardian of English literature, 582
[*I, being born a woman and distressed*], 446
I bring no throat-slit kid, 593
I came to represent the case, 1325
I can hear little clicks inside my dream, 1347
I caught a tremendous fish, 610
I did not fall from the sky, 1074
If an ant, crossing on the clothesline, 713
If any ask why there's no great She-Poet, 267
If "compression is the first grace of style," 314
I feel, 712
If I, like Solomon, 318
if our grandchild be a girl, 1121
If the year is meditating a suitable gift, 725
I had come to the house, in a cave of trees, 505
I had grieved. I had wept for a night and a day, 1427
I have a good deal of sympathy for you, mate, 936
I have been a stranger in a strange land, 1391
I have done it again, 1062
I have gone out, a possessed witch, 919
I have to thank God I'm a woman, 266
I have wanted excellence in the knife-throw, 1279
I knew too well, 871
I know not what to do, 289
I Know Why the Caged Bird Sings, 926
I lie by the pond in *utter nakedness*, 916
I'm fond, nereids and nymphs, unlike some, of the pig, 1426
In a Café, 619
Inamoratas, with an approbation, 782
In an Iridescent Time, 709
In Celebration of My Uterus, 924
Indissoluble Matrimony, 469
I needed fox, 978
In His Own Image, 1289
In human need, 593
In Memory of Constance Markiewicz, 885
In Mind, 862
In My Country, 1488
Innocence, 261
In our content, before the autumn came, 273
In Search of Our Mothers' Gardens, 1296
Instead of a cup of tea, instead of a milk, 1276
In the burned house I am eating breakfast, 1209
In the cold, cold parlor, 613
In the early springtime, after their tea, 301
In the middle of winter, middle of night, 496
In the Park, 832
In the vine-shadows on the veranda, 724
In the Waiting Room, 614
In Those Years, 977
In those years, people will say, we lost track, 977
Intifada, 881
Into whose ear the deeds are spoken. The only, 1374
Invitation to Miss Marianne Moore, 612
In your dream you met Demeter, 498
I put your leaves aside, 131
I ordered this, this clean wood box, 1052
I remember long veils of green rain, 594

Irish Patriarch, The, 521
I saw the first pear, 283
I saw you once, Medusa; we were alone, 643
I shall never get you put together entirely, 1048
I shall see justice done, 883
Ishtar, 724
I Sit and Sew, 171
I sit and sew—a useless task it seems, 171
Is it the boy in me who's looking out, 1275
Is not the woman molded by your wish, 274
I suppose it hasn't been easy living with me either, 1086
It begins quietly, 1284
It has to be loved the way a laundress loves her linens, 737
I thought, as I wiped my eyes on the corner of my apron, 457
It is dangerous for a woman to defy the gods, 260
It is not so much the song, 886
It is true, Martin Heidegger, as you have written, 915
[*I too beneath your moon, almighty Sex*], 457
I, too, dislike it: there are things that are important beyond all this fiddle, 311
It's a long way from the bedroom to the kitchen, 1277
It's the hour when everyone's drunk, 1397
It was not I who began it, 726
It wasn't bliss. What was bliss, 1391
It was only important, 920
It was taken some time ago, 1204
it will not be simple, it will not be long, 975
I've come to give you fruit from out my orchard, 507
I've stayed in the front yard all my life, 782
I want a red dress, 1395
I was not myself, myself, 1289
I was setting out from my house, 869
I went to the clinic. I twisted my foot I said, 1091
I went with Aunt Consuelo, 614
I will defy you down until my death, 495
[*I will put Chaos into fourteen lines*], 458
I will speak about women of letters, for I'm in the racket, 908
i wish for her, 1121
I woke up, and the surgeon said, "You're cured," 1273
It would not be true to say she was doing nothing, 1079
I write in praise of the solitary act, 1080

Jamaica Oman, 808
Jamaica oman cunny, sah!, 808
Jane Eyre and Wuthering Heights, 227
Jane, Jane, 303
Jen, Gish, 1436
Jewels, The, 716
Jilting of Granny Weatherall, The, 340
Jordan, June, 1093

Käthe Kollwitz, 649
Kathy my sister with the torn heart, 730
Kaufman, Shirley, 877
Kay, Jackie, 1487
Keel and Kool, 888
Kingston, Maxine Hong, 1228
Kincaid, Jamaica, 1339
Kissie Lee, 720
Kitchen Linoleum, 1075
Kizer, Carolyn, 907
Kumin, Maxine W., 912

Lady, Lady, 260
Lady, Lady, I saw your face, 260
Lady Lazarus, 1062
Lahiri, Jhumpa. 1498
Laing, Dilys, 591
Language of the Brag, The, 1279
Larsen, Nella, 360
Last Call, 1397
Last Quatrain of the Ballad of Emmett Till, The, 789
Last, walking with stiff legs as if they carried bundles, 497
Lavin, Mary, 619
Lazarus Standup: Shooting Script, 1361
Leave Me Alone a Little, 496
Leave me alone a little!, 496
Leda 3, 1123
Leda and the Cowboy, 1393
Le Guin, Ursula K., 940
Lessing, Doris, 809
Le Sueur, Meridel, 533
Let No Charitable Hope, 272
Letter, The, 129
Letter from Chicago, 642
Letter to Jeanne (at Tassajara), 1087
Letter to My Sister, 260
Letter to the Front, 647
Let Them Ask Their Husbands, 593
Levertov, Denise, 859
Lightly Bound, 585
Lineage, 718
Litany, 1425
Little cramped words scrawling all over the paper, 129
Little Josie buried under the bright moon, 723
Little Red Hen Tells All, The, 1219
Livesay, Dorothy, 594
Living alone the feet turn voluptuous, 714
Living in hell, as I do, 716
Living in the earth-deposits of our history, 972
Living long is containing, 729
Loba Priestess as Bag Lady Utters Ragged Warnings, The, 1092
Long afterward, Oedipus, old and blinded, walked the, 653
Long ago, I was wounded. I lived, 1287
Longing for Prophets, 881
Lord Barrenstock, 581
Lord Barrenstock and Epicene, 581
Lorde, Audre, 1069
lost baby poem, the, 1120
Lost "Beautifulness," The, 201
Lowell, Amy, 128
Loy, Mina, 250
Lullaby (Glück), 1287
Lullaby (Sitwell), 304

Madonna of the Evening Flowers, 131
Making the Jam without You, 913
Malcolm X, 790
Management of Grief, The, 1238
Man looking into the sea, 312
Man-Moth, The, 605
Mannequin, 499
Mansfield, Katherine, 319
Map of Places, The, 542
Marshall, Paule, 955
Marsh Languages, 1209
Master, The, 291
Master Bed, The, 1342
Mating Calls, 886

Maybe if I did not have this, 1281
McCarthy, Mary, 630
McCullers, Carson, 739
McGuckian, Medbh, 1366
Meditation at Kew, 265
Medusa (Bogan), 505
Meehan, Paula, 1428
Memories of a Catholic Girlhood, 631
Memory lifts her smoky mirror: 1943, 976
Men go to women mutely for their peace; 494
Men seldom make passes, 488
Message, The, 1263
Mew, Charlotte, 72
Mid-Channel, 834
Middle-aged, Middle-class Woman at Midnight, A, 496
Migraine Sonnets, 1277
Military Harpist, The, 520
Millay, Edna St. Vincent, 444
Mill Town, 497
Mirror, 1050
Miss Hamilton in London, 1079
Miss Jane jus hear from 'Merica, 805
Miss Ogilvy Finds Herself, 188
Mlle. Dias de Corta, 845
Molly Means, 718
Moment before the Gun Went Off, The, 874
Moments of Being, 233
Moore, Marianne, 307
More of a Corpse than a Woman, 645
Morning in the Burned House, 1209
Mornings after my father left for work, 1342
Morning Song, 1382
Morrison, Toni, 994
Mortal One, The, 1282
Moss of His Skin, The, 920
Most things are colorful things—the sky, earth, and sea, 259
mother, the, 781
Mother, I love you so, 583
Mother, mother what illbred aunt, 1047
Mother, one stone is wedged across the hole in our history, 1324
Mothers, Daughters, 878
Mother the Great Stones Got to Move, 1324
Mother Who Gave Me Life, 832
Mother who gave me life, 832
Moths, The, 1414
Mourning Song, 1379
Mr. Baptiste, 167
Mrs. Lazarus, 1427
Mrs. Spring Fragrance, 57
Mukherjee, Bharati, 1238
Municipal Gum, 830
Munro, Alice, 1026
Muse as Medusa, The, 643
Muse Mother, The, 1291
Must you leave, John Holmes, with the prayers and psalms, 922
Mutes, The, 866
My bands of silk and miniver, 272
My candle burns at both ends, 445
My daughter plays on the floor, 1205
my dream about being white, 1121
My Father Addresses Me on the Facts of Old Age, 853
My father laid me in a ring, 884
My father used to say, 313
My grandmother's name was Nora Swan, 712
My grandmothers were strong, 718
My Life, 1250

My mother had two faces and a frying pot, 1072
My mother looks at her watch, 1364
My mother's playing cards with my aunt, 1285
My mother was a romantic girl, 580
My mother, when young, scrubbed laundry in a tub, 709
My Sisters, O My Sisters, 638
Myth, 653
My widow pearls wet, 1291
My womb was sealed, 1323

Naked Girl and Mirror, 728
Names, 712
Naming, The, 1380
Nanny, 1323
Narrow Path into the Back Country, 1087
News Item, 488
New Year's Day 1:16 AM, 1075
Next to my own skin, her pearls. My mistress, 1424
Nichols, Grace, 1371
Nick and the Candlestick, 1060
Night Feeding, 647
Nightmare 7, 1090
Nightmare 12, 1091
Nin, Anaïs, 587
Nobody heard him, the dead man, 585
Nobody understood her cruelty to herself. In this life, cruelty begets, 1422
No Name Woman, 1229
Noonuccal, Oodgeroo (Kath Walker), 828
No Pasarán, 515
No Swan So Fine, 314
Not for their ice-pick eyes, 881
Not for these lovely blooms that prank your chambers did I come, 455
Nothing nastier than a white person, 1387
Not Waving but Drowning, 585
"No water so still as the, 314
Now I am slow and placid, fond of sun, 495
Now let no charitable hope, 272
Now That I Am Forever with Child, 1072

Oates, Joyce Carol, 1191
O'Brien, Edna, 1065
O'Brien, Kate, 509
O'Connor, Flannery, 892
O God, in the dream the terrible horse began, 509
[Oh, oh, you will be sorry for that word!], 445
[Oh, sleep forever in the Latmian cave], 453
Old daughter, small traveler, 913
Old Molly Means was a hag and a witch, 718
Old Nelly's Birthday, 522
Olds, Sharon, 1278
Olsen, Tillie, 659
Omen of Victory, 253
On a Night of the Full Moon, 1071
On Being Young—a Woman—and Colored, 524
One Art, 617
One day I forgot my sleeve and my heart pinned to my arm was, 1090
One garland, 869
One Girl at the Boys' Party, The, 1281
One narcissus among the ordinary beautiful, 1389
One Off the Short List, 810
One Perfect Rose, 488
One Person, 273
Only Here for the Bier, 936
On Not Shoplifting Louise Bogan's The Blue Estuaries, 1344
On the Border, 1082

Opal, 132
Orchard, 283
Oread, 284
Original, 790
Orpheus and Eurydice, 1375
O Sylvia, Sylvia, 923
Other Two, The, 43
O to Be a Dragon, 318
Our Bog Is Dood, 584
Our Bog is dood, our Bog is dood, 584
Out of Africa, 1373
Out of Africa of the suckling, 1373
Out of my flesh that hungers, 1071
Ozick, Cynthia, 931

Page, P. K., 735
Paley, Grace, 852
Papa Love Baby, 580
Paper Nautilus, The, 317
Parker, Dorothy, 487
Parsley, 1385
Pass Fe White, 805
Pastiche, 274
Path to the Milky Way Leads through Los Angeles, The, 1382
Paw Broon on the Starr Report, 1491
Periphery, 709
Persephone, Falling, 1389
Phantasia for Elvira Shatayev, 974
Photo after Pogrom, 253
Picasso, 163
Pig's-Eye View of Literature, A, 489
Pink Dog, 617
Pink Lane, Strawberry Lane, Pudding Chare, 1083
Pitter, Ruth, 520
Planet Earth, 737
Plath, Sylvia, 1044
Poem about Police Violence, 1095
Poem as Mask, The, 649
Poem in Praise of My Husband (Taos), 1086
Poem to My Uterus, 1122
Poetics of Sex, The, 1446
Poetry, 311
Poets in the Kitchen, 955
Pomegranate, The, 1293
Porter, Katherine Anne, 339
Portrait of a Nun, 254
Power, 972
Power of Suicide, The, 648
Prayer of an Ovulating Female, 593
Prichard, Katharine Susannah, 261
Pro Femina, 908
Professions for Women, 244

Quicksand, 362
Quiet House, The, 86
Quiet Woman, The, 495

Rape Fantasies, 1210
Razors pain you, 487
Reception, The, 1094
Recitatif, 996
Rendezvous, 455
Request to a Year, 725
Résumé, 487
Rhys, Jean, 498
Rich, Adrienne, 962
Richardson, Dorothy, 120
Richardson, Henry Handel, 87
Riding, Laura, 541
Right Maw, hen, 1491

Risen in a, 648
Rite of Passage, 1280
Rites for Cousin Vit, The, 786
Room of One's Own, A, 237
Roosters, 606
Rosa, 1390
"Rosina Alcona to Julius Brenzaida," 729
Royalty, 1124
Rukeyser, Muriel, 644
Runaway Lil Bit Poem, A, 1096
Runaways Café I, 1273
Runaways Café II, 1273

Safe upon the solid rock the ugly houses stand, 445
Santa Teresa, 510
Sarton, May, 637
School Among the Ruins, The, 979
School Children, The, 1283
Sea Anemones, The, 832
Sea-black virgin—being in love with you, 1368
Sea Poppies, 284
Second Fig, 445
Second-Hand Coat, 712
Second Time Around, 911
Semele Recycled, 909
September, 1997, 1425
Serenade: Any Man to Any Woman, 305
Seven ones are seven, 734
Seventeen Syllables, 835
Several Voices out of a Cloud, 508
Sexton, Anne, 918
Shall I say how it is in your clothes?, 915
Shawl, The, (Erdrich), 1409
Shawl, The, (Ozick), 932
She climbed toward the sky, 1343
She in whose lipservice, 860
She is in the Past, She has this Grace, 1364
She knows where to get cracked eggs, does Nelly, 522
She sits in the park. Her clothes are out of date, 832
She tripped and fell against a star, 261
She Unnames Them, 953
Silence, 313
Silko, Leslie Marmon, 1332
Since there's no help, come let us kiss and part; 1399
Sir Beelzebub, 302
Sisters, The (Lowell), 137
Sisters, The (Wright), 724
Sitwell, Edith, 300
Skinnydipping with William Wordsworth, 916
Smith, Stevie, 580
Snapshots of a Daughter-in-Law, 965
Sojourn in the Whale, 309
Somebody is shooting at something in our town, 1054
Some things I have to say aren't getting said, 1341
Sometimes DeLiza get so crazy she omit, 1096
Somewhere a shop of hanging meats, 1396
Somewhere in Africa, 922
Some women marry houses, 921
Some Words, 733
Son, The, 864
Song for Baby-O, Unborn, 1084
Song for Ishtar, 861
Songge Byrd, 254
song in the front yard, a, 782
Song of Absinthe Granny, The, 710
Song of One of the Girls, 488
Sonnenizio on a Line from Drayton, 1399
Sonnet in Primary Colors, 1390

Sonnet in So Many Words, 918
Sonnets from a Lock Box, 172
Sonnets from an Ungrafted Tree, 446
Sonnet to a Sister in Error, 591
Sorrow, 714
So she came back into his house again, 446
Souvenir de Monsieur Poop, 582
So you have swept me back, 285
Spark, Muriel, 790
Spelling, 1205
Spencer, Anne, 258
Stand off, daughter of the dusk, 786
Stasis in darkness, 1059
Steeple-Jack, The, 315
Stein, Gertrude, 141
Stenographers, The, 736
Stepping Westward, 865
Still Falls the Rain, 306
Still falls the Rain—, 306
Stings, 1053
Stone, Ruth, 708
Stones, 880
Stone Woman, A, 1098
Stop bleeding said the knife, 657
Storm Windows, 1343
Strangely assorted, the shape of song and the bloody man, 520
Street Song, 1083
Such a nice girl. Just what I wanted, 936
Summer Rain, 132
Sunday shuts down on this twentieth-century evening, 645
Sundays of Satin-Legs Smith, The, 782
Sur, 941
Swarm, The, 1054
Sweat, 349
Sweet Anne of Winchilsea, you were no hellion, 591
Sweetheart, 1084
Swenson, May, 654
Sylvia's Death, 923

Taggard, Genevieve, 494
Taking us by and large, we're a queer lot, 137
Tapahonso, Luci, 1392
Teaching the first lesson and the last, 979
Tell me, 130
Tell Me a Riddle, 660
Tell me something, 1095
Temporary Matter, A, 1498
Terminal Resemblance, 1286
That Half Is Almost Gone, 1421
That's what they ordered for the old man, 879
The ambulance men touched her cold, 1279
The art of losing isn't hard to master, 617
The bull on the poster speaks, 885
The children go forward with their little satchels, 1283
The cockroach, 1075
The cold felt cold until our blood, 974
[*The courage that my mother had*], 457
The dark soft languages are being silenced, 1209
The eyeless labourer in the night, 723
The fat black woman, 1372
The fat black woman want, 1372
The first horn lifts its arm over the dew-lit grass, 1385
The fitter said, "Madame, vous avez maigri," 456
The free evening fades, outside the windows fastened with decorative iron grilles, 507
The host of golden flowers at my feet, 1330
The kind of woman that men poets, 885

The map of places passes, 542
The moon is a sow, 861
Then fold up without pause, 497
The only legend I have ever loved is, 1293
The page opens to snow on a field: boot-holed month, black hour, 1365
The pin-swin or spine-swine, 318
The potflower on the windowsill says to me, 648
The red dawn now is rearranging the earth, 1382
There is a parrot imitating spring, 1385
There's in my mind a woman, 862
There Was Once, 1217
There were bizarre beginnings in old lands of the making of me, 717
The river in its abundance, 863
The sand is still hot in September, 881
These women crying in my head, 596
The smile folded as a marriage-veil, 254
The soundtrack then was a litany—*candlewick*, 1425
The summer that I was ten—, 655
The sun is blazing and the sky is blue, 617
The tall man, towering, 1089
The time comes when it can't be said, 918
The time I dropped your almost body down, 1120
The trouble of a book is first to be, 543
The weekly dietary scale, 1081
The white flesh quakes to the negro soul, 251
The woman is perfected, 1065
The woman took a train, 592
The woman who has grown old, 505
They are my secret food, 596
They came in to the little town, 828
They eat beans mostly, this old yellow pair, 787
They had never had one in the house before, 787
They made a plaster cast of my corpse, 1489
They, without message, having read, 737
Things I Say to Myself While Hanging Laundry, 713
This, 1281
This afternoon a man leans over, 1208
This Englishwoman, 581
This Englishwoman is so refined, 581
This Is a Photograph of Me, 1204
This is for the woman with one black wing, 1390
This is not I. I had no body once, 728
This is the easy time, there is nothing doing, 1056
This unphilosophic sight, 273
Thomas and Beulah, 1387
Those groans men use, 866
Those Various Scalpels, 310
Though the world has slipped and gone, 304
Though you have never possessed me, 251
Three Emily's, The, 596
Three Moments in Paris, 250
Three Summers since I chose a maid, 84
Through every night we hate, 878
Thunder in the House, 1430
Time to rest now; you have had, 1287
Tiptree, James Jr. (Alice B. Sheldon), 686
Tlilli, Tlapalli, 1255
To a Lady's Countenance, 273
To Another Housewife, 726
To a Snail, 314
To be a Jew in the twentieth century, 647
To conceive death as death, 543
Today is your, 1085
To Inez Milholland, 452
To me, one silly task is like another, 506
To Mr. William Wordsworth, Distributor of Stamps for Westmoreland, 1330
To My Last Period, 1122

Top Girls, 1137
To start off again with my tale: "The expatriates, 133
To the Days, 977
Toughest gal I ever did see, 720
Transvestism in the Novels of Charlotte Brontë, 886
Trial Path, The, 174
Trifles, 178
Tropical Death, 1372
Troubles of a Book, The, 543
True Story of Mortar and Pestle, The, 1422
Trying to open locked doors with a sword, threading, 309
Twas the voice of the Wanderer, I heard her exclaim, 584
Twenty-one Love Poems, 973
22 Hyde Park Gate, 217
Two Dreamtimes
Two Hanged Women, 88
Typists, 737
Tyrone married her this afternoon, 1093

Understand, Old One, 829
Understand, old one, 829
Under the House, 1304
Unless, 733
Unspeakable Things Unspoken, 1009
Up ahead, I know, he felt it stirring in himself already, the glance, 1375
Upon this marble bust that is not I, 452

Various sounds consistently indistinct, like intermingled echoes, 310
Venus Transiens, 130
View from under the Table, The, 1429
Viramontes, Helena María, 1414
Visiting Rainer Maria, 1367
Vita Nova, 1287
Voyage Out, The, 1081

Waiting, 1206
Walker, Alice, 1295
Walker, Margaret, 717
walking by the waters, 1488
Walking Woman, The, 66
Waltz, The, 490
Wanderer, The, 584
Warming Her Pearls, 1424
War was her life, with want and the wild air, 523
was the best view and the table itself kept the sky, 1429
was what my mother called the noise above, 1430
Wat a joyful news, Miss Mattie, 806
We Are Going, 828
Weather-Cock Points South, The, 131
Wedding, The, 1093
Well girl, goodbye, 1122
Welty, Eudora, 597
We Real Cool, 787
We real cool. We, 787
West, Rebecca, 468
We were dreaming on an occupied island at the farthest edge, 1383
We will crouch down then in a red earth, 1331
Wharton, Edith, 29
What Do Women Want?, 1395
Whatever "in love" means, 1425
What is green in me, 865
What is it made of? Guilt. Blame. Sometimes, 1489
What Were They Like?, 868

What witchlike spell weaves here its deep design, 172
When, 302
When he takes off his clothes, 1398
When I am the sky, 868
When I first saw a woman after childbirth, 724
When I grew up I went away to work, 721
When I saw my father for the last time, we both did the same thing, 1286
When I take my girl to the swimming party, 1281
When I wrote of the women in their dances and wildness, 649
When reading *Villette*, *Shirley* and *Jane Eyre*, 886
When the World As We Knew It Ended, 1383
When the world turns completely upside down, 270
When We Dead Awaken: Writing as Re-Vision, 982
When we were children old Nurse used to say, 86
When you came, you were like red wine and honey, 132
When you live in Jerusalem you begin, 880
Where are the women who, *entre deux guerres*, 1269
Where Are You Going, Where Have You Been?, 1192
Whirl up, sea, 284
White Night, A, 73
White sky, over the hemlocks bowed with snow, 452
White Things, 259
Widow's Jazz, The, 251
Who are these people at the bridge to meet me? They are the villagers, 1050
Who in One Lifetime, 646
Who in one lifetime sees all causes lost, 646
Whores, 721
Who's Irish?, 1437
Wickham, Anna (Edith Alice Mary Harper), 265
Widows, 1285
Wild Peaches, 270
Wintering, 1056
Winterson, Jeanette, 1445
Wit, 1454
Witch, 883
With Child, 495
Woman fear for man, he goes, 864
Woman Hollering Creek, 1400
Womanhood, The, 786
Woman's College from Outside, A, 231
Woman to Man, 723
Woman with Girdle, 921
Women (Bogan), 506
Women (Swenson), 657
Women and Horses, 917
Women and the Future, 123
[*Women have loved before as I love now*], 453
Women have no wilderness in them, 506
Women in uniform, 253
Women Laughing, 938
Women Men Don't see, The, 687
Women of Dan Dance with Swords in Their Hands to Mark the Time When They Were Warriors, The, 1074
Woolf, Virginia, 212
Words, 1064
Worn Path, A, 598
Would you jump into my grave as quick?, 1431
Wright, Judith, 722
Wylie, Elinor, 268

Yamamoto, Hisaye, 834
Yellow Woman, 1332
Yezierska, Anzia, 201

Yorkshire Wife's Saga, 523
You are clear, 285
You are flying to Dahomey, going back, 1087
You are ice and fire, 132
You are not wanted, 709
You beastly child, I wish you had miscarried, 585
You do not do, you do not do, 1057
You Don't Know What Love Is, 1398
You hailed a cab outside the nondescript, 1273
You, once a belle in Shreveport, 965
Your book surprised me on the bookstore shelf, 1344
Your coffin looked unreal, 1429

You're, 1049
You're entangled with someone more famous than you, 911
Your gray glasses are for playing the piano, 715
You rise, you dawn, 1292
Your midriff sags toward your knees; 921
You saved me, you should remember me, 1287
You see, they have no judgment, 1284
You uterus, 1122
You wouldn't believe all this house has cost me, 1366

Zami: A New Spelling of My Name, 1076